D1030822

JAMES A. MICHENER

TWO COMPLETE NOVELS

JAMES A. MICHENER

TWO COMPLETE NOVELS

ALASKA
HAWAII

WINGS BOOKS

New York • Avenel, New Jersey

This edition contains the complete and unabridged texts of the original editions.
They have been completely reset for this volume.

This omnibus was orginally published in separate volumes under the titles:
Alaska, copyright © 1959 by James A. Michener.
Hawaii, copyright © 1988 by James A. Michener,
cartography © 1988 by Jean Paul Tremblay.

All rights reserved.

This 1993 edition is published by Wings Books,
distributed by Outlet Book Company, Inc., A Random House Company,
40 Engelhard Avenue, Avenel, New Jersey 07001,
by arrangement with Ballantine Books.

Random House
New York • Toronto • London • Sydney • Auckland

Printed and bound in the United States of America

Library of Congress Cataloging-in-Publication Data

Michener, James A. (James Albert), 1907–
[Alaska]
Two complete novels/James A. Michener.
p.   cm.
Contents: Alaska—Hawaii.
ISBN 0–517–09151–8
1. Alaska—History—Fiction.   2. Hawaii—History—Fiction.
I. Michener, James A. (James Albert), 1907– Hawaii, 1993.
II. Title.
PS3525.I19A6   1993
813'.54—dc20   92–42529
CIP

8 7 6 5 4 3 2 1

CONTENTS

ALASKA

1

HAWAII

775

ALASKA

ACKNOWLEDGMENTS

In recent books I have named all who helped in my research, and this was appreciated. I intended doing so again, but this time, because so many provided information, the list became endless and could not be included. However, certain scholars, sometimes of world renown, went beyond the normal bounds of courtesy, and read portions of the manuscript or helped in other important ways and suggested clarifications. They must be thanked.

Dr. David Stone, University of Alaska, on terranes.
Dr. David Hopkins, University of Alaska, on Beringia.
Dr. Jean Aigner, University of Alaska, on early peoples.
Professor Frank Roth, Sheldon Jackson College, on Healy and Jackson.
Dee McKenna, Nome Library, on the gold rush in that city.
Dr. Timothy Joiner, foremost expert on salmon, on that fish.
Joe Horiskey, premier Denali guide, on mountaineering.
Jonathan Waterman, Denali Park official, on that mountain.
Elva Scott, Eagle, on life at minus-fifty-two.
David Finley, Wainwright, on education north of the Circle.

My research could not even have been started without assistance from the intrepid aviators of Alaska who flew me into all corners of their state: Ken Ward to abandoned salmon canneries; Layton Bennett to the site of the sinking of the Canadian steamer; Tom Rupert to a remote part of the Yukon River; Bob Reeve, long ago to the Aleutians; and especially the helicopter men who flew me into spots that would otherwise have been inaccessible: Officers Tom Walters and Pete Spence of the United States Coast Guard to Three Saints Bay; Randy Crosby and Price Brower of the Nome Rescue Service to the remote and desolate Will Rogers memorial.

To the many others whose unstinting help and sound advice were of such value, please accept my gratitude, especially my word-processing wizard, Kim Johnson-Bogart.

Lastly, and most particularly, to my hosts Mike and Mary Ann Kaelke at Sheldon Jackson College, Sitka, my warmest thanks for allowing my wife and me to occupy their log cabin for three seasons.

FACT AND FICTION

Though it is based on fact, this novel uses fictional events, places and characters. The following paragraphs endeavor to clarify which is which.

I. Terranes.   The various geological concepts in this chapter have been developed and verified in recent decades but are still being refined. Specific histories of the various Alaskan terranes have not yet been fully identified, but the great basics, like the existence, genesis, movement and collision of plates, are generally accepted. There could be no other explanation of the Aleutian Islands and their violent behavior.

II. Beringia.   Few geological theories are more solidly accepted than this, especially since it will probably return to existence within the next twenty-five thousand years. The movements of animals from Asia into North America is generally accepted, but the existence and functioning of the ice-free corridor into the rest of North America is more debatable. That the mastodons arrived well before the mammoths seems irrefutable.

III. Arrival of Humans.   The earliest physical evidence of the existence of human beings in any part of Alaska seems to lie on a small island off the Aleutians and is dated no earlier than 12,000 B.P.E. But other problematic finds of much earlier date in Canada, California, Mexico and South America cause many scholars to postulate human arrivals in Alaska as early as 40,000 and 30,000 B.P.E. Regardless of the earliest date, it seems certain that the order of arrival was the Athapascans first, much later the Eskimos and finally the Aleuts, who were probably an offshoot of the Eskimos. The Tlingits were pretty clearly an offshoot of the Athapascans.

IV. Russians, Englishmen, Americans.   Tsar Peter the Great, Vitus Bering, Georg Steller and Aleksei Chirikov are historical characters whose actions were pretty much as described. Though Captain James Cook and his junior officers William Bligh and George Vancouver did visit Alaska and the Aleutians at this time, they are shown here in a fictional setting, and quotations from their logbooks are imaginary. The American ship *Evening Star,* Noah Pym, and all its crew are fictional, as is the island of Lapak. The experimental shooting of eight Aleuts occurred.

V. Russian Orthodoxy and Shamanism.   The religious facts are historical, the religious characters are all fictional. Data regarding the settlement of Kodiak Island are historical. Aleksandr Baranov is a historical personage of great importance.

VI. The Settlement of Sitka.   Kot-le-an is a real Tlingit leader; Raven-heart is fictional. Prince Dmitri Maksutov, Baron Edouard de Stoeckl and General Jefferson C. Davis, USA, are historical figures presented faithfully. Father Vasili Voronov and his family are fictional, but a heroic Orthodox priest from the area was called back to St. Petersburg to become Metropolitan of All the Russias.

VII. The Period of Chaos. Captain Michael Healy and Dr. Sheldon Jackson are historical. The *Bear* was a real ship as described. Captain Emil Schransky and his *Erebus* are fictional. The legal difficulties of Healy and Jackson were real.

VIII. The Gold Rush. Soapy Smith of Skagway and Samuel Steele of the North West Mounted Police are historical characters as depicted, as are George Carmack and Robert Henderson, the discoverers of the Yukon gold field. All the others are fictional. The two routes to the gold fields—Yukon River and Chilkoot Pass—are faithfully presented.

IX. Nome. All characters are fictional. The Dawson–Nome bicycle adventure is based on a real trip.

X. Salmon. All characters are fictional, but details of the salmon industry as it operated in the early 1900s are based on historical accounts. The Ross & Raglan role in Alaskan shipping, merchandising and the canning industry is fictional and is not based on any historic company. Pleiades Lake and River are fictional, as is the cannery situated on Taku Inlet, which is real.

XI. Matanuska Valley. All American characters are fictional, but the locations and their settling and development are historic. Data regarding the Japanese invasion of the Aleutians are historic. Details of the 1971 land claims settlement are as stated.

XII. Rim of Fire. All characters are fictional, especially the Japanese and Russian experts on Alaskan prospects. The young woman schoolteacher and the two lawyers working the North Slope are totally invented and relate to no real persons. The Japanese team of mountaineers is fictional but the climb is real. The floating ice island, T-3, is historic and functioned as stated; T-7 is fictional. The data about tsunamis originating in Alaska are accurate, and although the one that closes the novel is fictional, it could become quite real at any time. The details of Eskimo life at Desolation Point, an imaginary village, are based on reality. The Iditarod Race occurs each year, and the Jones Act of 1920 still sends cruise ships to Vancouver rather than Seattle.

CONTENTS

MAPS

ARCTIC

POINT BARROW
Barrow
DESOLATION POINT
Desolation
WILL ROGERS
MONUMENT
ICY CAPE

CHUKCHI SEA

NORTH

Colville

SOVIET UNION

SIBERIA

Anadyr

CHUKCHI PENINSULA

ARCTIC CIRCLE

Point Hope

BROOKS

CAPE DEZHNEV

Pelek

DIOMEDE IS.

KOTZEBUE
SOUND

BERING STRAIT

Shishmaref

CAPE PRINCE OF WALES

Koyukuk

GULF
OF
ANADYR

Teller

Nome

Nulato

Kaltag

Yukon River

SOVIET UNION
U.S.A.

Kobuk

CAPE NAVARIN

180°

Gambell

ST. LAWRENCE I.

NORTON
SOUND

Unalakleet

A L A

St. Michael

INTERNATIONAL DATELINE

A L A

MTS.

60°

ST. MATTHEW I.

KUSKOKWIM

Kuskokwim

ALASKA

NUNIVAK I.

COOK IN

BERING   SEA

ILIAMNA

ST. PAUL
PRIBILOF ISLANDS
ST. GEORGE

BRISTOL BAY

SHELIKOF STRAIT

Kodiak

KODIAK
ISLAND

Three Saint
Harbor

ALASKA   PENINSULA

UNIMAK I.

Dutch Harbor
UNALASKA I.

UMNAK I.

COLD BAY

ALEUTIAN   ISLANDS

P A C I F I C

170°

Jean Paul Tremblay

160°

OCEAN

BEAUFORT SEA

150°
140°
130°
70°
120°

● Prudhoe Bay

S L O P E

R A N G E

A L Y E S K A   P I P E L I N E

Porcupine

● Fort Yukon

YUKON   FLATS

● Circle

● Eagle

Fairbanks ●

S K A

● Chicken

Tanana

MT. McKINLEY
(DENALI)
+

R A N G E

● Tok

● Talkeetna

Susitna

● Matanuska

Copper

● Anchorage

● Valdez

Kenai ●

KENAI PENINSULA

PRINCE WILLIAM SOUND

ST. ELIAS   MTS.

MT. ST. ELIAS +

KAYAK I.

YAKUTAT BAY

GLACIER BAY

ARCTIC CIRCLE

GREAT BEAR LAKE

Mackenzie

NORTHWEST

TERRITORIES

YUKON

TERRITORY

● Dawson

Stewart

Yukon

Macmillan

Pelly

C A N A D A

R O C K Y

ALCAN HIGHWAY

Teslin

M O U N T A I N S

Liard

● Whitehorse

BENNETT L.

CHILKOOT PASS

● Skagway

● Haines

INLET

● Juneau

C O A S T

BRITISH
COLUMBIA

Stikine

● Petersburg

ALEXANDER

● Wrangell

● Sitka

BARANOF I.

● Ketchikan

M T S.

ARCHIPELAGO

GULF   OF   ALASKA

YAK I.

OCEAN

QUEEN
CHARLOTTE
ISLANDS

130°

0   100   200   300 MILES

0   100   200   300 KILOMETERS

150°
140°

NOVAYA
ZEMLYA

B A R E N T S   S E A

FRANZ JOSEF LAND

SEVERNAYA
ZEMLYA

A R C T I C

Yenisei

S O
V I
E T

Lena

80°

NEW SIBERIAN
ISLANDS

•Yakutsk

ARCTIC CIRCLE

Kolyma

WRANGEL I.

70°

CHUKCHI SEA

CAPE DEZHNEV   DIOMEDE IS.

CAPE PRINCE OF WA

U
N
I
O
N

OKHOTSK

CAPE
NAVARIN

ST. LAWRENCE
I.

BERING
STRAIT

KAMCHATKA PENINSULA

60°

NUNIVAK I.

•
Petropavlovsk

BERING SEA

PRIBILOF IS.

A L E U T I A N   I S L A N D S

ALASKA PENINSU

50°

P A C I F I C

170°   Jean Paul Tremblay   180°   170°   160°

SPITSBERGEN

NORWEGIAN SEA

30° 20° 10° 0° 10° 20° 30°

GREENLAND

NORTH POLE

OCEAN

ELLESMERE I.

AXEL HEIBERG I.

DEVON I.

BAFFIN I.

MELVILLE I.

BANKS I.

VICTORIA I.

BEAUFORT SEA

Barrow

ARCTIC CIRCLE

GREAT BEAR LAKE

NORTHWEST TERRITORIES

BROOKS RANGE

Mackenzie

GREAT SLAVE LAKE

CANADA

Yukon

ALASKA

Tanana

YUKON
TERRITORY

C

ALASKA RANGE

ROCKY

ALBERT

KAYAK I.

Juneau

BRITISH

MTS.

Edmont

KODIAK I.

ALEXANDER
ARCHIPELAGO

COLUMBIA

GULF OF ALASKA

QUEEN
CHARLOTTE
ISLANDS

OCEAN

VANCOUVER
ISLAND

U.S.

Seat

150° 140° 130°

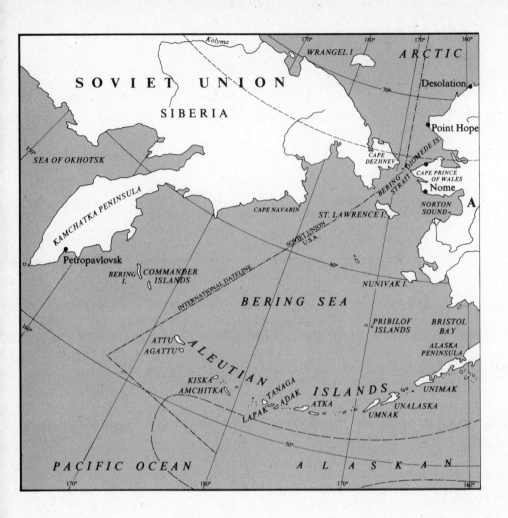

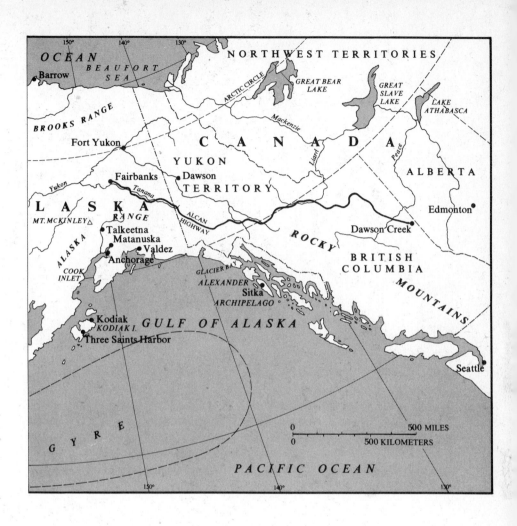

I

THE CLASHING TERRANES

About a billion years ago, long before the continents had separated to define the ancient oceans, or their own outlines had been determined, a small protuberance jutted out from the northwest corner of what would later become North America. It showed no lofty mountains or stern shorelines, but it was firmly rooted in solid rock and would remain permanently attached to primordial North America.

Its position, fixed though it was in relation to the larger landmass, did not long remain at what seemed the northwest corner, because, as we know from studies which flowered in the middle years of this century, the surface features of the earth rest on massive subterranean plates which move restlessly about, sometimes taking this position or that and often colliding with one another. In these ancient times the future North America wandered and revolved at a lively rate; sometimes the protuberance lay to the east, or to the north or, more dramatically, the far south. During one long spell it served as the temporary North Pole of the entire earth. But later it stood near the equator and then had a tropical climate.

It was, in effect, a fixed attachment to a wildly vagrant landmass, but it bore continuing relation to other would-be continents like Europe or, more significantly, to the Asia with which it would intimately be associated. However, if one had followed the errant behavior of this small jutting of rocky land attached to the larger body, one could never have predicted its present position.

The destiny of this persistent fragment would be to form the rootstock of the future Alaska, but during this early formative period and for long thereafter, it remained only that: the ancestral nucleus to which the later and more important parts of Alaska would be joined.

During one of the endless twists and turns, about half a billion years ago, the nucleus rested temporarily about where Alaska does today, that is, not far from the North Pole, and it would be instructive to visualize it as it then was. The land, in a period of subsidence after eons of violent uprising, lay not far above the surface of the surrounding seas, which had even yet not separated themselves into the oceans we know. No vast mountains broke the low profile, and since trees and ferns had not yet developed, Alaska, which amounted only to a minor promontory, was unwooded. In winter, even at these high latitudes, a phenomenon which would always characterize northern Alaska pertained: it did not receive much snow. The surrounding seas, often frozen, brought in so little precipitation that the great blizzards which swept other parts of the then world did not eventuate, and what little snow did fall was driven here and there by howling winds which swept the earth clear in many parts or left it lightly drifted in others.

Then as now, the winter night was protracted. For six months the sun appeared low in the sky, if it appeared at all, while the blazing heat of summer came in a season of equal length when the sun set only briefly. The range of temperature, under a sky which contained less relative moisture than now, was incredible: from 120° Fahrenheit in summer to the same number of degrees below zero in winter. As a consequence, such plants as tried to grow—and there were none that resembled anything with which we are now familiar—had to accommodate to these wild fluctuations: prehistoric mosses, low shrubs with deep roots, little superstructure and almost no leaves, and ferns which had adapted to the cold clung to the thin earth, their roots often thrusting their way down through crevices in rock.

No animals that we would recognize as such roamed this area, for the great dinosaurs were still far in the future, while the mastodons and mammoths which would at one time dominate these parts would not begin even their preliminary genesis for many millennia. But recognizable life had started, and in the southern half of the little promontory tentative forms moved in from the sea to experiment on land.

In these remote and formless days little Alaska hung in suspense, uncertain as to where its mother continent would wander next, or what its climate would be, or what its destiny. It was a potential, nothing more. It could become a multitude of different things; it could switch its attachment to any of three different continents; and when it enlarged upon its ancestral nucleus it would be able to construct miraculous possibilities.

It would lift up great mountains, the highest in North America. It would accumulate vast glaciers, none superior in the world. It would house, for some generations before the arrival of man, animals of the most majestic quality. And when it finally played host to wandering human beings coming in from Asia or elsewhere, it would provide residence for some of the most exciting people this earth has known: the Athapascans, the Tlingits and much later the Eskimos and Aleuts.

B UT THE IMMEDIATE task is to understand how this trivial ancestral nucleus could aggregate to itself the many additional segments of rocky land which would ultimately unite to comprise the Alaska we know. Like a spider waiting to grab any passing fly, the nucleus remained passive but did accept any passing terranes—those unified agglomerations of rock considerable in size and adventurous in motion—that wandered within reach. Where did these disparate terranes originate? How could blocks so massive move about? If they did move, what carried them north toward Alaska? And how did they behave when they bumped into the ancestral nucleus and its outriders?

The explanation is a narrative of almost delicate intricacy, so wonderfully do the various terranes move about, but it is also one of cataclysmic violence when the terranes finally collide with something fixed. This part of Alaska's history is one of the most instructive offered by earth.

The visible features of the earth, including its oceans, rest on some six or eight major identifiable subterranean plates—Asia is one, obviously; Australia another—plus a score of smaller plates, each clearly defined, and upon their slow, almost imperceptible movement depends where and how the continents and the oceans shall sit in relation each to the other.

At what speed might a plate move? The present distance from California to Tokyo is 5,149 miles. If the North American plate were to move relentlessly toward Japan at the infinitesimal rate of one-half inch per year, San Francisco would bump into Tokyo in only six hundred and fifty million years. If the plate movement were a foot a year, the transit could be made in about twenty-seven million years, which is not long in geologic time.

So the movement of a terrane from anywhere in Asia, the Pacific Ocean or North America to the growing shoreline of Alaska presented no insuperable difficulties. Given enough time and enough movement of the respective plates, anything could happen . . . and did.

IN ONE OF the far wastes of the South Pacific Ocean a long-vanished island-studded landmass of some magnitude arose, now given the name Wrangellia, and had it stayed put, it might have produced another assembly of islands like the Tahiti group or the Samoan. Instead, for reasons not known, it fragmented, and its two halves moved with a part of the Pacific Plate in a northerly direction, with the eastern half ending up along the Snake River in Idaho and the western as a part of the Alaskan peninsula. We can make this statement with certainty because scientists have compared the structure of the two segments in minute detail, and one layer after another of the terrane which landed in Idaho matches perfectly the one which wandered to Alaska. The layers of rock were laid down at the same time, in the same sequence and with the same relative thickness and magnetic orientation. The fit is absolute, and is verified by many matching strata.

Through the millennia similar wandering terranes seem to have attached themselves to the Alaskan nucleus. Frequently some enormous slab of rocky earth —sometimes as big as Kentucky—would creep relentlessly north from some-where and bang into what was already there. There would be a rending of the edges of the two terranes, a sudden uprising of mountains, a revolution in the existing landscape, and Alaska would be enlarged by a significant percentage.

Sometimes two smaller terranes would collide far distant from Alaska; they would merge and for eons would form an island somewhere in the Pacific, and then their plate would imperceptibly move them toward Alaska, and one day they would touch Alaska, so gently that even the birds inhabiting the island would not know that contact had been made, but the onetime island would keep remorselessly encroaching, grinding down opposition, overwhelming the exist-ing shoreline of Alaska or being overwhelmed by it, and no casual observer would be able to detect where or how the join of this new land to the old had been accomplished.

Now, obviously, after eight or ten such terranes had pushed against the ancestral nucleus, none of its original structure still touched the ocean, for it had been surrounded on all exposed sides by the incoming lands. A great peninsula, one of the largest on earth, was in the process of being formed, an immense proboscis reaching out toward Asia, which was also in the process of its forma-tion. About seventy million years ago this nascent peninsula began to assume a shape vaguely like present-day Alaska, but shortly thereafter it acquired a peculiarity with which we today would not be familiar.

A land bridge seemed to rise from the seas connecting Alaska to Asia, or the other way around, and it was so broad and permanent that it provided a continuous land connection between the continents. But at this time little advantage accrued to the change, for there were few animals and of course no humans at all on earth to profit from the bridge which had been so mysteriously exposed, but a few adventurous dinosaurs do seem to have used it for crossing from Asia.

In time the land bridge disappeared, overrun by the seas, and then Asia and Alaska were separated, with the latter still free to accept such wandering terranes as might come her way and thus to double or treble her size.

W E ARE NOW prepared to look at the specific formulation of the Alaskan land forms. When the northern half of the final outline was more or less set, but still awaiting the arrival of the final terranes, the Pacific Plate seems to have crashed into the continental plate on which the original Alaska rested, and the force was so great and persistent that a grand chain of mountains, to be known later as the Brooks Range, rose in an east-west direction. In the bleak and snowless area, north of the range, well beyond the Arctic Circle, would appear a multitude of small lakes, so many that they would never be counted.

The range itself, originally very high and mysteriously composed of slabs of limestone stacked one atop the other, would be eroded by wind, freezing, breakage and the action of summer rain, until the tallest peaks would stand at only six to eight thousand feet, the stumps of mountains that were once twice as high. But they would always be a noble range, the essence of the real Alaska.

South of them, spacious valleys spread out, garnering sunlight summer and winter, bitterly cold at times, delightful for much of the year. Here snow did fall, animals prospered, and all was readied for the appearance of man, and held that way eons before he finally appeared.

At a much later period a new collection of terranes from widely varied sources started moving in to complete the major outline of Alaska, and they arrived with such titanic force that an entire new mountain range was thrown up, about three hundred miles south of the older Brooks Range and parallel to it. This was the Alaska Range, a majestic row of rugged peaks which, because they are so much younger than the Brooks, have not yet been eroded down to stumps. Young, soaring, vivid in form, tremendous in reach, these peaks stab the frosty air to heights of twelve and thirteen, nineteen and twenty thousand feet. Denali, the glory of Alaska, soars to more than twenty thousand and is one of the most compelling mountains in the Americas.

Old Brooks and young Alaska, these two ranges form the twin backbones of the region and give Alaska a wilderness of mighty peaks, some of which have yet to feel the foot of man. Sometimes, when seen from the air, Alaska seems nothing but peaks, thousands of them, many not even named, and in such varied snow-covered profusion that Alaska could well be called the land of mountains.

And each one was formed by some segment of the Pacific Plate bulldozing its way into the North American Plate, submerging along the edge, and causing such tremendous commotion and movement of forces that the great mountains erupted as a consequence. When one looks at the glorious mountains of Alaska he sees proof of the power of the Pacific Plate as it noses its way north and east, and if today he visits Yakutat, he can observe the plate pushing into Alaska at the steady rate of two inches a year. As we shall see later, this produces large earthquakes in the area, and nearby Mount St. Elias, 18,008 feet, grows taller year by year.

But there is another region in Alaska which shows the operations of the great Pacific Plate at even more instructive advantage. West of what finally became mainland Alaska there was originally only water, and turbulent water it was, for here an arctic sea, the Bering, met an ocean, the Pacific, and dark waves signaled their meeting, a haunt of seal and walrus, of sea birds that skimmed the surface of the water seeking fish, and of one of the most delightful creatures nature provides, the sleek sea otter whose round bewhiskered face looks almost exactly like that of some roguish old man. In these waters, too, swam the fish that would ultimately make Alaska famous, the salmon, whose life story will prove compelling.

Here plates collided to produce a magnificent chain of islands, the Aleutians, and two of nature's most dramatic manifestations: earthquakes and volcanoes. In any century, considering the entire surface of the earth, of all the earthquakes that occur, three or four out of the ten most powerful will occur along the Aleutians or close to them, and some of the most destructive are those which take place deep within the bosom of the ocean, for then landslides of gigantic dimension displace millions of tons of submarine earth. This powerful disruption creates immense underwater waves which manifest themselves as tidal waves, more properly tsunamis, which course through the entire Pacific Ocean at speeds that can surpass five hundred miles an hour.

So a submarine earthquake in the Aleutians poses a potential danger to the Hawaiian Islands, because six or seven hours after it occurs in Alaska, its resulting tsunami can strike Hawaii with devastating power. Silently, never causing a surface wave much over three feet high, the tsunami transmits its power with vast radiating force, and if it encounters no obstruction on its way, it runs on and on until it finally dissipates. But if it does bump into an island, the waves that have been no more than three feet high come on quietly but relentlessly until they cover the land to a depth of five or six feet. This flooding, of itself, does little damage, but when these accumulated waters rush back off the land to regain the sea, the destruction and loss of life can be tremendous.

The earthquakes produced along the Aleutian chain are endless, thousands in a century, but most of them, fortunately, are only minor, and although many submarine ones produce tsunamis, only rarely are they of such magnitude as to threaten Hawaii, but, as we shall see, they do often produce local tidal waves of great destructive power.

The same tectonic forces which create situations conducive to earthquake activity produce volcanoes, and thus the Aleutians become one of the world's most active volcanic centers, with some forty volcanoes stringing along the chain. It is a rare island that does not have its crater, and some craters appear not in connection with established islands, but as lonely spots in the middle of the sea. Some stand on the verge of becoming islands, smoking above the surface for a hundred years, subsiding for half a century, then peeking their sulfurous heads above the waves to throw flames in the night.

Because of the profusion of volcanic activity along the Aleutians—a bubbling cauldron, really—Alaska holds an honored place, perhaps the preeminent place in the Rim of Fire, that unbroken chain of volcanoes which circles the Pacific Ocean wherever the Pacific Plate comes into violent contact with other plates.

Starting at Tierra del Fuego at the southern tip of South America, the volcanoes come up the western side of the continent (Cotopaxi, Lascar, Misti), then along Mexico (Popocatépetl, Ixtaccihuatl, Orizaba, Paracutín) and into the Pacific states (Lassen, Hood, St. Helens, Rainier), and then the Aleutians, where they are so ordinary that their names, often commemorating Russian sailors, are not widely known.

The Rim of Fire continues dramatically along the east coast of Asia, with many volcanoes in Kamchatka, Mount Fuji and others in Japan, a stunning array in Indonesia and on to New Zealand with its beautiful Ruapehu and Tongariro.

And, as if to prove the capacity of this area to breed violent activity, in the middle of the Pacific Ocean rise the two magnificent Hawaiian volcanoes Mauna Loa and Mauna Kea. Considering the platform from which they rise, far beneath the surface of the ocean, they are among the tallest mountains on earth and certainly the highest volcanoes.

But none of the many along the rim are more compactly arranged and fascinating to study than those dozens that cluster along the Aleutian chain; indeed, these islands could well be preserved as a universal park to demonstrate to the world the majesty of the volcano and the power of plate action.

WHAT IS THE future of Alaska, geologically speaking? For interesting reasons which will be developed, we can expect that at some distant time— perhaps twenty thousand years from now—Alaska will once again be joined to Asia by the historic land bridge, while land communication to the rest of the United States may be cut.

And since the great plates of the earth never rest, we can anticipate the arrival at Alaska of additional terranes, but these may not lurch onto the scene for several million years, if then. One future event will cause comment, if people are living then who remember history.

The city of Los Angeles is now some twenty-four hundred miles south of central Alaska, and since it is moving slowly northward as the San Andreas fault slides irresistibly along, the city is destined eventually to become part of Alaska. If the movement is two inches a year, which it often is, we can expect Los Angeles to arrive off Anchorage in about seventy-six million years, which was about the time that was required for some of the other terranes from the south to move into position against the ancestral nucleus.

So Alaska must be viewed as having two characteristics: great beauty but also implacable hostility. Its intricate mosaic of disparate terranes has produced lofty mountains, unequaled volcanoes and glaciers. But in the early days the land was not hospitable to settlers. Animals and human beings who came to this promontory had to adjust to profound cold, great distances and meager food supplies, which meant that the men and women who survived would always be a somewhat special breed: adventurous, heroic, willing to contest the great winds, the endless nights, the freezing winters, the cruel and never-ending search for food. They would be people who lived close to the unrelenting land both because they had to and because they reveled in the challenge.

Alaska would always call forth the best in a small handful of daring men and women, but those who did not relish the contest or who refused to obey the harsh rules which governed it would find the bitterly cold land repellent and would flee it if they could retreat before it killed them.

The number of settlers was never very large, for in the icy tundra of the north slope only a few thousand at a time would challenge the rigors; in the grand valleys between the mountain ranges not many would adjust to the radical alternations of climate; and even in the easier enclaves and islands to the south people would not cluster when with far less effort they could enjoy the more inviting climate of California.

But because Alaska lay at the crossroads joining North America and Asia, it would always be important; and since it dominated these crossroads, it would enjoy a significance which only the brightest intellects of the region would appreciate. There would always be a few Russians who understood the unique value of Alaska, a few Americans who appreciated its enormous importance, and upon these knowing ones would depend the history of this strange, compelling land.

II

THE ICE CASTLE

At various times in the ancient past, for a complex set of reasons which have yet to be untangled, ice began to collect at the poles in vast quantities, growing ever thicker and more extensive, until it created immense, ice sheets which encroached on surrounding continents. Snow fell at such a rate that it could not melt as it would have done under ordinary circumstances. Instead, it piled to unprecedented heights, and the pressure from that on top was so considerable that the snow at the bottom was turned into ice, and as snow continued to fall, ice continued to form, until it stood in certain places more than a mile and a half thick. The weight was so oppressive and inescapable that certain parts of the earth's surface, heavily encumbered, began to sink perceptibly, so that land which once stood well above the surface of the oceans was now depressed to sea level or below.

If in any given region this enormous accumulation of ice rested on a flat plateau, a huge and quietly spreading ice cap resulted, but since the surface of the earth, because of the violent way in which it had been formed, was irregular, with mountains and valleys predominating, the ice which found itself on a slope, as most of it did, began slowly to move, under the force of gravity, to lower elevations, and as it did, its weight was so great that it dragged along with it a mass of rubble composed of sand, gravel, rocks and, occasionally, boulders of gigantic size. This lateral transport of material occurred wherever the ice field was in motion, but when a snowfield accumulated on some high plateau and began to send glaciers down valleys which might have steep gradients, the consequences could be dramatic, for then the ice formed a moving glacier which routed out the bottom of the valley and scored the sides with streaks so pronounced that they would still be visible eons later.

These glaciers could not run forever; as they probed into lower and warmer land their ends began to melt, forming massive rivers which carried ice and silt and boulders to the sea. Such glacial rivers were a milky white, colored by the flecks of rock they carried, and as they dropped their stony burden, land was formed from the detritus of the melting ice field.

If the valley down which the glacier came ended at the shoreline, the towering face of ice would come right to the edge of the ocean, where in due time fragments of the glacier, sometimes as big as cathedrals, sometimes bigger, would break away with resounding cracks that would reverberate through the air for many miles as the resulting iceberg crashed into the ocean, where it would ride as an independent entity for months and even decades. Then it became a thing of majestic beauty, with sunlight glistening on its towering spires, with waves playing about its feet, and with primitive birds saluting it as they sped by.

In time, of course, the great icebergs would melt, adding their water to the ocean, and clouds passing overhead would lift this water, carry it inland, and deposit it as fresh snow upon the ever-growing ice field that fed the glaciers.

Normally, if such a word can be applied to any natural function which by its character must vary, an equilibrium between the formation of snow and its removal as it melted into water was maintained, so that the ice fields did not invade terrains which traditionally were not ice-covered, but during what have been called the ice ages, this equilibrium was disturbed, with ice forming much faster than it could be dissipated by melting, and for centuries learned men have been fascinated by the mystery of what caused this imbalance.

Seven or eight potential factors have been suggested to explain ice ages: the inclination of the earth's axis toward the sun, for if any portion of the earth was removed even slightly from the heat of the sun, ice would result; the wandering of the earth's poles, for they are not fixed and have been located in some periods close to the present equator; the elliptical path of the earth around the sun, which deviates so substantially that the earth's distance from the sun varies greatly during the course of a year; changes within the center of the sun itself causing the value of whatever heat is disseminated to vary; chemical changes in the atmosphere; physical changes in the oceans; and other inventive and enticing possibilities.

The time span of these variables can be as short as a calendar year or as long as fifty to a hundred thousand years, so to devise a theory which explains how they interact to produce an ice age is obviously complex and has not yet been solved. To take an easy example, if four different factors in an intricate problem operate in cycles of 13, 17, 23 and 37 years respectively, and if all have to coincide to produce the desired result, you might have to wait 188,071 years ($13 \times 17 \times 23 \times 37$) before everything fell together. But if you can get fairly satisfactory results when only the first two factors coincide, you could confidently expect that result in 221 years (13×17).

There is now an attractive theory that in relatively recent times, periods of extensive glaciation over Europe and North America have occurred in obedience to three unexplained cycles of about one hundred thousand years, forty-one thousand and twenty-two thousand. At these intervals, for reasons not fully understood, the ice begins to accumulate and expand, covering areas which for thousands of years have been clear of ice fields and glaciers. The causes are natural and may in time be understood; in fact, science-fiction writers dream that they may even become manageable, so that future ice ages need not extend so far south into Europe and North America as they have in the past.

Strangely, although a permanent ice cap came in time to cover the South Pole, which was a continent, none developed at the North, which was a sea. The glaciers which covered North America stemmed from caps in Canada; those that submerged Europe, from the Scandinavian countries; and those which struck Russia, from sites near the Barents Sea. And because the movement of ice in North America was mainly to the south, Alaska would never lie under a massive ice sheet; Wisconsin and Massachusetts would, and so would a dozen other states, but not Alaska. It would become known as a cold and barren land covered with ice and snow, but it would never know in all its millennia as much ice as a more habitable state like Connecticut had once known—or Massachusetts and New York.

The world has known many ice ages, two of which lasted an appalling number of millennia when much of Europe and North America lay crushed beneath monstrous thicknesses of ice. Then winds howled across endless wastes and freezing night seemed perpetual. When the sun did appear, it was unproductive, glistening down upon dead icy surfaces. All visible living things perished: grasses and trees, worms and insects, fish and animals. Desolation ruled, and during these vast periods of frozen waste it must have seemed as if warmth and life could never return.

But each protracted ice age was followed by joyous intervals of equal length when the ice mysteriously retreated to release from its frozen prison an earth bursting with energy and the capacity to restore life in all its manifestations. Grasses flourished to feed the animals that hurried back. Trees grew, some bearing fruits. Fields, nourished with minerals long unused, bore lavish crops, and birds sang. The future Wisconsins and Austrias exploded into life as the sun brought back warmth and well-being. The world had returned to abundant life.

These first two great ice ages began to evolve so very long ago, say about seven hundred million years, that they need not concern us, but some two million years ago when the historical record was about to begin, a series of much briefer ice ages arrived, and their dates, extents and characteristics have been so well defined that they have been given distinctive names: Nebraskan, Kansan, Illinoian, Wisconsin—in Europe: Gunz, Mindel, Riss, Würm—with the last segment in each group subdivided into three parts, making six in all. The names can be ignored; they will not be referred to again, but two significant facts cannot be ignored: the last of these six recent ice ages ended only fourteen thousand years ago, with glacial remnants existing as late as seven thousand years ago, so that the men and women then living in North America experienced one of the ice ages. And the normal extension and retraction of the polar ice cap indicates that about twenty thousand years from now we may anticipate another icy incursion to areas as far south as New York, Iowa and spots in between. But of course, if history is any predictor, Alaska at that time will be ice-free and a relatively attractive place in which the residents of our Northern states can seek refuge.

E VEN THOUGH ALASKA did escape being submerged by these vast weights of frozen water, it was attacked by isolated glaciers which formed in its own mountains, and some were of substantial size. In the northern areas during one of the lesser ice ages, an icy finger covered the Brooks Range, carving and readjusting those mountains and building beautiful valleys. Much later, glaciers of some size came into the Alaska Range to the south, and even today huge ice fields with their probing glaciers exist in the extreme southern regions, where constant precipitation brought in by Pacific winds keeps the fields covered with snow, which packs down to form ice just as it did when the first Alaskan ice fields formed.

But most of Alaska escaped the glaciers. North of the Brooks Range, there were none. In the vast middle section, between the mountain ranges, there were none, and in isolated parts of the region to the south, glaciers did not appear. At maximum, not more than thirty percent of the region was ice-covered.

However, the later ice ages did create in Alaska a result more dramatic than that which happened anywhere else in America, and for a reason which becomes evident once it is pointed out. If an ice sheet more than a mile thick is going to cover much of North America, the water it imprisons will have to come from somewhere, and it cannot come mysteriously from outer space. It cannot *arrive* on the surface of the earth; it can come only from water already here, which means that it must be stolen from the oceans. And that is what happened: dry winds whipping across the oceans lifted huge quantities of water that fell as cold rain over the high latitudes and as snow toward the poles. As it was compressed into ice it began to expand outward, covering hitherto barren sites, and causing more and more of the incoming moisture to fall as snow. This in turn fed the existing glaciers and created new ones.

In the recent period with which we are concerned, this theft of water continued for thousands of years, until the snowfields were immensely aggrandized and the oceans seriously depleted. In fact, when the deficiency was at its worst, only some twenty thousand years ago, the level of the world's oceans— all of them—was more than three hundred feet lower than it is now. All the American states that faced the Atlantic Ocean had shorelines that extended miles farther eastward than they now do; much of the Gulf of Mexico was dry; Florida was not a peninsula nor was Cape Cod a cape. Caribbean Islands coalesced into a few huge islands, and the shoreline of Canada could not be seen at all, for it was smothered in ice.

This sharp droppage in the level of the oceans meant that land areas which had previously been separated were now joined by necks of land which the subsiding waters revealed. Australia was attached to Antarctica by such exposed land, Ceylon to India, Cyprus to western Asia, and England to Europe. But the most spectacular join was that of Alaska to Siberia, for it united two continents, allowing animals and people to pass from one to the other. It was also the only one which acquired its own name, scientists having christened it Beringia, the lost land of the Bering Sea.

It was, perhaps, unfortunate that the phrase *land bridge* was invented by geographers to designate this phenomenon of revealed land connections, because the imagery connected with the word *bridge* is misleading. The Alaskan-Siberian connection was no bridge in the ordinary sense, a narrow structure across which one could travel; it was an exposed sea floor some sixty miles east to west, but a full six hundred south to north. At its widest, it covered about the distance from Atlanta to New York (in Europe, Paris to Copenhagen). It was four times wider than most of Central America from ocean to ocean, and if a man stood in the middle, he would hardly think of himself on a bridge; he would be on a substantial part of a continent. But it was an inviting passageway, and with its functioning the story of populated Alaska can begin. It starts with the earliest immigrants.

ABOUT THREE HUNDRED eighty-five thousand years ago, when the oceans and continents were in place as we know them today, the land bridge from Asia was open, and a huge, ponderous animal, looking much like an oversized elephant but with enormous protruding tusks, slowly made his way eastward, followed by four females and their young. He was by no means the first of his breed to lumber across the bridge, but he was among the more interesting, for his life experience symbolized the majestic adventure in which the animals of his period were engaged.

He was a mastodon, and we shall call him by that name, for he was a progenitor of those noble massive beasts who ranged Alaska. Obviously, a million years before, he had stemmed from the same source that produced the elephant, but in Africa, in Europe and later in central Asia he had developed those characteristics which differentiated him from his cousin the elephant. His tusks were larger, his front shoulders lower, his legs more powerful, and his body was covered with hair that was more visible. But he behaved in much the same way, foraged for the same kinds of food, and lived to about the same age.

When he crossed the bridge—less than seventy miles from Asia to Alaska —Mastodon was forty years old and could expect to survive into his late seventies, supposing that he escaped the ferocious wild cats who relished mastodon meat. His four females were much younger than he, and as was common in the animal kingdom, they could anticipate a somewhat longer life.

As the nine mastodons entered Alaska they faced four radically different types of terrain, varying somewhat from the land they had left behind in Asia. At the farthest north, facing the Arctic Ocean, lay a thin strip of arctic desert, a bleak and terrifying land of shifting sands on which little that was edible grew. During the dozen winter weeks when no sun appeared, it was covered by thin snow that did not pile up into high drifts but was whipped by intense winds across the barren landscape until it came to rest in low drifts behind some ridge or rock.

Since none of his breed could survive long in this desert, Mastodon intuitively shied away from the far north, and this left him three other areas to explore that were more rewarding. Just south of the desert and blending into it in various ways stretched another relatively narrow strip, a tundra, perpetually frozen twelve to twenty-four inches below the surface but rich in rooted plant life when the topsoil was dry enough to permit growth. Here succulent lichens abounded and mosses rich in nutrients and even an occasional low shrub with branches stout enough to provide leaves for grazing. No real trees grew here, of course, for summers were too short to permit flowering or adequate branch development, and this meant that whereas Mastodon and his family could eat well on the tundra during the long summers when nearly perpetual daylight spurred plant growth, they had to be careful to escape it when winter approached.

That left two rich areas between the northern and southern glaciers, and the first of these was a splendid, hospitable region, the great Alaskan steppe, an area of rich grass growing high most years and yielding some food even in poor years. Large trees did not customarily grow on the steppe, but in a few secluded spots that were protected from searing winds, clusters of low shrubs gained a foothold, especially the dwarf willow whose leaves Mastodon loved to crop. When he was especially hungry he liked to rip off the bark of the willow with his strong tusks, and sometimes he would stand for hours amidst a group of willows, browsing and eating a sliver of bark and striving to find among the low branches a bit of shade to protect himself from the intense heat of summer.

The fourth area he had at his disposal was larger than any of the previous three, for in these years Alaska had a predominantly benign climate which both allowed and encouraged the growth of trees in regions that had previously been denuded and would be again when temperatures lowered. Now poplar, birch, pine and larch flourished, with woodland animals like the spotted skunk sharing the forests with Mastodon, who relished the trees because he could stand upright and nibble at their copious leaves. After feeding, he could use the sturdy trunks of the pine or larch as convenient poles against which to scrape his back.

So between the largesse of the new woodland and the more controlled but assured richness of the steppe, Mastodon and his family could eat well, and since it was spring when they entered Alaska, he naturally headed for a region like the one he had known well in Siberia, the tundra, where he was certain that low shrubs and grasses waited. But now he faced an interesting problem, for the sun's heat that had enabled these plants to grow also melted the top eight or ten inches of the permafrost, turning the softening soil into a kind of sticky mush. Obviously, there was nowhere for the moisture to escape; the earth below was frozen solid and would remain so for countless years. As summer approached, thousands of shallow lakes thawed, and the mush thickened until at times Mastodon sank in almost to his knees.

Now he slipped and sloshed his way through the watery tundra, fighting off the myriad of mosquitoes that hatched at this time to torment any moving thing. Sometimes, when he lifted one of his huge legs out of the swampy mess in which it had slowly sunk, the sound of the leg breaking free from the suction echoed for long distances.

Mastodon and his group grazed on the tundra during most of that first summer, but as the waning heat of the sun signaled the approach of winter, he began drifting gradually south toward the waiting steppe where there would be reassuring grass poking through the thin snow. During the early days of autumn, when he was at the dividing line between tundra and steppe, it was almost as if the shrub willows that now appeared low on the horizon were calling him to a safer winter home, but the effect of the waning sun was the more important impulse, so that by the time the first snows appeared in the area between the great glaciers, he and his family had moved into the forested area which assured an ample food supply.

His first half-year in Alaska had been a spectacular success, but of course he was not aware that he had made the transition from Asia to North America; all he had done was follow an improved food supply. Indeed, he had not left Asia, for those solid sheets of ice to the east had made Alaska in those years a part of the larger continent.

A s THE FIRST winter progressed, Mastodon became aware that he and the other mastodons were by no means alone in their favorable habitat, for a most varied menagerie had preceded them in their exit from the Asian mainland, and one cold morning when he stood alone in soft snow, cropping twig-ends from a convenient willow, he heard a rustle that disturbed him. Prudently, he withdrew lest some enemy leap upon him from a hiding place high in the trees, and he was not a moment too soon, for as he turned away from the willow, he saw emerging from the protection of a nearby copse his most fearsome enemy.

It was a kind of tiger, with powerful claws and a pair of frightful upper teeth almost three feet long and incredibly sharp. Mastodon knew that though this saber-tooth could not drive those fearsome teeth through the heavy skin of his protected rear or sides, it could, if it obtained a secure foothold on his back, sink them into the softer skin at the base of his neck. He had only a moment to defend himself from this hungry enemy, and with an agility that was surprising for an animal so big, he pivoted on his left front foot, swung his massive body in a half-circle, and faced the charging saber-tooth.

Mastodon had his long tusks, of course, but he could not lunge forward and expect to impale his adversary on them; they were not intended for that purpose. But his tiny brain did send signals which set the tusks in wide sweeping motions, and as the cat sprang, hoping to evade them, the right tusk, swinging with tremendous force, caught the rear legs of the saber-tooth, and although the blow did not send the cat spinning or in any way immobilize it, it did divert the attack and it did cause a bruise which infuriated the saber-tooth without disarming him.

So the cat stumbled among the trees, then regained control, and circled swiftly so that it could attack from the rear, hoping with a giant leap to land upon Mastodon's back, from where the vulnerable neck could be punctured. The cat was much quicker than the mastodon, and after a series of feints which tired the larger animal as he tried to counter them, the saber-tooth did land with a mighty bound, not on the flat of the back where it wanted to be, but half on the back, half on the side. It struggled for a moment to climb to a secure position, but in that time Mastodon, with a remarkable instinct for self-preservation, scraped under a set of low branches, and had the cat not wisely jumped free, it would have been crushed, which was what Mastodon intended.

Repelled twice, the great cat, some nine times larger than the tiger we know today, growled furiously, lurked among the trees, and gathered strength for a final attack. This time, with a leap more powerful than before, it came at Mastodon from the side, but the huge animal was prepared, and pivoting again on his left front foot, he swung his tusks in a wide arc that caught the saber-tooth in midair and sent it sprawling back among the trees, one of its legs painfully damaged.

That was enough for the saber-tooth. Growling and protesting, it slunk away, having learned that if it wanted to feast on mastodon, it must hunt in pairs, or even threes or fours, because one wily mastodon was capable of protecting itself.

Alaska at this time contained many lions, huge and much hairier than the kind that would come later. These possessed no handsome manes or wavy tails, and the males lacked the regal quality that would someday be such a distinguishing characteristic; they were what nature intended them to be: great cats with remarkable hunting abilities. Like the saber-tooth, they had learned never to attack a mastodon singly, but a hungry pride of six or seven could badger him to death, so Mastodon never intruded upon areas where a number of lions might be hiding. Rocky tors covered with trees, deep vales from whose sides groups of lions might attack, these he avoided, and sometimes as he plowed noisily along, bending young and scattered trees to his will, he would see a group of lions in the distance feeding upon some animal they had run to earth, and he would change direction lest he attract their attention.

The water animal with which Mastodon occasionally came into contact was the massive beaver, which had followed him out of Asia. Of giant size and with teeth that could fell a large tree, these beavers spent their working hours building dams, which Mastodon often saw from a distance, but when work was done the great beasts, their heavy fur glistening in the cold sunlight, liked to play at rowdy games, and their agility differed so markedly from the ponderous movements of Mastodon that he was amazed at their antics. He never had occasion to live in close contact with the underwater beavers, but he noticed them with perplexity when they gamboled after work.

Mastodon had his major contacts with the numerous steppe bison, the huge progenitors of the buffalo. These shaggy beasts, heads low and powerful horns parallel to the ground, grazed in many of the areas he liked to roam, and sometimes so many bison collected in one meadow that the land seemed covered with them. They would all be grazing, heads pointed in the same direction, when a saber-tooth would begin stalking a laggard. Then, at some signal Mastodon could not detect, the hundreds of giant bison would start running away from the terrible fangs of the cat, and the steppe would thunder with their passage.

Occasionally he encountered camels. Tall, awkward beasts who cropped the tops of trees, they seemed to fit in nowhere, moving slowly about, kicking ferociously at enemies, and surrendering quickly whenever a saber-tooth managed a foothold on their backs. At rare times Mastodon and a pair of camels would feed in the same area, but the two animals, so vastly different, ignored each other, and it might be months before Mastodon saw another camel. They were mysterious creatures and he was content to leave them alone.

In this placid, ponderous way, Mastodon lived out his uneventful life. If he defended himself against saber-tooths, and avoided falling into bogs from which he could not scramble free, and fled from the great fires set by lightning, he had little to fear. Food was plentiful. He was still young enough to attract and hold females. And the seasons were not too hot and moist in summer or cold and dry in winter. He had a good life and he stumbled his gigantic way through it with dignity and gentleness. Other animals like wolves and saber-tooths sought sometimes to kill him for food, but he hungered only for enough grass and tender leaves, of which he consumed about six hundred pounds a day. He was of all Alaska's inhabitants in these early years the most congenial.

A CURIOUS PHYSICAL condition limited the movement of animals in Alaska, for Beringia's land bridge could exist only when the polar ice caps were so extensive that they imprisoned vast quantities of water which had previously sustained the oceans. Indeed, the prime requisite for the existence of the bridge was that the ice sheets be immense.

However, when they were, they crept across western Canada, and although they never reached Alaska in an unbroken mass, they did send forth probing glaciers, and in time these frozen fingers reached right down to the Pacific shoreline, forming a set of icy barriers which proved impassable to animals and men. Alaska was then easy to enter from Asia, impossible to leave for the interior of North America. Functionally, Alaska became a part of Asia, and so it would remain during vast periods.

At no time that we are aware of could any animal or man cross the bridge and proceed directly to the interior of North America; but since we know that eventual passage did occur, for mastodons, bison and sheep did move from Asia into mainland North America, as did men, we must conclude that such movement came only after an extended waiting period in Alaska's ice castle.

Proof of this can be found in varied data. Certain animals that came into Alaska remained there, while their brothers and sisters wandered on to the rest of North America during some interval when the barriers were removed. But the two strains became so totally separated when the barriers closed that over the thousands of years that they remained apart they each developed unique characteristics.

The movement of animals across the bridge was by no means always in one direction, for although it is true that the more spectacular beasts—mastodon, saber-tooth, rhinoceros—came out of Asia to enrich the new world, other animals like the camel originated in America and carried their wonderful capacities into Asia. And the intercontinental exchange which had the most remarkable consequences also moved westward across the bridge and into Asia.

One morning as Mastodon browsed among cottonwood trees near the edge of a swamp in central Alaska, he saw approaching from the south a line of animals much smaller than he had ever seen before. Like him, they walked on four feet; but unlike him, they had no tusks, no heavy covering of hair, no massive head or ponderous feet. They were sleek creatures, swift of movement, alert of eye, and he watched with ordinary animal interest and inspection as they approached. Not a single gesture, not one movement gave him any indication that they might be dangerous, so he allowed them to come near, stop, stare at him, and pass on.

They were horses, the new world's beautiful gift to the old, and they were on their wandering way into Asia, from where their descendants, thousands of years later, would fan out miraculously to all parts of Europe. How exquisite they were that morning as they passed Mastodon, pressing their way into the heartland of Alaska, where they would find a halting place on their long pilgrimage.

Nowhere else could the subtle relationships of nature be so intimately observed. Ice high, oceans low. Bridge open, passageway closed. The ponderous mastodon lumbering toward North America, the delicate horse moving toward Asia. Mastodon lurching toward inescapable extinction. The horse galloping to an enlarged life in France and Arabia. Alaska, its extremities girt in ice, served as a way station for all the travelers, regardless of the direction in which they headed. Its broad valleys free of ice and its invigorating climate provided a hospitable resting place. It really was an ice castle, and life within its frozen walls could be pleasant though demanding.

HOW SAD IT is to realize that most of these imposing animals we have been watching—as they lingered in Alaska during the last ice age and its intervals of friendly climate—passed into extinction, usually before the appearance of man. The great mastodons vanished, the fierce saber-tooth cats disappeared in mists that enclosed the bogs at whose edges they hunted. The rhinoceros flourished for a while, but then waddled slowly into oblivion. The lions could find no permanent niche in North America, and even the camel failed to flourish in the land of its origin. How much more enchanting North America would be if we had retained these great beasts to enliven the landscape, but it was not fated to be. They rested in Alaska for a while, then marched unknowingly to their doom.

Some of the immigrants did adjust, and their continued presence has made our land a livelier place: the beaver, the caribou, the stately moose, the bison and the sheep. But there was another splendid animal who crossed the bridge from Asia, and it survived long enough to coexist with man. It had a fighting chance to escape extinction, and the manner in which it fought that battle is an epic of the animal kingdom.

THE WOOLLY MAMMOTH came out of Asia much later than the mastodon and somewhat later than the animals of which we have been speaking. It arrived at a time of sharp transition when a relatively mild interval was ending and a harsher one beginning, but it adjusted so easily to its new environment that it thrived and multiplied, becoming one of the most successful examples of immigration and the archetypal Alaskan animal of this distant period.

Its remote ancestors had lived in tropical Africa, elephants of enormous size with long tusks and huge ears which they flapped constantly, using them as fans to keep their body temperature down. In Africa they browsed on low trees and pulled grass with their prehensile trunks. Admirably constructed for life in a tropical setting, they were magnificent beasts.

When such elephants moved slowly north they gradually converted themselves into creatures almost ideally suited to life in the high arctic zones. For example, their huge ears diminished in size to about one-twelfth of what they had been in the tropics, for now the animals did not require 'fanning' to enable them to live in great heat; they needed minimum exposure to the arctic winds that drained away their heat.

They also rid themselves of the smooth skin which had helped them keep cool in Africa, developing instead a thick covering of hair whose individual strands could be as long as forty inches; when they had been in the colder climates for several thousand years, they were so covered with this hair that they looked like unkempt walking blankets.

But not even that was enough to protect them from the icy blasts of winter Alaska—and remember that during the time we are now considering, the incursion of ice was at its maximum—so the mammoth, already covered with thick, protective hair, developed an invisible undergrowth of thick wool which augmented the hair so effectively that the mammoth could withstand incredibly low temperatures.

Internally also the mammoth changed. Its stomach adjusted to the different food supply of Beringia, the low, tough grasses, wonderfully nutritious when compared to the huge loose leafage of the African trees. Its bones grew smaller, so that the average mammoth, markedly smaller than the elephant, would expose less of its body to the cold. Its forequarters became much heavier than its hind and more elevated, so that it began to show a profile less like an elephant and more like a hyena: high in front, tapering off at the back.

In some ways the most dramatic change, but not the most functional, was what happened to its tusks. In Africa they had grown out of its upper jaw in roughly parallel form, curved downward, then moved straight ahead. They were formidable weapons and were so used when males contested for the right to keep females in their group. They were also useful in bending branches lower for browsing.

In arctic lands the tusks of the mammoth underwent spectacular change. For one thing, they became much larger than those of the African elephant, for in some cases they measured more than twelve feet. But what made them distinctive was that after starting straight forward and down, like the elephant's, they suddenly swept outward, far from the body, and down in a handsome sweep. Had they continued in this direction, they would have been enormous and powerful weapons for attack or defense, but just as this seemed to be their purpose, they arbitrarily swung back toward the central axis, until at last their tips met and sometimes actually crossed, far in front of the mammoth's face.

In this bizarre condition they served no constructive purpose; indeed, they hampered feeding in summer, but in winter they did have a minimal utility, for they could be used to sweep away snowdrifts so that mosses and lichens hiding below could be exposed for eating. Other animals, the bison for example, achieved the same result by merely pushing their big heads into the snow and swinging them from side to side.

Protected against the bitter cold of winter, adjusted to the plentiful forage of summer, the mammoth proliferated and dominated the landscape long after the much larger mastodon had vanished. Like all other animals of the early period, the mastodon had been subject to attack by the ferocious saber-tooth, but with the gradual extinction of that killer, the mammoth's only enemies were the lions and wolves that tried to steal young calves. Of course, when a mammoth grew old and feeble, packs of wolves could successfully chivvy it to death, but that was of no consequence, for if death had not come in that form, it would have in some other.

Mammoths lived to fifty or sixty years, with an occasional tough customer surviving into its seventies, and to a marked degree it was the animal's nature of death that has accounted for its fame. On numerous occasions in Siberia, Alaska and Canada—so numerous that statistical studies can be made—mammoths of both sexes and all ages stumbled into boggy pits where they perished, or were overcome by sudden floods bearing gravel, or died at the banks of rivers into which their carcasses fell.

If these accidental deaths occurred in spring or summer, predators, especially ravens, quickly disposed of the cadavers, leaving behind only stripped bones and perhaps long strings of hair, which soon vanished. Accumulations of such bones and tusks have been found at various places and have proved helpful in reconstructing what we know about the mammoth.

But if the accidental death took place in late autumn or early winter, there was always the possibility that the body of the dead animal would be quickly covered with a heavy layer of sticky mud that would freeze when hard winter came. Thus the corpse would be preserved in what amounted to a deep-freeze, with decay impossible. Most often, one has to suppose, spring and summer would bring a thaw; the protective mud would lose its ice crystals; and the dead body would decompose. Disintegration of the corpse would proceed as always, except that the freezing would have postponed it for a season.

However, on rare occasions, which could become quite numerous over a time span of a hundred thousand years, that first immediate freezing would for some reason or other become permanent, and now the dead body would be preserved intact for a thousand years, or thirty thousand, or fifty. And then, on some day far distant when humans ranged the valleys of central Alaska, some inquisitive man would see emerging from a thawing bank an object that was neither bone nor preserved wood, and when he dug into the bank he would find himself facing the total remains of a woolly mammoth that had perished in that bank thousands of years ago.

When the accumulation of viscous mud was carefully cleaned away, a remarkable object would be revealed, something unique in the world: a whole mammoth, long hair in place, great tusks twisting forward and meeting at the tips, stomach contents in the condition they were when it last grazed, massive teeth in such perfect condition that its age at death could be accurately calculated within five or six years. It was not, of course, a standing animal, plump and clean within a case of blue ice; it was flat, plastered with mud, disgracefully dirty, with leg joints beginning to come apart, but it was a complete mammoth, and it revealed to its discoverers a volume of information.

This next point is important. We know about the great dinosaurs who preceded the mammoth by millions of years because their bones have over the millennia been invaded by mineral deposits which have preserved the most intimate structure of the bone. What we have are not real bones, but petrified ones, like petrified wood, in which not an atom of the original material remains. Until a recent find in far northern Alaska, no human being had ever seen the bone of a dinosaur, but everyone could see in museums the magically preserved petrifications of those bones, photographs in stone of bones long since vanished.

But with the mammoths preserved by freezing in Siberia and Alaska, we have the actual bones, the hair, the heart, the stomach, and a treasury of knowledge that is incomparable. The first of these icy finds seems to have occurred by accident in Siberia sometime in the 1700s, and others have followed at regular intervals thereafter. A remarkably complete mammoth was uncovered near Fairbanks in Alaska not long ago, and we can anticipate others before the end of the century.

Why has it been the mammoth who has been found in this complete form? Other animals have occasionally been uncovered, but not many and rarely in the excellent condition of the best mammoths. One reason was the substantial numbers of the breed. Another was that the mammoth tended to live in those peculiar areas in which preservation by freezing mud was possible. Also, its bones and tusks were of a size to be noted; many birds must have perished in these areas in these times, but because they had no heavy bones, their skeletons did not survive to keep their skin and feathers in position. Most important, this particular group of mammoths died during a time of glaciation when instant freezing was not only possible but likely.

At any rate, the woolly mammoth served a unique function, one of inestimable value to human beings; by freezing quickly when it died, it lived on to instruct us as to what life was like in Alaska when the ice castle functioned as a refuge for great animals.

O N A DAY in late winter, twenty-nine thousand years ago, Matriarch, a mammoth grandmother, forty-four years old and beginning to show her age, led the little herd of six for which she was responsible down a softly rolling meadow to the banks of a great river later to be known as the Yukon. Lifting her trunk high to sniff the warming air and signaling the others to follow, she entered a grove of willow shrubs that lined the river, and when the others had taken their places beside her, she indicated that they might begin feeding on the sprouting tips of willow branches. They did so with a great deal of noise and movement, for they were glad to escape the meager rations they had been forced to subsist on during the recent winter, and as they gorged, Matriarch gave grunts of encouragement.

She had in her herd two daughters, each of whom had two offspring, heifer and bull to the elder, bull and heifer to the younger. Severe discipline on these six was enforced by Matriarch, for the mammoths had learned that the survival of their species did not depend very much on the great males with their tremendous showy tusks; the males appeared only in midsummer for the mating period; the rest of the year they were nowhere to be seen, so they took no responsibility for rearing and educating the young.

In obedience to the instincts of her race, and to the specific impulses which stemmed from her being female, she devoted her entire life to her herd, especially to the young. She weighed, at this time, about three thousand pounds, and to keep alive she required each day some hundred and sixty pounds of grass, lichen, moss and twigs, and when she lacked this ample supply of food she experienced pangs of biting hunger, for what she ate contained only minimum nourishment and passed completely through her body in less than twelve hours; she did not gorge and then ruminate like other animals, chewing her cud until every shred of value was extracted from it. No, she crammed herself with vast amounts of low-quality food and quickly rid herself of its remains. Eating had to be her main preoccupation.

Nevertheless, if in her constant foraging she caught even a hint that her four grandchildren were not getting their share, she would forgo her own feeding and see to it that they ate first. And she would do the same for young mammoths who were not of her own family but under her care for the moment while their own mothers and grandmothers foraged elsewhere. Even though her stomach contracted in emptiness and pain—with warning signals shouting 'Eat or perish!'—she would first attend to her young, and only when they had been provided with grass and twigs would she browse the birch tips and harvest the good grasses with her noble trunk.

This characteristic, which separated her from the other mammoth grandmothers, had developed because of her monomaniacal affection for her children. Years ago, before her youngest daughter had borne her first offspring, a once-prepotent older bull joined her herd during the mating season, and for some inexplicable reason, when the mating was completed, he remained with the herd when normally he should have left to join the other bulls who foraged by themselves until the next mating season came around.

Although Matriarch had made no objection when this old bull first appeared on the scene to care for her daughters—three at that time—she grew restless when he stayed beyond his welcome period, and by various ways, such as nudging him away from the better grass, she indicated that he must leave the females and their children. When he refused to comply, she grew actively angry, but she could do nothing more than show her feelings, because he weighed half again as much as she, his tusks were enormous, and he was so much taller that he simply overwhelmed her in both size and aggressiveness. So she had to be content with making noises and venting her displeasure by rapidly thrashing her trunk about.

But one day as she was eying this old fellow, she saw him roughly shove aside a young mother who was instructing her yearling daughter, and this would have been acceptable, for bulls traditionally commandeered the better feeding grounds, but on this occasion it looked to Matriarch as if the bull had also abused the yearling, and this she could not tolerate. With a high, piercing scream she lunged right at the intruder, disregarding his superior size and fighting ability—for he could not have bred Matriarch's daughters had he not been able to fend off other less able bulls who had also wished to do so—and she was so intent on protecting her young, that she drove the much bigger animal back several paces.

But he, with his greater strength and immense crossing tusks, quickly asserted his authority, and in a punishing counterattack, slashed at her with such great force that he broke her right tusk at about the halfway mark. For the rest of her life she would be an aging mammoth cow with a tusk and a half. Unbalanced, awkward-looking when compared to her sisters, she moved across the steppe with the short, jagged tusk, and the loss of its balancing weight caused her to compensate by tilting her massive head slightly to the right, as if she were peeking with her squinty little eyes at something that others could not see.

She had never been a lovely creature or even a graceful one. She did not have the impressive lines of her elephant forebears, for she was a kind of lumbering triangle, apex at the top of her high-domed head, base along the ground where her feet hit, a vertical coming down in front of her face and trunk, and most distinctive, a long, sloping, ugly drop from high forequarters to a dwarfed rear end. And then, as if to make her appearance almost formless, her entire body was covered with long and sometimes matted hair. If she was a walking triangle, she was also an ambulating shaggy rug, and even the dignity that could have come from her big, graceful tusks was lost because of the broken right one.

True, she lacked grace, but her passionate love for any younger mammoth who fell under her protection endowed her with a nobility of manner, and this huge and awkward creature lent honor to the concept of animal motherhood.

* * *

SHE HAD AT her disposal in these years when the ice age was at its maximum, a somewhat more hospitable terrain on which to feed her family than the harsher one the mastodons had known. It was still a four-part terrain: arctic desert at the north, perpetually frozen tundra, steppe rich with grasses, strip with enough trees to be called a woodland or even a forest. However, it was the steppe that had grown in size, until its mixture of edible grasses and nutritious willow shrubs provided ample forage for the mammoths who roamed it.

Indeed, the expanded area proved so hospitable to these huge, lumbering creatures that later scientists who would try to reconstruct what life in Alaska was like twenty-eight thousand years before would give the terrain the descriptive name 'the Mammoth Steppe,' and no better could be devised, for this was the great, brooding steppe, trapped within the ice castle, which enabled the slope-backed mammoths to exist in large numbers. In these centuries it looked as if the mammoths, along with the caribou and antelope, would always be the major occupiers of the steppe named after them.

Matriarch moved about the steppe as if it had been created for her use alone. It was hers, but she conceded that for a few weeks each summer she required the assistance of the great bulls who otherwise kept to themselves on their own feeding grounds. But after the birth of the young she knew that the survival of the mammoths depended upon her, so it was she who chose the feeding grounds and gave the signal when her family must abandon grounds about to be depleted in a search for others more rich in foodstuffs.

A small herd of mammoths like the one she commanded might wander, in the course of a year, over more than four hundred miles, so she came to know large parts of the steppe, and in the pilgrimages she supervised she became familiar with two perplexities, which she never solved but to which she did accommodate. The richer parts of this steppe provided a variety of edible trees whose ancestors the vanished mastodons might have known—larch, low willow, birch, alder—but recently, in a few choice spots protected from gales and where water was available, a new kind of tree had made its tentative appearance, beautiful to see but poisonous to eat. It was especially tempting because it never lost its leaves, long needlelike affairs, but even in winter when the mammoths had little to eat they avoided it, because if they did eat the attractive needles they fell sick and sometimes died.

It was the largest of the trees, a spruce, and its distinctive aroma both attracted and repelled the mammoths. Matriarch was bewildered by the spruce, for although she dared not eat its needles, she noticed that the porcupines who shared these forests with her devoured the poisonous leaves with relish, and she often wondered why. What she did not notice was that while it was true that the porcupines did eat the needles, they climbed high in the trees before doing so. The spruce, just as clever in protecting itself as the animals that surrounded it, had devised a sagacious defensive strategy. In its copious lower branches, which a voracious mammoth could have destroyed in a morning, the spruce concentrated a volatile oil which rendered its leaves unpalatable. This meant that the high upper branches, which the mammoths could not reach even with their long trunks, remained palatable.

In the few places where the spruce trees did thrive, they figured in the second riddle. From time to time during the long summers when the air was heavy and the grasses and low shrubs tinder-dry, a flash would appear in the heavens followed by a tremendous crashing sound, as if a thousand trees had fallen in one instant, and often thereafter fire would start in the grass, mysteriously, for no reason at all. Or some very tall spruce would be riven, as if a giant tusk had ripped it, and from its bark a wisp of smoke would issue, and then a little flame, and before long the entire forest would be ablaze and all the grassy steppe would erupt into flame.

At such moments, and Matriarch had survived six such fires, the mammoths had learned to head for the nearest river and submerge themselves to their eye-level, keeping their trunks above the water for air. For this reason lead animals, like Matriarch with her brood, tried always to know where the nearest water stood, and when fire exploded across their steppe they retreated to this refuge, for they had learned that if the fire ever completely surrounded them, escape would be improbable. Over the centuries a few daring bulls had broken through the fatal rim, and it was their experience which had taught the mammoths their strategy for survival.

Late one summer, when the land was especially dry, and darts of light and crashing sounds filled the air, Matriarch saw that fire had already started near a large stand of spruce trees, and she knew that before long the trees would burst forth in tremendous gusts of flame, trapping all living things, so with speed and force she herded her charges back to where she knew a river waited, but the fire spread so swiftly that it engulfed the trees before she could rush clear of them. Overhead she heard the oils in the trees explode, sending sparks down into the dry needles below. Soon both the crowns of the trees and the needled carpet below were aflame, and the mammoths faced death.

In this extremity, with acrid smoke tormenting her, Matriarch had to decide whether to lead her herd back out from among the trees or straight ahead toward the waiting river, and it could not be claimed that she reasoned: If I do turn back, the grass fire will soon entrap us. But she did make the right decision. Bellowing so that all could hear, she headed right for a wall of flame, broke through and found a clear path to the river, where her companions plunged into the saving water while the forest fire raged around them.

But now came the perplexing part, because Matriarch had learned that terrifying though the fire had been, she must not abandon this ravaged area, for fire was one of the best friends the mammoths had and she must now teach her young how to capitalize upon it. As soon as the actual flames abated—and they would consume several hundred square miles before they died completely—she led her charges back to the spot at which they had nearly lost their lives, and there she taught them how to use their tusks in stripping lengths of bark from the burned spruce trees. Now, purified by the fire which had driven off noxious oils, the spruce was not only edible but a positive delicacy, and the hungry mammoths gorged upon it. The bark had been toasted specifically for them.

When the fire was totally dead in all parts, Matriarch kept her herd close to the burned-over areas, for the mammoths had learned that rather quickly after such a conflagration, the roots of tenacious plants whose visible growth had been burned off sped the production of new shoots, thousands of them, and these were the finest food the mammoths ever found. What was even more important, ashes from the great fires fertilized the ground, making it more nutritious and more friable, so that young trees would grow with a vigor they would otherwise not have known. One of the best things that could happen to the Mammoth Steppe, with its mixture of trees and grass, was to have a periodic fire of great dimension, for in its aftermath, grasses, shrubs, trees and animals prospered.

It was puzzling that something as dangerous as fire, which Matriarch had barely escaped many times, should be the agency whereby she and her successors would grow strong. She did not try to solve this riddle; she protected herself from the dangers and luxuriated in the rewards.

In these years some mammoths elected to return to the Asia they had known in their early years, but Matriarch had no inclination to join them. The Alaska which she now knew so well was a congenial place which she had made her own. To leave would be unthinkable.

But in her fiftieth year changes began to occur which sent tremors, vague intimations, to her minute brain, and instinct warned her that these changes were not only irreversible, but also a caution that the time might be approaching when she would feel driven to wander off, leaving her family behind, as she sought some quiet place in which to die. She had, of course, no sense of death, no comprehension that life ended, no premonition that she must one day abandon her family and the steppes on which she found such ease. But mammoths did die, and in doing so they followed an ancient ritual which commanded them to move apart, as if by this symbolism they turned over to their successors the familiar steppe, and its rivers, and its willow trees.

What had happened to signal this new awareness? Like other mammoths, Matriarch had been supplied at birth with a complex dental system which would provide her, over the long span of her life, with twelve enormous flat composite teeth in each jaw. These twenty-four monstrous teeth did not appear in a mammoth's mouth all at one time, but this posed no difficulty; each tooth was so large that even one pair was adequate for chewing. At times as many as three pairs of these huge things might exist, and then chewing capacity was immense. But it did not remain this way for long, because as the years passed, each tooth moved irresistibly forward in the jaw, until it actually fell from the mouth, and when only the last two matching teeth remained in position, the mammoth sensed its days were numbered, because when the last pair began to disintegrate, continued life on the steppe would be impossible.

Matriarch now had four big matching pairs, but since she could feel them moving forward, she was aware that her time was limited.

WHEN THE MATING season began, bulls from far distances started to arrive, but the old bull who had broken Matriarch's right tusk was still so powerful a fighter that he succeeded, as in past years, to defend his claim on her daughters. He had not, of course, returned to this family year after year, but on various occasions he had come back, more to a familiar area than to a particular group of females.

This year his courtship of Matriarch's daughters was a perfunctory affair, but his effect upon the older child of the younger daughter, a sturdy young bull but not yet mature enough to strike out on his own, was remarkable, for the young fellow, watching the robust performance of the old bull, felt vague stirrings. One morning, when the old bull was attending to a young female not of Matriarch's family, this young bull unexpectedly, and without any premeditation, made a lunge for her, whereupon the old bull fell into a tantrum and chastised the young upstart unmercifully, butting and slamming him with those extremely long horns that crossed at the tips.

Matriarch, seeing this and not entirely aware of what had occasioned the outburst, dashed once again at the old bull, but this time he repelled her easily, knocking her aside so that he could continue his courtship of the strange heifer. In time he left the herd, his duty done, and disappeared as always into the low hills footing the glacier. He would be seen no more for ten months, but he left behind not only six pregnant cows but also a very perplexed young bull, who within the year should be doing his own courting. However, long before this could take place, the young bull wandered into a stand of aspen trees near the great river, where one of the last saber-tooth cats to survive in Alaska waited in the crotch of a larch tree, and when the bull came within reach, the cat leaped down upon him, sinking those dreadful scimitar teeth deep into his neck.

The bull had no chance to defend himself; this first strike was mortal, but in his death agony he did release one powerful bellow that echoed across the steppe. Matriarch heard it, and although she knew the young bull to be of an age when he should be leaving the family, he was still under her care, and without hesitating, she galloped as fast as her awkward hair-covered body would permit, speeding directly toward the saber-tooth, who was crouching over its dead prey.

When she spotted it she knew instinctively that it was the most dangerous enemy on this steppe, and she knew it had the power to kill her, but her fury was so great that any thought of caution was submerged. One of the young mammoths for whom she was responsible had been attacked, and she knew but one response: to destroy the attacker if possible, and if not, to give her life in an attempt. So with a trumpeting cry of rage she rushed in her clumsy way at the saber-tooth, who easily evaded her. But to its surprise she wheeled about with such frenzied determination that it had to leave the corpse on which it was about to feed, and as it did so it found itself backed against the trunk of a sturdy larch. Matriarch, seeing the cat in this position, threw her entire weight forward, endeavoring to pin it with her tusks or otherwise impede it.

Now the broken right tusk, big and blunt, proved an asset rather than a liability, for with it she did not merely puncture the saber-tooth, she crushed it against the tree, and as she felt her heavy tusk dig into its rib cage, she bore ahead, unmindful of what the fierce cat might do to her.

The stump had injured the saber-tooth, but despite its broken left ribs it retained control and darted away lest she strike again. But before the cat could muster its resources for a counterattack, she used her unbroken left tusk to batter it into the dust at the foot of the tree. Then, with a speed it could not anticipate or avoid, she raised her immense foot and stomped upon its chest.

Again and again, trumpeting the while, she beat down upon the mighty cat, collapsing its other ribs and even breaking off one of the long, splendid saber-teeth. Seeing blood spurting from one of its wounds, she became wild with fury, her shrieks increasing when she saw the inert body of her grandson, the young bull, lying in the grass. Continuing in her mad stomping, she crushed the saber-tooth, and when her rage was assuaged she remained, whimpering, between the two dead bodies.

As in the case of her own destiny, she was not completely aware of what death was, but the entire elephant clan and its derivatives were perplexed by death, especially when it struck down a fellow creature with whom the mourner had been associated. The young bull was dead, of that there could be no doubt, and in some vague way she realized that his wonderful potential was lost. He would not come courting in the summers ahead; he would fight no aging bulls to establish his authority; and he would sire no successors with the aid of Matriarch's daughters and granddaughters. A chain was broken, and for more than a day she stood guard over his body, as if she hoped to bring it back to life. But at the close of the second day she left the bodies, unaware that in all that time she had not once looked at the saber-tooth. It was her grandson who mattered, and he was dead.

Because his death occurred in late summer, with decomposition setting in immediately and with ravens and predators attacking the corpse, it was not fated that his body be frozen in mud for the edification of scientists scores of thousands of years later, but there was another death that occurred during the last days of autumn which had quite different consequences.

The old bull that had broken Matriarch's tusk, and had been a prime factor in the death of the young bull, strode away from the affair looking as if he had the strength to survive for many mating seasons to come. But the demands of this one had been heavy. He had run with more cows than usual and had been called upon to defend them against four or five lusty younger bulls who felt that their time to assume control had come. For an entire summer he had lusted and fought and eaten little, and now in late autumn his vital resources began to flag.

It began with dizziness as he climbed a bank leading up from the great river. He had made such treks repeatedly, but this time he faltered and almost fell against the muddy bank that impeded his progress. Then he lost the first of his remaining four teeth, and he was aware that two of the others were weakening. Even more serious was his indifference to the approaching winter, for normally he would have begun to eat extravagantly in order to build his reserves of fat against the cold days when snow fell. To ignore this imperative call of 'Feed thyself, for blizzards are at hand!' was to endanger his life, but that is what he did.

On the day of the first snowfall, a whipping wind blowing in from Asia and icicles of snow falling parallel to the earth, Matriarch and her five family members saw the old bull far in the distance, at what would later be known as the Birch Tree Site, his head lowered, his massive tusks resting on the ground, but they ignored him. Nor were they concerned about his safety; that was his problem and they knew he had many options from which to choose.

But when they saw him again, some days later, not moving toward a refuge or to a feeding ground, just standing there immobile, Matriarch, always the caring mother, started to move toward him to see if he was able to fend for himself. However, when he saw her intruding upon his satisfactory loneliness, he withdrew to protect it, not hurriedly, as he might have done in the old days, but laboriously, making sounds of protest at her presence. She did not force herself upon him, for she knew that old bulls like him preferred to be left alone, and she last saw him heading back toward the river.

Two days later, when thick snow was falling and Matriarch started edging her family toward the alder thickets in which they customarily took shelter during the long winters, her youngest granddaughter, an inquisitive animal, was off by herself exploring the banks of the river when she saw that the same bull who had spent much of the summer with them had fallen into a muddy crevice and was thrashing about, unable to extricate himself. Trumpeting a call for help, she alerted the others, and before long Matriarch, her daughters and her grandchildren were streaming toward the site of the accident.

When they arrived, the position of the old bull was so hopeless, mired as he was in sticky mud, that Matriarch and her assistants were powerless to aid him. And as both the snow and the cold increased, they had to watch helplessly as the tired mammoth struggled vainly, trumpeting for aid and succumbing finally to the irresistible pull of the mud and the freezing cold. Before nightfall he was tightly frozen into his muddy grave, only the top of his bulbous head showing, and by morning that too was buried under snow. There he would remain, miraculously upright for the next twenty-eight thousand years, the spiritual guardian of the Birch Tree Site.

* * *

MATRIARCH, OBEDIENT TO impulses that had always animated the mammoth breed, remained by his grave for two days, but then, still puzzled by the fact of death, she forgot him completely, rejoined her family, and led them to one of the best spots in central Alaska for passing a long winter. It was an enclave at the western end of the valley which was fed by two streams, a small one that froze quickly and a much larger one that carried free water most of the winter. Here, protected from even the worst winds, she and her daughters and grandchildren remained motionless much of the time, conserving body warmth and slowing digestion of such food as they could find.

Now once more her broken tusk proved useful, for its rough, blunt end was effective in ripping the bark from birch trees whose leaves had long vanished, and it was also helpful in brushing away snow to reveal the grasses and herbs hiding below. She was not aware that she was trapped in a vast ice castle, for she had no desire to move either eastward into what would one day be Canada or southward to California. Her icy prison was enormous in size and she felt in no way penned in, but when the frozen ground began to thaw and the willows sent forth tentative shoots, she did become aware—how she could not have explained—that some great change had overtaken the refuge areas which she had for so many years dominated. Perhaps it was her acute sense of smell, or sounds never heard before, but regardless of how the message reached her, she knew that life on the Mammoth Steppe had been altered, and not for the better.

Her awareness intensified when she lost one of her remaining teeth, and then one evening as she wandered westward with her family, she came upon a sight that confused her weak eyes. On the banks of the river she had been following stood a structure like none she had ever seen before. It was like a bird's nest on the ground, but hugely bigger. From it came animals who walked on only two legs; they were like water birds that prowled the shore, but much larger, and now one of them, seeing the mammoths, began to make noises. Others poured from the immense nest, and she could see that her presence was causing great excitement, for they made unfamiliar sounds.

Then some of the creatures, much smaller than herself or even the youngest of her grandchildren, began running toward her, and the speed with which they moved alerted her to the fact that she and her herd were about to face some kind of new danger. Instinctively she began to edge away, then to move rapidly, and finally to trumpet wildly as she started running.

But very quickly she found that she was not free to move as she wished, for no matter where she tried to go with her charges, one of the creatures appeared in the shadows to prevent her from escaping. And when day dawned, confusion intensified, for wherever Matriarch sought to take her family, these beings kept pace, persistently, like wolves tracking a wounded caribou. They would not stop, and when that first night fell they added to the terror by causing a fire to spring from the tundra, and this created panic among the mammoths, for they expected the dried grass of the previous summer to burst into uncontrollable flame, but this did not happen. Matriarch, looking at her children in perplexity, was not able to form the idea: They have fire but it is not fire, but she felt the bewilderment that such an idea would have evoked.

On the next day the strange new things continued to pursue Matriarch and her mammoths, and when the animals were exhausted, the newcomers finally isolated Matriarch's youngest granddaughter. Once the young animal was cut off, the pursuers closed in upon her, carrying in their front legs, the ones they did not use for walking, branches of trees with stones attached, and with these they began to beat the encircled mammoth and stab at her and torment her until she bellowed for help.

Matriarch, who had outrun her children, heard the cry and doubled back, but when she tried to aid her granddaughter, some of these creatures detached themselves from the larger group and beat her about the head with their branches until she had to withdraw. But now the cries of her granddaughter became so pitiful that Matriarch trembled with rage, and with a mighty bellow, dashed right through the attackers, and without stopping, lumbered to where the threatened mammoth was striving to defend herself. With a great roar, Matriarch flung herself upon the creatures, lashing at them with her broken tusk and driving them back.

Triumphant, she was about to lead her frightened granddaughter to safety when one of the strange beings shouted the sound 'Varnak!' and another, a little taller than the others and heavier, leaped toward the threatened mammoth, allowed himself to fall beneath her dangerous feet, and with an upward stab of whatever he was carrying, drove a sharp weapon deep into her bowels.

Matriarch saw that her granddaughter was not fatally wounded, but as the mammoths thundered off, seeking respite from their tormentors, it was obvious that the young one was not going to be able to keep up. So the herd slowed, and Matriarch assisted her granddaughter, and in this way the huge beasts made their escape.

But to their dismay, the little figures on two legs kept pace, coming closer and closer, and on the third day, at an unguarded moment when Matriarch was directing the others to safety, the creatures surrounded the wounded grand-daughter. Intending to crush these intruders once and for all, Matriarch started back to defend her grandchild, but as she strove to reach the attackers and punish them with her broken tusk, as she had done with the saber-tooth, one of them, armed only with a long piece of wood and a short one with fire at one end, stepped boldly out from among the trees and drove her back. The long piece of wood she could resist even though it had sharp stones on the end, but the fire, thrust right into her face, she could not. Try as she might, she could not avoid that burning ember. Impotently she had to stand back, smoke and fire in her eyes, as her granddaughter was slain.

With loud shouts, much like the triumphant howling of wolves when they finally brought down their wounded prey, the creatures danced and leaped about the fallen mammoth and began to cut her up.

From a distance that night, Matriarch and her remaining children saw once again the fire that mysteriously flamed without engulfing the steppe, and in this confusing, tragic way the mammoths who had for so long been safe within their ice castle encountered man.

III

PEOPLE OF THE NORTH

Some twenty-nine thousand years B.P.E.—Before the Present Era, which means before the reference year A.D. 1950, when carbon dating became established as a reliable system for dating prehistoric events—in that eastern projection of Asia which would later be known as Siberia, famine was rampant, and it struck nowhere with more ferocity than in a mud hut that faced the sunrise. There, in one big room excavated a few feet below the level of the surrounding earth, a family of five faced the coming winter with only a small store of food and little hope of finding more.

Their house provided no comfort except a slight protection from the howling winds of winter, which blew almost constantly through the half of the structure which rose aboveground and was formed of loosely woven branches plastered with mud. This hovel was no more than a cave-hut, but it did provide one essential: in the middle of the floor there was a place for fire, and here half-wet logs gave off the smoke which lent flavor to what they ate and endless irritation to their eyes.

The five people huddling in this miserable abode as autumn ended were headed by a resolute man named Varnak, one of the ablest hunters in the village of Nurik, who had as wife the woman Tevuk, twenty-four years old and the mother of two sons who would soon be able to join their father in his chase for animals whose meat would feed the family. But this year animals had grown so scarce that in some cave-huts the younger people were beginning to whisper: 'Perhaps there will be food only for the young ones, and it will be time for the old ones to go.'

Varnak and Tevuk would hear none of this, for although they had a very old woman to care for, she was so precious to them that they would starve themselves rather than deprive her. She was known as the Ancient One, Varnak's mother, and he was determined to help her live out her life because she was the wisest person in the village, the only one who could remind the young of their heroic heritage. 'Others say "Let the old ones die," ' he whispered to his wife one night, 'but I have no mind to do so.'

'Nor I,' Tevuk replied, and since she had no mother or aunts of her own, she knew that what her husband was saying applied only to his own mother, but she was prepared to stand by this resolute old woman for as long as life remained. This would be difficult, for the Ancient One was not easy to placate and the burden of tending her would fall almost solely on Tevuk, but the bond of debt between the two women was great and indissoluble.

When Varnak had been a young man, searching about for a wife, he fastened his attention upon a young woman of rare attractiveness, one who was courted by various men, but his mother, a woman who had lost her husband early in a hunting accident while chasing the woolly mammoth, saw clearly that her son would come to harm if he tied himself to that woman, and she launched a campaign to make him appreciate how much better his life would be if he allied himself with Tevuk, a somewhat older woman of common sense and unusual capacity for work.

Varnak, captivated by the younger, had resisted his mother's counsel and was about to take the seductive one, when the Ancient One barred the exit from their hut and would not allow her son to leave for three days until she was assured that some other man had captured the enchantress: 'She weaves a spell, Varnak. I saw her gathering moss and searching for antlers to pulverize. I'm protecting you from her.'

He was disconsolate at losing the wonderful one, and it was some time before he was prepared to listen to his mother, but when his anger subsided he was able to look at Tevuk with clear eyes and he saw that his mother was right. Tevuk was going to be as helpful when an old woman of forty as she was now: 'She's the kind who grows stronger with the seasons, Varnak. Like me.' And Varnak had discovered this to be true.

Now, in this difficult time when there was almost no food in the cave-hut, Varnak became doubly appreciative of his two good women, for his wife searched the land for the merest scrap for their two sons, while his mother gathered not only her grandsons but also the other children of the village to take their minds off hunger by telling them of the heroic traditions of their tribe: 'In the long ago our people lived in the south where there were many trees and animals of all kinds to eat. Do you know what south means?'

'No.' And in freezing darkness as winter clamped down she told them: 'It's warm, my grandmother told me. And it has no endless winter.'

'Why did those people come to this land?'

This was a problem which had always perplexed the Ancient One, and she dealt with it according to her vague understandings: 'There are strong people and weak. My son Varnak is very strong, you know that. And so is Toorak, the man who killed the great bison. But when our people lived in the south, they were not strong, and others drove us out of those good lands. And when we moved north to lands not so good, they drove us out of there, too. One summer we came here, and it was beautiful, and everyone danced, my grandmother said. But then what happened?'

She asked this of a girl eleven seasons old, who said: 'Then winter came,' and the old one said: 'Yes, winter came.'

She was surprisingly correct in her summary of the clan's history, and of mankind's. Human life had originated in hot, steaming climates where it was easy to survive, but as soon as sufficient people were assembled to make competition for living space inevitable—say after a million years—the abler groups started to edge northward toward the more temperate zone, and in this more equable climate they began to invent those agencies of control, such as seasonal agriculture and the husbandry of animals, which would make superior forms of civilization possible.

And then once more, in the time of the Ancient One's great-great-great-grandmother, or even further back, competition for favorable sites recurred, but now it was the less able who were forced to move on, leaving the most fit to hold on to the temperate zones. This meant that in the Northern Hemisphere the subarctic areas began to be filled with people who had been evicted from the more congenial climates. Always the pressure came from the warmer lands to the south, and always it ended with people along the edges being forced to live on cold and arid lands which could barely support them.

But there was another interpretation of this movement to the north, and the Ancient One related it proudly to her children: 'There were brave men and women who loved cold lands and the hunt for mammoths and caribou. They liked the endless days of summer and were not afraid of winter nights like this.' Looking at each of her listeners, she tried to instill in them a pride in their ancestors: 'My son is a brave man like that and so is Toorak, who killed the bison, and so must you be when you grow up and go out to fight the mammoths.'

The old woman was right about many of the men who came north. They thrilled to their contests with whale and walrus. They were eager to do battle with the white polar bear and the woolly mammoth. They fought the seal for his fur so that they might survive the arctic winters, and they mastered the secrets of ice and snow and sudden blizzards. They devised ways of combating the ferocious mosquitoes that attacked in sun-darkening hordes each spring, and they taught their sons how to track animals for fur and food so that life could continue after they were dead. 'These are the true people of the north,' the old woman said, and she might have added that a hardier breed never existed on this earth.

'I want you to be like them,' she concluded, and one of the girls began to whimper: 'I'm hungry,' and the Ancient One took from the sealskin tunic she wore in winter a piece of dried seal blubber and apportioned it among the children, retaining none for herself.

One day at the turning of the seasons, when there was practically no daylight in the village, the old woman almost lost courage, for one of the children who had gathered in the dark hut to hear her tales asked: 'Why don't we go back to the south, where there's food?' and in honesty she had to reply: 'The old people often asked that question, and sometimes they pretended to themselves and said: "Yes, next year we will go back," but they never meant it. We cannot go back. You cannot go back. You are now people of the north.'

She never considered her life in the north a penalty, nor would she allow her son or her grandchildren to think of it in that way, but as the hellish days of winter closed down—when days lengthened but cold increased and ice grew thicker—she would wait till the children were asleep, and then whisper to her hungry son and his wife: 'Another winter like this and we will all die,' for even now they existed by chewing sealskin, which provided them little energy.

'Where will we go?' her son asked, and she said: 'My father spent four days chasing a mammoth once. It led him east across the barren lands, and over there he saw fields of green.'

'Why not go south?' Tevuk asked, and the old woman told her daughter-in-law: 'The south never had a place for us. I'm finished with the south.'

So in those tantalizing days of early spring when winter refused to stop tormenting these people at the western end of the land bridge, the fine hunter Varnak, seeing his family slowly dying of hunger, began asking about the land to the east, and he came upon a very old man who told him: 'One morning when I was young and with nothing better to do, I wandered eastward, and when night came with the sun still high in the heavens, for it was summer, I felt no need to return home, so on and on I went for two more days, and on the third day I saw something which excited me.'

'What?' Varnak asked, and the old man said, eyes aglimmer as if the incident had occurred three days ago: 'The body of a dead mammoth.' He allowed Varnak time to fathom the significance of this revelation, and when nothing was said, he explained: 'If a mammoth saw reason to cross that bleak land, men would have a reason too,' to which Varnak said: 'Yes, but you said the mammoth died,' and the man laughed: 'True, but there was a reason for him to try. And you have just as good a reason. For if you remain here, you will starve.'

'If I go, will you go with me?' and the man said: 'I am too old. But you . . .' And that day Varnak informed the four members of his family: 'When summer comes we shall go where the sun rises.'

The route he would take had been available for the past two thousand years, and although some had used the bridge, they had not found it inviting. Across its six-hundred-mile width north to south harsh winds blew so constantly that no trees or even low shrubs had been able to establish themselves, while grasses and mosses were so sparse that big animals could not find forage. In winter the cold was so forbidding that even hares and rats stayed underground, and few men ventured upon the bridge, even in summer. Settled life upon it was unthinkable.

But it was by no means unpassable, since from west to east, the direction in which Varnak's people would be traveling if they attempted the crossing, the distance would be no more than sixty miles. Varnak, of course, did not know this; it could have been eight hundred miles, but all that he had heard of attempts to cross it led him to believe that it was shorter. 'We'll leave when day and night are even,' he informed his mother, and she approved of the plan so heartily that she spread the news throughout the village.

When it was known that Varnak was going to try to find food to the east, there was excited discussion in the cave-huts and several of the men concluded that they would be wise to accompany him. So as spring progressed, four or five families began to weigh seriously the possibility of emigrating, and in the end three came to Varnak with the firm promise: 'We'll go too.'

On that day in March which Varnak had selected, the one when day and night were equal in all parts of the earth, Varnak, Tevuk, their two sons and the Ancient One prepared to set forth, accompanied by three other hunters, their wives and their eight children.

When the nineteen gathered at the eastern edge of their village, they were formidable in appearance, since the men wore such massive pieces of fur clothing that they looked like hulking animals. They carried long pikes as if going to war, and their rumpled black hair drooped low above their eyes. Their skin was a dark yellow and their eyes a sparkling black, so that when they stared this way and that, as they often did, they seemed as predacious as eagles.

The five women had different styles of dress, featuring decorated skins with seashells along the hems, but their faces were surprisingly alike. Each was heavily tattooed with vertical blue stripes, some covering the chin, others running the length of the face beside the ears, which were pierced for rings carved from white ivory. When they moved, even the old woman, they did so with determined steps, and as the four sleds on which each family's goods would be carried were brought into position, it was these women who grasped the reins and prepared to do the hauling.

The ten children were like a collection of colorful flowers, for the clothes they wore were varied in design and color. Some wore short tunics with stripes of white and blue, others long robes and heavy boots, but all wore in their hair some ornament, some flashing bit of shell or ivory.

Any item of clothing was precious, for men had risked their lives to harvest the hides and women had toiled tanning them and preparing sinews for sewing. A pair of men's trousers stitched so carefully that they kept out cold and water would be expected to last most of an adult lifetime, and only a few men on this peninsula would ever own two such garments.

Most important, however, were the boots, some of which reached to the knee; each group of families had to have some woman skilled in making boots from heavy hides, or the male members of that group would freeze their feet when they hunted on ice. And this was another reason why Varnak wanted to keep his mother alive: she was the ablest maker of boots the village had known in two generations, for although her fingers were no longer nimble, they were strong and could still pull reindeer sinews through the thickest seal hide.

The men of this expedition were not tall. Varnak, the biggest, stood only five feet six, with the others noticeably shorter. None of the women was much over five feet, and the Ancient One was sharply under that mark. The children were small, the three babies tiny except for their big round heads, but when dressed in heavy clothing the young ones were balls of fur with insatiable appetites.

On small sleds with runners of antler and bone, the travelers dragged behind them the pitiful supply of artifacts their people had collected during ten thousand years of life in the arctic: ultraprecious bone needles, skins not yet sewn into clothing, shallow bowls carved from heavy wood or bone, longhandled cooking spoons of ivory; no furniture of any kind, but sleeping pads for everyone and fur blankets for each family.

But they did not leave Asia with only these meager physical possessions; in their heads they carried an extraordinary understanding of the north. Men and women alike knew hundreds of rules for surviving an arctic winter, scores of useful hints about finding food in summer. They knew the nature of wind and the movement of those stars which guided them in the long winter night. They had various tricks for protecting themselves from the mosquitoes, which would otherwise have driven them mad, and above all, they knew the traits of animals, and how to track them, kill them, and use even their hoofs when the slaughter was completed.

The Ancient One and the four young wives knew fifty different ways of utilizing a slain mammoth whenever their menfolk were lucky enough to bring one down, and at a killing the Ancient One was first at the carcass, screaming at the men to cut the body this way and that so as to ensure that she received the bones she needed for making more needles.

On their four sleds and in their minds they carried one other precious commodity without which no group of people can long survive: on the sled, tucked away in protected places, they brought with them bits of iridescent shell, or pieces of precious ivory carved in curious ways, or smoothed pebbles of attractive dimension. Such trinkets were in some ways more valuable than any other part of the cargo, because some of the memorabilia spoke of the spirits who supervised the life of humans, some referred to the lucky management of animals, assuring that food would be at hand when needed, some to the placation of great storms so that hunters would not be lost in blizzards, and certain pebbles and shells were treasured merely for their uncommon beauty. For example, the Ancient One kept in her secret hiding place the first bone needle she had ever used. It was not so long now as it once had been, and its original whiteness had aged to a soft gold, but its supreme utility through generations had invested it with such beauty that her heart expanded with the great joy of life whenever she saw it among her few possessions.

These Chukchis who walked to Alaska twenty-nine thousand years ago were a complete people. Their foreheads may have been low, their hairline close to their eyes, and their movements sometimes apelike, but people exactly like them in southern Europe were already creating immortal art on the ceilings and walls of their caves, composing chants for the fire at night, and creating stories that represented their life experience. If Varnak's people brought with them no physical furniture, they did bring a mental equipment which fitted them for the tasks they were about to face. If they brought no written language, they did bring into the arctic desert and steppe an understanding of the land, a respect for the animals that shared it with them, and an intimate appreciation of the wonders that occurred in any passing year. In later eons other men and women of comparable courage and ability would venture into their unfamiliar lands with a mental equipment no more competent than what these Asian stragglers carried in their dark heads.

Because emigrations like theirs would produce such tremendous consequences in world history—the opening up of two entire continents to the human race—certain limitations must be noted. Varnak and his companions were never conscious of leaving one continent to enter another; they could not have been aware that such landmasses existed, and had they been, they would have seen that in their day Alaska was far more a part of Asia than of North America. Nor would they have been interested in knowing that they were crossing a bridge, for the difficult land they were traversing certainly did not resemble one. And finally, they were impelled by no strong sense of emigration; their complete journey would cover only sixty miles, and as Varnak reminded them on the morning they left: 'If things are no better there, we can always return next summer.'

But despite these limitations, had there been a muse of history recording this fateful day, she might have looked down from her Olympus and exulted: 'How majestic! Nineteen little people bundled in furs moving onto the doorstep of two empty continents.'

B Y THE END of their first day, it was apparent to all the travelers except the very young that this journey was going to be extremely difficult, for in the course of that entire day they saw not a single living thing except low grasses which were permanently bent by the ceaseless wind. No birds flew; no animals watched the untidy procession; no streams flowed, with small fish huddled along their banks. Compared to the relatively rich land they had known before the hunger time struck, this was bleak and forbidding, and when they pitched their sleds against the wind that night, the runners worn from having no snow to glide upon, they could not avoid realizing what a perilous trip they were attempting.

The second day was no worse but the impact was, because the travelers could not know that they had at the most only five days of this before they reached the slightly improved terrain of Alaska; they were wandering into the unknown, and so it remained for the next two days. In all that time they came upon nothing they could eat, and the meager stores they had been able to bring with them were nearly depleted.

'Tomorrow,' Varnak said, as they huddled in the bare lee of their sleds on the third night, 'we shall eat none of our stores. Because I feel certain that on the next day we shall come to better land.'

'If the land is to be better,' one of the men asked, 'why not trust that we shall find food there?' and Varnak reasoned: 'If the food is there, we shall have to be strong enough to run it down, and fight it when we overtake it, and dare much. And to do all that, we must have food in our bellies.'

So on the fourth day no one ate anything, and mothers held their hungry children and tried to comfort them. In the warmth of the growing spring they all survived that trying day, and on the late afternoon of the fifth day, after Varnak and another had run ahead, drawing upon their courage and the spare fat from other days, they returned with the exciting news that yes, in another day's march there was better land. And that night, before the sun went down, Varnak distributed the last of the food. Everyone ate slowly, chewing until teeth met on almost nothingness, then savoring each morsel as it vanished down the throat. During the next days they must find animals, or perish.

In midafternoon of the sixth day, a river appeared, with reassuring shrubs along its banks, and on the spur of the moment Varnak announced: 'We camp here,' for he knew that if they could not find something to eat in such a favorable location, they had no hope. So the sleds were brought into position and over them the hunters raised a kind of low tent, informing the women and children that this was to be their home for the present. And to firm their decision to wander no farther until they found food, they started a small fire to keep away the insistent mosquitoes.

In the early evening of this day the youngest of the grown men spotted a family of mammoths feeding along the riverbanks: a matriarch with a broken right tusk, two younger females and three much younger animals. They remained motionless, well to the east, and even when Varnak and five other Chukchis ran out to watch, the animals merely stood and stared, then turned back to their grazing.

In the growing darkness Varnak assumed control: 'Tonight we must surround the beasts, one man in each direction. When dawn breaks we shall be in position to cut one of the younger animals off from the rest. That one we will run to earth.' The others agreed, and Varnak, as the most experienced, said: 'I will run to the east, to head off the mammoths if they try to return to some homeland pasturage,' but he did not move in a direct line, for that would have carried him too close to the animals. Instead, he plunged into the river, swam across, and went well inland before heading east. As he ran he kept the six huge beasts in sight, and with an expense of effort that might have exhausted a lesser man fortified with ample food, this starving little hunter, running breathlessly in the moonlight, gained the commanding position he sought. Swimming back across the river, he took his stance beside some trees, and now if the mammoths sought to flee eastward, they would have to run over him.

As night ended, the four Chukchis were in position, each man with two weapons, a stout club and a long spear tipped at the end and along the sides with sharp bits of flint. To kill one of the mammoths, they knew that each man must sink his spear close to some vital spot and then beat the wounded animal to death as it staggered about. From long experience, they knew that the initial chase, the culminating fight and the tracking of the wounded animal to its death might take three days, but they were prepared, because they either completed their task or starved.

It was a mild March day when they closed in upon the mammoths, and

Varnak warned them: 'Do not try to spear the old matriarch. She'll be too wise. We'll try for one of the younger ones.'

Just as the sun appeared, the mammoths sighted them, and began to move eastward, as Varnak had anticipated, but they did not get far, because when they approached him, he daringly ran at them, brandishing his club in one hand, his spear in the other, and this so confused the old matriarch that she turned back, seeking to lead her troop westward, but now two other Chukchi men dashed at her, until, in despair, she headed due north, ignoring spears and clubs and taking her companions with her.

The mammoths had broken free, but all that day as they ran in one direction or another, the determined hunters kept on their trail, and by nightfall it was apparent to both animals and men that the latter could keep in contact, no matter how cleverly the former dodged and ran.

At night Varnak directed his men to light another fire to keep away the mosquitoes, and he suspected correctly that this would command the attention of the exhausted mammoths, who would remain in the vicinity, and at sunrise on the next day they were still visible, but the camp where the Chukchi women and children waited was far in the distance.

All that second day the tiring mammoths tried to escape, but Varnak anticipated every move they attempted. No matter where they turned, he was waiting with that dreadful spear and club, and toward the end of the day he would have succeeded in isolating a young female had not the old matriarch anticipated *his* move and rushed at him with her broken tusk. Forgetting his target, he leaped aside just as the fearful tusk ripped by him, and with the old matriarch safely out of the way, he moved in, brandished his spear, and drove the young mammoth to where the other men waited.

Deftly, in accordance with plans perfected centuries before, the hunters surrounded the isolated animal and began to torment her so adroitly that she could not protect herself. But she could trumpet, and when her screams of terror reached the old matriarch, the latter doubled back, driving directly at the menacing hunters and scattering them as if they were leaves fallen from an aspen tree.

At this moment it looked as if the wise old mammoth had defeated the men, but Varnak could not allow this to happen. Knowing that his life and that of his entire group depended on what he did next, he dove headfirst, throwing himself directly under the feet of the young mammoth. He knew that one step of one powerful foot would crush him, but he had no alternative, and with a terrible upward thrust of his spear he jabbed deep into her entrails and rolled clear of her. He did not kill her, nor did he even wound her fatally, but he did damage her so seriously that she began to stagger, and by the time he rose from the ground, the other hunters were screaming with joy and starting to chase their prey. Unable to retrieve his spear, which dangled from the belly of the mammoth, he nevertheless ran after her, brandishing his club and shouting with the others.

Night fell and once again the Chukchis built a fire, hoping that the mammoths would remain within range, and the great beasts were so fatigued that they were unable to move far. At dawn the chase resumed, and guided by a trail of blood, and encouraged by the fact that it grew wider as the long day progressed, the Chukchis kept running, and finally Varnak said: 'We're getting close. Each man to his duty.' And when they saw the massive beasts huddling within a stand of birch trees, he grabbed the spear of the youngest Chukchi and led his men toward the kill.

It now became his duty to neutralize the matriarch, who was stomping the earth and trumpeting her determination to fight to the end. Bracing himself, he walked precariously toward her, he alone against this great beast, and for just a moment she hesitated while the other men crashed their clubs and spears against the exposed body of the wounded mammoth.

When the old grandmother saw this, she lowered her head and drove right at Varnak. He was in mortal danger and knew it, but he also knew that once he allowed that fierce old creature to rampage among his men, she could destroy them all and rescue her young charge. This must not be allowed to happen, so Varnak, showing a courage few men could have exhibited, leaped in front of the charging mammoth and jabbed at her with his spear. Confused, she fell back, giving the other men breathing space in which to finish off their prey.

When the wounded mammoth stumbled to her knees, blood streaming from many wounds, the three Chukchis leaped upon her with their spears and clubs and beat her to death. When she expired, they acted in obedience to procedures observed through thousands of years: they slit open her innards, sought for the stomach loaded with partly digested greens, and hungrily consumed both the solids and the liquids, for their ancestors had learned that this material contained life-giving nutrients which human beings required. Then, their vigor restored after the days of starvation, they butchered the mammoth, producing cuts of meat big enough to sustain their families into the summer.

Varnak played no role in the actual killing; he had given the mammoth the first wound and had driven off the old matriarch when the latter might have disrupted the hunt. Now, exhausted, deprived of food for so many days, and depleted of what little strength he had by the arduous chase, he leaned against a low tree, panting like a spent dog, too tired to partake of the meat already steaming on the new fire. But he did go to the immense carcass, make a cup with his hands, and drink of the blood he had provided his people.

W HEN THE HUNTERS finished slaughtering the mammoth, they made a traditional decision. Instead of trying to haul the mass of meat, bone and hide back to where their families waited, they decided to make their camp at a nearby stand of birch trees, so the two younger men were sent back to fetch the women, the children and the sleds.

The shift was made with ease, for the women were so starved for food that when they heard of the kill, they wanted to run off immediately, but when the men explained that the entire camp was to be moved, the taking down of the tentlike covering and the packing of the four sleds were completed quickly, and later that day when the women and children saw the slain mammoth, they shouted with joy and, abandoning their sleds, rushed for the fire where portions of the meat were roasting.

A group of hunters like Varnak's could expect to kill only one mammoth a year, but if they were unusually lucky or had at their head some hunter with exceptional skill, they might conceivably kill two. And since the taking of a mammoth was such a rare event, certain rituals for handling the carcass had evolved through the centuries. The Ancient One, as guardian of the tribe's spiritual safety, stood beside the severed head of the beast and apostrophized it:

'O Noble Mammoth who shares the tundra with us, who rules the steppe and runs the river, we thank thee for the gift of thy body. We apologize for having taken thy life, and we pray that thou hast left behind many children who will come to us in the future. Out of respect for thee, we make this prayer.'

As she spoke she dipped her right fingers in the blood of the mammoth, then placed them on the lips of all the women and children until their lips were red. For the four hunters on whom the continued existence of her people depended, she stroked with her bloodied fingers the forehead of the dead animal and then the foreheads of the men, beseeching the beast to impart to these worthy men a deeper understanding of her kind so that they might more effectively chase other mammoths in the future. Only when these sacred rites had been performed did she feel free to rummage among the entrails, seeking the strong gut that would be converted into sinewy thread for sewing.

Her son, meanwhile, was trimming away the meat from the right scapula, and when that stout shoulder blade was exposed, its bone white like ivory, he began working upon it with a stone burin that flecked away bits of the bone, until he held in his hands a sturdy scraper with sharp cutting edges which could be used in butchering the meat of the mammoth prior to storing it in cool places. His work with the burin was significant for two unrelated reasons: it produced a cutting tool which was useful now, and which, nearly thirty thousand years later, would be dug up by archaeologists to prove that human beings had once lived at the Birch Tree Site in the dawn of New World history.

Each of the nine adults had some special responsibility regarding the dead mammoth: one collected the bones to serve as ceiling ribs for whatever kind of house they would later build, another washed the valuable hide and began tanning it with a mixture of urine and the acid distilled from tree bark. Hair from the legs would be woven into a material suitable for caps, and the gristle which connected hoof to leg was saved to make a kind of mucilage. The Ancient One continued probing each piece of meat, intent on salvaging thin, strong bones for the making of needles, and one man sharpened stouter bones to be inserted at the tips of his spears.

Lacking any organized agriculture or the capacity to grow and hoard vegetables, the Chukchis were forced to depend upon their hunting skills, which were tremendous, and basic to everything else was the pursuit of the mammoth, a major source of food. So they studied its habits, placated its spirit to make it congenial, devised ways to trick it, and hunted it relentlessly. As they cut this one apart, they studied every aspect of its anatomy, trying to predict how it would have behaved in different circumstances, and when it had been absorbed into the tribe as a kind of deity, the four men agreed: 'The surest way to kill a mammoth is the way Varnak did. Fall under it and jab upward with a sharp spear.'

Fortified by this conclusion, they took their sons aside and taught them how to hold a spear in both hands, fall to the ground face upward, and jab at the belly of a thundering mammoth, trusting the Great Spirits to provide protection from the hammering feet. When they had instructed the boys, showing them how to fall and yet maintain control of their spears, Varnak winked at one of the other hunters, and this time when the oldest boy ran forward and threw himself on the ground face upward, this hunter, dressed in mammoth skin, suddenly leaped in the air, uttered a fantastic scream, and stamped his feet inches from the boy's head. The young fellow was so terrified by this unexpected explosion that he let the spear fall from his hands and covered his face.

'You are dead!' the hunter shouted at the cowering boy, but Varnak uttered the more serious condemnation of his cowardice: 'You let the mammoth escape. We shall starve.'

So the spear was handed back to the frightened boy, and twenty times he threw himself upon the ground, face up, as Varnak and the others thundered down upon him, stamping their feet close to his head, and reminding him each time as the charade ended: 'That time you had a chance to stab the mammoth. If it was a bull, he might have killed you, but your spear would have been in his belly, and we who were left would have had a chance to trail him and bring him down.'

They kept at it until the boy felt that when he encountered a real mammoth, there was a good chance he might succeed in wounding it so sorely that the others would have a later chance to complete the kill, and when they stopped their practice, Varnak congratulated him: 'I think you will know how,' and the boy smiled.

But then the men turned their attention to the second oldest boy, a lad of nine, and when they handed him a spear and told him to throw himself under the body of the charging mammoth, he fainted.

AT THEIR NEW campsite near the birch trees, the Chukchis unloaded their meager goods and prepared to set up their crude shelters, and since they were in a position to start afresh, they could have developed some improved style of living quarters, but they did not. They failed to invent an igloo made of ice, or a yurt made of skins, or aboveground huts made of stone and branches, or any of the other satisfactory types of dwelling. Instead, they reverted to the kind of hovel they had known in Asia: a muddy cave belowground, with a kind of dome above made of matted branches and skins plastered with mud. As before, the excavation had no chimney for the discharge of smoke, no window for the admission of light, no hinged door to keep away the small animals that wandered by. But each cave did constitute a home, and in it women cooked and sewed and reared their young.

The expected life span in these years was about thirty-one years, and from the constant chewing of meat and gristle, teeth tended to wear out before the rest of the body, so that death was hastened by literal starvation. Women often had three children who lived, three others who died at or shortly after birth. A family rarely remained in one place long, for animals would become wary or depleted, so that the humans must move on in search of other prey. Life was difficult and pleasures were few, but there was at this time no war between tribes or groups of tribes, mainly because units lived so far apart that there need be no squabbling over territorial rights.

Ancestors had patiently learned from a hundred thousand years of trial and error certain rules for survival in the north, and these were rigorously observed. The Ancient One repeated them endlessly to her brood: 'Meat that has turned green must not be eaten. When winter starts and there is not enough food, sleep most of each day. Never throw away any piece of fur, no matter how greasy it has become. Mammoth, bison, beaver, reindeer, fox, hare and mice, hunt them in that order, but never ignore the mice, for it is they that will keep you alive in the starving time.'

Long and cruel experience had also taught one fundamental lesson: 'When you seek a mate, go always, without exception, to some distant tribe, for if you take one within your own set of huts, fearful things result.' In obedience to this harsh rule, she had herself once supervised the killing of a sister and a brother who had married. She would grant them no mercy, even though they were the children of her own brother. 'It must be done,' she had cried to members of her family, 'and before any child is born. For if we allow such a one to come among us, *they* will punish us.'

She never specified who *they* were, but she was convinced that they existed and exercised great powers. They established the seasons, they brought the mammoth near, they watched over pregnant women, and for such services they deserved respect. They lived, she believed, beyond the horizon, wherever it chanced to be, and sometimes in duress she would look to the farthest edge of sky, bowing to the unseen ones who alone had the power to make conditions better.

There were among these Chukchis certain moments of transcendent joy, as when the men brought down a really huge mammoth or when a woman trapped in a difficult pregnancy finally produced a strong male child. On wintry nights when food was scarce and comfort almost unattainable, special joy came to them, for then in the northern heavens the mysterious ones hung out great curtains of fire, filling the sky with myriad colors of dancing forms and vast spears of light flashing from one horizon to the next in a dazzling display of power and majesty.

Then men and women would leave the frozen mud of their mean caves to stand in the starry night, their faces to the heavens as those others beyond the horizon moved the lights about, hung the colors, and sent great shafts thundering clear across the firmament. There would be silence, and the children who were summoned to see this miracle would remember it all the days of their lives.

A man like Varnak might expect to see such a heavenly parade twenty times in his life. With luck he might help to bring down the same number of mammoths, no more. And as he neared the age of thirty, which he was doing now, he could anticipate the swift diminution of his powers and their ultimate disappearance. So he was not surprised one autumn morning when Tevuk said: 'Your mother cannot rise.'

When he ran to where she lay on the ground beneath the birch trees, he saw that she was mortally stricken, and he bent down to give her such comfort as he could, but she required none. In her last moments she wanted to look at the sky she had loved and to discharge her responsibilities to the people she had helped guide and protect for so long. 'When winter comes,' she whispered to her son, 'remind the children to sleep a lot.'

Varnak buried her in the birch grove, and ten days later her grave was covered by the year's first snow. Winds whipped it across the steppe, and as it drifted about the cave-huts, Varnak wondered: Maybe we should winter in the place we left, and he went so far as to consult with other adults, but their counsel was unanimous: 'Better stay where we are,' and with this resolve these eighteen new Alaskans, with enough dried mammoth meat to keep them alive through the worst of the winter, buried themselves in their huts to seek protection from the coming storms.

V ARNAK AND HIS villagers were not the first to cross from Asia into Alaska. Others seem to have preceded them at different spots by thousands of years, moving gradually and arbitrarily eastward in their constant quest for food. Some made the journey out of curiosity, liked what they found, and stayed. Some fought with parents or neighbors and wandered off with no set purpose.

Others passively joined a group and never had the energy to return. Some chased animals so fast and so far that after the kill they remained where they were, and some were allured by the attractiveness of a girl on the other side of the river whose parents were making the journey. But none, so far as we can deduce, ever crossed over with the conscious intention of settling a new land or exploring a new continent.

And when they did reach Alaska, the same patterns prevailed. They never knowingly set out to occupy the interior of North America; the distances and impediments were so great that no single group of human beings could have lived long enough to complete the passage. Of course, had the route south been ice-free when Varnak and his people made their crossing, and had they been driven by some monomaniacal impulse, they could conceivably have wandered down to Wyoming during their lifetime, but as we have seen, the corridor was rarely open at the same time as the bridge. So had Varnak been intent on reaching the interior of North America—assuming that he could have generated such a purpose, which he could not—he might have had to wait thousands of years before the pathway was released from the ice, and this would mean that a hundred generations of his line would live and die before his descendants could migrate toward Wyoming.

Of a hundred Chukchis who wandered from Siberia into Alaska in Varnak's time, perhaps a third returned home after discovering that Asia was in general more hospitable than Alaska. Of the two-thirds who remained, all were imprisoned within the enchanting ice castle, as were their descendants. They became Alaskan; in time they remembered nothing but this beautiful land; they forgot Asia and were able to learn nothing about North America. Varnak and his seventeen never went back, nor did their descendants. They became Alaskans.

By what name should they be known? When their ancestors first ventured into the north they had been called contemptuously Those Who Fled the South, as if the residents knew that had the newcomers been stronger, they would have escaped eviction from those favorable climes. During one period when they could not find acceptable sites for their camps, they were known as the Wanderers, and when they finally came upon a safe place to live at the edge of Asia, they took its name and became Chukchis. An appropriate name would have been Siberian, but now that they had unwittingly committed themselves to Alaska, they acquired the generic name of Indians, later to be differentiated as Athapascans.

As such they would prosper across the middle section of Alaska and positively thrive in Canada. One sturdy branch would inhabit the beautiful islands forming southern Alaska, and improbable as it would have seemed to Varnak, some of his descendants thousands of years later would wander southward into Arizona, where they would become the Navajo Indians. Scholars would find the language of these Navajos as close to Athapascan as Portuguese was to Spanish, and this could not have happened by chance. There had to have been a relationship between the two groups.

These wandering Athapascans were in no way related to the much later Eskimos, nor must they be visualized as moving consciously onward in some mighty fanlike emigration, carrying their civilization with them to unpopulated lands. They were not English Pilgrims crossing the Atlantic in a purposeful exodus, with provisional laws adopted on shipboard before landing among the waiting Indians. It is quite probable that the Athapascans spread throughout America with never a sense of having left home.

That is, Varnak and his wife, for example, as older people, would be inclined to remain where they were among the birch trees, but some years later one of their sons and his wife might see that it would be advantageous for them to build their cave-hut somewhat farther to the east where more mammoths were available, and off they would go. But they might also maintain contact with their parents back at the original birch-tree site, and in time *their* children would decide to move on to more inviting locations, but they too would retain affiliation with their parents, and perhaps even with old Varnak and Tevuk at the birch trees. In this quiet way people can populate an entire continent by moving only a few thousand yards in each generation, if they are allowed twenty-nine thousand years in which to do it. They can move from Siberia to Arizona without ever leaving home.

Better hunting, an addiction to adventure, a dissatisfaction with oppressive old ways, motives like these were the timeless urges which encouraged men and women to spread out even in peaceful times, and it was in obedience to them that these early men and women began to settle the Americas, both North and South, without being aware that they were doing so.

In the process, Alaska would become of crucial importance to areas like Minnesota, Pennsylvania, California and Texas, for it would provide the route for the peoples who would populate those diverse areas. Descendants of Varnak and Tevuk, inheritors of the courage which had characterized the Ancient One, would erect noble cultures in lands that would rarely know ice or have any memory of Asia, and it would be these settlers and the different groups who would follow them in later millennia who would constitute Alaska's main gift to America.

FOURTEEN THOUSAND YEARS B.P.E., when the land route was temporarily submerged because of melting at the polar ice cap, one of the world's most congenial people lived in crowded areas at the extreme eastern tip of Siberia. They were Eskimos, those squat, dark Asian hunters who wore their hair cut square across their eyebrows. They were a hardy breed, for their livelihood depended upon their venturing out upon the Arctic Ocean and its attendant waters to hunt the great whales, the tusked walruses and the elusive seals. No other men in all the world lived more dangerously in a more inhospitable climate than these Eskimos, and none labored more strenuously in these years than a bandy-legged, sturdy little fellow named Oogruk, who was experiencing all kinds of difficulties.

He had taken as his wife, three years earlier, the daughter of the most important man in his seaside village of Pelek, and at the time he had been bewildered as to why a young woman of such attractiveness should be interested in him, for he had practically nothing to offer. He had no kayak of his own for hunting seals, nor any share in one of the larger umiaks in which men sailed forth in groups to track down whales that glided past the headland like floating mountaintops. He owned no property, had only one set of sealskins to protect him from the frozen seas, and what was particularly disqualifying, he had no parents to help him make his way in the harsh world of the Eskimo. To top it all, he was cross-eyed, and in that special way which could be infuriating. If you looked into his left eye, thinking that this was the one he was using, he would shift focus, and you would be looking at nothing, for his left eye would have wandered. And if you then hurried back to his right eye, he shifted that one, and once more you were staring at nothing. It was not easy to talk with Oogruk.

The mystery of why the headman's pretty daughter Nukleet was willing to marry such a fellow was solved rather soon after the wedding feast, for Oogruk discovered that his bride was pregnant, and at the boats it was whispered that the father was a husky young harpooner named Shaktoolik who already had two wives and three other children. Oogruk was in no position to protest the deception, or to protest anything else for that matter, so he bit his tongue, admitted to himself that he was lucky to have a girl as pretty as Nukleet on any terms, and vowed to be one of the best hands in the various arctic boats owned by his father-in-law.

Nukleet's father did not want Oogruk as part of his crew, for the hunting of whales was a perilous occupation and each of the six men in the heavy boat had to be an expert. Four rowed, one steered, one managed the harpoon, and these positions had long been spoken for in the headman's umiak. He led the way. Shaktoolik held the harpoon. And four stout fellows with nerves of granite manned the oars. In many expeditions against whales, these men had proved their merit, and Nukleet's father was not about to break up his combination simply to make a place for his lightly regarded son-in-law.

But he was willing to provide Oogruk with his own kayak, not one of the best but a sturdy craft which was guaranteed not to sink—'light as a spring breeze through aspen, watertight as a seal's fur'—regardless of how the waves assaulted it. This kayak did not respond quickly to paddle strokes, but it was many times better than Oogruk could ever have owned by himself and he was grateful; his parents, killed when a whale overturned their small boat, had left him nothing.

In midsummer, when great sea animals were on the move, Oogruk's father-in-law, aided by Shaktoolik, launched his umiak from the pebbled shore fronting the village of Pelek. But before they departed on what they knew might be a perilous excursion, they indicated with shrugs that Oogruk was free to use the kayak on the chance that he might creep up on some dozing seal and add both a needed fur and meat to the village larder. Standing alone on the shore, with the rude kayak waiting some distance to the east, he looked through squinting eyes as the abler men of the village set forth with prayers and shouts to try to intercept a whale.

When they were gone, their heads six dots on the horizon, he sighed at his hard luck in missing the hunt, looked back at his hut to see if Nukleet was watching, and sighed again to see that she was not. Walking dejectedly to his waiting kayak, he studied its awkward lines, and muttered: 'In that one you couldn't overtake a wounded seal.' It was large, three times as long as a man, and covered completely by watertight sealskin to keep it afloat in the stormiest seas. It contained only one opening, just big enough to accommodate a man's hips; the sealskin was secured snugly at the top around the hunter's waist and sewn to the kayak by lengths of whale tendons that were pliable when dry, an impermeable bond when wet.

After Oogruk eased himself into the opening, he pulled the upper part of the sealskin about his waist and tied it carefully, so that no water could seep through even if the kayak turned upside down. If that happened, all Oogruk would have to do would be to work his paddle furiously and the kayak would right itself. Of course, if a lone man lashed into the opening was foolhardy enough to tackle a mature walrus, the beast's tusks might puncture the covering, throw the man into the sea, and drown him, for Eskimos could not swim; besides, the weight of his bulky clothing, if it became waterlogged, would drag him down.

When the whale-hunting umiak vanished in the distance, Oogruk tested his aspen paddle and started out for the seas east of Pelek. He had little confidence that he would find any seals and even less that he would know how to handle a big one if he did. He was merely scouting, and if he happened to sight a whale surfacing in the distance, or a walrus lazing along, he would mark the beast's heading and inform the others when they returned, for if Eskimos knew for certain that a whale or a really big walrus was in a given area, they could track it down.

He saw no seals, and this did not entirely disappoint him, for he was not yet sure of himself as a hunter, and he wanted first to familiarize himself with the tricks of this particular kayak before he took it among a herd of seals. He contented himself with paddling toward that distant land on the other side of the sea which he had sometimes seen on clear days. No one from Pelek had ever sailed to the opposite shore, but everyone knew it existed, for they had seen its low hills gleaming in the afternoon sun.

He was well out from shore, some miles south of where the umiak must be by now, when he saw off to his right a sight which paralyzed him. It was the full length of a black whale riding the surface of the water, its huge tail carelessly propelling it forward. It was enormous, much bigger than any Oogruk had ever seen on the beach when the men butchered their catch. Of course, he was not an expert judge, for the hunters of Pelek had caught only three whales in the last seven years. But this one was huge, no one could deny that, and it was imperative that Oogruk alert his companions to the whale's presence, for he alone against this great beast was powerless. Six of the best men in Siberia would be required to subdue it.

But how could he notify his father-in-law? Having no other choice, he decided to stay with the whale as it lazed its way north, trusting that its course must sooner or later intersect the umiak's.

This was a delicate maneuver, for if the whale felt threatened by a strange object in its vicinity, it could with three or four flips of its mighty tail swim over and collapse the kayak or bite it in two, killing both the man and his frail canoe. So all that long afternoon Oogruk, alone in his boat, trailed the whale, seeking to remain invisible, cheering when the whale spouted, showing that it was still there. Twice the great beast sounded, then disappeared, and now Oogruk sweated, for his prey might surface at any spot, might even come up under the kayak accidentally, or be lost forever in one strenuous underwater plunge. But the whale had to breathe, and after a prolonged absence, the huge dark creature resurfaced, spouted high in the air, and continued its lazy way north.

About an hour before the sun swept low to the north in its reluctance to set, Oogruk calculated that if the men in the umiak had continued in their proposed direction, they must now be well to the northeast of where the whale was heading, and if so, they would miss it completely. So he decided that he must cut across the whale's path, paddle furiously, and hope to overtake the six hunters.

But now he had to determine which method of getting to the east of the whale promised the greatest likelihood of success, for he must not only avoid inciting an attack, which would destroy both him and the kayak, but he must also move in such a way as to conserve maximum time and distance. Remembering that whales, according to tradition, could see poorly and hear acutely, he decided to speed ahead, making as little noise as possible, and cut directly across the whale's path, doing so as far in front as his paddling would allow.

This was a dangerous maneuver, but he had far more than his own safety to consider. From his earliest days he had been taught that the supreme responsibility of a boy or man was to bring a whale to the beach so that his village could feast upon it, and use the huge bones for building and the precious baleen for the scores of uses to which its suppleness and strength could be put. To catch a whale was an occasion which might happen only once in a lifetime, and he was in position to do just that, for if he led the hunters to the whale, and they killed it, the honors would be shared with him for his steadfastness in trailing the great beast across the open seas.

In this moment of vital decision, when he was about to throw himself across the very face of the whale, he was sustained by a curious fact, for his doomed father who had left him so little did provide him with a talisman of extraordinary power and beauty. It was a small circular disk, white and with a diameter of about two narrow fingers. It had been made of ivory from one of the few walruses his father had ever killed, and it had been carved with fine runic figures depicting the ice-filled ocean and the creatures that lived within it, sharing it with the Eskimos.

Oogruk had watched his father carve the disk and smooth the edges so that it would fit properly, and since both realized from the beginning that when finished, this disk was to be something special, it was in no way foolish when his father predicted: 'Oogruk, this will be a lucky one.' Accepting this without question, the boy of nine had not winced when his father took a sharp knife made of whalebone, pierced his lower lip, and stuffed the incision with grass. As it healed and the opening grew wider, with larger plugs of wood inserted each month, his lower lip would form a narrow band of skin surrounding and defining a circular hole.

Halfway through this process, the hole became infected, as so often happened in these cases, and Oogruk lay on the mud floor stricken with fever. For three bad days and nights, while his mind wandered, his mother applied herbs to his lip and packed warm rocks against his feet. Then the fever subsided, and when he was again able to take notice, the boy saw with satisfaction that the hole had mended to just about the required size.

On a day he would never forget, Oogruk was taken to a sinister hut at the edge of the village and ceremoniously led inside one of the filthiest, most jumbled places he had ever seen. The skeleton of a man dangled from one mud wall, the skull of a seal from another. Dirty pouches sewn from sealskin lay about the floor beside a collection of stinking skins on which the occupant slept. He was the shaman of Pelek village, the holy man who uttered the prayers that controlled the oceans and conversed with the spirits who brought whales to the headland. When he loomed out of the shadows to confront Oogruk, he was formidable—tall, gaunt, with sunken eyes and missing teeth, his hair extremely long and matted with a filth that had not been removed in a dozen years. Uttering incomprehensible sounds, he took the ivory disk, looked at its elegance with obvious astonishment that a man as poor as Oogruk's father should possess such a treasure, then pulled down the boy's lower lip and with befouled fingers pressed the disk into the hole. The hardened scar tissue adjusted painfully to pinch the disk firmly in the position it would occupy for as long as Oogruk lived.

The insertion had been painful; it had to be if the disk was to stay in place, but when the beautiful object was properly seated, all could see, and some with envy, that the cross-eyed boy Oogruk who had so little was henceforth going to possess one treasure: the finest labret on the eastern shore of Siberia.

Now, as he sped his kayak across the path of the oncoming whale, he sucked in his lower lip, taking courage from the reassuring presence of the magical labret. When his tongue felt the ivory, carved on both faces, he could trace the talismanic whale carved there, and he was convinced that its companionship would assure him good fortune, and he was right, for as he sped past, so close that the whale could have made one thrust of its gigantic tail and leaped ahead to crush both kayak and man, the lazy beast kept its head underwater, not deigning to bother with whatever small thing was moving through the seas so close to it.

But when the kayak had safely passed, the whale lifted its huge head, spouted great volumes of water, and casually opened its mouth as if yawning, and Oogruk, looking back toward the sound of the spouting, saw how enormous the mouth was that he had escaped, and its size appalled him. As a young man he had through the years participated in the butchering of four whales, and two of them had been large, but none had a head or a mouth as big as this. For almost a minute the cavernous mouth remained open, a black cavelike recess that could have crushed an entire kayak, and then almost drowsily it closed, a desultory spout of water came forth, and the massive whale sank once more below the surface of the water, still headed toward where Oogruk suspected his companions in their umiak would be waiting. Clicking his lucky labret against his teeth, he hurried ahead.

He was now to the east of the whale, heading north, and he was so far at sea that the headlands of home were no longer visible, nor was the opposite shore. He was alone on the vast northern sea, with nothing to sustain him but his lucky labret and the possibility that he might help his people catch that trailing whale.

Since it was midsummer, he had no fear of a descending darkness in which the whale might be lost, for as he paddled he could from time to time see over his left shoulder the plodding creature, and in the silvery light of endless summer he remained reassured that the great beast was traveling north with him, but whenever he did see the whale, he saw again that monstrous mouth, that black cavern which bespoke the other world about which the shaman sometimes warned when he was in one of his trances. To travel north in the whispering grayness of an arctic midnight while a dark whale kept pace in the deep billows of the sea was an experience which tested the courage of a man, and Oogruk, even though he was determined to comport himself well, might have turned back had not the presence of his labret reassured him.

At dawn the whale was still heading north, and before the sun was much above the horizon where it had lingered through the night, Oogruk thought he saw off to the northeast something that could be an umiak, and he quit monitoring the whale and started paddling frantically toward the supposed boat. He was correct in his guess, for at one point both he and the umiak rode the crest of waves, enabling him to see the six men rowing and they to see him. Waving his paddle, he gave the sign which indicated that a whale had been sighted, and with pointing directions he indicated its course.

With surprising speed, the umiak cut westward, intending to intercept the leviathan and ignoring Oogruk completely, for it was the whale that was important, not the messenger. Oogruk understood, and with his own strokes he set his frail kayak on a course which would overtake the umiak just as it reached the whale, and now a three-part drama unfolded, with the men in the larger boat panting with excitement, the whale moving majestically ahead, oblivious of the danger about to assault it, and lone Oogruk paddling furiously, uncertain as to what his role in the forthcoming fray was going to be. And all about, in all directions, lay the gently heaving arctic sea, devoid of spring icebergs, devoid of birds, devoid of headlands and gulfs and bays. There in the vast loneliness of the north, these creatures of the north prepared for battle.

When the umiak first came in sight of the whale the men could not appreciate the size of this monster; they saw its head at times, its tail at other times, but they never saw the complete length of the beast, so they were able to convince themselves that this was just one more ordinary whale. However, when they drew closer, the whale, still unaware of their presence, suddenly breached; that is, for reasons unknown it arched itself completely clear of the water, exposing its entire body. Then, exercising tremendous power, it turned on its side as if wishing to scratch its back, and thundered back into the sea with a gigantic splash. Now the six Eskimos realized they were facing a master whale that, if it could be taken, would feed their village for many months.

Oogruk's father-in-law needed to give only a few orders. The inflated seal bladders, which would impede the whale's progress if they managed to harpoon it, were made ready. Each of the four rowers brought close to hand the spears they would use when they closed upon the whale, and in the prow of the umiak tall and handsome Shaktoolik stood erect, wedged his knees against the gunwales of the boat, his strong hands grasping the harpoon which he would thrust into the vitals of the whale. Far behind trailed Oogruk.

The harpoon which Shaktoolik tended so carefully was a powerful affair, its long shaft tipped with sharpened flint followed immediately by hooklike barbs carved from walrus ivory. But even this lethal weapon would prove ineffective if thrown, like a spear, with an overhand motion, for the force thus generated would be insufficient to penetrate the whale's thick, blubber-protected skin; the miracle of the Eskimo system was not the harpoon but the harpoon throwing-stick, which ingeniously imparted three or four times the penetrating power to the barbed shaft.

A throwing-stick was a carefully shaped, thin length of wood about two and a half feet long, so devised as to increase considerably the length of a man's arm. The rear end, which contained a kind of slot in which the haft of the harpoon rested, snuggled in the crooked elbow of the thrower. The length of the stick ran along the man's arm, extending well beyond his fingertips, and it was against this wood that the harpoon rested. Toward the front end there was a finger rest enabling the man to retain control over both the harpoon and the stick, and close nearby a smoothed place at which the thumb could steady the long harpoon as the man prepared to throw. Steadying himself, the harpooner drew his right arm bearing the stick as far back as possible, checking to ensure that the butt end was secure in its slot. Then, with a wide sweep of his right arm, parallel to the surface of the sea and not up and down as one might expect, he snapped his arm swiftly forward, released his hold on the nestled harpoon at the precise moment, and, thanks to the doubled length this gave his arm, released the flint-tipped harpoon at the whale with such force that it could drive through the thickest skin. In this intricate method the man slung the harpoon much as little David, twelve thousand years later, would sling his rock against big Goliath. It sometimes required years of practice before accuracy was obtained, but once the various tricks were synchronized, this slingshot harpoon became a deadly weapon.

It seems unbelievable that primitive man could have invented such a curious, complicated instrument, but hunters on various continents did: the *atlatl* it would be named after the example the Europeans encountered in Mexico, but all versions were similar. Somehow, men with no knowledge of engineering or dynamics deduced that their harpoons would be trebly effective if they were loaded into their atlatls and slung forward instead of being thrown. How awesome the intellectual force of this intricate discovery, but in assessing it, one must remember that for a hundred thousand years men spent most of their waking hours trying to kill animals for food; they had no occupation more important, so perhaps it is not remarkable that after twenty or thirty thousand years of experimentation they discovered that the best way to deliver a harpoon was with a sideways slingshot motion, almost like an awkward child throwing a ball.

On this day the Eskimo leader had calculated perfectly his approach to the target, and from a position a little to the right and close behind the lumbering beast, he planned to flash ahead on an angle which would enable Shaktoolik to strike at a vital spot just behind the right ear and thus provide the two paddlers on the left-hand side an opportunity to unleash their spears also, with the headman remaining available in the stern to plunge his spear somewhat behind the others. Using this maneuver, the four Eskimos on the left-hand side of the umiak would have a chance to wound this enormous creature, perhaps not mortally but certainly deeply enough to render it vulnerable to their subsequent attacks and ultimate victory. A battle of profound strategy was under way.

But as the umiak bore down, the whale became aware of its danger, and with an automatic response which astounded the men, wheeled on its midsection and swung its huge tail viciously. The leader, anticipating the destruction of his umiak if the tail struck, heeled his craft over, but this left the man in front, Shaktoolik with his harpoon, exposed, and as the tail swept past, one fluke struck Shaktoolik in the head and shoulders, sweeping him into the sea. Then, in what could only have been an accidental blow, the mighty tail smashed down, crushing the harpooner, driving him unconscious deep below the surface of the sea, where he perished. The whale had won the first encounter.

As soon as the headman grasped the altered situation, he acted instinctively. Drawing away from the whale, he looked about the sea for Oogruk, and when he saw the kayak just where it should have been, he moved the umiak in that direction and cried: 'Aboard!'

Oogruk was eager to join the fight, but he also knew that the craft in which he rode was the property of his father-in-law: 'The kayak?'

'Leave it,' the headman said without hesitation. Any boat was valuable, and this one was his, but the capture of the whale was of paramount importance, so the kayak was turned adrift as Oogruk climbed into the umiak.

It had long been understood in this crew that if either Shaktoolik or the headman was killed or lost, the principal rower, the one fore and left, would assume that vacant role, and this he did, leaving his own post empty. At first Oogruk assumed that he would move into that seat, but his father-in-law, knowing his limited skill, quickly reshuffled the men, leaving vacant the left rear seat, where Oogruk would sit under his direct supervision. There he could do the least harm, and in this new configuration, with almost no thought to the dead Shaktoolik, the Eskimos resumed their chase of the whale.

The leviathan, now aware that it was under attack, adopted various stratagems to protect itself, but since it was an air-breathing animal and not a fish, it had to surface from time to time, and when it did, these pestiferous little creatures in their boat tormented it. And they kept doing so, regardless of the fact that they were having no success, because they knew that if they could keep the whale reacting to their intrusions, they could in time wear it down and develop that critical moment when, tired from fleeing and exhausted by this constant sounding and spouting, it would leave itself vulnerable.

All that first day the uneven fight was waged, with the men fully aware that one sweep of that stupendous tail, one crushing of those vast jaws, would doom them. But they had no alternative; Eskimos captured their food from the ocean or they starved, and abandoning the fight never occurred to them. So when the sun moved toward the northern horizon, indicating that night, such as it was, had come, the men in the umiak continued their pursuit, and all through the silvery dusk which persisted in majestic beauty until it turned into a silvery dawn, the six little Eskimos chased the one great whale.

Toward noon of the second day the headman judged that the whale was tiring and that the time had come to attempt a master thrust, so once more he brought his umiak to a position slightly behind the whale, and again moved forcefully ahead so that his new harpooner would have a clear shot, as would he and the two left-hand rowers. As the run started, he kicked Oogruk in the back, growling 'Have your lance ready,' showing his contempt as his inept son-in-law fumbled around to find the unfamiliar weapon.

By the time the attack was launched, Oogruk had still not located his lance, and for the very good reason that the former occupant of the left rear seat had taken his with him when he moved forward and had not replaced it. Nevertheless, when the attack was made and the great whale slid past the right side of the umiak, the man ahead of Oogruk and his father-in-law behind stabbed skillfully, doing real damage, but Oogruk did not, and the headman, seeing this dereliction, began to berate him as the whale moved on, bleeding from its right side.

'Idiot! Had you stabbed it too, it would have faltered!' and as the day proceeded, the headman returned to this supposition so repeatedly that all in the umiak came to believe that Oogruk's inability to use his lance properly had been the sole cause of this second failure. Finally the censure became so strong that the cross-eyed fellow had to defend himself: 'I had no lance. I was given none.' And when the others inspected the umiak they had to know that this was true, but they were so eager to blame another for their own error that they continued to grumble: 'If Oogruk had used his lance properly, we would have taken that whale.'

During the second mystical night, with the whale occasionally visible as it raised its gigantic tail above the waves, the headman distributed fragments of food and allowed his men to take small drinks of water, and when all understood how meager the remainder of the ration was, they knew that on the coming day they must make their supreme effort. So early in the morning the headman brought the umiak once more into the position he favored—slightly behind, slightly to the east—and with great skill he positioned the forward harpooner right where he could do the most damage, but as the man delivered his blow, the point of the harpoon struck bone and was diverted. The man seated ahead of Oogruk again struck a good blow, a deep one but not fatal, and now came Oogruk's turn. As he rose, he felt his father-in-law kicking him, so he reached out with his borrowed spear, located it perfectly, and with all his strength bore down, driving the spear deep into the whale.

But he was inexperienced, and in this moment of triumph he forgot to brace his knees and feet against the side of the umiak, and even more important, he did not let go his spear, and he was dragged into the water.

As he splashed into the icy sea, caught between the umiak and the passing whale, he heard his father-in-law curse and saw him thrust his spear properly into the whale, protecting himself from falling as he deftly pulled the spear free, the way a man should, so as to plunge it deeper on his next try.

Aboard the umiak there was commotion as some cried: 'After the whale! It's wounded!' while others: 'Catch Oogruk! He's still alive!' and the headman, after brief hesitation, decided that since the whale could not escape and Oogruk could not swim, he had better attend to the latter. When Oogruk was hauled aboard, salt water dripping from his lucky labret, his father-in-law snarled: 'You've cost us the whale . . . twice.'

This was true only in part, because the whale was less seriously damaged than the men had at first supposed, and with its remaining strength it moved ahead so fast that by the close of that third day it was obvious to the Eskimos that they had lost it. In their despair at having been so near the capture of a champion whale, they again focused on Oogruk, berating him for their defeat, citing his failure to lance the whale and his falling overboard, and a legend was born there in the sullen umiak that they would surely have taken that whale had they not stopped to rescue Oogruk: 'Yes, clumsy fellow that he is, he fell right out of the umiak, and when we stopped to save him, our whale escaped.'

As he listened to the accusations, he bit on his labret and thought: They forget it was me who brought them the whale. And when his father-in-law, in a spell of truly ridiculous reasoning, began to scold him for having lost the kayak, Oogruk concluded that the world had gone mad: He ordered me to leave it. I asked twice, and he ordered me twice.

It was in these ugly moments, as bitter as a man could know, when the members of his community have turned against him and have for irrational reasons vilified him, blaming him for their own deficiencies, that Oogruk realized it was useless to try to defend himself against such irresponsible charges. But his silence did not win him respite, for now the men in the umiak faced another problem: How were they to make it back home in a trip that might require three days when they had no food and little water? In their extremity they renewed their attacks on Oogruk, and one crew member even suggested throwing him overboard to appease the spirits whom he had offended. From the rear of the umiak the leader said grimly: 'No more of that,' but he continued to voice his unfavorable opinion of the hapless one.

And then, to the east, the men saw for the first time the headlands of the country that lay on the opposite side, and in the late afternoon sunlight it looked inviting and a place worthy of attention. It was constructed, they saw, not of mountains like the ones they had known far to the west on their side of the sea, but of rolling hills, treeless but nevertheless attractive. They had no way of knowing whether the place was inhabited or not, and they had no assurance that there they would find food, but they did believe that there it would have water, and all agreed that the headman should turn the umiak toward the shore and begin seeking a safe spot at which to land.

It was with the gravest apprehension that the men neared the shore, for they could not anticipate what might happen if this otherwise appealing place contained people, and as they breasted a small headland protecting a bay, they saw with quaking hearts that within its shelter it did have a small village. Before the headman could stop the forward motion of the umiak, seven swift one-man kayaks sped from shore and surrounded the larger boat. The strangers were armed, and they might have discharged their spears had not Oogruk's father-in-law raised his empty hands high over his head and then dropped them to his mouth in a gesture of drinking.

The strangers understood, came close to the umiak and with their eyes searched it for weapons, and when they saw that Oogruk and another man were gathering the whaling lances and holding them aside in one bundle, they allowed the umiak to follow them ashore, where an elderly man, obviously their shaman, bade them a generous welcome.

They remained three days at Shishmaref, as the site would later be known, eating food much like what they had at home and learning words that were close to their own. They could not converse easily with these people of the eastern shore of the Bering Sea, but they could make themselves understood. The villagers, obviously Eskimos, said that their ancestors had lived in this bay for many generations, and it was clear from the bones used in building their houses that they lived on just about the same sea animals as did the people of Pelek. They were friendly, and when Oogruk and his fellow boatmen departed, farewells of real emotion were shared.

This visit to the east enabled the men of the west to survive the trip home, and on this long journey the old antagonism against Oogruk solidified, so that by the time they landed at Pelek the official judgment had become: 'Shaktoolik and Oogruk both fell overboard. Evil demons caused us to lose the good man and save the bad.'

Ashore they circulated this dogma so persuasively that those waiting in the huts accepted it, and Oogruk was ostracized, but now an enemy more powerful than anyone in the umiak rose against him, for the shaman, that mixture of saint, priest, necromancer and thief, began to circulate the theory that Oogruk, because of the insolent way he had crossed in front of the whale, had also been the specific cause of Shaktoolik's death, for that harpooner was known to be highly skilled and more than able to protect himself from normal dangers. It was obvious that some evil force had exercised an adverse spell against him, and the logical perpetrator had to be Oogruk.

And then the shaman, shaking his long and matted locks, betrayed the animus that motivated him in this attack: he whispered to various listeners that it was not proper for a pitiful man like Oogruk to possess a labret with magical powers, with a whale carved on one face, a walrus on the other, and he began to initiate those devious maneuvers which had worked to his advantage in similar situations in the past. His immediate goal, announced to no one, not even the spirits, was to gain possession of that labret.

He noisily bemoaned the death of the harpooner Shaktoolik, weeping in public over the loss of such a noble young man, and he tried to enlist the help of both Oogruk's father-in-law and Nukleet, the pretty daughter married to Oogruk. But there he ran into difficulties, because to everyone's surprise including her father's, Nukleet did not turn against her feckless husband; she defended him. And as she began to point out the various unfairnesses in the attacks upon him, she gradually convinced her father that Oogruk had in some ways been the hero of the expedition, not the villain.

Why did she do this? She knew that their daughter was not properly Oogruk's and that her father and most others had been distressed when she married the cross-eyed fellow, but as the years passed, four of them now, she had seen on numerous occasions that her husband was a man of great character. He was honest. He worked to his ability. He cherished their daughter, tending her as if she were his own, and always he had shared his meager possessions with her when young men of far greater favor treated their wives with contempt.

In these four years she had especially compared Oogruk's behavior with that of Shaktoolik, the real father of her child, and the more she had seen of that handsome man's behavior the more she had grown to respect her ungainly husband. Shaktoolik had been arrogant, he had abused his two wives, he had ignored his children, and had displayed his inherent meanness in a score of malicious ways. He stole other men's lances and laughed about it. He took their women and dared them to resist. Brave he was, all men agreed to that, but in all other human responses he had been an ugly man, and she admitted it if others did not. So when the shaman made a great fuss about Shaktoolik's death, she watched, and listened, and deduced what webs that evil man was weaving.

Characteristically, for although she now believed that Oogruk was good, she could still not admit that he was intelligent, she took her fears to her father and not to her husband: 'The shaman wants to drive Oogruk from Pelek.'

'Why would he do that?'

'He wants something that Oogruk has.'

'What could that be? The fool has nothing.'

'He has me.'

With remarkable instinct Nukleet had uncovered the shaman's other reason for getting rid of Oogruk. He did covet the beautiful labret, but that was merely to enhance his powers as a shaman; that would increase his public power. For himself, as a man living apart in a hovel on the edge of the village, he wanted Nukleet, and her daughter, and her favorable relationship to the headman. He recognized her as one of those women, not many in number according to him, who brought grace to whatever she did. Four years ago he had been perplexed as to why she would marry Oogruk instead of becoming Shaktoolik's third wife, but now he realized that she had done this through the force of her remarkable character and determination: She wanted to be first in line, not third. He convinced himself that if she now had an opportunity to become his woman, attendant to the most powerful man in the community, she would leap to the chance.

In a hundred ways this bizarre man deluded himself. Because the arctic world was a dangerous place where the successful capture of a walrus might mean the difference between life or death, the Eskimos had to placate the spirit of the walrus, and who could ensure this but the shaman? It was he who could turn the heavy blizzards away in winter, and bring rains to ease the droughts in summer. Only he could guarantee that a childless woman would become pregnant or that her child would be a son. With conviction he identified those Eskimos who were possessed by devils, and at a great price he exorcised the devils just before the clan rose up to punish the bewildered carrier of evil. In two extreme circumstances he had known that the clan's only hope of survival lay in appeasing the spirits and without qualm had identified the offending member who must be banished.

No one in Pelek would have thought of challenging this despot, for all knew that strange forces ruled the world and that the shaman alone knew how to master them, or at least propitiate them so they did minimum damage. In this way he served several useful purposes, for when an Eskimo died the shaman properly guided the spirit to its resting place through intricate rituals, reaffirming for the clan that malevolent forces would not roam the shore and drive away the seals and walruses. He was especially helpful when hunters went forth in their umiaks, for they found reassurance in his incantations for protection against malignant spirits that could bring disaster to the already dangerous hunt. In the depths of the coldest winters, when it seemed as if all life had disappeared from earth, the clan found renewed hope as he placated the spirits to prevail upon the frozen seas and bring the warm breezes of spring again to Pelek. No community could survive without a powerful shaman, so that even those who suffered at his hands conceded that their shaman's ministrations were essential. The most that anyone would say was: 'I wish he was a kinder man.'

The shaman of Pelek had begun to acquire his mastery of others in a quiet, almost accidental way. As a boy he had sensed that he was different, for he could look into the future when others could not. He was also sensitive to the presence of good and evil forces. But above all, he discovered early that the world is a mysterious place, that the great whales come and go according to rules which no man by himself can unravel, and that death strikes arbitrarily. He was concerned with these mysteries, as were all men, but unlike other men, he proposed to conquer them.

He did so by collecting lucky and powerful objects with which to excite his intuitions; that was why he longed for Oogruk's potent labret. He made himself a pouch of beaver skin, shiny fur outside, choice stones and bits of meaningful bone inside. He taught himself to whistle like a bird. He developed his powers of observation so that he saw conditions and relationships which others did not. And when he was satisfied that he had the capacity to be a shaman, and a good one, he mastered the art of speaking in different voices and even throwing his voice from place to place so that those who consulted him in their fears or anguish could hear the spirits addressing their problems.

He served his community well. Indeed, he seemed to have only one weakness, an insatiable craving for power and ever more power, and the young woman Nukleet was the first in the community to discover this terrible infirmity and identify it. She had started worrying about her good husband's helplessness before this forceful shaman, and quickly she had transferred that concern to herself. Now, perceiving the real danger, she asked her father to walk with her beside the sea, which was beginning to fill with ice: 'Can't you see, Father? It's not Oogruk or me. It's your power he's really after.'

The headman, a considerable force in any Eskimo community, ridiculed his daughter's fears: 'Shamans look after the spirits. Headmen look after the hunt.'

'If the separation is allowed to continue.'

'He would be no good in an umiak and hopeless in a kayak.'

'But if he controlled those who went in the umiak?'

She made no headway with her father, who was preoccupied with trying to bring in enough food before the winter closed in, and in the next weeks she saw little of him, for he and his men were out upon the great sea where the ice was forming, and to her relief and his, he succeeded in bringing home many fat seals and one small walrus. The shaman blessed the catch and explained to the people that the hunts had been successful because this time Oogruk had been left at home.

IT WAS A difficult winter. Without a whale on the beach the little village of Pelek lacked many necessities, and when the long night settled in, the sea froze solid along the shore and nearly so to a far distance out. Since Pelek perched on the extreme eastern tip of the Chukchi peninsula, it lay some distance south of the Arctic Circle, which meant that even in midwinter the sun shone briefly, a cold, reluctant orb which gave little warmth. Then, as if frightened by venturing so far north, after two meager hours it disappeared and twenty-two hours of freezing darkness returned.

The effect of this cold on the sea was spectacular, for not only did the sea freeze, it also heaved and fractured and disrupted itself so that enormous blocks of ice, taller than the tallest spruce to the south, rose eerily from the surface, standing about like structures thrown by some malevolent giant. The effect was staggering, a jagged, broken surface along which one could travel by sled for only a short distance before being forced to detour the monstrous towers of ice.

But interspersed among the great blocks were spacious areas where the frozen sea remained flat, and to such places men and women came with fishing lines, and with stout poles treasured from generation to generation they pounded on the ice until they broke their way to water, and down these holes they dropped their lines with the ivory hooks with which they caught their winter food. It was arduous work to dig the holes and a bitterly cold assignment to sit there hour after hour waiting for a fish to strike, but the people of Pelek had to endure it or go hungry.

In the long hours of darkness the Eskimos, like the prudent Siberians before them, slept much in order to conserve energy, but occasionally groups of men would venture far out on the ice to where free water stood, and there they endeavored to catch a seal or two, for the rich blubber was needed to supplement the deficient diet. When such a catch was made, the men responsible butchered the seal immediately, gorging on the liver, but the slabs of meat and blubber they carried home across the ice, shouting news of their success as they approached Pelek. Then their wives and children ran to the shore and far out onto the ice to help drag home the welcome meat, and for two unbroken days the people of Pelek feasted.

But mostly in these difficult winters the Eskimos of Pelek stayed close to their huts, periodically knocking away the snow that threatened to engulf them, and huddled by their meager fires. No Eskimos in this part of the north lived in igloos; those imaginative and sometimes beautiful ice houses with their splendid domes would come later and only in regions thousands of miles to the east. These Eskimos of fourteen thousand years ago lived in excavated huts with superstructures of wood and whalebone and sealskin, much like those which the Siberians of Varnak's day, fifteen thousand years earlier, had known.

In the dark winter, fears and superstitions flourished, and it was in this enforced and nervous idleness that the shaman could best work his spells. If a pregnant woman had a difficult delivery, he knew who was at fault and he was not loath to identify the evildoer. He had not the power of life and death—that was reserved for a community consensus—but he could influence the decision. Alone in his small hut at the edge of Pelek, and inland from the sea which he tried to avoid, he sat among his pebbles and his charms, his bits of bone and precious ivories, his aspen twigs which had happened to grow in premonitory forms, and cast his spells.

This winter he directed his spells against Oogruk first, and he did this for solid reasons: Oogruk with his gentle ways and crossed eyes is the kind of man who becomes a shaman. And that lucky labret might spur him, too. Better to force him from the village. The tactic was sensible, because there was little chance that when Oogruk fled, his desirable wife would go with him. She would stay behind, that was certain. And when the shaman had collected to himself whatever powers Nukleet had, her father would then be vulnerable to him.

These men and women of Pelek, twelve thousand years before the birth of Christ, eleven thousand years before the sophistication of Athens, thoroughly understood the drives which motivated men and women. They appreciated their relationship to the land, to the sea and to the animals which occupied both. And none comprehended these forces better than the shaman, unless it was this unusual young woman Nukleet, with whom he was obsessed.

'Oogruk,' she whispered in their dark hut, 'I think he'll make it impossible for us to live in this village another year.'

'He hates me. He turns all men against me.'

'No, the one he really hates is that one over there,' and she pointed to where her father slept. And she assured her husband that whereas he, Oogruk, was first on the shaman's list, while she was second, they were both no more than expendable targets by which the medicine man planned to attain his real goal.

'What's that?'

'The destruction of my father. The possession of his power.'

When Oogruk, tutored by his wife, began to unravel this ugly web, he saw that she was right, and a quiet fury began to build within him. But when he tried to devise some way to defend himself and Nukleet during the shaman's first assaults, and then to protect his father-in-law against the sorcerer's major attack, he found himself helpless. The shaman was essential to the village, and anything that damaged him endangered the entire community. So Oogruk remained paralyzed.

His initial fury was transmuted into a kind of dull ache, an uneasiness which never left his mind, and it produced a curious reaction. The cross-eyed fellow began to sequester in the snow surrounding his father-in-law's hut bits of whalebone, and spars of wood washed up by the sea during the previous summer. He acquired sealskins and lengths of sinew from the bodies of dead animals, and as he furtively collected these items a plan evolved. He visualized that congenial group of huts on the eastern edge of the sea, where he and his fellow hunters had been revived when they were without food, and he thought repeatedly: It would be better over there.

When he had surreptitiously assembled enough stray elements to consider seriously what might be done with them, he had to take Nukleet and her father into his confidence, and when he did, he revealed a revolutionary concept: 'Why not build a kayak with three openings? Men paddling front and back. Nukleet and the child in the middle?'

His father quickly rejected such nonsense: 'Kayaks have one opening. If you want three, you build yourself an open umiak.'

But Oogruk, slow-witted as he seemed to be, saw that necessity was more important than convention: 'In high seas an umiak can be swamped and everyone drowns. But a kayak, properly lashed down, can be rolled over and refloated. Then everyone lives.' When his father-in-law continued to insist upon an umiak, Oogruk said with startling force: 'Only a kayak can save us,' and the older man salvaged his pride by shifting the discussion: 'Where would we go if we had such a kayak?'

'Over there,' Oogruk replied without hesitating, and in that pregnant moment, with his left forefinger pointing eastward across the frozen sea, he committed himself and his family to the idea of leaving this village forever.

So Oogruk began to build a kayak, and when word of this reached the shaman's ears, that hairy fellow crouched among his magic pieces, his tattered garments rank from perpetual use and filth, and began to cast spells, asking penetrating questions throughout the community: 'Why is the kayak being built? What evil thing does cross-eyed Oogruk have in mind?'

The headman, hearing this insinuation, answered it boldly: 'My stupid son-in-law lost my good kayak when he chased the whale last summer. I'm making him replace it.' And by this lie the headman committed himself. He too was prepared to leave Pelek forever and test his fortunes in the world across the sea, even though he realized that over there he would no longer be a headman. The quiet glory of leading his people in decisions would be surrendered. Other men would stand in the stern of the umiak when the whale was pursued, and better men, younger and stronger, would fight the walrus and apportion the meat when the kill was made. More than either his daughter or her husband, the headman appreciated how much he was surrendering if this flight was made, but he also knew that he was powerless once the shaman turned his face against him.

When the necromancer learned that the new kayak, whose ribs now lay exposed in the snow, was going to have three openings, he deduced that all of the persons against whom he was plotting were preparing to escape his dominance, and in the last days of winter before the great sea melted to make the use of umiaks and kayaks feasible again, he decided that he must take action against the would-be fugitives, and now he stepped forth boldly to establish his authority.

'There has never been a kayak with three openings. The spirits frown on such contaminations. And why is it being attempted? The headman is preparing to sneak out of Pelek, and if he takes his hunting skills elsewhere, we shall starve.' When he uttered these words, all knew that he was threatening to sentence the headman to a cruel existence: he must remain in the village to guide the hunting, but in shame he must also surrender his leadership to the shaman. In the hunt he would be a free man, in all else a suspected prisoner.

It was a diabolical punishment made possible only by the unquestioned faith these Eskimos had in their shaman, and the only recourse either the headman or his children could envisage was flight. So construction of the kayak was hastened, and when in late spring the snows melted and the sea began to show signs of breaking free of its icy blanket, Oogruk and the headman worked strenuously to complete their craft, while Nukleet, who had in a sense initiated the strategy of flight, gathered those necessary things which she and her daughter would carry at their feet during the sea crossing. When she realized how pitifully small the cargo would have to be, and how much she must abandon, she felt sorrow but no lack of determination.

Had she been inclined to waver, or be in any way dissatisfied with her husband, she would have had, in these middle days of spring, ample excuse for quitting the conspiracy, because the shaman began to implement his plan for getting rid of Oogruk and rendering her father impotent. One day when the ice was fairly gone from the sea and flowers were beginning to show, he arrived at the headman's hut accompanied by three young men who carried in their arms a worn kayak with only one opening, and in a harsh voice, his head thrown back as if he were talking to spirits, he cried: 'Oogruk, whose evil ways allowed the great whale to escape, who brings additional disfavor to Pelek, it is the judgment of the spirits who guide us and of the men of this village that you leave us.'

Neighbors who had gathered from the surrounding huts gasped when they heard this harsh pronouncement, and even the headman, who had led these people in so many ways and with such proven skill, was afraid to speak. But in the fearful silence that followed, Nukleet moved to stand beside her husband, and with her free left hand brought her four-year-old daughter along with her, and with this simple gesture she let it be known that if Oogruk was expelled, she would go with him.

The shaman had intended that Oogruk leave immediately, but this unexpected development frustrated that plan, and in some confusion the visitors withdrew, carrying their kayak with them. But this temporary setback did not cause the shaman to relinquish his scheme for restructuring his village and finding himself a wife, so that night young men who were never identified crept up to the headman's house in the darkness and destroyed much of the new three-man kayak.

Nukleet, out early to gather firewood, was the first to find the vandalism, and when she saw what the shaman had caused to be done she did not panic. Aware that others might be spying upon her, since the hut she occupied was apparently doomed by the spirits that guarded the village, she continued on her way to the beach to see what driftwood the sea might have thrown up after the winter freeze, and when she had an armful she returned home. There she wakened her men, warning them to make no public lamentation when they saw what had happened to their kayak.

Quietly Oogruk and her father went out to inspect the damage, and it was the former who decided that the broken ribs could be replaced and the ripped skin repaired. In three days the two men had the kayak serviceable, but this time they moved it halfway inside their hut, with Oogruk sleeping upright in the hole that remained outside, his head resting on his arms folded over the rim of the hatch.

The Eskimos of this period, and of subsequent eras too, were a peaceful lot, and they did not engage in murder, so that although the shaman had declared war against these two men, he was not free to kill them or to have them killed. That would not be tolerated. But he was, as shaman, entitled to warn his people against persons who might bring disaster upon their village, and this he did with fervor and effectiveness.

He pointed out that Oogruk's malevolence was proved by the fact that he was cross-eyed, and when he ranted: 'How otherwise would the spirits make a man's eyes to cross?' he amused his listeners by crossing his own eyes for a moment and making his already ugly face quite hideous. In these tirades he carefully spoke no words against the headman; on the contrary, he praised him rather effusively for his able guidance of the hunting umiak, thus hoping to drive a wedge between the two men, and he might have succeeded had he not made one crucial error.

Driven by his increasing desire to gain Nukleet for himself, he came upon her one evening as she was gathering the first flowers of the year, and he was so taken by her dark beauty and the lyrical way she moved along the field, stopping here and there to study the spring growth, that he was impelled, against his better judgment, to run after her awkwardly and try to embrace her. When growing up, she had known several young men of considerable attractiveness, and for some months she had been a wife to Shaktoolik, the handsome one, so she knew what men were supposed to be, and not even by stretching her imagination could she conceive of the repulsive shaman as a partner. More seriously, she had discovered in Oogruk the kind of companion that women treasured, once they overlooked the obvious deficiencies. He was gentle yet brave, kind to others yet resolute when his mind was made up. In his defiance of the shaman he had shown courage and in his building of the new kayak skill, and in her more mature age, twenty-one, she knew how lucky she was to have found him.

So the greasy shaman with his matted hair and smelly rags had little to make him desirable except his acknowledged relationship with the spirits and the ability to make them work in his behalf. And when he grabbed at her now, she discovered that she was at last prepared to defy even those powers: 'Go back, you filthy one.' She pushed him away, vigorously, and then in the disgust of the moment she did a most unwise thing: she laughed at him, and this he could not tolerate. As he staggered back he swore that he would destroy this woman and all her companions, even her blameless daughter. The village of Pelek would know these malevolent ones no more.

Back in his isolated hut where he communed with the forces that ran the universe, he writhed in anger, devising one plot after another to punish this woman who had scorned him. He contemplated poisons and knives and sinkings at sea, but in the end his wilder passions subsided, and he decided that on the morrow, when the sun was up, he would summon the villagers and pronounce total anathema upon the headman, his daughter, her husband and their child. And in doing so, he would recite a calendar of the evil things they had done to bring discredit upon the village and incur the enmity of the spirits. He would make his accusations so violent that in the end his listeners might in frenzy decide to ignore the Eskimo aversion to killing and slay these four to save themselves from the retribution of the spirits.

But when, in the early dawn, he started to assemble the villagers and lead them to the headman's hut, where the denunciations would be made, he found most of them already gathered at the shore. When he elbowed his way among them, he saw that they were staring out to sea, where, on the horizon too far away to be apprehended by even the swiftest umiak, three figures nestling in the three protected holes of a new type of kayak were on their way to that unknown world on the far side.

BECAUSE THE GREAT sea was choppy, with a few vagrant icebergs still drifting southward, these daring emigrants in their fragile kayak were going to need three full days to make the crossing from Asia to North America, but in this bright dawn all things seemed possible, and they moved toward the east with a lightness of heart that would have seemed impossible to anyone not associated with the sea. When the headlands of Asia disappeared and nothingness lay ahead, they pushed on, with the sun streaming upon their faces. Alone on the great sea, uncertain as to what the next days might hold, they caught their breath as their kayak raced down into the trough of some powerful wave, then gasped with delight as it rose to the next oncoming crest. They were one with the seals sporting in the spray, they were cousins to the tusked walruses making their way north to mate. When a whale spouted in the distance and then sounded, flukes high in the air, the headman shouted: 'Stay out there. We'll come back for you later.'

Their precipitate departure from Pelek had produced two moments of such gravity that they summarized a life. Nukleet had returned from her encounter with the shaman white with shock, and when her father asked what had happened, she merely said: 'We must leave in the darkness.' Oogruk had cried: 'We can't,' and she had replied simply: 'We must.' She said no more, gave no explanation of how she had rebuffed and ridiculed the shaman, nor did she confess that she had brought such danger upon their hut that further occupancy was impossible.

The men, realizing that some forbidden line had been crossed, had asked only: 'Must it be tonight?' and she had started to nod, but had stopped, for she realized that she must give them the strongest possible reply, one that would allow no counterargument: 'We leave as soon as the village is asleep, or we die!'

The second moment of significant decision had come when the unwilling emigrants crept to the beach, father and son carrying the kayak silently, mother and daughter bringing with them the household goods. After the men had placed the craft in the water and had helped Nukleet into the center opening, where she would hold her daughter during their escape, the headman stepped naturally to the rear seat, the one from which the kayak would be commanded, supposing that he would lead the expedition. But before he could take that place, Oogruk stepped in front of him, saying quietly: 'I will steer,' and his father-in-law had surrendered the command.

Now, far from shore and safe from the retaliations of the shaman, the four Eskimos in their frail kayak settled into the routines that would govern them for the next three days. Oogruk at the rear, set a slow, steady pace, two hundred strokes on the right side, a grunted cry 'Shift!' and two hundred on the left. In the front seat, the headman applied his powerful muscles strenuously, as if their progress depended upon him alone; it was primarily he who pulled the canoe forward. And Nukleet, in the middle position, passed drinking water to her men fore and aft and gave them bits of seal blubber to chew upon as they paddled.

The little girl, always aware of the burden she placed upon her mother, sometimes tried to ride upon the rim of the hatch, but always Nukleet drew her back, with the warning: 'If you were up there and we turned over, how could we save you?' and heavy though the child grew, Nukleet kept her on her lap.

Travel did not stop at night, for in the silvery darkness it was important that forward motion be maintained, and both Oogruk and his father-in-law knew this, so when the sun finally went down in these first days of summer, they settled into a slow, steady stroke which kept the prow of the boat headed east. But no one could paddle incessantly, and when the sun rose, the men took turns dozing, first the headman, then Oogruk, and when they did, each was careful to slip his precious paddle inside the opening, jammed against his leg, from where he could retrieve it quickly.

Nukleet did not sleep during the first two days; she encouraged her daughter to do so, and when the child's drowsy head nestled against hers, she felt more like a mother than ever before, because on this great restless sea she, Nukleet, was all that protected her daughter from death. But she had two other sensations almost equally strong. Throughout the daring trip she kept her left foot against the sealskin that contained the water, assuring herself that it was there, and her right against the spare paddle which might become so necessary if one of the men should in an accident lose his. She imagined herself reaching down, retrieving the paddle, and handing it along to either her husband or her father, and there in the vast wilderness of the sea, she felt certain that if such an accident did occur, it would be her father and not Oogruk who would lose his paddle.

But on the morning of the third day she simply could not stay awake, and once when she dozed and realized that she had left her daughter unprotected, she cried: 'Father, you must hold the child for a while!' but as she started to pass the girl forward, Oogruk intervened: 'Bring her this way,' and as Nukleet fell toward sleep she thought, with tears in her eyes: She is not his daughter but she does fill his heart.

O N   T H E   A F T E R N O O N of that third day the eastern lands became visible, and this inspired the men to paddle more strongly, but night fell before they could reach the shore, and as the stars came out, seeming more brilliant because they shone not only with their own light but also with hope, the four silent immigrants moved purposefully ahead, with Nukleet again holding her child close, still keeping her feet against the reassuring water and extra paddle.

It was some while after midnight that the stars disappeared and a wind began to rise, and suddenly, with the swift change of weather that region so often provided, a storm was upon them, and in the darkness the kayak began to pitch and twist as it swept down vast chasms in the sea and rose to heights that terrified. Now the two men had to paddle furiously to keep their frail craft from capsizing, and just when they felt they could no longer bear the burning pain in their arms, Oogruk would cry 'Shift!' above the howling wind and they would in perfect rhythm change sides and maintain the forward motion.

Nukleet, feeling the kayak slip and slide, clutched her child more tightly, but the little girl did not cry or show fear; though she was terrified by the darkness and the violence of the sea, the only sign she gave of her concern was the increased pressure with which she grasped her mother's arm.

And then, as a giant wave came at them from the darkness, the headman shouted 'Over!' and the kayak was tumbled about, dipping far down on its left side and sinking totally under the great wave.

It had been agreed a thousand years earlier that when a kayak turned over, the man paddling it would, with a powerful sweep of his paddle and a vigorous twisting of his body, try to keep the craft turning in the direction in which it capsized; so now, submerged in dark, icy water, the two men obeyed these ancient instructions, straining against their paddles and throwing their weight to encourage the kayak to keep rolling. Nukleet automatically did the same, for she had been so indoctrinated since birth, and even the child knew that salvation lay only in keeping the kayak rolling, so as she clung ever more tightly to her mother, she, too, helped maintain the roll.

When the kayak was at the bottom of its submersion, with its passengers upside down in the stygian waters, the miracle of its construction manifested itself, for the exquisitely fitted sealskin kept water out and air in, and in this favorable condition the light little craft continued its roll, battled the terrific power of the storm, and righted itself. When the travelers brushed the water from their eyes and saw in the east the first signals of a new day, they saw also that they were nearing land, and as the waves subsided and calm returned to the sea, the men paddled quietly ahead while Nukleet clung to her daughter, whom she had protected from the depths.

They landed before noon, unaware of whether the village they had once visited lay to the north or south but satisfied that within reason it could be found. As the two men hauled the kayak ashore, Nukleet stopped them for a moment, reached into its innards, and pulled forth the spare paddle. Standing between the men, with the paddle erect in the bright morning air, she said: 'It was not needed. You knew what to do.' And she embraced them both, first her father, out of deep respect for all he had done in the old land and would do in the new, and then her gallant husband, because of the love she bore him.

In this way these dark round-faced Eskimos came to Alaska.

T WELVE THOUSAND YEARS ago—and now the chronology becomes somewhat more reliable because archaeologists have uncovered datable artifacts: stone outlines of houses and even long-hidden remains of villages—a group of Eskimos who were different from others of that remarkable race existed at various locations near the Alaskan end of the land bridge. The cause of their difference has not been ascertained, for they spoke the same language as the other Eskimos; they had managed the same adaptation to life in the coldest climates; and they were in some respects even more skilled in living productively off the creatures that roamed the earth and swam in the nearby seas.

They were somewhat smaller than the other Eskimos and darker of skin, as if they had originated in some different part of Siberia or even farther west in central Asia, but they had stayed in lands close to the western end of the land bridge long enough to acquire the basic characteristics of the Eskimos who lived there. However, when they crossed over to Alaska they dwelled apart and aroused the suspicion and even the enmity of their neighbors.

Such antagonism between groups was not unusual, for when Varnak's original group had reached Alaska they became known as Athapascans, and as we shall see, they and their descendants populated most of Alaska. Therefore, when Oogruk's Eskimos arrived to preempt the shoreline, they were greeted with hostility by the long-settled Athapascans who monopolized the choicer areas between the glaciers, and it became the rule that Eskimos clung to the seafronts, where they could maintain their ancient marine ways of life, while the Athapascans clustered in the more favorable lands, where they existed as hunters. Decades would pass without one group trespassing on the lands of the other, but when they did collide, there was apt to be trouble, contention and even death, with the sturdier Athapascans usually victorious. After all, they had occupied these lands for thousands of years before the Eskimos arrived.

It was not the traditional worldwide antagonism of mountain men versus seacoast men, but it was close to that, and if Oogruk's people found it difficult to defend themselves against the more aggressive Athapascans, this third wave of smaller, gentler newcomers seemed unable to protect themselves against anyone. So when it became doubtful that they could retain their foothold in one of the better areas of Alaska, the two hundred or so members of their clan began to question their future.

Unfortunately, at just this moment in their declining fortunes their revered sage, an old man of thirty-seven, fell so ill that he was unable to guide them, and things fell into drift, with important decisions either delayed or ignored. For example, the group had in its enforced wanderings settled temporarily in the desirable area south on the peninsula which had formed the westernmost tip of Alaska in those thousands of years when rising oceans had obliterated the land bridge. Now, of course, with the bridge exposed, there was no ocean within three hundred miles of the region, but instead, there was a natural resource even more copious and varied in its richness, and upon this largesse the group subsisted.

For reasons which have never been explained and perhaps never will be, in this period around twelve thousand years before the present, the wildlife of Alaska, and elsewhere across the earth, proliferated at a rate hitherto unknown. Not only were the species of animals extraordinarily rich in variety, but the numbers of the animals were almost excessive, and what was most inexplicable, they were invariably much, much bigger than their later descendants. Beavers were immense. Bison were like shaggy monuments. Moose towered in the air, with antlers bigger than some trees, and the shaggy musk ox was staggering in size. It was a time when great animals defined the age and when men were fortunate to live among them, for to bring down even one of these beasts meant that meat was ensured for many months to come.

Predominant as in the time of Varnak the Hunter were the mammoths, largest of the animals and still by far the most majestic. In the fifteen thousand years since Varnak had tracked Matriarch without succeeding in killing her, the mammoths had increased both in size and number, so that the area occupied by this group of Eskimos had so many of the huge creatures that any boy growing up along the eastern end of this land bridge had to become familiar with them. He would not see them every day, or even every month, but he would know that they, along with the huge bears and the crafty lions, were out there.

Such a boy was Azazruk, seventeen years old, tall for his age and Asian in every item of his appearance. His hair was a deeper black, his skin a browner yellow, his eyes more sharply narrow, his arms longer than those of his companions. That his ancestors had originated among the Mongols of Asia, there could be no doubt. He was the son of the old man who was dying, and it had been his father's hope that the boy would mature into the leadership he had exercised, but year by year it had become apparent that this was not to be, and while the father never berated his son for this deficiency, he could not hide his disappointment.

In fact, with the most hopeful intentions, the old man failed to identify any area in which his son could contribute to the clan. He could not hunt; he was unskilled at flicking sharp arrow points from cores of flint; and he showed no aptitude in leading men into battle against their oppressors. He did have a strong voice when he wanted to use it, so that leadership during discussions might have been possible, but he preferred to speak so softly that sometimes he seemed almost feminine. Yet he was a good young man, and both his father and the community at large knew it. The important question was: How would he exercise this goodness if a crisis demanded that he do so?

His father, a wise man, had seen that very few men who lived a normal life escaped the great testing moments. Born leaders, like himself, encountered them constantly, and in tracking animals or building huts or deciding where to lead the clan next, their decisions were held up to judgment by their peers. That was the burden of leadership which justified the privileges. But he had also observed that the average man, the one not remotely qualified for leadership, also faced these moments when all hung in the balance. Then a man had to act swiftly, without time for meticulous consideration or a careful calculation of possibilities. The mammoth pursued in a hunt turned unexpectedly, and someone had to confront it. The kayak upset in river turbulence, and when the paddler tried to right it in the ordinary way by increasing the speed of its toppling, a rock intervened, and then what? A man who did his best to avoid any unpleasantness was suddenly faced by a bully. Nor were women exempt from this requirement of instant judgment: A baby started from the womb in an upside-down condition, and what did the older women do? A growing girl refused to menstruate, and how should that be handled?

Since life within the ice castle of Alaska presented human beings with constant challenges, Azazruk by the age of seventeen should have developed clearly defined characteristics, but he had not, and his dying father could not guess what his son's future would be.

On a day in late spring when by ill chance Athapascans from the areas to the north made a sortie against the clan, the old man lay dying. His son was with him and not with the warriors who were rather futilely trying to protect their holdings, and as death neared, the father whispered: 'Azazruk, you must lead our people to a safe home,' and before the boy could respond or even let his father know that he had heard this command, death resolved the old man's apprehensions.

It was not a big fight that day, merely a continuation of the pressure the Athapascans exerted on all Eskimos regardless of where they settled, but when it coincided with the death of their longtime leader, it did confuse the clan, and the bewildered men sat before their huts in the spring evening wondering what to do. No one, and especially not those who had fought, looked to Azazruk for guidance or even suggestions. So he was left alone. Facing the mystery of death, and pondering his father's last words, he left the village and wandered away until he came to a stream which flowed down from the glacier to the east.

There as he tried to unravel the thoughts which tumbled through his head, he chanced to look down at the stream, and he saw that it was almost white because it carried myriad bits of stone flaked from rocks at the face of the glacier, and for some time he marveled at this whiteness, wondering if it represented some kind of omen. As he pondered this possibility, he saw protruding from the black mud that formed the bank of the river a curious object, golden in color and shining, and when he stooped to rescue it from the mud he saw that it was a small piece of ivory about the size of two fingers. Possibly it had broken off from some mammoth tusk or been brought inland from a walrus hunt ages ago, but what made it remarkable, even in those first moments when Azazruk held it in his hand, was that either by chance or the work of some long-dead artist, the ivory represented a living thing, perhaps a man, perhaps an animal. It had no head, but there was a torso, a joining of legs and one clearly defined hand or paw.

Turning the object this way and that in the fading light, Azazruk was astounded by the reality of this piece: it was ivory, of that he was certain, but it was also something living, and to possess such a thing created in the young man a sense of awe, of challenge and purpose. He could not believe that the finding of this lively little creature on the precise day of his father's death, when his clan was in confusion, could be an accident. He realized that the person whom the great spirits had led to this omen was destined for some significant task, and in this moment of discovery he decided to keep his find a secret. The figure was small enough to be hidden within the twist of deerskin he wore, and there it would remain until the spirits who had sent it revealed their intentions.

Then, just as he was about to leave the stream whose turbulent waters were still as white as the milk of a musk ox, he was halted by a choir of voices, and he knew the sounds emanated from the spirits who had sent him the ivory figurine and who watched over the fortunes of his clan. The voices announced in a beautiful whispering harmony which only he could have heard: 'You are to be the shaman.' And they sang no more.

A message like this, which might have produced tumults of joy in the heart of any ordinary Eskimo, since it would mean authority and constant intercourse with the spirits who controlled life, caused Azazruk only consternation. From his earliest days his sagacious father had found himself opposed to the various shamans who had been associated with his clan; he respected their unique powers and acknowledged the fact that he and his people had to rely upon their guidance in spiritual matters, but he resented their constant intrusion upon his day-to-day prerogatives. He had warned his son: 'Stay clear of the shamans. Obey their instructions in all matters concerning the spirits, but otherwise ignore them.' The old man was especially disgusted by the slovenly habits of the shamans and the filthy skins and matted hair in which they performed their mysteries and rendered their judgments: 'A man doesn't have to stink in order to be wise.' And the boy had had numerous opportunities to witness the justice of his father's strictures.

Once when Azazruk was ten, a scrawny Eskimo from the north had attached himself to the clan, proclaiming arrogantly that he was a shaman and offering to take the place of a wise man who had died. The deceased shaman had been somewhat better than average, so the inadequacy of the upstart miracle worker became quickly evident. He brought no mammoths or bears to the hunting areas, no male babies to the birthing beds. The general spirit of the village was neither improved nor mended, and Azazruk's father had used the unfortunate example of this inadequate man to condemn all shamans: 'My mother taught me they were essential, and I still believe it. How could we live with spirits who might attack us if we did not have their protection? But I do wish the shamans could live in the spruce forest and protect us from there.'

But now as Azazruk stood with the ivory figure hidden against his belly and heard the tumbling brook beside him, he began to suspect that his newfound treasure had been sent by the spirits to ratify their decision that he, Azazruk, was destined to be the shaman his people needed. He shivered at the implication and tried to dismiss it because of the heavy responsibility such a position entailed; he even contemplated throwing the unwelcome emissary back into the stream, but when he took the ivory from his waist and started to do so, the little creature seemed to be smiling at him, face or no face. And the unseen smile was so warm and congenial that Azazruk, tormented though he was by his father's death and these strange happenings, had to chuckle and then to laugh and finally to leap in the air in a kind of manic joy. He acknowledged then that he had been called, or perhaps commanded, to serve as shaman to his clan, and in this moment of spiritual acceptance of his obligation, the spirits showed their approval by causing a miracle to happen.

From the aspen trees lining the magical stream came a lonely rogue mammoth, not of exceptional size but huge in the evening shadows, and when it saw Azazruk it did not halt or shy away; instead it came forward, oblivious of the fact that it was inviting peril. When it reached a spot not four body lengths away, it stopped, looked at Azazruk, and remained rooted in place, its monstrous feet sinking slightly into the soft soil, and there it stayed, cropping aspen and willow leaves as if the Eskimo did not exist.

Slowly Azazruk withdrew, a step at a time, until he was well clear of the trees and the stream. Then, in a kind of mystical trance, he walked solemnly back to his village, where women were preparing his father for burial, and when various men, impressed by his grave mien, came to attention, he announced in sober tones: 'I have brought you a mammoth,' and the hunt was on. Four days later when, because of his ardent assurances to the men, they fought the great beast and killed it, the village realized that at the moment of his father's death that good man's spirit had passed into the body of his son, who predicted that the rogue mammoth would run east for two days after the first stabbings and come back the last two, seeking familiar haunts in which to die. Indeed, the creature returned to within a short walk of where Azazruk had found him, so that when he died his hulking carcass lay almost in the spot where it would be consumed. 'Azazruk has power over animals,' the men and women said as they butchered the mammoth and feasted on the rich meat.

And he seemed to have just that, for two weeks later when one of the village men was attacked by a pair of lionesses and badly clawed about the neck, everyone assumed that the man must die, for it was known that lions had so much poison in their claws that death was never escaped. However, this time Azazruk had run out, driven away the lionesses, and proceeded immediately to poultice the bleeding wound with leaves growing low in the forest and with moss, and the villagers were astounded to see the stricken man soon walking about and twisting his neck as if nothing had happened.

WHEN AZAZRUK ASSUMED spiritual leadership he made two innovations— which consolidated his control and made him more acceptable to his people than any other shaman within memory. He refused, utterly and with visible moral force, to accept any responsibility for military, governmental or foraging duties; he pointed out repeatedly that they were the prerogative of the leader, a daring, tested man of twenty-two and one for whom Azazruk had great respect. This man was brave, had a wide knowledge of animal habits, and asked no one to do what he himself was not prepared to do first. Under his leadership the clan could expect to protect itself at least as well as before, perhaps even better.

Second, Azazruk established practices that had never been tried before among his people. He saw no necessity for a shaman to live apart from others, and certainly no need to be filthy or unkempt. He continued to occupy his father's hut—a place half underground, half wood and stone above—and there he cared for his caribou trousers, his sealskin cloak. He made himself available to people with problems, and he especially attended to children in order to get them started in proper directions. Specifically, he assigned them tasks: girls were expected to be able to handle the skins of animals and the bones of mammoths and reindeer; boys were required to learn about hunting and the construction of implements used in the chase. He wanted the tribe to have a skilled flint-knapper, another who knew about the handling of fire, another clever in the tracking of animals.

Azazruk believed that most of his power derived from the fact that he understood animals, for whenever he moved about the vast lands between the glaciers he was attentive to the beasts that shared this paradise with him. Size was of no concern to him. He knew where the little wolverines hid, and how the badgers stalked their prey. He understood the behavior of the small foxes and the devices of the rats and tiny creatures that burrowed under the soil. Sometimes, when he himself hunted or helped others to do so, he felt momentarily like a wolf stalking a herd, but his major delight was always those larger creatures: the mammoth, the great moose, the musk ox, the tremendous bison and the powerful lion.

If man had a certain majesty because of his superior wit and cleverness of hand, these animals so much larger than he had their own majesty, and it derived from the fact that in this area of bitter winter cold they had found ways to protect themselves and to survive till spring warmed the air and melted the snows. They were as wise in their own ways as any shaman, and by studying them, Azazruk hoped he could perhaps detect their secrets and profit from them.

But when his study of the animals was concluded, and he had mixed their wisdom in with what he was learning about human beings, there remained another world of the spirit which neither he nor the animals could penetrate or inhabit. What caused the great winds to roar out of Asia? Why was it always colder to the north than to the south? Who fed the glaciers, when anyone could see that almost daily they died when their snouts reached dry land or the sea? Who called yellow flowers to birth in the spring and red ones in the fall? And why were babies born at almost the same time that old men died?

He spent the first seven years of his leadership in wrestling with these questions, and in that time he devised certain rules. The shiny pebbles he had collected, the oddments his mother had treasured, the sticks and bones which had omen-power were of profound assistance when he wished to summon the spirits and converse with them. From such dialogue he learned much, but always in the back of his mind there remained that vision of the piece of golden ivory shaped like an animal or a man, like a smiling man perhaps, even though it had no head. And he began to see his world as an amusing place where ridiculous things happened and where a man or woman could obey all the rules and avoid all the perils but still fall into some absurd situation at which their neighbors and the spirits themselves had to laugh, and not furtively either but with great guffaws. The world was tragic, and fine men and strong animals died arbitrarily, but it was also so preposterous that sometimes the crests of mountains seemed to bend together in laughter.

IN AZAZRUK'S NINTH year as shaman the laughter ceased. Illness brought in from the sea struck the village, and after the bodies were buried, the Athapascans invaded from the east. Mammoths left the area, the bison followed, bringing hunger, and one day when all things seemed to conspire against the clan, Azazruk summoned the village elders, more than half of them older than he, and said bluntly: 'The spirits send warnings. It's time to move.'

'Where?' the leader of the hunters asked, and before Azazruk could offer a suggestion, the men advanced the negative answers.

'We can't go toward the home of the Great Star. The people who hunt the whale are there.'

'And we can't go to where the sun rises. The people of the trees are there.'

'The Land of Broken Bays would be reasonable, but those people are fierce. They will drive us back.'

And so the logical options were discarded. It seemed that this unfortunate group, so small that it commanded no power, was wanted nowhere, but then a timid man, one who could scarcely be called a leader, suggested: 'We could go back to where we first came from,' and during a long silence the men considered this retreat, but to them the land their ancestors had left two thousand years before was not a viable memory; there were tribal recollections of a decisive trip from the west, but no one remembered any longer what that ancient homeland had been like or what strong reasons had compelled the old ones to leave. 'We came from over there,' an old woman said, waving her hand vaguely toward Asia, 'but who knows?'

No one did, and that first broaching of the subject came to naught, but some days later Azazruk saw a girl cutting a friend's hair with a clamshell, and he asked: 'Where did you find that shell?' and the girls told him that in their family there was a tradition that several such shells had been brought to the village in times past by strange-looking men who spoke their language, but in a curious way.

'Where did they come from?'

The girls did not know, but next day they brought their parents to the shaman's hut, and these older people said that they had not known the shell-bearers: 'They came before our time. But our grandmother told us they had come from that direction,' and both agreed from their different memories that the strangers had come from the southwest. They had not been like those in the village, but they had been likable visitors and they had danced. Everyone whose parents had heard the ancient stories agreed that the shell-bearers had danced.

It was this accidental intelligence, born of no sensible reasoning, which launched Azazruk in his contemplation of going to the place from which the shells had come. After much thought he concluded that since movement into no other area was practical and since continuation where his people were seemed destined to produce increasingly bad results, their only hope lay in lands that were unknown but which supposedly were habitable.

But he could not recommend such a perilous journey without ratification from the spirits, so for three long days he remained practically motionless in his hut, his fetishes spread before him, and in the darkness, when hunger had induced a kind of stupor, they spoke to him. Voices came from afar, sometimes in tongues he did not understand, at other times as clear as the bellowing of a moose on a frosty morning: 'Azazruk, your people starve. Enemies insult them on all sides. You are too powerless to fight. You must flee.'

This he had already accepted, and he considered it strange that the spirits should repeat the obvious, but upon reflection he withdrew that harsh judgment: They are moving step by step, like a man testing new ice. And after a while the spirits reached the core of what they wished to say: 'It would be better, Azazruk, if you went toward the Great Star to the edge of the frozen land and hunted the whale and walrus in the old way. So if you are brave and have many bold men, go there.'

Beating his hands against his forehead, he shouted: 'But our leader has no fighting men in sufficient number,' and the spirits said: 'We know.'

In total frustration Azazruk wondered why the spirits would recommend he go to the north when they knew it was so hazardous, but what they said next drove him to a frenzy: 'In the north you would build umiaks and go forth to hunt the great whale. You would chase the walrus and perish if he caught you. You would hunt the seal, and fish through the ice, and live as your people had always lived. In the north you would do all these things.'

The words were so insane that Azazruk started to choke. Air caught in his throat, and he fell forward among his fetishes in a faint. He remained thus for a long while, and in his frenzied dreams he realized that in giving these impossible orders, the spirits were reminding him of who he was, of what his life had been for generations untold, telling him that even though he and his clan had lived inland for two thousand years, they were still people of the frozen seas which lesser men would not dare to challenge. He was an Eskimo, a man of wondrous tradition, and not even the passage of generations could erase that supreme fact.

When he revived, cleansed of fear by the insistent messages of the spirits, they spoke calmly: 'To the southwest there must be islands, or how could the strangers have brought shells?'

'I do not understand,' he cried, and they said: 'Islands mean seas, and seas mean shells. A man can find his heritage in many different forms.' And they said no more.

On the morning of the fourth day Azazruk appeared before the worried people who had spent the previous night outside his hut, listening to the strange sounds coming from within. Tall, gaunt, clean, sunken-eyed and afire with an illumination he had not known before, he announced: 'The spirits have spoken. We shall go there,' and he pointed toward the southwest.

But back in his hut, where his people could not see him, his resolve faltered, and he was overcome by terror at what might happen on such a journey, over distances to strange lands that might or might not exist. Then he saw that the little ivory figure was laughing at him, ridiculing his fears and sharing with him in its timeless way the wisdom it had acquired when part of the tusk of a great walrus and when lying for seventeen thousand years in the muck of a glacial stream while a universe of dead fish and stricken mammoths and careless men drifted past: 'It will be joyous, Azazruk. You will see seven thousand sunsets, seven thousand sunrises.'

'Will I find a refuge for my people?'

'Does that matter?'

And as he tucked the little figure back in its pouch he could hear the laughter, the chuckling of the wind coming over a hill, the exhilaration of a whale breaching after a long submarine chase, the gaiety of a young fox chasing birds aimlessly, the wonderful, hallowed sound of a universe that does not care whether a man finds refuge or not so long as he enjoys the irreverent pleasure of the search.

THE NINETEEN YEARS during which Azazruk led his wandering people back and forth in southeastern Alaska were among the most glorious this part of the world would ever know. The animal kingdom was at its apex, providing an endless supply of noble beasts well suited to the stupendous land. The mountains were higher then, the surging glaciers more powerful, the wild-running rivers more tumultuous. It was an energetic land whose every feature struck notes of wonder, from the winters so cold that prudent animals went underground, to summers in which a multitude of flowers filled the plains.

It was a land in those years of enormous dimension; no one man could travel from one end to the other or traverse the multitude of glacial rivers and soaring peaks. From almost any spot a traveler could see snow-capped mountains, and when he slept at night he could hear powerful lions and huge wolves not far away. Of special interest were the brown bears, as tall as trees when they stood erect, which they liked to do, as if boasting of their height. In later years they would be known as grizzlies, and of all the animals that came close to camps where travelers halted, they were the most perplexing. If food was available, they could be as gentle as the sheep which inhabited the lower hills, but if they were disappointed or enraged by unexpected behavior, they could tear a man apart with one swipe of their tremendous claws.

In these days the bears were immense, sixteen and seventeen feet tall, and in the uninitiated they produced terror, but to Azazruk, as one who had learned to consult with animals, they were big, awkward, unpredictable friends. He did not seek them out, but he spoke with them when they appeared at the edges of his people's camps, and when he came upon them he would sit calmly upon a rock and ask them how the berries were among the birch trees and what the mighty bison were up to. The great bears, always big enough to bite him in two, would listen attentively, and sometimes come close enough almost to nudge him, and smelling that he was unafraid, never harmed him.

That was not the case with one young hunter, who, seeing a bear with the shaman and not knowing that a special relationship existed between the two, had attacked it. The bear, bewildered by this sudden change, fended off the hunter, but when the man attacked a second time, it swung its right paw, almost decapitating the young assailant, and lumbered off. This time the shaman's ministration with leaves and moss proved futile; the man was dead before words could be exchanged, and the camp saw that great bear no more.

Why did it take nineteen years for this ordinary group of Eskimos to locate their new home? For one thing, they did not speed to some established target; they drifted along, sampling this place and that. For another, rivers were sometimes in flood for two or three summers at a time and mountains intruded. But principally the fault was the shaman's, for whenever he came upon a likely spot, he wanted to believe that this was it, and he tended to remain with his choice until adversity became so great that survival dictated a further move.

Always the people allowed him to decide, for they were aware that in shifting so radically to new terrains, they must have the unqualified support of the spirits. Once in the later years when they were well established on the shores of a huge lake teeming with fish, they wanted to remain, and even when the spirits warned the shaman that it was time for his people to move, they spent two years dawdling along the shores of the lake, but when they reached the western extremity where a lively river left to seek the sea, they obediently packed their few belongings and moved on.

During the next year, the seventeenth of their pilgrimage, they were faced by problems far more crucial than usual, for even the most casual exploration proved that they were entering not merely upon new land but onto a peninsula bordered on both its narrowing shores by ocean. But the spirits encouraged them to test the peninsula, and when they again found themselves in close contact with the sea, after an absence of two thousand years, powerful changes began to take place, as if racial memories long subdued were surging back to the surface.

Responding to the salt air and the splashing of waves, these wanderers who had never eaten shellfish or caught fish in the sea found themselves enthusiastically doing both. Artisans began building little boats not much different from the kayaks their ancestors had known, and those craft which did not take well to waves were quickly abandoned, while others which seemed adapted to the sea were improved. In a score of little ways, many of them of apparent insignificance, these onetime Eskimos were becoming sea people again.

Azazruk, as fearful as any about forging ahead into a world so different, was encouraged to continue by the unwavering support of his fetishes, for when he spread them in his skin hut beside the ocean, they spoke only approvingly of this venture, and the most ardent encouragement came from the little ivory figure. 'I think,' Azazruk said to it one night as the waves of a rising sea thundered outside, 'that you wanted to bring us to the sea. Did you once live here?' And above the storm he could hear the little figurine laughing, and on later days, when the seas were calm, he was sure that he heard chuckles from that pouch.

The clan spent that year pushing ever westward, exploring their peninsula as if just around the next hill they would find the refuge they sought, but sometimes in the distance they could see smoke from unidentified fires and this meant they were not yet safe. In this uncertain state of mind, they reached the western end of the peninsula, and now they were confronted by a question, the answer to which would determine their history for the next twelve thousand years: should they try to maintain a foothold on the peninsula or should they plunge ahead onto the unknown islands?

Rarely does a people have an opportunity to make within a limited period a decision of such gravity; choices are made, of course, but they tend to creep up on a society over a much longer period of time or even to be made by refusing to choose. Such a moment would occur eons later when black people in central Africa had to decide whether to move south out of the tropics to cooler lands fronting the southern oceans, or when a group of Pilgrims in England had to decide if life was likely to be better on the opposite side of the Atlantic.

For Azazruk's clan their moment came when they elected, after painful deliberation, to quit the peninsula and try their fortunes on that chain of islands stringing out to the west. This was a daring decision, and of the two hundred who had left their relatively secure settlement eighteen years before, fewer than half had survived to enter the islands, but many had been born along the way. In a way this was fortunate, because it meant that the majority of those who would execute the decision would be younger and more prepared to adjust to the unknown.

It was a sturdy group that followed the shaman across the narrow sea onto that first island, and they would require both physical stamina and moral courage to exist in these forbidding terrains. In the chain there were more than a dozen major islands they might have chosen and more than a hundred lesser ones, some little more than specks. They were dramatic islands, many with high mountains, others with great volcanoes covered with snow much of the year, and Azazruk's people looked in awe as they moved along the chain. They explored the big one later to be known as Unimak, then crossed the sea to Akutan and Unalaska and Umnak. Then they tried Seguam and Atka and twisted Adak, until one morning as they probed westward they saw on the horizon a forbidding island protected by a barrier of five tall mountains rising from the sea to guard its eastern approaches. Azazruk, repelled by this inhospitable shore, cried to his rowers in the first boat: 'On to the next one!' but as the convoy passed the headland to the north, he saw opening before him a splendid wide bay from whose central plain rose a towering volcano of perfect outline and surpassing snow-capped beauty that had been sleeping peacefully for the past ten thousand years.

'This is to be your home,' the spirits whispered, adding a reassuring promise: 'Here you will live dangerously yet know great joy.' With this surety Azazruk headed toward the shore, but halted when the spirits said: 'Beyond the headland there is a better,' and when he explored further he came upon a deep bay rimmed by mountains and protected on the northwest, from where storms came, by a chain of islands curved like a protecting hand. Along the eastern side of this bay he found an estuary, a kind of fjord flanked by cliffs, and when he reached its head he cried: 'This is what the spirits promised us!' and here his wandering clan established their home.

The travelers had not been on Lapak even one full season before, on a much smaller island to the north, a tiny volcano, which reached not a hundred feet above the sea, exploded in a dazzling display of fiery fumes, as if it were an angry whale spouting not water but flame. The newcomers could not hear the sparks hissing as they fell back into the sea, nor know that on the far shore, beneath clouds of steam, a river of lava, apparently endless in supply, was pouring into the sea, but they did witness the continued display, which the spirits assured Azazruk they had organized as a welcome to his new home. And because the young volcano sputtered whenever it was about to explode, the newcomers named it Qugang, the Whistler.

Lapak had a broken, rectangular shape, twenty-one miles east to west at its widest, eleven north-south in its two extended arms. Eleven mountains, some reaching more than two thousand feet high, rimmed the outer circumference, but the shoreline of the two bays was habitable and in certain places even inviting. No tree had ever stood on the island, but a lush green grass grew everywhere, and low shrubs appeared wherever they found a valley offering protection from the wind. The salient aspect, apart from the two volcanoes and the protecting mountains, was the abundance of inlets, for this was, as the spirits had foretold, an island totally committed to the sea, and any man who elected to live on it knew that he must make his living from that sea and spend his life in obedience to its waves, its storms and its abundance.

Azazruk, surveying his new domain, noted with assurance the several small rivers that threaded inland: 'These will bring us food. On this island our people can live in peace.'

Prior to the arrival of Azazruk's people the island had never known inhabitants, although occasionally some storm-driven hunter in his solitary kayak or group of men in their umiak had been tossed on the island, and one morning some children playing in a valley that opened onto the sea came upon three skeletons of men who had died in dreadful isolation. But no group had ever tried to settle here, and it was generally supposed that no woman had ever set foot on Lapak before Azazruk's people came.

However, one day a group of men who had gone fishing in one of the rivers that came down from the flanks of the central volcano was overtaken by nightfall and sought refuge in a cave high on a mound overlooking the area of the Bering Sea subtended by the chain of islands, and when morning came they saw to their astonishment that their cave was occupied by a woman unbelievably old, and they ran to their shaman with cries of 'Miracle! An old woman hiding in a cave.'

Azazruk followed the men to the cave and asked them to wait outside while he investigated this strange development, and when he was well within the cave, he found himself facing the withered, leathery features of an ancient woman whose mummified body had been propped upright, so that she seemed to be alive and almost eager to share with him the adventures she had experienced in the past millennia.

He remained with her for a long time, trying to visualize how she had reached this island, what her life had been like and whose loving hands had placed her in this protected and reverential position. She seemed so eager to speak to him that he bent forward as if to hear her, and in a low voice he spoke comforting words to himself, as if she were uttering them: 'Azazruk, you have brought your people to their home. You will travel no more.'

When he returned to his hut by the shore and took out his stones and bones for guidance, he heard her reassuring voice directing his decisions, and much of the good that his people enjoyed on Lapak Island came from her sage advice.

WITH NO TREES and little space suitable for such agriculture as had been developed at this time, how did the immigrants expect to live? From the largesse of the sea, and it was astonishing how the oceans had anticipated the needs of these daring people and supplied them in abundance. Were they hungry? Every bay and inlet on the island teemed with whelks and shellfish and slugs and seaweed of the most nutritious kind. Did one hunger for something more substantial? With a string made of seal gut and a hook carved from whalebone, one could fish in the bays and be almost certain of catching something, and if a man found a pole among the flotsam, he could perch himself upon a protruding rock and fish in the sea itself. Did one require timbers for building a hut? Wait till the next storm, and onto the shore right before one's land would come an immense pile of driftwood.

And for one who dared to leave the land and venture upon the ocean itself, there was a richness no man could exhaust. All he needed was the skill to build himself a one-seated kayak and the courage to trust his life in this frail thing that even the smallest wave could crush against a rock. With his kayak a man could go two miles from shore and catch beautiful salmon, long and sleek. At ten miles he would find halibut and cod, and if he preferred, as most did, the heartier meat of the large sea animals, he could hunt for seals, or venture out into the body of the ocean and test his courage against titanic whales and powerful walruses.

It was easier to spot a whale than one might suppose, for the islands of the chain were so disposed that only certain passages were available to creatures of this size, and Lapak rested between two of them. Whales cruised so close to the headlands that they were regularly visible, but their hunting became an uncertain matter. The brave men of the island would chase a whale for three days and wound it grievously, but fail to bring it to shore. With tears in their eyes they would watch the leviathan swim away, although they knew it to be so stricken that it must die at sea and drift ashore at some distant spot to feed a group of strangers who had played no part in its capture. But then some morning a woman rising early in Lapak to gather kelp along the shore would see not far off an object floating on the sea, and it would be of such tremendous size that it could only be a whale, and for a moment she would think it a live wanderer that had ventured close inland, but after a while when it did not move, a surge of overpowering excitement would possess her and she would run screaming to her men: 'A whale! A whale!' and they would rush to their kayaks and speed out to the dead giant and attach inflated sealskins to its carcass to keep it afloat as they nosed it slowly toward their shore. And when they butchered it, with women beating on drums, they would see the fatal wounds inflicted by some other tribe and even find harpoon heads behind the whale's ear. They would give thanks to the unknown brave men who had fought this whale so that Lapak could eat.

It was some time before Azazruk's people discovered the real wealth of their island, but one morning as the shaman huddled in the middle of the island's first six-man umiak, built by a powerful hunter named Shugnak, the boat strayed among the chain of little islands leading to the small volcano. Since these rocky protrusions were dangerous, Azazruk warned Shugnak: 'Not too close to those rocks,' but the hunter, younger and more daring than the shaman, had seen something moving in the masses of matted kelp that surrounded the rocks, so he pressed on, and as the umiak entered the tangled seaweeds, Azazruk chanced to see a swimming creature whose appearance so startled him that he cried aloud, and when others asked why, he could only point at this miracle in the waves.

Thus the men of Lapak made their acquaintance with the fabled sea otter, a creature much like a small seal, for it was built similarly and swam in much the same way. This first one was about five feet long, beautifully tapered and obviously at ease in the icy waters. But what had made Azazruk gasp, and others too when they saw the creature, was its face, because it resembled precisely the face of a bewhiskered old man, one who had enjoyed life and aged gracefully. There was the wrinkled brow, the bloodshot eye, the nose, the smiling lips and, strangest of all, the wispy, untended mustache. From its appearance, exaggerated in the telling, would be born the legend of the mermaid, and in fact, this face was so like a man's that later hunters would sometimes be startled by the watery vision and refrain momentarily from killing the otter lest an involuntary murder take place.

In the first moments of meeting this amazing creature, Azazruk knew intuitively that it was special, but what happened next convinced him and Shugnak at the stern of the umiak that they had come upon a rare sea animal: trailing along behind the first otter came a mother, floating easily on her back like a relaxed bather taking the sun in a quiet pool, while on her stomach protruding above the waves perched a baby otter, taking its ease too and idly surveying the world. Azazruk was enchanted by this maternal scene, for he loved babies and revered the mysteries of motherhood, even though he had no wife or children of his own, and as the loving pair drifted past he called to the rowers: 'What a cradle! Look at them!'

But the hunters were staring at something even more extraordinary, for trailing behind the first two otters came an older fellow, also floating on his back, and what he was doing was unbelievable. Perched securely on his ample belly lay a large rock, and as it rested there, held in place by his belly muscles, he used his two front paws as hands, and with them he slammed down upon the rock clams and other similar sea creatures, knocking them repeatedly until their shells broke so that he could pick out their meat and stuff it into his smiling mouth.

'Is that a rock on his belly?' Azazruk cried, and those in the prow of the umiak shouted back that it was, and at this instant Shugnak, who was always tempted to throw his lance at anything that moved, swung his paddle so dextrously that the rear of the umiak moved close to the basking otter. With a skillful launching of his sharp lance, Shugnak pinned the unsuspecting clameater and dragged him to the boat.

Secretly he skinned the otter, throwing the flesh to his women for a stew, and after the skin had cured for some months, he appeared with it draped about his shoulders. All marveled at its softness, its shimmering beauty and unequaled thickness. Trade in sea-otter skins had begun, and so had the rivalry between Azazruk the benevolent shaman and Shugnak the master hunter.

The latter saw from the beginning that the fur of the sea otter was going to be treasured by men, and even though trade to far places was still thousands of years in the future, each adult on Lapak wanted an otter skin, or two or three. They could have all the sealskins they wanted, and they made admirable clothing, but it was the sea otter that the islanders craved, and Shugnak was the man who could provide them.

He quickly saw that to chase these otters in a six-man umiak was wasteful, and drawing upon tribal memories, he directed his men to build approximations of the ancient kayaks, and when these proved seaworthy, he taught his sailors how to hunt with him in groups. Silently they would prowl the sea until they came upon a family of otters, with some fat fellow cracking clams. On some lucky days his men would bring home as many as six, and the time came when the islanders discarded the flesh and kept only the pelts. Then the massacre of the otters became appalling.

Azazruk had to intervene. 'It is wrong to kill the otters,' he said, but Shugnak, a good man and in things other than hunting a gentle one, resisted: 'We need the pelts.' It was obvious that no one really *needed* the pelts, for seals were plentiful and the otter meat was found to be tough, but those who already had otter-skin garments reveled in them while those who lacked them kept urging Shugnak to bring them skins.

The hunter's view was simplicity itself: 'The otters are out there and they do no one any good, just swimming about and cracking clamshells on their bellies.' But Azazruk had a deeper understanding: 'The animals of land and sea are brought to earth by the great spirits so that man can live.' And he became so obsessed with this concept that one morning he climbed to the cave of the mummified old woman, where he sat for a long time in her presence as if consulting with her.

'Am I foolish in thinking that the sea otters are my brothers?' he asked, but only the reverberation of his voice responded.

'Could it be that Shugnak is right to hunt them as he does?' Again there was silence.

'Suppose we are both right, Azazruk to love the animals, Shugnak to kill them?' He paused, then asked a question which would perplex subsequent philosophers: 'How can two things so different both be right?'

Then, like all men and women throughout history who would consult oracles, he found the answer within himself. Projecting his own voice toward the mummy, he heard her speak back with warm assurance: 'Azazruk must love and Shugnak must kill, and you are both right.'

She said no more, but there in the silent cave Azazruk fashioned the phrase that would sing in his islanders' minds: We live off the animals, but we also live with them. And as he elaborated his perception of what the spirits intended, many listened, but most still yearned for their otter skins, and these began a whispering campaign against their shaman, alleging that he did not want the otters to be killed because they looked like human beings, whereas everyone knew they were only big fish covered with fur of great worth.

The island community split down the middle, with some supporting their shaman, others backing their hunter, and in thousands of these early communities in Asia and Alaska there were similar fractures, the dreamers versus the pragmatists, the shamans responsible for the spiritual well-being of their people versus the great hunters responsible for feeding them, and throughout all ensuing eons this unavoidable struggle would continue, for on this issue men of good will could divide.

On Lapak Island the conflict came to a focus one summer morning as Shugnak was preparing to take his one-man kayak out to catch sea otters and the shaman halted him at the shore: 'We do not need any more dead otters. Let the creatures live.' He was an ascetic, with a mystical quality which set him apart from other men. He was a quiet man, but on the infrequent times when he did speak, others had to listen.

Shugnak was entirely different: stocky, broad of shoulder and heavy of hand, but it was the savage look of his face that marked him as a great hunter. It was reddish rather than the yellow or dark brown of the typical islander and distinguished by three powerful lines parallel to his eyes. The first was a huge length of whalebone stuck through the septum of his nose and protruding past each nostril. The second was a fierce, bristly jet-black mustache. And the third, most impressive of all, was a pair of rather small labrets set in the two corners of his mouth and connected across his chin by three links of a chain intricately carved from walrus ivory. He was dressed in skins from sea lions he had caught, and when he stood erect, his powerful arms broadening his torso, he was formidable.

On this morning he did not propose to have the shaman interrupt his hunt, and when Azazruk tried to do so, he gently put him aside. Azazruk realized that Shugnak could knock him down with only a push, but his responsibility for the welfare of animals could not be surrendered, and he moved back to obstruct Shugnak's passage. This time the hunter grew impatient, and without intending any irreverence, for he liked the shaman so long as the latter tended his own affairs, he shoved Azazruk so sharply that he fell, whereupon Shugnak strode to his kayak, paddled angrily to sea, and continued his hunting.

A tenseness fell over the island, and when Shugnak returned, Azazruk was waiting for him, and for several days the two men argued. The shaman pleaded against what he feared might be the extermination of the sea otters, while Shugnak countered with hardheaded realism that since the creatures had obviously been brought to these waters to be used, he intended using them.

Azazruk, for the first time in his long years of leadership, lost his composure and inveighed rather ridiculously against all hunters and their prowling kayaks, and he became so offensive that the people started to turn away from him. And he realized that he had made himself so foolish in their eyes, had so alienated them, that he had no recourse but to relinquish his leadership. So one morning before the others were awake he gathered his fetishes, left his hut by the sea, and walked mournfully to the headwaters of a distant bay, where he built himself a mud-walled hut. Like a thousand shamans before him, he was learning that the spiritual adviser of a people had best remain aloof from their political and economic quarrels.

He was an old man now, nearly fifty, and although his people still gave him credit for having led them to this island, they no longer wanted him meddling in their affairs; they wanted a more sensible leader like Shugnak, who could, if he put his mind to it, learn to consult with spirits and placate them.

In his sequestered hut Azazruk would end his days in exile. From the shores of the bay he could collect enough shellfish and slugs and seaweed to survive, and after some days big-hearted Shugnak provided him with a kayak, and although he had not paddled much before, he now became reasonably skillful. Often he would venture far from shore, always to the north toward those waters which had perpetually lured his people, and there, deep in the waves, he would talk with the seals and converse with the great whales as they drifted by. Occasionally he might see a group of walruses plowing northward, and he would call to them, and sometimes in the warm days of summer he would spend the entire night—only a few hours long—under the pale stars, at one with the vast ocean, at peace with the sea.

But the times he treasured were those in which he found himself in the kelp close to some family of sea otters and he could see the mother floating on her back with her baby on her bosom, the pup's wide eyes gleaming at the new world it was discovering, or greet the happy old man with whiskers as he floated past with a rock on his belly and two clams in his fat paws.

Of all the animals Azazruk had known, and his friends were legion, from the towering mammoth to the crafty lion, he prized most highly these sea otters, for they were creatures of distinction, and as his years drew to a close he conceived the idea—for which he had no reasonable justification—that it was the sea otter who best represented the spirits that had guided him through his honorable and productive life: It was they who called me when we lived on those arid steppes to the east. It was they who came at night to remind me of the ocean where I and my people belonged. And one morning when he returned from a night voyage on that maternal ocean and sat among his fetishes and took them from their pouches so they could breathe and talk to him, he realized with joyous surprise that the headless ivory piece he had cherished had never been a man, but a sea otter lazing along on its back, and in that moment he discovered the oneness of the world, the unity of spirit among mammoth, whale, bird and man, and his soul exulted in this knowledge.

They did not find him until some days later. Two pregnant women made the long journey to his hut to enlist his aid in ensuring healthy babies, and when they stood near his door and called him without receiving an answer, they supposed that he was once more out on the ocean, but then one of them spotted his empty kayak well up on the shore, and she deduced that he must still be within his hut. When the women entered they found him seated on the earth, his body fallen forward over his collection of fetishes.

T HE CHAIN OF islands to which Azazruk led his clan would later be known as the Aleutians and their residents as Aleuts (Ahl-ay-oots) and a stranger, more complex collection of people would rarely exist on this earth. Isolated, they developed a unique way of life. Men and women of the sea, they derived their entire subsistence from it. Each group self-contained on its own island, they felt no necessity in these early days to invent war. Secure within the world governed by their benevolent spirits, they achieved a satisfactory life. Tragedy they knew, for at times starvation threatened, and most families lost fathers and husbands and sons when sudden storms swept the great seas upon which they depended. They had no trees, nor any of the alluring animals they had known on the mainland, and no contact with either the Eskimos of the north or Athapascans of the center, but they did live in close contact with the spirit of the sea, the mystery of the little volcano that sputtered off their shore and the vivid life of whales, walruses, seals and sea otters.

Later experts, looking at the inviting way in which the chain of islands reached out for Asia, constituting almost a land bridge of its own, would conclude that a particular tribe of Mongolians from Asia must have walked across this supposed bridge to the far western group of islands, populating each of the more easterly ones in turn. It did not happen that way. The Aleutians were settled east to west by Eskimos like Azazruk and his people, who, if they had turned north when they crossed the real land bridge, would have become indistinguishable from the Eskimos of the Arctic Ocean. Having turned south, they became Aleuts.

Azazruk, who would be revered in island legend as the Great Shaman, left two heritages of importance. For his trips on the ocean in the closing years of his life he devised an Aleut hat which would become perhaps the most distinctive head covering in the world. It was carved of wood, although baleen from a whale could also be used, and it came straight up in the back to a fairly high level. There it sloped downward in a broad sweep forward, stretching gracefully in front of the eyes and at a beautifully dropping angle, so that the sailor's eyes had a long visor to shade them from the glare of the sun. In this form alone the hat would have been distinctive, for it provided a lovely artistic form, but from the point where the erect back joined the long slope forward, Azazruk had fastened five or six graceful arching feathers or stems of dead flowers or bits of decorated baleen, so positioned that they arched forward above the visor. This wooden hat was a work of art, perfect in every proportion.

When a group of six or seven Aleuts, each in his own kayak, each with his Azazruk hat, visors sloping forward, feathers atilt, swept across the ocean, they were memorable; and in later days when European artists traveling with explorers sketched them, the hats became a symbol of the arctic.

The shaman's other contribution was more lasting. When children born on Lapak had pestered him to tell the exciting legends about the other land from which the clan had come, he always referred to it and its glaciers and fascinating collection of animals as the Great Land, for it had been great, and to leave it had been a sad defeat. In time those words came to represent the lost heritage. The Great Land lay back to the east, beyond the chain of islands, and it was a noble memory.

The Aleutian word for Great Land was Alaxsxaq, and when Europeans reached the Aleutian Islands, their first stopping point in this portion of the arctic, and asked the people what name the lands hereabout had, they replied 'Alaxsxaq,' and in the European tongues this became Alaska.

IV

THE EXPLORERS

On New Year's Day of 1723 a giant Ukrainian cossack stationed in the remote town of Yakutsk, most easterly of the Siberian posts, became so outraged by the gross tyrannies of the governor that he cut the man's throat. Immediately arrested by six junior officials, for no three could have handled him, he was beaten, manacled, and tied to an exposed pillar on the parade grounds facing the Lena River. There, after nineteen lashes from the knout on his bare back, he heard his sentence:

'Trofim Zhdanko, cossack in the service of Tsar Peter, may heaven preserve his illustrious life, you are to be conveyed in shackles to St. Petersburg and hanged.'

At seven the next morning, hours before the sun would rise in that far northern latitude, a troop of sixteen soldiers set out for the Russian capital, forty-one hundred miles to the west, and after three hundred and twenty days of the most difficult travel across the trackless wastelands of Siberia and central Russia, they reached what passed for civilization at Vologda, where swift messengers galloped ahead to inform the tsar of what had happened to his governor in Yakutsk. Six days later the troop delivered their still-shackled prisoner to a dank prison, where, as he was thrown into a lightless dungeon, the guard informed him: 'We know all about you, Prisoner Zhdanko. On Friday morning you hang.'

But at half after ten the next night a man even taller and more formidable than the cossack left an imposing house along the Neva River and hastened to a waiting carriage drawn by two horses. He was bundled in furs but wore no hat, his thick head of hair blowing in the frosty November wind. As soon as he was settled, four men on horseback, heavily armed, took positions before and after his carriage, for he was Peter Romanoff, Tsar of all the Russias, and destined to be remembered in history as The Great.

'To the prison by the docks,' he said, and as the coachman drove down one frozen alleyway after another, the tsar leaned forward and shouted: 'Aren't you glad it isn't spring? These streets would be hub-deep in mud.'

'If it was spring, Sire,' the man shouted back with an obvious touch of familiarity, 'we wouldn't be using these alleys.'

'Don't call them alleys,' the tsar snapped. 'They'll be rock-paved next year.'

When the carriage reached the prison, which Peter had prudently placed close to the docks where he knew that sailors from all the shipping nations of Europe would be brawling, he leaped out of his carriage before his guard could form, strode to the tightly barred portal, and banged on it clamorously. It was some moments before the sleepy watchman inside could muster himself and come complainingly to the tiny wicket, set in the center of the heavy gate, to ask: 'What noise at this hour?'

Peter, showing no displeasure at being stopped by such a functionary, said amiably: 'Tsar Peter.'

The watchman, invisible behind his wicket, betraying no surprise at this remarkable answer, for he had long known of the tsar's propensity for surprise visits, replied briskly: 'Open immediately, Sire!' and Peter heard the gates creaking as the watchman pushed them apart. When they were sufficiently ajar for the carriage to enter, the coachman indicated that Peter should jump in behind him and enter the prison courtyard in state, but the giant ruler was already striding forward and calling for the chief jailer.

The noise had awakened the prisoners long before their custodian was roused, and when they saw who it was that was visiting at this late hour, they began to bombard him with petitions: 'Sire, I am here unjustly!' 'Sire, look to your rascal in Tobolsk. He stole my lands.' 'Tsar Peter, justice!' Ignoring the criminals who did the shouting, but noting their complaints against any specific agent of his government, he proceeded directly to the heavy oaken door guarding the main entrance to the building, where he banged impatiently on the iron knocker, but he had done this only once when the watchman from the gate shuffled up, calling in a loud voice: 'Mitrofan! It's the tsar!' Then Peter heard vigorous activity taking place behind the massive doors constructed of wood he had imported from England.

In less than a minute, Jailer Mitrofan had his door opened and his head bowed low: 'Sire, I am eager to obey your orders.'

'You better be,' the emperor said, clapping his appointee on the shoulder. 'I want you to fetch the cossack Trofim Zhdanko.'

'Fetch him where, Sire?'

'To that red room across the way from yours,' and assuming that his order would be promptly carried out, he marched unguided to the room on which he himself had done the carpentering a few years before. It was not large, for in those first days of his new city Peter had visualized it as being used in exactly the way he now proposed, and it contained only a table and three chairs, for he had supposed that here prisoners would be brought for interrogation: one chair behind the table for the official, one at the side of the table for the clerk taking down the answers, and that one over there for the prisoner, who would sit with light from the window glaring in his face. At night, if such interrogations had to be conducted, the light would come from a whale-oil lamp on the wall behind the official's head. And to give it the solemnity its intended purpose required, Peter had painted the room a sullen red.

While waiting for the prisoner to be produced, Peter rearranged the furniture, for he did not wish to stress the fact that Zhdanko was a prisoner. Without calling for help, he moved the narrow table to the center, set one chair on one side and the other two facing it from the opposite side. Still awaiting the arrival of the jailer, he paced back and forth, as if his energy were so great that it could not be controlled, and as he heard footsteps coming down the stone corridor, he tried to recall the fractious cossack he had once sentenced to prison. He remembered him as a huge mustachioed Ukrainian, tall like himself, who after his release from jail had been dispatched to the city of Yakutsk, where he was to serve as military constable enforcing the orders of the civilian governor. He had been a worthy soldier up to the moment he fell into serious difficulty, and in memory of those better days the tsar now mumbled: 'Good fortune they didn't hang him out there.'

The latch rattled, the door opened, and there stood Trofim Zhdanko, six feet two, broad-shouldered, black-haired, fierce drooping mustache, huge beard which bristled forward when the owner jutted out his chin to argue a point. On the march to the interrogation room, surrounded by guards, the jailer had warned him who his nocturnal visitor was, so as soon as they entered, the big cossack, still manacled, bowed low and said softly, with no theatrical humility but with sincere respect: 'Sire, you do me honor.'

For just a moment Tsar Peter, who hated beards and had sought to prohibit them in his empire, stared at his hirsute visitor, then smiled: 'Jailer Mitrofan, you may remove the shackles.'

'But, Sire, this man is a murderer!'

'The shackles!' Peter roared, and when they jangled to the stone floor he added gently: 'Now, Mitrofan, take the guards with you as you go.' When one of the guards showed hesitancy at leaving the tsar alone with this notorious criminal, Peter chuckled and moved closer to the cossack, punching him in the arm: 'I've always known how to handle this one,' and the others withdrew.

When they were gone, Peter indicated that the cossack should take one of the two chairs while he, Peter, took the one on the other side. Having done so, he placed his elbows near the middle of the table and said: 'Zhdanko, I need your help.'

'You've always had it, Sire.'

'But this time I don't want you to murder my governor.'

'He was a bad one, Sire. Stole as much from you as he did from me.'

'I know. Reports on his misbehavior were tardy in reaching me. Didn't get here till a month ago.'

Zhdanko winced, then confided: 'If a man is innocent, that trip from Yakutsk to St. Petersburg in shackles is no Easter outing.'

Peter laughed: 'If anyone could handle it, you could.' Then he grew serious: 'I stationed you in Siberia because I suspected that one day I would need you there.' He smiled at the big man, then said: 'The time has come.'

Zhdanko placed both hands on the table, far apart, looked directly into the eyes of the tsar, and asked: 'What?'

Peter said nothing. Rocking back and forth as if perplexed by some subject too weighty for easy explanation, he kept staring at the cossack, and finally asked the first of his significant questions: 'Can I still trust you?'

'You know the answer,' Zhdanko said with no show of humility or equivocation.

'Can you keep important secrets?'

'I've never been entrusted with any. But . . . yes, I suppose.'

'Don't you know?'

'I've never been tested.' Realizing that this might sound impudent, he added firmly: 'Yes, if you warned me to keep my mouth shut. Yes.'

'Swear you'll keep your mouth shut?'

'I swear.'

Peter, nodding his satisfaction with this promise, rose from his chair, strode to the door, opened it, and shouted down the hall: 'Fetch us some beer. German beer.' And when Jailer Mitrofan entered with a pitcher of the dark stuff and two beakers, he found the cossack and the tsar seated side by side in the middle of the room like two friends, the table behind them.

When the first deep drafts had been drunk, with Zhdanko saying: 'Haven't had that in the past year,' Peter opened the conversation whose subject would dominate much of his life in the next months and all of Zhdanko's: 'I am much worried about Siberia, Trofim.' This was his first use of the prisoner's given name, and both were aware of the significance.

'Those Siberian dogs are difficult to train,' the cossack said, 'but they're puppies compared to the Chukchis out on the peninsula.'

The tsar leaned forward: 'It's the Chukchis I'm interested in. Tell me.'

'I've met up with them twice. Lost twice. But I'm sure they can be handled if you go at them properly.'

'Who are they?' Clearly, the tsar was temporizing. He was not concerned about the fighting qualities of these Chukchis perched on the far end of his empire. Every group his soldiers and administrators had encountered on their irresistible march to the east had been difficult at first, tractable when reliable government and resolute force were applied, and he was sure the Chukchis would prove the same.

'As I told you in my first report, they're closer to the Chinese, I mean in appearance, habits, than to you Russians or us Ukrainians.'

'But not allied to the Chinese, I hope?'

'No Chinese has ever seen them. And not too many Russians, either. Your governor'—there was a slight hesitation—'the one who died, he was deadly afraid of the Chukchis.'

'But you went among them?'

At this point Zhdanko had an invitation to play the hero, but he refrained: 'Twice, Sire, but not by choice.'

'Tell me about it. If you reported it, I've forgotten the details.'

'I didn't report it, because I didn't come off too well.' And there in the quiet room, toward midnight, he told the tsar about his two attempts to sail north from his headquarters in Yakutsk on the left bank of the great Lena River, largest in the east, and of his failure the first time because of opposition from the hostile Siberian tribes that infested the area.

'I'd like to know about the Lena.'

'Majestic river, Sire. Have you ever heard about the Mouths of the Lena? Maybe fifty little rivers all running into the Great North Ocean. A wilderness of water. I got lost there.'

Very gently Peter asked: 'But you certainly never met any Chukchis on the Lena or at its fifty mouths, as you call them.' He hesitated, then said: 'Everything I've heard puts the Chukchis much farther east.'

Zhdanko took the bait: 'Oh yes! They're out on the peninsula. Where the land ends. Where Russia ends.'

'How do you know that?'

The cossack leaned back and reached behind him for his beer, then, turning to face Peter, he made a confession: 'I've told no one, Sire. Most of the men involved are dead. Your officials in Yakutsk, like that damned governor, never cared, as if what I'd discovered had no value. I doubt if your other officials here in St. Petersburg would have cared, either. You're the first Russian who gave a damn, and I know exactly why you're here tonight.'

Peter showed no displeasure at this intemperate outbreak, this blanket castigation of his officials. Smiling, he said with the greatest conciliation: 'Tell me, Zhdanko, why am I here?'

'Because you think I know something important about those eastern lands.'

Peter smiled and said: 'Yes, I've suspected for some time that when you made that river journey north from Yakutsk, and of that part I was informed, you did much more than sail down the Lena River to its many mouths, as you reported.'

'Where do you think I went?' Zhdanko asked, as if he too were playing a game.

'I think you went out into the northern ocean and sailed east to the Kolyma River.'

'That I did. And I found that it also enters the ocean by many mouths.'

'I was told that by others who had seen the mouths,' the tsar said in a manner which indicated that he might be bored.

'But not by anyone who approached from the sea,' Trofim said sharply, and Peter laughed.

'It was on a second trip, about which I did not bother to inform your despicable governor . . .'

'You took care of him. Let his soul rest.'

'It was on this trip that I encountered the Chukchis.'

This was a revelation so significant, so pertinent to the hammering questions being asked in learned circles in Paris, Amsterdam and London, let alone Moscow, that Peter's hands began to tremble. He had heard from the greatest geographers in the world, men who dreamed about little else, two versions of what happened at the northeast corner of his empire, there at those capes shrouded in mist and frozen for more than half the year in great cakes of ice. Some in Paris had argued with him: 'Eminent Sire, at the Arctic Circle and just below, your Russia has an unbroken land connection with North America, so that the hope of finding a sea passage from Norway to Japan around the eastern end of Siberia is fruitless. In the far north, Asia and North America become one body of land.'

But others in Amsterdam and London had tried to persuade him differently: 'Sire, mark our words, when you find navigators brave enough to sail from Arkhangelsk past Novaya Zemlya and on to the mouths of the Lena . . .' He had not interrupted them, for he did not care to reveal that this had already been accomplished. 'You will find that they could, if they wished, keep right on sailing from the Lena to the Kolyma and around the easternmost cape and straight down to Japan. Russia and North America are not joined. A sea intrudes between them, and although it is probably frozen most of the year, it is still a sea, and as such, it will have to be open during the summer.'

In the years since his epochal travels in Europe and his work as a shipbuilder in Holland, Peter had accumulated all the shreds of information he could glean from suppositious accounts, rumors, hard evidence and the canny speculation of geographers and philosophers, and he had in this year of 1723 concluded that there was an ocean passage open most of the year between his most eastern possessions and North America. Having accepted this as proved, he was now interested in other aspects of the problem, and to solve them he needed to know more about the Chukchis and the forbidding land they occupied.

'Tell me about your second trip, Zhdanko. The one where you met the Chukchis.'

'This time, when I reached the mouths of the Kolyma, I said to myself: "What lies beyond?" and I sailed in good weather for many days, relying upon the skilled Siberian boatman who captained my ship, a man who seemed to have no fear. Neither of us understood the stars, so we don't know how far we went, but in all that time the sun never set, so we had to be well north of the Circle, that I know.'

'And what did you find?'

'A cape, and then a sharp turn south, and when we tried to land we found those damned Chukchis.'

'And what happened?'

'They turned us back, twice. Pitched battles. And if we had tried to force our way ashore, I'm sure we'd have been killed.'

'Could you talk with them?'

'No, but they were willing to trade with us, and they knew the value of what they had.'

'Did you ask them questions? I mean with signs?'

'Yes. And they told us that the sea continued south forever, but that there were islands just beyond in the mists.'

'Did you sail to those islands?'

'No,' and when the tsar's grave disappointment showed, the cossack reminded him: 'Sire, we were far from home . . . in a small boat, and we could not guess where the land lay. To tell you the truth, we were afraid.'

Tsar Peter, who realized that as emperor of a vast domain he was obligated to know what the situation was in all its parts, made no reply to this honest admission of fear and failure, but after a long swig of beer he said: 'I wonder what I might have done.'

'Who knows?' Zhdanko shrugged, and Peter was glad that he had not cried effusively: 'Oh, Sire, I'm sure you would have plowed on!' because Peter was not at all sure. Once, in crossing from Holland to England, he had been caught in a furious Channel storm and he knew what fear could do to a man in a small boat.

But then he clapped his hands, rose, and began walking about the room. 'Listen, Zhdanko, I already know all this about Russia and North America not touching. And I want to do something about it, but in the future, not now,' and the interrogation seemed to be ending there, with the tsar going back to his unfinished palace and the cossack to his hanging, so Zhdanko, fighting for his life, boldly reached out and grabbed Peter's right sleeve, being careful not to touch his person, and said: 'In the trading, Sire, I obtained two things which might be of interest to you.'

'What?'

'Frankly, Sire, I want to trade them to you, for my freedom.'

'I came here tonight to give you your freedom. You were to leave this place and take quarters in the palace near mine.'

Zhdanko stood up, and the two big men stared at each other across the narrow space which separated them, and then a big smile broke across the cossack's face: 'In that case, Sire, I shall give you my secrets freely and with thanks.' And he stooped to kiss the hem of Peter's fur-lined robe.

'Where are these secret things?' Peter asked, and Zhdanko said: 'I had them spirited out of Siberia and hidden with a woman I knew in the old days.'

'Is it worth my while to go to her tonight?'

'It is,' and with this simple declaration Trofim Zhdanko left his shackles lying on the prison floor, accepted the fur cloak the tsar ordered the jailer to give him, and side by side with Peter, passed through the oak door and climbed into the waiting carriage while the four armed horsemen formed up to protect them.

They left the river docks, where Zhdanko could see the gaunt timbers of many ships under construction, but before reaching the area leading to the rude palace they veered inland away from the river, and in the two-o'clock darkness searched for a mean alley, where they stopped at a hovel protected by a door without hinges. The drowsy occupant, when finally wakened, informed Zhdanko: 'She left here last year. You'll find her three alleys down, house with a green door.'

There they learned that the woman Maria still protected the valuable package the prisoner Zhdanko had sent her from Yakutsk. She showed neither surprise nor pleasure in seeing her friend Trofim again, and for the very good reason that when she saw the soldiers she supposed that this very tall man with Zhdanko was an official of some kind who was going to arrest the cossack for having stolen whatever was in the package.

'Here,' she muttered, shoving a greasy bundle into Peter's hands. Then, to Zhdanko, she said: 'I'm sorry, Trofim. I hope they don't hang you.'

Eagerly the tsar ripped open the package, to find that it contained two pelts, each about five feet long, of the softest, finest, strongest fur he had ever seen. It was a dark brown that scintillated in the weak light and much longer in each hair than the furs with which he was familiar, though dealers brought him only the best. It had come from the treasured sea otter inhabiting the icy waters east of the Chukchi lands, and these two pelts were the first of their kind to reach the western world. In his first moments of examining these remarkable furs, Peter appreciated their worth, and he could visualize, even then, the immense importance they would enjoy in the capitals of Europe if they could be supplied in assured quantities.

'These are excellent,' Peter said. 'Tell this woman who I am and give her rubles for having saved them for me.'

The captain of the guard told Maria as he handed her the coins: 'This is your tsar. He thanks you,' and she fell to her knees and kissed his boot.

Her gesture did not close this unusual night, for while she was still genuflecting, Peter shouted to one of his guards: 'Fetch it,' and before the man returned, the tsar had forced a startled Zhdanko onto the hut's only chair. When the guard produced a long, dull and murderous-looking razor, Peter cried: 'No man, not even you, Zhdanko, stays in my palace with a beard,' and with considerable force he proceeded to hack off the cossack's beard, taking with it a substantial helping of skin.

Trofim could not protest, for as a citizen he knew that the law forbade him to wear a beard, and as a cossack he must not flinch when the unsharpened razor pulled hair out by the roots or cut into his face. Stolidly he sat there until the barbering was completed, then he rose, wiped the blood from his newly revealed face, and said: 'Sire, keep hold of the empire. You'll never make a barber,' and Peter tossed the razor to a guard, who allowed it to fall to the floor lest it cut him. Placing an arm about his astonished cossack, the tsar led him to their carriage.

PETER THE GREAT was in no degree diverted from his main interest in far eastern Siberia by the fact that a new and wonderful kind of fur appeared to be available there. Of course, he had his tailor, a Frenchman named Des-Arbes, adapt the furs to three of his ceremonial robes, but then forgot about them, for his perpetual concern was with the actuality of Russia—where it was and how it related to its neighbors—and in safeguarding it for the future. And now, when occasional rushes of blood to the head warned him that even he with all his strength was mortal, he began to focus on three or four major projects which had to be given direction or consolidation. Russia still had no reliable seaport, and certainly no warm-water one. Relations with all-powerful Turkey were not good. The internal government of Russia was sometimes a disaster, especially in those districts far from St. Petersburg where a letter of instruction might take eight months for delivery and two years for a response to reach the capital if the recipient was desultory in conforming and replying. The road system was deplorable in all parts save a fairly reliable route between the two major cities, and in the far east, nobody in power ever seemed to know what was going on.

So, important though furs were, and much of Russia's wealth came from the brave men who trapped in the Siberian wilderness, the providential discovery that the waters off the Chukchi lands would provide a fur as resplendent as that of the sea otter was no cause for immediate action. Peter the Great had learned, more from his experiences in Europe than from what he saw in Russia, that in the far east his nation faced two potential dangers: China and whatever European nation ultimately controlled the west coast of North America. He already knew that Spain, through her ancillary agent Mexico, had a strong foothold on the part of America facing the Pacific Ocean and that her power extended unchallenged all the way down to Cape Horn. By his constant study of maps then available, and they were becoming more complete each year, Peter saw that if Spain attempted to project her power northward, as she probably would, she must ultimately come into conflict with Russian interests. He was therefore much concerned about Spanish behavior.

But with that intuition which so often assists great men, especially those responsible for the governance of homelands, he anticipated that other nations more powerful today than Spain might also extend their power to the Pacific coast of North America, and he saw that if either France or England, each with a foothold on the Atlantic, were to do so, he might one day be faced with pressure from such a country applying it in Europe on his western borders and in America on his eastern.

Peter loved ships, had sailed in them and believed that had his life developed differently, he might have made a fine sea captain. As a consequence, he was fascinated by the capacity of ships to move freely over the waters of the world. He was close to completing his grand design of making Russia a sea power in Europe, and his empire had derived so much advantage from this new posture that he was considering building a fleet in Siberia if conditions warranted. But first he had to know what those conditions were.

Accordingly, he spent much time planning a vast enterprise which would place a Russian ship of stout construction in the seas off Siberia with a commission to explore the area, not for any specific item of information but for the kind of general knowledge on which the leader of an empire could rely when making prudent decisions. Concerning the vital question of whether his Siberia touched North America, his mind was made up: it did not. But he did have considerable mercantile interests in the area. He already conducted profitable trade with China overland, but he wanted to know whether he could do better by sea. And he was most eager to trade with Japan on any terms, for the few goods which reached Europe from that mysterious land were of such high quality that they excited him as they did others. Above all, he wanted to know what Spain, England and France were doing in this important ocean and be able to estimate what they were capable of doing. Eighty years later the American president Thomas Jefferson, a man much like Peter, would want to know the same things about his newly acquired western possessions along the Pacific.

When his ideas were in a yeasty froth with no firm structure—often the precedent to man's most constructive thinking—he sent for this cossack he had come to trust, this rough, unlettered man who seemed to know more about Siberia than most of the more learned officials he had sent there to govern, and after preliminary sparring to satisfy himself as to Zhdanko's energy and continued interest, he reached a favorable conclusion: 'Trofim, you're twenty-two, great age to be. A man's approaching his apex then. By God, I wish I were twenty-two again.' Motioning Zhdanko to join him on a bench, he continued: 'I have in mind to send you back to Yakutsk. Beyond, maybe. Perhaps all the way to Kamchatka.'

'Place me under a better governor this time, Sire.'

'You'd not be under a governor.'

'Sire, what could I do on my own? I can't read or write.'

'You'd not be on your own.'

The cossack rose, walked about, and said: 'I don't understand,' and Peter said: 'You'd be on a ship. Under the command of the best sailor we could find.' Before Trofim could show his astonishment, Peter became all excitement, waving his hands about and talking louder each minute: 'You'd go to Tobolsk and pick up some carpenters, to Yeniseysk and get some men knowledgeable about tar, then on to Yakutsk, where you already know everyone and can advise what men to take to Okhotsk, where you will build your ship. A big one. I'll give you the plans.'

'Sire!' Zhdanko interrupted. 'I cannot read.'

'You shall learn, starting this day, and as you learn you will tell no one why you are learning.' Now Peter rose and stalked about the room with his arm linked in Trofim's. 'I want you to take a job at the docks. Where we're building ships . . .'

'I don't know much about timber.'

'You're not expected to bother about timber. You're to listen, to judge, to compare, to serve as my eyes and ears.'

'For what?'

'To advise me as to who the best man is down there. Who really knows ships. Who can handle men. Above all, Zhdanko, who is as brave as you proved to be.'

The cossack said nothing; he did not try with false modesty to deny that he had been brave, because it had been his daring feats in the Ukraine at age fifteen which had brought him to the tsar's attention. But Peter could only guess at what acts of courage had allowed this man who knew nothing of the sea to venture down the Lena River and along the coast to the land of the Chukchis and to protect himself along the way.

Finally, as they paced together, Peter said: 'I wish I were to be the captain of that ship, with you the officer in command of troops. We would sail from the coast of Kamchatka, wherever it is, to all of America.'

During the time that Trofim spent working in the shipyard at day and learning to read at night, he discovered that most of the constructive work being achieved in St. Petersburg, and a massive amount was under way, was being done not by Russians, but by able men from other European nations. His tutor Soderlein was from Heidelberg in Germany, as were two of the medical doctors at the court. Instruction in mathematics was in the hands of brilliant men from Paris. Books were being written on a variety of subjects by professors imported from Amsterdam and London. Astronomy, in which Peter took great interest, was in the hands of fine men from Lille and Bordeaux. And wherever practical solutions to problems were required, Trofim found Englishmen and Scotsmen, especially the latter, in charge. They drew the plans for the ships, installed the winding stairs in palaces, taught the peasants how to care for animals, and watched the money. One day as Peter and Trofim discussed the still shadowy expedition to the east, the tsar said: 'When you seek ideas, go to the French and the Germans. But when you want action, hire yourself an Englishman or a Scotsman.'

When Zhdanko delivered letters to the Academy in Moscow he found it populated by Frenchmen and Germans, and the porter who led him about the newly furnished halls whispered: 'The tsar has hired the brightest men in Europe. They're all here.'

'Doing what?' Trofim asked as he clutched his parcel.

'Thinking.'

In the second month of this training, Zhdanko learned one other fact about his tsar: the Europeans, especially the French and Germans, might do the thinking, but Peter and a group of Russians much like him did the governing. They supplied the money and said where the army would go and what ships would be built, and it was they who ran Russia, make no mistake about that. And this perplexed him, for if he was to help select the sailor who was to command the vast expedition that Peter had in mind, he felt obligated to identify some Russian capable of directing a task of such magnitude. But the more he studied the men along the waterfront and listened to reports about them, the more clearly he saw that none of the Russians was remotely capable of the task, and he was loath to tell Peter, but one day when asked how his thinking was going, he had to speak out: 'I hear of two Germans, one Swede and one Dane who might do. But the Germans with their mighty ways would be unable to control Russians like me, and the Swede fought against us three times in the Baltic wars before joining our side.'

'We sank all his ships,' Peter laughed, 'so if he wanted to continue being a sailor, he had to join us. Are you speaking of Lundberg?'

'Yes, a very good man. I'll trust him if you choose him.'

'And who was the Dane?' Peter asked.

'Captain-of-the-Second-Rank Vitus Bering. His men speak well of him.'

'I, too,' the tsar said, and the matter was discussed no further.

But when alone Peter spent careful hours reviewing what he knew about Bering: Met him that day twenty years ago when our training fleet stopped in Holland. Our admirals were so hungry for anyone with experience at sea that without examination they commissioned him sublieutenant. And they chose well, for he rose fast, Captain-of-the-Fourth-Rank, the Third and Second. He fought manfully in our war against Sweden.

Eight years younger than Peter, Bering had retired with honor at the beginning of 1724, taking up residence in the stately Finnish seaport of Vyborg, where he expected to live out the remainder of his life as a gardener and watcher of naval ships as they passed up the Gulf of Finland to St. Petersburg. In the late summer of that same year, he had been summoned to Russia to meet with the tsar: 'Vitus Bering, I should never have allowed you to retire. You're needed for an exercise of the greatest importance.'

'Your Majesty, I'm forty-four years old. I tend gardens, not ships.'

'Nonsense. If I weren't needed here, I'd go on the journey myself.'

'But you're a special man, Your Majesty,' and when Bering said this, a round little fellow with pudgy cheeks, a twisted mouth and hair drooping close to his eyes, he spoke the truth, for Peter was a good fifteen inches taller and possessed of a commanding presence which Bering lacked. He was a stolid, capable Dane, a bulldog type of man, who had attained a position of eminence by his rugged determination rather than because of any quality of dramatic leadership. He was what the English mariners liked to call a sea dog, and such men, when they fastened their teeth onto a project, could be devastating.

'In your own way,' Peter said, 'and in a way vital to this project, you too are special, Captain Bering.'

'And what is your project?' It was typical of Bering that from the start he allocated the project to the tsar. It was Peter's idea, whatever it was, and Bering was honored to be his agent.

Zhdanko did not hear what Peter said to Bering in reply to that question, but later he left a memorandum of some importance in which he said that Peter had spoken to Bering much as he had spoken to him, Zhdanko: 'He said he wanted to know more about Kamchatka, and where the Chukchi lands ended, and what European nations held what settlements on the west coast of America.' There was, Zhdanko felt sure, no discussion as to whether Russian territory was joined by land to North America: 'That was taken for granted by both men.'

For some weeks Zhdanko watched the fat little Dane moving about the shipyards, and then he disappeared. 'He's been called to Moscow to meet with some Academy men stationed there,' a workman told Zhdanko. 'Those fellows from France and Germany who know everything but can't tie their own cravats. He'll be in trouble if he listens to them.'

Two days before Christmas, a holiday that Zhdanko relished, Captain Bering was back in St. Petersburg and was summoned to a meeting with the tsar which Zhdanko was invited to attend. As the cossack entered the business room of the palace he blurted out: 'Sire, you've been working too hard. You don't look well.'

Ignoring the observation, Peter showed the men where to sit, and when a certain solemnity clothed the room, he said: 'Vitus Bering, I've had you promoted to Captain-of-the-First-Rank because I want you to undertake the major mission of which we spoke last summer.' Bering started to expostulate that he was unworthy of such preferment, but Peter, who had been continuously ill since leaping impulsively into the icy waters of the Bay of Finland to rescue a drowning sailor and who was now apprehensive lest death cut short his grand designs, brushed aside the formality: 'Yes, you are to cross overland to the eastern limits of our empire, build yourself ships in that spot, then conduct the explorations we spoke of.'

'Exalted Majesty, I shall consider this your expedition, sailing under your command.'

'Good,' Peter said. 'I'll be sending with you our ablest men, and as your aide, this cossack who knows those areas, Trofim Zhdanko, who carries with him my personal approval. He's a tested man.'

At this the tsar rose to stand with his cossack, and when fat little Bering took his position between the two giants, it was like a hill standing between two mountain peaks.

A month later, before he had an opportunity to spell out the details of the exploration, Tsar Peter, called properly the Great, was dead at the premature age of fifty-three. The governance of Russia fell into the hands of his widow, Catherine the First, an extraordinary woman who had been born into a Lithuanian peasant family, was orphaned young, and married at age eighteen to a

Swedish dragoon who deserted her after a honeymoon of eight summer days. Mistress of various well-placed men, she fell into the hands of a powerful Russian politician who introduced her to Peter, who, after she had borne him three children, married her gladly. She had been a stalwart wife, and now, with her husband dead, she desired only to execute the orders he had left unfinished. On 5 February 1725 she handed Bering the temporary commission he would hold during the expedition, Fleet Captain, and his orders.

The latter were a muddled set of three paragraphs which had been drafted by Peter himself shortly before his death, and although the instructions about crossing all of Russia and building ships were clear, what to do with those ships, once built, was most unclear. The admirals interpreted the orders to mean that Bering was to determine whether eastern Asia was joined to North America; other men like Trofim Zhdanko, who had spoken to Peter in person, believed that he had intended a reconnoiter of the coast of America, with a possibility of claiming that unoccupied land for Russia. Both interpreters agreed that Bering was to try to find European settlements in the area and to intercept European vessels for interrogation. No major explorer, and Vitus Bering was that, had ever set forth on a grand voyage with such imprecise orders from his patrons who were paying the bills. Before he died Peter had certainly known what he intended; his survivors did not.

THE DISTANCE FROM St. Petersburg to the east coast of Kamchatka, where the ships were to be built, was an appalling five thousand nine hundred miles, or, considering the unavoidable detours, more than six thousand. Roads were perilous or nonexistent. Rivers had to be used but there were no boats to do so. Workmen were to be picked up en route from remote little towns where no skilled hands were available. Large stretches of empty land which had never before been traversed by a group of travelers had to be negotiated. And what was to prove most irritating of all, there was no way whereby officials in St. Petersburg could forewarn their officials in far-distant Siberia that this gang of men was about to descend upon them with requirements that simply could not be filled locally. At the end of the second week Zhdanko reported to Bering: 'This isn't an expedition. It's madness.' And this was said during the good part of the trip.

Twenty-six of Bering's best men, driving twenty-five wagonloads of needed materials, set out ahead of him, and he followed shortly thereafter with six companions, including his aide Trofim Zhdanko, with whom he established the firmest and most productive relations. During the troika ride to Solikamsk, an insignificant village marking the start of the bleak lands, the two men had an opportunity to learn each other's foibles, and since this trip was going to require years, not months, it was important that this happen.

Vitus Bering, his aide discovered, was a man of sturdy principles. He respected a job well done, was willing to praise his men who performed well, and demanded the same kind of effort from himself. He was not a bookish man, which reassured Zhdanko, to whom the alphabet had been a problem, but he did place major reliance upon maps, which he studied assiduously. He was not overly religious but he did pray. He was not a glutton but he liked clean food and hearty drink. Best of all, he was a leader who respected men, and because he was perpetually aware that he was a Dane giving orders to Russians, he tried never to be arrogant, but he also let it be known that he was in command. He had, however, one weakness which disturbed the cossack, whose method of controlling his subordinates had been so different: at any critical moment Bering, like all the Russian officers in command, was expected to convene his subordinates and consult with them regarding the situation that faced them. When they had formed their recommendations they then had to submit them in writing, so that he would not have to assume the entire blame if things went wrong. What disturbed Zhdanko, Bering actually listened to the prejudices of his assistants and often acted upon them. 'I'd ask their opinions,' Zhdanko growled, 'then burn the paper they signed,' but apart from this deficiency, the big cossack respected his captain and vowed to serve him well.

For his part, Bering saw in Zhdanko a man of resolute courage who, at that time of crisis in Yakutsk, had been willing to risk his life by murdering his superior when that man's irrational behavior threatened Russia's position in Siberia. As Tsar Peter had revealed when informing Bering about Trofim: 'The man he killed deserved it. Zhdanko did my work for me.' Bering asked: 'Then why did you bring him to the capital in chains?' and Peter had explained: 'He needed cooling down.' Then he laughed and added: 'And I had always planned to use him later in some fine project. Yours.'

Bering recognized that this cossack had enormous strength, both physical and moral, and he found a special reason to like him, for as he said to himself: He did sail down the Lena River. He did test those northern seas. He saw further that his aide had a gargantuan appetite, a quick anger, an equally quick forgiveness, and a tendency always to choose the more difficult way of doing things if that way produced a challenge. He decided early in their trip that he would not look to Zhdanko for advice but he would certainly rely on him for assistance in troubled times. At Solikamsk he had an opportunity to put his theories regarding the cossack to the test.

Solikamsk was one of those minute stations at which travelers halted only for greasy food for themselves and very expensive oats for their horses. It contained only sixteen rude huts and a surly innkeeper named Pavlutsky, who began to complain as soon as Bering's men and wagons descended upon him: 'There's never been so many. How can I be expected . . . ?'

Bering started to explain that the new empress herself had ordered this enterprise, whereupon Pavlutsky whined: 'She may have told you but she didn't tell me,' and in this protest he was correct. The poor man, accustomed to a solitary post rider now and then heading from Vologda to Tobolsk, was overwhelmed by this unexpected influx: 'There's nothing I can be expected to do.'

'Yes there is,' Zhdanko said. 'You can sit right here and keep your mouth shut,' and with this he lifted the innkeeper and plopped him on a stool. Threatening to break the man's head if he uttered one word, the huge cossack then began ordering his own men and Pavlutsky's to break out what food there was, all of it, for the men and such forage as could be provided for the horses. When the way station itself could produce only a portion of what was needed, he ordered his men to search the nearby huts and fetch not only food but women to cook the meal and men to feed the horses.

Within half an hour Zhdanko had mobilized nearly everyone in Solikamsk, and the hours from sunset to midnight were frenzied with the running about of the villagers as they attended to the wants of the travelers. At one in the morning, when his two casks of ale were emptied, Pavlutsky, a much-humbled man, came to Bering, pleading: 'Who is to pay for all this?' and Bering pointed to Zhdanko, who placed his arm about the innkeeper's shoulder and assured him: 'The tsarina. I'll give you a paper which the tsarina will honor,' and in the light of a flickering oil lamp in a cruet, he wrote out: 'Fleet Captain Vitus Bering ate 33 meals and 47 horses. Pay to supplier Ivan Pavlutsky of Solikamsk.' When he delivered this to the bewildered host, he said: 'I know she'll pay,' and he hoped this would be the case.

From Solikamsk they traveled by troika over frozen fields to the important stopping place of Tobolsk, but east of there the snows were so formidable that they had to idle away almost nine weeks, during which Zhdanko ranged the countryside to requisition additional soldiers, overriding the protests of their local commanders. Bering, on his part, ordered a monk and the commissar of a small village to join too, so that when the troop marched north out of Tobolsk they numbered sixty-seven men and forty-seven wagons.

When they left this relatively comfortable town they had been on the road exactly one hundred days and had covered the respectable distance of nearly fourteen hundred miles in the dead of winter, but now the well-tended post roads began to vanish and they had to travel down rivers, across barren wastes and in the shadows of forbidding hills. The treasured troika with its warm furs gave way to carts, and then to horseback, and finally to booted feet trudging through snowdrifts.

In the early summer of 1725 they covered only two hundred and twenty miles—Tobolsk, Surgut, Narim—but finally they came upon a river system which allowed them to raft speedily. One day they reached the brooding frontier fortress of Marakovska Post, where Bering said prayers to the notable missionary Metropolitan Philophei, who had only a few years before converted the people in these parts from heathenism to Christianity. 'It is a noble work,' the Dane said to his aide, 'to bring human souls into the knowledge of Jesus Christ,' but Zhdanko had other problems: 'How are we going to get our men and all this baggage over the mountains to the Yenisei River?'

By the most diligent effort they accomplished this, and for a few weeks thereafter had easy going, for ahead lay a chain of rivers down which they could boat to the little town of Ilimsk on that greater river whose distant upper reaches Zhdanko had once explored, the Lena. But now another crushing winter was upon them and they had to abandon any further attempts to forge eastward. In miserable huts and with barely adequate food they survived the dismal winter of 1725–26, adding to their roster thirty blacksmiths and carpenters. They were now ninety-seven in all, and if they ever reached the Pacific with at least some of the building materials they were carrying, an unlikely possibility, they would be prepared to build ships. Not one of them, except Bering of course, had ever even seen a real ship, let alone built one, Zhdanko having sailed in improvisations, but as a carpenter named Ilya said when impressed into service: 'If a man can build a boat for the Lena, he can built a ship for whatever that ocean out there is called.'

Vitus Bering was a man rarely distressed by conditions he could not control, and now, locked into this miserable, snowbound prison, he showed Zhdanko and his officers what a stubborn man he could be. Prevented from moving north or east, he said: 'Let's see what's south,' and when he inquired, he was told that in the important town of Irkutsk, more than three hundred miles away, the present voivode was a man who had formerly served in Yakutsk, the town to which they were heading, and the one in which Zhdanko had murdered the commander. When Bering inquired of his aide: 'What kind of man was this Izmailov?' Trofim replied enthusiastically: 'I know him well! One of the best!' and with no other information, the two men set forth on this arduous journey to acquire whatever additional facts about Siberia the voivode might have.

It was a fruitless trip south, for as soon as Zhdanko met the voivode he realized that this man was not the Izmailov he had known. Indeed, the present governor had never stuck his nose into the lands east of Irkutsk and would be of no help for the impending travels into those areas. But the governor was an energetic fellow who wanted to be helpful: 'I was sent here three years ago from St. Petersburg, Grigory Voronov, at your service,' and when he learned that Zhdanko had once explored as far east as the Siberian village of Okhotsk, he interrogated him strenuously about conditions on the eastern marches of his command. But he was equally interested in what discoveries Bering might make: 'I envy you the chance to sail in those arctic seas.'

When the three men had talked for about an hour, Voronov summoned a servant: 'Inform Miss Marina that the gentlemen would appreciate tea and a tray of sweets,' and shortly into the room came a big-boned, handsome girl of sixteen, with flashing eyes, broad shoulders and a way of moving which proclaimed: 'I'm in charge now.'

'Who are these men, Father?'

'Explorers for the tsarina.' Then, turning to Bering, he said: 'Concerning the fur trade, I have good news and bad. Down at Kyakhta on the Mongolian border, Chinese merchants are buying our furs at phenomenal prices. On your travels, pick up all you can.'

'Is it safe to visit the border?' Bering asked, for he had been told that Russian-Chinese relations were strained, and it was Marina who responded in a voice trembling with excitement: 'I've been twice. Such strange men! One part Russian, one part Mongolian, best part Chinese. And the excitement of the marketplace!'

The voivode's bad news concerned the overland route leading to Yakutsk: 'Agents tell me it's still the worst journey in Siberia. Only the bravest attempt it.'

'I made it three times,' Zhdanko said quietly, adding quickly with a smile: 'That's a damned cold trip, I can tell you.'

'I'd love to make a trip like that,' Marina cried, and when the visitors left to prepare for their journey north, Bering said: 'That young lady seems willing to go anywhere.'

So back to Ilimsk, Vitus Bering and his company trudged, more than three hundred miles of tortuous terrain, and there they waited on the banks of the still-frozen Lena River, but when spring finally thawed the valleys and streams, they rafted nine hundred miles to the eastern stronghold of Yakutsk, where Trofim showed Bering with great excitement that portion of the mighty Lena he had twice navigated, and when the Danish sea captain saw that massive body of water so close, in a sense, to the Arctic Ocean, he gained a new respect for his energetic aide. 'I long to sail that river,' Bering said with deep emotion, 'but my orders are to the east,' and Zhdanko said with almost equal feeling: 'But if our journey prospers, may we not see the Lena from the other end?' and Bering replied: 'I would like to see those hundred mouths you spoke of.'

I⟶T REQUIRED THE entire summer of 1726 and into the fall to move the eight hundred miles from Yakutsk to Okhotsk, that bleak and lonely harbor on the huge sea of that name, for now the full meaning of the fearful word *Siberia* became clear. Vast wastelands without a sign of habitation stretched to the horizon. Hills and mountains intervened, with turbulent streams to ford. Wolves followed any body of men, waiting for an accident that would provide them with a defenseless target. Untimely snows swept out of the north, alternating with blasts of unexpected heat from the south. No man could plan a day's journey and expect to complete it on schedule, and to look ahead for a week or a month was folly.

When, on the lonely uplands of this forlorn area, one did meet a traveler coming from the opposite direction, he was apt to be one of two kinds: a man who spoke no known language and from whom no information could be got, or a cutthroat who had escaped from some terrible prison compound not visible from the trail. This was the Siberia which terrified wrongdoers or antiroyalists in western Russia, for a sentence to these unrelieved monotonies usually meant death. And in these years the very worst part of the entire stretch was the region which Fleet Captain Bering now had to negotiate, and at the end of autumn, when not even half his goods had reached the eastern depot, it began to look as if he would never become a true fleet captain because he seemed destined never to have a fleet.

The trips back and forth between the two towns that year were so awesome that when porters bearing heavy loads staggered into Okhotsk, they sometimes fell in a heap, for they were totally exhausted. Bering had to make the arduous journey on horseback, since wagons and sleds could not cross the mountains and muddy flats and even cargo sleds became snowbound. At first Zhdanko remained at the western end guarding the supplies, and then, in a burst of energy, he made two round-trip journeys.

When, worn to thinness, he dragged in the last of the timbers he supposed that he would be awarded with a rest, for he believed that he could not complete another journey, but just as the snows of early winter began, Bering learned that one small party of his men was still stranded in the badlands, and without his having to ask his constable to go rescue them, Zhdanko volunteered: 'I'll fetch them,' and with a few men like himself he went back over those snow-covered trails to bring in the vital supplies, and it was providential that he did, because it was this group of sleds that carried many of the tools the shipbuilders would need.

Bering and his men were more than five thousand miles from St. Petersburg, counting their detours and doubling back, and they were beginning their third winter on the road, but it was only now that their worst difficulties began, for without proper materials or experience, they were supposed to build two ships. And it was decided that this could be most expeditiously done not here in settled Okhotsk but far across the sea on the still-primitive peninsula of Kamchatka.

That dubious decision having been made, they now had to face the next step, a perplexing one: any hastily built temporary ship sailing from Okhotsk would land on the *western* shore of the peninsula, but departure for the exploration would have to be made from the *eastern*. So, on which shore should the ships be built? When, as was his custom, Bering consulted with his subordinates, two clear opinions quickly emerged. All who were European or European-trained recommended that he land on the western shore, cross over the high mountains of the peninsula, and build on the eastern: 'For then you will have clear sailing to your target.' But the Russians—especially Trofim Zhdanko, who knew northern waters—argued that the only sensible thing would be to build the ships on the western shore, the near one, and then use them to sail around the southern tip of Kamchatka and head north to the serious business.

Zhdanko's recommendation made maximum sense—for it would enable Bering to avoid that man-killing haul of building equipment across the backbone of Kamchatka where mountains soared to fifteen thousand feet—but it had one serious weakness: no one at that time knew how far south the peninsula ran, and if Bering followed his aide's advice, he might spend a fruitless year trying to breast the southern cape, wherever it was. Actually, it was about one hundred and forty miles from where the ships could be built, and it could have been breasted in five or six easy sailing days, but no map of that period was based on hard evidence, and those who guessed placed the cape hundreds of miles to the south.

Against Zhdanko's vigorous protests, Bering decided to land on the western shore at a lonely, wind-swept spot called Bolsheretsk, a settlement of fourteen mean huts, and there, as summer waned, this indomitable Dane, now forty-seven years old, launched an operation which stunned his men and staggered the imagination of those seafaring men and explorers who heard of it later. He decided that he could not afford to waste a fourth winter in idleness, so he ordered all the gear, including the timbers to be used for building the ships, to be transported by dogsled across the entire peninsula and over mountains that would be covered with snow. He did this so that he could build on the eastern shore and thus be ready to sail directly north when winter ended. Zhdanko, seeing the first of the heavily burdened men start out, shuddered when he visualized what lay ahead, and when, as planned, he brought up the rear with some of the most valuable equipment, he gritted his teeth and told his men: 'They have a hellish blizzard in the mountains ahead. Called the *purga*, and when it rages, each man to dig his own hole!'

He and his cadre were on the highest hills in February when the temperature dropped to minus-fifty, and despite the fact that winds usually did not blow at that temperature, a dreaded *purga* roared down from northern Asia, whipping snow and sleet ahead of it like bullets. Although Zhdanko had never before been caught in such a storm, he had heard of them, and shouted to his men: 'Dig!' and with fury they scooped out ten and fifteen and twenty feet of snow on the lee side of some huge rocks, and into these holes they crept while snow piled over the openings.

Zhdanko had to go down eighteen feet before he hit a solid base, and at that depth he feared he would be so totally covered as to be lost, so that as the storm raged, he constantly pushed himself up through the falling snow and sleet, and when dawn broke and the storm abated, he was able to break clear and begin to search for his companions. When they dug out of their burrows two of the men began urging that they return to their starting point, and others would have supported them had not Zhdanko, with that fierce pride which motivated so much that he did, lashed out with his right fist and knocked one of the men backward into the snow. Seeing him fall, he leaped like a mountain cat upon the man and started bludgeoning him about the head with his powerful hands, and it was obvious that he was going to kill the defenseless man, but one of the others who had said nothing quietly interceded: 'Trofim, no!' and the big man fell back, ashamed of himself, not for having rebuked the man but for having done so to such an excess.

Chastened, he reached down, helped the man to his feet, and said jocularly: 'You've worked hard enough today. Bring up the rear.' Then he added: 'But don't try to run back. You'll not make it.'

That journey across the peninsula in dead of winter was one of the most hellish in the history of exploration, but Bering held his men together, and when they reached the eastern shore, he immediately put them to clearing away snowdrifts so that they could start building. It was a forlorn spot that had been chosen for this improvised shipyard, but never in his adventurous life did Vitus Bering show to greater advantage. He seemed to build the ship himself, appearing at every danger spot whenever needed. He spent eighteen hours a day in the long spring twilights, and whenever an aspect of the plans drawn up in St. Petersburg seemed incomprehensible, he deciphered them or made up his own rules on the spot. And his gift for improvisation was incredible.

Tar for caulking the ships had been lost somewhere en route, and it was no use blaming any individual. Somewhere in the six thousand miles from the capital—perhaps on one of the handmade boats plying some unnamed river, or in the dreadful stretch east of Yakutsk, or during the two great blizzards in the Kamchatka mountain passes—the tar had been lost, and the *St. Gabriel*, as they decided to call their ship, could not go to sea, for if left uncaulked, the open seams in her sides would admit enough water to sink her in twenty minutes.

For the better part of a day Bering studied this problem, then gave a simple order: 'Cut down those larch trees,' and when a huge pile had been assembled, he had the trees cut into lengths and from their bark he distilled a kind of sticky substance which, when mixed with a heavy grass, made a passable caulking, and the shipbuilding proceeded.

However, it was with another invention that he gained popularity with his men. Telling them: 'No man should sail a ship that has no spirits for a cold night,' he directed them to collect various grasses, roots and herbs, and when he had an ample supply he set up a fermentation process which, after many false starts, finally produced a strong beverage that he designated brandy, and of which his enthusiastic men laid in a copious amount. More immediately practical, he set other men to boiling seawater to obtain extra supplies of salt, and he directed Zhdanko to catch all the fish possible so that an oil could be made to take the place of butter. Larger fish were cured to serve instead of meat, which was not available, and he directed men to weave strong grasses together to make substitute ropes to be used in an emergency. In ninety-eight days—4 April through 10 July—this energetic man built himself a seagoing ship in which to make one of the world's premier voyages of exploration, and after only four days' rest, he sailed forth. Then came one of the mysteries of the sea: the daring man who had braved so much, who had already spent three and a half years in this quest, sailed north for only thirty-three days, saw another winter approaching, turned about, and scurried back to his Kamchatka base, arriving there after a total cruise of only fifty-one days out and back, despite the fact that the *St. Gabriel* carried a year's provisions and medical supplies for forty men.

Once again on land, with heavy snows about to descend, the men huddled in improvised huts and passed the winter of 1728–29 accomplishing nothing. Bering did interrogate a group of Chukchis, who told him that in clear weather they had often seen a mysterious shore across the sea, but for Bering the weather remained so foul that he did not see this land.

When spring brought good weather, he launched the *St. Gabriel* again, sailed boldly east for three days, became disheartened, and sailed back to Okhotsk. This time, ironically, he did go south, as Trofim Zhdanko had suggested two years ago, and he did easily round the southern tip of Kamchatka. Had he followed that easy route the first time, he would have had months of cruising time in the North Pacific and would also have avoided that fearful crossing of the peninsula during the blizzards.

It was time to go home, and since he now knew the good parts and bad of the Siberian road-and-river system, he made it to St. Petersburg in a rapid seven months and four days. He had been absent on his heroic travels for more than five years but had been at sea on his explorations slightly over three months, and about half that was spent on return trips.

But since the instructions handed him had been vague, it cannot be said that his voyage was a failure. He did not, of course, confirm Peter's conviction that Asia and North America were not joined, nor did he sail far enough to encounter Spanish or English settlements. He did, however, excite both Russian and European interest in the North Pacific and he had taken the first tentative steps in making this bleak area a part of the Russian Empire.

V ITUS BERING, THE stubborn Dane, had been back in the capital less than two months when, despite the criticism and rebuke ringing in his ears because of his failure to sail either west to join the Kolyma River or east to prove that Asia was not joined to North America, he had the temerity to propose to the Russian government that he lead a second expedition to Kamchatka, and that, instead of using about a hundred men, as he did the first time, he would now do it on a scale that would ultimately require more than three thousand. With his recommendation he submitted a careful budget in which he proved that he could accomplish this for ten thousand rubles.

The grandeur of his behavior in this negotiation was that he blandly refused to admit that he had failed the first time, and when critics assailed him for his supposed deficiencies he smiled at them indulgently, and pointed out: 'But I did everything the tsar ordered me to do,' and if they said: 'You didn't find any Europeans,' he replied: 'There weren't any,' and he maintained pressure on the government to send him back.

But the sum of ten thousand rubles was not to be spent lightly, and as Bering himself admitted, the expedition he now had in mind could run to as much as twelve thousand, so the government officials began a careful reexamination of his qualifications, and after interviewing his senior assistants, they came to the cossack Trofim Zhdanko, who had seen nothing wrong with Bering's conduct of the first expedition and who, having no family or pressing business in western Russia, was prepared to go east again.

'Bering is a fine commander,' he assured the experts. 'I was in charge of troops and can tell you that he kept his men working and happy, and that isn't easy. Yes, I'd be proud to work with him again.'

'But what about the fact that he didn't go far enough north to prove that the two continents don't touch?' they asked, and he surprised them with his answer: 'Tsar Peter himself once told me . . .'

Their jaws dropped: 'You mean, the tsar consulted with you . . . ?'

'He did. Came to see me the night I was about to be hanged.'

The interrogators ended the meeting at this point to ascertain whether Tsar Peter had actually gone to a waterfront prison to conduct a midnight talk with a cossack prisoner named Trofim Zhdanko, and when Jailer Mitrofan verified that indeed the tsar had come on just such a mission, they hurried back to question Zhdanko further.

'Peter the Great, may his honored soul rest in peace,' Zhdanko began solemnly, 'was already thinking about the expedition in 1723, and what we discussed he must have told Bering later. He already knew that Russia did not touch America, but he was very eager to know more about America.'

'Why?'

'Because he was the tsar. Because it was proper for him to know.'

The learned men hammered at the cossack for the better part of a morning, and all they learned was that Vitus Bering had failed in no commission that the tsar had given him, except the finding of Europeans, and that Zhdanko was eager to sail with him again.

'But he's fifty years old,' one scientist said, to which Trofim replied: 'And able to do the work of a man twenty.'

'Tell me,' the head of the committee asked abruptly, 'would you trust Vitus Bering with ten thousand rubles?' and Zhdanko replied truthfully: 'I trusted him with my life, and I'll do it again.'

That interrogation, and others like it, took place in 1730, when Trofim was twenty-eight, and in the years that followed, an energetic debate developed as to whether such an expedition should be made entirely by sea, which would be both quicker and cheaper, or by land-and-sea, which would enable the St. Petersburg government to learn more about Siberia on the way. No decision was reached for two years, and it was not until 1733, when Bering was fifty-three, that he was able to leave St. Petersburg on the overland route.

Once more he and Zhdanko were immobilized for two dreary winters by the snows of central Russia, and once again he was held in Okhotsk, and then his real troubles began, because bookkeepers back in St. Petersburg submitted a devastating report to the Russian treasury: 'This Vitus Bering, who assured us that his expedition would cost ten thousand rubles or twelve at most, has already spent more than three hundred thousand before leaving Yakutsk. Nor has he placed his foot aboard his two ships. How could he? They haven't been built yet.' And the nervous accountants added a shrewd prediction: 'So a foolish experiment budgeted at ten thousand may ultimately cost two million.'

In a kind of dull and futile rage the authorities cut Bering's pay in half and refused him the promotion to admiral that he sought. He made no complaint, and when he fell a full four years behind schedule, he merely tightened his belt, strove to maintain the spirits of his men, and went ahead with the building of his ships. In 1740, seven years after leaving the capital, he finally launched the *St. Peter*, from which he would command, and the *St. Paul*, which his able young assistant Alexei Chirikov would captain, and on 4 September of that year he led the two ships forth for their great exploration of the northern waters and the lands that bordered them.

They sailed bravely across the Sea of Okhotsk, rounded the southern tip of Kamchatka, and put in at the recently established seaport town of Petropavlovsk, which would become so crucially important in the next century and a half. It lay at the head of a remarkable bay, protected on all sides and facing south away from storms. Long arms of land safeguarded ships at anchor and comfortable houses for officers and bunks for crew lined the shore. No civilians lived here yet, but it was a splendid maritime installation and in time would be an important place. Here Bering and Zhdanko settled down for their eighth winter, 1734 through 1741.

Among the men stationed in the houses hugging the shore was a thirty-two-year-old German naturalist of unusual ability, Georg Steller, who had been brought along with astronomers, interpreters and other scientists to lend the expedition intellectual dignity, and he better than any of the others was prepared to do just this. Avid for learning, he had attended four German universities—Wittenberg, Leipzig, Jena, Halle—leaving with a determination to extend human knowledge, so during the land part of the trip he had studied whatever materials were available on the geography, astronomy and natural life of Russia all the way from the Baltic Sea to the Pacific Ocean, and at the end of this tedious journey and its protracted delays, he was hungry to get to sea, to visit unknown islands and set foot on the unexplored shores of North America. In his unflagging enthusiasm he told Zhdanko: 'With luck, I will be able to find a hundred new animals and trees and flowers and grasses.'

'I thought all grass was alike.'

'Oh no!' and the German enthusiast, using broken Russian, explained to Zhdanko some two dozen varieties of grass, where they flourished, how animals used them, and the great good that could be accomplished if men cultivated them intelligently.

Eager to turn the conversation away from a subject in which he had little interest, Zhdanko pointed out: 'Sometimes you speak of birds and fishes as if they were animals.'

'Well, Trofim, they are!' And here came another lecture that lasted the better part of a morning. At one point the other man interrupted: 'To me a bird is a bird and a cow is an animal,' at which Steller applauded, crying almost joyously: 'And so it should be, Trofim! And to you an eagle is a bird. And a halibut is a fish. But a scientist sees that all such creatures, including man, are animals.'

Zhdanko, drawing himself erect, thundered: 'I am not a fish. I am a man.'

Steller, reacting as if the huge man were a bright child in a beginner's class, leaned forward and asked gently: 'Well then, Scholar Trofim, what would you call a chicken? In some ways it looks like a bird, but it runs on the ground.'

'If it has feathers, it's a bird.'

'But it also has blood. It reproduces sexually. So, to the scientist it is an animal.'

'What new animals do you propose finding?'

'That's a silly question, Trofim. How do I know what I'll find until I find it?' He laughed at himself, then added: 'But I have heard of a remarkable beast, the sea otter.'

'I once had two sea-otter pelts.'

Steller was eager to learn all that he could about this legendary animal, so Trofim related all he remembered about his two otter pelts and how he had given them to the tsar of blessed memory and how splendid the fur had looked on Peter's robes. Steller leaned back, studied the cossack, and said admiringly: 'Trofim, you should be a scientist. You noticed everything. That's quite wonderful, really.' And then he became a teacher of children again: 'Now, what would you call a sea otter? He swims like a fish, that you know. But he is clearly not a fish, that you also know.'

'If he swims, he's a fish.'

'But if I pitched you overboard right now, you'd swim too. Would that make you a fish?'

'I can't swim, so I'm still a man.'

THE TWO SHIPS remained tied up in Petropavlovsk harbor, delayed by frustrating accidents. To use the summer to advantage they should have sailed before the middle of April; they planned to depart the first of May, but at the end of that month workmen were still making repairs and alterations. Also, word was received that the expedition's supply of ship's biscuit, on which sailors lived, had become completely spoiled, so that sailing really should be delayed for one more winter. Since they had to wait for adequate provisions, they convened an emergency meeting in which a plan of action was proposed and ratified by the senior staff.

And now science, which the German Steller praised so highly, intervened to hamper the whole adventure. Some learned man, a century earlier or more, had acquired through rumor the idea that a vast land lay between Asia and North America. It had been discovered, legend said, by the indomitable Portuguese navigator Dom Joao da Gama in 1589 and was reputed to contain great riches. It had been named Terra da Gama, and since the nation which first laid hold on it would stand to gain enormously, the Russians hoped that Bering would find the island, map it, allow Steller to explore it for ores, and hide the facts from other nations.

Since the ships would not be able to leave harbor before June, and since the sailing season would be short, it was obvious that a majority of the good days would have to be spent in searching for Terra da Gama, with only a few reserved for the search for America, but nevertheless, on 4 May 1741 the wise men of this expedition, and there were many, agreed that their first duty was to find Terra da Gama, and to this decision they signed their names: Comandeur Vitus Bering, Captain Alexei Chirikov, Astronomer Louis De Lisle de la Croyère and seven others. Tragically belated, on 4 June 1741 they began their futile search for land that did not exist, named after a legendary Portuguese who had never sailed anywhere, for the substantial reason that he, too, never existed.

After having satisfied themselves that there was no Terra da Gama and could never have been, the ships headed eastward, but had the ill fortune to become separated during a blow, and despite the fact that each captain behaved properly during a frantic two-day search, the ships never saw each other again. Chirikov's *St. Paul* had not sunk; it sailed on ahead and Bering's *St. Peter* was not able to catch up. After thrashing about futilely, Bering resumed his sail to the east, and in this tandem formation the Russian ships approached North America.

Should Fleet Captain Bering, to use the title to which he had been temporarily promoted at the start of this unfortunate expedition, be blamed for the parting of his two ships? No. Before sailing, he had laid out the most minute instructions for maintaining contact, and he, at least, followed his rules. As in so many instances during his long probing of the eastern seas, he was plagued by bad luck; storms pushed the ships apart and heavy fogs made their reunion impossible. Misfortune, not malfeasance, was to blame, and the fact that both ships did proceed to the shores of North America proved that his orders were clear and obeyed.

And then, on 6 July, Bering's luck changed, and at half after twelve in the afternoon a light drizzle ended and out of the clearing mists rose a congregation of the grandest snow-covered mountains in America. They perched on what would be the corner of the future boundary between Alaska and Canada and they soared in white splendor sixteen and eighteen and nineteen thousand feet into the blue skies, with a score of lower peaks clustered about. It was a magnificent sight, a justification for the entire voyage, and it excited the Russians with a promise of what might come to pass if they ever attained sovereignty over this majestic land. It was an awesome moment when the mountain Bering named St. Elias, more than eighteen thousand feet high, soared into view. Europeans had discovered Alaska.

But the seas that guard this northern wonderland rarely permit prolonged investigation, and a few hours later the log of the *St. Peter* read: 'Passing clouds, air thick, impossible to get a bearing because the shore is hidden by heavy clouds.' And early next day it read: 'Heavy clouds, rain,' and later the familiar entry for any ship attempting to navigate in these waters: 'Heavy clouds, rain.'

On the third day, when exploration of the newfound land might have been expected to begin, the log read: 'Wind, fog, rain. Though the land is not far away, yet because of heavy fog and rain we could not see it.' So Bering, who discovered Alaska for Europe, never set foot upon the continent; however, four days after sighting Mount St. Elias he did come upon a long, skinny island which he also named St. Elias because it was the saint for this day. Later Russians would rename it Kayak Island because of its shape.

And now one of the unbelievable debacles of the Bering expeditions occurred. Bering, concerned primarily with the safety of his ship and getting back to Petropavlovsk, decided to inspect the island only casually, but Adjunct Steller, perhaps the most luminous intellect on either voyage, protested almost to the point of insubordination that his life for the past decade had been dedicated exclusively to this supreme moment when he would step upon a new land, and he made such a childish commotion that Bering grudgingly allowed him a brief visit ashore. But as he left the ship a trumpeter sounded a sardonic flourish as if some great man were departing, and the sailors jeered in derision. Steller took with him as his only helper Trofim Zhdanko, whom he had convinced of the importance of science. Upon landing, the two men initiated a frenzy of running about, grabbing rocks, staring at trees, and listening for birds. They tried to study everything at once, for they realized that the *St. Peter* might have to put out to sea at any moment, and they had spent only seven or eight hours collecting when a signal from the ship alerted Zhdanko to the fact that it was about to sail.

'Herr Doktor Steller! You must hurry.'

'I've just begun.'

'The ship is signaling.'

'Let it signal.'

'Herr Doktor, frantic signals.'

'I'm frantic.' And he had cause to be, for he had studied in Germany long years in preparation for an opportunity like this, and he had traipsed for eight years across Russia to get to Kamchatka, and lately he had been at sea for weeks, and finally he had landed on the American continent, or one of its islands less than three miles offshore, and he was being allowed less than a day to carry out his work. It was infuriating, inconsiderate and insane, and he told Zhdanko so, but the cossack, an officer of the ship in a manner of speaking, had learned to obey orders, and Fleet Captain Bering was signaling that the longboat must return immediately and fetch Steller with it.

Actually, what Bering said to those about him was: 'Signal him to come aboard at once or we sail without him.' He had his ship to consider, and although he could easily have given the German scientist two or even three days ashore, he was a nervous Dane and he kept always in mind the agreement reached prior to sailing: 'Regardless of what happens, the *St. Peter* and the *St. Paul* will return to Petropavlovsk on or before the last day of September 1741.'

'Adjunct Steller,' Zhdanko said sternly as he moved close to the sweating scientist whose arms were laden with samples of this and that, 'I'm going to the longboat, and you're going with me,' and he began to drag and push the protesting German off the island. That night, the following remarks were entered in the log:

> The yawl returned with water, and the crew reported having come across a fireplace, human tracks, and a fox on the run. Adjunct Steller brought various grasses.

Later, as Bering was preparing to sail for home, he sent Zhdanko and a few crew members back to St. Elias Island on a mission which symbolized his personal interest in doing a good job for his Russian masters, but this time he did not allow Steller to go, for he had learned of the German's refusal to quit his collecting at the termination of the first trip:

> The men who returned on the small yawl announced the finding of an underground hut, something like a cellar, but no people. In this hut they discovered dried fish, bows and arrows. The Captain Commander ordered Trofim Zhdanko to take to that hut a number of government things: 13 yards of green material, 2 knives, Chinese tobacco and pipes.

In this quiet and generous way began the lucrative trade that Russia would soon be conducting with the natives of Alaska. Georg Steller's summary of his day was more acerbic: 'I spent ten years of preparation to perform a task of some importance and was allowed ten hours to complete it.'

But if Bering did not appreciate what Steller had accomplished during the time allotted him, history does, for in those brief hours ashore he perceived the significance of North America, the character of its western ramparts and their potential importance to Russia. His work that day constitutes one of the finest applications of human intelligence within restricted confines.

V ITUS BERING WAS not the first Russian to see Alaska, for when his ship, the *St. Peter*, lost contact with the *St. Paul*, the captain of the latter, Alexei Chirikov, spent nearly three full days searching for his missing partner, and then entered in his log:

> At the fifth hour in the morning we gave up looking for the *St. Peter* and with the assent of all the officers of the *St. Paul* we went on our way.

In shipshape fashion the younger captain proceeded with his exploration, and on 15 July 1741, a day earlier than Bering had sighted the cluster of great mountains, Chirikov sighted land some five hundred miles to the southeast. Coasting northward, he passed close to the beautiful island which would later be occupied by Russians, Baranof, and the exquisite bay which would house their capital, Sitka. In doing so, they saw a snow-covered volcano of near-perfection, to be named by a later explorer of far greater reputation Mount Edgecumbe, but they did not tarry to investigate one of the choice areas of the region.

However, a short distance to the north Captain Chirikov did dispatch a longboat to another island, under the direction of Fleet Master Dementiev, who had ten armed men to assist him. The boat ducked in among a nest of small islands and was never heard from again. After six anxious days of being immobilized by bad weather, Captain Chirikov put three technical men in a second small boat—Bosun Savelev, Carpenter Polkovnikov, Caulker Gorin—and sent them to find the first crew. At the last minute Sailor Fadiev cried: 'I want to go along,' and he was allowed to do so.

This boat also vanished, and now the men of the *St. Paul* had to make fearful decisions. With no small boat of any kind by which food or water could be brought aboard, and only forty-five casks of water left, they faced disaster:

> At the first hour of the afternoon the officers reached the following decision, which they put in writing: go straight to the harbor of Petropavlovsk in eastern Kamchatka. Ordered the crew to catch rain water and commanded that it be rationed out.

Thus the great expedition proposed by Vitus Bering staggered to an inconclusive ending. No officer had set foot on Alaska proper; the scientific excursions had been aborted; no useful charting was done; and fifteen men had already been lost. The adventure which Bering had said could be completed for ten thousand rubles would ultimately consume the two million predicted by the accountants, and all that would have been proved which was not already known was that Alaska existed and Terra da Gama did not.

Now CAME THE worst. When Bering's ship, the *St. Peter*, headed west from its encounter with the great mountains, it followed more or less the lovely curve of the Aleutian Islands, but the ship was now so sluggish that it could make only sixteen or seventeen miles a day against the wind. From time to time the lookouts sighted one of the islands, and several of the grand volcanoes that dotted the chain were also visible, soaring perfectly into the sky and covered at their peaks with snow.

The sailors found little comfort in this beauty, for scurvy of the most virulent kind attacked them. Without fresh food and with inadequate water to accompany what biscuits they did have, their legs began to swell and their eyes to glaze over. They suffered violent pangs of hunger and unsteadiness in gait. Each day their plight worsened, until the entries in the log became monotonous and mournful:

> Frightful storm and great waves . . . all day waves from both sides washed over the deck . . . terrific storm . . . 21 men on sick list . . . by the will of God, Alexei Kiselev died of scurvy . . . 29 men on the sick list . . .

During the last days when ordinary activity was possible, the *St. Peter* hove to off the shore of Lapak Island, the one to which the Great Shaman Azazruk had led his emigrants twelve thousand years earlier, and here they encountered islanders who provided them with water and seal meat which helped sustain them during the month of September.

Since most of the junior officers were now incapacitated by scurvy, the yawl which went ashore was captained by Trofim Zhdanko, who requested that Adjunct Georg Steller assist him, and this was a fortunate choice, because the German had been ashore only a few minutes when he began scampering about and grabbing grasses. 'This is no time for such nonsense!' Zhdanko protested, but Steller waved a handful of grass in his face, shouting with glee: 'Trofim! This is an antiscorbutic! It can save all our men who are ill!' And off he went, enlisting three Aleutian children in his search for the acid-tasting grasses which he knew would combat the dreadful scurvy. Had he been given time, he might even have saved those members of the crew on whom death had already fastened his gaze.

But the man on whom this brief visit was to have the most lasting influence was Trofim Zhdanko, for when late in the day he came upon a hut dug deep into the ground in the old style but faced with stones carefully placed and covered with a solid roof made of whalebone and stout driftwood beams, he wanted to know more about the man who had built so carefully, and when finally the frightened fellow came tentatively forward, black hair down in his eyes, a big walrus bone stuck through his septum, Zhdanko handed him some of the goods Captain Bering had given him to appease the natives: 'Here, this Chinese tobacco, this hand mirror. Look at yourself. Aren't you handsome with that big bone in your face? This fine cloth for your wife, and I'm sure you have one, with that handsome face. And this ax, this pipe and this tobacco.'

The Aleut who received this largesse, which Captain Bering had wanted to get rid of before returning to Siberia, realized that he was being offered gifts; the miraculous mirror alone proved that, so in the custom of his people he knew that he must give this huge stranger, two heads taller than himself, something in return. But when he looked at the munificence of what Zhdanko had given, especially the ax made of metal, he wondered what possibly he could give that would not seem niggardly. And then he remembered.

Beckoning Zhdanko to follow him, they went to an underground storage area, from which the Aleut produced two walrus tusks, two sealskins and, from the dark rear, the pelt of a sea otter longer and more handsome than either of those Trofim had given the tsar. It was a full seven feet long and as soft and gentle as a handful of blossoms. It was magnificent, and Zhdanko allowed the Aleut to know he thought so.

'Have you many out there?' he asked, pointing to the sea, and the man showed his understanding by waving his arms in the air to represent plenty. And he indicated that his kayak resting on the shore was the best on this island for catching them.

Steller, meanwhile, had succeeded in collecting a large armful of weeds, some of which he was already chewing vigorously, and when the boatswain signaled that the longboat was leaving, he summoned Zhdanko and offered him a handful of the life-saving grass whose ascorbic acid would counteract the onslaughts of scurvy. When he saw the sea-otter skin he reminded Trofim of their conversation, and it was evident that he hoped that Trofim would give the skin to him to augment his meager collection. But the cossack would have none of that. Turning away, he said: 'Wonderful island. I wonder what it's called?'

Now the German showed how clever he was. Handing Zhdanko his armful of grass, he faced the Aleut, and using wonderfully orchestrated movements of hands and lips, he asked what name his people gave this island, and after a while the man said: 'Lapak,' at which Steller bent down, touched the ground, and then rose to embrace with his arms the entire island. 'Lapak?' he asked, and the islander nodded.

As Steller turned to view the island, he saw off its northern shore a splendid small cone of rock emerging from the sea, and by gestures he asked if it was a volcano, and the Aleut nodded yes. 'Does it explode? Fire? Lava flowing into the sea? Hissing?' Steller asked all these questions, and received answers. He was pleased that he had discovered an active volcano and tried to ascertain its name, but this was a concept one or two degrees too difficult for the language these men had invented in half an hour, and he did not learn that in the twelve thousand years since Azazruk had first seen the nascent volcano, then less than one hundred feet above the surface of the sea, it had erupted hundreds of times, alternately rising high in the air or falling almost beneath the waves. Now it was of intermediate height, about three thousand feet, and tipped with a light cover of snow. Its name in Aleut was Qugang, the Whistler, and as Trofim Zhdanko studied it, there in the near distance rising so handsomely from the waves, he told Steller: 'I'd like to come back here,' and the German replied as he gathered up his grasses: 'So would I.'

T HE ELIXIR THAT Steller brewed proved an almost perfect cure for scurvy, since it supplied all the nutrients missing in the belly-filling but blood-depleting diet of biscuit and salt-pork fat. But now one of the recurring ironies of the sea took place, for the very men whose lives could have been saved by imbibing the horrid-tasting stuff refused to try it. Steller drank it and so did Trofim, convinced at last that the German scientist knew what he was doing, and so did three junior officers, who saved their lives thereby. The others continued to refuse, and in this they were supported by Captain Bering himself, who growled: 'Take away that mess. Do you want to kill me?' And when Steller railed against this folly of rejecting the life-saving substance, some men whispered: 'No damned German can make me drink grass.'

By mid-October, long after the *St. Peter* was supposed to be safe in Petropavlovsk, the men wallowing about in the storm-stricken ship were dying from the dreadful effects of scurvy, and entries in the log were piteous:

> Terrific gale blowing. Today I became ill with scurvy but do not count myself among the sick.

> I have such pains in my feet and hands that I can with difficulty stand my watch, 32 on the sick list.

> By the will of God died the Yakutsk soldier Karp Peshenoi, and we lowered him into the sea.

> Ivan Petrov, the naval carpenter, died.

> The drummer boy Osip Chenstov, of the Siberian garrison, died.

> 10 o'clock died the trumpeter Mikhail Totopstov. Grenadier Ivan Nebaranov died.

On 5 November 1741, when the *St. Peter* hove to off one of the most miserable islands in the northern seas, far past the end of the Aleutians, Captain Bering, himself stricken with a severe case of scurvy, assembled his officers to consider objectively their tragic condition, and to open the meeting, Zhdanko read the report prepared by the doctor, who was too ill to participate: 'We have few men to handle this ship. Twelve are already dead. Thirty-four are so weak they may soon die. The total number of men strong enough to handle ropes, ten, and of them, seven can move about only with difficulty. We have no fresh food and very little water.'

Faced with such blunt facts, Bering had no option but to recommend that his ship, the one in which he had dreamed of accomplishing so much, be beached on this forlorn spot, there to build a refuge where the sickest seamen might have a chance to survive the bitter winter that was descending upon them. This was done, but of the first four men sent ashore, three died in the rescue boat—the canonneer Dergachev, the sailor Emilianov, the Siberian soldier Popkov—and the fourth man, the sailor Trakanov, died just as he was being handed ashore.

Then came that blizzard of sorrowful entries: Stepanov died, so did Ovtsin, Antipin, Esselberg, and then the pitiful notation:

> On account of sickness I had to stop keeping a regular journal and am just making notes like this.

On 1 December 1741, during the blackest single day of the journey, Captain Bering sought out his aide, and with a burst of energy that was remarkable in one so old and so ill, he moved about the camp, encouraging everyone and assuring them that this winter would pass as had the other difficult ones they had shared. He refused to admit that this situation was far worse than difficult, and when Zhdanko tried to tell him how perilous things were, the old man stopped, stared at his assistant, and said: 'I would not expect a healthy Russian to talk like that.'

Zhdanko, realizing that his captain's mind was wandering, gently led him to his bed, but he could not make the old lion lie down. Bering continued to move about, giving orders for the management of the camp. Finally he staggered, reached for things that were not there, and fell into Zhdanko's arms.

Unconscious, he was placed in the bed from which he would never rise. On the second day he slept, but on the third he asked for full details on what was being done aboard ship, and then he again lapsed into unconsciousness, which Zhdanko said was God's mercy because of the extreme pain the old fighter was experiencing. On 7 December, a bitter cold day, he wanted to be taken out to the ship, but this Zhdanko refused to do. In lucid moments, Bering discussed intelligently the work still to be done before the expedition could be considered a success, and he judged that the expedient thing to do would be to dig in for the winter, break the *St. Peter* apart, build from its timbers a tight small boat called a hooker, sail to Petropavlovsk when the weather was good, and there build a new ship with better strength in its timbers and return to explore seriously those inviting lands close to that great nest of mountains coming down to the sea.

Zhdanko encouraged him in all this dreaming, and on that night of 7 December he slept beside this extraordinary Dane whom he had grown to respect and love. At about four in the morning Bering wakened with a host of new plans, which, he told Zhdanko, he felt sure the authorities in St. Petersburg would approve; when he tried to explain them in detail he lapsed into Danish, but there were none of his Danes still living to understand.

'Go back to sleep, Little Captain,' Zhdanko said, and shortly before five o'clock on that storm-swept island the old man died.

But now the survivors took hold of themselves, as Bering had hoped they would, and despite blizzards and inadequate food, the gallant forty-six surveyed the island, reported on its possibilities, and did exactly what Bering had planned: from the wreckage of the ship *St. Peter* they constructed the hooker *St. Peter*, thirty-six feet long, twelve feet wide, five feet three inches deep. In this frail and crowded craft all forty-six sailed the three hundred and sixty miles to Petropavlovsk, where they landed on 27 August 1742, an appalling nine years, one hundred and sixty-three days after the departure from St. Petersburg on 18 March 1733.

When they landed they learned that their companion ship, the *St. Paul*, had had its troubles, too. Of her seventy-six officers and men who sailed in June, only fifty-four returned in October, four months later. They heard with sorrow of how the two boats with fifteen knowledgeable seamen had vanished near a beautiful island, and they understood what had been involved when a local officer reported: 'On the journey back to Petropavlovsk they were smitten with scurvy and many died.'

The harshest judgment on Vitus Bering was that he had been unlucky. All events seemed to conspire against him; his ships leaked; the stores that he anticipated did not arrive on time, or were lost, or were stolen. Many other captains conducted voyages of much greater extent both in miles and time than his from Kamchatka to Alaska and back without being struck by such a virulent outbreak of scurvy, but he was so adversely marked by fate that on this relatively brief cruise he lost thirty-six in one ship, twenty-two in another. And he died without ever having encountered the Europeans he sought.

And yet this doughty, stumpy Dane left a heritage of honor and a tradition of seamanship which inspired the navy of a great nation. He had sailed the northern seas with a vigor that excited the men who accompanied him, and in all the logs of his ships there is no entry which speaks of ill feeling against the captain or disturbances among the men under his command.

In the seas he wandered so ineffectively, two memorials remind us of his valor. The icy water that lies between the Pacific and Arctic oceans carries his name, the Bering Sea, and it seems to borrow its character from him. It is dour; it freezes hard; it is difficult to navigate when the ice crowds down; and it punishes those who miscalculate its power. But it also teems with a rich animal life and rewards good hunters and fishermen enormously. It is a sea deserving to be named after someone rugged like Bering, and in this narrative we shall meet it repeatedly, always with respect. At the close of the following century thousands will swarm to its shores and some will find in its magical sands the golden wealth of Croesus.

The Russians also named after him that forlorn island on which he died, and a more wretched memorial no good sailor was ever given. But there will always be critics to claim that he was not a good sailor and they will cry: 'No first-rate seaman ever attempted so much, managed it so poorly, and accomplished so little.' History does not find it comfortable to adjudicate such debate.

THE EXPLORATION OF Alaska was conducted by two contrasting kinds of men: either purposeful explorers of established reputation like Vitus Bering and the other historic figures we shall be meeting briefly, or tough, nameless commercial adventurers who often achieved more constructive results than the professionals who preceded them. In the early development this second wave of men in motion was made up of rascals, thieves, murderers and ordinary toughs who had been born in Siberia or served there, and their guiding motto as they began to probe the Aleutian Islands was brief and accurate: 'The tsar is far away in St. Petersburg and God is so high in heaven He can't see us. But here we are on the island, so let's do whatever's necessary.'

Trofim Zhdanko, miraculously alive after his winter of near-starvation on Bering Island, became through an odd combination of circumstances one of these commercial adventurers. Having made his way to Russia's eastern terminus at the seaport of Okhotsk, from which he supposed he would be sent home, he gradually realized, during a six-month waiting period, that he had no desire to go back: I'm forty-one. My tsar's dead, so what's in St. Petersburg? And my family's dead, so what's in Ukraine? The more he examined his limited prospects the more he was attracted to remaining in the east, and he started asking what his chances were of landing a government job of some kind, but he had made only a few inquiries when he learned a basic fact about Russian life: 'When there's a good job in any of the alien provinces like Siberia, it's always some official born in homeland Russia who gets it. Others need not apply.'

The best government job he could hope for as a Ukrainian in Okhotsk was as a laborer on the new harbor that was being built to accommodate trade with Japan, China and the Aleutians, if such trade ever developed, which seemed unlikely, since the ports of the first two nations were closed to Russian ships while the Aleutians contained no harbors. Despondent, and perplexed as to what ugly things might happen to him if he did return to St. Petersburg, now that new officials were in power, he was lazing in the sun one June morning in

1743, when a man, obviously a Siberian, with dark skin, Mongolian features and no neck, accosted him: 'The name's Poznikov, gentleman merchant. You look like a strong one.'

'I've met men who could best me.'

'Have you ever sailed?'

'I've been to the other shore,' and when he pointed toward America the merchant gasped, took him by the arm, and spun him around for closer examination.

'You were with Bering?'

'Buried him. A great man.'

'You must come with me. You must meet my wife.'

The merchant led him to a well-appointed house overlooking the harbor, and there Zhdanko met Madame Poznikova, an imperious woman obviously not Siberian. 'Why do you bring this workman to see me?' she asked her husband rather sternly, and he said with obvious meekness: 'He's not a workman, dearest, he's a sailor.'

'Where has he sailed?' she demanded.

'To America . . . with Bering.'

When this name was spoken, she moved closer to Trofim and, as her husband did in the street, swung him around to inspect him more closely, turning his big head this way and that as if she had perhaps seen him before. Then, shrugging, she asked with just a touch of scorn: 'You? You were with Bering?'

'Twice. I was his aide.'

'And you saw the islands out there?'

'I was ashore, twice, and as you know, we spent one whole winter there.'

'I didn't know,' she said, taking command of the conversation and asking Trofim to sit while she fetched a drink made from the cranberries which abounded in these parts. Before resuming her interrogation, she cleared her throat: 'Now tell me, Cossack. Were there really furs on those islands?'

'Wherever we went.'

'But I was told by the first ship that returned, Captain Chirikov's, that they saw no furs.'

'They didn't land, we did.'

Abruptly, she rose and stalked about the room, then sat down beside her husband, and with her hand on his knee as if seeking either his counsel or his silence, she asked very slowly: 'Cossack, would you be willing to go back to the islands? For my husband, that is? To bring us furs?'

Zhdanko breathed deeply, endeavoring to suppress the excitement he felt at being offered an escape from a dead life in western Russia: 'Well, if it could be done . . .'

'What do you mean?' she said sharply. 'You've already done it.' She waved her hand, brushing aside any questions: 'Crews, ships, that's what Okhotsk is for.' Suddenly she was standing before him: 'Would you go?' and he saw no purpose in delaying his enthusiastic acceptance: 'Yes!'

During subsequent discussions of how such an expedition could be organized, it was she who laid down the principles: 'You'll sail to the new harbor at Petropavlovsk, a thousand easy miles in a stout Okhotsk ship belonging to the government. There you'll be only six or seven hundred miles from the first island, so you'll build your own ship and sail forth in early spring. Fish and hunt all summer, come back in autumn, and when you reach here Poznikov will take your furs to Irkutsk . . .'

'Why so far?' Zhdanko asked, and she snapped: 'It's the capital of Siberia. All good things in this part of Siberia come from Irkutsk.' Then, with a show of modesty: 'I come from Irkutsk. My father was voivode there.' And as she uttered this word, she and Trofim pointed at each other and broke into laughter.

When Poznikov asked: 'What's so funny?' she choked, took Trofim by the wrist, and shook it vigorously: 'He *was* with Bering! I saw him with Bering!' and she drew back to study him: 'How many years ago could that have been?' and Trofim said: 'Seventeen. You brought us tea and your father told us of the fur trading in Mongolia.' After a moment's pause, he asked: 'Did you ever return to that trading post on the border?'

'I did,' she said. 'That's where I met him,' and she pointed to her stolid husband, showing no affection but great respect. Then she clapped her hands: 'Ivan, I hire this cossack here and now. He's to be our captain.'

I VAN POZNIKOV WAS in his fifties, hardened by the cruel winters of Siberia and even more by the harsh practices he had been forced to employ in his dealings with Chukchis, Kalmucks and Chinese. He was a big man, not so tall as Zhdanko but broader in the shoulders and just as powerful in the arms; his hands were immense, and on several occasions when facing ultimate danger his long fingers had clamped around an adversary's neck and remained there, tightening until the man fell limp in his hands and died. In trading he was equally brutal, but because through the years of their unequal marriage his wife had hammered at him, he allowed her to run their family and its business.

When Trofim met the Poznikovs that first morning he had wondered how this dynamic woman, daughter of a voivode sent out from the capital, had consented to marry a mere Siberian tradesman, but in the following weeks when he saw how this pair dominated the eastern fur trade he remembered the interest she had shown in it as a girl in Irkutsk. Apparently she had seen Poznikov as her main chance to learn the mysteries of eastern Siberia, so she had stifled her social ambitions, accepted him as her husband, and expanded his business sixfold. It was she who supervised the trading, making most of the major decisions, for as Poznikov confided: 'I do better when I listen to her.'

One day while the two men were working on plans for establishing a chain of trading posts in the Aleutians, Poznikov made a casual remark which indicated that perhaps the Madame, as both men called her, had done the proposing which resulted in their marriage: 'We were on the Mongolian border, and I was astonished at how thoroughly she knew fur prices, and I said: "You're wonderful!" and to my surprise, she said right back: "You're wonderful, Poznikov. Together we would make a powerful team." ' Neither man commented further.

When it became clear that it was going to require much longer to arrange the first trip to the Aleutians than planned, it was Madame Poznikova who suggested: 'Time's come for us to get our furs to Kyakhta on the Mongolian border,' and she proposed that Zhdanko hire six armed guards to escort them through the first five hundred miles of forbidding bandit country between Okhotsk and the Lena. But when details were completed, Trofim learned that he would be protecting not only the merchant and his wife but also their sixteen-year-old son, a brash, ill-mannered young man who bore the highly inappropriate name of Innokenti.

During their first hours together Trofim learned that the son was arrogant, opinionated, brutal in his treatment of inferiors, and miserably spoiled by his mother. Innokenti knew the answer to everything and volunteered to make all decisions. Because he was a large lad, his firm opinions carried more weight than they might have otherwise, and he took especial delight in telling Zhdanko, whom he considered little better than a serf, what to do. Since the distance to Yakutsk was about eight hundred miles, it was obvious that the journey with the pelts was not going to be a pleasant one.

To ease the tension as they plodded through the wastelands of Siberia, Trofim devised a nonsense rhyme like the ones his mother had sung in the Ukraine:

'Irkutsk to Ilimsk to Yakutsk to Okhotsk!
No one can handle such difficult names.
Okhotsk to Yakutsk to Ilimsk to Irkutsk!
When you're a cossack they're easy as games.'

'That's a stupid song,' Innokenti said. 'Stop it!' But the six guards were so attracted by the difficult names and broken rhythms that soon the entire column except the boy chanted 'Okhotsk to Yakutsk to Irkutsk,' and the tedious miles became more bearable.

When they were more than halfway to Yakutsk, Trofim was so pleased with the progress they were making and with the congeniality of the two older Poznikovs that one night as they camped on the barren side of a Siberian mountain, he beckoned the big merchant with the drooping mustaches and no neck, and in the moonlight whispered: 'I brought with me a special fur. I think it's valuable. Will you sell it for me when you get yours to Mongolia?'

'Glad to. Where is it?' and from his voluminous blouse Trofim produced the remarkable pelt he had acquired on Lapak Island. As soon as Poznikov felt its extraordinary quality, and even before taking it to a light, he said: 'This must be sea otter.'

'It is,' Trofim said, and the merchant whistled: 'I didn't know they grew so big!' and Trofim said: 'The seas out there are full of them.'

In the next moments Zhdanko learned why the bull-necked Siberian had been so successful even before he acquired his capable wife, for Poznikov adjusted the flickering light so that it illuminated the fur without revealing its presence to the six guards, who might be spying. Then, he lifted one tip after another, satisfying himself as to its quality by rubbing it between his fingers, tugging at it gently at first, to be sure it had not been glued onto the pelt, and when Zhdanko was not looking, giving it a tremendous yank. Satisfied that the fur was real, even though of a type with which he was not familiar, he pressed it against his face, then blew upon it to separate the hairs so that he might see the subtle variation of color along the length. Then suddenly, in a gesture which startled Trofim, he pressed both hands heavily upon the fur and pulled the hairs roughly apart so that the animal skin was revealed for him to judge of its health, and when all this was done, he stood up, walked away from the lamp so that no watcher but Zhdanko could see him, and holding his right hand high above his head, he allowed the full length of this gorgeous pelt to reveal itself.

When he returned to the light, he masked the fur, sat down beside Trofim, pressed the pelt into his hands, and whispered: 'Madame must see this,' and when he and Trofim slipped quietly into her tent, he told her: 'We've found a treasure,' and he indicated that Trofim was to show her and Innokenti the pelt. As soon as she saw it she tried to assess its value with a set of tricks totally different from the ones her husband had used. Standing erect and adopting the poses of a princess, this imposing thirty-four-year-old woman draped the pelt about her shoulders, took a few steps, wheeled, took some more steps, bowed before her son as if he had invited her to dance.

Only then did she give her opinion: 'This is a fine fur, worth a fortune,' and when Trofim asked hesitantly: 'How much?' she offered a figure in rubles that amounted to more than seven hundred dollars. He gasped and said: 'There are hundreds out there,' and she restudied the pelt, hefted it in her hands, then held it against her face: 'Maybe nine hundred.'

It was unfortunate that Innokenti had heard this, for he could not keep from boasting to one of the Siberian guards the next morning: 'We have a new kind of pelt. Worth more than a thousand rubles,' and as the days passed, this man told the other guards: 'In those bales they never open they have hundreds of pelts worth fifteen hundred rubles each,' and the Siberians began to hatch a plot.

As the little caravan entered a canyon girt by low hills, one of the Siberians whistled, whereupon all six turned on the Poznikovs and their personal protector, Zhdanko. Knowing that he was the one they must dispose of first, the three biggest guards fell upon Trofim with clubs and knives, expecting to kill him instantly, but with an instinct gained from many such encounters, he anticipated their thrusts, and calling upon his extreme strength, he held them off.

And to the amazement of the guards who had attacked the three Poznikovs, expecting an easy victory, the family turned out to be Siberian tigers, or worse. Madame Poznikova started screaming and beating about her with a walking stick, which she wielded with fury and direction. Her son did not run for cover, like an ordinary frightened sixteen-year-old; grabbing at one of the men, he caught him by an arm and swung him into a tree, and when the rogue stumbled, Innokenti jumped upon him and with his fists beat him senseless. But it was Poznikov himself who proved the most valorous, for after manhandling his own assailant, choking him with his huge hands, he sprang to help Zhdanko, who was still fending off his three attackers.

One of the men had a long, sharp knife pointed at Trofim's throat, and Poznikov, fighting off the other two, leaped on him but could not wrest the weapon from him, and the desperate man now plunged the knife deep into the merchant's belly, pulling it upward and to one side, leaving it there to complete its work. Poznikov, realizing from the terrible course of the knife through his vitals that he was mortally wounded, screamed in some old Siberian tongue to his wife, and she stopped flailing about with her stick and dashed to his side.

When she saw what had happened, assessing it, like him, as certain death, she grabbed at the handle of the long knife, ripped it from her husband's belly, and looked frantically about. Seeing the man that her son had fought off, she leaped on him as he lay on the ground and plunged the knife into his throat. Pausing only to jerk it out sideways, she turned toward the man whom her husband had downed, and with a wild yell she bent over him, stabbing him three times about the heart.

The four other guards, watching with horror what this frenzied woman was doing, started to flee, leaving the supposed cache of otter pelts behind, but Innokenti tripped one of them, pinned him when he fell, and shouted for his mother to give him the knife, which she did, and he stabbed the man many times.

Three Siberian scoundrels and Merchant Poznikov lay dead in the canyon, and after Trofim and Innokenti had buried the latter under a pile of stones, Madame in solemn words spoke the truth about the fight: 'Innokenti was very brave, and I'm proud of him. And I knew what to do when I grasped the knife.

But we would all have been dead if Zhdanko had not held off those first three . . . so long . . . so valiantly.' She nodded before him and told her son to do the same, in respect for his behavior as a true cossack, but the boy refused to do so, for he was lamenting the death of his father.

Maintaining watch against the three runaway guards lest they attempt to return with allies to capture the caravan, the travelers held counsel as to what they had best do to protect themselves and their precious cargo, and since they were well over halfway to the Lena River they agreed that it would be wise to push ahead through the remaining two hundred miles, and in the morning, after paying tearful farewell to the grave of Ivan Poznikov, merchant-warrior, they set forth across some of the loneliest terrain in the world: those barren upland reaches of central Siberia, when days were a forlorn emptiness with nothing visible to the horizon and nights a wind-howling terror.

It was in this testing land that Trofim came to appreciate the extraordinary family of which he had become a part. Ivan Poznikov had been fearless in life, courageous in death. His widow Marina was a remarkable woman, the equal of any man in judicious trading, an astonishing performer when turned loose with a long knife. Watching her adjust to the loss of her husband and the rigors of the march, he understood why Ivan had been willing to place in her hands the management of his business. Now, in the most dangerous parts of their journey, she offered to stand guard while her men slept. She ate as frugally as they. She tramped the difficult miles without complaint, helped tend the horses, and smiled when Trofim paid her a compliment: 'You're a cossack in dresses.'

Her son Innokenti was a problem, for although he had behaved astonishingly well during the attack on their caravan, fighting like a man thrice his age, he remained an unpleasant youth, and his killing of a man made him even more arrogant than before. He had a visceral dislike of Trofim, a distaste for his mother's leadership, and an inclination to do all those irritating things which caused elders to distrust him. Able he was, likable he would never be. And Trofim heard him complain: 'Three robbers dead, and the cossack didn't kill one of them. A woman and a boy saved the caravan.'

Madame Poznikova would have none of this: 'We know who protected us that night . . . who held off three . . . miraculously, I think.' And it was Zhdanko who guided them across these hazardous wastes. He selected the places to halt and then volunteered to stand the night watches. He kept an eye out for bears, went first into the streams that had to be forded, and in every way performed like a true cossack. But despite this constant exhibition of leadership, Innokenti refused to accept him as anything but a serf; he did, however, obey Trofim during the march, intending to be rid of him when it ended.

In this disciplined way, the three travelers completed their fourteen perilous days on the lonely trails and came to that hill from which, exhausted but still prepared to forge ahead, they looked down upon a most beautiful sight, the wide, flowing Lena River. Here they rested, and Zhdanko, gazing at the river, said: 'When you sell the furs, you'll have rubles instead of pelts. And then we'll have to worry about getting them safely back to Okhotsk,' but Madame said sternly: 'This time we'll hire honest guards.'

In Yakutsk she faced a different problem: finding honest merchants to barge her bales up the Lena River to the big markets on the Mongolian border; but calling upon old acquaintances of her husband's, she concluded a promising deal. Before dispatching them, she took the merchants aside and revealed the special pelt she was sending to market: 'Sea otter. Nothing else like it in the world. And I can provide an assured supply.' The men studied the exceptional fur and asked why her husband had not come with one so valuable, and she said: 'He came and was killed by our guards,' and she added: 'Help me to find six I can trust not to kill me on the way home.'

After they had provided reliable men from their own ranks, they said: 'Bring us all the sea otter you can catch. Chinese merchants will fight over such fur.' Smiling thinly, she offered them a guarantee: 'You'll see me often in Yakutsk,' and on the trip home she discussed with Trofim and her son how the Aleutian Islands could be exploited.

When they were back in Okhotsk, a town building itself into a city, she was in her house only one day before she summoned Trofim, to whom she said frankly: 'Cossack, you're a tremendous man. You have both courage and brains. You must stay with me, for I need your help to control the fur islands.'

'I have no mind to marry,' he said.

'Who said marry? I need you in my business.'

'I'm a seaman. We're no good at business.'

'I'll make you good.' Then she added pleadingly: 'Poznikov, rest the good man's soul, he'd been a merchant for years. Accomplished nothing, until I put iron in his backbone.'

'My job is in the islands.'

'Cossack, you and I, we could own those islands and all the furs they contain.' She moved to face him directly: 'But neither of us can do it alone.' Her voice rising to an irritated shriek, she cried: 'Cossack, I need you.'

But he knew what his destiny was: 'I shall go to the islands. And bring you furs. And you shall sell them,' and from this simple resolve he would not retreat. However, when she said in ill-disguised disgust: 'If you must go, take Innokenti with you. Teach him wisdom and control, for he has neither,' he assented: 'I don't want him. He's already ruined, I'm afraid, but I'll take him,' and she grasped his arm: 'To hell with wisdom and control. Teach him to be a reliable man, like his father, like you; otherwise, I am sore afraid he'll never be one.'

ANY SERIOUS SHIPBUILDER looking at the pitiful craft in which Trofim Zhdanko and the eighteen-year-old Innokenti Poznikov proposed to sail with eleven others from Petropavlovsk across the Bering Sea to Attu Island, westernmost of the Aleutians, would have been appalled. Green timbers had been used for the main structure of the boat, but not for the sides, which were of sealskin, some heavy enough to withstand real shocks, some so thin they could be punctured by any shard of ice that struck them. Since nails were almost nonexistent in Kamchatka, the few that were obtainable were used to bind main pieces of wood; for the other areas thongs of walrus and whale had to suffice, which made one practiced sailor groan: 'That thing wasn't built, it was sewed.'

The finished product was little more than a sealskin umiak somewhat strengthened and big enough to hold thirteen fur traders and their gear, particularly their guns. Indeed, there were so many firearms aboard as to make the boat resemble a floating arsenal, and their owners were eager to use them. But the chances that such a flimsy vessel would ever reach the Aleutians seemed improbable, and that it could get back loaded with bales of pelts, even more so. But Zhdanko was eager to test his luck, and on a spring day in 1745 he sailed forth to capture Alaska for the Russian Empire and riches for his motley crew.

They were a brutal lot, prepared to take risks and determined to win their fortunes in the fur trade. Forerunners of Russia's expansion to the east, they would set the pattern for Russia's behavior in the settlement of Alaska.

What kind of men were these? They were divided into three clear-cut groups: true Russians from the rather small tsardom in northwest Europe centering on two great cities, St. Petersburg and Moscow; adventurous men from all the other parts of the empire, especially Siberians from the east; and a curious group called by the difficult name *promyshlenniki*, which was comprised of petty criminals from anywhere who had been sentenced by the court to a choice between death or forced servitude in the Aleutians. Taken as a mass, they were usually all called Russians.

These ugly men were blessed with gentle winds that kept their improvised sail full, and after twenty rather easy days requiring little paddling, Zhdanko said: 'Tomorrow, maybe. Or next day.' They were heartened by the large number of seals they were seeing, and early one morning as Innokenti peered eastward he spotted, bobbing on the waves, their first sea otter.

'Trofim!' he called, for he continued to treat the cossack like a serf. 'Is that one?'

There was little space in the unroofed boat for movement, but Trofim edged his way forward, stared into the morning light, and said: 'I see nothing.' This irritated Innokenti, who shouted impatiently: 'There, there! Floating on its back.'

And now when Trofim looked he saw one of nature's strangest yet most pleasing sights: a female sea otter swimming along on her back with a baby nestled securely on her belly, both looking at ease and enjoying the shifting clouds in the sky. Trofim could not yet be sure they were sea otters, but he knew they were not seals, so he moved to the back, took the tiller, and steered toward the floating pair.

Unaware of what a boat was or a man, the mother otter continued her lazy swim as the hunters drew near, and even when Innokenti raised his gun and took aim, she attempted no evasive action. There was a loud bang, she felt a crushing pain through her chest and sank immediately to the far depths of the Bering Sea, dead and of use to no one. Her baby, left afloat, was clubbed by a heavy paddle, and then it too sank to the bottom. Of all the sea otters that would in the years ahead be killed by careless hunters firing prematurely, seven out of ten would sink to the bottom before being caught for their fur. With Innokenti's first gun blast, the extermination was under way.

Having lost what Trofim and the others certified as a true sea otter, the young fellow was not in a happy mood when later that morning one of the men shouted 'Land!' and the boy took no pleasure in watching as the lone island of Attu emerged from the mists that enshrouded it.

They had made landfall at the northwest corner of the island, and for an entire day they coasted along its northern face, encountering nothing but forbidding cliffs and the lifeless stare of what appeared to be barren fields, no tree or even a shrub. They did pass the mouth of one bay, but its flanks were so precipitous that any attempt at landing would have been foolhardy, and that night Innokenti prepared for bed with the whining observation: 'Attu's a rock.'

However, next morning, after breasting a low headland at the eastern tip of the island, they saw facing them a wide bay with inviting sandy shores and spacious meadows. Gingerly they made a landing, and supposing the island to be uninhabited, started inland. They had progressed only a short distance when they discovered the miracle of Attu. Wherever they moved they were faced with a treasure of bright flowers in the most profuse variety: daisies, red flamers, lupines in many colors, lady slippers, thistles, and two which astonished them: purple iris and gray-green orchids.

'This is a garden!' Trofim cried, but Innokenti had turned away, and suddenly wailed: 'Look!' and from the opposite end of the meadow, coming toward them, was a procession of native men wearing the distinctive hats of their island, long visor in front, straight back, and flowers or feathers stemming from the crown. They had never before seen a white man, nor had any of the invaders except Zhdanko seen islanders, so mutual curiosity ran high.

'They're friendly,' Zhdanko assured his men, 'until something proves different,' but it was difficult to convince them of this, because each islander had sticking horizontally through his nose a long bone and in his lower lip one or two labrets, which imparted such a fierce appearance that Innokenti shouted: 'Fire at them.'

Trofim, countermanding the order, moved forward, holding in his extended hands a collection of beads, and when the islanders saw their glittering beauty they whispered among themselves, and finally one came toward Zhdanko, offering him a piece of carved ivory. In this way the serious exploitation of the Aleutian Islands began.

The first contacts were congenial. The islanders were an orderly group: smallish men with dark Oriental-looking faces who could have come out of northern Siberia a year ago, they went barefoot, wore sealskin clothing, and tattooed their faces. Their language bore no resemblance to any that the men from the boat had ever heard, but their wide smiles showed their welcome.

But when Zhdanko and his crew made their way to one of the huts in which the islanders lived two things happened: the Attu men obviously did not want the strangers to approach their women and children; and when the Siberians forced their way inside one, they were repelled by the darkness of the underground cave in which they found themselves, by its confusion and by the awful smell of fish and rotting seal fat. In that moment the tension began, for one of Zhdanko's men growled scornfully: 'They're not human!' and this became the consensus.

Nevertheless, in several of the thirty-odd huts the newcomers did find small piles of sealskin, though with whom the islanders could be trading no one could guess, and in two huts they found well-tanned pelts of the sea otter. Their long quest—starting in Okhotsk and ending with their daring venture across the Bering Sea in their improbable boat—seemed assured of success.

It was not difficult for Zhdanko, who was an ingenious man, to explain to the men of Attu that if they brought him sealskins, he in turn would trade them for things they wanted from the boat; and that was preliminary to informing them that what the strangers really wanted were pelts of the sea otter. But that was a different matter, because through the centuries the islanders had learned that the sea otter was the rarest creature in their ocean and that to catch him was not easy. But the traders finally convinced the islanders that the latter must go forth in their kayaks and bring back furs, especially those of the otter.

The name of the young paddler who now took it upon himself to instruct Innokenti in island rites was Ilchuk, some five years older and a skilled hunter who had been instrumental in bringing to shore the only whale that Attu had captured in ten years; its baleen had been used by Ilchuk's sisters in the creation of numerous useful articles and a pair of baskets that were not only practical containers but also works of art.

When Trofim saw these baskets and other things made from whalebone and ivory, he began to alter his opinion of the Attu islanders; and when he and Innokenti were finally invited into Ilchuk's hut, he saw that they did not all live like animals. The hut was orderly and arranged much as a house in Siberia would be, except that it was mostly underground, and when the winds of winter began to blow, Trofim understood why the houses were kept so low; had they been any higher, the gales would have blown them away.

Now, in the dark winter, tensions between the two groups flared, because the newcomers, hungry for furs, wanted the island men to continue hunting regardless of weather, while the Attu men, well acquainted with the power of winter storms, knew that they must stay ashore till spring. The one who applied the greatest pressure was Innokenti, nineteen years old now and increasingly brutal in his relations with others. Always aware that it was his family that had built the fur trade, he found it impossible to accept an intruder like Zhdanko, so he placed himself in charge of the growing bales and of the operations which promised to bring in more. Trofim, a quarter of a century older than this callow youth, surrendered control of fur hunting but resolved to retain command of all else.

As soon as there was any cessation of storm, and sometimes two or three days in a row would be relatively calm, Innokenti ordered Ilchuk and his men to venture forth, and if they showed reluctance to do so, he raged until it became clear to the Attu men that they had somehow, by steps they could not now recall, become slaves of the strangers. This feeling was intensified when two of Innokenti's men appropriated young women of the settlement, with such pleasing results that a third man plucked off one of Ilchuk's sisters.

There was resentment, but on Attu relations between adult men and women were customarily easy, so that the tempers which might have flared elsewhere did not erupt here, but what did matter was Innokenti's unwavering insistence that the men go out to sea when all their instincts and long experience warned them to stay ashore. This radical alteration of their life systems they opposed, and when, on a clear day, Innokenti demanded that Ilchuk and four of his men go out, there was a momentary flareup, which ended quickly when Innokenti produced his gun and ordered the men with gestures: 'You go or I shoot.'

Grudgingly they went, pointing to the sky as if to say 'We warned you!' and before they were out of sight of land, a great wind blew in from Asia, bringing sheets of freezing rain that came parallel to the sea, destroying two of the kayaks and drowning their occupants. When Ilchuk led the surviving boats back to shore he began to rage at Innokenti, who stood quietly for several minutes, but when the other Attu men joined the recriminations, surrounding him on three sides, he lost his composure, raised his gun, and shot one of the protesters. Ilchuk, seeing the man fall and realizing that he was fatally wounded, started to leap at Innokenti, but he was seized by two of the Siberians, who threw him to the ground, then kicked him about the head.

Trofim, hearing the gunfire, ran from where he had been working on a driftwood house, and by virtue of his size and authority, brought order to what would otherwise have degenerated into a riot which might have caused the deaths of all the invaders. It was the last time he would exert his authority over the men, for when he shouted: 'Who did this?' Innokenti stepped brazenly forward: 'I did. They were attacking me,' and when the others supported this claim, thrusting their chins forward belligerently, Zhdanko realized that leadership of the expedition had passed to Innokenti. Almost lamely he said: 'Warfare has begun. Each man to protect himself,' but it was the younger man who gave specific orders: 'Bring our boat closer to our huts. And each man to sleep with us, not with his native woman.'

The man who had taken as his bed-partner Ilchuk's sister ignored this last instruction, and two mornings later, when the winter fog lifted, his body was found on the beach stabbed in many places.

Now the warfare became hateful, sullen, a thing of dark shadows and sudden retributions. With only twelve men left, including himself, Trofim tried to regain control by making peace with the more numerous islanders, and he might have succeeded had not an evil affair frustrated him. When Ilchuk, a wise islander who lamented the sad deterioration, came with two fellow fishermen to arrange with Trofim a kind of truce, Innokenti, who was watching nearby with four of his followers, allowed them to come close, then flashed a signal, whereupon the Russians leveled their guns and killed all three members of the peace team. Next day, when one of the island girls charged Innokenti with having murdered her brother in the ambush, he proved her correct by murdering her, too.

Vainly Trofim tried to halt the killings, and in quick succession six more islanders were slain, after which it was meekly accepted that a new order had come to Attu. When spring made orderly hunting of sea otters practical, Innokenti and his group had life on the island so rigorously organized that kayaks went out regularly, and came back with the furs the traders craved. It would be difficult to explain just how these eleven—five Siberians, three Russian petty criminals, two from other parts of the empire and the boy Innokenti—maintained control over the population of an entire island, but they did. Murder was a prime persuader—eight, two dozen, then thirty, all executed coldly and at such times and places as to create the most intimidating effect, till everyone on Attu knew that if fishermen-hunters were tardy in doing what the strangers wanted, someone was going to be shot, usually the delinquent fisherman and sometimes several of his friends.

Even more difficult to explain was how Trofim Zhdanko allowed all this to happen, but in the affairs of men under pressure, decisions are made as a consequence of events far beyond their control; chance determines, not planned thought, and each bloody incident on Attu strengthened Innokenti's hand and weakened Trofim's. Of all these episodes of killing, he participated in none, for as a cossack trained in killing at the tsar's command, he had learned that murder was justified only if it quickly brought a workable peace. On Attu, Innokenti's aimless slaughter brought no peace, only more furs, so by midsummer Trofim realized that the situation had degenerated so badly that the only sensible strategy was to leave the island with what furs had been accumulated and head for Petropavlovsk.

When he proposed this, many of the crew were so eager to leave Attu that he regained a modicum of leadership, but once more chance intruded to deny him that position, for when in mid-July 1746 he organized the men secretly for an escape, an island woman detected the strategy of flight and informed her men, who made plans to murder all the strangers before they reached their boat.

When the bales were aboard and the twelve survivors about to push off, the islanders tried to rush them, but Innokenti had anticipated this, and as the shouting men and women surged toward the boat, he ordered his men to fire straight into the middle of the crush and then to reload and fire again. They did, with terrible effectiveness.

As this first group of invaders from Russia to spend a winter in the Aleutians finally retreated to the safety of the Bering Sea they had slain, since the day of their first landing, sixty-three Aleuts.

THEIR SAIL HOME was a tale of horrors, for in their frail boat, with no deck and only a modest sail attached to a flimsy mast, they headed into adverse winds blowing out of Asia and had to confront in turn a broken spar, a near-swamp-ing, rotten food, a raving sailor close to insanity and closer to death at the hands of Innokenti if he did not stop his rantings, and interminable storms which threatened for days to capsize them. Trofim, as the only one aboard experienced in navigation, was given control of the pitiful boat, keeping it afloat more by courage than by skill; and when survival seemed impossible and some counseled 'Throw the bales overboard to lighten ship,' he might have done so had not Innokenti, with iron resolve, cried: 'Don't touch them! Better dead trying to make port with our furs than alive without them.' When the storm abated, the boat limped home with bales intact, and the Aleutian fur trade was under way.

As Trofim and Innokenti climbed ashore at Petropavlovsk they found a surprise awaiting them, for in their absence Madame Poznikova had moved her headquarters to this excellent new harbor and built on a prominent rise along the shore a spacious two-story house with a lookout on the top floor. When Trofim asked: 'Why so big a house?' she said bluntly: 'Because we three are going to live here.' He gasped, but she pressed on: 'You're getting to be an old man, Cossack, and I'm not getting younger.' He was forty-four that year, she thirty-seven, and while he did not feel old, he was aware, from his experience in losing the leadership of his men on Attu Island, that he was no longer the tireless young Ukrainian for whom the world was an endless adventure.

Asking for time to consider what she was suggesting, he roamed the waterfront, looked at the small boats resting there, and visualized the islands to which they would in time be sailing, and two facts remained rooted: Madame Poznikova is a remarkable woman. And I long for the islands and the lands to the east. He would be honored to have a woman like Madame for a wife and pleased to work with her in the fur trade, but before committing himself, certain things would have to be agreed upon, so he walked back to the new house, called her to the front room, where he sat rigidly like a nervous businessman asking a banker for a loan, and said: 'Madame, I admired your husband and respect what you and he accomplished. I would be honored to associate with you in the fur trade. But I will not ever again sail to the Aleutians without a proper ship.'

Astonished by this extraordinary response to her proposal that they marry, she burst into laughter, and cried robustly: 'Cossack, come see!' And she led him down the main street of Petropavlovsk to a formal shipyard which had not been there when he sailed out two years before. 'Look!' she said with pride. 'That's the ship I've been building for you,' and when he saw how sturdy it was, he said: 'Perfect for the Aleutian trade.'

After the wedding she forced her son Innokenti to take the name Zhdanko and to call Trofim *father*, which he refused to do: 'He's not my father, that damned serf,' and he bristled even if someone called him the cossack's stepson. His mother, embarrassed by such behavior, summoned the two to stand before her: 'From this day on we're all Zhdankos, a powerful new life for everyone. You two will conquer the islands one by one. Then on to America.' When Trofim protested that this might prove to be more difficult than supposed, she cried: 'We're destined to move east, always east. My father left St. Petersburg for Irkutsk. I left there for Kamchatka. The furs, the money are waiting for us out there.' And in this way the Ukrainian cossack Trofim Zhdanko acquired a ship he wanted, a wife he admired and a son he abhorred.

WHEN, THANKS TO the example set by Madame Zhdanko, the court at St. Petersburg discovered what a bonanza they could reap in the Aleutian fur trade, companies of adventurous men were encouraged to test their fortunes in the islands. These informal groups were composed mainly of cossacks, especially those trained in the harsh disciplines of Siberia, and a more cruel group of invaders never descended upon a primitive people. Accustomed to dispensing harsh discipline among the unlettered tribes of eastern Russia, they devised new barbarisms for dealing with the gentle, simple-minded Aleuts. The brutal precedents set by Innokenti Zhdanko during the first encounter on Attu Island became the norm as the cossacks pressed eastward, and more outrages were invented as the marauders approached the larger islands in the middle of the chain.

Of course, when the first group after Trofim and Innokenti came in their flimsy sealskin boat to Attu and tried to land, the enraged natives, remembering what had happened before, stormed down to the beach and slaughtered seven traders, an event which enshrined in Russian folklore the belief that the Aleuts were savages who could be tamed only by gun and knout. But when the second expedition sailed on to Kiska, the next sizable island in the chain, it encountered natives who knew nothing of white men, and here the cossacks initiated a reign of terror which produced many furs and more dead Aleuts.

On sprawling Amchitka, next in line, the islanders were quickly subdued by the relentless invaders. The natives had to remain mute when these men stole their women. They had to sail forth in all weathers to hunt for sea otters. Of the otters killed in the new and wasteful ways introduced by the Russians, far more than half sank useless to the bottom of the Bering Sea, but since those brought to shore fetched increasingly high prices when caravaned down to the Mongolian border, the pressure to continue hunting mounted, and with it the barbarities.

In 1761, Madame Zhdanko, eager to see the establishment of Russian control over the Aleutians and Alaska before she died, replaced Trofim's aging ship with a new one built with real nails, and in it she dispatched Innokenti, a mature man of thirty-four and ruthless in his ability to bring home maximum cargoes. To protect her investment in the ship, she suggested that Trofim captain it, even though he was fifty-nine: 'You look like a man of thirty, Cossack, and this ship is valuable. Keep it off the rocks.' The plea was not an idle one, for like the slain otters, of a hundred vessels built by the Russians in these parts, a good half sank because of faulty construction, and the half that remained afloat were apt to be commanded by such inadequate captains that a large number crashed on rocks and reefs.

In the decade ahead, the Zhdankos, father and stepson, leapfrogged many smaller islands in order to land directly on Lapak, the attractive one guarded by the volcano about which Trofim had spoken repeatedly when recounting his adventures with Captain Bering. When the boat hove to off the northern coast and Trofim saw the unforgettable land which he and Georg Steller had explored back in 1741, he reminded his crew of how generously he had been treated and issued stern orders; 'No molesting of islanders this time,' and as a result of this humane caution, the first weeks ashore saw none of the atrocities that had befouled the other islands. Trofim, searching for the native who had given him the otter skins, learned that he was dead, but one of the fur traders who had acquired a few words of Aleut on a previous mission informed Trofim that the man's son, one Ingalik, had inherited the old man's two kayaks and his leadership of the island clan. Hoping to make friends with the young man and thus avoid what had happened on the other islands, Trofim sought him out, and learned to his dismay that word of Russian behavior had now penetrated all the islands and that the people of Lapak were terrified as to what they might expect.

Trofim tried to placate the young man, and things might have got off to a good start had there not been among the traders a very rough cossack with shaved head and big red mustaches named Zagoskin who was so obsessed by otter pelts that he insisted the men of Lapak go out immediately to the hunting grounds. Young Ingalik tried to explain that there was little chance of locating any animals now, but Zagoskin would not listen. So at his command a pair of traders lined six kayaks on the shore, and their owners, not yet identified, were ordered to get into them and go out to hunt sea otters. When no one responded to this stupid order, Zagoskin grabbed an ax and raged among the kayaks, destroying their delicate membranes and crushing the frail driftwood frames on which they depended.

This destruction was so insane that various islanders, unable to comprehend such folly, began to mutter and move toward the frenzied cossack, who continued slashing. But Innokenti could not allow even the least sign of rebellion, so after ordering the Lapak men by sign language to retreat and seeing they were not going to obey, he stopped trying to dissuade them. Instead, he lifted his gun and ordered the rest of his men to do the same, and at a signal from his left hand, they fired.

Eight Aleuts died in that first volley and three more in a second, by which time Zagoskin, like a wild man, was prancing over their dead bodies and hacking at them with his ax. An awful hush fell over the beach, and then women began to wail, high-pitched, terrible wailing that filled the air and brought Trofim to the scene of carnage. Having come late, he could not apportion the blame for this tragedy, but he was certain that his son and Zagoskin had been primarily responsible, but who had done what he could not decipher. He was revolted, but before long, he would have to endure two more acts so vile that the once-honorable Zhdanko name would be darkly stained.

The first occurred only two months after the initial slaughter on the beach. Under evil encouragement from Zagoskin, Innokenti intensified his normal proclivity for atrocious actions, and in the weeks following the first batch of killings, there were several other isolated incidents in which either Zagoskin or Innokenti murdered Aleuts who were tardy in obeying them.

Both of these ugly men enjoyed participating in the exciting hunt for otters, and they ordered islanders to build them a two-seat kayak in which they could together engage in the chase. Zagoskin, because his arms were stronger, paddled in the rear, Innokenti in front. In the fourteen thousand years since Oogruk had navigated his kayak in pursuit of the great whale, the men of the north had developed an improved paddle, one with a blade at each end, so that the paddler did not have to reverse the position of his hands when he wanted to change the side from which he paddled. And both Zagoskin and Innokenti became expert in using these two-ended paddles.

Their kayak was not really needed in the hunt, and they realized that sometimes it seemed to do more harm than good, but the chase was so exhilarating that they insisted on participating. A hunt went like this. Some keen-eyed Aleut would detect what appeared to be an otter out toward Qugang, the whistling volcano, and signaling, he would speed directly to that spot while other craft would swing wide and take up positions forming a circle around where the otter was presumed to be. Then silence, no blade moving, and before long the otter, not being a fish, would have to come up for air. Then all would swarm down upon it; it would dive; and quickly the boats would form another circle, in the center of which the otter would surface. When this was repeated six or eight times, with the poor otter always forced to come up for breath in the midst of the tormenting kayaks, it would approach exhaustion, until, finally, it would surface almost dead. Then a club over the head, a swift grab before it sank, and the prized animal was lashed to one of the kayaks, its head smashed in, its fur undamaged.

Zagoskin and Innokenti had their greatest fun when the circle enclosed a mother otter floating on her back with her baby on her belly, the creatures moving along as if on a summer's outing. Then Innokenti, in the front, forced the mother to dive. But the infant could not stay under water as long as its mother, so as soon as the latter felt her child struggling for air, she returned to the surface, even though she knew that this meant danger for herself. Once more afloat, she became the target for the circling canoes, which, driven by In- nokenti's wild cries, closed in upon her again. Again she dived, again her child struggled for air, and again she rose amid the threatening kayaks.

'We have her!' Innokenti would shout, and with a burst of speed he and Zagoskin would virtually leap at the anguished mother, clubbing at her till the babe fell from her protective grasp. When the pursuers saw the little one afloat, Zagoskin would club it, reach out with a net, and pull it into the kayak. The mother, now bereft of her child, would begin swimming madly from one boat to another, searching for it, and as she approached each one, lamenting like a human mother, she suffered the blows that came from the gloating men and swam on to the next, pleading all the while in a high-pitched wail for the return of her child.

Finally, so weakened and so bewildered by her fruitless search that she dared not dive, she remained on the surface, her almost human face turned to her tormentors as she sought her baby, and thus she remained till someone like Innokenti bashed her over the head, knocked her senseless, pulled her into his kayak, and cut her throat.

One day as they returned to shore, after two such killings, some of the Aleut fishermen protested against the slaughter of the baby otter and its mother, pointing out to Innokenti in their sign language that if he and Zagoskin con- tinued doing this, the supply of otters in the seas surrounding Lapak Island was bound to be depleted. 'And in that case,' the protesters reasoned, 'we will have to go too far to sea to find the otters you seek.'

Innokenti, showing his displeasure with such an interruption, brushed aside their objections, but Trofim, when he heard about the argument, sided with the Aleuts: 'Don't you see what killing the mothers and babies will mean before long? No otters for us to use in trade or for them to use as always.'

This warning coming from his own stepfather infuriated Innokenti, who replied insolently: 'It's time they learned, that we all learned. Their job from here on is to kill sea otters. Nothing else. I want bales of those pelts, not a few handfuls.' And ignoring Zhdanko's counsel, he and Zagoskin initiated the harsh routine of sending the Aleut men out every day to hunt the otter and of disciplining them by means of blows and deprivation of food if they were not successful.

In the meantime the two leaders continued to sail forth, and with the forced assistance from others, to chase mother otters with their babes, and one after- noon when the sun was clouded Innokenti saw such a pair and shouted to the attendant Aleuts: 'Over here!' The chase ended as always, with the baby slain and the mother otter swimming almost into the arms of an Aleut, pleading piteously. This Aleut, a fine hunter, mindful of his relationship to all things living, refused to kill needlessly when neither food nor fur was really needed, and ignored Innokenti's shrieks of 'Kill her!' The Aleut allowed the mother to escape and looked in disgust as Zagoskin beat the water with his paddle in frustration.

When they reached shore, Innokenti rushed up to the man who had refused to kill the otter, berating him for his disobedience, and the man was so outraged that he threw down his paddle, indicating in terms that could not be misunderstood that he would no longer hunt otters, male or female, with the white men, and that from this day on neither he nor his friends would kill mothers and babes. Innokenti, enraged by this defiance of his authority, grabbed the islander by the arm, swung him around, and struck him so solidly with his fist that the man fell to the ground. The other islanders began to mutter among themselves, and soon there were signs of such general defiance that Zagoskin, frightened, fell back, and the Aleuts, judging mistakenly that they had made their point, now swarmed at Innokenti to persuade him to stop abusing them.

His reaction was radically different from what they expected, for Innokenti, calling for all his men to assist him, ran to fetch his and Zagoskin's guns, and when the Russians in tight assembly marched on the startled Aleuts, the latter retreated, having learned what guns were capable of. But Innokenti did not intend this show of power to end with a mere display, and when the islanders were cowed, he uttered that dreadful phrase which was so often resorted to in these years when civilized Europeans were meeting uncivilized natives: 'It's time we taught them a lesson.'

Utilizing three of the willing Russian traders, he had them choose at random twelve Aleut hunters, who were lined up one behind the other, with the man who had started the protest in front. When each Aleut was prodded forward, so that he stood tightly wedged against the man in front, Innokenti cried: 'We'll show them what a good Russian musket can do,' and he loaded his gun heavily, moved close to the head of the file, and took careful aim right at the heart of that first troublemaker.

At this moment Trofim Zhdanko came on the scene and saw the hideous thing that was about to happen: 'Son! What in God's name are you doing?'

His unfortunate use of the word *son* so infuriated Innokenti that with the butt of his gun he struck Trofim in the face. Then, with icy rage he fired, and eight Aleuts, one after the other, dropped dead while the ninth fainted, for the bullet had ended against his ribs. The final three stood transfixed.

Innokenti had taught the Aleuts a lesson, and it was as a result of this that he was able to establish on Lapak Island, once so pleasant a place to live if one loved the sea and was unaware that in other parts of the world trees existed, a dictatorship so complete that every man on the island, Russian or Aleut, had to work at his command and the women to serve at his pleasure. Lapak Island became one of the more ghastly places on this earth, and the honorable old cossack, Trofim Zhdanko, huddled alone in his hut, steeped in shame and powerless to oppose the evil his stepson had created.

A S THE EIGHTEENTH century drew toward a close, the governments of many nations learned of the riches available in the northern waters, and also of the vast territories waiting there to be discovered, explored, and claimed. The Spaniards, moving north from California, would send out a fleet of daring explorers, Alessandro Malaspina and Juan de la Bodega among them, and they would contribute significant discoveries, but since their government did not follow with settlements, they accomplished nothing lasting except the naming of certain headlands along the coast.

The French would dispatch a gallant man with a glowing title—Jean François de Galaup, Comte de La Pérouse—to see what he could find, and he left a record of daring adventure but little hard knowledge of the island-studded seas among whose reefs future navigators would have to move.

In 1778 the English sent to these waters a slim, nervous man of ordinary parentage who, by virtue of his maritime brilliance, resolute courage and general common sense, would make himself into the world's foremost navigator of that day and one of the top two or three of all time: James Cook. On two flawless voyages to the South Pacific he had in a sense cleaned up the map of the ocean, locating islands where they belonged, defining the shorelines of two continents, Australia and Antarctica, informing the world of the glories of Tahiti and finding in the process a cure for scurvy.

Before Cook, a British warship could leave England with four hundred sailors and expect one hundred and eighty to be dead by the time the voyage was over, and sometimes the toll reached the appalling figure of two hundred and eighty. Cook, unwilling to captain a ship that was little more than a floating coffin, decided in his quiet, efficient way, to change this, and he did so by instituting a few sensible rules, as he explained to his crew at the beginning of their memorable third voyage: 'We have found that scurvy can be controlled if you will keep your quarters clean. If you wear dry clothes whenever you can. If you follow our rule of one watch on, two off so that you get plenty of rest. And if you will each day consume your portion of wort and rob.'

When sailors asked what they were, Cook allowed his officers to explain: 'Wort is a brew of malt, vinegar, sauerkraut, such fresh vegetables as we can procure, and other things. It smells bad, but if you drink it properly, you will not catch the scurvy.'

'Rob,' said another officer, 'is an inspissated mixture of lime, orange and lemon juice.'

'What's *inspissated*?' someone always asked, and the officer would reply: 'Captain Cook uses the word all the time,' and someone would persist: 'But what's it mean?' and the officer would growl: 'It means "You drink it." If you do, you'll never get scurvy.'

The officers were correct. Any sailor who consumed his wort and rob was miraculously immune from the gray killer of the seas; in wort about half the ingredients were by themselves ineffective, especially the malt, but the sauerkraut, and particularly its fermented juice, worked miracles, and of course, although the lime and orange juice were of small account, lemon juice was a specific. The inspissation, in which Cook put so much store, had no effect whatever; it was merely a process which thickened the lemon juice and made it easier to transport and administer.

By his stubborn insistence that scurvy could be cured, this quiet man and devoted leader saved thousands of lives and enabled Britain to build the world's most powerful fleet. Now, in the years when England was fighting her American colonies in places like Massachusetts, Pennsylvania and Virginia, the British government had sent this great explorer forth once more to end speculation about the North Pacific, and he, having solved the various riddles of the South Pacific, eagerly accepted the challenge to confirm once and for all whether Asia did join with North America, whether there was a Northwest Passage across the top of the world, whether the Arctic Ocean was free of ice—because a learned scientist had proved that unless ice was somehow moored to land, it could not form in an open sea—and particularly, what the coastline of the newfound Alaska was. If he could solve these nagging questions, Great Britain would be in position to claim all of North America from Quebec and Massachusetts in the east to California and the future Oregon in the west.

On his famous Third Exploration, which would cover parts of four years, 1776–79, Cook would not only discover the Hawaiian Islands but also become the first European to explore properly the jagged coastline of Alaska. He would chart and name Mount Edgecumbe, that splendid volcano at Sitka; he would explore where the future Anchorage would locate; he would cruise the Aleutian Islands and position them properly in relation to the mainland; and he would run far north to where the frozen Arctic Ocean confronted him with a wall of ice eighteen feet high along its face, the ice that the earlier expert had proved could not exist.

It was a marvelous journey, a success in every respect, for although he did not find the fabled Northwest Passage which navigators had been seeking for almost three hundred years since Columbus discovered America, he did demonstrate that the supposed passage did not enter the Pacific in ice-free waters. In moving to the north to prove this point, Cook had to penetrate the wall erected by the Aleutians, and he did so by heading for the passage just east of Lapak Island. When he cleared the headland and looked west he saw rising from the Bering Sea the volcano Qugang, the Whistler, which now stood one thousand one hundred feet above the surface of the sea.

Cook, after surveying the construction of Lapak, was the first to deduce from its semicircular form that it had once been a volcano of immense dimension whose center had exploded and whose northern rim had vanished in erosion, but he was more impressed by the copious and inviting harbor, where he sent ashore a foraging party to procure such provisions as the islanders could provide. The two young officers in charge were men destined in later years to make resounding names for themselves. The senior was Shipmaster William Bligh; his assistant, George Vancouver. The first watched carefully everything that happened on the island, taking careful note of the two Russians who seemed to be in command, Zagoskin and Innokenti, whom he did not like at all and whose insolent manner he said he would correct in short time if the two served under him. Vancouver, a born navigator of unusual abilities, noted the position of the island, its harbor capacity, its capacity for provisioning large ships, and its probable climate insofar as that could be judged from a brief visit. It was obvious that Cook had picked his staff with care, for these two were among the ablest men sailing the Pacific that year.

The visit lasted less than half a day, for by midafternoon Cook felt that he must push the *Resolution* northward, but he took with him only a fraction of the information he could have had, and the fault was his. Amazingly, in view of his meticulous foresight in planning his cruises, on this one into northern oceans where it was known that the Russians had penetrated, he brought with him no one who could speak Russian, nor any dictionary of that language; authorities in London still refused to believe that Russia already had a sizable foothold in western North America and had every intention of enlarging it. However, Cook was able to make this entry:

> We came upon a promising chain of treeless islands whose occupants came to greet us in two-man canoes wearing the most enchanting hats with long visors and decorations. I encouraged artist Webber to make several depictions of both the men and their hats, and he complied.

> The chain of islands contained one called Lapak if we understood what its Russian occupants were saying. We mapped the whole and charted a fine harbor on the north coast, guarded by a beautiful dead volcano 1,100 feet

high six miles due north. It was named something like Lewgong, but when I asked a second time for the name they whistled at me, signifying what, I do not know. Perhaps it is their sacred volcano.

George Vancouver in the last hour of his stay ashore met up with the Russian named Trofim Zhdanko, and in this grizzled warrior he recognized a man much different from the two brash younger men whom both he and Bligh had disliked. Desperately he longed to share ideas with this wise old man, and the Russian just as eagerly wanted to ask these strangers how they had managed to get such a fine ship, how they had navigated it from Europe, and what they judged the future of these islands to be. Alas, the two could not converse except in the most fragmentary sign language.

When shots were fired from the *Resolution*, warning Bligh and Vancouver that sailing time was at hand, the old cossack did hand each of the officers who had been so congenial a sea-otter pelt, but unfortunately, he had, in his generosity, given them two of the best, and Innokenti, seeing this, unceremoniously grabbed the pelts from the hands of the English officers and substituted two of inferior quality. Vancouver, always a gentleman, saluted and thanked both father and son for their generosity, but Bligh glared at Innokenti as if he wanted to smash his insolent face. However, when the two men regained their ship, Bligh penned in his logbook a revealing entry:

On this Island of Lapak I met a most disagreeable Russian named, if I caught what he said, something like Innocent. He repelled me from the moment I saw him, and the longer I suffered his unwelcome attentions the deeper grew my loathing, for he seemed the worst type of Russian.

But when I observed the compliant manner in which the natives obeyed him and the enviable peace and order prevailing on his island, it was clear to me that someone in authority governed this place firmly, and that is always to be desired. I suspect that prior to our arrival, there may have been disturbances here, but prompt action on the part of someone quelled them, and if the credit goes to this Innocent, I withdraw my strictures against him, for order in any society is of maximum value, even if sternly achieved.

In this casual manner, and with such bland acceptances of what the Russian terror had achieved, the great English navigator James Cook crossed lanes with the Russian navigator Vitus Bering: each landed briefly at Lapak; each remained about the same amount of time; each sent ashore a subordinate who would gain fame on his own account—Cook sending two, Bligh and Vancouver; Bering only one, Georg Steller—and each sailed on, the Russian in 1741, the Englishman thirty-seven years later in 1778.

How different the two men were: Bering the bumbling, unlucky leader, Cook the impeccable captain with only one detectable flaw and that showing itself only at the end; Bering, who sailed under the most rigorous orders from his tsar or tsarina, Cook, who once he left sight of England sailed under his own orders; Bering the hesitant explorer who scurried back at the first sign of adversity, his tasks uncompleted, Cook the nonpareil who invariably went the extra mile, the extra continent; Bering, who advanced the art of navigation in no particular, Cook, who altered the definitions of the words *ocean* and *mapmaking;* Bering, who had grudging support from his government and no international acclaim whatever, Cook, who lacked for nothing in England and who heard the cheers of an entire world ringing in his ears for more than a decade; Bering often with no uniform and then a miserable one that fitted poorly, Cook with his prim hand-tailored officer's garb topped by an expensive cockaded mariner's hat. How differently the two men behaved and how different their careers and contributions.

When Cook sailed on his second of three great journeys, England and France were at war, and the fighting at sea was vigorous, but both warring nations agreed that James Cook in his *Resolution* be allowed free passage anywhere he chose to sail, for it was acknowledged that he was doing the work of civilization in general and would not fire upon an enemy French warship even if he met up with one. During his third voyage, the one to Alaska, England was at war with her American colonies and, by extension, with France also, but once more the three warring nations agreed among themselves to let James Cook sail where he would, for by his perfection of the cure for scurvy, which Georg Steller had pioneered, and his promotion of this treatment through the fleet, he saved far more lives than would have been gained in a victorious battle. This second safe-passage arrangement was masterminded in part by Benjamin Franklin, the practical-minded American ambassador to France, who knew an international benefactor when he saw one, and Cook was that.

It was said earlier that as a navigator Cook had only one failing. He was apt, when tired, to be short-tempered, so that when, in February 1779, he found himself in Kealakekua Bay on the Big Island of Hawaii surrounded by mildly hostile natives who could have been placated with gifts, he lost his patience and fired a gun into a threatening crowd, in which a Hawaiian of some importance had already been killed. In a flash the infuriated watchers fell upon Cook, clubbed him from behind, and held his head under water when he fell into the surf.

Vitus Bering and James Cook, two of the grandest names in Alaskan history, had mournful ends, the first dying of scurvy on a bleak, treeless, wind-swept island at the age of sixty-one, his life and his work incomplete. The second, having conquered scurvy and the farthest oceans, died at fifty-one because of his own impetuousness on a beautiful tropical island far to the south. The oceans of the world were made more available by the explorations of such men.

B UT THERE WAS in these years another kind of explorer, the commercial adventurer, and in 1780 such a one wandered almost accidentally into Lapak Bay in a small, incredibly tough little ship called the *Evening Star*, a two-masted, square-rigged whaling brig out of Boston. It was captained by a small, wiry man as resolute morally as his ship was physically. He was Noah Pym, forty-one years old and already a veteran of the dreadful gales at Cape Horn, the trading marts at Canton, the lovely coastline of Hawaii, and all the vast empty spaces of the Pacific where whales might hide, for if his ship was not big, it was valiant, and in it Pym was ready to challenge any storm or any group of hostile natives gathered on a beach.

Unlike Bering and Cook, Pym never left port with support from his government or cheering notice from his fellow citizens. The most he could expect would be a one-line notice in the Boston newspaper: 'On this day the *Evening Star*, Noah Pym with crew of twenty-one, sailed for South Seas, intended stay six years.' And as for the great nations agreeing among themselves to give this tough little fellow free passage, they were far more likely to sink him on sight in the supposition that he was sailing for the enemy. Indeed, he had in his time fought off the warships of both France and England, but this was a misnomer, for what he really did was maintain a sharp lookout and run like a frightened demon at the first sight of a sail that might prove threatening.

Zagoskin and Innokenti were out in their two-man kayak chasing sea otters when the *Evening Star* hove into sight off the south shore of Lapak Island, and they were astounded when a voice from the aft deck called out in good Russian: 'Ho there! We need water and stores.'

'Who are you?' Innokenti called, establishing that he was in charge.

'Whaler *Evening Star*, Boston, Noah Pym commanding.'

Innokenti, surprised that a ship from that far distance should have found Lapak Island, shouted back: 'Good harbor on the north shore south of the volcano!' and with Zagoskin paddling strongly from the rear seat, he led the way.

When the ship anchored between the shore and the volcano, Innokenti and Zagoskin climbed aboard and satisfied themselves in two minutes that whereas the *Evening Star* did carry one gun fore, it was not a warship. Neither man had ever seen a whaler before, but under the tutelage of the sailor who had called to them in Russian, they quickly learned what the procedures were, and just as quickly saw that Captain Noah Pym out of Boston was, though small, a leathery individual with whom it would not be profitable to quarrel accidentally.

They learned that this amazing little brig which had traveled so far—Cape Horn, China, a try at Japan, Hawaii—had in its crew sailors who could speak most of the languages of the Pacific, so that wherever the ship anchored, someone could conduct business with the natives. Only one man spoke Russian, Seaman Atkins, but he loved to talk, and for two rewarding days he, Innokenti and Captain Pym traded information on the Pacific.

Pym, once the ice was broken, enjoyed the swift interchange: 'Six men in Boston own the *Evening Star* and they award me a full share for serving as their captain.'

'Do you also receive pay?' Innokenti asked.

'Small but regular. My real pay comes from my captain's share of the whale oil we deliver and the sale of goods we bring home from China.'

'Do the sailors share?'

'Like me, small pay, big rewards if we catch whales.' Pym pointed to a sturdy young fellow, a New Englander almost as hefty as Zagoskin and with the same kind of scowl: 'That's Kane, our harpooner. Very skilled. Gets double if he succeeds.'

'Why have you come into our waters?' Innokenti asked, and Harpooner Kane frowned at the word *our*, but Captain Pym answered courteously: 'Whales. They must be up there,' and he pointed toward the arctic.

Zagoskin broke in rudely: 'We see them coming past here sometimes,' and he would have said more had not Innokenti signaled that this was privileged information. The baldheaded Russian was obviously irritated by this tacit reprimand, and both Pym and Atkins caught the warning, but neither commented.

On the third day the men of the *Evening Star* met Trofim Zhdanko, now in his late seventies and still unbearded out of his respect for the memory of Tsar Peter, and they liked him from the start, in contrast to their rejection of the two younger men. The old fellow, at last in the company of someone who could speak Russian, poured out his recollections of Captain Bering, that hard winter on Bering Island, and the remarkable accomplishments of the German scientist

Georg Steller: 'He went to four universities and knew everything. He saved my life because he made this brew of weeds and things that cured scurvy.'

'Now what might that be?' Pym asked. He had the habit of staring hard at anyone with whom he was speaking on important subjects, his small eyes closing almost to beads, his close-cropped head of brown hair bent forward.

'Scurvy is what kills sailors.'

' 'I know that,' Pym said impatiently. 'But what was in the brew this Steller made?' Trofim did not know exactly: 'Weeds and kelp, that I remember. First time I tasted it I spit it out, but Steller told me, right over there it was, behind that group of rocks, he said: "You may not want it but your blood does," and later on, when we spent that dreadful winter on Bering Island, I looked forward to the little amount of brew he allowed me each day. It tasted far better than honey, for I could feel it rushing into my blood to keep me alive.'

'Do you still drink it?'

'No. Seal meat, especially blubber and guts, they're just as good. You eat seal you never have scurvy.'

'What will happen up here?' Pym asked. 'I mean Spain, England, France, maybe even China? Don't they all have an interest in this area?' And he pointed eastward to the unknown area which the Great Shaman Azazruk had once called Alaxsxaq, the Great Land.

'It's already Russian,' Trofim said without hesitation. 'I was with Captain Bering when he discovered it for the tsar.'

On the evening before departure Captain Pym broached with Zhdanko the navigational problem which had brought him to Lapak, and it was premonitory that he did not reveal his questions to either of the two Russian leaders, for he already distrusted them: 'Zhdanko, what do you know of the oceans north of here?'

Since it was obvious that Pym was toying with the idea of sailing north, a difficult adventure, as Zhdanko had learned from his own explorations beyond the Arctic Circle, the cossack felt he must warn the American: 'Very dangerous. Ice comes crashing down in winter.'

'But there must be whales up there.'

'There are. They swim past here all the time. Going, coming.'

'Has any small ship . . . like ours . . . sailed north?'

Since Zhdanko did not know where Captain Cook had sailed after leaving Lapak Island, he could honestly warn Pym: 'No. It would be too dangerous.'

Despite this advice, Pym was determined to probe the arctic seas before other whalers would dare to venture into those icy waters, and he remained firm in his desire to explore them, but he did not share with Zhdanko his plans, for he did not want the other Russians to know them.

Next morning, Pym allowed himself an uncharacteristic gesture: he embraced the old cossack, for he saw in his noble bearing and generosity in sharing his knowledge of the oceans a man in the true tradition of seafarer, and he felt renewed for having been in contact with him. Summoning Atkins, he said: 'Ask the old fellow why he lives alone in this little hut?' and when the question was put, Zhdanko shrugged, pointed to where his stepson and Zagoskin were whispering, and said with resignation and repugnance: 'Those two.'

AFTER PYM, WITH no knowledge or charts to guide him, sailed his *Evening Star* north from Lapak, he entered a world into which no other American had ventured or would soon do so. Yankee ships had penetrated the rest of the major oceans, following quietly in the more spectacular wake of Captain Cook's ships. But the constant search for whales, whose oil for lamps, ambergris for perfumery and baleen for the stays in women's corsets would produce fortunes for shipowners and their captains, made exploration of untapped seas obligatory. To go north of the Aleutians was daring, but if whales existed in the area, the risk was worth it, and Noah Pym was a man to take that risk.

He lived a hard life. He was a devoted father, but he was away on his voyages for years at a time, so that when he returned home he scarcely knew his three daughters. But the results were so profitable to all concerned in his expeditions that both his owners and his crew urged him to sail yet again, and he did much sooner than he would have on his own account. He kept a cadre of reliable hands with him—John Atkins, who spoke both Chinese and Russian; Tom Kane, the expert harpooner without whom the ship would have been powerless when a whale was sighted; and Miles Corey, the Irish first mate, who was a better navigator than Pym himself—and even in bad weather he slept easily knowing that these men and others like them were in charge. He suspected that Corey was a crypto-Catholic, but if so, he created no problems aboard ship.

With the Aleutians left far behind, the *Evening Star* entered upon those dangerous waters which seemed so congenial in early spring, so fearful in October and November, when ice could form overnight, or come crashing down of an afternoon, already formed into great icebergs farther north and now cruising free on their own.

Noah Pym, in search of whales instead of knowledge, captured one whale south of that narrow strait where the continents seemed to meet, and having heard in Hawaii the rumor that Bering and Cook in their larger ships had proceeded farther north without incident, he decided to do the same. In the Arctic Ocean, Harpooner Kane struck a large whale, and when Pym laid his ship close to the dying beast, landing boards were laid to its carcass so that sailors could cut it up, searching for baleen and ambergris and throwing great slabs of blubber on the deck for reduction to oil in the smoking pots.

While the brig lay idle as the oil was rendered, Corey, in a voice that betrayed no panic, warned the captain: 'Should the ice start to move down upon us, we must be prepared to run.' Pym listened, but since he had no experience in such waters, he did not appreciate how swiftly the ice could strike. 'We must both watch it closely,' he said, but when the harpooner stabbed a second whale with a splendid shot, work on salvaging it became so exciting, with promise of full casks for the long sail home, that Pym forgot about the impending ice, and for several triumphant days attended only to the bringing aboard of baleen and blubber.

Then, like some giant menace looming out of a fevered dream, the ice in the arctic began to move south, not slowly like a wanderer, but in vast floes that made giant leaps in the course of a morning and stupendous ones overnight. When the floes appeared, almost out of nowhere, the free waters around them began to freeze, and it required only a few minutes for Captain Pym to realize that he must turn south immediately or run the risk of being pinned down for the entire winter. But when he started to give the order to hoist all sails, First Mate Corey said in a voice that still showed no emotion: 'Too late. Head for the coastline.'

The advice was sound, the only one that would enable the *Evening Star* to avoid being crushed by the oncoming ice, and with an adroitness that far abler navigators than they might not have been able to exercise, these two New England men used every breath of wind to shepherd their little whaler with its thrice-precious cargo toward the northern coastline of Alaska, and there at a spot almost seventy-one degrees north, later to be christened Desolation Point, they stumbled by sheer luck into an opening which led to a substantial bay, at whose southern end they found a snug harbor surrounded by low protecting hills. Here, shielded from pounding ice, they would spend the nine-month winter of 1780–81, and often during that interminable imprisonment the sailors would not curse Pym for his tardiness in leaving the arctic but praise him for having found 'the only spot on this Godforsaken shore where the ice can't crush us to kindling.'

They had barely started constructing a refuge ashore when Seaman Atkins, the one who spoke Russian, cried: 'Enemy approaching over the ice!' and with expressions of fear that could not be masked, the twenty other crewmen looked up from their work to see coming at them across the frozen bay a contingent of some two dozen short, dark-faced men swathed in heavy furs.

'Prepare for action!' Captain Pym said in low voice, but Atkins, who had a good view of the oncoming men, cried: 'They aren't armed!' and in the next tense moments the newcomers reached the Americans, stared in amazement at their white faces, and smiled.

In the days that followed, the Americans learned that these men lived a short distance to the north in a village of thirteen subterranean huts containing fifty-seven people, and to the vast relief of the whalers, they found that the villagers were peacefully inclined. They were Eskimos, lineal descendants of those adventurers who had followed Oogruk from Asia fourteen thousand years earlier. Six hundred and sixty generations separated them from Oogruk, and in the course of time they had acquired the skills which enabled them to survive and even prosper north of the Arctic Circle, which lay nearly three hundred miles to the south.

The Americans were at first repelled by the meagerness of the lives these Eskimos lived and by the tight meanness of their underground huts roofed by whalebone covered with sealskin, but they quickly came to appreciate the clever ways in which the chunky little people adjusted to their inhospitable environment, and were dumfounded by the courage and ability the men exhibited in venturing forth upon the frozen ocean and wresting from it their livelihood. The sailors were further impressed when half a dozen men from the village helped them build a long hut from available items like whalebone, driftwood and animal skins. When it was completed, large enough to house all twenty-two Americans, the men had reasonably comfortable protection against the cold, which could drop to fifty degrees below zero. The sailors were awed when they saw how much these short men, rarely over five feet two, could shoulder when helping to carry the *Star*'s supplies ashore, and when all was in place the Americans settled down for the kind of winter they had known in New England —four months of snow and cold—and they were astounded when Atkins learned from sign language that they could expect to remain frozen in for nine months or perhaps ten. 'Good God!' one sailor moaned. 'We don't get out till next July?' and Atkins replied: 'That's what he seems to be saying, and he should know.'

The first indication of how ably these Eskimos utilized the frozen ocean came when one of the powerful younger men, Sopilak by name, if Atkins understood correctly, returned from a hunt with the news that a monstrous polar bear had been spotted on the ice some miles offshore. In a trice the Eskimos made themselves ready for a long chase, but they lingered until their women provided Captain Pym, whom they recognized as leader, Seaman Atkins, whom they had immediately liked, and husky Harpooner Kane with proper clothing to protect them from the ice and snow and wind. Dressed in the bulky furs of Eskimos, the three Americans started across the barren ice, whose jumbled forms made movement difficult. Such travel bore no relationship to ice travel in New England, where a pond froze in winter, or a placid river; this was primeval ice, born in the deeps of a salty ocean, thrown sky-high by sudden pressures, fractured by forces coming at it from all sides, a tortured, madly sculptured ice appearing in jagged shapes and interminably long swells that seemed to rise up from the depths. It was like nothing they had seen before or imagined: it was the ice of the arctic, explosive, crackling at night as it moved and twisted, violent in its capacity to destroy, and above all, constantly menacing in the gray haze, stretching forever.

It was upon this ice that the men of Desolation Point set forth to hunt their polar bear, but after a full day's search they found nothing, and night fell so quickly in these early days of October that the men warned the seamen that they would probably have to spend the night far out on the ice, with no assurance that they would ever find the bear. But just before darkness, Sopilak came plodding back on his snowshoes: 'Not far ahead!' and the hunters moved closer to their prey. But it was a canny bear, and before any of them had a chance to see it, the first of its breed any American would encounter in these waters, night fell and the hunters fanned out in a wide circle so as to be able to follow the bear should it elect to flee in the darkness.

Atkins, who stayed close to Sopilak and who seemed to be learning Eskimo words by the score, moved about to caution his mates: 'They warn us. The bear is dangerous. All white. Comes at you like a ghost. Do not run. No chance to escape. Stand and fight and shout for the others.'

'Sounds dangerous,' Kane said, and Atkins replied: 'I think they were trying to tell me they expect to lose a man or two when tracking a polar bear.'

'Them, not me,' Kane said, and Atkins proposed that in the coming fight, the three Americans stay together: 'We have guns. We'd better be prepared to use them.'

The Americans and most of the Eskimos slept uneasily that night, but Sopilak did not sleep at all, for he had hunted polar bears before, with his father, and had been present when a great white beast, taller than two men when it reared on its hind legs, had crushed a hunter from Desolation with one smashing blow from its paw. It had driven the man right down against the ice and then torn at him with all four of its sets of claws. The man and all his clothing had been left in shreds, and that bear had not been taken.

There had been other hunts, some of them led by Sopilak himself, in which the monstrous beasts, more beautiful than a dream of white blizzards, had been tracked for days and brought to heel by wisdom and courage. Toward dawn Sopilak instructed Atkins: 'Tell your men to watch me,' and though the seaman tried to explain to the Eskimo that the Americans had guns, which would give them a sizable advantage if the fight did materialize, no matter how often in the darkness Atkins raised his arms and went 'Bang-bang!' Sopilak did not understand. He saw only that they had no clubs or spears, and he feared for their safety.

When a pale, silvery cold light broke, a scout far to the north signaled that he had the polar bear in sight, and none of the three Americans who experienced the next moments would ever forget them, for when they rounded a huge block of ice thrown high above the surface of the frozen sea on which they moved, they saw ahead of them one of the world's majestic creatures, as grand an animal as the mastodons and mammoths that had once crossed over to Alaska near this point. It was huge, so completely white that it blended with the snow, and agile with a lumbering grace that caused the human heart to hesitate, so overpowering was the sense of beauty and awkward energy the bear exhibited as it began to move away. A supreme example of animal majesty, it seemed to be at one with the ice sheet and with the frozen sky. A light snow that began to fall as day brightened enhanced the dreamlike quality of the hunt as Sopilak's men began their chase.

The polar bear, unique among its genus in color, size and speed, could easily outrun any one man, and it also had the capacity to dive headlong into those strange openings in the ice where water flowed free, swim vigorously to the other side, clamber with amazing ease onto the new ice, and scamper off to other frozen areas where the men could not pursue, since they could not cross the open water. But it could not outrun half a dozen pestering men, especially when with spears and clubs and wild shouting they prevented it from attaining open water. So the long day's fight was about equal: the men could harass it and keep it from open water; it could outrun them and swim short distances to new positions. But in the end their persistence and anticipation of its moves enabled them to stay close and to drive it so that it winded itself, and in this manner the fight continued.

But as day began to wane, and it was brief at this autumn latitude, the men realized that they must soon come to grips with the bear or run the risk of losing it in the long night. So two Eskimos, Sopilak and another, became much more daring, and in a pair of coordinated thrusts they ran at the bear, confused it, and with Sopilak's spear damaged its left hind leg, and when they saw that it was wounded, two other men dashed in from behind, evaded the deadly swipe of its forepaws when it turned, and struck again, in the same leg.

The bear was now seriously wounded, and knew it, so it retreated until its back was against a large block of ice which protected it in that quarter, and now the men had to attack from positions where it could spot them from the moment they began to approach, and in this posture it was formidable, a towering white giant, red-bloodied in one leg but the possessor of claws that could rip out a man's guts.

In this moment of equal battle, when the Eskimo who first charged knew that he stood a strong likelihood of being disemboweled, none of Sopilak's hunters volunteered to make the possibly sacrificial run, so the master hunter knew that it devolved upon him. He succeeded in striking the bear's undamaged right leg, but in endeavoring to escape, he fell under the bear's full glare, and a mighty swing of the right paw sent him sprawling flat upon the ice and exposed to the bear's revenge.

In this extremity, two Eskimos darted bravely out to incapacitate the bear, regardless of what happened to Sopilak, but they were so tardy that the bear had time to leap at its fallen enemy and would have crushed him and torn him apart had not Captain Pym and Harpooner Kane discharged their rifles at this moment to stagger the great white monster. With two bullets in it, an experience never known before, the bear stopped and gasped, whereupon Atkins fired his gun, and this bullet lodged in the bear's head, causing it to lose control and to fall powerless across the prone body of the master hunter.

There the marvelous bear died, this creature of the frozen seas, this magnificent giant whose fur was often whiter than the snow upon which it moved, and when the seven Eskimos saw that it was truly dead they did something that amazed the three Americans: they began to dance, solemnly and with tears streaming down their faces, and the man holding wounded Sopilak erect so that he too could participate began to chant a song that reached back five thousand years, and there as darkness fell the men of Desolation wept and danced in honor of the great white creature they had killed. Seaman Atkins, watching this performance, appreciated its meaning instantly, and in response to some ancient force that his ancestors in Europe had revered, he dropped the gun which had been instrumental in killing the bear and joined the dancers, and Sopilak took his hand and welcomed him to the circle, and picking up the rhythm, Atkins joined the chant, for he too honored the splendid white bear, that creature of the north that had been so majestic in life, so brave in death.

SOPILAK HAD A fifteen-year-old sister named Kiinak, and in the days following the kill of the polar bear she worked with her mother and the other women of Desolation in butchering and tending to the valuable bones, sinews and magnificent white skin. As she did so, she became aware that the young seaman from the *Evening Star* was placing himself near her, watching her. With the Eskimo words which he was acquiring so rapidly, he had been able to explain to Sopilak and his mother that he, Atkins, as one of the cooks aboard the American vessel, wanted to learn how the Eskimos handled the meat of the bear, the walrus and the seal that they caught in winter, and this explanation was accepted.

But the Eskimo men who had participated in the famous hunt of this bear also knew that it was only the bravery of Atkins and his leader, Noah Pym, that had saved the life of Sopilak, and since they had told the story of those culminating moments, the heroism of the young man was known throughout the village, and his attendance upon the butchering and Kiinak was accepted and even encouraged. Several times Sopilak told the villagers: 'The young one saved my life,' and whenever he said this, Kiinak smiled.

She was a vivacious girl, just under five feet tall, broad-shouldered, broad-faced, with a smile that charmed all upon whom it fell. But her outstanding characteristic was a heavy head of very black hair, which she kept cut so low that it obscured her eyebrows and shook from side to side when she laughed, which she did many times each day, for she loved the great nonsense of the world: the pomposity of her brother when he killed a walrus or captured a seal, the posturing of some young woman trying to attract the attention of her brother, or even the whimpering behavior of a child who was trying to enforce his will upon his mother. When she talked, she had the habit of using her left hand in a wide, careless sweep to brush the hair out of her eyes, and at such times she seemed quite gamin, and the older women of the village knew very well that this girl Kiinak was going to give the young men of the village much to think about as the time came for her to select a husband.

There was one other charming aspect, which John Atkins noticed the first time he saw her in the hut she shared with Sopilak and his young wife: Kiinak was not, like many Eskimo women, heavily tattooed about the face, but she did have two parallel slim blue lines coming down from her lower lip to the edge of her chin, and they gave her rather large, square face a touch of delicacy, for when she smiled the lines seemed to participate, thus making her warm smile even more generous.

When the butchering of the bear was completed on the spot where it had been slain, and the hundreds of pounds of rich meat lugged ashore for treatment in various ways, Atkins had no utilitarian reason for lingering about Sopilak's hut, but he did, and it was not long before the gossipy women of Desolation began predicting that something of interest was going to happen one of these days. And now came an amusing contradiction, the kind that confused many societies: the older women were romantics who reveled in watching how young girls attracted and bewildered young men, and they spent many hours speculating on who was going to go to bed with whom and what kind of scandal this might produce; but they were also rigorous moralists and protectors of village continuity.

Through long centuries they had learned that Eskimo society functioned best when girls postponed having babies until they had fastened themselves to some reassuring man who would provide for their children. Widespread flirtation and even bedding down with this attractive young fellow or that was permitted and even encouraged—for example, if two aunts had an ungainly niece who looked as if she might never catch a man; but if that niece had a child without first having found a husband, these same aunts would excoriate her and even banish her from their hut. As one wise old woman said while watching the courtship of Seaman Atkins and Sopilak's sister: 'It's always better when things go orderly.'

The romantic half of their concern was quickly resolved, for although Atkins had returned to his long hut half a mile away when the butchering ended, he remained there only two days, after which he came plodding back to Desolation on snowshoes, longing to see his Eskimo lass. He arrived at noon, bringing with him four ship's biscuits as a present to Sopilak, his young wife, Sopilak's old mother and Kiinak. Tasting the strange food outside their hut so as to enjoy the final few hours of faint haze before winter clamped a perpetual frozen darkness over all, they asked Atkins: 'Is this what you told us about? Is this what white people eat?' and when he nodded, they said, not contemptuously: 'Seal blubber is much better. Fat to keep you warm in winter,' and Atkins laughed: 'We'll soon find out. Our biscuits are almost gone.'

And within the next week the Eskimos were starting to provide the marooned sailors with seal meat, which they learned to enjoy, and with seal blubber, the part of the animal that enabled the Eskimos to live in the arctic, which the white men could not force themselves to eat. And one afternoon, as John Atkins helped bring the meat to the ship, accompanied by Sopilak, who had caught the seal, he returned to the Point and lived thereafter in Sopilak's hut, sharing a sealskin bed with laughing Kiinak.

WHEN THE LAST days of November brought total darkness to the icebound ship, the twenty one Americans living in the long hut—Atkins no longer being with them—settled into a routine which enabled them to withstand the terrible isolation. Most important, each day at what they judged to be high noon, Captain Pym attended by First Mate Corey marched to the rude ship's clock and ceremoniously wound it so that they could ensure having what they called Greenwich Time, which made it possible to calculate where they were in relation to London. The principle was simple, as Captain Pym always explained to each new sailor coming aboard his ship: 'If the clock shows it's five in the afternoon at the Prime Meridian in London, and our shot of the sun shows it's high noon here, obviously we're five hours west of London. Since each hour represents fifteen degrees of longitude, we know for certain that we're at seventy-five degrees west, which puts us in the Atlantic some miles east of Norfolk, Virginia.' Within a few years, wandering sea captains like Pym would have one of the new chronometers being perfected by English clockmaking geniuses, and with it they would be able to ascertain their longitude precisely; for the present, using the rough clocks available, they could only approximate. Latitude, of course, had been determinable with amazing accuracy for the last three thousand years: in daylight, shoot the noonday sun; at night, shoot the North Star. '159 degrees West Longitude,' Pym would chart each day as he completed winding, '70 degrees, thirty-three minutes North Latitude.' No other explorer had been so far north in these waters.

From the inadequate tables which mariners like Captain Pym carried with them, he calculated that at this latitude north the sun would quit the heavens sometime near the fifteenth of November and not reappear as even a sliver until sometime in late January. Harpooner Kane, hearing him speak of this, asked in a kind of stupor: 'You mean, no light at all for seventy days?' and Pym nodded.

But on the midday of November the sun was still faintly visible for a few minutes, low in the sky, and Pym heard Kane tell the others: 'Tomorrow it'll be gone,' but on the sixteenth it still lingered. However, two days later the merest edge of the sun appeared for two minutes, then disappeared, and the sailors battened down their minds and their emotions, going into the kind of hibernation which many of the other arctic animals followed.

They were surprised, however, by the discovery that even at this great distance north, a kind of magical glow did appear each midday, illuminating their frozen world for a few precious minutes, not with actual daylight but with something more precious: a wonderful silvery aura which reminded them that the loss of their sun was not going to be perpetual. Of course, when this ambient glow vanished, the ensuing twenty-two hours of pitch-black seemed more oppressive and the penetrating cold more devastating. But when things seemed at their worst, the aurora borealis appeared, flooding the night sky with colors the New England men had never imagined, and Seaman Atkins, on his casual returns to the long hut, informed them: 'The Eskimos say that the People Up There are holding festivity, chasing bears across the sky. Those are the lights of the hunters.' But when the temperature dropped to what Captain Pym estimated as colder than seventy-below, for even oil froze solid, the men ignored the lights and huddled by their driftwood fire.

A prudent captain, Pym insisted that his men rise from their beds at what would have been dawn if there had been a sun, and he wanted them to eat such food as they could assemble at stated meal hours. He asked Mr. Corey to maintain a watch around the clock, especially in the direction of Desolation Point, warning: 'Many ships in the Pacific have been taken by natives who appeared friendly.' He assigned tasks to keep his men occupied, and week by week he devised ways to make the long hut more habitable, and each afternoon, two hours after lunch, he and Corey and Kane hiked across the ice to check upon the status of the *Evening Star*. Each day they inspected the planking to see if ice pressures had broken the stout body of the ship, and they saw with relief that the sides were so properly sloped that the crushing ice found nothing solid to push against. When it did move in with such tremendous force that it would have destroyed any ship not carefully built, it found only the curved flanks of the *Evening Star*, and when it pressed against them it lifted the ship gently aloft, until the keel stood some two feet above the surface of where the unfrozen water would have been. The ship had been lifted right into the air, and there it stayed as if it were some magic vessel in a dark gray dream.

'She's still firm,' Captain Pym reported each afternoon as the inspectors returned.

But the solemn moment came at what would have been sunset, local time, when in the blackness of perpetual night Noah Pym gathered his sailors and by a whale-oil light conducted evening services:

'Oh, God! We thank Thee that our ship is safe through one more day. We thank Thee for the minutes of near-light at midday. We thank Thee for the food that reaches us from Thy sea. And we ask Thee to watch over our wives and children and mothers and fathers back in Boston. We are in Thy hands, and in the dark night we place our bodies and our immortal souls in Thy care.'

After such a prayer, delivered with surprising variation as he invited God's attention to their daily problems, he asked each of his sailors in turn, those who could read, to take the Bible which accompanied him on all his trips, and read some personally chosen selection, and rarely did the soaring words of this Book resound with more meaning than there in the long hut beside the Arctic Ocean as the sailors read the familiar verses they had learned as boys in distant New England. One night, when it was Tom Kane's turn to read, this normally violent man chose from Acts a selection of verses that seemed to speak directly to their marooning and their encounter with the Eskimos:

' "But not long after there arose against it a tempestuous wind . . . And when the ship was caught, and could not bear up into the wind, we let her drive. And running under a certain island . . . we had much work to come by the boat . . . But when the fourteenth night was come, as we were driven up and down . . . about midnight the shipmen deemed that they drew near to some country . . . Then fearing lest we should have fallen upon rocks, they cast four anchors out of the stern and wished for the day . . .

' "And when it was day, they knew not the land: but they discovered a certain creek with a shore, into which they were minded, if it were possible, to thrust in the ship . . . And falling into a place where two seas met, they ran the ship aground . . . And so it came to pass, that they escaped all safe to land.

' "And when they were escaped . . . the barbarous people shewed us no little kindness: for they kindled a fire, and received us every one, because of the present rain, and because of the cold." '

His constant remembering that he was still an officer of a church back in Boston and that he was, in a very real sense, responsible for the moral welfare of his sailors, often placed Captain Pym in difficult situations, as when he put his whaler into some island port and his men ran wild with the tempting girls with flowers in their hair who came at them skimming over the water on boards. Not being unnecessarily prudish, he looked aside while his men reveled, then reminded them of their perpetual duties when he had them back at sea attending his evening prayers. He also knew that they would raise hell when they hit ports like the one serving Canton, and he told himself: Stay clear. Let the Chinese bash heads.

But his magnanimity ended where marriage or its local equivalent was concerned, and when he saw how deeply Seaman Atkins was involved with Sopilak's sister, he realized that he could not ignore the moral problems which could result, and one morning in December when no hunting for seals was under way, he walked on self-made snowshoes to Desolation Point, where he sought the hut occupied by Sopilak, and once inside, he asked to meet with Atkins and the girl with whom he was living, but three others concerned in these matters insisted upon attending also: Sopilak, his mother and his young wife, Nikaluk. Seated in a circle on the floor, Captain Pym started his discussion of the timeless problems involving men and women.

'Atkins, God does not look with favor at young men who live with young women in an unmarried state—to the eventual detriment of those young women when the ship sails and they are left behind.'

Now developed a bizarre situation in which young Atkins, as the interpreter in the group, was required to repeat in Eskimo the castigation his captain had delivered, but the relations which had always existed between Noah Pym, one of the notable captains out of New England, with his men were such that Atkins felt obligated to translate honestly, and when he did, Sopilak's mother broke in vehemently: 'Yes, it is all right to make'—and here she used a gesture which could not be mistaken—'but to leave a baby behind and no man to feed it, that is no good.'

For the better part of two hours these six people on the edge of the mighty ocean, whose frozen blocks cracked and snarled as they spoke, discussed a problem which had confused men and women since words were invented and families came into being for the nurturing and rearing of new generations. The contradictions were timeless; the obligations had not altered in fifty thousand years; and the solutions were as obvious now as they had been when Oogruk sought refuge in these parts fourteen thousand years ago after family problems on the far shore.

The climax of the discussion conducted in such an awkward manner and with so many participants came when it was revealed that John Atkins from a little town outside Boston, a good Protestant and unmarried, was profoundly in love with the Eskimo girl Kiinak and she in turn was so lost in love for him that come midsummer she was going to have his child.

Interpreting of this last intelligence was not required, for when Kiinak pointed to her growing belly, her mother leaped from the ground, dashed to the door, and began shouting into the darkness: 'The bad one is going to have a baby and she has no man. Woe, woe, what is happening in the world?' Her cries attracted three other gossips her age, and now Sopilak's hut was filled with recrimination and noise and attacks against both the girl and her lover, and when the riot was sorted out, Captain Pym learned to his confusion that whereas it was completely wrong for Atkins to have got this fine young woman, fifteen years old, with child, it had been quite all right for them to have conducted all the steps leading up to that unfortunate development.

It was at the height of this complicated moral chaos that Pym first became conscious of the fact that Sopilak's wife was indulgently smiling at his confusion, as if to say: 'You and I are above this nonsense,' and he found himself blushing and awkwardly aware that they had formed a kind of partnership. Nikaluk was tall for an Eskimo, thinner than usual, and with an oval face unmarked as yet by tattoos. Her hair was jet-black and trimmed straight across her eyebrows, but she lacked the impishness of younger Kiinak, who had now moved close to Atkins as if to protect him from the condemnatory women who were shouting at him.

The impasse was settled when Atkins suddenly rose to announce in Eskimo that he wanted to marry Kiinak and that she had told him she wished to marry him. Now the four older women danced with glee, and embraced Atkins and told him what a fine man he was, with Captain Pym all the while standing aghast at this unexpected result his visit to Desolation Point had produced. But Nika-luk, still smiling condescendingly from the rear, made no attempt to quiet the confusion or give Pym any sign of reproof for the disturbance he and Atkins had created.

As the turbulent morning drew to a close, Pym told the crowd that he believed Atkins should return to the long hut with him and talk things over, and although the older women feared that this might be a device for preventing the promised marriage, they had to agree with Sopilak, who was the leader of their village, that it should be allowed, so after holding hands ardently with his young love, Seaman Atkins solemnly bound on the skis that Sopilak had made for him and followed his captain back to the long hut.

There Pym gathered the crew, informed them of what had transpired in the village, and awaited their amazed responses, but just as Harpooner Kane was about to make a suggestion, Pym interrupted: 'Mr. Corey, I believe we have missed winding the clock,' and after the two men gravely attended to this ritual, Pym restated their position at the edge of the Arctic Ocean: '159 degrees West Longitude . . .'

IN THE PUBLIC meeting to discuss the possibility that John Atkins might have to marry his Eskimo girl, the first alternative voiced was eminently practical: 'If she's pregnant, find some Eskimo to marry her. Give him an ax. They'll do anything for an ax,' and before Captain Pym could oppose such an immoral proposal, several other sailors pointed out how impossible it would be for a civilized man from Boston, and a good Christian, to take back with him a savage who had never heard of Jesus, and this sentiment was about to prevail when a surprise comment altered the whole course of the debate. Big Tom Kane growled: 'I know this girl and she'll make a damned sight better wife than that bitch I left in Boston.'

Several sailors whose minds were undecided happened to be looking at Captain Pym when these harsh words were spoken, and they saw him blanch, gasp, and then say sternly: 'Mr. Kane, we do not invite such comments in this ship.'

'We're not aboard ship now. We're free to speak our minds.'

Very quietly Captain Pym said: 'Mr. Corey, will you accompany me and Harpooner Kane in our inspection of the *Evening Star*? And you will come with us, Seaman Atkins.'

Across the ice the four men went, and once aboard their ship Captain Pym began the daily examination as if nothing untoward had happened. They saw that the ice, still pressing in from the ocean, had as before struck the sloping sides of the ship and lifted her higher in the air rather than crushing her against the shore; the sides were tight; the caulking held; and when the thaw came she would sink back into the sea, ready for the trip to Hawaii.

But when the inspection was completed, Pym said almost sadly: 'Mr. Kane, I was sore grieved by your intemperate outburst,' and before the big man could apologize, the captain added: 'We know of your tribulations in Boston and sympathize with you. But what shall we do about Atkins?'

Corey interrupted: 'What Tompkin said is true. She is a savage.'

Pym corrected him: 'In her own way she's as civilized as you or me. The way her brother catches bears and seals and walruses is as able as the way you and I catch whales.'

Corey, not silenced by this apt comparison, addressed his next remarks to Atkins: 'You could never take her to Boston. In Boston a dark savage like her would never be accepted.' And Atkins astonished the three men by saying rather innocently, as if he were in no way annoyed by this intrusion into his affairs: 'We wouldn't go to Boston. We'd leave ship in Hawaii. I liked what I saw there.' Before the men could respond, he nodded deferentially to the captain: 'Granting your permission, sir.'

There in the dark hold of the whaler, with the casks of valuable oil on all sides, Captain Pym considered this surprising development. Almost as if an act of God had descended upon his ship, he could in one sweep salvage his Christian conscience, help to save the soul of an Eskimo girl, and get rid of the consequences by putting the young couple ashore in Hawaii. On only few occasions in a navigator's life would he encounter an opportunity to do so many sensible things at one time and discharge the responsibilities of all concerned.

'You have my permission,' he said as ice pressed upon his ship and the timbers creaked.

Back in the long hut, he informed the crew that he would, as a captain legally entitled to do so, perform the wedding of his Seaman Atkins to the Eskimo lady, but he also pointed out that for the marriage to be acceptable, it would have to be conducted aboard his ship, for he was not entitled to act in that capacity elsewhere. And he then skied to the village to deliver the same message, and when he made it clear to the intended bride, who now spoke a bit of English, that a celebration was to be held to which the entire village would be invited, she ran through the huts, shouting: 'Everybody come!' and when she returned to where Captain Pym waited she kissed him warmly, as Atkins had taught her to do. Astounded by her boldness, Pym blushed furiously, and then he saw young Nikaluk smiling once again.

That wedding aboard the creaking *Evening Star* was one of the gentlest affairs in the long history of the white man's contact with the Eskimo. The Boston sailors decorated the ship with whatever bits of ornament they could construct, and that was not much: a scrimshaw here and there, a doll of stuffed sealskin, a striking block of ice carved with hammer and chisel by a carpenter, showing a polar bear rearing on its hind legs. When the Eskimos caught on to the idea of decorating the empty ship, they were far more inventive than the sailors, for they brought across the ice ivory carvings, things made of entire walrus tusks and the most wonderful items woven and constructed from baleen, until Captain Pym, comparing what they had done with what the Americans had accomplished, asked First Mate Corey: 'Now who is civilized?' and the dubious Irishman answered cogently: 'Taken together, what they've brought wouldn't signify in Boston.'

The service that Captain Pym conducted was a solemn affair, outlined in pages printed at the rear of his Bible, and it was made doubly relevant by a passage which he arbitrarily quoted from Proverbs:

' "There be three things which are too wonderful for me, yea, four which I know not: the way of an eagle in the air; the way of a serpent upon a rock; the way of a ship in the midst of the sea; and the way of a man with a maid."

'During this voyage we have seen eagles in the air and serpents on land. The way our ship escaped ice in the sea was truly mysterious, and which of us can understand the passion which has impelled our man John Atkins to take as his bride this lovely maid Kiinak?'

The ceremony made a profound impression on the Eskimos, for although they understood nothing of its religious significance, they could see that Pym took it with such high seriousness that this must be a true marriage. At its conclusion the older women attending Kiinak began to chant ritual words reserved for such occasions, and for a few precious moments there in the darkness of the *Evening Star* the two cultures met in a harmony that would not often be repeated in years to come, and never exceeded.

But of all the persons participating in this occasion and in the limited feast which followed, only pregnant Kiinak detected a collateral event which was going to have even greater significance, for as she watched the women during the feasting she observed her sister-in-law, and she whispered to her new husband: 'Look at Nikaluk! She's in love with your captain.'

And as the long, dark winter drew to a close, and the sun returned to the heavens, no more than a silvery shadow at first, peeking its head above the horizon for a few minutes, shivering and running away, Nikaluk was powerless to hide the abiding affection she felt for this strange man, so different from her husband, the notable hunter Sopilak. She was loyal to her husband and reverenced his skill in leading the villagers and keeping them provided with food, but she also recognized in Captain Pym a man of deep emotion and responsibility, one in touch with the spirits who ruled the earth and the seas. She observed how his men respected him and how it was he who made decisions and said the important words. More even than her admiration for his qualities was the fact that she thrilled to his presence, as if she knew that he was bringing to this lonely village at the edge of the icebound ocean a message from another world, one which she could not begin to visualize but which she knew intuitively must have aspects of great power and goodness. She had known two men from this world, Atkins, who had loved her husband's sister, and Captain Pym, who controlled the ship, and they were in their way as fine as her husband.

But there was also the fact that she was captivated by the idea of Pym, by the possibility that she might lie with him as Atkins had done so easily with Kiinak and with such joyous results. Driven by these impulses, she began to frequent the places where Pym would be, and she became the object of gossip in the village, and even the sailors in the long hut knew that their married captain, the one who took the Bible so seriously and had three daughters in Boston, had caused an Eskimo woman to fall in love with him, and she with a husband of her own.

Pym, an austere man who took life seriously, thrashed about in a blizzard of moral confusion: sometimes he refused to acknowledge that Nikaluk was in love with him; later, when he did confess to himself that complications threatened, he assumed no responsibility for them. In either case, he made not the slightest gesture toward Nikaluk, not even so much as giving her a glance, for he was absorbed in what he deemed a much more weighty problem. 'When,' he asked his officers at New Year's, 'can we expect the ice to melt?' and one of them who had read books written by Europeans about Greenland gave it as his judgment that the ice would not start to melt till May, but when Atkins asked among his wife's people, they gave an appalling date which translated into early July, and when Pym himself consulted with Sopilak, he was satisfied that this later date was probably correct.

Only then did despair settle upon the men of the *Evening Star*, for in autumn when the ice trapped them they had accepted their imprisonment, expecting it to last till the end of March, when spring thawed New England ponds. And at the onset of winter they were almost eager to see if they had the fortitude to withstand its historic blasts and were proud when they did. But now to greet a new year and to realize that summer would be more than six months distant was intolerable, and frictions developed.

Some wanted to shift their quarters to the ship, but the Eskimos warned vigorously against this: 'When ice melts, strange things happen. Maybe worst time.' So Captain Pym ordered them to remain ashore, and each day his inspections were more careful. He was considerate in dealing with men who gave trouble, assuring them that while he understood their anxieties, he could not tolerate even the slightest show of insubordination.

He was pleased, therefore, when the Eskimos organized hunting trips far out on the ice, which still showed no signs of melting, for then his more adventurous men could accompany them to share the dangers. He himself went once to where a long lane of open water had lured sea lions north, and he had shared in the dangerous task of killing two and then lugging them home over the ice. 'If we keep busy,' he told the men and himself, 'the day will come when we'll break free.'

As the day Captain Pym calculated to be the twenty-fourth of January approached, he encouraged his crew by telling them that the sun, still hiding beneath the horizon, would soon be returning to the Northern Hemisphere, and at a speed that would make the noonday twilight grow longer and brighter. And he explained to those sailors who knew no astronomy: 'Yes, the sun is heading north, and it will keep coming till it stands directly over the Arctic Circle. Then daylight will last twenty-four hours.'

'Tell it to hurry up,' one of the sailors said, and Pym replied: 'As with all things ordained by God, like the planting of corn and the return of geese, the sun must follow the schedule He gave it.' But then he added a curious bit of information: 'The ancient Druids, who did not know God, expressed their joy at the sun's responsible behavior with prayer and song, and since the Eskimos are also primitive people, I suppose we can expect the same.'

But he was not prepared for the things that happened at Desolation Point, for when on the twenty-third of January the sun threw unmistakable signals that on the next noon it would show its face, the villagers went wild, and children cried: 'The sun is coming back!' Drums were produced and tambours made of sealskin fastened to rims of driftwood, but what seemed to be the focus of attention and delight was a huge blanket woven years ago from precious fur spindled into thread and woven into a stout cloth. It was colored with dyes gathered along the shore in summer and from the exudations of sealskin and walrus.

That afternoon Sopilak and two other men in ceremonial garb came solemnly on their skis to the long hut to announce that on the morrow, at high noon when the sun would reappear, the sailors were invited to its celebration, and gravely they bowed as Captain Pym had done when conducting the wedding in his ship. First Mate Corey, speaking for the crew, promised they would be there, but when the Eskimos had gone he said, not spitefully but with a certain cynicism: 'Let's see what these savages are up to,' and half an hour before noon on the twenty-fourth he and Captain Pym led their entire complement of sailors over the frozen snow to Desolation Point.

In the silvery darkness they joined a solemn crowd, a group of people who had lived for many months without sunlight, and there was muffled excitement as the Eskimos looked to the east where the sun had regularly reappeared in years past, a hesitant disk bringing rejuvenation to the world. When the first delicate rays flickered briefly and a gray light suffused the sky, men began to whisper and then cry out in uncontrolled joy as shoots of flame came forth, heralding the true dawn. Watchers from the dark huts smiled, and even the sailors felt a surge of joy when it became apparent that the sun really was going to appear, for they had resented this strange dark winter even more than the Eskimos, and as the villagers gazed in awe when the sun itself peaked over the edge of the world to see how the frozen areas had sustained themselves during its absence, a woman began to chant, and one of Pym's sailors shouted: 'Jesus Christ! I thought it would never come back!'

Then, in the brief moments of that glorious day when hope was restored and men were assured that the world would move as it always had, at least for one more year, people began to cheer and sing and embrace, with the sailors jigging in heavy boots with old women in parkas who had not expected ever to dance again with a young man. And there were tears.

But now things happened that the sailors could not have imagined and which, perhaps, had never before happened at Desolation Point, unpremeditated acts which captured the essence of this glorious moment when life began anew. Along the beach, where great blocks of ice protruded like the backdrop to some drama enacted by the gods of the north, a group of girls, eight or nine years old, danced, and their little feet clad in huge fur-lined moccasins moved so gracefully as their bodies smothered in furs bent in unusual directions that the sailors fell silent, thinking of their daughters or little sisters whom they had not seen for years.

On and on the dancing of the little girls continued, elfin spirits paying respect to the frozen sea, feet clomping handsomely in the snow as they performed steps which had graced this day and this seashore for ten thousand years. It was a moment in time that would be frozen in the memory of all the Americans who saw it, and two big sailors, overcome by the sudden beauty of the spectacle, remained in the background but in their own clumsy way aped the movements of the little girls, and old women clapped, remembering those years long ago when they had greeted the returning sun with similar dancing.

But no one watching these little girls reacted in the way Captain Pym did, for as he followed their unaffected steps and saw the joy with which they smiled at the sun, he thought of his own three daughters and unprecedented judgments came to his lips: 'My daughters never showed such joy in their lives. In our home there was little dancing.' Tears came to his eyes, a symbol of his confusion, and he kept staring at the dance; he could not join it as his sailors did, but he understood its significance.

While the sun was still visible on its brief stop to say hello, excitement grew among the huts, where Eskimo men busied themselves with something that Captain Pym could not see, and after a few moments all the Eskimos cheered as Sopilak and his fellow hunters, mature men all, brought forth the big blanket which Pym had seen earlier but whose purpose he had been unable to guess. Laughter and excitement attended its passage to the spot where the girls had been dancing, but still none of the Americans could fathom why a mere blanket should be causing such a flurry. But then it was unfolded, and Pym saw that it had been made in the form of a circle with a rim strengthened to provide handholds, which most of the men in the village now grabbed. At signals from Sopilak, they simultaneously pulled outward, causing the blanket to form the surface of a huge drum, which was instantly relaxed and as quickly drawn tight again. Under Sopilak's skilled timing, the blanket pulsed like a living membrane, now loose, now taut.

When the men indicated their confidence that they could operate the blanket, Sopilak paused, turned to the crowd, and pointed to a rather pretty girl of fifteen or sixteen with braided hair, a large labret in her lower lip and prominent tattoos across her face. Obviously proud to have been chosen, she jumped forward, flexed her knees, and allowed two men to toss her in the air and onto the waiting blanket, which had been drawn tight to receive her. As watching women cheered, the girl waved to assure them that she would not dishonor them, and Sopilak's men began to make the blanket pulse, lifting the girl higher and higher, but as she had promised the women, she deftly maintained her balance, remaining erect on her feet.

Then, suddenly, the men tightened the blanket furiously, all pulling outward at once, whereupon the girl was tossed high in the air, perhaps a dozen feet, and there she seemed to hang for a moment before falling back to the blanket, upon which she landed still upright on her feet. The villagers applauded and some sailors shouted, but the girl, surprised at how high she had been thrown that first time and knowing that much more was to follow, bit upon the upper edge of her labret and prepared for the next flight.

This time she soared aloft to a considerable height, but still she maintained her footing; however, on the final toss she went so high that gravity and a spinning motion acted upon her heavily padded body and she came down in a heap, collapsing with laughter as the men helped her descend from the blanket.

Kiinak, clutching her husband's hand, told him: 'None went higher than me, but that was last year,' and he, always aware of her pregnancy, said: 'That was last year.' However, after two more saucy girls went flying up toward the sky, Sopilak relinquished his place on the blanket and came to stand before his sister, saying: 'To make the baby strong,' and gravely she took his hand and accompanied him to the blanket.

'Wait!' Atkins shouted, terrified at the prospect of his gravid wife's flying through the air and landing on the taut blanket with a thump, but Kiinak held up her right hand, indicating that he must stop where he was. Agitated as never before, he watched as she was lifted onto the blanket and her brother resumed his place in the circle of men holding it.

Gently, as if dealing with a baby already born, they started the rhythm of the blanket, chanting as they did, and then at a nod from Sopilak they imparted just the right gentle lift, and the pregnant girl rose slightly into the air and was expertly caught as she descended, suffering no shock whatever from her brief flight. When she rejoined her husband, she whispered: 'To make the baby brave.'

A very old woman, one who had soared to the sky when young, was similarly honored, but the lift was too modest for her tastes. 'Higher!' she shouted, and Sopilak warned her: 'You asked us to,' and his men applied just enough pressure to send the old one well into the air, where miraculously she controlled her feet so that she landed upright. The sailors cheered.

And now it was the villagers who did so, because gravely Sopilak stepped before his wife and invited her to leap upon the blanket, which she did without assistance. For some years, when she was sixteen to nineteen, Nikaluk had been champion of the village, flying with a grace and to a height which no other girl could match, for it was not the men alone who determined how high a girl on the blanket would rise; the use of her half-bent knees and the thrust of her legs helped too, and Nikaluk was bolder than most, as if she hungered for the higher air.

The rhythm started. The blanket pulsed. The excitement intensified as Nikaluk prepared for her first leap, and the sailors leaned forward, for they had been told by Atkins: 'The champion. None higher.' However, both Nikaluk and the men working the blanket knew that on her first three or four tries she was not going to rise very high, because both she and they had to test strengths and calculate just when to snap the blanket with maximum power, timing it with the bending of her knees.

So the first four tosses were experimental, but even so the rare grace of this lithe young woman was apparent, and the sailors stopped talking to watch the elegant manner in which she handled arms, legs, torso and head during her ascension, and upon no observer did her lovely motion have a greater effect than upon Captain Pym, who stared at her floating in air as if he had never before seen her.

Then, with no warning, she shot skyward at a speed and to a height which left him astounded: 'Oh! Goodness!' More than twenty feet above his head she hung motionless, every part of her body in delicate alignment, as if she were a renowned dancer in a Paris ballet, a creature of extreme beauty and grace. And now slowly, then gathering speed, she started downward in a posture that looked as if she would have to land awkwardly, but at the last moment she established control and landed on her feet in the middle of the blanket, smiling to no one and preparing herself and her knees for the next flight, which she knew would carry her even higher.

Coordinating with unspoken signals from her husband, she flexed her knees, took a deep breath, and soared into the air like a bird seeking new altitudes, and as she sped aloft, Captain Pym noticed a strange aspect of her flight: Those big fur boots she wears, her heavy clothing, they seem to make her more graceful, not less, and her control doubly impressive. She was a wonderful flying young woman, and there were not on the entire earth at that moment more than a dozen women, regardless of race, who could have equaled her performance and none who could excel. High in the air, with the sun about to bid her farewell, she hung at the apex of her art and she knew it.

On the last upward thrust of the blanket, she went higher than ever before in her life, and this was not because her husband pulled the blanket especially strongly but rather because she synchronized her whole body in one supreme effort, and she did this solely because she wanted to enchant Captain Pym, whom she knew to be staring at her, mouth agape. She succeeded in making a lovely arc through the sky against the quickly settling sun, and as she returned to earth like a tired bird, she smiled for the first time that morning and looked boldly at her captain in a gesture of triumph. She had been aloft where no woman of that village had ever been before; she had been one with the newly born sun and the great ice field whose days were limited, now that her earth was moving into warmth. And when she was lifted from the blanket she experienced such a surge of victory that she went not to her husband but to Noah Pym, taking him by the hand and leading him away.

THE CELEBRATION OF the sun lasted twenty-four hours, and three events in the course of that celebration became part of the tradition of the village of Desolation Point, some treasured, some better forgotten. The young woman Nikaluk went with the Boston captain Noah Pym to a hut where they made love throughout the night. The rough sailor Harry Tompkin from a seafront village near Boston crept down into the bowels of the *Evening Star* to tap a keg of Jamaica rum which had been stowed aboard for medicinal and other emergencies. With the dark, delicious fluid he and two of his mates got drunk, but what was more significant in the history of Alaska, in their generosity and general mood of celebration, they shared their alcohol with Sopilak, who was staggered physically and emotionally by its stupendous effect. And when the sun came up for a second dawning, certifying that its return was legitimate, the old women of Desolation gave Captain Pym a present which in time would strangle him in a remorse that would never dissipate.

The lovemaking was a beautiful experience, a splendid Eskimo woman, pride of her village, striving to understand what the coming of this ship to her shore signified, sought to hold on to such meaning as she could discern. She knew that Noah Pym was the finest man she would encounter in this brief life, and since she had for three months longed to be with him, she had deemed it proper to make her desires known at the celebration of the sun when she performed her ultimate act of reverence, the faultless leap to heights never attained before.

Her boldness in leading him to the twilight hut was not surprising in this Eskimo village, for although the older women disciplined the younger, forcing them to marry in an orderly way so that their babies could be protected and reared in security, no one assumed that marriage ended the desires of people, and it was not unusual for a young wife or husband to behave as Nikaluk had done; no stigma attached to it and life went on after such an affair pretty much as it did before, with no one the worse because of it.

But since sailors like those from the *Evening Star* went home from Eskimo land averring that 'this here husband offered our captain his wife, as hospitality, you might say,' the legend grew that the proffering of a wife to a traveler was Eskimo custom. It was not. About the same amount of affection between traveler and local wife developed at Desolation Point as in a rural community outside Madrid or one close to Paris, or London, or New York. Nikaluk the Eskimo sky-dancer from Desolation had sisters all over the world, and many of the good things that happened in the world did so because of the desire of these strong-minded women to know of the world before the world left them or they it.

But Sopilak's disastrous introduction to rum was not a universal experience. White men had distilled this drink, so exhilarating, so liberating, for many decades and they had introduced it to people all over the world, and Spaniards or Italians or Germans or American colonists could imbibe it moderately, celebrate immoderately, and be little affected next morning. But others, the men of Ireland and Russia, for example, or the Indians of Illinois, or the Tahitians whom Captain Cook respected so highly when they were not drunk, and especially the Eskimos, Aleuts and Athapascans of Alaska, could not accept alcohol one day and leave it the next. And when they drank, it did terrible things to them. On the morning that Sopilak, the great hunter, accepted the liquor from the unwitting Harry Tompkin, the long decline of Desolation Point began.

When Sopilak swished that first taste of rum about his mouth he considered it too biting and too strong, but after he swallowed it and felt its effect all the way down to the depths of his stomach, he wanted another sample, and with its warmth began that indescribable swirl of dreams and visions and illusions of endless power. It was a magical drink, that he realized in those earliest moments, and he craved more and then more. As spring returned he became the prototype of those myriad Alaskans who in later days became addicted to alcohol, prowling the beaches and waiting for the arrival of the next whaler out of Boston. They had learned that such ships brought rum, and no finer gift in the world existed than that.

It was a filthy business the good Christians of Boston were engaged in,

Captain Pym's brother and uncle among them: fabrics to hungry buyers in the West Indies, slaves to Virginia, rum out to the natives of Hawaii and Alaska, and whale oil back to Boston. Unquestionably wealth was created, but the slaves, the whales and the Eskimos of Desolation Point were destroyed.

The present that the old women of the village gave Captain Pym was delivered on the second morning after he had with a remorse never experienced before left the hut of love and taken Nikaluk to her own, where he found her husband lying in a drunken stupor on the ground. In that awful moment he saw two old women pointing at him and Sopilak, and he could deduce that they were praising him for having used sorcery on the fallen man so that he could enjoy his wife. They were criticizing neither Pym nor Sopilak; in a sense they were congratulating the former for a rather neat trick.

Then other women appeared bearing in their arms a garment on which they had been working for some time, and after they had raised Sopilak to his feet and slapped his face a couple of times, he took the garment from them, smiled sheepishly at the men who had gathered, and held out his arms to Captain Pym. John Atkins, who approved of all that was happening, translated:

'Honored Great Captain whose guns saved my life when we fought the bear, and who helped Tayuk and Oglowook to kill him when I could not, our village offers you this gift. Your men have been good to us. We honor you.'

Bowing, he allowed the garment to fall free, and the sailors who were still celebrating fell silent as they saw the noble cloak which their captain was receiving. It was pure white, heavy, long: the fur of the polar bear taken on that early hunt.

Everyone insisted that he put it on, and he stood embarrassed and ashamed as Sopilak and Nikaluk draped the glorious cape about his undeserving shoulders. He wore it all the way back to the long hut and even during the inspection of the ship, but that night as the time approached for evening worship he laid it aside, and when the men looked to him for prayer, he turned ashen-faced to his first mate and said: 'Mr. Corey, will you offer prayer? I am unworthy.'

P YM'S SURRENDER OF evening prayer to others had a constructive aftermath, for when the trying days of late April arrived, with permanent daylight but no indication that the frozen sea would ever relinquish its stranglehold on the *Evening Star*, the sailors grew at first restless and then downright belligerent. Fistfights erupted for no reason, and even when they were halted by Corey's quick attention, a general surliness prevailed.

When it looked as if real trouble might erupt, one of the ship's quietest men came to Captain Pym, saying shyly: 'Captain, sir, I've found proof in the Bible that God knows our plight and has promised rescue.' When Pym showed astonishment that the Lord should be concerned about this lost little ship and its sinful captain, the sailor asked: 'I was wondering if I might read Scripture tonight?' and Pym had to say: 'That's no longer my province. You must ask Mr. Corey,' and when the young man did, Corey gave quick assent, for if anything promised to ease tensions, he would try it.

So after evening meal, with the light as bright as it had been at midday, this frail young man, his voice throbbing with emotion, read from an obscure passage in the often overlooked book of Zechariah:

' "Behold, the day of the Lord cometh, and thy spoil shall be divided in the midst of thee.

' "And it shall come to pass in that day, that the light shall not be clear, nor dark:

' "But it shall be one day which shall be known to the Lord, not day, nor night: but it shall come to pass, that at evening time it shall be light.

' "And the Lord shall be king over all the earth: in that day shall there be one Lord, and his name one." '

Closing the Bible reverently, the sailor leaned forward to offer a brief emendation: 'Clearly, men, this prophecy pertains to us. When we sell our whale oil, the shares will be divided. When the ice melts, and it surely will, we shall be set free. Already we have continuous day, as the Lord ordained. And at evening time there is light, and the Lord our God does reign as king over all the earth. Since He has promised to save us, there is no need for bitterness now.'

Several sailors, grateful for what seemed like divine intervention, clapped hands as he finished, but Captain Pym, suspecting that he had outlawed himself from such dispensation, shivered and stared at his knuckles, but his remorse did not prevent him from spending hours and then days and finally nights with Nikaluk, so that when the ice did finally begin to melt, with the *Evening Star* slowly resuming her position as a ship floating in water, Nikaluk started asking the inevitable questions, using the patois which the sailors and their women had developed over the nine months of the marooning: 'Captain Pym, s'pose Atkins take Kiinak with him. Why not you?'

He told her frankly: 'You know I have a wife, children. You have a husband. Impossible.'

Without rancor, but with a realistic assessment of the situation, she said: 'Sopilak? He what you call drunk all time.' And she began insisting that Pym take her with him. She had no concept of either Hawaii, where Atkins was going, or Boston, where the others were headed, but she was confident and with good reason that she would fit in and find for herself and Noah an acceptable life, but for two conclusive reasons he found it impossible to consider taking her to Boston: I already have a family, and even if I didn't, I could never show her there. No one would understand.

He was nowhere near brave enough to share that second reason with her, especially since Atkins had had no hesitancy in marrying Kiinak, Boston or no, so he postponed telling her definitely that he would be leaving her behind when the ship sailed. Yet he could not break himself away from her, for he was ensnared in the great passion of his life, the one that awakened a man to what love and women and a life's destiny involved. She had already placed an imprint on his life that would never be erased, neither by time nor regret, and in a perverse way he found intense pleasure in strengthening the experience. He was in love with Nikaluk, and when he was away from her he could visualize her flying in the air, her heavy boots prepared for a sudden landing, her arms and hair outflung in a vision of wonder that few men ever had of their women. She was of the sky, and the ice, and the endless nights, and the quiet harmony of this village beside the Arctic Ocean. 'Oh, Nikaluk!' he sometimes cried aloud when he was alone. 'What will happen to us?'

He did not, like many American men who were in those days exploring the world and new societies, engage in sentimental reflection about the poor island girl left behind, as if she were going to cry her heart out while he went on to better things, unaware that she was going to handle the situation rather easily in her island paradise while he would be tormented about island memories when he returned to Philadelphia or Charleston. No, Pym saw Nikaluk as a human being equal to himself in all ways except the possibility of her living in Christian Boston. Corey had been right; she was, in so many respects that mattered, a savage.

But he continued to wear the polar-bear cloak and to luxuriate in its richness and the memories it held of those great days hunting on the ice. The long coat became his symbol as he moved about the *Evening Star* preparing her for sea. One morning Atkins brought his wife aboard, and when Captain Pym saw her, smiling and eager for adventure, his breath caught and he wished he were that young seaman bringing Nikaluk, so much more mature and lovely than Kiinak, aboard for the long voyage to the closing of his life.

The sun shone. The sea relaxed. The ice retreated, baffled for another summer but sullenly hoarding its strength for a swift return in autumn, and sails were set. All the people of Desolation came down through the mud to watch the departure, and it might have been a gala morning except that with the raising of the gangplank, this final severance from the shore that had treated the visitors so hospitably with seal blubber and dancing and loving women, Nikaluk ran from her husband, approached the departing ship, and wailed: 'Captain Pym!' Her husband ran after her, not to rebuke but to comfort, but he had that morning drunk the last of Harry Tompkin's rum, and before he could catch his wife he fell in the mud and lay there as the ship withdrew.

Land had scarcely been lost on the journey south to Lapak Island, where the whaler would replenish as best it could for the long run to Hawaii, when Captain Pym, on the bridge, suddenly called out: 'Mr. Corey, this polar bear is strangling me!' and with frantic hands he tore at the beautiful cloak, throwing it from him and kicking it into a corner when it fell.

When Harpooner Kane heard of the incident he went to the captain, saying: 'I, too, helped kill the bear. Can I have the cloak?' and Pym said hurriedly and with a sense of overpowering guilt: 'You are entitled to wear it, Mr. Kane. You have not covered it with shame.' And during the long, cold trip to Lapak Island, Noah Pym continued to refrain from reading the evening prayers, for he was indeed strangled: the bear, and Sopilak fallen in the mud, and Nikaluk flying magnificently in the air were all fragments of his agony, especially his memory of those little girls, so untouched by the coming of the *Evening Star*, dancing on the frozen beach to rejoice in the return of their sun.

THE ENFORCED STOP at Lapak Island was brief and terrible. When the little brig entered the familiar water between the volcano and the island and saw the Aleuts in their kayaks and elegant hats, Harpooner Kane cried: 'Home port!' but they had barely anchored when the sight of Kane in that rich white cloak excited the two reprobates, Innokenti and baldheaded Zagoskin, to start whispering among their men: 'That ship out there must be crammed with furs,' and after two days of adroit spying, prolonged by dilatory action in delivering provisions to the ship, the talk became: 'Properly led, sixteen determined men could take that ship.' When this was secretly discussed among seven ringleaders, Innokenti reminded his fellows of something he had spotted when the *Evening Star* stopped at Lapak on its way north: 'Captain Cook had soldiers aboard his ship. This one has none.' And now the plotting began.

No one had yet made a specific proposal of piracy, but Innokenti, remembering how Captain Pym had relished talking with Trofim Zhdanko, encouraged the New Englander to spend time in the old cossack's hut, and this necessitated the presence of the interpreter, Seaman Atkins, who took his wife along. The sessions were protracted, and Trofim had an opportunity to see what an excellent wife the young American had acquired in the Eskimo girl Kiinak, and he became especially concerned about her pregnancy: 'How wonderful that one of the first Americans in these waters found himself an Eskimo girl that he wanted to marry . . . before a priest . . . like decent human beings.' He returned several times to this theme, finally betraying his deeper concern: 'How much better these islands would have been if men like my son had taken Aleut wives.' He smiled at the young couple and said: 'You're beginning a new race. May God bless you.'

With Trofim was a boy named Kyril, son of a Russian brigand and an Aleut woman whom he had raped and later killed. The Russian had sailed off to an eastern island in the Aleutians, abandoning his son, who began to frequent Zhdanko's hut, where he helped the old man. Trofim was especially eager that Kyril see how easy and normal it was for a man like Atkins to marry an Eskimo woman like Kiinak: 'Let this be a lesson. Good lives come from good beginnings.'

'Are you married?' Captain Pym asked, and the old man said proudly: 'Most powerful woman in Siberia. She'd make a grand tsarina,' and he asked Pym: 'Have you a family?' and the captain flushed a deep red, giving no answer, but Trofim needed none; what the trouble was he could not guess, but that there was trouble he knew.

While these wandering conversations were under way in the hut, Innokenti and Zagoskin, defeated men in their advancing years who had accomplished nothing but destruction, were huddled with their fellow conspirators, coordinating their attack on the *Evening Star*: 'Tomorrow when the captain and the young couple go to talk with the old fool, you and you, keep them inside. Then Zagoskin and I, with you three, board the ship as if bringing them supplies. He goes below with one helper. I stay on deck with two. And all of you speed out in your kayaks. At this signal,' and he shouted in Russian, 'we take the ship.'

'And if they fight?' one of them asked.

'We kill as many as we have to.'

'The others?'

'Like the ones in the hut? We deal with them later. But get the ship, because then we can do almost anything.' It had been secretly agreed between Innokenti and Zagoskin that after capturing the ship, all survivors would be taken to nearby Adak and murdered, the blame being placed upon the Aleuts there.

The plot was uncomplicated and brutal, with an excellent chance for success, except that on the target day Captain Pym did not visit Trofim and Kyril; he stayed aboard ship and this meant that Atkins and his wife stayed too, but the conspirators were so sure of success that the plan went forward. At one in the afternoon the two leaders came to the *Evening Star*, accompanied by three traders, as agreed. They brought with them a substantial supply of stores, and as they began to deliver them, other men with more goods set out from shore.

Noah Pym, learned in the lore of ships' being taken by land-based natives, was below when the second contingent started to come aboard, and instinctively he rushed toward the door of his cabin, crying: 'Mr. Corey, what goes on?'

He was met by Zagoskin, who gave a loud bellow signaling that the fight had begun, and then clubbed Pym over the head, cracking his skull and knocking him to the deck. From that fallen position the dazed man raised himself on one elbow and tried to defend himself, but with a heavy boot Zagoskin kicked him in the face, whereupon Zagoskin's Siberian helper beat the little New Englander to death. He died trying to save his ship, which in his last moments he supposed he had lost. He uttered no final words, entertained no last thoughts. He was not even allowed time for prayer, which had been absent from his lips for so long.

Young Atkins and his wife, hearing the commotion in the captain's cabin, ran to his assistance, just in time to be clubbed to death by Zagoskin and his helper, who were then free to rush topside to help Innokenti clear the decks, but when they reached there they found far more confusion than they had anticipated, for First Mate Corey, an iron-tough Irishman, assumed that Pym was dead and that the salvation of the ship depended on him. Armed with pistol and sword, he killed two attackers and forced their leader Innokenti to stay back. But now, seeing huge Zagoskin coming at him, he shouted: 'Help! Help!' threw down his empty pistol and grabbed a belaying pin, determined to kill as many Russian pirates as possible before surrendering the ship.

At this moment a huge man in a long white cloak rushed on deck, wielding a long harpoon in each hand. It was Kane, shouting: 'Pym's dead. Kill them all!' And without stopping to take careful aim, he threw one of his lethal spears at the approaching Zagoskin. It sped through the air like a slim bolt of lightning, struck the Russian just above the heart and pinned him like a helpless seal to the mast.

Not satisfied that the harpoon had killed the man, Kane leaped at him as he stood speared and with his other harpoon stabbed him twice, once through the neck, once through the face. Then, failing to jerk the first harpoon loose, he abandoned it, grabbed the club with which Zagoskin had killed Atkins and his wife, and rampaged about the deck, striking with fury any Russians he encountered.

Joining with Corey, who was defending himself with only a belaying pin, Kane pointed to Innokenti and shouted to all the Americans within earshot: 'He's the bastard! Kill him!' and with that he launched his other harpoon at the instigator of the attack. He missed, and when Corey lunged at him, Innokenti deftly sidestepped and gained a moment to survey the deck where plans had gone so terribly wrong. He saw the dead Russians, his partner Zagoskin skewered against the mast, and both Kane and that damned Irishman summoning their men, so in one bloodstained second he made his decision. With a wild dive over the side he abandoned his cohorts and ignored the fact that he couldn't swim. With the superhuman power that men can often muster in the face of mounting disaster, this amazing scoundrel flopped about in the sea like a stricken fish, reached an empty kayak, upset it sideways, thrust his legs into one of the hatches, righted it, and with long skilled strokes fled toward shore. Corey, seeing him about to escape punishment, grabbed a pistol from a sailor and tried to shoot him, but missed.

After the Boston men had tossed overboard the corpses of Zagoskin and his fellow pirates, Corey said in controlled voice, as if nothing of importance had happened: 'Up anchor, prepare sails. Mr. Kane, you are promoted to First Mate. Report to me on the condition of the crew.'

The last sight the Russian fur traders had of this doughty little ship—which had explored the seas, chased whales, and survived being pinned down in an arctic winter—was a file of men standing at attention along the port gunwales while the new captain read solemnly from a Bible, and a big man in a long white cloak lifted three bodies, one by one—Captain Pym, Seaman Atkins, the pregnant Eskimo girl Kiinak—and pitched them into the Bering Sea.

But that was not all, for when the ceremony ended, the new captain ordered the ship's ineffectual gun unlimbered, pointed ashore, and fired. A cannonball of no great weight ricocheted across the rocky land of Lapak Island, coming to harmless rest close to the hut occupied by Trofim Zhdanko, who had watched the events of this day with shame and horror.

T HIS ATTEMPTED PIRACY occurred in the spring of 1781, and combined with the near-loss of the *Evening Star* in the ice pack off Desolation Point, it deterred other American whalers from adventuring into the Chukchi Sea and Arctic Ocean for half a century, but by 1843 the floodgates would be opened, and a few years later nearly three hundred whalers would brave these northern seas.

After the *Evening Star*, first of that gallant breed, escaped to the south and a memorial stone was erected to indicate where Zagoskin's pierced and mutilated body had drifted ashore, it seemed as if the fur traders were willing to dismiss the affair of the *Evening Star* as nothing more than a good risk which had gone astray. 'We came this close to taking that ship,' Innokenti said to the men who closed ranks around him. 'That damned harpooner.' He ignored Zhdanko when the old man asked: 'Why did you have to kill that fellow and his wife?' for his son felt that this could happen in any lively action. As for the killing of the captain, who had been so congenial during his two visits, that was also one of the accidents of war.

When his stepfather asked: 'But was it war?' Innokenti snapped: 'We are at war with anyone who thinks to take this new land from us,' and when Zhdanko asked further what made him sure that Americans would want an island like Lapak, with no trees and a diminishing supply of seals and sea otters, he said: 'Yes, this island is used up. The natives are no good. But there are others better than this farther east.' And it was this indication that his son planned to continue eastward with his slaughter, his piracy and his wanton killing that decided the old man.

On a fine overcast day with no rain or wind, perfect for hunting otters, Zhdanko surprised Innokenti by saying: 'Fine day. We've been enemies too long. With Zagoskin gone, let's see if we can catch some more furs,' and when they went to the kayak in which Zagoskin had sat in the stern so that Innokenti could club the otters forward, the old man said: 'I'll paddle here,' and his son shouted to some idlers on the beach: 'Come help us form the circle,' but only two others responded.

Trofim led the way, far from shore and into the shadow of Qugang, assuring Innokenti: 'I've seen otters out here,' and they came at last to a spot from which the actions of the three kayaks could not easily be followed by the men on the beach. Here they did find otters, and as Innokenti started the abbreviated circle in pursuit of a female with a babe on her belly, the mother proved surprisingly agile, dodging this way and that, aided of course by the fact that the circle did not contain enough boats.

Innokenti, infuriated by his stepfather's tardy response in adjusting to the otter's tactics, cursed at him and at the other paddlers, threatening the latter with beatings when he got them ashore: 'Form up! Come at her faster when I chase her your way!'

A few minutes later, when the hunters were grievously mispositioned, thanks to Trofim's ineptness, Innokenti turned to berate him again, when the old man, from his rear position, gave the kayak such a violent lurch that the front spun completely around, tossing Innokenti into the sea.

He did not panic. Cursing Trofim again, he did as before when he dove off the *Evening Star*, flailing his arms and thrashing out violently to grab the leading hole of the kayak, and he would surely have saved himself a second time, except that when he reached up, Zhdanko moved swiftly away, looked down at his son, and struck him full in the face with the blunt side of his paddle. Then, as if he were hunting a helpless mother otter who had to surface, he waited for Innokenti's head to rise above the surface, whereupon he moved swiftly to that spot and almost crushed his skull with a second blow.

Biding his time, he paddled gently, waiting for the bloody head to appear, and when it did he calmly pushed it back under, keeping it there for many minutes. Only then did he wave his paddle furiously and start shouting: 'Help! Innokenti has fallen.'

M ANY DAYS AFTER the body came ashore, so waterlogged and decomposed that no one could say what had happened during the otter hunt, the boy Kyril came to Trofim's hut, and after prolonged silences during which the old cossack thought: He's the same age as Innokenti was when I met him, but how different, the young fellow said hesitantly: 'I saw what happened when we chased those otters.'

Trofim made no response, and after a while the young man said: 'No one else saw but me. I was in front position.'

Tears came to the old man's eyes, not of regret but in response to the great contradictions of life. The young hunter did not notice them, for he was assailed by his own bewilderments—this old man whom he loved had killed his own son —but he did gain composure to say: 'He fell from the kayak because he turned too fast. Only he could be blamed. I saw it. I told the others.'

Again there was silence, during which each knew the other to be engaged in a deliberate lie, but to absolve their mutual guilt, Kyril added: 'He was a bad one, Old Father. To kill that girl who had treated us so gently. To kill so many islanders. He deserved to die, and if he hadn't drowned himself the way he did, I would have killed him.' He hesitated and the silence grew ominous: 'I don't know how, but I would have slain that one, Old Father.'

Zhdanko weighed most cautiously what he wanted to say next, because each separate word must convey its exact meaning, and he wasted perhaps half an hour staring at the volcano and speaking of inconsequential things, then in a low voice: 'Kyril, it is time again for me to take our pelts to Petropavlovsk. Madame Zhdanko will be waiting there with bales she's been collecting, too, and she'll have a ship to take me to Okhotsk and I'll have to go overland through the bad country to the Lena River.' Subtly he changed pronouns: 'Then we'll pole the barge toward Irkutsk. Now that's a fine town, believe me. And we'll go on to Mongolia and trade our pelts to the Chinese buyers, but you'll have to be careful with them or they'll steal your back teeth.'

He rocked back and forth in the cold sunlight, then asked: 'Would you like that?' and the lad cried: 'Oh, yes!'

'It could take three years, you know. And with the leaky ship we have we might not even reach Kamchatka, but it'll be worth the try. And when we sail back to Lapak we'll quit this miserable place and move east to Kodiak, which they tell me is rich in fur.'

Kyril considered this for a moment, then asked: 'But if you want to go to Kodiak, why don't we go now?' and Trofim explained: 'Because I must inform Madame Zhdanko that her son is dead. She's a most worthy woman and should hear this only from me.'

'Did she know . . . about Innokenti?'

'I think mothers always know.'

'Then how could she go on loving him?' and Trofim said: 'That's the mystery of mothers.'

And this old man of seventy-nine, who should have been long retired, sat dreaming of turbulent seas, and robbers in a storm-swept Siberian pass, and the arm-wrenching torture of poling a barge up the Lena River, and the excitement of haggling with Chinese over the value of an otter pelt, and he was impatient to wrestle once more with the old challenges and test his strength against the new in Kodiak.

For he knew that an explorer should dedicate his life to probing eastward, always eastward toward the sunrise: as a lad from a trivial Ukrainian village north of Lvov he had traveled east to serve Tsar Peter in Moscow, then across Siberia to meet Madame Poznikova, and on to the Aleutians, where he had known those honorable captains—Bering, Cook, Pym—and even to the coast-line of America, where he had aided the great Georg Steller. And always there had been the noble challenge of the next day, the next island, the next stormy sea.

'I have no son,' Trofim said quietly, 'and you have no father. Shall we load our leaky ship and take our furs to Irkutsk?'

V

THE DUEL

In that memorable year 1789, when France launched the revolution which would bring its people freedom from excessive tyranny, and the former American Colonies ratified their revolution by initiating a new form of government under a remarkable constitution ensuring freedom, a group of vicious Russian fur traders committed a great atrocity against the Aleuts on Lapak Island.

Two small boats appeared in the harbor, commanded by ruthless bearded traders who put into ruthless execution a cruel order: 'All males above the age of two, off to the boats.' When women came solemn-faced to the shore to ask: 'Why?' they said: 'We need them on Kodiak Island to hunt otter,' and when they asked: 'For how long?' they said: 'Who knows?' And when the two boats sailed that same afternoon, husbands and wives felt a panic which warned them: 'We shall never again see each other.'

When the lamentations ended, the women faced the hideous necessity of reorganizing their lives in ways never before contemplated. The islanders lived from the sea, but now there were none who knew how to hunt seals, or catch big fish, or go after the great whales that spouted past the island on their way north. Along the beach stood kayaks and harpoons and long clubs for knocking seals in the head, but no one remained who was practiced in using them.

The situation was not only perilous but also extremely frustrating, for the Aleutian Islands marked the line where the vast Pacific Ocean collided with the Bering Sea, and enormous upthrusting currents brought ocean edibles constantly to the surface: plankton thrived, so shrimp could grow fat, and when they did, salmon could feed upon them, and when the salmon were plentiful, seals and walruses and whales could feed well. Nature threw an abundance of seafood to the surface at the Aleutians, but only brave and daring men could harvest it, and now there were no men. When storm winds swept out of Asia, they seemed to be crying: 'Where are the hunters of Lapak?'

In executing this barbarous policy the Russians had to be aware that they were operating against their own long-term interests, for they needed the Aleuts to do their hunting and fishing for them, but if they removed and ultimately killed off all adult males, the population could not be replenished, for male two-year-olds would not have time to mature to an age at which they could father other children. However, they were spurred to this insane behavior because they still believed that the Aleuts were less than human, and the mechanics of their grisly plan did seem workable, for with men absent, the supply of food would diminish rapidly.

But there was one characteristic of Lapak and the other Aleutian islands which the Russians overlooked: people lived longer here than elsewhere in the world, and it was not too unusual for men or women to reach into their nineties. Reliance on a balanced diet focusing on seafood rather than meat had something to do with it, but so did clean air from the sea, an orderly life, hard work and a sturdy inheritance from ancestors who had crossed from Asia. At any rate, there was on Lapak in 1789 a great-grandmother of ninety-one who had a granddaughter of forty who had a lively daughter of fourteen, and this strong old woman decided not to die easily.

The great-grandmother was called by her family and friends Old One; her granddaughter was Innuwuk. The fourteen-year-old girl bore the lovely name of Cidaq, which meant *young animal that runs free*, and no more appropriate designation could have been awarded her, for to see this child was to see movement and vitality and grace. She was not tall, nor was she plump as some Aleut girls were at her age, but she did have the big round head which indicated an Asian heritage, the intriguing Mongolian fold to her eyes, the elegantly tinctured skin. In the left-hand corner of her lower lip she wore one delicate labret carved from an old walrus tusk, but what made her distinctive was her long, silky black hair, which reached almost to her knees and which she kept cut straight across her forehead, right down to her eyebrows, giving herself the appearance of wearing a helmet, and customarily she scowled from under it.

But often, for she loved the vitality of life, her round face would break into a smile as big as a rising sun: her eyes would squint almost shut, her white teeth would flash, and she would throw her head back to utter sounds of joy. Like most Aleut and Eskimo women, when she spoke she kept her lips close together, so that she seemed to mumble or perpetually whisper, but when she laughed with her head back she was Cidaq, the little deer, the young leaping salmon, the little whale skimming through the seas in the wake of its mother. She, too, was an adorable little animal, and she belonged to the land which sustained her.

Now she was about to starve. With all the richness that the two seas provided when they met, she and her people were about to starve. But one afternoon when Old One, who still moved about with ease, was looking at the pathway between Lapak Island and the volcano, she saw a whale gliding past, not moving rapidly but lazing along, sounding now and then, revealing its enormous length by the occasional flipping of its tail or a sporadic turn on its side. And she thought: One whale like that would feed us for a long time. And she decided to do something about it.

Exploring the beach with the aid of a driftwood cane that she had carved, she chose six of the best two-hatch kayaks and asked the help of Innuwuk and Cidaq in separating them. Then she moved among the women asking who knew how to operate a kayak, but she found none. A few had broken taboos by riding in them and some had even tried to paddle them, but none had studied the intricate principles of using them in hunting otter or seals, and it would have been unthinkable for them to go after a whale with their husbands. But they did know what the ocean was and were not afraid of it.

However, when Old One started to put a team together—six boats with twelve paddlers—she ran into opposition. 'What are we doing this for?' one cautious woman asked, and when she snapped: 'To kill whales,' this woman and others began whimpering: 'You know that women cannot go near whales, or touch the kayak that goes after them, or even let our shadow fall across one that is going after whales.'

Old One considered these objections for several days and, in consultation with her granddaughter Innuwuk, conceded that if things were normal, the troubled women could consult the shaman, and he would certainly advise them that the spirits would curse the island hideously if women trespassed on the path that whales took past the island, and that to touch a kayak about to be used in a hunt would be to ensure the escape of the whale and even, perhaps, the death of the men pursuing him. The evidence of ten thousand years was against the threatened women of Lapak Island.

But at the close of the third day of this speculation Old One stood firm, with the precept her grandmother had taught her long before the appearance of any Russians: 'Can do? Must do!' which meant that if a desirable thing could be done, you were obligated to try. When she proposed this operating principle to Innuwuk, the latter said with obvious apprehension: 'But everyone knows that women and whales have never . . .' In disgust the old woman turned to Cidaq, who stood silent for a moment, reflecting on the gravity of what she was about to say. When she spoke she did so with a firmness and a willingness to break old patterns which would characterize the remainder of her life: 'If there are no men, we'll have to break their taboos. I'm sure we can capture a whale,' and Old One, encouraged by this eager response, said: 'After all, men do certain things to catch a whale. It isn't all mystery. We could do the same things.' And the two agreed that it was nonsense to believe that spirits would want an island of women to starve to death because there were no men at hand to pursue whales in the traditional way.

Assembling the other women, Old One harangued them, with Innuwuk and Cidaq at her side: 'We can't just sit here and starve. Berries we have and shellfish from the lagoons and maybe a salmon or two in the fall. We catch birds, but it's not enough. We need seals and maybe a walrus if one comes along, and we must have a whale.' She invited her granddaughter to ventilate her fears, and this Innuwuk did, most ably: 'The spirits have always warned women to stay clear of whales. I believe they still want it that way.' This brought loud assent from those locked in tradition, but then little Cidaq stepped forward, tossed her long hair from one hip to the other, and said: 'If we must do it, we can do it. And the spirits will understand.' When the younger women nodded hesitantly, she turned to her mother, held out her hands, and pleaded: 'Help us,' and with a nudge from Old One, this perplexed woman submerged her fears and joined those who said that taboo or not, they would speed out to sea in the shadow of the volcano and try to catch a whale.

From that moment, life on Lapak changed dramatically. Old One never relinquished her determination to feed her island, and she convinced even some recalcitrants that the spirits would alter the old rules and side with them if they were working to save their lives: 'Think how it is when a pregnant woman is giving birth and baby starts out backward. Obviously the spirits intended that baby to die, but Siichak and I . . . we've done it many times . . . we turn the child around and thump on the belly and it comes out right, and the spirits smile, for we have corrected their work for them.'

When some still held back, the old woman grew angry and demanded that Siichak, the midwife, come and stand with her, and when this insecure woman did, Old One cried, grabbing her granddaughter's hand: 'Siichak! Did I not call you when this one was pregnant with Cidaq here? And did we not reverse the spirits, and bring forth this child properly?' And the midwife had to confess that Cidaq would have been born dead if she and the old woman had not intervened. After that the program to catch a whale went more smoothly.

Old One decided early in the process that she herself was too old to manage a harpoon, and when she looked about for someone who could, she concluded there was only one real candidate strong enough, her own granddaughter: 'Girl, can you be trusted to do your best? You have the arms. Have you the will?'

'I'll try,' Innuwuk mumbled with no enthusiasm, and Old One thought: She wants to fail. She's afraid of the spirits.

Now the six crews began to practice in the calm space between Lapak and the volcano, with various women recalling bits of the procedure. One knew how to tip the harpoon with flint, another how to make and inflate the sealskin bladders that would float behind the harpoon after it had been stuck in the whale, so that a visible trail would always be available. And still others recalled what their vanished husbands had said about this fight or that. They failed to recover all the knowledge they needed, but they accumulated enough to make a try.

But, as Old One had foreseen, her granddaughter failed miserably in her attempt to master the throwing-stick: 'I can't hold the stick and the harpoon at the same time, and when I try, I can't make the harpoon fly the way it should.'

'Try again!' the old woman pleaded, but it was no use. Since boy babies were instructed in the use of this intricate weapon from the age of one, it was absurd to think that an unpracticed woman could master it in a few weeks. So in the end the women agreed that when the whale came, they would paddle their canoes so close to it that Innuwuk could reach out and push her harpoon into the huge gray-black body. A sillier strategy had rarely been devised.

In late August a nine-year-old girl who kept watch came shouting: 'Whale!' and there in the passageway between the islands swam this monstrous creature, forty tons at least, and the prospect of untrained women going forth in frail canoes to give it battle was so unnerving that one crew member simply ran away. But this left five kayaks, and Old One could remember when her husband and one other craft managed to puncture a whale and harry it to its death.

So the five teams went solemnly to the beach, no one showing eagerness for this battle, and it had been agreed that Cidaq, a strong girl at fourteen, should sit in the rear of Innuwuk's kayak and guide her mother close enough to the whale for the harpoon to be driven home, but when they approached the beast and the women saw how tremendous it was and how pitifully small they were, all lost heart, even Cidaq, and not one craft came within stabbing distance of the whale as it moved sedately past.

'We were like tiny fish,' Cidaq confessed later as she spoke with her disappointed great-grandmother. 'I wanted to paddle closer but my arms refused.' Burying her face in her hands, she shuddered, then looked up from beneath her bangs and said: 'You can't imagine how big it was. Or how small we were.' And the old woman said: 'Yes, I can. And I can also imagine all of us dying here . . . eyes sunken . . . cheeks gone . . . and no one to bury us.'

THE PLAN TO catch a whale for Lapak was salvaged in a curious way. When the ten women scuttled back home without having come close to the whale, they were so ashamed of themselves that one young woman, who had been married only a short while before the men were taken away, said: 'Norutuk would have laughed at me,' and in the silence that followed, each woman visualized the manner in which her husband would have teased her: 'Imagine a bunch of women going after a whale!' and they longed to hear that teasing. But then the young wife added: 'But after he teased me, I think Norutuk would say: "Now go and do it right." ' And more even than Old One's determination, this voice of reassurance from the absent men they had loved put fire into the hearts of these women, and they resolved to catch their whale.

Heartened by this resolve, Old One resumed with terrible concentration training her teams, and hammered at them that next time they must go right into the face of the whale, no matter how big, and bring it back. And on the fifth day of their training she appeared with a three-hatch kayak, and she told her women: 'When the whales come, I ride here with my own paddle, Cidaq rides in back to steer, and Innuwuk sits up here with her harpoon, and we have taken a pledge that we will go into the jaws of that whale if we have to, but we shall lodge our harpoon in that whale.' However, even as she spoke, she doubted that Innuwuk would have the courage to do it.

Then came one of those revelations which enable the human race to progress, for as Innuwuk slept she dreamed with horror of the moment when she would be sitting in her kayak, reaching out with her harpoon to stab the great whale, and she woke bathed in sweat and terror, for she knew she could not do that thing. But as she lay in the darkness, trembling, she suddenly had a vision, a kind of synthesis of brain and imagination and kinesthetic control of her muscles, and in a blinding flash she understood how a harpoon-thrower worked. Again and again she drew back her right arm, feeling an imaginary stick and harpoon in place, and as she threw her arm forward she felt all parts of this marvelous machine harmonizing—shoulder, arm, wrist, fingers, stick, harpoon, flinted point—and she leaped from her bed, ran out to the shore, grabbed harpoon and stick, and with great swinging movements of her arm, flung the harpoon far and true. After the sixth proof that she had mastered the mysteries, she ran shouting to the others: 'I can do it!'

And in the dawn when they saw with what accuracy she could throw her harpoon, and from what a distance, they knew that next time a whale swam into their sea they would have a strong chance of landing it.

The six crews were ashore when the little girl watching the straits came shouting: 'A whale!' and then, as if she realized the terror her information would cause in some, she added: 'A little whale!' and the women ran to their kayaks.

They were very small, these women who presumed to attack leviathan, none over five feet one, and with Old One, who had masterminded the assault, at less than four-eleven and ninety-one pounds, one for each year of her adventurous life. Cidaq, watching her climb in with her driftwood paddle, knew that the frail old woman could contribute nothing to the speed, but everything to the courage of the other five crews. As for herself, Cidaq was determined to take her craft right up against the whale: 'Mother, be ready! This time we won't fail!' And trailing behind Old One, the other teams went forth to do battle.

The little scout had been correct, for this whale weighed only nineteen tons, a great deal smaller than the first giant, so that when the women saw it coming toward them, many thought: This one, maybe! and they moved ahead with a courage they had not known they had. From the rear of their canoe, Cidaq paddled with undeviating direction, assisted by counsel from Old One in the middle, who kept dipping her paddle from side to side, and both called to Innuwuk perched in the prow: 'Steady! You've proved you can do it.' And finally, with a slingshot thrust that was exceedingly powerful for an untrained woman, the harpoon was lodged, and from another kayak a safeguard was stabbed home, and the bladders streamed out, and for two days of grandeur and terror and hope the six groups, driven by Old One's indomitable zeal, trailed their stricken whale, and in due course towed it slowly, triumphantly back through the Bering Sea to the salvation of their island.

I N 1790, AFTER the women had proved they could survive for an entire year, a small, hull-wracked ship, the *Tsar Ivan*, put into Lapak to take on fresh water. It had been dispatched from Petropavlovsk by that indestructible entrepreneur Madame Zhdanko, who had crammed into it a horrible collection of dregs from Russia's jails who had heard the sentence popular with judges in those days: 'To the gallows or the Aleutians.' They had chosen the latter, permanent exile with no hope of reprieve, but with every intention of murdering island officials if they got the chance.

When the *Tsar Ivan* hove to, its crew, not realizing that the island had been abandoned by the Russian government, found the marooned women in a state of perplexity. They hoped that the ship was going to carry them to their husbands, but knowing the Russians, they feared new abuses, and as soon as the sailors spoke, they knew it would be the latter: 'No woman gets on this ship!' and there was stolid grief as the women realized that they really had been left here to die.

There was among the criminals a multiple murderer named Yermak Rudenko, thirty-one years old, big, burly, bearded, and a scoundrel almost impossible to discipline. Knowing that he had nothing more to lose, he swaggered about exuding so clearly the threat 'Don't touch me!' that officials let him alone. He had been ashore only a short time when shrewd Old One spotted him, and sidling up with Russian words she had acquired, she began speaking to him about this and that, but always mentioning her great-granddaughter Cidaq, and she started this man's thinking along such lines by arranging one day when the other men were loading water that Rudenko and Cidaq were left alone in the old woman's hut, and later that afternoon made her proposal: 'Why not take Cidaq with you to Kodiak?'

He was startled by the idea, but as the old woman pointed out: 'She speaks Russian. She's a wonderful child. And believe it or not, she's already helped kill her whale.' This last claim was so preposterous that Rudenko began asking about the supposed killing of a whale by a girl not much more than fifteen, and the women confirmed that it was true, and to prove it they showed him and the other Russians how the skeleton was being used in imaginative ways.

When Innuwuk learned what her grandmother was proposing, the sale of Cidaq to this rude sailor, she protested bitterly, but the old woman was adamant: 'Better she live in hell than never to live at all,' and she allowed no counterargument: 'I want this child to know life. I don't care what kind of life,' and when Rudenko showed interest in what Old One was proposing, she took Cidaq aside: 'I dragged you into the world by one foot. I slapped life into your lungs. I have loved you endlessly, more than my own children, for you are a treasure. You are the white bird coming from the north. You are the seal diving to escape. You are the otter defending her young. You are the child of these oceans. You are the hope, the love, the joy.' Her voice rose almost to an impassioned chant: 'Cidaq, I cannot see you perish on this forlorn island. I cannot see you, who were made for love, go down to lifeless leather like the mummies in the caves up there.'

When the terms of sale were agreed upon, with the women of Lapak receiving a few trinkets and some lengths of gaudy fabric, Old One and Innuwuk dressed Cidaq in her best furs, warned her to be on the watch for evil spirits, and led her to the shore where the three-hatch kayak awaited. 'We'll take you out to the ship,' Old One said as Cidaq carefully stowed the small bundle that contained her meager belongings. However, at the last moment a woman for whom the family had had little respect ran up with a labret handsomely carved and suited for the spot at the corner of the girl's mouth: 'I carved it from the bone of the whale you and I caught,' and before Cidaq stepped into the rear hatch of the kayak, she removed the gold-colored walrus labret she had been wearing and gave it to the surprised woman, inserting in its place the new white one from her whale.

It was now time for Old One to take her place in the middle, but before she did she created a great stir along the beach, for she had asked another old woman to bring to the departure objects whose unexpected appearance tugged at the heart of every woman in the crowd. Bowing gravely, Old One took from her accomplice three of the famous visored hats of Lapak, those made and worn by the hunters of that island, and handing one to each of the other two members of her family, she donned the third, an elegant affair of gray and blue with plumes of silvery baleen and sea-lion whiskers, and thus attired she directed Cidaq to head for the *Tsar Ivan*, but when the women ashore saw the splendid hats on the waves once more, they cried 'Ah me!' and 'Woe, woe!' and tears fell like mist for a scene that they would never again see: the men of Lapak going forth in their gala hats.

At the gangway to the ship Old One took Cidaq by the hands, ignoring the leering insults shouted by sailors along the gunwales. 'It's not a proper thing we're doing, Girl,' she said, gripping Cidaq's fingers tightly. 'And the spirits may frown. But it's better than dying alone on this island. In days ahead, Cidaq, never forget. Whatever happens, it's better than what you left.'

The *Tsar Ivan* had scarcely left the shadow of the volcano when Old One's pragmatic philosophy was put to the test, for Rudenko, who now owned her, dragged Cidaq below, ripped off her sea-otter garments and began the series of brutal acts which left her dazed and humiliated. What was worse, when he was finished with her, he passed her back and forth among his brutish friends, who abused her in ugly ways, keeping her stowed in the fetid hold of the ship and feeding her only intermittently after forcing her to submit to their indecencies. Since Rudenko acknowledged no responsibility for her well-being, her treatment degenerated so savagely that several times during the fifty-two-day passage to Kodiak she suspected that before the voyage ended, she might be tossed overboard as a nearly lifeless object of no further use.

It was as dark an experience as a young girl could have, for among the seven or eight men who slept with her, there was not one who developed any affection for her or any feeling that he should protect her from the others. They all treated her as inhuman, a thing of scorn. But she knew that on Lapak she had been a child of value, the leader of girls her age and the peer of the boys, and that the awful indignities she was suffering were the price she had to pay to escape from a situation that was even worse. Remembering her great-grandmother's words, she never once considered ending the abuse by throwing herself overboard, even when her tribulations became almost unbearable. Not at all! If this passage to Kodiak was her only chance for survival, she could endure it, but she did take careful note of the men who humiliated her and kicked her when they finished with her, and she vowed that when their boat landed at Kodiak, if it ever did, she would have certain scores to settle, and sometimes there in the darkness a sea-swept smile would take possession of her entire face, and with her tongue she would touch the new labret: If I helped kill that whale, I can handle Rudenko. And she devised so many heartening possibilities for revenge that the creaking of the ship and the hideous behavior of its passengers ceased to distress her.

The journey did end. Contrary to expectations, the rickety *Tsar Ivan* limped in to Kodiak Island, and when its stores had been unloaded to the cheers of the starving Russians stationed there, Cidaq was allowed to gather her pitifully small bundle and step into the barge that would ferry her into the turbulent life of this island colony. But even though she was now free, she could not leave this dreadful ship and its equally dreadful passengers without saying farewell, so when the barge pulled away she looked up to where the men who had misused her were laughing at her from the gunwales, and cried in Russian: 'I hope you drown! I hope the great whale drags you to the ocean depths!' And despite her fury she flashed that grim smile which seemed to warn: 'Watch out, Masters! We shall surely meet again.'

HER FIRST GLIMPSE of Kodiak Island told Cidaq that it was both similar to Lapak and much different. Like her home island it was barren, indented with bays and rimmed by mountains, but there the resemblance ended, for it contained no volcano; but it did offer something she had never seen before. In certain meadows there were alders, low-growing shrublike trees, and the manner in which their leaves and branches moved back and forth puzzled her. In a few protected spots clumps of cottonwoods with peeling white bark collected, and at the far end of the village in which she would be living rose a single majestic spruce whose towering height and dazzling green-blue color amazed her.

'What is that?' she asked a woman hauling fish from a boat.

'A tree.'

'And what's a tree?'

'There it is,' and Cidaq remained gazing upward at the spruce.

Three Saints Bay was a small collection of rude huts hugging the shore of a bay shaped like an upside-down capital L, but it provided safe anchorage for boats engaged in the fur trade, because it was further protected by a large island a quarter-mile offshore; but it had little hinterland for development, since it was pinched in at the foot of tall mountains.

It was two days before Cidaq, existing as she could from hut to hut, learned the major difference between Lapak and Kodiak: the people of her new home were divided into four distinct groups. There were the Aleuts like herself who had been imported here by the Russians; they were small in size, in numbers and in importance. Then there were the natives who had always inhabited the island, Koniags they were called, big, difficult, quick to anger and outnumbering the Aleuts twenty or more to one. One Aleut who had known Cidaq on Lapak told her: 'The Russians brought us in because they couldn't control the Koniags.' Next up the ladder came the fur traders, wild and horrible men stationed here for life unless they could contrive some excuse late in their lives to accompany a shipment of furs back to Petropavlovsk. And finally there were the few true Russians, usually sons of privileged families, who served here for a few years before they stole enough to retire to estates near St. Petersburg. They were the elite, and the three other castes behaved as they directed, and occasionally warships put into Three Saints to enforce the discipline they dictated.

What Cidaq lacked the experience to understand at this early date was that her Aleuts were slaves; there was no other word for it, because over them their

Russian masters exercised absolute power from which there was no escape, for if an Aleut tried to run away, hostile Koniags might kill him. With no women on hand to share their misery, and no children coming along to replace them, the Aleut men slaving on Kodiak were exactly like the Aleut women in isolation on Lapak: both were condemned to live brief lives, die, and speed the extermination of their race.

The fur traders were not much better off, for they were serfs, tied to the land without chance of betterment or the possibility of ever establishing a proper home back in the Russia from which they were exiled. Their only hope was to catch some native woman, or to steal one from her husband, and with her have children known as Creoles who might in time gain Russian citizenship. But for the most part, they were the property of the company, and until they died, were to toil endlessly to enhance the riches of the empire.

These cruel traditions were in no way exceptional, for all Russia was governed in this manner, and the superior officials who reached Kodiak saw nothing wrong in this pattern of endless serfdom, for that was how their family estates had been run in the homeland and that is how they expected things Russian to continue perpetually.

Life on Kodiak was hell, for as Cidaq was discovering, there was insufficient food, no medicine, no needles for sewing and no sealskins to be sewed. To her surprise, she saw that the Russians had adjusted to their surroundings on Kodiak far less intelligently than her Aleuts had done on Lapak. She existed outside official channels by hiding with one impoverished family after another and, close to starvation, watching as the strange life on Kodiak unfolded. She was spying, for example, one morning when Russian officials, supported by a pitiful ragtag of soldiers, rounded up most of the new fur traders who had shared the *Tsar Ivan* with her and forced them at bayonet point into a fleet of small boats which, with much commotion and cursing, was about to set forth on what an Aleut whispered to her was going to be the 'world's worst sea trip,' the seven hundred and eighty miles to the two remote Seal Islands, later to be known as the Pribilofs, where fur seals abounded in numbers that were unbelievable.

'Will they come back?' she asked, and the man whispered: 'They never come back.' And then she gasped, for at the rear of the line filing into the boats she spotted three of the men who had abused her, and she was tempted to call out to them in derision, but she did not, for at a short distance behind them, his hands in manacles, came Yermak Rudenko, hair awry as if he had been fighting, clothes torn, eyes flashing fire. He had apparently been warned of what life was going to be like on the Seal Islands, a sentence from which there would be no reprieve, and he was still refusing to comply.

'March tidy!' Cidaq heard the soldiers growl in Russian as they prodded at him, and for just a flashing second she thought: Aren't they glad he's in chains! And she amused herself by wondering what Rudenko would do to these skinny, undernourished men if his hands were unbound. But then she remembered him as the animal he had been and smiled to think that he was about to endure some of the punishment he had visited upon her.

A whistle blew. Rudenko and the other stragglers were shoved aboard, and the file of eleven small boats sailed forth on a voyage that would have been a test for one large, well-built one. Cidaq, watching the boats disappear, found herself alternately hoping that they would sink to give her revenge and praying that they would survive because of the poor Aleuts who were also being taken to lifelong imprisonment on the Seal Islands.

She had no such ambivalence about her own position, for each day she survived caused her to give more thanks that she had escaped the lonely terror of Lapak Island. Kodiak was vital; its people might be caught up in storms of hatred and frustrated vengeance, and its managers might be distraught over the decline in sea otters and the necessity to sail so far for seals, but there was energy in the air and the excitement of building a new world. She loved Kodiak, and even though she lived far more precariously than she ever had on Lapak, she constantly reminded herself that she was living.

And because she was now fifteen, with an intense interest in everything about her, she saw that things were not going well for the Russians, who faced open warfare with the Koniags and rebellion from natives on other islands to the east. Scores of men from Moscow and Kiev who had considered themselves superior in every way to the primitive islanders now died at the hands of those who showed that they had mastered night ambush and daytime surprise attack.

But what saddened Cidaq was the obvious deterioration of the Aleuts, who were being strangled by malnutrition, disease and abuse; their death rate was shocking, and the Russians did not seem to care. On all sides she saw signs that her people faced inexorable extermination.

For a brief while she lived with an Aleut man and a native woman—not married, for there was no Aleut community to arrange or give benediction to marriages—who strove to maintain a decent life. He obeyed the rules of The Company, going out day after day in search of otters, and he hunted with superior skills, conducting himself properly and living on what meager food The Company provided. He complained to no one lest he be sentenced to the Seal Islands, and his woman was equally obedient.

But then disaster of the most arbitrary and cruel dimension struck. The man was taken from his job of otter hunting and sent without warning to exile in the Seal Islands. One of the worst traders from the *Tsar Ivan* raged into the hut one night looking for Cidaq, and not finding her, beat the woman about the head, hauled her off to where four of his companions were roistering, and all abused her through three nights, strangling her at the end of their celebration. After two weeks of hiding alone in the hut, Cidaq was captured by the same five fur traders and raped repeatedly. They might eventually have slain her, too, at the conclusion of their sport had not an extraordinary man arrived quietly in Three Saints with a fiery determination to halt the slow death of his people.

He had appeared mysteriously one morning, a gaunt figure emerging from the forested area to the north as if he were a creature accustomed to woods and high mountains, and had the Russians seen him coming, they would surely have turned him back, for he was too old to be of service to them and too wasted to be of much use to anyone else. He was in his sixties, unkempt, wild-eyed, and brought with him only an outrageous collection of odds and ends at whose utility no Russian could have guessed: a pouch of agatelike stones polished by long residence in some riverbed, another pouch of bones; seven sticks of various lengths; six or seven bits of ivory, half from long-dead mammoths, half from walruses slain in the north; and a fairly large sealskin which covered a squarish bundle that gave him his unusual powers. It contained the well-preserved mummy of a woman who had died thousands of years ago and been buried in a cave on Lapak Island.

Slipping quietly into the northern edge of the village, he headed by instinct for the tall spruce whose spacious roots had been partly exposed by erosion. There he laid aside his precious bundle and started to dig among the roots like an animal burrowing. When he had produced a sizable excavation, he erected around and above it a kind of hut, and when it was finished he took residence inside, installing his bundle in a place of honor. For three days he did nothing, then quietly he began circulating among the Aleuts, informing them with funereal gravity: 'I have come to save you!'

He was the shaman Lunasaq, with experience on various islands where he had never accomplished much or attained real stature, for he had preferred living apart, communing with the spirits that govern mankind and the forests, the mountains and the whales, and helping where needed. He had never married, felt uncomfortable with the noises made by children, and did his best to avoid contact with the Russian masters, whose odd behavior bewildered him. He could not, for example, conceive how anyone in power could separate men from women, as the Russians had done in stealing all the men from Lapak Island and leaving the women behind to die. 'How,' he asked, 'can they expect to produce new workers for their boats?' Nor could he comprehend how they could kill all the otters in the sea, when by restraint they could ensure all they required, year after year to the end of time. Above all, he could not understand the crime of older men debauching the very young girls whom they must later marry if either the men or the girls were to survive in any meaningful existence.

In fact, he had seen so many things evil in the conduct of Russians on the various islands they occupied that he knew of no sensible thing to do but come to Kodiak, where The Company headquartered, to see if he could not bring some kind of relief to his people, for it grieved him to think that he must soon be leaving them in the sad conditions under which they now suffered. Like Thomas Aquinas, Muhammad and Saint Augustine, he felt driven to leave his world a little better than it was when he inherited it, and as he settled down amid the roots of the great tree that protected him, he realized that compared to the might of the Russian invaders with their boats and guns, he was almost powerless, except for one asset which he had and they did not. In his sealskin bundle he had the old woman, thirteen thousand years old and more formidable each year she existed. With her help he would save the Aleuts from their oppressors.

Quietly, like the stormless southern wind that sometimes blew in from the restless Pacific, he began to move among the little Aleut men who served so obediently the dictates of the Russians, always reminding them that he brought messages from the spirits: 'They're still the ones who rule the world, Russians or no, and you must listen to them, for they will guide you through these ugly days just as they guided your ancestors when storms tormented them.' He let it be known that among the tree roots at his hut he had the magical instruments which enabled him to communicate with those ever-present spirits, and he was reassured when men in twos and threes came to consult with him. Always he delivered the same message: 'The spirits know you must obey the Russians, no matter what insane orders they give, but they also want you to protect yourselves. Save bits of food for those days when none is issued. Eat some seaweed every day, for strength lies there. Allow the baby seals and baby otters to escape. You'll know how that can be done without the Russians' seeing. And abide by the old rules, for they are best.'

He helped when illness struck, placing the sick man on a proper mat and surrounding his head with shells so that the sea could talk with him, enclosing his feet with his sacred stones so that he might remain stable. And on those occasions when faced with problems for which he could find no answers, he produced the mummy, this withered creature whose sunken eyes in her blackened face stared out to give reassurance and counsel: 'She says that you will have to go to the Seal Islands, no escaping. But there you will find a trusted friend who will support you through life.' He never lied to the men sentenced to the islands, or assured them that they would find wives and have children, for he knew that this was impossible, but he did tell them that friendships of the kind that sustain life were possible, and that men of good sense sought them out, regardless of the terror in which they otherwise lived: 'You will find a friend, Anasuk, and a kind of work that only you can do. And the years will pass.'

Now when boats set out for the Seal Islands he appeared openly on shore to bid the Aleuts farewell, and during the latter part of the year 1790 the Russian officials became accustomed to this spectral figure, wondering occasionally where he had come from and who exactly he was. They never suspected that he was restoring a tiny shred of decency and integrity to their establishment, for from what they could see of their own people—Russian officials and trader-serfs alike—everything was going pretty much to hell.

In due course the shaman Lunasaq heard of one of the saddest cases of Aleut despair, the girl Cidaq, who was being passed from one criminal to another despite Company rules forbidding this, and one day while her current trader-serf was absent unloading a kayak filled with furs, he presented himself at the hut in which she was temporarily living, and when he saw her bedraggled hair, her wan face and the labret almost slipping from her lip, so emaciated had she become, he grasped her hands and pulled her toward him: 'Child! The good spirits have not abandoned you. They have sent me to help you.' And he insisted she accompany him immediately, and leave the moral squalor in which she had been living. Defying Company rules and the possibility that her Russian trader might beat him to death to recover his woman, he led her to his hut among the roots, and once they were inside, he uncovered his most precious treasure, the mummy.

Placing Cidaq before the wizened old face, he chanted: 'Girl, this old one knew far more terror than you ever have. Volcanoes in the night, floods, the raging of the wind, death, the endless trials that assail us all. And she fought on.' He continued in this way for some minutes, not aware that little Cidaq was trying hard not to laugh at him. Finally she put out both hands, one to touch his, the other to touch gently the lips of the mummy.

'Shaman, I don't need her help. Look at this labret. Whalebone. I helped kill this whale. The day will come when I'll kill every one of the Russians who have abused me. I am like you, old man, I am fighting every day.'

And then, in the dark hut, the connection of Cidaq and the mummy began, because the long-dead old woman from Lapak spoke to the young girl from her island. Yes, the mummy *spoke*. Through decades of practice Lunasaq had perfected his gift for ventriloquism until he could not only throw his voice a considerable distance but also make it resemble the speech of different characters. He could be a child appealing for help, or an angry spirit admonishing an evildoer, or, especially, the mummy with her vast accumulation of knowledge.

In the first of their many discussions these three spoke of Russian tyrants and sea otters and men sentenced to the Seal Islands, and particularly of the revenge that Cidaq was planning to visit on her oppressors: 'I can wait. Four of them, including the worst, are in the Seal Islands already. We'll never see them again. But three remain here in Kodiak.'

'What will you do to them?' the mummy asked, and Cidaq replied: 'I am willing to risk death, but punish them I will.'

'How?' the ancient one wanted to know, and Cidaq said: 'I could cut them when they're asleep,' but the mummy said: 'Cut one, and they cut you. Forever.'

'Did you face such problems?' Cidaq asked, and the old one said: 'Everyone does.'

'Did you get your revenge?'

'Yes. I outlived them. I laughed at their graves. And here I still am. But they? Long gone. Long gone.'

The hut was so filled with the sound of the mummy chuckling at her memories of retribution that no one hearing it could be aware of the skill with which Lunasaq used his voice to create the sound of laughter, nor when he had suddenly stopped being the mummy and spoke sternly in his own voice: 'I would remind you that Cidaq's problem is not vengeance but the continuation of her people. Her problem is to find a husband, to have babies.'

'Seals have babies. Whales have babies. Anybody can have babies.'

'Did you?' Cidaq asked, and the ancient one replied: 'Four. And it made no difference whatever.'

Again Lunasaq broke in: 'But you were living secure with your own people,' and the mummy said: 'No one is ever secure. Two of my children died of starvation.' And the shaman asked: 'How did they die and you survive?' and the old one explained: 'Old people can withstand shocks. They look past them. Young people take them too seriously. They let themselves be killed.' She then spoke rather brusquely to the shaman: 'You deal with this child too harshly. Let her have her revenge. You'll both be astonished at the form it will take.'

'It will come?'

'Yes. Just as the Russians will soon be coming to this hut to thrash us all. But Lunasaq, my helper, has taken care of that, and your big help will come in ways you cannot guess. Three ways, coming from many directions. But right now, hide me.'

The mummy was barely secreted when two trader-serfs broke into the hut and began thrashing the shaman so brutally that Cidaq supposed he would die. But immediately the beating started, a group of five Aleuts with clubs rushed into the little hovel, and in the confined space struck the attackers heavily about their heads, and they did such a thorough job that the roughest one stumbled out of the hut with his head smashed and fell dead, while the other man ran screaming, with two Aleuts flailing at him from behind.

Miraculously, the other Aleuts spirited away the corpse and disposed of it in a gully beneath a pile of rocks. The trader who survived his beating tried to incriminate 'some Aleuts who attacked me with clubs,' but his reputation and that of the dead man were so wretched that The Company was not unhappy to have the latter off their rolls, and a few days later they shipped the survivor off to a lifetime of duty with the seals. After watching with grim satisfaction as he was taken away, Cidaq returned to the shaman's hut, where, surprisingly, the mummy showed little interest in the incident: 'Of no consequence. Those two are no loss and you're no better off. What is important is that the three ways I promised you are about to come to pass. Prepare. Your life is changing. The world is changing.'

The shaman now made the mummy speak in a voice which created the illusion that she was retreating from the hut, but Cidaq pleaded with her to stay, and when she did linger, it was the shaman who interrogated her first: 'Will the ways be helpful to me, too?'

'What is helpful?' the old one snapped, almost impatiently. 'Is Cidaq helped because one oppressor was slain and the other exiled? Only if she does something herself to profit from it.'

Through the years the mummy had acquired a personality of her own, and with it she often voiced opinions contrary to the shaman's. It was as if a willful student had broken loose from the tutelage of her teacher, so that occasionally, on significant topics, the shaman and his obstinate mummy actually conducted a debate.

'But will not the new ways be harmful?' the shaman asked, and again she answered with a snappish question: 'What is harmful of itself? Unless we allow it to be?'

'Can I use the new ways? To help my people?' Lunasaq asked, and there was no reply, for the old one knew that the answer rested only with the shaman himself. But when Cidaq asked almost the same question, the mummy sighed and remained silent as if in deep recollection, then sighed again. Finally she spoke: 'In all the years, and I have savored many thousand, the ones I remember are the ones that brought me challenges—a husband I never appreciated until I saw the way he handled adversity . . . the two sons who refused to learn hunting but who became master builders of kayaks . . . the winter when all lay sick and only one other old woman and I had to catch the fish . . . that awful year when the volcano at Lapak exploded right out of the ocean, covering our island with ash two elbows deep, and my husband and I took survivors four days out to sea so we could breathe . . . and the peaceful nights when I laid plans for a better life.'

She stopped, and seemed to aim her voice directly at Cidaq, and then to shift it toward the shaman, the one who had ensured her continued existence through this present span of years: 'Three men are coming to Kodiak. They bring the world and all the world's meaning. And you are to receive them, each of you in your own way.'

Then, with a much softer voice, she spoke only to Cidaq: 'Did it feel good when you saw that Russian slain?'

'No,' Cidaq said. 'It felt as if it were over. As if something had ended.'

'And you didn't gloat?'

'No, it was just over. Something evil was ended, and I had little to do with it.'

'You're ready for those who are coming.' Then she asked her shaman: 'How did you feel when he was slain?' and Lunasaq replied honestly: 'For him, I was sorry that he had lived so poor a life. For me, I was glad, for I have so much more work to do here at Kodiak.'

'I am glad for you both. You're ready. But nobody has asked me how I feel. The three are coming to me too, with their problems.'

'How do you feel?' the shaman asked, for the mummy's well-being fortified his own, and she said: 'I told you the good years were those when something brought challenges. It is long overdue for something exciting to happen on this forsaken island.' And on that reassuring note she retired to prepare for the next confrontation in her thirteen thousand years.

THE FIRST OF the three arrivals was a man who was returning illegally. Nobody on Kodiak Island had expected to see him again, and he appeared on a mission which astounded those with whom he came in contact. He was Yermak Rudenko, the huge, hairy trader who had bought Cidaq, and he had escaped from the Seal Islands a man determined to do anything rather than go back. When The Company officials found out that he had stowed away on a boat returning with a shipment of pelts, they arrested him, and he stood in the rude office at the head of the harbor and asked with mock contrition: 'Do you know what it's like up there? Before, no one ever lived on the islands but seals. Now a handful of Aleuts, a few Russians. One ship every year. Little to eat. No one to talk to.'

'That's why we sent you there,' interrupted a young officer who had never known hardship. 'You proved incorrigible here, and you'll go back on the next boat, because that's your station now and forever.'

Rudenko blanched, and all the fury he had displayed when dominating the *Tsar Ivan* and the traders on Kodiak vanished. To face the awful loneliness of the Pribilofs for the rest of his life was more than he could bear, and he began to plead with the officials who controlled his destiny: 'Nothing but rain. Never a tree. In winter, ice binds all things, and when the sun returns, nothing but seals crowding the island. A boy of six could kill the quota in a week. Then nothing.'

From his huge body with its large muscles and heavy shoulders the fight seemed to drain and certainly the arrogance seemed to vanish. If the judgment was to be that he must get on a small boat and sail back to that bleak land, he knew that he would jump off en route or kill himself after he landed; to waste the years of his life in such barren futility was more than he could absorb: 'Don't send me back!'

The officials were obdurate: 'We sent you there because we could do nothing with you here. There's no place for you in Kodiak.'

In despair, a man flailing about for any escape, he uttered a plea which, though irrelevant, would engage Kodiak for the remainder of his violent life: 'My wife is here! You can't separate a believing Russian and his wife!'

The news astounded his listeners, who turned to one another, asking: 'Has anyone seen this man's wife?' and 'Why weren't we told of this?' The upshot was that the officer in temporary charge of Company affairs said: 'Take him away and let us look into this.'

The investigation was put in charge of a junior naval officer, Ensign Fedor Belov, who initiated inquiries while Rudenko was kept in chains, and as a result of tedious interrogations the young officer learned that the prisoner Rudenko had indeed purchased an Aleut girl on the island of Lapak and that although he had treated her poorly, he could be considered in some respects her husband. When Belov informed his superiors of this, they became actively concerned, for as the temporary head pointed out: 'We've been ordered by the tsarina to help Russians establish families in these islands, and she said specifically that if native girls converted to Christianity, marriage with them was to be encouraged.' And since the tsarina in question was Catherine the Great, Autocrat of Autocrats, whose probing fingers went everywhere, it was advisable that any ukase issued by her be enforced.

So Ensign Belov was sent back to work, and now the subject of his investigation was Rudenko's supposed wife. Did she exist? Was she a Christian? Could the marriage be solemnized by Kodiak's solitary Orthodox priest who was drunk most of the time? He tackled the last problem first, and when he found Father Pëtr, a broken-down clergyman of sixty-seven who had made repeated fruitless appeals for return to Russia, he found the old man ready to comply with any request made by The Company, to which he must look for his meals and lodging: 'Yes, yes! Our adored tsarina, whom God preserve, has instructed us, and our revered bishop in Irkutsk, whom God preserve, worthy man . . .' Mention of the bishop's name diverted his thoughts to the seventh appeal he was drafting to that worthy, praying for relief from his arduous duties on Kodiak. Now he lost this thread also, and with a blank stare coming from his heavily bearded white face, he asked humbly: 'What is it you want me to do, young man?'

'Do you recall the trader Yermak Rudenko?'

'No.'

'Big man, very difficult.'

'Yes, yes.'

'He bought a girl on Lapak Island. Aleut, of course.'

'Sailors will do that.'

'He's been on the Seal Islands for almost a year.'

'Yes, yes, a bad one.'

'Would you marry this Rudenko to his Aleut girl?'

'Of course. The tsarina told us to—yes, she did.'

'But only if the girl became a Christian. Would you baptize her?'

'Yes, that's what I was sent here for, to baptize. To bring heathens into the love of Jesus Christ.'

'Have you baptized any?'

'A few, they're a stiff-necked lot.'

'But you would baptize and marry this one?'

'Yes, that's what the tsarina ordered. I saw the order, sent out by our bishop in Irkutsk.'

It was apparent to Ensign Belov that this old fellow knew little of what he was doing or ought to be doing. He'd been in the islands several years, had baptized few, married even fewer, and learned none of the languages. He represented the Russian civilizing effort at its worst, and it was into the wide gap left by his lack of missionary zeal that shamans like Lunasaq had been able to slip.

'I'll forward your request to the bishop at Irkutsk,' Belov promised. 'And will you prepare to solemnize this marriage?'

'Thank you, thank you for sending the letter.'

'I asked about the marriage.'

'You know what the tsarina said, may heaven protect Her Royal Highness.'

So Ensign Belov reported to the officials that Rudenko did have a wife of sorts and that Father Pëtr was prepared to baptize and marry her, as the tsarina had instructed. When the officials asked if Belov had seen the young woman and did he deem her worthy to become in effect a Russian citizen, he answered: 'Not yet, but I believe she's here in Three Saints and I'll pursue the matter diligently.'

Making further inquiries, he learned that her name was Cidaq and that she was living, if that word could be so used, in a hut whose former owner had been killed in some way; the details were cloudy. To his surprise, she turned out to be a modest young woman, perhaps fifteen or sixteen, not pregnant, exceptionally clean for an Aleut and possessed of an adequate Russian vocabulary. Realizing that she was terrified by his presence but unaware that this was because she feared being implicated in the murder of the trader, a matter which had been quickly dropped, he strove to put her at ease: 'I bring good news, very good news.'

She took a deep breath, for she could not imagine what it might be. 'A great honor is to be bestowed upon you.' He leaned forward when he said this, and she leaned to hear: 'Your husband wants to marry you legally. Russian church. Priest. Baptism.' He paused, then said with great pomposity: 'Full Russian citizenship.' Holding his position, he smiled at her, and was relieved to see the huge smile that broke across her face. Grabbing her by the hands and suffused by his own joy, he cried: 'Didn't I tell you? Great news!'

'My husband?' she finally asked.

'Yes. Yermak Rudenko. He's come back from the Seal Islands.'

And here began the deception which would enable her to gain her revenge on Rudenko, for with the cunning of a knowing little animal, Cidaq masked any physical or verbal response which might betray her repugnance at the thought she might be rejoined to Rudenko, and in the pause she began to contrive a score of ways by which to pay back this horrible man. But realizing that she must know more before she could take the next step, she feigned delight at hearing about him: 'Where is my husband? How soon can I see him?'

'Not so fast! He's here in Three Saints.' Then the young officer said gravely, as if bringing ultimate dispensation: 'And The Company says that if you marry him properly, he can stay here.'

'Wonderful!' she cried, but then he added the caveat which would enable her to complicate things: 'Of course, you have to convert to Christianity before the church wedding can take place.'

Showing mock horror, she asked: 'Otherwise they'd send him back?'

'Might even shoot him.'

'You mean, he came back without permission?'

'Yes. He was burning to be with you again.'

'Christian? Marriage? Is that all that's needed?'

'Yes, and Father Pëtr says he's ready to supervise your conversion and marriage.'

Her round face radiant with feigned gratitude, Cidaq smiled at Ensign Belov, thanked him for his heartwarming news, and asked like a young woman deeply in love: 'And when can I see Master Yermak?'

'Right now.'

Three Saints Bay had no jail, which was not surprising, since it had little else that an organized society required, but there was in Company offices a room with no windows and a double door, both parts of which could be kept locked, and when the bolts were shot, the young officer led Cidaq into the dark room where her supposed husband sat in shackles. 'Yermak!' she cried with a joy which pleased but did not surprise the prisoner, for although he realized that he was taking a gamble in relying upon her to achieve his freedom, he was arrogant enough to believe that she would be blinded by this dazzling opportunity to become the lawful wife of a Russian and would forgive him all he had done to her in the past.

'Yermak!' she cried again, like a dutiful wife. Breaking away from Ensign Belov and running to her persecutor, she took his manacled hands, kissed them, and then, pushing her smiling face into his beard, she kissed him again. Belov, witnessing this emotional reunion of a Russian fur trader and the island girl who adored him, sniffled and went off to inform the authorities that the marriage should proceed.

A S SOON AS Cidaq was free of Rudenko and Belov, she hurried to the shaman's hut: 'Lunasaq! I must speak with your mummy!' and when the sealskin pouch was opened, Cidaq revealed with laughter the surprising opportunity that had chanced her way: 'If I marry him, he stays here, and if I don't, back he goes to his seals.'

'Remarkable!' the mummy said. 'Have you seen him?'

'Yes. Manacled. Guarded by a soldier with a gun.'

'And what did you feel when you saw him?'

'I saw him with my hands about his neck, strangled.'

'And what shall you do about this?'

In the time since she first saw Rudenko's hateful face she had perfected her devious strategy: 'I'll make everyone believe I'm happy. I'll let them think I'm going to marry him. I'll talk with him about our life here in Three Saints . . .'

'And you'll relish every minute?' the ancient one asked.

'Yes, and at the last moment I'll say "No" and watch as he's dragged back to his forever prison among the seals.'

The mummy, who had been a practical woman in life, which explained her long persistence thereafter, asked, 'But what reason will you give . . . for changing your mind?'

In response, Cidaq uttered words which would create the most intricate complications: 'I'll say I'm unable to surrender my old religion and become a Christian.'

At this frivolous statement Lunasaq gasped, for now religion, the essence of his life, was involved, and he foresaw the danger in playing such a game. The withered mummy was left to one side in her sealskin pouch, and Lunasaq, the endangered shaman, took sole control: 'Did you say you were thinking of turning Christian?'

'No, they said it. I'd have to join their church before I could marry Rudenko.'

'Surely, you'd not think of that?'

Continuing to play games, she said half humorously: 'Well, if he were a decent Russian . . . like young Belov, for instance . . .'

Gravely the shaman placed Cidaq on a stool and took a position facing her; then, as if he were summarizing his entire life, he began speaking: 'Young woman, have you not seen the Russian Christianity? Has it done anything for our people? Has it brought us the happiness they promised? Or the warm house? Or the food? Do they love us as their Book says they should? Do they respect us? Or allow us entrance to their places? Have they given us any new freedoms, or preserved the ones we built for ourselves? Is there anything . . . any one thing you can think of . . . any good thing their god has given us? And is there any good thing which we already had which they have not taken away?'

From her sack the mummy groaned at this accurate summation of Christian rule under the Russians, and fortified by this encouragement the shaman continued, his unkempt locks shaking whenever he made a persuasive point: 'Did we not in the old days on our islands know happiness with our spirits? Did they not keep food swimming past our islands, protect us in our kayaks, bring our babies safely to birth, bring back the sun each spring, ensure a harmony in our life, and enable us to maintain good villages where children played in the sun and old men died in peace?'

He became so agitated by this vision of the lost Aleutian paradise that his voice rose to a plaintive wail: 'Cidaq! Cidaq! You've survived great tribulation. The spirits have saved you for some noble mission. Do not at this time of crisis even think of embracing their ignoble ways. Cidaq, stay with your people. Help them to regain their dignity. Help them to pick their way honestly through these testing times. Help me to help our people.'

He was trembling when he finished, for his spirits, those forces which animated the winds and activated the sun, had vouchsafed him a glimpse of the future, and he saw the rapid and painful demise of his people if they abandoned the old ways. He saw the drunkenness increasing until men lay senseless; he saw strange illnesses slaying his dark Aleuts but never the white Russians; he saw vibrant young women like Cidaq debauched and discarded; but most of all, he saw the remorseless decline and eventual disappearance of all that had made life on Attu and Kiska and Lapak and Unalaska resplendent, saw it all dragged in the dust until even the spirits who had supervised that life would be gone.

A universe, an entire universe which had known its episodes of grandeur, as when two men alone on the vast sea, protected only by a sealskin kayak with sides that even a determined fish could puncture, went up against leviathan—they two hundred and fifty pounds in all, he forty tons—to fight him to the death. This universe and all it comprised was in danger of being extinguished, and he felt that he alone was responsible for its salvation. 'Cidaq,' he whispered, pleading and anguish almost stifling his voice, 'do not scorn the tested old ways which have protected you in favor of bad new ones which promise a good life and deliver only death.'

His words had a powerful effect on Cidaq, and she sat in a kind of trance as he produced from his bundles those revered symbols which had guided her life so far: the bones, the pieces of wood, the polished pebbles, the ivory harvested so painfully from the sea. Distributing them about her in the designs to which she was accustomed, he began chanting, using words and phrases which she did not understand but which were so potent that into the room came the spirits that governed life, and they spoke to her as in the days of her childhood: 'Cidaq, do not desert us! Cidaq, the others promise a good life but never produce it, not for our people. Cidaq, cling to the ways that enabled your great-grandmother to live so long and so bravely. Cidaq, do not transfer your allegiance to strange new gods that have only boasting and no power. Cidaq! Cidaq!' Her name reverberated from all corners of the hut until she feared she might faint, but then from the mummy sack came comforting words: 'First things first, Cidaq. Smile at Rudenko. Give him reason to hope. Then send him back to exile with the seals. After that we must grapple with the things that perplex our shaman, for they perplex me, too.'

The round-faced girl with the sunburst smile shook her head vigorously from side to side as if to clear it for the tasks ahead, then promised her shaman: 'I'll not allow them to make me a Christian, not a real Christian, that is,' and she left the hut, smiling once more and trying to imagine how Rudenko was going to look at the last moment when she refused to marry him and he realized that she had tricked him into going back to the seals.

T HE MUMMY HAD predicted that three men would arrive at Kodiak with disturbing or hopeful messages, and Rudenko had been the first, with news that was all bad; but now a second was approaching, with creative ideas, and he came not a moment too soon.

By 1790, Russian colonization of her American territories had stumbled to the lowest level achieved by any European nation in bringing its civilization to newly discovered lands. Spain, Portugal, France and England all performed better, and it would not be until Belgium behaved so atrociously along the Congo that any nation would come close to the malperformance of Russians in the Aleutians. They destroyed the reasonable systems by which the islanders had governed themselves. They depleted food supplies, so that people starved. They nearly exterminated the sea otter, so that a wealth which might have expanded forever almost vanished. And worst of all, they crushed old beliefs without substituting viable replacements. Drunken old priests like Father Pëtr at Three Saints converted less than ten Aleuts to Christianity in nineteen years, and even to these willing souls they brought no spiritual reassurance or worldly improvements. Conditions were so bad that an impartial observer would have been justified in concluding: 'Everything the Russians have touched, they've debased.' But now reform was coming, from Irkutsk.

During that winter of 1726 when Vitus Bering and his aide Trofim Zhdanko were snowbound on their way to Kamchatka, they made a voluntary detour to the regional capital at Irkutsk, not far from the Mongolian border, and there they consulted with the voivode, Grigory Voronov, whose able and forceful daughter Marina impressed them so favorably. This Marina married the Siberian fur trader Ivan Poznikov and later, after he was slain by brigands on the way to Yakutsk, the cossack Zhdanko. She had said, during her introduction to Zhdanko: 'All good things in Siberia come from Irkutsk,' and this was still true.

During the intervening years the town had blossomed, becoming not only the administrative and commercial focus of eastern Russia but also the center from which radiated those imaginative ideas which enrich society, and no agency was more energetic than the Orthodox Church, whose local bishop was determined to inject religious vigor into Kodiak, the most eastern and backward of his administrative areas.

When Bering and Zhdanko met Marina Voronova they were not aware that she had a younger brother named Ignaci, who had remained behind in Moscow when his father moved east to assume his governorship. This Ignaci had a son Luka, who in 1766 had a son Vasili, who, from his earliest days, showed an inclination toward holy orders. As quickly as possible after finishing his preliminary studies, this Vasili sought entrance to the seminary in Irkutsk and in 1790, at the age of twenty-four, he qualified himself for ordination. But now a vigorous debate occupied the Voronov family and Great-Aunt Marina Zhdanko from Petropavlovsk, eighty-one years old, had come all the way to Irkutsk to make her strong opinions known, which she did to the irritation of many.

The problem confronting the family was a curious one. In the Russian Orthodox Church, priests at the time of ordination were required to make a difficult choice, one which determined the future course and limits of their lives. A young man, his heart aflame with zeal, could elect to become either a black priest or a white, and this designation included priestly costumes proclaiming the decision. A white priest was one who elected to serve the public as head of some local church or as a missionary or as a lowly assistant in God's work. Significantly, he was not only allowed to marry but encouraged to do so, and when he did establish his family in the community he became inextricably affiliated with it. A white priest was a man of the people, and much of the good work of the church stemmed from his and his family's efforts. Luka Voronov, Vasili's father, had been a white priest serving the Irkutsk countryside, which meant that his son, growing up in this tradition, had been indoctrinated as to its merits.

But other young priests, fired with either ecclesiastic ambition or an honest desire to see their church well administered, chose to become black priests, knowing that this would prevent them from ever marrying but knowing also that to their care would be handed the governance of their church. Any boy aspiring to become a metropolitan in Russia or even in a major province like Irkutsk, must choose the black, take a vow of chastity, and adhere to these decisions through life, or he would find himself rigorously excluded from any significant position in the hierarchy. It was an ironclad rule, one admitting no exceptions: 'Church leaders come only from the black.'

Young Vasili was strongly inclined to follow in his father's footsteps, for no priest in the Irkutsk area was more highly regarded than Luka Voronov, not even the bishop himself, who was, of course, a black. And with considerable encouragement from his father, Vasili would have followed his father's example had not Great-Aunt Marina voiced firm opinions to the contrary: 'Child! It would be horrible to cut yourself off from eventual leadership of our church.

Don't even think of electing the white. You were destined from birth to be a leader, maybe even the supreme leader.'

Her nephew Luka, the young priest's father, reacted rather vigorously to this advice, which he felt visionary: 'My dear Aunt Marina, you know and Vasili knows that leadership in our church does not seek out priests from Siberia.'

'Now wait! Just wait! Because you forsook the high moral road, Luka, and turned your back on preferment, which I never understood, there's no reason why your gifted son should do the same. Look at him! Has he not been ordained by God Himself to be a man of leadership?'

When the family turned to stare at Vasili, dignified in his seminary robes, blond, tall, straight, handsome in appearance and reverent in manner, they saw in him a young man eligible for distinguished service in their church. He was, as his great-aunt properly observed, a man destined for greatness. But his father saw something else nobler than the possibility of preferment: he saw a young man born to serve, perhaps in the humblest position the church provided, perhaps as a metropolitan, but serving always the noble responsibilities of his religion, as he, Luka, had striven to serve. The young seminarian had that touch of grace which ennobles men, regardless of where chance assigns them; he had a calling, a demand from outside as sharp as a sergeant's insolent cry on a cold morning. He was called to do the Lord's work and was eager to do it wherever assigned.

So he was about to announce his preference for the white when Great-Aunt Marina astounded her family: 'Knowing the importance of this meeting, I took it upon myself to consult with the bishop, and I asked him to be waiting outside just about now, to give us guidance. Luka, see if his carriage has arrived.' And shortly the bishop himself appeared, bowing to the great lady whose ample funds had so often enabled him to complete work the church had started, especially in the islands.

'Madame Zhdanko, as I told you the other day, you grace Irkutsk,' and she said without embarrassment: 'As did my father before me.' Then, belatedly: 'And as Luka has, in his own way.'

She did not propose to waste the bishop's time in persiflage: 'Vasili thinks that if he is to serve the Lord, he must elect the white.'

'At his age I chose the black.'

'And were you able to perform the Lord's work just as capably?'

'Maintaining a healthy church is perhaps the Lord's most urgent desire.'

Marina did not gloat, but she did want more than platitudes: 'Bishop, tell me truthfully, if this young man takes the black, would you consider him for a post in the Aleutians?'

Members of the family gasped at the impertinence of this inquiry into church politics, but the old woman knew she had few years remaining, and in the islands which her late husband had loved, there was work left uncompleted. The bishop was not surprised at the old lady's frontal approach, for her past beneficences entitled her to some meddling, especially since a member of her own family was concerned. Asking for more tea, he balanced his cup, munched on a sweet, and said: 'Madame Zhdanko, I am, as you well know, profoundly worried about the posture of our church in the islands. The tsarina has placed on my shoulders responsibility for seeing that the Holy Word is disseminated there and that the savages are brought into the family of Christ.'

Staring at each family member in turn, he sipped from his cup, put it down, and said with what amounted almost to sorrow: 'And I have failed. I've sent one priest after another out there, good men in their time, but old men, too, who have banked the fires of ambition and zeal. They waste their lives and the church's funds. They drink, argue with Company officers, ignore their true charges, the islanders, and bring no souls to Jesus Christ.'

'You make my summary for me,' the fighting old woman cried with that intensity which had never diminished since it was ignited while she was a girl here in Irkutsk. 'We need real men in the islands. That is, if we're to build a civilization there. I mean, if we're to hold that new empire and not surrender it like cravens to the English or the Spanish, let alone those damned Americans whose ships are beginning to sneak into what ought to be our waters.' She was obviously prepared to sail to the islands right now, as either governor, admiral, general or head of the local church.

'I've considered the suggestion you made the other day, Madame Zhdanko, and yes, if this fine young man elects the black, he will do so with my blessing. He has a great future in this church. And he can start at no better place than the Aleutians, where he can launch a whole new civilization. Do well there, young man, and your opportunity for serving the church is unlimited.' Then, with a bow to Marina, he added a practical note: 'What I need to head the church in Kodiak is not some young fellow who will marry a local girl and subside into gentle drunkenness like his predecessors, but someone who will marry the church and build a strong new edifice.'

Encouraged by such words, Vasili Voronov, the most promising young man ever to have graduated from the Irkutsk seminary, chose the black, took vows of celibacy, and committed himself to the service of the Lord and the resurrection of His disreputable Orthodox Church in the Aleutians.

M ARINA ZHDANKO, ALTHOUGH over eighty, possessed such demonic energy that when she finished instructing her grandnephew Vasili as to how he was to conduct his religious life, she turned with great vigor to the straightening out of her own affairs. Since she was already in Irkutsk, where The Company of which she was a leading member kept its headquarters, she felt she ought to initiate certain changes in management, and the male members of the board were surprised when she stalked into their office with the firm announcement: 'I want to send a real manager to organize our Aleutian holdings.'

'We have a manager,' the men assured her, but she snapped: 'I want a man who will work, not whine,' and when they asked: 'Have you someone in mind?' she replied enthusiastically: 'I certainly have.'

There was at this time in Irkutsk an unusual businessman, one Aleksandr Baranov, in his early forties and the veteran of rugged Siberian mercantile wars. Marina had seen him occasionally, picking his way about the streets, head bowed as if contemplating some master move, and she had been intrigued by the stories men told about him: 'He's low-born, no family background at all. Has a wife that no one ever sees, because when he first came to Siberia she promised: "I'll join you soon," but she never did. He's served everywhere, honest as the sunrise but always wiped out by some disaster not of his making.'

'But he is honest?' she asked, and everyone agreed: 'None more so.'

'What's this I've heard about a glass factory?' she asked, and a most improbable story unfolded: 'I was with him when it happened. We were drinking beer when a maid, a real peasant, dropped a beer stein and broke it. Now, glass, as you well know, costs money in a frontier like Irkutsk, so the barman began to knock the poor girl about for having broken such a costly item. Pavel and me, we berated the man for his brutality, but Baranov sat there with fragments in his hands, and after a while he said: "We ought to make our glass here in Irkutsk. Not haul it all the way from Moscow." And do you know what he did?'

'I can't imagine,' Marina said, and another man explained: 'He wrote to Germany for a book on glassmaking, then learned German from a merchant so he could decipher his book, and with no practical experience, never saw one piece of glass blown, he opened a glass factory.'

'Did it fail, like his other dreams?'

'Not at all! He made fine glass. You drank from his work at dinner.'

'What happened?'

'Imports from big factories farther west began to stream in, much cheaper prices.' When Marina asked if this competition drove Baranov out of business, the men vied with one another to answer her question: 'Not Baranov! He looked at the imported glass and said: "This is better than I make," and he closed down his shop to serve as agent for the other people.'

'I'd like to meet a man with such good sense,' Marina said, and when Baranov was brought before her, she saw a short, unkempt, pudgy man, bald as an iceberg, hands clasped over his belly as if preparing to bow before some approaching superior, but with sharp, dancing eyes that betrayed his eagerness to explore any proposition that might be laid before him.

'Do you know the fur trade?' she asked, and for half an hour he described recent developments in the Aleutians, Irkutsk and China, with a recommendation as to how Aleutian furs could with improved routing be speeded to St. Petersburg.

Her next question—'Are you earning much as a salesman in the glass business?'—provided him with an opportunity for an oration on how the Aleutians could be developed by someone with imagination and a little assured capital.

Before the hour ended she was satisfied that he was the man to represent both Russia and The Company in the Aleutians: 'Hold yourself in readiness, Mr. Baranov, while I do some investigating,' and when he was gone she returned to her directors with a succinct recommendation: 'The man we need in the islands is Aleksandr Baranov.' When the men protested that he had failed in everything, she reminded them: 'But you all said he was honest. I'm saying he has imagination . . . and force of character . . . and common sense.'

'Then why has he failed?' they asked, and she said: 'Because he did not have an old hand like me setting policy and bright young men like you providing him with funds.'

No better summary of Russia's needs in her American adventure than this had so far been voiced, either in Irkutsk or St. Petersburg, and the directors recognized it, but one cautious man protested: 'Baranov may be too old.'

'I'm twice as old,' Marina snorted, 'and I'd sail out to Kodiak tomorrow if I had to.'

'You might as well bring him in,' the men said grudgingly, and after a few minutes of Marina's expert questioning, Baranov revealed himself as a man who had a clear view of future possibilities, and she complimented him on his astuteness: 'Thank you, Mr. Baranov. You seem to have three attributes we seek. A surplus of energy, boundless enthusiasm and a vision of what Russia might accomplish in her islands.'

'I hope so,' he said modestly, bowing slightly.

The directors, aware that Marina was rushing them into decisions they might not wish to make, were so resentful of her intrusion that they started to demonstrate the flaws in her nominee: 'Mr. Baranov, we're sure you understand that The Company has two obligations. It must make money for us directors here in Irkutsk. And it must represent the wishes of the tsarina in St. Petersburg.' When Baranov nodded enthusiastically, one of the directors pointed out acidly: 'But you've never turned a steady profit on anything you've attempted.' Without embarrassment, the chubby merchant smiled and said: 'Always I've made a good start, then run out of money. This time I'd have the same good ideas and your job would be to see that I had the funds.'

'But could you keep the tsarina happy?' they asked, and with a tradesman's simplicity he answered: 'Make money and you keep everybody happy.'

'Well said!' Marina cried. 'That could be the motto of our company.' But now the directors raised an even more subtle objection: 'If you did become, as Madame Zhdanko seems to be recommending, our representative in the Aleutians, you would be Aleksandr Baranov merchant, and for protection you would be forced to rely upon some naval officer of noble lineage.' No one spoke, and then, from an older man: 'And as you know, there can be on the face of this earth nothing more contemptuous than a Russian naval officer looking down his nose at a merchant.'

Another director agreed, then all leaned forward as he asked: 'Mr. Baranov, do you think you could handle a naval officer?'

With the simple grace that characterized this unusual man, he replied: 'I've never been vain. I've always been eager to concede the other man any rights to which he considers himself entitled. But I've never been diverted from the task which requires to be done.' Looking from one man to the other, he added: 'I am only a merchant, and nobility is far beyond my reach. But I have something the noble officers will never have.'

'And what is that?'

In the quiet of this office in Irkutsk, Baranov the indefatigable dreamer gave his answer: 'I know that Imperial Russia must use the Aleutian Islands as stepping stones to a great Russian occupation of North America. I know that the supply of sea-otter pelts is already dwindling and that other sources of wealth must be found.'

'Such as what?' one of the directors asked, and without a moment's hesitation this amusing little fellow with the trigger-quick brain revealed his compulsive vision: 'Trade.'

'With whom?' someone asked, and he replied: 'With everyone. With the Hudson's Bay Company at Nootka Sound, with the Spaniards in California, with Hawaii. And across the ocean to Japan and China. And with the American ships that begin to invade our waters.'

'You seem hungry to embrace the entire Pacific,' a director said, and he replied: 'Not me, Russia. I see a constant movement of our empire to all corners.'

His vision was so grand, so all-encompassing that on the morrow the directors, frightened by its implications, brought in an officer who represented the tsarina and the more responsible elements in her government: 'Mr. Baranov, these men tell me that you have soaring visions.'

'The future of Russia demands them.'

'But have you any comprehension of Russian policy? No? Well, let me explain, and I shall use no shadowy meanings or oblique references. Our policy is to defend ourselves at all costs from dangers in Europe. That means we must do nothing to alert or offend anyone in the Pacific. If you become our man in the Aleutians, you must not offend Britain in North America, or Spain in

California, or the United States or Japan or China or even Hawaii. Because the fate of Russia will not be determined in these waters. It will be determined only in Europe. Do you understand?'

What Baranov understood was that the temporary concerns of Russia might be in Europe but that her long-term interests lay in the Pacific, and a powerful foothold in North America would, in the future, be of the greatest significance. But he also knew that as a mere merchant, he had no power base or standing from which to put his grand designs into operations, so he dissembled: 'I understand my orders. If I'm sent, I'm to tend the islands and touch nothing else.'

Now he was to receive his first lesson in imperial diplomacy, for the officer looked about the room, lowered his voice, and said quietly: 'Now wait, Mr. Baranov. No one said that, not at all. If you're sent to Kodiak, you're to probe outward in all directions. A fort here if the natives will allow it. Trade with Hawaii if practical. Exploration deep into California when the Spaniards aren't looking. And above all, secure us a foothold on North America.'

In the silence that followed, Baranov did not say triumphantly: 'That's what I was saying.' Instead, he nodded to the official, then to each of the directors, and said: 'Excellency, you're a wise man, a prudent man. You show me horizons I had not seen before,' and the tsarina's officer smiled bleakly, like a winter sun in northern Siberia.

Few imaginative men in history were given diplomatic assignments more precisely tailored to fit their peculiar talents than this one handed to Aleksandr Baranov. As a lowly merchant with no social standing, he was to compete on equal terms with haughty naval officers from the nobility. In a dying fur market he was to earn a profit. In an ocean where he must not make any overt moves he was to extend Russian power in all directions. And burdened with a wife who was never with him, he was to civilize and educate the wild islands of the northern seas. Nodding to those who were about to send him on this impossible mission, he said with quiet dignity: 'I'll do my best.'

Next day he learned that he would have help, for at a luncheon arranged by Madame Zhdanko he met with the Bishop of Irkutsk, who said ominously: 'The tsarina is aware that the international reputation of Russia depends upon how successful we are in establishing a Christian church among the natives, and, frankly, we've not accomplished much. If the tsarina ever learns how remiss we've been, control of Russian America will be ripped away from The Company and you'll never see a pelt again.' He glared at Baranov as if he were responsible for past error, and thundered: 'We expect you to mend these matters.'

'I can't do it alone,' this practical man replied. 'And I certainly can't do it with the kind of priests you've been sending to eastern Siberia.'

The bishop surrendered to these blunt truths: 'To correct my church's past deficiencies I shall be sending with you a priest of true devotion and unlimited promise, Madame Zhdanko's nephew, young fellow named Vasili Voronov.' At this, Marina rang a bell, and a servant brought into the room the young man who had already garbed himself in the black robes of a priest whose life was to be dedicated to the welfare of his church, and for the first time these two conspirators, the aspiring young cleric determined to save souls in the islands and the energetic businessman afire with a desire to enlarge Russia's power, met. Neither man, at that moment, appreciated how important in his life the other was to be, but each knew that a partnership had been established whose purpose was to Christianize, civilize, explore, make money, and extend the might of Russia deep into North America.

* * *

FATHER VASILI VORONOV, who left Irkutsk months before Baranov could arrange his affairs, had not been in Kodiak a full day in 1791 before he identified the man with whom he would wrestle for the spiritual leadership of Russian America. He was walking about, exploring his parish, when he saw coming toward him a tall, gangling Aleut man of untidy appearance and haunted eye who appeared to be roaming aimlessly, with no apparent affiliation with The Company, and from his disheveled looks, with not even a home. He was the kind of person Vasili would normally meet only when visiting him in some pastoral capacity, like the distribution of alms or the extension of sympathy over a death, but this old man had such a penetrating gaze, and was obviously so interested in the new priest, that Vasili felt compelled to know more about him.

Nodding austerely, a gesture that was not returned, he hurried back to Company officials and asked: 'Could that strange-looking Aleut be a shaman?' and the Russian said: 'We think so,' but Vasili uncovered no substantial proof until he queried Ensign Belov: 'Yes, he's a known shaman. Lives in a dugout among the roots of the big spruce.'

Satisfied that he was on the track of the devil, Vasili asked to see the acting manager, who listened respectfully as the young priest warned about 'the presence of Anti-Christ in our midst,' and agreed that Voronov should 'keep a sharp eye on that one.' But the priest's attention was soon directed to his major task, for a Company official informed him: 'You arrive at a propitious moment. A young Aleut wants to join the church, so you have your first conversion waiting.'

'I'll see him at once,' Vasili said, and the official made a correction: 'It's a girl,' and when the young priest inquired into the matter, he discovered that this was a conversion with strings attached, for when he met with Cidaq to discuss what conversion meant, he found her strangely ambivalent. Obviously she was interested in becoming a Christian, for this would mean that she could enter the favored world of the Russians, but she lacked the emotional intensity of a real convert, and this dualism was disturbing. And even after three long discussions, with her looking soulfully into his eyes as if in search of enlightenment, he failed to discover that she was playing games with him, and had he learned that she was interested in Christianity only as a weapon with which to castigate her would-be husband, he would have been outraged.

But fortified by his innocence, Father Vasili forged ahead with his instruction, and the beauties of Christianity were so real to him that Cidaq, despite her original scorn, began to listen. She was especially impressed with his stories of how Jesus had loved little children, for this had been one of the attributes of her Aleuts which she sorely missed, and twice when the priest elaborated on this she found tears coming into her eyes, a fact which Vasili noted.

Unaware that in fencing theologically with Father Vasili, she was confronting a far more dangerous adversary than either Ensign Belov or old Father Pëtr, she found herself increasingly seduced by the Christian testimony on redemption, for this was completely alien to the teachings of the shaman and the mummy; for them there was good and evil, reward and punishment, and no vagueness in the dichotomies, and to learn that there was another view of life in which a human being could sin, repent, and gain redemption, with the sin being totally erased, was new and perplexing. After asking a few preliminary questions which revealed her honest interest, and which provided Vasili with an opportunity for an enthusiastic elaboration of this cardinal principle, she unwittingly asked the question that would entangle her in the real and very beautiful mysteries of Christianity: 'Do you mean that a man who has done really awful things can be redeemed?'

'Yes!' he replied with great excitement. 'It's exactly that man that Jesus came here to save.'

'Did he come to the Aleutians too?'

'He came everywhere. He came especially to save you.'

'But this man . . .' She hesitated, dropped her question, and sat for some moments staring out the window toward the spruce tree. Then she said in a low voice: 'He is a real man, this one. He did terrible things to me, and now he wants to marry me.'

Vasili jumped back as if he had been struck, for he had supposed that Cidaq was thirteen or fourteen, and in the society he had known at Irkutsk, girls that age did not marry. 'How old are you?' he asked in a state of shock, and when she said 'Sixteen,' he stared at her as if seeing her for the first time.

But her last statement had contained so many surprising revelations that he had to sort them out. 'You're sixteen?' Yes. 'And a man wants to marry you?' Yes. 'And he's been a terrible man?' Yes. 'What did he do to people?'

In a low, controlled voice she said: 'He did them to me,' and Vasili gasped, for up to this moment he had seen her as a child of some maturity who was perplexed by the arrival in her primitive community of the advanced concepts of Christianity; to discover that she was of marriageable age and bewildered by problems relating to that was confusing. Had he known that she was grappling in her own unsophisticated way with the most profound moral and philosophical problems—nothing less than the nature of good and evil—he would have been astounded.

Keeping the discussion on the only level he comprehended, he asked: 'What could he have done to you?' and his continuing innocence made him so attractive to Cidaq, that in her sympathy for him she realized that she was already much older and better informed than he.

'He was ugly' was all she thought him capable of understanding at this time, but Vasili pressed on, unaware that he was about to detonate a bomb that would shatter him far more gravely than it would her: 'In what way did he harm you? Did he steal? Did he lie?'

A half-smile sneaked across her face as she stared into the eyes of this earnest young man who was trying to bring her into his religion, and she recognized his goodness of spirit and his desire to help, but she felt it was time he understood aspects of life that apparently he did not know. In quiet, unemotional words she told him of the depopulation of Lapak and the intended death of the women remaining there, and by the daze that came over his face she saw that he could not believe his people capable of such brutality, and for a while she lost him as he contemplated Russia.

But when she resumed her narrative she brought him back with a force that sickened: 'So I was sold to this man on the *Tsar Ivan*, and he kept me in the hold of the ship, without much food, and when he was through with me he passed me along to his friends and there was no day or night.' Now Vasili closed his eyes and tried to close his ears, but she continued with her account of her life in Kodiak: 'So this evil man was shipped off to the Seal Islands and I was free of him, but others like him caught me here in Three Saints, and I might have been killed, but the shaman brought help and we killed the worst of the men who abused me.'

Once more the details cascaded so rapidly that Vasili could not absorb them: 'What do you mean by *abused*?' and she replied: 'Everything.'

'When you say killed, you don't mean you *murdered* someone!'

'Not exactly.' He sighed, then gasped anew when she added: 'The shaman fetched five Aleuts with clubs and they beat the man to death and we hid his body under rocks.'

He leaned back, clasped his hands, and stared at this child, and when the physical horror at her account had passed, the psychological shock remained: 'Twice you said that you went to the shaman. You mean that strange old man who lives among the tree roots?'

'He's the keeper of our spirits,' Cidaq said. 'He and the spirits saved my life.'

This was too much: 'Cidaq, his spirits do not control the world. The Lord God does, and until you and your people acknowledge this, you cannot be saved.'

'But Lunasaq saved me, and he was able to do it only because the mummy warned us that the men were coming to kill us.'

'The mummy?'

'Yes. She lives in a sealskin sack and is very old. Thousands of years, she said.'

'Said?' he asked incredulously, and she replied: 'Yes, she talks to us about many things.'

'Who are *us*?'

'Lunasaq and me.'

'It's a deception, child. Don't you know that wizards can throw their voices? Make anything talk, even old mummies? The Lord has brought me here to end the reign of wizards and shamans, to bring you into the salvation of Jesus Christ.' He stopped, resumed his position near her, and stared once more into her dark eyes: 'They tell me you wish to join His regiments.' The metaphor missed her, and she asked: 'What?' and he translated: 'They said you wanted to become a Christian.'

'I do.'

'Why?'

'Because they said I couldn't marry Rudenko, that's the evil man I told you about, unless I did.'

Again the statements were incomprehensible, but patient questioning elicited the truth: 'You're converting only to get married?' Yes. 'Why would you marry a man who had treated you this way?' and because she was an honest young woman, devoid of duplicity when she was not playing games, she told him: 'I discussed this with the shaman and the ancient one, and they approved when I told them that I would fool you Russians and make believe that I was becoming a Christian so that I could marry Rudenko.'

Vasili was completely lost, unable to believe that she could have devised such a strategy, and confused as to why: 'But what did you hope to gain by such trickery?'

Again she had to be honest: 'When that evil man's heart was joyed with the thought of escaping the Seal Islands, I wanted to look at him and all the Russians and say in a loud voice: "It was all a sham. I did it to torment you. I will never marry you. Now back to the seals . . . for the rest of your life." '

In that ugly moment of complete revelation, Vasili no longer saw her as a delightful, innocent child of thirteen. He heard her low voice as a wanton cry from some ancient past when horrible spirits roamed the earth and devastated souls. He was shattered to learn that such hardness of heart could exist in a young girl like Cidaq, and he felt his own secure world trembling.

Of the horrors she had endured in the hold of the *Tsar Ivan* he had no conception, and the slaying which had rescued her from a continuation ashore he was able to dismiss as one of those fractures of the peace to be expected among sailors, but her proposed use of Christianity to exact revenge was abhorrent, and the discovery that her shaman had encouraged her in this perversion strengthened his resolve to eliminate shamanism from Kodiak. From here on, it would be a battle to the death.

But first he must attend to the spiritual needs of this child, and the purity of his own soul, which had been nourished and kept untarnished by the simple country faith of his father and mother, enabled him to regard Cidaq for what she was: half-child, half-woman, brave, honest and surprisingly uncontaminated by what had happened to her. She was, like him, a pure spirit, but unlike him, she was in mortal danger because of her traffic with a shaman.

Putting aside other tasks, he directed his considerable spiritual energy to the salvation of her soul, and with extended prayer, and exhortation, and the telling of noble Bible stories, he showed her the ideal nature of Christianity, and having discovered that she was moved by Christ's relation to children, he stressed that aspect, and now, having learned that she had been forced into sin, he emphasized especially the theory of redemption. Christ was no longer one who could redeem the hypothetical sinner Rudenko; He could now redeem Cidaq.

After five unbroken days of this incessant pressure, Cidaq said, with no conviction but only to please the young priest: 'I feel called to Jesus Christ,' and he interpreted this as a true conversion, shouting to the members of his little world: 'Cidaq is saved!' He told the Company managers, the sailors, the uncomprehending Aleuts that the child Cidaq was saved, at which the trader who had escaped murder at her hands growled: 'That one's no child!'

On Sunday after service in his rustic church at the end of the world, Father Vasili informed his tiny congregation that Cidaq had elected to march under the banner of Christ, and that she would, in conformance to the law of the empire, take an honest Russian name: 'Henceforth she will no longer be called by her ugly pagan name, Cidaq, but by her beautiful Christian name, Sofia Kuchovskaya. *Sofia* means *the wise, good one* and *Kuchovskaya* is the name of a fine Christian woman in Irkutsk.' Kissing his convert on each cheek, he proclaimed: 'You are no longer Cidaq. You are Sofia Kuchovskaya, and now your life begins.'

W ITH THE PERPLEXING simplicity that characterizes many devout believers, Father Vasili became fixed upon a course of theological action which seemed to him completely rational, indeed, inescapable: Sofia has become a Christian, and with her love and faith she can redeem the prodigal son Rudenko. Together they can find a new life that will bring honor to Russia and dignity to Kodiak.

Eager to believe that Rudenko was no more than a repetition of the Biblical prodigal son who had perhaps drunk too much or wasted his patronage in what was euphemistically termed *riotous living*, and incapable of believing that any man could be inherently evil, the young priest saw that his next task was to convert him as he had Sofia, and since he had never met the criminal, he asked Ensign Belov to take him to the darkened room where Rudenko still lingered.

'Be careful of this one,' the young officer warned. 'He killed three men in Siberia.'

'It's just such men that Jesus seeks,' Vasili said, and when he sat with Rudenko, still in manacles and assigned to the next ship returning to the Pribilofs, he found the murderer still convinced that the girl he had purchased on Lapak was going to prove the agency for his rescue from the Seal Islands. Assessing Father Vasili correctly as one of those benign priests who could be convinced of anything, he saw that it was important for him to win the man's good graces, and he presented himself as submerged in contrition: 'Yes, the girl you now call Sofia is my wife. I did buy her, but I developed a sincere affection for her. She's a good girl.'

'What about that sinful behavior in the hold of the ship?'

'You know how sailors are, Father. I couldn't stop them.'

'And the same kind of behavior here at Three Saints Bay?'

'I suppose you know that one of them was killed by the Aleuts? He's the one that did it all. Me? My father and mother were followers of Jesus. Me too. I love Sofia and am not surprised she's joined our church, and I hope that you'll make us man and wife.' He made this final plea with tears filling his eyes.

Vasili was so affected by the prisoner's apparent transformation that the only matter which remained to be clarified concerned the murders in Siberia, and Rudenko was eager to explain: 'I was wronged. Two other fellows did it. The judge was prejudiced. I've always been an honest man, never stole a kopeck. I wasn't supposed to be sent to the Aleutians, it was a mistake.' Now, speaking of his deep love for his wife, he became even more unctuous: 'My whole aim is to start a new life in Kodiak with the girl you call Sofia. Tell her I still love her.'

He delivered these sentiments with such a display of religious conviction that Vasili had to suppress a smile, and even though the priest knew that Rudenko had committed the murders, he was disposed to accept the man's longing to begin a better life. Everything Vasili had been taught about the wishes of God and His Son Jesus made him want to believe that repentance was possible, and next day when he returned to talk with the onetime criminal, he asked that the manacles be struck from his wrists so they could talk as man to man, and at the end of the dialogue he was convinced that illumination had entered Rudenko's life.

Yearning to save what the prophet Amos called 'a firebrand plucked out of the burning,' Vasili reported to Sofia: 'God's wishes will be served if you marry him and initiate a true Christian home.' In saying this, he was viewing her not as an isolated human individual with her own aspirations but as a kind of mechanical agent for good, and he would have been astonished had someone pointed this out. It was no tortured chain of theological reasoning which produced this impersonal conclusion, but rather the teachings his parents had hammered into him: 'Even the lowliest sinner can be reclaimed.' 'God is forever eager to forgive.' 'It's a woman's job to bring her man to salvation.' 'Woman must be man's beacon in the dark night.'

So when Vasili spread his plan before Sofia, he told her: 'You are Rudenko's beacon in the dark night,' and she asked: 'Now what does that mean?' and he explained: 'God, who now has you in His care, loves every man and woman on this earth. We are His children and He longs to see each of us saved. I grant your husband has had a troubled past, but he's reformed and wants to start a new life obedient to Christ. To do so, he must have your help.'

'I never want to help that one. Let him go back to his seals.'

'Sofia! He's a voice crying in the night for help.'

'I was crying in the night, real tears, and he gave me no help.'

'God wants you to fulfill your promise . . . marry him . . . save him . . . bring him into eternal light.'

'He left me in eternal darkness. No.'

The proposal was so repugnant, so contrary to common sense that she allowed Vasili no time to develop it. Leaving him abruptly, she marched openly to Lunasaq's hut, unaware that in joining the Christian church she had obligated herself to forswear all others, and especially shamanism. When she came to what had been the source of her spiritual instruction, she cried: 'Bring out the mummy! I want to talk with a woman who knows about these things.'

And when the mummy appeared, Cidaq blurted out: 'They've made me change my name to Sofia Kuchovskaya so I can be a good Russian.'

The mummy laughed: 'You could never be a Sofia. You are forever Cidaq.'

'And they say I must go ahead and marry Rudenko . . . to save him . . . because their God wills it.'

The mummy sucked in her breath so sharply that she whistled: 'Suppose you do ruin your life to save his, what will that accomplish?' and Cidaq explained: 'It's called salvation, his, not mine.'

The shaman was bold and unrelenting in his rejection of all the priest stood for: 'Always the interests of the Russians come first. Sacrifice the Aleut girl to make the Russian man happy. What kind of god gives such advice?' And as he ranted on, he revealed his motives to Cidaq, who thought to herself: He's afraid of the priest, knows that the new religion is powerful, but even so, a shaman may know what's best for Aleuts, so she listened respectfully as Lunasaq concluded his diatribe: 'They crush us step by step, these Russians. The Company makes slaves of us, they bring in their priests to assure that everything is the way their spirits intended. And each day, Cidaq, we fall lower.'

Now came an example of how the shaman's utilization of the mummy had endowed the ancient relic with a character and mind of its own, for when Lunasaq pretended to be the old woman, he became one, drawing upon his long familiarity with how women thought and expressed themselves: 'On the islands women served their men, making their clothes, collecting the fish and the berries, chanting when the men went out to fight whales. But I never felt that we were lesser, only different and with different capacities. What man on what island could bear a child? But this new faith, it's quite horrible, to sacrifice a girl like you to a brute like Rudenko in order to make him feel better.' She surprised Cidaq by laughing: 'Once we had a man like your Rudenko. Bullied everyone. Beat his wife and children. Once when he didn't do his share he caused the death of a good fisherman.'

'What did you do about it?' the shaman asked, and the old woman replied: 'There was a woman in our village who caught the most fish and sewed the best sealskin pants. One morning she told us: "When the kayaks return tonight, you three join me when I go out to unload his fish, and while he is still in the canoe, watch me." '

'What happened?' Cidaq asked, and she said: 'He came in. We waded out to get his fish. And at this woman's signal, she and I pulled him from his kayak and the two others joined us as we held him under the waves.' She reported this without gloating: 'Sometimes that's the only way.' And Cidaq asked: 'The other fishermen must have seen you. What did they do?'

'They looked the other way. They knew we were doing their work for them.'

'And what should I do?' Cidaq asked, and the old woman replied in heavy words: 'These are troubled times, child.' Then, realizing that this was an inadequate answer, she added: 'Some evening when the kayaks come home through the mists, you'll discover whatever it is that must be done.'

'Should I let them marry me to that one?' and in posing this question she saw nothing wrong in seeking moral advice from the shaman and his mummy, because she still felt herself a member of their world. She would look to her new priest for guidance in ethereal matters, to her old shaman for instruction in practical affairs.

The shaman, seeing an opportunity to reinforce his control over her, leaped at her question: 'No! Cidaq, they're using you for their purposes. This is corruption, the destruction of the Aleuts.' Fighting to preserve the Aleut universe of sea and storm and walruses and salmon leaping up the stream, he cried: 'It is not Rudenko who should be drowned at dusk, but the priest who gives such advice. He's here to destroy us.' But the mummy had other counsel: 'Wait. See what happens. In my long years I've found that many problems are solved by waiting. Will the baby be a boy or a girl? Wait nine moons and you'll see.' And Cidaq, as she left the hut, knew that the shaman spoke only of this year, this body of contradictions, whereas the mummy spoke of all the summers and winters there were to be, and their joint counsel made more sense to her than Father Vasili's.

S OFIA'S BRAZEN RETURN to the shaman's hut, and to a religion she was supposed to have forsworn, alerted Father Vasili to the fact that the struggle for the soul of this young woman was far from decided. She had been baptized and was technically a Christian, but her faith was so wavering that he must take dramatic steps to complete her conversion. Inviting her to the driftwood building he called his church, he sat her on a chair he had made, and began: 'Sofia, I know the pull of the old ways. When Jesus Christ took His new faith to the Jews and the Romans . . .' She understood not a word he was saying. 'It is not I who has brought the true religion to Kodiak, it is God Himself, who has said: "It's time those good Aleuts were saved." I didn't come here. God sent me. And He did not send me to the island. He sent me to you. God longs to take you, Sofia Kuchovskaya, to His bosom. And even if you don't want to listen to what I say, you cannot escape listening to what He says.'

'How can He tell me to marry a man like Rudenko?'

'Because you are both His children. He loves you equally. And He wants you to serve as His daughter to save His son Yermak.' For more than an hour he pleaded with her to embrace Christianity completely, to forswear shamanism, to throw herself onto the mercy of God and the benevolence of His Son Jesus, and he was shocked when she finally halted the persuasion by throwing at him the arguments she had heard in the hut: 'Your god cares nothing for the woman, me, only for the man, Rudenko.'

He jumped back as if he had been struck, for in the harsh rejection of this island girl he was hearing one of the permanent complaints against the Russian Orthodox faith and other versions of Christianity: that it was a man's religion established to safeguard and prolong the interests only of men, and he realized that he had instructed this capable young woman in no more than half the basics of his faith. Humbled, he took her two hands and confessed: 'I've left out the beauty of my religion. I'm ashamed.' Fumbling for a clear way to express the aspect of his faith that he had overlooked, he mumbled: 'God especially loves women, for it is they who keep life moving forward.'

This new concept, beautifully developed by the ardent young priest, had a powerful effect upon Sofia, who remained fixed to her chair in a kind of trance as Vasili collected from his altar area those revered symbols which summarized his religion: a depiction of the crucifixion, a lovely Madonna and Child carved by a peasant in Irkutsk, a red-and-gold icon showing a female saint, and an ivory cross. Distributing them before her in almost the exact pattern that Lunasaq had used when displaying his icons, he began pleading with her, using words and phrases best calculated to summarize the exquisite significance of Christianity: 'Sofia, God offered us salvation through the Virgin Mary. She protects you and all other women. The most glorious saints are women who saw visions and helped others. Through such women God speaks, and they beg you not to reject the salvation they represent. Abandon the evil old ways and embrace the new ways of God and Jesus Christ. Sofia, their voices call you!' and from all corners of the rude chapel her name seemed to reverberate until she feared she might faint, but then came the compelling words: 'As God has sent me to Kodiak to save your soul, so you have been brought here to save Rudenko's. Your duty is clear. You are the chosen instrument of God's grace. Just as He could not save the world without the help of Mary, so He cannot save Rudenko without your help.'

When Sofia heard these radiant words she realized that her new Christianity had been made whole. Hitherto it had concerned only men and their well-being, but these new definitions proved that there was a place for her too, and in these transcendent moments of revelation came a wholly new vision of what a human life could be. Jesus became real, the Son of Mary through the benevolence of God, and through Mary's intercession women could attain what had for so long been denied them. The women saints were real; the cross was tangible driftwood that had come to whatever island it was that these women saints occupied; but above all the other mysteries and the precious symbols of the new religion rose the wondrous message of redemption and forgiveness and love. Father Vasili had brought to Kodiak a new vision of the universe, and Sofia Kuchovskaya at last recognized and understood it. 'I give my life to Jesus,' she said with soft simplicity, and this time she meant it. Her conversion was completed.

Because she was a young woman of integrity, when she left the chapel she went directly to the shaman's hut, where she waited until Lunasaq brought forth his mummy: 'I've seen a vision of the new gods. I'm reborn this day as Sofia Kuchovskaya, and I've come to thank you with tears in my eyes for the love and assistance you shared with me before I found the light.'

A kind of wailing filled the hut, emanating both from Lunasaq, who realized that he was losing one of the major battles of his life, and from the mummy, who had known for many seasons that the changes taking place in her islands boded no good: 'Cidaq, you're like a young walrus tumbling on dangerous ice. Beware!' This accidental reminder that her name signified a young animal that ran free brought to mind the immense loss she was facing, and she whispered: 'I shall tumble, no doubt. And I shall miss your comforting. But new winds are blowing across the ice, and I must listen.'

'Cidaq! Cidaq!' the mummy cried, and this mournful intonation was the last time this child of the islands would hear that precious name, for now she knelt before the shaman, thanking him for his guidance, and before the mummy, whose sensible support had been so important to her in times of crisis: 'I feel as if you were my grandmother's grandmother. I shall miss you.'

Eager to retain contact with this worthy child, the shaman caused his mummy to say with no show of anxiety: 'Oh, but you can still come talk with me.'

Then came the wrenching moment: 'No, I cannot, for I am now a new person. I am Sofia.' With that, she bowed once more to these ancestral forces in her life, and with tears in her eyes she left them, apparently forever. When the hut was bereft of her presence, the old shaman and the ancient one remained silent for some minutes, then from the sack came a scream of mortal anguish, as if the end of a life as well as the end of an idea had come: 'Cidaq! Cidaq!' But the once-owner of that name would no longer hear.

IT WAS A wedding which none who attended would ever forget. Huge black-scowling Yermak Rudenko appeared almost pale from his long incarceration, beetle-browed, hunched over, embittered by his previous treatment but relieved at having escaped a return to the Seal Islands; he resembled in no way a bridegroom, for he looked much as he had in his previous incarnation, a skulking murderer of defenseless travelers. Sofia Kuchovskaya presented a striking contrast. Young, exuberant, lacking even the slightest sign of her former mistreatment at the hands of her intended, her hair marvelously long at her back, neatly trimmed almost to her eyelashes in front, and with that big smile in place, she looked to be exactly what she was: a young bride somewhat bewildered by what was occurring and not at all certain that she was in control.

The guests were all Russian or Creole; not one Aleut had been invited, since this day was held by the officials to be one when a native girl was being allowed entrance to Russian society. For her the evil old days of paganism were dead; the bright new days of Orthodox faith were beginning, and it was assumed that she would be grateful for the improvement in her status.

Even Rudenko enjoyed the metamorphosis. He was no longer just another brutal convict sentenced to the Aleutians or a runaway from the Seal Islands; he was now the agency for performing a major mission for the tsarina, the bringing of an Aleut pagan soul into Christianity. He bathed in his newfound respectability and behaved like a real Russian settler.

Father Vasili was engulfed in emotion, for Sofia was the first Aleut woman he had converted and the first Aleut of either sex whose entrance into Christianity could be taken seriously. But to him Sofia was much more than a symbol of the change that would sweep the islands; she was an admirable human being, triumphant over disasters that might have deranged a lesser person, and gifted with a keen sense of what was happening to her people. In saving this young woman, Vasili said to himself as he approached the canopy under which he would stand as he read the wedding service, Russia's getting one of the best. And in his black robes he married them.

There were singing and dancing by the Russian sailors and speeches by officials, who congratulated Sofia Rudenko on her entry to their society and her husband Yermak upon his release from custody. But on the third day these celebrations were marred by the sudden intrusion of the disheveled old shaman, who left his hut, came onto Company property, and in a wild shaky voice berated Father Vasili for having conducted such an infamous wedding.

'Go back, old fool!' a guard warned, to no effect, for the old fellow persisted in his disturbing accusations until Rudenko, irritated by this interruption of festivities at which he was the central figure, rushed at the shaman, bellowing: 'Out of here!' and when the old man pointed a long finger at the bridegroom, crying in Russian: 'Murderer! Debaucher of women! Pig!' Rudenko became so angered that he began clubbing at him with his fists, and he struck him so often and so hard that Lunasaq, staggered, tried to steady himself by holding on to his assailant, then took two sharp knocks to the head and fell into the dust.

Now Sofia intervened. Pulling her husband away, she knelt beside her old counselor and gently slapped his face until he regained consciousness. Then, ignoring her wedding guests, she started to lead him to his hut, but to her surprise Father Vasili interceded, placed his own arms about his enemy's trembling body, and led him to safety. Sofia, watching the two men disappear, knew that she should be with them and began to run after them, but Rudenko, infuriated by what had happened and his wife's participation, grabbed her by the arm, spun her around, and struck her so heavily in the face that now she lay in the dust. He might have kicked her, too, had not Ensign Belov intervened, lifted Sofia to her feet, and brushed away the dust. The dark blood dripping from her chin, where Rudenko's fist had cut the flesh enclosing her ivory labret, he could not wash away.

YERMAK RUDENKO WAS not disciplined for beating his wife or thrashing the shaman, because most Russians considered Aleuts less than human and proper objects for brutal punishment. In lawless Kodiak, Russian opinion was that all native wives, Aleut or Creole, profited from a justified beating now and then, while the castigation of the shaman was seen as a service to the Russian community. But when Father Vasili heard of what Rudenko had done while he was helping the shaman to his hut, and saw during prayer services the extent of Sofia's cuts, he did not go to console her, but he did accost Yermak: 'I've seen what you did to Sofia. This must never happen again.'

'Mind your business, Black Robes.'

'It is my business. Humanity is my business.' The frail priest looked ridiculous, speaking thus to the huge trader, and both men knew it, so with a big paw, not a fist, Rudenko pushed Vasili away, and the priest's feet became so entangled that he fell. Others saw the accident, for that was how it should be defined, since Rudenko did not strike the priest, and they interpreted it as yet another thrashing their bullyboy had administered to an interfering priest, and when they saw that Vasili was afraid to take counteraction, they began to denigrate him, until it became general opinion that 'we were better off with drunk old Father Pëtr, who knew enough to stay clear of our affairs.'

Some days later, when Sofia appeared at prayer with her left eye bruised, Father Vasili knew he could no longer avoid taking action, and when service ended he approached the bully, and said in a voice loud enough for others to hear: 'If you ever abuse your wife again, I shall have you punished.'

The listeners laughed, for it was obvious that the priest had neither the personal strength to punish Rudenko nor the authority to demand that some official do so, and this pusillanimity indicated the low estate to which The Company had fallen.

But this situation was about to change, a third visitor was about to reach Kodiak, and his arrival would make a vast difference. On a day in late June 1791 a sailor, looking down the bay on whose shores Three Saints stood, spotted a small sailboat that looked as if it had been slapped together from bits of wood and sealskin. Unfit for ocean travel or even the crossing of a lake, it was struggling to make landfall before it disintegrated, and the sailor wondered if he should first hurry to the shore to try to save it or run for help.

Choosing the latter option, he dashed toward town, shouting: 'Boat arriving! Men aboard!' Assuring himself that he had been heard, he ran back to the shore and tried to haul the boat onto the rocky beach, but the near-dead sailors, beards salted white, were unable to help. When he tried to do the job alone he recoiled in horror, for in the bottom of the boat lay the corpse of a baldheaded man too old for such adventure.

The first islander to reach the stricken craft was Father Vasili, who shouted to those coming behind: 'Hurry! These fellows are near death!' And as others arrived he started to administer rites to the body in the bottom of the boat, but as he did so the man groaned, opened his eyes, and cried with delight: 'Father Vasili!'

The priest jumped back, looked more closely, and gasped: 'Aleksandr Baranov! What a way to report for duty!'

When the exhausted men were lifted ashore and given hot drinks, it was Baranov, miraculously revived, who surprised both his shipmates and those who had rescued him—brushing off his muddied clothes, pressing down his few strands of hair, and taking command of the impromptu meeting at the edge of the bay. His report was brief, its items recognized by all who sailed in Russian ships:

'I am Aleksandr Baranov, merchant of Irkutsk and chief manager of all Company affairs in Russian America. I sailed from Okhotsk in August last year and should have reached here in November. But you can guess what happened. Our ship was leaky, our captain was a drunkard, and our navigator put us onto rocks seven hundred miles off course, losing our ship in the process.

'We spent a dismal winter on an island with no people, no food, no tools and no maps. We survived principally because this fine fellow, Kyril Zhdanko, son of our lady director in Petropavlovsk, had island experience and courage. He built this boat, sailed it to Kodiak, and now receives promotion as my assistant.

'If Father Vasili, a friend of mine from Irkutsk, will lead us to his church, we will offer thanks to God for our salvation.'

But when the procession reached the pitiful shack that served the priest as his church, Baranov voiced loudly a decision which informed the islanders that a new man with strong ideas was now in charge: 'I will not give thanks in that pigsty. Not fit for the presence of God, or the work of a priest, or the attendance of a chief manager,' and under the open skies beside the bay he bowed his bald head, folded his arms over his sagging belly, and gave awed thanks to the various miracles that had saved him from drunken captains, stupid navigators and a winter's starvation. At the conclusion of the prayer, which not the priest but he gave, he reached for Kyril Zhdanko's arm and said: 'It was a near thing, son,' and before that day ended he issued what sounded like contradictory instructions. To Zhdanko he said: 'Begin planning immediately to move our capital to a more likely spot,' but to Father Vasili: 'We'll start building you a real church tomorrow.'

Zhdanko, who knew that he would be doing most of the work, protested: 'But if we're leaving this place, why not wait to build our new church at the other spot?'

'Because I have no commission more important than giving our church proper support. I want conversions. I want children learning Bible stories. And I certainly want a decent church, because it represents the soul of Russia.'

But when Zhdanko discussed this preposterous decision in greater detail, he found that what Baranov really wanted was some building, any building, that carried on top the comforting onion dome of a Russian church: 'Sir, I don't believe we have anywhere on Kodiak a man who can build an onion dome.'

'Yes, you do!'

'Who?'

'Me. If I could learn to make glass, I can learn to make a dome.' And on the third full day of his residence in Three Saints this energetic little man identified a building which, if its top were knocked off, would support an onion dome which he, Baranov, would build. Assembling woodmen to provide him with timbers and sawyers to cut curved planks, he scratched Kodiak for nails and commandeered the few crude hammers, and soon he had rising in the cool air beside the cottonwood trees a fine onion dome, which he wanted to paint blue, but since Kodiak had only brown, he settled for that.

At the dedication he revealed his strategy: 'I want every board to be numbered, in sequence, because when we move to our new location, we'll take our dome with us, for I do believe we've built a good one.'

The incident of the dome convinced the people of Kodiak that this dynamic little man, so like a gnome, so unlike a manager of frontier posts, was determined to make Russian America a vital center of trade and government, and his broad interest probed into all aspects of life in the settlement. For example, when the attractive young girl Sofia appeared with a black eye, he summoned Father Vasili: 'What happened to that child?'

'Her husband beats her.'

'Husband! She looks an infant. Who is he?'

'A fur trader.'

'I should have known. Have him brought here,' and when the hulking brute shambled in, Baranov shouted: 'Stand at attention, you dog!' And when it became possible to conduct a reasonable disciplinary interview, the new manager snapped: 'Why do you think you can smash your little wife about?'

'She . . .'

Moving very close to him, the little fellow bellowed: 'She what?' and before Rudenko could respond, Baranov shouted: 'Fetch me Zhdanko!' and when that no-nonsense Creole appeared, adopted son of the powerful Madame Zhdanko and future governor of the Aleutians, Baranov gave him one simple command: 'If this swine ever beats his wife again, shoot him.' Turning with scorn to Rudenko, he said: 'I'm told you like to kick priests about, too. Kyril, if he ever touches or in any way threatens Father Vasili, shoot him.'

So a kind of rough order was established at dissolute Three Saints, a kind of peace descended upon the Rudenko household, and under encouragement from Baranov the new religion flourished while the former receded ever deeper into the shadows. Chief Manager Baranov attended mostly to the task of moving Three Saints to a more favorable spot at the other end of Kodiak, but he had completed only the provisional planning when Rudenko, chastened by the threats of death that Baranov had made, came crawling in to curry favor: 'Sir, have you ever hunted the great bear of Kodiak?'

When Baranov replied that he had not even heard of such a bear, Rudenko fell over himself to offer expert guidance into the beautiful wooded area well to the north of Three Saints where mountains rose out of the sea to the majestic height of nearly forty-five hundred snow-capped feet. A party of six was arranged, and during its expedition Rudenko showed himself to such advantage, tending to all matters and working diligently, that Baranov concluded he must have seen the fur trader at a temporary disadvantage in that first meeting, so on the third night out he told Yermak: 'When you behave yourself, you can be an admirable man,' and Rudenko replied: 'Under your new rules I always behave.'

When they detected signs that one of the monstrous Kodiak bears was in a region of rolling foothills and spruce trees, Rudenko assumed command,

sending four skilled helpers in various directions until they had circled the still
unseen beast. Then, with everyone moving toward the center of the area thus
subtended, they approached what Rudenko assured Baranov in whispered instructions was going to be a massive one: 'Stay behind me, Chief Manager.
These bears can be terrifying.' With his left arm he pushed Baranov to the rear,
and it was fortunate that he did, because at this moment a hunter on the
opposite side of the ring made an unplanned noise, alerting the bear, which
started running right at Rudenko.

When it loomed out from a cluster of trees, stopped, and reared upward to
scout what lay ahead, Baranov gasped, for it was immense, a towering animal
with awesome claws. Instinctively, Baranov sought a tree behind which to hide,
but the nearest one was too far away for him to reach before the bear swiped
at him with a raking paw. The few steps the manager did succeed in taking saved
his life, for the terrible claws penetrated only the back of his parka, ripping it
with a sickening noise. However, because Baranov was so slow and the bear so
swift, another swing of that mighty paw would surely kill the man, but here
Rudenko boldly thrust himself between man and bear, brought his rifle up, and
pumped a bullet upward through the animal's throat and into its brain. The
bear staggered sideways, struggled for nearly half a minute to maintain its
footing, and finally collapsed in the snow. When a shaken Baranov and
Rudenko measured the dead beast, they found that erect, it would have stood
eleven terrifying feet, and Baranov asked: 'How can they grow so large?' and
Rudenko explained: 'Kodiak's an island. More berries than you ever saw. Lots
of grass too, and nothing to bother the bears. So they eat and grow and eat and
grow.'

Baranov ordered that after the beast was butchered, with edible parts being
sent back to Three Saints, the skin be salvaged and mounted for his office, and
it was this towering stuffed bear, looming down from his corner, that subsequently saved Rudenko's life, for after he gained the good graces of the new
manager, he wrongly believed that this restored his right to thrash his wife, who,
as an Aleut, merited no regard. In a sickening scene he accused her of some
trivial fault, and when in her customary style she not only denied his charges but
mocked him with her silence, he became enraged and beat her about the face.

When boys ran to the shaman's hut to inform him of what Rudenko had
done, he asked only one question: 'You said she was bleeding?' and they replied:
'Yes, all over her mouth,' and then he knew that he must intervene, for if the
Russian managers had visible proof of such misbehavior and refused to take
action, he must. So he bade the mummy farewell and marched forth to what he
suspected might be his last undertaking as a shaman, but one he could not
avoid.

Thin, unkempt, bent slightly forward, an old man burning with a determination to preserve his one true religion and fight evil influences that were
paralyzing his people, he walked boldly to Rudenko's hut, crying as he approached: 'Rudenko, the spirits place a curse upon you! Never again will you
see your wife! Never again will you abuse her!'

Inside the hut Rudenko was sharing with two companions a kind of beer
fermented from cranberries, young spruce needles and seaweed, and the noise
outside became an irritation, especially when Rudenko heard words which
threatened him. Going to the improvised driftwood door, he was disgusted to
see the wretched figure of the shaman: 'Begone! Let honest men drink in peace!'

'Rudenko, you are cursed! Evil of great dimension will fall upon you!'

'Stop your caterwauling or I'll thrash you.'

'Rudenko, never again will you abuse your wife. Never again . . .'

From the doorway Rudenko leaped upon the shaman, and as he did so, his two cronies tumbled out, eager to beat the old man, even kill him, but it was Rudenko's intention merely to scare the shaman and drive him back to his hut. 'Don't hit him!' Rudenko shouted, but he was too late, for his friends dealt such heavy blows at the old man that he reeled back, fought to control his feet, and stumbled off toward his hut, where he collapsed among its roots.

Father Vasili quickly heard what had happened, and although he had opposed all that the wizard did, he knew that Christian charity required him to help this man who had endeavored to hold his community together prior to the arrival of Jesus. Hurrying to the hut, he entered for the first time the shaman's dark world.

He was appalled by the gloom, the dank earthen floor, the bundles piled here and there, but he was more aghast at the condition of the old man, for he lay in a heap, hair disheveled, blood speckling his gaunt face. Cradling the shaman's head in his arms, he whispered: 'Old man! Listen to me. You'll be all right.'

For a long time there was no response, and Vasili feared that his adversary was dead, but gradually the fierce old battler recovered the energy which had kept him struggling against great odds for the past years of Russian occupation and the onslaughts of Christianity. When he finally opened his eyes and saw who his savior was, he closed them again and lapsed into a lifeless stupor.

Father Vasili stayed with him most of that afternoon. Toward dusk he called for children to fetch Sofia Rudenko, and when she stood in the doorway of the hut, anguished by what she saw, he said simply: 'He's been hurt. He needs attention,' and with a fearful glance about the filthy, disorganized place, he asked in wonderment: 'Sofia, how could you have thought there was illumination here?' Without waiting for an answer, he left her, unaware that he had been present as the old religion of shamanism was perishing in its struggle with Christianity.

Unfortunately, the children who were sent to summon Sofia were nearby when Rudenko returned home, bellowing: 'Where's my wife?' and they told him: 'She went to the shaman's,' and this infuriated him so that he shouted for his two drinking companions: 'Let's finish that old fool right now!' and the three stormed out to the hut among the roots, found Sofia there tending the shaman, and Rudenko struck her across the face before tossing her out. Then they dragged the old man to his feet, and as he toppled forward, Rudenko met him with a mighty smash to the face, knocking him to the floor. As he fell the men kicked him to death, and in this brutal manner the Russian Christians terminated their debate with a pagan religion they were fated to displace.

THE SHAMAN'S MURDER provoked confusion for Kodiak's two administrators. Father Vasili, hearing of the death, hurried to the hut, where he assumed control, as if it were an adjunct to his church, which in a way it had been. Feeling no sense of personal triumph in the defeat of his rival, he lit a candle beside the corpse, stared, nauseated, at the blood which stained the earth, and felt tears of compassion welling in his eyes as sailors finally carried the dead body away. But after he had knelt to pray for the departed soul of his misguided but valiant opponent, he rose with renewed determination to end this plague of shamanism. With the zeal that young men experience when they know they are doing right, he began to gather the ridiculous assembly of twigs and bits of carved wood and scraps of polished ivory and the stones with which the shaman had presumed to converse with spirits, and piling all this junk into a heap where the body had lain, he scattered inflammable spruce needles over it and with his candle set it afire.

As the pile began to blaze, people ran up, shouting: 'Father Vasili! Get out . . . quickly!' But as he started to leave he saw in a darkened corner a sack made of sealskin, and when he opened it he found that it contained a dark, leathery substance, and half-choking from the noxious fumes of the burning symbols, he muttered: 'This must be the mummy Sofia spoke about,' and when he pulled the bag apart he found himself facing this stubborn old woman of thirteen thousand years.

With a shudder at the heresy she represented, he was about to pitch her into the fire when Sofia dashed into the hut, saw what was happening, and, too late, she screamed: 'No! No!' Then she watched with horror as flames consumed the old woman whose spirit had refused to die.

'What have you done?' she cried, and when the priest left the hut she followed him into the night air, shouting at him, but she was soon silenced by her outraged husband. With a savage slap he struck her across the face, and she fell to the ground. For a long moment she lay there, staring at the flaming hut, and then she surrendered to the great confusions of her life. 'She's fainted,' Father Vasili cried, and two Aleuts picked her up.

At this moment Chief Manager Baranov arrived at the scene, and when he learned of the shaman's murder he was aghast, for he appreciated the complications that might arise. Like all Russians, he held shamans in contempt, but he also recognized that they were a constructive agency in keeping Aleuts under control. 'Who did this thing?' he asked, and then he saw Sofia Rudenko, held upright by the two men, her face a mass of bruises.

'Rudenko,' Kyril Zhdanko replied. 'He did both. Killed the shaman. Beat his wife,' and without being instructed to do so, he set off to apprehend the criminal, who had now committed his fourth murder.

When the bearded hunter was hauled into the temporary office of the chief manager for punishment, Baranov took one look at him and remembered his earlier threat to shoot Rudenko if he ever again beat his wife, and now, since that offense had been compounded by murder, he had double reason to act. But as he faced Rudenko, he saw in the corner behind the wretch the huge stuffed figure of the Kodiak bear, and he remembered that he was alive only because of this renegade's bravery. With disgust he handed down his verdict: 'Rudenko, you're a disgrace to Russia and mankind. You have no right to live, except one. You saved my life when that one attacked, so I cannot shoot you as I threatened. Instead, your marriage to Sofia Kuchovskaya is annulled, for it should never have occurred in the first place, and you will be taken back to the Seal Islands, the only place I can think of that God might want you to live.'

Refusing to listen to Rudenko's impassioned promises of reform, he told Zhdanko: 'Guard him till the next boat sails north,' and with a glance of repugnance toward Rudenko, he left to console Sofia with news that her infamous marriage to Rudenko was dissolved.

But he had not taken into account the priest, Father Vasili, whose devout parents he had known in Irkutsk and whom he respected for his piety. When he told Vasili: 'The marriage between Sofia Kuchovskaya and the brute Yermak Rudenko is dissolved, you should never have married them in the first place,' Vasili replied firmly, relying first on the Gospel According to Mark: ' "What therefore God hath joined together, let not man put asunder," ' and then on an equally powerful injunction from the Irkutsk countryside: 'Thunder and lightning shall not separate a man and his wife, even though God Himself sends the thunder.'

'I didn't mean that I was annulling the marriage,' Baranov apologized. 'I meant that since you performed the ceremony, you would do so.'

But Baranov underestimated the zeal with which this young priest adhered to the teachings of his Bible: 'A vow is a solemn engagement undertaken in the sight of the Lord. There is no way I could annul it.'

'You mean, this fine child . . . her husband banished to the Seal Islands . . . as a Christian she has to live alone . . . the rest of her life?'

In his reply, Father Vasili revealed the harshness of his Christianity, for when the practical problems of a human life, in this case the welfare of the innocent child Sofia Kuchovskaya, conflicted with the teaching of the Bible, it was the child who had to sacrifice: 'I concede that Sofia has known great sorrow in her life, the tribulations of Job, and now we place yet one more upon her. Well, God nominates some of us to bear His yoke so that others can appreciate His ultimate grace. That is Sofia's assignment.'

'But to waste her life . . . ?'

The priest was adamant: 'That's the cross she must bear,' and he would not deviate from this harsh judgment.

At this juncture it must have seemed to the people of Kodiak—Russian and Aleut alike—that in the great confrontation between the two religions, Father Vasili had triumphed. He had bested the shaman, who was dead, removed the pernicious influence of that provocative mummy, whose ashes were banished to a proper grave, and had won for himself a church with an onion dome, symbol of the best in Russian religion. But anyone who offered that hasty judgment would be ignoring the power of the Aleutian Islands to strike back.

Scientifically, the disaster could be easily explained, but to the Aleuts it was obviously the revenge that Lunasaq and the destroyed mummy exacted on Father Vasili.

A vigorous earthquake eighteen miles below the surface of the Pacific Ocean caused a massive submarine cliff three miles below the surface to collapse. The crumbling cliff spewed downward nearly a cubic mile of mud and rock, and this dislocation created a monstrous tsunami which sped eastward as a gigantic lateral surge of water moving deep within the ocean, never creating a visible wave of more than two feet at the surface but rushing with fearsome power toward Kodiak at a speed of four hundred and sixty miles an hour.

When it reached the mouth of Three Saints Bay it did not come as one engulfing tidal wave; its forerunners entered quietly, but the following waves kept coming and coming, and their speed was so great and the pressure so persistent that the water rose rather quietly ten feet, then twenty, and finally fifty-seven. For nine dreadful minutes it hung there, after which it rushed out of the bay with such gurgling force that it sucked all things along with it.

Father Vasili, scrambling over the rocks to save the precious icons of his newly domed church, had reached only a small hill when he saw a sight so infuriating that it made him question the justice of the God he served. The turbulent waters were not touching the lone spruce which had served as the shaman's temple, but they were tearing the Christian church from its foundations, tumbling it this way and that until it smashed to splinters on a cluster of rocks.

The loss of life at Three Saints, pinched in as it was along the bay, would have been tremendous had not young Kyril Zhdanko responded to the first sign of the incoming surge: 'Terrible danger! I saw this once on Lapak!' and he released the prisoner Yermak Rudenko to help rush people to higher ground. The powerful convict responded by dragging first the dazed Father Vasili and then Chief Manager Baranov up the side of a steep hill. Perching them like children on a rock that looked as if it might remain above the surging waters, he had gone back down the hill a third time to rescue others when a towering wave swept in, turned all things upside down, and sucked him to his death.

THE GREAT TIDAL wave of 1792 solved problems for one Russian at Three Saints but raised perplexing difficulties for another. Chief Manager Baranov had decided during his first hours at this spot that the location had not been well chosen and that an anchorage to the north would be more advantageous. The site he chose seven months before the wave demonstrated his mind-set, for spiritually and emotionally Three Saints had looked backward toward Russia and its affiliations with the past, while the town of Kodiak would look eastward toward the future and the looming challenges of North America. Three Saints carried an umbilical cord to old Siberia, Kodiak to new Alaska.

As he and Zhdanko labored over their plans for the new capital, he asked Kyril: 'Are you the natural son of Madame Zhdanko, of Petropavlovsk?'

'Adopted.'

'Was your father the trader they tell about?'

'My birth father must have been some Russian serving on Lapak Island. My true father, Zhdanko.'

'What happened to him?'

'He was eighty-three. We came home from trading furs. Walked from Yakutsk to Okhotsk . . .'

'I've done that.'

'He was tired, almost worn out, that I could see. When we reached Petropavlovsk, I said: "Father, let's rest," but he had always longed to see Kodiak. Wanted to control the peltries here. So we set forth when he was eighty-five.'

'What happened?'

'On the way he died. We bound him with rocks from the ballast and pitched him into the Bering Sea. Not far from the volcano that guards Lapak Island. As a boy I used to sit with him and watch its glow in the twilight.'

Baranov stopped in his planning, knocked on wood, and said fervently: 'By the grace of God, I'd like to see eighty-five. The building you and I could do!'

The second man whose life was sharply modified by the tidal wave was Father Vasili, for on the mournful day when the sixteen victims of the flood were buried, he mumbled when required to pray for the departed soul of Yermak Rudenko, for he could not in decency, when so many present knew the truth, embroider that brutal man's life with platitudes. And even had he been able to exalt charity over reality, he would have been deterred when he looked across the grave to where Sofia Kuchovskaya stood impassively staring at the rumpled soil which would cover her accursed husband.

In that accidental glance the young priest saw in vivid flashes the history of this valiant girl: her abandonment on Lapak, her hideous escape in the hold of a ship, the beatings and abuses, her fealty to an old religion, her embracing of the new. She was, he thought, a young woman of crystal character who had allowed nothing to sully her and who had represented the best of an old society that was dying to make way for a new. He saw her firm jaw, the dark knowing eyes, the controlled little body, and finally, as the grave was closed, the irrepressible smile, not in triumph over evil but in pleasure at the ending of an episode. He could almost hear her sigh as she looked about as if to ask: 'Now what?'

On the day after the funeral Baranov summoned Father Vasili to the ruins of his office to hand him a surprising commission: 'I consider myself responsible for every human being in these islands, Russian, Creole, Aleut, Koniag, makes no difference to me.'

'I feel the same way, Chief Manager.'

'But I intend doing something about it. How many children did the tidal wave leave without parents?'

'Fourteen, fifteen at least.'

'Start an orphanage for them. This afternoon.'

'But I have no funds. The bishop promised . . .'

'With you, Vasili, the bishop promises and never delivers. With me, it's The Company. "You'll have everything you need, Baranov," but the money never arrives.'

'Then how can I . . . ?'

'I will pay. The honor of Russia demands it, and if the gentlemen who run The Company are not considerate of Russia's honor, the merchant who runs Kodiak is.' And forthwith he provided the money for the orphanage out of his own meager salary.

'But who's to run it?' he asked the priest, and after some reflection, Vasili remembered how Sofia, during her conversion, had been so deeply moved by his tales of Christ's care for children, and he said: 'Sofia Rudenko would be ideal.'

'She's not more than fifteen, just a child, really.'

'She's seventeen.'

'I can't believe it,' but when she was sent for, and Baranov asked bluntly: 'Child, how old are you?' she said: 'Seventeen,' and he asked: 'Do you think you could run an orphanage?' and she asked: 'What's that?' When it was explained, she said: 'Father Vasili told me that Jesus said "Suffer little children to come unto me." Children are my joy,' and the Kodiak orphanage was established with Baranov's funds and Sofia's love.

Baranov, determined to see anything he launched succeed, told Vasili: 'Get her started properly,' and the young priest maintained supervision, teaching her the rudiments of her new job and instructing the orphans in their new religion. As he worked close to Sofia he was encouraged by the enthusiastic manner in which she became mother to the infants, older sister to the girls and boys. She was so influential with the youngsters that an older Aleut told Baranov: 'If she was a man, she'd be our new shaman,' but Sofia knew this was not accurate, for a real-life shaman had slipped into the remnants of Three Saints in an effort to keep the Aleuts away from Christianity, but his magic now seemed shabby, and compared with the spiritual miracles that Sofia at her orphanage and Father Vasili in his improvised church were accomplishing, he achieved nothing and left.

As Sofia worked at the orphanage, Vasili had repeated opportunities to observe how she was maturing as she entered her new life, and in multiple ways he was drawn to her. She was serious, yet always ready to burst into her warm smile. She was industrious, but available for rough-and-tumble play with her children, and above all, she made people of whatever age or racial background happy in her presence. And in the way that happens with certain fortunate women, as she approached her twenties she grew more lovely, more complete. A full inch taller now, her face less rounded, the whalebone labret slightly less conspicuous, she was what one visiting sea captain called: 'That adorable lass,' and one evening as Father Vasili left the lively warmth of the orphanage and walked under the stars to the bleak building serving as his church, he looked up at the shaman's spruce and cried aloud: 'I was never meant to be a black. I've been in love with her since the day I stepped on this island.'

He interpreted it properly as an inevitable development and in no manner as shocking as it would have been had he served in the Roman Catholic clergy, where celibacy was an act of faith and dedication; in the Orthodox branch, as he had observed in the case of his own father, far more than half the priests were whites who had married with the encouragement of their bishops, who, even though they were black and celibate, preached: 'Marriage is the normal condition of man.' To switch from black to white involved a change only in direction, not faith.

But even such a limited switch was not easy to accomplish, so on the day that Three Saints shut down, with all Company work moving to Kodiak, Vasili went to talk with Baranov, who was packing the one small box which held the few possessions he had been able to accumulate in the colony.

'Chief Manager, I seek a boon.'

'Granted. No manager ever had a better clergyman.'

'I want you to write to my bishop in Irkutsk.'

'He won't give you a kopeck. You'll have to make do.'

'I want him to release me from my vows.'

'My God! Are you leaving the church? Your parents . . .'

'No! No! I want to cease being a black. I seek to be a white.'

Baranov sat heavily upon his box and stared at the young cleric, and after a very long silence, he said in a voice so low that Vasili could scarcely hear: 'I've been watching you, Vasili, and I know your problem. I know because I, too, have fallen in love with an island woman. And I shall take her as my wife.'

Shocked by such a confession, the young man became once more a monitory priest: 'Aleksandr Andreevich, that's a terrible thing to say. You have a wife in Russia.'

'True, and she says she may join me one of these days, but she's been saying that for twenty-three years.'

'Aleksandr Andreevich, if you commit bigamy, I shall have to report you to St. Petersburg.'

'I'm not going to marry her, Father Vasili, just take her for my wife till my real wife comes.' Then he added in a low voice: 'Which will be never, and I cannot live alone.'

Vasili, who had come to consult about *his* problem, found himself engulfed in Baranov's: 'She's a wonderful woman, Vasili. Speaks Russian, has dutiful parents, is neat in the house and can sew. She promises she'll take the Russian name Anna and attend our church regularly.' Looking up from his box, his round face beaming, he asked: 'Have I your blessing?'

There was no way this young priest could sanction such cavalier treatment of the marriage vow, but on the other hand, to untangle his own affairs he had to have Baranov's letter to the bishop, so he temporized: 'Will you write to my bishop?' and by this digression he let it be known that he would not publicly castigate Baranov if the latter took a common-law wife: 'After all, Chief Manager, I'm not leaving the church. I just want to switch from black to white.'

'In order to marry Sofia?'

'Yes.'

'I'll write. If I was younger, I'd take her myself.' But then he broke into such irreverent laughter that Vasili blushed, thinking that Baranov was making fun of him. He was, but not in the way Vasili feared. 'Remember what you said when I wanted Sofia's marriage to Rudenko annulled?' And now he gave a good imitation of the serious young priest: ' "A vow is a solemn engagement undertaken in the sight of the Lord. There is no way I could annul it." Well, my young friend, you're certainly eager to annul your own vows.'

Vasili blushed again, so deeply that Baranov snapped his fingers at having made a discovery: 'You haven't asked her yet, have you?' and Vasili had to confess that he had not. 'Come along!' the energetic manager cried. 'We do it now.'

And on his stout little legs he ran to the orphanage, where he summoned its startled mistress. Facing her, with Vasili's hand in his, he said: 'Since I think of myself as your father, I must inform you that this young fellow has asked for your hand in marriage.' Sofia did not blush, or at least if she did, it was not visible through her golden skin, but she did bow, keeping her head down until she heard her priest saying softly: 'I labored to save your soul, Sofia, but equally to save you. Will you marry me?'

She now knew enough to understand the meaning of his black robes, which she reached out to take between her fingers: 'What of this?' and he said: 'I have thrown it off as you threw off your sealskin dress when you became a Christian,' and, with a smile that swept her face, she said: 'I would be proud.'

Since two or three years sometimes elapsed between the arrival and departure of a ship at Kodiak, there could be no quick response to Vasili's application to change from black to white, and even if permission had been obtained, it might be another three years before a priest arrived to conduct a wedding, so Baranov made a practical proposal: 'If I'm going to live with Anna as my wife, you should do the same with Sofia . . . that is, until a priest can come to straighten things out.'

'I couldn't do that.' But then Baranov cited the ruling theology of the distant Aleutians: 'The tsarina's in St. Petersburg, and God's high in the heavens, but we're here on Kodiak, so let's do what's necessary.'

In this bizarre manner the two leaders of Russian America, old manager, young priest, took their island wives. Cidaq Sofia Kuchovskaya Rudenko Voronova would become the mother of that later Voronov who would illuminate Russian America and bring into fruition Baranov's dreams. The gifted Anna Baranova would serve as the chief manager's mistress for years and give birth to two excellent children, one of whom would become the wife of a later Russian governor. Upon word of the death of the real Madame Baranova, never seen in Siberia or the islands, Anna would become Baranov's legal wife, whom he presented to all as 'the daughter of the former king of Kinai.' Visitors found no difficulty in accepting this legend, because she was indeed queenly.

IN THE PROTRACTED battle between shamanism and Christianity, the latter won, but it was a murderous victory, for when Vitus Bering's men first stepped ashore on the Aleutians in 1741, the islands contained eighteen thousand, five hundred healthy men and women who had adapted masterfully to their treeless but sea-rich environment. When the Russians departed, the total population was less than twelve hundred. Ninety-four percent had been starved, drowned, forced into slavery, murdered, or otherwise disposed of in the Bering Sea. And even those few who survived, like Cidaq, did so only by merging themselves into the victorious civilization.

VI

LOST WORLDS

Within the shadow of the lovely volcano that guarded Sitka Sound, the Great Toion lay dying. He had for thirty years dominated the multitude of mountainous islands which comprised his domain and had brought order among the headstrong, sometime mutinous Tlingit Indians, who were reluctant to follow the lead of anyone. They were a powerful lot, these Tlingits, resembling in no way the more placid Eskimos of the far north or the gentle Aleuts of the island chain. They loved warfare, enslaved their enemies when possible, and were afraid of no man, so that after the Great Toion died, relinquishing the power he had accumulated so craftily, the Tlingits knew that there might be a period of confusion, warfare and sudden death before the next toion proclaimed and established himself.

When the big slave known as Raven-heart became aware that his master was dying, panic captured him, for he realized that the very strengths which had made him the prime slave of the toion—his bravery in war, his alertness in defending his master—would condemn him to death, for when a toion died, it was the custom among the Tlingits to kill almost at that instant three of his finest slaves so that they could attend him properly in the world beyond the mountains. And since Raven-heart was by any judgment supreme among the toion's slaves, he would be awarded the honor of being the first to have the back of his neck stretched across the ceremonial log, while a smaller log, held by four men, was pressed down upon the front of his neck until life was crushed out—strangling him without marring his body for use in the next world.

The big fellow had never before been afraid. His history was one of constant struggle against odds, and in the mainland valley which his clan occupied he had been a principal defender against enemies who tried to invade from the higher lands to the east. He became known as a champion, the one on whom the valley Tlingits depended for their protection and their freedom, and even when the more powerful Tlingits from Sitka Island, led by the Great Toion, invaded in their canoes, sweeping all before them, when they came up against Raven-heart and his nine companions, they were halted, and it required two dozen of the invaders four bruising days to overcome Raven-heart's men. Three of his companions died in the battle, and he would have been among the dead except that the toion himself commanded: 'Save that one!' and he was entangled in vines cleverly thrown about him, immobilized, and hauled before the victorious chief, who asked: 'Your name?'

'Seet-yeil-teix,' he replied in a surly manner, using three Tlingit words that meant *spruce-raven-heart*, and when the toion heard that his conspicuous captive was a Raven he smiled, for he himself was an Eagle, and although this implied natural competition against the Ravens, he had to acknowledge that a warrior, if he was a good Raven, could be exceptionally clever and formidable.

'How did you win your name?' he asked, and his captive replied: 'I was trying to jump from this rock to that, fell into the stream. Wet and angry, tried again. Fell again. This time very angry, tried again. Just then a raven tried to pull loose something from a spruce limb. Slipped backward, tried again. And my father shouted: "You're the raven." '

'The third time, did you make the jump?'

'No. And the raven failed too. When I was bigger I jumped, and my name remained.'

Because of his unusual persistence, he had been valuable to his tribe when unusual tasks confronted them, and he succeeded so often that he acquired a daring approach to everything, whether in battling other clans in actual warfare, or in building a house, or decorating it with the proper totems when it was completed. It was this daring which had led to his capture, for when the Great Toion's army moved against Raven-heart's clan, the latter led the defensive sorties and raced so far ahead of his supporters that he was easily surrounded.

Now, as the toion gasped away his final moments, making death for Raven-heart inevitable, the captive made his boldest move. Slipping away from the wood-and-wattle big house in which the toion had lived since gaining ascendancy, Raven-heart moved carefully among the six tall totem poles that marked the place and edged toward the heavily forested area to the south. Cautiously he endeavored to slip into the deeper part of the forest, but was prevented by the noisy arrival of sixteen mourners coming from that direction. Jumping nimbly behind a large spruce, he heard them pass, lamenting the approaching death of their leader, but when they were gone, he leaped onto the path they had been following and dashed headlong into the saving comfort of the tall trees and the shady glens they protected. Once safe among the spruce, he began to run with an almost demonic fury, for his strategy required that he be removed as far as possible when the old man died.

He reasoned: If they can't find me at that moment, they can't kill me then. Of course, if they catch me later, they will kill me for having run away. But I have one good chance. If I can find an American ship and get aboard, I can tell them I was busy bartering, and they'll have to believe that. This strategy was not irresponsible or ill-founded, because he was one of the Tlingits who had learned enough rudimentary English to conduct trade negotiations with the Americans, whose ships stopped in Sitka Sound with considerable frequency.

So as he ran, he began calling silently upon those ships he remembered servicing with deer meat and fresh water when the Americans had come for peltries: *White-Dove*, come flying. *J.B. Kenton*, help me. *Evening Star*, shine to guide me.

But now the bad weather for which Sitka was famous descended like a feathery blanket, gray, thick and hanging but a few feet above the earth and the surface of the bay. It quickly became impenetrable, and any chance Raven-heart might have had of saving his life by attaching himself to some trader vanished, and for three agonizing days he hid among the spruce trees along the edge of the bay, waiting for the fog to lift.

On the evening of the third day, when he was hurting from hunger, he heard a muffled sound which electrified him. It seemed to be the firing of a cannon such as mariners used to create echoes from which they could deduce their approximate distance from the looming peril of rocky shores, but it was not repeated as would have been the case had this been such a probing shot. On the other hand, the cannon fire might have been so effective that only one shot was required, and with this hope to feed on he fell asleep in the lee of a fallen spruce.

In the early dawn he was awakened by the raucous voice of a raven, and no better signal from the other world could have been devised, because all Tlingits, from the beginning, had been divided into two moieties, the Eagle Clan and the Raven, and every human being on earth belonged to one or the other. Ravenheart was of course a Raven, which meant that he must defend that moiety in games between the two clans and in contests of a more serious kind, such as the providing of totem poles for the village commons or the bringing in of fish. As a Raven, he must marry only an Eagle, a provision established thousands of years earlier to protect the cleanliness of the race, but the child of a Raven man and a woman Eagle was an Eagle, and as such, was dedicated to the furtherance of that clan.

There was a belief among the Tlingits, and he subscribed to it, that although Eagles were apt to be more powerful, Ravens were by far the wisest, the wittiest and the cleverest in utilizing nature or in winning advantages over adversaries without recourse to fighting. It was known that mankind received water, fire and animals to feed upon through the cleverness of the First Raven, who outsmarted the primordial protectors of those boons to mankind. 'All the good things were kept apart,' his mother's brother had told him, 'and we lived in darkness, cold and hunger until the First Raven, seeing our sorrow, tricked the others into letting us share these good things.'

Now, when the raven cawed in the early dawn, he knew it was a signal that some rescue ship lay in the bay, and he ran to the water's edge expecting to see the vessel which might have fired the cannon the night before, if that was indeed the sound he had heard. But when he stared into the fog he saw nothing, and in his disappointment he could feel the crushing log upon his throat. Disconsolate and starving, he leaned against a spruce and glared at the invisible bay, still shrouded in gray, and in his extremity, very close to death, he again pleaded silently with the American ships to show themselves: *Nathanael Parker*, help me. *Jared Harper*, come close to save my life.

Silence, then the sound of iron against wood, and the arrival of a vagrant breeze which moved the fog a little; then, mysteriously, as if some powerful hand were drawing aside a curtain, the revelation of a shiplike form, followed by its quick submersion in the shifting mist. But the ship was there! And in desperation, ignoring the danger he placed himself in by revealing his position to searchers who might be trailing him, he ran to the shore and knee-deep into the water, crying in English: 'Ship! Ship! Skins!'

If anything could lure the Americans, assuming they were Americans, to shore, it would be the promise of otter skins, but there was no response. Edging deeper into the water, in which he could not swim, he cried again: 'Good Americans! Otter skins!' Again there was no response, but now a stronger gust of wind swept aside the fog, and there, not two hundred yards away, miraculously safe amid the dozen tree-studded islands that protected Sitka Sound, lay the Boston trader *Evening Star*, with which he had traded in the past.

'Captain Corey!' he shouted, dashing into the waves and flailing his arms, and making such a commotion that someone on the brig had to see him. An officer put a glass upon him and called to the bridge: 'Native signaling, sir!' and a boat was lowered and four sailors rowed it hesitantly shoreward. When Raven-heart, overjoyed at being saved, waded forward to meet it, he found himself facing two rifles pointed right at his chest and heard the stern command: 'Stand, or we fire!' Captain Miles Corey of the trader *Evening Star*, fifty-three years old and Pacific-hardened, having known too many commanders who had lost their ships, did not take any risks, anywhere, at any time. Before leaving the *Evening Star* in the skiff, the sailors had been warned: 'It's one Indian. But there could be fifty lurking in those trees.'

'Stand, or we fire!' the men repeated, and as Raven-heart froze, waist-deep in water, one of the four shouted: 'My God, it's Raven-heart,' and he reached out his paddle so that the Tlingit with whom he had traded before could make his way into the boat.

It was a gala reception that Captain Corey and First Mate Kane arranged for their old friend, and they listened attentively as he explained the predicament which had sent him alone into the forest. 'You mean,' Captain Corey asked, 'that you'd have been killed? Just because the old man died?'

In his broken English, Raven-heart pleaded with them: 'You say me on ship four days, eh? You say fog too much, eh? Four days.'

'Why is four days so important?' Kane asked, and Raven-heart turned to explain. The two men were of about the same size, each a muscular, fearless brawler, and for that reason Kane, the former harpooner, was attracted to the Tlingit, who explained: 'I suppose to be killed three days ago. Suppose run away, catched, killed now. But if I on ship, trading with you . . .' By lifting his hands as if relieving them of bonds, he indicated that with such an excuse he might be spared.

The omnipresent Sitka fog had once more descended upon the *Evening Star*, this time so heavily that even the tips of the two masts were invisible from the deck, so Corey and Kane assured the endangered slave: 'We'll probably be in this soup two more days. You're safe.' And to celebrate they broke out a bottle of good Jamaican rum, and there, in Sitka Sound, protected by the volcano and the circle of unseen mountains, they reveled. When Raven-heart felt the fine dark liquid exciting his throat, he relaxed and told the Americans of the many pelts he had helped assemble for them, and they were so pleased by this intelligence that they in turn showed him the goods that they had brought from Boston to enrich his Tlingits.

'These are the casks of rum,' Captain Corey said, indicating the eighteen barrels stowed in safety belowdecks, 'and what do you suppose these are?' Raven-heart, with a copper ring through the septum of his nose, studied the dozen squared-off rectangular wooden cases, and said: 'Me not know,' where-upon Corey ordered a sailor to draw the nails—'And save them'—from one of the lids, and there, nestled in oil-soaked rags, lay nine beautiful rifles, and below them, in similar ranks of nine, twenty-seven others. These twelve boxes, packed in orderly manner by the gunsmiths of Boston, contained four hundred and thirty-two first-class long-barreled rifles, and the kegs stowed behind had enough powder to last two years, along with supplies of lead for bullets and molds in which to make them.

Raven-heart, satisfied that no one could order him killed if he brought such power to his captors, smiled, grasped Captain Corey's hands, and thanked him profusely for the tremendous boon the Bostonians were bringing the Tlingits: rum and guns.

* * *

A MINOR OFFSHOOT from the powerful Athapascans who populated interior Alaska, northern Canada and much of the western United States, the Tlingits were a collection of about twelve thousand unique Indians who had moved far south into what would later be Canada and then fishhooked back north into Alaska, with their own language and customs. Divided into various clans, they occupied the southern littoral of Alaska and especially the big offshore islands, their principal location being the excellent land surrounding Sitka Sound on the island of that name.

The people of the dead toion had chosen for their center a conspicuous promontory in the sound, one which rose to a small hill that dominated every-thing. It was an excellent site, surrounded by at least a dozen rude mountains that formed a protective semicircle to the east, with the majestic cone of the volcano standing as beacon to the west. But as the Russian Baranov had learned when he first saw the sound some years before, one of its most attractive features was the horde of islands, some no bigger than a tea table, others of considerable size, which speckled the surface of the water, breaking up surging storm waves that would otherwise have roared in from the Pacific.

When the fog finally lifted, Captain Corey gingerly threaded his *Evening Star* through the islands, bringing her some hundred yards from the foot of the hill, and fired a cannon to inform the Indians that he was prepared to trade with them for pelts, but when the time came for such trade, the Americans found themselves in a predicament. Ever since the ambushing of Captain Cook in the Hawaiian Islands, captains and crews had remained on their trading ships and invited natives to come aboard with their goods, while sailors armed with rifles maintained watch. However, at Sitka the Tlingits were preoccupied with bury-ing their Great Toion, so the Americans launched a longboat, and with Raven-heart perched in the prow, they ignored custom and rowed ashore.

At first, the grieving Tlingits waved them away, but when those in charge of the ceremony saw the slave Raven-heart standing amongst the visitors, they announced that they had spent the last five days seeking him as one of the three slaves to be slain so as to provide the toion with servants in the next world. When Captain Corey and First Mate Kane realized that the Tlingits were determined to take Raven-heart from them and put him to death, they indicated that they would not allow this, but since they had only four sailors in the boat, and they without arms, they knew that the Tlingits could overpower them if they tried to make a serious protest. So with a sense of sinking shame at abandoning a good man who had placed his life in their care, they made no further objection when some of the elders seized Raven-heart and started hauling him to the ceremonial log.

But now an important man in Tlingit history stepped forward, the bold young chieftain Kot-le-an, a tall, sinewy fellow in his early thirties, dressed in shirt and trousers made from choice pelts and draped in a decorated white tunic of deerskin. About his neck he wore a chain made of shells and on his head the distinctive hat of the Tlingits, a kind of inverted funnel from the top of which streamed six ornate feathers. Like Raven-heart, he had a slim copper ring in his nose, but his brown-red features were made distinctive because of his drooping black mustache and neatly trimmed goatee. In height, slimness and mien he was visibly differentiated from the other Indians, and in voice, determination and willingness to act he displayed a moral force which made him the acknowledged military leader and principal aide to the toion.

The six Americans had not encountered Kot-le-an on previous trips to Sitka, for he had been absent on punitive forays against troublesome neighbors, but even had he been present they would probably not have met with him, because he felt that trade was beneath him. He was a warrior, and it was in this capacity that he now stepped forward to prevent the execution of Raven-heart. In words that the Americans did not understand and which were not interpreted for them, since Raven-heart had previously provided that service, the young chieftain voiced a decision that would soon prove to have been prophetic: 'One of these days we shall have to protect our land from either the Americans like these here today or Baranov's Russians gathering strength in Kodiak. As your leader in battle, I shall need men like Raven-heart, so I cannot let you take him.'

'But the Great Toion also needs him,' several of the old men cried. 'It would be indecent to send . . .'

Kot-le-an, a man who loathed oratory or extended debate, responded by nodding to the elders, then ignoring them and grasping Raven-heart by the hand, pulling him free of both the Americans and the funeral managers: 'This one I must have for when the battles begin,' and in this abrupt manner the life of the big Tlingit was saved.

The Americans then watched with horror as two male slaves, young men in their teens, were dragged down the hill to the seashore, where their heads were held under water until they strangled. Unmarred, their corpses were then hauled back up the hill and placed ceremoniously beside the dead body of the Great Toion, whereupon four of the stoutest Tlingits grabbed the slave who had been selected to replace Raven-heart, stretched him across the sacrificial block of wood, and placed across his neck a slim driftwood log, pressing it down until all twitching in the body ceased. Sadly, as if mourning the loss of a friend, they placed this third body across the toion's feet, and signaled to the watching Indians that the burial of their chief could proceed.

After the funeral ceremony was concluded, trading for the pelts collected by the Tlingits proceeded, and ten of the eighteen barrels of rum were exchanged, under the mediation of Raven-heart, for seal pelts. No sea otters, the fur that China, Russia and California wanted, were in evidence, and it looked as if the *Evening Star* would have to sail without trading the guns, which the Tlingits really sought. However, just as Captain Corey was about to give the signal 'Haul anchor!' Raven-heart and Kot-le-an drew up to the ship in a small wooden rowboat recently built in imitation of those used by American ships, and when the two men were aboard the *Evening Star*, Raven-heart showed the young chief who had saved his life the dozen boxes containing the guns, telling him in Tlingit: 'There they are. The guns you need.'

Kot-le-an, spotting immediately the box whose top had been removed earlier to show Raven-heart the guns, pulled the loose boards aside and saw the handsome dark-blue barrels and the polished brown stocks. Even had the guns had no practical purpose, they would have been beautiful, but as rifles capable of protecting the Tlingits from would-be invaders, they became objects of immense importance.

'I want them all,' Kot-le-an said, but when this was interpreted, Captain Corey demurred: 'We trade only for sea otter.'

When this was translated, Kot-le-an found it impossible to control his rage. Stamping the deck with his moccasined feet, he shouted: 'Tell him that we have enough men to take the guns!' but before Raven-heart could speak, Corey grabbed Kot-le-an by the arm, swung him about to indicate the four cannon on the port side pointing directly at the houses atop the hill, and then to the four on the starboard, which could be pivoted around. 'And tell him,' he snarled, 'that we have one aft and one forrard, ten in all.'

Translation was not necessary, for Kot-le-an knew what cannon were. One year ago an English ship, having fallen into dispute with Tlingits on the mainland, had lost a sailor in a brawl, and in retaliation had bombarded the offending village until only one house remained standing, and Kot-le-an knew that American whalers were even quicker to exact vengeance. Capitulating to Captain Corey's superior strength, he instructed Raven-heart: 'Tell him in five days, many otter pelts.'

When Corey saluted this information, as if Kot-le-an were the ambassador of a sovereign power, the Tlingits withdrew, and as they departed First Mate Kane assured them: 'We'll wait five days.' Within the hour the Americans saw numerous small boats set forth from Sitka Sound to visit outlying settlements, and during the next days they watched them returning much deeper in the water than they had been when departing.

'We'll be getting some otter pelts,' Corey assured his men, but even as he prepared to leave ship he ordered Kane: 'While Kot-le-an can see, train half our cannon on the hill, half on the shore where he'll be, and have the men stand ready.' Kot-le-an, watching these preparations, was satisfied that no surprise attack from his side was going to succeed, but he also knew that the Americans, having come so far from Boston, could not return with an empty hold. They needed furs as badly as he needed guns, and from this pragmatic base the barter proceeded.

When Corey stepped ashore and saw the enormous number of pelts assembled under duress, he realized that whereas the sea otter might be extinct in the Aleutians, the Pribilofs and Kodiak, it was still swimming vigorously in these southern waters, and at the end of two hours of close inspection, he saw that he could with great profit to his ship dispose of his entire dozen cases of guns. So the deal was struck: 'Tell Kot-le-an I will give him all the guns. You saw them, four hundred and thirty-two. But I want all these pelts and this many more.' Pulling aside nearly a third of the pelts, he indicated that this was the requirement, then stood back, allowing Kot-le-an time to digest this new demand.

As a warrior, the young chief did not relish bartering, he was more used to command, but his apprehensions about the future were so strong that he knew he must have those guns the *Evening Star* carried, so with a gesture which astonished Corey, in a low voice he issued orders to his men, who moved aside a beached boat to disclose a hidden cache of otter pelts half again as large as the additional demand being made by Corey. Showing his contempt, he started kicking the skins toward the pile already belonging to Corey, and when he had thus moved some dozen pelts he growled to Raven-heart: 'Tell him he can have them all.'

When the precious cargo was safely stowed upon the *Evening Star*, with a value many times the cost of the guns, Kot-le-an and Corey stood facing each other, and in a formality which the Tlingit had learned from English captains, he held out his right hand, and Corey took it. But the American was so surprised at the gesture and so pleased with the results of this barter that on the spur of the moment he told Raven-heart: 'Tell Kot-le-an that because he gave us extra fur, we shall give him extra lead and powder,' and he ordered his sailors to bring forth a substantial chunk of lead and nearly half a barrel of powder.

WITH WARM FEELINGS on both sides, the deal was concluded, and two days after the *Evening Star* sailed from Sitka with a fortune in otter skins to be traded in Canton for twice what Corey had calculated, the prudence of Kot-le-an in making this lopsided deal was confirmed. A small armada of Russian ships and Aleut kayaks came into the bay, passed insolently beneath the hill where the local Tlingits kept their headquarters, and threaded its way eight miles to the north, where, in a spot which seemed to be completely surrounded by protecting mountains, they proceeded to unload the material required for the building of a major fort.

The armada, headed by Chief Administrator Aleksandr Baranov, was not a trivial one, for it brought one hundred Russian men, some wives and nine hundred Aleuts to Sitka with the avowed purpose of establishing here the capital of Russian America, from which the mainland north of California could be developed as a major Russian holding. On 8 July 1799, Baranov led his people ashore, and his aide Kyril Zhdanko planted a Russian flag in the loamy soil beside a gently flowing river. Then Baranov asked Father Vasili Voronov, who had come with him to serve as spiritual mentor of the new capital, to offer thanks to God that although the long trip across the open ocean from Kodiak had experienced grave difficulties—scores of Aleuts dying from poisoned fish, hundreds perishing at sea—the Russians themselves had completed it safely, and that was what mattered. Prayers said, the chubby little master of Russian imperialism stood uncovered, wiped his bald head, and proclaimed: 'As the old century draws to a close and a bright new one, full of promise, is about to begin, let us apply all our energies to the building of a noble capital city for the greatness that is to be Russian America.'

With that, in a loud voice he christened the fort-that-was-to-be 'Redoubt St. Michael,' and Sitka's Golden Age was under way.

W HEN KOT-LE-AN AND his aide Raven-heart saw the Russian armada creep past their hill at the southern portion of the bay, their first impulse was to muster all the Tlingit troops and engage in whatever activities might prove necessary to repel the invaders and prevent them from landing, whatever their intentions. But when Kot-le-an took the first steps to put this plan into effect, a curious relationship, which would govern the rest of Raven-heart's life, came into operation. 'Tell me what to do,' he said to Kot-le-an, and by this statement he meant that whatever order was issued at any time, he was prepared to execute it regardless of danger to himself, because, as he said, 'I am already dead. The log is across my throat. I breathe only at your pleasure.'

'So be it,' the young chieftain said. 'What you must do first is scout out their positions and strength.'

So Raven-heart, keeping to the woods, crept up the eight miles to Redoubt St. Michael and set up an observation post, from which he took careful note of the Russian potential: Three ships, not strong like *Evening Star* but many, many more men than the Americans. About a thousand men, but only one in ten are Russian. The others, what can they be? He studied the non-Russians with care, reasoning that they could not be Tlingits or from any clan associated with the Tlingits: They're shorter, darker. They wear bones through their noses and some of them have that strange sloping hat. He noticed two favorable aspects: They know how to make boats and none of our people can handle paddles the way they do. He decided that in a fight on the water, these little men would be formidable, and that with eight or nine hundred such fighters in support of the three big ships, the Russians would give a strong account of themselves.

They're Koniags, he concluded, and rumor had swept through the islands in recent years that these men of Kodiak were able warriors, to be avoided if possible, but before he reported this to Kot-le-an he wanted to assure himself as to the facts, so one night when the moon was gone, he crept close to where the outlines of the fort had been dug and waited in the darkness till one of the workmen wandered out.

With a leap and a big hand about the man's face, he dragged the man back into the trees, where he gagged him with a handful of spruce needles and bound him with sinew thongs. Sitting on him till daylight, he then hefted him across his shoulders like a bundle of pelts and marched back to Sitka Hill with him. There, others who were familiar with the languages of the Bering Sea identified the workman as an Aleut, and when they interrogated him they learned that he had been born on Lapak Island and had been taken as a slave to Kodiak. He revealed further that all the non-Russians at the redoubt were Aleuts. When asked: 'Are your people happy to be working here?' he replied: 'It's better than the Seal Islands.'

Satisfied by further scouting that the cadre really was Aleut, Kot-le-an and Raven-heart decided that an attack in total force stood a good chance of driving off the Russians, for, as Kot-le-an pointed out, 'If the others were all from Kodiak, it might be difficult, but we know that in battle we can overpower Aleuts.' And an attack would have been mounted except that, to Kot-le-an's astonishment, the new toion, without adequate discussions among the warriors of his tribe, not only arranged a peace treaty with the Russians but actually sold them a portion of land at and around the growing fort.

Enraged by this supine surrender to what he properly perceived as a mortal threat to Tlingit aspirations, Kot-le-an assembled all who were disgruntled with this invitation to Russian interference in ancient ways, and harangued them:

'Once the Russians fix their fort on this bay, we Tlingits are doomed. I know them from what others say. They will never let go, and before we know it, they will demand this hill and this portion of the bay. They'll want the island there and the volcano and our hot baths and the shore beyond. All the otters will belong to them, not us, and for every American ship that comes here now to trade with us and bring us the things we need, six of theirs will come, and not for trade. With guns they'll steal everything we have.

'I am not happy with what I see as our fate if we let them stay unchallenged. Our totems will crumble. Our canoes will be driven from the bay. We will no longer be masters of our lands, for the Russians will smother us everywhere and in everything we want to do. I feel the terrible hand of the Russians pressing down upon us like the log that presses upon the throat of a condemned slave.

'I hear our children speaking not our language but theirs and I can smell the coming of their shaman among us and our souls will be lost to wander forever in the forests and the moaning will never end. I see these islands changed, and the seas lifeless, and the skies angry. I see the imposition of strange orders, new enforcements, totally different ways of life. And above all, I see the death of Tlingits, the death of all we have fought for through the years.'

His words were so powerful, and so predictive of the future which many of his listeners were beginning to fear, that he might have enlisted hundreds in his drive to eliminate the Russians and their Aleut allies had not the leader of the

Russians, this little man Baranov, anticipated such a ground swell. On a day in August, as summer was beginning to fade, this clever Russian, always attentive to the safety of his flanks, got in his biggest ship and had his sailors bring him down the bay to the Tlingit settlement, and as he approached the landing, where sailors carried him ashore through the waves, the sun came out in full radiance, so that he climbed the hill the first time on a day as beautiful as this part of Alaska provided.

It's an omen, he said to himself, as if he could foresee that he would spend the glory years of his life atop this fortuitous hill, and when he reached the lofty summit, with the new toion coming forth to greet him, he stopped, looked in all directions, and saw as if in a revelation the incredible majesty of this spot.

To the west swept the Pacific Ocean, visible beyond the hundred islands, the highway back to Kodiak, out to the far Aleutians and on to Kamchatka and the ramparts of Russia. To the south rose a squadron of mountains, marching backward in file to the end of the horizon, green then blue then misty gray, then almost white in the far distance. To the east, crowded close in, stood the glory of Sitka, the mountains that dipped their toes in the sea, big and powerful but also gentle in their green finery. They were mountains of infinite variety, of changing color, of surprising height to be so close to the sea. And to the north, where he was already building, he saw that splendid sound, island-dotted, ringed with its own mountains, some as sharp as needles carved from whale-bone, others big and comfortable and rounded.

He was so enchanted by the rich variety of this scene from the hill that he was tempted to cry out at its wonder, but his Russian merchant's canniness warned him not to reveal how struck he was lest his Tlingit hosts fathom his interest in their paradise. Dropping his head and keeping his arms folded across his belly, as was his custom, he merely said: 'Great and Powerful Toion, in appreciation for your many kindnesses in helping us to establish our little fort on your bay, I bring you a few humble gifts.' And motioning to the sailors who accompanied him, he had them unroll bundles which contained beads, brass, cloth and bottles. After these had been distributed he asked his men for the *pièce de résistance*—and he called it by just those words in French—and they produced a somewhat rusty, out-of-date musket, which he handed gravely to the toion, asking one of the sailors to provide powder and ball plus an exhibition of how the old gun should be fired.

When the sailor had everything in order, he showed the toion how to handle the gun, apply his forefinger to the trigger, and discharge the ball. There was a flash of fire as the excess powder burned away, a feeble blast from the end of the gun, and a slight rustle of leaves as the ball bounced its way harmlessly through the treetops below the hill. The toion, who had never before fired a gun, was excited, but Kot-le-an and Raven-heart, who had nearly five hundred first-class new rifles hidden away, smiled indulgently.

However, it was canny Baranov who seemed to triumph, for in response to these impressive gifts, offered with such voluntary good will, he was given the loan of fifteen Tlingits, who would move to the fort and supervise the Aleuts in catching and drying the multitude of salmon which had begun streaming into the small river to the north of the fort. Kot-le-an, infuriated by this easy capitulation of his toion to the blandishments of the strangers, did gain one advantage: he insinuated into this group of temporary workers his man Raven-heart, so that when Baranov returned to the fort with the salmon experts, he took also a spy with unusual powers of observation and deduction.

At the fort, Raven-heart performed like the other Tlingits, standing knee-deep at the mouth of the river with a wicker scoop, which he dipped among the multitude of fat thirteen-inch salmon as they returned to their natal stream to spawn and give rise to the new generation. They left the salt water like myrmidons, each fish in file behind another, fifty or sixty files across, so that at any one spot at the river mouth for these relatively few days, thousands of fish passed, driven only by their urge to return to the fresh water where they had been born years ago, and there to lay the eggs which would renew their species.

A blind man with a torn net could catch salmon at this spot, and when Raven-heart and his mates had thrown several thousand ashore, they showed the Russians how to spot females rich with roe and how to eviscerate the fish and prepare them for drying in the sun. Baranov, watching the stacking up of food in piles of unbelievable size, told his Russians: 'This winter nobody starves.'

In the evenings, when work was done and the Tlingits were left to themselves, Raven-heart utilized his time in memorizing details of the growing fort. He saw that the promontory was divided into two halves: one inland, consisting of a blockhouse that could be furiously defended from fixed gun emplacements and portholes through which rifles could be fired; the other half, a collection of small buildings outside the main blockhouse and not heavily defended. These sheds and barns, he concluded, were to be sacrificed in case of an attack, with all defenders withdrawing inside the fortress, which had to the rear, away from the seafront, a huge square yard with walls two feet thick. Invading and taking that fortress was not going to be easy.

But the more he studied the redoubt the more clearly he saw that a determined assault, which took first the outlying buildings without destroying them and then laid siege to the blockhouse, could succeed if some way were found to break into that huge enclosed yard at the rear, for then the attackers could nibble away at the central redoubt while enjoying protection from the very buildings provided by the Russians, and in time the latter would have to surrender. Redoubt St. Michael could be captured, provided the attackers were led by a man like Kot-le-an and staffed by determined aides like Raven-heart.

When the salmon season ended, in late September, the Tlingits were sent back to their hill, with the understanding that they would not be needed next year, since the Russians and Aleuts were now proficient in the business of catching and preserving the valuable fish. Fourteen of the Tlingits left the redoubt merely with memories of a reasonably pleasant stay, but Raven-heart departed with complete plans for capturing this fort, and as soon as he rejoined Kot-le-an, the two men drew up diagrams of the Russian installation and procedures for destroying it.

During the remainder of 1799 the impetuous young men were prevented from putting their scheme into operation by the hesitancy of their toion, who was awed by Russian power, and by the thoughtful leadership of Aleksandr Baranov, who anticipated and frustrated any Tlingit moves. Whenever it looked as if the Indians on their hill might be getting restive, he threw them off balance by offering them trades of surprising generosity, and once when several hundred of them threatened actual rebellion, he boldly marched among them, advising them to come to their senses. 'He's a brave one,' the Tlingits said, and in this manner Kot-le-an and Raven-heart were neutralized by Baranov's clever moves, even though they continued to regard him as their chief enemy.

In the summer of 1800, at the end of the first full year since the Russian arrival at Redoubt St. Michael, when Raven-heart's spying warned him that the fortress had been completed in good style and ahead of schedule, Baranov, to the surprise of all, loaded one of his ships with pelts from Sitka waters, hoisted sail, and set out for Kodiak, where his wife, Anna, and his son, Antipatr, waited in the big log house which served as the capitol of Russian America. He had gone to Kodiak expecting to load there with supplies forwarded from mainland Russia, but when he landed he heard the pitiful news: 'No ship has reached us in the past four years. We're starving.' So his attention was diverted from his outpost at Sitka and directed to the problem which would assail him all his life in Alaska: How can I increase the power of this colony if I'm ignored and neglected by the homeland?

With Baranov tied down in Kodiak, no help from that quarter could be forwarded to the new establishment at Sitka, and in the summer of 1801, Kot-le-an and Raven-heart suspected that the Russians would be so weakened that they would not be able to defend themselves. But just as the Tlingits were preparing their attack, the Boston trader *Evening Star* put into the sound on a return trip from Canton, and whereas on all previous visits it had anchored near the hill to conduct trading with the Tlingits, this time it sailed right past, as if acknowledging that now it was the Russian fort that was important. Seething with anger, Kot-le-an suffered the indignity of having to get into a boat and trail along behind the trader as if hungry for its favors, and then wait in the sound until the Americans had completed details with the Russians. 'I have been made a stranger in my own land,' the young chieftain fumed to Raven-heart, who took advantage of the enforced idleness to coach his leader in the steps that would be required when the attack on the redoubt took place. That it would occur, neither man doubted.

But it did not happen in 1801 because supplies from the *Evening Star* strengthened the four hundred and fifty Russians who now operated the place, making an assault at this time inadvisable. However, on its way out of the bay, the *Evening Star* did stop at the Tlingit stronghold, where Captain Corey and First Mate Kane proved their basic friendship for the Indians by showing them a corner of the hold in which they had hidden from Russian eyes the trade goods that the Tlingits really sought, casks of rum and flat boxes filled with additional rifles made originally in England and shipped to China.

'We saved the best for last,' Corey assured the Indians, and as before, Raven-heart scrambled among the small settlements scattered about the littoral, collecting the still-surprising harvest of sea-otter pelts. When the barter was concluded, Corey and Kane met with Kot-le-an on the hill, and as they shared a bottle of rum, the Americans drinking little but pouring generously for the Tlingits, Corey observed: 'Wouldn't it make sense to join these two settlements? Russians and Tlingits working together?'

'In Boston,' Kot-le-an asked with surprising acuity, 'do you and your Tlingits work together?'

'No. That wouldn't be possible.'

'Here, too, it is not possible,' and Corey, remembering the large number of guns he had sold these warlike Tlingits, looked at his first mate and with a gesture so slight that only Kane could see it, shrugged his right shoulder as if to say: 'What happens is their business, not ours,' and that afternoon he made final calculations on his cargo of whale oil and otter skins, weighed anchor, and headed for Boston, which he had not seen in six years.

When he was gone, Kot-le-an told Raven-heart: 'We'll wait. If you want to build your house at the southern salmon stream, do it now,' and this invitation, thrown off so casually, marked a turning point in the slave's life, for it released him, by implication, from servitude. Because if a Tlingit was free to build his own house, it meant he was also free to take himself a wife to help occupy that house, and for some time now Raven-heart had been eying with increasing excitement a Tlingit girl who bore the lovely name of Kakeena, a name of lost meaning belonging to her great-grandmother. She had not only the bland, open face which bespoke spiritual ease but also a nobility of bearing which warned the world: 'I shall do many things in my own way.' The daughter of a skilled fisherman, she was sixteen, and for some lucky reason had escaped both tattooing and the inserting of labrets into her lower lip. She was, in these early years of the new century, the self-confident yet modest type of young woman who, in these times of change, might be expected to marry with some Russian in exile, forming with him a bridge between past and present, between Tlingit and Russian.

But even as a child she had sensed that this was not going to be possible, for she was fiercely devoted to the Tlingit way of life, and she saw that the spiritual distance between the Tlingit village and the Russian fort was so great that it could not be honorably bridged unless the Tlingit woman surrendered her identity, and this she knew she would refuse to do. In recent months her parents had begun to wonder: 'What will become of our daughter?' as if they were responsible for her salvation and not she. They were pleased when several young Tlingit and Russian men displayed their lively interest in her, and during the latest visit of the *Evening Star* they had been aware that First Mate Kane had tried several times to get her into his bed, but she had rebuffed both him and the local lads for the good reason that she had, when she was only fourteen, identified the slave Raven-heart as the finest young man in the region. In subsequent years she had witnessed his sturdy courage, his loyalty to Kot-le-an, his ability in trading with the Americans and, above all, his comely manner, for she saw in his face the same kind of stately calm she had seen in her own when allowed to borrow one of the magical mirrors provided by Captain Corey.

So in this quiet summer of 1801, Raven-heart had three tasks, to the completion of which he could apply his entire energy: win Kakeena as his wife, build them a house on the banks of the salmon stream beneath the big spruce trees, and carve himself a totem pole like the ones that had graced his home village to the south in the days before his capture and servitude.

The various tribes of Tlingits were so different in nature that they scarcely seemed like members of the same family. The Tlingits at Yakutat to the north were almost savage, so intent were they on warfare, raiding and the killing of prisoners. Those like Kot-le-an on the hill above Sitka Sound were warlike enough to defend their terrain but also gentle enough to appreciate the rewards of peace, if it could be obtained on their principles. Those to the south, where Raven-heart had lived, existed along the borders of the Haida people, a distinct branch of Athapascans with their own language, and from them had acquired the gracious habit of carving for each village and prominent home a totem pole of red cedar, tall, stately, colorful and a record of events important to that village or that home. Kot-le-an's people rarely carved totems, and the Yakutats burned them when overrunning a village, but Raven-heart, living as he must in alien land, would not feel easy in any house which was not protected by its totem.

So with the vigor which characterized him, he launched all three of his assignments simultaneously. Asking Kot-le-an to accompany him, he marched to the fisherman's hut where Kakeena lived and solemnly asked her father: 'May I have the honor of taking your daughter to wife?' and before the father could respond, Kot-le-an assured him: 'This one can be trusted.'

'But he's a slave,' the fisherman protested, to which Kot-le-an replied: 'No more. Honor erases that,' and the marriage was arranged.

That afternoon, on the banks of the salmon stream a mile east of the hill in the heart of a noble stand of spruce trees, Raven-heart and Kakeena began felling the logs which would form their home, and in the early evening, when the outlines of their house had been staked out, they hauled ashore the cedar log from which he would carve his totem. Next day, with the help of Kot-le-an himself and three of his assistants, the log was lifted onto the supports which would hold it free of the ground while Raven-heart carved, a task which would occupy his spare time for nearly a year.

As he worked on the log, carving only the side that would be exposed in front, he incorporated a personal selection of those precious images which summarized the spiritual history of his people: the birds, the fish, the great bears, the boats that plied the waters, the spirits that directed life. But he did not do so haphazardly; in obedience to the same principles that had guided Praxiteles and Michaelangelo in fashioning their sculptures, he followed highly traditional patterns for relating forms and color so masterfully that the totem, as it gradually emerged, would be no mere illustrated pole standing before a house, but a forceful, sophisticated work of art, magnificent in its final appearance. He and Kakeena were pleased with it when it was finally ready for erecting into place, and they were honored when the toion, Kot-le-an and the shaman came south to honor and bless it as it rose in the air, a signal that in the house below lived a Tlingit family that took life seriously.

Married, with a house three-quarters built and a bright totem in place, Raven-heart was at work in June of 1802 when Kot-le-an and two of his men ran east to the salmon stream with exhilarating news: 'The Russians were never weaker. Now's the time to destroy them.' So Raven-heart was dispatched to complete his spying, and from a thicket east of Redoubt St. Michael he determined various significant facts: the dangerous adversary Baranov was not in residence; his trusted assistant Kyril Zhdanko was gone, too; with so many of the Aleuts returned to Kodiak, the total complement at the fort seemed to be about fifty Russians and only two hundred Aleuts, a number which could be defeated; and whereas the number of small, unprotected buildings along the shore had increased, the big fort itself and its attendant palisaded square had not been strengthened.

Reporting to Kot-le-an and his aides, Raven-heart said: 'Same as the plans we drew up before. Strike by boat from the bay, by land from the forest. Take the small buildings in the first blow, dig in, and then overwhelm the redoubt.'

'The first part easy?' Kot-le-an asked, and Raven-heart nodded. 'But the second part?' Kot-le-an asked, and his spy gave an honest answer: 'Very difficult.'

When the force of Tlingit boats left the southern part of the sound at eleven o'clock at night in late June, the sun had barely set, and as the quiet flotilla moved north, coordinating its movement with that of the warriors infiltrating through the forest, the fort was outlined in the silver glow of a midsummer Alaskan night in which darkness would never come. Silently the two forces converged, and at four in the morning, coincident with the return of the sun, they fell upon the Russian encampment, occupied immediately all the unprotected buildings, and swept into the palisaded yard, and then, following tactics which the spy Raven-heart had developed two years before, attacked the spots he had seen to be weakest, broke through, set the Russian buildings afire, and cut the throats of the defenders as they fled to escape the flames. Russians and Aleuts alike perished, and only those fortunate enough to be absent on fishing or fur-hunting parties escaped.

When the carnage was completed, Kot-le-an, its instigator, stood among the dead bodies and cried: 'Let this be a warning to the Russians! They cannot come and steal Tlingit land!' After burning the Russian ships and boats, the victorious Tlingits marched in triumph back to their hilltop home, conquerors of Sitka Sound, protectors of Tlingit rights.

ALTHOUGH ASTONISHED BY the ease with which he had eliminated the Russians, Kot-le-an did not even briefly suppose that a determined man like Baranov would allow such a humiliation to go unchallenged. What response the Russians would make and when, he could not anticipate, but certain that it must come, he initiated unusual precautions. Striding out to where Raven-heart and his wife were still at work on their new home, he announced bluntly: 'This is the best site on the island. Our fort must be here.' Raven-heart, who had spent considerable energy in building as much of the house as was finished and in carving his totem, started to protest this invasion, but was stopped by Kakeena, who stepped forward with a boldness that surprised him: 'Kot-le-an, we shall have no rest till we drive the Russians from our land. Take our house.' And when Tlingits arrived to convert their home into a military headquarters, she worked with them. Later, it was she who suggested that the whole area be enclosed in a high, thick, spear-studded palisade, and on the construction of this she also helped.

The completed fort—a collection of strong small buildings protected by a palisade—stood close to the salmon stream on the east and not far from the sound on the south. To the east it was guarded by a dense forest whose older trees fell in crisscross positions when they died, forming an impenetrable thicket. When all was done, Kot-le-an told his people: 'We cannot defend this hill. Russian ships could lie in the sound and bombard us with their cannon, but down on the point where we have our new fort, they'll not be able to get close enough to harm us.'

'When do we move there?' some women asked, but the toion replied: 'Not before the Russians come . . . if they ever do,' and Raven-heart, hearing this almost boastful statement, thought: Kot-le-an's right. A man like Baranov will return. He'll have to.

So the dream of Raven-heart and Kakeena was lost in the plans of war. The house was built, but it served as a military headquarters, and the totem was in place, but it stood before a Tlingit version of the Russian redoubt and not before a home.

'Can we hold it against the Russians?' Kakeena asked, and her husband equivocated: 'We built it strong. You can see that.'

'But can the Russians fight their way in? The way you did against them?'

'One of these days we'll see,' he replied, and a kind of nervous, passive waiting began. Then in September 1804, Russian ships crowded with fighting men began appearing in Sitka Sound, first the *Neva*, come all the way from St. Petersburg, then the *Jermak*, the *Katharina* and the *Alexander*. Three hundred and fifty two-man kayaks also reported at the end of a fearful crossing of the gulf that separated Sitka from Kodiak. Toward the end of the month the sound was dominated by a hundred and fifty Russians and more than eight hundred Aleuts, all well-armed and eager to avenge the destruction of Redoubt St. Michael two years before. Since it was assumed by the Russians that they would have to storm the hill the Tlingits had occupied in the past, on the night of 28 September, Baranov brought his ships close to the foot of the hill, with every intention of investing it under gunfire in the morning.

But when dawn broke next morning and the Russians began marching up the hill behind Baranov, a brave man prepared for battle, they found to their surprise an unoccupied fort; all the Tlingits had fled to their big new fortress a mile to the east, where the totem stood protecting the main gate, whose supporting walls were twenty inches thick. Announcing that he had won a victory, Baranov assigned troops to man the abandoned fort and hauled up seven cannon, which were emplaced so as to command all approaches. 'I don't know where the Tlingits are,' he told his men, 'but they will never again occupy this hill,' and he would enforce that decision for the remainder of his life.

The Tlingits, safe in their new fortress and satisfied that they could hold it against any Russian pressure, laughed when they heard how Baranov had attacked an empty fort, but their attitude became more grave when spies reported: 'They're beginning to load extra men on the four warships anchored at the foot of the hill.' This news did not frighten Kot-le-an, but it did make him wonder how much damage the guns on those four warships could do, so he dispatched Raven-heart to parley with Baranov and settle the terms under which the two groups could share this handsome bay and the riches it commanded.

With one young warrior at his side, and with a white flag atop a tall pole, Raven-heart strode down the path leading through the forest, expecting to spread before the Russians the terms which Kot-le-an would be proposing, and he was shocked when he reached the fort to be dismissed abruptly with the scornful words: 'Our commander does not deal with underlings. If your chief wishes to converse with us, let him appear in person.'

Humiliated and enraged, Raven-heart stormed back to Kot-le-an, informing him that there was no purpose in further negotiation, but during Raven-heart's absence, the young chief had become more convinced that peaceful sharing was better than open warfare, so in the morning Raven-heart, accompanied by a special emissary, returned to the hill, this time by water and in a ceremonial canoe. As Raven-heart brought the canoe to a landing place, the emissary began to chant a flowery message of peace:

'Mighty Russians, we of the Mighty Tlingit seek your friendship. You took our land for your redoubt, we took back your redoubt for our land. We stand even, toe to toe, hand to hand; so let us abide in peace.'

With that, the emissary threw himself from the canoe, lay in water up to his nostrils, and looked pleadingly at the Russian sentries, who whistled for officers to come. Down the steps leading from the hill marched two young men who when they saw the floating emissary began laughing. When they saw that Raven-heart was back again, they spat out the same contemptuous message: 'If your chief has a message, let him come in person,' and they were about to withdraw when Raven-heart unfolded before them one of the largest, silkiest sea-otter skins this area had ever produced. In English he cried: 'This is our present to the Great Baranov!' and the gift was so compelling that the officers led him up the stone steps to the fort, where Baranov accepted the pelt graciously, giving him in return a complete suit of woolen clothing.

In Tlingit the former slave, now a man of considerable dignity, said: 'Great Baranov, we seek peace,' at which the Russian spelled out his demands: 'You must leave two hostages with me. You must confirm our ownership of this hill and such surrounding territory as I shall designate for our headquarters. And you must remain peacefully in this area and trade with us.'

After asking for two repetitions of the demands, Raven-heart asked: 'You want all this land?' Baranov nodded. 'And you want us to live obedient to your commands?' Again the Russian nodded, whereupon Raven-heart drew himself up to his considerable height and said: 'I speak for our chieftain Kot-le-an and for our toion. We shall never accept such terms.'

Baranov did not flinch. Looking inquisitively toward Captain Lisiansky of the *Neva*, who nodded, he said almost casually: 'Tell Kot-le-an that our attack will begin at dawn tomorrow.' And by the time Raven-heart reached his canoe, where the emissary waited, the two Tlingits saw that Russian soldiers and hundreds of Aleut fighting men had started streaming toward the four ships and the kayaks.

O N 1 OCTOBER 1804 the four warships were ready to sail the short distance to the Tlingit fort and start bombarding it, but an infuriating calm settled over the sound, and the big ship *Neva*, on which the Russians must depend, could not be moved. However, the *Neva* was commanded by Captain Urey Lisiansky, a determined and resourceful fighter, and he resolved the impasse by lining up more than a hundred kayaks, which, by means of ropes attached to their sterns, pulled the heavy ship slowly into position. Kot-le-an, watching this herculean effort, whispered to Raven-heart: 'They mean to fight,' and stern preparations were ordered.

The efficiency of Captain Lisiansky was somewhat diluted by the fact that Baranov, fifty-seven years old and overweight, fancied himself a military genius with the right to lead into battle a force consisting of about one-half the effectives. Dubbed by his men the Commodore, he believed that his experience in Siberian brawls and minor island skirmishes qualified him as a tactician, and he shouted orders like a battle-tested veteran. However, buffoon though he seemed to some, his gallantry and lust for vengeance on the Tlingits who had destroyed his redoubt so inspired his men that they were prepared to follow him anywhere.

But before leading his men forward in the actual assault, Baranov, remembering battle stories he had read, believed he was honor-bound to offer his enemy one last chance to surrender, so he sent forward three Russians under a white flag. When they neared the Tlingit fort, the one in command cried in loud voice: 'You know our demands. Give us land. Hostages. And stay here peacefully to trade.'

From inside the fort came laughter and then a volley which rattled high in the trees over the negotiators' heads. These men, afraid that the next shots might be directed at them, scampered back to the *Neva*, where they told Baranov how they had been received. He did not rant, but to those about him he said: 'Now we take their fort,' and as agreed beforehand, Captain Lisiansky dispatched four small boats, heavily armed, to destroy all the Tlingit canoes left on the beach. The battle had begun.

Now Baranov, clad in a suit of wood-and-leather armor, sword held high, waded ashore at the head of his men, determined to assault the walls and demand surrender. Supported by three small portable cannon, he stopped to listen for sounds of Tlingits inside the fort, heard none, and cried: 'They've abandoned it, just like they did the hill,' and with a bold, peasant heroism he led his men right up to the walls.

But as soon as they came well within musket range, the walls erupted with fire from hundreds of good Boston rifles, and the effect upon the invaders was disastrous, for the unexpected volley struck many full in the face.

When the Russians retreated in disorder, the Tlingits broke from their central gate guarded by the totem pole and descended upon the disorganized men, killing and wounding without having to dodge any counterfire. And had not Captain Lisiansky sped to Baranov's relief, a general slaughter would have occurred. The first round, clearly won by the Tlingits, had been a disastrous defeat for Commodore Baranov.

Back aboard the *Neva*, he revealed to his officers a major wound in his left arm, and after he was put to bed under a doctor's care, Lisiansky summed up the fracas: 'Three of my men dead, fourteen Russians wounded and countless Aleuts, who fled like rabbits at the first gunfire. But we gained one victory. Baranov is wounded just seriously enough to keep him from marching forth again. Now let's organize this siege and blow that fort apart.'

But before the cannonading could begin, there was an ugly portent that this battle was to be a no-surrender affair like the earlier assault on Redoubt St. Michael, where all Russians present were slaughtered, for onto the beach almost in range of their enemy's pistol fire came six Tlingit warriors bearing spears aloft, on whose tips was impaled the body of one of the dead Russians. At a whistle from their leader, the Tlingits jabbed their six spears sharply upward, driving the points so far through the body of the corpse that the metal tips shone red with blood. Then, at another signal, they threw their spears forward, allowing the body to splash into the bay.

Minutes later the cannonading began, and when word reached the deck that a fourth Russian had died from his wounds, the fire intensified. For two days the bombardment continued, and a sortie in strength under Lisiansky ranged the area before the fort, killing any Tlingits they encountered, but in doing so, they saw that the great wooden fence constructed by Kot-le-an and Raven-heart had sufficient thickness to repel even the biggest cannonballs.

'We won't win by trying to knock down the fence,' Lisiansky told his men, and after this was reported to Baranov he consulted with his captain, the elevation of the guns was raised, and cannonballs of destructive size and frequency began raining down into the fort's interior.

Lisiansky, watching them land with rarely a miss, assured Baranov: 'They won't be able to tolerate this for long,' and grimly the fat little merchant smiled.

DURING THE FIRST days of the siege there had been great jubilation inside the fort, for then the Tlingit defenders gained three significant victories: their palisaded walls had proved to be impervious to Russian fire, they had repulsed the first land attack with heavy loss to the enemy, and without suffering any retaliation they had successfully taunted the Russians at the seashore, spearing the corpse and tossing the body into the waves. 'We can hold them off!' Kot-le-an cried in those moments of initial victory.

But when the cannonading began in earnest, with the Russians firing over the walls, the tides of war shifted dramatically. There were, inside the stockade, some fifteen separate buildings clustered about the house that Raven-heart and Kakeena had started, and with hellish luck the Russian cannonballs began striking these wooden buildings, smashing them apart and killing or badly wounding the occupants. Children shrieked as the destruction continued, and there was a terrible moment when three shots in a row struck the Raven-heart house, scattering embers and starting a fire which quickly consumed the entire building. Raven-heart, watching the raging flames, had a premonition that he was seeing the demise of all things the Tlingits cherished, for this house had been a symbol of his release from slavery and his acceptance into the strongest of the Tlingit tribes.

However, knowing he must not allow either Kakeena or Kot-le-an to see his apprehension, he passed among the fort's defenders with words of encouragement: 'They'll stop. They'll see they can't conquer us and they'll go away.' But as he uttered such words during the third day of the bombardment he was interrupted by a scream from Kakeena, and supposing that she had been hit by one of the cannonballs, he ran toward where he had last seen her, but when he reached her he found her standing, mouth agape and looking toward the sky. Unable to speak, she pointed heavenward, and then he saw what had caused her outcry: a shot from the *Neva* had struck his totem halfway up and had shattered it, knocking away the carefully carved top with the raven and leaving a jagged stump, still tall but forever decapitated. Remembering the legends of his people and their spirits which he had carefully carved in the pole, he was distraught, but still he did not allow himself to show his distress at the loss of yet another aspect of the life he loved and had hoped to defend. And the bombardment continued.

As daylight waned on the sixth day, Kot-le-an came to Raven-heart with a message the latter had not expected to hear: 'Trusted friend, take the white flag and go to them.'

'Asking for what?'

'Peace.'

'On what terms?'

'Any they propose.'

For some minutes, while Kot-le-an gathered a team of six to accompany his messenger, Raven-heart stood in the middle of the wreckage and felt the ground swaying under him. A dream was coming to an end, a world was being lost, and he had been selected to be the man to do the surrendering, but before putting into effect the signal of submission, his entire body revolted—eyes refused to see, feet to move, and mind to accept the horrid duty—and he cried to no one: 'I cannot!'

It was Kakeena, not Kot-le-an, who persuaded him: 'You must. Look,' and she pointed to the destroyed houses, the row of corpses not yet buried, the universal signs of loss. 'You must go,' she whispered.

Astonished that it was his resolute wife who was uttering these words of defeat, he turned to stare at her, and saw that she was grimly smiling: 'This time we've lost. Save what we can. Next time, when they've grown careless, we'll crush them.' And when he moved toward the gate through which he would lead his messengers of surrender, she walked beside him to the beach, where he called in English to the Russians, who halted their bombardment when they saw his white flag: 'Baranov, you win. We talk.'

Through a brass trumpet came a reply in Russian: 'Go to bed. No more bombardment. In the morning we will come.'

At these words, which meant that the siege was over and that Tlingit hopes of recovering Sitka were doomed, Kakeena began a high-pitched wail which Russian listeners interpreted as a lament for lost hopes; they would have been astounded could they have understood her words: 'Ai me, the waves have left our shore and only rocks remain. But like the rocks we will endure and in the years to come we shall return like the waves and smother the Russians.' And as the enemy sailors listened in the falling darkness, they heard one Tlingit voice after another join in the supposed lament until the shore was filled with what they construed as grief but which was, under Kakeena's leadership, a commitment to revenge.

When Raven-heart and his contingent returned to the fort, they were greeted by silence. The cannonading had stopped, but so had purposeful movement by the Tlingits. Standing in confused groups, they discussed what to do next, and as Raven-heart went from one gathering to the next, he found only consternation and lack of any plan as to what action they must take after the surrender, but toward midnight Kot-le-an and the toion assumed command, and their directives were short and brutal: 'We shall cut across the mountains and leave this island forever.' And as those fateful words were whispered through the fort, their awful meaning became clear, for to cross Sitka Island at any point was a monstrous undertaking, considering the jagged mountains and the lack of trails. But the Tlingits had decided to flee, and in the four hours after midnight there was in this destroyed fort a hurricane of activity.

Only Raven-heart and Kakeena had actually lived on this beautiful point between the salmon creek and the bay, so only they had mementos which they wished to take with them—for him, a fragment of the totem; for her, a shattered wooden plate—but all who prepared to flee carried recollections of their majestic hill overlooking the bay, and all were heavy-hearted.

As dawn approached, two groups of refugees had special and heartbreaking tasks: appointed men roamed through the fort killing all the dogs, especially those who had attached themselves to specific families, for to take them on the journey ahead would prove impossible, and there were moments of grief as some animal that had bounded with love at the sound of a child's voice was slain, but this sadness was soon forgotten, because a comparable team of women led by Kakeena was passing through the assembling crowd, killing all the Tlingit babies.

EARLY ON THE morning of 7 October, as the mists lifted and the bright autumn sun appeared, sailors from the *Neva* and the three other ships lined up on the beach behind Commodore Baranov and started their triumphal march to accept the surrender of the Tlingits, but as they approached the fort they saw no people, heard no sounds, and with uncertainty they drew closer, whereupon a cackle of ravens took to the air, and one superstitious sailor muttered: 'They feed on the dead,' and when Baranov peered past the sagging gates, knocked awry by some cannon shot, he saw the desolation, the litter of dead dogs and the tiny human corpses. It was a moment of dreadful victory, accentuated by the sudden appearance from a shattered house of two old women too ancient to travel who were guarding a six-year-old boy with a crippled leg.

'Where have they gone?' Baranov demanded of the women, who pointed to the north. 'Across those mountains?' the interpreter asked, and they said 'Yes.'

As they spoke, Kot-le-an, Raven-heart and the toion who had lost his kingdom were leading their people across rough land covered by immense spruce trees, each trunk as tall and straight as a line drawn in sand. The going was so difficult that only a few miles would be covered that day and it would be painful weeks before they reached the northern limits of Sitka Island. When they did, they would have to halt for the building of canoes to ferry them across Peril Strait, after which they would have to find some kind of refuge on inhospitable Chichagof Island, a place infinitely more brutal and unyielding than Sitka Sound.

But they persisted, and finally reached the northern edge of the island, and when they saw, across the strait, the mountains of their new home, some wept, for they knew they were making a miserable exchange. But Raven-heart, having been dispossessed before in his turbulent life, told Kakeena: 'I think we can make a home over there,' and as he spoke, a fish jumped in Peril Strait and he told his wife: 'Good sign.'

NOW CAME THE fifteen amazingly productive years, 1804 through 1818, which confirmed the reputation of Aleksandr Baranov as the father and chief inspirator of Russia's fragile empire in North America. Fifty-seven years old when his burst of energy began, he displayed the enthusiasm of a boy going after his first deer, the wisdom of a Pericles building a new city, the patience of an island Job.

As a builder he was indefatigable, for as soon as the last fragment of the Tlingit fort was burned, including all parts of the totem pole, he hurried his people back to start work on the hilltop, where he built himself a modest cottage from which he could survey the sound, the volcano and the surrounding mountains. During his lifetime that cottage would be rebuilt into a more imposing house of many rooms, and after his death, into a grandiose mansion three stories high and crammed with rooms of all sorts, including a theater. And even though he would never see or occupy it, it would always be known as Baranov's Castle, and from it Russian America would be governed.

At the foot of the hill he outlined a generous area including a large lake, and this he enclosed within a high wooden palisade; it would be the Russian town. But now a curious problem arose, for Baranov called his settlement New Arch angel, while ship captains of all nations, and the Tlingits and Aleuts who shared the site, continued to call it Sitka, the name by which it would ultimately be known. So the fine town would have two names used interchangeably, but only one important rule: 'No Tlingits allowed inside the palisade.'

But even as he proclaimed that law, Baranov made plans for the day when the Indians would return to help him build a greater New Archangel, and when a huge area adjoining the palisade was cleared, he explained to the townspeople: 'That's to be kept for the Tlingits when they start to come back. They're sensible people. They'll see we need them. They'll see they can live better sharing this spot with us than hiding out in the wilderness, wherever they are now.'

That crucial decision made—'Russians inside the walls, Tlingits outside'— Baranov turned his energies to the construction of a major town, and with the help of Kyril Zhdanko in a time so short it startled the workmen doing the building, he had a huge barracks for his soldiers; a school which, as in the case of the orphanage in Kodiak, he paid for out of his own meager salary; a library; a meeting hall for social affairs, with a treasured corner in which a piano imported from St. Petersburg was housed for the dances he sponsored and a stage for the one-act plays he encouraged his men and their wives to perform; plus a dozen other necessary buildings like sheds for the overhaul of ships putting in to New Archangel and shops in which their instruments of navigation and their cannon could be overhauled.

When these day-to-day essentials had been ensured, he turned to Father Vasili: "With this safe start behind us, Father, we'll now build you a church,' and with a zeal twice what he had shown before, he plunged into the construction of St. Michael's Cathedral, which he liked to call 'our cathedral.' Converted from an abandoned ship, it was a wooden affair, taller than any of the previous buildings, and when its lower stories were well finished, Baranov himself supervised the erection of a modified onion dome, and on the day of solemn dedication, with a choir chanting in Russian, he could truthfully tell the parishioners: 'With our fine cathedral in place, New Archangel becomes Russian forever and the center of our hopes.'

Some weeks after the dedication he received a confirmation of his dreams, which gave him profound joy, for an aide came rushing up the hill, shouting: 'Excellency! Look!' and when he ran to the parapet surrounding his cottage, he saw a score of Indians looking tentatively toward the palisade in the hope of permission to build houses in the space Baranov had set aside for them.

If the Russians on guard were perplexed by the arrival of these former enemies, Baranov was not; he had been expecting them, and now he shouted as he hurried down the hill: 'Bring food! Those old blankets! A hammer and nails!' And with gifts spilling out of his fat arms, he went to the Tlingits, forcing the goods upon them, and when an old man who spoke Russian said: 'We come back, better here,' Baranov had to fight back the tears.

However, this moment of exaltation was soon lost as he began to experience the frustrations which would cloud the remaining years of his life, and he himself caused the unpleasantness, because the more important he made New Archangel, the more frequently the Russian government sent naval ships to support the island, and this meant inevitably that Russian naval officers would be appearing in blue-and-braid to inspect 'what the merchant Baranov was doing out there.' And as he had been warned in that famous meeting in Irkutsk so many years ago, when he was being interrogated as to his ability to manage The Company's properties, 'there's nothing on earth more insolent than a Russian naval officer.'

The one that Tsar Alexander I selected in 1810 to prowl the Pacific in the warship *Muscovy* and torment local officials in Kodiak and New Archangel, especially the latter, was a prime dandy. Lieutenant Vladimir Ermelov, a brash twenty-five, was almost a caricature of the young Russian nobleman perpetually ready for a duel if his honor was in any way impugned: tall, thin, mustachioed, hawklike in countenance, severe in deportment, he considered enlisted men, servants, most women and all merchants as not only beneath contempt but also beneath civil courtesy. Brave in battle, a fairly good naval officer, and always prepared to defend his behavior with either sword or pistol, he was a terror on any ship he commanded and a dazzling white-uniformed cynosure wherever he came ashore.

Lieutenant Ermelov, scion of a noble family that had provided Russian rulers with some of their most pigheaded and ineffective counselors, was married to the granddaughter of a real grand duke, which gave her an unchallenged patent of nobility, and when she traveled aboard ship with her husband, both she and he believed that she served as personal representative of the tsar. Alone, Ermelov was formidable; when supported by his arrogant wife, he was, as a junior officer told Father Vasili without being reprimanded, 'damned near insufferable.'

When Ermelov sailed out of St. Petersburg in command of the *Muscovy*, he had known almost nothing about Aleksandr Baranov toiling away in the farthest east of the Russian possessions, but during this long voyage, which would take him around the world, he anchored in many ports, and in conversation with Russian or English or American captains who had stopped at either Kodiak or Sitka, he began to hear strange tales about this unusual man who had stumbled by accident, it seemed, into a position of some importance in the

Aleutians, 'those damned, fog-ridden fur islands, or was it Kodiak, which isn't much better,' and the more he heard, the more perplexed he was that the imperial government had placed such a man in charge of one of its increasingly important areas.

Madame Ermelova, who had been called Princess before her marriage to Vladimir and who was still authorized to use that title, was especially irritated by what she kept hearing about 'this damned fellow Baranov,' so that by the time the *Muscovy* left Hawaii in 1811, they were crammed with tales about 'that crazy Russian up in New Archangel, as they're calling it now,' and the Ermelovs were pretty well fed up with the man they both considered an interloper, Ermelov for political reasons, his wife for social: 'Vladimir, I know a dozen fine young men in St. Petersburg worthy of a position as governor, and it's damned irritating to think that a clown like this Baranov has outdistanced them.' Her irritation manifested itself in her first letter home from New Archangel; it was addressed to her mother, the Princess Scherkanskaya, daughter of the grand duke and a person attuned to social niceties:

Chère Maman,

We have arrived in Amerika and I can summarize our entire experience by telling you briefly what happened when we went ashore. From the
sea we recognized where we were by seeing the splendid volcano which
resembles so much the engravings we have on Fujee-yamma in Japan, and
soon after progressing past this entry point, we saw the little mount on
which our eastern capital stands. It is a promising site, and if the buildings
surmounting it were of appropriate construction and ornamentation, it
might in time prove to be an acceptable capital, but alas, although the area
consists of nothing but mountains, there is no stone for building, so what
happens? The low, rambling buildings without any sign that an architect
or an artist was involved in their planning consist of untempered wood
poorly put together and left unpainted. You would laugh at what they call
their cathedral, a gross, unplanned, ugly pile of wood topped by an
amusing construction which passes for a kind of onion dome, which can
be so handsome when done well, so pitiful when the various pieces don't
quite match.

But this 'cathedral' is a work of art compared to what the natives
proudly call their castle atop the hill. Again unpainted, unplanned, and in
a very real sense still unbuilt, it is a collection of barns, no less, one added
to the other in haphazard style and allowing no possibility of later improvement. A team of our finest St. Petersburg architects could not salvage this place and I'm quite certain it will grow worse as time passes and
new additions are added at random.

However, I must confess that on a clear day, and they do come
occasionally but mostly it's rain, rain, rain, the country surrounding the
hill can look supremely beautiful, like the best of the lake scenes we saw
in Italy, for in every direction mountains of surprising height come right
down to the water, forming a kind of rocky, tree-covered cocoon in which
New Archangel rests. And with that volcano standing guard, you have a
setting worthy of a master planner.

Instead, we have Aleksandr Baranov, a miserable merchant striving
ridiculously to be a gentleman, and I shall tell you only one thing about
this foolish and incapable man. When Volya and I were presented to him,
and we had not seen him before, he came forward, bowing low as was

proper, a fat little fellow with a round little belly and a costume sewn by some provincial tailor, because no two parts fitted. When he came closer I gasped, and Volya whispered to me, almost loud enough to be heard: 'My God, is that a wig?'

It was and it wasn't. It was certainly made of hair, but from what animal I would not care to guess, for it resembled no hair that I had ever seen before and I'm quite sure it wasn't human, unless it came from the beheaded member of some savage tribe. And obviously it was intended to serve as a wig, for it did rest upon his head, which I found later to be quite bald. But it was not that kind of wig which gentlemen and public officials in Europe can wear with such distinction, like Uncle Vanya's, for example. No, this was a kind of carpet, with a sickly color, no proper texture and absolutely no shape. It was a most sorry affair.

But now comes the unbelievable part. To keep it on his head, Monsieur Baranov used two strings of the kind you see French peasant women use to keep their bonnets on while milking their cows, and these strings he brought under his chin, where they were tied in a bowknot big enough to have served as his cravat. Later, when this fat little fellow with his absurd wig stood beside my dear Volya, receiving the sorriest lot of guests in all of Russia, not a gentleman among them, the comparison was preposterous and I almost cried from shame for the dignity of Russia. There he stood in his nightcap wig, and beside him stood Volya, erect, proper and never more worthy in his white uniform with the gold epaulets Uncle Vanya gave him.

We cannot leave New Archangel too speedily for me, and if the above is not enough, I now find that this tedious Baranov has a native wife whom he preposterously calls the Princess of Kenai, wherever that is, but when I protested about this disgrace to Russian dignity, my informant reminded me that the local priest, a man named Voronov, also has a native wife. What in the world is happening to Mother Russia that she is so careless with her children?

> With fondest thoughts, ever your loving daughter,
> Natasha

The *Muscovy* remained at New Archangel for nine tedious months, and week by week Lieutenant Ermelov and his princess became more openly contemptuous of Baranov, ridiculing him before his own men as a low merchant and castigating whatever moves he made to improve his capital. 'The man's an impossible dolt,' the princess observed loudly at one party, and in his frequent reports to St. Petersburg her husband wrote disparagingly on Baranov's intelligence, managerial ability and understanding of Russia's position in the world. More seriously, in three different letters Ermelov initiated those ugly questions concerning Baranov's use of government funds which would haunt him in subsequent years:

> When one considers the funds which our government has had to pour into New Archangel and then looks at the little which has been accomplished, one has to question whether this grubbing little merchant has not sequestered a fair share of them for his own selfish purposes.

These attacks on himself Baranov could accept, since he had been forewarned to expect them from any naval officer who was also of the nobility, but when

the Ermelovs began to vent their bile on Father Vasili, accusing him of impro-
prieties that were plainly ridiculous, Baranov had to intercede: 'Esteemed Princess, I really must protest. There is no finer clergyman in eastern Russia than
Vasili Voronov, and in that comparison I include His Reverence, the Bishop of
Irkutsk, whose piety is famous throughout Siberia.'

'Pious? Yes,' she granted. 'But isn't it offensive to have the leading church
figure in an area as big as this with a wife who was a short time ago a savage?
It's undignified.'

Under normal circumstances Baranov, never wishing to excite the animosity of the Ermelovs, would have allowed this condemnation to pass unchallenged, but in recent years he had become an intense defender of Sofia
Voronova, whom he saw as the epitome of the responsible Aleut woman whose
marriage to a Russian invader would form the basis of the new mixed race,
Russian-Aleut, which would populate and in time govern Russia's American
empire. As if eager to prove the correctness of Baranov's predictions, Sofia had
already given birth to a fine boy child, Arkady, but the underlying reason for
Baranov's predilection for this smiling, lovely woman lay in the fact that once
more he himself was without a spouse. For reasons he could not fathom, his
native wife, Anna, was behaving exactly like his Russian wife: she was refusing
to leave comfortable Kodiak to live with him in what she considered a less
desirable residence, New Archangel. Deprived of two wives, he brought his two
half-native children to Sitka, where he acted as both father and mother, and
resigned himself to the fact that he was one of those men unable to hold on to
a wife.

But in this loneliness he found increasing pleasure in watching the marital
progress of the Voronovs, and the more he observed the gentle, loving manner
in which these two people discovered fulfillment in each other, the more he saw
in them the emotional satisfaction denied him in his own marriage. Vasili
Voronov was proving to be an almost ideal clergyman for a place like New
Archangel. Courageous in battling frontier situations, loyal in supporting the
lay governor, and dedicated to the law of Jesus Christ on earth, he moved about
his enormous parish like the first disciples, and wherever he touched or paused
to give comfort, he produced an almost tangible Christianity. If the early fur
traders brought disgrace to the concept of Russian imperialism, Father Vasili
erased that stain by bringing love and understanding.

In this work he was supported by his Aleut wife, who continued to organize
and tend nurseries and orphanages and who formed a glowing bridge between
her pagan fellow Aleuts and her husband's Russian Christianity. She was,
Baranov thought, an ideal pastor's wife, and in his support of her efforts he
became a kind of father to her, so he was not disposed to allow Princess
Ermelova to denigrate her.

'I beg your pardon, Princess,' he said, after listening to the latest diatribe,
'but I have found Madame Voronova, whom you call a savage, to be a true
Christian; indeed, a jewel in our North American crown.'

The princess, not accustomed to rebuttal from anyone, looked down her
patrician nose at this ridiculous baldheaded man—Baranov wore his wig only
on ceremonial occasions—and said haughtily, as if dismissing some peasant:
'Monsieur Baranov, here in New Archangel, I see hundreds of Aleuts and they
are all savages, the priest's wife among them.'

Fully aware of the dangerous course he was pursuing, Baranov thrust his
fat little chin out and said: 'I see in those same Aleuts the future of Russian
America, and none is more promising than the priest's wife.'

Startled by this rude refutation, the princess snapped: 'Mark my words, you'll see that one slide back into the gutter. If she poses as a Christian, it's only to deceive men like you who are so easily fooled,' and when she next saw her husband, she stormed: 'Baranov spoke harshly when I reprimanded him for defending that pathetic Aleut woman attached to the priest. I want you to inform St. Petersburg that this Voronov is making a spectacle of himself with that little savage.'

Vladimir Ermelov had, in the wisdom that married men acquire so painfully, learned never to oppose his strong-willed wife, especially since she maintained close contacts with the tsar's family. But this time he did quietly ignore her fulminations against Sofia Voronova because in his dispatches home he simply had to report glowingly on the conduct of her husband, and it was these first assessments which were to pave the way for the extraordinary events which emerged later in the life of Father Vasili:

> The worse Baranov appears, and I have reported only his most glaring defects and malperformances, the better does his priest Vasili Voronov stand out as an exceptional churchman. In the perfection of his approach and accomplishment he is almost saintly and I commend him to Your Excellency's attention, not only because of his religious perfection but also because he represents Russia so ably. He has only one drawback that I have been able to detect: he is married to an Aleut lady of markedly dark complexion, but if he were to be promoted to a superior post, I suppose he could be released from her.

Now, when the princess railed against both Baranov and Sofia Voronova, Lieutenant Ermelov loudly agreed with her regarding the man but remained silent when Sofia was the target, and in this persistent way he continued to undermine Baranov's leadership of the colony, for as he told his wife and anyone else who wished to listen: 'Just as you cannot operate a naval ship with peasants, so you can't run a colony with merchants. In this world gentlemen are at a premium.'

As the *Muscovy* was preparing to quit New Archangel for the return trip to Russia, documents arrived confirming Ermelov's basic attitudes, for one set of papers brought severe rebukes to Baranov for his supposed laxity in minding The Company's funds and his tardiness in bringing order to his vast domain stretching from Attu Island in the west to Canada in the east, while another set informed Lieutenant Vladimir Ermelov that the tsar had authorized his promotion to lieutenant captain.

Baranov, mortified by the harshness of the criticism, sought counsel with Father Vasili, to whom he poured out the misery of his position: 'I had hoped that the next ship would bring me the funds to do the work required and perhaps a notice that I had at last been recognized with a title of some kind—nothing big, you know, just this or that of the third class, but with a ribbon testifying to the fact that I was now a member of the lesser nobility . . .'

Here he broke down, a sorely disappointed man in his sixties, and for some moments he fought against tears. 'There, there, Aleksandr Andreevich,' the priest whispered, 'God sees the worthy work you do. He sees your charity to children, the love with which you bring Aleuts into the bosom of His church.'

Baranov sniffed, wiped his eyes, and asked: 'Then why can't the government see it?' and Voronov gave the answer which had resounded through the centuries: 'Preferment is not dispensed in rational portions,' and after a thoughtful digestion of this truth, Baranov laughed, wiped his nose, and said: 'True, Vasili. You're six times a better Christian than the Bishop of Irkutsk, but who recognizes it?'

Then, self-pity laid aside, he took the priest's hands and said with great solemnity: 'Vasili, I'm an old man and very tired. This endless work eats at a man's soul. Twenty years ago I begged St. Petersburg to send a replacement, but none has come. That ship down there, it brings condemnation of my work but no money to help me do better and no younger man to take my place.' Now, dealing with real disappointments and not with transitory wounds to his vanity, he could no longer control himself, and tears of the most burning kind welled from his eyes. At the end of a long, distorted life he was a failure and a worn-out one to boot, so he sat before his priest, shoulders shaking, head bowed: 'Vasili, pray for me. I am lost at the end of the world. I know not what to do.'

But an even greater humiliation awaited. When Ermelov received notice of his own promotion, his wife initiated a gala celebration which would include all the ships in the bay, the multiple rooms atop the rock, and even the Aleut workmen inside the walls and the Tlingits outside; and the princess arranged it so that naval funds would pay for the ship festivities, while the celebrations ashore would be charged against Baranov's depleted treasury. When the chief administrator learned of this duplicity he was outraged: 'I *have* no treasury. I *have* no money.' But as the entertainments began and Baranov witnessed the jollity of the sailors and the Indians, he found himself caught up in the celebration, and at its height, when Lieutenant Captain Ermelov, straight and severe as an ash-tree harpoon, stepped forward to receive from Father Vasili the oath of allegiance, Baranov cheered with unfeigned generosity, even though both he and the priest knew that he was many times more effective as a commercial-political manager than Ermelov was as a naval geopolitician.

A LESSER MAN than Baranov might have been immobilized by the incredible position in which he now found himself: not only to be accused of stealing Company funds when The Company refused to send him any funds, but to be accused of diverting this Company money to his personal use at the very time when he was spending his own funds on work The Company should be doing, like caring for widows and orphans! It was insane, but he refused to let it disorient him, taking refuge in a comforting saying and an even more comforting visit south. The saying explained and forgave everything: 'That's Russia!' and the excursion soothed away mortal wounds.

Seventeen miles south of New Archangel, lost in a wilderness of islands and surrounded by mountains that rose from the sea, lay one of nature's miracles: a spring, rank with the smell of sulfur, which bubbled forth in a copious steaming flow that could be mixed with a trickle of icy water from a nearby stream, making it bearable to soak in. For a thousand years or longer the Tlingits had treasured this spring, hollowing out spruce trunks to serve as pipes to feed water from the spring and nearby stream into a stone-lined hole dug in the earth. Ingeniously, the Tlingits had fixed the cold-water pipe with a swivel so that it could be swung aside when the hot water was properly tempered.

It was a congenial place, hidden among trees, protected by mountains, but so situated that one could luxuriate in the tub and gaze out upon the Pacific Ocean. One of the constant regrets voiced by Kot-le-an and Raven-heart in their distant exile was: 'I wish we could go back to the hot bath,' and one of the first things the Russians did when they captured the hill was to sail south and build at the sulfur spring a proper housed-in bath with two real pipes to bring in the two kinds of water. In time they had a spa equal to any in the homeland, and as soon as Baranov had the area pacified he began his visits to the baths. Was Ermelov behaving outrageously? Off Baranov scuttled to the hot baths. Was his replacement seven years overdue? Down he went to the sulfur treatment, and as he lay back in the tub, working the two pipes with his toes, and the hot water steamed him to a rose-petal pink, he forgot the irritations which others wreaked upon him, and in his repose he visualized the great things yet to be done.

So on the happy day when the *Muscovy* finally sailed from New Archangel to carry Lieutenant Captain Ermelov back to Russia, Baranov stood on the shore, waving farewell with the obedient enthusiasm of an underling, but as soon as the ship was out of sight he called for an assistant: 'Let's go to the baths. I want to cleanse myself of that odious man,' and deep within the therapeutic waters he formulated those remarkable steps which would make his tenure in the east so productive and so remarkable to later historians.

When he sailed back to New Archangel after his visit to the baths, his shiny round head was bursting with new ideas, and he was pleased to see that yet another foreign ship had anchored during his absence. As he drew close enough for the letters on the bow to become readable he smiled—*Evening Star* BOSTON—and he supposed that Captain Corey was bringing in his hold much-wanted cargo, like food and nails, and just as much that was not, like rum and guns.

Relieved to see an easygoing American ship replace the stiff and disagreeable *Muscovy*, Baranov greeted Captain Corey and First Mate Kane warmly, inviting them to his home on the hill and learning from them the details of Napoleon's latest triumphs in Europe. With the generosity which marked all his dealing and which accounted for discrepancies in his accounts, if there were such, he told the Americans and Father Vasili as they dined together: 'Now I understand! Russia's been so frightened of Napoleon, the tsar hasn't had the time to bother about us out here. Or send us the money he promised.'

But as this first evening wore on, difficult questions existing between America and Russia began to surface, and Baranov said with considerable frankness: 'Captain Corey, this town is most delighted to see you back in these waters, but we trust you'll not be trading rum and guns to the Tlingits.'

Corey answered with a shrug, as if to say: 'Governor, we Americans trade as we can,' and Baranov, interpreting the shrug correctly, warned in an amicable way: 'Captain, I have orders to halt your trade in rum and guns. Such trade destroys our natives, makes them useless for any worthy purpose.'

Very firmly Corey replied: 'But our nation insists upon its right to trade anywhere on the high seas and with any goods we wish.'

'But this is not the high seas, Captain. This is Russian territory, just the way Okhotsk would be, or Petropavlovsk.'

'I think not,' Corey said without raising his voice. 'Where we sit tonight, yes. Sitka Sound is Russian.' Like most foreigners, he spoke only of Sitka Sound, never of New Archangel, and this added to Baranov's irritation. 'But the waters hereabout, they're open sea and I shall treat them as such.'

Very evenly Baranov replied: 'And my orders are to prevent you from doing so.'

Miles Corey was a small, grimly determined man who had spent his life contesting the seas and their harbors, and Russian threats did not alarm him any more than had the threats of Tahitians or Fijians: 'We honor without question your preeminence here in Sitka, but you have none in what we deem international waters.'

'So you intend to peddle your rum and guns to our natives?' Baranov asked, and Corey said with firm politeness: 'We do.'

It was curious, and a fact long to be debated by historians and moralists, that in these years the two Anglo-Saxon nations which presumed to follow the higher dictates of religion and public behavior, England and America, should feel themselves entitled by some moral justification which others could not discern to trade as they wished with what they called 'the backward nations of the world.' In defense of this inalienable right, England felt herself justified in forcing opium upon the Chinese; while America insisted upon the right to trade rum and guns with natives everywhere, even, it must be admitted, to her own warlike Indians in the West.

So when Aleksandr Baranov, this doughty little merchant, proposed to halt such trade in his territory, men like Captain Corey and First Mate Kane stated firmly that the rights of free men entitled them to trade with natives under Russian rule as they wished and without fear of retaliation from Russian arms. 'It's simple, Governor Baranov,' Corey explained. 'We sail north, well away from Sitka, and trade our goods for pelts, and no one's the worse off.'

'Except the natives, who remain drunk all the time, and we Russians, who have to spend vast sums to protect ourselves from those who now have guns,' and he pointed to the palisade which had to be maintained at such heavy cost.

The problem was not resolved that time. The superior American morality prevailed, and the *Evening Star* laid plans to sail north to dispose of its goods for the dwindling supply of sea-otter pelts. However, on the last night ashore, a conversation occurred which had a profound effect upon development in this part of the world, for while Captain Corey talked with the Voronovs about Tlingit and Aleut history, Baranov and onetime-harpooner Tom Kane sat off to one side, looking down upon the silvery gray beauty of the harbor, and the Russian said, 'Mr. Kane, New Archangel will never be the first-class city I plan until we have our own shipbuilding yard. Tell me, how difficult is it to build a ship?'

'I've never built one.'

'But you've sailed in them.'

'Sailing and building, two different challenges.'

'But could a man like you, who knows ships so well, do you think you could build a ship?'

'If I had the proper books, yes, I suppose I could.'

'Can you read German?'

'I was fifteen before I could read English.'

'But you did teach yourself?'

'I did.'

'So did I,' Baranov said. 'I wanted to start a glass factory, got a book from Germany and taught myself to read that language.'

'Was the factory any good?'

'Satisfactory. Look,' and he produced a German text on shipbuilding, an elaboration of the one Vitus Bering had used a century earlier.

Kane, hefting the volume and inspecting a few drawings, handed it back: 'A glass factory can work if it's merely satisfactory. A ship can't.' So he dismissed Baranov's implied invitation but he could not dismiss the man's penetrating vision of what Sitka might become, and when he asked about this, he knocked the top off a volcano from which erupted a lava flow of ideas.

'I want to build ships here, a score of them. And plant a colony in California, where the Spaniards accomplish nothing. I think we ought to trade with

China. And with a captain like you in his own ship, Hawaii would be wide open for trade and maybe even settlement.' Reaching out and taking Kane by the arm, he asked: 'What did you think of Hawaii?' And there at the edge of the Pacific, Kane was lured into disclosing his admiration, indeed his longing, for those heavenly isles.

'Somebody ought to take over those islands,' he said enthusiastically. 'If Russia doesn't, England or America will.'

Now Baranov became more pressing: 'Mr. Kane, a man your age . . . How old are you? Past fifty? You ought to be captain of your own ship.'

Kane smiled bitterly: 'Our first captain, fine man named Pym, promised to promote me along the line to captain one day. But he got himself killed at Lapak Island. So I stayed on with Captain Corey, thinking he'd promote me the same way. Never happened. So then I thought maybe one of these days the old fellow would die and I'd take over. But you can see for yourself, he's past sixty, strong as ever, and he told me the other day he'd decided never to die. So I work on.' He stopped, laughed, and admitted: 'He's a good captain and I'm not unhappy.'

So the *Evening Star* traded a few goods with Baranov's people, weighed anchor, and sailed on to the next island north, where they sought out Kot-le-an and Raven-heart, providing them with many guns and their followers with casks of rum. But when the time came to sail north toward Yakutat, where other Tlingits longed for guns with which to attack Kot-le-an's people, because Tlingits enjoyed nothing more than a good battle now and then—among themselves if no Russians were at hand—First Mate Kane stayed behind with Raven-heart, and when Corey sent a boat to fetch him, Kane said: 'Tell him I'm staying here,' and the ex-harpooner spoke so forcefully that no one cared to challenge him.

'What shall we do with your things?' the sailors asked, and Kane said: 'There are no things. I brought them with me.' And two days later he and Raven-heart were in a canoe paddling down to Sitka, where Kane informed Baranov that he had come south to start a shipyard, while Raven-heart used this opportunity to scout out the Russian defenses against the night when his Tlingits would attack once more.

WHEN TOM KANE of Boston, using a German shipbuilding manual whose words he never learned to read but whose drawings he followed, completed building four ships, *Sitka*, *Otkrietie*, *Chirikov* and *Lapak*, his employer, Baranov, was ready to make his long-planned moves in the Pacific. Commissioning a group of bright young men and giving them two ships, he sent them off to occupy a fine site north of San Francisco, and the Spaniards were so inattentive to this invasion of their territory that they allowed the Russians to gain a substantial foothold.

So a remarkable situation developed in this part of the world. Before cities like Chicago or Denver were even thought of, and while San Francisco had no more than a few score of residents and the future Los Angeles none, Sitka was a thriving town of nearly a thousand, with its own library, school, shipyard, hospital, navigation center, civil government and navy. In addition, it controlled a solid foothold in California, and under Baranov's prudent leadership, seemed destined to command the entire west coast of the Pacific down to San Francisco and probably beyond.

From that solid beginning, Baranov decided to reach into the central Pacific, for after Kane had finished with his shipbuilding, he was given command of the *Lapak*, with orders to establish good relations with King

Kamehameha in Honolulu. Since Kane and the king already knew each other favorably, the wooing of Hawaii proceeded so rapidly that other nations began to fear they might have to take steps to thwart it, but Baranov's astute guidance strengthened the friendship between Hawaii and Sitka and for a spell of years it looked as if the golden islands were destined to fall under Russian control.

But now hammer blows began to strike Baranov. Close to exhaustion, he pleaded with St. Petersburg for three boons: money to complete building his beloved capital at New Archangel, a replacement to serve as chief administrator and, at the end of one of the most productive public services in Russia, some small shred of recognition—a medal, a ribbon, a title no matter how mean— that would lift him out of the category of despised merchant and enable him to believe, no matter how briefly, that he had won by his energy and imagination a patent of minor nobility.

The money never came. But the distant government, acknowledging at last that Baranov was an old man, did appoint a replacement who would assume responsibility for the government, an able fellow named Ivan Koch who had compiled a good record as commander at Okhotsk. Baranov, delighted by the prospect of having free time to work at the things which really interested him and knowing Koch to be a good man, sent a letter of warm congratulations, which Koch never received, for while at Petropavlovsk on his way to his new duties he died with tragic suddenness.

Once more Baranov besieged St. Petersburg with appeals for a successor, and this time a much younger man with good credentials was shipped out to New Archangel aboard the *Neva*, a reliable ship familiar with the eastern Pacific. From the lookout room in his house Baranov watched with delight as the *Neva* approached the bay, then with horror as it ran into a storm off Edgecumbe volcano and sank within reach of land, taking to their death most of her complement, including the new governor.

It was a savage disappointment, worsened by the return of the notorious *Muscovy* under the command of Baranov's avowed enemy Vladimir Ermelov, who, since his wife the princess did not accompany him this time, arrived in a foul mood. Among his secret papers was one which instructed him to probe the rumors which he himself had circulated during his previous visit:

> You are to inquire as judiciously and secretly as possible into the financial deportment of Chief Administrator Baranov, who has been reported to us as having sequestered for his own use funds belonging to The Company. If in the process of your investigation you find him guilty of defalcations, you are hereby empowered to arrest and incarcerate him prior to his return to St. Petersburg for trial. In his absence you will serve as Chief Administrator.

But now the complexity of government in Russia manifested itself, for in the same mail pouch, directed not to Ermelov but to Baranov, was a letter which brought him great satisfaction. It came from a different branch of government, obviously, for it said:

> Know Ye All, We do confer upon said Aleksandr Andreevich the rank in the Civil Service of Collegiate Councilor, with social standing equal in rank to a Colonel in the Infantry, a Lieutenant Captain in the Navy,

an Abbot in the Church, and entitled to be addressed by all as Your Excellency.

Alexander I

The duty and privilege of announcing to the world that Chief Administrator Baranov was now His Excellency Collegiate Councilor Aleksandr Andreevich Baranov fell by tradition to the senior officer present, who happened to be Lieutenant Captain Vladimir Ermelov, commanding officer of His Majesty's warship *Muscovy*, and on a bright morning which would bring bile to the throat of that young nobleman, he had to preside on the hill when Baranov, his incredible wig tied under his chin, stepped forward to receive the great honor which the tsar had bestowed upon him. With taut lips and in a whisper so low that few could hear, Ermelov read in grudging terms those words which lifted Baranov into the nobility. It was then incumbent upon Ermelov to place about Baranov's neck the ribbon from which was suspended the shimmering medal he would henceforth be entitled to wear, and then came the worst moment of all, for by custom Ermelov was now required to kiss the recipient on both cheeks. He planted the first one with obvious repugnance, and as he made preparations to award the second, he grumbled in a voice suddenly so loud that all could hear: 'For the love of Jesus Christ, take off that wig.'

Two weeks later, when Ermelov was well on his way into the garbled books of the New Archangel office of The Company, he was required to discharge an even more disagreeable obligation, for one of his young officers, scion of one of Russia's noblest families, came to him with a request which stunned him:

'Respected Lieutenant Captain Ermelov, with your permission, sir, I want to marry a local girl of impecable reputation, and in obedience to custom, I beg you to represent me when I make my petition to the girl's father. Will you do me the honor, sir?'

Ermelov, aware of his responsibility to protect the noble families of Russia and to prevent hasty marriages which would damage them, sparred for time with the ardent young man. Holding himself very erect and looking his most severe, he asked: 'Surely you're mindful of the exalted position your family occupies in Russia?'

'I am.'

'And you know that you must not stain its impeccable reputation by an improper marriage?'

'Of course, my parents would be appalled if I behaved poorly.'

'So wouldn't circles at the court deem it imprudent if you were to marry some chit of a child here in New Archangel? Some Creole, no doubt?'

'I'd never do that. This young lady is the daughter of a princess. She's lovely and will glow in even the highest court circles.'

'A princess? I thought my wife was the only princess in New Archangel, and she's no longer here.' He coughed. 'Who is this paragon?'

'Baranov's daughter Irina.'

The cough turned into a choking sound, and then into a sputter: 'Do you believe that nonsense about Baronov's wife being the daughter of some stupid king somewhere?'

'Yes, Excellency, I do. Baranov showed me a paper signed by the tsar himself, legitimizing his second marriage, and another confirming his new wife in her title as the Princess of Kenai.'

'Why haven't I heard about such a ukase?' Ermelov stormed, and the young suitor explained: 'It arrived after you returned to Russia,' and when he borrowed the precious papers to show Ermelov, the reluctant officer had to honor them. So on a solemn summer day, with the sun reflecting from the many mountaintops, Lieutenant Captain Ermelov, in his best dress uniform, accompanied his aide to the hill, where they were met by His Excellency Baranov wearing over his ears his wig and upon his chest his medal. 'Your Excellency,' Ermelov began, the words sticking in his throat, 'my distinguished aide, a young man of excellent family well regarded by the tsar, seeks permission to marry your daughter Irina, lineal descendant of the kings of Kenai.'

Baranov, bowing before the man who was now of rank no higher than his own but of a more ancient lineage and therefore entitled to respect, replied in a low voice: 'You do our humble house great honor. Permission granted,' and the three men repaired to a balcony, from which they could look west to the volcano where the *Neva* had foundered, north toward the site where Redoubt St. Michael had stood before Kot-le-an and Raven-heart destroyed it, and then to the mountains where Raven-heart was plotting his revenge.

WITH HIS DAUGHTER married into the nobility and his own patent of nobility firmly about his neck—he wore it on all occasions, even when drinking beer at the close of day—Baranov should have been at the golden apex of his life, a man respected in New Archangel, valued at The Company offices in Irkutsk, and esteemed in St. Petersburg for his sagacity in handling problems in the Pacific, but as the months passed, it became obvious that Lieutenant Captain Ermelov was probing Company records to prove that the old man was a thief, and as the scandal grew, Baranov withered.

He was seventy now, resident in the islands for an unbroken twenty-six trying years, and his health had never been good since the day of his arrival, when he lay almost dead at the bottom of that improvised boat in Three Saints Bay. Four or five times subsequently he had been near to expiring, but he had struggled on, subduing adversities which would have collapsed a lesser man. He had brought order among the trader-hunters, utilized creatively the Aleuts, and conquered the warlike Tlingits. On a mountainous island at the edge of North America he had constructed a capital worthy of a vast territory, and above all, he had defended widows and cared for orphans, spending his own money in doing so. To end his life accused of petty thievery was almost more than he could tolerate and twice he contemplated suicide, but he was prevented from indulging in such negative actions by the unwavering loyalty of three trusted friends: Father Vasili and his wife, and his aide Kyril Zhdanko, who in these latter days stepped forth as his protector and the man who could be relied on to see that his grand designs moved forward.

As the rumored accusations of thievery intensified, he appeared infrequently in public and when he did he moved furtively, as if he realized that people in the settlement were speculating as to when he would be thrown into irons and bundled aboard the *Muscovy* for return to Russia in disgrace. Lieutenant Captain Ermelov did nothing to defuse these rumors; indeed, he encouraged them, waiting for the day when he could inform the man who would come out from St. Petersburg to replace Baranov: 'I think we have a case against him. We'll be leaving for Russia promptly.'

During this time, an American ship put in to Sitka Sound, where it traded openly with rum and guns, now that Baranov no longer had the energy to combat this evil traffic. Then the ship sailed north to the remote settlement in which Kot-le-an and his aide Raven-heart continued to collect rifles against the day when they could once more attack the Russians. But now when they learned from the Americans that their old foe Baranov was being shipped back to Russia in disgrace, they decided they had one last score to settle with the old man, and as soon as the ship departed, these two who had fought Baranov so assiduously climbed into a canoe and started paddling south to meet for the last time with their adversary.

They were spotted from a distance as they came into the island-studded sound, and as they glided resolutely through the myriad islands, word flashed through the capital that Tlingits in war dress were approaching the hill, and everyone who could rushed down to the waterfront, where with great dignity the two warriors were approaching the landing. When they were close enough for their identity to be established, a wild cry surged through the settlement: 'Kot-le-an is back! Here comes Raven-heart!' And Baranov himself came down the eighty steps that separated his house from the shore, ignoring those who fell back to whisper about him and going directly to where the canoe was being pulled ashore.

As soon as Raven-heart stepped on dry land he halted, raised his right hand, and launched into a ten-minute oration delivered in a deep, thundering voice. The highlights of his message were memorable:

'Chief Warrior Baranov, builder of forts, burner of forts, your two ene-mies who destroyed your fort to the north, who lost our fort down here, greet you. In all our battles, you were toion. You fought well. You behaved with generosity when you won. You have given our people who live beyond the palisade a good life. Manager Baranov, we salute you.'

With this, the two warriors, still big and powerful, moved forward to embrace their old enemy, and after warmly welcoming them, Baranov suggested: 'Let us climb the hill together,' and there on the porch of his hilltop house these three good men who were losing so much surveyed the noble theater in which they had played out their tragedy. 'Up there's the fort we drove you out of,' said Raven-heart, explaining how he had scouted the defenses while smoking salmon. 'And down there's the fort you Tlingits thought could not be taken,' Baranov said, and Kot-le-an surprised them both by saying: 'My heart broke when your cannon shattered our totem, because then I knew we had lost.'

They shared the saddest reversals an older man can know, the loss of dreams, and that evening dusk fell with a heavy sadness, but it was relieved somewhat when Baranov left them for a moment to fetch a most surprising gift.

Retiring to his room, he tied on his wig as ceremony required, placed about his neck the medal proclaiming his nobility, and lifted from a wooden trunk a bulky article in which he took considerable pride. It was the wood-and-leather suit of armor which he had worn when marching against the Tlingit fort. Holding it forth in both arms, he approached Kot-le-an and said: 'Bold Chief-tain,' but then his voice broke. For some moments he stood in the growing dark, striving to control his tears, and as his shoulders trembled his wig bobbed up and down, so that he was about as ridiculous as any make-believe commodore could be. Finally he controlled himself, but he dared not trust his voice, so in silence and with a kind of love for these men who had proved so valiant he handed them his armor, even though he had good reason to believe that at some future date, after he was gone, they would come storming back to try once more to destroy the Russians.

I N DISGRACE AND threatened with prison when he reached St. Petersburg— except that Father Vasili Voronov had volunteered to travel at his own expense to the capital to defend his friend from the insane charges lodged against him—Baranov left Sitka Sound a prisoner aboard a Russian warship, which wandered across the Pacific to Hawaii, whose wondrous islands he had almost brought into the Russian Empire, and then down to the unlikely port of Batavia in Java. Here, in one of the hottest, most feverish outposts of the Pacific, he was kept penned up aboard ship, until his frail body collapsed in final surrender.

He died on 16 April 1819 near the strait which separates Java from Sumatra, and almost immediately the sailors weighted him with iron, tied his beloved medal about his neck, and tossed him into the ocean.

Three men of noble bearing had wrestled with the Pacific Ocean and all had perished in their attempt. In 1741, Vitus Bering died of scurvy on a forlorn island in the sea named after him. In 1779, James Cook was slain on a remote beach in Hawaii. And in 1819, Aleksandr Baranov died of exhaustion and fever near Sunda Strait. They had loved the great ocean, had conquered it in part, had been destroyed by it, and had been consigned in death to the vast, consoling sea.

Baranov was not a great man and sometimes, as in his enslavement of the Aleuts, not even a good man. But he was a man of honor, and in the Alaska he molded his memory would always be revered.

I N 1829, TEN years after the death of Baranov, the old warship *Muscovy* put in to Sitka Sound, bringing as passenger from St. Petersburg a bright-eyed young university graduate who was returning to his home island after a course of study in which he had distinguished himself. This was in the time when his father's friend, Kyril Zhdanko, served as the interim chief administrator, a notable appointment in that he was the first Creole to occupy that powerful position.

The returning young man was Arkady Voronov, himself a Creole as the son of the Russian priest and the Aleut convert Sofia Kuchovskaya. Twenty-eight years old, he came with an appointment as assistant manager of trade affairs and with a passionate attachment to a young woman he had met during a visit to Moscow. So, after greeting his parents with the affection that had always marked his relationship to them, he paid his respects to Chief Administrator Zhdanko and then repaired to his room in the priest's quarters next to St. Michael's Cathedral, the little wooden church with the big onion dome and the pretentious name. There, as soon as his bags were stowed, he wrote to his beloved back in Moscow:

My darling Praskovia,

The voyage was simpler than the others had predicted. Five easy months, with a halt at the Cape and another in Hawaii, where I had expected to find many friends from Baranov's day. Alas, they are now our enemies because of errors made by others, and I'm afraid we've lost our chance to make those islands part of our empire.

Sitka Sound is as beautiful as I remembered it, and I long for the day when you stand here beside me enjoying its majesty of islands and mountains and lovely volcano. Please, please convince your parents that it is safe to make the trip, which really isn't so long, and then to live here in what's becoming a major city.

I have given your silhouette in its ivory frame the place of honor on my table, the first item to be unpacked, and I am now hastening to the offices of The Company to acquire data on New Archangel so that your parents can be reassured that it is a real city and not merely an outpost in the wilderness. I shall resume this letter before I go to bed.

When young Voronov left the cathedral and climbed the hill to the castle, where Zhdanko waited to instruct him as to his duties, he saw all about him the signs of a bustling town, not a city as he had described it to Praskovia, but a prosperous settlement which no longer depended solely on furs for its wealth. In one direction he saw the tall windmill that operated a grist mill; in another, the smoking fires where fat from various sea animals was being rendered for soap. There was a walk for spinning rope, a smithy for forging varieties of gear, a boilermaker who made his own rivets, a foundry for casting bronze, and all sorts of carpenters, sailmakers and glaziers.

What surprised him was one small shop for making and mending watches, and another for the repair of compasses and other nautical instruments. And for the general population, there was one tailor, three dressmakers, two doctors and three priests. There was also a school, a hospital, a place for public dining, an orphanage run by his mother, a library.

Stopping at a corner where the main road intersected with one perpendicular to the bay, he asked a man carrying boards: 'Is this place always so busy?' and the man replied: 'You ought to see it when an American ship puts in to trade.'

From Zhdanko himself he learned the facts about his new post: 'I'm proud to have at my right hand the son of two people who have been so important to me. Your father and mother, Arkady, are special, and I hope you remember that. But you asked for the facts. Total population inside the palisade, nine hundred and eighty-three. That's three hundred and thirty-two Russians with the right to return to the homeland, and a hundred and thirty-six of their wives and children. Then we have a hundred and thirty-five Creoles who do not have the right of return. We have forty-two children in the orphanage, a horrible number, but we do have accidents and parents do run off. To round out, we have inside the walls three hundred and thirty-eight Aleuts helping us with our hunt for sea otters and seals. Total, nine hundred eighty-three.'

'And do the Tlingits still live outside the palisade?' Arkady asked, and Zhdanko replied grimly: 'They better.' Then he summarized the Russian experience with this brave, intractable people: 'The Tlingits are different. You never pacify a group of Tlingits. They love their land and they're always ready to fight for it.'

'So you think the walls are still necessary?'

'Positively. We never know when those people out there are going to try once more to drive us off this island. Observe our cannon up there,' and when Arkady looked up at the hill he saw that three of its guns were aimed down at the bay to fend off any ships which might intrude unexpectedly, but nine were directed at the Tlingit village outside the walls.

What reassured him even more than the guns was the energy with which Russians, Creoles and Aleuts attacked the problems of daily living. A few educated Creoles like himself or trusted ones like Zhdanko supervised Company affairs, and Russian clerical types like Mr. Malakov kept accounts, but most were out in the sun conducting the businesses that one would expect to find in a thriving seaport. The average Creole did manual labor and most Aleuts went out regularly in their kayaks.

He did not find time to finish his letter that first evening, for Chief Administrator Zhdanko and his Creole wife invited him to the hill, where sixteen Russian men, each convinced that he could govern the colony better than the Creole, and their wives had joined to welcome young Voronov to his new post, and he was awed by the handsome new building which had replaced the house he had sometimes visited when Baranov occupied it. The place was now quite grand, with several stories, imported furniture and an even better view of Sitka Sound because obstructing trees had been removed. 'Everyone calls it Baranov's Castle,' Zhdanko explained, 'because we feel that his spirit still resides here.'

It was a gala evening, with a husband-and-wife team playing four-hand music on the two pianos and a set of surprisingly good baritone solos by Chief Clerk Malakov. He sang first a selection of arias from Mozart, then a rousing medley of Russian folksongs in which the guests joined, and finally, a most moving rendition of 'Stenka Razin' whose grand, flowing notes reminded his listeners of distant Russia.

Next night, after a day of inspecting the palisade and seeing the intricate gateway through which a limited number of Tlingits were allowed entry to trade, Arkady did find time to complete his letter:

I have now seen New Archangel inside and out, and I beg you, Praskovia, to gain permission from your parents to sail here on the next ship, for this is a complete little city. We have a good hospital, doctors trained in Moscow, and even a man who fixes teeth. The houses are made of wood it's true, but each year the city grows, and both the chief administrator and I expect it to have two thousand citizens before very long. Of course, it has that now if you count the Tlingits who live outside the walls.

And I must tell you one thing more, which I confide with great pride. My father and mother occupy a place of considerable honor in this part of Russia. He is known far and wide, through all the islands, for his piety, and he is loved by the natives because he has taken the trouble to learn their language and help them in their way of life before he ever importunes them to become Christians. If there is a saint walking this earth today, it is my father. Indeed, they call him a living saint.

And Mother is his equal. She is, as I told your parents most explicitly, an Aleut born, but she is now, I do believe, a better Christian than my father. Goodness radiates from her face and sanctity from her soul.

I was, as you may remember, awed by the notable traditions of your Kostilevsky family and said many times that you had a right to be proud of your heritage, but I feel the same about my father and mother, for they are establishing the new line of nobility for Russian America.

One terribly important fact, Praskovia. When you leave Moscow to come here, you must not think of yourself as going into exile at the ends of the earth. People leave here all the time to return to the mainland. Irkutsk is a splendid city where my family served in both government and the church. Hawaii is gorgeous with its wealth of flowers. And some travelers go back to Europe by way of America, which takes a long time if you round the Horn but which is, I am told, rewarding.

priest who had visited New Archangel offered
s sixty-three. She's probably in her mid-fifties.
seemed to be about that age.' He stopped, but
, he volunteered: 'A fine-looking woman, you
savage, not at all.'
to keep the discussion on the main theme, asked:
n order to reassume the black?' and an elderly
st's church, a man might do anything.'
arshly at the man and said: 'You may not believe
any things I would not have done to attain these
Well, would he take the black?'
who had served in Irkutsk. 'Service in the Lord's
l the opportunity to accomplish good is not to be

ay so,' the metropolitan snapped, and the cleric
I do mean power.'
power?' the old man asked, and one of his younger
neither sought nor avoided it. The man's a real saint,

the metropolitan muttered. 'In one family on a
rd of, we have a male saint and a female saint.
thers started to assure him that this was the case, he
asked the most difficult question of all: 'If we lure him
dazzling prize, will she let him go?' and the priest who
: 'She would understand if he were called to glory. He
her. She would, I'm sure, advise him to do the same
y the church.'
, the powers in St. Petersburg reached the extraordinary
he tsar, to bring into the highest office of the Orthodox
t from the parish farthest from the capital, Father Vasili
l's Cathedral in New Archangel. But the metropolitan,
ccessor had been selected but not eager to have the man
rg too soon, suggested: 'Let us appoint him Bishop of
Metropolitan next year, when I shall be too old to continue
en those energetic churchmen who wanted a new leader
promoting Father Vasili by easy steps was the preferred
gh the tsar wanted a new man quickly, he too capitulated
o protect himself, announced publicly that early next year
f the Orthodox Church would be retiring.
nd devious way, Vasili Voronov received secret notice that
lack, which he had abandoned thirty-six years before, he
l Bishop of Irkutsk, the town from which his family had
kelihood of further preferment later on. The naval officer
exciting information added, as he had been directed by the
f course this would necessitate a divorce. And if your wife,
people Russia is endeavoring to win over to Christianity,
shrugged his shoulders.
Vasili studied the confidential papers which verified this ex-
sal he had two reactions, which he could voice only to himself:
but if the church in its wisdom calls me, how could I refuse?
ately: But what would Sofia's role be in this? And without even
ofound problem with his son, he left his cathedral and walked

No one knew exactly, but a
a guess: 'We know her husband
I saw her several times and she
before anyone else could speak
know. On the short side but n

The metropolitan, wanting
'Would Voronov divorce her
churchman said: 'To lead Chr
The metropolitan looked h
it, Hilarion, but there were m
robes.' Then, to the others: '
'I think so,' said a cleric
cause would be enticing. An
lightly bypassed, either.'
'If you mean power, s
replied sharply: 'Very well,
'Does this Voronov seek
helpers said firmly: 'He has
I assure you.'
'Goodness, goodness,
remote island I never he
Remarkable.' But when o
looked at his advisers and
to St. Petersburg with our
had seen her at work said
broke his vows to marry
if he now seeks to marr
With that assurance
decision, applauded by
Church the saintly pries
Voronov of St. Michae
eager to know that a su
appear in St. Petersbu
Irkutsk this year and N
in the office.' And ev
now had to agree tha
route, and even thou
to this strategy, but t
the grand old man
In this strange a
if he resumed the b
would be appointe
come, with every l
who delivered this
tsar himself: 'But
as a member of a
objected ...' He
When Father
traordinary prop
I am not worthy
and then immedi
discussing the p

Thro
crisis
were s
accomp
sage to
one abou
Petersbur
of the prie
'One of th
resident in
consulted te
of Voronov
Church had p
fortunate use

Improbabl
of the church, s
force of Russia
forceful, devout
renowned for his
attention on Fathe
they investigated h
solution to their pr
the tsar, who appla

'It's understood,
Vasili accepts our inv
have to surrender his

'No difficulty, Ho
Irkutsk, he did so as a

'Why was it he cha

'Yes, when he had
Kodiak ...'

'Now I remember. Y

'On a busy day, Holi
remember.'

'Yes.' He reflected on
youth and to imagine distan
Aleuts ... well, they're paga

'This woman was, but s
Christian than the Christians,

'That's always a reassuring
guardian of his church, he jabbe
as saintly as you say, and her hu
on the black, will there not be an
her advanced age? How old is she

And if, as Baranov taught Zhdanko to do, we establish significant holdings on the North American continent, you and I could well be important factors in the new Russia. My heart beats with excitement at the possibility.

All my love,
Arkady

Through a bizarre twist, it was this letter which precipitated the final wrenching crisis in the Voronov family, because when Praskovia's parents received it, they were so struck by that forceful paragraph in which Arkady spoke of his father's accomplishments in Kodiak and Sitka that Kostilevsky senior showed the passage to church authorities in Moscow, who copied the paragraph, adding the one about Father Vasili's wife, Sofia, for circulation among the authorities in St. Petersburg. There Lieutenant Captain Vladimir Ermelov was asked his opinion of the priest Voronov in New Archangel, and Ermelov replied enthusiastically: 'One of the finest,' and he instructed the church fathers as to who else now resident in Moscow had knowledge of the eastern lands, and all who were consulted testified that Vasili Voronov, white priest from the noteworthy family of Voronov in Irkutsk, was about as strong a churchman as the Orthodox Church had produced in a long time. In the discussion thus launched, Arkady's fortunate use of words was often repeated: 'They call him a living saint.'

Improbable as it seemed at the time and unlikely as it seems now, the leaders of the church, spurred on by Tsar Nicholas I, who sought to revive the spiritual force of Russian Orthodoxy, decided that what St. Petersburg needed was a forceful, devout man from the frontier uncontaminated by churchly politics and renowned for his sanctity. For a host of intricate reasons they focused their attention on Father Vasili Voronov, wonder-worker in the islands, and the more they investigated his credentials the more satisfied they were that he was the solution to their problems. But no sooner had they announced their decision to the tsar, who applauded it, than a knotty problem arose.

'It's understood, of course,' the present metropolitan pointed out, 'if Father Vasili accepts our invitation to come to St. Petersburg as my successor, he will have to surrender his white robes and transfer to black.'

'No difficulty, Holiness. You'll remember that when he took orders in Irkutsk, he did so as a black.'

'Why was it he changed? To marry?'

'Yes, when he had assumed his first office, on that big island they call Kodiak . . .'

'Now I remember. You told me about this last week, didn't you?'

'On a busy day, Holiness. He fell in love with an Aleut woman, you'll remember.'

'Yes.' He reflected on this for some moments, striving to recall his own youth and to imagine distant frontiers about which he knew nothing: 'Aren't Aleuts . . . well, they're pagan, aren't they?'

'This woman was, but she's proved to be a most unusual type. More Christian than the Christians, they say. Charity among the children.'

'That's always a reassuring sign,' he said, but then, as the longtime spiritual guardian of his church, he jabbed his thumb down on the real problem: 'If she's as saintly as you say, and her husband must renounce his white robes and take on the black, will there not be an outcry against him and us if he leaves her at her advanced age? How old is she?'

No one knew exactly, but a priest who had visited New Archangel offered a guess: 'We know her husband is sixty-three. She's probably in her mid-fifties. I saw her several times and she seemed to be about that age.' He stopped, but before anyone else could speak, he volunteered: 'A fine-looking woman, you know. On the short side but no savage, not at all.'

The metropolitan, wanting to keep the discussion on the main theme, asked: 'Would Voronov divorce her in order to reassume the black?' and an elderly churchman said: 'To lead Christ's church, a man might do anything.'

The metropolitan looked harshly at the man and said: 'You may not believe it, Hilarion, but there were many things I would not have done to attain these robes.' Then, to the others: 'Well, would he take the black?'

'I think so,' said a cleric who had served in Irkutsk. 'Service in the Lord's cause would be enticing. And the opportunity to accomplish good is not to be lightly bypassed, either.'

'If you mean power, say so,' the metropolitan snapped, and the cleric replied sharply: 'Very well, I do mean power.'

'Does this Voronov seek power?' the old man asked, and one of his younger helpers said firmly: 'He has neither sought nor avoided it. The man's a real saint, I assure you.'

'Goodness, goodness,' the metropolitan muttered. 'In one family on a remote island I never heard of, we have a male saint and a female saint. Remarkable.' But when others started to assure him that this was the case, he looked at his advisers and asked the most difficult question of all: 'If we lure him to St. Petersburg with our dazzling prize, will she let him go?' and the priest who had seen her at work said: 'She would understand if he were called to glory. He broke his vows to marry her. She would, I'm sure, advise him to do the same if he now seeks to marry the church.'

With that assurance, the powers in St. Petersburg reached the extraordinary decision, applauded by the tsar, to bring into the highest office of the Orthodox Church the saintly priest from the parish farthest from the capital, Father Vasili Voronov of St. Michael's Cathedral in New Archangel. But the metropolitan, eager to know that a successor had been selected but not eager to have the man appear in St. Petersburg too soon, suggested: 'Let us appoint him Bishop of Irkutsk this year and Metropolitan next year, when I shall be too old to continue in the office.' And even those energetic churchmen who wanted a new leader now had to agree that promoting Father Vasili by easy steps was the preferred route, and even though the tsar wanted a new man quickly, he too capitulated to this strategy, but to protect himself, announced publicly that early next year the grand old man of the Orthodox Church would be retiring.

In this strange and devious way, Vasili Voronov received secret notice that if he resumed the black, which he had abandoned thirty-six years before, he would be appointed Bishop of Irkutsk, the town from which his family had come, with every likelihood of further preferment later on. The naval officer who delivered this exciting information added, as he had been directed by the tsar himself: 'But of course this would necessitate a divorce. And if your wife, as a member of a people Russia is endeavoring to win over to Christianity, objected . . .' He shrugged his shoulders.

When Father Vasili studied the confidential papers which verified this extraordinary proposal he had two reactions, which he could voice only to himself: I am not worthy, but if the church in its wisdom calls me, how could I refuse? and then immediately: But what would Sofia's role be in this? And without even discussing the profound problem with his son, he left his cathedral and walked from one corner of the palisaded area to the most distant, back and forth past the warehouses he had helped build, then past the stores that Kyril Zhdanko had helped start, out to where the Tlingits gathered on the other side of the palisade, and back to the church which would never have come into being without his hard work and that of his wife. And when her name or her image came up, he realized the cruel choice that was being offered him.

For three days he was unable to broach the subject with her, and he refrained for a good reason: he felt sure that if she knew of his chances in Irkutsk and later perhaps in the capital, she would encourage him to change robes and accept the opportunity, even though it would mean leaving her behind. And he did not wish in decency to place her in a position in which she must do the choosing. He alone would decide what was right, and he would then place his thinking before her and encourage her to oppose it if she felt she must.

Satisfied that neither of them would act selfishly or in haste, he spent a fourth day largely in prayer, which he uttered with that simplicity which had always characterized him:

'Heavenly Father, from the time I was a child I knew that I wanted to live my life in Thy service. Humbly I have striven to do so, and as a young man I took my vows without even considering any alternative. But inside three years I was altering those vows in order to marry a native girl.

'As Thou knowest, so well, she brought me a new vision of what Thy church and its mission can be. She has been the saint and I the servitor, and I could do nothing to injure her. But now I am called to a higher service in Thy church, but to accept it, I must once again revise my vows and commit a grave wrong against my wife.

'What am I to do?'

That night was the fifth in which he carried this extraordinary problem to his bed, and as before, he tossed fitfully, unable to close his eyes, but toward dawn he fell into a deep, replenishing sleep from which he did not break till nearly ten. His wife, aware that he had been under some kind of pressure brought by the most recent ship from Russia, allowed him to sleep on, and when he woke she stood waiting with a tall glass of tea and the comforting words: 'Vasili, you've been worried about some perplexing problem, but I see in your face that God has solved it during your sleep.'

Accepting the tea gently from her hands, he swung his feet onto the floor, took a long, thoughtful drink, and said: 'Sofia, the tsar and the church want me to move to Irkutsk as bishop, and from there in due course perhaps to head the church from St. Petersburg.' Without hesitation, for he was speaking from a vast reserve of faith, he started to say: 'And this would mean . . .' But she ended the sentence for him: 'It would mean that you would have to take the black robes again.'

'It would,' he said, 'and after consulting God, I've decided . . .'

'Vasili, you started life in the black robes. Would this be so great a change that you should be sleepless?'

'But it would mean . . .'

The two lovers, each of whom had molded his or her life to the other's, crossing bridges that lesser persons might have been afraid even to test, let alone leap upon, looked across the brief space which separated them, she a little Aleut woman less than five feet tall, dark of skin and with a whalebone labret in her lip, he a tall Russian in a nightshirt, white-haired and bearded and troubled. For a painful moment neither knew what to say, but then she took the tea glass from his hands and placed her hands in his, and with the strange and lovely pronunciation of Russian words which her Aleut upbringing and the presence of the labret produced, she said: 'Vasili, with Arkady here to protect me, and perhaps soon with a wife to help, I have no fear, no claim. Do as God directs,' and he said: 'Last night, after the midnight bell from the castle, I knew that I must go to Irkutsk.' He uttered the words softly, then pressed her hands and added: 'And may God forgive me for the wrong I commit against you.'

Once the decision was made, neither of the Voronovs reviewed it, and neither subjected it to harsh reconsideration or recrimination. Before noon that eventful day they asked their son to accompany them to the castle, where they sought a meeting with Zhdanko, and when the four were settled in porch chairs overlooking the bay and the mountains, Father Vasili said unemotionally: 'I have been selected Bishop of Irkutsk. This means that I must return to the black robes I wore as a young man. And that means that my marriage to Sofia Kuchovskaya must be dissolved.' Allowing time for this dramatic news to take effect, he reached out for the hands of Zhdanko and Arkady, saying as he did so: 'I must leave the care of this wonderful woman to you two men.' And during the next half-hour he did not speak again.

The others discussed a chain of obvious topics: Who would replace him at the cathedral? Where would Sofia live? What would be the responsibility of both Zhdanko and Arkady? And for that matter: What was Zhdanko going to do when his provisional term as chief administrator ended? And even: Is the palisade strong enough to withstand an attack by the Tlingits, an ever-constant threat? By these practical steps, which reminded everyone that life in New Archangel must go on, even if the spiritual head of the community was moved to a higher obligation, the three participants chose among the various options available to them, and they did so in highly sensible ways, as if acknowledging that Father Vasili was no longer a part of their lives. But when they were finished, with the course of Sofia's future life determined within reason, Father Vasili broke down, covered his face with his hands, and wept. He was leaving a paradise which he had helped create and whose spiritual values he had both defined and protected. He had helped build a world, and was now surrendering it.

He was a white-haired old man, somewhat stooped, somewhat slowed in his movements. He spoke with greater caution and was prone to reflect on his defeats rather than his triumphs. He had seen much of the world's folly, and although he had been forgiving, he did wish that he'd had more time to combat those aspects of life which were wrong. He was, to put it simply, closer to God than he had ever been before, and he believed that he was prepared because he had learned to do God's work in whatever position he finally found himself.

The ship which had brought the news of his elevation to bishop required eleven days to finish its duties in Sitka Sound, and during the latter stages of the stay Father Vasili completed all details relevant to his departure. But on the last day, when everyone knew that the ship would be sailing at eight the next morning, he had to face the fact that within a few hours he must say farewell to his wife forever, and this became increasingly painful as the sun set and the long hours of night loomed. Sitting with Sofia in the main room of the modest house next to the cathedral, he began by saying: 'I can't remember when I first saw you. I know it was at Three Saints and I know it involved the old shaman in some way.' He hesitated, then chuckled as he recalled his long duel with that frenzied man: 'All that really mattered between us, I can see now, was that my parents had introduced me to God and Jesus and his had not had an opportunity to do so.' She nodded: 'He was an obstinate one. I hope I can defend my beliefs as valiantly as he did his.'

They spoke of the tragic manner in which so many Aleuts had perished during the Russian occupation, and he said truthfully: 'Months go by, Sofia, without my ever thinking of you as an Aleut,' and she said quickly: 'I think of it every day. I mourn the world we lost, and sometimes at night I see the forsaken women on Lapak, too old and weak to venture out for their last whale. My heart breaks.'

Then they spoke of the good days they had known, the birth of Arkady and the dedication of the cathedral, and this set Vasili to laughing: 'It seems I'm to have a real cathedral, maybe even a scintillating one, but whatever form it takes, it can never be a more dedicated House of God than the one you and I built here in New Archangel.'

At the mention of this place, they thought of Baranov and of how it was his will power which had built the thriving little town. 'He thought of it as the Paris of the East,' Vasili said, and the darkened room grew silent. A saintly man was deserting his even more saintly wife, leaving her for the rest of their lives for no reason with which she was associated, and there was no more to say.

WHEN PRASKOVIA KOSTILEVSKAYA, daughter of the notable Kostilevsky family in Moscow, arrived in New Archangel, men working along the waterfront stopped to stare at her, for a young woman of her striking elegance and beauty was rarely seen in this frontier town. She was much taller than either the Aleut women or the average Creole, and her skin was markedly whiter, for she was one of those Russians with a strong admixture of German blood, in her case Saxon, which accounted for her blue eyes and lovely flaxen hair. She had a warm smile but also an unmistakable patrician manner, as if she knew how to be congenial toward superiors and haughty toward inferiors, but the general impression she created was one of competence and self-assurance.

When it became known that she was the young woman who had come this great distance to marry Arkady Voronov, cynics said: 'He's a Creole and he'll never be able to hold a woman like that.'

To give her time to comply with religious law, her marriage to Arkady had to be delayed for three weeks, and during that time she began to have doubts about New Archangel, for the weather was typical of this part of Alaska. The warm Japanese current which swept clear across the North Pacific came so close to shore that it produced heavy moist clouds which clung to the mountains, completely obscuring them for days at a time. After the nineteenth rainy day in a row Praskovia lost patience, and wrote to her family, using, as cultivated Russian women did, a host of French words to describe her emotions:

Chères Maman et Soeur,

I have now been on this rain-soaked island for nineteen days and have seen nothing but mist, fog, low clouds and the most gloomy aspect of nature a human being has ever witnessed. Everyone here assures me that when the sun reappears I shall be seeing a glorious congregation of mountains encircling us, with a beautiful volcano off to the west.

Now, I am willing to believe that not all the people here are prevaricators, so I suppose the mountains do exist, but I find that one must take that on faith, for the visitor rarely sees them. One dear lady, hoping to raise my flagging spirits, assured me yesterday: 'Rarely does an entire month go by without the clouds lifting for at least a day,' and with that hope I shall go to bed tonight, praying that tomorrow may be that one day in thirty.

Arkady is even more delightful to be with than we thought in Moscow, and I am divinely happy. We have purchased a small wooden house near the castle, and with imagination and ingenuity we shall transform it into our hidden palace, because on the outside it will not be much.

I'm not sure whether the exciting news about Arkady's father has circulated in Moscow, but he has been ordained as Bishop of Irkutsk, with every likelihood of becoming, before the year is out, Metropolitan of All the Russias. So you shall be seeing the father in your city while I entertain the son out here in mine.

And now the best news of all. Arkady has been appointed second-in-command to supervise the transfer of power from the temporary chief administrator to the permanent one, and when that's been done, to continue as second-in-command until such time as he becomes chief. For the time being, his mother lives with us, a wonderful Aleut woman under five feet tall and with a kind of ivory earring fixed in a hole at the edge of her lower lip. She smiles like an angel and will allow me to do no work, for she tells me in good Russian: 'When you're young enjoy your husband, for the years pass too quickly.' In a later letter I'll tell you what happened to her marriage, but maybe you can figure it out for yourselves.

When the tantamount widow Sofia Voronova heard her prospective daughter-in-law complaining about Sitka's weather—she preferred the Tlingit name for her town—she feared that the high-born young woman might prove an unsuitable wife for her son, and she watched carefully as Praskovia made her way about the colony. She knows what she's doing, Sofia said to herself, and when she saw Praskovia go outside the gate to talk with Tlingit market women, she thought: And she's not afraid. But intuitively this elderly Aleut who had witnessed so many dramatic turns in human life feared that any young woman as pretty as Praskovia, and from a city, must lead her husband a difficult life, and she awaited the forthcoming wedding with trepidation.

But then, as if this bright child from the social circles of Moscow had anticipated Sofia's fears, she came to visit her two days before the wedding to say: 'Mother Voronova, I know I must seem strange to you, and I'm not going to try to change your mind. But I also know this. Arkady could not be the fine man he is unless someone had taken charge of him and taught him manners and how to treat a wife. I'm sure it was you, and I thank you.'

Then, to Sofia's astonishment, for Russian women in Sitka had never been so bold, Praskovia asked: 'What do you call that thing you wear in your lip?' Sofia, appreciating this openness, replied: 'A labret,' and her visitor said pertly: 'All right, now you must tell me what a labret is.'

Sofia did, but Praskovia was still not satisfied: 'I suspect that one must be very special. Could you . . . ?' She let her question hang, and for a very long moment Sofia looked at her, wondering: If I told her, would she understand? And in the end she concluded that it did not matter whether this young stranger understood or not; she was going to be Arkady's wife, and the more she knew of his heritage the better. So in a quiet voice she began to tell of life on Lapak

Island, and of the death sentence on her people, and of how she and her mother and her great-grandmother had killed the whale: 'A woman in the village made this from the bone of the whale we killed, and gave it to me as I left the island.' Seeing that Praskovia was transfixed by the story, she added: 'Of all the women on Lapak, I was the only one who escaped, and I shall wear this labret till I die out of my love for my people!'

Praskovia sat silently for a long time, kept her hands over her face, and finally rose and left without uttering a word, but on the following day she came back, laughing in a bright youthful manner, to tell Sofia: 'In Russia the bride wears something her mother wore at her wedding. I wish I could wear that labret of yours for just one day,' and the two women embraced, each assured that there would never be trouble between them.

NOW WHEN THE citizens of New Archangel used the phrase *the Voronovs* they meant the young administrator and his attractive wife, and the older possessors of that name were largely forgotten. Nor was Baranov mentioned very often, and when Kyril Zhdanko was replaced by a permanent chief administrator from Russia, a man with a minor title, he too faded from conversation. A new generation had come in to run what amounted to a new town, and when the American shipbuilder Tom Kane died, the last of the old breed was gone, the arrival of a steam-propelled ship from San Francisco signaling the new day at sea.

Arkady Voronov had been in his position as general manager of Company affairs for only a brief period when his capacity for leadership was tested, because from the islands to the north the Tlingits under a new toion decided that the time was ripe for a renewed attempt to retake Castle Hill, throw down the palisade, and return the settlement to its original Indian owners. With careful planning, the accumulation of many weapons and the stealth for which they were famous, they began infiltrating southward at such a steady rate that soon they had a sizable army in the valleys east of the settlement.

With the heroic Kot-le-an dead, they were led by the tested old warrior Raven-heart, who was ardently supported by his implacable wife, Kakeena, and their twenty-year-old son who, because of the spectacular way they had developed, was known as Big-ears. Together the three would form a powerful fighting unit, with Kakeena urging her men forward and providing food and hiding places when they were either recuperating from wounds or plotting their next assaults.

Raven-heart decided to position his best men near the palisade gate through which the Tlingit women would enter with their goods for market. At the exact moment, he, Big-ears and six others would force their way through the gate and break it off its hinges, allowing a hundred or so warriors to flood the palisade. What happened after that would depend upon the degree of success attained by the first wave, but all were prepared to accept large losses at first in order to subdue the Russians.

At six in the morning the men hiding among the spruce trees north of Castle Hill heard the sound of the morning bugles, and at eight they watched as two Russian soldiers directed a half-dozen Aleut workmen to throw open the wicker gate. One Tlingit woman entered bearing clams. Another came with seaweed. And as the third moved forward with her fish, Raven-heart, his son and their bold companions dashed into the compound, killing one Russian soldier and forcing the other to flee. Within minutes the battle for New Archangel had begun, with the Tlingits enjoying what appeared initially to be a victory.

But Arkady Voronov, commanding from the hill, was the kind of young man who was not afraid to make instant decisions, and at the moment he saw the gate collapse he knew he must wipe out that threat, so without considering the consequence to his own people or the enemy, he shouted to his cannoneers: 'Fire!' and two iron balls of tremendous power ripped into the mass of people struggling at the gate, killing fifteen attacking Tlingits and seven Creoles—five men, two women—who had come there to barter with the pacified Tlingits.

When Raven-heart saw some of his best men crushed by the cannonballs, he was first enraged, then sobered by the realization that those nine great cannon on the castle walls were going to be used, and he shouted to his men: 'Take cover!'

For three hours the Tlingits remained inside the walls, wrecking whatever they could reach when outside the range of the cannon and defending themselves by taking positions in houses and doorways. It was brutal warfare, which could have continued till nightfall had not Voronov decided upon drastic measures. Dodging from one cover to another, he told his men: 'Engage them. Don't let them escape through the gate. But when you hear the bugle, run back like hell, because I'm going to fire those cannon.'

With that, he ran up the hill to the castle walls, where he trained six of his cannon on the heart of the fighting, that spot near the gate where Russians and Tlingits tangled in one indecipherable mass. 'Bugler!' he cried, and in the next instant the Russians fled the spot, all except one young fellow who tripped, tumbling down among the Tlingits. For a split second Voronov considered holding his fire to allow the fallen lad a chance to get away, but then he saw the milling Tlingits: 'Fire!' and six ricocheting balls swept through the confused mass of Tlingits, killing or maiming two out of three.

Raven-heart, alerted by the bugle call, escaped the fusillade, but as he made for the wall, seeking to follow his son with a giant leap, Voronov directed his cannoneers to fire again, and a huge ball struck the Tlingit leader full in the back, crushing his bones and throwing him against the fence that he had been about to climb. Pinned there by his own flesh and bones and tattered clothes, he hung limp for a moment, after which rifle fire from the windows of a nearby house cut him down.

Thus ended the attack of 1836 and with it the last hopes of the Tlingits . . . during this generation. Of Raven-heart's four hundred and sixty-seven men, fully a third had been slaughtered inside the compound, and he had died with them. The green hills, spruce-covered and lovely in either snow or sun, would know his breed of Tlingit no more.

Kakeena, a widow now, would take her son to a new refuge on an island more distant than Chichagof, and there he would remember this day and plot the manner in which he would lead his expedition for revenge, because no Tlingit like Kot-le-an or Raven-heart could ever accept defeat . . . and Big-ears, brooding on his island, would be such a Tlingit.

SOFIA VORONOVA, THE young commander's mother, watched the battle from the castle, and at first she was proud of the manly way in which her son was conducting himself, but when, with victory assured, the big guns continued firing at houses well outside the walls, 'to give the Tlingits a lesson,' she saw that peaceful Indians who had elected to live side by side with the Russians were being slain.

'Stop it!' she cried, rushing at the gunners. And her cry was so different from what her son and Praskovia were shouting in this moment of victory, that they were astonished. Turning away from the final salvos of the bombardment, they looked at her in amazement, and saw that she was staring at them as if she had never seen them before. In that moment a wall as high as Denali rose between them.

As soon as the cannons were silent, she turned away from her son, going down the steps to work among the wounded, inside the palisade and without, ministering to those who had lost an arm or a friend or a child, and as she did so she found that she was identifying not with the Russian victors but with the shattered Tlingits, as if she knew that the latter deserved her help while the former did not.

When the Tlingits convinced her that they had been as surprised by Raven-heart's attack as the Russians, she felt a surge of sorrow for these confused people who had surrendered a life of great freedom in order to live in a settled community next door to what her husband had called 'Christian civilization,' only to find themselves trapped in a war not of their own making but in which they suffered most. Recalling her own childhood when similar injustices happened, she concluded that it was the kind of thing that was bound to occur when patterns of life were in collision, and she moved back and forth between Tlingits outside the gate and Russians inside, assuring each that life could proceed as it had in the past and that guilt rested on no one.

She convinced few—her son telling her that the Russians might have to expel the Tlingits altogether; the people outside the gate rebuffing her with a threat to leave New Archangel and join up with the rebels in a new assault. Unwilling to accept such disillusionment and remembering how on Kodiak she had been instrumental in bringing Aleuts and Russians together, she persisted in her efforts to bind these two strong-minded groups into one workable whole, and gradually it was her view of the future that prevailed.

'Tell them out there,' her son said one morning, 'that we want them to stay. Tell them that when the gate opens tomorrow they'll be free to bring in their goods as usual.'

'You need them, don't you?' she asked, and he said: 'Yes, and they need us,' and that evening she went to the still-apprehensive Tlingits: 'The gate will be opened tomorrow. You must bring your food and fish as before.'

'Can we trust them?' asked a man who had lost a son in the fighting, and she replied: 'You must.'

Reassured, they clustered about her, and in a friendly manner started to question her. One asked: 'Were you an Aleut before the Russians came to your island?' and she laughed to brighten the evening: 'I still am.'

'But in those days you were not of their church?' and she said that she wasn't.

'But you are with them now, aren't you?' an inquisitive woman asked, and when Sofia said that she had been married to the tall man with the beard who had preached in the cathedral, several wanted to know: 'Is your new religion . . . ?' They did not know how to finish their question, until a man blurted out: 'Is there a god, like they say?'

She remained with them a long time that night, telling them of the beauty she had found in Christianity, of its gentle message where children were involved, of the benign role played by the Blessed Virgin and of the promise that God made regarding life eternal. She spoke with such simple conviction that for the first time, in their hours of distress, certain of the Tlingits perceived a religion that was gentler and more worthy than the one they had been following. It was a persuasive description of Christianity that she offered, for despite the fact that this religion had treated her poorly at the close of her life, taking her husband from her, it had still been the glory of those middle years which seemed to count more than the others.

But if she helped the confused Tlingits find a balance between old and new, she could not do the same for herself. At night, in the darkness of her room, she experienced a profound longing to be with the people of her childhood. At times her mind wandered, and she believed that she was once more on Lapak Island, or in the kayak with her mother and great-grandmother chasing the whale, and her yearning for the old days became so persistent that one morning she passed through the gate to speak with two Tlingit men she had come to know during the aftermath of the battle.

'Could you take me to the hot baths?' she asked, pointing south toward that congenial spot where she and her husband and Baranov and Zhdanko had so often gone for relaxation and restoration.

'The Russians will take you,' the men protested, afraid that any unusual act on their part might be interpreted as a renewal of hostilities, but she brushed aside their fears: 'No, I want to go with my own people,' and with those words she made the last important decision of her life. She was not Russian; she was not of their society; she was what she had always been, an Aleut girl of enormous courage, an Indian like the Tlingits, cousin to their leaders Kot-le-an and Raven-heart. If she journeyed to the springs which the Indians had been using for a thousand years, she wanted to go in the company of these gallant Tlingits of the coastal islands.

But to protect these men who would take her south, she instructed several women: 'When we're gone, go to the gate, ask for Voronov, and tell him: "Your mother has gone to the hot springs. She's all right and will be back by nightfall. If not, in the morning." ' And off she set for one of the finest parts of the Sitka region.

Picking their way through the myriad islands, keeping the great volcano well to the west, they wove in and out of narrow channels, with the mountains guarding them on the east and the placid Pacific smiling at them from beyond the little islands. It was a voyage as wonderful this day as it had been when she had first gone with her husband and Baranov, and she caught herself thinking: I wish it would never end. And then the more painful wish: When we get there, I'd like to see Vasili and Baranov and Zhdanko waiting. And with such thoughts she lowered her head, ignoring the rim of mountains that welcomed her to the ancient springs.

When the two Tlingits deposited her on the shore, she told them: 'I'll not stay long,' then she added hopefully: 'I'm very tired, you know, and maybe the springs will help.'

Slowly she climbed the easy hill to where the hot sulfuric waters bubbled from the earth, and when she entered the low wooden structure erected by the tireless Baranov, she threw off her clothes and eagerly immersed herself in the soothing water, which at first she found almost too hot to manage, but as she became accustomed to the heat, she luxuriated in its comfort.

After she had lain thus for some time, the waters reaching up to her chin and bringing their therapeutic smell as close as it could possibly come, she lapsed into a kind of dream world in which she heard a ghostly voice whispering her real name: 'Cidaq!'

Amazed, she opened her eyes and looked about, but there was no one else in the bath, so she dozed again, and once more from the arched ceiling came the shadowy voice: 'Cidaq!'

Now she wakened, splashed her face with water, and chuckled, remembering the day when her husband and Baranov had taken her to the hut beneath the big tree at Three Saints to convince her that the clever shaman Lunasaq had been able, by ventriloquism, to make his mummy talk. 'It was a trick, Sofia,' chubby Baranov had explained. 'I can't do it very well. No practice. But look at my lips,' and he had astonished her by keeping them almost closed while words poured out, seeming to come from a root which he kept tapping with a stick.

How they had laughed that day, the two men careful not to deride her for having believed in spirits, she exulting in the joy she felt in the brotherhood of her new faith. Now she laughed again at the thought of how she had been deceived. But then, with the hot water reaching almost to her lips, she drifted again, and desirous of communing once more with the old woman of Lapak, she spoke in a kind of hypnotic daze, talking alternately for herself and the mummy: 'Have you heard that they took my husband from me?'

'Young Voronov?'

'He's not so young anymore.' Then proudly she added: 'Metropolitan of All the Russias, that's something.'

'And now he's gone. And Lunasaq is gone. But you had a good life on Kodiak and Sitka, didn't you?' The mummy used the old names for these locations, not the new Russian ones.

'Yes, but at first, when I thought of losing you and Lunasaq, I could not be happy.'

'Does it really matter? Don't you suppose that he and I were mournful too, having lost you for a while?'

'I am not unhappy in my new religion.'

'Who said you were?'

'You just said you were mournful to have lost me.'

'As a friend. What do I care how you pray? What really counts, in the very old days and in all the days to come . . .' The dome became filled with the ancient one's voice: 'To live on this earth as a bride lives with her husband. To know the whales as brothers. To find joy in the frolics of a mother sea otter and her babe. To find refuge from the storm and a place to enjoy the sunshine. And to treat children with respect and love, for with the passing years they become us.'

'I've tried to do those things,' Cidaq said, and the old woman agreed: 'You did try, little girl, the way I tried and your great-grandmother. And now you're very tired from so much trying, aren't you?'

'I am,' Cidaq confessed, and the old one asked gently: 'Does it really matter?' and she was gone.

In the silence that followed, Cidaq lay back, allowing the water to grow increasingly hot and sulfurous, and as she stared upward, she thought: Her religion is of the earth, the sea, the storms, and it's necessary to a good life. Voronov's religion was of the heavens and the stars and the northern lights, and it's necessary too.

Images from her two lives filled the walls of the bath: the great tsunami knocking down Vasili's church but allowing the shaman's lone spruce to stand; shadows on Vasili's crucifix at dusk; that first whale that terrified the women sliding past, enormous even now; the cluster of children she had cared for after the tsunami; Baranov with his wig drifting to one side; the joy with which Praskovia Kostilevskaya from a noble family in Moscow stepped ashore to marry Arkady in distant New Archangel; and dominating everything else, the stately white volcano lifting its perfect cone into the sunset.

She knew she had been blessed to have been privileged to share these two worlds equally, and although she had lost both, for she had rejected the Russian way, she did retain the best of each, and for that she was grateful. The heat increased; the images became a kaleidoscope of the years from 1775 to 1837; and the voice sounded no more, for her final question had summarized it all: Does it really matter?

It does matter! Cidaq concluded. It matters enormously. But you mustn't take it too seriously.

After waiting on the beach for more than two hours, one of the Tlingit boatmen said: 'I wonder if something's happened to the old woman?' and he insisted that his partner accompany him up the hill so that an honest story could be told if things had gone wrong. When they reached the bath they found Sofia floating free upon the surface of the water, facedown, and the cautious one began to wail: 'I knew we'd get into trouble.' They wrapped her in her clothes, carried her down the hill and perched her in the center of the canoe, then started paddling home.

When they neared the landing at the foot of the castle they began waving their paddles, and people on the shore saw only the two men fore and aft and their priest's former wife sitting upright in the middle seat, but as the canoe neared the shore they realized that she was dead, and men began running toward the castle, shouting: 'Voronov!'

I**N THE YEARS** following the death of Sofia Voronova, the thriving town of New Archangel discovered, as had so many settlements in the past, that its destiny was being decided by events which occurred in locations far distant and over which it had no control. In 1848 gold was discovered in California; in 1853 war broke out in the Crimea between Turkey, France and England on one side, Russia on the other; and in 1861 a much bigger civil war erupted in the United States between North and South.

Gold in California excited people in all parts of the world, sent a jumble of them crowding into San Francisco, and altered alliances throughout the eastern Pacific. A totally unexpected development occurred in New Archangel, where the chief administrator sent his assistant on a scouting trip to Hawaii and California to ascertain what the influx of Americans to the west might mean to Russia's interests. Placing their children in the care of two Aleut nurses, Arkady invited his wife to accompany him, and under palm trees in the familiar town of Honolulu they heard for the first time a rumor which astonished them. An English sea captain, fresh from a trip to Singapore, Australia and Tahiti, asked casually, as if all Russians knew of the matter: 'I say, what will men like you elect to do if the deal goes through?'

'What deal?' Voronov asked, his interest piqued by any suggestion that trade involving Great Britain and Russia might eventuate.

'I mean, if Russia goes ahead and sells your Alaska to the Yankees?'

Arkady gasped, leaned back, and looked with consternation at his wife: 'But we have heard nothing about such a sale.'

'We heard talk of it more than once when we put into port,' the Englishman said, and Voronov asked pertinently: 'By English interests?' and the captain said: 'Nothing substantial, you understand, but those discussing it were from various nations.'

'But were there any Russians?' Voronov persisted, and the man replied without equivocation: 'Indeed there were. Usually they were the ones who broached the subject.'

Voronov leaned back and said quietly: 'I don't intend to boast, but for some years I've been second-in-command in New Archangel. My father was a leading force in the islands before he was promoted, and I can assure you from all of us that we have no intention of disposing of what is becoming a jewel in the Russian crown.'

'I'm told it's a splendid place, Sitka Sound,' the Englishman said quickly.

In Honolulu no more was said about the possible sale of Russia's American holdings, and after arranging for the continued shipment of Hawaiian fruit and beef to New Archangel, the Voronovs moved on to San Francisco, where on the third night at anchor in that glorious bay behind the headlands, a Russian ship captain had his men row him over to Arkady's ship, and within minutes of their greeting he was asking for details about the possible sale of Alaska to the United States.

'Nothing to it,' Voronov assured the worried man, but then he corrected himself: 'At least not in Alaska, and I think we'd be the first to know.'

So the matter was dropped, and next day Voronov went ashore to inspect the burgeoning city for himself, and as he sat sweltering in a waterfront saloon where sailors gathered, he heard one of the bartenders saying: 'What a place like this needs is someone to haul ice down from those mountains out there.'

'None forms that could be used,' a veteran of the high country explained. 'Snow falls, but it don't form ice.'

'Well, it ought to,' the sweating bartender said. Then he added the words which led to Voronov's enhanced reputation in the Russian colony: 'Somebody ought to bring ice down here from up north,' and that night, back on his ship, Arkady told his wife: 'I heard the strangest idea this afternoon.'

'That we're really going to sell Alaska?'

'No, that's dead. But this man in the bar, it was very hot, we were sweltering, he said: "Someone ought to bring ice down here." '

Praskovia, fanning herself with a palm frond brought from Honolulu, studied her husband for a moment, then cried enthusiastically: 'Arkady! It could be done. We have the ships, and God knows we have the ice.'

When they returned to New Archangel in early October they hurried to the rather large lake inside the palisade, and after asking a score of questions, learned that ice formed in late November, very thick, and lasted until well into March. 'Properly protected,' he asked the men advising him, 'how long into the summer would it stay frozen?'

'Look up there,' and on the mountains surrounding the sound, in nests protected from the sun, and even in gullies where the drifts had packed down, he saw ample supplies of snow which had lasted through a warm summer. 'Properly packed so air don't hit it, and kept in a barn so the sun don't strike, we keep ice around here through July.'

'Could you do that on a ship?'

'Better. Easier to keep it from the wind and sun.'

He spent three tingling days discussing his mad project with all the knowing men he could locate, and on the fourth he instructed the captain of a ship heading for San Francisco: 'Tell them that on the fifteenth of December, this year, I'll be sending down a shipload of the best ice they ever saw. Arrange for a buyer.'

The cold came early that year, and when the ice was thick on the big lake he and some clever Aleut workmen devised a system for cutting out perfect rectangles of ice, edges square, four feet long, two feet wide and eight inches thick. What these men did was build a horse-drawn gouger, not a cutter, with the left-hand drag merely a marker to keep the rows straight, the right-hand a sharp metal point which scored the ice in a long unbroken line. That done, the gouger was reversed, with the marker now retracing the line already cut while the metal point scored a parallel line two feet distant from the first. Then, moving the gouger to a position so that it could cut across the two scored lines, the outline of the rectangle was completed.

This done, pairs of men with huge trunks of spruce moved along the rectangles, dropping the trunks heavily upon them and breaking them loose into handsome blue-green blocks of ice, which were speedily hauled to the harbor and stacked into the waiting ship. When a hold was filled, with no way open for air to reach the closely packed blocks, heavy matting was tucked over the ice and topped with spruce branches, which formed pockets that would trap what air did seep through the decking. For no more than thirty-two dollars a ton, perfect New Archangel ice could be delivered in San Francisco.

Three weeks ahead of schedule, Voronov's first cargo of ice made its way south, where it sold for an amazing seventy-five dollars a ton. Arkady had launched a trade which, during the frozen months at least, promised to be more lucrative than peltries. And with the bonanza thus provided, the energetic young assistant administrator launched the building program which would make New Archangel the leading town by far in the North Pacific. He strengthened the palisade, improved his father's cathedral, made shore improvements to aid vessels, and erected a snowstorm of new buildings: stores, an astronomical observatory, a new library, a Lutheran church with an organ, and on the top floor of the castle, much enlarged, a theater for the presentation of plays or the exhibition of singing and orchestral talent by companies from ships putting into the harbor.

By the time all this was completed, New Archangel had accumulated a population of nearly two thousand, not counting the nine hundred Tlingits who still clustered outside the gates, and as Voronov observed at a castle dinner for the local notables: 'Any talk of selling this place to anyone would be preposterous.'

But in 1856 the Crimean War imposed such a burden on the Russian economy, and such a grievous threat to her security in Europe, that serious discussions were held at the highest levels of government regarding the practicality of ridding the empire of her far eastern holdings, and whereas from New Archangel, Arkady Voronov was able to submit the most cogent reasons why places as promising as Kodiak and New Archangel should be retained, in St. Petersburg, Baranov's old nemesis Vladimir Ermelov, now an admiral with a lofty if unearned reputation, smothered Arkady's reasoning with sharp and pertinent official documents:

Even if our present position in the Crimea were not so perilous, and even if conditions in North America were more stable and predictable, it would be advisable for His Imperial Majesty to rid himself of the incubus our eastern territories impose. The entire territory called in the popular vernacular *Alaska* should be sold if possible, given away if necessary. Four basic facts dictate this as the only practical solution.

First, Alaska is impossibly distant from the real Russia, months from Okhotsk, many dangerous weeks from Petropavlovsk. Communication by land is impossible, even from one part of Alaska to the next, and by ship dangerous, costly and time-consuming. To send a messenger from St. Petersburg to a place like New Archangel and wait for his return with a reply can take more than a year, and there is no possibility of speeding the process.

Second, with the demise of the sea-otter trade, for the animal is practically extinct, there is no feasible way to make money in Alaska. It has no natural resources except trees, and Finland near at hand has much better. It contains no metal reserves, no present trade, no skilled natives to make anything for future trade. It will always be a deficit possession and money will be saved by getting rid of it.

Third, conditions in North America are chaotic. The future of both the Canadian territories and the United States is precarious, and one can expect Mexico to launch a war of some kind to win back the territories stolen from her. For us to remain in Alaska is to invite certain trouble from various quarters.

Fourth, and I have saved this most important reason till last. Even though the United States shows signs of breaking apart, its citizens also show many signs of wanting to take under their control all of North America, from the North Pole to Panama, and if we retain holdings in that area which they have marked out for themselves, we must sooner or later find ourselves in conflict with that rising power. The United States doesn't realize it now, but its more forward-looking citizens already long for Alaska, and in the years ahead that desire will augment.

My most fervent advice is that Russia rid herself of this doomed holding now.

It is possible that a copy of this report, by clandestine means, found its way into the hands of President James Buchanan, former Secretary of State, with a warm regard for Russia which he acquired while serving as ambassador to that country in 1831. At any rate, by the time the Crimean War drew toward a close, many Americans in high places were aware that Russia was at least contemplating the sale of Alaska to the United States.

And now one of the more curious developments of world history evolved, almost by accident. On those hilly battlefields in the Crimea, soldiers of many European nations combined to fight against Russia, who stood them off alone. Again and again, outnumbered and outgeneraled, she lost on the battlefield, but in the courts of world opinion she had one stalwart supporter and friend: the United States. At every critical point, America, for reasons never explained, sided with Russia, and let it be known that she was doing so. She strove to prevent an even larger coalition from forming against the tsar. She sent many letters affirming her moral support, and she did nothing to embarrass Russia about the potential sale of Alaska. Of all the nations involved in the Crimean War, even peripherally, the two who formed the warmest alliance were Russia and the United States.

So it was natural, when that war ended, that those in Russia who wanted to divest themselves of what they deemed an incubus should look with favor toward the United States, and in the period of serious discussion no one in Russia spoke harsh words against the United States as a possible buyer, and had times been normal, it is quite probable that President Buchanan would have completed the sale sometime between 1857, when his incumbency began, and 1861, when it ended in the Civil War.

That dreadful war, so comprehensive in terrain and devastating in loss of life and disruption of commerce, made any foreign adventure like the purchase of an unknown part of the world impossible. The war dragged on; money became unavailable for anything else; and for two desperate years it looked as if the Union would be shattered, leaving no one in authority to talk purchase with Russia.

But now the second half of the curious development occurred, for when the fate of the Union seemed most precarious, with European nations eager to pounce on the remains, Russia sent her fleet into American waters, with the implied promise that she would help defend the North against any incursions by European powers, particularly Britain and France. One Russian flotilla steamed into New York harbor, another into San Francisco, and there they waited, saying nothing, making no boasts, just riding at anchor and waiting. Those ships were to the North in 1863 what the American letters of reassurance had been to the Russians in 1856, not tangible military assistance but perhaps something equally important: the knowledge in dark days that one does not stand alone.

When the war ended in the spring of 1865, the two nations which had supported each other in such times of crisis were prepared to effect the sale that had been discussed over so many years, and it was significant that each nation supposed it was doing the other a favor. The United States thought that Russia had to sell and was seeking a buyer; Russia was under the impression that everyone in Washington was hungry to grab hold of Alaska. How misinformed the two friends were!

D URING BOTH THE Crimean and the Civil wars, Arkady Voronov, a mature man now, and his gracious wife, Praskovia, continued to live and work in New Archangel as if the future of their part of Russia were engraved in marble. They refurbished the castle and began living in one of the new wings; they increased trade with nations of central and western Pacific, like Hawaii and China; and they improved almost every aspect of colonial life.

It was Praskovia's idea to send promising Creole boys to St. Petersburg for their education, and already some were returning as doctors, teachers or minor administrators. Inspired by the performance of her saintly father-in-law, she had led the way in imploring monasteries across Russia to contribute the treasure of icons, statues and brocades that now graced the cathedral, making it one of the richest artistically east of Moscow.

As if wishing to double the attractiveness of Alaska, St. Petersburg dispatched a dashing young prince to govern it, Prince Dmitri Maksutov, whose title reached back to the days when Tatars from central Asia invaded Russia, giving its people the Asian cast which differentiated them from other Europeans. He was a handsome, able man who had, during his services to the tsar, married an attractive woman whose father taught mathematics at the Naval Academy. After bearing three children, this gracious lady had died prematurely, so that when the prince arrived in Alaska he brought with him a charming young wife named Maria, who, as the daughter of the governor general of Irkutsk, was familiar with Alaskan affairs. She proved to be an ideal princess for this frontier post, a gracious woman interested in everything, and she headed a court in which the locals were honored to participate.

During the first day in their new home Prince Dmitri confided his plans to Maria: 'We'll be here ten or fifteen years. Make this place a capital in every sense. Then back to St. Petersburg for an additional title and a major promotion.' The couple had been in residence only briefly when they realized that to attain their ambition, they must rely on some trusted local aide, and it did not take them long to identify the one person qualified to give such assistance.

'This man Voronov,' the prince told his wife. 'Exceptional.'

'Isn't he a Creole?'

'Yes, but his father was chosen by Tsar Nicholas himself to serve as Metropolitan.'

'His mother? Wasn't she a native?'

'A saint, they say. You must ask about her,' and when the princess did, she learned from everyone she asked that Sofia Voronova had indeed been a saint, and she became Arkady's most ardent supporter. It was she who invited the Voronovs to the Maksutov quarters, and then entertained Praskovia so that their husbands could conduct a serious discussion.

It took place at a table bearing a collection of maps, and from the prince's opening remarks, it was clear that he was determined to translate those lines of the map into a reality they had never before had: 'Voronov, I am almost physically distressed whenever I hear the phrase you used in your last dispatches.'

'What, Excellency?' Voronov asked with a disarming simplicity, for as the older man and one with an unsullied reputation he was not awed by the new commander.

' "Russia's island empire in the east." '

'I apologize. I don't seem to understand your objections.'

'Island, island! If St. Petersburg thinks of us as a collection of islands, they'll think small. But Alaska'—he waved his hand toward the unknown mainland—'is a vast land, as grand maybe as all Siberia.' He slammed his hand down on one of the maps and said: 'Voronov, I want you to explore that land, to alert St. Petersburg as to what we really have.'

'Excellency,' Voronov said, moving the prince's hand from the map, 'I've already been just where you pointed,' and he indicated the forbidding land on which the future capital of Juneau would one day stand. 'It's just like the land here at New Archangel. A cramped foreshore, then nothing but mountains deep into what must be Canada.'

Impatiently, Maksutov pointed to where the castle stood: 'We built a fairly good place here. Why not the same over there?' and with his slim forefinger Voronov indicated the difference: 'Excellency, the land behind our town is beautiful wooded terrain. The land over there is one vast field of ice, forever frozen, forever throwing glaciers down into the sea.'

For a moment there in the comfort of the castle, Prince Maksutov experienced the stern reality of the land he had been sent to govern, because in various English and German books he had seen engravings which demonstrated what an obliterating force a glacier could be, but he had never suspected that monstrous examples existed less than a hundred miles from where he now sat. But he was not deterred by this knowledge; he had progressed in government not because he was a prince but rather because he was a stubborn man, and now, surrendering his concept of building a new town on the mainland, he moved his hand boldly to the north to where some enthusiastic Russian cartographer— using fragments of information provided on scraps of paper sent to St. Petersburg by ship captains, fur traders and missionaries—had sketched what he conceived to be the course of the great, mysterious Yukon River. The prince and Voronov studied this awesome stretch of nearly a hundred miles of shoreline where the Yukon degenerated into a tangle of would-be mouths, some of them finishing as dead ends. From either the river side or the sea, it would be impossible for an uninstructed traveler to identify the proper route, and to send any man, no matter how clever or brave, into that ugly snarl of river, channel and swamp was to condemn him to at least a year of thrashing about, but Maksutov was obdurate.

'Voronov, I want you to go far up the Yukon. Make sketches. Talk with our people, if you can find them. Tell us what we have.'

Arkady had inherited from his Orthodox ancestors both courage and a sense of commitment to whatever tasks his occupation required, and he now told his superior: 'I understand that you need to know what goes on up here,' and with a sweep of his hand he indicated on the map a huge frozen area. 'But I wonder if the approach should be through the mouth of the Yukon? Or better said, the mouths of the Yukon?'

'How else?' Maksutov asked, and Voronov evaded the question: 'Look, Your Excellency, at what happens if I do penetrate that tangle at the mouth . . . and who knows if I could identify the proper entrance?' While the prince watched attentively, Voronov traced that immense sweep to the south that the Yukon takes at the beginning of its course inland. 'A man could waste a year picking his way through that morass.'

'He could,' Maksutov agreed, but then he punched his right fist into his left palm, making a sound like a rifle shot: 'Damn it all, Voronov, I know that priests have gone up the Yukon to a mission outpost called . . .' He could not remember the name of the place but he did recall hearing that some priest currently reporting to his superiors at the cathedral had made exactly the kind of journey he was proposing to Voronov, and an Aleut messenger was dispatched to find the man.

While they waited, Voronov assured the prince: 'I want to go. I want to see the Yukon. But I prefer to do it from an orderly approach,' and Maksutov said: 'I'd not have it any other way.'

Now the priest, a bedraggled, incredibly thin fellow with an unkempt beard, watery eyes and of an uncertain age—he could have been forty-seven or sixty-seven—appeared before the two administrators and fell immediately into profuse apologies, but for what, the two managers could not ascertain. Cutting through the verbiage, the prince asked rather sternly: 'Name?' and the trembling man replied: 'Father Fyodor Afanasi.'

'Is it true you've been up the Yukon River?'

'Nine years.'

'How old are you?'

'Thirty-six,' and this simple statement told his inquisitors much of what they needed to know about the great river: it made young men old.

Dropping his voice to a more congenial level, the prince asked: 'Then you know the area well?' and the priest replied: 'I walked hundreds of miles.'

'Now look, you didn't walk up and down the Yukon. It's a river.'

'And most of the year it's frozen.'

'Most of the year?' the new chief administrator asked, and Father Fyodor nodded: 'September to maybe July.'

'How far up the river did you go?'

'Five hundred miles. To Nulato. That's as far as Russian troops have penetrated.' He hesitated, then added the unpleasant news: 'It's only the beginning of our territory, you know. Nulato's only a short way up the Yukon, really.'

Voronov whistled in amazement, then asked: 'How would I get to Nulato?' and both he and the prince were astonished by what happened next, for the priest—after asking meekly 'May I?'—shuffled through the maps until he found one covering much of the eastern Pacific: 'Your best approach, sail from New Archangel down to San Francisco . . .'

This was so preposterous that both listeners protested: 'But we want to head north to the Yukon, up this way,' and on the map they indicated that Sitka Sound lay well to the southeast of the Yukon, whereupon Father Fyodor said: 'Of course, but there are no ships going that way. So down you go to San Francisco, about twenty-eight days, then across the ocean to Petropavlovsk.'

'We don't want to go to Siberia,' the prince shouted. 'To the Yukon.'

'But that's the only way to reach the Yukon. About one month in transit.'

Voronov, who was jotting the elapsed time on a slip of paper, noted that he had now been at sea about two months and was still an ocean and a continent away from his target.

The priest droned on: 'From Petropavlovsk you will cross over to this little storm-swept harbor of St. Michael, maybe ten days.'

'But that's nowhere near the Yukon,' Voronov protested, and the priest, wincing, said: 'I know. I once got laid up there for two months.'

'Why?'

'Big ships can't enter the Yukon. You must wait at St. Michael for a skin boat to take you across the bay and into the Yukon.' Tracing this dangerous route on the map, he added: 'Boats capsize trying to make this crossing.'

Rather dry in the mouth, Voronov asked: 'But now at the end of three months we're in the river?'

'You are. And with any kind of luck and two months of hard rowing and poling, you may get to Nulato before the Yukon freezes.'

'What month are we in?' Voronov asked, and the priest said: 'Everything must be scheduled according to the Yukon. It's ice-free only briefly. So if you leave New Archangel in late March, you should get to St. Michael in late June, just right for the thaw. That would put you in Nulato safely before the freeze.'

'You mean I'm to stay in Nulato all winter? Till the ice goes out again?'

'Yes.' When Voronov totted up the time it would take him to get from New Archangel to Nulato and then back, he and Prince Maksutov realized that he would have to be gone at least a year and a half, and just to go from one Alaskan base to another. Both men were appalled.

But then Father Fyodor dangled a slight ray of hope: 'I once followed a much different route,' and Voronov cried: 'I'd like to hear it!' and back to his maps went the priest.

'Same first part. San Francisco, Petropavlovsk, St. Michael. But now, instead of heading south in a riverboat to the Yukon, you head north to this little place Unalakleet.'

On the map this was a dead end, leading to no river, no thoroughfare, and a good sixty miles from the Yukon, which at that point would be heading almost due north, but Father Fyodor relieved their apprehensions by assuring them: 'There is a trail across the mountains, some parts very high, and it intersects the Yukon about here.'

'How would I negotiate the trail?' Voronov asked, and the priest said: 'You'd walk.'

'And when I reached the Yukon?'

'You'd be in a party, of course. Have to be, or the Indians might kill you.'

'Are they like the Tlingits?' Voronov asked.

'Worse,' and with a long finger he pointed to various Russian installations where Eskimos or Athapascans had either murdered everyone or burned the place: 'Most often they did both. Here at St. Michael, many dead. At Nulato, where you want to go, three burnings, same number of murders. Toward the mouth of the Yukon, this little place, two burnings, six murders.'

Voronov cleared his throat and asked: 'From St. Michael to Nulato by your overland route, how many days?' The priest tried to recall his own experiences, for he had made the journey in both directions, then guessed: 'I left St. Michael once on July first, an excellent time except for mosquitoes, and reached Nulato on August fourth.' Voronov groaned, but then the priest added: 'Now, if you were willing to trust a dogsled, you wouldn't have to remain in Nulato for nine months. You could hire a sled, Indians have them and love to travel, and come right down the middle of the frozen Yukon and across the pass to Unalakleet and over to St. Michael.'

At this point Prince Maksutov, increasingly horrified by the difficulties involved in exploring his domain, cut a Gordian knot: 'Arkady, suppose I diverted one of our ships direct to Petropavlovsk, bypassing San Francisco? Commandeer a smaller ship there for the run across to this Unalakleet? Over the mountains on the dogsled, a short, swift visit of inspection at Nulato, and right back down the frozen Yukon, with the ship waiting for you off the mouths of the Yukon? What would that take?'

Jotting down new figures, and giving himself the benefit of the briefest delay at each junction point, Voronov announced with some pleasure: 'Supposing not one day's delay, about one hundred and fifty days. With normal disappointments, two hundred days.'

But Father Fyodor blasted such plans: 'Of course, when you reached the sea it would be frozen too, just like the river.'

'Till when?' Voronov asked, and the priest replied: 'Same schedule. Solid ice till about July . . . maybe the middle of June,' and the two administrators groaned.

But Prince Maksutov, more determined than ever to have a report on his dominions, told Voronov: 'We'll handle it however the ice allows. Pack your bags.' Arkady saluted, turned to leave, but stopped abruptly to offer a sensible suggestion: 'Father Fyodor, you know the area. Would you come along to show me the way?' and the priest replied enthusiastically: 'I would love to see my people again. I lived among them nine years, you know,' and he smiled at the prince as if the Yukon he knew were some Isle of Capri, a vacationland basking in the sun.

So the trip was scheduled, and Prince Maksutov, fulfilling every promise he had made, diverted a rather smart ship to Petropavlovsk. On it he sent a letter to the commandant there, requesting that Voronov be forwarded speedily across the Bering Sea to St. Michael, but when the time came for departure, Maksutov and Voronov were presented with a problem no one had anticipated: Praskovia Voronova announced that she would be accompanying her husband to Nulato. This occasioned much turmoil, for although Arkady was delighted with the prospect of having his intelligent and energetic wife along, Prince Maksutov put his foot down: 'The Yukon is no place for a lady!'

And there matters stood, until the impasse was resolved by strong advice from an unexpected quarter. Father Fyodor, hearing of the argument, announced in what was for him a bold voice: 'A woman on the Yukon? Splendid! The men would be delighted and so would I.'

'Why, in God's name?' Maksutov shouted, and the priest replied: 'Precisely! It's in His name I make the suggestion. Our Athapascan women should be allowed to see how a Christian woman lives.' Then, blushing, he added: 'How she looks,' and it was agreed that Praskovia would join the expedition.

NEW ARCHANGEL–PETROPAVLOVSK–ST. MICHAEL–UNALAKLEET, it was a journey to two continents, half a dozen cultures. The travelers passed great glaciers, a score of volcanoes, whales and walruses, terns and puffins, until they reached a bleak and barren shore where Father Fyodor spent three hectic days trying to find a team of natives to serve as porters while they crossed the high country leading to the Yukon. As the Voronovs traversed this barren but exciting land marked by low mountains, they learned how overwhelmingly vast inland Alaska was and how ferocious its mosquitoes, for at times they settled upon the travelers like a flock of sea gulls descending upon a dying fish.

'What do you do about these dreadful things?' Praskovia asked in despair, and the priest said: 'Nothing. In six weeks they go away. If this were September, you wouldn't be bothered at all.'

After they had been on the trail some days, one of the Indians who spoke Russian said: 'Tomorrow, maybe, the Yukon,' and the Voronovs rose early for their first glimpse of this great river whose name so fascinated geographers and others who speculated on the nature of the earth. 'It's a magical word,' Arkady told the priest as they breakfasted on smoked salmon, but Father Fyodor corrected him: 'It's a brutal word. It's a river that never allows you to travel it easily.'

But Voronov could not be discouraged by the reports of another man, so after breakfast he and Praskovia rushed ahead, and at the conclusion of a hard climb, reached a point from which they could look down into the broad valley that opened up below them. Since the mists which obscured it from time to time had cleared, Arkady and Praskovia could see clearly this great and powerful river, twice as wide as they had expected, much lighter in color because of the monstrous load of sand and silt it brought down from distant mountains.

'It's so big!' Arkady cried to Father Fyodor as the priest puffed up to the vantage point, but when the latter saw his old friend, his nemesis, he said matter-of-factly: 'In spate I've seen it reach from that hill to this one. And in late spring when the ice breaks up, chunks as big as a house come sailing right down the middle, and heaven help whatever they strike.'

The Voronovs remained on the hill till the rest of their party had passed, speculating on what the river must look like a thousand miles farther up, where the Canadians, those mysterious people the Russians never saw, had their footholds. They were enchanted by the Yukon, awed by its turbulent power and mesmerized by its incessant flow, this messenger from frozen lands, this symbol of Alaska.

'Come along,' Father Fyodor said. 'You'll see enough of it before we leave,' and this frank assessment was proved accurate when the party descended to the level of the river and started up its right bank, for their way was constantly impeded by many small rivulets that wandered down from the north to join the great stream; to cross these required wading, and since one seemed to appear each half-hour, the Voronovs had wet feet most of that first day, but at dusk they approached the small but important settlement of Kaltag, where dogs began barking as children screamed: 'Father Fyodor! He comes back!'

In the explosive moments that followed, the Voronovs gained a completely different impression of what life in central Alaska could be, for they were surrounded by a new kind of native, the taller, sturdier Athapascans whose ancestors had reached Alaska long before either the Eskimo or the Aleut and who served as progenitors to the Tlingits. Like the latter, they were a warlike lot, but when they saw that their onetime priest, Father Fyodor, was back, they swarmed about him with cries and presents and manifold expressions of their love. For two exciting days the travelers remained in the village, with the Voronovs getting an idea of what it was like to be a missionary on the frontier.

During this time Arkady had an opportunity to witness the wisdom of Father Fyodor's strange statement when Prince Maksutov objected to Praskovia's joining the expedition: 'Our Athapascan women should be allowed to see how a Christian woman lives,' for the Kaltag women trailed along with Praskovia wherever she went, marveling at her appearance and joining with her when she laughed. Those who spoke Russian asked innumerable questions, wanting to know specifically: 'Is your bright hair real?' and 'Why is it so different from ours?' and from the direct manner in which she answered even their most personal questions, they knew that she respected them and was meeting them as equals, and this friendliness encouraged them to ask more questions.

Arkady, watching her performance, said to himself: She likes this village and this river! and he loved her even more than before because of her willingness to see and accept Alaska as it was. When he mentioned this to her after one of her sessions with the women, she cried: 'I do love this strange land. I think I now understand Alaska.'

On the morning of the third day, when they were about to depart, Praskovia, with her practiced woman's eye, noticed that one Athapascan, no longer a girl but not yet a woman, was taking a special interest in the priest, bringing him the best bits of food and protecting him from the importunities of the children. Praskovia began studying the young woman, noticing her handsome carriage, the subtle coloring of her skin, the attractive way she wore her hair in braids, and she thought: That one was meant to be the mother of children, the custodian of a house.

So when the time came to leave the village, she went to Father Fyodor and said: 'That girl, the smiling one, she'd make a fine wife,' and the priest blushed, looked to where Praskovia pointed, and said, as if he had never seen the woman before: 'Yes. Yes, it's about time she was finding herself a husband,' and he nodded to Praskovia as if thanking her for her sensible suggestion.

The journey up the Yukon to Nulato required three days, and they were days the Voronovs would never forget, for as they progressed northward the river broadened out until it reached a mile and a half from bank to bank, a massive stretch of water pressing always toward the distant ocean, which now lay nearly five hundred miles away, counting all the twists and turns. On the bosom of the river, which seemed to move past the boat with rugged determination, the Voronovs felt themselves to be entering the heartland of a great continent, a feeling totally different from any they had previously experienced in their gentler part of Alaska where islands and stretches of open sea predominated.

'Look at those empty fields!' Praskovia cried, pointing to the land that reached down to the river's edge and seemed to stretch off to infinity.

'A field,' her husband said reflectively, 'makes you think of orderliness, as if someone had fenced in an area and tended it. The land up here goes on forever.' It did, and across much of it no human being had ever moved, and as they contemplated its awesome immensity the Voronovs began to comprehend the terrain they governed. For long stretches there would be no trees, no hills, no animals moving, not even any snow, just the boundless emptiness, so lonely and forbidding that Praskovia whispered: 'I'll wager there aren't even any mosquitoes out there,' and Arkady asked: 'You want us to let you off? Test your theory?' and she cried: 'No! No!'

Yet in a perverse way it was the brutal nothingness of this trip up the Yukon that enchanted the Voronovs. 'This isn't a garden along the Neva,' Arkady said, anticipating the sentiments of those thousands of men from all corners of the world who would soon be crowding into the empty spaces of Alaska. They would deplore the loneliness, the difficulties of travel and the dreadful experience of fifty-five degrees below zero, but they would also revel in the fact that they had been able to withstand and conquer this gigantic, forbidding land, and fifty years later, as their lives drew to conclusion, they would cherish above all their other accomplishments the fact that 'I traveled the Yukon.'

Toward the close of their third day on the river the Voronovs saw around a bend a sight which caused them to cheer: the tight little fort of Nulato, its two wooden towers defying the world, a Russian flag flying from a central pole. As they drew close and men ashore began firing salutes from rusty guns and an ancient cannon, Arkady felt a surge of emotion: 'This is the last outpost of empire. My God, I'm glad we came.'

The garrison, some twenty Russian traders and soldiers, were as delighted to see their old friend Father Fyodor as the people at Kaltag had been and ran to the shore to embrace him, but when they did so, they stared in amazement to find that a woman, and a pretty one at that, had come so far up the Yukon, and when Praskovia tried to debark, four men reached for her, lifted her high in the air, and with shouts and imitated bugle calls carried her into the fort, while her husband trailed behind, informing the garrison commander of his official position in the government and his interest in their fort.

It was a rough, frontier stronghold perched well back from the right bank of the Yukon, but so located as to command far reaches of the river in all directions. Built in the classic form of four lengths of long buildings joined to enclose a rather spacious central square, it was dominated by the two stalwart towers and protected by a double-strength palisade which surrounded the entire structure. Having been overrun three times in the past, with considerable loss of Russian lives, it was not going to be an easy target in the future, for during daylight hours one soldier manned each tower; two at night.

After samovars bubbled with hot tea, and toasts were drunk, and garrison members reported on their experiences with the surrounding Athapascans, a fierce lot according to them, the commanding officer, an energetic clean-shaven young lieutenant named Greko, signaled one of his men, who blushed, stepped forward, bowed to the Voronovs, and said: 'Gracious visitors, this humble fort at the edge of the world is honored by your presence. As a token of our respect, Lieutenant Greko and his men have prepared a special treat.' At this point he broke into uncontrollable laughter, which left the visitors bewildered, but now Greko took over.

'It was that rascal's idea, not mine,' he said, pointing to the young fellow, whom he now punched in the arm: 'Go ahead, Pekarsky, tell them what you and those others did,' and Pekarsky, after holding his hand over his mouth to stop his laughter, straightened up, bit his lower lip, and announced in a butler's manner: 'Come this way, *monsieur et madame,*' but the French, proving too much to handle under the circumstances, threw him into such convulsions that Lieutenant Greko had to intervene.

'The men have paid you a great honor, Excellency. I'm proud of them,' and he led the way out of the meeting and into the square, where soldiers, still hungry for a glimpse of the beautiful woman from Moscow, stared and nudged one another as she passed, her golden hair glowing in the darkness. They went to a low building outside of which lay stacked a huge pile of logs, which had been cut far upstream and floated here. *'Voilà!'* the young officer cried, and when he pulled open the door the Voronovs found themselves entering a typical thick-walled Russian bath, with an outer room in which to undress, a very small middle area nearly filled with logs, and an inner room lined with low benches facing a collection of red-hot rocks heated by wood piled on from below. There were also six buckets of water to be thrown on the rocks to provide clouds of steam, so that within minutes of starting a bath, one would be engulfed in a cleansing, relaxing vapor.

'We could not maintain a fort here without this,' Greko said, and he bowed to his distinguished guests and departed.

The promise of a good steam bath was so inviting that the two Voronovs almost raced to see who would reach it first, and when Praskovia won, for she had no high boots to unlace, she cried: 'Heaven at the end of an arctic trip!' and her husband replied with that accuracy which can be so infuriating: 'We're a hundred and twenty-one miles south of the Circle. I checked,' but as the steam rose about them she replied: 'It's arctic to me. I could feel the river preparing to freeze,' and without warning she burst into tears.

'Darling?'

'It's been so wonderful, Arkady. There we were, all those years at Sitka Sound with our beautiful volcano thinking we were in Alaska. I'm so glad you brought me.' She wept for some moments, then took her husband's hand: 'When we were on the river I had the feeling that we were heading into eternity. But then I saw the soldiers come running down to embrace Father Fyodor, and I realized that people lived here and that eternity was somewhere far beyond.' Her tears stopped, and she said: 'Quite far beyond, I think.'

S HE HAD BEEN correct about the coming of winter, for after they had explored this part of the Yukon, going some twenty miles farther on to where a large river debouched from the north, and after they had met with members of various Athapascan tribes coming to the fort to trade, Arkady announced one morning: 'I think we're ready to head downstream,' and he supposed that because they would be drifting with the current rather than poling against it, the five-hundred-mile trip could be made speedily, but Lieutenant Greko corrected him.

'You'd be right if this were the beginning of summer. Easy ride. Pleasant, really. But this is autumn.'

'If we started right away?'

'Fine. River's open here and it remains open for some time. But at the mouth it freezes early. The cold winds coming in from Asia hit there first.' Allowing time for these facts to register, he then said: 'Excellency, if you and Madame were to leave here now, you might very well be frozen in halfway down, and there you'd be, eight months in an arctic winter with no possible chance of escape.'

Arkady called for his wife to join him so that she could hear the lieutenant's warning, and long before Greko finished, she blurted out: 'We'll stay till the river freezes. Then return the way we came,' and Greko, hoping to forestall any reconsiderations, jumped at the suggestion: 'Good! You'll be most welcome here and we'll have time to find you a first-class dog team for the return.'

So the Voronovs, he the son of the Metropolitan of All the Russias, she the daughter of a socially prominent family in Moscow, dug in for the opening days of a real Alaskan winter, and they watched with fascination as the thermometer began its steady and sometimes precipitous descent. One morning Praskovia wakened her husband with a rough shake: 'The Yukon's freezing!' and they spent that whole day watching as ice formed along the shores, then broke away, then formed again, then vanished. That day it would not freeze.

But three days later, in mid-October when the thermometer suddenly plunged to three degrees above zero, the mighty river surrendered and ice began to rush across from shore to shore as if it operated under directions of its own, and two days later the Yukon was frozen.

Then came the exacting days of testing to see how thick the ice was, and Lieutenant Greko explained that no matter how cold it became, the bottom of the Yukon never froze: 'The current below and the protection of the snow on top prevent the cold from taking command. In mid-January it'll still be flowing down there.'

When various teams of dogs were brought in, Praskovia found delight in making their acquaintance: big gray-brown malamutes, white Eskimo dogs, mongrels with powerful bodies and inexhaustible energy, and others the Russians called huskies. They were dogs unlike any she had known in Russia, and although some snarled when she approached, others recognized her as a friend and showed their appreciation for her attention. But none became pets, nor did she try to make them so; these were noble animals bred for a particular purpose, and without them life in the arctic would have been difficult.

She found that she was loving the experience of extreme cold, but one night when the mercury thermometer dropped to minus-forty-two and quit, she was stunned by the force of weather at such temperatures, the way icy air sped down into the lungs, almost freezing them, and the curious manner in which a face could be fairly comfortable one minute and frozen the next. When she realized that the thermometer could not register below the low forties, she asked Greko what the actual temperature was, and he consulted his spirit thermometer and said: 'Minus-fifty-three,' and when she asked: 'Why don't I feel it to be that cold?' he said: 'No wind. No humidity. Just this heavy, heavy cold weighting everything down.'

It did not weigh her down. Every day she ran and leaped outside the fort, and not until she had exhausted herself, and felt the cold threaten her very bones, did she hurry inside. 'If I stayed out there,' she asked Greko, 'how long before I'd freeze?' and he called to a soldier, who showed her his wrecked ears and a big white scarlike place on his right cheek.

'How long did that take?' Greko asked, and the man said: 'Twenty minutes, about as cold as this.'

'Is your face permanently damaged?' she asked, and the man answered: 'The ears are gone, the face will be all right, maybe a brown spot later on.'

That night, in the heart of Alaska that few Russians would ever know, she had the most exciting experience of all, for over the fort at Nulato, where twenty-two Russians huddled against the bitter cold, the northern lights began their heaven-encompassing dance. The Voronovs joined Lieutenant Greko in the center of the frozen square, inside the protection of the wooden barracks and the double palisade, and there they watched the great ebb and flow of the colored lights as they pranced across the midnight-darkened sky. 'How cold is it now?' Praskovia asked, and Greko said: 'Maybe sixty-below,' but the Voronovs only huddled deeper within their furs, for they did not want to move inside while this fantastic performance filled the heavens.

Later, as they drank tea and precious brandy with Greko, Praskovia said: 'We've seen Alaska. Without your help we might never have known it existed,' and he said: 'There's three times as much that none of us has seen,' and he agreed that on the day after tomorrow they could safely begin their journey back toward Sitka Sound.

THERE WAS AN abrupt change in plans on the return journey, but it had only happy consequences. When they reached the village of Kaltag, where they would have to leave the frozen river in order to take the hill route to Unalakleet, Father Fyodor informed them, with embarrassment: 'I'll be staying here. They need a priest.' Arkady, although distressed at the prospect of continuing what was a dangerous journey without Father Fyodor's help, had witnessed the admirable manner in which this scarecrow of a man fitted into Yukon life, and he had to consent.

'Will you explain to the religious authorities at the capital?' the priest asked, and Arkady said: 'I can see this village needs you,' and was about to express his appreciation for the help he had given the party, when Praskovia marched up, holding by the hand the attractive Indian girl she had noticed on the earlier visit. Going to the priest, she said: 'You proved yourself to be a dear, good man, Father. But you'd be twice as effective with a wife,' and she placed the young woman's hand in his.

When it was understood by everyone, even the children, that Father Fyodor was taking a wife and staying in their village, the young bride said firmly: 'It would be wrong to make the Russian couple cross the mountains by themselves!' And with the help of her father she arranged for a team of dogsled men to carry the Voronovs and the priest and his bride across snow and ice to where the Voronovs would wait for the thaw and a ship that would take them back to New Archangel.

AS THEIR SHIP pulled into Sitka Sound the Voronovs saw running down from the castle, in a manner quite undignified for a noble chief administrator, the agitated figure of Prince Maksutov, who shouted, as soon as he saw the Voronovs: 'Go over to that English ship!' and as they veered course to pull alongside the merchant steamer, they saw Maksutov jumping into a small boat, which two sailors rowed to the English vessel.

When the Voronovs climbed aboard the visiting ship, they waited at the railing for Maksutov to join them, and when he did they saw that he was ashen-faced. 'I want you to hear the news they've brought!' and he hurried them toward the captain's quarters, where they were met by a plump, jovial Scotsman who introduced himself: 'Captain MacRae, Glasgow.'

In a fevered rush Prince Maksutov presented his two guests, then blurted out: 'Tell them what you told me,' and Captain MacRae said: 'It's such a bizarre story I'd like to have young Henderson along. He heard it first and checked it out after I'd heard it from a different source.' So while Henderson was sent for, the Voronovs waited, quite in the dark as to what had been happening during their long absence. Probably England and Russia at war again, Arkady said to himself, but when Henderson appeared to stand beside his captain, the two Britons delivered quite a different story.

'It seems,' Captain MacRae began, 'and we have it on unimpeachable authority both from the Americans in San Francisco and our consul there, that Russia has sold Alaska—land, company, buildings, ships, everything—to the Americans.'

'Sold?' Voronov gasped. Long ago he and Praskovia had heard rumors of a possible sale, but that was when Russia had her back to the wall in the Crimea and needed money. To sell now would be insane. He and his wife had just seen the grandeur and promise of Alaska, and could not imagine losing such a treasure. His agile mind leaped from one possibility to the next. In the end he asked an almost insulting question: 'Prince Maksutov, how do we know that these two men are not saying this to put us to some disadvantage? I mean, if there's war between our nations?' As soon as he saw the prince blanch he realized how intemperate his question had been, and he turned to the two British officers and apologized.

'Not at all!' MacRae said, his round face beaming. 'This gentleman is quite right. All we've brought you, as I warned you before, Prince, is a San Francisco rumor. A very solid one, as I said, but only a rumor until you receive official confirmation from your own people.' He invited the Russians to stay, then ordered a steward to bring drinks for everyone, and as the Voronovs sat in stunned silence, MacRae said almost jovially: 'Henderson here gave a damned good account of himself in the Crimea. Said you chaps were mighty handy with your heavy guns.'

For some time they talked about the affair at Balaklava as if it had been a cricket match played in the distant past with no rancor left behind, but when that gracious interlude ended, Voronov addressed Henderson: 'Please, sir, would you share with my wife and me exactly what happened?' and the young officer told of having been in a San Francisco waterfront saloon of the better type, with officers from another British ship and a French, when an American businessman asked: 'Any of you Johnnies headed for Sitka? I suppose you know it belongs to America now?' Henderson said that since his ship was heading for Alaska, he asked to know more, and a general discussion evolved into which several Americans were brought, and two of them had knowledge of the sale.

Henderson had then run back to his ship to alert Captain MacRae, who did not believe the yarn but who did hurry to the British consul, who said that although he had no solid knowledge of the transaction, he had been forewarned in the pouch from Washington that the sale had been confirmed by the American political leaders and that the price agreed upon had been $7,200,000.

'Good God,' Voronov gasped. 'How many rubles is that?'

'A little better than two to one, maybe eleven, twelve million rubles.'

'Good God,' Voronov repeated. 'The Yukon River alone is worth that much.'

'Have you been to the Yukon?' MacRae asked, and Praskovia replied: 'Far up. It's a treasure, and I refuse to believe it's been sold.'

MacRae, feeling sympathy for the difficult problems facing these Russians so far from home, invited them to join him for tiffin, during which he did his best to relax their tensions, but when he asked them what they might do if the rumors proved true, he received two sharply different answers. Prince Maksutov said with diplomatic propriety: 'I'm an official of the government. I'd stay here to effect an orderly transfer, salute as our flag came down, then sail home.'

'You wouldn't protest the action?'

'Six times in the past three years I've advised St. Petersburg to hold on to Alaska. If a contrary decision's been made, as you suggest, I'll have no more to say.'

'But you wouldn't continue to live here in Sitka Sound?'

'Under the Americans? Unthinkable.' Realizing the pejorative nature of that comment to a representative of a third power, he added: 'Nor under anybody else, including you British.' MacRae, appreciating the reason for the correction, said: 'I'd feel the same way.'

But now Praskovia broke in: 'Leave this lovely place? Never!'

'You'd surrender your Russian citizenship?'

Arkady, hoping to forestall an answer his wife might later regret, interrupted: 'How can we predict what the rules will be? If America has bought Alaska, she might want to kick us all out, so your question is premature.'

'Not at all!' strong-willed Praskovia snapped. 'America needs people. So much empty space. So many of their men killed in the war. They'll be begging us to stay.' Looking at each of her listeners in turn, she added: 'And the Voronovs will be staying. We've made this our home.' After she launched this challenge, the fire went out of her, and she looked only at Prince Maksutov: 'You did a terrible thing, sir, when you sent us to Fort Nulato. You allowed us to see Alaska. And we fell in love with it. Here we shall stay to speed its development, and I won't give a damn who owns it.'

'Bravo!' MacRae cried. 'I'll toast you both on later trips.' Trying her best to smile at this levity, she failed miserably, dropped her face into her hands, and wept.

THE TRANSFER OF Alaska from Russia to the United States formed one of those unbelievable incidents of history, because by 1867, Russia was nervously eager to get rid of it, while the United States, still recovering from the Civil War and immersed in the impending impeachment of President Johnson, refused to accept it on any terms.

At this impasse an extraordinary man monopolized center stage. He was not a Russian, a fact which would become important more than a century later, but a *soi-disant* baron of dubious background, half Austrian, half Italian, and a charmer who was picked up in 1841 for temporary duty representing Russia in the United States and who lingered there till 1868. In that time Edouard de Stoeckl, parading himself as a nobleman, although no one could say for sure how or when or even if he had earned his title, became such an ardent friend of America that he married an American heiress and took upon himself the task of acting as marriage broker between Russia, which he called his homeland, and the United States, his adopted residence.

He faced a most difficult task, for when the United States showed hesitancy about accepting Alaska, support for the sale withered in Russia, and later when Russia wanted to sell, half a dozen of the most influential American politicians led by Secretary of State William Seward of New York looked far into the future and saw the desirability of acquiring Alaska to serve as America's arctic bastion, yet the hardheaded businessmen in the Senate, the House and the general public opposed the purchase with all the scorn they could summon. 'Seward's Icebox' and 'Seward's Folly' were two of the gentler jibes. Some critics accused Seward of being in the pay of the Russians; others accused De Stoeckl of buying votes in the House. One sharp satirist claimed that Alaska contained nothing but polar bears and Eskimos, and many protested that America should not accept this useless, frozen domain even if Russia wanted to give it away.

Many pointed out that Alaska had no wealth of any kind, not even reindeer, which proliferated in other northern areas, and experts affirmed that an arctic area like this could not possibly have any minerals or other deposits of value. On and on went the abuse of this unknown and somewhat terrifying land, and the castigations would have been comical had they not influenced American thinking and behavior and condemned Alaska to decades of neglect.

But an ingenious man like Baron de Stoeckl was not easily diverted from his main target, and with Seward's unflinching support and admirable statesmanship, the sale squeaked by with a favorable margin of one vote. By such a narrow margin did the United States come close to losing one of her potentially valuable acquisitions, but of course, had one viewed Alaska from the vantage point of frozen Fort Nulato in 1867, with the thermometer at minus-fifty-seven and about to be attacked by hostile Athapascans, the purchase at more than $7,000,000 would have seemed a poor bargain.

Now the comedy intensified, became burlesque, for although the U.S. Senate had bought the place, the U.S. House refused to appropriate the money to pay for it, and for many tense months the sale hung in the balance. When a favorable vote was finally taken, it was almost negated by the discovery that Baron de Stoeckl had disposed of $125,000 in cash for which he refused to give an accounting. Widely suspected of having bribed congressmen to vote for land that was obviously worthless, the baron waited until the sale was completed, then quietly slipped out of the country, his life's ambition having been achieved.

One congressman with a keen sense of history, economics and geopolitics said of the whole affair: 'If we were so eager to show Russia our appreciation for the help she gave us during the Civil War, why didn't we give her the seven million and tell her to keep her damned colony? It'll never be of any use to us.'

So the sale was completed and the scene of the comedy moved to San Francisco, where a fiery Northern general named Jefferson C. Davis—no relative of the president of the Confederacy—was informed that Alaska was now American property and that he, Davis, was in command of the icebergs, the polar bears and the Indians. A short-tempered man who during the Civil War had gunned down a Northern general to whom he had taken a dislike—the other general died and Davis was forgiven on the grounds that he, Davis, did have a short temper—he had spent the postwar years chasing Indians on the Plains, and accepted his job in Alaska under the impression that his duty there would be to continue chasing Indians.

On 18 September 1867 the steamer *John L. Stevens* sailed from San Francisco bearing the two hundred and fifty soldiers who were to govern Alaska for the ensuing decades. One who left that day wrote a dismal account:

As we marched in battle gear to our waiting ship, no maidens stood on the corners to throw roses at us and no enthusiastic crowds gathered to cheer us on our way. The public was so disgusted with our purchase of Alaska that they showed only contempt as we passed. One man shouted directly at me: 'Give it back to Russia!'

When the *Stevens* reached Sitka a holy mess developed. The Russians follow a calendar which is eleven days behind ours, so everything was confused. Also, in Alaska they keep the Moscow day, which is one ahead of ours. You figure that out. At any rate, when we arrived the Russian commander said: 'You're here early. This is still Russia and no foreign troops can land till the American commissioners arrive,' and we poor soldiers have had to stay in our stinking ship's quarters ten days looking at a volcano off our port side, which I can see as I write. I don't like volcanoes and I certainly don't like Alaska.

Finally, the ship bearing the American commissioners came into the sound, and now the troops were permitted, belatedly, to land; they were a grumbling unhappy lot, but soon they were engaged in the formality of transfer, which to everyone's surprise took place that very afternoon.

It was not a well-managed affair. Prince Maksutov, who could have handled it beautifully, was prevented from doing so by the presence of a stuffy minor official sent from Russia to represent the tsar, while Arkady Voronov, who knew more about the Russian holdings than anyone else, was not allowed to participate at all. There was, however, a certain formality that pleased the few people who climbed the eighty steps to Baranov's Castle, where the Russian flag streamed from a ninety-foot pole made from a Sitka spruce. There were cannon salutes from the bay and a proper ceremony for the lowering of one flag and the raising of another, but a painfully silly mishap marred the ritual, as explained by Praskovia Voronova in a letter home:

Although we had already signified our intention of becoming American citizens, Arkady, as you would expect, wanted the farewell Russian performance carried out with proper dignity, as would befit the honor of a great empire. He rehearsed our Russian soldiers with great care in the lowering of our flag and I helped mend torn uniforms and supervised the polishing of shoes. I must say that our troops looked pipe-clay neat when Arkady and I were finished.

Alas, it came to naught. For when one of our most reliable men pulled the halyards to lower our glorious flag, a sudden gust of wind whipped it about the flagpole, fastening it so tightly that nothing could be done to dislodge it. The poor man with the rope looked woefully at Arkady, who indicated with his hands that he should give it a good tug. He obeyed, but succeeded only in ripping off the bunting which decorated the flag and tightening the flag even more securely to the pole. It was obvious that no amount of pulling was going to loosen that flag, and I almost broke into cheers, thinking it to be an omen that the sale would not take effect.

At this point Arkady left me, swearing under his breath, and I heard him tell two of his men: 'Get that damned thing down. Now!' They had no idea of how this could be done, and I am humiliated to confess that it was an American sailor who called out: 'Rig up a bosun's chair!' I couldn't see how this was done, but pretty soon a man was clambering up the pole like a monkey on a rope, and he broke our flag loose, tearing it further in his haste.

Freed at last, it fell ignominiously earthward, where it landed on the heads of our men, who failed to catch it in their hands, and then it became mixed up in their bayonets. I was mortified. Arkady continued to swear, something he rarely does, Prince Maksutov looked straight ahead as if there were no flag and no pole, and his pretty wife fainted.

I wept. Arkady and I are determined to remain here in Sitka, as it is now to be called, and to be the best citizens we can be of our new nation. He is staying because his mother and father had such close associations with these islands, and I shall stay because I have grown to love Alaska and its enormous potential, and when you come to visit us next year I believe you will see a city twice this size and twice as prosperous, for they assure us that when America assumes control, it will pour millions of dollars in here to make this a major possession.

It was not premature for Praskovia and the other Russians who were selecting American citizenship to announce their choice, because in the days before the transfer, Prince Maksutov had assembled the heads of families and explained in glowing terms the Russian-American treaty which would govern such matters. Standing in his crisp white officer's uniform and smiling warmly, he was obviously proud of the work his committee had done: 'Both countries deserve commendation for the excellent rules they've agreed to. Great statesmanship, really.' When a young teacher from the local college, one Maxim Luzhin, asked for details, Maksutov patiently explained: 'I helped draft the regulations, so I can assure you that you'll be fully protected, however you choose.'

'For example?' Luzhin pressed, and the prince said: 'If you want to go back to Russia, you can do so anytime within three years. We'll provide free transportation to your home district. If you elect to remain here and become Americans, your new government promises you full citizenship automatically, no restraints because you're Russian, and complete freedom of religion.' Smiling at people who trusted him, he told them honestly: 'Not often in life do you get two choices, each one excellent. Choose as you wish. You can't go wrong.'

So when the Voronovs participated in the transfer ceremonies they did so as American citizens, but their transition into their new homeland was a rude one, for no sooner had the American flag risen to the top of the pole on that first day than General Davis issued a startling order: 'All Russians on the hill to vacate their quarters before sunset!' and a major directed his soldiers to occupy the buildings.

Arkady went to the major, and in a quiet, respectful voice, explained: 'My wife and I have elected American citizenship. Our home is up there,' and he pointed to their quarters atop the castle.

'You're Russian, aren't you?' the major growled. 'Out by sunset. I'm taking those rooms.'

When Voronov, burning with indignation, informed his wife of the order, she laughed: 'The prince and princess have been tossed out of their quarters, too. General Davis wants their rooms.'

'I can't believe it.'

'Look at the servants,' and Arkady saw the Maksutov possessions being toted down the hill.

The Voronovs moved their goods into a small cottage near the cathedral, where they watched as their Russian friends made agonizing choices. Those who had enjoyed their life in Sitka longed to remain, willing like the Voronovs to trust their fate to American generosity, but friends in Russia applied such strong pressure for them to return home that most decided to sail on whatever steamer arrived to carry them to Petropavlovsk.

'What will happen to them when they get to Russia?' Praskovia asked, and Arkady replied: 'I wouldn't like to guess.' But now distraught neighbors, unable to decide for themselves, came to the Voronov cottage, asking Arkady what to do, and usually he advised: 'Go home.' And if a husband and wife differed in their choice, he invariably counseled a return to Russia: 'There you know what your neighbors are going to do.'

This repeated recommendation that people who harbored doubts should go back to Russia had a surprising effect on him, for although he had started with a firm resolve to stay in Alaska, his constant projection of himself into the minds and conditions of others revealed how insecure in his choice he was. One evening as he and Praskovia walked home from a meeting with the Maksutovs, who were reconciled to returning home and perhaps even eager to do so, Arkady said without warning: 'Praska, are we doing the right thing?' and she temporized, wishing to know the full range of his doubts: 'What do you mean, Arkady?' and he revealed his uncertainty: 'It's a fearful decision, really. The rest of our lives. We don't know Russia anymore, we've been away so long. And we don't know America, because we can't predict how they'll behave ten years from now . . . or even now, for that matter. This General Davis? I wonder if he has any concept of what Alaska is. I wonder if he's very bright.'

'I'm certainly not impressed with his first decisions,' Praskovia said, 'but he may get better.' She encouraged her husband to spread out all his fears, and as he ventilated them she saw that they were nothing more than the sensible alternatives that any people their age should consider when making a decision of such gravity: 'Go on, what's your greatest fear?' and he said gravely: 'That it's the last big choice we'll ever make. Not for me, really. I was never attached to Russia, you know. I'm from the islands. But you . . .' and he looked at her with the great love which had always been the mark of Voronov men. His great-grandfather and his grandfather, both in Irkutsk, had enjoyed the good fortune of loving their wives. His father, Vasili, had found in the islands a love with his Aleut bride that few men know, and he had been the same. From the first moment he saw Praskovia during his student days in the capital he had loved only her, and now he feared that he might be behaving as his father had done when he surrendered Sofia Kuchovskaya in order to accept soaring promotion in the church. He was thinking of himself and not of his wife, and very quietly he said: 'I'm an island man. I'm forcing you into a cruel choice.'

She did not laugh, or even smile at his ingenuousness, but she did take him by the arm and lead him toward the cathedral, where they entered together to find rude chairs in the back among the shadows, and there she informed him as to her vision of the future: 'Arkady, you're sixty-six. I'm fifty-eight. How many years are we gambling on this thing? Not many. An error, if we make one, won't be the wastage of an entire life.' Before he could respond, she said with great force: 'At Nulato, watching the Yukon sweep past, feeling the immense cold, getting to know those sled dogs and seeing how Father Fyodor was greeted in the villages . . .' She smiled and squeezed his hand: 'I made my choice then, whether Alaska remained Russian or not. This is my home. I want to be here to witness the conclusion of our great adventure.' Before he could speak, she concluded: 'Arkady, I do believe that if you elected to go home to Russia, I might stay here by myself.' Then she added in a confidential whisper: 'Truth is, but don't tell the prince, I actually prefer their American name Sitka to the Russian name New Archangel.'

After that revealing moment, Arkady stopped advising anyone what to do, nor did he volunteer any information as to what Praskovia and he would do when the first ship sailed, the one that would take Prince Maksutov and his wife away. Instead, the Voronovs bought a somewhat larger house that was being vacated by a family heading home, and in it they began accumulating those comfortable odds and ends that would mean so much to them when Sitka became a totally American city. 'It's to be a wonderful new life,' Praskovia said, but Arkady, who was witnessing each day the inability of the Americans to govern their new possession, had additional reasons for apprehension.

As Christmas approached in that fateful year 1867, the Maksutovs held a farewell dinner party to thank those trusted friends who had worked so hard for

Russia but who now elected to become American citizens. 'I cannot challenge your decisions,' he said gently, 'but I pray you will serve your new homeland honorably.' He explained that although he must remain two more weeks to complete the transfer, his wife would be sailing on the morrow. And then nature pulled a cruel trick. During these weeks of departure Sitka's normal fog and gloom had established a mood proper for farewell, but on the final day the mists lifted, revealing Sitka in its refulgent grandeur: there stood the noble volcano, the rim of snow-clad mountains, the myriad green islands, the green onion dome of the Orthodox cathedral, the trim neatness of the most congenial port in Russian America.

'Oh, Praska!' the princess cried as she embraced her friend. 'We're throwing away the most beautiful town in the Russian Empire,' and it was in bitterness that she made her departure.

Two weeks later the Voronovs formed an honor guard for Prince Maksutov as he marched in dignity down the hill to where a small boat waited to ferry him to his waiting ship: 'I leave Alaska in the hands of you Voronovs. You know it better than anyone else.' From atop the hill, General Davis, now ruling from Baranov's Castle, ordered a salute to be fired, and as the echoes reverberated through the mountains and valleys of Sitka, the Russian Empire in Alaska came to an end.

THE UNITED STATES assumed responsibility for Alaska on 18 October 1867, and by early January 1868 it was apparent to the Voronovs and the Luzhins that no sensible form of government—indeed, none at all, sensible or ridiculous—was going to be installed. General Davis and his soldiers were supposed to be in charge, but only a part of the blame could be placed on them.

The fault lay with the American Congress, which, remembering the irresponsible oratory opposing the purchase of Alaska, had claimed that the area was worthless and populated by no one meriting serious attention. So, incredible as it would seem to later historians, America refused to give Alaska any form of government. It refused even to give it a proper name: in 1867 it was called the Military District of Alaska; in 1868, the Department of Alaska; in 1877, the Customs District of Alaska; and in 1884, simply the District of Alaska. From the first day of ownership it should have been designated the Territory of Alaska, but that would have presupposed eventual statehood, and orators opposing the suggestion ranted: 'That icebox will never have enough population to warrant statehood,' so the area was initially denied the step-by-step learning experience of first being an unorganized territory with judges and sheriffs, then an organized one with its own legislature and emerging government, and finally a full-fledged state.

Why were normal rights denied the area? Because businessmen, saloon-keepers, trappers, miners and fishermen demanded a free hand in garnering the riches of Alaska and feared that any form of local self-government might pass laws restricting them. And especially because Alaska was then and would remain America's blind spot. No matter what happened here—what riches were uncovered, what triumphs achieved—the American people and their government would not believe. For generations this treasure would be left to float adrift in icy seas, like an abandoned ship whose planking slowly rotted.

By mid-January, Arkady Voronov began to fear that a kind of creeping paralysis had engulfed Sitka and the rest of Alaska, but he did not appreciate the depth of the confusion until he talked with the young teacher Maxim

Luzhin: 'Arkady, you can't imagine the situation! An enthusiastic businessman from California came north on the ship that brought the troops. He wants to move here and open some kind of trading business. But he can't buy land for a home and office because there is no land law. And he can't start his business because there is no business law. If he settles here, he can't leave his property to his children, for there is no office to legalize wills or enforce them.'

When the two Russians looked into other impediments, they were told: 'You can't call upon the sheriff to protect your rights, because there is no sheriff, no jail and no court to appeal to for redress, for there is no court, which is understandable, because there is no real judge.'

Together the two men climbed the hill to inform General Davis of the concern the Russians had for their safety amid such chaos, and when they met him at ease in his quarters, they were struck by how handsome and military he looked. Tall, lean, carefully erect, with a heavy black beard, a voluminous mustache and a romantic wealth of dark hair which covered much of his forehead, he looked a born ruler of men, but when he spoke the illusion was shattered: 'I'd like to enforce the law, but there is no law. And I can't make guesses about it because no one knows what Congress will do.' When they asked what form the new government would probably take, he said: 'Legally, I think we're a Customs District, so I guess when a customs officer arrives, he'll be in charge.'

Despite the perspicacity of their questioning, they could elicit no substantial explanations from the general, and they left the meeting both confused and disheartened, so they were not surprised when, upon the arrival of a passenger ship, well over half the local Russians decided to leave Alaska and head back to Siberia. When General Davis saw the huge number departing, he tried ineffectively to entice them to remain, but they'd had enough of American vacillations and would not listen.

Voronov and Luzhin, better able than Davis to estimate the high quality of those who were fleeing Sitka, consoled each other and their wives with the hopeful thought: 'Those of us who are staying will have extra work to do . . . and extra opportunities to do it,' and each of the four was determined to be the best possible American citizen.

T HE REST OF the Russian story is quickly and sadly told. After the first contingent of émigrés fled, the undisciplined American troops, with no clear mission to occupy them or any stern leader to keep them under control, began to run wild, and Voronov, like the other Russians who had stayed behind, became appalled at what was happening.

Aleut women who had worked as servants of Russian families transferred their duties to the barracks where the soldiers were billeted, and before the week was out three cases of the ugliest kind of rape were reported. When nothing was done to discipline the men, they went outside the palisade and raped two Tlingit women, whose husbands promptly killed a soldier in retaliation, but he was not one of the rapists.

This particular case was resolved by paying the aggrieved husbands twenty-five American dollars each and sending the mother of the dead soldier a medal and the news that her son had died bravely in action against the enemy.

But now the violence extended to Russian families, who began locking and barring their doors, and two of the men complained bitterly to General Davis, but nothing happened. However, Voronov assured his wife: 'This madness will stop.'

It didn't. When a gang of drunken soldiers staggered down to a nearby village and assaulted three women, the Tlingits retaliated with a series of hammering counterblows, which General Davis interpreted as a dangerous insurrection against American rule. Dispatching a gunboat to the offending village, he ordered the place to be chastised; it was totally destroyed, with heavy loss of Tlingit life.

This resulted in the rupture of contact between the occupation force and the Tlingits, which meant that little fresh food made its way into the town. Tempers ran high, and one afternoon as Praskovia returned from a visit with distraught Russian neighbors she saw something which sent her screaming for her husband.

When the Voronovs and the Luzhins reached the front door of their cathedral they saw that in the sanctuary, at the iconostasis and throughout the main body of the cathedral everything breakable had been smashed, paint was smeared over the walls, and the pulpit was destroyed. The cathedral was a wreck; it would take thousands of rubles to restore it, and even at that cost the icons hallowed by time could not be replaced. When General Davis was informed of the sacrilege, he shrugged his shoulders and absolved his men of any blame: 'No doubt some angry Tlingits sneaked in when we weren't looking.'

That night those Russians with administrative or mercantile experience met at the Voronovs' to discuss what could be done to protect their rights and perhaps their lives, and the consensus was that since General Davis would not assume responsibility for his troops, the only practical thing to do was to appeal to the captain of the first foreign ship putting into Sitka, and Arkady volunteered for the assignment.

It was a French ship and the captain was a man well versed in maritime tradition. After listening to Voronov's recitation of complaints, he fumed: 'No self-respecting general allows his troops to rape,' and he marched directly to the castle and made a formal protest. Davis was outraged at this interference, and his assistant, who took note of Voronov's name in the Frenchman's recitation, warned the Frenchman that if there was any further intervention from him, 'the cannon up here will know what to do.'

That night, perhaps by accident, perhaps by design, three soldiers went to Voronov's house while he was known to be absent at a protest meeting, and tried to rape Praskovia, who fought them off vigorously and ran from the house screaming for help. Before she could make good her escape, one of the men grabbed her, dragged her back into the house, and started stripping off her clothes.

Neighbors alerted Voronov, who came running home in time to find his wife practically naked in their bedroom, fighting and scratching and gouging at the three men, who were laughing maniacally. When they saw that three big Russians were crowding in behind the enraged husband, they beat a planned retreat through a back window, smashing it and as much kitchenware as they could.

The other Russians wanted to chase the soldiers, but Voronov would not allow this. Instead, he gathered his wife's clothes, helped her dress, and then hurriedly packed everything that could be crammed into three bags. In the dark of night he led Praskovia, the Luzhins and their children down to the shore, where he signaled the French ship, in vain. Throwing off his shoes and jacket, he entered the cold water and swam out, shouting as he approached the ship: 'Captain Rulon, we seek asylum!'

In the darkness the Voronovs and Luzhins fled Sitka.

VII
GIANTS IN CHAOS

American maladministration had a devastating effect on Sitka, for its lovely port, which had been the site of more than two hundred visits a year by ships of all nations, saw arrivals drop to nineteen stragglers with little to offer in trade and less money with which to purchase local goods.

The population of the town, once among the finest in North America, dropped from more than two thousand to less than three hundred, and with its skilled work force gone to Russia, Sitka saw its Custom House receipts decline from more than $100,000 a year in the heyday of Russian control to $21,000 under the Americans and then to a shocking $449.28.

And year by year, the leaders of the Tlingits, watching this debacle, grew bolder, moving out of the fastnesses to which they had retreated under Russian pressure, edging always closer to where the protective palisade had once stood but stood no more. Sitka was in terrible trouble.

But the lack of government had an even more destructive impact on the other parts of Alaska, as a chain of incidents will demonstrate.

WHEN THE CONSORTIUM of landbound wealthy New Bedford owners learned that their Captain Schransky wanted to christen their new brig the *Erebus*, they complained that this name, which bespoke underworld and hell, was improper for a whaler owned by God-fearing Christians. He told them sharply: 'It could bear no name more appropriate, for it will be sailing into the white hell of the arctic ice and snow,' but when he wanted to paint the ship a solid, funereal black, they demurred: 'Our forefathers sometimes gave their lives defending New England ships against pirates, and we will not have one of our ships sailing under that fearful color.'

When Captain Emil Schransky, six feet four inches tall, with Nordic white hair and heavy beard, insisted that black was the color he wanted—'If it's to be a hell ship, which it has to be to make money in these waters, let it have a proper hell color'—a compromise was reached: it was painted a blue so dark and snarling that from a distance it appeared black, and it was under this fearful color that the *Erebus* sailed south for dreaded Cape Horn, whose passage would throw her into the broad Pacific. There she would chase the bowhead whale into the Bering Sea, with yearlong expeditions against the fur seals of the Pribilof Islands and the walrus of the Chukchi Sea. Oil taken from the whales would be delivered to Hawaii; sealskins and walrus tusks would be sold in China, and in between such commercial forays the *Erebus* would prowl the Pacific, seeking any cargo of opportunity. The ominous dark ship commanded by the formidable captain with the white hair and beard never engaged in outright piracy, but Schransky would be prepared to do so should a likely opportunity safe from detection present itself.

He was forty-five years old when he assumed command of the *Erebus*, a huge man in every way. Born in Germany of Prussian-Russian parentage, he had been thrown out of his turbulent home at the age of eleven and had promptly shipped aboard a world-trader out of Hamburg. Educated in the cruel academy before the mast, he had been at the age of fourteen a bare-knuckle brawler, willing to take on and sometimes seeking out cabin boys four and five years older than himself. He was a gouger, a knee-er, an arm-wrencher and a terror who, after he reached his full height at twenty-two, rarely had to use his fists. He was not averse to doing so, but he was just as pleased to lean heavily upon some minor troublemaker and slowly muscle him away from the scene of trouble, saving his punishing fists for real enemies whom he felt he must destroy before they destroyed him.

Enraged, he could become a terrible foe, two hundred and forty-eight pounds of incarnate fury, all windmill arms and kicking feet and great white beard snapping in the breeze as he came roaring at whoever had in some way infuriated him. At such moments he struck for the kill, and although he had not yet actually slain an American sailor with his fists, two who had shipped with him, one from Maine, one from Maryland, had never recovered from the terrible beatings he gave them. The Maine man died five months later in Lahaina; the Marylander lived along the Santiago waterfront, his brains addled and his left arm useless. Others, less severely punished, recovered, with arms slightly atwist from the breakings or teeth missing in front.

He was a massive man with massive powers and massive enthusiasms, but it was his driving compulsions that made him something more than just another German-Russian sailor with gargantuan appetites. Any ship he stepped upon as captain was his ship, and the financial owners were not welcome aboard; it would be unthinkable for any of them to accompany him on a voyage, or even part of one. He sailed to make money, and he possessed an uncanny faculty for smelling out where it was going to be found. (He had once made a small fortune in sandalwood which other captains had bypassed.) And he despised all governing bodies, all restraints and rules. He kept his ships away from their home ports for four and five years because by doing so he could avoid interference from the owners, and as soon as he rounded the Horn, for he avoided the Cape of Good Hope, calling it 'the route home for milksops,' he seemed to breathe more easily, taking deep drafts of the salt air of the Pacific, which he sometimes referred to as 'the Ocean of Freedom,' for he was able to negotiate from Chile to China without surveillance from local policing agencies.

But it was when he penetrated the Aleutians and broke out into the Bering Sea that he began to operate with that abandon which characterized his captaincy. Prior to 1867, when Alaska and its surrounding seas passed into American control, he had been a scourge of the Russian masters of the Bering, for he had scorned their attempts to keep him away from the Pribilofs, where he would sweep in unexpectedly to harvest a whole shipload of forbidden sealskins. He also liked to rampage along the Siberian coast north of Petropavlovsk, trading with natives whom the Russians themselves were afraid to approach, or come storming down the western coast of Alaska in chase of bowhead whales, which he seemed able to catch when even the local Eskimos could not. He sometimes spent an entire year in and out of the Bering Sea, harvesting its riches and keeping them semifrozen until he decided to make port at Lahaina or Canton.

He kept honest books, and frequently sent huge amounts of money home to his New Bedford owners by way of some returning ship against which he had been competing for years, and when the time came for him to head back for New England, ship captains came to him, begging him to transport their profits, for he was known to be trustworthy. 'He's his own law,' a Boston captain said with great force, remembering his own contests with Schransky, 'and he's destruction to his enemies, but there's nobody I'd trust with my cargo or my cash sooner than Captain Emil.'

The Russians before 1867 and the American authorities thereafter did not hold Schransky in this high regard; to them he was a predator, a scoffer at rules, a thief in the night, a pirate where seals were concerned, and the scourge of the Bering. He seemed ordained by some evil power to prowl the arctic, for he had a sixth sense of when he must flee these unforgiving waters before ice grabbed his vessel, immobilizing it for eight or nine months, and whereas incautious captains were sometimes trapped for the winter, he never was. No better description of him was ever given than the admiring one offered by an Eskimo at Desolation Point as he watched the *Erebus* slip out of that northern anchorage just before the arrival of the ice pack: 'Cap'n Schransky, he's a polar bear in a black coat. The ice whispers to him "I'm comin'," and out he goes.'

In this harsh world he might have been considered an ideal captain, except for three ugly flaws which estranged him from other rough-and-ready types. He was known as a niggardly captain who kept his crew on meager rations while afloat and then encouraged them to gorge themselves at their own expense when they hit some Hawaiian port. However, his sailors put up with his penury because when the time came to split profits with his crew he was generous.

His second flaw was that he was contemptuous of the great sea animals on which his prosperity depended. He hunted them callously, sometimes wounding and losing through drowning two whales or walruses for every one he hauled up to his ship. If a mate protested this arrogant waste of animal life, he growled: 'The seas are endless. There'll never be a lack of whales or anything else,' and during the long hunting season of 1873 he put this philosophy in practice in several gruesome ways.

When the *Erebus* sailed through the protective arc of the Aleutians, always a magnificent moment, it was in the Bering Sea only two days when one of the men sighted a pod of nine magnificent bowhead whales, great slow-moving creatures making their way north to the colder seas they loved. In the old days, some hundred thousand of these noble animals had threaded through the northern seas; now there were less than ten thousand, and Captain Schransky's abusive manner of hunting them helped explain why.

'On the starboard beam!' he shouted to the mate at the wheel, and when the *Erebus* swung around to head off the whales, some of them forty feet long and weighing forty tons, the boats were launched and three teams of rowers and harpooners started in pursuit of the placid beasts, who were unaware of the dangers into which they were heading.

The hunters of the *Erebus* had two enormous advantages. The long harpoons they used had in their sharply pointed heads toggles which fitted snugly against the shaft as the harpoon stabbed into the flank of the whale, then sprang open to form a T inside the whale's body so long and strong that the whale could never dislodge it; and to the other end of the harpoon were fastened big inflated seal bladders which prevented the stricken whale from either diving or swimming rapidly ahead. Once a whale had four or five *Erebus* harpoons in it, with trailing bladders, it was doomed.

But if it managed to swim too far from the ship, Captain Schransky let it go; he did not pursue endlessly: 'It's gone! Get that next one!' So in this attack on the nine whales of the pod, his men killed three, but only one of them was captured for its oil and baleen; the other two wandered off to perish at a distance. However, that one proved a bonanza, for it rendered many casks of oil and, even better, immensely long strips of baleen, the bonelike substance that enabled the whale to filter out the plankton from the huge amounts of seawater it passed through its gaping mouth.

'Get all the baleen!' Schransky shouted as his men worked the whale, for he knew that in the fashion shops of Paris and London this whalebone, as it was called, was essential. He could afford to let the two stricken whales escape, for this one catch would bring him more than seven thousand dollars.

His hunting of the walrus was equally brutal: three huge beasts shot with rifles, only two and sometimes one retrieved for their ivory. But it was his treatment of the fur-bearing seal that was most ruthless. Evading American patrols with the same clever tricks that had fooled the Russians, he slipped into the Pribilof Islands, that remarkable pair to which most of the world's seals came to have their young. Watching for an opportunity, he landed swiftly on Saint Paul, the northernmost island, where his men armed with clubs rampaged among the defenseless seals, beating them over the head and crushing their skulls. It was not difficult work, because perhaps six hundred thousand seals clustered on this island, a slightly lesser number on southerly Saint George, so the killing could continue as long as the men's arms could wield their bloodied clubs.

In the time of the Russians, when perhaps two million seals had come to the Pribilofs, they appreciated the fact that they had an almost inexhaustible treasury here and policed the harvest so that the immense herd was sure to be replenished, but when avaricious men like Schransky were not restrained, the seals on the Pribilofs were threatened with extinction.

However, the real slaughter, the one that all the maritime nations of the world opposed and strove to abolish, was pelagic sealing, the kind that Schransky particularly enjoyed and from which he profited enormously. Pelagic hunting, derived from the Greek word *pelagos* meaning sea, as in *archipelago*, consisted of chasing down the seals, most of them gravid females, when they were in the open sea totally defenseless, slaughtering them with ease, and ripping from their wombs the partly formed young whose skins had a special appeal in China. It was an operation that sickened many sailors forced to engage in it, but it was remunerative, and if a captain had no conscience and a ship fast enough to elude Russian or British or American patrol boats, a tidy sum could be made from pelagic campaigns.

Captain Schransky was known as 'the King of the Pelagic Sealers,' and this year he was determined to sail into Canton with his holds full of choice pelts, so he kept two lookouts forward to spot, if possible, the areas in which the oncoming seals might show, and when one of the men shouted 'Seals, five on the port bow!' he sped the *Erebus* toward that spot, and when the boats were launched, the men rowed in among the defenseless seals and started stabbing and beating them to death. Since seals could not stay submerged indefinitely, and since a boat with four strong rowers could overtake them when they had to surface for air, the slaughter was concentrated and endless.

Especially vulnerable were the pregnant females; their mortality was above ninety percent in any area that the boats reached, and in time the Bering Sea was reddened with their blood. But again, a shocking eighty percent of all seals killed were not retrieved; they sank fruitlessly to the bottom of the sea as the *Erebus* signaled for its boats to return so that it could proceed on its way to China and the riches that awaited it there.

Captain Schransky's third flaw was the most serious, for its evil consequences would survive long after he departed these waters. Abstemious himself and allowing no drunkenness aboard his ship, he early discovered the enormous profits that could be made by filling his hold in New Bedford with casks of rum and molasses and pushing them on natives who had little or no experience with alcohol. The consequences in the lands bordering the Bering were disastrous; natives developed such a craving for rum or the hoochinoo rotgut they distilled from the molasses—named after the local tribe that first made the stuff and quickly abbreviated to *hooch*—that sometimes entire villages were wiped out because men, women and children destroyed themselves with incessant drinking.

It seemed that everyone in the arctic with good sense was opposed to this traffic: the Russians had outlawed it early and policed their shores vigorously; missionaries preached against it; and New England moralists deplored the sinful transactions in which these crews were involved. But captains like Schransky found the great wealth to be derived from the trade irresistible, so gradually, village by village, in both Siberia and Alaska, the natives were corrupted.

With the change of national ownership in 1867, the tough Russian captains who had maintained some kind of order in the Bering Sea turned over the responsibility to poorly trained American seamen in the Treasury's revenue cutter service, whose cumbersome ships, the *Rush* and *Corwin*, proved incapable of disciplining the *Erebus*. So for nearly eight years, 1867–75, Captain Schransky enjoyed unchallenged mastery of the northern waters, slaughtering seals as he wished and purveying hooch wherever he anchored. He had become dictator of the oceans, obedient only to his own law.

This year, 1875, he was only forty-eight, and it was while laying to off Cape Krigugon on the Chukotsk Peninsula in Siberia that he summarized the future as he perceived it: Three more returns to New Bedford, that could take maybe eighteen years. I'll be sixty-six. One grand final sweep . . . all the seals in the Pribilofs . . . all the rum our ship can hold. Then buy a home by the sea . . . maybe New Bedford, maybe near Hamburg. In his speculations it never occurred to him that a man might be coming into these waters almost as tall as he, almost as brave, almost as good a fighter and, because of his exceptional personal history, many times more determined.

I F IN THE whaling season of 1875, Captain Schransky had chanced to put in to the little settlement at Desolation Point on the Alaskan side of the Chukchi Sea, he would probably have prevented a murder, but since the summer was waning fast, he required none of the goods that Desolation could provide. Also, his inner compass–thermometer–ship's-wheel warned him that the freeze was going to strike rather sooner than it had in previous years when he had stopped there. So, keeping well out into the Chukchi, he hurried south.

As he disappeared, taking with him the last group of white men the region would see for nearly a year, the vengeful Eskimo Agulaak understandably felt that perhaps the time for retaliation had come, and he began to lay plans for the undoing of the missionary Father Fyodor, the Orthodox priest who had come north from the Yukon to open a mission here in 1868.

The priest was appreciated by the Desolation Eskimos, for he was a generous, understanding soul who lived in the Eskimo manner, using a timber-roofed underground dwelling until he and his wife and their young son had collected enough driftwood to build themselves a proper cabin; *proper* meaning a lean-to, with a stout wall facing the frozen sea and the great blasts of cold air coming out of Siberia, a crude fireplace with an improvised chimney, and a whole southern wall more or less open to the elements but protected in part by three caribou hides that served as flaps to be pushed aside, one after the other, when one wanted to enter.

The cabin was warm, well insulated with packets of moss stuffed in cracks, and a lively center for the informal meetings which occupied so much of Eskimo life. Here the young people of the village gathered for their informal courtships, and along its warm walls sat the older Eskimos, listening as one of their members told of heroic adventures in the olden days. It was a satisfying life, and when Father Fyodor's wife produced another child, a girl this time, the little cabin echoed with singing, for the priest and his wife had made themselves a central part of the community.

If the priest, forty-seven years old and one who never looked at another man's wife, had become the target of the would-be murderer Agulaak, what evil force had begun to prowl the Point, bringing Agulaak under its malevolent spell? It would have been fruitless to argue with the tormented Eskimo that no force was assailing him, for evidence to the contrary was overwhelming. On each of his last two walrus hunts, far out on the ice, he'd had a beast under his magic control, only to lose him at the critical moment: Something spoke to the walrus, warning him that I was there. I didn't hear the voice but I know it was whispering. Last spring, when the caribou came down from the northeast, as they so often did when making their rounds of the north, he had trailed the herd as always, had selected his spot where the bigger animals must pass, and had watched in despair as one after another of the sleek beasts came almost within range of his spears, then veered away. On a later hunt, when he took the rifle that he had acquired from the *Erebus* two years before when it came to trade, almost the same thing happened: the caribou appeared on the horizon in great quantity, came right down the slough they always followed, then swung away when someone or something warned them that Agulaak was waiting.

From a series of unprecedented defeats like this, it was easy for him to deduce that someone at Desolation Point was casting a spell upon him, and since the area had at this time no shaman whose incantations would solve the mystery, Agulaak was left to stew in his own twisted imaginings, and the more he brooded about the magic that had been directed against him, the more clear it became to him that this intruder, Father Fyodor, must be the man responsible.

He was, first of all, a Russian, which of itself awarded him unusual powers. Then he was a priest, which involved incantations, the burning of incense and behavior of the most suspicious kind. Most condemnatory was the fact that the man had an Athapascan wife, for it looked to Agulaak as if the priest had married her for the specific purpose of insinuating her into the Eskimo community at Desolation for its ultimate destruction. As a boy he had heard endless tales of how the Athapascans connived to cast spells upon Eskimos, and these recent events involving himself proved that some malefic force was operating in the village and on the hunting grounds.

At this point, when he had convinced himself that it was Father Fyodor's Indian wife, who had taken the Biblical name Esther, who was working against him, a curious transferral of guilt took place, for as a self-respecting Inupiat Eskimo trained in the rigors of hunting and warfare, he could not in decency direct his ire against a woman, regardless of how malevolent her spells, but he certainly could strike out at the misguided man who had brought her into the community. So his anger now focused on the priest, and the more he pondered the wrongs done him by this white man, the more embittered he became.

Agulaak decided that since Father Fyodor had to be the activating cause of everything bad that had befallen him, he must be destroyed. And once he had reached this verdict, he never looked back: his only problem was when and how.

He was a canny fellow, rather superior in his hunting skills when evil forces were not working against him, and while he did not try to contrive anything clever which would deceive the other villagers as to who had done the killing, for it was essential that everyone know that he, Agulaak, had cleansed the village of its evil agency, it was imperative that he find a time and a situation appropriate for the deed and one in which the priest's unquestioned powers would be at a disadvantage or perhaps totally neutralized. This required artful plotting.

Agulaak's twisted mind suggested a variety of actions which he dismissed, and then a maneuver which seemed positively brilliant when he weighed it. What he did was get his gun, load it heavily, march to the hut in which the mission church met on Wednesday evenings, and wait until Father Fyodor appeared with six parishioners at the close of service. Moving to within eight feet of his enemy, he suddenly produced his gun, took careful aim, and in the presence of six witnesses, shot the priest through the chest. Death was immediate, as Agulaak saw, for he remained at the murder site grinning vacuously at the witnesses.

And now the absurdity of Alaska in these lawless years manifested itself, for there was no governmental agency in the entire district that had authority to move into Desolation Point, apprehend the murderer, and carry him off to trial in an established court before a legally impaneled jury. The people living in or near Desolation did not feel qualified even to arrest Agulaak, let alone try him, and as for placing him in jail to prevent further outrage, there was none within almost a thousand miles. So this madman was allowed to roam free, and citizens took precautions to prevent his attacking them while they prayed that with the coming of spring thaw next year, some American ship might put in to Desolation with an officer aboard to exercise the rudiments of governmental authority.

This inability to handle an ordinary civic problem placed an unusually heavy burden on Father Fyodor's widow, for she was now an Athapascan intruder in the midst of an Inupiat Eskimo community, with two children, a boy, Dmitri, of nine and a girl, Lena, of two. A devout Russian Orthodox Christian, she continued to offer her hut for informal religious services, but in doing so, she intensified Agulaak's suspicions and animosity. Neighbors warned her of threats the madman was making against her as he wandered aimlessly about the village, but there was nothing she could do to protect herself against him.

Her son, however, had access to his dead father's Russian rifle, and he was old enough to appreciate the danger Agulaak presented, so one wintry day when there was a wisp of gray dawn for about an hour at noon, and he saw Agulaak approaching his mother's hut, Dmitri suddenly jumped in front of him, gun pointed at his chest, and cried: 'Agulaak! If you ever come one step closer to my mother, I'll shoot!'

The demented fellow, convinced that the dead spirit of the priest had come back to earth in the person of his son, was terrified of the lad, drew back from the Russian gun, and fled.

He was seen thereafter wandering about the edges of the village and sleeping sometimes in the wind-shadow of this hut or that. On the occasions when he spoke with villagers, he warned them about the ghost of Father Fyodor who had returned to seek vengeance, but he seemed unable to comprehend that if this were true, it would be himself, Agulaak, who would be in danger. He had never really understood that he had murdered the priest, but he continued to be terrified of little Dmitri, who rarely appeared in public without his gun.

In such sad, broken ways the remote villages of Alaska stumbled on without a government.

L IKE SOME DARK raven scavenging the northern seas, looking for the latest disaster upon which to feed, the *Erebus* coasted along the shore of Siberia, seeking some Chukchi village whose citizens it could defraud of their pelts trapped during the last winter, but the Siberians had become accustomed to Captain Schransky's harsh ways and remained indoors, hiding their furry riches until his sinister ship departed, with him standing, white-crowned and bare-headed, peering for an advantage.

Disappointed in this portion of his expedition, he coasted north to that cape which brought Asia closest to America, and there he headed east for the big, well-populated St. Lawrence Island, whose northern three villages had provided him with good pelts in the past. But he approached the towns with mixed feelings, because in recent years men of the villages had become aware of the value of their furs and demanded high prices in barter goods like cloth for their wives and saws and hammers for themselves.

Determined to put a stop to this sophisticated trading, Captain Schransky had decided long before sighting St. Lawrence that this time he would use less expensive tactics, so when he anchored off Kookoolik, principal settlement on the northern rim, he took ashore not the customary items of hardware and cloth, but a keg of rum, and with it he taught the people of St. Lawrence how barters were going to be conducted in the future.

Dispensing the rum liberally, he ingratiated himself with the natives, until there was nightly dancing and singing, then men and women lying inert till dawn. Swift affairs developed between the sailors and the village maidens while the girls' customary suitors lay drunk in corners. However, the salient outcome of the induced debauchery was that the islanders, always hungry for the alcohol, brought forth their carefully hoarded stores of sealskins and ivory tusks, which they traded for abominably low prices as calculated in rum.

At the end of three weeks, when Schransky had pretty well denuded Kookoolik of its treasures, he brought ashore two barrels of dark West Indian molasses, but after tasting the bittersweet fluid the islanders said that they did not care for it and wanted rum instead. Now Schransky initiated them into a new pleasure that would guarantee the destruction of their village: he taught two of the older men how to transform molasses into rum, and when the first heady distillate appeared, the islanders were lost.

In the season when they should have been at sea catching seals and storing both the pelts and the meat, they were reveling on the beach, and in the more arduous months when they should have been tracking the walrus for its ivory tusks and again for the meat which, when dried, would sustain them through the coming winter, they were drunk and happy and heedless of the passing season. There had never been so much unmindful happiness in Kookoolik as there was that long summer when they learned how to drink rum and then make more from the treasured kegs of molasses. Of course, when the *Erebus* sailed, all the valuables of the village went with it, and one old woman who did not like the taste of rum was already asking, vainly: 'When are you men going to go out and catch the food we'll need for winter?' No one paid any attention to the problem she raised or to its solution.

When the *Erebus* moved along to the village of Sevak at the eastern end of the island, the sailors came upon a people who loved to dance, so when they were introduced to rum and the fascinating secret of how to manufacture it, the village echoed with the sound of Eskimos singing old songs as they engaged in one of the world's most curious dance forms: men and women stood with their feet solidly planted on the floor, as if set in frozen lava, while their knees, middle, torso, arms and head twisted rhythmically in contortions that no ordinary human would imagine. If to the rest of the world the word *dance* meant *to leap or skip about in an artistic manner*, to these Eskimos it meant something quite the opposite: *keep your feet firm but move your body artistically*.

At first the sailors found the Sevak dancing monotonous, but after they had watched it for several nights, some of the more adventurous took to the floor, listened to the beat of the chanting, and stood with their feet firmly planted while they contorted their bodies in ways never tried before as some old women of lively spirit danced beside them. Toward dawn this glorious summer, the dancers fell drunk while walruses and whales passed the island unmolested.

A feature of all the celebrations on St. Lawrence that surreal summer was the tall austere figure of Captain Schransky standing off to one side as he watched the debauchery, taking a perverse delight in following the steps of the islanders' degradation: now that girl is going off with Adams; now that old woman is beginning to stagger; now the man with the missing teeth is about to collapse. Like an uninvolved Norse god, he watched the frolicking of his earthlings and found sardonic amusement in their destruction of themselves.

At the third village, Chibukak at the extreme western end of the island, he used a minimum of rum to acquire a maximum of pelts, for in the waters off this point seal and walrus were easiest to capture, and the villagers had accumulated a substantial store of furs that they would normally have traded with adventurous ships setting out from Siberia, but since Russians had been forbidden over the past century from taking alcohol to any part of Alaska, they could not bring to Chibukak the exciting goods that Captain Schransky offered.

Here the devastation was even more tragic than at the first two villages, for the riches of the sea were so abundant that prudent fishermen could lay in a rich store of food with a few weeks' work in late July and August, but this year the precious days were spent in revelry and song and concupiscence. Here no sage older woman warned the men of the dangerous track they were following, for the women, too, stayed drunk from one festivity to the next, and when the *Erebus* finally sailed, the grinning people of Chibukak lined the shore to bid their good friends farewell, as pelts of seals and walruses accompanied the ship southward.

When the dark *Erebus* was about to leave St. Lawrence, Captain Schransky spotted on the southern coast the tiny village of Powooiliak, and he judged that because of its isolation, it might never have been visited by Siberian traders. If so, it would probably have an accumulated store of ivory, and he was about to put in to investigate when a sudden shift in the weather warned him that ice was not far off, so he surrendered the ivory of Powooiliak and headed south toward the southern limits of the Bering Sea.

There, on a day in early autumn, he found himself drifting in the midst of a large movement of seals that had left the Pribilofs and were heading for the warmer waters in which they would winter, and although he knew that taking seals under such circumstances was forbidden, the temptation to fill his hold to the limit with pelts for trade in Canton was too great to resist, and he ordered his men to attack the seals, who in midocean were especially vulnerable. This was not true pelagic sealing, for it was occurring in autumn when the females were not pregnant, but it was outlawed by all nations bordering on the seal routes; however, since it was unlikely that any patrol ships would be in these waters at this time, the cruel harvest continued.

There was, however, by accident and not design, a slow, inadequate ship, the revenue cutter *Rush*, limping home from a mishap which had deterred it in the Pribilofs, and when its captain saw the *Erebus* slaughtering the seals, he fired a warning shot to alert the trespasser of his presence, but even as he did so he realized that beyond warning the poacher, there was not much he could do. When the *Rush* came slowly up to the sealing area, the *Erebus* insolently eased off at about the same speed, and for most of one morning the charade continued.

Finally, with all sails spread, the *Erebus* put on a burst of speed, maneuvered insultingly close to the impotent *Rush*, and hurried toward China with its riches. It was the dominator of these seas and it would comport itself as Captain Schransky determined, not some pusillanimous captain of an American patrol boat.

D URING THE LAST days of spring 1877 the Tlingit Indians, who clustered outside the palisade protecting Sitka, kept close watch upon happenings in the capital, and saw with amazement that the steamer *California* had anchored in the sound for the purpose of removing the entire army garrison, whose troops boarded the ship on the fourteenth of June and left Alaska forever on the morning of the fifteenth.

'Who will take their place?' one Tlingit watcher asked his companions, but no one knew, and it was as a result of this confusion that three thoughtful Tlingits, who would have been termed warriors in the old days, sequestered a canoe where the Americans in command, whoever they might be, could not observe it, and on a silvery night, when the sun disappeared only for a few hours, left Sitka, paddled due north to that maze of enchanting narrows which led to Peril Strait, and from there into noble Chatham Strait, which bisected this part of Alaska. At the northern tip of Admiralty Island, which lay to the east, they turned south through the lovely passage on which the future capital of Juneau would one day sit, and then, with a left turn toward Canada, they entered one of the choice small waterways of the region, Taku Inlet, from whose left bank, hidden amidst glaciers, debouched a beautiful mountain stream, Pleiades River, and there at the mouth of the river stood a cabin erected many years ago. It was to the redoubtable occupant of this rude dwelling that they had come seeking counsel.

'Halloo, Big-ears!' they shouted as they approached the cabin, for they knew from experience that he was prone to shoot at intruders. 'Ivan Big-ears, we come from Sitka!' And when the calls were repeated, a tall, big-boned Tlingit in his sixties, with white hair and erect posture, came to the cabin door, stared toward the riverbank, and saw men he had known forty years earlier when they fought the Russians in repeated battles that the Tlingits usually lost.

Striding down to the bank, he greeted his onetime companions, then asked them bluntly: 'What brings you here?' and his nostrils widened when he heard their reply: 'The Americans in Sitka. They grow weaker every day. The time's at hand, Big-ears . . .'

'Come! Let us talk,' and as they told him of the chaos in which the American occupation foundered, he listened grim-lipped, and by the time their mournful litany was finished, his mind was made up: 'It's time to strike,' but one of the messengers warned: 'I've thought so, too. We can surely defeat the fools who hold the hill now, but I'm worried about the rush of new soldiers who might be brought in,' and Big-ears had a sage response: 'Not a big battle with war cries. Slow pressure, day by day, until their spirit is broken and we regain our ancient rights.'

Like a Kot-le-an of a later day, he spoke as a wise man of his tribe, one who had spent his life brooding upon the unjust way in which his people had lost their glorious land at Sitka, and this report of degenerating American control inflamed his ardor but did not confuse his generalship: 'A big battle would produce big news, and ships filled with soldiers would speed up from the south, but each day more pressure, more advantage to us, and there will be no alarms.'

He was fortified in this strategy by an act of folly committed by the incompetent Treasury official who had assumed command at Sitka. A Tlingit living in a village on Douglas Island came hurrying up Taku Inlet in his canoe, with distressing news: 'Trouble in our village. Four white miners tried to abuse our women. We fought them. Now the warship is coming from Sitka to punish us, because they claim we attacked them.' The word in Tlingit for *warship* carried no implications of size: the approaching vessel could be either a huge man-of-war or a corvette, but the impression created was one of military power, and Ivan Big-ears, who had been forced to take a Russian first name in 1861 when he knew the tsar's power to be already fading, wanted to see for himself what American power was in the waning days of its control, so he and his visitors set forth in two canoes, moving quietly along the shore so as not to be seen by the approaching warship.

Accompanied by the messenger from the village about to be attacked, they slipped out of Taku Inlet, hid in the mouth of the strait that led to the settlement, and were concealed there when a small American ship steamed into the quiet waters, located the wrong village, and began shelling it so ineffectively that at the first salvo, which missed completely, the occupants fled to the surrounding forest, from where they watched as the fourth salvo finally struck their empty shacks, battering them to pieces. Triumphantly the ship patrolled the shoreline for about an hour, with no soldier brave enough to go ashore to assess the damage, and then, with a final salvo that merely ricocheted among the trees, it retired to report another American victory.

When it was safely gone, Big-ears and his companions, including the messenger from the village that should have been the target, paddled across the strait to the wreckage and explained to the bewildered villagers as they came out of the forest: 'They fired on the wrong place,' and from that settlement as well as the other, Big-ears enlisted Tlingit warriors, who agreed that the time had come to move against the incompetents who occupied Sitka, and in succeeding weeks men from the Taku Inlet area began quietly infiltrating the capital.

Had Arkady Voronov still been in residence at Sitka, he would have known of the increased Tlingit pressure within a week, but the Americans now in charge of the place drifted amiably on, unaware that they were surrounded by an enemy that grew stronger each passing month.

NOW CAME THE darkest period of the American occupancy of Alaska. The presence of the army, inadequate though it had been and preposterous as its commander, General Davis, had seemed to the citizens who were ruled by him, had nevertheless provided a semblance of government, and of a hundred typical acts it performed in the post-1867 period, some ninety were either constructive or neutral, and now to have even this inadequate symbol of government removed was to invite disaster.

First the outward signs of control disappeared from the streets of Sitka. Police, even the few who were present, exercised no authority. Port facilities deteriorated so badly that the few ships which did put in left quickly, with vows never to return to such poorly administered facilities, which meant that customs revenues declined month by month. Smuggling became endemic, and rum, whiskey and molasses flowed unimpeded into the settlements. Miners and fishermen did as they wished, evaded such laws as there were, and decimated the supplies that used to flourish near Sitka. Foreign ships trespassed on seal rookeries that were supposed to be protected, and threatened to exterminate walruses, whales and the frolicsome sea otters who had begun to make a comeback.

But the most ominous development surfaced when Tlingits like Ivan Big-ears started drifting in from outlying districts, joining up with local dissidents and indulging in pressure behavior that terrified the white citizens. There were no murders, no burnings, simply the reappearance of Tlingits into areas from which they had been expelled by Baranov. And to the average white man unfamiliar with the old days, the sudden appearance of a tall, powerful Indian like Ivan Big-ears could be both terrifying and a premonition that dreadful things were about to happen.

What the Tlingits wanted was well represented by Big-ears. 'We must be free,' he told his fellow conspirators, 'to live where we wish according to our ancient ways, to have the new government respect our tribal laws and customs.' Since there was no resident authority to which he could make these reasonable demands, he was forced to further them by insinuating his people into the daily life of Sitka, and when he did this, the locals felt that they must resist.

There was a family from Oregon living in Sitka at this time, the Caldwells —husband, wife, son Tom aged seventeen, daughter Betts aged fifteen—and they had come north through Seattle with the understanding that Mr. Caldwell could open a lawyer's office in the capital, and he came well prepared for such service to the frontier community. He brought with him three crates of lawbooks, especially those dealing with territories and new states, both of which he assumed Alaska would become in the near future. He was most disappointed to learn that law and courts were not major concerns of the little capital, and as for an office from which to practice, there was no legal way by which he could acquire land on which to build one, nor were there any spare buildings that one could buy with assurance of obtaining a title.

'What can I do?' he asked in growing frustration, and a man who had been living in Sitka since the Russian days said: 'I think your wife might be able to get a job teaching at the new school,' and in disgust Mr. Caldwell said: 'If there's a job open, I'll take it,' but then his problem became: 'But where will I find a place to live?' and the same adviser told him: 'There's a big house down the street. Used to be lived in by a Russian family. Great people, went back to Siberia.'

Mr. Caldwell said: 'I don't think we want to buy a big house,' and the man said: 'Good, because it ain't for sale. But a very nice Aleut woman married to a Tlingit fisherman runs it, and she takes in boarders.'

So in one day the Caldwells received the good news that they could rent rooms at the old Russian house, as it was still called, and the bad news that whereas there was a teaching job at the informal school, only a woman would be considered. As a result, Mrs. Caldwell became a teacher in a school that had no visible means of support, for it had no tax base, there being no agency to assess taxes, whereas her husband, with the ingenuity of a man who had wanted to leave settled Oregon for the adventure of the Alaskan frontier, devised five or six imaginative ways to earn a little money other than by being a lawyer. He did paperwork for citizens who had to communicate with offices back in the States. He served as agent for the few ships that steamed into port. He helped at the coaling station where those same ships acquired fuel for their trips north. And he was not above working as either a day laborer or a handyman. Neither he nor his wife had a steady salary, but with what they did earn, plus some money picked up by their son, who was just as adaptable as his father, the Caldwells survived, and when the father received small commissions from miners and fishermen, they came close to prospering.

But always Caldwell listened to rumors and actual reports as to when Sitka was going to have a court system, and Alaska a formal system of government in which a lawyer could make a decent living: 'When that time comes, Nora, there's not going to be anyone in Alaska who'll know more than I will about the ins and outs of commerce and customs and the importation of goods and the management of mining and fishing. Surely, things will have to be straightened out, and then the Carl Caldwells come into their own.'

Of course, during the dismal years of 1877 and '78, his hopes of action from Washington were disappointed, and instead of order coming to Alaska, grievous disorder came. Caldwell first became aware of impending danger when his wife came home from school one afternoon with perplexing news: 'One of our children who plays with Aleuts said that a famous Tlingit warrior who fought the Russians many times . . .'

'What about him?'

'He's come back to Sitka.'

'What does that signify?'

'I asked one of the other teachers, and all she said was that her brother had seen him at the edge of town. Name Ivan Big-ears, a famous warrior . . . like the child said.'

'Never heard the name,' Mr. Caldwell said, but during the next days when he made quiet inquiries he learned that Ivan Big-ears, if it was indeed he, had fought against the Russians and had fled to voluntary exile somewhere to the east. 'If he's come back,' one older white man said, 'it can only mean trouble. I was here when he battled the Russians. Never won but also never accepted defeat.'

Caldwell asked what this Big-ears looked like, and another man said with obvious fear in his voice: 'I think I saw him the other day. Tall, robust man in his sixties. White hair. Dark even for a Tlingit.'

About this time Caldwell noticed that the Aleut-Tlingit couple who ran the Russian house in which the four Caldwells stayed became aloof, unwilling to talk with their boarders, and when Carl tried to discover why the change had occurred, he discovered, through the kind of detective work that lawyers enjoy doing, that the owners of the house were entertaining secret guests at night, and when the three older Caldwells established a watch, the son saw four Tlingits slipping into the back of the house. 'Was one of them tall, older, white hair?' Carl asked in a whisper, and his son said: 'Yes. He's in there now.'

Carl swore the boy to secrecy: 'Important things may be involved. Speak to no one.' But he himself stayed up all night, keeping watch on the rear door, and toward dawn he was rewarded by a clear glimpse of a tall, handsome Tlingit who must have been Ivan Big-ears.

In subsequent weeks the four Caldwells, for now the daughter had joined the detective work, accumulated fairly solid evidence that the Aleut-Tlingit community was engaged in some kind of conspiracy which involved Ivan Big-ears and at least several scores of Indians from other settlements across the water. And once this distressing theory was formulated, this clever family amassed a disturbing amount of substantiating data—more secret meetings in the back of the house, Tlingit men who could not be identified as locals lurking along the edges of the town, a gun stolen here and there, a subtle arrogance among the natives which had not existed before. Carl Caldwell said: 'With the army gone and no agency to replace it, the Tlingits have grown bold. Something bad is bound to happen.'

His wife said: 'If the rumors I hear are true, enough Tlingits have filtered in to wipe us out.'

Tom said: 'The men at the dock told me more guns had been stolen,' and Betts reported that Tlingit children had begun to push white children off the footpaths.

Caldwell exploded: 'Dammit, if we can see trouble brewing, why can't the officials?'

But who were the officials? When it was agreed that Caldwell must go to them and present his suspicions about a possible uprising of the Indians, it became obvious that there was really no one in authority with whom he could conduct a meaningful conversation. The little customs boat which had shelled the wrong village near Taku Inlet still lay at anchor in the harbor, but its captain, having made a fool of himself at that bombardment, showed no disposition to do so again in response to the crazy suspicions of a man who had been in town less than a year.

So when Caldwell broached the subject, the captain stopped him with a rambling discourse: 'Were you here when General Davis was in command? No? Well, folks hereabout thought poorly of him, but when he left here he was assigned to the Oregon-California boundary where the Modoc Indians was actin' up. Real bad Indian named Captain Jack come out under a white flag and shot the American general, man named Canby. Davis was appointed to replace him, and with great courage captured Captain Jack and saw him hanged. At the end of the Modoc affair, he gained a commendation and spent his remainin' time in service chasin' Indians, who he despised. A real hero.'

Caldwell had not come to talk about a general he had never known, but when he tried to bring the conversation to a serious discussion of the impending crisis whose outlines he saw so clearly, he accomplished nothing and left the customs boat in despair. 'They didn't even listen,' he told his wife, and that night when Ivan Big-ears and five of his lieutenants crowded into the Russian house,

Caldwell managed to overhear their agitated conversation, but since it was conducted in Tlingit, he understood nothing except the spirit of the words, but the animosity in the voices could not be masked.

However, at several points in the Indian debate about timing and tactics, men did use individual English words or phrases, and from them Caldwell obtained such confirmation as he needed: *'ammunition, ship in harbor, early morning, three men running* and other words pertaining to military action, and toward dawn, when he had heard enough, he convened his own meeting to discuss the steps that would have to be taken: 'If the United States can't protect us, and if there isn't any government here to take action, the only practical thing we can do is throw ourselves on the mercy of the Canadians,' and this strategy his three listeners agreed to. But how to reach the Canadians with a plea for help?

Tom had kept a map of the approaches to Alaska which the steamship company bringing them to Sitka had provided, and from its imperfect data he calculated that the distance to Prince Rupert Island and the seaport of that name would be about two hundred and eighty miles: 'Three men in a good canoe could get there in four days, if they're good men.'

'Would you be one of them?' Caldwell senior asked, and Tom said: 'You bet.'

The question then became: 'Nora, if Tom and I have to go south to fetch aid, can you and Betts protect yourselves till we get back?' Before she could reply, he pointed toward the back of the house: 'With them scheming on the other side?'

'We'd go to the church,' she said calmly, 'find safety with the other women and their men,' and when she looked at her daughter, Betts nodded.

Tom's suggestion that to paddle nearly one hundred miles, the first half through open seas, would require at least three men was so sensible that his father had to agree: 'We must find a third man before we can set out,' and in the next days as he scanned the community, peering into white faces to calculate who might have courage, he settled upon a choice between two men who impressed him with their general bearing. One was an older fellow named Tompkins, who like Caldwell worked at various jobs; the other, a much younger man named Alcott, whom Carl had seen along the waterfront when he worked the ships.

His inclination was to approach Tompkins first, and this was a good hunch, because when he did, Tompkins surprised him by saying immediately: 'Of course there's bound to be trouble,' but he shied off when Carl suggested begging for help in Canada: 'Too far. They'd never help Americans, anyway. They want Alaska for theirself,' and it looked as if the Caldwells would not be able to enlist his help.

However, that very afternoon a group of Indians who had come into town from the north began acting in a rowdy manner in the center of Sitka, and so terrified newcomer whites that a general panic ensued, but the quick disciplining of the rambunctious Tlingits by other Indians associated with Big-ears quieted the affair, so that the general uprising which many now feared did not occur. That was enough for Tompkins, who came to report his decision: 'We've got to get to Canada for help.' In the meantime, however, Caldwell had approached Alcott at the waterfront, and this bright young fellow had accumulated his own strong evidence: 'Things got to blow to hell pretty soon. Canada? Hadn't thought of it, but there's no help around here,' and he insisted upon joining the expedition, making four.

It was not a canoe in the sense that a frail birchbark affair in Pennsylvania would be called by that name; the one that Tompkins provided was a sturdy, spruce-ribbed, solidly built craft which had every chance of surviving in the ocean part of the journey. It could, in calmer water, provide space for eight paddles and ample room for four, regardless of the waves, and when the men met to inspect the craft, it was young Tom who voiced their judgment: 'We can get to Canada in it,' and the adventure was under way.

The white men used as much craftiness in slipping out of Sitka as Ivan Big-ears had used when slipping in. Waiting for one of those gray, misty dawns when all things in Sitka, even the brooding mountains, seemed clothed in silvery garments which made them invisible, they took off undetected by the Tlingits, sped out of Sitka Sound, ducked in and out through the protecting islands for the first leg of the journey, then headed south for the first perilous reach of open ocean, where they found the waves frighteningly big but not overwhelming. It was a heroic trip, with muscles strained and stomachs taut, but in time they reached that wilderness of islands which provided an inside passage nearly to Prince Rupert. There was a final dash across unprotected ocean, but at last the weary messengers paddled into the safety of the Canadian harbor.

In one of the fortunate accidents which help determine history, equal in results to times with careful planning, when the four men from Sitka reached Prince Rupert they found in its harbor the Canadian warship *Osprey*, a vessel of no great size stationed there to protect Hudson's Bay Company outposts on the coast, and because Prince Rupert was at the western edge of Canada, its officials were in the habit of making up their own minds without seeking approval from some distant capital: 'You say the Indians are about to overrun Sitka? Why doesn't your own government take steps? You say there is no government? Unbelievable.'

So the first task of the Sitka men was to convince the Canadians that things were as bad in Alaska as they said, but Carl Caldwell was a persuasive man, and within an hour he satisfied the men of the *Osprey* that without their help, real tragedy threatened in Sitka, and by nightfall the little Canadian warship was steaming north to protect American interests.

WAS SITKA IN the closing days of February 1879 in the perilous situation that the Caldwell party reported? Probably not. Responsible Tlingit leaders like Ivan Big-ears had no plans to murder the white population in their beds; what they sought was fair ownership of the land, assured supplies of food and hardware and cloth, some kind of sensible control of salmon fishing, and a just participation in the lawmaking procedure. They were willing to do battle with whatever military force might oppose them, and men like Big-ears were pre- pared to die in defense of their beliefs, but in these delicate days when the *Osprey* hurried north to put down a bloody revolution, the attacking Tlingits had no plans for one. Indeed, any kind of responsible government in Sitka would have been able to parley with the Tlingits, resolve their concerns amicably, and avoid serious trouble, but of course there was no government.

The *Osprey* steamed into Sitka Sound on 1 March 1879, and its bold show of power, with guns at the ready and uniformed troops marching ashore, quieted even the remote possibility of Tlingit revolt. No lives were lost. The Caldwell women did not have to seek sanctuary in the old Russian church. And the Tlingits who had been meeting in the rear of their house gradually dis- sipated, with outside warriors like Ivan Big-Ears returning sadly to their isolated homes, aware that justice would be denied them for decades to come.

In this manner the legend was born that a Canadian warship had saved Alaska for the United States when no American agency was brave enough to assume responsibility. Caldwell, in a surge of emotion aboard the *Osprey*, helped launch the myth: 'It's been a dark day in American history. Even this General Davis they laugh at wouldn't have allowed this shameful thing to happen.' In April, when an American warship finally arrived, the Canadians courteously retired, taking with them the gratitude of the community.

Later, an able, quiet-spoken Commander Beardslee reached Sitka in the *Jamestown*, whose afterdeck became the capital of Alaska, with Beardslee issuing orders regarding things about which he knew little. Fortunately, he had the advice of Lawyer Caldwell, and many of the good rules the latter had sought were promulgated by Beardslee, who installed Caldwell as a kind of judge in an informal court.

It was not a good system of government and both men knew it, but it was the only one available, so for two years these well-intentioned men more or less ran Alaska, but neither believed such a system could prevail. 'It's a disgrace,' Beardslee growled one day when something had gone wrong, and Judge Caldwell agreed. But they did not take themselves too seriously, because at this time Sitka contained only one hundred and sixty whites and Creoles, plus about a hundred Indians, and all of Alaska had only thirty-three thousand people, counting everybody.

T HE IMPLACABLE COURSE of history and the nature of the human beings who enable it to evolve make it impossible for a condition like that of Alaska in the post-1867 period to continue. Either revolution churns the chaos, as the uprising of the Tlingits nearly did, or some alien power steps in, as Canada might have done, or some giant like Abraham Lincoln or Otto von Bismarck steps forward to take command and reshape things sensibly. Alaska in these crucial times was blessed in having two giants of dissimilar character come to its shores and assume responsibility; between them they brought a semblance of government to an abandoned region.

The first of these men was an irascible dark-browed mariner with the good Irish name Michael Healy, who had a foul vocabulary, an insatiable craving for strong drink and an inherited willingness to use his fists. A hulking six feet two with a temper he could not control, he was hardly the kind of man one would expect to evolve into a respected leader, but that's what happened in the frozen seas of the north. Born in Georgia, he hated the cold, but of all the American seafarers of his time, he better than any other mastered the arctic seas and tamed the wild coasts of Siberia and Alaska.

He had been a junior officer during that humiliating experience in 1876 when the inadequate revenue cutter *Rush* tried to discipline the semipiratical *Erebus* for illegal sealing, and he would never forget the oath he took as he watched the insolent white-haired captain of that ship glide away with an insulting grin. 'I'll get that bastard,' Healy swore, and the rest of what he vowed to do with the German when he caught him would be unprintable. He was so infuriated that an American vessel, a warship really, had been demeaned that he retired to his quarters, sneaked out his smuggled liquor, and got drunk. Late at night, when he sobered a bit, he promised the tame parrot he kept with him on his cruises: 'By the saints, we'll get that cocksure bastard. Somewhere when the ice is thick and he can't run from us . . .' and his dark right fist punched at air.

On duty in the little revenue cutters, Lieutenant Healy, Commander Healy and, finally, Captain Healy gained increasing praise from his superiors and repeated humiliation from the *Erebus*, but he did not lose these near-battles through incompetent seamanship or any lack of courage, but only because he sailed an inferior ship. Once while in charge of the *Corwin*, the better of the two revenue cutters, he caught the *Erebus* engaged in illegal sealing at the Pribilofs: 'We have him, men! Hard to!' But almost as if aided by divine winds, the big indigo ship unfurled its square sails and ran right away from the cutter. Pursuit was impossible, and the government ship had to limp off to other duties as Captain Schransky, standing on the bridge of his sleek vessel, laughed once more at Healy's frustration.

If the profane and hard-drinking Irishman failed repeatedly in his attempts to discipline the dark rogue ship, what did he accomplish on his tours of duty through the northern oceans? To find the answer, one must accompany him on one trip made in the late 1870s. In early spring, in command of the *Corwin*, he sailed out of San Francisco with a full crew and considerable implied powers, for he was the major American representative in Alaska and the surrounding waters. Putting in to Sitka on the way north, he listened to local complaints and summoned to his afterdeck scoundrelly men accused of selling hooch to Indians; these he fined, making careful duplicate copies of receipts showing his handling of the money involved.

From there, following the reverse of the historical course which had brought Aleksandr Baranov to immortality at Sitka, he crossed an arm of the Pacific that carried him to Kodiak, where a deputation of old-time Aleuts and newcomer Americans awaited his decision on a fishing-rights controversy which had embittered the two groups. Moving ashore this time, but taking a ship's scribe with him, he listened patiently as the contesting parties made their presentations, then surprised everyone by announcing: 'Let's think about this carefully,' and he invited the entire party back onto the ship, where a feast from the *Corwin*'s supplies was provided. There was no public drinking, of course, since a major responsibility of the *Corwin* or any other cutter was to end the illegal sale of alcohol to natives, but he did slip into his cabin for a healthy nip from the bottles he carried hidden there. At the conclusion of the feast he took the leaders of the two factions, some seven men, to the railings of the cutter and said: 'You Aleuts have ancient rights which must be respected. But you newcomers have rights too. Would it not be sensible if you shared the ocean in this way?' And when he handed down a verdict worthy of a judge, the combatants accepted it, for on Kodiak as elsewhere in these waters it was understood that 'the word of Cap'n Mike is as good as we'll ever get.'

From Kodiak he sailed westward to the Aleutians proper, putting in at Unalaska, where he learned from six daring shipwrecked sailors, who had made it through great hardship to that haven, that twenty of their mates were still marooned on the north coast of the big Unimak Island to the east. Diverting his cruise to that bleak island, he rescued the men, sailed back to Unalaska, and paid with government funds for the forwarding of all twenty-six sailors to Kodiak, where they would transship to San Francisco.

From Unalaska he sailed across the Bering Sea—for he always chose this in preference to the Pacific Ocean, since that sea was in a certain sense his body of water—to one of his favorite towns, Petropavlovsk, at the southern end of the Kamchatka Peninsula. In this beautiful land-protected harbor he met with old friends, learned from them what had been happening along the Siberian coast and where tribal wars were brewing. Since Russian officials looked upon him as an arm of their marine police, the last nights ashore were riotous and drunken affairs, with Mike Healy being lugged back aboard the *Corwin* in time for a dawn departure to the north.

His next stop, at Cape Navarin, far distant from Petropavlovsk, had great significance this year and would have even more for the years ahead. Heaving to off the forbidding coast, he fired a salute which brought ten or fifteen canoes speeding out to the *Corwin*, where normally there would have been only a sullen silence. But Healy had raised the American flag, and now men and women who had some years before rescued sailors from an American shipwreck clambered up the sides of the *Corwin* to greet these new Americans. When all were aboard, Healy lined them up as if they were dignitaries representing an alien potentate, then fired another salute and had his bugler blow assembly. In broken Russian, which only a few of the Siberians who spoke only Chukchi would have understood had it been perfect, Healy said with the visible emotion that possessed him at times of solemn significance:

> 'The Great Ruler in Washington always knows when someone of good spirit aids an American who is in danger. You and you and you went out into the sea to rescue our sailors from the doomed ship *Altoona*, and you kept them in your yurts for more than a year. You delivered them in good health to the rescue ship sent by the Russians, and the Great Ruler in Washington has told me to come here and thank you.'

He then asked that members of the visiting party line up before him so that each could receive a gift of considerable value—a saw, a set of tools, enough cloth for three dresses, a parka, a set of kitchen pots, a ceremonial hat with feathers for the chief. On and on the gifts appeared, each one personally chosen by Captain Healy, each one delivered personally by his hands. When the presentations were over, he mumbled to his first mate: 'Next time an American ship gets wrecked along this coast, the sailors will have no fear.'

But the lasting outcome of this good-will visit came by accident, for the Siberians were so gratified by this gesture of appreciation that they insisted upon taking Captain Healy back onshore with them, and while there, his restless imagination forced him to ask: 'How can you live so well on land that is so poor?' and he poked his forefinger into the fat that covered these healthy people, and they explained: 'Reindeer,' and they showed him how, at the edge of their village, they maintained pens made of wooden timbers, inside which clustered herds of reindeer, nine owned by one family, thirty to a group of families, perhaps sixty in a community-owned group.

'What do they eat?' and they pointed to a far hill where a shepherd boy tended a herd of free-roaming reindeer that grazed on the tundra moss, and he sent runners, one to replace the shepherd, one to bring him back to the village, and when the boy arrived Healy gave him the belt off his own trousers and said that the Great Ruler in Washington wanted him to have it for his brave behavior three years ago.

F ROM CAPE NAVARIN he proceeded up the Siberian coast past St. Lawrence Island and the Diomedes and into the Chukchi Sea, where he stopped at a lonely village whose residents had once traded with him, and they too had troubles which they placed before him, and in his dark-browed way he listened to words he did not begin to comprehend, but finally a sailor who knew some

Russian found a Siberian who knew a little, and they pieced together what the problem was and what a reasonable solution would be. Delivering this judgment, he resolved the matter for the time being at least, and one of his men said to him when they were back aboard the *Corwin:* 'The Russians at Petropavlovsk would be afraid to come up here and listen to a problem like that,' and he said with some truth: 'But this is my ocean. These are my people.'

He ran from Siberia across the Chukchi Sea to an anchorage he knew well, Desolation Point, where he learned with dismay and personal sorrow that a fine missionary, Father Fyodor, had been murdered by a demented man who still roamed loose after all this time because there was no jail in which to incarcerate him. When he was caught and brought before Healy on the *Corwin,* only a few questions sufficed to show that the poor fellow was incompetent, so he was locked in the brig, which all the cutters had. Healy then went ashore to visit with Mrs. Afanasi and her two children, and he heard how Dmitri with his Russian gun had protected his mother against the crazy man, and Healy said: 'I have aboard ship a medal for a brave lad like you,' and when the ship was about to sail southward to its other duties, Dmitri was rowed out and Captain Healy rummaged through his pile of gifts and came up with a medal he had bought along the waterfront in San Francisco. It showed an eagle, and as he pinned it on the boy's tunic he said in his deep, solemn voice: 'This belongs to a real hero.'

His next stop on this particular trip was at forlorn Point Hope, where winds from the north were incessant and where his lookout spotted a group of white men huddling among sand dunes, and when small boats were sent to investigate, they discovered something so terrible that when Captain Healy, back aboard the *Corwin,* was told of it, his face turned almost black as he thundered: 'I want no record of this. No entry in the log. We did not stop here,' but then impulsively he jumped down into the longboat, sped ashore and gathered the marooned men, treating them gently as if they were his children, and brought them to safety aboard his ship. Then he fled to the sanctuary of his cabin, where his first mate found him caressing his parrot and mumbling: 'Who knows? Who knows?'

'We know damned well who knows,' the mate said in great anger. 'They're cannibals. They ate the flesh of their own companions, and from what I can piece together, they probably killed some before they died naturally.'

'Who knows?' Healy mumbled, whereupon the mate grew bitter: 'I know, that's who knows. Henderson knows. And so does Stallings. They're goddamned cannibals and we won't have them aboard this ship.'

Almost pathetically, Mike Healy looked up at his righteous mate and asked: 'Who knows what you and I would do? Who goddamned bloody knows?' And during the remainder of the trip, till the marooned sailors could be handed over to other authorities, they ate apart, ostracized by the other men, but Captain Healy sat with them to talk of how they had lost their whaler in the ice pack, and he listened attentively as they told of how the timbers strained and cracked and tore apart as the relentless ice continued its crushing advance. Before the next stop he summoned the first mate and said: 'I want to make an entry in the log. "At Point Hope we rescued six sailors marooned when their whaler *Cassiopeia* out of New Bedford was lost in the ice." '

'Is that all? No dates? No disposition?'

'That's all,' Healy roared, and when the entry was made he signed it.

He next put in at Cape Prince of Wales, a place which was to be of great importance to him in later years and of a determining influence now, for when he was rowed ashore he found a sizable group of Eskimos starving because the catch of seals and whales had been disastrous, and no other food was available.

It was here, for the first time, that he said to his officers after they had fed the emaciated natives: 'How ridiculous? Over there in Cape Navarin the Eskimos —they must be the same people, you go back far enough—they had rolls of fat, with no more food from the land than these people over here. What's the difference? They have reindeer . . .' It was then that his great idea was born: 'Why not bring a hundred, a thousand reindeer over here? Our Eskimos would live like kings.'

From Cape Prince of Wales he drifted down to the mouth of the Yukon River, where he dispatched two ship's boats to go upriver thirty miles, dispensing medicines and news, and when he heard about life along the great river he said: 'I'd like to go up it about a thousand miles.'

He was now back in the Bering Sea, and with a long sweep toward the west he came to the north coast of big St. Lawrence Island, and when he anchored off the easternmost settlement of Sevak he expected to be greeted by many canoes, for the *Corwin* was known to these natives, but in the entire village there was no sign of life. He was in the prow of the first boat ashore, and what he found at first perplexed him and then aroused a bitterness beyond expression, for every single person in Sevak was dead.

As they walked about the village, trying to find out what had happened, one of the sailors pointed out that there were no seal bones lying about, no walrus or whale: 'They had nothing to eat, sir. They died of starvation. But why . . . ?'

The mystery was not solved at Sevak, or even at big Kookoolik, where many natives had lived; all there, too, were dead, and again there were no seal or walrus bones, but there were clear signs of kegs in which rum had been delivered and molasses distilled. But it was not until the *Corwin* reached Chibukak that the solution was found, for there a pair of natives from the village of Powooiliak on the southern coast, the one that Captain Schransky had wanted to visit but could not because of the storm, had come to prospect among the ruins, and they said: 'Much rum. Much molasses. All July, August dancing, lovemaking along the shore. No men in umiaks chasing whales. At end they come to us, begging food. We have none to share. They all die.'

'Who did this?' Healy fairly bellowed, standing amid desiccated corpses.

'Big dark ship, captain very big, white hair. He taught them molasses, took all their ivory.'

Healy did not ask his men to bury the corpses; there were too many. The major part of an island population had been wiped out, and the man responsible appeared to be outside the law, an empire to himself, bounded by the North Pole and Tahiti, by Lahaina in Hawaii and Canton in China. Now his apprehension became more obligatory than ever, for he was the defiler of a society.

But Healy in the *Corwin* was no match for Schransky in the *Erebus*, and when toward the finish of this year's tour of his domain, Healy saw the *Erebus* off to the west still shooting seals in midocean, he ignored the difference between their two ships and bore down upon him as if he would ram the poacher, but Schransky easily avoided him, moved off to the west, and told his first mate: 'The *Erebus* will never be disciplined by a goddamned nigger.'

CAPTAIN MICHAEL HEALY, Lord Protector of the Arctic Seas, was an American Negro. As a young man striving to make his way in the customs hierarchy, he had learned to wear a hat that covered his dark forehead and a large mustache that obscured the blackness about his mouth, so that many people knew him for some time before they realized he was a black man.

His father, Michael Morris Healy, was a tough-minded Irish plantation owner in Georgia who took as his wife a marvelous slave woman named Elisa. Together they had ten children of such extraordinary grace and promise that Healy said: 'It would be a crime to have children like ours grow up to be slaves,' which would have been the legal situation had they grown to adulthood in Georgia. Therefore, with tremendous personal effort Healy and his wife accomplished the impossible: they spirited their ten children out of Georgia, enrolled them in cooperating Quaker and Catholic schools in the North, and watched them develop into what was probably the outstanding group of black siblings in American history.

Four of the boys made historic names for themselves: one became a leading bishop of the Catholic church; another became a respected doctor of canon law; Patrick, the third son, early showed the unusual academic talents that carried him to the presidency of Georgetown University, and he was for some twenty years, in the latter part of the nineteenth century, one of America's leading and most respected educators; and the fourth son, Mike, ran away from school, went to sea, and became in time one of the most honored captains in the Treasury's revenue cutter service.

Three of the girls became nuns, one ending her career as Mother Superior in a major convent. It is interesting to speculate on where these extraordinary black children acquired their unusual talents, which were recognized by so many white people in so many diverse areas of performance. Certainly, from the courageous behavior of their father they could have inherited the strong character they manifested, but there seems little in this Irishman's background which would account for their intellectual preeminence, and one can speculate that perhaps this sprang from the remarkable slave girl Elisa. At any rate, they formed in these years one of the most distinguished groups of brothers and sisters in America, matched perhaps by a comparable group from the Adams family of Massachusetts, but one must remember that the Adams children enjoyed every advantage from childhood on and suffered from no fear of being stigmatized as slaves. The contribution the ten Healys made to America was incomparable, but none of the other children attained the headline prominence of Mike.

His feats in the northern seas became legendary, and newspapers reveled in writing about his heroics. Did a group of careless whalers tarry too long off Desolation Point and become icebound, with starvation threatening? Mike Healy in one of his frail cutters would speed through ice floes that would have crushed an ordinary ship six times over and miraculously find open tracks leading him to the stranded sailors. Did tragedy strike in some remote village on the Siberian coast? Mike Healy dauntlessly arrived on the scene to save the Russians. Did a whaler sink during a storm in the Bering Sea? Who rescued the castaways six months later but Mike Healy, who chanced to stop at their unpopulated Aleutian island on a hunch. And whomever he rescued, no matter in what lost corner of the arctic, that person could be relied upon to sing his praises when returning to civilization.

His popularity extended across the nation, and one Canadian in a small western town when asked who the President of the United States was, said without hesitation: 'Mike Healy. He runs everything.'

But knowledgeable maritime people were not fooled by the adulation he received from the unwitting public; they were aware that frustration gnawed at him because he proved powerless to drive Emil Schransky from the seas which

Healy had taken under his protection. Whenever men who knew the oceans gathered, they marveled at the impunity with which the German captain acted in the seal islands, the way he operated at will in the pelagic-sealing areas, and his flagrant abuse of alcohol and rum and molasses in devastating native villages. Not even the disaster on St. Lawrence Island, which by now was well known among seamen, deterred Schransky from repeating his performance elsewhere, and then running to Hawaii or China with his corrupt bounty. He was a thorn in Mike Healy's side, and the excuse was always given by Mike's apologists: 'If only he had a ship as good as Schransky's, the duel would be even. As it is, he has no chance.' And because of this imbalance, the image of the huge captain with the white mass of hair and beard continued to haunt the former slave from Georgia.

BUT HELP WAS forthcoming, through a route so intricate that no one could have planned it. Dundee, on the east coast of Scotland, was not a major shipbuilding city by any means, but in 1873 a shipyard there, with a reputation for constructing unusual crafts to specification, received an order to build a ship stout enough to withstand the ice fields off Labrador and Greenland, and as a result, in 1874 a stubby, rugged vessel was launched which would, when it finally sank eighty-nine violent years later, be remembered as one of the great small ships of history. It was christened the *Bear*, 198 feet 6 inches stem to stern, 29 feet 9 inches beam, 18 feet 8 inches draft, 1,700 tons displacement. Its construction was an eclectic marvel: hull of Baltic oak, ribs of a heavier Scottish oak, decks of Burma teakwood, prow and sides sheathed with Australian ironwood, bottom of American yellow pine, iron fittings cast in Sweden and the navigation instruments assembled from seven different European and North American maritime nations.

The *Bear* was a three-master rigged as a barkentine—big square sails on the foremast, deft little fore-and-aft sails on the main and mizzen masts—but what made it look like the awkward little powerhouse it proved to be was a full-fledged steam engine forward of the mainmast served by a huge, squat smoke-stack at midships. When it was delivered to its future owners for work in the North American ice field, its builders promised: 'Square sails will give you drive, fore-and-afts maneuvering quickness, and the engine the ability to plow through ice. But the real secret? Look at that prow!' It was treble thick, fortified by oak and ironwood, and capable, said the proud marine architects who devised it, 'of breaking its way through any ice it faces.'

At that moment, at the beginning of the *Bear*'s life at sea, it was thought that the ship would serve some routine purpose, but later, when it was dragooned into a rescue operation, it achieved fame on front pages across the world: the American arctic explorer Adolphus Greely had gone bravely into the northern waters of the Atlantic, lost his ship in a crushing ice pack and nineteen of his men in the ensuing attempt to walk back to civilization. All rescue efforts by normal ships having failed, the *Bear* was purchased by the American government for the huge price of a hundred thousand dollars and hurried to the supposed scene of the disaster.

Now an entirely different kind of ship was in the arctic, and its double-stout construction enabled it to break its way through ice fields that no other could have penetrated and, to great acclaim, to rescue Greely and six other survivors. In the aftermath, while the world was applauding this extraordinary ship, someone had the clever idea of transferring it to the revenue cutter service in Alaska, where it would be most useful.

Around the Horn it went in November 1885, arriving in San Francisco after only eighty-seven days at sea. By chance, when the *Bear* docked, Captain Mike Healy was available for a new command, and without much forethought he was given this well-regarded ship which already had a reputation as exalted as his own. It was a remarkable wedding of man and machine, for when he moved his gear into the captain's quarters and arranged a perch for his parrot and a hiding place for his booze, he said: 'This is home,' but it was only when he saw that amazing prow with its fantastic thickness of ironwood that he dared reissue his earlier oath: 'Now we drive that bastard from the seas.'

In 1886, Healy took his new command north, all the way to icebound Barrow at the tip of the continent, where he muscled his way through floes that no ordinary vessel would even have attempted, and luck was already sailing with him, for he rescued three groups of sailors whose ships had been crushed by the ice. When he delivered them back to San Francisco they spent half their praise on Healy, half on the *Bear*, and thus the legend of the ship was augmented: 'It can go anywhere. It'll save a thousand lives up there. And with Healy in command, the seas will be safe.'

In going to and from Barrow, the *Bear* passed in sight of St. Lawrence Island, and the memory of those three dead villages tormented Mike Healy's soul, and it infuriated him to think that the *Erebus* was still prowling these waters and breaking all laws with impunity. Time and again he would cast anchor off some village on the Alaskan coastline, only to find that the *Erebus* had already been there with its cargo of rum and molasses for which it had obtained two or three years' supply of ivory and pelts.

Powerless to punish the marauder or even catch him, he had to sail disconsolately back to San Francisco and report that 'the brig *Erebus*, Captain Schransky, out of New Bedford, has been selling rum to the natives and engaging in pelagic sealing and poaching the rookeries, but an attentive patrol failed to apprehend him.' Even with his more powerful ship, the Negro Healy could not catch the Nordic Schransky.

B UT WHEN A giant engages in valiant battle, and Mike Healy was a giant, he is often joined by another eager to lend support, and together the two, who might have been strangers six months earlier, achieve miracles. Such a second giant was approaching Alaska from the hilly region around Deadhorse, Montana, on a wintry afternoon in February.

Sheldon Jackson was that amazing man. Even though he had been warned in the last settlement that a blizzard might be brewing, he was traveling alone. Forty-three years old, he had a complete beard and heavy mustache to make his little face look more dignified, a matter which concerned him deeply, for he wished always to impress strangers favorably despite his diminutive stature. His exact height would always be a matter of debate, for his detractors, a numerous band, claimed that he was under five feet, which was preposterous; he referred to himself as five four, which was equally absurd; because he favored built-up shoes, he looked to be about five two. But whatever his height, he often looked a dwarf among men markedly taller than he.

Now he plowed ahead through the snow that was beginning to drift, but he had no worry about his ability to make his destination before dark. God wants me to get there, he assured himself, and this was more than enough to fuel his energy, for he was a missionary of the Presbyterian church, absolutely convinced that God intended him for some great work and increasingly suspicious that it might be outside America that he would perform his miracles of conver-

sion. Therefore, when he came to the top of a small hill from which he had been
certain, as he climbed it, that he would see the town of Deadhorse, population
381, and found before him no town lights, but only another hill, and this one
larger than the last, he merely adjusted his heavy pack, squared his frail shoulders, and said aloud: 'Well, God, You must have it hiding on the other side of
this one,' and down into the light but swirling snow he marched, stopping now
and then to clear his steel-rimmed glasses.

The dip was quite deep, but he interpreted this as a protection God had
placed around this town, and his enthusiasm flagged not one bit as he reached
the bottom and started the upward climb, for it was inconceivable to him that
Deadhorse would not lie just beyond the ridge. On his way to the top the snow
increased noticeably, but this gave him little concern, for he thought: It's good
that I'm almost there, because this storm could get bad, and upward he struggled, as secure in his faith as he had been when doing his missionary work in the
mountains of Colorado or the flatlands of Arizona.

As he neared the top of the hill he was hit by a blast of snow borne by a
strong wind that came howling over the crest, and for just a moment his little
feet lost their hold and he slipped backward, but he quickly caught himself,
struggled to the top, and saw below him, as he had known he would, the
flickering lights of Deadhorse.

But now a more serious problem arose, for instead of a town of 381, there
stood before him a village of eight houses, well scattered. He had been grossly
deceived by the Presbyterians at his last stop, but since they were Presbyterians,
he could not think ill of them: Perhaps they never made the trip here themselves.

He had in his pocket the name of the man to whom he was being sent, Otto
Trumbauer: Sounds more like a Lutheran than a Presbyterian. But when he
stopped at the first house and asked for the Trumbauers, he was told: 'You must
be that missionary fellow they said was comin'. Trumbauer's expectin' you. He's
two houses along,' and when he knocked on the Trumbauer door, it was flung
open with a hearty cry: 'Reverend, we've been holdin' supper for you,' and he
was pulled into the warm room.

Mrs. Trumbauer, a hefty woman in her forties, said as she closed the door:
'You got here just in time. Take off that pack and your coat.' A son in his
twenties and a thin young woman who was apparently his wife helped Jackson
get rid of his heavy garments and found a place for him at the waiting table.

At supper he learned the bad news, for the elder Trumbauer said: 'There has
to be some mistake. We got only eight families here, two of them are Catholic,
two are atheist, and of the other four, only three of us have any interest in
starting a Presbyterian church.'

Jackson heard the dismal report with only a slight wince: 'Jesus didn't start
out with twelve disciples. The church marches forward with what soldiers it has,
and you two men look like stout ones.' He insisted that the two other Presbyterian families be invited in that very night, so that the first meeting of the
Deadhorse Presbyterian Church was held while a small blizzard piled snow
outside.

The adult men, on whom the labor of building even a small church would
fall, were not eager to commit themselves to such a task, but Jackson was
adamant; he had been sent to Deadhorse to start a Presbyterian church and he
was determined to do so: 'I do believe I've organized more than sixty congregations and helped build at least thirty-six church buildings west of the Mississippi, and my commission now is all the Northern states starting west from
Iowa. Your fine town is in an ideal spot for a church which will bind this whole
area together.'

In succeeding weeks the two male Trumbauers were astonished by the physical and moral energy of this little man who had come on foot over the mountains to live with them during the building of their church. He worked like the strongest man present, and on Sundays he preached inspired sermons that ran for more than an hour, even though his entire congregation consisted of only three families. However, this changed when he visited the two atheist families and was informed that they were agnostic rather than atheist. 'Join with us on Sunday,' he pleaded. 'You don't have to believe, just hear the message.' Then, in what was supposed to be humor, he added in his awkward way: 'We won't take up a collection,' and he was so sincere in his invitation that one of the families did stop by the Trumbauer house to hear the next Sunday's sermon. It dealt with missionary work, and during the communal dinner that followed he revealed the sources of his surprising energy: 'In my freshman year at Union College back east I heard a call: "Sheldon, there are people overseas who do not know the Word of God. Go to them, take them My Holy Word." '

'You didn't go overseas. You said you worked in Arizona and Colorado.'

'When I graduated from Princeton Theological, I went before an examining board for the foreign missions, and their doctors said: "You're too frail and weak for service in foreign countries," so they sent me to Colorado and Wyoming and Utah, where I helped build church after church, and now I'm in one of the most demanding regions of all, Montana and Idaho.'

'What do you mean,' a young man asked, 'when you say "I heard a call"?' and Jackson replied with startling vigor: 'Sometimes to some people you're standing alone in a room or you've been praying, and Jesus Christ himself comes into that room and says in a voice so plain it sounds like a bell: "Sheldon, I want you for my work," and ever after your feet are headed in that direction and you are powerless to turn aside.' No one spoke, so he ended: 'That voice called me to Deadhorse where Jesus Christ wanted one of His churches to be built, and with your help, not mine, it will be built.'

He was being too modest, for his contribution to the small log building was tremendous; he worked nine and ten hours a day at the most difficult jobs of construction, and sometimes the women laughed when they saw him coming down the road carrying one end of a log while some huge young fellow struggled with the other end. He was good with a hammer if he could have the help of one of the homemade ladders, but always on Sunday he was prepared for his sermon, and had the ones he delivered at Deadhorse been collected in a small booklet, they would have provided a logical exposition of the philosophy that underlay the missionary effort.

But what staggered the three local families was that in addition to his day's labor and his Sunday sermons, the little man spent most of his nights after supper writing voluminous copy for a popular religious journal he had started in Denver and for which he still felt responsible. As the work on the log church neared completion, the Trumbauers and their Presbyterian friends recognized Jackson as a true man of God, a Christian without a flaw, and they were pleased to have known him. Mrs. Trumbauer said, as the time approached for his departure for some town in Idaho that needed a church: 'I've never had a man in the house, not even my own father or Otto's, who caused me less trouble. Sheldon Jackson is a saint.' And then she added: 'Hadn't we better tell him? It might break his heart to find out later.'

The families held private discussions in another home and concluded that if one balanced the honorable with the practical, the best course would be to finish the church, have a big dedication ceremony, and then tell him, and that was the plan that was followed.

When the time approached for committing this church to the service of Jesus Christ, Jackson went humbly to the nonreligious families and pleaded with them to help in the dedication: 'It's for the good of the whole community, not just a few Presbyterians,' and then, stifling his pride and his convictions, for he waged unceasing war against Catholics and Mormons, he went to the Catholic families and invited them also to the celebration, using much the same arguments: 'I will be dedicating a church. You will be helping the community to take a step forward.' He was so persuasive that on the Thursday, a day of the week that he specifically chose so that the agnostics and the Catholics would feel free to participate, which they did, he preached a sermon that was a marvel of friendliness and devotion. All his customary exhortation was muted, and to listen to him, the Presbyterian church had not an enemy in the world nor was there any other Christian denomination with which it was at odds. Most earnestly he wanted this church to be a force for good in a community which he was sure would be a growing one.

And at the feasting he moved from family to family, all eight of them, assuring them that with the opening of this church, a new day was dawning in Deadhorse, and he was so convinced by his own rhetoric that when he saw tears in the eyes of the Presbyterian women, he assumed that they were the joyous tears of Christian triumph.

They were not, but it had been agreed by the three families that they would wait till Jackson was packed for his move into Idaho before telling him the painful news, but one night when he was busy in the Trumbauer dining room finishing a report for his Denver publication—it dealt with the triumph of Jesus Christ's message in the town of Deadhorse, Montana, a settlement he refused to call a village—Otto Trumbauer coughed and said: 'Reverend Jackson,' and when the little fellow looked up he saw the entire Trumbauer family ranged before him. Obviously, something of moment had agitated these good people, but what it was he could never have guessed.

'Reverend Jackson, we've tried every way on earth to avoid this, but there's no way out. Us and the Lamberts, we're movin' back to Iowa. Our families have farms for us to work there, and we can earn a livin', somethin' we can't do here.'

Jackson dropped his pencil, looked up, wiped his glasses meticulously, and asked for confirmation of the astounding news: 'Iowa? You're leaving here?'

'We got to. No future for our children here. Nor for us.'

For the first time since he was trapped in the growing blizzard, Sheldon Jackson allowed his shoulders to sag, but then he tensed them for the Lord's work: 'Why, if you knew you were leaving . . . ?'

'Did we stay to help build the church?' Mr. Trumbauer finished the question, but he was not allowed to give the answer; his wife did: 'We discussed that, all the families, and we decided that you were a true man of God sent to us on a special mission.' She burst into tears, and it was up to her husband to add: 'We agreed that we would build the church and leave it as a beacon in the wilderness.'

Jackson squared his shoulders, rose, and grasped in turn the hands of all the Trumbauers: 'You were right in your decision! God always directs us in the right path! I started six, maybe eight churches in the Colorado mountains that never took hold, but there they stand, as you say, beacons in the mountains to remind those who will come later that Christians once labored here.' But then his indomitable optimism manifested itself: 'But this town will never become a wilderness! I see expansion, families moving here from the Dakotas, and when they arrive, there'll be your church waiting for them, for no collection of houses is ever a town without a church at its center.'

He left Deadhorse in a state of positive euphoria, a little man with a big pack, eyeglasses that collected mist and dust, and a conviction rooted in rock that the work he was doing was ordained by God and supervised by His Son Jesus Christ, but the judgment which Mrs. Trumbauer voiced as he departed—'Reverend Jackson, you're a saint without a flaw'—was far from true, for he had another side to his nature which had not had an opportunity to reveal itself during his constructive visit to Deadhorse.

ON THE SNOWY day that Sheldon Jackson left Deadhorse, Montana, to push westward, an informal gathering of the board which governed Presbyterian missions convened during a retreat in a rural setting overlooking the Hudson River in New York. A tall, worried clergyman, who obviously wanted to be fair, started the afternoon's discussion with an announcement which brought discomfort to all who heard it: 'As your chairman it's my duty to be scrupulously just in what I say, but I must advise you that our dear and respected friend Sheldon Jackson has done it again. We don't know where he is or what he's up to. After we took him out of Colorado, where he, as you know, was pursuing his own ways, he obeyed our orders for a while, taking proper steps to develop the area we assigned him.'

'Which was?' a minister asked.

'The Northern states and territories west of the Mississippi, but not including Dakota, the state of Oregon or the territory of Washington.'

'That's a vast area, even for Jackson. Where's he supposed to be?'

'We directed him to work in Montana. Where he actually is, who can guess.'

'Isn't it about time,' an impatient clergyman in his sixties asked, 'that we discipline this young man?'

'He's not so young, you know. Must be in his forties.'

'Old enough to behave himself.'

'That he will never do,' the chairman said as he produced a single sheet of notes. 'But before we take any action regarding this little hurricane, I want to bring before you eight aspects of his behavior, for he is consistent, and the first three refer to the finest attributes any missionary could exhibit. *First*, he is a born missionary. From his earliest days at Union College he had a specific calling to Christ, and whereas he is not loath to challenge the veracity of your calling or mine, he never doubts the authenticity of his. He is therefore by his definition a better missionary than you or I, and he is not afraid to point this out. *Second*, he has, from early childhood, been a committed Presbyterian. He believes without question that ours is the world's superior religion, and the doubts that assail the rest of us from time to time, the great debates about the nature of God and the paths to salvation never touch him. The two Johns, Knox and Calvin in that order, settled it for him!'

The clergymen discussed this second point for some time, and one man spoke for several: 'To have a faith as solid as that . . . maybe I envy him,' but another minister from New York cautioned: 'You may have used the wrong word, Charles. Not as *solid* as that, as *simple*. He knows what he's for and what he's against.'

'For example?' Charles asked, and the speaker ticked off his response: 'He's for Jesus Christ and against Catholics, Mormons and Democrats.' Charles did not laugh: 'I wish I knew even ten things for sure . . . no questions, no doubts. Jackson knows ten thousand.' And the second speaker said: 'And he's convinced that you and I don't know even three.'

The chairman continued: 'Out of this rock-solid conviction comes the third attribute you've all noticed, his remarkable gift for persuading others to listen to him attentively. Small, contentious, single-minded, you'd expect him to turn people away, but it's just the opposite. He attracts them the way honey attracts flies, and they'll listen to him discuss the basic principles of religion and particularly the work of missionaries.'

At this point the discussion stopped, and the clergymen reflected on the positive attributes of their difficult colleague; all granted him his piety, dedication and surprising ability to cooperate with the other Protestant denominations, but most had felt the lash of his venomous tongue, and after a pause, which included the nodding of heads in agreement with what had been said so far, the analysis continued:

'*Fourth*, and this fault had better be admitted up front, for it accounts for many of the problems we've had with Jackson and will have in the future. For a devout Christian, which he certainly is, and a man who has devoted his life to missionary work, he displays a singular skill in going for the jugular of anyone whom he considers an enemy. This accounts for the fact that if you take a hundred of his acquaintances in either Colorado, Washington or the church in general, you find fifty of them revering him as a saint, fifty reviling him as a serpent.'

This called for a show of hands among those present, and the score was saint three, serpent fourteen, with many of the latter eager to relate how Jackson had battled with them over points not worth the effort. But these same men nodded in agreement when one sagacious elder pointed out the fundamental fact about Jackson's place among the Presbyterians: 'He is our front-line general in the fight against darkness. He's the one, above all others, who ensures that our efforts in the field equal those of the Baptists and Methodists. Like him or not, he is our man.'

'I was coming to that,' said the chairman, who had been repeatedly savaged by Jackson, 'for he does have his virtues. *Fifth*, early in life, for reasons not easy to explain, he developed a conviction that if he wanted something, he should go right to the top. Have you ever visited Washington with him when he wants something important? He slams his way into someone's office—congressman, senator, cabinet ministers, the President himself. He told me once after having lectured a senator: "These are good men, but they need guidance," and he's ready to offer it anytime, anywhere, on any subject. I've often wondered why a man so small, so insignificant, can bully a senator six feet tall, but he does.'

Several men testified to Jackson's extraordinary power in Washington, and one said: 'He's made himself the voice of morality, especially Presbyterian morality, and that counts for something.'

The chairman now came to one of the fundamental talents of Sheldon Jackson: '*Sixth*, his power stems from his capacity to convince large numbers of women church members to support whatever program he's fostering at the moment. They'll write letters to Washington and, most important, contribute large sums of money for his various projects, like that extraordinary church newspaper he still publishes in Denver, although he hasn't been there for years. He depends upon these women, beseeches them for funds, and thus places himself somewhat beyond our control.'

A choleric minister who had often been the subject of Jackson's vituperative attacks said: 'I watched him address a group of women in Maine whom he'd never seen before, and he was using the approaches that he'd found productive in Western states like Colorado and Iowa. He warned them about the dangers posed by the Catholic church, but they'd heard enough of that in Massachusetts and Maine. He saw he wasn't getting anywhere, so he switched to a hard-hitting exposé of the Mormon church in Utah, but most of them had never heard of the Mormon church, so that fell flat. Obviously agitated—I could see he was perspiring—he suddenly launched into a heartrending account of guess what? Out of the blue, with no preparation whatever, he gave them a tearful account of how Eskimo girls in Alaska were being seduced at the age of thirteen by rascally goldminers, and his pictures were so vivid and lamentable that even I had tears in my eyes. Now, he's never been to Alaska, knows nothing about it, but he convinced those good Presbyterian women that unless they contributed heavily to the mission work he was planning for Alaska . . .'

'Who said we're sending him to Alaska?' an irate clergyman shouted, and the informant said: 'He did. That is, he didn't actually say we were sending him. He said he was going.'

Surveying the group almost belligerently, the chairman asked: 'Did anyone here mention Alaska to him?' and one clergyman said: 'The last place on earth we'd want him meddling. That's Oregon territory. Tell him to mind his own business,' and several members mumbled: 'Amen.'

So the chairman returned to his bill of indictment, but before he could speak to the next point he was interrupted by chuckling coming from the group's oldest member. 'Did I say anything improper?' the chairman asked, and the man said: 'Heavens, no! I was just recalling that I was on the committee that interviewed Jackson years ago when he wanted to be one of our overseas missionaries. I read him our verdict: "You're too frail for the hard work of an overseas post." ' When the gross inaccuracy of this prediction struck the meeting, everyone joined in the laughter.

'Seventh,' resumed the chair, 'he's displayed an insatiable appetite for publicity. From the first he's appreciated the power that can come to a man, particularly a clergyman, if he's seen by the press to be an agent for good. He saw early that this would protect him from bodies like ours who might not want to support his more outrageous plans. And he was never willing to leave good publicity to chance; as you know, he started or had others start some four or five religious newspapers or journals in which his good works are extolled and in whose columns it is always he who accomplishes things and not the hard-working missionaries who work in silence. Since he acquired that honorary degree from that little college in Indiana, and I have reason to believe he initiated it, he always refers to himself in his journals as Dr. Sheldon Jackson, and nine-tenths of the people who work with him are convinced that he really earned a doctorate in divinity.'

The board members discussed the little man's remarkable ability at promoting himself, and there were notes of envy as they recalled one illustrated article after another which spoke of his heroic efforts, but then the meeting closed with an almost irrelevant comment, Item Eight: 'Jackson has always been an ardent Republican who believes that when the United States government is in such hands, God smiles upon our nation, and that when Democrats come into power, the forces of evil are set loose. This outspoken devotion aids Presbyterianism when the Republicans are in control of the nation, as they have been for so long, but it could damage us if the Democrats ever took over.'

In the discussion that followed, it was agreed that since the Democrats were not likely to assume national power in the foreseeable future, the Presbyterians might as well run the risk of allowing Jackson to continue as their spokesman in Washington, but all were firm about the resolution which the board passed at the end of their meeting:

Resolved: that the Reverend Sheldon Jackson be complimented on his new missionary successes in Dakota, but that he be admonished to keep this Board informed of any future movements before he makes them. He is specifically directed not to move into Oregon or Alaska, since those areas are the domain of the Oregon church.

But even before these stern directions could be handed to a secretary for transmission to Jackson, a messenger arrived at the retreat with a communication from distraught church leaders in Oregon:

The Reverend Sheldon Jackson appeared in our midst without warning and proceeded to infuriate everyone. After creating a great disturbance, he left us for Seattle and Alaska. When we warned him that the latter was Oregon's responsibility, he told us bluntly that he read his commission to include everything from the Mississippi River to the Pacific Ocean and that it was time someone attended to Alaska. We informed him that our church already had missionaries in place in Wrangell, but he retorted: 'I mean a real missionary,' and he sailed north.

In this abrupt and unauthorized manner Jackson carried the Word of God and the salvation of Jesus Christ to darkest Alaska, and it was a curious fact that for the first seven definitive years of his mission he received not a penny of aid from the Presbyterian church, which was outraged by his insolent behavior. He paid the huge expenses of the Alaskan experiment, one of the most successful in American missionary efforts, solely from the funds turned over to him by adoring women whom he visited each winter on hortatory expeditions. At a time when he was accomplishing miracles in the frozen north, he spent half of each year back in various states imploring women's groups for help, or in Washington hectoring Congress for better laws and more money for Alaska.

He became the close personal friend of almost everyone in government who was destined for spectacular promotion, especially those who were Republican or Presbyterian, which was how he attached himself early to the coattails of Senator Benjamin Harrison of Indiana, who was both, and who, when he became President, would look to Jackson for counsel as to what should be done in Alaska. At a mere five feet two, with the stubby legs of a child, this Presbyterian minister had transformed himself into a giant.

WHEN DR. JACKSON arrived in Alaska, illegally his opponents said, he put his tremendous ingenuity to work, and achieved two brilliant successes: he persuaded his friends in Congress to grant him the resounding title of General Agent for Education for Alaska, which carried no salary and for the early years no government funds, but which did empower him to have impressive calling cards made which he used to bully anyone opposing his plans; and he hectored the Treasury Department into assigning him free passage aboard any of its revenue cutters that were sailing to any point that he wished to visit in the execution of his duties. With these assurances in his pocket and with the continued financial support of the women's clubs back home, he was prepared to set forth on his life's work: the humanization and education of Alaska.

In these beginning years Jackson led a frenetic life. During the spring and summer months he jumped aboard any available cutter to explore the arctic seas, engage in battle against alcohol, arrest malefactors, help dispense law, visit

Siberia, plan the development of Alaska, and with his own money provide many of the services which the government should have funded. Then, for the six months of fall and winter, he would be back in Washington or New York or Boston, lobbying and lecturing on the future of Alaska. During one typical twelve-month period he traveled 37,624 miles, and a fellow clergyman guessed that in that time he had given not less than two hundred lectures on behalf of Alaskan education: 'Sheldon's ready to launch into a lecture if he can find an audience of six.'

But whenever he was on the verge of achieving some improvement, he found himself frustrated by the fact that the United States still refused to provide Alaska with any kind of government or adequate tax base, and in his frustration he would roar back to Washington, breathing fire, to bombard Congress. It was there, with his traditional foresight, that he formed his close acquaintanceship with the promising senator from Indiana, Benjamin Harrison, grandson of the ninth President. The senator listened to his pleas for a law that would enable Alaska to govern itself, became convinced by Jackson's moral force, and in 1883 began to work in the Senate for such a law. In 1884, spurred vigorously by Jackson, Senator Harrison finally maneuvered through Congress an Organic Act, giving Alaska a civil government of sorts, with one judge, one district attorney, one clerk of court, one marshal—four deputies to bring law and order to an area of more than five hundred thousand square miles. It was pathetically inadequate, but a step in the right direction.

Jackson, of course, had hoped for self-governing territorial status, but Congress would not concede this, for it would have implied that sooner or later the territory would become a state, as all the other emerging sections of the United States were doing, and that, ranted the lawmakers, was preposterous: 'That icebox will never have enough people to become a state.' 'Self-government? Hell, the entire area has only nineteen hundred people, I mean white people of course.' 'If the Army don't govern it, the Navy should.'

But not even Jackson appreciated the almost fatal inadequacy of the bill he and Harrison had helped pass; he learned, however, when he returned that spring to Sitka, for he had not been in his summer home two hours before he was visited by an irate Carl Caldwell, the former lawyer from Oregon and now a leading citizen of Alaska: 'What did you allow Congress to do, Dr. Jackson?'

'We didn't allow it. Harrison and I forced it.'

'But the Oregon bit? That nullified everything.'

'Now wait,' Jackson said defensively. 'Congress refused to give us territorial status. Best we could get was that we should be governed by the same local laws as Oregon.'

At this, Caldwell leaped from his chair: 'If it was the laws of Oregon, it would be all right. What you gave us are the ancient laws of the territory of Oregon. It became a state in 1859. You're taking us back to the way Oregon was in 1858,' and when he spelled out the monstrous limitations this placed on Alaska, Jackson sat with mouth agape: 'We can't have jury trials in Alaska because Oregon territorial law said that to be eligible, jury members must be taxpayers.'

'Sensible rule,' Jackson said. 'Provides responsible men for jury duty.'

'But we have no taxes in Alaska; therefore, no juries.' When Jackson gasped, he continued: 'Many of the best laws in Oregon Territory related to counties, but we can't have any of those laws because we have no counties.'

'That's ridiculous,' the missionary who fathered the law grumbled, but Caldwell was far from finished with his critique: 'No one can buy land here, because Oregon's law made no provision for a land law. Worse, for the same reason, the great Homestead Act which has settled the West can't be used here to give settlers free land. But what really strangles us is that we can have no local legislature because Oregon in those days didn't have one.' On and on he went, sometimes showing Jackson chapter and line of the antiquated law, so that by the time he was finished, Jackson realized that with his help Congress had returned Alaska to a straitjacket; he saw that he would have to fight most of his battles all over again, and he began that night to flood Congress with new letters of advice and his women supporters with new appeals for funds, because when he engaged in battle, there was no truce, no surrender.

But it was not until the new officers authorized by the Organic Act of 1884 arrived in Sitka to take control of Alaska that he realized the jeopardy he was in, because President Chester Arthur, under almost unendurable pressures from office seekers, had appointed some of the most despicable rascals available at the time, and from the moment they arrived in Sitka they determined to get rid of the troublesome little missionary about whom miners, fishermen and rumrunners complained.

Ringleader of Jackson's enemies was the district attorney, a notorious drunk. His marshal was little better, but it was the federal judge, a man of enormous power, who was the real disaster. Ward McAllister, Jr., was the incompetent nephew of the man with the same name who served as social dictator of New York. All had received their appointments to good-paying jobs through the political pull of their friends and without regard to their competency, which was nil.

They had not assumed their offices long when, with the connivance of the district attorney and Judge McAllister, they issued in secret an indictment for the arrest of Jackson, then waited till a maximum number of local citizens were at the dock to see the departure of a steamer on which Jackson was to sail. At the last possible moment Deputy Marshal Sullivan went aboard with handcuffs to arrest the little missionary and haul him off to jail.

In the next weeks Jackson suffered indignities he could not have imagined, but in the end he was rescued by a most improbable source of justice. President Arthur, responsible for these infamous appointments, left office, and almost immediately after the Democratic reformer Grover Cleveland assumed the presidency, he canceled the Arthur appointments, replacing them with more standard politicians, who served Alaska well. One of the first things the new team did was quash the indictment of Sheldon Jackson, who nevertheless continued to believe that the nation was served best when Republicans were in power.

It was about this time that Jackson participated in one of the most farseeing acts of Alaskan history, one that was rarely if ever duplicated in other newly settled frontiers. Communicating with the leaders of other American churches, he proposed a mutually enforced division of Alaska into a dozen or so religious spheres of influence, each the preserve of one denomination into which proselytizing missionaries from other sects would not intrude. What he proposed was a grand religious truce, and primarily because his reputation as a man of integrity was so widely recognized, leaders of the other groups adopted his suggestion.

As he explained it to the people of Sitka: 'Because the Presbyterians were first on the scene, we get Sitka. But since this is the easiest part, we're also taking the most difficult, Barrow in the extreme north.' Modestly he added: 'It'll be the northernmost mission in the world.' When he spelled out other terms of the agreement, he sounded like some follower of Jesus in the Book of Acts apportioning the missionary responsibilities of the infant Christian church: 'Our good friends the Baptists are taking Kodiak Island and lands nearby. The Aleutian Islands, where much work needs to be done, to the Methodists. The Episcopal church picks up the work already done decades ago by their cousin church, the Anglicans of Canada, along the upper Yukon. The Congregationalists have volunteered to accept a most difficult area, Cape Prince of Wales. And a fine church you may not know, the German Moravians of Pennsylvania, are going to take God's Word along the Kuskokwim River.'

In a later wave of ecumenical enthusiasm, other churches volunteered to become part of this grand arrangement: the Quakers of Philadelphia, always in the forefront where such work was to be done, received Kotzebue and a mining area near Juneau; Swedish Evangelists got Unalakleet; and the Roman Catholics received the vast areas about the mouth of the Yukon which had once been served by the Russian Orthodox missionaries. It was an extraordinary example of ecumenism at its best, and much of the credit went to Jackson.

But verbal agreements, noble though they may be, and actual implementation are two vastly different things, and years passed before any of the major American churches implemented their promises. There were no Baptist missions, no Methodist, not even a Quaker. In despair, for he saw the natives of Alaska perishing because the Word of God was denied them, Jackson implored the major churches to get moving, but with no results. He went to Philadelphia to visit with the Quakers, whom he was sure he could persuade to move north, but he accomplished nothing, so in a kind of moral despair he spent a steaming hot night in August 1883 in the Quaker city drafting a letter to the Moravian church centered in nearby Bethlehem. He implored them to continue in Alaska the noble work they had begun with the Eskimos of Labrador, and once more he received for his labors nothing but silence.

But his letter must have had some effect on the stalwart Germans of Bethlehem, for during Jackson's visit to the United States in the following winter he received without any preliminary encouragement an invitation to visit Bethlehem and present his vision of Alaska's needs to the Moravians. Hastily boarding a train in Philadelphia, he journeyed north to the quaint and lovely old German city, where he delivered one of his most inspired orations, telling the audience: 'The Moravian church has always been in the forefront where missionary work is involved. It's your tradition, your soul. Now God's call reaches you one more time: "The Eskimos of Alaska are languishing for My Holy Word." Dare you say no?'

The solemn burghers who supervised the church agreed that night that they would send an exploratory mission to the Kuskokwim River by the end of 1885, and when the five young, devout farmers—three men, two wives—saw that great twin of the Yukon and the hunger among the people for medicine, education and Christianity, which they interpreted as the reason why white men prospered, the young missionaries wrote back to Bethlehem: 'We are needed,' and one of the finest groups of religious workers ever to reach Alaska followed in due course, and the logjam of indifference was broken. Quickly the Quakers took up their appointed areas, then the Baptists and the Methodists, and soon Alaska was dotted with those missions, often stuck away on remote sites, which would in time account for the civilizing of the Great Land.

ONE DAY WHEN Jackson was at work in Sitka, the new cutter *Bear* hove into the sound, and before it could be anchored, Jackson had made the decision which would determine so much Alaskan history: That's the kind of ship I'd like to sail in. By midday he had presented his authorization for passage to the first mate, who looked down his nose at the strange little man offering it and said: 'Captain'll have to clear this,' and for the first time the missionary was led into the quarters of Captain Mike Healy, who had begun to drink heavily the moment the *Bear* reached Sitka, and who now sat with his parrot on his shoulder.

Irritated by this unwarranted intrusion, he let loose a chain of his most violent oaths, glared at Jackson, and ended: 'Now what in hell do you want?'

Had the little missionary quailed before this onslaught, the possibility of any relationship between the two men might have died there, but Jackson was a truly fearless man, and drawing himself up to his most impressive posture, he shouted in his strongest oratorical voice: 'Captain Healy! I am a man of the cloth, and I do not allow such profanation of God's name in my presence. And I have also come to Alaska to stamp out the alcohol trade, and you, sir, are drunk.'

Startled by the little gamecock, Healy began to say 'You're right, Reverend . . .' when his parrot came forth with a few choice curses of its own, whereupon Healy cuffed him so that his feathers seemed to fly as he fled to the safety of his perch: 'Shut up, you!' He then turned his attention to his visitor: 'What does your paper say?'

'It's from the Treasury Department and it says that I'm to have free passage aboard your ship as long as I am in pursuit of my duties.'

'And what are your duties?'

'The bringing of God's Word to the Eskimos. The education of the children of Alaska. And the stamping out of the liquor traffic.'

To Jackson's amazement, Mike Healy, whose life had been saved by education, rose unsteadily, reached for his hand, and pledged a support which would last for twenty years: 'I'm for everything you're for, Reverend. Education saves souls, and strong liquor is the curse of the Alaskan native.'

'You seem to be well cursed yourself, Captain.'

'In my private life. As captain of this ship, one of my major duties, stamp out the trafficking in hooch.'

'And what is hooch?'

'Rotgut, booze, John Barleycorn. It kills Eskimos. It wipes out entire villages.' He fell back in his chair, reached for a glass which Jackson had not seen before, and finished his drink. Then he looked up with a roguish smile and said: 'Bring your gear aboard. We sail for Kodiak and Siberia at four.' And thus the partnership between these two unlikely men was initiated.

Healy was six feet two, five years younger and twenty years more powerful; Jackson was exactly a foot shorter, so that the top of his head came to Healy's windpipe. Healy was a believing Roman Catholic, with brothers and sisters occupying important roles in that religion; Jackson was a devout Presbyterian who, like John Knox before him, railed against Catholics. Healy was a Georgia Negro who legally should have been a slave; Jackson was the product of that social and religious ferment which had swept the rural area of upper New York State—Elizabeth Cady Stanton, Lucretia Mott and Joseph Smith, to whom the secrets of Mormonism were revealed, sprang from the same source—and he believed that Negroes, Indians and Eskimos were humans who deserved God's love but not social equality with white men. Healy was a man devoted to a profane vocabulary and booze; Jackson was a man of rectitude who felt it his duty to lecture miscreants and save them from their folly. Their differences were tremendous, and they were never hesitant about displaying them.

But they had three beliefs in common, and it overrode all these differences: they both believed that Alaska could be governed if one found men of good will to make the effort; they were prepared to volunteer for that duty; and both sought justice for the natives.

Their first cruise together sealed their friendship, because whatever difficulty they ran into, they seemed to perceive instantly its moral overtones, and to a startling degree, each approved of what the other recommended. Now it was no longer Captain Healy of some grubby revenue cutter dispensing rude justice along the shores of the seas; it was the noble ship *Bear* steaming into harbor, its engine puffing smoke, with a distinguished ship's captain aboard, supported by a self-appointed doctor of divinity. They formed a majestic pair, two giants moving into an area that had been pestered by midgets, and after the first visit of this *Bear* to a new village, the authority of Healy and Jackson was established.

On this first trip together they straightened things out at Kodiak, provided stores to the Russian garrison at Petropavlovsk, delivered and enforced a set of judgments along the Siberian coast, and wound up at Cape Navarin, whose settlers streamed out in canoes once they learned that Captain Healy was back, for they remembered the gifts with which he had been so generous on his last trip. It was here that Healy took Jackson ashore to inspect the reindeer herds upon which these Siberians lived so bountifully, but the missionary did not at first appreciate the significance of the visit, for he had not yet seen Alaskan Eskimos starving for lack of winter food.

'Reindeer!' Healy cried. 'You load the *Bear* with them, a good wind offshore, and two days later you land them in Alaska.'

'Would that be possible?'

'We could do it right now if we had the authority, and the money to pay these people for their surplus.' The two Americans became so excited by the prospect of utilizing Siberian experience to save Alaskan lives that they assembled the herders of Cape Navarin, and Healy harangued them about the possibility of a trans-Bering trade in reindeer, and when he told them what they would receive in return, they became so enthusiastic that Healy told Jackson: 'When you get to Washington, see if funds are available.'

'But are the reindeer that necessary?'

'You'll see.'

And when they crossed the Chukchi Sea and landed at a chain of settlements—Barrow, Desolation, Point Hope, Cape Wales—and Jackson saw the devastation that an uncertain food supply wreaked at these points, he reached a firm conclusion: 'Captain Healy, you and I must do two things to save the Eskimos. Bring them a mission which has a school attached, and bring them reindeer.'

On the way home the *Bear* diverted for a stop at St. Lawrence Island, where Healy showed his missionary friend the ruination wrought by the rum and molasses from the *Erebus*. Jackson was appalled when he saw the skeletons still lying about, and that night as the sturdy *Bear* plowed southward he sought out Healy as he conned the ship on its way through the Bering Sea: 'Captain, if you were the man who discovered the death of those villages, and if you knew the reason, how can you possibly go on drinking?'

'I'm not perfect,' Healy said. 'And if you were perfect, you wouldn't have so many good people mad at you . . . I mean, disgusted with you.'

'Drunkards, miners with no conscience, the riffraff of Sitka—I welcome their enmity, Captain.'

'But I'm talking about the good people. Oh, I learned a lot about you in Seattle before I met you.'

'I was put on earth by God to do His will, and I must do it my own way.'

'I was put on earth by who knows? I was put here to sail a ship, and I do it my way.'

So these two imperfect men, each of whom would have enemies as long as he worked in Alaska, sailed southward with visions of what they hoped to accomplish: to Christianize the Eskimos, to bring order to the oceans, to transfer deer from Siberia to Alaska, to educate, to educate. On this last ideal they both agreed, as the dramatic events of their second trip together would prove.

They were only a few days out when Jackson, under the cold northern stars of October, asked: 'Captain, you never mentioned the *Erebus* before we reached St. Lawrence, but it eats at your soul, doesn't it?'

'It does.'

'Would you care to tell me about it?' and in a flood of profanity Healy told of his endless struggle with this renegade ship, of the cruel way it flouted the laws that were supposed to protect not only Eskimos but walruses and seals: 'He lurks out there in the spring, against the laws of all nations, and he waits for helpless female seals, pregnant, swimming north to give birth, and he guns them down with rifles and rips out the baby seals to sell the soft skins to China.'

'He should be destroyed,' Jackson said, and Healy told him: 'With this ship under me, I could destroy him,' and he retreated to his cabin, where he got drunk.

In the latter days of the trip Jackson remained on deck a good deal, a small man decked out in sealskin garments obtained in Siberia. When sailors asked him what he was doing, he gave evasive answers, for he was on a kind of fool's chase: he wanted to spot the *Erebus*, a ship he had never seen but which he already hated, and late one afternoon he did spy a black ship, or so it seemed, far to the west, and he ran to inform Captain Healy.

'It's the bastard,' Healy cried. 'Look, you can see his white hair in the glass,' and there, commanding his outlaw ship, stood Emil Schransky, who had spotted the *Bear* long before the *Bear* had spotted him. He had heard that Captain Healy had a new cutter but he did not believe the tales told of it, and especially he scorned the man in charge of it: 'No damned nigger can outsail me!'

But at the moment when in the past he had unfurled his great black sails to play cat-and-mouse with the slow cutters that Healy had been using, he realized that he was facing a much different kind of ship. He saw the smokestack belching a black cloud, the oversize square sails opening to embrace the wind and, most frightening, that formidable prow double-sheathed in oak and ironwood.

Too late he shouted: 'Prepare to run!' for even as his sailors insolently broke out the last bank of canvas they saw to their consternation that the *Bear* had outsmarted them, had turned on a sixpence to head directly at them.

'He's trying to ram us!' Schransky cried in unhidden fear, and he was right, for Mike Healy, this despised black captain, was about to smash his terrible prow right into the midships of the *Erebus*.

'Hard aport!' Schransky bellowed to his steersman, and the man tried to turn the dark ship parallel to the course of the *Bear* so that the latter would glide harmlessly past, as in former duels.

But this time Healy possessed his old wiles plus a powerful new ship in which to perform them, and standing amidships with his parrot screeching on his shoulder, he gave precise orders to his helmsman, who whipped the *Bear* about to send her crashing thunderously into the splintering timbers of the *Erebus.* Grinding on, propelled by the engine, the prow locked tight in the vital innards of its great dark enemy.

Quietly Mike Healy, the loser in so many previous encounters, gave commands which he had rehearsed: 'Gunners, stand ready to rake their decks! Sailors, board!' And an astonished Schransky, rendered impotent by this combination of a superior ship captained by a superior mariner, had to stand mute in a posture of surrender as Healy's victorious men swarmed aboard.

As Healy left the *Bear* to stride onto the *Erebus*, he saluted its captain, as the rules of the sea required, and then, with his revolver at the ready, he smiled coldly at Schransky and sent his men rampaging through the bowels of the captured ship. His many previous humiliations were handsomely avenged, and both he and Schransky knew it.

His officers found the kegs loaded with rum and molasses; others came upon the holds filled with sealskins. 'All overboard!' Healy commanded, and Schransky's men had to watch in sullen silence as the heads of the kegs were bashed in and the contents poured into the scuppers. Up came the illegal sealskins, worth a fortune in Canton, and into the dark Bering Sea they went.

It was only at this point that Sheldon Jackson felt free to leave the *Bear* and step onto the *Erebus*, and when Captain Schransky saw him in his preposterous sealskin uniform he thundered: 'And who in hell is he?' and Healy replied: 'The man who brought us here, the one who spotted you first.'

'Throw him overboard too,' Schransky growled, but now Healy delivered his ultimatum: 'Look at my ship, Schransky. Study that prow which cut right through you, that engine. There's a new day in Alaska, Schransky. If I ever see you in the Bering Sea again, I'm going to overtake you and ram you and send you to the bottom, with all hands.'

As he stood there in the growing darkness, preparing to give the orders that would retract the *Bear* from the gaping hole in the *Erebus*, he was two inches shorter than the German, many shades darker, but he spoke with an authority that had come late in his life and after many defeats, but at long last he was in command of the Bering Sea, and he was determined to remain so. When he returned to his own ship he left Jackson behind on the *Erebus*, and there were many things about which the little missionary wanted to lecture the big blond captain, especially those destroyed villages on St. Lawrence Island, and he opened his mouth to start his preaching, but when he looked up at that mammoth head so much higher and tougher than his own, he judged that silence was advisable, so without speaking he stepped gingerly across the shattered timbers and returned to his quarters.

IT WAS JACKSON's second trip with Healy that changed missions from mud-roofed hovels into true churches and schools, for when the rugged *Bear* steamed out of Sitka Sound, its smokestack belching sparks, every available corner of the deck was crammed with lumber, and ready-made doors and roof beams. Behind it trailed an old schooner piled with additional timber.

This year the *Bear* did not stop at easy ports like Kodiak and Dutch Harbor; instead, it plowed ahead through heavy Bering Sea storms to a first stop at Cape Prince of Wales, where two Congregational missionaries had for two years tried to survive in a hovel half underground. When the *Bear* dropped anchor on the Fourth of July, these surprised young men saw three ship's boats setting out from the mother ship, laden with lumber and sailors, and when the latter climbed ashore and unloaded their cargo, they did not merely deposit it there for the missionaries to use; they turned to and began that afternoon building them a church and a school.

That evening, as if to celebrate the holiday, the trailing schooner pulled in with the bulk of the timber, and the next morning Captain Healy himself joined the work crew, while Dr. Jackson scurried about, helping to dig the foundation trenches for the walls. Every man aboard the *Bear* except the cook worked on this mission church, and at the end of eight days they turned over to the astounded missionaries a center from which they could begin to Christianize this area.

When the *Bear* moved on to Point Hope, one of the loneliest villages in the world, the sailors who went ashore to work on the mission building were introduced to the Alaskan mosquito: it came in three versions, one more ferocious than the next, each strain thriving about three weeks in late spring and early summer. They took turns, as if to say: 'We'll send in the little ones to make people nervous, then the medium size, and three weeks later the giants.' They were fierce enemies, able to penetrate any opening in the clothes and bite deeply, until they sent some men almost crazy.

'What do you do when these things hit?' a sailor asked the lone missionary, and he said: 'You give thanks they last only about nine weeks,' and the sailor whined: 'I want to go back to Cape Wales and civilization.'

On the second day at anchor, Healy and Jackson joined the workers ashore, and again a solid church was built, despite the mosquitoes, but the strongest wood was saved for the next anchorage, farthest Barrow, where the world ends and the Arctic Ocean piles its ice nine months of the year and the sun vanishes completely for three months and more or less for five. Here the sailors met a missionary who was striving to implement Jackson's vision of civilization advancing through the Word of God to the most remote corners of the world.

Through Captain Healy's energetic intervention, space was secured in a government building to serve as temporary school-mission until his sailors could erect a regular structure, one strong enough to withstand the rigors of Barrow, where in this year not one house rose more than three or four feet above the ground. So Healy and his men worked with special care to make this Presbyterian mission a building that would withstand the pressures of the arctic for decades. After eleven days they turned over to the young missionary a rural masterpiece, a church that would illuminate the little village to which whaling vessels came in June, and where they perished in ice if they lingered too long in October.

Not long after leaving Barrow, and firing a parting salute to the new church which loomed like a beautiful volcano above the shacks of the village, the *Bear* swung into shore and anchored off the little wind-swept village of Desolation Point, where the residents clustered on the shore to greet the captain who in the past had meant so much to the security and prosperity of their settlement.

Healy waved to them all, but not seeing a certain individual, he called out: 'Where's Dmitri?' and a villager said: 'He's Father Dmitri now. Here he comes,' and from up the shore came an umiak containing a young man and one passenger, a woman. When it came closer, Healy saw that the man was the same young man who as a boy some years ago had protected his mother from the madman Agulaak. He was twenty-three now, a self-ordained missionary who had assumed in Desolation the leadership position once filled by his murdered father.

When Jackson met him, the young man explained that he supposed he was responsible to the Russian Orthodox Church to which his father belonged, and now began one of the uglier demonstrations of Jackson's behavior in remote areas. When he went ashore with Dmitri and his mother he said bluntly: 'We've brought you a real church. The sailors will start building it tomorrow, but it's to be a Presbyterian church, so you really must become a Presbyterian missionary.'

'We're Russian,' the widow of the martyred Father Fyodor said, but Jackson overrode this: 'You're American, and there's no place in our society for a Russian church.' When he learned that Dmitri, who was revered as Father Dmitri by everyone in Desolation, was teaching the children in the village the Cyrillic alphabet, he said to the crew of the *Bear*: 'The wrong religion in the wrong language,' and forthwith he launched an unabashed campaign to persuade—and when this failed, to force—Dmitri to convert to Presbyterianism: 'After all, you must remember, Dmitri, that we Presbyterians were given responsibility for the northern reaches of Alaska.'

When Dmitri refused apostasy, in which he was supported by his mother even though she had herself been born of Athapascan parents who now favored Methodism, Jackson became unpleasant, threatening him with the loss of the church and school the sailors had begun to build: 'We didn't bring all that lumber here to build a church for Russians. It's an American church and it's to have an American missionary.'

The likelihood that his obstinacy might cost his village the bright new buildings it so badly needed caused Dmitri so much grief that he consulted with his mother, who surprised him by taking from the little store of treasures she kept wrapped in a cloth behind a log pole in their underground hut the medal that Captain Healy had given her son so many years ago: 'He gave it to you because you had been brave. You should still be brave and not allow the little one to make you surrender your father's religion.'

At her insistence, Dmitri waited till Reverend Jackson was busy with floor plans for the school, which he was prepared to build despite his threat not to do so, for he was convinced that Dmitri would eventually appreciate the tremendous advantage of turning Presbyterian, both for himself and for the village. Then, making sure that Jackson did not see him, Dmitri jumped into the small umiak he had used when the *Bear* first anchored, and before long he was aboard the ship. Asking for permission to speak with the captain, he was ushered into Healy's quarters, where he was startled both by the parrot and the fact that the captain was close to being drunk. But when Healy, a good Catholic, learned what his trusted friend, the little missionary, was up to—the conversion of a good Russian Catholic into a Presbyterian—he sobered in a hurry, jumped down into Dmitri's umiak, and ordered the young priest, or would-be priest, to take him ashore.

Once there, he hurried to where the school was being built, grabbed Jackson by the sealskin under his chin, and demanded: 'Sheldon, what in hell are you doing to this boy?'

There was a confused attempt at explanation, a charge of kidnapping by Mrs. Afanasi, who came running up, and a great embarrassment on the part of Dmitri, who had not wanted the incident to develop in this manner.

The debate between Jackson and Healy continued for two stressful days, with the missionary arguing that since he had provided the lumber for the buildings, he had a right to say what kind of structure they should go into, and the captain arguing with equal force that since it arrived on the ship which he commanded, he had the privilege of saying how it should be used. Unfortunately, he had an imprecise understanding of the Russian Orthodox priesthood, and when on the second day he learned that Dmitri was planning to marry a local Eskimo girl who was at best a pagan, he became completely confused. His brothers who had high positions in what he called the real Catholic church did not run around getting married, nor did his sisters who were nuns. There has to be something terribly wrong, he said to himself, in a church which allows its priests to marry.

Nevertheless, he felt obligated to defend any Catholic church, and he did so with vigor, but he had never before argued religion with a moral cyclone like Sheldon Jackson, and when the church and school were finished, they were consecrated as Presbyterian structures, with Father Dmitri taking passage on the *Bear* to Seattle, where he would, through the help of local Presbyterians, be converted into Reverend Afanasi, the first Inupiat Eskimo to bear that august title.

But during the trip south to Kodiak, Captain Healy argued with the young man so persuasively, defending Catholicism as the one universal church, that he almost prevailed upon Dmitri to leave the *Bear* in Kodiak, return by some other ship to Desolation, and operate the new buildings as Catholic structures. But then the matter of Dmitri's wedding came up, and Healy, who was now quite drunk, stopped trying to understand what was happening. Jackson, who had anticipated this moment, stepped in, took charge, isolated Dmitri from the captain, and kept him on board the *Bear*, which carried him to Seattle and the ministrations of the good Presbyterians in that city.

In this manner, Desolation Point became a fountainhead of Presbyterianism in the north.

D URING ONE OF Sheldon Jackson's later cruises, the *Bear* was at sea for more than six months, and the missionary became aware that two of the junior officers were showing signs of irritation about having to serve so long away from home port and with a black captain. He overheard one of the young fellows complaining as they finished work on the school at Cape Prince of Wales: 'Have you noticed that Reverend Jackson, who's supposed to distribute money and materials impartially, always favors any school run by Presbyterians? Damn little for Baptists or Methodists, but it's only natural, him being a Presbyterian and so vehement about it.'

After the *Bear* touched at Desolation Point, the other officer said: 'I'd like to see an accounting of Jackson's funds. He gave three times as much money to the young minister here, and when I asked him about that, he said: "This is my church," but what that meant he didn't explain and I didn't ask.'

The officers openly voiced their displeasure with Captain Healy when the *Bear* made a long detour to Cape Navarin for the ridiculous purpose of picking up Siberian reindeer for transplanting to Alaska to feed Eskimos who might otherwise starve. When one man asked: 'Why are we doing this?' the captain replied: 'To enable good people to stay alive,' and the other said: 'If God wanted reindeer to feed Alaskan Eskimos, He'd have put some on our side of the Bering,' and Healy replied without rancor: 'Dr. Jackson might argue that we're doing work that God overlooked.'

But the young men had cause for complaint, because when the *Bear* returned to those very natives to whom it had so generously given gifts in appreciation of their assistance in rescuing American seamen, and the ones who had promised they would sell reindeer to help Alaskan Eskimos, the herders grew massively protective of their animals and would not part with a single one. The officers watched with growing bitterness as Healy sailed the *Bear* more than a thousand miles along the coastline of Siberia, pleading in vain for the stubborn Asians to sell him reindeer, and the young men also noted that Jackson was just as ineffective in trying to buy animals. At the conclusion of this wasteful excursion, one of the officers wrote to his father:

> This trip has been a shameful waste of government time and money. I begin to suspect that Jackson and Healy are plotting to sell their reindeer, if they ever get any, for private gain. The U.S. Gov't. could well investigate this scandal.

Despite the fevered efforts of the two would-be humanitarians, they were able to purchase no reindeer at Cape Navarin, but farther north at Cape Dezhnev, where the Siberian coastline turned sharply eastward toward America, they came upon a village which allowed them to buy nineteen of their precious herd, but the same officer wrote:

> With persuasion so ardent that it was unbecoming in the representatives of a Great Democracy, they finally purchased nineteen animals, but at a cost per beast that was unconscionable. This whole affair smells.

On the choppy trip across the Chukchi Sea three of the reindeer died, but sixteen did survive to become the foundation of a herd in the Aleutians, with more to follow in later years.

T HE COURT-MARTIAL in which Captain Healy would soon find himself enmeshed was partly his own fault, because once he had delivered the reindeer, he should have headed back to his home port of San Francisco to allow his sea-weary crew shore leave. But he was so enamored of the Bering Sea that he decided to make one last, quick scout north—Jackson would ultimately make thirty-two different trips to the land of the Chukchis—and it was on this sortie that he spotted an American whaler, the *Adam Foster*, engaged in pelagic sealing. Running forward at full sail-and-steam, he drew alongside the offender and ordered his men to board, and when some thirty energetically obeyed, he and Jackson followed suit, leaping adroitly onto the captured ship.

However, the sealers, who stood to make a great deal of money if they could get their illegal catch to either Hawaii or China, put up a surprising defense, during which Healy suffered a wound to his left shoulder and a bleeding slash along his cheek. Infuriated by this act of what he deemed warfare, he urged his men to subdue the attackers, and when they did he calmed his temper and ordered three reprisals: 'All rum and molasses into the scuppers. All pelts into the Bering. These six ringleaders and those three who assaulted me, trice them up!'

Jackson did not know what this horrendous word meant, but the young officers did, and as it was uttered, one moved to Jackson's side and whispered: 'Oh, this should not be done! They're Americans.' He made this protest because, erroneously, he believed that in a crisis the clergyman would have to side with him against Captain Healy and his drunken, profane behavior, but in this supposition, as he was about to find out, he was wrong. Jackson was not his man; he was Healy's.

So, much to the officers' horror, the nine sailors were triced up, that is, their hands were handcuffed behind their backs and ropes were passed through the cuffs and over a yardarm. Crewmen from the *Bear* then pulled on the loose ends of the ropes, and the miscreants were hauled just far enough aloft so their toes could barely reach the deck, and there in fierce agony they remained dangling for seven minutes, after which they were dropped, some of them senseless, to the deck.

Standing over them, Healy said: 'You'll not take arms against a ship of the United States government,' and one of the officers whispered to Jackson: 'But they didn't take arms,' and the missionary, who believed that crime deserved punishment, defended Healy: 'The punished men were selling rum and killing pregnant seals.'

Back aboard the *Bear*, two relevant things happened: Mike Healy, agitated by the pain from his wounds and the excitement of boarding a ship in midocean, got drunk, and one of the officers sought out Sheldon Jackson for an impassioned discussion of the afternoon's events: 'No captain has the right to storm aboard another ship and trice up nine of its sailors.'

'Captain Healy serves under orders to do just that. Stop unlawful sealing. Punish men and ships that sell alcohol to natives.'

'But certainly not to trice men up by their wrists behind their backs. Reverend Jackson, that's inhuman!'

'It's the law of the sea. Always has been. An alternative to hanging. You ought to be glad he didn't keelhaul them.'

The officer, appalled that a clergyman should defend such behavior, was goaded into saying something which, had he been a more sensitive young man, he would have regretted later: 'You don't sound much like a Christian, defending a man like Healy.'

Jackson rose from where he was seated on the edge of his bunk, pulled himself to his full height, looked up into the young man's eyes, and said: 'Michael Healy in the Bering Sea reminds me of St. Peter on the Lake of Galilee. I'm sure Sailor Peter was a rough-and-tumble man, but he was Christ's chosen apostle on whom he founded his first church. The church in Alaska depends upon the good works of Captain Healy.'

This comparison was so odious that the officer cried: 'How can you say that about a man who blasphemes and gets drunk all the time?' and when Jackson snapped in reply: 'I dare say Peter used rough language aboard his ship, too,' the young man stormed from the cabin.

Late that night, when Healy was more or less recovered from his bout with the bottle, Jackson went to the captain's quarters, allowed the parrot to rest on his left shoulder, and said: 'Michael, I'm afraid you and I have constructed permanent enemies in your young officers. They can't understand why you don't behave like a storybook sea captain, and they certainly think I ought to be like every minister they knew back home.'

'They're young, Sheldon. Never had to captain a ship. Never chased the *Erebus* back and forth across the Bering Sea.'

'They think I ought to condemn you because of your blasphemy and your drinking.'

'I think you should, too. But on the other hand, I think you forgot you were a minister of the Lord when you made young Father Dmitri turn Presbyterian in order to keep the church we gave him.' To halt such lugubrious thoughts, Healy snapped his fingers: 'They want us to be gods, but we're only men.'

The two reprobates talked long into the cold night, speculating now and then on what the young officers might be plotting.

THEY SOON FOUND out, for when the *Bear* doubled back to Kodiak with three prisoners taken at the Pribilofs, the officers dispatched a telegram to the headquarters of the revenue cutter service in San Francisco, lodging serious charges against their commanding officer:

> Michael Healy, captain of the revenue cutter *Bear*, has been consistently drunk on duty to the impairment of his responsibilities, has repeatedly used vulgar and abusive language against his officers and men, and has behaved with extreme cruelty to nine American sailors from the whaler *Adam Foster*. As officers under his command, we request that he be court-martialed.

By the time the *Bear* returned to its duty station off the coast of Siberia, the *Adam Foster* had docked in San Francisco, giving the local newspaper people a horrendous account of its run-in with the *Bear* and of Captain Healy's unwarranted tricing up of nine American sailors.

However, in the scandal that developed in the California papers, a force much more powerful than the captain of the *Adam Foster* entered the guerilla warfare against Mike Healy. Mrs. Danforth Weigle, president of the San Francisco Woman's Christian Temperance Union, had been searching for some time to find a foolproof case against some ship's captain who abused his men while under the influence of John Barleycorn, and when she read the lurid accounts of Mike Healy's behavior, she and her entire membership lodged formal complaints against him, demanding that he be summoned home, court-martialed, and dismissed from the service. Now all the envious people who had felt that this Negro mariner was growing bigger than his britches united to call for his trial and dismissal.

Bowing to the public clamor and especially to the pressures brought by the W.C.T.U., Healy's superiors had no alternative but to wire him at Kodiak to return immediately to San Francisco to defend himself in a general court-martial against charges of drunkenness, gross and improper behavior toward subordinates and, in the case of nine American sailors, the use of cruel punishment long outmoded in the navies of civilized nations.

He had left Kodiak long before the telegram arrived and spent the summer in the far reaches of the northern seas. During his sail south at the end of the season he learned of the statements made against him, and discussed them with Reverend Jackson: 'They mean to do me in, Sheldon. The captain of the *Adam Foster* bringing charges! I should have had him hanged from his own yardarm.'

It was Jackson who foresaw the real danger in the threatened court-martial: 'The women, Michael. They'll prove the most powerful of your enemies. I've always found the women to be the final arbiters.'

'Can I count upon you for support?'

'To the end, but I am worried.'

'You'll come to San Francisco? Testify for me?'

'You're the best captain there's ever been in the Bering Sea, Russian or American.'

'James Cook was up here, you know.'

'I didn't include the English.'

So it was agreed that Healy and Jackson would make a united stand against the considerable forces arrayed against the former, but Jackson's promised testimony did not come to pass, because when the *Bear* put into Sitka to disembark him, the doughty little clergyman faced a kind of court-martial of his own, for a special investigator with plenipotentiary powers had been dispatched from Washington to check upon the numerous charges of malfeasance lodged against him. Although he was not thrown into jail this time, it was obvious that he would not be able to go to San Francisco to testify in defense of his friend, for he had to save his own neck.

THE COURT-MARTIAL of Michael Healy was a solemn, miserable affair. Five senior officers from the nation's armed services sat in judgment of a popular hero gone sour, and the very newspapers which had inflated his reputation as the savior of the north now seemed to revel in his debasement as a tyrant, a brute, a foul-mouthed rascal and a drunk, but this was understandable, because in the opening days of the trial the evidence against him was devastating. Clean-looking young sailors from the *Adam Foster* testified, one after another, that whereas they had done nothing wrong, 'merely tried to protect our ship, as you gentlemen would do, he comes aboard, abuses us, and trices us up.' They explained in harrowing detail what *trice up* meant, and one man showed the court scars that resulted from the seven-minute ordeal when handcuffs had cut into his wrists. The marks were vivid.

The nails were hammered into Healy's coffin by Mrs. Danforth Weigle, of the W.C.T.U., who had long visualized this trial as the triumph of her organization's fight against alcohol on American ships. A fine-looking woman, with a low, cultured voice and not a crusading harridan at all, she made an impressive witness, for her testimony was brief and to the point: 'American sailors have for too long been victimized by drunken brutes who have tyrannized their men once they sailed from port and left the protection of courts ashore. No case more savage than that of Captain Michael Healy has come to our attention, and we demand that he be sent to jail for his crimes and dropped from the service of the United States.'

She asked that members of her committee who specialized in legal aspects of the problem be allowed to testify, and these ladies completed the devastating case against the black officer. When the prosecution closed, most observers in the stuffy courtroom supposed that Healy's fate was sealed, and stories resembling obituaries appeared in the papers, lamenting this deplorable conclusion to a career which had had its moments of nobility, as when the *Bear*, on various rescue missions, saved many sailors whose ships were trapped in ice.

But traditions of the sea run deep, and when the prosecution rested, a parade of the ordinary seamen whose lives Mike Healy had saved from shipwreck came forward to testify in his behalf. Junior officers who had served under him were eager to tell of how his indomitable will had saved the *Bear* when crushing in the ice pack seemed inevitable. A representative of the Russian Empire told the court of how, when he was stationed in Petropavlovsk, his officers looked to Mike Healy and the *Bear* as their right arm along the Siberian coast, and there was a moment of terrible drama when a survivor of a shipwreck at Point Hope took the stand:

'We lost our ship when the ice come in sudden in October. We was nine men made it ashore. The rest went down.'

'Did you get any ship's supplies ashore with you?'

'Some.'

'How long were you marooned?'

'Till June next year.'

'How did you survive?'

'We built lean-tos against the wind. Driftwood.'

'I mean eat? What did you eat?'

'We shot two caribou. We rationed careful. We ate bacon rind, anything.' Here he paused, looked away from the court, and sought the eyes of his salvation, Mike Healy. 'Then he come with the *Bear.*'

'Go on. What then?'

In a very low voice, which did not reach to the back of the room, he said: 'He knew from lookin' that in April and May when there were no caribou, no stores, we'd been forced to eat the bodies of them as died.'

The last words were lost in whisper, and the court asked the sailor to repeat, but a man in the front row of the audience said clearly: 'They were cannibals,' and the room fell into confusion. When order was restored, the sailor said: 'Captain Healy knowed what we'd done . . . been forced to do, that is . . . and he took us under his wing like we was his children. No sermons, no lectures. I remember exactly what he said: "We are all men of the sea. We plow a fearful furrow." '

The room was silent as the sailor stepped down, and at that juncture it was clear that the five-man court was not at all as certain of Healy's guilt as it had been the day before, but he would still have been found guilty of at least certain charges had there not been a commotion at the rear of the court, with the marshal shouting: 'You can't go in there!' and a gruff voice responding: 'We're goin' in!' and into the proceedings came a six-foot-four mariner with a huge head of snowy white hair and beard, followed by two junior officers and an ordinary seaman.

'Who are you, barging in like this?' the president of the court demanded, and the intruder said: 'Cap'n Emil Schransky, *Erebus,* out of New Bedford,' and he said that since maritime matters were under judgment here, he demanded a right to testify.

'Would your testimony be pertinent?' the presiding officer asked, and he replied: 'It would.'

He was allowed to come forward, and without even looking at his old enemy, he began in a restrained voice: 'If there is any San Francisco newspaperman present, he'll be able to verify that for better'n ten years me and Mike Healy, the man on trial, fought each other up and down the Bering Sea. He was for the Eskimo, I didn't give a damn. He was against pelagic sealin', it was my gold mine. He fought anyone who brought rum or molasses to the Eskimos, I didn't. Year after year I outwitted him because I always had the best ship. Then he got the *Bear* with its steam engine and defeated me. Almost sunk me. Threatened to shoot me if I ever invaded his sea again. I said to myself: Schransky, you had the best ship and did what you pleased. Now he has the best ship and he'll do what he pleases.'

'But what did you do?'

'I said: "Let him run the Bering as he likes. The Pacific is a big place." I left.'

'Why did you come here today?'

'Because me and my men read what you were doin' to Mike Healy. What the people from the *Adam Foster* whined about. The *Adam Foster*! What a pitiful ship. What a ship to bring charges against anybody. My men wouldn't waste time spittin' at the *Adam Foster,*' and his three associates nodded.

'And these good women ravin' about his drinkin'. What did he do when he finally captured the *Erebus*? Dumped all our rum and molasses down the scuppers. Ask the *Adam Foster* what he did when he captured them. I'll bet they'll say first thing he did was dump their rum. Healy was fierce against alcohol for Eskimos.'

He concluded his testimony with a surprising statement: 'I fought Healy for a decade, and always I had the best ship. But he fought me like a tiger, because he represents the best traditions of the sea. Even a master ship like the *Bear* is no good unless it has a master like Healy. That damned nigger with his parrot drove me from the arctic seas, and no lesser man could've done it. And if we went to sea again, we'd still fight, and the man with the best ship would win.' From the witness stand he saluted his longtime enemy and retired to the back of the room followed by his men.

The judges filed out, returned after the briefest possible consultation, and rendered their verdict: 'The citizens who lodged charges against Captain Michael Healy did not do so frivolously. His actions must have seemed deplorable to them. But the sea is governed by noble traditions accumulated through centuries and from the experience of many nations. Unless they are enforced by captains like Michael Healy, no ship can sail safely. This court finds him Not Guilty on all charges.' The audience, divided sixty percent for conviction, forty for acquittal, groaned and cheered while Emil Schransky rose from his seat, uttered a wild yell, and saluted Healy once more.

When order was restored, the court continued with its verdict: 'But since not even the ablest captain can be allowed free rein for intemperate behavior at sea or for abusive language directed against his subordinates, this court must take into account that on three past occasions Captain Healy has received severe reprimands for drunkenness and misconduct, 1872, 1888, 1890. We recommend that he be deprived of command for a period of two years.'

But his turbulent life continued. In 1900, on his first trip after regaining his command, he escaped a most serious court-martial pertaining to his abuse of a woman passenger only when his protectors had him declared temporarily insane, and in 1903, at the conclusion of his final command, he was again reprimanded for 'unofficerlike and indecent language in the presence of his officers and crew.' Unrepentant, he moved ashore, and died a year later.

IN SITKA THE government's case against Sheldon Jackson rehashed old charges against him, but with new and more effective citizens making them. As the population of Alaska grew, the numbers of miners, businessmen and saloonkeepers increased proportionately, and these groups had always been violently anti-Jackson, but since their speakers were now more literate, they painted him in dark and dictatorial colors: 'He wants to tell everyone how to behave, but he himself is an unchristian, ungodly tyrant.' He had also acquired a new body of enemies, the members of the Russian Orthodox Church, who felt that if the little missionary wanted to declare war against their church and their language, which he obviously did, they would take up arms against him. Most telling was a voice not heard before, and therefore extra persuasive: 'If Reverend Jackson spends six months a year attending to personal business in Washington, and six months cruising with his drunken crony on the *Bear*, how much time per year has he left to mind his duties in Alaska?'

At the conclusion of this round of testimony, things looked gloomy for Jackson, but the investigator was no fool, and before issuing his conclusions he sought a secret meeting with Carl Caldwell, now a full-fledged judge in the Alaskan court, who confided: 'Everything his enemies say about Jackson is true. But his enemies say the same thing about me, and if you set up your office here, they'd lodge the same charges against you. Nobody can be neutral where Jackson is concerned. He often irritates me, and I'm sure he'd irritate you. But you must have deduced from the character of his enemies that he's one of the best forces in Alaska. He represents the future.'

Paralleling the court-martial in San Francisco, the government man in Sitka began by conceding that the charges against Jackson had been brought in good faith, and he said so; there were many reasons why men of serious mind could dislike this obstreperous little man, but like Mike Healy, he was necessary for the well-being of his society. So the verdict had to be: 'All charges dropped with prejudice,' which meant, as Caldwell explained: 'They can't be revived again.'

But of course that applied only to Alaska, because when Jackson returned to Washington, members of his own church conspired against him, bringing charges of misapplication of funds, disobedience to orders and arrogance in the conduct of his missionary efforts. But his defenders pointed out that while others sat in offices pondering the niceties of formal administration, he had been on the firing line, sleeves rolled up and winning souls to God. His loyal women, seeking to remind the public of his astonishing accomplishments, published a small pamphlet summarizing his work:

In unflagging dedication to God's work from Colorado to Arizona to Montana to Alaska, with yearly returns to Washington to instruct Congress, he traveled more than a million miles using every known form of transportation, including his own feet. He organized from scratch more than seventy congregations, for whom he personally built more than forty church buildings. He often gave four or five speeches in one day for a total that ran into many thousands, and church organizations launched by him collected for missionary and other religious work a proved total of $20,-364,475, for in the work of the Lord he was tireless. We shall not soon again see his like.

But perhaps the most revealing portrait of this contentious little man, who continued all his days to make friends and enemies in equal proportion, can be found in his battle with the Post Office Department, of which he was a paid official. It was his belief that since the Great Land was now American, its villages should carry respectable American names, and since he had the right to choose the names, he saw no reason why they should not honor the Presbyterians who had helped civilize the new territory. Accordingly, he dumped fine old Eskimo and Tlingit names and replaced them with ones like Young, Hill, Rankin, Gould, Willard and especially Norcross and Voorhees, good Presbyterians all, the last two being relatives of his whom he wished to honor. One of his most interesting switches was getting rid of Chilkoot, attached to a beautiful village west of Skagway; for it he substituted *Haines*, the name of the chairwoman of the Presbyterian Women's Committee, who had never seen Alaska but who had contributed generously to Jackson's support. His principal change, however, was to drop the historic old Tlingit name of Howkan in favor of his own, Jackson.

This caused a furor, for the residents did not want to lose their historic designation. Jackson, however, was adamant, and pestered Washington to ignore local complaints and retain the new name, which honored him. But when the Democrats assumed national leadership under Grover Cleveland, the Post Office Department restored the name but spelled it Howcan, at which Jackson, with a burst of spleen which proved he had no shame or sense of the ridiculous, deluged Washington with requests that Howcan be changed back to its proper name, Jackson. He accomplished nothing, but when the Republicans rewon the presidency, he sent a sharp letter to John Wanamaker, the new and Presbyterian postmaster general:

> With the Republicans again in power we expect to receive just considera-
> tion. . . . During Cleveland's administration the Democrats had it changed
> back to Howkan, out of opposition to myself. With our Republican
> victory, it became Jackson again. Now I hear there is a local movement to
> make it Howkan once more. Please notify the clerk in charge of these
> proposals that you wish it left Jackson, and greatly oblige.

But his foes prevailed, and changed the name back to a misspelled Howcan.

THE TWO AMERICAN giants in Alaska, Michael Healy and Sheldon Jackson, were in some ways reminiscent of the two earlier giants Vitus Bering and Aleksandr Baranov. In each instance the first of the pair was an imposing sea captain who exerted his will and his command over the northern oceans, while the second member was insignificant or even comic in appearance but gargantuan in determination to forge ahead despite opposition. Each of the pairs left an indelible imprint on Alaska, especially the second and less imposing members, but the greater similarity seems to be that each of these four explorers and dreamers was a badly flawed man. They were not resplendent conquerors like Alexander the Great or continent builders like Charlemagne. They were ordinary men who drank too much or were foolishly vain or who started things they did not finish or who were objects of ridicule to their colleagues. All four were subjected to official harassment or legal investigations or the censure of court-martial, and each ended his life in a kind of disgrace.

Alaska did not produce supermen, but in its formative periods it was served by men of character and determination, and it is a fortunate land which knows such public servants.

VIII

GOLD

The cataclysmic incidents which produced the scenic grandeurs of Alaska began at least a hundred and twenty million years ago, but the events which gave rise to the most dramatic development in Alaskan history started much earlier.

About eighteen billion years ago, insofar as science can determine from signals left behind, an explosion of indescribable magnitude took place, and what had previously been a void became occupied by gigantic clouds of cosmic dust. Different men with different insights or mind-sets have described this beginning of the beginning in different ways, but regardless of its cause, the event seems to have set our universe spinning; all that happened thereafter stemmed from its complexity and overpowering force.

We cannot reasonably guess what happened to the major portion of the dust thus set in movement, but about nine billion years ago a minor portion—staggering in size though only a fraction—began to coalesce into what would ultimately become the galaxy of which we are a part. In this galaxy some two hundred billion stars would form, the one we see rising each morning as our sun being one of the smaller. We must not take too much pride in our galaxy, wonderful as it is, because it is merely one of more than a billion; quite often the others are greater in dimension and larger in their starry populations.

About six billion years ago an immense agglomeration of cosmic dust within our galaxy began assuming the shape of a huge swirl much like the ones we will see in the heavens this night if we have a good telescope, for all the processes here mentioned are still being repeated in other parts of the universe. Out of this swirling mass of cosmic particles a star began to evolve and with it the nine or ten accompanying planets which together would make up our solar system. Our sun, therefore, is probably about six billion years old, with some of the planets slightly younger.

Now our figures become more precise. About four and a half billion years ago cosmic dust somehow related to what was happening in the sun began to agglomerate into what would ultimately become our earth. For the first billion years of its existence the earth seems to have been a turbulent cauldron in which violent physical and chemical alterations were taking place.

Composed at first mainly of hydrogen and helium, the interior of the earth accumulated such heat and pressure that nuclear reactions occurred, and out of them began to take form the more than one hundred distinct elements upon which the earth would be constructed. Iron, one of the principal elements, being heavier than most, concentrated in the central core, where in a part molten, part solid form it would exert the unifying force which held the earth together, determine much of its movement, establish the magnetic poles, and lend stability to the whole. Mixed with generous amounts of nickel, this central core of iron helped in manifold ways to keep the earth functioning.

At the center, in a heat inconceivable, under pressures never known on the surface and driven by nuclear reactions, the semiliquid components of the earth were sorted out, forming all the basic elements which would later comprise the earth as we know it. Essential substances as diverse as lead, sulfur, nitrogen and arsenic emerged, each with its peculiar atomic weight, each with its preassigned and unique position among its neighbors.

One of these elements, Number 79 in line with an atomic weight of 196.9, which made it conspicuously heavy, was a bright metal with an alluring appearance and a curious set of propensities. Gold, far from copious in its distribution throughout the mass of the earth, had a specific gravity nineteen times that of water, so that if any one of the major oceans had been comprised of gold rather than water, its sheer weight could have collapsed the system.

A major characteristic of gold was its reluctance to react with other elements, staying stubbornly to itself. In this respect it differed strikingly from the element carbon, which formed relationships with almost any substance with which it came into contact. Carbon formed more than four hundred thousand different compounds, gold almost none. Also, carbon metamorphosed itself into an almost endless chain of useful or valuable products: petroleum, carbon black, anthracite, graphite and limestone. A notable characteristic of carbon was its capacity to restructure itself late in the life of earth, when altered conditions produced altered forms. Thus diamonds, one of the spectacular manifestations of carbon, did not come into being until relatively late, when a unique combination of elementary material, heat and pressure transformed carbon into something quite dazzling.

Gold, on the contrary, began as gold, and remained gold, despite the hammering of heat, and atomic reactions, and the ever-present invitation of other metals to join them in exotic new combinations. Gold tended to associate with the heavier elements related to iron, but it also showed a slight affinity for sulfur. It combined occasionally with the exotic mineral tellurium, but refused to do so with oxygen, the way so many other minerals did. There would be no gold oxide. Gold did not rust.

Because of its insularity, gold was known as a noble metal, an adjective applied also to those rare gases which refused to combine with other gases. The word did not refer to lineage, or attractive appearance, or value; a metal or a gas was *noble* if it stood by itself, had great persistence and a reluctance to deform itself in union with another element. According to such definitions, gold was certainly a noble metal.

It seems to have moved upward from its originating cauldron by following fissures in rocky formations, depositing itself here and there in arbitrary and diverse patterns. At times, like any other liquid under pressure, it found some convenient crevice and spread laterally, coming to rest at various levels, never in great concentrations like lead or sulfur, but in areas so widely scattered that no logical reason could explain their placement.

When man succeeded in exploring most of the surface of the earth, he would find deposits of gold in places as varied as Australia, California, South Africa and on the banks of a trivial snowbound stream on the Canada-Alaska border, close to the Arctic Circle.

Gold could be found in two dramatically different circumstances. Like other metallic elements, copper and lead for example, it might rest well below the surface of the earth in concentrations laid down millions of years earlier. This gold would be mined, as metals have been mined for some four thousand years, and there would be no great difference between the mining of gold and the mining of the other metals. A deep shaft would be sunk; walls would be shored up by timbers; and at promising levels laterals would be sent out to explore veins.

What would be found in such a below-the-surface gold mine? Not concentrations of the noble metal, waiting to be dug out and brought to the surface. What was common was a quartz rock containing flecks of gold so minute that the unpracticed eye could scarcely recognize them. A find of tremendous value would be a hunk of quartz whose cross section showed traces of gold no larger than pinpoints—not pinheads—and so widely dispersed that the uninstructed would have to look twice to see them.

Such rock, broken loose from its underground hiding places and brought to the surface, would be crushed and sluiced with water, and now the weight of gold became important, for invariably it would sink to the bottom, where it would be trapped in riffles while the apparently heavier but lighter quartz rock was carried off by the water. To mine gold in this way required courage to delve into the earth, dynamite to break the quartz loose, and a constant flow of water to sluice the crushed mixture.

The second way of finding gold was the more exciting. Through millions of years as the upper crust of the earth shifted and rose and fell, veins of rock containing minute traces of gold were exposed to the elements, allowing abrasion to take place. Freezing winters fractured the quartz; incessantly dripping water broke down the rock; gravel at the bottom of swift-moving streams acted like sandpaper on wood; and volcanic displacement brought to the surface new deposits to be abraded.

As the suddenly released flecks of gold found their freedom, their fate was determined by their weight. They moved for a while with the motion of whatever stream was carrying them, then irresistibly they fell to the bottom, and as they came to rest, certain hydrodynamic forces dictated where they would accumulate. If a stream was tumbling headlong down an incline, they would seem to be almost internally driven to seek some quiet nook in which to escape the turbulence. If a quiet creek was meandering over fairly level land, its cargo of gold would fall into some outer curve where the relative speed of the water slowed. But all the flecks came to rest somewhere.

The finding of this surface gold was known as *placer* mining—the word rhymed with *gasser*—and the mark of the placer miner was a man with a beard holding a tin basin beside a creek, panning a load of gravel to see if it showed colors, flecks of gold, then building a crude sluice of some kind to bring lots of water to wash away lots and lots of gravel. To find gold locked in quartz, a man had to dig deep into the earth; to find placer gold in its easier locations, one sometimes had to dig only two feet and lift up not tons of rocks but only a covering of gravel or sand.

Through centuries of gold seeking, men had devised a dozen rules of thumb to guide them in locating where placer gold was hiding, and men who had been on the various gold fields became uncanny in their ability to find the noble mineral. If you brought onto a new field a gang of men practiced in the fields of Australia, California and South Africa, they would find the gold, while amateurs from Idaho, London and Chicago would not.

Three practical rules seemed to prevail. The first knowledgeable men on a new field preempted the good spots; those who arrived late found little or nothing. However, the second rule kept the hopes of the general public alive; just often enough some lucky prospector who knew nothing about gold stum- . bled upon colors, scouted about, and by sheer chance staked himself a bonanza. This did not happen often, but it did happen.

The third rule was not widely understood, but it accounted for some of the great finds. In seeking placer gold, one followed stream beds, because moving water was the only possible agency by which placers could be deposited. But since the gold had been laid down over millions of years, and since a stream could wander notoriously during even one man's brief lifetime, what the prospector should investigate was not necessarily the little stream as it existed today but the mighty one that might have existed a thousand years ago, or a hundred thousand, or even a million. Perhaps, along the Yukon River and its tributaries in 1896, the place to look for gold was not along the banks of the Klondike, that magical stream with the magical name, but on ridges hundreds of feet high where some river of significance had laid down its gold three hundred thousand years earlier.

IN THE SUMMER of 1896 a broken-down American prospector with an unfavorable reputation because of his propensity for lying, George Washington Carmack, happened to strike up an acquaintance with a dour, proper Scotsman born in Canada. Robert Henderson could have laid claim to the title *gentleman* had he preferred, for he favored strict personal behavior and austere business rectitude. Had he no weaknesses? He was an inveterate snob.

The two formed a solid but unlikely partnership, because although each was willing to work hard and undergo privation when seeking gold, there was one difference which superseded all others. Carmack was a squaw man, legally married to an Indian woman whose two shiftless brothers, Shookum Jim and Tagish Charley, occasionally helped him in his prospecting. Henderson did not countenance this; he was honor-bound to share information and potential profits with Carmack, even though Lying George, as he was called, did have an Indian wife, but he could not tolerate the two brothers-in-law. Therefore, when Henderson announced that he had made a find on a small tributary to the Thron-diuck River, which debouched into the Yukon, Carmack and his two Indians went over the hills to help him develop his find and share in the profits. But Henderson made things so unpleasant for the Indians, refusing insolently to sell them tobacco, that Carmack decided to reject his share of the claim and strike out on his own.

The three men, leaving Henderson to his modest find, climbed over the hills to the west and started their own prospecting on Rabbit Creek, an insignificant tributary to the Thron-diuck. There, on the afternoon of 17 August 1896, they sluiced the gravel from their pan and found settled on the bottom gold flakes and nuggets worth four dollars. Since a pan which showed gold worth ten cents was known as an exciting find, Carmack and his brothers-in-law realized that they had struck a bonanza. Hasty additional trials maintained the exhilarating average of four dollars a pan.

In the wild excitement, Carmack remembered that he had two obligations to discharge, one moral, one legal. Morally he must inform his partner Henderson of the find, but he was so irritated by the latter's treatment of the two Indians that he remained on his side of the mountain, leaving Henderson unaware of the stupendous discovery and unable to share in it.

Carmack's legal obligation could not be avoided. When a miner found gold he was required to do two things: file a proper claim with the government and immediately inform other miners as to where his find was and its probable richness, so that they could stake their claims. Carmack, leaving the Indians to guard his rights, sped down the Yukon to the old mining town of Fortymile on the left bank of the river, and there he staked his title to what would thereafter be known as the *Discovery Claim*, five hundred feet running along the bank of Rabbit Creek and across it on both flanks to the crest of the first rise.

His legal obligations discharged, he then proceeded to the saloon, where he announced at the top of his voice: 'The biggest strike of all!'

He also laid claim to three other five-hundred-foot sites: *Number One Above*, *Number One Below* and *Number Two Below*. Carmack, as the principal claimant, was entitled to *Discovery* and *One Below*, the other two were for Shookum Jim and Tagish Charley. Henderson's interest was not protected.

The habitués in the little settlement, accustomed to Carmack's lying ways, refused to believe that he had found anything. However, when he produced the empty rifle cartridge in which he kept his largest nuggets and dumped it onto the assayer's scales, the men's eyes widened. As prospectors long in the field—and meager scatterings of gold had been known in this region for a dozen years— they were familiar with the qualities of gold peculiar to each site along the Yukon. This came from none of the established mines. It was new gold; its quality was supreme; and the size of the nuggets suggested that it came from a major find, not from the weak tail of some small placer.

The great gold rush was on! Before nightfall, hungry prospectors from Fortymile were speeding upriver to stake their claims above and below Carmack's *Discovery*. When fresh hordes streamed in they rejected the traditional names of these trivial streams. The Thron-diuck, a name of maximum difficulty which no one could pronounce, was quickly changed to the Klondike. Carmack's little Rabbit Creek was given the traditional gold-field name Bonanza, while an even smaller contributor—which would prove richer than any of the others—was appropriately called Eldorado. It was these enchanting names that would flash around the world.

Almost every facet of this fabulous stampede, perhaps the largest in history, had its ironic aspect, none more striking than the one which launched the field. Said a Canadian in a letter home to his wife:

> We Canadians are resentful of the fact that our fellow countryman Robert Henderson, of Nova Scotia, New Zealand and Australia, has been so badly treated in these gold fields. We are certain that he made the first find and that the disreputable American, the squaw man George Carmack, and his Indian helpers defrauded him of his rightful claim to half their find.
>
> However, I must confide to you alone, and do not speak of this to anyone, but I think that maybe Henderson deserved what he got. I heard him say long before the find was made that 'I do not *(ugly words)* propose to let any *(ugly words)* Indian *(ugly words)* share in my finds of gold.'

We have reason to believe that Carmack's strike is so wonderfully rich that Henderson's refusal to work with Indians has lost him more than two million dollars.

A second irony of the great discovery on the Klondike was that although it occurred in mid-August 1896 and was widely known along the Yukon, verifiable word of its amazing richness did not reach the Outside until 15 July 1897. How could information of such a bonanza, to borrow the name of the creek where it happened, be so long concealed?

The Yukon River, 1,993 miles long with much of its course close to the arctic, freezes early, some parts in September, and thaws late, some segments not until June or occasionally July. So for those months, August 1896 till July of the next year, Carmack and his fellow millionaires were frozen in with their secret. But now a determined little Yukon River boat, the sternwheeler *Alice*, of meager draft, forced a passage through the June ice and puffed into Dawson City, the boomtown, which incoming miners from the region had hastily constructed at the mouth of the Klondike.

When the crew learned of the tremendous strike and saw the boxes and bundles of gold the lucky prospectors intended taking to the Outside, they quickly unloaded the life-saving fruit and vegetables they had brought to the near-starving community and turned their little craft around in hours, loaded it with the new millionaires, and headed downstream to where ocean liners would be waiting near the mouth of the Yukon. As the *Alice* pulled out of Dawson another sternwheeler arrived, so that all the miners who wished to return to the States found passage.

After a journey of nearly fourteen hundred miles, the two little boats reached the Bering Sea, where they turned north to deposit their historic cargo of men and gold at the entrepôt of St. Michael. There, after several days of vast dinners consisting of fresh fruit, vegetables and delicious canned foods, heavy in vitamins to fight off the incipient scurvy from which so many suffered, the argonauts with their gold were lightered out to either the *Excelsior*, bound for San Francisco, or the more famous *Portland*, for Seattle.

As the two steamers approached mainland United States, few passengers could anticipate the storm of publicity they were about to cause, for they assumed that news of their staggering finds must have percolated to the outer world. Word had been forwarded to Canadian officials, who dismissed it as just one more exaggerated report from the Yukon: 'We know there's gold up there. Always has been. But never in such amounts.' Also, a daring dog-team driver had made a heroic trip up the Yukon and across the forbidding Chilkoot Pass to alert American officials stationed in that area, but since these men could not believe the extent of the find, word was not sent south. And a Chicago newspaper received an account from one of its reporters, but since they did not trust him, they printed almost nothing.

The *Portland* achieved immortality by accident, for although she left Alaska first and made the long journey home in less than a month, and although her course was shorter than the *Excelsior*'s, she did not arrive in Seattle until two days after the latter had already docked in San Francisco. There was, of course, some excitement along the California waterfront, but its newspapers failed to appreciate the magnitude of what had happened at the Klondike.

William Randolph Hearst's fledgling *Examiner*, always eager for spectacular stories, almost ignored the arrival of the gold, and only cursory stories were circulated nationally by rival San Francisco papers, the *Call* and the *Chronicle*.

However, by the time the laggard *Portland* pulled into Schwabacher's Wharf in Seattle on the morning of 17 July, the citizens of that city had already been informed by San Francisco that adventurous men with great hoards of gold were coming home. An imaginative reporter, one Beriah Brown, who deserves to be remembered, had shown ingenuity by going out at dusk in a little boat to intercept the incoming ship and had through the night interviewed its passengers. Preparing his story for that day's papers, he pondered how most effectively to report this striking story, and he must have considered phrases like 'a huge amount of gold' and 'much gold' and 'a treasure trove of gold.' Discarding them all, he hit upon one of the memorable phrases of American journalism:

At 3 o'clock this morning the Steamer *Portland* from St. Michael for Seattle, passed up the Sound with more than a ton of solid gold aboard.

Those words, 'a ton of gold,' sped across a nation hungry for the metal and seriously in need of it. In banks, in small business houses, in homes where killing mortgages had to be paid off and in the hearts of men yearning for a more accommodating money system, the words 'a ton of gold' became an enchantment, a lure that could not be resisted.

How did men react to this thundering bugle call? In a small Idaho town one John Klope, unmarried and embittered by reverses, heard the summons and cried: 'At last! Gold for all!'

And in a cramped, rickety house in a mean quarter of Chicago, a man whose optimistic father had named him after a President of the United States, Buchanan Venn, was forty years old and disgusted by how sadly his life had deteriorated. Half afraid to voice the revolutionary thoughts which assailed him, he whispered to himself: 'Dear God! Perhaps!'

I N THE NORTHERN corner of Idaho's panhandle, not far from the Canadian border, lay the little town of Moose Hide. It was visited by no railroad, for the trans-Canada line ran to the north through Winnipeg and Calgary, while the nearest American road, from Chicago to Seattle, ran to a junction some miles to the south at Bonners Ferry.

News came late to Moose Hide, and good news sometimes not at all, so on the eighteenth day of July 1897, its citizens did not learn from their newspaper, for they had none, of the arrival in Seattle the day previous of a ton of gold. John Klope, a taciturn young man of twenty-seven, remained ignorant of an event which would in due course mean much to him.

Klope was the son of an Idaho farmer who had in the race of life kept just a few yards ahead of both the sheriff and president of the small bank in Coeur d'Alene to whom he had mortgaged his farm some years before. In order to help pay off this loan, son John had had to quit school at thirteen to work at any jobs available, but since these were years when the supply of gold in the United States was severely limited and the circulation of paper money even more so, the Klopes had a difficult time paying off their mortgage. But because they stinted themselves on the luxuries of life and many of the necessities, they succeeded. The farm was now theirs, but it represented not a bountiful life, only the victory of Slavic stubbornness.

Incredible as it might seem to others who took pride in their ancestry, John Klope did not know for sure where his ancestors had originated, or what their name had been in the old country. In school his mates had called him 'that

Polack,' but from something his father said one evening, he judged that he was not Polish; however, the alternative was not spelled out, and he concluded, correctly, that the original Klopes had lived in a territory near the Carpathian Mountains which had changed hands many times. He was satisfied with that status, which was good, because his father could not have clarified the ancestry had he wished, and his mother knew even less about hers.

He was John Klope, not a Pole, not a Scandinavian and not a German— merely an American and happy to be one, like many of his neighbors. In the Klope family one never heard the lament 'I wish I'd'a stayed in the old country,' because if vague fragments of memory did adhere to that cliché, they were not pleasant.

Klope did not resent the fact that because of poverty he had been denied an education, for he would have had little success in any subjects then being taught, but he did most furiously object to the stranglehold which banks and the money system imposed upon the lives of hardworking families like his, and had he chanced to live in some large city, Chicago or St. Louis, he might well have become radicalized. Sometimes in the evening when the young men of Moose Hide lounged on the street corner after supper, John would listen to those brighter than he explain the difficulties under which the local farmers suffered, and he would say nothing, but later, when the discussion had changed to girls, he would suddenly blurt out: 'The man who has the gold sets the rules.'

In 1893, when terrible panic gripped the nation and when the freight trains of the Great Northern chugging in to Bonners Ferry carried little cargo, Klope's preoccupation with gold seemed less arbitrary, for now neighbors who had not paid off their mortgages began to feel the icy sting of the nation's inadequate money system. Farm after farm was foreclosed, and many young people with whom he had associated when he still attended school had to move away to the slums of cities like Chicago and San Francisco.

This painful removal of people had an effect upon Klope that even he did not understand at the time. During his school years he had been vaguely aware of a small, lively farm girl named Elsie Luderstrom; he had never approached her and certainly he had never walked her home, but he knew that she was kindly inclined toward him and he felt that when they both grew older he might very well want to speak with Elsie. Before he could do so, her family farm was taken back by the bank and she was whisked away in the silence of the night, as it were, to Omaha.

He never saw her again, but with her departure went his chance for a normal life of awkward courtship at nineteen, marriage at twenty-two, children at twenty-four, and the inheritance of either his father's farm or hers in his thirties. Without his knowing it, Elsie Luderstrom had held the key to his life, and the key had been lost.

'Banks is what did them in,' he growled one night as the young men met, and from that solemn judgment, not entirely correct but still relevant, he began to focus upon the need for a man to control his own sources of wealth. A farm was not enough; what seemed at the moment to be a good job on the Great Northern was not enough; and even one's own responsible character was inadequate, for there were no better men in America than Klope's father and Elsie's. They had struggled; they had saved; they had been frugal; and they had been overtaken by this nationwide panic. If there was in all America one young man to whom the call of Klondike gold would seem imperative, it was John Klope.

On the afternoon of 20 July 1897 he heard about the strike. A business traveler from Seattle to Chicago had changed trains in Spokane and come up to Bonners Ferry and made the customary joke: 'Where's the ferry?' and old-timers had explained for the fiftieth time: 'It used to cross the Kootenai,' and later the jokester would refer to it as 'the Hootenanny which runs through Bonners Ferry.' Many local people would have been just as happy if such travelers stayed home, but this one brought sensational news, for he carried with him newspapers from Seattle, and when people in the rooming house read the headlines and asked if they could have one of the papers, he said: 'Keep it. I'm sure the Chicago papers will have the story.'

By afternoon of 20 July word had filtered up to Moose Hide, and it so excited John Klope that he dashed in to Bonners Ferry and asked to see the man who had brought the news. When he found him, he asked: 'They said you had two papers. Could I see one?'

'Here, with my compliments.' Then he laughed: 'If you go to the gold fields, good luck.'

On the way home Klope stopped three times to read the article about the ton of gold, and he became so excited that by the time he reached his farm he was prepared to leave immediately for the Klondike. There was nothing to stop him. He was not really needed to run the farm; his mother and father between them could have managed a place four times the size of their few acres. He was, if the truth were known, a drain on their resources and he knew it. He was not even peripherally involved with any young woman, so his departure would not prevent the formation of a useful marriage. He had no real friends, and even the young fellows on the corner had begun to think of him as 'that queer older man.' He was not only prepared to join the stampede to the Yukon, he was almost impelled to do so.

At that time, had Klope been a student of geography, he would have seen that he was already about as close to the Klondike gold fields as he would be if he moved to one of the other starting points like Seattle in Washington or Edmonton in Alberta. In a straight line he was only one thousand three hundred and seventy miles from the Klondike, not much farther than to Chicago, but had he tried to negotiate that distance, he would have found himself entangled in some of the most forbidding terrain in North America. Wisely, he decided, even before he reached home, to approach the Klondike by way of Seattle.

When he sat with his parents at supper and showed them the newspaper, he did not wait for them to digest the amazing story: 'I'm heading there tomorrow.' It was indicative of the Klope family that his father replied simply: 'I could let you have a hundred and fifty,' and John said: 'Added to what I have, it'll be enough.' Mrs. Klope did not speak, but she felt it high time her son got out of the house and took steps of his own.

John never looked back. He was not able to depart, as he had first said, on the next day, but early on the day after that his father drove him to Bonners Ferry, where they learned that a train would soon be heading south to Spokane and on to Seattle. After an awkward farewell, John said: 'You better head home, Pop. I'll be all right.' And off went the elder Klope, in no way unhappy that his son was making this move.

WHEN KLOPE REACHED Seattle he found the city in turmoil, for the entire population seemed to be concentrated in the area around Schwabacher's Wharf, from which steamers were leaving for Alaska, and rarely since the days when nondescript craft plied the Mediterranean had any port seen such an amazing variety of seagoing vessels. There were ocean liners the equal of many crossing the Atlantic, but there were also river tugs hastily fitted out for the relatively quiet Inside Passage to Juneau and Skagway. There were sternwheelers intended for use along the Mississippi and big, rickety sidewheelers which had been used as excursion boats on the placid waters near Seattle.

Regardless of what the individual ship looked like, all its space was taken by the time Klope reached the waterfront seeking passage to anywhere in Alaska. In two frustrating days, he found not a single berth available, and since each new train from the east brought fresh hordes like himself, the problem worsened. In his despair at being so close to gold but forestalled from grabbing for it, he asked at the store of the principal outfitters, Ross & Raglan, where he was purchasing his necessities: 'How can a man find passage to the Klondike?' and they told him: 'We have one ship, the *Alacrity*, but she's booked solid through March of next year.' The clerk, seeing his disappointment and knowing him as a man who spent money freely in buying his gear, said: 'If you go to the far end of the docks, I believe there's an old Russian ship being refitted. I forget the name, but anybody out there will show you where she's berthed.'

'And you think she won't be sold out?' Klope asked, and the clerk said: 'I doubt it.'

When he found the Russian ship, the *Romanov* of Sitka, he understood why her tickets had not been at a premium, for she was one of the most extraordinary ships presuming to make the run. Hastily built as a Russian sidewheeler for use in the protected waters of southeast Alaska, she had been purchased by Boston seafarers when Russia abandoned the area in 1867 and after long service in the sealing trade had been brought to Seattle, where she had for some years plied the quieter waters of the bays and inlets. Later she had been fitted with an additional boiler that burned coal and a spasmodic propeller that operated in conjunction with the two sidewheels. It thus had two completely different systems for propulsion and three instruments for shoving itself through the sea: two wooden sidewheels and a slightly bent metal propeller.

This ancient ship, leaking at many points but never enough to cause sinking, proposed to make the three-thousand-mile journey through rough open and often turbulent seas to St. Michael, the ocean port where passengers and cargo would transfer to smaller steamers for passage up the Yukon. The fare would be one hundred and five dollars for the proposed three-week run, and by the time of departure, every usable spot on the ship would be taken. During a gold rush such a statement did not carry its customary meaning; it did not mean that all berths were occupied; it meant that even sleeping room on the deck and in the cargo areas below was filled. A ship which in its most favorable days of 1860 could have carried perhaps fifty passengers would now set forth with one hundred and ninety-three.

An irony of the situation was that none of these American passengers spoke of themselves as 'heading for Alaska.' It was always 'We're off for the Klondike!' Alaska was an unknown entity, not yet acknowledged as being part of the United States, and as for the Yukon, that great river which they would have to travel if they sailed in the *Romanov*, few had ever heard of it, and those who had, supposed it to be Canadian. John Klope, a typical passenger, was stumbling into an area about which he knew nothing.

He sailed from Seattle on 27 July 1897, expecting to reach St. Michael in three weeks, which would have been ample time for one of the big steamers, and from there to move promptly into the Yukon on a smaller boat, landing in the Klondike not later than early September. It was indicative of his attitude toward life that during this sea passage he made friends with no one. He was not an

unapproachable man, and if some stranger had taken pains to make his acquaintance, he would have responded, but it was not his nature to strike up
conversations, share secrets, or form partnerships. He was John Klope, no
known ancestry, no special attributes, just a tall, somewhat thin, stoop-shouldered man, cleanshaven, neat in his ways, and content to remain aloof.

The *Romanov* plowed the seas with which she was familiar at a somewhat
slower speed than announced; in fact, she seemed to crawl along, as if her
diverse means of propulsion counteracted one another. A well-run modern
steamer should have made the three-thousand-mile run in nineteen days, and
several did, but the *Romanov* limped along at a speed which would require at
least a month. One passenger familiar with ships spread the report: 'We're
making no more than ninety miles a day. If we hit bad weather, we could take
five weeks.'

When she finally wheezed into St. Michael on 25 August 1897, three days
ahead of prediction, Klope and the other passengers began to learn the realities
of Alaskan travel, because there was no harbor waiting and certainly no wharf.
The *Romanov*, like all other vessels arriving here, had to anchor about a mile
offshore and wait till cumbersome barges worked their way out to unload
passengers, luggage and freight. And when these barges finally did reach land,
they usually stopped some yards from the shore, so that passengers had to wade
to safety; women were sometimes carried on the backs of men who acted as
informal stevedores.

Ashore, the people of the *Romanov* encountered a predicament which beset
even the newcomers from better ships: there were no riverboats available for the
long journey up the Yukon, and it seemed likely that none would arrive on their
downward journey in time to make another trip up before the freezing of the
river.

'Impossible!' some of the *Romanov* passengers stormed, but when they
talked with officials they learned that the mournful situation was true: 'The
Yukon is no ordinary river. It flows north of the Arctic Circle, you know. And
it freezes at different times at different places.'

'But not in September!'

'Especially in September, in some places. And if it freezes anywhere, it halts
all traffic . . . obviously.'

'When does it thaw in spring?'

'May, if we're lucky. More likely June. Last year, early July.'

'My God, it's only open . . . what? Three months?'

'Three and a half, if we're lucky.'

'How often are you lucky?'

'Not very often.'

Now an icy blast seemed to play upon the horde of gold seekers stranded
at St. Michael. The weather was still comfortably warm, but threatening ice
seemed to be moving closer, and when Klope heard that the *Romanov* was
heading straight back to Seattle lest it be trapped in arctic ice drifting down into
the Bering Sea, he asked: 'You mean, the whole sea out there freezes?' and the
locals said: 'Sure does. If a captain ain't spry, he can get trapped maybe in
September and certain in October.'

'What's he do?'

'Well, if he's lucky, he stays pinned there for nine months, right offshore
where we can see him. If he's unlucky, ice keeps coming at him, crushes his ship
and turns it into kindling, like over there.' And when, along the bleak, treeless
shore, Klope saw the remnants of various large ships which had been destroyed

by the impersonal, pounding ice, he became obsessed with a determination to get out of St. Michael and up the Yukon before the ice trapped him, too, but he found not a single riverboat available for the trip; three departed while he searched, but since each was crammed with men standing along the rails, not another passenger could be accommodated.

When it looked as if the *Romanov* people would be stranded in St. Michael, a town of less than two hundred, mostly Eskimo, Klope heard of a certain Captain Grimm, a boatowner familiar with the Yukon, who had a disabled craft which he was willing to put into the water if a boatload of passengers would pay in advance so that he might in turn pay for boiler repairs which his old stern-wheeler simply had to have before it could move a foot.

At first Klope was doubtful about such a transaction, for he suspected that the name Grimm depicted the captain's character: He's probably just another banker wearing a different suit, but when no alternative appeared, he was forced to consider Grimm's offer. As usual, he found it difficult to discuss anything with anybody, but fortunately, there were other would-be passengers willing to assume that chore, and an outgoing young man from California with mining experience moved through the small community asking pertinent questions, then reporting to the stranded gold seekers: 'Everybody says Grimm has a good reputation. And he really does need money. His boat can't sail unless it has a working boiler.'

With this provisional information, the passengers encouraged the miner, whom everyone called California, to pursue his investigations, and this time he returned with exciting assurances: 'They say Grimm's about the best captain sailing the Yukon. Knows every twist and turn. And they say that when you're on the Yukon, the twists and especially the turns become important.'

No vote was taken, but by general acclaim the castaways agreed to provide Captain Grimm with the funds he needed, and Klope was assigned to see that the money was spent only on repairs. He helped the three skilled Eskimos employed by Grimm, and in sixteen days they completed a job of extensive overhaul. On 13 September the river steamer *Jos. Parker*, Captain Grimm, pulled out of St. Michael with sixty-three fully paid passengers when it would ordinarily have carried thirty-two. Baggage and stores were so plentiful that temporary wooden sides had to be erected around the foredeck, and atop this cargo half the men would sleep.

From St. Michael to the mouth of the Yukon was seventy miles over the open Bering Sea, and night fell and the next dawn arrived before the little craft reached the amazing delta of the Yukon, where Klope learned that no real mouth of the great river existed; there were some forty mouths emptying into the sea over a distance of almost a hundred miles. 'The trick,' said Captain Grimm as he maneuvered his boat, 'is to find the right one,' and the passengers stood amazed as he picked his way through this tangle of swampland and tributaries and dead-end channels. At last he came upon the one channel in these parts that would enable him to move upstream toward the gold fields.

The Yukon had several peculiarities. It rose far to the south in mountains less than thirty miles from access to the Inside Passage, but instead of joining the sea there, it chose to travel one thousand nine hundred and seventy-nine miles before entering the icy waters of the Bering Sea. It started north like all the other great rivers of the arctic—Ob, Yenisei, Lena and Kolyma in Siberia, and Mackenzie, greatest of all, in Canada—but unlike them, it did not empty into the Arctic Ocean or its subsidiaries, for after crossing the Arctic Circle at Fort Yukon, it seemed to grow afraid of the frozen north. Turning sharply westward, it fled the arctic and wandered sometimes almost aimlessly toward the Bering Sea.

A major peculiarity was that for much of its distance it was a braided river —that is, it broke into many strands which meandered here and there, so that at some points there was not one Yukon but twenty, or even thirty—and only a good ship captain or an Indian long familiar with the river could pick his way in and out. The chance that a stranger could navigate the Yukon when it became braided was minimal.

It was this formidable river that Captain Grimm in his *Jos. Parker* proposed to battle, always against the current, for thirteen hundred and fifty-five increasingly cold miles. Since the *Parker* could make about eighty miles a day, if it could take aboard enough cords of wood along the way, the trip should require some seventeen days, but when the little boat reached Nulato, where the Russians had prospered, they ran into a peculiar difficulty which warned the passengers that their journey was sure to be prolonged.

As the *Parker* drew to shore where the old palisade had stood, Captain Grimm saw to his satisfaction that some nineteen cords of neatly cut wood, $4 \times 4 \times 8$, awaited him, enough, as he told passengers nearby 'to get us to Chicago if the Yukon ran that way . . . which one of these days it might . . . if it took it into its head.'

But when he tried to purchase the needed fuel, he was informed that most of the piles had been preempted for riverboats belonging to the Alaska Commercial Company of Seattle, while the rest had been spoken for by boats of Ross & Raglan of the same city.

'Can't I get even one cord? To carry us to the next depot?'

'All bespoken.'

'Can I hire someone to cut wood for us?'

'All engaged.'

When it became obvious that the only way the passengers aboard the *Jos. Parker* were going to reach Dawson before the river froze would be for them to cut their own wood, parties were arranged and men fanned out across the barren countryside to find what trees they could, and after a four-day delay, the boat continued upstream, but at the next depot it was the same story, and this time when Klope left the boat with his ax he grumbled: 'I didn't think I'd have to chop my way to the Klondike.'

But chop he did as the projected quick trip to the gold fields was agonizingly prolonged. As September waned, the man called California raised the question: 'At this rate, can we possibly reach Dawson before the river freezes?' But when he and a man known as Montana broached the subject with Captain Grimm, the latter gave his reassuring smile and said: 'That's my job.'

The attention of the worried passengers was distracted by the fact that they were about to enter the notorious Yukon Flats, a desolate and almost frightening area one hundred and eighty miles long in which the Yukon became hopelessly braided, as if some headstrong girl had purposely tangled her hair. Since the area was seventy miles wide, reaching out from both banks, it covered more than twelve thousand six hundred square miles and was about six times the area of Connecticut.

On first acquaintance it had not one redeeming feature: few trees, no surrounding mountains, no swift-moving streams, no villages clinging to the banks, merely an endless expanse of swampland, the overpowering Yukon Flats. John Klope, as a farmer who knew good land when he saw it, was appalled. But those familiar with the Flats developed an affection for them; here birds thrived in numbers unimaginable, and hunters from North Dakota to Mexico City were indebted to the summer breeding grounds thus provided for game birds which could have flourished nowhere else. Geese and ducks abounded. Wild animals of the most valuable kind proliferated: martin and mink and ermine and lynx and fox and muskrat and others whose names Klope would not have recognized. Larger game lived here, too: moose with enormous horns, caribou in winter, bears along the edges, savage mosquitoes by the billion.

But the pride of the Flats was the innumerable lakes, some little larger than a table, others as big as normal counties. At one spot the Yukon itself broadened into a lake of tremendous size, and occasionally fifty or sixty lakes would be linked together by minute streams, forming a chain of jewels resplendent in the cold sunlight.

How many lakes were there in the Flats? An explorer who had traveled the two major rivers which joined the Yukon here—Chandalar to the west, Porcupine coming in after a very long ramble through Canada—estimated that the area as a whole must contain at least thirty thousand independent clearly defined lakes: 'What amazed me most, as I reflect upon it, was the excessive number of oxbows, those almost circular streams cut off from any main body of water, no entry, no exit, proof that in times past a meander had been eliminated when a flood altered the course of some little stream.'

Riverboat captains had a less enthusiastic opinion of the Flats, for as Captain Grimm explained: 'If you choose wrong at one of the braids, you can travel for a day before you find yourself at a dead end. Then you waste another retracing your way back to the main channel, supposing you can find it.'

On 1 October 1897, Captain Grimm apparently lost his way in one of these landlocked braids, for after stumbling about during most of a long, cold morning, he confessed to his passengers: 'We seem to be lost,' and they knew that they were still fifty miles short of Fort Yukon, which they had to reach in order to obtain the next load of wood. Some men grumbled, and when Grimm decided to stay where he was and spend the night against the shore rather than retrace his course, two men came close to threatening him, but others provided sager counsel and no threats were voiced. During the argument Klope took neither side, for although he desperately wanted to reach the gold fields, he suspected that Captain Grimm knew what he was doing.

It was extremely cold that night, and in the morning the passengers were wakened by Montana, who was shouting about what was happening in their cul-de-sac: 'Look at those fingers of ice!' And when Klope reached the railing, he could see delicate probes reaching out from shore as the colder water there began to freeze.

Few travelers had ever had an opportunity to watch a great river actually freeze, and although the braid in which the *Parker* was trapped was not part of the main current, the process was the same. While the middle of the river remained free, with no indication that it was about to freeze, thin ice did form at a few spots where the water touched land, but for the moment these isolated incidents indicated little, for they were not extensive nor did they reach far enough into the river to constitute any menace. No man could have walked upon the fragile ice thus formed.

But as Klope watched, a miracle occurred, for without warning of any kind, no cracking or popping, an entire stretch along the shore suddenly congealed, and it would remain so until June.

Now the watchers grew apprehensive, and at a spot well ahead of the *Parker*, that is, up near the closed end of the braid, they saw a second miracle, this one of greater import, for as the icy fingers coming out from land grew more sturdy, they suddenly leaped outward from each shore, joining in the middle of the braid as if forming a congratulatory handclasp, and in that instant, that part of the Yukon was frozen. The process was mysterious, quick and beautiful.

By afternoon, with the temperature far below zero, ice began to move out from the waterline of the *Parker*, and Klope stood with California as its fingers groped for those reaching out from shore, but night fell before they could witness completion of the jointure.

By next morning, 3 October, most of the Flats were frozen shut and even the mighty river was sending out preliminary fingers. By nightfall this section of the Yukon would be closed to navigation.

'That's why I ran in here,' Grimm explained. 'I didn't tell you at the time, because you wouldn't have believed the river could freeze so swiftly. If we'd tried to finish the run to Fort Yukon, we'd have been locked in the big ice and most likely been crushed when it moved.'

'How long will we be trapped here?' California asked, and Grimm said: 'Till June.'

'Oh my God!' Montana cried, and Grimm said: 'We're only one of many. Take heart. I've chosen one of the safest spots on this river. Less wind. No fear of creeping ice.'

In a good winter the *Parker* might have provided a comfortable eight-month refuge for perhaps thirty men; any hope of keeping sixty-three content was impossible, and before that day was out some men were demanding refunds of their money. With his beard jutting out, his feet firmly placed, his eyes atwinkle, Olaf Grimm lined out the simple truth: 'I undertook to get you to Dawson. I didn't promise when. Now, all men will scour the area to find what trees there are and bring us some wood, because if you don't we'll freeze to death, and I'll do my share of the chopping.'

He explained where the privies would be built, 'and any man not using them will be shot.' He asked for volunteers to hunt for moose and caribou, 'and you must go out right now to catch what you can before the heavy snows.'

As this resolute man spoke he conveyed the impression that he had faced such situations before and intended to see that his passengers survived this one. He was conciliatory; he sympathized with men who were sorely disappointed; but he allowed no excuses, gave no exemptions from the work that he knew had to be done. When California complained, with reason: 'If you knew we were going to freeze in, why did you leave St. Michael?' he said truthfully: 'Because you people wanted to come. And we'd have made it on schedule if we'd been able to buy our wood on the way.'

THAT WINTER ELEVEN river craft were imprisoned in ice. None handled the situation better than the *Jos. Parker*, and when one of the passengers returned to the boat with news that he had killed a moose, he accepted the praise due him, then asked: 'Ever since I've been aboard this damned ship I've wondered why it was called the *Jos. Parker*. Comin' back just now, I understood. The name-board ain't big enough for a full first name.'

'That's right,' Grimm said, thankful for any diversion. 'Named after the father of the man who built it. Josiah Parker. Nice trim name, I always thought.'

On 4 October, John Klope, still burning to get to the gold fields, spoke with Captain Grimm: 'Living like this has got to get worse and worse,' and Grimm said: 'Yes.'

'Could I walk to Fort Yukon?'

'Fifty miles. Rough sledding. Take you maybe three, four days.'

'But it is just ahead, on the river?'

'Sure is.' The veteran hesitated, for he would not want it said later that he had encouraged men who had started up the river under his care to leave their boat at the beginning of an arctic winter. At other ships other captains were facing the same moral problem; from one ship a lone man with dogs would set out for a journey of twelve hundred and fifty miles and make it. From another, a man who liked to paint watercolors would go three hundred yards and freeze to death.

Captain Grimm said, very carefully: 'You and I, Klope, could make it. I've watched you. You're disciplined. But I wouldn't want to try it with some of those others. And don't you. Stay here and live.' It was a masterful statement, a warning not to leave the safety of the *Parker* but at the same time a challenge, and Klope, ignoring the former, embraced the latter.

When it was learned that he was going to trek overland to Fort Yukon, eleven other men volunteered, and in some cases demanded, to go along, and suddenly he found himself the leader of an expedition. The idea terrified him, because although he had no fear about succeeding on his own, he doubted that he could hold a disparate group of men together if they ran into trouble, nor did he want to. Cleverly, he handed the management of the expedition over to loud-spoken California, who enjoyed giving directions, and justifying Klope's decision, California proved to be resourceful and a good leader, although to Klope's taste, a trifle domineering.

Well bundled, the twelve who wanted to get to Fort Yukon bade farewell to the ice-locked *Jos. Parker* early on the morning of 5 October, expecting to cover no less than thirteen miles a day, which would put them safely in Fort Yukon on the late afternoon of the eighth, and since darkness did not come till about five-thirty, they assumed they would have ample light. What they did not anticipate was the extreme roughness of the route they had chosen.

The Yukon did not freeze flat and smooth like the lakes some of them had known in the States; because it froze in arbitrary ways at sharply varying times, its surface was uneven, crumbled at times, and broken by irregular upthrust blocks. California, distraught by the impediments thrown up by the Yukon, shouted: 'What in hell happened to this river?' and Montana explained what was obvious to an outdoorsman: 'It freezes here but not there. Free water floods in, covers the frozen ice and freezes. Then more free water comes in below, everything buckles.' He assured California that a level route could be found through the ice chunks, but the latter had had enough. Kicking at the blocks, he growled: 'Let's get away from this damned river.'

But when he led his team away, he soon faced the myriad lakes and the frozen swamps between. This tundra was dotted with large, round tufts of matted grass called by everyone in Alaska niggerheads. To cross such country, one had to lift one's legs high to step from low ground to high, and then take longer strides than usual to reach the next niggerhead. It was painful going.

By alternating between the jagged ice of the river and the uneven surface of the frozen swamp, the informal expedition moved at a painful pace that would cover not thirteen miles a day as planned, but no more than eight. The trip would thus require not four days but six, and since the men had geared themselves to an easy four-day dash over the kind of snowy roads they had known in states like the Dakotas and Montana, they were disheartened.

Fortunately, the cold was not yet excessive, and no wind blew, so that even the weakest of the men did not suffer, and when night came they were not so exhausted that they were unable to care for themselves, but they were thoroughly tired.

It had been planned that they would sleep with snow piled about them like a blanket, for this would deflect the wind and allow each man to hoard his body heat. They ate sparingly, for they had brought along only enough food for the projected four days, but as California said: 'Short rations won't hurt anyone. And we'll soon be there.'

The first night's rest was brief, for the men found it difficult to sleep in their snow beds, and while no one suffered from a lack of clothing, no one was properly clothed, either, for such exposure. As soon as dawn began to show, about six-thirty, the men were eager to resume their march, and with a day's practice behind them, they handled the difficult terrains more adeptly. But if California led them onto the river, they wanted to wander among the lakes, and if he acceded to that suggestion, they rather quickly asked for the river. At dawn some had predicted: 'Yesterday was learning. Today we'll do fifteen miles,' but they covered barely half that distance.

Klope slept soundly that second night. He had seen that when neither he nor Montana set the pace, the file would lag, so he stayed in front most of the time, yielding only when Montana saw that he was tiring. The two men never spoke of what they were doing or of their growing suspicion that some of them were not going to make it to Fort Yukon.

On the night of the fourth frustrating day, when three of the men became almost too weak to lift their legs high enough to negotiate the niggerheads, it was apparent to Klope that emergency measures must be taken, and he consulted with both California and Montana. The latter said: 'We got to put someone at the rear. Else we're gonna lose somebody back there.'

'They can see our trail,' California said, but Montana would not accept this easy answer: 'Trouble is, in this weather the man at the end says: 'I'll lie down for just a minute,'' and you never see him again. Frozen solid.'

Klope volunteered to walk last, and it was fortunate that he did, because the men detected as being weakest began to lag dangerously, and he spent a trying day urging them to keep moving forward. Twice the major file forged so far ahead that he had to shout at the top of his voice to make them slow down until his three flagging charges could catch up. By nightfall two others had fallen behind, and when California, whose courage and determination helped keep the men together, consulted with his two assistants, Klope reported: 'I'm not sure I can make them keep up for another day,' and to make things worse, that night the temperature fell precipitously.

Shortly after midnight California shook those still sleeping in the protection of the snow: 'Better start moving, men,' and in the shadowy light of a waning moon they started what they would later remember as the worst night and day of their lives.

That sixth day they elected to stay with the river, picking their way slowly past protruding blocks, and at times John Klope, bringing up the rear, thought that the silent figures ahead of him looked like ants moving across a white blanket, but such poetic comparisons were banished when one of the laggards simply fell in a heap, unable to respond to Klope's commands that he rise.

When helpers hurried back, they found to their horror that the man had not fainted; he had died. Yes, on the Yukon River some miles below the safety of the Fort, a bank clerk from Arkansas had died of exhaustion, and after his body had been placed under a blanket of snow, a subdued and sometimes terrified group of eleven resumed its slow march forward.

Klope was not unduly distressed by the death. He was aware that men died in arbitrary ways; on a neighboring farm a man he knew well had been strangled when the reins of a rearing horse caught around his neck, and once during a visit to Bonners Ferry he had heard men shouting at the railroad station, where a workman had been crushed between two boxcars. So he could absorb the shock of death. But when the party halted at noon for rations, he heard something that did frighten him tremendously. California, seeking to dispel the gloom attendant upon the death, was giving encouragement: 'It was fifty miles in all, and I calculate we've covered forty-two,' when a man from Ohio said: 'I heard Captain Grimm say: "It's only fifty or sixty miles to Fort Yukon." '

The possible addition of ten miles to what was already a hellish journey terrified Klope, for as rear man he had witnessed better than anyone else the utter exhaustion of the weakest members. When California and three other strong men moved apart to discuss the situation, Klope was impressed by the forthright manner in which the leader conducted himself: 'I want the four of us to pledge that we will not forge on ahead and forget the others. We'll stay with these men and get them to Fort Yukon.'

'But what if the time comes when one of us has to rush ahead,' Montana asked, 'to bring help?'

'You three can draw straws. I'll stay.'

'Could it have been sixty miles?' Klope asked, and California snapped: 'No.'

That afternoon the temperature dropped to ten degrees below, but mercifully no wind accompanied the fall; however, another man walking not far ahead of Klope collapsed and died, not instantly like the first, but in terrible, rasping pain over a period of forty minutes.

Klope buried him, and then the real horror of this forlorn journey began, because the Yukon became excessively humpy while the swamps were barricaded by niggerheads that were barely negotiable. At half past four what arctic daylight there was would begin to fade, and the men would face the punishment of a long, bitterly cold night without adequate protection.

Klope did not lose courage; he could never do that so long as the lure of gold pulled him forward, but as he estimated the waning strength of the laggards, he realized with deepening concern that as many as three could perish during the coming hours, and he called for the other strong marchers to join him. 'What shall we do?' he asked, and California replied: 'Keep moving ahead. All night. Otherwise we could all die.'

'And if those over there . . . ?' California studied Klope's forlorn group sitting numbly in the snow, either unaware of or indifferent to the fact that their lives were under discussion, then said: 'Keep them going as long as possible. If they die, don't stop to bury them.' And he returned to the lead, where he spurred the marchers on.

It was almost dusk on that terrible day when one of the weakest men espied an amazing sight, which he called to Klope's attention: 'Dog team!' And there to the north, picking his way carefully through the frozen swamps of the Yukon Flats and obviously headed toward Fort Yukon, came a man running behind a sled drawn by seven large, powerful dogs. He was dressed in Eskimo garb, his exposed face surrounded by the fur-lined hood of a parka, his body so swathed in heavy garments that he looked almost round. He had not yet seen the struggling men, and there was a chance that he might speed by without stopping, so with a wild shout Klope started running northeast in hopes of intercepting him.

The other men, hearing the shouts, turned and saw the speeding dogsled, and without a moment's hesitation California began running, too, and because he started from a better angle, it was he whom the sled-driver finally saw. Commanding his huskies to halt, he came forward to meet these strangers, and a moment's glance at the weary file whose men had taken rest in the snow satisfied the man that he had come upon a party of cheechakos in peril.

He was Sarqaq, half Eskimo, half Athapascan Indian, and he ran a dogsled out of Fort Yukon. He spoke little English but understood many words, and when he asked California: 'Fort Yukon?' he comprehended the answer.

'How far?' California asked, and he said, holding up one finger: 'Tomorrow.' But then California asked: 'Your tomorrow or our tomorrow?' and Sarqaq did not understand. Klope solved the problem by putting his hand on one of the dogs, a handsome white-faced animal fifth in line from the lead, and with his fingers imitated the four swiftly moving legs of a dog. Then, using his own feet, he plodded slowly forward: 'Dog one day? Man how many?'

Sarqaq, whose brown face was as round as if it had been drawn with a compass, laughed, showing white teeth: 'I now. You tomorrow.'

Klope was in no way a religious man, but he sighed: 'Thank God.' He and California and the others in strong condition could certainly survive till tomorrow night; the weakest could perhaps be taken to warm beds by the dogsled. Taking the driver by the arm, he pointed to the resting men: 'Two, three. Maybe die,' and with sign language he indicated men dying from lack of will.

Sarqaq understood immediately, and without even a minute's hesitation knew what he must do. Furiously he started throwing off his sled the piles of fur and caribou meat he was delivering to Fort Yukon, and when it became apparent that he was unloading cargo to provide space to transport the threatened men, Klope said: 'I go get,' but Sarqaq stopped him: 'I go,' and with curt commands he swung his dogs about, sped to the line of men, who uttered feeble cheers, and asked: 'Who go?' holding up three fingers taken from the mitten which protected them from freezing. The men waited for Klope to identify the three worst cases, and when he had done so, these men, barely aware of what was happening, were loaded aboard the sled.

Then came a moment of the most painful indecision, for the seven men left behind could not anticipate what might happen. Were these three alone to be saved? Was Fort Yukon really only one day away? Could they survive any more nights in this dreadful cold?

Sarqaq, anticipating their fears, smiled like a rising moon and said to Klope: 'Watch meat. Wolves.' And to the men from the *Parker* he said: 'Cut meat. Chew it. Wrap in furs. I come back. Many sleds.' And off through the darkening night he sped.

It was about four in the morning when one of the travelers, who was moving about to keep himself alive, heard from the east the sound of dogs. Listening for confirmation lest he deceive his companions, he heard the unmistakable sound of men cheering on their teams, and he began shouting: 'They're here! They've come back!'

From wherever they had been sleeping and in whatever postures, the survivors leaped to their feet and peered into the moonlit night. Slowly, like the vision in a narcotic dream, dogsleds began to appear upon the Yukon, with the figures of men running behind, and as they became reality the freezing men began to scream and shout 'Hurrah!' and weep.

IN 1897, FORT YUKON was no longer a fort, but when erected half a century earlier, it had been a rather formidable place, and a drawing made by the intrepid English explorer Frederick Whymper, in 1867, still showed the imposing four blockhouses, inside whose square nestled several homes, and two enormous barns for the storage of furs being bought and merchandise being sold by the Hudson's Bay Company, whose daring traders had established this most remote of their outposts.

In 1869, Fort Yukon provided an outstanding example of why Canada and the United States were such good and sensible neighbors: that was the year when young Otis Peacock and his army team proved that the Canadian Hudson's Bay Store was far inside American territory. Instead of raising a ruckus, Americans and Canadians had diplomatically moved the store—twice, because after the first move, it was still trespassing on American soil.

For some years Fort Yukon had been a thriving little settlement of about a hundred and ninety people who earned a modest living by collecting furs from Indians and by servicing the occasional riverboat like the *Jos. Parker* when one stopped by, but with the discovery of Klondike gold, the town had flourished and was now crowded.

When the Eskimo Sarqaq, as he was called despite his part-Athapascan blood, and the other sled drivers delivered the ten white men to the Fort, a curious situation developed. California, the man who more than any other had been responsible for keeping the travelers moving forward, suddenly lost his nerve, and when a third man died at the Fort, he took the blame upon himself. For three days he sat in a stupor, overwhelmed by the tragedy in which he had participated. Klope and others told him: 'You kept us going,' but he could not accept this; he felt compelled to take responsibility for the deaths of his three companions and the near-deaths of the others.

Klope was not being honest when he said that it had been California who had saved the expedition. Both he and Montana knew that they, too, had held the team together and that many more would have died had not Klope refused to let them do so. But he sought no accolade for having done what he considered his duty; instead, he sought out his rescuer, Sarqaq, and spent hours with the Eskimo's ten dogs.

Sarqaq was known as an Eskimo because that was an easier identification than half Eskimo, half Athapascan; besides, he looked like a prototypical Eskimo, with stocky build, round face and pronounced Oriental features. He was an amiable man, much given to grinning, which made his face shine like a full moon, and he enjoyed having Klope take an interest in his dogs.

He maintained ten, even though he preferred to use only seven on his sled; the extra three would be fed into the team as present members aged or grew refractory. For example, he had not much use for the dog that Klope had liked in those first moments of their meeting in the Flats, number five in line. By some instinct, Klope had identified the one dog that was not a pure husky, as if he had spotted some variation in character.

'Not husky,' Sarqaq said. 'Maybe half-half.' A white man who had once owned the dog had given it the name of Breed, indicating a mixed heritage, and when Klope heard that the dog was mixed, he supposed that this accounted for the difference he had noted.

Breed looked like a husky; he had the white mask, the extremely dark hair edging his eartips, the heavy coat and the powerful front legs. His eyes were framed in white and he also had a thin white stripe down the middle of his forehead. His body was a brownish gray and his whole attitude one of alertness. His weakness was that he did not fit in with the other dogs, and if he did not mend his ways and quickly, Sarqaq would have to replace him, because one difficult dog could ruin a team.

As Klope spent these October days with the dogs, he slowly acquired an understanding of these remarkable animals, so unlike the ones he had known in Idaho. The most important beast in a team was the lead dog, and Sarqaq's was almost unbelievable in its intelligence and its love of mushing at the head of six other dogs almost as capable. It was the lead dog who disciplined the others, who threw its total weight into the straps, who kept the sled always moving forward and who designated the track. It was responsive to Sarqaq's commands and even anticipated them, and although it could not be said that it loved its master, for it stayed aloof from humans, it obviously did love the job of leading the team and protecting the heavy sled they drew.

Dog number two in line was known as the swing, and it was its responsibility to transfer the leader's decisions to the dogs behind. Often when the lead dog died or became too old for continued service, the swing took over; in the case of Sarqaq's team, this would not occur, because although his swing was admirably suited to that job, it would not make a good leader; it was too amenable to suggestion.

Of an importance almost equal to the lead dog was the last in line, the wheel dog, for it was its task to see that the moves of the other dogs did not imperil either the safety or the progress of the sled. A knowing wheel could be worth the whole remainder of the team if it saw to it that their considerable efforts were properly applied to the moving sled, and Sarqaq had about the best wheel in the business.

That accounted for the three principal dogs; the others were lumped together as the team, and sometimes it seemed as if they did the hard work. Each dog had a name, but since these names were in some native dialect, Klope did not master any but Breed's. He was not an impressive dog when the sled was in motion, and when on three occasions Sarqaq allowed Klope to accompany him on short trips into the countryside, John saw that Breed lacked that strange mixture of respect for discipline and determination to pull regardless of sled weight which characterized the outstanding dogs. Breed was something else, a fierce animal yet one that seemed to crave human companionship, and in John Klope he found a man who had a similar need for animal friendship. A man to whom human associations did not come easily or warmly was developing a powerful affection for this dog.

He was therefore dismayed when, after a poor performance by Breed which caused the lines to tangle, Sarqaq said in disgust: 'No good dog. Maybe shoot.'

'Wait!' Klope pleaded, but that night when they were back at the Fort, another dogsled man who spoke fairly good English explained: 'Husky, malamute same. Good only for hauling sled. No good for that, get rid of them.'

'But would you shoot one of your own dogs?'

'No good, maybe better shoot. Dog's whole life, to be in traces, pulling. Lose that job, maybe dog want to be shot.'

'Wouldn't you keep it . . . as a pet?'

The driver, an Athapascan, laughed and called to two other drivers: 'He asks husky sled dog a pet?' And the men roared with delight at this further proof that Outsiders never understood the arctic.

In the days that followed, Klope spent more time with Breed, and with each passing experience he saw in him an animal capable of enormous affection and willing to share all experiences with this man who had taken an interest in him. Now when Klope came to where the dogs were tied overnight—for had they been allowed to run wild, they all might have disappeared—Breed strained at his link chain to reach him, and when Klope moved close the dog leaped upon him, and pawed him and tried to lick his bearded face. But such behavior intensified Sarqaq's belief that Breed had no place in an orderly string of working dogs.

It became unthinkable to Klope that such an animal should be destroyed merely because it did not serve obediently the whims of some man, and several times he tried to broach the matter with Sarqaq, who dismissed the subject almost scornfully.

As the survivors from the *Jos. Parker* recovered from their ordeal on the Yukon Flats and their courage returned, some started to think of trying to move south to their destination, but the managers at Fort Yukon dissuaded them: 'That's more'n three hundred miles. And it'll be bitter cold now. You fellers lost three men comin' only fifty miles, in what we call good weather.'

'But if we wait till this damned river thaws, all the good claims will be taken.'

'We wait every year,' the Fort Yukon men said. 'And besides, young feller, all the good claims was taken two years ago. You got plenty time to claim on nothin' land, so stay here where there's a hot stove and somethin' to eat.'

Such advice became more relevant when a dogsled driven by two Indians straggled in from the south with a horror story: 'Starvation in Dawson. People ordered to leave by the Mounted Police. They reached Circle City, pitiful condition. Frozen toes had to be cut off. Fingers gone. One man lost a leg.'

This portrait of conditions in the south so discouraged the *Parker* men that any thought of trying to reach the Klondike before the thaw made boat passage possible was discarded. That is, it was discarded by everyone except John Klope, who was still tormented by his gnawing mania to get to where the gold lay hiding. Each new hardship made him more determined to ignore difficulties, so that when the fugitives from Circle asked the authorities at the Fort whether a rescue mission of any kind could be mounted to get food to those trapped there and in Dawson, he said without hesitation: 'I'll go,' and the Indians laughed. They had meant: 'Is there any local dogsled man who will attempt it?' They said that the trip north had exhausted both them and their dogs; they had no intention of volunteering.

Two days after the request circulated, Sarqaq came to Klope: 'You say you go?'

'Yes.'

'You, me, maybe?' When Klope jumped at the invitation, the Eskimo asked: 'You pay?' and now Klope had to think. Carefully he explained that he had already paid the money intended for his fare to the captain of the *Jos. Parker*, and with signs he indicated that if he, Klope, wanted to stay in Fort Yukon till the river thawed, the *Parker* would be obliged to carry him to Dawson for no extra payment.

The explanation was painfully drawn out, but finally Sarqaq understood that Klope would not pay, and there the matter rested for two days. But on the third day, just as gold-hungry Klope was about to volunteer a limited fee for the trip, Sarqaq returned with his own proposition: the two men would load their sled with all the food that Fort Yukon could spare; they would hurry it to Dawson; and there they would sell it for a profit. There seemed to be no risk in such a venture: Sarqaq was certain his dogs could make the trip; he knew that he could and he suspected that Klope was the kind of white man who had just as much endurance as any Eskimo; and both men trusted that if they could get the food to Dawson, they would be sure to find customers who would pay for it.

All was set, except for one detail: Klope would have to buy the food from the commissary at Fort Yukon, and he would have to pay cash, relying upon the successful termination of the rescue mission for repayment. He considered this for several days, for unlike Sarqaq he could visualize many reasons why such a daring venture might fail, but in the end he was so determined to reach the gold fields before the rest of that year's crowd that he agreed to put up the money. On 20 November 1897 it was known throughout Fort Yukon that Sarqaq and the American were going to attempt the dash to Dawson, three hundred and twenty miles to the south over trails that were frozen deep and covered with snow, along a river that was filled with block ice. If they made twenty-five miles a day, they felt they could cover the distance, with rests for the dogs, in eighteen days, which would put them on the Klondike well before Christmas.

On the day before departure two things happened which heightened the tension of the men. Klope went to California, whom he admired, and said: 'You want to come along? You were the best man on the other trip.' But the man who had proved so valiant on the venture from the *Jos. Parker* had not yet regained his courage, or, more kindly, he had spent it all on that disastrous expedition when only his will power had prevented it from ending in total horror. Now he could do no more than shudder when Klope suggested a repetition. Drawing in his shoulders as if to prevent Klope from getting at his vitals, he shook his head. He had seen the Yukon in autumn and he could not imagine it in winter.

When Klope warned, 'The gold fields will be all taken,' he looked up in amazement, asking: 'Gold fields?' When the Yukon thawed he intended catching a boat downstream for St. Michael and Seattle; under no circumstance would he go upstream toward Dawson, either in the spring when the river opened or now when it was frozen tight, and only when Klope saw the terror with which the invitation was rejected did he acknowledge to himself the dangerous trip he was about to undertake.

Sarqaq heard a more frightening story. The two drivers who had reached Fort Yukon with news of starvation in Dawson related what had happened when a boat tried to rush supplies to that beleaguered town: 'Boat got lots of wood for burnin', extra food. Good captain, good Indian pilot through the channels. Everything good. If reach Dawson, save many people.'

'What happened?' Sarqaq asked, and the informant said: 'Him, me, we reach Circle one day before boat. No food there, no medicine. One hell of a time, I tell you.' At this point he looked to his fellow driver for confirmation, and the man nodded.

'Next day many cheers. Boat come in. But captain say: "This food for Dawson. People starving in Dawson." But people in Circle say: "People starving here, too. We take your food." Big words, maybe big fight. Men with guns. Captain say: "Okay, damn you, take food and let others starve." And men run all over boat, take all food. Boat stay there empty. Pretty soon, boat fast in ice. Never go to Dawson because captain say: "What the hell?" '

Then the first driver made his point: 'Sarqaq, s'pose you and dog team, food go to Circle, same men stop you. Same men take everything. No food can go past Circle, damn sure.'

The three drivers talked for some time, discussing routes which could be traversed without the men of Circle becoming aware that a dog team was in the vicinity, and on the night prior to departure Sarqaq informed Klope of his strategy: 'Not bad men, hungry men. We go . . .' and with his hands he indicated the town of Circle on the left bank of the river while a dog team headed far to the east on the right bank.

CALIFORNIA AND MONTANA were up early to help finish last-minute preparations, and by the time dawn arrived, almost the entire Fort was present and making predictions: 'They'll never make it' and 'No white man can go that far in winter' and 'If anyone can make it, Sarqaq can.' Klope, growing impatient at any delay, was about to stride off when an old woman, daughter of some early Canadian miner and an Athapascan squaw, came pottering out to stop him yet again. She brought with her an object which she obviously considered precious, a crock made of clay, inside which lay something wrapped in a damp cloth. A widow now, she served as cook for one of the merchant dormitories, and as she handed Klope her treasure she said, with the wisdom of decades in the north: 'It can never be a house without this. God would not allow.'

Klope thought the gift must be a Bible, but why have it in a damp crock? 'What is it?' he asked, and proudly, with fingers gnarled from much labor, she loosened the cloth, and when Klope peered inside the crock all he could see was a loose round ball of what looked like the dough from which his mother had baked German cookies.

'What is it?' he repeated, and the old woman said: 'Sourdough. Keep warm. Keep with you. It will make life . . .' She hesitated, for she could not think of one word that could describe the difference between having a good strain of sourdough and none.

Her family of sourdough dated back to 1847, when the Hudson's Bay people built the fort in which her grandmother had worked as cook. The dough had reached the Yukon after a perilous trip from eastern Canada, where its ancestry had come after a similar trip from Vermont, where the strain had already been kept alive for forty years, dating back to 1809. It was a gift of antiquity and civilization and love which the old woman was turning over to Klope, and it was a responsibility, too. In crocks like this, under damp cloths like this, the women of Vermont and Quebec and Fort Yukon had kept the strain of yeast viable, and now she was turning the job over to a new caretaker.

Weighing the crock in both hands, Klope said: 'I can't carry this all the way to Dawson,' but she warned him: 'Gold comes, goes.' With a sweep of her hand she indicated all the men of Fort Yukon: 'They look, they look. S'pose they find? Gamble it away. Pretty women.' Pressing the crock into Klope's hands, she said: 'But good sourdough . . . it goes on forever.' In the world she had been able to observe from the lonely fort on the Yukon, gold had accomplished very little, but a family with a reliable crock of sourdough was on its way to happiness.

This crock was obviously too heavy to lug all the way to Dawson City, but Sarqaq, immensely reverent where a strain of proved leaven was concerned, solved the problem. Calling for one of the little glass jars in which California farmers were now packing their cooked vegetables, he transferred the sourdough, and showed Klope how to carry it close to his body so the precious yeast did not freeze.

With the old woman's blessing and cheers from the men, the two daring travelers set forth, and as they pulled out of the Fort they presented sharply contrasting appearances. Klope was tall and thin, dressed in an American's version of what an arctic explorer should wear, which was about the same as what an American farmer in Idaho should wear: heavy clothes, heavy leather boots, heavy cap with very heavy earflaps. It was good clothing, appropriate for a day's hard work in cold weather, and he presented an impressive figure when he stepped behind the sled. An observer would have said: 'He's not one to fool with.' But how the clothing would serve for eighteen days when it could not be taken off at night, one could not guess.

Sarqaq, a short butterball of a man, wore clothing which his people had developed over thousands of years of arctic living. No item was heavy; all seemed to be composed of many layers of the thinnest and lightest skin possible. His boots were made of caribou leather, tanned to perfection, and lined not only with caribou but with the almost weightless fur of baby seal. His trousers were miracles of lightness and durability, stiff when he put them on, supple as he began to move. He wore five shirts and jackets, each seemingly thinner than the preceding one, and his hood was a marvel, a capacious cavern in which his head could hide from snow and sleet, and from whose edges he would gain both protection and warmth, for it was trimmed with wolverine hair that had the mysterious quality of not allowing ice to form along its tips.

The Eskimo's arctic costume had one further advantage, not a minor one: it was completely watertight, and would, if its wearer were suddenly pitched into some ocean wave or river, keep him dry for up to an hour. It was formidable gear, in which a man could work all day and sleep all night with the maximum comfort available in the arctic. One would suppose that with this advantage in clothing and with a superior knowledge of dogsleds and river trails that Sarqaq would outdistance Klope in everything, but that was not to be, for the big man knew how to husband his strength and how to pull 'courage from the gut,' as he phrased it.

An Eskimo with seven good dogs could harness them in either of two ways: some excellent drivers liked to have three pairs, each pair yoked side-by-side, with a lead dog in front, his chain locked into the chain which ran down the center and attached to the sled. If a man had seven or nine superbly trained dogs long accustomed to this hitch, that was the way to do it, but there was an element of show in such a harnessing.

Tough-minded men who liked to move a maximum weight of cargo hitched their seven dogs in tandem, one directly behind the other, with each dog's harness tying directly into that of his follower. Such a hitch had the advantage of allowing the three key dogs—lead, swing, wheel—to perform at maximum and to utilize whatever skills they had mastered. Sarqaq, who had done much hauling in the areas bordering on the Yukon Flats, preferred the tandem hitch and used it to perfection.

Regardless of which harnessing the driver adopted, his dogs pulled the same kind of sled. If the trip was for show, or for the conveying of young women or a well-to-do couple, the sled looked like an ordinary sleigh familiar in either Russia or the United States: a commodious and well-upholstered place for two persons to sit, a handrail for the driver in the rear to use when he caught a ride, and long after-runners for him to stand on when doing so. But when, as in Sarqaq's missions, the sled had to carry the maximum freight, it was a low sturdy vehicle with no frills, wide, heavy runners and no sides, the freight being kept in place by numerous rawhide thongs.

Either of these marvelous machines—for they constituted two of the world's most effective users of energy—required special conditions: in most snow where a trail had not already been established, the man in charge of the sled had to go in front, on snowshoes, to break a path; the dogs by themselves could not do this, for they would waste their energy fighting snow which might be so deep that it covered their nostrils. When a man drove a dogsled he worked.

Of course, if a driver was lucky enough to be traveling along a river whose ice had been frozen to a glassy smoothness, which happened occasionally even on the Yukon, he might ride for several hours, because the dogs loved such a gallop when only slight friction retarded their sled. But generally, in a typical day's travel of twenty-five miles, the man would run at least twenty, gliding over the snow on his big webbed shoes.

Since each dog weighed about sixty pounds of concentrated muscle and could haul about one hundred pounds over terrain that was not excessively rough, Sarqaq's seven dogs ought to haul a total weight of seven hundred pounds, but since the sled itself, severely trimmed, weighed ninety pounds, the effective weight of foodstuffs for starving Dawson could be a little over six hundred pounds, less the weight of dog and human food carried.

During the first hour out of Fort Yukon, Sarqaq established the patterns to be observed: 'Always that way,' indicating southeast. 'Start before daylight, stop after light goes,' or twelve hours at least a day. 'Try for twenty-five miles a day, with stops, rest,' this indicated by fingers and gestures. 'Five days, stop one day, dogs sleep,' because no dog could work as hard as a man nor as long. 'You, me walk. Maybe good time, ride,' but mostly they would do what Klope had called as a boy the dogtrot. 'Eat? You, me that,' and Sarqaq indicated the dried food on the sled, including pemmican made of caribou, moose and bear. 'Dog eat?' And there came the major problem.

Sarqaq's dogs worked extremely hard and were constantly hungry, but tradition said that they must be fed only at night. It seemed to Klope that a quarter of the sled's load was dog-salmon dried the previous summer; a pound and a half of this nutritious food heavy in oil would keep a big dog alive and able to work and, when mixed with just a little dried oats or meal, the salmon gave the dogs more energy than they required.

In the cold, salmon did not turn rancid and dogs never tired of it, gulping down great chunks even though it contained sharp tiny bones which might have killed less sturdy breeds. To carry so much cargo merely to feed the dogs was in one sense extravagant but in another not, for without dogs, there could be no safe human traffic over the vast expanse of the arctic.

To supplement the dried salmon, on which the dogs would be quite content to feed permanently, Sarqaq was always on the alert for animal tracks, because if he could kill a caribou or a moose, or perhaps a bear wandering from its hibernation, the dogs could be fed for two or three days with a healthy change of diet and no depletion of the dried salmon. In fact, Klope deduced after several days of travel that since Sarqaq had brought along insufficient salmon for the proposed eighteen days, he was gambling on supplementing the fish with a caribou now and then. Accordingly, each of the men kept an eye cocked for signs of game, and Sarqaq was quite willing to halt progress for an entire day while he tracked some animal, for he knew that whenever he caught one, he improved the chances for bringing this long and daring venture to a successful conclusion.

When either he or Klope departed on such a hunting excursion, two rules were in effect: the hunter would take with him the extra dogs to help drag home the kill, and after the man had been absent for three hours, the other man would light a smudge fire to indicate where the sled was waiting, for otherwise the hunter might have no clue as to where either he or the sled was.

It was strange, almost to the point of being unbelievable, but in this wind-less, almost treeless north, a fire giving off smoke would send a signal high into the air, almost half a mile straight up, with never a waver in the column. The smoke just hung there motionless until it gradually dispersed. A traveler could often tell where people were living, beyond the rise of a hill, by the column of steam which hung suspended over their outdoor privy; such a signal could be seen for miles.

It was during a foray for meat that Klope made the hesitant suggestion which modified this trip, for as he was about to set off in search of a moose whose tracks were visible along the river, he asked if this time he could take as his drag-dog not the extra animals, but Breed, who lay in harness like the six other members of the team.

'Maybe good,' the Eskimo said, and Klope went off with only Breed, leaving the extras behind.

It was a day Klope would never forget, gray-blue sky, hazy sun low on the horizon, snow bright but not enough to cause snow blindness, a probability of snaring a moose, and the joy of the dog at heel. Breed loved the chase, but he was well enough trained to respond when Klope gave even the softest signal. Breed was in the hunt, too, and he wanted to bring down the moose upon which he and the team could feed. It became a rare partnership, even on that first day, and toward dusk, which came at an appallingly early hour, they approached their moose. Now Breed remained at Klope's side as they both edged into position, and when the gun fired, he leaped like the discharge of a cannon to trap the moose by a leg lest it stagger on merely wounded.

Now the problem became how to drag this heavy carcass back to the sled, and where was the sled? Scouting the horizon before total darkness fell, Klope located the pillar of smoke, hitched Breed to the one-dog harness, and looped the free end about the moose's neck. It was problematic whether the dog could pull so heavy a load—some four hundred pounds—but with help from an initial push by Klope, the fallen animal began to edge forward, and through special effort which Breed knew was required, the dead animal began to slide across the snow.

Klope, watching in admiration, muttered to himself: 'He knows he's bringing home something important,' and that did seem to be the case, for the dog stepped high, ears alert, dark eyes peering from side to side, harness taut, handsome silver-brown body straining forward. It was such a triumphant return that as darkness fell, with Klope spotting the sled, he fired into the night an exultant shot which reverberated in the frozen air.

Soon there came sounds of excitement in the camp, the barking of other dogs, the welcoming cry of Sarqaq; then the butchering of the meat, the tossing of offal to the hungry dogs and the warm good of coming home at end of day. But in the morning there came the ugly moment when Klope saw that Sarqaq had harnessed his team without including Breed, who was thus demoted to serving merely as a spare.

Shoving the dog forward, Klope said: 'Here's Breed,' but Sarqaq growled: 'No damn good,' and Breed was dropped from the team.

Klope, realizing that he knew little about operating a dog team, said nothing, but he was sorely disappointed, and so, apparently, was Breed, who showed his displeasure at not being harnessed with his six mates. And since the spares were kept together in a small harness of their own to prevent straying, Breed could not even walk with Klope, and it would have been difficult to decide which was the more disappointed.

DURING THE FIRST leg out of Fort Yukon, Sarqaq kept to the river, picking his way across the rumpled ice, and one cloudless afternoon he came upon a long stretch of glaze ice as smooth as a mirror, and since this was the first time that Klope had experienced such ice, the Eskimo encouraged the white man to ride on the rear runners, and for about an hour, with Sarqaq lagging far behind, Klope and the seven huskies skimmed over the ice through the windless beauty of an arctic day. It was a thrill Klope could never have imagined, this timeless, placeless, noiseless movement through a world of white. When the ride ended, with the dogs showing no tiredness but lying happily on the ice, Klope wanted for one brief moment to shout, but shouting was not his style. 'Good dogs,' he said, rummaging in the cargo for bits of salmon to throw them.

But when the Yukon took a slight curve to the southwest, forming in effect a detour from straight-line passage, Sarqaq left the river and kept to the east. This deviation was practical only because the dreaded Yukon Flats tapered out at this point, providing the dogs with relatively flat land; it was made imperative because Circle and its hungry men lay in wait just ahead, and if Sarqaq and Klope tried to rush their cargo of food through that snare, they were going to lose everything. So well back from the river they ran, not pausing to hunt for game and missing one day of rest they should have allowed the dogs.

When they returned to the Yukon south of Circle, the temperature began to drop so precipitously that Sarqaq feared they might not be able to move ahead, and he began to look about for accumulations of snow in which the dogs could burrow if the cold became unbearable.

It did. It went down to thirty-below, where Sarqaq's thermometer ceased to register, then down to forty-two, then to forty-seven. Had a heavy wind also been raging, men and dogs would probably have frozen. As it was, the cold was almost clement; if you stayed out in it with face exposed, you ran the risk of losing a nose or an ear, but if you protected yourself and your dogs, survival was surprisingly easy. As Klope moved through the extreme cold he kept hugging his left elbow close to his side, for this enabled him to feel the jar of sourdough against his skin, and he developed the conceit that he was like one of the gods he had read about in fifth grade, the custodian of a sacred fire, and the idea gave him pleasure: The leaven may not be any good when we get it there, but it won't be frozen.

Survival for the dogs consisted of burying themselves like rabbits in the snow till only their black noses were visible; you could find them by watching for their frozen breath hanging in the silent, motionless air. For men it was much the same; at fifty-one-below they used their sled as a wall, piled snow about them as an added windbreak, and found as much comfort as they could.

As they lay immobilized, Sarqaq chastised himself for having been so stupid as to come back onto the river: 'Colder here,' and with his mittened hands he made the sign of wind blowing, but as Klope pointed out: 'No wind. None at all,' and the Eskimo agreed: 'No wind, but cold follows river,' and he showed with his mittens how the bitter cold moved up and down the Yukon as if propelled by some strong wind.

'How could that be?' Klope asked, and the Eskimo replied, in effect: 'You tell me. But it is colder, isn't it?' And it was.

When daylight came on the eighth day of their trip, Klope noticed that Sarqaq had his mittens off and was carving some small object. 'What are you doing?' he asked, and the Eskimo said: 'For you.' It was a pair of sun goggles to prevent snow blindness, for if a white man with his lack of pigmentation, but any man really, remained surrounded by snow when the sun shone, his eyes would fight against the glare so strenuously that he would go temporarily blind, or, if the cold was sufficiently intense, permanently so. To prevent this, the Eskimos had long ago learned to wear protectors carved from ivory, bone or wood, or even cut from caribou hide if nothing better was available; the guard covered the eye completely but provided a very narrow slit, less than a quarter of an inch vertically and not more than an inch horizontally, through which the traveler could see where he was going. Often the goggle was painted black to reduce glare to a minimum, and as Sarqaq delivered this valuable survival tool to his companion he warned: 'Sun strong, no more hunt,' for even with such a shade, continued exposure to the arctic sun as it beat against snow could be perilous.

When the intense cold relaxed, one of the worst Sarqaq had known, the men resumed their southern push, and the Eskimo received a lesson which startled him. That he had a high regard for Klope had been proved by his willingness to share this trip with him, but this did not prevent his holding all white men in gentle deprecation. 'They can't work the way we do,' he told his Eskimo and Athapascan fellow drivers. 'They can't move over the tundra like us. And they cry at cold weather.' Since all native people accepted such evaluations as an act of faith, the sled-drivers nodded.

But now, in the later stages of the run when the white man should have been exhausted, Klope was showing surprising strength, and during one day's run of twenty-seven miles he led most of the way, spent no time riding, and at the end of day was in much stronger condition than Sarqaq. The Eskimo, noticing this, supposed that it was because of something he, Sarqaq, had eaten, but since the two men had shared the same rough food, this theory didn't make much sense. And when on the third successive day Klope ran and worked somewhat better than the Eskimo, the latter said admiringly: 'You white man work good.' It was high praise.

They were on the river, fortunately, when they came upon those remarkably fine cliffs which hemmed it in at the old-time mining settlement that some hopeful prospector had christened Belle Isle and which later realists would call by the more appropriate name of Eagle. It was a noble spot, rimmed in by mountains which occasionally formed cliffs delineating the river. There was an island, which in summer, Klope conceded, might be pretty enough to warrant the *Belle*, but what he liked especially about Belle Isle was its sense of being a little universe of its own, and when he saw in rapid succession a moose, a pair of red foxes and a line of caribou, he supposed that the animals felt the same way.

The spot was memorable also because it was here, or close to it, that American territory along the Yukon ended and Canadian began. Beyond Eagle, John Klope would pass for the first time into foreign country, but he had no one to discuss this with because to Sarqaq, there were no boundaries from the North Pole to the South, it was all land which had to be dealt with in the same way. When the temperature dropped to minus-sixty-six, you dug in; when it rose to a comfortable minus-ten, you made as many miles a day as you could.

When they were about forty miles out of Dawson they were once more overtaken by severe cold, this time accompanied by a stout wind blowing up the Yukon from the north, and were forced to hunker down in an area of snow and scrub trees. Placing their sled against the direction from which the wind came, they cut trees to provide additional shelter and allowed the dogs to burrow into the drifts for what heat could be accumulated there.

When better weather prevailed, Sarqaq suggested they both hunt for moose or caribou to take into the starving town, and after making arrangements as to how each would return to the river in order to regain the sled, they set forth, Sarqaq with two of the spare dogs, Klope with the help of Breed and a one-dog harness with which to bring back meat if any was taken.

It was a bitterly cold, lonesome hunt, with both dog and man suffering from the extreme weather, and so forbidding was the cold that no animals were on the move. Klope shot nothing and returned to the Yukon, that great river locked in ice, in bad temper. Sarqaq was not there, and since darkness came each December day sooner than on the day before, it was obvious that unless he was found, and quickly, night would fall and the two men would face some eighteen hours apart.

The first thing Klope did was build a smudge fire, but the force of the wind soon dispersed what should have been the signal pillar; however, he added more wood in hopes that if Sarqaq smelled smoke, he would be able to trace it to its source. Registering carefully in his mind every turn he made, he moved out in widening circles, shouting for his companion but receiving no reply, and he was about to retrace his steps when Breed, with hearing more acute than his, began to whine and look to the north. There, after a demanding tramp, they found Sarqaq and his two dogs beside a dead moose whose unexpected death throes had wrecked the Eskimo's left ankle.

Stoically, Sarqaq had waited, certain that if any companion he had ever traveled with could find him, it would be this stalwart American. When Klope knelt over him he said: 'Kill moose. Run to knife. Head come around, horn smash ankle.'

Klope said: 'I'll help you to the sled,' but Sarqaq was too much a man of the tundra to allow that: 'We go, wolf eat moose. You get sled, I guard.' And he refused to leave the kill.

So Klope returned to the river, harnessed the dogs, and drove the sled to where Sarqaq waited. In the lowering darkness they butchered the moose, attended to Sarqaq's ankle, erected a protection against the bitter night wind, and settled in till dawn.

In brutal cold they made their plans. Sarqaq, hobbling about in tremendous pain, gave the impression of a man who had suffered a slight bump: 'We harness all dogs, even Breed.' When this was done with makeshift hitches, he insisted that all good cuts from the dead moose be stowed on the sled, which became possible because the dogs had finished the initial stores of dried salmon. Then he and Klope released the dogs, allowing them to gorge themselves on the offal and the scraps.

Now came an amazing decision. Klope had supposed that Sarqaq would ride atop the loaded sled and that the extra dogs would provide hauling power to carry both him and the moose, but the Eskimo, always mindful of his dogs and the purpose of this trip, refused to ride. With the aid of a stick and one hand on the sled, he proposed to walk the remaining miles to Dawson City.

He started valiantly, maintaining a pace that astonished Klope, but as Sarqaq pointed out: 'S'pose me alone? No help? Me walk all same.'

Drawing upon the inherited strength that had brought his ancestors across the Bering Sea and then enabled them to survive in the world's most inclement surroundings, Sarqaq maintained his pace for about an hour, but when they were safely back on the Yukon, he relaxed his terrifying determination and fainted.

Halting the dogs, Klope struggled to get him onto the top of the sled, tied him there, shouted to the dogs 'Hi!' and off they went.

They spent the two final nights on the river, cold and frightened as to what might happen to Sarqaq's leg, but next morning they had traveled only a short distance when they caught sight of Dawson, that turbulent city where thousands of men pinched themselves in between mountain and river. Klope stopped the dogs, leaned forward on the handles of the sled, and bowed his head from exhaustion. He had completed one of the world's most demanding trips: nearly four hundred miles by train to Seattle, three thousand miles by sea to St. Michael, seventy miles along the Bering Sea to the Yukon, nearly fourteen hundred miles up that stubborn river to Dawson. He had earned the right to find his place in that city and try his luck on its gold fields.

W HEN THEY BURST into Dawson, with desperate men firing off guns to welcome them, Klope acted vigorously: he sold the cargo of food, including the moose meat, for a small fortune; he persuaded Sarqaq to give him Breed, which the Eskimo did because he knew that this misbegotten dog, so useless in the traces, had saved his life; and he rushed out to the Klondike, to learn that every inch of both the Bonanza and Eldorado shorelines had long since been staked. When laughing men, secure on their own claims, told him that there might be free sites about four miles away, where there was no gold, he stormed back into town prepared to fight anyone bare-knuckle for a claim.

Men who had been on the fields for a couple of years had learned to stay clear of newcomers who were semiwild with disappointment like Klope, and since this particular specimen had that big Eskimo dog that bared its teeth, they gave him extra room. It was probable, the more experienced men thought, that this one would wind up with a bullet through his chest before long.

They did not know that John Klope was quite a different type of person; he did not propose to die in some blazing shoot-out in a Yukon alley. He was angry not at the men who had filed on all the promising sites, but at himself for having arrived so late. He did not stop to reflect that from the time he had heard of the Klondike, on 20 July 1897, to this sixteenth of December in the same year, he had wasted scarcely a day. The layover in Seattle had been minimal; the stop in St. Michael needed to rebuild the *Jos. Parker* had been inescapable; while the stay at Fort Yukon had been necessary for him to complete arrangements with Sarqaq. Even so, he cursed his luck.

Now his problem was: Where do I find a place to sleep? and there was no easy solution, for most of the town was housed in tents whose temperatures at night could drop to minus-forty. Rarely had so many men lived in such misery, and he could find no one to take him in, even though he had saved lives by bringing in the cargo of food.

The main thoroughfare of Dawson—the entire place had been empty swampland only a year and a half before—was a gaudy stretch called Front Street, with saloons galore, a theater, a dentist, a photographer and forty other kinds of establishments for the separation of miners from their gold. No spot along Front Street was hospitable to Klope and his dog, but there was another street parallel to Front, nothing more than a line of dives, called Paradise Alley, and here in ramshackle cribs lived the women who had come to service the miners.

Some had climbed the Chilkoot Pass, others had been brought up the Yukon on the *Jos. Parker* by their pimps, and some came as actresses, seamstresses or would-be cooks. Failing to find the employment they had hoped for, they wound up on Paradise Alley in whatever kind of pitiful housing they or their pimps could find.

In one of the more commodious cribs lived a large, noisy, blowzy Belgian woman in her early thirties. She was one of eleven professional prostitutes who had been conscripted as a gang in the port of Antwerp, brought across the ocean and across the United States to work the gold fields. They had been imported, the locals claimed, by an enterprising German businessman who knew what a gold rush needed, and they were some of the best workmen, to use an odd term, in the Klondike.

The lead woman in the biggest crib was known widely and favorably as the Belgian Mare, and when Klope complained openly about being unable to file a claim or find a place to sleep, an American in a bar told him: 'I spent four nights at the Belgian Mare's. She rents an extra bed.'

So down Paradise Alley, Klope picked his way to the Mare's crib, and she did have an extra bed and she was in the habit of renting it out. Of course, there were only flimsy walls separating the rooms, so that anyone renting the bed-room almost had to participate in the Mare's lively and repeated profession, but Klope, always a loner, was able to blot out the reality of the Mare's occupation.

He was, however, grateful to her for her generosity, and especially for her good will, because although she spoke no English, she did go out of her way to make him comfortable, as she did with all men. It was when he took her out to breakfast one morning—sourdough flapjacks and moose-meat patties—that he met the man whose claim he would ultimately inherit. He was Sam Craddick, a disgruntled miner from California, one whose father had struck it moderately rich in the Gold Rush of 1849, the real one they spelled in capital letters. Craddick had expected to find lodes of gold similar to those in California, and the idea of washing tons of sand to find flecks of placer gold disgusted him.

'Have you a claim?' Klope asked, and the man said: 'When I reached here last summer, all the good sites were taken. I met the Mare same way you did.'

'So you staked no claim?'

'Hell yes, I staked one. But not down on the streams where the gold is. High up on a hill overlooking Eldorado.'

'Why would you stake up there?'

And while the Mare wolfed her flapjacks, for she was a prodigious eater, Craddick used the slab-sided breakfast table on two trestles to explain mining theory to Klope: 'Today, yes, you find gold along the streams down here. And that's where you'll always find it, time out of mind, if it ain't in a lode like in California.'

'You think the mother lode lies under the hills?'

'I do not. I don't think there's a mother lode in the whole of Canada, or Alaska either.'

'Then why did you claim on a hill?'

The miner said: 'Today's gold, yes, it's found down here in the running stream you see. But yesterday's gold, and maybe the bigger lot—where was the stream that captured it?'

'You mean, there could've been another river?'

'That's what the experts say.'

'But wouldn't it be lower? Not higher?'

'Ten years ago it would be lower. But let's say a million years ago? Who in hell knows where it could've been?'

Klope asked: 'You mean it could've been much higher than today's river?'

'You ever see pictures of the Grand Canyon?'

'Everybody has.'

'Remember how that little river cut that deep canyon? Maybe it was some-thing like that.' Craddick stared at Klope, then asked abruptly: 'You want to buy my claim? The whole damned thing?'

'Why would you sell?'

'Because I'm fed up. This is hell country compared to California.'

Klope thought: He's saying just what that fellow from California said. Maybe the Klondike is too tough for these men. Out loud he asked: 'How big a claim?'

Craddick, aware that he had on his line a buyer on whom he might unload his mine, said honestly: 'Standard size. Five hundred yards parallel to the stream. Usual distance east and west.'

Klope interrupted the Belgian woman eating her pancakes: 'Is he a good fellow, yes?'

The woman laughed, embraced Craddick, and cried: 'Damn good man.' She called for other men in the tent restaurant to testify, and when with the help of hand signals she explained the question, the men confirmed her opinion: 'He is honest and he does hold a legitimate claim on the hills above Eldorado.'

But when the Mare started out to defend the reputation of a man whom she knew to be reliable, it was difficult to stop her, and now she left the restaurant, stood in the middle of the frozen street, and with her right fingers to her lips uttered a piercing whistle. From a store midway down the street a young man in the red and blue uniform of the North West Mounted Police appeared. When he saw, as he suspected he would, the robust figure of the Belgian Mare, he walked sedately down to see what was the matter this time.

He was a fine-looking officer, twenty-eight years old, clean-shaven, and with the frank, open manner that betrayed his origin in some small Canadian town far to the east. He was Sergeant Will Kirby, taller than the average member of his distinguished force but no heavier. Since his job had required him to learn French, he conversed easily with the Belgian woman, who told him that the American Klope was demanding references from Craddick, whom she knew to be a trustworthy man.

When Kirby called the men out from the saloon, for he had been taught by his superiors to avoid both saloons and brothels, he recognized the miner at once: 'Sam Craddick is a good man. I've known him more than a year.'

Klope asked: 'If he was here a year ago, why didn't he get one of the good claims?' and Kirby said: 'Even then it was too late.'

In no way did the officer suspect Craddick of trying to pull an illegal trick, for he was a decent man, but Kirby did think it best if he knew what was going on: 'Is he trying to sell you a claim?'

'Yes.'

'Where is this claim?' he asked Craddick, and when the latter said: 'On the hill at Eldorado,' Kirby said with guarded enthusiasm: 'That's a serious site. Good things have been happening around there.'

He did not want to know how much the seller was asking, but when the figure, fifty dollars, slipped out, he whistled and told Klope: 'If you don't take it, I will.' With that, he saluted the Mare and moved on.

Klope had the money and a burning desire to own a gold mine of any sort, so he said that he would buy, cash in hand, if the miner would show him the claim and sign a transfer of sale at the Canadian government's office.

Eager to dispose of what had been nothing but an irritation, the miner said: 'You know, you're getting a cabin, not finished altogether. That goes with the sale.'

'Let's go see it. Now.'

So Klope paid for the Mare's breakfast, untied Breed, and set out with the miner to walk the thirteen miles to Eldorado, and when they reached there,

Klope found that everything the man had said was true. He had a claim. It was atop a hill. He had started to dig deep into the frozen earth. And he had already built about three-fourths of a one-room cabin. It was, the man said, the best damn buy on the Yukon: 'I don't think there's a flake of gold down there, but it's a real claim in a real gold field.'

It was now late in the afternoon of the twenty-second, and neither man wished to take that long hike back to Dawson, so the miner suggested: 'Why don't we stay here?' and they made rude beds in the half-finished cabin. As the man was about to go to sleep, he suddenly cried: 'Damn near forgot!' and when Klope inquired, he explained: 'You got to start your mix at night if you want flapjacks in the morning,' and when he left his bed to rummage among his stacked goods for some flour, Klope asked: 'Do you put some sourdough starter in the flour?' and the man replied: 'No other way.'

Now Klope rose to make a hesitant proposal: 'I brought some sourdough all the way from Fort Yukon, and I was wondering if it was still any good.'

'Try it someday and see.'

'Could we try it now?'

Craddick studied this, then gave a judicious answer: 'Mine's run out. I borried some from Ned down the line. I know this is good. If we just try yours and it ain't, we got ourselves no breakfast.'

Klope considered this, then made his own proposal: 'Why don't we try both?' and the miner said: 'Now, that makes sense.'

In the morning he was up before Klope, whom he awakened with good news: 'Pardner, you got yourself some real live sourdough!' and he explained how a substantial pinch of old dough rich in proliferating spores of yeast, when mixed in with ordinary flour, a little sugar and water and allowed to ferment overnight in a protected place, would generate the finest cooking yeast in the world and produce a new dough that produced delicious flapjacks.

'Looks to me like your dough did three times as good a job as Ned's,' and when Klope studied the two pans of rising dough, he agreed.

The first pancakes made from his leaven were, he proclaimed forcefully, the best he had ever tried: chewy, tasty, excellent when flooded with the almost frozen syrup from a big can. 'They'd be even better with butter,' the miner said, but even he had to admit that just as they were, they were pretty good.

'You got yourself a good strain,' he said. 'It'll work well up here as you dig your shaft.'

After breakfast he instructed Klope in the intricacies of this type of mining: 'What we do, every man on this hill, is light a fire every night, from September when the ground freezes hard to May when it begins to thaw. The fire softens the ground, maybe eight inches. Come morning, you dig out that eight inches and pile it over here. Next night and every night, you build yourself another fire. Next morning and every morning, you dig out the eight inches of thawed earth till you have yourself a shaft thirty feet deep.'

'What do you do with the earth?' Klope asked, and Craddick pointed to a score of earthen piles, frozen solid: 'Come summer, you sluice all that earth and maybe you find gold.'

The miner shouted down the hill to a man working on a lower level: 'Can we see your dump?' and the man shouted back: 'Come ahead, but hold that dog.'

So Klope, Craddick and Breed climbed down to the lower level, halfway to the rich creek below, and studied the large pile of frozen muck. The owner said: 'Cain't tell as how there's much color in there, but Charlie, three claims down, says he believes he'll sluice forty, fifty thousand dollars outen his pile of mud.'

'How does he protect it when he's down below working?' Klope asked, and both miners laughed: 'There's millions lying around these diggings this wintry day. And it better stay right where it is, because if any man touches a thimbleful of my frozen muck, there's fifty men will shoot him dead.'

On their way up the hill they passed a grizzled man in his sixties who had a larger-than-average pile of frozen earth beside his cabin. 'Louie,' Craddick said, 'I hear you found real gold,' and the man said: 'Hasty assay said maybe twenty thousand dollars.'

'Could I see what real gold looks like?' Klope asked, and the old man kicked at his pile until he broke loose a frozen fragment, and when he and the California man looked at it their faces broke into glorious smiles, for they were seeing a rich deposit. But when Klope looked he saw nothing and his face showed his disappointment.

'Sonny,' the man said, 'it don't come in minted gold pieces like the bank has. It's them teeny-weeny flecks. My god, this is a rich deposit!' And now when Klope moved the chunk of earth in the sunlight, he saw the flecks, golden and pure and extremely small. So this is what he had come to find, these minute particles of magic?

Back at his own mine, Craddick took Klope down the square opening he had so laboriously cut through the frozen soil, and for the first time in his life Klope heard the word *permafrost*: 'Our curse and our blessing. We have to work like hell to dig it loose. But it's so permanent, here forever, that we don't have to timber our hole the way my pappy did in California. We dig a hole, it remains same size till doomsday or an earthquake. And when you do reach bedrock . . .'

'What's that?'

'Where the ancient river collected its gold . . . if there ever was a river, or gold.' He sighed over lost dreams, and added: 'When you reach bedrock, you just build more fires and melt sideways rather than down, and the permafrost holds everything together . . . even the roof of your cave.'

They were about seven feet down when the miner said this, and when Klope looked up he asked: 'How do I get my thawed earth up to the pile?' and from bitter memory the man laughed sardonically: 'You load it in this bucket which I'm givin' you and you climb out of the shaft, takin' this rope with you, and you haul it up and dump it, and then you climb down with the bucket and do it all over again.' He stopped and chuckled: 'That is, unless you can teach that dog of yours to haul up the bucket and dump it.'

'Is that how all those men . . . ?' and the miner nodded: 'That's how they all did it. The men like me who found nothin'. The lucky ones who took out half a million.'

The two men walked back to Dawson, with Breed in tow, and next morning they appeared at the Canadian registry office, where they met Sergeant Kirby filing a report. 'I bought the claim,' Klope said, and Kirby replied: 'You won't regret it.' And minutes later Klope had in his possession the valuable paper which stated that a transfer had been made and that he now owned 'Eldorado Crest, Claim #87 in Line, formerly in the legal possession of Sam Craddick of California, now belonging to John Klope of Moose Hide, Idaho, this 24th day of December 1897, $50.00 U.S.A.'

As night fell and a group of sentimental miners toured the frozen streets singing Christmas carols, Klope felt that he knew the rock-bottom fact about gold mining on the Klondike: Luck. I was lucky to get here alive. I was lucky to meet Sarqaq before it was too late. I was lucky to find a helpful woman like the Mare. And I was damned lucky to buy as good a lease as I did. I know the chances of finding gold in that hole are a thousand-to-one against, but no wiseacre back in Idaho will ever be able to laugh at John Klope: 'That fool farmer! Went all the way to the Yukon and never found hisself a mine.'

O N THE LAST day of July 1897 a tall elderly gentleman, garbed in the uniform of a Confederate general, complete with a big Robert E. Lee kind of hat and a pair of cavalryman's boots, was lounging in the offices of Ross & Raglan, one of Seattle's principal shipping firms. Idly inspecting the hordes of would-be gold seekers from all parts of the globe who cluttered Schwabacher's Wharf, his inquisitive eye fastened upon a family obviously from somewhere to the east, and even more obviouly ill at ease. 'They're running away from something.' he muttered to himself. 'They're nervous, but they do look decent.'

The man appeared to be in his forties, a wispy sort of fellow unsure of himself, as if he were waiting to hear directions from his employer. A clerk perhaps, the watcher thought. The wife was in her twenties, an undistinguished sort of woman, and their son, who seemed standard in every way, was probably thirteen or fourteen.

The man watching started to chuckle as the three argued among themselves as to whether they should all enter the shipping office or only one, with the wife making the decision. Placing her hand in the middle of her husband's back, she shoved him toward the open door and turned to watch him enter.

The onetime Confederate studied the husband as he tentatively approached the counter, then heard him say to the shipping clerk: "I've got to get to the Klondike."

'Everyone does,' the clerk said, 'but our big ships are sold out, every inch of space through the October sailings, when ice closes down all the major ports.'

'What am I to do?' the man asked in a kind of desperation, and the clerk said: 'I might find you space on a converted tugboat, seven hundred dollars, and grab it, because tomorrow it'll cost eight.'

When the man winced, the clerk showed a twinge of sympathy and said: 'Between you and me, pardner, the price is too high. Our big ships are the rich man's route. Take one of our little R&R boats to Skagway and climb over the Chilcoot Pass. Save yourself a bundle.'

Since the man was now confronted with conflicting decisions, he told the clerk: 'I better discuss this with my wife,' but as he was about to leave the office he felt his arm being grabbed by someone he did not know, and looked up to see the smiling face of a Confederate officer, who asked: 'Are you by any chance seriously considering entering the gold fields in one of their leaky saucepans?'

Startled both by the general's appearance and by his question, the man nodded, whereupon the stranger said: 'I shall offer you invaluable advice, and trust me, it's worth more gold than you'll ever find along the Klondike.' He introduced himself as the Klondike Kernel and produced three clippings from Seattle newspapers attesting to the fact that this honored veteran of a North Carolina regiment, who had fought with both Lee and Stonewall Jackson, had prospected in the Yukon from 1893 through the height of the discoveries in 1896, and had come south on the *Portland* 'with a gunnysack of gold bars so heavy two members of the ship's crew had to help him drag it to a waiting cab, which rushed him and the gold to the assayer's office.' The papers said that the Klondike Kernel, as he was favorably known among his fellow tycoons, refused to give his real name 'lest avaricious relatives descend upon me like a flock of vultures,' but his gracious ways attested to his good breeding in North Carolina.

He wanted to talk. Having been immured in lonely cabins for so long and having wasted so many years in fruitless search before striking it rich on Bonanza *Forty-three Below*, he was now eager to share his knowledge and counsel with others: 'Did I hear you say you had three in your party?' and when the nervous fellow said: 'I didn't say,' the Kernel explained: 'I saw you talking with your wife and son. Fine-looking pair.' Then with an all-embracing smile he added: 'I'd better meet them so you'll all understand the situation.'

When they stood together in the street the man said: 'We're from St. Louis,' and the Kernel said effusively, with a low bow: 'Ma'am, you are mighty young to have a boy that age.'

'He's a fine boy,' she said.

'Dear friends,' the Kernel assured them, 'I have nothing to sell. I seek to steer you to no store where I receive a commission. I'm a man who scratched his way from one end of the Yukon to the other. I loved every minute of it, and seek only to share my experiences so that good people like you don't make the same mistakes.'

'Why did you leave?' the man asked defensively.

'Have you ever seen the Yukon in winter?'

'If you have all this money, why don't you go back home?'

'Have you ever seen North Carolina in summer?'

He said he could save them both money and heartache if they would but listen, and he was so persuasive, so congenial in the way he seemed to be trying to protect them, that they accepted his invitation to lunch. The wife assumed he would take them to some fancy restaurant, and she was eager to go, for she had not eaten well on the journey west; prices on trains were too costly.

'I take my lunch at a little saloon down the way. Excellent food for twenty cents.' Stopping in the middle of the wharf, he said: 'I live as if I was a poor veteran of the war in a small town in Carolina in the year 1869, which was a very poor year indeed. I still cannot believe that my gold is in the bank. I'm sure I'll waken and find this all to have been a dream.'

That lunch lasted four hours, and repeatedly the Kernel assured his guests that they were doing him a favor: 'I like to talk, always did, kept my men moving forward in the darkest days of the war.'

'Were you a general?' the man asked, unable to resist the charm of this amiable man.

'Never higher than a sergeant. But I was the one who led the men.'

Starting in the second hour he instructed his guests as to just what they would find on the gold fields. Asking the waiter, whom he tipped five cents, for a pencil and paper, he drew with remarkable skill a detailed map of the path from the ship's anchorage at Skagway, across the mountains and down the twists and turns of the Yukon: 'Understand two things, my dear friends. In Alaska the ship does not land you. There are no docks to land at. It anchors way out here at the edge of a great sand flat. You have to work like animals to move your goods ashore before the tide engulfs them.

'Then you carry them, piece by piece, nine miles inland over roads that are merely trails. Then you come to this very steep mountain, not even horses can climb it, and in deep snow you lug every single pound of your goods up and over that mountain.' He shocked them with the angle of the climb: 'Thirty-five degrees. Inhuman.'

The boy studied the drawing and said: 'Any steeper, a man couldn't climb that in snow,' and the Kernel said: 'Even the way it is, many can't.'

Then, when his listeners seemed properly awed, he asked: 'And how much weight are you going to have to transport over that mountain? I mean each of you. You, Mrs. . . . I didn't catch the name.' When she offered no response, he accepted the rebuff: 'How many pounds of gear do you think your frail little arms are going to have to carry up that mountain and over?' Somberly he stared at each of the travelers, then said slowly: 'One ton. You will each have to carry one ton over the mountains. You, ma'am, will have to lift up one ton and carry it up an angle like this in the snow.'

Leaving his guests open-mouthed, he got up and started moving about the saloon, asking politely if this man or that would lend him his gear for a moment, and within a few minutes he had accumulated a small pile, with the owners standing in a circle watching his performance. Lashing many of the borrowed articles together, he said: 'I'd judge this to be about fifty pounds, wouldn't you?' and men who were expert at that sort of thing agreed that yes, that was about fifty.

'The reason we use fifty is that's about the best a man can do heading up that mountain. So if you've got to haul a ton across—'

'Why so much?' a watcher asked, and the Kernel turned to face him: 'Son, at the top of the mountain there's a Mounted Police station, and they will not let you enter their country unless you bring with you a ton of supplies.'

'Why not?'

'They don't want you starving to death in Dawson City. I went six days without food in Dawson, and some went longer. We buried them.'

He now turned to the boy: 'Young feller, can you divide fifty pounds into one ton?'

'How much is a ton?'

The Kernel stared at the boy's mother: 'Ma'am, don't you teach your son anything?'

She was not awed by this bearded stranger, for she recognized him as a man with a compulsion to talk, to share his experiences, so when he asked loudly, to impress the watchers: 'Ma'am, I'll bet you don't know how much a ton is,' she laughed and said: 'It's a lot, that I do know.'

'Young feller, it's two thousand pounds. Now, at fifty pounds a load, how many trips up that mountain will you have to make to hoist your tons of goods across?'

'Forty.'

'You pass. Grade of C.' And with that he hoisted the load of goods, borrowed a strap, and tied it to the wife's back: 'Now, young woman, I want you to walk out that door, down to the corner and back,' and he shoved her on her way.

When she returned she was not smiling. For the first time since leaving home she had some understanding of the adventure on which they had embarked: 'It's heavy. I don't think I could climb a mountain with it.'

'How about you, son?' and he strapped the burden onto the boy's back and sent him down to the corner. When he returned he, too, was subdued and willing to learn.

'I'm not going to send you, Mr. . . . What did you say the name was? Because if you can't handle fifty pounds straight up the face of that mountain, you have no right to leave Seattle.'

He spent the third hour sharing with them the secrets of survival: 'You must take with you two essentials besides the food. A good whipsaw for cutting the logs you'll need to build your boat at Lake Bennett, and be sure to buy the best, because whipsawing logs is the worst job in the world.' When the wife asked what it consisted of, he asked for more paper, tipped the waiter another nickel, and proceeded to draw an excellent sketch in perspective of a log whose bark had been removed. It was perched over a pit, with one man down in the pit holding to one end of an eleven-foot saw, while above him, on a low platform, stood his partner holding on to the other end: 'Up and down you go, the man on top swearing that the man below is not pushing the heavy saw back up, the one on the bottom cursing because the man on top isn't pulling his weight.' He turned to the couple: 'I hope the minister who married you tied a tight knot, because it's going to be tested when you whipsaw the boards for your boat.'

'What was the other essential?' the wife asked, and he said: 'A coal shovel. Because when you climb that mountain forty times, which you'll have to do, there's another route parallel to it, much steeper, so when you get to the top and stow your goods—'

'Who watches them?' she asked, and he said: 'Nobody. You make a little pile at the top and mark it as yours. A stick, a flag, stones, anything. That's yours, and as long as you work on that mountain your goods are safe, even though you're at the bottom and they're alone at the top.'

'There must be thieves.'

'Occasionally. Very occasionally.'

'What do you do about them?'

'In my day we shot them. Fifteen, sixteen miners in a cabin. Man in charge says: "This here fellow, name of Whiskey Joe, he stole Ben Carter's cache, Ben almost died. What's your verdict?" And we'd all say: "Shoot the son-of-a-bitch, stealing a man's cache" and two minutes later the thief was shot dead.' One of the men who had gathered near the table to listen said: 'He's telling the truth.'

'You ever shoot a thief?' the boy asked, and the Kernel said: 'No, but I voted to have it done and helped bury the body after. Son, if you ever stole anything wherever it is you came from, don't do it in the Yukon or you're going to be shot dead.'

'What is the shovel for?' the wife asked, and he nodded slightly, his beard brushing the table: 'Thank you, ma'am. Sometimes I wander. Buy the lightest-weight shovel you can find. Carry it up to the top every time. Because after you stow your goods at your cache . . . Now, you understand, there may be a thousand other caches up there alongside yours. It'll look like a Persian market on a busy day, and when the snow comes, it'll all be covered in white six feet deep.'

'So that's why you need the shovel.'

'It is not. When snow hits, people just push and shove and kick and scrape, and pretty soon their goods are uncovered, as good as new if they've been properly packed. The shovel, ma'am, is for coming down. You walk about fifty yards from where your goods are, and before you lies a very steep hill, you couldn't possibly climb it coming up. And you couldn't walk it going down. So what you do, you sit on your shovel, handle out forward between your legs, and you give a push with one hand, and zooooey! You get the damnedest ride down the face of that mountain.'

'Could two ride one shovel?' the boy asked, and the Kernel said: 'If you were both skillful,' and he sent one of the watchers to fetch a shovel, and since there were sixteen or eighteen establishments nearby specializing in the outfitting of would-be miners, a broad shovel was soon produced.

'Too heavy, much too heavy. But the size is right. Ma'am, you sit in front, knees drawn up if you can. Son, you fit this board under your mother's seat and let it stick out a little in back. You sit on it,' and when they were perched precariously on the shovel, he gave them an imaginary shove and cried: 'Zooooey, down we go!'

When the shovel had been returned, he said: 'Two other things are advisable. A good square. Very light, weighs almost nothing, but you'll need it when you build your boat. And at least three good books apiece. Tear the covers off to cut down weight, but get books of substance for the long days of waiting. There's much to be said for a long book.'

With the skill that he had manifested before, he drew a sketch of the boat they must build on the shores of Lake Bennett, and the wife complimented him: 'You draw very well.'

'General Lee said I should've gone into the Engineers, but I had no schooling.'

'You speak so well. You use bigger words than I do,' and he said: 'In the Yukon you read a lot. You might walk forty miles to trade books, and the man you're heading to visit is overjoyed to see you. One man had a dictionary, traded it to me for a novel by Charles Reade. A dictionary can be very exciting when the night is six months long.'

'How long is that boat you're drawing?' the man asked, and the Kernel penciled in the dimensions of a boat he had once used, 23′ long 5′ 6″ in the beam: 'It's got to carry three tons and three people. I do declare, ma'am, you're a slight woman to have a son as big and sturdy as this one.'

In the fourth hour he reached the core of his advice. Pushing back his chair, he asked: 'Would you good people care for a little food as we approach the real problem?' and he ordered four more twenty-cent meals. The food was copious and good, but when the waiter asked: 'Drinks?' the Kernel said: 'Never touch it,' and the waiter said: 'For the twenty-cent meal you're supposed to buy drinks, too,' and the Kernel said: 'Give four beers to those men over there and four more—that'll cover lunch—to those over there.'

He then turned solemnly to his guests, and in carefully chosen words, spread their options before them: 'Now, from what I've said, two things ought to be obvious, the first realistic, the second cruel.'

'Yes?' the wife said, leaning forward. He liked this tough-minded little woman and addressed his two explanations to her: 'First, if you sail to Alaska now, no matter where you go, St. Michael or Dyea, there is no way you can get to the gold fields this year. The lower Yukon will be frozen, so that way's blocked. And if you did succeed in getting over the Chilkoot Pass before the heavy snows, which I doubt, you'll find Lake Bennett and the others frozen up, so somewhere, at great expense of time and health and patience, you'll have to hole up for the winter.' He paused to let this harsh truth sink in.

'Is that the realistic thing or the cruel one?' she asked, and he said: 'That's realistic. Now, the cruel fact you must already have figured out for yourselves. When you do reach the gold fields next spring, which is the earliest you can get there, you'll find that every likely spot for digging gold has been staked out. I got there four days after the big strike in 1896, and I had to settle for *91 Below* on Hunker Creek. Turned out to be the poorest creek of the bunch. I don't know what the numbers will be next year. Maybe *291 Below, 310 Above,* if there's that much land available. And even if there is, it won't be land with any promise.'

'Then we're too late?' the man asked, his face ashen.

'Yes.'

'But you just said you started with a poor claim,' the wife said, boring in. 'And you came out with a fortune. The papers said so.'

'I started with a bad one on Hunker Creek. Wound up with that good one on Bonanza.'

'How did you do it?'

The Kernel patted her on the cheek: 'So complicated, that trade, I'd be ashamed to tell you.'

'Did you steal it?'

'The other man thought so.' He shook his head, partly in embarrassment, partly in disbelief that he had been able to conclude such a swap.

'Then our chances aren't good?' she asked, and he said: 'They are not, and any honest man who came south on the *Portland* with me will tell you the same, if he has any interest in your well-being.'

'Then why do the newspapers . . . ?'

'Seattle wants to keep this alive. To keep the stores open. The shipping companies. The bars like this one.' Then he added a sagacious observation: 'And it's people like you, streaming in, who help keep the rush alive.'

'Is it all a lie?' she asked, and now the Kernel rocked back and forth before his plate of savory stew. He wanted to explain an intricate fact, and he wished attention to be paid: 'Oh no! It's not a lie. It's just that the facts are different from what they say.'

'How do you mean?' she asked, and he explained: 'You'll not get any gold up there. Believe me, if you took a hundred men like me who knew the fields like a book, men of enormous experience . . . Only two or three of us out of a hundred found any gold to speak of.'

'But they came off the *Portland* in dozens, I saw the photographs.'

'They didn't photograph the hundreds who stayed behind, the old men in the tiny cabins, the young men freezing at the bend of the creek.'

Rapping the table with her spoon, she demanded: 'Tell us what you're trying to say.'

He bowed: 'Ma'am, you deserve a straightforward answer. You'll find no land worth claiming at the diggings, but smart people like you, if you have courage and even a little nest egg, you can find the real gold mine in Dawson City.'

'You mean a store? A hotel?'

'I mean opportunity unlimited. Men like me will be out there digging for gold. You and your husband can be waiting in Dawson to take it away from them. This may sound ugly, ma'am . . . Damn it all, what's your name?'

'Missy. My mother named me Melissa, and this is Buck, and this is Tom.'

'Pleased to meet you good folks. I don't mean to be harsh or mean-spirited. But Dawson is a tough place, except that the Canadian police do try to enforce some kind of limits. That gives bright people like you and Buck a fighting chance to earn a real fortune.'

'What would we need?' Missy asked, for since listening to the Kernel she had begun to surrender hope of finding gold in the customary way.

'Money,' the Kernel said. 'Here in Seattle and in Dawson the rule's the same. If you have ten dollars, you're infinitely better off than if you have only nine.'

'But if you don't have ten?' she persisted, and he ignored her, digging into his plate for more of the good stew. Finally he looked up: 'Can't you see the situation? Don't go to Alaska now. Wait till April, when the snows stop and the ice begins to thaw. And the boat fares drop.'

'And what do we do while we wait?'

'Work. Get jobs, all of you. Save every penny. So that when you do leave for the Yukon, you arrive with enough money to make a splash. If you're clever, and I think you are, you can double your money and then double it many times again.'

'How?' Missy insisted, and he said: 'Once you reach Dawson, you'll see a hundred ways,' and later, when she saw one of the photographs of the famous gold town she saw that one of its characteristics was the blizzard of carefully painted banners hanging from the false-fronted stores which provided some kind of service:

DOUGHNUTS AND HOT COFFEE 20¢
GOLD ASSAYS IMMEDIATE
LAUNDRY MENDING FREE
DR. LEE, TEETH PULLED

As Missy studied the photographs, Buck did some figuring: 'If we don't sail north till April . . . that's eight or nine months to wait. What should I do? What should any of us do . . . to earn money?'

'Aha!' the Kernel said without hesitation. 'You find the best-paying job you can . . . anything,' but Buck, remembering a year without employment of any kind, could not visualize getting work so easily, and it was here that the North Carolinian proved most helpful.

'Tom?' he asked. 'What can you do?'

'Deliver papers. I was good at that.'

'No, no! It doesn't pay enough,' and he was about to dismiss that possibility when the boy said with the enthusiasm that the Seattle waterfront engendered: 'I don't mean one door to the next. I mean this whole wharf area . . . going out to meet the ships coming in. Lots of new possibilities.'

'And what can you do?' the Kernel asked Buck, but Tom broke in: 'Pop can manage furniture accounts better than anybody.'

'What experience?'

'Hardware. Big furniture.'

'You're the man they need,' the miner cried, rising from his chair and dragging Buck three blocks toward the center of the city, with Missy and Tom following.

He took them to Ross & Raglan, the store that had outfitted him years before when he first went into the arctic and which now was crowded with goods required by gold seekers. Calling for Mr. Ross, the Kernel reminded that industrious Scotsman of who he was and displayed the newspaper clippings to prove his identity: 'I want you to hire this man, Mr. Ross. He knows goods. He can bring some order into this place.'

So many of Ross & Raglan's clerks were leaving for Alaska that the merchant was eager to find a responsible replacement, and after a series of inquiries as to Buck's capabilities, he asked: 'Can I write to your former employer for a reference?' and Buck said: 'No. We left St. Louis after a misunderstanding. But you can see that the three of us are responsible.'

'Are you married to this lady?'

'He certainly is,' the North Carolinian said, and the enthusiasm of this miner who the papers said had brought nearly sixty thousand dollars on the

Portland was so infectious that against his better judgment, Mr. Ross employed Buck on the spot.

The Kernel then took Tom to the offices of the *Post-Intelligencer* and insisted that the paper hire this intelligent lad to organize the distribution of the journal in areas that had been served only sporadically before: 'I mean the waterfront, the new bars, the ships coming in.'

Again, the excitement of the gold rush was so pervasive that the managers of the paper listened to a proposal that would have been dismissed as outrageous a year before. Tom got a job, on trial, and now the restless miner turned his attention to Missy.

It was not yet completely dark as he hurried the Venns along one of the major streets until he came to a fashionable restaurant, where he left Buck and Tom at the front door while he took Missy to the back. There, forcing his way into the kitchen, he asked to see the manager, and since in these frantic days Seattle was accustomed to bizarre behavior, the manager listened when the Klondike Kernel introduced himself, showed his credentials, and said: 'My young friend here is a master waitress, widely regarded in St. Louis. She's on her way to the gold fields and needs a job till April.'

'Can you do hard work?' the manager asked, and when Missy said, 'Yes,' he said, almost with a sigh: 'You can start right now.'

'I can start in an hour,' she said, and he said: 'Don't disappoint me.'

In slightly over an hour, the North Carolina miner had landed three good jobs for his new friends, and when, back at the bar, they asked why he had done this, he said: 'I wish I was thirty. Starting up the Chilkoot again, rafting down the Yukon in a thing I built myself. I want to see you do it right.' But as they rose to leave, he terrified them by placing his hands on the table, staring at each in turn, and saying: 'I like you three. People of character, and I'm going to help you all the way. But you have got to tell me who you are and why you're here.'

'What do you mean,' Buck stuttered, and the Kernel patted him reassuringly on the arm: 'When you came into that shipping office you were scared to death. Looked at me twice to see if I was a policeman or a detective. What have you stolen? What crime? What are you running away from?' Before the man could respond he turned to Missy: 'You! You're the salt of the earth, I can see that. But you can't possibly be the mother of this boy, can you? How old are you?'

'Twenty-two.'

'And you're not married to this one, are you?' When she began to remonstrate, he said: 'How do I know? You don't look married. You don't treat him as if he was your husband.' When she asked what this meant, he said: 'You treat him too nice.'

Now it was Tom's turn: 'And you, young fellow? Have they kidnapped you? Get you out of a reform school?' When Tom started to speak, the Kernel put his hand on his arm: 'Not now. Think it over. Decide if you can trust me. Half the people coming through here have secrets they'd rather not reveal.' He then looked seriously at each of the three: 'But if I am to help you any further, wherever you're from, and it certainly isn't St. Louis, you must tell me the truth.'

Badly shaken by the Kernel's final salvos, they convened at midnight, following Missy's stint at the restaurant, and leaped into an agitated discussion of their plight, with Missy saying: 'He was uncanny. Twice I remember him looking at me funny when I said something that wasn't exactly true.'

'But how did he know we weren't from St. Louis?' young Tom asked, and then Buck raised the real question, the one that each of the other two had wanted to ask but had been afraid to: 'Suppose he is a detective? Suppose the Chicago police telegraphed him with our descriptions?'

The tiny rented room fell silent as the three fugitives contemplated this frightening possibility, and with the sounds of life crashing down about their ears, they went to bed and tried to sleep.

IF THE KERNEL was a detective, he behaved in contradictory ways, for in the days that followed he did everything possible to help them start successfully in their new jobs, and after their working hours he reviewed item by item the things they must buy for their great adventure in the gold fields: 'Six thousand pounds and each ounce must mean something.' He arranged for Ross & Raglan to give Buck, as an employee, a discount on the purchases he made there and located a grocery that was eager to get rid of large supplies of dried goods before the New Year: 'Buy them, Buck. They'll keep.' But it was Buck himself who compiled the famous list that so many newcomers used as their buying guide. It itemized the hundred or so necessities a prudent gold seeker ought to purchase before he left Seattle. At the top the card said: 'You will find every piece of this equipment at Ross & Raglan,' and then he demonstrated his growing ingenuity by adding at the bottom a helpful reminder:

Ross & Raglan, always mindful of their customers' welfare, most urgently recommend that each prospector take with him a small kit containing medicaments sure to be needed.

Borax	Essence ginger	Laudanum
Iodine	Chlorate potash	Chloroform
Quinine	Toothache drops	Acetanilid
Iodoform	Spirits of nitre	Witch hazel
Paregoric	Belladonna plasters	Carbolic salve

Such a kit can be purchased for less than ten dollars at Andersen's Drug Store, which is connected in no way with Ross & Raglan. Andersen's also recommends that men take along Monsell's salts for hemorrhages, in quantities according to each man's susceptibility to attack.

The disclaimer that R&R had no financial interest in Andersen's Drug Store and received no return on this free advertising was only partially true, because Buck did collect a small commission on each medical kit he helped sell.

But whenever they met up with the Klondike Kernel they were aware that he was watching them with far more than casual interest, and they grew nervous when he invited them to take meals with him. 'You're my Seattle family,' he said, and when Missy asked: 'Haven't you any in North Carolina?' he parried: 'That place seems to grow ever more distant.' Then, instead of goading them to reveal their secrets, he confided his: 'When I left this harbor years ago for Alaska, I had one ambition. To show those bastards back in Carolina. And all the time I grubbed along the Klondike, I consoled myself with the thought that with my increasing hoard of gold, I'd show them back home.'

'What changed it?' Missy asked, and he said: 'North Carolina don't seem so important now,' but quickly he amended the statement: 'Fact is, there's no one there who would remotely understand what the Klondike meant.'

The three felt honored, in a way, that he had shared his thoughts with them, but this did nothing to alleviate their suspicions about him, for as Buck warned repeatedly when they were alone: 'He could still be their detective.'

Because each of them worked diligently, their savings grew, and this gave the two adults a happy feeling of security, but it was Tom who was enjoying himself most, for as he became familiar with the waterfront, meeting the dazzling steamships which came up from San Francisco or the old ones limping down from St. Michael, he began to sense what a magical city Seattle was. It dominated the extreme northwestern corner of the nation, with great trains arriving daily from various parts of the country; it also dominated trade with Alaska, which had no other outlet. It was a city built on a captivating waterfront, with lakes and islands and stretches of water reaching to the horizon north, south and west. It was girt with massive mountains both east and west, and what surprised Tom, as it did Buck and Missy, the city did not lie on the ocean, as they had always supposed; it lay some eighty miles inland along waterways that served both Canada and the United States.

'I like this city!' Tom often cried when he saw it from the deck of some incoming ship to whose passengers he had sold copies of the *Post-Intelligencer*, or when he met a decrepit scow, barely afloat, which had limped down from Skagway and Juneau bringing three men who arrived with gold and sixty-three with nothing.

He knew the operation of the Seattle waterfront as intimately as a boy could in the limited time he had worked it, and one night he went running to the restaurant where Missy worked: 'Wonderful news! The *Alacrity*, that little steamer owned by Ross & Raglan, they need a head stewardess for the Skagway run and they told me you can have the job.'

'When?'

'They sail tomorrow at four in the afternoon.'

'How much pay?'

'They said tips were plentiful . . . really generous.'

She told Tom to wait till she could leave work, then accompanied him to where the *Alacrity* was docked, preparing for her return run to Skagway. As they neared the trim little vessel, Tom said: 'A new ship like this, it makes the run to Skagway in six days, even with two stops.'

Nervously, but with pride, he took Missy to see the captain, who was in his nightshirt: 'Captain Reed, this is the one I told you about.'

'You a hard worker?'

'He told you I was, didn't he?'

'I mean really work. Get this crew in the dining room straightened out?'

'I can, but what's the pay?'

'The tips are very generous.'

'But from you? For getting things in order?'

Captain Reed considered this, then parried: 'I suppose you'll jump ship the minute we hit Skagway.'

'You know that my son will be here in Seattle.'

'He said he was your brother.'

'So, how much pay?'

'Two dollars a day. Your bunk. Your meals. And the tips have been very generous.'

'Three dollars and I'll take it.'

'I said two and I said you'd be treated generously. Take it or leave it.'

'I'll take it.'

'Be here at oh-seven-hundred.'

'He said you sail at four in the afternoon.'

'But we feed people at oh-eight-hundred. Be here.'

Now Missy faced three obligations: she must inform her present employer that she was leaving the restaurant, she must tell Buck that she would be on the *Alacrity* during the coming months, and she must in decency explain matters to the Kernel, who had been so helpful. Grappling with the easiest first, she asked Tom to walk back to the restaurant with her and wait outside while she talked with the owner. He understood: 'In Seattle everything happens. Good luck in the gold fields.'

'I'm not going there at once,' she tried to explain, but he said, not unpleasantly: 'When you go, you go.' To her astonishment he gave her an extra five dollars: 'We can use you when you come back broke.'

Explaining to Buck presented no problems at first, for he appreciated the fact that she would be earning substantially more than at the restaurant and that she would also be learning how prospectors reached the gold fields, but when she added that now they must level with the Kernel, he cried in real anxiety: 'Why? Why?' and she said: 'To clear things,' and he said: 'But suppose he really is a detective?' and she said: 'There is no way that good man can be evil,' and Tom supported her.

So at about one in the morning of the day she would make her first tour to the north, the three of them walked soberly to the saloon where the Kernel was sitting at his usual table, and Buck said: 'They want to talk,' and the Kernel rose, bowed politely, and said: 'Why have you decided so late at night?' and Missy said: 'I start work on an R&R ship tomorrow, and we owe you an explanation. You've been like a father to us.'

'I've tried to be,' and to his astonishment it was Tom who broke the ice, saying, 'It was during the starving time in Chicago. My grandmother, my father and me, we had no food at all, no jobs of any kind . . . nothing.'

'It was the Panic of '93,' Missy explained, and Buck, who was still ashamed of those days when he failed the family, remained silent, so Tom continued: 'Missy was in charge of charity for our church, and that's how we got to know her.' He looked at her with love, there in the smoky saloon, and she said: 'The minister came to me and said: "Missy, there's one of our families, the Venns, we haven't seen for three weeks. They may be starving in silence." And they were.'

Painfully the recollections of that terrible time returned, and in reluctant pieces the three told how she, Missy Peckham, had made contact with the Venns, how a few dollars of church money a week had kept them alive, and of how their courage kept them afloat, but Tom said something else: 'It was Missy who did it. I know that whenever the church money ran out, she gave us her own, and that's when we all fell in love with her.'

On this extraordinary clue, the Kernel raised his two forefingers, pointing one at Buck, who had not yet spoken, one at Missy. 'You also? You fell in love?'

'He had a wife,' Missy said, and before she could describe the situation, Tom broke in: 'A terrible woman. My mother, and a really terrible woman.'

'Now, that's a harsh thing for a boy to say,' the Kernel said reprovingly, and Missy said: 'But she was. She tricked Buck into marrying her because . . .'

'Do you really need to tell me so much?' the Kernel asked, for he realized that he was getting more answers than he had sought, but Missy said: 'Yes. You asked, and you're the only friend we have in the world.'

At last Buck felt free to speak: 'We thought you were a detective. Sent out from Chicago to trap us.'

'What did the pair of you do?' and again he pointed at each at the same time. 'Murder her?'

'No,' Missy said, 'but we might have. After Tom was born she abandoned him, ran away with two or three different traveling salesmen, a woman of great vanity.'

Again Tom broke in: 'She left me for eleven years, then when my father— he's not my real father but lots better than that—and Missy and I were a good family, she came back to Chicago and wanted to claim me as her child.'

'It was unfortunate,' Missy said. 'When she brought two lawyers around to make us give up the boy, Tom told them all to go to hell. Very wrong, because when the judge heard that a son had told his mother to go to hell, he became furious and said he would not only take Tom away from us, he would have Buck put in jail for adultery.'

'That was when we decided to flee to Alaska,' Buck said quietly. 'The judge handed down a court order, and we ignored it.'

The Kernel leaned back, ordered drinks for everyone and sandwiches, too; then, pointing to the crowded bar, he said: 'Half the men in there are probably under some kind of court order, and if they wanted to dig up my record in Dawson, I'd be under one, too.'

They spent the next two hours unraveling the tangled story of Chicago, one in which the three fugitives had been treated so very badly, and at one point the Kernel said: 'You know, Buck, I guessed some of this that first day when I saw you talking in the street with your family. You looked like a man who'd been defeated . . . carrying a terrible burden. And you, Missy, you looked like a bossy woman who had to provide backbone for three.'

'Not for me,' Tom said, but the Kernel looked at him indulgently and said: 'Yes, many a boy younger than you goes out to find a job when he has no father or the father he does have can't find one,' and Missy said sharply: 'Maybe you did, sir, in your day, but that wasn't 1893,' and very sternly she added: 'There were no jobs, and with the skimpiest church funds I tried to keep eleven families alive.' Placing her hand in Buck's, she said: 'We know. For us the gold fields will hold no terrors.'

At five in the morning, when the first rounds of breakfast coffee were being served, the Kernel gave the Venns some solid advice: 'What with Missy's new job and Buck's, you'll be making good wages. Save them in a bank, not a stocking somewhere that can be rifled by thieves or wasted when you think you need something. Go to the Klondike with money in your pockets, for then you can set your own speed.'

At six, as he and Missy stood in the middle of the street while Buck and the boy climbed to their quarters to fetch her bag, she asked: 'Why have you been so kind to us?' and he remained silent, for there were too many answers—his loneliness, his inclination always to back the underdog—but finally he selected one: 'You're the kind of people that Alaska was invented for. Down on your luck, struggling back.' Then he offered a strange one: 'And because you back your man so strong.'

'And you?' Missy asked. 'What drove you, years ago?' and again he had a score to choose from: lost battles, little country villages reduced to ashes, mortgages in peril, but he voiced one that truly pertained: 'You and I are cousins, Missy. Marry him,' but she said: 'We've done so much already, kidnapping and disobeying court orders, we don't need bigamy, too.'

'But isn't the other one divorced . . . and remarried?' and she said gloomily: 'She don't bother with things like that.'

At seven the three men walked her down to the *Alacrity*, where they kissed her goodbye as she boarded for her maiden voyage. 'You're my family,' the Kernel said. 'Behave yourselves.'

So through a chain of happy accidents the Venns found themselves locked in with the fortunes of the merchant shippers Ross & Raglan. Buck's excellent work for the firm assured his promotion and the offer of continued employment should he wish to stay in Seattle and forgo the gold rush. Missy was so able aboard the *Alacrity* that she, too, was promoted to jobs of greater responsibility.

Even young Tom had been drawn into the Ross & Raglan orbit, for as he enlarged his operations along the waterfront he had, as his service for the captain of the *Alacrity* proved, been of use to the smaller ships controlled by the firm. One morning as he delivered papers to Ross & Raglan's dockside office, the manager, Mr. Grimes, called from his desk: 'Young man?' And when Tom, a husky, well-mannered boy big for his age, reported to him, Grimes said: 'We could use a young fellow like you.'

'Doing what?'

'Running messages to the ships. Tracking down freight. Many things.'

'I like working down here.'

'I noticed that. You'd be suited for what I have in mind,' so Tom signed on with Ross & Raglan, but he also retained his lucrative newspaper route, starting at four o'clock each morning, finishing well before the ship office opened.

The Venns were now prospering so reassuringly that considerations for the future had to surface, and during the next layover of Missy's ship, the family held long discussions, in which Tom was the spokesman for staying in Seattle: 'We have good jobs. We've saving money. And Mr. Grimes said I could have free mornings if I wanted to go back to school.'

When the Kernel heard that Tom was talking of skipping the gold fields and staying in Seattle, he thundered: 'Son! What is the matter with you? The great adventure of the century, and you want to miss it?'

'But you've warned us a dozen times we'll find no gold.'

'Gold? Who's talking about gold? Four of the best men I ever knew in Dawson found no gold. I'd rely on those men any day of my life, and I'll wager they're just about as happy now as I am,' and Missy added: 'I see it on the Skagway run. Men who come out of the gold fields seem to carry a secret. "We did it. We were there." '

So it was agreed that come the middle of March they would take their savings out of the bank, catch a Ross & Raglan steamer to Skagway, go over the low ground to Dyea, and start up the Chilkoot. When they informed the Klondike Kernel of this decision he said: 'My heart explodes with happiness for you. You'll never regret it,' and a few days later he was gone. No one knew where he went, or even by what means he left Seattle. Missy was surprised, and said so frankly, that he had not bid them farewell or given Tom a going-away present, but a month later she received a registered letter from St. Louis, sent in care of Buck at the store. It contained two one-hundred-dollar bills, the first she had ever seen, a beautiful green on the face, resplendent gold on the back. Each had a brief note pinned to it, and one read: 'This is for you.' The other said:

> When you reach Dawson City, look out for a lady in the cribs on Paradise Alley called the Belgian Mare. Give her this and tell her the Klondike Kernel sent it.

On 15 March 1898 the Venns regretfully terminated their various jobs with Ross & Raglan, assembled their carefully chosen gear, and booked passage on the next trip of the *Alacrity* to Skagway. The fare, with a place to sleep and full meals, was thirty-four dollars for each adult, twenty-four for Tom, but when Buck went to pay for the tickets, Mr. Grimes said: 'Total bill fifty dollars, courtesy of Malcolm Ross, who hopes you'll all come back to work for him.'

Buck, who had never been on a ship before, stood transfixed at the railing as Missy explained which parts of the land were American and which Canadian. For him, this inland passage, with mountains to the east, large islands to the west and vast glaciers snouting their way into the ocean, was both a delight and a wild promise of greater scenes to come. He was sobered by the magnitude of the adventure they had undertaken and determined to succeed in it. As he contemplated the dreaded Chilkoot, the ominous rapids in the Yukon, he found himself thinking less and less of the gold that the Kernel had warned would not exist.

Tom deplored leaving Seattle, and as the *Alacrity* moved away from Schwabacher's Wharf with a steam-driven speed that really was alacritous, he felt tears coming to his eyes: This is a great city, I'd like to live in Seattle. I hope we find a million dollars in gold and bring it back here. As he stared at the receding profile of the town he had grown to love, he could identify almost every watery inlet along the broken shore, every hill that he had climbed with his papers. He could feel the vitality of this fine port hidden deep behind the protective mountains, and he loved even the strange sound of the name: *Seattle!* I'll be back!

O N THE EVENING of 23 March, prior to arrival off the Alaskan port of Skagway—navigable water ended about a mile from the town, which was approached over a wide sandy beach—Buck held a long family meeting to discuss a strategy for getting through the concentration of thieves without losing savings and property.

'It can be done,' Missy said. 'I've been to Skagway many times. Crooks everywhere, but if you stay clear, nothing happens.'

'I have the money sewed in my clothes,' Buck assured them. 'Talk to no one. Hire the horses and let's hurry across to Dyea.'

These precautions proved unnecessary, for at supper that night the captain of the *Alacrity* announced: 'Because there's a big buildup of people coming out of Dyea, we'll move the ship over there three days from now. Anyone wishing to disembark at Dyea is invited to stay aboard.'

So transiting the hellhole of Skagway was avoided, and during the two days the ship stood off that infamous port, Buck stayed in their cabin, guarding his family's funds and keeping his eye on their luggage stored on deck. But Tom wanted to see the notorious place, and to Buck's surprise, Missy said she was eager to chat with two women she had come to know while working the Skagway run, so on the second day she led Tom to the gangway, descended to the flats, and paid a sturdy man twenty-five cents to carry her through the low waves and deposit her ashore. Tom, refusing such aid, sloshed along behind her, watching everything: how lighters drawing only a few inches came out to unload the ship, how horses drawing carriages came far onto the sands, and how the little coastal town loomed up from below its crest of mountains.

Ashore, Tom found Skagway to be an intriguing place, for Missy kept warning him against practically every person they saw: 'He's not a minister. He's Charley Bowers. He talks sweet and steals every cent you have.' Later she said: 'He's not a real policeman. He's Slim Jim Foster, shoot you dead if you bump into you.' And according to her, the institutions in Skagway were as bogus as the people: 'See that bank; it really isn't one. They accept your funds and you never see them again.' Nor was the post office really a post office; letters dropped in its slot were never heard of again.

'Why doesn't someone report such stuff to the sheriff?' Tom asked, and she explained: 'There is a sheriff, sure. Right over there. But he's not really one, either. Uses anything you say as an excuse for stealing you blind.'

'What is real?' Tom asked, and she replied without hesitation: 'The saloons,' and when Tom studied the main streets, rough and unpaved, he saw at least three dozen whiskey joints.

Missy, however, was not awed by the boomtown, and with what Tom considered great courage she led him to a false-fronted building serving as the 317 Oyster Bar, with parlor attached. Marching boldly in, she said: 'My name is Missy Peckham. I'd like to see Soapy, if he's in,' and she indicated the back room where the notorious boss of Skagway held court.

A waiter stopped shucking oysters and disappeared, returning in a moment with a slim, fine-looking bearded man dressed in a business suit which would have passed muster in Denver, from whose worn-out gold fields he had come only a year before. He was about thirty-five years old, reassuring in appearance, and old-world polite in greeting Miss Peckham, in whose care he had once sailed.

'Tom,' she said as the man gravely bowed, 'this is Jefferson Randolph Smith, an important gentleman in this town.'

'You were so attentive to me aboard the *Alacrity,*' the famous gambler said, 'could I invite you and Master Tom to an oyster stew?' She said: 'We'd be honored, Mr. Smith, but Tom here wants to see the start of your White Pass.'

'He'll see that in due course, I'm sure.'

'No, we're entering by way of Dyea.'

At mention of this rival town, a hated competitor for the Klondike traffic, Soapy stiffened: 'Surely you're not going by that miserable route? Son, you climb that Chilkoot Pass once, you'd be exhausted for a week, and you'll have to climb it forty times! Do, please, for your own sake, Miss Peckham, take the easy route. Unload your baggage here at Skagway and let my people help you get organized.'

'Tom wanted to see White Pass. He wants to see everything.'

At this rebuff, Smith bowed graciously: 'My good and trusted friend, if your young man wants to see the start of our commodious trail, the only practical way to enter the Klondike, you and he shall go in comfort. You were very kind to me aboard your ship, and I can do no less when you're in my city.' He summoned from the back room a man named Ed Burns, who whistled for a henchman named Blacktooth Otto: 'Get out the horses and take these two for a ride.'

'Where to?'

'The start of White Pass.'

'They goin' over?'

'Shut up and get goin',' and soon Blacktooth appeared with three rather good horses.

In January 1897, Skagway had consisted of a few scattered houses; by July of that year, it was becoming an exploding tent city; and now, in March of 1898, it was a real Alaskan boomtown, with streets sometimes knee-deep in mud or ankle-deep in dust and with stumps two feet high in the middle; with timbered houses unpainted and often without windows; and with the inevitable false-front stores emblazoned with carefully and sometimes ornately lettered canvas signs proclaiming a score of different services. In these days the name of the town, derived from Indian words meaning *Home of the North Wind*, was most often spelled *Skaguay*, but the variation in name did little to erase the monotony of the ugly place.

Blacktooth Otto was a big stupid man who talked more than his employer might have liked, for as they rode toward a rocky canyon which led toward the pass over the mountains leading into Canada, he first said what he had been directed to say: 'You look, huh? This much better than Chilkoot, huh? You come Skagway you got no trouble.' But then he shifted to subjects which really fascinated him: 'Last week, five men shot in White Pass. Next corner, you look, huh?' And when Tom, riding ahead in the excitement of his first day ashore in Alaska, followed the trail around a nest of boulders, he saw dangling over the passage the swaying body of a hanged man.

'What did he do?' he asked, his voice close to shaking as he leaned away to avoid striking the corpse with his shoulder.

'Sheriff and those arrested him.'

Tom thought it strange that a legal arrest should have ended in a hanging along a trail, but Blacktooth Otto next revealed that 'the sheriff and those' had also been responsible for the five shootings, but Missy whispered the words which unlocked the mystery: 'Soapy Smith,' and as they rode deeper into the canyon their guide spoke of other incidents which could be attributed only to the nefarious Soapy.

Tom started to say 'Why doesn't somebody . . . ?' but Missy indicated that he should keep his mouth shut, and the boy dropped that question, asking Blacktooth: 'Why did the sheriff and those feel they had to shoot them?' and he explained: 'Mr. Smith looks after everything. Good man, huh?'

Now the attention of the travelers was diverted from Mr. Smith's curious system of government to a horror much more immediate, because as they entered the first stages of the White Pass trail, which they had to concede was much lower than what the snowy Chilkoot seemed to be in the famous photographs they had seen, the bodies of horses, apparently worked to death among the boulders that strewed the pathway, began to appear, first one with a foreleg broken and a bullet between the eyes, then an emaciated beast that had fallen and found itself unable to rise, and had simply died where it fell.

Tom was sickened by the sight of these once noble animals come to such disastrous ends, but then, at the next corner, they saw a defile which was literally crammed with the fallen bodies of dead horses. He counted seven, their legs at wry angles, their necks draped grotesquely over rocks, and finally they came upon four that had perished one atop the other, and he became sick.

Now a different horror surfaced: a short distance beyond, Blacktooth halted his tour: 'More better we go back.' Two men, partners since leaving Oregon, had come to the end of their expedition and to the end of their horses, for two of their three grotesquely loaded animals had fallen, and each man was kicking and cursing the beast for which he was responsible, and as the men slowly began to realize that these animals would never again rise, they started screaming at them, as if the horses were at fault and not the lack of oats and the poorly stowed burdens and the rocky trail. It was a scene of madness, which revealed the horrors of the trail, and as one of the men whipped out a revolver to shoot one of the fallen horses, his partner, remembering what they had paid for the beasts and still hoping to salvage their services somehow, tried to protest: 'Not my horse, damn you!' whereupon his partner turned his gun away from the fallen horses and shot his companion right through the head.

'We go back, huh?' Otto said, not in fear and not much worried by the incident. Tom and Melissa followed obediently, and for the rest of their journey the boy would have no complaint about the tribulations of the Chilkoot, for he had seen the alternative.

WHEN THEY RETURNED to the *Alacrity* that evening they faced still another change of plan, for the captain revealed that Soapy Smith had come aboard the ship with a warning that if it dared sail to Dyea to unload passengers heading over the Chilkoot, when it was supposed to land them at Skagway, where the Smith hoodlums could get a shot at them, he, Soapy, would direct his sheriff to prevent the ship from ever landing at Skagway again, and any crew members already ashore would be arrested and held in jail till Lynn Canal froze over. In furtherance of his ultimatum, Soapy posted his armed guard along the shore with orders to nab all sailors on shore leave.

Since it was obvious that Soapy held the commanding cards, the captain had acquiesced, announcing to the passengers who were still aboard: 'You must disembark here. Mr. Smith will arrange for the transfer of your baggage to the shore and then over the hill to Dyea,' and when some of the men, unaware of Soapy's reputation, began to demur, the amiable dictator smiled, pardoned himself for intruding in this abrupt way, and explained: 'It's a matter of law and order.'

So next morning the Venns had to supervise the unloading of their three tons of gear and its laborious delivery across the sandy flats to the chaotic shore, where vast mounds of goods lay stacked just far enough inland to escape the tide. When they had their gear assembled, quite a distance from town and some nine miles from the sister port of Dyea, Buck told Missy and Tom: 'We're in real trouble tonight. An officer on ship warned us that if Soapy Smith's men can't trick you in town, they'll rob you here on the beach or along the trail.'

Afraid to leave their goods unguarded on the beach, Buck decided to form a mutual protection arrangement with other stranded travelers, and had started to approach a stranger with such a proposal when he caught Missy's frantic signals to desist. Hurrying back to Missy and Tom, he learned that this was one of Smith's men sent to make just that kind of deal. 'If you'd gone along,' Missy said, 'he'd have steered us to some place where he could have knocked us down and stolen everything of value.'

So the Venns remained on the beach that night, guarding their goods and staying clear of the town where they would have been in greater danger. They were more fortunate than two brave miners with experience on the California gold fields, for when they slam-banged their way into town, willing to challenge anyone to molest them, two of Soapy's henchmen calmly shot each through the heart and left the bodies prone and bleeding in the dusty roadway, where they were ignored by passersby in the morning.

How could such blatant murder have been allowed? How could a boomtown clearly a part of the United States exist without law of any kind other than the smoking end of a revolver? Even the railroad boomtowns of Wyoming, the cattle towns of Kansas, the gold towns of California, the fledgling oil towns of the Southwest had not paraded their lawlessness with such flagrant disregard for organized society; some attempt was always made to preserve orderly government, and an honest sheriff or a powerful clergyman could usually be found to lead the community to a more respectable existence.

Alaska was different because its heritage was different. In the Russian days the Slavic forebears of Soapy Smith said: 'St. Petersburg is far away and God is up in heaven.' When the Americans finally assumed power, there was that incredible thirty-year period when the new owners made no attempt to govern, when there were no codified laws or courts to enforce them. No people in the organized states and, least of all, the members of Congress, could visualize the raw anarchy in which Alaska, this latest and potentially most important addition to the Union, was allowed to rot like a melon at the end of a very long vine. Soapy Smith, this tinhorn Colorado gambler whose crimes at Skagway were far worse than the Venns knew about, was the specific creature of the American system of governing its colonies. If he and his henchmen were a hideous blot on the United States, the culprit was not Smith but the American Congress.

In the morning the Venns, with their goods and their money fortuitously intact, sought to hire two of Smith's draymen to haul their gear the nine miles across the low hills to Dyea, and this transaction could also have produced danger and the possibility of losing everything had not Blacktooth Otto, prowling the beach to see what he might promote, spotted Missy and Tom and recognized them as Soapy's friends. Running to town, he burst into the 317 Oyster Bar with the news: 'Mr. Smith, that lady, that boy, yesterday. They're on the beach.'

Commanding Blacktooth and another henchman to fetch horses and a dray, Smith walked slowly down to the beach, greeting citizens as he went and studying with careful eye the various improvements that had appeared in the growing town since his last inspection. He liked what he saw, but he liked even more that vast accumulation of goods on the flats. If four hundred and fifty stampeders had landed in recent days, and if each had brought a ton of goods, the amassed pile of wealth on the shore was almost incalculable, and Soapy intended siphoning off his fair share, say thirty percent of everything.

When he found the Venns he was exceptionally courteous to Missy, whom he admired, and fairly courteous to Buck. He offered them both whatever assistance they needed, and said: 'I do hope you'll be taking our White Pass and not that dreadful affair at Chilkoot.' Buck, almost trembling with apprehension over being so close to Smith and bewildered by the man's graciousness, said firmly but without the least hint of aggression: 'We've decided to try the Chilkoot.'

'You're making a bad mistake, my friend.' Then Tom blurted out: 'We saw those dead horses in your canyon,' and Soapy replied, with just the slightest touch of irritation: 'Horses are not meant for our canyon. Men have no trouble.'

He asked if they would care to take breakfast with him, prior to their march to Dyea, but Missy replied, as if she were still a stewardess on the *Alacrity*: 'You were far too kind yesterday,' and he bade them goodbye with a flourishing kiss of Missy's hand and a stern admonition to Blacktooth: 'Take special care of these good people.'

They arrived at Dyea, a town much smaller than Skagway but free from the attentions of Soapy Smith and his gang, before noon on 1 April 1898, and there took stock of their situation. 'We can thank God,' Buck said, 'that we escaped Soapy Smith. Only five hundred and fifty miles to go, and most of it a soft ride down the Yukon.'

But they were not wholly free of Soapy Smith, because his man, Blacktooth Otto, lingered as they talked, and when they finished, he surprised them: 'I'm supposed to haul you on to Finnegan's Point.' This was a spot five miles farther up the trail, and since one had to cross and recross the little river running down the middle of the footpath, the assistance would be invaluable.

'We'll go,' Missy said immediately, and when Buck questioned her wisdom, she said wisely: 'Anything to get the gear closer to the pass.'

But after they crossed the corduroy bridge that carried them into Finnegan's, a problem arose which had perplexed every newcomer: there was no hotel, no orderly place to store goods, and no police protection. 'Are we supposed just to dump our goods here?' Buck asked, and Blacktooth said: 'Everyone else does.'

'Who guards them?'

'Nobody.'

'Don't thieves steal them?'

'They better not!' Blacktooth was unable to imagine his boss, Soapy Smith, as a thief, and he supposed that what happened on the trail out of Skagway was always the fault of some careless traveler. Saluting the Venns, he and his partner left the family on the trail, their little mountain of goods piled beside them.

'I'm not going to leave all this here without a guard,' Buck vowed as he began to pitch their canvas tent, but a man who had made many trips along this difficult roadway advised against such action: 'Believe me, pardner, go back to Dyea and get a good night's sleep in a hotel while you have the chance,' and on his own he ran ahead and whistled for Blacktooth to turn around and carry these good people back to Dyea.

The Venns now faced a dilemma: a good bed and a hot meal versus the protection of their cache, and Buck made the decision: 'Sooner or later we'll have to be in one place, our goods in another,' and their adviser said: 'That's talking sense, pardner. Look at all those other caches. That's how we do it.'

As they rode in comfort back to the hotel they could not avoid staring into the faces of gold seekers coming up the trail, and after a few such encounters, Missy could differentiate between them: 'This group coming next, they're on their first trip to Finnegan's. Bright eyes, looking this way and that, oohing and aahing over the snow-covered mountains. But look at these next three! They've been back and forth a dozen times. How can I tell? They look only at the ground to find the best place to step.'

Before depositing the Venns at the Ballard Hotel, Blacktooth Otto confided to Tom: 'You shoulda been in Skagway last night. Two men shot dead on the main street.'

'What did they do wrong?'

'It was dark. You couldn't see.'

Buck was up before dawn, goading his companions to hurry on to their cache, where a team of smiling Indians awaited them: 'We carry goods, Sheep Camp, five cents a pound.' With horror, Buck calculated the bill would be three hundred dollars for a distance of only eight miles, and from Sheep Camp to the summit would cost twice as much.

'We'll carry it,' Buck said, and the Indians predicted: 'You be sorry!'

Because this was not yet the sharp incline, Buck proposed that he try to carry sixty pounds, Tom forty and Missy thirty, and in that disposition they started out. Eight miles on level ground with no pack would have been a smart task, but over this rocky trail with its insistent upward grade it became a torment. Nevertheless, because they were eager and in good shape, they made two round trips that day. At sunset Buck was back at his figuring: 'One hundred and thirty pounds a trip between us. I don't think we can make more than two trips a day. To move three tons . . .' His face grew ashen: 'That's more than three weeks. Hotel bills and all, maybe we better get some Indians,' and when Missy set herself to the task, she found another team, husky young men, who would portage the lot to Sheep Camp for one hundred dollars. After that day's toil, Buck voiced no objection.

Five days later, when they were safe at the Scales, with their gear beside them waiting to be weighed, elevations became more important than distances. It was less than a mile to the summit, but when the Venns stared at that incredible ladder of twelve hundred steps carved out of ice, Tom consulted his map and informed the others: 'When we get there . . . three thousand seven hundred feet high,' and Buck shuddered: 'We've got to carry three tons to that height?'

Missy, the practical one, ignoring this talk of the terrifying climb, said: 'You know, a man could land naked at Dyea beach and outfit himself up here at seven cents on the dollar . . . or maybe for nothing,' and she pointed to a vast accumulation of stuff that had been discarded: 'A man or woman staring at those steps can decide in a hurry that they don't really need a folding table or a sewing machine,' and forthwith she began to identify those things she was sure they could do without.

That night the Venns saw, in all its ugliness, a demonstration of why the leaving of unguarded treasure on the trail was possible, for there was a commotion outside and cries of 'We caught him!' and then a deep voice shouting 'We got him red-handed!'

Even those already asleep piled out of the grubby tent hotels—there were eleven such places, one worse than the other—to witness the drumhead trial of a vagrant named Dawkins who had committed the one unforgivable crime along the trail. Murder in hot blood was acceptable if there was even a shadowy justification; desertion of a wife was not uncommon; and the lesser wrongdoings of a frontier society were tolerated, but on the arctic frontier, where to tamper with a man's cache might mean his death, theft was unforgivable.

Trappers would leave a month's supply of food in some cabin so far removed that you might think no one could ever reach it, but during an unexpected storm some forlorn man would stagger in exhausted, find the can of matches, the carefully cut branches, the pine needles and the food, and he would be saved. He could consume the entire month's supply of food if necessary, but he must replace it. He must cut new branches, ensure that there were matches ready, and leave everything in place for the next emergency. Even if he had to double back fifty miles to replenish the cache, he was honor-bound to do so, and because many a trapper or prospector owed his life to this tradition, it was sacred. In a lawless land this was the supreme law: never violate a cache.

Well, Dawkins had seen stacked at the edge of the Scales an extra parka that would nicely replace his worn and poorly lined affair. The parka had been neatly tied in a bundle and partly hidden in a growing pile of goods, so that no one could possibly believe it had been abandoned, but he had taken it. He had been seen and chased and caught, and now the sourdoughs in the crowd, the old-time Alaskan adventurers as opposed to the newcomer cheechakos, convened a miners' court, a fearsome affair that had become necessary because the government provided no control.

While a lantern was held close to the face of the accused, the men who had caught him stealing told their story, which Dawkins could not refute. 'Shoot him!' a grizzled sourdough cried, and several took up the cry, but a Presbyterian minister, on his way to the gold fields to try to bring a little morality to a corrupted land, protested: 'Men, a sentence like that would be excessive. Show compassion.'

'He showed none. Steal a cache, you murder a man.'

'Give me a gun,' snarled another man. 'I'll shoot him.'

The minister pleaded so earnestly that even some of the sourdoughs reconsidered, and a veteran stood before the clergyman, inches from his face, and offered a compromise: 'We'll give him thirty lashes.'

'Thank God,' the minister said, not guessing what the rest of the sentence was to be.

'But you must apply them. Or we shoot.'

Now Dawkins broke his silence, for he knew the sourdoughs meant business: 'Please, Reverend.'

So Dawkins was stripped, his hands were tied to a stake—which took the place of a tree, for there were none amid the snows—and a rawhide rope with a wooden handle and a big knot tied at the end was handed to the clergyman, while two sourdoughs said: 'We'll count.'

Ashen-faced, the minister accepted the improvised cat-o'-nine-tails, but recoiled: 'I can't.'

'Lash him,' a sourdough shouted, 'or I shoot.'

'Please!' Dawkins pleaded, and the trembling minister, biting his lip and closing his eyes at the crucial moment, swung the rawhide and brought the heavy knot across the man's back. Dawkins made no sound, and the watchers shouted 'Stronger!' But on the sixth lash, when the culprit's back was bleeding, the minister could see only the form of Jesus Christ being lashed by Roman soldiers on the way to Calvary, and he fell prostrate in the snow, his shoulders heaving as sobs wracked his body.

An old prospector, whose life had been saved by a cache north of the circle, snatched the rawhide, and as the solemn voices counted seven . . . eight . . . nineteen . . . twenty the punishment continued, but before the twenty-first blow fell, Missy Peckham threw herself upon the old man's right arm and the beating stopped. Dawkins, who had fainted, was cut down, dressed in his own parka and revived with snow. When he could walk he was headed down the hill to Dyea and told: 'Get going.' He was seen no more.

THE VENNS SLEPT late next day, for it was Sunday, but at about eight Buck began to build nine bundles of gear, with the admonition: 'Today we start up the steps. Endless daylight, so we'll try for three trips.' Then he made a most sensible decision: 'Forget what anybody else is trying to carry. For us, lighter loads. Me, fifty pounds, Tom thirty-five, Missy twenty-five.' At this news Tom did some more calculating: 'Oh! For three tons that's going to be fifty-five trips.'

'Fifty-five it'll have to be,' Buck said, but as he was about to heave Missy's onto her shoulders, men came into camp shouting: 'Avalanche! They're all dead!'

It was not a warning. It was fact. From the southern face of a mountain more than two thousand feet above the Chilkoot, a vast accumulation of snow and ice had come crashing down, burying a portion of the trail to a depth of twenty or thirty feet.

'How many trapped?' Buck shouted as he threw aside Missy's bundle and grabbed for one of the shovels.

'Mebbe a hundred,' and the messenger went shouting up and down the camp as volunteers grabbed whatever they could and rushed toward the avalanche, which was much bigger than the frightened crier had said and had engulfed even more people.

They did not all die. Cheechakos who had been on the trail only a few days, men and women alike, clawed at the snow and ice to make extraordinary rescues. Many had shovels, which were ably used, but one thoughtful man from Colorado, learned in the ways of avalanches, had brought a pole, which he used to probe through the snow till he struck something hard. Then others dug like moles where he indicated, often finding only rock but occasionally bringing to the surface someone still alive. This man and his pole saved more than a dozen.

In all, some sixty gold seekers perished that Sunday morning, but not even a disaster of such magnitude could diminish the passion with which the survivors hungered for gold or slow the incessant traffic up the mountain. Hordes from below had been set in motion, and it seemed that nothing could halt them, not even crushing death. Half an hour after the cascades of snow had obliterated the path to the top, gold-savage men had tramped out a new path, looked sideways at the site of the tragedy, and plodded on.

Because the Venns had spent half a day helping with rescue work, it was late afternoon when they eased their way into the line of prospectors climbing the stairs, and once they claimed a place in that struggling chain, there was no way to rest or turn back; they were on a steep, upward pathway to hell. If a man simply had to urinate, he could step aside and do so with no one noticing, but when he struggled to reenter the chain, he might try vainly for more than an hour. On Chilkoot, no one helped anybody.

The three Venns, clinging tenaciously to their places, approached the last sixty vertical steps as dusk fell, and for one fearful moment Missy wavered and looked as if she might have to surrender her place in the line, but, gasping for breath and nearly fainting with exhaustion, she clawed her way to the summit, looked back at the swarming humans mechanically following her, and thought: My God! To do that fifty-four more times!

In that act of climbing to the top of a mountain, where goods lay stacked in hundreds of different piles, some of them fifteen feet high, the Venns and the other stampeders entered an entirely new world. Arbitrary and chaotic it was, but it was also a world where reason and law prevailed. For this lofty point represented the boundary between American Alaska and the Yukon Territory of Canada. It was a line drawn in the snow with no legal authority to justify it; actually, the American boundary should have been quite a few miles to the east, but this high pass became the permanent boundary between the two nations because some remarkably stout-hearted men said it was.

They were a contingent of the North West Mounted Police, sent out to an undefined border to establish an undefined law. Few men in North America ever served their nation or their people better than these, for when they took one look at the preposterous situation that the Americans had allowed to develop, they said simply, but with great force: 'The law is going to be what we say it is.' And this law, eminently reasonable and just, was forthwith adopted, enforced, and accepted.

Indeed, many Americans struggling up the Chilkoot Pass from the moral swamp of Skagway were gratified to find at the crest of the mountain a body of resolute men who said: 'This is the boundary. These are the laws. And you will obey both.' Like wayward children who have been running wild without supervision but know inwardly that reasonable discipline is better, the cheechakos climbing over the pass embraced the law of the Mounties.

The rules as they evolved on the spot were practical: 'You cannot enter unless you bring in supplies for one year, particularly food. You must pay Canadian customs on every item you do bring in. You cannot sail down the first rough lakes and then the Yukon unless you build yourself a stable boat capable of carrying yourself and your gear. And each boat must be numbered so that we can track its successful passage to Dawson.' They justified this last demand by citing a sobering thought: 'When people went down the lakes in just anything and without proper numbering, scores drowned.'

In obedience to these rules, late on Sunday, 3 April 1898, the Venns placed their first load of goods under the protection of the Mounties, and for the first time since leaving Seattle they felt safe in doing so. But the next days in early April were shattering, for Buck's easy supposition that they could make three round trips a day was totally impractical. The ice stairs were so steep and the weights so punishing that two trips proved the maximum, and on some days the wait to get into line was so protracted that only one trip could be made, and one night Missy groaned as she crept into her sleeping bag: 'Oh God! We'll be at this all of April.'

But they strove diligently, up that icy stairway watching always for the next avalanche, taking not a single step in an upright position, always bent parallel to the earth from the waist up, legs failing, lungs collapsing, sodden eyes fixed to the ground but always vaguely aware of the man ahead, whose back was also parallel to the ground, for he too carried fifty pounds up those stairs of ice.

It was a human effort not matched in America by any of those star-led pioneers who had settled the continent. None had known a worse task than these thirty thousand who climbed the Chilkoot when the late storms of winter were still raging.

On one trip, when Missy and Tom reached the top, they found their earlier deposits under fifteen feet of sudden blizzard and could not even estimate where their vital treasures lay. In their desperation they were assisted by a handsome young sergeant of the Mounted Police, a clean-shaven, blue-eyed man from Manitoba in central Canada named Will Kirby, twenty-eight and determined to make a name for himself in the North West force. He loved the outdoors and had been both a trapper and a voyageur, one who canoed down remote rivers to explore trade possibilities.

When he saw Missy and Tom poking through the April snows, searching for their buried cache, he came to their aid: 'I don't want to see you fretting over a little snow like this. Last January it was seventy feet high up here.'

'That's impossible,' Missy snapped, not eager to be patronized after her exhausting climb, but he produced a photograph of himself and two other Mounties standing then right where they were today, and no sign of habitation was visible: 'It can snow up here. Now, what kind of cache had you been building?'

Mollified by the photograph, although she suspected it was a fake, Missy indicated about where the Venn goods lay and described what they looked like, and as the three shoveled and kicked snow and probed, Sergeant Kirby told them: 'There was a man last January, during the fierce storm, he did a clever thing,' and when he described what this inventive man had done, both Missy and Tom recognized immediately that it could work again. So when they found their cache, with Kirby's help, they hastened down the mountain and told Buck what they had heard. And he cried: 'It'll work!'

He would require several props: a securely fixed rock at the top of Chilkoot, and there were many of them; two sleds, which could easily be made from scattered bits of timber; a very long rope; and five additional men, the heavier the better. Buck saw quickly that he had available all the ingredients except the very long rope, but he had seen among the household goods discarded along the trail from Sheep Camp to the Scales several skeins of heavy rope, so he left

Missy and Tom at their depot and scrambled back down along the trail he had so recently climbed. He did not find the rope he had remembered but he found some of more recent vintage abandoned among the trunks, the furniture and the excessive household goods.

Grabbing the rope, he hurried back to the Scales, where he studied the laboring men about him, settling ultimately upon four likely candidates. Sergeant Kirby had recommended six in all, but Buck believed he could work more effectively with four others besides himself. Assembling them outside his tent, he divulged the plan: 'If we climb to the very top of the Chilkoot, fasten a self-made block-and-tackle to a rock that can't be budged, and build us two sleds capable of carrying us five men, see what we'd have?' And slowly the four listeners began to visualize what the Canadian Mountie had divulged to Missy and Tom: 'Hey, if we five got on one of the sleds and let ourselves slide down the mountain, the other sled packed with our gear would have to go up!'

It worked. They climbed to the top of the pass and found, with Kirby's help, an appropriate rock, to which they attached their crude block with the rope tackle passed through the pulley. When the sleds were attached, top one empty, bottom loaded with gear, the five men climbed to the top carrying very light loads, which they quickly deposited at their respective depots on the Canadian side. They then ran to the waiting sled, onto which they placed themselves so that they could push with their hands, and when the sled was eased to the top of the steep incline, Buck gave the signal and the fifth man, in back, started pushing the sled until it gained momentum. With a final shove which sent it downhill, he jumped aboard, and the men had the extraordinary satisfaction of feeling themselves sliding down the mountain while the other sled, loaded with the heavy baggage, crawled up the hill as if pulled by invisible hands.

The experiment was more successful than even Sergeant Kirby had predicted. Said he when Missy and Tom next reached the top of the mountain: 'It takes an American to build a machine,' and he was pleased as he saw how the men had perfected the operation. These particular Americans were going to negotiate the Chilkoot Pass the easy way.

In the meantime Missy and Tom were making their trips with what might almost be described as joy, for they carried to the top loads that were much diminished but which invariably contained a shovel, and when they unloaded their burdens at the Venn cache and saluted Sergeant Kirby, they moved away from Chilkoot proper, going instead to the very steep slope covered by many feet of snow. Here Missy placed a board on the shovel, pointed the handle downhill, then sat as far forward as possible. Tom, placing himself behind her and resting part on the shovel, part on the extended board, grasped her by the waist and down they sped like children on a painted sleigh.

The ride became so exciting, so refreshing with the cold wind blowing in their faces, that they found themselves actually hurrying up the last few icy steps of the Chilkoot so they could run over to the precipitous drop and hurl themselves downward on their magical shovel. Tom, holding tight to Missy, who half steered the shovel with her heels, felt that this was the most joyous thing he had ever done, exhilarating beyond words, but once when Kirby saw them speed off he became worried, and when they next climbed the pass he took them aside: 'I saw you steering with your heels, Mrs. Venn. I wouldn't do that, because at that speed, if your heel caught on anything, even a small piece of ice, your leg would bend back and it might even tear off. Surely it would snap.' So after that the rides were a little more circumspect, with both Missy and Tom preventing the shovel from descending too fast.

One evening, when Buck's sled and Missy's shovel reached the Scales at the same time, one of the men on the sled told Missy: 'We like the way your husband takes charge of things. You must be proud of him.' And when she talked with Tom during their hikes up the mountain, she said: 'Have you noticed, Tom, how much stronger your father seems to be? Other men show respect for him. He makes decisions and sticks to them.' And Tom replied: 'It's as if he was waiting all those years for this to happen,' and Missy, in a burst of affection for this maturing boy, grasped his hand and added: 'Same thing's happening with you, Tom. By the time we get to the gold fields, you'll be a man.'

Sergeant Kirby, watching this energetic team move its goods so adeptly, told his fellow Mounties one night: 'We've seen some pretty horrible Americans come up that slope. But have you noticed those three Venns? They make up for a lot of the others.'

One of the Canadians asked: 'Why do you look after them so much?' and he said: 'I have a boy at home, about half their boy's age. I'd be happy if he grew up as responsible.' He reflected on this for some moments, then added: 'And I have a lot of respect for a man like Venn who keeps things moving. Who maintains order,' and one of the older Mounties asked: 'You also have quite a bit of respect for Mrs. Venn, don't you?' And there the conversation ended.

The Chilkoot Pass had its photographers, too, men of daring and endurance who lugged huge cameras and heavy glass plates to the most remote locations so as to take three-minute exposures of tiny figures set against vast snowfields. One such bold experimenter was a twenty-one-year-old man born in Sweden but reared in Wisconsin, where at the age of fifteen he had opened a full-time professional photography studio. Mesmerized by the magnitude of the Klondike gold rush, he was one of those prudent men who perceived that his fortune was to be made not washing sand in some mountain stream but in making pictures of the men who were.

He seemed to be present everywhere, his industry combining with good luck to put him in the right place at the right time. For example, on that fatal Sunday when the avalanche struck, he was not far away, and three of his shots show Buck Venn and son Tom, among hundreds of others, digging for bodies. But one of his most memorable pictures, taken on that same day, shows Missy Peckham looking small, determined and appealing against the snow. She stands erect, in heavy boots, a jaunty Russian peasant's cap on her head. Her skirt is extremely full, falling in neat folds to her boot tops and gathered at her waist in a circle so tiny it seemed to divide her into two different halves. Her blouse, not unusually heavy despite the snow, fits very tight across the middle but is voluminous at the shoulders and topped by the neatest possible little collar. Six bright buttons adorn the front, but even such features are obscured by the determination that glows from her face. It is not a pretty face, in the advertiser's sense, but it is so marvelously controlled that it is almost heroic. The young woman who stares from this photograph intended getting to the gold fields.

On the day that the five-man team hoisted the last of its supplies into Canada, and the duties had been paid, the men parted, each following his own vision of how best to reach the gold fields. As the Venns prepared to take their cargo downhill in nine or ten easy sledloads, Sergeant Kirby took them aside for a curious message: 'When a man dies on the slopes, if he's alone, I have the job of looking after his belongings, and if he carried an address, we send his money and his papers home. His goods we sell . . . whatever we can get for them. An old man died up here the other day. Must have been sixty.'

'What's the problem?' Buck asked, and Kirby said: 'He didn't leave much but he did have this very good sail. He may have been connected with ships, because the sewing on the canvas is special.'

'I don't follow.'

'Mr. Venn, hasn't anybody told you? It's a long way to Lake Lindeman. When you get there it'll be frozen, and when you finish with it, there's a far distance to Lake Bennett, where you must build your boat for the river trip to Dawson. But if you mount a sail on your sled, what with the strong winds around here, you'll skim all the way to the lake.' He added: 'I'll sell you the sail for two dollars, and I advise you to take it.' When Buck handed over the two dollars, Kirby asked for a signed and dated receipt: 'We like to keep things strictly legal, seeing two different nations are involved.'

Descending the Canadian side of Chilkoot Pass was almost a pleasure; leaving Tom at the top to help with loading the sled, Buck took Missy down to the bottom of the steep incline to assemble the goods as he brought them down, and he traveled so fast that he often became airborne when vaulting over some bump in the snow. Missy, watching him come around the corner as he approached the rapidly building store of goods, cautioned him: 'Sergeant Kirby warned me not to stick my legs out at the speed Tom and I were going. You're coming down twice that fast. Be careful.'

Once the goods were down off the mountain, the nine miles to Lake Lindeman consisted of a gentle, easily negotiated slope, and now the dead man's sail became invaluable, for Buck built a small wooden box into which the bottom end of the mast could be stepped, and guyed with ropes to keep the top erect. With a yardarm in place, he could expose a huge amount of sail, and thus impelled, could almost sail over the packed snow.

Again the three Venns were separated: Tom guarding the cache at the foot of the mountain, Missy at the delivery point, and Buck either sailing happily downhill with a load of gear or trudging back with the empty sled.

On the last sail downhill from the top of Chilkoot Pass, Buck brought Tom with him, and when the careening sled pulled up where Missy waited, the boy saw that their goods were now stashed beside the first lake, a beautiful body of water whose shores contained a blizzard of white tents housing an informal town of thousands, with snowy roads and two improvised hotels which served hot meals. Gazing in awe at this improbable sight, Tom cried: 'The whole world seems to be white.'

The Venns were now at the spot where the Yukon River was supposed to begin and where Soapy Smith's route from Skagway joined. The repeated cargo trips down Lake Lindeman, about six and a half miles each way, were a dreamlike adventure, for the surface was frozen smooth, allowing the sled to skim along. The surrounding hills were deep in snow, the air was crisp, and there was a constant wind blowing away from the Chilkoot and directly toward where the travelers wished to go. 'This is the best journey we'll have,' Buck predicted as they moved through this world of winter beauty, modified by a strong hint of coming summer in the air.

On his third trip down Lindeman, Buck allowed his sled to slide rather far to the right, which threw him onto an unexpected rough patch in the ice. Wind, or the inflow of water from some unseen stream debouching from the mountains, had caused blocks of ice to erupt, marring the smooth surface. He tried kicking his sled away from them, and sprained his right foot. It was not serious, but he wished to avoid such a problem on his remaining trips, so when he dragged his sled back to the western end of the lake he asked Tom to see if he could find some kind of pole which could be used to maneuver among the ice blocks, and the boy found one about nine feet long and stout enough to protect the sled. On subsequent trips, the wind continued to push Buck toward the right bank, but with the pole he was able to shove the sled away from the blocks.

On his last trip he packed the sled with the remaining eight hundred pounds of gear and perched Tom on top. Lying back, guiding the sled by tugging on the lines holding the sail, they glided speedily down toward Lake Bennett—where they would build their boat for the Yukon—as Tom cried with glee: 'Not a single hill between here and Dawson. We can sail right to our gold mine.'

Then the boy suddenly shouted: 'Pop! Rough ice ahead!' and Buck called back: 'I see it. I know how to get past.' He swung his pole out, but this time the load was so heavy and the speed so great that the end of the pole caught in a huge block of ice, then wedged itself in a crevice.

When the pole began to bend in an alarming arc, Tom shouted: 'Pop! Let go!'

Too late. The pole snapped, the near end dangling uselessly from Buck's hands, the other, jagged and torn, springing forward like an arrow shot from some giant bow. It hit Buck in the middle of his chest, not like a sliver of steel but like the shattered end of a lance, tearing a hole big and crude and brutal.

When Buck saw the blood spurt out, he looked helplessly at his son, and Tom saw his father's wind-hardened face grow ashen. His hands left the pole and reached up, and he clutched at the wound. He looked once more at his son as a pulsating flow of blood gushed from his mouth; then he collapsed as the sled, sail aloft, sped serenely down the lake.

WILL KIRBY WAS policing the seven thousand boats being built along Lake Lindeman and the waterway leading to Lake Bennett when he heard that yet another prospector had been killed coming down from Chilkoot Pass, and with a sense of irritation with Americans who barged into dangers they did not comprehend, he hurried up to where reports said the accident had occurred. He was shaken to find that the dead man was Buchanan Venn, who had proved himself so reliable on the pass, and when he came upon the woman Missy and her son and found them shivering beside the lake, bereft and unable to focus upon the manifold problems that now confronted them, he felt great pity for them and did what he could to help.

'We'll look after you. We don't allow women to suffer disadvantage on this trail.' Taking Tom aside, he said firmly: 'Now we see whether you're going to be a man or not,' and he was gratified to watch the boy respond by taking charge of the sled that had killed his father.

Gathering them beside the lake, he said: 'It's my job, you know, to see that the dead man's goods are properly handled . . . a legal disposition, that is,' and he was startled by the amount of money Buck had carried, and he warned: 'Mrs. Venn, I can't just hand this money over to you. Much too dangerous. I'll ask Superintendent Steele to take charge of this till you reach Dawson.'

Kirby's statement raised two difficult questions, and Missy took each in turn: 'I'm not Mrs. Venn. But half the money Buck carried is mine. And I will not turn my half over to anyone.' Kirby nodded, but stood by his first judgment: 'We'll wait till Superintendent Steele gets here on his inspection.'

The search of Buck's property turned up two items which Missy and Tom would not allow him to keep. The first was an envelope containing the hundred-dollar bill for the Belgian Mare, which, as Missy explained, belonged to her: 'We have nothing to do with it except to deliver it.'

Sergeant Kirby smiled indulgently: 'But, ma'am, don't you see? It's just this kind of money we can't have floating around with a defenseless woman. I must keep it. She'll get it, I assure you.'

'But I must deliver it . . . personally. It's an obligation.'

'And so you shall.' But the envelope with the money he filed in his blouse.

There was no argument about the paper Tom defended: 'An engineer drew this for me. It's plans for the boat we'll have to build,' and when Kirby handed back the sketch, after surveying it, he said: 'That man could draw. Whoever he was, he knew boats.'

'If we build like that,' Tom asked, 'can we sail it to Dawson?'

And now the gravest problem of all arose, one that Will Kirby had had to face several times before: 'Sit down, please. I need your full attention.' Standing soldierlike and handsome before them in his proper uniform of striped trousers, neat jacket with ornaments and big hat, he was a figure of authority, and both Missy and Tom were prepared to listen to him.

'The question is: "Do you really want to go on to Dawson?" Now wait, don't answer too fast.' And then he outlined the disadvantages of their position: 'There's twenty thousand people along these lakes, waiting for the ice to melt. You'll be lost in a stampede. You have no man to help you. Anyone can ride over you. And even if you do get there, you must realize that all the good spots will be taken. And maybe I shouldn't say all the *good* spots, maybe I should say *all* the spots. Your goods will last maybe half a year. Your money will begin to run out. And then what will you do?'

Missy and Tom looked at each other, and she spoke: 'The man who gave us that money for the Belgian woman . . . the Klondike Kernel he called himself . . .'

'I've heard of him. Crazy sometimes, but very reliable.' He chuckled, then asked: 'Did he tell you what I just told you?'

'He did.'

'But you came anyway?'

'We did.'

'Mrs. Venn . . . Excuse me, the papers say you're Miss Peckham and he's young Mr. Venn. To go to Dawson with a man to protect and guide you is one thing. To go alone is quite another.' He felt it necessary to shock these people into considering reality: 'Surely, a woman like you . . . you're not planning to enter the cribs, are you?'

Missy did not flinch: 'I have not that intention.'

'Well, it's my duty to see that Mr. Venn's property is legally handled. I give you and his son the sled, all the gear, the boat-building equipment. The money and the papers other than the boat plans I must hold on to.'

To everyone's surprise, even his own, Tom rose and stepped forward: 'You can't do that. We saw what happened at Skagway.'

Kirby nodded, pleased rather than offended that the boy should take such protective action: 'You're right. You're entitled to verification.' And he sent Tom scouting around the end of the lake for other members of the North West Mounted Police, and when two young men in uniform reported to the Venn tent, Kirby returned their salute and explained the situation: 'From previous experience at Skagway, Miss Peckham and young Mr. Venn refuse to surrender the dead man's goods to our care until an adjudication can be made.'

'Oh, but you must!' the younger of the two officers said.

'How can we trust him?' Missy asked. 'How can we trust you?'

'Ma'am,' the officer said, 'if you can't trust Sergeant Kirby, you can't trust

anybody,' and the other one said: 'And if you go to Dawson . . . alone . . .
Ma'am, you've got to trust somebody.'

The two Mounties watched as Kirby wrote out a receipt, then they signed
it and handed it to Missy, but she passed it along to Tom: 'He's Buck's son,' and
one of them asked: 'But aren't you his wife?' and she said: 'No.'

Three days later, as thousands milled about at the lower end of Lake
Lindeman preparing for the dash to Lake Bennett and the building of their
boats, Sergeant Kirby brought to the Venn tent a hefty, mustachioed officer who
had won the reputation of being the Lion of the Yukon. He was Superintendent
Samuel Steele, incorruptible dispenser of frontier justice. Tall, deep-chested and
exuding a sense of power, he wore a large black cowboy hat and no visible gun;
every movement, every gesture bespoke authority but also compassion. He had
jurisdiction over a wild, almost ungovernable domain, with now more than
twenty thousand strangers about to descend upon a city which had not even
existed three years ago, and all men subject to his orders agreed that he was just.

He allowed a street of prostitutes, where the Belgian Mare ruled. He permitted saloons to run openly and gambling dens too, but the drinks and the wheels
had to be honest. Before any bank had opened in his town, he had served as the
repository for miners' funds, and no money was lost while in his care. He
insisted that Sunday be observed. There was no wild shooting on the streets, as
had become so prevalent in American boomtowns, and he outlawed murder. If
any man brazenly transgressed his rules, he himself went after him, faced him
down, and threw him out of Canada.

It was this man who now stood before Missy Peckham and the boy Tom:
'I am most grieved to hear of your tragic loss.' Missy said nothing; she was
hoarding her strength for the contest ahead. 'And I understand your reluctance
to have us take charge of your dead husband's money.'

'He wasn't my husband,' Missy said.

'To us he stood in that regard.' As he said this he nodded gravely, for Kirby
had informed him as to Missy's stalwart character.

'Now, ma'am, we've decided that the money involved is legally this young
man's.'

'I agree. It's certainly not mine.' But when Superintendent Steele started to
smile at this easy concession, Missy stopped him: 'But the half that's mine,
which I earned as a waitress and aboard the *Alacrity*, that I want.'

'And you shall get it,' Steele said. 'But not here. Not in this jungle where we
can't protect you.'

'Why not?'

'I'm not thinking about you so much, ma'am, as I am of my men. They can't
protect you from here to Dawson. The things you'll be going through . . .' He
stopped. 'You are determined to go ahead? We'll help you back over the pass,
you know, if you want to return home, like I think you should.'

'We're going to Dawson.'

'When you reach there, we'll deliver your money, safe and sound.'

Missy was close to tears. In the short time since Buck's death, she had made
herself into a resolute woman, aware of the dangers that would be facing her and
Tom in an unprotected trek to Dawson, but this constant pressure from the
struggle up the Chilkoot, from death, and now from these official-looking men
was almost too much: 'How do we know you're all not another gang of Soapy
Smiths?'

It was a frontal attack, and so relevant that Superintendent Steele fell back
a step. Yes, how did an unprotected woman know that there was a difference?

He gave a strange yet reassuring answer: 'Ma'am, I'd like to be in Skagway one week, with three or four men like Sergeant Kirby.'

She trembled, put her hand to her upper lip, and looked at the two men, whereupon Kirby told her an amazing fact: 'Did you know that on the day of the avalanche, Soapy dispatched four of his men to the scene to see what they could steal of the dead men's belongings? Ugly brutish oaf named Blacktooth Otto led them, and they made off with quite a bit, we're told.'

'How could you permit such a thing?' she asked, and Steele reminded her: 'That's Alaska, ma'am. Not our territory. That's how they do things over there. In Canada we don't allow it.' And Kirby said: 'Superintendent Steele and one of his men would handle Soapy in one afternoon. Wouldn't even last till nightfall.'

Reassured, she decided she could trust these men, and as they parted, Steele said: 'We never lose a customer. We'll see you in Dawson.' Then he added: 'Sergeant Kirby, see they build themselves a proper boat. And give it a lucky name. We need people like them in Dawson.'

They did not see Kirby again until they had painfully moved all their gear across the short distance from Lake Lindeman to the much more important Lake Bennett, which was, in some ways, the water equivalent to the snowy Chilkoot Pass, for here decisions of life and death were made. They concerned boats, because every traveler to Dawson City was required by the Mounties to build or buy a boat capable not only of sailing the five hundred and fifteen miles to Dawson but also sound enough to survive a fearsome canyon and several sets of violent rapids.

The reason they did not see Kirby was that it took him a while to find them. The shores of icebound Lake Bennett housed an exploding tent city of about twenty thousand would-be prospectors, each engaged in building a boat. Trees were felled at a speed which denuded the surrounding hills, and whipsaw pits were dug everywhere. The song of Lake Bennett was the rasping of saws, the hammering of nails, and this music continued around the clock. Men who had never been near water four months ago were now studying how to bend a length of wood to conform to the shape of a boat, and the results were staggering in their ineptitude and variety.

One group of men constructed a scow that could have handled a railroad train. A sole adventurer built himself a snug little boat about eight feet long; the Mounties would not allow it to enter the dangerous passages, so he hired an Indian to help him portage it six miles. Prudent men kept the sails with which they had come down the slopes and across Lake Lindeman, and those who knew something about rapids and rock-strewn gorges built very long, heavy oars which they mounted on the rear of their boats and called sweeps; a man with strong nerves operating a sweep could avoid a lot of trouble.

When Missy and Tom erected their tent on a preferred spot near the edge of the lake with a whipsaw pit already constructed, they were able to do so only because sharp-eyed Missy saw two men about to quit the place and move their finished boat, a twenty-two-footer, to a spot more favorable for quick launching. When she asked them if she could have the spot they were vacating, they said: 'Sure. But if you ain't started your boat yet, you're gonna miss the armada.'

That afternoon Missy and Tom started the formidable task of building their twenty-three-footer. He visited all the sites within walking distance, asking if anyone had extra planks to sell, or good nails, and in this way he accumulated more boards already sawn than he had expected. He then went into the remaining woods with his ax and felled trees till dusk, and since it was already spring, with the sun heading north, sunset did not come till nearly eight and darkness not till more than an hour later, so he was dog-tired when he quit.

Next morning they were both at work before sunrise, which came at half past four, and this was the way they passed the rest of April. Missy spent the morning cooking for men who paid her well for pancakes, bread and beans and in the afternoon she went into the woods, helping Tom drag home the logs he had felled. When they calculated they had enough to provide the planking needed for their boat, they gritted their teeth and began the cruel work of whipsawing out the boards required.

When they succeeded in maneuvering their first log into position over the pit, they faced the problem of who would work from the top, pulling the saw up, and who down at the bottom, pulling it down. Tom, believing the hardest work to be at the bottom end of the seven-foot whipsaw, volunteered for that spot; he was wrong about the difficulty of the work, for the person topside had to pull upward till his arms ached, but he was right in thinking that the bottom work was much more unpleasant, for down in the pit that sawyer was going to eat a constant supply of sawdust as it fell upon him.

How easy it seemed when one explained the process, how brutally difficult when one had to do it. At the end of the first long day, Missy and Tom had barely squared off the first log, and had done so with such ineptness, the line wandering as if the man who drew it was drunk, that they despaired. But when they faced each other in the tent that night, Missy said grimly: 'Dammit, Tom. We learn to cut the boards or we rot here while the others sail on.' He did not point out that much of their failure stemmed from the fact that she could not keep the saw in a straight line.

Next day they tackled their work with even more seriousness than they had shown before, and although Missy's line wavered more than it should, they did hack out three rather good boards, and went to bed satisfied that with determination they could master the whipsaw. Tom was so worn-out that he fell asleep before he could brush the sawdust from his hair.

For five dreadful days, as the ice in Lake Bennett prepared to soften, the pair kept to the drudgery of whipsawing. Their hands produced blisters and then callouses. Their back muscles tightened and their eyes grew dull, but on and on they went, stacking up the precious boards upon which their lives would soon depend.

On the day when Missy doubted that she could continue much longer, for she could barely lift her arms to pull the heavy saw, Sergeant Kirby found them after looking into some two thousand tents. 'You've done wonders,' he said, patting Tom on the shoulder. 'I see you have Missy up there where she belongs. Good for you.'

The exhausted sawyers were so glad to see Kirby that for the moment they forgot their pains and worked the great saw with a vigor, but he noticed that Missy was operating on courage alone, so he scrambled to the top of the structure, gently lifted her to the ground, and took the top handle. As soon as he did so, Tom could feel the difference. The saw came down with more strength, stayed closer to the line, and was pulled back up with authority. For about two hours the two men ripped down the squared-off log, producing planks at a speed Tom had not felt possible.

At the noon break Missy had soup ready, and Kirby stayed at the pit most of that afternoon. He returned next day to help Tom finish off the planking whose length had been determined by the Kernel's drawing, and that night Kirby stayed for supper.

When the actual building of the boat started, with a heavy keel neatly formed, Kirby appeared frequently to give not only advice but also his valued assistance in shaping the form of the boat. He took his meals there too, providing meat and vegetables from his own sources of supply, and late one afternoon Missy came to Tom with a curious request: 'Tom, could you maybe sleep over in the Stantons' tent tonight?' He stood stock-still, hands at his side, his head in a whirl. He was fifteen years old and Missy was twenty-three, and under no conceivable circumstances would he have said that he loved her, but he had admitted to himself many times in recent months that she was the best woman he had ever known. Never did he refer to her as a girl; a girl would be someone his own age and he had met several in school who were attractive, with every promise of becoming more so as the years passed. Missy was a woman; she had been the salvation of the Venns during the years of privation and the agent of his father's rejuvenation. She was a wonderful person, courageous, hardworking, amiable, and on those trips down the mountain on the shovel he had clung to her as if they were one person engaged in a great adventure. Recently, as they worked on the whipsaw, he had known how mortally tired she was, and he had wished that he might have done all the work himself. Indeed, he had pushed up and pulled down with doubled effort to spare her, and he did so almost joyously, for his affection for this strong-minded woman went beyond words. He felt they were a team, not one that conformed to any ordinary description, but a pair of like-minded, strong people. They would cut their planks, and build their boat, and guide it through the canyons and past the rapids, and what happened when they got to Dawson was a problem for another day. Now he was being asked to take his bedroll somewhere else, and he felt displaced.

But when Sergeant Kirby moved into Missy's tent, the building of the boat took a leap ahead, for the Mountie had had numerous experiences with the very rough waters that the stampeders would be facing as soon as they left placid Lake Bennett, and this knowledge caused the first rupture between him and Tom. When he saw that Tom proposed building the boat to the exact specifications laid down in the Klondike Kernel's sketch, he asked: 'Are you sure you want it that big? Two people could ride in something a lot smaller.'

'That's what he said. Look.' There the figures were: '23' long and 5' 6" in the beam' and that's what the boat would be.

'The point is,' Kirby said, 'there are two places which are extremely dangerous, Miles Canyon and Whitehorse Rapids. A lot of boats are lost there, lives too.'

'He said a boat like this would make it,' Tom said firmly, not designating who the *he* was.

'I'm sure he said it. But if you had a boat half that size, you could still pack all your gear, and when you came to the bad spots you could hire Indians to help you portage around. You have the money, I know that.'

'The boat has to be this long,' and it was remarkable to see this city boy, who knew nothing of either wood or shipbuilding, join the timbers to the keel and form them moderately well at the forward post. With help from Kirby and Missy at the difficult joins, and with constant reference to both the sketch the Kernel had provided and the thin metal square his father had bought, Tom built a boat that was better than nine-tenths of those put together by experienced men.

When it was finished, he was disgusted with the number of open chinks he had left where boards did not join accurately, but Kirby laughed: 'Tom, all boatbuilders leave chinks. That's why we have caulking.'

'What's that?'

'Oakum.'

'And what's that?'

'Hemp and tar. You hammer it into the open spots and make the boat watertight. Otherwise you'd sink.' And suddenly Tom and Melissa realized that in this leaky craft built by a fifteen-year-old boy they were about to trust their lives on a five-hundred-mile run down extremely dangerous waters.

'Where do you get the tar and the other?'

'You ought to have brought it with you, but you didn't. Your Kernel couldn't think of everything, could he?' But Kirby had an idea: 'We'll go to men finishing their boats and see if they'll sell us the caulking they have left over.' And when a bizarre collection of substitutes for real caulking was assembled— horsehair, forest moss, strips of linen, burlap—they tamped the mélange into the cracks, then sealed them with another outrageous mixture of wax, bear fat, tar and pitch, and when all was completed, young Tom Venn could send his first letter home to his grandmother:

> Pop was killed when a spruce pole doubled back and ran him through. He died brave. Missy and I are now in Canada so I think it's all right to give you our address, Dawson City, as I don't think anybody could arrest us here. I have built a boat twenty-three feet long and five and a half feet in the beam and in a test it floated like a duck. As soon as the ice clears the lake we head down the Yukon River, a fine easy trip all the way. I wish Missy had married Pop.

On Sunday morning, 29 May 1898, the thick ice which had held Lake Bennett in its cold embrace for nearly nine months relaxed its hold and started cascading down the narrow river, which, after ninety miles, tumbled first into a high, rock-walled canyon and then over stupendous rapids before it reached the relative calm of the soon-to-be-clear Yukon. Tom, watching the first open lanes of free water appear like jagged daggers across the surface, shouted: 'It's breaking up!' But Missy and Kirby did not hear his cry, because men in all parts of the vast tent city were shouting and firing their guns.

'Lake Bennett is bustin' open!' More than seven thousand homemade boats edged toward the shoreline as if everyone had to be first out of the lake and first to the gold fields of the Klondike. It was an armada such as had never been seen before, with hardly any two of the crazy boats alike, but into the icy waters of the lake they came, pushed and pulled by straining men who wondered why they had built them so big that ordinary men could not launch them. The great scows had to be wedged in; the one-man affairs—those that would be turned back before the canyon—could be carried down on the back of the solitary owner. But all that Sunday and the days that followed, the boats were launched, the sails were set, and the men floated toward their treacherous rendezvous with the rapids.

Each boat that set forth, regardless of size, had to carry a name, a number and, in the files of the Mounties, a list of all passengers, for during the previous year too many had been lost. When the time came to christen the Venn boat, which would be Number 7023, Sergeant Kirby had several appropriate suggestions for a name, but once more Tom interrupted to establish the fact that this was his boat: 'It's the *Aurora*. After the northern lights.'

It was not launched during the first mad scramble, since, as Kirby pointed out, 'you're not rushing to get to the gold fields themselves, let the others break their backs.' And then he said a revealing thing: 'We can drift down at our own speed.'

'Are you coming with us?' Tom asked, part of him hoping that the answer was yes, because he'd heard about the dangers of the canyon and the rapids, part hoping for a no, because he resented Kirby's relationship with Missy.

'I want to be sure you get through the bad parts,' Kirby said, and on the second of June he called for help from three other Mounties stationed at Bennett, and with many cries of encouragement, for Tom's boat was heavy, the *Aurora* was launched, the foremast was stepped and guyed, the big sail was made ready, and the long sweep which Kirby would operate from the stern was fitted into its slot.

'Good sailing!' Kirby's fellow officers shouted. 'Find yourself a gold mine!'

It was twenty-six miles to the exit from Lake Bennett, and the *Aurora*, despite her ample sail and the professional steering of Kirby, did not reach that spot before a kind of gentle semidarkness settled like a comforting blanket thrown over the water. Eager to get a fair start in the morning, and loath to tempt the turbulent water ahead in the night, Kirby nosed the *Aurora* into the right bank and asked Tom to make fast the line which he threw ashore.

They slept on the boat that night, and early next morning left Lake Bennett for the long run to the perilous segment of their voyage, the three-part terror where careless or boastful men without sure knowledge lost their lives. When the June sun was high, thawing snow on the surrounding mountains, Kirby pulled the *Aurora* into a small stream of melt-water seeping down from the heights, and there he spelled out what lay ahead: 'In the space of two and a half miles, so much happens, and so fast, that you can be forgiven if you lose your courage.'

'What is it?' Missy asked, for she knew that because she was a woman the decision would be left to her.

'First a canyon, deep and very swift. Water piles up six feet higher in the middle than on the sides. You catch your breath. Then a pair of rocky rapids.'

'Then what?'

'Then a peaceful sail downriver to Dawson.'

'Have you ever taken a boat through?'

'I have.'

'Then let's go!' Tom cried, but Kirby said: 'No. You can make this decision only after you've seen for yourself.'

'And if we turn coward?' Missy asked, and he whipped about as if he had been struck: 'Dammit, ma'am! Some of the bravest men in Canada and America take one look at that canyon and say "No, thanks." It's not because they're cowards. It's because they have the good sense to realize they don't know a damn thing about boats.' He glared at Tom: 'Do you know anything about boats?' And Missy replied: 'We don't, but you do.'

Subdued by the seriousness of what they were about to encounter, the three people in the *Aurora* moved swiftly downriver toward the entrance to Miles Canyon, first of the tests, but as they neared it, a group of men gathered on the right bank shouted to them: 'Better not try the canyon in a boat like that. You'll sink sure.'

Tom, who was steering through the easier water, headed for the shore, and the men, seeing a woman aboard, tried to frighten her: 'Ma'am, I sure wouldn't try that canyon in that there boat.' Kirby, aware that these men condemned all boats about to enter the canyon, called: 'What do you suggest?'

'We're practiced hands. We'll guide you through, safe and sound.'

'How much?'

'Only a hundred dollars.'

'Too much,' Tom cried, and the men yelled back: 'Then portage around. Indians'll do it for two hundred.'

'Thanks,' Kirby shouted. 'But we may risk it.'

'Ma'am, before you do, please go to the other bank, rest your boat, and climb up that little hill to see what awaits you in the canyon. Then come back and pay us ninety dollars, and we'll see you through, safe and sound, like we say.'

Kirby took over the sweep, and when they were well out from shore, he headed directly toward the other bank, as the men had suggested: 'I planned to do this anyway. You must see what faces you.'

When they were atop the cliff and looking down into the turbulent canyon, even Tom, who had been eager to try it, grew afraid, for below them rushed the icy waters flooding out from the lakes, and as they roared in they turned and twisted and threw white spume.

'Oh!' Missy cried, and when the others looked to where she was pointing, they saw at the exit a series of jagged rocks, barely above the waterline, onto which three or four small craft had foundered. All goods had been lost in the swift current, but it looked as if the passengers had saved themselves by clinging to the rocks.

Suddenly Missy and Tom lost much of their desire to test this canyon, but now a boat much like theirs came down the approach, manned by two bearded prospectors whose faces could not be clearly seen. They might have been in their twenties, but they could also be tested older hands in their forties. The would-be pilots on the bank hailed them, there was the same discussion, and the same rejection of the hundred-dollar offer. The two men would venture into the canyon relying upon their own skills.

They had no rear sweep, but they did appear to be powerful paddlers, and as their craft leaped toward the swirling waters where the canyon narrowed and the rushing water increased its speed, they paddled with fury and dexterity. Tom had never before seen skilled men handle a boat, and he was thrilled when the craft headed directly at a menacing cliff, then swung safely past as the men paddled heroically. In less than a minute and a half the boat shot out the far end, and Tom cheered.

But now the boat must clear the rocks on which former attempts had come to grief, and instinctively Tom shouted: 'Watch out!' As if obedient to his warning, the men paddled even faster than before and scraped by the rocks to which the marooned prospectors held. Their heavy boat dipped and darted, more like a bird skimming the calm waters of a lake than a small craft caught in big turbulence. It was a masterful performance, and both Tom and Missy were willing to try duplicating it.

'You ready?' Kirby asked, and Missy asked him: 'Can we do as well?' and Kirby said: 'That's why I've come along.' Then, to Tom: 'You're captain. It's your boat.'

'Let's go!'

'And if we make it, which I believe we can, do you want to head right into the other rapids?'

'Yes.' The boy felt certain that his father, had he lived, would have made the same choices.

So the three climbed down from their perch, returned to the boat, and pushed off as the men on the opposite shore shouted: 'Good luck! Hope you make it!'

The passage of the *Aurora* was almost a duplicate of the one made by the two skilled paddlers. Kirby stayed aft to work the sweep, Missy and Tom perched forward with paddles, but they had been in the canyon only a few yards when a rock, not visible before, threatened them from Tom's side, and instinctively he thrust out his paddle and shoved it against the rock. As he did, the paddle bent, and Missy screamed: 'Tom!' but he pulled away and no damage was done.

There was another variation. As the *Aurora* shot out of the canyon and neared the rocks on which the castaways were huddled, Sergeant Kirby, in line of duty, headed almost straight for them, cocking his sweep just so, and when he was abreast of the terrified people, but moving so fast that any rescue was impossible, he shouted: 'We'll be back to get you. Mounted Police.' No words along the Yukon trail could have been more reassuring, and as the *Aurora* sped past, the abandoned men waved and shouted, for now they knew they were to be saved.

WHEN KIRBY GUIDED them through the last set of breathtaking rapids, spume high at the prow and wrecked boats leering at them as if to warn: 'One false move of that sweep and you join us!' the Mountie headed the tested boat toward a point in the direction of Lake Laberge where he must leave them. As they pulled the nose of the *Aurora* onto dry land, he said approvingly: 'Tom, you built yourself a fine boat.'

'I was scared,' the boy said. 'Not in the canyon. You keep to the middle where the water bulges up, you make it. And it's all so swift. All you need there is courage. But in those rapids, there you have to know something. I couldn't have done that.'

'Well now,' Kirby said. 'Maybe you've said the wisest thing on this trip. Courage for the canyon. Knowledge for the rapids.' He stopped, winked at this boy who gave such promise of becoming a fine man, and said: 'Which is the important factor? What do you think, Missy?'

'I don't think you ever gain real knowledge unless you have courage to begin with.'

Tom had other ideas: 'Anybody can have courage. Just grit your teeth. But to handle a boat, or a gun, or someone like Soapy Smith . . . that takes knowing.'

'Let's not make this too serious,' Kirby said. 'Lots of men get through that canyon and the rapids.'

'And lots don't,' Tom said, remembering the wrecks.

The boy hoped that he could retain contact with this excellent man who knew how to meet contingencies. When they crashed through the final rapids with the *Aurora* almost vertical in the air, Kirby had calmly brought her around, then shouted to two Mounties who were checking the numbers of the boats that made it: 'Exit from the canyon. Men marooned. Send heavy boat through from the other side.' No heroics, no speeches. Find a heavy boat and get started. Tom could visualize how the rescue would be handled, the boat drifting past the rocks, the rope thrown, the kept end led ashore lower down, both ends fastened tight, the people working their way ashore while grasping the rope.

'It would be fun being a pilot through those waters,' Tom said, and Kirby replied: 'Three years ago not six canoes a year came through. Three years from now there won't be seven.'

'Won't the Klondike produce forever?'

'Nothing does.'

Tom sensed that Kirby's parting from Missy was going to be a painful affair, so he left the boat and walked along the shore while they said farewell. The sergeant told Missy of his son in Manitoba and of his wife. He reminded her of what an exceptional boy Tom was and he almost commanded her to look out for his welfare. He said that in some ways Dawson City was rougher than Skagway, but that Superintendent Steele could always be counted on. And he challenged her to find sensible employment: 'I'll be in Dawson one of these days. I don't want to see you down on your heels in mud.'

Then he said that he loved her, and he was heartsick that she had lost Buck Venn, who seemed one of the best men to come over the Chilkoot, and he wished her well. He hoped that her dreams would come true, whatever they were, and he ended with a statement she would cherish: 'You're strong. You're like the ravens.'

'What does that mean?' she asked, and he said: 'They survive. Even in the goddamnedest parts of the arctic, they survive.' And he said no more, moving away quickly to avoid the necessity of speaking with Tom again.

AT LAST THEY could relax. In Chicago they had been afraid of Tom's mother's lawyers, and in Seattle they were always looking over their shoulders lest her detectives track them down. In Skagway they feared Soapy Smith, and on the Chilkoot they had feared everything. Then death came and the horrors of the whipsaw, and then the canyon and the rapids. Now, by damn, they were drifting down the placid ice-free Yukon in just about the best boat on the river, and they took it easy.

Tom found special delight in being alone with Missy, as if the real voyage to the gold fields was back on target, and one afternoon as they drifted past the mouth of the Pelly, a large river coming in from the east, he asked abruptly: 'Did you know that Sergeant Kirby has a boy back in Manitoba?' and she replied: 'Yes, and a wife too, if that's what's bothering you.'

He thought about this for some minutes, then said: 'You know, Missy, if you keep going with men who have wives, you're never going to get married.'

'Tom, what's getting into you?'

'I was thinking how good it would be for all of us if you could marry Sergeant Kirby.' When she made no comment, he added: 'Then the three of us could stay together.'

Only then did she realize that Tom was disturbed about what they would do when they reached Dawson, and she confessed to him: 'Tom, I don't know what we'll do in Dawson. I'm as worried as you are. You remember this. We're a team. We won't be separated.'

'We better not be.'

'So you look after me, Tom, and I'll look after you.'

'Shake hands on that?' They shook hands, and she said: 'What's more, we'll seal it with a kiss,' and she leaned across the drifting boat and kissed him on the forehead.

In the last warming days of spring, when ice had left the rivers, they passed that series of streams whose waters joined to build the mighty Yukon: the White, the Stewart, the Sixtymile, and when Tom visualized the vast hinterland that had to be drained to form such rivers, he appreciated what an immense land this part of Canada was. America had seemed big when he and Buck and Missy crossed it by train, but it was broken into manageable units by the little towns and big cities along the way. From Dyea, which was nothing, to Dawson City, which hadn't existed at all three years ago, there was nothing, not a town, nor a train, nor even a road.

Some nights they dragged their boat onto the right bank of the Yukon and pitched a tent, especially if they wanted to do some cooking, but on others they simply drifted in the silvery light, for always as they moved further north the nights became shorter and the twilights so extended that sometimes there seemed to be no night at all, only deepened shadows through which the ever-present ravens flew.

As they lazed along they were sometimes passed by other boats whose passengers, hungry for the Klondike, were rowing through the arctic haze. 'Where you from?' a voice would hail, and Tom would shout back: 'Chicago,' and the voice would respond: 'Minnesota,' and somehow this simple recitation of names signified a great deal to the travelers.

At last the *Aurora*, showing almost no leakage, turned a bend in the river, and its owners saw ahead on the right the formless outlines of a tent city, much smaller than Dawson had been reported to be, and they were disappointed, but then Tom consulted the sketch the Kernel had provided: 'That's got to be Lousetown. And here's the Klondike coming in, and Dawson City will be dead ahead.'

And there it was, this fabulous place with more than a thousand boats occupying its riverfront and outlining the site. It was a dream city, composed of nothing, a nightmare city, perhaps, with more than twenty thousand residents now and another five thousand out on the diggings, and both Missy and Tom felt their hearts beat faster as the *Aurora* neared the end of its journey. They were excited not only by the imminence of the decision they would soon have to make but also by the limitless possibilities, and as Tom edged their boat toward the shore and then elbowed his way to a landing spot, Missy suddenly cried: 'Tom, we've made it! Tomorrow we'll find Superintendent Steele and be on our way!' She betrayed no doubt as to the success of their adventure.

It was three hectic days before they found Steele's headquarters, and then they learned that he was downriver at Circle, more than two hundred miles away. But a woman at the Mounted Police headquarters assured Missy that yes, the superintendent had alerted her that Miss Peckham would be stopping by, and yes, her money was safe. The superintendent would deliver it as soon as he returned.

In the waiting days Missy and Tom had ample opportunity to explore Dawson, but ten minutes would have sufficed to learn all that was needed. The streets were incredibly muddy, and peopled by men in beards and heavy dark clothing. Material of every description had been utilized in the making of huge white signs proclaiming all the services usually found in an ordinary town plus those unusual additional ones necessary in a mining boomtown. Dawson, it seemed to Missy, was a place in which thousands of men stood around doing nothing and in which everything was for sale. Six different emporiums announced WE SELL OUTFITS and four others announced that they bought them.

Each night Missy and Tom returned to the riverfront and the tent they had wedged in among a hundred others, and after the third aimless day of wandering these crowded, meaningless streets, they took serious counsel. Missy said: 'Tom, you and I will never find a place in the gold fields. That's for men who know what they're doing.'

'I'm willing to try.'

'No!'

Her curt dismissal annoyed him: 'If the men I see are clever enough to find gold, so are you and me.'

'Two years ago, yes. But now we'd have to go ten, fifteen miles into the country. Spend a winter there, maybe.'

'If I can build a boat, I can build a cabin.' The idea of spending a winter helping a woman like Missy was not distressing; it was downright agreeable.

But Missy, haunted by the doleful predictions of the Klondike Kernel, saw that he had been correct. The gold of the Yukon lay in servicing the great mass of men, not in competing with them. Sixteen lucky miners were making money that June on their fantastic finds; six hundred were coining gold from their stores, their rental of horses, their trading in leases, their medical or legal services. She saw also that enterprising women no more skilled or determined than she were doing extremely well with fortunetelling, the running of brothels, the selling of doughnuts and coffee. Three women had banded together to run a laundry, which was stacked with miners' clothing, and one seamstress seemed to be prospering from the sewing of shirts.

'What do we have to offer?' Missy demanded during the long twilight, and Tom replied: 'I can build boats.'

Unwisely she laughed, and when Tom flushed, she pointed to the riverfront where more than a thousand boats were for sale, their mission accomplished. Realizing the ridiculousness of his proposal, he, too, laughed: 'Anyway, I can build cabins.'

They talked on, rejecting one impractical alternative after another, but as they spoke, Missy kept looking at their nearby boat, and this gave her a viable idea: 'Tom, we have double rations in the *Aurora*. All our food and all of Buck's too,' and the more they considered this, the more appealing became the idea of opening a food shop of some kind and selling at profit their excess. The arrival this summer of regular boats up the Yukon from the Bering Sea meant that there would be no starvation in 1898 as there had been in '97, but there would be opportunities for enormous rewards.

Using the sail which Sergeant Kirby had sold them atop the Chilkoot Pass, Tom painted an enormous sign, one which dominated the waterfront: MISSY'S GOOD MEALS CHEAP, and the tent restaurant was in business—not along the main street where competition would have been severe, but along the river where thousands of men were almost forced to congregate in the first days of their arrival.

To his own surprise, Tom was not loath to knock apart the *Aurora*, which he had built with such care, and after some of her planks were converted into tables and benches he bought for almost nothing another boat, so poorly built that it practically fell apart.

The two proprietors slaved over their restaurant, Missy doing the cooking, Tom the washing-up and the procurement of additional food from various sources. Mostly they relied upon their own cargo of dried foods so carefully chosen by Buck and the Kernel, and the diet they served was heavy on starches and caribou or moose meat brought in by some hunter.

They learned to equate gold dust, which passed as currency in Dawson, with dollars, and although their banner proclaimed cheap prices, the rates were surprisingly high. Their specialty, a loss leader you might say, was a breakfast of pancakes and syrup, greasy caribou sausage and cups of steaming coffee for thirty-five cents. Hungry men who gorged on this bargain were apt to return for lunch and supper, on which Missy and Tom made a real profit.

They had been in successful operation some six weeks when Superintendent Steele returned, and hearing that they had arrived in Dawson, came looking for them along the riverfront. 'Hello,' he greeted Tom as he entered the tent. 'You remember me? I'm Samuel Steele, and I'm glad to see you prospering.'

'Hey! Missy! It's the superintendent!' And when she appeared, obviously involved in heavy work, Steele congratulated her on having, as he said, 'found your footing.'

He said that he had her money with him and was prepared to turn it over, but he wondered if she might not prefer to deposit it in one of the reliable banks that had opened since he had last met with her: 'I would advise it, ma'am.'

'I think so too,' she said, for as a businesswoman she was already beginning to wonder how she and Tom could protect the money they were raking in. 'But that special envelope . . . for the woman. I'd want to have that, because it isn't my money.'

'I brought it,' Steele said, and that afternoon Missy picked her way along Front Street, the main thoroughfare, then ducked off to a more famous street which paralleled it. This was Paradise Alley, where thoughtful men had built some seventy cribs for the prostitutes who were needed in any boomtown. Over the doors of many of the little huts, arranged in neat rows, hung boards proclaiming the names of the occupants:

TIGER FLO
THE MATCHMAKER
BETSY POO

On the largest crib, as befitted the situation:

THE BELGIAN MARE

Knocking sedately on the door beneath this sign, Missy called: 'Ma'am, are you in?'

The big woman inside, five feet ten inches tall, a hundred and seventy pounds, was surprised to hear a woman's voice following the customary rapping, and supposing it to be one of the other Belgian girls, she shouted in Flemish: 'Come in!' Missy, of course, could not understand the words and waited on the stoop.

When her invitation produced no results, the woman came to her door, and showed surprise at the type of person waiting there. Calling to another crib whose occupant spoke both Flemish and English, she asked: 'What does this one want?' and soon half a dozen of the unoccupied girls crowded into the Mare's crib, delighted with the unusual diversion.

'Tell her,' Missy said, 'that I bring something from the Klondike Kernel.'

The interpreter had arrived from Antwerp after the departure of the Kernel on that first boat down the Yukon with news of the strike, so she had not known the man, and at first her explanation made no sense to the Mare, but when Missy repeated the name the big woman's face broke into a beatific smile, and the way she reacted proved she had been unusually fond of the tough Carolinian.

'Ah! The colonel!' she cried in Flemish, and with a military flourish imitating a drum and bugle, she began a vivid march, as if she were one of Wellington's men leaving Brussels for the great battle at Waterloo. Other girls, remembering the Kernel, joined in, and for a few minutes there was jollity and military nonsense and the remembrance of old friends.

'She says,' the interpreter explained as the petite march continued, 'that Kernel, he was one damn fine man.' And another Belgian girl broke in to have the interpreter say: 'He was the lucky one. He found the gold. And he was good to us.'

The Mare, exhausted from her unusual activity, fell onto the second bed in her crib, and while she regained her breath, Missy said: 'Tell her that I liked her dance. She is an artist.' And when this was translated, the Mare sat straight up and said with great seriousness: 'I was an actress. But the fat, it grew too much. What does this one want?'

Missy wondered if it was prudent for her to display the amount of money the envelope contained, and she decided against it.

Standing so that the other girls could not see, she bent over the Mare, opened the envelope slightly, and allowed her to see the beautiful gold face of the hundred-dollar bill.

Her attempt to protect the Mare was useless, for the latter shouted in French: 'Oh my God! Look at what that dear man sends me!' And she ripped the bill from the envelope, showed it to the girls, then paraded it up and down before the other cribs, shouting in Flemish: 'Look what that dear man sent me!' and soon almost all the girls were in Paradise Alley, looking at the golden bill. A few customers stuck their heads out, wanting to know what the shouting was about, and after a while the procession halted and the Belgian girls returned to their cribs, while the Mare thanked Missy, calling for the interpreter again: 'What business is this one in?' And when she heard that Missy ran the new restaurant down by the river, the Mare went back into the alley and shouted: 'This kind lady runs that new restaurant down by the river. Tell the men to eat there.'

In this accidental way, Missy and Tom obtained customers they would not otherwise have had, and occasionally one of the girls from Paradise Alley would accompany some customer to the restaurant and share breakfast with him. One morning two girls brought with them a tall, dour miner who had been immured in a lonely cabin atop a hill for most of a year, and they told Missy: 'This is one of the loneliest sons-of-bitches in the world. He won't even come to the Alley, but he does bring us fresh meat now and then.'

'And what is your name?' Missy asked, and the man grunted through his beard: 'John Klope, ma'am.'

'From where?'

'Idaho.'

Missy laughed, saying: 'I didn't know anybody lived in Idaho,' and he replied as if she had asked a serious question: 'Quite a few do, ma'am.'

She noticed that although he seemed to be hungry, he toyed with his pancakes, and on two subsequent visits for breakfast he did the same, until out of curiosity she asked: 'Anything wrong with the cakes?' and he said: 'They're disgraceful.' When she winced, he added apologetically: 'No offense to you, ma'am. It's just that you ain't usin' a proper strain of sourdough.'

'What does that mean?'

'Ma'am, to make proper flapjacks, you got to have the right starter to begin with.'

'I use yeast. Bought it in Seattle.'

'You see? You got off on the wrong foot, and can't never recover.'

'What do you use?'

'I got my sourdough from an old woman in Fort Yukon. She'd had the same strain for more'n fifty years. I brought it by sled near three hundred and fifty miles, the way we came, in dead of winter. It makes real flapjacks.'

'I'd like to taste the difference.'

'I'll bring you some of my starter next time I'm in town.'

'Where's your claim?'

'El Dorado. On the Bench. Eldorado Crest, Claim Eighty-seven.'

'Ooooh, one of those millionaires?'

'No, ma'am. Bench means I'm up on the ridge.'

'Nothing?'

'Not yet.'

He made the tedious trip to his claim and back, just to bring Missy a batch of his sourdough starter, and when he showed her how to use it in preparing pancakes while conserving the strain by keeping it in a cool jug, she had to agree that his sourdough flapjacks were definitely superior to her ordinary pancakes. They were light, they browned well if a customer wanted them that way, and most did, and they were chewy, blending perfectly with either sorghum or honey. She said: 'I'm indebted to you, Mr. Klope, and I hope you strike it rich.'

'I will,' he said, but an even more important consequence of this second series of visits related to the fine dog he brought with him. Missy paid no attention to the well-formed husky, but Tom recognized immediately that this was a superior animal. He knew little of dogs, really, and nothing about the famous sled dogs of the arctic, but even so, he could see in this dog's bearing, in the intelligence which flowed in his eyes, that he was special.

'Where'd you get him?'

'He pulled our sled . . . down from Fort Yukon.' Almost hesitantly he added: 'I couldn't let him go. We went through a lot together.'

In the weeks that followed, when the miner should have been at his diggings above Eldorado, he lingered in Dawson, appearing each morning at the tent for his sourdough flapjacks.

One morning Superintendent Steele stopped by with some startling news for Missy: 'Remember how you suspected my man Kirby because of how Soapy Smith's men behaved at Skagway? And you asked me why I didn't do something about it? And I said I couldn't, because that was America, and America had to clean up its own messes?'

'What happened?'

'Just what I expected to happen. Good men exist everywhere in the world, and when they finally cry "Enough!"—watch out.'

'Was somebody brave enough to cry "Enough"?'

'Chap named Reid, if I have it right. Engineering fellow. When Soapy's gang stole the entire poke of a quiet fellow heading home out of the mountains, that was bad enough, but when the hoodlums rallied around and made fun of the little man, the poor chap appealed to the conscience of the community.'

'And?'

'And Mr. Reid shot Soapy dead.'

Missy did not exult, for the dead gambler had on several occasions been good to her and considerate of unfortunates she brought to his attention, but she knew enough of his criminality to realize that sensible people could not allow him to continue unopposed, and she was pleased that he had been stopped: 'I should think that Mr. Reid would be a hero in Skagway.'

'He's dead too. Soapy got him in the exchange of bullets.'

Missy sat down, and as she looked up at Superintendent Steele and saw the quiet determination he represented she realized that her man, Buchanan Venn, had been on his way to becoming such a person. Had the Venns stayed in Skagway, the day would have come when Buck would say "Enough!" and it would have been he who gunned down the petty tyrant.

'Tom, come here,' and when the boy stood facing Superintendent Steele, she said: 'You hear what he just told me? About Soapy Smith? Sometimes you have to stand up against such men. Remember that.'

Steele smiled at Tom, then asked if he could speak alone with his mother, using that word even though he knew it did not apply. He did this because of the nature of what he wanted to say next: 'Miss Peckham, it may seem none of my business, but believe me, it is. It's been my business many painful times.'

'Do I need a license or something?'

'I want to warn you against the woman you call the Belgian Mare.'

'She's been a good friend. Brings me business.'

Steele coughed, looked Missy right in the eye, and said: 'She's a horrible woman. It's not the German pimp who brings these Belgian girls here. She does. It wasn't the businessmen who built the new cribs. She did. She rents them to her girls, takes a huge slice of their earnings. Please, do not interrupt. These are things you must hear.' And he continued with a recital of the Mare's almost criminal behavior: 'When a girl is used up, and some last only a short time, she kicks her out. Even at best, they're treated like animals. If she's being kind to you, it's because she knows that lone women sooner or later run out of money. Then you work for her, on her terms.'

'Please, Superintendent Steele . . .'

'I tell you only the truth.'

'But if she's so terrible, why do you allow her in Dawson?'

'With the services her girls provide, there's no rape in my city.'

Aware that he had succeeded only in arousing Missy's indignation, he saluted and left, but he had not been gone long before his place was quietly taken by John Klope, who ordered nothing but who did occupy one of her four stools for nearly an hour, watching her as she worked. She was so busy that she forgot he was there until he suddenly spoke in a loud voice, all in a rush, uttering important words he'd been rehearsing for a week: 'You and Tom are people I like. Come out to Eldorado with me and help find the gold that has to be there.'

'Now what would the two of us do in a mining camp?' she asked lightly, and he lowered his voice, speaking carefully, as he would to a child: 'In the winter we build fires in the earth, to melt the frozen soil. Then we dig in the softened earth. And haul it by ropes to the top, like it was a well and we were drawing water. Because it's so cold, the wet muck freezes immediate, locking in whatever gold we found. Come summer and the thaw, we sluice the muck and find the gold. And then we're rich.'

'Have you found any gold yet?'

'No, but I have a feeling I'm getting close.'

It was obvious to Klope that his two listeners were still interested in gold and that having come so far, they did not want to return to civilization without having at least tried their hands at the great gamble of mining, so although they said nothing, he pressed his case: 'You can go on earning a living here in the tent, but if you come with me, share and share, you might make a fortune.' He hesitated: 'That's what you came here for, wasn't it? Isn't that why we all came?'

'Where did you come from?' Missy asked as she turned away from her cooking to listen to this strange, compelling man.

'Idaho, like I told you before. All washed up, sort of like you, I guess.'

'We were. But now we're safely started. We could have a good life here in Dawson.'

For the first time in their acquaintance John Klope smiled: 'Ma'am, can't you see? When the gold runs out, Dawson runs out. There's no future here for a tent restaurant. Only future in the Klondike is gold, and when it ends, you end. All of us do.'

Missy now left her side of the counter and came to sit on one of the stools: 'Just what do you mean, we come and help in your cabin?'

'I need help. I stand very close to gold, of that I'm sure. But when I dig out the softened muck, I need someone to haul it to the top and dump it. In the summer I need someone to help me sluice it. Your son here . . .'

'He's not my son. We . . . It would be too complicated to explain.'

'I could use him.'

'And me?'

'We'd both need someone to mind the cabin. You know, it's not a shack. It's got real sides and a window.'

They did not explore, at this first discussion, the role that Missy as a human being and a woman would play, but on subsequent mornings Klope did quietly intimate that he was not married and that he did not drink. There was nothing about his silent, austere manner which would tempt a woman to move in with him, regardless of the arrangement, and he, realizing this, did not press his case, and things might have ended on that tentative note had not two extraneous incidents muddied the situation of the Venns.

The impact of Klope's suggestion that they move to Eldorado fell most heavily on young Tom, for it caused him to think seriously about his future, and after long speculation and study of Dawson, he drafted a surprisingly mature letter to Mr. Ross back in Seattle:

I hope you will remember me. My father, Buck Venn, worked in your office and I think you respected him. He was killed in a freak accident. I hope you also remember my mother, Missy, who worked on your ship the *Alacrity*, but maybe you didn't meet her. I was the newspaper boy who became your helper on the docks. So our whole family was Ross & Raglan, and I hope you remember us well, because we tried to work well.

My idea is this. You have a lot of interests here in Dawson City and two of your riverboats come here. Why not let me organize things in Dawson so that you get more business for your boats and sell more of your goods after the boats get here? Everything must be done in three months while the river is open. If you lose time, you lose money.

I think you ought to open a serious store here and put me in charge, and your business will double or even double double. I am sixteen years old and understand business like a man. Please let me hear from you.

He was only fifteen when he wrote, but by the time his letter reached Seattle he would probably be the sixteen he claimed. However, all thoughts of such an opportunity were forgotten when Dawson experienced one of those periodic fires which at one time or another ravaged most boomtowns. This one, unlike the two more famous ones which would gut the heart of the city, merely roamed the tents and shacks along the waterfront, and one of the first it consumed was the Venn restaurant, whose canvas side walls, heavy with splatter grease, disappeared in minutes, leaving Missy and Tom with only the surplus goods still stacked in the half-demolished *Aurora*.

While the extensive blaze was still ravaging the huts along the riverfront, two men elbowed their way through the crowd explicitly to advise Missy Peckham. The first was Superintendent Steele, who said simply: 'Miss Peckham, this is the kind of disaster I warned about. I'm in charge of government emergency funds, which will allow me to ship you and the boy back to Seattle. Frankly, ma'am, I believe that's what you should do.'

Even as he spoke, the Belgian Mare came along the waterfront, assessing the damage and consoling those who had lost heavily. Waiting till Superintendent Steele went about other business, she sidled up to Missy and said, with the aid of one of her girls who spoke English: 'How sad. If you need help, let me know.' Saying no more, she patted Missy on the cheek and wandered on.

The second man to arrive was John Klope, with his dog Breed, and all he said was: 'Now you two need me as much as I need you.'

That dismal night, when Missy and Tom took shelter in the theater with some fifty other people deprived of their homes, they did not even try to reach any decisions, but in the morning when they returned to where their tent restaurant had been, they saw with sickening clarity that reopening it or anything like it was impossible. They never really said 'Klope's offer is all that's left,' but each recognized the inevitability, and Tom poked about till he found a handcart which a defeated miner was willing to sell for one dollar.

When Klope saw him pushing it along the waterfront he hurried up, took over, and then helped Missy pack the few things she had saved from the fire. By midafternoon they were on their way to Lousetown, Tom and Klope each pulling a rope tied to the front of the cart, Missy pushing from behind.

From Lousetown they followed the left bank of the Klondike till they came to Bonanza Creek, the tributary on which the squaw man George Carmack had made the first big discovery. Up it they trudged, past claims now famous around the world—*Seven Above, Nine Below*—until they reached the confluence with the Eldorado with its less famous but far richer claims, and after they had passed a score of these immensely productive sites along the stream, they climbed sharply to reach the upper ridge, far above the gold-producing placers, and there, on the high ridge, they came to John Klope's cabin.

It stood on a plot five hundred feet long, paralleling the stream below, by about fifteen hundred feet wide: this gave him about seventeen acres, but the effective portion would be an area close to wherever gold-producing muck was found. 'Technically,' he explained as they neared the hole which already went deep into the earth, 'what we're looking for is bedrock.'

'Do we have to blast solid rock?' Tom asked, and Klope said: 'No. The gold will be resting on the bedrock—the bottom of some old river.'

'How do you know a river used to run down there?'

'How did those fellows down there know the present river had gold? They panned. We dig.'

By gold-field standards his cabin was superior, but it was still a miserable affair: nine by twelve feet, four log walls, a solitary window cut into the logs and carefully caulked, a wooden floor, a single bed, stove, pegs jutting from the wall to dry the clothes which seemed always to be soaked, and a change of boots, which also seemed to be permanently wet and mud-caked. It had a chimney which carried away the smoke, but the long exposed run of the piping meant that when the stove was working, the heat inside the cabin was intense, often higher than eighty-five degrees; when the fire was out, the cold could drop to twenty-below.

Because Klope was essentially a neat man who attended to his appearance, he had built an outside stand for washing and shaving and had started his occupancy with a determination to remain clean-shaven, but this resolve had lasted less than a month, for shaving in the Klondike, whether in summer or winter, was a drudgery which he gladly avoided. Now his beard, which he often forgot to trim with his rusty scissors, was long and masked his true age; he could have been either a well-preserved forty or a determined twenty. Actually, he was twenty-eight that year and one of the most dedicated miners on any of the famous streams.

When Missy saw that the cabin had only one bed, she stiffened, but Klope eased the situation by stating: 'First thing, we've got to build two more beds,' and with Tom's expert help, this was promptly accomplished. However, the supplies they had brought with them could not all fit into the cabin, and this required some ingenuity on Klope's part. He found a solution by bringing the cart flush against one of the windowless walls and erecting over it a kind of sloping roof with two side walls. The front, of course, had to be left open, but none of the gold-field cabins had locked doors, and Klope said: 'No danger of anyone stealing things. The Mounties don't permit it.'

During the first months of the occupancy, each of the three kept to a separate bed, but as the routine settled into boredom, with Klope down in the hole nine and ten hours a day during the long, cold winter, and Tom topside managing the loads of muck that came up on the windlass, it became obvious that when Klope climbed the ladder at the end of his stint, he was interested in Missy as a woman and not only as the person who prepared his morning flapjacks. So one very cold February night, when the temperature hovered about the minus-thirty mark, Missy, quietly and without a gesture of any kind toward Tom, crept in with Klope, and shortly thereafter, while the men were working the mine, she moved her former bed out into the shed.

So for a third time young Tom was a bystander when this practical-minded woman moved in with a man to whom she was not married. His education in the ways of men and women had not been a conventional one, so he was not troubled by this, and he still felt that Missy was the most nearly perfect woman he had known. As the long months passed, with endless work and little promise of gold at the bottom of the deep mine, it was she who kept the spirits of the place buoyant, the cabin livable and the work moving forward.

In this she was abetted by a new friend whose support she could not have anticipated, the husky Breed. Different from most sled dogs, hence his name and the willingness of Sarqaq to part with him, he had more or less liked his three principal companions, Sarqaq, Klope and Tom Venn, but during the long hours when Klope and Tom were working the mine, he found himself increasingly with Missy. She fed him, summoned him to help her drag logs for the stove, played with him, and spoke to him twenty times to the men's one, so before long he was adjusting his life to hers. Always a dog who appreciated being with humans, he now focused his entire affection on Missy. He became her dog, and once when two miners from the lower claims along Eldorado appeared suddenly to make inquiries about whether Klope could supply them with meat, their moves toward Missy were too abrupt, and within two seconds Breed was at their throats, and only Missy's prompt intervention saved them.

'You ought to keep that one on a chain,' one of the men complained as he moved back.

'He's that way only if he thinks we're in trouble,' Missy said, hoping that the men would relay that information to the camps below.

'You got any surplus meat?'

'Not right now. But maybe Tom will get some the next few days.'

'We'd pay well.'

And so Tom and Breed went out on Sundays and after work to scout for deer or bear or caribou, and when they were lucky and had butchered the carcass, Missy peddled the cuts along the river.

She was doing this one wintry morning in 1899 when a Mountie came riding along the river, asking for her whereabouts, and when one of the miners shouted: 'Hey, Missy! Someone to see you!' she looked up to see Sergeant Kirby, as neat and trim as ever in his blue uniform.

He led his horse as they climbed the hill to Klope's shaft on the upper ridge, and when he saw the cabin with two beds inside and one stacked beside the cart, he asked no questions: 'I came to see Tom Venn, really. Important news for the boy. Startling news, really.'

Calling for Breed, she told the dog: 'Fetch Tom!' and before long the boy reported.

'Superintendent Steele wants to see you.'

'I haven't done anything.'

'Yes,' Kirby said, with a wide smile, 'I rather think you have.'

'I couldn't have, Sergeant Kirby. I've been here all the time.'

Kirby reached out, grasped the boy by the left arm, and said: 'Sit down. The news is very good. In fact, it's spectacular.' Then, winking at Missy, he asked: 'Did you mail a letter from Dawson City when you arrived?'

'Yes. To my grandmother.'

'And maybe one to a Mr. Ross in Seattle?'

'Yes, but I was only asking questions.'

'You're going to be amazed, young Mr. Tom, at his reply.' And he said that whereas Superintendent Steele would no doubt want to do the explaining, he, Kirby, could reveal that Ross & Raglan had jumped at the ideas proposed by Tom and were sending, on the first R&R steamer to break through the Yukon ice, supplies for a major trade depot at Dawson, along with a Mr. Pincus to run the place, provided Thomas Venn was ready to offer the services he spoke of in his letter of such and such a date.

Before Klope could climb out of the deep shaft—twenty-nine feet straight down, with no timber supports of any kind—Tom and Missy and Sergeant Kirby had agreed that the boy must leave immediately to arrange for space in which to open the R&R branch in Dawson. When Klope was informed of this *fait accompli* arranged in his absence, he behaved in his characteristic way. He scratched his beard, looked at Missy, then Kirby, then the boy, then said quietly: 'He's soon to be a man. Anyone would be lucky to hire a fellow as good as this one.'

But once he had established that Tom was free to leave if he wished, he sought to forestall action. 'Let's all sit down and talk about this,' and when the session began he laid out the relevant facts: 'Tom, you and Missy have earned part ownership of this claim, and I testify before the Mountie here that when I next get in to Dawson, I'll enter the transfer legally. But only if you stay and help work it.'

'It's time for him to go,' Missy said with great firmness.

'And you're going with him?' Klope asked.

'I'm staying here.'

'Good, because I'm convinced the old river must have run along where we're digging. We're at twenty-nine feet now, another fifteen feet, we've got to strike it.'

'Have you shown any color?' Kirby asked, for he had heard predictions like this from a hundred different men in a hundred different locations. The bedrock was always just a little farther down.

'No.'

'In all that frozen muck out there, not two cents to the pan when you wash it out this summer?'

'Probably not, but when men started on these creeks, ten cents a pan was enough to make them dream. Then Carmack found four dollars a pan, and the boom was on. Down at that claim you can see from here, eighty dollars a pan, and that far one, they hit a thousand dollars in one pan.'

'What he says is true,' Kirby affirmed. 'Sometimes the midnight bell did toll.'

'What I'm shooting for, and it's got to be down there, will be something like five or six thousand dollars a pan. That's what we're hoping for.'

His three listeners sat looking at their knuckles, each one afraid to bring him down to reality. Finally Tom said: 'I asked Mr. Ross to do something. He's doing it and I got to do my part.'

'You understand the gamble?' Klope asked, and when Tom said he did, the tall, gangling man said with no rancor: 'It's your decision, son. I couldn't have asked for a better helper.'

While Tom packed, with Missy throwing one useful item after another into his canvas bag, Kirby asked Klope: 'Have you any solid reason for believing there's gold down there?'

'The lay of the land.'

'But you can't see the lay of the land.'

'Every inch I dig deeper tells me something new.'

'And you're willing to risk everything . . . on those secrets?'

'I don't have much to risk, Officer.'

When the packing was done and Klope had paid Tom for his work in hauling up the muck, the time had come for goodbyes, and the boy went from Breed to Klope to Missy, close to crying as he bade farewell to those with whom he had shared a cabin on an authentic Klondike claim. He sensed that this departure marked a watershed in his life, like climbing the last six feet of Chilkoot Pass and looking down the other side toward Lake Lindeman and the thousands of boats at Bennett.

He said brave words, then knelt and kissed Breed. 'Well,' he said matter-of-factly when he rose, 'I guess we better be going.'

HE WAS WORKING in the new Ross & Raglan store on a bright June morning in 1899 when a commotion filled the main street, and he ran out to learn where the new strike had been made. It wasn't the finding of additional gold, it was the arrival of an extraordinary Klondiker come all the way from Edmonton, over the hideous route down the untamed Mackenzie River to a spot far beyond the Arctic Circle and then across hellish, barren heights to the Yukon Territory. When word flashed through Dawson that 'a tough little Irishman made it by the Mackenzie route,' hardened sourdoughs gathered to see the miracle man who had done what they would never have attempted.

Tom, from the edge of the crowd, saw a medium-sized Irishman in his early thirties, haggard as a hungry ghost but smiling roguishly at the men about him. He had dark, uncut hair which came down about his eyes, heavy clothes tattered from his ordeal north of the Circle, and a positive passion for talking: 'Name's Matt Murphy from a town west of Belfast. Five of us from London hurried to Edmonton as soon as we heard of the Klondike find. Set out down the Mackenzie in July 1897, got lost, one man drowned, one starved to death, one died of scurvy. That tall fellow you saw come in with me, he'd had enough. Kited right back to London. Me? I'm here to stay. Determined to find meself a gold mine.'

His listeners broke into laughter, not derisively but with a desire to straighten him out: 'Every good site taken three years ago.'

Tom saw with admiration how the stranger reacted to this shattering news: his shoulders drooped ever so slightly, he took a deep breath, then he asked almost jocularly: 'Any place a man can grab a beer?' and when one was provided, the first he had had in two years, he sipped it as if it were nectar, then asked quietly: 'Now, if there was to be new sites found, where would they be?' and solemnly the men replied: 'There won't be any.'

For just a moment Tom wondered if Murphy was going to faint, but then he flashed an irrepressible Irish smile and said softly: 'Your news is not comfortin'. I've come so far, so close to starvin' . . .'

The miners, ashamed that they had not acted sooner, led him to a tent restaurant where eggs, bacon and pancakes were available, and Tom, once more at the edge of the crowd, watched as the newcomer ate in a way Tom had never seen before. With infinite care, as if trying to hold back rearing horses, he cut his food into minute portions, eating them one by one like a dainty bluebird. 'Ain't you hungry?' asked the miner who was paying the bill, and the Irishman said: 'I could eat everything in this tent and in that one over there. I haven't seen food like this in two years.'

'Then eat up!' the miner bellowed, but the stranger said: 'If I did, I'd drop dead,' and he continued placing in his mouth one tiny morsel after another.

In the days that followed, Tom spent a good deal of time with the incredible Irishman, listening to his account of the epic trip north and of the dreadful deaths which had overtaken the gold seekers. 'My father died too,' he told Murphy. 'Pole doubled back on him while we were riding an ice sled with a sail.'

The boy was impressed by the self-discipline with which Murphy continued to handle his meals, still eating them piece by piece, but always as they ate, the Irishman asked questions about gold, and Tom could see that he was obsessed by his determination to find himself a site, any kind, at which he could go through the motions of panning or digging. Not wanting to dismay Murphy by reiterating that there were no more sites, Tom threw the burden onto the able shoulders of his friend Sergeant Kirby of the North West Mounted, who had dealt with many latecomers like Murphy.

'Spots to claim? The good ones were nailed down three years ago. Will there be any new ones? Not likely.'

When Murphy, gaunt as a bear coming out of hibernation in April, heard this confirmation from an expert, he masked his disappointment, whereupon Kirby made a suggestion: 'There's a chap named Klope out on a ridge. Digs day and night. Feels sure he's on to something good. He needs help.'

'How do I fit in? Do I buy part of the claim?'

'No, you work for him. He pays you wages, and when he runs out of money, maybe he'll offer you a share of the claim to keep you on the scene.'

'You're sayin' he's not finding any gold?'

'Down along the stream you pan the placers and know immediately if you've hit. Up on the benches, you dig, dig, dig and never know anything till you reach bedrock.'

Murphy, not yet strong enough to take hard knocks like this, sat down: 'You mean . . . I've come all the way from Edmonton . . . You can't know what that's like.'

'I think I can,' Kirby said. 'Half a dozen parties have straggled in. I've had to bury some of them.'

'Did any of the Edmonton men find gold?'

'Like you, they never even found a place to dig for it.'

For some moments Murphy sat with his face buried in his shockingly thin hands. Then he straightened his shoulders and stood erect: 'Where's this Mr. Klope's ridge? By God, I'm the one that came the Edmonton route that's going to make a try, at least.'

Kirby drew him a rough map, at the bottom of which he wrote: 'John Klope: This man has come from Edmonton. He knows how to work. Will Kirby, North West Mounted Police.'

When Murphy climbed the hill above Eldorado and presented his recommendation, Klope said: 'We've been at wit's end. I keep digging, but Missy here can't work the windlass and do the cooking both. We need you.'

So the Irishman started work for wages, and when Missy saw how emaciated he was, and yet how eager to take over the heavy labors that she had been performing, she felt it her duty to feed him generously, but he would not gorge himself, just carefully ate all those things which would send energy through his body and antiscurvy fluids down his legs. When he found that Klope had a good rifle, he remembered hunting tricks he had learned in Ireland, going far into the country and bringing back quarters of meat when other hunters were getting nothing.

When his strength returned, he proved a diligent laborer, hauling up the muck and getting it ready for the summer washing, so that after the second month Klope raised his pay from one dollar a day, which was standard in the mines that were producing nothing, to a dollar and a quarter, which encouraged Murphy to even greater exertion. But as he worked aboveground while Klope slaved away deep inside the frozen earth, he had an opportunity to spend hours each day with Missy, who became attracted to his witty stories of Ireland, his accounts of horse racing in that country, and especially his explanation of what had gone wrong with the Edmonton gold seekers: 'We were like men chasing the northern lights. We could see the golden colors dancing just beyond our reach, but when we struggled to catch them, we found ourselves lost in snow and ice.'

When he related his harrowing experiences, she said: 'I'm glad you told me this, Murphy. I was beginning to feel sorry for myself on the Chilkoot.'

Both Klope and Missy enjoyed the musical manner in which Murphy spoke and they marveled at his use of big words. 'You're a poet,' Klope said one summer night as the Irishman prepared to take his evening stroll with Breed. He took such a walk fairly regularly, wishing out of delicacy to be away from the cabin part of each night so that Klope and Missy could be alone, but of late in these pleasant ambles, with the twilight lasting for hours, he found himself thinking only of Missy. And one morning, halfway between breakfast and when Klope would be climbing out of his shaft for a bite to eat, while he and Missy were working together at the pile of muck which they would soon be sluicing, he very carefully laid aside his shovel, took Missy's away from her, and kissed her fervently.

She did not respond, nor did she rebuke him. Reaching for his shovel, she handed it to him, then took her own and said: 'We're after gold, and don't forget it.'

But on subsequent mornings she began placing herself so that Murphy had to pass near her, and they began kissing without the formality of putting aside the shovels, and by autumn, when it was clear that the painfully accumulated muck contained no gold whatever, it was also clear to them that John Klope's would-be mine was a lost hope and that he was lost too. Missy saw him as the big, unresponsive, unimaginative lout he had always been, and Murphy discovered that the poor man had almost no money left to pay anyone to help him dig his unproductive mine.

As the days shortened and Murphy recalled those two tragic winters when he was trapped in the arctic, he began to feel a repetition of that sense of doom, and one morning at breakfast he threw down his fork and said: 'I've got to get out of here, Klope. I see no chance of gold on your claim.'

'Maybe it's best,' Klope replied. 'I've little left to pay you with,' and then he descended with his hopes into his hole.

Murphy spent that morning packing while Missy worked the lift, but after lunch, when Klope was back at his digging, the two in the cabin drifted almost automatically into a passionate encounter, after which Missy said: 'I'm going with you, Matt,' and he said: 'We'll find something.'

They did not tell Klope that night, but he must have suspected something, for instead of staying in the cabin with Missy while Murphy went for a walk, it was he who left, and when he returned, silent and moody as ever, he went right to bed without conversation.

In the morning Missy prepared breakfast, ate none herself, and then informed Klope: 'We're going in to Dawson. I pray you'll find your gold, John.'

'Leaving?' he asked.

'Yes. It's better.'

'Coming back?'

'No. It's worked out, John.' He could not tell whether she meant that the mine was finished or her relationship with him. He looked at the Irishman and said: 'I could break you in half.' Then he shrugged his shoulders: 'What would be the use?'

Left alone in the late autumn sunlight, John Klope watched the travelers depart, with Murphy pushing the handcart Tom Venn had bought for the handling of their goods. When the sound of their departure was silenced, he walked purposefully to the hole, adjusted the bucket rope so that he could work the removal of muck by himself, and without any visible sign of emotion climbed down to the thirty-second foot.

Of all the gold seekers who had come up the Yukon River in 1897 on the *Jos. Parker*, not one had found gold. Of those few who had tried the Mackenzie horror, not one had even filed a claim. And of those who scaled the Chilkoot Pass with the Venns and braved the canyons in their wake, not one found gold. But all had participated in the great adventure provided by the dying century, and as Matthew Murphy said on approaching Dawson behind the cart: 'I dreamed of digging for gold, and I did.'

WHILE JOHN KLOPE, Matt Murphy and Tom Venn labored in anonymity seeking gold on the Yukon, there was another group of men who attained vast publicity from their participation in the rush. Jack London, the proletarian writer from San Francisco, would find here material for his most notable stories, while the Canadian poet—English born, Scottish reared—Robert W. Service would immortalize the sourdough with poems that may have been no more than jingles but which proved unforgettable:

> The Northern Lights have seen queer sights,
>   But the queerest they ever did see
> Was that night on the marge of Lake Lebarge
>   I cremated Sam McGee.
>
> Now Sam McGee was from Tennessee . . .

He misspelled Lake Laberge in order to find an attractive rhyme, but this and his other misconstructions did not matter, for he breathed into his yarns of the

Yukon a vitality and charm that will apparently never fade. Two remarkable facts highlight his career: he did not get to the Klondike until 1904, when the great days were long over, and he wrote his most famous poems about it, including those featuring Dan McGrew and Sam McGee, long before he had set foot in Dawson City.

Tex Rickard, famous fight promoter and friend of Jack Dempsey, spent time on the gold fields, as did Addison Mizner, notable wit and Florida real-estate genius, Nellie Bly, the famous New York reporter, and Key Pittman, a future senator from Nevada, notorious and a power in foreign relations.

But early in the existence of the Yukon fields, the flat-bottomed river steamer *Jos. Parker* puffed into Dawson City for an overnight stop, bringing a passenger who epitomized those visitors who stayed only briefly but who nevertheless added to the world's knowledge of the Klondike. He was dressed in Eskimo costume and at age sixty-three was one of the oldest men on the diggings.

His boat laid over in Dawson only one day, but in these twenty-eight hours the little cyclone moved up and down the dusty main street introducing himself to anyone he thought might be an authority: 'Hello, friend! I'm Dr. Sheldon Jackson, General Agent for Education for Alaska. I'd like to know what plans you have for schools in your gold camps.'

Like a little ferret he pried into the quality of the hotels, the system of paying for purchases in gold dust, and the condition of women, but he spent his major effort in learning about religion in the camps. He was welcomed by ministers as soon as he presented his imposing card:

> DR. SHELDON JACKSON
> *Moderator of the General Assembly*
> *The Presbyterian Churches of America*

Knowing clergymen would ask: 'Isn't that the highest office in your church?' and he would reply almost apologetically: 'Yes. Three of us contended for the post. Our former President, Benjamin Harrison, the millionaire businessman John Wanamaker, and me.' Then he would cough modestly: 'I won on the first ballot . . . overwhelmingly.'

He made a nuisance of himself that day, but next morning when the *Parker* headed down the Yukon, he carried with him knowledge enough to use the rest of his life in his popular lecture: The Gold Fields of the Klondike.

IX

THE GOLDEN BEACHES
OF NOME

No move by Captain Healy and Reverend Jackson to improve the quality of life in Alaska elicited the scorn of their enemies like their attempt to import Siberian domesticated reindeer to feed the starving Eskimos during winter famine. The stubborn do-gooders were accused of being idiots, thieves and secret agents for the Russians: 'You wait, when the books are inspected you'll find them two stole four-fifths of the money the government has poured into this hare-brained scheme.' And of course Jackson was denounced, with some justification, for having delivered most of the reindeer that did reach Alaska to his Presbyterian settlements up and down the coast.

In the spring of 1897 the Army command in Washington dispatched a Lieutenant Loeffler of its Supply Corps to look into these charges of gross mismanagement: 'Tell us whether the idea is practical.' In obedience to his orders, the lieutenant visited eight of the sites where Dr. Jackson had tried to establish his herds, and sent Washington a just summary of the situation:

> It is prudent for the Army to express interest in this experiment because the time could come when our troops operating in the arctic would want to rely upon reindeer as a major source of food.

> How has the experiment gone? Poorly. Many of the first imports died either during the sea crossing from Siberia or shortly thereafter because the Alaskan Eskimos had no concept of how they should be husbanded. Reindeer which had been accustomed to the most thoughtful care in Siberia and treated as if they were valuable cattle on some Iowa farm were turned loose as if they were wild caribou, with the result that many reverted to untamed ways and were seen no more, while others died for lack of attention and their customary food.

> The result? All the reindeer settled in the Aleutians are now dead or have disappeared. That experiment was a disaster. Most of those brought to settlements along the northern seacoast have fared poorly, so that one must look upon this adventure as having come to very little. The Army would be ill-advised to rely for the foreseeable future in any important way upon domesticated reindeer as a major source of food supply.

But in fairness, Lieutenant Loeffler did report upon one establishment where the Healy-Jackson reindeer imported from the Cape Dezhnev region of Siberia had prospered, and he must have liked what he saw, for he wrote of it with obvious enthusiasm:

> However, I did find one installation where, due to a peculiar set of circumstances, the reindeer experiment did work. At the western end of Seward Peninsula, a bleak place which has been named Port Clarence contains a settlement called Teller Station, and here a Norwegian named Lars Skjellerup, thirty-three years old and unmarried, has put together a team of three helpers who appear to know how to handle reindeer.
>
> When Skjellerup came to Alaska he brought with him a short, tough Laplander named Mikkel Sana, who can think like a reindeer. Because he anticipates what they're going to do, he guides them quietly but firmly around to his purposes.
>
> The second helper gave me problems. He is Arkikov, no first name, brought over from Siberia by Captain Michael Healy of the famed revenue cutter *Bear*. This Chukchi Eskimo may know reindeer but I found him surly, not given to following directions, and difficult to discipline. But when I asked Skjellerup: 'Why do you bother with this man?' he told me: 'Arkikov is a man, and from time to time in this work you need men.'
>
> The third helper was a shy Eskimo lad of nineteen, not tall and with a dark, round face. Skjellerup told me: 'Ootenai is special. He has no family, they died during one of the famines, so he appreciates our project as his only chance for a good life. One day he'll be head of this station.'
>
> Well, there they are, and should the Army ever be required to work with reindeer in Alaska, I recommend that our officers ignore all other stations and head directly for Teller.

After Loeffler submitted his report in the spring of 1897 he returned to his regular duty in Seattle, where, in the early autumn of that year, he handled the urgent telegram that came from Washington:

> DOZEN AMERICAN WHALERS TRAPPED IN ICE POINT BARROW STOP RATIONS SHORT STOP NO MEDICAL STORES STOP EVALUATE RESCUE OPERATIONS AND ADVISE IMMEDIATELY STOP

Since Loeffler had recently been in Point Barrow, he was assigned as second-in-command of the study group, and he spent his first three days along the Seattle waterfront trying to piece together the possible avenues whereby a covey of whalers stuck off Point Barrow could have alerted Washington, D.C., of their plight, and he learned that the owners of some of the stricken vessels had deduced from the nonarrival of their ships that they must be trapped in ice. Canadian officials at Prince Rupert had reached similar conclusions, but most important were appeals for help delivered over the northern snows by dog-team messengers heading south from Barrow.

Loeffler reported to the group: 'There is a crisis. The whalers are probably icebound already, and there's no way of breaking them loose till early next summer.' Then he added the ominous judgment: 'Since they cannot possibly have enough food to last them nine months, a rescue operation is imperative.'

The Army officials, with assistance from the Navy and private shippers like Ross & Raglan, began analyzing possible maneuvers, and none was too bizarre to be discarded out of hand. One Army officer said: 'I've always heard that Siberia and Alaska are only a few miles apart. Could we telegraph Russia and request them . . . ?'

A Navy man broke in: 'Southeast of Barrow that's true. How far apart do you think they are at Barrow?' and a former whaler who knew the northern oceans well broke in: 'About five hundred miles.' Rescue from Canada was equally impossible—about six hundred miles to the first tiny outpost, which would have no chance of providing enough food or medicine.

The group fell silent, then turned to Loeffler, who said tentatively: 'I've looked at every possibility. It's about five hundred miles from any of the nearest mining camps. To cover that distance you'd have to use dogsleds, and where would you get enough food to feed your dogs en route? And what mining camp would have a cache of food big enough for twenty ships?'

'What alternative have you in mind?' the chairman asked, and Loeffler coughed several times before daring to reveal the plan which had been slowly germinating. Then, with the aid of a big map, he said: 'Up here at Port Clarence Bay, at the far end of Seward Peninsula, there's a remarkable Norwegian, Lars Skjellerup, supported by a tough, capable team of three. One Siberian, one Laplander, one Eskimo.'

The chairman broke in: 'What do they have to offer? A superior dog team?' And a longtime sailor pointed out: 'By the time we loaded a ship here in Seattle, that place would be iced in,' but Loeffler said quietly: 'You ask what they have up there?' Pausing dramatically, he said: 'Reindeer.'

The word brought an explosion from the study group: 'We've heard about that fiasco.' 'How many are still alive? Six or seven?' and 'That missionary stopped by Seattle one year and gave us a lecture about how the reindeer was going to solve all Alaska's problems. Whatever happened to the little fraud?' Before Loeffler could explain himself, it was unanimously agreed by the others that the few scattered reindeer at Port Clarence represented no solution whatever.

But then with a patience that won the respect of his superiors, the young lieutenant developed his plan: 'Port Clarence has a huge herd of reindeer, actually. Under Skjellerup's professional guidance, the local Eskimos have acquired or bred well over six hundred fine beasts. Some are so domesticated, they serve in harness in place of dogs. And do you appreciate what that means? If we used reindeer, we wouldn't have to carry any food for the animals.'

'Why not?'

'Dogs eat meat. Lots of it. Reindeer feed on the moss and lichens as they go along.' Allowing time for this important fact to sink in, he added: 'And we wouldn't have to carry any food. Because when our reindeer team reached Barrow they'd be slaughtered, and the starving men would be fed.'

His arguments were greeted with silence, but now a secretary broke into the meeting with the latest telegram from Washington:

REPORT IMMEDIATELY PLANS TO RESCUE ICEBOUND WHALERS STOP NATION'S NEWSPAPERS DEMANDING ACTION

Now all the members of the group turned to face Loeffler, who said: 'I think the only practical thing to tell them is that I will sail immediately to Alaska with medicines, organize a dog team, and hurry overland to Teller Station, where

Skjellerup and his men will start at once for Point Barrow with a herd of four hundred or more reindeer.'

'How far would they be traveling?'

'About six hundred miles.'

'My God! Siberia's as close as that. Canada too.'

'But we have the reindeer, gentlemen, and the men to move them.'

With a caution born of long experience in the arctic, one of the shipowners asked: 'Is such an operation practical?' and Loeffler replied: 'I can't promise that, but what I can promise is this: there's more than three hundred American sailors up there who will die if we don't do something. And this offers our best chance. Let's do it.'

So a telegram was dispatched to the White House, with a reply arriving in Seattle that afternoon:

PROCEED WITH REINDEER AND MAY GOD SPEED YOUR EFFORTS STOP NATION IS WATCHING

It took Lieutenant Loeffler till the middle of January to reach the southern shore of Norton Sound, and when his dogs pulled into the primitive settlement of Stebbins he faced an open crossing of some ninety miles to the north shore, from which Teller Reindeer Station could be approached by land. The prospect of venturing to the other side on ice which might or might not be solidly frozen frightened him so much that he considered making a complete circuit of the eastern end of the sound so as to remain on land. But an old-time Eskimo who ran dogs assured him: 'All frozen. No trouble,' and when Loeffler still held back, the man said: 'I go with you,' and in days when the sun barely shone at noon, the two set out, traveling indifferently day or night.

When they reached the northern shore, the old man accepted the payment Loeffler offered him and started his long hike back across the ice, while the young officer speeded his dogs the remaining hundred and twenty miles west to Teller. As he approached where he judged the reindeer station ought to be, for he had previously come to it only from the sea, a sharp-eyed Eskimo outlook spotted him coming and sounded the alarm, so that when his dogs raced joyously into the station, four resolute men, whom he already knew, were waiting to greet him.

The Laplander Mikkel Sana was first to greet him with a vigorous handshake, then the dour Siberian Arkikov, then the dark young Eskimo Ootenai, and finally the tall, thin unbelieving Norwegian, Lars Skjellerup. 'How did you come with that dog team?' the latter asked, and Loeffler felt that he ought to deliver the news, as he said, 'plain and prompt': 'Washington wants you to drive a herd of three to four hundred reindeer to Point Barrow. A score of whalers stranded there. Three hundred sailors starving.'

The news was so dramatic that none among the four Teller men knew how to respond, so after a moment of silence, Loeffler said: 'Orders. From the President himself. How soon can we leave?'

Once the reality of the situation struck them, the four herders were eager to accept the challenge, for they knew well the scandals that had been circulated throughout Alaska and the United States regarding their deportment and that of other Laplanders and Siberians associated with the reindeer. Skjellerup, as the man in local command, was especially eager in order to demonstrate the capabilities of his reindeer: 'How many miles do you guess?'

'Six hundred, maybe,' Loeffler said. 'Can you do it in sixty days?'

'I think maybe fifty. If we go, we go fast.' He consulted with his men, and Arkikov said: 'Faster. Lead reindeer Siberian, not your kind.' He was referring to the softer Lapland reindeer that Skjellerup had imported by ship from Norway. The Norwegian ignored this implied slur, for he had become accustomed to Arkikov's conviction that only reindeer or herders from his Siberia were of much account.

Loeffler was delighted with Arkikov's estimate that the food and medicine could be delivered in less than fifty days, but his enthusiasm was dashed when Skjellerup said: 'We'll depart three days from now.'

'Wait a minute! I packed my gear in half an hour for my trip up here. Surely you men . . .'

Quietly Skjellerup reasoned: 'You ever try to round up over four hundred reindeer from their comfortable winter quarters . . . which they don't want to leave?' And in the next two days Loeffler learned how much shouting and shoving this entailed, but on Wednesday morning, 19 January 1898, the herd was gathered, the two sleighs were loaded with medicines and food for the trip, and the team was ready for its awesome dash north. Loeffler, watching them depart, called out the message from Washington: 'The President says: "God speed your efforts. The nation is watching."' And within the half-hour the reindeer, the four leading men, three Eskimo helpers and the sleds were indistinct on the eastern horizon. They would travel almost two hundred miles in that direction before they could turn north for the real drive into Barrow where the starving sailors waited.

I T WAS A heroic run, for the nights were bitter cold, the winds blew more than usual, and on several frightening occasions the deer could find no lichen or moss when they scratched or pawed the snow with their sharp hoofs. Sana warned: 'We must find moss. Maybe over there . . . maybe over here? Stop one day,' and when this was done the animals did find lichen and the trip could resume.

When long downhill vistas opened, the men urged the reindeer to run free, but always Sana and Arkikov, two of the best herders in the world, watched for shallow crevasses, and when the gallop ended, men and animals started the breath-strangling climb to the crest of the next hill. When they finally made the big turn from their east heading to north-by-northeast, they felt they were at last on the main part of their journey, the long run to Barrow, perched on the edge of the world. Men alone could not have made this punishing run, nor could dogs have traveled as relentlessly as the reindeer, and certainly the dogs could not have fed themselves. Only reindeer could have carried this burden of food over such terrain and across such distances.

When they were approaching the seventieth latitude, far above the Arctic Circle, they were confronted by a spell of weather so cold and blustery that the thermometer dropped to minus-sixty-two. Now came a real test of what the reindeer could do, for when they were turned loose at the end of a twenty-nine-mile run they pawed the frozen snow until food was uncovered, grazed for half an hour, their backs into the wind, then burrowed in the snow until protecting drifts piled up around them.

'We'd better dig in too!' Skjellerup cried as the gale raged, and both Sana and Arkikov drew their sleds into a bulwark position. With the wind howling over them, but deflected by the sleds, the seven men hunkered down, allowing the snow to build drifts over them.

They stayed there for two long days, their bodies warm and dry in the almost perfect gear they wore; even their feet remained comfortable inside their heavy caribou boots, while the porcupine fur around their heads and the mysterious wolverine tips about their faces kept out the cold and ice. Not many could have withstood that assault, but these men had been drilled since childhood in arctic survival, and it was a curious fact, which both the Lapp and the Siberian noticed, that the white man Skjellerup was as gifted in arctic lore as they who had been bred to it. He was an impressive man, and the others treated him not with reverence, for they were his equal, but with respect for his mastery.

When the storm abated they became lighthearted as children, for now Barrow lay only a hundred miles ahead, and with clear weather and adequate food for the deer, it seemed almost as if they could cover that easy distance in a day. It required several, of course, but on 7 March at about ten in the morning they participated in a moment of such beauty that no one who shared it would ever forget. From the north, out of Barrow, came three dog teams drawing empty sleds and traveling at high speed. From the south came hundreds of reindeer, moving at their own steady speed, and for more than half an hour each party could see the other and calculate its mode of travel and its speed.

Skjellerup cried to his men: 'They must have become desperate. They were going to try to break through!' and the men in the dog teams cried to one another: 'Thank God! Look at those reindeer.'

Closer and closer the two running teams moved, until the bearded men could discern each other's faces. Soon there was cheering and embracing and men weeping, and all the while the wonderful, powerful dogs lay panting in the snow and the reindeer pawed through the drifts for lichen.

T HIS TWELVE-HUNDRED-MILE round trip of rescue became significant in Alaska history not because of heroism or reindeer or the fact that the leaders came from four such divergent backgrounds, but rather because of a chance conversation which occurred on the return trip. Skjellerup and the Eskimo boy Ootenai were driving one of the empty sleds while Arkikov and Sana rode in the other, the one drawn by the Siberian deer, and it was Arkikov, of this we can be certain—because years later each man would so testify—who first broached the subject.

'Remember last spring? Me make trip east . . . take deer to miners' Council City . . . meet many men.'

'What were they doing?'

'Looking gold.'

'Where?'

'To east.'

'Did they find any?'

'Not yet. Soon maybe.'

'How would they find gold?'

'Along rivers . . . little streams. You dip. You wash. You find.'

That was the opening conversation, and on succeeding days as they drifted always southerly south-by-southwest, then due west, these two managed it so they rode together, and repeatedly Arkikov wanted to talk about the gold seekers, those ghost-driven men who prowled creeks, until Sana began to suspect that maybe ordinary men like Arkikov and himself had a chance of finding gold, but suspicious Lapp that he was, he dismissed the idea.

And yet: 'What creek do they dig sand from?'

'Any creek. Me hear men say Klondike . . . all creek.'

'Do you mean river? Like Yukon, big river?'

'No! Little river . . . maybe jump across.' From his conversations with prospectors the Siberian had acquired an accurate sense of what gold seeking consisted of, and he was obviously mesmerized by the possibility of finding gold in some creek along the way home: 'When sun higher . . . no snow . . . little streams run water . . . you, me find gold.'

'How could we . . . no papers . . . just Lapp, Siberian?'

These were practical matters, and to a methodical Lapp like Sana they were powerful enough to disqualify the whole endeavor, but to a Siberian they were meaningless, a temporary irritation to be sidestepped.

'You, me . . . money . . . we go . . . we find gold . . . sure.'

Arkikov gestured so wildly as he talked that in time Skjellerup, riding in the other sled, could not escape noticing it, so when they stopped to eat he asked: 'What's going on? You fighting?' Arkikov looked at Sana as if to ask: 'Shall I tell him?' and when the Lapp nodded the fateful words were spoken.

'Council City . . . all men look gold . . . little streams . . . maybe we look too?'

When the big Norwegian stared at his companions as if they were mad, Arkikov added seductively: 'We three . . . find gold . . . buy many reindeer.'

He said this so confidently, his round face smiling in sunlight as if the gold were already in his hands, that Skjellerup had to be impressed with the possibility of what was being proposed, and found himself saying: 'Well, we do have money enough for a year, even two years. We need no immigration papers.' Then his shrewd practicality asserted itself: 'We were all invited here by the U.S. government. And we have contracts which allow us to stay.'

Before the hasty meal was over he was planning how he and the other two could leave the station and strike out on a prospecting tour, and he became so excited by the prospect of huge riches that he told the others: 'Ootenai, you ride with Arkikov. I want to talk with Sana,' and when the switch was made, he asked: 'Mikkel, you have no wife, nor me. Would you be willing to leave the station, the reindeer . . . and go exploring?'

'Yes!' delivered emphatically.

'You're not worried about leaving Lapland?'

'You worried about Norway?'

'Not at all.' He considered this for a moment, then added firmly: 'I like Alaska. I liked this run. Maybe you . . . me . . . him . . .' As he said this he looked toward the other sled, and what he saw outraged him.

'Stop! Stop!' and when the sleigh was halted he rushed over, bellowing: 'What have you done with those traces?' and Arkikov pointed to his harness, now geared Siberian-style with the traces coming straight down between the front legs.

'I told you the other way!' His voice rose: 'The right way!'

'But these Siberian deer . . . like my way. Stronger now than when we start.' And since there was truth to what he said, Skjellerup relaxed: 'All right. For the rest of the run.' But his mind was still on gold, and once he placed himself in the Siberian's hands, all was lost.

'Mr. Skjellerup! You . . . me . . . him . . . powerful team. We look all streams. We dig all sand.' It was obvious that Arkikov had queried prospectors when he delivered the reindeer to Council City, and most desperately he wanted to be with them searching for something more rewarding than the few dollars he earned tending reindeer.

So on the impulse of the moment, the Norwegian called a halt for the day, to the amazement of Ootenai, who had just that morning been urged to forge ahead so that the journey could be completed within two days. Now Skjellerup was eager only to talk, so while Ootenai tended the deer, he conducted a serious discussion with Sana and Arkikov.

'You say men were looking for gold?'

'Plenty men . . . seven maybe eighteen.'

'But were they finding any gold?'

'Not there. But Koyukuk River, yes. Yukon, yes.'

'How do they get the right to look?' Sana asked.

Now the Siberian became an expert: 'Me ask men . . . "Me got to ask this man, that man . . . come on his land?" '

'What did they say?'

'They laugh. All free . . . every land free. You find, you keep.'

'Could that be true?' It was so alien to what Skjellerup had known in Norway, where land was a jealously protected commodity, that he found it difficult to believe. But in reply, Arkikov ran to a tiny streamlet coming out of rocks and dipped his hand in, washing his palms back and forth as if they contained gravel. 'Every stream free . . . to you, to him.'

Now Sana spoke in Norwegian: 'I heard a Canadian say the same about his country. No one owns the land, millions of acres, so you can mine where you wish. The land doesn't become yours, but the gold does. If Arkikov finds gold tomorrow, it's his. You, me, we can dig anywhere, if what they told me was true.'

When he translated this for Arkikov, the three men fell silent, for they were being called upon to make decisions of the gravest import. But there could hardly be three men more eligible to do so. Lars Skjellerup had run his deer to the very top of the world. Mikkel Sana had traveled across Lapland through some of the loneliest terrain on earth. And Arkikov had left his secure homeland in Siberia to trust his luck in Alaska, and had proved his fortitude on this impressive mercy run to Barrow. These were men of resolution, courage and good sense. They were also men jealous of their rights, as the Siberian had just proved in returning to a system of harnessing which he preferred. If one had searched a far territory, he could not have found three men more capable and appropriate than these to go on a prospecting tour. They knew nothing about mining but they knew themselves.

They were unmarried. Skjellerup was the oldest at thirty-four, Sana next at thirty-two, with Arkikov the baby at twenty-eight. In raw intelligence—say in the ability to herd forty reindeer for eight months and wind up with fifty-seven, or to find true north when little was visible—these men were superior. And of great importance, each man had all his teeth and the constitution of a bull. Mining in Alaska was invented for the benefit of such men.

'I think we should make a try,' said Skjellerup, and Arkikov, hearing these reassuring words, shouted: 'We go many rivers . . . find much gold!' And after that joyous but carefully pondered moment of decision, the three never looked back. In fact, when the delayed trip to the station resumed, Skjellerup looked dispassionately at the flying feet of his marvelous steeds who had performed so well, and thought: Who would believe it? I'm tired of reindeer.

THEIR SUCCESSFUL RESCUE trip to Barrow occasioned so much favorable publicity that both the Alaska government, such as it was, and the national were prepared to look into further uses of the reindeer, but Skjellerup could express no interest: 'It's time I moved on. Young Eskimos like Ootenai are more than capable.' When his superiors asked: 'What will you do?' he replied: 'I'll find something,' for he was not ready at this point to reveal that he was about to go prospecting.

Everyone who knew this capable man wanted to employ him, the most unusual proposal being that he become the Presbyterian missionary at Barrow. When he explained 'I'm a Lutheran,' they said: 'Doesn't matter. You're obviously a man of God.'

And he was, in his own way. He loved animals, he could work with anyone, and he revered the earth, which seemed to him a special gift from God. But he was also now at the age when he wanted to work at something which produced money: 'I've served Norway, Lapland, Siberia and Alaska. Now, by damn, I serve Lars Skjellerup.'

In this time of wild movement in Alaska, which had commenced explosively with the discovery of gold along the Yukon, passports and such impedimenta were not in much demand. Of course, both Skjellerup and Sana had documents but they were grossly out of date, and as for Arkikov, he had only his grin. He had been brought to America under unique circumstances and almost any week he could catch a boat back to Siberia, for travel between the two lands was still frequent, convenient and untrammeled.

So on a bright day in late July 1898 the three partners left the station and headed east, taking with them a sled and three Siberian reindeer. Since there was no snow, they allowed one of the deer to pull the empty sled, while their packs were slung across the backs of the other two. They made an interesting study as they set forth on their great adventure, with tall, angular Skjellerup in the rear, tough, lean Sana in the middle and stout, happy Arkikov in front, setting the pace and almost running to get to the first stream.

They were dressed differently too, the Norwegian having adopted the standard dark, heavy clothing of the American prospector, the Lapp retaining his colorful garb, and the Siberian choosing a mixture of the fur clothing used by all the northern peoples. Their gear was modest but extremely practical and almost entirely handmade. Even the hammers had been given their handles by Arkikov and the sieves had been made by Mikkel Sana.

They started their prospecting by moving east, and at one small stream Arkikov panned enthusiastically, failed to notice the minute colors, and shouted to his companions: 'No gold this one,' so the men moved on. In this casual way they dismissed one of the richest streams in world history, but they should not be ridiculed for having bypassed a fortune, because during this restive summer many others would do the same.

After covering more than a hundred miles eastward, they found themselves in the midst of seventy or eighty other prospectors, and turned back to a spot on the map labeled Cape Nome, which would always be a curious place. There was a Cape Nome, and a Nome River, far apart and in no way connected. Later there would be a Nome City, miles removed from either of the first Nomes. When Skjellerup's team reached the cape, there was of course no town in the vicinity, only a handful of tents, but here they camped, finding nothing. Edging gingerly to the west, they returned to Nome River and again found only disappointment. At this point Arkikov, who fancied himself the expert miner in the trio, insisted that they hurry back to Council City and establish a claim, good or bad, but Skjellerup dissuaded him, and without much hope they and their reindeer wandered on to where the Snake River entered the sea.

It was probably the animals that accounted for the good fortune which was about to overtake them, because on a day in late September three agitated Swedish immigrants, who knew even less about mining than they, came in whispers to consult with Skjellerup in broken English: 'You Norwegian? Like they say?' When he replied in good Swedish that he was the man who had made the rescue run to Barrow, they sighed with deep relief and asked: 'Can you keep a secret?'

'Always have.'

'Are you willing to help us? If we count you in?'

'What's happening?'

Peering about to be sure no one from the tents along the shore was looking, the leader of the Swedes produced in the palm of his left hand a spent cartridge, and when he removed the protective wrapper and tilted the cartridge, a flow of golden dust and small pellets rolled out into the palm of his hand.

'Is that gold?' Skjellerup asked, and the three Swedes nodded.

'Where from?'

'Sssshhhh! We found a creek. It runs with gold. It's unbelievable, really.'

'Why do you tell me?'

'We need your help.'

'To do what?'

Again the Swedes looked about: 'We found the creek, but we don't know what to do next.'

It was fortunate that they had come to Skjellerup, for he was the kind of man who knew a little about everything, but not the kind who was arrogant about any of it. He knew, and that was enough.

'I think that within a certain time you have to hold a public meeting, because others have a right to know. Give them a chance to stake their claims. And you have to stake your discovery claim with great accuracy. Then you file some papers. And if you fail in any one of these, you lose everything.'

'That's what we feared.'

'Who else knows?'

'Nobody, but men have been sneaking around up there. Soon everyone will know.'

Lars Skjellerup was one of the ablest men on the gold fields that year, and now he proved it: 'I'll help, but I want the right to stake my claim, and tonight.'

'That's what we intended,' the Swedes said with an honesty that could not be questioned, except that Skjellerup did question it, thinking: That's what they say now, since I've asked. Wonder what they'd have said if I hadn't?'

'And for my two partners. We're a team, you know.'

'Your name again? Skjellerup? Somebody warned us we can claim only one site each, two for me because I found it. The other claims have to go to somebody. Might as well be to you and your partners.'

One of the Swedes asked: 'And who are those partners?' When Skjellerup introduced the Lapp and the Siberian, the other Swedes muttered: 'Could be trouble. We're all foreigners.' It turned out that the leader and one other Swede were naturalized, but that did leave four foreigners among the first six claimants.

'I think the law is clear,' Skjellerup assured them. 'Anyone in good standing can file a claim. We'll soon find out.'

After a few casual inquiries, they learned that a mining district could be declared in a public meeting if six miners were present and if knowledge of the strike was circulated, but none of these six knew the precise procedures and especially not the intricacies of filing a claim. 'We must trust one other person,' Skjellerup said. 'You choose.'

By the great good luck that sometimes watches over Swedes and other sensible people, the leader chose an older mining man, down on his luck but a veteran of many honorable battles. Up to now he had always reached the next auriferous area, as a gold field was technically called, six months late. Fate was now about to knock on his door three days early.

John Loden, himself a Swede of some generations back, knew exactly what to do, and advised that it be done with dispatch: 'Announce the meeting. Publicize it. Have your claims in order. Then stand back as the stampede begins.'

The meeting was held in a tent at the spot where the Snake River emptied into the Bering Sea, and eleven selected men were present, word of promising developments having been quietly circulated. Loden chaired the session and asked repeatedly for assistance from the floor. Two of the prospectors knew more mining law than he, and it was merciful that they were present, because in the wild days to come, their testimony that everything had been done legally was going to be significant.

When the four newcomers heard the seriousness of the seven who were in on the secret, they became wildly excited: 'Where is the strike?' and 'Are there real colors?'

'In good time, gentlemen, in good time.'

When all details were in order, insofar as the members could determine, Loden turned to the major Swede and said: 'Tell them!'

'We have struck real colors, an important find, on Anvil Creek.'

'Where in hell's that?'

'Up where the big rock hangs over. Looks like an anvil.'

One of the listeners yelled, another cheered, and a third shouted: 'Jesus Christ, here we go!' The fourth man, more practical than the others, went to the door of the tent and fired his revolver three times in the air to alert everyone in the tents: 'Major strike! Anvil Creek!' and some forty wild-eyed miners rushed out into the October night to stake their claims under a harvest moon.

Five, *Six* and *Seven Above* were staked by the Norwegian Skjellerup, the Lapp Sana and the Siberian Arkikov, and while men along the little stream cheered and fired guns and danced jigs together, Arkikov, in the moonlight, panned the first sand from his claim. It left gold dust at the bottom worth seven dollars. The three partners were going to be very rich.

THE SITUATION IN the newborn town of Nome was technically much as it had been along the Klondike following that fabulous strike: gold had been found, but so late in the year that no ships could bring stampeders through the icebound Bering Sea. The big push would be delayed ten months; however, miners already in the region were free to rush in and stake claims, and this they did, so that a real town began to develop, with a narrow Front Street running along the bleak waterfront.

In July 1899, when the big ships began crowding in with prospectors, Nome quickly became the largest city in Alaska, with no less than eleven bars, each of which claimed to be 'the best saloon in Alaska,' so an enterprising newcomer opened a still bigger bar, naming it proudly 'Second Best Saloon in Alaska.' One of its noisy patrons was a braggart from Nevada called Horseface Kling, who boasted that he 'knew more about mining law than any son-of-a-bitch in

Alaska,' and he was so self-assured that hangers-on began taking him seriously.

'No Russian has the right to come over here and claim on good American mining sites,' he bellowed, and as soon as he saw that he was gaining support, he added: 'I'm gonna by damn 'propriate *Seven Above* which that Siberian is holdin' illegal.' When this appealing battle cry was cheered, he assembled an armed posse, marched to the creek, and took possession.

He apparently did know something about mining procedures, for as soon as he returned to town he gathered his gang about him, appointed a chairman, and convened a general miners' meeting on the spot, which enthusiastically authorized the takeover. 'You will all testify,' he said at the conclusion of the meeting, 'that everything was done legal.' And as his men shouted their approval, *Seven Above* was ripped out of Arkikov's hands and deposited in those of Horseface Kling.

The effect on Arkikov was staggering. He had come to Alaska under pressure of performing public service; he had behaved well here; he had participated in the famous mercy run to Barrow; and he had been instrumental in establishing and developing Anvil Creek, and now to have the rewards of his industry torn away was intolerable, and he began to haunt the saloons, asking: 'Can do this America?' and people told him: 'This ain't America, it's Alaska.'

The theft stood, and after days of fruitless appeal, he met with his two former partners, warning them: 'Me Russian . . . pretty soon they do same to you Lapp, then you Norwegian,' and seeing the reasonableness of his prediction, they began to carry guns and bought him one.

Sure enough, as soon as Horseface Kling had his possession of *Seven Above* digested, he began pestering folks in the Second Best Saloon with complaints against 'that damned Lapp, little better than a Russian, who came over here and stole our good claims.' This time he was arguing on behalf of his partner, one Happy Magoon, a big man who smiled constantly, and after another miners' meeting, Mikkel Sana was dispossessed of *Six Above*, and it was made pretty clear in the Second Best Saloon that the Norwegian Lars Skjellerup was going to be next.

It soon became apparent that Happy Magoon, now the owner of *Six Above*, was a stupid man not able to think clearly and that Horseface Kling had used him merely as a front for stealing a fine claim. When rumors started to circulate against 'that damned Norwegian,' Skjellerup and the three Swedes could see that they were going to be next, and that before long Horseface was going to be sole possessor of seven fine claims on Anvil Creek.

How could such flagrant lawlessness be tolerated? Because the United States Congress still refused to give Alaska a sensible government. The region continued to struggle along as the District of Alaska, but what it was a district of, no one could say, and it was still hamstrung by the old Oregon territorial law that had been outmoded at the time of its imposition. Had Congress said: 'Let Alaska have the same laws that pertain in northern Maine,' it might have made sense, for the two types of land and problems would have been roughly similar, but to equate Alaska with Oregon was preposterous. Oregon was an agricultural state with spacious fields; if there was any flat land in Alaska, it was probably terrorized by grizzly bears. Oregon had been peopled by God-fearing men and women who brought with them a New England Puritan dedication to organized life and work in settlements; Alaska, by drifters like John Klope from a run-down farm in Idaho and rascals like Horseface Kling from temporary mining camps. Oregon, in other words, was a beautifully controlled area which had aspired to be another Connecticut as soon as possible, while Alaska was determined to remain unlike any other American region as long as possible.

But you had to be on the scene to appreciate the real insanity of life in Alaska, and no better laboratory for analysis than Nome could have been found. Since the old Oregon territorial law had not provided for the establishment of new towns like Nome, the burgeoning boomtown could not elect a city government, and since the law did not provide for health services, none could be authorized in Nome; everyone in the town could throw his bathroom slops where he damned well pleased. Craziest of all was the circular insanity which still prevented courts from trying criminals. Oregon law clearly stated that no man could be a juror unless he proved that he had paid his taxes, but since there was no government in Alaska, no taxes were collected. This meant that there could be no trial by jury, which meant that ordinary courts could not exist.

And this preposterous state of affairs meant that criminals like Horseface Kling could commit their thefts with impunity. The famous boast of frontier brawlers in times past, 'No court in the land can lay a hand on me,' had become a reality in Alaska. The stolen mining claims now belonged to Horseface, and their former owners had no court to which they could appeal.

However, justice of another kind was available, and had an impartial observer familiar with frontiers studied the Anvil Creek dispossessions, he might have warned: 'Of all the men in this corner of Alaska to steal from, those three have got to be the most dangerous!' and he would point to the dour, self-reliant Norwegian, the steel-sinewed Lapp and the wildly imaginative Siberian to whom anything was possible. He would point out: 'These men have traversed great distances unafraid, slept unprotected in blizzards at sixty-below, and saved Barrow. It seems highly unlikely that they will allow a braggart from Nevada to dispossess them of rights which they gained the hard way.' But less sagacious men in the Second Best would point out: 'In Nome there is no law.'

On 12 July 1899, Horseface Kling was found shot to death at the entrance to his mine *Seven Above*, and shortly thereafter a grinning Happy Magoon was quietly told: 'You no longer own *Six Above*.' No one discovered who had done the shooting, and no one really cared, for by this time it was clear that Horseface had intended sweeping up everyone's claim, so his death was not lamented. And when the industrious Lapp, Mikkel Sana, recovered his ownership of *Six Above*, no one protested, for it was now recognized that he had more than earned the right to hold that claim.

However, when the Siberian Arkikov tried to move back onto *Seven Above*, the original protests were revived, and in a raucous miners' meeting it was again decreed that no Russian could hold a claim on Anvil Creek, and he was once more evicted.

This time the rugged fellow was completely distraught, and again he moved from bar to bar trying to elicit sympathy and support, but now a rumor started circulating: 'It was the Siberian who murdered Horseface,' and the very men who had applauded the death of the usurper resented the fact that a Siberian had slain an American, and he became something of an outcast. His two partners tried to console him with a promise that they would share their profits with him, but this did not pacify him, and he continued to rant about the fact that this should never have happened in America.

But he was at heart an incorruptible optimist, and after several days of venting his resentment, he grabbed his prospecting gear and started up the valley cut by the parent stream, Snake River, testing the gravel in even the tiniest tributary. He found nothing, and as dusk approached on the third day he came back to Nome disconsolate and seething.

What happened next can be appreciated only by another miner, but Arkikov had his prospecting tools—a fifty-cent pan and a sixty-cent shovel—he had plenty of time, and he certainly had a wild lust for gold, so with no further streams to prospect, he looked at the endless stretch of beach before him and he cried with the soul of a true miner: 'Whole goddamn ocean . . . me look.' And he began to sift the sands of the Bering Sea.

Such things had happened before. Some men, drifting down the Mackenzie from Edmonton, had prospected every creek along the way. Others, near death from starvation, had paused in the mountains to prospect some errant stream. And now the Siberian Arkikov was prepared to prospect the whole Bering Sea. It was irrational, but to him it made sense.

He did not have to move far along the empty beach, for in his second pan, there in the quiet dusk with curlews overhead, he came upon one of the strangest finds in the history of mining. His pan, when washed in seawater, showed colors, and not just flecks, but real, substantial grains of gold.

Unwilling to believe what he saw, he poured the gold into an empty cartridge, then dipped again and once more found colors. Again and again, almost insanely, he ran along the beach, dipping and testing and always finding gold.

July sunset at Nome in those days before time was fiddled with came at about nine-thirty, so all that evening, in the gray-silver haze while the sun toyed with the horizon, this wild Siberian ran along the beaches, dipping and testing, and when night finally fell he had a story to relate that would astound the world.

He whispered it first to his partners, at a table in the Second Best Saloon, for if they had been faithful enough to promise him a share of their wealth, he must reciprocate: 'No look round. No speak. Me find something.' Quietly he handed the cartridge to Skjellerup, who furtively inspected it, whistled softly, and passed it along to Sana, who did not whistle but who did raise his eyebrows.

'Where?' Skjellerup asked without changing expression.

'The beach.'

These two tested miners were the first to hear that the beaches of Nome literally crawled with gold, and like everyone who followed, they disbelieved. Clearly, Arkikov's misfortunes had addled his brain, and yet . . . there was the gold, clean and of a high quality. He had got it somewhere.

They would mollify him, urge him to keep his voice down, and when he was tranquil they would ask: 'What stream did you find it in?' But even after they had tried this tactic, they received the same answer.

'You mean the beach? The sea? Waves?'

'Yes.'

'You mean some miner lost his poke on the beach and you found it?'

'No.'

'What part of the beach?'

'Whole goddamn beach.'

This was so incredible that the two men suggested: 'Let's go to our digs and talk this over,' and when they did, Skjellerup and Sana found that Arkikov was locked into his story that the common, ordinary beaches of Nome teemed with gold.

'How many spots did you try?'

'Many. Many.'

'And all gave colors?'

'Yes.'

The two men considered this, and although they were inwardly driven to reject the report as improbable, there in the cartridge rested a substantial amount of gold. Putting half into his hand, Skjellerup held it toward the Siberian and asked: 'If the sands are filled with this, why hasn't anybody else found it?' and Arkikov gave the resounding answer that explained the mystery of mining: 'Nobody look. Me look. Me find.'

It was now midnight, and since the sun would rise at two-thirty, Skjellerup and Sana decided to remain awake and go out in the earliest dawn to test the truth of their partner's implausible yarn. 'We mustn't work near each other,' Skjellerup warned, 'and don't let anyone see us actually panning. Pick up driftwood maybe.'

Arkikov said he would not join them. He was tired from his days of prospecting and had to have sleep; besides, he knew the gold was there.

So the Norwegian and the Lapp eased themselves out of their bunks at quarter past two on the morning of 16 July 1899 and strolled casually along the beaches of Nome, stopping idly now and then to salvage driftwood, and at five in the morning Lars Skjellerup sat on a log, covered his face with his hands, and came as near to tears as he ever had: 'I am so happy for Arkikov. After what they did to him.'

Displaying no emotion, the two stragglers slipped back to their bunks and shook Arkikov: 'The beaches are full of gold,' and he said sleepily: 'Me know. Me find.'

That afternoon, following the most careful assessment of how the three partners could best protect their interests in this incredible find, Skjellerup called a miners' meeting at which he spoke with great force:

'Gentlemen, you know my partner here, Arkikov, who you call "that damned Siberian." Well, he's made a discovery that's going to make all of you millionaires. Well, maybe not that much, but damned rich.

'Now there's no law in Nome, and there's no example that we can apply in handling this stupendous find. The usual claim size just don't pertain. So we'll have to work out special rules, which I believe we can do.'

A miner off to the right called impatiently: 'What did he find?' and Skjellerup took from his pocket the cartridge, holding it high in his right hand and allowing the golden particles, some of which he himself had picked up that morning, to float down through the afternoon air and into his left palm. Even the men in the farthest corners of the Second Best could see that this was what they had come so far to find, placer gold.

'Where?' voices shouted as men edged toward the door to be the first to claim on the subsidiary sites.

'Like I told you, there's never been a gold field like this one. We need new rules. I'm proposing that each man gets . . . well, let's say ten yards to the side.'

This was so preposterously minute in relation to a normal claim—five hundred yards along the stream and across the flow to the top of the first bench —that the men howled.

'All right!' Skjellerup conceded. 'This is an organizing meeting and you set the rules. That's proper, so go ahead.'

'Like always, five hundred yards along the stream and bench to bench.'

'But there are no benches. There is no stream.'

'Where in hell is it?'

'Tell them, Arkikov.' And the smiling Siberian, all his white teeth showing, uttered the unprecedented words: 'Along the beach. Whole goddamn beach. Me find.'

Before his last words were pronounced, men were bursting out of the saloon, and within a minute only the three partners and one bartender, the one with a bad leg, were left. The real gold rush at Nome had begun.

THE BEACH STRIKE at Nome was unique in many ways. Because the gold was so readily available, prospectors who had missed earlier rushes now had a second chance; they had only to dig in the sand and take out ten thousand dollars or forty, and if they could devise some ingenious machine for sluicing large quantities of sand with seawater, they were in line to become millionaires. Also, the painful work that John Klope had had to do high on his unproductive ridge above Eldorado—burrowing down forty feet, building fires to thaw the frozen muck and hauling it to the surface—would be avoided at Nome, where a man could go out in the morning, test his luck through an easy day, and complain in the saloons that night: 'Today I panned only four hundred dollars.'

But there was a similarity between the two historic strikes. As on the Klondike, Arkikov made his discovery so late in the season that even though word did get to Seattle on the last ship south, the Bering Sea froze over before any other ship could come north. This meant that the relatively few men lucky enough to reach Nome before the freeze would have clear pickings from July 1899 through June 1900. But while they sieved, a tremendous backlog of would-be miners would be building up at San Francisco and Seattle, for word had swept the world that 'in Nome the beaches are crawlin' with gold,' and the handful of miners who went south on that last ship had pouches and bars to prove it. When the ice finally melted in the early summer of 1900, Nome's population was going to skyrocket to more than thirty thousand, and it would still be a city without laws.

THE YUKON RIVER presented its own problem, because the *Jos. Parker*, on its last trip upriver before the freeze, carried with it news of the unique find, and even before the boat docked at Dawson, a deckhand was shouting: 'Gold found on the beach at Nome!'

The effect was not electric, it was volcanic, because every miner who had missed the big strike on the Klondike knew that he had to get to the next one fast, and within half an hour after that first shout, eager men were crowding the riverfront seeking passage to Nome. As one old miner expressed it to Tom Venn, who was in charge of selling tickets for his R&R's *Jos. Parker*'s home-ward run back to St. Michael: 'Stands to reason, don't it? It's winter in Nome, just like here, and they cain't no ships get into Nome from Seattle till next June. If'n I kin get there on your boat, I got the field all to meself. This time I stake me a claim.' He was distressed when Tom had to tell him: 'No bunks left, mister. Last ones sold off fifteen minutes ago.'

'What kin I do?' the old man asked, and Tom said: 'Sleep on deck,' and the miner almost shouted: 'Gimme a ticket,' and with it clutched in his hand, he ran off to fetch his bedroll for the long trip.

The sleeping bunks had been preempted so quickly because within ten minutes of that first shout of 'Gold at Nome,' the Belgian Mare had called to her ten girls: 'Pack! We're off to Nome!' and she had rushed to Venn's office to grab eleven berths. Like the fabled rats whose departure signaled the sinking of the ship, this departure of the Belgians from their cribs gave notice that Dawson was doomed. For two years it had been a golden city; Nome would be the next thing higher than that.

Tom was preoccupied with trying to calculate how many more deck spaces he could sell on the *Parker* when he received a jolt from his manager, Mr. Pincus, an old R&R hand who had run stores at various locations for the big Seattle firm: 'Tom, chance of a lifetime. I'm going to ship everything we have down to Nome. I wish I could get approval from Mr. Ross first, but the motto of our company is "If it has to be done, do it." Dawson is finished. Nome will have fifty thousand people this time next year.' He smiled at the boy and asked, 'How old are you?' and when Tom replied 'Seventeen,' giving himself the benefit of a year, the manager said: 'You're old enough. You've seen what can happen in a gold field. Sail down to St. Michael with the *Parker*, then move your goods over to Nome, build a store, a big one, and give honest service.'

'You mean . . . ?'

'I do. Son, it's either you or me, and frankly, it's more difficult to close down a store than to open one. I'm needed here. You're needed there.'

As Tom started to tremble, overcome by the gravity of the proposal, the manager called him to his desk: 'A wise old man gave me these gold scales, Tom. I've used them on three different fields. There's no rust on them, is there?' When Tom studied the handsome little balances and the set of weights for weighing gold dust, he could see no rust. 'I mean moral rust. Tom, I do believe those scales have never weighed a dishonest poke. Keep them polished.'

Sailing of the *Parker* was delayed one day so that practically the entire stock of goods from the R&R store in Dawson could be crammed aboard, and while Tom was supervising the placement of the valuable wares for which he was now responsible, he heard such giggling from the cabins booked by the Belgian Mare that he concluded her fare was going to be repaid by the end of this first night in port.

In one important respect the delay was fortunate, for at dawn on the second day, three people of great importance to Tom appeared, two of them seeking passage. They were Missy Peckham, Matthew Murphy and, to Tom's amazement, tall, dour John Klope. Missy and Murphy were the ones who wanted to depart, but they had no money, the gold fields had not been good to them; and since Klope had found no colors deep in his shaft, neither did he.

They had come to throw themselves on the mercy of their common friend Tom Venn, and Klope did the speaking: 'Tom, you're like a son to me. I beg you like your father might if he was here today. Take Missy and Matt to Nome. Give them another chance.'

'I'd have to charge passage, company rules.'

This was a heartbreaking moment, for these three who had striven so valiantly, who had endured between them all the agonies of the gold rush, had nothing to show for their courage and toil. They were broke, dead flat broke, and two of them sought money to escape. For Klope, it seemed there would be no escape; he was locked into his futile shaft forever.

When Tom asked: 'Who helps you now?' he said: 'Sarqaq. His leg never healed. He can't run dogs no more, but he sells one now and then. We live.'

After these diversionary remarks, Tom had to give the waiting trio the bad news: 'The boat can take only one more,' and without hesitation Matt pushed Missy forward: 'She's the one,' but then Tom had to say: 'Her fare has to be paid . . . by someone.' In the discussion that followed, three things were clear: Missy had to get to Nome; Matt would follow later as best he could; and none of the three had the money required for passage.

Klope waited for one of the others to speak, then took Tom aside: 'She looked after you . . . when your father died, when you were a kid in Dawson, and at our mine. It's your job to look after her now,' and with that, he pushed

Tom back to confront the woman with whom his young life had been so closely intertwined.

'Missy,' he said in a fumbling manner, 'you were better than a mother to me. I'll pay your fare.' In silence Missy accepted the ticket, for her hard life on the gold fields had led her to expect no acts of generosity. However, she did look at Tom, wanting to mutter some words of thanks, but when she saw that he was equally embarrassed, she said nothing.

The journey had to be swift, for ice was beginning to form; there could be no more trips this year, and Captain Grimm snorted at the calls for speed: 'Two years ago, everybody in a great hurry to get to Dawson. Freeze my boat in the Yukon. This year, everybody in a hurry to get out. Maybe we freeze again.'

'Oh my God!' a miner cried. 'And miss the claims again?'

'Forced draft, if you'll load the wood promptly at the stops.'

Now, since the *Jos. Parker* had become part of a regular shipping line, when Grimm pulled into a wood depot the waiting cords were earmarked for him, as an R&R regular, so it was possible to maintain a forced draft. But even so, it was a touchy race, because as so many riverboat captains had learned in past years, the mouth of the Yukon often froze nearly solid while the upstream parts were still open. This year, however, he slipped through, but as he left the river for the Bering Sea he watched behind him as the great river closed down. His would be the last boat through.

P ASSENGERS FROM THE *Parker* were the last people into Nome before the winter freeze clamped fingers of ice over the town. The beaches now contained thirteen miles of canvas tents stretching to the west and another eleven miles reaching eastward toward Cape Nome. At some places the frozen Bering Sea edged to within ten yards of the tents, its icy hummocks towering above them. How will those poor men survive the blizzards? Missy asked herself when she saw the endless string of flimsy white tents, but then she laughed: Wrong question. How will I survive?

After much searching, she found a one-room shack in an alley, but now the question became: How can I pay for it? and the solution arrived in a curious way. For as she looked down at the pathway in front of her shack, she saw that the entire area was encased in a yellow glacier two feet thick composed of frozen urine, and as she stared in disgust at the icy sewage, men from the saloons on Front Street came out to use the alley as a toilet.

She was so enraged by this that she asked the owner of her shack: 'Aren't there any public closets in this town?' and he said: 'There isn't anything. No closets, no services, no law of any kind,' and she asked: 'Well, isn't there a doctor?' and he directed her to a tentlike affair in which a young man from Seattle struggled to tend the health problems of Nome.

Blustering into his tent, she asked: 'Do you know that the alley in front of my shack is two feet deep in frozen urine?' and he said: 'Look at the alley in back of my tent,' and when she did she saw a massive pile of human feces.

'Good God, Doctor! This town's in trouble,' and he said reassuringly: 'Not until the thaw. Then, of course, people will die of dysentery. And we'll be lucky if we escape epidemics of typhoid and diphtheria.'

'You need my help, Doctor. I can keep records and keep track of your medicines and help with your women patients.' The young man was barely earning enough to support himself, but was persuaded by Missy's strong plea: 'Just till my husband gets here. He's in Dawson, but he'll be down one of these days.' And in that way she acquired a job that would at least sustain her till Matt arrived.

During her first days at work, she was further shocked to learn that the few wells which had been dug for drinking water had been placed so that anything could flow into them, while the Snake River, from which most of the town's water came, also served as the town's sewer. When Missy protested the situation, the doctor said: 'Don't tell me! I saw it three months ago. I can't understand why half the population isn't deathly ill right now. A miracle must be protecting us, but don't drink a drop of water that hasn't been boiled.'

With no one responsible for streets, the thoroughfares of Nome were frozen cesspools into the cold morasses of which horses sometimes casually disappeared during a temporary thaw. Theft became common; the Belgian Mare opened her cribs right on the main street; children did not go to school; and there were three saloons for every grocery store. Not far wrong was the newspaper editor who cried: 'Nome is a hell on earth.'

Missy had been in town only a week when she had an opportunity to witness just how lawless the place had become. Near her shack clustered several canvas tents, each occupied by one man, and following the discovery of gold on the beach, it was likely that in any given tent there would be a small poke filled with the precious metal. Gangs of ruthless thieves had devised a bizarre method of stealing such gold: they scouted saloons until some lone miner rolled home, but since they knew that every miner went armed after the shooting of Horseface Kling, the gang did not attack him till he was in his tent and safely snoring. Then they crept up, slit the canvas near his head, and poked through the hole a long stick with a rag soaked in chloroform tied on the far end. When the miner succumbed to the vapors, the thieves entered casually, spent ten or fifteen minutes methodically taking the place apart, and in this way laid hold of much gold. It was a kind of painless theft, because when the miner woke up, all that was missing was his gold, and when he returned to the beaches he could replace that.

On the night involving Missy, things went wrong as two different gangs worked the tents. In the first one, either the victim had received an inadequate dose of chloroform or the thieves dawdled, because the man awakened, saw through the film over his eyes that two strange men were robbing his poke, and bellowed. This wakened Missy, who ran out in time to see the robbers escape with the gold. Seeing that the victim needed help, Missy ran for the doctor, who easily detected from the smell what had happened. Together they brought the miner back to full consciousness.

While the doctor stayed to care for the man, Missy went to check the other tents. Most of the occupants were still in saloons, but when she came upon a tent with a ripped canvas and peered inside, she saw lying on the cot an inert miner with a big wad of chloroformed rag over his face. Instinctively alarmed, she shouted: 'Doctor! Come here!' and when a crowd gathered in the cold November night they found the miner was dead. The fracas in the first tent had frightened the second group of thieves, and they had fled, but when they pulled away the long stick, the heavily dosed rag had fallen off, covering the miner's mouth and nostrils, and asphyxiated him.

When the doctor led Missy back to her shack she bolted the door and propped a chair against the window. 'This is a dreadful town,' she said as she sat unsteadily on the bed. 'You have to protect yourself every minute.'

However, after the miner was buried she had a chance to inspect Nome more carefully, and she concluded that two establishments were well run, the

Mare's cribs and the Ross & Raglan store, where Tom Venn, only sixteen but more mature than most of his customers, ran a taut shop. He was willing to buy almost anything that destitute miners wanted to sell and to offer it to others at decent prices. She saw Tom at his best one day in mid-November when he came running to her shack pleading for help.

'What's the matter?' Missy asked, and he blurted out: 'That idiot who had the little general store before I came down to set up R&R. Can you guess what he did?'

'Steal the funds?'

'Worse. He was stupid.' And he led her to an improvised warehouse about which he had just learned. The roof had blown off and a huge stack of canned goods shipped up from Seattle during the summer had been drenched by so many rains that the labels had soaked off.

'Look at them! Five hundred, six hundred cans. All from the same cannery. All alike. And nobody can tell what's in them.'

In disgust he applied a mechanical opener at random: 'Sweet corn, cherries, plums, sweet potatoes.' Missy inspected the four cans, and had to agree that they contained no outer clue which would help identify other like cans in the mess.

'What'll I do?' Tom wailed, but Missy was busy tasting the contents, which, with a smack of her lips, she pronounced delicious. And that's when Tom Venn proved capable of making a practical decision. Taking a huge square of cardboard, he worked in his rude office while Missy and a helper moved the stack of label-less cans to the roadway in front of the store, where they constructed an eye-catching pyramid in front of which Tom placed the sign:

DELICIOUS FOOD
GUARANTEED WHOLESOME
CONTENTS UNKNOWN
5¢ A CAN
TRY YOUR LUCK

Within the hour all the cans were gone and the drifters of Nome were telling one another what a good sport this young fellow who ran the R&R store was.

This imaginative action caught the attention of Lars Skjellerup and the other responsible men who were trying to maintain some kind of order, and despite Tom's youth he was invited to become a member of Skjellerup's informal governing team, as Tom explained in a letter that he dispatched to his superiors in Seattle:

Under the leadership of men like Skjellerup this town has enormous potential, and although Dawson proves that a gold town can go bust in one year, I find no similarity between the two places. Dawson is landlocked at the far end of the Canadian road, of no interest to anyone but miners. Nome is a seaport at the crossroads between Asia and America and must prosper.

During a clear spell I rode a reindeer sled out to Cape Prince of Wales and could see Siberian Russia only sixty miles away. Boats pass easily between the two coasts and I would expect traffic between them to multiply.

I must warn you about one thing. We are making huge profits, and when forty or fifty steamers lay to off our coast come June, we shall make more. But Nome has no government, none at all, and no system of fire prevention. If one building catches fire, the entire city will go up in flames. Therefore, I shall keep inventory low and remit all money to Seattle as promptly as possible, for one of these days I expect to see my beautiful store in flames.

However, there is hope that we shall soon be allowed to have a government. There's talk that Congress is about to pass a law giving Alaska two judges, and if that happens, one of them is to be stationed here. Then things must improve and I shall expect our young city to forge ahead.

As the last days of 1899 approached, the citizens of Nome, eager for any excuse to hold a celebration, decided to organize a slam-bang affair to welcome the birth of the twentieth century, even though sensible men knew that would not occur until midnight on 31 December, 1900, and during preparations Lars Skjellerup assured Tom: 'The days of no law in this city are passing. When the ice breaks next May or June, and the federal judge arrives, things'll begin to hum. No more claim-jumping, no more.'

'Can a federal judge do all that?' Tom asked, and Skjellerup had to admit that he did not know, but he did know a man called Professor Hale, a former schoolteacher who would. He was a cadaverous fellow with a huge Adam's apple and a thunderous voice who loved to give his opinion on everything, so on the festive day before Christmas an informal meeting was held in the Second Best Saloon, and Hale demonstrated his wide knowledge.

'In our American system a federal judge is about the finest official we have.'

'Better'n the President?' a miner shouted, and Hale snapped: 'In some ways, yes. The judge serves for life, and in the long history of our nation, no federal judge has ever been found corrupt. When all else fails, you turn to him for justice.'

'You mean, they're responsible only to Washington?' Skjellerup asked, and Hale replied: 'They're responsible only to God. Not even the President can touch them.' He became almost evangelical: 'Gentlemen, I thank you for inviting me here today. A year from now, with a federal judge on the bench, you won't recognize Nome.'

Skjellerup and Hale were wrong in jumping to the conclusion that the incoming judge would be from the federal bench but right in assuming that he would arrive with plenipotentiary powers. If he was the proper choice, he could bring Nome quickly into the ranks of civilized society.

'One thing he'll do for sure,' Professor Hale told Skjellerup, 'he'll restore *Seven Above* to your Siberian friend,' and as the old century ended, nearly everyone in Nome, except the chloroform gangs, was prepared to welcome the powerful judge. They were ready, and perhaps even eager, to be regulated in an honest way, for anarchy had sickened them.

NOME HAD CELEBRATED New Year's Day only three times. In 1897 the entire population, three unsuccessful miners, had gathered in a bitterly cold tent to share a hoarded bottle of beer. As 1898 began, again the whole population, only fourteen and still all men, had celebrated with whiskey and pistol shots, and as 1899 started, with the golden sands about to be discovered, a mixed population of more than four hundred, including the pioneers known by then as the Three Lucky Swedes and Lars Skjellerup's team, had had a high old time with songs in many languages.

But at the end of December this year, the three thousand citizens of Nome, aware that their number must soon explode to more than thirty thousand, brought out caches of whiskey which had been hidden in the big boxes that served as root cellars. Of course, it was impossible to have real cellars; the permafrost would not allow it.

On the last day of what men insisted on calling the dying century, one of Tom Venn's clerks asked: 'Everyone says Nome may soon have twenty or thirty thousand more people. How can they know that? If no news can't get in here, how can any get out?'

Tom became defensive: 'They don't know for sure, but if you want to know how I made my guess, just listen. When news of gold on the beaches trickled up to Dawson City, our riverboat, the *Parker*, was about to leave with sixteen passengers. Within half an hour we had more than one hundred, and when it sailed, nearly two hundred were aboard, and I do believe it could have picked up another fifty at Circle and fifty more at Fort Yukon, if it could've held them. People slept standing up!'

'What's that mean?' the clerk asked.

'It means you better get that addition finished, because I know in my bones that Seattle and San Francisco are filled right now with people aching to get to Nome.'

For a variety of reasons the Nome gold strike was trebly attractive. The gold was on American soil, not Canadian. A miner could get to it on a luxury steamer in no way inferior to those that sailed to Europe. And when he landed, all he had to do, he thought, was to 'sift sand and ship the gold bars home.' This was prospecting deluxe. And there was a final attraction: anyone who had missed the earlier strikes in Colorado, Australia and the Yukon could compensate in Nome.

There were drawbacks. Because thick ice captured the Bering Sea early and firmly, ships could operate only from June through September, and even then at grave risk, for the town had no docking facilities and could have none. And the hours of daylight available for gold seeking oscillated radically through the year: four hours in winter, twenty-two in summer; and since these endless winter nights could be formidable, the people of Nome welcomed any diversion, such as the beginning of a new year.

As the sun went down at two in the afternoon on the thirty-first of December, citizens began assembling in saloons, and at the Second Best, Lars Skjellerup assured everyone of three things: 'Congress will pass the law giving us a government. We'll get a good judge. And gold on the beaches will never run out, because it goes twenty or thirty feet deep. Any new storm, it uncovers new concentrations.'

His listeners spent much of the afternoon arguing as to how the Nome gold got to the beaches, for this had happened nowhere else on earth. One miner who had collected a small fortune said: 'The Bering Sea is filled with gold. The tide brings it our way.' Another reasoned: 'There's this small volcano ten miles out under the waves. It spews gold regular.' Others claimed that at some past time a river of lava had run out of a land volcano, now vanished, and had dropped its gold as the rock pulverized in the sea. It was Arkikov's idea, which he had trouble expressing except through wild use of his hands, that the gold was no different from that of the Yukon: 'Many years ago . . . little river . . . comes across rocks with gold. Many years . . . gold wash free . . . reaches shore . . . me find . . . me know.'

But his broken words failed to convince even his own partners, each of whom had his own bizarre theory. The gold of Nome was regular in every detail except in the way it finally came to rest . . . and its abundance.

When Tom Venn joined the celebration after closing his store for the year, someone shouted: 'A drink to the benefactor of Nome,' and men cheered.

'What did the young feller do?' asked a miner who had walked overland in November cold from his unrewarding diggings on the Kyokuk River, and another man told the story of the cans of good food which Tom had sold for five cents each: 'He'll be the John Wanamaker of Nome.'

At a minute to midnight the banker leaped upon the bar and whipped out his watch: 'We'll count down to welcome the greatest century Nome will ever have. Forty-five, forty-four, forty-three, forty-two . . .'

When he reached ten, all in the bar were shouting in unison, and as the new year dawned, men started kissing any women in sight and clapping new acquaintances on the back. Tom Venn sought out Missy Peckham and kissed her fervently: 'I've wanted to do that since 1893,' and Missy said: 'High time.'

IN THE THREE long months following the celebration, Nome went into its yearly hibernation, for life in a frozen mining camp could be unbelievably monotonous. Even Tom Venn, who preferred the town over Dawson, saw that it had disadvantages, which he was willing to discuss with his customers: 'It's farther north. Days are shorter. And Dawson never had that bitter wind that whips in from the sea. There's a lot wrong with Nome, but its spirit, that's for me!'

The things Nome did to entertain itself were ingenious, but two diversions were especially regarded. Professor Hale, who had never taught anything beyond grade seven, was prevailed upon to give readings from Shakespeare. Before large audiences of miners who packed one of the halls, he sat in a chair on a platform, clad in a togalike garment which reached to his toes, and with a tumbler of whiskey at hand to keep his voice lubricated, he read aloud in powerful tones the more popular plays.

He took all parts, all voices, and he had always had such a love for Shakespeare that as the action quickened, or when he came to some part he especially liked, he would rise from his chair, prance about the platform, and shout the words until the smoky hall echoed. When he was required to depict Lady Macbeth or any of the other heroines, he manipulated his toga in such a way that, combined with his high, querulous voice, he became a distraught murderess or a lovesick Juliet. Indeed, it was so much fun to hear Professor Hale that when the cycle of plays ended, the miners insisted that he start repeating them, but this he refused to do. Instead, he advertised a special evening in which he would 'deliver in sonorous voice the immortal sonnets of the Bard of Avon.'

The hall was filled when he came onto the platform, and those in front could see that in addition to a slim volume of the sonnets, he had brought with him a much larger tumbler than before: 'I am not at all certain, ladies and gentlemen, that I can make these sonnets, all to be read in the same voice, as interesting as the plays, but believe me, if I fail, the fault is mine and not Shakespeare's.'

He had not reached the great sonnets, those with the singing lines, before he began reading certain ones as if a young girl were uttering them, or an old man, or a warrior, and when he came to the final dozen, with his tumbler near empty and the audience enraptured by his flow of words, he began to let himself go, reading the sonnets as if they were the most powerful and dramatic of the Bard's writings. He was shouting, mouthing, posturing, leaping forward and slinking back, always maintaining the powerful voice which thrilled his listeners. Rarely had the sonnets been accorded such a rousing performance.

The second treasured re-creation was the Eskimo Dance, a bizarre and almost dreamlike affair which had been invented in response to one of Alaska's preeminent features.

For the greater part of its recent history, Alaska has had the problem of men's coming into the district without women, as when the Russian traders came in numbers but without women; or the western explorers probed the seas for years without seeing women of their own kind; or when merchant whalers from New England arrived, always without women; or, more recently, when the gold seekers poured into the area, always forty or fifty men to one woman.

As a consequence, the story of Alaska has had to focus upon the friendships between men, their trustworthiness, their tragedies, their triumphs at the conclusion of incredible heroics. When women did appear in these highly structured affairs they were apt to be prostitutes, or native women already married to some Eskimo, Aleut or Athapascan. In the mining camps, wherever enough men concentrated, the ritual of the evening dance developed, where men hungry for entertainment and any kind of association with women on even bizarre terms would hire a fiddler or two, most often native men who had more or less acquired the skill, and a dance would be announced. Admission: Men $1. Women free.

There might be in the area one white woman who would don her best frock and be expected to dance with each of the men; the rest of the women, perhaps as many as eight or nine, would be natives of any age from thirteen to fifty, and they would come shyly to the dance, often well after the fiddler had started, edging in and standing along the wall, never smiling or giggling or looking directly at any particular white man.

After a period of social thaw, one of the women would step away from the wall and begin a monotonous dancelike motion, mostly up and down but with her shoulders swaying, and when she had done this for a moment or two, some miner would step forward, face her, and without ever touching her, go through his own interpretation of a dance, and so they would move as long as this set of music continued.

Once the ice was broken, and that is not an inappropriate idiom, for the temperature outside might be thirty-below, other women would begin to dance in their own dreamlike way, and other men would join them, never touching, never speaking. Since the women did not remove much of their clothing, they looked like round furry little animals, and some added to that impression by dancing with babies strapped to their backs. It didn't matter, for the lonely miners had come to see women, and many onlookers who constituted most of the paying audience did no dancing themselves. They watched, for they were the kinds of men to whom prostitutes would be unthinkable and actual participation in the dance improbable, or, in extreme cases, absolutely out of the question. They were men desperately wanting to see again what women looked like, and they were content to pay for the privilege.

At about eleven the fiddlers would stop, silence would fill the hall, and one by one the native women would depart, each one receiving a dollar for that night's performance. On most nights no man would have spoken to any woman, or laughed with her, or touched even her arm, and it was customary, when the dance ended, for the women to be escorted home by their men, who had been waiting outside and who now preempted the dollar for family needs.

That was the famous Eskimo Dance, that curious symbol of man's loneliness and hunger for human association, and it came into being almost of necessity, because the men had persisted in coming into the arctic without their women.

At Nome the dance had a peculiarity which occasioned some difficulty for

Missy Peckham, for she was an attractive little white woman with whom the miners wanted to dance in the American mode, and they urged her to attend. It was flattering to have young men and some not so young lined up for every dance, but it also had its drawbacks, because during the course of any evening Missy would receive three or four invitations to move into the quarters of this miner or that, so she had constantly to explain that her man Murphy would be arriving from Dawson at any moment.

This caused merriment among her suitors: 'How's he gonna come down the Yukon? Swim?' They pointed out that Murphy, if he really existed, which they doubted, 'couldn't no way get here before the June thaw, no boats runnin'—so why waste the winter?'

She insisted that he would be arriving anytime now: 'He survived the Mackenzie River in Canada, and that's a lot tougher than the Yukon,' and like Penelope resisting the suitors who pestered her, Missy never deviated from her conviction that one of these days her Ulysses, through one device or another, would soon be joining her in Nome. But how he would accomplish this she did not know, and if someone had whispered to her what Matt's plan was, she would have thought the scheme plain crazy.

WHEN THE *JOS. PARKER*, last ship out of Dawson for Nome, departed with Missy Peckham aboard, it left Matt Murphy stranded ashore, with several unappealing options as to how he might overtake his lady and join her in exploiting the town where 'gold nuggets the size of pigeon eggs can be picked up on the beach.' He could wait nine months till the Yukon thawed in the spring and catch the first boat down, but by then all the good spots would be taken. Or he could associate himself with some party of men trying to hike down, but as a fiercely independent Irishman, he did not trust group adventures. But doing it alone would necessitate the purchase of a dog team, a sled and enough meat to keep the dogs fit for two months as they tackled the thousand-mile run.

Rejecting all these choices, he settled upon one so bizarre that only a mad Irishman down on his luck could have dared it. Since the Yukon River would soon be frozen almost solid all the way to the Bering Sea, why not use it as a highway and to hell with waiting for it to thaw so that boats could navigate it? The idea was a sound one, but what to use for transportation if walking was out and no money was available for gear?

There was in Dawson a grubby store run by a shopkeeper from San Francisco who had found no gold. He dealt in everything, a kind of minimal hockshop with a worn set of scales for weighing gold dust and, inside his door, hung on pegs on the wall which kept it off the ground, an almost new two-wheel bicycle made by Wm. Read & Sons of Boston. It was the top of their line and had sold in Seattle in 1899 for $105, which included a kit for mending tires, a clever tool for replacing broken spokes and twelve spare wire spokes.

Matt, entering the shop one day to pawn his last possessions for money to keep him alive during the Klondike winter, chanced to see this bicycle, and right then it came to him: 'A man could ride a contraption like that right down to Nome.' Only a man who had conquered the great Mackenzie River would entertain so daring a scheme for the Yukon.

'What would he use for roads?' the shopkeeper asked, and he was astounded when Matt said: 'The Yukon. Frozen all the way,' and the pawnbroker said: 'The Yukon don't go to Nome,' and Matt replied: 'But Norton Sound does, and it freezes solid too.'

Finally, after pawning his belongings, Matt asked: 'How much?' and the dealer said: 'That's a special bicycle,' and he showed Matt a paper which had come with it and which described the machine as 'Our New Mail Special model used widely by members of the Postal Service. $85.'

'Save it for me,' Matt said without hesitation, but the dealer said: 'It's a hundred and forty-five dollars,' and Matt said: 'It says here, plain as day, eighty-five,' and the pawnbroker said: 'That was Boston. This is Dawson.'

During the next weeks Matt, captivated by the concept of bicycling to Nome, returned often to the shop to check whether the bicycle had been sold, and he was always relieved to see that it had not. However, two impediments stood in his way. He lacked the money to buy the bicycle, and even had he been able to do so, the machine would have been of little use to him, for he had never sat astride one and had almost no idea of how it worked.

When the great river froze, forming a highway, as he had said, 'right down to Nome,' he became almost monomaniacal, badgering everyone in Dawson who had a spare dime to give him work. As October, November and December passed he painfully accumulated funds toward the purchase of the bicycle, and on 2 January 1900 he marched into the pawnshop and made a deposit of eighty dollars on the purchase. This done, he begged the owner to let him practice riding the contraption, and when the miners of Dawson saw him trying to pedal along their snow-covered roads, they said: 'We better lock him up to save his life,' and when they learned that he proposed making it all the way to Nome, they seriously considered keeping him in jail until his madness abated.

But by the middle of February he made his last payment, and with skill painfully acquired, rode out to the middle of the river, where, with the temperature at minus-forty, he waved goodbye to the doubting watchers. At this late point he was struck with an idea that was going to make the long trip a kind of triumph: abruptly he turned and returned to shore, ignoring the jeers: 'One taste of that cold, he don't want it! He's brighter'n we thought!'

He had come back to acquire copies of four newspapers then circulating along the Klondike with the latest political news from the United States: Dawson *Daily News*, Dawson *Nugget*, and the two with flaming red headlines, San Francisco *Examiner* and Seattle *Post-Intelligencer*. With these stowed in his gear, he returned to the middle of the river and set forth.

Once his wheels adjusted to the extreme cold, they functioned perfectly, and to the amazement of the onlookers, he quickly disappeared from sight. Like his machine, Matt was undaunted by the cold, which was surprising because he was not dressed as one might have expected—no heavy furs, no goggles, no immense sealskin cap with wolverine edging, no fur-lined mukluks. He wore pretty much what he would have worn on a cold, rainy day in Ireland: heavy boots, gamekeeper leggings, stout fur mittens, three woolen jackets, a scarf about his neck, an ingenious cap made of wool and fur with three big flaps, one for each ear, one to be pulled down to protect the eyes. As he pedaled out of Dawson, old-timers predicted: 'Absolutely impossible he can get to Nome. Hell, he won't even get to Eagle,' which was a mere ninety-five miles downriver.

Matt covered sixty-three miles that day, sixty-nine the next, and long before even he expected it, he pulled into Fort Yukon, and here his newspapers proved themselves, for the occupants of the rude hotel were so excited by the arrival of news from home that they stayed up all night reading the papers aloud while Matt slept, and in the morning the hotel manager would accept no money from him. Wherever he stopped along the river, and there was a surprising number of solitary cabins—sheds dedicated to mail drops and camps from which woodsmen went out to cut logs in preparation for the summer steamers—he and his bicycle were received with disbelief and his newspapers with joy. And even though this was midwinter, since the Yukon followed a course south of the Arctic Circle, there was a grayish light for five or six hours each day when the temperature rose to a comfortable minus-twenty.

Matt's New Mail Special performed even better than its builders in Boston had predicted, and at the halfway mark he'd had no trouble with his tires except that they froze solid at anything below minus-forty, and only one loosened spoke. During the first days his personal gear, strapped to his back, did cause chafing, but he soon solved that problem by adjusting his pack, and during his long, solitary ride down the Yukon he often amused himself by bellowing old Irish songs. The only thing that held him up was an occasional bout of snow blindness, which he cured with a day's rest in some dark cabin.

He kept going at more than sixty miles a day, and once when he felt he had to make up lost time after an enforced halt because of the blindness, he did seventy-eight. That night he shared a cabin with a toothless old-timer, who asked: 'You claim you come all the way from Dawson? How do I know that?' so Matt produced his newspapers with their dates of publication showing, and the old man said: 'So you think that git-up'll work on this 'ere river?'

'You don't have to carry food for dogs, or spend an hour cooking it at the end of the day,' to which the old man, recalling the hardships he had suffered with his dogs, replied: 'Yep, that would be an advantage.'

Rider and bike were in such excellent condition that when they reached Kaltag, the village which Father Fyodor Afanasi had served as missionary and in which he had married his Athapascan wife, Matt was emotionally prepared to face the difficult choice laid before him: 'You can continue down the Yukon, more than four hundred miles to the Bering Sea, or you can leave the river for a sixty-mile hike across the mountains to Unalakleet.'

'How do I get my bicycle across?'

'You carry it.'

Matt chose the mountains, and after finding an Indian to lug his gear, he dismantled his bicycle as best he could, lashed it to his back, and climbed the eastern slopes, then scrambled down to the welcome sight of Unalakleet perched on the edge of Norton Sound, which was, as he had anticipated, beautifully frozen all the way to Nome.

Glad to be riding again, he set out blithely on the final dash, a hundred and fifty miles as the crow flies, and on 29 March 1900 at about four in the afternoon he pedaled his way down Front Street in Nome. He was a man who had accomplished one of the remarkable travel adventures of the dying century: Dawson to Nome, solo, depth of winter, thirty-six days.

After turning his bicycle over to admiring bystanders and delivering his four newspapers to the editor of the local paper, he hurried to meet Missy Peckham, who embraced him ardently and informed him: 'All the good mining sites are taken, but I'm sure you can get a job somewhere. I did.'

D URING THE LAST week in February, while Matt Murphy and his bicycle were still on the Yukon, the testing time came for men and women living in northern Alaska. Existence was brutal. All through February wind howled in from the Bering Sea, and although little snow fell, it was so whipped about that a ground blizzard obscured buildings just half a block away. Now came the feared whiteout, when earth and horizon and sky blended into one gauzelike whole and trappers went blind if they lacked eye shields. What made this time more difficult were the huge blocks of ice that forced their way upward through the layers of ice already covering the Bering Sea, for they loomed ominously, casting weird shadows when either the midnight moon or the wan noontime sun shone upon them.

'I'll be glad when February goes,' Tom Venn said as he watched the sea from his store, but a knowing woman customer warned: 'March is the bad month. Watch out for March.'

She did not, during that visit, explain this strange statement, and when March did arrive, it brought such fine weather that Tom felt a surge of spring, and he was most pleased when the days began to lengthen and the sea started to look as if would soon relax its icy grip enough to allow ships to arrive. Four days later, when the weather was still perfect, the woman returned: 'These are the dangerous days. Husbands start to beat their wives, and men sharing one hut as mining partners begin to quarrel and suddenly shoot each other.'

Shortly thereafter, news of two such scandalous affairs reached Tom, and when he asked why they had happened just as winter was relaxing its hold, the same woman customer explained: 'That's the reason! In dark January and February, you know you have to remain strong. But in March and April, we have more daylight than dark. Everything seems to be brighter. But the fact is, we face three more long months of winter. March, April, May. The sun shines but the sea remains frozen. We feel life moving but the damned sea stays blocked, and we begin to shout at our friends: "When will this thing ever end?" Watch out for March!' And Tom found that he was reacting exactly as she had described: he felt winter should be over; ships ought to be coming in with new stores; and there stood the frozen sea, its great hummocks immobile in the ice as if winter would never end.

In his seventeen years he had never experienced a worse month than May when it was spring throughout the world, even in the arctic. Yet still the sea remained locked in the grip of winter. And then, as May ended, the Bering Sea began to break up into monstrous icebergs as big as cathedrals, and despite the fact that navigation was now at its most perilous, for one of these mighty bergs could crush any ordinary vessel, men began to speculate on how soon ships could begin to arrive.

How glorious it was, in an ordinary year, to be in Nome at the beginning of June and watch as the first of that season's vessels hove to in the roadsteads. Men would fire salutes, and study the ships' profiles, and run down to the shore to greet the first arrival of the year. It was the custom for the local news sheet to print in bold letters the name of the first man ashore:

HENRY HARPER, FIRST IN 1899

And each year the cry that greeted every newcomer as he stepped ashore was the same: 'You got any Seattle newspapers? You got any magazines?'

This spring of 1900 was to be entirely different, for the desire of many to reach Nome was so great that on 21 May a heavy whaler pushed its snout through the ice, and two days later a legitimate passenger ship arrived, to the astonishment of those who felt that to approach Nome before the first week in June was folly.

But it was what happened next that amazed the citizens, because in swift successsion two more passenger ships arrived, then three more, until, amidst the lessening ice, forty-two large ships lay at anchor. Since docking facilities could not exist on this turbulent roadstead, the ships sat about a mile and a half offshore, while improvised barges and lighters ferried back and forth to disgorge more than nineteen thousand newcomers. Nome, in those hectic weeks of thaw, was a more important harbor than Singapore or Hamburg.

And as the stampeders streamed ashore, eying the beaches already crowded with the bizarre machines of prospectors, each hopeful man tried to identify the spot to which he would hurry to pick up his share of the gold. Some had tents, which they erected quickly; others less prudent had to scrounge around for sleeping places; the Belgian Mare rented space, rotating four customers in a bed every twenty-four hours; and Tom Venn had to keep one employee watching the store at night so that men endorsed by the R&R office in Seattle could sleep on the floor.

As more and more ships arrived the chaos in Nome became indescribable, and now the lack of civil government posed a fearful threat, for as health problems mounted, so did crime, and for the same reason. Crime, like disease, can be kept under control in a crowded society only by the exercise of constant policing powers, and if those powers are not allowed to exist, tranquillity cannot exist either.

But one of the big ships arriving on 20 June, with sixteen hundred new miners, brought newspapers confirming the news for which men like Lars Skjellerup and Tom Venn had waited: Congress is about to pass an Alaska Code and the district will receive two additional judges, the more important one to be assigned immediately to Nome.

Sober men cheered the news and even drunks agreed that the time had come to bring order into this vast disorder. Skjellerup sent Sana searching for the Siberian, and when Arkikov stood before him, the Norwegian cried with unwonted enthusiasm: 'Arkikov! Your judge, he's coming. *Seven Above* will be yours again,' and a broad, robust smile illuminated the irrepressible reindeer herder's face: 'Me glad.'

I N A SMALL town in Iowa in the years prior to the Civil War, a mediocre lawyer developed such vaulting ambitions for his newly born son that he named him John Marshall, after the greatest of the Chief Justices of the United States. The boy could remember that when he was only five his father walked him past the county courthouse and predicted: 'Someday you'll be the judge in that building,' and during his early years the lad believed that the famous jurist was his grandfather.

John Marshall Grant, alas, had none of the qualities of that noble proponent of justice, for he was essentially a weak human being who developed none of the flinthard character a judge should have. He slouched his way through high school and did poorly in one of Iowa's small colleges. He played no games, avoided books as well, and was notable on campus solely because he became increasingly handsome as the years passed. He was tall, well formed, with even features and a head of wavy hair which photographed so handsomely that people said, when his proud father displayed the cards he carried with him: 'Simon, your son looks like a judge!'

At the University of Pennsylvania Law School, one of the best, the future judge did so poorly that in later years his classmates often wondered: 'How did John Marshall ever become a judge?' He became one because he looked like one. And as his father had predicted, he was installed in the little Iowa courthouse, dispensing a garbled kind of justice—but his decisions frequently had to be overturned by higher courts because he had failed to understand the simplest common law as applied in courts like his throughout the other forty-four states and in Great Britain.

He was so handsome and so pompous in Fourth of July orations that politicians began thinking of running him for major office, but he was so flabby and lacking in determination that no one knew whether he was Republican or Democrat, and those who knew his pathetic record joked: 'Whichever party loses him is to be be congratulated.' When some Republicans sought a safe candidate who could be elected to Congress, they asked the judge's father what party his son favored, and the old man said proudly: 'My son the judge wears no man's collar.'

He would probably have bumbled his way to innocuous obscurity, harming few because his worst errors could always be reversed, had he not been invited to address a legal convention in Chicago, where a noted lobbyist heard him speak.

Marvin Hoxey was at age forty-five a man difficult to forget, once he had buttonholed you and stared penetratingly into your eyes. Portly, crop-headed, careless in dress and characterized by a huge unkempt walrus mustache and a perpetual cigar, he derived his considerable power from the fact that he seemed to know everyone of importance west of the Mississippi or in the halls of Congress. Protector of the more powerful interests in the West, he could always find a friend willing to do 'a little something for Marvin.' He had parlayed his skills into a position of some importance. For his help in gaining South Dakota's admission to the Union in 1889, he had been named National Committeeman for the Republican party in that state, a position from which he orated about 'the growing power of the New West.'

He thought globally, a man without a college education who could have taught courses on political manipulation. He saw nations as either rising or falling and had an uncanny sense of what actions a rising nation like the United States ought to take next. It then became his job to see to it that only those steps were taken which would serve his clients.

He became interested in Alaska when Malcolm Ross, senior partner of Ross & Raglan in Seattle, employed him to obstruct any national legislation which might give Alaska home rule, for as Ross pointed out: 'The destiny of Alaska is to be governed by Seattle. The few people who are up there can rely on us to make the right decisions for them.'

At Ross's suggestion he had taken two cruises on R&R ships—one to Sitka, which he found disgracefully Russian, 'hardly an American town at all,' and one up the great river to Fort Yukon—as a result of which he knew Alaska better than most residents. He saw it for what it was, a vast, untamed area with a shockingly mixed and deficient population: 'Not in mental or moral ability, Mr. Ross, but deficient in numbers. I don't think the entire area has as many people, I mean real people, not natives and half-breeds, as my county in South Dakota, and God knows we're thinly staffed.' It was his opinion, stated loudly in Seattle and Washington, that 'Alaska will never be ready for self-government.'

Whenever Hoxey lobbied against legislation for Alaska he repeated the pejorative phrase *half-breed,* spitting it out as if the offspring of a hard-working white prospector and a capable Eskimo woman had to be congenitally inferior to someone purebred like himself with his Scots-English-Irish-German-Scandinavian-Central Asian heritage. He believed, and he worked hard to convince others, that since Alaska would always be inhabited by people of mixed derivation—Eskimo, Aleut, Athapascan, Tlingit, Russian, Portuguese, Chinese and God knows what—it must always be inferior and somehow un-American: 'Stands to reason, Senator, a land filled with half-breeds will never be able to govern itself. Keep things as they are and let the good people of Seattle do the thinkin'.'

During sessions of Congress, Marvin Hoxey sometimes single-handedly defeated the aspirations of Alaska for self-rule. It was not allowed to become a territory, that honorable preparatory step to statehood, because the firms profiting from conditions as they were could not trust what a self-controlled territorial government might do to diminish their advantages. It was not anything, really. For some years it had been known as a district, but mostly it had been simply Alaska, vast, raw and unorganized, and Marvin Hoxey was engaged to keep it that way.

At the legal convention in Chicago he had already buttonholed several delegates when he learned by telegraph from an aide in Washington that despite all his efforts, a bill was going to be passed giving Alaska a modicum of self-government—about one-fiftieth of what was justified—including two additional judges to be appointed by a superior court in California. There was some talk of choosing them locally, but Hoxey had that killed instantly: 'There aren't two half-breeds in all that forlorn region qualified to be judges. I've been there.'

He was wandering the halls of the convention, pondering how he could get the right kind of man appointed judge in the Nome district, when he happened to drift into the back of the room where Judge Grant was orating. His first impression was: I could make a man like that President . . . or an important judge, but it was not until he heard Grant deliver one of his typical sentences in praise of home that he realized that he had come upon something special:

'The American home is like a fort atop a mighty hill that keeps its powder dry in preparation for the day when assaults from the swamps below, and you can never know when these are going to come, the lawless conditions in our big cities being what they are and fights to resist the agencies of contamination, keeping the flag flying to ensure that it always has a constant supply of gunpowder to do such.'

As soon as the judge ended his speech, Marvin Hoxey hurried up, shoved his walrus mustache and cigar close to Grant's face, and said with great feeling: 'What a magnificent address! It's of the utmost importance that we talk.'

And there, at the rear of a public room in a Chicago hotel, Marvin Hoxey's plan was formally launched. It was magnificently simple: he was going to steal the entire Nome gold field. Yes, with the assistance of Judge John Marshall Grant of Iowa, he would steal the whole damned field. If what the papers said was true, it could amount to fifty million dollars, and if they continued to dredge gold by the bucketful from the beaches, it might run to eighty million.

'Judge Grant, the leaders of this nation are searching for a man just like you to save Alaska. It's a forlorn place that cries aloud for the staunch leadership that only a judge like you can give it.'

'I'm flattered that you should think so.' He asked for Hoxey's name and address and said that he'd think the matter over.

As the lobbyist bade Judge Grant goodbye, he caught a final glimpse of the handsome, white-haired figure: That's the phrase we'll use to get him the job. *Eminent jurist.* Even better: *Eminent Iowa jurist.*

Defeated in his efforts to kill this legislation favorable to Alaska, he left

Chicago for an urgent meeting in Seattle, where he placated his clients, especially Malcolm Ross, whose R&R ships and stores stood to lose some of their freedom under the new rules: 'Trust me, we lose a battle but we win the war. Our task is not to fight the new law but to use it to our advantage, and the first thing we have to do is to make sure we get our man into that judgeship governing Nome.'

'You have some local man in mind?' Ross asked, and Hoxey said: 'Too blatant. Never be blatant, Mr. Ross.'

'Who, then?'

'I have in mind an eminent Iowa jurist. Fine-looking man. Knows Western life.' This was a cliché of the period, that anyone who had ever been in Denver or Salt Lake automatically understood Alaska.

'Can we get him appointed?'

'That's my job.'

And as soon as he returned to Washington, the Eastern one, he launched his campaign. Every Republican leader he had worked with as a national committeeman heard confidential reports on the distinguished Iowa jurist John Marshall Grant, and repetition of that resounding name inspired such confidence that the White House began to receive calls supporting Grant for the appointment 'to this here new judgeship in Alaska.' By simply stating that his new friend was an eminent jurist, Hoxey was making him one.

In late June 1900, John Marshall Grant was assigned to the new court in Nome, and many newspapers applauded a decision free of even a suspicion of political influence, and shortly thereafter he and his mentor Marvin Hoxey sailed on the steamer *Senator* to his new duties.

On the evening prior to arrival at the Nome roadstead, Hoxey laid down the law that Grant was to follow: 'John Marshall, if you play your cards right in Nome, you'll attract so much favorable attention you'll become a United States senator. The name of this ship is an omen, Senator Grant, me and my friends will see to that.'

'How do you see the situation, Mr. Hoxey?'

'I've been to Alaska, you remember. Know it like the back of my hand.'

'And your judgment?'

'Nome is in a terrible mess. The claims are false as hell. Mining law was not followed in making them. They're not in legal form. And they should all be vacated.'

The eminent jurist, knowing nothing about mining law and having neglected to bring along any books which would unravel its arcane lore, listened attentively as it was explained according to the doctrine of Marvin Hoxey: 'What you must do, Judge, and do it fast, is to declare . . . let's say fifteen of the major claims invalid. Present owners are disqualified, on the best legal grounds. Then appoint me as the impartial receiver, not the owner, you understand. Oh, of course, you know all about that. What you do is appoint me receiver, and I watch over the property, as an agent of the government, till you decide later on after formal court cases who really has title.'

Hoxey stressed two facts: 'Speed is essential. New broom and all that. And the receiver must be appointed immediately, so as to protect the property.' Judge Grant said he understood.

Now Hoxey came to the ticklish part: 'One thing I don't like about the Nome situation—and you must remember that I know Alaska like the back of my hand—is that a bunch of aliens and half-breeds have grabbed up the best claims. Can you imagine a Russian citizen owning a gold mine in America? Or a Lapp, God forbid? Who in hell ever heard of Lapland . . . and their people coming over here and taking up our good claims? And Norwegians and Swedes aren't much better. You must remember that I come from South Dakota, some of my best friends are Scandinavians, but they have no right coming over here and taking up our best claims.'

'I thought two of them were naturalized citizens?'

'Subterfuge.' With that marvelous word, delivered with a sneer, he settled the goose of the Swedes, and neither man seemed to appreciate that they themselves were engaging in the greatest subterfuge of all.

So it was decided that Judge Grant would do three things immediately upon arrival: outlaw all foreigners, vacate the claims, and appoint Hoxey receiver. He would also make a speech affirming American values and reassuring the men that law and order had come, although belatedly, to Nome. Health law enforcement, land-title paperwork, legal collection of taxes and protection of the public weal would all come later, if ever; the important thing was to outlaw foreigners and clarify the ownership of the gold mines.

'I can see it now,' Hoxey said as he accompanied Judge Grant to the ship's bar. 'That sign over there is prophetic.' It was the crest of the ship done in ornate blue and gold hand-carved letters: *Senator*.

In view of the heinous things Judge Grant was about to do, it is proper to ask: How much did he understand of Hoxey's infamous plan? Not much. He never guessed that if he appointed his trusted friend Hoxey to the receivership of the mines, Hoxey would steal every bit of gold being produced and that such theft could quickly run into the millions. Outstanding men in American history had started their careers as small-town judges, but these men had used their time on the bench to hone their perceptions, to differentiate between the motives of good men and evil; each year such judges grew wiser, more judicial, more honest, until in the end they stood forth as some of the finest products of our nation. Judge Grant had had all the opportunities of an Abraham Lincoln or a Thomas Hart Benton, but he had squandered them. He was now prepared to initiate one of the blackest pages of American legal history.

When the *Senator* anchored well out in the roadstead, lighters sped out to start the unloading; the first one to arrive was commandeered by Marvin Hoxey on the grounds, which he announced discreetly, 'that Judge Grant must establish his court at the soonest possible, in obedience to personal instructions from the President.' So the eminent jurist and his mentor were ferried toward the shore, but the lighter had such a deep draft that it could not nose into the beach. Important passengers and goods had to be transported that remaining distance on the backs of porters, so now six strong Eskimos, three for Judge Grant, three for Hoxey, hoisted the two men high in the air and carried them ashore.

They were a striking pair as they set foot on the golden beaches: Judge Grant, handsome and severe; Marvin Hoxey, pudgy and red-faced, with that immense walrus mustache and the eyes which took in everything. Holding his cigar in his left hand, he waved it, signaling that it would be proper for the citizens of Nome to applaud the arrival of the judge who was bringing order to their community, and one man started a cheer: 'Hooray for the judge!' and with that cry ringing in his ears, Judge John Marshall Grant strode sedately to chambers in the Golden Gate Hotel.

He had barely supervised the placing of his luggage when he began issuing the sheaf of orders which Hoxey had recommended and sometimes drafted. After vacating the leases and appointing Hoxey receiver to protect their assets, Judge Grant let it be known that henceforth no Swedes, Norwegians, Lapps or

Siberians could hold claims and that the ones they currently did hold illegally must be turned over to the receiver. By nightfall of that first cyclonic day Marvin Hoxey controlled claims *One* through *Eleven Above*, with a combined capacity of producing nearly forty thousand dollars a month.

N O SOONER HAD Judge Grant vacated claims *One* through *Eleven Above* on his first day in Nome than he did one other thing that would have equally heavy consequences. Taking from his pocket a memorandum handed him by Malcolm Ross before the *Senator* sailed from Seattle, he read: 'When hiring staff in Nome, consult with our R&R man, Tom Venn, who will know the abilities of everyone.' Calling for Hoxey, he said: 'Can you get this fellow Venn to come to my quarters?' and very soon Tom reported to the Golden Gate Hotel.

'Judge Grant? I'm Tom Venn, Your Honor. Just got a note from Mr. Ross instructing me to find you a secretary. I've brought along the only candidate I think you'd be interested in, sir. She's waiting downstairs.'

'I'd like to see her,' and in this way Melissa Peckham, twenty-five years old, met Judge Grant.

'What's your name?' When she said 'Missy Peckham,' he scowled: 'Now what kind of name is that?' and when she said: 'It's really Melissa,' he said: 'That's better. A proper girl needs a proper name, especially if she's going to work for me.'

Judge Grant hired Missy to begin immediately, and Matt, again on Tom's recommendation, was hired by Hoxey to act as caretaker of the vacated claims. From her experience in Dawson and on the Eldorado ridge, Missy knew a good deal about mining, much more than Judge Grant, and she was so bothered by some of his early decisions that she began taking careful and secret notes of what was transpiring in this ugly business of depriving the discoverers of a field of their just property:

> Thursday 25 July. In the first batch of decisions the Siberian Arkikov, no first name, lost his claim to *Seven Above* on Anvil Creek. He is believed to be one of the discoverers.

> Friday 26 July. The Norwegian Lars Skjellerup notified that as a foreigner he cannot hold a claim on Anvil Creek, even though he is known to have been the organizer of the mining district.

Working late into the night to record the judgments of each day, Missy frequently heard, through the thin makeshift wall separating the judge's chambers from her desk, Hoxey discussing plans with Judge Grant. She discussed this growing pattern with Murphy, who said without reflection: 'I think this man Hoxey, he's mighty near a criminal. Keep an eye on him,' and now Missy inscribed in her small book not only what she thought the judge was doing but Murphy's suspicions as well, and the result was a document so devastating that Murphy told her one night: 'You better hide that,' and she did.

The impact of Judge Grant and Hoxey on Nome was so shocking that some miners who had been deprived of their rights spoke of lynching, but Lars Skjellerup, who had lost more than most, counseled restraint: 'Things like this won't be allowed in a free country. There must be something legal we can do to unmask these men.'

There was nothing. Clothed in the dignity of a law which local people had not called into being and supported by the might of a great but remote nation, Judge Grant and Hoxey were free to do as they wished, and now that the mines were working smoothly under their receivership, Hoxey was shipping out of Alaska more than two hundred thousand dollars a month.

When Skjellerup questioned this, he was told by Judge Grant: 'Mr. Hoxey is the legal receiver. That means he is to manage the mines as he sees fit until such time as the case against you is legally decided. Of course, you and I both understand that Mr. Hoxey is not to keep such money as his mines—'

'They're our mines.'

'The court will decide that, later on, but I must advise you that as an alien breaking the law—'

'Judge Grant! The jury is to decide that, not you. You're stealing our property.'

'You can go to jail for contempt, I suppose you know that.'

'I'm sorry. I mean Hoxey is stealing—'

'Mr. Skellerby, if that's how you pronounce your name, you don't seem to understand what a receivership is. Mr. Hoxey is there to protect you and the public . . . till the trial can take place. Not a penny of that money, I assure you, will ever accrue to him, except for a small managerial fee to which, even you must admit, he's entitled.'

'But it goes out of here on every ship. I've watched.'

'For safekeeping. Should the trial be decided in your favor,' this being said in a tone of voice which guaranteed that it would not, 'you would, of course, get back all the money, except for the managerial fee I spoke of.'

'Which is how much?'

'Twenty thousand a month. Set by the court.' When Skjellerup exploded, Judge Grant justified the fee: 'Mr. Hoxey is an important man in the United States. Adviser to presidents. Counselor to great industries. He can't work for shavings.'

Skjellerup had heard enough, and even though his strict Norwegian up-bringing had indoctrinated in him a grave respect for policemen, ministers, schoolteachers and judges, he was morally infuriated; his Lutheran sense of rectitude was outraged and he said so: 'Judge Grant, an evil thing is being done in Nome. In a democracy like the United States, this can't be allowed. I don't know how it will be stopped, but it will be stopped. You cannot steal a man's honest work.'

'Mr. Killerbride, or whatever. Do you know what a deportation order is? The judge signs a paper stating that you're a dangerous alien, and out you go, back to Lapland where you belong.'

'I'm Norwegian.'

'That's almost as bad. Miss Peckham, show this man out.' She did, making note of his name, the location of his mine and the threats made against him.

During most of these trying times Hoxey remained invisible, and men like Skjellerup, who now saw pretty clearly what the plot was—Judge Grant to issue improper orders, Hoxey to steal the property thus turned loose—suspected that the South Dakotan was hiding through fear of being shot, but that was not the case. Hoxey was kept indoors writing an unbroken stream of letters to senators, representatives and even the President, pointing out a mistake that had been made in the 1900 Alaska Code and lobbying for an immediate rectification:

We simply must have a new law which nullifies any mining claim filed by an alien illegally, namely, while he was an alien. As you are aware, I know

Alaska like the back of my hand, and few evils hold this area back like having Scandinavians and Russians holding title to mines on American soil. I urge you to correct this evil.

If passed, Hoxey's proposed bill would legally confirm the dispossession of aliens like Skjellerup and Arkikov and give sanction to his temporary receivership of the Nome holdings. After that, permanent possession would depend upon his ingenuity and Judge Grant's stupidity. With just a little luck and the continuance of Judge Grant's good health until all the claims had been thrown into receivership, Hoxey would be a millionaire before half a year was out and a multimillionaire in due course.

But to nail this down, he must convince Congress to pass his bill, and to make this happen, he must bombard Washington with a blizzard of letters. Obviously, he needed secretarial help, and since Judge Grant had little to do except write dispossession orders, Hoxey borrowed Missy, and this gave her an opportunity to obtain proof of the disreputable relationship between the two men, for boastfully Hoxey would say in some letters: 'In these matters we can rely on our good friend, the eminent Iowa jurist,' or even more damning: 'So far Judge Grant has handed down not one decision adverse to our cause, and I think we can depend on him for the same kind of help in the future.'

In the meantime, conditions in Nome worsened. The filth grew deeper in the streets. People began to die of strange diseases. There were robberies, and now and then a miner would be found dead near his claim, now occupied by Hoxey's men. Women were assaulted even in the twilight hours, and feared to move about at night.

One evening, though Missy and Murphy were still not sure they could confide in Tom Venn, they invited him to dinner: 'We're so pleased to have a little extra these days so we can show our gratitude.'

'I was happy . . . no, I was proud to recommend you to the two gentlemen who are doing so much to make Nome better. What do you think of them?'

'They work hard,' Missy said evasively. 'At least Mr. Hoxey does.'

'I thought you were working for the judge.'

'I am, but Mr. Hoxey has to write a lot of letters to Washington. To Seattle too, so he borrows me.'

Tom knew that he must not ask a secretary to break the confidence under which she worked, so he asked no more about the letters, but she did feel free to make a general observation: 'Mr. Hoxey seems to think that Alaska should be governed from Seattle.'

'I agree. They have the brains down there . . . the money . . . they know what's best for the nation as a whole. And my company, at least, does a grand job of protecting Alaskan interests.'

Murphy changed the subject: 'I've been thinking, Tom, that what Nome needs is not Judge Grant and Mr. Hoxey from Seattle, but Superintendent Steele and Officer Kirby from Dawson. Do you realize that those two men could clean this town up in a weekend?'

So the three shifted to that provocative topic, and they agreed that even one man like Steele, fortified by tradition and supported from Ottawa, could hammer Nome into shape. 'The cribs would be out of sight,' Murphy said. 'Those little buildings that project into the main street, they'd be gone by nightfall. The saloons that steal from newcomers, out! One man could clean up this town, if he was the right man.'

'That's certain,' Tom said. 'In Dawson we never worried about our R&R

money, and in the good days we had huge amounts. Superintendent Steele wouldn't allow theft. Here? Everyone at the store sleeps with a gun.'

'Would you use a gun?' Missy asked, and Tom replied: 'I'd avoid it as long as possible. Even if the other man struck me, I'd still try to calm him down, but if it was hopeless—'

'I'll tell you one thing Superintendent Steele would clear up,' Murphy broke in. 'What I know of Hoxey, he's got the claims in a real mess here. Three hundred men in town at the beginning, each allowed one legal claim, no proxies. But now they say that fifteen hundred claims were filed.'

'Impossible!' Venn cried, but Murphy insisted on his story. 'Fifteen hundred claim jumpers, and each one entitled to his day in court before Judge Grant.'

'This could go on forever,' Tom said, and Missy, knowing what she had seen in the two offices, said: 'That's what they intend.'

This further irritated Murphy, who broke in: 'You know how Superintendent Steele handled claim jumpers? I saw him in operation twice. A man near us on Klope's ridge had a perfectly good claim, but like us, no gold. When word circulated that gold was sure to be found on the ridge—it never was—this big, loud fellow from Nevada, I often wanted to punch him, he said he knew more about mining than anyone in Canada, he tried to jump our friend's claim. Superintendent Steele came up to settle the dispute, recognized the claimant, and said: "Sir, I been watching you for seven months. Even if your claim is valid, we don't want you in Dawson. It's half past two on Tuesday. If you're in town this time Thursday, you go to jail, and if you want to make a move for your gun, just try it." And he walked away.'

But then Murphy told a more representative story of how Steele operated, and how anyone like him could handle the situation in Nome: 'On the stream below us, *Eldorado Nine Below*, a man had a placer that wasn't producing, and he dug deep, came up with a winter's load of gold-bearing muck that froze solid beside his cabin. One day when I was there, Superintendent Steele came by with surveying instruments: "Sam, I got bad news for you. Your line's skewed. That portion over there's open for whoever claims it, and I've heard someone is going to file tomorrow. Wanted to warn you." And Sam cries: "Good God, sir, all my muck is on that property. Assayer said maybe thirty thousand." And Steele said: "You know the law. Muck goes with the claim." Sam grew so weak he had to sit down. A winter's work gone. The only strike he'd ever make. And all on somebody else's property: "My God, sir, what am I goin' to do?" and the superintendent considered for a while and said: "I'm supposed to have my office open at nine in the morning. Tomorrow I'll open at seven. If you can find a friend you can trust, have him claim on that piece and have him file early, because tomorrow afternoon will be too late." With that, he stalked off, because he didn't want to know what kind of deal was made.'

'What happened?' Tom asked, and Murphy said: 'Sam looked around, saw only me, and in despair asked: "Murphy, can I trust you?" and I said: "You better," and early next morning I was in Superintendent Steele's office and he took me to the registry and I claimed on *Eldorado Nine Below, False Portion* and I got it and here's the paper to prove it,' and from his pocket he produced a sweat-stained paper which proved that Matthew Murphy, Belfast, Ireland, had a valid claim to *Nine Below, False Portion:* 'I came to Canada to get me a mine, and by God's sacred word I did, and here's proof.'

'But what about Sam's muck?'

'I sold it to him for one dollar, but I kept the mine. His muck proved out at thirty-three thousand dollars and he gave me five percent. That's what Missy and I lived on when we couldn't get work in Dawson.'

'But your claim?' Tom asked. 'What about it?'

'It was only a tiny piece of land, covered with Sam's muck. On the stream, nothing. Below nothing. But I get great spiritual gratification from that certificate.'

'Why?'

'Fifteen hundred men left Edmonton to stake a claim—doctors, lawyers, engineers—and I'm the only one who staked his claim, and it was worth thirty-three thousand dollars . . . from seven in the morning one day till four that afternoon.'

'Why did Superintendent Steele protect Sam in that way? That illegal way, I might add.'

'When he handed me my certificate he said, off to one side: "Glad it was you, Murphy. Because the other claimant was a real swine." '

'Like I said,' Missy concluded, 'one Superintendent Steele could clean up this town.'

I N EARLY SEPTEMBER 1900 it seemed as if all nature had turned against the good people of Nome. Saddled with a corrupt judge, a cunning expropriator and rampant chloroform gangs, they looked with disgust as the wild summer drew to an end, for the experienced ones knew that with the arrival of the ice pack, they would be locked in with these criminals for eight or nine nearly sunless months. Their experience had been that as the sun receded and the roadstead iced in, the worst came out in what was already bad.

Tom Venn, in the cramped office of his R&R store, felt that he would have enough food supplies for the winter if the large steamship *Senator* could break through the ice one last time and discharge the enormous shipment it was supposed to contain. It would require the R&R barges six days just to unload the supplies onto the shore, and then teams of horses would need another six days to haul them into the store and the nearby warehouses.

As one of the principal businessmen in town, and the leader of those who looked to Seattle for guidance in all things, Tom was no longer happy with the judge and the receiver the men in Seattle had sent to Alaska, for he had begun to see almost daily proof of their deceptive behavior. 'It isn't that Seattle sent them. Most of the men R&R send us form the backbone of our country,' Tom told Matt and Missy. 'It's just that in this case Seattle chose poorly.'

As the days shortened, Missy, in her work with the two miscreants, had redoubled proof of their iniquities. In recent weeks, as Hoxey took possession of the many mines Judge Grant placed under his protection, there had been so much paperwork that Missy had worked ten hours a day for Hoxey and rarely saw Judge Grant, although her salary was being paid by the government on his behalf. And although she did not yet wish to bring her little notebook to Tom Venn, she said to Matt: 'You know, almost everything they do is corrupt. Last week the judge had to settle a simple problem, the transfer of property belonging to the widow of that workman killed when the boom on that cargo ship broke. It was a simple matter, I could have handled it. But no, he had to involve Mr. Hoxey, and by the time they were through with their mumbo jumbo, eighteen hundred dollars of the widow's money had disappeared.'

'You know what I think, Missy? Somebody's going to shoot Mr. Hoxey. I see things that would curl your hair.'

'Don't you get mixed up with any shootings, Matt!' After months of struggle and deprivation, this hardworking, reliable pair had an income at last, but her work was beginning to sicken Missy: 'Matt, what would you say if we quit? Just quit and ask Tom Venn if he would take us on in some capacity?'

'What could we do? We need money.'

'I could keep records, honest ones, for Tom, and you could run the warehouse so the freight's not backed up on the beach. And we could sleep at night.'

'Do you lie awake?'

'I do.'

'Jesus, Missy, a soul should never lie awake for what he done for someone else during the waking hours.'

'I'm scared, Matt. When the shooting starts, and it will, you might get hit. Or me.'

Her words were so solemn that half an hour after dawn on the tenth of September they were knocking on the door of Tom Venn's office: 'Tom, we want a job.'

'You have jobs. I went to a lot of trouble getting you those jobs.'

'We can't keep them any longer.'

'Why not?'

'Tom, do you remember what I said when you left us to go to work on your own for the first time? Up on Klope's ridge?'

Tom breathed deeply, then put his left hand over his mouth, then mumbled: 'You told me always to be honest.' He walked away from the pair, turned, and said: 'When I left Dawson last year to come down here, Mr. Pincus gave me those assayer's scales. Told me to keep them burnished. Warned me they would rust if I ever did anything dishonest for R&R.' For some moments he walked back and forth, kicking up dust. Then he stopped abruptly and looked back over his shoulder: 'They're not very nice men, are they.'

'No, Tom, they are not,' Missy said heavily, and no more was said on that subject.

'Well,' Tom said brightly as he came forward as if meeting them for the first time, 'suppose I did have a pair of jobs. What could you do for me?'

'I could keep your records,' Missy said, and Matt chimed in: 'I could take charge of your goods coming in on the barges.'

Only Tom himself could assess how much he owed these two fine people, how deep his debt was to Missy, who had saved his family back in '93 and who had taught him on the Chilkoot Pass what courage was. Only he knew the subtle effect Matt Murphy had had with his lyrical Irish ways, his gentler view of life and his indomitable spirit. Tom was beholden to Matt and Missy for the values which would guide him through life, and if they now needed jobs, he had no choice but to provide them, and then figure out how to explain it to his bosses in Seattle.

'You can't leave the judge and Mr. Hoxey in the lurch, you know. You'll have to give notice.'

'Of course,' Missy said. 'Would two weeks be honorable?'

'It would, and because it might look bad if you quit and then I hired you . . . What I mean, it might look as if I'd approached you. It will be better if I tell them myself. Lay my cards on the table.'

And that morning, as soon as their offices opened, Tom went to Judge Grant and suggested that Hoxey be called. When the three were together eating doughnuts, Tom said: 'Gentlemen, when you came here I recommended two very old friends of mine, Missy Peckham and Matthew Murphy . . .'

Judge Grant leaned forward, made a lascivious gesture with his fingers, and asked: 'Are those two . . . ? I mean, is he diddling her?'

'I wouldn't know,' Tom said. He turned to Hoxey: 'Winter's coming and the *Senator*, your old ship, is arriving with a huge shipment, and I could certainly use their help.'

'That is, you want to hire them away from us?' Hoxey asked belligerently.

'Well, yes. I can find you other help.'

'The Irishman isn't worth a damn,' Hoxey snarled. 'Take him, and good riddance. The girl, well, she's something else.'

'I thought she worked for you, Judge.'

'After-hours she helps me,' Hoxey lied.

'You find you can't let her go?' Tom asked, and when Hoxey said: 'I'd take it most unkindly, most unkindly. And when I take something unkindly, I usually do something about it. I am very close to your superiors in Seattle, Mr. Venn, and I would take it most unkindly.'

So Tom had to report to his old partners that whereas Matt could start working for R&R at the end of two weeks, Missy would have to stay with the judge: 'I'm sorry, Missy, but I'm discovering that few people in this world are ever their own bosses. Mr. Hoxey won't let you go.'

'If I could stand those rapids at Lake Bennett, I can stand Mr. Hoxey.' It was clear that she would be locked into her position during the interminable winter, and now as she worked she took even more careful note of all that he was doing. During the last two weeks when Matt would also be working for him, she queried Matt on every detail of the dealings at the mines. On the night of the thirteenth of September, she said to Matt: 'Remember that story you told us about Superintendent Steele protecting the miner who had his pile of muck on the other man's property? And the reason he gave for doing so, even though it was against the law, you might say?'

'Yes. Steele said: "Because the other claimant was a real swine." '

'These men we're dealing with are swine.'

On the fourteenth the *Senator* arrived in the roadstead off Nome with its huge cargo for R&R and the last batch of miners for the season. When the latter got ashore they would find all claims along the rich creeks taken and every inch of oceanfront bespoken, but ashore they would come, and by the end of the bitter winter, ten months off, they would have found some way to eke out a living. They would have survived, although not as they had envisioned.

They did not get ashore on the fourteenth, because a major storm brewing in the western half of the Bering Sea began to pile so much water against the Nome beaches that any lightering became quite dangerous, if not impossible. A picket boat did make it ashore with a ship's officer and an official from Ross & Raglan, but by the time they intended returning, the seas were so high that no one wanted to leave, they least of all.

They brought word that eight hundred and thirty-one newcomers were hankering to rush ashore and dig their millions: 'Some of them asked us to lay over three days so they could sail back to Seattle with their fortunes. One of our sailors made a tidy sum pointing out to them the choice spots along the beach —all of them taken, of course.'

The R&R man brought two bits of good news: that Tom's entire shipping list had been forwarded and lay out there in the *Senator* awaiting the barges, and that his salary had been upped by seven dollars a week. As he handed Tom the shipping list the man said: 'We're proud of the way you've handled things. Not many take charge as you have. And do you know what attracted major attention? The way you sold those cans without labels for five cents. Our accountant screamed: "Debit his account thirty cents a can. That's what they cost us." And do you know what Mr. Ross said? "Give the young feller a bonus. For the next forty years they'll talk about how generous R&R was with those perfectly good cans." '

Then the man added: 'There's a Mr. Reed, I think maybe he's from an insurance company in Denver. He's very eager to talk with you, Venn,' and from the way this news was delivered, it was clear to Tom that the R&R man might think that he was involved in some shady operation, because insurance inspectors did not come all the way from Denver just to say 'How's business?'

'Tom, do you know this Mr. Reed?' the R&R man asked. 'From Denver . . . in insurance?'

'Never heard of him. I don't carry insurance yet.'

'You should. Every young man who expects to get married one of these days should start an insurance plan. This fellow Reed did mention a Mrs. Concannon. Death claim or something. You know anything about a Mrs. Concannon?'

'I'm afraid not.' Then, most suspiciously, he did remember: 'Oh yes! Her husband was killed when a boom snapped on one of our ships. The *Alacrity*, I think.'

'Were we culpable?'

'Oh no! Act of God, as they say.'

'Was her claim in any way spurious?'

'No, couldn't have been. He was killed flat out.'

'Did you handle the paperwork on her insurance? I mean for R&R?'

'No.' Again he had to correct himself, and again he appeared duplicitous: 'I serve as sort of mayor or coroner or something in Nome. We have no government, as you probably know. All of us businessmen . . . Well, I did sign the Concannon death certificate.'

'No flimflammery? No complications on your part?'

Tom did not like the way this interrogation was going, and said so: 'Look, sir. Everything I do for R&R is open and aboveboard. Same in my private life.'

'Son, wait a minute! If tomorrow a man came in here, a responsible insurance detective from Denver with good credentials, and he started asking questions about me . . . Wouldn't you wonder what was up?'

'I suppose I would.'

'Well, Mr. Reed, an insurance inspector from Denver, was asking questions about you, and you're one of our employees. Naturally I perked up my ears. Son, you are turning pale. Do you want a glass of water?'

Tom fell into the chair and covered his face for some moments, then said: 'He wasn't from Denver. He's from Chicago. And he's not an insurance man. He's a private detective hired by my mother . . . that is, my other mother, the one I don't want.'

He was trembling so furiously that the R&R man sat down beside him and asked gently: 'Do you want to talk about it?' and Tom said: 'Only if Missy is here too,' and through the storm that was now beginning to lash Nome, he and the man ran to the Murphy shack, where Tom broke the news.

'One of those detectives we were running away from, Missy, he's found us.'

'Oh God!' She fell into a chair and remained silent. She had never told either Klope or Murphy of her flight from Chicago to avoid the law, and she had not the heart now to review that painful time.

But Tom did speak. He told of how Missy Peckham had saved his family

and of how his mother and her lawyers had harassed them and of how brave
Missy had been on the Chilkoot and of his father's death on Lake Lindeman.
As the passions of seven years swept over him he did not weep, but he could say
no more.

'What in hell!' the man from R&R, father of six, cried. 'You got nothing
to worry about. Your mother was a bitch, let's use simple words, and Mr. Reed
ought to be ashamed of himself. I'd like to punch a man like that in the nose.'
A little while ago he had been cautioning Tom against behavior that might bring
discredit to R&R, and now he was prepared to slug an insurance inspector.
Trying to restore some steel to Tom Venn's backbone, he resorted to comforting
old sayings: 'Let the dead past bury its dead. Tom, I'd defend you through every
court in this land. Besides, an honest man never has anything to fear.'

On the morning of the fifteenth, in the last week of summer, the people of
Nome awoke to find themselves assaulted by one of the greatest storms of the
decade, indeed, five or six decades, as a tremendous wind howled out of Siberia.
At dawn it measured forty-seven miles an hour; at eight o'clock it stood at
fifty-nine on the anemometer; and then it began to gust up into the seventies and
eighties.

Great waves pounded the unprotected shore, sucking rail huts and tents
into the sea. Relentlessly, the waves ate away the shore until they lashed at
houses and shops two hundred yards inland, and water came up to the steps of
the new R&R warehouses. By nightfall a quarter of Nome's houses were destroyed, and for three terrible days the storm raged. A minister, gathering his
flock, read passages from Revelation proving that God had come to Nome to
scourge the Antichrist, and the men with chloroform swabs looked only to their
own safety.

Tom Venn spent the three stormbound days with Missy and Matt, talking
over strategy for dealing with the detective and whatever problems he would
present. They were a mournful crew, and as squalls swept in from the sea, they
anticipated the typhoon of troubles which would soon engulf them. But then
Murphy, with his healthy peasant doubt, began to bring some sanity into the
discussion.

'Wait a minute! What do you really know about this Mr. Reed? You don't
even know who he is.'

'He asked about me. More than once, I think.'

'You don't even know whether he's an insurance man like he said or a
detective like you said. Or maybe neither.'

'He was looking into things, personal things.'

'You don't know whether he's from Denver or Chicago. Or again, maybe
neither.'

'What are you suggesting?' Missy asked, for in her time with Matt she had
learned to trust his common sense.

'That we wait till this damned storm dies down and your Mr. Reed can
come ashore and explain himself. In the meantime, it does no good to get
ourselves all worked up over things we don't know.'

This was such sober counsel that Missy and Tom stopped lacerating themselves, and while the storm increased in its fury, their fears subsided; the apprehensive pair could not escape their sense of doom but they could maneuver it
onto a plateau where it could be managed. And in this waiting period while the
storm raged, Tom offered various reflections: 'I owe so much to you two, I want
to see you happy. I want you to work with me at R&R. Judge Grant and Hoxey
will have to leave here soon, or as Matt says, someone is likely to shoot them.

Then Missy will be free and we can work together. Matt, why don't you marry her?' and Matt revealed to Tom what he had long ago told Missy: 'I have a wife in Ireland.' He said this so flatly and with such finality that comment was uninvited, and for some time the three sat, listening to the howling of the wind as it rose in fury to match the pounding rain.

'There'll be a lot of houses go down this morning,' Tom said, 'and when we rebuild, I'd like to see wider streets. Make this city something to be proud of.'

Matt said: 'Go careful, Tom. Men like you wanted better government and you got Judge Grant.'

'I don't think Nome can stay a big city. When the *Senator* sails, if it's ever able to unload, our committee has more than four hundred miners who want to sail with it. But they haven't a dime.'

'What will you do?'

'Our committee will give each one a blue ticket. Free fare south. And I'll bet four hundred others will be paying their own fare to sleep on deck, just to get out of here.'

'What will they do in Seattle?'

'Some'll mix in, most'll move on. Drift until they find work, and start over again. If a city is big enough, it can absorb men with no money. A small place like Nome can't.'

'Nome's pretty big,' Missy said. 'Biggest city in Alaska.'

Tom listened to the storm as it reached its howling peak, and he said: 'I had a vision last night, I guess you'd call it that. Couldn't get to sleep worrying about the detective . . .'

'You're not sure he is a detective,' Matt said again.

'And I saw Alaska as a huge ship, much bigger than the *Senator* lying out there, and it survived this storm only because it was firmly anchored. This gold rush has to die down, and when it does I think we must do everything possible to strengthen our lifeline to Seattle. As it goes, we go.'

But Missy said: 'I'm not so sure. Any good that comes to Alaska, will come from Alaska.'

On the evening of the seventeenth when the storm began to abate, Tom and Matt walked through the heavy rain to survey the damage, and were aghast at the large number of houses destroyed, the small number of tents left standing. Nome, with no protection of any kind against the Bering Sea, would have been erased from the map had it not been for the persistence of the miners who were prepared to rebuild their city of gold.

'What we must have, sooner or later,' Tom said, 'is a sea wall to give us protection against such storms.'

As they walked in the fading light they were joined by several businessmen, some of whose establishments had been completely washed away. Others found two feet of water in their stores, and only the better of the sixty-odd saloons were in any condition to reopen.

'The rain did some good,' one of the men said. 'At least the Golden Gate Hotel didn't burn again.'

It was when they came to the beach, to any part of its wild twenty-six-mile extent, that they appreciated the tremendous power of this storm, because not a single piece of gold-dredging equipment was visible. The little box sluices and the huge machines that gobbled up the sand and wrestled it for gold were gone, every one of them. The beach had been swept clean, without leaving a vestige of the great gold rush, and when one of the town's clergymen joined the group, he could not refrain from saying: 'Look for yourselves, men. It's as if God had grown tired of our excesses and had wiped the slate clean. There's your gold rush.'

'No,' a miner said. 'Out there's your gold rush, the men waiting on that ship to come ashore. Two days from now, the beach'll be covered with men the way a piece of venison gets covered with ants.'

'I agree with you, Reverend,' another miner said, 'but I reach a contrary conclusion. I think God sent the storm, but He did it to rearrange the placer rights. And to move in a fresh cargo of gold. I can hardly wait to get started again.' And as he spoke two older men, dragging behind them some monstrous contraption, came down to the beach, picked a spot where gold had once been abundant, and resumed dredging the sand for gold.

But the lasting image as the historic storm of September 1900 subsided was the large steamer *Senator* far offshore riding the turbulent waves and waiting to discharge the next influx of gold seekers. It held also a Mr. Reed, who was more impatient to get ashore than any of the would-be miners.

I F HE HAD been visibly restive at sea, he became almost unnoticeable ashore. Registering at the undamaged Golden Gate Hotel as Mr. Frank Reed, Denver, Colorado, he spent three days familiarizing himself with the lay of Nome, where its original claims had been along the streams and how the men who came swarming back to the beaches like flies established their rights to this stretch of sand or that. He visited the main stores to see what they were selling and tested the beer at several saloons, where he said nothing but did listen. He was appalled, as any sensible man would be, when he saw the way Nome handled its sewage, and he ate only sparingly those first days.

On his fourth day in town he began visiting the so-called leaders, and his questions were so diverse and unrevealing that three older men went to the Golden Gate asking to talk with him, and on the way they encountered Tom Venn and took him along.

'Mr. Reed, your activities have perplexed us.'

'You're no more perplexed than I am.'

'Who are you?'

The stranger considered this for some moments and his whole inclination was to reveal himself to these honest, worried men, but since long experience had warned him against being premature, he temporized: 'Gentlemen, I'm not at liberty to answer your questions yet, but believe me, I come meaning no embarrassment to men like you.' He knew they deserved to know more, so taking a document from his inside pocket, he said: 'You're Mr. Kennedy. I was told you were a man of honor. I came here to see you.' He read off two other names with similar comment, and then he turned to Tom: 'I don't believe I know you.'

'You didn't come for me?' Tom blurted out in tremendous relief.

'I didn't come for anybody.'

'I'm Tom Venn. Ross & Raglan.'

'Well, well!' Mr. Reed cried, evidencing a surprise which he could not mask. 'I had no idea you'd be so young. You're the man I wanted to see first.'

Tom felt his knees shake and his mouth go dry, but he had agreed with Missy that he would brave this thing out: 'What did you want to see me about?' and now Mr. Reed simply had to disclose part of his hand: 'The Concannon case.'

'Oh!' Tom sighed so heavily that if Mr. Reed had come to look into a major bank robbery, he would have had to judge by that sigh that Tom was the thief.

'You signed Mr. Concannon's death certificate, did you not?'

'Yes. We have no coroner, you know.'

'I know.'

'So they asked some of us . . . I think Mr. Kennedy here signed it too.'

'That's right,' Mr. Reed said. 'His name was on the document. Now let's sit down, gentlemen, and you tell me what you know about the Concannon case.'

He was like a ferret, dissecting even the most remote details of what had been a normal accident at sea when ships rolled and booms snapped: 'The *Alacrity* was an R&R ship, was it not?'

'A small one,' Venn said, 'built for the Skagway run but diverted when the great rush to the beaches began.'

'Isn't it rather strange that an employee of the company that owns a ship involved in a fatal accident should authenticate the death warrant?'

'At first I didn't even know he died on our *Alacrity*. I was just called in to sign the papers. Somebody had to, or Mrs. Concannon wouldn't get her insurance.'

'Yes, the people in Denver explained that.'

'Then you're not from the insurance company?'

'No. They alerted the authorities that something odd might have happened in the Concannon case, and it seemed to fit a pattern.'

'What fitted a pattern?' an older man asked, and Mr. Reed smiled: 'That's a penetrating question, sir, and it deserves an answer. But I can't give you one yet. I will repeat, I'm not here to inquire about any of you. We've had only the finest reports about you men. Now let's break up, and the less you say about this the better. I know you'll want to discuss it among yourselves, but please, please don't talk about it in public.' Then, as the men were about to leave, he added: 'Anything else you can tell me about the Concannon case, well, I'd appreciate hearing it.'

'Mr. Reed,' Tom said firmly. 'It could not have been murder.'

'Of that I'm sure,' Mr. Reed said.

O N THE FIFTH day after the storm Mr. Reed summoned that first group of leaders to the Golden Gate along with eight or nine others, including all the clergymen in town, and when they were settled he stood before them.

'Gentlemen, you've been very patient and I appreciate it. You have every right to know who I am and what I'm here for. My name is Harold Snyder. I'm a federal marshal from the California District, and I'm here to take action in the fraudulent conversion of property belonging to miners who had perfectly legal claims on Anvil Creek.' Before his listeners could even gasp, he rasped out orders like a spitting machine gun: 'I want the fullest details of what happened to claims *Five*, *Six* and *Seven Above*. And I should like to meet tomorrow with Lars Skjellerup, citizen of Norway, and with Mikkel Sana, citizen of Lapland. What nation would that be a part of?'

'Could be Norway, Sweden, Finland, or maybe even a tip of Russia.'

'And the Siberian known as Arkikov, no first name.' Then followed a barrage of instructions: 'Get me a plat of Anvil Creek. All papers relating to titles. A timetable of the various meetings. And a complete list of miners who attended the first two meetings.' He ended with a statement which electrified the businessmen: 'Before this session convened I stationed three of your members, including one clergyman, to watch every move that Judge Grant and Marvin

Hoxey make. These watchers will not allow them to burn any papers.' With that, he dismissed the meeting.

The next day the original claimants to *Five, Six* and *Seven Above* arrived, and when the doors were closed he conducted as minute an investigation as possible, using maps, diagrams, calendars for dates and lists of earlier testimony to nail down the frightful miscarriages of justice which officials in San Francisco had begun to suspect.

At the end of two days he had unequivocal evidence against the two thieves which convinced him but which, he was afraid, would not count for much in a court of law, and apparently Judge Grant and Hoxey knew this, for they continued to operate as usual, with the latter placing aboard the *Senator* a huge shipment of gold to go south to his account.

'The problem,' Mr. Snyder warned the committee, 'is that what these two rascals have done is almost impossible to prove to a jury. You men know better than anyone else that Judge Grant has been faithless to his oath as a judge, because it was your property he stole. But how do you prove it in court? You know that Hoxey stole your leases, but how are you going to prove it? Juries don't care much for paper rights. However, if we could nail them in the Concannon case . . .'

'What is the Concannon case?'

'We think they bilked a widow of her just insurance. The Denver people smelled a rat, but the rascals covered their tracks. We have nothing to go on, but if we could put a defenseless widow on the stand . . .' He stopped. 'Dammit, doesn't anybody know anything about that case?'

It was then that it occurred to Tom Venn that Missy could know something about Concannon. 'I can't be sure, Mr. Snyder,' Tom said, 'but I think Missy Peckham might.'

'Bring her here. Now.'

So Tom ran first to his store, where he grabbed Matt Murphy: 'Go to Judge Grant's—he mustn't see me—and fetch Missy.'

'Here?'

'No, the Golden Gate.'

When Matt reached Judge Grant's office he was stopped by the three guards watching the place: 'You can't go in there.'

'Mr. Snyder wants Missy.'

'Judge Grant won't let her go.'

'I'm going to count three, and then I'm damn well going in and get her.'

Missy was delivered, and when she and Tom and Matt sat with Mr. Snyder, the questioning was blunt.

'What do you know about the Concannon case?'

'Not suicide, not murder,' Missy said. 'Insurance policy. Judge Grant and Mr. Hoxey stole a lot of it.'

'How do you know that?'

'I just know.'

'Damn it all, everybody says "I just know" and nobody knows anything that can be used before a jury.'

'Well, I do know,' Missy said stubbornly.

'How do you know?' Mr. Snyder stormed.

'Because I wrote it all down.'

Mr. Snyder, feeling life flow back into the veins of his case, forced himself to ask in a low voice: 'You kept notes?'

'Yes.'

'Why?'

'Because after one week on the job I knew these two men were up to no good.'

'Two men?'

'Yes. I typed all of Mr. Hoxey's letters.'

Silence, then very cautiously Mr. Snyder asked: 'You took notes on Hoxey's dealings too?'

'I did.'

'And where are those notes?'

Now came a very long silence, for Missy was recalling Skagway when Soapy Smith's men dressed like clergymen to defraud, and like mail carriers to steal, and like freight forwarders to gain possession of goods which they never shipped. In those ugly days every man was suspect, and she could even see Blacktooth Otto scurrying like a rat up to the scene of that terrible avalanche to steal the packs of the dead. Like one of Soapy Smith's henchmen, Mr. Snyder could be an imposter brought to Nome by Judge Grant and Hoxey to ferret out and destroy any evidence against them. She would confide nothing further to this unknown man.

'Where are your notes?' Mr. Snyder repeated.

Missy was mute.

'Tell him,' Matt said, and his plea was so insistent that she turned in anguish to Tom and blurted out: 'It's just like Skagway. How can we know who he really is? How can we trust him? How do we know he isn't working for Hoxey?'

It was a cry that both Tom and Mr. Snyder understood, for when a society allows total chaos, it engenders total suspicion, and the normal processes by which any society is held on a steady keel—trust, dedication, reliability, penalty for wrongdoing—corrode, and things begin to fall apart, for the props are gone.

Patiently, forthright Harold Snyder, no longer a mysterious Mr. Reed, produced his credentials for Missy to finger and digest. He was indeed a federal marshal; he did have orders from the federal court in San Francisco to inquire into the malfeasance of a judge in Nome, and he did have the power to arrest. But still Missy was unconvinced: 'Soapy's men had documents. Soapy printed them himself.' Looking in turn at each of the three men, she asked: 'How can I really know?'

'Missy,' Tom said. 'Remember what Sergeant Kirby told you when Superintendent Steele wanted to protect your money? "If you can't trust Superintendent Steele, you can't trust anybody." Same situation.'

She saw that it was, that at some point in any crisis you simply had to trust someone, and she indicated that she would surrender her notebook, and with that, all the fight went out of this sturdy little woman. Too much had hit her in the face in too short a time, and she let her head fall heavily to the table and covered it with her arms.

Matt and Tom left her there, and after a hurried trip to the cabin, returned with the notebook, which Matt placed on the table unopened.

'Is this the famous book, Missy?'

'It is.'

'Now let's go over each item carefully.'

In the late afternoon Snyder asked: 'What does this entry mean?' and she said: 'Judge Grant had me claim for seven hours of extra work which I didn't do, but when I was paid he kept the money.'

Snyder pushed the book away as if its odor offended him: 'Jesus Christ, if a man had his salary, you would not expect him to cheat on his secretary.'

But it was when he reached the Hoxey entries that he became really enraged: 'I'm an officer of the law and I take it very seriously, but I find myself wishing that I could lock these two in a room with that big Norwegian, that Siberian and that tough little Lapp. I'll bet they could handle this case in fifteen minutes and save the taxpayers a lot of money.'

And then, on his second morning with Missy's notebook, he came upon the Concannon case, and he was sickened: 'A woman loses her husband in a crazy accident that cannot be explained, and two skunks defraud her of her insurance.'

He could read no further. Storming from the hotel, he went to where Judge Grant and Hoxey were skulking and slapped handcuffs on them. 'Where are you taking us?' Judge Grant whined, and Snyder said: 'Protective custody. So these people here don't lynch you.' Two days later, when the *Senator* sailed south, these two were aboard. They had been in Nome less than four months, but in that time they had smeared across the face of blindfolded American justice one of her most disgraceful stains.

T HE SAGA OF Nome ground to a stumbling halt. The Golden Gate Hotel burned again and was rebuilt. The glacier of frozen urine filled the alleys once more in winter and melted into the sea in summer. The golden beaches continued to throw up gold for another year and then were exhausted, while the placer mines along Anvil Creek continued modestly for several decades.

But there had been stunning if brief glory. In one twelve-month period alone, Nome produced $7,500,000 worth of gold, more than the price paid for all Alaska back in 1867. In all, more than $115,000,000 was taken out when gold was valued at $20 an ounce.

Claims *Five*, *Six* and *Seven Above*, once more controlled by their rightful owners, produced only modest fortunes because Marvin Hoxey had sequestered the best portion of the gold, and had hidden it so effectively that during his trial in San Francisco and his time in the penitentiary, the government was unable to find his two million in loot. He kept it all.

An outraged judge sentenced him to fifteen years, just punishment for a man who had defrauded so many of so much, but after three months President McKinley pardoned him on the grounds that his health was threatened by imprisonment, and besides, everyone knew he had been, in prior life, an exemplary citizen. He would function another thirty productive years as one of the most effective lobbyists in Washington, continuing to prevent any constructive legislation for Alaska's self-governance. Legislators listened to him, for he continued to boast: 'I know Alaska like the back of my hand and, to speak frankly, it's just not ready for self-government.'

Judge Grant's case had a surprising conclusion. As Harold Snyder had predicted, despite Missy's notebook, no specific charges could be proved against him, for with an almost animal cunning he had, during his frantic weeks in Nome, conducted his affairs so carefully and with such complete knowledge of what was happening, that he manipulated what evidence that did surface to condemn Hoxey while revealing himself as a forthright Iowa judge striving to do his best. Snyder, listening in court to the evidence, burst into laughter several times: 'All of us in Nome thought Judge Grant was the dummy. Used as a cat's paw by clever Marvin Hoxey. No, Grant was the smart one. He maneuvered it so that he went free and Hoxey went to jail.' At the end of one court session in which Judge Grant's evidence absolved him and damaged his partner, Marvin came over to Snyder and said: 'I was Hoxey, he was foxy.'

Declared 'Not guilty' by a federal jury, Grant returned to Iowa, where, after a lapse of two years during which he mended his fences, he resumed his position on the bench before which his father had practiced, and there he was known favorably as 'the eminent jurist who brought a system of justice to Alaska.' Repeatedly, while he was on the bench or delivering orations locally or in Chicago, admiring people would comment: 'He looks like a judge,' proving that in many circumstances it is more important to look like something than to be something.

Tom Venn prospered, as such dedicated and well-trained young men so often do. He kept his assayer's scales clear of rust, and when the R&R store in Nome was closed because of the catastrophic drop in population—32,000 in 1900, counting drifters; 1,200 three years later, counting almost no working miners—he was promoted to the big store in Juneau, the new capital of Alaska, where he tended to business as before, but also began looking carefully at all his younger female customers for a potential marriage partner.

The biggest change came in the lives of Missy Peckham and Matt Murphy. No, his wife in Ireland did not die so that he could remarry, and since they were Catholic, divorce was not possible, but one July afternoon after the Yukon thawed, a tall stoop-shouldered stranger arrived in Nome, taking a room not in the expensive Golden Gate but in one of the cheaper makeshift places, half wood, half canvas.

He registered, and threw his canvas duffel in a corner without unpacking. Then he started roaming the streets, and after a few inquiries, was directed to a miserable shack, where he knocked on the door and announced himself: 'I'm John Klope,' and Missy, showing no surprise, quietly said: 'Come in, John. Sit down. Can I get you coffee?'

He wanted to know what had happened to them, so Matt recalled his bicycle trip down the Yukon and he and Missy explained how they had fitted in with the famous gold rush: 'Got here too late, like always, for the good placers. Didn't even file a claim. Missed the beaches too. That was a madhouse. We found jobs, and I'm sure we did better than most of the people on the beach.'

'What kind of job?'

'Missy worked for that corrupt judge, what a mess. I worked for Tom Venn when the store got big.'

'Tom Venn! Is he in town?'

'Juneau. Big promotion.'

'How is Tom? How'd he do?'

'I just said, big promotion.'

'He was a fine boy.' He sipped his coffee, then pointed to the mean quarters they shared. 'Things not going too well?'

'After the gold stopped,' Matt said. 'You know how it is.'

'How's it with you, John?' Missy asked, for he, too, looked as if he had fallen upon bad times.

'You know how we dug that damned hole?'

'I sure do,' Matt almost groaned. 'You ever strike anything down there?'

'Lots of rock, no colors.'

'I'm sorry,' Missy said. 'You gave it such an honest try, but your claim was up so high . . . everybody knew the gold was down on the creek where the claims were already taken.'

The three oddly matched people, older now and sobered by their experiences, sat quietly cradling their cups, and after a while Klope said: 'That must have been a wild storm, the one that blew all the machines off the beach.'

'It was.'

'We saw pictures. Looked pretty awful.'

'Dawson must be a ghost town these days,' Matt said.

'You wouldn't recognize it. Not one tent left.'

'Remember ours? The grease on the canvas? Those good sourdough flap-jacks you taught us how to make?'

As they reminisced about the old days with affectionate nostalgia, Missy said: 'You remember the Belgian Mare? Her cribs here burned twice and were blown away once, and we were sorry for her till we found that she had sweet-talked miners into building them for her and she didn't lose a nickel. After each disaster she hiked her prices and made a fortune. One day she just left. Yep, John, she just up and left. Eight girls stranded on the beach without a nickel.'

'Where'd she go?'

'Belgium, to buy a farm near Antwerp.'

The day was wasting, and it was obvious to Missy that John Klope had something more important to talk about than the storm or the changing fortunes of the Mare. A startling thought exploded in her mind: My God, he's come here to ask me to marry him! And she began to draw back, because in Matt Murphy she had met a man of almost ideal temperament. He was kind, he was witty, he could smell out rascals and identify good people, and she loved sharing life with him, even if he could never seem to find a steady job. But since there was always need for her secretarial skills, she was more than willing to share her income with Matt.

Klope coughed, edged about in his chair, and diddled with his fingers. Finally he said: 'Haven't you heard?'

'About what?'

'About me?' When they shook their heads, he said with embarrassment: 'I always told you there had to be gold down there.'

'But you never found it. You said so.'

'Not in the hole the three of us worked. But when I got down to solid rock and threw out my laterals . . .'

'You did that while I was still helping,' Matt said.

'Yep, and I found nothing. But I got so mad with all that work, and I was so sure about the ancient river I talked about that I dug me another hole, way down. Didn't you hear?'

'What happened, John?'

'Sarqaq kept with me. Maybe we'd find something. Back down to bedrock, me thawing, him raising the muck, and this time when I sent out my laterals . . .'

He stopped and looked at his two good friends: 'First pan from the big crevice, nine hundred dollars . . . in nuggets . . . not flakes.'

Yes, before that one lucky lateral was exhausted, John Klope, assisted by the lame Eskimo Sarqaq, took out three hundred and twenty thousand dollars of some of the purest gold produced along the Klondike. His persistence had led him to the deposits laid down by a river that had flowed two hundred thousand years ago.

After Missy and Matt fell silent, emotionally exhausted from exploring all aspects of this tremendous stroke of good fortune, Klope was ready to make the awkward speech which had drawn him from Dawson to Nome on his way back to his farm at Moose Hide, Idaho: 'You two and Tom Venn were as much a part of that strike as I was. You kept me goin' in the bad days. Sarqaq, too. All the time I dug out that rich lateral and sent up that muck crawlin' with gold, I thought of you folks.'

His voice broke: 'You know, a man can't work underground for two years else'n someone believes in him. Here.' He thrust into Missy's hand an envelope, and when she opened it two drafts fell out, one to her, one to Matt, drawn upon a Canadian bank. Each check was for twenty thousand dollars. 'I'll mail Tom's to him in Juneau,' Klope said.

And he did one thing more. As he was about to leave the shack he took from his worn backpack a parcel, which he placed on the rude table: 'If you ever open another restaurant, you'll need this.' And when Missy removed the wrapper, she realized that Klope was placing in her care one of his prized possessions: the sourdough starter whose recorded history was now nearly a century old.

TWO DAYS LATER Klope was aboard a ship to Seattle, and as he left he epitomized all the lonely men who had come to Alaska in search of gold. He was one of the few whose dreams had come true, but only at terrible cost. He had braved the Yukon Flats in a blizzard; he had fought his way up the frozen Yukon past Eagle; he had slaved in the shafts atop Eldorado; he had lost Missy, the woman he loved, and Matt Murphy, a partner he had trusted. But he did get his gold.

And it changed him not at all. He did not walk any straighter. He did not suddenly read good books. He made no firm friends to replace the ones he had left behind, and his life had been altered neither negatively nor positively. As an honorable man, he had given twenty thousand dollars to each of the four to whom he knew he was indebted—Missy, Matt, Tom Venn, Sarqaq—but when he returned to Idaho he would do no spectacular thing with what was left. He would not form a bank for assistance to farmers, nor endow chairs at any of the Idaho colleges, nor start a library, nor finance a hospital. He had left Idaho in those first heady days of July 1897, lived through times of cataclysmic changes, and now he was returning home in the sputtering aftermath—the simple inarticulate man he was when he had come to the arctic. There were thousands like him.

Missy Peckham had developed in the Klondike and Nome into a woman of towering strength, beautiful in her integrity, and Tom Venn had grown from a callow youth into an amazingly mature man, but they had achieved this through hardship and failure, not success, and the lessons they acquired would last them through life. John Klope, like so many others, would bring home only gold, which would slowly slip through his fingers, until in old age he would ask: 'Where did it go? What did it accomplish?'

The rigs along Bonanza and Eldorado were closed down. The shacks that had protected miners along the Mackenzie during the arctic winters were slowly falling apart, and the marvelous golden beaches of Nome were once again mere sand. When new storms howled in from the Bering Sea they found no tents to destroy, for all was now as it had been before.

No more will be said about gold in this chronicle. Exciting small finds would continue to be made near the new town of Fairbanks, and one of the most rewarding of all operations would be the deep quartz mine across from Juneau, but there would never be another Klondike, another Nome. Through some miracle never to be fully understood, at those favored points gold had somehow risen to the surface and been eroded away, abraded by sand and wind and ice to be deposited arbitrarily in one place and not another.

The metal that drove men mad behaved as crazily as did the men, and in those frenzied years at the close of the century, turned the world's attention to Alaska, but its effect on the area was no more lasting than it had been upon John Klope.

There were, however, three men whose lives were changed by the miraculous gold of Nome. Lars Skjellerup became an American citizen, and one morning, while at the beach watching the arrival of passengers from a ship anchored in the roadstead, he spotted on the near end of the lighter bringing them ashore a wonderfully vivacious young woman, and he was so captivated by her smile, her look of eagerness and her general demeanor, that when sailors manning the lighter shouted to Eskimo porters: 'Come! Take the people ashore!' he ran quickly into the surf, offered himself to her, and shivered with a new excitement as she was lifted onto his back.

Step by careful step he carried her to the beach, his mind in a whirl, and after she was some fifteen yards inland she said quietly: 'Don't you think you could put me down now?'

Introducing himself somewhat awkwardly, he learned that Miss Armstrong had come from Virginia to teach school in Nome. In the days that followed he haunted the schoolhouse, and when everybody including Miss Armstrong was aware that he was smitten with her, he made the most extraordinary proposal: 'I'm taking the job as Presbyterian missionary at Barrow. Would you honor me to come along?' And in this way a young woman who had fled Virginia for the romance of Alaska found herself a missionary's wife in farthest Barrow, where her husband spent most of his time teaching Eskimos how to handle the reindeer replenishment stock he and his wife had driven north.

Mikkel Sana deposited his money in a Juneau bank and returned to Lapland for a bride, but could convince none of those cautious Lapp beauties that he was really a very rich man. He finally persuaded the third daughter of a man who owned three hundred reindeer to take a chance, and what a surprise she encountered when she accompanied Sana to Juneau and found that the bank account really did exist. After she learned English, which she did in six months, she became the town librarian.

In Arkikov's life, a wife did not feature, at least not at first. Having been abused because he was not an American citizen, and having lost *Seven Above*, he was determined to repair this deficiency, and as soon as his claim was returned after Hoxey's arrest, he started naturalization procedures. Of course, since Alaska still had no regular form of civil government, this proved so difficult that twice he almost gave up, but his partner Skjellerup persuaded him to continue, and after Lars became the missionary in Barrow, the letters he sent to Seattle in support of Arkikov's petition were so persuasive that citizenship was granted.

When a revenue cutter officer who came to Nome explained that in America, as opposed to Siberia, it was customary for a man to have first and last names, Arkikov asked: 'Me get what name?' and the man said: 'Well, some people like the name of their occupation.'

'My what?'

'Your job. If you were a baker in the old country, you'd take the name Baker. A goldsmith becomes Goldsmith. What were you in the old country?'

'What country?'

'Siberia.'

'Me herd reindeer.'

Since it was widely known that this fellow Arkikov now had some sixty thousand dollars in the bank, he had to be treated with respect, and the officer coughed: 'We don't hand out many names like Arkikov Reindeerherder. How about keeping Arkikov as your last name and putting two American names in front?'

'Maybe. What names?'

'Two pairs are very popular. George Washington Arkikov . . .'

'Who is he?'

'Father of this country. Fine general.'

'Me like general.'

'The other pair is just as good. Abraham Lincoln Arkikov.'

'What he did?'

'He freed the slaves.'

'What you mean slaves?' And when the man explained what Lincoln had done—Arkikov had never seen an American black—the choice was made: 'In Siberia got slaves. Me like Lincoln.'

So he became A. L. Arkikov, Nome, Alaska, and in time he took an Eskimo wife, and their three children attended the University of Washington in Seattle, for their father was a rich man.

X

SALMON

East of Juneau, Taku Inlet, a splendid body of water which in Scandinavia would be called a fjord, wound and twisted its way far inland, passing bleak headlands at one time, low hills covered with trees at another. On all sides mountains with snow-covered peaks rose in the background, some soaring to more than seven and eight thousand feet.

A notable feature of Taku was the family of powerful glaciers that pushed their snouts right to the water's edge, where from time to time they calved off huge icebergs which came thundering into the cold waters with echoes reverberating among the hills and mountains. It was a wild, lonely, majestic body of narrow water, and it drained a vast area reaching into Canada almost to the lakes which the Chilkoot miners traversed in 1897 and '98. To travel upstream in the Taku was to probe into the heart of the continent, with the visible glaciers edging down from much more extensive fields inland, where the ice cover had existed for thousands upon thousands of years.

Taku Inlet ran mainly north and south, with the glaciers crawling down to the western shore, but on the eastern bank, directly opposite the snout of a beautiful emerald glacier, a small but lively river with many waterfalls debouched, and nine miles up its course a lake of heavenly grace opened up, not large in comparison with many of Alaska's lakes, but incomparable with its ring of six or, from some vantage points, seven mountains which formed a near-circle to protect it.

This remote spot, which not many visitors, or natives either, ever saw, had been named by Arkady Voronov, during one of his explorations, Lake Pleiades, as his journal explained:

On this day we camped opposite the beautiful green glacier which noses into the inlet on the west. A river scintillating in the sunlight attracted my attention, and with two sailors from the *Romanov*, I explored it for a distance of nine miles. It would be quite unnavigable for even a canoe, because it came tumbling down over rocks, even forming at times small waterfalls eight and ten feet high.

Since it was obvious to us that we were not going to find a better waterway on this course, and since grizzly bears started at us twice, to be deflected by shots over their heads, we had decided to return to our ship with nothing but a fine walk for our labors when one of the sailors, who was breaking the path upstream, shouted back: 'Captain Voronov! Hurry! Something remarkable!'

When we overtook him we saw that his cry was not misleading, for ahead of us, rimmed by six beautiful mountains, lay one of the clearest small lakes I have ever seen. It lay at an elevation, I should guess from the nature of our climb, of about nine hundred feet, not much higher, and it was marred by nothing. Only the bears and whatever fish were in the lake inhabited this magnificent refuge, and we decided on the moment, all three of us, to camp here for the night, for we were loath to depart from such an idyllic place.

I therefore asked one of the men to volunteer for a hurried trip back to the *Romanov* to fetch tents and to bring with him one or two other sailors who might like to share the experience with us, and the man who stepped forward said: 'Captain, with so many bears, I think he should come too,' indicating his partner. 'And he better bring his gun.' I consented, for I realized that I, with my own gun, could protect myself in a settled spot, while they, being on the move, might attract more attention from the bears.

Off they went, and I was left alone in this place of rare beauty. But I did not stay in one place, as planned, because I was lured by the constantly changing attitude of the six mountains which stood guard, and when I had moved some distance to the east, I saw to my surprise that there were not six mountains but seven, and in that moment I determined the name of this lake, Pleiades, because we all know that this little constellation has seven stars, but without a telescope we can see only six. As mythology teaches, the visible six sisters each married gods, but Merope, the hidden seventh, fell in love with a mortal, and thus hides her face in shame.

Lake Pleiades it became, and on three subsequent visits to this eastern area I camped there. It remains the happiest memory of my duty in Alaska, and if, in future generations, some descendant of mine elects to return to these Russian lands, I hope he or she will read these notes and seek out this jewel of a lake.

In September 1900 one hundred million extremely minute eggs of the sockeye salmon were deposited in little streams feeding into that lake. They were delivered by female salmon in lots of four thousand each, and we shall follow the adventures of one such lot, and one salmon within that lot.

The sockeye, one of five distinct types of salmon populating Alaskan waters, had been named by a German naturalist serving Vitus Bering. Using the proper Latin name for salmon plus a native word, he called it *Oncorhynchus nerka,* and the solitary egg of that hundred million whose progress we shall watch will bear that name.

The egg which, when fertilized by milt, or sperm, would become Nerka was placed by its mother in a carefully prepared redd, or nest, in the gravelly bottom of a little stream near the lake and left there without further care for six months. It was abandoned not through the carelessness of its parents but because it was their inescapable nature to die soon after depositing and fertilizing the eggs which perpetuated their kind.

The site chosen for Nerka's redd had to fill several requirements. It had to be close to the lake in which the growing salmon would live for three years. The stream chosen must have a gravel bottom so that the minute eggs could be securely hidden; it must provide a good supply of other gravel which could be thrown over the redd to hide the incubating eggs; and most curious of all, it had to have a constant supply of fresh water welling up from below at an unwavering temperature of about 47° Fahrenheit and with a supersupply of oxygen.

It so happened that the area surrounding Lake Pleiades had varied radically during the past hundred thousand years, for when the Bering land bridge was open, the ocean level had dropped, taking the lake's level down with it, and as the different levels of the lake fluctuated, so did its shoreline. This meant that various benches had been established at various times, and Nerka's mother had chosen a submerged bench which had through the generations accumulated much gravel of a size that salmon preferred.

But how was the constant supply of upwelling water at a reliable temperature delivered? Just as some ancient river had existed where John Klope's present-day Eldorado Creek flowed, but at a much different level, so another subterranean river, emerging from deep in the roots of the surrounding mountains, surged up through the gravels of that sunken bench, providing the rich supply of oxygen and constant temperature that kept both the lake and its salmon vital.

So for six months, his parents long dead, Nerka in his minute egg nestled beneath the gravel while from below flowed this life-giving water. It was one of the most precise operations of nature—perfect flow of water, perfect temperature, perfect hiding place, perfect beginning for one of the most extraordinary life histories in the animal kingdom. And one final attribute of Lake Pleiades could be considered the most remarkable of all, as we shall see six years later: the rocks which lined the lake and the waters which flowed into it from the submerged rivulets carried minute traces—perhaps one in a billion parts—of this mineral and that, with the result that Lake Pleiades had a kind of lacustrine fingerprint which would differentiate it from any other lake or river in the entire world.

Any salmon born, as Nerka would soon be, in Lake Pleiades would bear with him always the unique imprint of his lake. Was this memory carried in his bloodstream, or in his brain, or in his olfactory system, or perhaps in a group of these attributes in conjunction with the phases of the moon or the turning of the earth? No one knew. One could only guess, but that Nerka and Lake Pleiades on the western shore of Alaska were indissolubly linked, no one could deny.

Still only a minute egg, he nestled in the gravel as subterranean waters welled up through the bench to sustain him, and each week he grew closer to birth. In January 1901, deep under the thick ice which pressed down upon the tributary stream, the egg which would become Nerka, along with the other four thousand fertilized eggs of his group, underwent a dramatic change. His egg, a brilliant orange color, showed through the skin an eye with a bright rim and an intensely black center. Unquestionably it was an eye, and it bespoke the emerging life within the egg; the unwavering supply of cold, fresh water welling up through the gravel ensured the continuance and growth of that life. But the natural attrition that decimated these minute creatures was savage. Of Nerka's original four thousand, only six hundred survived the freezing gravel, the diseases and the predation by larger fish.

In late February of that year these six hundred eggs of Nerka's group began to undergo a series of miraculous changes, at the conclusion of which they would become full-fledged salmon. The embryo Nerka slowly absorbed the nutrients from the yolk sac, and as the interchange occurred, he grew and developed swimming motions. Now he obtained the first of a bewildering series of names, each marking a major step in his growth. He was an *alevin.*

When his yolk was completely absorbed, the creature was still not a proper fish, only a minute translucent wand with enormous black eyes and, fastened to his belly, a huge sac of liquid nutrient upon which he must live for the next crucial weeks. He was an ugly, misshapen, squirming thing, and any passing predator could gulp down hundreds of him at a time. But he was a potential fish with a monstrously long head, functioning eyes and a trailing translucent tail. Rapidly in the constantly moving waters of his stream he began to consume plankton, and with the growth which this produced, his protruding sac was gradually resorbed until the swimming thing was transformed into a self-sufficient baby fishling.

At this point Nerka left his natal stream and moved the short distance into the lake, where he was properly called a *fry,* and in this condition he showed every characteristic, except size, of a normal fresh-water fish. He would breathe like one through his gills; he would eat like one; he would learn to swim swiftly to dodge larger predators; and it would seem to any observer that he was well adapted to spend the rest of his life in this lake. It would, in those first years, have been preposterous to think that one day, still to be determined by his rate of growth and maturation, he would be able to convert his entire life processes so radically that he would be completely adapted to salt water; at this stage of his development salt water would have been an inclement milieu.

Ignorant of his strange destiny, Nerka spent 1901 and 1902 adjusting to life within the lake, which presented two contradictory aspects. On the one hand it was a savage home where salmon fry were destroyed at appalling rates. Larger fish hungered for him. Birds sought him out, especially the merganser ducks that abounded on the lake, but also kingfishers and stiltlike birds with long legs and even longer beaks that could dart through the water with incredible accuracy to snap up a tasty meal of salmon. It seemed as if everything in the lake lived on fry, and half of Nerka's fellow survivors vanished into gullets before the end of the first year.

But the lake was also a nurturing mother which provided young fry a multitude of dark places in which to hide during daylight hours and a jungle of underwater grasses in which they could lose themselves if light, dancing off their shimmering skin, betrayed their presence to the larger fish. Nerka learned to move only in the darkest nights and to avoid those places where these fish liked to feed, and since in these two years he was not even three inches long, and most things that swam were larger and more powerful than he, it was only by exercising these precautions that he did survive.

He was now a *fingerling,* a most appropriate name, since he was about the size of a woman's little finger, and as his appetite increased, the comforting lake provided him, in its safer waters, nutritious insect larvae and various kinds of plankton. As he grew older he fed upon the myriad tiny fishes which flashed through the lake, but his main delight was twisting upward, head out of water, to snare some unsuspecting insect. Meanwhile, in the town of Juneau, a scant seventeen miles distant over a glacier-strewn route, impossible to travel on foot, forty miles by an easy water route, creatures of a much different life history were working out their own tangled destinies.

* * *

W HEN TOM VENN came down to Juneau to open the Ross & Raglan store in the spring of 1902, he found the thriving little town a joy after the bitter cold and raw lawlessness of Nome. The settlement which many had been proposing as the new capital of Alaska, replacing outmoded Sitka, which lay off to one side at the edge of the Pacific Ocean, was already an attractive place, even though it was cramped into a narrow strip between tall mountains to the northeast and a beautiful sea channel to the southwest.

Wherever Tom looked in Juneau he saw variation, for even nearby Douglas Island, which crowded in from the south, had its own distinctive mountains, while big ships from Seattle berthed a hand's breadth from the main streets. But the majesty of Juneau, which differentiated it from all other Alaskan towns, was the huge, glistening Mendenhall Glacier, which nosed its way to the water's edge west of town. It was a magnificent, living body of ice that snapped and crackled as it ground its way toward the sea, yet so available that children could take their picnics along its edge in summer.

Another glacier, less famous and visible, approached Juneau from the opposite direction, as if it sought to enclose the little town in its embrace, but the encroaching ice did not determine the temperature of Juneau, which was warmed by the great currents sweeping in from Japan. It had a pleasant climate, marked by much rain and fog but punctuated by days of the most enchanting purity when the sun made all components of the varied scene sparkle like jewels.

After he had been in town for only a few days, Tom selected the location for his store, a lot on Franklin Street near the corner of Front. It had the advantage of facing the waterfront, so that he could have easy access to the ships that docked there. But it also had a disadvantage, because a small hut already occupied it, and he would have to buy the shack if he wanted the land. In the long interests of his company, he decided to do so.

When the time came to close the deal, he learned that the land and the building had different owners. The land belonged to a gentleman from Seattle, the building to a local Tlingit who worked along the waterfront. So, after paying for the land, Tom found himself in negotiation with a fine-looking, dark-skinned Indian in his late thirties. An able fellow according to reports along the docks, he bore the unusual name of Sam Bigears, and as soon as Tom saw him he supposed that he was going to have trouble with this taciturn fellow. But that was not the case.

'You want house, I glad to sell.'

'Where will you go?'

'I have land, fine spot Taku Inlet. Pleiades River.'

'So you're leaving Juneau?'

'No. One day canoe trip, tassall.' Tom was to learn that Sam Bigears used this comprehensive word to dismiss a world of worries: 'Fish broke the line, got away, tassall,' or 'Rain seven days, tassall.'

Within fifteen minutes Tom and Bigears agreed upon a price for the shack —sixty dollars—and when Venn handed over the check, Bigears chuckled: 'Thank you. Maybe house worth nothing. Maybe belong Mr. Harris, along with ground.'

'Well, it was your house. You were living in it. And I'd be very happy if you stayed around to help me build the store.'

'I like that,' and the informal partnership was formed, with Sam Bigears assuming control of materials and the time sheets of the other workmen. He proved himself to be an intelligent, clever craftsman with a positive genius for devising new ways of performing old tasks. Since he was good at woodworking, he took charge of the doors and stairs.

'Where did you learn how to build a stair?' Tom asked one day. 'That's not easy.'

'Many buildings,' Sam said, pointing to Front and Franklin streets where stores and warehouses clustered. 'I work with good German carpenter. I like wood, trees, everything.'

One morning when Tom reported for work, having had a spacious breakfast in his hotel, he was astounded to find that a gigantic iceberg, much larger than his entire store and three stories high, had been driven into the channel by a westerly storm, and there it rested, right at his worksite, towering over the men hammering nails.

'What do we do about this?' Tom wanted to know, and Bigears replied: 'We wait till somebody tow it away,' and before noon a surprisingly small boat with a puffing steam engine hurried up, threw a lasso and chain around a projection from the iceberg, and slowly towed it out of the channel. Tom was amazed that such a small boat could dictate to such a monstrous berg, but as Bigears said: 'Boat knows what it's doing. Iceberg just drifting, tassall,' and that was the difference. Once the berg started slowly moving away from shore, the little boat had no trouble keeping it headed in the right direction, and by midafternoon the berg was gone.

'Where did it come from?' Tom asked, and Bigears said: 'Glaciers. Maybe our glacier. You ever see Mendenhall?' When Tom said 'No,' Sam punched him in the arm: 'Sunday we make picnic. I like picnics.'

So on Sunday, after Tom had attended the Presbyterian church and surveyed with satisfaction the progress of his building, he waited for Bigears to fetch him for the trip to the glacier, and to his surprise the Tlingit appeared in a two-horse carriage rented from a man for whom he had worked and driven by an attractive young Indian girl of about fourteen whom he introduced as his daughter: 'This Nancy Bigears. Her mother see glacier many times, stay home.'

'I'm Nancy,' she said, extending her hand, and Tom felt both that she was very young, and that she was quite mature in her solid posture toward the world, for she looked at him without embarrassment and handled the horses with confidence.

Bowing to the girl, Tom asked: 'Why Nancy? Why not a Tlingit name?' and Sam said: 'She got Tlingit name too. But she live with white people in Juneau. She have name of missionary's wife. Fine name, tassall.'

Nancy was an Indian, no doubt about that, with an even dark skin, black eyes and hair, and that saucy air of freedom which came from living in close association with the land. She wore Western clothes, but with a touch of piping or fur here and there to retain the Indian look, but the two things which typed her as Tlingit were the handsome dark braids which hung below her shoulders and the big decorated boots that covered her feet. They gave her otherwise slender body a heavy pinned-to-earth look which matched her pragmatic approach.

The ride to the glacier was extremely pleasant, with Bigears explaining where he lived, now that his shack had disappeared, and Nancy telling of her days in school. She was attending not a mission school for Indians but the regular white school, and apparently she was doing well, for she could converse easily on subjects like music and geography: 'I'd like to see Seattle. Girls tell me it's a fine place.'

'It is,' Tom assured her.

'Did you live in Seattle?' she asked as they approached the turn to the north which would take them to the glacier.

'Yes.'

'You born there?'

'No, Chicago. But I lived in Seattle half a year.'

'Many ships? Many people?'

'Just like your friends said.'

'I would like to see, but I would never want to leave Alaska.' She turned to face Tom: 'Which do you like, Seattle or Juneau?' and he replied truthfully: 'I long to get back to that city. Maybe with R&R, after my apprenticeship . . .'

'What's that?'

'The years when you learn how to work. When I know all about stores and ships and other parts of Alaska, maybe I'll be allowed to work in Seattle.'

'There she is!' Bigears cried as they reached a crest from which the great glacier first became visible, and it was both bigger and more impressive than Tom had imagined from the many photographs he had seen. It was not green-blue, as so many said, but a rather dirty white as centuries of snow, tight-packed, reached the breaking-off point where the crawling glacier died.

He was surprised that Nancy was able to drive the carriage almost to the entrance to a cave in the ice. Here Bigears stayed with the horses while Nancy led Tom inside to a deep cavern. As he stood there, looking about, he saw in the ceiling a spot thinner than the rest where the sun shone through the crystal ice, showing it to be the green-blue he had expected. It was radiant, a glorious touch of nature that not many would ever see, this splendid, vibrating cavern in which sun and ice met.

'My people say the raven was born in this cave,' she told Tom, and in his ignorance he asked: 'Is the raven something special . . . with you, I mean?' and she said proudly: 'I'm a raven,' and there deep within the birth-cavern of her totem he learned of how the world was divided between the eagles and the ravens, and he said, reflecting on his study of American history: 'I suppose I would be an eagle,' and she nodded: 'Ravens are more clever. They win the rope games, but eagles are necessary too.'

They did not, on Tom's first visit to the glacier, see any icebergs calve; Nancy thought that happened more frequently at other glaciers to the north, but when they left the cave and Tom threw rocks at the snout he could see fragments of ice break away, and he understood the mechanism of how the iceberg which had visited his store had formed and broken away.

Bigears had additional information, gathered by his people over many centuries: 'You didn't see no glaciers in Nome, did you? I tell you why. Not so much rain up there in summer, not so much snow in winter. North of Yukon, even north of Kuskokwim, no glaciers. Not enough snow. But down here, much rain, much snow, it fall, it fall, and never melt.'

'Where does the ice come from?'

'You pack snow down, this year, next year, many years, it cannot melt. Snow get hard, make ice. Hundred years, thick ice. Thousand years, very thick.'

'But how does it crawl along the valleys?'

'Ice comes, it stays, it says like the salmon: "I got to get to the ocean," and down it crawls, little bit each year, many years many big icebergs break off, but always crawling to the sea.'

'Next year, will that cave still be there?'

'Next week, maybe gone. Always crawling toward the sea.'

In the days following the trip to the glacier, Tom was distressed by the fact that Sam Bigears did not report for work, nor was there any word from him, and Tom had to proceed without him. One of the white carpenters, who had come to depend on Bigears for much of the important woodwork, said: 'You can't never rely on them Tlingits. Good people for the most part, but when you really need 'em they're never on hand.'

'What do you suppose has happened?' Tom asked with real concern, for he missed Bigears, and the carpenter said: 'Any one of fifty reasons. His aunt is ill, bad cold, and he feels he must be with her. Pollock have come into the area and he feels he must fish while they're here. Or most likely, he felt that he needed a walk in the woods. He'll probably come sauntering back, Tlingit style, one of these days.'

That was a fair prediction, because after two weeks' absence Bigears did come drifting back to resume his carpentering, and when he reported to work as if he had never been absent, he explained to Tom: 'I got to get things ready.' That was all he volunteered, and when Tom asked: 'What things? Where?' he said cryptically: 'Store look pretty good. Be finish soon. Then you, me, we go my home.'

'But we tore that shack down.'

'I mean my real home. Pleiades River.'

Tom noticed that he had not brought his daughter back with him, and this vaguely disappointed him, but he supposed that she had been left at the other home, and when the time came, in late August, that the store was, as Bigears had pointed out, in good shape, with only a few refinements left to be finished, Tom judged that he could with safety take a couple days off, so he told Bigears: 'We could leave tomorrow, if you can get your canoe ready,' and on a bright morning, with the sun rising over the great ice fields back of Juneau, the two set forth for the easy paddle to Taku Inlet.

But anyone in Juneau who took a sunny day for granted was a fool, and they had not progressed far down Gastineau Channel before rain began to fall. For some hours they traveled through it without complaint, for a Juneau rain was not like that of other places: it did not fall in big drops, or any drops at all, but came down as a kind of benevolent mist which permeated everything without getting any particular item really wet.

The canoe ride was a fresh experience for Tom, a trip of unusual beauty. Bigears was a strong paddler who kept the canoe thrusting forward and Tom added youthful vigor from the prow, from where he studied the changing landscape. Prior to entering the inlet, he saw about him the hills that protected Juneau on all sides, making its waterways alluring channels, but when they turned into the inlet the scene changed dramatically. Now they faced that chain of high peaks which crowned the Alaska-Canada border, and for the first time Tom felt as if he were entering one of the fjords he had read about as a boy. But most of all, he was aware that he was heading into a primitive wilderness, with not a sign of human occupancy anywhere, and his stroke grew stronger as they glided silently up the inlet.

They had not progressed far when Tom spied a sight so lovely and balanced that its parts seemed to have been placed where they were by an artist. From the west came down a small glacier, sparkling blue in color, in what seemed an attempt to meet a large rock which barely emerged from the middle of the inlet, while beyond rose the great mountains of Canada. 'This is something!' Tom called back, and Bigears said: 'Low water like now, we see the Walrus, high water no see.' When Tom asked what the Walrus was, Sam pointed to a half-submerged rock which did indeed resemble a walrus rising from the sea to catch a breath.

As they passed the face of the glacier Tom cried: 'This is a fine trip, Sam,' but to paddle nearly thirty miles, even when the water was relatively smooth, took time, and when sunset approached, Tom called back: 'Will we get there tonight?' and Bigears replied as he gave the canoe an extra thrust forward: 'Pretty soon dark come, we see lights,' and just as dusk appeared ready to encompass the inlet, straight ahead on the left bank Tom saw the last rays of sunlight striking the face of a glacier whose ice glistened like a waterfall of emeralds, while atop a headland on the right bank glowed the light coming from the windows of a log cabin.

'Halloo there! Halloo!' Bigears shouted, and on the headland Tom could see movement, but they were now at the southern end of the estuary formed by the entry of the Pleiades River, and they had to do some stiff paddling before they crossed it. As they did, Tom saw an Indian woman and a young girl coming down to the water's edge to greet them.

'This my wife,' Bigears said as his powerful hands dragged the canoe well onshore. 'You know Nancy.'

Mrs. Bigears was shorter than her husband and rounder. She was a taciturn woman who was never surprised at what her enterprising husband did; her task was to supervise whatever house they occupied, and it was clear that she had done a good job at this cabin, for the grounds about it were neat and the interior a model of traditional Tlingit habitation. She spoke no English, but with her right hand indicated that her husband's young guest would occupy a kind of alcove; Nancy, apparently, would have her own corner, while mother and father would take the large spruce-needled bed.

On the iron stove which Sam had purchased some years before in Juneau, various pots were producing an aroma which augured well, but Tom was exhausted from that long day's paddling and fell asleep long before the Bigears family was prepared to eat. They did not waken him.

In the morning, after a huge breakfast of sourdough pancakes and venison sausage, Nancy said: 'You must see where we are,' and she led him about the wedge of land on which her ancestors had built their refuge from the Russians. 'We have this protected hill. Across the inlet we see the green glacier. Down there the bay where the Pleiades River empties. And wherever we look, the mountains that watch over us.'

Tom was still admiring the site, so well suited for a cabin, when with a wide sweep of her arm she indicated the spacious land to the east: 'In these woods, deer to feed us. In the river, salmon every year. Soon we catch many salmon, dry them on those racks.'

As Tom looked toward the drying racks, he saw lying on the ground behind the cabin a large white object stretching a considerable distance, with many chips of some kind scattered about. 'What's that?' he asked, and Nancy cried with a mixture of delight and reverence: 'That's why my father wanted you to come,' and she led him to an extraordinary object—which was to have a permanent influence in his life.

It was the trunk of a large fir tree transported here from a considerable distance. Its bark had been carefully peeled away, exposing the pale-cream wood on which Sam had been working, and when Tom saw the kind of work his carpenter had been doing, he was awed. For this was a Tlingit totem pole in the making, a majestic work of art symbolizing the experiences of its people. In its present position, prostrate on the ground and stretching immoderately, it created a powerful impression, the figures comprising it seeming to flow and crawl and twist in a bewildering confusion.

Tom gasped: 'It's so big! Did your father carve it all?'

'He's worked on it for a long time.'

'Is it finished?'

'I think so. But it's not cut off at the top, so I don't know.'

'What do the figures mean?'

'We better ask Pop.' And when she called her father, Sam came out with the tools he had used to carve this masterpiece: an adz, two chisels, a gouge, a mallet, and now a saw for the final act of cutting away the top.

'What does it mean?' Tom asked, and Bigears laid his tools aside, all except the saw, which he kept in his right hand as a wand with which to indicate the twisting figures.

'First the frog who brought us here. Then the face of my grandfather-grandfather who built the fort at Sitka. Then the deer that fed us, the ship that brought the Russians, the trees.'

'And the man in the top hat?'

'Governor Baranov.'

'Wasn't he your enemy? Didn't he fight you and kill your warriors?'

'Yes, but he won.'

'And now he sits at the top of everything?'

'Not quite. Today I finish.'

And throughout that entire day Tom Venn sat beside Nancy Bigears as her mother brought food to her husband while he applied his tools vigorously to the wood at the top of the totem. First he sawed off the tip of the fir, leaving two feet of exposed wood. Then, with his rude gouge, he began to hack away the huge chunks that protruded from the top of Baranov's big hat, and his work appeared to be so aimless that Tom asked 'What are you doing, Sam?' but received no answer, for it seemed that the carver was working in a kind of trance.

By midafternoon, with a misty rain replacing the morning sunlight, Tom was completely mystified, but now Bigears began working with his adz, using strokes and cuts much less flamboyant than before. Gradually from the top of the fallen tree emerged the shadowy form of a bird—and no one spoke. Now, with rapid, sure strokes, the Tlingit artist gave vibrant form to his topmost figure, and in a triumphant conclusion he brought forth the raven, symbol of his tribe and his people. The Russians in their tall hats had triumphed momentarily, but in conformance with history, atop the Russians stood the raven. In their quiet way, the Tlingits had also triumphed.

'How are you going to get it upright?' Tom asked, and Bigears, willing to talk at last, indicated a raised spot from which the totem would be visible for miles up and down the inlet, and on the river too.

'We dig hole there, you, me, Nancy.'

'But how will we drag the totem there?'

'Potlatch.'

Tom did not understand either the word or its meaning, but he accepted the fact that a Tlingit miracle of some kind would move the totem to the top of the mound and then erect it in an upright position, but what this mysterious potlatch would consist of, he could not guess.

When the totem was finished, all its rough spots smoothed away, Bigears mysteriously disappeared in his canoe, and when Tom asked where he had gone, Nancy said simply: 'To tell the others,' and for six days they did not see him.

In the waiting period Nancy suggested that her mother pack a little bundle of food which she and Tom could take with them on an excursion to a lake at the head of the river: 'It's a beautiful place. Quiet. All mountains. Nine miles, easy walk.'

So off they started on a fine September morning, and as they hiked along, with Nancy showing the way on a footpath long used by her people, Tom experienced the quiet charm of this part of Alaska, so different from the bleak power of the Yukon and the vast emptiness of Nome and the Bering Sea. He liked the trees, the waterfalls, the ferns lending grace to the scene, and the ever-present rippling of the little river.

'Any fish in there?' he asked, and Nancy replied: 'A few salmon come all the time. But in September, many, many come.'

'Salmon? In this tiny stream?'

'They come to the lake. Soon we'll be there.' And at the end of their climb Tom saw one of the choice spots of southeastern Alaska, Lake Pleiades, rimmed by its six mountains.

'This was worth the effort,' he cried as he looked at the placid water with the mountains reflected in its surface. Beside its quiet shore they ate their lunch, and then Tom showed Nancy how he could skip flat stones across the surface of the water, and she said that he must have many skills.

On the way back to the cabin, with a bright sun winking at them as they passed the waterfalls, Nancy was in the lead, some twenty feet ahead, when Tom became aware that someone was coming up behind him, and supposing that it was some Tlingit on his way to the Bigears cabin, he turned to speak, and found himself facing a rather large grizzly bear approaching rapidly.

Since the bear was still some distance away, Tom erroneously supposed that he could escape by running from it, but as he started to dig in his toes and speed to safety he recalled a tale told one wintry night by an old man with half a face: 'No man can outrun a grizzly. I tried. It caught me from behind. One sweep of its claw. Look at me.'

Driven by an anguished fear, Tom increased his speed, heard the bear gaining, and screamed: 'Nancy! Help!'

When she heard his cry she turned and saw with horror that he had no chance of outrunning the bear, for the animal, reveling in the chase, was forging ahead with even greater strides and must soon leap upon Tom from the rear. She was terrified, for she knew that the bear would not stop until it had overpowered its target. With one swipe of a gigantic paw with its swordlike claws, it would rip away Tom's face and perhaps sever his windpipe.

In that instant Nancy Bigears knew what she must do, what her Tlingit ancestors had learned through the centuries when they confronted the grizzly on lands they shared with the fierce creature. 'You can do three things,' her grandmother had told her. 'Run away and be killed. Climb a tree and maybe live. Or stand and talk to the bear, making him think you're bigger than you are.'

There were trees at hand, but none close enough to run to, nor fit for climbing if one did reach them. The only hope lay in talking to the bear, and with almost spontaneous bravery Nancy dashed back toward Tom, who was close to being overtaken by the speeding bear, grabbed his hand, and brought him to a stop. Holding him firmly, she turned him to face the bear, who lumbered up, stopped abruptly about ten feet away, and blinked at the object that now blocked its path.

The bear had exceptional powers of smell, and these assured him that what it had been chasing was still at hand, but its eyesight was limited at best and often defective, so it could not determine what it was that stood before it. And then came that low, powerful, unfrightened voice in Tlingit: 'Sir Bear, do not be afraid. We are your friends and we mean you no harm.'

The bear remained motionless, cocking its ears to hear the reassuring sounds: 'Stop where you are, Sir Bear. Go your way and we shall go ours.'

Its small brain became confused. In chasing the man, it had been playing a kind of game, no more, and had it overtaken him, as soon it must, it would probably have killed, more in sport than anger. It knew it was not threatened by the man, whom it saw merely as an intruder upon its stream banks, and as long as Tom fled he remained an attractive target to be chased. But now everything was changed, for there was nothing to chase, no slim moving thing to be played with. Instead, there was this big immovable thing, these firm sounds coming from it, this sense of mystery and confusion. In the flash of a moment everything was altered.

Slowly the bear turned around, stared over its shoulder at the strange object in its path, and took a powerful first bound of its retreat. In its ears as it went it could hear those quiet but forceful sounds: 'Go your way, Sir Bear. Go to your salmon spot and may the fishing be good.'

Only when the huge bear was gone did Nancy relinquish her hold on Tom, for now she knew it was safe for him to relax. Had he run when the bear stood there facing them, or even moved conspicuously, both she and Tom might have been killed; now as she released Tom's hand she could feel him start to sag.

'That was close.'

'It was, for both of us.'

'I didn't know you could talk to bears.'

She stood in the sunlight, her round, placid face smiling as if nothing of moment had happened: 'He needed talking to, that one.'

'You were very brave, Nancy.'

'He wasn't hungry. Just curious. Just playing. He needed to be told.'

ON FRIDAY THE neighboring Indian families began to arrive, coming up Taku Inlet in their painted canoes or drifting down with sails set as the famous Taku Wind blew out of Canada, shoving their boats along. They were dressed not in work clothes but in festive garments, dresses heavy with beads, trousers trimmed in fur. They wore hats that Tom had not seen before, and children were adorned with shells and wore cloaks of decorated deerskin. They were a colorful group, and as each family arrived Nancy and her mother greeted them with the same words, which Nancy interpreted for Tom: 'We are honored that you have come. The master will soon be here,' whereupon the visitors bowed and moved off to inspect the prostrate totem, which they adjudged to be excellent.

Now there was excitement along the shore, and children ran down to greet Sam Bigears as he paddled his way home, his canoe full of purchases from Juneau. Eagerly the young people helped him unload, handing along from one to the other the parcels which would soon lend dignity to the potlatch. When they came to three small packages of surprising weight they asked impertinently: 'What's in here?' and he told them to tear away the wrappers. When they did they found three small cans of white man's paint, and these were taken to where the nearly completed totem lay on the ground.

Its major segments had already been colored in the subdued tones provided by the earth: a soft brown, a glowing blue, a quiet red. What Bigears now proposed was to highlight the pole with small areas of a vivid green, a scintillating carmine and a jet-black. Going directly to the totem without even pausing to greet his guests, he opened the three cans, gave two carvers as gifted as he their own brushes, and explained what he wanted: 'Frog got to be green, black spots. Hat black, what else? Faces red, wings of the other bird green, eyes of the beaver red, too.'

Deftly the men applied the finishing touches. Purists among them would have preferred that only natural colors be used, as in times past, but even they had to agree that the restrained touches of store-bought paint blended pleasingly with the rest of the design, lending it those accents of brightness which revealed the character of the man who had done the carving.

When the third coat was applied, with the sun beating down to bond it to the wood, the women came to applaud, and all agreed that Bigears had done his work like a carver of the old days. One woman pointed out that the totem in her village was taller, and another was not too pleased with the bright red touches, but in general it was approved: 'It will stand properly in this cove, facing the glacier, speaking to all who come up or down the inlet.'

Now the potlatch began. Seventeen families had come to participate in Sam Bigears' hospitality, and as the food and the gifts were presented to the visitors, it was acknowledged that Sam was just as generous as his forebears had been. Tom Venn was astounded at the lavishness of the celebration, and thought: This must have cost him a lot. Sam, as he moved among his guests, gave no indication that he considered his gifts extravagant, nor did he comment in any way upon the bountiful piles of food. When Tom, eyes wide, asked: 'Do you hold potlatch often?' Sam evaded a direct answer: 'I have luck. Good job. Good wife. Good daughter.'

Tom told him of the adventure with the grizzly, and Sam laughed: 'I wish I know sooner. I put bear on totem. Celebration.'

Suddenly Tom wanted to know many things: a celebration of what? a potlatch in honor of what? these friends assembled on what principle? the totem representing homage to what power? the force or spirit which bound these people together stemming from what? And as these questions pounded through his head, he realized how much he respected his carpenter and how impossible it was to ask him for an explanation.

But he could ask about the totem itself, and now as it lay for the last time on the ground where each part could be inspected at close hand, he moved along it, asking what role the turtle played, and why that bird rested the way it did, and why the raven's wings were added to the post and were not a generic part of it? Sam, obviously proud of his work and pleased with the way his three store-bought colors accommodated to the softer earth tones, was happy to speak of the totem in these hours before it was to be formally erected at the entrance to the cove; it was as if at that moment the totem would become the property of all and no longer his creation.

'No special man, no special bird, no special face. Just how I feel. Just how the rains fall.'

Rain was beginning to fall, so men brought canvases to protect the still-wet paint, and through that first night of the potlatch one man played a fiddle, women danced, and Tom Venn complained to Nancy: 'Nobody tells me what it is. A potlatch for what?' and watching the celebration as if from afar, she explained this ancient custom:

'When all goes well and there is money in the house and neighbors think kindly of you, maybe it's proper for you to give it all away and start over. Maybe you must prove yourself again. Maybe you must not rise too high above your neighbors. Look! They dance. They sing. And Sam Bigears grows bigger in their eyes, for he has made real potlatch.

'The missionaries hated potlatch. Claimed it was the work of the devil. Too much noise. Not enough praying. Lots of things happen at potlatch. Good things. Noisy things. Maybe seem wild. But the celebration . . .'

She nodded her head gently to the screeching of the fiddle and smiled as she watched her mother dance in a corner as if partnered by a ghost, dancing to a music which she alone heard.

On the morning of the third day everyone assembled at the totem to participate in the ritual of its erection. Since the pole was thirty feet long and ample at the base, this was going to present quite an engineering problem, but the Tlingits had, through the centuries, perfected a system for getting their massive totems into an upright position, and now came the test.

Bigears and Tom and Nancy had already readied the hole for the pole, lining it with rocks, so now a trench was dug leading on a gradual slope from the deep bottom of the hole out beside the pole to a distance of about one-third the length of the totem. When it was properly graded, the men applied muscle and rope to the task of easing the long pole sideways and down into the sloping trench. The top end of the totem—that is, the end not in the trench—was propped up at various points with stout logs, and all was ready, except that at the last moment men wedged into the waiting hole, along the far face, a large flat slab against which the bottom of the totem would abut, so that when the top was raised, this slab would prevent the totem from gouging out the soft earth as the end of the pole was forced against it.

Now ropes were applied at many points along the top of the pole, one of the most important being the one which would prevent it from swinging too far over when it was pulled upright. Other ropes were attached to keep the totem from weaving from side to side, and men experienced in raising poles began to shout orders while others hauled on the ropes. Women, watching in admiration as the handsomely carved totem began to rise majestically in the sunny morning, its painted surfaces reflecting light, began a chant, whereupon the men pulled more vigorously, and with those pulling back to prevent too rapid a rise straining to maintain a balance between speed and caution, the beautiful totem rose in the air, trembled for a moment as it approached the perpendicular, then shuddered and quietly slipped down into its hole. Tom Venn, pulling on one of the ropes which prevented sideways motion, felt the great log come to rest.

'Halloo!' the man in charge of the ropes shouted, and everyone let go, and as the ropes fell easily toward the tall pole, men and women alike cheered, for now Sam Bigears' totem stood alone and erect, facing the shore as if to greet all ships that might approach on the inlet.

The potlatch was over. Sam's neighbors carried their gifts to their canoes, each man aware that at some future time he would be expected to repay Sam with a gift of equal value, each woman wondering what gift she could sew or knit that would be as presentable as those Sam's wife had given. Thus the economy of the Tlingits was preserved and enhanced; goods were exchanged; wealth was redistributed; obligations were established which would continue into the indefinite future; and at the entrance to Pleiades River a man, his wife and their daughter preserved a way of life totally alien to the one developing in the town of Juneau, only seventeen miles away as the raven flew.

WHILE SAM BIGEARS was conducting his potlatch at the mouth of the Pleiades, what was happening in the lake at the head of the river to Nerka and his generation of salmon? By the beginning of 1903, even though he had completed two years, he was still so insignificant that he played no conspicuous role in the lake. Larger fish ate his brothers so incessantly that they were now depleted to a mere eighty. As the devastation continued and even intensified, it began to look as if the sockeye in Lake Pleiades must soon be exhausted, but Nerka, with a powerful urge for self-preservation, kept to the dark places, avoided the predatory larger fish, and continued as little more than a fingerling, unaware that upon the perseverance of other salmon like himself depended the survival of their breed.

In that winter of 1903, while Nerka's generation in Lake Pleiades dropped to two million, and Tom Venn was busy in his new store along Juneau's waterfront, the Ross & Raglan steamer *Queen of the North* docked with a large shipment of goods for the summer trade plus a red-headed gentleman who was about to revolutionize this part of Alaska. He was Malcolm Ross, fifty-one years old and surging with energy. 'I'm bursting with plans,' he said as he led Tom into the small office from which the Juneau branch of R&R conducted its business. 'And I'm warning you, Tom, I want to start now.'

Tom had not seen Mr. Ross since that day in 1897 when he began representing R&R along the waterfront, but in the intervening years he had witnessed the tremendous growth of the firm, and he took personal pride in the reports circulating through Alaska that Mr. Ross was a commercial genius.

'What do you have in mind?' Tom asked. 'A new store in Skagway?'

'Skagway's finished. The gold rush has ended. That new railway to White-horse may be good for a few years. But I can see no future for Skagway.'

'Where, then?'

'Here.'

Tom was stunned. His store in Juneau was doing well, but it did not warrant any enlargement, and the idea of a duplicate in some other part of town would be precarious at best and more likely a disaster: 'Mr. Ross, I know R&R rarely makes mistakes, but a second store here . . . it wouldn't be justified.'

'Thank you for an honest opinion, son. But I'm not thinking about another store. I want you to start right now, this morning, to build R&R a major salmon cannery.'

'Where?' Tom asked weakly.

'That's for you to find out. Let's start now.' When Tom protested that he knew nothing of fishing as an industry, let alone canning, Ross forestalled him: 'Neither do I. We start even. But I do know one thing. There's going to be a fortune made on salmon, and we've got to get our share.'

Tom had never seen anything like Malcolm Ross; not even Superintendent Steele of the Mounties had displayed the intensity and vigor of this handsome Seattle merchant who knew intuitively that salmon was certain to replace gold as Alaska's contribution to mainland wealth. By eleven that morning Ross had assembled four knowledgeable men, whom he entertained at a lavish lunch so that he and Tom could probe their secrets about salmon fishing.

'What you would need,' one of the men said, 'that is, if you wanted to do it right . . .'

'I'd do it no other way.'

'Well then, get out your pencil. To clean the fish, you need a huge shed. Bigger than anything you see around here. To cook them, you need another shed, not quite as large. To house the Chinese, because they have to be kept separate, they fight with everyone, you need a third shed, a bunkhouse. For the other workers, another dormitory. A mess hall divided one-third for the Chinese, two-thirds for the others. A carpenter's shop for making crates, a welding shop for making the tin cans. A warehouse next to a loading dock built out on pilings so you can tie up at either high or low tide.'

'That's a lot of money,' one of the other men said, and Ross replied: 'I think we can borrow it. But where do we get our fish to put in the cans?'

The first man resumed: 'Now we get down to the really expensive part. You would have to have a large ship under your own control, leased perhaps, but better if you owned it.'

'We have ships.'

'But not like the one out there. You need a ship to bring the Chinese north in the spring, and all the goods you need. And then it collects fish, brings them to the cannery, and at the end of the season hauls away the workers and the canned salmon.'

'What do you mean, season?'

'Salmon only run a few months each year. Summer. So you open two months early to get things ready and handle the slow early run. Then work your tail off. Take one month to close. Late fall and all of winter you're shut down.'

'Who stays at the cannery during the winter?'

'One watchman.'

'All those buildings, all that investment—and one watchman?'

'Mr. Ross, you don't understand. Your cannery will be way out in the country, along some small body of water, nobody around for miles except bears and spruce trees and salmon.'

'Where do I find such a place?' Ross asked, and now all the men wanted to talk at once, but the first speaker was not finished, so he silenced the others: 'So when you have your big ship to do the big jobs, you must have one or two small ships to move about the waters servicing the thirty-odd boats that do the fishing. You need a lot of boats, Mr. Ross.'

'I can believe that. But where?'

Carefully and with mature judgment, these men, well versed in the lore of the sea and its riches, eliminated the unpromising sites: 'Most scenic body of water hereabouts is Lynn Canal leading to Skagway, but it has few fish.'

'I have no interest in Skagway,' Ross said abruptly, 'and absolutely none in scenery.'

'There's good salmon fishing on Admiralty Island, but the best sites are taken.'

'I don't want second-class locations.'

'There are some very promising areas on Baranof Island . . .'

'Too far from Juneau. I want my headquarters here.'

'With good boats, it doesn't matter much how far away your cannery is. There are some great salmon streams to the south.'

'I've fixed my sights here.'

'Then there's only one untouched spot—good run of salmon, good anchorage for cannery boats.'

'Where?'

'But it has one drawback. The wind that roars out of Canada you won't believe.'

'We can build to protect ourselves against wind.'

'Not this wind. Eddie, tell him about you and the Taku.'

A nearby fisherman, who had been eating prodigiously, laid down his fork and said: 'Everybody hereabouts calls it the Taku Wind. It comes down off the mountains in Canada and funnels through Taku Inlet. In fifteen minutes it can beat up from dead calm to fifty miles an hour. Be careful in a Taku Wind.'

Ross dismissed the warning: 'What kind of salmon run the streams coming into this Taku Inlet?'

'Sockeye, mostly,' the men agreed, and with the utterance of this magic word, Ross made up his mind: 'We'll find a spot on Taku Inlet where there's protection from the wind,' and immediately after lunch he asked Tom to arrange for an exploration of that beautiful body of water.

They found Sam Bigears at work on an addition to the hotel, and he was delighted with the prospect of heading back up the Taku, so one of the small R&R coastal steamers already in Juneau was commandeered, and by noon the expedition was under way.

As soon as the steamer turned the corner into the inlet, Malcolm Ross became aware that he had come upon something special, for the fjord was far more beautiful than he had imagined from the accounts he had heard at lunch. 'This is magnificent!' he cried as the shimmering blue face of Walrus Glacier came into view. He was also impressed by the narrow defile between the glacier and Walrus Rock through which the ship nosed its way, and when the inlet broadened out, disclosing exciting new perspectives, his attention focused on the emerald face of Pleiades Glacier, one hundred feet high and gleaming in sunlight: 'This is stupendous!'

But then he looked to the east, and behind the headland on which Sam Bigears' cabin stood he saw his first Alaskan totem pole, its varied colors glistening in the sun as if to complement the glacier on the facing shore. 'Why would such a pole be erected up there?' Ross wanted to know. 'Nothing around but that one cabin.'

'That's Bigears' cabin,' Tom explained. 'He carved the totem. I helped put it in position.'

'I suppose the figures mean something. Pagan rites and all that.' So Bigears was called to the railing to explain his totem, and he did a much poorer job than his daughter would have done, until finally Ross, somewhat irritated, asked: 'Tell me, who's the man in the top hat?' and Bigears said with a big smile: 'A white man. Maybe Russian.'

'Don't you know?' Ross asked impatiently, and Sam said: 'Just a white man. He won.'

Ross could make nothing of this, and when he asked about the bird atop the totem, he received another ambiguous answer: 'Just a bird. Maybe a raven.'

Now Ross became conciliatory: 'That's a fine pole. And you have a good location here. Any salmon in the river?'

'Many sockeye,' Sam replied, and Ross made careful note of this fact, but his shrewd eye detected a fact of greater significance to a potential salmon cannery: 'Bigears, doesn't your headland jutting out and up like that . . . doesn't it protect that little bay from what they call the Taku Wind?'

'Maybe.'

'So if I built my cannery on that point to the south, opposite yours, I'd not have to worry too much about the wind, would I?'

'Maybe not.'

'Then why did you build your cabin up there where the wind hits?' and Sam replied: 'I like wind. It blow too hard, stay inside, build good fire.'

After several more twists, the steamer passed close to the sullen snout of Taku Glacier, immensely higher and wider than the earlier ones but lacking the intense blue color, its dirty ice standing in gray-brown pillars. They were, however, massively impressive, as if they were ready to tumble down upon any ship that came too close. As Ross watched, the captain came down to inform him that ships like this sometimes carried small cannon so that they could fire at glaciers, seeking to precipitate spectacular calving of icebergs, and he said: 'I'd bet a big one's about to let loose.'

'Have you a cannon?' Ross asked, and he was disappointed when the captain said that only passenger ships carried them. But the captain had another tactic: 'We'll go to just the right distance and give our whistle five or six short blasts. Sometimes that'll do the trick,' so the ship moved in surprisingly close, and when the blasts reverberated against the face of the glacier, the vibrations did cause a tall pillar of icy snow to break away and thunder down in a monstrous splash. It produced no lasting iceberg, for the snow was not tightly packed, but it did demonstrate how bergs were formed.

Passing the awesome glacier, the steamer ascended two more miles up near the head of the inlet, where a river tumbling out of Canada came into view, and Ross, watching the water churn and boil over huge boulders, asked: 'How can a salmon pick its way through that twisted affair?' and Bigears said: 'Coming home, they know every bend. Remember from when they came down as smolts,' and Ross said: 'Encourage them to breed well. They're the ones who'll fill our cans.'

The steamer turned around at a point much farther up the inlet than later navigators would be able to go; in their day silt coming out of Canada would accumulate so that big ships would not even be able to reach Taku Glacier, but during the first years of the twentieth century this clogging of the waterway had not yet occurred.

On the trip back down the inlet, Ross stood at the railing, imagining himself a fierce Taku Wind blowing out of Canada, and as the ship neared Sam Bigears' cabin atop the bluff, Ross could feel himself soaring high over the headland and not coming back down till well past the southern side of the Pleiades estuary. Pointing triumphantly at this southern point, so available to shipping yet so well protected, he cried: 'We'll build our cannery on that point,' but Tom said: 'I think we'd better call Sam Bigears over.'

'Why?' Ross snapped.

'Because I think he owns both sides of the cove,' Tom said.

'Sites are allocated in Washington,' Ross said, indicating that he did not want to discuss the matter with Bigears. 'I'll get my man in Washington to get working on it right away.'

As the steamer departed from Taku Inlet he looked back at the compact, enchanting waterway with its cliffs and mountains and scintillating glaciers, and said to those about him: 'It's a proper location for Ross & Raglan. Practically made to order.'

To Tom's surprise, Mr. Ross remained in Juneau for two weeks, supervising the purchasing of materials for a major cannery, even though he had as yet no assured location for it, but on the thirteenth day a telegram arrived informing him that he had been granted exclusive rights to the cove at the mouth of the Pleiades River. 'Full speed ahead!' Ross cried. 'Tom, rush that timber and machinery over to the cove. Start building like a madman, and have things ready to operate by April twenty-fifth.'

'Where do I get the boats?'

'That's my responsibility. They'll be here, believe me.'

'And what shall we call the place?'

Ross considered this for some moments. For some time now he had feared that the widely known name of Ross & Raglan was being attached to too many ventures; it could engender jealousy. Or a man who was angry at treatment he received aboard an R&R ship might stop trading at an R&R store. Then, too, customers in Alaska might grow resentful of the concentration of power in Seattle. For these and other good reasons he decided firmly against any further use of that designation: 'What we need, Thomas, is a name that echoes Alaska.

Make local people proud of their affiliation with this new cannery. Let me think about this tonight.'

An able man who had honestly striven to outfit thousands for Alaska in the gold-rush years, had provided good shipping and general merchandise needed in the growing communities, and now was planning a first-class cannery operation as opposed to certain fly-by-night enterprises which took money out of Alaska and plowed none back in, Malcolm Ross wanted his salmon venture to be an example of the best that enlightened capitalism could provide, and a name which proclaimed that quality was essential.

At breakfast he informed Tom that he had found the perfect solution: 'Totem Cannery. On the labels for our cans, a fine drawing of a totem pole like the one I made when we sailed up Taku Inlet that first day.' And from his pocket he produced a lively sketch of Sam Bigears' totem, but with the amusing white man in the top hat eliminated. In his place appeared a brown bear, with the original raven at the top.

Not only would Bigears' land at the mouth of the Pleiades be taken from him, but his totem would also be appropriated, and there would be nothing he could do about either theft. Malcolm Ross in Seattle and his agent in Washington would see to that.

I N THE DAYS that followed, Tom Venn had ample opportunity to observe just how remarkable his employer was, for two large R&R steamers sailed into Taku Inlet with lumber and hardware for the four main buildings which would have to be in operation by mid-May. Along with these supplies came sixty-five artisans from Seattle, plus tents to house them temporarily and a big portable kitchen. Within a week of landing, this army of men had dug the footings for the principal buildings and had unloaded from a barge the stone and cement that would form the foundations for the large structures whose vertical timbers would soon begin sprouting like a forest of growing stalks after a spring rain.

It was not preposterous for Mr. Ross to expect his buildings to be ready so quickly, for they were essentially barns in which a variety of machinery would be housed; no intricate architectural problems required to be solved. 'Get them up fast and strong,' he told the men whenever he visited the inlet, and when new ships arrived with the heavy iron retorts in which the stacks of filled cans would be cooked by steam pressure, a place was ready for them, and by the time they were installed, some thirty Indians had been hired to lug in the wood to stoke the fires.

The smaller building, in which wooden crates would be built for shipping the cans to Seattle and then to cities like New York and Atlanta, was erected in four days; *slapped together* would be a more appropriate term, perhaps. But the twin building in which the tin cans would be manufactured from raw stock required more time; it had to be sturdy enough to house the heavy tin-working machinery.

In the meantime, thirty-seven local fishermen had been hired to catch the salmon when the run began, and the two small steamers that would move among them to collect their haul and ferry it to the cannery were brought up from Seattle complete with crews. Along with them came a most useful vessel, a big, tough tug with a pile driver mounted on the stern, and on the deck several hundred long wooden piles which would be driven into the muddy bottom of Taku Inlet to form the wharf at which the large cargo ships would dock when loading the crates of canned salmon.

In early April the scene at Totem Cannery was one of intense activity of the most varied sort. Tom Venn, in charge of keeping the hours and pay scales for everyone working on the project, now had about nine different crews at their tasks twelve and fourteen hours a day. Mr. Ross had given specific orders: 'Spend money now and get the work done so that we can make real money in September.'

In mid-April he ordered all work on nonessentials to halt so that a long bunkhouse could be whipped into shape at breakneck speed: 'Just got word that our people in Seattle have found a gang of Chinese in San Francisco. They hired the lot and are shipping them north sooner than expected. I've been warned that keeping them happy is the secret of any good cannery operation, so we've got to have their sleeping area and mess hall ready in two weeks.'

But when Tom tried to decide which carpenters and builders could be taken from which jobs, he found that almost every building was just as essential as the bunkhouse, so he had to scout around for local artisans to fill in. His first thought was to approach his trusted friend Sam Bigears, but Mr. Ross had been told by his Washington lobbyist that 'no Eskimo, no Indian is worth a damn. Only white men can do the work needed to build in Alaska,' and this prejudice had become ingrained. Tlingit Indians in the Taku vicinity could be employed to dig trenches and unload cargo, but they must not be entrusted to build a bunkhouse, even though Chinese were to occupy it: 'I'll have no Indian carpenters, Tom. They can't be trusted.'

'Where did you get that idea?'

'Marvin Hoxey told me how they drink, work two days, then disappear.'

'Marvin Hoxey! He's never worked with Indians. All he knows are barroom stories.'

'He understands Alaska.'

Tom Venn, veteran of the Chilkoot Pass, the Yukon River, the frenzy of Dawson and Nome, had become a young man of twenty with the sound character of a man twice his age, and he was not going to have his hard-won wisdom dismissed by a man like Marvin Hoxey: 'Mr. Ross, I don't mean to contradict, because you know more about business than anyone I've met. But about Indians like the ones I'd hire for the bunkhouse, you've been given poor advice.'

'Hoxey has never let me down. Don't hire Indians for any important work on Totem Cannery.'

Tom laughed, and to his own surprise, took Mr. Ross by the arm: 'Who carved that totem pole over there that you admire so much? The Indian I want to hire. And who helped build your Juneau store in what you admitted was record time? That same Indian. Mr. Ross, Sam Bigears—you've met him, on the boat that first day—he's twice as good a carpenter as any of the men you brought up from Seattle.'

Malcolm Ross had not become the head of a major Seattle enterprise through ignoring the advice of strong-minded men, for he had always been such a man himself. When his partner Peter Raglan grew afraid of the speed at which the original Ross & Raglan store was expanding under the whiplash of Ross, Malcolm had promptly bought Raglan's interest in the firm. He had taken enormous risks in starting his shipping line, and he was taking greater ones today in trying to open this cannery in such a short time. If a young man who had proved himself as repeatedly as Tom Venn wanted to hire a Tlingit Indian to rush a building to completion, so be it: 'If he's as good as you say, get him on the job today. But don't come wailing to me when he shows up drunk tomorrow.'

Tom saluted, smiled, and refrained from informing his boss that it was the

Seattle carpenters who had smuggled whiskey ashore at the beginning of this hectic job and who mysteriously replenished their stocks whenever an R&R ship entered the inlet. Instead, he suggested that Mr. Ross accompany him in a skiff ride across the cove for an opportunity to see how a Tlingit Indian of noted rank lived.

'I'd like to do just that,' Ross said, and he perched in the rear of the skiff as two Indians who worked at unloading cargo took the boat across the cove to the informal landing place which Sam Bigears had scooped out for beaching his canoe and sailboat.

'Hey, Bigears!' Tom shouted as he and Ross climbed ashore. 'Boss man to see you.'

From the cabin atop the rise Sam appeared, standing for a moment between two doorposts carved and painted in totem style. When he saw Mr. Ross he called: 'Welcome. You build pretty fast over there.' He led them into his cabin, bare now because so many of its contents had been given away during the potlatch. However, the solidity of the structure was evident, and Ross asked: 'Did you build this?' and Bigears said: 'Wife and daughter help a lot.'

He called for Nancy, whose lovely oval face broke into a smile like her father's. Not deferring in any special way to Mr. Ross, she gave a slight bow and said in lilting English: 'Tom is very proud to work for you, Mr. Ross. We're proud to have you in our home. My mother speaks no English, but in Tlingit she says the same.'

'I came on business, Mr. Bigears. Tom tells me that you're a fine carpenter.'

'I like wood.'

'He wants me to hire you to build the big bunkhouse—right now, for the Chinese. They're coming soon.'

Sam Bigears said: 'Sit down, Mr. Ross,' and when the guests were seated, he asked bluntly: 'Why you bring in Chinese? Taku Inlet is Indian. Many Indians here work good as Chinese.'

'We've hired many of your people.'

'But not real work. Not building. Not making boxes. Not making cans.'

Ross was never loath to face inescapable unpleasantries: 'The fact is, Mr. Bigears, all the canneries have learned to rely on Chinese to do the major jobs —crates, cans, preparing the salmon.'

'Why Chinese? Why not Tlingits?'

'Because Chinese work harder than any other men on earth. They learn quickly what has to be done, and they do it. They work like hell, they save their money, and they keep their mouths shut. No cannery could succeed without Chinese.'

'Tlingits work like hell too.'

Ross was too considerate to say bluntly that yes, on a given day a Tlingit could work as well as a Chinese. He'd been told that by other cannery owners. But he had also been told that after two or three days of intense work, the Indian liked to draw his pay and go fishing—for himself, not for the cannery. Instead, he said: 'Will you help Tom build the bunkhouse?' and Sam Bigears replied: 'No. You bring in Chinese to take our jobs, so I not work for you. Not here at Pleiades. Not in Juneau no more.' With great dignity he led Ross and Venn to the door, and as they left he said quietly: 'Many Chinese here, many troubles.' And the interview ended.

With what skilled help Tom could find along the waterfront in Juneau, and with a large crew of Tlingits, the shell of the bunkhouse was hastily erected, and as work started on the tiers of wooden bunks in which the imported workmen would sleep during their five-month campaign with the salmon, Venn felt for the first time that this massive project was going to be finished on time. It was the complexity of the action that day which generated this optimism: at the waterfront, the pile driver was hammering home the tall poles on which the floor of the dock would rest, twenty-two feet above the water at low tide; in the cooking shed, the retorts were being installed; in the big gutting shed, tables were being built at which the Chinese would clean the salmon with long, sharp knives; a rude sawmill was cutting Sitka spruce for the boxmakers soon to arrive; and in the tin-can building, intense fires were being prepared for the melting of solder to seal the lids of the cans when the packing was completed. A gigantic operation was drawing to a successful climax; it had been an Alaska-type venture: big, undisciplined on many days, frenzied, exciting. As Tom said to one of the carpenters in the bunkhouse: 'You'd never do a job this way in Chicago.'

But what sealed this sense of euphoria was the arrival, from the printing house in Seattle, of the first hundred thousand labels to be glued onto the cans before shipping. They were a bright red, the color of a mature sockeye, and the words printed in heavy black read:

PINK ALASKAN SALMON
IT'S GOOD FOR YOU

and beneath that appeared the proud designation:

TOTEM CANNERY
Pleiades Glacier, Alaska

But what caught the eye was a Seattle artist's conception of a totem pole, well drawn and printed in four colors with a blue-green glacier in the background.

It was a striking label, and when Mr. Ross had three samples glued onto the cans of a competing cannery, everyone who saw the result agreed that this was one of the most effective labels so far devised. Indeed, Tom was so pleased with the cans' appearance that he asked to have one, which he took across the cove in hopes that when Sam Bigears saw what a fine product Pleiades Cove was going to produce, his animosity would be relaxed.

'Pretty fine, eh?' Tom said as he handed the can over to his friend. Sam accepted it, studied it for some time, and then handed it back, almost with contempt: 'All wrong.' When Tom showed that he did not understand what Sam was saying, the latter pointed to the label: 'My totem not on same side Taku with glacier. Man missing in totem. Look for yourself, no raven.' Tom was about to laugh, when Bigears voiced the real complaint of his people: 'Outside of can bad. Inside even badder.'

'What do you mean? Our salmon will be the freshest packed this year.'

'I mean inside have Tlingit salmon from Tlingit rivers packed by Chinese, and all money go to Seattle workmen, Seattle ship men, Seattle company.' Grabbing the can and holding it in the air, he said with great bitterness: 'Tlingit salmon make everybody rich but Tlingits. Seattle get everything, Alaska nothing.' Sadly, for he saw with cruel clarity the shape of the future, he handed the can back, and in that gesture cut himself off from his trusted friend. Both he and Tom knew that an unbridgeable alienation had risen between them. Tom henceforth would be of Seattle; Sam, of Alaska.

*   *   *

IN MID-MAY, when resin still seeped from the raw boards in the long bunk-house, an R&R steamer came into Taku Inlet, eased through the narrows, avoided Walrus Rock, and tied up alongside the newly finished dock. As soon as the gangplank was lashed tight, down streamed forty-eight Chinese who would get the cannery started. They were dressed in loose pajamas, black smocks, cheap rubber-soled shoes and no socks. About a fifth of the number wore pigtails, and these established the character of the group. They were alien, of a different color, unable for the most part to speak English, and with a much different appetite; along with them came the one essential necessary for keeping Chinese workers contented at a cannery: several hundred sacks of rice. And hidden away in various clever places came another essential almost as impor-tant: small glass vials not much bigger than a thumb, filled with opium. Since the forty-eight men would have no women with them, no opportunity for ordinary recreation, no respite from twelve- and fourteen-hour days of back-breaking labor, no fraternization with white fellow workers, opium and gam-bling were about the only relaxation available, and these they would pursue assiduously.

They were a silent, frightening crew as they came ashore, and it fell to Tom to lead them to their quarters. Ill-at-ease and not happy with the prospect of dealing through a long summer with these strange creatures, he walked in silence toward the newly finished bunkhouse, but he was stopped by a tugging at his sleeve and turned to face the one man on whom the success of this operation would come to depend.

He was a thin, frail Chinese who wore his hair in a thick pigtail that reached well down his back. Only slightly older than Tom and markedly shorter, he nevertheless had a commanding presence, and in that first moment of meeting, Venn noticed a peculiarity which he supposed would determine the man's behavior: His yellow face smiles, as if he knows that it will please me, but his eyes do not, because he doesn't give a damn what I think.

'My name Ah Ting. Work Ketchikan two time. Me bossman all Chinese. No trouble.'

Although suspicious of the man's motives, Tom was relieved to learn that someone at least spoke English, so he invited Ah Ting to walk with him, and even before they reached the bunkhouse it was clear that Totem Cannery was going to operate as Ah Ting directed, for the other Chinese accepted his leader-ship. When the line reached the building, the others waited till he allocated the plain board beds and distributed the two skimpy blankets to each man.

'We no eat on ship,' he said, and when Tom led the way to the mess hall reserved for the Chinese, Ah Ting quickly designated two cooks, who started at once to prepare the rice. After they had eaten, Ah Ting, and not Venn, divided the men into three groups. One would build crates; one would fabricate tin cans; and the main group, in addition to cleaning the buildings, would prepare the tables at which they would later behead and gut the salmon.

Tom could not guess how many of the forty-eight had worked in canneries before, but he found that he had to give instructions only once, and even though most of the Orientals could not understand his words, they showed an uncanny skill in catching his intention and jumped to do as he indicated. By two in the afternoon the work force was in place, with specialists identifying themselves and taking over the more important jobs, and by three, finished crates and tin cans were appearing.

For example, the making of tin cans to be shipped around the world was a precise task. The long rolls of tin had to be cut in strips for the body of the can, which then had to be rolled around a template and soldered carefully. Disks to close the bottom had to be punched out and then soldered firmly. Finally, disks of a different character were required for the top, and these would be set aside to be soldered in place when the can was filled with raw fish. A small opening had to be left for the suction machine to draw off remaining air and create a vacuum, and then that minute hole had to be soldered. By nightfall it was obvious that cans for Totem salmon were going to be first-class and in good supply.

As the end of May approached, all parts of this huge effort began to mesh: sixty-five white men from Seattle managed the offices, supervised the laborers, and commanded the steamers; the Chinese produced cans and crates for processing the fish; and the thirty natives continued to lift and carry. Now, also, the thirty small boats that would actually do the fishing and the seining—two white men to each boat except for three that were manned by Indians—moved into position, and on a bright morning in June a lookout on one of the large vessels shouted: 'Salmon are coming!' and when fishermen rushed to the railing to peer into the dark waters of Taku Inlet, they could see thousands of shadowy forms moving steadfastly up the waterway on their way to distant streams far inside Canada.

But those sailors who looked toward Pleiades Cove could see an impressive group of big sockeye separating from the main flow and heading for that beautiful cold stream down which they had come as smolt three years before.

'They keep comin'!' men shouted from boat to boat, and that year's harvest, the first for Totem Cannery, was under way.

When Nancy Bigears heard the cry she alerted her father, and he went out to inspect the quality of this year's returning salmon, and he was so pleased with what he saw that he sent his daughter back to the house to fetch his dip net, and he was about to cast for his first fishing of the season when a cannery warden with a loud voice shouted from the other side of the cove: 'Hey, there! No fishing in this river.'

'This my river,' Bigears called back, but the warden explained: 'This river and the lake too, it's now restricted to Totem Cannery. Orders from Washington.'

'This my river. My grandfather-grandfather fished here.'

'It's all different now,' the warden said as he climbed into a small boat to deliver the new instructions at closer range. When he climbed ashore, Bigears said: 'You better pull her higher. She'll drift away,' and when the warden looked back he saw that he would have lost his dory had Sam not spoken.

Consulting a paper, the warden said: 'You're Sam Bigears, I suppose,' and when Sam nodded, the man continued: 'Mr. Bigears, the cove has been deeded to us by the officials in Washington. We are to control fishing on this river and adjacent waters. We had to have that reassurance before we could spend so much money on the cannery over there.'

'But this my river.'

The warden ignored this, and in a tone of conciliation, as if he were granting a generous dispensation to a child, he said: 'We've notified Washington that we volunteer to respect your squatter's rights to your home over here plus six acres of land.'

'Squatter rights? What that mean?'

'Well, you have no title to your piece of land. It's not yours legally, it's ours. But we're going to let you occupy your cabin during your lifetime.'

'It's my river . . . my land.'

'No, things have changed, Mr. Bigears. From here on, the government will say who owns what, and it has already said that our cannery has the right to this river. And that naturally gives us the right to the salmon that come into our river.' When Bigears looked perplexed, the warden simplified the new instructions: 'You and your friends are not to fish in this river any longer. Only those who fish for the cannery. It is closed. The government says so.'

He stood at the spot where the river began, wanting to be certain that the Tlingit did not break the new law, and when he saw Bigears put up his pole and trudge back to his house in bewilderment, he said to himself: Now that's a sensible Indian.

When the first big catch was hauled into the gutting shed, with all parts of the cannery functioning as planned, thousands of tall one-pound cans began sliding off the soldering tables and over to the men who pasted on the bright red labels of Totem Cannery. Mr. Ross, hearing that his plant was operating even better than he had hoped, came north, and after a few days' inspection, told Tom: 'This place will pay for itself in three years. After that, enormous profits.' He felt so gratified with how smoothly things were going that he made several gestures to let the workmen know that they were appreciated: 'It's standard R&R procedure. Give everybody who does well an unexpected reward.' An extra ration of chicken and beef was issued to Ah Ting for his Chinese, who held in succession a feast, a gambling frolic and an opium session. Tlingit workers were given a small bonus and white workers a large one. Senior staff received chits entitling them to two weeks' extra vacation with pay at the end of the year's campaign, and Tom Venn was told: 'A raise for you, Tom, and when you've put everything to bed for the winter, Mrs. Ross and I want you to come down to Seattle for a well-earned rest.'

The prospect of visiting the city he admired so much set Tom to dreaming, and he speculated on the possibility that once at headquarters, he might be given a job there, or perhaps the management of one of the big R&R stores in Seattle. But before such a promotion could come to pass, he must perform the distasteful task which Mr. Ross now threw his way: 'Tom, I've generated a grudging respect for that Indian friend of yours. He seems to be a man of character. I want you to row over to his cabin and assure him that whereas he can no longer fish in our river, we're not going to be niggardly with a man who, as you reminded me, helped build our store in Juneau.'

'What do you mean, sir?'

'When the catch is in and the end of season in sight, we'll tell the warden to be sure that Bigears—well, see to it, Tom, that he gets a salmon or two. It's only fair.'

Mr. Ross directed Tom to make the initial gift of salmon right now, while he, Ross, was still at the cannery, and Tom was given two fat sockeye, brilliant red in their spawning color, to take to the Tlingit. He did not want this job, for he appreciated the irony of offering Sam Bigears two salmon when his family had for generations held the right to all the fish in the Pleiades; but the order had been given, and as he had done with previous orders, he obeyed it.

He felt uneasy crossing the cove, and acutely distressed when he landed and started up the path to Sam's cabin. Rehearsing possible words he could use to disguise the ugliness of what he must do, he was relieved when Nancy and not her father came to the door. In her cheerful way she said: 'Hello, Tom. We've been wondering why we haven't seen you.'

'In a new cannery, there's a new job every day.'

'I've seen the big ships stopping by to pick up the crates. You send out so many.'

'Thirty-two thousand before we close.'

'What's in your hand? Looks like a fish.'

'It's two fish. Salmon.'

'Why?'

'Mr. Ross wants your father to know that even though the river is closed and Indians can't fish here anymore . . .'

'We've heard,' she said gravely, and Tom was afraid that she was going to upbraid him, but she did not. She was fifteen now, a bright, knowledgeable young Indian girl who had enjoyed school and whose intuitions about the changing world of which she was a confused part were surprisingly shrewd. And now, even though she saw immediately the sad impropriety of what Tom was saying, she had to laugh, not scornfully, but with compassion for the fool that Tom was making of himself: 'Oh, Tom! You didn't come here to tell my father that even though you now own all his fish, you're going to let him have one or two each year? That is, if there's any left after you take what you need?'

Tom was shaken by the adroit way she had phrased her question, and he scarcely knew how to respond. 'Well,' he fumbled, 'that's exactly what Mr. Ross proposes.' When she laughed, he added lamely: 'But he did express it a little better.' Then, with force: 'He means well, Nancy, he really does.'

Now the girl's face grew as stern as those of her ancestors who had fought the Russians: 'Throw your damned fish in the river.'

'Nancy!'

'Do you think my father, who owns this river, would allow fish like those in our house? Under such conditions?' When Tom remained at the door with the two salmon in his hands, she reached out, grabbed his package, and smelled it disdainfully. 'You must know that these fish are old, spoiled, caught days ago —and now thrown to the Tlingits who watched over them while they were alive in our river.'

When Tom tried to protest, she said bitterly: 'No Bigears would feed those fish to his dogs,' and she ran down to the riverbank, drew back her right arm, and pitched the rancid fish into the stream.

When she returned to the house she washed her hands and offered Tom a cloth to wash his, and then she invited him to sit with her: 'What's going to happen, Tom? Each year your cannery will grow bigger. You'll catch more of our salmon. And pretty soon you'll be placing one of those new traps right across our river. And do you know what'll happen then? There won't be any more salmon, and you will have to burn your handsome cannery.'

Tom rose and moved uneasily about the room: 'What a horrible thing to say! You talk as if we were monsters.'

'You are,' she said, but then she added quickly: 'You're not to blame, I know that. Let's go up to the waterfall and watch the salmon leaping.'

'I have to get back. Mr. Ross is handing out final orders before he sails for Seattle.' Then, for some reason he could not explain, he said: 'He's invited me to spend my vacation there, after the season ends up here.'

'And you would be afraid to say no, wouldn't you?' There was such iciness in her voice that Tom said: 'I can do as I please,' and he took her by the hand, led her from the house, and started up the river to the waterfall where the brown bear had chased them and where the last salmon returning to spawn leaped like ballet dancers up the foaming waters, pirouetting on their tails as they gathered strength for the next leap.

'You see them jump,' Tom said. 'You can almost touch them. But you can't believe it,' and in that moment of confession that Alaska contained mysteries he could not fathom, he became precious to Nancy Bigears, who, in these days of confusion, was meeting only those white men who remained blatantly ignorant of her homeland and all it represented. Tom Venn was the kind of white man who could save Alaska, who could pick a sensible path through the tangle that threatened the land, but whenever he uttered the word *Seattle*, he did so in a way that revealed his longing for that more exciting world.

'If you go to Seattle with Mr. Ross,' she predicted, 'you'll not come back. I know that.'

Tom did not protest with specious assurances: 'Maybe it's men like Mr. Ross in Seattle who make the right decisions about Alaska. Look at the miracle he created here. In February he cried "Let there be a cannery on Taku Inlet," and in May he had it operating.'

'In all the wrong ways,' she said with such finality that Tom became irritated. 'For a thousand years,' he said, 'the salmon have been swimming up and down this river, doing no one any good. I guess they had baby salmon and then they died, and next year their babies died, and no one on this earth profited. Well, do you know where the salmon we packed last week are going? Philadelphia and Baltimore and Washington. Salmon that used to swim past your front door are heading for all those places to feed people. This year they're not heading up the Pleiades just to die.'

She had nothing to say to this; if he refused to understand the great swing of nature, in which the going and coming of the salmon was as important as the rising and setting of the moon, she could not instruct him. But she understood, and from the destruction she had watched at the mouth of her river—the salmon caught but never canned, the thousands of fish allowed to rot because the gutting shed was swamped—she knew instinctively that conditions could only worsen, and it saddened her that men like Ross and the foremen, and yes, even Tom Venn, refused to see the drift of the future.

'We'd better go back,' she said, adding a barb: 'Mr. Ross will be wondering what you've been doing with his two salmon.'

'You're in an ugly mood, Nancy. Maybe we should go back,' but as they started, a pair of sockeye coming home after long travels reached the low waterfall, and with a persistence that had few parallels in nature, they tore into the difficult ascent and almost gleefully leaped and twisted and gained precarious resting places, finally reaching the higher level.

I'm like those salmon, Tom thought. I aspire to higher levels. But it never occurred to him that he could attain those levels in Juneau, or even here along the banks of Taku Inlet.

As they reached the spot where Nancy had spoken to the charging bear, bringing the animal to a halt, they recalled that scene, and both of them began to laugh, and Tom saw her once more as that dauntless fourteen-year-old child who had lectured the bear and perhaps saved both their lives; but now she seemed so much more grown-up and golden and happy in her freedom that he took her in his arms and kissed her.

Now there was no laughter, for she had known that this would happen, and that it was proper for it to happen, but also that it would come to nothing, for they were on different rivers heading in different directions. For a brief spell during the potlatch of the totem raising he had been a Tlingit, appreciative of her people's values, and in the cave at Mendenhall Glacier he had accepted her as a white girl attuned to some new Alaska, but neither moment solidified, and these kisses, which could have been so meaningful, were not a beginning, but a parting.

In near-silence they walked back, feeling none of the elation which should have followed a first kiss, and when they reached the house Nancy called to her father, who had returned with a friend: 'Pop! Mr. Ross said we would be allowed to have a salmon now and then. The first two he sent us were rotten, so I threw them in the river.'

Sam, ignoring the bitter comment, asked Tom: 'Was the season as good as you hoped?' and Tom said: 'Better.' They left the matter there, but when the two young people walked down to Tom's dory, Nancy said: 'I'm sorry.'

'About what?'

'I don't know,' and she kissed him farewell.

T HE KISS WAS viewed by Mr. Ross, who had borrowed a pair of binoculars to see why his manager was so long delayed in delivering two fish across the cove, and when Tom anchored his boat and climbed back to the cannery, he was told that Mr. Ross wanted to see him. The Seattle merchant, disturbed by what he had seen, felt that here was a situation that had to be handled immediately.

'Tom, you have a bright future, a very bright future. But young men like you with everything before you, you sometimes stumble and lose it all.'

'I don't know what you mean.'

Mr. Ross hated dissembling and was always willing to speak bluntly when affairs of moment were involved: 'I mean girls. Indian girls. I borrowed these glasses to see what was keeping you, and I suppose you know what I saw.'

'No, I don't.'

'I saw you kissing that Bigears girl. I saw . . .'

Tom heard no more of the charge, for he was thinking: I did not kiss her. She kissed me. And what business is it of his, anyway? And then Mr. Ross explained in forceful terms just why a vagrant kiss was his business: 'Do you think I could let you keep running the Juneau store if you were married to an Indian girl? Do you think Ross & Raglan would ever bring you to headquarters in Seattle if you had an Indian wife? How could you and your wife meet with the other company officials? Socially, I mean.' On and on he went, repeating stories he had heard of the disastrous consequences which followed such marriages: 'And in our own experience, Tom, in our various stores, that is, we've seen only tragedy when we hired squaw men. It never works, because you can't mix oil and water.'

Tom bristled, and spoke with the same hard sense of integrity that had motivated his employer: 'In Dawson and Nome, I saw quite a few squaw men who led better lives than most of us. In fact, the whole Klondike field was discovered by a squaw man.'

'On a gold frontier there may be a place for such men, Tom, but we're talking about real society, which is what towns like Juneau will soon have. In real society, squaw men are at a terrible disadvantage.' He shook his head in sad recollection, then spoke with extra force: 'And another thing to think about, young man, their half-breed children are doomed from the start.'

'I think that settlements like Nome and Juneau will soon be filled with half-breed children,' Tom countered. 'They'll run those towns.'

'Don't you believe it.' And Ross was about to cite telling evidence about the total ineptitude of half-breeds he had known in the Northwest when loud shouting was heard from the main shed, and the white foreman bellowed: 'Help! The Chinks are running wild.'

Tom, who had for some time anticipated such an outbreak, leaped for the wooden causeway leading to the main shed, but Mr. Ross had reacted even more quickly, and as Tom ran toward the sound of rioting, he could see his boss plowing ahead like an enraged bear to join in the fray. As the two white men burst into the brawl, Tom thought: God help the Chinks if Mr. Ross gets really mad.

Inside the cavernous building they met total chaos, with scores of Chinese roaring among the tables where that day's catch of salmon was being gutted, and although at first Tom thought that this was merely one more brawl in which two workmen had fallen into a fistfight over jealously guarded positions at the worktable, when he ran toward the center of the fighting he saw to his horror that the Chinese were attacking one another with their sharp gutting knives.

'Stop!' he bellowed, but his order had no effect. Mr. Ross, having been involved in riots before, waded into the midst of the fighting, laying about him vigorously and crying: 'Get back! Get back!' a command which had no more effect than Tom's.

'Ah Ting!' Tom called, hoping to locate the leader of the Chinese. 'Ah Ting! Stop this.'

He could not spot the tough little man, nor did he see any evidence that anyone was trying to halt the melee, but then Mr. Ross, infuriated by this frenzied interruption in the canning process, started to grab one Chinese or another, and at first he was unsuccessful.

'Tom! Give me a hand!' And as Venn ran to assist his boss, who had grabbed the pigtail of one of the more vigorous of the fighters, he shouted: 'I'm here!' But as he did so, he saw to his horror that Mr. Ross had pinioned the arms of the man he held, rendering him unable to defend himself, and in this exposed position the terrified Chinese could only watch impotently as a fellow worker lunged at him with a long fish knife, jabbing it once into the man's heart and then into his stomach, which he ripped apart with a powerful upward thrust.

As Mr. Ross held the captive in his arms he could feel life seeping out of the tense body, and when the wounded man went limp, both Ross and Tom watched helplessly while three of the dead man's friends leaped upon the assassin, stabbing him many times until he, too, fell dead.

'Ah Ting!' Tom began to shout aimlessly, but the man who had been assigned to prevent just such outbursts could still not be found. But now he was not needed, for the shock of the two slayings caught the Chinese off guard, and they backed away, awaiting the restoration of order. Mr. Ross, still clutching the body of the man whose death he had caused, looked about in bewilderment while Tom continued to call for Ah Ting.

And then Tom saw the aggressive leader. He was pinned against a wall, surrounded by three men, all taller than he, holding their knives against his throat and heart. Some wild dislocation had swept through the cutting shed, something too big to be handled by ordinary procedures, and in its first moments these men, determined to see it to a conclusion, had isolated Ah Ting to prevent him from exercising his authority. Two murders had resulted, and now when Tom ran up to the men, shouting: 'Let him go!' they obeyed.

'Big fight, boss,' Ah Ting gasped as he shook himself free. 'Could not stop.'

Mr. Ross lumbered up, his hands red with the blood of the man he had been holding. 'Were you in charge here?' he blustered, and Tom interceded: 'This is Ah Ting. Leader. Good man. These three held him prisoner.'

Mr. Ross's first reaction was to shout 'You three are fired!' but before he could utter the words he realized how stupid they would sound, for there was no way of firing unsatisfactory Chinese working at a summer cannery. The men had come from Shanghai to America on a British boat. They had come from

San Francisco to Seattle on an American train. And some Ross & Raglan recruiter had placed them aboard an R&R steamer, which had conveyed them to Taku Inlet, where they had been deposited directly from the ship to the cannery. Supposing that Mr. Ross, in his obstinacy, went ahead and fired the three men, where could they go? They were miles from any settled area, and if they did reach some town like Juneau or Sitka, they would be refused entrance, for Chinese were not allowed. They were supposed to arrive by ship in late spring, work all summer at some remote outpost, and leave by ship in early autumn, taking their few dollars with them and surviving in some large, impersonal city till the recruiters summoned them again for the next canning season.

So instead of firing the men responsible for neutralizing Ah Ting, Mr. Ross scowled at them and asked Tom: 'What can we do?' and Tom gave the only sensible answer: 'Only thing we can do, trust Ah Ting to get the men back to work.'

'Do we call the police? There are two men dead over there.'

'There are no police,' Tom said, and in this statement he described the extraordinary position in which the District of Alaska found itself. There were men in towns like Juneau who were called policemen, but they had no real authority, for there was still no properly organized system of government, and for such improvised officers to venture into an area like Taku Inlet was unthinkable. Each cannery ran its own system of self-protection, which included drastic measures for handling disturbances, including crimes at the plant. Therefore, the murder of the two Chinese workers became Tom Venn's responsibility, and Mr. Ross was most interested to see how the young man proceeded.

He was favorably impressed by the fearlessness with which Tom moved among the agitated workers, directing them back to their tasks and checking to ensure the maintenance of an orderly flow of salmon from the arriving fishing ships. But when the time came for Tom to discipline the men who were seen to have done the stabbing, Mr. Ross was appalled to see that Venn turned the matter over to Ah Ting, and Ross was further dismayed when he watched how the leader of the Chinese handled it. Ah Ting reprimanded the guilty men, did nothing to punish the others who had immobilized him in the fracas, and blandly told the men to pick up their gutting knives and get back to work.

But it was what he did afterward that affected Mr. Ross most profoundly, for Ah Ting directed two men to fetch one of the large barrels used for shipping salted fish to Europe, and when the barrel was in position he himself poured in a three-inch layer of coarse rock salt. Then he leaned deep into the barrel to spread the salt evenly over the bottom, after which he drew himself out, brushed off his hands, and directed his two helpers to bring the first of the slain men. When the corpse lay on the floor before him, Ah Ting helped his men strip away all bits of clothing and then hoist the dead body into the barrel, where it was propped into a sitting position. Now the second corpse was undressed and carefully fitted into the barrel, also in an upright sitting position, facing the first man and adjusting to him.

'What in hell are they doing?' Mr. Ross asked, and Tom explained: 'Our contract requires us to ship any dead Chinese back to China for burial in what they call "the sacred soil of the Celestial Kingdom." '

'In a barrel?'

'Look!' And as they stared in disbelief, Ah Ting and his helpers packed every cranny in the barrel with rock salt, filling it so to the brim that no sign of the dead men remained visible. Even their nostrils were crammed with salt. And when the heavy lid was nailed tight, the coffin barrel was ready for shipment back to China, where the two slain men would attain whatever immortality this tradition ensured.

BACK IN THE manager's quarters, Mr. Ross was still agitated by what he had seen: 'A man murdered while I was holding him. His assailant stabbed half a dozen times. The man supposed to be in charge being held captive. And everything settled by packing the victims in a barrel and salting them down.' The more he reflected on this extraordinary behavior, the more distressed he became: 'We can't have Chinese in our cannery. You've got to get rid of them, Tom.'

'Nobody can run a cannery without them,' Venn said, and he reviewed briefly the disastrous experiences of operators who had tried to handle the great crush of salmon with other kinds of workmen: 'Indians refuse to work fifteen hours a day. White men are worse. You've seen that our Filipinos cause more trouble than the Chinese and do half the work. Mr. Ross, we're stuck with them, and I don't want today's incident to sour you, especially not in our first year.'

'What irritates me—no, it's worse than irritation, it's downright fear—is the way you and I are at the mercy of that Ah Ting. I think he let those men neutralize him. He didn't want to face those knife-wielding wild men.'

'But when he was freed, Mr. Ross, he did get the men back to work. I couldn't have done it.'

'I will not have a cannery of mine at the mercy of a Chinese scoundrel. We must do something.' And as he began to study his Chinese employees, what he saw caused further dismay: 'In the whole lot, only three speak any English. They're a tight clan living by their own rules, with their own food, their own customs. And for some reason I can't pinpoint, that Ah Ting unnerves me.'

'I've sometimes felt the same way, Mr. Ross.'

'What is there about him?'

'He knows he's indispensable. He knows this cannery couldn't handle a single salmon without him. And I think he's clever.'

'About what?'

'I'm sure he knew that serious trouble had become inescapable. He suspected there might be knifings and he wanted to be held prisoner while it took its course.'

'I want him off our property.' When Tom made no reply, Ross continued: 'It infuriates me to see him grinning at me, knowing that he's in command, not me.'

Tom, aware that there was no chance of dispensing with Ah Ting, neither this year nor next, ignored Ross's unhappiness, and three days later the two men stood together as a crane hoisted the burial barrel off the wharf and onto the deck of an R&R ship loading salmon to ship to a wholesaler in Boston. No Chinese workman bothered to bid the dual coffin farewell as it headed back to China, but as Tom started for his office he caught a glimpse of Ah Ting in the shadows. The wiry fellow was smiling, and Tom entertained a momentary suspicion that Ah Ting was not at all unhappy to have at least one of the men in that barrel disappearing from Totem Cannery.

But preoccupation with the Chinese was abruptly terminated when Mr. Ross learned that the fishermen on whom his cannery relied for its salmon were protesting their meager pay and refusing to take their small boats out unless that scale was increased. The fishermen did not engage in a formal strike; that would be against their principles of freedom and individual responsibility, for as one sailor said: 'Strikes are for factory people in Chicago and Pittsburgh. All we demand is fair pay for what we catch.' And when Mr. Ross told Tom Venn that additional pay was impossible, and Tom told the fishermen, boats stopped heading up Taku Inlet, and for two desperately long weeks Totem Cannery saw no salmon.

The Chinese workers in the carpentry shop kept building shipping boxes, but the larger number engaged in heading, gutting and cleaning the catch had nothing to do, and in their idleness they started having trouble with the Filipinos, who were also idle. The huge establishment at the mouth of the Pleiades River became such an uneasy place that Tom warned his boss: 'If we don't get some salmon in here right quick, there's going to be real trouble.'

It was then that young Tom Venn came to appreciate the difficulties of management, for he watched at close hand as Malcolm Ross, a determined and wealthy man of fifty-two who commanded hundreds of men and almost a score of ships, stood helpless before a gang of Chinese and a rabble of fishermen in small boats. He could not command his Chinese to behave if they had no work to do, nor could he halt their wages, and he had to continue feeding them, for they were prisoners at his cannery and could not move elsewhere if they wanted to.

And he was equally ineffective with the fishermen. Fiercely stubborn, they said: 'We can live off our savings or what we get peddling fish to housewives in Juneau. Mr. Ross of Seattle can go to hell.' Ross, unwilling to grant demands which he felt to be excessive, was powerless to make them fish and incapable of getting his salmon from any other source. Caught in this vise formed by Chinese in one jaw, illiterate white and Indian fishermen in the other, he felt himself so miserably squeezed that he spent one whole week fuming and contriving ways to put himself in a secure position which no Chinese, no fisherman could ever attack: 'We must make ourselves self-sufficient, Tom. We must never be forced to sweat out a season like this.'

He did not confide to Tom what he was devising, but during the closing days of the second painful week, when the cannery was losing great sums each day, he walked back and forth along the banks of Taku Inlet as if studying its fish-laden waters, and then through the cavernous buildings whose tables and ovens and canning sheds were silent. Only the hammering of the Chinese carpenters as they built boxes that might never be filled broke the solemn quietness, and out of these days of intense study, Malcolm Ross of Seattle constructed his vision and launched his plan to attain it.

'What we shall do before next year,' he told Tom almost bitterly, 'is surprise these scoundrels. Ross & Raglan will never again be held up by Chinese coolies and hard-drinking fishermen.'

'What do you have in mind?'

'To get rid of that grinning Ah Ting. To teach those insolent fishermen a lesson.'

'How?'

Ross swung into vigorous action: 'Tell the fishermen we'll accept their demands if they double their catch. Tell Ah Ting his sheds must run sixteen hours a day. Send a telegram to get our two biggest boats up here. In the remaining weeks of this season we're going to pack the way Alaska has never seen before.'

The fishermen, gloating over the way they had defeated the big man from Seattle, accepted the challenge he issued, and assured of the raise they sought, fished arduously to earn the bonus he promised. And as soon as the handsome loads of sockeye salmon arrived at the cannery dock, Ah Ting's Chinese crew accepted the extra rations Mr. Ross authorized and then worked sixteen productive hours each day, seven days a week.

The gutting tables were never free of fish. The great cooking ovens, made in Germany, received one batch of cans after another. Chinese tinsmiths worked in three shifts to build the great volume of cans required, while skilled men under Ah Ting's direction soldered the lids, and the packing crew stowed them in boxes, forty-eight to a box, and sent them down the slide to the waiting ships.

When the cannery was running at maximum speed, with all parts meshing as Mr. Ross had visualized a year ago, he saw it as an American miracle, an almost flawless operation which provided one of the world's most nutritious foods to eager buyers throughout the world at a price no other form of food could match. Taking one of the cans from the machine which pasted on the bright-red Totem label, he hefted it, tossed it to Tom Venn, and cried: 'A pound of matchless salmon. Sixteen cents in stores across America. And next year it's all to be under our control, Tom. No more Chinese. No more men in tiny boats commanding us what to do.'

In his euphoria he uttered a phrase which would dominate his actions for the remainder of his life: 'It's the job of Seattle businessmen to organize Alaska. And I promise you I'm going to show the way.'

'What am I to do?' Tom asked, and he said: 'Pay the bills. See that our last ship takes away the Chinese. Close the place down, and after the first of the year, catch one of our ships at Juneau and work with me in Seattle. Because next year we are going to astonish the world.' With that, he boarded an R&R ship at the Totem dock, waved farewell to the cannery whose first campaign was coming to an end, and watched approvingly as the ship's captain threaded his way toward the Walrus, out into the channel, and on to his offices in Seattle.

O N 5 JANUARY 1904 Tom Venn turned the management of R&R affairs in Juneau over to his assistant and took passage on one of his firm's smaller vessels headed for Seattle, thus fulfilling a desire which had gnawed at him since the day in March 1898 when he and Missy had left that enticing city for the Klondike gold fields. He was so excited about seeing Seattle again that he barely slept the first night out, and when the ship finally entered the quiet waters of Puget Sound he was perched on the railing hoping for a sight of Mount Rainier. When that majestic snow-clad peak appeared, he cried to no one in particular: 'Look at that mountain!' Later, when a woman passenger asked: 'What's that huge mountain?' he said proudly: 'Mount Rainier. It guards Seattle,' and the woman told him: 'Looks as if an artist painted it,' and he nodded.

It was an emotional homecoming for Tom, and as the familiar sights of the city rose from the water, he entertained bold thoughts: If in the next few years I show a profit on the salmon cannery, Mr. Ross will be almost obligated to promote me to the Seattle headquarters permanently. That'll be the day! Whispering to himself, he said: 'I'll use the money John Klope gave me to buy a home on one of those hills and watch as our ships sail home from Alaska.' As the words formed he could visualize the *Alacrity*, that small white R&R ship on which Missy had worked and on which he, Missy and his father had traveled to great adventure on the Yukon.

How far away those days of high daring seemed, and as he thought of them he resolved to perform as creditably at the cannery as Missy had done in Dawson and Nome: You'll be proud of me, Missy. One of these days you'll be proud of me.

His excitement grew as he left the ship, carrying nothing, and hurried along the dock where he had once sold newspapers. Searching for the familiar sign of the R&R dockside offices, he found that the old building had been replaced by a fine modern one, and when he burst through its doors, three older men inside recognized him: 'It's Tom Venn. Loaded with Nome gold.' After enthusiastic greetings they told him: 'You're to leave your bags aboard ship. We'll send them along.'

'Where am I to stay?'

'Mr. Ross left orders for you to go to the main office immediately. He'll give you instructions.'

It was ten in the morning when Tom arrived at the building on Cherry Street, its oak door bearing the neatly carved blazon ROSS & RAGLAN, and as on that first visit nearly seven years ago, he felt a pulse of excitement on entering the waiting room leading to Mr. Ross's office. The same austere lady, Ella Sommers, her hair now streaked with white, guarded the portals, and the same air of busy importance dominated the place, for this was the nerve center from which controlling ganglia spread out to all sections of northwestern America and Alaska.

'I'm Tom Venn, from Juneau. The men at the dock told me that Mr. Ross wanted to see me.'

'Indeed he does,' Miss Sommers said. 'You're to go right in,' and she nodded toward the door through which she allowed only a few to pass.

As soon as Tom entered the room he felt once more the spell of the powerful man who sat behind the big blond-oak desk. As before, the red-haired man fitted exactly the setting from which he operated, but this time the office was filled with three smaller tables, on which rested a bewildering array of small wooden models whose interlocking parts moved when Mr. Ross or one of the two men working in the room operated them.

'Tom, these men are from the university. They know salmon. Gentlemen, this is our Mr. Venn from the Totem Cannery, where your machines will be installed, if you ever get them to work.' And with these peremptory words the informal session began.

Moving to the largest of the three tables, Mr. Ross explained: 'This is Taku Inlet, and this feeder, shown by the blue paper, is our Pleiades River. Our cannery, obviously, is on this point. Professor Starling, show us how it's going to work.'

As the first words were spoken, Tom accommodated himself to the diagram; he was in the middle of Taku Inlet, and when the professor said: 'Now you must imagine yourself a sockeye swimming upstream to spawn on a warm July day,' Tom became a salmon, and from that moment on, he understood viscerally what Starling said.

'This is Taku Inlet as we know it now. The returning salmon, heading for either our Lake Pleiades over here, or to one of the hundred similar lakes upstream in Alaska or over the border in Canada, swim past this point, where your fishermen catch a fair proportion and bring them to the cannery over here.'

'The system worked pretty well last summer,' Tom said. 'And we're enlarging the cannery starting March first.'

'It was a respectable catch you canned,' the second professor said, a Dr. Whitman, 'but it could have been four times that size.'

'Impossible!' Tom said without hesitation. 'Mr. Ross knows that our boats worked overtime, barring the two weeks they fought about their pay.'

Mr. Ross broke in: 'These men have a way to help us escape the tyranny of the fishermen and, as they just said, quadruple our catch.'

'That would be miraculous,' Tom said bluntly, and Ross replied: 'It's only miracles that will save our industry, and we have three of them right here in this room. Study closely, Tom.'

'What we will do,' Professor Starling said, 'is throw this weir across a fair portion of the inlet and completely across the entrance to the Pleiades River,' and onto the middle portion of the table representing the historic waterway he placed a wooden construction which clearly dominated much of the inlet and all the river. When Tom gasped, protesting that no dam of that magnitude could be built in the deep waters of Taku, Starling laughed: 'That's what everybody says. That's what Mr. Ross said in this very room when I put the construction in place for him.' The professor looked at Ross, who smiled and nodded.

'What we do,' Starling explained, 'is float this entire central section out into the channel, anchor it, and then build these wings on the sides as permanent structures fastened to the bottom. And look what we have!'

Tom Venn, still swimming upstream as a salmon, found himself facing an obstruction in his familiar waterway, and when he came to one of its outreaching arms he naturally followed the slant to the left, and this threw him into the heart of the floating trap, which contained a restricted pen large enough to hold five hundred salmon. From it the struggling fish could be easily netted for transfer to the cannery.

'What we have,' Starling explained, 'is a three-part masterpiece. These long fingers reach out to guide the salmon our way. We call them *jiggers* because they jig the fish along in the direction we want. Then the trap itself, with these narrowing chambers into which the salmon can swim but from which they can't retreat. And finally the big holding pen, where the salmon collect until we process them in the cannery.'

When his contraption was fully explained, he stood back admiringly and said: 'Consider the virtues. Cheap to build. Cheap to repair. Guaranteed to catch every salmon heading up the Pleiades and a fair share of those heading for Canada.' Then came Ross's powerful assessment: 'And we can tell the boatmen to go to hell.'

Tom, still trapped in the holding pen into which he had swum exactly as Professor Starling had intended, said quietly: 'It's catching salmon without having to fish for them,' and the three older men applauded, for that was precisely what the weir and its outriding jiggers would make possible.

'We start building this in mid-February,' Ross said. 'The weir, the holding pen and the western jigger all float. The eastern jigger coming out from our shore, that we'll build permanently.'

And then Tom saw the fallacy of the proposed system: 'But no salmon can get through to spawn in Lake Pleiades. Three years, four years, you'll wipe out all our sockeyes.'

'Aha!' Ross cried. 'We've thought of that. Each Saturday afternoon we'll close down the trap, open the jiggers, and let all the salmon swimming upstream Saturday night and all day Sunday get through. Professor Whitman assures us that that will be enough to ensure ample stocks the following years.' And Whitman nodded.

'Now for the Chinese!' Ross cried as he moved to the second table, his eyes dancing with excitement. 'Look at this, will you?' And on a beautifully constructed model using real tin he demonstrated a clean, simple solution to the problem of making cans: 'A large wagon drawn by four horses comes onto the dock here in Seattle, delivering fifty thousand, a hundred thousand of these for shipment to Totem Cannery.' And he held in his left hand a small rectangular piece of flattened tin, which Tom could not visualize as a finished can, and said so.

'I couldn't either,' Ross said. 'When Professor Whitman showed it to me, I laughed. But watch!'

Wedging the piece of tin into position on the complicated machine, he pressed a lever, and slowly a plunger forced its way between what was now revealed as two layers of tin, and when it had made an entrance, another plunger took over, spreading out the welded tin into a perfectly formed can lacking bottom or top. 'Every ten seconds,' Ross cried triumphantly, 'you have a perfect can, ready for the bottom to be soldered on and the insides filled with salmon.' Handing the finished can to Tom, he said with great force: 'No more Chinese making cans. It will all be done here in Seattle, kept flat to save shipping space, and formed out with one of these machines at the cannery.'

'We'll still have to solder the bottoms and the lids,' Tom pointed out, and Ross snapped: 'You'll teach Filipinos how to do it. I've ordered ten of these machines.'

Exulting in his partial victory over Ah Ting and his fractious Chinese, Ross now moved to the final model, by far the most important of the lot: 'We don't have this perfected, yet, but Professor Whitman says we're getting close.'

'Correction!' Whitman interrupted. 'They told me yesterday they've eliminated the problem of adjusting to size.'

'They have?'

'Yes. I haven't actually seen the new version, but if what they told me is true . . . .'

'Let's go see!' Ross cried impulsively, and before they could protest he grabbed his coat, herded the other three out of his office, down the stairs and onto the street, where he hailed two horse-drawn cabs to take the men to a factory at the southern edge of the business district. Here, in a long, low building, two practical-minded wizards were at work on a machine which, if it ever worked, would revolutionize the salmon industry. Nervous with excitement, Ross led the men into the dark work area of the building and to a long table which contained a bewildering array of wires, moving levers and sharp knives.

'What is it?' Tom asked, and Ross pointed to a hand-lettered sign which some comedian had attached by string to the weird contraption: THE IRON CHINK.

'That's what it is,' Ross said. 'A machine that does everything a Chinaman does now,' and at his signal the two engineers opened a steam valve, whereupon various belts and levers began to operate, and with much creaking, went through a series of motions calculated to cut off the head of a salmon, cut away the tail, and with a special long blade gut it from gullet to anus and whisk out the entrails. Tom, watching the various movements, could visualize how the intricate invention was supposed to work, but he doubted that it would: 'Salmon don't all come in the same size.'

'That's been our problem,' one of the inventors said. 'But we think we have it solved,' and while the machine was still going through its clanging motions, he fetched from an icebox three salmon, two of about standard size, the third much shorter. Feeding the first of the standards into the machine as would be done at a cannery, he watched with obvious satisfaction as his machine took the fish, lopped off its head and tail, wasting not an ounce of good meat, then turned it on its side and with deft strokes gutted it, swept away the offal, and sent the beautifully cleaned fish on its way.

'That's wonderful!' Tom cried, and as he spoke the second standard salmon came creeping along, and it, too, was handled perfectly. 'Great! Great!' Tom shouted above the noise of the belts. 'We could sort the fish and send through only those of the same size.'

'But wait!' the second inventor shouted, and with an almost paternal affection he introduced into the machine the third, shorter sockeye. A part of the system which Tom had not noticed before came down, sized the fish and adjusted the knives accordingly, so that now the head and tail were cut off quite differently from before, with Tom cheering at the cleverness of the operation.

But when the salmon was turned on its side, the most important of the knives failed to adjust, and in an unguided flash cut the smaller fish to pieces.

'Oh, hell!' the first inventor cried. 'Oscar, that damn cam doesn't work.'

'It worked last night, didn't it, Professor Whitman?'

'I saw it. Adjusted perfectly.'

The disappointed man hammered at the offending cam, fixed it to his satisfaction, then said: 'Let's try two more fish,' and when the normal-sized one went through, the knives worked perfectly, but when the undersized one came through, the cam once more failed to adjust and once more the big knife shredded the fish.

'What can it be?' the man asked in almost tearful bewilderment, at which the second inventor said with painful honesty: 'We thought we could have it ready for the 1904 campaign. I'm sure we can fix it, Mr. Ross, but I can't let you risk it as it stands.'

'He's right,' the other man said. 'I'm positive I can work out a foolproof system, but we don't have it yet,' and his partner said ruefully: 'You'd better sign up your Chinese for one more year. But by 1905 this little beauty will be doing all your work for you.'

'You need any more funds?' Ross asked, and together the two men said: 'Yes,' and one of them added: 'We're very close, Mr. Ross. I have another idea for adjusting to the length of the fish. I preferred it to begin with, but it requires one extra part and I had hoped to keep it simple.'

'Keep it simple. Take time and keep it so simple that even a Filipino can fix it,' and he snapped at Tom: 'Hire the Chinese. One more time.' Then he added gruffly: 'But do not hire Ah Ting. Won't have him on the place.' And to his own surprise, Tom said firmly: 'We can't handle the Chinese without him,' and that afternoon he arranged for the employment of some ninety Chinese to handle the increased flow of salmon.

At dusk, exhausted by the long day's work, Tom asked: 'Where am I to stay?' and Ross replied: 'I've told the men to deliver your things to our house. You'll be staying with us,' and in the dark, wintry evening the two men rode behind R&R horses to the Ross mansion at the top of a modest rise from which could be seen the grandeur of the Seattle waterfront with its myriad bays and channels, islands and promontories. It was a marine wonderland made even more attractive by the height from which Tom saw it; he wanted to express how much it enchanted him, but prudence told him to remain silent lest Mr. Ross interpret his enthusiasm as a strategy for angling an assignment in the city. However, Ross spoke for him: 'Isn't this a grand view of a great city, Tom? I never tire of it,' and the two admired it for some moments before turning to face the mansion.

It was a nineteenth-century Gothic castle, not overly pretentious or grandiose in size but very definitely modeled on some forgotten Rhine structure, featuring small turrets, battlements and gargoyles. Had other less flamboyant buildings encroached, it would have seemed out of place, but since it stood alone among tall pines, it maintained a quiet grandeur. 'Highlands' he had named his castle in memory of that noble part of Scotland from which his father had been evicted in the mournful Clearances of 1830, and his neighbors in Seattle, who knew nothing of the past history of the Rosses, supposed that the name referred only to the height on which the castle stood and deemed it appropriate.

As with the office building in town, the castle was guarded by two heavy oak doors, and Tom said approvingly: 'You seem to like oak, Mr. Ross,' and the Scotsman replied: 'I certainly don't like white pine.'

Mrs. Ross, some years younger than her husband, was a gracious lady who wore simple clothes and ran the mansion with the help of only two servants. She exhibited no airs as she moved forward to greet the young workman who had been invited into her home with little consultation on her part. Having been informed of his excellent record on the Klondike, at Nome and now at the cannery, she was surprised at his youthfulness and said so: 'How could you have crammed so much into so few years?'

'A lot happens in a gold rush. I was there each time,' and she said: 'But salmon isn't gold,' and he said: 'It's Alaska's new gold. And bound to be much more important than the metal kind.' She smiled approvingly at the way he expressed himself.

For three happy days Tom Venn stayed at Highlands, working with Mr. Ross on schemes relating to Alaska and pointing out on large maps, often inaccurately drawn, where additional R&R canneries might profitably be placed. At the conclusion of their work, southeastern Alaska, the only part that mattered, was peppered with half a dozen proposed sites, and Ross said, as he looked down at the island world: 'Unlimited wealth in those cold waters, Tom. You're to build one new cannery a year as fast as we can get title to the sites. And the man is arriving tomorrow who will make it possible.'

He identified the stranger no further, but on Friday noon he and Tom went to the railway station, and were waiting there when the train from Chicago deposited the man on whom R&R would rely for the allocation of vital leases to land for its canneries and, what was much more important, exclusive rights to the salmon-bearing rivers.

Mr. Ross was delighted to see the newcomer descending the steps from the Pullman, but Tom was astounded. It was Marvin Hoxey, forty-nine years old, ten pounds heavier than he had been at Nome, and more ebullient and conniving than ever. On the ride from the station to the R&R offices he expounded grandiloquently on how he had lined up support throughout Congress for the new regulations which Seattle businessmen felt they needed in order to manage affairs in Alaska. And not once in his volcanic explanations of how the new laws would operate did he acknowledge that he had ever seen Tom Venn before, but as they stepped from the carriage to enter the R&R building, Mr. Ross said: 'This is Tom Venn, who'll be in charge of our canneries project,' and Hoxey said with a kind of noble condescension: 'Of course. Mr. Venn and I shared those unpleasant experiences in Nome, dreadful city, frozen tight most of the year.'

Later, when Hoxey had moved into the main guest room at Highlands, Tom said tentatively to Mr. Ross: 'You know, that man in there . . . he was put in jail, for what he did in Nome,' and Ross said with an almost icy formality: 'And McKinley pardoned him. Completely. The President knew Hoxey had been torpedoed by jealous political enemies.' When Tom started to explain that that wasn't the way it had been, not really, Ross cut him short with a piece of frontier advice long tested in the crucible of practicality: 'Tom, many times when you have a job that simply has to be done, the best man to use is a disbarred lawyer. He has to work hard.'

During that long weekend Tom paid close attention as Ross, Hoxey and three business leaders of the community laid plans which would bind Alaska and its fisheries indissolubly to Seattle, and in all the projected maneuvering, Malcolm Ross led the way: 'What we must do is enact in Washington a law which requires all goods headed for Alaska to pass through Seattle.'

'Congress would never pass such a law,' one of the other men protested, and Hoxey corrected him: 'Congress will pass any law dealing with Alaska that the Western states agree to. Your problem, gentlemen, is to decide what within reason you want.'

'We'll begin with the law I just proposed,' Ross said, 'but we will not present it to Congress in that form.'

'What form do you suggest?' the original protester asked with a touch of sarcasm.

'Patriotism, Sam. Our law will forbid ships of any other nation to conduct business directly with Alaska. They must transship all their goods through an American port, which will naturally be Seattle.'

'That makes sense,' Hoxey cried. 'It's reasonable. It's easy to understand. And it is, as Mr. Ross said, patriotic.'

'The advantage . . .' Ross began, then stopped to correct himself. 'There are really several advantages. Our local stevedores will get paid for unloading the foreign ship and then paid again for loading the goods into our ships. And since cheap competition will be eliminated, our merchants can pretty much establish their own prices. It's expensive to run ships into those cold, island-strewn waters.' He paused, looked at each of the men, and asked: 'Have you any idea how many ships are lost each year in Alaskan waters?' And when they replied 'No,' he ticked off the disastrous record, going back to the days when Russia owned the area, losing several ships a year on reefs and hidden rocks: 'And the Americans haven't done a lot better. Our company has already lost two.'

'Sounds like poor captains and faulty navigation,' one of the men suggested, but Ross rejected that charge: 'More like sudden storms, wild seas and submerged rocks that haven't been properly charted,' and he told them of the ferocious wind that could come roaring out of Canada down Taku Inlet, rattling the roof of the cannery and placing any fishing boat in jeopardy: 'Alaska is no place for weaklings. Mining gold was difficult. Mining salmon requires just as much daring. Any profit we make from Alaskan waters, we earn.'

'But how can we protect your access to the salmon?' asked a financier whom Ross had approached for funds to cover the rapid development of the canneries he was proposing.

'Tom, fetch that model of Taku Inlet,' and when Tom returned from the office with it, Ross said: 'Explain to the men how this trap will work.' But before Tom could begin, Ross said: 'Gentlemen, you are to visualize traps like this in every major salmon stream. Properly administered, they will control the entire production of salmon.'

'This isn't a design, or a plan,' Tom began. 'It shows a real cannery. Totem on Taku Inlet coming out of Canada, where a little river called the Pleiades comes in. Our salmon breed in this little lake up here, and in a hundred others along the Taku River system, most of them in Canada. Up and down Taku Inlet salmon move by the million. So here at this vantage point we float this trap. Costs very little to build, and then we line out these grabbers to steer the fish in. Jiggers we call them, and when they're in place every salmon coming up Taku Inlet becomes a possibility for our cannery here.'

It was a beautiful, easy-to-control system as Tom explained it, but one of the more experienced men listening to the details was quick to spot an important problem: 'But what about Canada? If the Taku salmon breed mostly in their waters? Won't they raise hell about an efficient trap like this intercepting fish headed for their river system?'

'Tom,' Mr. Ross directed, 'fetch that big map of the area,' and when it was unfolded the men were shown the amazing structure of the area they were discussing: 'Here's Juneau, the new capital of Alaska. And a score of miles over here is Canada. You could ride the distance in half a day with a good horse. Except for one thing. Look closely, gentlemen. These mountains along the border are more than eight thousand feet high, rising from sea level in that short distance. And on our side, this entire area is one vast ice field. If you set out on foot to walk from Juneau to Canada, you'd be on a glacier all the way, with crevasses and monstrous uprisings of ice, and it might take you three weeks, if you were lucky enough to get through alive.'

While the men studied the forbidding terrain, he dismissed with a wave of his hand all of Canada east of the salmon stations: 'Wilderness. Towering mountains. Ice fields. Wild rivers. Inaccessible. Not one settler in a hundred square miles. Not one cannery anywhere and none likely to exist for a hundred years.'

Again the men studied the map, that vast expanse of nothingness on the Canadian side, after which Ross summarized: 'In building our system of canneries and traps, we can ignore Canada. For our purposes, it doesn't exist.' And he turned to more pressing matters: 'Hoxey, it's up to you to prevent the government of Alaska, such as it is, from passing any laws that might restrict our access to the salmon. No taxes. No impositions. No inspectors snooping around our canneries. And above all, no legislation governing the operation of traps.'

When Hoxey said that that was how he understood his commission, Ross said: 'Good. Now execute it,' and to the businessmen he said: 'Gentlemen, in situations like this one at Taku Inlet—and Alaska has hundreds as good or better—we have a gold mine, a living, swimming gold mine, but we must harvest it with care. Maintain quality. Penetrate new markets. Make salmon the rich man's delight, the poor man's sustenance. Can we do it, Tom?'

'If those two professors can perfect the Iron Chink, the sky's the limit.'

'And what is this Iron Chink?' one of the prospective investors asked, and Ross said simply: 'A secret which must not go beyond this room. But two men at the university are about to perfect a machine which will make the use of Chinese labor no longer necessary.'

'What does it do?'

'An endless supply of salmon moves down the conveyor and automatically the machine cuts off the head and tail, then sizes the salmon and guts it beautifully. Without the help of one damned Chinaman, the fish is prepared for canning, and another comes along in nine seconds.'

'Does such a machine exist?'

'Not for this canning season. But sure as the sun rises in the east, by 1905, farewell to those Chinamen and hello to profits you haven't even dreamed about.'

But then came a sharp protest from one of the men who had been paying special attention to the Taku model: 'Hey, wait a minute! If we throw those weirs clear across the inlet to trap our fish, how are the baby salmon going to get out of the lake when they want to head for the ocean?'

Tom slapped himself on the forehead: 'I always forget to explain the most important things. The movable weirs are in position only during the part of the year when we're catching mature salmon coming upstream. When the young ones come down from the lake, they find the inlet open right to the sea.'

Hoxey left Seattle on Tuesday morning, a complete strategy for the control of Alaska in his satchel. According to the plan devised principally by Mr. Ross, the fabulous riches of the salmon run could be garnered by his and the other companies without involving more than a handful of Alaskan citizens: 'All the lumber for the new canneries is milled here in Seattle and the machinery is assembled here too. Then it sails north in our ships. They're installed by the Seattle workmen who sail with them. The fish are caught in traps built here in the city and placed in position by our men. No more arguments with Tlingit fishermen, or white ones, either. The cans are made here, packed flat, and opened up at the cannery. No more tinsmiths. And best of all, that big bunk-house filled with Ah Ting and his outfit, it will be filled with machines that'll work faster than that gang ever could and double our working area without adding another building.'

He smiled at Hoxey, then said: 'And when the cans are sealed and labeled, they come back here in our ships. And we send them throughout America and the rest of the world.'

IN THE TWO days following Hoxey's departure, Tom drafted plans for the coming season at the R&R headquarters, and whenever he looked at the map in Mr. Ross's office and saw the red stars indicting where future canneries were to be established, he had a sinking feeling which he could share with no one: I'm never to get back to Seattle! I'm to spend my life moving from one Taku Inlet to the next, always building some new plant, and he could visualize the locations: Some remote inlet. No town within fifty miles. No wives. No children. Just traps catching salmon and the Iron Chink processing them.

But then he reflected on the advantages of working with a man like Malcolm Ross, who seemed unquestionably the most effective human being he had ever known: He's not warm and eager like Missy Peckham, who was the most admirable person he had been privileged to watch, but he does have vision and he does get things done. He was content to keep his wagon hitched to Mr. Ross, and as he reviewed the decisions of the past few days, he found that he had no reason to oppose any of Ross's plans for Alaska. Worthy things were to be done and the interests of both R&R and Seattle were to be protected.

It simply did not occur to Tom to question the morality of Seattle's intention to keep Alaska in a kind of serfdom, without political power or the right of any self-determination. He ignored the fact that if the Ross-Hoxey plans were established in law, Alaska would pay some fifty percent more for any goods it imported through Seattle than the similar territory of Hawaii would pay for its freight through San Francisco. Nor did he question the design that would leave Alaska powerless to pass any regional law protecting its salmon, or its trees, or its mines, or even its citizens. He did not at this time know the word *fiefdom*, but the concept would not have worried him: Mr. Ross has a clear vision of how Alaska should be developed, and no one I've met in Juneau has a clue as to what should be done.

No sooner did he reach this conclusion than he felt a twinge of doubt: Maybe Sam Bigears on the other side of the Pleiades, maybe he has a vision of how he and his Tlingits ought to live. And then he thought of Nancy Bigears facing the grizzly bear and talking him down: Maybe she knows, too, and when he visualized Nancy, he experienced a pang of remorse, for she and her father were aspects of Alaska that he could not dismiss.

However, his attention after work was diverted to the study of Mrs. Ross, whose behavior perplexed him. She was, on the one hand, a social leader in Seattle society, the wife of one of the city's richest men and obviously a woman of power. She could be imperious, as a social leader sometimes had to be, and she could look down her nose with the best of them, but even when she was being dictatorial, which she was several times in his presence, she displayed a roguish sense of humor, which bubbled into her eyes and often caused her to laugh quietly—at either herself or at the inadvertent pomposities of her husband.

At the end of his first week sharing the intimacies of the Ross home, Tom blurted out at the dinner table: 'You are two of the nicest people I've ever met.'

'Why, that's very kind of you, Tom. Surely, though, you've met many kind people in all your travels,' and Mrs. Ross turned in her chair to study him.

'Well, I've met lots of nice people. Missy Peckham, who was like a mother to me, was about as good as a person could be. And I knew a goldminer on the Yukon. I'd go anywhere with him. But . . .'

'What are you trying to say?'

'Just that these were good people, maybe the very best, but things never seemed to work out for them.'

'How do you mean?' It was obvious that Mrs. Ross was sincerely interested in his perceptions.

'Well, for one thing they never met the right person to marry. And for another, whatever they tried seemed to fail.' He hesitated, then came to his significant point: 'You're the first people in my life where you're both . . .' He did not know how to finish the contrast between the failures he had known and this pair of well-adjusted, happy people. 'I guess what I mean is, I've known some wonderful people, but they were never married to each other.' With this confession he looked down at his plate.

Mrs. Ross cherished such moments of honest revelation; her life had been enriched by them and she had no intention of allowing this conversation to end on such a note: 'You mean to say, Tom Venn, that you've never before seen a happily married couple?'

'I never have.'

'What do you think makes us so different?'

'Well, you both have power, a lot of it, but you don't abuse it.'

'That's a wonderful compliment, Tom. I have to work very hard to keep Malcolm here from abusing the power he commands.' She winked at her husband. 'And he keeps me from being stuffy.'

Mr. Ross coughed and said: 'There's never been any need for that. Would you like to know why?' and Tom said 'Yes,' nodding eagerly.

'Well, son,' said Mr. Ross, 'Mrs. Ross is no ordinary woman. In the early 1860s when Seattle was just beginning, it was filled with adventurous men like my father who had come here after being kicked out of Scotland. Lots of such men and no women. So a far-seeing man named Mercer had this bright idea. He'd go to Washington to seek the government's help in financing a ship, then go to New England, which was suffering heavy losses of men in the Civil War, and invite several hundred young women who might otherwise find no husbands to sail to jobs in Seattle where lonely men abounded. The newspapers of the time gave his expedition such great publicity that when he reached Boston, he found scores of women eager to try their luck out west. A girl named Lydia Dart working in a factory was especially eager to escape from that drudgery.

'Mercer did succeed in convincing hundreds of young women to undertake this adventure, and found much moral support for his plan but had difficulty getting funds for the ship. He finally found a willing financier who agreed to back the venture and provide passage for five hundred passengers at a minimal fee. Well, everything was working fine. Looked like a perfect operation.' He stopped, smiled at his wife, and seemed hesitant to continue.

'What happened?' Tom asked.

'Some evil-minded newspaper reporters, they were bastards, really, they started the rumor that Mr. Mercer ran a chain of whorehouses on the West Coast, and that when the girls reached Seattle, he was going to shove them into these brothels. A great scandal exploded. Tears. Recriminations. Fathers and brothers locking young women in their rooms to keep them from sailing. Before Mercer could answer these nasty accusations, more than two-thirds of his potential travelers had changed their minds and refused to reconsider.

'In January 1866 the ship sailed with only a hundred passengers, and of those, fewer than thirty were young unmarried women. Satisfied that Mr. Mercer was honest, they stayed with him, suffered the Victorian scorn of their neighbors, and sailed around the Horn of South America to make their homes in the Northwest. Lydia Dart became their leader. Watched after them. Fended off reporters seeking to create more scandalous stories. And sort of mothered the younger girls when they reached Seattle.'

'What happened to them then?'

'They became the soul of the city. These were refined, educated women who had come to the frontier. Many of them became teachers, and within the year they were married to the best young men of Seattle. One, who never married, opened the city's first public school. All of them represented the very best of this city, and four of them are alive today, the grand old ladies of Seattle.'

'How was Mrs. Ross connected with them?'

'Aha! The young woman Lydia Dart was the last to marry. She wanted to study the field, and in the end she chose a promising young lawyer named Henderson. And their first child is the gracious lady with whom you're dining tonight.'

A huge smile spread across his face as Tom looked at Mrs. Ross and said: 'Then you're the daughter of one of those young women?'

'The Mercer Girls they're known as in Seattle history. Yes, I'm the daughter of one of them, and a finer group of women never hit a Western city.'

'If you had known Lydia Dart Henderson,' Mr. Ross said, 'you'd understand why my wife could never be pompous or lacking in a sense of humor. Tell him about the letter she wrote to the Boston newspaper.'

Mrs. Ross laughed at the outrageous thing her mother had done, but in relating the incident she obviously took delight in it: 'About ten years after the Mercer Girls had descended on Seattle, my mother convened a meeting of them. I remember it well, I was about seven years old, and here came these two dozen women, wives of doctors and lawyers and businessmen, and I listened to their stories. Not a bad marriage in the lot. And that night my mother posted her letter to the newspaper in Boston which had been foremost in creating the scandal about the houses of prostitution.'

'What did the letter say?' Tom asked, and Mr. Ross pointed to the wall behind Tom's head where a framed piece of newsprint held a place of honor. Indicating that Tom should take it down, Ross said: 'You'll find it amusing. I did when I first saw it.'

The editors of this journal have recently received an interesting correspondence from one Lydia Dart, formerly of this city, who ventured out to Seattle in 1866. We thought our readers might find it instructive.

To the Editor:

Last night twenty-five young women who braved public censure to emigrate to Seattle as the Mercer Girls celebrated the tenth anniversary of their adventure. Twenty-four of us are married to the civic leaders of the community and we have nearly ninety children among us. Lizzie Ordway chose not to marry, and she heads the biggest school in the city. All of us own our own homes and all our children of school age are doing quite well. Thirteen of our husbands either are or have been elected officials of our beautiful city.

We invite twenty-five of the young women who refused to come with us in 1866 to meet and send us a letter describing what they have been doing in the meantime.

Lydia Dart Henderson

'That's some letter!' Tom said as he rehung the document, and Mr. Ross said: 'My mother-in-law kept writing letters like that till she died. Much of what's good about this city grew out of her Mercer Girls.'

'Somebody ought to organize another ship like that for the men in Alaska,' Tom suggested. 'And they could use a couple of Lydia Darts in Juneau right now.' Mrs. Ross smiled and said: 'On Friday afternoon, Tom, you'll meet the newest Lydia Dart, except that she's added Ross to her name.'

At first Tom failed to catch the significance of what had been said, but when Mr. Ross nodded, it dawned on him that his hosts were speaking of their daughter, whereupon Mrs. Ross said: 'She's at school during the week. A convent school, where she's been doing rather well.'

'Was the original Lydia Dart a Catholic?'

'As a matter of fact, she was,' Mrs. Ross said. 'But when her church tried to prevent her from coming to Seattle, she more or less broke away. Then she married this strict Presbyterian from Scotland, and I was raised believing that I was both a papist and a John Knox Presbyterian. Never bothered me a bit, but I've always liked Catholic schools. They teach children something, and our Lydia can profit from their discipline too.'

So Tom Venn spent Thursday and Friday in a state of considerable excitement, wondering what Lydia would be like and how he was going to react to the granddaughter of the woman who had written that letter. He feared that he might make a fool of himself, but when he returned from the office late Friday his apprehensions vanished, because Lydia Ross, aged seventeen, was a slender, vivacious girl whose happy life encouraged her to meet everyone with a disarming frankness. Not for her were the torments of adolescence; she supposed that both her famous grandmother and her well-adjusted mother had enjoyed similar girlhoods, and she intended becoming a grown woman much like them. She also adored her father and was at ease with her younger brother, who was developing similar attitudes. When Tom Venn first saw her come swinging in the front door, her blond hair coiled about her head so that her strong neck was revealed, he sensed immediately that she was an extension of the happy family which had so impressed him during his visit.

'Hello!' she said easily as she stretched out her hand. 'I'm Lydia. Father has told me about how good you were in handling the murders at the cannery.'

'He told you about that?' Tom asked, showing his surprise that Mr. Ross should have discussed such an unpleasant fact with his daughter.

'He tells us everything,' she replied, tossing a strapful of books onto a hall table, where she intended leaving them till Monday morning. 'And he told me about your run-in with the grizzly bear.'

'It wasn't really a fight. You won't believe this, but an Indian girl told the bear to go back, and it went.'

'How big can a grizzly be? Our geography book said they're twice as big as ordinary bears.'

'This one was so-so. But a hotel in Juneau has one about ten feet tall. Stuffed, of course.'

'He would be quite an attraction if he wasn't.'

She was seriously interested in Alaska, emphasizing that she had not yet been allowed to visit there on her father's ships: 'What I want to see are the glaciers he tells us about. Are they as big as he says?'

'It seems that everything in Alaska is big. Bigger than you imagine,' and he told of the huge iceberg that had floated right to the doorstep of the Ross & Raglan store in Juneau.

'You mean right onto the main street?'

'In the water, of course. But yes, you could reach out and touch it with a pole.'

'What happened to it?'

'A fellow with a little tug threw a rope around one part and easily towed it away.'

'You mean a tug this little and an iceberg this big?' And the way she moved her hands was so expressive that Tom fell under the spell of her liveliness, her quick reaction to spoken words and her ingratiating smile.

Dinner with the Rosses now became a treasured ritual, and on Saturday night Lydia regaled the table with a burlesque description of how two of the Catholic sisters at her school hoodwinked the young priest who served as principal: 'He looked quite simple when they were through with him, so foolish, in fact, that we were sorry for him.'

'Did he know what was happening?' Tom asked, and she said: 'No. Actually, he never knows what's happening.'

Her brother, who was in a public grammar school, asked what kind of school Tom had attended, and Tom said apologetically: 'Just an ordinary school, in Chicago. But I had to drop out.'

'Tom has learned in the best school there is,' Mr. Ross interrupted. 'The kind my father attended. The school of actually doing it.' He asked for his son's attention, and said: 'The young man sitting across from you, Jake, was practically in charge of our store in Dawson before he was Lydia's age. And a year later he was head of everything in Nome.'

'You mean the gold fields?' the boy asked, and when Tom nodded, both the younger Rosses viewed him with more respect.

That weekend was the richest in human experience that Tom Venn had known up to this moment, for he witnessed how a well-organized family interacted, how children were allowed great freedom if they attended to the basic courtesies, and he was especially impressed by the fact that Mrs. Ross, who was obviously proud of her lively daughter, refused Lydia permission to go out on Sunday afternoon until she had finished her weekend homework. Down the books came from the table where Lydia had tossed them, but two hours later she was ready to take a walk over the wooded hills in back of the castle.

It was a walk Tom would never forget. The air was wintry but the sun was warm. Puget Sound glistened at first, then grew somber as a rain squall drifted in from the Strait of Juan de Fuca, and at one point Tom said: 'Look down there. It's almost as if the heart of the city lay exposed.'

'You use words well,' Lydia said, and Tom explained how, in both Dawson and Nome, he had studied books which Missy Peckham had provided.

'Who was she?' Lydia asked, and he replied: 'My mother, sort of,' and when she asked what that meant, for heaven's sake, he laughed uneasily and explained: 'My real mother . . . well, she ran away with another man . . . and my father sort of married Missy. She was a wonderful woman . . . is, I'd better say. She lives in Nome now.' He stopped, overcome by the contrast between Missy's chaotic life and the orderliness of the Ross household. He wanted to tell her how this good woman Missy Peckham had been unable to marry his father and was now unable to marry Mr. Murphy, and for much the same reason, but it was too complicated to unravel.

'Father thinks I ought to go on to college,' Lydia said, tactfully changing the subject. 'Mother has doubts.'

'Where would you go?'

'Here in Seattle. The university maybe.'

'That would be nice.'

'But Grandmother always remembered the Boston area with affection, and she told me before she died . . .'

'I thought she was fed up with Boston.'

'No! She wrote that letter to tease them. She loved the place, said it was the lighthouse of America. She wanted me to go back there to school.' Then Lydia stopped speaking, for powerful thoughts were coursing through her mind, and after a while she said: 'I want to be like my grandmother. I want always to be brave enough to try things. I think I'll need an education to achieve what I want to do.'

'And what is that?'

'I don't know. There are so many possibilities, I really can't decide.'

Tom had to laugh, because he faced the same quandary: 'Just like me. I love the work in Alaska. And I can see unbroken years of it ahead. But I feel more at home in Seattle and I can't see how I'm ever going to find a position here.'

'I should think that if you do a good job for Father up in Alaska, it would be only natural for him to bring you down here sooner or later. He has a very high opinion of you, Tom, and so does Mother.'

'But he also has a lot of work for me to do in Alaska.' He halted that line of talk: 'Have you ever met this Marvin Hoxey?'

'He's an awful man. Real slimy. Father knows it, but he says that sometimes you have to use whatever tool's at hand.' She kicked at a stone: 'Hoxey doesn't fool my father one bit.'

They had now swung around to the eastern side of the small hill; Puget Sound was no longer visible, but in its place stood the lakes and waterways which defined this segment of Seattle, and they were as attractive in their more subdued way as the more dramatic sound to the west. 'I've always liked this view,' Lydia said, 'less powerful but safer.'

'I don't think of you as someone looking for safety,' Tom said, and she corrected him: 'I'm not afraid of challenges, but I do appreciate safe havens at the close of day. My grandmother said the same. She told me once: "I didn't come west for adventure alone. I came to find a good man and build a solid home." Adventure and a safe haven, that's a good mix.'

On Monday morning she told Tom: 'Father says you'll be gone before I come back. It's been real fun talking to you. I can see why Father thinks so much of you, Tom.' And off she went, her hair down her back this time, her strapped books bouncing against her right leg.

On Tuesday, Mr. Ross said at dinner: 'I want you to supervise delivery and installation of the equipment for making tin cans. Our boat sails Thursday, and after Juneau it will lay over at the cannery. The men from the factory will help you with the machines and the new welding device.'

Tom was twenty-one now and amazingly poised for his age, so without embarrassment he suggested: 'Couldn't I take Monday's ship north and meet the men at the cannery?'

'Why would you do that?'

'Because I'd very much like to see Lydia again.'

A hush fell over the room, broken by Mrs. Ross, who said brightly: 'That's a sensible idea, Malcolm. I'm sure Lydia would like to see Tom again.' And without further words the decision was reached, with Mr. Ross showing no irritation at having been overruled; he liked Tom Venn and appreciated the young man's forthrightness.

The second weekend was more serious than the first, because all the Rosses, especially Lydia, were aware that Tom had stayed on for the express purpose of exploring further their friendship. She told him frankly, when they were alone, that she had broken two other engagements so that they could spend time together, and when he protested that she should not have done that, she said frankly: 'Oh, but I wanted to. So many of the young men I meet are clods.'

'They won't be when they're four years older,' he said, and she replied: 'They're already four years older and they're confirmed clods.'

Twice they walked on the hill, seeing Seattle and its environs in its varying moods, and they talked incessantly of school and Mr. Hoxey's political plans and the future of Ross & Raglan, and on Monday morning when Lydia again left for school, she stood in the hallway in the presence of both her father and her mother and kissed Tom goodbye. She did not want there to be any misunderstanding as to how she felt.

WHEN THE TIN-CAN machines were installed at Totem Cannery, Tom Venn and Sam Bigears, who had reluctantly agreed to serve as winter watchman over the vacant buildings, began to prepare for the arrival of the Filipino and Chinese workmen. Huge quantities of rice were brought in from Seattle, because both these groups would become difficult if the cannery tried to feed them potatoes, and additional bunks were built for the extra Chinese who would be coming. When Tom paddled across the estuary one day to visit with Sam, whose friendship he wanted to retain, he unwisely told him: 'This may be the last year we use Chinese.'

Sam, who could never bear a grudge, even though he had been disgusted after Tom's last visit, asked: 'Who else you gonna get? Tlingits never work no factory.'

Sensing potential trouble, Tom said no more, but on several later occasions Sam wanted to know who would be taking the place of the Chinese: 'We don't want no Japanese, no Eskimos brought into our territory. Be damned much better if Chinese and Filipinos both get out.'

'Maybe they will, someday,' Tom said, but in late April a big Canadian ship, the *Star of Montreal*, hove to off the mouth of the Pleiades River to deposit ninety-three Chinese workers, and as they began to stream down the gangplank, Tom saw what he had expected: Ah Ting was once more in command, his long pigtail trailing, his eyes more challenging than before, if that was possible. This year only one of his co-workers spoke English, and as Tom moved among the gang he suspected that more than half were recent arrivals from China, for they had no concept of what work they would be doing.

'I want two of your best men,' Tom told Ah Ting.

'What for?' the leader asked, implying, as usual, that he, Ah Ting, would decide who would work where.

'They're to work a new machine,' Tom said, and Ah Ting replied: 'I work the new machine,' but Tom said firmly: 'No, you're needed in here. To keep order.'

'That's right,' Ah Ting said with no animosity. He was the top man, and it was prudent that he work where he could supervise the largest number of workers. So he designated two good workmen, but when Tom led them away, Ah Ting insisted upon trailing along, for he considered it essential that he know what was going on in every part of the cannery; in fact, he acted as if it were his cannery, an assumption which irritated Tom, as it had Mr. Ross during the rioting last year.

As soon as Ah Ting saw the stacks of flattened cans and the machines which would expand them into usable form, he appreciated the threat this new system posed for his Chinese. Contemptuously he spurned the machines, saying: 'No good. No more Chinese working here.'

'We'll need two good men on the machines,' Tom assured him. 'Maybe two more to move the cans around.'

Ah Ting would have none of this. Last year he had supervised sixteen of his men in this section; this year there were to be four at most, and he was pretty sure that Mr. Venn would quickly cut that back to three or even two as the men became familiar with the operation of the new system. But what could he do other than sulk? And this he did, with every sign of becoming increasingly difficult as the season progressed.

Faced by this insubordination, Tom was tempted to fire Ah Ting on the spot, but he knew that no replacement could manage the scores of Chinese who would still be required to keep the cutting tables and the cooking ovens functioning. So against his better judgment, Tom bided his time, accepted Ah Ting's protests, and made small concessions on food and bunkhouse space to keep his tenacious manager happy.

And when this was accomplished, more or less successfully, he faced the wrath of the fishermen, for when Professor Starling and his crew came on the scene to erect their trap, and the local men saw the long jiggers stretching nearly across the inlet, they realized that their days of domination were ended, and they began to make trouble. Some of the rougher white men threatened to demolish the weir and cut the jiggers, while others said they would prevent the supply ships from landing at the dock or hauling away the cases of canned salmon. There were other threats too from the Tlingits, but in the end the great trap was built and the jiggers installed, and then the fishermen were both superfluous and powerless to oppose the swift changes that were sweeping their industry.

When the mature salmon began to flood into Taku Inlet, all hands watched carefully to determine whether the trap would collect enough fish to keep the gutting tables filled, and by the end of the first week it was apparent that the weir and its two jiggers were going to succeed even beyond the hopes of the men who had installed it. In fact, when Professor Starling reviewed the operation he spotted a problem which not even he had anticipated: 'It's working so well, Mr. Venn, that the holding pen is receiving more fish than it can handle. Your men are not taking the salmon out fast enough.'

'We can't handle any more in the gutting shed than we are right now.'

'When Dr. Whitman gets his Iron Chink perfected,' Starling said, 'we can speed up the chain. But what shall we do now?'

Even as he spoke, the efficient jiggers, blocking the movement of the salmon as they fought to reach their natal lakes, kept throwing so many big fish into the trap and from there into the holding area that there was only one solution: 'We'll have to let the weaker fish at the bottom die and let their bodies drift downstream with the current.'

This was done, and all that summer the trap at the Pleiades caught so many big sockeye that an appalling number of weaker ones were wasted. Now bald eagles from miles around gathered in the skies over Taku Inlet to feast upon the decaying fish, and thousands of fish which could have provided delectable sustenance to hungry people everywhere were allowed to rot and contaminate the lower waters of the Taku.

Even more ominous so far as the future of the industry was concerned, the trap was so effective that knowing fishermen began to wonder whether enough mature salmon were getting past the barrier to ensure perpetuation of the breed. 'We do open it up over the weekend,' Professor Starling assured the skeptics as he stopped in Juneau on his way back to Seattle, 'and if you saw the hordes of fish that get through on those two days . . .'

'A day and a half,' someone corrected, and he nodded: 'If you saw the hordes of salmon that escape in that period, you'd know their future was secure.'

'What about the fish you allow to die in the holding area?' another man asked, and Starling replied: 'There's a little wastage in any big operation. Unavoidable, and in the long run it does no substantial damage.' And back he sailed to lay plans for six more huge traps to be installed at future Ross & Raglan canneries.

Some concerned men in Juneau took Professor Starling's advice and sailed to the Pleiades River to inspect the operation of the trap, but when their little boat started to dock, Tom Venn appeared on the wharf to warn them that they were approaching private property on which they were not permitted to intrude. 'But your Professor Starling invited us to come out and see how the trap works,' and Tom said: 'He had no authority to do that,' but the hardened fishermen of Juneau were not to be so easily turned back.

'We're coming ashore, Venn, and you'll be asking for trouble if you try to stop us.'

Such confrontation was avoided, since inspection of the weir and jiggers could be accomplished without trespassing on Totem property. Tom directed the fishermen to take their boat downstream from the trap, from where they could watch the behavior of the salmon, and a stranger to Alaskan fishing would have been astounded at what they saw. The mature salmon swam in from the gyre not in dozens or hundreds but in thousands, three hundred in one solid block, six hundred resting with their noses all pointed against the current. At times the clear water in which the boat rested was solidly packed with salmon, ten or fifteen thousand crowding past, their sleek bodies shining in sunlight a few inches below the surface. It did seem, in such moments of abundance, that the supply was inexhaustible and indestructible.

But when this multitude approached the outreaching jiggers, they faced a situation unlike any they had encountered before. These weirs, these high fences were not like the waterfalls up which their ancestors had leaped for countless generations; these new devices were effective barriers, and after trying to circumvent them, the bewildered fish began taking the course of least resistance.

Aimlessly they drifted toward the central trap, and there they slipped into that maze which was so easy to enter, so impossible to escape. Step by step they moved more deeply into the maze, until at last they passed into the relative freedom of the big holding pen.

But now the crowding in the pen became so threatening that the weaker fish began to gasp for water to pass through their gills, and with astonishing rapidity the smaller salmon began to die off, their bodies sinking to the bottom of the pen while Tom Venn's workmen hoisted the survivors onto the track to carry them to the cutting shed, where Ah Ting's men prepared them for the ovens.

The Juneau fishermen who witnessed the magnitude of this revolutionary approach to salmon fishing could see at once that it involved a dreadful wastage which their older process would never have caused. Said one older man: 'They have no respect for the salmon. If they keep this up, I don't know what'll happen.'

But one of the boats stayed overnight to see what would happen on the weekend, and on Saturday afternoon when the trap was shut down and the jiggers raised, these men watched as the horde of fish came up the Taku, passed the trap, and swam on to their various home lakes along the Taku system. 'There's enough fish getting through to populate all Alaska and most of Canada,' one of the men said, and thus reassured, they viewed the situation differently.

'It's the modern way,' one of the fishermen conceded, and they agreed that despite the regrettable wastage of salmon, enough sockeye probably escaped during the free weekends to maintain the stocks.

IN 1904, AFTER the fishermen of Juneau had reached this erroneous conclusion about the safety of the salmon, Nerka, now three years old, had settled into a routine in fresh-water Lake Pleiades that looked as if it would continue throughout his lifetime. But one morning, after a week of agitation, he sprang into unprecedented action, as if a bell had summoned all the sockeye of his generation to the performance of some grand, significant task.

And then, for reasons he could not identify, his nerves jangled as if an electric shock had coursed through his body, leaving him agitated and restless. Driven by impulses he did not understand, he found himself repelled by the once-nurturing fresh water of his natal lake and for some days he thrashed about. Suddenly one night, Nerka, followed by thousands of his generation, began to swim toward the exit of his lake and plunged into the swiftly rushing waters of the Pleiades River. But even as he departed, he had a premonition that he must one day, in years far distant, return to this congenial water in which he had been bred. He was now a *smolt,* on the verge of becoming a mature salmon. His skin had assumed the silvery sheen of an adult, and although he was still but a few inches long, he looked like a salmon.

With powerful strokes of his growing tail he sped down the Pleiades, and when he was confronted by rapids tumbling over exposed rocks he knew instinctively the safest way to descend, but when waterfalls of more ominous height threatened his progress he hesitated, judged alternatives, then sprang into vigorous activity, leaping almost joyously into the spray, thrashing his way down, and landing with a thump at the bottom, where he rested for a moment before resuming his journey.

Did he, through some complex biological mechanism, record these waterfalls as he descended them, storing knowledge against that fateful day, two years hence, when he would be impelled to climb them in the opposite direction in order to enable some equally determined female sockeye to spawn? His return trip would be one of the most remarkable feats in the animal world.

But now as he approached the lower reaches of the river he faced a major peril, because at a relatively inconsequential waterfall which he could normally have handled with ease, he was either so tired or so careless that he allowed himself to be thrown against a rock protruding from the downward current, so that he landed with an awkward splash at the foot of the falls, where, awaiting just such mishaps, a group of voracious Dolly Vardon trout, each bigger than the salmon smolts, prowled the waters. With swift, darting motions the trout leaped at the stunned smolts, devouring them in startling numbers, and it seemed likely that Nerka, totally disoriented by slamming against the rock, would be an easy prey and disappear before he ever reached the salt water which was luring him.

But he had already proved himself to be a determined fish, and now in an instinctive, brain-clouded way he dodged the first attack of the trout, then dropped into protective weeds from which the larger fish could not dislodge him, and in this quivering manner evaded the hungry attacks of the trout.

Of the four thousand salmon born in Nerka's group in Lake Pleiades in 1901, how many now survived? That is, how many swam down the Pleiades River to fulfill their destiny in the ocean? The constant depletion had been so frightful and so constant that three thousand, nine hundred and sixty-eight had perished, leaving only thirty-two alive and ready for the adventure in the ocean. But upon those pitiful few the great salmon industry of Alaska would be built, and it would be Nerka and the other fighting, cautious, self-protective fish like him who would keep canneries like Totem on Taku Inlet so richly profitable.

At last, one morning Nerka, having fended off long-legged heron and diving mergansers, approached the most critical moment of his life so far: this fresh-water fish was about to plunge himself into the briny waters of the sea, not inch by inch or slowly over a period of weeks, but with one sweep of his tail and the activation of his fins. True, the change from lake water to sea had been in gradations, but even so, the leap from all-fresh to all-sea was momentous. It was as if a human being who had lived in benevolent oxygen were told: 'A week from now it's to be only methane gas.' No human could survive unless he could make his metabolism and physiological structure take a quantum leap, and that is what Nerka did.

Even so, when he entered the new medium it was an almost lethal shock. For several days he staggered about, recoiling from the salt, and in this coma-tose condition he faced a terrible danger. An immense flock of voracious white gulls and black ravens hovered low in a sullen sky, eager to dive upon the foundering smolts, catch them in their beaks and carry them aloft for feeding. The devastation wreaked by these screaming scavengers was awesome: thousands of would-be salmon perished in their sharp claws, and those that miraculously survived did so only by pure luck.

Nerka, slow to adjust to the salt water, was especially vulnerable, because from time to time he drifted listlessly on his side, an easy target for the diving birds, but sheer chance, not his own efforts, saved him, and after one near-miss he revived enough to send himself down deep toward the darkness he loved, and there, away from the predators, he worked his gills, forcing the unfamiliar seawater through his system.

Most of that summer Nerka and his fellows lingered in Taku Inlet, gorging themselves on the rich plankton blooms and accommodating to the salt water.

They began to grow. Their senses quickened. Surprisingly, they were no longer afraid to battle larger fish. They were now salmon, and gradually they worked their way toward the mouth of the inlet as their appetite made them hunger for the squid, shrimp and small fish that flourished there. And as they matured, they felt an urge to move out into the open ocean to their adventures in its great swirling waters.

Of his thirty-one companions who made it to the mouth of Taku Inlet, about a half perished before they reached the ocean, but Nerka survived, and he swam forward eagerly, scraping past the protruding rock of the Walrus, leaving Taku Inlet, and heading westward to the Pacific.

WHILE NERKA HEADED toward the Pacific Ocean, Tom Venn was making his first serious mistake in managing Totem Cannery. The Chinese workmen whom Ah Ting had nominated to run the new machines that turned flat slabs of tin into finished cans were not doing a good job. Through either ineptitude or malice they were causing the machines to malfunction, and Tom, convinced that it was a case of sabotage, dismissed them from the section in which they had been working and had the machines moved to the Filipino area, where four young men were instructed how to make cans.

When Ah Ting learned that the tin shop, which used to employ sixteen Chinese, now had jobs for none, he fell into a rage. His customary smile gone, he stormed into Tom's office, demanding that the machines be returned to the Chinese section and that six, not four, of his helpers be assigned to operate them. Such an intrusion into his prerogatives as manager Tom could not allow, and after listening to only the first sentences of Ah Ting's complaint, he said: 'I will say who works where. Now get back to the gutting shed.' But as Ah Ting retreated, Tom had a premonition that his curt rejection of the man's just complaint might cause trouble, and he started after him to explain more carefully the grounds for his decision. However, he was interrupted by the arrival of one of the Filipinos assigned to the canning operation, so he was unable to placate Ah Ting.

The question was a minor one: 'Mr. Venn, how do we get the finished cans to the packing line?' Ah Ting would never have allowed one of his men to ask such a silly question; he would have devised three or four ways to move the cans, tried each, and then reported to Mr. Venn which one was most efficient. But the Filipinos have to learn, Tom told himself, and when the problem was solved in exactly the way Ah Ting would have elected, he returned to his office. He had signed only a few shipping papers when he heard a wild commotion.

Dashing out to the sheds, Tom found that when two of the Filipino workers bringing finished cans to the line trespassed on what had always been Chinese terrain, Ah Ting's men had gone for them with knives.

The Filipinos were an able pair who had often tangled with Chinese in their homeland, where the two races maintained an uneasy truce, and they did not intend to let these Chinese oppress them. Grabbing whatever weaponry lay at hand, including a heavy hammer, the two men held off their attackers, screaming in Tagalog for reinforcements, and in less than a minute some dozen Filipinos had stormed into the building.

This could not be tolerated, for the Chinese considered their work area inviolate, and by the time Tom Venn reached the fray, he found men slamming each other across tables against the walls and slashing perilously close at one another's throats with their knives. Without regard to the danger he was inviting, he grabbed Ah Ting by the arm and shouted: 'We've got to stop this!' and in time, due largely to the effectiveness of his Chinese helper, he quieted the screaming and reduced the riot to snarling threats. Fortunately, neither side could understand the vilest charges made by the other, and the Filipinos retreated to their domain, satisfied that they had won a victory.

They had not, because in a carefully controlled meeting between Venn, Ah Ting and the leader of the Filipinos, a sensible man who, like many Manila citizens, spoke both English and Chinese, a truce was worked out whereby the Filipinos would continue to fabricate the cans but leave the transportation of them to the packing line to the Chinese who had been deposed from the tinwork area. In this way, Ah Ting recovered the four jobs he had lost, and when Tom next saw him the big toothy smile had returned.

However, the armistice did not long prevail, because the Filipinos working the two machines jammed first one and then the other, and no one in their section knew how to fix them. When Tom was summoned, he confidently approached the damaged machines but found himself unequal to the task, so with considerable embarrassment he had to call for Ah Ting, the inveterate fixer, to rescue him so that the work of the cannery could proceed.

With an insolent air, as if to tell both Venn and the Filipinos 'You can't run anything around here without my help,' this master of machines and people went to work, and within two minutes he had identified what needed to be done and within fifteen minutes he had both machines running like new; in fact, he had them working better than they had in their original condition, for he had corrected a design weakness.

Unfortunately, when he finished he said in Chinese, forgetting that the leader of the Filipinos understood that language: 'Now maybe even the stupid Filipinos can work the machines without wrecking them.'

When the Filipino foreman translated this slur to his companions, four of them leaped at Ah Ting, who defended himself with his tools, but had Tom not jumped forward to assist him, Ah Ting would have crumpled beneath the assault. That evening Tom drafted a letter to Mr. Ross in Seattle:

> So I have decided once and for all that we cannot work anymore with these impossible Chinese. I would fire them all tomorrow if there was some way to operate the cannery without them. How is that Iron Chink coming along? Can we rely on it for next year? I certainly hope so.

When Ross received the query he hurried over to Dr. Whitman's laboratory, whereupon Whitman sent for his colleague Professor Starling, who had installed the very successful trap at the Totem Cannery. When the three stood before the latest model of their Iron Chink, Ross asked bluntly: 'Can we risk it for next year?' and to his delight, the two men agreed that the former difficulties had been eliminated.

'This thing works!' Dr. Whitman said in a way that allowed no doubt, but Ross said: 'I'd like to see for myself,' so a batch of fish about the size of salmon was brought in, and when the steam-driven flywheel had the various leather belts operating the knives, Whitman began feeding the fish, some long, some short, into the machine, and unerringly the first knives cut off the heads and tails, while the device measuring the body of the fish adjusted faultlessly, enabling the third knife to gut the fish cleanly and send it on its way.

'It's wonderful!' Ross shouted, and after elbowing Whitman aside, he began feeding the assorted fish into the hopper, and for several minutes the Iron Chink made not a single mistake. 'When can we have this in Alaska?'

Dr. Whitman evaded that question: 'I want you to study the way we have it now. Half as many moving parts. Half as many things to go wrong. And look how sturdy the parts are that we do use.' Grabbing a small hammer, he beat upon the critical joints, demonstrating how they could withstand the considerable punishment they would receive when unskilled workmen used them in the field.

'That's good. That's all to the good,' Ross said impatiently. 'But how soon can we have them?' And Professor Starling said: 'I think we ought to move this prototype into position right now. See if it works in Alaska, which I'm sure it will. Make any adjustments by October first, and we can have your entire cannery using nothing but these machines by April first next year.'

'Agreed!' Ross said. 'How many machines do you think we'll need at Totem?' and Starling, who knew the installation well, said: 'Six will do the job as the plant now stands,' and Ross said: 'Perfect this one on the spot, and then build me eight. We're enlarging Totem.'

So in July the R&R steamer *Queen of the North* docked in Taku Inlet with three mysterious long boxes, and when they were hauled to a new shed which had been hastily built to accommodate the miracle machine, Tom refrained from informing Ah Ting what the equipment was intended to do. But as soon as the parts were unpacked, with boards nailed over the windows to prevent spying, Ah Ting was determined to find ways to penetrate the mystery, and what he saw disturbed him. Furtively inspecting all parts of the new machine, he deduced what its functions must be, and cleverly he identified how it would work. One night, when it was completely assembled, he sneaked into the new shed, and with the aid of matches stolen from the kitchen, he traced each step of the process, figuring out how the moving parts would operate. In the end he had almost as good an understanding of the whole as its inventors.

There in the darkness, his matches gone, he understood the reason for Tom's secrecy: No more Chinese. Tin cans gone to the Filipinos. Pretty soon salmon gone to this damned thing. He reflected on this sad state of affairs for several mournful minutes, then voiced the conclusion which concerned him most directly: 'Pretty soon no more Ah Ting.'

At nine next morning agitated Chinese stormed into Tom Venn's office, making gestures which he was able to interpret, to the effect that in their shed there was great trouble. Assuming that another Chinese-Filipino brawl had erupted, he grabbed a heavy length of wood much like a baseball bat and hurried to the gutting shed, where no work was being done, and there he learned the cause of the commotion.

Ah Ting was gone. His men were sure that he had not slept in the Chinese bunkhouse last night, and a thorough search of the cannery grounds, a considerable area now, had revealed no trace of him. And the rumor had started that during the night the Filipinos had murdered him.

This accusation Tom refused to accept, and calling for the other Chinese man who understood English, he warned: 'Tell your men not to say that. We'll have another riot on our hands. Ah Ting is around here somewhere.' He then hurried to the Filipino quarters, where he quickly satisfied himself that there had been no planned attack on Ah Ting. He liked the Filipinos and saw reassuring possibilities for them once the disturbing effect of the Chinese had been removed, and he told their leaders: 'No more work today. And do not any of you go near the Chinese sections.'

He then turned his attention to Ah Ting, and the more he investigated, the more frustrated he became. The man was not on cannery property, and if he had been murdered, Tom supposed Ah Ting's body could have been weighted and dumped in Taku Inlet, where it would remain hidden forever. By three in the afternoon he ordered everyone back to work, but posted white guards to see that the two Oriental crews remained apart. Ah Ting was gone, and there was no sense speculating any further as to what had happened. Venn himself took charge of the Chinese, and at night, after having tried vainly to settle the endless disputes that erupted within that work force, he sneaked over to the new shed, inspected the miraculous machine housed there, and muttered with grim satisfaction: 'We aren't going to get rid of them one day too soon,' and he went to bed convinced that 1905 would be a much better year than 1904.

WHEN AH TING decoded the mystery of the new machine hidden away in the new building, and realized that it signaled the end of his days at Totem Cannery, he spent about fifteen minutes considering what to do, and his principal decision was one he had never contemplated before: I want to stay here. Upon brief reflection he concluded that he liked Alaska, respected the people like Tom Venn that he had encountered, and had high regard for the few Indians he had known about the cannery. Most significant of all, he loathed the prospect of being sent back to China and his memories of San Francisco were deplorable.

So on the spur of the moment he did what resolute men had often done when faced by a situation they could not tolerate: he decided to strike out on his own and take his chances for a new life that was better than the one he had known in the past or was enjoying now. In addition to his courage, which was of a high order, he had certain self-assurances: Nobody, not even Mr. Venn, knows machines better than I do. No one can work harder. And I doubt if there are many who are willing to take the chances I took in getting out of China or beating off the murderers in San Francisco. If anybody can do it, I can.

He therefore quietly slipped out of the new building by the secret way he had gotten in—by removing a floorboard—left all his petty gear in the bunkhouse, and with only the clothes he wore, walked casually through the darkness to the mouth of the Pleiades River where it widened before joining Taku Inlet. He was clear of the cannery and for the moment safe from detection by anyone outside. Although he was in no degree guilty of any crime, all the Chinese had been warned that Alaska would not allow any Orientals to remain permanently within its borders: 'You must all sail back to Seattle in the fall or face arrest.'

But with the wisdom he had accumulated during his stay in America, he felt certain that no matter where he settled he could earn a living by fixing things. He estimated his value as a carpenter, a plumber, a builder to be high, and he knew that such people were always welcomed, no matter what the law said. He was, as before, willing to take his chances.

He had heard many times of Juneau, and from what the men who lived there said, he judged it to be an attractive place, precisely the kind of growing community that would provide work for a man of his talents. But how to get there he did not know. On several occasions he had made carefully veiled inquiries, but the white foremen had always said: 'We came by boat,' and he had no boat. He knew also that Juneau lay on the other side of the two glaciers with which he was familiar; Walrus he had seen three times when the Seattle ship transporting him back and forth had stopped off Walrus Rock to blow its whistle in hopes an iceberg would break off because of the resonance, but this had never happened; and of course he had seen Pleiades Glacier almost daily since his arrival at Totem. They were formidable barriers of ice, and he knew that above them the great ice fields continued for many miles, so he had no desire to trust his luck to such awesome terrain.

Three or four times during his work at Totem he had seen an older Indian workman visit the place, and by chance he had learned that this was the Tlingit with the strange name of Bigears. Because Ah Ting had an insatiable hunger for collecting information that might later be of use, he was able to recall hearing casual remarks which had led him to believe that Bigears was not entirely pleased with having the cannery so close to his home.

And where was that home? Again, by paying the most careful attention, Ah Ting had found out that it occupied that visible headland due north of the smaller point on which the cannery rested, and now in the darkness, when he knew of no friend anywhere that he could trust, he concluded that if he could reach this Bigears, he might find some way to get to Juneau.

Slipping far inland from the Totem dock, he found a spot where the Pleiades River narrowed, and there he waded at first, then swam the short distance to the northern shore. Waiting for an hour in the warm summer night till his clothes dried more or less, he started down the right bank of the river until he came in sight of Bigears' cabin. Seeing a light in the window, he took several deep breaths, committed himself to bold action, and knocked on the door.

Sam Bigears, the man he had seen at the cannery, did not appear, he was in Juneau; but his daughter, Nancy, did, and when she opened the door she betrayed no surprise at seeing a Chinese man standing before her.

'Hello! Trouble at the cannery?'

He understood the question and its implications, and he knew that he gambled his future on what he said next: 'I try to get to Juneau.'

'Did they send you from the cannery? Why didn't they give you a boat?'

'I run away. No more work cannery.' Nancy Bigears, who was also disgusted with the factory across the estuary, understood his plight. 'Come in,' she said. 'Mother, man here to see you.' And from a back room Mrs. Bigears walked calmly in, and like her daughter, expressed no surprise at seeing a Chinese facing her.

'His pants are wet,' she said in Tlingit. 'Ask him if he wants some tea.'

And in this way Ah Ting met the Bigears family, with whom he hid for three days until Sam returned from Juneau. When Sam heard the story, which Nancy had developed in detail, he greeted Ah Ting heartily, assured him that there would be a way for him to reach Juneau, and told him further that good workmen were needed on at least a score of building and repair jobs in the youthful capital.

On the second day of Ah Ting's visit with Sam Bigears, the Indian said frankly: 'I never like Chinese in Alaska. Good thing they go.'

'I work hard,' Ah Ting replied.

'That very important in Juneau,' Sam said, and that afternoon he took Ah Ting fishing well up the Taku.

It was during their absence that Tom Venn was rowed across the estuary to inquire whether the Bigears family had seen anything of the missing Ah Ting. 'He's done nothing wrong,' he explained to Nancy, whom he had seen only rarely since their romantic moment. 'He's needed at the cannery. He keeps the other Chinks in line.'

Without actually lying, Nancy indicated that neither she nor her mother had knowledge of the mysterious fugitive, and as she deflected Venn's inquiries she thought: If Ah Ting wants to escape that prison over there, I'll help him. So she told Tom nothing.

But since he had taken the trouble to cross the estuary, and since he had not seen Nancy for some months, Tom lingered and accepted the tea Mrs. Bigears offered. Still interested in Nancy's future, he asked: 'Are you still at school in Juneau?'

'Vacation.'

'Are you learning anything?'

'Two good teachers, four pretty bad.'

'The good teachers are men, I suppose?'

'All women. The principal is a man, a real dooper.'

'And what does that mean?'

'You wouldn't let him shovel snow at your store.'

'It's not my store anymore. Mr. Ross says I'm to spend my time opening new canneries.'

'All over?'

'As soon as he gets government permission.'

'And you'll steal the rivers? Like here?'

'We'll sell a million cans of salmon. Make everyone rich.'

She pointed in the general direction of the Totem Cannery: 'Nobody here gets rich from that one. You fired all the fishermen. Now I suppose you'll be firing all the Chinese, too.'

'Who told you that?'

'People talk. In Juneau they know everything pretty quick. Those two men from the university who came up three weeks ago. They had pictures of a new machine. What will the new machine do?'

'Who told you that?'

'The woman who works in the hotel. She saw the pictures. She knew they were a machine.' Nancy, realizing that it would be embarrassing and perhaps even dangerous if Tom Venn was still there when her father brought Ah Ting back, said abruptly: 'Well, I suppose you have to get back to work.'

'Yes, I'm going.' But as he started to walk toward the waiting boatman he felt dissatisfied with the way this visit had gone, so he returned to the house, and when Nancy appeared at the door he asked her to go with him to the totem pole, and in its shadow he said: 'What's wrong with you, Nancy? Have I done something to offend you?' And he asked these questions so frankly that she felt ashamed of herself for having treated him so brusquely.

'I thought last time that we agreed we were going separate ways. It's better.'

'But that doesn't mean we can't be friends. I admire your father. I admire you.'

And now Nancy wanted him to stay, regardless of whether Ah Ting stumbled in or not, and so for several minutes she leaned against the totem as if she were a part of it, and her gently rounded face and dark eyes made her an authentic image of the real Alaska.

'You're going to be a very beautiful woman, Nancy,' he said.

'You know many beautiful women last winter in Seattle?'

'I met one. Mr. Ross's wife. She's very special.'

'In what way?'

'She's like you. Natural in all she does. Forthright. She laughs like you, too.' He did not deem it necessary to reveal that he had also met Mr. Ross's equally attractive daughter.

Now Nancy grew even more eager for him to stay: 'What was it like, Seattle?'

'Two big bodies of water meet. Many islands, lakes, little streams. It's a fine city, really.'

'Will you be working in Seattle pretty soon?'

'Why do you ask that?' He, too, was leaning against the totem.

'Because your eyes always light up when you say Seattle.'

'I have a lot of work to do up here.' Since he was looking directly at her as he said this, he could not escape seeing in her eyes a sudden expression of dismay, and when he turned to see what had alarmed her, he found Sam Bigears and Ah Ting heading right for him.

'Hello!' Sam called as if nothing had happened. 'You know Ah Ting. I sail him to Juneau tomorrow.'

Tom was flabbergasted by at least half a dozen surprises cascading down on him, but he tried to avoid challenging Ah Ting or Sam or Nancy, who had lied to him so outrageously. Swallowing hard, he asked: 'What will he do in Juneau?' and Sam said: 'You know. Like what I did. Every town needs men to fix things.'

'He's very good at that,' Tom said weakly. 'But I'm sure he knows Chinese can't live in Alaska.'

'He won't be Chinese,' Sam said. 'He'll be workman everybody will need.' He looked admiringly at this courageous Oriental, laughed, and said: 'I tell him nobody notice if he cut off damned pigtail. But he show me how he tie it in knot under hat.'

'Why not cut it?' Nancy asked, relieved that Tom had not made a scene.

'Because it's part of him,' Sam said. 'Like those bangs are part of you.' Reaching out, he rumpled her hair and asked: 'Why you not cut your bangs?' and she said: 'Because all good Tlingits have bangs. You have them.'

Now Tom faced his Chinese foreman and asked: 'So you're going to Juneau?' and when Ah Ting nodded, Tom said, with his hand extended: 'I wish you luck.' Then he added: 'And if you don't have luck, come back. We'll always need you at the cannery.' But the way Ah Ting looked at him with half-smiling eyes and a sardonic grin twitching at his lips made Venn know that both of them knew the last statement had been hollow.

Impulsively Tom gripped the right hand of this very difficult man: 'I do wish you good luck, Ah Ting.' And without looking at Nancy, he hurried to his waiting boat.

S AM BIGEARS NOT only ferried his Chinese visitor to Juneau in late July 1904, but when they landed, Sam took Ah Ting to three different white men who had construction jobs under way, informing each that 'this here Chinaman good worker. Keep cannery Taku Inlet out of trouble.' And by the end of the week he had found Ah Ting a place to stay with a widow who took in boarders and who was willing to defer collecting rent until they started collecting wages. She did not have long to wait, for Ah Ting's skills were needed at many sites, and after four weeks on various jobs, workmen started the game that would be carried on in Juneau for as long as he resided there.

Some rowdy fellow would shout: 'Goddammit, you know we don't allow Chinks in here,' then he would playfully knock off the hat which Ah Ting wore outdoors and in, and down would tumble the coiled pigtail. Then some other man would grab the pigtail, not harmfully, and pretend to haul the Chinese out the door. He never protested. At the end he would recover his hat, show the men how he coiled his pigtail, and sit with them sharing their food. He never drank, but after hours he did enjoy any card game, and since he was brighter and quicker than most of the men he worked with, he usually won. The men liked playing with him, because at tense moments, when big money rested on the turn of a card, he would pray in Chinese and leap with joy if he won. But Ah Ting was a sensible man, and when he realized that he could win pretty much at will, he refrained from doing so. He wanted just enough to stay ahead, never enough to arouse envy.

While Ah Ting was establishing himself in Juneau, the only Chinese who managed to remain in Alaska, Tom Venn was quietly traversing the Pleiades estuary to visit with the Bigears family, and it did not matter much whom he found at home, for he took equal pleasure in talking with them all, even Mrs. Bigears. She was fun because of her propensity for humorous pantomimes of others' follies; she regaled Tom with legends of the Tlingits and accounts of this big man or that pompous woman who had come to grief, and although she spoke words he could not understand, he found that he could understand her imaginative gestures quite easily, and they laughed a good deal.

Her husband preferred talking politics and business, and his observations about the fumbling efforts of the new officials in Juneau were pithy. It was his opinion that Alaska had made an error in moving the capital from Sitka, but when Tom queried him on this, Nancy interrupted: 'It's only because the original Bigears lived in Sitka. Juneau is a lot better.'

But although Tom told himself that he didn't care which of the Bigears family was there when he called, he was really happiest when it was Nancy. She had matured in so many ways, especially in her ability to fathom the behavior of white men: 'They want to steal all Alaska, but they want to be sure they have God's blessing in doing it.'

'What do you mean?' Tom asked, and she said: 'What the principal says at school meetings, and what the minister says in church, they don't very often agree with what people actually do.'

'But what's this about stealing Alaska?' And she pointed out that Marvin Hoxey was back in town, with papers from the government that would give Ross & Raglan control of five more rivers.

As soon as Tom heard this, his interest focused not on the machinations of Hoxey, whom he despised, but on the locations which he proposed obtaining for R&R: 'What rivers did he have in mind? Did you hear any specific names?'

'What does it matter? It's stealing, that's all it is.'

'But it's very important to me. Because I'm supposed to build the new canneries, and I'd like to know where I'm to be working.'

Nancy could not understand how Tom could so loathe a man like Hoxey and at the same time be involved in the evil things he was doing: 'I don't like him, Tom, and I'm surprised you let him do business for you.'

But Tom was so concerned about his own future assignments, as if one bleak and lonely spot for a cannery was preferable to another, that he requisitioned one of Totem's small boats and had two workmen sail him to Juneau, where he learned what hotel Hoxey was staying in, and there, like some merchant trying to sell the great man a bolt of cloth for a new suit, he applied for an interview.

Hoxey, remembering well this capable young man from Nome and the R&R offices in Seattle, graciously received him, and when Tom wanted to know what sites he had acquired, Hoxey unrolled his maps and indicated the five proposed locations. 'I thought there were to be six,' Tom said, and Hoxey replied: 'There were. But a new firm called George T. Myers beat us to the best one of all in Sitkoh Bay. So we have five.' And with a forefinger neatly manicured, he indicated the remote and desolate spots at which huge installations requiring thousands of carpenters would soon be built, and from which millions of cans of salmon would be sent to all parts of the world.

'There's never been anything like it,' Hoxey said with unfeigned excitement. 'Always before . . . Take the cotton mills in New England—why, you had your factory near some town or even in the middle of it. Out here, look at our five spots! Not a settlement of any kind for fifty, eighty miles. Factories in the wilderness, and the obedient salmon swim right up to them.'

Tom asked about rumors that new laws might halt the placement of traps across waterways, or at least cut down the length of the jiggers, but Hoxey reassured him: 'It's our job to see that you men doing the work are not hampered.'

'No need for such laws,' Tom said. 'You should see how many salmon go through over the weekends.'

'There are always people,' Hoxey said expansively, 'who want to interrupt the flow of progress.' Then he asked: 'Will the new machine, what they call the Iron Chink, will it do the job?' And Tom spent the next minutes recounting his adventures with Ah Ting: 'If the Iron Chink does nothing else but get rid of the Chinese, it's worth the effort.'

When he returned to the cannery he had a fairly good idea of what his life was going to be like for the next years, and although he continued to long for Seattle, life on the frontier was not an unpleasing prospect; the challenges would be great and the rewards commensurate with his efforts. Besides, he found that he liked organizing men and equipment into a major operation in unlikely locations, and the grand openness of Alaska was alluring. But as a normal young man, he began contemplating how he was going to find a wife, and he began asking questions about how the managers of other canneries in southeastern Alaska handled this problem.

One white man who had worked at various sites said: 'The manager only has to be at the plant four or five months during the campaign. He's like a sailor. He can have a perfectly good marriage the other seven or eight months.' And another man told of two managers he knew who had brought their wives to small private houses attached to the plants: 'They brought their kids too, and they had a high old time.'

Without revealing any specific plans, Tom said to both men: 'I think I'd want my wife to live at the cannery,' and the first man issued a caution: 'You didn't ask me about that. But I saw a man down near Ketchikan try that once. A disaster. At the end of the campaign she ran off with the engineer in charge of the cooking boilers.'

But regardless of how the debate went, during his spare hours Tom traveled more and more frequently across the estuary to visit with the Bigears, and now he had his own skiff, which he operated with such skill that one day Sam said as he greeted him at the Bigears dock: 'You handle that like a Tlingit.'

'Is that good?'

'Best in Alaska. You ever see one of our great canoes?'

Tom had seen only the smaller ones at the potlatch, but some days later he had an opportunity, for scores of Indians gathered at the Bigears place, and on Saturday afternoon, when the trap was closed down for the weekend, two teams of Tlingits, each with a very long hand-hewn wooden canoe which could hold sixteen men seated on boards slung across the gunwales, held a set of races down Taku Inlet from the mouth of the Pleiades River, around the Walrus, and back to the starting line. As soon as the Chinese workers realized what was going on, they began placing very large bets, some preferring the canoe with a bright-red star on its prow, others backing the one with a carved eagle as figurehead.

Tom was surprised at the appearance of the Indians; they were darker than either Sam Bigears or his daughter, and shorter. But they were quite husky across the chest and their arms were powerful. They dressed almost formally, in heavy shoes, dark woolen trousers that looked rather bulky, and store-bought white shirts buttoned at the neck but without ties. However, when Sam Bigears shot his revolver to start the race, the Tlingits lost all sense of formality, digging their paddles deep in the water and pulling backward with brutal force.

Tom, standing with Nancy, could hardly believe it when Sam came over to say: 'See those two men back of eagle canoe? In very small canoe they paddle Seattle to Juneau. Right through high seas, rocks they couldn't see.'

When the races ended—the teams having been intermixed after each finish to make the betting more interesting—Tom stayed at the Bigears house, and in the shadow of the totem pole he met with the rowers, only a few of whom spoke English. 'They all understand,' Sam explained, 'just bashful with white man.' But as the evening progressed, several of the men became quite voluble, and learning that Tom was associated with the cannery, they wanted to know why Totem had decided to rely upon the trap rather than on fishermen like themselves. And as Tom started to give bland explanations, he found out that eleven of the men had formerly fished for the cannery but had been replaced by the trap.

'You come from Seattle. You take our salmon. You don't leave nothing.'

'But all Alaska will profit from the canneries,' Tom protested, but when Nancy heard this fatuous claim she burst out laughing, and the men joined.

That evening, inspired by the frivolity of the races and the good humor of the picnic that followed, Tom lingered with the Tlingits, and for the first time since he had arrived in Alaska he caught the full flavor of native life. He liked these men, their frank manners, their obvious love of their land, and he could see the stolid grandeur of their women, those round-faced, black-haired wives who remained observant in the background until some outrageous thing was said. Then they pounced on the man who made the foolish statement and goaded him until sometimes he actually ran off to escape their taunts. To be among a gathering of proud Tlingits was a challenging experience.

When the time came for the visitors who were staying with Bigears to drift off to bed, Tom and Nancy walked down to where his skiff had been dragged ashore, and there they stood for some time in the light of a late-rising moon. On the opposite side of the estuary rose the huge buildings of the cannery, only two lanterns throwing light at entrances. Tom had never before actually studied the immensity of this strange construction in the wilderness, and to see its many buildings now in silhouette, with the moon casting strange shadows from the east, was sobering.

'I never realized what a huge thing we've built,' he said. 'To be used for just a few months a year.'

'Like you said, it's a gold mine, except you mine silver, not gold.'

'What do you mean?' And before she could explain, he added: 'Oh yes! The silvery sides of the salmon. I never think of them that way. I see only those precious red sides of the sockeye. They're my salmon.'

He found no easy way to say goodnight, for having seen the Tlingit women at their best, he appreciated more than ever before the unique qualities of Nancy Bigears. He saw the beauty of her rounded face, the gamin appeal of her black bangs, the lilt in the way she walked. 'You are very close to the earth, aren't you?' he asked, and she said: 'I am the earth. You saw those men. They're the sea.'

Knowing that he must not do this thing, he caught her in his arms and they kissed, then kissed again. Finally she pushed him away: 'They told me you were in love with Mr. Ross's daughter.'

'Who told you that?'

'Everybody knows everything. They told me that you had paddled over to talk with Mr. Hoxey. To steal more rivers from us.' She drew away, leaning against a spruce tree that edged the water. 'There's no hope for you and me, Tom. I saw that tonight.'

'But I love you more tonight than ever before,' he protested, and she said with that frightening clarity which Indian girls like her often commanded: 'You saw us for the first time as human beings. It was the others you saw, not me.' And then she quietly stepped forward and kissed him gently on the cheek: 'I shall always love you, Tom. But we both have many things to do, and they will take us far apart.' With that, she went swinging back to her house, where her father and three cronies were singing in the moonlight.

A GYRE IS a massive body of seawater which retains its own peculiar characteristics and circular motion, even though it is an integral part of the great ocean which surrounds it. The name, pronounced *jire*, comes from the same root as *gyrate* and *gyroscope* and obviously pertains to the circular or spiral motion of the water. How a gyre is able to maintain its identity within the bosom of a tumultuous ocean poses an interesting problem whose unraveling carries one back to the beginnings of the universe. Certainly, in our day, the great Japan Current sweeps its warm waters from Japan across the northern reaches of the Pacific to the coasts of Alaska, Canada and Oregon, modifying those climates and bringing much rain. But this and all other ocean currents have been set in motion by planetary winds created by the differential heating of various latitudinal belts, and this is caused by the earth's spin, which was set in primordial motion when a diffuse nebular cloud coalesced into our solar system. This carries us all the way back to the original Big Bang which started our particular universe on its way.

A gyre, then, is a big whirl which generates at its edges smaller whirls whose motion increases its viscosity, forming a kind of protective barrier about the parent gyre, which can then maintain its integrity eon after eon. One professor of oceanography, name now unknown, striving to help his students grasp this beautiful concept, offered them a jingle:

> Big whirls make little whirls
> That feed on their velocity.
> Little whirls make lesser whirls
> And so on to viscosity.

The Pacific houses many of these self-preserving gyres, one of the most important being the Alaskan, which dominates the area just south of the Aleutian Islands. Reaching more than two thousand fluctuating miles from east to west, four hundred variable miles from north to south, it forms a unique body of water whose temperature and abundant food supply make it irresistible to the salmon bred in Alaska and Canada. This gyre circulates in a vast counterclockwise motion and the sockeye like Nerka who enter it swim with the current in this unvarying counterclockwise direction. Of course, the very fine salmon bred in Japan start from a contrary orientation, so they swim their ordained route clockwise, against the movement of the gyre. In doing so, they repeatedly pass through the larger number of Alaskan salmon, forming for a few hours a huge conglomeration of one of the world's most valuable fish.

For two years, starting in 1904, Nerka, accompanied by the remaining eleven survivors of his group of four thousand sockeye, swam in the Alaskan Gyre, eating and being eaten in the rich food chain of the North Pacific. Mammoth whales would swim past, their cavernous mouths able to sweep in whole schools of salmon. Seals, who had a predilection for salmon, sped through the gyre decimating the ranks. Birds attacked from the sky, and from the deeper waters came big fish like tuna, pollock and swordfish to feed upon the salmon. Each day consisted of a ten-mile swim with the current in an ocean literally teeming with enemies, and in this perpetual struggle the salmon that survived grew strong. Nerka was now about twenty-five inches long, seven pounds in weight, and although he looked almost immature in comparison with the huge king salmon of the Pacific or the even larger members of the salmon family living in the Atlantic, of his type he was becoming a superb specimen.

The reddish color of his flesh stemmed in part from his love for shrimp, which he devoured in huge quantities, although he also fed upon the larger forms of plankton, gradually shifting to squid and small fish. He lived, as one can deduce from these details of his existence, in a mid-range of the ocean hierarchies. Too big to be an automatic prey of the seal and the orca whale, he was at the same time too small to be a major predator. He was a tough, self-reliant master of the deep.

During his three and a half irregular circuits of the Alaskan Gyre, Nerka would cover a total of about ten thousand miles, sometimes swimming largely alone, at other periods finding himself in the midst of an enormous concentration. For example, when he reached the halfway point, where sockeye more mature than he began to break away and head back to their home streams, he was drifting along the lower edges of the Aleutian chain when a massive concentration of salmon composed of all five Alaskan types—king, chum, pink, coho and sockeye—began to form, and it grew until it contained about thirty million fish, swimming in the same counterclockwise direction and feeding upon whatever they encountered.

But now a large collection of seals heading for their breeding grounds in the Arctic Ocean came rampaging through the middle of the aggregation, devouring salmon at a rate that would have exterminated a less numerous fish. Two female seals swimming with amazing speed came right at Nerka, who sensed that he was doomed, but with a sudden twist he dove. The two seals had to swerve to avoid colliding, and he escaped, but from his vantage point below the turmoil he witnessed the devastation the seals wrought. Thousands of mature salmon perished in that ruthless onslaught, but after two days the seals passed beyond the outer fringes and continued on their journey north. But Nerka's group was now down to nine.

Nerka was almost an automatic creature, for he behaved in obedience to impulses programmed into his being half a million years earlier. For example, in these years when he thrived in the Alaskan Gyre he lived as if he belonged there forever, and in his sport with other fish and his adventures with those larger mammals that were trying to eat him he behaved as if he had never known any other type of life. He could not remember ever having lived in fresh water, and were he suddenly to be thrown back into it, he would not have been able to adjust: he was a creature of the gyre as irrevocably as if he had been born within its confines.

But in his second year in the great Alaskan Gyre a genetically driven change occurred in Nerka, compelling him to seek out his natal stream above Lake Pleiades. And now a complex homing mechanism, still not fully understood by scientists, came into play to guide him over thousands of miles to that one stream along the Alaskan coast. Though employing this inherited memory for the first time in his own life, Nerka did so instinctively and expertly, and thus began his journey home.

The clues guiding Nerka were subtle: minute shifts in water temperature triggered his response, or it could have been electromagnetic changes. Certainly, as he approached the coast his sense of smell, among the most sensitive in all the world's animals, detected trace chemical markers similar to those in his own Pleiades. This chemical distinction could have been a difference of less than one part in a billion, but there it was. Its influence persisted and grew, guiding Nerka ever more compellingly to his home waters. It is one of the strangest manifestations of nature, this minute message sent through the waters of the world to guide a wandering salmon back to his natal stream.

THE 1905 SUMMER campaign was the last that Tom Venn would spend at the Totem Cannery, since Mr. Ross wanted him to supervise launching the new R&R cannery north of Ketchikan. Tom would have enjoyed making the acquaintance of that distinctive area of Alaska, but the professors who were installing the Iron Chink machines at Totem insisted that a practiced hand like Tom remain there to handle the problems that would inevitably arise when instructing a new work force in such a radical procedure.

For a host of reasons the summer was unforgettable. Tom had spent much of February in Seattle with the Rosses, and had received intimations from both of Lydia's parents and from Lydia herself that as soon as she finished two years of university it might be possible to consider marriage. As if to demonstrate the seriousness of this possibility, in July, after the Iron Chinks were operating at top speed and with an efficiency not even their inventors had envisioned, Mrs. Ross and Lydia sailed to Taku Inlet aboard the Canadian luxury vessel *Montreal Queen*, and Tom had the pleasure of showing them around the cannery.

'I'm really surprised,' Mrs. Ross said. 'From the tales I'd heard Malcolm and you tell, I'd expected to see hundreds of Chinese, and I find none.'

'Well,' he reminded her, 'didn't you see us studying the Iron Chink that day in your sitting room?'

'That little thing, Tom? It was just a model, trivial, really. I never visualized it as a mechanical monster like this.'

He guided Mrs. Ross and Lydia to one side as he explained the workings: 'This one machine, and we have these three here, the other two slightly improved on this one . . .' He lost the thread of his reasoning. 'Well, as you can see, this Iron Chink as we call it has the capacity to handle a fish a second, but we don't like to run it that fast. At the speed you see, it can take care of more than two thousand salmon an hour.'

'Where do you get them all?'

From the window he showed the women the enlarged trap in the center of the inlet with its very long jiggers: 'We catch a lot of fish down there. See how the baskets are winched up out of the holding pen . . . And you can't see it, but another winch at the end of our dock lifts them right up to that conveyor over there.'

He showed them how, after the salmon were cleaned and slimed by the Iron

Chink, the raw flesh, bones and all, was cut by fast-moving machines into appetizing chunks which fitted precisely the famous 'tall can' designed for exactly one pound of fish and recognized worldwide.

'You can it raw?' Lydia asked, and he said: 'We sure do!' and he showed them how the filled cans passed under a machine which clamped the lid into place.

'That isn't safe,' Lydia said. 'There's air in there, and bacteria.'

'There sure is,' Tom agreed. 'As a matter of fact, there's even a small hole in the lid, but look what happens next!' And proudly he showed them a standard canning device which his cannery had improved upon: 'The filled can with a hole in its lid comes here, and a vacuum expels all the air that Lydia is worried about, and as soon as that happens, this next machine drops down this dab of solder, and whango! the salmon is locked in an airtight can.'

He then took them to another building where sixteen massive steam retorts stood in a row, huge ovens, really, into which whole trolley cars loaded with cans of salmon could be wheeled. When the massive iron doors clanged shut, whistling steam under great pressure was let into the ovens, and for a hundred and five minutes the salmon were cooked until even the succulent bones were edible.

'I always ask for the part with the bones,' Lydia said as they moved to a third huge building, in which so many unlabeled cans of cooked salmon were stored that the effect was dazzling. At the far end, teams of women, recently employed, applied the distinctive Totem label, now well regarded by better stores throughout the nation, since its cans carried only the superior pink sockeye of Taku Inlet.

Deftly snatching one of the finished cans from the production line, Tom held it before Mrs. Ross and said with pride: 'Some woman in Liverpool or Boston is going to appreciate this can when it reaches her kitchen. We do a good job here.'

Thousands of wooden boxes, each holding forty-eight cans of Totem salmon, two tiers of twenty-four each to the box, waited to be filled or stood ready for shipment south on an R&R steamer. 'How many boxes do you ship a year?' Mrs. Ross asked, and Tom replied: 'About forty thousand.'

'My goodness, that's a lot of salmon,' and Tom assured her: 'There's a lot out there.'

The Ross women could stay only two days, and then they had to leave by fast boat to catch the *Montreal Queen* as it sailed from Juneau. As they said farewell, they both invited Tom to spend Christmas with them this year, and once more Lydia kissed him warmly as they parted, a fact which would find its way to Nancy Bigears across the estuary.

Some days after they were gone, a most amusing contretemps occurred, for one of the Iron Chinks became temperamental, cutting heads and tails in a way that wasted half the salmon and gutting it so that the backbone was whisked away while the entrails remained attached, partially spilling out of the fish and making a gruesome mess. Despite his normal skill at handling emergencies, Tom was unable to correct the malperformance, and it looked as if he would have to send to Seattle for Dr. Whitman, but one of his workmen suggested that he see if Sam Bigears could do the job: 'He's very good with machines.' But when Sam sailed over to look at the Iron Chink he said: 'Too complicated. But I know man who fix.'

'Who?' Tom asked, and he was chagrined when Sam replied: 'Ah Ting.' However, Sam was so insistent that he took it upon himself to sail to Juneau to fetch the Chinese miracle worker, and Ah Ting saw nothing unpalatable in going back to work on the machine which had displaced him and the other Chinese.

Tom's reception of him at the dock was decidedly cool, which gave Ah Ting no concern. Smiling his buck-toothed smile as always, he lugged his tool kit into the former cutting shed where for two years he had reigned. 'Well!' he said as he watched the two functioning Iron Chinks slicing their way through hundreds of salmon. 'Good machine I think. Now what's wrong?'

Tom ordered his men to run half a dozen salmon through the malfunctioning machine, and in that first minute Ah Ting spotted the error, but how to correct it he could not determine so quickly. In fact, it took him about two hours to fix what at first had seemed only a simple problem, and as he lay on a piece of bagging under the Iron Chink he called to Tom: 'Much better this rod go over here,' but Tom shouted: 'Don't change anything!' However, Ah Ting had detected a much superior way to relay power to the cutting knives and at the same time protect them from what had disabled the machine. So without seeking further permission, he began hammering and sawing and making such a racket that Tom became distraught, but after some fifteen minutes of this, Ah Ting climbed out from underneath and said, with his usual confident grin: 'All right now. You want me fix other two?'

'No!' Tom said, and after paying Ah Ting, he shoved him along to Sam Bigears' waiting skiff. However, some weeks later, one of the other machines broke down in much the same way, and back came Ah Ting to correct the mistake in its design. This time Tom looked the other way when the clever Chinese crawled under the third machine and corrected it too. That night he drafted a letter to Starling and Whitman in Seattle, advising them that he had learned through hard experience that the power transfer under the knives of their Iron Chink could be much improved if they made the changes he outlined in the drawings which accompanied his note.

I N LATE JULY all kinds of good things seemed to happen, each more pleasing than the preceding. At the government offices in Juneau, where he had gone to consult with officials about extending the jiggers even farther across the inlet, Tom was working over maps when he heard a familiar voice, and when he turned to see who it was, there stood Reverend Lars Skjellerup of the Presbyterian Mission in Barrow, who had come south with his pretty Virginia wife to plead with the government to send schoolteachers, not to the mission, where he and his wife were doing a creditable job with the money he had earned in the gold fields of Nome, but to the Eskimos of the Barrow area in general.

Tom invited the Skjellerups to lunch, where he realized for the first time that one of the greatest joys of a human life is to learn, after a prolonged absence, how people with whom one had shared dangers were doing. Now, as he listened to the adventures of this man he had known so intimately in troubled days, he became almost effusive in his desire to recall old times.

'Lars, you'll never in a hundred years know who sat last year in that very chair you're in. He's advising our firm on land acquisitions.'

'Matthew Murphy?'

'No, but I'd sure like to see him. Hold on to your hat. It was Marvin Hoxey.'

With a shout that could be heard across the room, Skjellerup jumped up from the chair and cried: 'Is he out of jail?' and both he and his wife sat dumfounded as Tom told them how Hoxey had become an even greater force in Washington and the legislative adviser to Ross & Raglan.

He spent three days with the Skjellerups, learning how a man with no religious education could suddenly find himself a missionary in a frozen land, but he was even more impressed by Mrs. Skjellerup, who had reached that distant, frozen mission in such a curious way: 'You must have been very brave to go to the end of the earth where one winter night is three months long,' and she laughed off the suggestion: 'I'd be just as happy in Fiji.'

The idea astounded him. He knew nothing of Fiji and he supposed she didn't either, but it was about as far away from Barrow and the arctic ice as one could get: 'Do you mean that?'

'Of course I do. And it's the truth. Adventure. Hard work. Seeing good results. That's why we're put on earth.'

'Are you religious?' he asked. 'I mean, do you believe in God?'

'My wife and I believe in work,' answered the man who had driven reindeer to the top of the world, 'and I think that God does too.'

'Yes,' his wife broke in. 'I believe in God. I prefer to see Him as an old man with white hair who sits on a throne about six miles higher than the clouds. He sits there with a big book and writes down everything we do, but fortunately for people like me, He has very poor eyesight. You see, He's been writing like that for a good many years.'

The Skjellerups were well on their way back to Barrow, where the July midnights were a silvery gray, when Tom started for Taku Inlet, and as he was leaving Juneau's Occidental Hotel, he saw coming up the street from the wharf seven of the most improbable citizens of Alaska. In the forefront, giving orders as usual, came A. L. Arkikov, the Siberian reindeer herder, with his wife and three children, all of them wearing the winter clothing of Siberia. Behind them came two whom Tom had hoped to meet again more than anyone he had ever known, Matthew Murphy and his companion Missy Peckham, and *their* baby daughter.

He saw them before they saw him, and he ran quickly down the hotel steps, dashed into the street, and grasped Arkikov by the waist, dancing him about before any of the newcomers could identify him. Then, as he whirled past, Missy saw him, and she stopped dead in the street, put her hands to her mouth, and fought back tears. Murphy, when he recognized this stranger, joined the dance, and for some minutes, there in front of Juneau's major hotel, the four veterans of the gold fields celebrated in noisy joy.

Insisting that they all accompany him to the dining room, Tom ordered a feast, and once more he posed his riddle: 'Who do you think was sitting in that chair you're in, Missy, not too long ago?'

Lowering her gaze, she looked at Tom from beneath her dark eyebrows and asked: 'Not that son-of-a-bitch Marvin Hoxey?' and when Tom nodded enthusiastically, as if Hoxey were an old friend, Missy and Matt and Arkikov guffawed. So for the next hour they compared notes on Hoxey and his disciple Judge Grant, and the others became hilarious when they learned that the judge was now a respected member of the Iowa bench. 'Hooray for justice!' Matt cried, and the people who had suffered so grievously from the misbehavior of Hoxey and Grant laughed at the pretensions of those two scoundrels, and the bitterness of those frantic days was lost in merriment, after which they filled in the details of the last few years for one another.

Tom learned that Missy, Matt and Arkikov had decided that there was not much future in Nome, now that the seashore provided no more easy gold. 'We thought,' said Missy, 'that the future of Alaska would be decided here in Juneau, and we wanted to be a part of it.'

'What part?'

'Who knows? Did you expect to be running a salmon cannery?'

'Never came into my head. But neither did running a restaurant along the banks of the Yukon.'

'Weren't they the best pancakes? That John Klope!'

At the mention of their benefactor, Missy and Tom fell silent, and Matt proposed a toast to the man who had finally found his gold mine. And then Missy started to laugh, and she explained to the Arkikovs: 'John Klope had this marvelous sourdough, and I would mix up and cook maybe forty, maybe fifty pancakes, stack them outside in twenty-below and allow them to freeze. Anybody came in hungry, he took one of my frozen cakes, thawed it out, and had a good meal.'

Then she asked Tom: 'What do you suppose we brought to Juneau with us. Yep, that jar of sourdough. You're all invited to come over when we find a house.'

'But what are you going to do here in Juneau?' cautious Tom asked, and both she and Arkikov replied: 'Something will turn up.'

THE NEXT VISITOR to the Juneau area came on a more sober mission. Tom was in his office at the cannery during the final week of the campaign, casting up preliminary estimates of how the season had gone. His carpenters had built about fifty thousand boxes, of which more than forty-four thousand would be filled by the end of the run. At forty-eight #1 cans to the box, that meant that Totem would be shipping out well over two million individual cans. And since each sockeye, by no means the largest of the salmon family, would fill about three and a half cans, Totem had handled over six hundred thousand fish.

'The Iron Chink certainly did the job,' Tom said as he pushed back his calculations. 'We'll get about four cents a can and the final customer will pay about sixteen cents. Nowhere else can she get a food bargain like that.' The industry had recently published a widely circulated brochure which showed that salmon could provide the basic food requirement at twelve cents a pound, chicken at twenty-two cents, steak at thirty-three, and eggs at thirty-six, but as Tom conceded: 'That's the cheaper types of salmon. But even at sixteen cents a pound, our choice sockeye will be the housewife's best bargain.' He closed his calculations with a guess that for the 1905 campaign, Totem Cannery would show a profit of at least seventy thousand dollars, a stupendous sum for those days.

He was congratulating himself when he saw to his surprise that the _Montreal Queen_ was disembarking passengers at the Totem dock, and this was so unusual that he ran from his office to see what was happening. When he reached the dock he saw coming toward him a tall gentleman dressed in the handsome uniform with which Tom had been so familiar during the Klondike days. It was the uniform of the North West Mounted Police and the man wearing it was Sergeant Will Kirby, behind whom trailed a committee of five men in rather formal business suits.

As soon as Tom recognized Kirby, he ran forward to greet him, but to his surprise Will drew back, maintaining his posture of stiff formality: 'Mr. Venn, you are the manager of this cannery, are you not?'

Astonished at his friend's rigid decorum, Tom admitted that he was, whereupon one of the other men stepped forward to introduce himself: 'I am Sir Thomas Washburn, Canadian government. And these are members of our Fisheries Commission. I presume you've received word from Washington about our visit?'

'I know nothing.'

'I'm sure papers are on their way. Captain Kirby will show you our credentials when we're seated. And I assure you, we're here at the invitation of your government.' And when the committee was seated in the office, Kirby placed before Tom documents signed by officials in Washington asking all cannery operators in Alaska waters to cooperate with this 'commission of experts from our good neighbor Canada.'

'The purpose of our visit,' Sir Thomas said, 'is to ascertain the effect of your new traps on the movement of salmon up and down the various rivers, which, as you know, all start deep in Canada and run only short distances in Alaska. Your Taku River is a prime example of what we mean. May I show you our map?'

When Tom nodded, Sir Thomas asked Kirby to let Mr. Venn see the map which delineated the situation, but as soon as the map was unrolled, one of the committee members laughed: 'You've got the Stikine, Kirby,' and when Tom looked more closely he saw that the man was right. This map showed the Stikine River, which ran for many miles in Canada before spending less than twenty-five miles in Alaska to join the sea near Wrangell.

'Wait a minute!' Sir Thomas interrupted. 'Leave the map, Kirby. It will explain our problems rather nicely, I think.' And with his pencil he traced out the far reaches of the Stikine River system, indicating the many lakes it fed and the almost endless tributaries in which salmon bred. 'It's a salmon empire, you might say,' he concluded as he indicated the extremely brief length of the river in Alaska. 'But any dam or dams improperly placed in your small territory forcefully affects all of this.' Leaning back as if he had proved his point, he instructed Kirby to lay out the map of the Taku River system, and when this complicated network of rivers, creeks and lakes was displayed, even Tom had to admit that the relative situations were the same: 'I see what you mean, Sir Thomas. A great deal in Canada, much less in Alaska.' But he added quickly: 'However, as you must already know, our trap does not prevent the return of spawning salmon to Canada.'

Very dryly Sir Thomas said: 'I had rather thought that it did,' but Tom pointed out: 'To protect you, we keep the trap open, totally free passage, every weekend,' and Sir Thomas said: 'I'm sure that helps somewhat.' He paused just a moment, then added: 'Our task is to ascertain whether it helps enough.'

Since the canneries had guesthouses in which visitors and company inspectors could be made reasonably comfortable, Tom was quick to extend an invitation to the committee to remain overnight at Totem, but Sir Thomas said: 'I'm afraid we shall have to remain three days. We want to see how the weekend opening affects the fish,' and he directed Kirby to fetch their bags.

They spent the rest of Friday inspecting the trap itself and comparing the eastern jigger, which was permanently installed by means of pilings driven into the bottom, with the western jigger, which merely floated, and they were amazed that the latter seemed to be as effective as the former. They also checked, with some dismay, the number of salmon that drowned in the holding pen and were not impressed when Tom tried to dismiss the loss as relatively trivial.

When they inquired as to how many salmon Totem Cannery took out of the Taku system each summer, they were not startled by the total, some six hundred thousand, for as one of their experts said: 'Quite reasonable, provided enough are allowed to get through the trap to spawn,' and then he spotted a problem about which Sam Bigears had often worried: 'But the placement of your trap means that even if enough do get through on the weekends to supply the Canadian needs, it looks to me as if your Pleiades River is pretty well cut off from its replenishment,' and Tom said with a show of assurance: 'I'm sure enough go up that river, too.'

On Saturday afternoon the entire commission, including Captain Kirby, was in small boats watching the transit of salmon past the trap and under the jiggers, and so many handsome fish swam past, only a few inches underwater and therefore clearly visible, that Sir Thomas had to admit: 'Impressive, truly impressive,' and one of his team said: 'Problem's simple. Train the salmon to swim upstream only on Sundays,' and when the laughter subsided, Tom sought to allay the doubts that had bothered the other team to whom he had explained the system: 'You realize, gentlemen, that when the young salmon swim down from your rivers to reach the sea, they encounter no problems. Entirely different season, so the traps aren't operating.'

On Sunday morning, after another visit to the trap, the Canadians got down to business, and with their map on Tom's desk they demanded to know: 'What will you canners in Alaska be doing to protect our Canadian breeding grounds?' and Tom answered flatly: 'The canneries are here, Sir Thomas. In all your area' —he spread his hands over the Canadian part of the map—'you haven't a single cannery. You don't need the salmon. We do.'

Sir Thomas did not flinch: 'For the present what you say seems to be correct. But we must also consider the future when there will be many Canadians in these parts. Then an assured supply of salmon will be most important, and if you Alaskans prevent or destroy that supply, you will be doing us grave wrong.'

Tom would concede nothing: 'Throughout Alaska we shut down the traps, as you've seen. I'm positive enough fish get through.'

'But the wastage! The dead salmon.'

'Not excessive when you consider the numbers.'

Sir Thomas was somewhat irritated to be arguing with so young a man, but he had to be impressed favorably by Tom's ability to defend his company's interests, so after stating most emphatically Canada's intention to seek an international agreement protecting her interests in the salmon trade, he listened politely as Tom rebutted his arguments and said that he doubted the United States would ever submit to such an agreement.

Unwilling to prolong the debate when the positions were so contrary, Sir Thomas asked Kirby to pass him another file, and after searching through its papers, he found the document he wanted: 'Mr. Venn, do you happen to know a Mr. Marvin Hoxey?'

The surprise on Tom's face proved that he did, and the Canadian continued: 'He seems to be our principal stumbling block in Washington. Keeps citing statistics at us demolishing all our claims. We suspect his data are fraudulent. Can you tell us anything about him? Is he really an expert in these matters?'

Without blinking, Tom said: 'He certainly is.'

'Has he inspected these traps? I mean, your trap in particular?'

'He has.'

Sir Thomas said nothing, but he did ask for another paper, which he studied for some moments as if calculating how to use its information. Finally he cleared his throat, leaned forward, and asked in a most conciliatory voice:

'Now, is it not true, Mr. Venn, that in the Alaskan city of Nome in the year . . . Let us see, could it have been 1900? Yes, I believe it was. Were you then acquainted with Mr. Hoxey?'

'I was.'

'And did you not offer testimony that helped send him to prison?'

Very weakly Tom replied: 'I did.' But then quickly added: 'But you must also know that Mr. Hoxey received a full pardon from the President himself. It was all a political mistake.'

'I'm sure it was,' Sir Thomas said, and he dropped the matter.

It was not till late Sunday evening that Tom found a chance to talk alone with Captain Kirby, who, after exchanging reminiscences of the old days, asked frankly: 'Tom, what kind of man is Hoxey? He's giving us a lot of trouble.'

'Confidential?'

'Like in the old days.'

'You can use the information, but don't say I told you.'

'I think you know you can trust me.'

Looking Kirby straight in the eye, Tom said: 'If he had shown up when you and I were on the Klondike, after two days you'd have shot him.'

No more was said on that subject, but when the conversation returned to the old days, Tom said: 'You'd never guess who's in Juneau,' and when Kirby said he had no idea, Tom said: 'Missy Peckham!' and the two men leaned back and visualized that plucky woman climbing to the top of Chilkoot Pass, where she had first met Kirby. And they spoke of her whizzing down the snowy pass on the shovel, and of building their boat and of the days in the tent at Dawson and on Bonanza Creek.

'She never found any gold, did she?' Kirby asked, expressing regret for Missy's bad luck, and Tom said: 'She never did.'

'Damn,' Kirby said, banging his fist on the table. 'That woman has had bad luck all the way.'

'Not so bad,' and very quietly Tom told of how John Klope had come by Nome one day, bringing great gifts of gold to Missy, to Murphy and to himself.

'Well, I am glad. You say she's in Juneau?'

'Yes. She and Murphy told me they were going to settle there.'

'Doing what?'

'They had no idea. But knowing Missy, you can be sure it'll be something lively.'

Kirby considered this for a moment, then clapped his hands and asked: 'Tom, could you accompany us to Juneau? We have a boat picking us up tomorrow morning.' Tom hesitated, but Kirby persisted: 'If it's a problem with your boss in Seattle, I'll have Sir Thomas insist that you continue the interviews there. In writing.'

In the morning Kirby did deliver a formal request that Thomas Venn, manager-on-site of Totem Cannery, accompany the Canadian Fisheries Commission for further consultations in Juneau, and during the speedy trip to the capital Sir Thomas said: 'Mr. Venn, if I were the owner of a cannery, I'd want you for my manager.' Then he added: 'But you are dreadfully wrong in your interpretation of Canada's interest in this matter. We shall never rest till we arrange an equitable solution to the problem.' He did not inquire as to why Kirby had wanted him in Juneau, but when they reached the Occidental Hotel and he saw the delight with which the two younger men greeted the woman staying there with her husband and daughter, he judged that the reasons were substantial.

It was an emotional reunion, one in which Matt Murphy participated as eagerly as the other three. They had known heady days, vast disappointments. Then, in due course, the name of Marvin Hoxey came up, and Matt and Missy revealed the whole sickening story in such lurid detail that Kirby had to ask: 'Tom, how can you do business with such a man?' and Tom could only reply: 'I don't. The company does.'

'And you feel you have to be loyal to the company?'

'I do.'

Kirby said nothing, for he felt that he had to be loyal to the Mounted Police, and he knew the pressures that any kind of loyalty can exert. In his case the pressures were legitimate, those of the Canadian government; in Tom's case, illegitimate, as everything associated with Marvin Hoxey had to be. But thoughtful men acknowledged pressure, good or bad, and responded to it in different ways.

But now the conversation turned to the purpose of the Canadian visit, with Missy showing herself to be more than passively interested in the salmon fisheries, and gradually the facts unfolded: 'That's part of the reason Matt and I came down here. I don't mean salmon. I mean the rights of native people.'

'What do you mean by that?' Kirby asked, and she explained: 'Will, wherever we've been, Canada or Alaska, we've seen natives getting the bad deal. You ought to see Nome.'

'I can imagine.'

'And it seemed to Matt and me, seeing that we came from what you might call native Irish and native American stock . . . well, it seemed to us that we ought to be on the side of the natives. We ought to help them look after themselves better than they're doing now.'

Aware that he might be speaking against his own interests, Tom said impulsively: 'Isn't that somethin'! When Lars Skjellerup was down here a few weeks ago, he was pleading with the government for native schools. He said almost the same thing you did, Missy.'

'What do you mean?' Kirby asked as he turned to face the woman to whom he had once been so deeply attached. Now they met as mature adults, each striving to make his world a more orderly place.

Encouraged by his smile, Missy for the first time voiced in public the principles which would guide the remainder of her life: 'I see an Alaska which is not dominated by rich men in Seattle. I want an Alaska which has self-rule, its own laws, its own freedoms.'

Here she became almost vehement: 'Do you know that Matt and I can't buy land in Juneau? Why? Because the Alaska government hasn't been allowed to pass land laws, and the United States government won't.'

She passed from this grievance, one which infuriated all Alaskans, since it inhibited normal civic growth, to the broader canvas: 'We have been looking into the same problems you've come here to study, Kirby.' She stopped there, and Kirby asked: 'And what have you two concluded?' and she said: 'That all the salmon in these waters should be devoted to the welfare of Alaska, not to businessmen in Seattle.'

Kirby laughed and pointed to Tom: 'She's speaking about you.'

'No, I mean it. More than thirty canneries like Tom's operated this summer, I've found, and not one of them leaves a penny behind for us Alaskans.' Prior to that statement she had spoken of Alaskans as *they*, as if she wanted to protect *their* rights, but now, subtly, she had herself become an Alaskan, and so she would remain.

At the end of her animated discourse, Kirby asked: 'Does this make you and your old friend Tom enemies?' and she said: 'If he continues to work for Seattle businessmen, political enemies, yes,' and before anyone could respond, Kirby turned to beckon to Sir Thomas Washburn, saying: 'Sir Thomas, you ought to listen to this lady,' and when the chairman of the commission did, he was astounded at how close her opinions were to his: 'Young woman, you've quite a head on your shoulders.'

'I fought these battles in Chicago. Among the hopeless, but never without hope.'

They spoke for a long time, together, as if the others were not there, and the more they revealed of their aspirations the more clearly Tom Venn saw that they could attain what they wanted only at the expense of his employer, Malcolm Ross. Finally, somewhat provoked, he broke in: 'Sir Thomas, with your position and all that, how can you feel the way you do?' and the Canadian gentleman laughed: 'My father ran a little store in Saskatchewan. He would have applauded what this young woman is saying, because he used to tell me the same things.' And he turned abruptly away from Tom to resume his discussion with Missy.

T OM HAD LOOKED forward to spending Christmas with the Rosses, and renewing his friendship with Lydia. But though she greeted him warmly, he soon found that she was deeply involved with a rather polished young man of twenty-two named Horace whom she had met at the university. She seemed not to be actually engaged to him, but she had obligated herself to attend quite a few holiday functions with him. By no means did she cut Tom off, but she was so busy that he often found himself alone with her parents or with other older members of the firm.

From them he learned how profitable the 1905 season had been, how generously the United States Congress had treated the Seattle interests, and how well the plans for the new cannery at Ketchikan were progressing. He learned that he would definitely be in charge of its construction, starting in mid-January, and he surprised them with the information that he was planning to buy a home in Juneau. When they asked why, in voices intended to dissuade him, he said: 'I like the town. It has great character and the setting is almost as good as Seattle's. Besides, it's now the capital.'

A vice-president of R&R said: 'But if you work for us, you have to move around a good deal. We have a lot more canneries in the planning stage, and you're our expert on making them work,' and Tom said: 'I want the job, but I also want a home,' and he reminded them of how the normal cannery year went: 'Two months preparation, three months working like a dog, one month to close down, and six months to live. I don't want to spend those six months locked up on some remote spot at the edge of the woods.'

'You're right,' the vice-president admitted. 'And I suppose that pretty soon you'll want to get married. Your wife will probably think the way you do.'

The mention of marriage caused an uneasy gap in the conversation, and later that night when the other guests had gone, Mrs. Ross went out of her way to assure Tom that Lydia still thought highly of him and he must excuse her near-rudeness in spending so much time with Horace and so little with him. When she said: 'It's to be expected, the excitement of college and all that,' he told her: 'I understand.'

But this winter there were few walks to the hill with Lydia, and practically no extended conversations on even trivial matters, let alone important ones. His disappointment led to two conclusions: I've never met a woman more sensible than Mrs. Ross. If she's a sample of what Lydia will be at her age . . . mmmmm! and It looks as if Lydia has moved on to a different level. He did not try to pin down what that level might be or what the obvious difference consisted of, but he had a strong feeling that he had lost her, and not even the gay festivities of a Seattle Christmas Eve or the warm celebrations of the day itself modified his conclusions. He was out of place and he knew it.

Cutting short his vacation, he offered the excuse that he had to get back to Juneau to prepare for the move to Ketchikan, and when he departed, the older Rosses noted without surprise that this time their daughter did not kiss him goodbye.

When he returned to Juneau he encountered the contradiction to which Missy had referred in their meeting with Captain Kirby: Alaska had almost unlimited land, but the four southern towns of Juneau, Sitka, Ketchikan and Wrangell existed in such a pinched condition, clinging to a mere foothold on the edge of the ocean, that they gave the impression of meanness and certainly a lack of spaciousness. In fact, usable land was so scarce and precious in Juneau that Tom was unable to find either a house already built or land on which to build, and although he liked the town and considered the mountains which edged it into the sea picturesque, he began to despair of ever finding a place there in which to live.

But since Juneau had a population of only sixteen hundred—many times bigger than either Ketchikan or Wrangell, both of which had far less than a thousand—he was constantly meeting old acquaintances when he was in town, and gradually they found for him a small selection of available houses. They also kept him advised of what was happening in the capital, and when with Missy's help Tom finally decided on a house being vacated by a sea captain, he was ready to make a down payment, but Sam Bigears protested vigorously: 'Tom! More better you look back of house?' and when he and Sam explored that area with some care, Tom saw what his friend was warning against, for the land rose precipitously, almost in the form of a cliff. Now, this was common in Juneau, where some of the streets leading in from the sea were not ordinary streets but wooden stairs climbing straight up. Indeed, to live in Juneau one had better have strong legs, because climbing up and down was a part of daily existence.

At first Tom was not worried about the steepness of the rise, but then Sam pointed to the serious problem. Down a ravine, whose end pointed directly at the house Tom was considering buying, loomed a bank of snow so huge that it could be expected at some time or other to launch an avalanche that might bury the house. 'Look over there,' Sam cautioned. 'Used to be house, but last year snow let loose. Poof! No more house. Same happen here, maybe.'

Some days after this meeting with Bigears, Nancy appeared in Juneau, eighteen years old and ready to finish her schooling. She was one of the very few Indian children who had progressed so far, and her teachers, one of whom Tom met at the hotel, said that she was a precious find: 'Most of the Indians drop out in the seventh or eighth grade, but Nancy has unusual abilities. She can sing with the best and she knows the old Indian dances, but she can also write acceptable papers and she has almost a hunger to know American history and how Alaska came to be what it is.' When Tom questioned another teacher, the man said: 'I'm the only man in the school, bar the principal, and I don't have much patience with these Indians. I want my kids to study, to make something of themselves, and almost no Indians respond to such discipline, so I pretty much ignore them. But this Nancy Bigears, she's as good as any of the white boys, maybe better. She ought to go to college.'

So Tom began to see her again, and on a totally different basis from before. She was now a town girl, dressing and acting like the other students, except that she had a powerful new sense of her capacities. She was studying American history and applying all its lessons to Alaska, and one day as she spoke of the injustices her land suffered, Tom said: 'You ought to meet my friend Missy. She's older but her ideas are a lot like yours.'

So one January day he invited them both to lunch, and they lingered over their meal so long that darkness descended over the mountains and Gastineau Channel was shrouded before they finished. They spoke of Eskimo and Tlingit tradition, of the difficulties brought by the ways of the white man, of land ownership, and of all the problems that rose to the surface if one lived very long in towns like Nome and Juneau. The two women did most of the talking, and what they said infuriated Tom occasionally, for they made men like him out to be the villains, and this he could not accept.

Once in his anger he voiced for the first time the attitude that he and most white men like him espoused: 'Time's wasting. Work's to be done. Maybe the Eskimo up in Barrow can adhere to the old ways. But the Indians elsewhere, all of them, had better enter the twentieth century, and fast.'

'And what, pray, do you mean by that?' Missy asked contentiously, and he was not loath to explain: 'There aren't many real Americans in Alaska yet, white men and women I mean, but the future of this land, believe me, is to become another Oregon, another Idaho. Indians should receive every consideration and certainly title to their lands, but they have no option but to enter the mainstream, forget their tribal customs, and beat us at our own games.' Then, taking Nancy's hands, he said: 'And this young lady is the one with the capacity to lead the way for her people.'

'I second that!' Missy said enthusiastically, and Tom added: 'Mr. Wetherill told me the other day that Nancy was so good in her studies, she should go to college next year. California or Washington, or even back east. Now, what do you think of that?'

He was astonished at what Missy thought: 'Tom, that's the wrong answer! Nancy does not need college any more than I did. Her job is to stay here in Alaska, make a place for herself, show others how to adjust. She could become the greatest woman in Alaska, and don't you and Mr. Wetherill send her off to the States to be ruined.'

Tom was prepared to argue that his approach was the one that would save the Indians, but he was prevented from voicing his opinion when Sam Bigears came to the hotel looking for his daughter: 'Some people are coming over to Harry's, and they want you to help.' Obediently she rose, thanked Tom for the lunch and Missy for her support, and when she was gone, Missy said: 'It will always be like that, I'm afraid. There will be a party somewhere, and that comes first.'

And then, as they sat in the shadows, for the dining room was not yet open for the evening meal, she said quietly: 'I suppose you know, Tom?'

'That you and she are right? I don't know that at all.'

'No. That you're in love with her.'

Shocked at hearing these words spoken so openly, Tom sat silent, his thoughts in turmoil. A picture of Lydia Ross dismissing him so lightly came to his mind, then Nancy Bigears brimming with excitement here in Juneau, and he recalled the afternoons with her beside the family totem and along the path beside the Pleiades, and the morning she had taken him in her canoe across Taku Inlet to walk upon the emerald ice of Pleiades Glacier, and he realized that Missy was right.

'Seattle is a lost dream, Missy. I flew high and singed my wings.' He smiled ruefully as she listened in silence, unwilling to break the flood of thoughts she knew he needed to express. 'I'll stay here and work in one cannery after another, and always in the shadows there will be Nancy Bigears, growing more lovely every year, and finally when the years pass and there is nothing better to do, I'll ask her to marry me.'

But then he remembered Mr. Ross's harsh words that day when he had seen them kissing, and he wanted to share them with Missy: 'Do you know what Ross told me when he thought I might become involved with Nancy? "Venn, do you think Ross & Raglan would ever bring you to headquarters in Seattle if you had an Indian wife?" and he scared me away for the moment.'

'And then his daughter scared you away from the other direction?'

'How do you know that?'

'Tom, you're like a little boy in grammar school who's kissed a girl for the first time. All the other girls in the room know.'

Smiling brightly, as if to change the subject, he asked: 'What are you and Matt going to do here in Juneau?' and she said: 'We're in no hurry. Irishmen know how to take things as they come.' And she started to leave, but as he rose to escort her to the door, she touched his arm and said: 'You know you could, Tom.'

'Do what?' he asked, and she said: 'Marry a wonderful Tlingit girl. You're first-class, she's first-class. Together you could go to the stars.' And before he could respond, she was gone.

I N SUCCEEDING DAYS things began to work out as he had predicted to Missy: Nancy Bigears was always present in the shadows, and almost against his will he began to drift toward her. They met far more often than he intended, and when she directed their conversation into channels which concerned her, like Tlingit rights and the advisability of outlawing alcohol in Alaska, he found that she struck dissonant but powerful chords in his own reflections: rarely did he agree with her, but he had to acknowledge that she did not waste her life on trivialities.

One afternoon he said: 'I'd like to go out to the glacier again,' and she realized that he was saying this because he wanted to see her once more in the setting where he had first become aware of her, even though she had been only fourteen at the time.

'Are there many states in America,' she asked, 'where you can leave the capital and ride out to an active glacier?' and he said: 'Not many.'

It was a beautiful January day and the Japan Current brought enough warm sea air ashore to create a near-summer atmosphere, even though a small family of icebergs huddled in the channel, so they rode with the carriage windows open. At the glacier, whose former cave had been long obliterated by ice crashing down from the face above, they walked for some time along the front, touching the monstrous snout from time to time and even leaning against it when they stopped to talk.

'Missy told me the other day, Nancy, that I was in love with you.'

'I've always been in love with you, Tom. You know that. Since that first day in there,' and she pointed to where the blue-roofed cave had been.

'Could marriage . . . ?' He could find no words to express the careful definitions he had in mind. But she diverted his reasoning with a question which startled him: 'Did the boss's daughter in Seattle let you know she wasn't interested?'

Tom snapped his fingers: 'Did Missy tell you to ask that?' and she laughed: 'I don't need other people to tell me important things,' and from beneath her dark bangs she smiled so provocatively that he burst out laughing.

With Nancy he laughed quite often, and as they walked beside the glacier he thought: What I said was right. We'll drift along and one day I'll say: 'What the hell?' and we'll get married. But now she stopped and turned to face him, saying softly: 'It wouldn't work. Not in these years, anyway. Maybe later, when we all grow up . . . I mean when Alaska grows up . . .' She said no more, and she resumed walking back to where the horse waited, but he remained motionless, standing close to the glacier, and he felt that like it he was moving slowly, relentlessly in an age of ice.

In due course he overtook her, and as they rode back to Juneau, night came down upon the surrounding mountains and the breath of untimely summer vanished. At the edge of town she pointed to a house lying on its side: 'Like Father warned you. Sometimes the snow comes crashing down. As if we had our own little glaciers.'

In the morning he told Sam Bigears to stop trying to find him a house in Juneau: 'I'll live in Ketchikan while we're building the new cannery. After that . . . ?' And next day he sailed south to his new obligations.

A S TOM VENN headed for his future life in Ketchikan, the salmon Nerka was receiving signals in the far turn of the Alaskan Gyre, warning him that it was time he started for home, and the message was so compelling that even though he was far from Lake Pleiades, he began to swim no longer in aimless circles but with undeviating direction toward his natal water. Sweeping his tail in powerful arcs with a vigor not used before, he shot through the water not at his customary ten miles a day but at a speed four or five times that fast.

In his earlier circuits of the gyre he had always been content to string along with his fellows, male or female, and rarely had he distinguished between the two, but now he took pains to avoid other males, as if he realized that with his new obligations, they had become not only his competitors but also his potential enemies.

From his accidental position in the gyre when these signals arrived he could reasonably have headed for Oregon, or Kamchatka, or the Yukon, but in obedience to the homing device implanted in him years ago, he followed his signal—that wisp of a shadow of a lost echo—and from one of the most isolated parts of the Pacific he launched himself precisely on a course that would lead him to Taku Inlet and Lake Pleiades, where he would undertake the most important assignment of his life.

On the first of May he was still one thousand two hundred and fifty miles from home, but the signals were now so intense that he began swimming at a steady forty-nine miles a day, and as he sped through the gyre he began to feed prodigiously, consuming incredible numbers of fish, three or four times as many as ever before. Indeed, he ate ravenously even when not really hungry, as if he knew that once he left the ocean, he would never again eat as long as he lived.

In early September he entered Taku Inlet, and when he immersed himself in its fresh waters, his body began to undergo one of the most extraordinary transformations in the animal kingdom, an ugly one, as if he sought a frightening appearance to aid him in the battles he would soon be facing. Up to this moment, as he swam easily through the gyre, he had been a handsome fish, quite beautiful when he twisted in the light, but now, in obedience to internal signals, he was transformed into something grotesque. His lower jaw became ridiculously prognathous, its teeth extending so far beyond those in the upper jaw that they looked like a shark's; his snout turned inward, bending down to form a hook; and most disfiguring of all, his back developed a great hump and changed its color to a flaming red. His once svelte and streamlined body thickened, and he became in general a ferocious creature driven by urges he could not hope to understand.

With determination he swam toward his natal lake, but his course brought him to where the trap of Totem Cannery waited with its very long jiggers, making entry to the Pleiades River impossible. Bewildered by the barrier which had not been operating when he left the lake, he stopped, reconnoitered the situation like a general, and watched as thousands of his fellows drifted supinely along the jiggers and into the trap. He felt no compassion for them, but he knew that he must not allow this unusual barrier to stop him from fighting through to his river. Every nerve along his spine, every impulse in his minute brain warned him that he must somehow circumvent the trap, and he could do so only by leaping across the lethal jigger.

Swimming as close to the right bank as he could, he was encouraged by the cold fresh water that came from the Pleiades River carrying a powerful message from the lake, but when he attempted to swim toward the source of the reassuring water, he was once more frustrated by the jigger. Bewildered, he was about to drift toward the fatal center when a sockeye somewhat larger than he came up behind, detected a sagging spot in the jigger, and with a mighty sweep of his tail leaped over it, splashing heavily into the free water beyond.

As if shot from a gun, Nerka sped forward, activated his tail and fins and arched himself high in the air, only to strike the top strand of the jigger, which threw him roughly backward. For some moments he tried to fathom what had caused him to fail when the other fish had succeeded, then, with a greater effort, he tried again, and again he was repulsed by the jigger.

He lay for some minutes resting in the cool water drifting down from the Pleiades, and when he felt his strength returning he started swimming with great sweeps of his tail, and mustering all his strength, he sped like a bullet at the jigger, arched himself higher than before, and landed with a loud splash on the upstream side.

A workman from Totem Cannery, observing the remarkable leaps of these two salmon, called to his mates: 'We better add two more strands to the jigger. Those two who got across were beauties.'

It was crucial that Nerka survive to complete his mission, for of the four thousand who had been born in his generation, only six still survived, and upon them rested the fate of the Pleiades sockeye.

SINCE THE NEW R&R cannery at Ketchikan was being planned for a capacity half again as large as Totem, Tom was kept so busy from the middle of January on, he had little time to think about the mournful way his two conflicting love interests had collapsed. When he reached the site, the four major buildings had already been roughed out; they were enormous, and he gasped when he realized that it was up to him to finish off the eight or ten subsidiary buildings which would be required, and then fill all of them with the needed machinery. So he spent February and March installing crating areas, canning lines and the two great essentials: the Iron Chinks and the huge steam retorts for cooking. He did not like to think what this cannery was going to cost, perhaps four hundred thousand dollars, but he did know that once it started functioning, it would have the ability to pack sixty thousand cases a year, and that was a lot of salmon.

In mid-March when it became apparent that some of the bunkhouses might not be finished on time, he sent a distress signal to Juneau, and on the next trip south Sam Bigears appeared with four expert helpers. 'I still not work in buildings,' Sam said, 'but I work on them.' One of the men, to Tom's surprise, was Ah Ting, and when the local workmen saw him come onto the premises, they complained loudly that no Chinese were allowed in Alaska, but Tom explained that Ah Ting was an exception. They were not happy with the explanation, but when they saw how he could get the temperamental Iron Chinks operating when they could not, they allowed that he served a purpose.

During working hours Sam Bigears often paused to inform his friend Tom of happenings in Juneau, and certain bits of information were both pleasing and amusing: 'That crazy Siberian, what's his name, he got one of best houses in town and he and his wife have boardinghouse. He collect rent and she do all the work.' He said also that Matt and Missy had yet to find a house they wanted, but that Missy kept sticking her nose into everything: 'Call her Lady Governor, she tell everyone what to do.'

'Do they get mad at her?' Tom asked, and Sam said: 'No. They like what she say. Maybe like her interest,' and Tom said: 'She was always that way.' Sam said that she offered to work at one of the churches, but they wouldn't accept her because no one could be certain whether she was married to Murphy or not: 'But her girl go Sunday School that church.'

Tom never asked how Nancy was doing, because he could not be sure how much Sam knew about their feelings for each other, and he certainly did not want to say, but whenever Sam spoke of the girl, he listened attentively: 'She win big writing contest, which not surprise me. She good at writing, but she also win what they call oratory. That was surprise. She speak "Tlingit Land Rights" and I think she win because Lady Missy one of judges. She like what Nancy say. Me too.'

Thanks to Tom's driving energy, and the hard work of men like Bigears and Ah Ting, Ketchikan Cannery was ready on time, and since the runs of salmon in these southern waters were even more copious than those in Taku Inlet, the big buildings were soon working to capacity and the Juneau men returned home. As Ah Ting left, some of the older workers in the Iron Chink shed told Tom: 'It's good to see that one go. No place in Alaska for a Chink,' and Tom said: 'Aren't you from Seattle?' and they said they were, and Tom surprised himself by saying: 'Then it's not your problem, is it?' Ashamed of his curt retort, he returned to the men and said: 'You know we couldn't have had this place ready without his help,' and the matter was dropped.

His display of temper disturbed him, because on his jobs in Dawson, Nome and Juneau he had been known for his unruffled disposition, and he wondered what had caused him to change. But when he reviewed his recent behavior he came to several conclusions: I've been working at top speed for too long. I need a rest. But then a deeper reason surfaced: Working with Sam Bigears reminded me of what a great girl Nancy is. I want to see her again. And when he announced that he would be sailing back to Juneau with Sam, he accepted the fact that the unintended drift toward Nancy he had spoken of to Missy was under way, and he muttered: 'Let it happen.'

Before he completed arrangements for other men to run the cannery during his short absence, an R&R supply ship arrived from Seattle, and the captain had a personal message for Tom: 'Mrs. Ross is arriving on the next *Montreal Queen*, and her daughter will be with her. They want to spend the day inspecting the new cannery, and when they sail for Taku Inlet, Mr. Ross hopes that you will accompany them. They'll spend a few days there, then catch the *Queen* on its trip back to Seattle.'

Wondering what this assignment might imply—there had certainly been no hint of anything like this at Christmas—he felt a surge of excitement on realizing that he was going to see Lydia again, even though she had treated him so badly the last time. He tried to avoid thinking that the visit had any deeper meaning, but he did move about the cannery in a state of euphoria.

One decision was easily made: 'Sam, I won't be sailing with you back to Juneau.' He said this almost mechanically, as if his decision not to visit Nancy Bigears was a free act without moral or emotional meaning, and that was the case, for it never occurred to him that in turning down Sam in favor of Mrs. Ross, he was also rejecting Nancy in hopes that something better would develop with Lydia.

The citizens of Ketchikan felt a sense of pride when some big passenger steamer sailed in, and since the *Montreal Queen* was the finest, newest ship in the Alaskan service, they lined the dock when the sleek Canadian beauty edged in. As soon as the gangway was dropped into position and secured to the dock, Mrs. Ross appeared at its top, attended by an officer. He was Captain Binneford, a trim, imposing seaman from eastern Canada with years of experience on the Atlantic crossing. Handing her along to Tom Venn, who ran forward to greet her, Captain Binneford said: 'Take care of this good lady. We want her safely returned when we stop at Totem Cannery on the return.'

As Tom reached to give Mrs. Ross his arm, he saw behind her Lydia, dressed in a white suit with blue nautical trimming. She looked like some carefully chosen young woman posing for an advertisement depicting a European voyage to Paris or Rome: she was an eager traveler prepared to see the sights. 'Hello, Tom!' she called out with unladylike vigor, and to her mother's surprise, as well as Tom's, she ran to him as soon as she left the gangway and planted an enthusiastic kiss on his cheek.

They spent that long day seeing what Ketchikan had to offer, and the little town of six hundred went out of its way, with a band concert, a barbecue and a parade back to the ship, which sailed at dusk.

The Rosses had provided a stateroom for Tom, but he had barely entered it when Mrs. Ross asked him to accompany her as she walked the upper deck, and once again he was awed by the easy graciousness of this woman: 'It was Lydia's idea, this trip. She knew . . . well, the truth is, I gave her living hell for the way she treated you at Christmas. No, don't speak. These things happen sometimes, Tom, and we're powerless to stop them. But we can correct them. And that's what she wants to do.' She chuckled. 'I'm not sure she *wanted* to do it, but I made it very clear she had to.' They walked some more, and she added: 'That's when she suggested this cruise. What a brilliant idea!'

'I respect your daughter enormously, Mrs. Ross. I've never known anyone like her.'

'Nor I. She's special, if I say so myself. But then, as you know, so was her grandmother.'

'She didn't have to apologize.'

'She wanted to, when I pointed out how horrid she'd been.'

Later Tom walked the same deck with Lydia, and she too astonished him by the frankness of her comment: 'At Christmas, Tom, I thought I was very much in love with Horace. He seemed the proper answer to everything. Now he seems rather fake, and to tell you the truth, I very much wanted to see you again. Because, as Father told me at the time, you're real.'

He could not believe what he was hearing, but then she said: 'I doubt I'm in love with you, Tom. I doubt I'll be in love with anyone till I'm much older. But the talks I had with you on that hill, they're the best talks I've ever had, and when Horace blathered on about his family and his school and the keen fellows he knew, I couldn't help thinking of you . . . and reality.'

They made almost a complete circuit in silence, then Tom said: 'I wasn't really hurt at Christmas. I thought that that was the world you were entitled to and I knew I didn't belong.'

'Oh, Tom!' She burst into tears and stopped to lean against the railing. Reaching for his hand, she pressed it and said: 'Forgive me. It was Christmas and I got caught up in all the celebrations and thought that this was my world.' They resumed walking, and after a while she said: 'My world is considerably larger than that.'

But when they said goodnight, well after one in the morning with the mountains of Alaska looking down on them, she spoke with another burst of frankness: 'I don't know what this trip means, Tom. I really don't. Neither of us must take it too seriously, but you must take with great seriousness the fact that I want to keep you as a friend.' She laughed nervously, then added: 'And so does Father. It looks as if you're to be around for a long time, and I wanted to make peace.'

'The pipe is lit.'

She kissed him and went to her room.

WHEN THE *MONTREAL QUEEN* made her stately way up Taku Inlet, Tom Venn stood at the railing with the Ross women and explained the glaciers on the western shore. The best part of their adventure came when the big ship anchored at the very end of the inlet to disembark passengers for the twenty-minute walk to a hidden lake and the lovely twin glaciers, small and glistening, which fed it.

It was a sturdy walk uphill, but both the Rosses insisted upon taking it, and they were well worn when they reached the beautiful gemlike glaciers, so different from the others. Standing next to them, it was possible to imagine that they really were part of a living field of ice. 'They're the daughters of the old woman up there,' Lydia said, and they did indeed create that impression.

When they reached the cannery on the return trip down the inlet, Tom learned that Nancy Bigears was home for the school vacation, and when Sam came over to pay his respects, he informed Tom that Nancy still hadn't made up her mind what she was going to do. Mrs. Ross asked what options she had, and Sam said: 'Her teachers think maybe college,' and this so intrigued Mrs. Ross that she said: 'We've always wanted to educate bright young Eskimos.'

'We're Tlingits,' Sam said, and Mrs. Ross quickly said: 'I'm so sorry. Nobody has told me the difference,' and Sam said: 'No offense. Some my people not much to be proud of.'

'But I imagine you're very proud of your daughter.'

'I sure am.'

'Well, Mr. Bigears, if she's as good as you say, there should certainly be a way for us to get her into college. Could you ask her to come over while we're here?'

So on a bright summer's day, while the cannery was in full swing, Sam Bigears and Nancy came across the estuary to meet two women about whom she already knew a great deal. When they came into the office, Nancy, scowling apprehensively from beneath her sharply edged bangs, looked first at Mrs. Ross, who smiled at her reassuringly as if to make her feel at home, and then at Lydia, whom she was seeing for the first time and whom she knew to be her rival. Mrs. Ross, aware that the setting, with everyone staring at one girl and waiting to hear what she had to say, was too much like a legal procedure, sought to soften it: 'Nancy, sit here with me. We've heard such exciting reports about your work in school, we wanted the honor of meeting a girl who could do so well.'

Taking the seat indicated, Nancy thought: They keep calling me a girl. I'm older than any of them. But now Lydia, taking the cue from her mother, said: 'You know, there's a way you could attend the university,' and Mrs. Ross added: 'Alaska needs . . . in fact, we all need bright young people who will bring modern ways to everything.' Aware that this sounded condescending, she hurried on: 'Like Mr. Venn . . . managing this factory.' Nancy lost the analogy, for she was looking across the room at Tom, in such a way that Lydia Ross knew instantly that the Indian girl was in love with him.

Tom said: 'Mrs. Ross told me it would be a privilege to meet you, and I assured her she wouldn't be disappointed.'

Now Nancy was ready to speak: 'Are you the wife of the man who owns this cannery?'

'I am.'

'Well, you should tell him that he mustn't stop my people from fishing in our Pleiades as we've always done.'

Mrs. Ross, surprised by this frontal attack but not unnerved by it, turned to Tom and asked: 'Is what she says true?' and Tom had to explain that under the law, when a cannery obtained the right to place its trap at the confluence . . .

'It's wrong, Mrs. Ross, and it ought to be stopped. My family has fished this river for more than fifty years.' She continued with such a strong statement about native rights that Mrs. Ross found herself agreeing, but in the end she put a stop to it: 'Nancy, we wanted to find out two things. Would you like to attend the university? Have you done well enough in school to succeed if you do go?'

'I don't really know what a university is, Mrs. Ross. But my teachers keep telling me that I could go if I wanted to.'

After this frank self-assessment, Mrs. Ross began asking a series of questions calculated to identify the level of the girl's learning, and both she and Lydia were surprised at the mature manner in which Nancy responded. She apparently knew several good works of literature and had a much better than average knowledge of American history. She knew what the Sistine Chapel was and how an opera was structured. But when Mrs. Ross asked about algebra and geometry, Nancy said frankly: 'I'm not very good in arithmetic,' and Lydia chimed in: 'Neither was I,' but Mrs. Ross would not allow this easy escape: 'If you want to be first-class, Nancy, you really ought to know about proportions and how to solve for simple unknowns,' and Nancy replied with disarming frankness: 'That's what Miss Foster keeps saying.'

Mrs. Ross was disturbed to learn from Nancy and Tom that few Indian children ever persisted past grade six and that Nancy was the first Tlingit girl ever to reach senior year. 'She's set a good standard,' Mrs. Ross said, and Tom was as pleased as if he had been one of Nancy's teachers.

At this point no one doubted that Nancy could survive in a university, and Lydia said that she was already better educated than many sophomores: 'You could have a great time at the university, Nancy,' and Mrs. Ross assured both Nancy and her father that a scholarship of some kind would be forthcoming: 'It isn't that she needs the university. The university needs her.' But it was obvious that Nancy, who would be the first of her kind ever to undertake such a bold adventure, was uncertain about such a move.

'I don't know,' she said diffidently, but her father, proud of her deportment this day, said to no one in particular: 'If free, she take it,' and Mrs. Ross said quickly: 'Not exactly free. Could you help her with small funds?' and Sam said: 'I do now,' and everyone laughed.

At the conclusion of the interview, which had gone better than anyone had expected, the Ross family reached a decision which both surprised and ex-hilarated Tom Venn. Mrs. Ross announced: 'When the *Montreal Queen* stops by on its return trip this evening, I'm sailing to Seattle as planned. But Lydia tells me she wants to stay here a few days and catch our R&R supply boat on Friday.' Before anyone could comment, she turned to Sam: 'Mr. Bigears, could my daughter stay with your family till the ship comes? She certainly can't stay here with Mr. Venn.' She said this disarmingly, with such easy grace that everyone was placed at ease, and Sam asked Lydia: 'You ready for real Tlingit potlatch?' and Lydia replied: 'I don't know whether you eat it or sleep in it, but I'm ready.' So when the Canadian ship arrived, she remained on the dock with Nancy and Tom as her mother boarded.

Mrs. Ross was even more congenial than before as she stopped at the head of the gangway: 'Thank you, Mr. Bigears, for watching over my daughter. We'll see you in Seattle in September, Nancy. Tom, you've been a gracious host. And all you good people who work at the cannery, God bless you. We need your help.'

T HE *MONTREAL QUEEN*, pride of the Canadian line which sailed out of Seattle to Vancouver and the Alaskan ports, was more than 245 feet long, weighed a majestic 1,497 tons and was legally authorized to carry 203 passengers. But because many tourists wanted transportation to Seattle as the summer season drew to a close, on this trip she carried in hastily erected wooden bunks a total of 309 paying passengers plus a crew of 66. All but two spaces had been filled when the ship left Juneau on its homeward leg, and when it stopped at Totem Cannery to pick up the two Ross women, Mrs. Ross explained that even though Lydia would not be sailing with her, the Rosses would pay for two passages. The purser took the problem to Captain Binneford, who said that in view of Mr. Malcolm Ross's close affiliation with the line, no charge would be made for the unused quarters.

The ship left Totem Cannery in the silvery dusk of a late August day, and because it was somewhat behind schedule, it traveled rather faster than usual in an attempt to make up time and beat the ebbing tide past the rocky portions of the upper inlet. Captain Binneford knew well—for the route had been carefully spelled out by the revenue cutter service years before and partially marked by them—that in passing the Walrus it was obligatory to keep well to the west, that is, to keep the rock safely to port, and this he did, but for some reason never to be known, he cut the margin of safety, and at half after seven on Wednesday night, 22 August 1906, while there was still ample light, this fine ship plowed headlong onto a submerged ledge which reached out from the Walrus. The bow of the ship was punctured, and its forward speed was so great that a gash eighty-two feet long was made down the port side. Almost instantly the *Montreal Queen* was wedged onto the Walrus, its gaping wound exposed as the tide went out.

Mrs. Ross was still unpacking when the speeding ship slammed abruptly onto the ledge, and she was thrown forward, but she was such an agile woman that she protected herself and was not hurt. She was one of the first on deck and the one who best understood what had happened, for she assured her fellow passengers: 'My husband runs a shipping company in these waters, and accidents like this do happen. But we have wireless, and other ships will hasten to rescue us.' She saw no reason for fear, and said so repeatedly.

However, as she was speaking, Captain Binneford was sending and receiving messages which would exert a powerful effect on the fate of the *Montreal Queen*, for when his company headquarters received news of the grounding, they sent a reply which would become famous in Alaskan history:

IF DAMAGE NOT TOTALLY DISABLING, YOU ARE ORDERED TO AWAIT ARRIVAL *ONTARIO QUEEN* SPEEDING TO RESCUE ALL PASSENGERS. WILL ARRIVE FRIDAY SUNSET.

Had Mrs. Ross been allowed to see this message, she would, as the wife of a shipowner, have understood its implications, for what the parent company was doing was ordering the captain of the stricken ship not to allow any salvage effort by ships of another line or by adventuresome seamen based in Juneau or Ketchikan. Maritime law was such that if a disabled ship allowed any other vessel to aid it, that other craft established a vested interest in the wreck. In this case, easing the *Queen* off the rocks or towing her back to Juneau would be interpreted as providing help, which qualified for a share in the salvage.

If the *Montreal Queen* could hold on till her sister ship, the *Ontario Queen*, arrived from Vancouver, the Canadian company would save considerable money. And when Captain Binneford studied the condition of his ship, he made the gambling decision that it would remain safely wedged where it was throughout Thursday and Friday, by which time the *Ontario Queen* would arrive to carry the passengers on to Seattle. It was a risky decision, but it was not stupid, for it looked to all the officers in charge of the *Queen* that she was so tightly wedged that she must stay safely on the rock indefinitely.

Captain Binneford ordered his staff to so inform the passengers, who that night dined off badly tilted tables and slept in beds that kept rolling them to starboard.

News of the wreck did not filter back to Totem Cannery on Thursday morning until about an hour after word had reached Juneau, so by the time Tom Venn, Sam Bigears and others had launched all the cannery boats to effect a rescue of Mrs. Ross and all who could be crowded into the space available, many small boats from Juneau were already at the scene. Just as Tom and Bigears arrived at the Walrus, a coastal boat of some size which had been unloading at Juneau steamed up, enabling Sam to announce: 'We got enough boats here, rescue everybody.' It was agreed that they would whisk Mrs. Ross back to Totem, where she could wait for the Friday arrival of the R&R supply ship.

But when the various vessels—from the big one which had just arrived to the smallest boat from Totem—approached the stranded *Montreal Queen* they became enmeshed in that insane law. To protect his company from salvage claims, Captain Binneford refused to allow even one person, passenger or crew, to leave his ship into the care of another vessel, regardless of its size. This meant that the 309 passengers of the *Queen* could line the railing of their badly damaged ship and almost touch hands with their would-be rescuers, but they could not leave the ship to accept help.

Tom and Bigears located Mrs. Ross quickly, where she stood in the midst of many women passengers, assuring them that rescue was imminent; of all the women she showed the least strain. When she saw Bigears, she cried: 'Oh, Mr. Bigears! You are a most welcome sight.' And she started below to fetch her bags so that she could be one of the first off.

'I'm sorry, madam,' a polite Canadian officer apologized as he barred her way. 'No one can leave the ship.'

'But our cannery boat is alongside. It's our boat. It's our cannery, just a few miles back there.'

'I am most sorry, and so is Captain Binneford, but no one can leave the ship. We're responsible for your safety. Your rescue is imminent.'

Mrs. Ross, unable to understand the stupidity of such a rule, demanded to see the captain, but the officer told her, reasonably: 'Surely you appreciate the strain he's under. He has enough to do to work with the crew.' And she was forbidden even to throw her luggage into Tom's boat lest the legal position of the steamship company be compromised.

Tom and Bigears remained at the wreck all that Thursday, trusting that somehow common sense would prevail, but none did, and when a second even larger would-be rescue ship from Juneau arrived on the scene, and men from the various small craft climbed aboard to learn from its captain what the situation was, they were told: 'If we were allowed to take off all the passengers, it might cost the Canadian company as much as two thousand dollars.'

'Wouldn't the salvage rights to the ship itself also be involved?'

'Never. We're talking about two thousand dollars, at most.'

Without hesitation Tom Venn cried: 'I'll put up the two thousand,' and half a dozen others volunteered to contribute, for as one sailor accustomed to these waters warned: 'You can never tell when that Taku Wind will come roaring out of Canada. We better get them off before sunset.'

So the captain of the new arrival, the captain of the earlier ship and Tom Venn as representative of the Ross & Raglan line decided to approach Captain Binneford by bullhorn, and Tom served as spokesman in offering to pay all costs involved in disembarking the passengers immediately. Binneford refused even to consider the proposal, because in the meantime he had received a second set of instructions from the home office assuring him that the *Ontario Queen* would arrive at the Walrus two hours earlier than previously estimated. The wireless message had ended:

ALL PASSENGERS WILL BE SAFELY ABOARD *ONTARIO* BY FOUR FRIDAY AFTER-NOON.

Tom, feeling a personal responsibility for Mrs. Ross, remained near the stricken ship, because he still felt that Captain Binneford, whom he had found to be a sensible man during their brief acquaintance on the run from Ketchikan to Totem, would want to ensure his passengers' safety, regardless of instructions which might endanger them, and he wanted to be on hand to protect Mrs. Ross. He therefore sent Sam Bigears back to the cannery in another Totem boat, with instructions to assure Lydia that her mother was going to be all right.

But Sam's craft had barely left the stricken ship when a brisk wind came speeding down the inlet from Canada, and two experienced sailors warned: 'If this continues, we could have a full-scale Taku,' and because Sam was cautious where gales were concerned, he swung his boat in a full circle and headed back to be ready to disembark passengers if the winds worsened.

In her creaking quarters that Thursday night Mrs. Ross, along with quite a few other passengers, penned notes to relatives. Hers was to Lydia:

> This adventure proves one thing to me, and I hope it does to you too, Lydia. No disaster, and the wrecking of this ship is a disaster, justifies you to act stupidly. In fact, at such times you ought to act with superhuman intelligence, and I trust you will always do so.
>
> It is stupid to keep us passengers trapped on this ship, even if there is a modicum of assurance that the other ship will get here in good time. It is stupid to allow a few dollars to obstruct the operation of ordinary intelligence. And it is always very stupid, Lydia, to allow one minor consideration to obscure the right decision regarding a major concern. If we get off this pathetic craft alive, which I begin to doubt, I shall want your father, with the most ardent support from me, to see to it that Captain Binneford never again sails in Alaskan waters, for his behavior tonight as the winds begin to rise is indefensible.
>
> Yes, the wind has picked up considerably and the boat is creaking much more loudly than before. I see a dish start to move across my table as I write, and instead of stopping, it picks up speed. But I am glad I made this trip with you, Lydia. I think we both saw young Mr. Venn in new lights, and they were neither favorable nor unfavorable, just new. That Nancy Bigears is a gem, lecturing me before I could offer my help. See that she does well at the university. And take care of yourself. Make right choices and defend them.
>
> I'm far less apprehensive than this letter sounds. I'm sure we'll be rescued tomorrow.

When she went to the railing to throw her letter, properly weighted, down to Tom, an officer tried to prevent her from doing so, again saying the legal position of the ship would be compromised, but she pushed him away and said harshly: 'For God's sake, young man, don't be a damned fool.'

When Bigears reached the scene he sought Tom's boat, but could not find it among the scores of little craft eager to rescue the passengers, but later he saw Tom talking with Mrs. Ross, who was leaning down from the railing. Not wanting to alarm her with the news he was bringing, he waited till she withdrew, then he climbed into Tom's boat: 'I fear. So do men at cannery.'

'What's up?'

'Taku Wind comes. No doubt about it.'

'Big enough to push the *Queen* off the rocks?'

'If water rises, maybe.'

'Any chance?'

'Maybe yes.'

So Tom and Bigears moved among the waiting boats till they reassembled the two captains who had consulted with Captain Binneford earlier that day, and Tom told them: 'Sam Bigears here has lived on Taku Inlet all his life. Knows it better than anyone. And he says . . . Tell them, Sam.'

'Big Taku Wind coming. Maybe before sun rise.'

'Sweeping water down with it?'

'For sure.'

'And there'll be a pretty high tide too,' said Tom.

The two captains needed no more information. Keeping Tom and Bigears with them, they moved close to the *Queen* and shouted: 'We want to talk with Captain Binneford.'

'He's busy.'

One of the captains grew angry: 'You tell that stupid bastard he better get unbusy and come talk with us.'

'He wants no further interference.'

'He's goin' to get it. Because one hell of a big Taku Wind is goin' to blow his ass right off that rock.'

When the young officer refused to interrupt Captain Binneford, the captain grew furious, whipped out a revolver, and fired two quick shots over the *Queen*. This brought Captain Binneford on the run: 'What's going on, Mr. Proudfit?'

'Trouble,' the leader in the rescue boat shouted. 'Captain, there's a big wind risin'. You better get everyone off your ship.'

'The *Ontario Queen* will be here by four tomorrow afternoon.'

'It may find you missing.'

Captain Binneford started to leave the railing, but now the second captain shouted at him: 'Captain, this man here has lived on Taku Inlet all his life. He knows, and he says there's danger of a real big wind.'

In the darkness Captain Binneford, shaken by these words, stared at the man in the boat below as if he were prepared to listen, but at that moment Tom held a lantern to Bigears' face, and when the Canadian skipper saw that Sam was a Tlingit, he turned on his heel and left.

But Sam was correct in his estimate of this wind, because by midnight it had risen so sharply that most of the really small boats, whose skippers knew these waters, had headed for the safety of a protected cove north of Walrus Glacier. Tom and Sam felt they had to stay close to the *Queen* in case the captain came to his senses, but by three in the morning the blasts out of Canada were so powerful that Bigears warned: 'If we not go, we sink too,' so against his will Tom headed his boat toward a cove south of Walrus Glacier.

As they drew away from the *Queen,* he asked: 'What's going to happen?' and Bigears said: 'I think she go down,' and Tom asked: 'Will those two bigger ships be able to rescue them?' and Sam said: 'They got any sense, they leave now,' and in the darkness Tom saw with horror that the two larger boats were indeed running for shelter, because their captains knew that a gale strong enough to drive them onto the rocks had to strike the Walrus before long.

In her cabin, with the wind roaring and the ship listing at a more severe angle, Mrs. Ross wrote a final note, which, waterstained, would be delivered to her daughter some weeks later:

I am sure, Lydia, that your grandmother must have known moments like this when all seemed lost. Remember the harsh accusations that were made against her and other brave young women. They survived and so shall I. But the wind does grow stronger and we await the dawn in a kind of dumb terror. It is so sad. I can't hold back my tears, because this was all so unnecessary. Your father and I would have solved this problem in three minutes, and I beg you to develop the same kind of character and willingness to assume responsibility, for they are great virtues, maybe the greatest. I love you. Tonight my hopes must transfer to you.

When dawn broke on Friday morning, with all the rescue ships scattered but watching in horror as the gale increased, raking and churning the water as it swept down the inlet, Tom and Bigears moved out from their sanctuary and, braving the furious chopping swell, tried to approach the foundering *Queen*. But when the light was strong enough for them to see the ship listing perilously to port, the wind became so powerful that Tom cried: 'Turn back!' but Bigears shouted: 'We got to get Mrs. Ross!' and he kept their small boat plowing through great swells. Then suddenly a combination of intense gusting wind and pounding waves much higher than before rocked the *Montreal Queen* loose and turned her over on her gaping side.

Within minutes the beautiful ship disappeared in the dark waters of the inlet, and because of the tremendous sucking action it generated, not a single passenger of the 309 survived. To prevent a financial loss of two thousand dollars, everyone aboard the *Montreal Queen*, including the crew, perished.

TOM AND BIGEARS stood by the site of the sinking, hoping along with some dozen other small craft to save at least a few of the passengers, but it soon became obvious that there would not be anyone to rescue. Indeed, the capsizing had come with such a sudden rush that there were hardly any stray bits of wreckage to mark where the ship had been. So at about three in the afternoon, just as Tom was about to start back to Totem, Sam Bigears shouted: 'Look!' and Tom turned and saw the stately *Ontario Queen,* steaming up an hour early.

At the cannery, Tom was unable to tell the waiting women what had happened. Instead, Bigears climbed onto the dock, walked slowly toward the crowd that had gathered, and embraced Lydia Ross: 'Everyone go down. Everyone. Tom has letter.'

By the time Tom approached the crowd Lydia had herself under control, but when she saw this gallant fellow whom she had once treated so poorly, she ran to him, collapsing in tears and throwing herself into his arms.

Her father, when he met her on her return to Seattle, suspected rightly that she was being overly emotional when she announced that she was marrying Tom Venn, and he begged her to wait until she saw things more clearly, but she said: 'I did see things very clearly during that visit. If Mother had lived, she would have told you that I stayed behind because I did not want Tom to marry that Nancy Bigears, wonderful as you'll find her to be. I wanted him, and I wanted him for the best reason in the world. I love him.' Later she added: 'I saw him in the storm. He performed the way you would have, Father,' and Mr. Ross said: 'Most men behave courageously in a storm,' but she corrected him: 'Captain Binneford didn't.'

Her father did prevail upon her not to marry immediately: 'I don't give a damn for appearances, as you well know. But there is meaning to that old phrase *a decent interval*,' and she said: 'October tenth will be decent. Tom and I have things to do.'

Nancy Bigears, now a student at the university, attended the wedding, and although there was uneasiness between her and Lydia, there was none with Tom. She still loved him, and both Lydia and Tom knew this, and in return they loved her, for she was the first of the Tlingit women to test her luck in the white man's world and they wished her well. When she asked where they would be spending their honeymoon, Lydia said: 'At Ketchikan Cannery. Tom has work to do,' and Nancy kissed them both.

WHEN NERKA THE salmon leaped over Tom Venn's right-hand jigger in order to return to the Pleiades River, he faced the reverse of the problem which had threatened him three years earlier. Now, as a fish acclimated to life in salt water, he must relearn how to live in fresh, and this sharp alteration required two days of slow swimming in the new medium. But gradually he adjusted, and now the excess fat which he had acquired in his hump during his burst of prodigious eating became an asset, keeping him alive and strong enough to ascend the waterfalls of the river, for as we have seen, once he entered fresh water he would never again feed, his entire digestive system having atrophied to the point of nonfunction.

He had nine miles of upstream swimming to negotiate before he reached the lake, and this was a task immeasurably more difficult than swimming down had been, for not only did he have to leap over major obstacles, but he also had to protect himself from the large number of bears that lined the river, knowing that the fat salmon were coming.

At the first rapids he proved his ability, for he swam directly up the middle, breasting the full power of the stream and propelling himself forward with forceful strokes of his tail, but it was when he reached the first waterfall, about eight feet high, that he demonstrated his unusual skill, for after hoarding his strength at the bottom, he suddenly darted at the falling plume of water, lifted himself in the air, and leaped the full eight feet, vibrating his tail furiously. With an effort not often matched in the animal kingdom, he overcame that considerable obstacle.

His outstanding performance came with the third waterfall, not a vertical drop but a long, sliding affair of rapidly rushing, turbulent water some eighteen feet long and with such a sharp drop that it looked as if no fish could master it, and certainly not in a single bound.

Here Nerka used another tactic. He made a furious dash right at the heart of the oncoming flow, and within the waterfall itself he swam and leaped and scrambled until he found a precarious lodging halfway up. There he rested for some moments, gathering energy for the greater trial to come.

Trapped in the middle of the fall, he obviously could not build up forward motion, but rising almost vertically, with his tail thrashing madly, he could resume his attack. Once more he swam, not leaped, right up the heart of the fall, and after a prodigious effort he broke free to reach calm water, in which he rested for a long time.

The most perilous part of his homeward journey, insofar as external agencies were concerned, now loomed, for in his exhausted state he failed to practice the cautions which had kept him alive for six years, and in his drifting he came within range of a group of bears that had gathered at this spot because they had learned, centuries ago, that after the homecoming salmon finished battling that waterfall, they would for some time flop aimlessly about and become easy prey.

One large bear had waded some feet into the river, where it found success in scooping up exhausted salmon and tossing them back onto the bank, where others leaped upon them, tearing their flesh. This bear, spotting Nerka as the most promising salmon of this morning's run, leaned forward like an ardent angler, sent its right paw flashing through the water, caught Nerka full under the belly, and with a mighty swipe tossed him far behind it, like an angler landing a prize trout.

As Nerka flew through the air he was aware of two things: the bear's claws had ripped his right flank, but not fatally, and the direction in which he was flying contained some areas which looked like water. So as soon as he landed with a hard thump on dry land, with two large bears leaping forward to kill him, he gave a series of wild gyrations, summoning all the power his tail, fins and body muscles could provide. As the bears reached out with their powerful claws, he wriggled and flopped like a drunken fly trying to land on unsteady legs, and just as the bears were about to grab him, he leaped at one of the shimmering areas. It was a sluggish arm of the river, and he was saved.

Now, as he neared the lake, the unique signal composed of mineral traces, the position of the sun, perhaps the gyration of the earth and maybe the operation of some peculiar electrical force, became overwhelming. For more than two thousand miles he had attended to this signal, and now it throbbed throughout his aging body: This is Lake Pleiades. This is home.

He reached the lake on 23 September 1906, and when he entered the jewellike body of water with its protecting mountains, he found his way to that small feeder stream with its particular aggregation of gravel in which he had been born six years earlier, and now for the first time in his exciting life he began to look about him not for just another salmon but for a female, and when other males swam by he recognized them as enemies and drove them off. The culminating experience of his life was about to begin, but only he and two others of his original four thousand had made it back to their home waters. All the rest had perished amid the dangers imposed by the incredible cycle of the salmon.

Mysteriously, out of a dark overhang which produced the deep shadows loved by sockeye, she came, a mature female who had shared the dangers he had known, who had in her own way avoided the jiggers reaching out to trap her and who had ascended the waterfalls with her own skills and tricks. She was his equal in every way except for the fierce prognathous lower jaw that he had developed, and she, too, was ready for the final act.

Moving quietly beside him as if to say 'I shall look to you for protection,' she began waving her tail and fins gently, brushing away silt that had fallen upon the gravel she intended using. In time, employing only these motions, she dug herself a redd, or nest, about six inches deep and twice her length, which was now more than two feet. When the redd was prepared, she tested it again to ensure that the steady stream of life-giving cold water was still welling up from the hidden river, and when she felt its reassuring presence, she was ready.

Now the slow, dreamlike courtship dance began, with Nerka nudging closer and closer, rubbing his fins against hers, swimming a slight distance away, then rushing back. Other males, aware of her presence, hurried up, but whenever one appeared, Nerka drove him off, and the lyrical dance continued.

Then a startling change occurred: both salmon opened their mouths as wide as their jaw sockets would allow, forming large cavernous passageways for the entrance of fresh water. It was as if they wished to purify themselves, to wash away old habits in preparation for what was about to happen, and when this ritual was completed they experienced wild and furious surges of courtship emotions, twisting together, snapping their jaws and quivering their tails. When their marine ballet ended, with their mouths once more agape, the female released some four thousand eggs, and at that precise instant Nerka ejected his milt, or sperm, over the entire area. Fertilization would occur by chance, but the incredible flood of milt made it probable that each egg would receive its sperm and that Nerka and his mate would have done their part in perpetuating their species.

Their destiny having been fulfilled, their mysterious travels were over, and an incredible climax to their lives awaited. Since they had eaten nothing since leaving the ocean, not even a minnow, they were so exhausted by their travel up Taku Inlet, their battle with traps, their swim upstream against waterfalls, that they retained not a shred of vital force. Will power consumed by these tremendous exertions, they began to drift aimlessly, and wayward currents eased them along a nepenthelike course to the spot where the lake emptied into the river.

When they entered the lively swirls of that stream they were momentarily revived, and fluttered their tails in the customary way, but they were so weak that nothing happened, and the current dragged them passively to where the falls and the rapids began.

As they reached the fatal spot at the head of the long falls, where bears waited, Nerka summoned enough energy to swim clear, but his mate, near death, could not, and one of the biggest animals reached in, caught her in its powerful claws, and threw her ashore, where other bears leaped at her. In a brief moment she was gone.

Had Nerka been in possession of his faculties, he would never have allowed the long waterfall to grasp him and smash him willy-nilly down its most precipitous drops and onto its most dangerous rocks, but that is what happened, and the last shuddering drop was so destructive that he felt the final shreds of life being knocked out of him. Vainly he tried to regain control of his destiny, but the relentless water kept knocking him abusively from rock to rock, and the last he saw of the earth and its waters of which he had been such a joyous part was a great spume into which he was sucked against his will and the massive rock which lurked therein. With a sickening smash, he was no more.

He had returned to Lake Pleiades system on 21 September 1906. He had fathered the next generation of sockeye on the twenty-fifth, and now on the last day of the month he was dead. He had lived five years, six months and had discharged all obligations courageously and as nature had programmed.

For three miles his dead body drifted downstream, until waves washed it to sanctuary in a backwater where ravens, familiar with the habits of the river, waited. He reached their domain about four in the afternoon of an increasingly cold day when food was essential, and by nightfall only his bones were left.

Of the one hundred million sockeye born along with Nerka in 1901, only some fifty thousand managed to make it back, and since it is reasonable to assume that these were evenly divided between the sexes, this meant that some twenty-five thousand pairs were available for breeding. Since each female produced about four thousand eggs, a total of exactly one hundred million eggs would be available to ensure a generation born in 1907, and we have seen that this is the precise number required to maintain the lake's normal population. Any diminution in the number of survivors would imperil the chance for continuation.

If the jiggers were raised even higher next year, as planned, the number of breeding salmon able to avoid them would be further diminished, so that year by year the deficiency would worsen.

The greed of Tom Venn and his masters in Seattle had doomed the Lake Pleiades sockeye, one of the noblest members of the animal kingdom, to eventual extinction.

* * *

IN NOVEMBER WHEN the Thomas Venns, as they were now called, were in the process of closing down Ketchikan Cannery for the winter, after an excellent campaign, an officer from Ross & Raglan headquarters in Seattle stopped by with depressing news: 'Mr. Ross asked me to tell you that Nancy Bigears, after only a few weeks at the university, boarded one of our ships and sailed back to Juneau. When asked why she had quit her education, she said: "Those classes held nothing for me." '

'What's she doing?' Tom and Lydia wanted to know, and to be sure he gave an accurate answer, the officer took from his pocket a paper which Mr. Ross had given him: 'Two weeks after arriving in Juneau, Nancy married a Chinese handyman named Ah Ting.'

XI

THE RAILBELT

In the summer of 1919, when Malcolm Ross, age sixty-seven, lay dying, he knew that he was leaving his prominent mercantile establishment, Ross & Raglan, in the most profitable condition it had ever known. In the three areas to which it restricted itself—maritime service to Alaska; warehouses in Anchorage, Juneau and Fairbanks, with retail stores in most of the towns; the catching and canning of salmon—it was preeminent. R&R represented the finest forward-looking leadership in Seattle, and commentators were not far wrong when they said: 'R&R is Alaska, and Alaska is R&R,' for the relationship was profitable to both partners. R&R received money, a great deal of it, and Alaska received the goods it needed and a reliable transportation service to what was called the Lower Forty-Eight. Since there were no roads from Alaska to either industrial Canada or the United States, and no likelihood of any in the foreseeable future, any goods that Alaska needed had almost inevitably to reach the north in some R&R ship, and any travelers who wanted to leave Alaska for the south had to use that same route.

But Ross had for some time been aware of a potential weakness in his company's benevolent monopoly, and anxious to discuss the situation, he summoned his daughter Lydia to his bedside, asking her to bring along her husband, Tom Venn, who for more than a decade had supervised the company's chain of salmon canneries. When they stood beside him, and saw how frail he had become through overexertion during the closing months of the recent world war, they were alarmed, but he would allow no sentimentality: 'I'm not strong, as you can see, but my mind's as good as ever.'

'Take it easy, Father,' Lydia said. 'The men at the office have things under control.'

'I didn't call you here to talk about the office. I'm worried about the insecurity of our shipping lines to Alaska.'

'Traffic's impeccable,' Tom said, who at an energetic thirty-six had traveled the R&R ships more than any other officer. He knew the shipping line to be in first-class condition.

'For the present, yes. But I'm looking ahead, and I see danger.'

'From what?' Lydia asked, and after raising himself on one elbow, her father replied: 'Competition. Not from American companies, we have them in line and none of them can touch us. But from Canada, they're able traders. And from Japan, they're very able.'

'We have been seeing signs,' Venn conceded. 'We can hold them off, I'm sure, but what did you have in mind?'

'Cabotage,' the sick man said as he fell back. 'Do you know what it is?' When the young people shook their heads, he said: 'Find out!' and that launched their study of this arcane law of the sea and its coastal waters. The word came from the French *caboter* meaning *to coast along*, and through the centuries it had gained in diplomatic circles a specific application: the right to transport goods between two ports within the same country. As applied by mercantile nations, it meant that a Japanese ship built in Japan, owned in Japan, and manned by Japanese sailors was legally eligible to sail out of Yokohama laden with Japanese goods and sail to Seattle, where, if the proper duty was paid, the goods could be unloaded and sold in the United States. The ship could then pick up American goods and carry them back to Japan, or China or Russia.

But when the Japanese ship finished unloading at Seattle, it was forbidden to engage in cabotage, that is, it could not pick up either cargo or passengers in Seattle and carry them to some other American port, say San Francisco. And, specifically, it could not deliver American items to Alaska. Any goods or passengers traveling from one American port to another had to be transported in American ships manned by American sailors, and not even the slightest deviation was allowed. Businessmen in Seattle revered the principle of cabotage as if it were Scripture, for it ensured them protection from competition from Asian vessels whose poorly paid crews enabled them to move freight at the lowest cost. So the more deeply the two young Venns probed into the intricacies of cabotage, the more clearly they saw that the future of Seattle, and especially the profitability of their family firm, depended upon the retention, strengthening and strict application of cabotage.

When they next gathered at their father's sickbed to discuss the matter, he showed his pleasure at their quick mastery of the situation, but he was distressed at their failure to identify the next step Seattle would have to take to protect itself completely: 'Tom, the people of Alaska aren't going to support any strengthening of cabotage. In fact, they're going to fight against it. In Congress.'

Venn nodded: 'They would get their goods a lot cheaper if ships from Europe and Asia could haul them. Maybe even ships from Canada would be able to undercut us.'

'I'm especially afraid of the Canadians. So what you must do when Congress takes up the matter, which the people of Alaska will insist upon, is line up a type of support we've never had before.'

'I don't understand. Cabotage is a shipping concern. We're for it. The businessmen of Seattle are for it. West Coast shippers are for it. But who else?'

'That's where statesmanship comes in. Move away from the coasts. Enlist a whole new body of supporters in cities like Pittsburgh, Chicago and St. Louis.'

'And how do we do that?'

'Labor. Add one simple provision to the navigation bills and you'll have all labor shouting support for our cabotage bills.'

'And what is this magical provision?' Lydia asked, and her father replied: 'Require that the American ship, owned by American businessmen and staffed by American officers and seamen, be built entirely in American shipyards by American workers.' As he finished his prescription for the ensured growth of Seattle and the R&R shipping lines, he settled back on his pillows and smiled, for he was convinced that if such a bill could be shepherded through Congress, the possibility that Alaska might somehow evade control from Seattle would be eliminated.

But his clever son-in-law spotted the danger in relying upon Congress to pass a law which would aid the few and harm the many. 'Alaska will fight like hell to prevent a law like that,' he warned the old man, who merely nodded: 'Of course they'll protest. They've never understood, up there, that they must rely on us for their well-being. R&R has never taken one nickel out of Alaska that wasn't justified. It'll be the same way with the bill I'm talking about. We'll pass it to protect Alaska from herself.'

'How?' Tom asked, and he received a recommendation he did not savor: 'We'll do it as we've always done it. The West Coast hasn't enough power in Congress to do it alone, but we do have friends in the other states. We must mobilize those friends, and there's only one man can do that job for us.' Tom felt a sinking feeling in his stomach, and he was right to be apprehensive, for Ross said firmly: 'Get Marvin Hoxey.'

'But he's a crook!' Tom cried, recalling his distaste for this fraudulent operator.

'He still carries weight in Washington. If you want to protect our interests in Alaska, get Hoxey.'

This Tom was reluctant to do, but in the anxious days that followed, as the directors of R&R convened to decide whom to select as Malcolm Ross's successor as head of the company, it became clear that Ross was not going to bestow his blessing on Tom Venn unless the latter hired Marvin Hoxey, the proven lobbyist, to maneuver a new maritime bill through Congress. Her father warned Lydia, when she met with him alone: 'If Tom doesn't get Hoxey out here right away, I'll tell the board outright that he's not the man to replace me.'

'But Hoxey is an evil man, Father. He's shown that again and again.'

'He's an able man. He does what he says he'll do, and that's all that counts.'

'And you'll block Tom if he refuses?'

'I must think about the safety of my company. I must do what's right.'

'You call hiring a crook doing what's right?'

'Under the circumstances, yes.'

That night Lydia told her husband: 'I think you'd better telephone Hoxey.'

'I will not do that.'

'But, Tom . . .'

'I will not humiliate myself again in connection with that swindler.'

There was a protracted silence, after which Lydia said quietly: 'When Father dies, I'll be the principal stockholder . . . Mother's shares and the ones he'll leave me. So I must act to protect my interests. I'm calling Hoxey.' Tom, in disgust, left the room, but as he paced back and forth outside the door he realized that he was forcing a break between himself and his wife, and at a moment when she deserved his fullest support, so he returned to the room, just as Lydia finished putting in the call. Taking the telephone, he said with as much control as possible: 'Marvin Hoxey? This is Tom Venn. . . . Yes, we knew each other in Nome during the great days, and during the salmon leases. . . . Yes, I'm married to Lydia Ross. . . . Sorry to tell you that her father is quite ill. . . . Yes, he wants to complete one big job before he dies. . . . He needs you. Right away. . . . Yes, Alaska.' A long silence followed, during which the ebullient lobbyist delivered an oration. . . . 'Yes, I'll tell her.'

When he hung up, he looked sheepishly at Lydia: 'The old rascal! He'd already guessed what Seattle would want done on the maritime bill. Had already started visiting congressmen on the assurance we'd call.'

'What else did he say? During that one long spell?'

'He said he knew Alaska like the back of his hand and that everything was going to be all right.'

Shortly thereafter the wily old campaigner came to Seattle to consult with Malcolm Ross. Sixty-four years old, heavyset, florid of face and clean-shaven, he breezed into the sickroom, cocked his right forefinger as if it were a pistol, and fired an imaginary bullet at Ross: 'I want you out of that bed by nightfall. Orders.'

'I wish I could obey, Marvin. But the . . .' He tapped his chest and smiled. 'Draw up a chair and listen.' And as the dying merchant prince lay in bed, he plotted his last great strategy for the enhancement of Seattle.

In these years the state of Washington was represented in the Senate of the United States by a hardworking, amiable Republican named Wesley L. Jones, whose devotion to duty had elevated him to the chairmanship of the important Senate Commerce Committee. Always attentive to the interests of his home state, he had listened when Malcolm Ross consulted with him concerning ways to nail down permanently all traffic heading for Alaska. He agreed early and firmly that nations like Japan and Canada should be eliminated from the profitable trade, and he saw no good reason why the established state of Washington should not take precedence over the unformed territory of Alaska, but he cautioned Ross and his fellow Seattleites: 'It's not like the old days, gentlemen. Alaska is beginning to have a voice in our nation's capital. That little son-of-a-bitch Sheldon Jackson, no bigger than a pinpoint, he stirred up a lot of good Christians back there. We can't just run your bill through this time. We'll have to work on it, and work hard.'

It was in April of that year that the Seattle men had awakened to the opposition which existed in the industrial states and those along the Mississippi. At the last meeting he chaired before becoming bedridden, Ross had reported: 'You'd be astonished at some of the charges they're making against us. They say we're robbers, pirates trying to keep Alaska to ourselves. We've got to come up with some new tactic.'

Just who it was who had the clever idea of enlisting labor in the fight to keep Alaska a colony was not recorded; Ross had not been at the meeting when this was first proposed, but as soon as members of his committee brought the suggestion to his bedside, he had grasped its significance: 'Ride that one very hard. We're not trying to protect our interests. We're thinking only of the American workingman, the American sailor.'

Now, in the closing weeks of his life, he outlined to both Marvin Hoxey and Tom Venn the strategy that would enable Senator Jones to ramrod through a maritime bill in 1920, the one that would remain in force for the rest of the century, binding Alaska in the harshest, most restrictive fetters any American territory would know since the days of King George III's repressive measures which had goaded the Colonies to revolt.

No one in the entire American political establishment was more influential in getting this act passed than Marvin Hoxey. Only three years younger than Malcolm Ross, he had four times the explosive energy and ten times the shameless gall. It took him less than three minutes to perceive the brilliance of enlisting labor in the fight, and before that first meeting ended, he had devised a presentation which would capture the imagination of congressmen in all parts of the nation. It required him to patrol the halls in Washington, while Tom Venn visited those state capitals whose representatives would cast the deciding votes.

Tom did not appreciate the assignment, for it meant that he would have to telephone Washington every night to inform Hoxey as to how things were going, and he might have refused to serve as Hoxey's assistant had not Malcolm Ross taken a sharp turn for the worse. Informed of the situation, Lydia and Tom rushed to his bedside, and when the two stood before him he gave them their last commission: 'Any industry of magnitude faces moments of crisis . . . when decisions of life and death are in the process of being made. Choose right, up to the stars. Choose wrong, down to Avernus.' He coughed, then flashed that smile which had served him so well at other times when he was striving to convince people: 'And the hell of it is, usually we don't recognize that the decision is vital. We make it blind.' He coughed again, his shoulders shaking violently; now the smile left his drawn lips and he said softly: 'But this time we do know. The prosperity of this part of the nation depends upon getting Senator Jones's bill enacted.' He asked Tom to promise that for the next crucial months he would work with full vigor on this campaign: 'Let the company guide itself. You get out there and line up the votes.' Then he reached for his telephone and called Marvin Hoxey, telling him to catch a night train. But at midafternoon Tom placed another call: 'Marvin? Tom Venn. Cancel the trip. Malcolm died forty minutes ago.'

THE JONES ACT of 1920 passed with its three essential provisions in place: no ship of foreign ownership and registry could carry American goods from one American port to another; only ships owned and manned by Americans could do that; the ship itself, even if it was American-owned, had to have been built in the United States by American labor. The future of Seattle was ensured.

The effect of the Jones Act could best be illustrated by what happened to a modest grocery store in Anchorage. Sylvester Rowntree had invested his savings in a new store half again as big as the old one, and by the year 1923 it had again doubled, so that the owner could have profitably ordered, from suppliers across the United States, his goods in cargo lots. But this was not practical, because a custom had evolved whereby goods destined for Alaska had to be handled in curious ways by the railroads and in ways downright insane at the docks in Seattle. Even before Rowntree's cargo was ready for loading onto an R&R vessel he would be forced to pay fifty percent more freightage than if his goods had been destined for some West Coast destination like Portland or Sacramento.

But now provisions of the Jones Act came into play: to use the Seattle docks for shipment to Alaska cost almost twice what the same dock services cost for a shipment, say, to Japan. And when the R&R ship was loaded, the cost-per-mile of goods to Alaska was much higher than the cost of the same goods being shipped to other American ports by other lines. R&R had a monopoly which exacted a fifty-percent or better surcharge on every item freighted in to Alaska, and the territory had no escape from this imposition, for there were no other avenues by which goods could get in: no highways, no railroads, and as yet no airplanes.

'That damned Jones Act is strangling us,' Sylvester Rowntree wailed, and he was right, for the Act exercised its tyranny in the most unexpected ways. The forests of Alaska could have provided wooden boxes for the Alaskan salmon canneries, but the cost of bringing in American sawmill equipment was kept so excessive that it was much cheaper to buy the wood from Oregon than to use trees which stood fifty feet from a cannery, and tariffs kept out non-Americans.

In the years following passage of the Act, a dozen profitable extractive industries went out of business because of the exorbitant costs imposed by the new rules, and this happened even though scores of Canadian ships stood ready to bring heavy equipment in at reasonable cost and take finished products out at rates that ensured a good profit.

Such discrepancies were explained away by Marvin Hoxey, defending in public the Act which he had engineered, as 'inescapable minor dislocations which can be easily corrected.' When no attempt was made to rectify them, he told Congress: 'These are nothing more than the minor costs which a remote territory like Alaska must expect to bear if it is to enjoy the privileges of life within the American system.' In his old age Hoxey had converted himself into a revered oracle, forever prepared to justify the indecencies to which Alaska was subjected.

What infuriated Alaskans like grocer Rowntree was not the pomposity of Hoxey and the self-serving statements of Thomas Venn, president of Ross & Raglan, but the fact that Hawaii, much farther from San Francisco than Alaska was from Seattle, received its goods at substantially cheaper rates. Rowntree's seventeen-year-old son, Oliver, figured: 'Pop, if a grocer in Honolulu places a hundred-dollar order at the same time you do with a wholesaler in New York, by the time the two orders reach the West Coast docks, his has a total cost of $126, but yours is $147. Dockage fees being so different, by the time his goods get aboard they cost $137, but yours are $163. And now comes the rotten part. Because R&R rates are the highest in the world, by the time his goods reach Honolulu, they cost $152, while your goods landed in Anchorage cost us $191.'

The boy spent the summer of his senior year conducting similar studies regarding various kinds of in and out shipments, and wherever he looked he found this same terrible discrepancy, so that for his graduating paper in English he composed a fiery essay entitled: 'The Slavery Continues,' in which he drew parallels between the economic servitude under which Alaska now suffered and the governmental chaos of the 1867–97 period. Fortunately for him—as it turned out later—this lament did not appear in the school journal, but Oliver's father was so proud of his son's insight into Alaskan affairs that he had three unsigned copies made, sending one to the territorial governor, one to Alaska's nonvoting delegate to Congress and one to the Anchorage newspaper, which did print it. His arguments played a role in the continuing attack Alaskans made against the cruel provisions of the Jones Act, but nothing was accomplished because in Seattle, Thomas Venn, increasingly active as head of R&R, and, in Washington, the aged warhorse Marvin Hoxey prevented any revision of the Jones Act or even any orderly discussion of its harmful effect upon Alaska.

Young Oliver Rowntree, nursing his outrage, spent the summer brooding about what he could do to retaliate. And that fall, on his way to the University of Washington in Seattle—where he had won a scholarship—he evolved a plan. From then on, as he traveled back and forth on R&R ships, he began slowly and slyly to sabotage them. He stole silverware from the dining rooms and quietly pitched it overboard at night. He jammed pillowcases down toilets. He wrenched fittings off newel posts, messed up documents he came upon, and threw large amounts of salt into any food he could contaminate without being caught. On some trips, if he was lucky, he did up to a hundred dollars' worth of theft and breakage.

Whenever he committed one of his acts of retribution he muttered to himself: 'That's for stealing from my father . . . and the others,' and twice each year he continued his depredations.

When Tom Venn, from his headquarters in Seattle, studied reports of this sabotage he was at first perplexed, and at dinner one night he told his wife: 'Someone is conducting a vicious campaign against us, and we have no way of determining who it is,' but when she studied the records she said immediately: 'Tom, the worst cases seem to appear in autumn down to Seattle, in spring back to Anchorage.'

'And what's the significance of that?'

'Don't you see? Probably some student. Feels a grievance toward our line.'

Grasping at this clue, Tom initiated a study of passengers who sailed on the ships that had been attacked, and his staff came up with the names of eighteen young people who had sailed on at least three of the six affected voyages and seven who had been on all of them.

'I want a full report on each of the eighteen, with special details on those seven,' Tom ordered, and during the weeks when these were being compiled, Oliver Rowntree was doing some thinking on his own, and he had learned in a math class dealing with the laws of probability that there were many ways by which a shrewd mind could analyze data which seemed at first capricious: Some smart operator could look over the passenger lists and make correlations, and if he was really bright, he could identify four or five likely suspects and then narrow it down intelligently by legwork. Oliver knew that his name would be thrown up by such an approach and what there was in his background which would alert R&R detectives to his being responsible for the sabotage—his essay on the evils of the Jones Act: Damn! Anyone reading that would know it was more than an attack on the Jones Act. It was a blast at Ross & Raglan. And he was glad his father had removed his name from the article.

He was a senior at the university when he completed these deductions: I've been down four trips and back up three. And on each one I've raised hell with something or other. But there must have been others like me who made those same trips. So the problem is: How can I throw the R&R flatfeet off my trail?

For several anxious weeks in 1924 he plotted diversionary actions, and gradually began to see that the best thing he could do would be to enlist into his conspiracy someone who would commit an act of sabotage—the kind he had done—on a northward trip when he was not a passenger, while he followed blamelessly on a later ship. But whom to enlist? Whom to trust with such a delicate mission? Because in the act of explanation he would have to reveal his past culpability, and this would place him in jeopardy.

Looking about the university, he came upon several small groups of students whose homes were in Alaska, and naturally these young people came mostly from Anchorage and Fairbanks; he shied away from the former as being too close to his father's store, and felt no harmony with the latter, but there were four students from Juneau, and he felt both a harmony with them as being more his serious type and an assurance that they, at least one of them, would understand his unusual problem. He therefore started to socialize with them, finding them politically concerned because of the way in which Alaskan politics dominated their hometown, and as the spring term drew to a close he judged it expedient to confide in one of the girls.

She was a beautiful young woman, about nineteen, whose origin was difficult to identify. Her name was one of those alliterative ones popular in the early 1920s, Tammy Ting, which could have made her Chinese, except that she also looked almost completely Indian, so one day after he had spoken to her several times, he asked as they left a student meeting: 'Tammy Ting? What kind of name is that?' and she replied with a frank smile: 'Tammy Bigears Ting.' And she told him about her unusual father—'Only Chinese allowed to remain in Alaska after the big expulsion'—and her equally distinctive Tlingit grandfather —'His family fought the Russians for fifty years and now he fights the government in Washington.' And as she spoke young Rowntree was mesmerized.

'Can I trust you, Tammy? I mean, with something big?' He was older than she, a graduating senior while she was only a sophomore who was thrashing around from one course to another, trying to identify subjects that involved her sympathies: 'My mom came to Washington, back in the ancient days. Only Alaskan native in the university, but she stayed only a few weeks. When I left Juneau she warned me: "You come home without a degree, I break both your arms." '

'What a horrible thing to tell a daughter,' Rowntree said, but Tammy corrected him: 'The horrible part, she meant it. Still does.'

Reassured by such frank comment, Oliver decided he could trust this girl of the new Alaska, and before he finished laying his problem before her, she perceived both his predicament and its solution: 'You want me, on a different ship from the one you'll be on, to do everything you'd be doing?' When he nodded, she cried: 'Set me loose! I despise Ross & Raglan, the way they punish Alaska,' and the plot was hatched.

'Three trademarks,' Oliver said, and when he explained about the stolen cutlery, the rip-off of newel posts and the clogging of the toilets, she asked: 'But if you always did the same damage, didn't you realize they'd know it was always the same person?' and he said: 'I wanted them to know.' He hesitated: 'But I never wanted them to catch me. I wanted them to know that people in Alaska despised what they were doing with their rotten Jones Act,' and she said: 'Pop and Mom feel the same way. I'm your girl.'

At this point Oliver Rowntree leaves this part of the narrative. He graduated with honors from the University of Washington in 1925, sailed home to Anchorage on an R&R ship which he did not vandalize, so as to confuse anyone tracking his case, lived at home for the summer of 1925, and then left for a good job in Oregon, where he would marry in 1927 without ever returning to Alaska. His father had told him as he sailed: 'Don't come back, Oliver. The way those bastards in Seattle and D.C. have things rigged against us, it's impossible to earn a decent living up here in Alaska.' And in 1928 the older Rowntree also moved to Oregon, where, having escaped from the economic tyranny under which Alaska lived, he ran a highly profitable grocery store.

The case of Tammy Ting developed quite differently. On the R&R liner *Pride of Seattle*, which carried her north at the end of her sophomore year in 1925, she surreptitiously performed the three acts of sabotage which would earmark the perpetrator as the same one who had been pestering Ross & Raglan for the past four years, plus a couple of inventive and highly costly depredations of her own, but one evening as she was preparing to devastate an expensively carved newel post, a young man came upon her so unexpectedly that she had to dissemble in obvious embarrassment. 'I'm sorry I startled you,' he apologized, and when he looked more closely he saw that she was strikingly beautiful. 'Are you Russian?' he asked, and she said: 'Half Tlingit, half Chinese,' and as she began to explain how this could be, while they walked in the moonlight with the mountains of Canada on their right, he stopped her abruptly: 'Bigears! I've always known about your family. Your mother came to the university, didn't she? Stayed only a couple of weeks. Back at the turn of the century.'

'How do you know that?'

'My grandmother provided your mother with the scholarship she used.'

Tammy stopped, leaned against the ship's railing, and pointed a delicate finger at her young companion: 'Is your name Ross?'

'Malcolm Venn. Named after my grandfather Ross. He founded this line.' After they had discussed for some moments the improbability of such a meeting, young Venn said: 'You won't believe this either. But I'm on this ship as a detective. Some damned fool's been committing sabotage on the Alaska run, and Father sent me north to sort of watch things . . . that is, to report anything suspicious.' Before she could comment, he added: 'We have men like me on all the ships. We'll catch them.'

Innocently, Tammy asked: 'Why would anyone want to damage an R&R ship?' and he gave her a long lecture about how there were always misguided souls who refused to appreciate the good things that others were doing for them. He explained how the welfare of Alaska depended upon the benevolence of the industrial geniuses in Seattle who looked after the interests of everyone in Alaska. Pleased by having such an attentive and apparently brilliant audience, he progressed to explain how Alaska would never qualify for statehood but how, through the years, it could rely upon Seattle for constructive and parental leadership.

When she had heard enough of this nonsense, she interrupted: 'My mother's people, way back, fought against the Russians, then against the United States, and now against you people in Seattle. I think my children and their grandchildren will continue the fight.'

'But why?'

'Because we're entitled to be free. We're intelligent enough to run our own state.' Flashing fire, she stared at R&R's future owner and asked: 'Has your father ever told you how my father, an illiterate immigrant working for sixty dollars a year, solved the mechanical problems in your father's cannery? And then left to start a business of his own? And taught himself to read, and use a slide rule, and acquire lots and lots of land that no one else thought useful? Mr. Ross, if my father was bright enough to do all those things, he's certainly bright enough to run a state government, and I know a hundred others like him . . . in all parts of Alaska.'

And as she spoke, young Venn became so enchanted that he dogged her throughout the remainder of the trip, eager to share her vision of an Alaska about which he had never been told. She was flattered by his attention, but on the last night out, when others were celebrating, she detached herself from him, waiting cautiously for an appropriate moment, then tore away an expensive newel post decorating the grand stairway and tossed it into the icy waters of Cook Inlet.

The splash in the dark waters reflected light from one of the ship's portholes, and it had scarcely died when she felt herself caught by strong arms, whipped about, and kissed passionately on the lips. 'I've always thought,' Malcolm Venn said quietly as they walked the upper deck, 'that when my father spoke of those early days at Totem Cannery—the sinking of the *Montreal Queen*, the fight over the salmon in the Pleiades River . . .' He paused, afraid lest he say too much, but then he blurted out: 'I'm sure my father was in love with your mother.'

'Of course he was,' Tammy said. 'Everyone knew that. Mother told me: "Mrs. Ross understood the first moment we saw each other. And she wasn't going to let no goddamned Tlingit marry a boy her daughter might want!" '

Young Malcolm laughed at the idea of anyone's wanting to prevent a marriage with a girl like Tammy Ting, and they kissed again.

* * *

IN THE BITTERLY cold winter of January 1935 the small towns in the vicinity of Thief River Falls in western Minnesota, close to the Canadian border, were experiencing the full terror of the Great Depression. In Solway, John and Rose Kirsch with their three children were living on one meal a day. In the tiny village of Skime, Tad and Nellie Jackson, also with three children, were close to starving, and in Robbin, right on the border of North Dakota, Harold and Frances Alexander had four children to worry about, with no assured income of any kind. This part of Minnesota was being strangled.

In the crossroads of Viking, a mile or so northwest of Thief River, a tall, gawky farmer named Elmer Flatch left his wife, Hilda, and their daughter, Flossie, in their barren lean-to with its wood-burning stove and led his sixteen-year-old son, LeRoy—pronounced LEE-roy—into the woods north of town with a solemn warning: 'Son, we ain't comin' out of these woods withouten we got ourself a deer.' Grimly the two Flatches marched into the small forest, well aware that they were hunting out of season: 'If a warden tries to stop us, LeRoy, I'm a-gonna let him have it full in the face. Be ready.' And with these two determinations—to get a deer and protect themselves in doing so—the two hunters left the dirt road and plunged into the woods.

In the open spaces there had been drifts of snow, some quite deep, but in the scrub forest, last timbered in the early 1920s, the January snow was sparse, just thick enough to show tracks where animals had crossed it, so during the first hour and a half in the silvery shadows Elmer reminded his son how to identify the various animals that shared the woods with them: 'That'n's a hare, you can tell by the big hind marks. Elbow of the leg leaves a dimple. This'n? Maybe a wood mouse. This'n, for sure, a rabbit. That'n a fox, I do believe. Not many foxes in these parts.'

As the father probed the secrets of the forest, he felt a sense of well-being, even though he had not eaten a full meal in three days. 'Ain't nothin' better in this world, LeRoy, than huntin' on a winter's day. Yonder has got to be some deer.' From his earliest days in Minnesota he had been convinced that beyond the next rise there would be deer, and that he could find them. His assurance was justified by his remarkable record in bagging deer where others could not, and on this day, when venison was not sport but almost life-and-death, he tracked with exceptional care.

'Down thataway, not much, LeRoy. Over thisaway, maybe,' but as the morning passed without even a track showing where deer had been, the two men —for at sixteen, LeRoy was a responsible partner with a sure manner of handling his gun—began to feel the first signs of panic, not in wild gestures, for the Flatch family never engaged in such display, but in the tenseness which gripped the pits of their stomachs.

'LeRoy, I'm wore out. What do you think?'

'There's got to be deer. Vickaryous got one last month. They told me at the store.'

At the mention of his Finnish neighbor, Elmer Flatch stiffened. He did not cotton to the Finns, Norwegians and Swedes who clustered in this part of Minnesota; they were decent enough neighbors but they were not his kind. He stuck with people carrying names that were more American, like Jackson, Alexander and Kirsch. The Flatches, if he understood correctly, came originally from Kentucky, via Indiana and Iowa, 'American as far back as you can count.'

But now he asked his son: 'Where did Vickaryous say he got his deer?'

'I didn't see him, but the men in the store said it was at the edge of the clearing.'

Admitting a kind of failure, Elmer told LeRoy: 'Let's head for that clearing, the big one,' and his son said: 'That's the one, if I understood right.'

At the clearing they encountered nothing, not even tracks, and now the incipient panic intensified, for they simply dared not go home without something to eat: 'If'n we see rabbit or a hare, LeRoy, bag it. The women got to have somethin' they can chew on.' The boy made no response, but as shadows began to lengthen his fears increased, for he knew what despair there would be in the lean-to if they returned empty-handed. It had been more than a week since anyone in the Flatch family had tasted meat, and even the bag of beans no longer had sufficient contents to stand upright in the corner.

But twilight deepened, with no sign of deer, and what would otherwise have been fifteen minutes of snowy grandeur as night descended upon the Minnesota hills became instead a cause for anxiety. Elmer Flatch, a man whose major pride lay in his ability to go out with his gun and feed his family, faced the disastrous situation of not only failing to find meat but also being unable to buy the poorest canned substitutes at the Viking store.

It was now dark, but Elmer, who like most good hunters kept account of the moon, knew that what he called a 'three-quarters waner' would soon begin to show, and he instructed his son: 'LeRoy, we're stayin' out till we get us a deer,' and the boy nodded, for he was as reluctant as his father to return to the women of his family with no food.

The two men moved cautiously in the dark, with the father reminding his son: 'Don't leave my side. I don't want to be shootin' at you in the shadows, thinkin' you're maybe a deer.' What he really meant was: 'Don't wander over there among the trees and then blaze away at me when I make a sudden noise,' but mindful of his son's youth, he refrained from embarrassing him.

They came upon an open glade which ought to have had deer, but none showed, and when they returned to the woods they were in almost total darkness for about half an hour, but then, as they approached another opening, the waning moon rose above the surrounding trees, and a comfortable light suffused the scene, but it disclosed no tracks. At midnight, when the moon was climbing to its apex, the two were still surrounded by empty forest and the father began to grow weak, hunger overcoming him, but he tried to hide his condition from his son, pausing now and then to catch his breath, something he had never had to do before, given his lean frame and his capacity for endurance.

It was nearly two in the morning when the Flatches came upon a moonlit opening across which deer had recently traveled, and at the sight of tracks, Elmer felt a surge of strength, and with masterful commands he vectored LeRoy off to the right, keeping him in sight to prevent a shooting accident, and with great caution moved forward among the trees.

They saw the deer. Among the shadows it saw them and darted away. LeRoy almost wept as the animal's flag twisted and darted to safety, but his father merely bit his lower lip for a moment, then said: 'We're on their trail, LeRoy. Over there we catch ourself a deer.' And with a fortitude that astonished his son, Elmer Flatch started in pursuit of the deer he knew he must have: 'We'll follow it till sunset tomorrow if we have to.'

An hour before dawn the two Flatches came upon a solitary doe, handsomely framed in fading light from the declining moon. Mustering all his control, Elmer whispered to his son: 'Fire when my right elbow drops. Aim just a little forward in case she leaps ahead.' Then he added: 'Son, we got to get this one.'

Meticulously the two Flatches leveled their guns, protecting them from the moonlight lest a sudden glint startle the doe, and as Elmer signaled with his right elbow, the two fired, dropping her as if she had been struck by lightning. When Elmer saw her fall, he could feel himself falling too, from exhaustion and the sudden relief of having found food, except that as he started to go down, LeRoy caught him: 'Sit on the log, Pop. I'll cut her throat.' And while Elmer sat in the frozen moonlight, again close to fainting from hunger, LeRoy ran across the opening and began to prepare the deer for carrying.

It was a long walk back to the Flatch lean-to, and the sides of deer were heavy, but the two men walked as if joy were pulling them forward; they seemed to receive strength and sustenance from the mere presence of the bloody meat upon their backs, and as they approached their destination and saw the wisp of morning smoke coming from wood recently thrown upon the fire, LeRoy began to run, shouting: 'Mom! Flossie! We got us a deer!'

Unfortunately, his cries alerted the Vickaryous men on the farm nearby, and when the Finns learned that their neighbors had shot a deer, two men and two women came to the Flatch home: 'We ain't had food for three days, Mr. Flatch.'

The starving settlers studied one another, the four Flatches from back east, the two Vickaryous couples twenty years out of Finland. They were tall and straight, all eight of them, and lean and hardworking. Their clothes were presentable, especially the Finns', and they were at the end of their rope, all of them.

'You got to let us have something, Mr. Flatch,' one of the Vickaryous women said, and Hilda Flatch moved forward with a knife: 'Of course,' and she knelt down to cut off a sizable chunk of venison. As she did, one of the Vickaryous women burst into tears: 'God knows we're ashamed to beg. But in this cold . . .'

As the four women were butchering the deer, a guardian angel appeared as if sent by heaven to succor these families. He appeared in a used Ford, badly treated over the past fifteen years, and at first the men in the lean-to thought he might be a game warden. 'He don't get this deer,' Elmer whispered to the others, and one of the Vickaryous men told his group: 'Careful, but don't let him touch that meat. Just don't let him do it.'

The visitor was Nils Sjodin, from a government office of some kind in Thief River Falls, and he carried with him a remarkable message and the documents to back it up. Seated in the lean-to, with the eight people clustered about him, he said: 'Glad to see you got yourselves a deer. Food's scarce in these parts.'

'Who are you?' Hilda Flatch asked, and he replied: 'The bringer of good tidings,' and with that, he slapped upon the wooden table a pile of papers which he invited everyone to inspect. Since farmers in this part of Minnesota respected education, all in the shack were able to read, even young Flossie Flatch, and in the next moments they received first notice of the revolution that was about to engulf them and their neighbors in this northern part of the United States.

'Yep!' Mr. Sjodin said with the enthusiasm of a Methodist minister or a farm-equipment salesman. 'Every word it says here is true. Our government is going to select eight, nine hundred people from areas like this, people really down on their luck through no fault of their own, and we're going to ship you,

all expenses paid, to a valley in Alaska . . . cabbages weigh sixty pounds each
. . . never saw anything like it.'

'To what purpose?' Hilda Flatch asked. All her life she had dealt with
flimflam artists and she judged Mr. Sjodin to be the next in that engaging
parade.

'To start a new life in a new world. To populate a paradise. To build an area
of great importance to the United States—our new frontier, Alaska.'

'Isn't it all ice up there?' Elmer asked.

Mr. Sjodin had been waiting for just this question. Producing three new
publications, he spread them so that all could see, and for the first time in their
lives, the Flatches and the Vickaryouses saw the magical word Matanuska.
'Look for yourselves!' Sjodin said with a pride that would have been appropriate had he owned the area he was about to describe: 'Matanuska Valley. Set
down among great mountains. Girt by glaciers that run mysteriously out of the
hills. Fertile land. Crops like you never saw before. Look at this man standing
beside those cabbages and turnips. Look at this affidavit, signed by an official
of the United States government: "I, John Dickerson, U.S. Department of
Agriculture, do certify that the man standing beside these vegetables is me and
that the vegetables are real and not doctored in any way." ' In awe these farmers
looked at the produce of this Alaskan valley, then at the crest of glorious
snow-capped mountains which enclosed it, then at the sample house erected
beside a flowing stream. They were looking at a wonderland, and they knew it.

'What's the catch?' Hilda Flatch asked, and Mr. Sjodin asked everyone to
be seated, because he knew that what he was about to say was beyond belief:
'Our government, and I work for it, in agriculture, has decided that it must do
something to help you farmers who have been so roughly treated by the Depression. And this is what we're going to do.'

'Who are you?' Mrs. Flatch asked, and he said: 'From a family of farmers
just like you. Went to North Dakota State in Fargo. Farmed awhile myself in
Minnesota and was tapped by the federals. My present job? To help families like
yours move into a new life.'

'You don't even know us,' Hilda Flatch said, and Mr. Sjodin corrected her
politely but sharply: 'I've done a great deal of work on the Flatches and the
Vickaryouses. I know how much you owe on your farms, what you paid for
your machinery, what your credit is at the bank, and your general health
records. I know you're honest people. Your neighbors give you good reports,
and you're all absolutely dead broke. You know what the grocer in Thief River
told me: "I'd give them Flatches the shirt off my back. Honest as the day is long.
But I can't give them no more credit." ' The men in the two families looked at
the floor. 'So you've been selected. I think all of you can count on that.'

'Children too?' Hilda asked, and he said: 'Especially the children. We want
kids like yours to be the seed of the great new Alaska.'

Now that he had their attention, he spelled out the details: 'We will carry
you to San Francisco on the train, not a penny of expense to you. There we'll
place you on a ship to Alaska, not one cent of charge. When you land in Alaska
we'll convey you to Matanuska, our charge. There we'll assign you, with you
making the choice of location, forty acres. We'll build you a brand-new home
and a barn and give you a free supply of seeds and livestock. We'll also build
a town center with stores, doctors and a highway to market.'

'You mean,' Elmer asked, 'all this for free?'

'At the beginning, yes. You do not spend a penny. Even the stove comes free. But we do charge against your name three thousand dollars, on which you pay nothing while you're getting started. Beginning in the second year you pay three percent interest on your mortgage. That's ninety dollars a year, and with the way things grow in that valley, you'll be able to pay not only the interest but on the principal too.'

As he finished with a grandiloquent gesture, he smiled at the four Finns, as if he wanted particularly to convince them: 'The federal government has asked us to specialize getting Swedes, Norwegians and Finns, ages twenty-five to forty, farmers with children. You'd be perfect if you had children.'

'We have seven between us,' one of the Finnish women said, but before Mr. Sjodin could assure her that this pretty well assured the two families of selection, he was diverted by a soft thud behind him, and he turned to find that Elmer Flatch had fainted.

'He ain't had solid food for four days,' Hilda Flatch said. 'Flossie, start somethin' cookin',' and she asked Mr. Sjodin for help in lifting her bone-skin husband to a bed.

To THE AMAZEMENT of the two hundred and ninetynine Minnesota farmers that Mr. Sjodin selected in the winter of 1935 for this bonanza provided by the federal government, he kept every promise he made. A train designated the *Alaska Special* took them in relative comfort to the Southern Pacific Station in San Francisco, and at various stops local citizens, eager to see the New Pilgrims, crowded the railroad stations with canteens of hot coffee, sandwiches and doughnuts. Newspaper reporters flocked to query the travelers and wrote stories that fell into two distinct categories: either the Minnesota people were daring adventurers thrusting forward into unknown frozen frontiers, or they were shameless participants in another of President Roosevelt's socialist schemes destined to destroy the integrity of America. A few penetrating reporters tried to strike a balance between the two extremes, one woman in Montana writing:

> These hardy souls are not plunging blindly into some arctic wasteland where they won't see the sun for six months at a time. This reporter has looked up the climatic conditions at Matanuska and found them to be about the same as northern Maine or southern North Dakota. The valley itself looks a lot like the better parts of Iowa, except that it is surrounded by a chain of beautiful snow-covered peaks. In fact, there is reason to believe that these emigrants are headed for a kind of paradise.

> The big question is: Why them and not somebody else? The federal government is handing them all kinds of bonanzas at little or no cost, and the taxpayers of Montana will ultimately have to foot the bill. This reporter could find no justification for heaping this largesse on this particular group of farmers except that they were all from northern states, they were mostly Scandinavian, and they all looked as if they knew how to work. The people of our county who met them at the station wished them well, for they really are launched on a great adventure.

In San Francisco, Mr. Sjodin, as promised, had a ship waiting to carry them north, and even though it proved to be one of the ugliest ships afloat—the old army transport *St. Mihiel*, a slab-sided bucket with deep indentations in the railings fore and aft—it did float, it had abundant food, and each family had a place to sleep. In this first shipment of Matanuska settlers, there were no men without wives and almost no families without children. They were a homogeneous lot, these emigrants from an old world in Minnesota to a new life in Alaska: of similar age and similar background, any fifty of the men chosen at random seemed almost indistinguishable. The majority were of medium height, about a hundred and sixty pounds, clean-shaven and capable-looking. Their greatest similarity was in dress, for unlike the women, who wore varied clothes, these hardworking men all wore dark suits with trousers and jackets made of the same heavy woolen fabric. They wore shirt and tie, the former invariably white, the latter always of some subdued color, but what set them apart from the people they met in San Francisco and the other towns their train had passed were the workingmen's caps they wore, made of some woven fabric with a stiff brim. In appearance these adventurers were the drabbest group of men ever to have attempted settlement in a new locale: they compared in no way with the conquistadors from Spain who braved their way into Mexico and Peru; they wore none of the variegated clothing that characterized Jamestown in Virginia; nor had they the colorful dress of the Dutch who came to New York, or the handsome austerity of the Pilgrims in Massachusetts. They were men from Middle America venturing forth in that period when clothes were at their supreme dullest, and in their banal similarities neither the men nor the women looked as if they were bound for any great exploration.

However, once the *St. Mihiel* was under way, radical differences within the group began to surface. A minority of the passengers proved to be ordinary Americans like the Flatches and their friends, the Alexanders of Robbin, the Kirsches of Solway and the Jacksons of Skime, and almost automatically these families clustered together as if to protect themselves from the overbearing Scandinavians: the Kertullas, the Vasanojas and the Vickaryouses. The Scandinavians were not actually overbearing, they merely seemed that way—keeping to themselves, speaking in their native languages, and conducting themselves with the superior air of men and women many of whom had already taken sea voyages in getting to Minnesota. They moved about the *St. Mihiel* with such confidence that they seemed to own it.

Despite this factionalism, which manifested itself in all aspects of the voyage north, the trivial animosities were forgotten when the ship entered Alaskan waters, for then the great mountains which guarded the western shore of the peninsula shone in splendor, and like Vitus Bering two hundred years earlier and James Cook in the 1770s, these newcomers watched in awe as these majestic mountains and their glaciers came down to the Pacific. As Mr. Jackson said to the American group: 'This sure ain't Minnesota,' and Mr. Alexander replied: 'Hard to believe there's fields you could farm behind them mountains.' Elmer Flatch, staring at the great masses of rock, told the Kirsches: 'Have we been trapped? There can't be tillable ground in there.'

At Anchorage they were surprised when Mr. Sjodin, who despite his own Scandinavian background maintained good relations with both groups, moved them into the cars of a modern train, 'as fine,' he told them, 'as the Union Pacific.' They had expected dogsleds, but found themselves in railroad cars much better than the ones in which they had ridden from Minnesota to California. They were further surprised when they saw on the roads paralleling the train tracks a plentiful supply of automobiles that looked the same as the ones they had known in Minnesota. However, young LeRoy Flatch did notice one difference: 'Look how the fenders are all rusted. Why?' And Mr. Alexander, who knew automobiles, said: 'Salt spray, I'm sure.'

They left Anchorage at nine in the morning for the forty-mile run to Matanuska, and during the first three-quarters of the trip they saw nothing that indicated the possibility of farming: uninspiring salt beds lay to the west, forbidding mountains to the east, so that even the hardiest Scandinavians, accustomed to northern terrains, began to despair, while flatlanders like the Flatches and the Jacksons were ready to surrender. 'No man can farm that stuff,' Mr. Jackson said as he surveyed the western plains, devoid of both trees and grass, and Hilda Flatch agreed, and they were further depressed when the train approached the undisciplined Knik River, a mile wide and apparently six inches deep.

But as their car reached the middle of the bridge, young Flossie Flatch, staring to the east, cried: 'Mom, look! Hey, Pop, look!' and the Flatches saw opening before them the kind of prospect European travelers expected when they ventured into the Alps. First there was a nearly circular rim of resplendent mountains, their white caps glistening in the morning sun. Then came the trees, thousands upon thousands of them, hardwood and evergreen alike, a bounty so plentiful it could never be depleted. And then, to delight the farmers, spread the waiting fields and meadows, thousands of acres ready for the plow.

In their varied tongues the Scandinavians shared their assessments of this valley, and all agreed that they had come upon a wonderland as fine as anything in Norway or Sweden, and the magnitude of the components bedazzled them. One of the Vickaryous men, running back to where the Flatches clustered, gripped Elmer by the arm and cried: 'With land like this, anything!' And he kissed Hilda Flatch, who was astonished by his familiarity.

For about half an hour the train picked its way slowly along the western edge of the valley, allowing the passengers to see one marvel after another, and what pleased the newcomers especially was the plenitude of little streams cutting their way through the flatlands. 'Everyone can have their farm along a river,' Elmer said, but his wife cautioned: 'And get flooded out when all that snow melts.' Her husband did not hear her, for just then the conductor was shouting: 'Get everything ready. Almost there.'

'Is there any game out there?' Flatch asked him. 'Huntin', I mean?' and the conductor said: 'Anyone can't get hisself a moose or a bear in them hills, he ain't no hunter. Even my wife's brother Herman got hisself a moose.' So for the remaining moments of the trip to Matanuska, Elmer visualized himself prowling those uplands, so close to the flat fields, on the trail of moose.

When the train finally stopped, at a station called Palmer, it did so in three jolting hiccups, with the cars jamming forward one against the other, followed by a screeching halt. Then onto the wooden platform, much like what would have been found in Minnesota, the immigrants piled out, and one conductor said to another: 'Look! They really are different. Most of 'em have cardboard suitcases.'

From the train station the families looked across an empty field to where an amazing sight awaited them: Tent City, a collection of some half a hundred white military field tents, each with cots and a black stovepipe protruding from the top. 'There it is!' Mr. Sjodin cried enthusiastically. 'Your home till your houses are built.' When some of the Scandinavians began protesting, Sjodin cried: 'Look! They're fine tents. Your sons in the army use them all the time,' and the Scandinavians replied: 'But not in Alaska,' and Sjodin broke into loud laughter: 'Go up to Fairbanks! You'll find them in tents right now. Stayed in them all winter.'

'Are you living in one of them?' a Swede asked. 'I'll bet you have yourself a real house.'

'Tent Number Seven, right over there,' Sjodin said. 'You'll do a lot of business with me in Number Seven.'

The Flatches and the Jacksons were assigned a tent in the second row back from the road, Number 19, and since each family had a daughter of an age where she should not be sleeping in the same room with boys, they strung a rope down the middle of the tent and suspended sheets from it. On one side slept the four females, on the other side the five males, and similar arrangements prevailed in all the tents occupied by two families. As the groups were sorted out, Mr. Jackson observed: 'Not one case where real Americans are mixed in with the Scandinavians,' and this separation would prevail when it came time to draw lots for the land assignments.

This exciting day came relatively late in the settlement at Matanuska. The land had to be surveyed, parceled into reasonable holdings, and made available by the building of rough roads, but when all was in readiness, Mr. Sjodin and his three superiors announced that the lottery was ready to take place as planned. That afternoon Elmer Flatch went quietly to Tent Number 7 to consult with the man whose performance in getting the Minnesotans to Matanuska had been so exemplary.

'I'd like your advice, Mr. Sjodin.'

'That's what I'm here for,' and before Elmer could speak further, Sjodin said with great warmth: 'Remember that morning I met you. You and your son had just shot a deer. You were sharing it with the Vickaryous family. And now you're all up here in Alaska. Quite wonderful, isn't it?'

'Never figured it would happen,' Flatch said, 'but now Hilda and me, we got to choose our land. What do you advise?'

With an unusual gift for perceiving personal situations, a skill developed while serving as student manager of the football team at North Dakota State and later as county agricultural agent in Minnesota, Sjodin recognized that Elmer Flatch probably had desires and plans somewhat different from the other settlers, and he intended to respect them: 'Now, before I can advise you, Mr. Flatch, you must share with me your honest statement of what it is you hope to accomplish here in Alaska.'

'Well, like all the others . . .'

'I don't mean all the others. I mean you.'

For almost a full minute Elmer stared at the floor, his tense knuckles clasped under his chin, wondering if he could level with this Swede. Finally, acknowledging that he must confide in someone, he said slowly: 'We won't be movin' never again, Mr. Sjodin. This'n is it.'

'Glad to hear you say that. Now tell me the best that you can hope for, and let's see if it's possible.'

'I'm fed up to my ass with farmin'. It's a fool's paradise.'

'Not to a born farmer—like my father, or me. But for you, maybe yes. Go ahead.'

'I'm a hunter. I'm a rifleman. I want me a place near the woods. I want me a runnin' stream. I want to be close to where there's moose and bear and deer. But mostly I do want a runnin' stream.'

Before responding to this defensible ambition, Sjodin asked: 'But how will you earn a living? A wife and three children?'

'Two.'

'How?'

Again Flatch fell silent, then he said tentatively: 'I'll work for others.'

'What kind of work?'

'Any kind. I can do most any kind of work. Build houses, work on the roads.' And then came the most difficult revelation, the one at which Mr. Sjodin might laugh: 'Maybe I could sort of guide rich people who want to shoot theirself a moose.' Quickly he added: 'I can use a gun, you know.'

Nils Sjodin leaned back and thought of all the immigrants he had known, those daring men and women who had left Europe to brave the blizzards of the northern United States, and it occurred to him that almost every good one had been driven by some intensely personal image of what he or she could accomplish in a new world. They had not drifted into the snowbanks of the north; they had come impelled by great visions, noble aspirations, and although most of them fell short of their dreams, they would, through the years, be astonished at how many of those dreams had been realized. To Sjodin, Elmer Flatch's dream made sense.

'There's a couple of spots far out I've seen during surveying, I wouldn't mind having one of them for myself. But I have to stay near where the town's going to be. For you, with what you have in mind, perfect.'

He borrowed the staff car, a Ford truck, and with Flatch at his side, crossed the Matanuska River, which ran through the heart of the valley before joining the Knik, and after a long ride over almost nonexistent roads, they came to an enclosed valley protected by a magnificent mountain to the south, Pioneer Peak, more than six thousand feet high, with much higher mountains to the west. The kind of stream that Flatch longed for cut through the area: 'It's called Dog Creek. Flows out of a beautiful lake up there in the hills, Dog Lake. And up this way, in easy hiking distance, the great Knik Glacier. They tell me it's something to see when the lakes formed by the glacier break through their dam in summer.'

'Any sites here?'

'About a dozen. Good ones, that is.'

'Any taken?'

'Nobody wants them. Too far out. That's why you can get one without going through the lottery.'

As they were strolling about, along the banks of Dog Creek a moose came exploring to see what kind of creature had come into its terrain, this strange shiny object whose sides flashed sun signals. Preoccupied with the truck, it did not see the two men some distance away, so for perhaps six or eight minutes it nosed about, then majestically strolled back toward the hills.

'I'll take this one,' Flatch said, indicating the surveyed site at the confluence.

'I don't want you to do that, Mr. Flatch,' Sjodin said. 'When the creek and the river are both high, you'll have flooding. Look at those twigs in the trees.' And after Flatch inspected more closely, he asked: 'The water gets that high?' and Sjodin assured him that the records said it did.

So with the Swede's help, Elmer identified a site on the right bank of Dog Creek, facing Pioneer Peak, which seemed about to topple down upon it, with great glaciers, brown bears and wandering moose nearby. It was a spot of supreme natural beauty, one that any hunter would aspire to, and it was far enough from where the new town would be to provide privacy for decades to come. When he and Sjodin marked off the corners with their piles of rocks, Flatch had forty acres of a new life, arranged by the federal government, which would postpone any mortgage reduction for four years and then extend the payments over thirty years at the rate of three percent per annum. It was frontiersmanship on the grand scale, and all it required of the nine hundred and three settlers was hard work, the construction of some kind of economy, and the ability to withstand the Alaskan winter at 61.5° N, about the same latitude as southern Greenland.

* * *

As always in a pioneer settlement, the heaviest burden fell upon the women, and when Elmer Flatch eschewed a chance for one of the attractive lots near the center of town—the ones that would be invaluable within a few years—selecting instead the romantic one near the glacier, his wife realized that the task of holding her family together while a cabin was being built and the children established in school would be hers, and like many of the other immigrant women, she was finding the job even more onerous than she had expected. Her husband was a true frontiersman, always ready to cut a new batch of logs or help a distant neighbor who was cutting his. Problems were exacerbated by the fact that those who drew the good sites in town were having their new homes built for them by government carpenters as part of the three-thousand-dollar deal; stubborn outriders like Elmer Flatch had to build their own.

Marketing posed a special problem for Hilda, because one of those geographical accidents occurred which not even brilliant men can anticipate and over which they have no control. Since the settlement was in Matanuska Valley, the newcomers assumed that whatever town grew up to serve them would be called by that name, but a short distance to the north there already existed the trivial town of Palmer. It had but one asset: the Alaska Railroad had a station there and, as had happened so often before throughout the United States, it was the railroad, not the town fathers, that decided where civilization would center.

So, despite the fact that a village called Matanuska did take root, Palmer became the local metropolis. But it was far from the Flatch place and it would not be easy to get the doctor or the deliveryman to travel such a distance, especially since no reliable road would reach the Flatches for a long time. But Elmer insisted: 'This is where I want to be,' and he left it to Hilda to make adjustments. However, when one of the army emergency tents was erected on their plot, with a double lining to ward off the bitter winds sweeping down from the glacier, and she had a wood fire burning in her little iron stove, she found life quite tolerable and worked like a Belgian draft horse helping her husband clear the ground and level it for their cabin, which he swore to have under roof by the first heavy snow.

Sometimes at the end of an especially long day, Hilda would sit on a wobbly chair outside the tent, too tired even to worry about supper, and at such times she was tempted to complain, but she refrained out of respect for the other members of her family, all of whom declared repeatedly that 'this is sure a lot better than Thief River Falls.' But one day when everything went wrong, she was overcome by a sense of dismay and she couldn't help wondering if the Flatches were ever going to have a family home, and as she perched on her stool she decided that when Elmer and LeRoy returned from whatever they were doing—certainly they weren't doing any work on the house—she would give them an ultimatum: 'No more foolin' around. No more helpin' others till we get our own place finished.'

But her resolve vanished when at dusk her two men came roaring down from the mountains east of the campsite with astonishing news: 'Hey, Mom! We got a moose!'

Knowing that this signified assured food for a long time to come, she cried: 'LeRoy, I'm so proud of you.'

'You don't know the best, Mom. We got two!'

'Yep,' Elmer said as he marched proudly into camp with much the same stride that Roman generals adopted when they came home triumphant from having put down rebels along the borders of the empire. 'I got a big one up by the ice. But LeRoy, he got one half again as big. This boy can hunt!'

With this vigorous news, everything stopped, and Hilda assumed command: 'Flossie, you run down to the Vasanojas', see if they'll let us borry the horse tomorrow. LeRoy, run to the Kirsches', see if Adolf'll help us butcher tomorrow. I'm goin' in to those people with the six children, ain't been eatin' too well. If they'll help bring down the meat . . . Elmer, how far away are the two animals?'

He told her they were about three miles up toward the glacier, and for just a moment he considered that it might be proper for him to run down to the family with six kids, rather than his wife, but then he rationalized to himself: I been out chasin' moose all day, and she's probably not been doin' nothin' much. Let her go. Off she went to share the good news with her neighbors, and as she hurried westward, following the course of the Knik River, she thought: It's gonna be all right. If Elmer can do his huntin', we're gonna eat and he's gonna be happy.

The women like Hilda who labored so strenuously in building Matanuska, which grew more habitable every week, were aided considerably by an extraordinary old settler in Alaska, a woman of the widest experience who had been assigned by the Alaskan government to represent its interests in the new settlement. She was in her early sixties, white-haired, smallish and with an energy that staggered even proven workers like Hilda Flatch. Her name was Melissa Peckham but she was known as Missy, and in introducing her around the valley, Sjodin told each of the families two relevant facts: 'She don't need the job. Made a pile in the gold fields back in the nineties. And she's workin' for nothin', so don't throw your weight around, because she can knock any of you flat, and will.'

Missy was one of those women, the immigrant wives discovered, who could face up to any problem without flinching. She controlled a small sum of money provided by the territorial government which she used in dire emergencies and a somewhat larger sum which she provided from her own savings. She took up quarters in Tent Number 7 and made herself an invaluable aide to Mr. Sjodin, but what she did best was ride a horse, which she had bought with her own money, out to the edges of the settlement, where she worked with women like Mrs. Flatch and the mother down the line who had six children. It was also she who organized the Matanuska Lending Library, gathering from all the homes that would participate books no longer in use and placing them in a tent with a fifteen-year-old girl in charge. She helped churches get title to corner lots and then aided them in starting their rude buildings, but the women of Matanuska remarked that she did not attend any of the church services, and a rumor started that Missy had never been married to the Irishman with whom she lived and who helped her in her charities.

Two clergymen were delegated to visit with the Murphys, as they were called, and Missy answered their questions forthrightly: 'I escaped Chicago during the bad years. I had no husband, but that's beside the point. On the gold fields at Dawson, I met Matthew there, and his story is twice as interesting as mine. But that's another point. He was married in faraway Ireland. Left his wife. Never went back. We worked together in Nome and Juneau, we have a daughter, and we've been very happy.'

The Presbyterian minister was appalled by her story, but the Baptist, a man hardened in the oil fields of Oklahoma, was tantalized by her frequent reference to the dramatic history of Mr. Murphy, and when he made inquiries he learned that this Irishman had not only spent two winters on the Mackenzie River route but had then helped the miner John Klope find one of the great treasures at Dawson, after which he had bicycled — bicycled, mind you — from Dawson to Nome, more than a thousand miles in the dead of winter. The minister, who had been having some trouble with his parishioners who complained that they had to draw water by means of a large wooden crank that pulled a heavy bucket up from a considerable depth, had told them: 'All right! Use a shallower well and die of typhoid fever.'

Fed up with their self-pity, he went to Missy Peckham and asked: 'Would your husband . . . I mean, would Mr. Murphy . . . would he consent to telling our church about the Mackenzie River and the bicycle ride?'

'If you get him started, you'll not stop him,' Missy said, and that was how Matthew Murphy of Dawson, Nome and Juneau happened to speak one autumn night at the Matanuska Baptist Church. He said: 'We're all immigrants, aren't we?' and when his listeners nodded, a kind of strength came into his voice, nearly seventy years old, and an unaccustomed straightness to his back. He spoke of those exciting days at Edmonton when so many launched forth to conquer the gold fields, and he ticked off the hundreds who failed for one reason or another: 'If they went by land, they never made it. If they tried horseback, every horse was dead within five weeks. If they went up the easy rivers, they got lost in swamps. And if they did what we did . . .'

Turning to where the young were sitting, he said: 'Often in life you'll be offered a choice of two routes, the right one and the wrong one, and you may not know which is which. If you choose the wrong one, you can spend a couple years thrashin' around in the wilderness while those who choose right quickly get to their target.'

A Norwegian man interrupted: 'But Mr. Sjodin said that when you reached the Klondike, you found yourself a fortune.'

'I found nothin'. Of the hundreds who left Edmonton in search of sure gold, not one of us found a red cent. We all failed.'

'But they told us you were rich.'

'A man I worked for found it. Years after I left him broke, he come by our place in Nome and gave both Missy and me a lot of money. I think it was because he was always in love with Missy.'

This was hardly the way the minister had expected the talk to go. Coughing noisily, he said: 'Mr. Murphy, tell us about your bicycle ride.'

'Dead of winter, locked up in Dawson, no money. Had to get to the gold fields in Nome, a thousand miles away. Talked a Canadian storekeeper into sellin' me a bicycle cheap, and he said: "Hell, you can't ride"—if you'll excuse me, sir, but that's what he said. But in less than a week I had the hang of it, and I set out with some tools, spare chain and half a dozen spare spokes, and off I went to the next batch of gold fields—no roads, no trails, just the frozen Yukon River. I made about forty miles a day, one day sixty. A river tight frozen is better'n a highway. Of course, when great blocks of ice heave up at angles, it ain't so much fun. But the fact is, I made that thousand miles startin' on February twenty-second and arrivin' on March twenty-ninth, as this clippin' from a Nome paper proves.' And out came a yellow sheet which attested to the fact that Matthew Murphy, who had come to Dawson back in 1899, had traversed the entire distance from Dawson to Nome riding only a bicycle in thirty-six or thirty-seven days: 'You figure it out, but remember that the year 1900 which should have been a leap year wasn't. But those of you who live till the year 2000 will have a leap year that time.'

The minister feared that the man was wandering, but realized that was not the case when Murphy continued: 'Now, don't make too much over this bicycle trip. The next year, 1901, more than two hundred and fifty rode the Yukon. Next year a man named Levie made the thousand miles from Point Barrow to Nome in fifteen days. That's more than twice as fast as I traveled. Can you believe it? A bicycle on ice?'

The Murphys became a center of attraction in Matanuska, for when Missy's story was made known, about her sledding down the Chilkoot and braving the rapids on the Yukon system, the pair were recognized as admirable examples of the Alaskan spirit, but the story persisted that Matt had found himself a gold mine on the Klondike so big and rich that it still paid him dividends.

In 1937, THE second year of their occupancy in the cabin, Flossie became the cynosure of the Flatch family. Twelve years old, a handsome child with her father's love of animals, she was sitting at the window one afternoon when she saw a small brown bear come out of the woods leading to the glacier, and when she alerted her family: 'Hey, look at the bear!' her brother grabbed his rifle on the solid Minnesota principle that if anything out there was moving, shoot it. This time she stopped him, so instead of receiving a bullet through its forehead, this prowling bear came upon a young girl who moved toward it with two potatoes and a head of cabbage.

The bear stopped, studied her suspiciously, turned and lumbered off, but after some minutes, while she remained stationary, it came back. It could smell her, and the potatoes and the cabbage, and the mix was confusing, so again the bear fled. But it was an inquisitive type, and for the third time approached the place with the tantalizing smells. This time, in the middle of the path it was following, there was a raw potato, which it sniffed several times before chewing it to a tasty pulp.

On subsequent days the bear reappeared, always in late afternoon and always on the alert for this fearless child who approached it with things it liked. One day when she offered a head of cabbage it took it, and before the end of the second week of these visits it was obvious that Flossie had tamed a bear, and when the news circulated through the town, various people came to see the miracle. But it was Mr. Murphy who spoke sense: 'Bears can't be trusted. Especially not brown bears.'

'I thought it was a grizzly,' Flossie said, whereupon Mr. Murphy gave a short lecture on one of the peculiarities of Alaskan life: 'If'n a bear up here is found within fifty miles of the ocean, it's called a brown bear. If'n it's more than fifty miles inland, people like to call it a grizzly. Same bear, same habits.'

'I want my bear to be a grizzly,' Flossie said, and Murphy replied: 'Arms of the ocean touch us on all sides, it's got to be a brown.' Then, seeing her disappointment, he added: 'But there is a way of measurin' that would give you fifty miles to the ocean. So you can call it a grizzly. I'll bet you don't know its Latin name. *Ursus horribilis.* Sounds terrifyin', don't it?' She shook her head negatively: 'This grizzly is my friend,' and to Murphy's horror, that afternoon when the bear appeared, Flossie walked out to greet it, sat playing with it, and fed it some more cabbage. It seemed much bigger now than when it had first appeared, and had Murphy come upon it of a sudden along a wooded trail he would have been petrified.

As the year progressed, so did the friendship between the girl and her grizzly, but excitement at this development faded when something even more astonishing occurred at the Flatch cabin. Because of Flossie's constant visits with her bear, she began to sense that a much larger animal was in the region, and late one afternoon as her bear vanished up the trail, she saw coming down in the opposite direction an enormous black figure, and at first she suspected that a really huge grizzly was approaching her, but she had enjoyed such success with the first bear that she supposed she could do the same with this one. But when the animal came closer she saw that it was a moose with a body as big as a truck. It was a female, an immense ungainly creature that moved awkwardly but with a compelling majesty that arrested the attention of anything that saw her, animal or human, and Flossie assumed that when her tame bear encountered this massive creature, it would be the bear that stepped aside, not the moose.

On that first meeting the moose came within a few feet of the girl before halting. There was a long inspection by the moose, which had bad eyes, and a wealth of sniffing, then with an inquisitiveness that startled the girl, she came forward to smell more acutely; and once more the wonderful legend that woodsmen believed, and to which Flossie certainly subscribed, came true: 'Pop, this moose knew, from one smell, that I wasn't afraid. Maybe she could even smell that I had been playing with the bear, but she came right up to me. I think she knew I was her friend.'

Flossie had barely delivered this Matanuska version of the old legend when her father grabbed for his rifle, shouting: 'Where is it?' and when Flossie realized that he intended shooting her moose, she screamed: 'No!'

Her father was so surprised by this violent reaction that he fell back a step, dropped his hand from the door latch, and said quietly: 'But, Flossie, a moose has the kind of meat we can sell. We need . . .'

Again she screamed, the anguished cry of a girl who had grown to love all the animals that shared the edge of the glacier with her. She was one with the bear and knew that with patience she could tame this great moose, ten times her weight and half again as tall at the shoulders. Throwing herself in front of the door, she forbade her father to leave the house with his rifle, and after a tense moment when he considered lifting her aside, he surrendered. Allowing her to take the rifle from him, he grumbled: 'When you go to bed hungry, don't blame me,' and she replied: 'There are others up in the mountains,' and he said: 'But if'n he walks right up to our cabin, he wants to be shot. He's entitled to it.'

'It's a she,' Flossie said, and in the days that followed she met with the moose at various locations, and always the huge beast smelled assiduously until she was satisfied that this human being was the one she could trust. On about the seventh visit, Flossie tied a large piece of white ribbon to the hair behind the moose's huge left ear, and she spread word through the school and as much of the town as she could reach that the moose up by the glacier with the white ribbon was tame and belonged to Flossie Flatch.

Unfortunately, the white cloth flopping near her eye irritated the moose so much that by next evening when she came to visit, it had been rubbed off on a spruce branch. However, she approached Flossie with obvious affection and allowed the girl to tie another ribbon far back on her left flank, and this remained in place long enough for the Matanuska people to become familiar with the story of the pet animal.

Mildred the Moose posed certain problems, because when she appeared at the Flatch cabin she expected to be fed, and her appetite was insatiable: carrots, cabbage, lettuce, potatoes, celery, she took all of them in her big mouth, curling her immense upper lip over them and causing them to disappear down her capacious throat as if she were a magician. However, even if the expected meal turned out to be too meager, she did not display bad temper, and her friendly presence around the cabin made the place seem even more a part of Matanuska's natural wonder.

Flossie was distressed, therefore, when at school she heard from the Atkinson children a constant wailing about the hardships in the valley and protests against the federal government for having brought families into this barren wilderness. When Flossie rebuked the four Atkinsons for their lack of an adventurous spirit, they told her harshly that she was stupid to be playing with a bear and moose when the rest of Matanuska was suffering because the government was not living up to its promise of caring for the immigrants.

When Flossie told her parents of this, her father became quite angry: 'Them Atkinsons, when they lived in Robbin they didn't have a pot to pee in. Now they're puttin' on airs.' Hilda reprimanded him for speaking that way before his children, but he repeated his disgust at people who were offered a new start in life and then complained about little inconveniences.

He had a right to judge, because none of the newcomers had worked harder or longer to establish himself in Matanuska. He had built his own house on land that he had selected for his special purposes and, refusing to farm, he had devised a score of imaginative ways to earn his living. He carpentered for others, helped butcher, plowed fields with either horses or tractors provided by the owners, and drove into Anchorage with other men's cars to pick up important orders of medicine or tools. And he even worked now and then at the graveled Palmer Airstrip, helping to take wheels off airplanes and put on skis for winter travel into camps located in the high mountains. But most of all he hunted, bringing back to his cabin the carcasses of moose and bear and an Alaskan deer that natives called caribou, which he sold throughout the district.

One night when he returned with a quarter of a moose dragging behind him in the snow, Hilda said: 'We're expected at a meeting tonight. Harold Atkinson's makin' a formal protest or somethin',' and when she forced Elmer to accompany her into town, they sat in rigid silence as they listened to the Atkinsons and three or four other couples grumbling about every aspect of life in Matanuska. To hear their litany of disappointments was to realize how differently people could interpret the same conditions. 'At every point,' Harold Atkinson was lamenting, 'we've been defrauded by our government. No roads, no proper school, no agricultural help, no marketing plan for the crops we do grow, and no money in the bank which we can borrow.'

Missy and Matt, hearing these picayune complaints, could not restrain themselves, and in the absence of the senior camp officials, who had done a fairly good job so far, even though all schedules did seem to lag, they took the floor, standing together as they had done so often during their Alaskan years. 'Everything you say is true, Mr. Atkinson, but none of it has to do with the starting of a new town here in Matanuska. And to tell you the truth, it doesn't have to do with getting your family on a solid footing. I think things are ten times better here than they were in Dawson City in 1898 or Nome in 1900, and that's where Alaska got started.'

'This ain't 1898. It's 1937,' John Krull shouted from the rear. 'And what we got to put up with is a disgrace.'

This outraged Matt Murphy, who in his seventieth year saw all situations from a broad perspective. Avoiding any mention of his own heroics in conditions fifty times worse than what the Matanuska settlers were experiencing, he told in lilting voice of the starvation hardships that had driven his people from

Ireland during the great famines, and concluded by rebuking the Atkinsons: 'You have a right to complain about things promised but not delivered, but to blame the whole operation makes no sense.'

He succeeded only in so infuriating the protesters that the meeting broke up in a kind of fracas, and at the close of the next week the Flatches learned that the Atkinsons, Krulls and three other families had left Matanuska, abandoning everything, and were heading back to the Lower Forty-eight. Not long thereafter the settlement was flooded with newspaper clippings mailed by friends who said: 'It must be pure hell trying to live in a socialist settlement where everything has gone wrong.' One well-intentioned farmer who wrote to the Flatches said: 'I suppose we'll be seeing you back here one of these days. When you arrive, look me up. Things are a lot better in Minnesota than when you left and I'll be able to find you a real good farm at a bargain.'

What irritated those like the Flatches who stayed in Matanuska, and government people like the Murphys who were doing their best to make the huge experiment work, was the fact that one conservative newspaper after another, across the entire United States, picked up the complaints of the 'go-backs,' as they were called, and castigated both the Matanuska people and the Roosevelt administrators who had devised the program as communists who were introducing alien procedures into honest American patterns. By 1937 and '38, recovery from the Great Depression was so solidly under way that people forgot what conditions had been only a few years before, and scores of newspapers and magazines used the supposed failure of Matanuska as proof that socialism never worked.

If there were two human beings in all America less vulnerable to the charge of socialism than Missy Peckham and Elmer Flatch, they were not known to the general public. These two had, in the great tradition of American individualists, pioneered with pennies in their pockets, triumphed over enormous odds, and accomplished wonders in their own quiet way. In Matanuska they were doing the same. Missy, at the apex of her rambunctious life, was helping a new generation of adventurers establish a society in which families would own their own farms, sell their own produce, and educate their children to do the same. Elmer, having worked in Alaska as few men ever work anywhere, had watched as his forty governmental acres had grown to more than three hundred, and although some people had laughed at him when he had said at the beginning that he wanted to be a kind of guide to rich men who wanted 'to shoot theirself a moose,' by dint of making himself locally famous as the best hunter in Alaska, he had patiently attracted to himself exactly the type of big-city hunter who wanted to be shown the tricks that he had mastered. As the hunting season of 1938 approached, he was in such demand that he suggested to his wife: 'Why don't you serve meals to these hungry coyotes?' and people in places like Los Angeles and Denver began to talk about Elmer and Hilda Flatch.

And when one of his clients brought with him four clippings about the communist community sponsored by the government in Alaska, he felt that he must rise in defense of Matanuska, so with help from Missy Peckham he drafted a letter, which was mimeographed and mailed to some thirty Lower Forty-eight newspapers. The opening paragraph set the tone:

> I read in your paper the other day that we people in Matanuska are all communists, and since I don't know much about Russia, maybe it's true. But I want to tell you how we communists up here spend the day. We get up at seven, each family on the plot of land it owns privately, and some

of us milk the cows we own and others open the stores they paid for with
their own hard work, and our kids go to the school we support with taxes,
and at the end of the week we gather up our produce and ship it off to
Anchorage to a private wholesaler who cheats us like hell out of what we
think we ought to get, but when times get tight, we borrow money from
that wholesaler against our next crop.

The next paragraph explained what the Matanuska 'communists' did with their
spare time, and mention was made of Flossie and her pet animals and Irishman
Carmody at the airport who had saved his money to make a down payment on
a 1927 plane which he was using as a cargo carrier to serve the gold mines way
back in the hills. The mines were owned, Elmer said, by private prospectors,
some of whom had been searching fruitlessly for fifty years.

It was the final paragraph that was so widely quoted in the running debate
on the practicality of Matanuska; because of that first barrage of adverse
comment by men like Harold Atkinson, most readers in the Lower Forty-eight
considered the experiment a dismal failure. Of Atkinson and his fellow 'go-
backs,' Elmer and Missy said:

We know that when Columbus set out to discover America and ran into
trouble, many of his crew advised him to turn back. When settlers headed
for Oregon and California hit the great empty Plains and the hostile
Indians, lots of them turned back. And whenever anything of importance
has been tried on this earth, the fainthearted have turned back. How many
goldminers in 1898 took one look at the Chilkoot Pass and turned back?
Those who persevered found gold and built a new land. We're building a
new land up here, and ten years from now Matanuska will be a thriving
valley filled with big farms and healthy people and kids who wouldn't
want to live anywhere else. Watch the workers and see. Don't listen to the
'go-backs.'

While Elmer was busy drafting his defense of Matanuska, LeRoy was having an
exhilarating time in Palmer, where in the last days of his nineteenth year he was
being introduced to two of the most exciting experiences a young man could
have: girls and airplanes. He first met Lizzie Carmody at a grocery store, where
her red hair and Irish smile so captivated him that he furtively followed her
home, discovering that she lived in a shack at the edge of the large flattened field
which served as Palmer Airstrip. In the days that followed he learned that her
father, Jake Carmody, owned one of the planes that serviced the mines tucked
away in various canyons of the nearby Talkeetna Mountains. It was a small
plane famous in aviation history, a Piper J-3, dubbed the Cub, with wings
sprouting from above the pilot's head and in this instance an improvised enclosure for the cabin in which another person could sit. Its insides had been pretty
well torn out so as to accommodate the maximum amount of freight for the trips
into the mountains.

For some three weeks LeRoy could not decipher whether he hung around
the Palmer strip to see Lizzie Carmody or her father's airplane, but toward the
end of that period, the latter won out. 'What kind of plane is this?' he asked one
day as he sidled up to Carmody, and the Irishman said: 'A 1927 Survivor,' and
when LeRoy asked what kind that was, Carmody showed the various dents and
tears which symbolized his life as an Alaskan bush pilot: 'It's a Piper Cub that's
learned to survive. That long scar, landin' in a spruce tree in a fog. This'n,

landin' on a riverbank that turned out to be mud when I thought it was gravel. The big tear in the side, a spare dynamo busted loose from in back of my head when I landed too fast on a lake up in the hills.' The Cub showed so much damage that LeRoy said: 'It looks like flyin' is mostly tryin' to land,' and Carmody clapped him on the back: 'Son, you just learned all there is to know about aviation. Any damned fool can get a plane up in the air. Trick is to get it down.'

'Have you ever been in real danger?' LeRoy asked, and the bush pilot gave no reply; he simply pointed once again to the eight or nine heavy scars, each one of which represented a close brush with death. Awed, LeRoy said: 'You must be brave.'

'Nope. Just careful.' This seemed so contradictory, considering the condition of the Cub, that LeRoy had to ask: 'How can you be careful if you've had so many accidents?' and Carmody burst into laughter: 'Son, you really cut down to the quick. I am careful. I'm very careful never to crash before seein' a way to walk out alive. Any landin' is the right one if you walk away.'

'This plane's a wreck,' LeRoy said. 'Why don't you fix it up?'

'It still flies. Anyway, I carry mostly freight.' He studied his battered antique and said: 'I think I've about had Alaska. I'm plannin' on buyin' a Cessna four-seater and doin' my flyin' in California, or some other place Outside.'

'Where's Outside?'

Carmody laughed: 'You newcomers call down there the Lower Forty-eight. Us born here call it Outside.'

'What will you do with this one? If you do buy a new plane.'

'Lookey here,' Carmody said, pointing to a bolt. 'When I'm through, I pull that bolt and whoosh! the whole thing falls apart.'

One day when Carmody was satisfied that LeRoy was a decent lad with a sincere interest in both Lizzie and airplanes, he asked, as he was about to climb down after a freight run into the mines: 'Son, you ever been up in an airplane?'

'No, sir.'

'Jump in,' and in his bare-bones Cub, Carmody took LeRoy on the kind of flight that can reorder a young man's perceptions. Rising slowly from the little dirt strip, he flew north along the front of the snow-covered Talkeetna Mountains, allowing his passenger to peer into lovely canyons that would normally have been hidden: 'You've never seen Alaska till you see it from the air.' Then he cruised over the gleaming Matanuska Glacier, then westward deep into the glens of the soaring Chugaches: 'You couldn't survive in Alaska without an airplane. They were made for each other.'

As they returned homeward LeRoy shouted: 'Over there! That's our place!' and Carmody dive-bombed the cabin three times before Hilda appeared at the door, apron over her hands, and looked up to see her son screaming past, his blond head sticking out from the plane window.

E LMER'S IMPASSIONED DEFENSE of Matanuska brought a flood of letters from the Lower Forty-eight, sixty percent containing messages of encouragement, the rest condemning him as a communist. Missy Peckham, who handled the mail for the Flatches, burned the latter and paraded the endorsements through the valley, winning applause for Elmer, but it was short-lived because of a sad affair which reminded the immigrants of the nature of life in any frontier settlement. Matt Murphy, delighted by the attention given him because of his adventures in old-time Alaska, often spent his days at the Flatch cabin, helping them build a wing in which hunters could sleep overnight, or staking out a path to the glacier that overhung the valley. He found special joy in sharing with Flossie her work with animals, and whereas her grizzly resented his presence and sometimes growled at him, Mildred the Moose saw in him one more friend and would sometimes walk considerable distances with him, nudging him along with her nose.

One day she had guided him toward the shore of the Knik River, and he told Flossie: 'I think she wants us to go see the George Lakes,' and with only this shadowy suggestion the old Irishman organized an expedition to one of the treasures of Alaska.

As the four Flatches and the Murphys crossed the icy Knik with their lunch baskets and climbed its left bank toward the snout of Knik Glacier, Matt utilized the rest periods for a description of what they were going to see: 'Way up there is a closed-in valley. It ought to flow directly into the Knik, but the wall of the glacier blocks it off, so the backed-up water forms a chain of three beautiful lakes, Upper, Inner and Lower Lake George. And there they stay locked up all through the cold weather, because the frozen glacier serves as a stopper.'

At this point the climbers resumed their progress to the prominence from which they would be able to look down upon the marvel that Murphy had promised them, but at the next halt he explained what would be happening one of these days: 'When warm weather gets here, the ice in the glacier barrier, it sort of melts. Water in the three lakes, now really one big lake more than a hundred and fifty feet deep, tremendous pressure you can be sure, it begins to seep right through the glacier wall and weaken it. Finally, one day in July the time comes when the pressure from the lake grows so intense, *bang!* the lake breaks through, the walls of the glacier explode, and you have a gorge six hundred feet wide and more than six hundred feet deep.'

'Will we see that?' Flossie asked, and he said: 'You never know when the break will come. Not many see it. But the gorge stays open about six weeks. The lakes empty. And huge icebergs float down. Government engineers figured the flow. Two million seven hundred thousand gallons a second when the break comes. That's a lot of water.'

The Flatches had no concept of what they were to see when they reached the vantage point overlooking where the three lakes had been, but as Murphy led them to the top they could hear the roar of water below them, and he shouted: 'I think it broke through!' and finally they saw this miracle of nature, the only instance of its kind in the world, in which an immense lake exploded into the face of a soaring glacier and tore away chunks of ice bigger by far then the *St. Mihiel* on which they had come to Alaska.

Flossie was the first to speak: 'Look! That iceberg coming at us is bigger than our house!' Then her brother said quietly: 'And look at the one behind,' but they all fell silent when the rushing lake water cut off a whole side of the glacier, a cathedral of ice that remained upright for a hundred yards, then toppled slowly onto its side as it felt the full force of the flood. It was so immense it did not twist like the others but in supreme majesty made its way down the turbulent chute.

Far down the course of the river the Flatches saw the final grandeur of this extraordinary performance; there, enormous icebergs, having run out of sufficient water to keep them afloat, perched like stranded white seabirds while the more placid water moved quietly past them. It would require weeks of bright summer sun to make them disappear.

'Does this happen every year?' Flossie asked as they were hiking home, and Murphy said: 'As far as I know. It's been happenin' every year since I first saw it.'

'How long ago was that?' the girl asked, and Matt said: 'About a score of years. We came to Matanuska often in the old days. Huntin'. We knew then it was a choice spot. We knew good people would come to it one day.' And the old fellow cried: 'Now look who's comin' to meet us on this fine day!' And there came Mildred the Moose, stepping carefully along the path to greet the people she had grown to love. She was an admirable creature that sunny afternoon, bigger by far than a deer or a caribou, much heavier than her friend the grizzly, and awkward in the endearing way a thirteen-year-old girl can be when her legs seem so long and uncoordinated.

And then, with the sun on her, she lurched forward as a shot rang out from below. 'No!' Flossie screamed as she had that first day when her father had tried to shoot the moose, but as she ran forward, with Mildred still on her feet, there was a second shot, and the huge animal plunged to her knees, tried vainly to crawl forward toward the Flatches, and keeled over. She was still breathing, blood flecks spraying from her nostrils, but before Flossie could cradle her head in her arms, she died.

'You!' Matt Murphy shouted, and with surprising energy he started to run toward the two hunters, men apparently from Anchorage, judging from their expensive guns, but when they became aware that they had shot a tame moose, they scuttled off. Murphy, scandalized at their cruel behavior, chased after them, but he had covered less than a hundred yards when he collapsed, all at once and like the wall of the glacier, and while Flossie, distraught, tended her dead moose, Missy ran forward to care for her man lying on the rocky path.

When the other Flatches reached the fallen man, they saw that he was severely stricken, and Elmer shouted crisp commands: 'LeRoy, help your sister. Hilda, find me a couple of poles. Missy, loosen his clothes. Help him to breathe,' and with the efficiency he had always shown in moments of crisis, this skilled woodsman set his rescue party in motion, and when his daughter refused to leave her dead friend, this creature from the depths of the forest, he called wisely to his son: 'Stay with her as long as she needs,' and with the help of the two women, carried the old Irishman to the cabin.

Flossie and LeRoy did not reach the cabin before the old man died, and when the girl realized that not only had she lost her moose but that her much-loved old pioneer was also gone, she gave a mournful cry and fell to her knees, for she sensed in that awful moment that the old days were gone, the days when a girl could tame a moose at the edge of Matanuska, the days when children in church could hear a man explain what it was like to spend two long winters in a narrow lean-to in the heart of the arctic. And there on the floor she began to tremble.

ON A SCRAWLED piece of paper Matt Murphy had penciled his will: 'Everything to Missy Peckham, but five hundred dollars each to LeRoy and Flossie Flatch, trusted friends of my old age.' The Anchorage courts accepted this as a viable document, and just as John Klope's unexpected gift to Missy and Matt that day in Nome in 1902 remade their lives, so now Matt's gift to LeRoy restructured his, because the day after the probate judge awarded him his five hundred dollars, he hurried to Palmer Airstrip, sought out Jake Carmody, pointed to the beat-up Cub, and asked: 'How much?' and Jake said: 'I really hadn't planned to sell,' and LeRoy said: 'You told me you were leavin' . . . goin' to buy a new Cessna.'

'Three hundred dollars, it's yours,' and to the bush pilot's surprise, LeRoy peeled off six fifty-dollar bills, and took possession.

'Flyin' lessons thrown in,' Jake said, and that afternoon LeRoy started to learn the intricacies of keeping this old relic aloft. An apt pupil, he took his first solo flight that weekend, and after two more weeks of intensive instruction he felt himself qualified to offer his services to the various mining camps. After one week of such flying with never a mishap, he returned his attention to Lizzie Carmody, who gave many signs of being interested in the young pilot, but when he suggested that he take her up for a spin, Jake roared out of the room where the local pilots waited: 'Holy Christ! You're not takin' my daughter up in that crate, are you?' and he forbade Lizzie to go near the perilous junk. Two days later Jake did exactly what he had threatened to do for so long: he took his wife and three children down to Portland, where he bought a new Cessna and entered the local aviation circles.

LeRoy, now the pilot of his own plane and eager to display his talents to someone, asked his mother if she would go up with him, and she said: 'I go up with no one,' so he propositioned Missy Peckham, who almost leaped at the invitation. Together they flew up the Knik Valley to see from aloft the three George Lakes making their assault on the face of the glacier.

When they returned to a smooth spot near the cabin, LeRoy's parents gave him their only advice about his plane: 'Don't go killin' yourself.' More specific counsel was provided by an old veteran who flew into the Palmer strip one afternoon after a horrendous flight in the mountains: 'Young feller, we welcome recruits like you. But if you want to sit here when you're my age, remember one thing: There is bold pilots like you, and there is old pilots like me. But there ain't never been an old bold pilot.' When LeRoy looked perplexed, the man said: 'When I was comin' in, real cautious like, for I was still shook up by that fog in the mountains, I seen you actin' up with your plane. Real fancy. And when I landed I asked: "Who's that young duck with his pinfeathers showin'?" and they told me it was you tryin' out a plane you'd just bought.' He stared at LeRoy and wagged his finger: 'You're clever, but you ain't clever enough to break the rules.'

'What rules?'

'Not many. Five, six? Stay away from whirlin' propellers, they chop you into mincemeat. Never, never climb into your plane without checkin' the gas. An empty tank is remorseless. You'll be flyin' into strange areas without strips, so never, never land straight in. Circle to see whether the ice is frozen or the sand strip along the river is solid. On the way out, check every visible point, you'll need 'em comin' back. Don't hesitate to sleep beside your plane, because tryin' to find your way home at night in a fog ain't really productive. And for Christ's own sweet sake, tie down your cargo. Keep plenty of light rope in your plane and lash down them floatin' objects, or sure as hell they're goin' to smash right into the back of your head at sixty miles an hour.' As LeRoy tried to visualize the situations in which these instructions would apply, the old-timer added a special one for Alaska: 'And, LeRoy, maybe you wouldn't think of this, but in winter always keep an armful of spruce branches in the rear of your plane, tied down, of course.'

It was a magnificent world into which LeRoy Flatch entered with his Cub. It was a sturdy plane, so thoroughly rebuilt after its predictable series of accidents that not much of the original structure remained. Its engine, sixth in the series for this particular craft, was now a 75-hp Lycoming, but it too had been heavily recast after smashups. It gave good mileage to a gallon of aviation fuel, but it had also flown quite a few hours on various hideous mixtures, including one flight on half kerosene, half gasoline, and as the man who was flying it at the time said: 'Plus another half alcohol. But the alcohol was in me.'

It was a plane that had to be flown by muscle power, for it contained no automatic pilot or the sophisticated instrumentation that would make its successors much easier to operate. It responded slowly to instructions and its various surfaces could be activated only by brute strength, but it had one characteristic which made it revered by its longtime pilots: it could land on almost anything, remain upright, and fly out after repairs had been completed. It was almost an ideal plane for an Alaskan bush pilot, but after LeRoy had flown it several hundred hours he saw that for it to serve him as he intended, it needed two simple modifications, and he spent the remainder of Matt Murphy's bequest to engineer them.

'What I got to have,' he explained to Flossie when she flew with him to mining camps far in the hills, 'is a pair of pontoons so's I can land on water up in the lake country. A smooth lake is far better than a rough field. And I simply got to have a pair of skis for landin' on the snow in winter.'

Reflecting on this, she said: 'LeRoy, you'd be takin' your plane apart every four months. Now wheels, now pontoons, now skis,' and he said: 'It'd be worth it,' but when he scouted around for such gear he learned that it was not cheap, and finally he had to approach Flossie: 'Only way I can get the plane I need is you lend me the money to buy the other landing gear.'

She had the funds to make the loan, Matt Murphy's bequest would take care of that, but she was not satisfied that her brother was really serious about making his living as a pilot until he rushed home one afternoon: 'Floss! A man at Palmer is selling his plane, going to Seattle. He has a buyer who doesn't want the extra landing gear. A bargain, a real bargain!'

She accompanied him to the airfield, where she found that what he was saying was true, for an old-timer told her: 'Them's the best pontoons around here and the skis are practically new.'

'Could my brother get them on and off?'

'I'd teach him in ten minutes.'

It was a deal, and with his acquisition of pontoons and skis, LeRoy became a full-fledged bush pilot, able to land on ground, snow or lake, but as Flossie had predicted, switching them was hard work. However, the man who had encouraged Flossie to lend her brother the money now showed him how to approach this difficult task: 'You get yourself a long spruce pole, and a short oak stump for your fulcrum. Watch how easy it is to lift the Cub right up in the air!'

When the front end was high off the ground he said: 'Now edge this other stump under the middle, and let your pole down bitsy, bitsy, and you have your plane right up in the air where we can work on it.' And he showed LeRoy how to switch between wheels, pontoons and skis.

'Of course,' the old fellow said, 'each year you have to spend four mornings of hard work. Mid-March, off with the skis, on with the wheels. June, put on the pontoons for the lakes. September, you need wheels again, and in early December, back to skis.' With this relatively simple shifting back and forth, LeRoy had a most versatile machine, and he used it imaginatively, flying anywhere anytime in almost any weather, promoting new business and earning real income.

At Palmer Airstrip, where he kept his plane when it had wheels, he became acquainted with several young hotshots who performed amazing feats, flying onto glaciers with their skis, landing on remote, uncharted lakes, or carrying immense loads far beyond the stated capacity of their planes, and they were a glamorous lot until the night when they lost their way home and crashed, out of fuel, in a timbered area. If they were picked out of the tree next morning and if their plane could be rebuilt, they were talked about on all the airfields, while cautious farm boys like himself attracted no attention. But he noticed two important facts: the really great bush pilots, like Bob Reeve and the Wien brothers and Bud Helmericks, took none of these unnecessary chances, and the young bucks who tore the place apart, challenging the far north with their frail planes, invariably wound up dead. Gallant legends, the very heart of the bush pilot's charisma, but very dead.

It had now become standard practice for any Flatch who was at home when LeRoy set out on a flight to tell him: 'Don't go killin' yourself,' and he did not resent the implication, but even though he was a most careful pilot when he reached his twenties, he did not escape the normal adventures that seemed to lie in wait for all bush pilots. On one flight into a high lake in the Talkeetna Mountains north of Palmer where a man from Seattle had a hunting lodge, he was carrying a load of mail and groceries purchased at the local store. He had his pontoons on, and after twenty-two minutes he spotted the landmarks leading to the camp. With care he zeroed in, circled the lake to be sure its surface contained no unexpected additions like rafts or loose boats, and made a perfect landing upwind to help him stop his forward progress. Dropping the revolutions on his propeller to their lowest practical speed, he steered his Cub deftly up to the floating dock, where the owner of the camp and his wife awaited.

'LeRoy,' the Seattle man said, 'you make a better landing on this lake than any of the big boys. The minute you get yourself a four-seater, Madge and me are goin' to fly with no one else.'

He heard this refrain constantly: 'Get yourself a four-seater. You'd have three times the customers.' But a used four-seat Waco with pontoons and skis extra would cost not less than forty-five hundred dollars plus the Cub, and this he could not afford.

'I pick up the grocery trade,' he told the Seattle man. 'Or like when you built your new wing.'

When he made such deliveries, he tried always to be extra helpful in unloading the gear, doing most of the work himself to let the owners know he appreciated their trade, and always if he had time, when he was finished, he asked the wife: 'Ma'am, would you like to take a short spin to see the land around here?' and he almost never got a refusal.

Then he would climb into the pilot's seat, instruct the woman as to how she could manage the struts to climb in beside him, and after she was belted in he would take the plane slowly out to the farthest end of the takeoff area and tell her: 'Now, ma'am, I don't want you to watch me. I've done this lots of times and it's old hat for me. But you lean way forward, keep your face close to the window, and watch how we use the step.'

'The what?' she usually asked.

'The step. The pontoon isn't just straight, you know. Halfway back, it has a step, a break in the smoothness, and unless we can get this plane up on that step, where the adhesion of the water and the friction is less, we won't be able to lift off.' When he felt that she understood, more or less, he said: 'Watch! Here we go for the good old step.'

It was sometimes incredible the amount of lake LeRoy required before his plane went up on the step, and several times the watching wives shouted: 'Are we going to make it?' and always he yelled back: 'Sooner or later, up we go,' and always, when it seemed that the plane was never going to fly, it would mysteriously lift itself onto the step, and then the length of pontoon clinging to the water was diminished by half, and in a few moments, from this more advantageous posture, the plane finally broke completely loose, whizzed along throwing bits of spray, and rose grandly into the air while the passenger clapped and sometimes shouted with triumphant joy. The fact was, LeRoy also wanted to cheer every time this miracle of the seaplane took place; he couldn't believe that it required such a very long takeoff before the pontoons broke loose, and he was cautious about the maneuver because on three occasions, to his great embarrassment, his plane never did get onto the step, and twice he ran right onto the beach at the far end of his attempt. For that reason he added an extra precaution to the ones the old-timer had given him: 'When you start to take off from a lake, always study the far shore, because pretty soon you may be on it.'

Usually on a sightseeing trip he stayed aloft no more than fifteen minutes, but on this afternoon the lady wanted to investigate the entire area surrounding her family's holdings, so she called to LeRoy: 'Give me a real trip. I'll pay for the full hour,' and he was happy to comply, for he also enjoyed such exploration. It was a fine sunny day with just a hint of clouds moving in from the distant ocean, and the scores of lakes nestled among the hills glowed like emeralds when the sun struck them. Being careful to maintain his orientation among the mountains which protruded, he spent more than an hour aloft, and this took him well to the north.

'Wonderful!' his passenger shouted. 'Let's go home,' and when he landed the plane on her lake and ferried her to the dock, she told her waiting husband: 'Pay him double. I never realized we lived in such a gorgeous place!'

His unplanned excursion meant that he was delayed about two hours on his return trip south to Matanuska, but this posed no problem, for in late July there would be plenty of daylight—sunrise at 0314 in the morning, sunset not till 2057 at night—but the situation became somewhat more complicated when the dark clouds which had been hovering to the south began to speed in with that astonishing ability to move that made Alaskan weather so unpredictable. A sky could be warm and bright at five, cold and menacing at five-thirty. This evening it was menacing.

It was about eight at night when LeRoy approached the Matanuska area, which meant that he had almost an hour of light left, but this was somewhat irrelevant because he had fuel for not more than forty minutes and the finding of his home lake in light was obligatory. However, by the time he had located Knik Glacier and knew where he was, storm clouds of a rather violent nature rushed in to obscure the area and he knew that any attempt to either find his lake or land upon it was futile. He therefore began casting about for an alternative, and there were a dozen eligible lakes in the area, but now they too were closed down by this rampaging storm.

It'll pass in a hour, he told himself, but that won't do me much good. So he must either speed back northward, hoping to outrun the storm, and land on one of the lakes adjacent to Palmer, where several planes headquartered, or continue south and try landing on some arm of the Knik River or even the bigger Cook Inlet, but to attempt the latter would be risky, for if the storm contained strong winds, it might generate waves too high and powerful for the Cub to negotiate. The situation was becoming ugly.

What to do? He tightened his seat belt, relaxed his hands, shook them twice, then gripped the wheel even more firmly and gave himself time-tested instructions: Now's the time to take a deep breath, LeRoy. You know you can always land this bird on the ground. Chew up the pontoons, but they can be replaced. You can't.

Looking out, he saw to the right the menacing tops of the Talkeetna Range: Let's get out of here! and he swung sharply to the left, striving to gain as much altitude as he could, but when he did he could see nothing below.

In this extremity he sought no miraculous escape, no sudden revelation of a known lake. He was in dire trouble and he knew it. He would survive only if he flew in a manner that kept him alert to every chance condition like wind or sudden gusts or choppy water, and only if he flew with but one resolute purpose: Let's get her down. Eight minutes to go.

He would forever remember those eight minutes at the end of which his tank was empty. He flew south till he was certain the Knik River must be under him, within a mile give or take. He descended precisely as he would have done had the terrain been visible, and he trusted the strength of the storm to remain constant. Most of all, he kept control of his plane, adjusting to the wind as if he had wheels and a clear landing strip ahead. When his altimeter showed little free space beneath him, he did not grit his teeth and prepare for some unexpected shock: he continued to breathe evenly, kept his hands at the same pressure as before, and prepared to land in whatever lay below.

Not quite as fatalistic as that: I'll have some visibility. I'll see whether it's water or land, and if it's land, I'll have about two minutes to find water. He did not add that in those minutes it would be vital as to whether he flew north or south at low altitude to find his water.

At the end of the sixth minute he broke through the clouds at an altitude of forty feet and saw below him only land, and extremely rough land at that. To put his plane down in that mix of trees and hills would be insane, but in which direction lay the river? Calmly and for no reason that he could have explained, he estimated that it was behind him, to the north, so in an easy swing he brought the plane about in a 180° turn, dropped even lower, and at the last practical moment saw ahead of him the rippling waters of the river. Breathing just a bit more deeply, he steadied the wheel, judged that he was landing broadside to the wind, which did not seem excessive, and with almost the last cupful of gas he landed the Cub in a faultless approach, and without slowing the engines continued across the river until the front of the pontoons climbed up on grassy bank. Using the luggage ropes he always carried, he tied the plane to a group of trees and set out on foot to find someone to help drag it ashore.

IN MANY WAYS LeRoy derived his greatest pleasure from his Cub when it wore skis, for then, if a heavy snow had fallen, he would soar over central Alaska with the feeling that he could fly anywhere and land in almost any corner of his majestic world. In the first days of trial and error he learned the limits of altitude to which his little plane could go and the most effective ways of landing on drifted snow. 'Hey!' he shouted one morning as he flew into a blazing sunrise with snow covering everything. 'This is all mine!' But there was also a financial advantage to flying on skis, as one of his customers explained in a letter to his wife back in Maryland:

Since I was eager to see the Matanuska experiment, I went to a small airport in the area and asked who their best pilot was and they agreed that a fellow named LeRoy might not be the best but he was certainly the safest, so I engaged him. He had a small rickety-looking plane which he assured me never failed, and after I had inspected the famous valley he asked: 'You want to see our glaciers?' and I nodded. But we were still miles from them, flying over snow, when he suddenly shouted: 'Lookeeee!' and he dropped the plane in a sickening spiral, whipped open his window, reached for a shotgun from behind his ear, flew the plane with his knees while paying no attention to where we were heading.

'Look at that wolf!' he said, and with great skill he brought our plane about, leveled with the huge beast, and killed him with one shot. Then, swinging the plane about as if it were a leaf, he landed not ten feet from the dead wolf, ordered me out so that he could climb down to retrieve the animal, which he threw into the cabin behind us.

When we resumed flight we had been in the air only a few minutes when he yelled: 'Hey! There's his brother,' and down we dropped in that sickening spiral. Again he flew the plane with his knees and again he nailed his wolf with one shot. This time when I started to get back into the plane I said: 'There's blood all over my seat,' and he became most apologetic, producing from a little box a clean cloth with which he wiped my seat clean. I also noticed that he lashed down the two wolves as carefully as if they were cargoes of gold, and when I said: 'I hope you don't see any more wolves,' he explained: 'For flying you I get $40. For each of those wolves, $50 government bounty,' and I asked him where he had learned to shoot so professionally, and he said: 'I learned guns in Minnesota, airplanes in Alaska.' I later found that he'd had two weeks of flying instruction. Believe me, Elinor, flying in Alaska is a lot different from flying in suburban Baltimore.

It was a few days after this successful wolf hunt that LeRoy stumbled upon the adventure which was to modify his life in ways he could not have anticipated. He was idling at the Palmer Airstrip when a well-dressed, good-looking businessman in his mid-fifties came up: 'You LeRoy Flatch?'

'I am.'

'The fellow who made that remarkable river landing last summer?'

'Luck and a very strong plane got me down.'

'Could I see the plane?'

Bewildered as to why a stranger would want to see an old workhorse like his Cub, LeRoy said: 'That one over there . . . on skis. Lot of miles on it. Lot of savvy in it.'

The stranger studied the exterior of the plane for some minutes, then asked: 'Mind if I take a peek inside?'

'Be my guest,' and when the inspection was complete, the man asked: 'Son, why don't you get yourself a four-seater?'

'I'm savin' like the devil to get one.'

The stranger laughed, extended his hand, and said: 'I'm Tom Venn, Ross & Raglan, and my wife and I are building ourselves a hunting lodge up on the flanks of Denali. We need someone to fly in big batches of our gear.'

'I'd be interested. How far is it?'

'About eighty miles northwest heading. Could you handle that?'

'I could. But I'd want to top off with some aviation gas when I got there.'

'That can be arranged. When could you fly?'

'About ten minutes after you got your stuff here. Will you be flying along?'

'Yes. I want to do some exploring along the way and after we get there.'

'You know I'm not allowed to fly into the National Park.'

'There's a lot of land outside it,' and with that, Venn hurried into the building and phoned the truck waiting at the railroad siding to start bringing out the electrical gear. At half after one the Cub was solidly packed, with all the cargo tightly lashed. Venn, working inside the fuselage and sweating like a deckhand, asked: 'Can we throw out these branches?' and LeRoy shouted back: 'Not on your life. You remember carefully just where they are. Anytime you fly into mountains you may need them.'

The heavily loaded plane, with Venn flying in the right-hand seat, took off neatly from the Palmer Airstrip, rose purposefully to an altitude of four thousand feet and started on a 320° heading. After the routine was set Venn asked: 'By the way, have you ever flown in the Denali area?' and LeRoy said: 'No, but I've always wanted to,' and Venn said with no hint of sarcasm: 'Good, we'll explore together.'

They had flown about halfway to their destination when LeRoy gasped so audibly, Venn guessed correctly that his pilot had never before seen the extraordinary sight that lay ahead. Rising majestically above a cloud wreath that enclosed its lower elevations, stood that mass of great mountains—Russell, Foraker, Denali, Silverthrone, from southwest to northeast. Except for Russell, these were among the highest mountains in North America, and Denali was the highest.

They formed a stupendous white-crowned barrier across the heart of Alaska, and after gazing at them in awe for some moments, LeRoy told his passenger: 'You can come to Alaska forty times and travel around all sides of those mountains and never see Denali,' and Venn said: 'I know.' But there it was, in all its frozen glory, not only the highest peak on the continent but also the farthest north by a large margin. When you paid your respects to Denali, you were knocking on the door of the Arctic Circle, which lay less than two hundred and fifty miles to the north.

For about twenty minutes the great mountain stood in solemn majesty, a peak so grand that only two groups of mountaineers had ever mastered it, the first in 1913 when a Nenana clergyman made it to the top, the second in 1932 when a group of four especially daring men used skis and dog teams, an amazing combination, to master the howling winds and the crevasse-ridden slopes. As the plane approached the outer perimeter of the park, LeRoy explained: 'You know, Mr. Venn, the mountain isn't visible from down there,' and Venn said: 'It rarely is. I was here eight times before I ever saw the darned thing.'

So Flatch started to descend, but when he passed through the cloud cover that seemed always to cluster about the mountains as if perversely they refused to let their treasure be seen, he found that the clouds did not end but continued right down to the ground, which in this area was covered with snow of exactly the same coloration. Trying not to alarm his passenger, LeRoy said quietly: 'We seem to be caught in a whiteout. Tighten your seat belt.'

'Are we going to crash?' Venn asked with that coolness in the face of adversity which had always characterized him.

'Not if I can help it,' but when he started to drop cautiously it was clear that neither he nor any other pilot, no matter how skilled, would be able to determine where these snowlike clouds ended and the real snow covering the ground began. There was, in other words, no discernible horizon, and Flatch recalled the shocking number of Alaskan aviators who in such circumstances had flown their planes nose-first into the solid ground, not having a clue as to where they were or in what attitude relative to the earth. Always, of course, in such crashes, the plane exploded, and in only one or two cases could one of the young-bold pilots boast later: 'I flew it right into the snow cover and walked away.'

In an extremity like this it was essential that the pilot not panic, and Venn, watching LeRoy closely, was pleased to see that he was reacting with admirable calm. Three times Flatch tried to land on the snow, and three times he was thrown into total confusion, for he could not ascertain where clouds ended and snow-covered rock began, so he flew in what he was sure was an upward attitude, and when he had gained some height above what he assumed to be the ground, he told Venn: 'We must try to spot something on the ground. Anything. A caribou, a tree, just anything.'

So the two men strove to determine where the ground was, and failed. 'Mr. Venn, undo your belt, climb back and fetch those spruce branches.' After a struggle across the lashed-down luggage, Venn reappeared with a large armful of branches. 'Open your window, put your seat belt back on, and when I shout "Drop," start throwing out the branches, one at a time. Throw the ones with the most branches first.'

For some moments they flew in silence, each man breathing heavily, and then came the command: 'Drop!' Out from Venn's window the branches began to fall, but only the first one was required, for when LeRoy saw how quickly it came to rest, that is, how perilously close to the ground he was, he said only one word: 'Jesus!' But with the frail bit of directional information provided by the branch, he adjusted in his seat, pulled his plane almost straight up, then circled low until he was lined up with the fallen spruce branch, which stood out on the snow like a great beacon light. Rarely had he been so glad to see something solid.

'Seat belt tight? Good. This could be pretty rough, but we've got to suppose it's level snow,' and with no further attention to his passenger, who behaved well, Flatch lowered his flaps, dropped the nose of the Cub, and felt a surge of triumphant joy as the skis struck the smooth snow that stretched in all directions.

When the plane skidded to a safe halt, Tom Venn unfastened his seat belt, leaned back, and asked quietly: 'So what do we do now?'

'Send a radio signal to let everyone know we're safe'—which he proceeded to do—'and then wait here till this storm passes.'

'All night?'

'Could be,' and without further discussion of their plight, the two men settled down for a long wait.

They did have to stay overnight, and early next morning when the skies had cleared, a rescue plane flew over, dipped low to check whether Flatch and his passenger were safe, then flew in large circles while LeRoy revved up his engine, taxied to the end of what looked like a relatively level space, and in one-third of the distance it took the Cub to take off when its pontoons were on water, the skis attained a surprising speed, and the plane was in the air.

Perversely, Denali and its sister mountains stood forth in such clear beauty that Venn suggested: 'Let's stay up a while and see this area,' and LeRoy said: 'I have the fuel. I'd enjoy it,' so for about half an hour they surveyed that chain of remarkable glaciers which tumbled southward out of the massif, a sight thrilling and exhilarating to the spirit of anyone who loved nature. When Flatch finally brought his plane to rest on the snow alongside Venn's lodge in the lower hills, the Seattle millionaire congratulated him: 'You know how to handle a plane, young man,' and when Venn's wife, Lydia Ross Venn, ran out to greet them, a handsome gray-haired woman in her early fifties, he told her: 'This is

LeRoy Flatch, a most gifted pilot. You and I are going to finance him a four-seater and he'll be flying us in here regularly from now on.'

On this first trip LeRoy stayed with the Venns for three days, taking first one, then the other on exploration trips which enabled him to familiarize himself with the great mountains, and when the visit ended, Tom Venn asked: 'LeRoy, would you consider flying down to Anchorage to pick up our son and his bride? They're coming here for part of their vacation.'

'Glad to, you give me the instructions. But my plane only seats one.'

'Rent a four-seater. Try them all out and let me know which one suits this part of Alaska best.'

So LeRoy Flatch, in a rented Fairchild with only a few hours on it, reported to the air terminal in Anchorage and paged Mr. and Mrs. Malcolm Venn, and as soon as the young man appeared, LeRoy knew he must be Tom Venn's son, for the resemblance was striking, but he was not at all prepared for Mrs. Venn, who was not a white woman. She was nearly as tall as her husband, extremely slim, with very black hair, and he could not tell whether she was an Eskimo, an Aleut or an Athapascan, three tribes he was still trying to get organized in his mind, and he was too polite to ask. But young Venn solved the problem, for as he tossed their gear into the plane he said: 'My wife'll ride shotgun. She wants to see this land. She's half Tlingit and this is all new territory for her.'

Since the subject had been broached, LeRoy asked: 'And what's the other half?' and Malcolm said: 'Chinese. Good mix. Very intelligent, as you'll find out,' and by the time the Fairchild reached the Venn lodge at the foot of Denali the three travelers were respectful friends.

'What's that crazy name for your father's place?' LeRoy asked as they unloaded the plane.

'Why didn't you ask him?'

'I thought it might be nosy.'

'You asked me.'

'But you're not head of the company. He is.'

'He named it Venn's Lode.'

'Does Lode mean what I think it does?'

'Yes. He said that in the old days men came here probing for gold . . . trying to find their lode. He and Mother are here to find their own lode, happiness. He loves Alaska, you know. Tramped all through it in the old days.'

L EROY FLATCH WAS so busy in the fall of 1939 scrounging around to find a used four-seater that he could afford, even with help from the Venns, that he actually failed to realize that a major war had broken out in Europe. At the reasonable cost of three thousand seven hundred dollars he found a pretty good Waco YKS-7 which had been used in the Juneau district, and with it he discovered Alaska's hunger for aerial transport. American soldiers suddenly appeared asking for transportation to strange places, and gold mines already in being called for new equipment. Road building experienced a spurt, new stores opened everywhere, and wherever commerce or new building flourished, bush-trained aviators like LeRoy were in demand.

'What's going on?' he asked men who lounged about the airstrip, and one night in the winter of 1940 he found out. Friends hauled him off to a meeting at the schoolhouse in Palmer, where a trim young bullet-headed officer from the Army Air Corps gave a clipped lecture that brushed away the cobwebs: 'I'm Captain Leonidas Shafter, and I can lick any man who laughs at that first name.

My father was West Point and he named me after the Greek hero of Thermopylae. Lost his entire contingent and his head. I propose to do better.'

Aided by maps that had been converted by photography into color slides —which, when projected, filled a large section of blank wall behind him—he gave his audience of pilots, bulldozer operators and ordinary workmen fresh understanding of the war in Europe and Alaska's possible relation to it:

'The war over there may have subsided into what they humorously call the Sitzkrieg, with each side trying to outwait the other. But believe me, it's going to explode soon enough, and if past history is any guide, we'll be drawn into it.

'I cannot predict when or how our participation will come, but in one way or another it will have to involve Soviet Russia. The Communists are at present allies of Nazi Germany. This can't last long, but whether it does or not, can't you see how whatever Russia does will involve Alaska? Here at the Diomede Islands, the Soviet Union is a mile and a half from Alaska. All right, they're tiny islands and they don't matter. But across the Bering Sea from Russia to Alaska is trivial for a modern airplane. Contact is almost inescapable, and when that contact comes, your Alaska will be right in the middle of the war.'

A flier who had spent time in the Air Corps asked: 'Are you speaking of Russia as our enemy or our ally,' and Shafter snapped: 'I haven't said because I can't guess. The way things stand tonight, she's our enemy. But things won't continue as they are, and then she could become our ally.'

'Then how can you make plans?'

'In a case like this you plan for every contingency, and I'm certain that whatever happens, you good people will adjust to it.' To emphasize his point, he slapped the area where the Soviet and American frontiers met, and with that, he moved into the heart of his surprising talk:

'Look, please, at this map of North America and the eastern part of Siberia. Let's suppose that the Soviet Union continues to be our enemy. How can they most effectively strike at cities like Seattle, Minneapolis and Chicago? By streaming right across Alaska and Canada, a straight line to their industrial targets. The first battles, the ones that could decide everything, would be fought in places like Nome and Fairbanks and over the airfield on which we're sitting right now.

'But let's suppose that the Soviets turn on Hitler, as they should, and become our allies. How will we help supply them? How will airplanes built in Detroit get to Moscow? I think they'll fly a modified great circle route, across Wisconsin and Minnesota to Winnipeg, then, within six months, maybe over to Edmonton, Dawson, Fairbanks, Nome and into Siberia. Gentlemen, you could very well be using this gravel strip as an emergency landing field for huge bombers.'

While the men stared at one another in amazement, he showed a beautifully drawn map of the region between Edmonton and Fairbanks, and said: 'Whether the Soviet Union turns out to be enemy or friend, what we ought to do right now is build a highway capable of handling military equipment from here'—and he pointed to Dawson Creek, northwest of Edmonton—'where the railroad ends, right through this morass to here.' And, ignoring the terrible terrain, he marked a sweeping line across Canada and into the heartland of Alaska at Fairbanks. 'Don't tell me such a road has been tried before. Don't tell me it would impose all sorts of difficulties. Listen to me when I tell you it must be built.'

When a pilot asked 'Why?' Shafter grew impatient: 'Because the life and death of a great republic is at stake. Two great republics, the United States and Canada. We have got to move war equipment from Detroit and Pittsburgh to the shores of the Bering Sea.' And then he said something strange and prophetic, a stray idea that would always be remembered by the men who heard it. 'We've got to be prepared to drive off anyone who comes at us from Asia.' When this challenge was greeted by silence, he laughed at himself, slapped his right leg, and said jovially: 'They tell me the original Americans, Eskimos, everyone up here, they all came across the Bering Sea when it wasn't a sea any longer. Just walked across. Maybe the seas will drop again. Maybe they'll be coming at us across some land bridge. But they'll come, gentlemen, they will come.'

IN THE MONTHS that followed, LeRoy Flatch ignored the progress of the war in Europe and the frightening predictions of Captain Shafter, because he now had two planes to look after, the old two-seater Cub and the relatively new four-seater Waco. He kept pontoons on the former and berthed it at a nearby lake, and perfected a speedy way for switching the four-seater first to wheels and then to skis. With this two-pronged attack, which he used creatively, he was able to probe the center of Alaska about as effectively as any bush pilot then operating, for despite his youth, he had acquired a mature appreciation of what his airplanes would do if he kept them in good shape and filled with gas.

In any twelve-month period he would certainly land one of his planes on the following surfaces: wide macadam at an official airport like Anchorage, narrow bumpy macadam at a rural port like Palmer, gravel at one mining camp, loose gravel and dust at the next, grass at some strip beside a hunting lodge, gravel bank beside a river, mud and gravel beside some stream, ice, snow and—very dangerously—ice covered by a thin layer of snow, grass covered with sleet or grass covered with snow, sleet and light rainfall. He would also alight on lakes, rivers, ponds and other bodies of water too limited in length to permit a subsequent takeoff; then he would haul his plane onto dry land, walk out, and get some other daring aviator to fly him back in with a pair of wheels to replace the pontoons and some tools with which to chop down small trees and smooth out a runway.

And sooner or later he would also land in the branches of some tree; then he would scramble down, wait for a replacement wing to be flown in, bolt it carefully to the undamaged stub, and be off again. He was constantly in danger, considering the routes he flew, but with remarkable foresight he saw to it that any of the unavoidable accidents occurred with his old two-seater and not his new four-seat job.

His most enjoyable assignment came whenever he received a telegram asking him to meet one or another of the Venns at the Anchorage airport, for this always meant renewing acquaintance with this exciting family. He liked all of them: the cool, reserved father who ran an empire; the spirited mother who seemed to make many of the decisions; the young man who would one day inherit that empire; and especially the young wife, so pretty and secure in what she wanted to do. 'She's certainly not like any of the half-breeds you read about,' LeRoy said to his fellow pilots. 'Any man would be proud to have such a wife.'

'Not me,' an old-timer growled. 'Half-breeds, native women, sooner or later they all lead a man to hell.'

On pickup trips like the ones to Anchorage, LeRoy could never be sure just when the incoming plane would arrive; schedules in Alaska were subject to instant change, sometimes involving whole days. For example, when Bob Reeve flew his crazy planes out to the far end of the Aleutians, you were never certain when he would land on his return trip, because the weather out there was so unpredictable. One Reeve pilot told LeRoy: 'I kid you not, we were flying a normal route over Atka when a williwaw come up off the Bering Sea, calm one minute, tempest another, and turned us exactly upside down. Dishes, stewardesses, customers, all up in the air—and me too, if I hadn't been strapped in.'

'How long you fly that way?'

'About half a minute. Seemed like two hours, but the next blast of arctic air straightened us out.'

'I'd like to fly those islands with you someday.'

'Be my guest.'

On the long layovers, LeRoy liked to read accounts of the old bush pilots, the ones who had pioneered the routes he covered, and while the best stories dealt with the young men who flew out of the settled places like Sitka and Juneau, the most fascinating, it seemed to him, were about the men who brought aviation to the center of the country—Fairbanks, Eagle, the little settlements along the Yukon like Nulato and Ruby—and especially those intrepid pilots who carried the mail to the really minute villages on the southern and northern flanks of the great, forbidding Brooks Range—Beetles, Wiseman, Anaktuvuk and the camps along the Colville River.

Those guys really had guts, LeRoy thought repeatedly as he read of their exploits, but the tales had a mournful similarity. Harry Kane was about the best of the bush pilots. First man to land at a dozen different sites, field or no field. Loved riverbanks if the sand and gravel were not rippled. But if they were rippled, he landed anyway. Helped three different women have their babies at nine thousand feet. Never took chances. Always a bearcat for safety. You'd fly anywhere with good old Harry Kane, the best of the lot.

And then in the last two pages of the chapter you learned that one night, in a blinding snowstorm, good old Harry, best of the lot . . . kerplooie. Just once, LeRoy reflected, I'd like to read about someone who was the greatest of the bush pilots and who died in bed at the age of seventy-three.

With help from Tom Venn, LeRoy had rearranged the interior of his Waco so that an extra seat was provided back amidst the luggage, which meant that he could now meet the commercial planes flying up from Seattle and carry all four Venns out to their lodge, and once when the Seattle plane was late and he was delayed in reaching Venn's Lode he slept over, and in the morning Tom Venn said: 'You know, LeRoy, it's very gloomy to listen to the eight-o'clock news in Alaska.'

'Why? Just like the Lower Forty-eight, isn't it?'

'Not at all. Every morning there's this unbroken litany as to where the small planes have crashed the night before. "Harry Janssen's two-seater, at Lake This-or-That, west of Fairbanks. Twenty-eight hundred feet in snow. Signals indicate survivors." Or like the one they just broadcast. Some fellow named Livingston. "Four-seater at a lodge five miles west of Ruby. Snow. No signals. Plane looks to be severely damaged and on side." '

'Could that be Phil Livingston?' LeRoy asked. 'He's one of the best. He doesn't crash in a snowstorm. He doesn't even go out in a snowstorm.'

'He seems to have gone yesterday,' and when Flatch flew back to Palmer he learned that it was Phil Livingston, one of the best, and he began to listen to the eight-o'clock news with more attention, and the almost daily notice of which airplanes had crashed, where and at what altitudes, with or without visible survivors, brought home to him just how perilous it was to fly small planes in Alaska. 'Perilous but inescapable,' a veteran said in the pilots' room at Palmer as LeRoy was waiting for a passenger who wanted to explore the wonderful valleys that nestled among the glaciers streaming down from Denali.

But dangerous or not, bush flying in central Alaska was one of the world's most exciting occupations. The weather systems were monumental in extent, whole continents of air rushing madly out of Siberia. The mountains were endless, great armies of peaks many of them not even named, stretching to the horizons. The glaciers were, as one pilot trained in Texas said, 'not much like what you see on a flight out of Tulsa.' And the diversity of the people who populated the little villages or labored in the mining camps was endless and rewarding.

'Some of the craziest people in civilization,' the Texas pilot said, 'if you care to call this civilization, are up here in Alaska.'

LeRoy met some of them when he was commissioned to fly heavy replacement gear into a hopeless mining camp lost in a back corner of the Talkeetna Mountains north of Matanuska. He had never serviced this outfit before, but with the aid of a penciled map drawn hastily by a fellow pilot who had been there once, he found the place, and when he landed in the snow he saw three typical Alaska mountainmen waiting at the edge of their improvised airstrip: an old-timer from Oregon, a relative newcomer from Oklahoma and a young half-breed fellow with jet-black bangs hanging over his eyes. He had been born, LeRoy learned, in another mining camp well to the north, where his grandfather, a 1902 drifter from New Mexico, had married an Athapascan woman who could neither read nor write. Their son had hooked up with another Athapascan, so that their son, this Nathanael Coop, was really only one-quarter white, three-quarters Indian, but it was customary to call such a person a half-breed. His name was an oddity, for his New Mexico grandfather had arrived in Alaska with a name like Coopersmith or Cooperby, but his son was called by all his friends plain Coop, and it was thus that the name appeared on lists when the various head counts were made. Certainly his grandson was Nate Coop and had never been anything else.

Nate was in his late teens, a silent lad who seemed unrelated to his two older companions; his only friend was a big, surly brown dog named Killer, who had been trained to attack any stranger who trespassed on the mining property. He took an instant dislike to LeRoy, whom he attacked twice before Nate growled 'Down!' whereupon he leaped savagely at the snow skis, trying to grasp first one, then the other in his strong jaws before Nate growled a second 'Down!' Killer obviously loved his master, for at Nate's command he left the plane but positioned himself so that he could keep a bloodshot eye on both LeRoy and the Cub.

After the cargo was unloaded, LeRoy was informed that on the return trip he was expected to drop Nate off at a parent mine farther into the Talkeetnas: 'Nobody told me.'

'Nobody needed to. Ten bucks extra, you make the stop.'

'I have no idea where it is.'

'Nate'll show you,' and with the stub of a pencil the Oregon man added a few squirms and squiggles to the map and asked: 'Nate, you think you can figure it out?' and the young fellow said: 'I guess so.' With such preparation LeRoy prepared to fly deep into mountains he had never negotiated before.

'Hop in, Nate. If you know the landmarks, I'm sure we'll make it,' and Nate said with no concern: 'Never seen 'em from the air, but I guess they can't be much different,' and then to LeRoy's astonishment, Killer jumped in too.

'Now wait! I can't have a dog . . .'

'Stays on my lap, no trouble . . .'

Apprehensively, LeRoy allowed the dog to stay even though he could see that the hostility between them had not abated. As the plane climbed up off the snow, he happened to look sideways, and noticed how similar the dog and his master appeared, each with hair in his eyes: Nate and Killer, boy, they're a pair! When the plane achieved altitude, he warned the young miner: 'That dog still has it in for me. We could be in trouble if he tried to bite me,' but Nate said reassuringly: 'He's just protective.' But how Killer interpreted this commission, LeRoy could not guess, for although the evil-looking beast did stay on his side of the cockpit, secured in Nate's arms, he also kept his nose so close to LeRoy's right wrist that he could clamp down at the first false move. Killer was not a good passenger, and when the plane flew into rough mountain air which tossed it about, he started to whimper.

With two sharp taps on the dog's forehead, Nate said: 'Shut up, Killer,' and the complaints stopped.

In this uneasy posture Flatch flew deep into the mountains, his attention diverted by the snarling manner in which Killer maintained watch on him, and after some minutes of purposeful flight he told Nate: 'I'm lost. Where's the camp we're looking for?' Nate, no more worried than his pilot about being astray among great mountains in snowy weather, for that was an ordinary Alaskan experience, said blithely: 'It's got to be over here somewheres,' and, seeking to aid LeRoy, he opened his right-hand-door window to look down as they flew extremely low over a pass. But as he did, Killer saw the kind of chance he often leaped at when on the ground, an opportunity to escape from wherever he was being held, and with a powerful thrust of his legs he turned his back on the pilot he despised, left Nate's arms, uttered a triumphant bark, and jumped right out the open window.

LeRoy, on the left-hand side of the plane, did not see him go but he did hear the bark and Nate's anguished shout 'My God! There he goes!' and as the plane twisted in its course, the two occupants watched as big Killer, afloat in the cold air, intuitively spread out his legs to slow his fall and bring it under control.

'He'll be kilt!' Nate screamed. 'Do somethin'!' but there was nothing LeRoy could do except circle the plane and watch Killer smash onto the rocks below. However, the dog seemed to have some miraculous guidance system, for, with the bulk of his body parallel to the ground, and the fierce pull of gravity somewhat abated, he drifted and glided toward a snow-filled crevice, a kind of enclosed valley, high in the hills.

When the men saw him land, lie stunned for a moment, then rise and start to snarl, Nate said weakly: 'It's a miracle.' But now the problem became: 'How we gonna get that dog outta there?'

Even a moment's study convinced the two men that landing in that tight valley was an impossibility, for even though the plane did have its skis on, there was not nearly enough space for an approach or takeoff. Killer was marooned high in the Talkeetnas, and for the time being, there was no way to rescue him.

But they stayed over him for some minutes, loath to leave a pet, even an ugly-spirited one, in such a forlorn condition, and during one flyover LeRoy remembered the packet of sandwiches Flossie customarily put in the back of the plane whenever she knew her brother was off on one of his expeditions where food might be scarce, and now he directed Nate: 'Find that bundle. Paper tied with string. Break it loose.' And on their last flight over the bewildered animal, who had apparently landed uninjured, for he was thrashing about, Nate adroitly dropped the package not far from where the dog stood in the snow, his ugly face turned up toward the plane.

'I told you Killer had the brains of a man,' Nate exulted when the dog spotted the descending object, took note of its landing area, and ran to retrieve it. This was an act of such intelligence that LeRoy shouted: 'That dog's gonna live!' With Nate's guidance he turned the plane toward the camp.

By that evening all Alaska had been alerted to the drama of the 'parachuting' dog, and by the next day several determined outdoorsmen resolved to make a rescue effort, but the valley in which the dog was penned was so inaccessible that he could be kept alive only by food drops delivered from the Cub. Though overland hikes were clearly not feasible, suggestions poured into the camp from all parts of the territory.

The person who became most deeply concerned about Killer's fate was not his owner, Nate, but LeRoy's sister, Flossie, who had lost her tame moose so cruelly but whose considerable affection for animals was undiminished. So it was natural that the next day, when her brother and Nate were going out to feed the prisoner, she asked to go along, and they rigged a seat for her.

Killer had been in his mountain prison for three days when Flossie, on one of the routine flights, saw something that thrilled her: 'Nate! Look! He's heading over that hump and down into a better place.' And after LeRoy circled several times, they saw that the dog was indeed following the stream that led to the end of the valley, and they watched him cross over the divide and start down another stream that led to a snow-filled surface. Then LeRoy said: 'I think I could land in that one.'

That night avid listeners heard the heartening news that Killer, the marooned dog, had moved into an area from which it might be possible to rescue him, and newspapermen chartered an airplane at Palmer to interview LeRoy and Nate at the camp.

It was on this hectic night, when the mining camp was full of extra men, that LeRoy became aware that his sister was developing an unusual interest in Nate Coop. Impressed by the young man's devotion to his dog and his love for animals in general, and excited by his manly good looks—raven-dark hair, strong face with sunken spots beneath his cheekbones, gleaming white teeth when he smiled, flashing dark eyes—she could not hide her growing preoccupation with this young fellow who was becoming a hero, and she had even begun to speculate on what life would be like with such a man. She confessed to herself that she was seriously attracted to Nate, and once this was admitted she found herself powerless to hide the fact from her brother.

'He seems so decent' was all she said, to which LeRoy replied: 'He's a half-breed.'

'Aren't we all?' she asked, and there the philosophical part of the discussion ended, for LeRoy added a practical note: 'We better get you out of here, Floss. We're heading into a mountain blizzard.'

He now had an extra reason to speed the rescue, so on the morning of the fourth day they unloaded every bit of gear the Cub could spare and took off for the mountains. When they found Killer he was, as they had expected, down at a much lower level where there were areas of snow extensive enough for a ski plane to land, but the quality of the snow was dubious. 'It doesn't look packed,'

LeRoy told the others as he circled not far from where the dog waited, 'and it's certainly not flat.'

'You can do it,' Flossie said, and it was good that she spoke first, for Nate was quite sure that the snowbanks were so sloping that the plane could not land, while LeRoy was uncertain. In the silence that greeted her enthusiastic endorsement, Flossie said nothing. She was only sixteen that year, a quiet girl not given to expressing her ideas boldly in front of strange men, but now when it appeared that they might turn back, she repeated her verdict: 'You can do it, LeRoy. Over there. You've landed on worse,' so in silence the three adventurers approached the more-or-less-level space she had indicated, but when they saw it close up, even Flossie began to doubt that they could make it.

But at this moment Killer, aware that something special was under way, since no food had been dropped, began to leap and bark in wild excitement, and although they could not hear his cries of encouragement, they knew what he was doing, and Nate said: 'Let's go down.' Breathing very deeply to settle his nerves, and adjusting three or four different times to his pilot's seat, LeRoy asked quietly: 'Nate, you strapped in? Floss, you tied in with those ropes?' Clearing his throat and swinging his shoulders about to ensure that he would have relatively free movement if required, LeRoy brought his plane in for a mountain landing that would have daunted the average practiced pilot and frightened even the best Alaskan bush pilots.

Over a crest of rocks he brought the Cub down across a heavily rumpled field of snow and onto the fairly flat space where Killer waited. As the plane neared the ground the occupants saw that it was much more tilted to the right than they had anticipated from aloft, and for just a moment LeRoy judged that he ought to abort this dangerous landing, but from the rear Flossie shouted: 'It's all right! Better spot on ahead!' and with just a bit more gas her brother kept the plane aloft until he saw the place where he could land.

With a whoosh that terrified Killer waiting below, the plane's two skis reached for the snow while the Cub tilted perilously to the right, as if it were going to tumble down the slope, but then better levels were reached, the plane righted itself, and the skis glided to an easy stop. Before even the doors were opened, Killer was leaping upon the struts and barking his delight at seeing once more a thing he had despised.

Nate, of course, was first out, for the access door was on his side, and when Killer saw him alight the dog leaped into his arms and whimpered the equivalent of sobs of joy, and when LeRoy edged himself out of the plane, the dog ran to him too, licking at him as if past enmities were forgiven. But when Flossie descended, a person Killer had never seen or smelled before, he started at her with a menacing growl. Giving him a solid kick, Nate snapped: 'Down, you damned fool. She's the one who rescued you,' and to Killer's dismay, his master turned away from him and took Flossie in his arms.

WHEN THE TWO Flatches returned to their cabin at Matanuska, LeRoy convened an emergency session of the family, to whom he reported: 'Flossie's been kissin' a half-breed named Nate Coop.'

'He the one who owns the dog?' Elmer asked, and LeRoy said: 'The same,' and the whole weight of the family fell upon silent Flossie. Elmer pointed out that 'acrost the states of the two Dakotas and all of Minnesota, no marriage of a white man to no Indian woman, or vicey versey, has ever worked. It's agin the law of nature.'

Hilda Flatch, generous in most of her judgments, warned: 'You know him for four days! Ridiculous! Besides, Indians drink. They beat their wives and ignore their children.'

And LeRoy said, with a perspicacity that surprised everyone: 'Why would you bother with a half-breed when you have that perfectly good Vickaryous boy available?'

And suddenly Paulus Vickaryous, scion of the Finnish family about whom the Flatches had always been cool, became a paragon, a young man who knew how to farm and who had acquired land of his own, a responsible fellow who attended the Lutheran church regularly and saved money. He was, according to Flossie's family, about the finest young American or Canadian of this generation, and they began inviting him to dinner.

He was a tall young man with the attractive light-blond hair that nature had given the Finns, whose fair skin could attract even the slightest of the sun's rays that hit their forbidding land. He was well educated, well mannered and as good a farmer as Elmer had said. There was no conceivable reason why a girl like Flossie would not want to marry a man as promising as Paulus, except that she had lost her heart to Nate Coop, his mountains and his dog.

So after young Vickaryous had been rebuffed three or four times in ways so blatant that he could not fail to receive the message, he stopped appearing at the Flatch cabin, and the restrained fury of the Flatch family began to envelop poor Flossie. Day after day she heard stories of how Indian men mistreated their women, and of how no Indian could ever stay sober three weeks in a row, and of how, if you took a hundred miners, Indian or white, ninety-six of them never amounted to a damn. An outsider, listening to the Flatches berating their headstrong daughter, would have concluded that the girl was a delinquent who merited the scorn she was suffering. And certainly the listener would have supposed that young Flossie would never again be allowed to speak with her Indian half-breed.

But in this extremity she found a powerful champion, one prepared to sweep away the cobwebs of the past and misunderstandings of the present. The presumptive widow Melissa Peckham had remained at Matanuska as the representative of the Alaskan territorial government and it was often her counsel that enabled the teetering settlement to find a stable balance. She met with wives unable to accept the interminable winters: 'You should have seen the Klondike in February. I made fifty, sixty pancakes at a time. Stacked 'em outside the cabin, dealt 'em off one by one as the hungry men came in. Frozen solid—the pancakes, not the men. Thaw 'em out. Heat 'em up, douse 'em in syrup, and away we go. One stack would last maybe two weeks.'

To the husbands defeated by floods and freezes she said: 'Now, Mr. Vasanoja, do you think for one minute that life back in Minnesota would be one bit better for you if you returned? For the banker, already there with his millions stolen from the poor, yes, it would be better. And for the sheriff with his big Buick, yes, lots better. But for you, a Finn with no savings? Mr. Vasanoja, did I ever tell you about how my man Murphy rode a bicycle a thousand miles to find his gold mine, and found nothin'?' Missy had in her youth spoken flawless English, but in the gold fields she had on occasion adopted the language of the frontier until she sometimes spoke like the toughest woodsman.

It was this woman, a sixty-six-year-old social worker and mining-camp veteran, who now stepped in to defend Flossie Flatch. Meeting with the girl's distraught family, she glared at them and said: 'You remind me of law sessions they used to have in the gold fields before the North West Mounted moved in.

Some miner would do somethin' the rest didn't approve of, so they'd hold a court in a saloon, and eight men who'd done a lot worse things would pass judgment on him. Ridiculous.' She glared at the older Flatches and said: 'You're doin' the same with Flossie. You're really not qualified to judge. This is a new world with new rules.'

When she had their attention she said: 'Of course he's a half-breed, but so is most of Alaska, one way or another. I've seen a score of good marriages with full-blooded Eskimos and Indians. You, LeRoy, you fly the Venns around, don't you? Surely you've seen that young Venn's wife is a half-breed, haven't you? Chinese and Tlingit. And those very wealthy Lincoln Arkikovs down in Juneau—Siberian and Yupik. My daughter married an Arkikov, and I'm damn proud of her family.' And then she uttered the simple statement that summarized so much Alaskan life: 'You want to be happy up here, you better learn the rules.'

'But don't the Indians always drink too much?' Hilda Flatch asked, and Missy snapped: 'Sometimes. Alcohol and suicide, the twin curses of the native people. But in good marriages the risk is no greater than with white men and women in general.'

'But how would a half-breed like him ever find a steady job?' Elmer asked, and this infuriated the feisty older woman: 'Mr. Flatch, you amaze me. You want guarantees. I don't see you with a steady job. When my husband was alive he used to ask me: "Why doesn't a reliable man like Elmer Flatch get himself a steady job?" and I said: "Looks like to me he's makin' a better livin' than you are." '

Allowing this sharp attack to relax, she asked for a drink—'Anything handy'—and said with a gentleness much removed from her previous arguments: 'Now listen to me, you too, Flossie. Years ago, in Chicago, I was a fairly acceptable-looking young woman. Straight teeth, nice hair, a good education. I've never married. Always fell in love with men who already had wives. Great, wonderful men, best in the world, but never free to marry me. So . . . Life comes at you in a thousand different forms, and you better be prepared to accept it when it comes along. Because if you miss it, the years stretch out forever, bleak and lonely and meaningless.'

When no one commented, she said with a renewed brightness: 'So, you fine Flatches who aren't really as fine as you think you are, nor am I, nor are the Vickaryouses that you've been courtin' . . . It was an accident, a cruel accident perhaps, that this Flossie, who is such a good girl, flew into that mining camp and met Nate Coop. I know nothin' about him except that he took great pains to save his dog. You took your sister there, LeRoy, hotshot pilot, so the blame's on you. Could be the best thing you ever did, because I am going to do everything I can to help your sister marry that boy.'

But when she saw the truly tormented faces of all the Flatches but Flossie, she had to try to help them understand the situation: 'All right! I agree with you. According to LeRoy, he's an illiterate oaf with hair in his eyes and a grunt for hello. But he's lived in the woods with people who know no better. Marriage in Alaska is often a woman with good sense and an overdose of humanity marryin' a clod like this Nate and civilizin' him. So if your Flossie can tame a moose, she can sure civilize young Mr. Coop.'

When Missy finally stomped out of the house, she left expecting that the Flatches would make some kind of conciliatory gesture to their daughter, but what Hilda said was: 'If you marry that damned half-breed, your father will throw you out of this house . . . and I'll help.' But when Nate flew down to

Matanuska in the plane of another bush pilot to present himself to the Flatch family, they had to admit that he seemed like a manly young fellow, with good, though awkward, manners, but he was frighteningly dark-skinned and his features were hopelessly Indian. If Flossie were going to live in the wilderness, he might be acceptable as a son-in-law, but in ordinary town life with other people he was painfully inferior to Paulus Vickaryous. And he had made the grave error of bringing with him his dog Killer, who showed his growling dislike for all the Flatches, including Flossie. So when Nate in mumbling fashion asked for Flossie's hand, with Killer snarling in the background, all of the Flatches replied with a clear-cut 'No!'

U NWILLING TO ACCEPT this as a final answer, Nate remained in the vicinity for some days, then vanished. However, he did write to Flossie, but Mrs. Flatch appropriated the letters, and when this was discovered by Flossie's asking at the post office if any mail had come in for her, she so informed Missy Peckham, who stormed out to the cabin with some harsh news: 'Hilda Flatch, if you prevent United States mail from reachin' its intended owner, you can go to jail. You hand over those letters, right now, to me as an agent of the government. And don't be a damned fool.'

When the letters were delivered to Flossie, she carried them home unopened and told her mother: 'I'm not mad. You did what you thought was right. But I want to read them here in my own home with you watching,' and with a long kitchen knife she opened the letters, one by one, and read them in silence. As she finished each one she handed it over to her mother, sitting on the opposite side of the kitchen table, and that night she wrote to Nate.

As a consequence of this exchange of letters, Nate Coop flew down to Matanuska at the time of year when the three George Lakes could be expected to break through the great glacier wall; Flossie had told him that she wanted to see it actually happen this year and he had come to take her up the Knik River to witness it. He lodged at Missy Peckham's place and came to the Flatch cabin only twice, for when he appeared the second time the older Flatches made it clear that he was not welcome, and he left.

They were shocked, some days later, when Flossie disappeared, and no one could guess where she might have gone; Missy said her lodger had left too, and she supposed they might have flown to Seattle to get married, but when Hilda, who was especially opposed to Coop, ransacked her daughter's mail she found in one of Nate's letters a reference to the dramatic breakup of the lakes, with the comment: 'That would be a neat thing to see.' Shuddering, she called her son, but he was absent on a trip to Venn's Lode, and by the time he returned it was too dark for him to do anything about finding his sister.

But in the morning he acceded to his mother's wild laments, revved up his Cub, now on wheels, and set out to scout the surrounding countryside, and as he flew up the Knik River toward the glacier he saw, near the promontory from which the shattering collapse of the glacier would best be viewed, a white canvas tent. Dropping low, he buzzed the place, and was relieved but also distressed to see two young people emerge—obviously from sleeping bags, for their hair was disheveled and they wore what could be taken for pajamas or some kind of slapdash substitute. Although he could not identify the pair, he was pretty sure they must be Flossie and Nate, and his uncertainty was removed in a way which infuriated him: the dog Killer burst out of the tent and began yapping at the plane.

Signaling to them by dipping his wings, he made another circuit, now flying so low that he could see their faces, but at this moment his attention was distracted by a gigantic pillar of spume soaring high in the air. The ice plugs which had held the three lakes captive during the past ten months had exploded, and the long-imprisoned waters were now roaring free. LeRoy in his plane, his sister and Nate from in front of their tent, watched in awe as this titanic force broke loose, for as the waters struck the face of the glacier they carved away massive icebergs, which began their tortuous way down the tempestuous river, gouging out smaller icebergs as they ground and jostled and carved their way along. It was the most violent manifestation of nature any of the three had ever seen, and LeRoy circled over the cascading waters and the crumbling icebergs for half an hour, after which he buzzed the tent once more, dipping his wings to the lovers and their excited dog.

When he landed at Palmer he hurried out to the cabin, rushed in, looked at his apprehensive parents, and said: 'Well, now they got to get married.'

THE FOUR FLATCHES had been so preoccupied with their own affairs, they had remained oblivious to the irresistible manner in which world history had been creeping up on them. In June 1941 the prediction that Air Corps Captain Shafter had made at the Palmer Airstrip in the winter of 1940 came true; Nazi Germany declared total war against Communist Russia, and what Shafter had seen to be an illogical alliance came to an end. This meant, the other pilots at the airstrip pointed out, that 'Russia will probably be our ally, if we ever get into this thing.' And the more knowing, with whom LeRoy did not associate, began to look more closely at that very narrow stretch of the Bering Sea separating the Soviet Union from Alaska.

At about this time even LeRoy became aware that someone, Canadian or American, he could never tell which, was expressing interest in a chain of would-be airports—skimpy strips in the wilderness, really—linking Edmonton in Canada to Fairbanks in Alaska, and he wondered what was afoot. Once more Leonidas Shafter, a major now, appeared in Palmer with a request, or perhaps it was an order, that all bush pilots in the region meet with him:

'American participation in the war's inevitable. How we'll enter is any-body's guess. I think Hitler will do something stupid in Europe. The *Lusitania* all over again. But something. Or maybe Russia will begin to fall. When that happens, right here where you are in Alaska becomes of utmost importance.

'So what we're about to do in anticipation, is rush into being this line of airports, call them emergency landing strips, from Great Falls down here in Montana to Edmonton up here in Canada and over to Fairbanks in Alaska. Then we'll use the little Yukon River strips already existing from Ladd Field in Fairbanks to Nome. To accomplish this we must have the cooperation of you flyboys familiar with the territory.'

This time he had with him a map marked Secret, and after asking anyone not a pilot to leave the room, he tacked it onto the wall behind him. It was almost identical to one of those he had displayed on his previous visit, except that this time it had a linked chain of some dozen red stars glued to little-known villages or river crossings in northern Montana, western Canada and eastern Alaska:

'If you tried to walk the last part of that route, Edmonton to Fairbanks, it'd take about two years, supposing you had a good Indian guide and an airplane to drop supplies. To drive it, maybe fifteen years, granted that the two countries ever woke up to build a road through that wilderness . . . or could do it if they did decide. What we're going to do is build us eleven emergency fields, right now, and since there are no roads along most of this route, you men are going to fly the equipment in, right now.

'Of course, from the opposite end here in Edmonton, another group of guys just like you will be flying in their share of the cargo. So as of tonight, now, you are all enlisted in one of the damnedest projects Alaska has ever seen. Building airfields where there have never been any. We want you, and we want your planes. An office will be established in Anchorage and I've asked two officers to work out of here, starting right now. Captain Marshal, Army Air Forces. Major Catlett, Army Corps of Engineers. Start signing them up, Officers.'

The two officers were delighted to learn that LeRoy Flatch owned, more or less, two airplanes, the two-seater Cub and the four-seater Waco, but they were taken aback when he allowed as how he would lease out the four-seater and keep the two-seater for himself: 'It carries more. It can do more things. And when it crashes you walk away from it more often.'

So he dropped all other obligations, except for borrowing back his four-seater occasionally for a hurried flight to ferry the Venns into their camp at the base of Denali, and flew one tedious flight after another with huge loads of cargo for the incipient airstrips in the wilderness. The system of linked airfields, primitive and provisional though it was, bore the exalted title the Northwest Staging Route, and since its various components came into service at the most uneven times, with an extremely difficult base operational five months before a much easier one, flights along it were spasmodic, but workhorse pilots like Flatch became accustomed to stops like Watson Lake, Chicken and Tok, with occasional flights to unheard-of places between Fairbanks and Nome. 'When we get this damned thing finished,' Lieutenant Colonel Shafter told his crews at the various construction bases, 'we'll have a first-class route from Detroit to Moscow, because I can tell you the Russians are doing the same on their side of the Bering Sea.'

After LeRoy had been serving for six months on the Northwest Route, Colonel Shafter, who seemed able to work twenty-two hours a day when things were going smoothly, thirty-six at times of crisis, and to win a promotion every five months, flew into Palmer Airstrip with surprising news: 'Flatch, I've been watching you. They don't come any better. I want you to trade back your four-seater Waco. Give whoever has it your old Cub and become my personal pilot for the whole route, Great Falls to Nome.'

'Does this mean I have to join the Air Corps?'

'Not yet. Later on, when we get into this thing, probably.'

But his new job did mean that LeRoy had to learn to fly again, for Shafter's job required flying over such vast unexplored areas north of the tree line that the old safeguards of bush-piloting no longer prevailed. 'Son,' Shafter said in the midst of one dangerous flight, 'you got wheels on your crate and skis and you could have pontoons, but none of them is worth a damn if we have to land on tundra down there,' and two days later he had a pair of 'tundra' tires flown in. They were enormously wide balloonlike affairs inflated only partially, which enabled Flatch to land on humpy or even slightly marshy tundra. But the tires were so huge they altered the flight characteristics of any plane using them, and this required LeRoy to avoid things a prudent pilot would normally do.

A flier familiar with tundra tires instructed him: 'Since the tires can't be retracted, no tight turns at low or even moderate speed. The tundras will drag you into a spin. Your maximum altitude will be cut by about two thousand feet. When you land, don't rush things, just sort of skip along. And most important, the wind drag of these monsters cuts your maximum range on a full tank by a large factor.'

LeRoy said: 'You sound as if using the tundras converts the Waco into a whole new plane,' and the pilot said: 'You've learned your lesson. Now respect it.' But once Flatch adjusted to this plane with its monstrous tires, he gained the ultimate refinement in his career as a bush pilot. Now he really could land almost anywhere.

Confident but never cocky, he flew over the most forbidding terrain, landing occasionally at sites that would have caused the average pilot to shudder, and in the air he exercised stern command, for no matter what some frightened general shouted at him, he would say quietly: 'Sit back, sir. I'm gonna land on that stuff right below us, so keep your belt tight.' Half a dozen times he terrified Shafter, but after one such flight ended safely, Shafter said: 'You did the right thing, son. You bush pilots seem to operate under your own rules of aerodynamics.'

As paperwork for the route neared completion, Flatch underwent three emotional experiences. The first came on the Sunday when news of the bombing of Pearl Harbor reached the temporary base at Chicken at about the same time as a long American P-40 fighter plane reached that field on a multistop flight from a point near Pittsburgh. The war that Captain Shafter had so clearly foreseen had erupted, and that night, before a startled judge stopping over in Chicken, LeRoy Flatch was sworn into the Air Corps as a second lieutenant, ordinary requirements having been waived.

The second moment he would never forget came in the following January when he received word that his old two-seater Cub had crashed at Fort Nelson, over in Canada. He flew General Shafter there to investigate, and found that a young pilot straight from training camp in California had become engulfed in a whiteout: 'General, you couldn't see nothing. Sky, snow, ground all the same. We got two planes down by lighting fires. This boy never knew where he was, but he says calm as you please, I was on the radio: "Pretty soupy up here . . . everywhere," and two minutes later he comes roaring down, nose right into the snow, as you see it over there.' The plane was a wipeout, its loss more grievous because Flatch was certain that had he been at the controls, it could have been saved.

'You want a photograph of it?' the general asked, and LeRoy said: 'No.'

'Come on, lad. It was a part of your life. Fifty years from now you'll cherish the memory of this day,' and he led LeRoy to the shattered plane, indistinguishable as to make or number, and they were photographed together, the tough young general, the quiet young lieutenant and the 1927 Cub they had both respected.

The third experience was an extraordinary one, for when huge cadres of young Russian pilots began flooding into Ladd Field, Fairbanks, in late 1942 to pick up the American planes they would fly across to Siberia, General Shafter assigned Flatch to special duty at Nome, where a large segment of the historic gold field was converted into the last staging point prior to flight into Siberia.

Here LeRoy was to give the daring Russian fliers who would convoy the planes all the way to Moscow, then under dreadful siege, whatever assistance they required, and he was on duty one morning when an unusual Russian pilot came to him, speaking not perfect but very good English: 'I am Lieutenant Maxim Voronov. My ancestor Arkady Voronov turned Alaska over to you Americans, 18 and 67. No planes coming, I like to see maybe Sitka. You can take me, yes?'

The idea was so startling that Flatch tried to get in touch with Shafter, but when that proved impossible, he said to the Russian: 'General Shafter told me to do everything within reason to help you. If you make a formal request, we'll go.' So Voronov made his request; LeRoy wrote it down; an enlisted man at Nome Base phoned the message over to Fairbanks; and without waiting for a reply, Flatch and Voronov were on their way to the big base at Anchorage, where they obtained a seaplane for the flight to Sitka, which at that time had no landing facilities except in the sound.

It was a bright day, with the sun glistening off the glaciers and the manifold little islands shining in the Pacific like drops of crystal resting on blue satin. Voronov had apparently studied the history of Russian Alaska with some care, for when the seaplane was well aloft he told the pilot from the right front seat, which he occupied: 'I would to appreciate much if you show me Kayak Island,' and when the plane flew over that strange elongated island on which Vitus Bering's Russians had first landed, LeRoy, sitting in the back seat, saw that Voronov had tears in his eyes. Flatch, never having heard of Kayak Island and seeing it now only as a desolate place which no one would want to bother with, asked what the island signified, but Voronov, studying the terrain with unusual care, indicated that he would explain later.

The visit to Sitka, which LeRoy had seen only twice before when dropping down to pick up military guests for General Shafter, was a powerful experience for both men. Voronov tried to pick out the places where his ancestors had lived: he recognized the Russian church with its onion dome, and he very much wanted to go to the hill on which Baranov's Castle had stood, but during these war years, when an invasion by the Japanese was always a possibility, the mount was restricted to the few military personnel who manned batteries there and in the vicinity.

But Voronov astonished Flatch by knowing in the most intimate detail the conduct of the various battles that had marked the prolonged combat between Russian and Tlingit warriors, and the probable location of the palisades that had once enclosed the town. He knew where the old Tlingit village had been outside the walls and where the lake was from which one of his ancestors had cut ice for sale in San Francisco. He was particularly interested in where the ships had been built for the trade with Hawaii, and he quite startled both Flatch and the pilot of the seaplane by asking whether they could fly down to the famous hot springs south of Sitka.

Permission to do so was difficult to arrange, but an Aleut with a Russian name was designated to take the three travelers, and when the seaplane landed in the bay that fronted the hill from whose side the springs erupted, the pilot remained with the plane while the others climbed up the slope to the springs, where in a rickety house built decades before, they stripped and let themselves down into the hot and sulfurous waters.

As they luxuriated, Flatch thought how strange it was that a great war should have been the instrument which brought this Russian back to the land where his ancestors had served with apparent distinction, but it was the Aleut-

Russian guide who was most deeply moved. He spoke no Russian, of course, but he told Voronov of how *his* ancestors had served the Russians in Kodiak Island and then later just north of San Francisco, and Voronov listened attentively, asking many questions as to how the American possessors had treated the Aleuts when they occupied the area. The guide said: 'Pretty well. They let us keep our church here. Up till the 1917 revolution, our priest got his salary from Moscow,' and Voronov, splashing water on his face, nodded.

When the time came to depart Sitka a local woman who attended the Russian church came to Voronov with a curious reminder of the Russian days: it was an invitation to a dance held annually in Sitka, this one dated 1940, and it had been issued in the name of Prince and Princess Maksutov as if they still occupied the palace: 'When we dance, sir, we imagine that the nobility sits on the sidelines as in the old day up in the castle, watching us with approval.' She kissed Voronov's hand and said: 'We remember your great ancestor well. May you enjoy victory.'

When she was gone, Flatch asked: 'What great ancestor?' and Voronov explained: 'A Voronov who served in that church over there, wonderful man, in touch with God, I think. Served out here on the edge of nowhere and became so holy that they called him back to Moscow to become head of all the churches in Russia.'

'Catholic?' LeRoy asked.

'Not Roman, Orthodox. He married an Aleut woman, one of God's great messengers. So I'm part Aleut. That's why the man in the bath . . .' He surprised Flatch by asking: 'On the way back to Nome, could we to stop by the Totem Salmon Cannery, on Taku Inlet?'

'You know these waters better than I do,' LeRoy said, and Voronov replied: 'A son of the great religious leader—I think it was—he discovered that place where the cannery was. Our family has all the records.'

So they flew the short detour to Taku Inlet, and up toward the closed end, where the great glaciers came snouting down, Flatch saw the cannery buildings about which he'd previously had no knowledge. 'They're immense!' he shouted to the front seat.

'Want me to land?' the pilot asked.

'No need,' Voronov said. 'But I would like you to fly up that little river. One of my family, Arkady, wrote a poem about it. Pleiades the lake is called at the source.'

So the seaplane wound its way inland the short distance to Lake Pleiades, where the three men saw the seven lovely mountains and the cool waters in which salmon bred, and from there they flew along the chain of glaciers back to Anchorage, where Flatch's plane waited for the direct hop to Nome. There American pilots were delivering specially equipped planes for the Moscow front, and Lieutenant Maxim Voronov, twenty-two years old, climbed into one of them, listened to fifteen minutes of instruction, and took off for Siberia. He did not offer any emotional farewells to LeRoy Flatch, merely said: 'Thank you,' and was off to the wars. In succeeding days some forty of these special planes passed through Nome, and to each of the Russians who took them over, some American said: 'Give Hitler hell!' or 'Hold fast till we get there,' or something like that.

Next morning as LeRoy shaved he reflected on his somewhat perplexing experience with Lieutenant Voronov, and concluded that he had better report it to General Shafter: 'He said his name was Lieutenant Maxim Voronov and we had better record his name, for I'm sure he'll be back this way again,' but when he did not reappear, LeRoy assumed he had been killed in the air battles over Moscow.

E ACH MALE MEMBER of the Flatch family had his life seriously disrupted by World War II, and each made a signal contribution to the defense of Alaska, and thereby of the United States itself: LeRoy in the construction of the aviation lifeline which helped save Moscow; brother-in-law Nate Coop as a foot soldier in one of the most confused and demanding battles of the war; and father Elmer in an activity he could never have anticipated. The two young men participated in ways that were extensions of their civilian lives, aviation and outdoor activity, but Elmer was propelled into a life for which he had practically no preparation. He did know how to drive a car, and that was about it.

He was drafted into civilian service by Missy Peckham. As representative of the territorial government she appeared at the cabin one morning with astounding news: 'Elmer, the United States has wakened up at last. The dunderheads in Washington see that Alaska's of vital importance. Japanese might land here at any moment and cut our connections with Russia.'

'LeRoy's busy building them emergency airfields.'

'You're gonna be buildin' a lot more than a bunch of puny airstrips.'

'Like what?'

She evaded this direct challenge: 'Alaskans always dream of somethin' additional. When I was young we wanted a railroad, Anchorage to Fairbanks. Nothin' but empty land. But in 1923, President Harding himself came here to drive the golden spike. Of course, he died right after. Some blamed poisoned clams he ate here, others claimed his lady friend in California did him in.'

'And what do you want us to build now?'

'A highway for automobiles. Right across the worst land in the world. Bindin' us to the Lower Forty-eight.'

'And we always decided it was an impossibility. Have a beer?'

As they sat in the Flatch kitchen, with Hilda watching from her corner, Missy unrolled a map provided her by an army detachment based in Anchorage: 'We're gonna build a first-class military highway parallelin' the airstrips your son is buildin',' and she revealed the thin red line that would connect Edmonton down in Canada with all the airfields coming into being across the bleakest part of the northwest and into Fairbanks. If building the little airstrips in that wilderness had staggered General Shafter and his airmen, constructing a highway would present difficulties that were unimaginable.

'It can't be done,' Elmer said flatly, and Missy replied: 'In time of war, it can.'

On her map she showed him the results of Allied thinking about the highway that would forever link the United States and Canada, if it could be constructed: 'Canadians wanted it to be more or less a coastal road so it could serve their western settled areas, or so they told us at the briefing. The wild men who love the arctic, they wanted to follow that hellish route my man Murphy took in 1897, right up the Mackenzie River damned near to the Arctic Circle, then across mountains and into Fairbanks. The square-headed Americans said: "We'll take the middle way, the Prairie Route, where the airstrips are already in." And that's the road you'll be buildin', Elmer.'

'Me?'

'You and your truck. Report to Big Delta soonest with a full kit of tools, and start construction from this end.'

'I don't know anything about road buildin'!'

'You'll learn.' And she was off to enroll the older Vickaryous, Vasanoja and Krull men.

In all, some four hundred Alaskan civilians were conscripted more or less forcibly into the work force that would build over a thousand miles of roadway in Canada, more than two hundred miles in Alaska. They were ordered to complete this gargantuan task in no more than eight months. 'We expect to have army trucks filled with battle gear coming over this road by October first,' the colonel in charge of Elmer's segment roared whenever anything went wrong. To make this possible, the Americans would provide nearly twelve thousand men in uniform, the Canadians as large a contingent as their population would allow.

The Alcan Highway it was officially dubbed, a roadway that had always been dreamed about by those in the north and one which might have come into being, under normal circumstances, sometime in the early twenty-first century, for the cost was horrendous and the obstacles terrifying. In wartime it would be built, incredible as it seemed, in eight months and twelve days.

When Elmer Flatch reported to army headquarters in Fairbanks he was told to deliver his truck to the central depot and take personal delivery of a huge Caterpillar tractor big enough to knock down trees or haul heavily loaded ten-wheel trucks out of ditches. 'I never drove a thing like that,' he protested, and the lieutenant in charge of the depot growled: 'Start now.'

Three of the regiments assigned to duty in the Alaskan sectors were all-black except for white officers, and a big, slope-shouldered black man who had operated dozers in Georgia was in charge of instructing civilians like Flatch in the intricacies of handling the behemoths that would be chopping a roadway through terrain that had hitherto seemed impassable. This huge fellow, Sergeant Hanks, gave concise, sensible instructions in a pronounced Georgia drawl which the Alaskans found difficult to understand: 'Learnin' gear shift, chir'n do that. Learnin' stay alive, some you surely fail, we bury you.'

Hanks said, with endless repetitions and illustrations, that a driver had to feel in his ass, not his brain, when a slope was too tilted to be negotiated by this dozer: 'Not up and down slope, even chir'n handle that.'

'What in hell is chir'n,' a Minnesota Swede asked, and Hanks explained: 'Chir'n. Boys, girls. I got four chir'ns back home. How many you got?'

The perilous slopes that he warned against, the ones that killed careless men by the score, were those which tilted the Cat sideways, especially to the left: 'Cat fall right, maybe got a chance. Fall left, crush you ever' time.' He repeated that a driver had to feel in his ass, not his brain or with the aid of his eye, when the slope, left or right, was becoming too steep to be negotiated: 'You feel that message, back to hell out. And doan' try turnin'. Jes' back out like you back out from a dark room where you hears a ghost.'

Under Hanks's repetitious instruction Elmer Flatch, and other ordinary men like him, began to master the intricacies of the great Caterpillars, and after an indoctrination period that seemed perilously brief, they were sent forth to do the job. In early May, Flatch found himself ten miles east of the little town of Tok, where the road from Eagle drops down from Chicken, and he had been on the job only a few hours when a major in the Corps of Engineers started bellowing at him: 'You, there. With the coonskin cap. Take your Cat down there and help pull the other Cat back on its tracks.' And when Elmer obeyed, he came upon two machines bigger than his own mired in mud as they strove to bring back, upright, a small dozer which had slid down a small slope.

When his Cat was attached by wires to the fallen behemoth, and all three machines pulled in unison, the creature at the bottom of the slope slowly righted itself, whereupon the major screamed: 'Hold it! You, there, get the body!' and Elmer remained with his wires taut, as medical corpsmen pried the shattered body of the careless driver free from the seat into which he had been crushed. Watching the gruesome process, Elmer said aloud: 'His ass didn't send him the message.' Pause. 'More likely it arrived but he didn't listen.'

The most useful member of the team at Tok was neither wise Sergeant Hanks nor hard-driving Major Carnon, but a short, stubborn Athapascan Indian named Charley. He had a second name, of course, probably something English like Dawkins or Hammond after some early goldminer who had married his great-grandmother up by Fort Yukon, but no one knew what it was. Charley's job was to grease the Cats and dozers and help install new tracks when the old ones jammed or broke or wore out, but his principal value lay in his eagerness to inform majors and colonels and generals from the Lower Forty-eight when they were about to do something which worked very well down in Oklahoma or Tennessee but which simply did not function up in Alaska. So when he saw well-intentioned Major Carnon preparing to build his road east of Tok the way he had done so often in Arkansas, he felt he must warn the energetic fellow that he was making one big mistake: 'Major, sir, down there, maybe okay strip off the topsoil, make solid base. Up here we don't do that.'

'Keep those dozers moving forward!' Carnon bellowed, whereupon Charley said quietly, but with some force: 'Major, sir, we don't do that up here.'

'Keep moving!'

So Charley bided his time, returned to his work area, and resumed threading a new track on a dozer which had shattered its right tread in trying to knock down a nest of trees just a mite too big for it to handle. With a sense of disgust, the knowing Indian watched as Major Carnon stripped away the topsoil until a firm base was reached, and when this desecration continued, he sought out Elmer Flatch, whose dozer he had often serviced: 'Flatch, you got to warn the major, we don't do that up here.'

Another dozer man, from Utah, hearing the warning, broke in: 'You always clear away the soft topsoil till you get a firm base. Then you build. Otherwise you got nothin'.'

'Up here we do it different,' Charley warned, but still finding no one to listen, he resumed his work, satisfied that after the warm May sun did its work on Major Carnon's roadbed, the know-it-all white men would pay attention.

Charley's message was verified on the twenty-third of May. Early that morning, when Elmer reported to work, he encountered an amazing sight: his monstrous Cat had sunk six feet into the solid earth, leaving only the top of the cab visible. Well, the earth wasn't really all that solid; it had been, three days before when the topsoil was scraped off, laying bare the permafrost, but the sun had melted the frost at an alarming rate, turning what had been almost rigid soil —ideal for serving as a road base—into a quagmire. Not only had Flatch's Cat practically disappeared, but three others had begun to sink into the pit provided by the melting permafrost.

Three days of sheer hell ensued, for as the sun's heat intensified with the coming of summer, the permafrost continued to melt at lower levels, sucking the great machines down and down. Of course, where the topsoil had been allowed to remain in place, protecting the frost from the sun, the whole earth structure had preserved its solid nature, and this was merciful, because a contingent of smaller bulldozers could move in upon the still-firm ground and haul away at the stranded ones. But the suction of the mud, which seemed bottomless and determined to hold on to anything that fell into its maw, made recovery most difficult.

Cursing, swearing and groaning, the men of the black regiment struggled to rescue their precious Cats, and on some days they succeeded only in surrendering one or two new ones to the tenacious mud. Major Carnon spent three frantic days trying this trick and that to lure his great machines out of their viscous prisons and watching in despair as they sank always deeper into their glutinous graves.

On the third evening, when he seemed powerless to halt the devastation, he motioned Charley to sit with him: 'I didn't listen, Charley. You warned me. What is this stuff?' and the Indian told him about the problems that permafrost presented to builders in Alaska: 'Not everywhere. Only in the north. Hundred miles down that way, none,' and he pointed to the south.

'Why didn't we build down there?'

'Too close to the ocean. Japanese ships come, shell road, finish.' Careful not to gloat over the major's discomfiture, he added: 'This middle way definitely best. Use permafrost right, you get damn good road.'

'What is the right way?'

Ignoring the question, Charley told of his experiences as a builder's helper in Fairbanks: 'Strange city. Permafrost line runs right through middle, I think. Houses here, permafrost plenty. Same street, down here, none. Very important to know, because suppose you got permafrost under your concrete slab? Heat from human bodies, you don't need no furnace, nothin', just people. It collects in slab, begins to seep down into permafrost, begins to melt, here, there, house winds up on a slant. Sometimes big slant. Sometimes maybe have to leave house.'

'How do you avoid it?'

'Like on your road. Leave topsoil in place. Don't move nothin'. Far over to side, dig some more topsoil, pile on top road, high, high. Pack down. You know that thing they call *sheep hooves*?'

'Yes. Lots of little iron knobs, packs earth like sheep walking over it.'

'Pack down the extra, tight, tight. You get yourself good roadbed.'

As soon as Carnon heard the solution he saw the problem: 'How far from the roadbed would we have to go for our topsoil? Too close, the whole area would melt down.'

'Ah ha, Major Carnon! You one smart man. Some dig too close, everything melts. I like to go about a hundred yards.' He considered this for a while, then asked: 'You got lots of wire rope?'

'Never enough. But yes, we got some.'

'Tomorrow morning, put your good dozers way off the road. Solid footing maybe. They pull out the stuck ones.'

So in the morning three good dozers were placed about fifty yards from the muddy road where the stricken Cats lay buried, and long lines of wire cable were attached to one of the vanished giants. It happened to be Flatch's and he helped supervise the operation, satisfying himself as he stood almost waist-deep in mud that the wires were properly fastened, then moving back as the three pulling dozers began to apply their strength. Slowly, and with vast loud cracking sounds as the Cat broke loose, Elmer's machine began its magical climb out of its prison.

Men cheered as its superstructure became visible, and Major Carnon ran here and there, directing this dozer or that to tighten its pull, and after about an hour of mortal struggle, Flatch's gigantic machine crawled back to life. Caked solidly in mud, it was barely recognizable as a bulldozer, but there it was, ready to be washed down, its vital parts still serviceable.

That night, when all the machines were back in operation, Major Carnon had his scribe draft a report to headquarters in Anchorage requesting that letters of commendation be forwarded to the civilians Elmer Flatch and Charley . . . Here he dispatched a messenger to find out the Indian's name.

I T WAS A summer that those who worked on the Alcan would never forget. One black man with a science degree from Fisk University, who served as a private in the 97th Regiment, wrote to his fiancée in Atlanta:

> Our ship put us down in Skagway after one of the most magnificent voyages you could imagine. Great mountains coming down to the sea, glaciers throwing icebergs at us, beautiful islands left and right. But the best part of all was getting on a rickety old train at Skagway and riding right through the biggest mountains you ever saw to a place in Canada called Whitehorse. Come peace, you and I are going to take our honeymoon on that railroad. Save your money and I'll save mine, because there is nothing else like it in the world.
>
> That was the end of the good times. From Whitehorse we moved west to a section of the road you would not believe. Mosquitoes as big as saucers, swamps without bottom, whole forests to knock down with bulldozers, then on to the broken stumps with saws, and to bed in tents, with never a hot meal for days on end. Can you believe that in such circumstances we build four miles of road on a good day, two miles even if it's raining up to your armpits?
>
> I miss you. I long for you, but almost no one up here bellyaches. It's a road that must be built. Someday it could save the nation.

Elmer Flatch was one of those many Alaskans who did not bellyache about the terrible conditions under which the Alcan Highway was being built, for he better than most appreciated its significance.

At the height of the summer there were seven work groups spotted along the emerging highway at widely separated points, and each had half its force building to the east, half to the west, so that from the air, when work pilots like LeRoy Flatch's successors flew over, the Alcan looked like an endless succession of inchworms, each moving out in studied leaps to meet its neighbor. There were really fourteen separate roads being built that summer.

For Elmer Flatch, forty-five years old and beginning to feel the passing of the years, July and August of 1942 were the closest to hell that he would experience on this earth, for his fifteen- and sixteen-hour days were spent in an exhausting routine: drive through that copse of trees in a straight line, flattening evergreens big enough to produce spars for ships, attach wire ropes to the stumps and yank them out, push in topsoil from the surrounding areas, level the whole, ride back and forth in the interminable dust to compact the surface, fight mosquitoes all day long and especially at night, eat lousy food, and with the help of the able black troops and their efficient white officers finish off four miles before turning in to an exhausted but sometimes sleepless night.

One night as they worked not far from the Canadian border, Major Carnon, the indefatigable, proved that he was very fatigable indeed. As he sat with Elmer and Charley, surveying yet another bulldozer whose careless driver had ignored orders, sinking his machine in dark gumbo from which it might never return, tears came to his eyes and his voice broke. After a while he said: 'Forty years from now, if we win this war, this road'll be blacktopped, and people will whisk by here in their Cadillacs. We've been at this damned lake three mud-soaked weeks and we've accomplished damned little. They'll whiz by in three minutes and not even see it. But it had to be done.'

Next morning he lost his composure and shouted at another inept driver, who was failing pitifully to take any reasonable part in the rescue operation: 'Get down off that dozer. Let a real man handle it,' and he pointed to Elmer Flatch: 'Show him how it's done.'

Elmer knew only how to handle his own big machine; it had an inborn stability created by its sheer mass, and he did not feel at ease aboard a smaller machine which might have better maneuverability but also less reliability. Nevertheless, he climbed aboard the smaller machine, tested the controls, and gradually eased it back until he felt the two wire cables tighten. Waiting for the signal which would send the two other rescue dozers in motion, he adjusted himself to the unfamiliar seat and said: 'Ass, send me messages.'

The messages did come, warning him that he was placing the smaller bulldozer in a dangerous posture insofar as tension on the cables and torque from the treads was concerned, but it came in a version that Elmer did not immediately comprehend. Ignoring the signals, he applied more pressure, not wanting to lag behind the other two, and when the sunken tractor broke loose, almost springing out of its cavern, the other two drivers, well acquainted with their machines, relaxed tension immediately. Elmer did not. His bulldozer leaped backward, responded unevenly because of torque, and toppled sideways, pinning Elmer beneath it and crushing both his legs.

Major Carnon, seeing him fall under the dozer, was terrified that he might be dead, and it was he who first reached the spot where Elmer lay trapped, with great courses of pain running up and down his body.

'Get him out of there!' Carnon screamed, but it was obviously impossible to do so while the dozer lay atop him.

'Come around this side,' Charley shouted, and when the two other dozers were in position, he and Major Carnon attached the wire cables, but it was Charley who gave the effective orders to the two drivers: 'Once you start back, don't stop for nothin'. You got to keep pullin'. You stop, it falls back down on him, he gone.'

'Hold everything!' Major Carnon shouted. 'You understand what Charley just said?'

'We got it,' one of the drivers replied, and there in the bright sunlight for a brief moment the five actors in this dangerous drama froze: Flatch pinned in the mud, Major Carnon trying desperately to save his life, Indian Charley testing the wire cables, and the two dozer men preparing to move their machines slowly, purposefully backward.

'I'm going to count to three, then I'll yell "Go!" And for Christ sake, pull even. If it twists sideways, it'll grind him to pieces.'

Assuming a kneeling position by Flatch's head, so that he could protect him from anything that might slip or bounce off the downed machine, Carnon asked: 'You ready, Flatch?' and when Elmer nodded, the major in loud voice gave the preliminary count, then shouted 'Go!' The two drivers, obeying hand signals from Charley, eased the toppled bulldozer away, steadily and with no rotating motion. Flatch was saved, but his war was over. The medic who inspected his partially crushed legs said, almost cheerfully: 'You were saved by the mud. Hard soil, your legs would've been pulverized.' Examining him carefully and probing the tissues, he said: 'Marvelous luck. I'm sure they won't have to amputate, soldier.'

'I'm not a soldier,' Flatch replied, determined not to faint.

Of the fourteen hundred and seven miles of the Alcan Highway, he had been instrumental in building sixty-one. Twenty-two men like him had been killed on the job; seven airplanes had crashed trying to deliver heavy supplies to the various camps; and many black soldiers and white Canadians had suffered severe injuries.

But on 20 October 1942 at a Canadian creek so small it appeared on few maps, Beaver Creek in Yukon Territory, Major Carnon, working south from Alaska, moved forward with his black troops to greet Canadian workmen moving north. The great road, one of the marvels of modern engineering, had been completed, so that trucks bearing the men and armaments required for the protection of the continent could take position along the western reaches of Alaska.

Elmer Flatch, hospital-bound, could not be present to witness this triumph of the human will, but Indian Charley was, standing a few steps behind Major Carnon as the latter stepped forward to greet the Canadians. When the brief ceremony ended, Charley whispered to the major he had served so faithfully: 'Up here we do it different. But we get it done.'

O N   THE   MORNING of 3 June 1942, when Elmer and the black troops had barely begun building the life-saving Alcan, the people of the United States, and especially those living in Alaska, were shocked by the news that a daring Japanese task force, containing two aircraft carriers and hiding behind the storm clouds which clustered permanently in this area of the Aleutians, had crept close to Unalaska, one of the first big islands off the end of the Alaska peninsula, launched bombing planes precisely as its predecessor had done six months before at Pearl Harbor, and brazenly bombed Dutch Harbor.

No great damage was done this time, for in the preceding months America's 11th Army Air Force had secretly constructed undetected airfields in the Dutch Harbor region, so that when the Japanese planes from the carriers attacked, our fighters sprang off the unknown fields and drove them off. The enemy landing that had been planned could not take place, for the Japanese, learning that a frightening number of land-based planes were ready to attack, prudently withdrew, seeking protective cover under the storm clouds.

But enough damage was done by this attempted invasion to send a chill through the Alaskan command, because the generals knew that had the Japanese come in greater force and with more planes, they might well have established a foothold close to Anchorage from which they would be able to subdue all of Alaska, and thus place great pressure upon cities like Seattle, Portland and Vancouver. As then-Captain Shafter had predicted at his 1940 meetings throughout the territory, the invasion from Asia was under way.

The response was quick, but during the first three months, not very effective. Waterfront towns like Sitka constructed shore installations with which to hold off Japanese landing forces. The little airfields of the Northwest Staging Route were beefed up, and the big air bases at Fairbanks, Anchorage and Nome were patrolled twenty-four hours a day by dogs, jeeps and combat aircraft. The frontiersmen of Alaska enlisted in a group called the Alaska Scouts, an official branch of the American armed forces, and some of the more daring men, middle-aged or young, were sent on scouting missions involving extreme danger.

On 10 June 1942, a week after the bombing of Dutch Harbor, one of these scouts riding in a small plane radioed appalling news to headquarters in Anchorage: 'The big Japanese task force that bombed Dutch Harbor, it sailed west under cover of fog and captured Attu Island. . . . And it looks like they've captured Kiska, too.' American territory, a substantial chunk of it and strategically placed, had been occupied by enemy forces, the first time this had happened since the War of 1812, and all America shuddered.

This was the week that young Nate Coop, the half-breed son-in-law that the Flatches had considered illiterate, left Matanuska to volunteer for duty with the Alaska Scouts. The army officers serving as liaison with the scouts quickly determined that Nate was too poorly educated to be of much use in any demanding job, but as they watched how capably he handled himself, they concluded: 'He's tough. He seems to have guts. And he knows the land. He might make a good scout.' And four nights later a solemn-faced officer, a woodsman from Idaho, sat with the three most promising volunteers and issued their instructions: 'We must know what's happening on the islands between here and Attu and Kiska. I can't tell you our plans, and you wouldn't want to know them . . . in case you're captured. But you are entitled to know that we have no intention of allowing the Japs to hold those two islands. And if you're caught, you're free to tell them so.'

By this time the three young men could guess what their assignment entailed: 'Teschinoff, you know the Aleutians well. We're putting you on Amlia Island. Small boat launched from a destroyer escort. Middle of the night. Food. Radio. Code. Tell us what's happening.' When Teschinoff, who was almost pure Aleut except for that Russian great-great-grandfather, saluted, the officer added: 'We're sure everyone got off that island, but we need confirmation.'

Kretzbikoff, another Aleut, was dispatched to Atka, an important island. And now came Nate's assignment: 'We must have information about Lapak. Two of our scout planes reported people there. They could be very troublesome if they're Japs.' He studied the three scouts and thought: My God, they look young. Then he asked: 'You understand your missions?' When they nodded, he gave them one further command: 'Master your radios. If you don't send us reports in code, you'll be pretty useless.' But as they prepared to leave his office, a ramshackle affair that had been used for salting fish, he felt a deep, fatherly affection for these youngsters and gave them a promise: 'The army never leaves a scout stranded . . . never.'

Nate spent one more week at Dutch Harbor, mastering his radio and poring over two old, conflicting maps of Lapak Island, and in early August he gathered his gear, marched down to the shore where a small boat was ready to ferry him out to a waiting destroyer, and saluted the officers who had come down to see him off and who would be responsible eight days hence for recovering him from Lapak, always supposing that the Japanese, if they were there, didn't get him first. As he stepped into the boat, the officer from Idaho said: 'It has about a hundred and thirty square miles. Lots of room to hide, if they are there.'

Nate had never before been aboard a ship of any kind, and the severe weather of the Aleutians was hardly the kind one would have chosen for an initiation. Within an hour of leaving Dutch Harbor he was wildly seasick, but so were many of the crew. A sailor who was not gave him good advice as the destroyer dodged westward through heavy fog and heavier seas: 'Stretch out when you can. Eat a lot of bread, slowly. Stay away from things like cocoa. And if they serve anything like canned peaches or pears, eat a lot.'

When Nate asked, between vomiting spells, how this small warship could stay afloat in such seas, the sailor explained: 'This tub can stay upright in anything. No matter how far it heels over, it always comes back. Built that way.'

'Where do these waves come from?' Nate asked, and now he had hit upon a subject the sailor enjoyed discussing: 'Up there to starboard, the Bering Sea whipped by arctic gales into choppy swells. Down there, to port, the great Pacific Ocean with its endless reach and massive seas. Up above, a constant flow of stupendous clouds roaring in from Asia. Mix that all together, you got yourself one of the hairiest weather cauldrons in the world.'

At this point Nate had to hit the railing again, and when he saw those violent seas hammering at the destroyer, he accepted the fact that this was a breeding ground for horrendous weather. But the sailor had good news for him when he returned to lean against the outer wall of the captain's quarters: 'You be damned glad, soldier, you're not an aviator. Imagine flying in that stuff?' and he pointed aloft. About an hour later, when Nate heard a plane flying overhead through the incredible storm, the sailor came back: 'Let's say a prayer for the bastards involved in that one,' and Nate asked: 'What do you mean?' and the sailor replied: 'I don't know who has it worse, the guys in the plane or the ones in the sea.'

'I don't understand,' Nate said, and the sailor pointed toward the sound of the plane: 'PBY, big flying boat. If it goes out in weather like this, somebody's lost at sea. In these waters you rescue them in fifteen minutes or they're dead.' He listened to the droning engines of the big, slow plane and bowed his head.

The destroyer, following a jagged course to confuse any Japanese submarine that might be tailing it, waited for morning light so it could spot the location of Qugang Volcano, the one that guarded Lapak on the north, and when that beautiful cone showed clear, the navigator assured the captain: 'Course two hundred ten degrees straight in for the central promontory. Air cover promises no Japanese guns in that region.' So into the beautiful land-enclosed Lapak harbor the destroyer came, its guns ready to fire at any prying Japanese aircraft, and when it looked as if all was clear, a rubber boat with oars lashed to the locks was dropped over the side and held fast by a rope extending from the prow. Gingerly, Nate dropped into the rubber craft, adjusted his oars, and set out for shore.

As the destroyer pulled away, vanishing behind the eastern headland for its hurried return to Dutch Harbor, Nate rowed himself toward the central headland, and as he approached it, looking for the deep cove that was supposed to exist on its western face, he was startled to see a middle-aged man striding forward unafraid, attended by what seemed to be either a young boy or a girl in boy's clothing. For one dreadful moment he was afraid he might have to use his revolver if these two were Japanese, but the man shouted in good English: 'What in hell is all the secrecy about?'

When Nate got his craft onto the beach, the man and his young companion ran forward to drag it safely inland, and now Nate saw that the helper was a girl. 'I'm Ben Krickel,' the man said in some irritation. 'This is my daughter Sandy, and why in hell didn't that ship, whatever it was . . . ?'

Nate felt it prudent not to reveal that he had come from an American destroyer, but he did ask, 'Are you Americans?' and when the man snapped: 'We sure as hell are,' he confided: 'They wanted to know if the island had any people on it.'

This infuriated Krickel, who almost roared: 'Of course it's inhabited! They know that back in Dutch Harbor— You come from Dutch?'

Nate refused to answer this, so the man continued: 'The officials in Dutch know I have the lease on Lapak. Blue fox.'

'What?'

'I have the whole island. I grow fox here.'

'You mean . . . the little animals?'

'I lease the whole island. Let the fox run wild.'

'What do you do with them?'

'Ship them to St. Louis. They've been buying our Aleutian pelts for seventy years.'

Nate halted the conversation by asking: 'Where's the best place for me to stay?' and Krickel said: 'Our cabin. Down where the village used to be. Mind if we ride there with you?' so the rubber boat was refloated, the gear repacked, and the girl placed in the rear as the two men took oars and rowed swiftly down the bay, with the high mountains of Lapak guarding them. As they neared land, Nate informed his passengers: 'You know that the Japs bombed Dutch Harbor?' When they expressed shock, he added: 'And they captured Attu and Kiska.'

'Kiska!' Ben cried. 'I had my grays on Kiska. It's less than three hundred miles from here. Much less.'

And now for the first time the girl spoke. She was seventeen, with a big placid face that bespoke a native mother and a smile that warmed the island air. She was neither tall nor slim, but she did have a grace in the way she carried her head, cocked to one side as if she were about to laugh, that made her a delightful little elf, even in the rough clothes she wore. It was midsummer, and her man's shirt was carelessly buttoned, revealing a tawny skin that looked as if it was intended to be kissed. 'We're glad to have you here,' she said from the stern of the boat, and she smiled so engagingly that Nate knew he must clarify the situation right now: 'My wife has a smile like yours. But she's from Outside. I'm Athapascan.'

The girl laughed and pretended to spit in the bay: 'Aleuts, Athapascans not a good mix.'

'Are you Aleut?' Nate asked, and her father broke in: 'Is she! Her mother doted on the Russian Orthodox. Named Sandy for Alexandra, last Russian tsarina, the one they murdered in that cellar . . . What date was it, Sandy?'

'Ekaterinburg, 17 July 1918. Every year Mom made me dress in black and she did, too. She used to call me her little tsarina,' and Ben added: 'Her name was Poletnikova, my wife's, that is.'

When they reached the deserted cabin which Ben occupied when trapping his fox on Lapak, Nate explained just enough of his mission to quieten any apprehensions they might have: 'The government has removed all Aleuts to the mainland. Camps in the south. We think the Japanese have done the same on Attu and Kiska. Camps somewhere in Japan. I came to see if this island, and maybe Tanaga, is free.'

'If they're on Kiska,' Krickel said, 'they'll be coming here next. Maybe we ought to get out . . . now.'

Nate explained that the army men would not be coming back for eight days, at which Sandy chuckled with that freedom that was so appealing: 'Our boat wasn't due for eight weeks. If there's war, like you say, they'll probably never come.'

Krickel asked: 'What if the Japs move east before your boys move west?'

Nate showed them his radio: 'To be used only in extreme emergency. They promised they'd come get us . . .' As soon as he said this he stopped; there was no reason why these strangers should know of the two other explorations.

But Sandy caught the slip: 'Us?' and he said quietly: 'Yes, they meant if there were any people like you on the island.'

It was her father who said: 'If the Japs are that close, they might fly over at any time. We better hide your boat,' and he carried the oars as Nate and Sandy dragged the heavy rubber craft well inland and concealed it behind some trees and under a little nest of branches.

Two days later an airplane, followed by two more, flew low over the island, but they were from the 11th Air Force in Dutch Harbor, so Nate ran out and signaled them with two white handkerchiefs as he had been taught. His message was simple: 'No Japanese. No signs of any.' He had no prearranged signals for explaining the presence of the two Americans, but when the planes returned to check his message, he wigwagged: 'No Japanese. No signs,' and then led Krickel and his daughter to where they could be clearly seen. The lead plane dipped its wings alternately and flew back toward Dutch Harbor.

His remaining days on Lapak were some of the best Nate would know during this strange war, for he found Ben Krickel to be a fascinating raconteur about life in the Aleutians, while Sandy was a bright young woman who seemed to know a great deal about life in Alaska: 'The churches in Kodiak fight something awful. The Russian Orthodox, that's what I am, thinks it's so high and mighty. The Catholics know they're superior to everyone else. And the Presbyterians are quite impossible. Pop's a Presbyterian.'

Nate found his keenest delight in talking with Sandy and walking with her to the old sites on the island. One morning when they returned for lunch her father summoned them both before him in the old cabin: 'Nate, you told us honest that you were a married man. Seems mighty young to me, but so be it. You and my daughter, no foolin' around. You hear that, Sandy?' He said that Sandy's mother was dead and that if the war hadn't come, Sandy was to have attended Sheldon Jackson School in Sitka when they returned to Dutch Harbor with their furs: 'No foolin', you understand?' They said they did, but that afternoon such matters were forgotten, because when a lone plane flew over the island and they ran out to greet it, they saw that it bore strange markings, which had to signify that it was Japanese.

'My God!' Ben shouted. 'They've seen us!'

He was right, for the plane wheeled and came back low, its guns blazing. If there were people on Lapak, they had to be Americans and therefore the pilot's enemies.

He struck no one on that first run, but upon his second try he came perilously close to the cabin, and on his third, lower and slower, he would certainly have wiped them out had not at this moment two American planes sped in from the east. There was a furious air battle, with all advantages to the Americans, for they were higher and they flew in close tandem, one protecting the other. But the Japanese pilot showed skill and courage, and after throwing one of his pursuers off his track, he turned his nose upward, gave his engine an immense burst of gas, and tried to escape to the west, toward Attu.

But the second American plane had not been deceived by his maneuvering, and as he tried to speed past, this plane turned sharply and threw a full blast from his guns right into the fuselage and engine of the Japanese plane. It exploded and pieces fell across Lapak Island, the corpse of the pilot landing somewhere in the high western mountains. In a graceful sweep, the two American planes re-formed, turned west to authenticate the breakup of the enemy plane, then flew a salute to the three American watchers.

His brush with death, the first he had ever had to face as a real possibility, launched a major change in Nate Coop, but even if someone had pointed out what was happening, and especially why, he would not have believed it. The rough treatment he had received from the Matanuska settlers when he sought to marry one of their daughters had scarred him; he had accepted their assessment of half-breeds as worthless and not entitled to the respect accorded white people. In a score of insulting ways it had been hammered into him that he was of a lower category, and he had accepted this judgment. But now to see what a superior young woman Sandy was—wise, informed, neat when she wanted to be, and qualified in every way to take her place in Matanuska society or any other, despite her half-breed status—made him reevaluate himself, and what struck him with great force was that Sandy spoke excellent English while he could barely manage the language, and he swore to himself: If an Aleut can learn, an Athapascan can. And he saw both Sandy and himself as acceptable American citizens, real Alaskans tied to the earth and children of it, and in respecting her he came to respect himself.

On the night before the destroyer returned, Nate borrowed Ben Krickel's lantern and in its flickering light composed a letter to his brother-in-law, LeRoy, in which he spoke of meeting on a remote island a wonderful girl named Sandy Krickel: 'She's just the right age for you and you've got to meet her as soon as possible, because you'll never do any better.' Then he added a sentence which revealed his resentment of past treatment by the Flatches: 'You'll be surprised to hear that she's American-Aleut, like me, and I tell you this even though you gave your sister merry hell for going with me.' He ended with a prediction: 'When you see her, LeRoy, you'll grab her, and I'll be your best man, and later you'll thank me.'

But that was not the end of the letter, because when he showed it to Ben Krickel for his approval, Ben scratched a postscript: 'Young man, your brother-in-law is telling the truth. Signed, Her Father.'

On the eighth day, as planned, the destroyer returned to Lapak Bay and the fox trappers said farewell to the volcano. The captain, a very junior lieutenant commander, shouted at Nate as he climbed out of his rubber boat: 'Who in hell are those two?' and there was great excitement when Nate yelled back: 'Ben Krickel and his daughter Sandy. They farm foxes here,' and the captain said: 'They warned us anything can happen in the Aleutians.'

At supper that night the young officers insisted that Miss Krickel dine in their mess, a cubbyhole barely big enough for six places at table, and when Nate looked in from outside and saw how even the captain was paying court to Sandy, he muttered to himself: 'That little beauty will be able to handle herself anywhere.'

THE DREAMLIKE DAYS that Nate spent with the fox farmers were the last easy ones he would know for the next year. As soon as the destroyer landed him back at Dutch Harbor, his superiors interrogated him about the possibility of building an airstrip on Lapak. He told them, in his usual grunting monosyllables: 'No chance. Some good ground at beach, but no. Too much hills.' However, Ben Krickel was prepared to lecture them rhapsodically on Lapak, but after an hour of listening to his outbursts they reported: 'He knows a hell of a lot about foxes, nothing about airstrips. Lapak is out!'

They turned their attention to Adak, midway down the Aleutians and a big inviting island, but they knew little about it. Word was passed: 'Anyone here familiar with Adak?' and Krickel volunteered: 'I used to raise foxes there,' so a scouting team was organized under the direction of a gung-ho Air Corps captain named Tim Ruggles, known to his friends as 'a hero waiting to happen,' and he chose for his Alaskan guides Krickel and Nate Coop.

Because no one knew if the Japanese had already occupied Adak, the trio underwent intensive training in small arms, machine guns, map work, and the sending of coded messages by radio.

DURING THE TRAINING Nate learned of an unusual development in the case of Sandy Krickel: instead of being shipped south to an internment camp, like the other Aleuts, she had, because of her father, been temporarily classified as a Caucasian and given a job typing at headquarters, a low, long wooden building owned by a fishing company. Nate saw her twice and found her to be even more enchanting in her office dress than she had been in men's clothes on the island.

She was therefore in the office when General Shafter and two other generals from the Lower Forty-eight flew out to Dutch Harbor to complete plans for the occupation of Adak. The high brass had come to the Aleutians in General Shafter's plane, which meant that LeRoy Flatch was in the pilot's seat, so that when the generals entered the headquarters building LeRoy trailed along. While the officers moved into an inner room for their discussions, he was left in the reception area where Sandy was typing, and as he idly watched her from a chair propped against the wall, he thought: She must be the kind of half-Aleut Nate wrote about. If his girl's as lovely as this one, he showed good judgment. And he spent some time analyzing the pretty typist: You can tell she's Oriental. Gosh, you might even take her for a Jap. But she's not too dark and she sure has style. Those teeth and the smile to go with them. Wow!

He became so fascinated by who the girl might be that finally he rose, sidled aimlessly toward her desk, stopped, and said: 'Pardon me, ma'am, but could you be one of the Aleuts I've been hearing about?'

Smiling easily and with no sense of embarrassment, she said: 'I am. Aleut and Russian and I guess a little English and Scotch.'

'You speak . . . I mean, better than I do.'

'We go to school.' She typed a few words, then smiled again: 'What brings you out here to the end of the world? Secret, I suppose?'

'Yep.' He did not know what to say next, but he did not want to leave her desk, and after a silence which was painful for him but not for her, he blurted out: 'Were you here when this place was bombed?' and she said: 'No.' She was about to say that at that time she had been with her father on a remote island, gathering pelts from their blue foxes, and that would have disclosed that she was indeed the girl of Nate's letter, but at this moment Nate's scouting team, led by the feisty captain, tramped into the office on their way to be interrogated by the three generals, and Nate, surprised by the unlikely presence of his brother-in-law, cried: 'LeRoy! What you doin' here?' Then he stopped, stared at Sandy, and said: 'You've met?' When LeRoy nodded, Nate said: 'This is Sandy Krickel. And her dad, he added the stuff to my letter.'

'And I meant every word of it,' Krickel said as he disappeared into the smaller meeting room, dragging Nate along with him.

Since the generals remained at Dutch Harbor overnight, LeRoy had time to visit with Sandy, who was even more exciting than Nate had said. That evening the two Krickels, Nate and LeRoy borrowed the cabin of a civilian engineer in charge of putting together the gear that would be required for the airstrip, and with food assembled from various sources they prepared themselves a satisfying meal, during which it became obvious that LeRoy was already smitten with this girl of the islands who alternately fended off his unspoken approaches and encouraged them.

In the morning the generals wanted to see Adak from the air, and they insisted that Ben Krickel fly along to point out the features of the island as he remembered them from once having leased part of it for his run of ordinary red foxes. It was a turbulent day, with vast winds sweeping in from Siberia, and it seemed unnecessarily daring for three senior officers to be taking such risks, but LeRoy had learned that General Shafter, at least, was truly afraid of nothing, and he assumed the two other officers were of the same breed.

It was Ben who yelled from a back seat: 'Steady her up!' but that was impossible. However, LeRoy found some comfort from the fact that two heavier military planes, bombers no doubt, had joined up and were flying wing positions. But now, when the planes passed in and out of heavy clouds, and then ran into violent rain, he said to no one in particular: 'Be safer if they went home.'

At Adak they saw very little, for storm clouds hung low over the island, 'a foretaste,' one of the generals said, 'of what our boys will face when they try to land.'

'When they land,' General Shafter corrected, and the three officers, bouncing about as they tried to peer down through the clouds, laughed. Not Krickel. He called forward: 'I'm gonna be sick,' and LeRoy called back: 'That's your problem. Rule is, you got to clean it up when we land,' and Ben proceeded to be very sick.

Disappointed in the flight, one of the generals, who was going to be personally involved in leapfrogging out the Aleutians, suggested: 'Could we fly around a bit? Maybe there'll be a break.' LeRoy studied his fuel reserve and wished that he could consult with his wingmen, but radio silence had to be observed, so with hand signals he indicated to the man on his left flank that he was going to drop lower and circle, and the other pilot signaled: 'Okay.'

It was lucky they did, for after a tedious quarter-hour a break did come in the lower clouds, and for about ten minutes they had relatively clear flying over their target, and now Ben Krickel gathered himself together and shouted out the characteristics of one site after another: 'Yeah, here's where the flat land begins beachside. Up here, better elevation but not so long. I don't recognize this, must be lost. You can see the rocks over there, stay clear. Yeah, this is Adak, all right. You found the right island, pilot.'

The third general, not an airman, wanted especially to see the beach areas, and in the fleeting glimpse he was allowed he saw all he needed: 'Another hell spot. Wade ashore and hope the other side didn't get here first.' To some senior officers the enemy was invariably *he*, to others *the enemy*, and to this man, a football player at Navy, it was *the other side*.

They remained at Dutch Harbor that night, completing plans, and while they huddled with Krickel over maps, LeRoy and Sandy had a long talk together, and then a longer walk in the August moonlight, at the end of which they knew that they were joyously close to falling in love. He could see that she was as desirable as Nate had indicated in his letter, and she had already been convinced by her Lapak discussions with Nate that LeRoy was a serious young man from a good family and with unusual ability as a pilot. At the conclusion of their walk they embraced, and Sandy was so happy to have found a man she liked and would increasingly respect as she got to know him better, she lingered in his arms and whispered: 'You flew in here on a kindly wind,' and he whispered back: 'In these islands there are no gentle winds. I learned today . . . the hard way.'

In the morning, as the visitors were preparing to leave, the army general delivered some bad news: a Seattle review board had reclassified Sandy Krickel as a designated Aleut, so she had to be evacuated with the rest. No appeal. She would be sent to where a large collection of island people had been gathered. 'There are four we can choose from,' the local commander explained. 'All in the southern part of Alaska, what the natives call the Banana Belt. Good climate.' And as he rattled off the unfamiliar names, LeRoy stopped him: 'Did you say Totem Cannery?' The commander nodded. 'On Taku Inlet?'

'I think so.'

Turning to Sandy, LeRoy cried: 'I know it. Big. Not a bad place. I'll come see you there.' But when the plane was about to take off, General Shafter said: 'If the girl's leaving, why doesn't she fly to Anchorage with us?' and within a few minutes Sandy collected the few things she had in Dutch Harbor, kissed her father farewell, and headed for what would actually become an American version of a concentration camp.

D URING THE LAST week of August 1942 the American high command received so much solid intelligence that the Japanese were about to invade Adak Island and use it as a base for bombing mainland Alaska that they issued peremptory orders: 'Grab Adak immediately, rush an airstrip, and we'll bomb them instead.'

In less than an hour after the receipt of those instructions Captain Ruggles and his team were rushed aboard a destroyer, which plunged into the heaving waters of the Bering Sea, tossing about, Ben Krickel said, 'like a drunken walrus trying to find his way home.' Seasick and feeling his way cautiously ashore through knee-deep waves, Nate was afraid even to ask in whispers 'What now?' but Ruggles, like an eager Boy Scout, actually shouted: 'This way!' and he led them scrambling up a muddy incline to higher ground, where in one blazing instant gunfire erupted from all sides, with tracer bullets etching pathways through the darkness.

They had run into a Japanese team of four equally daring scouts who had been engaged in their own reconnaissance, and an intense, totally confused gunfight ensued, during which the enemy conducted a disciplined retreat to a different beach where a submarine awaited them. Ruggles, now free to probe about the island, rushed everywhere, and shortly after daybreak encoded the message which would authorize a massive invasion fleet to set sail: 'No Japanese on Adak. Locations Able, Baker or Roger eligible for bomber strip.'

Two days later they stood on an Adak promontory to greet an immense landing force as it streamed ashore with gigantic construction bulldozers that swarmed onto the island like an army of ants, and ten days later, when the first heavy bombers flew in on their way to bomb Attu, the three scouts stood at attention as medals were pinned to their tunics 'for heroic actions which speeded the capture of Adak Island.'

That night Ruggles and his men hit the hay early, exhausted by the fight and the following days of exertion, but before they fell asleep Ruggles said: 'They repeat brave words and hand out medals, but I wonder if they have any idea what it's like to climb up a slippery bank at midnight, not knowing if the Japs are waiting at the top?' and Krickel said: 'It ain't difficult. You take three deep breaths, plow ahead like a dummy, and when you see them . . .' He made the rat-tat-tat of a machine gun, after which the captain said: 'If I'm ever assigned to hit another beach, I want you men with me,' but Krickel cried: 'Don't volunteer!'

When the Americans had Adak operating as a powerful forward base, the Alaska Scouts had nothing immediate to do, so Nate Coop was assigned temporarily as driver and helper for a most unusual man—a thin, irascible civilian with the rank of corporal, a heavy black mustache, snow-white hair that stood upright in a butch job, very large glasses and a wry wit. One look at the informal way he dressed or one sound of his rasping, sardonic voice would have assured anyone that 'this one was not intended for military duty.' A wizard on the typewriter, which he banged with an odd assortment of fingers, he edited the mimeographed newspaper published for the troops, and Nate was responsible for driving him around to the various installations where he picked up news. He was in some ways difficult to work for, but in other ways it was a privilege to be with him, for he could see humor or contradiction or downright insanity in even the direst development.

What interested Nate was that wherever this unusual reporter went, there would be some one or two soldiers or airmen who knew him by reputation, and they would pester him with questions, listening attentively when he deigned to answer, which was not often. From these conversations, Nate concluded that this Corporal Dashiell Hammett had once worked in Hollywood, but since Nate had never even seen a movie, he obviously did not know what the man did.

'Is he an actor?' he asked some airmen as they finished talking with Hammett. 'No,' they said. 'Even worse. He's a writer.'

'What did he write?' The airmen thought it strange that a kid Nate's age had never heard of Hammett, so they rattled off the names of some of the films which had given him the reputation of being the hottest writer in town: 'Tough ones —The Glass Key, The Thin Man, The Maltese Falcon . . .'

'Never saw them.' The men were so astonished that they called: 'Hey, Mr. Hammett, your driver says he never saw The Maltese Falcon.'

The idea that this young fellow who had been so close to him for more than a week had not known who he was or what movies he had made, had not, indeed, ever seen one of them, fascinated Hammett, and during the remainder of Nate's assignment with him he probed the boy's background, and when he saw that Nate was semi-illiterate but also basically intelligent, he took a fatherly interest in him: 'What do you mean, you didn't go to school?'

'Back in the woods, the mines . . .'

'You say you've already landed on Lapak and Adak?'

'Yep.'

Hammett stepped back, looked at this taut, intense fellow just twenty, and said: 'I write 'em, you live 'em.' He asked if Nate had a girlfriend, and was surprised when the young man replied: 'I got a wife.'

Then Hammett became deeply interested in the problems that Nate presented of a half-breed marrying into one of the Matanuska families, and after this had been explored he wanted details about the valley's economic and social life, and when Nate proved ignorant of both, Hammett said: 'Jack London would have loved you, Nate.'

'Who was Jack London?'

'Never mind.'

Hammett accepted Nate as an authentic rough diamond, but when he saw some of Nate's notes, he exploded: 'Can you read? I mean big words? Can you write?' He excused Nate from work so that he could study materials the army provided its illiterates, and under Hammett's whiplash Nate began to learn ten new words a day and stand with his hands at his side and speak uninterrupted for five minutes on topics like 'How My Uncle Found a Gold Mine.' Belatedly, he was getting an education.

When Nate disappeared for two days, Hammett was furious: 'Where in hell you been?' But he was mollified when Nate explained: 'They're detaching me, Corporal.'

'What for?'

'Don't know. But maybe closer to Kiska. Maybe Amchitka.'

'Of course it's Amchitka. Everyone knows that. What's that to do with you?'

'Maybe me and Ben Krickel, scout again. Amphib landing.'

Hammett was appalled: 'Good God, you've scouted two islands. A man's luck runs out.' In a low fury he went to complain to the commanding officer, but was sharply rebuked for sticking his nose in where it wasn't wanted.

Nate saw this mercurial corporal only once more; when he was about to be sent off for intensive training regarding Amchitka, Hammett came to him and said gruffly: 'You have a real set of balls, Nate. I wouldn't have the guts for one expedition like yours, and you'll be going on your third.'

'Guess that's what us scouts are for.'

As Nate trained for the new task, he sometimes wondered why, if Dashiell Hammett was as bright as the younger airmen claimed, he was only a corporal, and he never found an answer to his perplexity. But then, in the second week of January 1943 he forgot Hammett, for his old team was reassembled— Captain Ruggles, Ben Krickel, himself—and once more they rowed out in a rubber boat to a waiting destroyer escort, which dodged through Aleutian storms till it reached the long, low, flat island that would provide a splendid airstrip for the bombing of Kiska and Attu, if the Americans were able to occupy the island before the enemy did.

Since Amchitka was only sixty miles east of the major Japanese air base at Kiska, the three scouts had to suppose that the enemy would be boating in his own patrols, and that proved to be the case. For three perilous days and nights Nate and his team moved about the island, hearing the Japanese at times and trying to avoid contact with them. In howling storms, with snow and hail whipping their faces, the Americans protected themselves while they scouted the island's beaches, and one night as they huddled in darkness Captain Ruggles said: 'The snow falls in Siberia, but it lands in Amchitka . . . parallel to the ground . . . eighty miles an hour.'

They faced the extra danger that came from the Japanese scouting planes which raked the island, bombing any spots where American spies might be hiding, and once when the three had to scramble to escape attack, they rushed shockingly close to a camp occupied by seven Japanese scouts. Gingerly, hearts pounding, the three Americans crept back and escaped detection.

It was difficult warfare, in its way, as difficult as any being conducted throughout the world: heaving seas, whipping blizzards, endless nights, and always great storms lashing at the beaches where any invader would have to land. But resolute men, American and Japanese alike, clung to Amchitka and sent their messages back to their headquarters. Said Ruggles in code: 'Jap aircraft overhead constantly. Will pose serious threat to landing craft.'

Nate was on lookout when the American armada approached the island, hundreds of ships of all sizes, and he expected Japanese planes to strafe them mercilessly, but now the storms became so violent that no planes could fly, and painfully the great ships moved close to shore. But even though the enemy planes were absent, the landing was hell. The *Worden* sank, drowning fourteen. One group storming ashore spotted the Japanese scouts, took them to be an advance force of a main Japanese army, and destroyed them with flame throwers. Another American team tried four times to make a landing, only to be forced back each time by mountainous waves thundering upon the beach, but as the long day passed into ominous night they kept on trying, and on their fifth attempt, aided by searchlights, they made it.

Next day Pacific Headquarters in Hawaii issued a brief communiqué: 'Yesterday our troops made a successful landing on Amchitka,' and reporters pointed out: 'A prelude to our retaking Attu and Kiska,' but no words indicated the hellish conditions the Americans had suffered in gaining this vital foothold in the brutal battle of the Aleutians.

From January till mid-March men like Nate and Ben Krickel worked like draft horses, hauling goods inland from the shore, storing them in piles, and slogging back knee-deep in icy water to break loose more cargo. It was back-breaking work, and usually it had to be done while a Siberian wind formed icicles on eyebrows. And when the gear was finally ashore, the amateur stevedores were transferred hastily to the flat area where the airstrip was emerging from the tundra. But wherever they worked, Nate and Ben lived miserably: food ships failed to arrive, and when they did stagger in they most often had food and clothing that had been destined for the tropics. For days in a row, when he was working at the far end of the airstrip, Nate would have no hot food, and when something was cooked up, it was frequently a type with which he was unfamiliar.

For example, one day Captain Ruggles went to great pains to steal a large bag of whole-wheat flour, the kind that made good, crunchy bread, but when the bakers turned it into loaves, Nate and the other men working with him refused to eat it. One farm boy from Georgia spoke for the group: 'Captain Ruggles, we got to be here in Alaska, it's our duty. We got to freeze our ass off, the enemy is just over there. And we got to eat cold food, because there ain't no stoves handy. But by God we don't got to eat dirty bread like that, it's nigger food. We want white bread.'

Ruggles tried to explain that whole wheat was twice as nutritious, twice as good for a man who wasn't getting enough roughage, but he was powerless to convince these well-intentioned country boys: 'Dirty bread like that, it ain't proper for no white man to eat.'

But what caused the most anguish to these men who worked on Amchitka was best expressed by the farm boy from Georgia: 'Tears your heart out. You work here at the airstrip, these fine kids climb in their planes, wave goodbye, fly over to Kiska or Attu, hit a storm. Christ, always there's a storm, and they fly right into some damned mountain, maybe three or four of them in one day, and you don't see them kids no more.'

The toll was dreadful, for as one frightened airman once added in despair at the end of a letter to his girlfriend which had been otherwise hopeful and of good cheer: 'There is nothing in this world like flying in the Aleutians, and we've lost so many of our men I'm scared to death to get into my plane, the chances are so poor.'

He wrote one more letter to her, two days later, apologizing for his outburst, and then no more.

It was under such conditions that Nate resumed his study of the textbooks Corporal Hammett had given him, and obedient to Hammett's dictum, he continued to memorize ten new words a day, until his vocabulary became civilized, but he still spoke in fragments, insecure in the substantial knowledge he was acquiring.

He did what he could to protect himself from the blizzards, but he refrained from making friends with the airmen who arrived on Amchitka all bright-eyed and ten days out of training school. He saw that they had special problems which ordinary grunts did not. He told himself: I got to bear this terrible weather. I learn tricks like findin' the buildins that are mostly underground. Wind can't whip you about. But those in the planes, they got to live in it. Right in the heart of it. And they don't live long.

Of course, he had his own nightmares, for when it was rumored that the next hit would not be nearby Kiska but distant Attu, he knew that the brass would want to put scouts ashore to ascertain just what the situation was. So he went to Captain Ruggles and said: 'They call for volunteers this time, I won't go.'

'Now wait a minute, Coop. You're the best man we have. You don't know what fear is.'

'Yes I do,' and to his own amazement and the captain's, his eyes filled with tears, and after a while Ruggles said quietly: 'Nate, I'm sure I'll be sent to Attu to see how soon we could have an airstrip after we land. I'd hate to go without you.'

'Maybe,' Nate mumbled, and when it became obvious that the same three men were going to be ordered to scout Attu, he felt real fear, and he told himself: You can't keep goin' to occupied islands without bein' killed. But he gnawed on his fingernails and kept his apprehensions to himself. One night the orders came: 'The PBY is off the southern shore. The pilots say they know a sure place to set you down. Easy paddle in, then you're on your own.' Trembling furiously, Nate trailed behind Captain Ruggles and Ben Krickel as they moved in the darkness, but the awkward job of climbing into the PBY so preoccupied him that his nervousness abated, and he spent the flight to Attu concentrating his strength and his courage for the extremely dangerous task ahead.

With great skill the PBY flew a route which evaded Kiska, ducked in and out of storms, and landed in the choppy sea less than a mile from the southern end of Massacre Bay, where the cossack Trofim Zhdanko had landed with his twelve fur traders in 1745. Climbing down into their rubber craft, the three men paddled through the heavy waves, made shore, and hid their boat under a tangle of twigs and low shrubs. Delighted with the ease of their landing, they started inland over the terrain the major landing parties would use in subsequent days, and came at last to a slight rise from which Ben could survey an area he had once known well: 'No defense positions here. Our men will get ashore. But up there where the Japs are'—and he pointed to the hills half a mile to the north—'very strong.' In the meantime, Captain Ruggles was inspecting with his glasses in the growing light the airstrip which the Japanese were struggling to complete before the expected assault began: 'Good! They'll have it in fair shape just as we drive in to take it over.'

Scout planes, looking for intruders like these three, flew overhead but saw nothing, and for two days of the most intense concentration the Americans took mental notes of what the conquest of Attu was going to entail, and they were sobered by their conclusions. Ruggles confirmed the plans he had heard at headquarters: 'The moment we land at Massacre, we must drive north to Holtz Bay. Hold them off there and clean out the pockets to the east.' He asked Ben and Nate to memorize the mountainous lay of the land, and when the second night fell, he and his men crept back to the boat and headed south for their midnight recovery.

When they were safe aboard the PBY, with mugs of hot bouillon to warm their hands, Ruggles poked Nate and said jokingly: 'Pretty much like a picnic, wasn't it?' and Nate replied: 'Always easy, the Japs stay clear. But when you hit Kiska, leave me out.'

THE AMERICAN RECONQUEST of Attu, which began on 11 May 1943, was one of the significant battles of World War II, for although it involved relatively few troops, it determined whether Japan had any hope of using an Alaskan foothold from which to attack the United States and Canada. The Japanese defenders of Attu were a resolute group of about 2,600 superior soldiers dedicated to the task of retaining this foothold on American territory. Led by officers of great daring and acumen, they had constructed a chain of positions that were the acme of defensive warfare. But there were other holes in the earth, dug almost casually, into which Japanese soldiers would climb knowing that they could never by any conceivable miracle escape. Deep two-man caves flanked the approaches the Americans would probably use, and there was one fiendishly clever line of positions that guaranteed the death of American attackers but also the certain death of the Japanese defenders. To rout heroic Japanese like these was going to be a hellish assignment conducted in arctic storms and Siberian gales.

To accomplish it, 16,000 American GIs plus a few Alaska Scouts and unlimited American air power would apply relentless pressure at merciless cost to both attacker and defender. On the eve of this strange battle, fought at the farthest ends of empire, the character of the entire war in the Pacific hung in the balance: Japan, the bold attacker, was about to become the stubborn defender, while America, the sleepy giant caught off balance, was belatedly gathering its forces for a series of crushing, annihilating blows. As the sun set that evening in a surly glow, no one could predict how the battle for Attu would evolve, but the men engaged on each side were of equal bravery, equal determination, and equally committed to their contrasting ways of life.

At dawn a most fearful armada loomed out of the mists, bearing down upon the northeast corner of Attu, and Nate and Ben, from their landing craft, watched in awe as the huge battleship *Pennsylvania* unlimbered its great guns to pulverize the foreshore where the troops would soon be landing. A hundred and fifty massive shells strafed the shore but killed not a single Japanese, for they had built their revetments so stoutly that only a direct hit would ravage them, and even then the damage would come mostly from flying debris which could be removed later.

The larger portion of the American armada appeared out of the mists enshrouding Massacre Bay, and here the huge ships were able to empty their cargo and their men without serious opposition. But once ashore, as Nate had predicted and as he now saw from his ship, the attackers had to swing sharply uphill toward Holtz Bay, around whose perimeter the Japanese had dug their positions. What had seemed at first an easy landing became a bitter, rainswept, mud-encumbered attack, with hundreds of Americans absorbing sniper bullets which either killed or maimed. Always the Americans died without having seen the enemy.

For nineteen terrible days, usually without respite and often without food, the Americans pressed on, and in this relentless attack Nate Coop and Ben Krickel covered each other, shared foxholes, or ran together to toss activated grenades into the mouths of caves from which sniper fire had come. 'It's always the same,' Ben said with heavy breathing after attacking a cave, 'you throw in your grenade and hear three explosions. The two men inside see it coming, know they're dead, and detonate their own grenades . . . they make the job clean, I guess.'

During one hellish period Nate's group cleaned out a whole hillside of caves, one at a time, most often with that sickening drumbeat of three explosions to each American grenade. In that time no prisoners were taken, little was eaten, and no attacker slept in dry clothes. It was a harrowing, hand-to-shadow battle, no bayonet work, not many mortar shots, just the dull, terrifying work of cleaning out installations that could not be attacked in any other way. No American men ever fought under more difficult conditions than these on Attu, no Japanese ever defended their positions with a greater sense of honor.

At the end of eight days of this cave-by-cave elimination, some fifteen hundred of the enemy were slain, but over four hundred Americans were also dead. Now came the final push when fifteen hundred more Japanese must die, and a hundred and fifty Americans. On both sides they would perish in chilling rain, blustery storms and mud. None died in a more fiendish way than the brave American officer leading Nate and Ben up a hill, nor the six Japanese responsible for his death.

Since Captain Ruggles was an airman, he was supposed to be aloft in some storm-battered plane, but because of his skill in detecting where airstrips should be located in the first few hours of a landing, he had slipped into a kind of permanent assignment to that most perilous of jobs, for when it was completed he became just one more foot soldier, except that his unusual bravery made him outstanding.

The responsibility Ruggles gave himself seemed routine. The American attackers were strung out along the bottom of a slope which climbed sharply to the north; the Japanese defenders were dug into a line of caves along the crest of the hill. At first glance it might seem that the task facing the Americans was impossible, but Ruggles had long ago devised a solution; it required exquisite timing.

Ruggles, with one or two trusted flank men, would move right up the center of the slope, depending upon a blanket of fire from their team to keep the Japanese away from the mouths of their caves. In the meantime, swift climbers far to the left and right would establish a kind of pincer movement that would carry them to a position well above the line of caves, from where they would creep down upon them from the rear and destroy the enemy with grenades tossed into the mouths.

Such a coordinated maneuver succeeded when all parts functioned perfectly, and Ruggles was one of the best at it: 'We finish off that line of caves and then look for some hot chow.'

But this time there was to be a subtle difference, because in the middle of the slope, not conspicuous from below, rose a slight but substantial mound, and looking at it, one would have supposed that the Japanese would have placed in it a series of caves pointing downhill to slow any Americans striving to climb up. But this the determined Japanese did not do; instead, they dug six caves on the far side of the mound, pointing *uphill*, and when they were ready, the colonel in charge said solemnly: 'The emperor asks for twelve volunteers,' and twelve young Japanese, far from home and bitingly hungry from lack of food, stepped forward, saluted, and moved two by two into the doomed caves.

They were doomed because the tactic they were to execute was suicidal from the start: 'You will allow the American attackers to pass over your positions. Wait till a sizable number have gone. And then open fire on their backs when they suspect nothing.' Many Americans would be killed in this way, but of course the twelve men in the caves would be slaughtered as soon as their positions were identified.

Ruggles, as one might expect, would lead the charge up the front face, with Nate on his left flank, Ben on his right and two skilled teams speeding up the far outside flanks to drop down upon the top caves from the rear, and everything went as planned, except that when Ruggles and his central core sped over the slight rise in the middle of the slope, they were allowed to proceed about twelve yards up the hill. Then from the hidden caves pointing uphill the Japanese fired point-blank into the backs of the attackers, and from habit, most of them aimed at the obvious leader, Captain Ruggles, who fell, cut to pieces by seven fusillades. One hit Ben Krickel in the left shoulder. Three other bursts killed two of Nate's companions, and yet another sped past Nate's ear.

Four Americans survived, including the wounded Krickel and Nate Coop, and for just a moment they were lost in confusion, but then Nate saw what had to be done: 'Ben! Back behind the mound!' And he led the remnants of the team to the down side of the mound where they could not be attacked by the men in the caves. There they regrouped, and when they saw their mutilated captain ten yards up the hill, a sullen rage overtook them, so that even Ben Krickel, seriously wounded, insisted upon being part of the next action. Accidently it seemed, Nate assumed charge: 'Creep up, belly down, prime grenades, and we'll reach over and slam them in.'

They did just this, four determined avengers, closing in upon the caves from the rear, ignoring bullets coming at them from the ridge, and thrusting the deadly grenades into the mouths of the caves, then falling back to hear the three explosions.

That left the two caves on the outer flanks still operating, and Nate shouted: 'I have this one! Ben, take over there,' but as he cried the words he saw that Ben had fainted, so he pointed to a young lad from Nebraska: 'Clean it out!'

But now these men had no more grenades, so two of them tore their shirts into long strips, and a third man doused them with the petrol he carried for such situations, and they were lighted and stuffed boldly into the mouths of the caves, and when four Japanese struggled out, gasping for air, they were brained with rifle butts.

The conquest of this hill represented one of the last orderly assaults by American forces on Attu, and that night, the men assumed that they had conquered the Japanese, but at midnight, with no one on watch, they heard a rustling on the side of a hill where no sensible Japanese would be, and then a patter of feet, and finally the wild shouts of men in a banzai charge, determined to kill or be killed. Now an inferno raged in that stretch of the undefined front. Japanese, maddened in what they knew to be their final moments, rampaged in all directions, grabbing rifles pointed at them, slashing with long knives, setting fire to whatever they could reach.

They were irresistible, overrunning positions that no ordinary human could even attack, let alone subdue. And as they came, they screamed, and it was nearly an hour before Nate and his men established some kind of defensive line. Then amazing things began to happen. One Japanese brandishing only the twig of a tree, not fifteen inches long, came directly at an American soldier armed with a gun, thrust the gun aside, struck the startled American in the face with his twig, screamed and disappeared in the darkness. Two other Japanese, with bayonets tied insecurely to the ends of sticks, rushed right at Ben Krickel, endeavoring to stab him with their flimsy weapons. They struck him, but the bayonets slid to one side, and with his good arm he killed both men with blows to the head.

A fourth Japanese was the craziest of all. Chanting a wild song and brandishing a deadly pistol, he overcame all obstacles and rushed right at Nate Coop, who was powerless to stop him. Thrusting his pistol in Nate's face, he screamed and pulled the trigger. There was a clicking sound; Nate thought he was dead; and then nothing happened. With a sharp thrust of his bayonet, Nate killed the Japanese, and when he studied the man's gun he found that it was a child's toy, filled with paper caps. Wresting the gun from the dead man's fingers, Nate pulled the trigger twice and sent popping echoes through the muddy dawn. The battle for Attu was over.

N OW ONLY KISKA remained, not nearly as big as Attu but far more heavily defended: intelligence reports gave twice as many Japanese on Kiska, 5,360, ten times the defensive capability. To subdue the island, more than 35,000 American troops were ferried out the Aleutian chain in by far the biggest, heaviest armada of this front. This time no scouting team was sent in to reconnoiter, for which Nate was grateful; it wasn't necessary; the powerful Japanese installations were visible from the air.

Instead, the 11th Air Force dumped an incredible amount of high explosives on the island, some of the planes flying eastward from the newly activated field on Attu. Also, from a printing press in Anchorage came a hundred thousand leaflets imploring the Japanese to surrender, but these had even less effect than the bombs, which accomplished nothing. Once again, for the last time in the Aleutians, the Japanese were dug in, and digging them out was going to be the brutal climax of this brutal campaign.

Ten weeks after the fall of Attu, the massive assault force was ready, and once again General Shafter flew to the Aleutians with Leroy Flatch as pilot to participate in the final planning. This time when LeRoy asked for his brother-in-law he found Nate morose and edgy: 'If the Japs start anything, I'm sure it'll be me and Ben to check them out if his arm's okay.'

'Where is Ben?'

'Field hospital. Mendin' his arm.' LeRoy was worried by Nate's listlessness, and asked: 'Anything wrong?' and Nate snapped: 'No! Why?' and LeRoy said: 'Well, all these battles . . . and Ben getting wounded,' and Nate said: 'It's a job.'

'Stay with it. Now I got to see Ben,' and they found the tired old fox farmer at a dressing station where final touches were being applied to his wound, and he looked much older than his fifty-one years, for, like Nate, he was bone-weary. But he showed surprise as LeRoy assumed an erect military posture, saluted, and said in formal voice: 'Mr. Krickel, I've flown all the way to this summer resort to ask for your daughter's hand in marriage.'

Years fell from Ben's battle-scarred face and pain from his wounded arm.

Staring at young Flatch, he asked in a quiet voice: 'Where is Sandy?'

'In Anchorage. With a good job. I used General Shafter's pull and got her sprung from the concentration camp, and we're getting married . . . with your permission.' When both Ben and Nate began pummeling him in their joy, he stopped them: 'Sandy said she'd never get married without your consent. Said you were her father and mother both.' He looked the old islander in the eye: 'So have I your permission?' and gravely Ben said: 'You have, son. Now let's get stinkin' drunk.'

They were not able to do this, because when a messenger came from the meeting of the generals, both Nate and Ben could guess what it meant. Yes, if Ben was up to it, they were to make one last sortie behind enemy lines: 'The Japs are behaving strangely. We've got to know how tough those Kiska beaches are going to be. You men have never failed us before.' The general in command jabbed at Ben's arm: 'Mended well enough for you to make the try?' and both Ben and Nate knew that even a moment's hesitation would excuse him from this perilous assignment, but the fox farmer said: 'It's ready,' and before dawn these two loyal frontiersmen, these prototypical Alaskans, were back in their rubber boat heading quietly for the waiting PBY that rose and fell on the dark Aleutian waves. With Captain Ruggles dead, they would be commanded by an enthusiastic young army lieutenant, Gray, who told them as they approached the beach: 'You'll get no rank from me. You know far more about this than I do.' Then, as if to reassure them, he added: 'But when you move out, I'll be there. You can count on it.'

As they rowed in darkness toward what might prove to be a blazing confrontation, Gray whispered: 'Wow! Landing on a little island occupied by a whole Japanese army!' and Ben, realizing that the young fellow was trying to maintain his courage, said quietly: 'Kiska's more'n a hundred square miles. Might be hard to find the Japs even if we wanted to.' Then, to ease the tension further, he added: 'Were you on Attu, Lieutenant?' and when Gray replied that he had led one of the clean-up assaults on Holtz Bay, Ben said with great warmth: 'You got nothin' to prove.'

And Ben was right, for in those first perilous moments when the three leaped upon the beach and started running, in those fateful seconds when hidden machine guns might have cut them literally in half, it was Gray who was in the lead, now a man without fear, and kept going until they found themselves well inland. But when they had traversed the beach in miraculous safety, a fearful thing happened. Gray, exulted by the fact that he had done well, turned to ask his adviser: 'What do we do now, Ben?' only to see that the fox farmer who had been so composed in the boat stood trembling—not nervously twitching, but shaking as if some fearful blizzard were engulfing him—and it was clear to both Gray and Nate that he was so emotionally exhausted he could no longer function as a member of their team.

For just a moment the young lieutenant was bewildered, for he realized that his group was in a hazardous position with one-third of its component immobilized, but Nate hid Ben behind a rock and said in a consoling whisper: 'It's all right. You wait. We'll be back.' Then he sought Gray and said: 'We split, very quiet, circle out and head for that big thing over there, whatever it is.'

With no sense of having had his position of leadership usurped, Gray said: 'Solid idea,' and he was off like a rabbit.

When the men met at what turned out to be a discarded generator, neither was bold enough to voice what was in his mind, but after poking about, Nate had to speak: 'I think nobody's here.'

Very quietly, Gray said: 'Me too,' but then echoes of his training surfaced. 'Men,' a gruff veteran of the first days of fighting on Guadalcanal had warned when he visited Gray's camp in Texas, 'the Jap soldier is the trickiest bastard on earth. He'll fool you in a dozen different ways. Booby traps, sharpshooters tied in trees, buildings left to make you think they're abandoned. You bite on his traps just once, you're dead . . . dead . . . dead.'

Ominous and lethal, the silent buildings ahead seemed a perfect example of Japanese perfidy, and Gray's knees grew weak. 'You think it's a trap?' he whispered to Nate, who replied: 'We better find out,' and then Gray resumed command.

'Cover me,' and with a bravery few men could have shown, he dashed right at a cluster of buildings that must have been a combined mess hall and laundry, and when he reached it, he jumped in the air, waved his arms, and cried: 'It's empty!'

Before Nate could overtake him he began running about, making a disgraceful amount of noise as he sped from one abandoned building to the next, finding each one vacant. Then, remembering that he was in command, but so excited that he could barely issue an order, he cried: 'Let's try that one, and if she's empty too, we flash our signal.'

So the two men crept toward what must have served as command headquarters, and when in darkness they found it cavernous and empty, Gray grasped Nate by the arm and asked: 'Dare we tell them?' and Nate said: 'Send the word,' and Gray activated his radio and shouted: 'They're all gone! There's no one here!'

'Repeat!' came the stern voice from the flotilla commander.

'There are no enemy here. Repeat. Nobody here.'

'Verify. Report back in ten minutes. Then return to ship.'

It was a strange ten minutes, there in the Aleutian night with the winds whipping in from Siberia and two bewildered Americans trying to figure out how an entire Japanese army could have slipped off this island while American boats patrolled the seas and American planes the skies. 'They couldn't all escape,' Gray cried petulantly. 'But they did,' and he ran about, savoring this great discovery, but when Nate Coop returned to the beach to sit with Ben Kriekel and saw the pitiful condition he was in, he, too, began to shake. Then Lieutenant Gray ran down shouting: 'Ten minutes up! We can verify,' Nate said: 'Go ahead,' but he took no joy in the dramatic news, and during the row back to the PBY he pulled mechanically, not fully aware of where he was.

So a fully equipped American-Canadian army of thirty-five thousand marched ashore against no opposition, but on the first afternoon an American bomber from Amchitka, having failed to get the news, continued his ordained run, saw what he supposed to be Japanese troops operating without cover below, bombed them. Two dead.

The generals, unwilling to believe that the Japanese had been able to evacuate an entire island while bombers were overhead on inspection flights, sent out heavily armed patrols to ensure that no remote pockets of Japanese hidden in caves were waiting to attack. This caution was advisable and it was carried out with proper care, but the men who had come so far to fight were so eager to do so that when one group heard suspicious sounds coming from another group on the other side of a slight rise, gunfire was begun by a nervous American corporal and returned by an equally nervous Canadian sergeant, and in the wild engagement that followed, twenty-five allies were killed by Allied bullets, and more than thirty were wounded.

That was the final battle of the Aleutian campaign. Japan's attempt to conquer America from the north had failed.

NO SOONER HAD peace in the Pacific been obtained than a war of equal importance to Alaska erupted. To appreciate its significance, one must follow what was happening to the two young married couples in the Flatch family in the months following the explosions of the two atomic bombs over Japan, and the subsequent collapse of the Japanese war effort.

Nate Coop, strengthened and deepened by his war experiences, now astonished everyone by announcing: 'I'm going to take my GI benefits and go to the university in Fairbanks.'

When the entire family seemed to ask at once 'What for?' he said: 'To study wildlife management,' and when they chorused: 'Where'd you get that crazy idea?' he explained cryptically: 'Corporal named Dash Hammett told me: "When the war's over, get off your ass and learn something." ' He would say no more, but after the first shock, he was supported by his wife, who remembered Missy Peckham's counsel: 'If you can tame a moose, you can civilize Nate,' and she accompanied him to Fairbanks.

LeRoy Flatch, now a captain in the Air Force, was urged by his superior, General Shafter, to remain in that service, with assured promotions to major and lieutenant colonel: 'After that it depends on the impression you make on your superiors, but I have confidence you could be a general one of these days . . . if you get yourself some education.' Despite similar recommendations from his fellow officers, LeRoy opted to retire so that he could resume his career as one of the leading bush pilots, and in pursuit of this ambition he decided to apply his bonus money as down payment on a used Gull-wing Stinson four-seater, total cost $10,000, whose former owner had been a mechanical genius. The plane, as he modified it, had both wheels and skis, permanently attached, which meant that he could take off, wheels down, fly to some snow-covered field high in the mountains, activate a hydraulic system, and retract the wheels through a slit in the middle of the big wooden skis. On the return home he could take off on skis, punch the hydraulic button, and feel the wheels come down through the slits. Of course, since the system was fixed, he could no longer attach pontoons for the summer lakes. So, to ensure maximum flexibility, he also bought an updated version of his old Waco YKS-7 which had pontoons, but he was shocked by the price increase. He had paid $3,700 for his first Waco, $6,300 for its replacement, which he kept on a lake near his cabin.

But he now had a wife, and the former Sandy Krickel, accustomed to the free and open life of the Aleutians, especially the field trips with her father to isolated islands like Lapak, did not look with favor on being cooped up in a Matanuska cabin with her in-laws.

Matanuska had proved such a signal success, despite the early negative publicity, that it seemed as if half the people who came to Alaska wanted to settle in the valley, which meant that LeRoy and Sandy could find nothing suitable. Sandy suggested acquiring some land up toward the glacier and building their own home, but LeRoy pointed out that with the purchase of two planes he could not swing a house too.

'Why not buy just one plane?' she asked, and he said firmly: 'Wheels, skis, pontoons, tundra tires, a guy like me has to have them all,' so the possibility of a house vanished.

At this point an old friend, or rather four old friends, helped him make a radical decision, one with which he was going to be quite happy. Tom Venn of Seattle, with his R&R ventures prospering in the peacetime business resurgence, was eager to reestablish himself at Venn's Lode at the side of the great glaciers issuing out of Denali: 'I want to spend more time there. So does Lydia. And the young ones, Malcolm and Tammy, insist. So, LeRoy, I want you to fly the stuff in and more or less look after the place when we're gone.'

'I'm a pilot, not a real estate agent,' LeRoy said brusquely, and Venn said: 'So you are. But I think that in the years ahead, bush flying is bound to center on some spot well north of Anchorage. Competition from the big planes will kill you if you stay in Matanuska.'

Since Venn had proved many times over that he had an acute business sense, LeRoy had to listen, and he attended carefully to what the older man said as they spread before them maps showing central Alaska: 'It's not badly named, this stretch between Anchorage and Fairbanks. "The Railbelt," because the railroad, such as it is, ties it all together. This is where the vitality of Alaska will focus in the future, and it's where you've got to focus now.' With an imperative finger Venn stabbed at the Lode: 'Our place is over here by the mountains. Matanuska, your place down here, is too far away for you to service us properly. Fairbanks is way too far north. But here in the middle is a delightful little town, Talkeetna, named after the mountains. Within easy distance to our place. Lots of mines in the area needing flights. Lots of lakes with one or two cabins along the shore needing groceries. The railroad runs through, but what keeps it good, the highway doesn't. Talkeetna stands off to one side. Quiet. Frontier.'

'You make some good points,' LeRoy said, and the wily businessman concluded: 'I've saved the most compelling for last. Move to Talkeetna and I'll finance your two planes, no interest.'

'Talkeetna has just become my headquarters,' LeRoy said. Then he reflected: 'You know, Mr. Venn, after you've been an Air Force captain in charge of big planes, you start to think big and you want to make something of your life. A wife and all. The best thing I can visualize, a real good bush pilot, master of this whole frontier,' and he spread his hands over the Railbelt, which would henceforth be his terrain, its remote fields, its whiteouts, its hidden lakes, its storms, its wonder.

Snapping his fingers, Venn rented a car and together they drove the eighty drab miles toward the sleepy, false-fronted, wooden-housed town of Talkeetna, population about one hundred, and during the trip LeRoy was apologetic for the bleakness of the land, but as they left the main highway for the Talkeetna cutoff they climbed a short hill, from the top of which there was a superb view of the great Denali range, high and white and severe, the guardian of the arctic, and the sight was so majestic, and so rare considering the clouds that usually prevented any view, that the two men halted the car, parked at one side, and luxuriated in this spectacular revelation of the Alaskan heartland: 'Looks like the mountains are sending you an invitation, LeRoy,' and the young veteran caught a reinforcing glimpse of what life could be like in this area during his mature years.

But even as they sat there on this day that seemed so perfect, a weather front began to scud in from Siberia at a furious speed, and within minutes the mountains were lost, and LeRoy was reminded that in moving his operations to Talkeetna, he was taking on a whole new set of challenges. He would still have to fly to remote lakes where old men lay dying or young women were preparing to give birth, and he would as always run the risk of being caught in sudden storms, but off to the northwest would rise that tremendous range of snow-capped mountains, and if he were to do a real job of flying, he would have to master them: land on skis at eight thousand feet to deliver and pick up mountain climbers, fly at sixteen thousand feet to scout the flanks of great Denali to locate where the dead bodies lay. It was the kind of flying a bush pilot not only accepted as a challenge but sought.

As the great mountains disappeared, those that would in the years ahead be his white beacons, he said quietly: 'I'll do it,' and Venn said: 'You'll never be sorry,' and the switch to Talkeetna with its earthen strip and convenient nearby lakes was done.

Sandy did not find a house they could afford, but with the loan from the Venns she and her husband were able to build one, and when they were ensconced it was she who volunteered to look after Venn's Lode while her husband did his flying. It was also she who purchased what she called 'this neat little radio job,' on which she could talk to her husband while he was flying out to some remote site or hurrying home ahead of a storm.

The move to Talkeetna was one of the best things LeRoy Flatch ever did, for it introduced him to the heartland of Alaska, the Railbelt that bound the major cities together. As an aviator he had previously been aware of the railroad only as a line of life-saving tracks to be followed when visibility was otherwise nil, but now, with daily trains stopping at Talkeetna, he occasionally had the opportunity to ride north to Fairbanks. Then he appreciated the superlative job his Alaskans had done in building this northernmost railbed. And he was especially pleased with the exceptional beauty that enveloped the land during a few trembling weeks in late August and September.

Then shrub alders turned a flaming gold, blueberry bushes a fiery red, while stately spruce provided a majestic green background against the pristine, icy white of distant Mount Denali. It was Alaska at its best, and LeRoy told his wife: 'You can see it only from the train. Looking down from a plane . . . just a blur,' and she replied: 'From wherever I stand, it looks pretty good.'

But later, when they flew to the Lode to dine with the Venns, they learned that others had quite different dreams of what Alaska might become. 'There's a lot of loose talk beginning to circulate,' Tom Venn said after dinner, 'about this crazy idea of statehood for Alaska.' He studied the two young people before him and asked: 'Do you support such nonsense?'

Since his question practically demanded a negative response, the best Sandy Flatch could do was temporize. Vaguely but not passionately in favor of statehood, she voiced an opinion which would be heard much in forthcoming months: 'I wonder if we have a big enough population?'

'We do not!' Venn said firmly. 'How about you, LeRoy?'

Since he still owed the Venns for the two planes and his house, and was dependent upon them for much of the business which kept his one-man company afloat, he, too, deemed it wise to be evasive, but in his case he believed rather strongly in the military judgment he now issued: 'Alaska's principal value to the United States, perhaps its only value, is to be a military shield in the arctic. With our limited resources we could never defend this territory against Asia. And with Russian communism on the march everywhere, they might be coming at us at any moment.'

'You've hit one nail on the head,' Venn said enthusiastically, but then he turned to his wife: 'Tell them the even bigger idea they missed, Lydia,' whereupon she entered the conversation with considerable vigor: 'My father saw it in the old days. I see it now. Alaska will never have the people or the power or the finances to operate as a free state, like the others. It must depend on help from the Lower Forty-eight.'

'And that means what it's always meant,' her husband broke in. 'Seattle.

We can assemble the money from the other states. And when we have it, we've always known what to do with it.'

'The point is,' Lydia said persuasively, 'my family, for example, we've always tried to do what's right for Alaska. We look after the people up here as if they were members of our own family. We help educate them. We defend their rights in Congress. And we treat their natives far better than they do themselves.'

For the better part of two hours the two Venns hammered away at the doctrine that had become almost sacred in Seattle: that statehood for Alaska would be wrong for the people of Alaska, wrong for the nation at large, wrong for the natives, wrong for industry, wrong for the general future of the area, and, although Venn never said so openly, not even at home, terribly wrong for Seattle. The two Flatches, who had entered this chance discussion with no strong convictions, left the Venns' house fairly well convinced that statehood was something to be avoided.

THE SECOND FLATCH family, fortified by its education at the university, took the other side in this battle. Flossie Coop had only vague and generally unpleasant memories of Minnesota, even though she had been ten during her last year in that state. 'It was bitter cold,' she told Nate, who had never visited the Outside. 'Much worse than Matanuska. And we never had enough food. And Father had to poach to get us a deer now and then. And I left it with no regrets, none at all.'

'What's your point?'

'So I was what they call disposed to like Alaska. For me it was freedom and enormous vegetables and a glacier right up the valley and a tame moose. It was excitement, and a new world being born, and great neighbors like Matt Murphy and Missy Peckham, and the feeling that you were taking part in history.' She stopped, tears came to her eyes, and she leaned over to kiss her husband: 'And what you did in the war.'

Suddenly embittered, she rose and stalked about the cabin: 'And what my old man did building that road. And the way LeRoy flew his airplanes everywhere in all kinds of weather. People have the nerve to ask me if we're ready for statehood? We were ready the day I stepped off that *St. Mihiel*, and we're a lot readier now.'

Nate Coop did not require his wife's surprising histrionics. Alone he had spied out the enemy on Lapak Island. Sometimes alone he had spied on Adak, Amchitka, Attu and Kiska. He rarely spoke of his adventures and never of the death of Captain Ruggles, one of the finest men he had known, but he did feel that from these experiences, and from his years as a miner in the heart of the territory, he knew something about what Alaska was and what its potential could be. He was for statehood. Men like him and his father-in-law working on the Alcan Highway and his brother-in-law flying those planes, they had earned statehood and a whole lot more. He rarely entered into the public discussions that were beginning to spring up across the territory, but if questioned, he left no doubt as to his basic opinion: 'I'm for it. We got the brains to run things.'

When peace came to Matanuska it modified the life of the elder Flatches very little. They continued to live in their original cabin, and even during the time they had to share it with LeRoy and his wife they felt no inconvenience, mainly because each of them was outdoors a great deal. Because Elmer's broken legs did not heal easily or strongly, the old man could not resume his life as a hunting guide for parties of rich men out of Oregon and California, and he was grateful when young Nate volunteered to replace him. There was trouble when they told Flossie of their plans, for she said: 'I want nothing to do with hunters who kill animals,' but Nate said: 'All you have to do is feed them,' and he encouraged her to start a section of the holding in which she kept orphaned animals and those wounded by careless shots.

It was during one of these hunts that Nate first felt emboldened to reveal openly his desire for statehood. He was guiding three well-to-do Seattle sportsmen in the Chugach Mountains; they had wanted to camp out in the old tent-and-blanket style, and rarely had he worked with a team which better exemplified the meaning of sportsmanship, for each man carried his full load of gear, each washed dishes in turn, and each chopped wood. They were a notable group, and on the third night, after the work had been done, one of them, a banker who had helped Tom Venn's Ross & Raglan finance recent expansion in Alaska and who had accepted enthusiastically Venn's interpretation of Alaskan history, said to his companions: 'It would be a shame to spoil this wilderness with some expensive nonsense like this statehood folly they're talking about. Keep this as the paradise it is.'

'Absolutely!' one of the hunters agreed, while the third, a man connected with the insurance of cargoes bound for Alaska, said: 'In a hundred years an area like this would never be able to support itself.'

The banker, who had fought in Italy in World War II, said: 'The important thing to remember is not dollars and cents. They can be negotiated. It's the military posture of our nation. We need Alaska up here as our forward shield. It should really be under the control of our military.'

Each of the three hunters had seen service during the war, but none had served anywhere near Alaska; however, each had strong opinions about the proper defense for the arctic. 'The great danger is Soviet Russia. People make a lot of the fact that at the two little Diomede Islands, one American, one Russian, communism is only a mile and a half from our democracy. That's insignificant, good propaganda but not much else. However, from the real Siberia to the real Alaska at one important spot is only sixty miles, and that's a real danger.'

The insurance man said: 'No way Alaska could defend itself if the Russkies decided to come over,' and the banker asked: 'What is the population of the place?' and the insurance man replied: 'I looked it up. Federal census 1940 showed a total population of seventy-two thousand. Single suburbs of Los Angeles have more than that,' and the banker concluded: 'Alaska is best seen as a basket case. It'll always need our help, and to give it statehood would be a criminal miscarriage.'

Nate, busy stowing gear while this conversation progressed, finally felt obligated to break in: 'We defended ourselves pretty well against the Japanese.'

'Wait a minute!' the third hunter protested. 'I was serving on Guadalcanal, and we were scared out of our minds when the Japanese captured your Aleutian Islands so easily. They had a real pincer movement going, South Pacific, North Pacific.'

'We drove them off, didn't we?'

The man from Guadalcanal, thinking that Nate meant the Alaskans alone had defeated the Japanese, said: 'You and about fifty thousand mainland troops to help,' and Nate laughed: 'Me and that fox farmer who scouted the islands didn't have much stateside help.'

The phrase *fox farmer* derailed the conversation because the Seattle men had to know what it meant. So Nate spent about half an hour explaining how, on the empty Aleutians, men like Ben Krickel leased entire islands, stocking them with one type of fox, 'maybe silver, they bring the most, or blue, they thrive pretty well, or plain red or even a pretty light gray.' He told how the Krickels, father and daughter, had harvested the blue foxes of Lapak Island and shipped them off to the dealer in St. Louis, and then he added: 'My brother-in-law became an officer in the Air Corps. He married Krickel's daughter.'

The insurance man was captivated by this story, and exclaimed with the kind of bubbling enthusiasm which enabled him to get close to people he was trying to sell policies: 'I'll be damned! Two marriages in your family, and in each, one person's a standard Minnesotan, the other, half Indian. Isn't that something?'

'I'm half Indian. Sandy Krickel's half Aleut.'

'Just by looking, can you tell one from the other?'

For the first time in this conversation Nate broke into a laugh: 'Me? I can tell an Aleut from an Indian at a hundred yards. But when I act up, Sandy says she can smell an Indian at a hundred and fifty. Not too much love lost among the various natives.'

'But they all have trouble with the white man?' the banker asked, and Nate evaded the question: 'You know, there's about half a dozen different kinds of Eskimos, too. And a Yup'ik won't take too kindly to an Inupiat.'

'Which is which?' the insurance man asked, and Nate said: 'Inupiat is north along the Arctic Ocean, Yup'ik is south along the Bering Sea. I prefer the Yup'iks, but they would both like to beat up on me, if they thought they could get away with it.'

'Which they can't?' the insurance man asked, and Nate said: 'Three of them coming at me together might.'

The banker looked up from the bed he was making: 'So with all those differences, you certainly don't want statehood, do you?'

'I do,' Nate said firmly, and the banker asked: 'With only seventy thousand population,' and Nate said: 'Like with me barroom-fighting Eskimos, up here one man counts double, or maybe triple.'

THE PERSON IN Matanuska who took the fight for statehood most seriously was Missy Peckham, the feisty seventy-five-year-old who had remained at Matanuska because so many of her friends now lived there. Partly because no one else in the region seemed eligible, the territorial governor had made her the local representative to a Statehood Committee whose job it would be to organize local support for statehood and to represent Alaskan aspirations at meetings in the Lower Forty-eight. For many, such an appointment was a kind of local honor involving no work and not much commitment, but for Missy it became the consuming passion in the remaining years of her life. For she had learned while climbing Chinook Pass or battling for justice at Nome that self-government was not a matter of population size or tax base or conformance to rigid rules, but rather the degree of fire in the human heart. And hers was ablaze, for she had witnessed at close quarters the zeal with which the Matanuska settlers had built a new world for themselves, and she had watched as ardent men constructed their highway through the wilderness. She knew that the people of Alaska were ready for statehood, and that their courage had established their eligibility.

So, taking her assignment seriously, she began to make herself Alaska's civilian authority on one small but important aspect of the problem: the salmon industry. She had never actually worked in a salmon cannery, but her long residence in Juneau had placed her in touch with some dozen operations like Totem Cannery on Taku Inlet, and from her experiences with both the Seattle owners of such places and the men who worked in them, she had a solid founding in the economics of this crucial industry. When she put her data together she was able to present a sickening portrait of an indefensible situation, as she did in her first impassioned presentation at a mass meeting in Anchorage:

'The facts are these. The canneries have always been owned by rich men in Seattle, only rarely if ever by anyone in Alaska. By remaining in cahoots with powerful interests in Washington, they've always avoided paying taxes to our government in Alaska. They import workers into our areas for the summer months but pay no taxes on their salaries. Oh yes! They do pay five dollars a head, five dollars, to a kind of school tax, but not nearly what they should pay for stealing one of our most valuable natural resources.

'What burns me up, and ought to burn you up, is the fact that with their fish traps and fish wheels they're destroying our salmon. In the state of Washington and in Canada they don't allow that wanton killing. So their salmon are increasing year by year. Ours are dying. Because the federal authorities have always been under the control of the Seattle interests, never under ours. Because we aren't a state, we have no senators or congressmen to fight for us.'

She spoke that first time for about fifteen minutes, making a tremendous impression because of the authority with which she had assembled the facts which condemned the present situation; later, when concerned experts began to feed her even more specifics, her standard salmon speech ran about twenty-five minutes, serving as what one admiring advocate of statehood termed 'our barn-burning speech,' but at the height of her popularity—a slight, battling woman with a most lively manner of speech—one of the experts warned: 'Missy, your talk is all facts and figures. If we send you to the Lower Forty-eight, you'll have to inject more human interest.'

Since she had never worked on a salmon boat or in a fishery, she was at a disadvantage, but by accident she received help from a source she could never have anticipated. One evening when she spoke in Anchorage, where the agitation for statehood was growing, she noticed in the audience a handsomely dressed woman in her late forties who leaned forward to follow acutely each of the charges Missy was making. Her presence was perplexing, since Missy could not determine what her race might be: she was certainly not Caucasian, but she was also neither an Eskimo nor an Athapascan: She's probably an Aleut. With those eyes.

At the end of the rally the strange woman did not depart with the others, but stood aside as several men and women surged forward to congratulate Missy on her stirring speech. And when the hall was nearly empty, the woman came forward, smiled warmly, and extended her hand: 'We used to meet in Juneau, Mrs. Peckham. I was Tammy Ting, Tammy Venn now.'

'You're Ah Ting's little girl? Sam Bigears' granddaughter?'

'I am. Ah Ting and Sam thought very highly of you, Mrs. Peckham.'

'Miss.' Suddenly, as if caught stealing cookies, she clapped her hand over her mouth and grinned: 'Did I say anything awful tonight? About the Venns, I mean?'

And then Tammy said something which would cement the friendship between the two: 'Nothing that I don't say. I'm a strong advocate of statehood, Miss Peckham.'

Missy stared at her, saw the lovely Chinese-Tlingit shadows which gave her face such a provocative expression, and suddenly leaned upward and kissed her. 'I think we better talk,' Missy said, and they returned to Tammy's hotel, where they discussed salmon and canneries and Ah Ting's and Sam Bigears' relations to both. 'It's always confused me,' Tammy said, 'but in English my father's name should have been expressed as Ting Ah. He was Mr. Ah, but he always went by Mr. Ting. So did I. I asked him about this one day, and he sneered: "Mr. Ah this, Mr. Ah that. Sounds if you're sneezing. Mr. Ting, sharp, businesslike." '

'He was certainly businesslike,' Missy said. 'Tell me what it was like at the cannery,' and the tales which Ah Ting and Sam Bigears had related to their families required hours to unfold. Thereafter, Missy's harangue on salmon took on a most personal touch, with stories of the visit of her old lover Will Kirby to Taku Inlet to try to persuade the Seattle owners to give the salmon a better chance to survive, and the dramatic sinking of the *Montreal Queen.* In fact, Missy's talk became one of the highlights in Alaska's drive toward statehood, for listeners went home and told their neighbors: 'You ought to hear the Peckham woman. She knows what for.'

The highlight of her personal campaign, insofar as salmon were concerned, came at a big meeting in Seattle, where it was essential to enlist the support of Senators Magnuson and Jackson. She telephoned Tammy Venn as soon as she got off the plane: 'Tammy, this is most important. I want to make a good impression and I need your advice.' She was astounded when Tammy answered: 'You'll have no trouble. I'm going to speak right after you. I'll cover for any mistakes you make.'

'You're going to speak in favor of statehood? In Seattle?'

'I certainly am.'

'Bless you.'

The two women, appearing toward the end of the program—the tough little social worker, the suave Chinese-Tlingit member of Seattle's high society —created a sensation, a powerful opening barrage for the statehood debate. The local papers, of course, featured the fact that Tammy Venn was the daughter-in-law of Thomas Venn, president of Ross & Raglan and an inveterate opponent of statehood for a backward area like Alaska, where so many of the Venn interests centered. Next morning, when reporters reached Venn for his reaction to Tammy's bombshell statement, he said austerely: 'My daughter-in-law speaks for herself, but since she left Alaska at a fairly early age, she has not been able to follow recent developments there.'

However, when the same reporters tracked down Malcolm Venn, he said: 'You mean, my wife came out publicly for statehood?' When they chorused 'Yes' he said: 'She's as loony as a bedbug. I'll have to speak to her about this.' Then he laughed: 'Have you ever tried to argue her out of anything?' When asked specifically: 'Then you're against statehood for Alaska?' he said seriously: 'I sure am. That wonderful area was meant to remain a wilderness. With seventy thousand population, it couldn't run a town council, let alone a state.'

Next morning the papers carried Tammy's rebuttal: 'I always suspected my husband knew very little about the place where I was born. The 1950 census figures show that we have 128,643 citizens, and I'm sure I'll convince him by the end of this month that we're entitled to statehood.' But that weekend the papers displayed a good-natured shot of Tom and Lydia Venn, accompanied by Malcolm, standing off to one side while saucy-looking Tammy posed with a banner that Missy Peckham had given her: STATEHOOD NOW.

The banter in the newspaper produced a most surprising dénouement: a fifty-year-old businessman in a blue-serge suit and highly polished black shoes came to Missy's hotel and introduced himself as Oliver Rowntree, in the freight-forwarding business in San Francisco and here in Seattle on some railroad negotiations important to the entire Pacific Coast. He was obviously surprised to see that it was such an elderly woman who was kicking up this fuss about statehood, but quickly got to his point: 'I'm with you a hundred percent, Miss Peckham. I have no position in government and no authority to wield, but I do have a lifetime of information, and it galls me to watch people like Ross & Raglan conspire with the railroads to deny Alaska statehood.'

'Why should you be concerned? Other than as a sensible citizen?'

'I was born in Alaska. Anchorage. I watched my father try to operate a grocery story there. One of the best, equal to anything in the Outside, as we called it then.'

'Lower Forty-eight now.'

'I do a lot of work with Hawaii. Out there they call it the Mainland. And it's my experience with them that has made me so bitter about Alaska. I want to see the people up your way get a fair break, at last.'

'You're doing this for your father, aren't you?'

'I suppose I am. I saw the way he had to struggle to earn a buck because his neck was in a noose. Came to Oregon where the laws were sensible, had no trouble at all in building the best grocery north of San Francisco, died a wealthy man with a chain of eight moderate-sized stores, each one a bonanza.

'Now let's get down to facts. I'm discovering that generalized emotion means little in this business. Starving Eskimos are no better now than starving Belgians were in World War One.'

The facts he unraveled were so startling that Missy asked him to go over them twice. 'Better yet,' he said, 'I'll send you some reports,' but when she received them they produced no substitute for the iron-hard recital he gave during their first meeting.

'It all starts with the Jones Act of 1920. Have you heard of it?'

'Vaguely. I know it's bad news for Alaska. Details? No.'

'Well, the father of that shipping man whose photograph was in this morning's paper, old Malcolm Ross, was instrumental in getting it passed. Senator Jones from Washington bird-dogged it through the Senate. What it did, in simple terms, was put Hawaii and Alaska in a straitjacket, but Alaska in far worse shape than Hawaii. It said that the only ships which could carry freight from West Coast ports to either Hawaii or Alaska were ships built in the United States, owned by United States companies, and manned by United States crews. That places Hawaii and Alaska at a considerable disadvantage over ports like Boston or Philadelphia, where European vessels and those under foreign registry can bring in goods from abroad. But Hawaii has it lots better than Alaska, because it has competing lines who work to keep costs down. Alaska has only R&R, and they've continued to strangle people up there the way they strangled my father.'

'I can't believe a nation would do this to one of its parts,' Missy said, and then Rowntree offered the clincher: 'Here's where I came into the picture in a big way. I bring an enormous lot of goods across country by train. Because of tricks the Seattle people slipped into the Jones Act, what costs me one dollar freight to San Francisco for shipment to Hawaii, costs you a dollar ninety-five to get it to Seattle for shipment to Alaska. So if you add up all the disadvantages under which Alaska suffers, it is something like three-to-one against.'

'Why does Hawaii get such a favorable break?' Missy asked in disgust, and Rowntree said, only half humorously: 'They're smarter. They've learned how to protect themselves in the clinches.' And Missy vowed: 'We're going to get some brains from Hawaii,' and she asked Rowntree's help in drafting and polishing the famous oration which she would deliver more than sixty times in all parts of the Lower Forty-eight, 'The Strangling of Alaska.'

Her first delivery, at a hall in Seattle, had an unforeseen consequence, for Tammy Venn appeared in the audience with her high-spirited husband in tow, and prior to the meeting, people who knew them joshed Tammy because Malcolm had described her in public as being 'as loony as a bedbug.' When pressed, he told a listening newsman: 'I have apologized most profusely for that statement. It was uncouth and almost indecent. What I should have said was that she's as loony as a pismire.' Together they explained in the best of humor that they disagreed on many things: 'Tammy's a Democrat, I'm a Republican. She wanted our kids to go to public school, I wanted one of the good private schools back east.'

'Who won?'

'Tie. Girl back east. Boy here in Seattle.'

'Who's going to win on the statehood issue?'

He replied: 'The senators of this great republic have enough sense not to pass that nonsense,' and as he spoke she put up behind his head, so the cameras could catch it, the index and little finger of her right hand, making them look like donkey's ears.

After the performance, which Tammy said was delightful and her husband a justification for citizen's arrest because of the way Missy slandered his father, they met with Oliver Rowntree, and at first greeting Oliver and Tammy stared at each other, snapped fingers, and cried: 'Hey! I know you!'

'How did that happen?' Malcolm Venn asked as they sat down for drinks, and Tammy began hesitantly: 'It's a long story, but do you remember, back in 1925, when you met me on that R&R ship heading for Alaska?' When he looked confused, she said: 'Remember? You were working as a private detective. To snare the scoundrel who was sabotaging your father's ships?'

'Of course! We had a damned romantic trip, if I say so myself. But I never did catch the saboteur.' Trying to repress a smile, Tammy pointed at herself, and when her husband shouted 'You?' loud enough for other tables to hear, she nodded, then appealed to Rowntree to substantiate her story.

'She's telling the truth. For seven passages I was the one who threw the newel posts in the sea and jammed up the toilets,' and Tammy broke in: 'He met me by accident at the university, told me he had to divert suspicion from himself, and asked me to do what he did when clearly he wasn't present. All the same clues and all that stuff.'

'But why?' Venn asked Rowntree, and the latter said simply: 'Because you people, with the Jones Act in your pocket, were strangling legitimate business in Alaska. My old man went broke because of your old man. Sabotage was the only revenge I could take.'

Malcolm Venn, soon to be president of R&R, stared at this stranger from the past, and broke into a warm smile: 'You son-of-a-bitch! I ought to have you arrested.'

'Statute of limitations.'

'And you helped him?' This to Tammy, who grinned and said: 'I sure did. My parents were pretty strong against R&R in those days. Later they relaxed.'

They talked a long time about the old days, and Venn said: 'My father worked with a real old reprobate named Marvin Hoxey to get the Jones Act passed, for the welfare of Alaska, and now I'll be working with some of the most honest businessmen in the world to combat statehood for Alaska, to protect that marvelous area from her own folly. There's no chance that you three can stampede this thing through, no matter how persuasively you speak, Miss Peckham. The good people of the United States are too clever to fall into your trap.'

IT SEEMED THAT once again the Western states knew what was best for Alaska, for in this early skirmishing, Congress listened to leaders like Thomas Venn and the industrial tycoons of Seattle, Portland and San Francisco, but even more damaging testimony came from Alaska itself, for in one public hearing after another its citizens rose to testify that their area was not ready for statehood, which they opposed for a variety of reasons. In one set of hearings convened by congressmen who flew all the way to Alaska to hear local sentiment, the following types of testimony surfaced:

General Leonidas Shafter, USAF (retired) living on the Kenai peninsula: 'You're right, Senator, I did help build the Alaskan airfields and I did serve in the Aleutians during World War Two. From that experience I know the military significance of Alaska. It's the highway through which Russia will one day attack North America, and it must stay under military control. Statehood would be disastrous to the safety of our nation.'

Thomas Venn, Seattle industrialist with a home near Denali: 'Because of my long association with Alaska and the years I lived and served here in various capacities, I must oppose statehood for this vast, unconnected, unpopulated virgin territory. Present arrangements, tested by time, have proved that they ensure the welfare of the few who live here and spur the development of areas as yet untouched.'

Mrs. Henry Watson, housewife, Haines: 'I don't know six taxpayers that want statehood. Of course, there are a few Indians and half-breeds who pay no taxes, and they're hot for it.'

John Karpinic, grocer, Ketchikan: 'Nobody down our way wants to fool around with state government. We got enough trouble with the feds.'

Opposed to this barrage in defense of the status quo, a few strong voices spoke up for statehood, and three voices were significant:

John Stamp, editor, Anchorage: 'I could give you eighty reasons why statehood for Alaska is overdue, but I cannot improve on the simple words of James Otis on the eve of the American Revolution: "Taxation without representation is tyranny." If your hearts do not respond to that embattled cry, you are false to the spirit of the great nation that arose from that cry. Why does Alaska not have the roads that other parts of America have? Because we have no congressmen to fight for them. Why were our railroads not properly subsidized by the federal government? Why do we not have the airfields which we so desperately need? Why do we not have the schools, the hospitals, the public libraries, the great courthouses? Because you have denied us the right to tax the industries which in other parts of the United States help pay for those services. Like the colonists of old, I cry for relief.'

Henry Louis Dechamps, professor of geography, University of California at Berkeley, an American citizen but educated at Canada's McGill University: 'Gentlemen, in trying to decide what to do about Alaska, I beg you, do not look only at Juneau and Sitka and think you are seeing the heart of Alaska. Don't look only at Anchorage and Fairbanks. Look, I pray you, to the northernmost part of this vast land where it touches the Arctic Ocean, for along those shores and in that icy sea will occur the history that will determine the fate of North America. We are lagging dreadfully in our knowledge of how to live and operate in the arctic. But I assure you that the Soviet Union is conducting constant exercises there and that her accumulation of knowledge far exceeds ours. We must catch up, for the Arctic Ocean is destined in the future to be not an icebound body of water, but a hidden sea in whose bowels submarines will prowl and other vessels that we cannot today envisage. It will be a highway for airplanes, a settlement for daring men prepared to make strikes against our communications, our forward bases, our shores and our very safety as a nation. Alaska, in the next century, will be one of the premier possessions of the United States. Ignore it and you endanger our nation. Develop it and you have an extra shield. Award it statehood now.'

Miss Melissa Peckham, housewife, Juneau (after explaining the monstrosities of the Jones Act and the abuse visited upon Alaska by the railroads and the shore installations at Seattle, she concluded as follows): 'I wonder if any single person who has testified before you during these three exciting days has had the wide experience of Alaska that I've had. Because I came young I was able to see the gold fields, the development of the Yukon River, the great salmon industry in the south, the growth of towns and cities, the noble experiment at Matanuska, the coming of the railroads, the building of the Alcan, the rise of aviation. Above all, I've seen the birth of a new people with new aspirations. We're fed up with being a colony. We want our own legislature to pass our own laws. We want to be freed from the condescending control of Seattle. We think we've earned the right to be considered full-fledged citizens with full-fledged rights.'

But in the long run the most effective testimony came from people with strange names and even stranger faces who paraded before the microphones with statements so simple, they echoed like gunfire from the walls of the frontier rooms where the meetings were held:

Saul Chythlook, Yup'ik Eskimo cabdriver, Nome: 'Demobilized San Francisco after duty on Iwo Jima. Worked awhile in country north of big bridge. Saw many small towns. Not so hot. They all self-governin', why not us?'

Stepan Kossietski, Tlingit teacher, Mount Edgecumbe school, Sitka: 'I have my A.B. from the University of Alaska at Fairbanks, my M.A. from the University of California at Berkeley. I must agree with the woman from Shishmaref who testified this morning. Many natives are not ready for statehood. But I imagine that in a state like South Dakota, there are quite a few who are not ready, either. They drink too much. They're lazy. They don't read the newspapers. But let me tell you, the good natives that I know, they're not only ready, they're impatient. Are they capable of running what would be the state of Alaska? Let me tell you they're a lot better prepared than some of the people you send us from the Lower Forty-eight to run it.'

Norma Merculieff, Aleut-Russian housewife, Kodiak Island: 'My husband fishes for king crab. He and two others own their own boat, a hundred and eighty thousand dollars, all paid, taxes too. You think they don't know how to run a town council? So if they're too dumb, we wives will run the council, let them run the boat. They're buying a new one next year, quarter of a million dollars, they're doing all right.'

THE ANTIS WON, and statehood for Alaska seemed dead, but then various things began to happen, some of nationwide significance, others of arbitrary and even foolish dimension. The citizens of the United States started to think globally, and many who had never before dreamed of Hawaii or Alaska began to realize that the sooner the nation grasped those precious outriders to its maternal bosom, the better. Also, many American men had served in the Pacific and had learned to appreciate both its magnitude and its significance. Those who had hopped islands had discovered how important a nothing island like Wake or Midway could be—sandspits on which the fates of nations were decided, specks invisible from ten miles away on which the airlines of the world would depend—and they were not about to give up substantial islands like Hawaii.

There was always more support for Hawaiian statehood than for Alaskan, and considering their relative populations and wealth, no wonder. But thoughtful men like Professor Dechamps, who had testified before the congressional committee, continued to speak about the significance of the northern lands; the military, too, had new globes now rather than flat maps, and they appreciated the enormous value of a northern defense perimeter. So there was also a growing constituency for Alaska.

But now politics began to assume major significance, and some very curious miscalculations erupted: the greatest experts got things completely backward. They reasoned that because Hawaii was fairly well settled with responsible men and women in charge, it would surely vote Republican if it ever got statehood; while Alaska, being a rambunctious frontier state, would probably vote Democratic. In the long run it turned out the other way, to the astonishment of many people, including the experts.

At this crucial point, the thoughtful military around Eisenhower and the conservatives from Seattle and the West somewhat overshot their hand; they convinced the President that Alaska, at least the ninety percent up north, should be kept in a territorial status under military control. One afternoon, persuaded by their arguments, he gave the Washington press an offhand judgment that while the populated southeast segment of Alaska—Juneau, Sitka, Ketchikan, Wrangell, Petersburg—might have enough people to warrant statehood some time in the distant future, the great empty areas to the north would probably never have enough.

This howling error enabled loyal Alaskans everywhere to rush into print with a startling correction: 'President Eisenhower may understand military affairs but he sure doesn't know much about Alaska. The preliminary census for 1960 shows that the southeast which he praises as being crowded with people ... you take the five towns down there, they have a total population of nineteen thousand, while the Railbelt, that's Fairbanks to Anchorage and down the Kenai Peninsula where our only railroad runs, it's going to show more than fifty-seven thousand. That's exactly three times as much. It's the Railbelt that's ready for statehood, not the general's favorite little burgs down in the forgotten corner.'

At this critical moment, when approval for statehood hung in the balance, one of those accidents erupted which sometimes help determine history. The governor of the territory was a gifted former medical student and journalist, Ernest Gruening from Harvard, who in 1928 had written the best book extant on the revolution in Mexico. His perceptive analysis having caught the attention of President Roosevelt, he had been appointed Director of the Division of Territories and Island Possessions, in which capacity he came to know Alaska and respect its potential for greatness. He spoke so often and so loudly in government circles about what Alaska might become that in 1939 he was appointed Territorial Governor, and was later elected to serve as make-believe senator to the United States Congress—allowed on the floor, but not allowed to vote—until such time as statehood was attained and real senators could be elected.

Having learned how much good the proper book at the proper time could achieve, Gruening, always the publicist, had approached a friend, the writer Edna Ferber, with a striking proposal: 'Come to Alaska and write a book about us. Do for us what you've just done for Texas.' Her immensely popular novel *Giant* had catapulted the foibles and grandeur of the Lone Star State into national prominence, and he supposed that a similar book by the same writer could do the same for Alaska.

Miss Ferber, having weathered the storm of adverse criticism that was rained down upon her by Texas loyalists, rather relished the idea of tackling another contentious problem, so she came to Alaska briefly and hurriedly wrote *Ice Palace*, which gained enormous readership. The consequences were precisely those that this clever man Gruening had anticipated. Of the book he would write later:

> *Ice Palace* made a strong case, in fiction form, for statehood. Some of the literary critics felt it was not up to her best work, but one of them referred to it quite correctly as 'the *Uncle Tom's Cabin* for Alaskan statehood.' Thousands who would never have been interested in any of our pro-statehood non-fiction magazine articles, of which I had written several for *Harper's*, *The Atlantic Monthly* and *The New York Times Magazine*, did read novels.

> In the closing weeks of our statehood drive scores of people asked me whether I had read *Ice Palace*. It was called to the attention of many Congressmen. I have no doubt that it changed quite a few votes.

In 1958, when the debate heatened, an elderly gentleman of excellent reputation stepped regally into a Senate hearing room in Washington prepared to testify against statehood for Alaska. He was Thomas Venn, seventy-five years old, here to protect the commercial interests of Seattle. White-haired and puritanically erect in bearing, he created the impression of a man who did not tolerate fools or their foolish opinions, but he was by no means repellent, for he could smile affably when his friends nodded, and he knew that this impression of gentility was heightened by the presence of his wife, Lydia Ross Venn.

As they took their places at one end of the row reserved for testifiers, Mrs. Venn whispered discreetly in her husband's ear, and he looked to the opposite end: 'My God! How did she get here?'

It was Missy Peckham of Juneau, whose fiery determination had helped keep the struggle for statehood on the front pages of newspapers. She had a puckish smile and quick wit, and was not at all overawed by either the Senate hearing room or the dignitaries now filing in to conduct the session at which she would testify for the last time regarding the crusade to which she had dedicated her waning years. Now she saw Tom Venn staring at her, and with an innocent smile she nodded as if to welcome him to her party. Stiffly, the color still absent from his face, he bowed. Then he took his seat and listened as his long affiliation with Alaska and Ross & Raglan was explained to the audience. Then, never raising his voice or engaging in polemics, he stated the case of those who opposed statehood, now and in the foreseeable future:

'Gentlemen, no man in this room can speak of Alaska with greater affection than I do. I've known every corner of that vast territory since 1898 when I climbed the dreaded Chilkoot Pass, and throughout the decades that followed I have always acted to promote the welfare of Alaska. I assure you that in my reasoned judgment Alaska is not ready for statehood, that it would be gross error to give it statehood, and that its future can best be assured by continuing the same benevolent custodianship it has enjoyed in the past.

'The military know how to protect Alaska. The businessmen of the West Coast know how to serve its industrial and banking needs. The sympathetic experts in the Bureau of Indian Affairs know best how to help the native peoples. And the Department of the Interior has proved that it can be relied upon to conserve the national resources. We have in place all the instruments required for a wise and protective system of government, one that has worked admirably in the past and will continue to do so in the future. Like thousands of thoughtful men and women who consider only the welfare of this great territory, I beg you not to encumber Alaska with a form of government it is incapable of handling. I urge you to reject statehood.'

As Venn stepped away from the witness chair he had to pass Missy, who had, in a certain sense, reared him, served as his mother, encouraged him in his work, and imparted to him her wonderfully stable set of values. If he had been asked at that moment, he would have said without hesitation: 'Miss Peckham taught me most of what I know.' As longtime friends they nodded and might even have embraced, for their debts, each to the other, were tremendous. But now she took his place at the table to refute everything he had said:

'Distinguished Senators. [Here she stopped and asked: 'Can this gismo be turned up? Can you hear me now? Good!'] Let's settle the biggest problem first. The previous speaker, a distinguished friend of Alaska, has claimed that we do not have a population sufficient to justify statehood. Well, when the fury of the Civil War was about to destroy our nation, President Abraham Lincoln realized that he simply must have two more Senate votes to protect his strategies for winning the war. How did he finagle them? Ignoring every rule for the creation of new states, he wrote his own rules and invited Nevada to become a state. He then bullied her acceptance through the Congress, and by this headstrong act helped save the Union. What was the population of Nevada at that historic moment? It says here: "Six thousand eight hundred fifty-seven." Right now Alaska has thirty-three times that number. And she is just as badly needed now as Nevada was then.

'Why do you need us? Because we will always be your gateway to Asia, we will always be your outpost on the Arctic. You need our expertise in living in and conquering the frozen north. The day will also come when you will need our natural resources: our vast supplies of wood pulp, our mineral deposits, our fish, and we may even have huge deposits of petroleum. My friend Johnny Kemper, who studied at the Colorado School of Mines, tells me we may have a large deposit way up on the Arctic Shelf.'

When she left the table she walked purposefully past her onetime charge, Tom Venn, who whispered: 'Thank you for not lambasting Ross & Raglan,' and she whispered back: 'We'll take care of you when we get statehood.' They smiled, nodded, and agreed to differ.

IN LATE JUNE 1958 it became apparent that Alaska had a strong chance of slipping into statehood ahead of Hawaii, the racial mix in the latter territory militating against acceptance. The House had already approved Alaska by a vote of 210 to 172, with an amazing 51 abstentions by congressmen who could not accept the idea that almost-empty Alaska should have two Senate votes while populous New York was restricted to the same number. Also, some opposed allowing what someone had termed 'a mongrel population trapped in an icebox' to attain full voting citizenship.

Now only the Senate had to approve, and for a while it seemed doubtful that it would do so. Some senators tried to limit Alaska to commonwealth status only: defeated 50 to 29. Others argued persuasively that the military were best fitted to decide Alaska's future: defeated 53 to 31, while a vocal contingent led by Senator Thurmond supported President Eisenhower's accidental proposal that the entire northern portion be excluded from statehood, even if the lower districts did attain it: defeated 67 to 16. It seemed to Missy Peckham, as she listened to the debate, that her enemies could cite fifty arguments against statehood, while she had only one in support: the time had come for the Union to embrace without restraint a worthy new member.

On 30 June the deciding vote could no longer be postponed by obstructive amendments, and as the roll call proceeded, striking anomalies became evident. Stalwart Southern conservatives like Harry Byrd of Virginia, James Eastland and John Stennis of Mississippi, Allen Ellender of Louisiana, Herman Talmadge of Georgia and Strom Thurmond of South Carolina, having stated publicly that they were against statehood, now voted against it. But so did conspicuous liberals like Sam Ervin of North Carolina, William Fulbright and John McClellan of Arkansas, and Mike Monroney of Oklahoma.

Two tormented pairs of senators handled their conflicting loyalties in contrasting ways. Warren Magnuson and Henry Jackson of Washington had been pressured heavily by their Seattle business constituents to come out against statehood on the grounds that the state of Washington would lose economic control of the territory. When the vote came, each man had to follow his conscience: 'Yes.' The two Texas senators, Lyndon Johnson and Ralph Yarborough, were unquestioned liberals who had frequently spoken in favor of statehood, but when the real crunch came they simply could not risk their political careers by voting to admit a huge new state which would relegate Texas to second place. On the day the vote was taken, each man reached the same decision: he dare not vote for Alaska, nor could he in good conscience vote against her; so both were recorded: 'Not voting.'

The final count: yeas 64, nays 20, 12 not voting. Alaska had become the forty-ninth state, 2.2 times as big as Texas with a total population about the same as Richmond, Virginia. When Tom Venn heard the final count he said: 'Alaska has doomed herself to mediocrity,' but Missy Peckham, celebrating with friends at an expensive Washington restaurant, rose unsteadily to her feet, raised her glass, and cried: 'Now we've got to show 'em!' and she spent the rest of that long night discussing the strange political and social innovations which would make Alaska unique among the states. Her own proposals were startling; 'I want a school available to every child in Alaska, no matter what it costs. I want housing for every Eskimo, every Tlingit. We must have control of our salmon and our moose and caribou. We've got to have roads and factories and a dozen settlements like Matanuska.' On and on she went, projecting those dreams which she had first voiced during the terrible Panic of 1893 and to which she had devoted her later life.

She became so excited, at age eighty-three, by this vision of an arctic utopia and by her unaccustomed intake of alcohol, that when her friends helped her to bed, she fell into a deep, contented sleep, from which she did not awaken. When her body was discovered, associates informed Thomas Venn, whom they knew to be her longtime friend, and he hurried to the modest hotel in which she had died, and for perhaps twenty minutes he stood beside her bed, remembering her as she had been in those far-off days when she had brought hope and food to a starving family. At last he bowed down and kissed her pallid forehead, then kissed her again for each of those men whose lives she had illuminated: Buchanan Venn, the betrayed husband in Chicago; Will Kirby, the lonely Canadian policeman; John Klope, the lost soul in the Klondike; Matt Murphy, the indefatigable Irishman.

'I know she would want to be buried in Alaska,' Venn said as he left. 'Send her to Juneau, and let me have the bill.'

XII

THE RIM OF FIRE

In 1969 the United States government began paying serious attention to the problem of how the ancient land rights of the Alaskan Natives could be honored and protected, and one honest principle motivated all decisions. It was best formulated by the senior senator from North Dakota, who said during debate:

> 'Regardless of how we approach this difficult problem of assuring justice to the various Alaskan Native tribes, we must do better than we've done with our Indians in the Lower Forty-eight. Whatever system we devise must avoid the reservation which is so destructive of Indian morale. It must assure the Native control over his ancestral lands. It must protect him against avaricious white men who would deprive him of those lands. And, if possible, it must enable him to preserve and practice his traditional patterns of life.'

In the private debates that followed, two contrasting terms predominated, *reservation* and *mainstream,* the latter used as a verb: 'I say the sooner we mainstream the Indian the better. Cut off all reservation support. Give him help where needed. But encourage him to enter the mainstream of our national life and find his own level.' In support of this recommendation, proponents cited horrible statistics stemming from the historic reservation policy:

> 'An Indian reservation is a ghetto, and no pious wishes can gloss that over. It destroys initiative, encourages drunkenness, and inhibits the attaining of maturity. To keep our Indians on reservations is to keep them in jail. Of a hundred young Indians who go to college under the most beneficent conditions—scholarships, guidance support, special classes—only three remain to begin their junior year. And why do they fail? Certainly not because they lack inborn intelligence. They fail because the horrible reservation system operates against their continuation, for when they return to it their peers scorn them and their parents whine: "Why go to college? You'll never get a good job even if you do graduate. The whites won't allow it."

'The only solution I can see is to shut down every reservation, throw the Indians into the mainstream, and allow each to sink or swim according to his or her ability. Granted, the first generation may encounter rough times. Those that follow will be ordinary Americans.'

Such draconian recommendations were quickly dismissed by those who felt, as congressmen had for the past century, that if only the reservations could be well managed, the present system would function:

'If you throw the Indian off his reservation, where a benign government endeavors to protect him, to preserve his ancient ways, and to enable him to live a decent life, where will he go? You've seen where he'll go. To the back alleys of Seattle, to the teeming warrens of Minneapolis and to the hopeless dregs of one small town after another. To throw him, as you phrase it, into the mainstream is to invite him to drown.'

The debate might have ended there, in the impasse which had persisted for the past century, had not two remarkable witnesses appeared to testify before the Senate. The first was a youngish Jesuit priest who served as principal of a Catholic school on a reservation in Wyoming:

'It is a bitter joy to see our Native boys and girls in their early teens. America has no young people better than these. The boys are manly, good at games, spirited and eager to learn. The girls? No more beautiful creatures exist in this country. As you teach them, boys and girls alike, they brim with hope and the promise of becoming adults who can help lead this great nation and improve it as they do.

'That's how they are at age fourteen. At twenty-eight the young women are still hopeful and prepared to work for a decent life, but their husbands have begun to drink, to lie about, and to degenerate. Often they come home drunk and beat their wives, who begin to appear with their eyes blackened and their front teeth knocked out. Then they, too, start drinking and before long all hope is destroyed and they both become prisoners of the reservation.

'At thirty-six they're lost, men and women alike, and they spin out their lives with tangled thread, producing nothing. It breaks the heart to see this remorseless decline, and please allow me to specify exactly what I mean. Four days ago reservation officials came to my office in Wyoming to discuss what to do about the children of John and Mabel Harris. His Indian name was Gray Bird and in normal conditions he would become a chief of some importance in our community.

'But he and his wife have become so addicted to alcohol that they can scarcely function. Their two children, a girl thirteen and a boy eleven, did what they could, with our help, to keep the family together, but it was becoming clear that they would fail, so with anguish I recommended that the children be taken from the Harrises and moved in with a more stable family. Everyone, including the children and the new family, agreed that this was the only solution, but I said: "A church school can't accept responsibility for taking children away from their parents, even though I personally recommend it," so the officials accepted the duty and took the children to their new home.

'That night John Harris, wildly drunk, went to the new family's house, shouting and ranting that he wanted his children. But the children themselves, not the foster parents, convinced him that they wanted to remain where they were. So off he stormed, staggered into the path of a reservation garbage truck that was sounding its horn wildly, and was killed.

'His own children, hearing the commotion, ran from the house and reached his mangled body in time to hear the truckdriver telling bystanders: "He was dead drunk. He was always dead drunk." And that night— three nights ago today—his wife shot herself. Drunkenness and suicide are the heritage we have given the Indians as a consequence of our laws in contiguous America. Do not reproduce those laws in Alaska.'

Indians, too, came before the various committees, pleading with Congress to establish in Alaska some system better than the one operating in states like Montana, Wyoming and the Dakotas: 'There must be a better way. It's your responsibility to find it.'

The second critical testifier was an Alaskan woman of forty-one who was about as far removed from a Jesuit priest as one could imagine. She was Melody Murphy, granddaughter of that famous Melissa Peckham who had come to the Klondike from Chicago in the 1890s and, via the wild gold fields of Nome at the turn of the century, to the capital at Juneau, where she had proved a thorn in the buttocks of any administration. Fighting always for the rights of the underdog, in 1936, Missy had turned up at the Matanuska settlement, where she had supported whites from Minnesota as vigorously as she had Aleuts from Kodiak. She had died in harness, fighting for statehood and enfranchisement for all Alaskans, and had bequeathed to her granddaughter not only her willingness to combat ignorance or injustice but also her indifference to marriage customs.

In fact, Missy Peckham had lived outside of wedlock with four different men, and by the time her longtime companion Matthew Murphy was finally free to marry her, neither she nor he saw much purpose in his doing so. Her granddaughter Melody, a handsome woman with four radically different strains in her background, had likewise avoided matrimony but not men, and by the time she was thirty she was known favorably as one of the great women of Juneau. Her mother, Melissa's daughter, had been more traditional and at an early age had married the son of a wild Siberian, Abraham Lincoln Arkikov, and his Eskimo wife. So Melody's four grandparents were the American woman Melissa, the Irishman Murphy, the Siberian Arkikov and the Eskimo woman Nellie, and there had not been a weakling in that quartet. And for reasons that she never explained, she early on took the last name of Murphy.

When she sailed into Washington at her own expense, having benefited from the profits of Grandfather Arkikov's uncanny skill in buying up unwanted Juneau real estate on the gut feeling that 'someone's gonna want this later,' she spread before Congress her vision of a much different Alaska from the one they had been considering:

'The informal census last year showed that we now have a population of two hundred ninety-one thousand eight hundred, and I assure you, it will double before the next one comes round. And if we strike oil big, as some are predicting, it could quadruple. We already have the most beautiful state in the Union and the one with the greatest potential for growth. I can see no end to what Alaska might become. But to get it started on the right path, we simply must get our land problems straightened out, and no part of that problem is more complicated than finding a way to assure our Native people their right to the lands they've always occupied.'

At this point a senator asked: 'Miss Murphy? It is Miss Murphy, isn't it?' and she replied: 'It sure is.'

'Tell us, Miss Murphy, are you a Native? Do you stand to gain if we allot land to the Natives?'

She laughed, the free and easy chuckle that might have come from any one of her Alaskan ancestors, and she was remarkably attractive as she leaned forward to help the senators: 'In the curious mixing way that operates in Alaska, I would be considered half Native. One grandfather was an Irish prospector on the Yukon. He found nothing. The other was a crazy Siberian who sought gold in Nome. He found a beach full of it. One grandmother was of English derivation, the other was Eskimo. Me? I'm Alaskan, and because my Siberian grandfather did find that gold, I can afford to be disinterested where my personal land rights are concerned, but I'm vitally concerned about land rights for others.' At this point the chairman had to rebuke the spectators for cheering.

'Of our total population, thirteen percent can be classified as Native, and they're roughly divided into Indians, Eskimos and Aleuts. But in Alaskan Native life, nothing is ever simple, because the Indians, who should properly be called Athapascans, are divided into various groups, one of the most important being the Tlingits. The Eskimos are also divided, Inupiat and Yup'ik. And even the Aleuts fall into two classes, the original Aleuts from the islands, the self-styled Aleuts from the mainland.'

When one of the senators asked: 'And what are you?' she said: 'My Eskimo grandmother was certainly a Yup'ik. My Siberian grandfather? Now there we have a nice problem. His ancestors way back must have been Athapascan stock. Later on they could have been progenitors of the Inupiat. And if you look far enough back into my English ancestors, God knows what you'll find. I like to think I'm part Pict.' Here the audience laughed quietly, but soon broke into guffaws as she concluded:

'Let's say I'm properly mixed. If I was a dog, you'd call me Rover and be damned pleased to have me.

'So Alaska has eight main Native groups—four Indian, two Eskimo, two Aleut—and we live together rather easily. By and large, any solution you come up with must apply equitably to all, and I assure you that the various groups will be prepared to accommodate, even though some of the small particulars might go against their own peculiar traditions. The basic problem? The Natives must have land. Next basic? They must be protected in their ownership until such time, maybe by some year in the next century like 2030, that they can make decisions about their land without these protections.'

At the end of her testimony one senator asked the question which perplexed them all: 'Miss Murphy, have you testified here today as a Native or as a non-Native?' and she replied: 'As I told you, gentlemen, I'm half and half. When

I took my oath to tell you the truth I was mindful that Alaska is eighty-seven percent ordinary Caucasian just like you, thirteen percent Native like the pure Eskimos and Athapascans. Your job is to find a solution that will enable both groups to move ahead in security and hope.'

The Alaska Native Claims Settlement Act of 1971 (ANCSA) was one of the more intricate and unprecedented bits of legislation to emerge from the American Congress, and its bountiful provisions were due primarily to the fact that the American people suffered from a guilt complex because of the shabby way they had treated their Indians. They were now determined to do better with their Alaskan Natives. It was a collection of laws of which the American people could be proud . . . as those laws were understood in 1971. ANCSA was not a solution for the ages, but it was a generous step forward at that time.

Alaska contained 586,412 square miles—an area 2.19 times larger than Texas—for a total of 375,303,680 acres. Of these the Natives were to be given 44,000,000—12 percent of all Alaska—plus a cash settlement of $962,500,000. So far so good. But to accomplish some of the goals Melody Murphy had espoused, and particularly to prevent extravagant behavior during the euphoria when Natives gained their own land, the vast acreage would not be distributed to them individually but would be delivered into the hands of twelve huge Native corporations located regionally so as to apportion the entire state among them, plus a remarkable thirteenth corporation to include all Alaskan Natives living outside the state and therefore not attached to any specific area of land.

Every Alaskan Native born before 1971 and living anywhere in the world would thus be assigned membership in one of the thirteen huge corporations and receive papers entitling him or her to a proportionate ownership of that particular corporation. For example, Melody Murphy, resident in Juneau, became a shareholder in the powerful Sealaska Corporation, one of the best managed and also favored in the quality of the land it received. Vladimir Afanasi up in remote Desolation Point became part owner of the vast Arctic Slope Regional Corporation with an acreage larger than many states. An interesting provision covered the corporation focusing on the heavily settled Anchorage area, for there most of the best lands had already passed into private ownership; the Native leaders here were allowed by Congress to select comparable government-owned lands in widely scattered parts of the United States, so that an Eskimo living in a village near Anchorage might find himself part owner of a federal building in Boston or an unused warehouse in Honolulu.

Land had been returned to the Natives, but individually they did not receive it, two provisions of the act governing this: no land accruing to the corporation could be sold or mortgaged or alienated prior to 1991, but on the other hand, no taxes could be collected from it by the state. Congress believed that this twenty-year dormant period would provide the Natives with time to master the intricacies of managing their assets in contemporary American society. It was hoped by all and predicted by some that during these two decades the Natives would prosper so outstandingly that at the end of the tutelage period they would not want to sell their shares in their corporation or in any other way dispose of their 44,000,000 acres.

But now, as if to make the chess game more demanding, Congress also encouraged the establishment of some two hundred subsidiary corporations which would control village lands and properties, and this meant that the large majority of Natives belonged to two corporations. For example, up in Desolation Point, Vladimir Afanasi belonged to the enormous Arctic Slope Regional Corporation with its vast holdings, but he also had shares in Desolation Management, the minute corporation which handled business affairs for that village.

Early in the new regime it became clear to him that sometimes the interests of the smaller corporation did not coincide with those of the bigger, of which it was a legal part, and he told his friends one day when they were far out on the ice hunting walrus: 'It would take an engineer from Massachusetts Tech and a manager from the Harvard School of Business to unravel these complexities.' Even though he'd had two years at the University of Alaska at Fairbanks, he felt himself incapable of plotting the course his two corporations should take: 'And I wonder if any other Eskimos are clever enough to do so with theirs.' The walrus hunters considered this for some time as they watched the icy sea, and one said: 'In twenty years our kids can learn, if somebody gives them the right kind of education,' to which Vladimir responded: 'They'll be the most exciting twenty years in Eskimo history.'

WHEN AVARICIOUS LAWYERS and business managers in the Lower Forty-eight learned that the Native tribes of Alaska, often illiterate and uneducated, were going to have nearly a billion dollars, plus all that land, to kick around, they developed a passionate interest in the arctic, and carpetbaggers from places like Boston, Tulsa, Phoenix and Los Angeles began to appear in remote villages, eager to guide the Natives through the intricacies of their new responsibilities, while collecting gigantic fees for doing so.

One fledgling with a bachelor's degree from Dartmouth in 1973 and a first-class law degree from Yale in 1976 had no intention of spending his life in Alaska; indeed, it was doubtful that he had spoken the name outside of grade-school geography, let alone given it serious attention. But when in the summer of 1976 he passed the bar examination with very high marks, his father gave him as a present the choice of a new car or a hunting trip into northern Canada. Jeb Keeler, who had prowled the New Hampshire hills north of Dartmouth in search of white-tailed deer, opted for the Canadian adventure. Heading due north from Dartmouth, he landed on Canada's remote Baffin Island, where he planned to shoot himself a caribou.

Probing boldly into the tundra north of the Arctic Circle, he accomplished nothing, but one night in July when there was no night he was lounging in the bar of the hunting lodge at Pond Inlet when a big, florid man wearing expensive hunting gear took a seat at his table without asking permission and said: 'Son, you look mighty glum.'

'I am. Came up here to get me a caribou . . . nothing.'

The uninvited visitor slapped the table and said: 'Remarkable! I came up here to do the same thing. And I got nothing. Name's Poley Markham, Phoenix, Arizona.'

'Somebody around here got a caribou. Look at it hanging over there.'

'That's mine,' Markham said proudly. 'But to bag it, I had to fly over to Brodeur Peninsula.'

'Where's that?'

'Smart distance due west.' He leaned back, studied his caribou, and said expansively: 'That could be one of the most important animals I've ever taken.' When Jeb asked what that meant, the Phoenix man called for a round of drinks and launched enthusiastically into a remarkable monologue which had so many unexpected twists that Jeb was enthralled:

'As you've found out, people say that caribou are very common. They're everywhere. But not when you want to shoot one. And they certainly weren't common when I tried to bag one in Alaska. Years ago up on the

Yukon River, I determined to get me the Big Eight, and I had seven of their heads on my wall in Phoenix, what hunters call "the hard ones," but damned if I could get the eighth, the easiest one of all, the caribou. ·

'The Alaskan Big Eight? Wonderful mix, a challenge for any serious hunter. The two tremendous bears, polar and Kodiak. I got them early on. Fierce effort in each case, but I did nab them. Then the two big land animals, moose and arctic muskox, difficult but it can be done. Then the two great mountain animals, maybe the most demanding of all, the goat and the Dall sheep. That's six, leaving the most difficult, the walrus, and the easiest, the caribou. ·

'Well, I flew up to a great site way north of the Arctic Circle, place called Desolation Point where there's a hunter I recommend if you ever head that way. Excellent fellow, Eskimo with a Russian name, Vladimir Afanasi. He had helped me get my polar bear and now he was going to lead me out to the walruses. Four difficult days, but I knocked down a majestic beast, and as we packed the head and tusks for shipping I said offhandedly: "Now I'll finish off with a caribou and I'll have my Big Eight."

'You know, I roamed northern Alaska searching for that damned caribou, never saw one. Someone said there were half a million caribou roaming Canada and Alaska, and I never even saw one except from a plane until the other day on Brodeur Peninsula.'

Jeb said: 'You call them the Alaskan Big Eight, but you shot your caribou in Canada,' and Markham said: 'It's the animal, not the place where you shoot it. I could well have been in Russian waters when I got my polar bear.'

Pleased by the manner in which young Keeler manifested his interest in hunting, Markham asked: 'Did you say you just passed your bar exams? From Yale? High marks? Young man, if I were you, you know what I'd do? I'd get on the first plane and fly to Alaska. And since you seem addicted to hunting, when I got there I'd keep right on flying till I got to Desolation Point.'

'Look, I'm just starting, and you're talking big bucks.'

'I am talking big bucks.'

'Nobody earns big money hunting. They spend big money.'

'Who's talking about hunting?'

'We are.'

'No,' Markham said. 'We're talking about Alaska, and after you earn your big bucks in Alaska, you spend your vacations collecting your Big Eight,' and as he uttered these words Jeb Keeler, twenty-five years old, blond, athletic, unmarried, visualized himself on the ice off Desolation Point hunting either bear or walrus and on the high ridges tracking Dall sheep and the exquisite white mountain goat. But how he would pay for such adventure before his fifties he could not guess.

Then the Phoenix man explained: 'Starting in 1967, I served as consultant to an ad hoc Senate committee on Alaskan Native land claims. Got my law degree at Virginia and always had an interest in Indian affairs. Point of my story, in 1971, Congress passed a land settlement act so complicated that no ordinary human being will ever be able to understand it, let alone administer it. On the evening of the day it was signed into law some of us lawyers met for dinner, and the oldest man present raised his glass for a toast: "To the law enacted today. It'll give us lawyers employment for the rest of the century." He was right. You ought to go up there and carve yourself a piece of the cake.'

'Why aren't you up there?' Keeler asked with the forthrightness that characterized his behavior either on the hunting ground or in class.

'I am. I'm consultant to one of the real big entities facing the Arctic Ocean. I spend three, four weeks trying to sort things out for them. Bond issues and the like. Then three weeks hunting and fishing. Then back home to Phoenix.'

'Can they afford to pay you? A bunch of Eskimos?'

'Son, have you heard of Prudhoe Bay? Oil! Those Eskimos are going to have so much money they won't know what to do with it. They'll need men like you and me to guide them.'

'Is this for real?'

'I'm doing it. So are several of the team I worked with in Washington. The Native corporations are flowing with money, and smart lawyers like you and me are entitled to our share.'

Markham was a big, fleshy man with what looked to be a flabby physique. But he loved the rigors of hunting and surprised the more athletic types when in the field, for he could outlast most of them when tracking an animal he wanted, and now, in pursuit of his hobby, he made a startling proposal: 'Keeler, I like you. I can see you understand hunting, and I'd be proud to help you bag your first caribou. I've been working hard in Alaska and I'd enjoy another trip into the field. Want to come along?'

He surprised Jeb by volunteering that he, Markham, would hire a local guide with a float plane and fly north across open sea to Bylot Island, where caribou could be expected at the foot of the glacier. It was a flight of great beauty if you liked desolate places and a feeling that the world was about to end; as they flew over the main part of Baffin Island they spotted several great herds of caribou, and Jeb said: 'How can there be so many down there, and so few when I want to find one?' Markham explained: 'That's the lure of hunting. Wait till you go out for your mountain goat.' He turned to study his young partner, then asked: 'You are going to shoot for the Big Eight, aren't you? Finest challenge in all of hunting, I think.'

'How about lions and tigers and elephants?'

'Hell, anybody can tramp through warm jungles on a safe safari. But you pit yourself against the arctic, against the Alaskan winter to get your polar bear, that's man stuff.'

When they landed, the guide took them to an area where he had often seen caribou during their yearly migrations: 'They swim right across that channel, or wait till it freezes. Fantastic animals.' On the third day, while the two lawyers were some distance from their tent, they came upon a fine buck with superior antlers, and Jeb was about to fire, but Markham restrained him: 'Good, but not perfect. Let's move quietly over there,' and when they did, they found just what this experienced sportsman had wagered: a huge buck stood at the edge of a small herd, and Markham whispered: 'Now!' With a perfect shot, learned at Dartmouth while hunting deer, Keeler dropped his trophy and tried to look nonchalant while the guide took a Polaroid of him posing beside it.

It was that photograph which determined Jeb Keeler's future, for as he was examining it during the flight back to Pond Inlet, he told Markham: 'I'd like to rack up my Big Eight,' and Markham said: 'If you come to Alaska, I'll help you get started. But the rules are a little tougher now. Guys from the Lower Forty-eight like you and me, we can't shoot walrus or polar bear or seals any longer. They're protected for the subsistence hunting of the Natives.'

'Then why did you tell me about them?' and Markham laid down the basic law of life in the north: 'In Alaska, there are ways to get around unpleasant rules that hem you in.'

'I'd like the challenge,' Jeb said, but Markham warned: 'The big-paying jobs with the major corporations have been taken, but you'll find lots of opportunities with the village corporations. Like that one at Desolation Point. I'll let Afanasi know that you're coming,' and by the time the plane landed, it was agreed that Keeler would put his affairs in order, kiss the girls from Wellesley and Smith goodbye, and head north to start his law practice in Alaska.

But on his return trip to the States, with the caribou head in the belly of the plane, he detoured to New Haven to consult with the man who had steered him through the law school and the bar exams. Professor Katz was one of those Jewish intellectuals who saw law as an interlocking of past human experience and future aspiration, and before Jeb could finish describing the Alaskan Natives' settlement, Katz stopped him: 'I followed that through the Congress. Disgraceful to make it so complicated. No way those Natives will be able to manage their corporations and defend them against greedy men from the States.'

'Then you agree with Mr. Markham that they need lawyers?'

'Indeed they do! They need guidance, technical support and meticulous advice on how to protect their assets. A bright young fellow like you could provide them with invaluable services.'

'You sound as if you'd take the job.'

'I would. For a spell, if I were younger. If you went into a New York law firm next fall, what experience would you have? An extension of what we gave you here at Yale. Nothing wrong with that, but it is limiting. However, if you go to Alaska, you'll be thrown into problems that haven't been defined yet. It's a real frontier, an opportunity to beat new paths.'

'That man from Phoenix made it sound exciting. You make it sound challenging. I'm going to think this over.'

When Professor Katz rose to accompany Jeb to the door he took him by the arm and held him close to his side, as he had done in those final weeks before the exams: 'Mr. Keeler, you're a grown man now, but you have the exuberance of youth, and in a frontier society like Alaska's, that could trap you into misbehavior. Laws for the white man are more flexible there, the rules more easily bent. If you do go to work straightening things out, take treble precautions to act honorably. I don't know any other word that applies. I don't mean honestly, because the law covers that. And I don't mean sagaciously, because that implies twisting things to your advantage. I suppose I mean honorably, the way a man of honor would behave.'

'I would hope that I've learned that from you, sir, and from my folks.'

'You never know whether you've learned it or not till you're tested by reality.'

It was under these conditions that Jeb Keeler left the East Coast for Alaska, taking with him his two hunting guns, his outdoor gear and the admonitions of his two advisers. Katz, his Yale mentor, had said: 'Act honorably'; Markham, his Phoenix mentor, had said: 'You can make a potful of money.' He intended to do both and bag the rest of his Alaskan Big Eight in the process. As a start toward his ambitions he already had that fine caribou and a first-class law degree. What he needed now were the seven other animals and an opportunity to put his legal talents to use in some constructive and rewarding way.

* * *

W HEN JEB REACHED Juneau to establish his lawyer's credentials at the state
capital, he found that Poley Markham had eased his way by enrolling him
as a member of his firm, which enabled Jeb to skip the local bar exam and get
to work within five days of leaving the airport. As Markham had warned, the
big jobs were taken, but two of the best-run Native corporations, Sealaska in
Juneau and massive Doyon in Fairbanks, found minor assignments for him,
and it was while working at these that Jeb learned the basics of serving as a
consultant in Alaska.

He had performed well in protecting the corporations' assets in a contract
with a Lower Forty-eight construction firm, and was about to submit his bill
when Markham flew in from Phoenix to supervise a business deal for his
operation on the North Slope. 'I'd be interested in checking your papers,' Poley
said. 'We want to keep things consistent.' When he saw Jeb's proposed bill he
gasped: 'You can't submit a bill like that!'

'What's wrong?'

'Everything!' and with a bold pen he struck out Jeb's modest figure, multiplied it by eight, and shoved it back: 'Have it retyped,' and when the new bill
was turned in, it was paid without demur.

As he worked about the state on these minor jobs, Jeb discovered that
Markham had served a long apprenticeship in such trivial work before landing
his present job with one of the major corporations. He had been everywhere and
had apparently offered Eskimo, Athapascan and Tlingit the brotherly kind of
help their small corporations needed in the early days. Jeb found that when he
mentioned Markham's name in the little villages, Natives invariably smiled, for
in his congenial way Poley had given these villagers not only guidance but also
a sense of worth. He had convinced them that they could manage their sudden
wealth, and one weekend when Jeb had business in Anchorage, he listened
attentively as Poley outlined his understanding of the enviable situation in
which lawyers from the Lower Forty-eight found themselves:

'Take the average village corporation, and there's more than two hundred
of them. There's certain things they have to do, the law demands it. And
there's nobody in the village able to do it. They have to incorporate, and
you know the paperwork that requires. Then they have to hold elections
for officers, with printed ballots and all. But they can't do this before they
have a complete enrollment of their members, and to achieve that they
must have forms and addresses and letters. When we know who's entitled
to the stock, the stock has to be printed and issued and registered, and that
requires lawyers.

'Now the fun begins, because the village has to identify the land it's going
to select, and that requires surveyors and legal conveyances and filings
with the government. Then we have audits for which we have to hire
C.P.A.s, the compiling of minutes, the arrangement for public meetings,
and most demanding of all, it seems to me, keeping the public and the
members informed regarding the operations of the new corporation.

'This is a lawyer's paradise, and not because we made it that way. Congress did. But since it's here and the money is in the bank, we're entitled
to drag down our share. What is our share? Well, the government gave the
corporations nearly one billion dollars. I'd say we were entitled to twenty
percent.'

'That would be two hundred million dollars!' Jeb gasped. 'Do you mean it?'

'I sure do. If you and I don't take our share, somebody else will.'

'You personally? What do you expect, I mean in real terms . . . what's possible?'

'What with one thing and another, I'll draw down not less than ten million.'

'Just what do you mean, Poley, "one thing and another"?'

'Oh, nothing really. Just the way all these deals shake out. But I do have some interesting things on the back burner, north of the Arctic Circle,' and Jeb realized that he was never going to obtain a clear picture of how this big, amiable man operated. He was about to conclude that Poley's manipulations tightroped along the edge of legality, when the Phoenix lawyer threw his arm about Jeb's shoulder and said with a laugh: 'The rule I follow is the rule you should follow: "If even eight cents in hard cash is involved, leave a trail of written receipts a yard wide." '

'I don't intend to steal.'

'Nor do I, but three years down the road some bastard will be trying to prove you did.'

Upon reflection later Jeb realized that Poley had not said forthrightly, like Professor Katz: 'Do nothing dishonorable.' What he had said was: 'No matter what you do, leave a trail of paper proving that you didn't do it,' but his attention was diverted from these moral euphemisms when Poley snapped his fingers and asked suddenly: 'Have you flown north to touch base with Afanasi? You haven't? How are you progressing on collecting your Big Eight?'

'Just that caribou you helped me bag.'

'Good. We'll fly up to Desolation and try to bag your walrus.'

'Didn't you say walrus was illegal for guys like us?'

'Yes and no.'

Poley insisted that Jeb clear his desk and accompany him to Barrow, where he introduced him to Harry Rostkowsky and his well-battered one-engine Cessna 185. 'Are we going to fly in that?' Jeb asked, and Poley replied: 'We always have. And two weeks from now it's going to fly your walrus head out.'

When Jeb learned that the distance from Barrow down to Desolation was only forty miles, he hoped that he could avoid flying in Rosty's crate, but when they were aloft, Poley pointed down to the bleak tundra below, with never a tree in sight, just mile upon mile of hummocks, near-swamps and shallow lakes: 'No road down there. Probably never will be. Up here you fly or you don't go.'

In preparation for landing at Desolation, Rostkowsky flew well out to sea, banked to the left, and as he came in low over the village of some thirty houses, a store and a school that was in the process of being built, Jeb saw to his amazement that despite the thousands of acres of unused land, the settlement was perched at the far southern tip of a spit of land exposed to the sea on one side, a large lagoon on the other. 'Snug, eh?' Rostkowsky shouted as he buzzed the place twice to alert the villagers, then dropped skillfully onto the graveled strip and taxied up to where people were beginning to assemble. Before anyone left the plane, he opened his window and tossed out two bags of mail and several parcels; then he unlocked the door and told his passengers: 'Yep. With God's help we made it again.'

When the citizens of Desolation saw their old friend Poley Markham climbing down, they began moving quietly forward, but no one made any gesture of excited welcome, and Jeb thought: If they treat an old friend with such reserve, how do they greet someone they don't like? But then he looked past Poley to the meager houses of his first Eskimo village and saw, standing off to one side, a short, round man in his mid-forties whose bare head showed that he wore his graying hair in a Julius Caesar cut, short and combed straight forward over his dark brow. Nudging Poley, he asked: 'Is that Afanasi?' and Markham said: 'Yep. He's not much for show.'

When all the villagers had greeted Markham, for he had performed many charitable services for this village, the two men walked over to greet the Eskimo who would be their guide for the walrus hunt, and Poley said: 'This is my young friend Jeb Keeler. Lawyer . . .'

'Don't you know anyone who works for a living?' Afanasi asked, and the men laughed.

In the days that followed, Jeb discovered that this quiet, capable Eskimo who owned the only truck in town was distinctive in a score of ways: 'You had two years at the university?' Yes. 'And you worked in Seattle two years?' Yes. 'And you subscribe to *Time* magazine?' Yes, three weeks late. 'And you're the head of the local school board?' Yes. And then came the question that perplexed Keeler but not Afanasi: 'Yet you prefer to live according to the old traditions of subsistence?'

In uttering this tremendously important word, Jeb Keeler catapulted himself right into the heart of contemporary Alaska, for a great battle had begun, and would continue during the rest of the century, between those Native Alaskans who accepted the inevitability of getting most of their food from store-bought cans but who also wanted to improve their lot by bagging a seal or a caribou now and then in the ancient manner, and those forces of government and modernity which sought to hammer the Native peoples into an urban, money-economy lifestyle. In the halls of Congress the struggle had been described as perpetuation of the reservation versus mainstreaming, and while this disjunction was relevant to the condition of the Indians in the Lower Forty-eight, in Alaska, which had never known formal reservations, it was not: here the struggle manifested itself as a choice between ancient subsistence versus modern urbanization. Afanasi, having experienced the best of both systems, strove to be an eclectic: 'I want penicillin and radio, but I also find great spiritual gratification in the subsistence way of life,' and Jeb was captivated when he learned what this entailed:

'You're going to hear a lot about subsistence if you work in Alaska, Mr. Keeler, so you better get the definitions lined up. In the Lower Forty-eight, I'm told it means just getting by with the help of government handouts. Subsisting on the poverty level. In Alaska the word has quite a different meaning. It refers to noble patterns of life that go back twenty-nine thousand years, back to when we all lived in Siberia and learned how to survive in the world's most difficult ambiance.'

Vladimir's use of this unusual word, and his vocabulary in general, caused Keeler to ask: 'Are you an Eskimo? You have such a wide-ranging vocabulary.' Afanasi laughed: 'I'm about as pure an Eskimo as you'll find these days,' which prompted Keeler to ask: 'But what about your Russian name?'

'Let's go back five generations, counting me as one. That's not difficult if you're an Eskimo. A Siberian married an Aleut woman, and they had a son who became the well-known Father Fyodor Afanasi, a spiritual light in the north. Rather late he married an Athapascan woman from a mission station where he had worked. His church sent him up here to Christianize

the heathen Eskimo, who promptly murdered him. His son, Dmitri, became a missionary himself, as did his son, my father. Me? I had no taste
for missionary work. I thought our problem was the challenge of the
modern world. But you asked what I was? One-sixteenth Russian without
being able to speak a word of that language. Same percentage Aleut and
equally illiterate there. One-eighth Athapascan, and not a word of that
language. Pure Eskimo, three-fourths, but when I say that twelve of my
ancestors were pure Eskimo, only God knows what that really means.
Maybe some Boston sailor blood in there, maybe some Norwegian.

'But whatever the truth, I'm an Eskimo committed to a life of subsistence.
I want to help my village take a whale or two each year. I want to go after
polar bears and walruses when I can. I want two or three caribou when
they come stampeding by. And we also live from the ducks, geese, seaweed
and salmon. And what's important these days, I want to range pretty far
afield to garner what I need to eat. And this puts me in conflict with
outside hunters like you. I don't want you flying up here to kill off my
game for trophies, taking the head back south and leaving the carcass to
rot.'

It was as succinct a summary of what subsistence meant to an Eskimo or an
Aleut or an Athapascan as Keeler would hear, and in subsequent days when he
and Markham went far out among the ice floes to hunt for walrus under
Afanasi's direction, his respect for this pattern of life was intensified. One night
as they cooked their evening meal in a tent pitched three miles from land, he
said: 'I've always considered myself a hunter. Rabbits as a kid. A deer in New
Hampshire. But you're a real hunter. You hunt or you starve.'

'Not really,' Afanasi said. 'I always have the option of going to Seattle or
Anchorage and working in an office. But is that a viable choice for an Eskimo?
Someone like me who has known what it means to be out here on the ice? Come
back when we're on a whale hunt and see the entire village join in the ceremony
of thanks to the whale. Then as we butcher our catch, everyone, even the oldest
women, stands by to receive their share of the ocean's gift, whale blubber, the
essence of life.'

On the fourth day out on the ice, when they had moved to the farthest edge
where blue open water showed in the distance, Poley Markham spotted what he
believed was a walrus hauling himself onto the ice, and when Afanasi put his
Zeiss binoculars on the spot he confirmed the sighting. Then, with a mastery
learned from his Eskimo uncles, he directed his team of three into an approach
which enabled the youngest member, Jeb Keeler, to put a heavy bullet into the
great beast's neck, but just as Jeb fired, both Afanasi and Markham, standing
well behind him, fired also, to ensure that a wounded animal was not left to
perish in the deep. The three shots were so beautifully synchronized that Jeb was
unaware that the other two had fired, and when he ran up to the fallen beast he
exulted as if he alone had slain this admirable specimen, but he had scarcely
reached the walrus when Afanasi started homeward to inform the villagers that
a walrus had been taken.

Jeb and Poley stayed out on the ice that night, protecting their kill, and in
the morning they were awakened by a file of villagers, men and women alike,
who had come to butcher the catch and haul the fine, nutritious meat homeward. It was a triumphal day, with even the children participating in the rejoicing, and when the meat was distributed several youngsters were on hand to run

portions of it to those who were bedridden. In the afternoon a dance was held, with the head of the walrus and his monstrous tusks occupying a place of honor, but now a shadow descended upon the celebration because a young Eskimo sidled up to Keeler and said: 'You know, you can't take the head home with you.'

'I can't?'

'Against the law. No sport killing of walruses.'

This so startled Jeb that he ran over to where Poley Markham was dancing a kind of jig with an elderly Eskimo woman and her husband, the three of them waddling about like ducks on land. 'They tell me I can't take the head back to Anchorage.'

'That's the law,' Markham said, leaving his dance.

'Then why did we fly up here? Just so we could say we'd shot a walrus?'

'We don't have to *obey* the law.'

'I don't want to get into trouble. A lawyer at the beginning of his career.'

'That's when you have to learn how to handle the stupid laws that legislatures keep passing,' Poley said, and when the walrus head mysteriously appeared at Jeb's flat in Anchorage, the young lawyer did not make inquiries as to how it had got there, but hung it in a place of honor.

As Jeb worked with the various village corporations throughout Alaska he observed two facts: wherever financial shenanigans were in progress he discerned the subtle orchestrations of Poley Markham, the Virginia–Phoenix–Los Angeles wizard. Suits against one corporation, legal processes in behalf of another, proxy challenges to protect this large corporation, proxy defenses to subvert the hopes of that small corporation—in all such legal battles Poley was involved, until it appeared that the man had no moral base whatever. His sole function, it seemed to Jeb, was to generate disputes between the Native corporations, then litigate them, and always at such phenomenal fees that it was rumored he was making about a million dollars a year, even though he was in Alaska only three or four months during that time. He was living proof of the prediction that the Native Claims Settlement Act of 1971 'was going to be a bonanza for the legal profession,' especially if, like Poley Markham, the lawyer seemed to have no moral compunctions.

But at the same time, whenever Jeb accepted Poley's help in garnering the next of this Big Eight, he found the man to represent the soul of generosity and sportsmanship. 'Why do you waste your valuable time helping me shoot a mountain goat?' Jeb asked one day as they were climbing the high mountains in back of Matanuska Valley.

'I love the high places,' Poley replied. 'The chase. I got as much fun watching you bag a Dall sheep as I did when I got mine.' He would permit no shortcuts in hunting; when you were out with Poley you didn't hire a helicopter, fly into some high point, duck out, and gun down a goat. Not at all. You followed Poley up steep inclines, puffing while he seemed to be tireless, and you staked out the spot where you thought the elusive creatures might pass. You waited, kept downwind of where the goats might be hiding, and you froze, and when you stumbled back without having even seen a goat, you appreciated the great respect Poley had for animals and the thrill of chasing them.

'Of the entire Big Eight,' he said one night after they had chased goats unproductively, 'I think the greatest excitement came with bagging my mountain goat.'

'Even more than the polar bear?' Jeb asked, for although under Poley's guidance he had bagged a big Kodiak, he had not yet managed a polar bear.

'I think so,' Poley said. 'To get your polar bear you just have to persist. Go out there on the ice floes. And in time you get him. But with a mountain goat you have to climb as high as he does. You have to be as surefooted. And you have to be one degree smarter. That's a tough assignment.' He considered this for some time, then added: 'I think maybe it's because he's such a handsome animal. Your heart skips a beat when you see a goat in your sights. So beautiful, so small, so high in the mountains.' He slapped his leg, pitched more logs in the fire, and said: 'Apply the attention test. I watched you when you were in my lodge in Phoenix. All the heads of my Big Eight on the walls. And what did your eyes come back to most often? That splendid white mountain goat. As if it represented the real Alaska.'

In three extended expeditions to various mountains in Alaska, Jeb and Poley failed to bring a mountain goat within range, so Keeler's campaign for the Big Eight remained stalled at six: caribou, muskox, Kodiak bear, walrus, Dall sheep and moose, in that order, had been taken, but not the polar bear or the evasive mountain goat. 'We'll get them,' Poley vowed, and his insistence upon helping kept him constantly close to young Jeb. This, in turn, led him to throw more legal business Jeb's way. For example, when the corporation centering on Kodiak Island staggered into horrendous legal battles over who had a right to sit on the board of directors, Poley was too busy with the oil companies developing the huge reserves at Prudhoe Bay to give the various proxy fights his full attention, so he passed the lucrative Kodiak case on to Jeb, who spent the better part of a year and nearly four hundred thousand dollars' worth of his time unraveling a problem which should never have arisen. At the end of his third year advising the Native corporations in their internecine brawling, he realized that before the age of thirty he was going to be a millionaire.

His real money came when Poley got him involved in the intricate legal battles centering on the great oil field at Prudhoe Bay, for then he flew to that remote location on the northern sea, walked out upon the floes that kept it ice-locked ten months in the year, and watched as men from Oklahoma and Texas kept the drills plunging downward twenty-four hours a day. His first visit to Prudhoe came in January, when there was no daylight and his body gave no advice on when to sleep; it was an eerie experience highlighted by his visit with the team from California which provided the living quarters for the men and the food: 'We've learned that to keep workmen from places like Texas up here, we have to provide three luxuries. Good pay, say about two thousand dollars a week. Movies twenty-four hours a day so that they can entertain themselves no matter when they get off work. And the dessert table.'

'What's that?' Jeb asked, and the concessionaire from California showed him: 'We keep the cafeteria open twenty-four hours, with breakfast constantly and a full dinner served whenever you want. But what makes life tolerable is the dessert table,' and he led Jeb to a large area at the end of the chow line. There, on something that resembled in size a big pool table, rested no fewer than sixteen of the most luscious desserts Jeb had ever seen: pies, pecan tartlets, cakes, blancmanges, fruit salads, 'and over here what they like best of all.' Beside the pool table, in a nest of ice, stood six fifty-quart steel containers, each filled with a different kind of ice cream: vanilla, chocolate, strawberry, butter pecan, cherry with whole cherries and a marvelous concoction called tutti-frutti. And to make the area truly seductive, on two huge plates beside the ice-cream cans rested piles of chocolate-chip or oatmeal cookies.

'Watch!' the concessionaire from California said with a degree of pride. 'That big fellow over there, he's already eaten enough dinner for three ordinary men, but now he'll hit the dessert table,' and when the Texas oilman did, he took a wedge of pie, a hunk of cake, a huge bowl of tutti-frutti and six chocolate chip cookies.

'If you keep their bellies satisfied,' the California man explained, 'they're satisfied. It's the cookies that turned the trick for us. The ice cream they expected. The cookies they appreciated as thoughtful extras.' With professional judgment he added: 'Men with a sweet tooth always take the chocolate-chips. Those attending to their health choose the oatmeal.'

On his second flight in to handle legal problems at Prudhoe Bay, Jeb was accompanied by Poley Markham, and the two lawyers had one of the most terrifying adventures in their lives. It was March, and daylight had returned to the arctic, but as was so often the case with aviation, this proved a hindrance rather than a help, for when the pilot learned from his radio range that he had to be approaching Prudhoe, he began his descent, but the light available was a silvery gray and the wind kicked up enough blowing snow to make the entire visible world one exquisite pastel, with no horizon, no sky, no snow-covered landing field. There was no time, no season, no hour of the day, no discernible anything, just this mysterious, lovely, potentially fatal whiteout.

Unable to detect in what direction—up, down or sideways—the land lay, the pilot was either unable or unwilling to deduce from his flight instruments where he was or in what attitude, so, cutting power drastically, he tried to edge himself down, and he was flying close to the ground when Poley Markham screamed 'Bulldozer!' and at the last moment the pilot pulled up in a grinding surge of power, just missing an enormous black dozer parked a hundred yards from the impoverished airfield.

Sick with fear, pilot and passengers circled in a grayness that had no definition, but gradually the omnipresent and inescapable force of gravity began to assert itself, and with the aid of his instruments, the pilot established his position relative to the snow-covered ground that lay somewhere below. Flying far out over the frozen ocean, he zeroed himself on the radio range and told Markham and Keeler: 'Keep watch. The signals are strong and good, thank God,' and gingerly the plane felt its way through the deadly grayness, and Jeb thought: I saw a picture like this in a storybook, years ago. The hero was approaching a castle, visor down on his helmet, seeing nothing. And there was a fog, a beautiful gray fog.

Jesus! The snowy field was fifty feet higher in the air than the pilot had anticipated. The plane struck while still in a flying attitude, bounced high in the air, came down again thirty feet before it was supposed to, bounced again, then rolled to a trembling stop. When the ground crew came out in a jeep riding on immense snow tires, the driver yelled up to the pilot: 'Land came up at you, eh?' and the pilot said: 'It sure did,' and the man said encouragingly: 'No pain, no strain.'

At lunch that day Jeb had a huge plate of tutti-frutti and four big oatmeal cookies.

J EB EARNED HUGE sums from his legal work at Prudhoe, and later, whenever he encountered Poley Markham on the latter's infrequent visits to Alaska, he would say: 'We still haven't nailed the mountain goat,' and Poley would remind him: 'It took me three years to get mine. Don't rush it,' and Jeb discovered that he and Poley were quite different in their attitudes. 'You like the chase, don't you?' Jeb said. 'But I want to round out my Big Eight and get it done with.'

Poley said: 'You never get it done with. Last month I took a young fellow hunting on Baranof Island, that's where Sitka is, trying to snag a goat, and it was as much fun as when I first went out on my own.'

'Poley,' Jeb said one day, 'I heard some men . . . that is, some local men from Barrow, white men, Eskimos, talking about your work over there. What's up?'

For the first time in their pleasant and rewarding acquaintanceship Poley became not just evasive, which he always was when he didn't want to answer a direct question, but almost shifty and edgy, as if he were ashamed of what he had been doing: 'Oh, they have some big ideas over there. They need counsel.' He would say no more, but in the months that followed, Jeb saw less and less of his mentor, and new men from the Lower Forty-eight began appearing in Anchorage and occasionally at Prudhoe Bay. They were a difficult lot to identify or fit into the Alaskan scene. If you saw in the airport at Fairbanks a trio of men who looked like oil-field men from Tulsa in Oklahoma or Odessa in Texas, you could bet that they were either headed for Prudhoe Bay or planning to open a short-order restaurant in Fairbanks for oil-field workers on vacation. But Poley Markham's visitors were a wildly mixed lot: a road builder from Massachusetts, a building contractor from Southern California, an electrical plant manager from St. Louis, and all of them apparently headed north of the Arctic Circle.

Then Markham disappeared for about half a year, and rumors filtered back that he was in Boston arranging bond issues of enormous magnitude: 'I got a letter from a friend associated with a small bank in Boston. He said Markham, and he had the full name, was finagling for a bond issue of three hundred million. My man didn't know what for.'

And that was the second discovery Jeb Keeler made regarding his friend: Poley was engaged in some very fancy footwork in relation to certain officials in Barrow, and the sums involved were staggering. At first Jeb believed that somehow Poley and his cronies had discovered a new oil field, but his contacts at Prudhoe Bay said: 'Impossible. We'd know about it within six hours.'

'What is he doing?'

'Who knows?' But then the oilman leveled: 'You know, Keeler, this oil field at Prudhoe pumps huge funds into the North Slope. Taxes, salaries. There's a lot of money kicking around up here, and Markham has always been the kind of man who's attracted to money.'

'So am I,' Jeb said defensively. 'So are you, or neither of us would be up here in this godforsaken place.'

'Yes,' the oil-field manager said reflectively, 'but you and I seem to work within defined boundaries. Markham doesn't.'

For almost a year Jeb had no opportunity to question Poley, for the latter spent all that time in Los Angeles and New York arranging financing for the huge operations taking place north of the Arctic Circle, but one day while Jeb was unraveling a legal bind at Prudhoe, he received an urgent letter from Markham: 'Meet me in Anchorage Friday. I think we may have your mountain goat.' Eagerly Jeb flew south on an ARCO plane, to find Poley waiting in a suite at the new Sheraton Hotel: 'Man phoned me that a large herd of goats has been seen in the Wrangell Mountains. Let's go.' They motored to Matanuska and then in to Palmer, where they both purchased nonresident hunter's licenses at sixty dollars each, with Jeb acquiring for an extra two hundred and fifty the metal tag which he would have to attach to the body of any goat he killed. Then, in a small plane which Markham had used in bringing down his own goat some years before, they flew in to the low hills at the base of the great sixteen-thousand-foot Wrangell range. The pilot, always looking to make a few extra dollars, suggested that he could land the two men well up into the mountains where the goats were likely to be, but Poley would have none of that: 'Put us where the law says we're supposed to be,' and when they were deposited with their tent and rifles, he led the way up toward the head of the valley where the goats had been reported.

When they reached the closed end of the valley, Jeb looked back and saw one of the loveliest sights of his hunting career: a herd of more than ninety nannies and their kids—not a billy in sight—grazing on rocky slopes interspersed with strips of succulent grass. One view like this, with nannies watching as their kids frolicked in bright sunlight, coats gleaming white, horns a jet-black, and the mountains looming protectively overhead, was worth a lifetime of hunting. 'Marvelous,' Jeb whispered as they drew closer to the herd, but then his hunting instinct prevailed: 'Where are the billies?'

'Hiding by themselves, even higher up,' and although he was fifteen years older than Jeb, Markham led the way out of the goat-filled valley and up a steep climb which would place them high on the flanks of Mount Wrangell, a thousand glacier-covered feet above the nannies.

'The trick with billies,' Markham explained for the third time, since Jeb had shot nothing on his previous two trips in search of goats, 'is to get well above them, because they keep looking for trouble from below, and this way we can get the drop on them.'

The tactic did not work, not that day, for the billies, who traveled in twos and threes after the rutting season ended in December, easily detected them and moved well beyond rifle range. Seeing them go, Markham said: 'Strange, isn't it? In season they fight one another furiously. Great gouges with those sharp horns, to the death if necessary. But when the passion wanes, old friends. Three weeks fighting and mating, forty-nine weeks traveling about buddy-buddy.'

'I wish some of them would buddy-buddy over my way.'

'By the way, Jeb, when does your own mating season come on track?'

As they trudged down the valley past the wonderful gathering of snow-white mothers and kids, Jeb said: 'I used to invite some pretty fine women up for the weekends at Dartmouth.'

'You mean girls?'

'The kind I invited didn't like to be called girls anymore. They made that very clear: "You're men, not boys. We're women, not girls." '

'Very tough to live with a girl like that. I've watched.'

'They're the only kind fellows like me would want to live with,' Jeb said, and Poley laughed: 'It ain't never easy, son. Regardless of what the current rules might be, it ain't never easy.'

'You divorced?'

'Not on your life! That way lies bankruptcy. My wife lives in Los Angeles, goes to cultural affairs at USC, and this may shock you, but she also takes care of our money.'

'They tell me at Prudhoe that you're making a killing on the North Slope.'

'Eskimos need guidance. They deserve the best advice they can get, and I provide it.'

'Like bond issues and proxy fights and lobbying in Congress?'

'If the United States says "Stop eating walrus blubber. It's time to move into the modern world," somebody has to show them how to make the move.'

They dropped the subject, and in the two remaining days, during which they never came close to a billy but did remain in contact with the nannies and kids, it was not reopened, leaving Jeb as uninformed as he had been when the hunt started, but as they packed to await the plane that would carry them back to Anchorage, Poley said: 'Jeb, you could do me and yourself a big favor. Vladimir Afanasi has asked me to come up to Desolation Point and sort out the problems in his village corporation. I simply haven't the time, but I owe Vlad a lot. Would you go up and see what needs doing?' Jeb said: 'I'd like to see that place again. Maybe get me my polar bear. Looks almost impossible to bag a mountain goat.'

'One problem, Jeb. I never charge Afanasi for the help I give him. He's sort of the charity that keeps me decent. And I don't want you to charge him, either. But of course, a lawyer can't work for nothing, so I'll pick up your tab,' and as the plane flew over the majestic Matanuska Glacier on its way to Anchorage, Markham wrote out a first check for ten thousand dollars.

I N THE EARLY years of Alaskan statehood, several contrasting groups of American citizens trekked northward in search of adventure and wealth. With the discovery of oil at Prudhoe Bay in 1968, roustabouts from Oklahoma and Texas flooded in to earn enormous salaries on the edge of the Beaufort Sea, a frozen arm of the Arctic Ocean. Notable were the lawyers and businessmen like Poley Markham and Jeb Keeler, who often spoke of taking up permanent residence but never did. In 1973, when President Nixon authorized the building of a gigantic pipeline from Prudhoe Bay to Valdez, construction workers poured into Fairbanks, from where they worked north and south to construct this miracle of engineering. And now the Flatch family of Matanuska entered the picture.

Son LeRoy, the aviator, was eager to become involved, but just when the oil companies at Prudhoe were sending out urgent calls for local planes to serve as couriers—spare parts needed at once, important visitors to be ferried in from Fairbanks, evacuation of an injured roustabout—LeRoy had the bad luck to crack up his postwar Waco YKS-7, so he could not participate in the bonanza.

When, in a degree of panic, he looked about to see what planes suitable for work in Alaska were available—and he insisted upon one fitted with the revolutionary improvement of permanent snow skis through the middle of which wheels could be let down—the best deal he could find was a new four-seater Cessna-185 at the frightening cost of $48,000, a price far beyond his means. Gathering his family, he said: 'I've got to have the Cessna. We're losing a fortune every day.' His wife suggested that he try to arrange a loan from a bank, but he feared that this would be impossible, since he had just cracked up his only collateral, and it looked as if the combined savings of the elder Flatches, LeRoy and his wife, Sandy, his sister, Flossie, and her husband, Nate Coop, would fall far short of the down payment.

But now the miracle of Prudhoe Bay intervened, for so many workmen were required at the site that even Elmer Flatch, crippled and in his seventies, was dragooned to serve as a paymaster at the oil rigs, Sandy Flatch was given a job as liaison in Fairbanks, assuring that workmen and their materials moved promptly to Prudhoe, while Flossie and her nature-loving husband received the best jobs of all.

'The head man came to see us particular,' Nate explained. 'He'd been hunting at our lodge and remembered the way Flossie understood bears and moose, and he offered us a deal in a way you'd never guess. He said: "Nature freaks are beginning to hammer us over the future of the caribou. They say if we build that pipeline right down the middle of their emigration routes, the caribou will be cut off from their natural habitats. They'll all die." He wants us to work with the naturalists from the university to see what can be done to help the caribou.' They were to start work immediately, and the various Flatches could save practically their entire earnings because food, lodging and transportation to the job would be paid in addition to their wages.

So it became a simple matter for LeRoy to borrow from all of them, fly down to Seattle, pick up his bright new Cessna-185 with permanent skis and retractable wheels, and fly it back to Fairbanks, where he became the busiest courier in the Prudhoe operation. With all maintenance and fuel costs covered by the company, he netted $165,000 the first year.

One night as Hilda Flatch totted up her family's income, which she banked for them, she broke into laughter, and when her husband asked: 'What's so funny?' she replied: 'Remember how they warned us when we were starving in Minnesota? "If you go to Alaska, you'll never grow nothin', and the polar bears'll eat you"?'

Salaries like these lured workmen from all over the United States, and Fairbanks was filled with the babble of strange accents as gape-mouthed laborers from Nebraska and Georgia paid $12.50-plus for a breakfast of one cup of coffee, one pancake, one egg and one strip of bacon. Dinner, of course, ran into the high twenties. Not many of these hastily imported workmen would remain in Alaska when the twin Golcondas of the oil field and the pipeline ended, but those who did remain added enormously to the vitality and excitement of Alaskan life. They tended to be outdoorsmen who loved the Alaskan patterns of life and served as the twentieth-century version of the frontiersmen. They were welcome additions.

Oil riggers, bulldozer drivers, welders for the pipeline, lawyers with vivid imaginations—such men continued the tradition of the gold-field immigrant, the daring men who built the first towns and the sailors who served on the *Bear* under Mike Healy, and once more Alaska created the impression that it was a land for men. But there were also women who sought their fortunes in this wild frontier, just as in the old days: nurses, wives, dance-hall girls, fugitives like Missy Peckham, and a few daring souls who simply wanted to see what Alaska was like.

In these years one young woman in particular experienced the lure of Alaska, and her coming north set many wheels in motion.

A FLAMBOYANT MAYOR of New York once opposed censorship by saying 'No girl was ever seduced by a book,' but in 1983 a young woman in Grand Junction, Colorado, was deceived by a magazine cover. Kendra Scott, twenty-five years old, was teaching her geography class about Eskimos of the Far North, when Miss Deller, the librarian, came to her room with two books Kendra had requested: 'I've checked these out in your name. You can keep them till April.'

Kendra thanked her, since good material on Eskimos was not easy to come by, and Miss Deller added: 'And I've brought you our latest copy of the *National Geographic*, the February issue, but you can have it for only two weeks. We have another request for it.'

Since Kendra already knew what was in the two books, she looked first at the magazine, and when she did, she was lost forever. On the cover was one of the most ravishing pictures of childhood she had ever seen. Against the white background of a blizzard in northern Alaska, a little girl—or it might have been a boy, for only the eyes were visible—was walking into the blowing snow, covered from head to toe in the colorful dress of her people: big fur slippers, blue denim trousers double thick, colorful smock edged with fur, bright beaded belt, two caps, one of white wool, the bigger one of heavy quilted corduroy edged in wolverine fur to repel ice and snow, and an enormous brown knitted scarf wrapped around her head three times. Her hands were protected in brightly decorated mittens, and Kendra could only guess that underneath the smock she must have had three or four more layers of clothing.

But what made the child adorable, and Kendra had convinced herself that it had to be a girl, was the resolute manner in which she pressed forward into the storm, her little body fighting the blizzard, her determined eyes, all that could be seen, staring ahead at the goal to be achieved despite the driving snow. It was a glorious portrait of childhood, a depiction of man's will to survive, and Kendra's heart went out to that child battling the elements.

And for a protracted spell she was not in a comfortable elementary school in Grand Junction but on the northern slopes of the arctic, and her class did not consist of middle-class white American children with a few interesting Mexicans thrown in, but a group of Eskimos living in darkness half the year and in bright sunlight nearly twenty-four hours a day the other half. Kendra had been taken prisoner by a little fur-bound child on a magazine cover and she would never again be the same.

For some time she had been aware that she ought to change, that her life was heading into such sterility that unless she made a radical shift, she was destined for a desolate, picayune existence. The responsibility was hers, that she admitted, but her mother, a distraught and frightened woman who lived with Kendra's father in Heber City, Utah, some thirty miles northeast of Provo, was a contributing factor. The Scotts were not Mormons, but they shared the stern discipline which that religion imposed, and when Kendra graduated from high school they enrolled her, without any input from her, at the respectable university in Provo, Brigham Young, where young men were taught to be FBI agents and young women to be God-fearing and obedient wives. At least, that's what Mrs. Scott believed.

'The good part about Brigham Young,' Mrs. Scott told her neighbors in Heber City, 'is that Grady and I can drive down most weekends to see how Kendra's doing.' And this they did, wanting to know what classes she was taking, whether her professors were 'decent, God-fearing men,' and checking particularly on her roommates, three girls with such disparate backgrounds that the elder Scotts had to be suspicious of at least two of them. One was a Salt Lake City Mormon, so she was all right, but another was from Arizona, where anything could happen, and the third from California, which was even worse.

But Kendra assured her parents that the two outsiders, as Mrs. Scott called them, were more or less respectable and that she, Kendra, would not allow them to corrupt her. This phrase, *corrupt her*, loomed large in the Scott set of values, for Mrs. Scott saw the world as an evil place, more than three-quarters of whose citizens were bent on corrupting her daughter, and she was morbidly suspicious of any men who hove within her daughter's orbit: 'I want you to tell me about any man who approaches you, Kendra. You simply must be on your guard against them, and a young girl is not always the best judge of a young man's character.'

So during her weekly visits to Brigham Young, Mrs. Scott pumped Kendra for a detailed report on any young man whose name surfaced during her long interrogations of her daughter: 'Where's he from? How old is he? Who are his parents? What business are they in? Why is he studying geology? What do you mean, he spent last summer vacation in Arizona? What was he doing in Arizona?' After eight or ten such grillings Kendra summoned up the nerve to ask her mother: 'How were you ever able to find a husband, if you had such endless suspicions?' and Mrs. Scott saw nothing impertinent in the question, for she felt this was a major problem for any young woman: 'Your father was raised in a God-fearing family in South Dakota and he was not contaminated by going to any college or university.' Kendra thought: Nor was he contaminated by anything else like books or newspapers or talk in a corner saloon. But as soon as she voiced this opinion to herself, she was ashamed of it. Grady Scott was a fine, trustworthy man who ran a good hardware store in Heber City, and if he lacked the courage to stand up against his wife, he had the character to run his business and his life honorably. During these long interrogations of his daughter in the Brigham Young dormitory, he rarely intruded.

In her four years at college, Kendra dated only two men, and they were so similar that they could have been twins: slight of build, washy-blond of hair, hesitant in speech and awkward in movement. The first young man had asked her out three times; the second, seven or eight. But the evenings were so painfully boring and unproductive that Kendra deemed them hardly worth the effort, especially when her mother asked at least fifteen questions about each young man and ended up by actually driving the forty-two miles south to Nephi to investigate the parents of the second young fellow. Mrs. Scott was most favorably impressed with the couple, classifying them as 'the best of Mormon society, and that's high praise.' She gave Kendra vigorous encouragement to pursue her friendship with the young man, but both he and Kendra were so embarrassed by the entire procedure—and so little interested in each other—that what Mrs. Scott called 'Kendra's courtship' ended with neither a bang nor a whimper. In fact, it didn't end at all. It just sort of tailed off like a slow groan.

Kendra graduated at age twenty-one with a B-plus average in education, and her choice of four or five good public schools in which to teach, and now came the first crisis in her life, for one of the schools was in Kamas, Utah, less than twenty-five miles from home, and both the elder Scotts felt that this was where Kendra should teach, at least for the first five or six years of her career, because, as Mrs. Scott pointed out: 'You could come home for weekends.'

In an act of defiance which startled and alarmed her parents, Kendra accepted, without discussing the matter with them, a job at the school that was farthest from home, in Grand Junction across the state line in Colorado, but even this was within striking distance of Heber City, and during Kendra's first autumn in her new school, Mrs. Scott drove the two hundred and fifty-odd miles on six different weekends to discuss with her daughter the problems she was facing, the women teachers with whom she was associating, and whatever men in either the school or the town she had come to know. It was Mrs. Scott's firm opinion that the men of Colorado were much more dangerous than those in Utah, and she advised her daughter to steer clear of them: 'Why you turned down that nice young man from Nephi, I will never know.'

'I didn't turn him down, Mother. I never had the opportunity. Nor did I seek it.'

Aware that their child was developing headstrong tendencies, the bedside prayers in Grand Junction now began to take subtle shifts: 'Almighty God, keep Your daughter Kendra mindful of Your precepts, protect her from arrogant and hasty judgments, and with Your constant supervision, help her to remain pure.'

*　*　*

THE LIBRARIAN, MISS DELLER, handed Kendra that copy of the *National Geographic* on a Tuesday morning, and during the next three days the little girl heading into the blizzard haunted the younger teacher. She did not turn the magazine over to her students, but kept it on her desk through Wednesday and Thursday, where she stared at it from time to time. On Thursday night she took it home with her, and studied it with great intensity before going to bed. On Friday she rose early, placed the magazine beside her mirror, and compared herself with that extraordinary child. In the glass she saw herself clearly and with neither exaggeration nor denigration; but whenever she compared herself with that child heading into the blizzard, she had to admit with great pain that she came off second best:

> I'm intelligent, always got good grades, and I know how to contribute to group projects. I mean, I'm not a dope, nor a recluse, nor anyone sick in the head. And although I'm not a cover girl, I'm not repulsive. Men do stare at me now and then, and I think that if I gave them encouragement . . . Well, that's neither here nor there.

> Good complexion, good posture, hair sort of blah but I've got to get rid of those braids, no cavities, thank God, not overweight, no disfiguring blemishes. Not much of a smile, but maybe one could be engineered. And I am liked by my students, I really am, and I think by the other faculty members too.

And then, with the child beside her, she broke into convulsive sobs and uttered words which shocked her as she said them and appalled her when she remembered them later: 'I'm such a horseshit fucking failure.'

Recoiling as if someone had struck her across the face, she stared at herself in the mirror, clapped her hand across her mouth, and mumbled: 'What did I say? What possessed me?' And then, when her passion subsided, she knew exactly what she had said and what had impelled her:

> In comparison with that child I'm a shameless coward. Disgustingly, I've allowed my mother to dominate me. I believe in God, but I do not believe that He sits there with a magnifying glass watching everything that an elementary-school teacher in Grand Junction is doing. I've been afraid even to go out in my snowfall, let alone my blizzard.

She grabbed the magazine, brought it to her lips, and kissed the little Eskimo girl in her heavy clothes edged with fur: You've saved my life, little one. You've given me what I never had before. Courage.

Dressing hurriedly, she marched boldly to Terrence's Tresses, the leading hair boutique of the region. Plumping herself grimly in the chair, she said: 'Terrence, you've got to cut off these damned braids.'

In some shock Terrence said: 'But, mam'selle, no one around here has braids as lovely as yours,' but she rebuffed him: 'My mother uses them to strangle me.' Since this obviously baffled Terrence, she added: 'Whenever she comes to visit me she insists on plaiting my braids—sitting me on a chair before her . . . to reinforce my captivity.'

'But what will mam'selle do to replace them? What style, I mean?' and she said: 'We'll settle that later,' and as the scissors snipped away she cried exultantly: 'Now I can breathe.'

Shorn of her burden, she and Terrence studied a score of photographs showing varied styles, and finally he said: 'If I may be so bold, mam'selle, that Dutch-boy bob would be perfect for you, clean and neat like your personality,' and she said: 'Go for it!' Deftly he applied comb and scissor and spray, producing a result which made Kendra look more sophisticated but at the same time more youthfully adventurous.

'I like it,' she said as she hurried off to school, skipped down the hall, and burst into the library: 'Miss Deller, I'm going to be very bold—'

'Kendra! I hardly knew you. What a marvelous hairdo! But what about those lovely long braids?'

'Thanks, but my problem is something quite different, and I'm embarrassed, really I am, to bring it up.'

'Shoot! I'm a good listener.' Miss Deller had short bobbed hair and a brusque manner of speech and movement; she came, Kendra thought someone had said, from Arkansas.

Kendra sat down, took a deep breath, and said: 'On the weekends, some weekends, that is, you go over to that lodge in Gunnison, don't you?'

'Several of us do. Special rates to teachers. We come from all around—Salida, Montrose.'

'What is it, exactly?'

'A kind of seminar. We invite lecturers from universities. People show slides of Arabia, Uruguay, that sort of thing. Sunday morning most of us go to church, and then we come home, refreshed.'

'Do you have to go . . . with a man, that is?'

'Heavens, no. Some do. And sometimes a teacher from here meets a keen guy from Salida, but that happens as the dice happen to roll.'

Taking a deep breath, Kendra asked: 'Could I go? I mean this weekend?'

'Of course! Some of us wondered about asking you before, but we felt you were rather . . . What shall I say? Aloof, maybe.'

'I was.' She said thanks so simply and with her head so low that Miss Deller, who was eight years older, left her desk and put her arm about Kendra's shoulder: 'What is it, kid?'

'My mother. She comes on so strong, like maybe a neutron bomb, new improved economy-size.'

'Yes, some of us have noticed.'

'I want to go with you to Gunnison. I'll leave a note on my door that I'm off for the weekend.'

'Tell her you've headed to Kansas City with a truckdriver.'

'Now wait, she's basically a good woman.'

'I'm sure that every neutron bomb is convinced that it's basically good and that whatever it does is for the betterment of mankind. Tell her to go to hell. Don't ask, just tell her you're going. We'll be expecting you.'

For just a moment Kendra feared that in asking for help from Miss Deller, she was getting in over her head. What did she know about the librarian? Was she, as her mother would have phrased it, 'a nice girl'? And what went on at the lodge in Gunnison? But Miss Deller, as if she knew what Kendra was thinking, squeezed her shoulder and said: 'It's never as bad as you think it's going to be, except when it's lots worse. If you ask me, Kendra, you better break loose.'

Returning to her desk, she snapped her fingers and said: 'I do believe you had the right idea. Just leave a note. Do that four or five times and she'll stop coming over.'

At the lunch break that Friday, Kendra ran home and typed a neat note, which read:

> Dear Mother,
>
>   I've had to attend a school seminar in Montrose. Sorry. Very unexpected.
>
>   Kendra

After hurriedly packing two changes of clothes, she gathered up her snow gear and hurried back to school, where she taught with verve about Eskimos.

FOUR TEACHERS DROVE the beautiful hundred and thirty miles of mountain road to Gunnison together—Miss Deller, a woman science teacher, an assistant football coach and Kendra—and they were a lively lot. The coach was married, but his wife had been to the Gunnison lodge and had small liking for snow sports or heady discussions, so she stayed home. After an analysis of what was wrong with the administration of the Grand Junction schools and a castigation of western Colorado politics, talk turned to national affairs, and all agreed that President Reagan represented a healthy turn to the right. Said the coach: 'High time we got some discipline in this country. He's on the right track.'

To Kendra's surprise, the other three were acutely interested in what a Mormon university was like, and since she had enjoyed Brigham Young she gave a good report, but the coach asked: 'Do they still discriminate against blacks? You know, you can't have a decent football team these days without them.'

'That's all in the past,' Kendra assured them. 'They didn't discriminate against me, and I'm not a Mormon.'

Fifteen minutes after arriving at the lodge, one of those things happened which proved once more how events that could have been set in motion only by chance had the power to alter lives: a young man who taught mathematics in Canon City, a hundred miles to the east, joined the group Kendra was talking with, carrying six mimeographed papers stapled together: 'Hiya, Joe! I followed your advice, wrote to the department of education in Alaska, and by return mail got all this.'

'What is it?' Joe asked, and the man said: 'Information. Application blanks, if you will,' and the group showed such interest in his material that he sat down, removed the staple, and passed out pages of his document from Alaska. As various Colorado teachers began reading aloud details from the pages they had received, groans, whistles and cheers filled the coffee shop: 'My God! Listen to this! "Three years experience in a good high school. Recommendations from university school of education. Rural school. You will teach all high school grades and subjects." ' At this reference to a system that had vanished fifty years ago in most of the world, the groans increased, and one man said: 'They want a miracle. Four different grades, eight different subjects, and I'll bet it's in one room.'

'It is,' the reader continued. 'Says so right here. "One general room but not overcrowded," ' and the protesting man groaned, but he was totally silenced by the next line: ' "Beginning yearly salary, thirty-six thousand dollars." '

'What?' The cry came from six different teachers, who started passing the incredible paper from hand to hand. Yes, the figure was accurate, $36,000 for a beginning teacher, with yearly increments thereafter to a level of $73,000 for high school, more for a principal. The Colorado teachers, and this was a superior experienced group, averaged $17,000, and for them to learn that in Alaska mere beginners earned more than twice as much—forget the conditions —was disturbing, and for Kendra Scott, whose salary as a novice was only $11,500, the differential was shocking.

But the single sheet which had wound up in her hands carried a message more profound than the level of salary. It came from an entity she had not heard of, the North Slope Borough School District, and it had been put together by a team of geniuses who had used all the tricks which cruise-ship companies had found useful in luring prospective passengers:

> You will fly to Seattle and board a sleek jet that will whisk you to Anchorage, where a representative of the Alaska education system will direct you to a modern hotel. There you will join fellow beginning teachers for a seminar entitled 'Introduction to the North' with colored films. Next morning the same friendly representative will deliver you to the airport, where you will board a smaller jet that will fly you past snow-tipped Denali, on to the northern metropolis Fairbanks and then to Prudhoe Bay, where oil gushes out of the ground, providing Alaska with its millions.

> From Prudhoe you will fly westward over the land of a million lakes, with an arm of the great Arctic Ocean at your right. You will land at Barrow, northernmost point in the United States. There you will spend three days visiting one of the finest high schools in the nation, after which a small, trim plane will fly you south to your school at Desolation Point, site of much Alaska history and an exciting Eskimo village whose citizens will be eager to make you feel at home.

By the time she reached the end of this paragraph, Kendra was so eager to fly off immediately that she quickly scanned the page for a phone number, and on the reverse side she found: Contact collect Vladimir Afanasi, Desolation Point, Alaska, 907-851-3305. The man's name set her guessing as to what history it summarized, and it was easily seen that the first name was Russian, but what the second signified she could not guess: Probably Eskimo, how musical! and she repeated it aloud several times. But it was the next two paragraphs that captured her imagination, and in just the way the insidious drafters had intended:

> You will not be teaching in some frontier shack. Not at all! Desolation Consolidated, one of the most modern and well-equipped schools in America, provides facilities for both elementary and high school and was built three years ago on a budget of $9,000,000. It sits atop a slight rise overlooking the Chukchi Sea and on a good day from your schoolroom you will see whales playing just offshore.

> But the thing that makes teaching at Desolation a rich experience—and don't be scared away by the name, because we love it and so will you— is the children. You'll have in your classes children of the most exciting

heritages: Eskimo, Russian, those who sprang from the New England whalers who used to frequent Desolation, and children like yourself who came from missionaries and occasional businessmen who settled here. To see your class in the morning, their faces bright in the arctic light, is to see a cross section of the best that America can provide, but if they are to attain the promise of which they are capable, they will need your help. Would you like to join us in our bright new school?

The invitation was so enticing that it dazzled her. She saw herself walking up the flight of steps leading to the big new school, which must have been built of marble to justify the budget of $9,000,000, and down the splendid corridors to her well-appointed room where some two dozen or more pupils of all colors awaited her, except that they all looked like the little girl on the *National Geographic* cover, with big fur hoods and wide scarves about their faces. Only their eyes peeked out at her, bright and very eager to learn.

When she left her quarters in the lodge to join the others for the Friday evening meal, she looked about for the young man from Canon City, and went up to him with a boldness she had never before displayed: 'Are you the man who wrote to Alaska?'

'Yes. Name's Dennis Crider, Canon City. Join us.'

She explained that she was with the contingent from Grand Junction: 'Kendra Scott, elementary school. May I have this chair?'

'You sure may. You interested in Alaska?'

'I didn't know I was when I came through those doors. But that correspondence you let me read! Wow! Are you thinking of going up there?'

'I'm thinking. That's why I wrote. And from the speed with which they responded, they must be interested too.'

'But how did you know whom to write to?' and he replied: 'Just State Education Department, Juneau, Alaska. Didn't even know if I had the right name or address, but they forwarded it to the Eskimo districts.'

'Are you considering it seriously?' and her questions became so pointed that both she and Dennis ignored the others at the table as they delved rather deeply into the possibility of chucking their jobs in Colorado and heading for the North Slope of Alaska, wherever that was; they had no map of the region, but deduced from things said that it was near the Arctic Ocean and that beyond it there was nothing but the North Pole.

They spent all Friday evening and most of Saturday analyzing seriously what steps would have to be taken if one were shifting to the far north, and the more they talked, the more practical it became for them to make the move. But Dennis pointed out a condition which had not appeared on Kendra's sheet: 'If you are accepted, you should plan to be on the job by the end of the first week in July so as to complete your plans for the winter.'

'That poses no problem,' Kendra said, but when she finally went to bed, she could not sleep. Ideas and images were thundering about tumultuously in her mind, and some of them were not flattering: What made me use those horrible words? Such words aren't a part of me. Or are they? She speculated on the possibility that she might be two people, the Kendra that her mother had groomed and pruned so carefully, acceptable to the world, and a subterranean Kendra of such tortured ambiguities that she was afraid to dig into them.

After a restless night, Kendra rose for an early breakfast, found Miss Deller sitting alone, and asked: 'Could I talk with you?'

'Yes, I noticed that you and Dennis Crider were in pretty deep consultation. Things getting pretty heavy between you two?'

'No, we were talking about Alaska. What I wanted to know, what's the time difference between here and Alaska?' Like many sensible people, Kendra assumed that a librarian knew everything, but the confusion which ensued would have disabused any listener. The two young women spent about ten minutes trying to decide whether Alaska was ahead of or behind Colorado, and then another fifteen minutes arguing heatedly as to what *ahead of* and *behind* meant. They even discussed seriously whether the International Date Line ran east or west of Alaska, and what it meant regardless of where it ran.

They were rescued by a pedantic geography teacher, a man from Montrose, who explained: 'Your question about the date line isn't foolish, not at all. Strictly speaking, it ought to cut the Aleutian Islands about in half. Eastern part Monday, western part Tuesday, the same as Siberia. But everybody agreed that it would be better if all of Alaska were on the same day, so the line takes a furious twist, first to the east so that all of Russia can be Tuesday, then an even bigger one to the west so that all of Alaska can be Monday. And then it jogs again to get on track.'

'But what about the time difference?' Miss Deller asked, and he replied: 'I can't explain anything that complex unless I explain it thoroughly.'

'Proceed, Dr. Einstein,' and he surprised them by admitting: 'I'm not sure I can give you the right answer,' and the librarian said with a friendly smile: 'But you sound as if you understand everything,' and he said: 'Trouble is, I know too much, and they've been changing the rules on me.'

Asking the waiter to fetch a sheet of paper from the desk, he took out the three colored pens he carried as part of his teacher's equipment, and sketched a surprisingly accurate outline of the Alaskan peninsula: 'At the university we had to make reasonable sketches of all the continents, but now I get just a bit hazy,' and he drew in eight lines of longitude. 'I know there ought to be eight of them from east to west, but how exactly they're numbered, I don't remember. Let's say the date line should run here. That's one-eighty, as you know.'

'I didn't know,' Miss Deller said, but he assured her that it was. 'That makes this one way over here next to Russia one-seventy east, and this one over here at the eastern edge of Alaska, one-thirty west. That is such a very wide span that it ought to have four different time zones. Geographically speaking, it's entitled to them. So Alaska ought to have the same difference in its times as the continental United States does. When it's twelve in New York it's nine in Los Angeles. When it's eight in eastern Alaska it ought to be five at the western tip in Attu.'

'Isn't it?'

'No. It's all screwed up. Alaska used to have three different time zones, with the eastern part the same as Seattle, and most of the rest something else and the Aleutians something else again. But I read the other day that they've changed everything around, so now I don't know what the score is. But I suggest we call the telephone company,' and when they did, they got hold of a bright girl who said: 'I haven't a clue, but I know how to find out,' and she called someone in Denver who said: 'Anchorage is two hours behind us. Nine o'clock here, seven o'clock in the morning there.'

When the geographer sat down, Kendra astonished them by saying: 'I'm going to call. He may not be out of bed, but he will be at home.'

'Call whom?' Miss Deller asked, and Kendra showed them the memo she had brought with her: Vladimir Afanasi, 907-851-3305. Call collect.

'Are you crazy?' Miss Deller asked, and as Kendra said: 'Maybe,' the librarian hailed Dennis Crider as he entered the breakfast room: 'What have you done to this perfectly normal young woman?' and when he heard Kendra's plan he said flatly: 'That's insane. It must be the middle of the night up there.'

'It's seven o'clock in the morning, and I'm calling Mr. Afanasi.' With that, she went to the pay phone, put in a dime, dialed zero, and said in a controlled voice: 'Person-to-person collect to Alaska,' and she gave the number. Within less than a minute a deep, husky voice came on the wire: 'Hello, this is Vladimir Afanasi.'

'I am calling about the teaching job,' Kendra said, and for the next five minutes she outlined her credentials, gave a list of people Mr. Afanasi could call if he wanted verification, and then stood with her mouth agape as Afanasi said with the most careful attention to his words: 'Before we go any further, I must inform you that I am not empowered to make you a specific offer of any kind. That must be done by our superintendent in Barrow, but since I'm president of the board, I think I can assure you that you sound like just the young woman we're looking for. You've read the details?'

'I've memorized them.' At this, Afanasi broke into laughter which concluded with a remarkable statement: 'Miss Scott, I think the superintendent will be offering you a job this afternoon.'

Clapping her hand over the phone, she turned and said: 'My God! He's offering me a job!'

Then came two questions she had not anticipated: 'Any conspicuous facial blemishes? Any crippling?'

She appreciated these questions for their frankness: 'If I were crippled, not badly, would you hire me?'

'If you could get around, more or less, it wouldn't make a damned bit of difference.'

'I want your job, Mr. Afanasi. I'm not crippled. I have no disfigurement. I'm a very ordinary person, in every way I think, and I love children.'

'Send me two photographs, and ask two of your professors at BYU—they have one hell of a football team—and your principal and clergyman to rush me references. If all's as you say, I'm sure the superintendent will offer you the job. You know the salary?'

'Thirty-six thousand. It sounds enormous.'

'Are you applying because of it?' He did not wait for an answer. 'There's a restaurant in Barrow up the line, hamburger with no onion, no cheese, seven dollars eighty-five cents. Enchilada with limited sauce, eighteen-fifty.' When she gasped, he said: 'But with your experience you'll qualify for forty-four thousand dollars, and that's what I'll be recommending to the superintendent.'

She bit her lip lest she say something foolish, then said softly: 'Mr. Afanasi, I won't be sending you a recommendation from my pastor. He would get my mother and the whole community lined up against my going.'

'You haven't told your mother?'

'No. And I mustn't till it's all settled.'

There was such a long silence in the booth, with Kendra's face indicating that no one was speaking, that her friends assumed that Mr. Afanasi had broken off communication, and they were about to console Kendra, when they could hear coming over the phone the conclusion to the interview: 'Miss Scott, if you didn't have problems, you wouldn't be interested in this job. Everybody who calls has problems forcing them to drastic behavior. I hope yours are manageable. If they aren't, don't come to the North Slope.'

Without hesitation Kendra said: 'I told you I was a very ordinary girl and my problems are ordinary.'

'I think you're telling me the truth. Now prove it.'

And that was how Kendra Scott of Heber City landed a teaching job at Desolation Point, Alaska, at a starting salary of $44,000.

H ER FLIGHT WEST from Prudhoe Bay introduced her to the vastness of her new home, for a tourist folder in the pocket before her said: 'Believe it not, Alaska has one million islands and three million lakes,' and as she looked down she saw the sun reflected from a wilderness mosaic of lakes, thousands of them and some not so small. I guess you have to accept their figures, she thought. Some country!

She landed at Barrow at ten-twenty on a bright July morning, and as soon as she entered the airport to claim her bags she was hailed by a rough voice: 'That you, Miss Scott?' and she saw coming toward her an unkempt man in his fifties. Extending his big hand, he said: 'I'm Harry Rostkowsky. I fly you down to Desolation.' When he saw her three big bags, he said brightly: 'You must be expectin' to stay awhile. Last one could take it only three weeks. That's why there's an opening.' 'But the brochure said there'd be an indoctrination period here at Barrow, three days in the new school,' and he laughed: 'Normally there is, but they need you in a hurry. Climb in.'

The brief flight at low altitude provided Kendra with an excellent introduction to her new home, for she saw below her only the bleak, treeless tundra with its myriad lakes between Barrow and Desolation and the dark, ominous Chukchi Sea beyond. In the entire flight between the two settlements she saw not a sign of human existence, and when Rosty spoke to her through the intercom, she responded: 'Emptier than I thought,' and he pointed with his left hand back toward the east: 'And it stays this empty all the way to Greenland.'

'When we land at Desolation, will you point out Mr. Afanasi for me?' and he replied: 'I won't need to. He *is* Desolation. And they're lucky to have him.' Then he added: 'He'll be your new boss, and you'll never have a better.'

Now came the long swing out over the sea, the swift drop in altitude and the sliding approach to the southern tip of the peninsula nomadic Eskimos had used as their base from time to time during the past fourteen thousand years. 'That's my new home!' she called to Rosty and she saluted Desolation Point, now an established settlement. She was astonished how vulnerable to the arctic sea its frail dwellings seemed to be, pinched as they were between the Chukchi on the west and a sprawling lagoon to the east. But she soon forgot their plight, for she was trying to spot the new nine-million-dollar school. She could not locate it among the scatter of small homes, so she supposed it must have been positioned inland to protect it from floods that might sweep in from the sea, but when she scanned the surrounding areas she still could not find it.

After Rostkowsky had buzzed the village twice, the entire population, it seemed, hurried to the landing strip, so that when the Cessna came to a halt, everyone who had business with the new teacher, and that included most of the village, was there to greet her. When she backed out of the plane, stepped gingerly upon the wing, and dropped down to the ground, there were gasps of approval when the villagers saw how young and attractive she was with her pageboy hairdo, her enthusiastic smile and her obvious delight and eagerness to meet the people she would be serving. It was an auspicious beginning, highlighted by a long, low whistle from an Eskimo boy who looked as if he might be a senior in the high school. Others cheered his boldness, and as Kendra was being introduced to members of the school board, one of them whispered to her neighbor: 'I think this time we got a good one.'

And then, from the back of the crowd, Vladimir Afanasi, bareheaded, gray-haired, clean-shaven and with an Asian face that was almost perfectly round, came forward: 'Welcome, Miss Scott. I'm Afanasi. We talked on the phone. Let's go to your quarters,' and he led her to what was called the Teacherage, a low, minimal frame building which had two side-by-side front doors. 'Mr. Hooker has this side with his wife. They're out fishing. This side is yours, all furniture and bedding are there,' and he banged open the door to lead Kendra into a compact apartment—bath, kitchen area, living room—which was smaller than any she had seen in either Utah or Colorado. But it was clean and it did have unobstructed wall space on which she could hang posters or maps or prints. It had the clear making of a comfortable home for a bachelor woman.

When Afanasi said with some pride, for he had ordered the building of this home for teachers: 'This could become a comfortable refuge for a young girl,' Kendra corrected him: 'I call myself a young woman,' and he laughed: 'Woman it will be. I've found that if people aren't self-proud, they don't amount to much.'

When her three bags were delivered and stowed in the middle of the empty room, she made no effort to deal with them; instead she said: 'Now, where is the school? I've been dreaming about it ever since that first phone interview.'

'That's it, there,' Afanasi said, taking her outdoors and pointing to a low, undistinguished one-story wandering building which, although new, already needed some repainting. To Kendra it looked like some nearly abandoned country store in a backwoods Colorado mining town that was down on its luck. Inadvertently she blurted out: 'Nine million!' and as soon as she uttered the pejorative words, Afanasi leaped ahead, turned to obstruct her passage, and thrust his face close to hers: 'It's crucial, from the first minute on, that you understand the Alaska to which you've come,' and he turned and pointed to each of the compass directions.

'What do you see, Miss Scott? Any trees? Any department stores? Any lumber warehouses? Nothing. The sea, where if we're lucky, we capture a walrus now and then, and maybe a whale. The sky which is dark half the year. And in this direction as far as the mind can reach, the tundra with not even a bush that could be burned.' In some agitation he led his new teacher into the bleak schoolhouse, which consisted of two large classrooms separated by a sturdy soundproof wall and a gymnasium much bigger than the rest of the school, a fact upon which she remarked.

'We need the gym. It's the heart of our community,' and then he began his instruction. Pointing to a nail which had been hammered into place, he said: 'This nail, that strip of wood, that pane of glass, where do you suppose they came from? We didn't go down to the hardware store to buy them, because there is no hardware store. Every item in this building had to be ordered specially from Seattle, had to be ferried up here by barge.'

'I didn't know,' Kendra said, as if making an apology for her insensitivity. Afanasi bowed, accepting the courtesy, then took her by the arm and explained the real disadvantage of being at the far end of a barge line in the arctic: 'You must understand, Miss Scott, that the barge from Seattle comes only once a year, late August usually. So if the builder of this school wants nails, he must anticipate that need almost a year in advance, for if they miss the yearly barge, he must wait a second year. Costs rise under such a remorseless system.'

'Couldn't the builder bring the nails in by airplane?'

'Ah, you see the possibilities, and believe me, Miss Scott, that calculation will form a major problem for you. You'll mull that one a hundred times next year.'

'I don't understand.'

'You can fly in almost anything you need. But your cargo, the keg of nails, for example, must be crated and taken to the Anchorage airport. From there it's flown to Fairbanks. There it transfers to the plane going to Prudhoe, where they're transshipped to Barrow. And from there Rostkowsky, in his little Cessna, flies them over the tundra to here. By barge the keg of nails, maybe thirty dollars. By airplane, maybe four hundred dollars.' He stared at her, allowing her time to digest this amazing discrepancy, and when it looked as if she understood, he pointed to various items which made the bleak school a little more congenial: 'We flew that in. We flew in the carved backboards for the basketball baskets. We flew in a great many things you'll appreciate, and in the end it cost nine million dollars.'

As he spoke she kept nodding her head, and her submission to the reality of Alaska was so genuine that he laughed and led her outside, where he pointed to the sixty concrete pilings on which the building stood: 'Why do you suppose we spend two million dollars to build those pillars before we lay a single board?'

'Floodwaters in the spring?'

'Permafrost four seasons of the year,' and he explained how, if a heavy structure was built flat on the ground, its accumulating heat would melt the permafrost and allow the building to sink right into the muck, then crack apart when the mud shifted.

He pointed to the Teacherage, in which she would be living: 'How much did it cost us to build that for you? Guess.'

When she was a child her family had lived in a modest house in Heber City and she remembered what it had cost, for her parents had agonized over what they considered an extravagance: sixteen thousand dollars. 'We had a house something like it in Utah,' she said quietly. 'Sixteen thousand dollars.'

'We spent two hundred and ninety thousand . . . so you could be comfortable when the winds howl,' and she saw that it had been built on a score of pillars.

'Did you make such decisions? As president of the board, or whatever?'

'The president of the board is in Barrow. But he listens to my recommendations.'

'Didn't it cause you some . . . ?' She fumbled for the right word, because even though she had talked with Afanasi for less than ten minutes, she could see that he was a man of strong convictions, one upon whom she must depend in the years ahead.

'You mean, did I wonder if I'd done the right thing? Never. Not even one twinge of remorse. The North Slope is getting millions of unexpected dollars from Prudhoe Bay, and I persuaded our people that the best way to spend this windfall was on education.' Leading her back to the Teacherage, he said with quiet pride: 'I gave a deposition in the Molly Hootch case.'

'The what?'

'A famous case in the Alaskan Supreme Court. Molly Hootch was a little Eskimo girl whose case clarified Alaskan law. Our constitution, which I helped write, said that every Alaskan child had the right to an education in his or her own community. But when I was young, if a child in a Native village wanted a secondary education, he had to leave home for a year at a time and go down to Sitka, and the emotional shock was fearful. The Molly Hootch consent decree changed all that, and now we have good schools all through the bleak regions, some with six students, some with twelve, but all with first-class teachers.'

'Is Desolation a Molly Hootch school?'

'We had a school of sorts here before the settlement. Molly Hootch provided us with the money to make it into a secondary school.'

'How many students do you have?' and she was amazed by the answer: 'In the high school, that's what you'll be teaching, three students, two boys and a girl. In the elementary school, that's where the principal, Kasm Hooker, and his wife . . . You'll like him, he's a teddy bear. He teaches the elementary school because he doesn't want the responsibility of the seniors who might know more than he does.'

'How many students do he and his wife have?'

'Grades one through eight, thirteen.'

Kendra was so astonished by these figures that she stopped short for a moment, and as Afanasi waited for her to catch up, she exclaimed: 'Sixteen students in a nine-million-dollar school?' and he said: 'That's Alaska. We put first things first.'

But a bigger surprise was in store for her, for when she and Afanasi returned to her apartment he pulled two chairs up to the built-in desk and shuffled through the papers that awaited her there: 'Yes, here it is, and we're almost out of time. But make out your order and I'll telephone it down to Seattle tomorrow. Just in time to catch the barge.'

Kendra understood not one word he was saying, but when he thrust before her a ninety-six-page catalogue, in fine print, she saw that it referred to groceries and household items like cleaners, toilet paper and toilet articles. 'Your supplies for the year. Ross & Raglan in Seattle have a branch that does nothing but ship goods north to people like you and me in the arctic,' and in the next two hours Kendra Scott, reared in civilized areas like Utah and Colorado, was inducted into life north of the Arctic Circle, because the time-tested R&R order forms covered everything that a normal individual or family might need during the next twelve months. In addition to the forms that dated back to the late 1890s, when Buchanan Venn compiled the first version, Kendra had the wise counsel of Vladimir Afanasi, who had helped several young teachers make out their first orders.

The amounts that Afanasi suggested staggered Kendra, who had been used to shopping twice a week for one person: 'Miss Scott, I firmly advise you to order four bushels of potatoes.'

'Where will I keep them?'

'In the cache,' and he rose, opened a door at the rear of the apartment, and showed her a storage room almost bigger than the room she was in: it was lined with shelves and had low platforms onto which barrels and kegs could be placed, and a superrefrigerator for storing meats and frozen goods. It was not until she saw the endless shelving that she appreciated the task in which she was engaged: 'I've got to order enough food for an entire year!'

'Not exactly. Like with the nails. You can, when you run out of something, ask R&R to ship it to you airmail. Can of sweet potatoes, two dollars in this order by barge, six dollars by air.'

When Kendra finished her list, Afanasi made a hasty calculation of the cost, and the barge bill came to about three thousand dollars. Kendra stared at the total, mouth gaping: 'I have no money to pay a bill like that,' and Afanasi said: 'That's why our school district pays you an advance right now . . . today,' and he handed her a check drawn on the bank in Barrow for five thousand dollars.

As he was leaving, he stopped and indicated the apartment next door, the one occupied by the principal, Kasm Hooker: 'Many people consider him one of the best teachers on the North Slope, an opinion with which I concur. Early forties, long string bean, married to a woman who adores him, came to us from North Dakota who knows how many years ago. His greatest value, Miss Scott, and never forget this, is what he does with basketball. Help him in that, and you'll make a grand contribution to our school.'

'He has a curious first name. Religious?'

'Oh, no. Hooker came from a very limited background. Not literary at all. In his first days in our school he referred to the "chasm that lies ahead," but he pronounced it with a soft *ch*, the way you say *church*. After he'd mispronounced it several times, for it was a word he relished—the entire world, in his opinion, faced chasms of the most fearful kind—one of his students came to me and said: "Mr. Hooker . . . he talks about chasms but he says it wrong,' so I had to come over to his room, he wasn't married then, and I told him outright: "The word is *chasm*, as if it was spelled *kasm*," and in his innocence when he met with his elementary classes next day he told them: "Last night Mr. Afanasi was kind enough to tell me that what I was calling *chasm* is really *kasm*," and thereafter everyone in town called him Kasm Hooker. You'll hear them cheer him at the basketball games. He's worth every penny of the ninety-four thousand dollars we pay him.'

Kendra, amazed at this figure, asked: 'And how much does his wife get?' and Afanasi said: 'She's had years of experience. Forty-nine thousand dollars.' When he was gone, she totted up the salary schedule for her school, and when she saw the total, gasped: 'One hundred eighty-eight thousand dollars for sixteen children!' And she was not yet aware of the additional $22,000 paid the part-time Eskimo woman called a 'Recognized Expert' who tried to teach the students their Inupiat language, which they ignored in favor of English, or the $43,000 paid the janitor who kept the new building operating. The grand total, which she would learn later, was $253,000, or nearly $16,000 per pupil just in salaries.

That night, the first in her new bed, she awakened at two-forty-five in the morning, sat bolt upright, and hurried to her desk, where the R&R order form lay flat beside its envelope. Grabbing a pen, she added—in the ample space provided for Miscellaneous—shelled pecans, eight pounds; heavy Karo syrup, eight one-quart cans; kumquats, one dozen cans. Then, feeling better, she returned to her bed and a sound sleep, even though it was bright daylight outside.

B Y THE TIME school opened in the fall, Kendra had ingratiated herself with two-thirds of the families in Desolation, for she proved to them that she was an outgoing enthusiast who liked children and who respected the traditions of the Eskimo. She moved from one small dark house to the next, answering questions about her childhood and what life was like in Colorado; but she also listened as local tales were told about walrus hunts and who in the village was best at tracking the great bowhead whales as they moved north and south with the seasons. However, what assured her acceptance in the community was the speech she gave one night in the gymnasium, to which most of the residents came to see how their new teacher conducted herself. The announcement billed it as 'Right and Wrong,' and some attendees were loath to appear because they thought it was going to be a missionary harangue.

How surprised they were! What Kendra did was stand before them as an unsophisticated, likable young woman from Utah and share with them the conceptions and misconceptions she had brought with her regarding Eskimo life:

> 'For some reason I'll never know, the American school system decided years ago that third grade was the ideal year to teach our children about the Eskimos. Books are written and study kits provided, and one company even sells equipment for building an igloo. I taught the Eskimo unit three times and I was real big on igloos. I had everyone living in an igloo. So when I fly in here in Mr. Rostkowsky's superjet, what do I find? Not one damned igloo.'

Her use of the near-swear word shocked some, delighted the majority, and on she went irreverently ridiculing her misconceptions about Eskimo life. In vivid words, gestures and appealing incidents, she made fun of herself, but when she had the audience laughing with her, she suddenly became serious:

> 'My study books also told me much that was true about you people. They told of your love of the sea, of the way in which your brave hunters go out to fight the polar bear and catch the walrus. They told me of your festivals and of your northern lights, which I have never seen. And I hope that in the years we shall be together that you will teach me the other truths about your way of life, because I want to learn.'

She made a special effort to make friends with her principal, and at first she found the tall, awkward man ill disposed to make friends with anyone, much less with a brash young teacher who might replace him as the leader of the school. Things remained so tentative that one day in late August, when she had been rebuffed more than once, she intercepted him on their common porch and said boldly: 'Mr. Hooker, will you come in for a moment?' and when he was seated uncomfortably in her bed-sitting room she said: 'Mr. Hooker . . .' and he interrupted: 'Call me Kasm.' She broke into laughter and said: 'They told me about your name. You handled that elegantly, I must say,' and he smiled thinly.

She said: 'I've come a long way to serve in your school and I can't do my job properly without a lot of help and guidance from you.' He nodded and said: 'You'll have my full cooperation,' but she would not accept this weak assurance: 'The children tell me that you lost your last teacher because you treated her as if she were a pariah.'

'Who said that?'

'Schoolchildren. They said you made her cry.'

'She was incompetent and Mr. Afanasi knew it. He was the one who suggested that she'd be better off in the Lower Forty-eight.'

'But you could have helped her, Mr. Hooker . . . I mean Kasm.'

The tall man sat with his hands gripping his knees in an attitude of jealous self-protection, then grudgingly admitted: 'Perhaps under different circumstances . . .'

'You'll not have that problem with me, Kasm. I like it here. I'm eager to teach, but even more eager to help you and Mr. Afanasi run a good school.' Her subtle use of Afanasi's name reminded Mr. Hooker of the fact that she had already built a solid friendship with that powerful citizen, and he began to relent, but just as he was about to say something conciliatory, the most important sound of the year echoed through the village, the belching smokestack of a vessel signaling its approach, and even staid citizens ran about the summer streets, shouting: 'Here comes the barge!' And there it was, a huge repository of goods hauled along by an old tugboat.

Its arrival launched two days of celebration, the pouring out of a vast cornucopia when the rewards of previous labors were delivered as if in obedience to some magic command: now came the cases of canned goods, a truck, a boat with an outboard motor, a forklift, stacks of clean lumber, the new hammers, the lengths of bright cloth, the books, the new lanterns with improved wicks for when the electricity failed. And always there were those modern inventions that made life in the dark months more livable: a television set, several tape recorders with two cases of batteries, a dozen basketballs and a shortwave radio. To watch the yearly barge disgorge itself at Desolation Point was to become a part of Eskimo life at a remote outpost, and Kendra was easily caught up in the activities. But she was not prepared for Mr. Hooker's gesture of friendship. When young men in their pickups began to bring from the shore the huge boxes and bundles assigned to her, he stepped forward, stationed himself in her cache, and supervised the orderly storage of her year's food. 'We want you to get started right,' he said.

The big surprise this year came on the second day toward the end of the unloading, when the supply of new snowmobiles came ashore. In Desolation even children had skidoos, as they were called, and it was not uncommon for a single family to have three of the noisy and dangerous machines. But after some dozen had been brought ashore, several watching boys whistled, for two deckhands came onto the ramp with a radically improved red-and-blue SnowGo-7, with wide treads, a molded plastic windshield and racing-type handlebars, four thousand dollars even.

'Who ordered that?' the boys cried in great excitement, and in response to many such queries, a handsome young fellow, graduated from school two years ago, stepped forward to claim the prize. A woman told Kendra: 'Jonathan Borodin. His father and uncle worked at Prudhoe. Earned a fortune.' Kendra recognized the name of a family she had not met, the proud Borodins who kept to the old ways, as opposed to Vladimir Afanasi, who accepted many aspects of the new. She wondered how the traditional Borodins had agreed to allow their son a snowmobile; it was a contradiction. But here the wondrous machine was, and as Kendra watched young Borodin push it proudly away she realized that it was going to monopolize both his imagination and his life. Turning to the woman, she asked: 'Did he do well in school?' and the answer came: 'Very well. He could have made it in college.'

'Why would his family waste so much money on a snowmobile? Instead of college?' and the woman replied: 'Oh, he went. Last year. To a fine college in Oregon. But after three weeks he got homesick. Missed "the smokin' and the jokin' " on our village streets at night. So back he came.'

Toward evening, after everything was carted away, the citizens of Desolation gathered at the shore to watch the barge weigh anchor and head north to Barrow, where it would unload the remaining cargo. How mournful it was to see the huge craft move off, to be absent for a whole year, the lifeline of the area, the big solid reminder that there was another world down toward Seattle. But especially meaningful was the moment when the barge sounded its foghorn in parting salute, for with this echoing sound the people of Desolation said to one another: 'Well, now winter begins.'

Kendra spent the rest of August and the first week of September continuing to familiarize herself with the village: the wind-beaten houses, the long, dark runways that served as protective entryways, the pits dug into the permafrost where meats were stored, the lake beyond the southern end of town from which fresh-water ice would be cut and melted later for drinking water—wherever she looked she found evidence that these Eskimos had been wrestling through the centuries with their arctic environment and had found acceptable solutions. So as she sat in the evenings playing Bingo with the women of the village, she studied them with admiration and never a shred of condescension.

They, in return, took it upon themselves to indoctrinate her properly, warning: 'You must have someone help you make clothes for winter.' As they said this they pointed back over their shoulders toward the Chukchi Sea, whose ice-free waves came to within a few yards of the village: 'Come December when the wind howls in off the ice, you got to be warm,' but Kendra was astonished at the prices she would have to pay for her gear. 'It starts with mukluks,' they said. 'Keep your feet warm, you win the battle.'

She learned that she could go two routes: 'You a beginning teacher, not much money, store sells cheap Sorrel Packs, made by machine, rubber, felt insoles and liners, pretty good. You want to be like Eskimo, you get mukluk, oogruk sealskin for soles, caribou for tops coming to the knee, mouton socks, total cost maybe two hundred fifty dollars.'

Kendra reflected only a moment: 'If I'm in Eskimo land because I wanted to be, let's go whole hog. Real mukluks.'

Her parka, the soul of the visible Eskimo costume, presented the same options: 'J.C. Penney makes a good commercial one, three hundred dollars, and lots of Eskimos wear them, because real ones too much.'

'How much?' and the answer made her head swim: 'Skins, sewing, trim to protect face . . .' On and on the list of strange items continued: 'Total about eight hundred dollars.'

The figure staggered Kendra, who had never been allowed to spend over forty-five dollars for a dress, so after a deep-breathing pause, she asked: 'Would I look silly wearing real mukluks and a store-bought parka?' The women consulted among themselves on this significant problem, then gave a unanimous answer: 'Yes.' Without further hesitation Kendra said almost happily: 'Then I'll go for the Eskimo parka.'

Not wishing to offend the Eskimo women with a question about money, she waited till she was alone with the Hookers: 'How can these poor women afford such prices? And the money they throw around at Bingo?'

Mrs. Hooker broke into laughter: 'Miss Scott, these women are loaded! Their husbands make enormous salaries when they work in the oil fields at Prudhoe. And of course, they all get that yearly bonus from the government.'

'What bonus?'

'We don't pay taxes in Alaska. The oil money flows so fast, the government pays us. I hear it'll be close to seven hundred dollars this year.'

Kasm broke in: 'Haven't you noticed that most Eskimo houses this far north have two or three abandoned snowmobiles in the front yard?'

'I was going to ask about that,' and Kasm explained: 'With the easy money it's cheaper to buy a new one than to have an old one repaired. So they cannibalize them. Steal parts from one machine to repair another.'

When the seamstresses decked Kendra in her new winter gear, with the fringe of the hood covering her face and her voluminous clothing masking the outlines of her body, she became one more Eskimo woman, a round, waddling, well-protected bundle, and she began to perspire. But the women assured her: 'In December it may not be warm enough,' and again they pointed ominously at the sea: 'The winds from Siberia. You'll see.' And now one of them said solemnly: 'Your name now Kunik. Means *snowflake.* She, me, all, we call you Kunik,' and as Kunik, the new teacher continued her campaign to understand Eskimo ways and be accepted in the community.

On opening day of her school, Kendra received a series of surprises, some pleasant, some not so. When she came into the cavernous room which could have supported forty high-school students, she found on her desk a bouquet made from seaweed and a kind of heather from the tundra, and never had she received any flowers that carried more emotional impact. Her breath caught as she tried to guess who had made this gesture of friendship, but she could reach no conclusion.

When a ship's bell on the schoolhouse roof rang and the sixteen students filed into the school, thirteen turned left for Mr. Hooker's elementary classes, while only three, a girl and two boys, came toward her section. When these three were seated at the front of the room, the place looked positively vacant, and she realized that it would be her job to fill it with activity and meaning. She was the schoolroom, not the books or the huge structure which had cost half of nine million dollars. Only she could make this inanimate place vital, and she was determined to do so.

These young people, round-faced, dark-haired, black-eyed and obviously eager, were prepared to help her breathe life into this cavern, but although she had come to know each of the three during the summer, she had not then appreciated how Asian they were in appearance when placed in a school situation. They were Eskimos and she was proud to be their teacher.

It was customary in many Eskimo schools for the teacher to address her collected students as 'You guys,' words which had a fine sense of familiarity, and from the beginning Kendra used the phrase freely. When she wanted to instill a feeling of comradeship she addressed her class as 'Hey, you guys, let's get on with the math problems.' But when she felt it necessary to establish discipline, she used 'Now listen here, you guys, knock off the horseplay,' and then they knew she meant business and order was restored.

Intuitively she liked her students, and after the first tentative questions and answers, she concluded that she had three above-average pupils, but before she could begin her serious teaching, there was an interruption which modified the whole day and indeed the entire year.

Vladimir Afanasi came into the room leading by the hand a frightened little Eskimo girl, fourteen years old, and before he had shown the terrified child where to sit, he took Kendra out onto the porch and said: 'Her name is Amy Ekseavik, last name in four syllables. Her parents are the pariahs of our village. They fish upriver six months at a time. Live in a hovel down at the far point. Amy's been in school at best seven, eight weeks a year.'

'Why is such a thing allowed?' and Afanasi said: 'It isn't. I put the Barrow police on them. She must go to school, so her parents have brought her here to live through the winter with Mrs. Pelowook.' Coming back into the classroom, he went over to the child and said: 'These are your classmates, Amy, and this is your teacher, Miss Scott.' With that he kissed the trembling child and indicated to Kendra that she, Kendra, must now take over.

But the teacher did not hear him, for at the moment when Amy first entered her room, Kendra had been struck by an overwhelming sensation: That's the little girl on the magazine cover! and the similarity between the child of six or seven and this maturing girl of fourteen was so striking that Kendra put her left hand to her face and bit her forefinger. It was a miracle, nothing less, that a replica of the child whose photograph had lured Kendra to this remote spot should now be entering her classroom. It was also a command: she had been called here to serve this child.

'You'll check her out,' Afanasi said as he prepared to leave. 'She can read and write some, but it's been a long time since the few weeks she was in school last year.' And with that, he was gone. When Kendra, too startled to react promptly, left her standing there, the girl in the class rose, went to Amy, and led her to a chair which one of the boys dragged into the circle; by that thoughtful gesture the strange child, reared alone at the edge of the world, was made welcome.

On Kendra's third day on the job she happened to find in one of her desk drawers a pamphlet which stated that the North Slope school district, of which her school was a part, contained 88,281 square miles with a total population of 7,600. Feeling already a sense of pride in what she called 'my northern turf,' she waited till school ended, then went next door to see if she could borrow Mr. Hooker's hand-held calculator, and he said almost gruffly: 'The school's supposed to supply you with one,' and he rummaged about in his desk until he came up with the fine one which had been intended for her. When she thanked him, he said: 'I probably got some more junk around here that's yours. I'll sort it out.'

The gift of the calculator surprised her, but the more she saw of this remarkable school, the more impressed she was with its generosity. Each child was given a free toothbrush, toothpaste, pencils, ballpoint pen, notebook, all reading material, a breakfast snack, a hot lunch and full health services. Teachers participated in the bonanza too: fully paid hospitalization, a life insurance policy of twice the yearly salary, no rent on housing, heating or electricity, plus the famous Thrift Plan, which Afanasi explained: 'You're invited to deposit six percent of your salary with us. Twenty-six hundred and forty dollars a year in your case. We add fifty percent to it, and on the total we pay you eleven percent each year. We don't want our teachers to go hungry.'

To test her calculator, she engaged in the kind of silly game that academic people find pleasure in pursuing: What state is about the same size as our school district; and how many of our smaller states would have to combine to be as big as we are? Using the almanac supplied by the school, she found to her intense delight that the state nearest in size was her own: 88,281 square miles for North Slope, 84,916 for good old Utah! and the thought that she was involved in a school district bigger than all of Utah staggered her.

She then proceeded to a second calculation, and found that North Slope was bigger than the ten smallest states combined, starting with Rhode Island and ending with West Virginia, but before gloating she did have the courtesy to question: Yes, but what about the population? and she found that these ten states had a combined population of more than 26,000,000 while North Slope had fewer than 8,000. Only then did she grasp the enormousness of her part of Alaska, and its emptiness.

Chubby-faced Amy Ekseavik, the newcomer, was proving to be a tough little customer; during her first two weeks in school she rebuffed any attempt to break down her reserve, and in her rugged self-determination she repelled students and teacher alike. As an only child living far from the village, she had never had friends, and the concept of being congenial with people or trusting them was alien; she had the gravest suspicions about her fellow students, and since her father and mother had treated her harshly, she could not imagine that Miss Scott was going to be much different, so for some time the atmosphere in the classroom was tense.

At this point Kendra consulted with her principal, and she discovered that where school matters were concerned, Mr. Hooker was a cautious, battle-scarred veteran who approached every problem from the point of view of 'How could this hurt me? And if there's potential trouble, how can it be defused?' With that strategy dominating, he was not at all happy to learn that the new teacher was having trouble with her new pupil, because he had reason to believe that Amy Ekseavik was for some reason or other the special concern of Vladimir Afanasi, a member of the North Slope school board, and therefore she was a child to be handled carefully.

'You say she's intractable?' Kendra was often surprised at Mr. Hooker's vocabulary, for although he had acquired an M.A. in education from Greeley, in Colorado, one of the best schools of its kind, he really was a boob, but one with latent possibilities, so she shared her apprehensions with him.

'Amy's like a wild creature, Kasm. I wonder if she was abused at home?'

'Not even a remote possibility. Afanasi doesn't like her parents, but he says they're not brutes. Eskimos never maltreat their children.'

'Then you think it's just the result of her being raised alone?'

'Possibly, and it might also be that she finds herself the youngest of your students. Maybe she would be happier, all around, if she dropped back to elementary school. I've been able to thaw out such children.'

Automatically, and with force she would not have used had she thought about how it might be taken, Kendra cried: 'Oh, no! She's where she should be. Her peers'll help her along, and I certainly aim to make her feel comfortable . . .' Suddenly realizing she was treading in a sensitive area, she backed out, saying 'help her learn,' at which Principal Hooker smiled with a depth of understanding that surprised Kendra: 'You mustn't identify with her too strongly, Miss Scott.'

'Please call me Kendra—that is, if you want me to call you Kasm.'

'Agreed. So you want to keep her? But is she learning anything?'

'She's very bright, Kasm. She shows a great capacity to learn.'

'Then stay with her. Congratulate her when she does something well, and don't be afraid to rebuke her when she stumbles.'

So during those haunting autumn days when the sun sank lower and lower in the sky, as if to warn the people of Desolation: 'Soon I shall be gone, soon night falls upon you,' Kendra worked to break down the reserve of this aloof, almost wild child who had been thrust into her life, and she was fortified in this difficult task by the fact that over her desk at home she had tacked that *National Geographic* cover showing the other Amy as a six-year-old, and the determination of that fur-bound little girl heading into the blizzard consoled her: Any child raised like that would have to be tough at age fourteen. My Amy's just the way she should be now, and it's my job to show her how much better she can be at twenty.

So the difficult educational process that all young animals must undergo if they are to be first-class polar bears or eagles continued, with Kendra applying constant love and pressure and tough little Amy resisting with all her might. The other three students, children of normal upbringing whose individual peculiarities had been knocked into conformity by contact with other children as opinionated as they, progressed rapidly under Kendra's guidance, so that Desolation High was functioning at a rate that had to be classified as far more than satisfactory.

At a church supper that marked in an accidental way the end of autumn and the beginning of the long night of winter, several parents told Kendra: 'We hear only good things about you. It was God's will that sent you to us,' but the people with whom Amy Ekseavik was boarding said: 'She never mentions school. Is she doing all right?' and Kendra said honestly: 'She seems to be coming along.'

IN SEPTEMBER, OCTOBER and early November the citizens of Desolation often referred ominously to 'the coming of winter,' and Kendra supposed they were referring to the problems of perpetual night, but one day in early November she learned the real meaning. Since the weather had grown cold, down to two degrees below zero with a light snow covering the ground, she had begun to wear her Eskimo garb, and very comfortable it was. But on this morning when she hurried from the Teacherage to the school building, she was struck by a wind of such cruel force that she gasped and puckered her face, and when her students came in swathed in protective clothing, they asked: 'How do you like real winter?'

The thermometer stood at minus-forty-two, but the howling wind roaring across the Chukchi from the wastelands of Siberia was so powerful that Barrow radio reported the wind-chill factor as 'minus-ninety-one and dropping.' It was a cold that Kendra had never imagined, let alone experienced: 'Hey, you guys. How long does this continue?' and they reassured her: 'Not many days,' and they were right, for after three bone-shattering days the wind subsided and she found that minus-twenty-two without a gale was quite bearable.

Now, in the depth of a real arctic winter when people had to draw together for survival, she learned what a superior educator Kasm Hooker was and what a superb citizen Vladimir Afanasi was, for now the gymnasium, which had accounted for more than half what it cost to build the school, became the focal point of the community. There were feasts at Thanksgiving and Christmas to which all the villagers except the parents of Amy Ekseavik brought frozen whale meat, smelts, tom cod and wonderful stews made of duck, goose or caribou. But above all, there were basketball games. Indeed, Kendra sometimes felt that the soul of Desolation Point, at least in winter, resided in the basketball games which attracted almost everyone in the community. But it was basketball as she had never seen it before, because Desolation High had only those two boys, and although they were quite good at dribbling and shooting, they did require at least three other players to make a five-man team.

The problem was resolved in this way: it was agreed by any team which played Desolation that two boys who had graduated earlier would be allowed to play, with Mr. Hooker serving as the fifth member, it being understood that he would not shoot or guard the best player on the opposing team. But whom could Desolation play? Barrow High School had a fully competitive squad of fifteen, but the six other small schools on the North Slope did not. What the school did was a tribute to the imagination of Vladimir Afanasi, who explained the situation to Kendra prior to the first big game: 'We have the money, so we pay the travel expenses of other schools to fly up here and play a set of three informal games, sometimes only two. The village goes crazy. Our boys have a great experience. And the players on the visiting teams have an opportunity to see what northern Alaska is like. Everybody profits.'

The first team imported under these conditions was from the little Yukon River town of Ruby. Eight players flew in along with the coach and the school principal, and for several days when no sun appeared, Desolation thought only of basketball, and since there was no difference between night and day, the games were scheduled for five in the afternoon, and they were something to behold, for the Desolation team consisted of Kendra's two high-school boys, Jonathan Borodin, the graduate who owned the snowmobile, another boy who had graduated two years earlier, and Mr. Hooker, six feet one inch tall and weighing one hundred and fifty-seven. They appeared in handsome warmup jackets that had cost ninety-seven dollars each and pale blue jerseys proclaiming in bright golden letters NORTHERN LIGHTS. Since three of the players were noticeably short, with Jonathan Borodin of average size and Mr. Hooker reaching toward the stars, they were quite a mixture to look at, but once the whistle sounded and Referee Afanasi tossed up the ball, a game of wild charges and changes ensued.

Kendra was amazed at how skillfully her two students could play, while Borodin was still the star shotmaker he had been when regularly enrolled in school, but at halftime the score was Ruby 28, Desolation 21. Of course, if Mr. Hooker had been allowed to shoot, or had he been permitted to guard the star of the Ruby team, the result would probably have been different. Nevertheless, Kendra was proud of her team and cheered lustily for it.

That night the Desolation team lost 49–39, but the next night the local team, even though it was a hodgepodge, sank shot after shot and won by the comfortable margin of 44–36. Next day, before the chartered plane came to take the Ruby players back to the Yukon, four hundred and forty miles due south, the two teams shared a huge breakfast of scrambled simulated eggs, a sausage made of various meats and muffins provided by Mrs. Hooker. All agreed that the Ruby visit had been a sensational success, and one of the visiting players said in a formal speech of thanks for the hospitality: 'I still believe that after we leave, the sun will come up,' and one of Kendra's boys, who had starred in the second game, responded: 'Come back in June, you'll be right!'

Now Kendra experienced the full wonder of life north of the Arctic Circle in the winter, those seemingly endless weeks of prolonged night, broken by a few hours of silvery haze at noon. Sometimes when the sun nibbled at the edge of clouds hanging over the Yukon River far to the south, Kendra would look out her schoolroom window and see shadowy figures, not distinct enough to be identified, moving slowly through the village, and she would think: I'm caught in a dream world, and none of this is real. But then the twenty-two hours of complete darkness would set in and she would say to herself: This is the real arctic. This is the one I came seeking. Then she would luxuriate in the blackness, as if only she of all the students who had graduated from Brigham Young could have the courage for such an adventure.

She was disposed, therefore, to enjoy the experience at Desolation, and whenever the women of the village arranged a festival of some kind, she helped them decorate the gymnasium and serve the refreshments, until all came to acknowledge her as a member of their community. Reports from her class were reassuring, except that dour Amy Ekseavik, the boarding pupil, volunteered no comment about her whatever.

In late December when Kendra surveyed her larder, she spotted those items which she had added to her order at the last moment, intending them to be a reward for her students, and now she dragged them forth, especially her pecans, Karo and cans of kumquats in heavy syrup. Enlisting the help of two women who had children in school, she made huge stacks of pecan-filled pancakes, links of canned sausage, piles of cookies which she decorated with the colored crystals she had ordered, and gallons of a sweet acid fruit punch made from powdered concentrate.

When all was ready, Kendra invited the entire school plus all the parents and the couple Amy lived with, and no attempt was made to bar curious neighbors who wanted to see what was happening in the school gym. Among those who gate-crashed was Vladimir Afanasi, who complimented Kendra on her gala affair and the friendly way in which she introduced the women of the village to kumquats, but the highlight of the affair for the children was the pecan-filled pancakes, and at the end of the feast even Amy Ekseavik admitted grudgingly: 'They were good.'

As Kendra watched Mr. Afanasi move off to talk with men of the village, she saw that he had in tow a stranger, and in her first glance at this white man, apparently from the Lower Forty-eight, she was swept by an impression which she would never forget: that he was someone of importance who had been sent to Desolation not by accident but in the completion of some grand design. He was young, medium tall, well groomed and had an engaging smile. He did not look her way, but his blond hair was so outstanding among the Eskimo men with whom he stood, that she could not help glancing at him, and when a break came in the entertainment the students had arranged, she wandered casually over to where Afanasi was speaking, and when he saw her coming he moved toward her as if he had divined her intentions, took her by the hand, and led her directly to the young stranger: 'Miss Scott, may I present my counselor-at-law, Jeb Keeler.'

'Welcome to our school festival, Mr. Keeler, Counselor . . . ?'

'Dartmouth and Yale Law,' Afanasi explained, 'and he's invaluable to this community.'

'You mean you work here?' she asked, and eager for the opportunity, Afanasi spelled out the unique relationship young Keeler had to the village and its citizens. Kendra was impressed and asked: 'Do you have a house here?' and Jeb replied: 'I stay with Mr. Afanasi. Most of my work is with him, and it's convenient.'

She lingered with the men several minutes more than necessary, then became aware of her intrusion and excused herself awkwardly, revealing the favorable impression the young lawyer had made upon her. But this was not an embarrassment, for she had made the same impression on him. He had once told his mentor, Poley Markham: 'I kissed the beauties at Wellesley and Smith goodbye,' and he had, but in neither Juneau nor Anchorage, where he continually met people in his legal work, had he met any women who interested him, and now to find in Desolation a young woman as attractive and able as Kendra seemed to be a dividend not to be ignored.

As the gala ended, he maneuvered his way toward where Kendra stood bidding the women of the village goodnight, and as the last of the guests left he asked: 'Would you have breakfast with me tomorrow? At Vladimir's, of course, but we cook up some mighty good chow.'

'I would like that,' she said with a disarming smile. 'But you know, Mr. Afanasi is my boss, and I have to be in my classroom at eight.'

'I'll pick you up at six.'

'But why so early?'

'I have a lot of questions I'd like to ask,' and she nodded.

She was up before five the next morning, and was waiting impatiently when at a quarter to six a knock came at her door, with Jeb Keeler standing on the stoop to escort her to Afanasi's for breakfast. As they walked through the dark, her arm linked in his, she sensed that he was just as eager for this conversation as she, and the idea pleased her enormously. It was her first real date between peers, a planned affair with excitement on each side, and she was gratified in some inexplicable way that it was occurring so far north of the Arctic Circle.

After breakfast Afanasi had the good sense to improvise a meeting on village matters, which took him quickly from his house.

'You come here on legal matters?' Kendra asked, and on this invitation Jeb explained his relationship to Poley Markham and the services the two lawyers had provided the Desolation corporation. From there he led her through the intricacies of the Native Claims Settlement Act, on which he had become something of an expert, so that when Afanasi returned, she was able to ask him: 'What do you think the result will be in 1991, when you Eskimos gain full title to your lands?'

'You've been talking heady stuff, eh?' He poured himself some coffee and sat with them for the next hour, discussing frankly the perplexing problems his people were facing: 'I'm happy about the condition of our local Desolation unit. With sober advice from Poley Markham at the beginning and Jeb here in recent times, we've protected ourselves. Haven't lost money, haven't made a great deal, but have held on to our land constructively. But the big corporations? Ah, now I'm worried. The good ones prosper, the poor ones are in danger of going under. And if they do, when 1991 comes around they'll be eager to sell out to business-men in Seattle.'

'Could that happen?' Kendra asked, and Jeb broke in: 'The wolves are gathered at the campfire. Just waiting for 1991 and a chance to grab millions of Alaska's finest acres. Once gone, the Natives will never be able to recover them. A whole way of life shot to hell.'

As they discussed this mournful prospect, Jeb's strategy became clear to Kendra, and she respected him for it: 'I think that about half the big corpora-tions are doomed. Technically they're in bankruptcy now, or close to it. I judge that those lands are already lost, unless the federal government steps in with some kind of rescue operation. But I do believe that many of the village corpora-tions can be saved and their lands protected far into the future, and that's what I'm trying to accomplish with the ones I work for.'

At this point Afanasi became almost poetic in his defense of the Eskimo's traditional relationship to his land: 'My land is not this empty tundra, measured in white man's acres. My land is the open ocean, frozen solid in winter, highway for walrus and seal and bowhead whale in spring and summer. Enough safe land for the houses of my village, enough free ocean to ensure the harvest of the sea on which we've always depended.' He snapped his fingers: 'Come on, Miss Scott, quarter to eight. You ought to be in your classroom!' and he led Kendra and Jeb to the school.

JEB KEELER'S COUNSELING with the corporation leaders required him to remain in Desolation for nine days, and each evening spent with Kendra deepened his interest in her; he found her an intelligent, alert young woman with concerns paralleling his own, and with the shy kind of humor that a man like him appreciated. He wanted a woman to be almost his equal in brain power, but not to be too aggressive about it. He particularly esteemed her maturing attitudes toward the Eskimos, a people he had taken under his protection.

'At first when I looked at their dark, scowling faces I thought: They hate the world, but then I discovered that they were merely marking time till they sized me up. Once I passed muster, they blossomed like peach trees in spring.' When he agreed that it took time to interpret the apparent reticence of the Eskimos, she wanted him to meet her four students, so he arranged his duties with Afanasi so that he could spend the afternoon in her class, and there he made a great hit with the three students from Desolation but no impact whatever on Amy Ekseavik, who glared at him as if he were the enemy.

This so challenged him that at the conclusion of his stories about hunting caribou in northern Canada and his skiing days at Dartmouth, he bade the three local students a warm goodbye but asked Amy to stay for further discussion. Dropping her head, she peered at him from behind dark bangs and reluctantly agreed.

'You said nothing in class,' he began, 'but I could see that you had more questions than any of the others, and I'm sure yours would have been the most interesting. Tell me, what was it you wanted to ask?'

Chin on her chest, hair covering her eyes, she mumbled: 'Do all men like you have white hair?'

'It isn't white. It's what we call blond. Sort of like Miss Scott's.'

'In magazines I see lots of women with hair like yours. Never no men.'

'There are a great many of us around, Amy.'

'Why you come here? What for?'

'I bring papers from the government in Juneau, in Washington. You know the big capital in Washington?'

'Sure.' The firmness of her response encouraged him to ask her a variety of questions well calculated to test the accumulated intelligence of a girl of fourteen, and both he and Kendra were surprised at the depth and scatter of her learning. Finally he turned to arithmetic, and again she surprised him with her facility: 'Amy, you're one of the brightest girls your age I've ever met. You see many things you never talk about, don't you?'

Obviously pleased but also deeply embarrassed at this probing of her secrets, she finally raised her face slightly, looked directly at Jeb, and gave him one of the widest, most encompassing smiles he had ever received. From that moment on, Jeb and Amy were partners, and whereas Kendra had been unable to thaw the self-frozen child, Jeb brought out all the hidden warmth that nestled in this taut bosom, and the more Amy revealed of herself and her extraordinary gifts of perception and understanding, the more Kendra and Jeb realized that they had discovered a burgeoning human being who could achieve almost anything to which she directed her unusual mind.

'We've got to organize it so she can get to college later on,' Jeb said, and Kendra agreed: 'She's practically ready now. I'm sure the University of Washington will have scholarships for a girl like this.'

That evening, Jeb's last in Desolation, they wandered for some time in the darkness, with the thermometer at minus-twenty-nine. The cold, with almost no humidity, was bracing rather than destructive and they almost reveled in it. 'Not many American lovers wandering about in minus-twenty-nine,' Jeb said, and she drew back: 'I didn't know we were lovers,' and he said: 'We could be, tonight.' And when they reached the Teacherage he wanted to follow her inside, but she rebuffed him: 'No, Jeb,' but then she weakened her answer by reasoning: 'Everyone in the village would know by morning,' and he said: 'Ah ha! You wouldn't mind if we were in some neutral place like Anchorage,' and her silence betrayed the fact that this was her precise attitude.

She embraced him with ardor and lingered on her doorstep so that he could respond again and again. He was by all odds the most desirable young man she had ever met, a lawyer with deep respect for the law, a friend to the Eskimo and, as he had proved in his adroit thawing out of Amy Ekseavik, an adult who could project himself into the world of children. She was in love with Jeb, and under different circumstances, where their privacy would be ensured, she would have been ready to prove it, but since she shared the Teacherage with her principal and the prying eyes of the villagers, she had to be constrained.

'Jeb, you're the most precious thing to enter my life in a score of years. Please, please let's keep in touch.'

'If you feel that way, and me the same, why not let me in?' and she said, with no great firmness: 'Here, it's not possible,' and he asked: 'But if you came to Anchorage on a visit? Would it be possible then?' and she said: 'Don't rush me,' which he interpreted properly as: 'Probably.'

HER ATTENTION WAS distracted by a chain of events engineered by Vladimir Afanasi, who seemed determined to prove that Alaska was both bizarre and unique. On the first of January he learned that payments from the oil fields at Prudhoe Bay were going to be several times what his board had anticipated, and he announced in public meeting: 'Good! It frees our hands,' and that afternoon he called for Harry Rostkowsky to fly him out to Barrow, where he caught the Prudhoe Bay plane to Anchorage. There he took a hotel room at the airport, visiting intensively with the local managers of all the dozen international airlines that flew over the North Pole to Europe, and in the end he found that the best price for what he had in mind would be with Lufthansa, which refused to allow German business to be lost to some other airline.

With a firm contract for at least as many round-trip tickets as he needed, he hurried back to Desolation, and at a big meeting in the gymnasium revealed his plans: 'Citizens of Desolation, by careful supervision and our good luck in having teachers like Kasm Hooker and Kendra Scott, we have in our village one of Alaska's finest Molly Hootch schools.' The crowd applauded as Mr. Hooker waved to them: 'But it's difficult to sustain morale and learning in the winter months that loom ahead.' He stopped here and allowed general discussion of this irrefutable truth: to run a school even this small was most difficult when there was no daylight.

'What you propose doin' about it?' a fisherman asked, and Afanasi evaded giving a direct answer: 'I have never wanted to run a parochial school here in Desolation.'

'What's *parochial*?' a man asked, and a woman replied: 'Catholic,' and Afanasi corrected her: 'It can mean Catholic, you're right, but in another sense it can also mean *narrow-minded* or *limited.*' As he paused to allow this to sink in, Kendra thought: What in the world is he leading up to? and she looked for a clue from her principal, who shrugged his shoulders, for he too had been left in the dark.

'We want our students to understand the world south of the Arctic Circle, don't we? Isn't that why we fly our basketball teams down to places like Juneau and Sitka? Why our dancers and Eskimo Olympians compete in Fairbanks? Well, this time we're going to broaden their horizons in a way not tried before. Ten days from right now, just about all of our students, two of our teachers, three of our board members and three mothers to act as chaperones are going to fly in a chartered plane to Anchorage, board a Lufthansa superjet and fly to Frankfurt, Germany, where we will have classes on the history of Central Europe, after which we'll fly to six other German cities to see what a major European nation is like.'

There were gasps, cheers, wild excitement among the schoolchildren, then a sobering question: 'Who's gonna pay for this?' and Afanasi's resounding answer: 'The school board. Our budget can stand it.' Then he recapitulated: 'We'll pay like I said. Twelve students. The five real young ones will stay here with Mrs. Hooker. Two teachers. Three board members. Three mothers as chaperones. That's twenty. And if some of the rest of you want to pay your own way, and it'll be a bargain, we can accept five more.'

Because the salaries at Prudhoe Bay had been spectacular in recent years, five volunteers shouted their names, with Kendra noting that Jonathan Borodin, the nineteen-year-old with the snowmobile, was among them. Before the meeting ended, all details of the safari to Germany were agreed upon; Kendra and Mr. Hooker compiled lists of vital data for Mr. Afanasi to take to the federal building in Fairbanks in the morning for the issuance of passports, and boys' suits and girls' dresses were hastily refurbished.

In their classes Mr. Hooker and Miss Scott dropped all other studies to conduct crash courses on German geography, history and music. One mother had old copies of the *Geographic* covering Germany and another had recordings of Beethoven's Fifth and selections from *Faust*. Children drew maps of Germany, and little Amy Ekseavik surprised everyone by drawing a fine map of Alaska, in the middle of which, displaying its insignificance in comparison with the North Slope and Yukon Valley, was shown Germany, East and West, drawn to the same scale. Amy would not tell the other students why she had done this, but after school she whispered to Kendra: 'I want to go, but it's no big deal.'

'There you're wrong, Amy. For two thousand years this part of Europe'— and her right hand almost obliterated Amy's Germany—'has dominated this part of the world. It isn't always bigness that counts.' And on a spur-of-the-moment impulse, she grasped Amy by both hands: 'You're a young girl, Amy. You could be so very much. Mr. Keeler said, "You could be anything you wanted to be. Anything."'

'You're in love with Mr. Keeler, aren't you?'

'I'm in love with Alaska, and all it stands for. I'm thrilled by the wonderful capacity you have stored inside of you. When you go to Germany, Amy, look, and weigh, and listen, and for God's sake, learn something.' She released Amy's hands and stepped back. From the door of the schoolroom Amy turned to stare at her teacher, recalling and evaluating all that had been said.

The expedition to Germany was a flawless success. The various planes took off on time. Lufthansa's publicity people peppered European papers with stories and photographs of the Eskimo schoolchildren. Museums, zoos, castles and industrial centers arranged special tours for the visitors, and one financial newspaper carried a long analysis of the financial structure of the North Slope and its petroleum bonanza. The reporter calculated that this commendable school adventure, which was apparently going so well, had cost Desolation Point not less than $127,000, all paid out of oil royalty funds. Afanasi issued a corrective: 'Only twenty of our people had their expenses paid by the school board, and this expenditure was roundly approved by the citizens. The other six paid their own fares, because they wanted to share in the experience.'

He was right in his numbers. There were twenty official members of the party, plus the five who had volunteered that first night in the gym, plus an unexpected traveler who asked to join the party when it reached Anchorage. Jeb Keeler, lawyer to both the Desolation corporation and the school board, had felt that he ought to come along as a counselor to Afanasi, and he did not deny to himself that the thought of spending time with Kendra in Europe influenced his plans. She was flattered by this proof of his sincere interest, and no two members of the expedition had more joy in the trip through Germany than they. In fact, their pleasure in each other became so obvious that one of the chaperones told the other two: 'We've been watching the wrong ones,' but everyone approved of the relationship, and speculation rose among the older students as to whether Mr. Keeler slipped in to Miss Scott's bedroom in the various inns at which they stopped.

One of the subjects that Kendra discussed with Keeler would have surprised the students: 'Jeb, I know this may infringe on the lawyer-client relationship, but I have to know. The way Afanasi throws money around, this trip for example, is he stealing from the corporation?'

Jeb gasped, then grabbed Kendra by her shoulders: 'That's a rotten question. Afanasi's the most honest man I know. He'd cut off his right arm rather than steal a penny.' Shaking her, he growled: 'And you can testify to the world that I said so.'

She was not rebuffed by his spirited defense of his friend: 'Then where does he get his money?' and he banged a table with his fist: 'Dammit, none of your people from the Lower Forty-eight believe it, but up here Prudhoe Bay money flows like water. Afanasi's school board has money. I have money. My partner Poley Markham has money—all of it legal, all of it verified by receipts. Now accept the facts. Up here money is very common.'

The observer who took the keenest interest in the sometimes stormy courtship was Amy Ekseavik, for her attachment to Jeb Keeler had intensified as she watched his courteous behavior in Germany, and she already had a proprietary interest in Miss Scott, because she, Amy, had been the first to detect that her teacher had fallen in love with the nice young lawyer. On several side trips Jeb and Kendra asked Amy to come along, and they were constantly amazed at her mastery of things German. 'Amy,' Kendra cried one day in the Munich Pinakothek, 'you're speaking German as if you'd studied it,' and she said: 'I have,' and she showed them the cheap phrase book which she had practically memorized. That night, after a romantic interlude which moved the lovers much closer to an open avowal of their plans, Kendra said: 'If we ever do get married, I want to adopt Amy,' and Jeb agreed: 'We'll send her to Dartmouth.'

The expedition provided two delightful surprises: the American ambassador invited the Eskimos to a formal luncheon in Bonn, and then arranged for a sleigh-ride outing in the nearby countryside, with a halt at a rustic German inn where musicians in costume played old German folksongs and danced with the Eskimos.

As the silvery days of the German winter passed, with the visitors thinking often of the bleak darkness back home, Kendra became aware of something she had not noticed before: Jonathan Borodin was a surprisingly able young man. She had known him only as a rather brash fellow who had no job but did have that very noisy snowmobile whose echoes seemed to disturb her class whenever she was trying to make an important point. During her first six months in the village she had not liked Jonathan, but now as she observed him on the trip, and saw how he cared for the younger children as if he were their uncle, she realized that the boy had possibilities, and she was so disturbed that he was not continuing with his education that during their trip into East Berlin she took a seat beside him in the bus and asked: 'Jonathan, why did you drop out of college?' and he replied in surly tones: 'I got hungry for village life,' and she said without inflecting her words: 'Like maybe "smokin' and jokin'"?' and he replied: 'It's our way of life.'

She bit her lip, for she knew that if she ridiculed his pathetically limited vision, she would lose him: 'But I've been watching you, Jonathan, and you have unusual talents.'

'Like what?' he asked, half offensively, half with a desire to hear more.

'You're an excellent manager. Get an education and you could work any-where, Anchorage, Seattle, maybe a congressman's aide in Washington.' When he looked at her in surprise, she said: 'I mean it. You have special talents, but if you don't develop them, they'll wither.'

He gave an arrogant answer, one that many young Eskimos might have given in these heady days: 'I can get a job at Prudhoe Bay anytime I need one. Make four times as much as you do teaching.'

She stiffened, for such kind of talk she would not accept: 'Who's talking money? I'm talking about the entire future of your life. You drift off to Prudhoe, work there three or four years, waste your salary, and what do you have for the rest of your life? Think about it, Jonathan,' and with obvious disgust she rose and stomped off to another seat.

He was a young fellow of some spirit, for later that day, when they were back in West Berlin, he looked for her and asked if he could take the chair next to hers in the restaurant. 'Please do,' she said, and he astonished her by revealing that he occupied a somewhat special place in Desolation: 'My grandfather, you don't know him, but you think Mr. Afanasi is the big man in the village. Corporation, yes. School board, yes. But the real man is my grandfather,' and he proceeded to share with her the remarkable gifts his grandfather possessed and the power he exercised over events like the birth of a child or the catching of a whale. Finally, she laid down her knife and fork, stared at him, and asked: 'Jonathan, are you telling me that your grandfather is a shaman?' She had heard the word several times since coming to Alaska, so she was well aware of the extraordinary powers shamans had once exercised in those northern parts, but she had never dreamed that a real, live shaman could have existed into the present. Desolation had a Presbyterian minister, eleventh in line since that fateful day when Captain Mike Healy of the *Bear* had put Dr. Sheldon Jackson ashore with timbers to build a Presbyterian mission and staff it with a converted Dmitri Afanasi. Everyone in the village was Presbyterian, always had been, and it was startling to think that a shaman from the ancient days coexisted with the church, conducting a subterranean form of religion to which the villagers sur-reptitiously adhered. It was heathenish. It was impossible. And it was exciting.

When the group returned to Munich, the German Tourist Board, delighted with the favorable notices the Eskimos were receiving, provided free tickets to the four high-school students, both teachers and the adults in the party to a performance of grand opera in the historic Munich opera house. 'I'm sorry it's not for an easy opera like *Carmen*,' explained the woman who would accom-pany the group, 'but its effects are magnificent, and I'll explain the action. Wagner's *Die Walküre*. Music you'll never forget.'

Amy Ekseavik, of course, procured a copy of the libretto and prepared both her fellow students and her elders for what they were about to see, and with assistance from the guide, the people from Desolation were able to follow the intricate story. Kendra, who had never seen an opera, sat behind the students, with Jeb Keeler on her left and Afanasi on her right, while Jonathan Borodin sat in front of her, but two seats away, so that she could see much of his face, and when the brooding music began and the ancient Norse customs started to unfold, it was clear that the effect upon Borodin was profound. No other student and none of the adults followed the mysterious grandeur of the Wag-nerian scene with the intensity that he did, and this prompted Kendra to ask Afanasi during the first intermission: 'Is it true that Jonathan Borodin's grand-father is a secret shaman?'

The question had an explosive effect on the wise, cultivated leader of the

Desolation community, for he turned abruptly to face Kendra, and asked with force: 'Who told you that?' and she pointed to where young Borodin sat alone in a kind of trance, staring at the great curtain which masked the stage.

Afanasi remained silent for some moments, then leaned toward Kendra so that Borodin could not hear what was being said: 'We live in a dual world. The Presbyterian minister reminds us of Christian values we've respected for the last hundred years. But the elders remind us of values we followed for the last ten thousand years.' He wished to say no more, but when Kendra said nothing, he grasped her by the hand and assured her: 'Shaman? In the ugly old sense of that word? No. Magic? Cures? Curses? None of that. But a conservator of valued ancient ways we've followed? Yes.'

And there the matter ended, except that during the last two acts of the opera, Kendra saw that Jonathan was transfixed by the majesty on the stage, the dominance of the gods, the wonder of the scenic effects and the power of the singing, the action and the invocations. Like all the Eskimos, including Afanasi, he was seeing an interpretation of northern life that was eerily foreign yet familiar. The guide had apologized when telling the visitors what the opera was going to be, but what she could not have known was that it would be one of the very best to show this group from another northern world.

As they filed out of the grand theater, the most impressive building the Eskimos had ever been in, Kendra found herself walking beside Borodin, and she asked him what he had thought of the opera, and he replied: 'They could have been Eskimos. It was like our story,' and when little Amy Ekseavik caught up with them, she said: 'They lived in a cold land too, didn't they?' and the magic of the performance continued to manifest itself throughout their late supper and the conversation that followed.

O N THE FLIGHT home, Kendra received tardy instruction concerning two verboten subjects of discussion in an Eskimo community, and the repressive warning came from the most worldly of the Desolation community, Vladimir Afanasi. Sitting beside him on a portion of the flight, she congratulated him on how successful the expedition had been, and said: 'You did it. When I first heard your proposal to take practically the whole school to Germany, I said to myself: "What a cockamamie idea!" Two days in Berlin straightened me out,' and he replied that it would not have been possible without the help of two teachers like Kasm and Kendra: 'People underestimate Mr. Hooker. He's one of those fortunate people in the world who find exactly where they want to be, and it's the place they ought to be. He wouldn't be any good in the high school, where you have to teach specific subjects, because investigators are going to be testing your students. Do you know what he teaches?'

'I've often wondered. When I get his students, they aren't up to speed, as I'm sure you know.'

'He teaches the glories of Eskimo life, the walrus hunt, the great whales. He's rather good at simple arithmetic.'

'I've noticed that.'

'But he despises things like poetry and history and traditional children's stories. Says they're all bunk. What he does stress is the glory of Notre Dame football. And he encourages his students to follow the old Eskimo arts, like carving and basketmaking and skin-work.' He reflected on this for some moments, while both he and Kendra studied the tall principal from the rear, then Afanasi said: 'In our Molly Hootch schools the curriculum tends to be whatever interests the teacher, and you just pray to God that he or she is interested in something. What, doesn't seem to matter much.'

This encouraged Kendra to say: 'You know, Mr. Afanasi, we have a near-genius in this little girl Amy Ekseavik.'

'You mentioned that before.'

'And she told me the other night in Frankfurt that she might have to drop out of school.'

'Why? She's doing superbly, what I hear.'

Kendra knew that what she was about to say was pejorative, but she had no warning that it was going to be as explosive as it proved: 'She told me that her father drinks too much and she might have to go back and help her mother.'

She could hear Afanasi suck in his breath and click his teeth: 'Miss Scott, there are two aspects of Eskimo life that we do not wish to have ventilated, especially not by strangers who come here from the Lower Forty-eight.' His dark face furrowed in anger, he pointed his finger at Kendra and said harshly: 'Do not comment on our drunkenness. Do not spread stories about our rate of suicide. These are problems which hide in the Eskimo soul, and we do not appreciate preaching from others. In your case in particular, still a stranger among strangers, I would advise you to keep your mouth shut.' Trembling with an old fury, for he had had to give this lecture to many white men and women who moved among the Eskimos, he left his seat and did not resume speaking to Kendra for the rest of the trip, but when they reached Desolation and the father of one of the high-school boys appeared at the plane too drunk to recognize his son, a common occurrence with that man, Afanasi pointed to him and said to Kendra: 'It's the canker that gnaws at our soul. But we have to bear it ourselves. You can add nothing, neither condemnation nor hope. So please do what I so rudely suggested. Keep your mouth shut.'

Tight-lipped, Kendra started looking more closely at the local situation, and she saw that beneath the good humor of the gymnasium meetings and the lively entertainments to which she invited the parents of her pupils, there was a silent undercurrent composed of the two dark streams that infected Eskimo life: the drunkenness that had been cynically introduced by the Boston whalers like Captain Schransky and his *Erebus*, and the general malaise that had been introduced with the best intentions by the missionaries like Dr. Sheldon Jackson, the bearers of the white man's law like Captain Mike Healy and his *Bear*, and the promulgators of education like Kasm Hooker and Kendra Scott.

Such a wealth of change, all of it defended as superior to the ancient ways of the Eskimo, had been too much to absorb in so few generations, so that this malaise, a sickness of the soul, evolved, with the all too frequent result that those who did not find refuge in drunkenness found release in suicide. Ignorant of the true situation, Kendra had not taken count of the men in Desolation who were drunks, nor had she the information to list the suicides over the past five years, but now that she had been alerted to the two dreadful burdens of the Eskimo, she compiled a sorrowful dossier.

One informant, an elderly woman, unknowingly revealed the cause of Afanasi's harsh reactions: 'His grandfather, missionary, he was man come from God, come to help us. He bring many good things. Many times he try to keep alcohol away from the village. But always white men bring it back. Much money. That Afanasi try to help lost ones. Always he say "turn to God," but nothing change. And his sons. They lost too. One, Vladimir's father. He always drunk. He should be strong hunter. But he die young. His brother Ivan, uncle to Vladimir, he become very quiet. No more talk. No more fish. No more hunt. Just stop. Then he shoot hisself.'

The woman halted her story, studied the young schoolteacher for some moments, and added: 'Eskimo sickness jump generations like salmon upstream. First Afanasi noble man, but both his sons destroy selves. Our Afanasi in next generation noble man, but you heard what happen to his son?'

'I didn't,' Kendra said, and she gasped when the woman said: 'One day, no reason, he shoot hisself.' Shaking her head, she concluded: 'Maybe someday Vladimir's sister in Seattle have a grandson, maybe noble man too.'

THAT FIRST WINTER ended with such a savage chain of days in which the thermometer stayed always below thirty and often forty, that Kendra sought to provide respite from the boredom that attacked her students. She told them of the wonders of Salt Lake City and Denver and tried to explain what a rodeo was, and when she learned that one of the Barrow teachers had brought back from a vacation in Honolulu some high-quality movies of the islands, she asked Mr. Hooker if he had funds to invite the teacher down to talk to their students, and he said: 'We'll throw it open to the whole community,' and it was a festive evening.

But along with the colorful shots of tropical flowers and hula dancers throwing fiery swords from one to the other, the film had an unusual segment which the teacher introduced with special care: 'We're now going to witness the dedication of a new high school. See the lovely murals . . . imagine a gymnasium with open sides . . . that's a bell tower. But what I want you to see is this old man—he's coming to bless the building before anyone can enter, reassuring the gods of the islands that all is in order. He's a kahuna . . . he speaks with the gods. He's what we would call a shaman.'

The film showed the solemn ceremonies, the mountains behind the new school, the wonderful craggy face of the kahuna as he asked for a blessing: 'But I want you to see especially those four men in black looking on . . . Catholic priests. They don't like kahunas but they've invited him to bless their school . . . and can you guess why?' And she stopped the film and said solemnly: 'I want you to study these next pictures carefully. Eight months before what you've just seen, an earlier version of the school was finished . . . students about to come to class. And someone warned the Catholic priests: "You better have the kahuna bless your school because if the gods aren't happy, it might burn down." The priests said: "Nonsense!" . . . and look what happened!'

She showed film taken earlier of the huge fire consuming the school, and after several minutes, when the fires abated and the ashes were visible, she said: 'The kahuna had warned them and they hadn't listened, so this time when their school was ready, they had him come in. He wears about his neck the leaves of a sacred tree, the maile. He prays to the god of fire: "Don't burn this school" . . . to the god of winds: "Don't blow down this school." And now he blesses even the priests who had fought against him: "Keep these good men in health and help them to teach." And now the old man blesses us all: "Help everyone to learn." And the school had no more troubles, for the Hawaiian shaman had protected it in the proper way.'

The effect of this film on Jonathan Borodin was so disturbing that he could not sleep, and toward two in the morning he came banging on Kendra's door.

'Who's there?' she called.

'Jonathan. I have to speak with you.'

'In the morning, Jonathan. I'm sleeping now.'

'But I must. I have to see you,' so against her better judgment she put on her robe, opened the door gingerly, and admitted the distraught young man.

His problem was unique. Both in Germany and in the film he had seen that sensible men and women revered the ancient ways, and that treasured beings like shamans survived in both cultures. 'What's wrong with my grandfather?' he asked, so abruptly and so combatively that she drew back and said quickly: 'Nothing at all, Jonathan. I hear he's a fine man. Mr. Afanasi said so.'

'Afanasi!' the boy repeated with contempt. 'In our little village he opposes everything my grandfather does. But in that big city they respect their shamans. They know they're needed.'

Suddenly, without any warning, he fell heavily upon her bed, trembling as if caught by some wracking force, and after several attempts to control himself, he said softly: 'I see things that others don't see, Miss Scott. I know when the whales are coming back.' When Kendra said nothing, he caught her hand and said quietly but with great force: 'That new girl you like so much, Amy, dreadful things are going to happen to her. She'll never go to college the way you want her to. I'm not going either. I'm going to be a shaman.'

With that, he rose, bowed toward where she stood, thanked her for her help, and said at the doorway: 'You're a fine teacher, Miss Scott, but you won't stay at Desolation very long. You represent the new ways, but with us the old ways never die.' Before she could respond he was gone, closing the door silently behind him.

He left a bewildered Kendra, aware that she should never have allowed him entrance to her room. As to his announcement that he intended to follow in his grandfather's steps and become a shaman, she understood the psychological impact the opera in Munich and the kahuna's performance in the film had had, but because her knowledge of Alaskan history was imperfect, she had no basis for judging whether his decision to become a shaman made sense or not. She was distraught and failed to sleep until nearly five in the morning.

She was inclined to report the night's bizarre events to Afanasi, but she judged that this would not be fruitful, for while the Eskimo leader had tried to be impartial in his judgment of shamanism, she had seen that he opposed it in even its mildest and most ineffective survival. What she really wished was that Jeb might have been there, for she knew that his appraisal would have been sober and relevant. In this unsettled frame of mind she prepared to complete her exciting first year of teaching, and sometimes in the late afternoon as spring approached the still-frozen north, she stopped young Borodin as he sped along on his snowmobile and tried to talk with him about returning to the university with the coming of summer.

Cryptically he referred to other interests, saying that he might look for a job at Prudhoe Bay, then adding: 'Anyway, whales will be arriving on their way north next week,' and with that prediction uttered so carelessly, she was catapulted into the heart of ancient Eskimo experience. For on Thursday the village exploded with excitement when scouts from Afanasi's umiak stationed at the edge of the landfast ice along the inshore lane of open water reported over their portable radio: 'Lookout at Point Hope radioed five bowheads heading our way.'

Afanasi, who had been waiting many days for just such a report, stopped by the school in his pickup, shouted for Kendra to join him, then waited impatiently while she slipped into her Eskimo gear. 'You'll see something now!' he cried exultantly as they went down to the edge of the ice, where a skidoo waited to skim him over the shore ice to the open water of the lane. 'I don't like these things,' he told Kendra, 'but jump on,' and over the rumpled ice they sped, picking their way through the hummocks.

When they reached water and the waiting umiak, they were greeted by Afanasi's crew of five tested whale hunters, and Kendra watched with admiration as Afanasi deftly eased himself into position, lest his heavy feet puncture the sealskin bottom.

The whale hunters of Desolation, and any man who took pride in his reputation wanted to be one, used two kinds of craft: the traditional umiak rowed by hand when the bowheads came close to the edge of the landfast ice, and an aluminum skiff with outboard motor when the lane water was wide and the whales stayed far from shore. Afanasi, as the conservator of old ways, abhorred the skiffs as much as he did the noisy skidoos. He was an umiak man.

Moving lazily north up the narrow lane of free water, hemmed in on both sides by thick ice, came four adult whales, two of them more than fifty feet long and weighing fifty tons each according to the rule 'One foot, one ton,' accompanied by a youthful one not more than twenty feet long, and in stately procession the whales approached the hunters. 'Oh!' Kendra gasped as she stood alone at the edge of the ice. 'They look like galleons coming back to England after a tussle with the Spanish.'

Now Afanasi, as the most practiced and respected hunter, took over, and from the rear of his umiak, not much different from those constructed in Siberia fifteen thousand years earlier, he and his five helpers set forth in freezing seas to harpoon themselves a whale. When the huge lead whale sounded, they knew from long experience that it might stay submerged as long as six or seven minutes, and they assumed that they had missed it. But on came the others, and when they too sounded at irregular intervals, Afanasi's men feared that they might have lost their opportunity. When the second fifty-footer reappeared, it had moved over to the far side of open water, where it slipped by unscathed, but one of the smaller ones, about forty feet long, sounded well south of where Afanasi and his umiak waited, and an Eskimo who had come to stand beside Kendra said: 'That one's gonna come up right where Vladimir wants it,' and about five minutes later the whale broke through the surface, spouted, and to the disgust of the men in the umiak and those watching from shore, immediately sounded again with its great flukes thrashing, and disappeared before any of Afanasi's men could attack it with any likelihood of success.

'Oh!' the man standing beside Kendra groaned with a pain that was obviously real, and when she looked at him for an explanation, he told her: 'The International Whaling Commission, Russia and Canada and them, wanted to halt whaling altogether. But our Alaska Eskimo Whaling Commission said: "Hey! It's our way of life. Allow us a few each year."'

'How many did they give you?'

'Desolation? Our quota? Two.'

'Per year?'

'Yep, and for the past two years how many do you think we landed? None.' He spat, looked out at the open water, so tantalizingly close, so inhospitable, and as he did, the third whale, still far off, broke the surface in a thunderous breach as if to tease Afanasi and his men.

'Has he lost them?' Kendra asked, and the man said: 'If anyone can catch us a whale, it's Afanasi. Lifetime he has nine. I have two. Nobody else has more than four. That's why he's headman in our village.'

Kendra turned to look at the man: 'You mean he's headman because he's brought in more whales than anyone else?'

'Miss Scott, in Desolation it don't count that he went away to college. And it don't count that he has more money and a Ford pickup. What does count is that he can take his umiak, which he mends himself in the summer season when the whales are finished, and go out and catch whales when the rest of us can't. In this village'—and he pointed back over his shoulder—'it's whales that make the difference.'

Now the second of the medium-sized whales surfaced unexpectedly at the tail end of the procession, but this time Afanasi was prepared to act. Signaling the two specialists who must kill the whale—the first man holding the harpoon, the second the high-powered rifle—he brought his umiak into exactly the proper position, and in the early years of the century it would have been the gunner who would have fired first. But too many whales were wounded and then lost in that procedure, so now the law prohibited the rifleman from firing until the harpoon had struck.

So, with the frail umiak positioned close to the monstrous whale, the harpooner drew back his right arm, brought it forward with great force, and landed the point of his harpoon just behind the whale's ear. Immediately two bright-red rubber floats four feet in diameter and attached to the harpoon's rope spun into the sea, forming a drag from which the whale would not be able to escape. One second after the point of the harpoon cut its way into the whale's neck, the heavy charge of explosive carried just below the point detonated, destroying much of the whale's muscular system. At that moment the rifleman fired a blast into the base of the whale's neck, and the great sea beast was mortally stricken. Harpoon point, explosive in the body, rubber floats and finally the devastating shot: it was too much for even a forty-ton whale to survive, and its blood quickly reddened the Chukchi Sea.

But now it showed why it was the leviathan of the oceans, for despite its terrible wounds, it continued moving north to rejoin the other members of its pod, and it kept on this course, always lagging farther behind, until it actually passed from the sight of the villagers watching on the edge of the ice. Miles up the coastline, when hunters from another umiak sped out to help finish it off with their explosive harpoon and rifle, the noble beast made one last effort to pull away from the braking bladders, failed, turned on its right side, and perished.

Afanasi, seeing the whale die, slumped on the rear bench of his umiak and felt no sense of triumph; it was the tenth successful whale hunt in his lifetime; he was the undoubted master of this northwestern coast; but he had lost a friend: 'Oh, gallant fighter! We honor you!' And he began to sing an old song out of respect to the whale who would bring food to all the citizens of Desolation Point. A thing of mystery had happened, the taking of a whale after two years of failure, and he was awed by the significance.

SINCE IT REQUIRED four hours for the men of the two umiaks to raft the dead whale back to Desolation, it was past midnight in a silvery light when the carcass finally approached the ice on which Kendra waited. Two huge block-and-tackle devices, each housing five stout pulleys, had been positioned about fifteen feet apart, with one massive rope roven through the pulleys back and forth. 'What are they doing?' Kendra asked, and a man interrupted his work to explain: 'When we pull six feet on that end of rope, the block and tackle . . . tremendous leverage . . . what you call mechanical advantage. You'll see the whale move maybe six inches.'

She could see nothing on the ice that would serve as an anchor for the inboard end of the device, and certainly no tree or post on shore to which to lash it, but now two teams of men began cutting very deep holes in the ice, about four feet apart, and when everyone was satisfied that the holes were deep enough, a skilled man let himself down into one of the holes and dug an ice tunnel from the bottom of one to the bottom of the other. Then, when another heavy rope was passed down one hole, through the tunnel and up the other, it provided an anchor that could not be dislodged.

The other block was run out to where the whale waited against the edge of the ice, fastened to its great hulk, and activated when Afanasi shouted: 'All hands! All hands!' Everyone from Desolation who was on the ice at that moment grabbed the free end of the rope and began straining to pull the whale's block toward the ice-fastened one, and as the man had predicted to Kendra, the mechanical advantage provided by five pairs of pulleys produced such force that slowly, unmistakably the great whale began to worm its way onto the ice and then across it toward safety.

One of Afanasi's team, watching his whale brought home, raised a flag which he traditionally flew at such moments—THANK YOU, JESUS!—and women knelt to pray.

'Come on!' Kasm Hooker shouted to Kendra as she stood watching. 'It's your whale too. Lend a hand,' and she took her place on one of the ropes, helping to haul the whale the final ten yards onto the landfast ice.

She would always remember the haunting quality of the next few hours— the pale spring light that suffused the arctic night; the excited concentration of almost everyone in Desolation as they pulled together on the huge ropes; an old man, bareheaded, solemnly raising a pennant in the wind to signify the taking of a whale, and the chanting of the old women singing songs inherited from their grandmothers and their grandmothers' grandmothers as the great whale was slowly pulled up onto the shore. Oh, night of triumph! And as Kendra watched the people about her she realized that she had never known them before. She had seen them only as semibewildered Eskimos, whom she had learned to love as they wrestled sometimes unsuccessfully with the white man's ways; now she saw them as masters in their world, finely tuned to their environment and following time-proven ways of survival in the arctic. She was in awe of anyone who could contend on equal terms with the arctic seas. The education of the Eskimo children had begun last September when they appeared before her for their schooling; her education began this May night when silvery light glistened on the ice.

Once the whale was secured, men with long poles tipped with sharp blades stepped forward for the butchering, but they hesitated until Afanasi, their peerless Eskimo, guide and protector of their district, made the first ceremonial cut, and as he drew his flensing knife across the tail and then a fluke, he was not a Native who had gone to college and worked successfully in Seattle and run a profitable village corporation; he was an Eskimo, his gray-sandy hair brushed forward till it reached his eyebrows, his hands red with the blood of the whale.

Cheers rose to grace his victory. The other men sped to the butchering. Young people rushed forward to receive their chunks of muktuk, the delicious wedge of chewy outer skin and succulent inner fat. And as full daylight broke over the spot on which Desolation rested, people rejoiced that they had once again proved their ability to take a bowhead whale. Kasm Hooker, thinking it time to take his young teacher back to her quarters, said with some surprise: 'Kendra! You're crying!' and she said: 'I'm so proud to be a part of this.'

But what she enjoyed most, even though it was less spiritually rewarding than the capture of the whale, came much later, in mid-July, when meat from the slaughtered whale was taken from the freezers and the four village umiaks were dragged ashore, tilted on their sides to provide protection against the bitter winds blowing in from the Chukchi, and rested there as gathering spots for the various groups into which the villagers had historically divided themselves. Mr. Hooker was invited as an honored guest into the shadow of Afanasi's umiak, Kendra into the one owned by Jonathan Borodin's family, and she was pleased when Jonathan was called forth to receive a ceremonial cut of meat out of respect for his having predicted when the whales would come past the point. 'How did you know?' Kendra asked him when he returned to her side, and he said: 'He told me,' and for the first time she looked up into the face of an old man who walked with a rude cane fashioned from a length of driftwood which had been washed ashore after some massive storm in Siberia.

The man was Jonathan's grandfather, convinced that his spells had brought the whales to Desolation, and she observed that he looked upon her with disfavor. The young man made no effort to introduce her, and silently the old man withdrew from the festivities.

It was a gala afternoon, an explosion of Eskimo spirits, with their foods, chanting and quiet, sometimes motionless dancing. At the height of the celebration, each umiak sent forward a young woman to participate in the highlight of the day. The men of the village gathered around a huge circular blanket made of several walrus hides stitched together, picked it up and pulled it taut. Then into the middle climbed one of the competing girls, and at a signal, with rhythmic movements which alternately loosened and tightened the blanket, the men all tugged outward, tossing the girl high in the air. The Eskimos had done this on the shore at Desolation for fifteen thousand years, and it still sent chills down the spine to see human beings fly aloft like birds.

But this day was to be special, for when the competition ended, Jonathan Borodin suddenly pushed Kendra Scott forward to the blanket, and a cheer went up urging her to try, and with a courage she did not know she had, she allowed herself to be moved toward the blanket, but she was much relieved when Afanasi came forward to caution the men: 'Not too high.'

Standing in the middle of the blanket, she felt its instability and wondered how she could maintain her balance, but once the up-and-down motion started she felt herself miraculously kept aloft by the blanket's rhythm. Then suddenly she was fifteen feet in the air, all arms and legs. Her composure gone, she descended in a heap.

'I can do better!' she cried as she sat up, and on the second try she did. Now I'm an Eskimo! she said to herself as she was lifted out of the blanket. I'm part of this sea, of this hunt, of this tundra.

A FEW DAYS after Desolation's celebration of the whale and while her mind still echoed with reverberations of that awesome capture, Kendra was vouchsafed an ugly glimpse of the flip side of subsistence, for one of her students dashed into school with exciting news: 'Miss Scott! Hurry to the shore. A new breed just floated in!' And before she could ask him what he meant he led her to the seashore, where the obscenity exposed repulsed her so acutely she nearly vomited.

'What is that dreadful thing?'

'The new breed.'

'What do you mean?'

'A walrus with no head.' And when she studied the sodden mass she saw that the boy was right. It was the corpse of a walrus, but it had no head and in its bloated condition it looked as if it had never had one.

'How did this happen?' she asked, and the boy said: 'The law says that because you're white, you can't kill a walrus. But because I'm an Eskimo who lives on walrus meat, I can.'

'Nobody lived on this walrus.'

'Or on any of the other new breeds. Eskimos kill them, like in the old days. But now they cut off only their heads. For ivory. The rest can rot.'

'How shameful!' and as details of contemporary hunting unfolded, the rotting carcass on the beach became increasingly repulsive. 'Does something like this happen very often?' she asked, and he replied: 'All the time.' He kicked at the wasted meat of the huge corpse: 'Kill them just for the ivory.'

As the months passed, Kendra found along the shores of the peninsula many such bloated remains of animals that had once majestically commanded the ice floes. In ancient days they had fed scores of people; today they fed no one, and the ugly process was defended by naïve sentimentalists who cried: 'The walrus must be preserved for the Eskimos who use him for subsistence.' But the great beasts were really used to fill curio shops with gimcrackery for tourists from the Lower Forty-eight.

When Kendra brought this hideous miscarriage of law to Afanasi's attention, she saw again what an excellent man he was, for he was prepared to admit the anomalies of the situation: 'We Eskimos take refuge in the word *subsistence* in contradictory ways revolving around the word *ancient*. We want government to respect our ancient rights to whale and walrus and polar bear. Also our rights to vast areas of land we hunted over in times past. And we demand special consideration where land rights are concerned.'

'You're a principal champion of such rights,' Kendra said admiringly.

'I am. They'll be the salvation of the Eskimo. But I also see the nonsense in the claims. My ancient hunters want to use radios to track whales, and skidoos to rush out to the edge of the whales' lane. And outboard motors when they get there. And explosive harpoons to help kill the whale, and the best block-and-tackle money can buy to haul them onto the landfast ice. And when they feast on their catch, they demand Coke and Pepsi to wash it down.'

'But could you return to the true ancient ways, even if you wanted to?'

'No. And if next year NASA devises some trick whereby whales can be spotted by lasers bounced off the moon, we Eskimos will enshrine that device as a time-honored segment of our revered ancient ways.' He laughed. 'Is it any different in Utah? Didn't your Mormons finally accept blacks as part of the human race only when they needed them for your football team?'

'I'm not a Mormon, and sometimes I suspect you're not an Eskimo.'

'Wrong again. I'm the new Eskimo. And with help from teachers like you, there'll soon be thousands like me.'

IN THAT TRYING period when spring had officially arrived but violent storms still gripped the tundra, all the widely scattered schools across the vast North Slope enjoyed a three-day holiday so that their teachers could convene for a Wednesday-to-Sunday professional seminar in Barrow, and Kendra especially looked forward to this opportunity to inspect the famous eighty-four-million-dollar high school in that town. It was arranged for Harry Rostkowsky to fly down to pick up Vladimir Afanasi, Kasm Hooker and Kendra Scott, but when another board member said that she would like to attend the sessions, a curious situation developed: Jonathan Borodin, the would-be shaman, stepped forward with the suggestion that since he was already planning to go to Barrow on his snowmobile, Kendra could ride with him the relatively short and safe distance of forty miles. With the same daring that had prompted her to try the blanket toss, she agreed to the proposal, and when both Afanasi and Hooker warned against it, she replied: 'I've always wanted to see the tundra, and Jonathan is an expert with his SnowGo.'

'The SnowGo is a great killer of cocky young fellows who think they know how to operate it,' Hooker said.

Nevertheless, early on Wednesday morning, when a wondrous light from the returning sun suffused the shoreline of the sea, the two adventurers set forth, with Kendra, her bag and two gallons of spare gasoline stowed behind Jonathan as they set out on a northeast heading for Barrow. Since his machine could do more than forty miles an hour at top speed, he and Kendra figured to be in Barrow well before Rosty left in his plane to pick up the others, and since he could also make well over forty miles to the gallon, they faced no danger of running out of gas in an area so bleak and forlorn that not a single sign of human occupancy would be visible during their entire trip.

Kendra reveled in the journey, and the fact that she was making it with Jonathan posed no problems, for she was six years older than he; a kind of mother-son relationship had developed between them, and he had shared with her many ideas and imaginings that he would never have told anyone else.

However, at the halfway point of their journey she became aware that he had quit the northeast heading which she knew they needed to follow to reach Barrow. He was heading almost due west, right toward the still-frozen Chukchi, and in some perplexity she tapped him on the shoulder: 'This isn't the way, Jonathan.'

Without turning to answer, he shouted: 'You're going to see something, believe me,' and after a run along the edge of the ominous sea he stopped at a monument rising from the bleak tundra, and without dismounting, Kendra read the solemn message:

WILL ROGERS AND WILEY POST
AMERICA'S AMBASSADORS OF GOOD WILL
ENDED LIFE'S FLIGHT HERE
AUGUST 15, 1935

'Did they crash here?' she asked in awe, and Jonathan replied: 'My grandfather was the one who ran in to Barrow to tell the people.'

'Do you know who Will Rogers was?'

'Someone important, I guess. They made a fuss about him.'

He was so insolent in his attitude toward the two men that she cried, with an intensity he had not seen her display before: 'Dammit, Jonathan, these were fine men. Who accomplished things. As you could if you put your mind to it. Don't you realize the opportunities you're throwing away?'

'Like what?'

'Like almost anything.' She spoke as the primordial teachers, the ones forty thousand years ago who had taught the progenitors of the Eskimos how to make better harpoons and use them more productively.

When Jonathan showed his usual indifference to what she was striving to accomplish with him, she lowered her voice and said pleadingly: 'When we reach Barrow you'll see Eskimos who lead their people. Study them. Because one day someone like you will have to take their place.'

Leaving him sullen and silent by his snowmobile, she went to the shore and gathered a handful of sea-washed rocks, which she arrayed about the base of the monument in homage to a man her father revered as a great American.

The greatest revelation for Kendra on the trip to Barrow stemmed not from the SnowGo ride or the lonely cenotaph by the sea, but from what happened when she reached the famous Barrow High School. From the outside the school looked quite ordinary, about what one would expect in Utah or Colorado in a community that had fallen on hard times; low, rambling, and of no distinguished architecture, it seemed like a makeshift patchwork, and Kendra was disappointed. But when she entered the building and saw the lavishness with which it had been equipped, she was amazed, for she had never before seen anything to compare with such luxury and abundance.

School was not in session, of course, but seniors had been delegated to show the visiting teachers around, and since Kendra was the first to arrive, she fell into the care of the young man who was president of his class. Dressed in a neat woolen business suit, he introduced himself as the son of a Lower Forty-eight electrical engineer who managed the governmental radar installations, and he took her first to a spacious section of the school devoted to electronics: 'We have, as you can see, a complete radio and television broadcasting setup, very popular with the students.' He then showed her the bank of computers: 'Here students learn how to encode and to service computers.' The shops where household appliances and automobile engines were torn apart and reassembled were impressive, and the wood shop was better than the average professional carpenter's shop: 'There's talk about having the students build a house each year, right in here, and selling it to someone outside. It could be done, you know.' The home-economics room was a delight, with every kind of equipment that students might come into contact with if they later on went to Anchorage or Fairbanks to work in the hotels and restaurants.

'Doesn't anyone study books in this school?' Kendra asked, and the president said: 'You bet. I do, and so do most of my buddies,' and he led her to the academic classrooms, the spacious library and the science laboratories which would have graced the average college, and she said: 'Well, the instruments of learning are certainly here, but does anyone learn?'

The young man was a scholar destined to go far; his parents were both university graduates, father from Berkeley, mother from San Diego State, and they had instilled in their three children a love of learning. But their son also had an acute mind where the political realities of any situation were involved, which probably accounted for his having been elected president: 'You seem interested, Miss Scott, and you'll appreciate what I have to say. But if you take all the equipment I've shown you and scale it from the most up-to-date to the least, and you come back here next week, you'll find that all the really advanced apparatus, like the television, the radio, the high-powered computers, they're all being used by white kids like me from the Lower Forty-eight whose parents work here for the government, while the older stuff that doesn't cost too much, like for machine overhaul and carpentry, it's all being used by the Eskimos.'

Kendra stopped in the hallway, turned to face her guide directly, and said: 'What a terrible thing to say,' and he replied without blinking: 'What a terrible thing to have to say.' But there it was: this fantastic school was, at great expense, training white students to take their places at Harvard and Chicago and Louisiana State, and training its Eskimo students, except for the unusual child who broke loose from village constraints, to be waitresses and bellhops and auto repairmen.

She sat on a bench in the hallway outside the library and asked her guide to join her, and this he was eager to do, for he was interested in the problems that concerned her. She mused: 'I wonder if it's different anywhere, if you look at things honestly. In Utah and Colorado, there were very few Mexicans or Indians mastering computers. And when I was in Germany, I was told that students were identified at age twelve as to which of three curricula they would follow to determine the rest of their lives. They said it was the same in France and Japan. Very bright guys like you to make decisions. Average guys for drones' work. Below average, laborers to keep the system running.' She reflected on this for some moments and said: 'I suppose it was the same in ancient Egypt . . . everywhere.' Then she touched him on the arm and asked bluntly: 'Are you ever ashamed to be in this school?' and he replied with no hesitation or embarrassment: 'Not at all. The money keeps pouring out of the ground. I think it's wonderful they had the guts to spend it on something like this.'

In the days that followed she saw the young man frequently, and it was at his insistence that they resumed their serious conversation. Then, on Saturday afternoon, he asked: 'Could some of us kids talk with you this afternoon?' and she replied: 'Yes, if I can bring along an Eskimo boy about your age,' and he said: 'Delighted.'

Seven of them met in the school cafeteria, where the students had prepared light refreshments, and the president asked, before introducing Kendra: 'Where's your Eskimo?' She said without emotion: 'Tooling around on his snowmobile,' and the session began.

Four of the seven local students were white children of specialists imported from the Lower Forty-eight, but the three who showed the keenest interest were Eskimos, two seniors of remarkable perception and a boy in his junior year whose reluctance to speak out did not indicate any lack of sharpness in his ability to follow the discussion. It started with the white students' wanting Kendra's opinion about which colleges to apply to, as if that were the major problem facing them, and they appreciated her knowing response. One girl asked a clever question: 'Considering that my hometown is Barrow, Alaska, what first-class university might want someone like me to demonstrate its geographical diversity?' and Kendra said without hesitation: 'The top ones. They'll be hungry for someone like you,' and the girl asked almost insolently: 'F'rinstance?' and Kendra rattled off: 'Princeton, Chicago, Stanford, and I hear good reports about Smith,' then she added: 'You guys are pretty hip. It's a pleasure to meet you.' But then she gently led the talk to the situation of the three Eskimos, and only when she had helped the dark-skinned, Asian-looking young people to feel at ease did she unload her blockbuster: 'Your president, Paul, when he was showing me around on the first day, pointed out that all the expensive, modern electronics and computer equipment is used almost exclusively by the white students from the Lower Forty-eight, while the less sophisticated stuff like carpentry and auto-repair tools are monopolized by the Eskimos. What about that?'

'It's true,' the Eskimo girl said, 'but our problems are different from their problems.'

'In what way?'

'They'll make their lives in the Lower Forty-eight. We'll make ours in Alaska.'

'You don't have to stay in Alaska.'

'But we want to,' the girl said, and she received surprising support from the reticent boy: 'I don't dream of going to Seattle. I don't even dream of going to Anchorage. I dream of working here in Barrow even after the oil money stops flowing.'

Moved by compassion for these young people, Kendra said very rapidly: 'But don't you understand that to accomplish anything in Barrow, anything important, that is, you'll have to have a college education? Don't you see that all the good jobs, those with good pay, go to educated people from the Lower Forty-eight? Or to the Eskimos who have gotten an education?'

Stubbornly the Eskimo boy replied: 'We'll do it the Eskimo way.'

'What will you do in Barrow?' she asked almost contentiously, and two years later, when she was a married woman floating around on an ice island five hundred miles north of Barrow, in the heart of the Arctic Ocean, she would remember each word of his amazing answer: 'Because the world is going to be interested in the Arctic Ocean, got to be—Russia, Canada, America. And I want to be here at the center.'

'What an amazing answer, Ivan. Where did you develop such an insight?' and he said: 'You look at a map,' and she thought, with tears coming to her eyes: Dear, wonderful boy! But without the education you despise, you'll never make it.

IN LATE MAY, when the Chukchi Sea remained frozen far out from shore, but with the snow beginning to vanish from the tundra, fearful news crept north from the lonely hut where the parents of Amy Ekseavik lived. A hunter came in to Desolation with a gruesome report: 'The old man got hold of some bad rotgut, got blind drunk, tried to murder his wife because she yelled at him, failed, jammed the rifle into the back of his mouth and blew his head off.'

Afanasi and Jeb Keeler organized a rescue party and found Amy's mother slightly wounded; a relative from farther south had come to take charge, and both women insisted that Amy leave school to assume responsibility for the hut. When Kendra heard this preposterous suggestion, she exploded: 'This girl will not leave my classroom. I forbid it.' Afanasi explained that if Amy was needed at home, which she obviously was, she would have to go there, that Eskimo custom demanded this, but Kendra cried: 'This child is brilliant. She can accomplish anything. I've written to the people at the University of Washington and they've shown great interest. Might even enroll her at age sixteen if she's as bright as I claim.' Her voice broke into a wail: 'Mr. Afanasi! Don't sentence Amy to a life of darkness!' Her plea was futile. Amy was needed at home and that took precedence over any other consideration.

On the day this wonderfully gifted child was to go home, Kendra walked with her for two miles across the bitter tundra where no tree sprouted and only the tiniest flowers bloomed. When they parted she embraced the girl, held her to her bosom, and fought to keep back her tears: 'Amy, you know that you have a remarkable mind. You've seen in school that you have special gifts. Look, I tell you the truth. You're way ahead of where I was at your age. You can accomplish anything. For God's sake, read the books I've given you. Do something with your life. Do something.'

'What?' the girl asked listlessly, and Kendra answered: 'We never know, Amy. But if we treasure our life, something turns up. Look at me, Amy. How in hell did I wind up in Desolation? Where will you wind up? Who knows? But keep moving. Oh, Amy . . .' There were a thousand relevant things she wanted to tell this girl in their last moments together, but all she could do was lean down and kiss the round brown face, an act which Amy accepted without emotion.

The next two weeks were bitter cold, more like midwinter than spring, and Kendra was as desolate in spirit as the storm-blown landscape, for she saw that regardless of how ably she and Kasm Hooker managed their school and encouraged their students, the harsh realities of Eskimo life established the limits of what could be accomplished, and one night she invited Afanasi and Keeler to her apartment in the Teacherage to discuss these matters with her and Hooker.

She began by posing a problem which depressed her: 'Mr. Afanasi, why are you the only Eskimo in Desolation with a world outlook . . . no, even an Alaskan outlook?'

'I had a good grandfather who taught me what to do, a father and uncle who taught me what not to do.'

'How can Kasm and I produce young people with the outlook and the capacities you have?'

'It happens by accident, I think. With Amy Ekseavik, you'd have had a chance. With Jonathan Borodin . . . well, you know, he should be exactly like me. Able to handle himself in the white man's world, a pillar in his Eskimo village. But somehow we missed, and now all he commands is a snowmobile.'

'He tells me he may want to become a shaman—in the ancient pattern, but a constructive one.'

Afanasi heard this news with great interest: 'Now, that's not a crazy idea, not at all. I've thought for some time that perhaps with the pressures of modern life, television, snowmobiles, clatter, that there might be a place for the revival of shamanism as my grandfather knew it.' He rose and walked about the apartment, picked at some food, then sat down close to Kendra: 'A hundred years ago, when Healy and his *Bear* came here with Sheldon Jackson, the shamans they met were a disreputable lot. Jackson's reports gave the system a bad name, but the shamans my grandfather worked with were a much different sort.' He rose and stalked the room again, concluding: 'Maybe that Borodin boy, you know he has unlimited talent, you saw that in school, Kasm. I'm going to talk with him.'

The conversation never took place, because three days later, in a swale that still contained deep snow, Jonathan Borodin, nineteen years old, got his rifle, his SnowGo-7 and five gallons of spare gas and headed far inland to get himself a couple of caribou, which his grandfather sorely wanted as the best food an Eskimo could eat. Dragging a cargo sled behind him to haul the meat, he rode speedily in an easterly direction toward where lakes and wandering rivers abounded, and in an area which he had often visited before, he shot two big caribou, slaughtered them on the spot, loaded the abundance of fresh meat on the sled and the horns on the back of his snowmobile.

On the way home he met with two disasters: a tremendous storm thundered in from the south, bringing new snow and whipping about the remnants trapped in the swale. When the blizzard struck, he was momentarily frightened, for the hunters of Desolation stood in awe of any storm coming at them from the south. If it were to continue at its present rate, he could be in trouble, but he felt sure that when it abated he could pick his way westward to Desolation. He never considered abandoning the sled he was dragging and speeding homeward as fast as possible: When I shoot me a caribou I bring it home.

But as he descended a moderate slope, with the bitter wind from the sea driving hard against his face, he realized that the remainder of his journey, some thirty-five miles, was going to be rough going: No worry. I have loads of gas. Then as he climbed the western side of the slope his motor began to cough, and at the very crest, where the wind was fiercest, it stopped entirely.

Again he had no immediate fear, for on his varied trips he had mastered the intricacies of his machine, and he assumed that he could repair it now. He could not. Some new defect, far more serious than before, had disabled his SnowGo, and with the gale whipping about him, he failed in one attempt after another to identify and repair whatever had stalled his engine. As the grayness of late afternoon fused into a whiteout, he realized that he was in peril of freezing.

Only his grandfather was aware that Jonathan did not return that night, and he felt sure that the boy had taken refuge behind some hillock, but when noon came and there was still no sign of Jonathan, the old man began to worry. But he did not alert anyone, because his mode of life kept him apart from others, so a second night passed with the boy still missing.

Early next morning the old man, trembling with fear, reported to the makeshift office from which Afanasi conducted his business, and there he delivered the appalling news: 'Jonathan, he went out, two days ago, caribou. He not come back.'

Afanasi leaped into action, and telephoned Harry Rostkowsky at the airfield in Barrow to fly south and east of Desolation toward the lakes to see if he could spot a missing SnowGo with a boy camped nearby. The area to be searched was due south of Barrow, and Rosty radioed the airfield three times to report that he had found nothing, and Barrow reported this by phone to Afanasi, but on a later pass Rosty saw the stalled machine and an inert body huddled beside it: 'Rostkowsky calling Barrow. Inform Afanasi Desolation SnowGo located atop ridge due east. Body nearby probably frozen.'

A party of four men and two snowmobiles was organized immediately, with Afanasi riding pillion on one, a highly regarded Eskimo tracker on the other. Rostkowsky, aloft in his Cessna, spotted them leaving town and signaled the direction they should take, and after nearly two hours, for they traveled slowly and cautiously, they came upon Jonathan Borodin's new SnowGo, his five gallons of spare gas, his two butchered caribou and his frozen corpse.

WHEN KENDRA SPOTTED the mournful cortege approaching the village from the east she knew what to expect, for everyone in Desolation had been alerted to the probability of tragedy, but forewarning did not make the death of this excellent young man any easier to take, and she ran to where the corpse lay, still in huddled, frozen posture. 'Oh my God!' she cried. 'What a terrible waste!' And that was the threnody that sounded throughout Desolation Point.

It was not until the school term ended that Kendra felt the full impact of the tragedies that had darkened the spring months when hope should have been so resurgent, and for two weeks she idled about the lonely school, filing her grocery order for the coming year and purchasing some two thousand dollars' worth of unnecessary specialties to be used for entertaining her students and their parents. But then Afanasi, who seemed to look after everyone in his village, came to her with an order: 'It's time to get you out of here. Go to Fairbanks or Juneau or Seattle. We have funds for teachers' travel, and here's a ticket to Anchorage with an extension for wherever within reason you want to go. Utah to see your folks? That would be okay.'

'Right now I do not care to see them,' she said firmly, but she accepted the tickets, one to Anchorage, one open, and as she flew south with minimum baggage, for her home was now Desolation Point and she was loath to leave it, she looked at herself coldly, as if she had a mirror before her face: I'm twenty-six, I've never been close to marriage, and that article by the woman researcher in Denver made it so clear that with every passing year after twenty-three, an educated woman has less and less chance of ever getting married, but I want to live in Alaska, I love the frontier, I thrill to the challenge of the arctic . . . Oh God, I'm so mixed up.

But of one thing she was certain, and this pertained to the nature of life itself, and as the engines of the jet droned on she continued talking to herself as if she were the subject of an analysis by an outside observer: I love people. Amy Ekseavik is part of my life. Jonathan Borodin—oh God, why didn't I talk to him more? And I do not want to live alone. I cannot face the endless years. The arctic night, I have no problems with it, for it passes, but loneliness of the spirit never passes.

Very slowly and with a recognized confusion she took from the mock-leather portfolio in which she carried her school papers a torn sheet on which was written an address in Anchorage, and at the airport she hurried to a cab, as if she feared she might change her mind, and thrust the paper in the driver's hand: 'Can you find this?' and he replied: 'I'd be fired if I couldn't. Biggest apartment house in town,' and although she was fully aware that she was doing a most dangerous thing, she took the elevator to the fifth floor, knocked on the door, and expected to see Jeb Keeler waiting for her when the door opened. He was, and as she embraced him she whispered: 'Without someone to love, I was lost in a blinding snowstorm,' and he said he understood.

Later that night as they lay together, she confided: 'Amy and Jonathan, they tore at my heart. We come to a place to teach, and the children teach us,' and Jeb said: 'It's the same with lawyers. We learn much more than we help others.'

She stayed with him for five days, and near the end of their time together she said: 'Afanasi suspected that I might be coming to see you. I think that's why he gave me the ticket to Anchorage. He says you're a man to be trusted. I asked him if he gave every lawyer that recommendation, and he laughed: "Not Poley Markham. I love him but I sure don't trust him," ' and Jeb said: 'He's wrong there. Poley's different, but I've found him to be completely honest. Never touches a dime that isn't his!'

The conversation then turned to talk of their future, and she said that perhaps at the end of the next school year, if Jeb still wanted to specialize in Alaskan law, particularly north of the Circle, they should consider marriage, with the understanding that Kendra wanted to continue teaching at Desolation, or perhaps move into Barrow. Jeb assured her that with his and Poley's leverage they could get her one of the jobs in Barrow, and she said, as she kissed him goodbye: 'Let's think about that. A good teacher with all that expensive equipment ought to be able to turn out some terrific Eskimos.'

At the airport, as she waited for her northbound plane, she watched idly the arrival of a Japan Air Lines plane from Tokyo as it discharged those passengers who would be stopping over in Anchorage, and saw five athletic-looking Japanese—three men and two young women—who were also going to have a very deep but much different interest in Alaska.

T HEY CALLED HIM *sensei*. Every Japanese addicted to mountain climbing, and they were legion, called him Takabuki-sensei, an honorific which could be translated as something like Revered-and-Beloved-Professor Takabuki. At forty-one his official position was professor of moral philosophy at Waseda University in Tokyo, but arrangements had been made with both the university authorities and the Japanese government for him to be absent on expeditions as often as the funding and a balanced, dependable climbing party could be arranged.

Japan's premier mountaineer, this small, wiry, normally clean-shaven man was familiar to newspaper and magazine readers from his photographs as a heavily bearded figure standing at the windblown, snowy apex of some great mountain. Because Japan lay relatively close to the great mountains of Asia, he had as a young apprentice climbed both Nanga Parbat and K-2, and in later years had led two assaults on Everest, one aborted at 27,000 feet by the death of two members, the other successful when he and two of his team stood on top of the world at 29,028 feet above sea level. The latter had been a classic performance without even one minor accident.

Encouraged by his successes, Japanese supporters had raised funds for him to lead lesser expeditions to Aconcagua in the Argentine, Kilimanjaro in Tanzania, the Matterhorn on the Italian-Swiss border, twice to Mount St. Elias in Alaska and once to Tyree in Antarctica. Even his German competitors agreed that Takabuki-sensei was a complete mountaineer. Said one German periodical specializing in alpinism: 'He can do anything he sets his mind to, and he has two salient characteristics. Even in adversity he smiles to keep the spirits of his fellow climbers high, and he brings them back alive. The two deaths that destroyed his 1974 assault on Everest occurred two thousand feet below where he was climbing close to the summit. Two members of his team, unroped, moved carelessly and plunged to their deaths.'

But in all his recent triumphs, another challenge gnawed at him, and in time his obsession grew so great that the mountain he had not yet conquered seemed to move about with him wherever he went, filling his mind. It can be done, he assured himself repeatedly. It's not a difficult climb. I could have mastered it when I was a boy. It's no more than a walk, really, but to take that walk requires a mixture of brute strength and infinite delicacy. At this point in his reverie he usually stopped, stood flat-footed, looked off into space, and questioned: If it's so simple, why do so many meet their death on that damned mountain?

He was in this frame of mind on the third of January when he was scheduled to meet with the mountaineering leaders of Japan, especially those industrialists who in the past had financed expeditions. When he and his associate Kenji Oda stood before them he realized that the Japanese New Year celebrations—wildest in the world, with even more alcohol consumed than at Scotland's Hogmanay roistering—had left these gentlemen somewhat hungover and bleary-eyed, but after some friendly joshing as to who had been drunkest—everybody in Japan, it seemed, having been so to some degree or other—they were as ready for business as they were going to be this day.

'How many would be in your team, do you think?'

'Five. Three men, two women.'

'Very small in comparison with your Everest teams.'

'A totally different climbing method.'

'In what way?'

'Fewer camps, much lighter gear.'

'But why does Denali fascinate you, Sensei?' Quickly the interrogator added: 'Because it does, you know.'

Takabuki's face hardened. His hands clenched and he disclosed what tormented him. 'Compared to the really great mountains of the world, Everest and Nanga Parbat for height, Matterhorn or the Eiger for rock work, Alaska's Denali is trivial.'

'Then why allow it to become an obsession?'

'Because of its challenge. Especially to a Japanese.'

'But you just said it was easy.'

'It is, except for three facts. It lies close to the Arctic Circle, less than two hundred and fifty miles . . .'

'In kilometers?'

'In Alaska they use miles. Everest is nearly two thousand five hundred miles farther south, and that difference in latitude makes Denali seem quite a few thousand feet higher than it really is.'

'Why?' a well-lubricated industrialist asked, and Takabuki said: 'At higher latitudes the air is thinner, just as it is at the higher altitudes. Everest, very high and moister. Denali, not so high, but very thin all the way up.' Satisfied that he had justified his basic respect for Denali, he moved on to his second point: 'It's true that Denali does not present us with much serious rock work, hardly any. And that's where the trouble comes for us Japanese and Germans. Because we're used to steep rock work and very high altitudes, we scamper to the top and yell back jubilantly "See! It was nothing!" And then on the way down, we grow careless in our euphoria, plunge over the edge or get lost in an avalanche, and no one ever sees us again.' He stopped, stared at his questioners, and added: 'They don't even find the bodies.' Halting again, he said painfully: 'Denali is a burial ground for German and Japanese climbers who come down the mountainside rejoicing,' and he asked Kenji Oda, who had studied with him at Waseda, to show the committee the map and chart they had drawn up. It displayed the mournful record of the arrogant Germans and the inattentive Japanese.

'Here is a team of four Germans, great climb, record speed I believe. No challenge whatever, they said later. That is, the two who didn't die on the way down.' He indicated another group of five Germans: 'A masterful team. I climbed with three of them in the Alps. They could go straight up any rocky face. Two more dead.' He pointed to the record of a team of seven that had lost two, a team of five that had lost one.

'How could a relatively easy mountain like Denali exact such a heavy toll on experienced climbers?' asked a manufacturer who had climbed with Takabuki-sensei in earlier years, and the dean of mountaineers added his third significant fact about this tall, beautiful and terrible mountain: 'Because it lures you, like the sirens of Ulysses, but when you're up there on its peak, triumphant, it's apt to send forth storms of hellish magnitude. Winds of a hundred miles an hour, temperatures of minus-ninety with chill factors to below a hundred and twenty, and when a storm strikes, if you don't burrow into a snow cave like an animal, you perish.'

The listeners said nothing, but finally the man who had done some climbing with the sensei pointed out: 'But you said the Japanese were careless. If you're hit by a storm like that, it doesn't sound much like carelessness.'

And now Takabuki became almost solemn, as if he were the undertaker in some small rural town: 'You're right, Okobi-san. Our people dig in, protect themselves from the storm, but when it's over they come romping down the slopes, fail to keep their ropes taut, and over the edge they go.'

'How do you know that?' a man asked, and Takabuki replied: 'We don't. We're guessing. All we know are the terrible figures. Show them, Oda-san,' and the next doleful summary was displayed. 'Look at that record! Eleven Japanese dead, and we've not recovered a single body. They vanished. Into a crevasse here? Over the side there? We don't know. They toiled, they conquered, and they vanished. And Denali refuses to tell us how it conquered them.'

At this point he stopped, his hands clenched with suppressed anger, and only Kenji Oda, looking at the man he worshiped, knew what ugly fact Takabuki was going to reveal next: 'Gentlemen, we Japanese have performed so poorly on Denali. Going up we're unbeatable, coming down we're . . .' His voice trembled; he mastered it and said bitterly as he pointed at the ridge from which his predecessors had vanished: 'Look what they call this place! Come up and look!' and when the men did they saw that American cynics had given the ridge where so many Japanese fell a hideous name. Since most of the committee could read English if not speak it, Takabuki did not translate, but two members asked: 'What do the words mean?'

'The Orient Express,' he said grimly. 'The place where we Japanese roar out of sight,' and there the mocking words stood on a map which had become semiofficial.

'It is my job,' he said quietly when discussion resumed, 'mine and Oda's here, to lead a Japanese expedition which will demonstrate what we can do, how we can discipline ourselves. We've been so careless in the past, so one-man daring and contemptuous of risk, that the people around Denali, the real mountaineers . . . Do you know what they call us when we appear at Talkeetna to climb into the planes that fly us to the mountain? The Kamikaze Crowd. Well, this expedition will not be a banzai charge. Have I your permission? And the necessary budget?'

Before an answer could be given, the chairman brought up a problem which perplexed mountaineers in many nations: 'The maps name your mountain McKinley. You climbers call it Denali. I don't understand.'

'Very simple,' Takabuki said. 'It's always been Denali. Real Alaskans and climbers call it nothing else. Honored Indian name, very ancient, meaning the High One.'

'Then where does the McKinley come from?'

'In 1896, I believe'—and the sensei looked for confirmation to Oda, who nodded—'the Democratic party nominated for the presidency a minor politician from Kansas, I think it was, man named McKinley. Nobody knew him nationally or thought much of him locally. The party needed some big event to give him prominence, and some politician dreamed up the idea of naming this great mountain after him. Very popular . . . with the Democrats.'

The committee members laughed, and one said: 'Same sort of thing happens in Japan. Why don't they go back to the real name?' During the discussion which followed, Kenji Oda, who had studied in America, spoke quietly to the chairman: 'I could never contradict the sensei in public. Or private either, for that matter, but McKinley was a Republican, their conservative party. Not a particularly bad man. And he came from Ohio, not Kansas.'

'Will his name remain on the mountain?'

'Everybody with good sense is trying to remove it.'

T**HE SEASON FOR** climbing Denali was rigorously defined: before the first of May the snow, storms and cold were too severe; after the middle of July the heat made the snow so rotten that avalanches came thundering down and bridges over crevasses collapsed. So in early June, Takabuki-sensei and the four members of the expedition took the short flight from Tokyo to Anchorage, where they reported to the shop of furrier Jack Kim, who served as liaison for all Japanese climbers. A Korean with a winning smile and a sharp knowledge of Alaskan business, he knew Takabuki by reputation, and after a brief discussion, had the team and their small mountain of equipment packed in a big station wagon headed north for the 133-mile drive to Talkeetna.

At a spot some miles south of the little town, the young man driving swerved to the shoulder of the road, slammed on the brakes, and cried: 'There it is!' From the almost level plain rose the three great mountains of the Alaska

Range: Foraker to the left, Denali in the center, Silverthrone on the right, with off to one side the remarkable black cube called Mooses Tooth. They formed a majestic march across the blue sky, a line of mountains that would have been commendable in any terrain; here, where the surrounding plain was so low, with an elevation not much above sea level, they soared enormously, white-capped, inviting but filled with subtle menace.

'Each mountain in the world is different,' Takabuki-sensei told his team. 'And each is precious in its own way.'

'What's different here?' one of the women asked, and he said: 'The surrounding terrain is so ordinary, so low, and the range of mountains so very high and so close together. They are like conspirators, up where the winds blow, and they are plotting storms. For us.'

At Talkeetna, like many Japanese teams before them, they sought out LeRoy Flatch, who now made a business of flying mountain climbers onto the 7,200-foot elevation of the southeast fork of Kahiltna Glacier. With the rear seats of his Cessna-185 removed, he could accommodate, as he said, 'three chubby Americans or five trim Japanese.' With wheels retracted and skis in place, he had delivered many young Japanese climbers to the starting point of their great adventure, flying back to meet them nineteen or twenty days later when they descended. Of course, if they became cavebound during some monumental snowstorm, he awaited a radio message from the park rangers and came for them after twenty-seven or even thirty days. He was their lifeline for getting on and off the mountain.

When Flatch assured them that he was ready and that weather reports for the next few days looked good, the Takabuki team repaired to the hut provided for visiting climbers, spread each item of their voluminous gear on the deck for a final check, and listened attentively as their sensei reviewed his instructions:

'There is only one purpose for this expedition. To restore the honor of Japan. And there is only one way to accomplish that. To put three men on the top of that mountain and to get five of us back here safely. It is our task to erase the opprobrium of that insolent phrase the Orient Express.

'So, the rules. We'll portage high and sleep low. That means climb diligently all day to get our gear up the mountain, but hurry back down at night so that we acclimatize gradually and in an orderly way. We'll take five days to our camp at eleven thousand feet. Very careful around Windy Corner and up to the last two camps at fifteen thousand and sixteen thousand nine hundred.

'Skis to eleven thousand, crampons the rest of the way. Roped three in my group with me, two in Oda-san's, and no slack. At our last stop we build a solid base which can be extended into a snow cave if a storm comes, and from there the three men ascend to the top, up and back fast in one day while the two women maintain supplies and gear at the camp. Only three thousand feet to cover, and more than a mile, very steep. We'll climb light and hurry back.

'Now'—and here his voice dropped to a whisper—'having attained the summit, the easy part, our real task begins. To get back to this hut, all five of us, in good shape, with no call to the rangers or the air force planes to rescue us, and no disappearances. I want each of you to look at this map.'

At this point he spread the offending chart before them, and each of his four climbers read in English the insulting legend the *Orient Express,* and each swore privately that this time there would be no Japanese cascading down those steep slopes to oblivion.

TAKABUKI'S TEAM HAD been cleverly composed. He, of course, was one of the world's premier climbers, experienced in almost everything that could happen on a mountain. His endurance was extraordinary, a slim man weighing less than a hundred and sixty who could lug up the tallest mountains in the world not only a protective uniform that would stagger most men, but at the same time carry a cleverly packed and disposed backpack weighing just under sixty pounds. Takabuki-sensei was determined to climb Denali, up and down.

Equally determined was Kenji Oda, who had served as base-camp commander in the second Takabuki assault on Everest, the one that succeeded. The third man, Yamada, had not participated in previous expeditions, but was a superb athlete and had a reputation for endurance in various punishing sports. Of the two women, only Sachiko had any experience in mountain climbing; Kimiko, Takabuki's daughter, had begged her father to let her join this expedition, and at the last minute he had consented.

'Women will do the cooking and mind the camp,' the sensei had said at the conclusion of his instructions. 'Men will set up camp and carry the heavier loads.'

The five-man team with all its gear was ferried to the starting station on Kahiltna Glacier in two easy flights in LeRoy Flatch's snow-ski Cessna, and the first afternoon, at 7,200 feet on the face of the snowy glacier, was spent getting the gear in order. When that job was half finished, the sensei said: 'Let's run the first load up,' so the three men suited up, put on their skis, hefted the huge loads onto their backs, and started smartly up the first part of the climb while the two women finished setting up the camp. In ninety minutes the men were back, wet with perspiration and ready for a rest. Excellent though their condition was, the altitude had forced them to breathe heavily and they were not unhappy to have the women prepare the evening meal.

Patiently, during the next days they lugged their packs upward, losing in weight only what they ate, and after the most cautious preparation, as if they were heading for the top of Everest, they reached the 11,000-foot mark, where they cached the first of their gear, their skis. Next morning, when they prepared to put on heavy steel crampons, they were reminded of a critical rule of mountain climbing: 'Keep your head clear and your feet warm.' If a climber faulted either of those commands, he or she was already in deep trouble, so Takabuki himself supervised how his team was shod. On bare feet which had been allowed to breathe during the night, each member put on a pair of finely woven, extremely expensive socks made of a silk-polyester-like material, a fabricated stuff that would lead perspiration away from the body. Over them came a second pair of very thin socks, then a third pair of heavy, loosely knit socks which provided warmth and protection from jarring and jabbing. On top of this came one of the lightest, most flexible shoelets one could imagine, in part some exotic metal, in part a canvas made from some newly invented material. This was the secret of the Japanese climber, this flexible, extremely strong, resilient shoe which gloved the foot and readied it for the very heavy Koflach plastic boot that was pulled on over it, forming a massive protection and also a kind of air-conditioned comfort.

A casual observer, seeing that the foot was now encased in five different layers of cloth and metal and space-age materials, might have concluded: 'Now you can clamp on the metal crampons,' but that would have been premature, for over the Korean boot was drawn a heavy, flexible insulated legging which made it impossible for snow to drift down into the boot or up the pantleg. Only when this was tied in place was it permissible to attach the crampons by means of heavy lashings. When this was done, a climber had on nearly four hundred dollars' worth of footwear so effective that without it there would be little chance of getting to the top and back down without serious frostbite, but so heavy that to lift one leg after another, kicking footholds up the steep icy incline, required unusual strength, even without a sixty-pound pack.

Not one person on the Takabuki team would suffer from frostbite that year; not one toe would have to be amputated by the doctors in the hospitals near the foot of Denali.

The climb went well. The three men proceeded boldly along the Orient Express and straight up the last slope to the peak, where amid snow and ice each man photographed the other two. Finally the sensei propped his camera on packed snow at an angle, set the self-timer and shot a picture of all three, with Takabuki proudly raising the banner of the Waseda University Alpine Club atop the world at 20,320 feet.

On the critical descent, things continued to go well, and when they reached the camp at 16,900 feet at about noon, they considered starting down immediately, but Takabuki, not liking the look of the clouds rushing in from the west, said: 'I think we'd better get out the two shovels,' and by the time the June blizzard struck—for blizzards could hit Denali on any day throughout the year—the five Japanese were snug in their snow cave, where they huddled for three storm-swept days.

There was only one untoward incident. Kimiko stepped outside, intending to move only a few steps to relieve herself, but when her father saw the terrible thing she had done he screamed in a way she had never heard before: 'Kimiko! No rope!' And Oda-san reached out and grabbed her by the leg. When they had her safely inside the cave, Takabuki said quietly: 'It is just stepping outside, no rope, that kills,' and after apologizing for her error, Kimiko said: 'I still have to go outside,' so she roped up, and Oda-san held the rope around an ice pick jammed into the snow inside the cave, and she was safe.

When the storm abated, they descended to a lower level and started setting up their last major camp, but Takabuki-sensei, mindful of the fact that deadly errors resulted when climbers were tired, personally tested the snow for safety and only then allowed the strong nylon tarp on which the tents would be placed to be laid out. In accordance with Takabuki's iron-clad rule 'No fire in the big tent'—scores of teams having lost their tents, their provisions and sometimes their lives in fires—the crew erected a simple cook tent nearby, and into it went Kimiko to prepare hot rations. After a few moments Sachiko went to help, but almost immediately came out, screaming: 'She's gone!'

The next twenty seconds were an exercise in iron discipline, for Takabuki moved gently before the exit, arms extended to prevent anyone from running out into what might be mortal danger, for if some terrible mishap had befallen his daughter, the same might engulf anyone who went chasing after her. 'By the book,' he said quietly, still barring the passage.

Kenji Oda had reacted within seconds, instinctively wrapping a rope about his body, tying knots in strange and powerful ways, reaching for a spare ice pick and handing the far end of the rope to Sachiko and Yamada. Then, moving the sensei aside, he went gingerly outside the tent to see what had happened, certain that behind him Sachiko and Yamada would keep his rope taut, so that he would not drag them to their deaths if he fell into some deep crevasse.

Peering into the cook tent, he at first satisfied himself that Kimiko had not by some freak accident fallen through the heavy nylon flooring. But when he explored the area just to the left of the entrance he gasped and returned to the big tent, ashen-faced: 'She's plunged into a crevasse.'

No one panicked. The sensei crept into the cook tent, probed with his ice ax, and saw the mysterious hole through which Kimiko had dropped to a depth unknown. Oda, continuing to act swiftly and effectively in unbroken movement, placed the wooden handle of his ice pick at the edge of the hole so that when his rope cut at the edge, the handle would prevent it from digging into the snow and perhaps starting a small avalanche which would engulf the person below. Where Kimiko was, and in what condition, no one could guess.

Without a moment's hesitation Oda eased himself into the opening down which Kimiko had plunged, and deftly lowering himself along his rope by using a figure-eight device to brake his fall, he descended deep into the crevasse.

It was a monstrous, gaping hole, yards wide and with no discernible bottom, but by the grace of the forces which had carved it, the sides were not unbroken smoothness but a series of broken ledges onto which a fallen body might plummet. But Kimiko was not to be seen, and even when Oda switched on his lamp and looked at the terrible icy formations, he saw nothing.

Then he heard a moan, and on a ledge about thirty feet below he saw the outline of Kimiko's body in the dim light, and with rope signals devised decades ago he let the others above know that he had at least seen her. Again without hesitating, he lowered himself deeper and deeper. When he was but a few feet above her he could see that the violent plunge had not only knocked her unconscious but had also wedged her tightly into a constricted area from which she had no way of extricating herself.

'Kimiko!' he called as he drew closer to her, but there was no response. Then, as he waited for the rescue rope to reach him, he considered how he might attach it with maximum effectiveness, but before he started he tied her so securely to himself that if anything happened within the next minutes, she would at least be prevented from falling to her death.

Only then did he grasp the second rope, and with a bewildering series of knots designed for just such emergencies, he tied her into a sling from which she could not fall. But when he tried to pull her loose, he found that she was so firmly wedged into her corner that he could not do so. However, a pull from above, if strong enough, might do the trick, so he signaled for one, and as the three above tugged on the second rope, having secured the first, Oda saw with relief that Kimiko was being eased out of her prison.

As soon as she was freed, he signaled for the hauling to stop, and there in the icy mists of the crevasse, with evening light filtering down, he pinched her face and compressed her shoulders to bring her back to consciousness, but the second part of his therapy was exactly the wrong one, for in her fall she had dislocated her right shoulder, and his pressure was so great that she revived, saw him holding her, and sobbed with pain.

At that moment Alaska had a population 460,837, which meant that perhaps 75,000 young people were of an age at which they might fall in love or consider marriage. Indeed, 6,422 marriages did take place that year, but none was founded upon a troth more extraordinary than the one pledged between Kenji Oda and Kimiko Takabuki as they dangled forty-seven feet inside a crevasse on the frozen slopes of Denali. As she reached over to kiss him, they both saw that had she missed slamming onto the projection which dislocated her shoulder she would not have bounced across the chute and onto some other ledge lower down. She would have plummeted to a depth unfathomed.

This time the Orient Express claimed no Japanese victims.

WHEN KENDRA SCOTT returned to Desolation Point after her unpremeditated visit to Jeb Keeler's Anchorage apartment, she became vaguely aware that a newcomer had moved into an abandoned shack north of the village, where he was said to be living in squalor with thirteen beautifully trained malamute and husky sled dogs. The rumors were correct. He was one more of that inexhaustible breed of young American men, graduates of good colleges like Colgate, Grinnell and Louisiana State, who had been trained to take over their fathers' businesses, but who quit after five dreary years, leaving both an excellent job and often a wife just as superior, to try their luck racing sled dogs in the wilds of Alaska. You found them on the outskirts of Fairbanks, Talkeetna and Nome, working like slaves unloading barges or other cargo during the summer shipping season to earn the huge salaries that they spent in the winter feeding their fifteen or sixteen dogs. They usually refrained from shaving; sometimes they picked up a little money offering dogsled excursions to tourists; and quite often adventurous girls, from colleges like Mount Holyoke and Bryn Mawr, who also wanted to experience the arctic worked as waitresses and moved in with them for longer or shorter periods.

The dream of each of these men, and they numbered in the scores, was to run the Iditarod, not to win it, for God's sake, just to complete the course which was rightfully considered the world's most demanding organized competition. In the depth of the arctic winter, with blizzards howling out of Siberia and temperatures down to minus-forty, some sixty-odd intrepid dogsled drivers left Anchorage and ran a punishing course to Nome, a distance which was officially stated as 1,049 miles—1,000 miles plus the 49th state—but which actually varied between eleven and twelve hundred miles over incredibly tough terrain. 'It's like running from New York City to Sioux Falls, South Dakota, before there were roads,' Afanasi told Kendra, 'and contrary to what many think, the driver does not usually catch a ride on the rear runners of his sled. He runs behind it four-fifths of the time.' Kendra could not understand why any sane person would dump so many thousands of dollars into dog food and pay a $1,200 entry fee to be so abused, especially when first prize was only $50,000, but Afanasi said: 'I ran it when I was younger, and the glory of gliding up to that finish line, win or lose, lasts a lifetime.'

Of course, the young men from the Lower Forty-eight who came north to compete usually ran the grueling course only once; then they returned home, married, and resumed managerial work in their family business. But behind their desks, as they grew older, hung that framed certificate proving that in 1978 they competed in the Iditarod, and finished—and that separated them from the local athletes who had shot a hole in one at the local course in 1979.

The young man who had moved into the shack at Desolation, wanting to give his dogs the experience of the real arctic, was in many respects a typical example of these intruders—Stanford University graduate, thirty years old, five years of work in the family business, divorced from a socialite wife who, hearing that he had decided to emigrate to the Arctic Circle with thirteen dogs, told her friends that he suffered from a mental disorder—but in certain important respects he was unique. First, he was Rick Venn, scion of the powerful family that controlled the Ross & Raglan interests in Seattle; second, of all the newcomers, he alone had historic ties with Alaska; and third, because he was the grandson of Malcolm Venn and Tammy Ting, he had Tlingit and Chinese blood, which made him part Native. His complexion was so dark and his features so reminiscent of Asia that he could easily pass as another of the half-Russian, half-Native young men of Alaska.

He also differed from the others from the Lower Forty-eight in that whereas he kept his cabin as chaotic as theirs, he did maintain his personal appearance much as he would have in Seattle: he shaved; he cut his hair with his own barber's shears; and he washed a tubful of clothes once a week. But he was like the others in the affection he showed for his dogs and the loving care with which he worked them—in the sand when there was no snow, in the deepest drifts when there was.

Polar was a seven-year-old husky with a strain of wolf from some generations back and, more recently, some malamute. He was not overly big, several of the other dogs in the team being larger, but he was unusually intelligent and the unchallenged leader among them. Perfectly attuned to his master, Polar quickened to Rick's commands. Sled dogs were trained to turn to the right at 'gee,' to the left at 'haw,' while half a dozen other calls each carried a particular meaning. But Polar had the remarkable ability to anticipate Rick's intent almost before he shouted a command, and would deftly lead the other dogs in just the right direction.

Though they ran well as a team, it was not uncommon when the dogs were waiting impatiently in their harnesses for two of them to leap at each other, fangs bared, and if someone didn't stop them quickly, the confrontation could rapidly degenerate into a savage, bloody fight. Of course, if Rick was present, he halted the nonsense immediately, but if he wasn't, Polar stepped back, uttered a deep snarl, and the dogs broke off. He also nipped at the heels of any dog he suspected of malingering, and it was always he who leaped forward with greater energy when Rick called for more speed. He was an exceptional dog, and when the snow arrived he found joy in leading his team on ten- and twenty- and even thirty-mile training runs across the tundra to the east.

There being no tourist restaurants in Desolation, no adventurous young waitress from the Lower Forty-eight had moved in with Rick, but when he brought his team into the village for an exhibition on sand, and when the crowd had gathered, he noticed Kendra Scott standing near Vladimir Afanasi. He recognized her as the kind of young woman he would probably enjoy knowing, so after the demonstration he sought out Afanasi and asked who she was.

'Best teacher we've had in a long time. Comes from Utah.'

'A Mormon?'

'Maybe so. Maybe that's why she wanted to explore the north.'

'Could I meet her?'

'I don't see how you could avoid it.'

So one sunny afternoon Afanasi took Kendra out to the tumbledown shack, where she started to laugh as soon as she stepped from Afanasi's truck, for a rather neatly painted signboard proclaimed THE KENSINGTON KENNELS, as if this were an expensive boarding place for pampered dogs. When the owner stuck his head out the door to ascertain the cause of laughter, Kendra saw a good-looking, neat young man, somewhat older than herself, dressed in blue coveralls: 'What's going on?'

'I like your sign. You board dogs?'

'Sure do. Thirteen of them,' and he pointed to where his huskies and malamutes were tethered, each to his own stake, on a short length of chain which prevented him from molesting the other twelve.

'For the Iditarod?'

'You've heard of it?'

'You must be crazy to attempt a race like that,' and he said: 'I am,' but it was not until he left his shack and came forth to shake hands that she realized how wacky he was, for across the chest of his coveralls was emblazoned the kind of motto that quixotic college students loved: REUNITE GONDWANALAND!

'What's your war cry?' she asked, and he explained that he had been a geology major at Stanford and this had been their rallying cry.

'But where is it?' and he said: 'Land mass that broke apart a quarter of a billion years ago. The South Pole was part of it, I believe,' and she said: 'You can enroll me in your crusade.'

In the following days, the more she heard about the rigors of the Iditarod, the more interested she became in the procedures whereby Rick trained his dogs, and when snow came she began to spend her Saturdays and Sundays out at the shack, bringing it into some semblance of respectability, but she avoided any romantic involvement, for she still considered herself in some vague degree engaged to Jeb Keeler. Certainly, when the young lawyer visited Desolation on business with Afanasi he practically lived at Kendra's apartment, staying until three or four in the morning. But when Rick, observing this, asked if she and Keeler were engaged, she said: 'It's difficult to make up your mind when you're so far from home.'

At least once a week, when the snow was adequate, Rick took her for a long training ride in his sled, and it was a magnificent experience to sit perched there, bundled in blankets, and to head off for a ten-mile run toward the frozen lakes, with Rick running behind and jumping from time to time onto the tail end of the long runners, shouting directions to Polar and encouraging the other dogs occasionally. 'I can see why the race fascinates young men,' Kendra said one day as they rested at the halfway mark.

'Not men only,' Rick said, reminding her that women older than she had won the race in recent years.

'You mean eleven hundred miles? They must be amazons,' and he corrected her: 'For this race you don't need brawn. You need brains and stamina.'

Brains were required because each racer had to arrange with some airplane pilot to drop large caches of dried salmon or other kinds of food along the way for the famished dogs as well as for himself, and the scheduling of these drops required both judgment and money. Many a newcomer spent his entire year's savings, plus money from home, merely to cover expenses for the Iditarod.

'Where'd the name come from?' Kendra asked one day, and Rick said: 'Name of an old mining camp. A trail used to run through there, and our race hits it every other year.'

For several weeks in the early days of winter Kendra existed in a kind of dream world, fixing up the shack, working with the dogs, reveling in long weekend training trips, and she began to feel that this glorious experience on the endless whitened tundra in gusty blizzards and the wonderful assurance that Rick knew what he was doing would go on endlessly. The possibility of their falling in love had not yet surfaced, for he was still gun-shy from the wreckage of his first marriage and she considered herself more or less bound to Jeb Keeler, but both she and Rick were increasingly aware that after the Iditarod, certain decisions could become inescapable. But for the moment they drifted along.

During one of their casual training trips over the snow to the south she was reminded of how close to disaster the Inupiat Eskimos of the arctic lived, for as they were coasting along quite a few miles distant from Desolation, Rick spotted an old-style earthen dwelling with wooden sidewalls and a heavy sod roof. Without thinking that they might be intruding, he shouted 'Gee!' to Polar, who instantly headed the team toward the hut. When the sled drew up before the door, Kendra realized with horror that this was where her prize student, Amy Ekseavik, had been reared and where she now lived, helping her widowed mother, for the girl appeared in the darkened doorway, glared at the dogs from beneath her heavy bangs, and then saw her teacher ensconced in blankets.

It was an icy reunion, for Amy had lost even the slight concession to humanity that she had allowed to develop under Kendra's care. She kept the visitors at arm's length, and when they asked to see her mother she said nothing, but stepped aside.

From the widow, Kendra learned that some kind of fol-de-rol had been exercised whereby the mother was supposed to be teaching her child at home, and this satisfied state law, even though good schools were available at Desolation to the north and Wainwright to the south. But it was obvious that the flame that had finally been ignited in this miraculous child in school the year before had gone out, or was sputtering in such a sickly manner that it must soon be extinguished.

Sick at heart that she had intruded upon Amy and her insoluble problems, Kendra bade the girl an awkward farewell and headed back north, her eyes filled with tears most of the way. When they stopped at one point to rest, she said to Rick: 'My heart could break. Really, it's too awful,' and she collapsed, sobbing, against his parka. When he asked what this meant, she told him of Amy's frozen arrival at school last year and her gradual thawing into one of the brightest, most promising girls of her age Kendra had ever seen: 'We may have done a dreadful thing, Rick. Stopping there and reminding her of lost worlds.' Kendra's fears were justified. Three days later, word trickled in to Desolation that Amy Ekseavik, fifteen years old and with a brilliant future, had left her home-study workbook open on the rough table in the dim light of the sod hut, taken her father's gun, stepped outside, and committed suicide while her mother slept.

THE HISTORY OF Kendra's first year north of the Circle was surprise at local customs, attaining plateaus on which she congratulated herself: Now I understand Alaska, followed by explosions which caused her to confess: I really know nothing. But none of the big revelations were more astonishing to her than the arrival in Desolation of a tall, determined woman who lived with her family in a log cabin some two hundred miles to the east in one of the most forlorn corners of the state, where they ran a hunting lodge from which visitors made spectacular catches of fish and bagged big game.

She was accompanied by her son, and she had a remarkable proposition: 'I've been teaching my boy at home—with Calvert study courses mailed from the United States—since he was a child. Although it's a mite early, I think he ought to take the SATs, because I'm convinced he's college material.'

Then she introduced her son, Stephen Colquitt, six feet one inch, shy, but with eyes that darted here and there like a hawk's, absorbing everything. 'What I came to ask you . . .' she explained nervously to Principal Hooker. 'We've heard good reports of Miss Scott here as a teacher who really knows how to teach math. And we wondered if she would tutor Stephen in algebra.'

Hooker fumbled: 'That would be highly irregular . . . maybe impossible . . . enrolling him in our school when he doesn't live in our district.'

'Oh! We didn't mean enroll him in your school. We meant we wanted special outside tutoring,' and before the principal could respond, she added: 'We'd be prepared to pay—for the outside help, that is.'

'I'd not charge anything,' Kendra said. 'I'd enjoy brushing up on my own algebra.'

'And trigonometry,' Stephen added, and Kendra said: 'We'll have a fling at that too.'

The next weeks were so productive that Stephen's triumphant gallop through algebra, geometry and trig drove away somewhat her guilt about Amy's death, and one night Kendra told Afanasi and Hooker: 'What this mother accomplished with home-teaching units from Maryland is incredible. When Stephen takes the SATs, stand back, because he's going to bust the system.'

Kasm Hooker was impressed by quite a different accomplishment of the young man: 'His father played a little basketball in college and they have a regulation basket on flat land beside the river. You wouldn't believe the moves this kid knows.'

In the pickup games the village held when no visiting schools were available, it was agreed that Hooker would play Colquitt one-on-one, and in the first game the boy astounded both the principal and the villagers by displaying an ability to tap the ball in on a follow-up without bringing it down to the floor for a wasteful dribble, but what evoked shouts of praise was Steve's adroit use of the double pump, in which he made believe to shoot, thus tricking Hooker into jumping to block his shot, while he, Steve, kept hold of the ball and shot just as Hooker came down and was out of position.

'Where did you learn that?' the winded principal asked during one time-out, and Steve said: 'Father has a satellite dish and I used to watch Earl the Pearl.'

But it was when Steve's SAT scores came in that everyone realized what Mrs. Colquitt had known all along. 'This kid can go to any college,' Hooker said, accustomed to scores of less than four hundred, and he forthwith dispatched letters to a variety of schools, attaching a recommendation also from the Fairbanks coach:

Kasm Hooker of Desolation and I played some good ball at Creighton in the days when we had a team, and I assure you that this six-foot-one boy of sixteen, who is sure to grow, is ready for the big time right now. He's had to train alone, no chance to play on a team. Given that chance, he'll be another Magic Johnson. Charge me double if I've deceived you.

In the spring Harry Rostkowsky flew in letters from nine leading universities and colleges offering Stephen Colquitt full academic scholarships—Yale, Virginia, Trinity in San Antonio among them—and another six wanted him for basketball. His mother and Kendra sorted out the offers and chose Virginia, which satisfied both Hooker and Steve, since they knew it favorably from the days when Ralph Sampson played there.

On the night they finished completing the entrance forms Kendra could not sleep, for she was trying to fathom how this gaunt woman, living in a remote cabin with not a single advantage except the Calvert correspondence materials and a television saucer, could have produced such a genius: Seems you don't need eighty-four-million-dollar high schools. Then again, maybe they help.

But as she laughed at this conclusion, Kendra suddenly began shivering and a terrible sickness of mind overwhelmed her, and in only her nightgown she ran from her quarters and banged furiously on Kasm Hooker's door. After a long silence, for it was near two in the morning, Mrs. Hooker came to the door and cried: 'My God, girl! What is it?'

When Kendra slipped inside, trembling as if assailed by some mysterious fever, it was obvious to the Hookers that she could not control herself: 'Kendra, sit down! Throw this robe about you. Now, what in hell goes on?'

It was not until Mrs. Hooker made her some hot chocolate that Kendra regained partial composure: 'I was thinking of Stephen and his good luck.'

'That's no cause for tears,' Kasm said. 'Martha and I were rejoicing.' Then he added almost sourly: 'But that was three hours ago.'

'So was I, but in the middle of my congratulations . . . to myself and to him . . . I thought of Amy . . . dead in the mud,' and she broke into wracking sobs. The Hookers, used to dealing at least once each term with some catastrophe, let her weep, and after a while she looked up piteously and asked: 'Why does a white boy with a determined mother reach the stars, and a girl just as brilliant but with an Eskimo mother fail?' She looked accusingly at the Hookers: 'Even you wrote letters to help him. Nobody stepped forward to help her.'

'You were magnificent with her, Kendra,' Mrs. Hooker said. 'Kasm told me.'

'It seems so unfair. So awful . . . socially and morally.'

Kasm lit a pipe, tapped its stem against his teeth, and said: 'Kendra, if you allow school tragedies to affect you so deeply, maybe you ought to consider leaving teaching. I mean it.'

'Don't you take them seriously?'

'Seriously? Yes. Tragically? No. Do I allow them to strike at my inner life? I do not.' Before Kendra could protest this inhumanity, he sat beside her, and while his wife brought a fresh cup of chocolate he took one of her hands in his and said: 'From high school on, I have never been in a school or teaching position but what some kid hasn't done himself or herself in, or died in some terrible accident.'

'What did you do?'

'Bury them, comfort the parents, and get on with the job. Because such things cannot be prevented. They can only be adjusted to.'

'I refuse to adjust to such unfairness.'

'Then, Kendra, what my husband says makes sense. If you allow your students' lives to affect you so deeply, maybe you ought to quit teaching. If you stay on, it'll destroy you.'

Kendra reacted to this sage advice, culled from years of school experience, with a renewed attack of shivering so vigorous that Mrs. Hooker sat down and took her other hand: 'How old are you, Kendra?'

'Twenty-eight.'

'It's very important that you get married. Afanasi told me that his young lawyer, that Keeler fellow, thinks highly of you. And I see the dog man at the north end of the village moseying around. Take one of them while you have the chance. You stay in Alaska as an old-maid schoolteacher worrying about every Eskimo disaster, you'll break your heart.'

But Kendra seemed not to hear her: 'It all seems so unfair to the young Eskimos.'

'Everything is unfair to young people. Years ago when I taught in Colorado it was fast cars and marijuana.'

'And a very important point,' Mrs. Hooker said. 'Eskimos don't like it when good-hearted teachers like you show too much interest in their family troubles. They actually resent it. Death is something that happens, always has, and they don't want you or me snooping around and weeping in public.'

Together the Hookers returned Kendra to her room, and in the morning Mrs. Hooker brought her more hot chocolate.

IN MARCH ALL attention in Desolation was centered on Vladimir Afanasi's high-powered shortwave radio, which brought hourly reports from Anchorage on the progress of the Iditarod. In favorable weather, for a change, the sixty-seven teams sped out of Anchorage on a course which this year covered eleven hundred and forty-three miles, with twenty-seven optional stops indicated at which teams could have food, dogs' and drivers', delivered by air. Rick had bought huge amounts of dried salmon for his dogs and Kendra had baked a big batch of rich, chewy high-energy brownies, filled with her pecans, for him. He also favored dried prunes, with pits he could suck on when the flesh was gone. At a designated spot, each team was obliged to rest dogs and drivers for an entire twenty-four hours, and here veterinarians inspected the animals. In recent years two women had won the race—the second, in the astonishing time of eleven days and fifteen hours—and at the camps there was much speculation as to whether a man could reclaim the trophy and the first-prize money of fifty thousand.

Rick, one of the twenty-six novices trying their luck this time, knew he had no chance of winning against the canny experts who had raced many times since the competition started in 1973, but he did confide to Kendra that he hoped 'to finish with a "single-digit-fifteen," ' that was, within the first nine in not over fifteen days.

During the first week of the race everything seemed to happen. Moose, driven southward by blizzards, strayed onto the marked course, became irritated by the dogs, and leaped among them, thrashing out with their hoofs and killing half a dozen dogs, whose drivers then dropped from the race. A bitterly cold storm blowing straight down from the north, an unusual direction, encouraged seven other mushers to quit, and this same storm prevented nearly a dozen airplanes from delivering dried salmon to supply stations along the route. Thus deprived of fuel, as it were, some competitors were forced to quit the race. At Ruby a Nome musher won two thousand dollars for being in the lead at the halfway mark, but Rick noticed that by now, eighteen racers with teams as good as his had dropped out.

Up in Desolation, Afanasi, Hooker and Kendra maintained a twenty-four-hour watch on the shortwave, Vladimir monitoring it during school hours, the teachers riding herd at night, and they picked up enough fragments of news to know that Rick was still among the active competitors, but where exactly in the standings he stood, they could not determine. Then, on the thirteenth day, as Kendra was teaching algebra to her students, a man in the village who had his own radio burst into her classroom with exciting news: 'When they left Unalakleet, Venn was in third place!' Shortly after, Afanasi ran to the school with confirmation: 'My God, no beginner has a right to be in third spot,' but Kendra said: 'Polar may be the best lead dog in the whole race,' and with Mr. Hooker's ardent approval, they dismissed school for the day and accompanied Kasm and Vladimir to the shortwave, where they heard in snatches the account of one of the most dramatic incidents in any Iditarod.

Afanasi explained the situation to Kendra: 'You mustn't think of this as an Olympic race with all the runners bunched. In the Iditarod they're scattered out. The Nome man in the lead is ahead by almost half a day. No one will catch him. The sixteenth man may be a day and a half behind. And the last man? Maybe a whole week.' Hooker interrupted: 'But this time it does seem as if the group behind the leader is bunched,' and he was correct.

A woman who had never before placed higher than fourteenth was, surprisingly, in second place, but as she sped her dogs onto the ice of Norton Sound, a moose testing the shoreline nearby panicked, darted in among the dogs, struggled free, and kicked the woman in the stomach and about the legs, wounding her seriously. Rick, well to the south in third place and already safe on the icy stretch leading to the finish at Nome, saw this happening as he came up, and whereas five other racers who also saw it hurried on to claim their spots among the coveted first nine, Rick turned aside, urged Polar to maximum speed, and arrived in time to fend off the enraged moose and place the battered woman on her sled.

With two of her dogs killed, there was no way she could continue as a competitor, but she insisted that she could limp into Nome under her own power, so she thanked Rick for stopping to help, hugged him, and urged him: 'Be on your way. You're still in this thing.' But he simply could not leave her with the dead dogs still in harness and herself needing attention, so he left the race for about two hours, unharnessed the dead dogs, tended her wounds, and sent her on toward Nome.

He never made up the time lost by this gallant gesture, and as the other racers sped past, he realized that he had lost any chance at third position and probably his place within the first nine. Actually, he finished thirteenth, but when he came to the finish line he was greeted with cheers, the woman having told a reporter stationed along the way what had happened. One drunk came out of his Nome bar to make the most pertinent observation: 'I never thought I'd see the day when I'd cheer for any son-of-a-bitch associated with Ross & Raglan, but this one knew what for,' and Rick's noble performance became the toast of the town that night.

The winner, a tough veteran from Kotzebue, had finished in fourteen days, nine hours, three minutes and twenty-three seconds, but the race could not be declared over till a week later, when the forty-sixth musher stumbled in to win the honored red lantern, symbolic of the light that used to shine from the caboose of railroad trains to prove that the last boxcar had passed. A college boy from the University of Iowa, he had taken twenty-one days and eighteen hours for this grueling race, and he was almost as proud of his red lantern as the winner was of his fifty grand.

WHEN RICK RETURNED to Desolation with Polar and the twelve other dogs, he was a hero, and many villagers crowded out to Kensington Kennels to pay tribute to the team that had conducted itself so ably and with such honor in the Iditarod. His gallantry had been the subject of articles in the Seattle and New York newspapers, and his picture appeared in *Time* magazine above the caption 'Winning Isn't Everything.' This spate of publicity brought a long letter from his grandfather, Malcolm Venn, chairman of the board of Ross & Raglan in Seattle. It was the first Rick had heard from his grandfather in more than two years.

He showed the letter to Kendra when she lingered that first evening after the others were gone. She liked the manly phrasing, the obvious pride the older man took in his maverick grandson:

> When you went north I told you to mimic your great-grandfather. Don't be afraid to try anything, and if you start, finish in style. We followed your progress in the odds and ends of news we got on local television and cheered your prospect of a fifth or even possibly a third, but we were far more proud of your thirteen.

'I don't get letters like that from my parents,' she said without self-pity, and as she looked at him—the certificate proving he had finished thirteenth in the Iditarod hanging just behind him on the wall—she saw him in a much clearer light than ever before: she admired the way he handled his dogs, with love and sternness, instilling in them a fierce and loyal drive to compete; she enjoyed his irreverent humor; and she appreciated the portrait she gleaned from his grandfather's letter of a family that was closely bound together in a long-standing tradition of mutual respect; and above all, she saw him as a stronger, more consolidated man than Jeb Keeler, and something of her thoughts must have shone in her eyes, for as she was about to leave the shack to return to the Teacherage, he reached out for her and said quietly: 'Don't you think it's time you stayed here?' and she whispered: 'Yes,' for she had found a man she could love.

Back in her own quarters the next afternoon, Kendra did what an honorable person would feel compelled to do: she wrote a frank letter to Jeb Keeler in Anchorage, thanking him for his valued friendship and explaining that she had fallen in love with another man: 'It looks as if any chance of our getting married has vanished, and I'm terribly sorry. On your next visit to Desolation let's talk about it, for I yearn to keep you as a friend.'

When she had sealed the envelope she said aloud, with the confidence that many young women have voiced in such circumstances: 'Well, that takes care of that.'

JUST ABOUT THIS time, in Washington, D.C., things were occurring that would eventually disrupt the lives of quite a few people in the village, the most dramatically affected being Kendra. The sequence of events began when the United States government awoke belatedly to the fact that Soviet Russia, Canada and even Norway were leaping ahead in the acquisition of knowledge about the arctic. In a somewhat frantic effort to catch up, a prestigious committee on arctic affairs had been appointed by the President, and it had assembled a consortium of American universities to sponsor and supervise a concentrated research attack on not only how to survive in arctic conditions but also how to utilize the arctic in either peace or war. Once the decision was made and the funds provided, this assembly of very bright men and women concluded that one of the first steps they ought to take was the furtherance of studies begun years ago on T-3, the floating ice island. As soon as that was agreed upon, the scholars in charge began to look about for arctic hands who'd had practical experience on T-3, and this threw them right into the lap of Vladimir Afanasi, who, as a young Eskimo with a university education, had been in charge of maintenance and operations on T-3 for three years.

The telephone call came from the President's scientific adviser in the White House: 'This Vladimir Afanasi? The one who served on T-Three? . . . How old are you now, Mr. Afanasi? . . . Can you still operate in real cold weather? . . . Would you be prepared to reactivate T-Three? . . . Right now? . . . Of course, I know that T-Three itself has long since vanished but its successor . . . maybe we'll call it T-Seven. I think that's next in line. . . . You would be prepared? . . . That's very good news, Mr. Afanasi. You cannot imagine how highly you've been praised by the men associated with this project. . . . By the way, you are an American citizen?'

'Is this top secret or anything?'

'Mr. Afanasi! Would I be using an open phone line if it were? We know what the Soviets are doing, they know what we're doing or about to do. Welcome aboard. You'll be hearing from us.'

Three days later a committee of three leading arctic specialists—one from Dartmouth, one from Michigan, one from the University in Fairbanks—met in Desolation with Afanasi, and for three hammering days they worked on the reactivation of a research station on what they called T-7. Maps of the arctic were spread everywhere. Old manifests of material required on T-3 were updated, formal agreements were drafted, and at the conclusion of the meetings Afanasi, by far the oldest man present, said: 'I want the right to hire my own assistant.'

'If he's qualified. If he can be cleared for security.'

'He's both. Very knowledgeable in arctic matters. Graduate of Stanford with a fine record. And available, that's important.'

'Is he in these parts?'

'He's at the edge of town. I'll take you to meet him.' So the four men drove out to the Kensington Kennels, where they were greeted by the agitated yapping of thirteen handsome dogs, whom they stopped momentarily to admire.

They found Rick Venn stretched out on his bed reading one of the great books about Antarctica, Apsley Cherry-Garrard's *The Worst Journey in the World,* and the fact that a man of Venn's age knew this classic endeared him in the hearts of the three scholars. 'You informed on Scott's tragedy?' the man from Dartmouth asked, and Rick said: 'Only the usual. Amundsen's accounts, some of the recent studies.'

'You a Scott man or an Amundsen man?' the scientist from Michigan asked, recalling the bitter animosities that had tormented the two polar explorers, and Rick said: 'Strictly Amundsen. He was a professional; Scott, a romantic.'

'Let's have nothing more to do with this young fellow,' the man from Michigan said. 'Rotten to the core.'

'Wait,' Venn said as he pulled on his trousers. 'If I was writing a poem about Antarctica, I'd choose Scott every time.'

The man from Michigan laughed: 'Not a preferred type, but acceptable. Go ahead.'

It was Afanasi who spoke, and Rick was impressed by the way these scholars deferred to the wise old Eskimo: 'Rick, we used to have an Arctic Research Lab in Barrow. Run by the Navy. Accomplished lots but the government closed it down. To save nickels and dimes. Russians leaped ahead of us in arctic knowledge, so to catch up we're going to reactivate the research we had been conducting on T-Three.'

'I read that it melted away, long since.'

'The very words I used when they broached the subject. This is a new island. They're calling it T-Seven this time. They want me to serve as kind of factotum. I want you to come along as my right hand.'

'How long? Two years, three years?'

'Who knows?'

Rick Venn was speechless, for this was what young men of ability dreamed about when they were graduate students: to be at the heart of some great enterprise in their field, to be surrounded by the top intellects of the preceding generations, to be applying all that had been learned in the past grueling years and to project learning forward. Those were the hopes of young medical students, geologists, literary critics or geographers. And rarely did an opportunity like T-7 come along.

'I'd be proud to work with you men,' he said finally, and the man from Dartmouth asked: 'What will you do with your dogs?'

'I'll cry a little and kiss each one goodbye, then pass them along to someone else.' He looked out at them: 'They carried me to thirteenth place in the Iditarod, you know.'

'I heard you could have finished about third,' the Michigan man said.

'You read about it? Third place? Who knows?' Suddenly he turned away from the dogs: 'Is this in any way secret?'

'No.'

'And you are going ahead? This is a job offer?'

Afanasi looked at the other three, and the chairman of this ad hoc committee, the man from Dartmouth, said, extending his hand: 'It is.'

On the flight back to Barrow in Rostkowsky's Cessna the Dartmouth man said: 'Did you notice, neither of them asked about salary,' and the Michigan man replied: 'This is their world. They love the north and they're a part of it. We're damned lucky to have found them.'

That afternoon, over maps left behind by the committee, Rick described his new job to Kendra, who felt a pang of apprehension on learning that the one man she loved was about to leave for an assignment of unlimited duration: 'For the past fifty or sixty thousand years, and probably much longer, over here at the northernmost tip of Canada, Ellesmere Island, immense glaciers occasionally calve icebergs that are so monstrous you can't really call them icebergs. They're ice islands, maybe three hundred square miles, a hundred and fifty feet thick.'

'That's unbelievable.'

'Everybody says that when they first hear about them. Well, they're real, and they circulate clockwise up there in the Arctic Ocean for several years before they drift off into the Atlantic. One of them sank the *Titanic* back in 1912.'

He showed her the track of the famous T-3 which had circulated north of Alaska for many years, and she asked: 'Why didn't it stay put?' and he said: 'Because it's floating in an ocean. Nobody seems to understand that the word arctic refers to an ocean; Antarctic, to a continent. But that's what they are.' And then he told her the most remarkable fact of all: 'The islands are so big and so flat that it's quite easy to level off an airfield right down the middle for as long as you need. You can land something as big as a 747 on an ice island, and the Russians do.'

'Do they have certain of these floating islands? And we have others?'

'Not really, not officially. But it works out that way. Or did.' And now he came to the critical reasons the Americans had decided to reactivate a research station on an ice island: 'Russia is way, way ahead of us in its ability to use the arctic. They've had men on ice islands continuously. We had one spurt, then quit. Fact is, we've pretty well surrendered the arctic to them.'

'And the three men who flew in here?' At Desolation Point, even children knew if an important letter arrived. 'They're going to start up again?'

'Yes. And they want Vladimir to supervise the day-to-day operations.'

'And he wants you to help?'

'He does.'

'And you've accepted?'

'I have.'

Desperately she wanted to cry 'What about us?'—but she intuitively knew that the sure way to lose a strong man like Rick Venn was to lasso him with tears or pin him down with a sense of obligation; he would fight against that and fly off. She also suspected that he was still unprepared to make a lifetime commitment, so she approached her problem obliquely and in a most beguiling way: 'What are you going to do about the dogs?'

'I was hoping you'd look after them, and find someone who'll care for them.'

'You mean sell them?'

'If you can. If not, give them away. But only to someone who'll run them.' He looked at the dogs who had served him so well. 'They're champions. They deserve to compete. It's in their blood.'

These words had a special meaning for Kendra; she saw Rick as a champion, destined to compete, and the ice island was an appropriate challenge, but this acknowledgment still left her isolated, and she felt like all women who have let one good man go to try for a better, only to lose both in her gamble.

'So I'm supposed to linger here, year after year, looking after your dogs.' It wasn't going the way she had intended, but it was to his eyes, not hers, that tears came: 'Kiddo! I've found me a real woman! I'll be back.'

'And you're sure I'll wait two years, or whatever. You're sure that Jeb won't come knocking and I'll say "Oh, what the hell?" and marry him?'

'I'm sure,' he said simply, and with repeated promises that he would be back to marry her, he closed the shack where they had been so happy, turned over his dogs, and flew with Afanasi to Barrow and then four hundred miles north over the open Arctic Ocean to where a floating ice island, eleven miles long and three wide, awaited their tardy experimentation.

THERE WERE EXPERTS other than the United States Commission on the Arctic who were interested in the complexities of the North Pacific, and two of the best-informed lived in small Asian villages where they spent their days and many of their nights immersed in studies which would have impact upon Alaska, either immediately or at some time in the distant future, for these two men, better than any Americans, appreciated the fact that Alaska's position, as the keystone of the great arch that encloses the North Pacific, gave her world importance.

The two men, one Japanese, one Russian, did not know each other, nor did they even realize that the other existed, but each kept on the wall of his study a large map showing all the nations bordering the Pacific, from Chile at the southeastern tip through Mexico and the United States on the east, across to Siberia and Japan on the west, and down the southwest to Indonesia, Australia and New Zealand. It was a glorious stretch of terrain made more so by the proliferation of red and black dots which peppered the circumference of this vast ocean: indeed, the map looked as if a hundred bees had stung places like Colombia, Kamchatka and the Philippines, raising ugly red welts. These were the clusters of volcanoes, dead and active, that gripped the Pacific in a rim of fire. These were the soaring, explosive mountains, with lyrical names like El Misto, Cotopaxi, Popocatepetl, Mount Shasta, Fujiyama, Krakatoa, Vulcan and Ruapehu, that bespoke the violent character of these areas.

The black dots, far more numerous, indicated where in historic times huge earthquakes had shaken the land, with heavy black crosses indicating the quakes that had leveled parts of Mexico City in 1985, San Francisco in 1906, Anchorage in 1964, Tokyo in 1923, New Zealand in 1931. The most casual glance at these maps revealed the constant attack of lava and trembling earth along the edges of the Pacific, a record of the tremendous relentless forces of the wandering plates.

Thus, when the Nazca Plate subducted under the continental plate, the edges shattered and parts of Mexico City collapsed in ruins. When the Pacific Plate ground along the North American Plate, San Francisco caught fire, and when the opposite side of the Pacific Plate subducted under the Asian Plate, Tokyo's buildings fell apart. And when, in its northern reaches, the Pacific Plate hammered its way down under the shallow continental Bering Sea, the world's most concentrated chain of volcanoes rose gloriously in the sky, while the earth's most incessant family of earthquakes shook the land and, if they were submarine, sent great tsunamis radiating through the Pacific.

Alaska, occupying the crown of this fiery rim, had a position not only of geographical dominance as the link between Asia and North America, but also of potential economic and military importance, and in these closing years of the century the Japanese expert was concerned primarily with the economic, the Russian with the military.

In a beautiful mountain village some twenty miles west of Tokyo on the minor Tama River, Kenji Oda, the able mountaineer who had rescued Kimiko Takabuki from her fall in the crevasse, pursued his studies. Tamagata, a village of graceful wood and stone houses in the traditional Japanese style, had been chosen by the powerful Oda family as the site of their research operations. The family had many commercial interests, but son Kenji, oldest and ablest of the third generation, had concentrated on the family's wood-pulp holdings, and to perfect himself in this international specialty, he had made himself familiar with the pulp forests of Norway, Finland and Washington State in the United States. While working with paper interests in Washington he had climbed Mount Rainier in the dead of winter with a team of American fanatics.

At thirty-nine he enjoyed his seclusion at Tamagata because it provided a serene environment in which to reflect at a distance on the balancing of these world markets, and also, easy access to the international flights that left Tokyo almost hourly for all parts of the Oda empire: the factories in São Paulo, the newly acquired hotels in Amsterdam and the forest leases in Norway and Finland. But the more he studied the world paper problems and Japan's diminishing access to major forests, the more clearly he saw that the almost endless forests of Alaska had to become a prime target for anyone interested in the making and distribution of paper.

'In many practical ways,' he told his study group, 'the forests of Alaska are closer to Japan than they are to the major centers in the United States. A manufacturer in the eastern United States can get his wood pulp more easily from the Carolinas, Canada or Finland than from Alaska. Our big Japanese ships can put in to Alaskan ports, load with pulp, and come back across the North Pacific to our paper and rayon plants here in Japan a lot cheaper than the Americans can handle the same wood pulp by truck or train.'

A representative of the Oda shipping lines—freight only—pointed out that the maritime distance from Japan to Sitka was rather longer than Kenji had indicated, whereupon the latter chuckled: 'You have good eyes. But if we go ahead with this, we're not going to Sitka. I have my eye on a rather substantial island just north of Kodiak, on this side of the bay,' and he indicated a densely forested island which could supply the Oda Paper Works for the next fifty years.

'On our mountain-climbing trips to Denali,' he explained to the men, 'our plane broke out of the clouds right about here, and below I saw this undeveloped island. Since we'd started our descent into Anchorage, we were low enough for me to see that this was prime forest, probably spruce, easy to log, easy to reduce to pulp, easy to ship back to our plants in liquid form.'

'Any chance that we can get long-term control? I don't mean outright ownership.'

Before replying to this critical question, Oda became reflective, and looking at the big map dominating the wall facing the men, he pointed to Alaska: 'Strategically speaking, this area is more a part of Japan than it is of the United States. Every natural resource Alaska has is more valuable to us than it is to America. The oil at Prudhoe Bay ought to be coming straight across the Pacific to us. The lead, the coal and certainly the wood pulp. The Koreans aren't stupid. They're moving in everywhere. China is going to show enormous interest in Alaska; Singapore and Formosa could use Alaska's resources to tremendous benefit.'

When the attractive hostesses interrupted the discussion to bring morning tea and rice cookies, Kenji took advantage of the break to suggest that they move into the garden, where the beauties of the Japanese landscape, so manicured compared to the wildness of Alaska, put the men at ease, and there he said as the meeting resumed: 'You can understand Alaska best if you view it as a Third World country, an underdeveloped nation whose raw materials are to be sold off to the more developed countries. The United States will never utilize Alaska properly, never has, never will. It's too far away, too cold . . . America has no concept of what it has, and very little interest in finding out. That leaves the marketplace open to us.'

'What can we do about it?' one of the men asked, and Kenji replied: 'We've already done it. On my last trip back from Denali, I started negotiations to lease that wooded island. Well, not the land, you understand. They'd never allow that. But the right to cut trees, build a chip mill, erect a dock for our ships.'

'Any luck?'

'Yes! I'm delighted to inform you that after several months of the most difficult negotiations . . . The Alaskans are far from stupid. I think they see their position just as clearly as we do. They know they're orphans in their own land. They know they have to cooperate with their Asian markets. And they know . . . at least the people I negotiated with knew how intimately they were going to be affiliated with both China and Russia. They can't escape it. So I had no trouble in gaining their attention. I think they'd prefer to trade with Japan, their wood, their oil, their minerals for whatever we can supply in return.'

The group, most of whom had motored up to Tamagata before breakfast, relaxed in the sun, munched sembei and drank tea. One of the men, who taught geography as a part-time consultant to a university, said: 'I don't want to play the big geopolitician, but that map back there . . . Could we take another look at it?' When they were seated as before, he continued: 'We and China enjoy a lucky advantage in our potential dealings with Alaska. But look at how close Alaska is to Soviet Russia! At these two little islands, which don't show on this map, the two superpowers are about a mile and a half apart. If commercial air travel were permitted between the two areas . . . up here where the two big peninsulas jut out, maybe sixty miles apart, you could fly it in maybe ten minutes.'

'What's your point?' Oda asked, and the man said: 'I think we can predict that Alaska and the Soviet Union will always be suspicious of each other. No trade, no amity possible. Also, what Alaska has, Siberia also has, so they are not natural trading partners. On the other hand, what Alaska has is what we need, what Formosa and Singapore need, not to mention China.'

'Your conclusion?'

'Build the pulping plant. Send our tankers to . . . What's the name of the island?'

'Kagak. Old Aleutian word, I believe, meaning something like *rich horizons.'*

'Send our tankers to Kagak. But while we're doing so, let's not overlook the copper mines, the oil which in common sense ought to come our way, and anything else that great empty land will be able to provide in the future.'

Now Oda took command: 'For some time it has been clear to me that the role of the Third World nations is to provide the technologically and educationally advanced nations with raw materials at a fair price. Allow countries like Japan and Singapore to apply intelligence and mechanical skill to those materials and pay for them by sending back to the Third World countries our finished products, especially those that they will never have the ability to invent or manufacture for themselves.'

When several young men well informed on international trade protested that such a simplistic exchange might not be indefinitely possible, Oda pointed to the calculator his financial expert had been using: 'Watanabe-san, how many controls on your computer, which as you others can see is about the size of a large playing card?' It took Watanabe more than a minute to summarize the wonderfully intricate capabilities of the thirty-five keys on his hand-held calculator: 'Ten keys for the digits and zero. Twenty-five others for various mathematical functions. But many keys can provide up to three different functions. Grand total: thirty-five obvious keys, plus sixty-three hidden variable functions, for ninety-eight options.'

Oda smiled and said: 'When I bought my progenitor of Watanabe's miracle gadget, it offered me ten numerals and the four arithmetic functions. It was so simple that it could be handled by anyone. But when you add eighty-eight additional function keys, you move it forever beyond the capacity of the untrained, and most Third World citizens will be in that category. They'll have to rely on us to do their thinking, their inventing and their manufacturing.'

'Just a minute,' one of the team protested. 'I visited the University of Alaska at Fairbanks on our last visit. They have scores of students in engineering who can handle bigger computers than Watanabe's.'

'Exactly!' Oda agreed. 'But when they graduate they'll have to find jobs in what they call the Lower Forty-eight. Their absence will leave Alaska a Third World nation, and let's remember that. Courtesy, assistance, modest stance, listen more than talk, and provide at every turn the help Alaska needs. Because our relationship with that great untapped reservoir can be magnificently helpful, to both of us.'

It was on these principles that Kenji Oda and his wife, Kimiko, who knew Alaska from the inside as it were, moved to the island of Kagak north of Kodiak to establish the big United Alaskan Pulp Company. Significant was the fact that the word *Japanese* appeared nowhere in the title or the printed materials of this

firm, nor were Japanese workmen involved in building the large and complicated plant which reduced Kagak spruce trees to a liquid pulp for tankering
across the Pacific to Japan. And when the plant was ready for operation, no
Japanese crews appeared to slash down the trees, and only three Japanese
engineers settled in Kagak to supervise the intricate machinery.

Kenji and Kimiko did take residence in a modest house on Kagak Island,
and they did rent a modest office in Kodiak, to which highly skilled technicians
from Tokyo flew in from time to time to inspect and supervise procedures. After
the first few months, at an enterprise which involved some nineteen million
dollars, there were only six Japanese on the scene and at least half the ships that
ferried the pulp to Japan operated under some flag other than the Rising Sun,
for if the great industrialists of Japan were determined to take over the development and utilization of Alaska's raw materials, they did not want to be flagrant
about it or generate local animosities.

In such behavior the Odas were exemplary. Kenji performed no act which
drew adverse attention to himself, but many which added to his sober reputation in the Kodiak community. Was a string quartet to be invited in from
Seattle? He contributed at a level just below the three leading local citizens.
Were local literary lights producing a fine outdoor spectacle about Baranov and
the Russian settlement of the Aleutians and Kodiak? As a paper expert he
contributed all costs for printing the programs. On two occasions he invited
leading Kodiak officials to fly with him and Kimiko for a vacation in their
wooded village at Tamagata, and on another occasion he underwrote the expenses of two college professors from the University of Alaska at Anchorage to
attend an international conference in Chile on the Pacific Rim. As a result of
such contributions, he and Kimiko became known as 'those fine Japanese who
have such a creative interest in Kodiak and Alaska,' and someone listening to
that assessment would add: 'And they both climbed Denali, which is more than
we can say for any of the Americans hereabouts.' But during his absences from
the pulp mill at Kagak, when he was not vacationing at Tamagata or attending
conferences in Chile, Oda was quietly probing into the remote areas of Alaska,
seeking out sites like Bornite, where copper might be found, or Wainwright,
which had rich seams of coal. Once he heard of a distant mountainside in the
northwest arctic whose assays looked as if it might contain promising concentrations of zinc, and after shipping to Tokyo samples of ore taken from various
spots in the area, he arranged for a ninety-nine-year lease on a vast area. When
questioned about this on his next visit to the research headquarters of his
family's operations at Tamagata, he said frankly and with as honest an assessment as he could muster: 'Japan does not want to "take over" Alaska, as some
critics suggest. All we want is to do with the other raw materials what we're
already doing so successfully with wood pulp at Kagak. And let me stress, in
case the subject comes up when I'm not available, Alaska profits from our
present deal equally with us. It's what you might call the perfect relationship.
They sell raw materials they haven't the capital to develop themselves and we
get the raw materials which we can process and on which we can earn substantial profits.'

'Can we do the same with Alaskan lead and coal and zinc?'

'Better. Their bulk is smaller, potential profits greater.'

The wise men of Japan contemplated this for some minutes, for this was the
way in which their island empire—no raw materials, excessive manpower,
superexcessive brainpower—functioned, but then one older man, who had
experienced the great revulsion the world had expressed toward a similar Japan

in the 1930s, asked quietly: 'But why should the United States allow us to operate in this manner?' and Oda gave the only sensible explanation: 'Because they started back in 1867 when they bought Alaska with the idea that the area was worthless, and in the first half century of ownership they totally ignored what they had, unable to perceive it as having any real value. Those injurious misconceptions persist. They contaminate a nation's thought processes. And it will be well into the next century before the leaders of America awaken to what they have in their "icebox." In the meantime, Alaska must always be visualized as part of Asia, and that brings it neatly into our orbit.'

And on this very day when the Japanese were laying their far-ranging plans to utilize the unattended riches of Alaska, similar industrialists in Korea, Taiwan, Hong Kong and Singapore were reaching the same conclusions and taking comparable steps to bring Alaska into their orbits.

THE SECOND ASIAN intellectual who was contem-plating Alaska with assiduous care in these days was a man of sixty-six who lived in a small village south of Irkutsk on the way to Lake Baikal. There he had assembled a treasury of family papers and imperial studies relating to the Russian settlement and occupation of Alaska, and with the encouragement of the Soviet government, was making himself into the world's unchallenged authority on the subject.

He was Maxim Voronov, heir of that distinguished family who had provided Russian Alaska with able men and women leaders, including the great churchman Father Vasili Voronov, who took as his wife the Aleutian Cidaq and who left her to become Metropolitan of All the Russias.

Now, in the later years of his life, still slim and erect but with a shock of white hair which he combed back with his fingers, this Voronov had retired to the Irkutsk of his ancestors, where he presided over Russia's outstanding collection of data on her Aleutian discoveries and her governance of Alaska. Since he knew more than any other Russian about these subjects, he certainly knew more than any American, and in the course of painfully analyzing the historical record, spending the years 1947 to 1985 in doing so, he reached certain interesting conclusions which had begun to attract the attention of the Soviet leadership. During the summer of 1986, when the weather in eastern Siberia was almost perfect, a team of three Russian foreign policy experts spent two weeks in protracted discussion with Voronov in which Alaska was kept in constant focus. The three men were all younger than Maxim and they deferred to his age and scholarship, but not to the interpretation of his data.

'What would be your conclusions, Comrade Voronov, as to practical timetables?'

'What I'm about to say should be of crucial importance to your thinking, Comrade Zelnikov.'

:That's why we came to see you. Please proceed.'

'Barring unforeseen disruptions of the greatest magnitude, I cannot see a propitious moment arising much before the year 2030. That's forty-five years down the road, and of course it could be longer.'

'What's your thinking?'

'First, America will probably remain strong till that time. Second, the Soviet Union will not yet have acquired the superiority in either strength or moral leadership to make the move practical. Third, it will take Alaska about that many years to fall so far behind that our move will be both sensible and inviting to her. And fourth, the rest of the world will require about that long to accommodate itself to the practicality and historical justification of our move.'

'Will your studies, the basic groundwork, that is, be in better shape in 2030?'

'I won't be here, of course, but whoever follows me will have been able to refine my studies.'

'Have you a successor in mind?'

'No.'

'You better find one.'

'Then you're prepared—that is, Moscow thinks enough of this . . .'

'It's vital. The pot's far on the back of the stove, as they say in America, but it must be kept quietly bubbling. Comrade Petrovsky could be alive in 2030, and if not he, somebody else.' Petrovsky smiled and said: 'Let's suppose that I am still alive. What sequence of thought should I be pursuing in the interval?'

Patiently, slowly and with great conviction Maxim Voronov spelled out his vision of the future relationship between the Soviet Union and Alaska, and as he spoke his visitors from Moscow realized that through eight generations the Voronovs of Irkutsk had never ceased thinking of the Aleutians and Alaska as an inherent part of the Russian Empire.

'We start with the fact, not the assumption, that Alaska belongs to Russia by the three sacred rights of history: discovery, occupation, established governance. And by the right of geography, because Alaska was as much a part of Asia as it was of North America. And by the fact that Russia gave the area responsible government when we had it and the Americans did not when they took it over. And most persuasively, we have proved that we can develop our Siberia creatively while America lags far behind us in developing her northernmost part of Alaska.

'In their discussions of the future the Americans have invented a highly applicable word, the *scenario*, borrowed from the theater. It means *an orderly scheme governing how things might work out*. What we now require is a Soviet scenario whereby we can regain the Alaska that is rightfully ours and do it with a minimum of international disruption.'

'Can there be such a scenario?' Comrade Zelnikov asked, and Voronov assured his listeners that there not only could be, but that there was an actual plan which would bring Alaska back into the Russian orbit.

'We use two great concepts, Russia in the historic past, the Soviet Union in the present, and there is no discontinuity between them. They are one moral entity and neither is in conflict with the other. I shall use the word *Russia* when speaking of the past, the *Soviet Union* when referring to the present or future. Our task is to bring Alaska back into the bosom of timeless Russia, and our Soviet Union is the agency through which we must work. The scenario is simple, the rules governing it implacable.

'First, in the decades ahead we must never disclose our objective, not by word or deed or even the most casual thought. If the United States government learns of our design, they will move to block us. I discuss these plans with no one, which is why I have no indicated successor. You three must keep your own plans just as secret.

'Second, we must never make even the most tentative overt move prematurely. World conditions, not our hopes, will determine when the time is ripe for us to make our intentions and our claims known. Eighty years would not be too long to wait for the propitious moment, because I am positive that it will in due course arrive.

'Third, the significant signal will be the decline of American power and, more important, the gradual wasting away of American will power.'

'Can we anticipate such decline? Zelnikov asked, and Voronov replied: 'Inescapably. Democracies grow weary. They lose momentum. I can foresee the time will come when they might want to rid themselves of Alaska.' He paused: 'Just the way we wanted to get rid of it in 1866 and '67.' These obiter dicta brought him to his major strategy:

'Now we forget Russia and focus sternly on the Soviet Union. Our argument must invariably be that the men who so cravenly gave away Alaska were not entitled to do so. They did not speak for the Russian people. In no way did they represent the soul of Russia. The sale was corrupt from the moment it was conceived. It had not the slightest validity. It transferred no rights to America and its terms will be reversed by any impartial international court or by the perceived wisdom of the rest of the world. The sale of Alaska was fraudulent, without moral base, and is subject to reversal. Alaska was, is and shall be Russian. The entire logic of world history demands this.'

The three visitors, not knowing enough historical detail to judge the merits of Voronov's claim that the transfer had been basically illegal, asked for substantiation, and he cited the three solid bases for the Soviet Union's claim to Alaska:

'I warn you gentlemen and those who follow in your place. Indeed, I've drawn up my most important *aide-memoire* on just this point, and you must keep it on file for your successors and mine. You must base our claim on legal principles, never on force, and I assure you that our legal claim is impeccable. It must prevail in the court of world opinion.

'First, the Russian government as it then existed was incompetent to speak for the Russian people. It was a corrupt tyranny from which the huge bulk of the Russian people were excluded. Since it possessed no authority, its acts were illegal, especially those involving the disposition of territories over which it exercised no moral control. The transfer became illegal at the moment of sale, which was itself totally venal and therefore unenforceable.

'Second, the agent who maneuvered the sale and without whose infamous participation it could not have gone forward was not a Russian; he was not formally authorized to conduct negotiations; and he could not possibly have been construed as acting on behalf of the Russian people. Baron Edouard de Stoeckl, as he liked to style himself, had no right to the title he paraded; he was either a Greek adventurer or an Austrian lackey who interposed himself in the negotiations, God knows how, if you'll forgive an old folk expression, and in much of the affair he acted solely on his own without consultation with St. Petersburg. It was his sale, not Russia's.'

At this point Maxim showed the men from Moscow three shelves of books in some seven or eight different languages dealing with Baron Edouard de Stoeckl and a set of two notebooks in which he, Voronov, had chronicled the life of this shadowy man month by month for a period of nearly four decades. But he had long ago decided that it would not further the Soviet Union's claim to Alaska for him to publish his materials now: 'It's all here, gentlemen, in these note-books. You can publish a devastating biography of De Stoeckl whenever you care to.' He laughed nervously: 'I'd appreciate it if you'd cite me in one of the footnotes.' And now he was ready with one of his most telling points:

'Third, there is the ugly business of the missing two hundred and fifty thousand dollars. I have facts in this second pair of notebooks, and a miserable set of facts they are. I have traced with infinite detail, accounting for nearly every kopeck, the money that De Stoeckl handled in this malo-dorous affair, and without the slightest ambiguity or juggling of figures, I have proved that De Stoeckl had in his control not the hundred and fifty thousand dollars which American scholars cite, but nearly twice that much. So what happened to it? American historians have long suspected that Baron de Stoeckl used this money to buy votes in the American House of Representatives, but they've never been able to prove it. I have. With the greatest care and discretion I've bought family records, old accounts, newspaper suspicions and hard proof. American documents, English, German consular reports—and they're a clever lot, those Ger-mans—and this row of Russian sources. Taken together, they prove without question that De Stoeckl corrupted the American Congress to an unbelievable degree.'

Here he stopped dramatically, smiled at each of his visitors, and hammered home his major point:

'Do you understand what this means? That the sale was corrupted from the moment of its completion in Congress. The American government in its wisdom did not want Alaska. It knew those remote areas were no part of its territory. The vote was consistently against either purchasing our land or paying for it when it was purchased. But De Stoeckl, this evil adventurer from nowhere, he forced America to take it, and he accom-plished this coercion by paying United States congressmen to vote against the national interest. America's acquisition of Alaska was totally corrupt and must be rescinded.'

In the discussion that followed, Voronov proposed that some Soviet scholar, not himself 'because that might attract unwanted attention to what I'm doing,' be authorized to publish a small hard-hitting volume which might be titled *What Happened to the Quarter Million?* It would reveal the surprising data ac-cumulated here in Irkutsk, name the congressmen who accepted the bribes, and establish in world circles the solid footing upon which the Soviet Union's later claim for Alaska would be based. But Comrade Zelnikov had for some time been developing his own scenario for the ultimate recapture of Alaska, and he counseled patience: 'I assure you it would look suspicious if Soviet scholars reopened this subject now. I agree with you, Voronov, it would awaken world scholarship to the facts, and it would build a solid foundation for our later claims, but I fear we would lose far more in the long run than we would gain in the short. Keep your notebooks for 2030, when we'll use them and everything else with devastating effect.'

Maxim Voronov came from a family of fighters and he was not prepared to accept a reversal so easily: 'Could we encourage foreign scholars to do our work for us?'

'I don't see how. Anything surreptitious we did would be bound to leak out.'

'But scholars in the United States and especially in Canada are already probing into these muddy waters to see if they can locate carp hiding at the bottom,' and here he showed the men half a dozen remarkable publications, barely known in the West, in which Canadians and Americans dredged up some of the easier facts that he had been uncovering since the end of World War II. Any one of these writers stood on an elevated platform of learning from which he or she could take off and reach the higher levels already occupied by Voronov, but the four plotters could devise no strategy whereby the Soviet Union could encourage or underwrite the necessary studies. 'It would be too risky,' Zelnikov warned, at which Voronov snorted: 'Russians can't do it, and Canadians and Americans can't be pushed. So the truth can only be very slowly revealed. And may be lost if too much time passes.'

'Not with your notebooks in existence,' Zelnikov said. 'And I want to take photocopies back to Moscow with me. We'll start shooting them as soon as we can get an army photography team in here.'

'We have good copy machines right here,' Voronov said, and Zelnikov smiled: 'Would you trust your notebooks to just anybody? The CIA probably runs your machines.'

So the time bomb on Alaska began ticking in both Irkutsk, where the individual tiles of the groundwork were being assiduously pieced together by Voronov, and in Moscow, where clever operatives like Zelnikov and Petrovsky were contemplating the geopolitical moves that would be necessary if Alaska were to be successfully reclaimed. All who worked on this sensitive project kept in mind Maxim Voronov's closing statement at the Irkutsk meeting: 'The time for our action will never be ripe unless the whole world sees great changes. But century by century such changes do occur, and we should be prepared when the next one arrives.' Neither he nor Zelnikov believed that the United States would willingly or even unwillingly surrender its grasp on Alaska. 'Those people labored too hard to extend their territory from their foothold on the Atlantic to the Pacific to relinquish anything,' Voronov predicted, but Zelnikov corrected him: 'They won't do the surrendering. World opinion, world conditions will dictate it, and they'll be powerless to resist.'

THERE WAS A third expert, not in Asia, who kept his eye trained on Alaska. He was an Italian-born volcanologist who had spent his early days on a farm in the shadow of Mount Vesuvius, and since he was a precocious child, by the age of fourteen he had become something of an expert on volcanoes and earthquakes. At fifteen he enrolled at the University of Bologna, where he excelled in science, and at twenty at the California Institute of Technology, where he earned a doctorate in seismology, his American citizenship and an appointment to a federal seismological station in the Los Angeles region. There he mastered the intricacies of earthquake measurement, assessment and prediction, knowledge in the first two fields being far more sophisticated than in the latter.

Giovanni Spada, forty-one, found himself in the small Alaskan city of Palmer, where the Flatches had done their marketing and where LeRoy had flown his first planes. There, on a quiet street lined with trees, he supervised operations in an inconspicuous white building of the Tsunami Research Center. On behalf of the governments of the United States, Canada, Japan and the Soviet Union, Spada surveyed the behavior of the volcanoes, earthquakes and devastating tsunamis that originated along the northern apex of the Rim of Fire. It was his responsibility, among other tasks, to alert the northern Pacific areas from Japan to Hawaii to Mexico and all points north when the volatile arc of the Aleutians generated a tsunami that might sweep with mounting force across the ocean toward a distant shore.

In the summer of 1986, wishing to impress upon a new group of associates assigned to the Tsunami Center the power of earthquakes to generate huge marine disturbances, he flew his team down to Lituya Bay, some four hundred and fifty miles to the southeast. There he led them to a spot high in the surrounding mountains where they could see the beautiful bay below: 'Observe that it's a long, thin bay with steep sides and a narrow opening to the Pacific.'

When his younger colleagues had familiarized themselves with the terrain, he told a story which astounded them: 'On 9 July 1958 an earthquake registering a massive eight on the Richter scale struck about a hundred miles north of here in the Yakutat area. The jolt was so strong that about forty million cubic yards of rock and earth were dislodged from that little mountain over there at the head of the bay and plunged all at once into the bay. The resulting splash created the greatest wave the world has seen in recorded history, and you can see for yourselves the magnitude of devastation it produced.'

As they looked down they slowly began to see that this wave, penned in as it was into the narrow bay, had risen tremendously high, uprooting every tree it encountered, and Spada suggested: 'Will someone who's had surveying experience calculate how high on the flanks of the mountainside the wave rose?' and a young man from the Colorado School of Mines laid out with his thumb and forefinger strata from sea level to the line of denudation, and after a while said in an awed voice: 'My God, that's more than a thousand feet high!' and Spada said quietly: 'Actually, that wave rose one thousand seven hundred and forty feet. That's the kind of tsunami a submarine earthquake can generate in a closed area.'

At Palmer, with his battery of delicate seismographs probing the earth's crust, and with instantaneous connections to similar watch stations in Canada, California, Japan, Kamchatka and the Aleutians, Spada monitored the restless plates which ground together deep below the surface of the ocean, now advancing, now submerging, now fracturing and often slipping and sliding one against the other to produce the submarine earthquakes which gave birth to the devastating tsunamis. He was especially responsible for any tsunamis originating in the Aleutians, for they had proved their capacity to overwhelm cities, towns and villages along the coast thousands of miles away, and when the stylus on his seismographs shuddered, indicating that something had slipped somewhere, he alerted some sixty stations throughout the Pacific that a tsunami might be on its way.

But Spada also monitored those earthquakes which were not submarine, or those which transmitted their power directly to inland locations. Thus, in 1964 he had caught the first tremors of that violent quake which struck Anchorage, dropping sections of the city forty feet, raising others, and creating havoc across a wide area. More than a hundred and thirty lives were lost in that quake which first registered on the Richter scale as 8.6 but which was later calculated to have been 9.2, the greatest ever recorded in North America. It was about ten times greater than the quake which had destroyed San Francisco in 1906.

Spada maintained a master map, one that showed in extended detail the supposed structure of the Aleutian chain, and whenever an earthquake struck in that region he filled in with red crayon that portion of the Aleutian arc. To his assistants he said, when his map was completed: 'Gradually, since 1850, we've noted the areas where the plates have shifted,' and he pointed to nine different arcs which filled in spaces on his map. 'At each of these sites an earthquake has eventuated. The plates have readjusted.' He allowed his assistants time to digest the data, then added: 'So in these three gaps . . .' He need say no more.

From Lapak Island to the west where it joined Tanaga and out to Gareloi, there was a neat arc of red dots; a big earthquake at the beginning of the century had resulted from the shift that occurred in the plates there, but east of Lapak to Adak and Great Sitkin the map was cadaverously white, which meant that the great readjustment of the plates had not yet occurred along that gap. A new man aboard asked: 'Can we expect a big quake out there one of these days?' and Spada said: 'We can.' He had been on solitary duty that night of 19 September 1985 when the Nazca Plate slipped violently, subducting under the bordering South American continental plate. His eye caught the vigorous activity of the tracing arm before the audible signals sounded, and he said to himself: That's rather big, and when he consulted his backup seismographs he whistled: Seven-point-eight! That's got to have consequences.

By now his assistants, roused by the electronic signals flashing in their bedrooms, rushed to the Tsunami Center. 'Any likelihood of a movement north?' a new man asked, and Spada said: 'Seven-point-eight could give us repercussions anywhere.'

'Where's the epicenter?' the young man asked, and Spada said: 'We can't pinpoint it yet,' but now reports from nearly a dozen other monitoring stations allowed him to triangulate the direction and place the locus of the earthquake fairly accurately at a spot well out in the Pacific Ocean and southeast of Mexico. 'It's far enough offshore not to pose any threat to land areas,' he said with some confidence, 'but the entire Pacific coastline could be vulnerable to a tsunami.'

However, within minutes, reports came rushing in of a massive earthquake beneath Mexico City, and Spada was aghast: 'To exert so much power so far from the slippage! It must have been much bigger than seven-eight,' and after he had assembled reports from around the world, it was he who first calculated that the Nazca shift had produced a quake of 8.1 on the Richter scale, much stronger than at first supposed.

This time a tsunami did not eventuate; only inland Mexico suffered the full force of this titanic disruption, and even before accurate casualty reports from Mexico City trickled in, Spada warned his team: 'There will be many dead,' and more than ten thousand were. But three days later his attention was diverted by a modest rumbling of Qugang Volcano on Lapak Island, in an area that generated disturbances of one kind or another. He dispatched a plane to inspect the activity, and relaxed when the report arrived: 'Six passes, six different elevations. No sign of major activity and no indication that anything major might develop.'

Spada occasioned in his superiors both respect and amusement. He had an uncanny sense regarding volcanoes, earthquakes and tsunamis, as if his childhood experiences near Vesuvius had acclimated him to their behavior, and he was invaluable to Russians, Japanese and Canadians alike for the thoroughness of his watch on their frontiers. He insisted upon calling himself a *vulcanologist*, the Italian and perhaps original spelling of the word rather than the more popular *volcanologist*. As a classicist—his father having been a teacher of Latin and Roman mythology—he believed that the older word related the phenomena with which he dealt to a whole nest of primordial causes, while the latter specified too narrowly its emphasis on volcanoes.

In his spare time, when he climbed the Talkeetna Mountains or explored the fascinating Matanuska Glacier with his American wife, they sometimes rested on a knoll and drank iced tea, munched on sandwiches, and contemplated the violence that marked the North Pacific: 'Great ice sheets grind down the mountains. The seas freeze over and throw up huge blocks of ice. Volcanoes like Qugang erupt, spewing millions of tons of lava and ash into the air. Earthquakes devastate cities, and deep in the sea tsunamis are unleashed to sweep away towns.'

His wife once responded to these reflections with a sober one of her own: 'And all the time, at the poles, ice begins to accumulate, until the glaciers spread relentlessly again to engulf all we've done.' As she poured more tea she said: 'When you live in Alaska, you live with change,' and then laughed at her own pomposity: 'Wouldn't it be hilarious, twenty thousand years from now, when the Bering land bridge is open again, if we all walked back to Asia?'

And so the speculation continued. In his vacation sessions at Tamagata west of Tokyo, Kenji Oda conjectured on the economic future of Alaska; in his cottage east of Irkutsk, Maxim Voronov tried to predict when his beloved Russia, whether Soviet or not, would be strong enough to win back Alaska; and in his austere white building in Palmer, Giovanni Spada tracked the behavior of volcanoes, earthquakes and tsunamis.

And deep within the heart of the Arctic Ocean on T-7, Rick Venn struggled to help the United States catch up with the experts of other nations in a comprehensive understanding of the arctic seas, and the rifts in the ocean floor from which new worlds were being built, and the wandering terranes which would one day construct a modified Alaska, and the Rim of Fire which dictated life in the Pacific, and the slowly growing ice caps at the poles, south and north, which would one day engulf so much of the world in another age of ice.

'There's so much to learn,' he said to Afanasi as they studied the polar stars. 'So much to fit together.'

U NBEKNOWN TO THESE civilian geniuses in Japan, Siberia and Alaska, there were in the latter jurisdiction three powerful groups whose duty it was to monitor whatever happened in arctic areas. From Elmendorf Air Force Base near Anchorage and Eielson near Fairbanks, two of the most powerful in the world, pilots flew night and day keeping watch on Russian air movements, and from time to time these sentinels sent back coded messages: 'Two invaders over Desolation Point,' and American fighter planes would scramble aloft to let the Russians know they were under surveillance. Of course, Russian planes kept similar watch from secret bases in Siberia.

And out on distant Lapak Island, where so much history had occurred since the first arrival of men and women twelve thousand years ago, rose a great black windowless building ten stories tall. It contained secret devices understood by only a few hundred experts throughout the United States (plus some twenty clever analysts in Moscow) and served as America's principal intellectual shield against surprise Communist attacks. Had the ancient mummy still occupied her cave on Lapak, she would have enjoyed this great black building and approved the novel use to which her island was being put.

In this quiet, restless manner the perpetual duel of brilliant minds—Japanese, Korean, Chinese, Russian, Canadian and, sometimes most effective of all, American—continued, with all playing the tantalizing game of 'What's going to happen next in the arctic?'

I T WAS AUTUMN when LeRoy Flatch experienced a temporary blackout—which frightened him, for his unconsciousness lasted several moments. Fortunately, he was not flying his Cessna, but when he came to he cried aloud: 'Jesus! Suppose I'd been trying to land!' And when he discussed the incident with his wife, she said firmly: 'LeRoy, time to quit flying,' and she started asking around as to who might want to buy their Cessna-185.

LeRoy was sixty-seven years old that year and not in the best of shape. Some old-time bush pilots flew when they were in their eighties, but they were lean and sinewy men who had cared for themselves, if not for the planes which they kept cracking up. Flatch was not of this breed; he liked beer and greasy Mexican food too much to keep his weight down, and his excesses added about fifteen years to his apparent age, so he listened to his wife's advice, even consulting with the prospective buyers for his plane.

But he was delayed in disposing of what his wife called 'your death trap' because of two seemingly unrelated events which involved him again in serious charter flying. In early October word flashed through Talkeetna of an extraordinary discovery near an archaeology dig called the Birch Tree Site, where a lone hunter rafting down a river saw protruding from the bank at his eye level the brown water-stained tusk of a mammoth that must have been trapped there twelve or thirteen thousand years ago. The hunter had attended the university in Fairbanks for two years and from a couple of good geology courses had learned to appreciate the significance of such a find. So, marking the area carefully on his map, he scrambled back to his raft and hurried on to Talkeetna, where he contacted the university: 'I'm no authority, but I picked about in the mud enough to think that this one still has most of its skin and hair intact.'

The response was electrifying, with two different teams of investigators flying in to Talkeetna and wanting to hire bush pilots to take them to the site. In this way, LeRoy Flatch was lured back into flying to take the college professors and their cargo the fifty-eight miles to the riverbank where, with unusual speed to escape the freeze, the scientists uncovered the complete, unmutilated carcass of a mammoth who could be carbon-dated to 12,800 years $\pm$ Before the Present Era. Of course, the remains didn't look like an erect, living mammoth, for eons underground had compressed the carcass into a flat, pancakelike mass, drenched in mud, but there was great excitement when even the novices could see that here was a complete animal, entire hide, with vital organs in place, so that investigators could ascertain what it had been feeding on in the hours before its death.

Flatch was quietly pleased when the scientists selected his plane as the one to fly the mammoth out to Talkeetna, and when the precious body was safely stowed, for there were only a few mammoth finds in either Alaska or Siberia in such condition, he muttered to himself as he prepared for takeoff: 'Don't black out now.' The flight was uneventful; the carcass was delivered to the much larger plane that would fly it on to Fairbanks, and respectful farewells were exchanged between Flatch and the scientists. Back in Talkeetna, he told his wife: 'Isn't every day a man delivers a cargo of meat maybe fourteen thousand years old,' and she said: 'I want you to get rid of that plane before New Year's.'

He was not able to do so, because when the newspapers heard of the remarkable discovery, their reporters streamed into Talkeetna asking LeRoy to fly them to the site, so he was kept busy in November taking his ski plane out to Birch Tree, but when in flying three science writers from the Lower Forty-eight he came close to blacking out, he pulled his nerves together and with little safety margin landed at Talkeetna. Turning away from his plane, he walked the short distance to his office, speaking to no one but feeling in his chest a warning that he might faint again. Inside the cramped little office Flatch pulled off his flight cap and hung it on the wall for the last time. LeRoy was one bush pilot who would die in bed.

WITH RICK VENN absent on T-7, Jeb Keeler had the courtship field to himself whenever he flew in to Desolation on corporation business, and he proved an ardent suitor, bringing Kendra flowers, a cherished rarity in the arctic, and pressing her to marry him. He pointed out what Kendra already knew, that 'Rick could be up there three, four years—and what happens to you?'

But attractive though Jeb Keeler was, she still could not erase from her mind the picture of Rick Venn skimming over the drifts on his thousand-mile chase in the Iditarod, and whenever such images appeared, she realized that fundamentally she wanted two things: to spend her creative years in the arctic and to share her life with Rick Venn.

So in the depth of winter she drafted an extraordinary message to T-7 which she sent by open radio from Afanasi's kitchen, for she had reached a point where she did not care who heard it:

> RICK VENN, T-7, ARCTIC OCEAN. I'M GETTING MARRIED IN JUNE AND I HOPE IT'S TO YOU. KENDRA.

The result was electric. Someone in Barrow monitoring radio traffic to T-7 was so delighted with this unusual message that he passed it along to a Seattle newspaper, whose newsmen were alerted by the name Venn, and they put it on the wire, so that people across the nation learned of plucky Kendra Scott's proposal to a very wealthy young man hiding out on an ice island. A wireless message resulted:

> RICK VENN, T-7, ARCTIC OCEAN. IF YOU'RE LUCKY ENOUGH TO FIND A GIRL LIKE HER, BE THERE IN JUNE. I'LL BE YOUR BEST MAN. MALCOLM VENN.

It was a memorable wedding, held in the school gym, with all of Desolation and a good deal of Barrow and Wainwright in attendance. Mrs. Scott, accompanied by her husband, flew in from Heber City and was astounded to learn who Rick was, and what an admirable young fellow he seemed to be, although as she pointed out to the Eskimo women with whom she sat at the ceremony: 'God does not approve of divorce.' She told them of several other things about which God had strong opinions, and one old woman whose men had for generations sought the walrus and the whale told the Eskimo woman sitting next to her: 'She sounds like a missionary.' Malcolm Venn, who in his sixty years of dealing with Alaska in almost every imaginable capacity had never before been north of the Arctic Circle, had gallons of ice cream and several dozen yellow roses flown in and served as his grandson's best man.

Kendra could not depart Desolation without paying her respects to the

Eskimo women who had been so considerate of her when she arrived among them as a stranger, so she invited them all to her quarters for a final breakfast, and afterward she walked alone through the village, staring out at the Chukchi Sea and confessing to herself an honest assessment of her three-year stay in Desolation: I've accomplished nothing. None of my students are going on to college. None of them have awakened to the potential of which they're capable. I couldn't make them study. I couldn't make them write papers the way kids do who are going to be productive, who are going to be leaders. I couldn't even make them come to school regularly or stop walking around aimlessly at night. I came, took my salary, and gave nothing in return. Four more years and I'd be a Kasm Hooker, jollying them along, leaving them no better than when I met them.

Tears started in her eyes, and to control them she snapped: 'To hell with their learning and ambitions. The two I loved, I couldn't even save their lives,' and when she thought of Amy and Jonathan she cried out in despair: 'Wasted years. Wasted lives.' Had some villager whispered to her at this moment, 'But, Kendra! The people of this village, the men who tossed you in the blanket, we'll remember you as long as we live, for your spirit walked with us, and we felt it,' she would not have believed her.

A s soon as she adjusted to the fact that she was the only woman on the island, Kendra's life on T-7 became as exciting as she had hoped it would be. Afanasi, as manager of the station, assigned her a paid job of supervising the paperwork streaming into and out of the offices, a task which the senior scientists were happy to have her perform. At first she was not happy with the apparent assumption that as a woman, secretarial work was all she was capable of performing, and she complained to Rick: 'It's not exactly what a liberated woman has in mind these days.' But when she found that monitoring the flow of information placed her in a critical position, because she knew the latest news before anyone else, she conceded: 'A job like mine does have certain advantages.' And gradually she inserted herself as an aide to anyone who could utilize her, and thus made herself invaluable.

But the more profound reward she garnered from her bold decision to propose to Rick over public radio and her later insistence that she accompany him back to his ice island came from the long, unstructured discussions these great scientists held during the endless hours when the perpetual darkness of November to February made human contacts and the dissection of human problems almost essential. Kendra frequently found herself in conversation with several scientists at a table in the mess, and one of them would casually say something like: 'Suppose that the Soviet Union were somehow to gain total control of Norway. She would then dominate exactly fifty percent of the Arctic Ocean,' and another would counter: 'But if Alaska, Canada and Greenland can maintain a union of mutual interest, they'll control the half that's nearest the North Pole, and that provides its own advantages for domination.'

Almost always the debate called for maps, and Kendra kept folded in her pocket a dog-eared copy of the *National Geographic* map which had accompanied the issue containing that compelling portrait of the little Eskimo girl on the cover, so quite often the scientists, although they had government maps of their own, gathered about Kendra, looking at hers. From such discussions she learned that the group of islands named Svalbard, which she had known as Spitsbergen, was vital to any military use of the Arctic Ocean, and everyone predicted that it would be used, because only in the trough off Svalbard were the seas deep enough to allow sophisticated submarine warfare; all other exits were much too shallow. 'And,' explained a scientist with military training, 'since the Svalbard Trough connects with the Atlantic, that ocean will be twice as important as the Pacific.' When the Pacific experts challenged this, he admitted: 'I'm speaking of submarine warfare only, as it relates to major shipping lanes. Think of the haven the Arctic Ocean will be if submarines can lurk here, dart out into the Atlantic, and control traffic between North America and Europe!'

This comparison of the two oceans led Kendra to ask: 'Why is it that the Pacific is rimmed by active volcanoes and the Atlantic not?' and this led to the suggestion that they invite Giovanni Spada, the volcanologist from Palmer, to fly north to conduct a seminar for them on recent developments in his field.

In these years T-7, in its ordained peregrinations, lay closer to Barrow than to any other American-Canadian point with a usable airfield, so it was a relatively simple matter for an air force plane to ferry Spada and his charts to Barrow and thence to the ice island, where he was greeted warmly by men who had worked with him in the past. His visit was surprisingly rewarding because he had the latest details of the earthquake which had produced the destruction in Mexico City and educated guesses as to when Mount St. Helens might let loose again.

But now discussion focused on copies of the map he had distributed, showing the disposition of volcanoes clustering about the rim of the Pacific, and he warned: 'If I'd had space to show each of the volcanoes along our Aleutian arc, there'd be sixty, and more than forty of them have been active since 1760. This chain of fire, guarding the approaches to the Arctic Ocean, is incomparably the most active in the world insofar as island building, submarine earthquakes and volcanic activity are concerned.'

'Is Alaska that volatile?' a scientist from Michigan asked, and Spada offered a somber statistic: 'Take any time span you wish—a decade, a score of years, a century—and list all the major earthquakes in the world, all the gigantic volcanic eruptions, and four out of the ten top disturbances, earthquake or volcano, occurred in Alaska. This is incomparably the world's most volatile segment. Plate tectonics make it so.'

Everyone but Kendra knew this term, and when she asked: 'What's that?' Spada gave a brilliant half-hour summary of how in the middle of the Pacific Ocean—'and also in the Atlantic, because in this part of the puzzle we're not unique'—magma flowed up through an extensive fissure. 'Believe it or not, this erupted material spreads the ocean floor outward, forming the great plates upon which the surface of the earth rests, including the tallest mountains and the deepest oceans. Accept that and the rest becomes simple.'

Using his hands he showed how the Pacific Plate collided with the North American Plate along the line of the Aleutians, with the former subducting under the latter: 'And *voilà*! Where this great clashing occurs, volcanoes are born, earthquakes help discharge the tensions.'

The scientists at T-7 queried him for several hours on recent refinements of accepted theories, and he flashed about the Pacific, laying out data from New Zealand, South America, the Antarctic, but coming always back to the Aleutians and his specialty, the Tsunami Warning System, which protected the people of Japan, Siberia, Alaska, Canada and the Hawaiian Islands from the disasters that used to strike them without warning when vast submarine earthquakes launched outward in all directions what used to be called tidal waves.

There, in the continuous darkness of winter, with their island moving imperceptibly in clockwise motion as if held in orbit by an invisible thread attached to a nonexistent North Pole, the scientists listened as Spada told of the event which had modified the marine history of the Pacific:

'April Fool's Day 1946. Qugang Volcano, out here on Lapak Island, erupted. No great deal. Ashes from the fiery belch didn't even reach Dutch Harbor, let alone the mainland. But a little while later one hell of a submarine earthquake occurred on the south side of the island. Displaced millions of tons of soft, sliding earth.

'It gave birth to a tsunami of epic dimension. Not a tidal wave rearing its head high in the air, but a lateral displacement of tremendous force headed for the Hawaiian Islands. Three ships that day had it pass right under them and only one even noticed it. "Sudden rise ocean surface, but less than three feet," read the log. But five hours later when it hit the town of Hilo on the north coast of the Big Island, at a speed of four hundred eighty miles an hour, it just kept coming and coming and coming. But it did no damage. However, when the runoff back to the ocean came, it sucked cars and houses and nearly two hundred people to their deaths.

'A tsunami from somewhere wiped out the first Russian settlement on Kodiak Island in 1792. And you've heard about Lituya, where the water level rose more than seventeen hundred feet.'

The scientists wanted to know if such things were likely to be repeated, and Spada said: 'Absolutely not. The Rim of Fire will act up, of that we can be sure, but the consequences will always be different. If the April '46 earthquake had been pointed two degrees differently, its tsunami would have missed Hawaii by hundreds of miles. And even so, it wasn't of maximum size, only seven-point-four on the Richter.'

Here Kendra broke in: 'Everybody talks about the Richter scale, but nobody ever says what it is,' and Spada offered a succinct description: 'It's an imprecise but helpful rule of thumb. It's a measurement taken about sixty miles from the point of origin and is reported on a logarithmic scale, which means that each major division is ten times more powerful than the one before. Thus, a four-point Richter has ten times the magnitude of a three-point, which is so weak that humans might not even feel it, while a nine-point Richter, which tears the place apart and is close to the maximum so far recorded, has a magnitude a million times that of a three.'

He told them what they must remember in their studies was that Alaska did have those sixty-odd potentially active volcanoes, and that the word *active* meant that each one was capable of exploding at any moment: 'So in this part of the world we must be prepared for anything. I'm uneasy about being away from my warning system even for an instructive meeting like this, because a significant volcanic eruption or major slippage of the ocean floor could happen at any time.'

The more the scientists interrogated Spada, the more Kendra saw that their worlds and his interlocked, and that in the Arctic Ocean, while it presented unique features, mainly a permanently frozen body of water, the ever-changing ice followed patterns of its own, just as the edges of plates, where they clashed, established their own bizarre rules. 'But nobody's told me yet,' Kendra said, 'why it's the Pacific that's rimmed with fire and not the Atlantic,' and this provoked considerable guesswork, with some reminding her that Mont Pelée and Etna and Vesuvius had not been trivial volcanoes in their day, but the answer that she preferred came from Spada: 'I've considered two theories. It could be that the size of the Pacific Plate, its sheer magnitude, releases greater forces when it collides with the various continental plates. But a more likely explanation would be that the Atlantic Ocean does not ride upon its own plate. It's not surrounded by fracture zones.'

On this satisfying note she was about to go to bed, but as she left the mess hall alone, Rick being on duty monitoring ocean-current recordings, she saw in the night sky the most tremendous display of the aurora borealis she had witnessed in Alaska. Running back to where the others still debated, she summoned them outside, where in a mild and windless minus-twenty-four degrees, they witnessed what even they admitted was an incomparable show of vast heavenly arcs, undulating waves and shifting colors.

When the others returned to their work or their beds, for clocks were of little significance in January, Kendra remained behind, trying to correlate these towering cathedrals of the northern lights, the eruptions of the Rim of Fire, the altering salinity of the various parts of the ocean, and the relationships between the Soviet Union and Norway, each of whom claimed with historic justification the ultracrucial Svalbard islands, past which the submarines would have to go in time of trouble.

As she stood there, she became aware that someone had joined her, and she saw that it was Vladimir Afanasi, who said: 'It's breathtaking. Maybe twice in a lifetime, spectacles like these.'

She led him to a bench, and as they sat there in the arctic night he said: 'Kasm told me that you took Amy's death . . .' He faltered.

'Amy and Jonathan . . . it pains me even to say their names. Sometimes I feel that my stay in Desolation was full of heartbreak.'

'The heartbreak never ends, Kendra.' He fell silent and remained so for some time, but it was obvious he wanted to say much more, and so Kendra began, and with her sympathy for people she touched the precise nerve that was troubling him: 'I heard you say once, Mr. Afanasi, that your father and uncle taught you what not to do. But you never explained.'

'They were tragic figures who tried to do the impossible. Stand with one leg in the Eskimo world, one in the white man's. Can't be done.'

'You do it.'

'No, no! I've never really left the Eskimo. At the university I was an Eskimo. That's why I didn't graduate. At work in Seattle, always an Eskimo. Here on the T-Seven, I'm the Eskimo, me and the polar bears.'

'What happened with your father and his brother?'

'It really happened with their father, Dmitri Afanasi, my grandfather. Remarkable man. Born and dedicated a Russian Orthodox priest, had no trouble whatever becoming a Presbyterian missionary. But his Athapascan wife was a powerful influence on the boys. She was Russian Orthodox and refused to change. No fuss. No public argument. "Just leave me alone as I am." So my father and uncle were Russian and Eskimo, Orthodox and Presbyterian, white man's world, Eskimo's world. And they both died.'

'Are you afraid of the word suicide?'

'No. Not afraid. My son committed suicide, just like the others. My father and uncle were murdered by the dreadful changes in their world.'

'It seems to skip generations, the impact I mean. Your grandfather had no problems. His two sons did. Your generation had no problems. Your son did.'

'It's never that simple, Kendra. My brother, a wonderful lad, committed suicide at nineteen.'

'Oh Jesus! What a terrible burden!' She choked, lifted her hands to her lips, then turned to embrace this sterling Eskimo who had brought so much meaning to her life. As new cathedrals were built, great towering edifices constructed of movement and light and heavenly design, they sat side by side on the bench, speculating on the dark significance of the north.

HISTORY OFTEN REPEATS, but rarely does it make a complete closed circle, yet that is what happened to Malcolm Venn when he was called upon to reverse his family's efforts of over half a century ago.

The Ross and Venn families of Seattle were among the most respected on the Pacific Coast. Self-educated, principled, concerned always with the advancement of society and generous with their charities, they demanded only one thing: a monopoly on trade with Alaska. Once assured of that, and satisfied that it was protected by legislation in Washington, the Ross & Raglan heirs were about as worthy public citizens as the nation produced.

They had a sense of humor too, so that when Venn, a distinguished-looking man in his late seventies, received the preposterous assignment from his fellow industrialists in Seattle, he was more than aware of its sardonic overtones: 'Gentlemen, if I accept this job, and make any public statements about it, I'll be the laughingstock of Seattle, and Alaska too!' They agreed, but pointed out: 'This is a crisis situation, and no one has the credentials you do for dealing with it.' So, reluctantly, he agreed to place his head upon the chopping block.

Accompanied by his lovely wife, Tammy Ting, the outspoken Chinese-Tlingit beauty from Juneau, he arrived by plane in Sitka, rented a suite overlooking the gorgeous bay, and sat for several hours each day glued to his window with a pair of high-powered binoculars pressed against his face. It was July, and he was watching the arrival in Sitka Sound of an unending sequence of the most beautiful cruise ships in the world. Each morning at six, two or three of these graceful floating hotels would put into Sitka, about a thousand excited passengers would stream ashore from each one to see the old Russian town and spend huge amounts of money, then return to their ship for the conclusion of one of the finest tours in the world: the seven- or eight-day cruise of the fjords and glaciers of southeastern Alaska. If one wanted to see happy and contented tourists, one came to Sitka in the summer, for it was the general conclusion that 'we got the best bargain available anywhere.'

For his first two days in town Venn was content merely to call off the names of the great ships as they arrived: 'That's the *Royal Princess*, of the great P & O Line in London. I forget what the initials mean, but it was the famous line that is supposed to have given us the word *posh*. Legend claims that people of standing, on their cruise from London to Bombay, had their tickets stamped POSH, port out, starboard home. That kept them in the shade, escaping the sun. I'm told the handsomest ship of all, inside, is that *Nieuw Amsterdam* of the Dutch line. But the Chalmers told me: "If you ever take the Alaska cruise, take that one over there." ' And against the dark peaks that rimmed the bay stood the *Royal Viking*, and beyond it the French *Rhapsody*, a more modest ship.

Tammy Venn, recording the names of the vessels as her husband called them off, said: 'They're all foreign. Why aren't there any American ships out there?' and Malcolm replied: 'That's what we're up here about. They are all foreign. They're all making simply potfuls of money. And not a cent of it is passing through Seattle.'

'Where do they come from?'

'Vancouver. Every damned one of them.'

Since her husband rarely used even mild profanity, Tammy knew he was angry, but she asked sweetly: 'Why don't you do something about it?' and he growled: 'I propose to.'

When he felt that he had a preliminary grasp of the situation, he visited commercial shops in Sitka and learned that during the summer season—no cruise ship would dare head north in winter—some two hundred and sixteen of the sleek ships put in to Sitka, with an even greater number, two hundred and eighty-three, docking at Juneau, where there were extraordinary tourist attractions like the great ice field in back of town and the glories of Taku Inlet with its own more typical glaciers.

Local experts calculated that, counting the smaller vessels, an average of about one thousand passengers arrived on each ship—'There's never an empty bed on one of the good boats. The crew has rakes to drag in the money'—which meant that more than a quarter of a million well-heeled tourists a year were coming to Alaska, always through Vancouver, never through Seattle. Counting the time most of them spent in Vancouver hotels, restaurants, nightclubs and taxicabs, the amount of money lost by Seattle in this traffic was astronomical.

Seeking to nail down a defensible figure, on his third day in town Malcolm Venn started visiting the lovely ships, all so clean and polished for display in the old Russian capital, and he happened to tour first the exquisite little *Sagafjord*, a jewel of the crusing trade. As onetime head of his own shipping company, Ross & Raglan having exited the field some years back, he was welcomed aboard, and learned to his astonishment that on this superior ship the fare for the Alaska cruise could run as high as $4,890, but when he gasped, the captain personally took him to a fine small cabin at a mere $1,950.

'What's an average?' he asked, and the captain said: 'That's easy. We've had a full ship, so you just multiply the figures,' but he warned that his figures were not representative of the trade in general: 'You want to study one of the really huge ships,' and just coming into the harbor was the stately *Rotterdam*. It carried more than a thousand passengers, all berths taken, of course, at what the pursers said was an average rate of $2,195.

Back in his room, Malcolm multiplied the *Rotterdam* figures by the estimated number of Sitka visitors, and got a result of close to $400,000,000. Adding in the money spent ashore at Vancouver, he stared at a total topping half a billion dollars: And every damn cent of it ought to be passing through Seattle!

In succeeding days he learned things about Alaskan cruising which caused him to whistle in admiration at the brilliance of the European operators who had put together this gold mine. 'You've seen it yourself, Tammy. Take that splendid English ship, the *Royal Princess*. She's really five separate ships. Officer cadre, exclusively British. Best men afloat. The dining room, exclusively Italian, no other. Deck crew, Pakistani. Everyone belowdecks, Chinese. And the entertainment team, sixteen or eighteen real stars, all American.' Tammy nodded to confirm each description, then said: 'And the *Nieuw Amsterdam*, the same divisions, with its own variations. Officers all Dutch. Dining room, what? Italian too, or French? Deckhands all Indonesian. Belowdecks, I think Chinese. Singers, band, all that nonsense, Americans.'

With each of the great ships it was the same: wonderfully trained European officers ran them, Italians and Frenchmen provided elegant menus, Asians of one kind or another cleaned and maintained the ship, Chinese kept the engines operating, and Americans provided the fun. A whole world of enterprise had been wrested from the Americans and turned over to foreign experts who performed like magicians. Considering everything, the glaciers, fjords, wildlife and frontier towns along the shore, the Alaskan cruise was indeed the best bargain in the world.

Why had the Americans allowed this bonanza to slip through their fingers? In a series of small, intense meetings attended by both Malcolm and Tammy, he opened the first session: 'Gentlemen, we face a shipping crisis in Alaska and on the West Coast. Your tremendous Alaskan tourist trade, which I calculate to gross well over half a billion dollars a year, is all passing through Canada, Vancouver in particular, when it ought to be passing through the United States, Seattle to be specific.' There was at this point a very slight disturbance; someone in the back of the room was laughing, and not courteously, but Malcolm plowed ahead: 'You and I both know the cause of this disaster.' He paused dramatically, then blurted out: 'The Jones Act.'

For just a moment the room was quiet, then the man in the back guffawed and pretty soon the whole room was echoing with laughter to hear the president of Ross & Raglan excoriating the Jones Act, which that company had engineered, protected, and extended through years of political skulduggery and generations of most cruel and unfair pressures on Alaskan economic hopes.

'Jones Act!' somebody from the side repeated, and the crowd really roared. Venn had foreseen the reception he would get in Alaska, had indeed predicted it before he left Seattle, but his colleagues had reasoned: 'Your saying it will make it more effective. What have you to lose, personally or for your company? Be a sport.'

He proved to be just that. Holding up his hands, he cried: 'All right! All right! My grandfather, Malcolm Ross, thought up the Act. My father, Tom Venn, kept it alive. And later I myself lobbied Congress to keep it on the books. I've always supported it, but the time has come . . .'

At this point Tammy Ting, always an irreverent woman, dipped her handkerchief in her glass, wet it with ice water, rose, and wiped off her husband's forehead as the crowd bellowed.

It was just the touch that was needed, for when the raucous laughter subsided, her husband said: '*Mea culpa*, and if you had a gutting knife, I'd slash my wrists. But now we face not a theory but a situation. An act which made sense in 1920 when we had American ships manned by American men makes no sense at all today when we have no American ships. We're saddled with the Jones Act, can't seem to force Congress to rescind or modify it, and what's the result? Do you know there is not an American ship afloat under the proper ownership required by the Jones Act that could bring passengers from Seattle to Alaska? None. We've given away the oceans.'

He asked a man who knew more about these problems than himself to explain further: 'The world's changed. Have any of you been aboard that perfectly splendid English ship the *Royal Princess*? Where in hell do you suppose she was built? With labor problems what they are in England, incessant strikes and industrial sabotage, you can't build a ship in England anymore. Scotland's worse. The *Royal Princess* was built in Finland, because in the socialist country company schedules are rigorously honored and the craftsmanship is so fine that the next three ships in the British tourist fleet will be built in Finland too.'

He said that in common sense the United States should do, if the Jones Act could be revoked, what the English did with the building of their modern fleet: 'Go into all the world's markets, find the best builders, the best sailors, the best officers, and invite them to sail the best ships at the cheapest rates from Seattle to Sitka or anywhere else they damned well please to sail.'

The audience cheered.

During his last two days in Sitka, Venn employed a secretary, who did a fine job transcribing his notes and putting them into condition worthy of being presented to his peers in Seattle. The two effective paragraphs were:

I submit these conclusions as the grandson of Malcolm Ross, who engineered the Jones Act, as the son of Tom Venn, who guided it through the Congress, and as myself, for more than sixty years the recipient of advantages from the Act. It was a good Act when passed. It served a worthy purpose, and it created wealth for Seattle. But it has outlived its usefulness. The tenets upon which it was based no longer apply. Today our city loses as much as half a billion dollars a year because the Act prevents normal traffic from using our wonderful port. It must be rescinded and it should be rescinded now. I recommend we mount a massive effort to rescind the Jones Act and I offer my services as spokesman. My family created it. It's my family's job to eliminate the damned thing.

I would be less than fair, however, if I did not report to you that our Canadian cousins in Vancouver, seeing the opening we have inadvertently left them, have leaped into it with imagination, brains, ample financing to accommodate some of the finest cruise ships in the world. We should encourage American tourists to enjoy these splendid ships, even though we're not getting a penny from them, for as my father always said: 'Whatever is good for Alaska is good for Seattle,' and this Alaskan cruising is about the best there is. Now we're entitled to get our share, but to do so we must kill the Act my family and I sponsored.

IT WAS WHAT you might call a typical experience in Alaskan aviation. On Thursday afternoon the governor told his assistant in Juneau: 'Washington's sending a man up here to talk to Jeb Keeler about that North Slope debt. See if he can be in my office Monday at noon.' It took the telephone operator about twenty minutes to track Jeb down, but she finally found him at Desolation Point, where he was in serious conversation with Vladimir Afanasi in an attempt to arrange a walrus hunt far out on the Chukchi Sea as soon as it froze.

'Jeb? This is Herman. Big boss wants to know if you can meet with him and one of the Feds from Washington. Our office. Monday at noon.'

'I've told you guys, I'm clean. I mean it.'

'That's what the governor told them, and they said you must be the only man in Alaska who is. That's why they want to ask you some questions. Can you make it?'

'Sure. I'll hop out of here Friday. Catch Mark Air to Prudhoe Bay and on in to Anchorage. The 0905 Monday morning will put me in to Juneau in good style.' The phone fell silent for a moment, then: 'You're leveling with me? They're not coming up here to put me on the griddle for something I've never done?'

'Jeb, you know what I know. They could be lying to us, but I do believe this is aboveboard. They're just trying to find out how the North Slope debt could have ballooned so high so fast.'

'I'll be there.'

It was dark when Jeb reached Anchorage, but a cab carried him swiftly to his apartment, where he spent some time in the shadows staring at that irritating blank spot reserved for his mountain goat. Pointing his right forefinger at the vacancy, he said: 'Starting tomorrow, bub, we bag you.'

On Monday morning his alarm sounded at six. Jumping up, he showered, shaved, and ate a frugal breakfast of orange juice, freeze-dried coffee and whole-wheat toast. Sorting through the papers he suspected the Washington investigator might want to see, he made three phone calls to people he was supposed to interview on Tuesday, telling each: 'I'm flying down to Juneau on the morning plane. I'll be back on the evening flight, and I'll see you tomorrow as planned. I'm calling just in case.' He then called the agent who looked after his airline tickets: 'Morning down, evening back. Like always, A down, F back.' She said the tickets would be at the airport.

He was always meticulous about his seating on this flight, because even though the skies were almost always either clouded or foggy between Anchorage and Juneau, if there happened to be a clear day, which occurred about once every twenty flights, the scenery inland to the east was spectacular. 'Not interesting,' he told strangers, 'mind-shattering.' So invariably he asked for Seat A southbound, Seat F northbound, and on rare occasions he was allowed to see a wonderland.

Then, just before leaving his apartment, he reached for his Gurkha Traveling Kit and checked its contents: shaving gear, pajamas, clean shirt. Through years of bitter experience he had learned never to board an Alaskan airliner without the wherewithal to spend the night in some unpremeditated bed.

At the huge Anchorage airport, where planes from many different nations stopped on their flights between Asia and Europe, some of them heading almost directly over the North Pole to Sweden, he was told: 'Takeoff on schedule. Slight chance of fog at Juneau.' He dismissed the information, since there was always a likelihood of fog at Juneau. Rumor had it that when there wasn't a fog, they fired off a cannon in celebration, but of course, this disturbance brought in the fog, so that you wound up, even on a good day, with a window of about fifteen minutes in which to land. Flying in to Juneau was not for the fainthearted.

His A seat was useless on this Monday morning, for when he looked out he saw only fog, and not an indifferent gray kind of fog but one so solid that had the window been opened, he might have been able to walk upon it. 'Damn,' he told the man riding in Seat B. 'No fun landing in Juneau in a fog like this!'

'Not to worry,' the man said. 'We won't even try in this soup.'

'That's a hell of a thing to say,' Jeb replied, half seriously. 'I have a meeting in Juneau. Important one. The Feds may be throwing me in jail.'

'You'll sleep in Seattle tonight,' the man said.

'You heading for Seattle?'

'I seem to go there twice a month. But not on purpose. I aim for Juneau, but we often miss it.'

The man was right, because when the plane approached Juneau it made a valiant effort to land, dropping lower and lower among the mountains as the radar emitted signals which gave precise locations. When Jeb's knuckles were clasped so tight that no blood showed beneath the skin, he heard the pilot put on the gas as the big Boeing 727 wheeled sharply up and to the right. Nobody in the cabin spoke, but when the pilot went back to his starting point to try again, Jeb asked his seatmate: 'Are you as scared as I am?' and the man said: 'No. If it's too bad, he'll fly up and off. You'll know.' And once more the plane came in lower and lower into that nest of mountains which protected Juneau from storms and airplanes. For just one fleeting moment the fog cleared enough for Jeb to see the waves only a few feet below the wing and the tall dark cliffs menacingly close to the wingtips. 'Jesus Christ!' he whispered to the man. 'We're walking on water!' But again the pilot rejected the idea of landing, and up and around he went.

'Really,' Jeb said, striving to control his nerves, 'he's not going to try again, is he?' and the man said: 'He often makes it on the third try.'

But not this time. In the plane came, skimming the water and dodging the mountains, but at the final moment there was no visibility, so as Jeb tried to keep from fainting the plane rose high and safe into the upper air, far above the mountains, and headed for Seattle. There were forty-nine passengers aboard the 727 with important meetings in Juneau, the state capital, but no one complained to the stewardesses: 'We should have tried again.' None of them wanted to spend Monday night in Seattle, but on the other hand, none of them wanted to test their fate against that fog in Juneau.

Very close to Seattle's Sea-Tac Airport there was a Vance Hotel which provided good rooms at a reasonable rate for airplane passengers hit with an emergency, and there Jeb unpacked, climbed into his pajamas, and watched *Monday Night Football.* At intermission he thought to call the governor's aide: 'I'll be there on tomorrow's noon flight,' and the official assured him: 'No great loss, Jeb. The man from Washington is staying over. As you suspected, FBI, but you're not the subject of the investigation. You're just another source. Like me.'

So on Tuesday morning, Keeler and forty-eight other Alaskans trooped over to the airport and boarded the return flight to Juneau. The plane made its scheduled landings in Ketchikan and Sitka without event, but as it approached Juneau, the weather was so bad that after three spine-tingling but fruitless passes, the 727 had to continue on to Anchorage, with Keeler sitting in his precious Seat F looking out into a fog which was, if anything, even thicker than the one the day before.

After two days of travel, and 2,876 miles of useless flight, Jeb was back in his apartment, but a phone call to Juneau assured him that the weather bureau was predicting clear weather for Wednesday: 'We all wish you'd give it a try, Jeb. The you-know-who says your information could be vital.' So early on Wednesday, with a fresh shirt in his bag, Jeb went out to the airport, saw that whereas there was some fog, it was clearing so fast that the lovely Chugach Mountains were visible. 'I'm sure it's going to be a great flight south,' the attendant at the counter said as she gave him Seat A. 'You know, it does happen!'

Alaska Airlines was a well-run outfit, with cabin personnel who endeavored to put their passengers at ease. This morning an affable steward announced: 'Clear weather all the way to Juneau. Glorious flight. Your stewardesses are Bubbles, Ginger and Trixie, and if anyone smokes in a nonsmoking area, the flight engineer will invite you to step outside.'

When the plane rose in the air, Jeb gasped, for the great mountain ranges glistened with such majesty that all who looked at them were dumfounded. He had the good fortune this morning to have beside him in Seat B an older woman who taught geography, and even though she leaned across him to glimpse the mountains out of his window, he did not mind, for she knew the mountains by name and could identify the vast glaciers that swept down from them to tumble into the sea.

'That's the Chugach Range. Not excessively high, but look at them! Eight thousand feet right out of the sea.' Then she caught her breath, for directly below them lay the pipeline terminus of Valdez with an ice field of enormous dimension behind it. 'There must be . . . How many glaciers would you say were down there?'

'Maybe half a dozen.'

'Goodness, you have no eyes. There must be twenty,' and when he looked more carefully he saw that out of this one field sprouted at least twenty icy rivers winding through the valleys, scouring the sides, grinding the rocky beds, and finally meeting the sea.

'I never realized so many different glaciers could spring from one source,' he said, and she explained that it was only this southern part of Alaska that had glaciers: 'The far north doesn't get enough rain to make snow. Very little snow up north. But down here the Japan Current. You know what that is?' When he nodded like a bright schoolboy, she said: 'Throws a lot of water on these mountains. So high and so cold, it can't melt. So it builds up into glaciers that flow very slowly down to the sea.'

He was about to ask her how she knew so much, when she said gently: 'Here's one of the parts I love most. I teach my students to revere this part. See that lovely mountain? Nearly eleven thousand feet high? Mount Steller. And that enormous glacier at its feet? Bering Glacier. Do you appreciate the significance of that pairing? Steller and Bering?' When he said 'No,' she told him briefly of the relationship between these two remarkable men who had discovered Alaska for the Russians: 'One German, one Dane. They didn't understand each other, but there they stand, forever locked together in ice.'

Jeb was about to respond when she clutched his arm: 'Here they come! My God, I've never before seen them so glorious! Oh!' But before she could explain what had justified this outburst, the pilot came on the intercom to announce: 'Ladies and gentlemen, only rarely do we see what's out there to our left. Mount St. Elias, eighteen thousand feet, the first view the Russians had of the mainland. Behind it Mount Logan in Canada, nearly twenty thousand feet. Down their sides flow forty or fifty glaciers, including the great Malaspina.'

The teacher blew her nose, drew back from leaning across Keeler, and said softly: 'Can you imagine? Vitus Bering in a small leaky ship. Seeing that. Wondering what it signified? And Georg Steller beside him whispering: "It's got to be a continent. It's got to be America." '

The pilot came back on the intercom: 'A day like this should not be wasted. Because the sky is so perfect we're going to take a little detour and swing over to the east so you can see the Fairweather Range, very high and beautiful. And then real low over Glacier Bay—you'll see it as few ever do. Then, over the great Juneau ice field with its score of glaciers, and on to our landing in Juneau, where the tower is reporting clear skies and light winds coming out of the southeast. Enjoy the view, ladies and gentlemen.'

The next minutes were magical. The Fairweather Range, which few travelers ever saw, had a plethora of very high snow-clad peaks rising right from the sea, and enclosing one of the glories of North America, the quiet, gentle, mountain-girt Glacier Bay, into whose waters great chunks of ice thundered off the glaciers as they made their imperceptible return to the sea, alerting the bears that prowled the shores. It was a magnificent bay, with a score of arms reaching far inland, and so many glaciers that no one, even in an airplane, could see them all.

'And now comes what might be the best of all,' the teacher said. 'Look!' And as the 727 made a grand slow turn to the east, Jeb saw the vast Juneau ice field extending far into Canada, with the ominous Devils Paw mountain reaching up as if to catch the plane and drag it to an icy death. From this field came a score of glaciers, including those that crashed down into Taku Inlet on the south. It was a fitting curtain to a drama that could have been equaled nowhere else, for as the teacher said when they came in for their landing: 'On a clear day, this ninety minutes from Anchorage to Juneau must be the most spectacular on earth. I'm told the Himalayas can be stupendous, but do they have this mix of ocean, great mountains, wild ice fields and endless glaciers? I doubt it.'

'I wish I'd had you for a teacher,' Jeb said, and when she turned to thank him for the compliment she snapped her fingers and said: 'Didn't I see your picture in the papers? Aren't you the fellow whose girl proposed to the other chap by open radio?' and when Jeb said: 'The same,' she said: 'That girl must've been crazy,' and Jeb said: 'I thought so.'

On this, Jeb's third try, they landed at Juneau in fine style, but by late afternoon when he wanted to fly home to Anchorage, the fog from the Japan Current had swept back in, closing down all airport operations. Relying once more upon the pajamas in his Gurkha bag, Jeb spent the night at the Baranof Hotel in Juneau and flew home the next morning, occupying his precious seat in hopes of seeing the glaciers again, but of course the clouds were impenetrable.

So his brief two-hour meeting with the government investigator in the state capital had consumed four complete days, Monday morning through Thursday afternoon. One never took a trip to Juneau lightly.

IN A PERVERSE way, the four-day trip was worth it, because his interrogation was attended not only by the man from the Department of Justice, but by two local FBI agents and an expert from the state government. When he saw the panel lined up across the table he began to perspire, but the man from Washington saw this and became remarkably conciliatory: 'Mr. Keeler, we want to quiz you on some ugly matters, but we assure you at the outset that we're not interested in you personally. Your record, at least as uncovered by these FBI men, is impeccable and we congratulate you on it.' He reached over and shook Jeb's hand, which was shamefully sweaty.

'Mr. Keeler,' began the Alaska official, 'what do you know about the North Slope?'

'I've worked in many parts of it—Prudhoe Bay for the oil companies . . . Desolation Point and its local corporation . . . an occasional job for the big Native corporation, but as you know, Poley Markham handles most of their affairs.'

'We do know,' the man from Washington said, almost ominously. 'But have you ever done any legal work—drafting of commercial contracts, for example —for the North Slope Borough?'

'No. Only the big corporation and its little satellites. Never the borough.' He was referring to an Alaskan phenomenon, a vast, empty township larger than a state like Minnesota but with a population of less than eight thousand. What it also had was an income of nearly eight hundred million dollars in taxes paid by the oil companies at Prudhoe Bay, or about a hundred thousand dollars in cold cash for every man, woman and child in the borough.

'A sudden influx of money like that tempts people to do crazy things,' one of the FBI men said, and from a typed sheet he read off a few of the more malodorous cases in which unexpected wealth had courted local officials into bizarre behavior: 'A heated subway to protect utility lines—projected cost, one hundred million; finished cost, three hundred and fifty; real cost, in Oregon let's say, eleven million. New high school—projected cost, twenty-four million—'

Jeb interrupted: 'I know about that one. Finished cost, seventy-one million.'

'Wrong,' said the FBI man. 'It's not finished yet. When it is, maybe eighty-four million.'

'What would it have cost in the Lower Forty-eight?' Jeb asked, and the man said: 'We had some school construction firms fly in from California and they gave us the figure three million, two.' But now the Alaska official broke in: 'In California, yes. Let them try to build it on the North Slope, with every nail coming in by barge or aircraft.'

The FBI man bowed: 'The California men said the same thing. So I asked them what the school should have cost in Barrow, and they said: "It should have been done for about twenty-four, twenty-six million." '

The man from Washington growled: 'That was the original estimate, the one that's exploded to eighty-four.' In disgust he indicated that the FBI man should terminate his recitation of horror stories. Instead, he took a piece of blank paper, scribbled on it, and passed it facedown to Jeb: 'In addition to their eight hundred million dollars in tax money, which they've spent, how much do you think those dreamers up there have borrowed on the New York and Boston markets, all of it spent, all of it representing outstanding debt?'

Jeb studied the matter, and from what he had heard about the generosity of borough dealings, he concluded that the indebtedness might be as much as half of what the income had been: 'Maybe half the eight hundred million. Maybe four hundred million in bonds sold by the Eastern banks.'

'Look at the paper,' the Washington man said, and when Jeb turned it over he saw the staggering figure: $1,200,000,000.

'My God!' he gasped. 'More than a billion dollars! How could a bunch of Eskimos who never went to college . . . ?'

And then the questioning became short and sharp and brutal: 'Do you know of any involvement Poley Markham had with North Slope Borough?' He was involved with everything in Alaska. 'Did he arrange for these bond issues?' He helped all the corporations with their borrowing. 'Did Markham own any of the contracting companies that got the big jobs?' I don't think he ever invested in other people's companies. He was his own man. 'In your opinion is Poley Markham a crook?' In my opinion he's one of the most honest men I know. I go hunting with Poley quite often, and a man's character reveals itself on an ice pack or a mountain slope. 'What would you say if we told you that Poley Markham has banked more than twenty million dollars from his Alaska fees?' I would believe it. And I'd bet he had signed vouchers for all of it. He told me years ago the money was lying around up here and could be picked up honestly. 'Do you think he earned his share honestly?' Yes, sir, as far as I know. I'm positive he did.

The men thanked him for his responses and reiterated that he himself was not under investigation: 'We have no solid proof of wrongdoing up there by anyone, and I will confess that we can find nothing on your friend Markham. But when two billion dollars floats around, we have to look for sticky fingers.' That night when Jeb reached his apartment in Anchorage, he tracked Poley down at a country club in Arizona: 'The Feds are after you real big, Poley.'

'They've been questioning me down here. And they're not after me. They're after the whole incredible setup on the North Slope. Eight thousand Eskimos spending about two billion dollars, all told.'

For just a moment an image of the Natives at Desolation flashed through Jeb's mind, and he could not visualize these hunters, who lived by the ways of the frozen sea, incurring such debts, but then he remembered Poley: 'Are you clean in this debacle?'

'Jeb, every penny I banked came by check . . . legal fees legally documented.'

'That's what I told the fellow from Washington.'

'A man with red hair and granny half-spectacles?'

'The same.'

'He left here unconvinced. I'm sure he left you unconvinced. But he'll find no trail of sleaze with me.' There was a moment of silence, and then Poley added: 'Of course, I recommended my friends in California and Arizona for the fat contracts. But they paid me nothing, Jeb. No kickbacks, no hunting lodges built for me in the mountains.'

'But two billion dollars! Poley, there has to be something not right somewhere.'

'Has there been any with you? No. Any with our friend Afanasi? Never. Any with me? Not on your life. I was mixed up in everything, as you know, but you also remember my golden rule: "If even eight cents of real money is involved, leave a trail of receipts a mile wide." '

'The Feds told me they'd tracked more than twenty million dollars of those receipts,' and Poley laughed: 'I'd never do it otherwise,' and Jeb said: 'That's what I told them.'

BECAUSE POLEY MARKHAM had to fly to the North Slope to give his clients support during the FBI investigation, he stopped over in Anchorage to verify whatever it was that Jeb told the investigators at the interrogation in Juneau, and he arrived at Jeb's apartment just as there was a flurry on Alaska television. Giovanni Spada, at the Palmer Tsunami Center, had issued an alert that out on the Aleutian chain, Qugang Volcano off the north coast of Lapak Island had begun erupting, with huge clouds of lava dust heading eastward toward Anchorage: 'However, the distance is so great that we can expect most of the dust to dissipate before it reaches the Anchorage area.'

Nevertheless, by late afternoon there was a cloud of ash in the air, and Poley suggested: 'Let's get out of here. A guide told me there were some mountain goats in a cove on the Pacific coast just north of the government lands at Glacier Bay.' So they packed their gear, rented a four-seater, and flew down to a primeval area which few people ever saw, and there in air so clear that even a raindrop seemed like an intruder, they trekked in to where they saw, in an area far below them this time, a trio of billies with small handsomely formed horns.

Poley slapped his thigh: 'At last we've struck it lucky. This time they're below us, not above. If we move down cautiously, you'll get one of those beauties,' but when he inspected the steepness of the descent, he altered his plan: 'We'd be bound to dislodge rocks and spook them. Better wait here and let them come up to us,' and his judgment was sound, for gradually the goats began working their way up the slope, but so very slowly that the two men had about an hour to wait. This they spent in whispered discussion of the crucial problem which governed Alaskan matters at the moment and the much more important one that would come to a head in 1991. Of the first, Poley said: 'Isn't it peculiar? The two states that irritate each other the most are the two that are most alike,' and when Jeb asked what that meant, he explained: 'Alaska and Texas. When we sent out a call for experienced hands to come in and help us with our oil, seemed like two out of three came from Texas, and I do believe that half our new permanent residents are Texans who stayed on.'

Jeb reflected on this and said: 'You do see a lot of them in Fairbanks,' at which Poley added: 'And like in Texas, up here you never hear a bad word said about OPEC. We want those Arabs to keep the price of oil as high as possible. They do our work for us.'

But both men agreed that with the disastrous drop in oil prices, the glory days of Alaskan development were ending, just as they seemed to be declining in Texas: 'We were lucky to get here when we did, Jeb, and I hope you saved your money, because come 1991, there'll be opportunities up here like you never saw before, and the prudent man who has eight or ten million in hard cash is going to be able to buy himself a major portion of this wonderful state. I can hardly wait.'

'You mean when the restrictions on the Settlement Act come to an end?'

'I do.'

Only a fellow Alaskan could have appreciated the ominous nature of Poley's response. It meant that he had tracked the operations of the thirteen huge Native corporations, the ones that really owned the land, and had concluded that many of them were in such pitiful shape financially that the Natives who owned them would have to sell to white men from Seattle and Los Angeles and Denver who had the money to buy them out and the know-how to make a fortune on the land when properly managed. Obviously this meant that well-intentioned Eskimos like Vladimir Afanasi were in danger of losing the land upon which their forefathers had depended for thousands of years, but when Jeb, who saw in Afanasi the salvation of Alaska, asked about this, Poley said reassuringly: 'I think the North Slope corporation is one that can survive. Even with the huge debt and the collapse of oil prices, we built some very solid social and political structures up there, but of the other twelve, I have good reason to believe that at least five are doomed. They're the ones we'll move in on.'

And now, on that lonely mountainside overlooking the Pacific, the wedge that would drive between the two friends manifested itself, for Jeb Keeler, despite his disappointment in losing Kendra Scott, had grown honestly to love Alaska and to see it as a unique blending of white newcomers like himself and longtime natives like the Eskimos, the Athapascans and the Tlingits for whom he had worked. He wanted the groups to coexist in harmony, he told Poley, to develop this wonderland mutually, and to trade its natural resources to countries like Japan and China in return for consumer goods. Specifically, he wanted the Natives to retain ownership of their land so that they could, if they wished, continue their subsistence style of life, and when he stated that conclusion he placed himself athwart the ambitions of Poley Markham, who revealed his plans with astonishing clarity.

'I don't see it your way at all, Jeb. The Natives can never govern their own lands, not in the modern world of airplanes, snowmobiles and automobiles, not to mention supermarkets and television sets. Even the six or seven corporations which are viable today could wither by the end of the century. And men like me will be on hand to pick them off.'

For some moments Jeb reflected on this gloomy prediction, whose probability of coming true he had to concede, but before he could comment on what he saw as a tragedy, Poley added a revelation which proved what a Machiavellian character he had: 'Why do you suppose I've worked so hard with these corporations? Not for the money—that is, after I solidified my nest egg. I wanted to know the capacity of each one, where the good lands were, what the likelihood of collapse was. Because I realized from day one that the crazy organization Congress established in ANCSA could not survive this century. And that meant that the lands would have to come into the hands of people like you and me.'

'Not me,' Jeb said firmly. 'I'll help the Natives petition Congress for an extension past 1991. We won't allow the lands to be alienated from the Eskimos and the Indians.'

Poley drew back to study this young man he had befriended in so many ways, had inducted into the fraternity of Lower Forty-eight experts who knew what was happening in Alaska, and he could not believe what Jeb was saying: 'Son, if you go that route, you and me is gonna cross swords.'

'I've seen it coming, Poley. I want to keep Alaska unique, a modern wonderland. You want to make it one more Southern California.'

'Face it, son,' and with the use of this word he had used when talking to Jeb years ago in northern Canada, he indicated the distance that had been reestablished between them, 'what is Anchorage but San Diego North?'

'Anchorage, I can surrender,' Jeb conceded, 'but the rest must be protected from men like you, old friend.'

Poley laughed: 'Impossible. The next census will show Anchorage with more than fifty percent of the population. Then its representatives will storm down to Juneau and begin to pass laws that bring this state into the modern world. Probably move the capital up to Anchorage, where it should have been long ago.'

'The more you say, Poley, the more I realize that I'll have to fight almost everything you'll be trying to do.'

If the two debaters had had their radio turned on, they would have heard an urgent broadcast by Giovanni Spada sent to all the nations bordering the North Pacific: 'This is a tsunami alert. I repeat, a tsunami alert. There has been a massive submarine earthquake off Lapak Island in the Aleutian chain registering eight-point-four on the Richter scale. All coastal areas are advised that a wave . . .'

Instead of hearing the warning which might have influenced their actions on that vulnerable coast, they were preoccupied with the goats that had begun to behave as Poley had predicted, but before the final stages of the hunt started, Poley wanted to assuage the political differences that had erupted between them, and he switched subjects completely: 'You know, Jeb, your mountain goat isn't a goat at all. It's an antelope, misnamed.'

Surprised, Jeb turned to face his future adversary: 'No one ever told me,' and for some moments he considered this strange news: 'Suppose the goat had been named *snowy antelope* or *arctic antelope*. It'd be twice as attractive,' and Poley growled: 'Not for me. I like things simple and honest.' Then he became the ruthless director of the hunt, the role for which he was predestined: 'Jeb, you've got to nail one as they come up that draw. Once you let them get above us, they're long gone.'

So Jeb, having lost half a dozen goats when he followed his own tactics, slipped silently down the protected side of the ridge, taking precautions that he not be seen by the approaching goats, and when he had positioned himself so that he could intercept them as they came up the other side, he realized that he would be allowed only one shot at whichever of the three billies first poked his head above the skyline. Looking back for confirmation from Poley, he was gratified when from a considerable distance above him Markham signaled an 'A-okay' with his right thumb and forefinger forming a circle. The stage was set for the best chance Jeb would ever have to bag the last of his Big Eight.

He held his breath, waited for one of the goats to appear, then experienced the great joy of seeing a billy, snowy white and with perfect black-spiked horns, emerge right onto the crest of the ridge and stand there for a moment. 'For

Christ sake, shoot!' Poley whispered to himself, frightened lest the merest sound alert the goat, and in the next moment he was relieved to hear the report of Jeb's rifle. The goat lurched forward, trembled, and fell backward out of Jeb's sight on the far side of the ridge.

But Poley from his higher vantage could see clearly that the goat had been killed and had plunged rather far down into the cut on the other side. 'Jeb!' he shouted. 'You got him but he's well down in the gully. Fetch him and I'll start down with the gear.' When Jeb descended to where he had last seen the goat, he took his gun with him, but Poley shouted again: 'Leave your gun, I'll get it. He's pretty far down the hill,' and when Jeb saw where the goat's body had landed, quite far below him, he appreciated the wisdom of Poley's advice and propped his gun against a rock where Poley could easily spot it. Almost as if the two men were attached by invisible bands, they began to descend together, Poley from his outlook spot to where the gun rested, Jeb from his gun down to where the goat's body had lodged.

As they scrambled down in this triumphant tandem, Jeb kept his eyes fixed on the goat, a magnificent specimen he was convinced, but Poley, from his higher vantage, was able to survey the entire setting: the Pacific Ocean near at hand, the two headlands marking the beginning of the little fjord, the steep flanks on which the three billies had been exploring, and the V-shaped head of the bay into which Jeb was descending to claim his prize. It was almost an artist's miniature stage setting for what would be an ideal Alaskan coastal painting.

But Poley also saw a sudden and persistent suction of water from the bay, and he knew instinctively that something ominous and terrible was happening.

'Jeb! Jeb!' he began to scream, but in Jeb's eagerness to get to his goat he had hurried ahead out of earshot. Nevertheless, the older man continued screaming, for now he saw the water sweeping back into the bay, inexorably piling up as if pushed from behind by some malevolent titan.

'Jeb! Come back!'

And now it became obvious that the dark waves, never very high but with tremendous pressure behind them, were not going to stop before they had filled the valley and flooded upward to some incredible spot seven or eight hundred feet above ordinary sea level, and when Jeb finally became aware of his peril, the water was so high, and piling up so rapidly, that he was incapable of doing anything to save himself. He saw the churning water snatch the goat and toss it about, submerging it in foam, and then the relentless waves were upon him, throwing him sideways and engulfing him as they climbed the sides of the valley faster than the goats had done. His last sight was not of his final trophy, which was mangled in the deep, but of Poley Markham scrambling desperately upward to gain the really high ground which even the Lapak Island tsunami could not reach.

As he was about to perish, Jeb saw that Poley was probably going to make it, and he cried: 'Go it, Poley. You win!'

FOR NOW, IT seemed that Alaska would be going the way Poley Markham wanted it, not as Jeb Keeler and Vladimir Afanasi and Kendra Scott in their various ways had visualized it.

HAWAII

To

All the peoples who came to Hawaii

This is a novel. It is true to the spirit and history of Hawaii, but the characters, the families, the institutions and most of the events are imaginary—except that the English schoolteacher Uliassutai Karakoram Blake is founded upon a historical person who accomplished much in Hawaii.

CONTENTS

I

FROM THE BOUNDLESS DEEP

Millions upon millions of years ago, when the continents were already formed and the principal features of the earth had been decided, there existed, then as now, one aspect of the world that dwarfed all others. It was a mighty ocean, resting uneasily to the east of the largest continent, a restless everchanging, gigantic body of water that would later be described as pacific.

Over its brooding surface immense winds swept back and forth, whipping the waters into towering waves that crashed down upon the world's seacoasts, tearing away rocks and eroding the land. In its dark bosom, strange life was beginning to form, minute at first, then gradually of a structure now lost even to memory. Upon its farthest reaches birds with enormous wings came to rest, and then flew on.

Agitated by a moon stronger then than now, immense tides ripped across this tremendous ocean, keeping it in a state of torment. Since no great amounts of sand had yet been built, the waters where they reached shore were universally dark, black as night and fearful.

Scores of millions of years before man had risen from the shores of the ocean to perceive its grandeur and to venture forth upon its turbulent waves, this eternal sea existed, larger than any other of the earth's features, vaster than the sister oceans combined, wild, terrifying in its immensity and imperative in its universal role.

How utterly vast it was! How its surges modified the very balance of the earth! How completely lonely it was, hidden in the darkness of night or burning in the dazzling power of a younger sun than ours.

At recurring intervals the ocean grew cold. Ice piled up along its extremities, and so pulled vast amounts of water from the sea, so that the wandering shoreline of the continents sometimes jutted miles farther out than before. Then, for a hundred thousand years, the ceaseless ocean would tear at the exposed shelf of the continents, grinding rocks into sand and incubating new life.

Later, the fantastic accumulations of ice would melt, setting cold waters free to join the heaving ocean, and the coasts of the continents would lie submerged. Now the restless energy of the sea deposited upon the ocean bed layers of silt and skeletons and salt. For a million years the ocean would build soil, and then the ice would return; the waters would draw away; and the land would lie exposed. Winds from the north and south would howl across the empty seas and lash stupendous waves upon the shattering shore. Thus the ocean continued its alternate building and tearing down.

Master of life, guardian of the shorelines, regulator of temperatures and heaving sculptor of mountains, the great ocean existed.

Millions upon millions of years before man had risen upon earth, the central areas of this tremendous ocean were empty, and where famous islands now exist nothing rose above the rolling waves. Of course, crude forms of life sometimes moved through the deep, but for the most part the central ocean was marked only by enormous waves that arose at the command of the moon and wind. Dark, dark, they swept the surface of the empty sea, falling only upon themselves terrible and puissant and lonely.

Then one day, at the bottom of the deep ocean, along a line running two thousand miles from northwest to southeast, a rupture appeared in the basalt rock that formed the ocean's bed. Some great fracture of the earth's basic structure had occurred, and from it began to ooze a white-hot, liquid rock. As it escaped from its internal prison, it came into contact with the ocean's wet and heavy body. Instantly, the rock exploded, sending aloft through the 19,000 feet of ocean that pressed down upon it columns of released steam.

Upward, upward, for nearly four miles they climbed, those agitated bubbles of air, until at last upon the surface of the sea they broke loose and formed a cloud. In that instant, the ocean signaled that a new island was building. In time it might grow to become an infinitesimal speck of land that would mark the great central void. No human beings then existed to celebrate the event. Perhaps some weird and vanished flying thing spied the escaping steam and swooped down to inspect it; more likely the roots of this future island were born in darkness and great waves and brooding nothingness.

For nearly forty million years, an extent of time so vast that it is meaningless, only the ocean knew that an island was building in its bosom, for no land had yet appeared above the surface of the sea. For nearly forty million years, from that extensive rupture in the ocean floor, small amounts of liquid rock seeped out, each forcing its way up through what had escaped before, each contributing some small portion to the accumulation that was building on the floor of the sea. Sometimes a thousand years, or ten thousand, would silently pass before any new eruption of material would take place. At other times gigantic pressures would accumulate beneath the rupture and with unimaginable violence rush through the existing apertures, throwing clouds of steam miles above the surface of the ocean. Waves would be generated which would circle the globe and crash upon themselves as they collided twelve thousand miles away. Such an explosion, indescribable in its fury, might in the end raise the height of the subocean island a foot.

But for the most part, the slow constant seepage of molten rock was not violently dramatic. Layer upon layer of the earth's vital core would creep out, hiss horribly at the cold sea water, and then slide down the sides of the little mountains that were forming. Building was most sure when the liquid rock did not explode into minute ashy fragments, but cascaded viscously down the sides of the mountains, for this bound together what had gone before, and established a base for what was to come.

How long ago this building took place, how infinitely long ago! For nearly forty million years the first island struggled in the bosom of the sea, endeavoring to be born as observable land. For nearly forty million submerged years its subterranean volcano hissed and coughed and belched and spewed forth rock, but it remained nevertheless hidden beneath the dark waters of the restless sea, to whom it was an insignificant irritation, a small climbing pretentious thing of no consequence.

And then one day, at the northwest end of the subocean rupture, an eruption of liquid rock occurred that was different from any others that had preceded. It threw forth the same kind of rock, with the same violence, and through the same vents in the earth's core. But this time what was thrown forth reached the surface of the sea. There was a tremendous explosion as the liquid rock struck water and air together. Clouds of steam rose miles into the air. Ash fell hissing upon the heaving waves. Detonations shattered the air for a moment and then echoed away in the immensity of the empty wastes.

But rock had at last been deposited above the surface of the sea. An island —visible were there but eyes to see, tangible were there fingers to feel—had risen from the deep.

The human mind, looking back upon this event—particularly if the owner of the mind has once stepped upon that island—is likely to accord it more significance than it merits. Land was finally born, yes. The forty million years of effort were finally crowned by the emergence of a pile of rocks no larger than a man's body, that is true. But the event was actually of no lasting significance, for in the long history of the ocean many such piles had momentarily broken the surface and then subsided, forbidden and forgotten. The only thing significant about the initial appearance of this first island along the slanting crack was the fact that it held on and grew. Stubbornly, inch by painful inch, it grew. In fact, it was the uncertainty and agony of its growth that were significant.

The chance emergence of the island was nothing. Remember this. Its emergence was nothing. But its persistence and patient accumulation of stature were everything. Only by relentless effort did it establish its right to exist. For the first ten thousand years after its tentative emergence, the little pile of rock in the dead, vast center of the sea fluctuated between life and death like a thing struck by evil. Sometimes molten lava would rise through the internal channels and erupt from a vent only a few inches above the waves. Tons upon tons of material would gush forth and hiss madly as it fell back into the ocean. Some, fortunately, would cling to the newborn island, building it sturdily many feet into the air, and in that time it might seem as if the island were indeed secure.

Then from the south, where storms breed in the senseless deep, a mighty wave would form and rush across the world. Its coming would be visible from afar, and in gigantic, tumbling, whistling, screaming power it would fall upon the little accumulation of rocks and pass madly on.

For the next ten thousand years there would be no visible island, yet under the waves, always ready to spring back to life, there would rest this huge mountain tip, rising 19,000 feet from the floor of the ocean, and when a new series of volcanic thrusts tore through the vents, the mountain would patiently build itself aloft for another try. Exploding, hissing, and spewing forth ash, the great mountain would writhe in convulsions. It would pierce the waves. Its island would be born again.

This was the restless surge of the universe, the violence of birth, the cold tearing away of death; and yet how promising was this interplay of forces as an island struggled to be born, vanishing in agony, then soaring aloft in triumph. You men who will come later to inhabit these islands, remember the agony of arrival, the rising and the fall, the nothingness of the sea when storms throw down the rock, the triumph of the mountain when new rocks are lifted aloft.

For a million years the island hung in this precarious balance, a child of violence; but finally, after incredibly patient accumulation, it was established. Now each new lava flow had a solid base upon which to build, and inch by inch the debris agglutinated until the island could be seen by birds from long distances. It was indeed land, habitable had there been existing men, with shelters for boats, had there been boats, and with rocks that could have been used for building homes and temples. It was now, in the real sense of the word, an island, taking its rightful place in the center of the great ocean.

But before life could prosper on this island, soil was needed, and as yet none existed. When molten lava burst upon the air it generally exploded into ash, but sometimes it ran as a viscous fluid down the sides of mountains, constructing extensive sheets of flat rock. In either case, the action of wind and rain and cooling nights began to pulverize the newly born lava, decomposing it into soil. When enough had accumulated, the island was ready.

The first living forms to arrive were inconspicuous, indeed almost invisible, lichens and low types of moss. They were borne by the sea and by winds that howled back and forth across the oceans. With a tenacity equal to that of the island itself these fragments of life established themselves, and as they grew they broke down more rocks and built more soil.

At this time there existed, on the distant continents visited by the ocean, a well-established plant and animal society composed of trees and lumbering animals and insects. Some of these forms were already well adapted for life on the new island, but were prevented from taking residence by two thousand miles of open ocean.

Consequently, there began an appalling struggle. Life, long before man's emergence, stood poised on distant shores, pressing to make new exploratory journeys like those that had already populated the existing earth with plants and animals. But against these urgent forms stood more than two thousand miles of turbulent ocean, storm-ridden, salty, and implacable.

The first sentient animals to reach the island were of course fish, for they permeated the ocean, coming and going as they wished. But they could not be said to be a part of the island. The first nonoceanic animal to visit was a bird. It came, probably, from the north on an exploratory mission in search of food. It landed on the still-warm rocks, found nothing edible, and flew on, perhaps to perish in the southern seas.

A thousand years passed, and no other birds arrived. One day a coconut was swept ashore by a violent storm. It had been kept afloat on the bosom of the sea by its buoyant husk, traveling more than three thousand miles from the southwest, a marvel of persistence. But when it landed, it found no soil along the shore and only salt water, so it perished, but its husk and shell helped form soil for those that would come later.

The years passed. The sun swept through its majestic cycles. The moon waxed and waned, and tides rushed back and forth across the surface of the world. Ice crept down from the north, and for ten thousand years covered the islands, its weight and power breaking down rocks and forming earth.

The years passed, the empty, endless, significant years. And then one day another bird arrived on the island, also seeking food. This time it found a few dead fish along the shore. As if in gratitude, it emptied its bowels on the waiting earth and evacuated a tiny seed which it had eaten on some remote island. The seed germinated and grew. Thus, after the passage of eons of time, growing life had established itself on the rocky island.

Now the passage of time becomes incomprehensible. Between the arrival of the first, unproductive bird, and the second bearing in its bowels the vital seed, more than twenty thousand years had elapsed. In another twenty thousand years a second bit of life arrived, a female insect, fertilized on some distant island on the night before a tremendous storm. Caught up in the vast winds that howled from the south, she was borne aloft to the height of ten thousand feet and driven northward for more than two thousand miles to be dropped at last upon this new and remote island, where she gave birth. Insects had arrived.

The years passed. Other birds arrived, but they bore no seeds. Other insects were blown ashore, but they were not females, or if they were, not pregnant. But once every twenty or thirty thousand years—a period longer than that of historic man—some one bit of life would reach the island, by accident; and by accident it would establish itself. In this hit-or-miss way, over a period of time that the mind can barely digest, life populated the island.

One of the most significant days in the history of the island came when a bird staggered in from some land far to the southwest, bearing in its tangled feathers the seed of a tree. Perched upon a rock, the bird pecked at the seed until it fell away, and in the course of time a tree grew. Thirty thousand years passed, and by some accident equally absurd, another tree arrived, and after a million years of chances, after five million years of storms and birds and drifting sea-soaked logs bearing snails and borers, the island had a forest with flowers and birds and insects.

Nothing, nothing that ever existed on this island reached it easily. The rocks themselves were forced up fiery chimneys through miles of ocean. They burst in horrible agony onto the surface of the earth. The lichens that arrived came borne by storms. The birds limped in on deadened wings. Insects came only when accompanied by hurricanes, and even trees arrived in the dark belly of some wandering bird, or precariously perched upon the feathers of a thigh.

Timelessly, relentlessly, in storm and hunger and hurricane the island was given life, and this life was sustained only by constant new volcanic eruptions that spewed forth new lava that could be broken down into life-sustaining soil. In violence the island lived, and in violence a great beauty was born.

The shores of the island, weathered by the sea, were stupendous cliffs that caught the evening sun and glowed like serrated pillars of gold. The mountains were tall and jagged, their lower levels clothed in dark green trees, their upper pinnacles shod in ice, while the calm bays in which the grandeur of the mountains was reflected were deeply cut into the shore. Valleys and sweet plains, waterfalls and rivers, glades where lovers would have walked and confluences where towns could have been built, the lovely island had all these accouterments, these alluring invitations to civilization.

But no man ever saw them, and the tempting glades entertained no lovers, for the island had risen to its beauty long, long before the age of man; and at the moment of its greatest perfection it began to die. In violence it had been born; in violence it would die.

There was a sudden shudder of the earth, a slipping and a sliding, and when the readjustment was ended, covering a period of thousands of years, the island had sunk some twelve hundred feet lower into the ocean, and ice nevermore formed upon its crests. The volcanoes stopped, and no new lava poured forth to create new soil to replace that which had sunk into the sea. For a million years winds howled at the hills, the ocean gnawed away at the ramparts. Year by year the island withered and grew less. It began to shred away, to shatter and to fall back into the ocean from which it had sprung.

A million years passed, and then a million more, and the island which had grown so patiently at the northwest tip of the great crack in the ocean floor slowly, slowly vanished. The birds that had fed upon its hills went elsewhere, bearing in their bowels new seeds. From its shore fertilized insects were storm-blown to other islands, and life went on. Once every twenty or thirty thousand years some fragment of nature escaped from this island, and life went on.

But as the island subsided, a different form of life sprang into increased activity. In the warm, clear, nutritious waters that surrounded the shores, coral polyps began to flourish, and slowly they left behind them as they died their tiny calciferous skeletons, a few feet below the surface of the sea. In a thousand years they built a submerged ring around the island. In a thousand more they added to its form, and as the eons passed, these tiny coral animals built a reef.

Ice melted in the north, and the coral animals were drowned in vast weights of unexpected water. The seas changed temperature and the animals died. Torrents of rain poured down from island hills and silted up the shoreline, strangling the tiny coral. Or new ice caps formed far to the north and south, pulling water away from the dying island. Then the coral were exposed and died at once.

Always, like everything to do with this island, throughout its entire history, the coral lived precariously, poised between catastrophes. But in the breathing space available, the coral built. And so it was that this tiny animal, this child of cataclysm, built a new island to replace the old as it gradually wore itself away and sank into the sea.

How terrible this passage of life and death! How meaningless that an island that had been born of such force and violence, that had been so fair upon the bosom of the great ocean, so loved of birds, so rich in trees, so willing to entertain man, should he ever arrive . . . how wasteful it was that this island should have grown in agony and died in equal agony before ever a human eye had seen its majesty.

Across a million years, down more than ten million years it existed silently in the unknown sea and then died, leaving only a fringe of coral where sea birds rest and where gigantic seals of the changing ocean play. Ceaseless life and death, endless expenditure of beauty and capacity, tireless ebb and flow and rising and subsidence of the ocean. Night comes and the burning day, and the island waits, and no man arrives. The days perish and the nights, and the aching beauty of lush valleys and waterfalls vanishes, and no man will ever see them. All that remains is a coral reef, a calcium wreath on the surface of the great sea that had given the island life, a memorial erected by the skeletons of a billion billion billion little animals.

While this first island was rising to prominence and dying back to nothing-ness, other would-be islands, stretching away to the southeast, were also strug-gling to attain brief existence followed by certain death. Some started their cycle within the same million years as did the first. Others lagged. The latest would not puncture the surface of the sea until the first was well into its death throes, so that at any moment from the time the first island began to die, man, had he then existed, could have witnessed in this two-thousand-mile chain of islands every sequential step in the process of life and death. Like an undulating wave of the sea itself, the rocky islands rose and fell; but whereas the cycle of an ocean wave is apt to be a few minutes at the most, the cycle of the rising and falling of these islands was of the nature of sixty million years.

Each island, at any given moment of time, existed certainly and securely within that cycle: it was either rising toward birth and significance, or it was perishing. I do not mean that man, had he been able to witness the cycle, could have identified which part of the cycle a given island was in; there must have been periods of millions of years when no one could have ascertained that condition. But the impersonal, molten center of the earth knew, for it was sending that island no new supplies of lava. The waiting sea knew, for it could feel the cliffs falling into its arms a little more easily. And the coral polyps knew, because they sensed that it was now time to start erecting a memorial to this island which would soon be dead . . . that is, within twenty or thirty million years.

Endless cycle, endless birth and death, endless becoming and disappearing. Once the terrifying volcanic explosions cease, the island is already doomed. Peace and calm seas and the arrival of birds bearing seeds are pleasant to experience, but the residence of beauty is surely nominated for destruction. A song at night of insects, the gentle splash of surf against the sand, and a new ice age is beginning which will freeze out all life. Limitless cycle, endless change.

T OWARD THE END of the master cycle, when the western islands were dying and the eastern were abuilding, a new volcano pushed its cone above the surface of the ocean, and in a series of titanic explosions erupted enough molten rock to establish securely a new island, which after eons of time would be designated by men as the capital island of the group. Its subsequent volcanic history was memorable in that its habitable land resulted from the wedding of two separate chains of volcanoes.

After the parent volcano had succeeded in establishing an island, its mighty flanks produced many subsidiary vents through which lava poured; whereupon a greater volcano, separated from the first by miles of ocean, sprang into being and erected its own majestic construction, marked by an equal chain of events.

For eons of time the two massive volcano systems stood in the sea in fiery competition, and then, inevitably, the first began to die back, its fires extinguished, while the second continued to pour millions of tons of lava down its own steep flanks. Hissing, exploding, crackling, the rocks fell into the sea in boundless accumulations, building the later volcano ever more solidly, ever more thickly at its base on the remote floor of the ocean.

In time, sinking lava from the second master builder began to creep across the feet of the first, and then to climb its sides and finally to throw itself across the exposed lava flows that had constituted the earlier island. Now the void in the sea that had separated the two was filled, and they became one. Locked in fiery arms, joined by intertwining ejaculations of molten rock, the two volcanoes stood in matrimony, their union a single fruitful and growing island.

Its soil was later made from dozens of smaller volcanoes that erupted for a few hundred thousand years, then passed into death and silence. One exploded in dazzling glory and left a crater looking like a punch bowl. Another, at the very edge of the island, from where it could control the sea approaches, left as its memory a gaunt headland shaped like a diamond.

When the island was well formed—and what a heavenly, sweet, enchanting island it was—some force of nature, almost as if by subtle plan, hid in its bowels a wealth of incalculable richness. It could not be diamonds, because the island was 250,000,000 years too young to have acquired the carboniferous plant growth that produced diamonds. It could not be either oil or coal, for the same reason. It wasn't gold, for neither the age nor the conditions required for the building of that metal were present on this island. It was none of these commonly accepted treasures, but it was a greater.

The volcanic basalt from which the island was built was porous, and when the tremendous storms which swept the ocean struck the island, the waters they disgorged ran partly out to sea in surface rivers, seeped partly into the heart of the island. Billions of tons of water thus crept down into the secret reservoirs of the island.

They did not stay there, of course, for since the rock was porous, there were avenues that led back out to sea, and in time the water was lost. But if any animal—a man perhaps—could penetrate the rocks, he could intercept the water and put it to his use, for the entire island was a catchment; the entire core of the island was permeated with life-giving water.

But that was not the special treasure of this particular island, for a man could bore into almost any porous rock on any island, and catch some water. Here, on this island, there was to be an extra treasure, and the way it was deposited was something of a miracle.

When the ice came and went, causing the great ocean to rise, when the island itself sank slowly and then rebuilt with new lava—when these titanic convolutions were in progress, the south shore of the island was alternately exposed to sunlight or buried fathoms deep in ocean. When the first condition prevailed, the exposed shore was cut by mountain streams which threw their debris across the plain, depositing there claylike soils and minute fragments of lava. Sometimes the sea would wash in bits of animal calcium, or a thundering storm would rip away a cliff face and throw its remnants over the shore. Bit by bit, over a hundred thousand years at a time, the shore accumulated its debris.

Then, when next the ocean rose, it would press down heavily upon this shelving land, which would lie for ages, submerged under tons of dark, green water. But while the great brutal ocean thus pressed down hydraulically, it at the same time acted as a life-giving agent, for through its shimmering waves filtered silt and dead bodies and water-logged fragments of trees and sand. All these things, the gifts both of land and sea, the immense weight of ocean would bind together until they united to form rock.

Cataclysmically the island would rise from the sea to collect new fragments washed down from the hills, then sink beneath the waves to accumulate new deposits of life-building slime. But whenever the monstrous ocean would beat down heavily upon the shore for ten thousand years at a time, new rock was formed, an impermeable shield that sloped down from the lower foothills and extended well out to sea. It was a cap rock, imprisoning in a gigantic underground reservoir all that lay beneath it.

What lay trapped below, of course, was water. Secretly, far beneath the visible surface of the island, imprisoned by this watertight cap of rock, lay the purest, sweetest, most copious water in all the lands that bordered upon or existed in the great ocean. It lay there under vast pressure, so that it was not only available, should a man deduce its secret hiding, but it was ready to leap forth twenty or thirty or forty feet into the air, and engulf with life-giving sweetness any man who could penetrate the imprisoning rock and set it free. It waited, an almost inexhaustible supply of water to sustain life. It waited, a universe of water hidden beneath the cap rock. It waited.

The adventurous plants and insects that had reached the earliest northwest island had plenty of time in which to make their way to the newer lands as the latter rose to life. It might take a million years for a given grass to complete its journey down the chain. But there was no hurry. Slowly, with a patience that is difficult to comprehend, trees and vines and crawling things crept down the islands, while in other parts of the world a new and more powerful animal was rising and preparing himself for his invasion of the islands.

Before the two-volcanoed island with its trapped treasure of water had finished growing, man had developed in distant areas. Before the last island had assumed its dominant shape, men had erected in Egypt both mighty monuments and a stable form of government. Men could already write and record their memories.

While volcanoes still played along the chain, China developed a sophisticated system of thought and Japan codified art principles that would later enrich the world. While the islands were taking their final form, Jesus spoke in Jerusalem and Muhammad came from the blazing deserts with a new vision of heaven, but no men knew the heaven that awaited them on these islands.

For these lands were the youngest part of the earth's vast visible surface. They were new. They were raw. They were empty. They were waiting. Books which we still read today were written before these islands were known to anyone except the birds of passage. Songs which we still sing were composed and recorded while these islands remained vacant. The Bible had been compiled, and the Koran.

Raw, empty, youthful islands, sleeping in the sun and whipped by rain, they waited.

Since, when they were finally discovered, they were destined to be widely hailed as paradises, it is proper to study them carefully in their last, waiting moments, those sad, sweet, overpowering days before the first canoes reached them.

They were beautiful, that is true. Their wooded mountains were a joy. Their cool waterfalls, existing in the thousands, were spectacular. Their cliffs, where the restless ocean had eroded away the edges of great mountains, dropped thousands of feet clear into the sea, and birds nested on the vertical stones. Rivers were fruitful. The shores of the islands were white and waves that washed them were crystal-blue. At night the stars were close, great brilliant dots of fire fixing forever the location of the islands and forming majestic pathways for the moon and sun.

How beautiful these islands were! How shot through with harmony and peace! How the mind lingers on their pristine grandeur, a grandeur that nothing so far devised could permanently destroy. If paradise consists solely of beauty, then these islands were the fairest paradise that man ever invaded, for the land and sea were beautiful, and the climate was congenial.

But if the concept of paradise includes also the ability to sustain life, then these islands, as they waited in the time of Jesus and Muhammad, were far from heavenly. They contained almost no food. Of all the things that grew on their magnificent hillsides, nothing could be relied upon to sustain life adequately. There were a few pandanus trees whose spare and bitter fruits could be chewed for minimum existence. There were a few tree ferns whose cores were just barely edible, a few roots. There were fish if they could be caught and birds if they could be trapped. But there was nothing else.

Few more inhospitable major islands have ever existed than this group. Here are the things they did not have: no chickens, or pigs, or cattle, or edible dogs; no bananas, no taro, no sweet potatoes, no breadfruit; no pineapple, or sugar, or guava, or gourds, or melons, or mangoes, no fruit of any kind; no palms for making sugar; no food. The islands did not even have that one essential, that miraculous sustainer of tropical life, the coconut. Some had drifted to the shores, but in salty soil along the beaches they could not grow.

Any man who came to the islands would, if he wanted to live, have to bring with him all food. If he were wise, he would also have to bring most of the materials required for building a civilized society, since the islands had no bamboo for decorating a home, no candlenuts for lamps, no mulberry bark for making tapa. Nor were there any conspicuous flowers: neither frangipani, nor hibiscus, nor bright croton, nor colorful orchids. Instead of these joy-giving, life-sustaining plants there was a hidden tree, useless except that its wood when dried yielded a persistent perfume, and this was the tree of death, the sandal-wood tree. Of itself, it was neither poisonous nor cruel, but the uses to which it would be put on these islands would make it a permanent blight.

The soil of the islands was not particularly good. It was not rich and black like the soil which Russian peasants were already farming, nor loamy and productive like that known to the Dakota and Iowa tribes of Indians. It was red and of a sandlike consistency, apparently rich in iron because it had been formed of decomposed basalt, but lacking in other essentials. If a farmer could add to this soil the missing minerals and supply it with adequate water, it had the capacity to produce enormously. But of itself it was not much, for the minerals were absent, and so was the water.

Tremendous quantities of rain did fall on the islands, but it fell in an unproductive manner. From the northeast, trade winds blew constantly, push-ing ahead of them low clouds pregnant with sweet water. But along the north-east shores of each island high cliffs rose, and mountains, and these reached up and knocked the water out of the clouds, so that it fell in cascades where it could not be used and never reached the southwest plains where the red soil was. Of the flat lands that could be tilled, fully three fourths were in effect deserts. If one could capture the wasted water that ran useless down the steep mountainsides and back out to sea, bringing it through the mountains and onto the flat lands, then crops could be grown. Or if one could discover the secret reservoirs waiting in the kidneys of the islands, one would have ample water and more than ample food. But until this was accomplished, men who lived on these islands would never have enough water or enough food.

And so these beautiful, inhospitable islands waited for some breed of men to invade them with food and courage and determination. The best that could be said of the islands, as they waited, was that they held no poisonous snakes, no fevers, no mosquitoes, no disfiguring diseases, and no plagues.

There was one additional aspect that must be remembered. Of all the growing things that existed in these islands at the time of Jesus, ninety-five out of every hundred grew nowhere else in the world. These islands were unique, alone, apart, off the main stream of life, a secluded backwater of nature . . . or, if you prefer, an authentic natural paradise where each growing thing had its opportunity to develop in its own unique way, according to the dictates and limitations of its own abilities.

I spoke of that adventurous bird that brought the first seed in its bowels. It was a grass seed, perhaps, one whose brothers and sisters, if the term may be used of grasses, stayed behind on their original islands, where they developed as the family had always done for millions of generations. On those original islands the grass maintained its standard characteristics and threw forth no venture-some modifications; or, if such mutations were offered, the stronger normal stock quickly submerged them, and the dead average was preserved.

But on the new islands the grass, left alone in beauty and sun and rain, became a different grass, unique and adapted to these islands. When men looked at such grass, millions of years later, they would be able to discern that it was a grass, and that it had come from the original stock still existing elsewhere; but they would also see that it was nevertheless a new grass, with new qualities, new vitality, and new promise.

Did an insect from one of the huge continents reach these islands? If so, here he became a different insect, his legs longer or his nose more adapted to boring. Birds, flowers, worms, trees and snails . . . all developed unique forms and qualities in these islands.

There was then, as there is now, no place known on earth that even began to compete with these islands in their capacity to encourage natural life to develop freely and radically up to its own best potential. More than nine out of ten things that grew here, grew nowhere else on earth.

Why this should have been so remains a mystery. Perhaps a fortunate combination of rainfall, climate, sunlight and soil accounted for this miracle. Perhaps eons of time in which diverse growing things were left alone to work out their own best destinies was the explanation. Perhaps the fact that when a grass reached here it had to stand upon its own capacities and could not be refertilized by grasses of the same kind from the parent stock, perhaps that is the explanation. But whatever the reason, the fact remains: in these islands new breeds developed, and they prospered, and they grew strong, and they multiplied. For these islands were a crucible of exploration and development.

And so, with these capacities, the islands waited. Jesus died on a cross, and they waited. England was settled by mixed and powerful races, and the islands waited for their own settlers. Mighty kings ruled in India, and in China and in Japan, while the islands waited.

Inhospitable in fact, a paradise in potential, with almost no food available, but with enormous riches waiting to be developed, the islands waited. Volcanoes, still building the ramparts with fresh flows of lava, hung lanterns in the sky so that if a man and his canoe were lost on the great dark bosom of the sea, wandering fitfully this way and that, he might spot the incandescent glow of the under side of a distant cloud, and thus find a fiery star to steer by.

Large gannets and smaller terns skimmed across the waters leading to land, while frigate birds drew sharp and sure navigation lines from the turbulent ocean wastes right to the heart of the islands, where they nested. If a man in a canoe could spot a frigate bird, its cleft tail cutting the wind, he could be sure that land lay in the direction toward which the bird had flown at dusk.

These beautiful islands, waiting in the sun and storm, how much they seemed like beautiful women waiting for their men to come home at dusk, waiting with open arms and warm bodies and consolation. All that would be accomplished in these islands, as in these women, would be generated solely by the will and puissance of some man. I think the islands always knew this.

Therefore, men of Polynesia and Boston and China and Mount Fuji and the barrios of the Philippines, do not come to these islands emptyhanded, or craven in spirit, or afraid to starve. There is no food here. In these islands there is no certainty. Bring your own food, your own gods, your own flowers and fruits and concepts. For if you come without resources to these islands you will perish.

But if you come with growing things, and good foods and better ideas, if you come with gods that will sustain you, and if you are willing to work until the swimming head and the aching arms can stand no more, then you can gain entrance to this miraculous crucible where the units of nature are free to develop according to their own capacities and desires.

On these harsh terms the islands waited.

II

FROM THE SUN-SWEPT
LAGOON

I have said that the islands along the rupture in the ocean floor were not a
paradise, but twenty-four hundred miles almost due south there did exist an
island which merited that description. It lay northwest of Tahiti, already populated with a powerful, sophisticated people, and only a few miles from the island
of Havaiki, the political and religious capital of the area.

It was Bora Bora, and it rose from the sea in sharp cliffs and mighty
pinnacles of rock. It contained deep-set bays and tree-rimmed shores of glistening sand. It was so beautiful that it seemed impossible that it had arisen by
chance; gods must have formed it and placed the bays just so, an illusion which
was enhanced by the fact that around the entire island was hung a protecting
necklace of coral on which wild ocean waves broke in high fury, trying vainly
to leap inside the placid green lagoon, where fish flourished in abundant numbers. It was an island of rare beauty—wild, impetuous, lovely Bora Bora.

Early one morning, while in Paris the sons of Charlemagne quarreled
among themselves as to how their late father's empire should be ruled, a swift
single-hulled outrigger canoe, sped along by sturdy paddlers and a triangular
sail, swept across the open ocean leading from Havaiki and sought the solitary
entrance to the lagoon of Bora Bora, on whose shores a lookout followed the
progress of the urgent canoe with dread.

He saw the steersman signal his sailors to drop sail, and as they complied
he watched the canoe pivot deftly in high swells that sought to crash it upon the
reef. But with enviable skill the steersman rode with the swells and headed his
canoe toward the perilous opening in the coral wall.

"Now!" he shouted, and his paddlers worked feverishly, standing the canoe
off from the rocks and speeding it into the channel. There was a rush of water,
a rising of huge waves, and a swift passionate surge of canoe and flashing
paddles through the gap.

"Rest!" the steersman called quietly, in audible relief. Gratified with his
minor triumph, he looked for approval to the canoe's solitary passenger, a tall
gaunt man with deep-set eyes, a black beard, and long thin hands in which he
clutched a staff carved with the figures of gods. But the passenger offered no
commendation, for he was lost in the contemplation of certain mighty processes
which he had helped set in motion. He stared through the steersman, past the

paddlers and onto the towering central rock that marked the heights of Bora Bora.

It was from a point partway up the slopes of this rugged mountain that the lookout now rushed down steep paths leading to the king's residence, shouting as he went, "The High Priest is returning!" The instinctive dread which the lookout felt was transmitted in his cry, and women who heard the message drew closer to their men and looked at them with new affection across dark, palm-thatched huts.

Although the agitated lookout delivered his frightening message to the general community, he was actually speeding to alert one man, and now as he darted along in the shade of breadfruit trees and palms, he kept whispering to himself, "Gods of Bora Bora, speed my feet! Don't let me be late!"

Dashing up to a grass house larger than its neighbors, the lookout fell to the ground, shouting, "The High Priest is in the lagoon!" From the grassy interior a tall, brown-skinned young man, courtier to the king, poked a sleepy head and asked in some alarm, "Already?"

"He has passed the reef," the lookout warned.

"Why didn't you . . ." In great agitation the young man grabbed a ceremonial tapa robe made from pounded bark, and without waiting to adjust it properly went running toward the palace crying, "The High Priest approaches!" He hurried past other courtiers like himself and right into the royal presence, where he prostrated himself on the soft pandanus matting that covered the earthen floor, announcing with urgency, "The august one is about to land."

The man to whom these agitated words were addressed was a handsome, large-headed man of thirty-three whose close-cropped hair showed gray at the temples, and whose unusually wide-spaced eyes were grave with wisdom. If he experienced the same dread at the High Priest's return as did his underlings, he masked it; but the tall young courtier nevertheless observed that his master moved with unaccustomed alacrity to the treasure room, where he donned an ankle-length robe of light brown tapa bark, throwing about his left shoulder and around his waist a precious cordon made of yellow feathers, his badge of authority. He then adjusted his feather-and-shell helmet, while around his neck he placed a chain of shark's teeth. At this appropriate moment the tall courtier issued a signal, and drums along the shore began to throb in royal rhythms.

"We go to honor the High Priest," the king announced gravely, waiting while an impressive train of tanned warriors, naked to the waist and wrapped in brown tapa, formed behind him. Almost against his will, the king found himself urging his men, "Hurry, hurry! We must not be tardy," for although everyone acknowledged that he was supreme on Bora Bora, he had found it prudent never to be wanting in courtesies to the spiritual ruler of the island, especially since the attributes and requirements of the new god, Oro, were not yet clearly known. The king's father had underestimated the power of the new deity, and during a solemn convocation in the temple of Oro, his high priest had suddenly pointed at him as one failing in reverence, and the king's brains had been clubbed in, his body dragged away as the next human sacrifice to red Oro, the all-powerful, the uniter of the islands.

But in spite of the king's care, when the royal procession left the palace the tall young courtier had to warn, "The august one already approaches the landing!" whereupon the king and all his retinue began to run, holding onto their various badges as they did. The king, aware of the ridiculous sight he presented, yet unwilling through fear to go more slowly, glared at the tall courtier whose information had been delivered late, and the aide, who was having difficulty keeping his tapa cloth straight as he ran, began to sweat and prayed beneath his breath, "If there is to be a convocation, O gods of Bora Bora spare me!"

The king stumbled on in the hot morning sun, angry, muttering, damaged in pride. But he did reach the landing place a few moments before the canoe, and although he could not have known it at the time, his sweaty embarrassment helped rather than hurt, for from the outrigger the High Priest noticed with satisfaction the king's discomfort and for a moment allowed a smile to creep toward his lips. But it was quickly suppressed, and the priest resumed his aloof study of the mountain peak.

Gently, the steersman brought his canoe to rest, careful lest any untoward accident draw the priest's attention, for the paddlers knew what message the religious man was bringing from the temple of Oro, and on this day it behooved all men to be careful. When the canoe was secured, the High Priest disembarked with imperial dignity, his white-bark cape with its fringe of dog's teeth shining against his long, black hair.

He was a powerful symbol of Oro as he moved with his god-carved staff to meet the king, genuflecting slightly as if to indicate that he acknowledged the latter's supremacy. Then, recovering his posture, he waited grimly while King Tamatoa, the supposed ruler, bowed low and held a subservient position long enough to impress all witnesses with the fact that power had somehow been mysteriously transferred from his hands into those of the priest. Then the king spoke.

"Oh, blessed of the gods!" King Tamatoa began. "What is the wish of Oro?"

The pressing crowd, handsome men and fine women, naked to the waist and dark-eyed, held its breath in apprehension, which the High Priest sensed and relished. He waited, while soft winds from the green lagoon tugged at palms that lined the shore and made the dark green leaves of breadfruit sway. Then he spoke solemnly: "There will be a convocation!" No one gasped, lest he draw fatal attention to himself.

The High Priest continued: "A new temple is to be erected in Tahiti and we shall convene to consecrate the god who is to live in that temple." He paused, and visible fear crept over the faces of his listeners. Even King Tamatoa himself, who could with reasonable assurance count on being spared, felt his knees weaken while he waited for the dread details that completed any announcement of a general interisland convocation at Oro's temple.

But the High Priest also waited, appreciating that the longer his terror continued, the more effective it would be in impressing the sometimes recalcitrant Bora Borans with the temper and might of their new god. On this day he would maneuver the king himself into asking the fatal questions.

Flies that had been feeding on dead fish along the lagoon shore now turned their attention to the bare backs of the waiting crowd, but no man moved lest in the next dreadful moments he become conspicuous. The king waited. The priest waited. Finally in a hushed voice Tamatoa asked: "When is the convocation?"

"Tomorrow!" the High Priest said sternly, and his news was instantly interpreted as he had intended. Thought the king: "If the convocation is to be tomorrow, it must have been decided upon ten days ago! Else how could the news reach Tahiti in time for their canoe to return to Havaiki tomorrow? Our High Priest must have been in secret consultation with the priests of Oro during all those ten days."

The flies stung perspiring backs, but no man moved, awaiting the next ominous question. Finally Tamatoa asked, "How many men for Oro?"

"Eight," the priest replied, impersonally. Placing his staff before him, causing watchers in the muted crowd to fall back, the gaunt dark man in shimmering white robes moved off toward his temple, but when it appeared that he had finished with the crowd he suddenly whirled about, made a terrifying sound in his throat, and thrust his staff directly at the steersman who had brought him into the safety of the lagoon.

"And this one shall be first!" he screamed.

"No! No!" the steersman pleaded, falling to his knees on the sand.

Implacably, the great gaunt priest towered over him, pointing at him with the staff. "When the seas were upon us," he intoned mournfully, "this one prayed not to Oro for salvation but to Tane."

"Oh, no!" the sailor pleaded.

"I watched his lips," the priest said with awful finality. Attendants from the temple gathered up the quaking steersman and hauled him off, for his legs, surrendering to terror, could not be forced to work.

"And you!" the dreadful voice cried again, thrusting his staff at an unsuspecting watcher. "In the temple of Oro, on the holy day, your head nodded. You shall be second." Once more the attendants closed in on the culprit, dragging him away, but gently lest Oro be offered as a human sacrifice a man who was bruised or in any way imperfect.

Solemnly the High Priest withdrew and King Tamatoa was left with the miserable task of nominating the six additional human sacrifices. He asked, "Where is my aide?" and from a spot toward the rear of the crowd, where he had hoped to remain unnoticed, the tall and trembling courtier stepped forth.

"Why was I late in greeting the sacred one?" the king demanded.

"The lookout stumbled. It was he who was tardy," the aide explained.

From the rear of the crowd a woman's voice inadvertently blurted, "No, that is not true!" But the woman's husband, a small man of no marked intelligence, was dragged before the king, where he shook like a torn banana leaf, and the king surveyed him with disgust. "He shall be third," the king commanded.

"Oh, please, no!" the lookout protested. "I ran true. But when I reached the palace," and he pointed to the aide, "he was asleep."

The king recalled his earlier impatience with the young courtier and announced peremptorily: "He shall be fourth. The rest shall be taken from the slaves." With this he strode back to the palace, while the lookout and the tall courtier, already pinioned by the priests, stood in limp amazement, appalled by the catastrophe in which each had so accidentally involved the other.

As the frightened crowd dispersed, each congratulating himself that for this convocation he had escaped the insatiable hunger of Oro, a young chief clothed in golden tapa, which indicated that he was of the royal family, stood bitter and silent in the shade of a breadfruit tree. He had not hidden himself through fear, for he was taller than most, better muscled than any, and marked by a lean, insolent courage that no man could mistake. He had remained apart because he hated the High Priest, despised the new god Oro, and was revolted by the incessant demand for human sacrifice.

The High Priest, of course, had immediately detected the young chief's absence from the welcoming throng, a breach of conformity which so enraged him that during the most solemn part of the ceremony his penetrating gaze had flashed this way and that, searching for the young man. Finally the priest had found him, lounging insolently under the breadfruit tree, and the two men had exchanged long, defiant stares that had been broken only when a golden-skinned young woman with flowing hair that held banana blossoms tugged at her husband's arm, forcing him to drop his eyes.

Now, with the ceremony ended, the stately wife was pleading: "Teroro, you must not go to the convocation."

"Who else can command our canoe?" he asked impatiently.

"Is a canoe so important?"

Her husband looked at her in amazement. "Important? What could there be more important?"

"Your life," she said simply. "Wise navigators do not sail when the clouds are ominous."

He dismissed her fears and strode disconsolately to a fallen log that projected into the lagoon. Falling angrily upon it, he dipped his brown feet into the silvery waters, and kicked them viciously as if he hated even the sea; but soon his placid wife, lovely in the fragrance of banana blossoms, came and sat beside him, and when her feet splashed in the cool green waters, it was as if a child were playing, and soon her husband forgot his anger. Even when he stared across to the small promontory on which the local temple sat, and where the priests were dedicating the eight doomed men to Oro, he spoke without the animal anger that had possessed him during the ceremonies.

"I'm not afraid of the convocation, Marama," he said firmly.

"I am afraid for you," his wife replied.

"Look at our canoe!" he digressed, pointing to a long shed near the temple, under which a mammoth twin-hulled canoe rested. "You wouldn't want anyone else to guide that, would you?" he teased.

Marama, whose priestly father had selected the sacred logs for the craft, needed no reminder of its importance, so she contented herself with pointing out: "Mato from the north can guide the canoe."

Then Teroro divulged his real reason for attending the dangerous convocation: "My brother may need my help."

"King Tamatoa will have many protectors," Marama replied.

"Without me events could go badly," Teroro stubbornly insisted, and wise Marama, whose name meant the moon, all-seeing and compassionate, recognized his mood and retreated to a different argument.

She said, "Teroro, it is you mainly that the High Priest suspects of being disloyal to his red god Oro."

"No more than the others," Teroro growled.

"But you're the one who shows your disbelief," she argued.

"Sometimes I can't hide it," the young chief admitted.

Furtively, Marama looked about to see if any spy had crept upon them, for the High Priest had his men in all places, but today there was none, and with her feet in the lagoon she resumed her careful reasoning. "You must promise me," she insisted, "that if you do go to Oro's temple, you will pray only to Oro, think only of Oro. Remember how the steersman's lips were read."

"I've been to three convocations at Havaiki," Teroro assured her. "I know the dangers."

"But not this special danger," his wife pleaded.

"What is different?" he asked.

Again Marama looked about her and again she saw nothing, so she spoke: "Haven't you wondered why the High Priest spent ten extra days at Havaiki?"

"I suppose he was preparing for the convocation."

"No. That must have been decided many days earlier. To permit canoes from Tahiti and Moorea to return to Havaiki by tomorrow. Last year a woman from Havaiki confided to me that the priests there consider our High Priest the ablest of all, and they plan to promote him to some position of prominence."

"I wish they would," Teroro grumbled. "Get him off this island."

"But they wouldn't dare make him paramount priest so long as his own island is not completely won over."

As Marama talked, her husband began to pick up a thread of importance, which often occurred when the wise, moon-faced woman spoke, and he leaned forward on the log to listen. She continued: "It seems to me that the High Priest will have to do everything possible in this convocation to prove to the priests of Havaiki that he is more devoted to Oro than they."

"In order to make himself eligible for promotion?" Teroro asked.

"He must."

"What do you think he will do?" Teroro asked.

Marama hesitated to utter the words, and at that moment an unexpected wind blew across the lagoon and threw small waves at her feet. She drew her toes from the lagoon and dried them with her hands, still not speaking, so Teroro continued her thought: "You think that to impress others, the High Priest will sacrifice the king?"

"No," Marama corrected. "It is your feet he will place upon the rainbow."

Teroro reached up and tugged at the tip of a breadfruit leaf and asked thoughtfully, "Will the killing then stop?"

"No," his wife replied gravely, "it will go on until all of your friends have left the lagoon. Only then will Bora Bora be safe for Oro."

"Men like Mato and Pa?"

"They are doomed," Marama said.

"But you think not the king?"

"No," the queenly young woman reasoned. "Your brother is well loved by the kings of Tahiti and Moorea, and such a bold step might turn not only those kings but people in general against the new god."

"But offering me to Oro would be permitted?" Teroro pursued.

"Yes. Kings are always willing to believe the worst of younger brothers."

Teroro turned on the log to study his beautiful wife and thought to himself: "I don't appreciate her good sense. She's a lot like her father." Aloud he said, "I hadn't reasoned it out the way you have, Marama. All I knew was that this time there was special danger."

"It is because you, the brother of the king, still worship Tane."

"Only in my heart do I do that."

"But if I can read your heart," Marama said, "so can the priests."

Teroro's comment on this was forestalled by an agitated messenger, his arm banded by a circle of yellow feathers to indicate that he belonged to the king. "We have been looking for you," he told Teroro.

"I've been studying the canoe," the young chief growled.

"The king wants you."

Teroro rose from the log, banged his feet on the grass to knock away the water, and nodded an impersonal farewell to his wife. Following the messenger, he reported to the palace, a large, low building held up by coconut-tree pillars, each carved with figures of gods and highly polished so that white flecks in the wood gleamed. The roof consisted of plaited palm fronds, and there were no floors or windows or side walls, just rolled-up lengths of matting which could be dropped for either secrecy or protection from rain. The principal room contained many signs of royalty: feather gods, carved shark's teeth, and huge Tridacna shells from the south. The building had two beautiful features: it overlooked the lagoon, on whose outer reef high clouds of spray broke constantly; and all parts of the structure were held together by thin, strong strands of golden brown sennit, the marvelous island rope woven from fibers that filled the husks of coconuts. Nearly two miles of it had been used in construction; wherever one piece of timber touched another, pliant golden sennit held the parts together. A man could sit in a room tied with sennit and revel in its intricate patterns the way a navigator studies stars at night or a child tirelessly watches waves on sand.

Beneath the sennit-tied roof sat King Tamatoa, his big broad face deeply perturbed. "Why has a convocation been called?" he asked peremptorily. Then, as if fearing the answer, he quickly dismissed all who might be spies. Drawing closer on the tightly woven mat that formed the floor, he placed his two hands on his knees and asked, "What does it mean?"

Teroro, who did not see things quickly himself, was not above reciting his wife's analyses as his own, and now explained, "It looks to me as if our High Priest must be seeking promotion to the temple in Havaiki, but in order to be eligible he has to do something dramatic." He paused ominously.

"Like what?" the king asked.

"Like eliminating the last signs of Tane worship in Bora Bora. Like sacrificing you . . . at the height of the convocation."

"I'm fearful of just such a plot," Tamatoa confessed. "If he waits till we're in convocation, he could suddenly point at me the way they pointed at our father, and . . ." The troubled king made a slashing swipe at his brother's head, adding dolefully, "And my murder would be sanctified because Oro had ordained it."

"More likely the High Priest," Teroro corrected.

Tamatoa hesitated, as if probing his younger brother's mind, and then added petulantly, "And my death would go unavenged."

Self-pity was so alien to Tamatoa, whose warlike capacities and prudent leadership had kept little Bora Bora free from invasion by its larger neighbors, that Teroro suspected his brother of laying some kind of trap, so the younger man fought down his inclination to confess his own plans for the convocation and observed idly, "The canoe will be launched at noon."

"Will it be ready by sunset?" the king asked.

"It will, but I hope you won't be on it."

"I am determined to go to this convocation," Tamatoa replied.

"Only evil can befall you," Teroro insisted.

The king rose from his mats and walked disconsolately to the palace entrance, from which he could see the majestic cliffs of Bora Bora and the sunswept lagoon. "On this island," he said with deep emotion, "I grew in joy. I have always walked in the shadow of those cliffs, and with those waves clutching at my ankles. I've seen the other islands, and the bays of Moorea are lovely. The crown at Tahiti is good to see, and the long beaches of Havaiki. But our island is man's heaven on earth. If I must be sacrificed to bring this island into harmony with new gods, then I will be sacrificed."

The images evoked by Tamatoa's memories of the Bora Bora of their youth accomplished what his guile had been unable to do, and Teroro cried, "Brother, do not go to Havaiki!"

"Why not?" Tamatoa asked, flashing around and moving back to the mats.

"Because your departure to the gods will not save Bora Bora."

"Why not?" Tamatoa demanded, thrusting his face close to Teroro's.

"Because when the club falls, I shall kill the High Priest. I will rage through all Havaiki and destroy it. Then the other islands will destroy us."

"As I thought!" the king cried sharply. "You have a plan to riot. Oh, Teroro, it will accomplish nothing. You cannot go to the convocation."

"I will be there," Teroro muttered stubbornly.

The king stood grave in the morning shadows and pointed his right fore-finger at Teroro. "I forbid you to leave Bora Bora."

At this moment the warrior-king Tamatoa, burly and serious-faced, was a symbol of overpowering authority to his younger brother, and the projecting finger almost made Teroro tremble; for although he wanted to grasp his brother by that finger, and then by his hand, and finally by his strong arm and thus pull him down onto the mats for an honest conversation, the young chief could never have brought himself to touch the king, because he knew that the king was the instrumentality whereby the gods delivered mana—the spiritual sanctification of the heavens—to Bora Bora, and even to touch the king or pass upon his shadow was to drain away some of that mana and thus imperil not only the king but the entire society.

Yet Teroro's desire for words with his brother was so great that he pros-trated himself on the matting, crept on his belly to him, and pressed his face so close to the king's feet, whispering, "Sit with me, brother, and let us talk." And while the flies droned in morning heat, the two men talked.

They were a handsome pair, separated in age by six years, for a sister had been born in between, and each was aware of the special bond that linked him to the other, for as boys their wrists had been opened one solemn day, and each had drunk the blood of the other. Their father, dead as a sacrifice to Oro, had named his first son Tamatoa, the Warrior; and then when a younger brother was born the family had reasoned: "How fortunate! When Tamatoa becomes king he will have his brother to serve him as high priest." And the younger child had been named Teroro, the Brain—the intel-ligent one, the man who can divine complex things quickly. But so far he had not proved his name to be appropriate.

Tamatoa, of course, had developed into a classical island warrior, rugged, big-boned and grave. Like his dedicated ancestors he had defended Bora Bora against all cabals and concentrations. Six times in his reign of nine years he had been called to beat back invaders from powerful Havaiki, so that the sudden supremacy of that island's new god, Oro, was especially galling; the ancient enemy seemed about to conquer by guile what it had never been able to take by force. Teroro, on the other hand, had not lived up to his name, and showed no signs of becoming a priest. Tall and wiry, with a handsome thin face, he loved brawling, had an impetuous temper and was slow to grasp abstract ideas. But his greatest failing was that he could not memorize genealogies or sacred chants. His love was navigation and the challenge of unknown seas. Already he had driven his canoe to distant Nuku Hiva, while a run down to Tahiti was familiar play.

"I am afraid it is for you the gods will send the rainbow," Tamatoa whispered.

"We have stood against them in the past, we can do so again."

"In the past they had canoes and spears. Now they have plans and plots. I don't feel hopeful."

"Are you afraid?" Teroro asked bluntly.

"Yes," the king confessed. "New ideas are afoot, and I can't seem to grasp them. How has the High Priest succeeded in manipulating our people so successfully?"

"New gods are popular, I suppose," Teroro hazarded. "When our people see many sacrifices they know the gods listen. It makes the island seem safer."

The king studied his brother for a moment, then asked cautiously, "Would it not be possible for you to accept their new god?"

"Impossible," Teroro said flatly. "I was born with the blessing of Tane. My father died defending Tane, and his father before him. I will never consider another god."

The king breathed deeply and said, "Those are my thoughts, too. But I'm afraid the High Priest will destroy us, Teroro."

"How can he?" the impetuous young warrior demanded.

"By tricks, by plans, by clever ideas."

"I'll trick him!" Teroro cried in frustration. Slashing his hand across his knee he muttered, "I'll trick his head into a mass of coconut jelly."

"That's why you mustn't attend this convocation," Tamatoa said.

Teroro stood humbly before the king, yet spoke stubbornly: "Beloved brother, that is why I must go." Then he moved about the palace mats and said prophetically, "The High Priest will not destroy us. If we go down, he goes down with us. The whole island goes down. Brother, I swore to our father that I would protect you. I'm going to the convocation, to protect you. But I will give you my promise not to riot unless they strike you."

"They won't strike me, Teroro. They'll strike you."

"They had better strike with the speed of a hungry shark," Teroro laughed, and with this he walked out into the glorious high noon of Bora Bora, when the sun blazed overhead and filtered through palm fronds and breadfruit leaves, making soft patterns in the dust. Naked children called back and forth in their games, and fishermen hauled their canoes onto the beach. The soporific haze of noon, compounded of sunlight and dust, was upon the island, and all things were beautiful. How restful this moment was, when the sun hung for a moment in mid-heaven, casting no shadows; flies droned and old women slept.

Through the beautiful and dusty heat Teroro moved slowly to where the great ceremonial canoe of Bora Bora rested, and as he went he called, "Into the water! Into the water!"

From various grass houses along the lagoon, men appeared, drowsily wrapping themselves in tapa and swallowing the last bits of coconut. "Send for the priests to bless our canoe," Teroro called, and soon four holy men arrived, pleasure on their faces, for among all the functions of this island, there was nothing that exceeded in common joy the returning of the ceremonial canoe to its natural element. Palm fronds that had enclosed the seaward end of the long shed were taken down, and the twin hulls of the immense canoe were edged carefully toward the water. Then a rare old priest named Tupuna, his long white hair piled on his head and stuck with skewers, separated his beard, and with his eyes on the lagoon and on the open sea beyond, cried:

"Ta'aroa, god of the dark and sweeping sea,
Ta'aroa, master of tempest and gentle calm,
Ta'aroa, protector of men with vision of the reef,
Ta'aroa, take *Wait-for-the-West-Wind* to thy bosom,
Take it to Havaiki and to Moorea and to Nuku Hiva,
To the Black Shining Road of Ta'aroa,

To the Black Shining Road of Tane.
To the Road of the Spider,
To the Much-traveled Road of Ta'aroa.
God of the dark and sweeping sea,
Accept as thy gift, this canoe."

In silence and in spiritual exaltation, Teroro pulled away the last prop that bound his glorious canoe to land, and slowly it began to taste the lagoon, to dip its high-tiered stern into the gentle waves, and finally to ride upon the bosom of Ta'aroa, which was its home.

The young chiefs who would paddle the canoe that night now leaped into the two hulls and adjusted the movable seats that slid back and forth along the dugout sections. Teroro, grabbing his personal god-carved paddle, gave the canoe a mighty shove that sent it far into the lagoon, with him trailing his feet aft in the green waters. "Hoist sail!" he cried. "We'll test the wind." And when a noonday breeze dropped down from the cliff, it caught the sail and began to move the great double-hulled canoe, and men paddled briskly, and soon with lightning speed *Wait-for-the-West-Wind* hurtled across its home lagoon.

It flew like a special albatross, just dipping into the waves. It went like the wind-caught leaf of a breadfruit tree, skimming the waters. It went like a young woman hurrying to meet her lover, like the essence of the god Ta'aroa majestically inspecting the ramparts of his ocean. It sped like the spirit of a warrior killed in battle, on its swift journey to the everlasting halls of Tane. And it flashed across the lagoon like what it was: a miraculous, slim, double-hulled craft of Bora Bora, the swiftest ship the world at that time had ever known, capable of doing thirty knots in bursts, ten knots for days at a time, hour after hour; a huge, massive craft seventy-nine feet long, with a tiered stern twenty-two feet high and a solid platform slung across the hulls on which forty men or the statues of forty gods could ride, with pigs and pandanus and water stowed safely in the hidden innards.

"Wait for the west wind," the men who built the canoe had advised, "for it blows strong and sure from the heart of the hurricane." The north wind cannot be depended upon, and the east wind is no treasure, for it blows constantly, and the south wind brings nothing but irritating minor storms, never those that shake the earth, not storms that last for weeks at a time and which can be counted upon to drive a canoe to the farthest points of earth. Wait for the west wind! It blows from the heart of the hurricane. It is a wind to match this great canoe.

On this day, it was an ordinary eastern wind. Some of the world's sailors might even have counted it a considerable breeze, but to Bora Borans who longed for the westerly gale that could carry them even to distant Nuku Hiva, the day's wind was really nothing. But it did bear a hint of invitation, and so on the spur of the moment Teroro cried, "Through the reef!"

Wait-for-the-West-Wind was already doing better than fifteen knots, and a prudent navigator usually took his craft through this perilous reef at slowest speed, but on this sun-swept day Teroro shot his precious craft directly at the small opening that marked the dividing line between the placid green waters of the lagoon and the thundering blue ocean which pounded outside.

The canoe seemed to anticipate the impending crash of giant waves, for it tensed in the wind, cut a little deeper into the lagoon, and leaped toward the passageway through the reef. For an instant the crew could glimpse the cruel fingers of gray coral clutching at the defiant craft, but this danger was quickly forgotten, for ahead loomed the towering waves.

With a song crying from its sail, with vigor to match that of the young chiefs who manned it, the swift canoe shot into the combers, lost its nose in a great gray-blue wave, then rose triumphantly onto the crest and sped away into the very center of the wind and the rousing waves and vast blue sea of Ta'aroa.

"What a canoe!" Teroro exulted, the spray whipping his black hair about his face.

It was with special exhilaration that the thirty paddlers tasted the last moments of freedom with which Teroro had provided them, for each man knew that at nightfall he would embark upon a different journey: solemn, joyless, with the constant threat of death impending. In their imagination they could see the altar where the blood would be. They could visualize the dreadful sacrificial clubs. But worse, each man knew positively that when *Wait-for-the-West-Wind* touched Havaiki's shore at dawn tomorrow one of today's crew would be struck down forever.

So in the day's bright sunlight, with spume about them and the sound of sea birds, they experienced momentary joy as they drove their swift canoe, champion of the islands, with the assurance that only competent men ever know. To their wishes the canoe responded; to their efforts it leaped forward; and now as they turned it in the free and joyous ocean, it responded as they willed, exactly to the inch as they intended, and found once more the opening through the reef, and came at last to shore. How competently these island men had built and mastered their canoe; how securely it obeyed their will.

B Y NIGHTFALL *Wait-for-the-West-Wind* had assumed a much different aspect. The upswept sterns were decorated with flowers and pennants of yellow tapa. The permanent platform which held the two hulls together was covered with polished planks. At the forward end stood an ultra-sacred grass-thatched temple, toward which a solemn procession of priests in sacerdotal attire now moved in dread silence.

The High Priest, clad in white and with a fringe of shark's teeth about his ankles, a skullcap of red feathers on his black hair, proceeded to the grass temple and paused, at which all Bora Borans, king and slave alike, fell to the ground and hid their faces, for what was about to occur was too sacred for even a king to behold.

The feather-figured statue of Oro himself, woven of sennit and with sea shells as his eyes, was about to be placed inside the temple for its journey to Havaiki. From his white robes the High Priest produced a wrapping of ti leaves, which hid the god, and holding the bundle high above him, he prayed in terrifying voice, then kneeled and placed the god inside the temple. He moved back, struck the canoe with his staff and cried, *"Wait-for-the-West-Wind,* take thy god safely to Havaiki!"

The prostrate crowd rose, no man speaking, and the paddlers assumed the positions they had held earlier that day. Next the seers of the island, old men of wisdom, stepped onto the polished platform wearing solemn brown tapa and skull-caps edged with dog's teeth. Some carried gourds with which to divine portents, while others studied the dying sun for auguries which they shared with no one.

Teroro, robed in yellow and wearing a warrior's helmet of feathers and shark's teeth, took his place in the prow, while the king, in precious yellow robes which covered his ankles, stood amidships. Silence resumed, and the High Priest announced that he was ready to accept the sacrifices.

Servants of Oro came forth with palm fronds which they spread in careful patterns, aft of the temple, and on these were laid strange gifts: a large fish from the lagoon, a shark caught at sea, a turtle taken on a special island, and a pig that had from birth been dedicated to Oro. These four dead sacrifices were not placed side by side, but about eighteen inches apart, and were promptly covered with additional palms.

Now, at the last moment, priests led forth the eight human sacrifices, and the people of Bora Bora, in awful silence, watched their neighbors depart for the last time. They saw the steersman who had been trapped praying to the old god Tane. And the man who had dozed in the temple. And the tardy lookout, and the sleepy young courtier. With grief the citizens watched them go. They were followed by four slaves, those unspeakable, untouchable things, known even in life as foul corpses.

As the intended victims were shoved aboard, the wife of one of the slaves, if a slave's woman could be so dignified, uttered a piercing scream. "Auwe! Auwe!" she lamented, reciting that heart-tearing word of the islands that has always been reserved for moments of supreme anguish.

Her outcry was such an appalling breach of discipline, especially on the part of a slave, that all in the canoe shivered with apprehension at such an evil omen. Teroro thought: "Now our island is truly disgraced. The king will surely be sacrificed." King Tamatoa thought: "The High Priest will have a right to be outraged. My brother is doomed." The thirty paddlers thought: "They may have to sacrifice two of us tomorrow."

The High Priest thought nothing. He was too astonished by this infraction of the tabu to do anything but point his staff at the offending woman, whereupon four priests grabbed her, rushed her to the lagoon, and pinioned her head under water. But with demonic strength the slave broke loose from their grasp, got her head free, and wailed prophetically: "Auwe! Auwe, Bora Bora!"

A priest struck her in the face with a rock, and when she staggered backward, two other priests leaped upon her and held her under the water until she died. But this did not compensate for the broken tabu, and the High Priest cried, "Whose woman was she?" Someone pointed to one of the slaves in the canoe, and the High Priest nodded slightly.

Swiftly, from the rear of the platform a burly priest, custodian of this job for many years, stepped forward and with a mighty swing of a knobbed war club crushed the skull of the unsuspecting slave. The body slumped, but before its blood could stain the canoe, it was pitched headfirst into the lagoon, where the swimming priests gathered it up as a sacrifice for their local altar. Automatically, from the shore, a substitute slave was whisked aboard, and amid such disasters and ominous portents, *Wait-for-the-West-Wind* headed out to sea. This time, as if sharing the guilt that had settled upon the passengers, the canoe did not spring lightly toward the reef but moved reluctantly, so that by the time the stars had risen for Teroro to steer by, *Wait-for-the-West-Wind* had covered only a small portion of its gloomy journey to the temple of Oro on the island of Havaiki.

Toward dawn, when the constellation which astronomers in other parts of the world had long since named the Lion was rising in the east, the seers whose responsibility it was to determine such things, sagely agreed that the time was near. The High Priest was consulted, and he confirmed the fact that the red-tipped hour of dawn, sacred to Oro, was at hand. He nodded, and a huge, slack-headed drum was struck in slow rhythm, sending its cry far out to sea.

The rest of the world was silent. Even the lapping waves and birds who customarily cried at dawn were supposed to cease their murmuring at the approach of dread Oro. There was only the drum, until, as night paled and red streamers rose in the east, Teroro caught the sound of another drum, and then a third, far in the distance. The canoes, still invisible to one another, were beginning to assemble for the solemn procession into the channel of Havaiki. Now the drums increased their beat, until a vast throbbing was set up—hammering, hammering—and the red dawn increased, and over the silent sea one could begin to spot tall sails and mournful pennants hanging in the breezeless air. The High Priest moved his hands faster, and the drummers speeded their beat, and the paddlers began to move the canoe, always in silence, toward the gathering place, and as the red sun burst from its pit in the horizon, eleven canoes, brilliant in color and sacrificial gifts, stood forth and formed two majestic lines, each headed for the temple of Oro; but as they moved and as Teroro studied them carefully, he concluded with satisfaction: "No one has a canoe like ours."

The drums abruptly stopped, and the High Priest began an agitated chant, into the middle of which a terrifying, inhuman sound intruded: it was the frenzied beating of a very long, small-headed drum which gave an anguished cry, and as it rose to its climax, the High Priest screamed, and the burly executioner swung his studded club and crushed the head of the tall young courtier who had slept when he should have been awake.

Reverently, priestly attendants caught the corpse while others removed the palms that had covered the earlier sacrifices: the fish, the shark, the turtle and the pig. It now became obvious why spaces eighteen inches wide had been left between these offerings, for into the first gaping slot was carefully fitted the dead body of the courtier.

The chanting resumed and the dreadful drum began a new lament for the feckless lookout. The club fell with great fury, and the body was tenderly slipped in between the shark and the turtle. Three more times the frenzied little drum was beaten, and in the red light of dawn the awful club crashed down upon some head, so that when day commenced, the fore part of the platform was filled with Bora Bora's diocesan statue of Oro, wrapped in ti leaves and wreathed in golden feathers, surveying the five fresh human sacrifices that lay interspersed with the fish, the shark, the turtle and the pig. Each of the other ten canoes, their wild drums wailing, had offered identical sacrifices, and all now moved the last half mile to the temple.

The travelers in *Wait-for-the-West-Wind* had varied thoughts as they approached the sacred landing, but on one thing all agreed: it was reasonable for a god to require special sacrifices on days of particular solemnity; and as for the customary four slaves, no one was concerned about their deaths, especially since one of their congregation had broken a tabu so shamelessly. Slaves were ordained for sacrifice.

The High Priest reasoned, in these last minutes, that considering Bora Bora's stupid persistence in allegiance to Tane the more sacrifices made to Oro the better, particularly when one of them happened to be yesterday's steersman, a man notoriously dedicated to Tane. "Weed them out, root and branch," he muttered to himself. He did not consider the five men so far sacrificed an unusual number, nor did he think that the four more who were marked for sure death, nor the slave and his wife, nor the chance ones that would be killed at the convocation itself exceeded a reasonable limit. Oro was a powerful god. He had accomplished what no other god before him had attained: the consolidation of all the islands; it was only appropriate that he be honored. Prayers, respect and observance of tabus had always been accorded all gods, but a master god like Oro merited supreme sacrifices like sharks and men. Far from feeling that a quota of nine was excessive, he was already dreaming of the time when Bora Bora could invade some outward island and return with thirty or forty captives to be offered up at one sublime ceremonial. "We must impress the islands," he mused.

King Tamatoa's thoughts were different. To be sure, he felt no regret or responsibility for the death of his tardy look-out and his one-time courtier. They had failed, and death was customarily the penalty for failure. Nor could he lament in any way the four foul corpses; slaves were born to be sacrificed, but he was personally ashamed that one of his slaves had been so weak as to cry out merely because her man was being taken to Oro. Tamatoa looked upon a reasonable number of sacrifices as the simplest way of obtaining a steady flow of mana, but he nevertheless felt considerable uneasiness over the fact that the total of sacrifices for any given convocation had now been established as nine, plus more perhaps according to the chances of the day. Bora Bora was not a large island. Its men were numbered, and if in the past they had maintained their freedom it was because of their superior courage. The king wondered: "Is this sudden conversion to Oro a device by the wise men of Havaiki whereby they can depopulate my island and thus accomplish by guile what they have always been unable to do by battle?" He was deeply perplexed by a further haunting possibility: "Do you suppose the priests at Havaiki are teasing our High Priest along with promises of promotion only until such time as he has disposed of Teroro and me?" Then, for the first time he expressed in words his real perplexity: "It is very difficult to be king when the gods are changing."

Teroro saw things more simply. He was outraged. His thoughts were forthright and purposeful. The death of slaves he could condone, for that was the law of the world, on every island. But to execute for trivial reasons the best fighters on Bora Bora, merely to appease a new god, was obviously wrong and disastrous. "Look at the body of Terupe, lying there between the shark and the turtle! He was the best steersman I ever had. And the High Priest knew it. And Tapoa, useless beside the shark. He was wise and would have made a good counselor." Teroro was so furious that he did not trust himself to look either at his brother or at the High Priest, lest he uncover his thoughts. Instead, he contented himself with staring ahead at the impressive canoes and listening to the mournful drums, speaking of death. He thought: "Unless we settle the High Priest now, these drums are the requiem of Bora Bora." He saw clearly that the death of eight or ten more key warriors would lay the island open to assault. "I'll work out a plan," he swore to himself.

The minor priests looked with some satisfaction upon the sacrifices already consummated and those about to occur. With the advent of Oro, each priest had faced an inner struggle: "Shall I go over to the new god, or shall I remain faithful to Tane?" It was gratifying to know that one had chosen the winner. The priests acknowledged that there remained some dissidence in the island, but they had observed that after each convocation, adherence to Tane weakened. "Sacrifices help us attract the attention of Oro," they rationalized, "and then he sends us mana." Their conclusions were influenced perhaps by the fact that as priests they could be reasonably sure that they would not be sacrificed to obtain mana; their role in the upcoming ceremonies was simple and known: to hoist the sacrifices into place, to eat the sacrificial roast pig, also the boiled bananas, the baked taro and the salted fish. And when the convocation ended, they had to throw the human bodies into the sacred pit. There was an exhilaration about Oro that other gods did not have, and they felt gratified that they had been among the first to join his side.

The thirty rowers had only one thought: "Will it be I?"

And the three remaining slaves had no thoughts . . . none, that is, that would have been remotely comprehensible to the non-slaves in the canoe; for curiously, these three men, even though each had known from birth that he was doomed, had exactly the same fears, the same sick feeling beneath their hearts, and the same unaccustomed sweat in their armpits as did the men who were not slaves. But this would never have been believed.

The palpitations of the slaves did not continue long, for on the instant that Teroro touched his canoe onto the beach of Havaiki, the burly priest flashed his brutal club and killed first one, then two, then three. Their bodies were pitched onto the runway up which the canoe was to be drawn, and soon every passenger who had come in the canoe, even the king and the High Priest, bent himself to the hallowed task of hauling the mighty craft ashore and onto a small plateau where it would be consecrated for the coming year.

At the precise moment when the canoe came to rest, the High Priest whirled in the morning sunlight and dipped his staff toward one of Teroro's most trusted companions, and before the man could move, the awful club descended and his skull was cleft in two. His body was strung from the stern to stand guard during the ceremonial days. The surviving crewmen, aghast at the rank of the man who had been slain, tried in deepest shame to prevent the thought that rose to their hearts: "It was not I."

The convocation was planned to last three days, during which no sound but the problems of priests should be heard. Assemblies took place in an extensive, roofless rock temple perched on a magnificent plateau overlooking the ocean across which the participating canoes had come. It was a low, sprawling edifice paved with blocks of black lava, from which even blades of grass had been swept. At one end an inner temple, thatched with palm, had been constructed, and in it reposed the ark which housed the holy of holies, the ultimate statue of Oro.

The exposure of this source-god, the essential being of Oro himself, was so solemn an undertaking that not even kings or their brothers could witness the ceremony; they were excluded during the first august meeting when Oro was taken from his ark.

There were, however, witnesses. From each canoe the five human sacrifices had been hauled to the temple, plus five from Havaiki itself, and had been stacked in a pile for Oro's approval. When through his highest priest Oro granted assent—the priest-as-man thinking: "It's impressive, seeing so many bodies at once. Proves the islands are beginning to demonstrate their love for Oro"—lesser priests stepped forward and engaged in one of the convocation's most solemn rituals.

With long bone needles, threaded with golden sennit, they pierced the left eardrum of each corpse, thrust the needle on through the dead brain, and jerked the sennit out through the right ear. Then, fashioning a long loop, they strung each of the sixty corpses onto trees surrounding the temple, and for the succeeding hours these sacrificial men were free to gaze with dead eyes upon what not even kings could witness.

Tamatoa was required to sit apart with his brother kings, absolutely silent for seven hours, for spies supervised the kings to note any who failed in just homage to Oro; but in truth this was not necessary, for the twelve kings appreciated that their divinity derived from some august ultimate source beyond themselves, and their reservoirs of mana required constant replenishment through sacrifice and prayer. The world itself, in terrified silence, now paid reverence as mana flowed into both island statues and island kings.

The temple grounds were not entirely silent, and had this fact been ascertained by spies, those who were secretly breaking the tabu would have been instantly sacrificed; but Teroro knew this, and for his hushed conversations with his twenty-nine remaining crewmen he had chosen a remote glade ringed by palms.

"Are we willing to speak with frankness?" he asked.

"What risk do we run?" a fiery young chief named Mato asked. "If we talk they will kill us. If we remain silent . . ." He bashed his fist into his hand. "Let's talk."

"Why should so many of our men be given to Oro?" another asked.

Teroro listened to the complaints and then said, "I have been willing to run the risk of getting you here, because it doesn't matter whether there's a spy among us or not." He stared at each of his men and continued: "If one of you is a spy, inform the High Priest, because that will scare him from carrying out what I think is his plan. If no one betrays us, we're even better off."

"What is your plan?" Mato, from the north side of Bora Bora, asked.

Teroro held a small length of sennit, which he twisted and untwisted, saying slowly, "I think the High Priest intends to offer our king as a supreme sacrifice to Oro. He wants to impress the other priests with his control over Bora Bora. But he's got to give the signal himself, because if he kills by stealth, where would be his political advantage? So we must watch the High Priest constantly."

The young chiefs sat silent, because whatever Teroro divulged as his plan was bound to involve maximum danger. Then a lesser noble pointed out: "It isn't today we have to worry about."

"That's right," Teroro agreed. "Today they're occupied." And he indicated the ghastly circle of dead men dancing in trees.

"But what about the general meeting tomorrow?"

Teroro untwisted the sennit and nodded judiciously. "If I were the High Priest," he said, "with his plans, I'd strike tomorrow."

Mato was in a reckless mood, for during an awful moment that morning he had felt sure that the High Priest was going to nominate him as the skull-split guardian of the canoe. He said sternly, "I think that if the priest even begins to point at Tamatoa, we must surround the king and fight our way to the canoe."

"I think exactly the same thing," Teroro said abruptly.

There was a long silence as the other twenty-eight men contemplated what such a bold step involved, but before any could turn away in cowardice Teroro threw down the sennit and spoke rapidly: "To succeed we must insure three things. First, we must somehow move our canoe to the top of the hill so that we can rush it into the water without cutting down our speed."

"I'll take care of that," Hiro the steersman promised.

"How?"

"I don't know."

Teroro liked his honest answer but nevertheless pushed his face to within a few inches of the steersman's. "You know that if the canoe is not in position, we will all die?"

"I do," the young chief said grimly.

"Next," Teroro said, "we must have two very determined men sitting on the rocks at the temple exit."

Brash Mato cried, "I'm one, and I want Pa for the other."

A wiry shark-faced man with no chin, Pa, the Fortress, stepped forward and announced: "I'm the other."

"You may not escape," Teroro warned them.

"We'll escape," Mato swore. "Men of Havaiki have never . . ."

"The third requirement," Teroro said impatiently, "is that each of the rest of us be prepared to kill instantly anyone who moves toward Tamatoa."

"We know the executioners," Pa growled.

"And once we make a move, we must sweep Tamatoa up and with an unbroken rush get him to the canoe." He paused and then added softly, "It sounds dangerous, but once we are seaborne, *Wait-for-the-West-Wind* will be our safeguard."

"They will never catch us," the steersman promised.

"And if they did, what could they do?" Mato boasted, and as the men talked it was apparent that all wished they were in the certainty of the canoe and not in the temple grounds of Oro, which were alien and unknown.

"This will be the signal," Teroro said. "You will watch me, and the moment I move to defend the king, the steersman must dash for the canoe and you men must see that he gets through the exit."

"Who will disarm the executioner?" Mato asked.

"I will," Teroro said coldly. Then, to inspire his men, he boasted, "No club will fall tomorrow swifter than my arm."

The men appreciated this assurance, but Mato killed their ardor by stating, "There is one grave fault in this plan."

"What?" Teroro asked.

"Yesterday, before we sailed, Marama took me aside and said, 'My husband is sure that the High Priest plans to kill the king. But I am certain that Teroro himself is the target.' I think your wife is right. What do we do if she is?"

Teroro could not reply. He could see only his patient, worried wife moving among the men, enlisting their promises to protect him. He looked at the ground, recovered the sennit he had been twisting, and placed it in his belt. It was shark-faced Pa who spoke. "Marama spoke to me, too," he said, "and our duty is clear. If they strike at the king, everything goes as planned. But if they strike at Teroro, you, Mato, with your men save the king and I with mine will rescue Teroro."

"I am not the important one," Teroro said honestly.

"To us you are," his men replied, and they proceeded with their plans.

But there was a mind at work that night much keener than either Mato's or Pa's, and it belonged to the High Priest. During the most solemn part of the convocation he had been thinking, and when great Oro was returned to the ark, the High Priest called his assistants to him, and they sat cross-legged in a shadowy corner of the great temple, with the bodies of men dancing above them in the night air.

"Have you noticed anything today?" he began.

"Only that you are right," a young priest reported. "Teroro is our mortal enemy."

"What makes you say that?"

"As you directed, I studied him constantly. Four separate times I caught him struggling against the will of Oro, terrible be the name."

"When?"

"Principally, when the king's courtier was slain. He drew back, markedly."

"I thought so, too," the High Priest agreed.

"And when one of his crew was sacrificed to guard the canoe."

"He did?"

"And it seemed to me that when it came time for Teroro to lead the king away from the temple, while we came in, he acted joyously rather than in sorrow."

"We thought so, too," several priests chorused.

"But what confirms it is that this afternoon Teroro must have held some kind of meeting with his men."

"Is that correct?" the High Priest snapped.

"I can't be sure, because as you know, I had to leave him when we entered the temple, but immediately after Oro was returned to the ark, I slipped out to check on our men."

"What did you find?"

"Nothing. They had vanished."

"How could they?" the High Priest demanded.

"I don't know, but they had vanished."

"Was the king with them?"

"No," the spy reported. "He sat properly with the other kings."

"Can we be sure that Teroro held a meeting? If we were sure . . ."

"I searched everywhere," the young spy insisted, "and in my own heart I am sure."

For a long time the High Priest contemplated this unwelcome news, fingering his staff and driving it into the ground. Finally he mused: "If we could be certain that a meeting was held, we could eliminate the entire canoe. We would . . ." But when he weighed all consequences he apparently decided against this, for he suddenly turned to his burly executioner and said softly, "Tomorrow I don't want you at any time to stand either near the king or near Teroro. Keep completely away. You, Rere-ao," and he addressed his spy, "are you as swift of club as you once were?"

"I am."

"You are to place yourself inconspicuously so that at an instant's signal you can kill Teroro. You are to watch him constantly. If he makes even the slightest move. Anything . . ."

"Do I wait for a signal from you?" Rere-ao asked.

"No, but as you strike I will point at him, and his dead body will be sacred to Oro."

The High Priest moved on to discuss their roles with others, but he soon returned to Rere-ao and asked, "You understand? You don't wait for a signal. You kill him if he moves."

"I understand."

The High Priest concluded his meeting with a long prayer to Oro, at the end of which he told his men, "One way or another, tomorrow will see Bora Bora finally delivered to Oro. The old gods are dead. Oro lives."

His assistant priests breathed deeply with excitement, for their struggle to implant their new god on the backs of Tane and Ta'aroa had not been easy, and for several months they had longed for some positive event of magnitude to assure them that they had won. Their leader, sensing this desire for the spectacular, cautioned them: "There are many roads to ultimate victory, my brothers.

Oro has many paths by which he can travel to triumph. Tomorrow one of them will result in his final capture of Bora Bora, but you must not anticipate which one. That is up to Oro."

With this the High Priest folded his hands, took off his skullcap, and inclined his head toward the inner sanctuary of Oro. His fellow priests did likewise, and in the deep silence of the night, dimly lit by distant fires and the glow of shimmering stars, the holy men prayed to their all-powerful god. It was a solemn moment at the end of an exciting day, a moment sweet and meaningful, with the essence of immortality hovering above the assembly, the sacrifices in place, great Oro brooding over his faithful, and all the world subdued in silent reverence to him. At such a moment, with the greatness of Oro pulsing in the night and throbbing in the veins more powerfully than the beat of a drum, it was incomprehensible to the priests that anyone should cling to old gods when the new deity was so powerful, so rational and so benevolent.

Next morning Hiro the steersman was up early, and with a sharp rock hidden in tapa he slashed several of the sennit strands that bound *Wait-for-the-West-Wind* together, shuddering with regret as he did so, then burying the rock and hurrying to the priest in charge of the canoe's welfare to announce: "We must have scraped coral."

The priest hurried to the canoe, which rested under the surveillance of the dead crewman lashed to the stern, and studied the broken sennit. "It can be mended with fresh cord," he said, hoping to get the accident repaired before the High Priest blamed him for it.

"Yes," the crewman agreed, "and we ought to do it while we are all under the protection of Oro."

Such sentiment charmed the priest, and he was therefore receptive when Hiro suggested, "Wouldn't it be easier to drag the canoe out here, where the sun can tighten the new sennit?" And they edged the canoe into the exact position Teroro required.

"Will the mending take long?" the priest asked.

"No," Hiro assured him. "I mustn't miss the convocation of Oro."

"You must not," the priest agreed, recalling the High Priest's assurances of the night before that on this day Oro would consolidate his victory over Bora Bora, and it seemed a good omen that Hiro, one of Teroro's prominent supporters, had thus voluntarily signified his affection for Oro.

The convocation began with a startling scene, so that all who later reviewed the day agreed that it had been doomed from the beginning, although at the time that was not apparent, since the priests had quickly converted an error into a blessing. The assembly had seated itself on rocks stretching out from the main altar, and the first two pigs were being disemboweled when a boy of seven came running into the temple, crying for his father who sat near the altar.

"Father!" the lost little child shouted.

The man, a lesser chief of Havaiki, looked in horror at the approach of his son, for the boy had committed so vast a sin that no excuse could pardon it. No woman, or child, or animal had ever strayed into the temple, and the father's arms trembled as he gathered the handsome little fellow to his heart.

"I was looking for you, Father," the lost child whimpered.

In austere silence the priests at the altar, their sacrifices to Oro interrupted, stared at the offending child. His father, aware of the tabu his family had broken, rose haltingly with the boy still in his arms. Suddenly, in an act of total dedication, he thrust his son toward the altar, the child's hair falling over his father's strong left arm.

With anguished but unfaltering conviction the man spoke: "Take this child and sacrifice him to Oro! For the consecration of the temple has been broken by him, the thread of our union with Oro has been entangled. He is my son. I begat him. But I do not weep in losing him, for he has outraged Oro."

At first the priests ignored the man and left him standing with the boy in his arms while with haughty indifference they finished slaughtering the pigs. Then, with fresh blood for Oro on their hands, two priests picked up a pair of stout bamboo rods. Holding one pair of ends rigidly together, they opened the others and formed a giant pincers which they deftly dropped over the child's head, one bamboo catching him at the nape of the neck, the other across the throat. With remorseless force they closed the pincers and held the little boy aloft until he strangled. Then, with one swift slash, the High Priest laid open the child's stomach and ripped out the entrails, placing the body reverently on the highest altar, between the pigs.

"This father does well," the priest droned. "All do well who honor Oro. Great Oro, bringer of peace."

The incident unnerved Teroro, because he recognized it as an omen for this faithful day, but how to interpret it was beyond him, and for a moment in his perplexity he forgot his brother whom he had come to protect. "What could such an omen signify?" he asked stubbornly, but no answer was forthcoming, so he breathed deeply and attended to his business; yet when he looked across the temple square toward the steersman Hiro, to check the man's position, he came upon a second omen which had to be interpreted as ominous; the present steersman sat directly under the swaying body of the earlier steersman who had been killed at the whim of the High Priest, and the corpse's distended belly, already disintegrating in the tropical heat, hung heavy over Teroro's accomplice.

In confusion Teroro dismissed all omens and watched first the High Priest and then the king, for he was totally resolved to defy Oro, even if it had to be done in the very seat of the red god's omnipotence. But he was not prepared for the High Priest's strategy, for while Teroro was anticipating an entirely different tactic, the priest suddenly whirled and pointed his staff at one of the least offensive members of Teroro's crew, and one of the finest warriors.

"He ate of the sacred pig of Oro!" the accuser shouted, but the young chief did not know why he died, for the burly executioner had anticipated the charge and had already crushed the man's skull.

Priests from other islands, gratified that Oro was being protected from apostasy, chanted: "All-powerful is Oro, the peace-giver, Oro of the united islands."

As they continued their droning, Teroro sat stunned. The young chief had been his special friend, an unassuming warrior who could not possibly have eaten sacred pig. Why had he been sacrificed? Teroro could not focus upon the problem. He had a fine plan to protect King Tamatoa, and he knew that if he himself were menaced, Mato would save him. But he had not foreseen the High Priest's clever assault upon lesser members of the Bora Bora community.

In dismay Torero looked at the steersman, who stared with equal dismay at him. No answer was available there, so Teroro tried to catch the eyes of Mato and Pa, at the exit, but they were obsessed by the altar, where the body of their companion now lay. The other members of Teroro's plot were equally stunned, and in mounting confusion their leader stared at the polished rocks which formed the platform on which they had convened.

Of the Bora Bora contingent, only one man saw clearly in these awful moments. Tamatoa, like many successful kings, was gifted not with marked intellectual ability but with a powerful, stolid insight; and he realized that the High Priest had determined not to assassinate Tamatoa and his brother, but to drive them from the islands by irresistible pressure, constantly applied. "He will avoid a direct confrontation," the king reasoned. "There will be no battle. Patiently and with cunning he will alienate and terrify my people, and we will have to go."

Tamatoa was confirmed in his analysis when the High Priest whirled his staff of death at another member of Teroro's crew, and the terrible club of death descended once more. Sick at heart, King Tamatoa looked at his younger brother and saw Teroro befuddled and distraught. The king thought: "He probably had some grandiose plan to save my life today, and probably the High Priest had spies who told him the whole plot. Poor young man."

In his compassion, the king kept his eyes fixed on his brother until, bedazed, the latter looked up. Almost imperceptibly the older man shook his head, cautioning his brother not to act, not in any way. Teroro, catching the message, sat numb in fury.

It was at this moment, in the sacred temple of Oro, with the bodies of his finest men dangling before him and strewn upon the altar, that King Tamatoa whispered in his heart: "Oro, you have triumphed. You are the ultimate god, and I am powerless to oppose you." When he had said these words of contrition, a great peace came over him and he saw, as if in a revealing vision, how foolish he had been to combat the will of the inevitable. New gods were being born, and new gods conquer; but what Tamatoa did not realize was that the contentment of soul which his confession induced was merely the prerequisite for a decision toward which he had been fumbling for some months, but from which he had always hitherto retreated. Now that he had accepted the obvious—that Oro had conquered—the next obvious conclusion was easy to reach, and in the stillness of the morning Tamatoa said the fatal words for the first time, and in uttering them an enormous burden was lifted from his heart: "We will depart from Bora Bora and leave it to you, Oro. We will go upon the sea and find other islands where we can worship our own gods."

During the rest of the convocation, King Tamatoa did not confide his decision to anyone, not even to Teroro. In fact, he avoided his hotheaded younger brother, but he did summon Mato, to whom he spoke harshly: "I hold you responsible for my brother's life, Mato. If he has plots afoot, I am sure you are part of them. He must not die, even if you have to tie him to the canoe. He must not die. I need him now more than ever."

So when Teroro convened his bewildered companions to dream up some new fantasy, Mato spoke first: "We must go back to Bora Bora and plan our revenge."

"We'll go back and work out a plan," shark-faced Pa seconded.

With the decision taken from his hands Teroro could only mutter, "We will have revenge! That we will have!" and thinking only of some utter destruction and disaster, he bided his time.

WHEN A CONVOCATION ended, the priests wisely withdrew and encouraged the population to release its tensions in a wild, spontaneous celebration that sometimes lasted for three days. Now women were free to join their men, and musicians crowded the night with echoes. Beautiful girls, flashing bits of brown radiance dressed in skirts of aromatic leaves, swept into the mad hula of Havaiki and danced provocatively before the visitors of other islands, as if to challenge: "Do the women of Tahiti have soft breasts like ours? Can they move their knees to music the way we can?"

One spectator watched the dances and muttered to himself, "May the women of Havaiki be damned." Teroro would take no part in the celebration. Neither the magic hammering of the excited drums, nor the sweet voices of older women chanting love songs, nor the beauty of the girls enticed him to join the dancers. When special beauties, their bodies illuminated by palm-frond torches and etched in smoke from the fires where pigs roasted, danced past him in direct invitation, he would look at the ground and mutter to himself, "I will destroy this island. I will kill every priest of Oro. I will desolate . . . ."

His men could not maintain such powerful resolve. One by one the young chiefs threw aside their spears, wiped their hands on their bare chests and leaped into the dancing circle, shouting and entering into the wild gyrations of the Havaiki hula. When they had driven themselves into an ecstasy, they would leap high into the air, slap their thighs and prance for a moment before their equally frenzied partners. Then each would pause, look at the other, and break into laughter, whereupon the girl would unconcernedly start to walk idly toward the shadows, her partner following with equal unconcern until at the last they gave a cry and rushed together to the seclusion of some protected glade.

As they disappeared, old women in the chanting circle were free to shout encouragement, usually of the grossest kind, at which the general audience roared with approval.

"He'll be tired before she is!" one old woman predicted.

"Show him what Havaiki's famous for, Rere," another screamed.

"Don't let him stop till he begs for mercy," the first added.

"Auwe!" another cried. "Make the moon hide its face for shame!"

"Remember what I taught you, Rere!" the first chanter shouted. "Don't make him do all the work."

When the advice became almost unbearably clinical, the general audience collapsed into gales of merriment, the music halted, and everyone rolled about the earth in animal joy. What delight the wildness of sex brought with it. Then the tiniest drum—no more than eight inches of hollowed-out branch beaten with a wand—would begin a wild, high rhythm that could almost compel a man to dance, and larger drums would pick it up, and soon some other of Teroro's men would begin dancing with a dark Havaiki girl, and they too would go into the shadows, accompanied by ribald advice from the lusty old women, for an island hula was meaningless unless at its climactic moment a man and woman so desired each other that they were propelled explosively into fulfillment.

Teroro alone was not captured by the mystery and joy of this night. He did not even look up when the leading heckler shouted, "I always thought there was something wrong with the men of Bora Bora. Tetua, dance over there and tell me if he's capable!" A marvelous young girl of fifteen danced almost on Teroro's toes, flashing her body very close to his. When he ignored her, she ran laughing into the middle of the fire-rimmed circle and shouted, "He can't do!"

The old woman cackled above the drums, "I keep wondering how they have babies on Bora Bora. Men from Havaiki must swim over at night!"

At this sally Teroro had to look up, and against his will he had to smile at the raucous old woman, for islanders loved wit and liked to acknowledge it, even when directed against themselves. The old chanter, seeing that she had pierced Teroro's indifference, cried passionately, "Auwe! If I were only twenty years younger, I'd explain to you what men were made for!" When the crowd roared she shouted, "I can even yet!" And she started an outrageous hula, moving toward Teroro with her white hair dancing in the night and the memory of great sexual feats animating her hips. She was prepared to make a great fool of Teroro, but at this moment a famous chief of Havaiki, fat Tatai who guarded the temple, appeared and said quietly, "We would like you to eat with us, Teroro." And he led the young chief away from the fires, but not away from the old woman's biting tongue, for as the two men disappeared she screamed, "Oh, now I understand. It's men he likes."

Fat Tatai laughed and said, "Only death will silence that one's tongue." He led Teroro to the outskirts of the village, where his imposing family grounds had for centuries been enclosed on three sides by a rock wall head-high, the fourth side free to open on the ocean. As he entered the enclosure, Teroro saw dimly eight or nine grass houses and he could identify each: the main sleeping hall, the women's hall, the women's cook house, and the separate houses for each of Tatai's favorite wives. It was to the men's area that fat Tatai took his guest, and there, in moonlight and to the music of waves, the feast was spread.

Teroro had barely finished licking burnt pig fat from his fingers when to the west of the compound a tiny drum, beaten frantically with a length of wood, began its persuasive chatter, followed by the steadier throbbing of several big drums as the musicians entered. "I wonder why Tatai bothered to set such a feast for me?" Teroro mused, pushing away the food. He wandered to a group seated by a fire and watched casually the figures that began to materialize from the night's soft shadows. They were the women of the Havaiki chiefs, and in tones less raucous then Teroro had recently heard in the village square, they began the haunting strains of old island love songs, and the bitterness went out of his heart:

> *"When the rolling surf*
> *And the rising moon*
> *And the swaying palm*
> *And the high white bird*
> *And the lazy fish*
> *All speak of love,*
> *I cry in the night:*
> *Where are you, love?"*

It was to the strains of this languorous island song that Teroro saw approaching him, in the gentle rhythms of a chief's hula, a slim, wiry-hipped girl of fourteen with midnight-black hair that fell to her knees. She swayed delicately, her dark eyes fixed on the ground, but when the plaintive old song ended, she raised her right finger about two inches from the fall of her ti-leaf skirt, shimmering in the flares, and indicated a swifter beat, which the drums initiated.

Now she danced on her toes, her knees and elbows out in an excitingly awkward position, with the fronds of her ti-leaf skirt whirling about her handsome legs. In this dance she allowed her face to show, and it was remarkably beautiful, and she brought it close to Teroro's, her full young breasts almost brushing his hands.

Against his will Teroro gazed back at her dark eyes and for a moment was inspired to leap to his feet and join her in the dance; but he felt that he must ignore Havaiki women, since he would one day destroy this evil place. He felt no burning sexual desire, for on Bora Bora he had always been allowed almost any girl he wanted; like all young chiefs, at puberty he had been handed over to an older woman who had instructed him long and intimately in the proper behavior of men and what pleases women, and it was this preceptor who had selected his first four partners. Later, after long consultations with a genealogist, the instructress had decided that moon-faced Marama was the girl he must marry. "She will fit you appropriately in all ways," the older woman had decided, and she was right. His subsequent girls Teroro had picked for himself, and sex had been as natural to him as swimming, so that now he was constrained to ignore the dancing girl before him, except that when he saw the look of intense disappointment on her face he felt ashamed, and against his better judgment, looked at her and smiled. And in that instant he saw her framed against palm trees, with long black tresses glistening in the fires, and on some surging impulse he leaped to his feet, whirled into the dancing area and positioned himself before her, swinging his body in the frenzied postures of the even more erotic Bora Bora hula.

Now the beautiful young girl acted as if she had never seen her new partner before. Dancing impersonally, her eyes far away, she led the drums to faster rhythms until in mounting fire her entire body quivered and a soft glow of perspiration reflected from every angle of her golden brown skin. She bent her knees and danced close to the ground. Then, in the most characteristic passage of the Havaiki hula, she spread her knees as if entertaining a man in love, whereupon the drums retarded their beat to allow her movements to become slow and madly provocative. She closed her dark eyes and held her head far back. With one hand she caught the ends of her hair and passed them between her teeth.

Over her a savagely aroused Teroro danced until with a fiery leap he sprang high into the air, descending with his toes not inches from hers. He now bent his body, spreading his knees, and for at least a minute the two bronzed bodies swayed until a woman shouted, "Auwe!" and the drums rose to new violence and the dancers entered upon the final wild gyrations.

Then, magically, everything stopped. There was dead silence, and the young girl, walking slowly like a sea goddess come ashore, moved demurely toward the shadows that marked the sleeping areas of the compound. When she had vanished, Teroro with maximum indifference stooped to throw a driftwood brand into the fire. Then tardily, like a boy summoned to a temple, he started edging toward the shadows, but this was too much for one of the chief's women, and she called in a wild, penetrating voice, "Take your skirt off, Tehani, I can't make you another."

He found her waiting for him in the far corner of the compound, before a small house which her family had reserved for her on her thirteenth birthday, for island parents encouraged their daughters to experiment with many young men and to learn the ways of love, since potential husbands did not like to marry any girl who had not already proved that she could bear children.

"This is my house," she said simply.

"What is your name?"

"I am Tehani, Chief Tatai's daughter."

"Tehani," Teroro interpreted. "The little darling."

The girl laughed nervously and replied, "My mother was beautiful." With a swift passage of his arm about her hair-hidden waist, Teroro swept Tehani into the air and carried her into her house. Happily, she twisted her long tresses about his face and pressed her lips to his. When he had placed her on the soft pandanus mats she pulled away her skirt of ti leaves and said, "It was my mother who warned me not to tear the skirt." And she pulled Teroro onto her and wrapped her arms about him, twisted and sought him, pressing him ever more strongly to her. But later, as he lay in the starlight that drifted in through the doorway, he swore to himself: "I will destroy this compound . . . this whole island."

But in the morning, after he had eaten in the men's house, where his adventure with Tehani occasioned no comment, he returned to the girl's secluded house, and after a while the two lovers began idly toying with the famous Havaiki slapping game, wherein to an ancient chant each gently tapped the other's finger tips, then shoulders, then sides, then thighs; as the game progressed the slaps grew in intensity, until perversely they dropped away to the tenderest of caresses, so that a gesture which started as a quick slap might end as a long embrace. At last Tehani lingered so gently over one slap, that Teroro caught her skirt and pulled it from her. Completely naked, she continued the game, chanting a few haphazard bars and attempting a few more desultory slaps, now grown breathless and passionate, until with a cry of soft triumph she surrendered the game and rolled into Teroro's arms, pushing him back onto the matting.

Later she whispered, "This is the way we fight on Havaiki." When Teroro laughed she asked, "Can girls of Bora Bora fight with their men like this?" Teroro was not pleased with the question, and although Tehani sensed his irritation she nevertheless pursued: "Is it true that on tiny Bora Bora you still pray to Tane?" The manner in which she pronounced *tiny* and *Tane* betrayed the contempt with which people of her island had always regarded Bora Bora.

Teroro did not rise to the insult. With studied courtesy he said, "We pray to Oro, which is why, even though we are so small, we invariably defeat Havaiki in war."

Tehani blushed at the memory of her island's humiliations and asked, "Did you wonder why my father came for you last night? And why I danced for you?"

"I thought about it. It looked planned."

"And why I brought you here?"

"At first love-making a man sometimes wonders," Teroro said. "At the second, he no longer bothers."

"And at the third," Tehani whispered, "he decides to stay with this girl . . . to make his home here . . . to become a man of Havaiki."

Teroro pulled away and said. "For a warrior there is only one home, Bora Bora."

It was an ancient island custom that high-born women could seek their husbands, and Tehani now did so. "I plead with you, Teroro. Stay here with me."

"If you want to be my wife," he said, "you'll have to come to my island."

"You already have a first wife there, Teroro. Live here, and I will be your first wife."

The young chief held the girl off and studied her marvelous face. "Why do you ask this, Tehani? You could have any man on Havaiki."

The girl hesitated, then decided to speak the truth. "Your island is doomed, Teroro. You must escape. Come here. Be loyal to Oro. We can have a good life."

"Has your father suggested this?"

"Yes."

"What evil is he planning?"

"I dare not say," she answered. Taking Teroro's hands, she knelt before him and pleaded softly, "I have shown you how sweet Havaiki could be because I want to save your life. Here you can become a powerful chief. My father has many lands, and Oro is generous to warriors like you."

"I belong to Bora Bora," Teroro said with passionate conviction. "I will never leave that island," and he started for the canoe, but pleading Tehani caught him by the legs, and he stayed with her that second night, so that on the next morning when the conch shells told of departure, he was reluctant to go.

"There are no women like you on Bora Bora," he confessed.

"Stay here with me," she pleaded.

At this moment he was almost tempted into confiding to her the revenge he had been formulating in his mind, but he fought back the impulse and said, "If I ever did come back to Havaiki, you would be my woman. A man could enjoy you."

"Come soon, Teroro, for Bora Bora is doomed."

Certainly, when the eleven visiting canoes departed the temple and stood out to sea, each breaking off from the column for its own destination, it seemed that the days of Bora Bora's greatness had vanished, for it was a dispirited group that occupied *Wait-for-the-West-Wind.* King Tamatoa acknowledged that in the game of power at the temple, he had permanently lost. All strength now lay with the High Priest, and abandonment of the island to Oro was the only sensible course. Teroro, surveying his depleted ranks, brooded on revenge, but had to recognize that the priest had outwitted him and had stricken down enough of his men to demoralize the rest. The crewmen sensed that their chiefs were disorganized and that ultimate power now lay with the High Priest, but they did not know by what political contrivances the power would be transferred; while the junior priests were so excited by the obvious victory of Oro that they had volunteered, while still on Havaiki, to assassinate both Tamatoa and Teroro and thus to settle the island's problems once and for all.

To their surprise, the High Priest had not assented to this; in fact, he had condemned his overeager assistants and had reasoned: "If we dispose of the king and his brother in this manner, the people will lament their passing and might even rise against us, but if we continue as we have been doing, then the people themselves will discover that their king is powerless against the wishes of Oro, and they will either force him to Oro's will, or they will desert him."

"But what if the king is obstinate?" an old priest had asked, recalling the record of Tamatoa's father, against whom Havaiki, Tahiti and Moorea had united in war, fruitlessly.

The High Priest had looked up at the sacrifices dangling in the moonlight and had observed: "Tamatoa may remain obstinate, but his people won't. Have you been watching how his men are even now confused and bitter? Where is Teroro, their leader, right now? Idling in the hut of Tehani!"

The old priest, not certain that Tamatoa would abdicate, had argued: "Whom shall we select to rule Bora Bora if we do depose the king?"

The High Priest had hoped that this question would not be raised, because he did not wish to stand forth among his followers as the originator of a plan that had indeed been devised by the generality of priests, so he had equivocated and said, "Oro has chosen a successor."

"Who?" the old man had pressed.

"Oro has chosen Tehani's father, the great chief Tatai."

There had been a long silence as the enormity of this decision struck the priests, for they were Bora Bora bred, and what was proposed was nothing less than the submission of their island to the ruling house of Havaiki, a thing never accomplished in the past by siege or war or contrivance. The High Priest had known that this intelligence must at first be repugnant, so before anyone could speak, he had added, "It is Oro who has chosen Tatai."

The invocation of Oro's name among men who had only recently staked their lives on this god, effectively halted comment, and the High Priest had continued: "That is why Tatai has urged his daughter Tehani to become the wife of Teroro. He will move to Havaiki and take with him most of his vigorous supporters, and they will soon become swallowed up among the men of Havaiki. Tatai, when he becomes king of Bora Bora, has agreed to leave his wives behind and to marry our women. In this way, Oro will be supreme." He had not added that when this was accomplished, he hoped to move his own headquarters to the great temple at Havaiki, and that at such time he would take along with him those Bora Bora subordinates who most heartily supported his master plan. But none of his listeners required to be told this, and with these exciting thoughts coursing through their minds the holy men returned to Bora Bora.

The twenty-seven surviving crewmen had few coherent thoughts. They had watched, helpless, while their original number was decimated by the power of Oro, and they had shared their leaders' confusion. Contrary to what the High Priest believed, they were gratified rather than disturbed by the fact that Teroro had spent his time with Tehani, for Mato had spread the news that Teroro must be got back to Bora Bora alive. They suspected that King Tamatoa had some solid plan of revenge, and they hoped to be a part of it. But beyond animal revenge they could not see.

There was one emotion which all in the boat shared, for at the end of the day, just before entering the home lagoon, the travelers saw the sun sink toward the west, throwing rich golden lights upon their magic island, and each man, no matter what his plots, instinctively felt: "This is the beautiful island. This is the land upon which the gods have spent particular care."

For to see Bora Bora at the end of a journey, with sunset upon the peaks, with dark night drifting in upon the valleys, and with sea birds winging home-ward; to see the red line of sunset climbing the mountain faces until the top was reached, and darkness, and to cry, "Hold! Hold! Let it remain day until I touch the shore!" and to catch within the lagoon the sounds of children at play and the echoes of home, while outside the reef the ocean roared—to have known Bora Bora at such a moment was to have known beauty.

It was with enhanced regret, therefore, that King Tamatoa led his brother to the palace and bade him recline on the pandanus mats, whereupon the king carefully lowered the matting walls, and when he was thus protected from spies, lay down facing Teroro. Secretly and in a low voice he delivered the striking words: "I have decided that we must leave Bora Bora."

Teroro was stunned. He had never even contemplated such a retreat, for he still did not appreciate the untenable position into which he and his brother had been maneuvered. "Why should we leave?" he gasped.

"There is no place for us here any longer."

"We can fight! We can kill . . ."

"Whom shall we fight? The people? The other islands?"

"We could . . ."

"We can do nothing, Teroro."

"But where can we go?"

"To the north."

This simple phrase carried implications that were difficult for Teroro to digest, and as the idea climbed from one level of his consciousness to another he could only repeat his brother's startling words. "To the north?" He recalled that other canoes had left for the north centuries before, legendary canoes which had never returned. There existed, however, a mysterious old chant which purported to give sailing directions to a distant land that lay under the Seven Little Eyes, the holy constellation whose ring launched the new year, and some said that this chant implied that at least one of the legendary canoes must have returned, and words from the chant came to his mind:

Sail to the Seven Little Eyes,
To the land guarded by Little Eyes.

But as soon as he spoke the words he grew angry, for they conjured up a picture of him fleeing Bora Bora.

"Why should we go?" he blustered.

"Don't take refuge in empty words, Teroro," the king snapped impatiently. "When you sailed to Nuku Hiva, did you find any certain knowledge of any of the canoes that have sailed to the north?"

"No."

"I understand there's an old sailing chant."

"No one knows for sure where it came from."

"What does it say?"

"If I remember, it says to sail until you come to land that lies under the Seven Little Eyes."

"How many days?"

"Some men say thirty, some say fifty."

"Teroro, if we decided to sail with the next big storm that brings us a west wind, how many people could we carry on our canoe?"

"Would they let us take *Wait-for-the-West-Wind*?"

"If not, we would have to fight for it."

"Good!" Teroro grunted, for now he could begin to see specific action.

"How many men?" Tamatoa pressed.

"About sixty."

"And all supplies?"

"Everything."

"And a house for our gods?"

"Yes."

The brothers lay on the matting with their faces at arm's length apart, whispering, and finally Tamatoa asked, "Who should join us?"

Teroro quickly rattled off the names of many warriors: "Hiro, Mato, Pa . . ."

"We aren't going to battle," Tamatoa corrected. "We are going to the north . . . forever."

In the hushed room the word overcame Teroro. "Leave Bora Bora forever?" He leaped to his feet and cried, "We'll kill the High Priest tonight!"

Tamatoa grabbed him by one leg and hauled him down to the matting. "We are concerned with a great voyage, not revenge."

But Teroro cried, "At the convocation I and my men were ready to fight all the islands if anyone touched you, Tamatoa. We would have strewn the temple with bodies. We feel the same way now."

Tamatoa smiled and said, "But the High Priest outsmarted you, didn't he?"

Teroro pressed his fingers into a tight knot and mumbled, "How did it happen? Our plan was so good."

"Oro has triumphed," the king said sadly. "We had better take our gods and go."

Teroro growled, "I should like to be set free on Havaiki one night before we go. They'd never put out the fires."

"Is there anyone on Bora Bora who knows the directions north?"

"Our uncle. It was Tupuna who taught them to me."

"Is he loyal to Oro?" Tamatoa asked.

"Yes, but I think he is also loyal to you."

"Impossible," Tamatoa objected.

"For wise old men like Tupuna, many things are possible," Teroro laughed. "Do you want me to call him?"

"Wait. Won't he be in session with the others?"

"They don't pay much attention to him," Teroro explained. "They suspect he's loyal to you."

"We wouldn't dare take so long a voyage without a priest," Tamatoa said gravely. "To be alone on the ocean for fifty days . . ."

"I would want a priest along," Teroro agreed. "Who would read the omens?" And he sent a messenger to fetch old Tupuna.

In the interim the brothers resumed their positions and their planning. "Can we gather all we need?" the king asked.

"We can get spears and helmets . . ."

"Brother!" Tamatoa cried impatiently. "For the last time, we are not going forth on some adventure. What I mean is can you get breadfruit shoots that will survive? Seed coconuts? Bred sows? And some good eating dogs? We would need a thousand fishhooks and two thousand lengths of sennit. Can you get those things?"

"I'll get them," Teroro said.

"Keep thinking about whom we shall take with us."

Again Teroro rattled off the easy names and again the king interrupted: "Find a man who can make knives, one who can strip pandanus, a good fishhook man."

"Well, if we take sixty men it ought to be easy . . ."

"I've been counting the spaces in my mind," Tamatoa reflected. "We can take only thirty-seven men, six slaves, and fifteen women."

"Women," Teroro gasped.

"Suppose the land to the north is empty," Tamatoa mused. "Suppose there are no women. We would watch our friends set their feet upon the rainbow, one by one, and each man as he left would be forever irreplacable. There would be no children."

"Will you take a wife?" Teroro asked.

"I will take none of my present wives," the king replied. "I'll take Natabu, so that we can have royal children."

"I'll take Marama."

The king hesitated, then took his brother by the hands. "Marama may not go," he said gravely. "We will take only women who can bear children."

"I would not want to go without Marama," the younger man said. "She is my wisdom."

"I am sorry, brother," the king said with complete finality. "Only women who can bear children."

"Then I won't go," Teroro said flatly.

"I need you," the king replied. "Don't you know any young girl to take?" Before Teroro could reply, the flaps parted and his uncle, old Tupuna of the white topknot and the flowing beard, came into the palace. He was nearly seventy, a remarkable age in the islands, where a man of thirty-three like the king was already an elder, so he spoke with exceptional authority.

"I come to my brother's sons," he said gravely, taking a seat on the matting near them. "I come to my own children."

The king studied the old man carefully, and then said in a low voice, "Uncle, we place our safety in your hands."

In a striking voice mellowed by years and wisdom Tupuna said, "You're planning to leave Bora Bora and want me to join you."

The brothers gasped and looked about lest any spies should have lingered, but the old man reassured them. "All the priests know you're planning to leave," he said benevolently. "We've just been discussing it."

"But we didn't know ourselves until we entered this room an hour ago," Teroro protested.

"It's the only sensible thing to do," Tupuna pointed out.

"Will you join us?" Tamatoa asked directly.

"Yes. I told the priests I was loyal to Oro, but I could not let my family depart without an intercessor with the gods."

"We couldn't go without you," Teroro said.

"Will they let us take *Wait-for-the-West-Wind*?" the king asked.

"Yes," the old man replied. "I pleaded for that in particular, because when I was younger I helped consecrate the trees that built this canoe. I shall be happy to have it my grave."

"Your grave?" Teroro asked. "I expect to reach land! Somewhere!"

"All men who set forth in canoes expect to reach land," the old man laughed indulgently. "But of all who leave, none ever return."

"Teroro just told me that you knew sailing directions," the king protested. "Somebody must have returned."

"There are sailing directions," the old priest admitted. "But where did they come from? Are they a dream? They tell us only to sail to land guarded by the Seven Little Eyes. Perhaps the chant refers only to the dream of all men that there must be a better land somewhere."

"Then we know nothing about this journey?" Tamatoa interrupted.

"Nothing," Tupuna replied. Then he corrected himself. "We do know one thing. It's better than staying here."

There was silence, and then Teroro surprised the king by asking, "Have they agreed to let us take our gods, Tane and Ta'aroa?"

"Yes," the old man said.

"I am glad," Teroro said. "When a man gets right down to the ocean's edge . . . when he is really starting on a voyage like this . . ."

He did not finish, but Tupuna spoke for him. He said, in a deep prophetic voice, "Are there people where we go? No one knows. Are there fair women? No one knows. Will we find coconuts and taro and breadfruit and fat pigs? Will we even find land? All that we know, sons of my brother, sons of my heart, is that if we are in the hands of the gods, even if we perish on the great ocean, we will not die unnoticed."

"And we know one thing more," the king added. "If we stay here we shall slowly, one by one, be sacrificed, and all our family and all our friends. Oro has ordained it. He has triumphed."

"May I tell the High Priest that? It will make our departure easier."

In complete humbleness of spirit, King Tamatoa replied, "You may tell him."

At this moment there came from the beach a sound which thrilled the three plotters, converting them at once from mature men into the children that they essentially were; and as each heard the exciting message, his eyes widened with joy and he threw off whatever badges of position he might have been wearing and ran toward the palace door, looking out into the starry darkness with the same pulsating thrill he had known as a boy.

For there along the waterfront, in the midnight hour, the citizens of Bora Bora, without king or priest, had assembled with drums and nose flutes for a night of wild merriment. The apprehensions of the convocation were ended and childish revelry was again in command. Therefore, with only the rank of commoners, Tamatoa, Tupuna and Teroro hurried eagerly to the beach. A raucous old woman was yelling, as they came, "Let me show you how our great helmsman Hiro steers a canoe!" And in superb mimicry she became not an old woman with few teeth, but a malicious lampoon of young Hiro steering his canoe; in a dozen ways she caught his mannerisms: the way he looked out to sea, and his swagger; but what she steered was not the canoe's tiller but the make-believe male genitals of another old woman who was playing the part of the canoe. When the steering was done, the first woman screamed, "He's very smart, Hiro!"

The crowd bellowed, particularly when they saw Teroro applauding the vicious mimicry of his helmsman. "I'll bet she really could steer a canoe!" he shouted.

"You'd be surprised at what I could do!" the lascivious old woman replied. But the crowd left her antics and started to applaud as blunt Malo, from the other side of the island, suddenly wrapped a bit of yellow tapa about his shoulders and made believe he was fat Tatai of Havaiki, executing ridiculous steps to the music and lampooning that chief's pompous ways. To the great joy of the assembly, King Tamatoa nimbly leaped into the smoky arena and took his place beside Malo, and both imitated Tatai, each more foolishly than his competitor, until at last it was difficult to say which was Malo and which the king. The foolish little dance ended with Tamatoa sitting exhausted in the dust, laughing madly as if he had no cares.

Again the crowd looked toward a new clown, for shark-faced Pa had grabbed a leaf-skirt and was crying in a shrill high voice, "Call me Tehani!" And he pirouetted grotesquely but with uncanny skill, evoking the Havaiki girl, until Teroro asked himself, "How could he have seen her dance?" But his preoccupation with Pa was broken when he saw his own wife, Marama, leap into the dance in hilarious burlesque of her husband. "It's Teroro!" the crowd applauded as the skilled woman ridiculed her man, gently and with love, but also with keenest perception. As she danced Teroro wondered: "Who told her about Tehani?"

Marama and the shark-faced man were the night's success. Pa was so ugly and his features so preposterous that he could make them seem like those of any man; and he could be both gentle, as in his mimicry of Tehani, and savage, as in his next burlesque of the High Priest. With a bit of black tapa for a wig and a breadfruit branch for a staff, Pa gyrated furiously in demented manner, whirling about and pointing his stick at first one islander and then another. As he did so, Marama, dancing behind with a feather bag, played the burly executioner, clubbing down one victim after another. Finally, in mock frenzy, the crazy dancer Pa gyrated directly up to King Tamatoa and pointed his stick at him, whereupon Marama rushed along, swung her feather bag, and brought it within an inch of the king's face. The victim fell as if his skull had been crushed, and lay in the sand, laughing, laughing.

As the long wild night progressed, every item of island life was brought under ridicule, with chinless Pa as the ringleader. He possessed what islanders loved: a child's sense of fairy tale, and to watch his amazing pointed face move from one characterization to the next was endless joy. Toward dawn, when the fears and repressions of the past weeks were dissipated, a group of old women approached King Tamatoa and began pleading with him, obviously seeking some special boon for the people, until at last he gave assent, whereupon the delegation's leader leaped withered-legged into the center of the crowd, screaming the good news: "Our great king says tonight we play the gourd game!" With hushed excitement the men and women separated into facing groups as King Tamatoa ceremoniously tossed toward the men a feathered gourd which glistened in the firelight. A chief reached out and caught it, danced a few ritual steps, then pitched it in a high, shimmering arc toward the eager women. A young girl who had long lusted after this man leaped into the air, snatched the gourd and dashed with it to the man who had thrown it. Clutching him by the waist, she rushed him passionately into the shadows, while the feathered gourd flew back and forth, determining the sleeping partners for that wild night.

Teroro, although he had the island to choose from, elected his own wife, Marama, the penetrating clown, and as they lay quietly in the gray-and-silver dawn, with the timeless waves of the lagoon once more established over the night's loud revelry, Teroro confided, "Tamatoa has decided to leave the islands."

"I suspected he had reached some grave decision," Marama said. "He was so eager to laugh."

"What I don't understand is, the High Priest has agreed to let Tupuna join us. And also to let us take *Wait-for-the-West-Wind.*"

Marama explained: "He's wise. He knows that islanders like to avoid direct conflicts that humiliate others. It's good procedure."

Her words were so in conflict with his plans for revenge that he asked, "What about the humiliation we suffered at Havaiki? Would you forget that, too?"

"I would," she said firmly. "When we're safe on some other island we can afford to forget Havaiki."

He started to explain that she would not be going on the voyage, but he could find no words to do so gracefully; in cowardice he fell asleep, but after a while he half-woke and mumbled, "You were very funny tonight, Marama. You were really wonderful."

W HEN THE DECISION to depart from Bora Bora was whispered from one village to the next, the island became a curious place, because no one admitted officially that the king was leaving. The High Priest continued to pay public deference to Tamatoa, and old Tupuna officiated at daily prayers to Oro. Young chiefs who had determined to join the expedition embraced wives who were obviously going to be left behind; but under this surface of indifference, all were preoccupied with one job: loading a canoe for an unknown voyage.

Particular care was given to food supplies. It was relatively easy to prepare food that was to be consumed on the voyage; it was dried in the sun and compacted into small bundles tied with ti leaves. What required special thought was the selection of roots and saplings for a new land. Experts sought taro roots that would produce the gray-blue tuber which made the best poi, and coconuts that came from the strongest trees, and breadfruit that did not grow too high but which did produce big heads rich in starch and glutinous sap. White-haired Tupuna spent three days selecting chickens that would yield meat and dogs that would bake well, for he constantly reminded his charges that they were heading for land that might be very spare, indeed.

Then came the day when departure could no longer be politely masked, for with a saw made from a large sea shell, Teroro boldly cut eleven feet from each of the canoe's high sterns. "We cannot risk such high adornment on a long trip," he explained.

"Auwe!" cried men and women along the shore. "The great canoe of Bora Bora is being desecrated." Gently Teroro handed down the god-carved sterns, and priests bore them to the temple. The crowd watched while he used dried shark's skin to smooth the ends of the truncated stern, and he kept his back to the watchers as he worked, for he was praying, *"Wait-for-the-West-Wind, forgive me for this mutilation,"* and out of his humiliation at having to cut down his own canoe, an obsessive rage was generated which was to make his departure from Bora Bora an event ever to be remembered in the islands.

His rage increased when he left his deformed canoe and went to his own hut, where he threw himself on the floor and hammered the pandanus mats. Marama came to sit with him and assured him: "When we have found a new home we will find big trees and we can make new pillars for our canoe."

"No! They'll remain as they are! A signal of our shame."

"You talk like a boy," the placid-faced woman chided.

"When I was a boy," he corrected, "if anyone insulted me, I beat him on the head. But now I'm a man, and Havaiki insults me without risks."

"Teroro," his wife pleaded. "Look at it sensibly. What has Havaiki really done? They've invented a new god, and the world seems to prefer him. They haven't . . ."

Teroro grasped his wife by the arm. "Haven't you heard the whispers?" he asked bitterly. "When Tamatoa goes, who is to be the new king? Fat Tatai of Havaiki."

Marama gasped. "Have they gone so far?" she asked.

"Yes!" Teroro snapped. "And do you know what they had the insolence to do? They proposed that I desert my brother and leave Bora Bora. I was to marry Tatai's daughter . . . trade places with him!"

"Why didn't you tell me this?"

"It was only now that I figured it out," he replied sheepishly. And as always, when he felt humiliated, he decided upon a plan of swift action. "Marama," he said hurriedly, "go across the mountain and assemble all who have agreed to paddle the canoe."

"What are you planning?" she asked suspiciously.

"To take *West Wind* for a trial, on the ocean. To see if the new stern works. Tell anyone who asks, that's what we're doing. But whisper to each man that he must also bring his best war club."

"No, Teroro!"

"Do you want us to creep away, unavenged?"

"Yes. There's no dishonor in that."

"Not for a woman, perhaps," Teroro said.

Marama considered what was involved, the possibility of death and the chance that Havaiki might send canoes in retaliation, thus ending escape to the north, but after she had considered for a long time she said, "Since men are what they are, Teroro, you ought not to go unavenged. May the gods protect you."

So, toward midafternoon two days before the intended departure for Nuku Hiva, and while a good wind blew from the west, promising a later storm of some dimensions, thirty determined paddlers, plus the steersman Hiro and the navigator Teroro, set forth from Bora Bora to test their canoe. It moved sedately across the light green waters of the lagoon and stoutly into the dark waters of the outer ocean, already whipped by the wind into sturdy waves. The canoe moved back and forth in speed tests, then hoisted sail and darted into a long leg down wind. When it had left the lee of the island Teroro asked, "Are we agreed?"

"We are," Mato said, pulling his war club into position.

"To Havaiki!" Teroro shouted to the steersman, and *West Wind* tore into the waves and its paddlers strained as darkness fell over the impartial sea.

For generations out of mind Bora Bora had been known among the islands as the land of the muffled paddles, for since it was the smallest of the major islands, its men were required to practice added caution. Now, with the dying moon not yet risen, they paused to wrap their paddle handles in tapa, so that they could creep silently, leaving barely a ripple on the sea, toward the hallowed landing of Oro, where only a few weeks before they had been so deeply humiliated.

Gently, gently, the double canoe was beached before any outlook spotted it, and thirty resolute men, leaving two to guard the canoe, slipped into the night toward the village where fat Tatai, the intended king of Bora Bora, slept. The avengers had almost reached the village when a dog barked, causing a woman to cry, "Who's stealing breadfruit?" She sounded an alarm, but before effective action could be taken, Teroro and his men had fallen upon the village and were seeking out all who had insulted them, and most particularly fat Tatai, the nominated king.

It was Teroro who led the avengers to Tatai's compound. There he and shark-faced Pa swept into the main hut, smashing and crashing all they encountered. A girl's voice, soft and petulant, whispered, "He is not here, Teroro!"

Then she screamed in pain, for Pa's great club struck her, and from the floor she whimpered, "He is not here."

Pa was about to crush her skull when Teroro pulled him away and with his left hand dragged her to safety. From a flare set ablaze by the frugal woman who was determined to protect her breadfruit, Teroro saw that Tehani was naked except for a hastily grabbed skirt which she held before her, and he rediscovered her spectacular beauty. From a distance came his brother's voice: "Don't you know any young girl?" and on the impulse of the moment he brought Tehani's face to his and rasped, "Will you go north with me?"

"Yes."

"Are you hurt?"

"My shoulder."

"Broken?"

"No."

"Wait for me at the canoe." He thrust her toward the shore and then caught her again, muttering, "We have come to kill your father. Do you still want to go?"

"I'll wait at the canoe," she said.

Now he heard Mato shout, "We've found him!"

"Save him for me," Teroro pleaded, swinging his club, but when he reached the prostrate figure of Tatai he saw that Pa had already killed him. Grabbing a handful of thatch from a roof he spread it about the dead man's head. "The new king of Bora Bora!" he cried derisively.

"To the canoe!" the steersman shouted.

"Not before we destroy this place!" Teroro cried, and grabbing from the woman's hand the brand by which she was inspecting her breadfruit, he swept it along the thatch of a nearby house; the rising wind ripped the flames along, and soon the sacred channel of Oro and the environs of his temple were ablaze. In this light, the men of Bora Bora retreated.

At the canoe a battle raged; only prompt reinforcement saved the craft, for one of the guardians was already dead and the other was badly wounded. As the Bora Borans drove back the attackers and leaped into the truncated canoe, Tehani ran from a clump of palms, crying, "Teroro! Teroro!"

"Traitor!" the defeated Havaiki warriors cried, already inventing an explanation that would excuse their defeat. They launched their spears and in their frustration would have killed her, except that Teroro left the canoe, leaped into the surf, and ran back to rescue her.

"We are in danger!" the steersman warned, standing the canoe out into the channel.

But Teroro continued running until he intercepted the girl and swept her into his arms. Then, dodging spears, he dashed for the beach and into the surf. He might not have made the canoe, except that Mato dived into the channel and took the girl, whose shoulder was so damaged that she could not swim. Together they lifted her into the canoe and set their course for Bora Bora, but before they had left the shadow of Havaiki, Teroro said to the girl, "We found your father."

She replied, "I know."

The return trip was one of intense excitement, marked by psychological relief at having struck a blow at Havaiki and at the just punishment of a stranger who had presumed to rule Bora Bora. And there was the ironic joy of knowing that before Havaiki could retaliate—if indeed they ever dared try—all involved would be on the open sea, far from Bora Bora.

But above all, there was great animal joy in realizing that during the strike at Havaiki, the promised storm had actually formed and that it now blew with real force, for although the unexpected strength of the westerly made the journey back to Bora Bora difficult, it also meant that the one essential requirement for a long journey to the north was at hand.

"This storm will blow for days!" Teroro assured his men.

At daybreak it became possible to turn and run before the wind safely into the lagoon, and as they reached its protection Teroro drilled his men in the story they must tell: "We took West Wind for a trial. The storm came up. We saw we couldn't get back. So we laid over in the channel at Havaiki." He repeated the sequence and added, "In this storm no one from Havaiki would dare come here with the true story."

"What about the girl?" Pa asked.

Everyone looked at Tehani, huddling wet in the hull, and it was immediately apparent, especially to Tehani, that the simplest solution to the difficulty she presented would be to knock her on the head and throw her into the storm. Pa was ready to do this, but Teroro stopped him.

"She's my girl," he said bluntly. "We'll take her to my house."

"She'll betray us."

"She won't. We'll say that while we were in the channel I went ashore to get her for the journey north."

"Do you intend taking her?" Mato asked.

"Yes. She's my girl."

"What about your wife Marama?"

"She can't bear children. She can't go."

"This one will betray us!" Pa warned.

Teroro reached down into the hull and pulled Tehani to her feet. Thrusting his face into hers he said, "Until we leave Bora Bora you will speak to no one about this night. No one."

"I understand," she said, sinking back into the canoe.

"It is you I will take north," Teroro promised her.

As the canoe neared shore, Mato cried, "What a storm! We went all the way to Havaiki."

Of all the listeners, only Marama knew the full significance of this statement: that some great revenge had been carried out. Swiftly she counted the canoe and saw that the young chief Tami had been lost. "Where is Tami?" she called.

"He was lost reefing sail in the storm," Pa lied.

A man called, "Why did you go all the way to Havaiki?"

Pa answered, "Teroro went to fetch the girl he will take north with him."

From the bottom of the hull, where she had lain hidden, Tehani slowly rose, and it was in this way, with the west wind of the storm beating in her face, that Marama learned she would not be accompanying Teroro to the north. No sound escaped her lips. She stood in the wind with both hands pressed against her sides, her hair whipping about her shoulders, her great placid face, handsome as a moon on the thirteenth night, staring at the stranger in the canoe.

She thought: "A man is dead. Some dreadful event has occurred that will contaminate the islands for years. Brave stupid men like my husband have gained their revenge, for what it matters. And a young stranger takes my place in the canoe." Patiently she studied the newcomer and thought: "She is beautiful and her body is well formed. Perhaps she can have children. Perhaps it's better." But then she looked at Teroro, and her heart broke.

Hiding her tears she turned to go home, but her degradation was not completed, for her husband called, "Marama!" She returned to the canoe and he said, "Take Tehani home," and Marama reached down and took the girl's hand and led her home."

In its second night the storm rose to an intensity that quite precluded any departure on the day planned, and as the winds howled, those responsible for the voyage had a few last hours free for dreaming. The visions of Teroro were agitated, and toward dawn he saw two women standing by *West Wind,* and the canoe had no mast on which to hang its sail. He awoke in fright, shook his head vigorously, and realized that the two women were merely Marama and Tehani and their standing by the canoe signified only that each wanted to go north with him, so he wakened Marama, explaining, "The king will allow only one woman to go, Marama, and he insisted that I take a younger."

"I understand," she said dully.

"It isn't that I've grown tired of you," he whispered.

"Tupuna explained," she replied.

"You understand how it is?" he pleaded.

"I understand that I have given you no children."

"You've been a good wife, Marama, but the king . . ."

He fell asleep, but before the birds had wakened, he dreamed again and saw his canoe with no mast, and this time the two women spoke, Marama in a deep voice crying, "I am Tane!" and Tehani singing in a lilting voice, "I am Ta'aroa!"

Teroro woke trembling and cried, "Why should the gods speak to me on such a night?" And for a long time he tried to decipher the dream, for he knew that before a voyage each dream meant something, but he could not find the key. So he rose in the gray light of dawn, while winds howled and drove rain across the island, and hurried, almost naked, to the hut of old Tupuna.

"What did such a dream mean?" he pleaded.

"Did the voices sound like those of gods?" the bearded old man queried.

"No, they were women's voices, and yet Tane's was deep as it should be, and Ta'aroa's was high and piercing like his voice in a storm."

The old priest sat gathering his wisdom and listened to the roaring wind that must take them on their way. Finally he announced: "It is very clear, Teroro. Tane and Ta'aroa speak most forcefully when they speak in the wind. You must obey them."

"What do they want me to do?"

"There was no mast in your dream canoe, and no sail?"

"None."

"Then it's simple. The gods wish you to take down your single mast and to raise instead two masts, one in each hull."

It was such an obvious explanation that Teroro laughed. "I've seen canoes like that. One came to Nuku Hiva from the south."

"It's natural," Tupuna explained. "When Tane, who rules the land, and Ta'aroa, who rules the sea, speak to a navigator in unison, they must be referring to the element that they rule together, the wind. They want you to erect two sails so that you can catch the wind better."

"I will do so," Teroro said, and forthwith he called his men together, and even though departure could not be far off, he ripped down the mast, found a matching tree, and erected one in the right hull, which he named Tane, and the other in the left, which he called Ta'aroa. Then he lashed each with sennit shrouds, so that by nightfall a man could climb to the top of either and not tear it loose. It would have been unthinkable for a navigator not to obey the gods.

On the third night of the storm it was the king's turn to dream, and he witnessed a fearful sight: two planets in the western sky at sunset, fighting with the sun and pushing it from the sky, whereupon one moved anxiously east and west, while the other roamed north and south. This dream was so ominous that the king summoned his uncle immediately and lay facing him in dead of night, imploring counsel.

"Does it mean that we are doomed?" Tamatoa asked in distress.

"Which of the wandering stars went searching east and west?" Tupuna inquired.

"The great star of evening."

"And they were both searching?"

"Like a dog combing the beach or a woman seeking a lost tapa."

"This is not a good omen," Tupuna said gravely.

"Could it mean . . ." the king began, but the concept was too foreboding to be put into words.

"Failure?" Tupuna asked bluntly. "You think it means that our canoe will wander north and south, east and west, until we perish?"

"Yes," Tamatoa answered weakly.

"It cannot mean that," Tupuna said consolingly, "for Tane and Ta'aroa themselves spoke to Teroro last light, and he governs the canoe."

The king was not relieved, for he confided: "My other thought is just as bad."

"What is it?" the old man asked.

"I wonder if the two stars do not represent Tane and Ta'aroa, and the thing they are looking for is Oro. I wonder if they acknowledge Oro as supreme and do not want to go in our canoe unless he goes along?" He dropped his head and muttered, "Uncle, I am sick with fear that we are doing something wrong."

"No," Tupuna assured him, "I've studied every omen. There is no indication of failure. Remember that Tane and Ta'aroa brought us significant advice, the need for two masts. Would they trifle with us?"

"But these searching stars?"

"I'll confess, not a good omen. But I am sure that all it means is that in some manner your preparation for the voyage is incomplete. You have forgotten some vital thing."

"What shall I do?"

"You must unpack everything and then repack it, and when you have accomplished this, you will know what oversight has displeased the gods."

And so, on the third day of the storm, King Tamatoa did an unprecedented thing: he threw open his tabu palace to the boat's crew, and they assembled, on mats which the day before it would have been death to touch, each item that was to go north, and before the king's careful eye they unwrapped and repacked their treasures.

"Have we our tools?" Tamatoa inquired, and his men brought forth the basalt stones used for cooking, and the sand. They produced bundles of sticks, some hard, some pithy, for making fire. Fishlines of sennit, fishhooks of pearl, nets and spears for sharks, all were in order. There were bluish-green adzes, stone chisels, pounders for crushing taro and others for making cloth. Some chiefs produced digging sticks, harder than many stones and covered with mana from long use in planting taro. There were gourds and calabashes and cups for cooking. Men hauled in bows and arrows, and slingshots with pouches of special stones. There was a long pole with sticky gum for catching birds, a conch shell for calling to prayer, and four heavy stones to serve as sea anchors. The women who had been designated to go, proudly presented fine mats, tight in structure and waterproof. There were bailers to keep the canoe dry, paddles to speed it forward, and extra mats to use as sails. During the passage of a thousand years these wandering island people had, without the assistance of any metal or clay, perfected an intricate civilization and its tools. In one double canoe they were now ready to establish that culture on a distant island. The king was satisfied.

"Have we cared for the plants and animals?" he next inquired. Tenderly, the farmers from the group unwrapped the seed-things that would, in time, sustain life in new lands. Taro corms were kept dry and twisted inside pandanus leaves until such time as they could be plunged into soft, wet mud for a new harvest.

Banana shoots, on which the voyagers must depend for quick crops, were wrapped in damp leaves and kept cool, while choice coconuts, their eyes un-opened, had to be kept dry lest they launch their shoots. Sugar cane, which all loved, had been cut into joints and was kept alive inside dark bundles made of leaves.

"Where is the breadfruit?" Tamatoa asked, and four men dragged onto the mat large bundles swathed in leaves and mud. These contained the breadfruit shoots, most delicate of the cargo, whose fruit was so loved by the islanders. When the shoots lay exposed, the king called for his uncle to bless them anew, and the group prayed for their safe transit.

Men now hauled two squealing sows into the palace. "Have they been bred?" the king asked.

"To our best boar," the men replied, hauling into the august presence an ugly, protesting beast, followed by two bred bitch dogs and a male, two chickens and a rooster.

"Have we feed for these animals?" the king inquired, and he was shown bags of dried coconut, mashed sweet potatoes and dried fish. "Place these living things before me, and their food," Tamatoa commanded, and when the assemblage was completed he cried in terrifying voice, "These are tabu! These are tabu! These are tabu!"

In solemn chant the witnesses repeated, "These are tabu!" Then Tupuna blessed them with long prayers of fertility, ending with his own warning: "These are tabu!" It was not just a word that was being used; it was a divine inhibition, and it signified that a man on this trip could see his woman die of starvation, but he could not hand her one morsel of the tabu food, nor eat any himself, for without this seed even those who did reach land would perish.

Teroro now brought in the rations: breadfruit partially dried and rolled into wads for fermentation; pandanus flour made by baking and grating the untasty fruit, just barely palatable but useful on long trips; dried sweet potatoes, shell-fish, coconut meat, bonito hard as rock; more than eighty drinking coconuts; three dozen lengths of watertight bamboo filled with clear water. When the food was assembled all could see that it did not bulk large, and Tamatoa studied it with apprehension.

"Have we enough?" he asked.

"Our people have been starving themselves for weeks," Teroro replied. "We can live on nothing."

"And have they been drinking little?"

"Barely a cupful a day."

"Are your fishermen prepared to catch us extra food along the way?"

"They have prayed to Ta'aroa. There will be fish."

"Then let us bless this food," Tamatoa said, and Tupuna recited the long chant which dedicated these rations to the gods. He hoped that the deities would allow his companions to eat the food while searching for a new land, and if it was found, the gods would be rewarded with an endless supply of pigs.

"Let us check the canoe," the king said, and he led his subjects into the storm, where they went over each portion of *Wait-for-the-West-Wind*. The two hulls were not made from single hollowed-out trees, but were built up by butting together three separate sections, each about twenty-five feet long. This meant that the canoe had to be tied together at the joints, and it was here that Bora Bora's skill with sennit showed itself to greatest advantage, for the huge canoe was as rigid as if carved from a single log, yet it was composed of many pieces, lashed intricately together, and it was these joints that the king now inspected.

They leaked, of course, and without constant bailing the canoe would sink, but they did not leak much. The strakes which formed the sides of the two hulls were also lashed on, and were also nearly water-tight. The two halves of the canoe were held together, about four feet apart, by eleven stout beams that passed through the inside wall of each hull, and were again bound by powerful sennit, while to them was lashed the long, solid platform upon which the passengers and the gods would ride. This left, in each hull, a narrow space between the edge of the platform and the outer edge of the hull, where the paddlers sat on small movable seats which they shifted back and forth until they found a place amid the cargo where their feet could reach the bottom of the hull.

"The canoe is fine," Teroro assured his brother, and the crowd waited in silence while the two brothers and their uncle studied the storm. Finally Tamatoa said, "If the omens are good, we will leave tomorrow at dusk. We must be at sea when the stars rise."

When the others had gone, Tamatoa led Tupuna back to the palace and sat disconsolately upon the matting. "What have we overlooked?" he fretted.

"I saw nothing missing," the old man said.

"Have we forgotten some vital thing, Tupuna?"

"Nothing that is apparent."

"What does it mean?" the king cried in deep perplexity. "I have tried so desperately to arrange this correctly. Where have I failed?"

His uncle said quietly, "I noticed that as we inspected the goods, when we were through, each man tied his bundles up a little more tightly. At the canoe they fastened the sennit just a bit more strongly. Perhaps that is what the gods wanted us not to forget. The last effort that insures success."

"You think it could have been that?" Tamatoa asked eagerly.

"It's been a long day," Tupuna evaded. "Let us all dream one more night, and if the omens are good, that must have been the meaning."

So on the fourth night of the storm all men who would make the voyage assembled at the temple according to ancient custom, there to acquire their last flow of mana and to sleep in terror, awaiting the omens that would lay bare the future. Once more Teroro dreamed of his canoe, and again Marama called that she was Tane and again Tehani was Ta'aroa, and just before he wakened, each woman was transformed into a mast, so that the omen was obviously hopeful. Teroro was so pleased that he risked a powerful tabu and crept out of the temple and went to the bed of Marama, lying with her for the last time and assuring her that it was only the king's command that kept him from taking her, and in the last stormy darkness, she wept. He consoled her by taking from his pouch the length of sennit that he had picked up at the temple in Havaiki, and taking Marama out into the storm, he upturned a large rock and carefully placed the sennit under it. "When I have gone for a year, turn the rock aside and you'll know whether I survived," for if the sennit still lay clean and straight, the canoe had reached land; but if it were twisted . . .

King Tamatoa woke from his dream and beat his matting with fists of joy, for incredible as it seemed, he had seen the Seven Little Eyes. He had seen them! They had actually hung over Bora Bora and moved off with the canoe. "Oh, blessed Tane!" the king cried in ecstasy. And for the rest of the night he did not sleep, but stood in the doorway of the temple surveying the storm, with the rain in his face, and in those solemn hours he knew an abiding content: "Our boat is well loaded. We have good men. My brother knows the sea and my uncle knows the chants. On this day we shall set forth."

But the dream that actually launched the voyage occurred in the hut of old Tupuna, for he saw in dream-spun heavens a rainbow standing directly in the path the canoe must take, and a worse omen than this there could not have been, but as he watched, Tane and Ta'aroa lifted the rainbow and placed it abaft the canoe, where it shone brilliantly on the waters. The omen was so auspicious, evil changing to positive good by the action of gods, that the old man did not even wake to record his dream. In the morning he was suffused with delight and told the king, "Some wonderfully good thing took place last night. I forget what it was, but we will sail tonight."

He went directly to the altar and took down the final precious essentials for the journey: one stone was black and white with flecks of yellow, and round, the size of a fist—it was Tane; the other stone was long and thin and greenish—it was Ta'aroa, god of the oceans on whom they must now depend. Tupuna wrapped each in a small cloth made of yellow feathers, and bearing his deities, he went to the canoe. In a small grass hut erected on the platform just abaft the masts, he placed Tane toward the right mast and Ta'aroa toward the left. The canoe could now be loaded.

Aft of the gods' house the platform provided an open space which Tupuna would occupy during the entire voyage, tending the deities. Behind him was sleeping space for those members of the crew who were not paddling, and behind them a large grass hut for the twelve women who had been chosen to accompany the crew. Aft of them sat Natabu, silent and sacred, the wife of Tamatoa, accompanied by red-eyed Teura, the wife of Tupuna and seer of the voyage; it was her duty to read omens. At the rear of the house, alone, sat Tamatoa beside a small doorway leading aft, from which he could watch the stars and check the steersman. The captaincy of the canoe lay with Teroro, who stood farthest forward with Tehani at his side; but the actual life and death of this bold adventure rested with the king. Only he could say turn or stay.

As the stormy day progressed it seemed inconceivable that any sensible man would venture outside the reef, but all knew that only in such a westerly gale could a canoe go forth with much chance of success, so when the winds kept strong, so did the hearts of the voyagers. They spent the day in prayer and in stowing the canoe. The slaves, the animals and the heavier bundles went into the left-hand hull, whose lead paddler would be Mato, upon whom the beat and rhythm would depend. Into the right-hand went the food, the trees and the extra mats. This would be headed by Pa. At the rear of this hull, cornerwise from Mato, the steersman Hiro would stand.

The afternoon wore on and the crew said good-bye to wives they could not take, and to their children. Teroro went for the last time to see grave Marama in the little house where they had been so happy. She was dressed in her finest tapa, yards and yards of it about her handsome body, and her hair was marked with flowers.

"Guide the canoe well, Teroro," she said softly. "I shall pray for you."

"You will always be in my heart," he promised.

"No," she corrected. "When you are gone you must forget me. It would not be fair to Tehani."

"You are my wisdom, Marama," he said sorrowfully. "When I see things clearly it is always because you showed me the way. I need you so much."

"Be quiet, Teroro," she said, and as they sat on the matting for the last time she tried to share with him all the things she had forgotten to tell him. "Never go against the counsel of Mato. He sometimes seems stupid because he comes from the north side of the island, but trust him. If you get into a fight, rely on Pa. I like Pa. The man you prefer is Hiro. He's fun, but can you trust him in an emergency? Listen to your uncle Tupuna. His teeth are yellow with wisdom. And, Teroro, never again go on a journey of simple vengeance."

"Would you have had us depart in shame?" he countered.

"Well," she admitted, "one can never defeat Havaiki enough." She caught her breath and confided, "It would have been unbearable to have a Havaiki man for king." Then she added quickly, "But mere revenge, especially when the king does not give consent. That must be past."

For the last time she talked with her man, and as the time came when he was forced to go she thought: "There is so much more he needs to know." When he took his first step toward the door she fell on the matting and kissed his ankles, and heard him say haltingly. "Marama, when we sail, please don't come on shore. I could not bear it," at which she rose full height and cried sharply, "Me! Stay hidden indoors when my canoe is leaving? It is my canoe. I am the spirit of the sails and the strength of the paddlers. I will take you to land, Teroro, for I am the canoe."

And when the men climbed aboard *Wait-for-the-West-Wind*, Marama, with her beautiful hair in the storm, guided them with her spirit and blessed them, and said to young Tehani, "Take care of our husband. Fill him with love." But at the last minute she was thrust aside by a most unexpected arrival. It was the High Priest, come down to the launching with a long retinue of assistants, and he went to the canoe and cried, "Great Oro bids you safe journey!"

Grabbing hold of the bowsprit, he stepped aboard, clutching the mast Tane as he did so. Kneeling before the gods' house, he pushed aside the grass door and deposited inside a sanctified statue of Oro, made of sacred sennit woven with his own hands and clothed in feathers. In haunting voice he cried into the storm, "Great Oro, bless this canoe!" And as he stepped ashore, Teroro saw that a smile of enormous relief had come upon the face of his new wife, Tehani. She had been willing to go upon the seas with strange gods, but now that Oro was with her, she knew the journey would succeed.

And so the double canoe, *Wait-for-the-West-Wind*, loaded and creaking with king and slave, with contradictory gods and pigs, with hope and fear, set forth upon the unknown. At the prow stood Teroro, ill-named the wise one, but at this fateful moment he was wise enough not to look back at Bora Bora, for that would have been not only an evil omen, but folly as well, for he would have seen Marama, and that sight he could not have borne.

When *West Wind* reached the reef, and stood for a moment in its last stretch of easily navigable water, all in the canoe experienced a moment of awful dread, for outside the coral barrier roared the storm on slashing waves and tremendous deeps. Just for an instant Mato, lead paddle on the left, whispered, "Great Tane! Such waves!" But with prodigious force he led the paddlers into a swift rhythm that bore them directly into the heart of the storm. The canoe rose high in the sea, teetered a moment with its shrouds whistling, then ripped down, down into the valley of the waves. Spray dashed across all heads and the two halves seemed as if they must tear apart. Pigs squealed in terror and dogs barked, while in the flooded grass house women thought: "This is death."

But instantly the powerful canoe cut into the waves, found itself, and rode high onto the crest of the ocean, away from Bora Bora of the muffled paddles, away from the comforting lagoon and onto the highway that led to nothingness.

I N   S U C H   W E A T H E R   King Tamatoa led his people into exile. They did not go in triumph or with banners flying; they fled at night, with no drums beating.

They did not leave with riches and in panoply; they were rudely elbowed off their island with only enough food to sustain them precariously. Had they been more clever, they would have held their homeland; but they were not and they were forced to go. Had they perceived the deeper nature of gods, they would never have fallen prey to a savage deity who tormented them; but they were stubborn rather than wise, and the false god expelled them.

Later ages would depict these men as all-wise and heroic, great venturers seeking bright new lands; but such myths would be in error, for no man leaves where he is and seeks a distant place unless he is in some respect a failure; but having failed in one location and having been ejected, it is possible that in the next he will be a little wiser.

There was, however, one overriding characteristic that marked these defeated people as they swept into the storm: they did have courage. Only if they had been craven could they have swallowed their humiliation and remained on Bora Bora; this they would not do. It is true that they fled into the dusk, but each man carried as his most prized possession his own personal god of courage. For Teroro it was the mighty albatross that winged its way over distant seas. For King Tamatoa it was the wind that spoke to him in tempests. For Tupuna it was the spirit of the lagoon that brought fish. And for his ancient bleary-eyed wife, Teura, the keeper of omens, it was a god so powerful that she scarcely dared mention its name. But it followed her in the ocean, her great and sweet and powerful deity, her courage in the unknown.

When they had reached, more swiftly than ever before, a point off the north coast of Havaiki, Teroro crawled over to where Mato paddled and said, "I am going to speak with the king about our feeling. Promise me that you will support me."

"I promise," Mato said.

"Even if it means death?"

"Even then."

Precariously, Teroro made his way aft to consult with his brother, laying bare a wish that startled the king: "I cannot sail with Oro in this canoe. Let us throw him into the ocean."

"A god!"

"I cannot sail with him."

Tamatoa summoned old Tupuna, who struggled aft with difficulty and sat with the brothers. "Teroro wants to throw Oro into the ocean," Tamatoa explained.

The thought was even more repulsive to the old man than it had been to the king, and he warned in powerful voice that such a thing had never been done. But Teroro was adamant: "We have suffered enough from Oro. My men cannot sail this canoe with such a burden."

"If we were on land . . ." Tupuna protested.

"No!" the king said firmly. "It is impossible."

But Teroro would not surrender. He shouted forward for Mato, who soon appeared. Tamatoa was grave and said, "Teroro wants to throw the god Oro into the ocean."

"It must not be done!" Tupuna warned.

"Let Mato speak!" Teroro demanded.

"Teroro is right," the stocky warrior said. "We have known only terror from this red god, deep, humiliating terror."

"But he is a god!" Tupuna protested.

"We must not carry such poison to a new land," Mato insisted.

Tupuna warned: "If you do such a thing, the winds will tear this canoe apart. The ocean will open to its depth and swallow us. Seaweed will grow in our hair."

"I would rather be dead," Mato shouted back, "than to install Oro in a new land."

At this point Teroro faced Tupuna and cried, "You say Oro will punish us? I say this to Oro." And he flung his head back, howling into the wind, "Oro, by your sacred pig, by your length of banana shoot, by the bodies of all men sacrificed to you, I condemn you and declare you nothing. I curse you and revile you and cast excrement in your face. Now strike me down. If you control the storm, raise your bloodstained hands and strike me down."

He stood motionless as the others listened in horror, waiting. When nothing happened he fell to his knees and whispered, just loud enough for the others to hear, "But, gentle Tane, if you guide this canoe, and powerful Ta'aroa, if you control this storm, forgive me for what I have just said. Forgive me especially for what I am about to do. But I cannot go forward with Oro as a passenger in this canoe."

He rose like a man in a dream, bowed low to his brother, and made dutiful obeisance to the priest. "Forgive me," he said in a choking voice. "If in the next moment we are swept to death, forgive me."

He stumbled forward in the storm, but when he reached the gods' house itself he was powerless to open the rain-sodden door. Inherited fear of gods, plus what he remembered of his early training when it was hoped he would become a priest, rendered him incapable of action and he returned to the rear. "I cannot act without your approval, brother," he confessed. "You are my king."

Tamatoa cried, "We shall be lost if we destroy a god."

Teroro fell on the platform and clutched his brother's feet. "Command me to destroy this evil thing."

"Don't do it, Tamatoa!" his uncle warned.

In this moment of indecision, when the ultimate values of the canoe were laid open on the stormy deck, it was tough Mato who acted. He shouted, "King Tamatoa, if we take Oro with us, when you land you will kill more people to show him gratitude, just in case it was he who brought us there. And once started, we will kill more, and more. You, Tupuna, you love gods, but we must save you from the temptation of growing to love this one!"

And he rushed to the gods' house, uncovered the sennit-and-feather form of the avenging god and raised it high into the storm. "Go back to Havaiki where you came from!" he shouted. "We don't want you. You've eaten our men. You've driven us from the home of our ancestors. Go away!" And with a vast sweep of his arm, Mato threw the god far out to sea.

But winds caught at the feathers and for an awful moment held the god aloft, so that it kept pace with the canoe. "Auwe!" shrieked the priest. "Auwe! See, Oro follows us!"

King Tamatoa, perceiving this miracle, fell to the platform in prayer, but Teroro, awakened from his indecision, grabbed a spear and with fury launched it at the god. It missed, but the shaft brushed the feathers and deflected the deity into the turbulent deep. Calmly, he turned to the prostrate king and said, "I have killed the god. You may do with me as you wish."

"Go to your post," the king mumbled, stricken with fear.

As Teroro moved forward upon the canoe whose burden of terror he had helped diminish, he felt his craft sweep into the storm with new vigor; the stays sang a sweeter song; and he could see from their smiles that his men were assured. But when he passed the gods' house and recalled how powerless he had been at the vital moment, he looked across to where Mato sat, stubbornly paddling to keep the canoe right with the storm, and he wanted to clasp the man in brotherhood, but only Mato's shoulders were free, and no man would dare touch another's shoulders, for they were reserved for the personal god to perch on when he inspired a man with courage; so Teroro merely whispered into the storm, "You were the brave one, Mato," and the sturdy paddler replied, "The canoe feels lighter."

When Teroro recovered his post he found Tehani, the daughter of Oro, weeping. He knelt beside her and said, "You must try to forgive me, Tehani. I killed your father and now I have killed your god." He took her by the hands and swore: "I will never offend you again." The dazzling girl, storm upon her face, looked up. She was bereft of the very foundations of her being, and although she tried to speak she could say nothing; but from then on Teroro treated her with extra kindness.

It was at this moment, when the captains of the canoe were most agitated, that Tane and Ta'aroa conspired to present them with an omen that erased from all hearts memories of what had just happened. The rain came heavily for about fifteen minutes, followed by strong winds that blew clouds scudding ahead in darkness until the clouds parted and the fine stars of heaven were momentarily revealed.

Then it was that the wisdom of Tupuna in setting forth at dusk on the new day of the month became apparent, for there, rising in the eastern sky and with no bright moon in competition, sparkled the Seven Little Eyes. It was their first twilight appearance of the year, their reassuring return which proved that the world would continue for at least twelve more months. With what extraordinary joy the voyagers greeted the Little Eyes. From the grass house women came forth and filled their hearts with comfort. Those crew members who had to keep the canoe headed with the wind found new resilience in their tired muscles, and Teroro knew that he was on course.

Then, the miracle vouchsafed, Tane drew the clouds once more across the heavens and the storm continued, but contentment beyond measure settled upon the canoe, for it was at last apparent that the company moved in accordance with divine laws. How sweet the roar of the wind that bore them on, how consoling the motion of the waves that carried them into the unknown; how appropriate the world, how well ordered and secure the heavens. On the canoe, that daring and insignificant bundle of wood lashed together by sennit and men's wills, all hearts were deep in peace, and the onwardness of their journey sang contentedly in all parts of the craft, so that when old Tupuna crawled back to his watching point abaft the gods' house, he called softly to Teroro ahead, "The king is content. The omen proves that Oro was caught by Ta'aroa and conveyed safely to Havaiki. All is well." And the canoe moved on.

The most critical part of any twenty-four-hour period came in the half hour just before dawn, for unless the navigator could catch a glimpse of some known star and thus check course he would have to proceed through an entire day with only the unreliable sun to steer by; for while it was true that master astronomers like Teroro and Tupuna could follow each movement of the sun and take from it their heading, they could not use it to determine their latitude. For that they depended upon the stars; their sailing directions reminded them which stars culminated over which islands, and to pass the last moments of night without seeing any constellations was not only an omen of bad luck in the future, it was also proof of present difficulty, which, if it persisted for several days, might develop into catastrophe.

For example, after their first fleeting glimpse of the Seven Little Eyes, Teroro and his uncle had waited anxiously for Three-in-a-Row, which other astronomers then living in distant deserts had already named Orion's Belt, for the sailing directions said that these stars hung over Nuku Hiva, their replenishment point. But Three-in-a-Row had not appeared during the night watch and Teroro had been unable to determine his latitude. Now the conspicuous stars were setting without having been seen, and the navigator was worried.

He had, however, observed on earlier trips that it was a peculiarity of his ocean that in the last few minutes of morning twilight, some star, as if determined to aid mariners, pushed clouds aside and showed itself, and he thought there was still time for this to happen.

"Three-in-a-Row will appear there," Tupuna announced confidently, but Teroro wondered if the night's strong wind might not have blown the canoe rather farther north than his uncle suspected.

"Maybe they will be closer to that cloud," Teroro suggested.

The difference of opinion was not to be resolved, for clouds continued to streak out of the west to meet the sun rising on the other side of the ocean. On this day dawn was neither inspiring nor refreshing, for the sun straggled reluctantly up behind many layers of cloud, half illuminated the ocean with dull gray and proved to the voyagers that they did not know where they were.

Teroro and Tupuna, having accomplished all they could, fell into immediate sleep in the stormy daylight; and it was then that the latter's wife, wizened, red-eyed old Teura, paid for her passage. She climbed out of the grass house, splattered sea water over her wrinkled face, rubbed her bleary eyes, threw her head back and started studying the omens. In nearly two thirds of a century of living with the gods, she had unraveled many of their tricky ways. Now she watched how Ta'aroa moved the waves, how the spume rose, how the tips fell away and in what manner they tumbled back into the troughs. She marked the color of the sea and the construction of the basic swells that underlay the more conspicuous waves.

At midmorning she saw a land bird, possibly from Bora Bora itself, winging its way out to sea, and from its flight she was able to determine the bird's estimate of how long the storm would continue, and it confirmed her own. A bit of bark, washed out to sea days before from Havaiki, was of particular interest to the old woman, for it proved that the ocean had a northerly set, which was not apparent from the wind, which blew more toward the northeast.

But most of all the rheumy-eyed old seer studied the sun, for although it was well masked behind layers of cloud, her practiced eye could mark its motion. "Star men like Tupuna and Teroro don't think much of the sun," she snorted, but when she placed her observations of its course beside the deductions she had made from earlier omens she concluded: "Those men don't know where they are! We're far to the north of our course!"

But what Teura particularly appreciated were those unexpected messages from the gods which meant so much to the knowing. For example, an albatross, not large and of no possible importance as food, happened to fly past the canoe and she saw with gratification that he kept to the left, or Ta'aroa's side, and since the albatross was known to be a creature of that god's, this was a refreshing omen; but when the bird insisted upon returning to the canoe, also from the left side, and finally perched on the mast of Ta'aroa, the coincidence could no longer be termed as an omen. It was a definite message that the god of the oceans had personally sent to an old woman who had long honored him, and Teura looked at the sea with new love, and sang:

> "O, Ta'aroa, god of the boundless deep,
> Ta'aroa of the mighty waves
> And the troughs that lead down to blackness,
> We place our canoe in your hands,
> In your hands we place our lives."

Contentedly, the old woman gathered her many omens, and they were all good. The men of her canoe might be lost, and the stars remain hidden, and the storm continue, but Ta'aroa was with them and all was well.

In the late afternoon, Tupuna and Teroro, before resuming their duties, came aft to find out from Teura where they were, and she advised them that they rode much farther north than even Teroro had suspected.

"No," the men reasoned. "We've been to Nuku Hiva. Directions don't call for a turn yet."

"Head for the pit from which Three-in-a-Row climbs," she warned with stubborn finality, "or you'll miss Nuku Hiva."

"You wait till the stars come out," Teroro challenged. "You'll see we're on course."

Teura would not argue. For her any problem was simple: either the gods spoke or they didn't, and if they did, it was useless to try to explain to someone else how the message was delivered. "We are far to the north," she snapped. "Turn."

"But how can we know?" Teroro pleaded.

"The gods said so," she muttered and went to bed.

When she was gone, the two men reviewed her various omens, but the only one upon which they were willing to place much reliance was the albatross. "You can't have a much better omen than an albatross," Tupuna reasoned.

"If Ta'aroa is with us," Teroro concluded, "we must be on the right course."

From the grass house old Teura stuck out her head and snapped, "I've noticed that Ta'aroa stays with a canoe only as long as its men keep it on course. Turn."

That night it could not be proved that Teura was either right or wrong, for no stars appeared, neither in the darkness of midnight nor in the anxious dawn, and Teroro steered solely by running directly before the wind, with only a small section of sail out, trusting that the storm was steady and not blowing in circles.

On the third starless night, when the canoe could have been in real danger, Teroro reached a major decision. While consulting with Tupuna he said, "We've got to believe that the storm is blowing true."

"Arrival of the albatross is best proof of that," Tupuna pointed out.

"Then I think we'd better take full advantage of it."

"You intend hoisting the sails to the peak?"

"Yes. If it is the gods who are sending us, we ought to go forward as fast as we can."

When they presented their proposal to King Tamatoa, he showed his disturbance over the lack of stars and pointed out that the night crew's estimate of position did not jibe with that of the old woman, but he also appreciated the good sense of his brother's proposal. "I am much impressed by that albatross," Tamatoa reasoned. "Teura confided one fact to me that she didn't tell you. When the bird came back the second time to land on the mast of Ta'aroa, it landed with its left foot extended."

The astronomers whistled, for this was a most propitious omen, since it confirmed the leftness of the bird's intentions and its peculiar inclination toward the mast of Ta'aroa. "I can only conclude," the king reasoned, "that Ta'aroa, for some reason of his own, has sent us this unusual storm. I agree with Teroro. Hoist the sails."

So Teroro sent Mato and Pa up the masts, and in complete darkness, while the canoe was already speeding forward into deep swells, the two young chiefs lashed fast the sturdy matting sails and with shouts of accomplishment slid down and began to play out the sails until they trapped the wind and whipped the canoe forward. Through the rest of the night and into the third disappointing dawn the canoe raced ahead on a course no man knew, for King Tamatoa realized that there came a time on any voyage when a man and his canoe had to trust the gods and to run forward, satisfied that the sails had been well set and the course adhered to whenever possible; but when all precautions failed to disclose known marks, it was obligatory to ride the storm.

At daylight, gnawed by uncertainty, the men went to sleep and old Teura came forth to gather omens. A white-bellied petrel wheeled in the sky but said nothing. Fishermen forward caught bonito, which helped conserve food but told nothing about position, and several fine squalls deposited calabashes full of sweet water trapped by the sails.

At noon when Teura advised the king that things were going well, he shrewdly asked, "Any omens of position?"

"None," she replied.

"How is the ocean running?"

"No signs of land, no islands ahead, the storm will blow for five more days." In such brief report she summed up two thousand years of study by her ancestors, and had she been required to explain why she knew that there was no land ahead, she would have been unable to do so. But there was none, and of this she was absolutely certain.

"Has the albatross returned?" the king asked anxiously.

"No omens," she repeated.

It was now seven days since the storm had risen on the night of Bora Bora's revenge against Havaiki, and three complete days that the canoe had been at sea, but true to Teura's prediction and to the amazement of all, the gale continued, and when the evening watch took over, Teura and the king wondered if the sails should not be lowered, for there were not going to be any stars that night, either. But in the consultation Teroro said, "I am convinced we are going forward," and since there was no one with superior knowledge to contradict him, Tamatoa asked, "You are willing to keep the sails aloft tonight?"

"We must," Teroro said. And through that starless night and into the starless dawn, he ran with the storm, insisting upon this because of his canoe's name. More than a century ago a wise man had named the predecessor of the predecessor of this canoe *Wait-for-the-West-Wind* because he had found that when Bora Borans went forth driven by the western hurricane, they went well. And until the stars had a chance to prove the contrary, Teroro was willing to abide by this ancient wisdom.

He was somewhat shaken however on the fifth night when Tupuna crept up to the prow and whispered, "I have never known a storm from the west to blow so long. We are entering the ninth night. It surely must have veered.''

There was a long pause in the darkness and Teroro looked down at the slim body of his wife, curled against the mast. He wondered what she would say to this problem, but she was not like Marama; she had no ideas. So he wrestled with the alternatives alone and felt irritated when Tupuna pressed him: "Can you recall a constant wind of such duration?"

"No," Teroro snapped, and the two men parted.

But toward dawn of the fifth day, when it seemed probable that no stars would show, Tupuna became frightened: "We must drop the sails. We don't know where we are."

He insisted upon a conference with the king and Teura, which produced three voices against Teroro, for it was obvious that the canoe was lost and that to persevere blindly without some confirmation from the stars would be folly. But Teroro could not accept this reasoning.

"Of course we're lost," he confessed. "But Ta'aroa sent his bird to us in the storm, didn't he?"

"Yes," they had to agree.

"This isn't an ordinary storm," he argued. "This is an unheard-of gale sent to the canoe of Bora Bora. From the oldest days, what has been the name of our canoe?"

"But we are lost!" the king reasoned.

"We were lost from the moment we set forth," Teroro cried.

"No!" Tamatoa cried, refusing to be enticed by his brother's rhetoric. "We were headed for Nuku Hiva. For fresh water and new supplies."

"And to listen once more to the sailing chants," Tupuna added cautiously.

"We must lie to," the king announced firmly. "Then, when we catch a glimpse of Three-in-a-Row, we will know where Nuku Hiva is."

It was under this pressure that Teroro broached his bold plan. He spoke quietly and without gestures, saying, "I am not lost, brother, because I am riding with the desires of Ta'aroa. I am heading with a great storm, and I am content to ride that storm."

"Do you know how to get to Nuku Hiva?"

Teroro looked at each of his companions and replied, "If we are concerned only with Nuku Hiva, I am lost. If we are going to Nuku Hiva only to get additional food and water, I am lost. But in all sense, brother, do we need to go to Nuku Hiva?"

He waited for these strong words to sink into the hearts of his seafaring companions, and he saw that he had used words they understood. Before anyone could speak he added, "What is there for us in Nuku Hiva? To get water we have to fight with those who live there, and some of us will be killed. Do we need water? To get food we must take great risks, and if we are captured, we are cooked alive and eaten. Do we need food? Hasn't Ta'aroa sent us fresh fish in abundance? Have we not disciplined ourselves as men have never done before so that each eats only a shred each day? Brother Tamatoa, if the storm is with us, what extra things do we need?"

Tamatoa resisted his brother's eloquence and asked, "Then you are lost. You can't take us to Nuku Hiva?"

"I cannot take you to Nuku Hiva, but I can take you to the north."

As if in support of his bold plan, a sudden force of wind ripped across the waves and spilled into the sails, whipping the canoe along in a burst of speed. Spray leaped, and dawn, still blotting out the stars and all certain knowledge, came upon the men of Bora Bora.

"We are alone on the sea," Teroro said solemnly. "We are engaged in a special voyage, and if it takes us past Nuku Hiva, then I say good, for we are doubtless being sped by the gods on some great mission. Brother, I beg you, let us keep the sails aloft."

The king would not present this dangerous request to the opinion of the group, for he knew that the old people, Tupuna and Teura, would insist upon caution, and he suspected that perhaps now was a time when caution was not required. Weighing all possibilities, he sided with his brother and said, "We should get some sleep."

So for two more nights, the sixth and seventh of the voyage, the canoe sped on, safe in the mighty arms of Ta'aroa, and in those somber, critical days, all eyes were kept on the left mast, for it was obvious that not the man Teroro but the god Ta'aroa was in command of this canoe. And then, on the late afternoon of the seventh day, red-eyed Teura spotted an omen. On the left side of the canoe came five dolphin, a propitious number in itself, followed by an albatross of some size. The creatures of Ta'aroa had come to celebrate the deliverance of this canoe from the storm, but before Teura could alert her companions to this fine intelligence, an event of transcendent importance occurred. A shark appeared not far from the canoe and followed it lazily for a moment, trying to catch Teura's attention, and when she saw it her heart cried with joy, for this great blue beast of the sea had long been her personal god; and now, while the others were blind with their work, it swam along the left side of the canoe, its blue head above the waves.

"Are you lost, Teura?" it inquired softly.

"Yes, Mano," she replied, "we are lost."

"Are you searching for Nuku Hiva?" the shark asked.

"Yes. I have said that it was . . ."

"You will not see Nuku Hiva," the great blue shark advised. "It is far to the south."

"What shall we do, Mano?"

"Tonight there will be stars, Teura," the shark whispered. "All the stars that you require."

In perfect contentment the old woman closed her tired red eyes. "I have waited for you for many days," she said softly. "But I did not feel completely lost, Mano, for I knew you must be watching us."

"I've been following," the shark said. "Your men were brave, Teura, to keep the sails aloft like that."

Teura opened her eyes and smiled at the shark. "I am ashamed to tell you that I argued against it."

"We all make mistakes," the blue beast said, "but you are on the right course. You'll see when the stars come out." And with this consoling assurance, he turned away from the canoe.

"There's a shark out there!" a sailor cried. "Is that a good omen, Teura?"

"Tamatoa," the old woman said quietly, "tonight there will be stars." And as she spoke two land birds with brown-tipped wings flew purposefully toward the south and Tamatoa saw them and asked, "Does that mean that our land is far to the south?"

"We shall never see it, Tamatoa, for we are safe on a new heading."

"Are you sure?"

"You will see when the stars come out."

* * *

With what excited apprehension Tupuna and Teroro waited for the dusk. They knew that when the Seven Little Eyes peeked above the eastern horizon, the canoe's course would be apparent; and when Three-in-a-Row appeared, they could deduce where Nuku Hiva lay. With what apprehension they waited.

Exactly as Teura had predicted, toward dusk the clouds disappeared and the evening sun came out. As it sank, a tremendous exhilaration filled the canoe, for trailing the sun was the bright star of evening, visible even in twilight and soon accompanied by a second wandering star of great brilliance, and like the two gods on whom the canoe depended, the stars marched grandly toward the rim of the ocean and vanished in their appointed pits of heaven.

On the platform old Tupuna called all passengers to silence as he threw back his white head and intoned a prayer: "Oh, Tane, in our preoccupation with the storm of your brother Ta'aroa we have not thought of you as often as we should. Forgive us, benevolent Tane, for we have been fighting to stay alive. Now that the heavens are restored to remind us of your all-seeing kindness, we implore you to look with favor upon us. Great Tane, light the heavens that we may see. Great Tane, show us the way." And all prayed to Tane and felt his benevolence descend upon them from the nearer heavens.

Then, as darkness deepened over the still heaving ocean, and as the winds died momentarily from the gallant outstretched sails, the stars began to appear; first the mighty golden stars of the south, those warm familiar beacons that showed the way to Tahiti, followed by the cold blue stars of the north, scintillating in their accustomed places and competing with the quarter moon. As each star took its position, its friends in the canoe greeted it with cries of recognition, and an assurance that had been absent for many days returned.

The critical stars had not yet risen, so that in spite of their joy, men could not suppress the questions that often assailed voyagers: "What if we have sailed away from heavens we knew? What if the Little Eyes do not rise here?" Then slowly and uncertainly, for they were not brilliant stars, the sacred group arose, precisely where it should have been, climbing up out of its appropriate pit.

"The Little Eyes are still with us!" Tupuna shouted, and the king raised his head to offer a prayer to the guardians of the world, the core around which the heavens were built.

The astronomers then met to read the signs, and they concluded that the storm had blown fairly steadily from the west, but apparently there had been, as Teura had guessed, a definite drift of the sea northward, for the Little Eyes were going to culminate much higher in the heavens than would be proper were the canoe on course to Nuku Hiva; but to say specifically how serious the drift had been, the navigators would have to wait until Three-in-a-Row appeared, which would not be for another two hours.

So the three plotters waited, and when Three-in-a-Row was well up into the heavens it became self-evident that the canoe was far, far north of the course to Nuku Hiva and was thus committed to an unknown ocean with no opportunity to replenish stores. It was therefore a solemn group that went aft to report to the king: "The storm has carried us even more swiftly than Teroro imagined."

The king's face showed his distress. "Are we lost?"

Uncle Tupuna replied, "We are far from Nuku Hiva and will see no land we know."

"Then we are lost?" the king pressed.

"No, nephew, we are not," Tupuna said carefully. "It is true that we have been carried into far regions, but they are not off our course. We seek lands which lie beneath the Seven Little Eyes, and we are nearer to them tonight than we had a right to expect. If we do not eat too much . . ."

Even though Tamatoa had given permission to keep the sails aloft, and even though he had known that the canoe thus ran the risk of missing Nuku Hiva, he had nevertheless hoped that they would stumble upon that known island, and perhaps find it congenial, and possibly establish homes there. Now he was committed to the greater journey, and he was fearful.

"We could still alter course and find Nuku Hiva," he suggested.

Teroro remained silent and allowed old Tupuna to carry the argument: "No, we are well on our way."

"But to where?"

Tupuna repeated the only chant he had ever memorized for sailing to the north. In effect it said: "Keep the canoe headed with the storm until the winds cease completely. Then turn into the dead sea where bones rot with heat and no wind blows. Paddle to the new star, and when winds strike from the east, ride with them westward until land beneath the Seven Little Eyes is found."

The king, himself an adequate astronomer, pointed due north and asked, "Then the lands we seek are there?"

"Yes," Tupuna agreed.

"But we go this way?" and he pointed eastward, where the winds of the dying storm were driving them.

"Yes."

The course seemed so improbable, to head for a promised land by fleeing it, that the king cried, "Can we be sure that this is the way?"

"No," the old man confessed, "we cannot be sure."

"Then why . . ."

"Because the only knowledge we have says that this is the way to do it."

The king, ever mindful of the fact that fifty-seven people were in his care, grasped Tupuna by the shoulders and asked bluntly, "What do you honestly think about the land that is supposed to be under the Little Eyes?"

The old man replied, "I think that many canoes have left these waters, some blown by storms, others like us in exile, and no man has ever returned. Whether these canoes reached land or not, we do not know. But some man, with a vision of what might be, composed that chant."

"Then we are sailing with a dream for our guide?" Tamatoa asked.

"Yes," the priest answered.

Gloom was not allowed to capture the canoe, for the reappearance of the stars had excited the paddlers and the women, so that even while the astronomers were consulting, shark-faced Pa had handed his paddle to another and had grabbed a length of tapa which he had wrapped around his shoulders, masking his head. Now imitating a very fat man, he pranced up and down the platform, shouting, "Who am I?"

"He's the headless king of Bora Bora!" Mato cried.

"Look at fat Tatai coming to be our king, with his head knocked off!"

In wild burlesque, Pa ridiculed the coronation of the headless would-be king. Paddlers stopped and began to beat rhythms on the canoe, and a woman produced a little drum with a high, almost metallic sound, and the night's revelry was launched.

"What is this new dance?" Tamatoa inquired.

"I've never seen it before," Tupuna replied.

"Do you know what he's doing?" the king asked Teroro.

"Yes," the younger man said hesitantly. "Pa is . . . Well, Tamatoa, some of us heard that fat Tatai was to be king after we left . . . and . . ."

Tamatoa looked at the headless dancer and asked, "So you sneaked over to Havaiki . . . some of you . . ."

"Yes."

"And now Tatai has no head."

"Well . . . yes. You see, we felt . . ."

"You could have ruined the entire voyage, couldn't you?"

"We could have, but we figured that Tatai's village wouldn't come over to Bora Bora very soon . . ."

"Why not?"

"Well, when we left there wasn't any village."

In the light of the quarter moon King Tamatoa looked at his daring young brother, and there was much that he would have said, but the sound of ancient drumming stifled his logical thoughts, and with a stirring leap he whirled forward to where Pa was dancing and entered into the ritual dance of the kings of Bora Bora. Like a boy, he gestured and postured and told forgotten stories, until toward the end he grabbed Pa's tapa and threw it over his head and did the now popular dance of the headless king from Havaiki. When the drums had reached a crescendo he threw off the tapa, stood very straight in the night wind, and exulted: "We did not go like cowards! I, the king, was afraid to strike at those evil worms, those faces of excrement, those vile and awful dead fish of the stinking lagoon. I was afraid to endanger the coming voyage. But Pa here was not afraid. And Mato was not afraid. And my brother . . ." In gratitude Tamatoa looked aft to where Teroro stood in darkness. The king did not finish his sentence. With demonic energy he leaped into a dance of victory, shouting, "I dance in honor of brave men! Let's have the celebration you were denied!" And he ordered extra rations of food to be broken out, and more drums, and all the water anyone wanted.

Like children careless of the dawn, they reveled through the night, got drunk on laughter, and feasted on food that should have been conserved. It was a wild, wonderful night of victory, and each half hour someone shouted, "Pa! Do the dance of the headless king!" Then, one by one, in savage triumph, they rose and screamed classic island insults at the vanquished.

"Havaiki is the strong scent of spoiled meat!"

"The worthless trash of Havaiki take pleasure in their shame."

"Fat Tatai trembles in fear. The hair on his head trembles. He crawls away and hides like a hen in a secret place."

"The warriors of Havaiki are the froth of water, boys playing with mud balls."

Teroro, succumbing to the excitement, shouted, "Fat Tatai is a sneaking little dog, excrement of excrement." But as his voice shrieked in the wind, he happened to look forward to where beautiful Tehani huddled against the masts, weeping as her father was reviled. Then he also saw Mato, from the left hull, touch the girl's shoulder.

Mato said, "This is the way of victory. You must forgive us." From the rear new voices rose with foul invective, and the drums beat on.

In the rainy dawn, of course, King Tamatoa took gloomy stock of what the celebration had cost and for a moment he thought: "We are children. We discover we're lost and half an hour later we eat enough food for a week." Contritely, he issued stringent orders that what had been wasted must be made up by austere rationing. "Even though we have plenty of water," he warned, "each must drink only a cupful a day."

* * *

So, with the remnants of the tempest at their back and with victory in their hearts, the voyagers sailed eastward for the ninth night, and the tenth, and the fifteenth. Their swift canoe, fleetest large craft that ever up to then had plied the oceans of the world, averaged two hundred miles a day, better than eight miles an hour, day after day. They sailed more than halfway to the lands where Aztecs were building mighty temples, and well onto the approaches of the northern land where Cheyennes and Apaches built nothing. In the direction they were then headed they could encounter no land until they struck the continent itself; but before that happened they would have perished of thirst and starvation in the doldrums. Nevertheless, they carried on, according to Teroro's plan. There was fear each dawn when the sun rose; there was momentary joy each night when the stars reappeared to tell their progress; for day was the enemy, crowded with uncertainty and the hourly acknowledgement of their forlorn position; but night was consolation and the spiritual assurance of known stars, and the waxing of the fat moon through its many stages, and the soft cries of birds at dusk. How tremendous an experience this was, at the end of a long day which had provided only the unstable sun, to watch the return of night and to discover, there in the west where the sun went down, the evening star and its wandering companion, and out of the vastness to see the Little Eyes come peeping with their message: "You are coming closer to the land we guard." How marvelous, how marvelous the night!

A S THE CANOE reached eastward and the storm abated, the daily routine became more settled. Each dawn the six slaves stopped bailing and cleaned out the canoe, while farmers moved among the animals and fed them, giving the pigs and dogs fish caught in the early hours, plus some mashed sweet potatoes and fresh water trapped in the sails. The chickens got dried coconut and a fish to pick at, but if they lagged in eating, a slim, dark object darted out from among the freight and grabbed the food away, unseen by the slaves, for as on all such trips, some rats had stowed aboard, and if the voyage turned out badly, they would be the last to die . . . would indeed sustain themselves for many drifting days on those who had already perished.

After the women in the grass hut had wakened, the female slaves would move inside, throw out the slops and do the other necessary chores. Particularly, they kept clean that corner of the hut which had been cut off by lengths of tapa and reserved for those women who were experiencing their monthly sickness, for it was a tabu entailing death for there to be any communication between men and women at such time.

In general, however, the tabus which were rigidly enforced on land had to be suspended aboard a crowded canoe. For example, had any of the rowers while ashore come as near the king as all now were, or had they stepped upon his shadow, or even the shadow of his canoe, they would have been killed instantly, but in the canoe the tabu was suspended, and sometimes when the king moved, men actually touched him. They recoiled as if doomed, but he ignored the insult.

The tabus which centered upon eating were also held in abeyance, for there was no one aboard of sufficient status to prepare the king's food as custom required; nor had the keeper of the king's toilet pot come on the journey, so that a slave, terrified at the task, had to throw into the sea the kingly bowel movements, rather than follow the required custom of burying them secretly in a sacred grove, lest enemies find them and with evil spells conjure the king to death.

Women upon such a trip did not fare well. Obviously, the food had to be reserved for men who did the hard work of paddling. The pigs and dogs also had to be kept alive to stock the new land; which left little for the women. That was why, at every opportunity, they set fishing lines and tended them carefully. The first fish they caught went to the king and Teroro, the next to Tupuna and his old wife, the next four to the paddlers, the seventh and eighth to the pigs, the ninth to the dogs, the tenth to the chickens and the rats. If there were more, the women could eat.

With great niggardliness, the prepared foods were doled out, a piece at a time, but when they were distributed, how good they tasted. A man would get his stick of hard and sour breadfruit, and as he chewed on it he would recall the wasteful feasts he had once held, when abundant breadfruit, fresh and sweet, had been thrown to animals. But the food that gave most pleasure, the master food of the islands, came when the king directed that one of the bamboo lengths of dried poi be opened, and then the rich purplish starch would be handed out, and as it grew sticky in the mouth, men would smile with pleasure.

But soon the poi was finished and the bundles of dried breadfruit diminished. Even the abundant rain ceased and King Tamatoa had to reduce his rations still further, until the crew were getting only two mouthfuls of solid food, two small portions of water. Women and slaves got half as much, so that unless the fishermen could land bonito, or trap water in the sails, all existed at the starvation level.

Early in the dry period the king and Teroro made one discovery, a tormenting and frustrating one made by all similar voyagers: when the tongue was parched and the body scorched with heat, when one's whole being craved only water, an unexpected squall often passed a mile to the left or right, dumping untold quantities of water upon the sea, just out of reach, but it was no use paddling furiously to overtake the squall, for by the time the canoe reached the spot where the rain had been falling, the squall had moved on, leaving all hands hotter and thirstier than before. Not even an expert navigator like Teroro could anticipate the vagaries of a rain squall and intercept it; all one could do was to plod patiently on, his lips burning with desire and his eyes aflame, trying to ignore the cascades of water that were being dumped out of reach; but one could also pray that if one did continue purposefully, in a seamanlike manner, sooner or later some squall would have to strike the canoe.

On a voyage such as this, sexual contact was expressly tabu, but this did not keep the king from gazing often at his stately wife Natabu; and old Tupuna saw to it that Teura got some of his food; and in the heat of day Tehani would dip a length of tapa into the sea, cool it, and press it over her husband's sleeping form. At night, when the stars were known and the course set, the navigator would often sit quietly beside the vivacious girl he had brought with him and talk with her of Havaiki, or of his youth on Bora Bora, and although she rarely had anything sensible to say in reply, the two did grow to respect and treasure each other.

But the most curious thoughts between men and women involved the twelve unassigned women and the thirty-four unattached men. Perhaps the word *unassigned* is not completely accurate to describe the women, because some of them in Bora Bora had been specific wives of individual men, but on such an expedition it was understood that upon landing, any such woman would accept as her additional husbands two or three of the men who had no wives, and no one considered this strange. So on the long voyage men with no women began cautiously to do two things: to form close friendships with men who had women, establishing a congenial group of three or four who would later share one woman as their common wife; or to study the unmarried women in an effort to decide which one could most satisfactorily be shared with one's group; so that before the voyage had consumed even fifteen days, groups had begun to crystallize, and without anything definite having been said, it was remarkably well understood that this woman and these three men would build a house for themselves and raise common children, or that that husband and wife would accept those two friends of the man into complete and intimate harmony, thus populating the new land. It was further understood that each woman, until she reached the age when children no longer came, would be kept continuously pregnant. The same, of course, was true of the sows and the bitches, for the major task of all was to populate an empty, new land.

On the eleventh night occurred an event which, in its emotional impact upon a people who lived by the stars, had no equal on this voyage. Even the abandonment of Oro had failed to generate the excitement caused by this phenomenon.

As the *West Wind* crept constantly northward it became obvious to the astronomers on board that they must lose, and forever, many old familiar stars which lay below what astronomers would later call the Southern Cross. It was with sorrow, and even occasionally with tears, that Tupuna would follow some particular star which as a boy he had loved, and watch it vanish into the perpetual pit of the sky from which stars no more rise. Whole constellations were washed into the sea, never to be seen again.

Although this was cause for regret, it did not occasion alarm, for the men of Bora Bora were exceptional astronomers. They had developed, from careful observation, a year of 365 days, and they had found that from time to time an extra day was required to keep the seasons aligned. Their ritual life was organized around a moon-month of twenty-nine and a half days, which is the easy way to build a calendar; but their year of twelve months was founded on the sun, which is the right way. They could predict with accuracy the new appearance and subsequent motion of the wandering stars, while the merest glimpse of the moon told them in what phase it stood, for each night of the moon-month bore its own special name, derived from the progress of the moon through its cycle. Men like Tupuna and Teroro even knew, by counting ahead six months, in what constellation the sun stood; so they were prepared, as they sailed north, to lose some of their familiar stars; conversely, they knew that they would come upon new stars, and it was with the joy of discovery that they identified the hitherto unseen stars of the north. But in all their wisdom, they were not prepared for what they discovered on the eleventh night.

Having set their course, they were surveying the northern heavens when the old man saw, bobbing above the waves, a new star, not of maximum brightness like the vast beacons of the south—for the voyagers found the northern stars rather disappointing in brilliance in comparison with theirs—but nevertheless an interesting newcomer.

"See how it lies in a direct line from the two stars in Bird-with-a-Long-Neck," Tupuna pointed out, referring to stars which others called the Big Dipper.

At first Teroro could not catch the bright star, for it danced up and down on the horizon, now visible above the waves, now lost. Then he saw it, a bright, clean, cold star, well marked in an empty space of the sky. Speaking as a navigator he said, "That would be a strong star to steer by . . . when it rises a little higher."

Tupuna observed, "We must watch carefully, the next few nights, to see which pit of heaven it goes into."

So on the twelfth night the two men studied the new guidepost, but as dawn appeared each was afraid to tell the other what he had seen, for each realized that he had stumbled upon an omen of such magnitude that it did not bear speaking of. Each keeping his own counsel, the two astronomers spent the last minutes of darkness watching the new star with an apprehension that bordered upon panic, and when daylight ended their vigil, they licked their dry lips and went to their beds knowing they would not sleep.

It was no more than midafternoon on the following day when the two men took their positions to study the heavens. "Stars won't be out for many hours," Tupuna said warily.

"I'm watching the sun," Teroro lied, and when Tehani brought him his water and stood smiling by the mast of Tane, her preoccupied husband did not bother to smile back, so she went aft with the women.

Swiftly, at six in the evening, and not lingeringly as at Bora Bora, the sun left the sky and the stars began to appear. There were the Seven Little Eyes, blessing the canoe, and later Three-in-a-Row, now well to the south, and the very bright stars of Tahiti; but what the men watched was only the strange new star. There it was, and for nine hours the two astronomers studied it, unwilling to come to the conclusion that was inescapable. But when they had triangulated the sky in every known way, when they had proved their frightening thesis beyond doubt, they were forced, each working by himself, to the terrifying conclusion.

It was Tupuna who put it into words: "The new star does not move."

"It is fixed," Teroro agreed.

The two men used these words in a new meaning; they had always spoken of the bright wandering stars that moved in and out of the constellations like beautiful girls at a dance; and they had contrasted these with the stars of fixed position; but they realized that in a grand sense the latter also moved, rising out of pits in the east and falling into the pits of the west. Some, who hurried around the Southern Cross, rose from one pit and quickly dropped into another, and there were even a few that never disappeared below the waves; but all moved through the heavens. The new star did not.

"We had better consult with the king," Tupuna advised, but when they went aft they found Tamatoa sleeping, and no man would dare waken another suddenly, lest the sleeper's spirit be out wandering and have no time to slip back in through the corner of the eye. A man without a spirit would go mad, but Tamatoa slept soundly and his uncle grew nervous, holding as he did the news of the ominous fixed star.

"Could you cough?" he asked Teroro. The navigator did, but with no results.

"What would let him know we are waiting?" Tupuna asked petulantly. He went outside the grass house, took a paddle and tapped the side of the canoe, whereupon the king, like any captain who hears a strange noise aboard his ship, rolled uneasily, cleared his throat and gave his wandering spirit ample time to climb back into his eye.

"What's happening?"

"An omen of terrible significance," Tupuna whispered. They showed Tamatoa the new star and said, "It does not move."

Anxiously, the three watched for an hour and then summoned old Teura, advising her: "Tane has set a star in the heavens which does not move. What can it signify?"

The old woman insisted upon an hour in which to study the phenomenon for herself, at the end of which she decided that the men were correct. The star did not move, but how should such an omen be read? She said, haltingly, "Tane is the keeper of the stars. If he has placed this miracle before us, it is because he wishes to speak to us."

"What is his message?" the king asked apprehensively.

"I have never seen such an omen," Teura parried.

"Could it mean that Tane has put a barrier, fixed and immovable, before us?" Tamatoa asked, for it was his responsibility to keep the voyage harmonious with the will of the gods. Others could afford to misinterpret omens, but not he.

"It would seem so," Teura said. "Else why would the star be set there, like a rock?"

Apprehension gripped them, for if Tane was against this voyage, all must perish. They could not go back now. "And yet," Tupuna recalled, "the chant says that when the west wind dies, we are to paddle across the sea of no wind toward the new star. Is this not the new star, fixed there for us to use?"

For many minutes the group discussed this hopeful concept and concluded that it might have merit. They decided, therefore, that this should be done: continue for the coming day along the course set by the westerly wind and consult again at dusk, weighing all omens. The four went to their appointed places and discharged their various tasks, but in the remaining moments of the night Teroro stood alone in the prow studying the new star, and gradually a new idea germinated in his brain, tentatively at first, like a drum beating in the far distance, and then with compelling intensity.

He began softly: "If this new star is fixed . . . Suppose it actually does hang there night after night and at all hours . . . Let's say that every star in the new heavens can be associated with it in known patterns . . ." He lost the thread of some compelling thought and started over again.

"If this star is immovable, it must hang at a known distance above the horizon . . . No, that's not right. What I mean is, for every island, this fixed star must hang at a known distance . . . Start with Tahiti. We know exactly what stars hang directly over Tahiti at each hour of the night for each night of the year. Now if this fixed star . . ."

Again he was unable to draw together the threads of his thought, but he sensed that some grand design of the gods was making itself manifest, so he wrapped one arm around the mast of Tane and concentrated his entire being upon the new star. "If it hangs there forever, then every island must stand in some relationship to it. Therefore, once you see how high that star is, you know exactly how far north or south you must sail in order to find your island. If you can see the star, you will know! You will know!"

Suddenly, and with dazzling clarity, Teroro saw an entirely new system of navigation based on Tane's gift, the fixed star, and he thought: "Life must be sweet indeed for sailors in these waters!" For he knew that northern sailors had what southerners did not: a star which could tell them, at a single glance, their latitude. "The heavens are fixed!" he cried to himself. "And I shall be free to move beneath them." He looked happily to the west where the Little Eyes blinked at him prior to dawn, and he whispered to them, "The new land you lead us to must be sweet indeed if it exists in such an ordered ocean beneath such an ordered sky."

And for the rest of the voyage, through the terrible days that lay ahead, Teroro alone, of all the canoe, knew no fear. He was sure. He was secure in his conviction that Tane would not have hung that fixed star where it was except for some high purpose, and he, Teroro, had divined that purpose. Up to now he had given no one cause to think that he merited his name, the Brain; certainly he could never be a knowledgeable priest like his uncle Tupuna, and that was a pity, for priests were needed. Nor had he wisdom in political counsels like his brother; but on this night he proved that he could do something that none of his companions could: he could look at the evidence planted in the universe and from it derive a new concept, and a greater thing than this no mind can accomplish. On what Teroro foresaw that night the navigation of the islands ahead would be built and their location in the ocean determined. In his joy of discovery Teroro wanted to sing, but he was not a poet.

Yet in his very moment of triumph, he experienced an emptiness that had been with him for many days and which apparently was not going to dissipate. When he finally grasped the significance of the fixed star, he wanted to discuss his concept with Marama, but she was absent and there was not much use talking about a thing like this with Tehani, for whereas Marama would have grasped the idea at once, beautiful little Tehani would have looked at the heavens and asked, "What star?" It was curious the way in which Marama's last cry persisted in Teroro's ears: "I am the canoe!" In a most strange way, she was, for she was the on-going spirit of the canoe; it was her grave face that Teroro often saw ahead of him on the waves, and when *Wait-for-the-West-Wind* in its swift flight overtook the vision in the waters, Marama smiled as the canoe swept past, and Teroro felt that all was well.

Into the arid heat of the doldrums they plunged. The sun beat upon them by day and the rainless stars mocked them at night. Now not even distant squalls passed with the tantalizing hope that rain might come. They knew it would not.

Teroro planned so that Mato and Pa, the two sturdiest paddlers, would not work at the same time; also, after an hour's stint in the right hull, which tore the muscles of the left shoulder, the paddlers would shift sides and wear out their right shoulders. At each shift six men would drop out and rest. But onward the canoe went, constantly.

From time to time the stronger women would take paddles, whereupon the shift was shortened to half an hour; while in the bottom of each hull the artisans and the slaves worked constantly baling the water that seeped in through the calked cracks where the pieces of log which formed the hull had been tied together.

It was ironic, and a fact remarked by all, that in the storm when fresh water was plentiful, the sails did most of the work, whereas now, when men sweated and strained endlessly with the paddles, there was no water. The king ordered it to be doled out in ever-decreasing portions, so that the harder the men worked, the less they had to drink.

The women, with scarcely any water, suffered miserably, while the slaves were near death. The farmers had an especially cruel task. Tenderly they would hold open the mouth of a pig and drop water inside to keep the animal alive, whereas they needed the fluid more than the animal; but the death of a farmer could be tolerated; the death of a pig would have been catastrophe.

Still the canoe bore on. At night Teroro, with his lips burning, would place on the platform near the prow a half coconut, filled with placid sea water, and in it he would catch the reflection of the fixed star, and by keeping this reflection constant in the cup, he maintained his course.

At daybreak, red-eyed Teura would sit in the blazing heat, her old body almost desiccated by the sun, and speculate upon the omens. Hour after hour she muttered, "What will bring rain?" The flight of birds might indicate where islands were, and water, but no birds flew. "Red clouds in patches in the eastern sky bring rain, for certain," she recalled, but there were no clouds. At night the moon was full, brilliant as a disk of polished Tridacna, but when she studied the moon she found no ring around it, no omen of a storm. "If there were a wind," she muttered, "it might bring us to a storm," but there was no wind. Repeatedly she chanted: "Stand up, stand up, the big wave from Tahiti. Blow down, blow down, the great wind from Moorea." But in these new seas her invocations were powerless.

Day followed day of remorseless heat, worse than anyone in the canoe had ever previously experienced. On the seventeenth day one of the women died, and, as her body was plunged into the perpetual care of Ta'aroa, god of the mysterious deep, the men who were to have been her husband wept, and through the entire canoe there was a longing for rain and the cool valleys of Bora Bora, and it was not surprising that many began to deplore having come upon this voyage.

Hot nights were followed by blazing days, and the only thing that seemed to live in the canoe was the dancing new star as it leaped about in the coconut cup which Teroro studied; and then late one night as the navigator watched his star, he saw on the horizon, lighted by the moon, a breath of storm. It was small at first, and wavering, and Mato whispered, "Is that rain?"

At first Teroro would not reply, and then, with a mighty shout, he roared into the night, "Rain!"

The grass house emptied. The sleeping paddlers wakened and watched as a cloud obscured the moon. A wind rose, and a light capping of the sea could be seen in starlight. It must be a substantial storm, and not a passing squall. It was worth pursuing, and everyone began to paddle furiously. Those with no paddles used their hands, and even the king, distraught with hope, grabbed a bailing bucket from a slave and paddled with it.

How desperately they worked, and how tantalizingly the storm eluded them. Through the remaining portion of the night, the canoe sped on, its men collapsing with thirst and exhaustion, in pursuit of the storm. They did not catch it, and as the blazing day came upon them, driving the clouds back to the horizon, and then beyond, an awful misery settled upon the canoe. The paddlers, their strength exhausted in the fruitless quest, lay listless and allowed the sun to beat upon them. Teroro was of no use. Old Tupuna was near death, and the pigs wept protestingly in the waterless heat.

Only the king was active. Sitting cross-legged on his mat he prayed ceaselessly. "Great Tane, you have always been generous to us in the past," he cajoled. "You have given us taro and breadfruit in abundance. You brought our pigs to fatness and birds to our traps. I am grateful to you, Tane. I am loyal to you. I prefer you above all other gods." He continued in this way for many minutes, hot sweat upon his face, reminding the deity of their close and profitable relationships in the past. Then, from the depth of his despair, he pleaded: "Tane, bring us rain."

From a short distance forward, red-eyed Teura heard the king praying and crept back to him, but she brought him terror, not assurance, for she whispered, "The fault is mine, nephew."

"What have you done?" the king asked in spittle-dry tones.

"Two nights before we left Bora Bora I had a dream and I ignored it. A voice came to me crying, 'Teura, you have forgotten me.'"

"What?" the king rasped, catching his aunt's withered arm. "That was my dream."

"A voice crying, 'You have forgotten me!' Was that your dream, too?"

"No," the king replied in ashen tones. "Two stars, combing the heavens, looking for something I had forgotten to put into the canoe."

"Was that why you unpacked everything at the last?" Teura asked.

"Yes."

"And you discovered no lack?"

"Nothing." The two wise people, on whom the success of this voyage now depended, sat despondent. "What have we forgotten?" They could find no answer, but they knew, each now fortified with substantiation from the other, that this voyage was conducted under an evil omen. "What have we forgotten?" they pleaded.

In bleak despair they stared at each other and found no answer, so Teura, her eyes already inflamed from watching the merciless sun, went out to the lifeless platform and prayed for omens, and as she gave her whole being to this duty, the great blue shark came beside the canoe and whispered, "Are you afraid that you will die, Teura?"

"Not for myself," she replied calmly. "I'm an old woman. But my two nephews . . . Isn't there anything you can do for them, Mano?"

"You haven't been watching the horizon," the shark admonished.

"Where?"

"To the left."

And as she looked, she saw a cloud, and then a disturbance ruffling the ashen sea, and then the movement of a storm, and rain. "Oh, Mano," she whispered, afraid to believe. "Is the rain coming toward us?"

"Look, Teura," the great blue shark laughed.

"Once before it looked the same," she whispered.

"This time follow me," the blue beast cried, and with a shimmering leap he splashed into the sea, her personal god, her salvation.

With a wild scream she cried, "Rain! Rain!" And all rushed out from the house, and dead sleepers wakened to find a storm bearing down upon them.

"Rain!" they mumbled as it marched across the ocean nearer and nearer.

"It's coming!" Tamatoa shouted. "Our prayers are answered." But old Teura, laughing madly as the benign water struck her face, saw in the heart of the storm her own god, Mano, his blue fin cutting the waves.

Almost as if by command, the near-dying voyagers began to throw off their clothes, their tapa and their shells, until each stood naked in the divine storm, drinking it into their eyes and their blistering armpits and their parched mouths. The winds rose, and the rains increased, but the naked men and women of Bora Bora continued their revel in the slashing waves. The sails came down and the mast of Ta'aroa was almost carried away, and the dogs whined, but the men in the canoe swept the water into their mouths and embraced each other. Into the night the storm continued, and it seemed as if the sections of the canoe must break apart, but no one called for the storm to abate. They fought it and drank it and washed their aching bodies with it, and sailed into the heart of it, and toward morning, exhausted in sheer joy, they watched as the clouds parted and they saw that they were almost under the path of the Seven Little Eyes, and they knew that they must ride with the easterly wind that had brought the storm. Their destination lay somewhere to the west.

I T WAS A long leg to windward they took. For nearly two thousand miles they ran before the easterlies, covering most days more than a hundred and fifty miles. Now the fixed star remained at about the same height above the horizon, on their right, and they followed close to the path of Little Eyes. At sunset Teroro would tilt his coconut cup backward to catch the bright star that stood near Little Eyes as they rose in the east. Later, as the constellation which men in the deserts had named the Eagle sank into the west, he would steer by its bright star, shifting back and forth between it ahead and Little Eyes to the rear, thus keeping always on course.

It was on this long westward leg that King Tamatoa's earlier insistence on discipline preserved the voyage, for now food had run perilously low and for some perverse reason the numerous fish in these strange waters would not bite; Tupuna explained that it was because they lived under the influence of the fixed star and that the Bora Bora fishhooks had not been adjusted to this new consideration. Every woman and all men who were not paddling kept lines, long and short, in the sea, but to no avail.

There was a little coconut left and a small amount of breadfruit, but no taro. Even the pigs, absolutely essential to the success of the journey, were famishing. But in this extremity the thirty paddlers, who worked constantly, survived amazingly. Their stomachs had long since contracted into hard little fists, shrunk to nothing under tight belly muscles. Their strong shoulders, devoid of even a trace of fat after nearly a month's steady work, seemed able to generate energy from nothing. With neither food nor adequate water, the men sweated little; through sun-reddened eyes they constantly scanned the horizon for omens.

It was old Teura, however, who saw the first substantial sign; on the twenty-seventh morning she saw a small piece of driftwood, torn away from some distant tree, and Teroro avidly directed the canoe toward it. When it was pulled aboard it was found to contain four land worms, which were fed to the astonished chickens.

"It has been in the ocean less than ten days," Teura announced. Since the canoe could travel five or six times faster than a drifting branch, it seemed likely that land lay somewhere near; and old Teura entered into a period of intense concentration, clutching at omens and interpreting them hopefully by means of old prayers.

But *West Wind* was not to be saved by incantations. It was Mato, a trained sailor, who late one afternoon saw in the distance a flock of birds flying with determination on a set course westward. "There's land ahead. They're heading for it," he cried. Tupuna and Teroro agreed, and when, a few hours later, the stars rose, it was reassuring to see that the Seven Little Eyes confirmed that they were near the end of their journey.

"A few more days," Teroro announced hopefully.

And two days later, aching with hunger, Mato again spotted a bird, and this one was of special significance, for it was a gannet, poised seventy feet in the air; suddenly it raised its wings, dropped its head toward the waves, and plunged like a thrown rock deep into the ocean. It looked as if it must have split its skull on impact, but by some mysterious trick, it had not, and in a moment it flew aloft with a fish in its beak. Deftly it flipped the food into its gullet, then plunged again with head-splitting force.

"We are surely approaching land!" Mato cried. But many on the platform thought of the gannet not as a harbinger of land, but rather as a lucky bird that knew how to fish.

In the early morning of the twenty-ninth day a group of eleven long black birds with handsome cleft tails flew by on a foraging trip from their home island, which lay somewhere beyond the horizon, and Teroro noted with keen pleasure that their heading, reversed, was his, and while he watched he saw these intent birds come upon a group of diving gannets, and when those skilled fishers rose into the air with their catch, the forktailed birds swept down upon them, attacked them, and forced them to drop the fish, whereupon the foragers caught the morsels in mid-air and flew away. From their presence it could be deduced that land was not more than sixty miles distant, a fact which was confirmed when Teura and Tupuna, working together, detected in the waves of the sea a peculiar pattern which indicated that in the near distance the profound westerly set of the ocean was impounding upon a reef, which shot back echo waves that cut across the normal motion of the sea; but unfortunately a heavy bank of cloud obscured the western horizon, reaching even to the sea, and none could detect exactly where the island lay.

"Don't worry!" Teura reassured everyone. "When the clouds do lift, watch their undersides carefully. At sunset you'll see them turn green over the island. Reflections from the lagoon." And so convinced was Teura that they were approaching some small island like Bora Bora with a lagoon, that she chose the spot from which the wave echoes seemed to be generating and stared fixedly at it.

As she had hoped, toward dusk the clouds began to dissipate, and it was Teura who first saw the new island looming ahead. Gasping, she cried, "Oh, great Tane! What is it?"

"Look! Look!" shouted Teroro.

And there before them, rearing from the sea like an undreamed-of monster, rose a tremendous mountain more massive than they had ever imagined, crowned in strange white and soaring majestically into the evening sunset.

"What a land we have found!" Teroro whispered.

"It is the land of Tane!" King Tamatoa announced in a hushed whisper. "It reaches to heaven itself."

And all in the canoe, seeing this clean and wonderful mountain, fell silent and did it reverence, until Pa cried, "Look! It is smoking!" And as night fell, the last sight the men of Bora Bora had was of a gigantic mountain, hung in the heavens, sending fumes from its peak.

The vision haunted the voyagers, for they knew it must be an omen of some proportions, and in the quiet hours of the night old Teura dreamed and woke screaming. The king hurried to her side, and she whispered, "I know what it was we forgot."

She went aft with her nephew, to where no one could hear, and she confided: "The same dream returned. I heard this voice crying, 'You have forgotten me.' But this time I recognized the voice. We have left behind a goddess whom we should have brought."

King Tamatoa felt a sick quaking near his heart and asked, "What goddess?" for he knew that if a goddess felt insulted, there was no restriction on the steps she might take in exacting revenge; her capacity was limitless.

"It is the voice of Pere, the ancient goddess of Bora Bora," the old woman replied. "Tell me, nephew, when your wandering stars were searching the heavens, were they not attended by specks of fire?"

The king tried to recall his haunting premonitory dream and was able, with extraordinary clarity, to conjure it, and he agreed: "There were specks of fire. Among the northern stars."

They summoned Tupuna and told him the burden of his wife's dream, and he acknowledged that it must have been the goddess Pere who had wanted to come on the voyage, whereupon his nephew asked, "But who is Pere?"

"In ancient days on Bora Bora," the old man explained as the thin-horned curve of the dying moon rose in the east, "our island had mountains that smoked, and Pere was the goddess of flame who directed our lives. But the flame died away and we supposed that Pere had left us, and we no longer worshipped the red-colored rock that stood in the temple."

"I had forgotten Pere," Teura confessed. "Otherwise I would have recognized her voice. But tonight, seeing the smoking mountain, I remembered."

"And she is angry with us?" the king asked.

"Yes," Teura replied. "But Tane and Ta'aroa are with us, and they will protect us."

The old seers went back to their places, and the king was left alone, in the shadow of his new land now barely visible in the misty moonlight. He was disturbed that a man could take so much care to satisfy the gods, and that he could nevertheless fail. He could study the omens, bend his will to them, and live only at the gods' commands; but always some small thing intruded; an old woman fails to recognize the voice of a goddess and disaster impinges upon an entire venture. He knew the rock of Pere; it had been retained in the temple for no known reason, both its name and its properties forgotten; it was no longer even dressed in feathers. It would have been so simple to have brought that rock, but the facts had eluded him and now he felt at the mercy of a revengeful goddess who had been deeply insulted, the more so because she had taken the trouble to warn him. He beat his hands against the poles of the grass hut and cried, "Why can we never do anything right?"

If the king was perplexed by his arrival at the new land, there were other passengers who were terrified. In the rear of the left hull, the slaves huddled in darkness, whispering. The four men were telling the two women that they had loved them and that they hoped the women were pregnant and that they would bear children, even though those children would be slaves. They recalled the few good days they had known on Bora Bora, the memorable days when they had chanced upon one of the king's stray pigs and had eaten it surreptitiously, for to have done so openly would have meant immediate death, or the days when the high nobles were absent from the island and they had been free to breathe. In the fading darkness of the night, for a day of great terror was about to dawn, they whispered of love, of human affection and of lost hopes; for the four men knew that when the canoe landed, a temple would be built, and when the four corner post holes had been dug, deep and sound, one of them would be buried alive in each, so that his spirit would forever hold the temple securely aloft, and the doomed men could already feel the taste of the earth in their nostrils; they could feel the pressure of the sacred post upon their vitals; and they knew death.

Their two women, soon to be abandoned, could taste worse punishment, for they had come to love these four men; they knew how gentle they were, how kind to children and how alert to the world's beauty. Soon, for no ascertainable reason, the men would be sacrificed, and then the women would live on the edge of their community, and if they were already pregnant, and if their children were sons, they would be thrown under the prows of canoes to bless the wood and to be torn in shreds by it. Then when they were not pregnant, on strange nights men of the crew, their faces masked, would rudely force their way into the slave compartments, lie with the women, and go away, for if it were known that a chief had had contact with a slave woman, he would be punished; but all had such contact. And when the children of these unions were born, they would be slaves; and if they grew to manhood, they would be ripped to pieces under canoes or hung about the altars of gods; and if they grew to comely womanhood, they would be ravished at night by men they never knew. And the cycle would go on through all eternity, for they were slaves.

In the early light of morning it became apparent that the smoking mountain and its supporting island lay much farther away than had at first been supposed, and a final day of hunger and work faced the paddlers; but the visible presence of their goal spurred the famished men so that by nightfall it was certain that next morning the long voyage would end. Through the last soft tropical night, with the luminous mountain ahead, the crew of the *West Wind* followed their rhythmic, steady beat.

As they approached the end of a trek nearly five thousand miles long, it is appropriate to compare what they had accomplished with what voyagers in other parts of the world were doing. In the Mediterranean, descendants of once-proud Phoenicians, who even in their moments of glory had rarely ventured out of sight of land, now coasted along established shores and occasionally, with what was counted bravery, actually cut across the trivial sea in voyages covering perhaps two hundred miles. In Portugal men were beginning to accumulate substantial bodies of information about the ocean, but to probe it they were not yet ready, and it would be six hundred more years before even near-at-hand islands like Madeira and the Azores would be found. Ships had coasted the shores of Africa, but it was known that crossing the equator and thus losing sight of the North Star meant boiling death, or falling off the edge of the world, or both.

On the other side of the earth, Chinese junks had coasted Asia and in the southern oceans had moved from one visible island to the next, terming the act heroism. From Arabia and India, merchants had undertaken considerable voyages, but never very far from established coasts, while in the undiscovered continents to the west of Europe, no men left the land.

Only in the north of Europe did the Vikings display enterprise even remotely comparable to that of the men of Bora Bora; but even they had not yet begun their long voyages, though they had at their disposal metals, large ships, woven sails, books and maps.

It was left to the men of the Pacific, men like cautious Tamatoa and energetic Teroro, to meet an ocean on its own terms and to conquer it. Lacking both metals and maps, sailing with only the stars and a few lengths of sennit, some dried taro and positive faith in their gods, these men accomplished miracles. It would be another seven centuries before an Italian navigator, sailing under the flag of Spain and fortified by all the appurtenances of an advanced community, would dare, in three large and commodious ships well nailed together, to set forth upon a voyage not quite so far and only half as dangerous.

* * *

At dawn Teroro brought his canoe close to land at the southeastern shore of the vast volcanic island that rose from the southeast end of the rupture in the ocean floor. When the shoreline became visible, the voyagers had many thoughts. Teroro reflected in some disappointment: "It's all rocks. Where are the coconuts? Where's the water?" Mato, who paddled in the hull nearest the land, thought: "No breadfruit." But King Tamatoa mused: "It is the land Tane brought us to. It must be good."

Only Tupuna appreciated the profound problems which the next few hours would bring. In trembling apprehension he thought: "The children of my brothers are about to step upon new land. Everything depends on the next minutes, for this island is obviously filled with strange gods, and we must do nothing to offend them. But will I be able to placate them all?"

So he moved with agitation about the canoe, endeavoring to arrange things so that the unknown gods would be offended as little as possible. "Don't pick up a single stone," he warned. "Don't break a branch or eat a shellfish." Then he went to the gods' house and called Pa to his side, handing him a square of flat stone. "You will follow me," he said, "because you are extremely brave." He adjusted the king's feather cape, handed Teroro a spear, and lifted into his own shaking hands the two gods, Tane and Ta'aroa.

"Now!" he cried, and the canoe touched land.

First to disembark was Tamatoa, and as soon as he had made one footprint in the sand, he stopped, kneeled down, and took that earth into his hands, bringing it to his lips, where he kissed it many times. "This is the land," he chanted gravely. "This is a man's home. This is good land to settle upon, a good land on which to have children. Here we shall bring our ancestors. Here we bring our gods."

Behind him, in the prow of the canoe, stood Tupuna, his face upraised. "Tane, we thank you for the safe voyage," he whispered. Then, in penetrating voice, he called, "You unknown gods! You brave and gentle gods who hold this island! You fine and generous gods of the smoking mountain! You forty gods, you forty thousand gods, you forty million gods! Allow us to land. Allow us to share your treasures, and we will honor you." He was about to step ashore with his own gods, but the idea of invading a new land was too overpowering, so he shouted once more, "Terrible, all-seeing gods, may I please land?"

He stepped upon the land, expecting some awful omen, but none came and he told Pa, "You may bring the rock of Bora Bora onto its new home," and the shark-faced warrior leaped ashore with the only lasting memorial of home: a square of rock. When he stood beside the king, Tupuna cried, "Now you, Teroro, with your spear."

But when it came time for Teroro to leave the canoe, he did not worry about the new gods. He placed his two hands on the prow of *Wait-for-the-West-Wind* and whispered, as gently as if he were speaking to Marama, "Beautiful, lovely ship. Forgive me for cutting away your glory. You are the queen of the ocean." And he leaped ashore to guard his brother in the next fateful moments.

Tupuna left three warriors at the canoe to guard it, while the others strung out in line and formed the solemn procession that would invade the island. At the head of his nervous column marched Tupuna, and whenever he came to a large rock, he begged the god of that rock to let him pass. When he came to a grove of trees he cried, "God of these trees, we come in friendship."

They had gone only a short distance inland when a passing cloud dropped misty rain upon them, and Tupuna shouted, "We are received! The gods bless us. Quick! See where the rainbow ends!"

It was Pa, holding the stone of Bora Bora, who saw the arc come to earth, and Tupuna cried, "There will be our temple!" And he hurried to the spot, crying, "Any evil that is here, Tane, push it aside, for this is to be your temple!"

The foot of the rainbow had fallen on an inviting plateau over-looking the ocean, and Tamatoa said, "This is a good omen indeed." Then he and his white-bearded uncle began their search for a high male rock, for both knew that the earth itself was female, and therefore polluted, but that solid rocks of impermeable stone were male, and therefore uncontaminated, and after a long search he found a large protrusion of male rock coming erect out of fine reddish soil, and when Tupuna saw it he said, "A perfect site for an altar."

So Pa placed upon this male rock his slab of Bora Bora stone, and with this symbolic action the new island was occupied, for upon the flat stone Tupuna reverently placed the fine old gods Tane and Ta'aroa. Then he climbed back to the sea with a coconut cup which he filled with water, and this he sprinkled over the temple area, over the gods, and over every human being who had come in the canoe, flicking it into their faces with the long finger of his right hand. "Now let us purify ourselves," he said, leading every living thing into the ocean: king, warrior, pig, chicken and breadfruit bundle. In the cool sea the voyagers replenished themselves and a canny woman cried, as soon as the job was done, "Do you know what I stood on? Hundreds of shellfish!" And all who were purified fell back into waves and began routing out succulent shellfish. Prying the sweet snails loose, they popped them into their mouths and grinned.

When they were satiated, Tupuna announced, "Now we must design the temple," and the slaves began to tremble. The old man led everyone back to the plateau, and while they watched, he and Tamatoa laid out the four sacred corners of the temple, and large piles of rock were collected about deep holes which the farmers dug.

The king signaled his warriors to bury the four quaking slaves, but Teroro prevented the sacrifice. Placing himself before the slaves, he pleaded: "Brother, let us not launch our new island by more killing."

Tamatoa, astonished, explained: "But the temple must be upheld!"

"Tane doesn't require that!" Teroro argued.

"But we have always done so."

"Isn't that why we left Havaiki and red Oro?"

"But that was Oro," the king rationalized. "This is Tane."

"Brother! I beg you! Don't start this killing!" Then, remembering how his best men had been sacrificed, he pleaded: "Ask the men!"

But this was not a question on which Tamatoa could take a vote. It concerned his relationship to the gods; perhaps the entire fortune of the voyage depended on these next few minutes. "Your words are ill timed," he said stubbornly.

Tupuna supported him, grumbling petulantly, "From the beginning of time, temples have been held up by men."

"Bury the slaves!" Tamatoa ordered.

But again Teroro spread his arms before them and cried, "Brother, don't do this thing!" Then an idea came to him and he pleaded, "If we must sacrifice to Tane, let us sacrifice the male pig."

For a moment the idea was appealing; all knew that Tane loved pig sacrifices more than any other. But Tupuna killed the suggestion. "We must keep the boar to breed more pigs," he said flatly, and all agreed.

But Teroro, impassioned by his desire to start the colony correctly, cried, "Wait! Long ago when we had no pigs, we gave Tane ulua, the man-of-the-sea!"

When Tamatoa looked at his uncle for confirmation, the old man nodded. "The gods are pleased with man-of-the-sea," he admitted.

"Give me half an hour," Teroro pleaded, and he took six of his best fishermen, and they waded onto the reef and cast their lines and Teroro prayed, "Ta'aroa, god of the sea and of the fish that live therein, send us ulua to save men's lives." And when they had caught eight, two for each corner, they returned to the plateau, and Tamatoa looked at the big handsome fish and said, "For three of the corners we will use the man-of-the-sea. But for the essential corner we will use a man."

"Please . . ." Teroro began, but the king roared in anger, "Silence! You are in command of the canoe, but I am in command of the temple. What would Tane say if we begrudged him his due?" So, in anxiety of spirit, Teroro left the scene, for he would not be partner to what was about to occur, and if the priest and the king conspired to kill him for his offense, he did not care. He sat on a distant rock and thought: "We flee an evil, but we bring it with us," and he knew bitterness.

When he was gone the king said to Mato, "Bury the fish," and they were placed in three of the holes. Then he directed: "Mato, bring us one of the slaves." And the warrior went to the six who huddled apart and said bluntly: "I am sent by the king to select one of you to be the spirit for the temple."

Although the slaves were gratified that only one had to die, they were anguished that the choice of that one was forced on them. Looking at one another, they asked, "Which of us shall go to die for our masters?" The six wept, and one who had a position of leadership finally pointed and said, "You, perhaps."

The man identified gasped and steeled himself for his ordeal. First he moved to the leader who had named him and rubbed noses with him, signifying that he went to his death with no hatred. Then he rubbed noses with the other two men, saying to each, "It is better that of the two of us I should die. Between you and me, good friend, it shall be I." But when he came to the second woman, whom he loved, and when he rubbed noses with her for the last mournful time, he could not speak, and he marched from her to the pit, where he was thrown in, with the stones crushed down upon him, and where earth was pounded about him and over him, and where in silence he met dark death.

When the consecration of the temple was completed, and when mana had again begun to flow from the gods into King Tamatoa, so that he could function as king, Tupuna organized his second expedition, and with all save four who guarded the canoe and the animals, he probed deeper into the unknown in search of food. It was not a productive journey, for there was almost no food available. They did come upon a fern whose inner core was just barely edible, and to the fern Tupuna said, "Oh, secret god of this sweet fern, we are hungry. Allow us to borrow your trunk, and we will leave the roots so that you will grow again."

They came upon a taller tree than any they had known in Bora Bora, and Pa observed: "One tree like that would build a house," so Tupuna reverently prayed, "Mighty tree, we need your wood to build a house. Please let us borrow your strength. See, I plant at your roots a rich ulua for you to eat, and when you are finished, may we come and use your wood?"

If they did not find food, they did come upon something almost as good: a cave well up from the reach of the sea, and dry. At its entrance Tupuna buried his last ulua and prayed: "Gods of this cave, please take away any dark things you have left hiding here. Allow me to sprinkle holy water that this place may be sanctified." Then he entered and called back: "This will be our home."

At this point there came a shout of laughter from the shore, where the pigs had been turned loose, and it was obvious that the old boar still had sea legs, for he would take a few steps, wait for the canoe to surge beneath him, adjust his legs to meet it, and then fall snout-first into the sand. Looking dazed, he would grunt loudly and adjust his wobbly legs for the next roll, only to fall on his face again. The watchers roared with glee and forgot the haunting uncertainties that perplexed them, for the infuriated hog brought them the therapy of laughter, so that when Tupuna cried, "Move everything to the cave!" they responded willingly, and in labor ignored the danger, threatening all of them, that in their new home there might be no food.

But when they got to the cave with their burdens, two farmers reported: "There are many birds on this island, good ones," and as if to prove this claim, overhead flew a line of terns, which ate clean fresh fish, so that when baked they tasted like delicious chicken and bonito, mixed. Tamatoa, looking at the terns, said, "Tane would never have brought us here if there were no food. It may not be the food we have known, but it's here. Our job is to find it."

Now, with the temple established and the gods at home, with the great canoe properly beached, and all treasures stowed in the cave, the hungry men who had completed this long voyage began to look at their women, and one by one the emaciated but handsome girls of the long black hair were led into the bushes and cherished, and strange multiple marriages were begun, and new life was launched on the island.

But of the women, the fairest could not find her man, for Teroro was brooding by the sea, reflecting on the sacrifice of the slave and its dark portent for the new homeland, so Tehani left the cave and walked down to the sea, crying in vain, "Teroro, Teroro!" until Mato, who so far had no woman of his own and who had sat close to Tehani all the way north, thus seeing her in many lights and appreciating her quality, heard her and ran through the woods until he could, as if by accident, encounter her along the shore. "Can't you find Teroro?" he asked casually.

"No."

"Perhaps he has important business," Mato suggested.

"Where?" Tehani asked.

"I don't know. Maybe . . ." He took Tehani's hand and tried to lead her back into the trees through which he had just run, but she pulled away.

"No!" she insisted. "I am a chief's daughter and a chief's wife."

"Are you Teroro's wife?" Mato chided.

"What do you mean?" she demanded, her long hair flashing across her delicate breasts as she turned her head sharply.

"I sat very near you on the trip, Tehani," Mato explained. "It didn't look to me as if Teroro thought of you as his wife."

"I was tabu," she explained.

"But thinking of you wasn't tabu," Mato said. "Teroro never thought of you, Tehani. I did."

He took her hand again, and this time she held on to the rugged young chief, because she knew that what he said was true. "I am very alone," she confessed.

"Do you know what I think, Tehani? I think you will never be Teroro's wife. I think he is hungry for his old wife Marama."

Since Tehani shared this suspicion, she experienced a moment of recognition and felt strongly drawn toward Mato and allowed him to pull her into the dark glade away from the shore, and to slip her leafy skirt from her, until in her nakedness she looked at him and realized how desperately she wanted this young man who did not reject her; and he, looking for the first time at her exquisite beauty, diminished though it had been by the voyage, felt a pang of sorrow that such a girl should have been given to a man who did not want her. Gathering her in his arms he whispered, "You are my woman, Tehani."

But when she actually felt his body against hers, and when she heard his words, she grew afraid, for she knew that she was not his woman, and she broke away and ran back to the beach, adjusting her skirt as she went. Before Mato could overtake her she saw Teroro and ran up to him, crying nervously, "You must make peace with your brother."

And she led her husband back along the ocean front, past where Mato stood bitterly watching her, and onto the plateau where King Tamatoa surveyed the rude temple. At first neither man spoke, but Teroro, looking over his brother's shoulder, could see the ominous stones resting on fresh earth. He was dismayed but said grudgingly, "This is an appropriate temple, brother. Later we will build a better." The king nodded, and it was then that Tehani of the long tresses and the flashing eyes led her bewildered husband into the darkness, knowing in her heart that it was another who should have accompanied her.

The sexual life of the king was much too important to be conducted in darkness and hidden glades, so on the next day, after the fishermen had brought in their first substantial catch and women had boiled their unpromising pandanus drupes, Tupuna announced that his wife Teura had ascertained that the time of the month was propitious and that their king, Tamatoa, would that afternoon lie with his wife Natabu. That grave and stately woman was then brought forth from beneath a tree, where she had been secluded, and a temporary shelter, made of cut saplings stuck into the ground and covered with the most consecrated tapas, was erected according to ancient custom.

When the tent was completed, sedate Natabu, who rarely spoke and who was, by a peculiar combination of omens and good circumstances, the most holy of all the voyagers, was blessed by Tupuna and led into the nuptial area and placed according to ancient custom upon the woven mats. The king was then blessed, and the entire company, including even the five slaves, surrounded the tapa house and chanted. Then, with the prayers and blessings of all the community, the king was taken to the sanctified house, placed inside by the priest, and hidden by the lowered tapa. At this point the prayers mounted in frenzy.

The woman with whom the king lay was his sister Natabu. It had been discovered anciently in the islands that for a king to breed a proper heir to the throne, one who would combine the finest lineage and utmost sanctity, he must mate only with his full-blood sister, and although both Tamatoa and his sister Natabu might later take other spouses, their principal obligation was the production—under circumstances of the most intricate propriety, and under the surveillance of the entire community—of royal descendants.

"May the union be fruitful," old Teura chanted as her niece and nephew lay inside the tapa tent. "May it produce strong kings and princesses blessed with godlike blood." The crowd prayed: "May this union produce for us a king," and although they had prayed thus on occasion in the past, when the nuptial tent had been raised over Tamatoa in hopes of breeding an heir, they had never prayed with equal fervor, for it was apparent that in a strange land an heir of the most impeccable lineage was essential, for who else could represent them before the gods if Tamatoa died?

In the late afternoon, when the king and his sister left the rude tent, the eyes of the people followed them, and the chants continued, and all prayed that a good thing had been accomplished on that auspicious day.

When the nuptial tent was taken down and all omens pertaining to it examined, King Tamatoa faced another major obligation, for he was led by Tupuna to a field into which the farmers had diverted a small stream. This would become the taro bed upon which the community would depend for its basic food, and already the mud walls surrounding it imprisoned a foot of water, making the bottom of the field a deep, soft mass of mud. Standing at the edge, where the stream entered, Tamatoa cried, "May the mana of my body pass through my feet and bless this field!" Whereupon he stepped knee-deep into the muddy water and began trampling the bed. He was joined by Tupuna, Teroro, Mato and Pa, the men with most mana, and for hours they passed back and forth over every inch of the taro patch, hammering the mud into a watertight basin, sealing it with their mana. When they were done Tamatoa shouted, "May this bed be forever sealed. Now plant the taro!"

And according to customs more than two thousand years old, the people planted not only the taro, but the breadfruit and the bananas and the pandanus; but for no crop were they as fearful of failure as when they planted coconuts, for to a large extent their entire manner of life was intertwined with this extraordinary tree. When the nuts were young they gave delicious water; when old, a precious oil or a sweet milk. Palms from the coconut thatched many of the houses; hard shells formed cups and utensils, fibers from the husks yielded sennit. Timber from the trunk was used for building and for carving gods; the wiry fiber that grew in the crown was woven into fabric; ribs of the fronds when dried were suitable for starting fires, and sharper ribs, from the leaves, were used in making darts. But most of all, the coconut gave food, and the vocabulary of these people contained twenty-eight different names for the maturing stages of this marvelous nut; from the time when it contained a just-formed, jelly-like substance eaten with scoops by the old or ill to the day when it was a firm, sweet nut.

Therefore, when a coconut was planted, the people placed about the nut a baby octopus to hold the resulting tree erect and prayed: "May the king have done a good job this day."

When the crops were planted, a question arose as to what the island should be named, and the warriors, who knew little of omens, agreed that it ought properly to be called Bora Bora; but a great surprise was in store for them, for when Tupuna of the ancient mane heard the report he was outraged. "There is only one name for our island," he announced stubbornly.

"What?" the warriors asked.

"Havaiki," he replied.

The settlers were aghast at this suggestion and began to swear that the hated name Havaiki would never exist in their new-found refuge: and both King Tamatoa and Teroro agreed, but the old priest, his white beard long and blowing in the breeze, began the most ancient chant of his people, and no interruption of the king could stay him until he had explained, in words more precious than coconuts, for they summarized the race-experience of his people, and were its soul, who the settlers were: "In ancient times, when great Tana lay with a goddess, the people of the swift canoes were born. They lived then in Havaiki, but it was not the Havaiki we know. It was Havaiki-on-the-Great-Land, and from there King Tamatoa's father's father's father, back to forty generations, led his people in a canoe, and they went to Havaiki-Where-the-Animal-Is-Like-a-Man, and there they lived for many generations, until King Tamatoa's father's father's father, back to thirty generations, led his people in canoes to Havaiki-of-the-Green-Lagoon . . ." And in a wild soaring voice he recalled the search of his people, wandering from one land to another, always seeking an island where they would find peace and coconuts and fish. Always, wherever they landed with their burning hopes, they called their new home Havaiki, and if the new Havaiki treated them badly, it was appropriate that they set forth in search of a better, as their parents had done from time immemorial. Thus, in parables, he spoke of the migration of his ancestors from the interior of Asia, to the north coast of New Guinea, through the Samoan islands and out to distant Tahiti; later men, reconstructing the voyages, would discover more than a dozen Havaikis, but none closer to the ancient dream than the island about to be dedicated.

"For us there is only one name," the old man insisted in a burst of rhetoric. "Havaiki of the manifold riches, Havaiki of the brave canoes, Havaiki of strong gods, and courageous men and beautiful women, Havaiki of the dreams that led us across the endless oceans, Havaiki that has lived in our hearts for forty and fifty and sixty generations. This is the island of Havaiki!"

When he was finished, King Tamatoa, who had forgotten his own history, spoke solemnly: "This will be the island of Havaiki, and if you have evil memories of old Havaiki let it be remembered as Havaiki-of-Red-Oro, but our land is Havaiki-of-the-North." So the island was named Havaiki, the last successor in a mighty chain.

It was only when Teroro, accompanied by Mato, Pa and three others, had sailed completely around Havaiki, requiring four days for the explorations, that the settlers appreciated what a magnificent island they had found. "There are two mountains, not one," Teroro explained, "and many cliffs, and birds of endless number. Rivers come down into the sea, and some of the bays are as inviting as Bora Bora's lagoon."

But it was blunt Pa who summed up what they had learned: "It looked to us as if we had picked our cave on the worst land in Havaiki." Gloomily, Mato agreed; but King Tamatoa and his aunt and uncle looked at the newly planted crops and at the temple and said stubbornly, "This is where we have established our home"; but Mato and Pa thought: "If anything should happen, we know where the good land is."

And then the forgotten one appeared. It was on a hot, dusty afternoon when Teroro had gone into the forest seeking birds, that he turned to avoid a tree and found a strange woman confronting him. She was handsome in figure, dressed in a fabric he had not seen before, and her hair, of a strange material that glistened in the sun, stood out like wild grass. She was of his race, yet she was not. With most mournful and condemning eyes she stared at Teroro until he felt his head swimming, but she did not speak. When, in unaccustomed fright, he started to run, she ran with him, and when he stopped, she stopped; but always when he paused, she stared at him in reproach. Finally, she departed in silence, whereupon Teroro regained some of his bravery and ran after her, but she had disappeared.

When he returned to the settlement, he was shivering, but for some reason which he could not explain he did not confide his experience to anyone; but sleep did not come to him that night, for he could see the deep-set, fanatic eyes of the woman staring at him in the darkness, so that on the next morning he took Mato aside and said, "I have found some birds. Let's go into the woods," and the two young chiefs moved through the trees, and Mato asked, "Where are the birds?" And suddenly the gaunt, distracted woman stood before them.

"Who is this?" Mato asked, astonished.

"She came to me yesterday. I think she wants to speak."

But the woman said nothing, content merely with admonishing the young men by her wild stare, so that Teroro said to his companion. "When we move, she will move with us." And certainly, when the warriors started walking under the trees, she walked with them, her garments disheveled and her strange hair glistening in the sun. Then, as they watched, she vanished.

"Where did she go?" Mato cried.

"Woman! Woman!" Teroro called, vainly.

The two young men consulted as to whether they should advise the others, and it was finally decided that they should, so they went first to old, red-eyed Teura and said, "In the trees we met a strange woman with different hair . . ."

Before they could finish, the old woman burst into a long wail, "Auwe, auwe! It is Pere! She has come to destroy us."

The old woman's husband hurried in and she announced: "They have seen Pere, of the burning fire!" And when the king arrived at the commotion she warned him: "The forgotten one has come to punish us."

"Auwe!" the king mourned, for he perhaps best of all understood the unforgivable error they had committed in abandoning a goddess who had warned them beforehand that she wished to accompany them, and he decided that the entire community must assemble at the temple to pray for respite from the goddess. But the prayer was not uttered, for at this moment the earth began to shake violently.

In a manner unknown to the strangers, the red earth of Havaiki rose and fell, twisted and heaved, and cracks appeared through the heart of the settlement, and pigs squealed. "Oh, Pere!" the king cried in terror. "Spare us!" And his prayer must have had power, for the trembling stopped, and the horrified voyagers huddled together to decipher this mighty omen.

They did not succeed, for a much greater was about to envelop them. From the mountain that reached high above their heads volumes of fire began to erupt, and rocks were thrown far into the air. Scattered ash fell back onto the earth and settled on the king's head and on the newly planted banana shoots. All day the fires continued, and into the night, so that the undersides of the clouds that hung over the islands shone red, as if even they were ablaze.

It was a night of terror, fearful in its strangeness and paralyzing in its power. The settlers gathered at the shore and hovered near *West Wind,* thinking that if the land caught fire, they might escape in it, and when the eruptions grew worse, Tupuna insisted that the king and Natabu, at least, be sent out to the safety of the sea, and it was because of this foresight that the colony was saved, for Teroro dispatched Hiro and Pa with the canoe, and when it was a mile out to sea, lighted by the blazing mountain, a great ocean wave sped toward shore, and if the canoe had not already reached the sea, its appropriate element, the onrushing wave would have destroyed it.

As it was, the water swept far inland, and tore down the temple and uprooted many of the crops. In its swirling return to the sea, it dragged with it one of the pigs, most of the bananas and old, red-eyed Teura. The goddess had warned her, but she had failed to interpret the dream correctly, so that when the turbulent sea reached far inland to grab her, twisting her this way and that, she was not afraid. Committing herself entirely to the gods, she whispered into the engulfing waves, "Great Ta'aroa, keeper of the sea, you have come for me and I am ready." As she was dragged across the reef, the green water rushing over her, she smiled and relaxed, for she was certain that somewhere out beyond the coral she would encounter her personal god, Mano, the wild blue shark. "Mano!" she cried at last. "I am coming to talk with you!" And she was carried far from land.

When dawn rose, accompanied by new explosions of ash and flame, King Tamatoa studied his stricken community, and he could explain the ravages, especially the fallen temple, only by the fact that no slaves had been planted alive at three of the corners, but Teroro would not tolerate such reasoning.

"We are punished because we forgot our most ancient goddess, and because we built in the wrong place," he insisted.

How wrong the place was would now be proved, for Mato came running with the news that up on the side of the mountain a creeping wall of fire was slowly descending toward the settlement. A dozen men went back into the trees and climbed toward where Mato had pointed, and they saw a fearful thing: above them, and marching over all obstacles on its way to the sea, came a relentless wall of fiery rock and molten lava, turning over and over upon itself, devouring trees and rocks and valleys. Its ugly snout, thirty feet high, was not ablaze and seemed dead, until it struck a dried tree, whereupon flames leaped mysteriously into the air. At intervals long tongues of molten rock spurted through the ominously creeping front and spread out like water. It was obvious that the crawling monster must soon devour the entire community.

"It will be upon us by tomorrow," the men calculated.

When he was satisfied with the news, King Tamatoa reacted without fear, for his brother's bold words had strengthened him. He commanded: "We will first pray for the old woman Teura," and he blessed her to the gods. When this was finished he said calmly, "All planted things will be dug up immediately and wrapped carefully, even if you must use your own clothes." Then he showed the slaves how to load the canoe, and when, at a distance of less than three miles, the molten lava began pouring over a low cliff, like a flaming waterfall, he studied it for a long time. Then he said, "We will stay ashore tonight and get all things ready. In the morning we will leave this place. Pa says he has found a promising land to the west."

Through the night the settlers worked, seeing one another in the dim flares of the volcano, and when dawn came they were ready to go. They had recovered much of their seed, and had saved their gods, their pigs and their canoe. With these they escaped, but when they were safe at sea, they saw the vast, fiery front of the lava break through onto their plateau, where it ate its way impersonally across all things. The temple site was burned away in a flash; the fields where crops had rested were gone; the taro patch was filled with fire; and the cave disappeared behind a wall of flame. From the plateau, the cascade of fire found a valley leading down into the sea, and after building its strength aloft, it plunged down this avenue and poured into the ocean. When it struck the water it hissed and groaned; it threw columns of steam into the air and exploded the waves; it sent noisy reports of its triumph and filled the sky with ash; and then, conquered by the patient and accommodating ocean, it fell silently into dark caverns, as it had been doing here for the past thirty million years.

The men of Havaiki, seeing for the first time the incredible fury of which their new land was capable, sat awestruck in their canoe and watched for a long time the cataclysm that had destroyed their home; but a gust of wind, stronger than the rest, carried down from the crest of the volcano a wisp of hair, spun by the breezes from the molted lava, and Teroro caught the hair and held it aloft, where the sun played on it, and he saw that it was the hair which the strange woman in the forest had worn, and he announced: "It was the goddess Pere. She came not to frighten us but to warn us. We did not understand."

His words gave the people in the canoe great hope, for if the goddess had thought enough of her erring people to warn them, she must retain some love for them; and all was not lost. The hair of Pere was given to the king as an omen, and he placed it upon the neck of the only remaining bred sow, because if this animal did not live and deliver her litter it would be as bad an omen as the volcano.

In this manner, but bearing only half the cargo with which they had arrived, and a bred sow clothed in Pere's hair, the voyagers started for a new home; and Pa and Mato had chosen wisely, for they led their companions around the southern tip of the island and up the western coast until they found fine land, with soil that could be tilled, and water, and it was here that the settlement of Havaiki began in earnest, with new fields and a new temple built without sacrifices. When the sow threw her litter, the king himself watched over the young pigs, and when the largest and strongest reached a size at which he could have been eaten—and mouths had begun to water for the taste of roast pig— the king and old Tupuna carried the pig reverently to the new temple and sacrificed it to Tane. From then on the community prospered.

WHEN THE SETTLEMENT was established, Tupuna took the steps which were to give it the characteristics which marked it permanently. He said one day to the king, "Soon I shall follow Teura, but before I go upon the rainbow, we ought to protect the life of our people. It is not good that men roam freely everywhere, and live without restraint."

Teuoro, listening, argued: "We had too many restraints in Havaiki-of-Red-Oro. Here we ought to be free. I like our life the way it is."

"For a few months, perhaps," the priest argued. "But as the years pass, unless a community has fixed laws, and patterns which bind people into their appointed place, life is no good."

"But this is a new land," Teroro reasoned.

"It is in a new land that customs are most necessary," the priest warned, and the king supported him, and out of their discussions the tabus were established.

"Each man lives between an upper, which gives mana, and a lower, which drains mana from him," Tupuna explained in words that would never be forgotten. "Therefore a man must plead with the upper to send him mana and must protect himself from the lower, which steals mana from him. That is why no man should permit a slave to touch him, or to pass upon his shadow, or to see his food, for a slave can drain away a man's entire mana in an instant, for a slave has no mana.

"The way for a man to obtain mana is to obey his king, for it is the king alone who can bring us mana directly from the gods. Therefore no man may touch the king, or the garment of the king, or the shadow of the king, or in any way steal his mana. To break this tabu is death." Tupuna then enumerated more than five dozen additional tabus which protected the king in his suspension between the upper gods and the lower men: his spittle may not be touched; his excrement must be buried at night in a secret place; his food must be prepared only by chiefs; his reservoir of mana must be protected; he is tabu, he is tabu.

Men with mana required protection from defilement by women, who usually had none. Since men were of the light, and women of darkness; since men were outgoing and strong, and women intaking and weak; since men were clean and women impure; since it was nightly proved that even the strongest man could be slyly drained of his power by a clever woman, dreadful tabus were set about the latter. They must never eat with men, nor see men eating, nor touch food intended for men, on pain of death. Each month they must spend the moon-days locked up in a tiny room, on pain of death. They must eat none of the good foods required to keep men strong: no pig, no sweet fish, no coconuts, on pain of death. "And since the banana has obviously been created by the gods to represent man's fertility," Tupuna wailed, "no woman may even touch a banana, on pain of instant strangulation."

The days of the moon, the turning of the season and the planting of crops were all placed under tabu. So were laughing at improper moments, certain sex habits, the eating of certain fish and the ridicule of either gods or nobles. Tabu was the temple, tabu were the rock-gods, tabu was the hair of Pere, tabu was the growing coconut tree. At some seasons, even the ocean itself was tabu, on pain of death.

In this manner, and with the approval of the people, who wanted to be organized within established levels, the tabus were promulgated and patterns were developed whereby each man would know his level and none would transgress. What had been a free volcanic island, explosive with force, now became a rigidly determined island, and all men liked it better, for the unknown was made known.

It is not quite true to say that all men were content. One was not. Teroro, as the king's younger brother, was the logical man to become priest when old Tupuna died. He had inherited great sanctity and was growing into an able if not a clever man; there was no greater astronomer than he, and it was tacitly understood that he would in time become guardian of the tabus.

But he was far from the dedication required for this exacting job. Instead of the equanimity that marked the king, Teroro was torn with uncertainties, and they centered upon women. Day after day, when he wandered in the woods, he would come upon Pere, her shining hair disheveled and her eyes deep-sunk. She said nothing, but walked with him as a woman walks with a man she loves. Often, after her appearance, the volcano would erupt, but what lava flows there were, went down the other side of the mountain and did not endanger the growing settlement, where many pigs roamed, and chickens, and sweet, succulent dogs; for Tamatoa and Natabu had done their work well and had produced a son.

Only Teroro did not prosper; often he would turn the corner of a well-known footpath, and there would be silent Pere, hurt, condemnatory and yet speaking her love for her troubled young chief. Always, in the background of his mind, there was Pere.

Yet his real agony concerned not a shadowy goddess, but a substantial woman, and this was Marama, his wife whom he had abandoned in Bora Bora. He thought: "How wise of her to speak as she did on that last day!" For he could hear her voice as clear as it had been a year ago: "I am the canoe!" It seemed to him almost godlike wisdom on Marama's part to have used that idiom; for she was the canoe. Her placid face and sweet wisdom had been the continuing thread of his life; over all the waves and through the storms she had indeed been the canoe. And for the first time, here on remote Havaiki, Teroro began to understand how desperately a man can remember a strong, placid, wise woman whom he had known before. She was the symbol of earth, the movement of waves, the song at night. Hers was the weight that rested in memory; her words were recalled. He could see the movement of her skirts, and the way she wore her hair; once on Bora Bora when he had been sick she had washed his fever and he could recall her cool hands.

In consternation he remembered that on the canoe young Tehani had done the same; but it was different. He had never known with older Marama one fifth of the sexual excitement he had experienced with Tehani; and yet his mind was tormented by his wife. He would see her at night when he returned from his silent walks with Pere. In his dreams he would hear Marama speak. And whenever he saw *Wait-for-the-West-Wind,* that perfect canoe, he would see Marama, for she had said, "I am the canoe!" And she was.

It was in this mood that one morning he dashed from his thatched hut where Tehani slept and ran to Mato, at the fishing grounds. Grabbing the surprised chief by the hand he dragged him to the hut, and jerked Tehani to her feet. "She is your woman, Mato," he shouted with unnecessary force.

"Teroro!" the young girl cried.

"You are no longer my woman!" Teroro shouted. "I watched you on the canoe. Mato never took his eyes from you. All right, Mato, now she is yours." And he stalked from the scene.

That afternoon, in torment of spirit, he sought out his brother and said simply, "I shall go back to Bora Bora."

The king was not surprised, for he had been watching his brother and news of his rejection of Tehani had been discussed with old Tupuna, who had said that Teroro was ill in spirit. "Why will you go?" Tamatoa asked.

"I must bring Marama here," the younger man said. "We need more breadfruit, more dogs, everything. We need more people."

A council was held and all agreed that a trip south could prove helpful, especially if foodstuffs were brought back. "But who can be spared for such a long voyage?" Tupuna asked, and Teroro replied that he could sail *West Wind* to Bora Bora with only six men, if Pa and Hiro were two of them.

"I'll go," Mato insisted, but Teroro growled, "We have treated Tehani badly. You stay with her." And he would not take Mato, his greatest friend.

So the return trip was authorized, and the community began assembling its pitiful stores of spare food. This time there was no dried taro, no coconut, no breadfruit, no bamboo lengths to carry water. There were, fortunately, some bananas, but they did not dry and carry well. Dried fish there was in plenty, and on this the men would exist.

When the food was collected, Teroro divulged his plan. Drawing a rough pattern of the trip north, he pointed out that the canoe had sailed far east, then north, then far west. With a bold line in the sand he cut across this pattern and said, "We will sail directly south, and we will find the island."

"There will be no storm winds to aid you," Tupuna warned.

"We will ride with the currents," Teroro replied, "and we will paddle."

On the last day before departure, Teroro was sitting alone when one of the village women came to him and said plaintively, "On the return, if there is room in the canoe, will you please bring one thing for me?"

"What?" Teroro asked.

"A child," the woman said.

"Whose child?" he inquired.

"Any child," the woman replied, adding softly, "It is woeful to be in a land where there are no children."

It was impractical to bring a child so far, and Teroro said so, and dismissed the woman, but in a little while another came to him, saying, "Why should you bring pigs and breadfruit, Teroro? What our hearts ache for is children." And he sent her away.

But the women came again, and while they did not weep, there were tears in their throats as they spoke: "We are growing older, all of us. You and the king and Tupuna and all of us. There are babies, to be sure, but we need children."

"There are no children playing along the shore," another said. "Do you remember how they played in our lagoon?" And suddenly Teroro could see the lagoon at Bora Bora with hundreds of brown, naked children in the green waters, and he realized why Havaiki-of-the-North had seemed so barren.

"Please," the women pleaded, "bring us back some children."

Then, on the night of departure, for Teroro insisted upon leaving when the stars were visible, he confided to his brother: "I am not going solely for Marama. I am going to bring back the stone of Pere. I think an island should have not only men gods, but women, too."

On the long voyage south, while his men starved and grew parched in the doldrums, Teroro put together the rough chant that would be remembered in the islands for generations after his death and which served to guide subsequent canoes from Tahiti to the new Havaiki:

> Wait for the west wind, wait for the west wind!
> Then sail to Nuku Hiva of the dark bays
> To find the constant star.
> Hold to it, hold to it,
> Though the eyes grow dim with heat.
> Hold to it, hold to it,
> Till wild Ta'aroa sends the winds.
> Then speed to the clouds where Pere waits.
> Watch for her flames, the flames of Pere,
> Till great Tane brings the land,
> Brings Havaiki-of-the-North,
> Sleeping beneath the Little Eyes.

But when the chant was finished, Teroro realized with some dismay that finding the home islands was not going to be easy, and he missed them altogether at first, reaching all the way down to Tahiti before he discovered where he was. Then, beating his way back north, he found Havaiki-of-Red-Oro, and there at sea, in the gently rolling swells, the seven men held a council of war. Teroro posed the problem simply: "If we sail into Bora Bora without a plan, the High Priest, who must know about our attack on Oro, will command his men to kill us."

"We've got to risk it," Pa growled.

"We are very weak," Teroro pointed out.

"We can still fight," Pa insisted.

"There is a better way," Teroro argued, and with a newly developing sense of guile he reasoned: "Since we're not strong enough to fight the High Priest, we must outsmart him." And he suggested a way, but his men thought of other things when in the dawn they saw once more the pinnacles of Bora Bora and the wild cliffs dropping away to the lagoon.

Pa muttered, "We must have been insane to leave this place for Havaiki-of-the-North." And each man in the canoe acknowledged the fact that he had surrendered earth's paradise in exchange for a harsh new land.

As soon as *Wait-for-the-West-Wind* was spotted standing off the western entrance into the lagoon, the residents of its home port began to line the shores and shout with joy at the return of their people. It was this joy that Teroro counted upon to give him ten minutes' respite to develop his plan, because he believed that the islanders' spontaneous acceptance of the canoe would prevent the High Priest from ordering the crew's immediate death, and in that interval Teroro would have time to accomplish his mission.

As the canoe neared land he warned his men again: "I'll talk, but you must look pious."

And promptly the bow of the canoe struck land, he leaped ashore and cried, "We seek the High Priest!" and when that dignitary, older and more solemn, with flecks of white in his beard, approached, Teroro made deep obeisance and cried for all to hear, "We come as servants of Oro, seeking another god for our distant land. Bless us, august one, and send us another god."

The plea took the High Priest so by surprise, coming as it did even before any narration of the journey, that he was unable to mask his pleasure, and the staff with which he could have directed the sacrifice of the crew remained rooted in the ground, and he listened as Teroro spoke rapidly: "Under Oro we have prospered, august one, and our community grows. But life is difficult and we live scattered. That is why your servant old Tupuna requires additional gods. When we have borrowed them from you, we will depart."

The High Priest listened, and then stood aside as the new king of Bora Bora appeared, and Teroro saw with intense pleasure that the man was not from Havaiki, as planned, but from Bora Bora. "King," he cried, "forgive us for our midnight assault on Havaiki before our departure. We did this thing not to dishonor great Oro, but to prevent a Havaiki man from becoming king of Bora Bora. Forgive us." And Teroro was so weak, and so urgently in need of food and help, that he kneeled in the dust, and prostrated himself before the king, and then before the High Priest, and to his deep satisfaction he heard from the canoe the pious voice of Pa intoning: "Now let us go to the temple of Oro and give thanks for our safe voyage."

But as the men marched, Teroro caught sight of a woman at the edge of the crowd, a tall, solemn, patient woman with a face like a moon, and he thought no more of gods or kings or priests, for the woman was Marama, and solely by looking at each other, intently and with the love that consumes two thousand miles of ocean, she knew that he had come to take her with him, and while he prayed to a god whom he detested, she went to her grass house and started packing.

When the prayers were over he joined her there, and they sat in silence, profound communion passing between them, and she was both forgiving and consoling in the disappointing moments when they found him too exhausted with famine even to make love with her. She laughed softly and said, from the edge of the house, "See what happened on the last night we made love." And she took from a maid's arm a boy nearly a year old, with wide eyes and dark hair like his father's.

Teroro looked at his son, and at the wife he had left behind because she could bear no children, and in his embarrassment he began to laugh. Marama laughed too, and teased: "You looked so ridiculous out there, praying to Oro. And Pa putting on that long face! 'Now let us go to the temple of Oro!' It was a good idea, Teroro, but it wasn't necessary."

"What do you mean?"

"Haven't you noticed how much older the High Priest looks? He has been very badly treated."

"That's good news. How?"

"After all his scheming to banish you and Tamatoa, so that he could become the chief priest at Havaiki . . ."

"You mean, they were just using him? To subdue Bora Bora?"

"Yes. They had no intention of making him chief priest. After you killed your wife's father . . ."

"She's not my wife. I gave her to Mato."

Marama paused for a moment and looked at the floor. Quietly, she added, "The men of Havaiki tried to give us a new king, but we fought."

"Then why do you keep the High Priest?"

"We need a priest," she said simply. "Every island needs a priest." And they fell silent, listening to the soft waves of the lagoon, and after a long while Teroro said, "You must find a dozen women who will go with us. It's a hard journey." Then he added, "And this time we'll take some children with us." His voice brightened. "We'll take the little fellow."

"No," Marama said. "He's too young. We'll trade him for an older boy," and in the island tradition she went from house to house, until she found an eight-year-old boy she liked, and to his willing mother she gave her son. When Teroro saw the new boy, he liked him, too, and after the child was sent away to wait for the canoe's departure, he took his wife in his arms and whispered, "You are the canoe of my life, Marama. In you I make my voyage."

At the consecration of the new idol of Oro, the High Priest insisted upon killing a slave, and Teroro hid his face in shame, for he and his men knew that once the reef was breasted, the idol would pitch into the sea, so that when the High Priest delivered the god to the becoming-priest Teroro, the latter took it gravely, not as an idol but as a symbol of the needless death of a man; and whether he or the crew liked the statue or not, it had somehow become a thing of sanctification, and Teroro treated it as such, for it spoke to him of blood. At the same time it reminded him of the difficulty which now faced him: he had to get the red-rock statue of the goddess Pere from the temple without exciting the High Priest's suspicion that that had been the real reason for the return. In secrecy he held council with Pa and Hiro to canvass the ways by which Pere might be kidnapped.

Pa suggested: "You fooled the priests with your talk of Oro. Fool them again."

"No," Teroro replied. "We were able to fool them about Oro because they wanted to believe. To mention a forgotten goddess like Pere would arouse their suspicions."

"Could we steal it?" Hiro proposed.

"Who knows where it is?" Teroro countered. They discussed other possibilities and agreed upon only one thing: to return to Havaiki-of-the-North without

Pere would be insane, for since she had warned them once with such a disastrous wall of fire, the next time she would obliterate them altogether. It was then that Teroro proposed: "I shall talk with Marama. She is a very wise woman."

And it was Marama who devised the plan. "The island knows that you have come back for me," she pointed out, "and they recall that my ancestors were priests. When the women for our voyage have been gathered, two of us will go to the High Priest and tell him that we want to take one of the ancient Bora Bora gods with us."

"Will he allow it?" Teroro asked suspiciously.

"He is a priest of Oro," Marama pointed out, "but he is also a Bora Boran, and he will understand our love of this island."

It worked exactly as she planned, but when the time came for delivering the feather-draped red rock of Pere, the High Priest could not bring himself to place such a treasure in the hands of a woman, insisting upon transferring the goddess directly to Teroro, and when the latter at last had the soul of Pere in his possession, the wild, passionate soul of the fire goddess, the mother of volcanoes, he wanted to shout in triumph, but instead he lay it aside as if it were only a woman's god, a whim of his wife's, and the High Priest thought the same.

The men were fattened and the food was packed. Twelve women were selected and put on starvation diets to prepare them for the voyage. King Tamatoa's favorite wife was included, for everyone agreed that since their king had produced with his sister a royal heir of greatest sanctity, he should be encouraged to import at least one woman he loved. For seed crops the crew emphasized pigs, bananas and breadfruit. "How we yearn for sweet breadfruit," they explained.

When all was ready, Teroro was startled to see Marama lugging toward the canoe a large bundle wrapped in leaves. "What's that?" he cried.

"Flowers," his wife replied.

"What do we want with flowers?" Teroro protested.

"I asked Pa and he said there were no flowers." Teroro looked at the other crew members, and they realized for the first time that Havaiki-of-the-North owned no natural blooms. Even so, the bundle seemed excessively large.

"You simply can't take that much, Marama," he protested.

"The gods like flowers," she replied. "Throw out one of the pigs."

The idea was so offensive that the crew would not consider it, but they did compromise on this: they would put back one of the smaller breadfruit, but they all considered Teroro's woman demented.

Then came the task, most joyous and exciting of all, of selecting the children. The men wanted to take only girls, while the women wished only boys, so that the compromise of half and half pleased no one but did have certain sense to commend it. The ten children selected ranged from four years old to twelve: dark-haired, deep-eyed, grinning, white-toothed children. Their very presence made the canoe lighter.

But when all had stepped aboard, Teroro was unaccountably depressed by the gravity of the task he had undertaken, and this time with no guile he went gravely to the High Priest and pleaded: "Bless our journey. Establish the tabus." And the High Priest arranged the gods on the side of the voyagers and cried in a high voice, touching the food for the animals, "This is tabu! This is tabu!" And when he had finished, the canoe somehow seemed safer, and it set forth for the long voyage north.

It had barely escaped from the lagoon when Pa, the shark-faced, went for the offensive statue of Oro, to throw it into the deep, but to his surprise, Teroro restrained him and said, "It is a god! We will place it reverently on the shore of Havaiki-of-Red-Oro," and when he had led the canoe to that once-hated island, slipping ashore where no lookouts could intercept him, he placed Oro in a sheltered position among rocks, and built a palm-leaf canopy; and he was overcome with the awareness that never again would he see Havaiki, from which he had sprung, and while the canoe waited, he stood on the shore of the ancestral island and chanted the story of the brave, lost people of Havaiki-in-Asia, who had set out upon innumerable voyages, never to return. This was his land, his home, and he would know it no more.

Pa and his rugged crew were further surprised when it came time to set the course back to Havaiki-of-the-North. This time Teroro would not permit them to follow his earlier reckless path far out to sea; he required them to take the cautious route to Nuku Hiva, where in all prudence they replenished their stores, so that in the heart-baking doldrums they had adequate food and water, especially for the children, who suffered intensely in the heat, for try as they might, they could not make their stomachs into tight hard knots. They were hungry and they said so.

At last the stars of the Little Eyes were overhead, and the canoe turned joyously westward before the wind. Now Teroro conducted daily lessons for every man and boy aboard the canoe: "You know the island lies ahead. What signals will prove the fact?" And every male above the age of six became a navigator, and Marama, taking the place of old red-eyed Teura, became the seer, collecting omens; and one day a boy spotted a black fork-tailed bird attacking a gannet, who had caught a fish; and Teroro showed all how to read the wave echoes as they bounced back from unseen Havaiki; but the most solemn moment came when Marama, reading her clouds, saw fire upon them, and she knew that the goddess Pere had lighted a beacon for her voyagers, and it was to this cloud of fire that Teroro directed his canoe.

As the craft neared shore Teroro faced one last odious job, but he discharged it. Moving among the men and women he told each: "The children are no longer yours. They must be shared with those on shore, and each child shall have many mothers."

Immediately a wailing set up, for on the long voyage men and women in the canoe had grown inordinately attached to the children, and the wild young things had found mothers and fathers whom they liked. "He is more than my son!" a woman cried, holding to her breast a nine-year-old boy with a broken tooth.

"No," Teroro said firmly. "If it had not been for the women on shore, pleading for children, I would not have thought to bring any. They must have their share. It is only just."

So when the canoe landed, there was a moment of intense anguish as the women from shore, too long without the sound of children, hurried down and saw the boys standing awkwardly by the mast and the little girls holding onto men's hands. The women on shore could not see the new pigs or the promising breadfruit or the bananas. All they could see were the children, and when the first child stepped ashore, a woman ran frenziedly to him with food, but the child drew back.

It was in this manner that Teroro, bearing in his hands the rock of Pere, stepped ashore to become the compassionate and judicious priest of Havaiki, with his gentle wife Marama as associate and seer, and with the volcano goddess as his special mentor. The pigs and the breadfruit and the children increased. Marama's flowers burst into brilliance. And the island prospered.

III

FROM THE FARM OF
BITTERNESS

Athousand years after the men of Bora Bora had completed their long
voyage to the north, a thin, sallow-faced youth with stringy blond hair left
an impoverished-looking farm near the village of Marlboro, in eastern Massachusetts, and enrolled as a freshman at Yale College in Connecticut. This was
the more mysterious for two reasons: to look at the farm one would never
suppose that its owners could afford to send any of their ten children to college;
and, having decided to do so, the parents must have had deeply personal reasons
for sending a son not to Harvard, which was only twenty-five miles away, but
to Yale, which was more than a hundred miles to the south.

Gideon Hale, a gaunt man of forty-two who looked sixty, could explain
each matter: "Our minister visited Harvard and he assures us that the place has
become a haven for Unitarians, deists and atheists. No son of mine shall be
contaminated in such a den of iniquitousness." So seventeen-year-old Abner
was packed off to Yale, which remained a haven for the honest if austere
precepts of John Calvin as expressed in New England Congregationalism.

As for the money, gaunt Gideon explained: "We are practicing Christians
adhering to the word of Calvin as preached by Theodore Beza in Geneva and
by Jonathan Edwards in Boston. We do not believe in painting our barns in
worldly displays of wealth, nor in painting our daughters to parade their concupiscence. We save our money and apply it to the betterment of our minds and
the salvation of our souls. When my son Abner graduates a minister from Yale,
he will glorify God by preaching the same message and exhibiting the same
example. How did he get from this farm to divinity school? Because this family
practices frugality and avoids worldly exhibit."

In his senior year at Yale, emaciated Abner Hale, whose parents did not
allow him enough money to live on, experienced a spiritual enlightenment which
changed his life, impelling him to unanticipated deeds and imperishable com-
mitments. It was not what the early nineteenth century called "conversion," for
Abner had undergone this phenomenon at eleven, while walking at dusk from
the far fields to the milking shed. It was a wintry Marlboro night, and as he
walked through the crackling stubble, frost on his breath, he heard a voice cry
distinctly, "Abner Hale, are you saved?" He knew he was not, but when he
replied, "No," the voice kept repeating the inquiry, and finally a light filled the

meadow and a great shaking possessed him, and he stood in the fields transfixed, so that when his father came for him he burst into wild tears and begged: "Father, what must I do to be saved?" In Marlboro his conversion was held to be a minor miracle, and from that eleventh year his pious father had scrimped and borrowed and saved to send the predestined boy to divinity school.

What thin-faced Abner experienced at Yale was far different from conversion; it was spiritual illumination on a specific point and it arrived through a most unlikely person. A group of his worldly classmates, including his roommate, the young medical student John Whipple, who had once smoked and drunk, came by his room as he was writing a long report on "Church Discipline in the City of Geneva as Practiced by Theodore Beza."

"Come along to hear Keoki Kanakoa!" his rowdy classmates shouted.

"I'm working," Abner replied, and closed his door more tightly against temptation. He had come to the part of his paper in which Beza had begun to apply the teachings of Calvin to the general civil life of Geneva, and the manner in which this was done fascinated the young divinity student, for he wrote with some fervor: "Beza constantly faced the problem which all who govern must face: 'Do I govern for the welfare of man or for the glory of God?' Beza found it easy to give his answer, and although certain harshnesses which the world condemned did unavoidably occur in Geneva, so did the Kingdom of God on earth, and for once in the long history of civilization, an entire city lived according to the precepts of our Divine Father."

There was a rattling at his door and wiry John Whipple stuck his head in and called, "We're saving a seat for you, Abner. Seems everyone wants to hear Keoki Kanakoa."

"I am working," Abner replied the second time, and carefully he closed his door and returned to his lamp, by whose amber light he wrote painstakingly: "The Kingdom of God on earth is not easy to attain, for mere study of the Bible will not illuminate the way by which a government can acquire sanctity, for obviously if this were the case, thousands of governments that have now perished and which in their day attended to the Bible would have discovered the godly way. We know they have failed, and they have failed because they lacked a man of wisdom to show them. . . ." He bit his pen and thought of his father's long and gloomy battle with the town fathers of Marlboro. His father knew what the rule of God was, but the fathers were obstinate men and would not listen. It was no surprise either to Abner or to his father when the daughter of one of these perverse men discovered that she was going to have a baby out of wedlock, although just what this sin involved, Abner did not fully know.

"Abner!" a stentorian voice called from the hallway. "It is your duty to hear Keoki Kanakoa." The door was thrust open, revealing a chunky little professor in a waistcoat too tight and a stock too dirty. "In the interests of your soul you should hear the message of this remarkable young Christian." And the man came over to the desk, blew out the light, and dragged his reluctant pupil to the missionary lecture.

Abner found the seat which handsome John Whipple had saved for him, and the two young men, so unlike in all ways, waited for the chairs on the college platform to be occupied. At seven-thirty President Jeremiah Day, calm but glowing with spiritual fire, led to the farthest chair a brown-skinned, white-toothed, black-haired young giant in a tight-fitting suit. "It is my honor to present to the students of Yale College," President Day said simply, "one of the most powerful voices in the world today. For when Keoki Kanakoa, son of a ruler of Owhyhee speaks, he speaks to the conscience of the world; to you young men who have already committed yourselves to Christ's ministry, the voice of Keoki Kanakoa brings particular challenges."

At this, the young giant, standing about six feet five and weighing more than two hundred and fifty pounds, rose and graced his audience with a dazzling smile, after which he raised his hands like a minister and prayed: "May the good Lord bless what I am about to say. May He open all hearts to hear."

"He speaks better than I do," John Whipple whispered, but Abner was not amused, for he wished to be back at his books, feeling that he had come close to the heart of his essay on Theodore Beza when his professor insisted upon dragging him to the lecture by this barbarian from Owhyhee.

But when the brown-skinned giant launched into his message, not only Abner Hale but everyone else in the auditorium listened, for the engaging young savage told how he had run away from an idol-worshiping home, from polygamy, from immorality, from grossness and from bestiality to find the word of Jesus Christ. He recounted how, after landing from a whaling ship in Boston, he had tried to gain entrance to Harvard but had been laughed at, and how he had walked to Yale College and had met President Day in the street and had said to him, "I come seek Jesus." And the head of Yale had replied, "If you cannot find Him here, this college should be dissolved."

Keoki Kanakoa spoke for two hours. Sometimes his voice fell away to a whisper as he spoke of the evil darkness in which his beloved islands of Owhyhee festered. Again it rose like a thundering sea when he told the young men of Yale what they could do for Christ if they would only come to Owhyhee and circulate the word of God. But what had captured earlier audiences throughout New England, and what now completely absorbed the men of Yale, so that no one stirred even at the end of two hours, was Keoki's impassioned story of what it was like to live in Owhyhee without Christ. "When I was a boy," he began softly, in the fine English he had mastered in various church schools, "we worshipped dreadful gods like Ku, the god of battle. Ku demanded endless human sacrifices, and how did the priests find victims? Before a sacred day, my father, the Governor of Maui, would tell his assistants, 'We require a man.' Before a battle he would announce, 'We require eight men,' and his assistants would then gather and say, 'Let's take Kakai. I am angry with him,' or perhaps, 'Now would be a good time to get rid of that one and take his lands.' And at night two conspirators would creep secretly from behind while a third would walk up boldly and say, 'Greetings, Kakai, how was the fishing?' and before he could reply . . ."

At this point giant Keoki had been coached by his missionary preceptors to pause dramatically, wait, then hold aloft in his enormous hands a lethal length of coconut-fiber rope. "While my father's agent smiled at the victim, one conspirator crept up and pinioned his arms. The other slipped this rope around his neck . . . like this." And slowly he twisted his two great hands together, compressing the rope into a tight knot. Making a strangling noise in his throat, he allowed his big head to fall on his chest. After a pause, while his enormous frame seemed to burst from its ill-fitting American suit, he slowly raised his head and disclosed a face masked in pity. "We do not know Jesus," he said softly, as if his voice were coming from a sepulcher.

Then he swept into his peroration, his voice hammering like thunder and tears splashing down like rain, so that the terror of his youthful days became clearly visible throughout his body. "Young men of God!" he pleaded. "In my father's islands immortal souls go every night to everlasting hell because of you! You are to blame! You have not taken the word of Jesus Christ to my islands. We hunger for the word. We are thirsty for the word. We die for the word. Are you, in your indifference, going to keep the word from us forever? Is there no man here tonight who will rise up and say to me, 'Keoki Kanakoa, I will go with you to Owhyhee and save three hundred thousand souls for Jesus Christ'?"

The gigantic man paused. In deep and honest grief his voice broke. President Day poured him a glass of water, but he brushed it aside and called, through choking sobs, "Will no one go with me to save the souls of my people?" He sat down, quaking in his chair, a man shattered by the revelation of God's word, and after a while President Day led him away.

The impact of Keoki Kanakoa's missionary sermon struck the roommates Hale of divinity and Whipple of medicine with stunning force. They left the lecture hall in shocked silence, brooding upon the misery depicted by the Owhyheean. In their room they did not bother to relight the lamp, but went to bed in darkness, weighed down by the indifference with which Keoki had charged them. When the awfulness of this indifference finally penetrated his conscience, Abner began to weep—for he had grown up in an age of weeping —and after a while John asked, "What is it, Abner?" and the farm boy replied, "I cannot think of sleep, seeing in my mind those human souls destined for all eternity to everlasting hell." From the manner in which he spoke, it was evident that he had been watching each separate soul plunge into eternal fire, and the misery was more than he could bear.

Whipple said, "His final call keeps ringing in my ears. 'Who will go to Owhyhee with me?' " To this Abner Hale made no reply.

Long after midnight, when the young doctor could still hear his roommate sobbing, he rose, lit the lamp, and began dressing. At first Hale pretended not to know what was happening, but finally he whipped out of bed and caught Whipple by the arm. "What are you going to do, John?"

"I am going to Owhyhee," the handsome doctor replied. "I cannot waste my life here, indifferent to the plea of those islands."

"But where are you going now?" Hale asked.

"To President Day's. To offer myself to Christ."

There was a moment's hesitation while the doctor, fully dressed, and the minister, in nightgown, studied each other. It was broken when Abner asked, "Will you pray with me?"

"Yes," the doctor said, and he kneeled beside his bed.

Abner, at his, prayed: "Father Almighty, tonight we have heard Thy call. From the starry wastes of the sky Thy voice has come to us, from across the boundless deep where souls rot in evil. Unworthy as we are to serve Thee, wilt Thou nevertheless accept us as Thy servants?" He continued for several minutes, issuing a prayer to a distant, living, full-bodied, vengeful yet forgiving God. If at that moment he had been asked to describe the Being to Whom he prayed he would have said, "He is tall, rather thin, with black hair and penetrating eyes. He is very serious, marks every transgression, and demands all humans to follow His precepts. He is a stern but forgiving Father, a harsh but just disciplinarian." And he would have described Gideon Hale in exactly the same terms. If anyone, at the end of his summary, should have asked, "Does this Father ever smile?" the question would have astonished young Abner as one he had not yet considered, but upon careful reflection he would have answered, "He is compassionate, but He never smiles."

When the prayer was ended John Whipple asked, "Are you coming with me?"

"Yes, but shouldn't we wait till morning to speak with President Day?"

" 'Go ye into all the world, and preach the gospel to every creature,' " the young doctor quoted, and Hale, acknowledging the aptness of this admonition, dressed.

It was four-thirty when they knocked at President Day's door, and with no visible surprise he admitted them to his study, where he sat in coat and muffler hiding his nightgown. "I surmise that the Lord has spoken to you," he began gently.

"We are offering ourselves for Owhyhee," John Whipple explained.

"Have you considered this grave step?" Day asked.

"We have often discussed how we should spend our lives in God," Abner began, but he was taken by a fit of weeping, and his pale young features became red and his nose runny. President Day passed him a handkerchief.

"Some time ago we decided to dedicate our lives to God," Whipple said forcefully. "I stopped smoking. Abner wanted to go to Africa to rescue souls, but I thought I would work among the poor in New York. Tonight we realized where it was that we really wanted to go."

"This is not then the decision of the moment?" President Day pressed.

"Oh, no!" Abner assured him, sniffling. "My decision goes back to Reverend Thorn's sermon on Africa three years ago."

"And you, Mr. Whipple? I thought you wanted to be a doctor, not a missionary."

"I vacillated for a long time between medicine and seminary, President Day. I chose the former because I thought I could serve God in two capacities."

The president studied his two able students and asked, "Have you prayed on this grave problem?"

"We have," Abner replied.

"And what message did you receive?"

"That we should go to Owhyhee."

"Good," Day said with finality. "Tonight I was inspired to go myself. But my work remains here."

"What shall we do now?" Whipple asked, as spring dawn came over the campus.

"Return to your rooms, say nothing to anyone, and on Friday meet with the committee of the American Board of Commissioners for Foreign Missions."

"Will they be here so soon?" Abner gasped in obvious delight.

"Yes. They have found that they are often needed after Keoki Kanakoa speaks." But noticing the joy in the young men's faces he warned, "Reverend Thorn, the leader of the group, is most adroit in uncovering young men who are guided by emotion and not by true dedication to Christ. If yours is not a profound commitment strong enough to sustain you for a lifetime, don't waste the time of Eliphalet Thorn."

"We are committed," Abner said firmly, and the two young men bade their president good night.

On Friday, John and Abner peered from behind curtains as the committee from the American Board of Commissioners for Foreign Missions gravely marched into Yale to hold sessions with various young men whose imaginations had been captured by Keoki Kanakoa. "That's Reverend Thorn," Abner whispered as the leader appeared. He was a tall, thin man, in a frock coat that reached his ankles and a black beaver hat that stretched far in the opposite direction. He had bushy black eyebrows, a hooked nose and a forbidding chin.

He looked like a judge, and the two young scholars were afraid.

But John Whipple's fear was misguided, for he had an easy time when he faced Eliphalet Thorn. The intense, gaunt face leaned forward, while the four lesser ministers listened, and Whipple heard the first kindly question: "Are you the son of Reverend Joshua Whipple, of western Connecticut?"

"I am," John replied.

"Has your father instructed you in the ways of piety?"

"He has." It was apparent that the committee recognized Whipple for what he was: a forthright, appealing, quick-witted young doctor from a God-fearing rural family.

"Have you experienced conversion?" Reverend Thorn asked quietly.

"When I was fifteen," John said, "I became much concerned about my future, and I vacillated between medicine and the clergy, and I chose the former because I was not certain in my heart that I understood God. I did not feel myself a pious youth, even though my father so reported me to the church. And then one day as I was trudging home from school I watched a whirling-broom of dust as it became larger and larger, and I am certain that I heard a voice say to me, 'Are you prepared to serve Me with your life?' and I said, 'Yes.' And I shook as I have never shaken before and the cloud of dust hovered about me for some time, but did not get into my nostrils. From that time on I have known God."

The five austere clergymen nodded approval, for this kind of sudden discovery of God had grown commonplace in New England, following the Great Awakening of 1740, and no man could guess how another would experience conversion, but Reverend Thorn bent his icy face forward and asked, "If you were originally confused, Mr. Whipple, between medicine and clergy, and if your confusion rose from the fact that you were not certain that you knew God, why, after God spoke directly to you, did you not change your decision and study for the ministry?"

"I was perplexed by this problem for a long time," Whipple confessed. "But I liked medicine and I concluded that as a doctor I could serve God in two capacities."

"That's an honest answer, Mr. Whipple. Return to your studies, and you will receive a letter from us within the week."

When John Whipple left the interview he was in a state of such exaltation that he neither looked at his roommate nor spoke to him. In fact, it was the most completely sublime moment in his life up to then and the one in which he felt closest to God. He had committed himself totally to God's work and he was certain that no power on earth could ever divert him from that commitment. Without speaking, he told his roommate that he had been accepted.

Abner Hale had an entirely different experience with the committee, for when he appeared with his ill-fitting suit, his stringy blond hair pasted down, his sallow face flushed and his pinched shoulders bending forward too eagerly, one of the more worldly of the ministers asked himself, "Oh, Lord, why dost Thou choose for Thy work such mangy men?"

"Are you converted?" Reverend Thorn asked impatiently.

"Yes," Abner said, but his explanation grew long-winded and turgid. He spent a good deal of time explaining just where the meadow was and how it lay in relation to the milking shed. But there was no doubt that he personally knew God.

"Why do you wish to serve as a missionary?" Reverend Thorn asked.

"Because ever since my conversion I have been determined to serve the

Lord," Abner affirmed hastily, too eager to convince, and it was apparent to the other members of the committee that the young man was making a bad impression on Thorn, who was chairman because he had done work in Africa and knew the problems faced by missionaries. After a previous meeting with would-be missionaries from Williams College he had told his committeemen, "The type of man we must avoid is the unbalanced young gentleman who is so certain of his personal relationship with God that he refuses to accept his subordinate role in the mission community at large. If we can weed such excitable men out now, we will save the mission much expense in money and confusion later." It was apparent that he was about to do some weeding, for he interrupted Abner's flow of piety and pointed out: "I asked you why you wanted particularly to be a missionary. You haven't explained."

"I always wanted to serve God," Abner repeated, "but I did not know that I was called to the mission field until the night of August 14, 1818."

"What happened then?" Reverend Thorn asked impatiently.

"You spoke on Africa, at the Congregational Church of Marlboro, Massachusetts. I date my true awakening from that night." Eliphalet Thorn then dropped his head and pinched his long nose, wondering what to ask next.

"What particularly did Reverend Thorn say that impressed you?" the worldly minister inquired waspishly.

"It is easy to answer that, sir, because ever since, his words have lived in my heart as an ideal. He spoke of the mission in Africa and said, 'We were as one family in Christ, each contributing his gifts, each dedicating himself to the common cause of saving souls.' From that night I started to train myself to become a member of such a family in Christ. I have learned to saw straight and to build, against the day when I was sent where there were no houses. I've taught myself to sew and to cook, and to keep accounts. From the time Reverend Thorn spoke I have never thought of myself only as a college student or as a seminary scholar. I have been in solemn training to become one humble member of a family sent to some far place to serve Christ."

The young man's statement was so unexpectedly contrite and so choked with the spirit of Christ's discipleship that even the worldly minister who had earlier classified Abner as mangy, which he decidedly was, awoke to his possibilities. "One of the members of the faculty," this minister said, gracefully concealing President Day's name, "has reported to us, Mr. Hale, that you are vain of your sanctity."

"I am," Abner confessed bluntly, "and I know I must fight against it, but none of my brothers or sisters are pious. Most of the young men here at Yale are not. From these comparisons I did acquire a sense of vanity. I said, 'The Lord has chosen me, but not those others.' I am ashamed that even my teachers saw this failing in me. But, sir, if you ask them again, I think you will find that they were speaking of me as I used to be. I have repeated over and over again the text, 'Every one that is proud in heart is an abomination to the Lord,' and I have taken it to heart."

Reverend Thorn was deeply impressed by the changes that seemed to have taken place in this young minister's character, for Abner's reference to August 14, 1818, awakened in the older man vivid reflections. He well remembered that meeting, for he had reported on it to his companions in Boston: "I spent the evening addressing a group in Marlboro, and I was distressed by the smug indifference of these well-stuffed farmers from their well-stuffed farms. I might as well have been preaching to their cattle, for all they understood of missionary zeal." Yet in that indifferent audience there had been one sallow-faced youth acquiring the dedication which now brought him before this committee. The coincidence was too great, Reverend Thorn thought, and on the sudden he saw Abner not merely as a stringy-haired, pasty-faced young man with obvious tendencies toward identifying himself with God, but as a heaven-sent answer to a most pressing problem within the Thorn family. So the leader of the committee of inquiry leaned far forward and asked, "Mr. Hale, are you married?"

"Oh, no, sir!" the young man replied with what could have been interpreted as distaste. "I have never sought the companionship . . ."

"Were you aware that the Board will send no minister abroad who is not married?"

"No, sir. I told you that I had learned to sew and cook . . ."

Reverend Thorn pressed his inquiry. "Do you perchance know some dedicated young female, someone who has experienced conversion, who has thought of going . . ."

"No, sir. I know no females."

Reverend Thorn appeared to sigh with relief and indicated that he had no further questions, but after the committee had advised Abner to wait at Yale for a week, pending their decision on his case, their leader made a slight correction: "It may take us longer than a week to discover our minds in your case, Mr. Hale. Don't become impatient." And after the young man had returned to his room, somewhat dazed by the complexity of the questions he had been asked, he found worse confusion, for his roommate reported how relatively simple his examination had been.

"They asked me a few questions about my faith," John Whipple recounted, "and then told me to get married as soon as the letter arrived next week."

"Whom will you marry?" Abner asked.

"My cousin, of course."

"But you've never spoken to her!"

"I will. Whom will you marry?"

"The committee treated me much differently," Abner confessed. "I really don't know what was in their minds."

A knock came at the door, and when Whipple answered it, towering Reverend Thorn, his Adam's apple dancing, said, "Will you please excuse us, Mr. Whipple?"

"Please sit down, sir," Abner stammered.

"I shall only be a moment," the gaunt reverend replied, and then with the directness of which he was noted, asked, "I wish to verify my report. I understand that if the Board nominates you for Owhyhee, you know of no young female whom you could invite . . ."

Abner was appalled at the idea that his careful life's plan should be frustrated in the bud because he knew no girls, so he said quickly, "Reverend Thorn, if that's all that's going to keep me . . . Reverend, I know I could ask my father . . . He's a very strong judge of character, sir, and if he picked a girl . . ."

"Mr. Hale, please. I didn't say that you would be forbidden to go. I didn't even say that you could go in the first place. I merely asked you, 'If we select you, do you know some appropriate female whom you could marry . . . well, rather promptly?' And you said no. All right."

"But, Reverend Thorn, if you would give me only two weeks," Abner pleaded, near tears, "I know my father . . ."

"I am much impressed with your piety, Mr. Hale," the older man began, on an entirely new tack.

"Then there's a chance?"

"What I wanted to speak to you about, Abner," said the tall, stern man in as kindly a manner as he could command, "is the fact that my sister in Walpole happens to have a daughter . . ." He paused in some embarrassment, hoping that Abner would anticipate his message and make its full delivery unnecessary. But honest Abner, with his hair pasted flat over his temples, could not imagine why the forbidding missionary was speaking of his sister, or his sister's daughter, and he looked with disarming innocence at Reverend Thorn, waiting for him to proceed.

The tall missionary swallowed his Adam's apple several times and wiped his forehead. "So, if you know of no young female . . ." he began.

"I'm sure my father could find one," Abner interrupted.

"And if the Board selects you . . ." Eliphalet Thorn doggedly continued.

"I pray it will!" Abner cried.

"I was wondering if you would entertain it kindly if I were to speak to my niece on your behalf?" The tall reverend swallowed heavily and stared at the sallow young man.

Abner gaped, then blurted, "You mean that you would help me to find a wife? Your own niece?" He thrust his hand out eagerly and pumped Reverend Thorn's for almost a minute. "That would be more than I dare ask," he cried joyously. "Really, Reverend Thorn . . ."

Withdrawing his hand, the gaunt missionary interrupted the effusive flow and added, "Her name is Jerusha. Jerusha Bromley. She is a year older than you, but a most devout young woman."

The mention of a specific name, and attributing to that shadowy name a corporeal being with a given age, quite overcame Abner and he started to weep, but quickly he mastered himself and said, "Reverend Thorn, too much has been happening today. Could we pray?" And in the small room at Yale College the experienced missionary and the emotional boy stood with their heads raised to heaven as Abner prayed: "Dear gentle and supervising Lord, I am unable to comprehend all that has occurred today. I have talked with Thy missioners, and they have said that perhaps I may join them. One of Thy servants has volunteered to speak to a young female of his family on my behalf. Beloved and powerful God, if these things come to pass through Thine aid, I shall be Thy servant to the end of my days, and I shall carry Thy word to the farthest islands." He dropped his head in humility and Reverend Thorn breathed a husky "Amen."

"It will take about two weeks," he said as he left.

Tact was something Abner Hale would never have. "John Whipple said that he would know within a week," he reminded the committeeman.

"Your case is different," Thorn replied.

"Why?" Abner demanded.

Reverend Thorn wanted to blurt out the truth: "Because you're an offensive, undernourished, sallow-faced little prig, the kind that wrecks any mission to which he is attached. There's not a man on my committee that really thinks you ought to be sent overseas, but I have a niece who has got to get married one of these days. And maybe if I can talk to her before she sees you, possibly I can force her into marrying you. That, young man, is what requires two weeks." Instead, with the self-control he had acquired in Africa, the sagacious minister recovered quickly and offered what he considered a rather clever explanation: "You see, Mr. Hale, Dr. Whipple will be going to Owhyhee as missionary doctor. If we accept you, and if you can find a bride, you will be going as an ordained minister. That's why your case requires more careful investigation."

The answer was so reasonable that Abner accepted it at once, and when John Whipple received his letter of acceptance and immediately dispatched both an acknowledgment to the Board in Boston and a proposal of marriage to his cousin in Hartford, Abner smugly smiled at his roommate's excitement, repeating over and over to himself the reassuring thought: "Anyone can be a missionary doctor. But to be a fully ordained minister requires careful investigation." But whenever he indulged in this vanity he invariably recalled his Biblical antidote and he recited this, too: "Every one that is proud in heart is an abomination to the Lord," after which he recalled the powerful words from Job: "Behold every one that is proud, and abase him. Look on every one that is proud, and bring him low." Thus his two natures warred.

REVEREND THORN, AS soon as his interrogations at Yale College were completed, hurried back to Boston and caught the stage running out to Marlboro, Massachusetts, to make inquiries as to the character and prospects of Abner Hale. Even as the coach neared Marlboro, he felt his old distaste for the village returning. The smug white barns in the smug spring landscape bespoke generations of thrifty, cautious people, proud of their possessions and deaf to the teachings of the Lord. His earlier impressions were fortified when he found the townspeople as smug as the outlying barns.

The school principal reported, airily: "Abner Hale! Ah, yes! There are so many Hale children it's rather difficult to keep them separated in one's mind. Abner, stringy hair, no good in games, worse in math, but rather gifted in the verbal processes that mark the cultivated mind. An austere young man who never pared his nails. Had good teeth, though."

"Was he pious?" Thorn pressed.

"To a fault," the airy schoolteacher replied. Then, sensing that this could be construed by his visitor to be a slur against piety, he quickly added, "By that I mean he was inclined toward priggishness, which I hold to be a fault, for does not the Bible counsel us: 'Dead flies cause the ointment of the apothecary to send forth a stinking savor: so doth a little folly him that is in reputation for wisdom and honor'?" And he held his hands up and smiled ingratiatingly.

"Would he make a good missionary?" Thorn asked in some anger, for he had been unable to follow the Biblical citation.

"Ah, yes!" the teacher cried. "To plunge into the unknown. To carry the good Word to the heathen. Yes, I think Abner Hale . . . Do I have the right boy? He was Gideon Hale's oldest? Bad complexion . . . really, an unlovely child? Yes, that's the one. Oh, yes! He'd make a fine missionary. Likes odd places and being alone."

The local minister was no better, and Reverend Thorn, schooled in the hard fields of Africa, could quickly spot where Abner had learned to weep. The doddering old man wheezed: "Little Abner Hale! I remember the year he found the Lord. It was in his father's meadow, and he stood transfixed . . ."

"Would he make a good missionary?" Thorn interrupted.

"Missionary!" the old man snapped. "Why should he leave Marlboro? Why not come back here and take my place, where he could do some good? Somebody ought to send some missionaries to Marlboro. Atheism, Deism, Unitarianism, Quakerism. Pretty soon there won't be a decent follower of John Calvin in all New England. If you want my opinion, young man, and I can see by your red face that you don't, you oughtn't to be coming here seducing our young men to go to Ceylon and Brazil and such places. Let 'em stay here and do some missionary work. But I haven't answered your question. Abner Hale'd make a wonderful missionary. He's gentle yet obstinate in the right. He's hard-working yet poetic in his love of nature. He's pious and he respects his parents. He's much too good to be sent to Ceylon."

On the dusty walk to the Hale farm, Reverend Thorn just about decided to give up his complex plan of first convincing the Board that they ought to take Abner and then convincing his niece Jerusha that she should do the same. All he had so far heard about the boy confirmed his committee's suspicions that Abner was a difficult, opinionated young man who was bound to cause trouble wherever he went, but then the gaunt missionary came upon the home of Abner Hale, and his mind was quickly changed.

From the road a line of maples led along a narrow lane to a wandering New England farmhouse with barn attached. For nearly a hundred and fifty years the buildings had known no paint and now stood grayish brown in the New England sun, which instead of brightening what could have been a lovely grassed-in square served instead to underscore the bleakness of the buildings. It was, recalled Reverend Thorn, the kind of Christian house in which he had been raised, the archetype in which to produce true piety. He understood Abner better from having seen merely the harsh outlines of his home.

Gideon Hale, angular and hard, completed the picture. Wrapping his skinny left leg completely around his right, so that one ankle locked into the other, he put his guest at ease by saying, "If you take Abner for Owhyhee you aren't getting an unmixed blessing, Reverend Thorn. He's not an average boy. He's not too easy to handle, either. He was pretty reasonable until he found conversion. Then he was certain that it was he and not me that was to interpret God's will. But he has enormous character. If you saw his marks in the Marlboro School, you'd find he started out poor in figures. But have you seen what he accomplished at Yale College? Only the best. In many ways he's an indifferent boy, Reverend Thorn, but where the right is concerned he's a rock. All my children are."

At supper Eliphalet Thorn saw the kind of granite from which Abner had been hewn. The nine little Hales, with no dirt on their faces and dressed in the cheapest kind of homespun, filed dutifully in and sat at a table marked by spotless cleanliness and very little food. "We will say prayers," wiry, hawk-eyed Gideon announced, and all heads were bowed. One by one the nine children recited appropriate verses from the Bible, after which Mrs. Hale, an almost dead bundle of bones, mumbled briefly, "God bless this house," which was followed by a five-minute prayer from her husband. These preliminaries over, Hale said, "And now will our guest consent to bless us with a word of prayer?" And the scene was so reminiscent of his own childhood that Reverend Thorn launched into a ten-minute blessing in which he recalled the pious highlights of his youth in a Christian family.

After the meager meal Gideon Hale took his entire brood into the front room, where a particularly dank smell proved that no fire was ever wasted, and he proposed formal evening prayers. His wife and daughters led in a spirited version of "All hail the power of Jesus' name," after which Gideon and the boys sang a hymn quite popular at the time: "Oh, for a closer walk with God." When they came to the stirring verse about idols, Reverend Thorn joined in forcefully, for the words could almost serve as the dominant motive of his life:

"The dearest idol I have known,
Whate'er that idol be,

Help me to tear it from Thy throne,
And worship only Thee."

Prayers by Gideon and his oldest boy followed, then an invitation to the visitor to say a few words. Reverend Thorn spoke long and passionately of the influence a Christian home can have upon a young man, or, as he remembered his sisters and the strong women into which they grew up, upon a young female. "It is from homes like this," he said, "that God picks those who are to carry forward His work on earth." And in the fullness of his talk he committed himself to sponsoring Abner Hale, for he knew then that while it must be granted that the young man was unpleasant now, in the future he was going to be a great and solid implement of the Lord.

When prayers were ended, and the children dismissed, the reverend asked Gideon for a sheet of paper on which to report to the Board. "Will it be a long letter?" Gideon asked anxiously.

"A short one," Eliphalet replied. "I have happy news to report."

Gideon, therefore, prudently tore his letter paper in half and handed his visitor one portion. "We waste nothing here," he explained, and as the tall missionary began his letter: "Brethren, I have visited the home of Abner Hale and have found that he comes from a family totally dedicated to God . . ." he happened to look at the narrow shelf where books were kept, and he saw with pleasure that they much resembled the books his family had collected—a battered copy of Euclid, Fox's *Book of Martyrs*, a speller of Noah Webster's, and a well-worn edition of John Bunyan standing beside a family Bible.

"I see with some pleasure," Reverend Thorn interrupted, "that this Christian family does not surrender to loose poetry and the novels which are becoming so popular in our land."

"This family is striving toward salvation," Gideon replied bleakly, and the thin-faced missionary finished the letter which would send Abner Hale to Owhyhee.

As Eliphalet Thorn stepped into the cool spring air, Mr. and Mrs. Hale accompanied him to the bright road that shimmered in moonlight. "If it were raining," Gideon said, "or if there were no moon, I'd saddle the horses . . ." Instead, he pointed the way to Marlboro with his powerful right arm. "It's not far," he assured his guest.

Reverend Thorn bade the couple good night and started off toward the dim lights of Marlboro, but after he had gone a short distance he stopped and turned to survey once more the bleak and arid home from which his protégé had come. The trees were in line; the fields were well trimmed; the cattle were fat. For the rest of the farm, one could see only penury, a complete lack of anything relating to beauty, and an austerity of purpose that was positively repellent, except that it so obviously called to the passer-by: "Here is a home that is dedicated to God." And as if to underline that fact, it was less than two hours after Reverend Thorn's departure that Abner Hale's oldest sister rushed weeping into her mother's room and stood trembling in the moonlight, crying, "Mother! Mother! I was lying awake thinking of the poor Africans about whom Reverend Thorn spoke tonight, and I began to shake, and I heard God's voice speaking directly to me."

"Did you have a sense of overwhelming sin?" her mother asked, slipping into a long coat which she used as a night wrap.

"Yes! I saw for the first time that I was hopelessly and utterly damned and that I had no escape."

"And you felt willing to surrender yourself totally to God?"

"It was as if a great hand were shaking me, violently, bringing me to my senses at last."

"Gideon!" the girl's mother cried in ecstasy. "Esther has been initiated into a sense of sin!"

The news was more pleasing than any other that Gideon Hale could have heard, and he cried, "Has she entered into a state of grace?"

"She has!" Mrs. Hale cried. "Oh, blessed Beulah Land, another sinner has found you!" And the three Hales knelt in the moonlight and gave ardent thanks to their bleak and forbidding Protector for having disclosed to still another member of their family the remorseless weight of sin under which mankind lives, the nearness of the inextinguishable fires to which ninety-nine out of every hundred human beings are forever and hopelessly committed, and the joyless, bitter path of salvation.

Within three days Reverend Thorn approached one of the most gracious villages ever to have developed in America: the tree-lined, white-clapboarded, well-gabled village of Walpole, near the Connecticut River in southwestern New Hampshire. It was a village to gladden the heart, for its glistening church steeple could be seen from afar, and the rolling hills that surrounded it were prosperous. It was to Walpole that Reverend Thorn's oldest sister Abigail had come when she had stubbornly insisted upon marrying the young Harvard lawyer, Charles Bromley, whose family had lived in Walpole for several generations.

Reverend Thorn had never approved of either the Bromleys or their village, for both bespoke good living rather than piety, and he rarely approached Walpole without a definite feeling that God must one day punish this sybaritic place, a conviction which deepened when he neared the Bromley home, a handsome, large, white three-storied house with many gables. He could hear, with some dismay, his sister playing English dances on the family organ. The dance terminated abruptly and a bright-faced, round-cheeked woman of forty rushed to the door, crying, "It's Eliphalet!" He, avoiding her kiss and looking about anxiously, was gratified to see that his niece Jerusha was not at home.

"Yes, she is!" Abigail corrected. "She's upstairs. Brooding. She's doing very poorly, but if you ask me, it's because she wants to. She refuses to get him out of her mind, and just when time is about to solve the problem, a letter reaches Boston from Canton or California, and she goes into a decline again."

"Have you thought of intercepting the letters?" Eliphalet asked.

"Charles would never permit that. He insists that any room which an individual holds within a house is that individual's castle. And foreign powers, even though they be corrupt, have an inalienable right of communicating with that castle."

Reverend Thorn was about to say he still could not understand why the Lord did not strike Charles Bromley dead, but since he had been wondering this for the past twenty-two years, and since the Lord stubbornly refused to do anything about it, he left his hackneyed observation unvoiced. What did gall him, however, was the fact that the Lord went out of his way to bless Bromley's various occupations.

"No," he said stiffly when his sister asked if he would stay with her. "I shall stop at the inn."

"Then why did you come so far?" Abigail asked.

"Because I have found an opportunity whereby your daughter may be saved."

"Jerusha?"

"Yes. Three times I have heard her say that she wanted to surrender her life to Jesus. To work wherever He sent her . . . as a missionary."

"Eliphalet!" his sister interrupted. "Those were the words of a young girl disappointed in love. When she spoke thus she hadn't heard from him for a year."

"It is in moments of disappointment that we speak our true thoughts," Thorn insisted.

"But Jerusha has everything she wants right here, Eliphalet."

"She wants God in her life, Abigail, and here she lacks that."

"Now, Eliphalet! Don't you dare . . ."

"Have you ever discussed with her the things she has told me?" Reverend Thorn pressed. "Have you had the courage?"

"All we know is that if she has recently received a letter from him, she's in heaven on earth and wants to get married as soon as he docks at New Bedford. But if six or seven months of silence have gone by, she swears she will become a missionary and serve in Africa . . . like her uncle."

"Let me speak to her now," Eliphalet proposed.

"No! She's in a fit of depression now and she'd agree to anything."

"Even, perhaps, to the salvation of her immortal soul?"

"Eliphalet! Don't talk like that. You know that Charles and I try to live good Christian lives . . ."

"Nobody could live a good Christian life in Walpole, New Hampshire," he muttered with disgust. "Vanity is all I see here. Look at this room! An organ not used for hymns. Novels. Books of lascivious poems. Money that should be going to missions going into ostentatious decoration. Abigail, a young Massachusetts man, dedicated to God, is about to sail as a missionary to Owhyhee. He has asked me to speak to you regarding Jerusha's hand."

Mrs. Bromley fell back in her damasked chair, then collected herself and called a servant. "Go fetch Mr. Bromley immediately," she ordered.

"I did not come here to talk to your husband," Eliphalet protested.

"It is my husband, not God, who is Jerusha's father," Abigail replied.

"Blasphemy!"

"No, love!"

The brother and sister sat in hateful silence until Charles Bromley, rotund, jovial, successful and overfed, came into the room. "Family fight?" he asked robustly.

"My brother Eliphalet . . ."

"I know who he is, dear. Just call him Phet." He laughed and added, "I've found in these matters that if you can get the litigants to start off on an informal basis it's so much better. If you call a man 'My brother Eliphalet,' why, out of self-respect you've almost got to wind up in court. What'r'ya up to, Phet?"

"A fine young man in the divinity school at Yale College is about to depart as a missionary to Owhyhee . . ."

"Where's Owhyhee?"

"Near Asia."

"Chinese?"

"No. Owhyheean."

"Never heard of it."

"And he was much impressed with what I had to say about my niece Jerusha."

"How did her name come up?" Bromley asked suspiciously.

"It's humiliating," Abigail sniffed. "Eliphalet's going around peddling our daughter. To get her married."

"I think it's very generous of him, Abby," Bromley exploded. "God knows I haven't had much success peddling her. One week she's in love with a sailor, whom she hasn't seen for three years. Abby, did that sailor ever even kiss her?"

"Charles!"

"And the next week she's in love with God and self-punishment on some distant island. Frankly, Phet, if you could find her a good husband I'd be obliged. I could then spend my efforts on her two sisters."

"The young man of whom I speak is Abner Hale," Thorn said stiffly. "Here's what his professors think of him. I visited his home . . ."

"Oh, Eliphalet!" his sister protested.

"In the guise of satisfying myself as to his Christian upbringing."

"And was it a good Christian home?" Bromley inquired.

"It was," Eliphalet replied. "In every respect."

Charles Bromley paced the handsomely decorated room for several moments and then said unexpectedly, "If you say it was a good Christian home, Phet, I'm sure it must have been horrible indeed. I can see young Abner Hale right now. Skinny, bad complexion, eyes ruined through too much study, sanctimonious, dirty fingernails, about six years retarded in all social graces. And yet, do you know, as I watch life go past here in Walpole, it's often those boys who in the long run turn out to be the best husbands."

In spite of himself, Reverend Thorn always admired the acuity of his brother-in-law's mind, so now he added what he had never intended saying: "Charles and Abigail, this young man is all the things Charles has just predicted. But he's also a dedicated man, extremely honest with himself, and one who is going to grow in grace. I wouldn't want him as a son-in-law now, but in ten years he'll be the best husband a woman could have."

"Is he as tall as Jerusha?" Abigail asked.

"Not quite, and he's a year younger."

Mrs. Bromley began to cry, but her gruff husband joshed her. "You know how it is, Phet! This sailor that Jerusha fell in love with . . . Some ridiculous dance here in Walpole . . . He's a cousin of the Lowells, I think . . . I've always thought it was her mother who fell most completely in love that night. These tall men with commanding eyes!" He patted his own rotund belly and coaxed his wife away from her tears.

"It amounts to this," Eliphalet said bluntly. "You have a daughter and I have a niece. We both love her very much. She's twenty-two, and she grows more confused each day. We must find her a husband. We must help her choose a way of life. I offer both."

"And I appreciate the offer," Charles said warmly. "God knows I've been helpless."

"Do you still wish to speak with her, Eliphalet?" Abigail asked, swayed by her husband's reactions.

"No, Abigail," her husband interrupted. "This is your problem, not Phet's."

"It is, isn't it?" Mrs. Bromley sniffed. "But what can I tell her about the young man?"

Eliphalet, having anticipated this, handed her a neatly written dossier on Abner Hale, including a minute description of the young minister, a transcript of his marks in college, an essay he had written on Church Discipline in Geneva, and a sketchy genealogy of the Gideon Hales of Marlboro, descendants of

Elisha Hale of Bucks, England. There was also a separate sheet which indicated that confidential letters could be addressed to John Whipple and President Day at Yale, to several Christian citizens at Marlboro, Massachusetts, and to Abner's sister Esther on the family farm. Abigail Bromley peeked first at the physical description: "Fine clear complexion but sallow; fine teeth."

Bad news she could have taken, but these hopeful comments collapsed her and she sobbed, "We don't even know where Owhyhee is." Then she accused her husband of lacking parental love: "Are you willing to send your daughter . . ."

"My dear," Charles said firmly, "the only thing I'm not willing to do is to abandon my child to fits of depression and religious mania in a small upstairs room. If she can find love and a rich life in Owhyhee, it's a damned sight better than she's doing in Walpole, New Hampshire. Now you go up and talk with her. I believe she's in a religious swing of the pendulum this month and she'll probably jump at the chance of marrying a minister and going to Owhyhee."

Therefore, as a result of Reverend Eliphalet Thorn's importunate trip to Marlboro and to Walpole, young Abner Hale, sweating the June days nervously at Yale, finally received his letter from Boston: "Dear Mr. Hale: As a result of careful inquiries conducted on our behalf by Reverend Eliphalet Thorn, the American Board of Commissioners for Foreign Missions is happy in the will of God to advise you that you have been chosen for mission duty in Owhyhee. You and your wife will depart Boston on September first in the brig *Thetis*. Captain Janders." There was enclosed a printed list of some two hundred articles that venturing missionaries were urged to carry with them:

3 razors	1 parasol	1 nest Hingham boxes
1 compass	3 scissors	1 pair bellows
21 towels	4 mugs	3 stone jugs
1 washbasin	3 chambers	1 pair andirons
1 calash	1 lantern	1 crane and hooks . . .

There was also a much shorter letter which said simply: "You would be well advised to present yourself in late July at the home of Charles and Abigail Bromley in Walpole, New Hampshire, there to meet their daughter Jerusha, a Christian girl of twenty-two. It occurs to me that you may require some few necessities to make yourself additionally presentable for this important meeting, so I enclose herewith three dollars, which you need not repay me." This letter was signed: "Eliphalet Thorn, of the African Mission."

IN THESE YEARS of the early 1820's there were many young ministers destined for Owhyhee, who, absorbed in study, found no time to make the acquaintance of marriageable young women and who were unexpectedly faced with the positive necessity of getting married within the space of a few weeks, for the A.B.C.F.M. resolutely refused to send an unmarried man to the islands and advised all such who wished to labor there for the Lord to inquire of their friends to see if a suitable female might be found, and there is no record of failure. Of course, some young ministers were rejected by the first nominees of their friends, but sooner or later all found wives, "not because the young fellers was handsome, but because New England turns out so danged many old maids. Our best boys is all out to sea." There was much argument as to whether the decision of the A.B.C.F.M. to reject unmarried men stemmed from understanding of what errors men living alone might fall into; or from specific knowledge of what life in Hawaii was like, and it seems probable that the latter was the case, for many whalers had often returned to New Bedford and Nantucket, if they bothered to come home at all, with faraway tales of generous maidens, endless supplies of coconuts and thatched houses in magnificent valleys. In all seaports one could hear the sad refrain:

> *"I want to go back to Owhyhee,*
> *Where the sea sings a soulful song,*
> *Where the gals is kind and gentle,*
> *And they don't know right from wrong!"*

From listening to such songs the Board concluded that, conditions being what they were, it would be prudent to require even young men who lived in a state of grace to take their own converted women with them. More potent however was the conviction that women were the civilizing agents, the visual harbingers of Christian life. The A.B.C.F.M. therefore required females, not only to keep the young missionaries in line, but also because a devoted young wife was herself a missionary of the most persuasive kind. And so the young men scattered over New England, meeting shy, dedicated girls for the first time on Friday, proposing on Saturday, getting married after three Sundays had elapsed for banns, and departing for Owhyhee immediately thereafter.

But none of these amorous odysseys was stranger than the one conducted by Abner Hale. When he left Yale in early July, duly ordained a minister in the Congregational Church, he was five feet four inches tall, weighed one hundred and thirty-six pounds, had a most sallow complexion, a somewhat stooped bearing, and stringy blond hair which he parted in the middle and pasted down with water, bear grease and tallow. He wore the black claw-hammer coat favored by ministers, had a skimpy cotton stock about his neck, and a new ten-inch-high beaver stovepipe hat which tapered inward about five inches above his head and then flared out to a considerable expanse of flatness on top. In his meager luggage, tied together in a box, he carried a small brush which he had been told to use in grooming his hat, and this was the one vanity of dress he allowed himself, for he reasoned that this hat, more than anything else, heralded him as a clergyman. His cowhide shoes, black with elastic webs, he ignored.

When the coach landed him at Marlboro, he stepped primly down, adjusted his tall hat, grabbed his box, and set out on foot for home. To his disappointment, no one in Marlboro bothered to congratulate him on having attained the ministry, for in his tall hat no one recognized him, and he reached the tree-lined lane leading to his home without having spoken to anyone, and there he stood in the hot dust, greeting, as he felt, for the last time, this bleak, unkindly home in which generations of Hales had been born, and it seemed to him so marked with love that he bowed his head and wept. He was standing in this manner when the younger children spotted him and led the whole family out to welcome him home.

They had barely assembled in the austere front room when Gideon Hale, brimming with pride at having a son who was ordained, suggested, "Abner, will you lead your first prayer in this house?" And Abner took as his text Leviticus 25:10, "And ye shall return every man unto his possession, and ye shall return every man unto his family," and poured forth a minor sermon. The family glowed, but when services were over, shy, gangling Esther took her brother aside and whispered, "The most wonderful thing has happened, Abner."

"Father told me, Esther. I am deeply pleased that you have entered into a state of grace."

"It would be vain of me to speak of that," the eager girl said, in blushes. "That wasn't what I meant."

"What then?"

"I have received a letter!"

"From whom?"

"From Walpole, New Hampshire."

It was now Abner's turn to blush, and although he did not wish to display unseemly interest he nevertheless had to ask, haltingly, "From . . ." But he could not bring himself to utter the name he had not yet spoken to anyone. It seemed to him so improbable that he should even know of Jerusha Bromley, let alone be on his way to propose to her, that he would not profane her name by mentioning it.

Esther Hale took her brother's two hands and assured him, "It is from one of the sweetest, most considerate, gentle and Christian young women in all New England. She called me sister and asked for my prayers and guidance."

"May I see the letter?" Abner asked.

"Oh! No! No!" Esther protested vigorously. "It was sent to me in confidence. Jerusha said . . . Isn't that a sweet name, Abner? It was Jotham's mother's name in Kings. She said that everything was happening so rapidly that she had to confide in a trustworthy friend. You would be amazed at the things she asked me."

"About what?" Abner asked.

"About you."

"What did you say?"

"I wrote a letter of eighteen pages, and although it was a secret letter between my sister and me . . ."

"Your sister?"

"Yes, Abner. I'm convinced from the manner of her letter that she intends marrying you." Esther smiled at her confused brother and added, "So although it was a secret letter, I made a copy of one of the eighteen pages."

"Why?"

"Because on that page I listed every single one of your faults, as a young woman would assess them, and in sisterly love, Abner, I would like to give you that important page."

"I would like to have it," Abner said weakly, and he took the finely composed page, with its flowing penmanship, to his room and read: "Dearest Jerusha, whom I hope one happy day to have the right of calling sister, thus far I have told you only of my brother's virtues. They are many and I have not exaggerated them, for as you can guess, living in close harmony in the bosom of a large and closely bonded family provides even the dullest intellect with ample opportunity to penetrate even the most secret recesses of another's mind and temperament. Against the day, therefore, when we may meet as true sisters, and desirous of having you judge me as having been completely honest with you in true Christian principle as enjoined by our Lord in Ephesians 4:25, 'Wherefore putting away lying, speak every man truth with his neighbor: for we are members one of another,' I must now advise you of the weaknesses of my devout and gentle brother. First, Jerusha, he is not skilled in pretty manners and will surely disappoint you if you seek them foremost in a husband. That he could learn to be more gracious I feel sure, and perhaps under your patient counsel he might one day become almost civilized, but I doubt it. He is rude and honest. He is thoughtless and forthright, and from having watched my mother deal with such a husband I know how trying it can be at times, but in all of my life I have not seen my father make much change, so I must conclude that this is something which women prize but which they rarely find. Second, he is thoughtless where women are concerned, for I have lived with him in closest intimacy for nineteen years, and I have shared his secrets and he mine, and never in that time has he thought to give me a present other than some useful object like a straight-edge or a journal. I am sure he does not know that flowers exist, even though our Lord saw to it that His temple in Jerusalem was constructed of finest materials and sweet woods. In this also he is much like his father. Third, he is not a handsome young man and his habit of stooping makes him less so. He is not careful of his clothes, nor of his person, although he does wash his mouth frequently to avoid giving offense in that quarter. On any day in Marlboro I see young men who are more handsome than my brother, and I suppose that one day I shall marry one of them, but I have not the slightest hope that this handsomer man will have the list of favorable attributes which I have just enumerated. But I know you will often wish that Abner stood a little straighter, wore linen a little whiter, and had a more commanding presence. He will never have these graces and if you seek them primarily, you will be grievously disappointed. Finally, sister Jerusha, for I make bold to call you this in the most fervent hope that you will accept my brother, for the spirit of joy I find in your letter is one that Abner sorely needs, I must warn you that he is both grave and vain, and if he were not destined for the ministry these would be insufferable traits, but his gravity and vanity spring from the same cause. He feels that God has spoken to him personally, as indeed He has, and that this separates him from all other men. This is a most unpleasant trait in my brother, and I can now say so because God has spoken to me, too, and I judge from your letter that He has come to you, and I find neither in you nor in myself the vanity that mars my brother. I have found in God's presence a sweetness that I never knew before. It makes me gentler with my sisters, more understanding of my little brothers. I take more joy in feeding the chickens and churning the butter. If only Abner could surrender his vanity in the presence of the Lord, he would be a near-perfect husband for you, Jerusha. As it is, he is a good man, and if you should elect him, I pray that you will keep this letter with you and that you will find as the years pass that your unseen sister told you the truth."

There was another letter waiting at Marlboro. It came from Reverend Eliphalet Thorn and said simply: "While you're at your father's, work each day in the sun with your hat off. If Jerusha accepts you, I'll perform the ceremony."

So for two weeks Abner worked in the fields as he had as a boy, and in time he grew bronzed and the sallow skin under his deep-set eyes tightened, so that when it came time for him to say farewell to his large and loving family he was as close to being handsome as he would ever be, but the relaxation from grimness that his sister Esther had sought to encourage had not taken place. This was partly because the young minister had a presentiment that this was the very last time on earth that he would see these eleven people, this barn, that meadow where he had known conversion, this warm fellowship of a Christian family. He shook hands with his mother, for he was never much of an embracer, and then with his father, who suggested cautiously, "Since you're leaving, maybe I ought to hitch up the wagon."

He was obviously relieved when his son replied, "No, Father. It's a good day. I'll walk."

"I'd like to give you a little money to go away with, Abner," his father began, hesitantly.

"That's not necessary," Abner replied. "Reverend Thorn kindly sent me three dollars."

"That's what Esther told me," Gideon Hale replied. Thrusting out a well-worn hand, he said stiffly, "May the Lord go with you, son."

"May you continue to live in grace," Abner replied.

He then said good-bye to Esther and for the first time realized that she was growing into quite a fine young woman. He had a pang of regret and thought: "I ought to have known Esther better." But now it was too late, and he stood in a welter of confusion when she kissed him, thus paving the way for each of his other sisters to do the same.

"Good-bye," he said chokingly. "If we do not meet again here on earth, we shall surely reassemble at His feet in heaven. For we are heirs of God and joint heirs of Jesus Christ to an inheritance uncorrupted, undefiled and limitless and which fadeth not away." With this he sternly moved away from his bleak parents and their bleak home with its unpainted boards and unlovely windows. For the last time he walked down the lane, out into the dusty road, and on to Marlboro, where the coach picked him up for New Hampshire and an adventure which he dreaded.

Arrived at the Old Colony Inn at Walpole, Abner washed and took from his papers one that had been written by his sister. Numerous items were set forth, and numbered, the first being: "Upon arrival wash, brush yourself thoroughly, and have the messenger deliver this note to Mrs. Bromley: 'My dear Mrs. Bromley, May I have the pleasure of calling upon you this afternoon at three?' Then sign your name and the name of the inn, in case one of the family should deem fit to come to escort you in person."

The letter had scarcely been dispatched when Abner heard a hearty male voice crying: "You got a young fellow from Massachusetts staying here?" And before Abner had time to read his sister's careful instructions for the first visit, his door was burst open and he was greeted by a generously filled-out New Hampshire gentleman who laughed, "I'm Charles Bromley. You must be nervous as a colt."

"I am," Abner said.

"You look a lot browner and tougher than everybody said."

"Reverend Thorn told me to do some work in the fields."

"Do me a lot of good to do the same. What I came for, though, was to tell you that we won't hear of you waiting around this inn till three o'clock. Walk right across the common with me, and meet the family."

"It won't be an imposition?" Abner asked.

"Son!" Lawyer Bromley laughed, "We're as nervous as you are!" And he started to lead young Hale home, but on the spur of the moment stopped and called to the innkeeper, "What are the charges here?"

"Sixty cents a day."

"Hold the bill for me. These young ministers don't earn much money." He then took Abner out into the midsummer perfection of Walpole. There was the village church, glistening white in its pre-Revolutionary splendor, the massive houses, the giant elms, the marvelous green common with a fretwork bandstand in the middle where Charles Bromley often delivered patriotic addresses, and straight ahead the lawyer's residence from which Mrs. Bromley and her two younger daughters peered like spies.

"He's not as bad as they said!" Charity Bromley whispered to her sister.

"He's not very tall," Mercy sniffed. "He's more your size, Charity, then Jerusha's."

"Now be composed, girls," Mrs. Bromley commanded, and all sat primly in large chairs. The door was kicked open in Charles Bromley's familiar way, and a young man in black carrying a large stovepipe hat entered the room. He walked firmly across the carpeting, bowed to Mrs. Bromley, and said, "I am honored that you would invite me to your home." Then he looked at Charity, nineteen and pretty, with curls to her shoulders, and said with a tremendous blush and a deep bow, "I am especially pleased to make your acquaintance, Miss Bromley."

"She's not Jerusha!" young Mercy squealed, attacked by a furious set of giggles.

Mr. Bromley joined the laughter and said, "You know how girls dawdle, Abner. You've got sisters. You'll know Jerusha when she comes down. She's the pretty one."

Abner felt a wave of paralyzing embarrassment sweep over him. Then he became aware that Mrs. Bromley had addressed a question to him: "Do you have a sister Mercy's age? She's twelve."

"I have a brother twelve," he fumbled.

"Well, if you have a brother twelve," Mercy said brightly, "you can't very well have a sister twelve, too."

"Could be twins," Charity laughed.

"No twins," Abner explained precisely.

"So then he doesn't have a sister twelve!" Mercy triumphed.

"What Mrs. Bromley was going to say, Abner," explained Mr. Bromley, "was that if you did have a sister of twelve, you'd understand why we sometimes would like to drown this little imp."

The idea startled Abner. He had never heard his parents say such a thing, even in jest. In fact, he had heard more joking in these first few minutes with the Bromleys than he had heard in his entire family life of twenty-one years. "Mercy looks like too fine a child to be drowned," he mumbled in what he took to be gallantry, and then he gaped, for coming down the stairs and into the room was Jerusha Bromley, twenty-two years old, slim, dark-eyed, dark-haired, perfect in feature and with gently dancing curls which framed her face, three on each side. She was exquisite in a frail starched dress of pink and white sprigged muslin, marked by a row of large pearl buttons, not flat as one found them in cheaper stores, but beautifully rounded on top and iridescent. They dropped in an unbroken line from her cameoed throat, over her striking bosom, down to her tiny waist and all the way to the hem of her dress, where three spaced bands of white bobbin lace completed the decoration. Abner, looking at her for the first time, choked. "She cannot be the sister they thought of for me," he thought. "She is so very lovely."

With firm step she came across the room and offered Abner her hand, saying in a low gentle voice, "The wisest thing I have done in my life was to write to Esther. I feel as if I already know you, Reverend Hale."

"His name's Abner!" Mercy cried, but Jerusha ignored her.

It was a long, hot, enchanting afternoon from one o'clock to six. Abner had never before encountered such wit and relaxed laughter, marred only by the fact that upon his dusty arrival at the inn he had drunk enormous quantities of water, so that from four o'clock on he needed more than anything else a chance to go to the privy, a predicament which had never before faced him and with which he was incapable of coping. Finally, Mr. Bromley said openly, "Just occurred to me, we've been keeping this young man talking for five hours. I'll bet he'd like to visit the outhouse." And he led the blushing young minister to the most enjoyable relief he had ever experienced.

At dinner Abner was aware that the entire Bromley family was watching his manners, but nevertheless he felt that he was conducting himself fairly well, a fact which gave him some pleasure, for although he thought it was stupid to judge a man by his manners, he suddenly realized that he wanted this pleasant family to think well of him.

"We were all watching to see if you took the cherry pits out of your mouth with your fingers," Mercy teased.

"We learned not to do that at college," Abner explained. "At home I used to spit them out." The family laughed so merrily that Abner discovered he had made a joke, which had not been his intention.

At eight Mr. Bromley asked if Abner would lead evening worship, and he did so, taking for his text one that Esther had selected, after much study, for the occasion, Genesis 23:4: "I am a stranger and a sojourner with you: give me a possession of a buryingplace with you, that I may bury my dead out of my sight." Charles Bromley found the passage excessively gloomy for a beginning preacher of twenty-one but he had to confess admiration for the adroitness with which Abner converted death into a glowing assurance of life. Abner, for his part, held that the manner in which Mrs. Bromley played the organ for hymns and the way in which her three daughters sang them were both unnecessarily ornate. But granting these differences, the service was a success.

Then Mr. Bromley said, "To bed, family! These youngsters must have much they want to discuss." And with a wide sweep of his arms he projected his brood upstairs.

When they were gone, Jerusha sat with her hands folded, looking at the stranger in her house, and said, "Reverend Hale, your sister told me so much about you that I feel no need for asking questions, but you must have many that perplex you."

"I have one that surpasses all others, Miss Bromley," he replied. "Do you have unshaken confidence in the Lord?"

"I do. More than my mother or father, more than my sisters. I don't know how this happened, but I do."

"I am pleased to hear that you are not a stranger to our Lord and Master," Abner sighed contentedly.

"Have you no other questions!" Jerusha asked.

Abner looked startled, as if to say, "What other questions are there?" But he asked, "Are you willing, then, to follow blindly His grand purpose of life, even if it takes you eighteen thousand miles away from home?"

"I am. Of that I am quite certain. For some years now I have had a calling. Of late it has grown most powerful."

"Do you know that Owhyhee is a pagan land, barbarous with evil?"

"One night I heard Keoki speak at church. He told us about the dark practices of his people."

"And you are nevertheless willing to go to Owhyhee?"

Jerusha sat extremely primly for several moments, fighting down her natural inclinations, but she could not do so, and finally she blurted, "Reverend Hale, you're not hiring me to go to Owhyhee! And you're not investigating me to see if I should be made a minister! You're supposed to be asking me if I want to marry you!"

From his chair some few feet away, Abner swallowed very hard. He was not surprised by Jerusha's outburst, for he was aware that he knew nothing of women, and perhaps this was the way they were expected to act. So he did not panic. Instead he looked at his hands and said, "You are so beautiful, Miss Bromley. You are so much more lovely than I had ever a right to expect, that I cannot even now comprehend that you might consent to marry me. I am astonished that you would bother with me, so I have been thinking that you must have some powerful call to the Lord. It seemed safe and reasonable for us to talk about that."

Jerusha left her chair, walked to Abner and kneeled on the floor so that she could look up into his eyes. "Are you saying that you're afraid to propose to me, Reverend Hale?"

"Yes. You are so much more beautiful than I expected."

"And you're thinking, 'Why isn't she already married?' "

"Yes."

"Reverend Hale, don't be embarrassed. All my family and friends ask the same question. The simple truth is, three years ago, before I came to know the Lord, I was in love with a New Bedford man who came here on a visit. He was everything you aren't, and immediately everyone in Walpole decided that he was a perfect husband for me. But he went away and in his absence . . ."

"You used God as a substitute?"

"Many think so."

"And now you wish to use me as a substitute, too?"

"I imagine that my mother and sister think so," Jerusha replied quietly. The moment of emotion having passed without Abner's even having touched her hands, she rose demurely and returned to her own chair.

"Yet my sister Esther thought that your letter was sincere," Abner reflected.

"And when she thought so," Jerusha said wryly, "she did her best to convince me to marry you. If Esther were here now . . ."

Aloofly, two strange lovers, like continents undiscovered, sat apart, with oceans of uncertainty between them, but as the unique day drew to an end, Jerusha found that Abner Hale really did believe on the Lord and that in his heart he was truly afraid to take a woman to wife who was not wholly committed to God; whereas Abner learned that it was unimportant whether Jerusha Bromley was in a state of grace or not; what counted was the fact that she was willing to remain an old maid forever unless marriage brought her the honest passion of which life was capable.

On these mutual discoveries the first interview ended, except at the door to the Bromley home Abner asked quietly, "May I be so bold as to grasp your hand tenderly before I go . . . as a token of my deep esteem for you?" And when he first touched the body of Jerusha Bromley, spinster of Walpole, in what was for him the most daring gesture of his young life, a surge of such power sped from her finger tips to his that he stood for a moment transfixed, then hurried in confusion across the sleeping common and to his inn.

Before eight the next morning all the kitchens of Walpole—at least all whose members attended the local church—knew of the precise state of the Hale-Bromley courtship, for little Mercy had been spying, and now she went from house to house relating breathlessly, "Well, he didn't really kiss her, because that would have been improper on a first visit, but he did take her hand in his, like in an English novel."

At eight-thirty, Mercy and her sister Charity called at the inn and advised their possible brother-in-law that he was about to be spirited away on a family picnic, and he asked impulsively, "Is . . . Miss Bromley attending?" And Mercy replied, "Jerusha? Naturally. How else is she going to become engaged?" But Abner, foreseeing another day spent far from a privy, refused to eat any breakfast or drink either milk or water, so that by the time the picnic baskets were opened on a New Hampshire hill, he was famished and ate prodigiously, after which he and Jerusha went for a walk along a stream, and he asked, "How do you find it possible to leave such a lovely place?" And she replied cryptically, "Not all of those who followed Jesus were peasants."

He stopped by a bending tree and said, "I could not sleep last night, Miss Bromley, thinking that I managed badly in our conversation, but then it seemed that I hadn't managed so poorly after all, because as a result of our talking I came to know you and to appreciate your qualities. Any fool could see that you were beautiful, so there was no sense talking about that, but in other circumstances we might have said a great deal last night without having discovered as much as we did."

"What we found out," Jerusha replied, holding onto a branch, "is that we are both stubborn people, but that we both honor the Lord."

Standing more than six feet from her, he asked, "Would you be willing to go to Owhyhee . . . on those conditions?"

"I would, Reverend Hale."

He swallowed, scratched at the tree trunk and asked, "Does this mean we are engaged?"

"It does not," she said firmly, holding onto her branch and swinging back and forth provocatively.

"Why won't you marry me?" he asked in great confusion.

"Because you haven't asked me," she said stubbornly.

"But I said . . ."

"You said, 'Would you be willing to go to Owhyhee?' and I said, 'Yes.' But that certainly didn't mean I'd be willing to go all the way around Cape Horn to Owhyhee with a man who wasn't my husband."

"Oh, I never intended . . ." Abner crimsoned in dismay and tried to make several different apologies, with no success. Finally, he stopped and looked at the slim girl in the silky summer dress, swinging on the bough so that she seemed to be dancing, and without her teasing him more, he discovered what he should say. He left the tree trunk and kneeled in the dust beside the faltering stream. "Miss Bromley, will you marry me?" he asked.

"I will," she replied, adding nervously, "I was so afraid, Reverend Hale, that you were going to say, 'Will you marry me and go with me to Owhyhee?' That would have spoiled it all."

She held down her hands and helped him to his feet, expecting to be embraced, but he dusted his knees and said in a burst of real joy, "We must advise your parents." Smiling wryly, she agreed, and they went back to the picnic area, but Mr. and Mrs. Bromley were sound asleep. Mercy and her sister were not, and could guess what had happened, so Mercy asked, "Are you engaged?"

"Yes," Jerusha said.

"Has he kissed you?"

"Not yet."

"Abner! Kiss her!" the sisters cried, and in the hot sun of a late July day, Abner Hale kissed Jerusha Bromley for the first time. It wasn't much, as kisses go, and the audience was nervously distracting, but when it ended he amazed himself by grabbing first Charity and kissing her and then Mercy, and crying, "You're the dearest sisters in the whole world!" Then he sat down, dazed, and confessed, "I never kissed a girl before but now I've kissed three of them!"

Mercy awakened her parents, screaming, "They've done it!" And there were more deep greetings, after which Charity produced a piece of paper on which she had outlined numerous dates: "We can post the banns on Sunday, that's the fifth, and on Monday the twentieth you can get married."

Mercy cried, "We'll turn Daddy's office into a sewing room and the cloth we've bought can be made into dresses and sheets . . ."

"You've bought the cloth?" Abner asked.

"Yes," Charity confessed. "Three weeks ago Jerusha decided to marry you, after she read Esther's letter. She told us, 'We'll let him come to visit just in case his sister's a wicked little liar.' But we all knew she wasn't. Anyway, Daddy must have got fifteen different letters about you, and we knew."

"Did all of you read all the letters?" Abner asked in embarrassment.

"Of course!" Mercy cried. "And the part I liked best is where you learned to cook and sew and keep house . . . in case you became a missionary. I told Jerusha to marry you quick, because then she'd never have to do any work at all."

But that evening, as the two younger sisters took their new brother-in-law-to-be back to the inn so that he could wash up before supper, Mercy pointed to a large white house and said, "That's where the sailor came to visit. He was a very handsome man, although I was only nine at the time, so he may have seemed taller than he really was."

"What happened?" Abner asked cautiously, and he saw Charity pinch her sister's arm.

"Ouch! Charity's trying to make me keep still, Abner, but I thought somebody ought to tell you. He was much handsomer than you are, but not as nice."

"Jerusha would never have married him, anyway," Charity added.

"Why not?" Abner asked.

"It takes a certain type of girl to marry a sailor," Charity said.

"What type?"

"The Salem type. The New Bedford type. Women who are willing to have their husbands away for years at a time. Jerusha is not that kind of woman, Abner. She lives on affection. Do be sweet with her."

"I shall be," he said, and on the marriage morning, when Reverend Thorn arrived by coach from Boston to conduct the ceremonies for his niece, he found his young minister friend from Yale in a state of gentle hypnosis. "I can't believe that I am going to marry this angel," Abner exploded, eager for someone to talk with after the three weeks of sewing and parties and meeting friends. "Her sisters have been unbelievable. Eighteen women were at their home all last week making me clothes. I've never known . . ."

He showed the tall missionary six barrels of clothing made by the women of Walpole, books donated for the mission in Owhyhee, and crockery. "I have experienced an outpouring of the spirit in this town that I never knew existed," Abner confessed.

"My sister Abigail is a girl who always made friends quickly," Eliphalet Thorn admitted. "I am so glad that you and Jerusha have found each other in God. Now if you'll excuse me, I'll step along to the house to complete arrangements with Charles."

But as he left Abner's room, the innkeeper called him and said, "If you're heading for Bromley's, you can take along this letter which just came in the mail," and he handed the missionary several sheets of paper folded upon themselves to form an envelope, and it was from Canton, in China, and had been on the sea for many months to London and to Charleston in South Carolina and to New Bedford. It was addressed to Miss Jerusha Bromley, Walpole, New Hampshire, and was written in a strong, fine hand. Reverend Thorn studied the letter for a long time and rationalized: "What chance is there that the innkeeper will mention this letter before Jerusha leaves Walpole? Not very much, I should think. But there is still a chance, so I must not burn it. Besides, to do so would be a sin. But if I now honestly declare, 'Eliphalet Thorn, you are to deliver that letter to your niece, Jerusha Bromley,' my intentions will be clear. Then, if I tuck it deep inside my inner pocket, like this, it would be only logical for me to forget it. Three months hence I can post it to my sister with apologies. And with Jerusha already married, why would Abigail want to bother her daughter with such a letter? Abigail's no fool." So he hid the letter and said in a loud voice as he walked across the common, "I must give this letter to Jerusha immediately I see her."

That afternoon Abner Hale, twenty-one, married Jerusha Bromley, twenty-two, whom he had known two weeks and four days, and on the next morning the young couple, accompanied by fourteen barrels of missionary goods, set out for Boston and the hermaphrodite brig *Thetis,* 230 tons, bound for Owhyhee.

The mission party assembled for the first time on August 30, 1821, in a brick church on the Boston waterfront. When Abner and Jerusha entered, John Whipple saw them and gasped with surprise at the beauty of the young woman who stood hesitantly in a fawn-colored coat and a pale blue poke bonnet that neatly framed her dancing brown curls and flashing eyes.

"Amanda!" he whispered to his wife. "Look at Abner!"

"Is that Abner?" the tiny bride from Hartford asked. "You said . . ."

"Hello, Abner!" Whipple called softly. When the couples met, Whipple said, "This is my wife, Amanda."

"This is Mrs. Hale," Abner replied, and they proceeded to meet the other nine mission couples.

Of the eleven young men convened in the church, all were under the age of twenty-eight, and nine were less than twenty-four. One had been married for two years, another for almost a year. The remaining nine had been married much as Abner and Jerusha. Friends had dispatched hastily written word pictures of unmarried girls of known piety, and weddings had been abruptly arranged, usually on the first meeting between the young people. Of these nine hurried marriages, only John Whipple and his tiny cousin Amanda had known each other for more than four days before banns were announced. Of the remaining eight couples, six, when it came time to sail, had not yet relaxed sufficiently for husband and wife to call each other by their first names, and that included Reverend and Mrs. Hale.

Few pilgrims have ever set forth upon great adventure with clearer directions than those promulgated by the American Board of Commissioners for Foreign Missions in the little brick church. Tall, godlike Eliphalet Thorn, drawing upon his hard years in Africa, said bluntly, "Brothers, you are about to immerse yourselves in one of the most difficult of all ventures, mission work in a pagan land. You are severely admonished to abide by these rules. First, all property is to be held in common. You are a family, and as a family you will receive from us here in Boston regular supplies which belong to no man or woman, but to the family in general. If you who are farmers raise fruit and sell the surplus, the proceeds belong to the family. If you who are good seamstresses sew clothing and sell it to the sailors in Owhyhee, the returns belong to the family. You are a family in Christ, and it is as a family that you own your houses, your lands, your schools and your churches.

"Second, you are abjured from interfering in the government of the islands, for you must constantly repeat to yourselves the injunction of our Lord, as found in Matthew: 'And they brought unto him a penny. And he saith unto them, Whose is this image and superscription? They say unto him, Caesar's. Then saith he unto them, Render therefore unto Caesar the things which are Caesar's; and unto God the things that are God's.' You are specifically abjured from participating in government. You are sent not to govern but to convert. You are directed to accomplish two divine missions: bring the heathen to the Lord and civilize him. How he governs himself is his concern. How he learns to know Christ and the alphabet is your concern, for remember that until he learns to read, he cannot know the Bible and God's redeeming word. Therefore, to speed this worthy end we are sending with you three full fonts of type, and you are to put into the language of Owhyhee the Holy Bible and such other learning as the Owhyheeans are capable of mastering. Provide them with a written language, and they will glorify the Lord.

"Third, there is an inborn inclination on the part of all New England men to trade, and I suspect from the natural abilities which I have found among you as I have studied your careers, that many of you would do conspicuously well in business, but you have been called to serve the Lord, and it is to this business that you must attend. You will receive no salary, and you are expected to earn none. Your sole job is to serve the Lord, and if you do this with all your ability, you will have no vain and idle time for business pursuits.

"Finally, you are to lift up the heathen step by step until he stands with you. Within the passage of years the schools you build must be taught by him, and before you leave the scene, the pulpits you erect and from which you deliver the word of God must be filled by him. You are setting forth to save immortal souls for the harvest of God."

After Reverend Thorn had taken up questions concerning medical practices to be followed, an elderly, white-haired minister who had worked in many parts of America and in Ceylon spoke briefly. "Brothers in God," he said simply, "you are not entering upon a limited mission. You are to aim at nothing less than the complete regeneration and salvation of a society. If children now die, they are to be saved. If minds are now ignorant, they are to be enlightened. If idols flourish, they are to be supplanted by the word of Jesus. And if a road is mired and useless, it is to be paved and made straight. If there is among you any man or woman with a hundred capacities, he will find in Owhyhee full outlet for all of them. Spend yourselves in Christ so that in later years it may be said of you, 'They came to a nation in darkness; they left it in light.' "

O N THE LAST day of August the mission family was introduced to the ship on which they would live during the six months required for the slow passage to Owhyhee. Reverend Thorn led them from the brick church, where they had engaged in morning prayers, onto the dock where a large three-masted ship lay anchored while her cargo of whale oil was being unloaded.

"That's a substantial ship," Jerusha observed to some of the other women. "A person shouldn't get too seasick on that," she added hopefully.

"That's not the mission ship," Reverend Thorn corrected. "Yours lies ahead."

"Oh, no!" one of the women gasped as she saw the squat and ugly little brig *Thetis.* It looked scarcely large enough for a river boat.

"Are we sailing in that?" Abner asked shakenly of John Whipple.

"It says *Thetis,*" Whipple replied dourly.

The brig was almost the smallest two-master that could successfully round Cape Horn at the farthest tip of South America. It was seventy-nine feet long, twenty-four feet wide, and drew only a dozen feet when loaded. Jerusha, upon inspecting it more closely from the quay, confided to Amanda Whipple, "It looks as if it might sink if twenty-two missionaries step aboard."

"You're free to inspect the *Thetis,*" a rough voice called, and for the first time they met Captain Retire Janders, a rugged forty-year-old master with a circle of sandy beard that framed his clean-shaven face from one ear, down the jaw line, under the chin and up to the other ear, making him look like a ruddy-faced boy peering through a hedge.

As Reverend Thorn led his family aboard he introduced each couple formally to Captain Janders. "The captain has been instructed to look after you on this long and tedious voyage," Thorn explained. "But his first job is to run his ship."

"Thank you, Reverend," Captain Janders growled. "Sometimes folks don't understand that a brig at sea ain't like a farm in Massachusetts." He led the missionaries forward to where a hatch stood open, and deep in the bowels of the brig they could see their boxes and books and barrels. "It's impossible, absolutely and forever impossible for anybody to touch anything that's down in that hold before we get to Hawaii. So don't ask. You live with what you can store in your stateroom."

"Excuse me, Captain," young Whipple interrupted. "You pronounce the name of the islands Hawaii. We've been calling them Owhyhee. What is their accurate name?"

Captain Janders stopped, stared at Whipple and growled, "I like a man who wants to know facts. The name is Hawaii. Huh-va-eee. Accent on second syllable."

"Have you been to Hawaii?" Whipple asked, carefully accenting the name as it should be.

"You learn well, young man," Captain Janders grunted. "I've sure been to Hawaii."

"What's it like?"

The captain thought a long time and said, "It could use a few missionaries. Now this hatchway aft is where you come up and down from your quarters," and he led the twenty-two down a dark, steep and narrow flight of stairs so that each wife thought: "If the boat rolls I'll never be able to manage this."

They were little prepared for what Captain Janders now showed them. It was a gloomy, grimy, 'tween-decks area twenty feet long—less than the length of four grown men—and fifteen feet wide, out of which a substantial portion had been stolen for a rough table shaped in the form of a half-circle, through the middle of which rose the brig's mainmast. "Our public living area," Captain Janders explained. "It's a mite dark at present but when a stout storm comes along and rips away our sails, we'll take that extra suit from in front of the portholes, and things'll be a bit lighter."

The missionaries stared numbly at the minute quarters and Jerusha thought: "How can twenty-two people live and eat here for six months?" But the real astonishment came when Captain Janders kicked aside one of the canvas curtains that led from the public quarters into a sleeping area.

"This is one of the staterooms," Janders announced, and the missionaries crowded their heads into the doorway to see a cubicle built for dwarfs. Its floor space was exactly five feet ten inches long by five feet one inch wide. It had no windows and no possible ventilation. The wall facing the canvas was formed by the brig's port side and contained two boxed-in-bunks, each twenty-seven inches wide, one atop the other. One of the side walls contained two similar boxed-in bunks.

"Does this mean . . ." Amanda Whipple stammered.

"Mean what, ma'am?" Captain Janders asked.

"That two couples share each stateroom?" Amanda blushed.

"No, ma'am. It means that four couples fit in here. One couple to one bunk."

Abner was stunned, but Jerusha, faced with a problem, moved immediately toward the Whipples, seeking them as stateroom partners, only to find that little Amanda was already telling the captain, "The Hales and the Whipples will take this room, plus any other two couples you wish to give us."

"You and you," the captain said, arbitrarily indicating the Hewletts and the Quigleys.

The others moved on to receive their assignments while the first four couples, knocking elbows as they stood, started making decisions which would organize their lives for the next six months. "I don't mind an upper bunk," Jerusha said gallantly. "Do you, Reverend Hale?"

"We'll take an upper," Abner agreed.

Immanuel Quigley, a small, agreeable man, said at once, "Jeptha and I will take an upper."

Practical Amanda suggested: "On the first day of each month those on top come down below. What's more important, the bunks along this wall seem longer than these. John, climb in." And when Whipple tried to stretch out, he found that whereas Amanda was right, and the bunks running along the wall of the ship were nine inches longer than the others, both were too short.

"Those who start with the shortest bunks," Amanda announced, "will switch to the longer ones on the first of each month. Agreed?"

And the eight missionaries formed their first compact, but long after it was forgotten, the one that Abner was about to suggest would mark the missionaries. Looking at the seven distressed faces in the little room he said, "Our quarters are not large and there will be many inconveniences, especially since four among us are females, but let us remember that we are indeed a family in Christ. Let us always call each other by true family names. I am Brother Hale and this is my wife, Sister Hale."

"I am Sister Amanda," the saucy little girl from Hartford promptly corrected, "and this is my husband, Brother John."

"Since we are only now met," Abner countered soberly, "I feel the more formal appellation to be the more correct." The Hewletts and Quigleys agreed, so Amanda bowed courteously.

"How's it look?" Captain Janders called, shoving his head through the canvas opening.

"Small," Amanda replied.

"Let me give one bit of advice, young fellow," Janders said, addressing Whipple. "Stow everything you possibly can right in here. Don't worry about having space to stand. Pile it bunk-high, because it's going to take us six months to get out there, and you'll be surprised how grateful you'll be to have things."

"Will we get seasick?" Jerusha asked querulously.

"Ma'am, two hours after we depart Boston we hit a rough sea. Then we hit the Gulf Stream, which is very rough. Then we hit the waters off the coast of Africa, which are rougher still. Finally, we test our brig against Cape Horn, and that's the roughest water in the world. Ma'am, what do you weigh now?"

"About a hundred and fifteen pounds," Jerusha replied nervously.

"Ma'am, you'll be so seasick in your little stateroom that by the time we round Cape Horn, you'll be lucky if you weigh ninety." There was a moment of apprehensive silence, and Abner, feeling a slight rocking of the ship, was afraid that he was going to start sooner than the rest, but the captain slapped him on the back and said reassuringly, "But after we round the Horn we hit the Pacific, and it's like a lake in summer. Then you'll eat and grow fat."

"How long before we get to the Pacific?" Abner asked weakly.

"About a hundred and fifteen days," Janders laughed. Then he added, "I'll send a boy in here with a screwdriver. Cleat your trunks to the deck. You don't want em' sloshing about in a heavy sea."

When the missionaries saw the boy in their cramped stateroom, they were both amused and delighted, for he was so tall he had to bend over. "It's Keoki Kanakoa!" John Whipple cried. There were hearty greetings as the massive Hawaiian explained, "The American Board is sending me home to help Christianize my islands. I'm working for Captain Janders only because I like ships."

When the tiny cabin was finally packed, no floor was visible; there was no place to sit; there was only one solid layer of luggage upon the other, and four bunks so close together that the toes of one missionary couple were only eighteen inches away from the toes of the next pair.

Early on the morning of Saturday, September 1, in the year 1821, the mission family assembled on the wharf. Gaunt, God-stricken Reverend Eliphalet Thorn conducted service, crying above the sounds of the port, "Brothers in Christ, I command you not to weep on this joyous day. Let the world see that you go forth in fullness of spirit, joyously to a great and triumphant duty. We who send you upon this mission to far lands do so in joy. You who go must evidence the same exaltation, for you go in the spirit of Jesus Christ. We will sing the mission song." And in a clear voice he started the anthem of those who venture to far islands:

> "Go, spread a Saviour's fame:
> And tell His matchless grace
> To the most guilty and depraved
> Of Adam's numerous race.

> "We wish you in His name
> The most divine success,
> Assur'd that He Who sends you forth
> Will your endeavors bless."

Reverend Thorn then spoke his final word of encouragement: "I have personally helped in the selection of each man in this group, and I am convinced that you will be adornments to the work of Jesus Christ. In storms you will not grow weary, in disappointments you will not question the ultimate triumph of your cause. Through your administration the souls of millions yet unborn will be saved from eternal hellfire. I can think of no better parting hymn than the one which sent me forth on such a mission some years ago:

> 'Go to many a tropic isle
> On the bosom of the deep
> Where the skies forever smile
> And the blacks forever weep.'

You are to still that weeping."

Another minister issued a long prayer, not much to the point, and the service should have been ended on this high religious plane, with each of the twenty-two missionaries attentive to Reverend Thorn's injunction that they show no sadness, but the elderly wife of one of the supervising ministers, upon looking at the pretty young brides about to depart, and knowing that some would die in childbirth in Hawaii and others would waste away and others would lose their grip on reality because of back-breaking work and insufficient food, could not restrain her motherly emotions, and in a high piping voice she began one of the most truly Christ-like of all church hymns. Its old familiar strains were quickly picked up, and even Reverend Thorn, unable to anticipate what was about to happen, joined lustily in:

> "Blest be the tie that binds
> Our hearts in Christian love;
> The fellowship of kindred minds
> Is like to that above."

All went well in the first verse, and also in the second, but when the singers came to the succeeding thoughts, one after another began to choke, and at the end all the women in the audience were weeping:

> "We share our mutual woes;
> Our mutual burdens bear;
> And often for each other flows
> The sympathizing tear."

Reverend Thorn, his voice strong and clear to the end, thought ruefully, "Women ought not to be permitted to attend leave-takings," for in the general sobbing that now overtook the congregation he witnessed the collapse of his plans for an orderly departure. Instead of triumphant testimony, the morning had become a sentimental shambles, the victory of common human love over black-coated respectability.

Nevertheless, and not by plan, the morning did end on a note of high religious emotion, for Jerusha Hale unexpectedly moved forward and in her fawn-colored coat and live poke bonnet stood before Reverend Thorn, saying in a clear voice so that all could hear, "I speak to you not as my Uncle Eliphalet, nor as Reverend Thorn of Africa, but as an officer of the American Board of Commissioners for Foreign Missions. We place our futures in your hands. The eleven men here take no money with them, only those things required for life on a savage island. It would not be proper for me to take worldly wealth, either, and so I turn over to the Board the small inheritance I received from my loving aunt. It was to have been spent on my marriage, but I have married the work of the Lord." And she handed Reverend Thorn a packet containing more than eight hundred dollars.

Penniless, uninformed, ill at ease with their suddenly acquired partners, but strong in the Lord, the missionaries climbed aboard the brig *Thetis,* and Captain Janders cried, "Break out the sails!" and the tiny ship flung aloft her nine new sails and began moving slowly toward the open sea. Standing on the port side of the vessel, Abner Hale had the distinct premonition that he would never again see America, and he uttered a short prayer which invoked blessing for all those who lived on that bleak, ungenerous little farm in Marlboro, Massachusetts. If he had been asked at that solemn moment what mission he was setting forth upon he would have answered honestly, "To bring to the people of Hawaii the blessings that I enjoyed on that farm." It could never have occurred to him— as indeed it never did—that a better mission might be to bring to Hawaii the blessings that characterized the solid white home facing the village common in Walpole, New Hampshire, for although he had said nothing about this to anyone, he could not believe that the levity, the profane music, the novels and the deficiency in grace that marked the Bromley home were in any sense blessings. In fact, he rather felt that in bringing Jerusha onto the *Thetis* he was somehow saving her from herself.

She was now tugging at his arm and saying, "Reverend Hale, I think I'm going to be sick." And he took her below and placed her in one of the short berths, where she was to stay for most of the time during the first four months. Abner, to everyone's surprise, proved a good sailor, for although he constantly looked as if he were about to vomit, he ate ravenously and never did.

It was he, therefore, who led prayers, did the preaching, studied Hawaiian with Keoki Kanakoa, and frequently took care of eighteen or twenty seasick missionaries. Some of them came ungenerously to detest the wiry little man as he moved briskly among their sickbeds, assuring them that soon they would be up like him, eating pork, biscuit, gravy, anything. And yet grudgingly they had to admire his determination, particularly when Captain Janders began to rail against him.

Janders started with his first mate. "Mister Collins, you've got to keep that pipsqueak Hale out of the fo'c's'l."

"Is he bothering the men?"

"He's trying to convert 'em."

"Those monsters?"

"He's got his dirty little fangs into Cridland. I found the boy weeping last night and I asked him what was wrong, and he told me that Reverend Hale had convinced him that death and eternal hellfire were the lot of everyone on this ship who did not confess and join the church."

"Maybe he's right," Collins laughed.

"But in the meantime we have to run a ship."

"Have the men complained, sir?"

"No, that they haven't. Cridland says they sort of like to have the little squirt around. Makes them feel as if someone was interested in 'em."

"I'll tell him to stay clear of the men," Mister Collins promised.

Captain Janders knew precisely when the message was delivered, for two minutes later Reverend Hale, sputtering with rage, was 'tween decks, hammering on the half-circle table. "Do I understand, Captain Janders, that I have been ordered not to go into the fo'c's'l?"

"Not an order. A request."

"Then you were a partner to this request?"

"I was."

"And you are consciously setting yourself athwart my efforts to save the souls of these forsaken men steeped in evil and abomination?"

"These are just good ordinary sailors, Reverend Hale, and I don't want 'em upset."

"Upset!" Reverend Hale beat the table more loudly, so that all the seasick missionaries could hear the argument, whether they wished to or not. "You call the conversion of an immortal soul to God's grace upsetting! Captain Janders, there are some aboard this brig who would profit from some upsetting, and I am not referring exclusively to those in the fo'c's'l." Thereafter, however, he stayed out of the men's cramped quarters forward, but he did lie in wait for them as they went about their duties, until Captain Janders had once more to call in the first mate. "Damn it, Mister Collins, now he's meddling with the men when they're trying to change sails. Warn him about it."

This led to further protests from the missionary, which Captain Janders patiently entertained. Finally Hale cried, "I don't believe you care, Captain Janders, whether you run a Christian ship or not. The men tell me that you issue rations of rum after a storm. That you never try to get them to take the pledge. Obviously, you try to impede me in every way possible."

"Reverend Hale," the captain pleaded, "I'm trying to get this ship to Hawaii. You seem to be trying to get it to Beulah Land."

"I am," Hale replied.

"The two ports are incompatible."

"Not in God's eyes, Captain Janders. You've forbidden me the fo'c's'l. Now you forbid me talk to the men on duty. Are you also going to forbid me the right to conduct Christian services on Sunday?"

"No, Reverend Hale, I aim to run a God-fearing ship, and when no ministers are aboard, I conduct services myself. Short ones. I'd be pleased to have you carry on for me. I'm in favor of church, at sea or ashore."

Later, when talking with the first mate, the captain asked, "Why do you suppose it is, Mister Collins, that with all these intelligent young men aboard, and with eleven damned attractive young women, it has to be Hale who is always well enough to eat with us? Why don't he get sick and his wife come to dinner?"

"Divine providence is sometimes malign, Captain Janders," the mate replied. But how malign, he was not to know until Reverend Hale preached his first Sunday sermon on the afterdeck. The *Thetis* rolled so sorely that no other missionary could appear above decks, but there stood Abner Hale, with a heavy Bible in his left hand, preaching into the winds.

"I have chosen for my text James, chapter 4, verse 8: 'Draw nigh to God, and He will draw nigh to you. Cleanse your hands, ye sinners; and purify your hearts, ye double minded.'" And he launched into one of the most violent attacks on the moral dangers faced by sailors that the crew had ever heard, for he charged that all who sailed before the mast were peculiarly tempted, that those who led them were apt to be insensitive brutes, that their employers who remained safe at home in Salem and Boston were determined to corrupt their vessels, and that every port they touched harbored instruments of evil that stay-at-home citizens could only dream of. Abner painted the men before him as the blackest, most evil and forlorn group of reprobates in Christendom, and the men loved it. Throughout his fiery sermon they nodded approvingly, and even Captain Janders and the first mate agreed that except in the part where Abner belabored them individually, he was close to the truth. But the result of his sermon was rather the opposite of what Abner had intended, for throughout the rest of the day the young sailors whom he wanted to reach most—for he felt that Janders and Collins were past saving—strutted with extra swagger as if in sudden realization of the fact that they "were among the evilest human beings known." They had suspected this for some time, and they derived positive pleasure from being told so by an expert. Only Cridland, a pathetic, undernourished boy with an overpowering sense of guilt, caught anything of Hale's message, and he appeared red-eyed and perplexed as Abner was about to go below, asking, "What must I do to be saved?" And from his question Abner knew that his sermon had been a success.

"You must pray. You must study the Bible. And you must try to save the souls of your mates in the fo'c's'l," Abner explained. He handed young Cridland his own Bible and said, "You may keep this tonight. I brought along eight seamen's Bibles, and I'll give you one at Sabbath service but it is only a loan from God to you. Only when you get some friend in the fo'c's'l to ask for his Bible, will you have started upon your true salvation."

At supper Captain Janders growled, "The mate says he saw your large Bible in the fo'c's'l, Reverend Hale. I thought it was understood that you were not to annoy the men down there any more."

"I have kept severely to my promise, Captain Janders, but since I am forbidden entrance into that pit of depravity, I feel sure that you will not object to my sending there, as my messenger better able to discharge my obligations than I myself, the holy word of God. If you wish to throw the Bible out of your ship, do so, Captain, and your name will become imperishable in the roll call of mariners."

"Please, Reverend Hale, don't preach sermons down here. I only asked if you had violated your agreement to stay out of the fo'c's'l."

"I have never violated an agreement," Abner cried. "Oh, I shall stay out! Never fear! But by next Sunday, Captain Janders, eight of my Bibles will be down there."

In spite of their arguments with the difficult missionary, both Captain Janders and Mister Collins were impressed by the fatherly way in which he tended his sick companions. Each dawn he went from one sickbed to another, collecting the night's slops, hauling them away and bringing fresh water to cleanse lips foul from vomiting. Before breakfast he visited each man and woman and read to them from the Bible. Men who wanted to shave were provided with hot water from the cook's galley, and women who required fresh linen could indicate to Abner which boxes were to be hauled out and opened. At mealtimes he took to each sick friend those portions of greasy food which had a chance of staying down in retching stomachs. He argued the captain into allowing him to cook up batches of oatmeal gruel for the women. And each evening, no matter how sick the missionaries were, they were hauled out of bed and made to attend divine worship conducted by Abner in the tiny, crowded cabin. If he saw that a man or woman could remain upright only with difficulty, he would conclude his prayer in half a minute and say, "The Lord has marked your presence, Joshua. You had better return to bed." Then, when the sick had mercifully departed, he would involve the others in long discussions, sermons, prayers, hymns. He was especially fond of one hymn which contained a verse which he held applicable to the *Thetis:*

"He'll shield you with a wall of fire;
With flowing zeal your hearts inspire,

> *Bid raging winds their fury cease,*
> *And hush the tempest into peace."*

But after the eighth rendition of this hopeful assurance, John Whipple, barely able to stand, said shakily, "Abner, you keep singing that the tempest is going to subside, but it gets worse."

"When we reach Cape Verde, we reach fine weather for certain," Abner assured everyone, and as the creaking little ship plunged sickeningly on through the North Atlantic swells, he grew more cheerful and more helpful.

"He'd make a wonderful cook's helper," Captain Janders observed to the first mate one night.

"Have you stopped to think what this cabin area would be like without him," Mister Collins reflected. "Twenty-one sick missionaries on our hands."

It was therefore not surprising that long before the storm abated, Abner Hale was recognized by all on board as the unofficial father of the mission family. There were men who were older, and men who were wiser, but he was the one to whom all looked for aid and decision. So, when he announced on the fourth Saturday that the storm had sufficiently abated to hold next day's service topside, and that all who could possibly do so must attend, there was a general effort to drag bruised and smelling bodies back into some semblance of order.

In his own stateroom, Abner kneeled on boxes and assured the four sick women there that when Sunday came, he would do everything required to help them dress and climb topside to worship the Lord. Amanda Whipple agreed, as did the two others, and he laid out their things for them, but Jerusha, after trying to rise, subsided and whimpered, "I cannot even raise my hand, Reverend Hale."

"I will help you, Mrs. Hale. I have brought you some broth from the meat, and if you will drink this now, by morning you will be stronger."

Jerusha drank the greasy broth, and only with difficulty kept from throwing it back into the smelly stateroom. "I am so dreadfully ill," she insisted.

"In the morning you will be better," Abner assured her, and while she slept he went aloft under the first stars of the voyage. As he was standing by the starboard railing of the brig, two shadowy forms came to him and he heard Cridland say, "I've been talking all week with Mason, sir, and he wants a Bible."

Abner turned in the darkness and saw the indistinct form of a young sailor. "Do you wish to be saved?" he asked.

"I do," the boy replied.

"What has led you to this decision?" Abner asked.

"I've been listening to the older hands speak of a sailor's life ashore, and I'm afraid," the boy whined.

"You're a wise young man, Mason," Abner said. "The Lord has spoken and you have listened."

"No, sir, begging your pardon. It's been Cridland who's been speaking. He's made me see the error of my ways."

"Tomorrow after service, Mason, I'll hand you your Bible, when Cridland gets his. But it is only a loan from God to you. To keep it, you must get some friend in the fo'c's'l to acknowledge God and to ask for his Bible."

"Would you say a prayer for us, Reverend Hale?" Cridland begged.

"The Lord always provides wisdom for those who seek," Abner replied. And in the darkness he raised his head to the stars and prayed: "Lord, we are afloat on a great ocean in a little boat. The winds and the storms harass us, but we trust in Thee. Tonight we are only three praying to Thee: a young boy on his first voyage, a sailor who seeks guidance, and a beginning minister who has never had a pulpit of his own. Great Father in heaven, we are insignificant in Thine eyes, but guide us in Thy divine ways. For if we are only three tonight, later we shall be more, for Thy wisdom permeates all things and saves all souls."

He dismissed the two sailors and stood for a long time watching the stars and waiting till the midnight hour heralded the first Sabbath on which a substantial number of the missionaries could attend formal service. As the holy day crept across the meridian of night, Abner prayed that the Lord might make this day one of special significance. Then he went below and whispered to his unnerved wife, "My dearest companion, you would not believe what has happened. Tonight two sailors came voluntarily requesting evening prayers. The spirit of God is beginning to permeate this forsaken ship."

"That's wonderful, Reverend Hale," his wife whispered, lest they waken the three other couples who had been sick most of the evening.

"And tomorrow our family will celebrate its first holy service," Abner sighed. "But I forget. It's already Sunday. I studied where the tarpauling is to be hung. We're going to have a very handsome church, Mrs. Hale, on the bosom of the deep."

"I won't be able to go up the stairs, Reverend Hale, but I'll pray with you," she whispered.

"You'll be well enough," he assured her, and he crept into the short narrow berth beside her.

But in the morning she was no better, and the sight of little Amanda swaying back and forth on the piled boxes made her more ill, so that when Abner returned from checking all his charges he found his wife not dressing, but lying in bed pale and exhausted. "I'm awfully sorry, Reverend Hale," she sighed, "but I'll have to miss service this morning."

"Not at all," he protested cheerily. "I'll help you."

"But I'm sure I can't stand," she protested.

"Now, Mrs. Hale . . ." And he forcibly brought her slim legs down onto the boxes and caught her in his arms when she proved unable to maintain her balance. "Some breakfast will strengthen you. Then we'll have service. You'll see the sun. And you'll be fine."

In trying to get out of the little heaped-up stateroom she almost fainted, weakness and nausea combining to make her deathly ill, but again Abner helped her and maneuvered her through the canvas opening and on into the cramped and smelly cabin, where Keoki Kanakoa was spreading a breakfast consisting of cold suet beef, mashed beans and watery rice, left over from the night before. Jerusha closed her eyes when the sodden food was placed before her and kept them closed as Abner asked one of the older ministers to bless the day. Then Keoki prayed in Hawaiian, to familiarize the missionaries with the language, and the meal was begun.

Jerusha could manage a little hot tea and one bite of suet beef, but the clammy lard in the latter revolted her, and she rose to leave, but Abner's firm hand caught her wrist and she heard him saying, "A little longer, Mrs. Hale, and you'll conquer it." So she sat in agony as the cold lard slipped down into her stomach and nauseated her whole body.

"I'm going to be sick!" she whispered.

"No," he said insistently. "This is our first meal together. This is the Sabbath." And she fought her rising illness, with the smell of food and two dozen people crowding in upon her nostrils.

She was pale when the meal ended, and staggered toward her berth, but

Abner refused to let her go, and with his strong hold on her arm, marched her up the stairs and onto the gently sloping deck, where a canvas had been hung to form a rude chapel. "Our first worship as a family," he announced proudly, but the entire family was not to participate, because one of the older ministers took one look at the slanting deck, rushed to the railing, relieved himself of his breakfast, and staggered white and gasping back to his berth. Abner stared at him as he left, interpreting the poor man's involuntary actions as a personal rejection of God. He was especially irritated because several of the sailors, who were idling the Sunday morning away by hanging on ropes to catch their first glimpse of the mission family, laughed openly as the distraught minister threw up his breakfast.

"There'll be more," one of the sailors predicted ominously, and his mates laughed.

Services were conducted by Abner, as the only one who was likely to be able to finish them, and the family, resting comfortably under canvas strung from the mainmast, sang as cheerfully as circumstances permitted, the fine old Sunday hymn of New England:

> "Another six days' work is done,
> Another Sabbath is begun;
> Return, my soul, enjoy thy rest—
> Improve the day thy God has blessed."

Abner then spoke at some length on various passages from Ephesians, chapter 3: " 'For this cause I bow my knees unto the Father of our Lord Jesus Christ, Of whom the whole family in heaven and earth is named, . . . That Christ may dwell in your hearts by faith; that ye . . . might be filled with all the fullness of God.' " He pointed out that the family of love within which they lived was open to all who were willing to confess their sins and work toward a state of grace. He was obviously preaching to two audiences: his brother missionaries, to remind them of the family within which they operated; and the eavesdropping sailors, tempting them to join this family of Christ; but his message to the latter was somewhat destroyed when Jerusha, experiencing a dreadful wave of nausea, tried to stagger to the railing, failed, fell on her knees and vomited over the deck.

"Watch out, lady!" a sailor called derisively, but Cridland and Mason, the two young men who were to get Bibles that day, quickly jumped forward, caught Jerusha by the arms and carried her below. Abner, infuriated at the disruption of his charge to the sailors, concluded his sermon in rather a jumble, and turned the prayer over to an associate. He was confused and angry, because he had arranged the entire service so that it would end dramatically with his presentation of the Bibles to Cridland and his friend, thus symbolically welcoming them into the Lord's family, but when the time had come to do this, those two were below decks, and Abner was painfully aware that his first major effort had ended like that of so many ministers: looking for a logical place to stop. Finally he had just quit.

When service ended, members of the family made a pretense of commending Abner for his sermon, but both the extenders of congratulations and the recipient knew that they were hollow. In an unruly fit of temper and disappointment, Abner started to go below, but he was met at the top of the hatchway by Cridland and Mason, who reported, "Your wife is very sick, sir."

"Thank you," he replied curtly.

"The minister who got sick first is helping her," Cridland said.

Abner started down but Mason stopped him and asked, "Have you our Bibles, sir?"

"Next week," Abner snapped, and was gone. But when he saw his wife, and how ashen white she was, he forgot his own problems and fetched water to wash her perspiring face.

"I'm sorry, my cherished partner," she said wanly. "I'll never make a sailor."

"We'll get you above decks just a few minutes each day," he said reassuringly, but even the thought of facing that slanting deck again brought back her nausea, and she said, "I'm going to weigh even less than Captain Janders predicted."

At noon, when the day's big meal was served, Janders saw with pleasure that seventeen of his passengers were at last able to eat. "On each trip," he observed, "as we approach Cape Verde, our sick ones get better."

"Shall we be stopping at the islands?" John Whipple asked.

"Yes, if weather permits." The news was so good that Abner rose from his pork-and-suet pudding and called into any staterooms where sick missionaries lay, "We'll soon be touching at Cape Verde. Then you can walk about on land and get fresh fruit."

"By the way, Reverend Hale," the captain added, "that was a good sermon you preached today. There is indeed a heritage that the Lord provides those who serve Him, and may we all come into it." The missionaries nodded their approval of this sentiment, whereupon Janders launched his harpoon: "Seems to me your message got a little tangled up at the end."

Since all knew this to be true, they looked at their plates and thought: "Our captain is a clever man." But Abner looked at him boldly and said, "I count a sermon a success if it contains one good Christian thought in it."

"I do too," Janders said heartily. "Yours had several."

"I hope we can all take them to mind," Abner said piously, but secretly he wished that services could have ended as planned. Then the ship would have heard a sermon.

After lunch Captain Janders invited the missionaries to tour the ship with him, and John Whipple asked, "I don't understand why, if we're bound west for Hawaii, we sail east almost to the coast of Africa."

"Mister Collins, break us out a chart!" And Janders showed the surprised missionaries how it was that ships wanting to double Cape Horn sailed from Boston on a heading which took them not south for the Horn but far to the east, almost to the coast of Africa. "It's so that when we finally turn south for the Horn, we can run in one straight line, down past Brazil and Argentine, straight on to Tierra de Fuego," Janders explained, and the chart made this clear.

"Are the Cape Verde islands pleasant?" Whipple asked.

"You watch! Some of our boys jump ship there on every trip. We'll be leaving Verde with a couple of Brava boys as replacements."

While the captain was explaining these things, Abner was on another part of the deck talking seriously with Cridland and Mason. "I did not give you your Bibles today because you did not earn them," he chided.

"But we had to take Mrs. Hale below decks," Cridland protested.

"The work of the Lord required you to be present topside," Abner said stubbornly.

"But she . . ."

"Others could have cared for her, Cridland. Next Sunday I shall give you your Bibles. I am going to preach from Psalms 26, verse 5: 'I have hated the congregation of evil doers; and will not sit with the wicked.' When I have finished my sermon, I shall hand each of you his Bible." Then he recalled what he had said earlier and, staring at Mason, asked, "But have you earned your Bible? I thought you were to have brought another soul to God."

"I am about to do so," Mason reported happily. "I have been reading the tracts you gave us to one of the older men. He had led an evil life, but last trip on a whaler he was swept overboard and was saved only by a miracle. Of late, he has been weeping very much and I shall keep talking with him. Perhaps by next Sabbath . . ."

"Good work, Mason," Abner replied, and although another might have thought it strange that the religious ardors of the two sailors were not dampened by their disappointment over the Bibles, particularly when their dereliction arose from their humane treatment of a woman, and she the wife of the minister himself, Abner Hale was not surprised. As he pointed out to the young men: "The Lord is a jealous master. You cannot approach Him at your determination. He tells you when you may come into His presence. And if you have been faithless in even small things, the Lord will wait until you have proved yourself worthy." For Abner knew that easy salvation was never appreciated; Cridland and Mason already treasured their forthcoming Bibles doubly because they had once failed to attain them.

If Abner's first Sunday sermon was something of a failure, his second was a stunning success, marred only by the fact that his wife Jerusha was unable to witness it. He had got her to breakfast, had forced a little cold pork and rice into her racked body, and had even carried her limply onto the deck, but one look at the wallowing waves put her stomach into gyrations, and she was hurriedly taken below by Amanda Whipple and Mrs. Quigley. The intellectual highlight of Abner's sermon came when he spent fifteen minutes on the congregation of evildoers that the devil had thrown together aboard the "hamferdite" brig *Thetis.* Like all the missionaries, he called it a hamferdite, not knowing exactly how to pronounce, spell or define the longer and more accurate word, since it was in none of the mission dictionaries. But according to Abner, few ships that had ever sailed the Atlantic knew such a congregation of evil, and his catalogue of what these sailors lounging idly on deck had perpetrated in their short and unspectacular lives was terrifying. The dramatic climax, of course, came when he announced to his startled missionaries and surprised ship's crew that God had been at work even in this den of vice and that three souls had already been saved, whereupon he produced Cridland, Mason and a beat-up old whaler with bad legs whose catalogue of sin actually surpassed Abner's conjectures. Some of the old man's friends, who had spent time ashore with him in Valparaiso, Canton and Honolulu, expected lightning to play upon the waves when he touched the Bible that Abner extended to him. Captain Janders shuddered and said to his first mate, "Mark my words, Mister Collins, you'll be up there next week."

That Sunday the noonday meal was an unalloyed triumph. Captain Janders said it was one of the best sermons he had ever heard afloat, although he was satisfied that Reverend Hale must have been talking about some other ship, and Mister Collins confessed, "It's a strange phenomenon, but no matter what the ship, the closer it gets to Cape Horn, the more religious everyone becomes. It's as if all aboard sensed at last the futility of man in the face of God's awful power. I'm not sure that I would be even a moderately Christian man, which I hold myself to be, if I had never rounded Cape Horn." Captain Janders added, "I agree. No man by his own power could accomplish the transit we shall soon face."

No comment could have pleased Abner more, for like all the missionaries he had been contemplating with some dread the trial they would encounter as Cape Horn approached, and although it still lay eight weeks in the future, he felt that he would make no mistake in undertaking reasonable preparations. He therefore said, "I have observed, Captain Janders, that you spend your Sundays reading . . ." He found it difficult to say the word, and hesitated.

"Novels?" Janders asked.

"Yes. Profane books. I was wondering, Captain Janders, if you would entertain it kindly if I were to give you, from the mission stores, several books of a more appropriate and edifying nature?"

"Richardson and Smollett are edifying enough for me," Janders laughed.

"But when you have in your care some four dozen souls . . ."

"In those circumstances I rely on Bowditch and the Bible . . . in that order."

"Do I understand that you would not take it kindly . . ."

"I would not," Janders said stiffly.

"The mission family had decided," Abner said abruptly, having talked with no one of this project, "that starting with today we shall hold both morning and afternoon services on deck, weather permitting."

"Fine," Janders said. Then, always eager to keep the young minister off balance, he asked, "By the way, how's Mrs. Hale?"

"Poorly," Abner said.

"I should think you would spend some time with her," Janders suggested.

"I do," Abner snapped. "I pray with her morning and night."

"I meant, play games with her, or read her an interesting novel. Would you entertain it kindly if I were to offer you, from my own library, several novels of an entertaining nature?"

"We do not read novels," Abner retaliated. "Especially not on Sundays."

"In that case, when you do get around to seeing your wife, you can tell her that on Tuesday we'll land at Brava, and she can walk ashore. It'll do us all wonders."

Jerusha was elated by this news, and on Monday, when the calmer waters in the lee of Cape Verde were reached, she ventured on deck for an hour and the sun diminished her pallor. On Tuesday, when the islands were clearly in sight, she clung to the railing, praying for the moment when she could step ashore, but she was to be sorely disappointed, for a stiff breeze came up offshore, followed by heavy low clouds, and even before the *Thetis* began to roll in deep troughs, it became apparent that to beat into Brava would be too difficult a task, whereas to run before the mounting storm would carry the little brig so far on its westward heading that any attempt to recover Brava would be wasteful. Nevertheless, Jerusha stood in the rain, praying that some miracle would enable the ship to make land, and it was not until Captain Janders himself passed and said, "We're going to run before the wind, ma'am. There'll be no Brava," that she admitted sorry defeat. Then she discovered that she was very seasick, and began retching at the rail so that Janders shouted, "You, there! Take this poor woman below!"

It was a gloomy family that met that night in the swaying cabin for a supper of gruel and hard cheese. Half the missionaries were unable to leave their staterooms. The others wore bleak faces in recognition of the fact that a chance to step ashore had been missed, and that no other would present itself for many days. How lonely and mean the cabin seemed as the whale-oil lamp swung in the creaking night, as the latrine smelled up the fetid atmosphere, and as friends retched in new despair. Keoki, coming in with the food, said, "I would like to offer the evening meal prayer," and in rich Hawaiian he praised the open ocean as compared to land, for on the former one was required to know God, whereas on land there were many diversions. Therefore, reasoned Keoki, it was better this night to be on the *Thetis* than to be in Brava.

Of all the listeners, only Abner knew enough Hawaiian to piece together the message, and he thought it so felicitous that he interpreted it for the mission family, and then he surprised everyone by standing and uttering his first prayer in Hawaiian. It was halting, but it was the native tongue of the islands, and it helped acquaint God with the strange tongue in which this family was to work.

O**N THE FORTY-FIFTH** day of the voyage, Monday, October 15, the groaning *Thetis* crossed the equator in brilliant sunshine and on a glassy sea. The first victim was Reverend Hale. Since the day was hot, Captain Janders casually suggested at noon that his passengers ought to wear old clothes, and not too many of them. When he was satisfied that no one was wearing his best, he winked at Keoki, who passed a signal aloft.

"Oh, Reverend Hale!" a voice cried down the hatchway. "Cridland wants to see you!"

Abner hurried from table, grasped the handrail leading aloft, and swung up the narrow ladder. He had gone only a few yards forward when he was completely drenched in a bucket of sea water thrown down from the shrouds. He gasped, looked about in dismay, and felt his muscles contracting in useless fury. But before he could speak, Mister Collins winked at him and said, "We've crossed the equator! Call Whipple!" And Abner was so startled by the experience that he found himself calling, "Brother Whipple! Can you come?"

There was a movement at the hatchway as Whipple ran into a full bucket of water. "Equator!" Abner giggled.

John wiped himself off, then looked up into the shrouds where two sailors were dizzy with delight and reaching for fresh buckets. On the spur of the moment Whipple shouted, "Whales!" and stood back as several passengers from below came storming up the ladder and into their initiation. Soon the deck was choked with laughing missionaries, and Captain Janders announced that the crew would now initiate the sailors who had not yet crossed the line. But when one of the young men who had doused Whipple came up for his diet of gruel, whale oil, soap and grease, John shouted, "Oh, no! I'm to feed this one!" And to everyone's surprise he leaped into the middle of the fray, got himself roundly smeared with grease, and fed the laughing sailor, whereupon there was great hilarity and the captain ordered all hands an issue of rum, at which point the missionaries solemnly withdrew. An hour later Abner had visible proof of the horrors of ardent spirits, for Keoki Kanakoa begged him to come forward into the fo'c's'l, where the old whaler who had accepted the Bible had somehow collected six or eight extra rations of grog and was now cursing vehemently and bashing his head into a bulkhead. With some difficulty Abner got him into his foul bunk and sat consoling him. When the man was sober enough to speak coherently, Abner asked, "Where is your Bible?"

"In the box," the old whaler replied contritely.

"This one?"

"Yes." Primly, Abner opened the box, ignored the filth and disarray, and lifted out the Holy Book.

"Some men do not deserve Bibles," he said sternly, and left.

"Reverend! Reverend!" shouted the sailor. "Don't do that! Please!" But Abner was already far aft.

The strange day ended with a sight of incomparable beauty, for from the west, heading to the coast of Africa, came a tall ship with many sails, out of the sunset, and the *Thetis* spoke to her and lowered a longboat to greet the stranger, taking mail which could be returned to Boston; and as the longboat prepared to stand off, Captain Janders, in the stern, shouted, "Whipple! They might appreciate prayers!" And John swung down into the boat, and all aboard the *Thetis* watched as their men rowed into the sunset to visit the strange, tall ship, so beautiful in the dusk.

Jerusha was brought on deck, and although she tried to control herself, fell into tears at the sight of this curious meeting of two ships in the first shadows of night. "My beloved companion," she sighed, "it's the most beautiful thing I have ever seen. Look how the sunset rests on the waters. The sea is a mirror."

Amanda, not wishing to be alone at such a still moment, came to stand with the Hales and whispered, "It was almost unbearable, to see Brother Whipple rowing away like that. It's the first time we've been separated. He has been my dear companion and close friend. How lucky we are to be spending our first days of marriage like this."

But when the longboat returned to the *Thetis,* and when the tall ship had resumed its passage, with night upon it and the noiseless sea, Amanda saw that her husband sat in the prow biting his lip, while Captain Janders sat in the stern, riveted in hatred. Even the sailors, New England men all, were harshly silent, their mouths pursed into tight lines. Only Captain Janders spoke. "By God!" he cried. "At such moments I wish we were armed. I wished to Almighty God we had sent that damned foul thing to the bottom." In fury he threw a handful of letters at the missionaries' feet. "I would not entrust your letters to such a ship. A slaver."

Later, John Whipple reported to the missionaries: "It was horrible. They had not secured the chains below, and you could hear them swinging in the swell. It was a dark ship. Abner, would you pray?" And in the hot cabin, on their first night across the equator, the missionaries prayed and Abner said simply, "Where there is darkness, Lord, allow the light to shine. Where there is evil, substitute goodness. But let us not concern ourselves only with distant evil. Remind us always that our first responsibility is the evil that occurs within our immediate environs. Lord, help us not to be hypocrites. Help us to do Thy work day by day."

He was so moved by this chance brush with the slaver that he could not sleep and spent the night on deck, peering off into the direction of Africa, hoping that God would vouchsafe him a flash of light indicating that the blackbirder had exploded. Toward morning he was visited by Keoki Kanakoa, who said, "Reverend Hale, you worry so much about Africa. Did you not know that there are also slaves in Hawaii?"

"There are?" Abner asked in astonishment.

"Of course. On my father's island there are many slaves. We call them foul corpses, and they may touch nothing that we touch. They are kapu. Not long ago they were kept for the human sacrifices."

"Tell me about them," the stunned young missionary said, and as Keoki explained the various rituals and kapus involving the foul corpses, Abner felt an impatient fury mounting in his throat, so that before Keoki finished he cried, "Keoki, when I get to Hawaii there will be no more slavery."

"It will be difficult," the giant Hawaiian warned.

"Keoki, you will eat with the foul corpses." He told none of the other missionaries of this resolve, not even Jerusha, but as dawn came he knew in his heart that that strange tall ship, that cruel Brazilian slaver, had been sent across his path at the equator for a purpose. "There will be no more slavery in Hawaii," he swore as the sun rose.

It was on the long, dreary run to Cape Horn, more than six thousand miles in almost a straight line, that the famous "missionary's disease" struck in earnest, so that long after seasickness was forgotten, missionary families would recall with embarrassment and discomfort the illness which really prostrated them.

They called it, in a blush of euphemism, biliousness, and day after day Jerusha would inquire cautiously, "Reverend Hale, do you still suffer from biliousness?"

He would reply, "Yes, my dear companion, I do."

Since all the other couples were conducting similar inquiries, with identical responses, the missionaries began to look with truly jaundiced eyes at their doctor, as if Brother Whipple ought by some miracle to be able to dispel the tormenting biliousness. He studied his authorities, especially the *Family Medical Book,* and prescribed various time-honored cures. "Two tablespoons of ipecac and rhubarb," he advised.

"Brother Whipple, I've been taking ipecac for weeks," a worried missionary reported. "No good."

"Have you tried two grains of calomel, Brother Hewlett?"

"It helps at the moment . . . but . . ."

"Then it'll have to be castor oil . . . and walking."

"I can't take castor oil, Brother Whipple."

"Then walk."

So the dreadfully constipated missionaries took ipecac and rhubarb and calomel and castor oil. But mostly they walked. After breakfast all who were able would stride purposefully up and down, up and down the cramped after-deck, turning on the animal pens at one end, and the foremast at the other. Sometimes they walked for hours, trying to shame their recalcitrant intestines into action, but nothing really cured the biliousness.

The after quarters contained one latrine, unbearably foul, and if each missionary occupied it for only fifteen minutes at a time, which was not excessive in their condition, five and a half hours were automatically consumed, and the day was half spent with no time allocated for emergency cases on the part of those who in extreme desperation had taken a master dose of ipecac, rhubarb, calomel and castor oil, all together.

It therefore became necessary for Brother Whipple, with Captain Janders' amused consent and with able help from Keoki Kanakoa, to rig an unclosed improvised privy aft of the stern. At stated intervals all females would go below decks, and one minister after another would test his good fortune on the open seat, his hands wrapped desperately about the timbers Keoki had hammered into place, his pallid white bottom winking at the whales.

Day after day they walked. The boisterous sailors, whose bodies were kept functioning by the extraordinary amount of work they had to do, irreverently made bets as to which of the brothers would next try his luck on the precarious perch, and they referred to the constant walking as "the missionary waltz."

One day, in despair, poor, tied-up Abner demanded of Brother Whipple,

"Why is it that God afflicts us so and does nothing to those impious sailors?"

"It's simple, Brother Hale," the doctor laughed. "We all got seasick and cleaned our lower quarters completely. Then we ate little and allowed it to compact itself. Lacking fruit and vegetables that compacting became harder. But most of all, we did no work. Sailors work, so God looks after their bellies."

Abner wasn't sure but what Brother Whipple had indulged in blasphemy, but he was too uncomfortable to argue, so he merely said, "I feel dreadful."

"Let me see your eyes," Whipple ordered, and when he saw the bleary yellow stains he said, "You are dreadful."

"What can I do?" Abner pleaded.

"Walk," Whipple commanded, and the missionary waltz resumed.

Brother Whipple took most of his walks at night, when the stars were out and when his interest in science could be freely indulged. His long discussions with the mates over astronomy came so to occupy his mind that he frequently absented himself from evening prayers, a dereliction which caused Abner to detail two brothers to investigate.

"We are a family, as you know, Brother Whipple," they said. "Our prayers are family prayers."

"I am sorry I was forgetful," Whipple apologized. "I'll attend prayers." But as soon as the first worshiper cried, "Amen!" the young doctor was up the hatch and talking astronomy.

"How does a mariner feel when he crosses the line and sees that the North Star has vanished?" he asked.

"Well," Mister Collins reflected, "no matter how well you know the southern stars, it's a wrench to see old reliable go down over the horizon."

From his work with the mates, Whipple learned to work Bowditch for both latitude and longitude, and occasionally his calculations coincided with those of Captain Janders, which led the latter to predict, "You'd make a better navigator than you ever will a missionary."

"We'll trap your soul yet," Whipple retorted. "If I could get Brother Hale up here . . ."

"Leave him where he is!" Janders urged.

Nevertheless, Captain Janders had to admit surprise at the success Abner was enjoying in converting the crew. He had five Bibles out and two more pending. Six men had been cajoled into signing temperance pledges, at which Janders growled, "Easiest thing in the world is to get sailors on board to become temperance. Trick is to do it in port."

The sailors appreciated Abner's curious gift of raising exactly those questions they had often pondered, so that even men who were not religious would stand about as he argued: "Suppose this voyage occupies four years. On the first week you are away, your mother dies. You don't hear about it. Now what is your relation to your mother during the next two hundred weeks? She is dead, yet you think of her as living. She is dead, yet she has the capacity to help you. Is it not possible that she is indeed living? In Jesus Christ?"

"I didn't think about it that way, Reverend," an unbeliever said. "But in another way I did. Suppose I'm married, and when I leave Boston my wife is . . . well . . . if you'll excuse me . . . expecting. Now I never see that baby for four years, but when I come home he looks like me, has my habits, and in some unknown way has come to love me."

"Only sometimes he don't look like you," the old whaler observed from his own experience. "What then?"

"Have you converted Captain Janders?" Cridland asked.

"No," Abner replied sorrowfully. " 'The fool hath said in his heart, There is no God.' "

"Wait a minute, Reverend!" an old hand corrected. "Cap'n believes. When you ain't aboard he conducts services."

"True believing requires that you submit your will entirely to God's," Abner explained. "Captain Janders will not confess that he lives in a state of abject sin."

"I don't classify him as no sinner," the old whaler reflected. "Not a proper, hard-working sinner, that is. Now you take a man like Cap'n Hoxworth of the whaler *Carthaginian* . . . I seen Cap'n Hoxworth get four naked Honolulu girls into his cabin at one time . . . Well, as a sinner, our cap'n just don't compare."

Nevertheless, Abner waged relentless campaigns against Captain Janders, particularly in the matter of novels, which the captain read ostentatiously immediately after each Sabbath sermon. "You will learn to call such books abominations," Abner mournfully predicted.

Janders fought back with irony: "You converting any more old whalers, Brother Hale?"

The question infuriated Abner, symbolizing as it did the world's pernicious habit of rejoicing over the downfall of sanctimonious men. Actually, he could have turned the tables on the captain, so far as the old whaler was concerned, for the man was agonizingly eager to win back his Bible before reaching Cape Horn. "Many's a sailor's been lost at the Horn, Reverend," he constantly pleaded. "Don't make me round the Horn without a Bible!"

But Abner had absorbed one fundamental lesson on this trip: the established church must not be maneuvered into a position of danger by the backsliding of fools who were never truly saved in the first place. It is such who have the greatest power to damage the church and they must be denied the opportunity of doing so. Frequently, on the long leg south Abner would sit on a trunk in his stateroom and analyze this case with his seven companions: "I was too prompt to accept this man . . . too eager for merely another number rather than for a secured soul. We must never repeat this foolish mistake in Hawaii."

And then, on the evening of November 24, just as Keoki placed on the half-moon table the Saturday night suet pudding, an unexpected gale from the southwest struck the *Thetis* port-side and threw her well onto her beam ends. Since the storm had come without warning, the after hatch had not been closed and torrents of cold gray water cascaded into the cabin. The lamp swung parallel to the decking. Food and chairs and missionaries were swept into a jumble and buried in new floods ripping down the hatchway. There were screams, and from the stateroom where Jerusha lay ghastly ill, Abner heard a plaintive cry, "Are we sinking?"

He stumbled to her and found her berth drenched with water, and everything in confusion. "We shall be safe," he said firmly. "God is with this ship."

They heard the hatchway being hammered into place and smelled the loss of air. Then the cook shouted, "Cape Horn is rushing out to meet us."

"Will the storm last long?" Brother Whipple inquired.

"Maybe four weeks," the cook replied, picking up the debris of his meal.

On Sunday, November 25, Abner ventured on deck to survey the damage, and reported breathlessly, "All the livestock was swept away. That first big wave almost capsized us." One by one the missionaries, those who were not confined to their bunks, viewed the storm and discovered what the cook meant when he said that Cape Horn had come to meet them. A cold, dismal fog enveloped the ship where the warm waters of the Atlantic met the icy wastes of the Antarctic, and the waves rose high in the gloom, falling away into icy depths.

"I'm fearfully cold," Jerusha told her husband, but there was nothing he could do. The little *Thetis* kept probing southward toward the Cape itself, and each day took her into colder waters. The thermometer stood at thirty-nine degrees, with no fires allowed on board. Bedding was wet from the dousing and all gear was molding in unaired boxes. Most of the time the hatchway was covered, so that no air swept into the dank confined cabin, and with no freedom for walking, griping biliousness overtook the missionaries.

On Tuesday, November 27, John Whipple hurried below with heartening news. "We can see Staten Island to port, so we must be approaching the Cape. The waves aren't as big as we feared." He led his companions aloft to view one of the bleakest, loneliest lands on earth, lying off the tip of the continent. Through partial mist its low treeless hills were visible, and Whipple said, "We are seeing it in summer. Imagine what it must be like in winter." But the missionaries were looking not at Staten Island, but rather at the terrifying waters that lay ahead.

There, at the southern tip of the habitable world, in a latitude of fifty-five degrees, the earth-girdling southern currents that thundered in from the lower Pacific crashed into the turbulent swells of the Atlantic, and the missionaries could see that the resulting waves were mountain-high and clothed with fog and fear. If a sailor were lucky enough to hit Staten Island with an easterly at his back, he could penetrate these monstrous waves with some hope of success, but when, as in late November of 1821, both the set of the Pacific and the bearing of its winds were from the west, there was slight chance of doubling the Cape.

But Captain Janders, face grim within the rim of sandy whiskers, was stubbornly determined to prosecute every chance. "I'll not be the captain who has to write in his log, 'Today abandoned hope of doubling Cape Horn and turned back across the Atlantic to try Cape Good Hope.' If you write that in your log, they never let you forget it. You're the Yankee who couldn't double the Cape." So he gambled that either the wind would veer to the east and blow him through, or that the Pacific swell would somehow abate and allow him to beat into the wind, no matter where it stood.

"I am convinced that one or the other will happen," Janders repeated doggedly. But on the evening of Thanksgiving Day he stumbled down into the cabin and said dourly, "If any of you missionaries have personal knowledge of God, I would appreciate your prayers now."

"Do the winds continue against us?" Abner asked.

"Never seen 'em so bad," Janders growled.

"Will we have to turn back?" one of the wives inquired.

"No, ma'am, we won't!" Janders said firmly. "There'll be no man say I tried the Cape and failed."

When he was gone back to the deck John Whipple said, "I see no fault in supporting him with our prayers."

"Nor do I, Brother Whipple," Jerusha said, and Dr. Whipple prayed: "Let us recall the reassuring words of Proverbs: 'I neither learned wisdom, nor have the knowledge of the holy. Who hath ascended up into the heavens, or descended? who hath gathered the wind in his fists? who hath bound the waters in a garment? who hath established all the ends of the earth? what is his name?' Brethren, we who stand at the ends of the earth, where the winds are gathered in God's fist against us, let us not forget that it is the just man whom God tries.

The evil man passes and repasses this Cape with no concern, for he has already been tested. It is you and I who have not been tested. Let us pray that these winds abate in our favor, but if they do not, let us doubly rely upon the Lord."

By Saturday, December 1, the *Thetis* had spent seven full days negotiating a distance of one hundred and ten miles. During breaks in the storm, the forlorn missionaries had seen blunt and brutal Tierra del Fuego to the north and had retired to freezing berths, huddling together in fear and seasickness. The tempest from the west did not abate.

On Sunday, December 2, the *Thetis* turned due west to find a channel which would carry them north of Cape Horn itself, perched on an insignificant island to the south, but this day the waves from the Pacific were terrifying even to Captain Janders. Once, when the *Thetis* heeled far over onto her beam ends, he looked in dismay at Mister Collins, who was brave enough to say, "I've never sailed in a worse sea, Captain. We'd better run for it." In an instant Captain Janders swung his tiny brig about and sent her running before the violent storm, eastward past dangerous rocks, and within three hours, at the amazing speed of nearly thirty knots, the little *Thetis* lost all the westward progress she had acquired in eight days.

On December 3 Mister Collins asked the fatal question: "Shall we run across the Atlantic, sir, to Cape Good Hope?" and Captain Janders replied, "We shall not!" and he trimmed his sails once more for the westerlies that roared in upon the great Pacific swells. At noon of that day John Whipple reported startling news to the frightened and freezing missionaries: "I think we're right where we were eight days ago! I'm sure that's Staten Island to the south and the point of Tierra del Fuego to the north." His wife asked weakly, "You mean to say that we're being driven backward?" When her husband nodded, she said softly, "John, I have to fight so hard to stay in my berth that my elbows are bleeding. Do see how poor Sister Hale is." And when John looked, he saw that her elbows and knees were bleeding, too. But there was nothing anyone could do but lie in his cold, wet berth and fight the frantic rolling of the ship.

On December 4 the *Thetis* reached far to the south, so that the sun barely set at all, and night consisted only of a mysterious ashen haze, holding low upon the turbulent sea. And when it looked as if there might be better wind toward the Antarctic, Captain Janders tried his next trick. Running boldly on a tack that carried him away from the protecting island behind which mariners customarily doubled the Cape, he led his tiny brig into the waters of the Drake Passage, roughest in the world. It was a gallant move, but toward morning a vast Pacific accumulation swirling with sleet and snow swept down on the *Thetis,* lifted her high, and threw her sideways, so that water rushed into the terror-stricken cabin and filled the lower berths. "Abner! Abner!" bruised Jerusha screamed from the floor, forgetting his proper title. "We're drowning." He replied calmly, picking her up gently and moving her into John Whipple's upper bunk, "No, my beloved companion, God is with this ship. He will not abandon us." The terrifying shaking continued, accompanied by fresh torrents of water slopping aft from some ruptured forward area. "We cannot stand this!" a hysterical wife screamed. "God is with this ship," Abner quieted her, and in the weird darkness, with water about his ankles and the sobbing of those who thought they would soon be dead, he prayed in a strong voice and reminded the missionaries that they had come on this voyage to do God's work and it was notorious that God tested His chosen and that their way was never quick or easy. "We shall ride through this storm and see the pleasant valleys of Hawaii," he affirmed. Then he went to each freezing stateroom and helped lift luggage out of berths into which it had been swept. No attempt was made to serve meals, but when Captain Janders looked below and saw the work Abner was doing, he shouted to the cook, "Bring some cheese aft to these poor people." Abner asked, "Are we rounding the Cape?" and Janders replied, "Not yet, but we will be." However, toward six in the evening it became apparent that the night's waves were to be even more tumultuous, so he said at last to Mister Collins, "We'll run for it," and once more within less than an hour they lost all they had gained in two days.

On December 5 the wounded brig *Thetis,* coated with ice, was back at the Atlantic entrance to the waters that guarded the Cape, and there was no sign of either an easterly wind or an abated swell, so Captain Janders kept his ship tacking idly back and forth, waiting, and about ten o'clock at night it looked as if the big chance had come, for the wind seemed to veer. Crowding sail, the captain lashed his ship into the swells and for the remaining two hours of that gray day the *Thetis* chewed awkwardly into the heavy seas and apparently made some progress.

On December 6 the brig actually accomplished forty-eight miles into a snowstorm, bucking a sea as choppy and as sickening as any the missionaries had so far experienced. There was not the abstract terror of the ship on beam ends, but there was the constant rise and fall, wallow and recovery that made even inanimate objects like the trunks and boxes creak in misery. The cold, intensified by the sleet and snow, grew worse, and wives huddled beneath wet blankets, shivering and convinced that death would be preferable to two more weeks of Cape Horn. But Brother Whipple reported heartily to all that at last the brig was making headway.

On Friday, December 7, the wind perversely returned to its former heading; the seas became more confused; and once again the *Thetis* stood on her beam ends. This time she came perilously close to foundering. Heavy trunks that had been cleated down tore loose and piled brutally into berths. Timbers creaked ominously as if they could bear no more, and the little brig fell sickeningly into a trough out of which it seemed it might not recover. "Oh, God! Let me die!" Jerusha prayed, for a trunk had pinned her against the bulkhead. Other women were crying, "Brother Hale! Can you move this box?" for they knew that he was the only missionary then capable of constructive work.

It was some minutes therefore before he got to Jerusha, and he found her wandering in speech. "Let me die, God. It wasn't Abner's fault. He was good to me, but let me die!" she whimpered. He pulled the trunk away and felt her limbs to see if they were broken, but as he did so, he heard her prayer for death. "What did you say?" he asked, appalled. "God, let me die!" she prayed blindly. With a violent slap he thrashed her on the cheeks and cried, "Mrs. Hale! You may not blaspheme!" He continued slapping her until she recovered her wits, and then he sat beside her and said, "I am afraid, too, my beloved companion. I am afraid we are going to drown. Oh!" And he braced himself for a wild ride down the hollow of a wave, and the shattering pause, and the groaning climb. "Do even you think we are lost?" Jerusha asked softly. "I am afraid," he said humbly, "but we must not blaspheme, even if we are deserted." She asked, "What did I say, dear husband?" He replied, "It's best forgotten. Mrs. Hale, will you pray?" And in the cold, dark 'tween-decks he coached her in what he thought would be their last prayer.

At that moment above decks, Captain Janders was shouting in fury, "God-damnit, Mister Collins, we can't make it!"

"Shall we run for Good Hope, sir?"

"We shall not."

"We'll founder, sir," Collins warned.

"Turn around, and we'll lick our wounds in the Falklands," Janders replied.

"And then?"

"We'll go through the Strait of Magellan."

"Yes, sir."

So THE HAMFERDITE brig *Thetis,* seventy-nine feet long, two hundred and thirty tons out of Boston, was finally turned away from Cape Horn, and on a northeast heading, which took advantage of the strong winds, it shot up to the Falkland Islands, which hung in the South Atlantic off the coast of Patagonia.

The Falklands were a group of rocky, wind-swept, treeless islands used by whalers—and those who could not double the Cape—for recuperation, and when the forbidding group hove into view on December 10 they seemed to the bruised missionaries like fragments of Beulah Land, and as soon as the *Thetis* had anchored in a rocky cove, all hastened to be among the first ashore. All through the brief, gray starless night John Whipple inspected the cold ground, and at dawn he hailed the brig with good news: "There are geese and ducks here and some small cormorants. Bring all the guns!" He organized a hunting party that was to provide the *Thetis* with fresh food for many weeks. Mister Collins led another group that found sweet water to replenish the barrels and stacks of driftwood that had reached the islands from the coast of Argentina.

"We'll keep fires going for ten days," he promised the missionaries. "We'll dry you out proper."

Wives decked the *Thetis* with laundry, since none had been done for more than a hundred days, but it was energetic Abner Hale, tramping to the highest spot of the island, who made the big discovery. There was another ship hugging one of the northern harbors, and he and two sailors ran down to it. It was a whaler just in from the Pacific, and before long its skipper and Captain Janders were comparing all the charts they had on the Magellan passage.

"It's a horrible passage," the whaler said, and he showed Captain Janders and Abner how the island of Tierra del Fuego, which they had tried to pass by the southern route, stood a narrow distance off the mainland of South America, so that the Strait of Magellan was actually the northern alternate route around Tierra del Fuego.

Nobody aboard either ship had ever penetrated that strait, but many recollected stories. "In 1578 Francis Drake made the passage in seventeen easy days," a historical expert recalled. "But in 1764 it took the Frenchman Bougainville fifty-two days. Record is two Spaniards who fought Magellan's route for a hundred and fifty days. But they finally made it."

"Why is it so difficult?" Abner asked.

"It isn't," the whaler explained. "Not until you reach the other end."

"Then what happens?" Abner pressed.

"See these rocks? The Four Evangelists? That's where ships perish."

"Why? Fog?"

"No. Westerlies from the Pacific pile up tremendous waves all along your exit from the passage. In trying to break out, you run upon the Evangels."

"You mean it's worse than where we just were?"

"The difference is this," the whaler explained. "If you try to double Cape

Horn in adverse conditions, you might have fifty days of mountainous seas. It just can't be done. At the Four Evangelists the waves are worse than anything you've seen so far, but you can breast them in an afternoon . . . if you're lucky."

"Where is it precisely that so many ships go on the rocks?" Janders reviewed.

"Here on Desolation Island. It's not bad of itself, but when a ship thinks it's breasted the Evangelists, it often finds it can't maintain position. In panic it turns and runs, and Desolation grabs it. Fifty . . . hundred ships."

"Any survivors?" Mister Collins asked.

"On Desolation rocks?" the whaler countered.

"What is the trick?" Mister Collins pressed.

"Find yourself a good harbor toward the western end of Desolation. Go out every day for a month if necessary and try to breast the Evangelists. But always keep yourself in position so that when you see you've got to run back to harbor for the night, you'll be in command and not the waves."

"That's exactly as I understand it," Captain Janders agreed.

"Is this an easterly coming up?" Mister Collins asked hopefully. "Seems to me if we caught a reliable easterly we'd be in luck. It would push us right through the strait."

"There's an error!" the whaler snorted. "Because while it's true that an easterly will help you a little in the first part of the transit, by the time the wind has built up a sea at the western exit, it simply creates added confusion around the Four Evangelists. Then you really have hell."

"But even so, the waves can be penetrated?" Janders inquired.

"Yes. Dutchmen did it. So did the Spaniards. But remember, go out every day from Desolation and come back every night till you find the right sea. And you do the steering. Not the storm."

The whaler, sensing that Abner might be a minister, asked him if he would consent to conduct divine services as a guest, and this pleased the missionary very much, for he looked at Captain Janders as if to say, "Here's one sea captain who acknowledges God," but Janders could never willingly permit Abner complete triumph, so in snakelike tones he destroyed Hale's paradise by commenting, when the whaler went below to rouse the men, "He's probably run the vilest ship on the seas. Probably has crimes on his head no man could measure. Ask him what he did in Honolulu? Once these whalers get back around the Cape and near Boston, they all beg for one good prayer to wash away their accumulation of evil."

Nevertheless, a surly, husky lot of men and officers assembled for worship, and Abner flayed whatever crimes they had committed, with this text: "Leviticus 25, verse 41: 'And shall return unto his own family.' And upon returning, will his conscience return with him?" In impassioned words, heightened by Captain Janders' goading, he analyzed the condition of a man who had been away from both the home of the Lord and the home of his family for four years, the changes which had occurred both in him and in his home of which he could not be aware and the steps which must be taken to remedy those changes, if ill, and to capitalize upon them, if favorable. The whalers listened with astonishment as he laid bare their half-expressed thoughts, and at the end of the service three men asked if he would pray with them, and when the prayers were over, the captain said, "That was a powerful sermon, young man. I should like to give you a token of our ship's appreciation." And he surprised Abner by delivering to the *Thetis'* longboat a stalk of handsome green bananas. "They'll ripen and be good for many days," he said, "and the sickly ones will enjoy them."

"What are they?" Abner asked.

"Bananas, son. Good for constipation. Better get to like them, because they're the principal food in Hawaii." The whaler showed Abner how to peel one, took a big bite, and gave the stub to Abner. "Once you become familiar with 'em, they're real good." But Abner found the penetrating smell of the skin offensive, whereupon the whaler bellowed, "You damn well better get to like 'em, son, because that's what you'll be eatin' from now on."

"Were you in Hawaii?" Abner asked.

"Was I in Honolulu?" the whaler shouted. Then, recalling the sermon just concluded, he finished lamely, "We took a dozen whales south of there."

On Tuesday, December 18, after Captain Janders had copied all the charts that his fellow skipper could provide of the Magellan passage, and had compared them with his own, finding that no two placed any single island in the passage even close to where the others did, the *Thetis* weighed anchor and headed back for Tierra del Fuego, but this time to the northern end of the island, where it abutted onto South America, and where the forbidding passage discovered by Magellan waited sullenly. As its bleak headlands came into view on the morning of December 21, Captain Janders said to Mister Collins, "Take a good look at 'em. We're not comin' back this way." And with stubborn determination he plunged into the narrow strait which had defeated many vessels.

The missionaries were fascinated by the first days of the passage and they lined the rails staring first at South America and then at Tierra del Fuego. These were the first days of summer, and once a band of natives clad only in skins was spotted. At night Abner saw the fires that had given the large island its name when Magellan first coasted, for in spite of the fact that all was bleak, it was also interesting.

The *Thetis,* aided by the easterly wind, sometimes made as much as thirty miles in a day, but more often about twenty were covered in slow and patient probing. After the first westward thrust was completed, the brig turned south, following the shoreline of Tierra del Fuego, and the days became somnolent, and there was scarcely any night at all. The missionaries sometimes slept on deck, wakening to enjoy any phenomenon that the night produced. When winds were adverse, as they often were, the *Thetis* would tie up and hunting parties would go ashore, so that for Christmas all hands had duck and thought how strange it was to be in these gray latitudes instead of in white New England. There was no seasickness now, but one passenger was growing to hate the Strait of Magellan as she had never hated any other water.

This was Jerusha Hale, for although her two major sicknesses had departed, another had taken their place, and it consisted of a violent desire to vomit each time her husband made her eat a banana. "I don't like the smell of the oil," she protested.

"I don't like it either, my dear," he explained patiently, "but if this is the food of the islands . . ."

"Let's wait till we get to the islands," she begged.

"No, if the Lord providentially sent us these bananas in the manner he did . . ."

"The other women don't have to eat them," she pleaded.

"The other women were not sent them by the direct will of God," he reasoned.

"Reverend Hale," she argued slowly, "I'm sure that when I get off this ship, where I've been sick so much, I'll be able to eat bananas. But here the oil in the skin reminds me . . . Husband, I'm going to be sick."

"No, Mrs. Hale!" he commanded. And twice a day he carefully peeled a banana, stuck half in his mouth, and said, against his own better judgment, "It's delicious." The other half he forcefully pushed into Jerusha's, watching her intently until she had swallowed it. The procedure was so obviously painful to the sickly girl that Amanda Whipple could not remain in her berth while it was being carried out, but what made it doubly nauseous was that Abner had strung the ripening bananas from the roof of their stateroom, and there they swung, back and forth, through every hour of the passage, and as they ripened they smelled.

At first Jerusha thought: "I'll watch the bunch grow smaller," but it showed no effect of her efforts to diminish it. Instead it grew larger, more aromatic, and swung closer to her face at night. "My dear husband," she pleaded, "indeed I shall be sick!" But he would place his hand firmly over her abdomen until the day's ration was swallowed, and he refused to allow her to be sick, and she obeyed.

After one such performance John Whipple asked, "Why do you like bananas so much, Brother Hale?"

"I don't," Abner said. "They make me sick, too."

"Then why do you eat them?"

"Because obviously the Lord intended me to eat them. How did I get them? As a result of having preached a sermon. I would be an ingrate if I did not eat them!"

"Do you believe in omens?" the young scientist asked.

"What do you mean?" Abner inquired.

"Superstitions? Omens?"

"Why do you ask that?"

"I was thinking. Keoki Kanakoa has been telling me about all the omens under which he used to live. When one of their canoes went out to sea, they had an old woman who did nothing but study omens. And if an albatross came, or a shark, that meant something . . . a god had sent them . . . you could learn what the god intended . . . if you could read the omen."

"What has that got to do with me?" Abner asked.

"It seems to me, Brother Hale, that you're that way with the bananas. They were given to you, so they must have been sent by God. So if they were sent by God, they must be eaten."

"John, you're blaspheming!"

"Blaspheming or not, I'd throw those bananas overboard. They're making everybody sick."

"Overboard!"

"Yes, Reverend Hale," Jerusha interrupted. "Throw them overboard."

"This is intolerable!" Abner cried, storming onto the deck, from which he speedily returned to the stateroom. "If anyone touches those bananas! They were sent by God to instruct us in our new life. You and I, Mrs. Hale, are going to eat every one of those bananas. It is God's will." So as the *Thetis* crept agonizingly ahead, the bananas danced malodorously in the stateroom.

The brig had now left Tierra del Fuego and was amidst the hundreds of nameless islands that comprised the western half of the passage. The winds veered and the dreary days ran into dreary weeks and Captain Janders wrote repeatedly in his log: "Tuesday, January 15. Twenty-sixth day in the passage. Land close on both hands. Beat all day into adverse wind. Made 4 miles but toward sunset lost on every tack. Could find no hold for anchor on sloping shores. Ran back and moored where we anchored last night. But hope this westerly gale continues, for it will smooth out waters at 4 Evangels. Shore party shot fine geese and caught 2 pailsfl. sweet mussels."

Day followed day, yielding a progress of four miles or six or none. Men would tow the *Thetis* from anchorage out into the wind and gamble that they would sleep in the same spot that night. Two facts preyed increasingly on their minds. The land about them was so bleak that it could not possibly support life for long, especially if summer left, and it was leaving. And all thought: "If it is so difficult here, what will it be when we reach Desolation Island? And when we have reached there, what must the Four Evangelists be like?" It seemed that inch by painful inch they were approaching a great climax, and this was true.

On the thirty-second day of this desolate passage an easterly wind sprang up and whisked the little brig along the north shore of Desolation Island, a location made more terrible by the fact that sailors spotted the stern boards of some ship that had foundered on the rocks. The sea grew rougher, and eighteen of the missionaries found it advisable to stay below, where the smell of bananas added to their qualms. That night Jerusha declared that she could not, on pain of death, eat another banana, but Abner, having heard such protests before, gallantly ate his half, then forced the remainder into Jerusha's mouth. "You may not get sick," he commanded, holding her stomach in his control. But the ship lurched as the first fingers of the Pacific swell probed into the passage, and neither Jerusha nor Abner could dominate her retching, and she began to vomit.

"Mrs. Hale!" he shouted, clapping his other hand over her mouth, but the sickness continued until the berth was fouled. "You did that on purpose!" he muttered.

"Husband, I am so sick," she whimpered. The tone of her words impressed him, and tenderly he cleaned away the mess, making her as comfortable as possible.

"I'm not doing this to torment you, my dear companion," he argued. "God sent us these bananas. Look!" And he took down one of the yellow fruits, which he had grown to detest, and ate the entire thing.

"I'm going to be sick again!" she cried, and again he washed away the filth.

The next morning showed that the *Thetis* had run to the end of Desolation Island and had completed more than ninety-nine hundredths of the Magellan passage. All that remained was to effect the short dash past the Four Evangelists, four cruel and unpopulated rocks that guarded the western entrance to the strait. So at dawn on Tuesday, January 22, 1822, the little brig left the protection of Desolation Island to test the meeting ground of storms, the wave-racked confluence of the easterly moving Pacific and the westerly moving Atlantic, and as the whaling captain had predicted, the good winds that had accompanied the *Thetis* on her last days now accounted for a turbulence that no man aboard the ship had hitherto experienced.

Gigantic waves from the Pacific lashed in with terrifying force, apparently able to sweep all before them, but the choppier sea from the Atlantic rushed like a terrier into the thundering surf and tore it into a thousand separate oceans, each with its own current and direction. As his small craft approached this multiple maelstrom Captain Janders ordered, "All hands on deck lash your-selves to the ship," and lines were secured about waists and chests, and hand holds were quickly improvised, and the *Thetis,* all openings closed, plunged into the tremendous confusion.

For the first fifteen minutes the tiny brig was thrashed about as if the terriers of the sea had left off tormenting each other and had turned on her. She was lifted up and thrown down, ripped along on her port beams, then wallowed over and thrown backwards. She slipped and slid, and no man not tied to her decks could have survived aloft.

"Do you keep your eye upon the Evangelists, Mister Collins?" Captain Janders shouted above the fury.

"I do, sir."

"Can we take more seas, Mister Collins?"

"We cannot, sir."

"We'll turn and run."

"Mind the rocks, sir."

And the *Thetis,* whipping around, slashed into the violent seas coming from the Atlantic, and sped like a wounded sea animal back to Desolation Island. Below, the missionaries prayed. Not even the sick were able to remain in their berths, so violent the shaking and pitching had been.

Suddenly it was calm, and Captain Janders hid his little craft in a snug harbor whose shoreline was shaped like a fishhook. And each morning for the next week, Abner Hale, John Whipple, two other missionaries and four stout sailors rowed ashore with long ropes attached to the prow of the *Thetis.* Running around to the tip of the fishhook, they would strain and dig into the sand, pulling until the brig began to move. Slowly, slowly, they would tow it out to the entrance of the main passage, and then run back to the rowboat and overtake it.

And each day for a week the *Thetis* nosed its way carefully into the meeting ground of the oceans, tested them, tried, valiantly probed, and courted destruction. The turbulence was so majestic that there seemed no possibility of subduing it, and the sailors lashed to the masts wondered if the captain would turn and head back through the strait for Good Hope. But each evening Captain Janders swore, "Tomorrow we'll break the spell. Tomorrow we'll be free." In his log he wrote: "Tuesday, January 29. Tried again. Gigantic swells from Pacific clashing with choppy sea from Atlantic caused scenes of most frightful violence. Surges so high no ship could master them. Ran for same harbor."

On the thirtieth day of January the winds veered to the west, which in the long run was a good thing in that they would now stop supporting the Atlantic choppiness and turn to stabilizing the unhampered Pacific; but their immediate effect was to prohibit any further assault on the exit. Therefore, the *Thetis* remained tied to shore in her snug fishhook harbor while Captain Janders, Mister Collins, Abner and John Whipple climbed a small hill to survey the wild confluence of the oceans. They could not see the Four Evangelists, but they knew where they were, and as they studied the pattern of the giant waves, Abner said, "Have you thought, sir, that perhaps you are being held back by God's will?"

Captain Janders did not growl at the young man. "I am willing to consider anything, if only we can breast that damned mile of ocean."

"It occurred to me last night," Abner said, "that your insane refusal to dispose of your worldly novels has cursed this ship."

Mister Collins looked at the young minister with blank astonishment and was about to make an obscene expostulation when Janders silenced him. "What did you have in mind, Reverend Hale?"

"If we missionaries can pray, and if we can get this ship through the barrier, will you then dispose of your worldly literature, and as the captain of a ship that needs God, accept books from me?"

"I will," Janders said solemnly. And the four men, standing on a hill at the end of the world, entered into a compact, and when the missionaries were gone, Janders justified himself to his first mate: "I am determined to pass this point. I've never seen such seas as we encountered at Cape Horn. Now this. Call me superstitious if you will, but it's bad luck for a ship to carry a minister. We've got eleven of 'em. If they're the cause of the bad luck, maybe they can also be the cause of good luck. I'll try anything."

That night Abner assembled the missionaries and told them of the compact. "God has been holding this ship back to teach us a lesson," he assured them, "but our prayers will lift the curse." To John Whipple and others, this seemed like medievalism, and they would not pray, but the majority did, and at the end of the prayer Whipple asked if he might pray, too, and Abner assented. "Lord, strengthen the hands and the eyes of our mariners," Whipple prayed. "Abate the wind, lower the waves and let us pass."

"Amen," Captain Janders said.

After prayers, Abner visited Jerusha, still bedridden, and shared a banana with her. When she protested that it was this which was keeping her abed, he pleaded: "We are placing our destiny in the hands of God tonight. Please bear with me, beloved companion, and if we pass the barrier tomorrow, you will not have to eat any more bananas."

"Is that a sacred promise?" she asked.

"It is," he assured her. So she mastered her gorge, felt her husband's firm hand on her stomach, and ate.

At four o'clock in the morning the entire ship met for prayers, and after the missionaries had spoken long, Captain Janders prayed, "Lord, get us through."

It was not yet five when Abner and John rowed ashore with their six regular towing companions, and the small craft edged its way into the main channel, but when the rope men were hauled back on board, Abner announced: "This day I want to pray on deck."

"Lash yourself to the mast," Janders grunted. To Collins he said, "The waves are as big as ever, but the sea is steadier and we have a wind we can cut into."

"As good a day as we'll get," the mate calculated.

"We're away!" Janders cried, and the *Thetis* probed far out to sea, well south of the Four Evangelists and into the wildest part of the ocean.

These were the hours of decision. Two days ago the problem had been to ride with the helpful wind from the stern, trying to accumulate sufficient speed to penetrate the massive waves. Now the wind was full in the face, and the *Thetis* had to tack first north, then south, then north, trying always to gain a few hundred yards of purchase in the sea, so that on one great burst to the north the tiny brig would at last clear the Evangelists. The grave danger involved was that on the vital run to the north, the *Thetis* would not hold its advantage, but would be swept sideways by the waves, and onto the rocks, crashing in final and hopeless destruction.

The hours of early morning passed, and the *Thetis* made one fruitless tack after another. Often on her beam ends, she fought vainly for leverage against the sea, but Abner could feel her slipping away, back toward Desolation Island, away from the line of safety that would permit a long tack past the Four Evangelists.

The hours of midday came and went, and the little brig fought on. Now she gained a mile and entered a more turbulent part of the ocean, where the full and mighty Pacific lashed out at her, and the timbers creaked and the masts swayed and Abner watched the whiskered face of Captain Janders, peering ahead, calculating the wind.

At three in the afternoon the pounding became almost unbearable on deck, and all not lashed down would have been washed away by the gigantic seas, so that Abner prayed, "Dear God, care for those below. Let the air they breathe be sweet." And he could smell the foul air of the staterooms and pitied the missionaries.

At four o'clock, but with no fear of encroaching dusk, for the summer sun would not set till nearly ten, the position of the *Thetis* was perilous. For Captain Janders was required either to stand farther out to sea and thus surrender all hope of running safely back to Desolation Island, or to abandon this day's attempt. He was loath to do the latter, because he had got closer to position than ever before, so for some minutes in the height of the gale he pondered.

"There's only half a mile more of turbulence," he shouted to Mister Collins.

"Hardly that, sir."

"Do you keep your eye on the Evangelists?" Janders cried.

"I do, sir."

"How many points more to windward must we head to pass the rocks, Mister Collins?"

"Three, sir."

"Can we hold such a course?"

The question was an unfair one, and both Janders and Collins knew it, for the captain was trying to tempt his mate into making the ultimate life-or-death decision. Mister Collins looked doggedly ahead and said nothing.

"Can you ease her three points into the wind, Mister Collins?"

"That I can, sir!" And the creaking *Thetis* bit more directly into the storm.

"If we hold this tack, will we clear the rocks, Mister Collins?"

"Yes, sir. If we hold this tack."

The two men stood tensely, trying to detect any notice of the brig's slipping in the great troughs, but she held firm. A minute passed, then two, then three, and finally Captain Janders shouted to all topside, "We'll run for the rocks. Stand ready to cut yourselves loose and tend the ropes."

Rarely did a group of men sailing a ship face a more clearcut problem. If the winds held, and the keel maintained its cut into the waves, this long tack would throw the *Thetis* just outside the Four Evangelists, and the penetration would have been accomplished, for on the southward tack the little ship could sail all night if necessary, until the last turbulence was cleared.

"Now's the time to pray, Reverend Hale," Janders shouted above the wind, and Abner, lashed to the mainmast at both the armpits and waist, prayed only that the present relationship of ship and ocean and wind be maintained.

Then came Mister Collins' calm warning: "She's slipping, sir."

"I feel her slipping, Mister Collins," Captain Janders replied, his stern face hiding his fear.

"Shall we raise the topsail a little more into the wind?"

"Raise her all the way, Mister Collins."

"She may carry away, sir, in this wind."

Captain Janders hesitated, studied the way in which his brig was losing purchase, and cried, "We've got to have that sail! If it holds, we'll make it. If it carries away, no matter. We were lost anyway." And he whipped around toward where his men were lashed, shouting directions that sent them hauling ropes which started the after topsail higher into the wind, where it could counteract the sideward set of the ocean. But as the men hauled, their lines caught in the top block, and the triangular topsail whipped dangerously in the wind, and the *Thetis* appeared doomed.

"You and you, clear the top block!" Janders shouted. And from the stormy deck, where they had been lashed to save themselves, Cridland and the old whaler cut themselves loose and grabbed for the ropes leading to the top of the mainmast.

They climbed like monkeys, four secure hands, four certain feet clinging to the ropes as the mast whipped back and forth in the freezing storm. Higher and higher they went, as their ship drifted toward the rocks. "May God protect them," Abner prayed, as they dangled far above his head.

The *Thetis* now entered a segment of the sea where the waves were of special violence, for they were rebounding from the Evangelists off to starbound, and as the little brig rolled from one beam end to the other, torn this way and that, the top of the mainmast, where the two sailors worked, slashed swiftly in great arcs of more than a hundred degrees. At the extremity of each swing the tall mast whipped sharply, whistling in the wind, as if determined to dislodge the men that annoyed its ropes. On one such desperate passage Cridland lost his cap, and in grabbing for it with his right hand, he seemed, as viewed from below, to have been swept away, and Abner screamed, "God save his soul!" But it was only his hat that was gone.

"Try the ropes again!" Captain Janders shouted.

"They don't pull clear yet," the second mate yelled above the storm.

"Are we drifting toward the rocks, Mister Collins?"

"We are, sir."

"Shall we send more men aloft?"

"Nothing any more can do," Collins replied.

So the two mariners stared ahead in the late afternoon storm, feeling the ship, praying. "Try the ropes again!" Janders cried, but again they failed to respond. Clasping his hand behind him, Janders took several deep breaths and said with resignation, "We've about eight more minutes, Mister Collins. This was a sane try."

At this point Abner forgot the navigators near him and focused only on the two sailors, who continued to fly through great sickening arcs of heaven. Freezing rain and howling winds were upon them; the violence of the pitching ship seemed concentrated at the point where they labored; and Abner recalled the plea of the old whaler: "I would not like to round Cape Horn without a Bible." And he began to pray for the salvation of these two brave men on whom the safety of the brig now rested. And as they flashed through the gray sky, riding high in the heart of the storm, his agonized prayers went with them.

"Try the ropes again!" Janders called at the expiry of two of his vital eight minutes, and this time the sailors shouted madly, and the ropes moved, and the after mainsail crept slowly up the swaying mast, and wind was mysteriously trapped in its triangular expanse, and the sliding shoreward stopped.

"I feel her steady on course," Janders shouted.

"She is steady on," Collins repeated.

"Will she clear the Evangels?" Janders checked.

"She will clear them," Collins replied dully, hiding the exultation his heart felt.

And as the last fearful moments passed, the little brig *Thetis* maintained her northward tack into the storm, until at last she neared the perilous rocks, and all on deck saw that she would pass them by a margin of dreadful precision.

"The Lord God of Hosts is with us!" Abner shouted in unministerial joy.

But Captain Janders did not hear, for he kept his eyes fixed ahead, refusing to look at the Evangelists. He was seeking the ocean area where it would be safe for him to swing the *Thetis* onto her new and final tack. Minutes passed, then a quarter of an hour, then a half hour, and still he kept his eyes monotonously fixed on the great, heaving ocean, until finally, in swift alteration, he heeled the brig over, and cut her back on a southward tack that would carry her through the last mountainous waves and down the final vile troughs. Then he shouted, "Bring the men down." And Cridland and the old whaler came down from their dizzy perch and found footing on the deck. "May God be praised," Abner mumbled.

Yet at this exact moment, when he was entitled to share in the ship's jubilation, Abner was grave, as if in a trance, thinking: "Two days ago when a comforting wind was at our back, we were unable to accomplish anything. But today, with the gale right in our faces, we were able to fight it." He studied the little brig to discover the secret whereby a New England ship could cut directly into the heart of a storm, combating the elements each inch of the way, and although he did not understand the technique Captain Janders had utilized, he understood the man, and all men, and himself. "How strange," he reflected in the howling wind, "that when the storm is in your face, you can fight it."

Later, when Captain Janders unleashed Abner, the mariner said, in a kind of daze, "I would not want to be the captain of whom it was said in Boston, 'He tried to round the Horn, but ran instead for Good Hope.'"

"No one will say that of you, Captain," Abner said proudly.

The hatches were broken open and Mister Collins shouted the good news to the missionaries: "We are safe!"

All below who could stand piled on deck, and in the cold wind Captain Janders said, "Reverend Hale, through God's grace we broke through. Will you pray?" But for the only time on the voyage, Abner was numbed into silence. His eyes were filled with tears and he could think only of Cridland and the whaler, whipping through distant space, working to save the ship, and of Captain Janders fighting the storm, so John Whipple read from the sweet thundering passages in the Psalms that sailors love:

"God is our refuge and strength, a very present help in trouble.

"Therefore will not we fear, though the earth be removed, and though the mountains be carried into the midst of the sea;

"Though the water thereof roar and be troubled, though the mountains shake with the swelling thereof. . . .

"The Lord of Hosts is with us; the God of Jacob is our refuge. . . .

"They that go down to the sea in ships, that do business in great waters;

"These see the works of the Lord, and His wonders in the deep.

"For He commandeth, and raiseth the stormy wind, which lifteth up the waves thereof.

"They mount up to the heaven, they go down again to the depths; their soul is melted because of trouble.

"They reel to and fro, and stagger like a drunken man, and are at their wit's end.

"Then they cry unto the Lord in their trouble, and he bringeth them out of their distresses.

"He maketh the storm a calm, so that the waves thereof are still.

"Then are they glad because they be quiet; so He bringeth them unto their desired haven.

"Oh that men would praise the Lord for His goodness."

It was then noticed that Captain Janders had disappeared during the reading, and he now climbed from the hatchway with an armful of books. "Yesterday I promised Reverend Hale that if his prayers could get us through this barrier, I would forsake my books for his. Richardson . . . Sterne . . . Smollett . . . Walpole." One by one he tossed them into the Pacific, already beginning to merit its name. Then he added, "From December 21 to January 31 we were forty-two days in these straits. I have never known such a passage, but we have made it safely. God be praised."

Abner's triumph was tempered by defeat, for as the missionaries were watching the worldly books disappear, they were attracted by the sight of Jerusha Hale climbing on deck followed by Keoki, who lugged the remnants of the bananas. Walking unsteadily past her husband, she found the railing of the ship and threw the bananas, one by one, far out to sea. That night she told her husband, in a berth already quieter, "You bullied me, Abner . . . No, I shall use your name from now, for to me you are Abner. You bullied me through your sin of overzealousness. Never in our life again will I submit to your bullying, Abner, for I am as good a judge of God's will as you, and God never intended a sick woman to eat so hatefully." When Abner showed his surprise at this ultimatum she softened it by adding the truth: "While you were away talking with the men tonight, Captain Janders said that at the worst part of the passage, he felt comforted that a man of your courage was with him. What is more important, Abner, is that I am comforted that a man of your courage and piety is with me." And she kissed him.

Before she could kiss him again, Keoki came to the cabin, saying, "Reverend Hale, the old whaler needs you. In the fo'c's'l."

"Is he drunk again?" Abner asked suspiciously.

"He needs you," the Hawaiian repeated, and he led Abner to where the rugged old man lay in his filthy bunk, mumbling.

"What is it?" Abner asked quietly.

"Can I have my Bible back, now?" the whaler asked.

"No. The church gave you a Bible once, and you defiled it. You brought scorn and ridicule on us all."

"Reverend Hale, you saw me in the ropes today. You know how I feared going aloft at Cape Horn . . . without a Bible, that is."

"No, the Lord is harsh with backsliders," Abner said sternly.

At this point Cridland, who had shared the perils with the old man, suggested, "Reverend Hale, suppose you didn't have to give him the Bible. Suppose I gave him mine. Would you then . . ."

"Give you another! Never! Cridland, the Lord has said, 'The backslider in heart shall be filled with his own ways.' It is these men, more than sinners, who damage the church."

"But, Reverend Hale, in the storm it was this man who saved us all. I tried to break the sail loose, but I couldn't. He did it all."

"It's true, Reverend," the old whaler confessed. "I saved the ship, and I want my Bible back."

"No," Abner said. "While you were aloft, I prayed for you. And I pray for you now. If you saved this ship, we all thank you gratefully. But run the risk of having the entire ship laugh at the church again? No. That I cannot do." And he stalked aft.

It was not until Saturday night that Abner noticed Jerusha without her

Bible. He was conducting prayers and saw that his wife was reading from Sister Whipple's, so when they had returned to their quarters he asked quietly, "Where is your Bible, my dear wife?"

She replied, "I gave it to the old whaler."

"To the old . . . How did you hear of him?"

"Keoki came to me, weeping for the evil old man."

"And you sided with Keoki against your own husband . . . against the church?"

"No, Abner. I simply gave a brave old man a Bible."

"But, Mrs. Hale . . ."

"My name is Jerusha."

"But we discussed this in the cabin. How backsliders are the ones who do the church greatest damage."

"I didn't give my Bible to a backslider, Abner. I gave it to a man who was afraid. And if the Bible cannot dispel fear, then it is not the book we have been led to believe."

"But the position of the mission? The foundation of our church?"

"Abner," she said persuasively, "I'm sure that this old man will backslide again, and he may do us damage. But on Thursday night, when he climbed down from that mast, he was close to God. He saved my life, and yours. And the idea of God has no meaning for me unless at such times He is willing to meet even an evil old man with love."

"What do you mean, the idea of God?"

"Abner, do you think that God is a man who hides up there in the clouds?"

"I think that God hears every word you are saying, and I think He must be as perplexed as I am." But before he could continue his charges, Jerusha, with her liquid brown curls dancing beside her ears, kissed him once more, and they fell into their narrow bunk.

It was long after midnight when Abner Hale, troubled as never before, left his bunk and went on deck, where a few bright stars were strong enough to dominate the dim, gray Antarctic night. He was troubled, first because Jerusha had given the old man her Bible, against his orders as it were, but more because of his deep and growing appetite for his wife's consoling body. Three times on this trip major arguments with Jerusha had ended by her laughingly drawing him into the narrow bunk, across whose opening she lowered the curtains, and each time during the next dazzling half hour he had forgot God and the problems of God. All he knew was that Jerusha Bromley Hale was more exciting than the storm, more peaceful than the ocean at rest.

He was convinced that such surrender on his part must be evil. He had often listened, in the cramped stateroom, to John and Amanda Whipple whiling away the hours, and he had marked their sudden cessation of whispering, followed by strange noises and Amanda's curious, uncontrollable cries, and he had judged that this was what the church meant when it spoke of "sanctified joy." He had intended discussing this with Jerusha, but he had been ashamed to do so, for now and again his own great surges of "sanctified joy" had left him morally stunned. Anything so mysterious and powerful must be evil, and surely the Bible spoke frequently of women who tempted men, with disastrous results. So on the one hand, Abner's imperfect knowledge of life inclined him to think that as a minister he would be far better off with Jerusha not so close to him. She was too intoxicating, too instinct with "sanctified joy."

But as soon as he reached this confused yet understandable conclusion, he was faced with the undeniable fact, clear to even a fool, that for a minister to live without a wife was nothing but popery, and if there was one thing he wished with all his heart to avoid it was popish ways. "The great men of the Old Testament had wives," he reasoned, "and it is not until you reach St. Paul that you get such admonitions as, 'I say therefore to the unmarried . . . , It is good for them if they abide even as I. But if they cannot contain, let them marry: for it is better to marry than to burn.' What does such a passage signify?" he asked himself throughout the strange half-night.

He walked back and forth for several hours, and the night watch joked, "He really has to do the missionary waltz!" but being of simpler minds, and particularly of minds that had long ago settled this difficult problem of man and woman—"The reason Honolulu's the best port on earth is that in Honolulu the women climb aboard the ship already undressed and ready to work"—they would have been unable to comprehend his real perplexities.

"Do I love Jerusha too profoundly?" he asked the gray night. But whenever he came near concluding that he ought to love her less, he would think of her overwhelming loveliness and he would cry, "No! That is the Romish way!" and he would return to his dead center of confusion. Thus in the night hours he wrestled with his sweet, perplexing temptation.

Sunday rose brisk and clear, and for the first time on the voyage, the entire missionary family was able to attend topside service in the cold, bracing air which swept up from the Antarctic. Since it was to be an occasion of special celebration, the four wives in Abner's stateroom asked their husbands to move elsewhere while they helped one another dress.

For this thanksgiving day Jerusha modestly changed from the two-piece red flannel underwear she had been wearing for some weeks into a fresh set, over which she laced a stout corset held in position by a two-inch-wide busk of polished birch. Long hand-knitted black stockings were pinned to the bottom edge of the corset, and a corset cover, starched long ago in Walpole, was fitted into place, after which pantaloons, also starched, were drawn up. Thus properly founded, Jerusha now climbed into a woolen underpetticoat, a starched linen petticoat and finally a cambric petticoat, all lashed securely at the waist. A small bustle was added, over which a hooped broadcloth dress was hung, its alternate patterns of black and purple providing a properly subdued color.

Next Jerusha adjusted a paisley shawl about her shoulders, fitted a saucy poke bonnet about her pale face, slipped a knitted bag over her arm, tucked a handkerchief into one cuff of her dress, jammed her fingers first into silk mittens and then into woolen ones, and stood while Amanda Whipple held her coat for her. She was then ready for morning service, and after she had helped the other women into their coats, the four missionary wives climbed the hatchway ladder and appeared on deck.

NOW CAME THE days of gold, the memorable days when the *Thetis* rolled gently in the sun, all canvas set, and dolphins chased flying fish that shone in iridescence as they leaped. The little brig was away on an unbroken leg of more than seven thousand miles from Cape Horn to Hawaii, and slowly the ugly cold of the south gave way to the increasing warmth of the north. The new stars of Tierra del Fuego began to disappear and the old familiar constellations of New England crept back into place. But most of all, the mission family became fused into a single organized and dedicated group. Some, who forgot how sick they had been and how Abner alone had kept the family functioning, protested at his assumption of leadership, and one sharp-tongued wife was heard to say, "You'd think he was the Lord's anointed," but her husband quieted her by remembering, "Someone had to make decisions . . . even in a family."

As the equator neared, the daily lessons organized by Abner became more meaningful, and many mornings were spent, after the missionary waltz had ended, with group sessions discussing Wayland's *Moral Philosophy* or Alexander's *Evidences of Christianity.* Keoki Kanakoa also gave lectures on the condition of the islanders, but when he cried, "In Hawaii women are forbidden on pain of strangulation from eating bananas!" his point was somewhat dulled by Jerusha, who whispered loudly, "I count that no great privation." But the most solemn moment in any session came when someone, usually a woman, intoned the first line of their most cherished hymn: " 'Blest be the tie that binds' "; for at such times the mission family was indeed bound together in a Christian brotherhood that few discover in this world.

With the Pacific more placid and daily walks more congenial, seasickness vanished and constipation diminished, but a strange new illness began to take their place. At the beginning of the day women passengers would often suddenly feel an overwhelming nausea attack them, and they would have to vomit, just as if the ship were rolling in its former manner. It soon became apparent to Dr. Whipple that of the eleven wives aboard the *Thetis,* at least seven and possibly nine were pregnant, and he was proud when his own wife became the first to acknowledge openly that she was, as she phrased it, "expecting a small messenger from heaven." Her handsome husband perplexed the missionaries by remarking cryptically, "It's not surprising. I've know her since she was seven."

Jerusha's pregnancy was one of the latest to be certified, but it was also the one which was most enjoyed by the mother, for she was almost unmissionary in her delight. "It is a great solace to me, Abner," she said, "to think that I am going to become a mother in a new land. It's beautifully symbolic . . . as if we were destined to accomplish great things in Hawaii." Abner, like the other husbands, was bewildered, for like them he knew practically nothing about having babies; and then a frightening discovery was made: of the eleven women aboard the *Thetis* not one had ever had a child, nor had any ever attended a birth. Neither had the men, excepting Dr. Whipple, and he suddenly became a most important man, breaking out his *Practical Handbook of Midwifery,* which everyone studied with care; and it was then that the first substantial shadow fell across the mission family, for women began to realize that when they reached Hawaii, Dr. Whipple would be assigned to one island and they would go to another, and when their time came, the mission's only doctor would be inaccessible, and birth would be given under primitive conditions with only such help as a wife's husband could muster. It was then that wives looked at their husbands with greater affection, knowing that upon these men depended the family safety; and in this way the cabin of the *Thetis* became a kind of obstetrical seminar, with Brother Whipple as instructor and his medical books as texts.

It was early one Sunday morning that the missionaries heard the first mate cry, "Whaler to starboard!" Jerusha and Amanda, experiencing morning dizziness, did not go on deck, but the other wives did and saw looming out of the morning mists a magnificent three-masted ship, all sails set and riding the waves majestically like a queen. Smoke from the oil pots had darkened her sails, proving her to be a whaler, and now one of her whaleboats was approaching the *Thetis.*

"What ship are you?" Mister Collins hailed.

"Bark *Carthaginian,* Captain Hoxworth, out of New Bedford. And you?"

"Brig *Thetis,* Captain Janders, out of Boston."

"We bring you mail to carry back to Hawaii," the whaler's mate explained, as he climbed deftly aboard. "And we'll take yours to New Bedford." Then, seeing the missionaries in their tall hats, he asked, "Are these men ministers?"

"Missionaries, for Hawaii," Captain Janders replied.

The whaler hesitated momentarily, then nodded deferentially and asked, "Would one or two of you come aboard and conduct Sabbath services for us? We haven't had any for months . . . really it would be years. We'll be home soon, and we'd like to remind ourselves . . ."

Abner, recalling his good work aboard the earlier whaler at the Falklands, quickly volunteered, and so did John Whipple, but principally because he wanted to see one of New England's great whaling ships at close hand. They were lowered into the whaleboat and started off, whereupon Abner as an afterthought shouted, "Tell our wives we'll be back after service."

At the *Carthaginian* the young missionaries were greeted handsomely. A tall, wiry, powerful man with a whaler's cap far back on his head shot out a big hand and cried in a deep, commanding voice, "I'm Rafer Hoxworth, out of New Bedford, and I'm mighty glad to see you good men coming aboard. We could use some prayers on this bark."

"Have you had a good trip?" Whipple asked.

"Whales are scarce," Hoxworth replied, cocking a long leg on the railing. "Our capacity is thirty-two hundred barrels, but we have only twenty-six hundred. Rather disappointing." Then he added, "But of course, we've already shipped twenty-two hundred barrels on ahead, so I don't think the owners will be unhappy."

"Have you been away from New Bedford long?"

"Coming four years," Hoxworth replied, rubbing his powerful chin. "That's a long time . . . a very long time."

"But the oil you have, plus what you sent home . . . does make it a good trip?" Whipple pursued.

"Oh, yes! Good enough so that our share will permit several of us to get married."

"Including you?" Whipple asked.

"Yes."

"Congratulations, Captain Hoxworth. Abner!" and he called his sallow-faced companion, who was already arguing salvation and temperance with some of the crew. "Abner! Captain Hoxworth's going to get married when he gets home."

The scrawny little missionary with the pale stringy hair looked up at the rugged whaler and said, "And after four years of doing whatever he wanted to in Honolulu, he now hopes to get back into Christian ways, and asks our assistance."

The big captain tensed his right fist and pressed his foot strongly into the railing, but kept his temper. To himself he muttered, "By God! These missionaries are all alike. All over the world. You try to meet them halfway . . ." And John Whipple thought: "Why can't Abner just accept the day's events as they transpire? If a whaler heading home desires a Sabbath service, why can't we simply have the service?"

Then Whipple heard Captain Hoxworth's booming voice break into laughter. "Yes, Reverend . . . What was the name? Hale. Yes, Reverend Hale, you're right. Us whalers hang our consciences on Cape Horn when we head west, and then pick 'em up three years later when we come back home. We'd kind of like to have you ready us up for the job of catching 'em as we glide past."

"Do you glide past Cape Horn?" Abner asked in some confusion.

"Certainly."

"How long did it take you to double Cape Horn coming out?" Abner continued.

"What was it?" Hoxworth asked one of the men, a scowling, evil-looking rascal with a long scar across his cheek. "Oh, you weren't with us. We picked that one up in Honolulu when our cooper jumped ship. You, Anderson! How long did it take us to double the Cape coming out?"

"Three days."

Abner gasped. "You mean you got around Cape Horn in three days?"

"It was like glass," Captain Hoxworth boomed. "And it'll be like glass for us when we go home. We run a lucky ship."

"That's the truth!" Anderson laughed. "If there's whales, we get 'em."

Abner stood perplexed in the sunlight, trying to rationalize the fact that an obscene whaler—for he was convinced that this was a hell ship—could double the Cape in three days whereas it had taken a group of missionaries almost eight weeks, and he concluded to himself, "The mysterious ways of the Lord with His appointed are beyond understanding."

"We'll pray aft," Captain Hoxworth announced, leading his men and the missionaries to an afterdeck that seemed as spacious as a village common compared to the cramped *Thetis*.

Abner whispered to Whipple, "You lead the singing and the prayers, and I'll give the sermon I gave on the other whaler," but just as the crew began singing, "Another six days' work is done," the lookout bellowed, "Thar she blows!" and the assembly disintegrated, some rushing for the whaleboats, some for glasses and some up the lower rigging.

Captain Hoxworth's deep-set eyes glistened as he spotted the blowing whales off beyond the *Thetis,* and he strode past the missionaries. "Get those boats away swiftly!" he boomed.

"Captain! Captain!" Abner protested. "We're having hymns!"

"Hymns hell!" Hoxworth shouted. "Them's whales!" Grabbing a horn, he shouted directions that sent the whaleboats far out to sea and watched with his glass as they closed in upon the mammoth sperm whales that were moving along in a colony of gigantic forms.

At this point John Whipple faced a major decision. He knew, for he was a missionary like Abner, that since this was the Sabbath he was bound not to participate in this desecration of catching whales; but he also knew as a scientist that he might never again have a chance of watching a crew fight a great sperm whale, so after a moment's indecision he handed Abner his tall hat and said, "I'm going up into the rigging." Abner protested, but in vain, and during the ensuing seven exciting hours, he stood glumly aft and refused steadfastly to look at the whaling operations.

Brother Whipple from his vantage point in the rigging saw the three whale-boats from the *Carthaginian,* each with sail aloft, a harpooner, a helmsman and four rowers, sweep down upon the massive whales.

"They're sparm!" Captain Hoxworth exulted. "Look at 'em!" and he passed Whipple a telescope. In the glass John spied the enormous beasts, wallowing in the sea and spouting a mixture of water and compressed air more than fifteen feet into the air.

"How many whales are there out there?" Whipple asked.

"Thirty?" Hoxworth suggested cautiously.

"How many will you try to take?"

"We'll be lucky if we get one. Sparm's smart whales."

Whipple watched the lead boat try to sneak up on a particularly large monster, but it moved aggravatingly off, so the mate directed his whaleboat onto a substitute, a huge gray-blue sperm that lazed along in the sun. Creeping up to it from the rear and on the right side, the mate maneuvered his prow deftly into the whale's long flank, and the harpooner, poised with left leg extended securely into the bottom of the boat, right cocked precariously against the gunwales, drew the harpoon back in his left hand and then flashed it with incredible might deep into the whale's resistant body.

At this first agonizing moment the great beast flipped out of the water, the harpoon lines trailing, and Whipple cried, "It's bigger than the *Thetis!*" For the men of the *Carthaginian* had hooked into a mammoth whale.

"It'll make eighty barrels!" a seaman cried.

"If we take him," Hoxworth cautioned. Grabbing the glass from Whipple, he watched the manner in which the whale plunged in its first attempt to shake off its tormentors. "He's sounded," the captain reported ominously, waiting to see how the first mad dash of the monster would be handled by the crew.

Whipple could see the rope whirring out of the harpooner's tub, with a sailor poised ready with an ax to chop it free—thus losing the whale if trouble developed—and it seemed as if the leviathan must be probing the very bottom of the ocean, so much rope went out. The minutes passed, and there was no sign of the whale. The other two boats placed themselves out of the way, yet ready to assist if the whale surfaced near them.

Then, in an unexpected quarter, and not far from the *Carthaginian,* the whale surfaced. It came roaring up through the waves, twisted, turned, flapped its great flukes, then blew. A tower of red blood spurted high into the air, a monument of bubbling death, and poised there for a moment in the sunlight as if it were a pillar of red marble, falling back at last into the sea to make the waves crimson. Four more times the huge beast spouted its lungs' burden of blood. Hoxworth, noting the color, shouted, "He's well stuck!"

Now came the most tense moment of the fight, for the anguished whale hesitated, and all knew that if it came out of this pause in the wrong direction it might stove the whaleboats, or crush them in its powerful underslung jaw, or even crash headfirst into the *Carthaginian* herself, sinking her within minutes, in the way many whalers had been lost. This time the whale ran true, and at a speed of thirty miles an hour, rushed through the open ocean, dragging the whaleboat along behind. Now the sail was furled and the four rowers sat with their oars aloft, while their mates aboard the *Carthaginian* shouted, "There goes the Nantucket sleigh ride!"

In this way six men in a little rowboat fought an enormous whale to death. The beast dived and paused, spouted blood and dived again. It ran for the open sea, and doubled back, but the harpoon worked deeper into its flank, and the rope remained taut. When the whale moved close to the boat, the oarsmen worked feverishly hauling in rope; but when the beast fled, they played it out again; and in this wild red game of take in and play out, the whale began to sense that it would be the loser.

Now a second whaleboat crept in, and its harpooner launched another cruel shaft of iron deep into the whale's forward quarter, and the chase was on again, this time with two whaleboats on the sleigh ride. Swiftly, they were hauled through the bloody sea, and swiftly their ropes were brought close in when the whale rested. Back and forth, up and down the leviathan fought, blood choking his lungs and beginning to paralyze his flukes.

"He's a monster, that one!" Captain Hoxworth said approvingly. "Pray God he doesn't catch one of the boats."

The minutes passed and then the quarter hours, and the whale fought on, bleeding profusely and seeking the safer depths; but always he had to surface, a great bull sperm whale in agony, until finally, after a last mighty surge through the red waves, he rolled over and was dead.

"Got him!" Captain Hoxworth shouted, as the third whaleboat moved in to attach its line to the second, and in this manner the three crews slowly began to tow the whale back to their mother ship. The *Carthaginian,* meanwhile, manipulated its sails so that it could move with equal caution toward the oncoming whale.

Aboard ship there was much activity. Along the starboard side a section of railing was lifted away, and a small platform was lowered six or eight feet above the surface of the sea. Men brought out razor-sharp blubber knives with twenty-foot handles. Others laboriously lugged huge iron hooks, each weighing almost as much as a man, into position for biting into the blubber and pulling it aboard. Where Abner was to have preached, the cook and his helper piled dry wood for firing the try-pots in which the whale oil would be rendered, while forward the scarfaced cooper supervised the opening of the hatch and the airing of barrels into which that blubber would be stowed that could not be immediately cooked. Just as these preparations were completed, with John Whipple noting each step in the process, and Abner Hale trying not to do so because all was being done on a Sunday, the whale was brought alongside and Whipple cried, "It's longer than the *Thetis,*" but Captain Hoxworth, who like all whalers never referred to the length of a whale, growled, "He'll make eighty, ninety barrels. A monster."

When the great sperm was lashed to the starboard side of the *Carthaginian,* and when the frail platform was adjusted, a black Brava sailor, from the Cape Verdes, nimbly leaped onto the whale's body and with a slashing knife tried to cut at the blubber so as to attach the giant hooks that were being lowered to him. Deft as he was, he could not make the enormous hooks fast, and when the *Carthaginian* took a sudden shift to windward, the Brava was struck in the chest by one of the swaying hooks and swept off the whale's flank and into the ocean, whereupon a dozen sleek sharks who had been following the blood stormed down upon him, but the men on the platform slashed and cut at the raiders and drove them off, so that the Brava climbed back on the whale, cursing in Portuguese, and this time, dripping in blood from whale and shark alike, he caught the brutal hooks into the blubber, and the unwinding was ready to begin. But before it could start, the whale's great head—twenty-six feet long and weighing tons—had to be cut away and fastened to the after end of the ship.

"You, Brava!" Captain Hoxworth shouted. "Tie this hook into the head!" And the sinewy black man leaped nimbly onto the whale's head, securing the hook, after which his mates with extra sharp knives on long poles sawed away the mammoth head.

When it drifted clear, they directed their knives to the body of the whale, slashing the thick blubbery skin in sloping spirals that started from where the head had been and ran down to the huge tail hanging limp in the sea. As the skilled workmen cut, they frequently paused for sport and slashed their deadly knives deep into some shark that had come to feed upon the carcass, and when the knife was withdrawn the shark would twist slightly, as if a bee had stung him, and continue feeding.

Now the men on the lines leading to heavy hooks began to haul, and slowly the whale rolled over and over upon itself while the blanket of blubber unpeeled in a huge spiral and was hauled aloft. When more than a dozen feet hung over the deck, one iron hook was cut free from the top and hooked into position lower down. Then the other was cut away and fastened beside the first, allowing the end of blubber to fall free upon the deck, where it was cut away, hacked into pieces, and thrust at first into the boiling try-pots, and when they were full, into the temporary barrels. Then the lines were hauled tight once more, and the thick blanket of blubber continued to unwind and swing aboard, as men on the swaying platform cut it free from the body of the slowly revolving whale.

At last, the tail was reached, and in the final moments, before the monstrous carcass was set free for the sharks, the Brava leaped back onto it and cut away a dozen steaks of fresh whale meat. "Get some liver, too," a sailor shouted, but the Brava felt himself slipping toward the sharks, so he grabbed a line and swung himself back aboard the platform. With a final slash of their scimitar-like knives, the workmen cut the whale loose and he drifted away to the waiting sharks.

Next the giant head was cut into three sections and hauled aboard, where near-naked men scooped out of its vast case more than two dozen precious barrels full of spermaceti, which would be converted into candles and cosmetics.

At dusk, when the head sections, now empty of their treasure, had been dumped back into the sea where twelve hours before they had held a tiny brain which had steered the goliath through the waves, Captain Hoxworth shouted, "Through the generosity of the Lord, our prayers have been delayed. Let the try-pots tend themselves. We'll pray." And he assembled all hands onto the oily deck, but Abner Hale would not participate in the services, so John Whipple conducted both the prayers and the singing and delivered an inspired sermon on a passage from the 104th Psalm: "O Lord, how manifold are Thy works! . . . The earth is full of Thy riches. So is this great and wide sea, wherein are things creeping innumerable, both small and great beasts. There go the ships: there is that leviathan, whom Thou hast made to play therein. . . . The glory of the Lord shall endure for ever." In his peroration he preached quietly: "From the turbulent deep God has raised up leviathan. From the wastes of the ocean He has brought us His riches. But from the wastes of the human ocean, constantly He provides us with riches greater still, for the leviathan of man's spirit is immeasurable and its wealth is counted not in casks or spermaceti. It is counted in love, and decency, and faith. May we who have trapped the great whale trap in our own lives the greater leviathan of understanding."

Captain Hoxworth was visibly moved by Whipple's sermon and shouted, "Cook! Break out some good food, and we'll celebrate!"

"We ought to be getting back to the *Thetis,*" Abner warned.

"Forget the *Thetis!*" Hoxworth boomed. "We'll sleep here tonight." And he led the missionaries down into his quarters, and they were stunned. The cabin was spacious, with clean green cloth upon the table. The captain's retiring room was finished in fine mahogany and decorated with numerous examples of carved whale bone, while his sleeping quarters featured a commodious bed, furnished with clean linen and hung on gimbals, so that even though the *Carthaginian* rolled in a storm, its captain slept in a steady bed. Along the wall was slung a bookcase, filled with works on geography, history, the oceans and poetry. Compared to the mean and meager *Thetis,* this ship was luxurious.

And the food was good. Captain Hoxworth said, in a low strong voice that carried his magnetism through the cabin, "We fight hard for our whales. We never finish second best, and we eat well. This is a lucky ship, and, Reverend Whipple, at the conclusion of this voyage I'll own two thirds of her, and at the end of the next, she'll be mine."

"These are fine quarters," Whipple replied.

"I had the mahogany put in at Manila. You see, I'm bringing my wife aboard on the next trip." He laughed apologetically and explained, "When a captain does that, the crew calls the ship a 'Hen Frigate.' Some whalers won't ship aboard a 'Hen Frigate.' Others prefer it. Say the food and the medicine are apt to be better."

"Do captain's wives ever get seasick?" Whipple asked.

"A little, at first," Hoxworth boomed. "But on a bigger ship, like this, they get over it quickly."

"I'd like to see Amanda and Jerusha as captains' wives," Whipple laughed.

"Did you say Jerusha?" the captain asked.

"Yes. Jerusha Hale, Abner's wife."

"Excellent!" the big man cried. "It's Jerusha I'm marrying, too." And he reached out to grab Abner's small hand. "Where's yours from, Reverend Hale?"

"Walpole, New Hampshire," Abner replied, unhappy at mentioning his wife's name in a whaling cabin.

"Did you say Walpole?" Hoxworth asked.

"Yes."

Big Rafer Hoxworth kicked back his chair and grabbed Abner by the coat. "Is Jerusha Bromley aboard that brig out there?" he asked menacingly.

"Yes," Abner replied steadily.

"God Almighty!" Hoxworth cried, shoving Abner back into his chair. "Anderson! Lower me a boat!" With fury clouding his face he grabbed his cap, jammed it on the back of his head, and stormed aloft. When Abner and John tried to follow he thrust them back into the cabin. "You wait here!" he thundered. "Mister Wilson!" he bellowed at his mate. "If these men try to leave this cabin, shoot 'em." And in a moment he was on the sea, driving his men toward the brig *Thetis*.

When he swung himself aboard, refusing to wait for a ladder, Captain Janders asked, "Where are the missionaries?" but Hoxworth, dark as the night, roared, "To hell with the missionaries. Where's Jerusha Bromley?" And he stormed down into the smelly cabin, shouting, "Jerusha! Jerusha!" When he found her sitting at the table he swept all the other missionaries together with his giant arms and roared, "Get out of here!" And when they were gone he took Jerusha's hands and asked, "Is what they tell me true?"

Jerusha, with an extra radiance now that she was both recovered from seasickness and in the first happy flush of pregnancy, drew back from the dynamic man who had wooed her four years ago. Hoxworth, seeing this, slammed his powerful fist onto the table and shouted, "Almighty God, what have you done?"

"I have gotten married," Jerusha said firmly and without panic.

"To that worm? To that miserable little . . ."

"To a wonderfully understanding man," she said, drawing herself against a small section of the wall that separated two stateroom doors.

"That goddamned puny . . ."

"Rafer, don't blaspheme."

"I'll blaspheme this whole goddamned stinking little ship to hell before I'll let you . . ."

"Rafer, you stayed away. You never said you would marry me . . ."

"Never said?" he roared, leaping over a fallen chair to grab her to him. "I wrote to you from Canton. I wrote to you from Oregon. I wrote from Honolulu. I told you that as soon as I landed in New Bedford we'd be married, and that you'd sail with me on my ship. It'll be my ship soon, Jerusha, and you're sailing with me."

"Rafer, I'm married. To a minister. Your letters never came."

"You can't be married!" he stormed. "It's me you love, and you know it." He crushed her to him and kissed her many times. "I can't let you go!"

"Rafer," she said quietly, pushing him away. "You must respect my condition."

The big captain fell back and looked at the girl he had been dreaming of for nearly four years. It is true that he had not, on that first wild acquaintance, asked her to marry him, but when the whales were good and his future known, he had written to her, three separate times, cautious lest any one letter not be delivered. Now she said that she was married . . . perhaps even pregnant. To a contemptible little worm with scraggly hair.

"I'll kill you first!" he screamed. "By God, Jerusha, you shall never remain married . . ." And he lunged at her with a chair.

"Abner!" she cried desperately, not knowing that he was absent, for she was certain that if he were aboard the *Thetis,* somehow he would rescue her. "Abner!" The chair crashed by her head and the wild sea captain was upon her, but before she fainted she saw Keoki and the old whaler leaping down into the cabin with hooks and clubs.

Later, the missionaries comforted her, saying, "We heard it all, Sister Hale, and we hoped not to intervene, for he was a madman and we trusted he would recover his senses."

"I had to club him, Mrs. Hale," Keoki apologized.

"Where is he now?"

"Captain Janders is taking him back to his ship," one of the wives explained.

"But where's Reverend Hale?" Jerusha cried in deep love and fear.

"He's on the other ship," Keoki explained.

"Captain Hoxworth will kill him!" Jerusha wailed, trying to get onto the deck.

"That's why Captain Janders went along," Keoki assured her. "With pistols."

But not even Captain Janders was able to protect Abner that night, for although Rafer Hoxworth quieted down on the cooling trip to the *Carthaginian,* and although he was a model of politeness to John Whipple, when he saw Abner, and how small he was and how wormy in manner, he lost control and leaped screaming at the little missionary, lifting him from the deck and rushing him to the railing of the ship, where the blubber had been taken aboard, and possibly because he slipped unexpectedly on grease, or possibly by intention, he raised Abner high into the night and flung him furiously into the dark waves.

"You'll not keep her!" he screamed insanely. "I'll come back to Honolulu and rip her from your arms. By God, I'll kill you, you miserable little worm."

While he was shouting, Captain Janders was desperately maneuvering his rowboat, warning his men, "After they cut a whale there's bound to be sharks." And the rowers saw dark forms gliding in the water, and one brushed Abner, so that he screamed with fear, "Sharks!"

From the dark deck of the *Carthaginian,* Captain Hoxworth roared, "Get him, sharks! Get him! He's over on this side. Here he is, sharks!" And he was raging thus when John Whipple reached into the vast Pacific and pulled his brother aboard.

"Did the sharks get you, Abner?" he whispered.

"They took my foot . . ."

"No! It's all right, Abner. A little blood, that's all."

"You mean my foot isn't . . ."

"It's all right, Abner," Whipple insisted.

"But I felt a shark . . ."

"Yes, one hit at you," Whipple said reassuringly, "but it only scraped the skin. See, these are your toes." And the last thing Abner could remember before he fainted was John Whipple pinching his toes and from a dark distance Rafer Hoxworth screaming futilely, "Get him, sharks! He's over there. Get the stinking little bastard and chew him up. Because if you don't kill him I'll have to."

That was the reason why Abner Hale, twenty-two years old and dressed in solemn black, with a beaver hat nearly as tall as he was, limped as he prepared to land at the port city of Lahaina on the island of Maui in Hawaii. The shark had not taken his foot, nor even his toes, but it had exposed the tendon and damaged it, and not even careful John Whipple could completely repair it.

THE ACTUAL LANDING of the missionaries was a confused affair, for when the *Thetis* drew into the famous wintering port of Lahaina, there was great commotion on shore, and the missionaries saw with horror that many handsome young women were throwing off their clothes and beginning to swim eagerly toward the little brig, which apparently they knew favorably from the past, but the attention of the ministers was quickly diverted from the swimmers to a fine canoe which, even though it started late, soon overtook the naked swimmers and drew up alongside the *Thetis*. It contained a man, a completely nude woman and four attractive girls, equally nude.

"We come back!" the man cried happily, boosting his women onto the little ship.

"No! No!" Keoki Kanakoa cried in a flood of embarrassment. "These are missionaries!"

"My girls good girls!" the father shouted reassuringly, shoving his handsome women aboard as he had done so often in the past. "Those girls swimming no good. Plenty sick."

"Heavenly Father!" Abner whispered to Brother Whipple. "Are they his own daughters?"

At this point two of the girls saw the old whaler who had saved the *Thetis* off the Four Evangelists, and apparently they remembered him kindly, for they ran across the deck, called him by name, and threw their arms about him, but he, seeing Jerusha Hale's dismay, tried to brush them away as a man keeps flies from his face when he is eating.

"Go back! Go back!" Keoki pleaded in Hawaiian, and gradually the four laughing daughters and their beautiful naked mother began to realize that on this ship, unlike all others, they were not wanted, and in some confusion they climbed back into the canoe, which their family had acquired by providing such services to passing ships. Sadly, the man of the house, his day's profits gone, paddled his employees back to Lahaina, and whenever he came to groups of girls swimming to the *Thetis* he called in bewilderment, "Turn back! No girls are wanted!" And the convoy of island beauties sadly returned to the shore and dressed.

Aboard the *Thetis*, Abner Hale, who had never before seen a naked woman, said dazedly to his brothers, "There's going to be a lot of work to do in Lahaina."

Now from the shore came out two other Hawaiians of sharply different character. Abner first saw them when a large canoe, with vassals standing at stern and prow bearing yellow-feathered staffs, became the center of an extraordinary commotion. Islanders moved about in agitation as among them appeared two of the most gigantic human beings Abner had so far seen.

"That's my father!" Keoki Kanakoa shouted to the missionaries, and by choice he came to stand with the Hales, repeating to Abner, "The tall man is my father, guardian of the king's estates."

"I thought he was King of Maui," Abner remarked with disappointment.

"I never said so," Keoki replied. "The people in Boston did. They thought it impressed the Americans."

"Who is the woman?" Jerusha inquired.

"My mother. She's the highest chief in the islands. When my father wants to ask her a question of state, he has to crawl into the room on his hands and knees. So do I." Along the railing the missionaries studied the enormous woman who half climbed, half relaxed as her subjects heaved her fantastic bulk into the canoe. Keoki's mother was six feet four inches tall, stately, long-haired, noble in every aspect, and weighed three hundred and twenty pounds. Her massive forearms were larger than the bodies of many men, while her gigantic middle, swathed in many layers of richly patterned tapa, seemed more like the trunk of some forest titan than of a human being. By her bulk alone it could be seen that she was a chief, but her most conspicuous features were her two splendid breasts, which hung in massive brown grandeur above the soft red and yellow tapa. The missionary men stared in wonder; the women gazed in awe.

"We call her the Alii Nui," Keoki whispered reverently, pronouncing the title Alee-ee. "It is from her that our mana flows."

Abner looked at his young Christian friend in amazement, as if some foul error had corrupted him. "It is from God and not from an alii nui that your spiritual consecration flows," he corrected.

The young Hawaiian blushed, and with attractive candor explained, "When you have lived a long time with one idea, you sometimes express better ideas in the same careless way."

Again Abner frowned, as if his labors with Keoki were being proved futile. "God isn't what you call a *better idea,* Keoki," he said firmly. "God is a superlative fact. He stands alone and brooks no comparisons. You don't worship God merely because He represents a better idea." Abner spoke contemptuously, but Keoki, with tears of considerable joy in his eyes, did not recognize that fact and accepted the words in love.

"I am sorry, Brother Hale," he said contritely. "I used the word thoughtlessly."

"I think it would be better, Keoki," Abner reflected, "if from now on you referred to me in the old way. Reverend Hale. Your people might not understand the title Brother."

Jerusha interrupted and asked, "Didn't we agree that we were to call one another Brother and Sister?"

"That was among ourselves, Mrs. Hale," Abner explained patiently.

"Isn't Keoki one of ourselves?" Jerusha pressed.

"I think the term *ourselves* refers principally to ordained ministers and their wives," Abner judged.

"When you have been ordained, Keoki, it'll be Brother Abner," Jerusha assured the young Hawaiian. "But even though you are not yet ordained, Keoki, I am your Sister Jerusha." And she stood beside him and said, "Your father and mother are handsome people."

With great dignity, and with yellow feathers on the staffs fluttering in the wind, the long canoe approached the *Thetis,* and for the first time the Hales saw the full majesty of Keoki's father. Not so large in bulk as the Alii Nui, he was nevertheless taller—six feet seven—and of striking presence. His hair was a mixture of black and gray. His brown face was cut by deep lines of thought and his expressive eyes shone out from beneath heavy brows. He was dressed in a cape of yellow feathers and a skirt of red tapa, but his most conspicuous ornament was a feathered helmet, close-fitting to the head but with a narrow crest of feathers that started at the nape of the neck, sweeping over the back of the head and reaching well in front of the forehead. By some mysterious trick of either history or the human mind, Kelolo, Guardian of the King's Estates, wore exactly the same kind of helmet as had Achilles, Ajax and Agamemnon, but because his people had never discovered metals, his was of feathers whereas theirs had been of iron.

Seeing his tall son on the deck of the *Thetis,* giant Kelolo deftly grabbed a rope as it was lowered to him, and with swift movements sprang from the canoe onto a footing along the starboard side of the *Thetis* and then adroitly onto the deck. Abner gasped.

"He must weigh nearly three hundred pounds!" he whispered to Jerusha, but she had now joined Keoki in tears, for the affectionate manner in which giant Kelolo and his long-absent son embraced, rubbed noses and wept reminded her of her own parents, and she held her lace handkerchief to her eyes.

Finally Keoki broke away and said, "Captain Janders! My father wishes to pay his respects," and the tough New England sea captain came aft to acknowledge the greeting. Kelolo, proud of having learned from earlier ships how properly to greet a westerner, thrust out his powerful right hand, and as Captain Janders took it, he saw tattooed from wrist to shoulder the awkward purple letters: "Tamehameha King."

"Can your father write in English?" Janders asked.

Keoki shook his head and spoke rapidly in Hawaiian. When Kelolo replied, the son said, "One of the Russians did this for my father. In 1819, when our great king Kamehameha died."

"Why did he spell it Tamehameha?" Janders asked.

"Our language is just now being written for the first time," Keoki explained. "The way you Americans have decided to spell it is neither right nor wrong. My father's name you spell Kelolo. It would be just as right to spell it Teroro."

"You mean the truth lies somewhere in between?" Janders asked.

Eagerly Keoki grasped the captain's hand and pumped it, as if the latter had said something which had suddenly illuminated a difficult problem. "Yes, Captain," the young man said happily. "In these matters the truth does lie somewhere in between."

The idea was repugnant to Abner, particularly since he had been increasingly worried about Keoki's apparent reversion to paganism as Hawaii neared. "There is always only one truth," the young missionary corrected.

Keoki willingly assented, explaining, "In matters of God, of course there is only one truth, Reverend Hale. But in spelling my father's name, there is no final truth. It lies between Kelolo and Teroro and is neither."

"Keoki," Abner said patiently, "a committee of missionaries, well versed in Greek, Hebrew and Latin studied in Honoruru for more than a year deciding how to spell Hawaiian names. They didn't act in haste or ignorance, and they decided that your father's name should be spelled Kelolo."

Thoughtlessly Keoki pointed out: "They also decided the town should be called Honolulu, but its real name is closer to Honoruru, as you said."

Abner flushed and was about to utter some sharp correction when Captain Janders rescued the moment by admiringly grasping Kelolo's tattooed arm and observing, "Tamehameha! A very great king. Alii Nui Nui!"

Kelolo, confused by the earlier argument, smiled broadly and returned the compliment. Patting the railing of the *Thetis* he said in Hawaiian, "This is a very fine ship. I shall buy this ship for Malama, the Alii Nui, and you, Captain Janders, shall be our captain."

When this was translated by Keoki, Captain Janders did not laugh, but looked steadily at Kelolo and nodded sagely. "Ask him how much sandalwood he can bring me for the ship."

"I have been saving my sandalwood," Kelolo said cautiously. "There is much more in the mountains of Maui. I can get the sandalwood."

"Tell him that if he can get the sandalwood, I can get the ship."

When Kelolo heard the news he started to shake hands in the American manner, but cautiously Captain Janders held back. "Tell him that he does not get the *Thetis* until I have carried the sandalwood to Canton and brought back a load of Chinese goods, which shall be my property to sell."

"That is reasonable," Kelolo agreed, and once more he proudly held forth his hand to bind the bargain. This time Captain Janders grasped it, adding prudently, "Mister Collins, draw up an agreement in three copies. State that we will sell the *Thetis* for a full cargo of sandalwood now, plus an equal amount when we return from China." When the terms were translated, Kelolo solemnly agreed, whereupon Mister Collins whispered, "That's a hell of a lot of sandalwood."

Replied Janders, "This is a hell of a lot of ship. It's a fair deal."

While the towering chief was concluding the deal, Abner had an opportunity to study him closely, and his eye was attracted to the symbol of power that Kelolo wore about his brown neck. From a very thick, dark necklace, apparently woven of some tree fiber, dangled a curiously shaped chunk of ivory, about five inches long and an inch and a half wide, but what was remarkable was the manner in which, at the bottom, a lip flared out and up, so that the entire piece resembled an antique adz for shaping trees.

"What is it?" Abner whispered to Keoki.

"The mark of an alii," Keoki replied.

"What's it made of?"

"A whale's tooth."

"It must be heavy to wear," Abner suggested, whereupon Keoki took the missionary's hand and thrust it under the tooth, so that Abner could test the surprising weight.

"In the old days," Keoki laughed, "you would be killed for touching an alii." Then he added, "The weight doesn't bother him because the necklace of human hair supports it."

"Is that hair?" Abner gasped, and again Keoki passed his friend's hand over the woven necklace, which, Keoki explained, had been made of some two thousand separate braids of plaited hair, each braid having been woven from eighty individual pieces of hair. "The total length of hair," Abner began. "Well . . . it's impossible."

"And all from the heads of friends," Keoki said proudly.

Before Abner could comment on this barbarism a considerable commotion occurred at the side of the *Thetis* and the missionaries ran to witness an extraordinary performance. From the mainmast two stout ropes had been lowered over the canoe which still held Malama, the Alii Nui. The ends of the ropes were fastened to a rugged canvas sling that was customarily slipped under the bellies of horses and cows, hoisting them in this fashion onto the deck of the ship. Today, the canvas sling was being used as a giant cradle into which the men in the canoe gently placed their revered chief, crosswise, so that her feet and arms dangled over the edges of the canvas, which insured her stability, while her enormous chin rested on the hard rope binding which kept the canvas from tearing.

"Is she all settled?" Captain Janders asked solicitously.

"She's squared away," a sailor shouted.

"Don't drop her!" Janders warned. "Or we'll be massacred."

"Gently! Gently!" the men working the ropes chanted, and slowly the gigantic Alii Nui was swung aboard the *Thetis.* As her big dark eyes, ablaze with childish curiosity, reached the top of the railing, while her chin rested on the edge of the canvas and her body sprawled happily behind, she waved her right hand in a grand gesture of welcome and allowed her handsome features to break into a contented smile.

"Aloha! Aloha! Aloha!" she said repeatedly in a low, soft voice, her expressive eyes sweeping the row of black-frocked missionaries in their claw-hammer coats. But her warmest greeting was for the skinny yet attractive young women who stood sedately in the rear. It would have taken almost four Amanda Whipples to equal the bulk of this giant woman as she lay in the canvas sling. "Aloha! Aloha!" she kept crying in her musical voice as she swung over the women.

"For the love of God!" Janders shouted. "Take it easy now. Gently! Gently!" As the ropes were eased over the capstans, the canvas swing slowly dropped toward the deck. Instantly, Captain Janders, Kelolo and Keoki rushed forward to intercept the sling, lest the Alii Nui be bruised in landing, but her bulk was so ponderous that in spite of their efforts to hold the sling off the deck, it pressed its way resolutely down, forcing the men to their knees and finally to a sprawling position. Undisturbed, the noble woman rolled over on the canvas, found her footing, and rose to majestic height, her bundles of tapa making her seem even larger than she was. Quietly, she passed down the line of missionaries, greeting each with her musical "Aloha! Aloha!" But when she came to the storm-tossed women, whose voyage she could imagine and whose underweight she instantly perceived, she could not restrain herself and broke into tears. Gathering little Amanda Whipple to her great bosom she wept for some moments, then rubbed noses with her as if she were a daughter. Moving to each of the women in turn, she continued her weeping and smothered them in her boundless love.

"Aloha! Aloha!" she repeated. Then, facing the women and ignoring their husbands as she did her own, she spoke softly, and when her son interpreted the words, they said: "My adorable little children, you must think of me always as your mother. Before, the white men have sent us only sailors and shopkeepers and troublemakers. Never any women. But now you come, so we know that the intentions of the Americans must at last be good."

Malama, the Alii Nui, the most sacred, mana-filled human being on Maui, waited grandly while this greeting was being delivered, and when the missionary wives acknowledged it, she moved down the line again, rubbing noses with each of the women and repeating, "You are my daughter."

Then, overcome both by the emotion and the exertions of getting aboard the *Thetis,* Malama, her great moon-face sublime in new-found comfort, slowly unfastened the tapas that bound her great bulk. Handing the ends to her servants, she ordered them to walk away from her, while she unwound like a top until she stood completely naked except for a hair necklace from which dangled a single majestic whale's tooth. Scratching herself in gasping relief, she indicated that she would lie down, and chose the canvas sling as a likely place, but when she stretched out on her stomach the missionaries were appalled to see tattooed along the full length of her left ham the purple letters: "Tamehameha King Died 1819."

"Did the Russians do that, too?" Captain Janders asked.

"They must have," Keoki replied. He asked his mother about the memento, and she twisted her head to study it. Tears came into her eyes and Keoki explained. "She was the nineteenth wife of Kamehameha the Great."

Jerusha gasped, "Why she was no better than a concubine!"

"In many ways," Keoki continued, "Malama was the favorite of the king's last years. Of course, since she was the Alii Nui, she was entitled to other husbands as well."

"You mean she was married to your father . . . at the same time?" Abner asked suspiciously.

"Of course!" Keoki explained. "Kamehameha himself consented, because my father was her younger brother, and their marriage was essential."

"Throw some water on that woman!" Captain Janders shouted, for one of the missionary wives, overcome by Malama's nudity and marital complications, had fainted.

Keoki, sensing the reasons, went to his mother and whispered that she ought to cover herself, for Americans hated the sight of the human body, and the great sprawling woman assented. "Tell them," she said enthusiastically, "that henceforth I shall dress like them." But before Keoki could do this she quietly asked Captain Janders if he could provide her with some fire, and when a brazier was fetched she fed into its flames the tapas she had been wearing. When they were consumed she announced grandly: "Now I shall dress as the new women do."

"Who will make your dress?" Abner asked.

Imperiously, Malama pointed to Jerusha and Amanda and said, "You and you."

"Tell her you'd be happy to," Abner hastily whispered, and the two missionary women bowed and said, "We will make your dress, Malama, but we have not so much cloth, because you are a very big woman."

"Don't make her angry," Abner warned, but Malama's quick intelligence had caught the burden of Jerusha's meaning, and she laughed.

"In all your little dresses," she cried, indicating the mission women with a sweep of her mighty arm, "there is not enough cloth for my dress." And she signaled her servants to fetch bundles from the canoe, and before the startled eyes of the mission women, length after length of the choicest Chinese fabric was unrolled. Settling finally on a brilliant red and a handsome blue, she pointed to the housedress worn by Amanda Whipple and announced quietly, "When I return to shore, I shall be dressed like that."

Having given the command, she went to sleep, her naked bulk protected from flies by servants who swept her constantly with feathered wands. When she woke, Captain Janders inquired if she would like some ship's food, but she refused haughtily and ordered her servants to lift great calabashes of food from the canoe, so that while the mission wives perspired over the tentlike dress they were building, she reclined and feasted on gigantic portions of roast pig, bread-fruit, baked dog, fish and three quarts of purple poi. Midway in the meal her attendants hammered her stomach in ancient massage rituals so that she could consume more, and during these interruptions she grunted happily as the food was manipulated into more comfortable positions inside her cavernous belly.

Keoki explained proudly, "The Alii Nui has to eat huge meals, five or six times a day, so that the common people will see from a distance that she is a great woman."

Into the evening the missionary women sewed while their husbands prayed that Malama would receive them well and allow them to lodge a mission at Lahaina; but the seamen of the *Thetis* prayed no less devoutly that soon both the missionaries and the fat woman would leave so that the girls waiting anxiously on shore could swim out to the brig and take up their accustomed work.

At ten the next morning the enormous red and blue dress was finished, and Malama accepted it without even bothering to thank the mission women, for she lived in a world in which all but she were servants. Like an awning protecting a New England store, the great dress was lowered into position over her dark head, while her streams of black hair were pulled outside and allowed to flow down her back. The buttons were fastened; adjustments were made at the waist, and the great Alii Nui jumped up and down several times to fit herself into the strange new uniform. Then she smiled broadly and said to her son, "Now I am a Christian woman!"

To the missionaries she said, "We have waited long for you to help us. We know that there is a better way of living, and we seek instruction from you. In Honolulu the first missionaries are already teaching our people to read and write. In Maui I shall be your first pupil." She counted on her fingers and announced firmly: "In one moon, mark this, Keoki, I will write my name and send it to Honolulu . . . with a message."

It was a moment of profound decision, and all aboard the *Thetis* save one were impressed with the gravity of this powerful woman's determination; but Abner Hale perceived that Malama's decision, while notable in that an illiterate heathen of her own will sought instruction, was nevertheless a step in the wrong direction, so he moved before her and said quietly, "Malama, we do not bring you only the alphabet. We have not come here merely to teach you how to write your name. We bring you the word of God, and unless you accept this, nothing that you will ever write will be of significance."

When the words were translated to Malama her enormous moon-face betrayed no emotion. Forcefully she said, "We have our own gods. It is the words, the writing that we need."

"Writing without God is useless," Abner stubbornly reiterated, his little blond head coming scarcely to Malama's throat.

"We have been told," Malama answered with equal firmness, "that writing helps the entire world, but the white man's God helps only the white man."

"You have been told wrong," Abner insisted, thrusting his stubborn little face upward.

To everyone's surprise Malama did not reply to this but moved to face the women, asking, "Which one is the wife of this little man?"

"I am," Jerusha said proudly.

Malama was pleased, for she had observed how capably Jerusha managed the work of making the big dress, and she announced: "For the first moon, this one shall teach me how to read and write, and for the next, this one," indicating Abner, "shall teach me the new religion. If I find that these two learnings are of equal importance, after two moons I shall advise you."

Nodding to the assembly, she went gravely to the canvas sling, commanding her servants to unbutton her dress and remove it. Then she ordered Jerusha to show her how to fold it, and in massive nakedness lay down crosswise upon the canvas, her feet dangling aft, her arms forward, with her chin resting upon the rope edging. The capstans groaned. The sailors hefted the ropes and swung them over the eaves, and Captain Janders shouted, "For Christ's sake, things are going well. Don't drop her now!"

Inch by inch the precious burden was lowered into the canoe until finally the Alii Nui was rolled off the canvas and helped into an upright position. Clutching the new dress to her cheek she cried in full voice, "You may now come ashore!" And as the ship's boats were lowered to convey the missionaries to their new home, they fell in line behind Malama's canoe, with its two standard-bearers fore and aft, its eager servants brushing away the flies, and with tall, naked Malama holding the dress close to her.

Prior to Malama's arbitrary choice of the Hales as her mentors, there had been some uncertainty as to which missionaries should be assigned to Maui and which to the other islands, but now it was apparent that the first choice, at least, had been made, and as the boats neared shore, Abner studied the intriguing settlement to which he was now committed. He saw one of the fairest villages in the Pacific, ancient Lahaina, capital of Hawaii, its shore marked by a fine coral strand upon which long waves broke in unceasing thunder, their tall crests breaking forward in dazzling whiteness. Where the surf finally ended, naked children played, their teeth gleaming in the sunlight.

Now for the first time, Abner saw a coconut palm, the wonder of the tropics, bending into the wind on a slim resilient trunk and maintaining, no one knew how, its precarious foothold on the shore. Behind the palms were orderly fields reaching away to the hills, so that all of Lahaina looked like one vast, rich, flowering garden.

"Those darker trees are breadfruit," Keoki explained. "They feed us, but it's the stubby ones with the big heads that I used to miss in Boston . . . the kou trees with their wonderful shade for a hot land."

Jerusha joined them and said, "Seeing the gardens and the flowers, I think I am at last in Hawaii."

And Keoki replied proudly, "The garden you are looking at is my home. There were the little stream runs into the sea."

Abner and Jerusha tried to peer beneath the branches of the kou trees that lined the land he spoke of, but they could see little. "Are those grass houses?" Abner queried.

"Yes," Keoki explained. "Our compound holds nine or ten little houses. How beautiful it seems from the sea."

"What's the stone platform?" Abner asked.

"Where the gods rested," Keoki said simply.

In horror Abner stared at the impressive pile of rocks. He could see blood dripping from them and heathen rites. He mumbled a short prayer to himself, "God protect us from the evil of heathen ways," then asked in a whisper, "Is that where the sacrifices . . ."

"There?" Keoki laughed. "No, that's just for the family gods."

The boy's laugh infuriated Abner. It seemed strange to him that as long as Keoki remained in New England, lecturing to church audiences about the horrors of Hawaii, he had sound ideas regarding religion, but as soon as he approached his evil homeland, the edge of his conviction was blunted. "Keoki," Abner said solemnly, "all heathen idols are an abomination to the Lord."

Keoki wanted to cry, "But those aren't idols . . . not gods like Kane and Kanaloa," but as a well-trained Hawaiian he knew that he should not argue with a teacher, so he contented himself with saying quietly, "Those are the friendly little personal gods of my family. For example, sometimes the goddess Pele comes to talk with my father . . ." With some embarrassment he realized how strange this must sound, so he did not go on to explain that sharks also sometimes came along the shore to talk with Malama. "I don't think Reverend Hale would understand," he thought sadly to himself.

To hear a young man who hoped some day to become an ordained minister speak in defense of heathen practices was unbearable to Abner, and he turned away in silence, but this act seemed cowardice to him, so he returned to the young Hawaiian and said bluntly, "We shall have to remove the stone platform. In this world there is room either for God or for heathen idols. There cannot be room for both."

"You are right!" Keoki agreed heartily. "We have come to root out these old evils. But I am afraid that Kelolo will not permit us to remove the platform."

"Why not?" Abner asked coldly.

"Because he built it."

"Why?" Abner pressed.

"My family used to live on the big island, Hawaii. We had ruled there for countless generations. It was my father who came here to Maui . . . one of Kamehameha's most trusted generals. Kamehameha gave him most of Maui, and the first thing Kelolo did was to build the platform you saw. He insists that Pele, the volcano goddess, comes there to warn him."

"The platform will have to go. Pele is no more."

"The big brick building," Keoki interrupted, pointing to a rugged edifice rising at the end of the stunted pier that edged cautiously out to sea, "is Kamehameha's old palace. Behind it is the royal taro patch. Then, you see the road beyond? That's where the foreign sailors live. Your house will probably be erected there."

"Are there Europeans in the village?"

"Yes. Castaways, drunks. I worry about them much more than I do about my father's stone platform."

Abner ignored this thrust, for his eyes were now attracted by the most conspicuous feature of Lahaina. Behind the capital, rising in gentle yet persistent slopes, cut by magnificent valleys and reaching into dominant peaks, stood the mountains of Maui, majestic and close to the sea. Except for the ugly hills at Tierra del Fuego, Abner had never before seen mountains, and their conjunction with the sea made them memorable, so that he exclaimed, "These are the handiwork of the Lord! I will lift up mine eyes unto the hills!" And he was overcome by an urge to say a prayer of thanksgiving to a Lord who had created such beauty, so that when the little mission band stepped ashore for the first time on the beach at Lahaina, he convoked a meeting, smoothed out his claw-hammer coat, took off his beaver hat, and lifted his sallow face toward the mountains, praying: "Thou hast brought us through the storms and planted our feet upon a heathen land. Thou hast charged us with the will to bring these lost souls to Thy granary. We are unequal to the task, but we beseech Thee to give us Thy constant aid."

The missionaries then raised their voices in the hymn that had recently come to summarize such efforts around the world, "From Greenland's icy mountains," and when the surging second verse was reached, each sang as if it had been written with Hawaii alone in mind:

> *"What though the spicy breezes*
> *Blow soft o'er Ceylon's isle,*
> *Tho' every prospect pleases,*
> *And only man is vile;*
> *In vain with lavish kindness*
> *The gifts of God are strown.*
> *The heathen in his blindness*
> *Bows down to wood and stone."*

It was unfortunate that this was the first hymn to be sung in Lahaina, for it crystallized a fundamental error in Abner's thinking. As long as he lived he would visualize Lahaina as a place "where every prospect pleases, and only man is vile." He would perpetually think of the Hawaiian as both heathen and blind; and now, as the singing ended, Abner saw that he and his mission band were surrounded by a huge crowd of naked savages, and he was instinctively afraid, so that he and his friends huddled together for mutual protection.

Actually, no missionaries in history had so far visited a gentler or finer group of people than these Hawaiians. They were clean, free from repulsive tropical diseases, had fine teeth, good manners, a wild joy in living; and they had devised a well-organized society; but to Abner they were vile.

"Almighty God!" he prayed. "Help us to bring light to these cruel hearts. Give us the strength to strike down each heathen idol in this land where only man is vile."

Jerusha, however, was thinking: "Soon these people will be reading. We will teach them how to sew and to clothe themselves against the storm. Lord, keep us strong, for there is so much work to do."

The prayers were broken by the noise of men running up with a canoe, one that had never touched the sea, for it was carried aloft by ten huge men with poles on their shoulders. With ceremony they deposited it before Malama and she climbed in, for since the Hawaiians had not discovered the wheel they had no carriages. Standing aloft, Malama unfolded her new dress and ordered her servants to slip its enormous folds over her head. As it cascaded past her huge breasts and the tattooed shank with its memory of Kamehameha, the Alii Nui wiggled several times and felt the blue and red masterpiece fall into place. "Makai! Makai!" squealed the women in the crowd, approving their Alii Nui in her new garb.

"From now on I shall dress like this!" she announced solemnly. "In one moon I am going to write a letter to Honolulu, because I have good teachers." Reaching down, she touched Abner and Jerusha, indicating that they must join her in the canoe. "This man is my teacher of religion, Makua Hale," she announced, and in Hawaiian style she called his name Halley, by which he was known thereafter. "And this is my teacher of words, Hale Wahine. Now we will build my teachers a house."

The bearers raised the canoe aloft, adjusted the poles to their shoulders, and at the head of a mighty procession containing feathered staffs, drums, court attendants and more than five thousand naked Hawaiians, the Hales set forth on their first magical journey through Lahaina, with Keoki trotting along beside the canoe, interpreting for his mother as she identified the subtle beauties of her island.

"We are now passing the royal taro patch," Keoki explained. "This little stream brings us our water. This field is a choice location, because it has so many fine trees, and this is where Malama says we are to build your house."

The bearers carried the Alii Nui to the four corners of the proposed dwelling, and at each she dropped a stone, whereupon servants began immediately to lay out a grass house, but before they had accomplished much, Malama grandly indicated that the procession must now move to her palace.

"This is the main road," Malama pointed out. "Toward the sea are the fine lands where the alii live. Toward the mountains are lands for the people. In this great park lives the king when he is in residence."

"What are all those little grass buildings . . . like dog houses?" Abner asked.

When his question was interpreted, Malama laughed vigorously and said, "Those are the people's houses!"

"They don't look big enough to live in," Abner argued.

"The common people don't live in them . . . not like the alii in their big house," Malama explained. "They keep their tapa in them . . . sleep in them if it rains."

"Where do they live the rest of the time?" Abner asked.

Spreading her huge arms grandiloquently to embrace the entire countryside, Malama replied, "They live under the trees, beside the rivers, in the valleys." And before Abner could reflect on this, the canoe came to a spacious and beautiful park, set off by a wall of coral blocks three feet high, inside of which stretched an extensive garden of flowers and fruit trees, interspersed with a dozen grass houses and one large pavilion looking out over the sea. It was to this building that Malama and the Hales were carried, and as the huge woman climbed out of the canoe, she announced: "This is my palace. You will always be welcome here."

She led the way into a cool spacious room outlined by woven grass walls, handsome wooden pillars and a narrow doorway which permitted a view of the sea. The floor was made of fine white pebbles covered by pandanus matting, upon which Malama with a gasp of relief threw herself, propping her big chin on her hands and stating, firmly, "Now teach me to write!"

Jerusha, who could not even recall how she herself had been taught, sixteen remote years ago, stammered, "I am sorry, Malama, but we need pens and papers . . ."

Her protests were silenced by a voice as soft as polished bronze. "You will teach me to write," Malama commanded with terrifying majesty.

"Yes, Malama." Jerusha trembled. Looking about the room, she happened to see some long sticks with which Malama's women had been beating intricate designs onto tapa and beside them several small calabashes of dark dye. Taking one of the sticks and a length of tapa, she smeared out the word MALAMA. As the giant woman studied it, Jerusha explained, "That is your name."

When Keoki translated this, Malama rose and inspected the word from varying angles, repeating it proudly to herself. Grabbing the stick rudely, she splashed it in the dye and started to trace the cryptic symbols, sensing fully the magic they contained. With remarkable skill she reproduced the word exactly. "Malama!" she repeated a dozen times. Then she drew the word again and again. Suddenly she stopped and asked Keoki, "If I sent this word to Boston, would people there know that it was my word, Malama?"

"You could send it anywhere in the world and people would know that it was your word," her son assured her.

"I am learning to write!" the huge woman exulted. "Soon I shall send letters to all the world. The only difference between white men who rule everything and us Hawaiians is that white men can write. Now I shall write, too, and I will understand everything."

This error was too profound for Abner to tolerate, and he interjected, "I warned you once, Malama, that a woman can learn to write words, but they are nothing. Malama, I warn you again! Unless you learn the Commandments of the Lord, you have learned nothing."

The walls of the grass house were thick, and not much light entered the area where Malama stood with her length of stick, and in the shadows she seemed like the gigantic summary of all Hawaiians: powerful, resolute, courageous. Once on Hawaii in the days of her husband Kamehameha's war she had strangled a man much larger than the puny, sallow-faced individual who stood before her, and she was constrained now to brush him aside as her servants brushed away the flies, but she was impressed by his dogged insistence and by the power of his voice. More important, she suspected that he was right; the mere trick of writing was too easy; there must be additional hidden magic that enforced it; and she was about to listen to the little man with the limp, when he pointed his finger at her and shouted, "Malama, do not learn merely the outlines of the words. Learn also what they mean!" His manner was insufferable, and with a sweep of her immense right arm, thicker than his entire body, she knocked him off his feet. Returning to the tapa she wrote furiously, splashing her name across it.

"I can write my name!" she exulted, but even as she did so, Abner's persuasive words plagued her, and abruptly she threw down the stick and went to where he lay sprawled on the tapa. Kneeling beside him, she studied his face for a long time, then said softly, "I think you speak the truth, Makua Hale. Wait, Makua Hale. When I have learned to write, then I will come to you." Then she ignored him and in her silky voice commanded Jerusha: "Now teach me to write."

The lesson continued for three hours, until Jerusha grew faint and would have stopped. "No!" Malama commanded. "I have not much time to waste. Teach me to write!"

"I am growing dizzy in the heat," Jerusha protested.

"Fan her!" Malama ordered, and when the young woman indicated that she must halt, Malama pleaded: "Hale Wahine, while we waste time, men who can read and write are stealing our islands. I cannot wait. Please."

"Malama," Jerusha said weakly, "I am going to have a baby."

When Keoki explained the meaning of these words to Malama, the great Alii Nui underwent a transformation. Thrusting Abner from the large room, she ordered her servants to carry Jerusha to an area where more than fifty of the finest tapas had been piled to make a day bed. When the slim girl had been placed on the pile, Malama swiftly felt for her stomach and judged, "Not for many months," but without Keoki in the room she could not explain this conclusion to the white woman. She could see, however, that Jerusha was exhausted and she blamed herself for what had been a lack of consideration. Calling for water, she ordered Jerusha's white face bathed, and then lifted her in her arms, a mere child against her own huge bulk. Rocking back and forth, she nursed the tired mission woman to sleep, then placed her once more gently on the tapas. Rising quietly, she tiptoed to where Abner waited and asked in a whisper, "Can you also teach me to write?"

"Yes," Abner said.

"Teach me!" she commanded, and she kneeled beside the little New England missionary as he began logically, "To write my language requires twenty-six different letters, but you are fortunate, because to write your language requires only thirteen."

"Tell him to teach me the twenty-six!" she commanded Keoki.

"But to write Hawaiian you need only thirteen," Abner explained.

"Teach me the twenty-six!" she said softly. "It is to your countrymen that I wish to write."

"A, B, C," Abner began, continuing with the lesson until he, too, felt faint.

WHEN THE TIME came for the *Thetis* to depart, almost the entire population of Lahaina appeared to bid the ship farewell, and the foreshore was dark with naked bronzed bodies following each movement of the departing missionaries. At last the twenty who would go to other locations assembled at the small stone pier to sing their sweet blend of mournfulness and hope, "Blest be the tie that binds," and as their dedicated voices rose in unison, the watching Hawaiians could detect not only an inviting melody but a spirit of the new god of whom Abner Hale and their own Keoki Kanakoa had already begun to preach. When the hymn spoke of tears, the eyes obliged, and soon the vast congregation, led by the missionaries, was weeping.

In one respect the sorrow was not formal but real. When Abner and Jerusha watched John Whipple prepare to sail they could not mask their apprehension, for he was the only doctor in the islands, and with him absent, Jerusha knew that when her term of pregnancy was ended, the success of her childbirth would depend upon how well her youthful husband had mastered his book lessons. Whipple, sensing this concern, promised, "Sister Jerusha, I shall do everything possible to return to Maui to help you. But remember that on the other end of the island Brother Abraham and Sister Urania will be living, and since her time does not coincide with yours, perhaps you shall be able to visit by canoe and help each other."

"But you will try to come back?" Jerusha pleaded.

"I will do my best," Whipple swore.

Jerusha Hale and Urania Hewlett then sought out each other and shook hands solemnly: "When the time comes, we'll help each other." But they knew that they would be separated by miles of mountains and by treacherous seas.

Now the wailing increased, for from the shaded road that led southward to the homes of the alii, Malama's canoe advanced, borne on the shoulders of her men, and she, dressed in blue and red, wept more than any. Descending from her strange palanquin, she moved to each of the departing missionaries and said, "If elsewhere in the islands you find no home, come back to Lahaina, for you are my children." Then she kissed each in turn, and wept anew. But the gravity of the situation was somewhat marred by the fact that as the mission people rowed out to the *Thetis* they met, swimming back, more than a dozen naked girls, their long black hair trailing in the blue waters; and when they reached shore, each carrying a hand mirror—more precious here than silver in Amsterdam—or some lengths of ribbon or a hammer which they had stolen, Malama greeted them exactly as affectionately as she had the departing Christians.

And then, to the eastward where stout waves broke on the coral reef, thundering shoreward in long, undulant swells whose tips were spumed in white, the missionaries witnessed for the first time one of the mysteries of the islands.

Tall men and women, graceful as gods, stood on narrow boards and by deftly moving their feet and the gravity of their bodies, directed the boards onto the upper slopes of the breaking waves, until at last they sped with frightening swiftness over the waters. And when the wave died on the coral beach, somehow the swimmer and his board subsided back into the water, as if each were a part of the Hawaiian sea.

"It's unbelievable!" Dr. Whipple cried. "The momentum creates the balance," he explained.

"Could a white man do that?" Amanda asked.

"Of course!" her husband replied, excited by the vicarious sense of speed and control created by the deft athletes.

"Could you do it?" Amanda pressed.

"I'm going to do it," John replied, "as soon as we get to Honolulu."

One of the older missionaries frowned at this intelligence, marking it down as one more proof of their doctor's essentially trivial attitude toward life, but his adverse opinion was not reported to his companions, because from a point forward of the *Thetis* a new board swept into view, and this one bore not a mere swimmer, but a nymph, a nude symbolization of all the pagan islands in the seven seas. She was a tall girl with sun-shot black hair streaming behind her in the wind. She was not grossly fat like her sisters but slim and supple, and as she stood naked on the board her handsome breasts and long firm legs seemed carved of brown marble, yet she was agile, too, for with exquisite skill she moved her knees and adjusted her shoulders so that her skimming board leaped faster than the others, while she rode it with a more secure grace. To the missionaries she was a terrifying vision, the personification of all they had come to conquer. Her nakedness was a challenge, her beauty a danger, her way of life an abomination and her existence an evil.

"Who is she?" Dr. Whipple whispered, in hushed amazement at her skill.

"Her name Noelani," proudly explained a Hawaiian who had shipped on whalers and who had mastered the barbarous pidgin of the seaports. "Wahine b'long Malama. Bimeby she gonna be Alii Nui." And as he spoke the wave subsided near the shore; the fleet rider and her board died away from vision and returned to the sea, yet even when the missionaries looked away they could see her provocative presence, the spirit of the pagan island, riding the waves, so that a blasphemous thought came to the mind of John Whipple. He was tempted to express it, but fought it down, knowing that none would understand his meaning, but at last he had to speak and in a whisper he observed to his tiny wife: "Apparently there are many who can walk upon the waters."

Amanda Whipple, a truly devout woman, heard these strange words and caught their full savor. At first she was afraid to look at her scientifically minded husband, for sometimes his thoughts were difficult to follow, but the implications of this blasphemous conclusion no one could escape, and at last she turned to look at John Whipple, thinking: "One person can never understand another." But instead of censuring the young doctor for his irregular thoughts she looked at him analytically for the first time. Coldly, dispassionately, carefully, she looked at this strange cousin who stood beside her in the hot Hawaiian sunlight, and when she was finished studying him, she loved him more than ever.

"I do not like such words, John," she admonished.

"I had to speak them," he replied.

"Do so, always, but only to me," she whispered.

"It will be very difficult to understand these islands," John reflected, and as he and his wife watched the sea, they noticed the nymph Noelani—the Mists of

Heaven—paddling her board back out to the deeper ocean where the big waves formed. Kneeling on her polished plank, she bent over so that her breasts almost touched the board. Then, with powerful movements of her long arms, she swept her hands through the water and her conveyance shot through the waves faster than the missionary boat was being rowed. Her course brought her close to the *Thetis,* and as she passed, she smiled. Then, selecting a proper wave, she quickly maneuvered her board, and finding it properly oriented, rose on one knee. From the missionary boat John Whipple whispered to his wife, "Now she will walk upon the waters." And she did.

When the *Thetis* sailed, Abner and Jerusha, feeling dismally alone, had an opportunity to inspect the house in which their labors for the next years would be conducted. Its corner posts were stout trees from the mountains, but its sides and roof were of tied grass. The floor was pebbled and covered with pandanus, to be swept by a broom of rushes, but its windows were mere openings across which cloth from China had been hung. It was a squat, formless grass hut with no divisions into rooms. It had no bed, no chairs, no table, no closets, but it did have two considerable assets: at the rear, under a twisting hau tree, it had a spacious lanai—a detached porch—where the life of the mission would be conducted; and it had a front door built in the Dutch fashion so that the bottom half could remain closed, keeping people out, while the top was open, allowing their smiles and their words to enter.

It was into this house that Abner moved the furniture he had brought out from New England: a rickety bed with rope netting for its mattress; rusted trunks to serve as closets; a small kitchen table and two chairs and a rocker. Whatever clothes they might require in years to come they would get only through the charity of Christians in New England, who would forward barrels of cast-off garments to the mission center in Honolulu, and if Jerusha needed a new dress to replace her old one, some friend in Honolulu would pick through the leftovers and say, "This one ought to fit Sister Jerusha," but it never did. If Abner required a new saw with which to build even the minor decencies of living, he had to hope that some Christian somewhere would send him one. If Jerusha needed a cradle for her babies, she could get it only from charity. The Hales had no money, no income, no support other than the communal depository in Honolulu. Even if they were fevered to the point of death they could buy no medicine; they had to trust that Christians would keep replenished their little box of calomel, ipecac and bicarbonate.

Sometimes Jerusha, recalling either her cool, clean home in Walpole, its closets filled with dresses kept starched by servants, or the two homes that Captain Rafer Hoxworth had promised her in New Bedford and aboard his ship, understandably felt distressed by the grass hut in which she toiled, but she never allowed her feelings to be discovered by her husband and her letters home were uniformly cheerful. When the days were hottest and her work the hardest she would wait until evening and then write to her mother, or to Charity or Mercy, telling them of her alluring adventures, but with them, even though they were of her own family, she dealt only in superficialities; increasingly it would be to Abner's sister Esther, whom she had never met, that she would pour out the flood of deeper thoughts that swept over her. In one of her earliest letters, she wrote:

"My most Cherished Sister in God, Dear Esther. I have been strangely mournful these days, for sometimes the heat is unbearable in Lahaina, whose name I find means Merciless Sun, and no appellation could be more appropriate. Possibly these have been unduly difficult weeks, for Malama has pressed me endlessly to teach her, and although she cannot pay attention to lessons for more than an hour at a time, as soon as her interest flags she calls for her servants to massage her, and as they do, commands me to tell her a story, so I tell her of Mary and Esther and Ruth, but when I first spoke of Ruth's leaving her home to dwell in an alien land, I am afraid that tears fell, and Malama saw this and understood and drove the massaging women away and came to me and rubbed noses with me and said, 'I appreciate that you have come to live with us in a strange land.' Now whenever she wants a story she insists like a child that I tell her again of Ruth, and when I come to the part about the strange land, we both weep. She has never once thanked me for anything I have done for her, considering me only an additional servant, but I have grown to love her, and I have never known a woman to learn so fast.

"For some curious reason I had been impelled, these last few days, to talk with you, for I feel that of all the people I remember in America, your spirit is closest to my own, and I have wanted to tell you two things, my beloved sister in God. First, I thank you daily for having written to me as you did about your brother Abner. Each day that passes I find him a stronger man, a finer servant of God. He is gentle, patient, courageous and extremely wise. Sharing his burdens, in this new land which he is determined to resurrect, is a joy that I had never in America even dimly anticipated. Each day is a new challenge. Each night is a benediction to good work either started or completed. In my letters to you I have never spoken of love, but I think that now I know what love is, and my dearest wish for you is that some day you may find a Christian gentleman as worthy as your gentle brother. His limp is much improved, but I massage his muscles each night. To be more correct, I *used* to massage them, but lately a very plump Hawaiian woman who is known to be highly skilled in the lomilomi, the medicinal massage of the islands, insists upon doing the job for me. I can hear her now, a huge motherly woman announcing, 'Me come lomilomi little man.' I tell her repeatedly that she must refer to my partner and guide as 'Makua,' which means Father, but this she will not do.

"The second thought I would share with you is my growing sense of working directly under the will of God. At one time I did not know whether I had a true vocation for mission work or not, but as the weeks go past and as I see the transformation that we are accomplishing in these islands, I am doubly convinced that I have found for myself the one satisfying occupation on earth. I rejoice to see each new dawn, for there is work to do. At five o'clock in the morning, when I look out into our yard, I see it filled with patient, handsome brown faces. They are willing to remain there all day in hopes that I will teach them how to sew or talk with them about the Bible. Malama promises me that when *she* has learned to read and write, I can start to teach her people to do the same, but she will not allow any of them to master the tricks until she has done so. However, she has consented to this. In her afternoon lessons she allows her children and those of the other alii to listen, and I find that her beautiful daughter Noelani is almost as quick as Malama herself. My dear husband has great hopes for Noelani and feels certain that she will be our second Christian convert on the island, Malama of course being first. Darling Esther, can you, in your mind's eye, picture the intense wonder that comes over a pagan face when the clouds of heathenish evil and illiteracy are drawn away so that the pure light of God can shine into the seeking eyes? What I am trying to tell you, dearest sister, is that I find in my work a supreme happiness, and although what I am about to say may seem blasphemy—and I can say it to no other but my own dear sister—in these exciting fruitful days when I read the New Testament I feel that I am reading not about Philemon and the Corinthians but about Jerusha and the Hawaiians. I am one with those who labored for our Master, and I cannot convey even to my dear husband the abounding joy I have discovered in my grass shack and its daily circle of brown faces. Your Sister in God, Jerusha."

While Jerusha was teaching Malama, Abner was free to explore the village, and one day he noticed that all the men and many of the stronger women were absent from Lahaina, and he could not discover why. The alii were present, and in their large grass homes south of the royal taro patch they could be seen, moving about beneath the kou trees or going to the beach in order to ride their surfboards on the cresting waves. It was good to be an alii, for then one's job was merely to eat enormous calabashes of food so as to grow large, and to play at games, so as to be ready if war came. Year by year the alii grew greater and more skilled in games, waiting for a war that came no more.

But one of the alii was missing, for Kelolo had not been to visit the missionaries for some days. He had sent food and three planks out of which Abner had hacked shelving for rude closets, but he himself had not appeared, and this handicapped Abner, because only Kelolo could say where the church was to be built. Then, when the missionary had reached the height of impatience, he discovered that Kelolo was out at the edge of town, digging a deep, wide pit. Keoki was not present to translate when Abner found the excavation, and all Kelolo would say was, *"Thetis,"* measuring the deep pit with his arms extended.

Abner was still perplexed when he saw, staggering along the beach, a procession of more than two thousand men and women, the dust from their movements filling the sky. They were goaded along by royal lieutenants, and they were burdened heavily by bundles of logs cut into six-foot lengths and slung from their backs by vines. The yellowish wood was obviously precious, for if even a small piece fell, sharp-eyed lieutenants struck the careless carrier and directed trailing women to salvage the dropping, for this was sandalwood: aromatic as no other, choice in the markets of Asia, the life-blood of Hawaiian commerce, and the goal of all Americans. It was the treasure and the curse of Hawaii.

Deep in the forests the trees hid, less than thirty feet high and marked by pale green leaves. Years ago, before their worth was known, the trees had flourished even in the lowlands, but now all those of easy access were gone, chopped down by the alii for whom they were kapu. Kelolo, if he wanted the two shiploads that would pay Captain Janders for the *Thetis,* had to drive his servants high into the mountains and on into remote corners of the island. Now, as the heavily burdened men staggered to the pit, Abner understood. On that first day while he had been instructing Malama, Captain Janders had laid out a pit the exact size of the *Thetis'* hatch, and when the pit was filled with sandalwood twice over, the ship would be Kelolo's.

As the precious logs tumbled into the excavation, Kelolo's men jumped in and laid them close together, for Janders had insisted many times, "No air! No air!" and Abner realized that these men had been in the mountains for some days. He was therefore disturbed when Kelolo ordered them back into the forests immediately. Summoning Keoki, Abner argued: "Your father shouldn't take his men back at once. What will happen to the taro beds? Who will catch the fish?"

"They're his men," Keoki explained.

"Of course they are," Abner agreed. "But it's in Kelolo's own best interests that they be given a rest."

"When an alii smells sandalwood, the mind turns and thought departs," Keoki replied.

"I must see your father," Abner insisted.

"He won't want to see you now," Keoki warned. "His mind is concerned only with sandalwood."

Nevertheless, Abner donned his black claw-hammer, tall hat and best stock, his invariable uniform when delivering the word of the Lord. In the heat of the day he strode southward past the king's quarters and out to the cool kou trees and the great grass houses of Malama and her consort-brother. He heard his wife Jerusha instructing huge Malama in the writing of letters, American style, but he paid no attention, for he wished to see only Kelolo, and he found him playing in the surf.

The chief, seeing Abner's official uniform, and not wanting a lecture at this time, refused to come out of the water, so Abner had to pick his way gingerly along the sandy shore, shouting above the waves as they washed in. "Kelolo!" he cried like a prophet from the Old Testament. "You have broken every promise to me." Imitating his instructor's voice, Keoki repeated the words.

"Tell him to go away!" Kelolo grunted, splashing water into his big face and rolling about in deep pleasure.

"Kelolo! You have not set aside the land for the church."

"Oh, I'll give you land for the church . . . one of these days," the sybaritic nobleman shouted back.

"Today!" Abner demanded.

"When I finish with the sandalwood," Kelolo promised.

"Kelolo, it is not sensible to lead your men back into the forests right away."

The big man scratched his back on a coral head and growled, "You've got to get sandalwood when you can find it."

"It is wrong to demand so much of your men!"

"They're my men!" the chief insisted. "They'll go where I tell them to go."

"It is wrong, Kelolo, to hoard sandalwood when the taro patches and the fish ponds remain unattended."

"The taro will take care of itself," Kelolo said grimly, diving deep to be rid of the irritating voice.

"Where will he come up?" Abner asked.

"Over there," Keoki replied, and the missionary ran along the sand, holding onto his tall hat, so that when the chief surfaced, there was Abner staring at him.

"Kelolo, God says we must respect all who work."

"They're my men," the huge nobleman growled.

"And that platform," Abner continued. "It's not been taken down."

"Don't touch the platform!" Kelolo warned, but the missionary was disgusted with the chief's behavior and ran awkwardly across the sand to the offending platform of old gods and reached down to throw aside the rocks of which it was composed.

"No!" warned Keoki, but Abner would not listen, and began tossing the ancient stones into the sea. One rolled near Kelolo, and when he saw his own handiwork thus destroyed, he uttered a wild cry, leaped from the surf and dashed inland, grabbing the lame little missionary by his claw-hammer coat and throwing him violently to one side.

"Don't touch the rocks!" he roared.

Abner, stunned by the suddenness of the attack, rose unsteadily to his feet and studied the naked giant who guarded the platform. Recovering his hat, he placed it firmly on his head and moved resolutely toward the collection of rocks. "Kelolo," he said solemnly, "this is an evil place. You will not let me build a church but you hold onto your evil old gods. This is wrong." And with his right index finger extended as far as it would reach, he pointed directly at the chief. "It is hewa."

The naked warrior, hero of battles, was inspired to pick up this worrisome little man and crush him, but the solemnity of Abner's manner stopped him, and the two stood there under the kou trees, staring at each other, and finally Kelolo temporized: "Makua Hale. I promised you land for a church, but I must wait until my king sends word from Honolulu."

"Shall we tear down this evil place?" Abner asked quietly.

"No, Makua Hale," Kelolo said firmly. "This is my church in the old fashion. I will help you build your church in the new fashion."

Quietly Abner said, "When I stand beside these rocks, Kelolo, I can hear the voices of all the victims who were sacrificed here. It is an evil memory."

"It was not that kind of temple, Makua Hale," Kelolo said forcefully. "This was a temple of love and protection. I cannot surrender it."

Abner had the sense to bow to this decision, but he did so in a way that Kelolo never forgot. Lifting one of the stones reverently, the little missionary looked at it and said, "If you consider this a rock from a temple of mercy I can understand why you wish to preserve it. But I shall build a church that will truly be a temple of mercy, and you will see the difference. To your temple, Kelolo, only the strong alii could come. In my temple it will be the weak and the poor who will find mercy. And when you see the mercy that spreads out from my temple, Kelolo, believe me, you will come to this shore and throw every rock in this pile far out to sea." And Abner strode to the shore in as impressive a manner as his limp would allow, and at the edge of the sea he drew back his arm and pitched the solitary rock far into the waves. Then, holding his hat, he came back to Kelolo and said, "We will build my church."

The tall chieftain kept his promise. Wrapping his tapa about him, he marched through the hot sunlight to a fine piece of land north of the mission grounds, where he paced off a generous area and said, "You can build your church here."

"This is not enough land," Abner protested.

"Enough for one god," Kelolo replied.

"Your own temples have more land," Abner argued.

"But they also have more gods," Kelolo explained.

"My God is bigger than all the gods in Hawaii."

"How much land does he require?"

"He wants a church of his size," Abner insisted, and Kelolo was astonished.

But when the marking out was completed, he said, "Good. I will call the kahunas to determine how the church should be arranged."

Abner did not understand Keoki's translation and asked, "What's he going to do?"

"Call the kahunas," Keoki explained.

"What for?" Abner asked in astonishment.

"The kahunas have to decide where the door should be, where the people will sit," Keoki explained.

Kelolo, sensing Abner's repugnance, hurried to explain, "You must not build a church without permission from the kahunas."

Abner felt dizzy. Frequently since his arrival on Maui he had been confronted by positive confusion. Malama and Kelolo both eagerly wanted Christianity for their island, and each had given substantial signs of surrendering a good deal to the new religion, but repeatedly they indicated that they considered it not a new religion, not a truth that would shatter old ways and introduce salvation, but merely a better religion than the one they had. Once Kelolo had reasoned, "If Jesus Christ can give you big ships with many sails, and Kane gives us only canoes, Jesus Christ must be much better. He is welcome." Malama, impressed always with the power of the written word, had corrected her husband. "It is not ships that Jesus Christ brings. It is the mana there in the black box," she said, indicating the Bible. "When we learn to read what is in the box, we will know the secret of mana, and we too will be strong."

"Jesus does not bring either ships or books," Abner had patiently explained. "He brings light that illuminates the soul."

"We'll take the light, too," Kelolo had agreed, for he was tired of his smoky oil-nut candles when the white man's whale-oil lamps were so obviously superior.

"I do not mean that kind of light," Abner had started to say, but sometimes the Hawaiians were too much for him. Now, however, he was adamant. "No kahuna, no evil, heathenish priest is going to say how we shall build the church of God."

"But kahunas . . ." Kelolo began.

"No!" Abner shouted. "The door will be here. The steeple will be here." And he placed big stones at the critical orientations. When he was finished, Kelolo studied the intended building for a long time. He looked to the hills and beyond them to the mountains. He studied the pathway of the little stream and the distance to the sea, but mostly he studied the rise and fall of the land, as if it consisted of human hands waiting to receive the building which would soon rest within the palms.

Finally he shook his head sadly and said, "The kahunas won't like it."

"The kahunas will never enter it," Abner said stiffly.

"You'll keep out the kahunas!" Kelolo gasped.

"Of course. This is a church for those who obey Jehovah and keep his Commandments."

"But the kahunas are eager to join," Kelolo protested. "They all want to find what power it is your god has that enables his people to build boats and make new lights that are better than ours. Oh, you'll have no better people in your church than the kahunas!"

Again the dizziness—the crazy irrationality of Hawaii—attacked Abner and he explained slowly, "I have come with the Bible to wipe out the kahunas, their gods and their evil ways."

"But the kahunas love Jesus Christ," Kelolo cried. "He is so powerful. I love Jesus Christ!"

"But you are not a kahuna," Abner countered.

Slowly, Kelolo raised himself to his full austere height. "Makua Hale, I am the Kahuna Nui. My father was the Kahuna Nui, and his father, and his father all the way back to Bora Bora."

Abner was stunned by this intelligence, but he felt that the moment was critical and that he must not surrender his position. "I don't care if your great-grandfather Bora Bora was a kahuna . . ."

"Bora Bora is an island," Kelolo said proudly.

"I never heard of it."

Now Kelolo was astonished. "In Boston they did not teach you about . . ." He stopped, thought a moment, and then placed his right foot on the stone indicating the door to Abner's church. "Makua Hale, we are in the time when gods are changing. These are always difficult times. When I argue as a kahuna, I am not defending the old gods of Hawaii. They have already been defeated by your god. We all know that. But I am speaking as the kahuna who knows this land. I have often spoken with the spirits of Lahaina and I understand the hills. Makua Hale, believe me when I tell you that this door is wrong for this land."

"We will build the door here," Abner said resolutely.

Sadly, Kelolo studied the obstinate man who understood so little about churches, but he argued no more. "Now I will lead my men back to the sandalwood trees. When we have returned three times, I will direct them to build your church."

"Three times! Kelolo, the crops will be ruined by then."

"They are my men," the huge chief said stubbornly, and that evening he led two thousand of them back into the hills.

O N THE THIRTIETH day after the arrival of the missionaries at Lahaina, Malama, the Alii Nui, had her handmaidens clothe her in the new China silk dress that Jerusha Hale had sewed for her. She put on shoes for the first time —heavy sailor's shoes with the laces untied—and covered her wealth of long black hair with a wide-brimmed straw hat from Ceylon. Then she ordered her servants to lay new tapa with extra care, and when this was done she lay prone on the floor, directed the fanning to begin, and spread before her a sheet of white paper, an ink pot and a China quill. "Now I shall write!" she announced, and in a clean, disciplined hand she composed this letter in Hawaiian for her nephew in Honolulu:

"Liholiho King. My husband Kelolo is working hard. He is going to buy a ship. Aloha, Malama."

When this exacting task was completed, the huge woman heaved a sigh and pushed the letter toward Jerusha and Abner. Then women came in to lomilomi her, and she smiled proudly from the floor as Jerusha said, "I have never known a person to learn as fast as Malama." When Keoki translated this, his mother stopped smiling and brushed away the lomilomi women, saying, "Before long I shall write to the king of America . . . in your language . . . and I shall use all twenty-six letters."

"She'll do it!" Jerusha said proudly.

"Now, little daughter," Malama said, "you have taught me well. You must go home and rest. It is Makua Hale who shall teach me now." Dismissing Jerusha she rolled over on her belly again, propped her chin in her hands, stared at him intensely and commanded, "Tell me about your god."

Abner had long anticipated this holy moment, and he had constructed a patient, step-by-step explanation of his religion, and as he began to speak with Keoki's help, he sensed that the huge woman on the floor was passionately eager to know all that he knew, so he worked with special care, choosing each word exactly and consulting often with Keoki as to its translation into Hawaiian, for he knew that if he could win Malama to the side of God, he would automatically win all of Maui.

"God is a spirit," he said carefully.

"Can I ever see him?"

"No, Malama."

She pondered this for some moments and said, "Well, I could never see Kane, either." Then she added suspiciously, "But Kelolo has often seen his goddess, Pele of the volcanoes."

Abner had sworn to himself that he would not be led down by-paths. He was not here to argue against Kelolo's miserable assortment of superstitions. He was here to expound the true faith, and he knew from experience that once he started on Kelolo's gods he was apt to get tangled up in irrelevant arguments.

"God is a spirit, Malama," he repeated, "but He created everything."

"Did he create heaven?"

Abner had never confronted this problem, but he replied unhesitatingly, "Yes."

"Where is heaven?"

Abner was going to say that it is in the mind of God, but he took the easier course and replied, "Up there."

"Are you certain in your heart, Makua Hale, that your god is more powerful than Kane?"

"I cannot compare the two, Malama. And I cannot explain God to you if you insist upon comparing them. And don't call Him my God. He is absolute."

This made sense to Malama, for she had witnessed the white man's superior power and knew instinctively that his god must also be superior, and she was gratified to hear Abner proclaim the fact. On this principle she was ready to accept his teaching completely. "God is all-powerful," she said quietly. "Then why did he bring the sailors' pox to infect our girls? Why does he make so many Hawaiians die these days?"

"Sin is permitted by God, even though He is all-powerful, for it is sin that tests men and proves them in God's eyes." He paused, and Malama indicated to one of her many servants that they must keep the flies off the missionary, too, and soft feathers swept his neck and forehead. Although he appreciated the attention, he felt that Malama's instructions had been an interruption consciously commanded by the woman to provide time for her thinking, so he added gravely, looking directly at the chieftain, "If you continue in sin, you cannot know God." Pausing dramatically and bringing his face close to hers, he said with great force, preparing the way for the great decision that would later become inevitable, "Malama, to prove that you know God you must put away sin."

"Is it possible that the Alii Nui herself is sinful?" Malama asked, for her religion took care of this problem by postulating that the acts of the alii were the acts of gods.

But she was to discover that in Abner Hale's new religion the answer was strikingly different. Pointing his forefinger at the prone woman he said firmly, "All men on earth are totally depraved. We abide in sin. Our natures are permeated and corrupted in all parts of our being." He paused, then fell to his knees so that he would be closer to the Alii Nui, and added, "And because kings have greater power, their sin is greater. The Alii Nui is the most powerful woman in Maui. Therefore her sin is greater. Malama," he cried in the woeful, desperate voice of John Calvin, "we are all lost in sin!"

A child cried in one of the surrounding huts, and Malama asked, "Is that baby filled with sin, too?"

"From the moment that child was born . . . No, Malama, from the moment it was conceived, it was steeped in sin. It was drowned in mortal vice, horrible, perpetual, inescapable. That child is totally corrupt."

Malama pondered this and asked tentatively, "But if your god is all-powerful . . ." Then she stopped, for she was willing to accept Abner's earlier answer. She thought aloud: "God has arranged sin to test us."

Abner smiled for the first time. "Yes. You understand."

"But what will happen, Makua Hale, to that baby if it is not rescued from sin?"

"It will be plunged into fire everlasting."

"What will happen to me, Makua Hale, if I am not saved from sin?"

"You will be plunged into fire everlasting." There was a pause in the grass house as Malama shifted her weight on the tapas. Rolling over on her right side, she leaned her jawbone on her right hand and motioned Abner to sit on the tapa near her.

"What is the fire like?" she asked quietly.

"It leaps about your feet. It tears at your eyeballs. It fills your nose. It burns incessantly, but you are constantly recreated so that it can burn you again. Its pain is horrible beyond imagining. Its . . ."

Malama interrupted, asking weakly, "Once I traveled with Kamehameha to the edge of a burning lava flow, and I stood with him when he sacrificed his hair to appease Pele. Are the fires worse than that?"

"Malama, they are much worse."

"And all the good Hawaiians who died before you came here, Makua Hale? Are they living in that perpetual fire?"

"They died in sin, Malama. They now live in that fire."

The huge woman gasped, took away her right elbow and allowed her head to fall onto the tapa. After a moment she asked, "My good uncle, Keawe-mauhili? Is he in the fire?"

"Yes, Malama, he is."

"Forever?"

"Forever."

"And my husband Kamehameha?"

"He is in the fire forever."

"And that baby, if it dies tonight?"

"It will live in the fire forever."

"And my husband Kelolo, who swears he will never accept your religion?"

"He will live in the fire forever."

"And I will never see him again?"

"Never."

The remorselessness of this doctrine overcame Malama, and for the first time she sensed the truly awful power of the new god, and why those who followed him were victorious in war and could invent cannon that swept away tribal villages. She fell to sobbing, "Auwe. Auwe!" and thought of her good uncle and her great king wasting in fires eternal, and her servants brought cool cloths to ease her, but she brushed them away and continued weeping and beating her huge breasts. Finally she asked, "Can those of us who are still alive be saved?"

This was the question that had once given Abner most trouble: "Can all be saved?" and it stunned him to hear it coming so precisely from the mouth of a heathen, for it was the touchstone of his religion, and he replied, "No, Malama, there are many whom God has predestined for eternal hellfire."

"You mean they are condemned even before they are born?"

"Yes."

"And there is no hope for them?"

"They are predestined to live in evil and die into hellfire."

"Oh, oh!" Malama wept. "Do you mean that that little baby . . ."

"Perhaps."

"Even me, the Alii Nui?"

"Perhaps."

This awful concept struck Malama with great force. It seemed a lottery of life and death . . . a god throwing smoothed pebbles into a rock hole . . . and sometimes missing. But it was the god who missed, and not the pebble, for unless the god had wanted to, he need not have missed. With pebbles he was all-powerful.

Then Abner was speaking: "I must confess, Malama, that all who slide into evil do so by the divine will of God and that some men are destined from birth to certain fire, that His name may be glorified in heaven because of their destruction. It is a terrible decree, I do confess, but none can deny that God foresaw all things for all men before He created them. We live under His divine ordinance."

"How can I be saved?" Malama asked weakly.

Now Abner's face became radiant, and his infusion of spirit transferred itself to the weeping woman, and she began to feel in the grass house a consolation that would never depart. "When God foredoomed all men," Abner said forcefully, "His great compassion directed Him to send to us His only begotten son, and it is Jesus Christ who can save us, Malama. Jesus Christ can enter this house and lift you by the hand and lead you to cool waters. Jesus Christ can save us."

"Will Jesus save me?" Malama asked hopefully.

"He will!" Abner cried joyously, clasping her huge hands in his. "Malama, Jesus Christ will enter this room and save you."

"What must I do to be saved?"

"There are two things required, Malama. The first is easy. The second is difficult."

"What is the easy one?"

"You must go down on your knees before the Lord and acknowledge that you are totally corrupt, that you live in sin, and that there is no hope for you."

"I must confess those things?"

"Unless you do, you can never be saved." Now the little missionary became once more the stern teacher, for he withdrew his hands, moved away from the prone chieftain and pointed at her: "And you must not only say the words. You must believe them. You are corrupt, Malama. Evil, evil, evil."

"And what is the second task?"

"You must work to attain a state of grace."

"I don't know what grace is, Makua Hale."

"When you have honestly confessed your corruption, and when you plead for God's light, some day it will come to you."

"How will I recognize it?"

"You will know."

"And when I have found this . . . What is the word, Keoki?"

Her son explained again and she asked him, "Did you find grace?"

"Yes, Mother."

"Where?"

"On the stone pavement in front of Yale College."

"And was it a light, as Makua Hale says?"

"It was like the heavens opening up," Keoki assured her.

"Will I find grace?"

"No one can say for sure, Mother, but I think you will, for you are a good woman."

Malama pondered this for some time, and then asked Abner, "What things have I been doing that are sinful?"

For a moment Abner was tempted to believe that this was the instant when he must excoriate the evil ways of the Alii Nui, but a more sober judgment prevailed and he restrained himself, saying, "Malama, you learned how to write in only thirty days. It was a miracle. Therefore I think you can perform the greater miracle that awaits."

Malama, loving praise and steeped in it since her first days as the Alii Nui, firmed her jaw and asked, "What is required?"

"Will you take a walk with me?"

"Where?"

"Through your land . . . through the land you rule."

Malama, exhilarated by her success in learning, agreed, and summoned her land canoe; but with all the able men in the mountains seeking sandalwood, there were none to man the carrying poles, and Abner raised his first disturbing question: "Why do you allow your workingmen to toil like slaves in the hills?"

"They're after sandalwood," Malama explained.

"For what?"

"For Kelolo's ship."

"Is the ruin of a beautiful island worth a ship?" Abner asked.

"What do you mean, Makua Hale?"

"I want you to walk with me, Malama, and see the fearful price Lahaina is paying for the sandalwood that Kelolo is seeking in the mountains." So Malama summoned her maids-in-waiting, and a procession was formed that would, in time, modify the history of Hawaii. The little missionary limped in front, accompanied by towering Keoki. Behind them marched gigantic Malama in a blue and red dress. On her right walked the handmaiden Kalani-kapuai-kala-ninui, five feet tall and two hundred and fifteen pounds, while on the left puffed Manono-kaua-kapu-kulani, five feet six inches and two hundred and eight pounds. Side by side, the three alii women filled the road as Abner began his perambulatory sermon.

"A ship at this time, Malama, is merely a vanity. Look at the walls of the fish pond. Crumbling."

"What does it matter?" Malama asked.

"If the fish escape, the people will starve," Abner said.

"When the men come back . . . from the sandalwood . . ."

"The fish will be gone," Abner reported dolefully. "Malama, you and I will rebuild the fish pond." And he stepped into the mud, calling her after him. Quickly, she perceived what he was teaching and ordered her handmaidens to help, and the three huge women plunged into the fish pond, pulling the back hems of their new dresses forward and up between their legs like giant diapers. Giggling and telling obscene jokes which Abner could not understand—among themselves they called him "the little white cockroach"—the alii mended the breaks, and when they were finished, Abner hammered home his lesson: "The wise Alii Nui commands the fish ponds to be patrolled."

A little farther on he pointed to a grass house that had burned to the ground. "Four people died there, Malama. A wise Alii Nui would outlaw the use of tobacco."

"But the people like to smoke," Malama protested.

"And so you let them burn to death. Since I came to Lahaina, six of your people have burned to death. A wise Alii Nui . . ."

"Where are you taking me?" Malama interrupted.

"To a spot a little farther under the kou trees," Abner explained, and before long he had Malama and the women standing beside a small oblong of freshly dug earth, and she recognized it immediately for what it was. She preferred not to speak of this little plot of earth, but Abner said, "Beneath here lies a baby girl, Malama."

"I know," the Alii Nui said gently.

"The child was placed here by her own mother."

"Yes."

"Alive."

"I understand, Makua Hale."

"And while the child was still alive, the mother covered it with earth and stamped upon the earth until the little girl . . ."

"Please, Makua Hale. Please."

"A wise Alii Nui, one who sought grace, would order this evil to be stopped." Malama said nothing, and the procession marched on until it reached the spot where three sailors were buying whiskey from an Englishman, and on the arms of the sailors were the four pretty girls whose father had paddled them to the *Thetis* on its arrival. "These are the girls who will soon die of sailor's pox," Abner said mournfully. "A wise Alii Nui would outlaw whiskey and keep the girls from going to the ships."

They passed the taro patches, rank with weeds, and the little pier with bales of goods from China waiting in the sun and rain. No men were in the fishing boats. When the circuit was at last completed, the little missionary pointed at the platform of stones in Malama's own front yard and said, "Even at your door you harbor the evil old gods."

"That's Kelolo's temple," Malama said. "It does no harm."

At the mention of the absent chief, Abner knew that the ultimate moment had come, the one toward which he had been building. He asked Malama to dismiss her attendants, and when they were gone he led the huge chieftain and Keoki to a smooth spot under the kou trees, and when all were comfortably seated he said forcefully, "I have taken you on this walk, Malama, to show you that God appoints a woman His Alii Nui for a reason. He gives you great power so that you may produce great good. More is expected of you than of ordinary people."

This made much sense to Malama, for the tenets of her old religion were not markedly different . . . only the interpretation. If a man was an alii, he was expected to die in battle. A woman alii must appear noble and eat enormously so that she seemed bigger than she was. In all religions there were duties, but she was not prepared for the one which the little missionary was about to propose.

"You will never enter a state of grace, Malama," Abner said slowly, "so long as you commit one of the gravest sins in human history."

"What is that?" she asked.

Abner hesitated, and the concept he now had to discuss was so loathsome to him that he rose, drew back a few steps and pointed at the Alii Nui: "You have as your husband your own brother. You must send Kelolo away."

Malama was appalled at the suggestion. "Kelolo . . . why he . . ."

"He must go, Malama."

"But he is my favorite husband," she protested.

"This relationship is evil . . . it is forbidden by the Bible."

At this news a benign light of comprehension shone over Malama's face. "You mean it is kapu!" she asked brightly.

"It is not kapu," Abner insisted. "It is forbidden by God's law."

"That's what kapu means," Malama explained patiently. "Now I understand. All gods have kapu. You mustn't eat this fish, it is kapu. You mustn't sleep with a woman who is having her period, it is kapu. You mustn't . . ."

"Malama!" Abner thundered. "Being married to your brother is not kapu! It's not some idle superstition. It's a law of God."

"I know. I know. Not a little kapu like certain fish, but big kapu, like not entering a temple if you are unclean. All gods have big and little kapus. So Kelolo is a big kapu and he must go. I understand."

"You don't understand," Abner began, but Malama was so pleased with her comprehension of this aspect, at least, of the new god, that she was spurred to action, and she summoned her servants in a loud voice.

"Kelolo will not live in this house any more! He will live in that house!" And she indicated one of the compound quarters about twenty feet removed from his previous residence. The law promulgated, she beamed at Abner.

"That is not enough, Malama. He must move out of the compound altogether."

At this, Malama said something to Keoki which the young man was too embarrassed to translate, but Abner insisted, and Keoki, blushing, explained, "My mother says that she stopped sleeping with her four other husbands years ago and you need have no fear that she will misbehave . . ." Keoki stopped, for he did not have the words. "Anyway, she says that Kelolo is a kind man and she hopes he can stay within the compound."

Angrily, Abner stamped his foot and shouted, "No! This is an evil thing. Tell her it is the biggest kapu of all . . . Wait, don't use that word! Tell her merely that the Lord says specifically that Kelolo must move outside the compound."

Malama began to cry and said that Kelolo was more to her than either a husband or a brother and that . . . Abner interrupted and said simply, "Unless he moves, Malama, you will never be able to join the church."

She did not understand this and asked, "I will not be allowed inside the big new church Kelolo is going to build?"

"You may come inside," Abner said gently. "Even the worst sinner may come and listen. And you may sing, too. But you may never join the church . . . the way Keoki has joined."

Malama considered this for a long time, concluding brightly, "Very well. I'll sing and keep Kelolo."

"And when you die," Abner said, "you will burn in hell forever and ever."

Malama knew she was being maneuvered into a corner, so with tears in her big deep eyes she said to Keoki, using sly words that Abner would not be able to detect, "I do not want to burn in hell, so you must build Kelolo a small house outside the compound, but brush the path well so there are no leaves, and at night he can tiptoe back to my room and God will not hear him." Then, in a loud voice she announced: "Makua Hale, I am going to write a new letter."

When she was sprawled once more on the floor of her palace, she tore up the earlier message, bit her pen and wrote:

"Liholiho King. I have told Kelolo he must now sleep outside. He is buying a ship. I think it is a foolish thing to do. Your aunt, Malama."

She handed Abner the letter, and when he had read it she said, "Tomorrow and tomorrow and the day after that I want you to come here to talk with me about the duty of an alii nui. After one moon I shall find a state of grace."

"It cannot be done in that way, Malama."

"When can I find it?"

"Perhaps never."

"I will find it!" the great woman roared. "You will come here tomorrow and teach me how to find it."

"I cannot do that, Malama," Abner said resolutely.

"You . . . will . . . do . . . it!" she threatened.

"No man can find grace for another," Abner stubbornly insisted.

Malama leaped to her feet with strange agility and grabbed her little mentor by the shoulders. "How shall I find grace?" she demanded.

"Do you really want to know, Malama?"

"Yes," she replied, shaking him as if he were a child. "Tell me!"

"Kneel down," he commanded, and he did so himself, showing her how to pray.

"What do I do now?" she whispered, turning her big eyes at him.

"Close your eyes. Make a temple of your hands and say, 'Jesus Christ, my master, teach me to be humble and to love Thee.' "

"What is humble?" Malama asked, her voice lower.

"Humble means that even the greatest alii nui in Maui is no more than a man who catches mullet from the fish pond," Abner explained.

"You mean that even the slave . . ."

"Malama," Abner said in ashen voice, overcome by his own perception of God's law, "it seems to me that right now the lowliest slave hauling sandalwood from the forest has a better chance of finding grace than you do."

"Why?" the kneeling woman begged.

"Because at any moment he may find God, for he has a humble spirit. But you are proud and argumentative, and unwilling to humble yourself before the Lord."

"You are proud, too, Makua Hale," the huge woman argued. "Do you humble yourself before the Lord?"

"If He told me tomorrow to march into the waves until they overcame me, I would do so. I live for the Lord. I serve the Lord. The Lord is my light and my salvation."

"I understand," the Alii Nui said. "I will pray for humbleness." And when he left, she was still kneeling with her hands forming the steeple of a church.

For the next several days Abner did not see Malama, for serious riots were sweeping Lahaina, and with Kelolo and the men gone, only Abner was left to combat them. Trouble started when three whaling ships, in from the Off-Japan grounds, sent more than eighty men ashore on overdue leave. The first place they visited was Murphy's grog shop, and from there they branched out through Lahaina, fighting, debauching, and at last murdering. Emboldened by the lack of police to discipline them, they formed mobs and began sacking Hawaiian homes, searching for girls, and when they found any, they dragged them to the ships, not waiting to discover whether these were normal ships' girls or not, and in this way many faithful wives of men off on the sandalwood expedition were raped.

At last, Abner Hale put on his black claw-hammer, his best stock and his tall beaver hat, and went down to the pier. "Row me out to the whalers!" he commanded the useless old men who were lounging along the shore, and when he reached the first ship he found that the captain was gone, and at the second ship the captain was locked in his room with a girl and would not speak with the missionary, cursing him through the door, but at the third ship Abner found a captain who sat below drinking whiskey, and to him Abner said, "Your men are debauching Lahaina."

"That's what I brought 'em here fer," the captain said.

"They're raping our women, Captain."

"They always do, in Lahaina. The women like it."

"Last night there was a murder," Abner continued.

"You catch the murderer and we'll hang him."

"But he could be one of your men."

"Probably was. Eight of my men deserve hangin'. I'd love to see 'em all swingin' from an arm."

"Captain, have you no sense of responsibility for what is going on ashore?"

"Look, Reverend," the captain said wearily, "for the last two nights I been ashore meself. Only reason I'm not there now is I'm too damned old . . . for three nights in a row, that is."

There was a great cry from ashore, and one of the grass houses went up in flames. From the captain's quarters Abner could see the blaze and it seemed near his home, and he was panicked for fear that Jerusha might be in danger. Pointing his finger at the captain he threatened: "Captain Jackson, of the *Bugle* out of Salem, I shall write to your church, Captain, and advise your minister of how one of his members conducts himself in Lahaina."

"By God!" the captain roared, pushing away his grog. "If you mention my name in your letters . . ." He lunged at Abner, but was drunk and missed him, his huge bulk crashing into the wall.

"You cannot be two men, Captain," Abner said solemnly. "A beast in Lahaina and a saint in Salem. You must stop the rioting."

"I'll strangle your dirty little chicken neck!" Captain Jackson shouted, clutching for the missionary, who had no trouble evading him. "You get off this ship! Lahaina was a good port till you came along."

Ashore another house went up in flames, and as Abner reached the deck he could see four sailors chasing a girl who had thus been routed out for their sport. "May God forgive them," Abner prayed. "But with such leaders . . ." He swung himself down into his canoe and returned to shore, determined at least to protect Jerusha, lest the violence disturb her pregnancy, but before he could get to her, there was a new commotion, and now even the stragglers along the shore became excited, for three large sailors had been prowling about the back area of Malama's compound and had discovered her young daughter Noelani, and were now dragging her through the dusty streets until they could find a comfortable spot in which to rape her, and she was screaming in Hawaiian, while the sailors cursed in English.

A few old men, too weak to be with the sandalwooders, proved themselves loyal to their alii and tried to stop the rapists, but they were laughingly pushed aside, for in justice to the sailors they could not distinguish between an ordinary girl, with whom such conduct was customary, and an alii, with whom it was sacrilege. Other old men tried to intervene, but they also were bowled over with shocking jolts to the jaw, and the drunken sailors proceeded with their captive.

At this point Abner Hale limped up, holding onto his top hat, and he pointed his right hand in the faces of the sailors and cried, "Set loose that girl."

"Get out of the way, little man!" the sailors warned.

"I am a minister of God!" Abner warned them.

The first two sailors stopped at this, but the third swaggered up to the missionary and shouted, "In Lahaina there is no God."

Abner, who weighed only half of what the sailor did, impulsively slapped the man in the face. "God is watching you!" he said solemnly.

The slapped man quickly squared off, British fashion, to demolish Abner, whereupon the two other sailors released the girl and grabbed their partner, but when they saw fair Noelani run away, the most beautiful girl they had so far found, they became infuriated and started to strike and punch and kick at Abner. He was saved by Malama herself, for the great alii had seen the abduction of her daughter and had hurried up with what men and women she could command.

"It's the queen!" one of the sailors shouted, and as big Malama waded into the midst of the riot, the men withdrew from beating Abner and ran, cursing, to assemble their mates. Soon more than forty sailors, most of them drunk, crowded the dusty street and shouted imprecations at the missionary and the women who were protecting him. "Come over here, you coward!" they challenged, but whenever an especially bold one spoke, Malama went bravely to him and damned him in Hawaiian, so that after a while the sailors dispersed, and Abner saw with horror that from the shadows two ship's captains had watched the affair with approval.

"What kind of men are they?" he wondered, and when the mob had gone back to Murphy's grog shop and Malama was attending his bruises, he said quietly, in broken Hawaiian, "Do you see what happens when the men are away gathering sandalwood?"

"I see," Malama said. "I will send the women to the hills."

That night was one of terror, for the sailors, goaded by their captains, could find no girls, so they surrounded Abner's home and cursed him vilely till midnight. Then they burned another house and finally found three girls, whom they hauled off to the ship. At two in the morning, when the rioting was its worst, Abner said to Jerusha, "I will leave Keoki and the women here with you. I am going to speak with Pupali." And by a back route he scurried to the home of Pupali, the ardent canoeist whose occupation it was to paddle his own wife and four daughters to incoming whalers.

He sat on the floor with Pupali, no light showing, and asked in broken Hawaiian, "Why do you take your own daughters to these evil men?"

"I get cloth and sometimes even tobacco," Pupali explained.

"Don't you see that some day your daughters may die from the sailors' disease?" Abner pleaded.

"Some day everybody dies," Pupali rationalized.

"But is a little money worth this to you?" Abner argued.

"Men like girls," Pupali said truthfully.

"Do you feel no shame in selling your own wife to the sailors?"

"Her sister takes care of me," Pupali said contentedly.

"Are you proud when the sailors burn down the houses?" Abner pressed.

"They never burn my house," Pupali replied.

"How old is your prettiest daughter, Pupali?"

Abner could hear him suck in his breath in pride. "Iliki? She was born in the year of Keopuolani's illness."

"Fourteen, and probably already sick to death!"

"What do you expect? She's a woman."

On the spur of the moment Abner said, "I want you to give her to me, Pupali."

At last something was happening that the rough old man could understand. Smiling lasciviously he whispered, "You'll enjoy Iliki. All the men do. How much you give me for her?"

"I am taking her for God," Abner corrected.

"I know, but how much you give me?" Pupali pressed.

"I will clothe her and feed her and treat her as my daughter," Abner explained.

"You mean, you don't want . . ." Pupali shook his head. "Well, Makua Hale, you must be a good man." And when morning dawned, Abner, in the dust of riots, started his school for Hawaiian girls. His first pupil was Pupali's most beautiful daughter, Iliki, and when she appeared she wore only a thin slip about her hips and a silver chain around her neck, from which dangled a whale's tooth handsomely carved with these words:

> Observe the truth; enough for man to know
> Virtue alone is happiness below.

When the other island families saw what an advantage Pupali enjoyed by having his daughter as an observer within the missionary household, for she could report on the strangest occurrences, they offered their girls, too, which nullified Pupali's superiority, so that he countered by enrolling his other three daughters, and when the next whaling ship touched port, matters were different. Before, sailors had instructed the Lahaina girls in profanity in the steaming fo'c's'ls; now Jerusha taught them cooking and the Psalms in the mission garden, and her ablest pupil was Iliki, Ee-Lee-Kee, the Pelting Spray of Ocean.

A BNER WAS NOT present to congratulate Iliki on the August afternoon when she first wrote her name and carried it proudly to her father, for that morning had brought an exhausted messenger to Lahaina. He had run across the mountains from the other side of the island, blurting out so bizarre a story that Abner summoned Keoki to translate formally, and the young man said, "It is true! Abraham and Urania Hewlett have marched all the way from Hana, at the opposite end of Maui."

"Why didn't they take a canoe?" Abner asked, puzzled.

Keoki rapidly interrogated the gasping messenger and then looked blank as the man explained. "It's hard to believe," Keoki muttered. "Abraham and Urania set out yesterday morning at four o'clock in a double canoe, but at six o'clock the waves were so great that the canoe broke apart, so Abraham brought his wife ashore through the surf. Then they walked forty miles to Wailuku, where they are now."

"I thought that trail was impossible for women," Abner argued.

"It is. The worst on Maui. But Urania had to make it, because next month she is due to have her baby and they wanted to be with you."

"What can I . . ." Abner began in bewilderment.

"They are afraid she is dying," the messenger said.

"If she's dying . . ." Abner was sweating and nervous. "Well, how did she get to Wailuku?"

With gestures, the messenger explained, "The paddlers from the wrecked canoe tied vines under her arms and pulled her up the gullies. Then, when it came time to go down the other side, they grabbed the vines . . ."

Before the tired messenger could finish, Abner knelt in the dust and raised his hands. He could visualize Urania, a dull woman and frightened, undergoing this tremendous trip, and he prayed, "Dear Heavenly Father, save Thy servant, Sister Urania. In her hours of fear, save her."

The messenger interrupted and said, "Abraham Hewlett says you must bring your book and help him."

"The book?" Abner cried. "I thought . . ."

"They need you now," the messenger insisted. "Because when I left she seemed about to have the baby."

The idea of assisting at a birth appalled Abner, but he hurried out to the garden where Jerusha was teaching her girls, and from his frightened look she knew that some new island crisis had occurred, but she was not prepared when he said, "Sister Urania was trying to reach us for help, but she has had to stop in Wailuku." The Hales had never spoken of Urania's pregnancy, just as, for reasons of delicacy, they had never mentioned Jerusha's, trusting that by some miracle the baby would either be born without trouble or wait until Dr. Whipple happened along. Now, under the coconut trees, they had to acknowledge imminent facts.

"I will take Deland's *Midwifery* and do what I can," Abner said dully, but what he wanted to cry was: "I will be with you, Jerusha! By the will of God, I will see that your baby is well born."

And she replied, "You must help Sister Urania," but what she intended was: "I am afraid, and I wish my mother were here."

So the two young missionaries, each so desperately in love but lacking capacity to speak of it to the other, because they judged that Congregationalism would not approve, looked at each other in the noonday sunlight, and then looked away; but it was Abner who broke, for when they had gone inside to pack Deland it was he who could not control his hands, and the package fell awry and the crucial book fell onto the dusty floor, and when he kneeled to recover it he hid his face in his hands and sobbed, "Sister Urania, may God spare you!" But it was another name he longed to say.

The journey on foot from Lahaina to Wailuku, on the other side of Maui, took Abner and the messenger high into the mountains, and as they hiked over barren and rocky fields, with sweat pouring from them, they came upon a cloud of dust, and it was Kelolo and his lieutenants, driving their men down to the plains with a vast cargo of sandalwood. For an instant Abner was infuriated and admonished the chief: "While you cut sandalwood, your town diminishes." But before he heard Kelolo's justification—"These are my men. I do with them as I please."—he saw that many of the servants were carrying not sawed trunks from grown trees but saplings and roots grubbed out of the soil.

"Did you take even the new trees?" Abner asked in disgust.

"It is my sandalwood," Kelolo explained.

"You faithless servant," Abner cried and limped on.

When they reached the topmost ridge and could see the houses of Wailuku below, Abner paused to wipe away his sweat and thought: "If it is such hard work for us to climb this little hill, how could Urania have borne her journey?"

In the village of Wailuku they found out. When the canoe in which they were journeying broke up, Abraham had pushed and hauled his wife more than forty miles overland in an effort to join with the Hales at Lahaina, and this had precipitated her labor pains. Now they were bogged down in a trader's shack, helpless in panic.

It was a miracle that Urania, after such a trip, was still alive, but it was a greater miracle that Abraham had not thought to enlist the aid of Hawaiian midwives at his home mission, for they were some of the most highly skilled in the Pacific and within ten minutes would have diagnosed Urania's case as one of simple premature birth brought on by exhaustion. Had the Hewletts relied on them, they would have produced a clean birth and a healthy baby; but for the Hewletts to have accepted their aid would have meant admitting that a heathen, brown-skinned Hawaiian knew how to deliver a Christian white baby, and such an idea was unthinkable.

"I was sorely tempted to call in the local midwives," Brother Abraham confessed to Abner, when he ran up to meet the limping traveler, "but I was ever mindful of Jeremiah 10, verse 2: 'Thus saith the Lord, Learn not the way of the heathen.' So I have brought my wife to her own people."

Abner agreed that he had acted wisely, and for a moment the two young men congratulated themselves on their righteousness, but then Abner asked, "How is Sister Urania?"

At this question poor Brother Abraham was seized with a blush of respectability which made it almost impossible for him to say the words, but finally he blurted out: "She seems to have lost a great deal of her water."

In the growing dusk Abner looked sickly at his companion, then started feverishly unpacking his handbook. Thumbing it awkwardly he found a section titled "The Dry Delivery," and as he read it hurriedly, he became quite ill in the stomach, for the news was ominous, but when he looked up and saw how hopeless Brother Abraham was, he gritted his teeth and said boldly, "I should like to see Sister Urania."

Hewlett led him toward a low grass hut in which the Englishman who traded at Wailuku lived, but both the man and his wife were absent in Honolulu, and the house was surrounded by fifty or sixty natives, sitting on the ground and watching the amazing white men. Abner made his way through them, and with his medical book under his arm, went into the mean house to greet the frail woman with whom he had shared the tiny stateroom on the *Thetis*. "Good evening, Sister Urania," he said solemnly, and she replied bravely, "It is so consoling to meet again one with whom we journeyed on the small ship." And for a moment they spoke of happier days.

Then Abner asked, "Sister Urania, when did your . . ." He paused in acute embarrassment, and then finished with a rush: "Your labor pains, how long have they been occurring?"

"They started at six this morning," Urania said. Abner stared at her blankly, but his mind thought fiercely: "Oh, God! That was when she was climbing the last gullies!"

He mopped his forehead and said slowly, "That was twelve hours ago. Presumably then, Sister Urania, the child will be born at midnight." He consulted his watch: six hours to go.

Aching with embarrassment, he asked, "Your pains. Have they been frequent?"

"I don't think so," she replied.

"Excuse me," he said, and fumbled for his book of instructions, but the light was so bad that he could not read, and he directed Brother Abraham to fetch a kukuinut lamp, and by its flickering, wavering light he picked out the words that would guide him. "Have we a sheet of tapa?" he asked, and when one was found, he cut it into halves, twisted them to make ropes, knotted one end and tied the other to the foot of the bed. "You must pull on these knots, Sister Urania," he instructed her. "In a dry delivery you will be called upon for extra work."

Instantly he was sorry he had said these words, for Urania looked up in terror and asked, "Have I done something wrong?"

"No, Sister Urania," he assured her. "With God's help we shall do well."

Instinctively, she took his hand and whispered, "My cherished husband and I are so glad that you came." But when Abner, blushing like a child, wanted to examine her stomach, as the handbook directed, both he and the Hewletts thought it proper that she first cover herself with all of her personal clothing plus a stout sheet of tapa. Feeling through the several layers, Abner gravely announced: "There seems nothing awry."

But his head was snapped back by a sudden scream from the bed and an automatic tightening of the ropes. He hurried to the sputtering lamp and studied his watch. In four minutes another cry and another straining. Sweating, he leafed through his book and found reassuring news. Hurrying back to the bed, he announced happily: "Sister Urania, things are going well. Now time will work with us."

At this news Brother Abraham grew a ghastly white and it was obvious that he was going to be very sick, so Abner left the straining woman and ran to the door of the delivery room, crying in Hawaiian, "Somebody come in here and take care of Reverend Hewlett!" Two experienced midwives, who understood husbands, laughed hilariously and rescued the missionary, who was, as they predicted in obscene asides to the gathering, conspicuously nauseated, but while the midwives comforted him other Hawaiians whispered, "Isn't this a strange way to do things? Our best midwives outside the hut caring for the husband, while a man who knows nothing is inside, caring for the mother."

"It's the way they do it in America," a listener explained.

Suddenly the midwives dropped Hewlett and listened acutely to Urania's cries, and it was sardonic that through the night these women, merely by listening, knew better what was occurring inside the hut than Abner, who was there with his book.

Hewlett, stabilized after his sickness, wiped his watery blue eyes and made his way back into the hut, demanding, "When will the child be born?"

"Brother Hewlett!" Abner cried in exasperation. "Unless you can make yourself to be of service, you will have to remain outside."

"When will the child be born?" the distraught man begged. Once more Abner went to the door and called for the midwives, who recovered Abraham and made him stay with them.

The pains now came at constant intervals, and Abner, checking his book constantly, found occasion to say, "Sister Urania, it does seem as if God were supervising us tonight."

"I am now in your hands, Brother Abner," the weak woman replied. "You must do with me as you require."

Later, Abner recalled that she had said these words with marked lassitude, and shortly thereafter he loked at her with horror and realized that she had not experienced a pain for some time and that she was still. Panic captured him, and he felt her wrists, but they seemed cold, and he ran to the door, shouting, "Brother Abraham! Come quickly!" And when the husband stumbled into the room, Abner reported, in a ghastly voice, "I fear she is dying."

Abraham Hewlett uttered a low sob and knelt at the bed, holding his wife's hand, and this unexpected movement caused Urania to shift her shoulders, and Abner in amazement cried, "Can she be sleeping?"

Outside, the midwives, listening intently, had already told the crowd, "She's sleeping. She'll probably stay that way for an hour or more. Then when she awakens, she'll begin all over again."

"Is it a good sign when a woman already in labor sleeps?" the crowd asked.

"No," said the midwives.

"Why not?" a man asked.

"It means she's weak," the woman said.

"What should they do . . . in there?" the man asked.

"They ought to be gathering herbs," the midwives explained.

"Why herbs?"

"To stop the bleeding, later on . . . since she is a weak woman."

Inside the shadowy house Abner and Abraham went frantically through their handbooks and could find nothing about sleeping at the eighteenth hour of delivery, and Abner began to experience an overpowering trembling and fear. "Somewhere in here there must be an explanation," he muttered, but his awkward fingers could not find it. "Brother Abraham, do you find anything?"

Then, mysteriously, the labor pains started again, rhythmically and in full force, but they gave Abner little help, for it was not Urania who was experiencing them, but her husband Abraham. It was pathetic to see the undernourished missionary grip at his stomach, following the exact course of a woman's pain, and for the third time Abner had to run to the door and beg the Hawaiians to take his assistant away. "And keep him away!" Abner snapped.

At two o'clock in the morning Urania Hewlett wakened and at five she had diminished her cycle of pain to intervals of a minute and a half, whereupon the listening women outside predicted, "The birth will be soon." Abner, still fumbling with his book, his eyes bleary, came to the same conclusion, but his next half hour was one of special trial, for not knowing that Urania was undergoing a typical labor, he had leafed through the diagrams in the back of the book where unusual births were explained, with black-lettered titles, and he was possessed by one diagram: "Abnormal Birth: Shoulder and Arm Presentation." Turning rapidly to the associated text, he discovered how difficult his immediate task was going to be if he was, indeed, faced by such a presentation. It was therefore absolutely essential that he prepare for the actual birth, if only to anticipate an abnormality; but this he could not do, because Urania still lay swathed in bedclothes and tapa, and he could not in propriety either remove them himself or ask her to do so. So he went to the door, where streaks of morning light were beginning to penetrate the palm trees, and asked for Brother Abraham, who was sleeping. One of the midwives started toward the door, but Abner recoiled from her in honest horror, so Abraham was wakened and Abner said to him, "Brother Abraham, you must now undress your wife. The hour is at hand."

Abraham looked dumbly at his associate and started toward the bed, but his own labor pains returned with violence, and he had to flee the delivery room, but Abner's problem was solved by a vigorous movement on the bed, where Sister Urania, caught in the violence of birth, was kicking her clothes away and screaming for Abner to help her. Abner, swallowing like a schoolboy and shaking with embarrassment, approached the bed, and then strangely all of his uncertainty vanished, for he thought with boundless thanks to God: "That is surely the head, It is a normal presentation."

Outside, when the wail of the child was first heard, the two midwives said gravely, "He had better have the herbs ready."

Abner, preoccupied with the baby boy he held in his hands and with the nerve-racking job of cutting the cord and then tying it, summoned desperately every memory of his midwife's textbook and did a creditable job. Then he stood for a moment in the shadows, perplexed, holding the new child in his hands, and knowing not what to do, but finally he went out into the dawn and handed the child to a native woman, whom the Hawaiians had summoned twenty-four hours before, certain that she would be needed, and this woman placed the child to her breast.

The first midwife said: "He ought to be watching the mother."

The second replied: "I wonder if he is massaging her stomach to help her throw out the afterbirth."

And the first asked: "Do you suppose he would want these herbs?" And she indicated a brew that her people had used for two thousand years to stop bleeding.

But the second replied: "He would not want them."

Inside the shack Abner now feverishly thumbed his book, refreshing himself as to what he must do next. He cleaned the bed, washed the mother, listened to her breathing, and then saw with alarm that something was happening that the book did not tell about. "Brother Abraham!" he called in fear.

"What is it?" the sick husband replied.

"I am afraid she is bleeding more than she should."

Brother Abraham knew nothing, but he quickly looked through his book, and while the two well-intentioned missionaries tried vainly to catch the shreds of knowledge that would have saved a life, on the rude bed Sister Urania grew weaker and weaker. The long day's exertions and the long night's exhaustion were inexorably exacting their toll, and her face grew gray.

"She should not be sleeping so soundly," Abner cried in panic.

"What can we do?" Hewlett moaned. "Oh, God! Don't let her die now!"

Outside, the midwives said, "They ought to be massaging her stomach, but they seem to be talking, instead." And gradually over the large crowd of natives that had stayed through the night, crept the knowledge that the frail white woman was dying. The idea came upon them like the rays of the morning sun, sweeping down from the coconut palms, so that the Hawaiians, to whom birth was a mystical matter, were already weeping before the missionaries knew that Urania had bled to death.

Later, sitting exhausted under a kou tree, Abner said dully, "Brother Abraham, I did all I could to save your dear wife."

"It was the will of God," Hewlett mumbled.

"And yet," Abner cried, hammering the medical text with his fist, "there must have been something in here we didn't read."

"It was the will of God," Hewlett insisted.

The Hawaiians, watching, said, "How strangely the white men do things."

"They are so smart about reading and guns and their new god," an old woman observed, "that you'd expect them to have found a better way than this to birth a baby."

"What is most curious," pointed out another, "is that in America men do the work of women," but the old woman who had been most critical of the midwifery was the first to acknowledge: "Even so, they make fine children."

After the burial of Urania—the first of many mission women to die in childbirth or from physical exhaustion due to overwork—Abner arranged with natives to care for Abraham Hewlett, his newborn son and the latter's wet nurse for the next two months until the difficult return journey to Hana at the tip of Maui was practical, and when these details were completed, Abner and the messenger climbed the hilly path to home; but they had not gone far when they heard a voice calling them, and it was Brother Abraham, pleading that they take his child with them.

"In Lahaina there will be people to care for the boy," he argued desperately.

"No," Abner refused. "It would be unnatural."

"What can I do with the boy?" Brother Abraham begged.

The question was abhorrent to Abner, who replied, "Why, Brother Abraham, you will care for him, and bring him up to be a strong man."

"I don't know about these things," Brother Abraham mumbled.

"Cease!" Abner cried sternly. "It is your duty to learn," and he turned the distracted missionary around and sent him back to Wailuku and the responsibility of his child. When the ungainly man had left, Abner remarked hotly to the messenger, who could not understand, "I think that if he had had courage, his wife need not have died. If he had kept her at Hana, and done the best he could, all would have been well. Sister Urania was killed by the long climb to Wailuku. And the poor thing, eight months with baby."

These thoughts drove him to the contemplation of his own wife, and he became afraid that news of Urania's death in childbirth might have an adverse effect upon her, so he devised an illogical plan for suppressing the news. He reasoned, more from hope than from common sense: "It will be some time before word of this bad business reaches Lahaina. I shall say nothing of it to my dear wife." He entered into a solemn compact with himself and even called God to witness, but when he reached home and saw the way in which Jerusha's six little curls fell beside her face, and the manner in which she leaned forward in eagerness to greet him after their first days of separation since marriage, his words were faithful to the pledge, but his actions could not be, and he looked at her with such love and apprehension that she knew instantly what had happened. "Sister Urania died," she cried.

"She did," Abner confessed. "But you will not, Jerusha." And for the first time he called her by her name.

She started to ask a question, but he grasped her harshly by her two wrists and looked hard into her brown eyes. "You will not die, Jerusha. I promise you by God's word that you will not die." He released her and sat on a box, holding his tired head in his hands, and said, half ashamed of what he was about to admit, "God protects us in the most mysterious ways, Jerusha, and although my thoughts may in some respects seem horrible, nevertheless they are true. I believe that God took me to the death of Sister Urania so that I would be prepared when your time came. Now I know what to do. I know what Brother Abraham should have done. Jerusha, I am prepared, and you will not die." He leaped to his feet and screamed, "You . . . will . . . not . . . die!"

More than anything else in life he wanted, at that moment, to sweep his wife into his arms and embrace her with kisses, wild bellowing kisses like the sounds of animals in the meadows at home, but he did not know how to do this, so all of his love expressed itself in this one profound resolve. "You will not die," he assured his wife, and from that moment on, no woman in a remote outpost, far from help, ever faced her last days of pregnancy with a sweeter resolution.

BUT IF ABNER thus found spiritual triumph in his missionary home, he encountered a fairly solid defeat at Malama's grass palace, for when he went to give the Alii Nui her day's lesson, he found that Kelolo had not moved to the new house built for him, but lived as usual with his wife. "This is an abomination!" Abner thundered.

The two huge lovers, well into their forties, listened in embarrassment as he explained again why God abhorred incest, but when he was finished, big Malama explained quietly, "I built the house for Kelolo outside the walls, and it is a good house, but he doesn't want to stay there alone." She began to cry and added, "he tried it for two nights while you were away, but when I thought of him sleeping alone, I didn't like it either, so on the third night I walked out to the gate and called, 'Kelolo, come inside where you belong.' And he came and it was all my fault. I am to blame, Makua Hale."

"You will never be a member of the church, Malama," Abner warned. "And when you die, you will suffer hellfire forever."

"Tell me about the hellfire again, Makua Hale," Malama begged, for she desired to know exactly how much risk she was taking, and when Abner repeated his awful description of souls in eternal torment, Malama shivered and began asking specific questions while tears crept into her big eyes.

"You are sure that Kamehameha the king is in such fire."

"I am positive."

"Makua Hale, once a Catholic ship kapena came to Lahaina and spoke to me about God. Are Catholics in the fire too?"

"They are in the fire forever," Abner said with absolute conviction.

"And the same ship kapena told me about the people in India who have not heard of your god."

"Malama, don't speak of him as my God. He is God. He is the only God."

"But when the people of India die, do they go into the fire, too?"

"Yes."

"So that the only people who escape are those who join your church?"

"Yes."

Triumphantly, she turned to Kelolo and said, "You see how terrible the fire is. If you keep that platform out there, hanging onto old gods the way you do, you will live in everlasting fire."

"Ah, no!" Kelolo resisted stubbornly. "My gods will care for me. They will never let me burn, for they will take me to their heaven, where I will live beside Kane's water of life."

"He is a foolish man!" Malama reflected sadly. "He's going to burn and he doesn't know it."

"But, Malama," Abner pointed out, "if you continue to live with Kelolo in such horrible sin, you also will live in everlasting fire."

"Oh, no!" the big woman corrected. "I believe in God, I love Jesus Christ. I am not going to live in fire at all. I will keep Kelolo with me only until I begin to feel sick. We have agreed that before I die I will send him far away, and then I shall be saved."

Then Abner played his trump card. Pointing his finger at her, he boldly faced her and warned: "But it is your minister alone who can let you enter the church. Have you thought of that?"

Malama pondered this unexpected news and studied her tormentor. He was a foot shorter than she, less than half her age, and weighed about a third as much. Cautiously she probed: "And it will be you who judges whether I have been a good woman or not."

"I will be the judge," Abner assured her.

"And if I haven't been . . ."

"You will not be accepted into the church."

Malama reviewed this impasse for some time, looking first at Abner and then at Kelolo, until finally she asked briskly, "But maybe you won't be here at the time, Makua Hale. Maybe there will be some other minister."

"I will be here," Abner said firmly.

Malama studied this gloomy prospect, sighed in resignation, and then changed the subject abruptly. "Tell me, Makua Hale, what things must I do if I am to be a good Alii Nui for my people?"

And Abner launched into the work which would have great political consequence in Hawaii. At first only Malama and Kelolo attended his daily instruction, but gradually the lesser alii reported, and when King Liholiho, or his regent-mother Kaahumanu were in residence, they too appeared, questioning, rejecting, pondering.

Constantly, Abner reiterated a few simple ideas. "There must be no slaves," he said.

"There are slaves in America," the alii countered.

"It is wrong in America, and it is wrong here. There must be no slaves."

"There are slaves in England," his listeners insisted.

"And in both America and England good men fight against slavery. Good men should do the same here." When his moral arguments bore no fruit, he resorted to exhortation, crying, "I was afloat on the ocean on my way to Hawaii, and we passed a ship at sundown, and it was a slave ship, and we could hear the chains clashing in the dismal holds. How would you like it, King Liholiho, if your hands were chained to a beam, and your back was cut with lashes, and the sweat poured down your face and blinded your eyes? How would you like that, King Liholiho?"

"I would not like it," the king replied.

"And the alii should see to it that no more babies are killed," Abner thundered.

Malama interrupted. "How should we greet captains from foreign warships when they come ashore at Lahaina?"

"All civilized nations," Abner explained, using a phrase that was especially cherished by the missionaries, "conduct formal relations with other civilized nations. The captain of a warship is the personal representative of the king of the nation whose flag he flies. When he comes ashore, you should fire a small cannon, and you should have four alii dressed in fine robes, wearing pants and shoes, and they should present themselves to the captain and say . . ."

There was no problem on which Abner was unprepared to give specific advice. This puny boy from the bleak farm at Marlboro, Massachusetts, had not in his youth foreseen that every book he read would one day be of value to him. He could recall whole passages about medical care in London, or the banking system in Antwerp. But most of all he remembered the studies he had conducted regarding the manner in which Calvin and Beza had governed Geneva, and it often seemed prophetic to him that each problem encountered by John Calvin in Switzerland now had to be faced by Abner Hale in Lahaina.

On money: "You should coin your own island money, and protect it against counterfeiters."

On wealth: "Money is not wealth, but the things you make and grow are. It is supreme folly for you to allow individual chiefs to trade away your precious sandalwood. And for any man to grub up the very roots of young trees is insane. The greatest wealth you have is your ability to service the whaling ships as they come into Lahaina and Honolulu. If the alii were wise, they would establish port dues for such ships and also tax each merchant who supplies the whalers."

On education: "The surest way to improve the people is to teach them to read."

On an army: "Every government needs a police force of some kind. I grant that if you had had a respectable army in Lahaina the whaling sailors would not have dared to riot. But I am afraid a large army such as you propose is ridiculous. You cannot fight France or Russia or America. You are too small. Do not waste your money on an army. But get a good police force. Build a jail."

On the good alii: "He is courageous. He protects the week. He is honest with government money. He listens to advice. He dresses neatly and wears pants. He has only one wife. He does not get drunk. He helps his people as well as himself. He believes in God."

On Hawaii's greatest need: "Teach the people to read."

But often when he returned to the mission he would cry dejectedly, "Jerusha, I truly believe they didn't understand a word I said. We work and work and there is no improvement." Jerusha did not share his apprehensions, for in her school it was obvious that she was accomplishing miracles. She taught her women to sew, to cook better and to raise their own babies. "You must not give your children away!" she insisted. "It is against God's law." She was pleased when they nodded, but her greatest joy was young Iliki, who had once run off to the whalers but who now could recite the Psalms.

In teaching boys and men Keoki was indefatigable. He was both a devout Christian and a skilled instructor, so that his school was one of the best in the island group, but where he excelled was in his daily sermons, for he had the innate oratorical gift of the Hawaiian and exercised it in robust imagery and appropriate incident. So realistic was his description of the Flood that his listeners watched the sea out of the corners of their eyes, expecting engulfing waves to sweep in from Lahaina Roads.

But in long-range importance the most effective school was Abner's, where the alii studied, and his choice pupil was Malama's daughter, Noelani, whom he had rescued from the sailors. This girl was, by birth, entitled to be the next alii nui, for her blood strain was impeccable. Her parents were full brother and sister, each noble in his own right, so that she inherited the glory of numberless generations of Hawaiian greatness. She was clever and industrious, an ornament in any society. In a report to Honolulu, Abner said of her, "She is almost as good a student as her mother. She can read and write, speak English and do the easier sums. And I feel certain that she is dedicated to the way of God and will be one of our first full members of the church." When he told the girl this, she was radiant.

Teaching Malama was more difficult. The great alii was stubborn to a point of obstinacy. She required everything to be proved and she had that irritating quality which teachers deplore: she remembered what the instructor had said the day before, for after each visit she recalled the steps of his reasoning, so that when he reappeared she was able to present him with his own contradictions. Few classes in the history of education were more stubbornly hilarious than those which occurred when Abner tutored Malama alone. She would lie prone on her enormous belly, her round moonlike face propped on her hands, demanding, "Teach me the way to attain grace."

"I cannot do that," Abner invariably replied. "You have got to learn it for yourself."

What made the lessons difficult was not Malama's intellectual intransigence, which was pronounced, but her insistence upon answering all questions in broken English, which she quickly identified as God's chosen language, since the Bible was written in English, and since those who were dear to God conveyed their thoughts in that language. She was determined to learn English.

Abner, on his part, was equally insistent that the lessons be held in Hawaiian, for he saw that if he was to make progress in Christianizing the islands, he would have to speak in the native tongue. It was true that many of the Honolulu alii knew English, but it was not only to the alii that he intended speaking. Therefore, whenever Malama asked him a question in broken English, he replied in worse Hawaiian, and the lesson staggered on. For example, when he inveighed against eating dog, the conversation went like this:

"Dog good kau kau. You no like for what?" Malama asked.

"Poki pilau, pilau," Abner explained contemptuously.

"Pig every time sleep mud. You s'pose dog he make like that?"

"Kela mea, kela mea eat pua'a. Pua'a good. Poki bad."

If each had used his own natural tongue, conversation would have been simple, for each now understod the other's spoken language. But Malama stubbornly insisted that she be the first on Maui to speak English, while Abner was equally determined to preach his first sermon in the new church in flowing Hawaiian.

What irritated him most was that whenever he succeeded in backing big Malama into a logical corner, so that her next statement would have to be a confession of defeat, she would call for her maids to lomilomi her, and while they pounded her stomach, moving her enormous meals about, she would smile sweetly and say, "Go on! Go on!"

"So if civilized nations don't eat dogs, neither should Hawaiians," Abner would argue, and Malama would call sweetly for her maids to brush his face with feathers: "Kokua dis one man face. Fly too many on it, poor t'ing." And while Abner fought with the infuriating feathers his argument would die away.

But the two antagonists respected each other. Malama knew that the little missionary was fighting for no less than her entire soul. He would be content with no substitute, and he was an honest man who was willing to face any adversary, and she sensed that through her he intended to capture all of Maui. "That would not be a bad thing," she thought to herself. "Of all the white men who have come to Lahaina"—and she recalled the whalers, the traders, the military—"he is the only one who has brought more than he took away. After all, what is it he is trying to get me to do?" she reflected. "He wants me to stop sending the men into the forests for sandalwood. He wants me to build better fish ponds and to grow more taro. He wants me to protect the girls from the sailors, and to stop baby girls from being buried alive. Everything Makua Hale tells me is a good thing." Then she would pause and think of her kapu husband, Kelolo. "But I will not give up Kelolo until just before I am going to die." And so the warfare between Malama and Abner continued, but if a morning passed when duties kept him from the grass palace, Malama was uneasy, for her arguments with Abner were the best part of her day. She sensed that he was telling her the truth, and he was the first man who had ever done so.

When the time came for Jerusha's baby to be born she was faced by unwelcome news from Dr. Whipple: "I have been detained on Hawaii, where three mission wives are expecting babies, and it will be totally impossible for me to come to Lahaina. I am sure that Brother Abner will be able to handle the delivery capably, but nevertheless I beg your forgiveness. I am sorry." She grew afraid.

At one point she even went so far as to suggest: "Perhaps we should ask one of the local women to help us." But Abner was adamant and quoted Jeremiah: " 'Thus saith the Lord, Learn not the way of the heathen,' " and he pointed out how unlikely it was that a heathen woman, steeped in idols and vice, would know how to deliver a Christian baby, and Jerusha agreed. But this time stubborn little Abner had so memorized Deland's *Midwifery,* and Jerusha was finally so content to rely on him, that her boy was born without difficulty, and when Abner held the child for the first time he rather stolidly congratulated himself on having done such a good job of doctoring, but when the time came to place the boy in Jerusha's left arm and apply the infant's mouth to his wife's breast, the floods of emotion that he had so long imprisoned within his tight heart burst loose, and he fell onto the earth beside the bed and confessed, "My dearest companion, I love you more than I will ever be able to explain. I love you, Jerusha." And she, hearing these words of comfort in an alien land, the words she had so longed for, fed her child and was content.

"We will call the boy Micah," he announced at last.

"I had thought some sweeter name, perhaps David," she suggested.

"We will call him Micah," Abner replied.

"Is he strong?" she asked weakly.

"Strong in the goodness of the Lord," Abner assured her, and within two weeks she was teaching her classes again, a slim, radiant missionary woman sweating in a heavy woolen dress.

For one of the peculiarities of the missionaries was that they insisted upon living in tropical Hawaii exactly as if they were back home in bleak New England. They wore the same heavy clothing, did the same amount of tiring work, ate the same heavy meals whenever they could be obtained. In a land rich with Polynesian fruits, their greatest joy was to obtain from some passing ship a bag of dried apples, so that they could enjoy once more a thick, sweet apple pie. Wild cattle roamed the hills, but the missionaries preferred salt pork. There was an abundance of fish in the shallows, but they clung desperately to dried beef shipped out from Boston. Breadfruit they rarely touched, and coconuts were heathenish. In all his years on Maui, Abner Hale would never once do any of God's official work unless costumed in underwear, heavy woolen pants, long shirt, stock, vest, heavy claw-hammer coat and, if the meeting were outside, his big beaver hat. Jerusha dressed comparably.

But what was impossible to comprehend was the fact that each year, on the first of October, when the Hawaiian summer was hottest, mission families regularly climbed into heavy woolen underwear. They had followed this custom in Boston. They would follow it here. Nor did they ever find relief by swimming in the cool lagoon, for Bartholomew Parr's *London Medical Dictionary* specifically warned them: "NATATIO. Swimming is a laborious exercise, and should not be continued to exhaust the strength. It is not natural to man as to quadrupeds, for the motions of the latter in swimming are the same as in walking."

All these conventions resulted in one of the most serious breaches between the Hawaiians and the missionnaries. The former, who loved to bathe and who rarely did even twenty minutes' work without sluicing themselves afterwards, found the missionaries not only dirty people but actually offensive in smell. Sometimes Malama, irritated by their sweaty odors, tried to suggest that Abner and Jerusha might like to swim on the fine kapu beach of the alii, but Abner rejected the invitation as if it had come from the devil.

So all the accumulated wisdom of the islanders was ignored by the mission families. Perspiring in unbelievably heavy clothing, eschewing the healthful foods that surrounded them, they stubbornly toiled and grew faint and lost their health and died. But in doing so, they converted a nation.

*   *   *

IN 1823, WHEN the building of the church was two thirds completed, Kelolo approached Abner one evening with his final plea. "We can still change the entrance," he argued. "Then the evil spirits will be sure to keep away."

"God keeps evil from His churches," Abner replied coldly.

"Will you come with me to the grounds?" Kelolo begged.

"Everything has been arranged," Abner snapped.

"I want to show you a simple way . . ." Kelolo began.

"No!" Abner cried.

"Please," the tall chief insisted. "There is something you must know."

Against his better judgment, Abner threw down his pen and grudgingly walked in the night air to the church grounds, where a group of elderly men sat on their haunches, studying his church. "What are they doing?" Abner asked.

"They are my praying kahunas," Kelolo explained.

"No!" Abner protested, drawing back. "I do not want to argue with kahunas about a church of the Lord."

"These men love the Lord," Kelolo insisted. "Ask them. They know the catechism. They want the church to be built strong."

"Kelolo," Abner explained patiently, drawing near to the solemn kahunas, "I understand perfectly that in the old days these kahunas accomplished much that was good. But God does not require kahunas."

"Makua Hale," Kelolo pleaded, "we have come to you as friends who love this church. Please do not keep the door where it is. Every kahuna knows that that is wrong for the spirits of this location."

"God is the supreme spirit!" Abner argued, but since the night was pleasant, with a pale crescent moon in the west and occasional clouds sweeping in from the roads, he sat with the kahunas and talked with them about religion. He was surprised at how much of the Bible they knew, and at the skill with which they could accommodate it to their ancient beliefs. One old man explained, "We believe you are correct in what you say, Makua Hale. There is only one God, and we used to call Him Kane. There is a Holy Ghost, and we called Him Ku. There is Jesus Christ, and He is Lono. And there is the king of the underworld, and he is Kanaloa."

"God is not Kane," Abner reasoned, but the kahunas merely listened, and when it came time for them to speak they said, "Now when Kane, that is God, wishes a church to be built, he supervises it. He always did when we built our temples."

"God does not personally supervise the building of this church," Abner explained.

"Kane did."

"But God is not Kane," Abner patiently repeated.

The men nodded sagely and continued: "Now, since Kane is concerned about this church, and since we have always loved Kane, we thought it proper to advise you that this door . . ."

"The door will be where it now is," Abner explained, "because that is where the door to a church has always been. In Boston the door would be here. In London it would be here."

"But in Lahaina, Kane would not like it to be here," the kahunas argued.

"Kane is not God," Abner stubbornly repeated.

"We understand, Makua Hale," the kahunas politely agreed, "but since God and Kane are the same idea . . ."

"No," Abner insisted, "God and Kane are not the same."

"Of course," the kahunas agreed heartily, "their names are different, but we know that Kane would not like this door here."

"The door has to be here," Abner explained.

"If it is, Kane will destroy the church," the kahunas said sorrowfully.

"God does not go about destroying his own churches," Abner assured the men.

"But we know that Kane does, if they are built wrong, and since Kane and God mean the same thing . . ."

The solemn kahunas never lost their tempers with the stubborn little stranger who did not quite understand religion, so far as they could judge, and Abner had learned not to lose his, so the argument about the door lasted for several hours, until the moon had vanished from the west and only low dark clouds scudded across the mysterious and silent sky. With nothing agreed, but with the kahunas feeling very sorry for their misguided friend who insisted upon building a doomed church for Kane, the meeting broke up and Kelolo said, "After I bid the kahunas good night I will walk back home with you."

"I can find my way alone," Abner assured him.

"On a night like this . . ." Kelolo said speculatively, looking at the low clouds over the coconut palms, "it would be better, perhaps . . ." And he bade the kahunas a hasty farewell so that he could hurry down the dusty road and overtake the missionary, but they had progressed only a few hundred yards when Abner heard the kahunas walking behind them, and he said, "I don't want to argue with them any more," but when Kelolo turned to tell the kahunas so, he saw nothing. There were no kahunas. There were no walking men. There was only an ominous echo under the scudding clouds, and suddenly Kelolo grabbed Abner in a vise of death and muttered in horror, "It is the night marchers! Oh, God! We are lost!" And before Abner could protest, Kelolo had caught him about the waist and had swept him precipitately over a hedge and thrown him into a ditch, where foul water drenched him. When he tried to rise, Kelolo's mighty arm pinned him to the wet earth, and he could feel that the huge alii was trembling in terror.

"What is it?" Abner sputtered, but Kelolo's giant hand clasped his mouth, accidentally forcing grass and mud into his lips.

"It is the night marchers!" Kelolo whispered, his lips quivering in horror.

"Who are they?" Abner whispered back, pulling Kelolo's hand from his mouth.

"The great alii of the past." Kelolo trembled. "I am afraid they are coming for me."

"Ridiculous!" Abner grunted, trying to break free. But his captor held him pinioned in the ditch, and he could feel the awful tenseness of the big man's muscles. Kelolo was terrified.

"Why are they coming for you?" Abner whispered.

"No one knows," Kelolo replied, his teeth chattering. "Perhaps because I gave the land of Kane for your church."

With the greatest circumspection he lifted his huge head until it was even with the top of the hedge, looked for a moment up the dark path, and shuddered. "They are marching toward us!" he gasped. "Oh, Makua Hale, pray to your god for me. Pray! Pray!"

"Kelolo!" Abner grunted, smothered by the pressure on his chest. "There is nothing out there. When alii die they remain dead."

"They are marching," Kelolo whispered. And in the silence of the night, with only wind rustling through dead palm leaves, there was indeed a sound of feet. "I can see them coming past the church," Kelolo reported. "They carry torches and feathered staves. They wear golden robes and feather helmets. Makua Hale, they are coming for me."

The giant alii pressed himself into the ditch, hiding Abner beneath his ample form, and the missionary could hear the man praying, "Oh, Pele, save me now; I am your child, Kelolo, and I do not want to die tonight."

The sound grew louder and Kelolo engaged in violent actions, almost smothering Abner, who mumbled, "What are you doing?"

"Undressing!" Kelolo grunted. "You cannot speak to the gods with clothes on." When he was completely naked he resumed praying in an agitated voice, but suddenly he grew calm and Abner heard him say, "The little man I am hiding is Makua Hale. He is a good man and he brings learning to my people. He doesn't know enough to throw off his clothes, so please excuse him." There was a long silence, after which Kelolo said, "I know the little man preaches against you, Woman of Whiteness, but even so he is a good man." There was another protracted silence, and then the sound of imminent feet, and Kelolo trembled as if a great wind tormented him and then he spoke: "Thank you, Pele, for having told the marchers I am your child."

The wind subsided. Only fitful sounds came from the topmost crowns of the coconut palms, and there was no echo of marching feet. It could have been the kahunas going home, Abner thought. It could have been a group of dogs. Or wind along the dusty footpath. Now there was no sound; the low scudding clouds were gone, and the stars shone.

"What was it?" Abner asked, as he wiped the mud from his mouth.

"They were marching to take me away," Kelolo explained.

"Whom were you speaking to?" Abner inquired, spitting the gravel from his teeth.

"Pele. Didn't you hear her tell the marchers that we were her children?"

Abner did not reply. He brushed the sand from his clothes and wondered how he would get the muddy portions of his clothing cleaned, and he was brushing his knees when Kelolo grabbed him and spun him around, demanding, "You did hear Pele, didn't you? When she protected you?"

"Did she mention my name?" Abner asked quietly.

"You heard her!" Kelolo cried. "Makua Hale, it is a very good sign when Pele protects a man. It means . . ." But his joy at having been saved from the revengeful night marchers was so great that he could not express his gratitude, either for her aid in saving him or for her unprecedented benevolence in protecting the little missionary. "You are my brother," Kelolo said passionately. "Now you see that it would have been foolish for me to have torn down my platform to the gods. Suppose Pele had not come to help us tonight!"

"Did you see the night marchers?" Abner pressed.

"I saw them," Kelolo replied.

"Did you see Pele?" the missionary continued.

"I often see her," Kelolo assured him. Then in a burst of passion he caught Abner by the hands and pleaded: "It is for these reasons, Makua Hale, that I beg you not to keep the door where it is."

"That door . . ." Abner began. But he did not bother to finish his sentence, and when he reached home and Jerusha cried, "Abner, what have you been doing?" he replied simply, "It was dark and I fell in a ditch." And the door was built where he intended.

Then, when it seemed as if the mission were gaining control of Lahaina, the whaler *John Goodpasture,* out of New Bedford, put in with a record tonnage of oil from the recently discovered Off-Japan whaling grounds, and Jerusha's school for girls was suddenly interrupted by the excited cry from the road:

"Kelamoku! Too many sailors inside boat! Come right away here!"

Since the *John Goodpasture* was well and favorably known in Lahaina from previous visits, the intelligence created much excitement, especially among the four daughters of Pupali, who spent the next few minutes darting significant glances at one another. Finally, they rose as a team and marched out of class. When Jerusha tried to stop them, the oldest girl explained that their youngest sister felt ill: "Poor Iliki head all come sore," and amid loud giggles they disappeared.

At first Jerusha did not appreciate what had happened, but later when one of her students blurted out, "Kapena aloha Iliki. She swim ship, see kapena," it became obvious that the mission's moral teaching had been outraged, and Jerusha dismissed class. Wrapping a light shawl about her shoulders and placing her poke bonnet firmly on her brown locks, she marched down to the waterfront in time to see the four girls, largely naked, climbing eagerly aboard the *John Goodpasture,* where sailors who had known them before greeted them with cheers.

Running up to an elderly American sailor who was scrimshawing a whalebone beside Kamehameha's old brick palace, she cried, "Row me out to that boat!" But the sailor continued carving the whalebone and drawled, "Ma'am, it's best if you don't fight the laws of nature."

"But Iliki is only a child!" Jerusha protested.

"First law of the sea, ma'am. If they're big enough, they're old enough," and he looked out into the channel, where the girls' pleased squeals filled the air.

Appalled by this indifference, Jerusha ran over to an old Hawaiian woman who sat on a rock guarding the four mission dresses which the girls had discarded. "Aunty Mele," Jerusha pleaded, "how can we get those girls back?"

"You stop one time. Bimeby ship go," Aunty Mele assured her. "Wahine come back, same like always."

In frustration, Jerusha grabbed at the besmirched mission dresses, as if to take them home with her, away from the contaminated waterfront, but Aunty Mele held onto them grimly, saying, "Hale Wahine! Bimeby wahine come back, I make ready dress for dem." And like the good friend she was, she remained on the rock, holding the girls' apparel until such time as they might need it once more for resumption of their missionary lessons.

That night it was a gloomy mission household that reviewed the day's defeats. "I cannot understand these girls," Jerusha wept. "We give them the best of everything. Iliki in particular knows what good and evil are. Yet she runs off to the whaling ship."

"I brought the matter up with Malama," Abner reported in deep confusion, "and she said merely, 'The girl is not an alii. She can go to the ships if she likes.' So I asked Malama, 'Then why were you so angry when the three sailors tried to take Noelani to their ship?' And Malama replied, 'Noelani is kapu alii.' As if that explained everything."

"Abner, I shudder to think of the evil that flourishes in Lahaina," Jerusha replied. "When I left the waterfront, where nobody would do anything, I went into the town to ask for help, and at Murphy's grog shop I heard a concertina. And girls laughing. And I tried to go in to stop whatever was happening, and a man said, 'Don't go in there, Mrs. Hale. The girls have no clothes on. They never do when the whalers are in port.' Abner! What is happening to this town?"

"For some time I have known it to be the modern Sodom and Gomorrah."

"What are we going to do about it?"

"I haven't decided," he replied.

"Well, I have," Jerusha said firmly. And that very night she marched down to Malama's palace and said in her able Hawaiian, "Alii Nui, we must stop the girls from going out to the whaling ships."

"Why?" Malama asked. "The girls go because they want to. No harm is done."

"But Iliki is a good girl," Jerusha insisted.

"What is a good girl?" Malama asked.

"Girls who do not swim out to ships," Jerusha replied simply.

"I think you missionaries want to stop all fun," Malama countered.

"Iliki is not engaging in fun," Jerusha argued. "She is engaging in death." And this Malama knew to be true.

"But she has always gone out to the ships," she said sadly.

"Iliki has an immortal soul," Jerusha said firmly. "Exactly as you and I."

"You mean to claim that Iliki . . . wahine i Pupali . . . like you or me?"

"Exactly like you, Malama. Exactly like me."

"I cannot believe it," Malama said. "She has always gone to the ships."

"It is our job to stop her. To stop all the girls."

Malama would do nothing that night, but on the next day she assembled the alii then in residence, and Reverend and Mrs. Hale presented their arguments, with Jerusha pleading: "You can tell a good town by the way it protects its babies and young girls. You can tell a good alii by the way in which he protects women. You are not good alii if you permit your own daughters to go out to the ships. In London the good alii try to stop such things. In Boston, too."

Kelolo contradicted this assertion by pointing out: "Kekau-ike-a-ole sailed on a whaler and he got to both London and Boston and he has often told us of how there were special houses filled with girls. Everywhere he went there were such houses."

"But the good alii in all cities try to control this vice," Jerusha argued bitterly.

It was Abner, however, who delivered the aching blow. "Do you know what happens if you alii of Lahaina permit your girls to be debauched in this way?" he asked ominously.

"What happens, Makua Hale?" Malama asked, for she trusted him.

"When the ships sail back home, the men laugh at Hawaii."

There was a long silence as this ugly accusation was digested, for the alii of Hawaii were proud people, desperately hungry for the world's approval. Finally, Malama asked cautiously, "Would the alii of Boston allow their girls to swim out to a Hawaiian ship?"

"Of course not," Kelolo snapped. "The water is too cold."

There was no laughter, for this was an honest observation, and Abner quickly added, "Kelolo is correct. The water in Boston is not so sweet and warm as here, but even if it were, no girls would be allowed to swim out to Hawaiian ships. The alii of Boston would be ashamed if that happened."

Malama asked quietly, "Do you think the sailors laugh at us, Makua Hale?"

"I know they do, Malama. Do you remember the whaler *Carthaginian* when it was here? I was aboard the *Carthaginian* on the whaling grounds, and the sailors were laughing about Honolulu."

"Ah, but Honolulu is known to be an evil place," Malama admitted. "That is why I will not live there. That's why the king keeps his capital here at Lahaina."

"And they laughed at Lahaina," Abner insisted.

"That is bad," Malama frowned. After a while she asked, "What should we do?"

Abner replied, "You should build a fort, by the roads, and each night at sunset a drum should beat, and any sailor who is ashore should then be arrested and kept in the fort till morning. And any girl who swims out to ships should be put in jail, too."

"Such laws are too harsh," Malama said, and she dismissed the meeting, but when the other alii had gone she took Jerusha aside and asked querulously, "Do you think the sailors laugh at us, because of the girls?"

"I laugh at you!" Jerusha said firmly. "To think of people debauching their own daughters!"

"But they are not alii," Malama insisted.

"You are the conscience of the people," Jerusha replied.

That night the Hales argued long as to whether the daughters of Pupali should be admitted back into the mission school, and Abner was for dismissing them permanently, but Jerusha held that they should be given another chance, and when the *John Goodpasture* left the roads, the four delinquent girls, dressed neatly in new dresses, came penitently back. The more Jerusha preached to them about the miserableness of their sin, the more heartily they agreed. But when, some weeks later, a child heralded the arrival of the whaler *Vashti* with the exciting cry, *"Vashti* iron hook fall now, plenty kelamoku," the four girls bolted again, and that night Abner insisted that the older three at least be expelled. They were, and since these were the years when whalers came to Lahaina with increasing frequency—seventeen were to arrive in 1824—the three older daughters of Pupali did a good business. They no longer had to go out to ships, for they became the dancers at Murphy's grog shop and kept little rooms aft of the small dance floor, where they were permitted to keep half of the coins they earned.

Iliki, the fairest of the daughters, was allowed to stay in the mission school, and under Jerusha's most careful guidance grew to understand the Bible and to forswear whaling ships. She was slim for a Hawaiian girl, with very long hair and flashing eyes. When she smiled, her handsome white teeth illuminated her face, and Jerusha could appreciate why it was that men wanted her. "When she is twenty," Jerusha said, "we will marry her to some Christian Hawaiian, and you mark my words, Abner, she'll be the best wife in the islands."

When Jerusha spoke thus, Abner was not listening, for he had erected for himself, out of rough ends of timber gathered here and there—for nothing in Lahaina was more precious than wood—a small table upon which papers were spread in seven or eight neat piles, each with a sea shell placed on it to preserve order. For he had begun, in co-operation with the other missionaries throughout the islands, the work which would be his most lasting contribution to Hawaii. He was translating the Bible into Hawaiian and sending his pages as they were finished to the printer in Honolulu, where they were being published a little at a time.

Nothing that Abner applied himself to in these years gave him greater pleasure, for he kept before him his Greek and Hebrew texts, Cornelius Schrevelius' *Greek-Latin Lexicon,* plus those versions of the Bible he had studied at Yale. He was happy, like a plowman who turns furrows in a field without stones, or a fisherman who sets his nets for known returns. Usually he worked with Keoki, laboring over every passage with the most minute attention, and as the years passed he reached those two books of the Bible which he cherished most. The first was Proverbs, which seemed to him a distillation of all the knowledge man could hope to know. It was especially appropriate for Hawaii, since its crystallizations were in simple language, easily understood and long remembered, and when he came to the glorious closing pages in which King Lemuel describes the ideal woman, his pen truly flew along the ruled pages, for it seemed to him that Lemuel spoke specifically of Jerusha Bromley: "Who can find a virtuous woman? For her price is far above rubies. The heart of her husband doth safely trust in her, so that he shall have no need of spoil. . . . She is like the merchants' ships; she bringeth her food from afar. . . . She stretcheth out her hand to the poor; yea, she reacheth forth her hands to the needy. . . . Strength and honor are her clothing; . . . Many daughters have done virtuously, but thou excellest them all."

When he finished translating Proverbs he left the last pages exposed, so that Jerusha might read them, and he was disappointed that she did not take notice of them, for she had learned not to interfere with his Biblical studies; so at last he was forced to hand her the pages of King Lemuel's conclusions, and she read them quietly, saying only, "A woman would do well to mark those pages." He was constrained to cry, "They were written about you, Jerusha!" but he said nothing, and put them along with the rest and forwarded them to Honolulu.

In the decades that were to follow, more than six committees would have occasion to polish this first translation of the Bible into Hawaiian, and in the portions contributed from the big island of Hawaii, or from Kauai, or Honolulu, the scholars frequently found understandable errors in translation or emphasis. But in the portions for which Abner Hale had been responsible, they rarely found an error. One expert, with degrees from both Yale and Harvard, said, "It was as if he had been in turn a Hebrew and a Greek and a Hawaiian." Abner did not hear this praise, for it came long after he was dead, but he reaped his full enjoyment from his great task when it came time to translate Ezekiel, for there was something about this strange book—a contrapuntal melody of the most banal observations and the most exalted personal revelations—that spoke directly to him and epitomized his life.

He loved the recurring passages in which Ezekiel, who must have been a rather boring man most of the time, laboriously set down the specific dates on which God spoke to him: "Now it came to pass in the thirtieth year, in the fourth month, in the fifth day . . . that the heavens were opened, and I saw visions of God. . . . The word of the Lord came expressly unto Ezekiel." The assurance with which Ezekiel spoke on all matters, and his confidence that the Lord personally directed him, gave Abner great consolation, and whenever he copied out Ezekiel's blunt statements of his correspondence with God, he felt that he, too, was participating in it: "In the sixth year, in the sixth month, in the fifth day . . . , as I sat in mine house, and the elders of Judah sat before me, . . . the hand of the Lord God fell there upon me." It was, to Abner Hale, clarity itself that the prophet Ezekiel, sitting in counsel with the elders of Judah, was markedly similar to the prophet Abner, sitting in counsel with the alii of Maui, and if the latter prophet sometimes spoke with an authority that the Hawaiians had difficulty in accepting, Abner felt that the elders of Judah must have had the same difficulty with the preachments of Ezekiel. Yet there it was in imperishable writing: "Again the word of the Lord came expressly unto me." A man required no greater authority than that.

* * *

IN 1825, JERUSHA had a second baby, the saucy little girl Lucy, who was in later years to marry Abner Hewlett, whom her father had also delivered. As Kelolo's big church neared completion, a serious problem confronted Abner, for he was determined above all things that when it was dedicated the Hawaiians who entered it must be dressed as proper Christians. "There will be no nakedness in this church," he announced. "There will be no wreaths of maile branches, with their distracting fragrance. Women will wear dresses. Men will wear pants."

But even as he promulgated the law, he wondered where enough cloth would be found to convert these heathens into Christians. The alii, with access to cargoes from China, were well taken care of. They had worn proper clothing from the first, and in recent months many visiting naval captains had been astonished by the gigantic and solemn noblemen who greeted them at the small stone pier. "They would do credit to the city of London," one Englishman reported to his superiors. "The men were dressed in black coats, proper trousers and yellow capes. The women wore strange but becoming dresses with a yoke at the neck, and an unbroken fall of expensive material from the tops of their bosoms to their ankles. When they moved, men and women alike seemed like gods, so straight and arrogant were they. They confided to me privately that a missionary from Boston had told them how to greet incoming ships properly, and if he has done as well with their souls as with their deportment he is to be commended, but this latter I doubt, for I have rarely seen so much open debauchery in any principal port as at Lahaina."

It was cloth for the poor people that worried Abner, and then from the coasts of China appeared his salvation. The hermaphrodite brig *Thetis* returned from its sandalwood expedition loaded with wares for sale in local markets. Captain Retire Janders, already committed to selling his ship to Kelolo, had determined to enter the trading business with a flourish and had gambled every farthing of his sandalwood sale in Canton on things he thought the Hawaiians might like. It was therefore an exciting moment when he opened his store next to Murphy's grog shop and started unloading the bales from China.

For men there were sturdy gabardine, shimmering silk shirts, knee-length black pants such as had been popular in France thirty years earlier, silk-ribbed stockings and shoes with fancy buckles. There were cigars from Manila, brandies from Paris, and one entire box filled with ready-made suits of which Captain Janders had told the Canton tailors, "Make each one big enough to hold three Chinese. These are for Hawaiians."

For the women the captain's lures were irresistible: bolts of fine brocades, lengths of satin, whole dresses made of velvet, yard upon yard of green and purple cloth, with boxes of lace edging. There were glittering beads, and bracelets and rings; fans for hot nights, and perfumes from the Spice Islands.

What the alii particularly prized, however, were the full-length mirrors, transshipped from France, and the massive mahogany furniture constructed in Canton from English patterns. Each noble family felt that it had to have a secretary, with two round rests for lamps and numerous pigeon holes for filing papers. The delicate china ware was also appreciated, especially that in blue and white, but more treasured than tableware were the gleaming white chamber pots, decorated with raised roses, etched in pink and blue and green.

And for the common people there were hundreds of bolts of turkey-red cloth, with some brown and white samples intermixed. It was this commodity that attracted Reverend Hale and led him to propose the strategy that laid the foundation for the Janders fortune.

"You have many bolts of good cloth here, Captain," Abner pointed out. "I have long dreamed of having my congregation properly clothed when the church opens. But the people have no money. Will you extend them credit?"

Captain Janders tugged at the rim of beard that still fringed his face and said, "Reverend Hale, long ago you taught me to revere the Bible. I have got to stand on Proverbs 22, verse 26: 'Be not thou one of them . . . that are sureties for debts.' Thus saith the Lord, and it's good enough for me. Cash! Cash! The rule of this establishment."

"I know that cash is a good rule," Abner began.

"The Lord's rule," Janders repeated.

Abner said: "But it doesn't have to be money cash, does it, Captain?"

Janders said: "Well . . . if something could be converted . . ."

Abner said: "A lot of whalers come into these roads, Captain. What do they need that my natives could supply?"

Janders countered: "Why are they your natives?"

Abner replied: "They belong to the church. What could they bring you?"

Janders mused: "Well, the whalers are always demanding tapa cloth for calking. And I could use a lot of olona twine."

Abner proposed: "If I could supply you with regular amounts of tapa and olona? Would you trade the cloth?"

So Janders sealed the deal which became one of the principal foundations of his fortune, for the explosion of whalers into Lahaina Roads was about to occur—42 in 1825; 31 in 1826—and when they arrived, Captain Retire Janders cannily waited to service them with products supplied by Reverend Hale's natives: tapa, olona, pigs, wild beef. At one point Kelolo protested: "Makua Hale, you used to fight with me when I took my men into the mountains for sandalwood. For me they worked only three weeks at a time. For you they work all the weeks." But Abner explained to the simple-minded man: "They do not work for me, Kelolo. They work for God." Nevertheless Kelolo insisted: "They still work all the time."

In one sense Abner did profit: he got each of his parishioners properly dressed for the opening of church, and on the Sunday when the sprawling edifice was consecrated, curious processions from miles around marched through the dust in their unaccustomed finery from Captain Janders' store. The alii, of course, made a respectable showing, the men in frock coats and black hats, the women in handsomely gored dresses made from rich, thick stuffs from Canton. But the common people, even though they had watched the alii shift from tapa breechclouts to London jackets, had not quite caught the niceties of western dress. Women seemed to have found the easier solution: prim high collars on tight-fitting yokes which encased the bosom and from which hung copious folds of cloth; long sleeves hiding the offensive nakedness of the wrists; this costume was the essence of practicality and ugliness, and that beautiful women should have submitted to it was incomprehensible. It was completed by a broad-brimmed hat of woven sugar-cane leaves, decorated with imitation flowers, for real ones were not allowed in church lest they exhibit vanity and distract the congregation.

Men faced more confusing problems, for each felt honor-bound to wear some one article from the Janders store, so that the first who entered the church after the alii wore a pair of shoes, a Bombay hat and nothing more. The second wore a man's shirt with his legs pushed through the sleeves and the collar tied around his waist with a strand of olona twine. When Abner saw these ridiculous worshipers he was inspired to send them back home, but they were so eager to enter the new church that he allowed them to do so.

The next pair were brothers to whom Janders had sold a complete Canton suit; one wore the coat and nothing else; his brother wore the pants and white gloves. Now a man came wearing a woman's dress, complete with a wreath of maile leaves about his head, and this time Abner was stern. "No flowers or pagan-smelling leaves in church," he commanded, tearing away the wreath and throwing it to the ground, whence the fragrance penetrated to the church. Some men wore only shirts with tails flapping over enormous brown buttocks, and some wore grass breechclouts and silk neckties, but in deference to the white man's God, who refused to share his mysteries with the naked, all wore something.

The interior of the church was impressive: a perfect rectangle with handsomely matted grass walls, an imposing stone pulpit, and not a shred of other furniture except one wooden bench for Jerusha and Captain Janders. The multitude, more than three thousand of them, spread individual pandanus mats on the pebbled floor and sat tailor fashion, elbow to elbow. Had Abner studied the climate for even a moment, he would have built his grass walls only a few feet high, leaving open space between them and the room so that air could circulate, but churches in New England were built foursquare, and so they were in Hawaii, with no air stirring and the congregation sweltering in the natural heat, plus the radiation of three thousand closely packed bodies.

The singing was magnificent: spontaneous, joyous, instinct with worship. The reading of the Scriptures by Keoki was impressive, and when Abner rose to deliver his two-hour sermon, the audience was thrilled to hear him speak in acceptable Hawaiian. He chose for his topic, Zephaniah 2, verse 11: "The Lord will be terrible unto them: for he will famish all the gods of the earth; and men shall worship him, every one from his place, even all the isles of the heathen."

It was a sermon almost ideally suited for the occasion. Phrase by phrase Abner interpreted Zephaniah's words. He defined the Lord and his powers, spending fifteen lyrical minutes in identifying the new god of the islands. It was a god of mercy and compassion that he expounded.

Then he described the terribleness of Jehovah when His anger was aroused, and he lingered over floods, pestilences, thunder and lightning, famines and the tortures of hell. To his surprise the Hawaiians nodded understandingly, and he heard Kelolo whispering to Malama, "The new god's just like Kane. Very difficult when he's mad."

Abner next turned to the specific gods of Lahaina whom the new God was determined to destroy. He specified Kane and Ku, Lono and Kanaloa, Pele and her attendants. "They shall perish," Abner shouted in Hawaiian, "both from Lahaina and from your hearts. If you try to hide these evil gods in your hearts, you will be destroyed, and you will burn in hell forever and ever."

After this he analyzed what the word *worship* meant, and here for the first time before the general public he expounded his view of the good society. "A man worships God," Abner said, "when he protects his women, when he does not kill girl babies, when he obeys the law." At one point he cried, "A man who grows better taro to share with his neighbors praises God." At another he came close to expounding pure New England doctrine when he suggested, "Look about you. Does this man have good land? God loves him. Does that man's canoe catch more fish? God loves that man. Work, work, work, and you will find that God loves you." Finally, with considerable courage, he stared directly at the alii and expostulated his concept of the good ruler, and the entire congregation, all but thirty of them commoners, heard a bold new concept of government. The sermon ended with one of the dramatic touches that Abner, like St. Paul before him, loved. He cried, "In the kingdom of God there is no higher and lower, there is no alii and slave. The lowliest man stands bright in the sweet gaze of God." And he summoned from the doorway, for the man would not otherwise have dared enter the edifice, a slave and he brought this slave to the pulpit area and put his arms about the man and cried, "You have previously called this man a foul corpse, one of the living dead. God calls him an immortal soul. I call him my brother. He is no longer a slave. He is your brother." And inspired by the awfulness of this iconoclastic moment, Abner leaned up and kissed the man on the cheek and made him sit on the ground, not far from Malama, the Alii Nui.

But the highlight of the dedication services came after a series of hymns led by Keoki, for Abner rose and announced, during the third hour of worship: "Entrance into the kingdom of God is not easy. Entrance into His church here on earth is not easy, either. But today we are going to allow two of your people to start their six months' trial period. If they prove good Christians, they will be admitted to the church." There was much excitement in the audience and open speculation as to who the chosen pair should be, but Abner stilled it by raising his hand and pointing to Keoki, tall, wiry and handsome.

"In Massachusetts your much loved alii, Keoki, was made a member of the church. He is the first Hawaiian to join. My dear good wife, whom you know as teacher, is also a member. So am I. So is Captain Janders. We four have met and have decided to test two others for membership. Mrs. Hale, will you rise and bring forth the first?"

Jerusha rose from her mat on the side, walked forward to the alii area, reached down and grasped the hand of the slave. In slow, careful Hawaiian she said, "This kanaka Kupa is known in all Lahaina as a saintly man. He shares his goods with others. He cares for children that have no parents." By her forceful enumeration of the man's extraordinary virtues, which were acknowledged by all, Jerusha made the consecration of the slave logical to the congregation. "In your hearts, people of Lahaina, you know that Kupa is a Christian man, and because you know him to be such, we are going to accept him into the church of God."

Abner took Kupa's hand and cried, "Kupa, are you prepared to love Jehovah?" The slave was so terrified by the experiences the missionaries were forcing upon him that he could only mumble, and Abner announced: "In six months you will no longer be Kupa the Foul Corpse. You will be Kamekona." And he gave the slave this treasured name, Solomon.

The audience was stunned, but before there could be any murmuring against the radical move, Abner said in his powerful and persuasive voice, "Keoki Kanakoa, rise and bring forth the second member of the church."

And it was with the greatest excitement and joy that Keoki rose, went to the alii area and reached down for his sister Noelani, the Mists of Heaven. That morning she was dressed in white, with a yellow feather lei about her head and white gloves on her capable hands. Her dark eyes were ablaze with sanctity and she moved as if God and not her brother had reached down to touch her. From a distance she heard the joyous acceptance of her nomination as the Hawaiians whispered, and then she was aware that Abner was addressing her: "You have been faithful to the Lord's ways. You have studied and learned to sew, for all women, alii and commoner alike, should know how to sew, for does not the Bible say of the virtuous woman, 'She seeketh wool, and flax, and worketh willingly with her hands.' But more than this, Noelani, you have been an inspiration to this island. In six months you will become a member of the church."

In her sweet resonant voice Noelani replied, "I shall make the learning and the law of Jehovah my guide," and Abner hid his irritation at the way these stubborn alii still insisted first upon the alphabet.

That night Malama summoned Abner, and when he was perched cross-legged on the tapa before her reclining bulk she said solemnly, "For the first time today, Makua Hale, I understood what humility was. I saw, even though imperfectly, what a state of grace would be. Makua Hale, I have sent Kelolo to live in the other house. Tomorrow I am willing to lead a procession through the streets and announce the new laws for Maui. We must have a better way of living here. Will you have the laws ready for us to study at dawn tomorrow?"

"Today is the Sabbath," Abner said flatly. "I cannot work today."

"An island waits to be saved," Malama commanded. "Bring me the laws in the morning."

"I will," Abner surrendered.

And on his way home, he stopped at the new house outside the wall and said, "Kelolo, will you work with me tonight?" And the outcast husband agreed, and they gathered Keoki, too, and Noelani and went to the mission house.

"The laws must be simple," Abner said with a show of statesmanship. "Everyone must understand them and approve them in his heart. Kelolo, since you will be the man who will have to organize the police and enforce the laws, what do you think they should be?"

"The sailors cannot roam our streets at night," Kelolo said forcefully. "It is at night that they do their damage." So Lahaina's first and most contentious law was written into Abner's rudely folded book: "A drum will sound at sunset, at which signal all sailors must return to their ships on pain of instant arrest and incarceration in the Lahaina jail."

"The next law?" Abner asked.

"There must be no more killing of girl babies," Noelani suggested, and this became law.

"The next?"

"Should we stop the sale of alcohol altogether?" Jerusha asked.

"No," Kelolo argued. "The storekeepers have already paid for their supplies and they would be ruined."

"It is killing your people," Abner pointed out.

"I am afraid there would be riots if we stopped the sale," Kelolo warned.

"Could we stop the import of new supplies?" Jerusha proposed.

"French warships made us promise to drink lots of their alcohol each year," Kelolo pointed out.

"Could we forbid sales to Hawaiians?" Jerusha asked.

"French warships said we had to make the Hawaiians drink their alcohol, too," Kelolo explained, "but I think we should refuse to do so any longer."

Without ever insisting upon his own opinion, Abner extracted from his group a short, sensible body of law, but when it was finished he saw that one of the most typical of all Hawaiian problems had been overlooked. "We need one more law," he suggested.

"What?" Kelolo asked suspiciously, for he feared some action against kahunas and the old gods.

"The Lord says," Abner began in some embarrassment, "and all civilized nations agree . . ." He paused, ashamed to go on. After a moment's hesitation he blurted out: "There shall be no adultery."

Kelolo thought about this for a long time. "That would be a hard law to enforce," he reflected. "I wouldn't want to have to enforce that law . . . not in Lahaina."

To everyone's surprise, Abner said, "I agree, Kelolo. Perhaps we could not enforce it completely, but could we not get the people to understand that in a good society, adultery is not encouraged?"

"We could say something like that," Kelolo agreed, but then a look of considerable perplexity came over his features and he asked, "But which adultery are you talking about, Makua Hale?"

"What do you mean, which adultery?"

Kelolo, Keoki and Noelani sat in silence, and Abner thought they were being obstinate until he realized that each was thinking very seriously. In fact, he saw Kelolo's fingers moving and judged that the big alii was counting. "You see, Makua Hale," the tall nobleman said, "in Hawaii we have twenty-three different kinds of adultery."

"You what?" Abner gasped.

"And this would be our problem," Kelolo carefully explained. "If we said simply, 'There shall be no adultery,' without indicating which kind, everyone who heard would reason, 'They don't mean our kind of adultery. They mean the other twenty-two kinds.' But on the other hand, if we list all the twenty-three kinds, one after the other, somebody will surely say, 'We never heard of that kind before. Let's try it!' and things would be worse than before."

"What do you mean, twenty-three kinds?" Abner asked weakly.

"Well," Kelolo replied, from expert knowledge, "there is a married man and a married woman. That's one. Then there's the married man and the wife of his brother. That's two. Then the married man and the wife of his son. That's three. Then we have the married man and his own daughter. That's four."

"That's enough," Abner protested.

"It goes on through brothers and sisters, boys and their mothers, almost anything you could think of," Kelolo explained matter-of-factly. "As long as one of the pair is married, we call it adultery. So how can we stop it?" he asked, palms up. "If we name all twenty-three kinds we're going to have more trouble than we already have."

It was long after midnight and Abner sat chewing his pen. Like every religious leader in history, he knew that a good society started with a stable home, and that stable homes—either by design or accident—were usually founded on the disciplined sexual relationship of one man and one woman joined after due consideration of the world's accumulated judgment on such matters. It was not good for a man to marry his sister. It was not good for families to interbreed endlessly. It was not good for girls to be taken when they were too young. But how could this accumulated wisdom be summarized for the Hawaiians?

Finally, he came up with an answer so simple, so sweetly right, that generations of Hawaiians smiled every time they heard Abner Hale's profound directive. They smiled, because they understood exactly what he meant. It was a law that covered their experience on a tropical island, and of all the minor things Abner accomplished on Maui, this happy choice of words was most affectionately remembered among the people. For his final law read: "Thou shalt not sleep mischievously."

On Monday morning Abner presented his simple forthright laws to Malama, and she studied them. Two she threw out as too meddling in the lives of her people, but the rest she liked. Then she summoned her two maids-in-waiting, and the three enormous women, dressed in fine China silks and broad-brimmed hats, formed a procession which was headed by two drummers, two men sounding conch shells, four with feathered staves, Kelolo in charge of eight policemen, Keoki, Noelani and a brassy-voiced herald. Abner and Jerusha stayed away, for this was the work of Hawaiians for Hawaiians.

The drums began to beat, and when the conches sent their shrill blast through the kou trees, Malama and her two attendants started walking past the fish pond, along the dusty road beside the alii's houses, and into the center of town. Whenever more than a hundred people assembled, coming running from all sides, Malama would command the drums to cease and direct her herald to cry: "These are the laws of Maui. Thou shalt not kill! Thou shalt not steal! Thou shalt not sleep mischievously!"

The drums resumed, leaving people gasping in the morning sunlight. Fathers, who had been earning their poi by rowing their daughters out to the whalers, were stunned and some tried to argue with Kelolo, but he silenced them and marched on.

At the little pier Malama halted and had the bugle blown four times, assembling such sailors as were available at that hour. Two captains were present, and stood with their caps in their hands, listening to the astonishing news: "Sailors shall not roam the streets at night. Girls shall not swim out to the whaling ships."

"By God!" one of the captains muttered. "There'll be hell to pay for this."

"You'll find it was the missionary who did it," the other predicted.

"God help the missionary," said the first, running by a back way to Murphy's grog shop, but he had barely exploded the news when Malama and her two stout ladies hove majestically into view with the rumpled paper containing the new laws. This time, as the drums finished beating before Murphy's establishment, there were two special laws promulgated: "Girls shall no longer dance nude in Murphy's grog shop. From today no more alcohol may be sold to Hawaiians." The drums resumed beating. The bugles sounded, and Malama and her two enormous ladies-in-waiting retired. The laws had been handed down. It would now be Kelolo's job to enforce them.

That night there were riots. Sailors from several ships stormed through the town fighting with Kelolo's inadequate policemen. Girls were ripped away from their beds and hauled against their wills out to the ships. And toward midnight a body of some fifty sailors and Lahaina merchants gathered at the mission house and began cursing Abner Hale.

"He done the laws!" a sailor howled.

"He talked the fat lady into it!" another cried.

"Let's hang the little bastard!" a voice called, and cheers greeted the suggestion.

No immediate action was taken, but someone in the crowd started throwing rocks at the grass house, and occasionally one would ricochet into the room and fall harmlessly to the floor. "Let's burn his damned house down!" a voice screamed.

"We'll teach him to meddle in our affairs!"

"Come out here, you damned little worm!" a harsh voice called.

"Come out! Come out!" the crowd roared, but Abner kept huddled on the floor, protecting Jerusha and the two babies with his body lest the increasing storm of rocks find them.

The long night progressed with its vile insults, but toward morning the crowd dispersed, and as soon as the sun rose, Abner hurried to consult with Kelolo. "It was a bad night," the big alii said.

"I think tonight will be worse," Abner predicted.

"Should we discard the laws?" Kelolo asked.

"Never!" Abner snapped.

"I think we had better ask Malama," the tall chief suggested, but when they found her, townspeople were already there, bombarding her with their fears, and it was then that Abner realized what a tremendous woman she was. "Malama has spoken," she said sternly. "The words are law. I want you to assemble all the ships' captains in this room within an hour. Get them!"

When the Americans appeared, rough, rugged, good-looking veterans of the whaling grounds, she announced in English, "The law, me I gib you. More better you t'ink so, too."

"Ma'am," one of the captains interrupted. "We been comin' to Lahaina for a dozen years. We always had a good time here and behaved ourselves pretty well. I can't say what's goin' to happen now."

"I can say!" Malama cried in Hawaiian. "You are going to obey the laws."

"Our men got to have women," the captain protested.

"Do you riot in the streets of Boston?" Malama demanded.

"For women? Yes," the captain replied.

"And the police stop you, is that not right?" Malama pressed.

The captain wagged his forefinger and threatened, "Ma'am, no police on this pitiful island better try to stop my men."

"Our police will stop you!" Malama warned. Then she changed her tone and pleaded with the captains: "We are a small country, trying to grow up in the modern world. We have got to change our ways. It is not right that our girls should swim out to the ships. You know that. You have got to help us."

"Ma'am," one of the captains growled stubbornly, "there's gonna be trouble."

"Then there will be trouble," Malama said softly and sent the captains away.

Kelolo wanted to back down. Keoki was afraid there would be serious rioting, and Noelani counseled caution, but Malama was obdurate. She sent messengers to summon all the biggest men from the outward areas. She went in person to the new fort to see if its gates were strong, and she told Kelolo, "Tonight you must be ready to fight. The captains are right. There is going to be trouble."

But when her people had gone about their tasks, and when they could not spy upon her, she summoned Abner and asked him directly, "Are we doing the right thing?"

"You are," he assured her.

"And there will be trouble tonight?"

"Very bad trouble, I am afraid," he admitted.

"Then how can we be doing the right thing?" she pressed.

He told her of a dozen incidents in the Old Testament wherein men faced great adversaries in defense of God's way, and when he was through he asked her in a low voice, "Malama, do you not know in your heart that the laws you read were good?"

"They are part of my heart," she replied cryptically.

"Then they will prevail," Abner assured her.

Malama wanted to believe, but the cowardice of her other advisers had infected her, so now she towered above Abner, stared down at him and said, "Little mikanele," using the Hawaiian pronunciation of missionary, "tell me the truth. Are we doing the right thing?"

Abner closed his eyes, raised his head toward the grass roof, and cried in the voice that Ezekiel must have used when addressing the Jewish elders: "The islands of Hawaii will live under these laws, for they are the will of the Lord God Jehovah."

Assured, Malama turned to other matters and asked, "What will happen tonight?"

"They won't bother you, Malama, but I think they may try to burn my house. Can Jerusha and the children stay with you?"

"Of course, and you too."

"I'll be in the house," he said simply, and as he limped away, Malama loved her stubborn little mikanele.

That night the streets of Lahaina were a shambles. At dusk a drunken sea captain, in conjunction with Murphy, led a group of men to the fort and dared the policemen there to blow the conch shell. When the warning to sailors sounded, the mob grabbed every policeman in sight and threw them into the bay. Then they stormed back to Murphy's, where Pupali's three oldest daughters were dancing in the nude to wild shrieks of joy. As bottles were passed, sailors shouted, "Drink up. When this is done, the missionary says we can't have no more." The reiteration of this cry so maddened the mob that someone shouted, "Let's have done with that little pisser for all time." And they stormed into the street, heading for the mission house, but on the way someone proposed a better plan: "Why bother with him? Why not burn his goddamned church? It's made of grass!" And four men scurried through the night with torches, pitching them high onto the grass roofing. Soon the night breezes had whipped the flames across the top of the structure and had started them down the sides.

The great beacon thus lighted had consequences that the rioters had not foreseen, for the people who had worked upon this church had grown to love it as a symbol of their town, and now that it was ablaze, they rushed to save it. Quickly the area around the church was filled with sweating, silent, urgent men and women who beat at the walls to keep them from going up in flames, and by the incredible labors they performed that night, they saved more than half the walls, drenching them with water and beating at them with brooms and bare hands. The sailors, aghast at the bravery with which these illiterate islanders worked, withdrew and watched in wonder.

But when the people of Lahaina saw how little was left of their beloved church, where words of great hope had been preached to them, they became furious to the point of hysteria, and an islander cried, "Let us throw the sailors into jail!" The fire fighters greeted his challenge with cheers, and a wild manhunt was launched.

Wherever a sailor was spotted, three or four big natives crashed down upon him, often leaving him unconscious under some heavy woman who sat on him, banging his head while her men went off in search of others. Bo's'ns, captains, common sailors were treated alike, and any who resisted had their arms or jaws broken. When the assault was over, Kelolo sent official policemen around, searching for bodies which he pitched into the new jail. Then, with the foresight of a politician, he went personally among the piles of Americans and searched out all the captains, saying to each in his most fatherly voice, "Kapitani, I sorry inside me. We no see good, we t'ink you crew, we boom-boom good too much. No pilikia, I take care of you." And he took them to Murphy's and bought each man a drink, but as they pressed their broken lips to the glass, he was pleased to see how badly scarred they were.

At the next dusk, the conches sounded and a good many sailors climbed into boats and returned to their ships. Those that didn't were chased through the town, not by policemen, but by infuriated gangs of Hawaiians bent on thrashing them. But whenever a sailor was caught, some policeman was ready to rescue him, and by eight o'clock the jail was full. On the third night, most of the sailors who were caught ashore after curfew sought out the police, to whom they willingly gave themselves up, preferring that to the coursing mobs. And by the fourth night, order was restored in Lahaina. Kelolo's police were in command.

On the next day, Malama, at Kelolo's suggestion, summoned the whaling captains to her grass palace, where a feast had been spread. She greeted each bruised skipper with personal warmth and commiserated with him over the rude behavior of her people. She fed the captains well, offered them fine whiskey, and then proposed: "Our lovely church is burned. It was an accident, I am sure. Naturally, we want to rebuild it, and we will. But before we do, we want to do something for the fine Americans who come to Lahaina. Therefore we are going to build a little chapel for sailors. It will give them a place to read, and pray, and write letters home to their dear ones. Will you kind men set the example and give a few dollars for the chapel?" And by her daring charm she wheedled more than sixty dollars from the astonished captains, and another of Abner Hale's dreams, one that he had entertained since that day off the Four Evangelists when the sailors went swinging through the arcs of heaven, was realized: the Seamen's Chapel at Lahaina.

B Y 1828 IT seemed that Abner's world was at last beginning to be well organized. He had a rude desk and a whale-oil lamp by which he translated the Bible. He had three schools functioning with increasing success, and the day seemed not too far distant when Iliki, Pupali's youngest and loveliest daughter, would be married in church to one or the other of the established Hawaiian men who were trying with increasing regularity to peek into Jerusha's school. Captain Janders' return to Lahaina and his announced decision to settle down as a ship chandler, with his wife and children coming out from New Bedford, gave Abner a polished mind with whom he could conduct discussions; while the captain's happy knowledge that young Cridland, the devout sailor from the *Thetis,* was footloose in Honolulu, where the ship's company had been disbanded, encouraged Abner to direct a letter to the youth, asking him to throw in his lot with the Seamen's Chapel, so that Cridland was now employed there, giving guidance to the younger sailors who arrived in Lahaina on the rapidly increasing whaling fleet—45 whalers in 1828; 62 in 1829.

Malama was rapidly approaching a state of grace, so that it seemed assured that she would be accepted into the rebuilt church when it was dedicated, and there were really only two difficulties looming on the broad and lovely horizon at Lahaina. Abner had anticipated the first, for when it came time to rebuild the church, Kelolo announced that the kahunas wished to consult with Abner again, but he replied, "The door will stay where it was. All this talk in the community that the kahunas knew the church would be destroyed irritates me. Some drunken sailors burned it and that's that. Your local superstitions had nothing whatever to do with it."

"Makua Hale!" Kelolo protested gently. "We did not wish to speak about the door. We know your mind is made up, and we know that your church will always be unlucky. But there is nothing we can do about that."

"What did the kahunas want to see me about?" Abner asked suspiciously.

"Come to the church," Kelolo begged, and when Abner met with the wise old men they pointed to the two-third walls and the absent ceiling and made this proposal: "Makua Hale, it has occurred to us that the last church was very hot indeed, what with more than three thousand people huddled on the floor and no wind to cool them off."

"It was warm," Abner agreed.

"Would it not therefore be a wise thing if we did not build the destroyed walls any higher? Would it not be better, indeed, if we could pull them down even farther? Then we could erect high posts and raise the ceiling as it was before, so that when the church is finished, the winds will move across us and cool us as if we were on the shore."

It took some minutes for Abner to comprehend this radical suggestion and he tried to piece its various components together in his mind. "You mean, tear the present walls down to here?"

"Even lower, Makua Hale," the kahunas advised.

"Well . . ." Abner reflected. "Then raise the pillars as before?"

"Yes, and hang the ceiling from them, as before."

"But you wouldn't have any walls," Abner protested.

"The wind would move over us, and that would be better," the wise men explained.

"But there would be no walls. A man sitting here," and he squatted on the ground, "could look up and watch the sky."

"Would that be wrong?" Kelolo asked.

"But a church always has walls," Abner replied slowly. He thought of every church he had ever seen in New England. The very essence of a church was that it have four rugged, square walls and a steeple above them. Even the pictures he had seen of churches in foreign lands showed four walls, and those that did not were clearly popish, so he said firmly, "We will build the church as before."

"It will be very hot," Kelolo warned.

"A church must have walls," Abner said, and he left the wondering kahunas.

The second difficulty could not have been foreseen, at least not by Abner Hale. It concerned Keoki Kanakoa, whose school was accomplishing wonders in bringing Hawaiian boys from the Stone Age into the present. Half the sailors aboard the *Thetis,* as it plied from Lahaina to Honolulu on weekly trips, were young men trained by Keoki. The boys who worked at the mission printing press, publishing the Bible, were his boys, too. In community life he was a rugged, dependable tower of Christian strength, and his Bible readings in formal services were inspiring. It should not have been surprising therefore—but it was—when Keoki appeared in Abner's grass house one day and asked, "Reverend Hale, when can I hope to be ordained a full minister?"

Abner rested his pen and looked at the young man in astonishment. "A minister?" he gasped.

"Yes, I was told at Yale that I must return to Hawaii and become a minister to my people."

"But you already work with them, Keoki," Abner explained.

"I believe I am ready to have a church of my own," Keoki suggested. "In some new part of the island where the people need God."

"But there can't be a church without a missionary, Keoki."

"Why not?" the handsome Hawaiian asked.

"Well . . ." Abner began. He threw down the pen. "I have no plans for ordaining Hawaiians," he said bluntly.

"Why not?" Keoki pressed.

"Well . . . It's never even been considered, Keoki," Abner explained. "You do excellent work in the school . . . of course . . . but a full-fledged minister? Oh, no! That would be ridiculous. Impossible."

"But I thought you missionaries came here to educate us . . . to get us ready to take care of ourselves."

"We did, Keoki!" Abner assured him. "You have heard me talk with your mother. I insist that she govern every aspect of the island. I touch nothing."

"You have been fine about that," Keoki acknowledged. "But the church is more important than the government."

"Exactly," Abner jumped. "The government could fail because of your mother's errors, and that would be no irremediable harm, but if the church failed because of your error . . . Well, Keoki, the damage could never be repaired."

"But how will you know whether I am strong enough to do God's work unless you test me?" Keoki pleaded.

"With the life of the church at stake, Keoki, we can take no chances."

"Does that mean that I can never become a minister? Here in my own land?"

Gravely, Abner leaned back in his chair and thought: "Somebody better tell him the facts." So he said coldly, "Would you have the strength, Keoki, to discipline your fellow Hawaiians as God requires? Would you seek out those who lead a lewd life and announce their names on Sunday? And track down those who drink? Would you dare to expel the alii who smokes? Could I trust you to use the right words in explaining the Bible? Or to refuse bribes when the alii want to join the church? Keoki, my dear son, you will never have the courage to be a true minister. For one thing, you are too young."

"I am older than you were when you became a minister," the Hawaiian pointed out.

"Yes, but I grew up in a Christian family. I was . . ."

"A white man?" Keoki asked bluntly.

"Yes," Abner replied with equal frankness. "Yes, Keoki, my ancestors fought for this church for a hundred years. From the day I was born I knew what a heavenly thing, what an inspired, divine thing the church was. You don't know yet, and we can't trust the church in your hands."

"You are saying very bitter things, Reverend Hale," Keoki replied.

"Do you remember aboard the *Thetis*, when I gave the old whaler in the fo'c's'l the Bible, and how he brought ridicule on the Bible and on me and on God? That's what happens when we risk the welfare of the church in the wrong hands. You must wait, Keoki, until you have proved yourself."

"I have proved myself," Keoki said stubbornly. "I proved myself at Yale College, when I stood in the snow begging an education. I proved myself at Cornwall, where I was the top student in the mission school. And here in

Lahaina I have protected you against the sailors. What more must I do to prove myself?"

"Those acts were your duty, Keoki. They qualify you for church membership. But to qualify for the ministry itself! Perhaps when you are an old, tested man. Not now." And he dismissed the arrogant young man.

He was rather startled when, in discussing these matters with Jerusha, she sided with Keoki, arguing, "Your commission, Abner, from the American Board that sent you here was to train up the Hawaiians so that they could organize and run their own churches."

"Organize them and run them, yes!" Abner instantly agreed. "Soon we will take in more members and institute a board of deacons. But to make a Hawaiian a minister! Jerusha, it would be complete folly. I couldn't tell poor Keoki, but he will never become a minister. Never."

"Why not?" Jerusha asked.

"He's a heathen. He's no more civilized than Pupali's daughters. One good hurricane, and he would lose all his veneer of civilization."

"But when we are gone, Abner, we shall have to turn the church over to Keoki and his fellows."

"We shall never go," Abner said with great solemnity. "This is our home, our church."

"You mean to stay here forever?" Jerusha asked.

"Yes. And when we die, the Board in Boston will send out others to take our places. Keoki running a church! Impossible!"

But Abner had acquired the habit of listening to his wife, and long after their discussion ended he brooded about what she had said, and at last he found a reasonable solution to the impasse over Keoki, and he summoned the young Hawaiian. "Keoki," he announced happily, "I have discovered a way whereby you can serve the church as you desire."

"You mean I can be ordained?" the young man cried joyfully.

"Not exactly," Abner replied, and he was so preoccupied with his satisfactory answer to Keoki's problem that he failed to observe how disappointed the latter was. "What I'm willing to do, Keoki, is to make you the luna of the church, the top deacon. You move among the Hawaiians and find out who is smoking. You check to see who has alcohol on his breath. Each week you hand me a list of people to be admonished from the pulpit, and you draw up the names of those to be expelled from church. At night you will creep quietly through Lahaina to let me know who is sleeping with another man's wife. I am willing to have you do these things for the church," Abner concluded happily. "How do you like that?"

Keoki stood silent, staring at the little missionary, and when the latter asked again for his response Keoki said bitterly, "I sought a way to serve my people, not to spy upon them." And he stalked from the mission, remaining in seclusion for many days.

If Jerusha and Keoki could not stand up to Abner's arguments against the Hawaiians, a visitor was about to descend on Lahaina who not only marshaled all of Jerusha's doubts and expressed them in vigorous English but who also brought along many of his own. It was Dr. Whipple, lean and brown from years of work on distant outposts, who came in one day on Kelolo's ship, the *Thetis.* He hurried immediately to the mission house and shouted, "Sister Jerusha, forgive me for not being here when you were pregnant. Good heavens! I forgot you have two children. And pregnant again!"

The years had mellowed Whipple and given him a strong no-nonsense vernacular. He had witnessed too much death—wives, children, black-frocked men who worked themselves to death—to bother any longer with the niceties of expression that had characterized the *Thetis*. "I had the same stateroom coming over. Only four other men in it with me, and I felt lonely. Sister Jerusha, how's the medicine box?" And he yanked the black box down and checked its contents against the new medicines he had lately received from Boston. "I'm giving you lots of ipecac," he advised. "We find it very good for children's fevers. And tonight you and Brother Abner and I are going to have a big dinner with Retire Janders in his new store. And because I was seasick on the damnable *Thetis* again, I'm going to have some whiskey. You'll be seasick too, when you go back to Honolulu."

"Are we required to go?" Abner asked, for like Jerusha he preferred to remain in Lahaina, finding Honolulu, at the yearly meeting of the missionaries, a dirty, dusty, ugly little collection of hovels.

"Yes," Dr. Whipple said sadly, "I'm afraid it's going to be a difficult meeting, this one."

"What's the matter?" Abner asked. "They going to discuss pay for the missionaries again? I explained my position last time, Brother John. I shall always be unalterably opposed to salaries for missionaries. We are here as God's servants and we require no pay. My mind will not change on this."

"That isn't the subject," Whipple broke in. "I don't agree with you on the salary question. I think we ought to be paid wages, but that's beside the point. We've all got to vote on the case of Brother Hewlett."

"Brother Abraham Hewlett!" Abner repeated. "I haven't heard from him since his baby was born. And he's on the same island with me. What is the question about Brother Abraham?"

"Haven't you heard?" Whipple asked in astonishment. "He's in trouble again."

"What's he done?" Abner asked.

"He's married a Hawaiian girl," Whipple said. There was a long, shocked silence in the grass house, during which the three missionaries stared at each other in amazement.

Finally, Abner took out his handkerchief and wiped his forehead. "You mean to say he's actually living with a native woman? A heathen?"

"Yes."

"And the meeting is to decide what to do about him?"

"Yes."

"There's nothing to decide," Abner said flatly. He went for his Bible and thumbed it for a moment, finding the text that applied to the case. "I think Ezekiel 23, verses 29 and 30, covers such behavior: 'And they shall deal with thee hatefully, and shall take away all thy labor, and shall leave thee naked and bare: and the nakedness of thy whoredoms shall be discovered, both thy lewdness and thy whoredoms. I will do these things unto thee, because thou has gone a whoring after the heathen, and because thou art polluted with their idols.' " He closed the Bible.

"Are they determined in Honolulu to throw him out of the church?" Jerusha asked.

"Yes," Dr. Whipple said.

"What else could they do?" Abner demanded. "A Christian minister marrying a heathen. 'Gone a whoring after the heathen!' I do not want to go to Honolulu, but it seems my duty."

Dr. Whipple said, "Would you excuse us, Sister Jerusha, if we walk down to the pier?" And he led Abner along the lovely paths of Lahaina, under the gnarled hau trees and the palms. "You are fortunate to live here," Whipple reflected. "It's the best climate in Hawaii. Plenty of water. And that glorious view."

"What view?" Abner asked.

"Don't you come down here every night to see the best view in the islands?" Whipple asked astonished.

"I wasn't aware . . ."

"Look!" Whipple cried, as a kind of poetry took command of him, tired as he was from seeing so many bleak Hawaiian prospects. "To the west the handsome rounded hills of Lanai across a few miles of blue water. Have you ever seen gentler hills than those? Their verdure looks like velvet, thrown there by God. And to the north the clean-cut rugged mountains of Molokai. And over to the south the low hills of Kahoolawe. Wherever you look, mountains and valleys and blue sea. You lucky people of Lahaina! You exist in a nest of beauty. Tell me, do you ever see the whales that breed in the channel here?"

"I've never watched for any whales," Abner replied.

"A sailor told me, as I was cutting off his arm, that one night at Lahaina he saw a dozen whales with their babies, and he said that all his life he had been harpooning whales and had thought of them only as enormous, impersonal beasts so huge that the ocean was scarcely large enough to hold them. But when his arm was gangrenous and he knew that he was going to lose it, he, for the first time, observed whales as mothers and fathers, and they were playing with their babies in the Lahaina Roads, and he told me . . . Well, anyway, he won't be throwing a harpoon any more."

Abner was not listening. He was doing something he had not done before: he was looking at the physical setting in which his whaling town existed. To be sure, he had seen the hills behind the town, for he had walked over them, but he had not appreciated the glorious ocean roads: jeweled islands on every side, the deepest blue water, white sands and the constant scud of impressive clouds. He understood why the whaling ships were content to anchor here, for no storm could get at them. From all sides they were protected, and ashore they had Lahaina for water, and fresh meat and cool roads.

"This is rather attractive," Abner admitted.

"I was sorry to hear your view on Brother Hewlett," Dr. Whipple began when he had found a comfortable rock.

"It's not my view," Abner replied. "It's the Bible's. He went whoring after a heathen."

"Let's not use that old-style language," Whipple interrupted. "We're dealing with a human being in the year 1829. He isn't a strong human being and I never liked him much . . ."

"What do you mean, Brother John? Old-style language?"

"He wasn't whoring after heathens, Brother Abner . . . Do you mind if I quit this brother calling? Abner, this man Abraham Hewlett was left alone at Hana with a baby boy and not a damned thing to guide him in the care of that child."

"Brother John!" Abner exploded. "Please do not offend me with such language. And besides, Brother Abraham had as much . . ."

"And the Hawaiian girl wasn't a heathen. She was a fine, Christian girl . . . his best student . . . and I know, because I delivered her baby."

"She had a baby?" Abner asked in a whisper.

"Yes, a fine baby girl. She named her Amanda, after my wife."

"Was it . . ."

"I no longer count the months, Abner. They're married now and they seem very happy, and if there is any system of morality which requires a lonely man like Abraham Hewlett . . ."

"I hardly comprehend your words any longer, Brother John," Abner protested.

"I have buried so many people, cut off so many legs . . . Many of the things we used to worry about at Yale don't worry me any more, ancient roommate."

"But surely you would not allow a man like Brother Hewlett to remain in the church? With a heathen wife?"

"I wish you would stop using that word, Abner. She's not a heathen. If Amanda Whipple were to die tomorrow, I'd marry such a girl any day, and Amanda would want me to. She'd know at least that her children had a good mother."

"The others will not think as you do, Brother John."

"Immanuel Quigley does, I'm proud to say. And that's why I've come to Lahaina. We want you on our side. Don't drive poor Hewlett from his church."

"The Lord saith, 'Thou has gone a whoring after the heathen.' " Dully, Abner closed the discussion, but in doing so he began to wonder about John Whipple. What the doctor said next erased the wonder and confirmed the doubt.

"I've been doing a great deal of speculation recently, Abner," he began. "Do you think we've done right in bursting into this island kingdom with our new ideas?"

"The word of God," Abner began, "is not a new idea."

"I accept that," Whipple apologized. "But the things that go with it? Did you know that when Captain Cook discovered these islands he estimated their population at four hundred thousand? That was fifty years ago. Today how many Hawaiians are there? Less than a hundred and thirty thousand. What happened to them?"

To Whipple's surprise, Abner was not particularly shocked by these figures, but asked casually, "Are your facts correct?"

"Captain Cook vouches for the first. I vouch for the second. Abner, have you ever seen measles strike a Hawaiian village? Don't. Ppppsssshhhh!" He made a sound like fire rushing through the grass walls of a house. "The entire village vanishes. For example, do you make your church members wear New England clothes?"

"I have only nine members," Abner explained.

"You mean that in this entire . . ." Dr. Whipple threw a pebble into the blue waters and watched a near-naked Hawaiian riding the surf onto the kapu beach. "On Sundays, for example, do you require a man like that one out there to wear New England clothes?"

"Of course. Doesn't the Bible specifically state, 'And thou shalt make them linen breeches to cover their nakedness'?"

"Do you ever listen to the hacking coughs that fill the church?"

"No."

"I do, and I'm terribly worried."

"What about?"

"I'm afraid that in another thirty years the Hawaiians will be not a hundred and thirty thousand but more likely thirty thousand. Out of all those who were here when we came, twelve out of thirteen will have been destroyed."

"Lahaina was never any bigger," Abner replied prosaically.

"Not the town, perhaps, but how about the valleys?" Whipple, as was his practice in touring the islands, called an old man to the seaside and asked in Hawaiian, "In that valley, did people used to live?"

"More t'ousand was stay before."

"How many live there now?"

"T'ree. Ikahi, ilua, ikulu. T'ree."

"In that valley over there, did people used to live?"

"More two t'ousand was stay before."

"How many live there now?"

"All dis fellow stay before, now make . . . die," the old man answered, and Whipple dismissed him.

"It's that way in all the valleys," he said gloomily. "I think the only thing that will save Hawaii is some radical move. There has got to be a big industry of some kind. Then we must bring in some strong, virile new people. Say from Java, or perhaps China. And let them marry with the Hawaiians. Maybe . . ."

"You seem beset with doubts," Abner marked.

"I am," Whipple confessed. "I am terribly afraid that what we are doing is not right. I am certain that we are sponsoring the spread of consumption and that these wonderful people are doomed. Unless we change things right away."

"We are not concerned with change," Abner said coldly. "Hawaiians are the children of Shem, and God has ordained that they shall perish from the earth. He has promised that their lands shall be occupied by your children and mine, Genesis 9, verse 27: 'God shall enlarge Japheth, and he shall dwell in the tents of Shem.' The Hawaiians are doomed, and in a hundred years they will have vanished from the earth."

Whipple was aghast, and asked, "How can you preach such a doctrine, Abner?"

"It is God's will. The Hawaiians are a deceitful and licentious people. Even though I have warned them, they continue to smoke, they circumcise their sons and abandon their daughters. They gamble and play games on Sunday, and for these sins God has ordained that they shall be stricken from the face of the earth. When they are gone, our children, as the Bible directs, shall inherit their tents."

"But if you believe this, Abner, why do you remain among them as missionary?"

"Because I love them. I want to bring them the consolation of the Lord, so that when they do vanish it will be to His love and not to eternal hellfire."

"I do not like such religion," Whipple said flatly, "and I do not aspire to their tents. There must be a better way. Abner, when we were students at Yale, the first tenet of our church was that each individual church should be a congregation unto itself. No bishops, no priests, no popes. Our very name bespoke that conviction. The Congregationalists. But what do we find here? A system of bishoprics! A solemn convocation to throw a poor, lonely man out of the ministry. In all these years you've allowed nine people to join your church as full members. Somewhere, Abner, we've gone wrong."

"It takes time to convert the heathen to true . . ."

"No!" Whipple protested. "They are not heathen! One of the most brilliant women I have ever met or read about was Kaahumanu. I understand you have one like her here on Maui, your Alii Nui. Heathen? The word doesn't mean anything to me any more. For example, have you admitted any of your so-called heathen to the ministry? Of course not."

Abner, finding the turn of Whipple's argument most distasteful, rose to go, but his old roommate grasped him by the hand and pleaded: "You have nothing more important to do today than talk with me, Abner. I find my soul wandering from its moorings, and I seek guidance. I had hoped that when you and Jerusha and Captain Janders and I sat down together, something of the spirit that animated us on the *Thetis . . .*" His voice trailed off, and after a while he confessed, "I am sick with God."

"What do you mean?" Abner asked quietly.

"The spirit of God fills my brain, but I am dissatisfied with the way we administer His word."

"You are speaking against the church, Brother John," Abner warned.

"I am, and I am glad that you said so, for I was ashamed to."

"It is the church that has brought us here, Brother John. It is only through the church that we build our accomplishments. Do you think I would dare to speak to the alii as I do if I were plain Abner Hale? But as the instrument of the church I can dare all things."

"Even wisdom?" Whipple inquired.

"What do you mean?"

"If your mind suddenly comprehended a new wisdom . . . some radical new concept of existence . . . well, could you as a servant of an all-powerful church dare to accept that new wisdom?"

"There is no new or old, Brother John. There is only the word of God, and it is revealed in the church, through the instrumentality of the Holy Bible. There can be no greater than that."

"No greater," Dr. Whipple agreed, "but there can be a different."

"I do not think so," Abner replied, and he wished to hear no more of this argument and left. But that night, in the warm fellowship of Captain Janders' excellent dinner, with good wine, and whiskey for the doctor, the old friends relaxed and Janders said, "Lahaina's becoming a first-rate city, thanks to Abner Hale's exertions."

"Who is that girl who's bringing in the dishes?" Abner asked, for her face seemed familiar, yet he did not recognize it.

Captain Janders blushed ever so slightly, in a way that Abner missed but which Dr. Whipple had seen often in the islands. "I understand you're bringing Mrs. Janders and the children out from Boston?" Whipple said by way of rescue.

"I am," Janders replied quickly.

"We need all the Christians we can get," Abner said heartily.

"Do you intend remaining here?" Whipple asked directly. "In Lahaina, that is?"

"It's the jewel of the Pacific," Janders replied. "I've seen all the towns, and this is best."

"You'll be in trade, I judge?"

"I see great opportunity for ships' chandlery here, Doctor."

"Do you suppose there is any way . . . it would be difficult I grant you . . . but do you suppose that if a man with good native connections could get some canoes at Hana . . . well, if he had some fine land there and energy, do you suppose he could grow things and sell them to you . . . for the whalers, that is?"

"You speaking of Abraham Hewlett?" Janders asked abruptly.

"Yes."

"If he could grow hogs . . . beef . . . I might buy 'em. He ever think of growing sugar? We could use a lot of sugar."

"I'll speak to him about sugar," Whipple said thoughtfully.

"You expect him to be giving up the church at Hana?" Janders inquired.

"Yes. I fear the Honolulu meeting is going to expel him."

Captain Janders sat very thoughtfully for some moments. He did not want to offend Reverend Hale, with whom he must live in intimacy, and yet he had always liked young John Whipple's honest approach to life. "Tell you what I'd be willing to do," he said slowly. "If Hewlett could get his stuff to me in the whaling season . . . on time and in good shape . . . well, I judge I could use everything he produces. But I want one thing he may not be willing to give."

"What's that?" Whipple asked.

"I hear his wife has claim to a nice piece of land at Hana, more than Abraham could possibly farm. Isn't he the scrawny fellow with big eyes that slept in your stateroom? He's the one I had in mind. I want him to enter into a contract with me so that I manage that land. I'll tell him what to grow and he won't ever have to worry about where his next meal's comin' from," Janders promised.

When it came time for the *Thetis* to carry the missionaries to Honolulu, Abner discovered the thrill that ugly memories yield when they have receded with their pain, for he was to bunk in his old stateroom and John Whipple would share it; but his pleasure was considerably dampened when a canoe arrived from the other end of Maui bearing the missionary Abraham Hewlett, his handsome little boy Abner, and his Hawaiian wife, Malia, the native pronunciation of Mary.

"Are they sailing with us?" Abner asked suspiciously.

"Of course. If we don't have them, we don't have a trial."

"Won't it be embarrassing if Hewlett's on the same ship with us?"

"Not for me. I'm voting for him."

"Do you think he'll be put in our stateroom?"

"He shared it with us once," Whipple replied.

The two missionaries looked with interest as Mrs. Hewlett, if anyone so dark could be given that name, came aboard the *Thetis*. She was taller than her husband, very broad-shouldered and grave of manner. She spoke to the little boy in a soft voice, and Abner whispered in disgust, "Is she talking to that child in Hawaiian?"

"Why not?" Dr. Whipple asked.

"My children are not allowed to speak a word of Hawaiian," Abner replied emphatically. " 'Learn not the way of the heathen!' the Bible directs us. Do your children speak Hawaiian?"

"Of course," Whipple replied with some impatience.

"That's very unwise!" Abner warned.

"We live in Hawaii. We work here. Probably my boys will go to school here."

"Mine won't," Abner said firmly.

"Where will you send them?" John asked with some interest, for he often discussed the matter with his wife.

"The Board will send them to New England. Then to Yale. But the important thing is that they never come into contact with Hawaiians." Dr. Whipple watched the Hewletts cross the deck and go down the hatchway aft, and the manner in which the Hawaiian woman watched over little Abner Hewlett proved that whereas she might have crept into the father's bed by some trick or other, she certainly loved the child.

"Boy's lucky," Whipple said. "He's got a good mother."

"She doesn't look the way I expected," Abner confessed.

"You expected a painted whore?" Whipple laughed. "Abner, once in a while you ought to look at the reality of life."

"How did she become a Christian?" Abner pondered.

"Abraham Hewlett took her into the church," Whipple explained.

There was a thoughtful pause, and then Abner asked, "But how could they have been married? I mean, if Hewlett was the only minister, who could have married them?"

"For the first year nobody did."

"You mean, they lived in sin?"

"And then I came along . . . on one of my regular trips. I was in a Russian ship."

"And you married a Christian minister to a heathen?" Abner asked, aghast.

"Yes. I'm probably going to be censured, too," Whipple said dryly. "And I have a suspicion in here," and he touched his heart, "that I won't accept the censure. I stand with St. Paul: 'It is better to marry than to burn.' Can anyone seriously doubt that Abraham is better off today than he was when you left him in Wailuku?"

The meeting in Honolulu went as expected. At first Abraham Hewlett made a sorry spectacle of himself, confessing that in marrying the Hawaiian girl Malia he had sinned against the decrees of God, thus bringing degradation upon both himself and the church. He begged forgiveness, asking the brethren to remember that he had been left alone with an infant boy; and at the recollection of his misery in those lonely days he wept. Later, when it was suggested that perhaps the sly Hawaiian woman had been responsible for his downfall, he recovered a portion of his dignity by avowing that he loved this gracious, tender girl and that it was he who had insisted upon the marriage, "and if the brethren think they dare imply censure of Malia, they are indeed mistaken."

The vote was an easily predicted condemnation and expulsion, only Whipple and Quigley speaking in defense. The meeting thought it best that the Hewletts leave the islands: "For your presence here would be a constant humiliation to the church. But it is recognized that it would be equally disgraceful for a Christian minister—an unfrocked one, that is—to return to America with a Hawaiian wife, for there are many in America who are eager to castigate missionaries, and your appearance among them would merely add ammunition to their blasphemies. It is therefore concluded that you and your family ought . . ."

At this point Abraham's tears were dried and he interrupted bluntly: "It is not within your province to advise me in these matters. I shall live where I wish."

"You will receive no sustenance from us," the meeting reminded him.

"I have entered into a compact to raise pigs and sugar cane for the whaling ships at Lahaina, and beyond this you are required to know nothing. But before I go I must point out that your mission is founded upon an impossible contradiction. You love the Hawaiians as potential Christians, but you despise them as people. I am proud to say that I have come to exactly the opposite conclusion, and it is therefore appropriate that I should be expelled from a mission where love is not." Dr. Whipple thought that when the scrawny man with the big eyes finally left the judgment room, he departed with some dignity.

The meeting then turned to the doctor's case and condemned him for having married the pair, thus constituting himself, as one minister pointed out, "the agency, if not the cause, whereby our miserable brother from Hana fell into temptation and sin."

Dr. Whipple retorted, "I should rather have thought that I was the agency whereby he fell out of sin."

This sally, being both witty and cogent, furthered the case against the doctor, and all the missionaries except Quigley joined in a vote of censure. Whipple was reproved and advised to be more circumspect in the future. To Abner's surprise, his roommate accepted the condemnation and sat without even a look of resentment as the meeting turned to less weighty matters, including assignments of the mission family to new posts.

But when it came time for the *Thetis* to return to Lahaina, Abner was surprised to find Dr. Whipple, his wife Amanda, and their two boys ensconced in the stateroom. "I thought you were directed to go to Kauai," Abner remarked.

"Where I am directed to go and where I go are two vastly different matters," Whipple said easily, and Abner was relieved to notice that they had no luggage, so apparently they were on a short visit to one of the way islands, Molokai or Lanai. But when these ports were cleared, the Whipple family was still aboard, and at the pier in Lahaina, John grabbed Abner's hand and said, "Don't leave. I want you to witness exactly what happens. There's Jerusha. I'd like to have her come along, too, because I don't want contradictory reports circulated regarding what I'm about to do."

And with his wife and children in tow, he led the Hales to Captain Janders' store and said boldly, "Captain, I have come to throw myself on your mercy."

"What do you mean?" Janders asked suspiciously.

"You're doing a large business here, Captain, and with more whalers coming each year, you'll need a partner. I want to be that partner."

"You leaving the mission?"

"Yes, sir."

"Over the Hewlett affair?"

"Yes, sir. And others. I happen to believe that men who work should get a just salary." He tugged at his ill-fitting trousers, pointed at Amanda's dress and said, "I'm tired of going down to the mission grab bag in Honolulu to see what scraps the good people in Boston have sent us this year. I want to work for myself, get my own wage, and buy my own things."

"Does Amanda feel the same?" Captain Janders asked.

"She does."

"Do you, Amanda?"

"I love the Lord. I love to serve the Lord. But I also love an organized home, and in these matters I am with my husband."

"You got any money to put into the venture?" Janders asked warily.

"My family comes to you with absolutely nothing," the handsome dark-haired doctor, then twenty-nine, replied. "We have these clothes, picked from the rag bag, and that is all. I have no medicine, no tools, no luggage. Certainly I have no money. But I have a knowledge of these islands that no other man on earth has, and that's what I offer you."

"Do you speak the tongue?"

"Perfectly."

Janders thought a moment, then stuck out his rugged hand. "Son, you're my partner. On the *Thetis,* when you asked so many questions, I remarked you."

"I have only one request, Captain," Whipple said. "I want to borrow enough money . . . right now . . . ."

"We'll fix you up with clothes and a place to live."

"Enough money to buy my own medical outfit. And anyone who wants medical advice from me can get it free. For I am a servant of the Lord, but I am determined to serve Him in my way, and not some other."

By the end of the week the Whipples had moved into a small grass shack, which Kelolo gave them along with a substantial square of land in return for medical care for Malama, whose exertions on behalf of the new laws had taxed her strength, and at the start of the next week the first of many signboards that were to become famous throughout Hawaii appeared on the dusty main streets of Lahaina: "Janders & Whipple."

ABNER'S DISTURBING EXPERIENCES in Honolulu, where both Abraham Hewlett and John Whipple had challenged the missionary board, confirmed his natural suspicion that there was inherent danger from too close relationships with the Hawaiian savages, and it was under the impetus of this fear that he built a high wall around his entire establishment, leaving an extra gate at the rear through which Jerusha could exit to her girls' classes, held in an open shed under the kou trees. Within the wall not a word of Hawaiian was spoken. No Hawaiian maid was allowed to enter unless she knew English, and if a deputation of villagers came to see Abner, he would carefully close the door leading to where his children were, and he would take the Hawaiians to what he called "the native room," where their voices could not be heard by the little ones.

"We must not learn the ways of the heathen!" Abner constantly warned his family, for what Abraham Hewlett had suggested in Honolulu regarding all missionaries was particularly true of Abner: he loved the Hawaiians, yet he despised them. He was therefore not in very good humor when Kelolo came to visit him one night, which forced him to close off the children's room, lest they hear Hawaiian being spoken.

"What is it you want?" he asked testily.

"In church the other day," Kelolo said in Hawaiian, "I listened to Keoki read that beautiful passage from the Bible in which this man begat that man, and the other man begat another man." The big chief's face was radiant with pleasant memory of the Biblical message which Hawaiians loved above all other. "The Begats," they called it among themselves.

Abner had long been curious about this partiality for the chapter in Chronicles, for he felt sure the Hawaiians could not understand it. "Why do you like that passage so much?" he probed.

Kelolo was embarrassed, and looked about to see if anyone was listening. Then he confessed somewhat sheepishly, "There is much in the Bible we do not understand. How could we? We don't know the many things the white man knows. But when we hear 'The Begats,' it is like music to our ears, Makua Hale, because it sounds just like our own family histories, and for once we can feel as if we, too, were part of the Bible."

"What do you mean, family histories?" Abner asked.

"That is what I came to see you about. I see you at work translating the Bible into my language, and we appreciate your hard work. Malama and I were wondering, if before she dies . . . No, Makua Hale, she is not well. We wondered if you would write down for us in English our family history. We are brother and sister, you know."

"I know," Abner mumbled.

"I am the last one who knows the family history," Kelolo said. "When Keoki should have been learning it, he was learning about God. Now he is too old to memorize the way I did when I was studying to be a kahuna."

Abner, a learned man, instantly saw the value of preserving old fables, and asked, "How does a family history sound, Kelolo?"

"I want you to write it as if Keoki were saying it. I am doing this for him, so that he will know who he is."

"How does it begin?" Abner pressed.

It was dark in the grass house, with only one feeble whale-oil lamp swaying with its retinue of shadows, when Kelolo, seated cross-legged on the floor, began: "I am Keoki, the son of Kelolo who came to Maui with Kamehameha the Great; who was the son of Kanakoa, the King of Kona; who was the son of Kanakoa, the King of Kona who sailed to Kauai; who was the son of Kelolo, the King of Kona who died in the volcano; who was the son of Kelolo, the King of Kona who stole Kekelaalii from Oahu; who was the son of . . ."

After Abner had listened for a while, his curiosity as a scholar overcame his initial boredom at this tedious and probably imaginary ritual. "How did you memorize this genealogy?" he asked.

"An alii who doesn't know his ancestry has no hope of position in Hawaii," Kelolo explained. "I spent three years memorizing every branch of my family. The kings of Kona are descended, you know, from the . . ."

"Are these genealogies real, or made up?" Abner asked bluntly.

Kelolo was amazed at the question. "Made up, Makua Hale? It is by these that we live. Why do you suppose Malama is the Alii Nui? Because she can trace her ancestry far back to the second canoe that brought our family to Hawaii. Her ancestor was the High Priestess Malama who came in that second canoe. My name goes back to the first canoe from Bora Bora, for my ancestor was the High Priest of that canoe, Kelolo."

Abner suppressed a smile as the illiterate chief before him tried to establish relations with some mythical event that must have occurred ten centuries before, if at all. He thought of his own family, in Marlboro. His mother knew when her ancestors reached Boston, but no one could recall when the Hales had got there, and here was a man who could not even write, claiming . . .

"You say you can remember the canoes in which your people came?"

"Of course! It was the same canoe on each trip."

"How can you remember that?" Abner demanded sharply.

"Our family has always known its name. It was the canoe *Wait-for-the-West-Wind.* It had Kelolo as navigator, Kanakoa as king, Pa at one paddle and Malo at the other. Kupuna was the astronomer and Kelolo's wife Kelani was aboard. The canoe was eighty feet long by your measures and the voyage took thirty days. We have always known these things about the canoe."

"You mean a little canoe like that one at the pier? How many people did you mention? Seven, eight? In a canoe like that?" Abner was contemptuous of the man.

"It was a double canoe, Makua Hale, and it carried not eight people but fifty-eight."

Abner was dumbfounded, but once more his historical sense was excited, and he wished to know more about the myths of these strange people. "Where did the canoe come from?" he asked.

"From Bora Bora," Kelolo said.

"Oh, yes, you mentioned that name before. Where is it?"

"Near Tahiti," Kelolo said simply.

"Your people came in a canoe from Tahiti . . ." Abner dropped the question and said, "I suppose the family history ends there?"

"Oh, no!" Kelolo said proudly. "That is not even the half-way mark."

This was too much for Abner, and he stopped abruptly calling it a family history. He realized that he had got hold of one of the classic myths of the Hawaiian islands, and he said bluntly, "I'll copy it down for you, Kelolo. I would like to hear the story." He adjusted the swinging lamp, took fresh sheets of paper, and laid aside for some nights his Bible translation. "Now tell me very slowly," he said, "and don't leave out anything."

In the darkness Kelolo began to chant:

"The time of the birth of the tabu chief,
The time when the bold one first saw light,
At first dimly like the rising of the moon
In the season of the Little Eyes in the ancient past.
The great god Kane went into the goddess Wai'ololi
And the offspring of light were born, the bringers of men,
Akiaki who dragged the islands from the sea
And gentle La'ila'i who made the flowers and the birds,
And in the evening of the long day Akiaki knew his sister,
And the man was born, bringer of honor and war . . ."

And as Kelolo chanted the historic summary of his people the little room was filled with the clash of battle, the birth of gods, the abduction of beautiful women and the explosions of ancient volcanoes. Men in yellow capes, carrying spears, marched from one lava flow to another; queens fought for their children's rights and brave men perished in storms. In time Abner fell under the spell of the fabulous events, these made-up memories of a race, and when Kelolo and Malama and the canoe *Wait-for-the-West-Wind* made their second journey from Bora Bora to Hawaii the little missionary caught a momentary thrill of the vast ocean and its perils as Kelolo, sitting in the darkness, chanted what purported to be the song of directions for that imaginary voyage:

"Wait for the west wind, wait for the west wind,
Then sail to Nuku Hiva of the dark bays
To find the constant star.
Hold to it, hold to it
Though the eyes grow dim with heat."

But whenever Abner found his mind prepared to accept some small aspect of the narrative as true, ridiculous legendary events intruded, like Kelolo's account of how his ancestor in Bora Bora left for the trip north at the height of a hurricane, with waves forty feet high.

"Imagine a Hawaiian canoe even venturing out of port in a strong wind!" Abner laughed to Jerusha as he recounted some of the more fantastic passages in the history. "Just look! Right here we have more than forty generations of supposedly historic characters. Now if you allot twenty years to each generation, and that's conservative, Kelolo wants us to believe that his ancestors came here more than eight hundred years ago and then went back to get a second canoeload. Impossible!"

When Kelolo finished his genealogy—128 generations in all—Abner prudently made a copy of what he termed "this primitive and imaginary poem" and sent it to Yale College, where it formed the basis for most accounts of Hawaiian mythology; scholars appreciated in particular the detailed descriptions of the conflict between the Bora Bora god Kane and the Havaiki god Koro. Abner himself had slight regard for his work, and when he summoned Keoki to present the original he said condescendingly, "Your father claims it's a family history."

"It is," Keoki bristled.

"Now, Keoki! More than a hundred and twenty-five generations! Nobody can remember . . ."

"Kahunas can," Keoki said stubbornly.

"You sound as if you were defending the kahunas," Abner suggested.

"In the recitation of family histories, I am," Keoki replied.

"But this is ridiculous . . . mythology . . . fantasy." Abner slapped the manuscript with disdain.

"It is our book," Keoki said, clutching it to his bosom. "The Bible is your book, and these memories are our book."

"How dare you, a man who presumes to ask when he will be made a minister?"

"Why is it, Reverend Hale, that we must always laugh at our book, but always revere yours?"

"Because my Book, as you improperly call it, is the divine word of God, while yours is a bundle of myths."

"Are 'The Begats' any more true than the memories of the kahunas?" Keoki challenged.

"True?" Abner gasped, his temper rising with his astonishment. "One is the divinely revealed Word of the Lord. The other . . ." He paused in contempt and ended, "Good heavens, do you consider them equal?"

"I think there is much in the Old Testament that is merely the work of kahunas, nothing more," Keoki said firmly. Then, to repay Abner for his arrogance, he asked in confidence, "Tell me, Reverend Hale, don't you honestly think that Ezekiel was mostly kahuna?"

"You had better go," Abner snapped icily, but he felt some shame for having goaded the boy, so he put his arm about his shoulder and pointed to a canoe on the beach. "Keoki," he reasoned quietly, "surely you must know that a canoe like that could not carry fifty-eight people for thirty days . . . all the way from Tahiti."

Keoki moved so that he could see the broad, silvery passageway that lay between Lanai Island and Kahoolawe, leading south. "Reverend Hale, do you recall the name of that stretch of water?"

"Don't they call it Keala-i-kahiki?" Abner replied.

"And have you ever heard the name of that point at Kahoo-lawe?"

"No."

"It's likewise Keala-i-kahiki Point. What do you suppose Keala-i-kahiki means?"

"Well," Abner reflected. *"Ke* means *the; ala* means *road; i* means *to;* and I don't know what *kahiki* means."

"You know that what we call *k,* the people to the south call *t.* Now what does *kahiki* mean?"

Against his will, Abner formed the older word, of which *kahiki* was a late corruption. "Tahiti," he whispered. "The Way to Tahiti."

"Yes," Keoki said. "If you sail from Lahaina, pass through Keala-i-kahiki Strait and take your heading from Keala-i-kahiki Point, you will reach Tahiti. My ancestors often sailed that way. In canoes." And the proud young man was gone.

But Abner refused to accept such claims, and by consulting many Hawaiians he proved to his satisfaction that the word *kahiki* meant not Tahiti but any distant place, so he added his own note to the Yale manuscript: "Keala-i-kahiki may be translated as 'The Path to Far Places' or 'The Beyond.'" Then, as if to prove that Abner was right, the Hawaiian captain of Kelolo's ship *Thetis* got drunk, stayed in his cabin during a storm, and allowed his sturdy old veteran of many seas to climb upon the rocks off Lahaina, where it rotted through the years, a visible proof that Hawaiians could not even navigate in their own waters, let alone penetrate distant oceans.

IT WAS WHILE Abner was drafting a letter to Honolulu, advising the mission board that his assistant Keoki Kanakoa was behaving strangely, so that perhaps the board ought to consider Keoki's reassignment to some post of lesser importance, that the news was shouted through the still morning air that was to disrupt Lahaina for many days. Pupali's oldest daughter came screaming to Jerusha's school: "Iliki! Iliki! It has arrived! The *Carthaginian!*" And before the startled Jerusha could intercede, the bright-eyed beauty had leaped over the bench and dashed madly away with her sister. Together they swam out to the sleek whaler, with the dark sides and the white stripe running lengthwise, where naked and shimmering in the sunlight they were both gathered into the arms of the bark's tall captain and led below to his quarters, from which he shouted, "Mister Wilson, I don't want to be interrupted till tomorrow morning. Not even for food."

But he was interrupted. Kelolo dispatched three policemen to the *Carthaginian* under orders to drag Pupali's daughters off to jail, but when they climbed aboard the whaler, Mister Wilson met them on the afterdeck, shouting, "Get away! I'm warning you!"

"We come fetch wahines," the officers explained.

"You'll get broken jaws!" Mister Wilson threatened, whereupon one of the policemen shoved out his elbows, knocked the first mate aside and started for the after hatchway. Mister Wilson, thrown off balance for a moment, tried to lunge at the intruder, but another of the policemen grabbed him, which became the signal for a general scuffle, in which, because most of the men were ashore, the three rugged policemen appeared to be winning.

"What the hell's going on here?" came a roar from the lower deck, followed by a lithe form, tall and muscular, leaping up the ladder. Captain Hoxworth was dressed only in a pair of tight sailor's pants, and when he saw what was happening on his ship, he lowered his head, lunged at the first policeman and shouted, "Into the ocean with 'em!"

The agile officer saw Hoxworth coming, sidestepped with agility, and brought his right forearm viciously across the back of the captain's neck, sending him sprawling across the deck, where the New Englander cut his lower lip on his own teeth. Wiping the blood onto the back of his hand, Hoxworth glimpsed the red stain, and from his knees cried ominously, "All right!"

Rising slowly, testing his bare feet on the decking, Hoxworth moved cautiously toward the policeman who had poleaxed him. With a deceptive lunge to the right, followed by a snakelike twist to the left, Hoxworth brought his powerful right fist into the policeman's face. Then, with the Hawaiian's head momentarily snapped back, Hoxworth doubled up his own head and shoulders and drove into the man's stomach like a battering ram. The surprised policeman staggered backward and fell onto the deck, whereupon Hoxworth began kicking viciously at his face, but remembering, from the pain in his bare feet as they crashed into the man's head, that he wore no shoes, he quickly grabbed a belaying pin and started to thrash the fallen islander, thundering solid blows onto the man's head and crotch, until the policeman fainted. Still Hoxworth continued hammering him until sounds from other parts of the deck called him to activity there.

Brandishing his brutal pin, he whipped about to help Mister Wilson, who was having a bad time with a large policeman until Captain Hoxworth brought down with all the force in his bare arms the rugged belaying pin across the man's skull. The big islander fell instantly and Hoxworth instinctively kicked him in the face, then set off for the third officer, but this man, having witnessed Hoxworth's savage attacks upon his mates, prudently abandoned the battle and leaped into the bay. With a well-directed throw, Hoxworth spun the belaying pin through the air and caught the man in the face, cutting open a huge gash across his forehead. At once the man sank below the waves, leaving a patch of purple where he had gone down, and one of Hoxworth's sailors shouted, "He's drowning."

"Let the bastard drown!" Hoxworth shouted violently. "And let these swine join him." Alone he picked up the first unconscious victim, strained as the man's feet slowly cleared the railing, and then with a mighty heave tossed the policeman toward the general direction of the first, who had now dazedly regained the surface in time to help his battered and inert companion.

Now Hoxworth grabbed the feet of the third policeman and Mister Wilson the hands, and with a one-two-three prepared to toss him overboard, but one of the man's hands was bloody, and on the three count, Mister Wilson lost his grip, so that when Hoxworth threw the legs mightily over the railing, the first mate failed to do so with the hands, and the policeman's face struck the wood with great force, breaking his jaw and cheekbones before he pitched into the bay. There he floated for a moment, then dropped slowly to the bottom, from which he was recovered a day later.

"I'm afraid he's drowned," Mister Wilson said apprehensively.

"Let him drown," Hoxworth growled, licking his damaged lip. Then, grabbing a horn, he shouted ashore, "Don't anybody try to board this ship . . . now or ever." Tossing the horn to his mate, he brushed off his sweating chest, stamped his bare feet to knock away the pain and growled at Mister Wilson, "I was disgusted with your performance."

"I stood them off, one after the other," the mate protested.

"You fought all right," Hoxworth admitted grudgingly, "but you had stout shoes on, and when I had the bastards down you didn't kick them in the face."

"It didn't occur to me . . ." Mister Wilson began apologetically.

Quickly, furiously, Captain Hoxworth grabbed his mate by the jacket. "When you fight a man aboard ship, and he knows he's licked, always kick him in the face. Because forever after, when he looks in a mirror, he'll have to remember. If you let him go without scarring him, sooner or later he begins to think: 'Hoxworth wasn't so dangerous. Next time I'll thrash him.' But if he constantly sees the memory of solid leather across his jawbone he can't fool himself." Seeing that his mate was shaken by this advice, he pushed him away and added coldly, "Keeping control of a ship is difficult duty, Mister Wilson, and until you nerve yourself to it, you'll never be a captain."

Abruptly, he swung himself down the after ladder, shouting, "This time I don't want to be disturbed." And he rejoined Pupali's daughters.

Ashore there was consternation. On the one hand, Kelolo was appalled that Americans would dare to kill one of his policemen in sight of the entire community, and he hurried to Malama to ask her what ought to be done. She was suffering from major ills and lay back on the floor, wheezing in the day's heat, but when she heard Kelolo's ominous report she called her attendants and with real effort rose and dressed. Then, with her two ladies-in-waiting, she went into the town, and after assembling all available policemen, she proceeded to the pier.

On the other hand, the various ships' captains who had been chafing futilely against the new laws saw in Hoxworth's bold action a chance to re-establish their control over Lahaina and to restore the good old days. Accordingly, they too assembled at the pier and passed the word to their men: "If they try to arrest Captain Hoxworth, we'll all fight." And as the sailors gathered, they armed themselves with stones and where possible with substantial clubs.

Malama pointed to the *Carthaginian* and said quietly, "Kelolo, arrest that captain."

Obediently, though with some apprehension, Kelolo adjusted his police-man's cap, picked three unwilling helpers, tested his two muskets, and set out for the whaler, but he had gone less than half the distance when Captain Hoxworth, alerted by Mister Wilson, rushed on deck with a brace of pistols and began firing madly at the rowboat.

"Don't you come a foot nearer!" he shouted, reloading and blazing away again. This time the bullets struck perilously close to the boat, and Kelolo did not have to order his men to cease rowing. They did so automatically, stared at the infuriated captain, then quickly retreated. To the surprise of all the watchers, and to the cheers of the sailors, Captain Hoxworth unexpectedly, perhaps even to himself, now swung barefooted over the side of the *Carthaginian,* one re-volver in his left hand, one jammed into the belt of his trousers, and started rowing furiously ashore. The other sea captains formed a reception committee both to welcome and protect him. Before he had touched shore he was shouting, "Captain Henderson! Is that a cannon I see on the *Bay Tree?*"

"It is. I'm headin' for China."

"Got any balls?"

"I have."

Content, Hoxworth leaped ashore and strode up to Kelolo. Then seeing Malama in the background, he thrust the police chief aside and stormed over to the Alii Nui. "Ma'am!" he growled. "There's not goin' to be any more interference with the whalers in this port."

"The new laws have been announced," Malama said stoutly.

"The new laws be goddamned," Hoxworth stormed. The sailors cheered, so he left Malama abruptly and advised them, "Do any goddamned thing you like!"

The whaling captains applauded and one cried, "Can we bring whiskey ashore?"

"Whiskey, girls, any damned thing you want," Hoxworth roared. Then, seeing Kelolo's two assistants who carried the muskets, he rushed over, ripped the arms from them and fired twice into the air.

At this moment the crowd separated and onto the pier stepped Abner Hale, dressed formally in claw-hammer and top hat but still limping slightly from his old wound received at the hands of the blusterer who now threatened Lahaina's peace. Kelolo drew back, as did the bewildered policemen whose arms had been taken from them. "Good morning, Captain Hoxworth," Abner said.

The violent whaler stepped back, looked at the little missionary and laughed. "I threw this miserable little bastard to the sharks once. I'll do it again," he roared, and the captains, all of whom despised Abner as the author of the sumptuary laws, shouted encouragement.

"You will send the girl Iliki back to school," Abner said forcefully. The two men stared at each other for a long moment, and then almost unconsciously Captain Hoxworth's real intention in coming to Lahaina manifested itself. He wanted to see Jerusha Bromley. Desperately, driven by powerful memories and dreams of revenge, he wanted to see this brown-haired girl. He lowered his pistols, jammed them back into his pants, and said, "We can talk better at your house."

"Shall we bring the whiskey ashore?" one of the captains shouted.

"Of course!" Hoxworth snapped. "There are no laws."

"We'll meet at Murphy's!" the captains yelled.

"Where is your house?" Hoxworth asked.

"There," said Abner, pointing past the taro patch.

For a moment Captain Hoxworth stared aghast, and in his incredulity Abner perceived for the first time the really miserable hovel in which he and Jerusha lived. "Does Jerusha live there?" Hoxworth gasped, staring at the low grass roof, the rain-tattered walls and the Dutch doorway.

"Yes," Abner replied.

"Jesus Christ Almighty, man!" Hoxworth ejaculated. "What's the matter with you?" With huge strides the barefooted, barechested captain strode up the dusty road, kicked open the wooden gate in the high wall, and brushed into the grass house. Standing on the earthen floor he adjusted his eyes to the darkness, and finally saw, in the doorway that separated the children's quarters from Abner's study, the girl he had wanted to marry. He looked a long time, at the tired face, the hair not quite tended, the red hands. He saw the cast-off dress that did not fit, and the coarse shoes also second-hand, a size too large and scuffed from long years in the dust. Possibly because of the darkness, possibly because he did not wish to recognize such things, he did not see the persuasive radiance that shone from Jerusha's tired eyes nor did he sense the peace that encompassed her.

"My God, Jerusha! What has he done to you?" The harsh voice caused one of the children to whimper, and Jerusha left the doorway for a moment, but she soon returned and said, "Sit down, Captain Hoxworth."

"Where, for Christ's sake?" Hoxworth stormed, beside himself with anger and bitterness. "On a box? At a table like this?" With extreme violence he smashed at Abner's rickety table, sending the Bible translations into the wind. "Where could I sit down if I wanted to? Jerusha, do you call this a home?"

"No," the self-possessed woman replied, "I call this my temple."

The answer was so final, and implied so much, that Hoxworth set adrift his first fleet of compassionate thoughts and established in their place an overpowering desire to hurt Jerusha and her husband. Kicking at the fallen table he laughed, "So this is the senate from which the laws are handed down?"

"No," Abner said cautiously, recovering the fallen Bible, "this Book is."

"So you're going to rule Lahaina by the Ten Commandments?" Hoxworth asked with a hysterical laugh.

"As we rule ourselves," Abner replied.

Again Hoxworth kicked at the table, bruising his foot as he did so. "Does the Bible direct you to live like hogs? Does it say you have to work your wife like a slave?" Impulsively, he grabbed Jerusha's hand and held it aloft, as if he were selling her, but patiently she withdrew it and straightened her dress.

Her action infuriated Hoxworth and he backed away from the missionaries, lashing them horribly with insulting words, towering oaths and threats which he had the capacity to enforce. "All right, you goddamned sniveling little worms. You can pass the laws, but you can't make the fleet keep them. Reverend Hale, there's going to be women aboard those whalers by noon."

"The women will not be allowed to go," Abner said stubbornly.

"My men have been at sea for nine months," Hoxworth said. "And when they reach shore they're going to have women. All the goddamned black-assed Hawaiian women they want. Me. I always have two. One fat one and one skinny one."

"Will you go to the church, Jerusha?" Abner asked.

"She'll stay here!" Hoxworth shouted, grabbing her once more by the hand. "Let her hear how a real man lives." He had a consuming desire to abuse her mind with ugly pictures, to humiliate her. "Now when I get hold of a fat one and a skinny one, ma'am, I like to lock the door for about two days and I undress completely—that's why you find me only in pants; I was interrupted and had to kill a man—and when I'm undressed I like to throw myself back on the bed and say to the girls, 'All right, the first one of you who can . . .' " His explanation was halted by a stinging blow from Abner's open palm against his bruised lip.

He stopped in astonishment, then thrust out his big right arm and caught Abner by the wrist. Turning it until the missionary had to kneel in the dust of his own home, Hoxworth retained his hold on Jerusha and finished. "I tell the two girls that the first one who can make me get hard can climb aboard, and when she does the other one has to blow on me."

Jerusha kneeled in the dust beside her husband, and Rafer Hoxworth looked down with contempt at the two miserable creatures. "What're you doing, Jerusha?" he tormented. "Tending your little man?"

"I am praying for you," Jerusha said, in the dust. Impetuously, Hoxworth threw them both across the room and then stood over them, threateningly.

"There's a cannon aboard the *Bay Tree*, and by the guts of God, if there is any interference with the whaling fleet, I'll blow this house to pieces." He started for the open door but felt compelled to turn and laugh at the fallen missionaries. "You'll be interested to know that of all Pupali's daughters the young one, Iliki, is the best. Iliki . . . the Pelting Spray of the Sea! I started with Pupali's wife and worked my way right through his girls, but Iliki is my choice. And do you know why? Because you taught her such nice manners. Here at the mission. When she climbs on top of me she says, 'Please.' "

When he left, the two missionaries remained on their knees for some minutes, praying, and then Jerusha helped her husband rebuild the rickety table and collect his manuscript. Realizing that Captain Hoxworth meant his threats about the cannon, she took her two children over to Amanda Whipple's, but did not divulge the scenes that had taken place at the mission. Then she returned to Abner, desiring to be with him if further trouble developed.

It did. The general whaling fleet saw in Hoxworth's bold defiance a chance to abolish forever the restrictive laws, and they coursed through Lahaina tearing, raping and destroying. They drove policemen into hiding and then congregated at the new fort, where Kelolo and a last group of trusted subordinates were determined to make a stand.

"Rip down the fort!" sailors who had been jailed there shouted.

"Don't come any closer!" Kelolo warned. But before he took action, he climbed down from the frail ramparts and asked Malama what she thought he ought to do.

"What do you think is wisest?" Malama, breathing heavily, countered.

"I think we must defy them," Kelolo said gravely. "We have started good laws, and we must not surrender them now."

"I agree," Malama said, "but I do not want you to get hurt, my dear husband."

Kelolo smiled warmly at her use of this unexpected term, for he knew that she had been forbidden by the missionaries to use it in respect to him. "Do you feel better now?" he asked solicitiously, as if he were a courtier and not a husband.

"I feel very ill, Kelolo. Do you think they will fire the cannon? I should not like to hear the noise of such a great gun."

"I think they will fire," Kelolo said. "And then they will be ashamed of themselves. And after a while they will stop."

"Do you think they will kill anyone?" Malama asked fearfully.

"Yes."

"Kelolo, I hope above all else that they do not kill you. There could be no finer husband than you have been to me." The enormous woman tried to find an easy position and then asked, "Did they harm the missionaries?"

"I don't know," Kelolo said.

"Isn't it strange?" Malama asked. "The little man spends so much time telling us how the Hawaiians ought to behave, but it is always his people who do the wrong things."

There was fighting at the gate and Kelolo was called away to make decisions. He told his men not to fire their few guns, lest a hopeless riot be initiated, but he did encourage them to use poles to push away the ribald attackers, so that from the *Bay Tree* Captain Hoxworth could see through his glass some of his own men from the *Carthaginian* being knocked off the walls, at which he grew agitated beyond control, and personally wheeled the cannon into position, ordering a charge to be fired. The forty-pound ball whistled high through the palm trees near the fort and he shouted, "Down twenty feet!"

The next ball crashed into the fort and threw bits of rock high into the air. The third ball struck the gate area and demolished it, so that hundreds of sailors were free to storm inside, where they elbowed Kelolo aside and threatened Malama.

"See that missionary house?" Hoxworth shouted, elated at his success with the cannon. "Up there to the left. Smash it."

Again the first ball was high, and Hoxworth danced barefooted with excitement as he directed the sights lowered. The fifth shot of the day tore completely through the mission house, as did the sixth and seventh. "By God," the captain screamed, "that'll end the laws!"

And then, as if he had been struck by some terrible unseen hand, he clasped his breast, cursed at the gunners and knocked them about like stones in a child's game. "Goddamn you!" he screamed. "What are you doing?" And leaping into the bay, he swam furiously ashore. Dripping wet he rushed past the breached fort, where sailors were abusing the chief of police and the fat woman, and onto the mission grounds, where the splintered wood from the shattered grass house appalled him. Bursting into the room he had visited only shortly before, he cried in anguish, "Jerusha! Are you hurt?"

He did not find her and started looking under the fallen beams—frail bits of wood hauled patiently from the mountains—and then from the inner room he heard sounds, and he smashed open the niggardly woven door and saw Jerusha and her husband praying in the dust of their destroyed home. "Oh, thank God!" he yelled with joy, grabbing Jerusha to his bare and salty body. She did not resist, but passively looked at him with horror which was heightened when she saw that her husband was approaching him with a broken knife.

"No!" she found strength to scream. "God will do it, Abner!" And with relief such as she had never known before in her life, not even when Abner alone and sweating had delivered her first baby, she saw her husband drop his arm. Quickly, Captain Hoxworth wheeled about, saw the knife, and smashed his fist into Abner's pale face. The little man doubled up and flew backwards against the grass wall and through its weakened portion. From inside the room he could hear his wife struggling with the sea captain. Before he could regain his feet he heard her screams and then the captain's cry of rage as she bit into the great salty hand. By the time he could get back into the room, brandishing a club, he saw Hoxworth standing at the front door, what was left of it, sucking his fiercely bitten hand. And then, as if nothing had happened, the huge sea captain said sorrowfully, "It is a dreadful place that your husband has brought you to, Jerusha. When did you last have a new dress?" He started to go, then added almost in tears, "Why is it that we always meet when you are pregnant . . . by this goddamned fool?"

The rioting continued for three more days, and girls who had been well along in Jerusha's school, standing midway between the savage and the civilized, reverted to the insane joy of sleeping, six and eight and ten at a time, in the hot fo'c's'ls of the whaling ships. Murphy's grog shop rollicked with songs. Old men who tried to keep sailors out of their homes were beaten up, and their daughters taken. And at the palace, tired, bewildered Malama ordered all women to the hills and found it increasingly difficult to breathe.

It was on the third day of the riots that she summoned Abner and asked with difficulty, "How did these things happen, my dear teacher?"

"We are all animals, Malama," he explained. "Only the laws of God keep us within the confines of decency."

"Why have your men not learned those laws?" Malama asked.

"Because Lahaina has itself been so long without the law. Wherever there is no law, men think they can do as they will."

"If your king knew about these days . . . the cannon and the burning of the houses . . . would he apologize?"

"He would be humiliated," Abner affirmed.

"Why is it that the Americans and the English and the French are so determined that we sell whiskey in our stores . . . and allow our girls to go to their ships?"

"It is because Hawaii has not yet established herself as a civilized nation," Abner explained.

"Are your men civilizing us?" Malama asked wearily. "By firing the cannon at us?"

"I am ashamed for our men," Abner said in despair.

This was the moment Malama had been waiting for, and after a long pause she said softly, "Now we are equal, Makua Hale."

"In what way?" Abner asked suspiciously.

"You have always told me that I could not achieve a state of grace without humility, without admitting to God that I am lost and totally evil. You would not accept me into your church because you claimed I was not humble. Makua Hale, I will tell you something. I wasn't humble. And you were right to keep me out of your church. But do you know why I could not be humble?"

"Why?" Abner asked carefully.

"Because you were not humble. Your ways were always right. Mine were always wrong. Your words were always white. Mine were black. You tried to make me speak Hawaiian because you wanted to learn Hawaiian, and I would not beg to join your church, because you spoke of humility but knew it not. Today, Makua Hale, with the fort destroyed and your home knocked down by your own people, we are equal. I am humble at last. I am unable to act without God's help. And for the first time I see before me a humble man."

The great huge woman began to weep, and after a moment she rose painfully to her knees, pushing aside her sorrowful attendants and making a prayer-temple of her hands. From that position she said in total contrition, "I am lost, Makua Hale, and I beg you to accept me into your church. I am going to die and I want to speak with God before I do."

From the *Bay Tree* some fools were firing the cannon again at the house of a man and wife who would not give them their daughter, and at the western end of town a building was ablaze. There was a dance under way at Murphy's, and three of Pupali's daughters were in Captain Hoxworth's cabin. It was under these conditions that Abner said, "We will baptize you into the church of God, Malama. We will do it on Sunday."

"We had better do it now," Malama suggested, and one of the waiting-women nodded, so Abner sent for Jerusha, Keoki, Noelani, Kelolo, Captain Janders and the Whipples. They came through the rioters, who jeered at Janders for not being a real sea captain and at the Whipples for being missionaries, but when Dr. Whipple saw Malama he was greatly concerned and said, "This woman is very ill," at which huge Kelolo began to sob.

It was a mournful crowd that formed a semicircle around Malama, who lay flat on the floor, wheezing painfully. The cannon sounded in the distance, and half a hundred hoodlums who had trailed the Whipples jeered outside the palace gates. Without a Bible, Abner recited from memory the closing passages of Proverbs, and the words had a special application to Malama, the Alii Nui: " 'Strength and honor are her clothing; and she shall rejoice in time to come. She openeth her mouth with wisdom; and in her tongue is the law of kindness. She looketh well to the ways of her household, and eateth not the bread of idleness.' "

Then he announced to the gathering: "Malama Kanakoa, daughter of the King of Kona, having entered into a state of grace, seeks baptism into the holy church of God. Is it your wish that she be accepted?"

Keoki spoke first, then Janders and the Whipples, but when it came time for Jerusha, who in the last days had appreciated for the first time the courage Malama had shown in governing Maui, she did not speak but bowed down and kissed the sick woman. "You are my daughter," Malama said weakly.

Abner interrupted and said, "Malama, you will now put aside your heathen name and take a Christian one. Which do you wish?"

A look of supreme joy came over the sick woman's massive face and she whispered, "I should like the name of that dear friend of whom Jerusha has often told me. My name will be Luka. Jerusha, will you tell me the story for the last time?"

And as if she were talking to her own children at dusk, Jerusha began once more the story of Ruth—Luka to the Hawaiians—and when she came to the part about the alien land she broke down and was unable to continue, so Malama concluded the story, adding, "May I like Luka find happiness in the new land to which I shall soon go."

After the baptism, Whipple suggested, "You'd better leave now. I have to examine Malama."

"I'll die with the old medicines, Doctor," Malama said simply, and she indicated to Kelolo that he must now bring in the kahunas.

"Are kahunas proper, when we have just . . ." Abner began, but Jerusha pulled him away, and the little procession marched back to the center of town, where Amanda Whipple suggested, "You had better stay with us, Jerusha and Abner."

"We will stay in our house," Jerusha said firmly, and when they were there, after the riotings had subsided and the ship captains were beginning to feel ashamed of themselves, for natives were whispering that sailors at the fort had killed Malama, or had caused her near-death, Captain Rafer Hoxworth, fully dressed, with polished cap and buttons, came up the pathway to the mission house, followed by five sailors with armloads of gifts.

Tucking his hat under his arm, as he had long ago been taught to do when addressing a lady, he said gruffly, "I apologize, ma'am. If I have broken anything I want to replace it. The other captains have contributed these chairs and this table . . ." He paused in some embarrassment and then added, "And I've gone among the ships and got this cloth. I trust you'll make yourself some decent . . . I mean some new dresses, ma'am." He bowed, placed his hat on his head, and left the mission grounds.

At first Abner was intent upon demolishing the furniture. "We'll burn it on the pier," he threatened, but Jerusha would not permit this.

"It has been sent to us as an act of retribution," she said firmly. "We have always needed chairs and a desk."

"Do you think that I could translate the Bible . . . on that desk?" Abner asked.

"Captain Hoxworth did not send it," Jerusha replied, and while her husband watched, she started arranging the chairs in the damaged room. "God has sent these things to the mission," she said, "and not to Abner and Jerusha Hale."

"I'll give the cloth to Malama's women," Abner insisted, and to this Jerusha agreed, but when he was gone, and the town was once more quiet, she sat in one of the new chairs at her new kitchen table and composed this letter:

"My dearest Sister Esther in God. You alone of all the people I know will have the grace to forgive me for what I am about to do. It is an act of vanity and one, under the circumstances of my life, truly unforgivable, but if it is sinful, it must rest on me alone, and I am powerless to avoid it. Dearest sister, do not smile at me and above all tell no one of my vanity.

"You have often asked me if there might be some small thing that you could send me, and I have always replied that God provided for my dear husband and me, and that is the truth. The mission board has sent us all that we require, but lately, as I grow older, I realize with some dismay that it has been many years since I have worn a dress that was made particularly for me. Quickly I must add that those which they send us from the charity barrels are good, and in fine style, but I find myself desiring just once more a dress of my own.

"I should like it to be russet in color, with either blue or red trimming, and I would be especially grateful to you if it could have the full round sleeves that seem to be in popular style today. I saw such a dress some years ago on a woman heading for Honolulu, and I thought it very becoming. But if the styles have changed substantially, and if there is now a fashion that I do not know of, I would rather wish you to follow the newer style. Hats I do not need, but if you could find it in your heart to send me a pair of gloves, with lace as in the old days, I should be most deeply appreciative.

"I do not need to tell you, dearest Esther, that I have no money wherewith to pay you for this extraordinary request, for I have not seen a dollar in over seven years and do not require to see any; and I appreciate that this is a vain and costly imposition to place upon a friend. But I pray that you will understand.

"I am not as stout as I used to be, and seem not to be as tall, so do not make the dress too large. I would judge from what your dear brother tells me that I am now about your size, but I do not want one of your dresses or anybody's. The cloth must be wholly new and mine. And may you find the charity in your heart to forgive me for this begging letter. Your sister, Jerusha."

When she went to Janders & Whipple's store to post the letter she discovered that the *Carthaginian* had sailed and that lovely Iliki, Pupali's youngest, had joined the captain. She felt sorrier for this than for anything that had happened in the past days, and she could not refrain from tears. "She was an adorable child," Jerusha said mournfully. "We shall not find another like her. Already I feel her departure as a great loss, for I had come to think of her as my own daughter. I do hope the world is good to Iliki." And she tried to dry her eyes, but the tears would not cease.

O NE OF THE last public acts Malama performed was to climb into her land canoe, adjusting herself painfully on piles of tapa and directing her bearers to carry her through the damaged streets. Wherever she went she said simply, "The laws we gave are good laws. They must be obeyed." She stopped to encourage policemen, and at Murphy's grog shop again announced, in short gasps: "No more alcohol may be sold to Hawaiians. Girls must stop dancing here undressed." And the force of her words, coming as it did so soon after the riots, was four times what it had been before, and gradually Kelolo's policemen retrieved the control they had lost, and gained more besides. In her ludicrous canoe, followed by her two enormous ladies-in-waiting and the men with feathered staves, Malama became a figure of considerable dignity.

Both Abner and Jerusha noticed that on this strange canoe journey Malama's children, Keoki and Noelani, were drawn closely to her, and at the fort, where the largest congregation had assembled, Malama went so far as to announce: "I am going to die. My daughter Noelani will be the Alii Nui." There was no applause, but the citizens studied the handsome young girl with increased respect.

Abner now observed that the important kahunas of the island were gathering about Malama and arguing with her fervently, and he assumed that they were trying to cajole their renegade leader into abandoning her new religion, but this was not the case. The kahunas were satisfied with Christianity and were willing to acknowledge that its god was patently superior to their own, so prudence alone directed them to respect the potent newcomer; but they were also eager to overlook nothing in protecting their calm and massive alii in her last days, so as Abner prayed to Jehovah, they silently prayed to Kane. They massaged Malama with special care, sought traditional herbs to soothe her, and prepared favorite foods, on which she continued to gorge, feeling that only in this way had she any chance of recovering her strength. She ate four times a day, and sometimes five, and at a normal meal consumed a pound or two of roast pig, part of a dog, some baked fish, a substantial helping of breadfruit and not less than a quart of poi and oftentimes two or three, after which the lomilomi women would kneed her stomach to spur her faltering digestion. Dr. Whipple stormed: "She's eating herself to death, but she started doing so when she was twenty. Such fantastic meals!"

When word reached the other islands that Malama, daughter of the King of Kona, was dying, the alii assembled, as they had at deathbeds for untold generations, and in after years whenever an American who had been in Lahaina at the time was asked for his most vivid impression of the island, he never referred to the cannonading but to this last mournful gathering of the alii: "They came from distant Kauai in ships and from Lanai in canoes. They came singly and in groups. Some came in western clothes, I recall, and some in yellow capes. But they all landed at our little pier, walked gravely past Kamehameha's old palace and eastward along the dusty road beneath the kou trees. I can see them now. What giants they were!"

Queen Kaahumanu, regent of the islands, came attended by Queens Liliha and Kinau, both of enormous girth. From Hawaii came Princess Kalani-o-mai-heu-ila, heavier by forty pounds than Malama, and from Honolulu, Kauikeaouli, the boy king. The great men of the islands were there: Paki and Boki and Hoapili and the leader called by westerners Billy Pitt; and Dr. Whipple, seeing them assemble, thought: "In one lifetime they lifted their islands from paganism to God, from the Stone Age to the modern. And to do so they had to fight off the Russians, the English, the French, the Germans and the Americans. Every time a civilized warship came to their islands it was to make them turn over girls for the sailors or rum to the natives." They were an amazing race, the old alii of Hawaii, and now as they gathered in formal panoply for the death of Luka Malama Kanakoa they seemed to be mourning for themselves.

Dr. Whipple observed to Abner: "They are like echoes of the great animals that once roamed the world and marched slowly to their death as changes overtook them."

"What animals?" Abner asked suspiciously.

"The monstrous ones before the ice ages," Whipple explained. "Some scientists think they vanished because they became too huge to be accommodated on the changing earth."

"I have no interest in such speculation," Abner replied.

In her grass palace Malama greeted each of the great old friends. "Aloha nui nui," she repeated constantly.

"Auwe, auwe!" they wept. "We have come to weep with our beloved sister."

When extreme pain in breathing attacked her, she bit her lower lip and gasped through the corners of her big mouth, resuming her smile as soon as the pain passed, while around her, in a vast semicircle, hunched the alii, whispering to themselves and praying.

Now Kelolo decided that it was time to move the woman he had loved so deeply onto the bed where she would die, so he sent his men to the hills to fetch bundles of fragrant leaves—api for protection against evil spirits, ti for healing, and mysterious maile whose penetrating aroma was the best loved—and when these leaves arrived, redolent and reminiscent of courtship days on Hawaii, Kelolo gently broke the back of each one so as to release its odor, and he arranged them in a formal pattern over the tapa blanket. Over this fragrant bed he placed a softly woven pandanus mat, and then a soft tapa, and over all a sheet of Cantonese silk embroidered with golden dragons. And whenever giant Malama moved on this bed, she caught the smell of maile.

Next, Kelolo went to the beach and had his fishermen procure fresh ahole-hole, which in the old custom of the islands he cooked himself. He grated coconuts and saw to the baking of breadfruit, and in her last days she ate not a morsel except from his fingers. In the long hours of the night it was he who waved the soft feathered wands to keep away the flies from the great sleeping body that he had loved so well, and he never approached her except on his hands and knees, for he wished to remind her that she was the Alii Nui, the one from whom his mana came. But what pleased her most was the morning, when Kelolo would leave her for a while and then come creeping back to her on his elbows, for his arms would be filled with red lehua blossoms and ginger and yellow hau. He brought them to her with dew still upon them, as he had done years ago, before the clashing battles of Kamehameha had interrupted their lives.

She died looking at Kelolo, seeing him as he had been in their youth, before strange gods and missionaries had intervened between them, but her last words reflected the new society which she had been instrumental in launching: "When I die no one must knock out his teeth. No one must blind his eye. There must be no furious lamenting. I shall be buried as a Christian." Then she summoned Kelolo and whispered to him for the last time, raising herself upon her elbow to do so, so that when she expired she fell backwards, a mighty surge of lifeless flesh, crushing the maile leaves.

Malama's wish was granted, and she was accorded a Christian burial in a cedar box on an island in the center of a marshy area where the alii had often gone on outings. Abner preached a moving graveside sermon, and the towering alii, standing beside the first Christian grave that many of them had ever seen, thought: "This is a better way to bury a woman than the old way," but the common people, not allowed onto the kapu island, stood on the shores of the river and wept piteously in the old fashion. None of them, however, knocked out their teeth or gouged their living eyeballs as they had done in the past when an alii nui died. Instead they watched in awe as the funeral procession formed: Makua Hale and his wife in front, intoning prayers for their beloved friend, followed by Captain Janders and Dr. Whipple and their wives. Then came the kahunas wreathed in maile and secretly muttering old heathen chants to themselves, followed by the towering alii, weeping in massive grief. Eight of the men, wearing yellow capes, carried poles on which was placed the cedar box. It was covered with maile and lehua blossoms and by a huge silken coverlet embroidered in purple dragons.

When the silent mourners reached the actual grave, the alii began to cry, "Auwe, auwe for our eldest sister." And the noise became so pitiful that Abner, attending to the Christian burial that was to expel heathen rituals, failed to observe that Kelolo, Keoki and Noelani did not approach the grave, but remained apart, conspiring with the major kahunas. What Kelolo confided was this: "When Malama whispered to me at her death she said, 'Let them bury me in the new way. It will help Hawaii. But when the missionary is finished, do not let my bones be found.'"

The plotters stared at each other gravely, and as Abner commenced his long prayer an old kahuna whispered, "It is right that we should respect the new religion, but it would be a shameful thing to the house of Kanakoa if her bones were found."

Another whispered, "When Kamehameha the Great died he gave those same instructions to Hoapili, and at night Hoapili crept away with his bones, and to this day no man knows where they are hidden. That is the way of an alii."

And while Abner pleaded, "Lord, take Thy daughter Malama!" the oldest kahuna whispered hoarsely to Kelolo, "Such a deathbed wish is binding above all others. You know what you must do."

At the grave the three missionary couples raised their harmonious voices in "Blest be the tie that binds," while each member of Kelolo's mysterious group whispered in turn, "It is your duty, Kelolo," but no such confirmation was really necessary, for from the moment Malama had whispered to her husband, he had realized what he must do. Therefore, when the singing at the graveside ended and Abner led the congregation in final prayer, Kelolo prayed: "Kane, guide us in the right way. Help us, help us." And the first Christian burial in Lahaina ended.

But as the funeral procession returned to the boats, Kelolo gently held his son's hand and whispered, "I would be happy, Keoki, if you would stay."

This was an invitation which the young man had anticipated, even though he had hoped to escape it. Now that it had come, he accepted and said, "I will help you." In this quiet manner, his appalling decision was made.

For some time he had sensed that a trap was closing about him, for he had been unable to hide from his father and the kahunas his bitter disappointment over Reverend Hale's refusal to accept him as a minister, a resentment which deepened when both Dr. Whipple and Abraham Hewlett quit the calling, proving that from the start they had had less dedication to God than he. The kahunas had whispered, "The missionaries will never allow a Hawaiian to join them." On the other hand, from the moment of his conversion in the snow outside Yale College, he had been totally committed to God and still stood willing to suffer the humiliation of seeing men with less vocation than he admitted to the ministry. He loved God, knew Him personally, spoke with Him at sunset. He was willing to devote his entire life to God's desires and he was ashamed of himself for having wondered, "Why should I remain faithful if the missionaries reject me because I am Hawaiian?"

In a curious way he had been content with his ambivalent position of loving God while hating His missionaries, for so long as he remained in that delicate balance he could escape making definite choices; but with the death of his great mother he had been subtly drawn by both Kelolo and the kahunas to a fundamental reconsideration of his beliefs. The cannonading of Lahaina and its debauch by Christian Americans had already pushed him to a stark question: "Is this new religion good for my people?" Now, on the evening of his mother's burial, as the pagan sun sank behind the fawn-colored hills of Lanai, lighting the sea roads with shimmering gold as it had in the days before Captain Cook, Keoki made his choice between the religions. "I will help you," he told his father.

When darkness fell, Kelolo, Keoki and two strong young kahunas proceeded to the fresh grave of their Alii Nui and carefully lifted aside the flower leis that covered it. Then they produced digging sticks which had been hidden earlier that day, and they uncovered the cedar box, pried away the top and reverently lifted out the black Bible that lay on top. Then they saw once more, wreathed in maile, their great alii. Gently they rolled the vast inert body onto a canvas sling and returned to repair the grave.

"You will cut the banana trunk," Kelolo directed, and Keoki went to the center of the island and cut down a leafy trunk which from time out of mind had represented man to the gods, and when he had a length as tall as Malama, he returned to the coffin, and it was placed inside, lest the Lord God Jehovah be angry, and the Bible was put in place, and the grave was resealed, with the flowered leis scattered upon it. Then the four strong men lifted the canvas and carried Malama to her true burial.

In darkest night they rowed to the shore where none could see them, then started a mournful march toward the hills of Maui. Toward morning they reached a secluded valley, where as soon as light came they dug a shallow grave and filled its bottom with porous rocks, upon which they placed banana leaves and ti. When all was ready, they tenderly put Malama into the grave, covering her with a sacred tapa and then with moist leaves and grass. Next they piled the grave high with such sticks as they could find, and lighted it. For three days they kept the fire slowly burning as the kahunas chanted:

> "From the heat of living to the cool waters of Kane,
> From the desires of earth to the cool waters of Kane,
> From the burdens of desire to the cool retreats of Kane,
> Gods of the many islands, gods of the distant seas,
> Gods of the Little Eyes, gods of the stars and sun,
> Take her."

On the fourth day Kelolo opened the grave whose burning heat had baked away Malama's flesh, and with a sharp knife he severed her head from her gigantic skeleton. Carefully scraping the skull to remove all desiccated fragments, he wrapped it in maile leaves, then in tapa and finally in a closely woven pandanus mat. For so long as he lived, this would be his perpetual treasure, and as he grew older, in the evenings he would unwrap his beloved's head and talk with her. He would recall that before the Christians came she had loved tobacco. He would light his pipe and when the smoke was good, he would blow it into her mouth, knowing that she would appreciate his thoughtfulness.

Next he cut away one of the huge thigh bones, and this he gave to Keoki both to scrape and to keep, and the young man proceeded with his ancient task as if voices from the past were calling him.

Now Kelolo cut off the other leg, and scraped the thigh bone for Noelani, the Alii Nui, so that she would always have with her some reminder of the source from whence came her greatness, and when these jobs were done, Kelolo gathered the remaining bones and embers and handed them to one of the kahunas who had brought with him a curious bag of sennit, so constructed that it looked like a woman, and into this receptacle Malama's final remains were put. The sennit bag was handed to Kelolo, and with it under his left arm and the wrapped head under his right, he started forth alone on his final pilgrimage.

He walked through the heat of day far up the valley from which the whistling winds sometimes came to strike Lahaina, over the saddle, along the crest of hills and on to a cave which he had discovered while gathering maile. Here he stopped and, crawling carefully inside, collected lava rocks with which he built a small platform. Here, safe from the corrupting earth, he deposited the last royal remains of his wife. Then, as in the old times, he prayed. When this was done he sat for more than an hour staring at the desolate and hidden pile of rocks.

"Oh, Kane!" he suddenly screamed, repeating the anguished shout until the cave echoed and until he became hysterical with grief. He threw himself against the platform, took a fragment of rock into his lips, ground it between his teeth until his whole body was racked with ugliness and despair. Beating the stones with his fists he screamed, "Malama, I cannot leave you. I cannot."

When he regained composure, he started a small fire beside the platform, then raved afresh as pungent smoke filled the cave. Grabbing a piece of bark he formed a tube which he held in the flames until it was ablaze, whereupon he jammed it against his cheek until he could feel the flesh burning in a small circle. Again and again he did this, seeking to scar his face so that all who saw him would know that he mourned the death of his alii.

Then, when the pain of burnt flesh was great, he grasped a pointed stick and jammed it between his two big front teeth. With a heavy rock he began to pound the opposite end, but his teeth were strong and would not break. In the quietness of the cave, with the smoke about him, he cursed his teeth and struck the stick with enormous force until he felt a horrible wrenching in his upper jaw. The bone had broken and the tooth dangled free. Clutching it with his fingers he jerked it loose and placed it upon the lava rocks, whereupon with demonic power he knocked its companion out with the stone itself, gashing his lips as he did so.

"Oh, Malama! Malama! Cherished of my heart, Malama!" In his misery he wept for some moments. Then with superhuman resolution he took the stick again and placed its dulled point next to his nose and in the corner of his right eye. With a sudden inward thrust followed by a lateral pull, he scooped away his eye and threw it onto the grave. Then he fainted.

It was ten days before the powerful chief Kelolo Kanakoa reappeared in Lahaina. He came walking erect, proudly, but removed, as if he were still in contact with his gods. About his shoulders he wore a lei of maile leaves, its fragrance reminding him of his departed wife. His right eye socket, a horrible wound, was covered with morning-glory leaves, bound in place by olona and ti. His cheeks were scarred with ugly blisters and his lips, when closed, were thick with wounds; when opened they disclosed a lacerated jaw. He moved like a man set free from grief, a man who walked with love, and as he passed, his Hawaiian friends, knowing what he had done, stepped aside with respect; but his American friends stopped with horror, wondering how he could have borne so much.

It was important that he warn Reverend Hale, but when Jerusha saw him she screamed, but he was not offended, saying through lisping lips, "The whistling wind is coming. It always does at the death of an alii."

"What is the wind?" Jerusha asked, trying to compose herself, for she realized that he was speaking with great conviction.

"The whistling wind is coming," he repeated and stalked off, a man apart.

When Jerusha told her husband of the message, and of Kelolo's appearance, Abner held his head in his hands, lamenting, "These poor, bewildered people. Thank God we gave her a Christian burial." And Jerusha agreed, saying, "We should be grateful that Malama forbade heathen practices."

They grieved for obstinate Kelolo, and finally Jerusha asked, "What was the wind he spoke about?"

"One of his superstitions," Abner explained. "He's probably in a trance because of the horrible things he did to himself and is convinced that since an alii died, there will have to be some supernatural occurrence."

"Is the wind rising?" Jerusha asked.

"No more than usual," her husband replied, but as he spoke he heard a weird whistling coming down from the distant valleys that led to the crests of the hills where Malama, unknown to them, now lay.

"Abner," Jerusha insisted, "I do hear a whistling."

Her husband cocked his ear, then ran out into the dusty roadway. Dr. Whipple and Captain Janders were already listening to the ominous sound, while Hawaiians were running out of their houses and huddling under trees. "What is it?" Abner cried.

"Not like anything I ever heard," Janders replied, and the moaning whistle increased in pitch while high in the coconut palms dead branches began to tear loose. A Hawaiian sailor, who had swum in panic from one of the whalers, abandoning the ship to its fate, dashed by, wet and frightened and shouting in Hawaiian, "The whistling wind is upon us!"

"Should we go inside?" Abner asked hesitantly, but the same sailor yelled back over his shoulder, "No stay in house! Bimeby come plenty pilikia." And the three Americans remarked that the Hawaiians, who seemed to know what the wind could do, had abandoned their huts. Abner was already on his way to collect his children when Murphy, the saloon-keeper, rushed up and shouted, "This wind is a killer! Get out of your houses!" And while the three men scattered, the first important gust of wind struck Lahaina.

It bent the palm trees level, ripped off the roofs of several houses, then roared out to sea, where it threw great clouds of spume across the roads and tore away the masts of two whalers. During its destructive passage the whistling increased to an intense shriek and then subsided. Under the protection of a clump of kou trees Janders asked, "Where's the rain?"

None came, but the wind howled down from the mountains in new gusts, knocking down trees and throwing pigs into ditches. From the little stream before the mission house it picked up water, flinging it upon the trees, then passed out to sea, where it dashed three moored whalers together, staving in the sides of one and leaving it in perilous condition.

Still no rain came, but the winds increased, rising to even more furious levels than before, and now it became evident why the Hawaiians had left their homes, for one after another the little huts went flying through the air, crashing into the first solid object that intervened. "Will these trees hold?" Abner asked anxiously, but before anyone could assure him he saw a dark object hurtling through the air and cried, "The church!"

"It's the roof," Whipple shouted, astonished at what he saw. "It's the entire roof!" Majestically, the roof sailed over the town of Lahaina and plunged into the sea. "The walls are going down!" Whipple cried as the wind utterly destroyed the building.

But before Abner could lament his new loss, a woman shrieked, "The whaling boats are sinking!" And she was correct, for in the roads the demonic wind, still with no rain, had whipped up a sea that the rugged whalers could not survive. The unfortunate ones were those who were torn loose from their anchorages and dashed across the roads to the island of Lanai, on whose steep and rocky shores no rescue was possible. In that manner four ships and seventy men perished, and as they died, the Hawaiians of Lahaina mourned, "They are the sacrifices for the death of our Alii Nui."

Therefore, the sailors whose ships capsized off Lahaina would also have perished at the feet of the fatalistic Hawaiians had not Abner Hale limped among them, shouting, "Save those poor men! Save them!" But the Hawaiians repeated, "They are sacrifices!" until in frenzy Abner rushed up to one-eyed

Kelolo, screaming above the storm, "Tell them, Kelolo! Tell them Malama does not require sacrifices! Tell them she died a Christian!"

There was a moment's hesitation during which the old man, weak from his vigil in the cave, looked out at the sickening sea. Then, throwing aside his tapa breechclout, he plunged into the waves and began fighting them for the bodies of sailors. Ashore Abner organized rescue parties which waded, tied together by ropes, onto the reef from which most of the water had been blown by the fantastic winds. At the end of each line swimmers like Kelolo battled the turbulent waters to haul foundering sailors across the jagged reef's edge, delivering them into the hands of rescuers. Without the work of Kelolo and Abner, the loss of American sailors would have been not seventy but nearly three hundred.

Toward the end of the struggle, Abner was limping about the reef, shouting encouragement, when he received from the hands of a swimmer the already dead body of a cabin boy, and he was overcome by the ceaseless tragedy of the sea and he started to pray: " 'They that go down to the sea in ships, that do business in great waters; These see the works of the Lord, and His wonders in the deep.' " But his prayer was halted when he looked into the violent storm and saw that the swimmer who had handed him the boy was Kelolo, who was shouting to the other Hawaiians, "Pray to Kanaloa for strength." And Abner could see that the swimmers were praying.

When the whistling wind subsided, Abner sat limply beneath the kou trees, watching Dr. Whipple treat the rescued sailors, and when the doctor came to him for a rest, Abner asked, "These things couldn't have had any connection with Malama's death, could they?" When Whipple made no reply, he continued, "John, you're a scientist." From the day Whipple left the mission, Abner had never again referred to him as Brother. "How do you explain such a wind? No rain? Coming not from the sea but from the mountains?"

Even while helping to rescue the whalers, Whipple had been perplexed by this problem and now suggested, "The mountains on the other side of our island must form a curious kind of funnel. I would judge there must be wide-open valleys up which the trade winds rush. When they roll over the tops of the mountains, the entire volume is compressed into this one narrow valley leading down into Lahaina."

"That wouldn't have anything to do with the death of an alii, would it?" Abner asked suspiciously.

"No. We can explain the wind as it roars down this side of the mountain. We know that's a force of nature. But of course," he added slyly, "it's entirely possible that the wind on the other side of the mountain blows only when an alii dies." Shrugging his shoulders he added, "And if that's the case, why you have just about what Kelolo claims."

Abner started to comment on this but instead changed the subject. "Tell me, John, how did you feel, at the very height of the storm, when you were on the reef rescuing the sailors . . . seeing the whalers that had so recently been tormenting us . . . well, seeing them destroyed by the Lord?" Dr. Whipple turned to study his companion, staring at him in disbelief, but Abner continued: "Didn't you feel that it was something like . . . well, I thought it was like the Egyptians at the Red Sea."

Whipple got up, disgusted, and called his wife, who was tending wounded sailors. "I don't think the alii sent the wind, and I don't think God sank the ships," he growled and left.

But he had not waited for Abner to develop the full meaning of his speculations, as they had matured on the coral reef, so Abner chased him and said,

"What I wanted to ask, John, was this: 'At that moment of what I have called God's revenge for the cannonading, did you feel any actual sense of revenge against the sailors?' "

"No," Whipple said flatly. "All I thought was, 'I hope we can save the poor devils.' "

"I thought the same thing," Abner said frankly, "and I was astonished at myself."

"You're growing up," Whipple said sharply and left.

O NE UNEXPECTED BENEFIT came from the whistling wind that leveled much of Lahaina in 1829. When the damage was cleared away, Kelolo for the third time helped Abner rebuild his church, but this time the kahunas refused even to argue where the door should be. They put it where it should have been in the first place, where the local gods ordained, and the famous stone church they built that year stood for more than a century.

Now Lahaina, most beautiful of all Hawaiian towns, prospered as the national capital. The business center of the kingdom was Honolulu, to be sure, for foreigners preferred living near their consulates, but the alii had never liked Honolulu, finding it hot, cheerless and commonplace, so that even though it was true that the boy king and his regents had to spend more and more time there, he returned whenever possible to his true capital, Lahaina, and his women often remained in the cool grass houses under the kou trees even when he was called to the larger city.

Whaling vessels, their crews now better behaved, came to Lahaina in increasing numbers—78 would come in 1831, 82 in 1833—and because each stayed for about four weeks in the spring and four in the autumn, there were sometimes many tall-masted ships in the roads; and since the famous whistling wind of Lahaina blew only about twice a century, they rested in security within the charmed pocket of islands. The important thing to Janders & Whipple was that every whaler who came into the roads paid them a fee for something or other. Did the ship need firewood? J & W had it. Salt pork? Dr. Whipple found out how to salt down island hogs. Salt itself? J & W had a monopoly on the fine salt evaporated from the sea in flat lava-rock beds. Did a ship's captain insist upon fresh pork at sea? J & W could provide healthy live pigs and bundles of ti leaves for fodder on long trips. Sweet potatoes, oranges that had been introduced by Captain Cook, and fish dried by Dr. Whipple . . . J & W had them all. And if a ship required balls of olona twine, strongest in the world, or even cables woven of it, J & W controlled that monopoly, too.

It was John Whipple, however, who devised one of the simplest money-making schemes for the firm. When a whaler put in with an unwieldy amount of whale oil, not enough barrels to warrant sailing all the way home, but so many that there seemed no purpose in returning to the Off-Japan Banks, Whipple arranged for the captain to leave his entire cargo at Lahaina, under the care of J & W, who, when they had assembled half a dozen such cargoes, would argue some New England captain into running the entire lot back to New Bedford. In this way J & W made a profit on storing the barrels of oil, on shipping them, and on chartering the ship that did the work. It therefore seemed to Whipple that the next logical step ought to be for his firm to buy the odd lots of oil outright and to hold them on speculation.

Accordingly, he proposed that J & W acquire its own ships and take over the whale-oil business, but cautious Captain Janders, tugging at his red beard, was adamant. "Only one way to make money in this world," he judged. "My motto: 'Own nothing, control everything.' Own a batch of oil outright? Never! Because then you worry about the market. Let someone else own it. We'll handle it, and we'll make the better profit. But to own a ship. That is real madness. I've watched the tribulations of shipowners. They have to trust a rascally captain, a worse mate and a depraved crew. They've got to feed the lot, insure the vessel, live in anguish when there's a storm, and then share whatever profits there are with the crew."

"You bought the *Thetis*," Whipple argued.

"Sure!" Janders agreed. "I bought her, but did you see how fast I sold her? On an earlier trip I had watched Kelolo's mouth watering for such a ship, and I knew I could turn a quick profit. Me operate a ship on my own responsibility? Never!" And he pointed to the rotting hulk that still hung on the reef. "Whenever you want to buy a ship, John, always remember the *Thetis*."

Still Whipple was not satisfied, for he argued, "Somebody makes money on ships. I thought it might as well be us."

Janders agreed, in part, for he said, "I grant that properly handled a ship can make a little money, but if you and I learn how to manage the business and the lands right here, John, we'll make a fortune that will stagger the shipowners. Own nothing, control everything."

In the fields Captain Janders had determined to control, he was a master trader, sending meat to Oregon, picking up furs for Canton; sending hides to Valparaiso and tallow to California. He made a quick profit on each exchange and was always on hand when men were in trouble, for then money was free. Gradually, the whalers found that they could trust him with any transaction, and he became their agent. If a ship's captain wanted to risk the dying sandalwood trade, having heard that Captain Janders had made his fortune on it, J & W gladly accumulated the precious cargo and provided letters of introduction to the Canton merchants who would buy it. If another felt convinced that he could turn a handsome profit running fresh beef to Oregon, then ice to California, J & W would supply the live cattle, sending the crazy young cowboys of Lahaina up into the hills to lasso the wild animals that had been introduced into the islands by Captain Vancouver in 1794.

To win the good wishes of the mariners, J & W also provided many free services. If a sailor wanted to marry a native girl, there was no point in applying to Reverend Hale to conduct the ceremony, for he frowned on such alliances and invariably spent at least an hour praying with the sailor and pointing out that God had long ago warned against the sin of whoring after the heathen. Dr. Whipple, however, had been given the right by Kelolo to solemnize such marriages, and many families who were destined to live in Hawaiian history, producing the powerful half-caste politicians who organized the islands, sprang from marriages which started in the J & W store, where Reverend Whipple used Amanda, Captain Janders and his wife Luella as witnesses. Abner, of course, held that all participants in such marriages were living in whoredom, and he told them so.

J & W also served as mail drop for the fleet, and sometimes musty letters would lie in their bins for years before sailors came rolling up the wooden stairs and along the porch, shouting, "Any mail for me?" The wiry wanderer would sit in one of the J & W chairs and read of family affairs that had transpired forty months ago. Then he would ask John Whipple for a piece of paper, and the doctor would explain, "That building at the corner. It's a writing room for sailors, and if you ask for Mr. Cridland, he'll take care of everything."

Frequently, ship captains would transmit from the distant whaling grounds requests to J & W for a half-dozen replacements for their crews, to be picked up when the ship reached Lahaina. Captain Janders knew that whalers preferred stout Hawaiian boys, and he provided them at five dollars a head, but when none were available, he would visit Kelolo and tell the one-eyed, toothless police marshal, "Round up eight or ten deserters for next month," and Kelolo would move his men through the countryside, dragging in as worthless a lot of murderers, cowards, shipjumpers, adulterers and hopeless drunks as any nation of the day could have provided. No American deserter could be so degenerate or worthless but that some kind Hawaiian family would give him refuge; they even fought the police to keep the murderers from arrest, but when the rogues were finally lodged in jail, Mr. Cridland, from the Seamen's Chapel, would move among them, explaining, "If you're taken back to America in chains, you'll be tried and sent to jail. But if you volunteer, you'll not only get wages but also escape trial." And with Abner's help, usually in the form of long prayers with the dissolute rogues, Cridland would whip the men into reasonable shape, and as soon as the shorthanded whaler hove into sight, Kelolo would release the imprisoned vagabonds, and Captain Janders would march them to the pier, where he would announce to the incoming captain: "A fine lot of men here for you to choose from!" And on every such recruitment J & W would make its small commission.

Other letters of more personal content sometimes arrived, and one day in 1831 Captain Janders sent Whipple through Lahaina, seeking the Hawaiian Pupali, for a letter awaited him from Valparaiso and it appeared to contain a substantial sum of money. When fat Pupali came to the store, Janders explained, "I no savvy, Pupali! One lettah for you, but."

"Me no savvy read," Pupali grinned.

"Okay. You lissen for me. I speak for you dis papah," Janders said.

"Alu, alu," Pupali nodded, his eyes bright with anticipation.

When Janders opened the Valparaiso letter, a handful of British pound notes fluttered to the floor, and Pupali jumped upon them, pinning them down one after another, like a man swatting cockroaches. "Pehea dis money? It b'long for me?" he grinned.

"We'll see," Janders said, pressing out the thin paper on which the letter was written. " 'To my good friend Pupali, of Lahaina,' " Janders began. "Well, at least the letter's for you. Now we'll see about the money," Janders announced, and fat Pupali laughed at the large circle that had now gathered at the startling news that one of their men had received a document from Valparaiso.

"Who's it from?" an onlooker asked, and Captain Janders carefully smoothed down and inspected the last few lines of the message. "It's from Captain Hoxworth!" he said with some surprise. At the name of the feared whaler, some of the Hawaiians drew back, for the memory of Hoxworth's cannonading was still vivid in their memories.

"Wha kine talk he make?" Pupali asked.

"I am sending you herewith, my long and trusted friend, the sum of forty-five pounds sterling, which is a goodly sum of money and which an English ship captain whom I bespoke off the Japan Coast gave me as a present when I gave him your daughter Iliki. He was a fine-looking man and promised to treat her well and said he would take her home with him to Bristol when his cruise was over. Since Bristol is on the other side of the world, you will probably not see Iliki again, but when I last saw her she was happy and in good health. I could not bring her back to Lahaina as I had made a full cargo off Japan and was sailing directly home, where a girl like Iliki would not be well received. Since I had to do something, it seemed to me better that I pass her along to a decent English captain than leave her in Valparaiso, where she would certainly get into trouble. I am sending you his entire gift, less five pounds which I gave Iliki for herself, because I think it good for a woman to have some money of her own in a strange country. I hope to see you again soon. Give my love to your wife and your other daughters. They are all good girls. Your trusted friend, Rafer Hoxworth."

It was the island consensus that Captain Hoxworth had behaved rather well in this matter, for all who knew Valparaiso and New England agreed that a girl like Iliki would not have prospered in either locale, and while it seemed likely that the English captain would pass her along to some other ship when the time came for him to return to Bristol, there was always the chance that he might grow fond of the lively girl and take her with him. Lahaina believed implicitly that the gift had indeed been fifty English pounds and that Captain Hoxworth had accounted honestly for all of it. His foresight in sequestering five pounds for the girl herself was widely praised, and carefree Pupali was suddenly looked upon as a wealthy man.

But the transaction was forcefully condemned by Reverend Hale, who, as soon as he heard of it, hurried to J & W to satisfy himself that the letter was authentic. He then sought out Pupali and charged in Hawaiian: "You cannot keep that money, Pupali. For a father to profit from the sale of his own daughter would be infamous."

"Is it a great kapu?" the fat Hawaiian asked, with his wife and three daughters at his elbows.

"A kapu so horrible that there is no word for it," Abner explained.

"But you just used a word for it," Pupali hopefully pointed out.

"I used several words," Abner snapped. "What I mean is that civilized languages are not required to have a single word because such an act . . ." He stopped in confusion and started over by stating flatly, "It is a horrible act, Pupali. You cannot keep that money."

"What shall I do with it?" Pupali asked.

"I think," Abner said after due reflection, "that you should turn it over to the church . . . absolve yourself of the sin of which you are now a part."

Pupali got the money, laid it out carefully and studied it. Then he shook his head negatively. "No," he reasoned, "if this money is as kapu as you say, isn't it better that it harm only me and not something as fine as your church?"

Abner coughed and explained, "It has always been the job of the church to correct the wrongs in any society, Pupali. If you give the money to a worthy cause, its kapu will be washed away."

"On the other hand," Pupali argued, "your fine church has already been destroyed twice because the spirits of the land were angry at the way you built it . . ."

"It was a fire and a wind," Abner corrected.

"And now if you make even your own god angry at the church, it would surely burn down again," Pupali reasoned triumphantly. "So I cannot let you run this risk, Makua Hale. I will keep the money." In fact, things had worked out so well for the shiftless man through the sale of Iliki, that he now started introducing his three other daughters to as many whaling captains as possible, but they had grown fat and careless and found no takers.

*   *   *

IN SPITE OF many such defeats, these were good years for Abner and Jerusha. They now had four children, two boys and two girls, each apparently gifted with superior intelligence. Abner was disappointed that the young ones could not play with the Janders and Whipple children, but since both Mrs. Janders and Amanda stubbornly allowed their offspring not only to associate with Hawaiians but actually speak that lascivious language, the Hale youngsters were kept rigidly alone within their walled garden. They appeared at church each Sunday, handsomely scrubbed, and often at twilight Abner would lead them to the waterfront, where they would study the marvelous islands that rimmed Lahaina Roads, and the clever children would play the game of "Spot the Whales!" in which at proper seasons of the year they would try to detect mother whales and their babies. The family came to enjoy these end-of-day respites as the finest part of the week, and much of the poetry of speech that marked the children derived from these hours when they watched the sunsets and the islands. In December the sun set almost over the middle of Lanai, as if it were a fireball going back to sleep in the dead volcano of that gracious island, but in June the great fiery sun sank off the coast of Molokai, rushing with crimson and orange streamers into the blue ocean. Then, with daylight fading, the children would listen for the talking owls and the gentle motion of the rising wind in the coconut palms.

What they loved best, however, was when their father pointed toward the rotting hulk of the *Thetis* and said, "I remember when your dear mother and I sailed from Boston in that brig." And he convinced the children that they belonged to three precious fraternities: "You are the children of God. All men are your brothers. And you are descended from the bravest group that ever came to Hawaii, the missionaries that sailed aboard the *Thetis.*" One night Micah whispered to his mother, "Father tells us that all men are brothers, but the ones who sailed on the *Thetis* are a little better than the others, aren't they?" And to the boy's surprise his mother said, "Your father is correct. The world holds no finer people than those who sailed aboard the *Thetis.*" But Micah noticed that year by year, in his father's stories of that fateful voyage, the waves got higher and the space in the little stateroom more cramped.

Jerusha found abiding joy in these days, for her nine years in Lahaina had taught her how to master life within a grass house. Her two great enemies were bedbugs and cockroaches, but scrupulous cleanliness controlled the first and meticulous care in wrapping every edible crumb in time dismayed the roaches so that they marched away to some more careless house. Even so, the grassy walls, lined though they were with smooth and fragrant pandanus matting, were convenient hiding places for all kinds of insects, and often at night one would roll over on his pallet and hear the squashing sound of some hard-shelled vermin being crushed. Nor could the dust from the pebbled floor ever be adequately controlled. But life was possible, and at times even palatable.

There was some talk between Amanda Whipple and Luella Janders that their patient sister Jerusha was killing herself in the damp grass shack, and together they sent a petition to the mission board in Honolulu begging for some lumber. "Our husbands have volunteered to build a decent house for this Christian and long-suffering woman, if you will but supply the timbers," they wrote. But since one of the signatories was Amanda Whipple, who was known to have encouraged her husband when he abandoned the mission, and since Whipple had twice been additionally censured for marrying American sailors to Hawaiian girls, the petition came to naught, and Jerusha continued to live and work inside the dark, damp grass shack.

Abner, had he known of Amanda's move, would have been outraged, for he stubbornly maintained his original conviction: "We have been sent here as the servants of God. Through gifts to the mission, He will provide for us as He deems best." It was, however, trying to Jerusha to see her four children clothed only in such remnants as the mission board could send her from the charity barrels, and she tried her health still further by constantly ripping apart gift clothing, smoothing out the larger pieces of cloth thus provided, and sewing them into new garments for her children. On one point, however, she was adamant: "We have got to have books for Micah. If you don't write to the Board demanding them, I shall have to." She was not above stopping whaling captains on the streets and begging them for any books which they might have done with and which her brilliant son could read. "I am trying to teach him all he requires for entrance into Yale," she explained. "But he reads so fast and understands so well . . ." In one way or another she got the books.

Each year Jerusha had had one moment of complete motherly happiness; it coincided with the arrival of the annual gift box from her parents in Walpole, New Hampshire. Each November they dispatched it, but she could never be certain when a ship's captain would knock on her Dutch door, saying, "We've a box for you, ma'am." How exciting it was to get that message, but how infinitely more exciting to see her family standing in a circle as Abner ripped away the top. There were dried apples, and spiced pears and hard dried beef. "These pants will be for Micah," Jerusha would say carefully, lingering over each item. "And this dress will fit Lucy. David can have this and Esther this." On the succeeding Sunday, at least, Jerusha could look back over her shoulder as her children marched to church in their new clothes, and she could be proud of them. She always allowed the box to stay in the house long after it was empty, and whenever she looked at it she could recall the cold winters of New Hampshire and the smell of cider.

A major reason why Abner would have found it impossible to accept aid from the Whipples was this: a phrase of John's kept running through his mind and seemed to him to summarize the apostasy into which his former roommate had fallen. At strange times Abner would hear ringing in his ears John's sharp pronouncement: "I don't think the alii sent the wind, and I don't think God sank the ships." The more he reflected on this the more contemptible it sounded. "In simple terms," Abner rationalized, "what he has done is to equate heathen idols of the alii with God himself. How appalling!" And increasingly he kept away from John Whipple, for without either man's being aware of the fact, as Whipple's financial fortunes grew, so did Abner Hale's deepening reliance upon the Lord; and since in Lahaina as elsewhere these lines of development are not parallel but are actually divergent, so that the distance between them increases, the two men grew not to comprehend each other.

Nevertheless, Whipple remained interested in Abner's welfare, and it was with both amazement and relief that he heard one day from a Salem captain, lately sailing from Boston, that a preposterous yet tantalizing thing was occurring on the wharves of that city. "Matter of fact, it's no doubt completed by now," the incredulous captain explained. "There was this man named Charles Bromley, out of New Hampshire, and he was building a complete two-storied wooden house right on the dock within spitting distance of the bay. No cellar, but everything complete, even to window cords. As soon as it was done, carpenters went over the entire thing with paint brushes and numbered every piece of wood in the house. Draftsmen drew pictures of everything, and indicated the numbers. Then what do you suppose happened?" the captain asked dramatically. "Damned if they didn't start knocking the whole house down and carrying it aboard this ship, plank by plank."

"What ship?" Whipple asked.

"*Carthaginian,* Captain Hoxworth, out of Bedford," the captain said.

"I would deeply appreciate it, Captain, if you'd keep this matter a secret," Whipple said.

"As a matter of fact," the man said, "the house is headed for these islands. Honolulu, probably. I was so fascinated I spoke to this fellow Bromley. He didn't want to talk but he did say that the idea was Captain Hoxworth's. The captain came to him and said that this mission family in Honolulu . . . living like swine . . . you know, grass house, bedbugs, cockroaches. Why Bromley was building the house I didn't get clear."

"Will you promise me?" Whipple pleaded.

"Of course," the captain agreed.

"I assure you, Captain," Whipple said, "you will be protecting a wonderful woman from hurt if you will keep your mouth shut about this. And I shall, too."

Dr. Whipple's preoccupation with anything so minor as a new house was superseded when Abner became aware of mysterious events occurring in Lahaina without his being able to identify them; and since he considered himself arbiter of all that happened in the community, he was irritated to think that Hawaiians would wish to conduct important affairs behind his back. To the meeting in Honolulu he reported: "I first became aware of this unusual secretiveness four days ago when returning from inspection of a home that burned because the owner smoked tobacco, and after having admonished him for his sin, I happened to peer into Malama's old palace grounds, where I spotted several kahunas I knew, and they were supervising the building of a large new house.

" 'What are you building there?' I called.

" 'A small house,' they replied evasively.

" 'What for?' I inquired.

" 'The other houses have grown musty,' they lied.

" 'What other houses?' I prodded.

" 'Those over there,' they said, waving their arms in some vague direction.

" 'Exactly which ones?' I insisted.

"This question they did not answer, so I pushed my way into the compound and inspected the new house, finding it spacious, with real doors, windows and two Chinese mirrors. 'This is a very substantial house,' I said to the kahunas, but they shrugged me off by saying, 'It's a pretty small house,' so I left the deceiving rogues and went in turn to each of the other houses and smelled them, and not one was musty, so I challenged the kahunas and asked, 'Tell me what you are building,' and they replied, 'A house,' and I left the conspirators, convinced that something suspicious is afoot, but what it is I do not know."

Abner was pondering these exasperating mysteries when he saw from his Dutch door a line of seven natives coming down from the hills bearing maile branches and great bouquets of ginger flowers. Leaving his Bible-translating, he hurried to the roadway and demanded, "Why are you bearing maile and ginger?"

"We don't know," the Hawaiians replied.

"Who sent you to the hills?" Abner insisted.

"We don't know."

"Where are you taking the flowers?"

"We don't know."

"Of course you know!" he fumed. "It's ridiculous to say you don't know where you're going," and he limped after them to the waterfront, where they wandered off, each in his own accidental direction.

Infuriated, Abner stood for some minutes in the hot sun trying to piece together his various clues. Then, jamming his hands into his coat pockets, he stomped over to J & W's and said brusquely, "John, what's going on in Lahaina?"

"What do you mean?" Whipple parried.

"I just encountered seven natives bringing down maile and ginger. Why are they doing that?"

"Why didn't you ask them?"

"I did, and they'd tell me nothing."

"Probably some kind of ceremony," Whipple guessed.

Abner both despised and feared this word, for it conjured up forbidding rites and heathen sex orgies, so he asked tentatively, "You mean . . . pagan ceremonies?"

Then Whipple remembered. "Now that you bring it up, two days ago some of the whalers wanted extra supplies of tapa for calking. Usually I can find a hundred yards by snapping my fingers, but I went to a dozen homes, and they were all making tapa, but no one had any for sale."

"What were they doing with it?" Abner pressed.

"They all said the same thing. 'It's for Kelolo.' "

At this, Abner placed before the doctor the various bits of evidence he had collected, and when they had studied the facts, he asked, "John, what's going on?"

"I don't know," Whipple replied. "Have Kelolo and his children been in church recently?"

"Yes, as pious as they ever were."

"I'd keep my eye on Kelolo," Whipple laughed. "He's a wily old shark." And for the rest of that day Abner brooded over the fact that an event of obvious significance had been masked from his surveillance; but his present exasperation was nothing compared to what it became when in the late afternoon he heard as if from a distant valley the muffled, haunting throb of a pagan drum. He listened, and it stopped. Then it began again, and he cried, "The hula!"

Without even informing Jerusha of where he was going, he started out in search of the long-forbidden hula, and he followed the echoes from one area to the next, until at last he pinpointed them as coming from a house on the edge of town. Hurrying along a winding footpath, he was determined to catch the lascivious revelers and punish them, when suddenly from behind a tree a tall native casually stepped into the middle of the path, asking, "Where are you going, Makua Hale?"

"There's a hula in that house!" Abner said ominously, but the man must have been a sentry, for when Abner reached the place from which the drum had echoed, he found only a collection of sweet-faced men and women practicing hymns, with never a drum in evidence.

"Where did you hide them?" he stormed.

"Hide what, Makua Hale?"

"The drums."

"We had no drums, Makua Hale," they said with the most winning simplicity. "We were singing hymns for Sabbath."

But when he reached home again, he heard once more the sound of drums, and he told Jerusha, "Something is happening in this town, and it drives me mad that I can't find out what it is." He ate no supper, but later, as the moon was rising, he announced sternly: "I shall not go to bed till I discover what evil is afoot."

Against Jerusha's protests he donned his white shirt, best stock, claw-hammer coat and beaver hat. Then, fortifying himself with a stout cane, he went out into the warm tropical night and for the first several minutes stood silent under the stars and the sighing palms, trying desperately to detect what was occurring in his parish, but he heard nothing.

He wondered if Murphy had revived the hula in his grog shop, but when he crept past the saloon it was orderly. He then went to the pier, suspecting that whalers might have conspired with Kelolo in organizing a debauch, but the ships were silent in the ghostly moonlight.

And then, as he stood at the far end of the pier, staring at the ships, he happened to see out of the corner of his eye a flickering light along the shore some distance to the south. He dismissed it with the thought: "A night fisher-man with his torch on the reef," but it did not move as a fisherman's should, and he muttered, "That's not one torch. It's several." And with this he remembered the new grass house at Malama's, and he recalled the kahunas, and like a fish drawn to the torches, he limped off the pier and started walking along the edge of the coral reef, past the fort, past the great alii homes and out toward Malama's, and as he walked silently through the sand, the torches grew brighter and it became obvious that a considerable celebration was in progress, one at which he was not welcome. He therefore moved stealthily, slipping from one coconut palm to the next until at last he came upon a hidden spot from which he could spy upon the palace grounds, and the first thing he saw was a concen-tration of guards at the gate that led from the public road into the compound, and he thought with satisfaction: "Those guards are there to keep me out. What evil are my people up to?"

He had not long to wait, for from a crowd of men who had been feasting on roast pig, Kelolo stepped forth in brilliant yellow robes, accompanied by six kahunas in feathered capes. Kelolo dropped his hand, and from an area near the beach a night drum began to sound, and then another, and finally a high-pitched variant which established a throbbing, disciplined rhythm. Suddenly, from the crowd, six women whom Abner had seen in the house singing hymns moved forth, naked to the waist and with red flowers in their hair, necklaces of polished black nuts about their shoulders and anklets of shark's teeth which clicked as they began an ancient hula.

Abner, who had often railed against this dance, had never seen it, and now as the swaying skirts made of ti leaves moved in the faltering shadows, he noticed how solemn and graceful the dance was, for the women seemed to be disembodied spirits, undulating in response to night winds: a movement would start in their heads, work its way along their supple arms, and pass to their hips in one unbroken symphony of motion. "This isn't what I expected," Abner muttered. "I understood that naked men and women . . ." But this fleeting concession was interrupted by what now took place, for he stood appalled as a chanter leaped before the dancers and began to cry mournfully, yet in exultation:

> *"Great Kane, guardian of the heavens,*
> *Great Kane, guardian of the night,*
> *King of the gods, ruler of all men,*

Kane, Kane, Kane!
Attend our ceremony, bless our shore!"

And as Abner stared in disbelief, from the new grass house Kelolo appeared, bearing in his reverent hands the ancient stone of Kane. It should have been long since destroyed, but it had survived through Kelolo's love, and now he placed it upon the low stone altar near the shore. When it was in position he shouted, "Great Kane, your people welcome you home!" Over the crowd a deep silence settled as each Hawaiian filed past Kelolo to deck the altar with flowers, and when this was done the kahunas chanted. Then at a signal from Kelolo the drums hammered out a new and wilder rhythm; the hula dancers swayed more joyously; and the people of Lahaina welcomed back their ancient god.

In spite of Abner's hundred sermons and two hundred hymns about destroying heathen idols, this stone was the first he had seen, and he stared at it with unholy fascination, for the curious combination of reverence and ecstasy it inspired in these worshipers bespoke its real force, and through it the little missionary comprehended much of Hawaii that he had not known before: its persistent religious passions, its abiding sense of history, and its mysteriousness. With all his heart he longed to rush forth and strike down the altar that kept these un-Christian forces alive.

But his attention was diverted from the idol to the figure of a man who now appeared from the new grass house. It was Keoki Kanakoa, in a golden trance, his mechanical movements betraying the deep hypnosis into which he had fallen. He was naked to the waist, his body rubbed with oil; about his loins he wore a brown tapa and across his left arm a feathered cape. His helmet was in the old style, with an elevated comb sweeping from the base of the neck to the forehead, and he wore a necklace of human hair from which dangled a huge whale's tooth fashioned into a hook.

As he walked toward the statue of Kane, a priest chanted: "He comes, the perfect man. His hair is dark and reddish, his figure is commanding, triangular from shoulders down, with narrow hips. He bears a straight back, has no deformity, no blemish. His head is squared from molding while an infant. His nostrils flare. His neck is short and muscular, and his eyes are intoxicating like the tree that lures fish into the ponds. He is the perfect man and he comes to worship Kane!"

In a trance, the young alii moved to the altar, bowed and cried: "Great Kane, forgive your son. Accept him once more." And from the shadows Abner prayed: "Forgive him, Almighty God! He is in the possession of evil men and knows not what he does."

Abner now had to suffer a sharper blow, for from the grass house appeared Noelani wearing a golden tapa and Malama's famous whaletooth necklace. She bore flowers in her hair and moved solemnly toward the altar, while the priest cried: "She comes, the perfect woman. Her skin is flawless, soft and melting like the waves of ocean, lustrous and smooth like the banana blossom. She is fairer than the lehua petal, lovelier than the opening buds of breadfruit. Her nostrils flare from her straight nose. Her brow is clean and low. Her lips are full and her back is straight. Her buttocks are rounded, with cheeks like the bursting moon, solid like the foundations of Maui. She is the perfect woman, and she comes to worship Kane."

Abner, stunned by this double apostasy, began to mumble: "They can't go back to Kane! They know the catechism. Keoki's been to Yale. They're Congregationalists. They're members of my church and I forbid it."

But the apostasy, complete though it was, formed merely the prelude to an event of much greater significance, for from the group of kahunas, whose night of triumph this was, a tall priest stepped forward bearing a black tapa, such as Abner had not seen before, and after a passionate prayer to Kane, this priest swirled the tapa wide in the night air, and when it was completely unfolded, brought it down about the shoulders of the brother and sister, crying: "From this moment on, you shall share forever the same tapa!" And he led the couple toward the waiting house.

The drums leaped to wild rhythms. Dancers created violent gestures which erased memories of earlier beauty, and the kahunas chanted: "Noelani and Keoki are married." Abner could tolerate no more. He leaped from his hiding place, swinging his stout club and shouting, "Abomination! Abomination!"

Before the astonished gathering could apprehend him, he leaped to the altar and with a mighty swipe of his club sent the sacred stone of Kane spinning into the dust. In fury he kicked at the maile branches and the ginger. Then, dropping his club, he marched solemnly to the married couple, ripped away the black tapa, and cried, "Abomination!"

By now the Hawaiians were recovered from their amazement, and Kelolo, aided by two kahunas, pinioned Abner, but they treated him gently, for they knew he was the priest of the other god, and what he had done was only his duty. So Kelolo pleaded softly, "Dear little friend, go home. Tonight we talk with other gods."

Abner broke loose and pointed his finger at Keoki, crying, "In God's eyes this is an outrage." Keoki looked at him glassily, and Abner cried, "Keoki, what has happened?"

The giant young alii stared at his old friend and mumbled, "I begged you, Reverend Hale, to make me a minister. If your church doesn't want me . . ."

"A minister?" Abner shouted, and suddenly the hideousness of this night—the hulas, the living stone, the drums and the kahunas—overwhelmed him and he began to laugh hysterically. "A minister?" he repeated several times, until Kelolo placed his hand gently but firmly over the missionary's mouth and had him dragged away from the ceremonies, but the God-driven little man struggled loose and rushed back almost to the bridal couple before he was apprehended.

"Keoki!" he shouted. "Are you proceeding with this marriage?"

"As my father before me," Keoki replied.

"Infamous!" Abner moaned. "It puts you outside the pale of civilized . . ."

"Hush!" an imperious voice commanded, and Abner drew back. It was Noelani who came close to him and said softly, "Beloved Makua Hale, we are not doing this to hurt you."

Abner looked at the beautiful young woman with flowers in her hair and he argued, with equal control, "Noelani, you are being tempted by these men to commit a grave sin."

The Alii Nui did not argue, but pointed instead toward the dark hills, saying, "In former days we followed our own gods, and our valleys were filled with people. We have tried following yours, and our islands are sunk in despair. Death, awful sickness, cannon and fear. That is what you have brought us, Makua Hale, although we know you did not intend it to be so. I am the Alii Nui, and if I die without child, who will keep the Hawaiian spirit alive?"

"Noelani, dear little girl of my hopes, there are dozens of men . . . right here . . . who would be proud to be your husband."

"But could their children be designated Alii Nui?" Noelani countered, and this line of pagan reasoning so infuriated Abner that he drew back and cried in dismal voice, "Abomination! Malama would curse you from her grave!"

Later, Kelolo confessed that he should have kept silent, but he could not, and asked tauntingly, "What directions do you think Malama gave me when she whispered on her deathbed?"

In horror the little missionary, his pale face and watery blond hair shining in the torchlight, stared at Kelolo. Could what the alii said be true? Had Malama commanded this obscenity? The repulsiveness of this possibility was more than he could accommodate at the moment, and he stumbled from the compound while the kahunas restored Kane, and the drums resumed their nuptial beat.

Bedazed, Abner moved along the dark and dusty road whose stones in recent years had witnessed so many changes. He saw the shadowy houses of the king and the wooden stores of the Americans who had scorned God and fought the mission. In the roads the whalers were snug-anchored, his permanent enemies, and at Murphy's grog shop somebody was playing a lonely concertina. How alien these things were to his lacerated spirit.

In the deep night he left the town and climbed a barren field strewn with rocks, and when he stumbled upon a clump of dwarfed trees he sat among their roots and looked back at his silent parish as if he were no longer responsible for it. To the south he could see the monstrous torches of the pagans. In the roads he could spot the swaying nightlights of the whalers, and between lay the grass-roofed shacks of the people. How miserable and grubby this town really was, how pitiful. What a minimum impression he had made upon Lahaina, how inconsequential his accomplishments. Malama had tricked him. Keoki had betrayed him. And Iliki was God knows where. Now even the gentlest of them all, Noelani, had turned against him and had rebuked his church.

For nearly ten years he had worn only one coat; God had not once sent him a pair of trousers that fitted; he had acquired only such learned books as he could beg from distant Boston; his wife had slaved in a wretched hut; and he had accomplished nothing. Now, as dawn began breaking over his little town, he studied in humiliation of spirit the shimmering sea, the mocking whalers and the palace grounds where the torches were slowly burning out. And he wished ardently that he could call down upon this entire congregation, saving only the mission house and its uncomplaining occupants, some awful Biblical destruction.

"Floods! Winds from the hills! Pestilence! Destroy this place!" But even as he begged God to inflict such punishment, the perverse lesser gods of the vicinity were preparing to launch what would be his crowning humiliation, for in the night that was to follow, the goddess Pele herself would visit once more her devotee Kelolo, and the upshot of this ghostly convocation would haunt Abner Hale for many months.

When John Whipple, rising early to sweep out the store, saw Abner staggering down from the hills back to town, he ran out and grabbed the little man, asking, "Abner, what has happened?"

Hale started to explain, but he could not pronounce the vile words. He hesitated dumbly for a moment, his eyes failing to focus properly, and then he pointed at a group of Hawaiians coming along the road from the palace. They wore maile in their hair, and a light step; they carried a drum and walked in triumph as they had a thousand years before, and Abner said weakly, "Ask them." And he stumbled off to bed.

Later that day he dispatched a letter to the missionaries in Honolulu, reporting: "At four o'clock this morning, January 4, 1832, in the old palace of Malama the kahunas triumphed and the dreadful deed was done."

In daylight, when the auguries were studied and the kahunas were satisfied that a good marriage had been launched, they assured Keoki: "This night you have done a fine thing for Hawaii. The gods will not forget, and when your child is born you will be free to go back to your own church once more and become a minister." But Keoki, shivering from the burdens which the gods throw upon some shoulders, knew that this could not be.

At the following dusk Kelolo, gratified that he had protected the succession of his family in these heavenly islands, walked among the shadows and as he did so he met, for the last time on earth, the silent, delicate form of Pele, keeper of the volcanoes, dressed in silken robes, with strange glasslike hair standing out in the night breeze. She obstructed his pathway beneath the palms and waited for him to approach her, and Kelolo could see that her face was radiant with contentment, and when she took her place beside him, walking mysteriously through whatever trees came into her way along the narrow path, he felt tremendous consolation. And they continued thus for some miles, each happy in the other's company, but when the walk ended, Pele did what she had never done before. She paused dramatically, raised her left hand and pointed south, directly through the Keala-i-kahiki Channel and onto Keala-i-kahiki Point, and she stood thus for some minutes, as if commanding Kelolo with her fiery yet consoling eyes.

He spoke for the first time and asked, "What is it, Pele?" but she was content merely to point toward Keala-i-kahiki, and then, as if wishing to bid farewell to this great alii, her dear and personal friend, she brushed past him, kissing him with fiery lips and vanishing in a long silvery trail of smoke. He stood for a long time, engraving in his memory each incident of her visit, and that night when he returned to his solitary shack outside the palace grounds he took down his two most sacred treasures: the whitened skull of his wife Malama and a very old stone, about the size of a fist, curiously shaped and well marked. It had been given him more than forty years before by his father, who had averred that the occult powers of the Kanakoas derived from this stone, which one of their ancestors recovered on a return trip to Bora Bora. It was, his father had sworn, not merely sacred to the goddess Pele; it was the goddess; she was free to roam the islands and to warn her people of impending volcanic disasters; but her spirit resided in this rock, and it had done so for generations out of mind, long, long before even the days of Bora Bora. And through the night Kelolo sat with his treasures, trying to unravel the divine mystery of which they were the most significant parts. In the morning his confusion was clarified, for a swift ship sped into Lahaina Roads with news that a massive surge of the volcano on Hawaii was threatening the capital town of Hilo and the citizens prayed that the Alii Nui Noelani would enter upon the swift ship and return to stop the flow of lava that must otherwise wipe out the town.

When the news was brought to Noelani, her impulse was to send Kelolo instead, for he was the friend of Pele. Furthermore, her discussions with Dr. Whipple had satisfied her that volcanoes were the result of natural forces whose eruption could almost be predicted scientifically, and she realized that the island stories of Pele were nonsense, but before she could discuss these conclusions with the messengers from Hilo, Kelolo hurried up and said, "You must go, Noelani. If Pele is destroying Hilo, it must be in punishment, and you should go where the lava is white-hot and remind her that Hilo loves her."

"You are the friend of Pele," Noelani replied. "You must go."

"But I am not the Alii Nui," Kelolo said gravely. "Here is a chance for you to win the people to you forever."

"I cannot believe that Pele has anything to do with this lava," Noelani objected.

"I saw her last night," Kelolo said simply. "I talked with her."

Noelani looked at her father in amazement. "You saw Pele?" she demanded.

"I walked with her for two miles," Kelolo replied.

"Did she give you any message?" Noelani asked incredulously.

"No," Kelolo lied. "But of course she warned me of the volcano on Hawaii. Yes, she pointed toward Hawaii." But he knew that she had not done this; she had pointed in quite a different direction.

"And you wish me to go to Hilo?" Noelani asked.

"Yes, and I will entrust to your care a stone that will enable you to halt the lava," Kelolo assured her.

And it was in this way, in the year 1832, that the Alii Nui Noelani Kanakoa left Lahaina with the curse of Abner Hale in her ears—"This is madness, an abomination"—carrying a sacred stone and traveling by ship to the port town of Hilo, where from the bay she could see the overpowering advance of glowing lava, rolling slowly upon itself and crushing in fiery embrace all it encountered. The town was obviously doomed; by the next night the lava must encompass it, and from shipboard there seemed no use for a young woman to try to stop it.

But the local kahunas breathed with relief when they saw Noelani alight, laden with the mana that heals, and start her painful climb to the lava face. Behind her streamed the entire population of the town, save only the local missionaries who were outraged by this heathenish performance. Up through the palm trees at the edge of town, through the nau bushes, and on into the scrubby brush marched the solemn, hushed procession. Now only a few yards ahead lay the crawling, crackling snout of lava: as each new flow cascaded down the mountainside it sped over former flows that in the meantime had cooled, using them as a passageway to lower ground, and as the living white-hot flow came to the dead tip of old lava, it poised a moment in the air, then rushed out in many new directions, consuming here a tree, there a house and beyond a pigpen. There would be a hissing and crackling of fire, and the doomed object would burn away in a sudden, fatal gasp. Then, as the ugly snout cooled, it formed a channel for the next burning flow.

It was to this creeping, crawling, devouring face that the young woman Noelani journeyed, and as she approached the living fire she underwent a transformation, for what she had been summoned to do was no less than to confront the fire goddess herself and to challenge her in a work that had been carried on by volcanoes since long before the coming of the Polynesians, and in the mystery of these last moments, in the awful inner fires that were burning away at her reason, Noelani lost all sense of ever having been a Christian. She was a daughter of Pele, one in whose family the very being of the goddess had resided, and now, returning to the suzerainty of the fire goddess, Noelani planted her feet before the on-surging lava and decided that here she would stand and if need be, die.

Holding the sacred rock of Pele aloft, she cried, "Pele! Great goddess! You are destroying the town of those who love you! I pray you to halt!"

And standing there with the stone aloft, she watched new fires reach the ugly snout and start to gush forward toward the town of Hilo, and as the fires trembled, she threw into them tobacco, and two bottles of brandy which flamed furiously, and four red scarves, for that was a color Pele loved, and a red rooster and finally a lock of her own hair. And the fires of Pele hung in the snout, consumed the tobacco, and slowly froze into position. The flow of lava had halted at Noelani's feet, but there were no cheers, only the soft prayers of all who had trusted that Pele would never destroy the town of Hilo. The fires went out. The probing fingers consumed no more homes, and in a daze of glory and confusion Noelani returned to her ship and went once more to Lahaina, there to await the birth of the child who, when she was gone, would take her place as intercessor with the gods.

This halting of the lava was the worst single blow Abner Hale experienced in Lahaina, for coming so quickly after the defection of Keoki and his sister, it was interpreted as confirming their marriage; while Noelani's demonstrated ability to influence the ancient gods convinced Hawaiians that they still survived, and many began drifting away from the Christian church. But what hurt Abner most was the hilarity with which Americans greeted the miracle. One profane captain kept shouting, "From here on count me a firm believer in Madame Pele!" Another promised, "Now if Noelani will only take care of the storms, I'll join her church, too."

Abner, suffering at each defection from his church and wincing at the American jibes, became obsessed with the lava incident and went about arguing with anyone who would listen: "The burning rock came so far and stopped. What's so miraculous about that?"

"Ah, but who stopped it?" his tormentors would parry.

"A woman stands before a nose of lava as it's about to die down, and that's a miracle," he snorted contemptuously.

"Ah, but what if she hadn't been there?" the logicians queried.

After some weeks Abner went at last, and grudgingly, to consult with John Whipple, and the young scientist reassured him. "When the internal pressures of a volcano become powerful enough, they erupt into violence. Depending solely upon the interior forces within the earth, and nothing more, lava is spewed forth and rolls down mountainsides. If there's enough lava, it's got to reach the ocean. If there isn't, it stops somewhere en route."

"Are these things known?" Abner asked.

"By anyone with a grain of intelligence," Whipple replied. "Look at Lanai. Anyone can see it was a volcano once. Look at our own Maui. At one time it had to be two separate volcanoes, gradually coalescing along that line. I would guess that at some time all the separate islands we see from this pier were one great island."

"How could that have been?" Abner queried.

"Either the islands sank or the sea rose. Either explanation would do."

The grandeur of this concept was too difficult for Abner to accept, and he retreated to certainty: "We know that the world was created four thousand and four years before the birth of Christ, and there is no record of islands having risen or fallen." The idea was repugnant to him.

Whipple was going to ask about the Flood, but he changed the subject and casually remarked, "Abner, why did you put yourself in such a bad light at the marriage of Keoki and Noelani? You surrendered a lot of influence that week."

"It was an abomination, unnatural, unclean!" Abner stormed.

"I've been thinking about it a great deal," Whipple reflected. "What's so dreadful about it? Now really, don't quote me incidents from the Bible. Just tell me."

"It's abhorrent and unnatural," Abner stormed, still hurting from the actions of his two preferred Hawaiians.

"What's really so abhorrent about it?" Whipple pressed.

"Every civilized society . . ." Abner began, but his companion grew impatient and snapped: "Damn it, Abner, every time you start an answer that way I know it's going to be irrelevant. Two of the most completely civilized societies we've ever had were the Egyptians and the Incas. Now, no Egyptian king was ever allowed to marry anybody but his sister, and if I can believe what I've heard, the same was true of the Incas. They prospered. As a matter of fact," Whipple continued, "it's not a bad system, scientifically. That is, if you're willing to kill off ruthlessly any children with marked defects, and apparently the Egyptians, the Incas and the Hawaiians were willing to do so. Have you ever seen a handsomer group of people than the alii?"

Abner felt that he was going to be sick, but before he could react to Whipple's astonishing reflections, the doctor said, "Noelani has asked me to attend her at the birth of the baby."

"Of course you rebuked her," Abner said with assurance.

"Oh, no! A doctor could practice an entire lifetime and not meet such an opportunity," Whipple explained.

"You would be partner to such a crime?" Abner asked, stunned by the prospect.

"Naturally," Whipple said, and the two men walked back from the pier in silence, but when Abner reached home and sent the children out into the walled yard he confided in whispers to his wife the nauseating news that John Whipple was preparing to attend Noelani, but to his surprise Jerusha replied, "Of course. The girl deserves all consideration. This must be doubly frightening for her."

"But John Whipple, a consecrated Christian!"

"The important thing is that he's a doctor. Do you suppose I ever rested easily, knowing that a totally untrained man would be my attendant when the children were born?"

"Were you so afraid?" Abner asked in surprise.

"I began by being," Jerusha said, "but my love for you made it possible to control my fears. Even so, I'm glad that Brother John is going to tend the girl."

Abner started to rant, but Jerusha had in these months of his defeat heard enough, and now she said firmly, "My dearest husband, I am afraid you are making a fool of yourself."

"What do you mean?" he gasped, rising and walking with agitation to the door.

"You are fighting the kahunas, and Kelolo, and Keoki and Noelani, and even Dr. Whipple. In church you speak without benevolence. You act as if you hated Lahaina and all that was in it. You've even withdrawn from your children, so that Micah told me, 'Father hasn't taught me Hebrew for two months.' "

"I have been sorely tried," Abner confessed.

"I appreciate the shocks you've suffered," Jerusha said tenderly, pulling her tense little husband into one of the whaling chairs. "But if, as I think, we are here engaged in a tremendous battle between the old gods and the new . . ." She saw that this phraseology hurt Abner, so she quickly modified it. "What I mean is, between heathenish ways and the way of the Lord, then we ought to fight with our subtlest resources. When the old seems about to reconquer the islands, we ought to combat it with . . ."

"I've warned them all!" Abner shouted, rising from his chair and striding about the earthen floor. "I told Kelolo . . ."

"What I meant was," Jerusha said gently, rising to be with her agitated husband, "that in these crucial times you ought to be calmer than usual, quieter, and more forceful. You've told me how you pointed at the evil three, Keoki, Noelani and Kelolo, and told them in turn, 'God will destroy you!' But you haven't told me or shown me how with Christ's gentle love you have tried to guide the people in these confusing times. I've watched you become increasingly bitter, and, Abner, it must stop. It is you who are destroying the good you have accomplished."

"I feel as if I had achieved nothing," he said from the depths of his spiritual humiliation.

Jerusha caught her husband's passing hand and imprisoned him, turning his pinched face to hers. "My dearest husband," she said formally, "if I were to recount your accomplishments in Lahaina it would take the rest of my life. Look at that little girl in the sunlight. If you had not been here, she would have been sacrificed."

"When I see her," Abner said with racking pain in his heart, "I can see only little Iliki, that sweetest of all children, being passed from one whaling ship to another."

The words were so unexpected, for Abner had not spoken of Iliki for some time, that Jerusha, recalling her dearest pupil, felt bitter tears welling into her eyes, but she fought them back and said, "If in losing Iliki we impressed the islanders . . . and, Abner, they were impressed!" She stopped and blew her nose, concluding her remarks with a firm command: "My dearest counselor, you are to smile. You are to preach about great and lofty subjects. You are to win these people to the Lord with bonds of charity so profound that the islands will be God's forever. You . . . must . . . preach . . . love."

With this master theme drummed into his ears by Jerusha, week after week, Abner Hale launched into the series of sermons which completed the winning of Lahaina, for as he spoke of the good life and the effect of God's love upon mankind, he found that whereas he had believed that the islanders had turned away from the Lord, following the example of Kelolo and his children, exactly the contrary was the case; for the common people sensed that in Kelolo's reversion to the old ways there was no real hope for them; and Abner's thoughtful, quiet words of consolation found their way into many hearts that had rejected his earlier ranting.

He preached a doctrine which was new to him . . . "The Holy Word of God as Interpreted by Jerusha Bromley, Modified by the Mysteries Encountered in an Alien Land." He continued to hammer forcefully at man's inescapable sin, but his major emphasis was now upon the consoling intercession of Jesus Christ. And what held his listeners doubly was his return to the tactic he had used as a very young man when preaching to the whalers on the Falklands: he addressed himself exactly to those problems which were perplexing his congregation, so that when he spoke of Christ's compassion he said bluntly, "Jesus Christ will understand the confusions faced by His beloved son, Keoki Kanakoa, and Jesus will find it possible to love his erring servant, even as you and I should love him."

These words, when they reached Keoki in the grass palace, shattered him and drove him to the seashore, where he walked for hours, pondering the nature of Christ, as he recalled Him from the early, secure days in the mission school at Cornwall, in distant Connecticut. Then Jesus was perceptible reality, and the eroding loss of this concept agonized Keoki.

* * *

When it was known that Noelani was approaching her time of delivery and that her child must be born the next Sabbath, Abner took public cognizance of this fact, and instead of ranting against the circumstances in which the child had been conceived, he spoke for more than an hour and a half on the particular love Christ has for little children, and he recalled his own emotions at the birth of his two sons and two daughters, of his love for the child Iliki, who was now lost —for as he receded from the facts of Iliki's disappearance, she became younger and younger in his memory—and of the joy that all Lahaina must feel that their beloved Alii Nui was about to have a child. Since Hawaiians loved nothing more than children, with whom they were gentle and understanding, the two thousand worshipers sniffled quietly during the last fifteen minutes of the sermon, so that without quite knowing how he had accomplished the strategy, Abner found that his words of compassion had quite won Lahaina away from Kelolo and his kahunas, whereas his earlier ranting had been driving the Hawaiians back to the old gods. It was with confusion, therefore, that Lahaina awaited the birth of its next Alii Nui: as loyal Hawaiians they rejoiced that their noble line was to be continued; as Christians they knew that an evil thing had been done by Kelolo and his children.

Noelani bore twins, and Dr. Whipple, after he left the grass palace, reported to his waiting wife, "We must prepare ourselves for an ugly moment, Amanda. The boy was a handsome child, but the girl was deformed. I suppose they will abandon her before morning." And when it was whispered through the town that Keoki Kanakoa, with his own hands, had taken his malformed daughter, and had placed her at the edge of the tide for the shark-god Mano, a wave of revulsion swept through the town.

On Sunday the Lahaina church was jammed with nearly three thousand people, as in the old days, but on the way to service Jerusha said quietly to her husband, "Remember, my beloved husband, God has spoken on this subject. You are not required to." And on the instant Abner threw away the text on which he was prepared to thunder, Luke 23, verse 34: "Father, forgive them; for they know not what they do," and spoke instead from those majestic words of Ecclesiastes which had been much in his mind of late: "One generation passeth away, and another generation cometh: but the earth abideth for ever. The sun also ariseth, and the sun goeth down. . . . All the rivers run into the sea; yet the sea is not full; unto the place from whence the rivers come, thither they return again . . . The thing that hath been, it is that which shall be; and that which is done is that which shall be done and there is no new thing under the sun. . . . There is no remembrance of former things; neither shall there be any remembrance of things that are to come."

He spoke of the permanence of Maui, of how the whales came back each year to play in the roads, and of how the sunset moved majestically through the months from the volcano of Lanai to the tip of Molokai. He referred to the whistling wind that could blow down churches and of the dead past when Kamehameha himself had trod these roads in mighty conquest. "The earth abideth forever," he cried in soft Hawaiian, and Jerusha, listening to the inspired flow of images, knew that the hatred he had recently held for Lahaina was now discharged, for he passed on from the physical world that endures to the human society which occupies the world. "With all its imperfections it endures," Abner confessed; but promptly he went on to his permanent vision of Geneva as it had been ruled by Calvin and Beza, and by suggesting many unspoken comparisons, he led his huge congregation to the truth he himself was seeking: some forms of human behavior are better than others; and at this point he returned to an idea which had, through the years, become a passion with him:

that a society is good when it protects children. "Jesus Christ loves even children who are not perfect," he preached, and on this awful contrast he concluded.

"What did he say about the baby?" Keoki asked nervously, fingering his maile leaves in the old grass palace as his spies reported to him.

"Nothing," the men replied.

"Did he rave about our sin?" the agitated young man pressed.

"No. He spoke of how beautiful Maui is." There was a pause and the men explained, "He did not speak either of you or of Noelani. But at one point I thought he intended saying that if you ever want to return to the church, he will forgive you."

The effect of these words upon Keoki was startling, for he began to tremble as if someone were shaking him, and after a while he retired with his confusions to a corner of his room, placing himself formally upon a pile of tapa, as if he were already dead, and saying, "Go away." As his friends departed they whispered among themselves, "Do you think he has decided to die?"

The question was seriously discussed, for the Hawaiians knew that Keoki was tormented by doubts arising from two religions in conflict, and that whereas he had reverted with apparent willingness to Kelolo's native gods, he had not easily cleansed himself of Abner's God, and the incompatible deities warred in his heart. They also knew, as Hawaiians, that if Keoki ever decided to die, he would do so. They had watched their fathers and uncles announce, "I am going to die," and they had died. Therefore, when one young man repeated his question: "Do you think Keoki has decided to die?" the group pondered it seriously, and this was their consensus: "We think he knows that he cannot survive with two gods fighting for his heart."

A CTUALLY, THE QUESTION was of no importance, for Lahaina was about to be visited by a pestilence known as the scourge of the Pacific. On earlier trips to Hawaii this dreadful plague had wiped out more than half the population, and now it stood poised in the fo'c's'l of a whaler resting in Lahaina Roads, prepared to strike once more with demonic force, killing, laying waste, destroying an already doomed population. It was the worst disease of the Pacific: measles.

This time it started innocently by jumping from the diseased whaler and into the mission home, where immunities built up during a hundred generations in England and Massachusetts confined the disease to a trivial childhood sickness. Jerusha, inspecting her son Micah's chest one morning, found the customary red rash. "Have you a sore throat?" she asked, and when Micah said yes, she informed Abner, "I'm afraid our son has the measles."

Abner groaned and said, "I suppose Lucy and David and Esther are bound to catch it in turn," and he took down his medical books to see what he should do for the worrisome fever. Medication was simple and the routine not burdensome, so he said, "We'll plan for three weeks of keeping the children indoors." But it occurred to him that it might be prudent to see if John Whipple had any medicine for reducing the fever more quickly, and so he stopped casually by J & W's to report, "Worse luck! Micah seems to have the measles and I suppose . . ."

Whipple dropped his pen and cried, "Did you say measles?"

"Well, spots on his chest."

"Oh, my God!" Whipple mumbled, grabbing his bag and rushing to the mission house. With trembling fingers he inspected the sick boy and Jerusha saw that the doctor was perspiring.

"Are measles so dangerous?" she asked with apprehension.

"Not for him," Whipple replied. He then led the parents into the front room and asked in a whisper, "Have you been in contact with any Hawaiians since Micah became ill?"

"No," Abner reflected. "I walked down to your store."

"Thank God," Whipple gasped, washing his hands carefully. "Abner, we have only a slight chance of keeping this dreadful disease away from the Hawaiians, but I want your entire family to stay in this house for three weeks. See nobody."

Jerusha challenged him directly: "Brother John, is it indeed the measles?"

"It is," he replied, "and I would to God it were anything else. We had better prepare ourselves, for there may be sad days ahead." Then, awed by the gravity of the threat, he asked impulsively, "Abner, would you please say a prayer for all of us . . . for Lahaina? Keep the pestilence from this town." And they knelt while Abner prayed.

But men from the infected whaler had moved freely through the community, and on the next morning Dr. Whipple happened to look out of his door to see a native man, naked, digging himself a shallow grave beside the ocean, where cool water could seep in and fill the sandy rectangle. Rushing to the reef, Whipple called, "Kekuana, what are you doing?" And the Hawaiian, shivering fearfully, replied, "I am burning to death and the water will cool me." At this Dr. Whipple said sternly, "Go back to your home, Kekuana, and wrap yourself in tapa. Sweat this illness out or you will surely die." But the man argued, "You do not know how terrible the burning fire is," and he sank himself in the salt water and within the day he died.

Now all along the beach Hawaiians, spotted with measles, dug themselves holes in the cool wet sand, and in spite of anything Dr. Whipple could tell them, crawled into the comforting waters and died. The cool irrigation ditches and taro patches were filled with corpses. Through the miserable huts of the town the pestilence swept like fire, burning its victims with racking fevers that could not be endured. Dr. Whipple organized his wife, the Hales and the Janderses into a medical team that worked for three weeks, arguing, consoling and burying. Once Abner cried in frustration, "John, why do these stubborn people insist upon plunging into the surf when they know it kills them?" And Whipple replied in exhaustion, "We are misled because we call the fever measles. In these unprotected people it is something much worse. Abner, you have never known such a fever."

Nevertheless the little missionary pleaded with his patients, "If you go into the water, you will die."

"I want to die, Makua Hale," they replied.

Jerusha and Amanda saved many lives by forcing their way into huts where they took away babies without even asking, for they knew that if the fevered infants continued their piteous moaning their parents would carry them to the sea. By wrapping the children in blankets and dosing them with syrup of squill, thus encouraging the fever to erupt through skin sores, as it should, the women rescued the children, but with adults neither logic nor force could keep them from the sea, and throughout Lahaina one Hawaiian in three perished.

In time the measles reached even Malama's walled-in compound, where it struck Keoki, who welcomed it, and his baby son Kelolo. Here the Hales found the shivering Kanakoa family, and Jerusha said promptly, "I will take the little boy home with me." And there must have been a great devil near Abner's heart, for when his wife had the dying child in her arms he stopped her and asked, "Would it not be better if that child of sin . . . ?"

Jerusha looked steadily at her husband and said, "I will take the boy. This is what we have been preaching about in the new laws—All the children." And she carried the whimpering child and placed him among her own.

When she was gone, Abner found that Keoki had escaped to the seashore where he dug a shallow grave into which salt water seeped, and before Abner could overtake him he had plunged in, finding relief at last. Abner, limping along the reef, came upon him and cried, "Keoki, if you do that you will surely die."

"I shall die," the tall alii shivered.

Compassionately, Abner pleaded, "Come back, and I will wrap you in blankets."

"I shall die," Keoki insisted.

"There is no evil that God cannot forgive," Abner assured the quaking man.

"Your God no longer exists," Keoki mumbled from his cold grave. "I shall die and renew my life in the waters of Kane."

Abner was horrified by these words, and pleaded, "Keoki, even in death do not use such blasphemy against the God who loves you."

"Your god brings us only pestilence," the shivering man replied.

"I am going to pray for you, Keoki."

"It's too late now. You never wanted me in your church," and the fever-racked alii splashed his face with water.

"Keoki!" Abner pleaded. "You are dying. Pray with me for your immortal soul."

"Kane will protect me," the stricken young man insisted.

"Oh, no! No!" Abner cried, but he felt a strong hand take his arm and pull him from the grave.

It was one-eyed Kelolo, who said, "You must leave my son alone with his god."

"No!" Abner shouted passionately. "Keoki, will you pray with me?"

"I am beginning a dark journey," the sick man replied feebly. "I have told Kane of my coming. No other prayers are necessary."

The incoming tide brought fresh and colder waters into the grave, and at that moment Abner leaped into the shallow pit and grasped his old friend by the hands. "Keoki, do not die in darkness. My dearest brother . . ." But the alii drew away from Abner and hid his parched face with his forearms.

"Take him away," the young man cried hoarsely. "I will die with my own god." And Kelolo dragged Abner from the grave.

When the pestilence was ended, Abner and Jerusha brought the baby Kelolo, now healthy and smiling, back to the palace, where Noelani took the child and studied it dispassionately. "This one will be the last of the alii," she predicted sadly. "But it may be better that way. Another pestilence and we will all be gone."

Quietly, Abner said, "Noelani, you are aware that Jerusha and I love you above all others. You are precious to God. Will you return to His church?"

The tall, gracious young woman listened attentively to these contrite words and for herself was inclined to accept them, for she had never taken the kahunas seriously, but when she thought of her dead brother her resolve was hardened, and she replied with bitterness, "If you had shown Keoki half the charity you now show me he would not be dead." And it was coldly apparent that she would never return to the church . . . at least not to Abner Hale's church.

* * *

ONE DAY IN early 1833, after John Whipple had recovered from his exhaustion due to the pestilence, he was accosted by a sailor who asked, "You Doc Whipple?"

"I am," John said.

"I was directed to hand you this personally," the sailor explained.

"Where are you from?" the doctor asked.

"*Carthaginian.* We're in Honolulu."

Eagerly, yet with apprehension, Whipple opened the letter, which said simply:

"Dear Dr. Whipple. You have good sense. Can you get Abner and Jerusha Hale out of Lahaina for a week? I intend to build them a house. Your trusted friend, Rafer Hoxworth."

"Tell your captain yes," Whipple said.

"When can he arrive?" the sailor inquired.

"Next Monday."

"He will be here."

So Whipple fabricated an intricate plot, whereby Abner was called to what the missionaries called "a protracted meeting" at Wailuku, where long ago he had tended Urania Hewlett at her death. To Abner's surprise, the Whipples said, "Amanda and I need a rest. We will join you, for holiday."

"The children?" Jerusha asked, frightened, for she had never left them during a single night since Micah's birth.

"Mrs. Janders'll care for the children," John insisted, and although both Abner and Jerusha thought it perilous to risk their offspring to a woman who allowed the Hawaiians to nurse her babies, they at last consented, and the four who had known one another so well aboard the *Thetis* began their pleasant hike to Wailuku, but when they reached the summit of the pass that divided the two halves of the island, John Whipple stopped and stared sadly back at the additional valleys that had been depopulated by the measles and said, "Abner, somehow we've got to get a virile new people into these islands. Because if dying Hawaiians were able to marry strong newcomers . . ."

"Whom could you get?" Abner asked, mopping his forehead.

"I used to think other Polynesians would do," Whipple replied. "But recently I've changed my mind. It'll have to be Javanese. A totally new blood stream." As he paused he idly compared the parched leeward areas he had just left with the green windward area they were approaching. "Curious," he mused.

"What is?" Abner asked.

"I was looking at the two halves of this island," Whipple replied. "The rain falls over here, where it isn't needed, but it never falls on our side, where the big fields lie barren. Abner!" he cried with positive delight. "Why couldn't a man bring the useless rain over to where it's needed?"

"Do you seek to correct God's handiwork?" Abner snorted.

"In such matters, yes," John replied.

"How could you bring rain through a mountain?" Abner challenged.

"I don't know," Whipple mused, but he kept staring at the contrast between rainy windward and parched leeward.

They were not long on their journey before the *Carthaginian* hove into Lahaina Roads and Captain Rafer Hoxworth strode ashore. One-eyed Kelolo and a band of able policemen met the fiery whaler at the pier and leveled six guns

at his chest. "Dis place kapu for you, kapena! We no aloha for you, you damn
hell!" the old alii warned, in his best pidgin.

Hoxworth, brushing aside the guns, announced: "I come only to build a
house."

"No girls on the ship!" Kelolo said sternly.

"I want no girls," Hoxworth assured him, striding briskly up to the mission
house. To his following sailors he said, "Get every movable thing out of that
house. And be careful!"

The removal took only a few minutes, and when Hoxworth saw how
pitifully little the Hales had—their only substantial furniture being the chairs
and tables he had provided them—he held his big right hand over his mouth,
for he was biting his lip with incredulity. "Cover it up," he said, and when this
was carefully done, he applied a match to the old grass house, and in a moment
it blazed into the air, with its burden of insects and memories. When the ground
was cleared he said, "Dig."

The cellar was broad and deep. It would be cool in the blazing hot summers
at Lahaina, and when it was done Captain Hoxworth lined it with building
stones hewn from coral, and these he continued some distance above the earth,
so that when he started to erect the house itself, it had a solid foundation. Now
he ordered his sailors to bring him the corner posts, each numbered, and he
began the fascinating task of reassembling the house exactly as it had been when
standing on the wharf in Boston.

In three days the job was well launched and obviously on its way to success,
and it was while lounging in the offices of Janders & Whipple, that Captain
Hoxworth, having told Pupali and all his women to go to hell and leave him
alone, heard the story of Keoki Kanakoa and his sister Noelani. "You mean
that tall, handsome girl I saw skimming naked past my ship one day on a
surfboard?" he asked quizzically.

"Yes. All this happened to her," Janders said gloomily.

"Why, hell!" Hoxworth growled. "She's the best-looking girl the islands
ever produced. You mean she's out there in that grass shack . . . alone?"

"She has the usual women-in-waiting," Janders explained.

"I know," Hoxworth said contemptuously, making huge circles with his
hands to indicate the women who usually attached themselves to the alii. "I
mean . . . she's just there?"

"Yes."

"That's a hell of a way to live!" he boomed. "Just because she got mixed
up with a lot of crazy nonsense. Janders, I'm going out there."

"I wouldn't," the older man said. "They don't remember you well in this
town."

"To hell with memories!" Hoxworth cried, slamming his big fist into the
arm of his chair. "I'm thinking of staying in Honolulu, Janders. Sail my ship to
Canton in the China trade. Maybe build a couple of ships. Could I get cargoes
here?"

"If your charges are low enough," Janders replied cautiously. "I've got a lot
of skins I'd like to get to China."

"I think you'll get 'em there," Hoxworth said, and he strode out of the office
and along the main road to the grass palace of the alii. At his approach, guards
ran to inform Kelolo, but before the old man could prevent Hoxworth from
doing so, the bold captain had bowed graciously, shoved open the gate, and
marched into the grass palace where he found Noelani.

"Ma'am," he said, extending his big right paw, "I've been wanting to meet you ever since I saw you riding naked past my ship. That must have been thirteen years ago. You were a dazzling beauty in those days, ma'am. You're lovelier now."

"Have you come to find someone else to sell?" Noelani asked coldly.

"No, ma'am. I've come to find me a wife. And I feel in my bones that you're the one."

Noelani started to reply to this abrupt assertion, but before she could do so, Hoxworth thrust upon her a bolt of choice Canton silk and a flood of words: "Ma'am, I suppose you know why I came back to Lahaina. My actions last time have preyed upon my conscience, and I deplored seeing an American man and woman living as those two did. If I offended you on my earlier visit, I now apologize, but with that out of the way, ma'am, I want to tell you that I propose running my ship henceforth in the China trade. I've bought a house in Honolulu, and for some time I've been looking for a wife."

"Why did you not find a wife in Boston?" Noelani asked coldly.

"Tell you the truth, ma'am," Hoxworth replied . . . But at this moment Kelolo rushed up with some guards and burst into the room to save the princess; but she, in turn, dismissed her father and said that she wished to talk with the captain.

"Truth is," he continued as if there had been no interruption, striding back and forth before the doorway leading to the garden, "I proposed once to one of those peaches-and-white-linen women of Boston, and I failed to win her. Since then I've come to prefer the lustier women of the islands."

"Where is Iliki?" the alii asked.

"I hope she's in good hands," Hoxworth said bluntly. "Where would she be if she were here?"

The question caused Noelani to reflect, and to gain time she asked, "When will the house be finished?"

"In two days, ma'am, and that's why I think it important that you dine with me tonight aboard ship. I want you to see your quarters . . . in case you should ever decide to join me on one of the trips to Canton."

The sound of this word, this distant city from which had come her clothes and her furniture and which she had never expected to see—nor had she any reason to see it—so captivated Noelani that she betrayed her excitement, where-upon Hoxworth said bluntly, "Noelani, you've had a bad time here, caught up in things of which you were no part. Why not leave it all? It's a sad, messy business that you will never conquer. I offer you a wild, exciting life."

"I have a son, you know," the proud woman said tentatively.

"Bring him with you. I've always wanted a tyke of my own aboard ship."

"He belongs to the people . . ." she hesitated.

"Then leave him with the people," he said firmly, and before she could protest, he had caught her by the hand and drawn her to him, kissing her harshly upon the mouth and pulling at her garments.

"Please," she whispered.

"Go to the door and tell the women to guard it. You're entertaining your husband-to-be."

She pushed him away, stood solemnly before him and asked, "Could you forget that I was once married to . . ."

"Noelani!" he chided. "How many of the girls of this village have I kept in my cabin? That's also past. Now I need a wife."

"I meant, that it was my brother who . . ."

He pondered this question for a moment, then laughed again and said reassuringly, "With me each day that dawns begins a new year. I have no memories."

The tall captain's words were warm in her ear, the kind of bold, sweet words an alii liked, and she thought: "This kapena is much like an alii. He is tall, eager to fight, and he is the leader of his men. He is tired of running after waterfront women. He owns an important ship and he was willing to take my son as his own. He is not pious, but I think he is honest. The day of the Hawaiian is dead, but the years of the white man are upon us." To Hoxworth she said quietly, "I will go with you to the ship."

He kissed her again and felt her wealth of hair cascading upon his hands, and it aroused him as the kisses of dark island girls had always done, and he whispered, "Tell the women to guard the door," but she refused and said, "Not in this room. It is a center of the old ways. I will go with you to your ship." And the town of Lahaina was astonished to see Captain Hoxworth and Noelani, the Alii Nui, walking down the dusty road beneath the palm trees, talking idly as if they were lovers. But they were more astonished when the tall girl, marvelously beautiful now that she was seeing daylight again, climbed into the captain's rowboat and went out to the *Carthaginian,* where she stayed till dawn, and when at parting she looked at the handsome, well-kept cabin which was to be hers, she thought: "He is a real man, and I will be faithful to him. I will eat his food to please him. I will dress as he prefers, so that other men shall look at him and say, 'Kapena is the lucky one.' I will never say no to him"—and then a soft smile came to her face as it would later come to the thousand Hawaiian girls who would marry Americans—"for I know that with my own words I can win him to a gentler life."

Noelani saw Captain Hoxworth on each of the next two days, and on the last day of his visit to Lahaina, while his men were dragging a complete set of furniture from the *Carthaginian* to the new mission house, she was alone in the grass palace wrapping in tapa cloth two heavy thigh bones; one Keoki had given her before his death, and the other she had received directly for herself. Taking the bundles in her arms, she went out to her father's small house and said to him, "Kelolo, my beloved father, I am leaving Lahaina, and I dare not take these oppressive gifts with me. You must return them to their grave. We cannot any longer live with such memorials haunting us."

Reverently, he accepted the two great thigh bones, placing them tenderly on the earth before him. "Are you determined to go to Honolulu with the American?" he asked.

"Yes. I am seeking a new life."

"May it be a good one," he said gently through his broken and lisping lips. He did not rise to bid her good-bye, for although he understood the pressures which were forcing her to act as she did, he could not condone them; and he was certain that she was rejecting the only true vocation and happiness she would know on earth. "May the goddess Pele . . ." he began, but she hushed his wish, unable to bear any further invocations.

Yet on her part she said, "May the gods be good to you, Kelolo. May the long canoe ride swiftly until the rainbow comes for your departure." She studied his worn old figure with its circular scars about the face and its gaping eye socket, and then she left, to board the ship, but when she reached the pier the sailors told her, "The kapena is not aboard yet," and they directed her to the mission house, where, looking into the bright new room, she saw her intended husband sitting on a kitchen chair, turned backward, its arched back under his chin, and he staring moodily at the floor; and as she watched he rose and carried the chair with him, and set it down three or four times with great violence, making the entire house shudder with his fury. And for some minutes he stood there, pounding the chair into the floor and holding his head down, with his eyes closed and knots standing out on his forehead in dark passion; and she recalled his earlier words and thought: "He can boast that he has no memories, but I am pleased that he has. I thought he remembered only trivial things like selling Iliki." And after he had thrashed the chair into the floor a dozen more times, to control himself from kicking the entire house into splinters, he carefully returned it to its place, gave the small wooden room one last lingering look and came out into the bright sunlight.

"We'll go," he said, and villagers, who had heard of the impending marriage, followed them to the pier, where they watched as the big captain caught Noelani in his arms and lifted her into the longboat.

On the way home from Wailuku, John Whipple and his wife, as soon as they reached the summit of the trail, began gazing into the distance so markedly that Abner finally asked, "What are you looking for?"

"A great surprise," John explained mysteriously, but the four had reached the last small hill before he was able to spot, beneath the branching trees, the roof line of the new mission house. "I see it now!" he cried. "Can you?"

The Hales looked futilely at the outlines of Lahaina and saw nothing. There was the broad reach of sea, the hills of Lanai, the dusty trails. And then Jerusha gasped, "Abner! Is that a house?"

"Where?"

"At the mission! Abner! Abner!" And she broke into a run and dashed down off the hill, with her bonnet flying behind and her skirts causing dust, and when she reached the road she rushed on ahead, not waiting for anyone to catch her, crying all the time, "It's a house! It's a house!"

Finally, gasping with excitement, she stood beside the stream and looked across the walled-in yard to where the old grass house had stood, and there rose, as in a magic story, a New England farmhouse, snug and secure. She put her left hand to her mouth and looked dumbly first at the house and then at the approaching three, and finally she ran desperately to Abner and kissed him in public. "Thank you, my dearest friend and companion," she said weakly.

But he was more surprised than she and looked at Whipple for enlightenment, and for the time being John thought it permissible to tell only part of the truth, so he explained: "Your father sent it out from Boston, Jerusha. We wanted to surprise you." Later, when the association with Captain Hoxworth was fully developed, the two missionaries were so happy with their home that neither made complaint. They took the gift as having come from Charles Bromley, in Walpole, and they thought it proper to ignore the intermediary by whom the gift had been delivered, and who in fact had initiated the idea. Jerusha thought it a marvelous house in these respects: it did not harbor bugs; it did not have an earthen floor; it had a proper cellar for storing food; it had separate rooms for the children; it had a desk where Abner could work; and it had a kitchen. Jerusha was proud when the Hawaiians came to see it.

The first official visitor was Kelolo, bringing with him a large square of paper which he had got from J & W and on which he wanted Abner to print the name NOELANI, after which for no apparent reason that could be ascertained at the time—although later his purpose became clear—he sat on and on until Abner felt that he might have to ask the one-eyed old man to go. He recalled how his wife Malama had always loved the church, how Keoki had wanted to become a minister, and Noelani's happy marriage in Honolulu. There seemed much more that he wished to say, but he did not say it, and at sunset when Jerusha interrupted, "Kelolo, my dear friend, we are about to have our sea biscuit and salt beef. Will you join us?" he gripped her hands passionately and wished her a world of luck. Finally, when he stood alone with Abner, he predicted, "Your church will last when you and I are both upon the rainbow, Makua Hale. It is a fine church, and through it you have done much good in Lahaina." He then inquired if he might embrace the little missionary, and in the Hawaiian manner he rubbed noses and said farewell.

It was not yet dark when he walked down the dusty road, past the taro patch and the royal grounds over the little bridge where the whaling boats came for clear water and onto the grounds that Malama had loved. As he walked he thought happily: "There is always a chance that the night marchers may come along to take me away," and he listened hopefully for the footfalls, but in vain. The walk did not tire him particularly, but he did feel himself to be an old man, and when he reached his small house he rested for a while before wrapping in the paper the three treasured objects he intended for his daughter: Malama's necklace, the whale tooth hung on the hair of his hundred friends, his feathered cape, and the ancient red stone of Pele.

When this was done, he placed the package in the middle of the room and proceeded to gather up his four remaining treasures: the skull of Malama, her right thigh bone which he had given Keoki, and her left, which had been Noelani's heirloom now rejected; and most significant of all, the sacred stone of Kane, which he had protected from the missionaries for so many years.

He carried these objects to the altar by the sea, where a canoe waited, unmanned and with a solitary paddle. Reverently, he moved the three bones onto a low tapa-covered table perched in the prow. Then, ceremoniously, he covered them with maile leaves, whose memorable fragrance marked the night. This ritual completed, he placed the sacred stone on the platform which had so infuriated Abner, and here for the last time he spoke with his god.

"We are not wanted any longer, Kane," he reported frankly. "We have been asked to go away, for our work is done. Malama is dead with a different god. Keoki is gone, and Noelani spurns you. Now even the kahunas worship elsewhere. We must go home.

"But before we leave, great Kane," the old man pleaded quietly, "will you please lift from your children in Hawaii the burdens of the old kapus? They are heavy and the young no longer know how to live with them."

He started to carry the god to the canoe, but as he did so the awfulness of his act oppressed him and he whispered to Kane, "It was not my idea, gentle Kane, to take you from the islands you have loved. It was Pele who pointed to Keala-i-kahiki, the way that we must go. Now we shall go home."

So speaking, Kelolo gathered up the god and wrapped him in a cape of yellow feathers, placing him in a position of honor in the prow. He then turned and looked for the last time at the grass palace, where he had known Malama, greatest of women and the most complete. "I am taking your bones back to Bora Bora," he assured her, "where we shall sleep in peace beside the lagoon." Bowing to the house of love, and to the rocky altar, and to the kou trees whose shade had protected him, he climbed into the canoe and started paddling resolutely toward Keala-i-kahiki, and as he stood out into the ocean itself, he chanted a navigational song which his family claimed had been composed by some ancient ancestor on his way from Hawaii to Bora Bora:

"Sail from the Land of the Little Eyes,
Southward, southward
To the oceans of burning heat . . ."

By morning he had entered exactly those oceans, and without water or food he paddled resolutely into them, a near-blind, toothless old man, bearing his god and the relics of the woman he had loved.

JERUSHA ENJOYED FOR less than three years the clean wooden house her father had sent her, for perversely, although she had managed to maintain her health in the grass shack, she could not do so in her comfortable home. "She's worked herself to death," Dr. Whipple said bluntly. "If she'd allow Hawaiian women to care for her children . . ."

Abner would not hear of this, so Whipple suggested, "Why not send her back to New Hampshire? Three or four cold winters with lots of apples and fresh milk. She'd recover." This time it was Jerusha who was adamant.

"This is our island, Brother John," she insisted stubbornly. "When I first saw it from the railing of the *Thetis,* I was afraid. But through the years it has become my home. Did you know that some time ago Abner was invited to Honolulu, but it was I who refused?"

"Then I can give you only one medicine," Whipple concluded. "Less work. More sleep. More food."

But with four children and a girls' school, Jerusha found little time for resting, until at last she awakened one morning with her entire chest in a viselike grip that she could not adequately describe, except that she found much difficulty in breathing. Abner placed her beside an open window and hurried to fetch the doctor, but when Whipple reached the room, Jerusha was gasping horribly.

"Put her to bed, quickly!" John cried, and when he lifted his friend's wife, he was appalled at how little she weighed. "Amanda," he thought, "weighs more than she." And he sent the children, running by themselves, to Captain Janders' home, and then he said quietly to Abner, "I am afraid she's dying."

There was no need to whisper, for Jerusha sensed that she was near death, and she asked if Amanda and Luella could come into the room, and when the women were there she sent for her children and said that she would like to hear, once more, the great mission hymn, and all in the room, including the dying woman, chanted:

"From Greenland's icy mountains,
From India's coral strand;
Where Africa's sunny foundations
Roll down their golden strand;
From many an ancient river,
From many a palmy plain,
They call us to deliver
Their land from error's chain."

"We have labored to do so," Jerusha said wanly, and seeing that death was strangling at her throat, Amanda Whipple began to whisper the hymn that had launched them on their individual adventures on the golden strands. "Blest be the tie that binds," Amanda began, but Abner could not join in the painful words, and when the wavering voices reached the poignant second verse, which seemed written particularly for those who travel in God's work to far places, he fell into a chair and held his hands before his face, unable to look at the frail figure on the bed who sang in the perfect fellowship of which she was the symbol:

> *"We share our mutual woes;*
> *Our mutual burdens bear;*
> *And often for each other flows*
> *The sympathizing tear."*

"My beloved husband," she gasped in great pain, "I am going to meet our Lord. I can see . . ." And she was dead.

She was buried in the Lahaina church cemetery, with a plain wooden cross, and with her children at the graveside, watching the white clouds sweep down from the mountains; but after the ceremony was ended, and the crowd dispersed, Amanda Whipple could not rest content with the niggardly marking of her grave, and she had carved in wood, which was later reproduced in stone, an epitaph which might have served for all missionary women: "Of her bones was Hawaii built."

In later years it would become fashionable to say of the missionaries, "They came to the islands to do good, and they did right well." Others made jest of the missionary slogan, "They came to a nation in darkness; they left it in light," by pointing out: "Of course they left Hawaii lighter. They stole every goddamned thing that wasn't nailed down."

But these comments did not apply to Jerusha Hale. From her body came a line of men and women who would civilize the islands and organize them into meaningful patterns. Her name would be on libraries, on museums, on chairs of medicine, on church scholarships. From a mean grass house, in which she worked herself to death, she brought humanity and love to an often brutal seaport, and with her needle and reading primer she taught the women of Maui more about decency and civilization than all the words of her husband accomplished. She asked for nothing, gave her love without stint, and grew to cherish the land she served: "Of her bones was Hawaii built." Whenever I think of a missionary, I think of Jerusha Hale.

In the hours following Jerusha's death, the Americans in Lahaina held long discussions as to what should be done with the four Hale children, and it was tentatively agreed that Mrs. Janders should take them until such time as a ship could be found to carry the youngsters back to the Bromleys in Walpole, but since these plans had been worked out without consulting Abner, they were obviously not binding on him, and to the general surprise he announced, when Mrs. Janders offered to take the children, that he would continue to care for them; and they stayed inside the mission wall—Micah, aged thirteen; Lucy, ten; David, six; Esther, four—while their father tended their needs. In this he was much aided by Micah, a sallow, serious child who read voraciously and who had a vocabulary even greater than his erudite father's, for often while the Whipple and Janders children were roustabouting near the mission grounds, Micah Hale, with nothing better to do, sat hunched inside the wall reading for pleasure either a Hebrew dictionary or Cornelius Schrevelius' *Greek-Latin Lexicon*. The two little girls were dressed as Abner thought appropriate, in fitted basques with full-length sleeves, plain flowing skirts, pantaloons to the ankle, and flat straw hats with ribbon streamers, all dredged up from the bottoms of the charity barrels, and they too became extremely fast readers with vocabularies that astonished their elders. Only on Sundays did the general population see the Hale children, for then their father washed and polished them, easing them one by one into their best apparel and leading them solemnly behind him to the big church. At such times many mothers in the community observed, "They are so pallid. Like their mother."

All might have gone well, however, for Abner was a father who demonstrated deep love for his children, except that in the spring of 1837 the *Carthaginian* put into Lahaina on a routine visit to pick up Janders & Whipple furs for an intended run to Canton, and while the handsome ship was loading, Captain Hoxworth idly roamed the tree-lined streets of the town; suddenly he snapped his fingers and asked a Hawaiian, "Where is Mrs. Hale buried?" Stepping briskly, the tall, powerful captain strode to the cemetery, stopping only at a wayside house to buy some flowers; and his intentions were peaceful, but when he reached the grave he had the great bad luck to find Abner Hale there, tending the grass that had grown up beside Amanda Whipple's improvised marker; and when the whaler spotted Abner, the author of his constant grief, he flew into a dark and savage rage, shouting, "You goddamned little worm! You killed this girl! You worked her like a slave in this climate!" and he dove for Abner, catching him below the knees and bearing him violently onto the grave, where he began punching him about the head. Then, struggling to his feet while Abner was still prone, he started raining kicks at the little man, crashing his heavy boots into Abner's head and chest and stomach.

Under such treatment, Abner fainted, but to lose the hateful enemy thus infuriated Captain Hoxworth additionally, and he grabbed him from the grave and began throwing him down again with tremendous force, shouting, "I should have kept you among the sharks, you dirty, dirty, dirty bastard."

How far the dreadful punishment would have continued is uncertain, for natives, hearing the fight, hurried in to rescue their beloved little minister, but when they reached him, they thought him dead. With love they carried him to the mission house, where unthinkingly they allowed the four Hale children to see their father's mutilated figure, and the three younger ones began to weep, but sallow-faced Micah kneeled over his father's battered face and began washing away the blood.

In the days that followed, it became quite apparent to Dr. Whipple that Abner had suffered severe damage in the head, Captain Hoxworth's huge boots having either displaced a piece of bone or dislodged a set of nerve ends; and for several days Abner looked blankly at his commiserating friends, who said, "We have told Hoxworth he can never again come into this port."

"Who is Hoxworth?" Abner asked dully.

But under Whipple's care, the missionary recovered, although ever afterwards the people of Lahaina would frequently see him stop on his walks, joggle himself up and down as if resetting his brain, and then continue, an uncertain man who now required a cane. There was one particularly uncomfortable moment during his recovery when he discovered that his four children were not with him, but were lost somewhere among the heathen of Maui. He began to rant, and his voice raised to a wailing lament, but Amanda produced the children, for she had been tending them in her own home, and he was pacified.

Both the Whipples and the Janderses were surprised, upon his recovery, to find that not only did he insist upon keeping the children with him; the children much preferred their life within the mission confines to the freer existence outside; and as soon as he was able, Abner re-established the curious, walled-in household on the mission grounds.

Then, in 1840, an unexpected visitor arrived in Lahaina, and the pattern of life was permanently broken, for the arrival was a tall, emaciated, very striking-looking Congregational minister dressed in jet-black and wearing a stovepipe hat that made him seem twice his natural height. At the pier he announced, "I am Reverend Eliphalet Thorn, of the American Board of Commissioners for Foreign Missions, of Boston. Can you lead me to Reverend Hale?"

And when the gaunt old man, spare and effective as a buggy whip, strode into the mission house, he was instantly aware of all that must have transpired, and he was appalled that Abner had tried to keep his children with him. "You should either find yourself a new wife, or return to friends in America," Thorn suggested.

"My work is here," Abner replied stubbornly.

"God does not call upon his servants to abuse themselves," Thorn countered. "Brother Abner, I am making arrangements to take your children back to America with me."

Instead of arguing against this sensible decision, Abner asked carefully, "Will Micah be able to enter Yale?"

"I doubt that the boy's preparation is adequate," Thorn countered, "living so far from books."

At this, Abner summoned his scrawny, sallow-faced son and bade him stand at attention, hands at sides, before the visitor from Boston. In a steady voice Abner directed, "Micah, I want you to recite the opening chapter of Genesis in Hebrew, then in Greek, then in Latin, and finally in English. And then I want you to explain to Reverend Thorn seven or eight of the passages which cause the greatest difficulty in translation from one language to the next."

At first Reverend Thorn wanted to interrupt the exhibition as unnecessary, he would accept Abner's word that the boy could perform this feat, but when the golden words began to pour forth, the gaunt old missionary sank back and listened to their pregnant promises. He was struck by the boy's feeling for language and was unhappy when he stopped, so that he asked, "How does such a passage sound in Hawaiian?"

"I can't speak Hawaiian," Micah explained.

When the boy was gone, Thorn said, "I'd like to meet some of the Hawaiian ministers."

"We have none," Abner replied.

"Who is to carry on the work when you go?" Thorn asked, in some surprise.

"I am not going," Abner explained.

"But the vitality of the church?" Thorn pressed.

"You can't trust Hawaiians to run a church," Abner insisted. "Has anyone told you about Keoki and his sister Noelani?"

"Yes," Eliphalet Thorn said coldly. "Noelani told me . . . in Honolulu. She has now four lovely Christian children."

Abner shook his head, trying to keep all things in focus, but for a moment he could not exactly place where he had known Eliphalet Thorn before, and then it became clear to him, and he recalled the manner in which the grave, gaunt man had gone from college to college in the year 1821. "What you must do, Reverend Thorn," Abner explained eagerly, "is go back to Yale and enlist many more missionaries. We could use a dozen more here at least."

"We have never intended sending an unlimited supply of white men to rule these islands," Thorn replied severely, and his accidental use of the word *rule* reminded him of his major responsibility in visiting Hawaii, but the subject was difficult to broach, and he hesitated.

Then he coughed and said bluntly, "Brother Abner, the Board in Boston is considerably displeased over two aspects of the Hawaiian mission. First, you have set up a system of bishoprics with central control in Honolulu, and you must know that this is repugnant to Congregationalism. Second, you have refused to train up Hawaiians to take over their churches when you depart. These are serious defects, and the Board instructed me to rebuke those responsible for these errors."

Abner stared coldly at his inquisitor and thought: "Who can know Hawaii who has not lived here? Reverend Thorn can throw down rebukes, but can he justify them?"

Thorn, having met the same kind of stubborn resistance in Honolulu, thought: "He is accusing me of intemperate judgment on the grounds that I know nothing of local conditions, but every error begins with a special condition."

Eliphalet Thorn was not at ease in delivering rebukes, and having warned Abner, he turned to happier topics, saying, "In Boston the tides of God seem always to run high, and I wish you could have witnessed the phenomenal changes in our church during the past few years. Our leaders have brought to the fore God's love and have tended to diminish John Calvin's bitter rectitude. We live in a new world of the spirit, Brother Abner, and although it is not easy for us older men to accommodate ourselves to change, there is no greater exaltation than to submit to the will of God. Oh, I'm convinced that this is the way He intends us to go." Suddenly, the inspired minister stopped, for Abner was looking at him strangely, and Thorn thought: "He is a difficult, custom-ridden man and cannot possibly understand the changes that have swept Boston."

But Abner was thinking: "Jerusha instituted such changes, and greater, in Lahaina seven years ago. Without the aid of theologians or Harvard professors she found God's love. Why is this tall man so arrogant?" A single conciliatory word from Thorn would have encouraged Abner to share with him the profound changes Jerusha had initiated in his theology, but the word was not spoken, for Thorn, noticing Abner's aloofness, thought: "I remember when I interviewed him at Yale. He was excitable and opinionated then. He's no better now. Why are the missions cursed with such men?"

Then, driven by that perverse luck which often frustrates full communion, Thorn stumbled upon a vital subject, and the manner in which it developed confirmed his suspicion that in Abner Hale the Church had acquired one of those limited, stubborn men lacking in capacity for growth who are such impediments to practical religion. "Brother Abner," the questioning began, "I have come here to join you in ordaining any Hawaiians who are ready for the ministry. Will you assemble your candidates?"

"I have none," Abner confessed.

Thorn, already satisfied that he had identified Abner's character, did not raise his voice. "I'm not sure I understand, Brother Abner. When young Keoki betrayed the church, didn't you immediately recruit eight or ten better prospects?"

"What I thought was," Abner began, but his head felt out of balance, and he jogged himself from the right hip. With compassion Reverend Thorn waited, and Abner continued: "I felt that since the church had suffered such a terrible disgrace, it would be better if . . ." Then he caught a vision of Keoki standing before the altar of Kane, with the maile leaves about his shoulders and the whale's tooth. "Well," he concluded, "I thought the most important thing was to protect the church from another such debacle."

"So you conscripted no potential ministers?" Thorn asked quietly.

"Oh, no! You see, Reverend Thorn, unless you live with the Hawaiians you can't really understand . . ."

"Brother Abner," the visitor interrupted. "I have brought with me two fine young men from Honolulu."

"Missionaries?" Abner cried excitedly. "From Boston?"

"No," Thorn explained patiently, "they're Hawaiians. I'm going to ordain them in your church, and I would be particularly happy if you could nominate some young man of Lahaina who seems destined for the church . . ."

"The Hawaiians in Lahaina, Reverend Thorn . . . Well, I don't even allow my children to associate with the Hawaiians in Lahaina. There's this man Pupali, and he had four daughters, and his youngest, Iliki . . ." He stopped and his mind became brutally clear and he thought: "He would not understand about Iliki."

The ordination ceremonies impressed Lahaina more deeply than any previous church activity, for when the congregation saw two of their own people promoted to full responsibility for Christianizing the islands, they felt at last that Hawaiians had become part of the church, and when Reverend Thorn promised that within a year some young man from Lahaina itself would be ordained, there was little discussed in the next days except one question: "Do you suppose they might choose our son?" But on the next Sunday came even more welcome news, for Thorn announced that the missionary board in Honolulu had decided that one of the two ordained Hawaiians, Reverend Jonah Keeaumoku Piimalo, should remain in Lahaina to preach in the big church and assist Reverend Hale.

When Thorn sensed the joy that this announcement occasioned, he happened to be looking at John Whipple, who turned sideways to his little wife, Amanda, and shook her hand warmly as if the family had long discussed this move, and Thorn thought: "Isn't it perverse? I like Whipple, who left the church, much better than Hale, who stayed. With his doctoring the poor and building a good business, Whipple is much closer to my idea of God than the poor little fellow sitting here beside me."

On the next morning Reverend Thorn sailed back to Honolulu, en route to Boston, taking with him the four Hale children, and when they left their father at the pier Abner said solemnly to each, "When you have learned the civilized manners of New England be sure to come back, for Lahaina is your home," but to his brilliant son Micah he added, "I shall be waiting for you, and when you return a minister I shall turn my church over to you." Thorn, overhearing these words, winced and thought: "He will forever regard it as his church . . . not God's . . . and surely not the Hawaiians'."

It now came time for Thorn to bid good-bye to the missionary whom he had inducted into the service nineteen years before, and he looked compassionately at the halting little man and thought: "What a profound tragedy. Brother Hale has never even dimly perceived the true spirit of the Lord. If the score were tallied, I suspect he has done far more harm than good."

Abner, his mind now beautifully clear, looked at his imperious inquisitor and saw him once more as the black-frocked judge he had been on that visit to

Yale in 1821. He thought: "Brother Eliphalet moves about the world dispensing advice and thinks that by coming to Lahaina for a few days he can detect where we have gone astray. What does he know of cannon? Has he ever faced a rioting mob of whalers?" And with a sense of deep sorrow Abner discovered: "He will never know." Then, his mind still competent, he developed an equally haunting thought: "I doubt that anyone will ever know . . . except Jerusha and Malama. They knew."

"Farewell, Brother Abner," Eliphalet Thorn called.

"Farewell, sir," Abner replied, and the packet stood out to sea.

IN THE YEARS that followed, Abner became one of the human signposts of the old capital, an increasingly befuddled man, limping about the city, stopping to adjust his brains and clicking his head sideways to relieve passing darts of pain. He no longer lived in the mission house, for others came to assume the major responsibilities of the church, but he frequently preached in flowing Hawaiian, and whenever it was known that he would occupy the pulpit, the church was crowded.

For all official duties he continued to wear the shiny old claw-hammer coat he had bought in New Haven and the black beaver hat. His shoes and other apparel he got as best he could from the charity barrels, and in time his life settled into a perfected routine, marked by three recurring highlights. Whenever a new ship anchored in the roads, he would hurry down to the pier and ask its people whether, in their travels, they had come upon the Hawaiian girl Iliki. "She was sold from here to an English captain and I thought that perhaps you might have intelligence of her." No one had.

His second calendar-marking moments came when, from the rude desk in the grass house in which he now lived, he released for printing another of his metrical renderings of the Psalms in Hawaiian, and when the printed sheets appeared, he would distribute the Psalms to his parishioners, and at the next church service would lead them in singing their praises.

The final triumph, of course, came whenever he received mail from his children in America. His sister Esther, now married to a minister in western New York, cared for the two girls, while the boys were the responsibility of the Bromleys. Each of the children's portraits had been drawn in black pencil at a studio in Boston, and they now looked down gravely from the grass wall: handsome, sensitive, alert faces.

Micah, having graduated with top honors from Yale, was already a minister, preaching in Connecticut, but the most exciting news was that Lucy had met young Abner Hewlett, studying at Yale, and had married him. It was Abner's intention to send his old friend Abraham Hewlett a brotherly letter of congratulation upon the joining of the two mission families, but he could not forget the fact that Abraham was married to a Hawaiian, nor could he forgive; and the subsidiary fact that the Hewletts were prospering exceedingly with their lands, and were now wealthy, did not alleviate Abner's distrust of anyone who would consort with the heathen.

One of the saddest aspects of these years was the fact that all who witnessed the visible impairment of Abner's faculties could at the same time observe John Whipple's cultivation of his. Always a handsome young man, he now flowered into an enviable maturity: he was tall, lean, sharp-eyed, and bronzed from surfing. His jaw was prominent, and the fact that he had a heavy beard, which he shaved twice each day, gave him a dark, manly look, which he accentuated by wearing dark suits very closely fitted with six-button waistcoats. His black hair, at forty-four, was untouched by gray, whereas Abner's was actually whitened, so that to see the two men of equal age side by side was shocking, and this was partly the reason why islanders always referred to Abner as the old man.

Whipple also prospered in trade, for whalers now jammed the roads—325 in 1844; 429 in 1845—and they had to buy from J & W. Following Captain Janders' driving precept, "Own nothing, control everything," John had become a master in manipulating the lands and wealth of others, and if an upstart attempted to open a major industry in Lahaina, it was usually Whipple who discovered the tactic whereby the man could be either bought out or squeezed out. When Valparaiso begged for more hides, it was Dr. Whipple who recalled seeing huge herds of goats on neighboring Molokai, and it was he who organized the expeditions to the windward cliffs. As honest as he was clever, he paid any man he employed a fair wage, but when his most skilled huntsman was tempted to organize a goat-shooting team of his own, selling the hides and tallow directly to an American brigantine for extra profit, the man suddenly found he could hire no boats to transport his hides, and after three months' labor had rotted away on Molokai, the venture was abandoned and he returned to work for J & W. Abner never understood how John Whipple could have learned so much about business.

Once, on a trading mission to Valparaiso, Whipple's schooner was laid over for two weeks in Tahiti, and John, as was his custom, improved the wasting hours by studying something of Tahitian ways and words, and it was out of this casual experience that he wrote the essay which dominated Polynesian research for some decades: "The Theory of Kapu," in which he made this provocative suggestion. "In our concern over why the Tahitian says *tabu* and the Hawaiian *kapu* we are apt to digress into theories which, while entrancing, are probably irrelevant. What we must remember is that a group of learned English scientists transliterated the Tahitian language and set it into western ways, while a body of not so well-trained American missionaries did the same job for Hawaiian. In each case we must suspect that the visitors crystallized what was not really there. Would it not be wiser to believe that when the English spelled their word *tabu,* what they actually heard was something quite different—somewhere between *tabu* and *kapu,* but slightly inclining toward the former—whereas when the Americans wrote their word *kapu,* what they heard was also something quite different—somewhere between *tabu* and *kapu,* but inclining slightly toward the latter? Much of the difference that we now observe between written Tahitian and written Hawaiian must be accountable for not by the actual differences between the languages but by the differences in the ears of the men who transliterated them.

"Thus we have many words for *house: whare, fale, fare, hale,* but they are all one word, and we should like to know how many of these differences can be attributed to the defective ear of the white man, whose system of spelling did much to crystallize error. I recall an educated Hawaiian who said to me one day in his native tongue, 'I am going to see Mr. Kown.' I replied, 'Kimo, you know his name is Mr. Town,' and he agreed, pointing out, 'But in Hawaiian we have no letter T, so we can't say Town.' And he pronounced the name perfectly. We had imposed limits on his speech that did not exist before we arrived on the scene.

At the same time, however, the visitor from Hawaii to Tahiti is visibly struck by the changes that occurred when Polynesians from the latter islands journeyed north. In Hawaii their stature increased. Their skin became lighter. Their speech became sharper. Their tools underwent obvious changes, and of course their gods were transmuted. Most spectacular was the transformation of the bold, angular and oftentimes lascivious Tahitian hula into the languorous, poetic dance of Hawaii. Change occurred in all things: religion changed from wild vitality to stately formalism; government became stable and self-perpetuating; and what in Tahiti was merely ornamental featherwork became in Hawaii a subtle art of rare beauty. Thus the development of Tahiti's god of the sea, Ta'aroa, into Hawaii's god of hell, Kanaloa, becomes a change in both orthography and theology, but the latter is the greater.

"In our studies of Polynesia we should start from this premise: Nothing that came to Hawaii remained unchanged; flowers, processes, words and men there found new life and new directions. But we must not be deceived by outward appearances, and especially not by word forms, into estimating the differences to be greater than they actually are. Scratch a Hawaiian, and you find a Tahitian."

Abner's avocation was the Seamen's Chapel, where he would often sit for hours with Chaplain Cridland, the sailor whom he himself had brought to God, and he thought: "Of all things I have accomplished, that accidental conversion of Cridland has borne the most fruit." He felt that no life was more difficult or more fraught with temptation than that of sailors, and he was happy that he had been instrumental in erasing Lahaina's brothels and grog shops.

He existed on a pittance sent by the mission board, for he was no longer a full-fledged missionary, but Dr. Whipple kept close watch upon him, and if he required pocket money, either Janders or Whipple saw to it that he got a little. Once, a visitor, seeing the lonely grass shack, adorned only with the portraits of his children, asked compassionately, "Have you no friends?" And Abner replied, "I have known God, and Jerusha Bromley, and Malama Kanakoa, and beyond that a man requires no friends."

Then, in 1849, exhilarating news reached Lahaina and transformed Abner Hale into a spry, excited father, for Reverend Micah Hale wrote from Connecticut that he had decided to leave New England—it was too cold for his taste—and to live permanently in Hawaii, "for I must see once more the palm trees of my youth and the whales playing in Lahaina Roads." Many mission children, after their years at Yale, wrote the heartening news that they were coming home, for the islands generated a persuasive charm that could exert itself across thousands of miles, but what qualified Micah's letter as unusual was the fact that he was determined to cross overland to California, for he wanted to see America, and he predicted that sometime near the end of 1849, he would be boarding a ship out of San Francisco.

Consequently, Abner, found a map of North America and hung it on the grass wall, marking it each day with his son's imaginary progress across the vast continent, and from deductions that were remarkably accurate, he announced one day to the crowd in the J & W store in late November of 1849, "My son, the Reverend Micah Hale, is probably arriving in San Francisco right now."

When Micah climbed down out of the Sierra Nevadas and started along the Sacramento to the booming San Francisco of the gold rush, he was a handsome, tall young man of twenty-seven, with dark eyes and brown hair like his mother and the quick intelligence of his father. The sallowness and delicate stature of his youth had been transmuted into an attractive bronze, and his chest had filled out from his long hike in the company of gold-seekers crossing the continent. He stepped forward eagerly, as if anticipating excitement at the next tree, and he had won the respect of his fellow travelers by preaching a simple Christianity characterized by God's abiding love for his children, and the respect of the muleteers by nipping straight whiskey when the nights were cold.

In wild and vigorous San Francisco he made acquaintance with many adventurers who had come from Hawaii to the gold fields and was asked to preach in one of the local churches, where after a brief reading of the Bible he captivated his audience by predicting that one day "America will sweep in a chain of settled towns from Boston to San Francisco, and will then move on to Hawaii, to which the American democracy must inevitably be extended. Then San Francisco and Honolulu will be bound together by bonds of love and self-interest, each advancing the work of the Lord."

"Do you consider the Americanization of Hawaii assured?" a San Francisco businessman probed, after the sermon.

"Absolutely inevitable," Micah Hale replied, reflecting his father's love of prophecy. Then, grasping the man's hands in his own, he said forcefully, "My friend, that a Christian America should extend its interests and protection to those heavenly islands is ordained by our destiny. We cannot escape it, even if we would."

"When you use the word we," the businessman asked, "are you speaking as a citizen of Hawaii or as an American?"

"I'm an American!" Micah replied in astonishment. "What else could I be?"

"Reverend," the Californian said impulsively, "you're alone in the town and I'd esteem it a signal honor if you'd have dinner with me. I have a businessman from Honolulu visiting me, and he used to be an American. Now he's a citizen of the islands."

"I'd like to meet him," Micah agreed, and he drove with his new friend through the excitement of the city to a point overlooking the bay. There they left their team and climbed a steep hill on foot until they reached a prominence which commanded a scene of far-stretching beauty.

"My empire," the man said expansively. "It's like looking out on creation!" He led the young minister inside and introduced him to a tall, powerfully built man with eyes set wide apart and a wealth of black hair that grew long at the ears. "This is Captain Rafer Hoxworth," the Californian said.

Micah, who had never before seen his father's enemy, drew back in loathing. Hoxworth saw this and was challenged by the fact that the young man might insult him by refusing to shake hands. Accordingly, he activated his considerable charm, stepped forward and extended his huge hand, smiling compassionately as he did so. "Aren't you Reverend Hale's son?" he asked in an extra deep, friendly voice.

"I am," Micah said guardedly.

"You look very much like your mother," Hoxworth reflected, as he held onto the minister's hand. "She was a beautiful woman."

Repelled by the sea captain of whom he had heard so many ugly reports, yet fascinated by the man's calculated vitality, Micah asked, "Where did you know my mother?"

"In Walpole, New Hampshire," Hoxworth replied, releasing Micah's hand, but holding him at attention with his dynamic eyes. "Have you ever been to Walpole?" And he launched into a rhapsody on that fairest of villages, and as he spoke he could see that he was whittling away at Micah Hale's resolve, and then with a sense of animal delight he saw that the young man was not listening to him but was looking over his shoulder at someone who had entered the room, and instinctively he wanted the young man to become fascinated, involved, hurt.

In fact, Micah was staring at two people who stood inside the doorway. The first was Noelani Kanakoa Hoxworth, whom he had last seen in his father's church at Lahaina, and if she had been beautiful in those days, she was now radiant, in a dress of jet-black velvet, her hair piled high and as shimmering as a polished kukui nut, and wearing about her slim brown neck a single gold chain from which dangled a glistening whale's-tooth hook. Micah hurried over, grasped her hand and said, "Noelani, Alii Nui, I am so pleased to see you." The tall woman, who now knew Hong Kong and Singapore as well she had once known Lahaina, bowed graciously.

But it was not really Noelani that Micah had rushed to greet, for behind Mrs. Hoxworth stood the most beautiful girl Micah had ever seen. She was as tall as he, very slender, with wide shoulders and tapered hips over which a tight-waisted gown of many gores was fitted. She wore her dark hair piled on her vivacious head, and her complexion was set off thereby, for it was absolutely smooth and of a brownish-olive cast. Her eyes were unusually sparkling and her lips showed white and even teeth. At her ear she wore a large California flower, and when her father said, "Join us, Malama. This is Reverend Hale, from Lahaina," she moved gracefully into the room, bowed slightly, and extended her hand in the American manner.

"Meet my daughter, Malama," Captain Hoxworth said, and he was grimly pleased to mark her effect upon the young minister.

That dinner was the most exciting in which Micah had so far participated, surpassing even those held at Yale when the president of the college conversed brilliantly with his students, for Captain Hoxworth spoke of China; the Californian told of his trip southward to Monterey; and Mrs. Hoxworth, unlike the disciplined women who had often eaten with Reverend Hale in New England, was effusive in her recollections of storms at sea and the adventures one could experience in ports like Bangkok and Batavia.

"Do your ships go everywhere in the Pacific?" Micah asked.

"Wherever there's money," Hoxworth replied bluntly.

"Have you ever sailed with your parents?" Micah asked the girl at his side.

"This is my first trip," Malama replied. "Up to now I've been at the Oahu Charity School in Honolulu."

"Are you liking San Francisco?" Micah continued.

"It's much more vigorous than Hawaii," she replied. "But I miss the sunny rainstorms at home. A visitor from Philadelphia came to Honolulu not long ago and asked how to get to J & W's and he was told, 'Go down to the first shower and turn left.'" The dining companions applauded the story, and young Malama blushed prettily, but what everyone waited to hear was Micah's account of crossing the prairies, and under the excitement of Malama's obvious interest in him, he expanded on his theme in a manner he had not intended.

"The land reaches for a thousand miles in all directions, a waving, wonderful sea of possibilities," he exclaimed. "I dug into it a dozen times, and it was rich, dark soil. A hundred thousand people could live there. A million, and they would be lost in its immensity."

"Tell us what you said about the movement of America to San Francisco and on to the islands," the Californian suggested, and at this, Rafer Hoxworth leaned forward and chewed on his expensive Manila cigar.

"I can see the day," Micah expounded, "when there will be wide and well-traveled roads connecting Boston and this town. People will occupy the lands I saw, and enormous wealth will be created. Schools, colleges, churches will flourish. Yale College couldn't begin to accommodate the millions . . ." He was prophesying, like Ezekiel.

"What was your idea about Hawaii?" Captain Hoxworth interrupted impatiently.

"When that takes place, Captain, there will be a natural impulse for America to leap out across the Pacific and embrace Hawaii. It will happen! It's got to happen!"

"Do you mean that America will go to war against the Hawaiian monarchy?" Hoxworth pursued, edging his hands forward on the table.

"No! Never!" Micah cried, intoxicated by his own visions. "America will never employ arms to extend its empire. If this excitement over gold continues to crowd California with people, and if Hawaii flourishes, as it must one day, the two groups of people will naturally see that their interests . . ." He stopped in some embarrassment, for he sensed that whereas Captain Hoxworth agreed with what he was expostulating, Mrs. Hoxworth did not, and he said, "I beg your pardon, ma'am. I'm afraid I presumed when I explained what the Hawaiians will think at that moment."

To his relief, Noelani replied, "There is no need to apologize, Micah." Then she added, "It is clear that Hawaii must one day fall prey to America, for we are small and weak."

"Ma'am," Micah assured her with explosive confidence, "the people of America will not tolerate bloodshed."

Quietly, Noelani reported, "We have been assured that there will shortly be bloodshed within your own country . . . over slavery."

"War? In America?" the young minister replied. "Never! And there will never be war with Hawaii, either. It is equally impossible."

"Young man," Captain Hoxworth interrupted on the spur of the moment, "my ship is departing for Honolulu in the morning. I'd be proud to have you accompany us." Then he added the explanation calculated to inspire the heart of any minister: "As my guest."

Micah, who instinctively knew that he should have no intercourse with this family enemy, hesitated, but at that moment, to Captain Hoxworth's sardonic satisfaction and to Micah's confusion, Malama placed her hand on his and cried, "Please join us!"

Micah blushed and stammered, "I had planned to visit San Francisco for some days."

"We won't wait!" Hoxworth boomed, in his calculated impression of a robust older friend. "We're making so much money running food from Lahaina to the gold fields that a day lost is a fortune foundered."

"You can see San Francisco later," Malama said winsomely, and when Micah looked into her deep Polynesian eyes he felt logic pass into confusion, so that even though he had hiked three thousand miles to see the phenomenon of the west he said weakly, "I'll move my things aboard . . . even though it is the Sabbath."

On the *Carthaginian,* Micah did not spend much time discussing America with Captain Hoxworth or Hawaii with his wife. Instead, he tagged along wherever Malama moved, and with her he watched the stars and the dolphin and the changing clouds. The first days were cold, and she wore an Oregon fur that framed her face in caressing beauty, and once when the night wind was blowing the edges of fur about her eyes, Micah felt positively impelled to raise his hand and brush the fur away, whereupon she accidentally leaned upon his fingers, and he felt how remarkably soft her skin was, and he kept his hand near her cheek and then almost unknowingly allowed it to slip around behind her neck, pulling her lips to his. It was the first time he had kissed a girl and he felt for a moment as if a family of dolphin had struck the ship, and he drew back amazed, at which the tall island girl laughed and teased: "I do believe you've never kissed a girl before, Reverend Hale."

"I haven't," he admitted.

"Did you enjoy it?" she laughed.

"It's something that should be saved for a starry night aboard ship," he said slowly, taking her properly into his arms.

Rafer Hoxworth, who had planned these events, watched with gratification as young Micah Hale became increasingly entangled with Malama. Nevertheless, he experienced contradictory emotions toward the boy: he despised him and wanted to hurt him in some tormenting way; yet at the same time he saw constantly how much the young minister resembled Jerusha Bromley, and when at meals the young fellow spoke so intelligently of America's destiny, Hoxworth was proud; so that on the seventh day he announced unexpectedly to his wife, "By God, Noelani, if the boy wants to marry Malama, I'll say, 'Go ahead.' We could use him in the family."

"Don't intrude into the Hale household again," his wife pleaded. "Besides, what would you do with a minister in the family?"

"This one won't be a minister long," Hoxworth predicted confidently. "Too much get-up-and-go."

That afternoon Captain Hoxworth called his daughter to his booklined cabin and said, "Malama, you intending to marry young Hale?"

"I think so," she replied.

"My blessing," Hoxworth said, but when his daughter brought her suitor, trembling, into the cabin to plead for her hand, Hoxworth subjected the young man to a humiliating examination, focused primarily on money and the inevitability that a clergyman would never have enough of it to support a ship captain's daughter, particularly one who had expensive tastes, and after about fifteen minutes of this, Micah Hale, who had boxed at Yale and who had worked hard in the wagon train crossing the prairies, lost his temper and said, "Captain Hoxworth, I didn't come in here to be insulted. A minister has a fine, good life, and I will hear no more of your abuse."

He stamped out of the cabin and ate his next three meals with the crew, and when Malama, in tears, came to find him he said proudly, "I'll come back to your table when the captain of this ship personally apologizes." After another day had passed, during which Noelani and her daughter cajoled Captain Hoxworth with assurances that Micah had acted correctly, the gruff captain surrendered, rammed a cigar into his teeth, and of his own accord sought out the young minister. Thrusting forth a huge hand he said with a show of real acceptance, "Glad to have a man like you in the family, Mike. I'll perform the ceremony tomorrow morning."

He hated the young man, yet he wanted him for a son. Partly because he knew that such a marriage would infuriate old Abner Hale and partly because he sensed that a half-caste girl like Malama required a strong husband, he proceeded with the ceremony, and as the ship passed into tropical waters, he assembled all hands aft, stood Malama and her mother to starboard and young Micah Hale to port, and bellowed forth a wedding service which he had composed himself. At the conclusion he roared, "Now if the groom will kiss the bride, we'll issue a triple ration of rum for all hands. Mister Wilson will divide the crew into halves. One half can get blind-drunk now, but the other half must wait till nightfall." It was a wild, joyous ocean wedding, and when the *Carthaginian* reached Honolulu, Captain Hoxworth immediately transshipped the newly married couple to Lahaina, for he was still not allowed to visit that port.

As the island boat entered Lahaina Roads, boxed in as it was between the glorious islands, Micah caught his breath and looked alternately at the wild hills of Maui, the soft valleys of Lanai, the barren rise of Kahoolawe and the purple grandeur of Molokai. He whispered to his wife, "As a little boy I was brought to that pier to see the whales playing in these roads, and I always thought of this water as the reflection of heaven. I was correct."

Now the packet began discharging its passengers into the crowd of islanders who regularly jammed the little pier to greet any casual ship, but before Micah and his wife could disembark, some men at the rear shouted, "Let him through!" And with intense joy, Micah discovered that the newcomer was his father, whom he had not seen for nine years.

"Father!" Micah shouted, but Abner had not been told that his boy was aboard the packet, and kept moving forward in his accustomed way, limping more, cocking his white head on the right side and stopping occasionally to adjust his brains. Coming upon a sailor he grabbed him by the shirt and asked, "On your travels did you by chance come upon a little Hawaiian girl named Iliki?" When the sailor said no, Abner shrugged his shoulders and started back to his grass hut, but Micah vaulted over the railing that separated him from the crowd and rushed to overtake his father. When the white-haired clergyman— then only forty-nine years old—realized that it was his son who stood before him, he stared for a moment, approved his handsome appearance and said, "I am proud, Micah, that you performed so well at Yale."

It was a curious greeting, this reference to Yale above all other values involved at the moment, and Micah could only grasp the diminishing shoulders of the old man and embrace him warmly, whereupon Abner's mind cleared perfectly and he said, "I have waited so long for you to take over the preaching in our church." Then, behind his son's elbow, he saw a tall, lovely olive-skinned young woman approaching and instinctively he drew away.

"Who is this?" he asked suspiciously.

"This is my wife, Father."

"Who is she?" Abner asked, afraid.

"This is Malama," Micah explained with tenderness.

For a moment the beloved old name confused Abner Hale, and he tried to clarify his thoughts, and when he had done so he bellowed, "Malama! Is she Noelani Kanakoa's daughter?"

"Yes, Father. This is Malama Hoxworth."

The trembling old man retreated, dropped his cane and slowly raised his right forefinger, leveling it at his daughter-in-law. "Heathen!" he croaked. "Whore! Abomination!" Then he looked in dismay at his son and wailed, "Micah, how dare you bring such a woman to Lahaina?"

Malama hid her face and Micah tried to protect her from his raving father, but scarifying, unforgivable words poured forth: "Ezekiel said, 'Thou hast gone a whoring after the heathen!' Get out! Unclean! Abomination! Foul, foul in the eyes of God. I will never see you again. You contaminate the island."

There was no halting the fiery old man, but in time Dr. Whipple rescued the bridal couple and led them to the refuge of his home, where he bluntly explained to the weeping Malama that Reverend Hale sometimes seemed insane, probably due to the fact that her father had once kicked him in the head. "I am so ashamed," she replied. "I will go to him and assure him that I understand."

Micah could not stop her, and she hurried along the brook, past the mission house and up to the grass shack into which she saw Abner Hale disappear in tottering rage. "Reverend Hale!" she pleaded. "I am sorry that . . ."

He looked out from his shack and saw a woman who seemed much like Noelani, more like Rafer Hoxworth, and she was his son's wife. "Abomination!" he rasped. "Whore! Contaminator of the islands!" And as she gazed in horror, he limped over to the wall, reached up and ceremoniously ripped away the pencil sketch of his elder son. Tearing it into shreds, he threw them at Malama, whimpering, "Take him from Lahaina. He is unclean."

Those were the circumstances under which Micah Hale, most brilliant of the mission children, resigned from the ministry and became partner with Captain Rafer Hoxworth, a man he feared and who hated him, but they formed a brilliant pair—Hoxworth bold and daring, Hale most far-seeing of the Hawaii traders—and in time all ports in the Pacific became familiar with the trim ships which flew the blue flag of the H & H line.

IV

FROM THE STARVING VILLAGE

I n the year 817, when King Tamatoa VI of Bora Bora and his brother Teroro fled to Havaiki-of-the-North, there to establish a new society, the northern sections of China were ravaged by an invading horde of Tartars whose superior horsemanship, primitive moral courage and lack of hesitation in applying brute force quickly overwhelmed the more sophisticated Chinese, who vainly and at times only halfheartedly tried to resist them. As the difficult years passed, Peking fell, and the coastal cities, and it became apparent that the Tartars had entered China to stay.

The effect of the invasion fell most heavily upon the great Middle Kingdom, the heartland of China, for it was these lush fields and rich cities that the Tartars sought, so toward the middle of the century they dispatched an army southward to invest Honan Province, some three hundred and fifty miles below Peking and south of the Yellow River. In Honan at this time there lived a cohesive body of Chinese known by no special name, but different from their neighbors. They were taller, more conservative, spoke a pure ancient language uncontaminated by modern flourishes, and were remarkably good farmers. When the Tartar pressures fell heavily upon their immediate neighbors to the north, those neighbors supinely accepted the invaders, and this embittered the group of which I now wish to speak.

In a mountain village, in the year 856, the farmer Char Ti Chong, a tall, thin man with a handsome high-boned face and a profusion of black hair which he wore in an unruly manner, swore to his wife Nyuk Moi, "We will not surrender these good lands to the barbarians."

"What can you do?" his stolid, sensible wife countered, for in her twenty-three years with Char she had heard some fairly far-reaching promises, most of which had come to nothing.

"We will resist them!" Char proposed.

"With grain stalks as an army?" Nyuk Moi asked wearily. She was a thin, angular woman who seemed always on the verge of complaining, but her life was so difficult that she rarely wasted her strength in whining. Her hopeful father had named her after the most beautiful object he had seen, a scintillating pendant resting among a rich man's jewels; unfortunately, she had not lived up to this name, Nyuk Moi, Plum Jade, but she possessed what was better than beauty: an absolutely realistic evaluation of life. "So you are determined to fight the invaders?" she asked.

"We will destroy them!" her husband repeated stoutly, certain that his boasts had already made his lands more secure.

They were not good lands, and in other parts of the world they would hardly have been deemed worthy of defense, for although the Middle Kingdom contained many rich fields, farmer Char had none of them. His three acres lay tilted skyward at the point where the rocks of the Honan mountains met what might charitably be called the arable fields. There was no running water, only sporadic rainfall, and the soil was not markedly productive. But largely because of Char's endless effort, this land did sustain a family of nine: Char, his wife Nyuk Moi, his old and battleworn mother, and six children. The living was not good, for the Chars had no ducks or chickens, and only two pigs, but it was no worse than that enjoyed by most of the other families in the mountainous village.

What the invading Tartars would have done with this walled-in village, had they ever got to it, was a mystery, for they could scarcely have squeezed out of it a single grain of wheat more than it already yielded, and if they took much away, the village would starve, but it became a fixation with Char and his friends that the Tartars, after satiating themselves with Peking, were certain to burst into this ancient village, so that the farmers formed the habit of convening each night in the farmhouse of their wisest member, General Ching, to discuss plans for the defense of their land, for now there was no government to protect them.

This Ching was not a real general, of course, but merely a stocky, red-faced wanderer who had chanced to be near Peking one day when the emperor's henchmen required an army in a hurry. Ching had been swept up, and in a long campaign found that he liked military life, which was a disreputable fact in itself. After the war, which proved fruitless, for the Tartars quickly overran the very areas Ching had been pacifying, he returned home to the mountain and to his resolute, stubborn associates, regaling them month after month with stories of his campaigns in the north.

"We will place men here and here," stout-hearted Ching proposed. He was a courageous man of whom it was said, "He can march forty miles in a day and fight that evening." He had a broad, resolute face, and in many of the things he did in the years following his impromptu military service he displayed great fortitude, so that although he was clearly a braggart, men did not begrudge him his title of general and listened when he predicted: "The Tartars will approach our village by this route. What other way would a sensible general choose?"

But before General Ching's theories could be tested, an enemy far worse than the Tartars, and far more familiar, descended upon the village. The rains did not fall as required, and a hot sun blazed remorselessly in the copper sky. Seedlings withered before the middle of spring, and by midsummer even drinking water was at a prohibitive premium. Families with old people began to wonder when the ancient fathers and mothers would die, and babies whined.

Farmer Char and his wife Nyuk Moi had lived through four famines and they knew that if one practiced a rigid discipline and ate the roots of grass and chewy tendrils dug from the forest, there was always a chance that one's family would survive. But this year the famine struck with overpowering force, and by midsummer it became apparent that most of the village families must either take to the road or die among the parched and blazing hills. Therefore, when the sun was most intense, Char and his wife fetched mud bricks from the almost vanished village stream and walled up the entrance to their home, placing a cross of black sticks where the door had been. When the house was almost sealed, Char went inside and weighed for the last time the little bag of seed grain upon which life would depend when his family returned next spring. Hefting it in his hand, he assured his miserable group: "The seed grain is now locked inside. It will wait for us."

He then climbed out and swiftly closed the opening. When this was done, he turned his back sorrowfully upon his home and led his family out of the walled village and onto the highway. For the next seven months they would roam over the face of China, begging food, eating garbage where there was any, and trying to avoid selling their daughters to old men with food. Twice before, Char and Nyuk Moi had experienced the wandering months and had brought their brood home intact and they felt confident that they could do the same this time, for as they started on the dreadful pilgrimage Char swore hopefully, "In seven months we will be back here . . . all of us." But this time Nyuk Moi was not so hopeful, and Char noticed that his wife kept her two pretty daughters close to her, day and night.

Concerning only one thing did the Chars have no fear. During their absence their house would be inviolate. Highwaymen might murder them along the road. Slave buyers in cities might try to filch their daughters. Possibly, soldiers would wipe out all the wandering families in a general massacre. And corrupt officials might trick any family into slavery. But no one in China would break into a house that had been sealed with mud and across whose door sticks had been crossed, for even an idiot knew that unless the house was there when the travelers returned, and unless the seed grain was secure, life itself—and not only that of the family in question—would perish. So while the Chars wandered across northern China, seeking almost hopelessly for food, their house stood sacrosanct.

In the autumn of 856 in a city on the northern borders of Honan, farmer Char was bitterly tempted. There the rains had been good and the crops were fine. For several weeks Char and his family went out to the harvested fields at night and crawled across them, on hands and knees, smelling out lost grains that even the insects had missed, and in this cruel way they had uncovered just enough hidden morsels to stay alive. Nyuk Moi cooked the gleanings with a kind of aerated mud, some grass, and a bird that had not been dead too long. The resulting dish was not too bad.

But when a spell of four successive days passed with no gleanings to be found and when no birds died, at least not within reach of the starving family, the servant of a rich man came to the tree where the Chars were sleeping, and he carried in a bag a bundle of freshly baked cakes, whose aroma drove the smaller Char children mad with hunger, for they were the kind of cakes Nyuk Moi had often baked, and the servant said bluntly, "My master would consider buying your oldest daughter."

Char, at the point of starvation, found himself asking seriously, "Would he keep her for his own?"

"Perhaps for a time," the servant said, rustling his package. "But sooner or later he sends most of the girls on to the city."

"How much would he give us?" Char asked pitifully.

The servant grew expansive and said, "Cakes, enough grain to live on till the spring."

"Come back in an hour," Char said, and as the man disappeared, swinging his tempting bundle of aromatic cakes, Char assembled his family, saying frankly, "The owner of the fields has offered to buy Siu Lan."

Nyuk Moi, who had foreseen that this must soon happen, drew her quiet child to her and, placing the girl on the ground between her bony knees, asked, "Is there no other way?"

"The gleanings are no more," Char said despondently. "Winter comes soon. This time we'll be lucky if we get home with any children."

Nyuk Moi did not rail at her husband, for she knew of no alternative to propose, not even one, and the family had about agreed to sell Siu Lan, Beautiful Orchid, when they heard a whistling, and some stranger was whistling a song long familiar in their village and not known much elsewhere. "Who's out there?" Char cried.

The stranger, recognizing his village's accent, shouted, "General Ching!" And in a moment he hurried up, square-faced, sallow with hunger, but as ebullient as ever. "How goes the famine with you?" he asked boisterously. "With me not so good."

Char said sadly and without explanation, "We are meeting to decide about selling our oldest daughter, Siu Lan."

"I'd buy her!" General Ching cried, bowing gallantly to the frightened girl. "Anybody'd buy her!"

"The rich man's servant is coming back within the hour to hear our answer," Char added.

General Ching's agile mind swept into military action. "Servant? Rich man?" he snapped, his hungry eyes darting about in the darkness. And in an instant he had a complete plot. "We will tell the servant that we will sell the girl. I'm your older brother. I make the decisions. Then you and I and Nyuk Moi and your older boy will deliver her. As soon as the servant gets close enough to the house so that we know where the rich old man lives, we kill him, take everything he has and send the booty back with the boy. We then enter the house, present Siu Lan, and as the rich old man steps forward to take her, we murder him. There may be a fight, so each of you, Char, Nyuk Moi and Siu Lan must be prepared to kill. Siu Lan, do you think you could kill a man?"

"Yes," the frail girl said.

"Good," General Ching said, rubbing his fleshless hands.

"Will the plan work?" Char asked.

"If it doesn't, we will die of starvation anyway," the general replied.

"If they catch us, what will they do?" the oldest boy asked.

"They will put us in cages," General Ching explained, "and starve us to death and carry us from village to village so that other starving people will see what happens if farmers kill to get food, and at the end, when they see we are almost dead, they will take us out of the cage and cut us up into three hundred little pieces and hang our heads on the town gate. So, you understand the risks?" he asked coldly.

"Yes," the Chars replied.

"Ssssshhhh," General Ching whispered. "Here comes the servant."

The man bustled up, officious and well fed, still rustling his bundle of cakes, and said, "Have you made up your minds?"

"I am the older brother," General Ching announced. "We have discussed it and have agreed to sell." Whereupon the servant led Siu Lan and her mother Nyuk Moi and the oldest boy and Char and the general back toward his master's house, and when they had gone far enough so that everyone saw clearly how the rich man's home was laid out, and where the entrances were, the general strangled the servant and threw the cakes to the boy, who ran back with them to the starving children and the old grandmother.

"Now it takes courage," Ching said solemnly. He led the way into the rich man's house, presented Siu Lan, and said, "Master, we have produced the girl."

"Where is Ping?" the man asked suspiciously.

"He is giving the cakes to the starving children," square-faced Ching said gently. "Master, have you ever seen your own children starve?"

"No," the man swallowed hard, trying not to look at Siu Lan, who was most temptingly beautiful.

"I have," Ching said softly. "In this famine I have buried three of my children."

"Oh, no!" Nyuk Moi gasped, and something in the manner by which she betrayed the fact that she did not know of General Ching's misfortune uncovered the plot to the rich, canny old man, and he tried to pull a bell which would summon servants, but General Ching coldly intervened, grasped the man's fat arm and bent it backwards.

"Three of my children have died," Ching repeated slowly, "and now you will die." With tremendous force, he closed his bony hands about the man's throat and strangled him, but in dying the man who bought girls for the city managed to utter a cry, and a servant rushed in with a weapon, trying to slash at General Ching, but Char leaped upon the man and the weapon fell to the floor, whereupon Nyuk Moi grabbed it and killed the intruder.

When the two bodies were kicked into a corner, General Ching said, "I have buried my children, and I have lived on clay, but tonight I am going to feast." And he ransacked the house, bringing forth all the food and wine he could find. Then he sent Siu Lan to fetch the children, and the feast lasted till midnight, with the general and Char's old mother singing mountain songs. Then, almost drunk with wine, the general said, "All the time we have been drinking I have been wondering, 'How can I help Char's family escape? With six children and a grandmother?' I'm sure I could manage for myself, but with so many in your family I don't know what to suggest. Shall we scurry to the city and try to lose ourselves there? Or shall we hide in the hills?"

It was then that tough-minded Nyuk Moi proposed: "This is a time of war, and soldiers are everywhere. So I believe that when the authorities discover these deaths they will first cry, 'Soldiers did this!' So they will waste valuable time looking for soldiers, and we will march far into the hills. Later, when they change their minds and say, 'It must have been starving farmers,' we will be so far away it won't be worth their while to follow us, for some new battle will engage them. Therefore we must hurry to the hills."

"Would you feel better if I stayed with you?" General Ching asked.

"Of course," Nyuk Moi replied. "You are now our brother."

"But will our plan work," the general asked, "if we have to take along the old grandmother?"

"We will take her," Char said firmly.

The general frowned and said, "Well, anyway, I will join you, for this famine has killed my entire family."

So the little band struggled back toward the mountains, planning their route so as to arrive home in time for spring planting, but as they approached their walled-in village scarifying news awaited them, for in their absence the Tartars had come and had broken open the inviolate seals and had stolen the seed grain. When Char stood before the sanctuary he had so carefully sealed and saw its shattered door, he experienced a bitterness he had never before known, not even in those moments when he was preparing to sell his daughter. He wanted to fight and slay, and in his anger he cried, "What kind of men are they, that they would break open a sealed house?"

Futilely he looked at General Ching, then dashed about the village summoning all the outraged farmers. Pointing at his trusted friend, he cried, "General Ching has shown us how to dispose our men so that when the Tartars come back we can annihilate them. I have found that Ching is a fine military strategist, and I think we had better adopt his plan. Let us kill these damnable barbarians . . . all of them."

General Ching, quivering with excitement at the prospect of military action, made a great show of assigning his troops to strategic points, but as he did so he heard Nyuk Moi's cold rational voice asking, "What are we fighting to protect? This village? We have no seed to build this village up again."

And as the farmers considered this fact, and as they felt hunger come upon them, even in the clement spring, they began to wonder, and at this moment a solitary outpost unit of the Tartars—two brutal men in furs and on big horses —swept into the village, rode briskly about, and reined up before Char's house. The men were so obviously conquerors that General Ching's bold strategies were not even attempted, and the villagers listened as the invaders shouted in barbarous Chinese, "You have three days to abandon this village. All men above the age of fifteen will join the army. Women may go where they like." The men pulled back on their horses, wheeled madly in the dust, and rode off.

That night General Ching proposed his plan. "When I was in the army I heard of a place they call the Golden Valley. In the morning we start marching there, and everyone who can walk will accompany us. For here there is no hope."

Char asked, "What do you mean, everyone who can walk?"

And Ching replied, "The old folks will have to stay behind. They cannot encumber us on the road."

Families looked in apprehension at their older members and a mournful silence fell across the village, so that General Ching was forced to move from family to family, saying bluntly, like a solder, "Old man, you cannot come with us. Old woman, you have seen your life."

When he reached Char's family he pointed directly at Char's mother and said harshly, "Old woman, you were brave the night we murdered the rich man, so you will understand."

Char remonstrated, "General, it is not within our religion to abandon a mother. Confucius is strict in this regard: 'Honor thy parents.' "

"We are going on a long journey, Char. Maybe a thousand miles over mountains and rivers. The old cannot come with us."

One of the frightened men of the village edged into the conversation and asked, "Have you ever been to what you call the Golden Valley?"

"No," Ching replied.

"Are you sure it is where you say?" the man continued.

"No, I have only heard tales about it . . . while I was in the army. Good land. Gentle rivers."

"Do you think we can get there from here?" the doubtful one asked.

General Ching grew impatient and pulled up his rags so that he looked more like a soldier. "I don't know the pathway, or whether we will be accepted when we get there. I don't know how long the journey will take. But by the demons of hell I know that I do not want to live any longer in a land where men break into sealed houses and where you starve three years in every ten." Suddenly sweeping his arms to include all the village, he stormed: "I don't know where we're going, but Siu Lan is going with me, and the rest of you can rot in hell."

Quickly he wheeled about and faced Siu Lan, the girl he had rescued from the old man, and he bowed before her as a proper general would, and said softly, "May the felicitations of a thousand years rest upon you." Then he turned gravely to Char and explained: "Old friend, I am not pleased to marry your beautiful daughter in this rude and uncivil way. I would like to send you a thousand cakes and a hundred pigs and barrels of wine. I would like to dress her in brocades from Peking and send a horse for her and musicians. But, Brother Char, we are starving to death and I at least am going south. Forgive me for my rudeness." He then faced Nyuk Moi and said gallantly, "Char's wife, let us make believe the famine is not upon us. I shall go to my house for the last time and wait there in the darkness. Will you consent, please, to bring your daughter to me in formal style?" He bowed low and left.

Farmer Char organized the marriage procession, and from the low stone houses streamed out the old people who had been condemned to stay behind, and they marched behind the bride, and one man played a flute, but there were no gifts and no brocades. At the door of General Ching's house, where there had once been many children, Char knocked twice and cried, "Awake! Awake! It is dawn, and we bring your bride!" It was nearly midnight, of course, and when the general appeared he was dressed in rags, but he had seen proper weddings and he bowed gravely to Siu Lan, and the flute played madly, and everyone pretended to exchange the customary gifts, and the general took his bride.

At dawn next morning, in the spring of 857, Char, then forty-four years old, assembled his family and said to them, "On our journey we must listen to General Ching, for he is a sensible man, and if we have any hopes of reaching a better land, it will be because of his genius. Therefore we must obey him."

When the rude army mustered, the Chars were first in line, followed by two hundred starving men and women ready to follow General Ching on the exodus south, but when it came time to bid farewell to this parched and inhospitable combination of rock and reluctant soil, the women in the procession could not control their tears. There was the memorable rock where the farmer Moo, a man much set upon by fate, had finally killed his wife. Here was the tree where the soldiers had hanged the bandit who had stayed hidden by the village for six weeks. There was the house where babies were born. It was a lucky house, that one, perpetually filled with children. And outside the village walls stood the fields where men and women toiled. How sweet this village had been. If there was food, all shared. If there was none, all starved together, and women wept at the memory of those days, now gone forever.

But there were certain houses at which not even the reminiscing women dared look, for they held the old people, and one house held not only two old women but also a baby that could not be expected to live; out of respect for the feelings of the departing army the old people remained hidden inside. They would stay in the village awhile. The Tartars would abuse them, and they would die.

In the entire army only one person dared look at the houses where the old people were left, and that was General Ching. He was not really a military man, in the honest sense of the word, but he had seen a great deal of fighting and much killing, and now as he stood at the village gateway, he was not ashamed to look back at the living tombs, for they held men and women who had been kind to him in days past. One old woman had given him her daughter, the mother of the three children who had starved to death, and for these patient old people he felt a compassion wider than the plains of China.

Suddenly he raised his arms to the cloudless spring heavens and shouted, "Old people inside the walls! Die in peace! Be content that your children shall find a better home! Die in peace, you fine old people!" And biting his lips he led his band down onto the plains.

But they had gone only a few miles when by prearrangement, from behind a rock on the trail, stepped forth Char's old mother, and Char announced firmly, "I have told her that she can come with us."

General Ching rushed up and thrashed his hands in the air, screaming, "This isn't military! She has got to stay with the others."

Char looked at the general coldly and said, "Who hid you in the fields after our triple murder? Who had courage that night?"

"Don't speak to me of murders!" Ching roared. "You are murdering the chances of the entire army."

"Who ever said that you were a general to lead an army?" Char shouted, and the two men, almost too weak to march, began fighting, but their blows were so weak that neither damaged the other, so that soon Nyuk Moi had pulled off her husband Char, and Siu Lan had pacified her new husband, the general.

"Brother Char," the general said patiently between gasps, "from the beginning of history there have been soldiers, and soldiers have rules."

"General Ching," Char replied, "from the beginning of history there have been mothers, and mothers have sons." These simple words were to live in Chinese history as the filial words of Char the farmer, but at the moment they did not much impress General Ching.

"She cannot come with us," he commanded icily.

"She is my mother," Char argued stubbornly. "Does not the old man Lao-tse tell us that a man must live in harmony with the universe, that he must give loyalty to his parents even before his wife?"

"Not even a mother can be allowed to imperil our march," General Ching responded. "She will stay here!" he cried dramatically, pointing to the rocks behind which she had been hidden.

"Then I shall stay with her," Char said simply, and he seated his old mother on a large rock and sat beside her. To his wife and five children he said, "You must go on," and the assembly began to disappear in the distant dust, so that Char's mother said, "Faithful son, the other old people were left behind. It is only right that I too should stay. Hurry, catch up with Nyuk Moi."

"We shall stay here and fight the Tartars," Char said stubbornly, but as he sat he saw a figure running back from the disappearing mob, and it was General Ching.

"Char," he said, in surrender, "we cannot go without you. You are a stalwart man."

"I will rejoin you, with my mother," Char replied.

"You may bring her," General Ching consented. "She will represent all of our mothers." Then he added, "But I will not accept you, Char, unless you apologize to the entire body for having made fun of me as a soldier."

"I will apologize," Char agreed. "Not from shame, but because you really are a very fine soldier."

Then General Ching said to the old woman, "Of course you know that you will not live to see the new land."

"If a journey is long enough, everyone must die along the way," the old woman replied.

A S GENERAL CHING'S resolute group moved south from Honan Province they acquired people from more than a hundred additional villages whose sturdy peasants, like Ching's, refused to accept Tartar domination. In time, what had started as a rabble became in actuality a solid army, with General Ching courageously willing to forge ahead in any risks while his lieutenant, General Char, guarded the rear and fought off bandits and stray bands of Tartars who sought to prevent the exodus.

Across great mountain ranges the travelers moved, down swollen rivers and past burned villages. Winter came and deep snows, summer and the blazing heat of central China. At times General Ching was forced to lay siege to large cities, until food was given, and had China been at peace, imperial troops would undoubtedly have cut the marauders to shreds and crucified the leaders, but China was not at peace, and the great trek continued.

Years passed, and the stolid, resolute men of Honan struggled southward, a few miles a day. Sometimes they bogged down at a river bank for two or three months. The siege of a city might delay them for a year. They ate, no one knew how. They stole from all. In the high mountain passes in winter their feet, wrapped in bags, left bloody trails, but everyone was constantly on the alert to fight. More than a thousand children were born, and even they fell under the simple rules of General Ching: "No old people can join us. You must submit to the government of Ching and Char. We never break into a sealed house."

There was only one element in the army that successfully defied General Ching, and that was Char's old mother. Like a resilient field hoe whose suppleness increases with age, the wiry old woman thrived on the long march. If there was plenty of food, she was able to gorge herself without the stomach sickness that assaulted the others at such a time; and if there was starvation ahead, she apparently had some inner source of strength that carried her along. General Ching used to look at her and swear, "By the fires of hell, old woman, I think you were sent to torment me. Aren't you ever going to die?"

"Mountains and rivers are like milk to me," she replied. And she became the symbol of the group: an indomitable old woman who had known starvation and murder and change. She refused to be carried, and often when her son, General Char, rejoined the group after some rear-guard action against local troops who were trying to disperse the army, he would throw his sword upon the ground and lie exhausted beside his mother, and she would say, "My years cannot go on forever, but I am sure that you and I will see a good land before I die."

The years passed, and this curious, undigested body of stalwart Chinese, holding to old customs and disciplined as no other that had ever wandered across China, probed constantly southward, until in the year 874 they entered upon a valley in Kwangtung Province, west of the city of Canton. It had a clear, swift-running river, fine mountains to the rear, and soil that seemed ripe for intensive cultivation. "I think this is what we have been looking for," General Ching said as his minions stared down at the rich promise below them. "This is the Golden Valley."

He held a consultation with General Char and his lieutenants, and then

called in Char's fantastically old mother. "What do you think?" he asked her
solemnly.

"From what I can see, it looks good," she said.

The general rose, cupped his hands, and faced north. "You old people, dead
back there in the walled village!" he shouted. "Your children have found their
new home." Then he glared at Char's mother and said, "You can die now. It
is really outrageous how long you have lived."

The occupation of the valley was not so simple a task as General Ching and
his advisers had hoped, for the river bed was occupied by a capable, fiercely
compact group of southerners whom Ching and his cohorts held to be not
Chinese at all, for they spoke a different language, ate different food, dressed
differently, followed different customs and hated above all else the old-style
Chinese from the north. At first, Ching attempted to settle the problem directly,
by driving the southerners out, but their troops were as well trained as his. so
his army had little success. Next, he tried negotiation, but the southern
more clever than he and tricked him into surrendering what advantage
already gained. Finally, when military occupation of the entire valley proved
unfeasible, the general decided to leave the lowlands to the southerners and to
occupy all the highlands with his people, and in time the highlanders became
known as the Hakka, the Guest People, while the lowlanders were called the
Punti, the Natives of the Land.

It was in this manner that one of the strangest anomalies of history developed, for during a period of almost a thousand years these two contrasting
bodies of people lived side by side with practically no friendly contact. The
Hakka lived in the highlands and farmed; the Punti lived in the lowlands and
established an urban life. From their walled villages the Hakka went into the
forests to gather wood, which their women lugged down onto the plains in
bundles; the Punti sold pigs. The Hakka mixed sweet potatoes with their rice;
the Punti, more affluent, ate theirs white. The Hakka built their homes in the U
formation of the north; the Punti did not. The Hakka remained a proud, fierce,
aloof race of people, Chinese to the core and steeped in Chinese lore; the Punti
were relaxed southerners, and when the lords of China messed up the government so that no decent man could tell which end of the buffalo went forward,
the Punti shrugged their shoulders and thought: "The north was always like
that."

In addition to all these obvious differences, there were two of such gravity
that it could honestly be said, "No Punti can ever comprehend a Hakka, and
no Hakka cares whether he does or not." The upland people, the Hakka,
preserved intact their ancient speech habits inherited from the purest fountain
of Chinese culture, whereas the Punti had a more amiable, adjustable language
developed during two thousand years spent far outside the influence of Peking.
No Punti could understand what a Hakka said; no Hakka gave a damn about
what a Punti said. In certain pairs of villages, they lived within three miles of
each other for ten centuries, but Hakka never spoke to Punti, not only because
of inherited hatreds, but because neither could converse in the other's language.

The second difference, however, was perhaps even more divisive, for when
the outside conquerors of China decreed that all gentlewomen, out of respect for
their exalted position, must bind their feet and hobble about like ladies on cruel
and painful stumps, the Punti willingly kowtowed to the command, and Punti
villages were marked by handsome, well-dressed wives who sat through long

years of idleness, the throbbing pain in their feet only a distant memory. In this respect, the Punti village became a true portrait of all of China.

But the self-reliant Hakka women refused to bind the feet of their girl babies, and once when a general of the imperial army strode into the High Village and commanded that henceforth all Hakka women must have small feet, the Hakka began to laugh at his folly, and they continued to ridicule the idea until the general retreated in confusion. When he returned with a company of troops to hang everyone, the Hakka women fled to the mountains and were not caught. In their resolve to be free they were fortified by their memories of three resolute ancestors: General Char's old mother, who had lived to be eighty-two and who survived the long trek south in better shape than most of the men; her practical daughter-in-law Nyuk Moi, who had ruled the Golden Valley for a decade after her husband's death; and the gentle, iron-willed Siu Lan, the learned widow of General Ching, who ruled the area for another decade after Nyuk Moi's death. They were revered as the ideal prototypes of Hakka woman-hood, and for anyone to think of them marching with bound feet was ridiculous. Furthermore, as Ching the seer prudently pointed out in 1670: "If our women bind their feet, how can they work?" So the Hakka women laughed at the government edicts and remained free. Of course, the Punti ridiculed them, and on those rare occasions when a Hakka woman wandered into Canton, the city people stared, but these resolute, difficult, obstinate guests from the north refused to be dictated to.

Of course, not all of General Ching's army settled in the Golden Valley, but all the Chars and the Chings did, and they built on the sides of the mountain a group of U-shaped low houses inside a mud wall, and this came to be known as the High Village; whereas the village along the river bank, in which the Punti lived, was always known as the Low Village; and in the two, certain sayings became common. When Punti children played, they taunted their fellows: "Quack like a duck and talk like a Hakka," but in the High Village people frequently cried, with adequate facial gestures: "I am not afraid of heaven. I'm not afraid of earth. But the thing I do fear is listening to a Punti trying to speak Mandarin." There were other folk sayings in the two villages that got closer to the fundamental differences between Hakka and Punti; for in the High Village, Hakka mothers would warn their daughters: "You continue as lazy as you are, and we'll bind your feet and make you a Punti." But in the Low Village, Punti mothers threatened their sons: "One more word out of you, and I'll marry you to a Hakka girl." This latter was held to be a rather dreadful prospect, for Hakka girls were known to make powerful, strong-willed, intelligent wives who demanded an equal voice in family matters, and no sensible man wanted a wife like that.

The High Village and the Low Village had only one thing in common. At periodic intervals, each was visited by disaster. In some ways the perils of the Low Village were the more conspicuous, for when the great river rose in flood, as it did at least once every ten years, it burst forth from its banks with a sullen violence and engulfed the farmlands. It surged across fields of rice, swept away cattle, crept high up the walls of the village houses, and left a starving people. Worse, it threw sand across the fields, so that subsequent crops were diminished, and in the two years after a flood, it was known that one lowland person in four was sure to perish either from starvation or from plague.

What the Hakka, looking down on this recurring disaster, could never understand was this. In the year 1114, with the aid of nearly sixty thousand people, Hakka and Punti alike, the government built a great spillway which started above the Low Village and which was intended to divert the flood waters away from that village and many others, and the idea was a capital one and would have saved many lives, except that greedy officials, seeing much inviting land in the bottom of the dry channel and along its sides, reasoned: "Why should we leave such fine silted soil lying idle? Let us plant crops in the channel, because in nine average years out of ten, there is no flood and we will make a lot of money. Then, in the tenth year, we lose our crops, but we will already have made a fortune and we can bear the loss." But over a period of seven hundred years the Hakka noticed that the escape channel for the river was never once used, and for this reason: "We can see there is going to be a flood," the officials argued, "and a great many people are bound to be killed. But if we open the floodgates to save the villages, our crops in the channel will be destroyed. Now let's be sensible. Why should we allow the waters to wash away our crops in the one year when we will be able to charge highest prices for them?" So the gates remained closed, and to protect one thirtieth of one per cent of the land around the villages, all the rest was laid waste. Flood after flood after flood swept down, and not once were the gates opened to save the people. The backbreaking work of sixty thousand peasants was used solely to protect the crops of a few already rich government officials, whose profits quadrupled when the countryside was starving. This the Hakka could never comprehend. "It is the way of China," Ching the seer explained, "but if it were Hakka fields being destroyed, I am sure we would kill the officials and break down the floodgates."

The Punti, on the other hand, were unable to understand Hakka behavior when drought struck the High Village. One Punti woman told her children, "There is no sensible way of explaining a people who wall up their houses with mud, place crossed sticks before the door, and then wander about the country-side for six months eating roots and clay." The Punti did learn one thing about the Hakka, however, and that was never to touch the walled-up houses or disturb the seed grain. During the great famine of 911 a body of Punti had invaded the deserted High Village and had carried away the seed grain, but there was much death when the theft was discovered, and this did not happen again.

For eight hundred years following the settlement in 874, the Hakka and the Punti lived side by side in these two starving villages—as they did throughout much of southern China—without a single man from the High Village ever marrying a woman from the Low Village. And certainly no marriage could be contracted the other way around, for no Low Village man would want to marry a woman with big feet. When it came time for a man in the High Village to marry, he faced something of a problem, for everyone in his community was named either Char or Ching, after the two famous generals who had led the Hakka south, and to contract a marriage within such close relationships would have been incestuous; the Chinese knew that to keep a village strong required the constant importation of new wives from outside. So in late autumn, when the fields were tended and time was free, missions would set out from the High Village to trek across the mountains to some neighboring Hakka village twenty miles away, and there would be a good deal of study and discussion and argument and even downright trading, but the upshot always was that the High Village committee came home with a pretty fair bundle of brides. Of course, at the same time missions from other Hakka villages were visiting the High Village to look over its women, and in this way the Hakka blood was kept strong. Two additional rules were followed: no man could marry into a family into which his ancestors had married until five generations had elapsed; and no girl was accepted as a potential bride unless her horoscope assured a bountiful relationship with her proposed husband. By these means the Hakka perfected one of the most rigid and binding family systems in China. Pestilence, war, floods and Punti threatened the group, but the family continued, and every child was proudly taught the filial words of Char the farmer: "From the beginning of history there have been mothers, and mothers have sons."

In 1693 a Punti man of no standing whatever ran away with a Hakka woman, the first such marriage ever recorded in the Golden Valley, and a brawl started which lasted more than forty years. No similar marriages were attempted, but serious fighting between the Hakka and the Punti erupted on many occasions, and during one terrible campaign which involved a good deal of southern China, more than one hundred thousand people were massacred in scenes of horror which dug one more unbridgeable gulf between the two peoples. In surliness, in misunderstanding and in fear the two groups lived side by side, and no one in the area thought their enmity strange. As Ching the seer pointed out: "From the beginning of history, people who are not alike have hated one another." In the Low Village the sages often explained the bitterness by asking, "Do the dog and the tiger mate?" Of course, when they asked this question, they threw out their chests a little at the word *tiger* so that no one could misunderstand as to who the dogs were.

IN THE YEAR 1847, when young Reverend Micah Hale was preaching in Connecticut—the same year in which Dr. John Whipple sailed to Valparaiso to study the export of hides—Char, the headman of the High Village, had a daughter to whom he gave a name of particular beauty: Char Nyuk Tsin, Char Perfect Jade, and it was this girl's destiny to grow up in the two decades when Hakka fortunes degenerated in scenes of great violence. Nyuk Tsin was not a tall child, nor was she alluring, but she had strong feet, capable hands and fine teeth. Her hair was not plentiful, and this bothered her, so that her mother had several times to reprimand her, saying, "Nyuk Tsin, it doesn't matter how you dress your hair. You haven't very much, so accept the fact." But what the little girl lacked in adornment, she made up in quick intelligence. Her father had to tell her only once the famous saying of the Char family: "From the beginning of history there have been mothers, and mothers have sons." When Char spoke of family loyalty, the conspicuous virtue of the Hakka, his daughter understood.

She was therefore distressed when many people in the High Village began to whisper that headman Char had gotten into serious trouble and had run away. She could not believe that her father had the capacity to be evil, but sure enough, in due time, soldiers invaded the High Village and announced: "We are searching for the headman Char. He has joined the Taiping Rebellion, and if he dares to come back to the village, you must kill him." The men kicked Nyuk Tsin's mother several times and one of them jabbed a gun into the girl's stomach, growling, "Your father is a murderer, and next time we come back it's you we're going to shoot."

Nyuk Tsin was six that year, 1853, and she saw her father only once thereafter. Well, that is not entirely correct, but let us grant for the present that she saw him only once, for he did return to the High Village late one night and mysteriously. The first thing he did was embrace his skinny little girl and tell her, "Ah, Jade, your father has seen things he never dreamed of before. Horses of his own! I captured an entire Punti city . . . not a village like that one down there.

Jade, they all bowed as I came in. Low, girl. Like this!" Later he embraced her as if she were his beloved and not his eight-year-old daughter, and he took her with him to watch his Hakka friends enlist in his great venture. Pointing at the frightened would-be soldiers, he said, "To begin with, all soldiers are afraid, Nyuk Tsin. Me? I trembléd like a bird gathering seeds. But the important thing is to have loyalty in your heart. When General Lai tells me, 'General Char, occupy that city!' do you suppose I stop to question, 'Now what is General Lai up to?' No, indeed. I occupy the city, and if I have to kill fifty thousand enemy to do it, I kill them. Jade," he cried warmly in the mountain darkness, "we are headed far north. I may never see you again." He swept the quiet girl into his arms and held her close to him. "Take care of your mother," he said, and the men dashed down the mountainside after him.

Nyuk Tsin did see her father again. In 1863, when she was a thin, extremely well-organized girl of sixteen, capable of bearing huge loads of wood and of caring for her mother and the rest of her family, General Wang of the imperial forces marched into the High Village and commanded his drummer to roll the drum a long time, so that all the villagers assembled. Then, with the aid of an interpreter, for such a general would never know how to speak Hakka, he ordered a herald bearing a black object to read an official announcement.

The man kept the black object in his left hand, stepped forward and read in a high nasal voice: "The Taiping rebel chief named Char, who was captured at Nanking and brought under guard to Peking, having confessed that he was a fellow conspirator with Lai Siu Tsuen, who himself has falsely assumed the title of General of the North, was tried and put to death last month by being slowly cut into three hundred small pieces over a period of nine hours, according to just law, and his head was exposed at the city for three days as a warning to all."

Having said this, the herald passed the decree to another, and with his free hand drew away the black covering, disclosing in a wire cage the head of General Char. Ants had gotten to it, and flies, so that the eyeballs were gone and the tongue, but the dedicated man's features were clear, and the head was fixed to a pole in the middle of the village, after which General Wang announced sternly: "This is what happens to traitors!" Then he demanded: "Where is the widow of the traitor Char?" The villagers refused to identify the wife of their great leader, but Nyuk Tsin's mother put her children aside and announced proudly, "I am his wife."

"Shoot her," General Wang said, and she fell into the village dust.

Later the High Village remembered sardonically General Wang's platitudes about traitors, for it was hardly less than two weeks after his brave appearance in their village that he studied the various opportunities confronting him and decided to become a traitor himself.

The year 1864 was therefore a truly terrible one in the Golden Valley, for half the time General Wang was rampaging through the villages seeking loot, while during the other half government troops were in pursuit of the traitor. Wang, having discovered the High Village, rarely passed it by, and in time even enlisted a good many Hakka into his band. This gave the government troops title to whatever they could find in the High Village, and they often shot Hakka farmers for the fun of it. Nyuk Tsin, by virtue of not looking too pretty and of working long hours hauling wood to the lowlands, which made her seem much older than she was, escaped rape, but many of the other Hakka girls did not.

At this time Nyuk Tsin was living meagerly in the home of her uncle, who, following the execution of her father and mother, was required by village custom to take her in. This uncle, a hard, unhappy one, reminded her constantly of two dismal facts: she was already seventeen years old and unmarried; and because she was her rebellious father's daughter the soldiers might at any time return to the High Village and shoot both her and her uncle. These two conditions were cause enough for her uncle to cut down on her food rations and increase the bundle of wood she was required to lug down onto the plain.

Nyuk Tsin was not married because of a most unfortunate event over which she had no control. Her horoscope, which had been carefully cast when envoys from a distant Hakka village came seeking wives for the Lai family, showed the thin girl to be doubly cursed: she was born under the influence of the horse and was therefore a headstrong, evil prospect as a wife; and she was clearly a husband-killer, so that only a foolish man would take her into his home. There were, of course, favorable aspects to her future, such as a promise of wealth and many descendants, and these might have encouraged an avaricious husband to discount the peril, except that her horoscope divulged an additional disgrace: she would die in a foreign land. Adding together her willfulness, her husband-killing propensity and her burial in alien soil, the Hakka of the High Village knew that in Char Nyuk Tsin they had an unmarriageable girl, and after a while they stopped proposing her to visiting envoys.

She therefore worked her life away in the near-starving village. She had two items of clothing: a dark-blue cotton smock and a pair of dirty cotton trousers to match. She also had a conical wicker hat, which she tied under her chin with a length of blue cord, and big strong feet for climbing down to the valley with huge burdens of wood; as far as she could see into the future, this was going to be her life. And then, on the festive night before the holiday of Ching Ming, when the Low Village required extra firewood for the great celebrations that were in progress, Nyuk Tsin left the High Village at dusk and started down the steep trail. She had barely reached the plain when a group of four men sprang at her from behind rocks, scattered the wood, slipped a gag into her mouth, jammed a bag over her head, and kidnaped her. When day broke, and her uncle found that she had not returned, he uttered a brief prayer that something permanent had happened to her, and it had. She was never again seen in the High Village.

It must not be assumed that during these troubled times the Punti fared any better than the Hakka. In fact, since the traitorous troops of General Wang disliked climbing mountains, there was a good deal more raping and kidnaping in the Low Village than in the High; but this was halted whenever the wild river went into its periodic flood and starvation threatened to wipe out the village completely.

These were bad years, but they were terminated in early 1865 by the arrival in the Low Village of a man reputed to be fantastically rich, and within six weeks this amazing Punti had broken open the floodgates so that the river was diverted and the village spared, had bought off the traitor General Wang and then betrayed him to government forces, and had made the village not only secure but happy. The man who accomplished these miracles was a wiry, clever Punti, Kee Chun Fat, whose name meant Spring Prosperity and who had been born fifty-two years earlier right there in the Low Village. In 1846 he had emigrated to California, where he had worked in the gold fields, acquiring the eleven thousand dollars which made him, according to Low Village standards, one of the richest men in the world.

As he moved about the village, making many decisions regarding the extensive Kee family of which he was now the effective if not titular head, he wore a long pigtail, a black skullcap edged in blue satin, a gray silken coatlike garment that fell to his ankles and was tightly buttoned at the neck and heavy brocaded shoes. His lean frame kept him from making an imposing, patriarchal figure, but his evocation of energy made him the unquestioned dictator of the village. In California he had learned to read English but not Chinese, and he could figure percentages, so that as soon as he unpacked he started lending money to his relatives at forty per cent interest per year.

When the Kee family asked admiringly, "How could a man like you, who is not a soldier at all, be so brave as to argue with General Wang?" he laughed slyly and explained, "When you've had to live by outsmarting Americans, it's very easy to manage a fool like General Wang." Of course, this answer was meaningless to the Punti, so they said, "We still don't understand how you did it."

Kee Chun Fat had an explanation for everything, so he replied, "In Peking a man is emperor, but I have found that in the world money is emperor."

"Did you give General Wang money?" the villagers pressed.

"I gave him enough to keep him hanging around," Uncle Chun Fat explained. "Then I told the government troops where he was, and promised them money if they would hang him, and they did."

There was much discussion among the Kee family as to how Uncle Chun Fat had made his great fortune in America, and one had only to pose the question for the head of the family to explain: "America has gold fields where money is easily made. There are gangs of men laying telegraph wires, and money is easy there, too. But where do you suppose the money is easiest of all? Where they're building railroads. Tell me, do you think that I brought home with me only the money you have seen here in the Low Village? Oh no, my good friends! I made that much in the gold fields in one year. Washing for the miners. Cooking food. My real money is in an English bank in Hong Kong." And he produced a book to prove it but only he could read the writing.

Uncle Chun Fat's stories of America were tantalizing. Once he said, "The best part of California is not the money but the women. A man can have three Indian wives and any number of Mexicans. But not at the same time." Young men with their lips watering asked more about this, but Uncle Chun Fat had already passed on to other matters. "What I would like to do," he explained to his assembled family, "is to restore the ancestral hall until it is known as the finest in China. We will do honor to our great ancestor, Prince Kee Tse of the Hsiang Dynasty, from whom we are sprung." As he said these words he recalled the illustrious prince who had invaded Korea nearly three thousand years before, and he told his clan, "It is strange to live in America, where most men do not even know who their grandfathers were. We shall make the name of Prince Kee renowned once more throughout China." Chun Fat had an older brother who had never amounted to much; nevertheless this Kee Chun Kong was still nominal head of the family, and Chun Fat was careful not to usurp any of his moral prerogatives. But time was short, and in practical matters the energetic Californian had to make one swift decision after another, for which he was forgiven in view of the fact that he was paying for everything. Therefore, as the yearly festival of Ching Ming approached, when honorable men pay obeisance to their ancestors, he dispatched runners with this command: "All members of the Kee family shall return to the ancestral hall to celebrate Ching Ming." He then spent nearly a thousand dollars beautifying the low tile-roofed building which was the spiritual focus of the Kee clan.

One of his messengers traveled as far south as the evil little Portuguese city of Macao, across the bay from Hong Kong, and there in the Brothel of Spring Nights he delivered his command to a handsome, sharp-eyed young man who cooked for the brothel and helped in other ways. Koe Mun Ki was twenty-two at the time, a clever opportunist, with a brisk pigtail, quick gambler's hands and an ingratiating smile. His father, hoping that his son would mature into a solid, gifted scholar, had named him Pervading Foundation, but he had wandered from academic pursuits, finding himself skilled at luring young girls into the brothel and in gambling with European sailors who frequented Macao. When the messenger from the Low Village arrived, young Mun Ki was in the midst of an impressive winning streak and showed no intention of leaving the Portuguese city. "Tell my father," he explained, "that this year I must miss the feast of Ching Ming. Ask him to offer prayers to our ancestors on my behalf."

"It was not your father who sent for you," the runner explained.

"Is he dead?" the young gambler asked in apprehension.

"No, he's well."

Relieved, Mun Ki asked, "Then who presumes to send for me?"

"Your uncle, Chun Fat," the messenger explained.

The young brothel assistant could not remember his uncle, who had left the Punti village when Mun Ki was only three, so again he dismissed the command. "I can't return this year," he explained. "Business is good here in Macao." He pointed to the freshly painted brothel and to the red dragons on the gambling hall nearby.

Then the messenger delivered the striking news that was to modify the young pimp's life. He said, "Uncle Chun Fat has come back to our village with several million American dollars."

"He's rich?" the adroit young nephew asked.

"He's very rich!" the messenger replied in an awe-filled voice.

"We'd better leave at once," Mun Ki said forcefully. He went in to see the brothel keeper and reported, "My father summons me home to the Low Village." That sounded impressive.

"Then you must go," piously replied the Punti who ran the house. "Children must honor their parents. But if you find any extra girls in the village, bring them back. We can always use extra Punti."

As Mun Ki and the messenger hiked along the river bank to their village, the soft airs of spring brushed over them, and they were deeply moved by the sight of rice fields just bursting into a limpid green; but when they came within sight of home, they saw the bright red paint that had been lavished on the ancestral hall, and Mun Ki whistled: "Oooooh, he must be very rich," and he hurried home to report to his uncle on the Eve of Ching Ming.

Uncle Chun Fat was thoroughly impressed by his nephew, for he recognized in Mun Ki his own quick shrewdness. "How is work in the brothel?" he inquired.

"Good," his nephew dutifully replied. "You can always steal a little something from the Europeans. But I make most of my money gambling with the sailors."

Uncle Chun Fat studied the boy's hands and said, "You ought to go to America."

"Could I prosper there?"

"Prosper! My dear nephew, any Punti who cannot make his way in America must be very stupid indeed." Encouraged by the boy's attentiveness, Chun Fat expatiated upon his favorite theme: "It's ridiculously easy to make a fortune in America if you remember two things. Americans understand absolutely nothing about Chinese, yet they have remarkably firm convictions about us, and to prosper you must never disappoint them. Unfortunately, their convictions are contrary, so that it is not always easy to be a Chinese."

"I don't understand what you are saying," Kee Mun Ki interrupted.

"You will in a moment," his uncle replied. "First, the Americans are convinced that all Chinese are very stupid, so you must seem to be stupid. Second, they are also convinced that we are very clever. So you must seem to be clever."

"How can a man be stupid and clever at the same time?" the young pimp pleaded.

"I didn't say you were to *be* stupid and clever. I said you had to *seem* to be."

"How is that possible?" the handsome young gambler inquired.

"I left America with forty-one thousand dollars in gold because I discovered the answer," Uncle Chun Fat gloated.

"For example?" the student pressed.

"Take the gold fields," the Californian began. "For two years they watched me travel from camp to camp, observing everything. But they thought: 'He's a stupid Chinaman and he don't see anything.' And I will confess I did my best to look stupid. When I had learned as much as possible, I went into San Francisco . . . Mun Ki, when you do go to America, be sure to go to San Francisco. What a marvelous city! So much happening!"

"Where did the clever part come, Uncle?" the young man interrupted.

Chun Fat liked the boy's attention to detail, and continued: "In San Francisco I went to all the newcomers and told them, 'I can tell you which land to buy,' and they always said to one another, 'These Chinese are very clever. If anybody knows where the good land is, they do.' And I got rich."

"Stupid and clever," the young man mused. "That's difficult."

"Not necessarily," his uncle corrected. "You see, the Americans want to believe, so you don't have to work too hard. It's difficult only when you want to convince the same man, on the same day or even at the same instant, that you are both stupid and clever. Like on the railroad gang."

"What happened there?" Mun Ki inquired.

His uncle began to laugh heartily and said, "There was this big American boss. When you go to America, Mun Ki, never try to be the boss, not even if they ask you to, which they won't, because you can always make more money by not being the boss. Well, anyway, if I wanted to run the restaurant for the gang, at my own prices, I had to get permission from this big American, and I simply could do nothing with him until on a certain day when he cried in desperation. 'You stupid goddamned Chinaman!' And then I knew things would pretty soon be going my way, because if you can get the boss to yell at you, 'You stupid goddamned Chinaman,' everything is going to be all right."

Uncle Chun Fat never finished this particular narrative because he was reminded that the household must rise next morning at cockcrow in order to pay proper respect to the dead; and as the village lay sleeping beside the river, with the ghosts of its ancestors ready to assume their positions for the day of celebration, an old watchman who had long performed this ceremony gathered his gong and beater and waited till the third hour of the night. Then, as the first cock crowed, the old man went out into the dark streets and began beating his gong.

"Ching Ming!" he called to the living and the dead alike. Walking down the winding road that led to the ancestral hall, he continued to beat his gong, and he saw with pleasure lights coming on in the low houses; a young attendant hastened to light torches at the hall, and before the first shimmering darts of sunrise began to sweep in from the east, the Low Village was awake, and Mun Ki's ineffective father took his position of superiority at the ancestral hall, but it was brash Uncle Chun Fat who hurried busily about, telling the Kees what he wanted them to do.

Kee Mun Ki, from the brothel in Macao, left his home and walked solemnly to the hall, where a flight of nine scrubbed steps led to the pavilion in which the ancestral tablets were kept. Here he deposited his gifts and made obeisance to those from whom his family honor had descended. He then left the pavilion and joined the members of his family, standing at attention while his father prayed and while his uncle began a bombastic speech: "I am going to buy land on this side, and some more on this side, and what you have seen so far is really nothing. There will be a spacious hall, and where our tablets now stand, we will have not wood but the finest stone. The Kees will be known for their magnificence." And then his crafty eyes fell upon the extensive family gathered before him and he sighed to himself: "All those poor idiots starving here year after year when they could be making their fortunes in America." But he knew from experience that the Kees were not the kind of people who would venture forth to unknown lands, and he became lost in admiration of himself for having had the courage to do so.

He was therefore in a receptive frame of mind when a surprising event occurred in the Golden Valley, one totally without precedent. It was on April 19, 1865, when the fields were beginning to recover from the flood, that a merchant from Canton appeared in the Low Village, leading an American. Normally, any stranger who wandered from the quays of Canton would have been executed, but this man was different, for as a scholar he had requested freedom to travel inland, and it had been granted, so that now he stood in the bright spring sunlight, looking with an appreciative eye upon the strange world thus uncovered to him.

It took the Cantonese merchant about four seconds to recognize that in this village Uncle Chun Fat was the man to deal with, so he said directly, "The stranger has come all the way from the Fragrant Tree Country to hire people to work in the sugar fields."

Chun Fat stood enraptured, and his mind leaped back to that memorable day when his ship had stopped in Honolulu and he had been allowed to come on deck to see the great green hills behind the city. How marvelously beautiful those few hours had been, for storms had swept down from the heights and Chun Fat had watched the copious rain spread out like a blanket of benevolence over the rich land. "The Fragrant Tree Country!" he cried. "To go there would be like going to heaven itself."

Excited with a wild joy he ran into his house and reappeared with a sandal-wood box which he had purchased in Canton for the preservation of his silks, and he passed it around his family, explaining: "Smell it! In the country of which he speaks the air is like this twenty-four hours a day."

"Is it better than America?" his nephew asked.

Chun Fat hesitated. He had loved the wild cold mountains of California, and the lusty grandeur of San Francisco and the Mexican women with their songs, but he could not forget the Fragrant Tree Country. "It is a softer land," he said.

"Could a man make money there?" Mun Ki pressed.

"It's gentler," his uncle replied, and Mun Ki's mind was made up in that instant, for he thought: "If my uncle loves a land more for its beauty than for its money, it must be a wonderful land indeed."

Mun Ki was therefore the first to step forward and volunteer. "I'll go to the Fragrant Tree Land," he announced firmly, and when the American in the dark suit held out his hand, the Cantonese merchant shouted in Punti, "Take the hand, you idiot! Take it!"

This infuriated Uncle Chun Fat, who snapped: "We do not require a Cantonese fool who has shoes like rags to tell us how to act. Stand back or I'll break your head." Then, to the American, he said, in English, "Me Chun Fat, long time California. My boy, he go."

The American again extended his hand graciously and said, "I am Dr. John Whipple. I would like to hire about three hundred men for the sugar fields."

Uncle Chun Fat looked at the slim, gray-haired American in the expensive suit and instinctively recognized him as a big boss. "How much you offer to pay that one?" he asked, indicating with contempt the Cantonese.

"I'm afraid that's none of your business," Dr. Whipple replied. "But what did you have in mind?"

Chun Fat did some fast calculating. In the Kee family alone there were more than one hundred and forty able-bodied men. "Boss, I get you all men two dollars each man."

Now John Whipple did his own calculating. The Cantonese merchant whom he had brought with him could speak English, and had helped in that regard, but he had no sense of how to enlist labor. It was pretty obvious that this wily fellow from California knew what was required. But two dollars a head? "I'll give you one dollar and a half a head," he proposed.

Uncle Chun Fat studied this for some time, then replied slowly, "Who gonna argue with women? Who speak everything right?" He enumerated a long list of tasks he could be counted on to perform. "Two dollars," he said firmly.

"One-seventy-five," Whipple countered.

"Boss," Uncle Chun Fat smiled sweetly, "I top man here. Unless I speak, they no go."

"Two dollars," Dr. Whipple surrendered. Instantly Uncle Chun Fat thrust his hand out and grabbed Whipple's shouting to his people in Punti, "When you shake hands like this, by god, you believe what you say! I'm warning you, everyone of you!"

He was appalled, however, by Dr. Whipple's one stipulation: "Sir, I do not agree to this bargain unless half the men you send are Hakka."

Chun Fat looked at the stranger blankly. Finally, he repeated dully, "Hakka?"

"Yes, you know. Hakka. Up there."

"How in the world did he know about the Hakka?" Chun Fat thought despairingly. "Did that foul Cantonese . . ." To Dr. Whipple he said, "Why you want Hakka? No good Hakka."

Dr. Whipple looked him sternly in the eye, and his forty years of trading for J & W fortified his judgment. "We have heard," he said slowly, "that Hakka are fine workmen. We know that the Punti are clever, for we have many in Hawaii. But Hakka can work. Shall we go up to that village?"

Uncle Chun Fat faced a desperate impasse. He could see as clearly as he could see his hand those lush valleys of the Fragrant Tree Land. Good heavens, a hard-working Chinese set loose there could make a million dollars if he were clever! And think of the advantage to the Low Village to have three hundred

Kees working there and sending money back home regularly. Uncle Chun Fat could be sure of getting not less than fifteen cents out of every incoming dollar. It would be a calamity, a disaster worse than a flood, for the Kees to miss such an opportunity. But this stern, straight man had mentioned the Hakka . . .

"Dr. Whipple," Uncle Chun Fat began cautiously, "maybe Hakka work well but too much fight."

"I will go to the village alone," Dr. Whipple said sternly.

"How you talk with Hakka?" Chun Fat asked slyly.

Dr. Whipple smiled superiorly at the wily negotiator and said simply, "My friend from Canton will do the translating."

"But he no speak Hakka," Uncle Chun Fat said evenly, smiling back at his visitor.

With no evidence of frustration Whipple asked, "Do you speak Hakka?"

"Only one man speak Hakka. My boy Kee Mun Ki. In army he learn few words."

"I suppose you want two dollars for each Hakka, too?" Whipple suggested hesitantly.

"Yes, because speak Hakka very difficult."

"Let's go," Whipple said with a resigned shrug of his shoulders, and then from the manner in which Chun Fat hesitated he realized with amazement that no one from the Low Village had ever climbed to the High Village. "You've never been up there?" he asked.

"Hakka up there," Chun Fat shuddered.

When Dr. Whipple saw how difficult it was proving to be to reach Hakka country, he was momentarily inclined to forget the matter and was about to surrender and allow Chun Fat to supply only Punti, but then his scientific interest asserted itself and he reflected: "I came here to initiate an experiment to see who would best satisfy our labor needs on the plantations, Punti or Hakka, and I'm not going to be bluffed out of that study now." So he said firmly, "If you can't lead the way, I will." And for all his sixty-six years he was as spry as the Chinese, and after a sturdy climb the travelers came at last to the gateway of the walled village, and as they entered and saw the frugal U-shaped homes and the brooding, worm-eaten pole in the central square, on which perched the skull of Char the rebel, Whipple looked about him as if he had come upon familiar terrain and thought: "The climb was worth it. This feels like a New England village. I'm home again, in China." The feeling was intensified when strong, sullen and suspicious Hakka began cautiously gathering about him, and he could see in their conservative faces portraits in yellow of his own ancestors. Motioning to Kee Mun Ki to interpret, he said, "I have come to take one hundred and fifty of you to the sugar fields of the Fragrant Tree Country." There was much subdued discussion of this, heightened by Uncle Chun Fat, who officiously passed among the Hakka his sandalwood box, with the assurance: "Where you're going smells like this."

In the end one hundred and thirty Hakka were conscripted for the Whipple plantations, with promises of twenty more to be gathered from other mountain villages, and as the deal was being formalized with much cautious nodding, Whipple happened to notice that these upland women did not bind their feet, and he pointed to one woman and asked Uncle Chun Fat, "Why are their feet normal?" And the Californian replied, "They Hakka. Not got good sense." And Whipple asked, "Would women be allowed to come to the Fragrant Tree Country?" And Chun Fat replied, "Maybe Hakka women. Not proper Punti women." At the moment Whipple said no more about it, but he thought to himself: "Some day we'll need many Chinese women in Hawaii. Be a good idea to bring these Hakka in. They look strong and intelligent."

WHEN DR. WHIPPLE and his Cantonese guide had returned to Hong Kong, there to wait in Whipple's ship for the arrival of the three hundred plantation hands, Uncle Chun Fat engaged in a flurry of action. He assembled his extensive family in the open area before the newly painted ancestral hall, and on its steps he had an imposing chair placed, in which he sat, wearing his satin skullcap, expensive gown and brocaded shoes. To his right, but a little behind him, sat his legal wife, a woman of fifty, while to his left and farther behind sat the two attractive unofficial wives to which he, as a wealthy man, was entitled. The meeting got right down to business, with Uncle Chun Fat informing his four hundred-odd relatives: "This is an opportunity that may never come again. Think of it!" and he leaned back so that the Kees could see him in his days of lassitude. "A young man goes to the Fragrant Tree Country, works a dozen years, sends his money home to the Low Village, where his wife is bringing up fine sons, and after a while he returns a very wealthy man and takes two or three young wives. He is happy. His wife is happy because she no longer has to work. The young wives are happy because they have a rich man. And," he said dramatically, pointing casually behind him with his thumb, "he can build a respectable ancestral hall in honor of his distinguished family."

He allowed this recipe for earthly happiness to mature in the minds of his listeners and then said, "I am distressed that Dr. Whipple would not take his entire shipload from our village, for we could have supplied him, but even so our opportunity is historic. I am going to point to the strongest young men, and you are the ones who will start for Hong Kong . . . in three weeks."

Uncle Chun Fat rose, passed through the crowd, and arbitrarily nominated eighty-six Kees to volunteer for the journey. Some did not want to go, but they were powerless, for wasn't Chun Fat the richest man in the world? Who could argue with such a man? When this job was done their Uncle Chun Fat asked, "We now have remaining sixty-four places for the Low Village. Who should fill them?" And there was public discussion of this important point until the gambler Kee Mun Ki, who was proving to be a rather clever young man, pointed out: "Why not take the men who are about to marry girls from our family?" But Uncle Chun Fat rejected this, for it would take money from the village, and made an even wiser proposal, which the family recognized at once as a sound course of action: "We will send everyone who owes us substantial sums of money. And their wages will come to us." In this way the list was completed. Of the one hundred and fifty Punti who were sent, one hundred and ten did not want to go.

Following the nominations, there was a moment of relaxation during which Uncle Chun Fat studied his vast family with care, and when the mood was right he coughed twice, and the crowd dutifully lapsed into silence to hear what the great man had to say. Chun Fat, looking thoughtfully over the heads of the gathering, said slowly, knowing that what he was about to propose would come as a surprise to his clan, "I want everyone who, for the honor of his family, has volunteered to go to the Fragrant Tree Country to get married before he leaves this village."

A blizzard of excitement struck the Kee family, and many young men who had been forced by Uncle Chun Fat to accept exile to the sugar fields now indicated that they did not propose further to wreck their lives by hastily taking a wife. Grandly, aloofly, Uncle Chun Fat allowed the storm to rage, and when it had reached a climax, he coughed again, and somehow the quiet cough of a rich man is louder than the braying of six paupers, and the great family grew silent. "For example, in my brother's family I have decided that his son Kee Mun Ki should marry at once, and I have consequently been in contact with . . ." And here he paused dramatically to allow the family to savor his next words, and no one listened with more apprehension than the young gambler Mun Ki, for no one had told him he was about to marry. "I have been consulting with the Kung family of the next village and they have agreed to betroth their daughter Summer Bird to my nephew. Negotiations are already under way to celebrate this marriage, and, Mun Ki, I must congratulate you."

The young gambler gave a silly grin, accompanied by the required show of joy, for he recognized that Uncle Chun Fat had done a good thing for him. The Kungs of the next village, though not so rich as the Kees of this, were nevertheless a distinguished family, the principal difference being that their leader had gone not to California but only to Canton and had returned not with more than forty thousand dollars but with six. Nevertheless, it was a match that all in the Low Village approved, even though no one had yet seen the intended bride.

"So I insist that every young man marry," Chun Fat concluded. "Families can start sending out messengers at once to find likely girls, and I think it would be proper if celebrations were combined, so as to save money." Now that the marriages were agreed upon, and the families realized that they must actually set out to find wives for their departing sons, a new storm of agitation swept over the Kees, and again Uncle Chun Fat waited grandly in his satin skullcap until it had pretty well run its course. Then, with the grandeur of the ancestral hall looming behind him as if to fortify his edicts, he coughed quietly and gave the young men certain assurances. "You young travelers, like Mun Ki, must not think that because you are required to marry here in the Low Village that you may not also take wives in the new land. Oh no, indeed! There is only one reason why you must get married here, and establish your home here, with your legal wife waiting patiently for your return. If you do these things, then no matter where you go, you will always think of this village as your permanent home. You will yearn for the day when, like me, you stride up these sacred steps," and sweeping his expensive gown about him, he marched into the ancestral hall, from which he cried with real passion, "and you will bow humbly before the tablets of your ancestors. For your home is here." Gravely he bowed before the memorials of the ancients whose energies had built this village, and in deeply moving syllables he said, "When the white man abused me in California, I remembered this pavilion with my family tablets, and I gained strength to endure their abuse. When the snows were unbearable in Nevada, I remembered this ancestral hall, and they became endurable. Marry a girl from this valley, as I did thirty years ago. Leave her here with your home, and no matter where you go, you will come back." Then, adding a more immediately practical note, he reminded them: "And you will always send money back to this village."

Grandly, he left the ancestral tablets and returned to his chair, from which he reasoned directly: "But we know that it is always better when a Chinese man has some woman with him, so it would be wise, if, when you get to the Fragrant Tree Country, you took a wife there too. And the reason I say this is that while I was in America I noticed again and again that the Chinese men who made the most money were those with women. You might think it ought to be the other way around, but as long as I had no woman I did rather poorly . . . gambling . . . bad houses . . . and I may as well confess it, I got drunk every night for almost a year. Well, anyway, I found this Mexican woman and pretty soon I had her washing for the miners and cooking their food. And consider this, you Kees who are departing for a strange country. Even though I had to pay much money for her food, for she ate like a pig, and even though she was always wanting a new dress, it was only because of her that I saved any money. Therefore, it seems to me that if a bright young man like my nephew Mun Ki wee to marry the Kung girl here, and then also find a strong wife for himself in the Fragrant Tree Country . . . but be sure to get one who can work . . . well," and Uncle Chun Fat coughed modestly, hiding his lips with his silken-sleeved hand, "it would not surprise me at all if he were to return to this village a much richer man than I am."

With a new flush of modesty he dropped his eyes and allowed this dazzling prospect to capture his family. Not for a summer's moment did he believe that Mun Ki or anyone else would come close to his record of more than forty thousand dollars, but from the corner of his eye he saw with assurance that some of the young men were instinctively looking out across the fields and planning where, among the hills, they would build their cemeteries when they returned with staggering riches. But from the rear of the family came a nagging question: "When Mun Ki returns a wealthy man, does he bring his strange wife back to this village?"

"Certainly not," Uncle Chun Fat said evenly.

"What does he do with her?"

"He leaves her where he found her."

A buzz of admiration swept over the crowd, for the solution was both right and simple. The Low Village would be contaminated if it had to accept wives with strange customs, and while the elders were congratulating Chun Fat on his perspicacity, he quieted them and told the sprawling family: "The other wives will be able to care for themselves. When I left California I had three wives. A Mexican in San Francisco and two Indians in different parts of the mountains. They had helped me, so I helped them. I gave each one a thousand dollars." The crowd gasped at Chun Fat's compassion, and he concluded: "Because the important thing in a man's life is to return home to his village, to find his patient wife waiting, and in his old age to acquire two or three beautiful young girls of good family." Behind him his three wives smiled gently as he said, "Believe me, under those circumstances a man's joy is great."

When the young gambler Mun Ki accepted the betrothal his uncle had arranged for him, Chun Fat sent the Kungs in the next village not the customary thousand cakes—"Your daughter is worth one thousand pieces of gold, but please accept these poor cakes"—but two thousand and forty-three, the idea being that the number really could have been as large as he wished. Each cake was the size of a plate: soft sponge cakes, cakes stuffed with chopped nuts and sugar, hard flat cakes, cakes lined with rich mince, and others decorated with expensive sweetmeats. He also sent sixty-nine pigs, four chickens with red feathers, and four large baked fish. Then, to prove his munificence, he added forty-seven pieces of gold, each wrapped in red paper. The procession that carried these things to the Kungs was a quarter of a mile in length.

From two of the ceremonial pigs the bride's family cut off the heads and tails, wrapped them in silk and returned them to the Kees, indicating that the largesse had been both humbly and impressively received by the bride's family. But on her own account she sent three gifts to the groom: an embroidered red cloth which he would use as a belt, a wallet for the worldly wealth which she would help him earn, and two pairs of pants.

It was obviously going to be a tremendous wedding, and it dwarfed the thirty-one others that were proceeding at the same time. Two weeks before the Kees were scheduled to depart for the ship waiting at Hong Kong, the ceremony took place amid all the grandeur the two Lowland villages could provide, and when the days of celebration ended, young Kee Mun Ki brought his bride home and tried mightily to impregnate her before the time for sailing, but he failed.

On the morning when Uncle Chun Fat assembled his hundred and fifty Punti for the three-day hike to Canton, where they would board a river steamer for Hong Kong and the American ship, he saw before him a rather bleary-eyed, sexually exhausted group of men. "A good march along the river will toughen them up," he reassured himself, because he realized that if he could deliver his volunteers in good condition, he had a right to expect that subsequently Dr. Whipple would commission him to conscript many more, all at two dollars a head. He therefore moved among his troops encouraging them to spruce up, but when he came to his nephew Kee Mun Ki, he scarcely recognized him. The young gambler had been drunk for two weeks, hardly out of bed for ten days, and looked as if he might collapse during the first hundred yards of the march to Canton. Realizing that he had to depend upon this youth for transmitting orders to the Hakka, Uncle Chun Fat started slapping him back and forth across the cheeks, and slowly the young man's eyes began to focus. "I'll be all right," the gambler mumbled. "In Macao once I was drunk for three weeks. But not with a fine wife like the Kung girl." And Chun Fat saw with pleasure that when his nephew's services were really required, the brash young gambler would be ready. "You'll do well in the Fragrant Tree Country," Chun Fat reassured the young man. "I expect to," the young husband replied. It was just a little insulting, the way in which he spoke to his uncle on a man-to-man basis, as if they were equals.

Now came a moment of intense excitement, for down from the hills marched the contingent of Hakka, thin men, dressed in rude, tough clothing, their pigtails long and their faces tanned. Two months before, the arrival of such a group would have signified war; now it occasioned only mutual disgust. Defiantly, the Hakka marched up to where the Punti stood, and against his own prejudices Uncle Chun Fat thought: "They'll do well in the new country." Because he was making two dollars a head on the Hakka, and hoped to make more in the future, he wanted to go up to them and bow in greeting, but he realized that this might be interpreted as Punti subservience and would never be forgiven by his family, so he glared at them as custom required. For a long moment the two groups stood staring insolently at each other. During nearly a thousand years they had lived side by side without ever speaking; they had met only in death and violence; there had been only one marriage. Now, with their inherited hatreds, they were going to travel in a small ship to a small island.

Mun Ki broke the spell. Pulling himself together, he stepped forward and said to a man named Char, leader of the Hakka, "We will start to Canton now. Some of your men look tired already."

Char studied the young Punti to see if this was intended as an insult, and replied evenly, "No wonder they look tired. They've been drunk for two weeks . . . like you."

"I got married," Mun Ki explained.

"So did they," the Hakka Char said, and the antagonists smiled.

The contingents started forward, but as they did, the Punti looked for the last time at their Low Village and its bright red ancestral hall. This was their home, the soil of their heart, the abiding place of their ancestors. Their wives were here. Many had sons whose names were already on the tablets in the pavilion. The graves where the ghosts of their forefathers walked at night were in this land, and to leave the Golden Valley even for a few years was punishment almost beyond the bearing. "I will come back soon!" Mun Ki called, not to his wife, nor to his domineering uncle, nor to any living person. "I will come back!" he called to his ancestors.

It took three days to reach Canton, the Punti moving together in one group, the Hakka in another, and during this vigorous exercise Kee Mun Ki whipped himself back into his customary lean condition. His eyes cleared and his wits sharpened, and as he entered the great city, seeking out Dr. Whipple to deliver the workers, he wondered if he could slip away for a few hours for some intense gambling with the British sailors at the quay, but unfortunately Dr. Whipple had a river boat waiting and herded his charges directly aboard. When they were assembled he spoke to them in quiet English, and his interpreter explained: "The American has discovered that if he tries to take you men out of China by way of Hong Kong, where his ship is visible in the bay, the government will execute every one of you. For daring to leave China. So we are sailing to Macao, where it will be possible to depart without being killed."

Quickly Mun Ki moved up to the interpreter and said, "In Macao I must see my old employer and bid him farewell. Please tell the American."

There was some discussion and the interpreter said, "All right. But the others must stay overnight inside a compound until the ship arrives from Hong Kong."

Mun Ki congratulated himself and began daydreaming of the great fortune he would make on his last hours at the gambling tables, when the interpreter returned and dashed his fantasies by announcing: "The American remembers that you are the only one who can speak with the Hakka, so you will not be allowed to leave the compound."

Mun Ki tried to appeal this unfair decision, but the interpreter, after discussing the protest with Whipple, said bluntly, "You will stay inside the compound."

When the coastline of Macao appeared, with its low white Portuguese buildings shining in the sunlight, and its military guard loafing about in European uniforms, the Punti and Hakka workers lined the river boat to study the strange port: a foreign city nestling on the coast of China, a city with one European for every two hundred Chinese, a curious, lawless enclave that was neither China nor Portugal but the worst of each. But to Mun Ki, well versed in the evil ways of Macao, it was a pragmatist's paradise. He saw the tiled roofs of the Brothel of Spring Nights and thought tenderly of some of the girls he had helped to bring there, strong, happy girls who enjoyed their work. Farther on he saw the gambling halls, where he had known both success and failure, and as the river boat drew closer to the shore, so his excitement mounted, until at last he moved swiftly among the Punti, whispering, "Lend me your money! I am going to the gambling halls and I will return with two for one." Some were suspicious of their brash cousin; others respected him for his daring, and in time he had a considerable number of coins. "I'll see you tomorrow," he whispered. "Say nothing to the fool from Canton."

So when the river boat touched the quay, and there was much jostling among the Chinese and calls back and forth between the Portuguese officials, Mun Ki slipped deftly away, disappeared into the piles of merchandise stacked along the quay, and hurried up a back alley to the Brothel of Spring Nights. "You must have celebrated the festival of Ching Ming as never before," the brothel keeper observed icily.

"I got married," Mun Ki explained.

"Ah, that's very good!" the keeper expounded. "Every man should have a loyal and patient wife. I count the beginning of my happiness from the day I married and began having a large family."

"I am also leaving China for the Fragrant Tree Country," Mun Ki said honestly. "I've come to get my things."

"You're leaving me!" the proprietor stormed. "After I've spent all this time and money training . . ." Suddenly he stopped ranting and asked, "Did you say the Fragrant Tree Country?"

"Yes. Sugar fields."

"Now that's really strange!" the brothel keeper cried, tapping his knee with his forefinger. "I have some rather important work that requires doing in that country. Yes." He went to a file of papers and sorted out one from a Punti who had gone to the Fragrant Tree land some years before, and this man, remembering how well the Brothel of Spring Nights had been run in Macao, had written to the proprietor asking for certain assistance. Holding the letter between his teeth, Mun Ki's superior studied the young gambler and then asked, "Would you be willing to execute a rather difficult commission for me?"

"Do I get paid?" Uncle Chun Fat's nephew asked bluntly.

"You do."

"I'll do it."

"I thought you would."

"What's the job?"

"I've got a girl tied up in the little room. Been planning to ship her to Manila. We can't use her here, as you'll see. Will you deliver her to my friend in the Fragrant Tree Country?"

"I will. Which room?"

"The one where the Russian girl used to be."

Mun Ki forgot his gambling for a moment, walked down a narrow hall, and kicked open the familiar door. Inside, the blinds were drawn, and in the darkness, on the floor, lay a trussed-up girl, knees lashed to chin, almost unconscious from hunger and lack of water. With his foot Mun Ki rolled her over and saw that she was dressed in a cheap blue cotton smock and trousers; her big feet proved that she was a Hakka. In disgust Mun Ki slammed the door and returned to his employer.

"Who wants a Hakka?" he demanded.

"Nobody," the brothel keeper agreed. "I paid some of General Wang's soldiers to kidnap half a dozen girls, and they brought back this one. I was going to send her to Manila. Over there they don't know the difference."

"How much for me if I take her to the Fragrant Tree Country?" Mun Ki asked.

"Twenty Mexican dollars," the proprietor replied.

"Paid now? I'd like to double it in the gambling rooms."

"Half paid now," the canny brothel keeper agreed.

He gave Mun Ki the ten Mexican dollars, and the young man was about to dash over to the gambling, but the proprietor suggested, "Maybe you better feed her. She's been tied up for two days. The soldiers seem to have treated her rather badly before they turned her in, and I was afraid she might run away after I had paid for her."

"Did you give much?" Mun Ki inquired.

"For a Hakka? That I couldn't use?"

The young gambler returned to the room, yelled for a maid to bring him some hot tea and rice, and then parted the curtains. He saw at his feet a young Hakka woman of about eighteen. Even when her face healed she would probably not be a pretty woman, and the manner in which she was gagged and trussed did not permit any estimate of her general appearance. Therefore, more in a spirit of investigation than humanity Mun Ki kneeled down and started to untie the merciless ropes. As he loosened one after the other, he could hear the girl groaning with relief, but he noticed that even so her limbs did not automatically stretch out toward their normal position, for they had been constricted so long that some of their muscles had gone into spasm. Again motivated by investigation, he started gently to unfold her hands and pull her arms down along her body. He pushed her shoulders back and could hear joints creaking in protest. She groaned deeply and fainted, but then the maid brought the tray, and he applied tea to her lips and gradually she regained consciousness and began to drink. She was so desperate for liquids that even Mun Ki was impressed, and he sent for more tea. As its warmth circulated through her body, the girl began to return to an awareness of where she was, and she looked in terror at the man who held her, but the manner in which he started to feed her the rice, waiting until she had chewed each grain lovingly, lest someone steal it from her . . . this made her think that perhaps he might not be like the others who had captured her that night before the Ching Ming festival. The things they had done in the three weeks they had dragged her and their other captives through the country-side she had already forgotten, for they were too terrible to remember. Instinctively she felt that this man would not treat her so.

Char Nyuk Tsin was the first Hakka the young gambler had ever touched, and it was with instinctive loathing that he now did so, and yet it was a strange fact that her response to his kindness moved him and made him want to be kinder yet. He held her shoulders in his left arm and fed her warm rice with his right, and when the maid brought in some cabbage broth, he gave her the spoon and encouraged her to eat, but her wrists were so swollen from the ropes that she could not do so. He therefore started to massage them, and gradually blood circulated to her fingers and she could hold the spoon, but she could not operate her shoulders. So he massaged her back and neck, and instinctively his hand slipped forward over her shoulders and he felt her hard little breasts. Almost against his will there came a moment of awakening, and he felt memories of his soft young wife from the Kung village come flooding over him, and he lifted away Nyuk Tsin's smock and caressed her body, and then he slipped off her trousers, and when her knees and ankles remained in their rigid, muscle-locked condition, he gently massaged them until they relaxed, and he saw with increasing pleasure how slim and beautiful this girl's body was. Reminded of his bride, he quickly slid out of his clothes and threw them against the door, saying to the Hakka girl as he did so, "I will not hurt you."

When he had been with her for some time the proprietor came back to the little room to advise him on how to deliver the girl to the brothel keeper in Honolulu, but when he pushed open the door a little way and saw what the young people were up to, he advised in Punti, "Use her as you wish, but tie her up again when you're through."

The voice of the boss awakened Mun Ki to his responsibilities, and with real fright he grabbed at his pants to see if while he had been engaged with the girl some clever man had stolen his gambling money in the way that he, Mun Ki, had sometimes picked the pockets of preoccupied customers in the Brothel of Spring Nights. His money was secure, so he quickly dressed and said to the naked girl, "I must go to the gambling. Put your clothes on."

And as he waited for her to do so, he picked up the cords, and when she turned to face him she saw the cruel, biting cords and tears came into her eyes and she pleaded with Mun Ki and took his hands and promised, "I will not run away."

He held the ropes and studied her, and something in the manner in which she looked at him convinced him that she would not flee; so, still grasping the ropes, he led her to his room in a hovel in back of the brothel, where he sat her upon the floor. Dangling the ropes before her terrified face he seemed to ask: "Am I required to use these?" and she looked at him as if to promise: "You do not need the cords." Against his better judgment, he started to leave, but to do so with the girl unbound was obviously ridiculous, so he decided upon a sensible solution. With one end of a fairly long rope he tied the Hakka girl's left wrist; the other end he attached about his own waist, and when this was done he said, "Come."

When he passed the desk of the brothel the proprietor saw what he was doing, and said, "A good idea." Then the man asked professionally, "Will she make a good girl for my friend?"

"Yes," Mun Ki assured him, and he led his captive to his favorite gambling hall. But when they were in the street he stopped and asked her, "What is your name?" and she answered, "Char Nyuk Tsin," and he replied, "Perfect Jade! That's a good name." To himself he thought: "In a brothel it's a very good name. A man can remember it when he comes back the next time."

The gamblers were playing fan-tan, in which from a large pile of snowy-white ivory buttons the dealer withdrew a handful, whereupon the crowd bet as to whether the number to be left over at the end was one, two, three, or none. Or, if the gamblers wished, they could bet simply on whether the ivory buttons would turn out to have been odd or even. When the bets were placed, the amazingly deft dealer started to pull his buttons away from the pile in lots of four, and it was striking how skilled the players were in discerning, while the pile of buttons still contained fifty or sixty, what the number left over at the end was bound to be.

Using his own and other Punti money, Mun Ki had a satisfactory run at fan-tan, and he felt that perhaps the fact that he had been kind to the Hakka girl had brought him good luck, so he took his earnings to the mah-jongg room, where the clattering ivory tiles evoked their perpetual fascination. When at the beginning of each game the players built their wall, it was customary for them to slam the tiles down with maximum force, creating an echo that accentuated the natural excitement of the game, and likewise, when a player scored a coup and exposed his pieces he slammed them onto the noisy table. Mah-jongg as played in Macao was a wild, exhilarating game, and now Mun Ki decided to test his luck at a table where real gamblers played for high stakes. Placing Nyuk Tsin behind him, and twitching the cord now and then to be sure she was still tied, he joined three waiting men. Two had long, wispy beards and costly gowns. The other was more like Mun Ki, a young, aggressive gambler. At first one of the older men protested, "I do not wish to play in a room where there is a woman," but Mun Ki carefully explained, "I am taking her to a brothel in the Fragrant Tree Country and am responsible for her." This the men understood; in fact, the man who had protested thought: "Probably he will have his mind on the girl and will lose more quickly."

But Mun Ki had not entered the game to lose. Mah-jongg, unlike fan-tan, did not depend so much on luck as on the skill with which one played the pieces luck sent him; and the young gambler, thinking that this might be his last day in a big mah-jongg contest, breathed deeply as he used both hands to help mix the 144 tiles at the start of the game. With loud energy he banked his pieces down to make the wall and then watched carefully as he rolled his dice to help determine where that wall should be broached to begin the gambling. With intense excitement he grabbed his tiles in turn and remembered Nyuk Tsin only when he leaned forward to reach the tiles and felt her rope tugging at his waist. When his tiles were arranged—and he had long since learned to keep them in haphazard formations from which his clever opponents could deduce nothing —he was ready to play, but the bearded man who had originally protested against Nyuk Tsin, said, "She has got to sit on the floor where she can't spy." So before the game began in earnest, the Hakka girl sat on the floor, but this was not entirely satisfactory to Mun Ki, who was afraid that she might slip away, so he forced her to sit under the table, against his feet, and there she remained for the long hours during which the four players slammed down their tiles with great force.

From her position under the table Nyuk Tsin noticed that she could detect when Mun Ki was attempting some daring coup, holding back tiles in hopes of building them into some fantastic combination that would win him much money, for then his ankles became tense, the little bones stood out and his feet began to sweat. At such times she prayed for his success, and she must have been attuned to some powerful god of good fortune, for her man won. At dusk he tugged on the rope and said, "We'll go home." But as they returned to the dusty streets of Macao, hawkers swarmed about them, attracted by the rumor: "The young fellow from the brothel was a big winner." They brought flowers and bits of cloth and steaming kettles of food, and Mun Ki found real pleasure in playing the role of a generous winner. Fingering the torn cotton fabric of his girl's smock he said, "This one needs a new dress, believe me." And with grandilo-quent gestures that all could admire, he announced: "We will have four lengths of that!" He was even more generous when it came to food, and hungry Nyuk Tsin had black eggs, dried fish, noodles and crystallized ginger. As they lounged beneath a dentist's sign he announced to the crowd: "I am really a very lucky gambler. I can see what's in the other man's mind."

As the night wore on, he drew the cord tighter to him, so that Nyuk Tsin could not stray, and he bought bits of food for worthless characters he had long known in the Portuguese city. When the civil guard passed by, he nodded to them, and when one asked, "why do you have the girl tied up?" he replied in the patois of the port city, "I am delivering her to a brothel in the Fragrant Tree Country."

The police nodded approvingly, and then one stopped. "Are you sailing on that American ship in the bay?"

"I suppose so," Mun Ki replied.

Instantly the policeman grew confidential, and whispered, "I'd better warn you, then. The American who bought you in the village came to us today to have you arrested. You'd better hide."

"I'm reporting in the morning," Mun Ki assured him. "But thanks." And he gave the policeman a coin.

"Thank you, Mun Ki!" the official bowed. "That's a nice girl you're taking with you."

"She's only a Hakka, but she brings luck," Mun Ki replied.

Finally he led his captive back to the Brothel of Spring Nights, where he showed his former boss how he had multiplied the ten Mexican dollars eight times. "This girl brings luck," he said.

"Are you going to tie her up again in the little room?" the proprietor asked.

"She'll sleep with me tonight," Mun Ki explained.

"All right," the prudent businessman replied, "but remember what you learned here about breaking girls in. Feed them and beat them."

"I'll take care of her," Mun Ki assured him. "Were the police here for me?"

"Of course," his boss replied. "Your ship's sailing tomorrow."

"I'll be there."

Tugging the cord, he led Nyuk Tsin down the narrow hallway, out the back door of the brothel and on to the hovel where he slept. Locking the door, he untied the rope from his waist, but fastened it even more securely about Nyuk Tsin's wrist. She explained that she needed to attend to her bodily functions, so he opened the door and allowed her to go outside while he lounged in the doorway, testing the rope now and then to be sure that she was still secured. When she returned he said, "Now we must pack for the journey."

He had provided a wooden tub into which he jammed his accumulated treasures: a teapot, five bamboo cups, two good rice bowls, a metal pot, a porcelain tea set with a small copper strainer, a bamboo tray for steaming vegetables and a large knife. The incense burner, the kitchen god and the ancestral tablet which proved who he was were tucked into place, followed by his extra clothes and a pair of good sandals. Over this tub he now tied securely a piece of canvas stolen from a Dutch ship.

In a wicker basket Nyuk Tsin packed the food for the trip: soy vinegar, pickled cabbage, spices, dried fish, seeds to chew on and several chunks of flattened duck. The implements for cooking also went into the basket: chopsticks, a charcoal stove, one old cup and two old rice bowls.

The little room now contained only a bed and a poem. The former would be rolled up in the morning; the latter, which explained the manner in which the names of one Kee generation followed another, was contained in a red-lined book in which the genealogy was kept, and as the most precious of Kee Mun Ki's possessions, it would be the last to leave and would be carried by Mun Ki himself.

Surveying the quarters in which he had lived with reasonable happiness, and from which he had moved out to become a skilled gambler, Mun Ki sighed. Then, seeing Nyuk Tsin standing forlorn in the middle of the dimly lit room, he said, "You may undress now," and when she untied her wrist and dropped away her clothes, and when he saw that the cord marks were disappearing from her body, he smiled and indicated that she could sleep with him. Since she had expected to be tied up again and thrown onto the floor, she came to him gratefully and was not afraid when he began quietly to enjoy her. He was the first man who had ever touched her with what could even remotely be termed affection, and she found herself reciprocating. They had a vigorous passage of love and Mun Ki thought: "In some way she's better than my Kung wife." When they were through he remembered to reach for the cord to tie her to him, but when he took her wrists she pleaded: "It is not necessary." He was tempted to believe her, but he knew that if she ran away he would not only look the fool but would also be required to refund the ten Mexican dollars plus whatever his boss had paid the kidnapers, so he lashed her wrists to his; but he did allow her to sleep beside him.

In the morning, when they were dressed, he finally threw away the rope, for he thought: "If I report to Dr. Whipple leading this girl by a rope, he will hardly believe my story that I am married to her," and on his ability so to convince the American depended the success of this voyage. But when the rope fell in the dust of the little room, Nyuk Tsin stooped down and retrieved it for tying her basket of food. When they left the room, Nyuk Tsin carried the tub and the heavy basket. Mun Ki carried the feather-light bedroll and the genealogy book, but after he had stepped into the filthy yard behind the brothel, Nyuk Tsin called to him and pointed to the wall above where the bed had stood and where a sign now hung that she could not read. Mun Ki whistled at his forgetfulness and recovered the omen of special good fortune: "May This Bed Yield a Hundred Sons!" Tucking it under his arm, he led his woman to the waiting ship.

At the quay Dr. Whipple stood ready to berate the only man he had who could converse with the Hakka, and as soon as Mun Ki appeared, the Cantonese interpreter started shouting at him, but he ignored the man and marched contritely up to the American. Bowing his head in feigned apologies he said softly, "I am a thousand times humble, sir, for having run away." Then, producing the overburdened Nyuk Tsin, he said simply, "I had to find my good wife."

"Your wife!" the interpreter stormed. "No women are allowed on this . . ."

Dr. Whipple, noticing the girl's big feet, asked, "Isn't she a Hakka?"

"Yes," Mun Ki replied, and the American scientist, remembering how he had once idly considered the desirability of importing some Hakka women to Hawaii, asked, "Do you wish to take her with you?"

When this was interpreted, Mun Ki piously nodded and explained: "I could not bear to leave her behind."

"I'm willing to try it," Whipple announced. Then he warned Mun Ki: "But when she gets to Hawaii, she's got to work."

"She'll work," Mun Ki assured him.

At this moment the hundred and fifty Hakka men saw Char Nyuk Tsin for the first time since her abduction on the Eve of Ching Ming, and they began to cry to her, and Mun Ki knew that if they explained who she was, his fanciful story would be exploded, but he also realized that no one on the quay but he could understand what they were saying, so he nudged Nyuk Tsin and told her, "Speak to them." Pushing her toward the Hakka, he followed behind and cried to the men, "This girl is my wife." And the Hakka saw about his waist a red marriage belt and they began to wonder what had happened. "Are you indeed married to the Punti?" they shouted. Mun Ki jabbed his girl in the back and whispered, "Tell them you are." So Nyuk Tsin informed her countrymen, none of whom had ever befriended her after her parents' death, "He is my husband." And the Hakka looked at her in scorn and would have no more to do with her, for their parents had often warned them about what had happened to the disgraceful Hakka girl who had married a Punti man in 1693.

This problem settled, quick-thinking Mun Ki now faced one far more serious, for Dr. Whipple was calling, through his interpreter, for the married couple to join him, but when Mun Ki and Nyuk Tsin started to do so, they had to pass through the Punti contingent, and these men were even more outraged at Mun Ki than the Hakka had been. They, too, had been well drilled in the evil that had befallen the Punti man who had dared to marry a Hakka girl back in 1693, and they drew away from Mun Ki as if he were unclean, but as he passed each group he muttered to those from whom he had borrowed: "Last night. Big winnings. Lots of money for you." And this softened their anger.

When he reached Dr. Whipple, the American said, "We will have to ask the captain of the ship if he will accept another passenger. And if he says yes, you will have to pay passage money for your wife."

He therefore sent a sailor in search of the captain, and in a moment a towering American loomed among the Chinese, a man in his seventies, with stout muscles and a sea cap jammed on the back of his head. He had fierce, dynamic eyes and looked at the men about to board his ship as if he hated each one of them with deep, personal anger. Brushing them away as he strode through their groups, he came up to Whipple and asked, "What is it, John?"

"Captain Hoxworth," the trim, gray-haired scientist began, "I find one man who wants to bring his wife along."

"You willing to pay five dollars' passage money?" Hoxworth asked.

"Yes. I'll get it from the man."

"Then it's simple," the captain growled. "She can come."

Dr. Whipple conveyed this news to Mun Ki, who grinned happily, explaining to the interpreter, "A man would not like to leave his wife in Macao." Dr. Whipple was impressed by this sentiment and asked Captain Hoxworth, "Where will the couple sleep?"

"In the hold!" Hoxworth snapped with some surprise that the question should have been asked. "Where the hell do you suppose they would sleep?"

"I thought," Whipple began, "that with her the only woman, and three hundred men . . ."

"In the hold!" Hoxworth shouted. Then, addressing the Chinese, who could not possibly understand him, he roared, "Because when this ship sails I don't want to see one goddamned Chinee anywhere but locked up in the hold. I'm warning you."

"Rafer," Dr. Whipple began again. "In the case of this couple, couldn't they stay with . . ."

Captain Hoxworth turned quickly, pointed his long forefinger at his missionary friend, and snapped: "They'll stay in the hold. How do I know this rascal isn't a pirate? How do you know he's married? There'll be no pigtailed Chinee anywhere on this ship except locked up below."

Reluctantly Dr. Whipple explained to Mun Ki that if he insisted upon bringing his wife along, she would have to share the hold along with two hundred and ninety-nine other men, but to his confusion Mun Ki evidenced no surprise and Captain Hoxworth observed: "It's nothing to them. They live like animals."

The moment had now arrived when the Chinese were to board the *Carthaginian* as it lay alongside the Macao quay, and Portuguese officers, in brilliant uniforms, took their places at the gangplank, checking off numbers rather than the names. The Cantonese interpreter said farewell, and the three hundred Chinese men and their one woman were left alone in two hostile groups, Hakka and Punti, with no one who could converse with the Americans who ran the ship and with only one man, Mun Ki, who could make himself understood to both contingents. However, their thoughts were diverted from their plight by the natural excitement involved in climbing aboard the schooner from whose mast flew the blue H & H flag. When the first Chinese stood at the top of the gangplank and saw before him the great open ocean, he hesitated in natural apprehension, which was increased when a sailor grabbed his pitiful store of belongings to stow them aft. The Punti started after his precious bundle, but he was halted by Captain Hoxworth, who grabbed him by the pigtail, spun him around and with a forceful kick sent him stumbling across the deck. "Get down into the hold, you stupid Chinee!" Hoxworth roared, and when the uncomprehending Punti stood in bewilderment, the captain kicked him again. The Chinese staggered backward toward the open hold, missed the ladder and plunged headfirst fourteen feet into the dark interior of the ship.

Instantly the remaining Chinese became tense, and Captain Hoxworth sensed this, for he whipped around, grabbed a belaying pin and took three determined steps toward the men climbing up the gangplank. Cursing them in a language they could not understand, he grabbed the arm of the next Punti, swung him about, and launched him toward the ladder. When the Chinese had sense enough to climb down, the big American roared, "There's gonna be no trouble aboard this ship!" And he brandished his belaying pin as the future plantation hands disappeared into the dark hold.

As they went below, the Chinese caught a last glimpse of their homeland, and unconsolable sorrows assaulted them, for it was a miserable thing when a man left China, and some sensed that never again would they see this great land; no matter how harshly China had treated them it was still the Middle Kingdom, the heavenly land suspended between mere earth and the residence of the gods: the sweeping plains, the rice fields in the spring, the glorious mountains, and the wild, cruel rivers. It was a land men could love, and for each who now deserted it, there came a memory of the village where his ancestral pavilion waited his return.

Just before it was Nyuk Tsin's turn to enter the hold, a thoughtful Punti climbed back out to advise Captain Hoxworth that the first man who had been thrown into the ship had broken his ankle, but when the good Samaritan reached the deck Hoxworth became furious and clouted the man with his belaying pin, knocking him back into the hold, where his friends caught him. "Don't any of you goddamned Chinee pirates come up onto my deck!" the captain bellowed.

Nyuk Tsin was the last person down the ladder, and as she prepared to descend, she saw Dr. Whipple smiling at her while Captain Hoxworth monitored her with his belaying pin. Beyond them she caught a last glimpse of China, and when she thought of the brutal way in which this land had murdered her parents, and of the near starvation in which she had lived, and of the archaic terror she had known with her kidnapers, she was glad to see the end of China. Since she was only a woman, her name appeared in no ancestral hall and there were no ties binding her to the mountains other than the memory of the animal-like loads her uncle had piled upon her, so as she saw her homeland for the last time she whispered to herself, "Farewell, cursed land. I shall never see you again."

Then she saw at the bottom of the ladder the young gambler, Mun Ki, the only person in many years who had been kind to her, and gladly she climbed down to be with him, and she was gratified when he extended his hand to help her; but she did not know that he was doing so to prevent her from breaking a leg, for an accident like that would seriously diminish her value when it came time to sell her in Honolulu.

As she reached bottom, the ladder was hauled out and heavy boards were dropped across the opening. When it became apparent that the hold was to be completely closed, the Chinese began a loud wail of protest, and Captain Hoxworth shouted, "Get the muskets!" When they were produced he ordered three sailors to kneel along the edge of the hold, and then he shouted, "Fire!" Shots whistled past the pigtails and crashed into the bulkheads. The terrified Chinese fell to the floor and the last boards of the covering were hammered into place. Now only a faltering light filtered in through a narrow grating, and there was no air, but a sail was rigged on deck so that when the ship was in motion, a breeze would be trapped and funneled below. There was no regular supply of water, only one foul bucket for slops, and such bedding as each man had brought of his own, nor were there any blankets for those who tried to sleep. It was in these quarters that Nyuk Tsin started housekeeping with her gambler, Mun Ki, and his two hundred and ninety-nine companions.

One thing was settled quickly. The Punti took their position forward and the Hakka aft, for naturally neither group wished to contaminate itself with the other, and for Nyuk Tsin there was a moment of hesitation when she felt that perhaps she ought to settle down with her own people, but they showed that they wanted nothing to do with a Hakka girl who had married a Punti; and at the same time the Punti made no effort to welcome her, so she took her position in a corner of the Punti terrain, and there she was left alone with her husband. The Punti did, however, bring to her their fellow with the broken ankle and they suggested in signs that she repair the damage. She studied the man's leg and concluded that the break was not complicated, so she made a splint of chopsticks and lashed it in place with ends of cloth. Then she borrowed bedding from others and made a rude mattress on which the man rested. If there had been water, she would have washed his face, too.

Now there was a motion of the ship, a swaying in the offshore breezes and finally the slow, steady roll of the ocean itself. Before long the hold was a confused agony of seasickness, with men vomiting everywhere and then rolling indifferently in it. Nyuk Tsin became so nauseated that she hoped the ship would sink, and in this stench the first awful night passed.

At dawn a sailor opened the grating to pass down some buckets of water, shouting to his mates, "You want to smell the other side of hell?"

His friends came over and took a whiff. "How do they stand it?" they asked.

The first explained, "They're Chinee. They like it that way," and he jammed the grating back, forgetting to reset the deck sail so that fresh air could funnel in. The day grew increasingly hot and there was insufficient water to wash away the appalling smell, so that most of the three hundred got sicker than before. They sweated, retched, went to the toilet, filled the foul bucket and then used the floor. The heat grew unbearable and the man with the broken ankle started to rave about going home.

In the afternoon a little more water was passed down and the sailor shouted, "For Christ's sake, now smell it!" And his mates agreed that with a hold full of Chinee you could do nothing. This time, however, someone remembered to tip the sail into the breeze, and by evening the hold was beginning to settle into the routine that would be followed for the next forty-six days. At eight in the morning and at four in the afternoon kettles of rice were lowered into the hold, along with stray ends of salt beef. There was no point in trying to serve vegetables or fish. Water was never plentiful, but a system was devised whereby at signals the slop bucket would be hauled up on a rope and emptied. The deck sail was tended so that a minimum breeze was funneled in, but never enough to permit a man a full breath of clean, cold air. The awful smell never abated, a mixture of urine, sweat, bowel movements and seasickness, but it was surprising that even those with especially sensitive stomachs did in time grow accustomed to it, for the odor seemed to represent them, forming a vital part of their foul, cramped quarters.

Providentially Mun Ki had brought with him some playing cards, and when his seasickness abated he set up a gambling corner where each day, as long as sunlight filtered through the grating, he tried to win back the money he had paid his Punti friends. He was adept with cards and won small amounts from most of his adversaries, announcing often, as he patted the back of his pigtail: "I'm a very lucky fellow. I understand the run of cards." When an opponent lost his stake, the nimble-witted gambler suggested: "I'll lend you some so the game can continue," and strict accounts were kept of who owed whom and how much. Significantly, no Punti ever promised: "Mun Ki, when we get to the Fragrant Tree Country I will pay you what I owe you." Instead, they assured him: "When I earn some money, I will send it to Uncle Chun Fat in the Low Village." For that was home. That was where accounts were kept, the permanent address of a man, the known anchor.

One evening when the faltering light no longer permitted gambling, Mun Ki looked at the girl he was convoying to the brothel keeper in Honolulu and reflected: "Perfect Jade! Not exactly perfect with those ugly feet." In comparison he recalled his soft young wife from the Kung village, well brought up and with small feet, and he would recall the enchanting manner in which a girl with bound feet walked, not like a man at all, but swaying in the ambient light like a flower, her hips moving in a special way calculated to drive a man crazy with desire. Thinking of the subtle poetry with which his young wife moved, he next recalled his memorable days of playing with that delectable girl, and he reconstructed the things they had done together in the silken bed. He became tumescent, and before night fell with its utter darkness, he studied Nyuk Tsin and thought: "But she can be fun, in her own way, too." He drew her to him and tried to slip his hands under her clothes, but the Punti were so crowded in the filthy hold that instinctively she drew away, for many were watching her. "They are looking," she whispered.

This irritated Mun Ki, so impulsively he stood and announced: "I am a married man and it is outrageous that I cannot sleep with my wife. I am going to build a corner." He unrolled all of his bedding, and with the point of a knife began tearing slivers of wood from the bulkhead until he got two stout ones started upon which he could hang his partitions, and before night fell completely, he had cut off a private corner, and when he brought Nyuk Tsin inside he told her that now she could undress, and when they lay locked together on the rough boards of the floor he told her, "Except for your disgraceful feet, you are almost as good as my Kung wife."

Thereafter, whenever the gambling declined in interest and the long dreary days ended in shadows, Mun Ki would announce: "Well, I am building our corner again!" And the other men, Punti and Hakka alike, honored his arrangement and during the daylight hours treated Nyuk Tsin with increased respect. On the bulkhead Mun Ki hung his good-luck sign: "May This Bed Yield a Hundred Sons." And although he was unaware of the fact, the sign was effective, and in due course Nyuk Tsin would bear him a son.

* * *

A T THE BEGINNING of the second week it became obvious that the broken ankle of the Punti man was not going to heal, for some of the splintered bones had caused wounds that were now well festered, and a dangerous blue line had begun to form along the man's leg. Therefore, one morning when the grating was opened to haul up the slop bucket, one of the Punti men swung himself aloft with the intention of asking the sailors for help, but when they saw his ominous yellow face and the long pigtail appearing on deck, they panicked and began to shout, "Mutiny! Mutiny!"

The first mate came rushing forward, grabbing a pin as he ran, and Captain Hoxworth left the bridge, leaping swiftly down the ladders onto the deck. By this time one of the sailors had swung a powerful fist at the startled Punti, knocking him toward the first mate, who brought his pin down across the man's skull with full force. This knocked the Chinese unconscious and into the path of the onrushing captain, who, when he saw the fallen mutineer, began to kick him in the face, driving his heavy leather shoes into the inert man's cheekbones until there was a sickly collapse of the man's facial structure.

When the terror ended, the captain shouted to his sailors, "You, there! Throw this damned pirate back in the hold." Two sailors grabbed the inert Punti and tossed him headfirst down the opening.

"Goddamnit!" Hoxworth shouted in frustration. "We should never have sailed without someone who can speak Chinee." He stormed for a moment, then commanded: "Mister Aspinwall, fetch the guns." When they were produced, Hoxworth directed his men to fire into the bulkheads over the cowering Chinese.

"Don't ever try to mutiny my ship!" Hoxworth stormed, cursing the coolies and stalking back to his bridge.

He was met there by an ashen-faced Dr. Whipple, who demanded bitterly, "Was such brutality necessary, Captain Hoxworth?"

The tall seafarer, fleshy and prosperous, stared ahead over the prow of his ship and said, "John, you'd better keep out of this."

"I can't be partner to such brutality," the gray-haired doctor said firmly.

"You afraid of blood?" Hoxworth asked. "Or afraid of losing your investment?"

Dr. Whipple refused to acknowledge this insulting query, and continued as if he had not heard it: "As a Christian I cannot tolerate your behavior toward men I conscripted in good faith."

The older man continued conning his ship and said calmly, "Dr. Whipple, how many vessels do you think were mutinied last year by Chinese pirates who smuggled themselves aboard?"

"I don't know," Whipple replied.

"Eleven," Captain Hoxworth said evenly. "That is, eleven that we know about. We haven't the remotest knowledge of what's lurking in that hold. Pirates . . . cutthroats . . . mutineers. You guess. All I'm saying is, that a Hoxworth & Hale ship is never going to be mutinied by any Chinee. That's why I personally supervised this little adventure."

"But to kick an unconscious man!"

"Dr. Whipple, I respect your principles. I like the way you carry out your business. But in my business, the minute a captain is either afraid or unwilling to kick his enemy to a pulp, he's on the verge of losing his ship. I have nineteen ships now, and I don't propose to lose a damned one of them to a bunch of murderous Chinamen."

Dr. Whipple studied these remarks in silence, then moved to the doorway leading from the bridge. In resolute, unhurried words he said, "Captain, although I respect your fears, I must dissociate myself from your actions. They were brutal and indefensible."

The doctor considered this statement a morally crushing one and left the bridge, but big Captain Hoxworth bounded after him, caught him by the arm, swung him around, and growled, "Once a missionary, always a missionary. Doctor, you don't know a goddamned thing about running a ship, and you ought to keep your nose out of it. This is not work for a missionary. It's work for a man." Shoving Whipple away in contempt, he stalked back to the bridge, from which he ran his ship and from which, figuratively, he ran his entire line of prosperous vessels.

John Whipple did not allow his anger at such treatment to obscure his judgment. In years of trading around the Pacific he had often met obstinate men and the cruel situations which they produce, and he had learned that in such confrontations his only chance of winning lay in doing exactly what in conscience ought to be done. It was by reliance upon this conviction that he had quietly made his way in such disparate jungles as Valparaiso, Batavia, Singapore and Honolulu. Now he went calmly to his cabin, next door to the one where the captain had kept the two young Chinese girls during the Hong Kong layover, and took up his doctor's kit. Checking it as he had learned to do more than forty years before, he carried it sedately to the locked grating and said to the sailor on guard, "Open it and let me in."

"The captain would . . ."

"Open it," Whipple commanded. "There's a man dying down there." And he took a belaying pin and started knocking away the wedges that held the grating in place. When it had swung free, he saw that no ladder could be fitted into it, so he held his bag between his knees, grabbed the edge of the opening, and swung himself down into the stinking hold. "What a horrible smell!" he mumbled through clenched teeth as he joined the three hundred and one Chinese.

Compared to the brightness of the day on deck, all was gloom and shadowy darkness in the hold, and as his eyes slowly became accustomed to the tenebrous hell, and his nose to its rankness, he saw that two men lay stretched out in the middle near where he had landed, while the others stood huddled in two clearly separated groups. He thought: "They will be the Punti and the Hakka." And he could not be certain when they might leap at him, as in justice they were entitled to do. But each of three hundred had seen him before, in the villages, and therefore he seemed like an old friend, which he now proceeded to prove he was.

Ignoring both the uncertainty and the danger of his position, he knelt beside the man whose face had been kicked in, checked the extent of damage, and spread beside him objects that the Chinese could see were medicines. Carefully, by keeping one thumb pressed inside the unconscious man's mouth, first at one place and then at another, he began to mold the bones back into line, thinking: "It's merciful that he is still insensible." He next medicated the open wounds where the heavy boot had cut the skin and saw with some pleasure that the man's eyes were not badly damaged. Looking up at the circle of inquisitive faces, he communicated his real joy at this discovery, and the Chinese understood.

At this point, Nyuk Tsin came to him and directed his attention to the man with the broken ankle, and he studied with admiration the splint made of chopsticks. Again he demonstrated his approval, and again everyone understood, so that Nyuk Tsin gained even greater acceptance than she had before enjoyed. But it was also apparent to Dr. Whipple that the injured Chinese could well lose his leg unless quick remedies were effected, so he shouted through the grating, "Send me down some hot water, right away." But when the sailor opened the grating, everyone below could hear the captain's great voice shouting, "Who in the hell ordered you to touch that grating?" And the sailor replied, "Dr. Whipple is down there tending the sick Chinese." There was a moment of ominous silence, the sound of heavy feet striding across the foredeck, and an echoing slap across someone's face, followed by a deluge of scalding water down the grating.

"There's his hot water, by God! And I'll teach you to open a grating!" There were ugly sounds, such as the Chinese had heard before, but this time, looking at Whipple amongst them, they could be sure that it was an American who was receiving a beating.

Then, in the mournful semi-darkness, a face that could not be clearly discerned pressed close to the grating and bellowed, "John Whipple, are you down there with those goddamned Chinee pirates?"

"I am giving them medical care," Whipple said.

"Well, if you love the Chinee so much, you can stay down there!" and he ordered the new sailors who assumed the grating-watch: "If he makes a single move to get out, bash him in the face with a board."

In the next hour John Whipple made one of the two or three fundamental discoveries of his long and scientific life. He found that men of good will who could understand not a single word of the other's language, could nevertheless communicate with reasonable accuracy and with profound perceptions that were neither logic nor sentiment. If a man wanted strongly enough to be understood, he was, and before sixty minutes had passed, Dr. Whipple had somehow explained to both the Hakka and the Punti that the damaged ankle could be saved if he could use their sparse reserves of water, that the unconscious man need not die, that the slop bucket should have the rim washed each day with the remnants of what water was left, and that only one section of wall away from the wind should be used for urinating, whether the man was a Hakka or a Punti, and when in the late afternoon it came time for him to urinate, he used that designated spot and saw with some satisfaction that the urine ran quickly out of the hold along a break in the floor. He smelled the area closely and concluded, "With this heat it'll be horrible in two days, but better than before."

To punish the mutineers for actions which, in Hoxworth's opinion as he reported in his log, could well have led to the loss of the *Carthaginian,* no food or water was passed down through the grating that day, nor was the slop bucket hauled up, and as twilight fell and the card games ceased, John Whipple settled down for his first long night of hell in the crowded hold, but as he prepared to lie upon the bare boards, Nyuk Tsin moved among the Hakka men and found a few extra cloths. Vermin had already begun breeding in the rags, but Whipple used them and thanked their owners. But the smell of the hold nauseated him.

It was not until four o'clock the following afternoon that the grate was opened and some water sent down, and Whipple was astonished at the sensible discipline imposed at this moment by the gasping Chinese. Kee Mun Ki stood forth as the leader of the Punti, and a tall, rugged man as spokesman for the Hakka, and the water was justly divided and apportioned, after which Dr. Whipple shouted, "Will you send down four more buckets of water, please?"

There was a hushed convocation aloft to consider this request and after a moment the heavy sound of boots. Through the grating Captain Hoxworth shouted, "What is it you want?"

"We require four more buckets of water," Whipple replied evenly.

"What you require and what you get are two different matters," Hoxworth stormed. "I'm dealing with a mutiny."

"Will you have your men haul up the slops?" Whipple pleaded.

"No!" Hoxworth replied, and marched off.

During the second awful night there was both hunger and acute suffering from lack of water, but Dr. Whipple explained to the Chinese that Captain Hoxworth was mentally unbalanced and that everyone, including Whipple, must be careful not to exasperate him. The stench was worse that night, if possible, for not much breeze came through the grating, but next morning four extra buckets of water were sent down and some food. When Whipple was given his share, his stomach revolted and he thought: "Good God! Do we serve them this? To eat?" The long day passed, and Dr. Whipple, unable to occupy himself merely by tending the broken ankle and the crushed jaw, found himself thinking: "No one who journeys to a distant land ever has it easy. Things were better on the *Thetis,* but were they really much better? At least in the Pacific there isn't constant seasickness. Now if this were the Atlantic . . ."

But the Chinese, in these same empty hours, were thinking: "I'll bet a rich American like this one never knew such things before." And although Whipple and his Chinese friends could talk about many things, on this fundamental fact of emigration they could never communicate. Even when each had the full vocabulary of the other, this basic fact of brotherhood—that all have known misery—could not be shared, for just as Abner Hale had refused to believe that the Polynesians had suffered heroic privation in getting to Hawaii, so the Chinese of the *Carthaginian* would never accept the fact that the wealthy white man had known tribulation too.

The day droned on. The smells lessened when Dr. Whipple showed the men how he wanted the slop bucket washed down. It helped, too, when he sloshed a full bucket of water in the urinal corner. The man with the broken face moaned less often, and the ominous red streaks up the groin of the other sick man diminished. There were card games and some shouting among the Punti over an incident which Whipple did not understand, and suddenly Mum Ki rose and announced something, whereupon he and his wife started hanging rude blankets across a corner of the hold.

"Goodness!" Dr. Whipple said to himself when he discovered what the contrivance was for. And the meaningless day passed into meaningless night. But before the light vanished, the grating was kicked aside and Captain Hoxworth shouted abruptly, "You ready to come up, Whipple?"

"I brought these people aboard this ship," the doctor said quietly. "I'll stay with them till the sores are healed."

"As you wish. Here's some bread." And a loaf of bread banged down into the hold. The Chinese, to whom Whipple offered some, did not like it, but Whipple observed that it was mainly the Hakka who were willing to try something new.

On the third day the grating was kicked aside, some of the boards of the hatch covering were removed, and a ladder was thrust down into the hold. Armed sailors stood guard as Dr. Whipple slowly climbed up and adjusted his eyes to bright daylight. Before he departed, the Chinese signified that they were sorry to see him go, and he replied that he would send them more water and better food. Then the boards were hammered home again.

Whipple's meeting with Captain Hoxworth was a painful one. For the first two hours the captain avoided him, but at lunch they had to meet, and Whipple said flatly, "Rafer, we have got to give those people more water."

"We will," Hoxworth grunted.

"And they must have better food."

"At the price we agreed to haul them, Doctor, that's impossible."

"It isn't impossible to keep filth out of the rice."

"Our cook ain't trained in this Chinese stuff, Doctor."

"He's got to feed them better."

"Not at these prices," Hoxworth replied stubbornly.

Dr. Whipple, now sixty-six, was afraid of very little, and without throwing down a blunt challenge, observed: "Two days ago you accused me of being a missionary. It's been many years since I thought of myself as such, but as I grow older I'm increasingly proud to accept the charge. I am a missionary. I've always been one. And, Rafer, do you know the truly damnable thing about a missionary?"

Hoxworth suspected that he was being challenged by a man at least as smart as he was, and replied cautiously, "I think I know the worst about missionaries."

"No, Captain, you don't, because if you did you would never treat me as you have the past two days. You have never learned the one respect in which missionaries must be feared."

"What?" Hoxworth asked.

"They write."

"They what?"

"They write. They have an absolute mania for taking pen in hand and writing a book, or a memorial, or a series of letters to the newspapers." Icily he stared at the big sea captain and said, "Rafer, I have never written, yet, of what I think of the way you treated Abner Hale, your partner's father, because that was a personal thing and could possibly be excused. But unless you feed these Chinese better, when we get to Honolulu I am going to write. I am going to write a series of letters, Rafer, that will forever cast a stigma upon the blue flag that you love so well. Whenever an H & H ship puts into port, someone will have heard about those letters. Because missionaries have one terrible power, Rafer. They write. They are the conscience of the Pacific."

There was an ominous silence, broken finally by Hoxworth's slamming his fist onto the table till the dishes rattled. "Why, goddamn it, this is nothing but blackmail."

"Of course!" Whipple agreed. "Blackmail is the only refuge of the literate man against barbarism. And you're a barbarian, Rafer."

"What is it you want?" the captain growled.

"Twice as much rice a day. And decent meat. Water three times day. The slop bucket to come up three times a day. And I will be free to go down into the hold once a day to check the sick."

"I will not run the risk of having this ship mutinied," Hoxworth stormed. "I will not uncover that hold till we reach Honolulu."

"I'll go down through the grating," Whipple countered.

"You'll get back as best you can," Hoxworth warned.

"The Chinese will lift me back."

"You seem very fond of . . ." Hoxworth did not finish this insult but asked confidentially, "Tell me, Doctor, what's happening with the Chinese girl? Do the men take turns?"

"She's the wife of one man," Whipple replied coldly. "They live in one corner of the hold."

"Tell me, does this man, well, does he . . ."

"Yes. Behind a sheet which he hangs from the bulkhead."

"Well, I'll be damned!" the captain mused. "You wouldn't find three hundred American sailors letting a man get away with anything like that. No, sir!"

"Maybe the Chinese are more civilized," Whipple said and left.

It was with pride that he accompanied the first additional ration of water into the hold. He was there when the improved food came down, and by this time the awful stench had abated somewhat, for he had taken upon himself the job of setting the deck sail properly so as to wash fresh air down into the noisome hold. The poison was now abated from the broken ankle, and the second man's face was healing. Some of the Punti, directed by Whipple, were fraternizing with the Hakka, and Mun Ki, on one special day toward the end of the voyage, actually wanted Nyuk Tsin for herself alone, and not because he had been daydreaming of his naked Kung wife. He was finding Nyuk Tsin a most pleasurable and hardworking woman.

On one particularly hot day the Chinese were startled to hear a terrifying sound forward, as of chains running out, and they thought some disaster had overtaken them, for they knew nothing of ships, but it immediately became apparent that the motion of the *Carthaginian* had ceased; at last the ship was home. After much coming and going on deck, the boards covering the hold were knocked away and the ladder was dropped down. One by one the Chinese climbed back into daylight, rubbed their eyes in pain, and gradually saw the white shoreline of Honolulu, the palm trees, the distant majesty of Diamond Head, and far behind the flat land the mountains rising green and blue and purple, shrouded in misty storms. As was customary on almost each day of the year, a rainbow hung in the valleys, and the Chinese thought this a particularly good omen to mark their arrival at the Fragrant Tree Country. How beautiful, how exceedingly marvelous the land seemed that day.

There were others, too, who felt that the arrival of the *Carthaginian* was a good omen, for the Honolulu *Mail* carried a report which stated: "We are told on good authority that Whipple & Janders, utilizing the H & H schooner *Carthaginian,* will shortly be depositing in Honolulu a new cargo of more than three hundred Celestials destined for the sugar fields. These ablebodied hands, for we have been assured that Dr. John Whipple went personally to China to secure only strong young males—many of them Hakka this time—will be available on five-year contracts at the rate of $3 cash a month, food and found, plus three Chinese holidays a year. At the end of ten or fifteen years of work in our fields, it is confidently expected that the Chinese will return to their homeland, especially since they have not brought their own women with them, and it can hardly be supposed that they will find any here.

"Sugar men who have already utilized Chinese on our plantations say this of them. For all kinds of work they are infinitely superior to the shiftless Hawaiians. They eat less, obey better, are not subject to illness, are more clever in mastering new jobs, make fine carpenters when trained, and have a noticeable affinity for agricultural life. The employer must be stern, not beat them too often, and above all must not show signs of vacillation, for like all Orientals, the Chinese respect and love those who exercise a firm authority and despise those who do not.

"We are fortunate in acquiring such admirable workmen for our plantations and we are sure that after these industrious Chinese have worked out their terms and have saved their wages, they will return to China, leaving in these islands an enviable reputation for industriousness while taking back to China wealth they could not otherwise have dreamed of. The sugar industry welcomes these Celestials, and we feel confident that the true prosperity of our islands will date from this day."

On such truly amicable terms the Chinese went ashore at the Fragrant Tree Country, but in their disembarkation there was this profound difference among them: the Punti thought: "This will be a good home for five years, and then I will see the Low Village again," and no Punti had this determination to a greater degree than Kee Mun Ki; but the Hakka thought: "This is a good land to make a home in, and we shall never leave," and no Hakka thought this more strongly than Char Nyuk Tsin.

If the Chinese sometimes irritated Hawaii by refusing to call the new land anything but the Fragrant Tree Country, the islands retaliated in a rather striking manner. Inside the hot customs shed an immigration official was shouting, "All right! Attention! All Pakes over here!" No one moved, so he shouted again, this time pronouncing the word slowly: "Pakays, over here." Again there was no response, so he yelled, "You Chinks! Line up!"

It was said that when the first Chinese landed in Hawaii the islanders asked them, "What shall we call you?" And the most sedate of the travelers replied, "It would be proper if you called me 'Pak Yeh,'" which meant Older Uncle. And from that time on, the Chinese were called Pakes.

As it came Kee Mun Ki's turn to face the interpreters he trembled, for he knew that soon he must make a fundamental decision concerning the Hakka girl Char Nyuk Tsin, but any perplexity over her was driven from his mind when an official, a large Hawaiian with a few phrases of Chinese, scowled at the man in front of Kee Mun Ki and growled, "What's your name?"

The Punti stood silent in fear, so the huge Hawaiian shouted, "What's your name?" Still the man remained awestruck, so that a Chinese scholar employed for the purpose hurried up and said in good Punti, "Tell the man your name."

"Leong Ah Kam," the Chinese replied.

"Which of the names is the important one?" the Hawaiian asked.

"Leong," the interpreter explained.

"How'd you spell it?" the Hawaiian asked.

"Well," the scholarly interpreter hedged, "in English this name Leong is rather difficult. It could be made into Lung or Long or Ling or Liong or Lyong."

The big official studied the problem for a moment. "Lung sounds silly," he growled, not because he was angry at the Chinese standing before him but because he was bedeviled by this constant problem of finding names for immigrant Chinese. Suddenly his face brightened into a generous smile and he pointed a big, pudgy finger at the laborer Leong Ah Kam, and fastening upon the last two names, he announced: "From now on your real name is Akama. And don't you forget it."

Carefully he printed the name on a white card: "This man's official name is L. Akama." It was in this manner that the Chinese got their Hawaiian names. Ah Kong became Akona. Ah Ki became Akina, and sometimes the simple Ah Pake, The Honorable Chinese, became Apaka. As in the past, Hawaii still modified all things that came to it, and the Punti laborer Leong Ah Kam became L. Akama.

It was now Kee Mun Ki's turn, and when the interpreter asked him his name he said firmly, "Kee Mun Ki, and I want to be known as Kee."

"What did he say?" the Hawaiian asked.

"He said that he wished to be known as Kee."

"How would you spell it?" the Hawaiian asked. When he heard the reply he tested the named several times, found it satisfactory, and printed: "This man's official name is Kee Mun Ki," and the tricky little gambler felt that he had won a victory. But before he had time to savor it, he was faced by two new problems, for outside the fence of the immigration area a thin, sharp-eyed Chinese was calling in whispers to him, and the young gambler knew by instinct that this was a man he did not wish to see; but the calling continued and Mun Ki had to move toward the fence.

"Are you the one who brought the girl?" the wiry man asked in Punti.

"Yes," Mun Ki replied honestly.

"From the Brothel of Spring Nights?"

"Yes."

"Thank the gods!" the nervous visitor sighed. "I need a new girl badly. It looks like she's a Hakka."

"She is," Mun Ki replied.

"Damn!" the visitor snapped. "Did he knock off the price? Her being a Hakka?"

"There is no price," Mun Ki said carefully.

The wiry man's face grew stern. "What?" he asked.

"I am going to keep her for myself," Mun Ki replied.

"You thief! You robber!" The man outside began to make such a protest that officials came up on the inside of the fence and shouted at him. "That is my girl!" the infuriated Punti shrieked, forgetful of the fact that he was incriminating himself. One of the Punti interpreters called a Hakka clerk and together they addressed Char Nyuk Tsin.

"The man outside says that you were sold to him," the Hakka interpreter explained.

"What man?" Nyuk Tsin asked in bewilderment.

"That small, nervous man," the official replied, and from the manner of the questioning, and from the look of the excited little man, and from the great embarrassment of her husband, Nyuk Tsin slowly realized that she had been brought to Hawaii to be sold into a house no different from the Brothel of Spring Nights. She could feel once more the ropes about her wrists, and although it had been some weeks since she recalled the hideous nights with her kidnapers, she could now remember. She did not panic, but with real courage fought down the terror that welled into her throat. Brushing aside the Hakka interpreter, she went boldly to Mun Ki and stood before him so that he would have to look at her.

His downcast eyes saw her big feet, her strong body, her capable hands and finally her unpretty but appealing face. He looked directly in her eyes for some moments and thought: "She is worth whatever she may cost. This one can work."

And with a clear voice, whose words Nyuk Tsin could understand, Mun Ki said, "This girl is not for sale. She is my wife."

No Hawaiians or Americans had so far become involved in this quarrel between two Chinese men, and as always the various interpreters were determined that the misunderstanding be settled within the Chinese community. So the Punti interpreter said, "That's all very well, but the man outside says he paid fifty dollars for this girl."

"He is correct," Mun Ki said. "And I will give him my own fifty dollars." He untied his wedding belt, dipped down into a pouch that his Kung wife had embroidered for him, and produced fifty Mexican dollars. It was like giving up part of his immortal spirit for Mun Ki the gambler to surrender these dollars, for he had intended to multiply them many times, but he passed them through the fence.

"It's better to handle everything among ourselves," the Punti official whispered, but the brothel proprietor began screaming that he had been robbed of an important asset, whereupon Mun Ki leaped to the fence, thrust his right arm through and caught the nervous little man by the neck.

"I will thrash you!" he cried. "I owed you money and like an honest man I have paid it."

"What's going on over here?" Dr. Whipple called.

"Nothing," the Chinese officials blandly replied.

"You, out there? What's the fighting about?"

"Me no fight!" the brothel keeper exclaimed, looking astonished that anyone should have thought that he was involved in trouble.

"What name did they give you?" Whipple asked Mun Ki. "Let's see the paper. Yes, Mun Ki. That's a fine name. Sounds Hawaiian. Interpreter, will you tell this man that I would like to have him and his wife work for me. Ask him if he can cook."

"Can you cook?" the Punti asked Mun Ki.

"I was the best cook in the best brothel in Macao," the gambler replied.

"I don't think the American missionary would understand," the Punti thought. To Whipple he said, "The man says he can cook."

"Explain to him that if he works on the sugar plantation he earns three dollars a month, but as a cook boy only two dollars. His wife gets fifty cents a month. But there are many advantages."

"What?" Mun Ki asked.

"You learn English. You become skilled. And you live in town, so that if later you want to open a store . . ."

"I'll be your cook," Mun Ki said, for although the explanations given by Whipple were interesting, the young gambler had swiftly foreseen an additional advantage that outweighed all the rest: in the city he would be closer to the big gambling games.

It was for these reasons that Kee Mun Ki and his Hakka wife Nyuk Tsin became the household servants of the Dr. John Whipples; but as the Chinese stooped to recover their luggage, Mun Ki taking the light bedroll and Nyuk Tsin the heavy tub and basket, she saw tied to the latter the rope with which she had been lashed up in the Brothel of Spring Nights, and it reminded her that it was the quick, clever man who walked ahead who had saved her from such things and who, with his own cherished gold pieces, had purchased her freedom. So as she tagged along behind him, weighed down with burdens, she thought: "May that good man have a hundred sons."

ON CLOSER INSPECTION, Honolulu of 1865 proved far less glamorous than its physical setting. Because Hawaii could provide no lumber, nor skilled stonemasons to work the product of its quarries, the houses of the city were meanly built, each foot of timber being conserved for practical rather than aesthetic use. Buildings were therefore low, formless and hastily put together. In the central area they crowded in upon each other and were usually not painted.

Streets were unpaved and very dusty, and although a few business thoroughfares had rude sidewalks made of granite ballast hauled from China, in most
areas pedestrians had to use the fringes of the road. There were, however, a good
police force and an active fire department, but judging from the numerous scars
that showed where flames had gutted whole rows of attached buildings, the
latter seemed to enjoy only a modest success.

Business establishments occupied big rambling buildings, often made of
brick carried as ballast from England, and stores sprawled aimlessly over many
haphazard counters. At the corner of Fort and Merchant streets in a bright new
brick building distinguished by green cast-iron shutters, Janders & Whipple had
the town's largest emporium, but the most impressive commercial building
stood on an opposite corner: Hoxworth & Hale's huge shipping headquarters.
Sharp-eyed Mun Ki, comparing Honolulu's grubby appearance with the grandeur of Canton, where impressive stone buildings lined the waterfronts, was
frankly disappointed in the contrast.

Meanwhile, other Punti from the *Carthaginian* were discovering that the
lush tropical growth of the island was confined to the inaccessible mountains,
whereas the land on which they were to work was really more bleak and barren
than that which they had fled in China. This depressed them and they thought:
"Uncle Chun Fat lied to us. Not even a Chinese can make his fortune on such
a barren island." Out of a hundred average fields surrounding Honolulu, not
less than ninety were desert, for on them no rain fell. The vast acreages west of
Honolulu, which belonged to the Hoxworth family through inheritance from
the last Alii Nui, Noelani, were practically worthless, thirsting for water. But
scattered across the island there were small valleys in which an occasional
bubbling stream fed the fields, and here the Chinese were put to work. Some
grew rice for the booming California market. Others worked on small sugar
plantations. A few lucky men were taught to ride horses, and became cowboys
on the parched rangelands, and many were put to work growing vegetables; but
as they started their new tasks, each man carried in his memory an exciting
picture of Honolulu's close-packed streets and dusty enterprise, and all thought:
"I've got to get back to Honolulu. That's where the life is."

Hawaii's reception of the Chinese was somewhat dampened by Captain
Rafer Hoxworth's frightening account of his heroic escape from mutiny, and the
newspapers were peppered with predictions from other seafaring men that
Honolulu had entered upon a period of maximum danger, when the possibility
of an armed Chinese uprising, with all white men murdered in their beds by
slinking Celestial fiends, was a distinct possibility. Captain Hoxworth volunteered several interviews with the press in which he contended that only his swift
reaction to the first attempts at mutiny had preserved his ship, and thereafter he
became known as the intrepid captain who had quelled the Chinese mutiny.

The friends of Dr. John Whipple were therefore apprehensive when the
doctor took into his home the Kees to serve as cook and maid, and men stopped
him several times on the street to ask, "Do you think it wise, John, to harbor
in your home such criminal characters?"

"I don't find them criminal," Whipple responded.

"After the mutiny?"

"What mutiny?" he always asked dryly.

"The one that Rafer Hoxworth put down on the *Carthaginian*."

Dr. Whipple never openly refuted the captain's story, for he knew that what
is mutiny to one man is not to another and it was his nature to make generous
allowances, but he often did observe sardonically: "Even very brave men some-

times see ghosts." He was content to have the Kees working for him.

On the day of their arrival Dr. Whipple piled their luggage into his dray and then led his two servants on foot leisurely up Nuuanu Street toward his home, and although he could not speak Chinese, he explained the structure of the city to the young couple. "The first street we cross is Queen, Queen, Queen." He stopped and drew a little map in the dust and made them repeat the name of the cross street. At first they failed to understand what he was doing, so deftly he drew a ship and pointed back to the *Carthaginian,* and immediately they caught on, for it was Dr. Whipple's conviction that any man not an imbecile could be taught almost anything.

"Merchant, King, Hotel," he explained. Then he left big Nuuanu Street and took a detour to the corner of Merchant and Fort to show his Chinese the J & W store. "This is where I work," he said, and his servants were impressed, the more so when he picked up several bolts of dark cloth and handed them to Nyuk Tsin.

Finally he came to the broad east-west street named in honor of Great Britain, Beretania, and when he had taught the Chinese how to say that important name, he showed them that they stood on the corner of Nuuanu and Beretania. They understood, and then he pointed to a substantial picket fence that surrounded a large property on the ocean-western corner, and when he had reviewed with them just where this stood, he opened the gate and said, "This will be your home."

They smiled, three people with three different languages, and the Chinese looked in awe at the Whipple homestead. Set amid three acres of land, it was built on coral blocks and consisted of a large one-story wooden building completely surrounded by a very wide porch. All interior rooms were thus dark and cool and were accessible to the veranda. The coral base of the house was masked by luxuriant croton plants, recently brought to Hawaii by the captain of an H & H ship, and these produced large varicolored leaves, iridescent in rain or sunlight, so that the sprawling house nestled in tropic beauty.

Dr. Whipple called, and from the front door his wife appeared, a small, white-haired New England woman wearing an apron. She hurried across the porch and onto the lawn, extending her hands to the Chinese. "This is my wife," Dr. Whipple explained formally, "and this is the cook Mun Ki and the maid Mrs. Kee." Everyone bowed and Mrs. Whipple said, "I should like to show you to your new home," and she demonstrated how the Whipple dining room stood at the rear of the big wooden house, and how there was a covered runway from it to an outside kitchen, where all the food was cooked, and another runway leading off to a small wooden house, and this was to be theirs. She pushed open the door and showed them a compact, clean room, which she herself had dusted that morning. Leading off from it was another, and while they stood there conversing they knew not how, the dray arrived with their luggage and stores of food, utensils and bedding.

"These are for you," Mrs. Whipple said warmly, taking Nyuk Tsin's hand and leading her to the boxes. That afternoon one of the Hewlett women asked, "Amanda, how will your Chinese learn to cook if they can't understand a word you say?"

"They'll learn," Amanda replied forcefully, for she shared her husband's New England conviction that human beings had brains; so for the first four weeks of their employment, the Kees went to school. Little Amanda Whipple was up at five, teaching Mun Ki how to cook American style, and she was impressed both with his clever mind and his fearful stubbornness. For example, on each Friday during the past four decades it had been Amanda's ritual to make the family yeast, and for the first two Fridays, Mun Ki studied to see how she performed this basic function in American cookery. He watched her grate the potato into a stone jar of almost sacred age and add a little salt and a lot of sugar, after which she poured in boiling water, allowing all to cool. Then, ceremoniously, she ladled in two tablespoonfuls of active yeast made the Friday before, and the strain continued. For forty-three years Amanda had kept one family of yeast alive, and to it she attributed her success as a cook. She was therefore appalled on Mun Ki's third Friday to enter the cookhouse full of ritualistic fervor, only to find the stone jar already filled with next week's yeast.

With tears in her eyes, she started to storm at Mun Ki, and he patiently listened for some minutes, then got mad. Flashing his pigtail about the kitchen he shouted that any fool could learn to make yeast in one week. He had been courteous and had studied for two weeks and now he wanted her out of the kitchen. Not understanding a word he was saying, she continued to mourn for the lost yeast, so he firmly grabbed her shoulders and ejected her onto the lawn. On Monday the new batch of yeast was as good as ever and she consoled herself philosophically: "It's the same strain, sent forward by different hands." Suddenly, she felt the elderly white-haired woman she was.

Mun Ki also had difficulty understanding why Americans ate so much, and he would consistently omit dishes to which the robust appetites of the white men had become accustomed. A typical Whipple dinner, served at high noon in the heat of the day, consisted of fish chowder, roast beef with Yorkshire pudding, creamed cabbage cooked in ham fat, delicious chewy biscuits made of taro and drenched in butter, mashed potatoes, candied yams, pickled mango, alligator pear salad with heavy dressing, French bread with guava jelly, banana pie marvelously thick and rich, followed by coffee with cream, and cigars. If guests were present, two extra vegetables were served and French brandy.

Later, the Chinese would eat steamed cabbage with no fat, a little fish cooked with soybean sauce, a bowl of rice and some unsweetened tea, and it was often remarked that Hawaii must agree with the Orientals, because even though they worked harder than the white men, they lived longer.

When she finished supervising the preparation of food, little Amanda Whipple, in her sixties, turned her attention to Nyuk Tsin and taught the hard-working Chinese girl how to care for a large house. Dusting was particularly stressed and caused some difficulty, because in China, Nyuk Tsin's mother had waited for a likely omen before bothering to dust, whereas energetic Mrs. Whipple demanded that it be done regularly every day. The floors had to be dusted, the flowered china lamps, the chandelier, the rosewood love seat with its multiple curlicues, the endless embroidered decorations, the peacock chair from Canton and the bamboo furniture that never looked clean. Nyuk Tsin's special nightmare was the great fish net on the parlor wall from which shells, leis and other keepsakes were hung. In fact, there was scarcely an inch of the Whipple house that did not contain some gimcrack whose main purpose was gathering dust.

In comparison, the Kee household contained one table bearing the genealogy book, a flint lighter, a candle and a wine bottle. There was also a rope bed above which hung the impressive sign: "May This Bed Yield a Hundred Sons."

According to the agreement reached by Whipple and his Chinese, Mun Ki received two dollars a month and his wife was to have received fifty cents, but when Mrs. Whipple saw how excellent Nyuk Tsin's work was, from five in the morning till nine at night, seven days a week, her generosity was touched, so she paid the girl a full dollar each month, and from this salary of $36 a year the two Chinese were required to clothe themselves, pay for the birth and education of their children, provide for entertainment and luxuries, and send money home to the official wife in China. They did all these things, but their problems were eased a bit by the unnecessary generosity of the Whipples. Unexpected gifts here and there added to the family treasury, and the allotment of an acre of good land which Nyuk Tsin could farm for herself allowed the couple to earn some real money, for Nyuk Tsin was a fine farmer and soon appeared on the streets of Honolulu with a bamboo pole across her shoulders and two baskets of fresh vegetables slung from the ends. She hawked her wares mainly among the Chinese, accumulating from them a growing store of American dimes, Australian shillings and Spanish reals, for Hawaii had wisely decided that any of the world's money could circulate freely within the kingdom.

The Kee funds were further augmented by some shrewd enterprise on the husband's part, for each day as soon as breakfast was finished, he hurried down Nuuanu Street to Chinatown, where nondescript shacks huddled together in ugly profusion and where white men rarely went. His destination was a particularly disreputable hovel in which sat an elderly Chinese with wispy beard and a brush and book in which he entered bets as they were offered. Behind him, on the wall, hung a luridly colored sketch of a man, with twenty-eight parts of his body indicated: nose, ankle, knee, elbow . . . The game which had captured Mun Ki's whole imagination consisted of placing a bet as to which of these words would appear in the sealed capsule that stood under a glass on the table before the game's operator. Most of the Chinese in Hawaii played the game, at odds of thirty to one, which gave the player an advantage, except that if there were too many winners the prize was proportionately lowered; the bank never lost. Nevertheless, the odds were enticing, and each day upon rising, families would inquire of one another: "Did you dream of an elbow last night?" Careful attention was also paid to any sudden pain, or to an accident involving any part of the body. But mostly it was dreams that brought good fortune, and it was uncanny how the dreams of Mun Ki kept pointing the way to the lucky word.

"You here again with the winning word?" the game's manager asked sourly.

"Today it's bound to be chin," Mun Ki assured him. "I woke last night with my chin itching furiously, and I can read through the glass and see the word written on the paper."

"How much are you betting?"

"Two dimes."

The proprietor's face betrayed his displeasure as he brushed the entry into his book. "You're a clever man, Mun Ki," he grumbled. "Why don't you join me in this business?"

"I'm a cook," Mun Ki replied. "It's better to win from you than work for you."

"What I have in mind," the older gambler proposed, "is for you to collect bets at the far end of town and bring them in here by ten each morning."

"Then I couldn't bet for myself, could I?" Mun Ki asked.

"No, then you'd be part of the game."

From one of the towers along the waterfront a clock struck eleven, people crowded in from the alleys of Chinatown, the excitement grew intense, and the proprietor ceremoniously lifted away the glass to uncover the capsule. To prevent the quick substitution of a word on which no one had bet that day—

a trick that had often been tried in the past—a man was selected at random, and under the most careful scrutiny he opened the capsule and shouted: "Chin!" Mun Ki leaped with joy and cried, "I had two dimes bet, because I woke with a definite itch on my chin." He explained to everyone the precise minute at which he had wakened and his thoughts at that propitious moment. With his two dimes and his dream he had won two months' normal wages.

He was about to leave the gambling shack when the old proprietor caught his arm and said, "You ought to join me. Today you made a lot of money, but I make it every day."

"You do?" Mun Ki asked.

"Every day. If too many win, I cut the prize. I send hundreds of dollars back to China."

"Could I?" the younger gambler asked.

"Easily. If you worked with me."

It was in this way that the cookhouse of the missionary home at Nuuanu and Beretania became one of the principal outposts of the chi-fa word game. Mun Kit kept on hand a supply of the gaudy posters which showed the twenty-eight parts of the human body that might be named; and for each bet he took he got six per cent from the bank and fifteen per cent of the prize money from the winner, if the ticket won; and he became one of the chi-fa's best operators, for as he had proved by paying the brothel operator full price for Nyuk Tsin, he was meticulously honest with both his employer and his customers. His chief return, however, came from his happy idea of having the chi-fa poster printed in Hawaiian and in enlisting dozens of native gamblers. They enjoyed doing business with him, and bought so many tickets that soon there were chi-fa drawings both at eleven and at four. With the money he made, Mun Ki slipped away two or three afternoons a week for the wild fan-tan and mah-jongg games that run uninterruptedly in Chinatown. He was a fierce competitor, and his store of dimes and reals and shillings grew steadily.

The only disagreement the Kees had with the Whipples occurred when it became obvious that Nyuk Tsin was going to have a baby. For some months she had hidden the fact behind her loose smock, so that when Mrs. Whipple finally did discover it she said, "You must do no more housework, Mrs. Kee. Rest." But that same afternoon she saw Nyuk Tsin trudging down Nuuanu with two huge baskets of vegetables at the ends of her bamboo pole. Amanda stopped her carriage, climbed down, and commanded her maid to drop the burden and wait till Mun Ki could be sent to pick it up; but when the cook arrived he studied the situation in astonishment and said, "Swinging the bamboo pole is the best thing a pregnant woman can do. It gets her ready."

That night Dr. Whipple went out to the Chinese house and said, "I'll make arrangements to deliver the baby." He was disturbed when Mun Ki explained in the little English he had picked up: "No need doctor. I bring baby." It was a rather difficult point to argue, since neither man was proficient in the other's language, but Dr. Whipple got the distinct impression that Mun Ki was arguing: "In China husbands always deliver their wives' babies. Who else?"

"I think I'd better get an interpreter," the confused doctor interrupted. He went to fetch the scholarly man who served as unofficial Chinese consul, and explained: "I'm afraid my servant here is intending to deliver his wife himself."

"Why not?" the consul asked.

"It's preposterous! I'm a doctor, living right here." Then, fearing that perhaps money might be the problem, he assured the consul: "I'll do it without charge."

Patiently the consul explained this to Mun Ki, who was awed by the presence of an official and who wanted to avoid trouble. "My wife and I don't need the doctor," he said quietly.

"Explain that there will be no charge," Whipple began, but he was interrupted by the consul, who, after listening to Mun Ki, explained: "If this man were in China, and if his other wife were pregnant, he would deliver her."

"What other wife?" Whipple asked in bewilderment.

"The wife here is only his number two wife. The real wife stays at home with the ancestors in China."

"Do you mean to say . . ." Whipple spluttered, but again the consul interrupted to explain: "Mun Ki says that his Uncle Chun Fat has three wives in China, two in California and one in Nevada."

"Does he also have children?" Whipple asked.

There was some discussion of this, and Mun Ki reported: "Seven in China, four in California, two in Nevada."

"And did this uncle deliver all of his thirteen sons?" Whipple snorted. "I'm sure they must have all been sons."

"Of course," the consul replied blandly.

"Of course he delivered them, or of course they were sons?"

This confused the consul, and he suggested: "Maybe we had better start again," but Dr. Whipple had had enough. Pointing at Mun Ki he snapped: "Do it your uncle's way. He seems to have had more experience than me." And he left.

Working by himself, Mun Ki produced a fine boy, but everyone in the white community was outraged to think that the barbarous Chinese would follow such a custom. "And to think," one of the Hewlett girls cried, "all the time not fifty feet away there was one of the best doctors in Hawaii! Really, the Chinese are scarcely human." And it was generally agreed that for a stubborn man to insist upon delivering his own wife when practical, proved assistance from a real doctor was available, was proof that the Chinese were not civilized.

The Whipples got another shock when they asked what the chubby, healthy little boy was to be called. "We haven't been told yet," Mun Ki replied.

"How's that?" Whipple asked.

Mun Ki said something about not yet having taken the poem to the store to find out what the child's name would be. Dr. Whipple started to ask, "What poem?" but he felt he'd better not, and said no more about the name, but some days later Mun Ki asked Mrs. Whipple if he and his wife could be absent for a few hours, and when Amanda asked why, he explained: "We must take the poem to the store to find out what the baby's name is." Mrs. Whipple called her husband and said, "You were right, John. The Kees are taking a poem to the store so as to get a name for their baby."

"I'd like to see this," Dr. Whipple said, for such things were of concern to him, and Mun Ki said he would be honored to have such a distinguished man assisting at the naming of his first son, but before they started to the store Whipple asked, "Could I see the poem?" And from the precious genealogical book Mun Ki produced a card containing the poem from which all names in the great Kee family were derived. It was an expensive, marbled, parchment-like cardboard bearing in bold poetic script fourteen Chinese characters arranged vertically in two columns. "What is it?" Whipple asked, his scientific curiosity aroused, but Mun Ki could not explain.

The Chinese store to which the trio headed stood at the corner of Nuuanu and Merchant streets and was known simply as the Punti store, for here that language was spoken and certain delicacies favored by the Punti were kept in stock. The storekeeper, an important man in Honolulu, recognized Dr. Whipple as a fellow tradesman and ceremoniously offered him a chair. "What's this poem my cook is talking about?" Whipple asked, whereupon the Punti said, "Not speak me. Him. Him."

And he pointed to a scholar who maintained a rude office in the corner of the store, where he wrote letters in Chinese and English for his Punti clients. Gravely the letter-writer picked up the poem and said, "This belongs to the Kee family. From it they get their names."

"What's it say?"

"That's not important. This one happens to read: 'Spring pervades the continents; earth's blessings arrive at your door. The heavens increase another year; and man acquires more age.' "

"What's it got to do with names?" Whipple asked.

"The answer is very complicated, and very Chinese," the scholar replied. "But we are very proud of our system. It is probably the sanest in the world."

"Can you explain it?" Whipple asked, leaning forward in his chair.

"In China we have only a few family names. In my area less than a hundred. All one syllable. All easy to remember. Lum, Chung, Yip, Wong. But we have no given names like Tom or Bob."

"No names?" Whipple asked.

"None at all. What we do is take the family name, Kee, and add to it two ordinary words. They can be anything, but taken together they must mean something. Suppose my father were a Kee and believed that I would be the beginning of a long line of scholars. He might name me Kee Chun Fei, Kee Spring Glorious. That's the kind of name we seek for your cook's boy."

"Where does the poem come in?" Whipple pressed.

"From the poem we receive the mandatory second name. All men in the first generation had to be named Chun, Spring, from the first word in the poem. All their offspring in the second generation had to be named Mun, Pervades. And all in the third generation, like the boy we are considering today, must be named from the third word in the poem, Chow, Continent. There is no escaping this rule and the benefit is this. If your cook Kee Mun Ki meets a stranger named Kee Mun Tong, they know instantly that they are of the same generation and are probably cousins."

"Sounds sensible," Whipple admitted.

"So the naming of this man's son has got to start Kee Chow, because that's what the poem says."

"Then why doesn't he just add any third name he likes?"

"Ah!" pounced the letter-writer. "There's the problem! Only a scholar can be trusted to pick that third name, for on it depends the child's entire good fortune. I'll ask Mun Ki who gave him his third name." There was a furious exchange of Chinese, after which the letter-writer reported triumphantly: "His parents summoned a learned priest from Canton. The man spent three days pondering his name. He consulted oracles and horoscopes, and finally the right name was selected. You see, a man's name can influence his entire life."

"So the Chinese in Hawaii consult with you because you are a scholar?" Whipple asked.

"Alas, there are some who are so ignorant they do not even know their family poems, and such people don't care what they name their sons. But Mun Ki comes from a strong family. They saw to it that he carried his family poem with him."

The scholar now ignored Whipple and began a long conversation with Mun Ki, and after fifteen or twenty minutes he returned to Whipple and explained: "I have been inquiring of Mun Ki what his hopes are for his son, for this is important in choosing a name."

The discussion continued for some time, and gradually the scholar began getting some paper in place and a Chinese brush, and after about an hour of speculation on the name, he reported to Whipple: "We are beginning to narrow it down. We are trying to find a word which will harmonize with Kee and Chow but at the same time add dignity and meaning. It must be a word that sounds well, looks well when written, has its own peculiar meaning, and combines well with the second word in the name. It must also express the father's hopes for his son, so you will excuse me if I concentrate on this and propose several possibilities."

With his brush he began drafting a variety of Chinese characters, and some he rejected as too feminine for a strong son like Mun Ki's, and others because they had alternative readings that might offend. Sometimes Mun Ki refused a name, and gradually the scholar began to confine the possibilities to a few choices. At last, in triumph, he announced the boy's name: "Kee Chow Chuk, the Kee who Controls the Center of the Continent."

He asked, "Isn't that a splendid name?" and Dr. Whipple nodded, whereupon the scholar took Mun Ki's genealogical book and on the appropriate page wrote down the bright new name, filled with parental hope. The scholar studied the handsome characters with obvious pleasure and told Whipple, "There's a name that looks good from any angle. It's what we call auspicious." He then took a sheet of writing paper and asked Mun Ki, "What's your village?" and when the cook replied, the letterwriter made a few swift strokes addressing the letter to that village, advising the elders that Kee Mun Ki was dutifully reporting the fact that he had a son whose name was Kee Chow Chuk, and in the ancestral clan book that name should be recorded. The family was going on. In remote Hawaii there was now a Kee who paid respect to his ancestors, who would in due time start sending money home, and who finally would return to the village, for to live elsewhere was unthinkable.

And then, as Kee Mun Ki and Nyuk Tsin were leaving the Punti store, the scholar made a dramatic gesture which changed the entire history of the Kees in Hawaii. As if a vision had possessed him, the name-giver cried, "Halt!" And with slow, stately gestures he tore up the letter to the Low Village, scattering its shreds upon the floor. Trancelike he approached Mun Ki, took away the genealogical book and splashed black ink across the propitious name he had just composed. Then, in a low voice, he explained: "Sometimes it comes like a flash of lightning on a hot night. After you have pondered a name for many hours you catch a vision of what this child can be, and all the old names you have been considering vanish, for a new name has been written across your mind in flame."

"Have you such a name for Mun Ki's boy?" Whipple asked respectfully.

"I have!" the scholar replied, and with bold strokes of his brush he put down the fiery name: Kee Ah Chow. He repeated it aloud, awed by its splendor.

"I thought it had to be Kee Chow Ah," Dr. Whipple suggested.

"It does!" the scholar agreed. "But sometimes rules must be broken, and this child's name is surely Kee Ah Chow."

The scholar handed the new name to Mun Ki and explained in Punti: "As you were leaving the store I had a sudden vision of your life. Your family is bold and you will venture far. You will have many sons and great courage. The world is yours, Mun Ki, and your first-born must have a name that signifies that fact.

So we shall call him Kee Ah Chow, the Kee who Controls the Continent of Asia. And your next sons shall be Europe and Africa and America and Australia. For you are the father of continents."

Mun Ki smiled deprecatingly, for the words were sweet. He had always imagined himself as rather special, a man nominated by the gods, and it was good to hear a scholar confirming the fact. Giving Nyuk Tsin an imperative shove, he started to leave the store, but again the scholar stopped them, pointing imperatively at Nyuk Tsin and crying, "And her name shall be Wu Chow's Mother, for she is to be the mother of continents."

This prophetic announcement caused embarrassment, and Mun Ki had to explain in Punti: "She is not my wife. My real wife is a Kung girl in China. This one is merely . . ."

The scholar folded his hands, studied Nyuk Tsin, and replied in Punti, "Well, that's the way of China. Maybe it's better, seeing that she's a Hakka." He shrugged his shoulders and turned to go, then paused and added, "Let her be known as Wu Chow's Auntie." Mun Ki nodded and told his wife her new name.

Dr. Whipple was perplexed by this exchange of words he could not understand, but he judged the matter under discussion was one of importance and from the manner in which Nyuk Tsin stood, the blood of shame rising to her ears, he guessed that they were talking about her, but no one explained what was being said. Finally Mun Ki bowed. Wu Chow's Auntie bowed. Together they recovered the poem and the name book, and when Mun Ki handed them to Nyuk Tsin to carry he touched her hand and said proudly, "We are going to have many sons."

The scholar, for his important role in naming the Kee's firstborn, received a fee of sixty cents, and Mun Ki considered the money well spent, for he was certain that his child was properly launched; but Dr. Whipple, who was then much concerned with the manner in which his own children and grandchildren were occupying themselves in Hawaii, was even more deeply impressed by the incident. He recognized it as symbolizing one of the strengths of the Chinese: "They exist within a hierarchy of generations. Their names tell where they belong, and remind them of their parents' hopes for them. A Chinese lives within a defined system, and it's a good one. No matter where he goes, his name is listed in a village, and that's home. We Americans drift where we will. We have no name, no home, no secure address. I'd like to know more about the Chinese."

So although he was then sixty-seven years old and preoccupied with important matters, John Whipple began his last scientific work: a study of the Chinese whom he had brought to Hawaii, and much of what we know today about those early Orientals—those strange, secret people imported to work the sugar—we know from what he wrote. It was Whipple who cast a shadow of fear across the other sugar planters by publishing an article in the Honolulu *Mail*: "We are deluding ourselves if we persist in the belief that these intelligent, thrifty and hard-working people will long be content to stay upon the plantations. Their natural destiny is to work as accountants and mechanics in our cities. They will be excellent schoolteachers and I suppose some will become bankers and enterprisers of great force. As soon as their indentures are discharged, they are flocking to our cities to open stores. More and more, the commerce of our countryside will fall into their industrious hands. Therefore, it behooves us to look about and find other workmen to take care of our cane fields for us; for the Chinese are not going to persist in a condition of servitude. They will learn to read and write, and when they have done this, they will demand a share in the government of these islands.

"There may be some who decry this development, but I for one applaud it. Hawaii will be a stronger community when we use our Chinese to their fullest advantage, and just as I would never have been content to be merely a field hand, doing the same chore over and over again, so I am gratified when I see another man who, like me, is determined to better himself. At one point, when I was engaged in the business of bringing Chinese to these islands, I believed that when their indentures were discharged they would return to China. Now I am convinced that they will not do so. They have become part of Hawaii and we should encourage them to follow in our footsteps. Let them become educated. Let them initiate new industries. Let them become fellow citizens. For through them the dying Hawaiian race will be regenerated."

Honolulu's reaction was simple and dramatic: "The sonofabitch ought to be horsewhipped!"

Captain Rafer Hoxworth stormed: "We brought those damned Chinamen here under the specific understanding that after five or ten years in the sugar fields they'd go home. Good God! Whipple wants them to stay! It's by God downright indecent."

Captain Janders' son, and now Dr. Whipple's partner in J & W, said, "The old man must be out of his mind! Why, one of our biggest problems in running the plantations is that as soon as the Chinese get a chance they leave us and open a store in Honolulu. I can take you to Nuuanu Street and show you half a dozen shops started by men who ought to be working for me right now, growing cane."

But what infuriated Hawaii most was the sly manner in which the Chinese, who had no women of their own, had been stealing Hawaiian women, and marrying them, and having babies by them. In spite of the fact that the babies were some of the most handsome ever bred in the islands, extraordinarily intelligent and healthy, the white community was outraged and passed laws to stop these criminal marriages. One edict forbade any Chinese from marrying a Hawaiian girl unless he became a member of the Christian church. The speed with which Chinese men learned the catechism was staggering, and one Chinese passed along to another the correct answers to the critical questions, so that it was not uncommon for a Chinese to utter, as his first words in broken English, the complete Nicene Creed plus explanations of the Trinity, the Virgin birth and Calvin's doctrine of predestination. One minister, after examining several such impromptu scholars, told a fellow Calvinist, "With my own ears I heard these men answer every important question correctly, and at the end I was tempted to ask one more, 'What does it all mean?' but I have never dared to ask even my Boston friends that fearful question, and I eschewed doing so here."

Actually, the Chinese made good Christians and did so without reservation. They were determined to have women, and conversion seemed a cheap price to pay. Those lucky ones who married Hawaiian girls with land and who grew to great wealth from manipulating that land, founded substantial Christian families and supported the large churches that were built by other Chinese; but when a male grandson was born, these prudent men went quietly to the Punti store and worked out a proper Chinese name for the boy, and sent that name back to the village hall, where it was written in the clan book.

As for the Hawaiian women, they preferred Chinese husbands to any other, for there were no men in the islands who loved women and children more than the pigtailed Chinese, and it was not uncommon to see a thin, bedraggled Chinese man, who had slaved all day on the docks for H & H, come home to where a hugely fat Hawaiian wife watched in idleness as he did the laundry, washed the children and cooked the evening meal. A Chinese husband brought presents and spent time educating his sons. He saw that his daughters had ribbons, and on Sunday he would take his whole brood to church. It became recognized in the islands that the very best thing that could happen to a Hawaiian girl was to catch herself a Chinese husband, for then all she had to do was laugh, wear fine brocades and rear babies.

But there was a subtler reason why the Hawaiians tolerated Chinese marriages: they saw with their own eyes that Chinese-Hawaiian children were superb human specimens. When the first such girls began to mature Honolulu was breathless at their beauty. They had long black hair with just a suggestion of a wave running through it, olive skin, a touch of mystery about their eyes and handsome teeth. They were taller than their Chinese fathers, much slimmer than their copious mothers, and they combined the practicality of the Chinese with the gay abandon of the Hawaiian. They were a special breed, the glory of the islands; and practically every writer from America or England who took part in launching the lively fable of the beautiful Hawaiian girl, had in his mind's eye one of these first Chinese-Hawaiian masterpieces; and they justified all that was written about romantic Hawaii.

The boys were promising in another way. They were quick to learn, good at games, very good at business and best of all at politics. They had a shameless charm in soliciting votes for their candidates, were gifted in repartee, and had a basic honesty which the public grew to respect. So the Hawaiians, who had been a vanishing race—400,000 in 1778, 44,000 in 1878—suddenly received a vital impetus from the Orient and began to re-establish themselves through the Chinese-Hawaiian mixture, until in later years the part-Hawaiian was to become the fastest-growing component in the islands.

Captain Rafer Hoxworth, watching the beginning of this miracle, spoke for all his Caucasian friends except Dr. Whipple when he said, "Any Chinese who leaves a plantation to become a peddler should be immediately deported, but any who touches a Hawaiian girl should be hung."

In the Honolulu *Mail* the Hewletts reported more moderate reactions: "Hawaii is ruined. The Chinese are fleeing the plantations, and who will raise our sugar?"

Dr. Whipple, having gained only contumely from his last public writing on the Chinese, confined his subsequent thoughts to his diary: "It was on the island of Oahu in 1824 that I first saw measles sweep through a Hawaiian village, leaving eighty per cent of the people dead, and it was soon after that I began considering what we could do to infuse new life into this lovable race which I had grown to cherish so dearly. I foresaw that only the introduction of some vital new blood could prevent the annihilation of these fine people. Erroneously, I thought that stronger Polynesians from the south might accomplish the reversal, but we imported such Polynesians and nothing happened. Later, I trusted that Javanese might suffice, and perhaps they would have, but we were unable to acquire them. And now the Chinese have arrived and they have served exactly as I long ago predicted they would. For my part in effecting this salvation of a race, I am humbly proud. At present the temper of the time is against me in this matter, so I keep my own counsel, but I am confident that the judgment of the future will support me. The best thing I ever did for Hawaii was to import Chinese."

As he wrote in his lamplit study, Mun Ki and his wife, in their small house nearby, were starting another son, the Continent of Europe.

NYUK TSIN AND her husband had been in Hawaii about a year when the entire Chinese community was aroused by news filtering into Honolulu from the island of Maui, where many Chinese workers were engaged on plantations. As the Chinese got the news, this is what happened: toward dusk one hot day an elderly clergyman with a limp and carrying a cane forced his way into one of the temporary Chinese temples erected there for the use of the laborers, and disrupted worship. One woman who had been in the temple at the time reported: "The little man struck everything with his cane, knocked down the statue of Kwan Yin, tore up the golden papers and shouted words at us. When we refused to leave the temple, for it was ours and built with our effort and none of theirs, his great anger turned toward us, and he tried to strike us with his cane, shouting at us all the time. But since he was an old man, it was easy for us to avoid him."

The Chinese generally felt that this was but one more evidence of the hard life they were to have on the plantations, and much indignation resulted from the old man's unexpected attack. Asked the Chinese, Punti and Hakka alike: "Don't the white men respect gods?" And the divergence between the Chinese and the Caucasian increased.

To the white men, the incident at the Buddhist temple was deplorable, and planters both on Maui and on the other islands quickly got together small sums of money which they handed to the offended Chinese, so that some of the damage growing out of the attack was rectified. Dr. Whipple, as spokesman for the planters, went personally to Maui to mollify the laborers, and after a period of tension, reasonably good relations were restored, and all whites who employed Chinese took special pains to assure the strangers that they were free to worship as they pleased. Thus, in the mid-1860's, a true religious freedom was established in the islands: Congregationalists, Catholics, Episcopalians, Mormons, Buddhists and Confucianists worshiped side by side in relative harmony.

When peace among the Chinese had been restored, the white planters took up the problem of wizened Abner Hale, and younger offspring of the old families, men like the Hewletts, the Whipples and the Hoxworths, convened in Honolulu to see what to do about the old man. Reported one of the Hewletts, honestly: "That pitiful fanatic, bursting in that way with his cane and his shouts of 'Abomination! Corruption!' almost ruined everything we've accomplished with the Chinese. We've got to make the old fool behave."

"Years ago he did the same thing with the Hawaiians, as I understand," Bromley Hoxworth explained. "One famous night when my mother was getting married to her brother, he burst into the ceremony and lashed about with his cane, destroying idols and raising merry hell. He still thinks he's fighting the old Hawaiian gods."

"Somebody's got to advise him that things have changed," one of the Whipple boys insisted. "Knocking down Hawaiian idols when it does no harm is one thing, but destroying Buddhas when we're trying to keep our Chinese help happy is quite another."

The group turned to David Hale and suggested: "Can you talk to him, Dave?"

"I'd rather not," the alert young man evaded. "I've never been able to make much sense with Father."

"What we really ought to do is to get him off Maui altogether," Brom Hoxworth proposed. "Truly, he oughtn't to be there alone. He messes up the Seamen's Chapel and interferes with the Chinese. He's really a dreadful nuisance, and I agree with the others, Dave, that you've got to talk with him. Convince him that he ought to live in a little house here in Honolulu . . . where we could watch him."

"I've tried that. So has Micah. The old man simply won't listen to any proposal which requires his leaving Maui. If you raise the question, he says stubbornly, 'My church is here, and my graves are here.' And that's that."

"Whose graves?" Brom Hoxworth asked.

"My mother's grave, and your grandmother's," the intense younger Hale explained. "He plays gardener for them, and insists now and then upon preaching in the old stone church that he built. But I'm sure the minister would be delighted to see him get out of Maui."

One of the Whipple boys spoke: "Looking at the whole thing frankly, the fact that he's left alone on Maui reflects on all of us, really. It looks as if we had cut the old man off . . . didn't want him, because he's sort of wandering in his mind. Now, I know that's not the truth. I happen to know definitely that my father invited Reverend Hale to live with him, and your mother, Brom, did the same, and of course we all know that both Micah and David asked him to live with them. So our skirts are clean, as it were, but even so we get a good deal of opprobrium for allowing him to stay in that filthy little house of his."

"And now if he's going to start meddling with the Chinese," young Hoxworth pointed out, "he's really got to be cleaned out."

The group therefore proposed that Dr. Whipple be dispatched once more to Lahaina to reason with Abner, and with some reluctance the trim, white-haired leader of Janders & Whipple climbed aboard the *Kilauea* and ploughed his way through the rough channel to Maui. He had barely started down the pier when he saw his rickety old friend pecking his way among the crowd and accosting one of the sailors from the ferry.

"Did you happen to hear any news of a little girl named Iliki?" he asked querulously.

"No, sir," the patient sailor replied, for he was asked this question at each arrival of the *Kilauea*.

Sadly the old man shook his head, turned and started for his home, but Dr. Whipple called, "Abner!" and the lame missionary stopped, turned about in the sunlight and studied his visitor. At first he could not quite understand who the thin, erect man in the black suit was, and then his mind cleared momentarily.

"John," he said softly, still refusing to accord the apostate his former title of Brother.

"I've come over to talk with you," Whipple explained patiently.

"You've come over to reprimand me for smashing the heathen temple," Abner replied contentiously. "Don't waste your words. If the bloody sacrificial rocks of the Hawaiians were evil and worthy to be destroyed, the gaudy red and gold temples of Buddha merit the same treatment."

"Let's walk along to our offices," Whipple suggested.

"We used to talk here, John, and this is still good enough for me." He sat down on a coconut log, under the kou trees, where he could see the roads. "Not many whalers come here any more," he mused. "But do you see that skeleton of a ship on the reef over there? The *Thetis*. How long ago we shipped on that rare vessel, John! You and Amanda, I and Jerusha. Later, you know, it was Malama's ship. Now it rusts on the rocks, like you and me."

"That's what I wanted to see you about, Abner," Dr. Whipple said quietly. "All of your friends, and I in particular, want you to leave Lahaina and come over to Honolulu to live with us. You are rusting on the reef, Brother Abner, and we want to take you home."

"I could never leave Lahaina," the old man said stubbornly. "Jerusha is here, and so is Malama, and I couldn't leave them. My church is here and all of the people I have brought to God. I see the *Thetis* every day . . ." and with mention of the old ship that had brought him to his triumphs and his troubles his mind grew dim, and he added pathetically, as if he were aware that he was losing the thread of his argument, "And I expect Iliki to come back soon, and I should not like to be absent on that day." He looked up in childish victory at his old friend, as if this line of reasoning were irrefutable.

Dr. Whipple, who had seen a good deal of the death of minds and men, showed no irritation with his old friend's obstinacy. "Abner," he reasoned patiently, "the younger men who run the plantations are most determined that you not be allowed to disrupt their good relationships with the Chinese."

"Those pigtailed heathens worship idols, John. I tell you I have seen it with my own eyes!"

"The Chinese are rather difficult to handle at best, Brother Abner," John quietly agreed, "but when you smash their temples, wholly extraneous problems are introduced."

"John, you and I labored for many years to erase the evils of heathenism from these islands, and in our old age we certainly can't sit idly by and see our victory snatched from us."

"Brother Abner," the doctor rationalized, "the Chinese problem is different from what we faced with the Hawaiians."

Abner's mind cleared and he stared coldly at his old friend. "Different?" he asked.

Dr. Whipple noticed that Hale's eyes had lost their film, and he thought to make the most of these moments of lucidity, so he spoke rapidly: "The Chinese religion is an old and distinguished form of worship. Buddha and Confucius both existed long before the birth of Christ, and the systems of ethics which they evolved have dignity. They must not be confused with the raw, pagan rituals that we found here on Hawaii when we arrived. Furthermore, the Hawaiians were steeped in ignorance and required leadership to the light, but the Chinese had a flowering civilization while Massachusetts was still a wilderness, so they do not need the same kind of spiritual instruction that we had to give the Hawaiians. But what disturbs the younger men most, including your sons Micah and David, who commissioned me to come here to talk with you, is that the Hawaiians were never really a part of our society. They lived on the outskirts, as it were, but the Chinese we need. Our whole economy depends upon harmonious relations with them, and anything which runs the risk of driving them from the plantations cannot be tolerated." He had ended his comments with a threat which he had not intended when he started, but there it was.

Abner missed the threat, for halfway through his friend's monologue he had clearly caught its central theme, and now he drew back appalled at the ravages which years and success can effect in a man who had originally launched his career in honor and dignity. The lame little missionary studied his visitor with contempt, and pity, and said finally, with the sorrow of Jeremiah and Ezekiel in his voice, "Dear John, I am ashamed to see the day when wealth and concern for a sugar plantation could force you to come to Maui and tell me, 'It was all right to destroy the gods of the Hawaiians, because they didn't work in our fields, but we need the Chinese to make money for us, so their heathen gods we must honor.' I am ashamed to witness such corruption in the soul of a good man, John, and I now think you had better get back on the boat and go home."

Dr. Whipple was stunned by the turn the conversation had taken, and he again resorted to threats: "Your sons say that if you don't . . ."

With some dignity old Abner Hale rose to his unsteady feet and dismissed his visitor: "I was not afraid of the whaling captains, nor of their rioting sailors, and I am not afraid of my own sons. There is good in the world, John, and there is evil. There is God in the universe, and there are heathen idols, and I have never been confused as to whose side in the great Armageddon I fight upon. An idol is an idol, and if a Christian is tempted to make money from an idol, then that idol above all others ought to be destroyed, for as Ezekiel commanded: 'Thus saith the Lord God, Repent, and turn yourselves from your idols; and turn away your faces from all your abominations.' I wish to talk with you no further upon these matters, John, but when you have left I will pray that before you die you will recover once more the sweet, clean soul you brought to these islands . . . but lost somewhere among the sugar fields."

The little missionary turned his back on his old friend and limped off to his small and dirty shack. When Dr. Whipple tried to overtake him and reason with him, saying, "Abner, you must come to Honolulu with me," the missionary brushed him away and would not speak, and when Whipple followed him right to the door of the filthy hovel in which he was spending his last days, Abner slammed that door against him and Whipple could hear him kneeling against a chair and praying for the corrupted soul of his one-time roommate on the *Thetis.*

Dr. Whipple returned to Honolulu and issued instructions to his managers on Maui that they must assume responsibility for keeping Abner Hale away from the Buddhist temples, for it was imperative that the Chinese be protected from any additional disturbances. The Hale boys sent regular funds to Lahaina, in care of the plantation managers, so that their father could be insured good food and medical care. Twice a year they begged the weak old man to come to Honolulu and live with them, and twice a year he refused.

It was in 1868 that Nyuk Tsin and the Chinese community throughout Hawaii finally realized how strange and barbarous the white man's society really was, for word came into Honolulu that the ancient father of the Hales had died alone, ignored and untended on the island of Maui. The news was difficult to believe, and Nyuk Tsin gathered with her Hakka friends at the Hakka store, while Nun Ki sat on his haunches in the Punti store trying to get the appalling news into focus. In both stores this was the news:

"You say the father of all these famous and rich people was allowed to die in poverty?"

"Yes. I was there, and I saw them find his old worn-out body in the cemetery."

"What was he doing there, this old man?"

"He had gone to care for his wife's grave, and then he was doing the same for the grave of some Hawaiian lady. It looked as if he had died late in the afternoon, falling over the Hawaiian grave, and he was there all night."

"You say he lived in a pitiful little house?"

"So small and dirty you wouldn't believe it."

"And here his children have such big houses. Have you seen the houses of his children?"

"No. Are they good and fine?"

"Li Lum Fong works for his son Micah, and he says Micah's house is one of the best in Honolulu. The old man's first daughter is married to Hewlett, and they have much wealth. His second daughter is wed to one of the Whipples, and they have a big house, and his second son also married a Whipple, so he is very rich."

"Have his children grandchildren among whom the old man could have lived?"

"The families have two grandchildren, and five, and five, and six."

"And he died alone?"

"He died alone, caring for the graves, but no one cared for him."

When this was said, this harsh summary of the white man's fundamental unconcern for human values and respect for one's ancestors, the Chinese in the various stores sat glum, bewildered. Some of them, reminded of their longing to see some ancestral hall in a remote Chinese village, would rock back and forth on their haunches, trying vainly to comprehend a family with four big houses and eighteen grandchildren who had allowed an old man to die alone and untended. How could the families be indifferent to the bad luck attendant upon such an untended death? In such discussions the Chinese often wanted to speak, to say, "How I long to see my father in the High Village!" but no words came, and they returned to their gloomy discussion of Abner Hale's death.

"Wasn't he the old man who knocked down the Chinese temples?"

"Yes. I saw him once running in with a club. He limped, but when he was knocking down temples he was extremely vigorous, and the plantation managers had to put a guard on him, every day, and if the little old man started for a temple the guard would shout, 'Here he comes again!' and white men would run out and capture him and take him home."

"You would think, under those circumstances, that it would be the Chinese who wanted to see him dead, and yet it is we who are mourning him, and his own family cares nothing about his death."

But in the big houses there was profound, silent grief. A Mormon missionary told Micah Hale: "On the last day your father met the ferry and inquired after the girl Iliki. He then picked some flowers and I met him on the road leading to the church graveyard. He shook his stick at me and cried, 'You are an abomination. You should be driven from the islands.' If I had had my thoughts about me, I should have followed him then, for he seemed weak and faltering, but so often we do not do that which we should, and I passed him by, keeping away from his stick. He certainly went on to the church and tried to get the pastor to allow him to preach again on Sunday, but as you know, he wandered so much that preaching was hopeless, and the minister put him off. That was the last anyone saw of him. He was found fallen across the grave of an alii nui of Maui, a woman, I believe, that he himself had brought into the church.

"That night I had a clear premonition that I had done an un-Christian thing in passing your father by, and once I started to see if he had gotten home correctly, but I failed to do so, but on my morning walk I stopped by his house to wish him well, and he was gone. I hurried out to the cemetery, expecting to find him fallen along the way, but as I explained, he had died at the grave.

"Mr. Hale, I'll not mince words. There were, as you are well aware, harsh comments made concerning your father's death alone in Lahaina, but I know and all like me know how hard you tried to make his last days easier. He was an obstinate man and would permit no kindness. I suffered from his sharp tongue, so I know. I want to reassure you that the true facts are known, and only the fools of the city condemn you."

* * *

As I have said, there was profound grief in the four Hale houses, for the children could remember how their father had cared for them, and loved them, and taught them, and changed their sheets when they had fevers and sacrificed his life for them, that they might be worthy children. They could see him, a father of terrible wrath, keeping them tightly confined to the small, walled-in garden; and they remembered his dreadful lamentations when Reverend Eliphalet Thorn took them away from his care. From that day on, each of the four Hale children had tried vainly to return to his father the love he had spent on them, but he would not accept it. He rejected his oldest son Micah for having married a part-Hawaiian. He scorned David for refusing to become a minister. He despised Lucy for having married young Hewlett, who although he was pure white was nevertheless half-brother to half-castes. And he ignored Esther, his baby, for having married a Whipple who had publicly made fun of missionaries. The sorrow of his four children was deep.

But they were also New Englanders, and when the Honolulu community whisperingly condemned them for having abandoned their poor old dim-witted father, allowing him to die in a filthy shack in distant Lahaina, the Hales felt it imperative that they appear in public. They accepted the scorn and walked proudly as if there were no whispers following them. When aggravating hostesses tempted them with invitations to see how they were bearing up, they accepted, and they moved normally in Honolulu society, grimly bearing the charges made against them. It was their duty.

But the Chinese servants, seeing this, were more perplexed than ever, and in the stores they added to the whispers: "Li Lum Fong told me that last night Micah Hale and Mrs. Hewlett and Mrs. Whipple all went to a party. Now please tell me, please explain how a family that allows their poor old father to die in poverty, untended, can be so shameless as to appear in public, drinking alcohol and laughing? Even before the first year of mourning has ended."

"You will never understand these heartless people," the Chinese agreed.

WHEN MUN KI'S son Asia started growing into a bowlegged, chubby-faced little toddler, he was promptly joined by the Continent of Europe and later Africa, who rioted around the kitchen floor as their parents prepared meals for the Whipples; and with the coming of these children a curious transformation occurred in the relationship between Mun Ki and his wife. Many centuries earlier Confucius had pointed out that the harmonious existence of husband and wife was most difficult to sustain: "Between the two let there be respect."

It was common, therefore, in Chinese families for a husband never to hand his wife anything, for to do so seemed to imply: "I wish to give you this. You must take it." Instead, he placed the object near his wife and she picked it up at her own time. Some ignored this particular convention, but there was another that all observed. As the scholar at the Punti store had explained to Dr. Whipple, a respectful husband never spoke his wife's name, neither in public nor at home. As soon as a girl married she became simply Mun Ki's wife; that was her profession and her personality. But when children arrived, special care was taken to hide her name from them, and there was scarcely a Chinese growing up in Hawaii who knew his mother's name. It was never spoken.

In Mun Ki's case the problem was further complicated by the fact that his Hakka girl was not properly a wife at all, but merely a concubine, and she must never be called Mother; to do so would be offensive. It is true that she had borne the three sons, but their real mother was the official Kung wife who had remained dutifully behind in the Low Village. By Chinese custom his first wife would be the legal mother of any children Mun Ki might have, anywhere in the world.

So the scrawny Hakka girl became Wu Chow's Auntie—the Auntie of the Five Continents—and by this name she was known throughout the city. She considered herself fortunate, because in many families concubines like her were known contemptuously as "That One" or more simply "She," but Mun Ki was not willing to give her those names, for he was impressed by the Punti scholar's prediction that his Hakka wife was going to bear many sons and that they would share the continents. So whenever the tricky little gambler addressed his wife as Wu Chow's Auntie, he felt a special love for her.

Not one of her children or many grandchildren would ever know her name, nor would they think of her as Mother, for as Mun Ki sternly reminded the boys: "Your mother lives in China." And the boys became convinced that in the Low Village their mother waited for them, and it was to her they owed their devotion. In time a photographer traveled out from Canton, and in some villages he was stoned as a sorcerer attempting to steal men's spirits with his magic, but in the Low Village, Uncle Chun Fat, who had been in California, said to his nephew's pretty wife, "Get your picture taken and send it to the Fragrant Tree Country." She did, and the Kee boys grew up with this brown-tinted picture of a regal-looking, well-dressed Punti woman staring down at them from the wall; and this photograph evoked in them a sterner sense of filial responsibility than Nyuk Tsin ever did.

She was not concerned with these matters, for as a Hakka she was governed by two supreme drives: above all else she wanted an education for her sons, and to attain it she would sacrifice anything; after that she wanted to own some land. To attain either of these goals she required money, and she had been in Honolulu only a few weeks before she started hawking vegetables. Now, without telling the Whipples, she took in the laundry of unmarried Hakka men, but one day Dr. Whipple asked his wife, "Amanda, what's all that blue clothing doing on the back lawn?"

"We don't have any blue clothing," she replied, and they investigated.

"No more laundry!" Dr. Whipple ordered, but by that time she had already earned her beginning store of coins.

She then switched to serving meals on the side to bachelor Chinese, and this proved fairly profitable until Amanda Whipple grew suspicious of the many strange men who were trailing up Nuuanu and slipping through the back garden gate. "John, forgive my evil mind," she said one night, "but do you think our maid is . . . well . . . all these men?"

"After all, she is only the cook's second wife, and I suppose that if he thinks he can earn a little more money."

"John! How horrible!"

They agreed that something must be done and Dr. Whipple appointed himself detective. Some days later he staggered into the sitting room, choking with laughter. "Ah, these evil Chinese!" he chuckled. "Amanda, Captain Hoxworth should see what's going on in our back yard. It'd prove every suspicion he ever had."

"John! What is it?"

"Mrs. Kee, horrible thought, is serving hot meals. To unmarried men."

Mrs. Whipple broke into an embarrassed laugh and ended by asking, "Why do our servants try so many ways to make extra money? We pay them good wages."

"They are determined to educate their children," Dr. Whipple explained.

"Good for them, but not by running a restaurant on our property." Again Nyuk Tsin was ordered to desist, but again she wound up with more coins than when she started.

Her big venture came when she discovered that two acres of swampland on the Whipple property could be converted into money. This time she went to Dr. Whipple and in the barbarous pidgin that all Honolulu spoke, conveyed to him the following: "Could I use this swampland?"

"What for?" he asked.

"To grow taro."

"Do you Pakes eat taro?"

"No. We will make poi."

"You don't eat poi, do you?"

"No. We will sell it to the natives."

Dr. Whipple made some inquiries and found that Nyuk Tsin had a good idea. The Hawaiians were now working for wages in livery stables and mechanics' shops and no longer wanted to waste their time making poi, so that the profession had fallen into the hands of Pakes. The bizarre idea appealed to Whipple and he told Amanda, "I've owned that swampland for years but it took a Pake to show me what to do with it. The more I see these people, the better I like them."

As the days passed he became increasingly impressed by what Nyuk Tsin could accomplish with land. Whenever she found a few minutes' respite from her long hours as maid, she would hurry down to her taro patch, tie her conical hat under her chin, roll up her blue trousers and plunge barefooted into the soft mud. She built dikes better than most men and constructed ingenious waterways that drained the land so it could be tilled and later flooded for taro. Dr. Whipple, watching her beaver-like industry, thought: "She has a positive affinity for the land." He was not surprised, therefore, when she came up to him one hot day, wiping her muddy hands on a bunch of grass, to ask, "Will you sell me the swamp?"

"Where would you get the money?" he teased.

She astounded him by disclosing how much she had already saved. "The rest I will get from selling poi, and year after year I will pay you the money."

This pleased Whipple, for it was the kind of frugal bargaining his own New England ancestors had probably engaged in when they wanted to send their sons to college; but he had to disappoint her. "This land's too close to our house to sell. But there's some up the valley I might let you have."

"Can we go see it?" Nyuk Tsin asked. "Now?" Her lust for land was such that she would have walked miles to see a field. For nearly fifty generations her Hakka people had yearned for rich valley lands, and here she stood among the choicest, determined to own some. That day it wasn't convenient for Dr. Whipple to take her up the valley to see the useless swampland he had in mind and later he forgot, but Nyuk Tsin never did.

Her progress to ownership was deterred by two setbacks. First her husband vetoed the idea of buying land, explaining: "We won't be here long. It would be foolish to buy land that we would have to abandon when we sailed back to China."

"I want a field," Nyuk Tsin argued in her stubborn Hakka way.

"No," Mun Ki reasoned, "our plan must be to save every dime we can get and take our wealth back to the Low Village. When we reach there, I'll send you on up to the High Village, because you wouldn't feel at ease among the Punti and my wife wouldn't want you around."

"What will happen to the boys?" Nyuk Tsin asked.

"Well, since they're really Punti, with Punti names, they'll stay with their mother." Seeing her shock he added hastily, "Of course, I'll give you a little of the money we've saved and you can buy yourself a piece of land in the Hakka village, and probably we'll see each other from time to time along the road."

"I would rather have the land here," Nyuk Tsin pleaded.

"Wu Chow's Auntie!" Mun Ki snapped. "We're not staying here."

Her second setback involved poi, for clever as the Chinese were, they could not master the trick of making this island staple. Nyuk Tsin raised the taro beautifully, and Dr. Whipple said he had rarely seen better. She harvested it correctly, removing first the dark green leaves to sell as a spinach-like vegetable. Then she peeled the stalks for cooking like asparagus, the flowers having already been sold to be eaten like cauliflower. This left the big, dark corms for the making of poi. In the raw state they contained bitter crystals of oxide that made them inedible, but when boiled and peeled they were delicious, except that they looked like Roquefort cheese. It was these boiled corms that Nyuk Tsin hauled to her poi board, a six-foot-long trough in which she hammered the taro with a lava-rock pounder, smashing and gradually liquefying the mass until finally a glob of sticky, glutinous paste resulted. This was poi, the world's most remarkable starch: it was alkaline rather than acid; it was more easily digestible than potatoes, more nourishing than rice; an infant of two weeks could eat poi with safety, while an old man whose stomach was riddled with ulcers could enjoy it with relish. Dr. Whipple, who amused his associates by having poi at his meals instead of bread or potatoes, termed it: "The only perfect food."

Hawaiians loved poi and were relieved when the Pakes took over the grueling work of manufacturing it, but they could not learn to like poi the way Nyuk Tsin and her husband made it. On days when poi was ready to be sold, it was an island custom to hang along the street a small white flag, and when Nyuk Tsin first displayed hers she had many pleased customers, but later they complained that her product lacked quality. Her poi was not the bland, neutral food they craved, and with apologies they inquired if she had been careful to keep her utensils clean, for whereas in ordinary living the Hawaiians were fanatics about cleanliness, in the making of poi they were maniacs. If a fly lighted on a poi bowl, they would throw the contents out, and the damning word was passed along that Pake poi wasn't clean. Worse, it had lumps.

A further complication developed. The dollar that formed the basic currency of the islands was broken down into three conflicting coin systems: ten American dimes equaled a dollar; so did eight Spanish reals; so did four English shillings. The latter could be chopped in half with a cold chisel to make eight sixpences to the dollar. Since dimes and reals were of about the same size, the Hawaiians tried to convince the Chinese that a dime worth ten cents was just as good as a real worth twelve and a half, whereas for her part Nyuk Tsin tried to collect reals and pay back dimes, so there was constant warfare.

When the Kees made up their fifth batch of poi, the white flag flapped outside for a long time before any customers appeared, but finally a big Hawaiian woman ambled in, dipped her finger into the purplish paste and tried it upon her tongue. With obvious disgust she grumbled, "I'll take three bundles, for half price, in dimes."

This was too much for Nyuk Tsin. Weighing hardly one third as much as her huge customer, she leaped forward and started shoving the woman back into the roadway, while the big Hawaiian started slapping at her as if she were an irritating fly. A considerable row ensued, which brought Dr. Whipple into the yard with an edict: "No more poi to be sold."

This embittered Mun Ki, who foresaw the loss of much money, and he condemned his wife for being so stupid as not to know how to make poi; but a worse humiliation was to follow. The Kees now had several gallons of the ugly-looking paste and frugal Nyuk Tsin ordered everyone to eat it instead of rice. As her husband bravely gulped the unpalatable starch he made wry faces and then discovered with dismay that his sons preferred it to rice.

Banging down his bowl he cried, "This settles it! We're going back to China as soon as our contract ends."

"Let's sign for five more years," Nyuk Tsin pleaded.

"No!" Mun Ki stormed. "I will not tolerate the day when my own sons prefer poi to rice. They're no longer Chinese." And he made a motion to throw out the poi, but Nyuk Tsin would not permit this. "All right, Wu Chow's Auntie," he grumbled. "I'll eat the poi, but when it's finished, I'm going back to China." Uncle Chun Fat had undoubtedly made a million dollars in California, but it was obvious that his nephew wasn't going to emulate him in Hawaii.

However, one good did come from the poi fiasco. Nyuk Tsin, always an experimenter, discovered that if she cut the stalks of her taro plants into short segments and packed them in heavy brine, with stones loaded on top of the barrel to keep the brew compressed, in time the stalks became pickled. With steamed fish or pork they were delicious, and as a result of her invention she acquired unexpected funds from her taro patch. She sold the flowers as vegetables, the leaves for spinach, and the uncooked roots to the king's poi factory on Fort Street. But the stems she kept for herself, and when they properly pickled she loaded them into her two baskets and slung her bamboo pole across her shoulder. Barefooted, she went through the town hawking her Chinese sauerkraut. Dr. Whipple, observing her buoyant recovery from defeat, said to her one day, "Mrs. Kee, do you remember that field that I spoke about?"

Nyuk Tsin's eyes grew bright and Whipple marked how eagerly she awaited his next words, so he said slowly, "I've looked it over, and it isn't worth much, so I'm not going to sell it to you." Nyuk Tsin's face became a study in yellow despair, and Whipple was ashamed of his trick, so he added quickly, "I'm going to give it to you, Mrs. Kee."

Nyuk Tsin was only twenty-two at the time, but she felt like a very old woman who had lived a long life, hoping for certain things that were only now coming to pass. Her almond-shaped eyes filled with tears and she kept her hands pressed closely to her sides. To herself she thought: "The land could have been mine, rich land in the Fragrant Tree Country," and at this thought a pair of tears rolled down her cheeks. Aloud, she said as a dutiful wife, "We Chow's Father tells me I must not bother with land in this country. Soon we shall be returning to China."

"Too bad," Whipple replied, ready to dismiss the subject as one of no importance.

But in the mind of the stubborn Hakka woman the land hunger that she had inherited from generations of her forebears welled up strongly. In a kind of dumb panic she stood on the Whipple lawn and watched Dr. Whipple walking away from her, taking with him her only chance of salvation—the promise of land—and in response to a force greater than herself she called, "Dr. Whipple!"

The elderly scientist turned and recognized the agony through which his serving girl was going. Returning to her he asked gently, "Mrs. Kee, what is it?"

For a moment she hesitated, and tears splashed down her sunbrowned face. Unable to speak, she stared at him and her mouth moved noiselessly. Finally, in a ghostly voice, she whispered her decision: "When Wu Chow's Father returns to China, I shall remain here."

"Oh, no!" Dr. Whipple interrupted quickly. "A wife must stay with her husband. I wouldn't think of giving you the land on any other terms."

The shocking probability that she was going to lose her land after all emboldened the little Chinese woman, and she confessed in a whisper: "He is not my husband, Dr. Whipple."

"I know," he said.

"He brought me here to sell me to the man you saw that day outside the fence. But he grew to like me a little, so he bought me for himself."

Dr. Whipple recalled the scene at the immigration shed and he sensed that what Nyuk Tsin was saying was true. But he was a minister at heart, and he now advised his maid: "Men often take women for strange reasons, Mrs. Kee, and later they grow to love them, and have happy families. It is your duty to go back to China with your husband."

"But when I get there," Nyuk Tsin pleaded, "I will not be allowed to stay with him in the Low Village. He would be ashamed of my big feet."

"What would you do?" Whipple asked with growing interest.

"I would have to live up in the Hakka village."

Dr. Whipple's conscience had often been stung by the inequities he witnessed in life, but he was convinced that obedience to duty was man's salvation. "Then go to the High Village, Mrs. Kee," he said gently. "Take your sons with you and lead a good life. Your gods will support you."

With cold logic she explained: "But my sons will be kept in the Low Village and I will be banished from them. They would not want it known that I was their mother."

Dr. Whipple walked away from the Chinese maid, kicked at the grass for some minutes, and returned to ask her several questions: How did she meet Kee? Was it true that he had brought her to Hawaii to sell her? Was it true that if she returned to China she would be banished from both her husband and her sons? Where were her parents? When he heard of her kidnaping and of her bleak future he thought for some time, then said bluntly, "We'd better go look at the land."

He opened the wicker gate and led the barefooted woman with the basket hat about a mile up the Nuuanu Valley until they came to a low-lying field, an ancient taro patch now fallen into disuse. Much of it consisted of a swamp running down to the banks of the Nuuanu Stream, but as Whipple and his Chinese servant looked at it that day they could visualize it as it might become: the far end would raise fine taro; the dryer land would be good for vegetables; in that corner a woman could have a little house; and in years to come, the city of Honolulu would reach out to encompass the area. It was an interesting piece of land, worth little as it stood; worth a fortune when energy and planning had been applied to it.

"This is your land, Mrs. Kee." The strange-looking couple shook hands and walked back to the Whipple mansion.

Nyuk Tsin did not divulge this compact to her husband, nor did she tell him of her intentions to remain in Hawaii when he left, for Mun Ki was a good man. As long as he was with his concubine in a strange land he was both kind and considerate, but as a realist he knew she could share no part of his life when he returned to China, and it never occurred to him that this future fact would in any way influence his present relationship. He loved Nyuk Tsin and treasured her four sons. She was pregnant again and he was happy. He was doing well as a runner for the chi-fa game and had established himself as one of the principal mah-jongg gamblers in Honolulu. He particularly liked the Whipples, who were exacting but just employers, and once he observed to the doctor: "It looks as if my six-year cycle began with my arrival here."

"What's the cycle?" Whipple asked, for although he was appalled at the callousness shown by Mun Ki in his proposed treatment of Nyuk Tsin when they returned to China, he liked the brash young man and found him interesting.

"The Chinese say, 'Three years of bad luck, six years of good,'" Mun Ki explained.

After the cook had passed along to other work, Dr. Whipple stood reflecting on this chance phrase, and it explained much about the Chinese. He observed to Amanda: "We Christians focus on the Old Testament: Seven fat years have got to be followed by seven lean ones. The world balances out. Good luck and bad equate. It summarizes the Jewish-Christian sense of remorseless justice, one for one. But the Chinese envisage a happier world: 'If you can stick out three bad years, six good ones are sure to follow.' That's a much better percentage, and it's why the Chinese I meet are such indefatigable optimists. We Anglo-Saxons brood on the evil that has to follow good. The Pakes know that good always triumphs over evil, six to three."

One afternoon he entertained an insight that struck him like a vision: "In fifty years my descendants here in Hawaii will be working for the Chinese!" At the time when this thought came to him he was watching Nyuk Tsin rebuilding her waterways after a storm, patiently leading the runaway waters back home to her taro patch, and as he saw the muddy stream bringing richness to her soil, he pounded his fist into his palm and said, "I've been talking about it for nearly fifty years. Now I'm going to do it."

He drove down to the J & W offices and summoned all the young Janderses and Whipples and showed them a map of Oahu Island. "Four fifths of it's a desert," he said crisply, reminding them of something they already knew. "It grows nothing but cactus and you can't even raise decent cattle on it. The other fifth over here gets all the water it needs, but the land is so steep you can't farm it, so the water runs out to sea. Boys, I've often talked about building a ditch to trap that water over there," and he pointed to the rainy windward side, "and lead it over here." And he banged his fist down on mile after mile of barren acreage. "This week I'm going to start."

One of his own sons was first to speak, saying, "If God had wanted the water to fall on these dry lands, He would have ordered it, and any action contrary to God's wish seems to me a reflection on His infinite wisdom."

Dr. Whipple looked at his son and replied, "I can only cite you the parable of the talents. God never wants potential gifts to lie idle."

One of the Janders boys, a profound conservative, argued: "J & W is overextended. There's no money for chancy adventures."

"A good firm is always overextended," Whipple replied, but seeing that the younger men would surely vote against his using J & W funds, he quickly added, "I don't want you to put up any of your own money, but I'm surely going to gamble all of mine. All I want from you is lease rights to your worthless land on the dry side."

When he had control of six thousand acres of barren soil, he hired two hundred men and many teams of mules and with his own money launched the venture that was to transform his part of Oahu from a desert into a lush, succulent sugar plantation. With shovels and mule-drawn sledges, he dug out an irrigation ditch eleven miles long, maintaining a constant fall which swept the water down from high mountainsides and onto the arid cactus lands. When his ditch faced some deep valley that could not be avoided, he channeled his water into a narrow mouth and poured it into a large pipe which dropped down to the valley floor and climbed back up to the required elevation on the other side, where it emptied out into the continuation of the ditch. Water, seeking its former level, rushed down the pipe and surged back up the other side without requiring pumps.

When the ditch was finished and its effect upon the Whipple fortunes evident, he convened the J & W men and showed them the map of Oahu, with arable areas marked in green. "We're bringing water about as far as we can in ditches. Yet look at this map. We're using less than twenty per cent of our potential land. Ninety per cent of our rainfall still runs back into the ocean. Gentlemen, long after I'm dead somebody will think of a way to pierce these mountains and bring that water over to this side, where it's needed. I beg of you," the white-haired scientist pleaded, "when the project becomes feasible, and sooner or later it must, don't hesitate. Pool your funds. Go into debt if necessary. Because the man who controls that water will control Hawaii."

One of the more conservative Janderses, who chafed at working under Whipple, whispered, "They always get dotty in their old age." And the firm became so preoccupied with making money from John Whipple's ditches that they quite forgot his vision of a tunnel through the heart of the mountains.

W HILE NYUK TSIN and her husband were suffering reversals in the manufac-
ture of poi, they observed that difficulties were also visiting their favorite guest. Captain Rafer Hoxworth, when he dined at the Whipples, showed in his face the strain that had overtaken him with the illness of his gracious wife, Noelani, the tall and stately Hawaiian lady whose charm was so much appreciated by the Chinese. In 1869 it became apparent to Nyuk Tsin, as she served the big dinners, that Mrs. Hoxworth needed medical care, and as the year progressed, the tall Hawaiian woman grew steadily less able to sit through a long dinner without showing signs of exhaustion, and Nyuk Tsin grieved for her.

The haoles, as Caucasians were called in the islands, were not able to understand what had brought their beloved friend so close to death, but the kanakas, as the Hawaiians were known, understood. Of their declining sister they said, "Ho'olana i ka wai ke ola.—Her life floats upon the water." But if Noelani herself was aware of this sentence, she betrayed her reactions to no one. She gave the appearance of a placid, pleased Hawaiian woman, graceful in motion and relaxed in countenance. She seemed like a secure brown rock facing the sea and richly clothed in sunlight; about her whispered the waves of her husband's affection and that of her friends.

Like a true alii, Noelani slept a good deal during the day in order to conserve her strength, but as evening approached she came alive, and when her two-horse carriage with its imported English coachman drove up to the big Hoxworth house on Beretania Street she displayed all the excitement of a child. Stepping grandly into the carriage she commanded the Englishman: "You may take me to the Whipples. But hurry." When she arrived she was a figure of striking beauty. Already tall, she accentuated the fact by wearing high tortoise-shell combs in her silvery white, piled-up hair and a dress with a train of at least three feet which trailed as she entered. In the middle of this train was sewn a loop which could be passed over the fingers of her left hand, the kanaka loop it was called, and guests enjoyed watching how deftly Noelani could kick her train with her right foot, catching the kanaka loop with her left hand. Her dresses were made of stiff brocade edged with delicate Brussels lace. She wore jade beads that blended marvelously with her dark skin, jade rings and jade bracelets, all purchased in Peking. Near her heart she wore a thin gold watch from Geneva, pinned into place by a jeweled butterfly from Paris, while in her right hand she customarily carried a Cantonese fan made of feathers and pale ivory. Over all, she wore her Shanghai stole, four feet wide, embroidered in red roses that stood off from the fabric, and edged with a two-foot fringe of Peking knots. Captain Hoxworth, who loved buying her gifts, once said, "A smaller woman would be dwarfed by such an outfit, but Noelani's always been a giant." When she entered a room, her dark eyes flashing, she was a very noble lady, the symbol of a valiant race. And she was dying.

She loved her clothes and parties and having her children about her, for if an evening passed when less than a dozen friends were in attendance, she felt lonely, as if in her last days her Hawaiian friends had deserted her. Then she would tell her husband, "Rafer, drive down to Auntie Mele's and see if there's anyone having a talk." And if there was, the entire group would be brought up to the Hoxworths' to visit with Noelani, who found breathing increasingly difficult.

Her children had married well, and she found great delight in her fourteen grandchildren. Malama, her oldest daughter, had of course married brilliant Micah Hale. Bromley and Jerusha had each married one of the Whipple children, while Iliki had married a Janders, so that when the Hoxworths were assembled, most of the great island families were represented, and there was much talk of Lahaina in the good old days. In these autumnal hours Noelani enjoyed most her discussions with Micah Hale, who now played such an important role in Hawaii, for he was not only head of H & H, he was also a nobleman with a seat in the upper house of the legislature, a member of the Privy Council, and the administrator of the Department of Interior. Often Noelani reminded him: "I was recalling our first conversation, Micah, on that Sunday in San Francisco when you and I were both so certain that America would absorb our islands. Well, it hasn't happened yet, nor will it in my lifetime. Kamehameha V will not sell one foot of land to the United States."

"We will unite," her bearded son-in-law assured her. "I am more positive than ever, Noelani, that our destiny will be achieved shortly."

"You've been telling me that for twenty years and look what's happened. Your country has been torn apart by civil war, and mine has drifted happily along, just as it always was."

"Do not believe it, Noelani," Micah reproved, stroking his copious beard as if he were addressing a legislature. "Each wave that reaches the shores of these islands brings new evidence that we will shortly be one land. I expect it to happen within ten years."

"Why are you so sure?" Noelani pressed.

"For one simple reason. America will need our sugar. In order to safeguard the supply, she will have to take over the islands."

"Are you working for that purpose, Micah?" the elderly woman asked.

"Indeed, as are all men of good sense."

"Does the king know this?"

"He appreciates the problem better than I do. He prays that Hawaii will remain independent, but if it cannot, he prefers that the United States absorb the islands."

"I'm glad I shall not live to see it," Noelani said wearily as the Chinese servants began bringing in the food.

When the Hoxworths dined with the Whipples the thing that impressed Nyuk Tsin was the extraordinary gentleness with which Captain Rafer cared for his wife. Throughout the Chinese community he was the favorite haole, for although he had abused the coolies on their voyage to Hawaii, and cursed them for leaving the plantations, in other respects he had proved a just friend. The man whose face he had kicked in got a good job, and the one whose ankle was broken when he was pitched into the hold was given money to import a wife into the islands. Whenever an H & H ship arrived with a cargo of special food for the Chinese, Captain Hoxworth was there to supervise the unloading, for he loved the smell of faraway places, and he was a familiar visitor to both the Punti and the Hakka stores. He slapped women on the backside and joked with men. If he happened to be carrying a bottle of whiskey, which he often was, he would knock off the cork, take a swig, wipe the bottle with his wrist, pass it to the Chinese, and then take another swig when it returned to him. He had a free and easy way that the Chinese appreciated and a capacity for suddenly imposing his will upon them which they respected. In private he railed against the Chinese peril; in public he treated them decently.

It was his obvious love for his Hawaiian wife which impressed them most, and the tall, rugged old captain with his white sideburns never looked more appealing than when he was gently helping Noelani into her carriage for a visit to some friend's for dinner. At such times he hurried before her to the carriage carrying her cashmere blanket, which he fixed on the rear seat. Then he waited and held out his strong right arm for her to lean on as she climbed painfully into the conveyance. Next he tucked the blanket about her feet and then adjusted her stole over her shoulders. Then he walked sedately in front of the horses—never around the rear of the carriage—and patted them on the flanks and on the noses. Then he came back to the rear door of the carriage and climbed in beside his tall Hawaiian wife. Giving his English driver a signal, he would sit back with her and nod to the evening strollers while his horses pranced through the dusty streets. Apart from the king, Captain Hoxworth was the most dignified and memorable man in Hawaii, and he knew it.

November nights can be cold in Hawaii, for then the days are short and the sun is low in the heavens, and as November, 1869, progressed, it became obvious to all that Noelani must soon be confined permanently to bed in her last lingering illness, for Dr. Whipple said, "I can't find what's wrong, but obviously she ought to stop going out so much." To this, Captain Hoxworth replied, "Noelani's not an ordinary woman. She is the Alii Nui of these islands and she will continue to ride with me as long as her strength permits, for she thinks it proper to move about among her people."

The nights grew colder and Captain Hoxworth wrapped his wife in more shawls. Once, when she seemed extremely weak and bordering on collapse, he asked her, "Would you prefer, my dear, to stay at home this night?"

"No," she said. "Why should I?"

So he helped her into the carriage and they drove not directly down Beretania but by way of King Street and Nuuanu and he pointed out various sights to her, as if she were a tourist seeing Honolulu for the first time. "That's where we're building the new H & H receiving warehouses," he explained, "and I propose buying land here for our office building. Over there's where the Chinese are opening a store for vegetables and meat."

He kept his sensitive finger on the pulse of Honolulu as it throbbed toward new life, but at the same time he kept close to his wife as she spent her last energies. At dinner that night, at the Hewletts', he altered the seating arrangements so that he could stay near her, and when she faltered he said calmly, "This may be the last time Lady Noelani will dine with friends." But she had rallied, and as December came she told her husband that she enjoyed more than anything else her evening drives with him, so on the eighth night in December he had the carriage roll up to take her to the Whipples' for dinner, but when Nyuk Tsin saw her enter the dining room, like a tall, shrunken brown ghost, she gasped.

At dinner that evening Captain Hoxworth shocked everyone but Noelani by saying a terrible thing: "When Noelani's mother, the great Alii Nui of Maui lay dying, her husband used to creep in to see her on his hands and knees, bringing her maile from the hills. I think it a shame and lacking in dignity to see a sweet Hawaiian lady with no maile chains about her, so I have asked some of my men to fetch us maile from the hills, and I should like to bring it to my Alii Nui."

He went to the door and whistled loudly for his coachman, and the Englishman ran up with maile chains and Captain Hoxworth placed the fragrant vines about his wife's shoulders. Then he took a chair far from her and said slowly, "The first time I saw Noelani must have been in 1820, when she was a girl. And I saw her on a surfboard, standing up with not a stitch of clothes on, riding toward the shore like a goddess. And do you know when I saw her next? In 1833. I walked out to her home, knocked on the door, and the first words I ever said to her were, 'Noelani, I've come to find me a wife.' And do you know what her first words to me were? 'Captain Hoxworth, I will go with you to the ship.' So we went aboard the *Carthaginian,* and she never left." He smiled at his wife and said, "Looking at the way people get engaged and married today, I'd say they had very little romance in their bones." he winked at her and then looked at the guests.

"To you young men who aren't married, I've only one bit of advice. Hang around the shore till you see a beautiful Hawaiian girl surfing in, completely naked. Marry that one, and you'll never regret it."

He took the sick woman home that night, and she never appeared on the streets of Honolulu again. Her death was a strange passing, a mysterious disappearance. No doctor could explain why she was dying, but it was obvious that she intended to do so. Like the poetic race of which she was the noblest part, she drifted casually away, and in late December she announced: "I will die in early January." The sad news spread through the Hawaiian community, so that all during the festivities of that season big women appeared at the Hoxworth door, barefooted and with flowers, explaining: "We have come to grieve with our sister." For hours they would sit about her bed, saying nothing, and at dusk, like ponderous, doomed creatures, they would slip away, leaving their flowers behind. Before Noelani died she summoned her son-in-law, dark-bearded Micah Hale of the Privy Council, and she directed him: "Look after Hawaii, Micah. Give the king good advice."

"Each time, before I counsel with him, I pray that God will direct me in the right way," he assured her.

"I don't want you merely to be pious," she said. "I want you to be right."

"It is only through prayer that I can discern the right," he countered.

"Are you as determined as ever to take Hawaii into the Union?" she asked.

"I will see it happen," he insisted.

Noelani began to weep and said, "It will be a sad day for the Hawaiians. On your day of triumph, Micah, be gentle and understanding with your wife. Malama will support you, of course, but on the day you exterminate the Hawaiian kingdom, she will also hate you."

Austere Micah Hale wanted to be lenient at this moment, the last during which he would see his powerful mother-in-law, but like a prophet from the Old Testament he was forced to add, "In the affairs of nations there is a destiny, Noelani, and it cannot be avoided."

She replied, "In the affairs of races there is a destiny, too, and ours has not been a happy one." He bowed and started to leave, but she called him to her bedside and said, "I should like to pray with you, Micah." He kneeled and she intoned: "God, survey the actions of this headstrong young man with the beard. Inspire him with gentleness as well as rectitude."

At her funeral in the old Makiki burial grounds Captain Hoxworth caused excitement by refusing to leave her grave. He remained there for several hours, not weeping or carrying on, but standing beside the grave and looking down across Honolulu toward the ships and out to Diamond Head. At Waikiki the surf was rolling in, and he could see the little figures of men riding upon the waves, and the skies were blue with cloud racks piled upon the horizon, and below lay the sea, the restless, turbulent sea upon which his life had been led.

"How wonderful it's been," he thought. "I wouldn't change a day of it. Even now, somewhere out there, the sperm whales are breeding, and I'm part of them. Go to it, whales! Soon enough somebody like me'll come along and stick a harpoon in you. Have fun while you can!"

Captain Hoxworth had never taken great pleasure in his children, allowing them to develop as they would, but now with Noelani gone he suddenly transformed himself into the benevolent old head of the family, and it became his habit to convene his son and his three daughters with their families and to sit benignly at the head of his table, dispensing charm and affection. He spoke of the old days in the South Pacific and of his adventures in China. It was his opinion that a man had to wait until he was dead to know the meaning of God, unless he happened to have known the sea in his youth.

"To sail before the mast when you're thirteen, to know the abuse of wind and foul captains, to find the spiritual solace that arises from the fo'c's'l, and then to drive yourself inch by inch to the captaincy and then the ownership of the vessel, these are the ultimate tests of a man. It's in such contests with fate that a man comes to know exactly how he stands with God. And don't you forget it, you young men who came to your positions the easy way," and he looked sharply at his son Bromley and his sons-in-law: Janders, Whipple, Hale.

He had already spotted Micah as by far the ablest of the group, and at his family dinners, to which the younger men willingly came, he talked more and more to Micah. "Any enterprise of moment is like commanding a ship, Micah. There are plots against the captain, and he's got to put them down ruthlessly. You may not like to kick a man in the face, I never did, but it may be the only way you can maintain control of your ship. And that's what's important. Control."

It was his opinion that the next decade would produce a series of fundamental crises which would determine the future of Hawaii, and, more important, the future of the powerful firms that sought to control the business enterprise of Hawaii. "Disregard the dear, fat, old kings. They are of no consequence whatever and should be kept around to amuse the people. The important thing is Hoxworth & Hale and Janders & Whipple and Hewlett's. Keep them on the right track, and the kings'll have to follow suit."

When he talked thus he was disturbed to find that Micah Hale did not agree with him. "We must settle this problem of the foolish kings," Hale insisted. "It is infuriating to see them wasting the substance of this kingdom, and I am more determined than ever to do something about it."

"Micah!" Captain Hoxworth reproved. "You be content with making H & H the most powerful company in the Pacific, and the kings'll take care of themselves. Remember what I say. Hell, son, you'll be the real king, the one that matters."

"It is not the destiny of Americans that they should live under kings," Micah repeated stubbornly.

"I'll tell you what the destiny of America is," Hoxworth boomed, thrusting his handsome, white-haired head forward among his children. "If Hawaii prospers and makes money, America will suddenly discover that we're part of its destiny. But if you allow the firms to fool around and squander our inheritance, America won't give a damn for us."

In these discussions with Micah the wiry old captain tended to ignore his ineffective son, Bromley, and when Micah argued against him on the matter of Hawaii's civil government, falsely holding it to be of more importance than the profitable governance of H & H and the other big companies, Hoxworth noticed that among his listeners one quick intelligence matched his own, and without ever directing himself purposely and obviously at this attentive listener, he began tailoring his comments so that Bromley's thirteen-year-old boy, Whip, could understand, and he was gratified to see how soon this wiry, quick boy with the sharp eyes caught on.

"I have always held," he said, speaking ostensibly to the boy's uncle, Ed Janders, who had married Iliki—it was curious the way in which Captain Hoxworth named his own children after women he had loved: Jerusha, Bromley, Iliki; but his wife had understood—"I've held that a man's life should begin at thirteen. He should go to sea, or engage in great enterprises. His mind should already have grappled with the idea of God, and he should have read half the fine books he will read in his entire lifetime. Any single minute lost after you're thirteen is an hour irretrievably gone." It was interesting to the old captain that Iliki's husband didn't understand a word he was saying, but his grandson Whip Hoxworth understood it all.

The captain therefore formed the habit of taking the high-spirited boy with him as he rode about Honolulu, and that year the community became accustomed to seeing handsome Captain Hoxworth parading the streets with his alert grandson, introducing him formally to his business associates and explaining shipping customs to the boy. One day the minister asked, "Captain, isn't the boy attending school any more?" And Hoxworth replied, "What I'm teaching him he can't get in school."

He took his grandson down to the wharves to see the H & H ships come in from Java and China, and he made the boy stay down in the fo'c's'l for entire days while he went about other work, saying, "If you've got a good imagination, and I think you have, you can construct what it must have been like to sail before the mast." He also said, "There is one thrill of the sea that every man must discover for himself, the arrival at some strange port after a long voyage. Whip, remember this. Travel about the world. See the forbidden cities and dive into them."

He said this while standing 'tween decks in a converted whaler, and in the half-darkness he added, "Whip, the two greatest things in life are sailing into a strange port and thinking, 'I can make this city mine,' and sailing into the harbor of a strange woman and saying, 'I can make this woman mine.' Whip, when I'm dead I don't want you to remember me as I was in church or as I looked sitting at the big table at night. I want you to remember me as I was."

He left his gig at the wharves and walked westward from the bustling docks until he and his grandson came to a section of evil-smelling little houses strung along a network of alleys. "This is Iwilei," Captain Hoxworth explained. "Rat Alley, Iwilei, and down here I'm king." But if his words were true, he was a king incognito, for no one in the alleys of Iwilei spoke to him. A few Chinese who had made money that week gambling, a few sailors, a few minor men from the smaller businesses of Honolulu ambled past, intent upon their business, and the first thing young Whip Hoxworth noticed was that in Iwilei even men who knew each other did not speak, as if by magic a man was invisible because he wished to be so.

"This is where I often come," the old captain explained, and he led his grandson into a dark and inconspicuous shack, the inside of which was well lighted and tastefully decorated. A Chinese who imported his girls from Macao, ran the place; he nodded deferentially to Hoxworth, who said, "I want to see all the girls."

A truly motley crew lined up in bathrobes and slips: a Spaniard from Valparaiso with no high combs in her hair; an Italian girl from Naples who had shipped into Honolulu on a whaler; an Irish girl from Dublin who knew Captain Hoxworth and who gave him a kiss—young Whip liked her and she smiled at him; two Chinese girls and one Javanese, who seemed forbidding and aloof. "Who's the youngest girl here?" Captain Hoxworth asked.

"This China girl," the curator of masterpieces replied.

"Can she speak English?"

"No. She don't have to."

"Today she have to," Hoxworth replied. "You go out and find me the youngest girl you can, but she's got to speak English. I want her to explain things to my boy here." When the proprietor left to scurry about among the sinks of Iwilei, the Chinese and Javanese girls retired, but the others who could speak English gathered about the captain and his charge, admiring the young man.

"How old is he?" the pleasant Irish girl asked.

"Thirteen," Hoxworth replied, putting his virile arm about the questioner. "And at thirteen it's high time a man gets to know what delicious things women are. How old were you, Noreen, when you discovered the fun in men?"

"I was thirteen," the happy Irish girl replied.

"And you, Constanza?"

"I was twelve, in back of the cathedral in Naples."

"I was fourteen myself," Hoxworth apologized. "And it happened in your home city, Raquella, and that's why I've always treasured Valparaiso. I had shipped on a whaler . . . well, you wouldn't be interested, but I spied on the sailors to see where they were going with such determination, and I marched in after them and said, 'Me, too!' And everybody roared with laughter as I plunked down my shillings, but thereafter they treated me with more respect. And, Whip, they'll treat you with more respect, too. Not because they'll know you were here. That's got to be kept a secret. But because you'll know something the others don't know. And this knowledge is what makes some men men, while the lack of it keeps other men boys . . . all their lives. I'm afraid that your uncles and your father are boys. Goddamnit, I want you to be a man."

The brothel keeper returned with a Chinese girl of uncertain age, but she seemed younger than the rest. She wore a black silk smock covering white pajama pants. She was barefooted and had her hair in a long braid, so that she looked completely alien to the boy who was intended to be her guest. He looked at her with frank curiosity, and when she saw his confused yet eager face, she smiled and took a step toward him. "I like to show him things," she said.

Young Whip was momentarily afraid, and although he did not draw back, neither did he step valiantly forward, so his grandfather benignly put his left arm about the little Chinese girl and his right about his grandson. "Remember what I said about ships sailing into strange ports? Anybody can be brave enough to love a girl of his own color, but to be a man, Whip, you've got to stare right into the eyes of the brown girls and yellow and whatever you meet up with, and say, 'You're a woman and you're mine.' Because what a man's got to discover is that there's no gain in loving a particular woman. It's the idea of woman that you're after. Now you be real sweet with this pretty little Chinese girl. Because she can teach you the first steps in this grand discovery."

Giving the curious pair his benediction, he pushed them gently toward the darkened hallway that led to the private rooms, and as they disappeared, hand in hand, he grabbed the Irish girl and cried, "Goddamn, Noreen, it's exciting! Imagine! The first time!"

The Chinese girl led Whip to a stall and showed him the furnishings. "Pretty, you think?"

"It's real nice," he stammered, holding tighter to her warm hand.

She pushed him away from her, turned to face him and said, "It's possible have much fun with a woman. You see?" And slowly she pulled her smock over her head, and when she had tossed the rustling silk onto a chair she smiled at Whip, placed her small brown hands under her breasts and moved her shoulders sideways in a slow rotary motion. "These made for men," she explained, and without further instruction young Whip moved forward, pulled her hands away and replaced them with his own. Instinctively he lifted the small breasts to his lips, and as he was doing so the girl slipped off her trousers. It would have pleased Captain Hoxworth could he have witnessed how little instruction his grandson really required.

But in other matters the boy needed substantial guidance. He was a wild-willed lad with only an average record at school, and his grandfather surprised him by insisting that he read long and difficult books like *Pendennis* and *Jane Eyre,* while the students at Punahou were struggling with *Oliver Twist* and *The Legend of Sleepy Hollow.* Captain Hoxworth also drilled his grandson on the necessity for showing a profit on anything one went into in the line of business, and his business principles were simple: "If you sell something, never give samples away. Make the bastards pay. And keep an eye on the help or they'll steal the company right out from under you."

There was one lesson, however, which the ramrod-straight old captain impressed upon his tough-minded grandson above all others: "Living seventy years is a tremendous adventure. You're thirteen now. You've probably only got fifty-seven Christmases left. Enjoy each one as if you would never see another, for by God the day soon comes when you won't. You've only got about two and a half thousand more Saturday nights remaining. Get yourself a girl and enjoy her. Never take a girl lightly. You may never sleep with another. Or she may be the one you'll always remember as the best of the lot. But god-damnit, Whip, don't be a weak old man before your time. Don't be like your father and your uncles. God, Whip, you can't even imagine what Hawaii's going to be like in twenty years, or fifty. Maybe nobody'll be growing sugar. Maybe they won't need ships any more. Maybe this whole city and the hills behind will be part of China. But be courageous about guessing. Be on top of the wheel as it turns, not dragging along at the bottom."

At this moment in his grandfather's harangue young Whip made the old man extremely happy. The idea that Hawaii might one day be part of China did not entirely impress young Whip, but the mention of that country reminded him of Iwilei and he said, boldly, "I'd like to see that Chinese girl again."

"So would I!" the old man roared, and he hitched his horse and led his grandson down into Rat Alley, but when they got to the Macao man's place, the Chinese girl could not be found, so Whip smiled as before at the Irish lass, who was heavier than he was, but his grandfather roared, "No, by God! No-reen's mine." And he rustled up Raquella from Valparaiso, and the Spanish girl was so pleased with the idea of being with a bright-eyed young boy that when she had him alone she tore at him like a tigress, and he fought with her, tearing a red welt across her back until with a tempestuous sigh of joy she pulled him onto the floor and taught him things no boy in Honolulu and few men knew.

And it was strange, but when he left Iwilei that day he was not thinking of women, but of strange ports, and the insatiable fighting of the world, and of ships—his ships—traveling to all parts of the globe to bring home strange people and stranger produce. "I don't want to go back to Punahou," he announced that evening at his grandfather's big table.

"What do you want to do?" asked his proper father, whose main job in life was hiding the fact that he was half-Hawaiian.

"I want to go to sea," young Whip replied.

"That you shall!" his grandfather promised, but this was a promise that was most difficult to keep, and for a while it seemed as if the stuffy uncles, who did not know the wild, free girls of Iwilei, would triumph.

"The boy has got to finish Punahou and go to Yale," Bromley Hoxworth insisted.

"To hell with Yale," Captain Hoxworth shouted. "Yale never did good for any man who wasn't already formed by his own experiences. Your son is a different breed, Bromley. He's for the sea."

"He's got to get an education to prepare him for his later responsibilities with H & H," Bromley insisted.

"Listen to me, you blind, blind men!" Hoxworth stormed. "That is exactly my purpose in sending him to sea. So that he can obtain the education in the world that he will require if he is going to run your companies well. It is for your sakes that I want him to sail before the mast. Because there has got to be somebody in this timorous outfit who has developed courage and a free new way of looking at things." He slumped back in his chair and said, "I'm growing tired of arguments."

The uncles supported Bromley, bearded Micah proving especially effective with his contention that a new day had arisen in Hawaii, one that required the exercise of prudence and conservative management. "It is our job to hold onto our position and consolidate our good fortune while we ponder what can be done about bringing these islands into the American orbit. Caution, hard work and intellectual capacity are what we require. Bromley's right. The place to acquire those virtues is at Yale."

"Colossal horse manure!" Captain Hoxworth responded from his slumped position at the head of the table. "The abilities you're reerring to, Micah, can always be bought for fifteen hundred Mexican dollars a year, and do you know why they can be bought as cheaply as that? Because your goddamned Yale College can always be depended upon to turn out exactly that kind of man in bigger supply than the market can possibly absorb. But a man of daring, schooled at sea and in commerce and in knockdown fights . . ." He rose from the table and left in disgust. "Such men don't come cheap. Nobody turns them out in large quantities."

The uncles kept young Whip sequestered from his grandfather, lest the stubborn old man ship the boy on one of the many H & H cargo carriers about to sail from Honolulu. To balk what they suspected was the old captain's plan, they prepared to ship Whipple back to New England, where in rather quieter quarters he could prepare himself for Yale; but one March morning in 1870 Captain Hoxworth ferreted out where his grandson was being kept, and he drove there hurriedly in his gig and told the boy: "Hurry, Whip, we've got only a few minutes."

"For what?"

"You're shipping to Suez."

The stalwart young fellow, now almost fourteen and tall for his age, smiled at his erect old grandfather and said, "I have no clothes here."

"Come as you are. You'll appreciate clothes more if you have to work for them."

They drove rapidly to the docks, where Whip automatically headed for a large H & H ship which seemed ready to put out to sea, whereupon his grandfather caught his arm, wheeled him about in the sunlight, and asked scornfully, "Good God, Whip! Do you think I'd ship you on one of my own boats? There's what you ride in, son!" And he pointed to a three-masted weather-beaten old whaler from Salem, Massachusetts. The years had not been good to this ship, for she had entered the whaling trade after its peak had been reached, and without ever finding her logical place among the wandering ships of the world, she had stumbled from one occupation to another. Three times she had changed her rigging and now sailed as a barkentine, bound for a speculative run to Manila for an overload of mahogany which the Khedive of Egypt required for a palace he was building. She had already waited at the pier half an hour beyond her announced time of departure, but since she had consistently missed the master schedule by which the oceans of the world operate, this was no new experience. Nevertheless, her captain chafed and he was not in a good humor when Rafer Hoxworth hurried up with his grandson.

"This is the boy I told you of," Hoxworth said.

"Looks strong," the surly captain snarled. "Get below."

"I'd like a minute with him," Hoxworth said.

"You can have six," the captain agreed.

Quickly Rafer Hoxworth swung himself down into the fo'c's'l, grabbed his grandson by the arms and said hurriedly, "Once you leave this harbor, Whipple, that evil-tempered man topside has the absolute power of life and death over you. His word is law, and he's no puny Yale professor. He's a tough, cruel man, and you'll get no sympathy from either him or me if you play the coward.

"Now, Whip, if you get into a fight, and you will, remember one thing. Fight to kill. There's no other rule. And when you've got a man fairly licked and on the deck, always kick him in the face so that when he gets up he can't contend that he almost had you down. Bruise him, scar him, mutilate him so that he can never forget who's boss. And when you've done this, help him up and be generous.

"Whip, you've tasted Chinese girls and Spaniards. There are a thousand more to sample. Try 'em all. That's the one thing you'll do in life that you'll never regret. Whip, I want you to come home a man."

As the fleeting seconds passed, the youth wished vainly that he could prolong this moment endlessly, for he felt deeply attached to this wild old grandfather of his, but the last question he asked was so surprising both to himself and to his grandfather that Rafer Hoxworth fell back a few steps: "Grandfather, if you liked the girls at Iwilei so much, how did you feel about Noelani? I can't get this straight."

There was a moment of silence, and then Rafer said, "When Noelani's mother died she weighed close to four hundred pounds. Your great-grand-mother. And every day her husband crawled into her presence on his hands and knees, bringing her maile chains. That's a good thing for a man to do."

"But how can you love a lot of girls and one woman, too? At the same time?"

"You ever study the skies at night, Whip? All the lovely little stars? You could reach up and pinch each one on the points. And then in the east the moon rises, enormous and perfect. And that's something else, entirely different."

He shook his grandson's hand and scrambled topside, waved to the surly captain, and leaped down onto the dock. The old whaler creaked and groaned as her ropes were loosened. A fresh wind came down off the mountains in back of Honolulu, and a voyage was commenced.

When it was discovered what Hoxworth had done with his grandson, the entire community was outraged. Bromley Hoxworth and his brothers-in-law talked for a while of dispatching one of the H & H ships to intercept the dirty old whaler and take the boy off, but Hoxworth pointed out: "He signed papers, and if you know the captain of that ship, the only way that boy will ever get off is either to die at sea and be buried feet-first under a scrap of canvas, or serve his time properly like a man."

Later, Honolulu softened toward the resolute old captain and the citizenry began to speak of him with amused affection, recognizing him for what he was: the leading resident of the islands. If he entered a bank, he was treated with deference. In church he was bowed to by the pastors, and at the library, which he had always supported with generous gifts, he was accepted as the patron saint of learning. The Chinese of Honolulu referred to him as "that courtly, sweet old man."

He died in June, 1870, full of years and public acclaim. At his deathbed were Hales and Whipples and Janderses and Hoxworths—the leaders of Hawaii—but the surviving mortal on whom his thoughts rested was his grandson Whip, happily bedded down in a Manila brothel with an agile little Co-chinese lately imported from Saigon.

O N THE AFTERNOON of Captain Rafer Hoxworth's funeral, Dr. John Whipple, then seventy-one years old but spare and well preserved, returned from the cemetery to his home, where he found the pregnant Nyuk Tsin waiting for him, and he supposed that finally she had surrendered her prejudices and had come to ask his medical advice upon her condition, but that was not the case. She said, "Mun Ki him sore leg, you help," and she requested a medicine to stop the itching that had arisen from her husband's work in the taro patch. Dr. Whipple was acquainted with this curious irritation that sometimes resulted from the immersion of one's legs in a taro bog, so he handed Nyuk Tsin a small jar of unguent, but as he did so he had the clear thought: "I'm getting careless as I grow older. I really ought to see the man's leg for myself." Months later he was to chide himself for this oversight, but in the days immediately following he did not.

Nyuk Tsin applied the unguent to her husband's itching leg, and as she had predicted, within a few days the irritation disappeared, and he proceeded with his work as cook. On the fourth day Dr. Whipple happened to remember about the salve he had prescribed, and asked casually, "Leg, how he come?" And Mun Ki assured him, "Good too much."

But some time later the cook again experienced strange sensations in his right leg and the beginnings of the same in his left, and once more it was apparent to him that American doctors understood very little about the human body, so this time he tonicked himself with Chinese herbs—at night so that none could watch except his wife, who brewed them—and this time the medicine was effective, and the irritation left for good. Mun Ki was pleased, and vowed that thereafter he would fool no more with Dr. Whipple.

But in July he noticed a new sore on the big toe of his right foot, and this one did not respond to normal Chinese medication. When he pointed this out to his wife, Nyuk Tsin argued: "Try the white doctor's unguent," and although Mun Ki knew this to be folly, he allowed his wife to smear it upon the toe, and to Mun Ki's confusion, the sore healed perfectly, and he was perplexed. "You watch!" he warned his wife. "This white man's medicine cures nothing. Next week the sore will be there again."

And to his personal gratification, he was right. The sore reappeared, and worse than before. He therefore drank more Chinese herbs and to a certain extent the sore improved, but now a dreadful itching occurred, and before long it passed over to his left foot as well. Then, to his dismay, a very small lesion opened on his left forefinger, and nothing either drove it away or subdued it, and he hid this fact from Dr. Whipple but he could not hide it from his wife.

Nyuk Tsin could never remember, in later years, just how the horrible, unspoken word first passed between herself and her husband, but she could remember the growing dread that filled their days—still with no words spoken and with life proceeding casually between them—until one morning, when she heard her husband scratching his legs, she went to him boldly, took him by the hands and said, "Wu Chow's Father, I must go to see the Chinese doctor." He dropped his eyes away from hers, sat staring at the floor and finally agreed: "You had better see him."

After the noonday meal was served, Nyuk Tsin slipped out through the garden gate and hurried downtown to the Chinese temple, where after much bowing she lighted incense before the compassionate picture of Lu Tsu, to whose wisdom she confided these facts: "Wu Chow's Father has an itching that will not go away, and his finger is sore. We are afraid, Lu Tsu, and hope that you who know all medicines will aid us." She prayed for a long time, then sought out the priest, a shaven-headed man with a kindly face and a bamboo holder containing nearly a hundred numbered slivers of wood. Carefully he moved the bamboo in an arc, repeating old prayers of proved efficiency, and gradually one of the sticks worked itself loose from the others, and it was number forty-one, a number which contained elements of hope. On a small piece of paper the priest wrote "Forty-one" and for a dime he gave it to Nyuk Tsin.

She took her prescription across the river to a dirty little drug shop in Rat Alley, and when she handed it to the herb doctor he said, "Ah, forty-one is a very good medicine. You're lucky today." Behind him he had row after row of boxes containing precious herbs, and from box forty-one he measured out a spoonful and said, "You must brew a strong tea and drink it with a prayer. Is it for pregnancy?"

"No," the honest woman replied, "it's for Wu Chow's Father."

The doctor's expression did not change, but he thought quickly: "Aha! Another one who is afraid to come in person!" To Nyuk Tsin he said casually, "This is a fine medicine for itching legs."

"I'm glad," Nyuk Tsin said, not noticing that it was not she who had introduced the subject of itching legs.

Then, as she was about to leave, the doctor said in an offhand manner, "I'm sure this will cure your man, but if it doesn't, remember! I know all the medicines. Remember." And as soon as Nyuk Tsin had gone, the doctor ran into another alley and cried, "Look Sing! Look Sing! Follow that one."

"Which one?" the loafer asked.

"The Hakka woman, with the big feet." But Nyuk Tsin was hurrying home by a different route, and that day the spy did not overtake her. When he reported his failure to the herbalist the latter shrugged his shoulders and said, "She'll be back."

Medicine forty-one was completely ineffective and the growing agony in Nyuk Tsin's mind could not be put to rest. "Wu Chow's Father," she implored, "you must come with me to the Chinese doctor."

"I am afraid," Mun Ki said.

"He told me he knew all the medicines," Nyuk Tsin assured him, so when the dishes were washed and the four babies placed in the care of another Chinese woman, Nyuk Tsin led her husband slowly, and in breathless fear, down Nuuanu Street and across the river to Rat Alley. As they approached their meeting with the doctor, they formed an unusual pair, for Nyuk Tsin in her black smock and trousers did not hobble obediently behind her pigtailed husband, as Punti custom required; she marched side by side with him in the Hakka way, for she was his wife, and if what she suspected was true, in the days to come Mun Ki was going to need her as never before; and he sensed this need and was content to have his strong wife walking beside him.

When they reached Rat Alley, and saw the row of shacks where the girls lived, Nyuk Tsin experienced an abiding gratitude toward the man who had kept her for himself instead of selling her to the brothel keepers, and in apprehension of what her life would have been like had Mun Ki not bought her, she drew closer to him, and when the alley narrowed she even took his hand, and at first he was constrained to throw it back, but he held onto it, and he could feel her fingers softly protecting the unmanageable sore on his index finger, and in that wordless moment a compact was built, and each understood it, for Nyuk Tsin was saying: "No matter what the doctor reports, I shall stay with you."

When the doctor saw them entering his shop he knew what their fears were, and he was certain that this meant money for him. He therefore held his soft, thin hands together professionally and smiled at the worried couple. "Did the medicine cure the itching?" he asked in Punti.

"No," Nyuk Tsin replied. "And now Wu Chow's Father has a sore on his toe."

"I would like to see it," the doctor replied, but when he had drawn a curtain aside so that sunlight could fall upon the floor where Mun Ki's foot stood, and when he kneeled down to inspect the unhealed lesion and the sickly white flesh around it, he instinctively recoiled in horror, even though he had known, when he knelt down, what he was going to see, and Nyuk Tsin marked his action.

"Are there other sores?" the doctor inquired in a subdued voice.

"On his other toes, and this finger, and his shins hurt," Nyuk Tsin explained in broken Punti.

Gravely the doctor examined each of these lesions. Then he rubbed his hands as if to cleanse himself of some terrible scourge. Nyuk Tsin watched this gesture, too, and asked bravely, "Is it the mai Pake, the Chinese sickness?"

"It is," the doctor whispered.

"Oh, gods of heaven, no!" Mun Ki gasped. He shivered for a moment in the gloomy office and then looked like a thrashed boy pleading with his father. "What must I do?"

Now the doctor's natural cupidity subdued any humane reactions, and he assumed his best professional manner—for he was not a doctor at all but a field hand who hated hard work—and assured Mun Ki: "There's nothing to worry about, really. For the mai Pake I have an unfailing remedy."

"You do?" Mun Ki pleaded with animal ferocity. "You can cure these sores?"

"Of course!" The doctor smiled reassuringly. "I have several patients, and not one has had to surrender himself to the white doctors." But Nyuk Tsin was studying the man carefully, and she knew that he was lying. She therefore said, openly, "Wu Chow's Father, this man has no cure. Right now we should turn ourselves in to the white doctors." Her husband caught the phrase, "turn ourselves in," and his wife's implied promise that she would share the illness with him was more than he could at that moment bear, and he began to weep.

"Come," Nyuk Tsin said bravely. "We will go now and talk with Dr. Whipple."

But the Iwilei doctor, fearing to lose a patient who seemed to have money and a good job, protested, in rapid Punti: "Are you, a respectable Punti gentleman, going to give up a chance of escape simply because a stupid Hakka wife thinks she knows more about the ami Pake than I do? Sir, have you thought of what it means if you report to the white doctors?" And he began conjuring up evil pictures: "The police coming to capture you? The little boat at the pier? The cage on deck? The journey to the island? Sir, your wife is pregnant now. Suppose it is a son. Why, you'll never see your own son. Have you thought about that? And all the time I have a certain cure right here."

Of course Mun Ki had thought of these extremities, and now to hear his fears paraded openly had an appalling effect upon him, and he collapsed against the doctor's table, mumbling, "Is it really the mai Pake?"

"It is the mai Pake," the doctor repeated coldly. "The Chinese sickness. You have it; and in another month unless you cure yourself with my herbs, your face will begin to grow big, and your eyes will have a film upon them, and your hands and feet will begin to fall away. Look even now, you poor man!" And he grabbed Mun Ki's index finger and pierced it with a dirty needle, and Mun KI could feel no pain. "You have the mai Pake, my friend," the quack doctor repeated, and as he saw his patient quivering with fear, he added, "The disease that the white doctors call leprosy."

"You are sure?"

"Any white doctor will see that you have leprosy, and you know what they will do then? The cage on the little boat."

"But can you cure me?" Mun Ki pleaded in terror.

"I have cured many patients of the mai Pake," the herbalist replied.

"No, Wu Chow's Father," Nyuk Tsin pleaded, knowing in her heart that this doctor was a fraud, but the herbalist realized that only a little additional pressure was required to make Mun Ki one of his most profitable patients, so he interrupted forcefully: "Be silent, stupid woman. Would you deprive your husband of his only chance of salvation?"

This challenge was too reasonable for Nyuk Tsin to combat, so she retired to a corner and thought: "My poor, foolish husband. He will waste his money with this evil man, and in the end we shall have to run away to the hills anyway."

So Mun Ki, in the silence, made his decision. "I will try your cures," he said, and the quick-witted doctor replied: "It will take a little time, but trust in me and you will be cured. How much money did you bring with you?" Mun Ki, in panic, opened his purse and showed the doctor his meager store of dimes and shillings and reals, and the doctor said happily, "Well, this will more than pay for the first bundles of herbs, so you see it isn't going to cost much, after all." But when Nyuk Tsin started to draw back some of the reals, the doctor prudently slipped his hand over the coins and suggested: "I'll give you more herbs so you won't have to come all the way back to Iwilei so soon."

"The herbs will cure me?" Mun Ki pleaded.

"Without fear," the doctor reassured him, and with their cloth-wrapped bundle of herbs Mun Ki and his wife left the medical man and walked home.

But now they were a different couple, for the unspoken fears that had haunted them when they journeyed to Iwilei had become realities: Mun Ki was a leper, and the law said sternly that he must give himself up, and be exiled for the rest of his life to a dismal lepers' island. He was different from all men, for he was irretrievably doomed to die of the most horrible disease known to man: His toes would fall away and his fingers. His body would grow foul, and from long distances it would be possible to smell him, as if he were an animal. His face would grow big and thick and scaly and hairy, like a lion's; and his eyes would glass over like an owl's in daylight; and then his nose would waste away, and his lips fall off, and the suppurating sores would creep across his cheeks and eat away his chin until at last, faceless, formless, without hands or feet, he would die in agony. He was a leper. Those were the thoughts of pigtailed Mun Ki on the hot July day in 1870 when he walked bedazed and in mental anguish back from Iwilei.

His wife, walking boldly beside him and keeping his doomed fingers in her protecting hand, had a much simpler thought: "I will stay with him, and if he must hide in the hills, I will hide with him, and if he is caught and sent to the leper island, I will go with him." In these simple thoughts she found solace, and never once in the months that followed did she deviate from them.

When she led her stupefied husband back to the kitchen at Dr. Whipple's she did exactly as the quack doctor had ordered: she brewed the ugly-smelling herbs and made her husband drink the broth. Where the doctor had pierced the finger with his dirty needle, she cleaned the wound, sucking it with her lips. Then she put Mun Ki to bed and cooked the evening meal, serving it by herself.

"Mun Ki not well," she explained in the spacious dining room.

"Shall I look at him?" Dr. Whipple asked.

"No," she said. "He be good quick."

Nyuk Tsin had to keep her diseased husband—for the quack's medication did no good whatever—away from public view, for that year there had been a general roundup of lepers, and some one hundred and sixty had been shipped off to the leper island to perpetual banishment and slow death; suspicious watchers had perfected tricks whereby to trap unsuspected lepers. One man boasted: "I can look at the eye of a leper and spot the disease every time. There's a certain glassiness you just can't miss."

Another argued: "What you say's true, but that comes late in the disease. The trick is to spot it early, before others can be contaminated. The way to do this is to look for thickening of the facial skin. That's the sure sign."

"No," the first man countered. "There's only one sure sign. When you shake a man's hand, dig your fingernail into his flesh, and if he doesn't wince, you've got a leper every time."

Nyuk Tsin, watching her husband carefully, felt relieved that neither his eyes nor his facial skin yet betrayed the secret ravages of the disease, but she also noticed that he shivered more noticeably than before and that the sores on his feet were growing. "Somebody will see them, and they will tell the police," she thought. To prevent this she went to the Chinese temple, and ignoring Lu Tsu, who had betrayed her, she knelt before the statue of Kwan Yin, the goddess of mercy, and prayed: "Help me, gentle Kwan Yin, to keep Wu Chow's Father free. Help me to hide him."

These were evil years, indeed, in Hawaii. Before the coming of the white man, leprosy had been unknown. Then, in some unfathomable way, the alii contracted it, possibly from a passing sailor who had become infected in the Philippines, and from 1835 on, the great ravager had swept through the nobles of the island, so that the disease was secretly known as the mai alii, the sickness of the nobles, but coincident with the arrival of the Chinese, the virulent killer attacked the common people, who therefore gave it a permanent name: the mai Pake. In the areas from which the Hakka and Punti had come, leprosy was rarely known and it had never been a conspicuously Chinese disease, but the unfortunate name was assigned, and it stuck, so that in 1870 if a Chinese was caught with it, the measures taken against him were apt to be more stringent than those taken against others; so spies were more active among the Chinese, since rewards were greater.

These were the years when an otherwise decent man would study his enemy's face, and when he saw a pimple or impetigo or eczema he would denounce his enemy, and the man would be hunted down, arrested and thrown into the cage. There was no appeal, no hope, never an escape. The doomed man had only one chance to enjoy even the meanest decencies during the long years of his exile: if some unafflicted person, fully aware of her actions, volunteered to accompany him to the leper settlement, she was free to go in expectation of making his inevitable death a little easier. The saintly persons who stepped forward to share the hell of leprosy became known as the kokuas, the helpers. Mostly they were Hawaiian women who thus surrendered their own lives to aid others, and sometimes they themselves contracted the awful disease and died in exile; so that from those agonizing years the word kokua was to gain a special meaning, and to say of a woman in Hawaii, "She was a kokua," was to accord her a special benediction unknown in the rest of the world.

Therefore, in the middle of September, when Nyuk Tsin was pregnant with her fifth child and when it became wholly apparent to her that Mun Ki would not be cured and that the quack's herbs were of no use whatever, she waited one day until the evening meal ended and then she sent the children away and knelt before her husband, sharing with him the resolve she had made more than a month before: "Wu Chow's Father, I shall be your kokua."

For some minutes he did not speak, nor did he look at the woman kneeling before him. Instead, he slowly picked up one of her needles and stuck it carefully into each finger of his left hand. When he had tested his fingers twice he said, "There is no feeling."

"Shall we hide in the hills?" she asked.

"No one has spied upon me yet," he replied. "Maybe next week the herbs will work."

"Wu Chow's Father," she reasoned, "the doctor is a quack."

He put his hand upon her lips and said, "Let's try once more."

"We have almost no money left," she pleaded. "We must save it for the children."

"Please," he whispered. "I feel sure that this time the herbs will work."

So she took the last precious dimes and reals of her family and plodded down to Iwilei in the hot September sunlight, and when she entered Rat Alley, she noticed that two men watched her carefully, and first she thought: "They think I am one of the girls," but quickly she realized that they were not looking at her in that way, and she gasped: "They're spies, watching to see who visits the doctor. If they report Mun Ki they'll get a little money." So she hurried down a different alley and then up another and finally slipped into the doctor's office.

He was happy and hopeful. "Is your Punti husband getting well?" he asked graciously. And something in the man's manner that day cautioned Nyuk Tsin, and she lied: "He's very grateful to you, Doctor. All the sores have gone and much of the itching in his legs. It's been a wonderful relief to us."

The doctor was surprised at this news and asked, "But nevertheless you wish a few more herbs?"

"Yes," Nyuk Tsin replied, sensing a great evil about her. "A little for the legs, and he'll be cured."

"He'll be cured?" the doctor repeated curiously.

"Yes," Nyuk Tsin explained, feigning happy relief. "It seems not to have been mai Pake after all. More like a sore from the taro patch."

"Where does the cured man live?" the doctor asked casually, as he filled the jar, and the manner in which he spoke convinced Nyuk Tsin that he was in league with the spies outside, and that he was turning over to them the names of his clients, so that after the afflicted Chinese had used up all their funds on herbs, he could squeeze a few more reals from the government as a reward for turning them in to the leper authorities.

"We live at Malama Sugar," Nyuk Tsin said quietly.

"Nice plantation," the doctor replied casually. "Which camp?"

"Number Two Camp," Nyuk Tsin replied, but when the cautious, probing doctor handed her the herbs and started to pick up her family's last coins, she could no longer tolerate him, and she swept the coins back into her own hand and grabbed a blue jar and knocked the top off and shoved the jagged glass into the doctor's face, and when the glass cut him and his own quackery entered his eyes, causing them to pain, she threw the money in his face and whispered in a hushed, hate-choked voice: "Did you think you fooled me? I know you are reporting secretly to the police. You pig, you pig!" In uncontrollable fury she smashed half a dozen pots of herbs to the floor, kicked them about with her bare feet, and then grabbed the broken blue jar to assault the doctor again, but he fled whimpering to the rear of his office, so she hurried away down a side alley, but she paused long enough to peer back at the doctor's shack, and when that man's cries had continued for a moment, the two spies hurried up and went inside to rescue their conspirator, while Nyuk Tsin returned, by a devious path, to Dr. Whipple's. When she reached home, she did not immediately go inside the gate, but walked on, stopping now and then to see if she were being followed. Then she went empty-handed to her husband and said, "The doctor was a spy. He was going to report us tonight, because his helpers were there, waiting."

"What did you do?" Mun Ki asked.

"I hope I cut his eye out," Nyuk Tsin replied.

That night she matured her second plan, for when the evening meal was over, she left the Whipple grounds and moved quietly about the Chinese community, going to families which had come to Hawaii with her in the hold of the *Carthaginian,* for all such men were brothers, and she said to each, "Will you take into your home one of the sons of your brother Mun Ki?"

Almost invariably the Chinese would listen, say nothing, look at Nyuk Tsin, and finally ask, "Is it the mai Pake?" and without fear, for she knew that no *Carthaginian* man would betray his brother, she always replied honestly, "It is." Then the man would ask, "And are you going to be his kokua?" And when Nyuk Tsin replied, "I am," the man said either, "I will take one of your children," or, "I can't take a child myself, but let us see Ching Gar Foo, because I am sure he'll take one." But she noticed that they shuddered when they came near her.

By midnight Nyuk Tsin had disposed of her four sons and her household goods and had made arrangements with a cook for one of the Hewlett families that when her unborn child arrived, Nyuk Tsin would return it to Honolulu by ship from the leper island to be cared for by that cook. She was therefore in a relieved if not hopeful mood when she returned to tell her husband that his sons would be cared for, but when she reached the Whipple grounds she saw an unaccustomed light in her quarters, and she started running toward where Mun Ki was supposed to be sleeping, but when she burst into the little wooden shack she saw Dr. Whipple standing beside the bed with a lamp in his right hand.

The American doctor and the Chinese woman looked at each other in silent respect, and she saw that tears were running down the white-haired man's face. He lifted Mun Ki's hand and pointed to the lesions, and Nyuk Tsin, following the course that Dr. Whipple's finger took across the doomed hand, had to look away. "It's leprosy," the doctor said. Then he held the lamp before his maid's face and asked, "Did you know?"

"Yes," she said.

"I understand," he replied. Then, putting the lamp down he started to question her, but she asked, "Did bad men whisper you?"

"No," Whipple replied. "It occurred to me that I hadn't seen Mun Ki for some time and I recalled his itching legs. I was in bed, Mrs. Kee, and it suddenly came to me: 'Mun Ki has leprosy,' so I came out here, and I was right."

"Morning come next day he go away?"

"Yes," Dr. Whipple said matter-of-factly, but the terror of his words overtook him and he said in a shaking voice, "Mrs. Kee, let us all pray." And he kneeled in the little shack, and asked his maid to do the same, and he formed Mun Ki's doomed hands into a Christian temple, and prayed: "Compassionate and merciful God, look down upon Thy humble servants and bring courage to the hearts of these needful people. Help Mun Ki to face the next days with a fortitude of which his gods would be proud. Help Mrs. Kee to understand and accept the things that must be done." His voice broke and for some moments he could not speak; then, through tears that choked him he begged: "Compassionate God, forgive me for the terrible duty I must discharge. Forgive me, please, please forgive me."

When the prayer was said he slumped upon the floor and seemed not to have the strength to rise, but he did so and asked Nyuk Tsin, "Do you know what I must do?"

"Yes, Doctor. Tomorrow police."

"I must," he replied sorrowfully. "But you can stay here as long as you wish, and all your children," he assured her.

"I kokua," she said simply.

He had to look away from her face as the crushing force of this word struck him, for he knew what it meant: the banishment, the horrors of the leper settlement, the sons lost forever . . . He thought: "I would not have the courage." Then he recalled that it had been Mun Ki's plan to abandon Nyuk Tsin as soon as they got back to China, and to take her children from her, and now she was volunteering to go kokua with him. Slowly he raised his head and looked at Nyuk Tsin. She was a small Chinese woman with not much hair, slanted eyes, brown wrinkles about her mouth, but she was his sister, and he stepped forward and kissed her on each cheek, saying, "I should have known that you would go kokua." He turned away to staunch his tears and then asked brightly, like a minister, "Now, what can we do about the children?"

"Tonight I fix one boy here one boy here one boy here, all fix." She told him which families would take whom, and when this was explained she asked, "Tomorrow police?"

"Yes, I must. In God's mercy I must."

"I know, Doctor. Long time ago I speak my husband, 'Police go,' but we hope."

"God will forgive those who hope," the old man said.

As soon as he was gone, Mun Ki was out of bed, explosive with energy. "We will run to the hills!" he swore. "The police will never find us there."

"How will we eat?" Nyuk Tsin pleaded.

"We'll take food," Mun Ki explained excitedly. He had visions of a free life in the mountains. He and Nyuk Tsin would work for nobody and maybe even the sores would go away. "Hurry!" he cried. "We must be gone before the police come."

Nyuk Tsin looked at her husband with incredulity. How could he hope to lose himself in the hills back of Honolulu, when the police would be on his trail within six hours and when every Hawaiian who saw two Chinese struggling through the trails would know they were mai Pake? It was ridiculous, insane, as impractical as the reliance upon the quack doctor, and she was about to tell him so, but then she looked in a new way at her quixotic husband and saw him as a temporary assembly of earth and bone and confused desire and a pigtail and hands that would soon fall apart with leprosy. He was a man who could be very wise and the next minute quite stupid, as now; he was a human being who loved children and old people but who was often forgetful of those his own age. He was a mercurial gambler charged with hope: he had hoped that the quack doctor could cure him; now he hoped that somehow the forests would hide him. But above all he was her man: even though he was a Punti he had chosen her as his woman, and she loved him more than she loved her own sons. If he had this crazy desire to try his luck once more in the hills, she would go with him, for he was an obstinate man and sometimes a foolish one, but he was a man who deserved to be loved.

It was two o'clock in the morning when Nyuk Tsin finished hiding in high places anything that might hurt her children. Then she went to each child as he slept on the long polished board and fixed his clothes, so that in the morning when the boys were discovered, they would be presentable, and she straightened her bed. Then she took her husband's hand and led him out the Whipple gate and up toward the mountains back of Oahu. She did not depart unnoticed, for Dr. Whipple, unable to sleep, had kept watch on the Chinese quarters, suspecting an attempted flight, but when it eventuated, and he saw the thin little Chinese woman guiding her doomed husband toward the hills, he could not bring himself to stop them or to sound an alarm, and when she carefully returned to close his gate lest his dogs escape, he prayed: "May God have mercy upon those who hope." At first he was inclined to go down and bring the Chinese babies into the house, but he thought: "That might arouse somebody. Anyway, I'm sure Nyuk Tsin left them in good condition." So he sat by the window, guarding the house where the babies slept.

But after a while his New England conscience, undaunted by forty-eight years in the tropics, made him reason: "The children must not be left in that contaminated house another minute. Rescue now might save them from the disease, whereas an hour's delay might give it to them," so in the darkness before dawn he led his wife to the Chinese house, gently wakened the children so as not to frighten them, undressed them so that not a shred of their old garments came with them, and carried them into the Whipple home.

When this was done, Dr. Whipple studied his watch and thought: "Nyuk Tsin and her man have had two hours' lead. It will be all right to call the policemen," and he sent a servant after the officials. When they arrived he reported: "Mun Ki has leprosy. We must burn the house and everything in it," and with his own matches he ignited both the Chinese house and the cooking shed. Then, pointing to the Nuuanu Valley, he said, "I think they headed for those hills."

Throughout the morning he expected the police to appear with the two Chinese, but their capture was delayed. The afternoon also passed, and so did the evening, without the Whipple servants' being apprehended. This seemed strange to the doctor, and early next morning he inquired of the police what had happened.

"There's no trace of them," the officers explained.

"I'm sure they went up the Nuuanu," Dr. Whipple assured them.

"If they did, they vanished," the police replied.

An ugly thought came to the doctor and he asked, "Did you look at the foot of the Pali?"

"We thought of suicide," the police assured him, "and we studied the Pali rocks, but they didn't jump."

Day by day the mystery deepened. Nyuk Tsin and her dream-spinning husband had accomplished the miracle Mun Ki had relied upon: they had fled to the mountains and had somehow disappeared. Fortunately, the quack herbalist and his two spies had had the good luck to report Nyuk Tsin's suspicious behavior to the police before Dr. Whipple did: "We are sure she is hiding her husband, who is mai Pake." So they got their reward, and the herbalist often pointed out to his friends: "If I had waited till next morning, the leper would have been gone and I would have received nothing. This proves that it is always best to perform your duty promptly and let the sluggards lie abed lazily till the next convenient day."

At the end of a week the police came again to Dr. Whipple and confessed: "We've been to every grass house between here and the other seacoast. No Chinese. We've been wondering if your servants could have doubled back and gone into hiding somewhere right around here. You spoke of arrangements made by the woman to give her children away. Which families did she choose?"

A minute search of those premises also failed to reveal the fugitives, so the police said, "We are faced by a mystery. Somehow Nyuk Tsin and her husband have made themselves invisible." And so as far as active energy was concerned, the official search for the leper ended.

On the night that Nyuk Tsin led her husband through the Whipple gate, and then turned back to close it lest the dogs escape, she walked rapidly toward the mountains, and as she stepped boldly forth Mun Ki, trailing a few paces behind, could not help seeing her big, unbound feet and he thought: "On a night like this it's all right for a woman to have such feet." But reflection on this ancient problem that separated the Punti and the Hakka served to remind him of the mournful fact that he would never again see his village, and he grew disconsolate and lost his optimism and said, "It will soon be morning, and they will find us."

His wife, who originally had advised against this ridiculous attempt to escape, now became the one who urged her husband on, assuring him: "If we can get even to the lower hills before dawn, we will be safe," and she began to formulate stratagems, one of which she put into effect as dawn broke.

"We will hide beneath those thickets," she said, "close to the road where no one will look."

"All day?" her irresolute husband asked.

"Yes. There's a trickle of water running through and I have some balls of cold rice."

They approached the thicket from a roundabout way, so as not to leave footprints leading into it, and when daylight brought travelers to the road, no one saw the leper and his kokua. Nor did the police when they hurried past. Nor did the children on their way to school. All day stout-hearted Nyuk Tsin kept her man hidden, and for long periods they slept, but when Mun Ki was sleeping and his wife was awake, she was distraught by the manner in which her man shivered, for leprosy seemed to be accompanied by a slow fever that kept an infected man forever cold and stricken with trembling.

That night Nyuk Tsin wakened her husband, counted her rice balls, and started on up the mountainside. She did not know where she was going, for she was impelled by only one driving consideration: the longer they evaded the police, the longer they were free; and such a simple doctrine anyone could understand. They grew hungry, cold and weak, but she drove them both on, and in this manner they escaped capture for three days, but they approached starvation and exhaustion.

"I have no more strength to walk," the sick man protested.

"I will lend you my shoulders," Nyuk Tsin replied, and that night, with Mun Ki hanging on to his wife's back, but using his own sick legs to walk whenever he could, they made some progress toward their unknown goal, but it was cruelly evident that this was the last night Mun Ki could move, so when the morning came his wife bedded him down in a hidden ravine, washed his face with cold water running out of the hills, and set forth to find some food.

That day it rained, and while Nyuk Tsin sloshed through the mountains gathering roots and trying vainly to trap a bird, her afflicted husband shivered on the cold ground while surface water crept in below his shoulders and hips, soon making him wet and colder still. It was a dismal, hungry night, with a handful of roots to chew and not even a remnant of hope to rely upon; and it became Mun Ki's intention, when morning came, to crawl out to the highway and wait until the searching police found him.

But Nyuk Tsin had other plans, and in the hour before dawn she told her shivering husband, "Wu Chow's Father, stay here and I promise you that I shall return with food and help." She smoothed the damp earth about him and saw with dismay that it was going to rain again that day, but she told him to be of cheer, for she would soon return. Crawling carefully among the trees parallel to the highway, she looked for narrow trails leading off into the hills, and after a while she came upon one, well trod, and this she followed for several hundred yards until she came upon a clearing in which an almost-collapsed grass shack stood, with a three-hundred-pound Hawaiian woman sitting happily in front. Cautiously, but with confidence, Nyuk Tsin walked down the path to greet the huge woman, but before the Chinese maid could speak in explanation of her unexpected appearance in the clearing, the big Hawaiian woman asked, "Are you the Chinese who is mai Pake?"

"My husband, hidden in the ravine, is the one," Nyuk Tsin replied in Hawaiian.

The big woman began to rock back and forth on her unsteady chair, lamenting, "Auwe, auwe! It is so terrible the mai Pake." Then she looked at the Chinese and said, "For three days the police have been here every day, searching for you."

"Could you please let us have some food?" Nyuk Tsin begged.

"Of course!" the big woman cried. "We don't have much. Kimo!" she called unexpectedly, and from the lowly grass house a big, fat, lazy Hawaiian man appeared, with no shirt and a pair of almost disintegrating sailor's pants held up by a length of rope. He was not shaved or washed and apparently he had slept in his pants for several months, but he had a huge, amiable, grinning face.

"What is it, Apikela?" he asked, using her Biblical name Abigail.

"The mai Pake is hiding in the ravine," Apikela explained. "He hasn't eaten for four days."

"We better get him some food!" Kimo, the Biblical James, replied. And he hurried back into the grass house and soon reappeared with a ti leaf full of poi, some baked breadfruit and a few chunks of coconut. "No rice," he joked.

"I'll take it to the sick man," Nyuk Tsin replied.

"I'll go with you," Kimo volunteered.

"It isn't necessary," Nyuk Tsin protested, for she did not want to involve these kind people with the police.

"How are you going to carry him back here?" Kimo demanded.

Nyuk Tsin could scarcely believe the words she was hearing. Without looking at Kimo she asked softly, "Then I can hide him here . . . for a few days?"

"Of course!" Apikela laughed, rocking back and forth. "Those damned police!"

"It's a terrible thing to catch sick men and send them to a lonely island," Kimo agreed. "If a man's going to die, let him die with his friends. He's soon gone, and nobody is poorer." He wrapped up the food and said, "Show me where the poor fellow is."

But now Apikela rose and said, "No, Kimo, I'll go. If police are on the road it will be better if I am the one they question. Because I can claim I'm on my way to work, and if they come here it will look less suspicious if you are asleep in the house as usual."

Kimo considered this logic for a moment and agreed with his shrewd wife that things would give a better appearance if the day's routine were not broken, so he went back to bed; fat Apikela marched slowly down the path; and Nyuk Tsin kept up with her by creeping through the rain forest, and the two women had progressed only a little way when Apikela stopped, motioned to the Chinese and said, "It would seem more reasonable if I had two chains of maile about my neck. Go back and ask Kimo for them." And when the huge woman had placed the spicy maile leaves about her shoulders, the procession resumed.

Her strategy was a good one; for when she reached the highway, with Nyuk Tsin cowering behind in the forest, police came by on horses and asked, "Have you seen the mai Pake Chinese?"

"No," she replied blandly.

"What are you doing abroad so early, Apikela?"

"Gathering maile vines, as usual," she said.

They saw the vines and believed. "If you see the Chinese in your clearing, come out to the road and report them."

"I will," the gigantic woman agreed, and slowly she moved on down the road.

Now Nyuk Tsin ran ahead, and it was fortunate that she did so, for when she reached the spot where she had left her husband, she saw that Mun Ki had disappeared, and she experienced a moment of despair, but she was soon able to pick up his tracks through the muddy leaves and she guessed that he was headed toward the highway, to give himself up. In panic Nyuk Tsin followed his trail and saw him just as he was about to climb an embankment and cry to passing strangers. Leaping ahead, she dashed up behind him and caught his legs, grappling with him and dragging him back down into the forest. "I have brought you food," she gasped.

"Where?" he asked, sure that his wife's empty hands proved the hoax.

"There!" Nyuk Tsin replied, and through the trees that edged the highway she pointed to the figure of a huge woman, rolling and wheezing along in a tentlike brown dress made of Boston fabric. She wore maile chains about her neck and an unconcerned, happy smile upon her enormous brown face.

"Who's that?" Mun Ki whispered.

"Apikela," his wife replied, and darted out to haul the Hawaiian maile-gatherer into the forest. The big woman looked at the leper's sad condition and tears came into her eyes. Handing Nyuk Tsin the bundle of food, she gathered the scrawny Chinese to her capacious bosom and whispered, "We will take care of you."

For nearly a month Apikela and her slothful husband Kimo sequestered the Chinese, sharing with them their meager supplies of food. Because there were now four to feed, Apikela had to go each day into the forest to gather maile, which her husband prepared for market by skillfully slitting the bark, cutting out the pithy core, and leaving a fragrant supple vine that could be woven into leis. Periodically he lugged the maile into Honolulu, peddling it among the flower merchants. With the money thus gained he would shoot a few games of pool, buy some breadfruit, a little pork and some rice. Since Hawaiians rarely ate rice, this purchase occasioned comment, which Kimo rebuffed by observing,

"I'm switching to rice so I'll be smart, like a Pake."

Once when big, lazy Kimo ambled home with rice, Nyuk Tsin bit her lip and asked, "Why do you do this for us, Kimo?" And Apikela interrupted, saying, "When we were children going to the church we were often told of how Jesus loved the lepers, and it was a test of all good men how they treated those who were sick. And no leper ever came to Jesus without receiving aid, and no leper will come to the house of Kimo and Apikela to be turned away."

"How much longer can we hide here?" Nyuk Tsin asked.

"Until the man dies," Apikela said resolutely.

And they lived like this for another week, and then a spy in the Honolulu store put two and two together, reasoning: "Kimo never before sold such amounts of maile. And he never bought rice, either. It is Kimo who is hiding the mai Pake Chinese!" And this man hurried to the police and told them, "I am certain that Kimo and Apikela, in the clearing up toward the Pali, are hiding the mai Pake." So the spy got a good reward for his ability to think cleverly, and that afternoon the police crept in upon the clearing. When they charged out, Nyuk Tsin grabbed a frail stick and tried desperately to fight them off, and big Apikela tried to wrestle with them, and Kimo shouted, "Who was the evil man who betrayed us?" But weak and shivering Mun Ki walked out of the little near-collapsing grass shack and gave himself up. The police were so pleased with having taken the fugitives that they started immediately to hustle them away, but Nyuk Tsin cried in Hawaiian, "Let us at least thank these good people," but she was not allowed this courtesy, and as she was dragged down the path and onto the highway she looked back and saw the two enormous Hawaiians weeping as their friends were hauled into final custody.

When Dr. Whipple heard that his Chinese servants had been captured, he hurried to the leper station, where the afflicted were assembled for shipment to their outcast island, and sought out Nyuk Tsin and her husband. "I wish you had escaped," he told them in Hawaiian. "I am sorry to see you here."

"Have you taken the children to their homes?" Nyuk Tsin asked.

"Are you determined to be a kokua?" Whipple countered.

"Yes."

"You're free to leave here, if you wish. Until the boat sails." He drove her to his home and showed her the four children, fat and happy in American clothes. She started to laugh and said, "They don't look like Chinese." She gathered them up and said that she would walk with them to their new homes, but Dr. Whipple piled them into his carriage, and they started forth on their unpleasant mission. At the first house, a Punti's, she delivered a son and said, "Bring him up to be a good man." The Punti replied, "It will be difficult, but we'll try."

At the second house, a Hakka's, she said, "Teach him to speak all the languages," and the Hakka grudgingly took the child. At the third, another Punti's, she begged: "Bring him up to honor his father." And at the last house, another Hakka's, she warned again: "Teach him to speak all the languages." Then she asked the doctor to drive her to the Hewlett home, and there she found the cook and his wife and spoke of the child that was not yet born, and she said to these Punti, "You are to keep this child as your own. Give it your name. Teach it to revere you as its just parents."

"When will the child get here?" the people asked.

"As soon as a ship leaves from the leper island," Nyuk Tsin replied, and the intended parents shivered with apprehension.

On the way back to the quarantine station, Dr. Whipple drove a short distance up Nuuanu Valley to the land which he had given Nyuk Tsin. Placing stones at the corners of a seven-acre field, he assured her, "Mrs. Kee, I have entered this plot at the land court and paid taxes on it. When your husband dies, because he can't live much longer, you come back here and start a little garden and get your children back with you."

From the carriage Nyuk Tsi looked at the wet land, and it seemed impossibly beautiful to her. "I will remember this land," she said in Hawaiian.

But when Dr. Whipple started to turn the horses around, he saw coming toward him two huge Hawaiians, and when they detected Nyuk Tsin in the carriage, they cried, "Pake, Pake! We have come for the children!"

They ran as fast as their enormous bulk permitted and caught hold of their friend's hands. "Surely you will let us keep the children for you," they pleaded.

"You have such a small house," Nyuk Tsin protested.

"It's big enough for children!" Apikela cried expansively, opening her arms like swinging gates. "Please, Pake wahine! You'll let us have the children?"

Nyuk Tsin spent some time considering this strange request, and she wished that Mun Ki were present to help her, but she was sure he would approve her conclusion: "The Punti and the Hakka families might grow weary of our children, even though we are all from the *Carthaginian.* But Apikela and Kimo will love them forever." So Nyuk Tsin spoke for her family: "We will give the children to you." And she asked Dr. Whipple to drive back to the houses where the children were and she explained to the Chinese: "It will be better this way because Apikela and Kimo will be able to keep all the children together. But I hope, for my husband's sake, that you will give them some money from time to time."

"Money? For keeping children?" fat Apikela asked in astonishment, and Nyuk Tsin thought how strange it was that Chinese families with good jobs always found it difficult to accept one strange child, but Hawaiians who had nothing could invariably find space for one child, or three, or five. She last saw her boys heading back up the Pali, one baby in Apikela's arms, one in Kimo's and the two older boys trudging happily behind.

When the time came for the panel of doctors to certify that Mun Ki was indeed a leper, and therefore subject to banishment for life without right of appeal, they reported: "Aggravated case of leprosy. Lesions both external and internal. Banishment to Kalawao imperative." The papers were signed. The three doctors left, and Whipple said to the condemned man, "Mun Ki, wherever a human being goes, there is a challenge. Be the best man you can, and your gods will look with favor upon you. And may my God in His heaven protect you. Good-bye." Bowed with the grief that comes upon all men who watch the swinging changes of life, Dr. John Whipple went home.

Two days later forty condemned lepers were assembled and marched through the streets of Honolulu toward the pier where the leper ship, *Kilauea,* waited. As the ghostly men and women walked, the citizens of the city drew back in horror, for some hobbled along on feet that had no toes and others stared vacantly ahead from horrible faces that had no cheeks and whose lips and noses had fallen away. In silence the doomed lepers approached the *Kilauea,* a small, snout-nosed little craft of four hundred tons with a grimy smokestack and filthy decks. Forward, some cattle had been tethered for the short, rough haul to the leper colony, and as the ship rocked slowly these beasts lowed mournfully. When the lepers appeared, a gangplank was lowered and nauseated policemen herded the doomed men and women aboard; but when the final moment came when the lepers were to be cut off forever from their families, a monstrous wailing began.

"Auwe, auwe!" howled women whose husbands were being dragged away.

"Farewell, my son!" an old man shouted, his face bathed in tears.

"We shall meet in heaven, by the cool waters!" wept a sister whose brother was being shoved onto the ugly ship, this unimpressive ferry to hell.

"Auwe, auwe!" mourned the multitude of watchers as they watched the stricken ones slowly climb the gangplank, overcome by terror and shaking.

In a sense, the lamentation of those on shore was traditional and formalized; but the sounds that now emitted from the decks of the *Kilauea* were not, for the hopeless lepers lined the railings of the ship and cried back their piteous farewells. Condemned women waved with hands that bore no fingers. Men cried good-bye from faces that had no recognizable features. Some of the lepers were too far progressed in the disease to be able to stand by themselves, and they wailed without purpose, adding their cries to the general lament.

But occasionally, among the forty victims, one would appear whose countenance or character aroused in all an instinctive outburst of sorrow. The first such harrowing case was that of a bright little girl about ten years old who had left the pier with not a member of her family present to bid her farewell. On her face beginning sores were visible as she hurried up the gangplank, and it was obvious to all that she would soon be completely ravaged by the disease, but in wonder and confusion she stepped onto the gently swaying deck of the *Kilauea,* not able to comprehend the awful step she was taking. Out of compassion an older woman, also condemned to exile, leaned down to comfort the girl, but when the child saw the awful chinless face coming toward her, she screamed, not realizing that soon she would look the same.

The next case was that of a man well known for his swimming prowess, a big, handsome fellow with broad chest and strong arms. Many came to see him leave for the island from which no leper had ever returned, and as he stood at the head of the gangplank, turning back to wave his hands at his friends, showing them fingers with the first joints already eaten away, the misery of his condition infected everyone and cries of "Auwe, auwe!" sounded. This communion of sorrow affected him, and he hid his face, whereupon the weeping increased.

But the third case was entirely different, so dreadful that it occasioned no public display of sorrow. It was that of a very lovely young wife, with flowers in her hair, on whose body no one could identify the fatal marks. Her feet were clean and her fingers, too. There was no infection on her face, but her eyes were glassy, so the well-informed crowd knew that here was one in whom the sickness lay accumulating its strength inside, ready to erupt generally in one massive sore. The death of this girl would be horrible, a total disintegration, and those who watched her walking slowly and with grace up the gangplank kept their sorrow to themselves.

But she was not to depart in peace, for her husband broke from the crowd of watchers and tried to dash up the gangplank after her, shouting, "Kinau, Kinau, I will be your kokua." Guards restrained him, and his wife Kinau, named after one of Hawaii's most able queens, looked back down the gangplank and with visible compassion cried, "You may not join me, Kealaikahiki." And with considerable dignity she stepped onto the *Kilauea* and ordered the guards to drag her husband away. Impassively, she watched him go, and if she heard his frantic cries, she did not indicate the fact, and he disappeared from the dock altogether, crying, "Kinau, Kinau! I shall be your kokua."

When the doomed Hawaiians were all aboard, the police produced the Chinese Kee Mun Ki, and since the disease from which he suffered was known as the mai Pake, the crowd somehow understood that he personally was the cause of this day's tragedy, and they mumbled strongly against him. Alone, looking neither right nor left, he passed through the hostile groups until at last he stood at the gangplank, and then two huge Hawaiians hurried forward to bid him good-bye. They were Kimo and his wife Apikela, and without fear they embraced the leper, kissed him on the cheeks, and bade him farewell. With some relief, the thin, shivering Chinese man walked up the gangplank. He had hoped, on this last journey, that Dr. Whipple would be present to bid him good-bye, but the doctor could no longer suffer the sight of people whom he had helped condemn taking their last farewells. Among the group sailing that day were more than twenty upon whose investigating boards he had sat, and he could not bear to see them go, partly at his command. On days when the *Kilauea* sailed, he stayed home and prayed.

When Mun Ki was safely aboard, the captain shouted, "Open the cage!" And two sailors went aft to a wicker cage that had been built on the deck of the leper ship, and they swung back on its hinges a latticed gate, and when it was open, other sailors, careful not to touch the lepers, growled, "All right! All right! Get in!"

The cage was not large, nor was the door high, and one by one the condemned people stooped, crawled in, and found their places. The wicker gate was lashed shut, whereupon the captain called down reassuringly, "There will be a man stationed by you at all times. If we start to sink, he'll cut open the gate."

While this encagement of the lepers was under way, two other sailors had appeared with buckets of soapy water and now proceeded to wash down the handrails of the gangplank, after which normal passengers were allowed to board, and when they had hurried below to escape the smell of the forty caged lepers the captain shouted, "All right! Kokuas board!"

From the wailing crowd some dozen Hawaiians, men and women alike, stepped forward and in a kind of spiritual daze groped for the clean handrails of the gangplank. They were the kokuas, that strange band of people who in Hawaii in the later years of the nineteenth century proved that the word love had a tangible reality, and as each Kokua reached the deck of the *Kilauea* a police marshal asked carefully, "Are you sure you know what you are doing in volunteering for the lazaretto?" And one man replied, "I would rather go with my wife to the lazaretto than stay here free without her."

No one, looking at the kokuas, could have predicted that these particular people would have been so moved by love. True, there were some old women whose lives were nearly spent and it was understandable that they should join the leprous men with whom they had lived so long; and there were older men who had married young women who had fallen prey to the disease, and it was also understandable that these men might prefer to remain with their girls; but there were also men and women of the most indiscriminate sort who climbed the gangplank to embrace other women and men of no apparent attraction whatever, so that the people on the dock had to ask themselves: "Why would a man in good health volunteer for the lazaretto in order to be with such a woman?" And to this question there was no answer except the word love.

No kokua came to stand beside the little ten-year-old girl, and none came to be with the beautiful Kinau. But there was general surprise when the police dropped their arms and allowed the Chinese woman, Nyuk Tsin, to join her husband, and as she reached the gangplank, once more the two huge Hawaiians, Kimo and Apikela, stepped forward to embrace her, and Apikela placed about the sloping shoulders of her yellow-skinned friend a chain of maile, saying, "We will love your children."

The gangplank was hauled aboard. The cattle tethered forward began lowing pitifully. The crowd ashore started shouting, "Auwe, auwe!" and the *Kilauea* stood out to sea with its horrible burden. When Dr. Whipple, inland in his study, heard the whistle blow farewell, he prayed, "Oh, may God have mercy upon them." For he alone, of all who heard the whistle blowing, understood what lay ahead for Nyuk Tsin and Mun Ki. He had seen the lazaretto.

T HE ISLAND OF Molokai, to which the caged lepers were heading, was one of the most strangely beautiful islands in the Hawaiian group. It lay in the blue Pacific like a huge left-handed gantlet, the open wristlet facing westward toward the island of Oahu, the cupped fingers pointing eastward toward Maui. The southern portion of Molokai consisted of rolling meadowland, often with gray and parched grasses, for rainfall was slight, while the northern portion was indented by some of the most spectacular cliffs in the islands. For mile after mile these towering structures rose from the crashing surf, sometimes reaching more than three thousand feet into the air, their faces sheer rock, their flanks marked by dozens upon dozens of shimmering waterfalls. These cliffs formed, at their bases, delectable valleys that probed inland half a mile to end in soaring walls of granite, but narrow and restricted though they were, these valleys were perhaps the finest in Hawaii. Upon the cliffs white goats ranged, so that a boat coasting the north shore of Molokai passed constantly beneath magnificent cliffs, trembling waterfalls and the antics of a thousand goats. Sailors, when the days were idle, would discharge guns aimlessly at the cliffs to make the goats scamper up walls of rock that no man could have negotiated. Thus, the uninhabitable north coast of Molokai was completely cut off from the gentle meadows of the south coast, where some two thousand normal islanders lived.

Jutting out from the isolated yet magnificent northern coast stood the thumb of the gauntlet, a small, verdant peninsula that had been formed millions of years later than the main island, for when the initial volcanoes that accounted for Molokai had long since died away, an afterthought-eruption occurred offshore. It did not rise from a major volcano, nor did it build a major island; it was content merely to add a peninsula of lovely proportions, from whose grassy shores one could look west and east toward the towering cliffs. It was a majestic spot, a poem of nature, and from the earliest memories of Hawaiian history, fortunate fishermen had lived here, building themselves a good community and calling it Kalawao.

Then in 1865, the year in which the Kees left China, the Hawaiian government tardily faced up to the fact that in the strange new disease called mai Pake it faced an epidemic of the most virulent sort. It was ironic that leprosy should have been named the Chinese sickness, for the scourge neither came from China nor did it especially affect the Chinese, but some kind of quarantine was necessary, and the heavenly peninsula of Kalawao was nominated to be the lazaretto. It was generally known that leprosy was contagious but no one knew of a cure; so in frenzied eagerness to take some kind of action, the government's medical advisers said: "At least we can isolate the afflicted." In desperation the lepers were hunted down; the Hawaiians living at Kalawao were exiled forever from their peninsula; and the *Kilauea* started its dismal voyages to the lazaretto. In the previous history of the world no such hellish spot had ever stood in such heavenly surroundings.

On the first day of November, 1870, the ferry *Kilauea* stood off the eastern edge of the peninsula, dropped anchor some hundred yards from the cliff-lined shore and rolled with the surf beneath the leaping goats. The captain ordered one section of the deck railing removed, and sailors began shoving into the sea huge casks of salt beef, cured salmon and dehydrated poi. When the cargo was thus thrown into the waves, lepers from Kalawao swam out to the ship and started guiding the stores to shore, for the colony had no pier at which supplies could be landed in an orderly way.

Now from the front of the ship cattle were led aft, and amidst great bellowing were shoved into the ocean where swimming lepers leaped upon their backs and guided them to shore. Occasionally a frightened cow would toss her rider and head for the open sea, but stout swimmers would overtake her and force her toward the land. A sailor, tiring of the sport provided by the swimmers, discharged his musket aimlessly at the cliffs, and from their cage the lepers saw wild goats leap up the cliffs like the flight of song, flying from crag to crag, and these white animals became the symbol of a freedom forever lost to them.

A longboat was lowered, with three sailors at the oars, and the police marshal who had accompanied the lepers, ordered the cage opened, and called off names, and saw each afflicted man and woman into the boat. There the government's responsibility ended, for the policeman did not enter the boat himself. He watched it move toward the shore, dump its human cargo on the beach, and return. Then he checked off another complement, and in this way the forty lepers were thrown ashore with no stores of clothing, no money, no food and no medicine.

When the condemned were all ashore, the marshal announced formally to the kokuas: "You are now free to accompany your husbands and wives, but you do so of your own free will. The government has no concern in what you are about to do. Is it your wish to go ashore and live with the lepers?"

The kokuas, staring with horrified fascination at the lazaretto, could barely scrape their tongues with words. "I am willing," an old man rasped, and he climbed down into the boat. "I am willing," a young wife reported, and with trepidation she went down. Finally the marshal asked Nyuk Tsin, "Do you do this thing of your own free will?" and she replied, "I am willing." The longboat set out for shore, and Nyuk Tsin approached the leper settlement at Kalawao.

She was surprised to see, as the green peninsula drew near, that it contained practically no houses, and she asked one of the rowers, in Hawaiian, "Where are the houses?" And he replied, unable to look her in the eyes, "There are no houses."

And there were none . . . to speak of. There were a few grass huts, a few remnants of homes left by the Hawaiians who had been expelled five years before, but there were no houses as such, nor any hospital, nor store, nor government building, nor functioning church, nor roads, nor doctors, nor nurses. In panic Nyuk Tsin stared at the inviting natural setting and looked for signs of community life. There were no police, no officials of any kind, no ministers, no mothers with families, no one selling cloth, no one making poi.

The prow of the longboat struck shore, but no one moved. The sailors waited and then one said, as if ashamed to be part of this dismal scene, "This is Kalawao." Appalled by what faced them, the kokuas rose and left the boat. "Aloha," the sailor cried as the boat withdrew for the last time. The *Kilauea* put back out to sea, and Nyuk Tsin, trying to find Mun Ki among the stranded lepers, cried to no one: "Where is the hospital?"

Her plea was heard by a big, tall Hawaiian man known to the lepers as Kaulo Nui, Big Saul of the Bible. He had no nose and few fingers, but he was still a powerful man, and he came to Nyuk Tsin and shouted in Hawaiian, "Here there is no law. There is nothing but what I command."

The newcomers were as frightened by this state of affairs as was Nyuk Tsin, but Big Saul ignored them, and pointing his mutilated hand at the Chinese couple, said, "You brought the mai Pake! You will live apart."

"Where?" Nyuk Tsin asked boldly.

"Apart," the big man said. Then his eye fell on the young wife Kinau, who still had flowers in her hair, and he moved toward her, announcing: "This woman is for me."

Kinau drew back in horror from the huge, noseless man whose hands were so badly deformed. She shuddered, and Big Saul saw this, so to teach her the required lesson, he grabbed her by the left arm, pulled her to him, and kissed her on the mouth. "You're my woman!" he announced again.

Nyuk Tsin expected to see someone—who, she could not guess—step forward to knock the big man down, but when none did, the awful fact of Kalawao slowly dawned upon her, as it did upon all the others. Big Saul, holding onto the shuddering Kinau, glared at the newcomers and repeated the news: "Here there is no law."

Nor was there any. In all of Kalawao there was no voice of government, no voice of God, no healing medicine. In the houseless peninsula there was not even a secure supply of water, and food was available only when the *Kilauea* remembered to kick into the sea enough casks and cattle. In truth, the lepers had been thrown ashore with nothing except the sentence of certain death, and what they did until they died, no man cared.

If any of the newcomers thought differently, they were disabused by what happened next, for Kinau was an uncommonly pretty girl, and the fact that she had no open lesions made her extraordinary in the doomed community, so that Big Saul and his rowdier companions became excited by her beauty and could not wait till nightfall, when such things usually occurred, and three of them dragged her behind a wall that still stood, a remnant of a house where a family of fishermen had once lived, and the two who joined Big Saul were among the most loathsome of the group, for their bodies were falling away, but they thought: "We have been thrown away by Hawaii. No one cares and we shall soon be dead." So they dragged Kinau behind the wall and started, with their fragmentary hands, to tear away her clothes.

"Please! Please!" she begged, but nothing could be done to interrupt the three hungry men, and when she was naked they admired her, and pinched her body and explored it and laughed, and then in turn two held her down while the other mounted her, and in time she fainted.

For five days Big Saul and his cronies kept her to themselves, after which any others who thought themselves strong enough to force their way into the group were free to join, and when they saw the naked Kinau, as yet unblemished, they were hungry with old memories of the days when they were whole men, and they cared nothing about what they did.

Occasionally Big Saul left the girl, to make decisions as to how the lepers should dispose themselves, and he was adamant that the Chinese must stay apart, so Nyuk Tsin and her husband were forced to live at the outer edge of the community of six hundred dying men and women. For the first six days they slept on bare earth; and they found an abandoned wall against which they built a rough lean-to, using shrubs and leaves, for there was no lumber of any kind. For their bed they had only raw earth, and when rain came it crept under them so that Mun Ki, already shivering with ague, came close to dying of pneumonia. Then Nyuk Tsin, using her bare hands, for there were no implements, scraped together a platform of earth and covered it with twigs and leaves, and this made a bed into which the water could not creep unless the rainfall was unusually heavy.

The two outlawed Chinese were forbidden access to the food barrels until all others had partaken, and even then Big Saul decreed that they live on half-rations, and if it had not been for Nyuk Tsin's resourcefulness they would have starved. On the reef she found small edible snails, and in one of the deserted valleys she discovered dry-land taro that had gone wild. With twigs she collected from the cliffs she built a small underground oven in which she baked the taro, so that life apart from the others had minor compensations. Certainly, the Kees lived better than the pathetic lepers who could no longer walk.

In Kalawao in 1870 there were over sixty such unspeakable persons: their feet had fallen away, their hands were stumps, and they crawled about the settlement begging food which they themselves could neither obtain nor prepare. Horrifying echoes of humanity, they often had no faces whatever, excepting eyes and voices with which to haunt the memories of those who came upon them. There was no medicine for them, no bed, no care of any kind. They crawled along the beach of Kalawao and in God's due time they died. Usually they did not even find a grave, but were left aside until their bones were cleaned and could be laid in a shallow ditch.

Sometimes the authorities in Honolulu forgot to send the *Kilauea* with replenishments of food, and then the settlement degenerated into absolute terror. Big Saul and his cronies commandeered whatever supplies remained, and protected their rights with violence. The death rate soared, four or five cases each day, and a legless woman might lie in the path all day screaming for food or water, and no one would listen to her, hoping that in the cold night she would die. And usually she did, and her tormented body might lie there, just as she had left it, for a day or even three, until Big Saul commanded someone to remove it.

There was no law in Kalawao and there was almost no humanity. What made the situation doubly terrible was that regularly the ugly little ferryboat *Kilauea* appeared offshore with an additional cargo of lepers, and when they were thrown ashore with nothing, Big Saul would move among them telling them the ultimate, terrifying truth: "Here there is no law."

After six weeks of keeping the beautiful young wife Kinau a prisoner, during which time more than eighteen men enjoyed her unmarked body, she was turned loose for whoever wanted her. She was allowed one flimsy dress, but the way in which she wore it proved that she had by God's grace lost her mind. She could remember nothing of what had happened to her, and she walked in a daze, unable to focus on the present, so that for a space of three or four months whatever man wanted her simply grabbed her and took her to where he slept on the cold earth and played with her for as long as he wished. Then he shoved her along, and she moved like a ghost, her dress askew and no flowers in her matted hair, until some other man wanted her, and then she was his. The women of Kalawao felt sorry for her, but each had her own problem, so that no one tended the poor crazy girl.

In the fourth month, in February of 1871, that is, the virulent leprosy that abided in Kinau broke loose, and within the space of a few weeks she became a horribly riddled thing, a walking corpse with a thick, bloated face, shivering lips about to fall away and sickening illness in her breasts. Now men left her alone, but in her dementia she took off her flimsy dress and exposed the sores of her body. She walked slowly from Big Saul to his first lieutenant and then on to his second, whimpering, "Now I should like to lie with you again." She became such a sore on the community that men could not stand seeing her approach, her body falling apart, and finally Big Saul said, "Somebody ought to knock that one on the head." So on a dark night, somebody did, and she lay dead in the path for two days before she was finally dragged away for burial."

Of course, no woman was safe on Kalawao, for Big Saul and his men were free to take whom they liked, and those who arrived on the beach with no men to protect them suffered grievously, for they were usually women not far advanced in the disease, and to be raped repeatedly by men with no faces or with hands eroded to stumps was unbearable, but there was no escape, and Kalawao was filled with women who fell into a kind of stupor, crying to themselves, "Why has God punished me?"

It must not be assumed that women were blameless for the degeneration that overtook Kalawao, for there were many presentable women who felt: "I have been abandoned by society. There is no law here and no one cares what I do." Such women helped the men brew a raw and savage liquor from roots of the ti plant, or muddy beer from stewed sweet potatoes, and for weeks at a time, whole sections of the leper population stayed madly drunk, coursing loudly through the settlement, brawling, screaming indecencies at the general population and winding up in some public place naked and lustful, there to indulge themselves with one another to the applause of cheering witnesses. Those who inflamed these orgies and who seemed to enjoy them most were women, and it was not uncommon in those days, when no priests or ministers or government officials were present to protect order, to see a half-naked woman, at the end of a nine-day drunk, stagger into a public place and cry, "I can have intercourse with any four men here, and when I'm through with them, they'll be half dead." And volunteers would leap at the offer, and there would be a wild, insane testing to see if she could make good her challenge, and when she was finished, she would fall asleep in a drunken, exhausted stupor, right on the ground where she lay, and the night rains would come and no one would cover her, and after a few years she would die, not of leprosy, but of tuberculosis.

If anyone in those years had wished to see humanity at its positive lowest, humanity wallowing in filth of its own creation, he would have had to visit Kalawao, for not only was the peninsula cursed by leprosy; it was also scarred by human stupidity. The peninsula had two sides, an eastern where cold winds blew and rains fell incessantly, and a western where the climate was both warm and congenial; but the leper colony had been started on the inclement eastern shore, and there the government insisted that it be kept while the kindly western shore remained unpopulated. The eastern location, being close to the towering cliffs, received its first sunlight late in the day and lost it early in the afternoon; but on the western slope there was adequate sun. Most ridiculous of all, even though the cliffs threw down a hundred waterfalls, none had been channeled into the leper settlement. At first a little had been brought down by an inadequate, tied-together pipe, but it had long since broken, so that all water had to be lugged by hand several miles, and often dying people with no kokuas to help them would spend their last four or five days pleading helplessly for a drink which they were never given. For six indifferent years no official in Honolulu found time to concern himself with such problems or allocate even miserly sums to their solution. In ancient times it had been said, "Out of sight, out of mind," and rarely in human history had this calloused apothegm been more concisely illustrated than at the Kalawao lazaretto. The government had decreed: "The lepers shall be banished," as if saying the words and imprisoning the leprous bodies somehow solved the problem.

IT WOULD NOT be fair, however, to say that during these appalling first years no one cared. Brave Christian ministers from other islands sometimes visited Kalawao to solemnize marriages of dying people who did not wish to live their last days in sin. Catholic priests and Mormon disciples occasionally made the rough crossing to the lazaretto, and their arrivals were remembered long after they had left. Dr. Whipple had come, at the age of seventy, to see what the settlement needed, and he reported: "Everything." At one point a group of religious lepers had actually started a church, and leafing through their treasured Bible had come upon that glowing passage of hope in which the Apostle John reported: "And as Jesus passed by, he saw a man which was blind from his birth. And his disciples asked him, saying, Master, who did sin, this man, or his parents, that he was born blind? Jesus answered, Neither hath this man sinned, nor his parents: . . . He spat on the ground, and made clay of the spittle, and he anointed the eyes of the blind man with the clay, And said unto him, Go, wash in the pool of Siloam. . . . He . . . washed, and came seeing." The lepers called their church—it had no building, for Honolulu could spare no lumber— Siloama, and it kept their hope alive, for every leper was convinced that somewhere in the world there must be a pool of Siloam, or a medicine, or an unguent that would cure him.

Because Nyuk Tsin was pregnant, she escaped the attentions of Big Saul and his ruthless gang, but as her birth time approached she forgot him and suffered apprehensions of a different nature. For one thing, the lack of water troubled her, and she wondered what her husband would do when the baby came, for he had only one small receptacle for water and no fire at which to heat it. Mun Ki promised: "I'll ask some of the Hawaiian women to help, and they'll have buckets." But Big Saul would permit no one to go near the Chinese shed, and on the final day Nyuk Tsi gave birth to her fifth son under conditions that would not have been permitted had she been an animal; no water, no clean clothes waiting for the child, no food to speed the mother's milk, no bed for the infant except the cold ground; there was not even clean straw upon which the mother could lie. Nevertheless, she produced a ruddy-faced, slant-eyed little fellow; and then her great worries began.

No one knew at that time how the contagion of leprosy operated, for it was a fact that many kokuas like Nyuk Tsin lived in the lazaretto for years in the most intimate contact with lepers without ever acquiring the mai Pake, so mere contact could not be the explanation; but she had learned that if children below the age of eight stayed very long in contact with leprosy, they were sure to catch it; so she nursed her infant as best she could and prayed for the arrival of the next *Kilauea*. While she waited, she did many things to make her son prematurely strong. She exposed him daily to the winds so that he would know them; she fed him constantly to build health; she slapped him vigorously to make him resist shock; but at night she cuddled him warmly between her shallow breasts, and she loved him desperately.

When the *Kilauea* finally arrived, she was filled with excitement and a determination to act carefully. Therefore, as soon as the first longboat arrived with its cargo of lepers she went down to the landing and called to one of the rowers, "My baby is to go back on your ship," and she made as if to enter the longboat with the child, but the sailors of the *Kilauea* were perilously afraid that some day the Kalawao lepers might try to capture their ship and escape, and Nyuk Tsin's motion seemed as if it could be the beginning of such an attempt, so the sailor swiftly knocked her down with an oar and shouted to his mates, "Push off! Push off!" But when they were safely at sea, Nyuk Tsin, protecting her son, struggled back to her feet and called again, "It is my baby who is to go back on your ship."

"We'll ask the captain," shouted back one of the sailors, and on the next trip in he yelled, "Where's the Pake with the baby?" and Nyuk Tsin almost stumbled she ran so fast to give her reply, but she was near tears when the sailor shoved the baby back and said, "Captain wants to know where the baby goes." Nyuk Tsin eagerly explained: "He goes to Dr. Whipple, in the big house."

"Doc Whipple died last month," the sailor growled, and prepared to shove off.

Nyuk Tsin was staggered by this news and sought frantically for an alternative. "Give the baby to Kimo and Apikela, the maile gatherers," she cried eagerly.

"Where in hell's that?" the sailor asked, and they rowed back to the ship. On the next trip they advised the agonized Chinese woman that they thought they'd better not take the child, because they had no idea what to do with it when they got to Honolulu, and since there was no wet nurse aboard on this trip, the baby would have no food for a full day. Nyuk Tsin tried to explain that the captain could give the child to any Chinese, and as for food, she had made little bags filled with poi which he could suck. But the longboat pulled away, and in complete panic Nyuk Tsin saw the *Kilauea* prepare to steam off, so without knowing what she was attempting she walked out into the surf, with her child in her arms, and she started vainly to attempt swimming to the departing ship, but as soon as she was in the water the fine Hawaiian swimmer who had shared the leper cage with Mun Ki saw her plight, and leaped in beside her, grasped the infant in his left arm and started swimming strongly toward the ship. The captain saw him coming and halted the engine for a moment until the powerful brown man caught hold of a rope and with a heave pulled himself up and threw the child into the arms of a waiting sailor. Then, with the same movement, he dropped back into the sea and started a long, easy stroke which carried him back to the leper settlement. The *Kilauea* sounded its whistle. The white goats sprang higher up the cliff sides. And Nyuk Tsin stood with her husband Mun Ki as their son Australia vanished; but all who stood with them watching the ship go, knew that no matter where the child was taken, or to whom, it was better off than it would have been on Kalawao.

IN THE SEVENTH month of their stay on Kalawao, the depredations of Big Saul and his cronies finally threatened the Chinese, because Nyuk Tsin was recovered from her pregnancy. Therefore, the men began to study her, saying among themselves, "A man could have a good time with her, and she's not diseased at all."

Accordingly, three of them swooped down one night on the grassy shack and grabbed for Nyuk Tsin. But she and her husband had long ago prepared themselves for this event, and the invaders were met by two fighting Chinese armed with sharply pointed sticks. It was a bitter, silent fight, with doomed Mun

Ki rising from his bed of leaves to battle desperately with Big Saul, while Nyuk Tsin, with pointed sticks in her hands, slashed and jabbed at the other two.

Once she was caught around the waist by arms that had only fragmentary hands, and she could smell the foul breath of a leper dragging her to him, but she jabbed backward with her sticks, and he screamed with pain and released her. Now there were two Chinese against two invaders, and like a jungle animal she instinctively ignored her own assailant and sprang for the jugular of Big Saul, the leader, and with great force she jabbed her remaining stick at the side of his head and it must have struck either his ear and gone in there or the soft part of his temple, for it pressed inward . . . long and sharp and pleasingly. At the same time Mun Ki ripped upward with his sharp stick, and Big Saul gasped.

Clutching his two vital wounds, he staggered away into the night and began shouting. "The Pakes have killed me!" This diverted his unwounded helper, who ran to assist his chief while the third man stumbled in the darkness with three inches of stick protruding from his left eye.

"The Pakes have killed me!" Big Saul bellowed, and he awakened all the community, so that by the time he actually did stagger mortally wounded into a circle of torches, all who could walk were present to witness his gasping, clutching death. Silently they withdrew from the ugly corpse. There were few who had not suffered at the hands of Big Saul, and now that they saw his leprosy-riddled body in the dust, they were content to leave him. His blinded crony slipped away into the night, and silence fell upon the lepers of Kalawao.

For the two Chinese it was a dreadful night. They could not know that the community at large approved the death of Big Saul and the blinding of his bully companion. They could not know, huddling alone together in the dark night, that no one in Kalawao was ignorant of how the huge man had met his death. "He went to rape the Pake girl, and her husband killed him. Good for the Pake."

Toward morning it began to rain, and the mournful drops, falling upon the leafy roof and creeping across the floor, first in tiny traces and finally in a small river, added to the misery, and Nyuk Tsin whispered to her shivering companion, "We did the right thing, Wu Chow's Father. The others should have done this years ago."

"Have we any sticks left?" Mun Ki asked.

"I lost both of mine," his wife confessed.

"I have one left, and there's another hidden under the leaves. I think that when they come to seize us in the morning, we should fight until we are dead."

"I think so, too," Nyuk Tsin replied, and she went to the corner of the miserable hut and from the muddy earth picked up the other weapon. In the lonely silence not knowing when Big Saul's men would re-attack, they waited, and Nyuk Tsin said, "I am glad, Wu Chow's Father, that I came with you. I am humbly honored that tonight you fought to help me."

"I have forgotten that you are a Hakka," he replied.

The rain increased, and for a moment the couple thought they heard the noise of lepers assembling to attack them, but it was only the rustle of water ꞏdown the sides of the cliff, so Nyuk Tsin asked: "Do you forgive me for my ungainly feet?" And her husband replied, "I don't see them any more."

They huddled together in the cold, dark night and Mun Ki said, "You must promise, Wu Chow's Auntie, that if you ever escape from here, you will be sure to send my real wife in China as much money as possible."

"I promise," Nyuk Tsin replied.

"And you must enter my boys' names in the village hall."

"I will do so."

"And when you send the news to the hall, you don't have to mention that you are a Hakka. It would embarrass my wife."

"I will not say anything to the letter-writer," Nyuk Tsin promised.

"And you must promise to bury me on the side of a hill."

"I shall, just as if we were in China."

"And you must promise to bring my sons to honor my grave."

"I shall do so," Nyuk Tsin agreed, and Mun Ki said, "When dawn comes we will die, Wu Chow's Auntie, and the promises you have made mean nothing, but I feel better." Through the long, rainy night they waited and when the gray, cold dawn arrived, Mun Ki the gambler said, "Let's wait for them no longer. Let's march out to meet them." And the two Chinese left the foul grass lean-to, each with a jagged, sharp piece of wood in his right hand.

It was with horror that they saw, slumped in the rain-filled path, the dead body of Big Saul, for they knew that this doomed them to retaliation from the others of the gang, but as they cautiously approached the village, their sticks ready for the final fight, they saw with amazement that the Hawaiian lepers did not draw back in enmity, but moved forward in conciliation, and slowly the deadly sticks were lowered and at last the two Chinese stood surrounded by dying men and women who said, "You did a good thing." And one woman who had been sadly abused by Big Saul and his gang, but who had stubbornly refused to go insane, said quietly, "We are determined that Kalawao shall be a place of law."

The resurrection of this dreadful lazaretto, where for six years condemned human beings had been thrown upon the beach to die without a single incident of assistance from the society that had rejected them, dated from that morning when the determined woman whose spirit had not been broken by leprosy, or rape, or indignities such as few have known said solemnly, "Kalawao shall be a place of law."

A rude organization was evolved, consisting of people responsible for parceling out the food, a team to bring water into the village, and informal policemen who were to stop the aimless rape of unprotected women. Girls who arrived on the beach unattached were ordered to pick a man quickly, and to stay with him; and when a young wife argued: "But I am married, and I love my husband," older women told her sternly, "You have left the world. You are in a waiting station for hell. Pick a man. We warn you." So some women passed in turn from one dying man to another, but in an orderly fashion and not according to the rule of rape.

Children, banished without their parents, were given to kokuas who took them as their own, and fed them. And one law was paramount: when an old man or an old woman was clearly about to die, he must no longer be left in the open fields; he must have some kind of shelter.

Even when the settlement thus disciplined itself, the government in Honolulu gave little help. Lepers were still thrown upon the beaches to die, and there was no medicine, no lumber, no consolation. But in mid-1871 a Hawaiian who had read many books arrived in the lazaretto, and he launched a more formal government, one of whose first decisions was that the two Chinese must no longer be banished to the foot of the cliff but must be allowed to live among the others. This decision was applauded among the lepers, since it was generally agreed that the coming of limited humanity to Kalawao dated from the night when Mun Ki decided to protect his wife from the rapists, or die. A rude hospital was started, with no doctors but with leper nurses; and women who could read opened a school for children born in the lazaretto. A committee begged the government to send regular supplies of food—five pounds of fresh meat a week for each inmate plus twenty pounds of vegetables or poi—and sometimes it arrived. Gardens were started and a water supply, and the women insisted: "Kalawao shall be a place of law."

There were, of course, still no organized houses in the leper settlement, and over half the afflicted people slept year after year under bushes, with no bedding and only one change of clothing. These naturally died sooner than even the ravages of leprosy would have dictated, and perhaps this was a blessing, but even the most horrible crawling corpses somehow longed for homes of their own, a shack with a grass roof where they could preserve the illusion that they were still human beings.

Therefore, in June, 1871, Nyuk Tsin, after five weeks of living inside the community, but on the bare ground, decided: "Wu Chow's Father, we are going to build ourselves a house!" Her shattered husband had already begun to lose his toes and fingers and could not be of much help, but she made believe that it was he who was doing the work, and to keep his interest focused on the future, she discussed each step of the building with him. Daily she trudged to a ruined Hawaiian house built a century before and hauled back heavy stones, standing with them in her arms while he decided exactly where they should be placed. In time a wall was built, and the two shivering Chinese had at least some protection from the winds that howled across Kalawao in the stormy season.

Next she sought the ridgepole and the few crossbeams that were essential for the roof, but this was a difficult task, for the government in Honolulu had consistently forgotten to ship the lepers expensive lumber, which had to be imported all the way from Oregon; for although the leaders of the state were practicing Christians and although their consciences bled for the lepers, they instinctively thought: "Those with mai Pake will soon be dead. Why, really, should we waste money on them?" So to get her precious timbers Nyuk Tsin stationed her husband along the shore, where he prayed both for the arrival of driftwood and for the speed to grab it before someone else did. Once he hobbled proudly home with a long piece of timber, and the ridgepole of the roof was slung into place. Now, when the two Chinese lay in their house abuilding, they could look up through the storm and see that promising ridgepole and think: "Soon the rains will be kept away."

While her husband guarded the shore, Nyuk Tsin taught herself to climb the lower cliffs that hemmed in the leper peninsula, and after a while she became as agile as a goat, leaping from one rock to another in search of small trees that could be used as crossbeams; but goats had roamed these cliffs so long that few trees survived where once forests had stood; but wherever the agile Chinese woman spotted a fugitive she climbed for it, as if she were racing the goats for treasure.

These were days of alternate exhilaration and despair. It was good to see Mun Ki taking an active interest in life, such as it was, and Nyuk Tsin often felt a surge of personal pride when she uprooted a tree high on the cliffs; but in the afternoons when the couple gathered pili grass and braided the panels for their future roof, exasperation would overcome them, and Mun Ki often cried, "We have the grass panels finished, but nowhere can we find the crossbeams on which to tie them." Those were the days when the missionary advisers to the king, in Honolulu, argued: "We must not waste money on Kalawao."

One day a whole board, long enough if carefully split to provide crossbeams for an entire roof, washed ashore from some distant wreck, and for a moment Mun Ki thought that he had secured it for himself, but a big man named Palani, whose feet were still sound, rushed down and captured it. So the Chinese continued to sleep under the open roof, with the rain upon them night after night; but they were luckier than many, and they knew it, for they had side walls to protect them from the wind; they had the solid ridgepole of their roof; and they had the piligrass panels finished and waiting to be slung into position.

More, they had a rude kind of spiritual peace. Mun Ki, sitting on the rocks by the sea, waiting for driftwood, often looked toward the cliff where his sure-footed wife risked her life daily in search of timber, and a change came over him. He was not aware of it, but Nyuk Tsin began to sense that her husband no longer felt inwardly ashamed of her Hakka strength. Once he had even gone so far as to admit grudgingly, "I watched you climbing on the high rocks. I would be afraid to climb there." This gave her much consolation, but the spiritual repose derived principally from another development. As long as the two Chinese had been total outcasts, even among the lepers, there had been a kind of enforced loyalty between them, for if either fought with the other, there was truly no hope left, so they were bound together by bonds of ultimate despair. But now that they were accepted into the full community, and were recognized for the prudent, loyal people they were, they were free to be ordinary people, husband and wife, and they could argue about how the house should be built, and sometimes Mun Ki, his patience strained by his stubborn Hakka wife, would stomp off in anger, hobbling on his toeless feet to the beach, where he would sit with dying Hawaiian men and confess to them: "No man can understand a woman," and the suffering men would recount their defeats at the hands of women. Then, when the day was done, he would hobble back to his home and wait for Nyuk Tsin, and when he heard her coming his heart was glad. At one such conciliation he confessed: "If you were not my kokua, I should be dead by now," and with no pride of either Punti or Hakka he looked at her in the tropical dusk and said, "Dr. Whipple was right. Wherever a man goes he finds a challenge. Today the committee asked me to handle the distribution of food, because they know I am an honest man. In fact," he admitted proudly, "I am also on the committee itself."

They suffered one major worry: what had happened to their baby? In questioning the sailors from the *Kilauea* they discovered nothing. Someone vaguely remembered that the child had been handed to a man on the dock at Honolulu, a Chinese perhaps, but he was not sure. With Dr. Whipple dead there was no way for Nyuk Tsin to send an orderly inquiry, so the two Chinese spent some months of quiet anxiety, which was heightened when an incoming leper said, "I know Kimo and Apikela. They gather maile, but they have only four Pake children." The parents fretted, but Nyuk Tsin often repeated: "Wherever the boy is, he's better off than here."

Mun Ki found escape from his worry through a fortunate discovery. One day while keeping guard at the beach, hoping for another timber, he happened to notice that some of the small black volcanic pebbles that lined the shore resembled the beans used in the game of fan-tan, and he started to gather them, and when he had well over a hundred of matched size he spent a long time searching for a completely flat rock, and although he did not find one, he did stumble across a slab which could be made reasonably smooth by polishing with another stone held flat against the surface. When it was ready he spread upon it the bean-like pebbles and began picking them up in his damaged hands, slamming them back down on the flat rock, and counting them out in fours. In time he became so skilled in estimating his initial grab that he could guess with fair accuracy whether the residue would be one, two, three or four; and after he had done this for some days he called to some Hawaiians and showed them the game. For the first days he merely tested his wits against theirs, and it was one of the Hawaiians who suggested, "We could play a game with those pebbles," and Mun Ki replied casually, "Do you think so?"

Since no one had any money, they looked along the beach to find something they could use as counters, and they came upon some hard yellow seeds dropped by a bush that grew inland, and it was obvious that these would make good substitutes for coins, and in this way the historic fan-tan game of the lepers at Kalawao began. When Mun Ki was banker it was uncanny how, using his two stumps of hands, he could grab a number of pebbles, apparently at random, and estimate whether the total was even or odd; and when bets were placed he was able to hide one of the pebbles, catching it between the base of his thumb and the heel of his damaged hand. If most of his adversaries had their yellow buttons on even, he would drop the hidden pebble, make the residue come out odd, and pocket the profits; but if the bets were concentrated on the odd, he would retain the palmed counter and win again.

The game continued for weeks, and more than a dozen men became so excited about it that as soon as the sun was up, they hurried to the beach where the sharp-eyed Pake gambler was willing to stand off their challenges. They played for nothing, only yellow seeds, but they developed agonies of hope over large bets, and in time one of their number, the big excitable man named Palani, the Biblical Paul, began to accumulate most of the buttons. When Mun Ki saw this he was pleased, and on the day when Palani finally cornered the seed-wealth of the lepers his Chinese adversary reported to Nyuk Tsin: "Palani is getting caught, just as we planned. Pray for me."

In the following days Palani began to lose. If he bet on evens, Mun Ki would drop the hidden pebble in his palm and throw down an odd number, and whenever the Hawaiian decided to risk a lot of seeds and go for a big win on a specific number, say three, it was a simple matter for Mun Ki to make the pebbles come out even, so that they couldn't possibly yield a three. The residue might be two or four, but never three.

Slowly Palani's pile diminished, but Mun Ki knew from the past that the cultivation of a sucker demanded patience and skill, so on some days Palani triumphed; but over the long haul he lost, and the afternoon came when Mun Ki ruthlessly drove him down to a mere handful of seeds. Excitement among the lepers was great as the fan-tan game progressed, and many were standing about when the Chinese finally broke his adversary completely, whereupon the Hawaiian spectators started joshing the loser, which was what Mun Ki wanted. When the joking was at its height, the Chinese said casually, "Palani, why don't we play this way. You have the ridgepole for your house, and I have one for mine. It's ridiculous for neither of us to have a complete roof, so I'll play for your ridgepole against mine."

There was an excited hush about the flat rock, and Mun Ki prayed that the Hawaiian would rise to the challenge, but when the big man did so he added a stipulation which left the Chinese stunned. To begin with, Palani said simply, "All right, I'll play for the timber . . . tomorrow," and Mun Ki tried to mask his joy, but then the big man added, "And tomorrow we won't pick up pebbles by hand. We'll scoop them up in a cup. And you won't count them, Mun Ki. Keoki over there will count them."

"Don't you trust me?" Mun Ki pleaded.

The big Hawaiian stared at the little gambler and said, "We'll scoop them up in a cup." And he marched off with his friends.

Mun Ki sat alone for a long time glumly staring at the pebbles on the fan-tan rock. Carefully he capitulated each incident in his relationship with Palani: "It all goes back to that day when I saw the big timber first. But he had good feet, so he dashed out and got it for himself. I must have shown my temper. So all along he's known what I've been planning. Letting him win and then making him lose. That evil man! All the time I was teasing him, he was really playing with me, letting me make him win and then letting me make him lose. So that while I thought I was trapping him into gambling for his roof, he was trapping me into gambling for mine. These damned Hawaiians."

Distraught, he hobbled home, looked up at his precious ridgepole and threw himself upon his wife's mercy. "Tomorrow we may lose our roof," he said solemnly.

"We have no roof . . . yet," Nyuk Tsin replied.

"We have the ridgepole," Mun Ki replied glumly. "And we're going to lose it."

"Our ridgepole?" his wife shouted.

"Nyuk Tsin, be quiet!" he pleaded.

"What have you been doing?" she shouted again, pushing him against the wall. "Did you gamble away our timber?"

"We still have a chance," he assured her, and then he explained how while he was leading big dumb Palani into a trap, the wily Hawaiian had really been leading him into one.

"Oh, husband!" Nyuk Tsin cried, and she began to weep, but he comforted her, and all night the two Chinese tried to figure out what their chances were, now that Palani had insisted that they play the game honestly.

As dawn broke, the sleepless Mun Ki was figuring with a stick in the wet sand and suddenly he looked up toward his wife with a beatific smile upon his thick, leprous lips. "Our good luck is beginning today," he assured her, and his sweating over the ridgepole ceased. "Three years ago we started the taro patch, and that was the beginning of our bad luck. We lost our money, got sick, were tricked by the Chinese doctor, and had to leave home. But the three years are over. Now our good-luck cycle is beginning, Nyuk Tsin!" he cried triumphantly. "We have six years of good luck ahead of us. Today I'll win Palani's ridgepole and tonight we'll sleep under our own roof!"

In an ecstasy of hope he led Nyuk Tsin down to the fan-tan rock, where Palani and his Hawaiians were waiting. The pebbles were on the flat surface, and beside them stood a metal cup with a handle. After some discussion it was agreed that the game should be played in this way: Palani would scoop a cupful of pebbles, and the umpire Keoki, closely watched by Nyuk Tsin, would count them out in fours until the residue was known. Mun Ki, in the meantime, would bet on odd or even and would also stipulate a specific number. Thus, if he nominated even and four, and if the pebbles left a residue of four, he would win two points for his even guess and four points for having guessed the exact number. On the other hand, if he wished to hedge his bets, he could nominate even and three, which would still yield him four points if three came up. Then he would scoop up the pebbles, and Palani would name his bets, and the first man to win one hundred points would win the other's roof.

Palani, content that he now had the Chinese in an honest game, was satisfied that he would win, but Mun Ki, joyous in the start of his six-year cycle of good luck, was positive that he would triumph. He watched the big Hawaiian scoop the pebbles, hold them aloft, and wait for his guess. "Odd and three," Mun Ki cried, and the pebbles were deposited before the umpire. Eagerly the circle of faces closed in for the count.

It was a ghoulish crowd that watched the battle for the ridgepoles. Some men had no hands and some lacked feet. The lips of some had fallen away and there were many noses missing. From the group arose the unmistakable stench of the leper, and brown skins were often marked with huge sickly-white areas. Hair had fallen out and sometimes eyes. These were the caricatures of men, those cursed by a malevolent nature so remorseless that few in the world who were not lepers could imagine. These fan-tan players were indeed the walking corpses, the crawling souls so foul that sound men, seeing them, could only shudder. They were the dead, the bodies thrown onto the beach at Kalawao, the forgotten, the abominated.

But now in the bright sunlight they laughed merrily; and if the judge had inadequate fingers with which to count in fours, he was allowed to keep his job because he was known as a trustworthy man. "Odd and one," he cried. "Two points to the Pake." The crowd cheered.

When it came time for Mun Ki to scoop the pebbles a difficulty presented itself. Although he had been able to play the game with his stumps, he did not have enough fingers to grasp the handle of the cup, so after two trial attempts he appealed to the crowd, and his request was granted: he passed the cup to Nyuk Tsin, and she scooped the pebbles. "Odd and three," Palani cried.

When the judge had counted, he announced: "Even."

"It's our lucky year!" Mun Ki shouted joyfully, and then he stopped to explain how a Chinese has three bad years followed by six good ones. "The good ones started last night!" he chuckled, and on Palani's next scoop he scored six points, for he bet on even and two, and that's how the pebbles fell.

At the midway mark Mun Ki was leading by a score of fifty to thirty-nine, and it was indeed uncanny how he picked up points. "It's our lucky year!" he exulted, and as the sun grew hot it became apparent that Palani was bound to lose his roof. Nevertheless, he played his numbers stolidly to the end, and when the Chinese gambler had fairly won, one hundred to eighty-three, the big Hawaiian jumped up, stretched and said, "I myself will carry the timber to your house!" And the Hawaiians formed a procession, those who could walk, and when they got Palani's driftwood to the stone walls which Nyuk Tsin had built, they cut it into lengths for crossbeams, and men who were agile leaped onto the top of the walls, lashed the beams in place and began tying down the pili grass that others passed to them. By midafternoon the roof was done, and Mun Ki, appraising it proudly, explained to all: "This is really my lucky year."

But Nyuk Tsin saw disappointment in big Palani's misshapen face, and without consulting her husband she went to the man and said, "In our new house there is room for another," and she took Palani by the hand and led him inside. The crowd cheered her generosity and then watched Mun Ki to see what he would do, but he cried, "This is the beginning of my six lucky years."

Taking the dying man Palani into their home was one of the best things Nyuk Tsin ever did, for he had been a sailor and he was a great liar; during a storm he would sit in the dark hut and tell the Pakes of distant lands, and it seemed wonderful to Nyuk Tsin that one man could have had so many experiences. "Asia, Africa, America!" he cried. "They're all fine lands to see." And as he talked, Mun Ki and his wife began to visualize the distant continents and to appreciate what a surpassing treasure their sons were going to inherit. One night Mun Ki said, "When you go back to the boys, Wu Chow's Auntie, make them learn to read. They should know about the things that Palani has been telling us." Once he actually said, "I am glad I came to the Fragrant Tree Country. A man should have great adventures."

Palani's fo'c's'l yarns also awakened Nyuk Tsin's imagination, and she saw how much better it was to live closely with her neighbors rather than apart as she had had to do as a Hakka wife, and sometimes at night, when rain fell over their roof, the three strange companions found a positive joy in sitting together, and this was the beginning of Nyuk Tsin's remarkable service to Kalawao. When big Palani died she helped bury him and then brought into her roofed house a man and wife, and when they died she buried them. She became known as the "Pake Kokua," and whenever a new ferryload of lepers was dumped ashore on the terrible and inhospitable beaches of Kalawao, she went among them and showed them how to obtain at least some comfort during the first weeks when they had to sleep in the open. She taught them to build houses, as she had done, and day after day she climbed the cliffs seeking out short timbers for others. Her most particular contribution was this: when the ferry threw ashore some young girl she would keep the girl in her house for a week or so, and there the girl was safe, as if she had come upon one of the ancient and holy sanctuaries maintained by the Hawaiians before the white man came, and during these days of grace Nyuk Tsin would bring to the girl a chain of possible husbands and would say sternly, "You have come here to die, Liliha. Do so in dignity." And many marriages, if they could be called such, were both arranged and consummated in Nyuk Tsin's house, and word seeped back to Honolulu about the Pake Kokua.

For his part, Mun Ki reveled in his time of good luck. He kept his fan-tan game running and was delighted one day to find that the leper ferry had brought him a Cantonese man, near death, who had managed to hide out in Iwilei for two years before the quack herbalist turned him in, and who was as good a gambler as he. They would play fan-tan by the hour, with Mun Ki insisting, "Pick up the pebbles in the cup, please."

And then the leprosy, which had been accumulating in enormous reserves throughout his body, burst forth horribly in many places and he could not leave the stone house Nyuk Tsin had built for him. She could provide him with no medicine, neither for his awful sores nor for the pneumonia that attacked him. She could get him no choice food . . . just salt beef and poi. There were no blankets to ease the hard earthen bed. But there was Nyuk Tsin's patient care, and as the ghastly days progressed, with death extremely tardy, she sat with her husband and attended to his last instructions.

"You are obligated to send money to my wife," he reminded her. "And when the boys are married, send word to the village. Try any ventures you wish, for these are my lucky years."

As death approached, he became unusually gentle, a poor wasted shadow of a man, a ghost, and he told the self-appointed governor of the settlement, "The fan-tan game belongs to you." At the very end he said to Nyuk Tsin, "I love you. You are my real wife." And he died.

She scratched his grave into the sandy soil, choosing the side of a hill as she had promised, where the winds did not blow and where, if there was no tree, there was at least a ledge of rock upon which his spirit could rest on its journeys from and to the grave.

Nyuk Tsin now turned her house into a hospital, and no longer were stumps of human beings seen abandoned in open fields. She cared for them until they died, and there were sometimes five or six days in a row when she never saw a whole living person. She cared for those who were beyond the memory of God, and there was no human being so foul in his final disintegration but that she could tend him. In Honolulu the government could find no way to send medicine to the abandoned, nor bandages nor even scalpels to cut away lost members, but Nyuk Tsin devised tricks of her own, and many Hawaiians blessed her as the Pake Kokua. If anyone had asked her: "Pake, why do you work so hard for the Hawaiian lepers?" she would have replied: "Because Kimo and Apikela took me in."

In these days she formed one habit. As each dusk came she sat apart and took off all her clothes. Starting with her face she would feel for signs of leprosy, and then her breasts, and then her flanks. She studied each hand with care and then inspected her legs. Finally she lifted her big feet and looked at each toe in turn, and when she was satisfied that for another day she was free of leprosy, she dressed and went to bed. She had to perform this inspection at dusk, for the government in Honolulu could not find the funds to provide the lepers with lamps and oil, so that when night fell, the utter blackness of hell descended upon the lazaretto, and ugliness rode the night. But Nyuk Tsin, even though she was now an unattached woman, was left alone, and she slept in peace, for she knew that so far she was not leprous.

In early 1873 word was sent to Nyuk Tsin that in reward for her help at Kalawao she would be permitted to return to civilization, provided that upon her arrival in Honolulu three doctors would certify that she was free of leprosy. The news excited much discussion among the lepers, but one reaction dominated: although all were sorry to see her go, none begrudged her the right. So in the period between ships this twenty-six-year-old Chinese girl moved about the peninsula of Kalawao. She climbed up to the crater where the volcano which had built the island had once flourished, and she crossed over to the westward side of the peninsula where, in her opinion, the tiny settlement at Kalaupapa offered a much better home for future lepers than the eastern side at Kalawao. But mostly she looked at the towering cliffs that hemmed in the peninsula, and she watched the wild white goats leaping in freedom. To herself she said, "I never expected to leave Kalawao. May those who are left behind find decency."

On the day of Nyuk Tsin's departure from the lazaretto the little *Kilauea* chugged into position beneath the cliffs; casks and cattle were kicked into the surf; and a longboat came in with its first load of condemned; and although Nyuk Tsin had decided to go out to the ship on the first return trip, she now changed her mind and moved among the quivering newcomers, explaining conditions to them in her broken Hawaiian; and when the last incoming boat arrived the sailors had to warn her: "Hey, Pake! More better you come, eh?" As she went to the boat she met climbing out of it a small, white-faced man in black priest's clothing. He wore glasses and his eyes were close together. His hair was combed straight forward like a boy's; his trip among the cattle had made him dirty, and his fingernails were filthy. Now, as he stepped ashore at Kalawao he was breathing deeply, as if in a trance, and he stared in horror at what he saw. To the self-appointed governor he said in an ashen voice, "I am Father Damien.

I have come to serve you. Where is a house in which I may stay?"

Nyuk Tsin was so surprised to think that a white man would volunteer to help her lepers that she did not find words to cry, "You may have my house!" By the time she thought of this, the sailors were already pulling her into the longboat, and so she left, but as she went she could see the lepers explaining to the priest that in Kalawao there were no houses and that he, like any other newcomer, would have to sleep as best he could on the bare ground under a hau tree.

W HEN NYUK TSIN returned from the lazaretto she was dominated by one desire, to recover her children, and as soon as the *Kilauea* docked she hurried off, a thin, sparse-haired Chinese widow of twenty-six wearing a blue smock, blue trousers and a conical bamboo hat tied under her chin and reaching out over her closely wound bun in back. She was barefooted, and after an eventful life of eight years in Hawaii, owned exactly what she wore—not even a toothbrush or a smock more—plus seven undeveloped acres of boggy land left to her by Dr. Whipple. As she plodded up Nuuanu Valley she did not pause to study the land, but as she went past she did think: "I shall have to start spading it tonight."

She was on her way to the forest home of Kimo and Apikela, and when at last she reached the footpath leading off the highway and into the dense vegetation, she broke into a run, and the wind pulled her basket hat backward, so that it hung by the cord around her neck, and at last she burst into the clearing where her children ought to be, but the family was inside the house, and she got almost to the door before Apikela saw her. The big hawaiian shouted, "Pake! Pake! and hurried over to embrace her, lifting her clear off the ground, but even while huge Apikela was holding her, Nyuk Tsin was looking over the woman's shoulder and counting. There were only four boys, from seven years down to four, standing in the shadows, frightened by this intruder.

"Where's the other boy?" Nyuk Tsin finally gasped.

"There's no other boy," Apikela replied.

"Didn't you get the baby from the ship?"

"We heard of no baby."

Nyuk Tsin was tormented by the loss of her child, yet overjoyed to see her other sons, and these dual emotions immobilized her for a moment, and she stood apart in the small grass house looking first at big Apikela, then at drowsy Kimo, and finally at her four hesitant sons. Then she forgot the missing child and moved toward her boys, as if to embrace them, but the two youngest naturally drew back because they did not know her, while the two oldest withdrew because they had heard whispers that their mother was a leper. Nyuk Tsin, sensing this latter fear, hesitated, stopped completely and turned to Apikela, saying, "You have cared well for my babies."

"It was my joy to have them," the huge Hawaiian woman laughed.

"How did you feed them?" Nyuk Tsin asked, feasting her eyes on her robust sons.

"You can always feed children," Kimo assured her. "Sometimes I worked. Sometimes the Pakes gave us a little money."

"Do they have the other child?" Nyuk Tsin asked.

"They never spoke," Apikela replied. Then the big woman noticed how frightened the boys were of their mother, and with a gigantic, embracing sweep of her huge arms she gathered them up as she had often done before. When they were huddled against her warm and ample body, she gave her belly a sudden flick, opened her arms and ejected a tangle of arms and legs at Nyuk Tsin. The scrawny little Chinese woman was engulfed, and then a strange thing happened. It was she who feared the leprosy, and instead of embracing her sons, she withdrew as if she were unclean, and the boys stared silently at their mother while she drew her hands behind her, lest she touch one of them.

"I am afraid," she said humbly, and Apikela withdrew the children.

After a noisy meal during which the boys chattered with Kimo, and Apikela asked a dozen aimless questions about Kalawao, Nyuk Tsin said, "I must go down to look at my land," and she set off for the four-mile jog back down the valley to where the boggy land lay, but again she passed it without stopping, for she was on her way to see the Punti and Hakki families, but none of them knew of her son. Because they were *Carthaginian* families, they felt obligated to help Mun Ki's widow, so they scraped together a set of garden tools, some seeds, a bag of taro corns and a bamboo carrying-pole with two baskets attached. With these Nyuk Tsin returned to her land, and there she worked till nearly midnight.

The low and boggy section she enclosed in dikes, for there taro would prosper. Furthermore, building the taro bed also drained the intermediate land, uncovering good alluvial soil, which she tilled for Chinese vegetables. This left a smaller, but still adequate high area where vegetables for the haoles could be grown. Thus, from the first night, Nyuk Tsin stumbled upon the system she was to follow for many years: taro for the Hawaiians, Chinese cabbage and peas for the Orientals, lima beans, string beans and Irish potatoes for the haoles. For she knew they all had to eat.

At dawn each day she slung her bamboo pole across her shoulder, hooked on the two baskets, jammed her conical basket hat upon her head, and set out barefooted for her garden. As her vegetables ripened, she loaded her baskets and began her long treks through Honolulu, and no matter how much business she produced at any one house, she was never as concerned with the money as she was to see whether this family happened to have a Chinese boy about four years old. She didn't find her son, but she developed a vegetable business that was becoming profitable.

When night fell, Nyuk Tsin continued working, putting her field in order, and after the stars had come out she would carefully place in her baskets those vegetables which she had not sold. Swinging them onto her shoulder, she would begin her four-mile trek back up the valley to the clearing where her sons were already asleep. There were many days when she never saw them, but as she sat in the night darkness with Kimo and Apikela she talked mostly of their future, and one night, when she had trudged up the valley in a heavy rain, she arrived home cold and wet and she was driven to recall the days in the lazaretto when the leper Palani told them of the world. So she woke her sons and stood before them, muddy and wet, and they rubbed their heavy eyes, trying to understand what she was saying. They could hardly speak Chinese and she was not adept in Hawaiian, but she explained: "Somewhere in Honolulu you have a brother, and his name . . . ." The boys began to fidget, and she commanded them to stand still, but they could not understand.

"Eh, you Kanaka!" Apikela shouted. "Shush! Your auntie speak you! Damned Pakes!" And the boys stood silent.

Slowly Wu Chow's Auntie spoke: "Your father wanted you to share the entire world. He wanted you to study . . . to be bright boys. He said, 'Work hard and the world will belong to you.' "

She took her first son by the hand and drew him into the middle of the room, saying, "Asia, you must honor your father by working hard." The sleepy-eyed boy nodded, quite unaware of the commission he had been given.

To each of her sons she repeated this paternal command: "Work hard." And when they stood at attention, she added, "And you must help me find your brother Australia."

"Where is he?" Asia asked.

"I don't know," Wu Chow's Auntie replied, "but we must find him."

When the confused and sleepy boys returned to bed, the little Chinese woman sat for a long time with the two Hawaiians, trying to decide which of her sons promised to be the most intelligent, and this was important, for Nyuk Tsin realized that she would be able to give only one a full-scale education in America and it was essential that the right one be identified early and concentrated upon. Now she asked Kimo, "Which do you think is best?"

"I like Europe," Kimo replied.

"You like him," Nyuk Tsin agreed, "but who is cleverest?"

"America is cleverest," the big man said.

Nyuk Tsin thought so too, but she checked with Apikela. "Do you think America has courage for a fight?" she asked.

"Africa is the most stubborn fighter," Apikela replied.

"But which one would you send to the mainland?"

"America," Apikela replied without hesitation.

By 1875 Nyuk Tsin had saved nearly twenty-five dollars, and if such a rate of income were to continue, she could obviously afford to educate all of her sons, but she knew that there was heavy obligation upon this money, so when it reached the even twenty-five-dollar mark she bundled it up, took her four sons with her, and marched formally down to the Punti store. "I want you to understand what we are doing," she said several times, and when she reached the store, she lined the boys up so that even six-year-old America could follow the transaction that was about to occur.

In those years the Chinese did not use banks, for there were no Chinese establishments, and what Oriental could trust a white man in the handling of money? Wealth was kept hidden until a responsible accumulation was made, and then it was carried, as on this day, to the Punti store or to the Hakka store, and there, in complete confidence, it was handed over to the storekeeper, who, for three per cent of the total, would manage, by ways only he knew, to transmit the balance either to the Low Village, as in the present case, or to the High Village if the recipient were to be a Hakka. Wars came and revolutions. Hawaii prospered or suffered loss. Men died and ships were captured by pirates, but money sent from the Punti store in Honolulu invariably reached the Low Village.

"This money is for the wife of Kee Mun Ki," Nyuk Tsin explained to the storekeeper. When he nodded she said, "A widow in the Low Village. Tell her that as dutiful sons her four boys send the money. And they send as well their filial respect." Again the storekeeper nodded and began to write the letter.

When it was completed, in strange Chinese characters that few in Hawaii could read, Nyuk Tsin proudly handed it to each of the boys and said, "You are sending money to your mother. As long as she lives you must do this. It is the respect you owe her." Gravely the little pigtailed boys in clean suits handled the letter, and each, in his imperfect way, could visualize China, with his mother sitting in a red robe and opening the letter and finding his money inside. When the letter was handed back to the storekeeper for transmitting, Nyuk Tsin stood her boys in line and said, "Remember! As long as your mother lives, this is your duty." And the boys understood. Big Apikela was like a mother in that she sang to them and kissed them; and Wu Chow's Auntie was sometimes like a mother because she brought them food; but their real mother, the one that counted, was in China.

Since the day on which the money was taken to the Punti store was already ruined, Nyuk Tsin decided to explore something that she had heard of with great excitement. She led her four bright-faced boys back up Nuuanu Valley, taking them off into a smaller valley where in a field a large building stood. It belonged to the Church of England, for as soon as the Hawaiian alii discovered the gentle and pliant religion of Episcopalianism with its lovely ceremonies, they contrasted it to the bleak, un-Hawaiian Calvinism of the Congregationalists, and before long most of the alii were Church of England converts. They loved the rich singing, the incense and the robes. One of the first things the English missionaries did was to open the school which Nyuk Tsin now approached, and to the surprise of the islands the Englishmen announced: "In our school we will welcome Chinese boys." The idea of having Orientals in any large numbers in the big, important school at Punahou would in 1875 have been repugnant, and also prohibitively expensive to the Chinese, so the ablest flocked to Iolani, where Nyuk Tsin now brought her sons.

She was met by one of the most unlikely men ever to inhabit Hawaii, Uliassutai Karakoram Blake, a tall, reedy Englishman with fierce mustaches and a completely bald head, even though he was only twenty-eight. His adventurous Shropshire parents had been with a camel caravan heading across Outer Mongolia from the town of his first name to the town of his second when he was prematurely born, "jolted loose ere my time," he liked to explain, "by the rumbling motion of a camel which practically destroyed my sainted mother's pelvic structure." He had grown up speaking Chinese, Russian, Mongolian, French, German and English. He was now also a master of pidgin, a terrifying disciplinarian and a man who loved children. He had long ago learned not to try his Chinese on the Orientals living in Hawaii, for they spoke only Cantonese and Punti, and to him these were alien languages, but when Nyuk Tsin spoke to him in Hakka, it sounded enough like Mandarin for him to respond, and he immediately took a liking to her.

"So you want to enroll these four budding Lao-tses in our school?" he remarked in expansive Mandarin.

"They are not Lao-tses," she corrected. "They're Mun Ki's."

Uliassutai Karakoram Blake, and he demanded of his acquaintances his full name, looked down severely at Nyuk Tsin and asked, "Is there any money at all in the coffers of Mun Ki, y-clept Kee?"

"He's dead," she replied.

Blake swallowed. He liked this practical woman, but nevertheless he tried to smother her with yet a third barrage of words: "Have you any reason to believe that these four orphaned sons of Mun Ki have even the remotest capacity to learn?"

Nyuk Tsin thought a moment and replied, "America can learn. The others aren't too bright."

"Madam," Uliassutai Karakoram cried with a low bow that brought his mustaches almost to the floor, "in my three years at Iolani you are the first mother who has even come close to assessing her children as I do. Frankly, your sons don't look too bright, but with humble heart, I welcome Asia, Europe,

Africa and America into our school." Very formally he shook the hand of each child, then roared in pidgin, "Mo bettah you lissen me, I knock you plenty, b'lee me." And the boys did believe.

In later years, when Hawaii was civilized and lived by formal accreditations, no teacher who drifted off a whaling boat one afternoon, his head shaved bald, no credentials, with mustaches that reached out four inches, and with a name like Uliassutai Karakoram Blake could have been accepted in the schools. But in 1872, when this outlandish man did just that, Iolani needed teachers, and in Blake they found a man who was to leave on the islands an indelible imprint. When the bishop first stared at the frightening-looking young man and asked, "What are your credentials for teaching?" Blake replied, "Sir, I was bred on camel's milk," and the answer was so ridiculous that he was employed. If Blake had been employed in a first-rate school like Punahou, then one of the finest west of Illinois, it wouldn't have mattered whether he was capable or not, for after Punahou his scholars would go on to Yale, and oversights could be corrected. Or if the teachers in the school were inadequate, the parents at home were capable of repairing omissions. But at Iolani the students either got an education from the available teachers, or they got none at all, and it was Blake's unique contribution to Hawaii that with his fierce mustaches and his outrageous insistence upon the niceties of English manners, he educated the Chinese. He made them speak a polished English, cursing them in pidgin when they didn't. He converted them to the Church of England, while he himself remained a Buddhist. He taught them to sail boats in the harbor, contending that no man could be a gentleman who did not own a horse and a boat. Above all, he treated them as if they were not Chinese; he acted as if they were entitled to run banks, or to be elected to the legislature, or to own land. In these years there were many in Hawaii who looked apprehensively into the future and were frightened by what they saw. They did not want Chinese going to college or owning big companies. They were sincerely afraid of Oriental businessmen and intellectuals. They hoped, falsely as it proved, that the Chinese would be perpetually content to work on the plantations without acquiring any higher aspirations, and when they saw their dream proving false, and the Chinese entering all aspects of public life, they sometimes grew panicky and talked of passing ridiculous laws, or of exiling all Chinese, or of preventing them from entering certain occupations. What these frightened men should have done was much simpler: they should have shot Uliassutai Karakoram Blake.

For when the first Chinese plantation worker saved, through bitter labor, the few pennies needed to send his son to Iolani, a kind of revolution was launched which nothing in world history had so far proved capable of reversing. When Blake taught the first Chinese boy the alphabet, the old system of indentured labor was doomed. Because a boy who could read would sooner or later come upon some book that would give him an idea, and a boy with an idea could accomplish almost anything. During these years in Hawaii, the Chinese were not particularly well treated. Hell-raising lunas on the plantations—gang foremen—often thought it hilarious to tie two Chinese together by their pigtails and abuse them both at the same time. Other lunas, on a drunk, found delight in tying the pigtail of a passing Oriental to the tail of a horse, and lashing the horse into a gallop. The Chinese retaliated until it became a standing rule among lunas: "Never go into a field where more than six Chinese are working with cane knives. Never." And one night an infuriated Chinese, for no reason that anyone ever developed, screamed into the bedroom of the French consul and with a long knife massacred him. These were not easy years, and the Chinese were by no means the docile Orientals that the Honolulu *Mail* had reported on their arrival. They were apt to be mean, fearfully quick to revenge insults, and positively unwilling to extend their contracts at three dollars a month for fourteen hours of hard work a day. Deep tensions were created, and the Chinese experiment might have failed, except that Uliassutai Karakoram Blake was quietly teaching his boys: "The same virtues that are extolled in China will lead to success in Hawaii. Study, listen to your parents, save your money, align yourselves with honest men." He also laid great emphasis upon the wisdom of conforming to the mores of the majority. "Cut your pigtails," he counseled, "and dress like Americans. Join their churches. Forget that you are Chinese."

A boy asked, "But if we ought to drop Buddhism, why don't you?" And Uliassutai replied, "When I leave Hawaii, I shall return to England, where freedoms of all kind are permitted. But you will not leave these islands. You will have to live among Americans, and they despise most freedoms, so conform." He was a difficult, opinionated man, and he transformed a race.

In these days, when Nyuk Tsin came to work in the early morning twilight, she led her four sons with her, and for the hours before school opened, they labored in the field with her. As schooltime approached, she dipped a rag in the muddy water of the taro patch and cleaned her sons, sending them off to their lessons. When day ended, they were back among the vegetables, and after nightfall they all reached home, where big Kimo had a hot supper waiting for them. After a year of this severe regime Kimo, exhausted by the amount of work the Chinese were doing, suggested, "Why don't we all leave this house and build a little house down the valley? We'll keep this land for a vegetable field. Then nobody will have to walk so far, and I'll be close to the poolroom."

Nyuk Tsin considered this for some time and said, "I don't like to give up even an inch of the vegetable field for a house."

"But look!" Kimo argued. "For a little corner of the vegetable field, you'll get a whole lot of land up here."

"If we do that," Nyuk Tsin countered, "Apikela will have to walk great distances for her maile. And I can walk better than Apikela."

"What I had in mind," Kimo explained, "was that Apikela should stop bothering with the maile and help you with the vegetable field down there. That way, the boys can study longer for their school."

The plan was so reasonable that next day Nyuk Tsin invited Kimo to accompany her to the vegetable field, and the huge man explained how little land would be taken off by the house, and he reminded her how much forest land she would be getting in exchange, and on the spur of the moment she said, "Good."

They took down the upland house and for several nights slept in the open while the lowland house was building, and after a while the first of the famous Kee houses stood on Nuuanu Street. This one was a ramshackle affair, neither waterproof nor tidy, but it comfortably housed five Chinese and two Hawaiians. In a way, it was also responsible for the good fortune of the Kees, for one day when Nyuk Tsin was trudging up the valley toward her new fields, which because they were so high did not produce as well as the lower, she was stopped by a handsome young man of twenty who was riding in a gig and who called, "You the Pake who has the field in there?" She said that she was, and he reined in his horse, climbed down, and extended his hand. "I'm Whip Hoxworth," he said, "and I'd like to see your field, if I may." He tied the horse to a tree and tramped in with her, kicked the soil, rubbed some through his palms, and said, "Pake, I'd like to make a deal with you. I brought back with me from Formosa, nearly lost my head doing it, about a hundred pineapple plants. I've tried growing them in low fields, and they don't work. Seems to me a field at this elevation might be nearer to what they knew in Formosa. Tell you what I'll do. I'll give you all the plants that are now living. And if you can make them grow, you can have them. All I want is some of the fruit and some of the seed."

"Can you sell pineapple?" Nyuk Tsin asked suspiciously.

Whip Hoxworth turned and pointed expansively back down the valley, and although trees cut off his view, that did not disturb him. "Every house you can see down there will want to buy your pineapples, Pake. Is it a deal?"

It was, and young Whip Hoxworth had made a shrewd guess, for Nyuk Tsin's upper field was exactly the soil needed for the Formosa pineapple, which was markedly sweeter and in all ways superior to the grubby degenerates that had been introduced into the islands half a century before. Now Nyuk Tsin hiked out of her upper Nuuanu fields day after day, her back loaded with pineapples which she hawked through the city. Her vegetables from the lower field also prospered, but best of all, her four sons were learning their necessary lessons.

In only one venture was Nyuk Tsin failing and that was, as before, her taro bed, for not satisfied with selling the brutish bulbs to the natives, and the leaves to anyone who wanted to steam them for vegetables, while keeping the stalks to herself for pickling and serving with fried mullet, thus exacting three profits from the accommodating taro, she allowed Kimo and Apikela to talk her into boiling down the roots and converting them once more into poi. This time the procedure worked exactly right, and the resulting poi was a rich, gooey, purplish color that made the mouth of any Hawaiian water when he saw it, and a considerable market developed for this Pake poi, as it was called. But very few Hawaiians were able to buy any, for big Apikela and bigger Kimo worked so hard at cultivating the taro that when mealtime came they were famished, and Nyuk Tsin, gobbling a few handfuls of cold rice with perhaps a bit of pickled taro stalk, sat by aghast at the amounts of poi her two gigantic housemates consumed. Kimo, now weighing nearly three hundred and fifty pounds, would lumber over to the poi buckets, ladle himself out a quart or more and serve Apikela an equal amount. Pecking at half a dozen fish, some cold pork, a baked breadfruit and what was left of a can of Oregon salmon, they would dip two fingers, held scooped like loose fishhooks, into the poi, twirl them around the sticky mass, and swing them deftly to their mouths. With a sweet sucking sound they inhaled the delicious paste, and looked happily at each other as they did so.

With dismay, Nyuk Tsin realized that none of her poi was getting onto the market. Yet she did not complain, for these great placid people had adopted her children when she was with the lepers. Even now Nyuk Tsin felt that she could not get along without them, for they tended the boys, did the laundry, brought the gossip home from the poolroom, and took care of the poi. But in prudence Nyuk Tsin felt she had to protect herself, so at last she said to Kimo, "I would like to buy your upper fields."

"Buy?" Kimo asked in astonishment. "You can have them."

"Maybe it's better if I buy them, properly."

"They're yours," Apikela insisted.

"Could we go to the land office and sign the papers?" Nyuk Tsin asked. "And I'll pay you."

Big Apikela lifted her Chinese friend in the air and sat her on her lap, saying, "Kimo and I have no use for the land. We have no children."

"You have the four boys," Nyuk Tsin corrected.

"Good idea!" Kimo cried. "We'll give the land to our boys." So the three of them went down to the land office and registered the sale of the upper fields to the Kee boys, and when the white man asked, through his interpreter, "And what fee changed hands?" the two huge Hawaiians looked confused, and the official explained, "There has to be a recognized fee, or the sale isn't legal."

Nyuk Tsin began to say that she had a bagful of dimes and reals and Australian gold pieces saved for her sons' education and she was willing, but Kimo interrupted, and with a grand gesture said, "We sell this Pake our land in return for all the poi we can eat." And that was what Nyuk Tsin had been thinking about in the first place, and that was how the deed was registered.

It was a strange and yet typical Hawaii-like life that Nyuk Tsin now led. Her four sons spoke mainly Hawaiian and English, and she communicated with them only in broken Hawaiian. They were carefully taught to think of the shadowy woman in China as their mother, but they considered Apikela their mamma, just as she thought of them as her sons. Nobody in the household even knew Nyuk Tsin's name, the Hawaiians always calling her merely the Pake, and her children knowing her as Auntie. In food, language and laughter the establishment was Hawaiian. In school-book learning, business and religion it was American. But in filial obedience and reverence for education it was Chinese.

Nyuk Tsin's years fell into an almost sacred routine. On the first of March she went to the land office and paid her taxes on her two properties, and her most valued physical possession became a box in which she kept her receipts. For her they were a kind of citizenship, a proof that she had a right to stay in the Fragrant Tree Country.

In September and June she washed her one suit of clothes with special care, dressed her hair with a fresh cloth, and accompanied her four sons to discuss their education with Uliassutai Karakoram Blake, who found delight in talking Chinese with her and who said that her sons were doing well. Her insistence upon this was fanatical, and whenever she talked with Blake she hammered one question: "Which of my four sons has the best mind?" And the big, fierce man would reflect and reply, "America." She was so pleased to know that her brilliant son was doing well in school, for she loved to visualize the day on which he would set out to the mainland for his advanced schooling, to be supported by all the others.

In April and October, Nyuk Tsin faithfully trekked down to the Punti store with an appropriate number of dollars and sent them off to Kee Mun Ki's family in the Low Village. Always she took her four sons with her, even though it meant keeping them out of school, for she impressed them with this: "Even more important than education is filial duty, and you are four brothers who must work extra hard to pay the respect due your father and his family." She made each of the boys actually finger the money as it was turned over, and each of them touched the resulting letter. "Now you can go back to school," she said. Sometimes she thought it strange that she should be inculcating these ancient Chinese virtues not in the powerful Hakka language but in a broken Hawaiian pidgin. However, the virtues were self-evident and the boys understood.

Such was the year of Nyuk Tsin, the Pake Kokua, the Auntie. For herself she had one blouse, one pair of trousers, no shoes and one basket hat. She had a bamboo carrying-pole, two baskets, a poi factory that made no money, and two parcels of land that would one day be worth more than a million dollars. But the revolution in which this slim-hipped Chinese woman was involved stemmed mainly from the fact that she had four bright boys in Iolani, and when they were ready to move into Honolulu's economic life, fortified by Uliassutai Blake's inspired learning and their Auntie's frugal common sense, there would be little that could stop them.

And then one day in 1879, as Nyuk Tsin was leading her sons to the Episcopal church, she saw a Hawaiian family entering with seven children, and one of the boys looked Chinese. She began studying this child and concluded that he must be about eight years old, which would be the age of her missing son. She was not sure that he was Chinese, for he blended perfectly with his Hawaiian brothers and sisters, but when service ended she sent her sons home with thirteen-year-old Asia and quietly followed the Hawaiian family to their residence. She found it to be a large, rambling house on Beretania Street far out Diamond Head way, and the eight-year-old boy seemed fully at home there. She tried to ask a passer-by what the family's name was but could not make the man understand.

She now revised her peddling routes and walked miles out of her way to keep check on the big Hawaiian house, and in time she found that the Chinese boy went to school, seemed normally bright, and was known only by a Hawaiian name. Once she lugged her pineapples onto the veranda of the house itself and tried to engage the mother of the household in conversation, but the latter wanted no pineapples. When she had exhausted all her own ingenuity, she decided to discuss the matter frankly with Apikela, but as she was about to do so, her intuition warned her that the big Hawaiian woman would sympathize with her fellow Hawaiian who now had the child, rather than with its rightful mother Nyuk Tsin; furthermore, she concluded that this was the kind of adventure that would appeal to Kimo, who considered himself not exactly fitted for other kinds of work. Accordingly, she took the big, shirtless man aside and said, "Find out who those people are."

"I don't have to find out," he replied simply. "That's Governor Kelolo Kanakoa's house."

"Find out where they got the Pake child."

"Good," Kimo grunted, and he set off to the poolroom and in a short time reported: "The governor was on the docks one day when a ship came in with a little baby boy, and no one knew what to do with it, so naturally the governor said, 'I'll take him,' and he did." Kimo shrugged his shoulders as if to say, "Isn't that simple?" And then he saw what Nyuk Tsin was driving at. "The boy belongs to Kelolo!" he warned. "He fed him. He brought him up."

"But he's a Pake," Nyuk Tsin argued. "He's mine."

"Of course!" Kimo agreed. "He's your boy, but he belongs to the governor."

Patiently, but with swelling emotion, Nyuk Tsin reasoned: "I did not give the child to the governor. I sent him to you, to keep for me till I got home."

"But what did it matter who got the child?" Kimo reasoned back. "The boy has a home and parents who love him. He has others to play with and enough food. What does it matter?"

"I want him to grow up to be a Chinese," Nyuk Tsin argued, growing nervous.

"I don't understand," Kimo said blankly. "When I was young my father always had two or three sailors who had fled their ships, hiding out in our fields up there. Swedish, Americans, Spaniards, it didn't matter. Sometimes they had babies with my sisters, and where are the babies now? I don't know, neither do my sisters. And are they Spanish or Hawaiian? Who cares?"

Nyuk Tsin found herself making no headway with Kimo, so against her better judgment she enlarged the debate to include Apikela, and as she suspected, the big Hawaiian woman instinctively sided with the boy's Hawaiian mother. "You must think of how much the governor's wife has grown to love this boy," Apikela reasoned.

"But she has six children of her own!" Nyuk Tsin replied in growing despair.

"They aren't all her own!" Apikela replied triumphantly. "Some were left in the street and one I know comes from Maui."

"I am going to get my son," Nyuk Tsin said stubbornly.

"Pake!" Apikela warned. "He is no longer your son."

Nyuk Tsin spoke unwisely: "Are the other four boys no longer my sons, either?"

Softly Apikela replied, "No, Pake, they are not yours alone. They are now my sons too." She did not have the words to explain that in the Hawaiian system the filial-parent relationship was completely fluid, and son-ship derived not from blood lines but from love. No child was ever left abandoned, and some of the most touching narratives of Hawaiian history stemmed from the love of some peasant woman who heard the cries of an unwanted girl baby whom the alii had left beside the sea to perish, and the peasant woman had rescued the child and had raised it as her own until war came, or some other great event, and then the child was revealed in full beauty. It had happened again and again. Apikela was unable to explain all these things to her Pake friend, but she did add this: "In all the Hawaiian families you see, there will always be one child that was found somewhere. A friend gave the child to the family, and that was that."

Stubbornly Nyuk Tsin repeated her question: "Then my boys are not my sons?"

"Not yours alone," huge Apikela repeated. The little Chinese woman, steeled in the Hakka tradition of family, stared at her big Hawaiian friend, reared in the softer tradition of love, and each woman typified the wisdom of her race, and neither would surrender, but as always, it was the copious Hawaiian who made the overture of peace: "Surely, Pake, with four boys we have enough for two mothers." And the big woman was so persuasive that even though Nyuk Tsin despised the concept being offered, and saw in it an explanation of why the Hawaiians were dying out and the Chinese were thriving, she could not ignore the testimony of love that she saw in the happy faces of her sons. Even if they did have to live suspended between Hawaiian love and Chinese duty, they were thriving; so at last Nyuk Tsin allowed herself to be drawn into Apikela's great arms and cherished, as if she were a daughter and not an equal. Then the big woman said, "Now that our tempers are at peace, let us go see the governor's wife."

Sedately, she and Kimo and the Pake walked down Nuuanu to Beretania and then out toward Diamond Head, and when they got to the governor's big house, Apikela said softly, "I will speak," and as if she were an ambassador from the court of the Nuuanu taro patch to the high court of Beretania Street, she explained to the governor's wife: "The Pake thinks your seventh child is hers."

"Probably is," Governor Kelolo's wife agreed easily. "I think my husband found him on a boat."

"The Pake would like to take the boy home with her," Apikela said softly.

The governor's wife looked down at her hands and began to cry. Finally she said gently, "We think of the boy as our own."

"See!" Apikela said, and she withdrew from the interview, for there was obviously nothing more to say.

But Nyuk Tsin was just beginning. "I appreciate what you did for the boy. He looks very clean and intelligent. But he is my son, and I would like to . . ."

"He is very happy here," the governor's wife explained.

"He is my son," Nyuk Tsin struggled. She felt as if she were engulfed in a mass of cloud or formless foam. She could push it back, but always it returned to smother her. The three big Hawaiians were falling upon her, strangling her with love.

Again the governor's wife was speaking: "But we think of him as our son, too."

"If I went to court, what would the judge say?" Nyuk Tsin threatened.

Now both the governor's wife and Apikela began to weep, and the former said, "There is no need to involve the judges. Apikela said that you had your four sons with you. Why not leave the fifth boy with us? We love him very much."

"He is my son," Nyuk Tsin stubbornly argued, but the phrase really had little meaning to the three Hawaiians. Obviously, the attractive boy was a son in many more ways than this thin Chinese woman could understand.

At this point the governor himself entered, a tall, handsome man in his late forties. He was generous in his attitude toward everyone and listened patiently, first to Apikela, then to his wife, and finally to Nyuk Tsin. When he spoke he said, "Then you are the Pake Kokua?"

"Yes," Nyuk Tsin replied.

"Every Hawaiian owes a debt to you, Kokua." He formally extended his hand. Then he remembered: "It was about eight years ago. I was at the docks on some kind of business. I wasn't governor then, had just come over from Maui. And this ship came in with a sailor who had a screaming baby, and he said, 'What shall I do with it?' And I said, 'Feed it.' And he said, 'I got no tits.' So I took the boy and brought him home." He paused significantly, then added, "And we made him one of our sons."

"Now I want him," Nyuk Tsin said forcefully.

"And it would seem to me," the governor said, ignoring her, "that it might be a very good thing if this Chinese boy continued to grow up in this house, among the Hawaiians. We two races need to understand each other better." Then he stopped and said bluntly, "I love the boy as my own son. I don't think I could let him go."

"The judge will give him to me," Nyuk Tsin said coldly.

Tears came into the big man's eyes and he asked, "Have you no other children of your own?"

"I have four," Nyuk Tsin replied.

"Then leave the boy with us. Please don't speak of judges."

The governor's wife brought in tea, and Nyuk Tsin was invited to sit in the best brocaded chair, and Kimo asked if they happened to have any poi. The meeting lasted for four patient hours, and the little Chinese woman was positively beat down by love. When her son was summoned she saw that he was big and bright and strong. He was not told that the strange Chinese woman in the smock and trousers was his mother, for he called the governor's wife that, and after he was dismissed, many proposals were made, and Nyuk Tsin consented to this: her fifth son would continue to live with the governor, but he must be told who his real mother was . . . And here Nyuk Tsin began to get mixed up, because she also insisted that the boy be given the Chinese name Oh Chow, the Continent of Australia, and that twice each year he accompany his brothers to the Punti store when the money was sent to his real mother in China.

"His real mother?" the governor asked.

"Yes," Nyuk Tsin explained. "His real mother is in China. I am merely his auntie."

"I thought you gave birth to the boy in Kalawao," the governor checked.

"I did," Nyuk Tsin assured him. "But his mother is in China."

The governor listened patiently and asked, "Could you please explain this again?" and as Nyuk Tsin repeated the curious rigmarole he realized that he was comprehending very little of it.

So Nyuk Tsin took Australia to the Punti store, where his name was duly forwarded to the ancestral hall in the Low Village, while he continued to be known in Hawaii as Keoki Kanakoa, the son of the last governor of Honolulu. He met his brothers, Asia, Europe, Africa and America, and then returned to the big rambling house. He called Nyuk Tsin, whose name he never knew, Auntie, and he vaguely understood that in China he had a real mother, to whom it was his duty to send money twice a year.

There was one other thing that Nyuk Tsin insisted upon. Four acres of Governor Kanakoa's choicest upland in Manoa Valley, then a wet, forested wilderness, were officially deeded over to the boy Australia Kee, otherwise known as Keoki Kanakoa, and after these were cleared, Nyuk Tsin grew pineapples on them. She was now thirty-two years old, and except for a really gaunt thinness and a lack of hair she was what one might call an attractive woman; but even though there was an appalling lack of women for Chinese men—246 women; 22,000 men—none of the latter ever considered Nyuk Tsin as a wife. She had proved herself to be a husband-killer and she was probably also a leper.

So she lived spiritually apart from her sons and her community. Each night after the others were in bed, she stripped herself naked and with a small lamp inspected each area of her body, and when she had finally cleared even her big feet of suspicion she sighed and said to herself, "Still no leprosy." And if she avoided this, nothing else mattered.

WHEN WHIPPLE HOXWORTH returned to Hawaii in 1877 he had brought with him only a hundred pineapple plants and a bag of miscellaneous seeds to show for his seven years abroad, but he had already become the man who was destined to rebuild the structure of the islands. He was tall, wiry-thin, quick both in muscle and wit and unusually well trained in the use of his fists. He had the insolent assurance of his paternal grandfather, Captain Rafer Hoxworth, plus the distinguished bearing that had characterized his maternal grandfather, Dr. John Whipple. He also exhibited certain other behavior patterns of those two men.

Like Captain Rafer, young Whip had an insatiable desire for women, and following quickly upon the Chinese girl who had taught him lessons at the age of thirteen, he had enjoyed the wild companionship of strange women in most of the world's major ports. His entire earnings for seven years had been spent freely on these women, and he regretted not a penny of his loss, for he had made an essential discovery: he had it within his power to make women happy.

Sometimes at a formal party, when as a budding second mate he was invited to a home of distinction in Perth or Colombo or Bangkok, he would enter the room and physically feel the lines of communication establishing themselves between him and certain women, and as the night wore on he would stare quietly, yet with insolent power, at the most likely of these companions, and he would seek her out for a dance and say certain modest yet fire-filled things to her, and the atmosphere often became so charged with passion that when he had maneuvered to find himself alone with the woman, she would thrust herself into his arms and encourage him to do with her as he wished, even though a few hours before they had not known of each other's existence. Whenever he entered a party he hesitated a moment at the doorway and thought: "Who will be in there tonight?" For he had found that there was always someone.

In his reflections during long days at sea young Whip never thought in polished terms of "milady's glove" or "my dear Miss Henderson." He thought of girls as strong young animals, naked and stretched out on a bed. That's how he liked women and that's how they liked to be when they were with him. They were utterly enjoyable playmates, and to think of them otherwise was a waste of energy. He made no distinctions as between married or unmarried women; he derived no special pleasure from cuckolding a married man; nor did he find women of any particular nationality or color especially desirable. If he could not gain entrance in Suez to the soiree of a French nobleman, he was quite content to pay down his livres at an established house and take his pick of the professional companions, but even though he often preferred this simple and direct method of acquiring a partner, he had also learned to be a professional gallant, and if he came upon some shy young lady who seemed worth the effort, he stood willing to humble himself before her as a traditional suitor out of a book, sending her flowers and candy, writing her short notes in his vigorous style, and dancing a rather impressive attendance upon her; for he always remembered his grandfather's advice: "When your great-grandmother Malama lay dying, she weighed over four hundred pounds, and her husband crawled in to see her every morning on his hands and knees, bringing her maile. That's not a bad thing for a man to do." Young Whip loved women passionately. He knew that they complemented his life and he was willing to do almost anything to make them happy.

As might be expected, his behavior when he returned from his seven years' cruise took Honolulu rather by surprise. He completely terrified the Hale and Hewlett girls by professing to each in turn his Persian-Egyptian type of love, acquired, as he intimated, by long travels in a camel caravan toward ruined cities of antiquity. The poor girls never really understood what the dashing young man was talking about, but they did discover that he had a great determination to get their underwear off as quickly as possible, so that pretty soon it was agreed among the missionary daughters that they would prefer not to be escorted by their Cousin Whip. He discovered early that one of his full cousins, Nancy Janders, was amenable to his attentions, and they entered into a disgraceful series of performances that ended with Whip being caught in her bedroom completely stripped at five o'clock one morning. Nancy was not to be bullied by her parents and cried that a girl had a right to get to know young men, but that very night young Whip's gig was left stranded at the entrance to Rat Lane down at the Iwilei brothels because a violent fight had broken out over an Arabian girl, and Whip had got cut across his left cheek with a sailor's knife. The next day Nancy Janders' father packed her off to the mainland and young Whip started fooling around with a Portuguese-Hawaiian girl, a great beauty whose grandfather had reached the islands via the Azores. She and Whip engaged in a brilliant courtship, marked by her riding openly with him through the gayer streets of the city and then hustling secretly off to California to have a baby.

By this time some of the younger men of town had given the young seafarer his permanent name. It was bestowed following a brawl in which Whip fought three English sailors outside the impressive H & H building on Fort Street. His austere father rushed down from his offices above the street in time to see his lithe son stretched out cold from a combination of a British blow to the side of the head and a stiff British kick to the groin. While the handsome boy lay in the dusty street, a nearby bartender doused him with a bucket of cold water, but as the fallen fighter gradually began to feel the throbbing pain in his crotch, he bellowed, "Somebody hit me again!" He looked up to see his father's beard staring down at him and he wanted to faint from humiliation and pain, but he scrambled to his feet and hobbled off.

From then on they called him "Wild Whip," and he seemed dedicated to the principle that every man must prove his right to whatever nickname has been bestowed upon him. He did not drink much, nor did he engage in fist fights willingly. In many respects he was a clean, handsome young man. But if he did not seek trouble, neither did he avoid it, and he developed a characteristic gesture, when a fight loomed, of shrugging his shoulders and ambling a few lazy steps forward before exploding into furious action. Normally he would have lost his nickname as he grew older, for he became content to by-pass general brawls, and that aspect of his wildness diminished; but as it regressed, his passion for women increased, and it was his adventures in this field that constantly lured him back into trouble. He often recalled his grandfather's apt simile: "Girls are like lovely little stars. You could reach up and pinch each one on the points." Wild Whip's capacity for reaching and pinching was insatiable, and in this he was a true grandson of Rafer Hoxworth.

But he also resembled in many ways his maternal grandfather, Dr. John Whipple, for in addition to that gallant man's physical handsomeness young Whip had inherited his abiding interest in science. Wherever he had gone during his seven years at sea, Whip had studied plants, grown to love local flowers, and collected specimens of trees and fruits that looked as if they might do well in Hawaii. But three particular discoveries had given him almost as much pleasure as leaping stalwartly into bed with a new girl. He had found the jungle orchids of Malaya positively enchanting, and he had gathered several dozen prime specimens of purple and crimson and burnt-gold beauties which he had shipped home by way of an H & H freighter out of Singapore. They now flourished in a lath house which he had constructed in back of the Hoxworth home on Beretania Street, and it was a major characteristic of their owner that as soon as they established themselves in Hawaii, they were given freely to others who might fancy them. Young Whip made his money running ships and working plantations; the rare plants he brought into the islands were free to anyone who would care for them as diligently as he, so that in later years when Hawaii became famous for its orchids, that fame was but an extension of Whip Hoxworth's personal concern with beauty. He also brought in ginger flowers, and two varieties of bird-of-paradise, that strange, almost unbelievable exotic which produced a burnished blue and red canoe out of which sprang a fantastic flower construction in purple and gold. All these Whip gave away.

He was also responsible for both the Formosa and the New Guinea pineapple, establishing the former through the help of the Chinese vegetable huckster,

Mrs. Kee. The latter, which was more acid and therefore much tastier, he failed to perpetuate. Twice in later years he endeavored to make this contrary pineapple grow, but with no success. He had his agents looking for a new strain which could combine the virtues of the Formosa and New Guinea types, but he did not find any.

But his major contribution at this period was a tree which later came to bear his name. He found it growing near Bombay, and when he first tasted its fruit he cried, "This tree we've got to have in Hawaii." Accordingly, he shipped four saplings home, but they died. He ordered four more and directed them to be planted in Kona on the big island, but they also died. He got four more, each in its own washtub of Bombay soil, and it was these that grew. When they produced their first fruit—a handsome hard rind that turned gold and red and speckled green, inside of which rested a big flat seed surrounded by delicious yellow meat—his neighbors asked what strange thing he had this time.

"Watch!" he said crisply. "You're about to taste the king of fruits." He gripped one, took out his knife and gashed a complete circle around the long axis. Then he spun the knife, point-over-end, into the tree and with two hands gripped the halves of the fruit, twisting them in opposite directions. The fruit tore apart and for the first time the people of Hawaii tasted Whip's luscious discovery.

"Like baked nuts with a touch of apple," one man judged.

"Something like a peach with a trace of turpentine," another said.

"What is it, Whip?"

"A Bombay mango," Hoxworth replied.

"We used to have mangoes around here years ago," the man replied. "But as I recall they were stringy. Couldn't hardly eat 'em."

"There are mangoes and mangoes," Whip agreed. "Trick is, to find the good ones. Then take care of them."

In later years many people grew to despise Wild Whip Hoxworth, for he developed into the ruthless operator his grandfather had been. The extension of H & H from merely a strong shipping line into the dictator-company of the islands was not accomplished easily, and if men hated Wild Whip they had a right to, but no one ever failed to remember with keen appreciation his first major gift to Hawaii. Whenever a hungry man reached up, knocked down a Hoxworth mango, circled it with his knife and sucked in the aromatic fruit, he instinctively paid tribute to Wild Whip. Other varieties came later, but the Hoxworth remained what its discoverer had once claimed it to be: "the king of fruits."

When Whip saw his mangoes established and had given several hundred saplings away to his friends, he turned his attention to the affairs of H & H, whereupon he ran headfirst into his bearded uncle, stern Micah Hale, a symbol of rectitude and a man determined not to have the H & H empire sullied by the escapades of his wild young nephew. Consequently, there was no opening for Whip. When he applied for a job, his grim-faced uncle stared at him over his copious beard and said, "You've outraged all the girls in our family, young man, and we have no place for you."

"I'm not applying for a wife," Whip snapped. "I'm applying for a job."

"A man who isn't appropriate for a husband, isn't appropriate for a job . . . not with H & H," Uncle Micah replied, enunciating one of the firmest rocks of his company's policies, for like most of the great emperors of history, the

Hales and Whipples and Janderses realized that an institution had to go forward on two levels: it produced intelligent sons to carry on when the old men died, and it produced beautiful daughters to lure able young husbands into the enterprise. It was an open question as to whether the great families of Hawaii prospered most from selling sugar at a good price or their daughters to good husbands. "There's no place for you in H & H," Uncle Micah said with finality.

When Whip appealed to his father, he found that sensitive and confused weakling quite unwilling to fight with Micah, who now controlled the family ventures. "Your behavior has been such . . . ." Whip's father began plaintively, whereupon his son said, "Stow it."

There was a good deal of argument within the family, but Uncle Micah said firmly, "Our success in Hawaii depends upon our presenting to the public an attitude of the most strict rectitude. There has never been a scandal in the big firms, and there won't be as long as I control them. I think that Whipple ought to go back to sea. We'll reward him justly for his part ownership of the business, but he must stay out of Hawaii."

And then clever Micah thought of a happy solution. Recalling his nephew's interest in growing things, he suggested a compromise: Wild Whip would divorce himself completely from all H & H enterprises, and an announcement of this fact would be made public so as to absolve men like Micah Hale and Bromley Hoxworth from responsibility for his future actions, and in return Whip would be given four thousand acres of the family's land to do with as he wished. When the assembled Hoxworths and Hales delivered this ultimatum to their errant son, Wild Whip smiled graciously, accepted the four thousand acres and said evenly, "Jesus, are you goddamned missionaries going to regret this day!"

He harnessed up two good horses and started westward to survey the lands he had been given. He drove some distance out of town, shaking the dust from his nose and staring at the bleak, grassless hills that rose to his right. Above them stood the barren mountains of the Koolau Range, and as far as he could see nothing grew. He drove past Pearl Harbor and out to where the land began to level off between the Koolau Mountains to the right and the Waianae Range to the left. Ahead lay his land. It was bleak, barren, profitless. Looking at it he recalled his Uncle Micah's description of the deserts of western America when that young minister traversed them in 1849: "They were lands where nothing grew, not even grass."

Grimly amused, Wild Whip tied his horse to a rock, for there were no trees, and got out to study his inheritance at closer quarters. When he kicked away the surface growth of lichen and dried scrub grass, he found that the soil was a rich reddish color that his Grandfather Whipple had once explained as the result of the gradual breaking down of volcanic rocks. "It's rich in iron," Whip mused. "Probably grow things like mad if it could get water."

He looked back at Pearl Harbor and saw the wide expanse of salt sea water, useless to a farmer. He looked up at the sky and saw no clouds, for few arrived here with rain, and then he happened to look toward the Koolau Range to his right, and above its peaks he saw many dark clouds, riding in upon the trade winds that bore down constantly from the northeast, and he could almost smell the water falling out of those clouds. It fell, of course, on the other side of the mountains and gushed furiously down steep valleys and back out to sea. His Grandfather Whipple had trapped a little in his ditches, but the bulk was as useless as the salt water of Pearl Harbor.

It was then that his great design came to him. "Why not build a tunnel right through the mountains and bring that water over here?" He visualized a system of ditches and dikes, all serving to bring the rich waters of the other side down to his parched lands. "I'll build that tunnel!" he swore. "I'll make this land so rich that by comparison Uncle Micah's boats will be worth nothing." He pointed his lone right forefinger at the Koolau Range and announced to those impassive giants: "Some day I'm going to walk right through your bowels. Be ready."

Curiously, Whip's great fortune was built in quite a different manner. When he saw that he was not wanted in his family's business, and when he had finished inspecting his imperial and useless acres, he decided to leave Hawaii, and he did so in memorable fashion. He had never forgotten how relatively pleasant it had been sleeping surreptitiously with his responsive cousin, Nancy Janders, still banished to the mainland, and now as he was about to leave he began paying deadly court to her saucy younger sister Iliki. It was a whirlwind affair, interspersed with wild nights in Rat Alley with a little French girl, and it culminated in pretty Iliki's slipping into men's clothes as a passenger aboard a British freighter whose captain married her to Whip on the journey to San Francisco. When the joint families heard of the scandal, they prayed that young Iliki would find a happiness which they felt sure would escape her; but when, in America, Iliki's older sister Nancy heard of the marriage she cried, "Damn them, damn them! I hope they both live in hell."

Wild Whip didn't, because he found considerable joy in his lively cousin, but Iliki did, for she discovered to her consternation and embarrassment that her husband had no intention of being loyal to her or of giving up his customary visits to local brothels. In San Francisco he had dashing affairs with several married women of otherwise good repute, and a running relationship with two popular Spanish courtesans from a waterfront institution of ill fame. In other ways he was a good husband, and when his son was born in 1880, he insisted that the boy be named Janders Hoxworth after his wife's father. He proved himself to be a doting husband and was obviously pleased to parade on Sunday after church with his wife on his arm and his son surrounded by lace in the perambulator which he proudly pushed.

But in late 1880 Iliki's sister visited them on her way back to Honolulu, and Nancy was now a striking New York beauty, and it was not long before Nancy's hatred of Wild Whip became once more the passionate love she had earlier known for this gallant gentleman. At first Whip sneaked away to Nancy's hotel, where they fell into wild, tormenting embraces. All the longing of three years rushed back upon poor Nancy Janders, and she abandoned restraint. She would lie in bed completely undressed, waiting for Whip to bound up the hotel stairs, and as soon as he burst into the room and locked the door, she would spring upon him and kiss him madly, throwing him onto the bed with laughter that welled up from her entire being. Sometimes she kept him imprisoned for a whole day, and it became obvious to her sister Iliki what was going on.

At first the gay little wife could not imagine what she ought to do; she wondered whether she was supposed to break into the hotel room and confront the guilty pair or whether custom required her to weep silently, but her problems were resolved when on a day which took her shopping she returned unexpectedly to find that bold Nancy had trailed Whip to his own home, had undressed in Iliki's room, and had pulled Whip into bed with her. When Iliki arrived, they stared up at her from her own sheets. Nobody made a scene. Nancy pouted: "I had him first. He's decided to stay with me."

"Put some clothes on," Iliki said, amazed at her restraint. When they were dressed Nancy announced defiantly, "Whip and I are going to live together."

Iliki did not bother to argue with her husband, for she knew that no matter what he promised, it was of no consequence. He was not like other men, and with deep sorrow—for she loved him very much—she saw that he was destined to bounce from one woman to another without ever resting with one, and she thought: "He'll have a very lonely life."

She left San Francisco with her son Janders and returned on an H & H liner to Honolulu, where she lived a long, full life as a divorcee, doing much good in the community. The natural history museum flourished largely because of her energies.

Her husband Whip and her sister Nancy enjoyed a wild time in San Francisco. Whip got a formal divorce but did not bother to marry Nancy, because, as he pointed out, "I'll never make a good husband." Nancy, finding in sex a complete gratification, was content to tag along on whatever terms he proposed, nor was she distressed when she uncovered suspicious circumstances that seemed to prove that her companion was also the consort of several well-known waterfront girls. What she liked best, however, apart from the passionate moments when he came home after a long absence, were the intense days when he took her with him to talk with men who had built tunnels. They were an odd, dedicated group of experts, willing to tackle nature on any terms, and they convinced Whip that if he could scrape together enough money, they could penetrate the Koolau Mountains and bring water to his dusty lands. Surreptitiously, he sent one of the engineer geologists to Hawaii, and in the guise of bird-collecting this keen fellow tramped the Koolaus and satisfied himself that tunneling them would present no unusual problems. "As a matter of fact," he reported, "it looks to me as if the mountains were built in layers tilted on end. If that's true, when you drill your tunnel you'll not only collect all the water you trap in outside ditches to lead into your tunnel, but the porous rock above the tunnel will probably deliver an equal amount of its own. This could be a profitable undertaking, so far as water's concerned."

"How long would the tunnel have to be?"

"Eight, ten miles," the engineer replied.

"Can you build a tunnel that long?" Whip asked.

"Any tunnel is simply a function of money," the engineer replied, "If you've got the money, I can get the dynamite."

"In this case, how much?"

"Four million."

"Don't forget my name," Whip said.

This report seemed to be the final answer to Whip's land problem. He didn't have the four million dollars then, but there was always a chance he might one day have it. He therefore decided to return to Hawaii, but Nancy Janders said, "I wouldn't, Whip."

"Why not?"

"Well, Iliki's there. That'll be embarrassing for you. And I certainly can't go back with you."

"I don't think you should," Whip said coldly, and a few days later he added, "You ought to be looking for a man for yourself, Nance."

"You through with me?" Nancy asked.

"No place for you in Hawaii," he said truthfully. "How you fixed for money?"

"The family sends me my share," she assured him.

"Nance," he said in his most friendly manner, "I sure hope you have a wonderful life from here on out. Now you better get some clothes on."

*   *   *

She had been gone only a few hours when there was a knock at his hotel-room door, and a little man in an overcoat that reached down to his ankles entered. "My name's Overpeck, Milton Overpeck, and I hear you're interested in drilling a tunnel."

"That's right," Whip said. "Sit down, Mr. Overpeck. You like whiskey?"

"I like anything," Overpeck said.

"You a tunnel man?"

"Well, yes and no," the little man replied, gulping a huge draft of whiskey. Coughing slightly he asked, "I understand you're drilling your tunnel in order to get water."

"You've followed me around pretty well, Mr. Overpeck. Another whiskey?"

"Look, son, if you calculate on getting me drunk and outsmarting me, quit now, because you simply can't do it."

"I'm offering it in hospitality," Whip assured him.

"I never accept hospitality unless the host joins me. Now you gulp one down and catch up, and we can have a fine talk."

The two men, Whip Hoxworth twenty-four years old and Milton Overpeck in his early fifties, guzzled straight whiskey for several hours, during which the little engineer fascinated the Hawaiian landowner with a completely new theory about water. The doughty drinker, whose eyes were bright and clear after three quarters of a bottle, apparently knew more about Hawaii than Whip did, at least about the island of Oahu.

"My theory is this," he explained, using pillows, books and newspapers to build his island. "This volcano here and this one here built Oahu. That's perfectly obvious. Now, as they built, one surely must have overflowed the rightful terrain of the other. I judge all volcanic rock to be porous, so in Oahu it seems to me you have got to have a complex substructure, the bulk of it porous. All the fine water that falls on your island doesn't run immediately out to sea."

"Well, the engineer I sent out there did say that he thought the mountains were probably porous," Whip remembered.

"I'm not interested in the mountains you see above land," Overpeck snapped. "I'm interested in the subterranean ones. Because if, as I suspect, there was a rising and a falling of the entire mountain mass . . ." He stopped, studied his friend and said, "Sorry, you're drunk. I'll be back in the morning." But as he was about to leave he said, "Don't sleep on a pillow tonight. Leave everything just as it is."

Whip, through bleary eyes, tried to focus on the turmoil in his room and asked, "What's all this got to do with tunnels?"

"I wouldn't know," Overpeck replied. "I'm a well man myself."

He appeared at seven next morning, chipper as a woodchuck, his long overcoat flapping about his ankles in the cold San Francisco weather. He surprised Whip by completely dismissing the intricate construction of pillows, books and newspapers. "Best thing is to show you," he said cheerily. "Wells'll be the making of Hawaii." And he led Whip down to the foot of Market Street, where grimy ferries left for the other side of the bay, and when after a long walk through Oakland they stood before a well he had recently dug he pointed with unconcealed admiration at a pipe protruding from the ground, from which gushed a steady volume of water that rose fourteen feet into the air.

"Does it run like this all the time?" Whip asked.

"Day and night," Overpeck replied.

"What does it?"

"Artesian, that's what it is. Artesian."

"How many gallons a day?"

"A million four."

"How long will it last?"

"Forever."

This was what Wild Whip had been dreaming of, a steady source of fresh water, but he had imagined that the only way to get it was to drive a tunnel through the mountains. If Overpeck were correct, where the water really lay was at his feet, but in business Whip was both daring and cautious. He was willing to take almost any gamble to obtain water, but he wanted assurance that he had at least a fair chance of winning. Carefully he asked, "Why did you have to bring me all the way over here to show me this well? Why didn't you show me one in San Francisco?"

"Artesian water don't happen everywhere," Overpeck replied.

"Suppose there isn't any on my land in Hawaii?"

"My job is to guess where it is," Overpeck answered. "And I guess it's under your land."

"Why?"

"That's what I was explaining with the pillows and the newspapers," he said.

"I think we better go back to the hotel," Whip said. "But wait a minute. How did you get the well down there?"

"A special rig I invented."

"How far down did you go?"

"Hundred and eighty feet."

"You want to sell the rig?"

"Nope."

"I didn't think so." The two men returned to the ferry, and as Whip studied the cold and windy hills of San Francisco, imagining them to be Hawaii, he became increasingly excited, but when little Mr. Overpeck assured him that a layer of cap rock must have imprisoned enormous stores of sweet water under the sloping flatlands of Oahu, Whip could feel actual perspiration break out on his forehead.

"What kind of deal can we make, Overpeck?" he asked bluntly.

"You're sweating, son. If I find water, I'm handing you millions of dollars, ain't I?"

"You are."

"I'm a gambler, Mr. Hoxworth. What I want is the land next to yours."

"How much?"

"You pay for getting the rig over there. You give me three dollars a day. And you buy, before we start, one thousand acres of land. If we get water, I buy it from you for what you paid. If we don't, you keep it."

"Are the chances good?"

"There's one way we can test my theory without spending a cent."

"How?"

"Think a minute. If there really is a pool of inexhaustible water hiding under your land, the overflow has got to be escaping somewhere. Logically, it's running away under the sea level, but some of it must be seeping out over the upmost edge of the cap rock. Go out to your land. Tell people you're going to raise cattle. Walk along the upper areas until you find a spring. Calculate how high above sea level you are, and then walk back and forth along that elevation.

If you find half a dozen more springs, it's not even a gamble, Mr. Hoxworth. Because then you know the water's hiding down below you."

"You come out and check," Whip suggested.

"People might guess. Then land values go up."

Whip reflected on this shrewd observation and made a quick decision. "Buy yourself a good bull. Bring him to the islands with you and we'll announce that you're going to help me raise cattle. Then everybody'll feel sorry for me, because lots of people have gone bust trying that on the barren lands. Takes twenty of our acres to support one cow, and nobody makes money."

Three weeks later little Mr. Overpeck arrived in Honolulu with a bull and announced to the Honolulu *Mail* that he was going to advise Mr. Whipple Hoxworth in the raising of cattle on the latter's big ranch west of the city. He led his bull out to the vast, arid, useless acres, and as soon as he got there he told Whip, "Buy that land over there for me." And Whip did, for practically nothing, and the next day he concluded that he had been victimized by the shrewd little man, for they tramped both Whip's acres and Overpeck's, and there were no springs.

"Why the hell did you bother me with your nonsense?" the young man railed.

"I didn't expect any springs today," Overpeck said calmly. "But I know where they'll crop out after the next big storm up in the mountains," and sure enough, three days after the rain clouds left, along the line that Overpeck had predicted, he and Whip discovered sure evidences of seepage. They stood on the hillside looking down over the bleak and barren acres, Whip's four thousand and Overpeck's one, and the little man said, "We're standing on a gold mine, Mr. Hoxworth. I'm mortally certain there's water below. Buy up all the land you can afford."

Eight weeks later the little man reappeared in Hawaii without any cattle, but with nine large boxes of gear. This time he informed the *Mail:* "It looks as if Mr. Hoxworth's investment in cattle is going to be lost unless somehow we can find water on those acres."

He set up a pyramidal wooden derrick about twelve feet high, at the bottom of which were slung two large iron wheels connected by an axle upon which rope could be wound when the wheels were turned by hand. This rope went from the axle and up to the top of the derrick, where it crossed on a pulley and dropped down to be lashed to the end of a heavy iron drill. Laboriously Overpeck cranked the heavy wheels until the iron drill was hauled to the top of the derrick. Then he tripped a catch and jumped back as the drill plunged downward, biting its way through sand and rock. Laboriously he turned the wheels and lifted the drill back into position; then a swift whirrrrr, and the next bite was taken.

"How long will this take?" Hoxworth asked, amazed at the effort required.

"A long time."

"Have you the strength?"

"I'm boring for a million dollars," the wiry little man replied. "I got the strength."

Days passed and weeks, and the determined engineer kept hoisting his drills, breaking their points on almost impenetrable hard pan, sharpening them by hand, and hoisting them once more. "You ought to have an engine," Whip growled as the work made slow progress.

"When I get some money, I'll get an engine," Overpeck snapped.

Now Whip saw the little fighter in a new light. "All your life you've been broke, haven't you?"

"Yep. All my life I was waiting for a man like you."

"Are we going to hit water?"

"Yep."

At two hundred feet the drills were hammering their way through cap rock, once soft ocean mud but now, millions of years later, rock as hard as diamonds. Whip grew despondent and was afraid to pass through the streets of Honolulu, where people already hated him for the way he had treated his former wife, Iliki Janders, and where they now laughed at him for his folly in trying to raise cattle on his barren acres. At first, when those who had sold additional land saw Overpeck's drilling rig, there had been consternation: "Has Whip bamboozled us? Did he know there was water below that rubble?" Such fears relaxed when it was apparent that no water existed. "He's down to two hundred and fifty feet and is running out of rope," spies reported.

And then on the fourteenth of September, 1881, Milton Overpeck's plunging drill crashed through the last two inches of cap rock, and up past the iron, past the rope, gushed cold sweet water at the rate of one million three hundred thousand gallons a day. When it gurgled to the top of the well it kept rising until it reached the apex of the twelve-foot derrick and stood a steady fourteen feet in the air, hour after hour, month after month.

When Whip saw the glorious sight he became agitated and cried, "We must save that water!" But little Mr. Overpeck assured him, "Son, it'll run forever." They scooped out a large depression in which the water was impounded and then pumped to wherever it was needed. They drilled additional wells, all by hand, and Whip said, "Overpeck, it's ridiculous for you to do so much work. Let's buy an engine that'll do it for you," but the determined little man replied, "I finish these wells, I'm never going to work again. I'm going to get a hotel room, lease my land to you, and live easy."

He did all these things, but he had failed to anticipate the natural future of a man like Overpeck in Hawaii. One of the unmarried Janders girls smelled him out, checked the land records to be sure he owned the land he said he did, and married him. Thus his thousand acres was brought safely back into the grand alliance of Hoxworth-Whipple-Hale-Janders-Hewlett.

Whip worked like a maniac organizing his own acres, now six thousand, plus the thousand he leased from Overpeck, and by means of pumps and ditches brought water to all of it. He bought out the old Malama Sugar Plantation and transferred its name and operation to his new lands. Then, with the touch of genius that characterized his business dealings, at the age of twenty-six he turned the entire management of his sugar lands over to Janders & Whipple, and he set out to see more of the world.

In late 1883 he returned to Honolulu with a cargo of new orange trees from Malaya; some excellent coffee beans from Brazil; the amazing torch ginger flower, a red slashing thing; and a tall, dark Spanish wife Aloma Duarte Hoxworth, who quickly bore him a son whom she insisted upon calling Jesus Duarte Hoxworth and whom Honolulu called Jadey, derived from his initials. Aloma Hoxworth was a sensation in the islands, for she was by nature an exotic creature and she quickly announced to her husband that his days of roistering on Rat Alley were ended. But it was easier for her to issue such instructions than to enforce them, so one night when Whip came home from delightful hours with a Chinese prostitute, Aloma Duarte tried to carve him up with a long knife. She gashed him badly across the scar in his left cheek, but before she could strike again he kicked her in the stomach, knocked her breathless against the wall, and proceeded to break her jaw and wrist.

"No one comes at me with a knife," he explained publicly, and when the once-beautiful woman was mended she decided to bring brutality charges against him in the Honolulu courts, but against her stood the mute testimony of the jagged gash in Wild Whip's cheek, and her lawyers advised her to drop charges. When she did so, Micah Hale, Bromley Hewlett and Mark Whipple visited her and advised her that they were ready to provide her with a small but adequate annuity if she would agree to leave the islands.

"There's no place for you here," Micah explained.

"I'm taking Jadey with me," she threatened.

"Whip won't allow that," her father-in-law warned.

"Jadey is for me!" Aloma Duarte stormed.

"He belongs in the islands," Micah reasoned with her, and in the end she left exactly as the family had originally planned, with exactly the annuity they had suggested. In New York she told a friend, "I was more afraid of the three bearded ones than I was of my husband. He comes at you with his fists, but they soft-talk you to death. In Hawaii they run things pretty much their own way. But they were generous."

And west of Honolulu, the once barren lowlands that had formerly required twenty acres to nourish a cow, blossomed into the lushest, most profitable agricultural lands in the world. When the sugar cane stood eight feet tall, bursting with juice, for mile after mile you could not see the red volcanic soil, nor could you see the water that Wild Whip had brought to it. All you could see was money.

IN 1885 NYUK TSIN could no longer postpone decision about her sons, and as she studied Ah Chow, Au Chow, Fei Chow, Mei Chow and Oh Chow she realized both how difficult her job was going to be and how important. At Iolani, the Church of England school, she was giving the boys the best education available to them on the islands. Had they been able to get into Punahou, they would have learned more and would have associated with the missionary children who were destined to rule Hawaii, but for both financial and social reasons, entry there was forbidden, and they had done well at the second-rate school.

But now the older boys were ready for advanced education, and it was clear that each merited college and university. They were bright boys, well behaved, industrious and alert. Their pigtails were well tended and they had learned to keep their nails clean. They had good teeth and clear skins. They were reasonably good at games and spoke four languages with skill: Punti, Hakka, Hawaiian and English. Each was above high-school ability in mathematics and abstract reasoning, and to choose among them the boy on whose shoulders the entire burden of the family should fall was difficult indeed.

Nyuk Tsin was confused as to which of her boys ought to go to America, nor could she decide what he ought to study when he got there. In early 1885, therefore, she began her long inquiry, starting with Uliassutai Karakoram Blake, and he wasn't of much help because he vigorously espoused two directly conflicting criteria. As an Englishman he swore: "No boy is worth educating unless he's proved himself good at games. Europe is the one. He has spirit and quickness of hand. He looks you in the eye when he gives you an answer. Fine, clean-cut lad to be trusted. Grow up to be a substantial man." That much was easy to understand, but when Uliassutai had said that—sort of in deference to British tradition—he promptly added, "But of course England's the only place in the world where a man can get ahead simply because he has good character and the brain of an ass. Everywhere else you have to have intelligence, and let's face up to it, Wu Chow's Auntie, your son Europe is an ass, and I'm afraid that's done it. The only one who shows the quick intelligence required in a scholar is America. But he's so appalling at games I can never take him seriously. Probably turn out to be a pretty poor sort in the end, a thinker and all that. I'd never waste me money on him, but in France he'd likely end up in the cabinet."

Nyuk Tsin pretty well agreed with Uliassutai in his analysis of the two boys. Europe was going to make friends wherever he went and was a fine, congenial boy, not too good at books, but an admirable son. America was clearly the ablest but he had a shy, withdrawing quality that sometimes frightened her. She concluded that what Blake was saying, in his cryptic way, was that he could not make the final choice.

Apikela and Kimo were certainly not obscure. "The only one is Australia," they said firmly. "He speaks such good Hawaiian he sounds educated already." When Nyuk Tsin tried to press them on things like character, ability to work, or insight in business they gave a quick, easy answer: "Only one's Australia. When he sings a song, you can hear the words so beautifully." Nyuk Tsin pointed out: "You two are with the boys more than I am. What do you see in them?" And again the answer was direct: "Australia is the one who will lead a happy life, because he has such a handsome smile and he knows how to laugh." Whenever the boy visited the Kee house, slipping away from his Hawaiian parents, Nyuk Tsin would hear him joking with Kimo and Apikela, and once when she said to him, "Maybe you will go to America for your education," he had replied, "I like it here." His friends were divided into four almost equal groups: Punti, Hakka, Hawaiians and Haoles. At Iolani he was elected president of his class and sang in the glee club. "Then you would send Australia to college?" Nyuk Tsin pressed, and big Apikela replied, "Oh, yes! He'd have a lot of fun at college." Nyuk Tsin pointed out: "But we're sending him to study," and the Hawaiians laughed, "Give him just as much as his tired little head will take, and forget the rest."

The Chinese community was again fairly clear in its recommendation. Partly because Asia was the oldest son and therefore to be respected unless he proved himself inadequate, but mainly because he had already opened a restaurant on Hotel Street that did a good business, he was their overwhelming choice. The Punti said, "This boy can be trusted. He buys wisely and sells with intelligence. At nineteen he's already a better businessman than my son at twenty-five. I wish he were my boy." The Hakka told Nyuk Tsin: "We have watched your boys for some years, and the others sometimes seem more Hawaiian than Chinese, but Asia is different. He has a real Chinese understanding, and he will do well." Few Chinese deviated from this strong recommendation, and when Nyuk Tsin arranged a marriage for him with a Punti wife whose father owned land, he built himself even more solidly into the Chinese community. Asia Kee was bound to become a powerful man.

That left Africa, the middle son. He excelled neither in games nor in books, nor was he inclined toward business or singing. His face was rather squarish and unlike his brothers he wore his pigtail tied at the end in a blunt knot. He would fight anyone who got in his way, but he was not offensively aggressive. His principal characteristic was hesitancy in making up his mind, accompanied by a bulldog tenacity when he had done so. His personal affections were kept well masked: he had no special regard for either Uliassutai Blake, Apikela or Wu Chow's Auntie. He studied each of them and knew their strengths but not their love. His brothers rarely shouted to him to join them in a game, but they often asked him the schedule for the next day's lesson. His mother studied him with a good deal of care and concluded: "In his stubborn, square-faced way, Africa is deeper than the others."

She had almost as much trouble trying to decide what the chosen son should study if he got to America. Here Uliassutai Blake was clear-cut in his advice: "The world is run by those who can manipulate, Wu Chow's Auntie. There are only two decent vocations open to a man of talent. He should become a messiah and lead us into eternal darkness, or he should study to be a lawyer, and then God alone knows what he may accomplish. If I were a lawyer I would run for Parliament. If your son becomes a lawyer he will coach you in how to cheat the government, and heaven knows, that's to be learned by all of us. Lawyer, Wu Chow's Auntie, nothing less." When she asked him, "Who would make the best lawyer?" he replied without equivocation, "America." She thought the same.

Kimo and Apikela were of no help. They pondered the problem for a long time, their great brown bodies wrestling with strange ideas, and finally Kimo asked, "Why should fine boys like this be anything? Asia has a restaurant. Europe has a store. Australia has more friends than anyone in school. They like Hawaii. They fit in. Why bother them with all these big ideas?" Nyuk Tsin, who appreciated the insight of these huge friends, asked, "But which do you like better, a lawyer or a doctor or a dentist?" The two Hawaiians studied this for some time and replied, "For a Hawaiian a lawyer is better because he makes such wonderful speeches, but for a Pake maybe a doctor is better because he makes so much money."

The Chinese community was more practical. The Punti almost to a man advised medicine: "A doctor is always respected. He gets paid. He becomes a leading man in the city, and we need Chinese doctors." The Hakka pointed out: "It takes two more years to become a doctor. Leave that to the haoles. Your boy should be a dentist. Quicker and in the long run just as much money."

One hot July day in 1885 Nyuk Tsin was hurrying down Nuuanu, her two baskets of pineapples balancing on her carrying-pole the way conflicting advice balanced in her mind, and she was thinking of lawyer versus doctor and Asia versus America when two horses pulling a J & W dray reared in the air, dashed down Hotel Street, and threw their wagon against one of the poles that held up the roof of Asia Kee's Chinese restaurant. The first pole snapped off and the sudden weight thrown upon the second caused it to collapse, allowing the roof to fall into Hotel Street. No one was hurt and a Hawaiian caught the reins of the runaway horses and easily brought them to rest.

Asia, who was inside the restaurant, exploded onto the street shouting curses at the horses who had so unexpectedly plunged his dining room into chaos. Nyuk Tsin hurried up, adding to the confusion by shouting, "I saw them! I saw them!" And the Hawaiian policeman agitated everyone by roaring, "Don't bring those horses back this way! Turn them around and get them out of here!" When the beasts reared he bellowed, "Turn them around!" A man from J & W hurried up to assure everyone that the driver was at fault because he had stopped to watch a pool game, and was going to be fired; and then amidst the confusion Nyuk Tsin, herself in great agitation, saw her son Africa, who had been helping wash dishes at his brother's restaurant, moving among the crowd and quietening the Chinese. "All right, Wu Chow's Auntie!" he said forcefully. "No more shouting. Nobody's hurt. Did you see what happened? Where were you standing?" And while the policeman fought with the man who had caught the horses, making him turn them around lest they stampede again, Africa Kee quietly got the names of all who had witnessed the accident. "The driver was nowhere to be seen?" he asked repeatedly. "You saw the wagon hit the pole?"

By the time Africa reached the J & W man, the latter's story about the driver's having been in a poolroom had been changed. It was now quite a different story, but Africa had the names of everyone who had heard the first version. The extent of the damage was not great, and the cash award grudgingly given by J & W did not amount to much, but restitution was made and the money went into the fund that would send Africa Kee to Michigan . . . to become a lawyer.

He was seventeen years old when Wu Chow's Auntie made her decision, and the family had practically no spare cash to spend on their living in Hawaii, let alone to send a boy to America. Yet in those important days Nyuk Tsin started many ventures. She made Asia and Europe, who were already in business, borrow money to pay Africa's ship passage. She sold pineapples and vegetables six hours a day, tilled her fields eight hours and kept two for scouting around. Finally, one evening when the scholar at the Punti store assured her that the time was auspicious, she washed her muddy feet, brushed her one blue uniform, tied a widow's cloth about her sparsely haired head and topped it with her wicker hat. Brushing her cheeks with her hands so that she might look as presentable as possible, she left home without speaking to anyone, and walked resolutely down Nuuanu, where she purchased a bag of brown, chewy candies covered with poppy seed.

Clutching the candy in her hand, she entered busy Hotel Street, in the heart of Chinatown, and turned right, walking past Asia's restaurant and Europe's vegetable stand, while she looked for a narrow alley that cut back among a maze of Chinese shacks. At last she found it, and with a prayer to Kwan Yin for mercy on her mission, she ducked beneath the bamboo poles that suspended drying laundry completely across the alley. Finally she reached a kitchen door which belonged to a house somewhat more pretentious than the rest, yet one of which few haoles could have known the existence, for it was well hidden by hovels. This was the home of Ching, Honolulu's wealthiest Hakka, and it was presumptuous of Nyuk Tsin to be calling there. She knocked and waited obediently until the tall, well-fed mistress of the house appeared and looked out in the darkness to identify her impecunious visitor. The taller woman did not speak, and Nyuk Tsin said deferentially, "May a thousand benedictions fall upon you on this auspicious night, my dear mother-in-law." The phrase was an honorary one and implied no relationship, so the wealthy woman accepted it imperiously and said, "Come in, my dear sister-in-law. Have you had your meal?"

This again was a formality, so Nyuk Tsin replied, as custom required, "I have eaten, but how about you?"

She was impressed by the munificence of the kitchen and its close attention to detail. The two windows were sufficiently high so that the Ching money could not leak out; the doors were not in a straight line, which kept the dragon of happiness from escaping; and the land leading up to the doors did not slope away from the house, so that good fortune did not drift away. The kitchen had a brick stove on which a permanent teapot rested, and now the Chinese woman poured Nyuk Tsin a cup of the stale stuff, not too big a cup, which would have accorded Nyuk Tsin an esteem she did not merit, nor too small, which would have brought reflections of niggardliness upon the Chings.

"Be seated, my dear sister-in-law," the wealthy woman said. In her outward appearance, nothing betrayed the fact that she controlled a good deal of money. She wore no jewelry, no paint, no combs in her hair. Her simple dress was the same as Nyuk Tsin's and she also was barefooted; but to her visitor's calculating eye Mrs. Ching was obviously a person of wealth: her kitchen was crowded with food! Three hams hung from bamboo poles, and five glistening dried ducks, their bills hanging downward with drops of redolent oil gathering at the tips. There were bunches of white cabbage, baskets of vegetables and bags of nuts. Throughout the kitchen there was the grand confusion loved by people who have money, and Mrs. China grandly swept aside some of the clutter that hid her table, making a small space on which Nyuk Tsin placed her bag of candies. Neither woman spoke of the bag, but each was painfully aware of its presence, and as the conversation developed, they stared at the candies with positive fascination.

"Why do you come to my poor house on such an auspicious night, my dear sister-in-law?" the older woman asked with studied sweetness.

Nyuk Tsin sat with her stubborn, hard-working hands folded in her lap and her brown feet on the floor. Bluntly she said, "Since I am not as wealthy as my honored mother-in-law, I cannot afford to hire a go-between, so I have been shameful and have broken the rules of decent behavior. I have come to ask for your daughter, Siu Kim."

Mrs. Ching showed no surprise, but unconsciously she drew back and took her hands far from the candies. Nyuk Tsin detected this and was hurt, but she continued to smile frankly at her hostess. Finally, after an awkward moment, Mrs. Ching said in a silken voice, "I thought your son Ah Chow already had a wife."

"He does, my dear mother-in-law," Nyuk Tsin replied evenly, launching her first barb of the evening. "I arranged a very fine marriage for him with the Lam girl."

Mrs. Chin said, "A Punti, I believe?"

Nyuk Tsin dropped her eyes modestly and confessed: "A Punti, yes, but she brought a good deal of gold with her and now my son owns his restaurant."

"He owns the building?" Mrs. Ching inquired in surprise.

"Completely," Nyuk Tsin said with firmness, "but of course our family controls it."

"It was my understanding that your second son was intending to marry a Hawaiian."

"He is," Nyuk Tsin confessed. She waited so that Mrs. Ching could react with distaste, then added quietly, "I was able to find him a Hawaiian girl with several large pieces of land."

"Indeed! And does the land now belong to your family?"

"It does."

"Mmmmmm," Mrs. Ching mused. She leaned forward ever so slightly and the talk resumed. She said, "I observe that your youngest son plays mainly with Hawaiians. I suppose that one day he will marry one."

"There are many Hawaiian girls who seem to like my son, and fortunately they all have large land holdings," Nyuk Tsin said. Then, to establish herself on an equal footing with Mrs. Ching, she added boldly, "Since my family will not return to China, I think it best that the boys find wives here."

"So that you were even willing to allow your oldest son to marry a Punti?"

Nyuk Tsin was not going to be stampeded by this woman. With a good deal of self-possession she said, "I want my family to live in the new style. Not as in the High Village that you and I knew as girls."

Mrs. Ching sensed a rebuke in these words and said bluntly, "What you mean is that you are building a family into which a decent Hakka girl, like my daughter Siu Kim, would hardly want to marry and into which I would not permit her to marry."

This was an important speech, for although it was harsh, Nyuk Tsin did not know whether Mrs. Ching was formally ending negotiations or whether she was trying legitimately to undermine Nyuk Tsin's bargaining position so that when final discussions of money came up, the girl's side could drive a harder bargain. At any rate, Nyuk Tsin felt that the time had come for her to detonate her first bomb, so she dropped it gently, letting it explode among the hams and glistening dried ducks. "I realize, my dearest mother-in-law, that a wealthy woman like you would have objections to marrying a fine girl like Siu Kim into a poor family like ours, but there is one thing you have overlooked. Yesterday the scholar at the Punti store cast my son Africa's horoscope," and she placed on the crowded table, beside the bag of candy, a slip of paper, "and when it was done, the scholar gasped for sheer pleasure, for he said, 'I have never seen a finer horoscope for a young man in my entire life.' That's what he said."

The two women, neither of whom could read, studied the precious slip of paper, and Mrs. Ching asked cautiously, "Are you sure this is your son's?"

"It is."

"And it speaks well?"

Modestly Nyuk Tsin looked down at her feet. In a soft voice she said, "Money, knowledge, a position even better than a scholar in China, a long prosperous life with many children—those were the words for my son."

The two women sat in silence, for each knew what a rare thing was before them. They stared at the premonitory paper and slowly Mrs. Ching rose. "My dear sister-in-law, I think I had better make some more tea." With bounding joy Nyuk Tsin heard these words, for they erased any that had been said earlier, but modestly she kept her eyes down and did not watch Mrs. Ching as she brewed fresh tea—not the old stuff waiting on the back of the stove—and poured it into a fine China cup. This was, up to then, the moment of greatest triumph in Nyuk Tsin's life, and she tasted the fine fresh tea.

"Siu Kim," Mrs. Ching began on a fresh tack, "is an unusual girl and she has been asked for by more than a dozen men, some of them with considerable wealth." Nyuk Tsin sipped her tea and courteously allowed Mrs. Ching to run up the bargaining price for her daughter. Over the edge of her cup, the rude-mannered younger woman studied the bag of candies and thought: "I will let her talk about her daughter for five minutes, and then I'll explode my next cannon."

When Mrs. Ching finished explaining why, in common decency, she had to save Siu Kim for a wealthier man than Africa Kee was apt to be, Nyuk Tsin said bluntly, "It is not every day that an average Hakka girl like Siu Kim has a chance to marry a man who is going to graduate from a fine college in America and become a lawyer. I should think, as her mother, that you would jump at this opportunity and throw in a good dowry as well."

Mrs. Ching was stunned by this news, but she was no mean negotiator. She did not raise an eyebrow but asked in a silky voice, "How can a vegetable woman possibly send her son to America?"

Meticulously Nyuk Tsin counted off: "We own the land up Nuuanu. We own the land in the forest. We own very fine fields in Manoa. Asia owns his restaurant and Europe has paid large sums toward the building where his vegetable store is. Each of my sons works, as do I, and I am sure that right now we have enough money to send Africa to Michigan."

Mrs. Ching was visibly jolted by this narration and she now wheeled into position her heaviest ammunition: "Your son's prospects sound . . . well, interesting. But of course his father was a leper."

Nyuk Tsin did not flinch: "The main reason why I was able to make such a favorable marriage with the Hawaiian girl, who brought us so much land, was that the Hawaiians know me as the Pake Kokua, and they have said that if Africa does become a lawyer, they will send all their business to the son of the Pake Kokua."

The two tough-minded Hakka women glared at each other in mutual respect, and as they did so, Mrs. Ching made her decision. Imperceptibly, she allowed her right hand to steal across the table. She extended two fingers and slowly encircled the bag of brown candy dusted with poppy seeds. Noiselessly she pulled it toward her, and Nyuk Tsin, witnessing these climactic gestures, thought: "I must not cry." And she fought back her tears, lest they spill out of her sloping eyes and betray to the Ching woman her great joy. With this acceptance of the candy, the marriage was agreed upon.

Up to this time Nyuk Tsin had not yet seen Siu Kim, and of course Africa Kee was not even aware that his auntie was planning his marriage. Neither he nor Siu Kim was told anything, especially since the basic financial negotiations were to consume the better part of a year, but one day Nyuk Tsin saw the attractive girl for whom she had been bargaining, and she admitted to Mrs. Ching: "Your daughter, Beautiful Gold, is even more desirable than you told me." But as she said these words, she happened to look past Siu Kim, who was then thirteen, and in the doorway behind, wearing a blue and gold Chinese dress, stood Siu Kim's eleven-year-old sister, Siu Han, and Nyuk Tsin sucked in her breath with pleasure. "What is that one's name?" she asked, and Mrs. Ching replied simply, "Siu Han, Beautiful Girl, but she will be saved for a very wealthy man." Nyuk Tsin smiled at the little girl and remembered her name.

These were exciting years in the Kee house. The original grass shack had been replaced by one of the ugliest buildings in Honolulu: an unadorned two-story bleak wooden house, to which had been appended as afterthoughts a collection of lean-to sheds. A mango tree and a coconut palm gave some shade, but there was no lawn nor any flowers. Pigs were kept in the yard and chickens in the kitchen, but the dominant occupants were enormous Kimo, who did all the cooking for the family, and sprawling Apikela, who did the washing and made the poi. There was a running battle between Nyuk Tsin on the one hand and everyone else on the other: she liked rice and Chinese food; they insisted upon poi and American-style food. When, at the end of a long day's work she begged for rice, big Kimo at the stove shrugged his shoulders and the boys yelled, "Oh, Auntie! Who wants rice?" If she did, she had to cook it herself because Kimo refused to bother.

Her two married sons lived with her, of course, one family to a room, and Apikela took care of the babies that began to arrive regularly. What with the pigs and the chickens and the babies it was a noisy, happy island home. There were many like it, for Chinese and Hawaiians lived together easily. At the poolroom one day Kimo came upon a new importation from Portugal, a ukulele, and like a boy he badgered Nyuk Tsin until she bought him one. Then Apikela demanded one, and Europe's wife, and songs from the Chinese house filled the valley.

In the middle of 1886, when Africa Kee was eighteen, it was announced that early next year he would marry the wealthy Hakka girl, Ching Siu Kim. He started looking about the city to see who she was, and one day he saw her walking in Aala Park, but he could not be sure that she was the girl picked out for him, and he thought: "It would be pleasant if she were a girl like that one."

The wedding was an impressive affair, with many guests, for the Chings were important, and before Africa Kee finally climbed aboard the ship to go to Michigan, he was already the father of three children. Dutifully he took the family genealogical book and the poem to the scholar in the Punti store, and there the man gave his sons their names. The poem showed that the name of this fourth generation must be Koon, Earth, and accordingly the two boys' names were Koon Chuk, the Center of the Earth, and Koon Yuen, the Essence of the Earth Which Produces All, but their parents called them simply Sam and Harvey. The Chinese names were duly forwarded to the Low Village, so that when twenty-one-year-old Africa finally enrolled at Michigan he was not only head of a burgeoning family left behind in Honolulu, but also the member of a powerful clan whose existence had continued in the Low Village for thousands of years, but the memory which recurred most often to Africa as he studied law in Michigan concerned an event which took place on his last morning in Honolulu.

Nyuk Tsin assembled her five sons and led them to the letter-writer at the Punti store. There she delivered fifty dollars that the family in Honolulu desperately needed for its various ventures. Asia and Europe gasped to see this amount of money being stolen from the Kees, and certainly Africa could have used it in Michigan, but Nyuk Tsin said, "Your mother in China may need this money. It may be a bad year for the crops. It is your duty above everything else to pay respect to your mother." If, at Michigan, Africa Kee excelled at law it was partly because he understood the fundamental fact that law directs the ongoing of society. It is rooted in the past, determines the present, and protects the future. Better than any other student in the law school, Africa appreciated these conservative principles.

On the day he sailed to America on the H & H liner *Molokai,* Nyuk Tsin climbed aboard a little island steamer and made her first pilgrimage to her husband's grave at the leper settlement of Kalawao, for she, too, was imbued with this sense of continuity, and if her ablest son was that day setting forth for a new world, it was only because the dead gambler Kee Mun Ki had been good to her. This time the island steamer did not swing around the peninsula and throw its passengers brutally ashore into the cold and unprotected hell of Kalawao. The vessel sailed directly to the pier at Kalaupapa, on the kindly side of the peninsula, and discharged its cargo decently. Doctors and nurses were on hand to assist the new lepers, and the big white Missionary Home for Lepers provided them a place to sleep. At the Missionary Hospital they still found no medicine that combated the disease itself, but they found charitable care that protected them from pneumonia and tuberculosis, which had once been so prevalent.

Nyuk Tsin walked through the clean new settlement and up past the volcano crater. Then she stopped and an ache past understanding assailed her, for she looked down upon the most beautiful sight she had ever seen. It was more dramatic than the hills of China, lovelier than the valleys of Honolulu. In the distance rose the soaring cliffs of Molokai, with white spray beating upon their rock bases and gossamer waterfalls leaping from their summits to fall three thousand silvery feet. The ocean was blue and the small islands that clustered offshore formed handsome patterns. The fields of Kalawao, now empty of lepers, were soft and green as they had been a thousand years before that horrible disease was known in the islands. Two vacant churches, one Protestant and one Catholic, stood where once there had been terror. The house she had built with her own hands no longer had a roof. "How sweet," she thought, "were the days Mun Ki and Palani and I spent there. Oh, how I wish I could see those two good men once more." In her mind's eye she saw them not with noses and lips falling away and with stumps of hands, but as men. "How I would like to see them once more playing fan-tan on the shore."

That night she spent at Kalawao in the home of a Kokua she had known years before, and on the next morning at cockcrow, in the third hour, she left the house and went to her husband's grave, so that she would be there when his spirit rose to walk about the valley. In the moonlight she carefully replaced any rocks that had fallen away. She brushed the earth and pulled weeds. Carefully she erected a slab on which his name, Kee Mun Ki, had been printed in gold letters. Then she undid a bundle and ceremoniously placed a fine set of new dishes about the grave, putting into them the three required delicacies: roast pig, chicken and fish. On saucers she placed oranges, boiled rice, little cakes with caraway, and brown candies with poppy seeds. Then she lit a small candle, so that its incense would infuse the atmosphere and make it congenial to the ghost, and when these preparations were completed, she waited for the dawn.

When her husband's ghost appeared he found no tree to roost in, as he would have expected in China, where trees were plentiful and where they were kept near graves for just that purpose, but he did find a perching place on the rocky cliffs that rose behind his grave, and there in the warm sunlight, away from the cold ocean breezes, he sat with his dutiful wife.

She explained in a quiet voice: "Three of the boys are married, Wu Chow's Father, and although I was not able to arrange perfect marriages with huge dowries, I did as well as could be expected. Mrs. Ching, as you would expect, argued very strongly against me, and at the last she even brought up an unpleasant fact. 'Your husband died of leprosy,' she said, but I didn't lose my temper, for there was more important business at hand, and at last she gave in.

"Ah Chow has four children, Au Chow has three and Fei Chow three. I am going to try very hard to get Mrs. Ching's youngest daughter to marry Oh Chow, but I may have a good deal of trouble there, for the girl is a beauty and will be able to command a high price.

"At the house things go well. Kimo and Apikela look after things for us all, and they are precious people. The fields yield as before, and pineapples continue to sell well. Ah Chow has a fine restaurant that is always busy and Au Chow has a good vegetable business.

"But the good news, Wu Chow's Father, is that your son Fei Chow is already on a ship going to Michigan to study to be a lawyer. When I put him aboard the vessel I could see you and Palani in our little house down there, dreaming of going around the world and seeing strange places.

"Think! Think! Our son, our own child, is going to be a scholar!"

In gratitude for this great boon Nyuk Tsin fell silent and tears trembled on her lids, and the sun rose higher in the heavens, and she stayed by the grave. At eleven she asked, "Is it not hot on those rocks? You really ought to have a tree, Wu Chow's Father." And in the later afternoon she left the grave and the meal she had set for the ghost.

On her walk back toward Kalaupapa she passed the old graveyard and saw a new stone, larger than the others, and she wondered who of her friends lay buried there, so she waited until a Hawaiian leper came by with hardly any face, and she asked him, "Who lies in that grave?" And the man said, "Father Damien. He died one of us."

When she reached Kalaupapa she found that while she was talking with her husband the settlement had discovered who she was, and she returned to see many people waiting for her. "Pake Kokua!" they called, and many came to greet her who had known her in the evil days. Some she recognized, for the disease had been kind to them, but others no eyes but God's could see as human beings. "Pake Kokua!" they all cried. "It's good to have you back."

She sat down on a rock, a little Chinese woman with a sunburned face, and they gathered around. A priest came up and asked in Hawaiian, "Are you the one they call the Pake Kokua?" She said that she was, and he said, "You are remembered in this place." She asked if it was true that Father Damien had died of leprosy, and the priest said, "Only last spring." "Did he suffer?" Nyuk Tsin asked, and the priest replied, "Here everyone suffers." She said, "Kalaupapa is better than Kalawao used to be," and the young man said, "When the people in Honolulu wakened to their responsibility, it had to become better." She asked, "Have you found any drug that cures?" And he replied, "The infinite mercy of God has not yet shown us the way, but He will not permit a thing like leprosy to continue without a cure. Meanwhile, we pray."

In late 1889 Nyuk Tsin spent most of her spare time arguing with the Ching family about terms on which their youngest daughter, Chin Siu Han, might be given to her youngest son Australia. She told Mrs. Ching frankly, "The boy is very good at school, and I don't worry about him in that regard, but having grown up with Hawaiians he is more like them than a Chinese. He's got to marry a Chinese girl. Otherwise he will be lost to us."

Mrs. Ching pointed out: "You allowed Au Chow and Mei Chow to marry Hawaiian girls."

Nyuk Tsin argued: "Those girls brought much land with them, and the marriages were good for the boys. But Oh Chow's problem is different. He doesn't require land. He requires a strongminded Chinese wife." But her antagonist felt that Siu Han, being rather prettier than average, ought to be saved for a better prospect than Australia.

At this time Siu Han, who was now a sparkling Chinese girl of fifteen, had begun to show her headstrong nature and had broken away from the severe old Chinese custom which required girls to hide at home. While her sister, Africa's wife, tended her three babies, Siu Han liked to walk up and down Hotel Street, and because she was unusually attractive this caused much comment in the Chinese community. On one such trip she met Nyuk Tsin, who said to her, "Have you ever seen my son Australia?"

"No," the girl said.

"He's in his brother's restaurant. Let's have a bowl of noodles together."

So Nyuk Tsin and the pretty young girl went into Asia's place and sat down, and in a moment Australia appeared and was astonished to see them, for Wu Chow's Auntie had never before entered the place. He sat down with them, and Nyuk Tsin asked bluntly, "Don't you think your brother's wife's sister is attractive?" Obviously, Australia did, and after a few minutes Nyuk Tsin found occasion to leave the table and talk with her son Asia, who said, "It's disgraceful to bring a girl like that in here."

In the weeks that followed, Nyuk Tsin often asked Australia, "Why don't you help your brother at the restaurant?" And whenever her only unmarried son did so, Nyuk Tsin managed to find Siu Han somewhere in Chinatown, and she would bring the two together, so that before the year was out it was not Wu Chow's Auntie who was arguing with the wealthy Chings that they permit their only remaining daughter to marry Australia; it was the daughter herself who did all the talking. "My rascal girl," Mrs. Ching called her. Nyuk Tsin prudently dropped out of the picture, and in early 1890 a marriage was announced.

At the wedding Nyuk Tsin, then forty-three years old but looking closer to sixty, sat silent and thanked the Hakka gods that they had been so good to her; then her attention was attracted to a Hakka woman who had brought as a gift a small sandalwood box, carried from Canton, and as Nyuk Tsin smelled that aromatic present she thought: "This is indeed the Fragrant Tree Country."

B Y THE TIME the last decade of the nineteenth century opened, Wild Whip Hoxworth was concentrating his considerable energy on two projects: women and making Hawaii part of the United States. For a while his performance in the former field was the more spectacular, for after his divorce from the Spanish woman Aloma Duarte he spent his free time with a strange assortment of creatures who could be counted upon to drift ashore from passing ships. They were women without faces, but with memorable bodies, and it was uncanny how as soon as they touched shore they made a direct line to Wild Whip, as if he had the capacity to send out messages that he could be found lolling on the porch of the Hawaiian Hotel. Quickly, these drifting women moved their luggage— they never had much—into the rooms Whip occupied and after a while each moved along to Manila or Hong Kong. Many would have enjoyed staying, but Whip was too smart to allow that.

From time to time he spent his weekends in Rat Alley, across the river in Iwilei, and one of the most common sights at the Hawaiian Hotel, built by the king for the entertainment of important guests, was the deferential appearance of some Chinese brothel keeper with news for Whip that a new girl had come in or that an old one wished particularly to see him. It was understandable that women liked Whip, for at thirty-three he was tall and lean, with knife scars across his left cheek and black hair that rumpled in the wind. He had flashing white teeth and slow, penetrating eyes. He was careful of his appearance, and when he rode horseback along the dusty roads of his sugar plantations, he could speak to his hands in masterful pidgin, with appropriate touches of Chinese, Japanese, Hawaiian or Portuguese to fit the individual workman with whom he talked, but for all sentences, regardless of language, he adopted the lilting accent brought to the islands by Mexican cowboys, so that each statement ended with an upward song: "Eh, you Joe! What you theenk? You holo holo watah?" The words *think* and *water* were heavily accented and given an ingratiating melody. While his men were in the fields, tending the cane, Wild Whip often stopped by their homes to talk with their women, and it naturally happened that occasionally these women would appreciate his courtly manners and he found great pleasure in suddenly leaping into bed with them and having a wild few minutes, after which he called, as he rode off, "Eh, you Rosie, me? Take care you boy he come home, he one fine man I theenk." Twice he had been slashed at with machetes, and when he reflected upon that occupational hazard he supposed that some day he would die in a scene of wild brutality and the sanctimonious newspapers of the islands would scream the scandal, and at the prospect he laughed, thinking: "What a great way to die!"

Then, in late 1892, Wild Whip became galvanized into even wilder action in a completely different arena, for the United States was beginning to show signs of once more discriminating against the importation of Hawaiian sugar. The great planters of cane in Louisiana were determined to end the reciprocity arrangements whereby Hawaii sent sugar to the mainland tax-free while the United States was allowed to send certain goods into Hawaii and also to use

Pearl Harbor as a naval base. Cried the Louisiana sugar men: "We don't need their sugar and we don't need Pearl Harbor."

For thirty years the New Orleans sugar tycoons had been waging war against Hawaii, and they had managed to hold the profits of Hawaiian planters like Wild Whip Hoxworth to reasonable limits, but they had failed to kill off the industry. Now a new factor had entered the battle against Hawaii: the huge western states of Colorado and Nebraska were beginning to grow beets and to grind them into sugar, and they, too, wanted to destroy Hawaiian competition. Within a few years it was likely that a coalition of Louisiana, Alabama, Mississippi, Colorado and Nebraska, plus such new states as Wyoming and Utah, would form to drive Hawaiian sugar forever out of the market, and when this happened sugar planters like Wild Whip would see their massive fortunes begin to vanish.

"In sugar, there's only one rule," Whip told the sugar planters he had assembled. "Either we sell to the United States, or we don't sell. Our sole aim must be to protect that market."

"We're losing it," John Janders pointed out. "Right now I represent eleven of your major sugar plantations, and with the way those bastards from Louisiana and Colorado are trying to strangle us, I can see nine of your eleven outfits going into bankruptcy. One more serious cut in our American market, and I don't know what we'll do."

"Excuse me, John," Whip interrupted. "You're right in what you say, but I'm afraid you're mincing words. I happen to have the figures, and by God, nobody can listen to these without panic. Since the McKinley Tariff every damned sugar man in Louisiana and Colorado has been getting a subsidy of two cents a pound, whereas sugar imported from Hawaii has been penalized. What's it all mean? During the first twelve months of this McKinley abortion our profits have dropped five million dollars. I don't mean the profits of Hawaii. I mean the profits of the nine men sitting in this room. Now as to the actual invested value of our plantations, they've lost twelve million dollars. And it's going to get worse and worse."

He paused to allow discussion of the peril in which the Hawaiian sugar men found themselves, for up to the moment of this meeting, the great planters had known they were in danger but no one had had the courage to accumulate the depressing figures; now under Whip's lashing they had to face facts. Companies were going to go bankrupt and men were going to lose plantations their fathers had built.

"What do you think we should do?" John Janders asked. He was a year older than Whip and eight centuries more conservative.

Whip parried the question and observed, "Obviously, John, unless we do something we're going to lose Hawaii. It's going to subside into the barren, useless batch of islands it was in 1840." There was a hush, and Whip continued: "Those aren't just words, either. Two more bad years, John, and you'll be bankrupt. Absolutely pau. Dave Hale may be able to hold out a little longer, but Harry Hewlett can't." Then he thumped himself on the chest and added, "I'm good for eighteen months, and then I'm bankrupt. Gentlemen, I don't propose to go bankrupt."

It was a sober group of Hales, Hewlett and Janderses who listened to these gloomy but accurate words. Finally Dave Hale asked, "How you going to escape, Whip?"

With carefully studied words Whip replied, "I've asked that the doors be closed, gentlemen, because what you and I are about to do is ugly work, so if any of you have weak kidneys I'll give you time to go out and take a piss right now. And don't bother to come back." He waited in silence and could see that the sugar men were breathing hard. "I'll give you two more minutes," he said, "and after that, there's no turning back." He put his watch on the table, and when the seconds had passed he said simply, "Gentlemen, we are now duly constituted as the Committee of Nine and no one here must have any illusions. This afternoon I want you quietly to buy up all the available guns in Honolulu." He put his left hand to his chin and with his thumb rubbed the scar that crossed his face like jagged lightning. When the shock of his first command had been absorbed he added, "Yes, we're going to launch a revolution, win control of these islands, and turn them over to the United States. Once we've done that, Louisiana and Colorado can go to hell. They'll be powerless to destroy us."

"Do you think the United States will accept us?" Dave Hale asked timorously.

Wild Whip dropped both hands on the table and said harshly, "Gentlemen, the days ahead are going to be damned difficult. But there is one thing we must never doubt. The United States is going to accept Hawaii." He thundered his fists on the table and repeated, "We are going to be part of America."

"How . . ." Dave Hale began.

"I don't know how!" Whip interrupted. "But we're going to join America and we're going to make all the goddamned money growing sugar that we want to."

John Janders spoke quickly: "Whip, you know I'm even stronger for sugar than you are, because I've got more to lose. But take my advice on one thing. Don't organize this revolution around sugar. Among ourselves, here in the committee, all right. But don't let the outside world know. For them you've got to have an idea bigger than sugar."

Young Hale added, "John's right. The big American newspapers will never support us if our revolution is built on sugar."

One of the Hewlett boys, who owned the biggest sugar plantation of all, suggested: "Somehow we've got to work in the word democracy. Red-blooded Americans on these islands are sick of living under a corrupt monarchy."

"That's it!" John Janders cried. "Something the American Congress can get hold of. American citizens yearning to be free."

Wild Whip smiled at his associates. "You fellows have a lot of sense. I agree with you that if we stand forth as a sugar revolution, the bastards in Louisiana and Colorado would crucify us. I can hear them now, bleeding for the monarchy. But I have a better idea, gentlemen. You and I are going to start this revolution, and we're going to direct it, and when everyone else gets scared, we're going to fire the guns. But," and he paused for effect, "not one of us is going to appear before the public."

"Who will?" Dave Hale asked.

"We'll get the lawyers who handle our plantation affairs, and the newspaper people and some schoolteachers and a couple of ministers," Whip snapped. "This is going to be the most respectable revolution in history. You're going to hear more highflown sentiments than you thought existed, because I've decided on the ideal man to stand before the public."

"Who you thinking of?" Hale probed.

Whip looked directly at the young man and said, "Your Uncle Micah."

David Hale gasped and said, "He'll never revolt against the monarchy. He's a citizen of Hawaii and takes it very seriously."

"We're all citizens of Hawaii," Whip replied, "and we all take it seriously. That's why we're going to save these islands."

"But Uncle Micah's been an adviser to the crown, a personal friend of all the kings. He's an ordained minister . . ."

"For those very reasons we've got to have him," Whip interrupted. "He won't support us willingly. He'll preach against us, and he'll despise our revolution, but the force of circumstance will make him our leader. Believe me, it'll be Uncle Micah Hale with his long white beard who will send the final letter to President Harrison: 'Hawaii is yours.' "

At this point John Janders threw some very cold water upon the revolution: "I got a letter from Washington which said that everyone there thinks Grover Cleveland will be elected again this year."

At the mention of this portly, strong-willed Democrat, the Committee of Nine grew glum, for in his previous administration Cleveland had delivered several staggering blows against Hawaiian sugar and it was likely that he would do so again; but more important, the idealistic reformer had come out strongly against the spirit of manifest destiny then popular in America. "The United States wants no empire," Cleveland had proclaimed, and it was the shadow of this great bulk that fell across the incipient revolution. But not even Grover Cleveland frightened Wild Whip Hoxworth: "To hell with his mealy-mouthed nonsense about international morality. We'll start the revolution right away. Wind it up fast. And have Uncle Micah throw the islands to Harrison before the next election is held. By the time Cleveland's President, we'll be part of America."

"Can we do it in the time available?" one of the Hewlett boys asked.

"If we work," Whip replied. The Committee of Nine broke up their first meeting and each man took upon himself three jobs: buy all available guns; find respectable citizens to stand before the public as front men of the revolution; and test every friend to see who could be depended upon to help overthrow the Hawaiian monarchy. When the frightened, but determined, sugar planters were gone, Whip Hoxworth was left with the most difficult job of all. He had to find some way of making white-bearded, righteous old Micah Hale assume leadership of the revolt.

It was not a strong monarchy to begin with. In 1872 the great Kamehameha line had ended in sickness and frustration, to be followed by a succession of amiable but incompetent alii. One had sought to revive paganism as the consolidating force of Hawaiian life; another had tried to abrogate the constitution and take Hawaii back to an absolute monarchy unrestrained by any middle-class legislature; there had been palace revolutions, the election of kings according to their personal popularity, and a shocking scandal in which one king was caught trying to peddle an opium concession twice over to two different Chinese gamblers. This sad decline of the Hawaiian state had caused deep concern among the missionary families, and although some men of rectitude like Micah Hale loyally supported the royal line, they were grieved when attempts were made to legalize opium and lotteries.

Even so, had the customary succession of amiable and handsome kings continued and had they allowed their iron-willed New England advisers to run the kingdom, Micah Hale and his responsible associates would probably have been able to keep the tottering monarchy viable; but on January 29, 1891, royalty of a far different sort ascended the throne and trouble was inescapable. Queen Liliuokalani was a short, moderately stout woman of regal bearing. She had large, determined lips, a high pile of graying hair, and wrists laden with jewels. In black satin fringed with ostrich feathers and bearing a feathered ivory fan, she was an imposing woman with a stubborn will. It was her custom to deliver important messages seated in front of a golden-yellow cape of feathers, both because this was an antique royal custom which set off her dignity and because she was slightly crippled and did not move with grace. For many years she had been plain Lydia Dominis, strong-minded wife of a slim haole of Italian descent, with whom she lived in a large white mansion called Washington Place. Upon the death of her brother, the king, she ascended the throne, bringing with her a desire to reverse the trend toward haole domination and a determination to cast aside New England influences like Micah Hale.

She was a highly intelligent woman and had traveled to the courts of Europe, where the role played by Queen Victoria impressed her, and she had a love of political power. Had she acquired the throne immediately after the passing of the Kamehameha, she might have made Hawaii a strong and secure monarchy, for she had a lively imagination and much skill in manipulating people; but she attained ultimate power too late; republicanism had infected her people; sugar had captured her islands. And although she did not know it, her enemy was no longer the stately political leader Micah Hale; it was the gun-running, determined plantation owner Wild Whip Hoxworth. Against the former she might have had a chance; against the latter she was powerless.

Without ever identifying her enemies, this headstrong, imaginative woman tried to combat republicanism, Congregationalism and sugar, but she succeeded only in driving those disparate forces together in a coalition. Hawaiians who were tired of the monarchy and its silly pretensions conspired against the queen, although most who joined the coalition did so in hope of currying favor with the Americans. Missionary families came out boldly against the corruption, absolutism and paganism of the monarchy, but many who cried loudest in public against these evils also owned businesses that would prosper under American rule. And lawyers were forceful in their arguments against the excesses of the monarchy and in defense of human rights, but mostly they fought to protect sugar. As the queen's obstinate reign continued, the coalition against her became more powerful.

In early 1893 the headstrong woman determined to eliminate the influence of men like the statesman Micah Hale and his insolent nephew Whip Hoxworth. Accordingly, she let it be known that she indended to abrogate the present constitution, which hampered her absolute power, to put the legislature under royal control, and to revoke the voting rights of many citizens and generally restore the ancient prerogatives of the monarchy. She was a notable figure when she made this disclosure: queenly, posed against yellow feathers dating back two hundred years, a lei of plumeria about her shoulders and a train of satin four feet long piled about her crippled foot. As she spoke she did not make it clear, but it was her intention to take Hawaii back to the good old days that France had enjoyed in 1620.

That afternoon Wild Whip Hoxworth summoned the Committee of Nine, and his conspirators convened in an upper room of Janders & Whipple on Merchant Street, an earlier proposal that the members meet at Hoxworth & Hale having been vetoed because of the fear that Micah Hale, still stoutly attached to the monarchy, might hear of the plot. Wild Whip was concise in his opening statement: "Our headstrong queen is to be congratulated. Her silly acts have made revolution obligatory."

The Hewlett boys were fearful of overt action and counseled caution, but straightforward John Janders said gruffly, "We've got to overthrow the monarchy in the next two days or lose our last opportunity to capture the government."

"Do you mean to incite a bloody revolution?" David Hale asked.

"If necessary," Janders replied, and no further vote was taken.

"Then it's revolution!" Whip Hoxworth announced, issuing a statement rather than a question. The committee cheered, and Whip said, "Our plan must be to strike quickly and to gain control of all the main points in the city."

"What about the other islands?" one of the Hales asked.

"To hell with the other islands," Hoxworth snapped. "The post office, the banks, the palace, the armory. We win them and we control Honolulu. Win Honolulu and we have Hawaii. Janders, tell the committee what you learned today."

John Janders rose, coughed, and spoke formally: "This morning I had a two-hour talk with the American Minister, and we studied the law with great care. It is quite clear, he advised me, that if the revolution quickly acquires control of the major points in Honolulu, so that an observer could logically say, 'the committee controls the city,' the United States will have sufficient cause to contend that we are the *de facto* government. The Minister will promptly recognize us. The monarchy will be at an end. And we will be on our way to incorporation within the United States."

"But what about the American troops in the harbor?" one of the Hewlett boys asked. "Will the ship captains send their troops ashore to fight against us?"

A broad smile came over the scarred face of Wild Whip as he lounged at the head of the table. The committee looked at him, satisfied that he had uncovered some trick for neutralizing the American forces, but he did not divulge the plan. "Tell them what we arranged, John," he said.

Burly John Janders explained: "We have entered into a solemn agreement with the American Minister and with the ship captains that as soon as we start the revolution, they will send ashore the maximum number of troops. Their orders will be simple: 'Protect American lives.' "

"But we're Hawaiian citizens," David Hale protested.

"We're also Americans," Janders replied blandly, "and we're the Americans who are going to be protected."

Fighting back a sardonic smile, Whip leaned forward across the table and said, "It's a plan that can't fail. We launch our drive against the ten key targets. Immediately fighting begins, American troops storm ashore. What can the Hawaiians think? They'll reason, 'The American troops have come to fight against the queen!' So they'll throw down their arms and we'll capture the ten key spots. And as soon as we control them the American Minister will announce: 'The United States formally recognizes the *de facto* government.' At that moment what in hell can the queen do?"

John Janders cried, "How can we lose?"

Soberly David Hale pointed out, "We can lose easily . . . if Uncle Micah appeals to the world powers against our revolution."

"He will not do so," Whip promised.

"He's a man of great honor," Hale insisted. "And he's sworn allegiance to Hawaii."

"It's my job to get Uncle Micah on our side," Whip said flatly. "He'll be there."

The Hewlett boys consulted, and one said, "We'll leave the revolution unless we can depend on Micah Hale to represent us before the world."

"He will be with us," Whip promised. "Not in the fighting. He's too old a man for that. But when it's over, he'll step forth as our leader."

"Can we depend on this?" the Hewlett boys asked.

Whip leaped up and crashed his chair aside. "Goddamn it!" he yelled. "If our whole success depends on Micah Hale, do you suppose I'm going to let him escape? Of course you can depend upon it. He'll be with us."

Then Janders spoke: "Whip's got to take care of that. We've got to stir up public enthusiasm for the revolution. What we need is a big mass meeting on Monday. Lots of speeches about human decency and men's inalienable rights."

"But I don't want to see any of this committee making speeches," Whip warned. "Get some of the lawyers and men like Cousin Ed Hewlett. He's part-Hawaiian and rants well."

Things seemed to be going so well that the Committee of Nine—that is, eight of them—began to relax: the revolution was at hand; the ten key spots were invested; the American Minister had recognized the new government; President Harrison had accepted it as part of the Union; and sugar was more profitable than ever. But Wild Whip brought the conspirators back to reality, pointing out in icy tones: "At the mass meeting on Monday I want everyone to be within quick reach of his guns."

"Will there be trouble?" one of the Hewletts asked.

"Not if we're ready for it," Whip replied.

As the others quietly left the cellar and circulated through the agitated city, dropping ideas here and there, Wild Whip walked eastward on King Street toward the Hale mansion across from the palace, and when he reached the white picket fence and the wide green lawns in which Malama Hale took such pride, he nodded graciously to that stately half-Hawaiian lady and asked, "Is Uncle Micah in?"

"He's in his study," Malama said gently.

Whip entered without knocking, and before he spoke he closed the door. His uncle was surrounded by his father's missionary books, brought over from Lahaina, and by a substantial theological and legal library. As principal adviser to four kings he had been required to give many legal opinions, and his fine mind found pleasure in doing so. From the 1870's on he had paid little attention to the ventures of H & H, leaving that to the Hoxworths and his nephews; he had gladly accepted his proper share of the firm's enormous profits and had applied his income to the betterment of Hawaii. The Missionary Home for Lepers at Kalaupapa, the library, Punahou and the church had benefited from his charities, but mainly he had spent his income on helping to run the government efficiently. When one of the kings took a grand tour around the world, stopping off in most of the major capitals, it was Micah Hale who accompanied him at his own expense and who paid for many of the essentials. Most of the legal books owned by the cabinet were also purchased by Micah, for he constantly harangued his contemporaries: "We are all of mission extraction, and until Hawaii is completely stable, the job of our fathers is not completed." No island throughout the Pacific ever had a better public servant than Micah Hale, for if he was liberal with his money, he was thrice generous with his energy. Of the fine laws that were often cited in Europe to prove that Hawaii was civilized, an astonishing proportion had sprung from his energetic mind; and what was remarkable in that period was his capacity to rise above personal interest: any laws passed in his regime that favored either sugar planters or shippers were proposed not by him but by the Janderses, the Whipples and the Hewletts who proliferated in the government. Four kings had thought of Micah Hale as their one trustworthy American adviser, yet each had known that he favored the ultimate submission of Hawaii to the United States. The present queen knew of his stand, and it had irritated her and she had dismissed him from all of his offices. He was seventy years old, of better than medium height, stately in bearing and with a long, spadelike white beard. He dressed only in white, including white-powdered shoes, and in public refused to wear glasses. This was the man that faced Whip Hoxworth on the night of Saturday, January 14, 1893.

"Uncle Micah," Whip began forthrightly, refusing the chair offered him, "there's bound to be a revolution within the next two days."

"Have you fomented it?" the spare old man asked.

"Yes, sir, I have. And the Hale boys and the Hewletts and Janderses. The Whipples have also joined us and my brother. There can be no retreat."

Micah leaned back in his office chair and studied his nephew. "So there's going to be a revolution?"

"Yes, sir." Whip was accustomed to addressing older people in the style he had been taught aboard the whaler.

"How old are you, Whip?"

"Thirty-six."

"How many wives have you had?"

"Two."

"How many knife battles in Iwilei?"

"Twenty, thirty."

"How many illegitimate children?"

"I'm supporting half a dozen or more."

"Do you know what they call you around town, Whip?"

"Wild Whip. They call me that to my face. I don't care."

"I wasn't thinking about what they call you to your face. I was thinking of the other name."

"What other name?"

'The Golden Stud. That's how you're known, Whip. And you consider yourself qualified to step forth as the leader of a commune dedicated to the overthrow of a duly constituted government?"

"No, sir, Uncle Micah, I don't."

"I thought you said your group was plotting the revolution."

"We are. And I'm directing it. And when I say, 'Fire,' by God, sir, we'll fire. So don't be in the way. And I'm well qualified to direct a revolution, Uncle Micah, because there's nothing on this earth I fear, and within two days I'll have a new government in Hawaii. But I am not qualified to step forth as the public leader of the revolution. You're right on that, and I know it."

"Who is to be the leader?"

"You are." As Micah gasped at this suggestion, Whip sat down.

The two men, so unalike, stared at each other, and each sensed the tremendous New England force of the other. Micah Hale lived by a code of fierce rectitude and he persuaded those who associated with him to do the same, while Whip Hoxworth had never outgrown the brawling fo'c's'ls of the Pacific. He knew that all men were swine and that they enjoyed being kicked into line; yet on the eve of the revolution he also knew that certain focal points of history required a man better than himself to stand forth as leader. There were limits to what even Whipple Hoxworth could attain without the assistance of decency.

"This is pretty much a sugar revolution, isn't it, Whipple?" Micah asked.

"From my point of view, yes, sir. From yours, no, sir."

"How can there be two interpretations of an evil act, Whipple?"

"If there weren't two interpretations of our necessary act, Uncle Micah, I wouldn't be here pleading with you. I want a revolution so that sugar will be forever made safe in these islands. You want it so that the islands can join the United States in accordance with a destiny that you foresaw fifty years ago. Uncle Micah, you've always been right, and you are tonight. Hawaii is doomed unless it contrives some trick to make America accept these islands. And I control that trick. Sir, the only way your dream will ever be realized is through me."

"Not so, Whipple. The day will come when Washington will see the inevitability of annexation."

"Never! Only actions make things inevitable."

"Justice and dawning conscience produce inevitability. Slowly, Washington will see what the right step is. And we must rely upon Washington to take it."

"No! If you live to be a hundred, you'll die talking about the slow inevitability of justice. There's going to be a revolution, my revolution, and you're going to lead it so that your dream of justice can come true."

Micah Hale rose slowly and stared down at his vigorous young nephew. "I am appalled, Whipple, that you so misjudged me as to think that I would be partner to such an evil action. I will not divulge your plans, although I should. But now you had better go."

To his surprise, his scar-faced nephew did not rise. Insolently he kept his position, raised one foot to kick his uncle's chair into place, and said, "Now we understand each other. Sit down, Uncle Micah, and let's talk about revolution. Let's forget everything we've said so far. And you might as well forget about threatening to divulge our plans to the government. Charley Wilson knows about them and wanted to arrest us all, but the cabinet didn't have the guts to back him up. So let's see what you and I can do for one another. You despise my position and I think yours is pathetic. Okay, let's not revert to that again. Uncle Micah, there's going to be a revolution in two days. You can't possibly stop it. We've got the American Minister waiting on the edge of his chair to recognize our *de facto* government. We've got American troops out there in the harbor just itching to swarm ashore and protect decent Americans against Hawaiian savages. We've got our targets pinpointed and our schedules laid. Even if you were to inform the queen herself, you'd only move up the timetable by the hours you stole from us." He leaned forward and looked hard into his uncle's eyes. "It's a revolution, Uncle Micah."

Micah Hale was not the kind of man to find his lips going dry at moments of crisis. He had weathered too many abortive revolutions when only his courage had saved the government from irresponsible outrage, and he did not sense any unusual quickening of his pulse now. With eyes as hard as his nephew's, but from a different cause, he said, "You've thought of everything."

"Let's accept the revolution as accomplished," the young sugar planter proposed. "I'm not the man who ought to stand before the bar of world opinion and explain why it was necessary. My record wouldn't read very well in London or Berlin. So let's say my part of the revolution has been successful, and that all it represents is my personal greediness . . . sugar . . . land. What happens then? America won't accept us. Maybe Japan would."

The idea that Wild Whip was developing had several other subsidiary clauses, but bearded old Micah Hale did not hear them, for with the mention of the word Japan he was suddenly transported to the mysterious city of Tokyo in the year 1881, when he served as privy councilor to the last king of Hawaii on the latter's triumphal journey around the world. The royal party was stopping in a Japanese mansion that contained no chairs; the floors were of the most exquisite wood polished by centuries of use and the sliding doors were joyous to behold. It was March and a horde of busy gardeners scurried about pruning pine trees with gnarled red branches. A row of plum trees showed white blossoms, cherries were eager to burst into bloom, and as the first warm days of the year approached, the Hawaiian party relaxed to enjoy the gracious scenery.

Suddenly Micah had looked up and asked, "Where's the king?" No one knew. At first there was excitement; then, as the hours passed, there was panic, on the part of both the Americans and the Japanese, for the King of Hawaii was clearly missing. No one had seen him leave the spacious grounds of the mansion and a frantic search revealed no betraying signs of foul play. He had vanished, a great hulk of a man dressed in conspicuous western clothes and a long black London-tailored coat. It was one of the few times that Micah Hale had experienced real dread, for he was aware that in relatively recent years Japanese samurai, outraged at the invasion of foreigners, had sliced off the heads of several. Consequently he knelt in the chairless room and prayed: "God, save the king! Please!"

In the third hour of panic, the king appeared, in jovial mood, holding his shoes. He had obviously been crawling through the stream that separated the mansion from the Imperial Palace, and he had obviously been having a rare time. He refused to explain where he had spent the missing three hours and he went to bed that night highly pleased with himself. In the morning the emperor's chamberlain waited until the king was occupied with other matters and then quietly slipped in to see Micah.

"Utterly extraordinary," the little man in the shiny black London morning coat said in good English. "Yesterday afternoon we heard this strange noise at the Imperial Palace, and the guards were about to shoot an intruder when I saw that it was your king. He was barefooted, muddy, laughing. His great brown face was wet with perspiration when he pushed aside the shoji, walked with his dirty feet over the tatami and said, 'I'd like to talk with the emperor.' We were appalled, because nothing like this had ever happened before, but Mutsuhito is a superb man and he said, 'I'd like to talk with you.' And they went into Mutsuhito's private audience chamber. And what is astonishing, they stayed there for nearly three hours."

Micah Hale wiped his forehead and straightened out his beard. "Believe me, Excellency, it was not I who sent the king."

"Hardly," the chamberlain replied. "In view of what he talked about."

"What did he speak of?" Micah probed.

"Don't you know?" the Japanese asked.

"No."

"The king said, 'Hawaii is tired of being pushed this way and that by America and England and Russia. It is a Pacific power and must remain so.'" The chamberlain paused for effect and it became apparent that Micah was expected to pursue the inquiry.

Instead he relaxed, bowed to the chamberlain and said, "I am grateful to you for having looked after my king."

"Are you a subject of his Majesty?" the Japanese asked.

"Yes. When I took service with the government, I swore allegiance to Hawaii."

"How interesting. Would you care to join me in a cup of English tea?"

"I'd be delighted," Micah said. They walked through lovely pine-laden gardens and came to a small rustic house, where a serving-maid waited.

"What your king proposed," the Japanese said, afraid that Micah was not going to ask, "was that the heir to his throne, the Princess Kaiulani, be given in marriage to the son of the emperor, so as to bind Japan and Hawaii closer together."

Micah lost his aplomb. He choked on his tea, spilled it, slammed the cup down, and gasped, "What did you say?"

"He proposed an alliance of mutual interest, to be sealed by the marriage of the princess to one of our princes. When I heard the facts, Mr. Hale, I choked, too."

The two diplomats stared at each other, aghast. Finally Micah stammered, "What had I better do?"

"You'd better get the king out of Japan immediately."

"Of course, of course. But I mean . . . with the emperor?"

"A formal offer of marriage has been extended. It's got to be considered by the Imperial family . . . and the staff. In a year or so we'll send an answer."

"Excellency, please take pains to insure that the answer is no."

"It is now beyond my control. How old is your princess?"

"Let me see, she's six."

"We have time."

That night Micah completed plans to whisk his unpredictable king out of Japan, but as they sat at supper, the king still having said nothing concerning his impromptu visit with the emperor, Micah studied his fat, jolly face and thought: "I wonder what transpires in that surprising brain? How did he think up a state marriage with the Japanese royal family? Where did he get the idea for an alliance with Japan? Such a thing would destroy all hope of eventual union with America! My goodness, what can we expect him to do when he gets to Europe!" From that prophetic day, Micah Hale had appreciated the inherent danger that Hawaii might one day associate itself with Japan. He had therefore fought against the importation of Japanese farmers onto the sugar plantations, but greedy men like John Janders and the Hewlett boys had insisted upon it. He was frightened by the adroit manner in which the little Japanese, who had begun arriving in the 1880's, accommodated themselves to Hawaiian life, and he had tried to pass laws forbidding them to leave the plantations and open stores. When alone with friends he often referred to the "Yellow Menace," and he foresaw that the Japanese would multiply and grasp for political power in a way that the more easygoing Chinese never would. Therefore he had constructed an international-relations platform that had only two planks: "Make Hawaii American. Keep the Japanese away."

Consequently, when Wild Whip uttered the phrase, "It begins to look as if Japan might . . ." vibrant chords were struck in Micah Hale's memory. "What was that last point, Whip?" he asked his nephew.

"I was saying that if you want to see your basic dream come to pass, you can do it only through me."

"I mean about Japan," Micah explained, and suddenly Whip realized that his uncle had heard nothing of his last statements. He had been day-dreaming about some forgotten incident that Whip didn't know about, but with sure instinct, Whip knew that his uncle's reverie concerned Japan and that it had produced fear. He therefore decided to play upon that fear.

"I was saying about Japan, that there is a good deal of evidence that the Yellow Menace would be glad to take Hawaii if the United States doesn't."

"Do you think so?" Micah asked fearfully.

"What more natural?" Whip asked, shrugging his shoulders.

"Do you think Japan would extend herself so far from her own islands?"

"Not by design, but if we don't get Hawaii into the United States, she'll have to."

"I am terribly afraid of that," Micah admitted. "And if not Japan, then England or Germany."

"Obviously, if we allow the islands to lie around unwanted, someone will surely grab them."

"But suppose the monarchy cleansed itself," Micah temporized. "Suppose we got rid of Liliuokalani and put somebody else on the throne?"

Wild Whip saw that his uncle was clutching at straws, so he hammered home his points: "The revolutionists will tolerate no Hawaiian monarch. None that you could propose, Uncle Micah, would be acceptable."

His nephew's position startled the white-bearded old man and he said, "Then even though you are uncertain of what comes next, you're determined to overthrow the monarchy?"

Whip was not to be trapped into such an admission of irresponsibility. Suavely he replied, "But we are certain of what comes next, Uncle Micah. You come next. You justify us before world opinion and lead us into the United States. It's what you've always wanted. It's what you know is right."

The two men fell into silence, as Micah, a leader on whom all the glories and perquisites available to the kings of Hawaii had been visited, considered what he must do. He was caught in wild currents of confusion, and any antagonist other than Wild Whip Hoxworth would have retired at this moment and allowed his uncle to study the matter through the remainder of the night, but now the mark of Whip's character stood out. He rose from his chair, went to the door, stretched as if he were leaving, looked out at the stars dancing over Diamond Head and turned back toward his uncle. Lifting a chair and placing it so that its back faced Micah, he sat with his arms folded across the top of the back and his legs straddling the seat. This brought his scarred face close to his uncle's, and he said coldly, "Uncle Micah, so far we've been sparring. Now we've got to get down to the bedrock base of this revolution. There's no escape. You've got to stand before the public."

Micah replied: "I cannot betray the Hawaiians who have befriended me."

Whip said: "But you're ready to betray the Americans who own these islands."

Micah replied: "When I took my oath of allegiance to Hawaii, I believed what I was doing. I became a Hawaiian."

Whip said: "I didn't. I remained an American. I'm going to call on American warships to protect my property for me."

Micah replied: "You can act that way. I can't."

Whip said: "That is not the action we're talking about, Uncle Micah. I'm saying that I am determined to lead a revolution against a weak and corrupt form of government. I'm going to win my part of the revolution. But only you can carry it to its logical conclusion: union with America."

Micah replied: "And that I refuse to do."

Whip said: "If you shared your stubborn conclusion with the silly queen, she'd applaud. But if you told Aunt Malama how you were wasting the tides of history and allowing them to slip away from you, even though she's Hawaiian she'd say you were stupid."

Micah replied: "I cannot betray these good people."

Whip said: "Then you will allow the forces of history to betray them to Japan."

Micah replied: "That's a risk we'll have to take."

Whip said: "It's not a risk, Uncle Micah. It's a certainty. These islands are doomed. There is only one way to save them. Pick up your revolution and lead it to a good end."

Micah replied: "I will not prostitute myself to protect a gang of sugar robbers."

Whip said: "Unless you protect us, every good thing you have ever wanted for Hawaii will be lost."

Micah replied: "I would relinquish even union with America rather than attain it as a result of unchristian acts."

Whip said: "I am surprised you speak of Christianity. Are you willing to abandon these islands to opium, lotteries, debauchery, with streets unsafe for women?"

Micah replied: "These are problems we must solve within the framework of established government, not by revolution."

Whip said: "Where was the framework of your established government when the late king used to convene his Ball of String Society?"

Micah replied: "That was an aberration. God has surely punished him for that."

Whip said: "It was the mark of the monarchy. The old fool stood facing a crowd of beautiful women and threw a ball of string at them. He held one end and the girl who caught the ball followed him obediently to bed."

Micah replied: "I hardly expected you to preach morality."

Whip said: "I'll preach anything that will end the monarchy."

Micah replied: "The one evil thing I did in my life was to ally myself with your grandfather against my own father. God has never forgiven me for this, and I often wake at night in dreadful sweat and lie there for hours reflecting upon the devilish compact I made with Captain Hoxworth. Now you ask me to make a worse with his grandson. I can't risk any more sleepless nights, Whipple."

Whip said: "The alliance between you and old Rafer Hoxworth may have been unholy in its inception. But look at the good it's done Hawaii. The building, the jobs, the ships, the fields. Somebody had to accomplish those things, Uncle Micah. Your influence in doing them the right way was fundamental. Now you have got to ally yourself with me to insure a proper culmination to our revolt."

Micah replied: "Must a good man always use such evil instruments as you and your grandfather?"

Whip said: "Yes. Because good men never have the courage to act. You can only direct and safeguard movements already set into motion by men like me."

Micah replied: "I will not compound the evil I did once. I will not help you, Whip."

Whip said: "You do not hurt me, Uncle Micah, but you destroy the future of these islands."

He bowed and left his austere uncle. It was nearly three in the morning when he walked down the path to King Street, and his last view of Micah was of the white-bearded old man sitting erect at his desk, staring at his books.

* * *

At the secret meeting of the committee held the next day, Sunday, January 15, Wild Whip reported frankly to his conspirators: "Uncle Micah will not join us."

"Then I can't either," said David Hale. Two of the Hewletts also withdrew.

John Janders suggested: "We'd better not try to force the revolution. If Micah Hale's against it, he might inflame public opinion against us. Then we'd be lost. I'm going to call off tomorrow's mass meeting."

There was a buzz of excitement and Wild Whip could feel the resolve of the would-be revolutionists ebbing away like the surf after a high tide. Men in groups were discussing how, having just coached Ed Hewlett in what to tell the mob tomorrow, they must now cancel his oratory.

"You may have misunderstood me," Whip said quietly. The revolutionists stopped retreating, eager to hear any words of direction. "I meant to say that Uncle Micah will not join us willingly. What I didn't say was that I shall force his hand, and make him join. Everything goes ahead as planned. In two days, gentlemen, Hawaii will be a republic, and the men in this room will govern it. With Micah Hale as our face to the world."

"How do you propose accomplishing that?" one of the Hales asked. "If Uncle Micah makes up his mind . . ."

"Your uncle is a patriot," Whip replied. "He loves Hawaii and is loyal to it. He will never see these islands disintegrate into formless revolution. He'll be with us."

"How will you force his hand?"

"I think we can get the American troops to march ashore tomorrow night . . . just after the mass meeting. This will accomplish two ends. It will encourage our side and scare the hell out of the monarchists. We occupy the government buildings, throw the queen out, and on Monday morning Micah Hale will have to join us."

"Are you certain of this?" one of the trembling Hales asked.

"I am going to begin drafting the proclamations now," Whip replied, "for him to sign, and I want David Hale and Micah Whipple to help me."

The revolution that overthrew the Hawaiian monarchy and passed the government into the hands of the sugar planters was under way. In her palace, the wild-willed queen shuddered as she saw American troops file ashore to invade her territory. She was disposed to fight them, for she knew that this was a cruel perversion of the ordinary relationships between sovereign nations, but the sugar planters quickly immobilized her loyal troops, and she was left defenseless, a stubborn, anachronistic woman in her mid-fifties, regal in appearance but totally unaware that the nineteenth century was ebbing to a close and taking with it the concepts of government to which she adhered.

However, in the dying moments of her reign she was not completely without support, for after her troops were disbanded without firing a shot, a squad of volunteer loyalists materialized from the alleys of Honolulu and marched out to defend their queen. In their ranks, and typical of their quality, waddled the old kanaka maile gatherer, Kimo. He had a musket that he had grabbed from a man in a pool hall and he held his uniform—a pair of sagging pants and that was all—about his waist with a length of red rope. His hair had not been combed for some days, he needed a shave and he was barefooted, but like his companions he gave every evidence of being willing to die for his queen. The sparkling American troops with new rifles watched in amazement as the volunteers marched up to give them battle, but a courageous officer in whites ran unarmed to the leader of the irregulars and said, "There's no war. The queen has abdicated."

"She's what?" the leader of the loyalists asked.

"She's abdicated," the young American said. Then he shouted, "Anybody here speak Hawaiian?"

A haole bystander idled up and asked, "What you want, General?"

"Tell these men that there is to be no war. The queen has abdicated.

"Sure," the haole agreed. Turning to Kimo and his men he said, "Eh, you kanaka! Liliuokalani pau. She go home. You pau too. You go home."

And so far as the actual fighting was concerned, in this manner the revolution ended. Kimo trundled his unused musket back to the poolroom and listened to the gibes of his friends. Then in great disturbance of spirit, for he knew that he had participated in the death of a world he had loved—the horses prancing in gold tassels, the royal guard marching in bright uniforms, the queen going forth in a gilt carriage—he walked slowly down Beretania Street and up Nuuanu to the small house where he lived with his wife Apikela and his Chinese family. He went directly to bed and lay there without talking or laughing until he died.

The provisional government, with Micah Hale as ostensible head and the sugar planters directing from behind, swept away the seventeenth-century anachronisms proposed by Queen Liliuokalani. Each act of the efficient new government was directed toward one clear goal: union with America. David Hale and Micah Whipple were rushed to Washington to force a Treaty of Annexation through the Senate before congenial President Harrison and his Republicans left office on March 4, because it was known that the newly elected President, Grover Cleveland, opposed what had been happening in Hawaii; and soon frantic appeals for moral support were speeding back to Honolulu, for the treaty commissioners Hale and Whipple reported: "There is considerable opposition to the manner in which the revolution was carried out. Cannot Micah Hale make a strong statement, relying upon his faultless reputation to give it force? Else we are lost."

It was under these circumstances, in February, 1893, that Micah Hale retired to his study on King Street and wrote for a New York journal: "Any sane man looking at these islands today has got to admit that they require supervision by the United States of America. The indigenous citizens are for the most part illiterate, steeped in idolatry, committed to vain shows of monarchical display and totally unsuited to govern themselves." In these harsh but true words, the son of a missionary, in his seventy-first year, summarized what his group had accomplished; but since he wrote as a profound patriot and as one who loved Hawaii above all else, he did not understand what he was saying. Furthermore, he went on to point out a great truth that others both in Hawaii and America were overlooking: "Hawaii cannot lie idle and unwanted in the middle of the Pacific. The islands seem to lie close to America, but they also lie close to Canada and on the route from that great land to Australia and New Zealand. There is every reason for Hawaii to become Canadian. They also lie close to Russia-in-Asia and except for an accident of history might even now belong to that great power. And to anyone who has sailed from Honolulu to Yokohama or to Shanghai, these islands lie perilously close to Japan and China. For more than half a century I have believed that their destiny lies with America, but it is not as I once thought an inevitable destiny. If at this crucial moment of history, our logical destiny is frustrated, an illogical one will triumph and

Hawaii, the gem of the Pacific, will belong to Canada or to Russia or to Japan. It is to prevent such a catastrophe that we pray for the United States to accept us now." This widely reprinted article was taken from the Hale mansion on King Street by Wild Whip Hoxworth and delivered to one of his ships waiting in the harbor, but as old Micah Hale handed it to his nephew, he was freshly appalled that he should be using such an evil agent to accomplish so good a purpose.

Micah's plea achieved nothing, for Louisiana and Colorado sugar interests prevented the lame-duck Senate of February, 1893, from jamming the Treaty of Annexation through, and five days after Grover Cleveland assumed the Presidency he sternly withdrew the treaty and rebuked those who had sought to foist it upon the American public. Now doleful news reached Hawaii. The Secretary of State wrote: "The United States will not accept the Hawaiian Islands on the terms under which they have been offered. It would lower our national standard to endorse a selfish and dishonorable scheme of a lot of adventurers. I oppose taking these islands by force and fraud, for there is such a thing as international morality."

President Cleveland was of a similar opinion and personally dispatched an investigator to Honolulu to inquire into America's role in the unsavory revolution, and by one of the tricks of history the investigator turned out to be a Democrat from Georgia and a member of a family that had once held slaves. When preliminary news of his appointment reached Hawaii, the Committee of Nine were apprehensive lest he report against them, but when his slave-holding status was revealed, they sighed with visible relief. "As a good Southerner he'll understand our problems," John Janders told the conspirators, and they all agreed.

But Whip Hoxworth, considering the matter carefully, judged: "We may be in for deep trouble. Since Cleveland's investigator comes from Georgia, he probably despises niggers."

"Of course he does," Janders agreed. "He'll see through these Hawaiians right away."

"I doubt it," Whip cautioned. "Granted that he hates niggers. As a sensible human being he'll try to compensate and prove that he doesn't hate other people with dark skins."

"Why would he do that?" Janders demanded.

"Don't ask me why!" Whip replied. "Just watch."

And when the investigator arrived he did exactly as Whip had predicted. Hating Negroes at home, he had to like Hawaiians abroad. It was a profound compulsion and it permitted him, a Georgia man, to understand the revolution better than any other American understood it at the time. He talked principally with Hawaiians, was bedazzled by the idea of speaking directly with a queen, became an ardent royalist, and suppressed evidence given by white men. His report to President Cleveland was a crushing rebuke to the sugar men; they had, he discovered, conspired with the American Minister to overthrow a duly constituted government; they had worked in league with the captain of an American vessel; they had deposed the queen against the will of the Hawaiian people; they had done all this for personal gain; and it was his opinion that Queen Liliuokalani, a virtuous woman, should be restored to her throne.

His report aroused such a storm in Washington that David Hale and Micah Whipple saw there was no hope of forcing the United States to accept Hawaii, and they returned to Honolulu with the glum prediction: "We will never become part of America while Grover Cleveland is President. His Secretary of State is already asking, 'Should not the great wrong done to a feeble state by an abuse of the authority of the United States be undone by restoring the legitimate government?' There's even talk of restoring the queen by force of American arms."

"What would happen to us?" members of the committee asked.

"Since you're American subjects," a consular official explained, "you'd be arrested, hauled off to Washington, and tried for conspiring to overthrow a friendly power."

"Oh, no!" the conspirators protested. "We're Hawaiian subjects. Our citizenship is here."

September and October, 1893, were uneasy months in Hawaii, and Wild Whip's gang maintained power by only a nervous margin. Each arriving ship brought ominous news from Washington, where sentiment had swung strongly in favor of Queen Liliuokalani, and it was generally assumed that she would shortly be restored to power; but just before this was about to occur the obstinate woman committed an act so appalling to the Americans that she forever discredited the monarchy. What Wild Whip had been unable to gain for himself, the queen won for him.

Late in the year President Cleveland dispatched a second investigator to check upon the specific terms under which Liliuokalani should be returned to her throne, for as Cleveland pointed out, America never wished to profit from the misfortunes of her neighbors. The new investigator plunged the Committee of Nine into despair by announcing that the annexation of Hawaii by America was no longer even under discussion, whereupon he entered into formal discussions with the queen as to what steps she wanted America to take in restoring her crown.

No difficulties were encountered, and the investigator had to smile when the queen pointed out, "One of the charges made against us most often, sir, was that we were a small kingdom overly given to a love of luxurious display. To this charge I must plead guilty, because from the first our kings selected as their advisers men of the missionary group, and we found that no men on earth love panoply and richly caparisoned horses and bright uniforms and medals more than men who have long been dressed in New England homespun. I have four pictures here of state occasions. You see the men loaded with gold and medals. They aren't Hawaiians. They're Americans. They demanded the pomp of royalty, and we pampered them."

"Speaking of the Americans," the investigator asked, "what kind of amnesty will you provide for the revolutionists?"

"Amnesty?" Queen Liliuokalani asked, inclining her large and expressive head toward the American. "I don't understand."

"Amnesty," the investigator explained condescendingly. "It means . . ."

"I know what the word means," Liliuokalani interrupted. "But what does it mean in this circumstance?"

"Hawaii's undergone some unfortunate trouble. It's over. You're restored to your throne. President Cleveland assumes that you'll issue a proclamation of general amnesty. It's usually done."

"Amnesty!" the powerful queen repeated incredulously.

"If not amnesty, what did you have in mind?"

"Beheading, of course," the queen replied.

"What was that?"

"The rebels will have to be beheaded. It's the custom of the islands. He who acts against the throne is beheaded."

The American investigator gasped, then swallowed hard. "Your Excellency," he said, "are you aware that there are over sixty American citizens involved?"

"I did not know the number of traitors, and I do not think of them as Americans. They have always claimed to be Hawaiians, and they shall be beheaded."

"All sixty?" the investigator asked.

"Why not?" Liliuokalani asked.

"I think I had better report to President Cleveland," the perspiring investigator gulped, excusing himself from the august presence; and that night he wrote: "There are factors here which we may not have considered adequately in the past." After that there was no more talk of restoring the monarchy.

Thus, in late 1893, it became apparent that the United States would neither accept Hawaii in view of the besmirched character of the men who had led the revolution nor restore a monarchy that threatened to behead more than sixty American citizens. So the islands drifted year by year, ships without moorings. Hawaiians grew to hate the Haoles who had defrauded them of their monarchy, and haoles despised the weak-kneed American senators who refused to accept their responsibilities and annex the islands. Sugar planters suffered, and it looked as if Colorado and Louisiana would keep Hawaiian sugar out of the mainland permanently. The great ships of the H & H carried less cargo, and both the British and the Japanese began wondering what, in decency, they ought to do about this rudderless ship drifting across the dangerous Pacific. In desperation the sugar men proposed a treaty which would allow them to peddle their accumulating sugar to Australia, and it was predicted that Hawaii would soon have to join the British Empire.

At this juncture Micah Hale saved Hawaii, and he was well prepared for his role. Years before in Lahaina his missionary father had kept him penned up in a walled garden where he had done nothing but study history, the Bible and his father's fierce sense of rectitude. Particularly, he had served two apprenticeships which now fortified him in the job of building a new government: he had watched his father translate the book of Ezekiel, so that the stern phrases of that obdurate prophet lived in his mind; and he had listened when his lame little father explained how John Calvin and Theodore Beza had governed Geneva in accordance with the will of God.

The first thing Micah Hale did was to deprive Wild Whip Hoxworth of any connection with the government. Next he insisted upon moral laws and fiscal responsibility. But above all, like a true missionary, he wrote. For the newspapers he wrote justifications of his government. For magazines he explained why the Hawaii revolution, which he had not wanted, was similar to the uprisings that had brought William and Mary to the English throne. To Republican senators he wrote voluminously, providing them with ammunition to be fired against the Democrats, and to long-forgotten friends across America he wrote inspired letters, begging them to accept Hawaii. He lived solely for the purpose of making his islands part of the United States, and his pen, as it pushed across paper in the quiet hours after midnight, was the only real weapon the islanders had left.

It was not a liberal government that Micah founded. When the wealthy men who were to draw up a new constitution met, he lectured: "Your job is to build a Christian state in which only responsible men of good reputation and solid ownership of property are allowed to govern." Explicit property qualifications were set for all who served and all who voted to have them serve. No man could be a member of the senate who did not own $3,000 worth of property untouched by mortgages, or who did not possess a yearly income of $1,200. In order to vote for a senator, a man was required to own $3,000 worth of property or to have an income of $600. Explained Micah: "In other parts of the world the uneducated workingman raises his voice in anger against his superiors, but not in Hawaii." Wherever possible, advantages were given to plantation owners, for upon them rested the welfare of the islands.

On one point Micah was adamant: no Oriental must be allowed to vote or to participate in the government in any way. "They were brought to these islands to labor in the cane fields, and when their work was done they were supposed to go back home. There was no intention that they stay here, and if they do so, there is no place in our public life for them." Therefore, at Micah's suggestion, cleverly worded literacy tests were required for suffrage, and no Chinese or Japanese, even if he were wealthy and a citizen, could possibly pass them.

In many respects Micah's government was too liberal for the sugar men who had thrown it into power, and there were many Hales and Whipples and Hewletts among the missionary group who opposed his radical liberalism, while the Janderses and Hoxworths considered him insane with French republican principles; for once the electorate had been restricted to the well-to-do, Micah was lenient and just in all other matters. He insisted upon trial by jury, the rights of habeas corpus, freedom of religion and all the appurtenances of an Anglo-Saxon democracy. But when in the later stages of the constitutional convention he was asked, "What kind of government are you building here?" he replied quickly, "One that will mark time decently until the United States accepts us."

From this great basic principle he never wavered. A lesser man than Micah might have been tempted by his power, but this austere New Englander was not. He awarded himself no medals, erected no fanciful structures of power about his erect white-suited figure. In the five years following the revolution of 1893 this ordained minister never once let a day pass without getting down on his knees and praying, "Almighty God, bring our plan to fruition. Make us part of America."

Micah's training as a Calvinist enabled him to face many crises with an absolute conviction that he was right, and when ugly decisions had to be made, he was willing to make them. In 1895 an armed revolution broke out against his government, and with unequivocating force he put it down, then arrested Queen Liliuokalani for her supposed complicity in it. When weak-livered men counseled caution in dealing with the fiery queen, Micah said, "She will be tried on charges of treason against this republic." And he stood firm when a jury subservient to the sugar men brought in a verdict of guilty. Of course, any other jury would have had to do the same, for the queen, refusing to honor the usurpers from America who had stolen her thrown, naturally worked against them and, although there were conflicting reports on the matter, probably also encouraged her followers to open rebellion; the new nation had no recourse but to try her for treason, and when the sugar men found her guilty, it was Micah's responsibility to imprison her.

The powerful, headstrong woman was incarcerated in an upper room of the palace, and while her imprisonment was rigorously policed, it was never physically unpleasant, and before long her adherents were circulating the greatest state paper ever produced by a sovereign of the islands. It was a song transcribed by Liliuokalani while in prison, and although she had composed it some years before, it had gained little notice; now its lament swept the island and the world, "Aloha Oe": "Gently sweeps the rain cloud o'er the cliff, borne swiftly by the western gale." One of the missionary men said of this song: "While she was free Queen Liliuokalani never did a thing for her people, but when she was in jail she expressed their soul." Micah Hale, hearing the melody, said, "Let her go free," and she left for Washington, there to fight against him bitterly.

When the revolution was put down and the new government stabilized, it seemed for a brief interval as if President Cleveland and the Democrats might accept Hawaii. Mainland newspapers were beginning to write: "The moral stature of Micah Hale has gone far to correct the evils perpetrated by younger Americans during the revolution." At last Micah reported to his cabinet: "I am beginning to see hope."

And then Wild Whip Hoxworth exploded across the front pages of America, and editors wrote: "The violent young man has served to remind us of the viciousness whereby men like himself stole Hawaii from Queen Liliuokalani." And hope of annexation evaporated.

The trouble started during a three-day orgy at a Chinese brothel on Rat Alley in Iwilei. Whip had driven down to see a Spanish girl picked off a ship just in from Valparaiso, and he was enjoying himself when one of the sailors from the ship appeared with a claim that the girl belonged to him by right of purchase. A dreadful brawl ensued in which the intruding sailor was well whipped and kicked about the face. When he recovered, he stormed back into the brothel with two friends armed with knives, and they started to carve pieces out of Whip's face, but the Valparaiso girl sided with Whip and crashed a stool into the face of the leader, who, already weak from the beating Whip had earlier administered, collapsed, whereupon Whip kicked him about the head so furiously that the man nearly died.

Wild Whip was not arrested, of course, not only because the affair had happened in Iwilei, which was more or less outside police jurisdiction, but also because there were many witnesses to the fact that three men had come at him with knives, and he had two scars to prove that they had cut him before he had manhandled them. This affair might have passed without more than local notice except that the wounded sailor was a man of obstinate character, and as soon as he was discharged from the hospital he bought himself a gun, waited for Whip in a Hotel Street bar, and shot him through the left shoulder as he walked by.

It was news of this shooting that reached America, where it vitiated much that Micah Hale had been accomplishing, but insofar as Hawaii was concerned, the worst was yet to come, for at the height of the scandal, Wild Whip got married, and this was almost insupportable, for the girl he married—with his left arm in a sling—was Mae Forbes. She was a beautiful girl of twenty, with long black hair, sinewy charm and perfect complexion. She had a soft low voice and was known to be of impeccable reputation, for her father, recognizing her beauty, had brought her up with extra care. Normally, the marriage of a vigorous young man like Wild Whip to a beautiful girl like Mae Forbes would have been acclaimed, especially as it was a love match and there was some hope that Mae might tame the fiery Hoxworth.

Instead, the marriage was so offensive to Hawaii that it overshadowed all of Wild Whip's former behavior, because Mae Forbes sprang from a rather curious parentage. Her grandmother was the daughter of one of the lesser alii families from Maui, and her grandfather, Josiah Forbes, was a strong-minded, able Englishman from Bristol, who had jumped ship on the Big Island to make a small fortune pressing sugar. Later he married his Maui sweetheart, a fine Hawaiian woman, and they had a pert daughter, but she was a headstrong girl who liked to do as she wished, and at the age of nineteen she married a Chinese farmer named Ching, so that her daughter who went by the name of Mae Forbes was really Ching Lan Tsin, Perfect Flower Ching, and her marriage to Whipple Hoxworth was the first example of an Oriental, or part-Oriental, in her case, marrying into a major island family. It was a terrifying foretaste of the future, and Wild Whip was ostracized.

Even though his behavior had damaged Hawaii he would probably have been allowed to remain in the islands except for a public brawl he engaged in with the Hewlett boys. It arose when he found that some of the Committee of Nine had developed second thoughts about the revolution and were now preaching against union with America: "Somebody pointed out that as soon as we come under American law, our contracts for forced labor will be declared void, and we won't be free to import any more Japanese."

"Anything wrong with that?" Whip asked scornfully.

"How can we grow sugar without contract labor?"

"Frankly, and all sentiment aside, what good does contract labor do you?"

"Well, they've got to work where we say, at a fixed wage, and if they don't we can depend on our judges to make them."

"Well, I'll be goddamned!" Whip snorted. "Don't you men ever read the papers? Of course our labor laws will be rejected by America."

"Then we don't want to join America," one of the Hewlett boys said.

"What do you propose?" Whip asked politely.

"Join England. She allows contract labor. Or go it alone."

Whip was stunned. The revolution was slipping away from him. First Cleveland frustrated it and now the original conspirators were talking of union with England. "Look," he said carefully, "you don't need the old labor contracts. For the last eleven years I've not dragged one of my men into court. If they want to leave, okay. I give them good food, a fair deal, a little humor, and they make more sugar for me than they do for all of you put together. Believe me, that's the pattern of the future."

One of the Hewlett boys was offended by this vision and added, unwisely, "There's one more thing you do for the men, Whip."

"What?"

"You also sleep with their wives."

Like a volcano about to build a new island, Wild Whip erupted from his chair, lunged at the Hewletts and would have maimed the man who had insulted him had not other committee members pinioned him.

That night Micah Hale summoned Whip to his study on King Street. "You must leave the islands, Whipple."

"But the revolution's falling apart!" Whip protested.

"Revolutions always do," Micah replied.

"These poor bastards are talking of joining England, or going it alone. Just to make a few more dollars on their labor contracts."

"That's all beside the point, Whipple. You're contaminating the new nation, and for the good of all, you've got to go."

"But I'm determined to fight this insidious idea of surrender. I'll not let this revolution . . ."

"Get out!" Micah thundered. "I'm trying to save Hawaii, and I can't do it if you're here. You're an evil, corrupt bully, and these islands have no place for you. Go!"

The old man shoved Whipple from the door, so in the vital years that followed, Wild Whip traveled abroad with his Chinese-Hawaiian wife, his two facial scars offsetting her crystalline beauty; and from a distance he followed the affairs of home. He was in Rio when word arrived of McKinley's election to the Presidency, and he paused in his work long enough to tell Ching-ching, as he called his wife, "In two years the islands'll join America. Thank God it's over."

"Shall we return for the celebrations?" Ching-ching asked.

"No," Whip scowled. "It's Uncle Micah's show. All I did was get him started." He said no more about annexation, for he was on the trail of something that was to have almost as profound an effect upon Hawaii as her union with the United States. One morning he burst into his wife's room in their hotel in Rio de Janeiro, crying, "Ching-ching! I want you to taste something."

"What are you doing?" she laughed, for she was not yet out of bed and he was wheeling in a small table bearing one dish, a knife and a fork.

"I'm bringing you one of the most delicious things yet invented. Tuck a towel under your chin." He threw her one of his shirts and tied the sleeves about her pretty olive throat. Then from a paper sack he produced a large, golden, barrel-shaped pineapple. Holding it aloft by its spiny leaves, he asked, "You ever see a more perfect fruit than this?"

"Very large for a pineapple," Ching-ching remarked. "Where'd you get it?"

"More than six pounds. They tell me ships bring them down here regularly from French Guiana. They're called Cayennes, but wait till you taste one." With a large, sharp knife Wild Whip proceeded to slice away the hard outer skin and the series of eyes. Soon a most delicious aroma filled the room and a golden juice ran down off the tip of the knife, staining the tablecover.

"Watch out, Whip!" his wife cautioned. "It's dripping."

"That's what makes it smell so good," he explained. With a sturdy cut across the middle of the pineapple he laid it in half, then sliced off a perfect circle of heavy, golden, aromatic fruit. He slapped it onto the plate, handed Ching-ching a fork and invited her to taste her first Cayenne.

"That's heavenly!" she cried as the slightly acid juice stained her chin. "Where did you say they grow?"

"Up north."

"We ought to plant these in Hawaii," she suggested.

"I propose to," he replied.

When Micah Hale was approaching seventy-six and was more tired than he dared admit, word reached Honolulu that in Washington the House of Representatives had finally approved annexation by a vote of 209 to 91. That night Micah's vigil began, for at dinner he said to his wife Malama, "We have two more weeks to wait, and then we'll know what the Senate is going to do."

"Are you confident?" his gracious Hawaiian wife inquired.

"If prayer to an understanding God is efficacious, then I am confident."

The Hales ate in candlelight and sat across from each other so that verbal communication was quick and direct. Malama, in her sixty-fifth year, was stately rather than vivacious. She had not gone to flesh as had so many of her Hawaiian sisters, and her silvery gray hair was complemented by the pale light. She retained her saucy manner of tilting her head quizzically when an idea amused her, and now she said softly, "It will be proper for Hawaii to submerge itself in America. We're a poor, weak group of islands, and anyone who had really wanted us in the last fifty years could have snatched us. It's better this way."

Micah, momentarily relaxed by the good news from Congress, asked, "Do you know, Malama, how sorry I am that it had to be your husband who did the things of the last five years?"

"It had to be somebody," she said to the erect, austere missionary.

"Of all the Hawaiians, you understood most clearly," he said. "But I suppose that's to be expected. Noelani's daughter and Malama's granddaughter." At the mention of these distinguished names he unexpectedly found tears in his eyes, and he wanted to hide his face in his hands, but Malama saw them, and if she had been sitting beside her husband, she would, Hawaiian-fashion, have comforted him, but on this important night they sat apart and only ideas sped between them, not love. Micah said, "It would have been so much better if you had been queen and not Liliuokalani. You would have understood, but she never could."

"No," Malama said slowly, "it was better that we had a headstrong, volatile Hawaiian. Let the world see us dying as we actually were."

"Dying?" Micah repeated in surprise.

"Yes, dying," Malama said with subtle firmness. "Soon our islands will be Oriental and there will be no place for Hawaiians."

His wife's comments were strange, and Micah pointed out: "But in the constitution we were careful to put up safeguards against the Japanese."

"That's only a paper, Micah," she pointed out. "We Hawaiians know that we're being pushed over in the canoe."

"You'll be protected!" Micah cried.

"We had an earlier constitution that was supposed to protect us," Malama said, "but it didn't prevent the sugar robbers from stealing our lands . . . and then our country."

"Malama!" Micah gasped. "Are you contending that only cupidity directed this revolution? Do you refuse to see the forces of American democracy at work here?"

"All I can see is that when our fields were barren no one wanted us, when they were rich with sugar, everyone wanted us. What else can I conclude?"

Micah was disturbed by the turn this conversation was taking and he went far back into memory: "Do you recall the first time I ever saw you? In San Francisco? And I said then, before I ever saw a sugar field, 'Hawaii must become a part of the United States?' I thought so for moral reasons, and my motivations have never changed."

"Not yours, Micah. But others' changed. And in the end you were pitifully used by a gang of robbers."

"Oh, no, Malama! As it worked out, it was I who used them. Hawaii's going to be annexed, on my terms."

"It was stolen by fraud," Malama said coldly. "We poor, generous Hawaiians were abused, lied about, debased in public and defrauded of our nation."

"No!" Micah protested, rising and walking around the table to be with his wife.

"I would rather you did not touch me now, Micah," she said without bitterness. "What do you think I have felt, when I met with my Hawaiian friends, and they asked me, 'How could Micah Hale write the things he did about us?' "

"What things?" Micah cried, returning disconsolately to his chair. "I never wrote anything about you."

To his surprise, Malama took from her pocket, where in bitterness she had kept it until this moment should arise, a clipping from one of his major articles, and in sorrow she read it: " 'The indigenous citizens are for the most part illiterate, steeped in idolatry, committed to vain shows of monarchical display and totally unsuited to govern themselves.' What abominable words."

"But I wasn't writing about you," he protested. "I was writing to help make these islands a part of America."

"You were writing about Hawaiians," Malama said quietly.

Micah, in his white suit, sat staring at the tablecover brought years ago from China. He was astonished at his wife's position in this matter and he thought of several lines of explanation that might be helpful in describing the choices he had faced, but when he looked up at her grave, accusing face, he realized that none would be of use. Therefore he said, "I am sorry if I have offended you, Malama." And she replied, "I am sorry, Micah, if I have brought up unpleasant subjects on your night of triumph. But we must not fool ourselves by words. Hawaii was stolen. Its liberties were raped." In stately manner this daughter of the alii rose, kicked her train behind her, and left the dining room. Micah, disconsolate, watched her depart, then dropped his head on the table for some minutes, after which he rose and walked to his study, where he composed a long and passionate letter of instructions to his representatives in Washington, telling them: "You must see every senator at least once a day. Tell him that the manifest destiny of America consists of an extension of God's grace to these islands. We cannot delay much longer, for the Japanese and English are beginning to make unpleasant moves and tardiness is suicide. Plead with them. Leave no argument to chance, and if the senators from Louisiana and Colorado fight with dirty weapons, fight back. We have got to make these islands American in this session. To your hands I commit the fate of Hawaii."

During the days that followed, Micah and Malama Hale avoided each other as much as possible. With each elating letter from Washington, for chances in the Senate looked increasingly good, the distance between the American missionary and the Hawaiian alii grew greater, and it was borne home to Micah a thousand times how sorrowful a thing it is to destroy a sovereignty. It was right that Hawaii become American. It was inevitable, and he was increasingly proud of his role in accomplishing this benediction; but it was also tragic, and in these last days the tragedy was greater than the joy.

On July 6, 1898, the American Senate finally accepted Hawaii by a vote of 42 to 21. In the Senate gallery David Hale, Micah's personal emissary to Congress, wept, and his assistant Micah Whipple said, "This is the beginning of America's greatness in world politics." One week later, on July 13, the news reached Honolulu, and an excited sailor discharged a gun. Nerves were on edge and some thought this might be the beginning of a counter-revolution, but soon the electrifying word swept through the city and men ran out into the streets and embraced one another. It was a wild, joyous day, with enough noise to be heard around the globe, but Wild Whip Hoxworth, in the jungles of French Guiana, did not hear the news for almost two months. When he did he said to Ching-ching, "Well, we're Americans at last. You feel any different?"

"You may be an American," Ching-ching replied. "I'm still a Chinese. I don't think your country will ever want me."

On August 12, 1898, by proclamation of President McKinley, Hawaii joined the United States, but in the islands this happy event seemed more like a funeral than a birth. No Hawaiians appeared that day, for they mourned in secret, but a good many Americans in tight coats, brown plug hats and patent-leather shoes roamed the streets wearing gaudy badges that showed Uncle Sam entering into matrimony with a Negro woman—the mainland manufacturers having been unable to visualize a Hawaiian—accompanied by the rubic: "This is our wedding day."

Out of deference to the Hawaiians, the day's ceremonies were kept brief. Soldiers marched and sailors came ashore from an American warship. At eleven forty-five a distinguished group of men responsible for the revolution appeared on the grandstand, led by Micah Hale. As he took his place, he looked out upon the gathering and saw Americans, Chinese, Portuguese and Japanese, but never a Hawaiian. When the once-impressive band began the Hawaiian anthem, the gasps that came from the horns would not have done justice to a group of beginners, for one by one the weeping Hawaiian members of the band had crept away, refusing to play the final dirge of their nation. The anthem ended in a sob and Micah began reading: "With full confidence in the honor, justice and friendship of the American people . . ." He had first dreamed of this day while crossing the Nebraska prairies in 1849. Now, almost half a century later, he had made it come to pass.

On the platform that day there was one Hawaiian, Malama Kanakoa Hale, for Micah had pleaded with her: "It is your duty," and as an alii she had understood these words. Dressed in regal black and purple, with a flowery hat and an ivory fan, she was an imposing figure, the final symbol of her defeated race. Even when the warships boomed their salute of twenty-one guns and when the flag she had loved so well came down, she had the fortitude to stare ahead. "I will not let them see me weep," she muttered to herself.

But when the ceremonies were ended, a most shameful thing occurred, and to Malama it would always epitomize the indecency by which her nation had been destroyed. As the Hawaiian flag fell, an American caught it and, before he could be stopped, whisked it away to the palace cellar where, with a pair of long shears, he cut the emblem into strips and began passing them out as souvenirs of the day.

One was jammed into Micah's hand and he looked down to see what it was, but his eyes were so strained from writing letters on behalf of Hawaii that he could not easily discern what he held, and imprudently he raised it aloft. Then he saw that it contained fragments of the eight stripes symbolizing the islands of Hawaii and a corner of the field, and he realized what a disgraceful thing had been done to this proud flag. Hastily he crumpled it lest his wife see and be further offended, but as he pushed the torn cloth into his pocket he heard from behind a cry of pain, and he turned to see that his wife had at last been forced to cover her face in shame.

As THE NINETEENTH century drew to a close, and as Hawaii accustomed itself to being a part of the United States, it gradually became apparent to the residents of Honolulu that in the Kee family Hawaii had another of those great, intricate Chinese units which were destined, by force of numbers alone, to play an important role in the community. There was old Mrs. Kee—known to the family simply as Wu Chow's Auntie—now fifty-two years of age and bent from arduous work. There were her five clever sons, Asia, Europe, Africa, America and Australia, and their five wives, a prolific brood with a total of thirty-eight children and a promise of more to come. Thus, as the century ended, there were already forty-nine Kees in the family, many of them approaching marriageable age. In two more decades the Kees would probably number more than two hundred.

To Nyuk Tsin, who still sold pineapples and taro-stem pickles through the town barefooted, her two baskets hanging down from her bamboo carrying-stick and her conical woven hat darting along the alleys of Chinatown, the multiplication of her offspring was gratifying indeed, and whenever on her daily huckstering trips she reached the point where Hotel Street crossed Maunakea, in the heart of Chinatown, she felt a glow of satisfaction. Years ago she had made a cold calculation that of her five sons—who shared the world among them—it would be Africa who would grow into the ablest. He had been given the education, and now at the age of thirty-one he was a leader in the Chinese community: Africa Kee, Lawyer. The sign in gold letters said so, but what it did not say was that the building in which his office stood was also his and that several of the stores in Chinatown belonged either to him or to his brothers.

Actually, the specific title to these buildings was of little consequence, for although to outward appearances it was Asia Kee who owned the profitable restaurant on Hotel Street, it was really owned by the Kees as a family. Under Nyuk Tsin's guidance, the five brothers had formed a combination known in Hawaii by the expressive term hui, pronounced hooey—"Them Kees got a hui workin' "—and it was this informal corporation, the great Kee Hui, that effectively controlled the family income. If Australia's lovely wife, the Ching girl acquired from her family a small inheritance, it did not go to Australia or to his children. It went into the hui, for no member of the Kee family could begin to identify the benefits he himself had already drawn from the hui. His clothes, his education, the education of his sons, his home, his start in business: all these things had been paid for by the hui; and if he were willing to hand over everything he was to earn for the rest of his life, he still could never discharge his debt to the hui.

No one felt this obligation more than Africa. It was through the energies of his four brothers that he had received his legal education at Michigan. To maintain him in law school they had deprived themselves; yet they never complained, for they agreed with Nyuk Tsin that the ablest of their group must be educated, to help protect the rest. And Africa Kee did just that. At present the Kee hui controlled seven businesses, and Africa guided each along the narrow path between conservative prudence and radical recklessness. He financed every new venture and advised when earlier ones should be liquidated. He selected which real estate to buy, what corner to lease for a store, and which mainland college the Kee grandsons should be sent to. For the present he was the central brain power of a trivial Chinese empire of dirty little shops, grubby efforts to make money and small landholdings. But it was not his intention that the Kee empire should remain small, and whenever he met with his brothers—they in pigtails and Chinese dress; he shorn and in the clothes he had learned to wear at Michigan—he preached one doctrine: "This hui has got to grow." To make it do so, Africa gambled in a manner that would have pleased his father, and the Kees rarely held property for even a week before borrowing heavily on it to buy more property, on which they also borrowed as soon as possible. All the Kee stores bought on credit, but obligations were carefully met as such came due. The hui never had any cash; it always owed debts that would have staggered a haole; and under Africa's calculating guidance it was beginning to prosper.

Nyuk Tsin, pleased with the manner in which he was taking hold of business problems, did not dominate her family, except in three particulars. Every Kee child had to be educated, and during the year 1900 this apparently impecunious Chinese family was preparing to send three grandsons to college in America— doctor, dentist, lawyer—and within the next decade fourteen more Kees would be ready to go. Nyuk Tsin herself went barefooted in order to save money to pay mainland tuitions, and it did not matter to her if her sons' wives were forced to do the same. The sprawling family lived with terrifying frugality in order to pinch off each fugitive penny that might be saved to provide some sparkling grandson with an education.

In this profound resolve Nyuk Tsin was constantly abetted by the wild-eyed Englishman, Uliassutai Karakoram Blake, who enjoyed walking down from the Church of England school to visit with her in Chinese. He said, "I used to curse the Yankee threat to Hawaii, and at one time I wanted to take arms against America, but when annexation took place I shrugged my shoulders and said, 'America's no worse than England. They're both bloody robbers, and if I can stand one I suppose I can stand the other.'"

He encouraged Nyuk Tsin to educate her grandchildren to their maximum capacity. "Have you ever stopped to figure, Wu Chow's Auntie, what it cost you to make Africa a lawyer? And how much you've already got back in return? Well, be assured that in the future the rate of return will be even greater." He was a flamboyant man and his ferocious mustaches flourished in the little Nuuanu room as he spoke of the future: "Science, mathematics, speculation! Who knows where they will lead? But wherever they take us, Wu Chow's Auntie, only the educated man will be able to follow." She always felt better after a talk with Uliassutai Blake; she wished she had gone to school to such a teacher. For his part, the eccentric Englishman found real joy in talking with one of the two people who understood his dynamic interpretation of the world. The other was a thin, hawkeyed young revolutionary then seeking refuge in Hawaii: Sun Yat Sen. Even better than Nyuk Tsin, he comprehended what his teacher Blake was talking about.

The second particular in which Nyuk Tsin dictated to her family was the matter of houses; she considered it a waste of money to build pretentious homes, especially since reliable people spent their time working outside. Therefore she kept as many of her sons jammed into the bleak clapboard house and its sprawling sheds as possible. Obviously, not all forty-nine Kees could crowd into even that commodious shack, but an astonishing number did. Asia and his family were excused to live in back of the restaurant; Europe and his brood were permitted to live over the vegetable store, but all the others crowded somehow into the Nuuanu residence. There the Hawaiian wives cooked fairly regular meals and the grandchildren learned to talk pidgin and eat poi. By 1899 Africa could well have afforded a home of his own, but even though Nyuk Tsin allowed him to juggle every cent the hui commanded, she did not consider him capable of deciding where he wanted to live, so at thirty-one with a wife and five children, he stayed on at the old house. "It saves money," she said. The bulging house now owned four ukuleles, and fat Apikela, white-haired and benevolent, taught all her grandchildren how to strum the little instrument. It was a noisy house, with a Hawaiian mother and a hard-working, silent Chinese auntie.

The third particular in which Nyuk Tsin dominated her family was in the purchase of land. Her Hakka hunger for this greatest of the world's commodities would never be satiated, and she was haunted by a recurring nightmare: she saw her constantly increasing brood and there was never enough land for each Kee to stand upon and to raise his arms and move about. So whenever the Kee hui had a few dollars left over after paying education bills, she insisted that they acquire more land. To do so in Honolulu was not easy, for generally speaking, land, Hawaii's most precious resource, was not sold; it was leased. Nor was it parceled into acres or lots; it was leased by the square foot. The Hoxworths owned tremendous areas of land, inherited from the Alii Nui Noelani, and so did the Hewletts, inherited through the old missionary's second wife. The Kanakoa family had huge estates; and the Janderses and the Whipples, although they owned little, controlled enormous areas through leases. Whoever owned land grew wealthy, and it was the ironclad law of the great haole families never to sell. Hawaiians were willing to sell, but their land was usually in the country. Therefore, when the bent little Chinese woman Nyuk Tsin decided to get enough Honolulu land for her multiplying family her interests threw her directly athwart the established wealth of the island.

I remarked some time back that if the haoles in Hawaii had wanted to protect themselves from the Chinese they should have shot Uliassutai Karaako-ram Blake. That chance passed, and the Chinese got their education. In 1900, if the haoles had still wanted to maintain their prerogatives, and apparently they did, they should have shot Nyuk Tsin; but none had ever heard of her. They thought that the guiding force behind the Kee family was the lawyer, Africa, and they kept a close watch on him.

In late 1899 Africa found himself hemmed in, unable to make a move, and he had to report to his auntie: "It's getting almost impossible to buy land. The haoles simply won't sell."

"How much money does the hui have?" Nyuk Tsin asked.

"Four thousand dollars in cash, and we could convert more."

"Have you tried to buy business land toward Queen Street?"

"No luck."

"Leases?"

"No luck."

The Kee empire, almost before it got started, was stalemated, and it might have remained so had it not received dramatic assistance from a rat.

On Thanksgiving day in 1899 the blue-funneled H & H steamer *Maui* put into harbor after an uneventful trip from Bangkok, Singapore, Hong Kong and Yokohama. As its seamen curled their landing lines artfully through the air and then sent heavy hawsers after them, this brown rat that was to salvage the fortunes of the Kee hui scuttled down from ship to shore, carrying a hideful of fleas. It ran through some alleys and wound up in the grimy kitchen of a family named Chang.

On December 12, 1899, as the old century lay dying, an old man named Chang, also lay dying with a dreadful fever that seemed to spring from large, purplish nodules in his armpits and groin. When young Dr. Hewlett Whipple from the Department of Health picked his way through the alleys to certify that the man had died of natural causes, he studied the corpse with apprehension.

"Don't bury this man," he ordered, and within ten minutes he had returned, breathless, with two other young doctors, each of whom carried a medical book. In silence the three men studied the corpse and looked at one another in horror.

"Is it what I think it is?" Dr. Whipple asked.

"The plague," his associate replied.

"May God have mercy on us!" Whipple prayed.

The three doctors walked soberly back to their Department of Health, trying to mask from the general public the terror they felt, for they knew that in Calcutta the plague had once killed thousands in a few weeks; there was no known remedy, and when this dreadful disease struck a community, the epidemic had to burn itself out in frightful death and terror. When they reached their Department office, the three doctors closed the doors and sat silent for a moment, as if trying to muster courage for the things they must now do. Then Dr. Whipple, who had inherited his great-grandfather's force of character, said simply, "We must burn that house immediately. We must set aside a special burying ground. And we must inspect every house in Honolulu. It is absolutely essential that not a single sick person be hidden from us. Are you agreed?"

"There will be protests against the burning," one of the other doctors argued.

"We burn, or we face a calamity of such size that I cannot imagine it," Dr. Whipple replied.

"I'd rather we talked with the older doctors."

They did, summoning them in fearful haste, and the older men were sure that their junior colleagues must have been panicked by some ordinary disease with extraordinary developments. "It's unlikely that we have the plague in Honolulu. We've kept it out of here for seventy years."

Another argued: "I think we ought to see the body," and four of the established physicians started to leave for the grimy little shack in Chinatown, but Dr. Whipple protested.

"You'll create consternation among the Chinese," he warned. "I went and hurried away for my associates. Now if you appear, they'll know something is wrong."

"I'm not going to announce that we have the plague in this city until I see for myself," a big, solidly built doctor said, "and I want two experienced men to come along with me."

"Before you go," Whipple asked, seeing that they were leaving without medical books, "what symptoms would convince you that it is truly the plague?"

"I saw the plague in China," the older doctor evaded haughtily.

"But what symptoms?"

"Purplish nodules in the groin. Smaller ones in the armpits. Marked fever accompanied by hallucinations. And a characteristic smell from the punctured nodules."

Dr. Whipple licked his lips, for they were achingly dry, and said, "Dr. Harvey, when you go, take a policeman along to guard the house. We must burn it tonight."

An ominous hush fell upon the room, and Dr. Harvey finally asked, "Then it is the plague?"

"Yes."

There was an apprehensive silence, a moment of hesitation, followed by Dr. Harvey's stubborn insistence: "I cannot authorize the required steps until I see for myself."

"But you will take a policeman?"

"Of course. And you can be talking about what we must do next . . . in the unlikely event that it is indeed the plague." He hurried off, taking two frightened companions with him, and it was a long time before he returned; and during this interval the three younger doctors on whom the burden of a quarantine would fall were afraid that their older confreres would refuse to sanction emergency measures until the plague had established itself, but in this uncharitable supposition they quite underestimated Dr. Harvey.

After an hour he rushed into the Department of Health, ashen-faced and with the news that it was the bubonic plague. He had searched all houses in the immediate vicinity and had uncovered another dead boy and three cases near death, so on his own recognizance he had alerted the Fire Department to stand by for immediate action of the gravest importance. "Gentlemen," he puffed, "Honolulu is already in the toils of the bubonic plague. May God give us the strength to fight it."

That night the terror began. The determined doctors summoned government officials and told them coldly: "The only way to combat this scourge is to burn every house where the plague has struck. Burn it, burn it, burn it!"

A timorous official protested: "How can we burn a house without permission of the owner? In Chinatown it'll take us weeks to find out who owns what. And even if we don't make mistakes we'll be subject to lawsuits."

"Good God!" Dr. Harvey shouted, banging the table with his fist. "You speak of lawsuits. How many people do you think may be dead by Christmas? I'll tell you. We'll be lucky if our losses are less than two thousand. Whipple here may be dead, because he touched the body. I may be dead, because I did, too. And you may be dead, because you associated with us. Now burn those goddamned buildings immediately."

The government summoned the Fire Department and asked if they had perfected any way to burn one building and not the one standing beside it. "There's always a risk," the fire fighters replied. 'But it's been done."

"Is there wind tonight?"

"Nothing unusual."

"Could you burn four houses? Completely?"

"Yes, sir."

"Don't do anything. Don't say anything." Nothing happened that night.

For three agonizing days the debate continued, with the doctors appalled by the delay. In the unspeakable warrens of Chinatown they uncovered three dozen new cases and eleven deaths. Old men would suddenly complain of fevers and pains in their groin. Their faces would become blanched with pain, then fiery red with burning temperatures. Their desire for water was extraordinary, and they died trembling, a hideous smell enveloping them whenever one of their nodules broke. It was the raging, tempestuous plague, but still the finicky debate continued.

At last Drs. Harvey and Whipple announced the facts to the general public: "Honolulu is in the grip of an epidemic of bubonic plague. The death toll cannot at this time be predicted, and the most severe measures must be taken to combat the menace."

Now general panic swept the city. A cordon was thrown around Chinatown and no one inside the area was allowed to move out. Churches and schools were suspended and no groups assembled. Ships were asked to move to other harbors and life in the city ground to a slow, painful halt. It was a terrible Christmas, that last one of the nineteenth century, and there was no celebration when the new year and the new century dawned.

During Christmas week the fires started. Dr. Whipple and his team showed the firemen where deaths had occurred, and after precautions were taken, those houses were burned. Chinatown was divided roughly into the business area toward the ocean and the crowded living areas toward the mountains, and although the plague had started in the former area, it now seemed concentrated in the closely packed homes. Therefore the doctors recommended that an entire section be eliminated, and the government agreed, for by burning this swath across the city, a barrier would be cut between the two areas. The condemned area happened to include Dr. John Whipple's original mansion, now crowded by slums, and his great-grandson felt tears coming to his eyes when he saw the old family home go up in flames that he himself had set. It was a ghastly business to burn down a city that one had worked so hard to build, but the fires continued, and patrols kept back the Chinese who sought to escape the doomed areas and circulate generally throughout the city. Refugee camps were established in church grounds, with tents for those whose houses had been burned and sheds for cooking food. Mrs. Henry Hewlett supervised one camp, Mrs. Rudolph Hale another, and Mrs. John Janders a third on the slopes of Punchbowl, the volcanic crater that rose on the edge of the city. Blankets were supplied by teams that searched the city, Mrs. Malama Hoxworth having taken charge of that effort. David Hale, Jr., and his uncle Tom Whipple set up the field kitchens and ran them, riding from one camp to the other on horseback.

Inspection teams were organized and every room in Honolulu was visually checked twice each day, to be sure that no new cases of the plague went unreported, and consonant with the missionary tradition from which they had sprung, it was the Hales and the Hewletts and the Whipples who volunteered for the particularly dangerous work of crawling through the Chinatown warrens to be sure no dead bodies lay hiding. It was a dreadful sight they saw, a fearful condemnation of their rule in Hawaii.

The streets of Chinatown were unpaved, filthy alleys that wound haphazardly past open cesspools. The houses were collapsing shacks that had been propped up by poles in hopes of squeezing out one more year's rent. Inside, the homes were an abomination of windowless rooms, waterless kitchens, toiletless blocks. Stairwells had no illumination and what cellars there were stood crowded with inflammable junk. No air circulated that was not filthy. After only two generations of use, Chinatown was overcrowded to the point of suffocation, all made worse by the fact that those whose homes had already been burned had managed, by one trick or another, to slip through quarantine cordons so as to remain with their friends rather than suffer banishment to the refugee camps, and with them they brought the plague. If one had searched the world, seeking an area where a rat bearing the fleas which bred bubonic plague could most easily infect the greatest number of unprotected people, Honolulu's Chinatown would have stood high on the list. The police had known of the pitiful overcrowding; the Department of Health had known of the unsanitary conditions; and the landlords had known best of all the menace they were perpetuating; but nobody had spoken in protest because the area was owned principally by those who were now inspecting it: the Hales, the Hewletts and the Whipples; and they had found that Chinese did pay their rents promptly. Now from this open sore the plague threatened to engulf the island, and as the inspectors bravely toured the infected areas day after day, exposing themselves to death and sleeping at nights in restricted tents lest they contaminate their own families, they often thought: "Why didn't we do something about this sooner?"

By January 15, 1900, eight substantial areas had been completely razed and innumerable rats that might have carried their infected fleas to uncontaminated sections of the city were destroyed; and it seemed as if a general eruption of the plague had been mercifully prevented. Three thousand Chinese were already in refugee camps from which they could not spread contagion, but unknown thousands were hiding out in the narrow warrens to which they had fled and they now began to accomplish what the rats could not. As the reports came into headquarters that night, each with tales of fresh death and new infection, it became hideously apparent to Dr. Whipple that the epidemic was not halted and that the fate of Honolulu hung in a precarious balance.

On the sixteenth he convened his doctors again, a group of exhausted men who understood how fearful the next week could be, for by their own inspection they had proved that the plague stood poised in upper Chinatown, ready to explode across the entire city, and they knew that on this day they must either take final steps to drive it back or surrender the general community to its ravages; and the only cure they knew was fire. Dr. Whipple was first to speak: "Our teams found twenty-nine new cases yesterday."

"Oh, hell!" Dr. Harvey cried in acute frustration. He folded his arms on the table and bowed his head upon them, retiring from this part of the discussion.

"All the cases this week, and most of the deaths, have been concentrated toward the mountains," Whipple explained, pointing to a map, "and we can thank God that they seem to be leading out of the city rather than in toward the heart."

"That's the only good news we've had," snapped an older doctor who had found seven cases in the mountain area.

Dr. Whipple hesitated, then said, "Our obligation is clear."

"You mean to burn that entire outlying area?"

"I do."

"Jesus, they'll explode. They just won't permit it, Whipple."

Dr. Whipple pressed his hands to his forehead and pleaded: "Have you an alternative?"

"Look, I'm not arguing one way or another," the older man explained. "I'm just saying . . . Hell, Whipple, there must be five hundred homes in that area!"

"And every one infected with the bubonic plague."

"I want no part of this decision!" the older doctor protested.

"Nor me!" another cried. "Christ, Whipple, that's half the city!"

From his position with his head on his arms, Dr. Harvey asked harshly, "If your arm is infected with blood poisoning that is certain to destroy your entire body, what do you do?"

There was no answer, so after a moment he slammed his fist onto the table and shouted, "Well, what in hell do you do? You cut it off! Burn those areas. Now!"

"Only the government can make this decision," Whipple said in slow, terrified tones. "But it's got to make it."

"We are withdrawing from this meeting," two of the doctors warned. "Let it be recorded."

Dr. Harvey shouted, "And let it be recorded that I did not withdraw. Burn the goddamned city or perish."

On the eighteenth of January, 1900, the emergency committee decided to burn a very substantial area of Honolulu in a last prayerful attempt to save the general population, and when the doomed areas were marked in red two facts became apparent: they were not in the center of town but in the residential district; and almost everyone who lived in the area was Chinese. Two members of the cabinet, as they faced the map, were in tears, and a man named Hewlett, who had a good deal of Hawaiian blood, asked, "Why does misery always fall on those least able to bear it?"

"You burn where the plague has fallen," a cabinet member named Hale replied. "And it's fallen on the Chinese."

"Stop this talk!" the chairman cried. "There's already an ugly rumor that we're burning Chinatown as punishment because the Pakes left the sugar fields.

I don't want to hear any of that libel in this room. We're burning Chinatown because that's where the plague is."

Hewlett, part-Hawaiian, felt that he was being unduly hectored, so he asked, "Would you burn here," and he banged the haole areas of the map, "if that's where the plague was? Would you burn your own houses?"

"The plague didn't come to our houses," the chairman replied. "It came to the Chinese."

On the nineteenth of January the Fire Department gave all its men the day off and advised them to sleep as much as possible in preparation for a hard day's work on the twentieth. The Honolulu *Mail* in its edition that day reported: "We beg all citizens of our city to be especially alert tomorrow and to watch for flying sparks, because although the able laddies of our Fire Department have proved over and over again that they know how to set fire to one house and save the next, the very magnitude of the job they now face increases the ever-present danger of a general conflagration. Brooms and buckets of water should be at hand throughout the city."

When word of the proposed burning reached Chinatown, it created panic and many tried vainly to force their way through the cordons that kept everyone within the plague area. Those whose homes were to be razed were rounded up and solemnly marched away to a refugee camp on the slopes of Punchbowl, where they could look down at their doomed homes, and this last view of buildings which they had worked so hard to acquire inspired them with a dumb rage, and that night there were many unpleasant scenes. One Chinese who knew a little English rushed up to Mrs. John Janders, the supervisor of the Punchbowl camp, and screamed, "You doing this on purpose!"

"No," she said quietly, "it is the plague."

"No plague!" the furious Chinese cried. "Your husband own my store. He say all time, 'More rent! More rent!' I not pay so he decided to burn."

"No," Mrs. Janders argued reasonably. "Mr. Apaka, it is the plague. Believe me, it would not otherwise be done." But the Chinese knew better, and through the long night of January 19 they watched the mysterious lights of the city and waited in bitterness for the fires to begin.

Fortunately, the twentieth was a calm day with no wind that might have agitated the planned blaze. At eight in the morning the firemen, according to a schedule worked out to provide maximum protection for the rest of the city, poured liberal amounts of kerosene over a small shack diagonally across from where the Whipple mansion, burned earlier, had stood. The shack certainly merited destruction, for it had already caused the deaths of five plague victims and the illness of three others. At eight-ten a match was applied to the kerosene, and the filthy hovel exploded in flame.

As it blazed, a slight breeze started blowing from the northeast. It crept down from the mountains and as it funnelled into the valleys that led into Honolulu it increased in speed, so that by the time it reached the flaming shack it was prepared to blow the sparks in exactly the opposite direction from that intended by the Fire Department. Within three minutes half a dozen shacks not on the list were ablaze, but they were easily evacuated and were of little value, so the fire-fighters simply surrounded them and beat out any sparks that might escape toward the center of the city where property was of real value.

Then at eight-thirty the capricious wind blowing down from the hills arrived in an unpredicted gust and whipped a flurry of sparks high into the air.

Fortunately, the land across from the fire had already been razed, so there was no danger of spreading the flames in that direction, but the wind seemed sent from hell, for it suddenly veered and deposited many active sparks on the large Congregational church that had been completed in 1884 directly across from where the old Whipple mansion had stood. The church had two soaring steeples, for the king had reasoned: "A man has two eyes so he can see better and two ears so he can hear better. My church has got to have two steeples so it can find God better." Now the steeples were in peril, and firemen noted that if any of the embers flamed to life in those tall spires, the rising wind would surely whip sparks clear across the areas previously burned and throw them down into the valuable center of the city, so two brave Hawaiians scrambled up the sides of the church seeking to reach the steeples, and one man arrived in time to stamp out the fires beginning on his, but the other did not, and when he pulled himself onto the upper ledge of his steeple, he found it already ablaze and he barely escaped.

In a few minutes the great tall church became a torch. Its bell plunged to the basement, clanging through the flames. The famous pipe organ, imported from London, melted into lumps of useless metal, and stained-glass windows crashed into the fire. As the church burned furiously in the morning wind, many who had helped build it with their dimes and personal labor gathered to weep. But what was most important was not the loss of the church, but the fact that its unusual height made it a target for every gust that blew down the valley, and even as the people gathered at its foot to mourn, far over their heads the wind was scattering a multitude of sparks. Had the fire occurred at night, the sight would have been one of fairylike splendor, with stars of fire darting across the dark sky; but in an ominous daylight the passage of the flames occasioned no beauty and only dread. For they sped high in the air across the already burned-out areas, a few falling harmlessly on charred land but most flying on into the very heart of the city, where they descended upon dried-wood roofs, there to ignite the fires that were to destroy almost all of Chinatown. With Old Testament accuracy the embers which flew out from the Christian church fell only upon heathen homes. If the Christians of Honolulu had righteously planned to destroy every Chinese building in the city, they could have accomplished the fact no more skillfully than did the sparks erupting from their doomed church.

The first blaze in downtown Chinatown occurred at nine-forty, when a sizable ember fell upon a closely packed area of houses and ignited a central one. Gangs of firemen quickly surrounded the house to extinguish the fire, and after considerable effort succeeded in doing so; but while they were at that job, another ember struck a house of somewhat special nature. On the outside it looked like an ordinary home, but when it started to burn, all the Chinese nearby fled, and Hawaiian firemen alone were left to fight its flames.

"Come back!" an old Chinese man kept wailing in a language the firemen could not understand. Grabbing a young Chinese he shouted, "Tell them to come back!"

A group of daring Chinese hurried forward toward the burning house, grabbed the firemen by the hands and pulled them away. "Mo bettah you come back!" they yelled.

The firemen, who were terribly afraid of the Chinese after the troubles of the night before and who had been cautioned that the Orientals might attempt to riot when the burnings started, interpreted this strange behavior as the start of communal rioting, and stopped fighting the fire in order to protect themselves from the Chinese, and it was fortunate that they did so, for as they left, the house exploded. In a golden, smoky gasp of flame, the little house simply disintegrated, and then the firemen understood: it was one of the closed sheds in which some trivial Chinese merchant had kept his kerosene. But what the firemen did not understand was that the explosion, frightful though it had been, was merely the beginning of something worse; for now from the ruins a series of fantastic fiery rockets exploded through the city. Some threw stars into the air. Others pinwheeled through streets, and still others went up with a crazy, violent zigzag through the morning sky, falling at last on the roof of some new house, there to burn with vigor until its shingles too were ablaze; for the shed had harbored not only kerosene but also a store of fireworks for the Chinese New Year.

With the explosion of the shed, any hope of saving downtown Chinatown was lost, and for the next seven hours the anguished Chinese on the Punchbowl hillside, huddling behind the barbed wire of their refugee camp, could spot the progress of the huge blaze from one of these kerosene dumps to the next. All day the little sheds exploded with violence, throwing their flames into new areas, and wherever the fire went, sooner or later it found out a horde of fireworks, and when they soared into the air with their burdens of flame they seemed invariably to fall back onto areas that were not yet ablaze. And to make the destruction of Chinatown certain, the vagrant wind kept blowing from its unusual quarter in the hills. By midafternoon, it was apparent that hardly a Chinese house in mid-city would be spared.

When it became obvious that all was doomed, the Chinese fell into panic. Old men who could barely walk after forty-five years of work in the cane fields began running into burning houses to salvage some item of family life which they prized above any other, and they soon appeared in the crowded streets hauling carts, or running with bamboo carrying-poles, each with some useless treasure. No one thought to bring blankets or food, both needed in the refugee camps, and soon the streets leading out from Chinatown were jammed with a miscellaneous horde: barefoot old women in blue smocks, men in laboring shirts, pretty young girls, their hair in braids, and round-faced babies. From a Japanese tea house two geisha girls, their faces ashen with talcum powder, hurried nervously in pin-toed, mincing steps that kept their brightly colored kimonos swaying in the smoke, while old Punti women hobbled behind on stubby feet. The pigtailed men tried to lug burdens which would have staggered horses and which soon staggered them. The escape routes became a litter of lost wealth and it was pitiful to see families who had never owned much, stooping as they ran, picking up valuables they had always coveted, only to abandon them later in the same breathless way as their owners had had to do.

Now the major tragedy of the day approached, for as the fleeing Chinese, with flame and firecracker at their back, sought to break out from Chinatown they ran into solid rows of impassive policemen whose merciless job it was to hold them back within the plague-ridden area. There was no intention whatever —absolutely none, the police commissioner later swore—to trap the Chinese within the fiery area, but there was an ironclad insistence that they move out by established routes that would take them not into the uninfected parts of Honolulu but into the barbed-wire refugee camps, where doctors could watch them for new outbreaks of the plague.

"They won't let us out!" a poor, dimwitted Chinese woman began screaming. "They want us to burn, in the houses they set afire."

She made a futile attempt to dash past a policeman, but his orders required him to push her back toward the burning area, from which there was an orderly escape route, could she but find it.

"He's pushing me into the fire!" the woman screamed, and men who had been free from panic suddenly realized that they were not going to be allowed out of the doomed area, and they began a concentrated rush toward the policeman.

"They're breaking out!" the officers called, and behind them, from the parts of the city where there was no plague, white volunteers rushed up bearing clubs and crowbars and guns.

"Get back!" they shouted. "There's a safe way out!"

At this point, when a deadly general riot seemed inevitable, the United States army marched onto the scene with several hundred trained soldiers, guns at the ready, and they were moved into position along all the main exit routes from Chinatown. "Under no circumstances are you to fire unless I give the order," their captains said, and they marched stolidly on until they stood shoulder to shoulder with the police.

To the distraught Chinese, bombarded by their own fireworks, the arrival of the soldiers was intolerable. To them it meant that any who tried to escape the burning area were to be shot, and because language between the groups was such a difficult barrier, no one could explain that the soldiers were there merely to halt the spread of infection. There was a way out of Chinatown, and it led to safety, but tempers were growing so violent that it seemed unlikely that this way would ever be found.

"They're coming at us again!" a corporal cried, as sixteen Chinese prepared for a mass dash through the lines.

"Don't fire!" the captain of that sector shouted. "Don't you dare fire."

"What am I supposed to . . ." There was a wild crush. Policemen beat at the pigtailed bodies while soldiers jammed at their bellies with the butts of their guns. The defense line sagged for a moment until volunteer reserves rushed up with boards torn hastily from picket fences. Lustily they clubbed the panicky Chinese over the head, driving them back toward the fire.

"We can't hold next time!" the corporal warned, and as if to accent the peril of the moment, a large store of fireworks exploded, adding to the frenzy of all.

"Don't you fire!" the captain warned each of his men.

"By God, if I go down beneath a bunch of damned Chinks I'm gonna fire!" the corporal shouted, disregarding the cautions of his superior, and it was then apparent that on the next charge from the Chinese a general massacre must surely begin.

At this moment, when the frightened captains were licking their lips and preparing to give the only sensible order they could: "Fire to repel rioters," Dr. Hewlett Whipple rushed up and shouted, "Let me through! And for Christ's sake, don't fire!"

He forced his way through the police lines and ran into the middle of the central group of terrified Chinese. Putting his arms about the shoulders of the ringleaders he pleaded: "Don't try to break out of here! Don't run toward the lines again. Please, please!"

"You want us die?" a laundryman screamed at him.

"We won't die," Whipple said as calmly as he could, and something in the unexpected manner in which he said "we" disarmed the Chinese and they listened. "We're going to run up Nuuanu," he explained. "We can all get out there." And pushing the principal rioters before him, he started running up Nuuanu, and the plague-ridden Chinese ran behind him, and in time the riot abated and the trembling young soldiers, wiping their ashen foreheads, returned their guns to safety and marched away.

* * *

Of the Chinese families that were stricken on that awful day of January 20, 1900, when Chinatown was burned—by the will of God, the haoles said; by plan, the Chinese claimed—none was struck so hard as the Kees. When the first kerosene depot exploded, its flames burned down Africa Kee's office and destroyed his records. A whole barrage of firecrackers ripped through Asia Kee's restaurant and the resulting fires leveled it. Europe's Punti store was completely lost and so was America's dry-goods emporium. Every business building owned by the Kees was burned, including the homes of two of the brothers. Their families escaped with what they wore and little else. Only the cluttered house up Nuuana was saved, but even its occupants—except Nyuk Tsin, who was working in the forest fields—had been herded into the concentration camps.

When Nyuk Tsin came barefooted out of the hills, with her two swaying baskets filled with pineapples, and found that much of Honolulu had been destroyed, including all the possessions of the Kee hui, and when she found that her family was dispersed—many of them dead, she supposed—she experienced a sullen terror, but she fought against it and said, as she stared at her empty home, "I must find my sons."

Fortunately, by force of habit she kept with her the swaying baskets of pineapples, so that when she had climbed the steep sides of Punchbowl and had come to the refugee camp the guards were pleased to see her and shouted, "Thank God, at last a Pake with food!" They let her pass, and after an hour of milling through the crowd she succeeded in collecting four of her five sons. No one had seen Asia leave his restaurant after the firecrackers had ripped it apart and it was reported that he was dead.

On the hillside overlooking Pearl Harbor, where the night lights of distant ships could be seen coming on, Nyuk Tsin convened her dazed family. They sat on rocks and looked down upon the desolate ruins of Chinatown, and in the silence of their crushing defeat Nyuk Tsin's Hakka instinct warned her that now was the time for her clan to pull courage out of its spasmed belly. As a woman she knew that on such nights of despair men were apt to surrender to the fate that had overtaken them, but it was a woman's job to prevent them from doing so. In the fading twilight she could see in the sensitive, shocked faces of Europe and America a willingness to declare the Kee empire ended. Blunt-faced Africa showed some of the fighting spirit to be expected in an educated man, but not much, while young Australia was burning with outrage because a soldier had struck him in the gut with a rifle. It was not much of a family that Nyuk Tsin had that night, nor was she herself in condition to inspirit her sons, for inwardly she was grieving for Asia, lost in the fire.

But she said quietly, so that no one else could hear, "It is unthinkable that the government will ignore what has happened."

"They destroyed all of Chinatown," America said with anguish in his voice. "They burned our stores on purpose because we wouldn't work on their sugar plantations."

"No," Nyuk Tsin reasoned, "the wind came by accident."

"That isn't so, Wu Chow's Auntie!" Europe cried, ugly with despair. "The merchants wanted this done. Last week they threw all the food I had ordered from China into the bay. They were determined to wipe us out."

"No, Europe," Nyuk Tsin calmly argued, "they were afraid your shipments might bring more of the plague."

"But they didn't throw the haole shipments overboard!" Europe shouted, with tears in his voice. "They came from China, too."

"They're afraid," Nyuk Tsin explained. "Men do strange things when they're afraid."

"I never want to see Honolulu again," America groaned. "They burned our stores on purpose."

"No," Nyuk Tsin patiently reasoned, "they were afraid that . . ."

"Wu Chow's Auntie!" America cried. "Don't be a fool!"

There was a harsh slap in the night and Nyuk Tsin said, "Behave yourself." Then she drew her sons closer about her and began again: "It is inconceivable that we will be left without compensation. Surely, surely we must believe that the government will pay us for what has happened."

For the first time Africa spoke. Cautiously and with the slow accent of a lawyer he asked, "Why do you think so?"

"I knew Dr. Whipple," Nyuk Tsin replied. "The old one. And men like him, Africa, simply do not allow injustice to stand."

"It was men like him who burned our stores on purpose," America whined. There was another harsh slap and Nyuk Tsin cried furiously, "No more words about the past! There was fire. We have lost everything. Now we are going to gain everything."

Africa's studious voice asked, "Wu Chow's Auntie, do you think that men like old Dr. Whipple will be listened to in the days to come?"

"Perhaps they won't be," Nyuk Tsin admitted, "but there is something new in Hawaii. The United States cannot afford to see us treated badly. Out of pride . . . or to show the world that they look after their people . . ." Her voice trailed off and she reflected for a moment. Then she said vigorously, "Sons, I am absolutely convinced that either our own government or the United States will pay us back for this fire. Let's not argue about it another minute."

"What you are thinking of," Africa said slowly, thinking aloud, "is that we must protect ourselves and see to it that we get our share of whatever money is distributed to those who have lost, regardless of where the money comes from."

Nyuk Tsin thought: "No matter how much we paid for his education, it was worth it." And she was also pleased at the way in which Africa's sensible statement of the problem awakened in her sons their old hui spirit; the Kee hui was again in operation. "I think," she said, "that Africa must devote his whole time to organizing a committee right away for just payment to all of us who have lost in the fire. Make the world realize that there is no question of whether claims will be paid. It is only a question of how much. Africa, you must appear on every platform. Whenever there is a meeting, you must speak. You must become the voice of all the Chinese. You will represent everybody and you will let it be known that you refuse to accept any fees. Work, work, work. Give statements to the paper and let them print your picture. But always speak as if you were positive that the money will be paid. Soon you will have others saying it, and in time they too will believe it." She paused, then added, "The money is absolutely going to come."

Europe broke in to ask, "How much can we claim for?"

"How many buildings did we have?" America asked.

The hui waited while Africa counted up in his mind. "We would have a very substantial claim," he said finally. "The restaurant, the stores, the houses, my office. The Kee claim could be one of the biggest."

"Oh, no!" Nyuk Tsin interrupted. "Because if that were the case, you could never stand forth as the leader of the claims committee. We will put in some of our claims as Wu Chow's Auntie. And wherever possible we will claim in the names of your Hawaiian wives. The Kee claim itself must not be large. Africa, it's your job to see that it isn't. Use the Chings, anybody, if you have to."

At this point Australia made one of the most pregnant observations of the night: "I don't think I ever want to see Chinatown again. After what they did to it today."

Coldly, yet with compassion for those with less courage than herself, Nyuk Tsin remarked, "There will be many in the next weeks who feel as you do, Australia. Today will be a memory too terrible to accept. They will decide to surrender their land in Chinatown. And if they do, we will buy it."

There was a long silence as the brothers looked down at the scarred city, visible now, and then through the low clouds of smoke that hung in the valleys. On the ocean beyond, the long surf came rolling in, impartially as it had for millions of years, and the Kee boys somehow understood what their mother was urging them to do. From despair hope rises; from defeat victory. There are only three bad years, followed by six wonderfully rich ones. The city is burned, but it must be rebuilt. The family is nearly destroyed, but if there is one man left alive, or one woman, it must go on. Night falls with the smell of destruction, but day rises with the smell of wet mortar . . . and building resumes.

Nyuk Tsin added: "We must never try to convince any man that he wants to leave Chinatown. We must be careful to drive no unfair bargains. And although we can't pay much now, we can promise to pay a great deal in the future. Our credit is good. They know a Kee will pay."

Nyuk Tsin added: "If two pieces of land are for sale, try to buy the one nearest the ones we already own, because stores in the future will be bigger, and we can put our parcels of land together and make each one more valuable than it was before."

Nyuk Tsin added: "Africa, in the last stages of the committee you must insist that you cannot serve on the board that will actually distribute the money. Because if you are on that board, you could not rightfully give substantial amounts to the Kees, but if you are not on it, everyone who is will say, 'If it hadn't been for Africa, we wouldn't be here today.' And they will be generous on our behalf."

Nyuk Tsin added: "As I came through the burned areas I saw that the only thing that was left standing anywhere was the iron safes. The haoles will think them no longer of use. Australia, it will be a good job for you to buy them all. Then figure out some way to make them work again." When her youngest son protested: "Wu Chow's Auntie, I've never worked on safes," she replied sharply, "Learn."

Toward daybreak Nyuk Tsin added: "If we succeed, people will hate us for owning so much land and they will say we stole it from people after the fire. Ignore them. A city belongs to those who are willing to fight for it."

Finally, Nyuk Tsin added: "I have a little money saved and many vegetables. All of our women and girls must work as servants with haole families, for that will feed the women and also give us money. Europe and America must start to visit every haole store tomorrow, begging for supplies on easy credit so that they can open new stores. Do it tomorrow, while the haoles are sorry for what happened today, for they will give you terms tomorrow that you will not be able to get next week." She smiled at her four sons and said, "We must work."

But at dawn Uliassutai Karakoram Blake puffed up the hillside with a list of names of men who were safe at another camp on the other side of Nuuanu River, and when he read in loud Chinese syllables: "Asia Kee, who runs the restaurant," then Nyuk Tsin dropped her head in her hands.

V

FROM THE INLAND SEA

In the year 1902, when the reconstruction of Honolulu's Chinatown was completed, one of the isolated farm villages of Hiroshima-ken, at the southern end of Japan's main island, stubbornly maintained an ancient courtship custom which everyone knew to be ridiculous but which, perhaps for that very reason, produced good results.

When some lusty youth spotted a marriageable girl he did not speak directly to her, nor did he invite any of his friends to do so. Instead, he artfully contrived to present himself before this girl a dozen times a week. She might be coming home from the Shinto shrine under the cryptomeria trees, and suddenly he would appear, silent, moody, tense, like a man who has just seen a ghost. Or, when she returned from the store with a fish, she would unexpectedly see this agitated yet controlled young man staring at her.

His part of this strange game required that he never speak, that he share his secret with nobody. Her rules were that not once, by even so much as a flicker of an eye, must she indicate that she knew what he was doing. He loomed silently before her, and she passed uncomprehendingly on. Yet obviously, if she was a prudent girl, she had to find some way to encourage his courtship so that ultimately he might send his parents to the matchmakers, who would launch formal conversations with her parents; for a girl in this village could never tell which of the gloomy, intense young men might develop into a serious suitor; so in some mysterious manner wholly understood by nobody she indicated, without seeing him or without ever having spoken to him, that she was ready.

Apart from certain species of the bird kingdom, where courtship was conducted with much the same ritual, this sexual parading was one of the strangest on earth, but in this village of Hiroshima-ken it worked, because it involved one additional step of which I have not yet spoken, and it was this next step that young Sakagawa Kamejiro found himself engaged in.

In 1902 he was twenty years old, a rugged, barrel-chested, bowlegged little bulldog of a man with dark, unblemished skin and jet-black hair. He had powerful arms which hung out from his body, as if their musculature was too great to be compressed, and he gave the appearance of a five-foot, one-inch accumulation of raw power, bursting with vital drives yet confused because he knew no specific target upon which to discharge them. In other words, Kamejiro was in love.

He had fallen in love on the very day that the Sakagawa family council had decided that he should be the one to go on the ship to Hawaii, where jobs in the sugar fields were plentiful. It was not the prospect of leaving home that had aroused his inchoate passions, for he knew that his parents, responsible for eight children and one old woman, could not find enough rice to feed the family. He had observed how infrequently fish got to the Sakagawa table—and meat not at all—so he was prepared to leave.

It happened late one afternoon when he stood in the tiny Sakagawa paddy field and looked out at the shimmering islands of the Inland Sea, and he understood in that brilliant moment, with the westering sun playing upon the most beautiful of all waters, that he might be leaving Hiroshima-ken forever. "I said I would go for only five years," he muttered stubbornly to himself, "but things can happen. I might never see these islands again. Maybe I won't plough this field . . . ever again." And a consuming sorrow possessed him, for of all the lands he could imagine, there could be no other on the face of the earth more exciting than these fields along the coastline of Hiroshima-ken.

Kamejiro was by no charitable interpretation of the word a poet. He was not even literate, nor had he ever looked at picture books. He had never talked much at home, and among the boys of the village he was known to be a stolid fighter rather than a talker. He had always ignored girls and, although he followed his father's advice on most things, had stubbornly refused to think of marriage. But now, as he stood in the faltering twilight and saw the land of his ancestors for the first time—in history and in passion and in love, as men occasionally perceive the land upon which they have been bred—he wanted brutishly to reach out his hand and halt the descending sun. He wanted to continue his spiritual embrace of the niggardly little field of which he was so much a part. "I may never come back!" he thought. "Look at the sun burning its way into the sea. You would think . . ." He did not put his thoughts into words, but stood in the paddy field, mud about ankles, entertaining tremendous surges of longing. How magnificent his land was!

It was in this mood that he started homeward, for in the Japanese custom all rice fields were gathered together while the houses to which they pertained clustered in small villages. Thus arable land was not wasted on housing, but the system did require farmers to walk substantial distances from their fields to their homes, and on this night little bulldog Sakagawa Kamejiro, his arms hanging out with their powerful muscles, walked home. Had he met some man who had earlier insulted him, as often happened in village life, he would surely have thrashed him then and there, for he thought that he wanted to fight; but as he walked he happened to see, at the edge of the village, the girl Yoko, and although he had seen her often before, it was not until then—when she walked with a slight wind at her dress and with a white working-woman's towel about her head—that he realized how much like the spirit of the land she was, and he experienced an almost uncontrollable desire to pull her off the footpath and into the rice field and have it over with on the spot.

Instead, he stood dumb as she approached. His eyes followed her and his big arms quivered, and as she passed she knew that this Kamejiro who was earmarked for Hawaii would watch her constantly throughout the following days, and she began to look for him at strange locations, and he would be there, stolid, staring, his arms hanging awkwardly down. Without ever acknowledging by a single motion of her own that she had even seen him, she conveyed the timeless message of the village: "It would not be unreasonable if you were to do so."

Therefore, on a soft spring night when the rice fields were beginning to turn delicate green, the sweet promise of food to come, Sakagawa Kamejiro secretly dressed in the traditional garb of the Hiroshima-ken night lover. He wore his best pair of trousers, his clean straw zori and a shirt that did not smell. The most conspicuous part of his costume, however, was a white cloth mask which wound about his head and covered his nose and mouth. Thus properly attired, he slipped out of the Sakagawa home, down a back path to Yoko's and waited several hours as her family closed up the day's business, blew out the lights and threw no more shadows on the shoji. When he was satisfied that Yoko had retired, with a reasonable chance that her parents might be sleeping, he crept toward the room which from long study he had spotted as hers, and in some mysterious way known only in the villages, she had anticipated that this was the night he would visit her, so the shoji had been left unlocked, and in a moment he slipped bemasked into the room.

Yoko saw him in the faint moonlight, but said nothing. Without removing his mask, for that was essential to the custom, he crept to her bed and placed his left hand upon her cheek. Then he took her right hand in his and held her fingers in a certain way, which from the beginning of Japan had meant, "I want to sleep with you," and of her own accord she changed the position of his fingers, which timelessly had signified, "You may."

With never a word spoken, with never a mask removed, Kamejiro silently slipped into bed with the intoxicating girl. She would not allow him to remove her clothing, for she knew that later she might have to do many things in a hurry, but that did not inconvenience Kamejiro, and in a few stolid, fumbling moments he made her ready to accept him. Not even at the height of their passion did Yoko utter a word, and when they collapsed mutually in blazing gratification and he fell asleep like an animal, she did not touch the mask, for it was there to protect her. At any moment in the love-making she could have pushed him away, and he would have had to go. The next day they could have met on the village street—as they would tomorrow—and neither would have been embarrassed, for so long as the mask was in place, Yoko did not know who was in her room. So long as the mask protected him, Kamejiro could not suffer personal humiliation or loss of face, for no matter what Yoko said or did, it could not embarrass him, for officially he was not there. It was a silly system, this Hiroshima courtship routine, but it worked.

When Kamejiro wakened, there was a moment when he could not recall where he was, and then he felt Yoko's body near his and this time they began to caress each other as proper lovers do, and the long night passed, but on the third sweet love-making, when the joy of possession completely captured them, they grew bolder and unwittingly made a good deal of noise, so that Yoko's father was awakened, and he shouted, "Who's in the house?"

And instantly Yoko was required to scream, "Oh, how horrible! A man is trying to get into my room!" And she continued to wail pitifully as lights flashed on throughout the village.

"Some beast is trying to rape Yoko-san!" an old woman screamed.

"We must kill him!" Yoko's father shouted, pulling on his pants.

"The family is forever disgraced!" Yoko's mother moaned, but since each of these phrases had been shouted into the night in precisely these intonations for many centuries, everyone knew exactly how to interpret them. But it was essential for the preservation of family dignity that the entire village combine to seek out the rapist, and now, led by Yoko's outraged father, the night procession formed.

"I saw a man running down this way!" the old woman bellowed.

"The ugly fiend!" another shouted. "Trying to rape a young girl!"

The villagers coursed this way and that, seeking the rapist, but prudently they avoided doing two things: they never took a census of the young men of the village, for by deduction that would have shown who was missing and would have indicated the rapist; nor did they look into the little barn where rice hay was kept, for they knew that the night fiend was certain to be hiding there, and it would be rather embarrassing if he were discovered, for then everyone would have to go through the motions of pretending to beat him.

In the hay barn, with chickens cackling, Kamejiro put on his pants, knocked the mud off his zori, and tucked away his white mask. When this was done, he had time to think: "She is sweeter than a breeze off the sea." But when he saw her later that day, coming from the fish stall, he looked past her and she ignored him, and this was a good thing, for as yet it was not agreed that Yoko would marry him, and if she elected not to do so, it was better if neither of them officially knew who had attempted to rape her. In fact, during that entire day and for some days thereafter Yoko was the acknowledged heroine of the village, for as one old woman pointed out: "I cannot remember a girl who screamed more loudly than Yoko-san while she was defending herself against that awful man . . . whoever he was." Yoko's father also came in for considerable praise in that he had dashed through every alley in the village, shouting at the top of his voice, "I'll kill him!" And farmers said approvingly to their wives, "It was lucky for whoever tried to get into that house that Yoko's father didn't catch him."

So THE LAST days before the ship's departure were spent in this make-believe manner. Kamejiro, the object of much admiration because of his willingness to go to Hawaii, worked hard in the family rice field, not because his labor was required, but because he loved the feel of growing rice. Neighbors, whose ancestors had farmed nearby fields for thousands of years, came by to say farewell, and to each he said, "I'll be back." And the more he said these words the more he believed that only death would prevent him from returning to the tiny, mountain-shaded, sea-swept fields of Hiroshima-ken.

Three or four nights a week he donned his magic mask and climbed more or less surreptitiously into bed with Yoko, and they found each other so completely enjoyable, and so mysterious in the unknowing night, that without ever facing up to the problem, they drifted into a mute understanding that one day they would marry. Kamejiro, finding endless delight in the girl's soft body, prayed that she might become pregnant, so that he would be forced to marry her before he left for Hawaii, but this was not to be, and as the final week began, he spoke haltingly with his mother.

"When I have been in Hawaii for a little while, and after I have sent you a lot of money, I think I may get married." He blushed a deep red under his dark skin and prepared to confide: "At such time, will you speak to Yoko-chan for me?" But his mother had long waited for this opportunity to advise her favorite son, and now she poured forth her fund of Hiroshima wisdom.

"Kamejiro, I have heard that it is a terrible thing for a man to travel overseas the way you are doing. Not that you will be robbed, because you are a strong man and able to handle such things as well as any." She was in her fifties, a small, stoop-shouldered woman with deep wrinkles from endless hours in the sun. She loved rice and could eat four bowls at any meal, but she could never afford to do that, so she remained as skinny as she had been in her youth, when Kamejiro's father had crept into her sleeping room.

"What mothers worry about, Kamejiro," she explained, "is that their sons will marry poorly. Every day that you are gone I shall be anxious, because I shall see you in the arms of some unworthy woman. Kamejiro, you must guard against this. You must not marry carelessly. When it comes time to take a wife, appoint prudent friends to study her history. Now these are the things I want you to bear in mind.

"The best thing in the world is to be a Japanese. What wonderful people the Japanese are. Hard-working, honest, clean people. Kamejiro, your father and I have heard that in Hawaii the people are careless and very dark. If you were to marry one of them . . ." She started to weep, real, mournful tears, so after a while she went to the hanging bucket at the fire and took herself a little rice in a bowl. Thus fortified, she continued. "If you were to marry such a woman, Kamejiro, we would not want you back in this village. You would have disgraced your family, your village, and all Japan."

Kamejiro listened carefully, for in these matters his mother was wise. She always collected gossip and in the last three weeks had walked fifteen miles to talk with people who had heard various bits of news about Hawaii. "Never marry a Chinese," she said firmly. "They are clever people and there are many of them in Hawaii, I am told, but they don't wash themselves as often as we do and no matter how rich they get, they remain Chinese. Under no circumstances can you return to this village if you have a Chinese wife.

"Kamejiro, many men from Hiroshima-ken are tempted to marry girls from the north. You've seen some of those pitiful women down here. They can't talk decently, and say zu-zu all the time, until you feel ashamed for them. I have no respect at all for girls from the north, and I have never seen one who made a good wife. I will admit that they're a little better than Chinese, but not much. If you are even tempted to marry a northern girl, think of Masaru's wife. Zu-zu, zu-zu! Do you want a girl like that?" she asked contemptuously.

Using chopsticks to flick the rice grains into her wrinkled but vigorous mouth she proceeded. "A good many men try wives from the south, too, but what respectable man really wants a Yamaguchi-no-anta? Do you, in your heart, really respect Takeshi-san's wife? Do you want a woman like that in your home? Would you want to present such a girl to me some day and say, 'Mother, here is my wife.'? And when I asked where she was from, would you feel satisfied if you had to confess, 'She's a Yamaguchi-no-anta?' "

Now the wise old woman came to the most difficult part of her sermon, so once more she fortified herself with a little rice, filling up the bowl with tea and a garnish of dried seaweed. "I would be heartbroken," she began, "if you married a northern girl or a southern girl, but to tell you the truth I would try to be a very good mother to them, and you would not curse me for my actions. But there are two marriages you may not make, Kamejiro. If you do, don't bother to come home. You will not be welcome either in the village or in this house or in any part of Hiroshima-ken." Solemnly she paused, looked out the door to be sure no one was listening, and proceeded.

"If you marry when I am not at hand, Kamejiro, ask your two closest friends to seek out the girl's history. You know the obvious problems. No disease, no insanity, nobody in jail, all ancestors good, strong Japanese. But then ask your advisers this: 'Are you sure she is not an Okinawan?' " Dramatically she stopped. Putting down her rice bowl she pointed at her son and said, "Don't bring an Okinawa girl to this house. If you marry such a girl, you are dead."

She waited for this ominous statement to wind its way through her son's mind, then added, "The danger is this, Kamejiro. In Hiroshima-ken we can spot an Okinawan instantly. I can tell when a girl comes from Okinawa if I see even two inches of her wrist. But in Hawaii I am told people forget how to do this. There are many Okinawans there, and their women set traps to catch decent Japanese. I wish I could go with you to Hawaii, for I can uncover these sly Okinawans. I am afraid you won't be able to, Kamejiro, and you will bring disgrace upon us."

She started to cry again, but rice stanched the tears, and she came to the climax of her warning: "There is of course one problem that every devoted son looks into before he marries, because he owes it not only to his parents but also to his brothers and sisters. Kamejiro, I said that if you married an Okinawa girl you were dead. But if you marry an Eta, you are worse than dead."

The wave of disgust that swept over Kamejiro's face proved that he despised the Eta as much as his mother did, for they were the untouchables of Japan, the unthinkables. In past ages they had dealt in the bodies of dead animals, serving as butchers and leather tanners. Completely outside the scope of Japanese civilication, they scratched out horrible lives in misery and wherever possible fled to distant refuges like Hawaii. A single trace of Eta blood could contaminate an entire family, even to remote unattached cousins, and Kamejiro shuddered.

His mother contiued dolefully: "I said I could spot an Okinawan, and I could protect you there. But with an Eta . . . I don't know. They're clever! Crawling with evil, they try to make you think they're normal people. They hide under different names. They take new occupations. I am sure that some of them must have slipped into Hawaii, and how will you know, Kamejiro? What would you do if word sneaked back to Hiroshima-ken that you had been captured by an Eta?"

Mother and son contemplated this horror for some minutes, and she concluded: "So when it comes time to marry, Kamejiro, I think it best if you marry a Hiroshima girl. Now I don't like girls from Hiroshima City, itself, for they are too fancy. They cost a man money and want their photographs taken all the time. I've seen a lot of girls from Hiroshima City, and although I'm ashamed to say so, some of them don't seem much better than an ordinary Yamaguchi-no-anta. And from what I have seen, a lot of the girls from the other end of Hiroshima-ken aren't too reliable, either. So don't be taken in just because a strange girl tells you she's a Hiroshima-gansu. It may mean nothing.

"And be careful not to marry into any family that has ever had an undertaker. Avoid city families if you can. To tell you the truth, Kamejiro, it would be best if you married a girl from right around here. Of course, I don't think much of the families in Atazuki Village, for they are spendthrift, but I can say there are no finer girls in all Japan than those in our village. So when the time comes to marry, go to a letter-writer and have him send me a message and when it is read to me, I'll find you a good local girl, and trust me, Kamejiro, that will be best." She paused dramatically, then added in an offhand manner, "Say, a fine strong girl like Yoko-chan." Kamejiro looked at his mother and said nothing, so she finished her rice.

When it came time for him to bid his parents farewell he assured them that he would never do anything to bring disgrace upon them, or upon Japan. His gruff father warned, "Don't bring home an Okinawan or an Eta." His mother summarized a larger body of Hiroshima morality by reminding him, "No matter where you go, Kamejiro, remember that you are a Japanese. Put strength in your stomach and be a good Japanese. Never forget that some day you will return to Hiroshima-ken, the proudest and greatest in all Japan. Come home with honor, or don't come home."

Then his father led him to one side and said quietly, "Be proud. Be Japanese. Put power in your stomach."

As he set forth from the village he saw by the shrine the flowering girl Yoko-san and he wanted to leave his weeping parents and rush over to her, shouting, "Yoko-chan! When I have made money I will send for you!" But his stocky legs were powerless to move him in that direction, and had he gone his voice would have been unable to speak, for officially they did not know each other, and all the exciting things that had transpired behind the darkened shoji had not really happened, for he had never removed his mask.

So he departed, a tough, stalwart little man with arms hanging down like loaded buckets, yet as he passed the shrine, looking straight ahead, he somehow received Yoko's assurance that if he cared to write for her, she would come; and a considerable happiness accompanied him on his journey.

For the first two miles his path lay along the Inland Sea, and he saw before him the shifting panorama of that wonderland of islands. Green and blue and rocky brown they rose from the cool waters, lifting their pine trees to the heavens. On one a bold crimson torii rose like a bird of God, marking some ancient Shinto shrine. On others Kamejiro saw the stained stone outlines of Buddhist temples, perched above the sea. How marvelous that footpath was! How the earth sang, while the rice fields swept their ripening grain back and forth in the winds creeping inland from the sea.

With every step Kamejiro encountered some unexpected beauty, for he was traversing one of the most glorious paths in the world, and the singing of that day would never leave his ears. Once he stopped to stare in wonder at the multitude of islands and at the magnificence of their position within the sea, and he swore, "A little time will pass and I will return to the Inland Sea."

WHEN THE *KYOTO-MARU* landed him in Honolulu he advised the immigration interpreter: "Stamp my paper for five years." Fortunately, he could not understand the official when the latter muttered to his assistant, "I wish I believed these little yellow bastards were gonna stay only five years."

There were others in Hawaii, however, who welcomed the Japanese ungrudgingly, for that day the Honolulu *Mail* editorialized: "Janders & Whipple are to be congratulated on having completed plans for the importation of 1,850 strong and healthy Japanese peasant farmers to work our sugar fields, with prospects for as many more at later intervals as may be required. We journeyed to the *Kyoto-maru* yesterday to inspect the new arrivals and can report that they seemed a sturdy lot. Lunas who have worked earlier crews of Japanese state unanimously that they are much superior to the unfortunate Chinese whom they are replacing. They are obedient, extraordinarily clean, law-abiding, not given to gambling and eager to accomplish at least eighty per cent more honest labor than the lazy Chinese ever did.

"Japanese avoid the Chinaman's tendency to combine into small and vicious groups. Themselves an agrarian people, they love plantation work and will stay in the fields, so that the trickery whereby in recent years crafty Orientals fled from honest work in the cane fields, so as to monopolize our city shops, can be expected to end. Japanese are notoriously averse to running stores, but J & W have taken the added precaution of importing only strong young men from rural areas. There are no wily Tokyo dwellers lurking ominously in their gangs. Plantation owners can expect a rapid improvement in the appearance of their camps, too, for Japanese love to garden and will soon have their buildings looking attractive.

"In two respects we are particularly fortunate in getting these Japanese. First, we have been assured that their men do not contract alliances with women of any other race but their own, and we can look forward confidently to a cessation of the disgraceful scenes of aging Oriental men marrying the best young Hawaiian girls of our islands. Secondly, because of the feudal structure of Japanese society, in which every Japanese is loyal unto the death to his master, firms like J & W are going to find that their new laborers will probably be the most loyal available on earth. Lunas who have worked them say they love authority, expect to be told what to do, respond promptly to crisp if not abusive treatment, and are accustomed to smart blows from time to time when their work is not up to par. Unlike their Chinese cousins, they neither resent honest correction nor combine secretly against those who administer it.

"All in all, we think that future history will show that the true prosperity of Hawaii began with the importation of these sturdy workmen, and when, at the end of their employment, they return to Japan, each with his pocketful of honestly earned gold, they will go with our warm aloha. Today we welcome them as fortunate replacements for the Chinese who have turned out so badly. Aloha nui nui!"

O F THE 1,850 Japanese laborers who debarked that September day in 1902, most were assigned to plantations on Oahu, the island that contained Honolulu, and they were depressed by the barren ugliness of the inland areas. They had not seen cactus before, but as farmers they could guess that it spoke ill of the land upon which it grew, and the dull red dust appalled them. They judged that no water came to these parts, and although they had not themselves grown cattle, they could see that the spavined beasts which roamed these desolate acres suffered from both thirst and hunger. They were disappointed in the parched land which showed so little promise, and one farmer whispered to his friends, "America is much different from what they said."

But Kamejiro Sakagawa was not to be disappointed, for he was among a batch of workers dispatched to another area, and when he reached it he saw immediately that this new land was among the fairest on earth. Even the glorious fields along the Inland Sea of Japan were no finer than the area which he was expected to till. To reach this veritable paradise young Kamejiro was not marched along the dusty roads of Oahu; he was led onto a small inter-island boat which at other times was used for the transport of lepers, and after a long, seasick night, he was marched ashore on the island of Kauai. At the pier a tall, scarfaced man waited impatiently on a horse, and when the captain of the boat was inept at docking, he shouted orders of his own, as if he were in command. At his side ran a little Japanese, and as his countrymen finally climbed down out of the boat, this interpreter told them, "The man on the horse is called Wild Whip Hoxworth. If you work good, he is good. If not, he will beat you over the head. So work good."

As he spoke, Wild Whip wheeled his horse among the men, reached down with his riding crop and tilted upward the face of Kamejiro Sakagawa. "You understand?" he growled. The little interpreter asked, "Ano hito ga yutta koto wakari mashita ka?" When stocky Kamejiro nodded, Whip lowered the riding crop, reached down and patted the new laborer on the shoulder.

Now he wheeled his horse about and moved into position at the head of the line. "We march!" he shouted, leading them off the pier onto a red-baked road where a group of sugar-cane wagons, hitched to horses, waited. "Climb in!" he yelled, and as the Japanese crawled into the low wagons whose sides were formed of high stakes bound together by lengths of rope, he moved to the head of the train and shouted, "On to Hanakai!" And the procession left the port town and moved slowly northward along the eastern coast of the island.

As the men rode they saw for the first time the full grandeur of Hawaii, for they were to work on one of the fairest islands in the Pacific. To the left rose jagged and soaring mountains, clothed in perpetual green. Born millions of years before the other mountains of Hawaii, these had eroded first and now possessed unique forms that pleased the eye. At one point the wind had cut a complete tunnel through the highest mountain; at others the erosion of softer rock had left isolated spires of basalt standing like monitors. To the right unfolded a majestic shore, cut by deep bays and highlighted by a rolling surf that broke endlessly upon dark rocks and brilliant white sand. Each mile disclosed to Kamejiro and his companions some striking new scene.

But most memorable of all he saw that day was the red earth. Down millions of years the volcanic eruptions of Kauai had spewed forth layers of iron-rich rocks, and for subsequent millions of years this iron had slowly, imperceptibly disintegrated until it now stood like gigantic piles of scintillating rust, the famous red earth of Kauai. Sometimes a green-clad mountain would show a gaping scar where the side of a cliff had fallen away, disclosing earth as red as new blood. At other times the fields along which the men rode would be an unblemished furnace-red, as if flame had just left it. Again in some deep valley where small amounts of black earth had intruded, the resulting red nearly resembled a brick color. But always the soil was red. It shone in a hundred different hues, but it was loveliest when it stood out against the rich green verdure of the island, for then the two colors complemented each other, and Kauai seemed to merit the name by which it was affectionately known: the Garden Island.

For out of its lush red soil, teeming with iron, grew a multitude of trees: palms that clung to the shore; pandanus that twisted itself into dense jungle; banyans with their thousand aerial roots; hau and kou, the excellent trees of the islands; swift-growing wild plum that had been imported from Japan to provide burning fagots for the laborers; and here and there a royal palm, its moss-pocked trunk rising majestically toward the heavens. But there was one tree specially dedicated to Kauai, and it made both life and agriculture on the island possible. Wherever the powerful northeast trades whipped sea and salt air inland, killing everything that grew, men had planted the strange, silky, gray-green casuarina tree, known sometimes as the ironwood. Groves of this curious tree, covered with ten-inch needles and seed cones that resembled round buttons, stood along the shore and protected the island. The foliage of the casuarina was not copious and to the stranger each tree looked so frail that it seemed about to die, but it possessed incredible powers of recuperation, and what it thrived on most was a harsh, salty trade wind that whipped its fragile needles into a frenzy and tore at its cherry-bark trunk; for then the casuarina dug in and saved the island. The sea winds howled through its branches; its frail needles caught the salt; the force of the storm was broken; and all who lived in the shadow of the casuarina tree lived securely.

As the Japanese rode through this verdant wonderland, a storm flashed in from the sea, throwing tubs of water over the land, but Wild Whip, holding his prancing horse under control, shouted to his interpreter, "Ishii-san, tell the men that on Kauai we don't run from storms!" The frail little interpreter ran from wagon to wagon, shouting, "On this island it rains a dozen times a day. Soon the sun comes out. We never bother." And as he predicted, after a few minutes the wild storm moved on to sulk in a valley until a rainbow was flung across it, and it was toward this rainbow that Kamejiro and his companions rode.

They had come to the valley of Hanakai, the Valley of the Sea, but they were not yet aware of that fact, for the highway upon which they rode was at this point more than a mile inland; but leading off from it, to the right and toward the sea, appeared a spectacular lane. It was marked by twenty pairs of royal palms, gray-trunked and erect, that Whip had sent home from Madagascar on one of the H & H ships, and these magnificent sentinels guarded the road as stone lions had once stood watch for the Assyrians. Entering the deep shade of the lane, the workmen sensed that they were approaching something special, and after a while they came upon twenty pairs of Norfolk pine, those exalted sculptural trees that had originally grown on only one South Pacific island, from which Whip had some years ago recovered two hundred young trees which he had scattered throughout Hawaii. Beyond them came the beauty of the Hoxworth lane: to the left and north stood an unbroken line of croton bushes imported by Whip from Guadalcanar in the Solomons, and of all that grew on his plantations, these were his favorites, these low sparkling bushes whose iridescent green and red and purple and gold and blue leaves were a constant source of wonder; but to the right ran a long row of hibiscus trees, low shrublike plants that produced a dozen varieties of fragile, crepelike flowers, each with its own dazzling color; Whip's favorite was the bright yellow hibiscus, bigger than a large plate and golden in the sunlight.

The lane now turned sharply south and entered upon a huge grassy area. As was the custom in Hawaii at that time, no specific roadway led up to the Hoxworth mansion. Over the spacious lawn, guests drove as they wished, for no matter how badly the grass was scarred by such usage, the next day's inevitable rain and sunlight cured it. On the lawn there were only two trees. To the right stood an African tulip tree with dark green leaves and brilliant red flowers scattered prodigally upon it, while to the left rose one of the strangest trees in nature, the golden tree which Whip had found in South America. Each year it produced a myriad of brilliant yellow flowers, and since it stood some fifty feet high, it was a spectacular exhibit.

The house was long and low, built originally in China of the best wood, then taken apart and shipped in an H & H cargo ship to Hanakai. It ran from northeast to southwest, and its southern exposure consisted of eight tall Greek pillars supporting a porch upon which the life of the mansion took place. For at Hanakai the view from the lanai—the open porch—commanded attention. A soft green grassy lawn fell away to the edge of a steep cliff some three hundred feet above the surface of the sea, which here cut deeply inland forming the bay of Hanakai. When a storm of major proportions fell upon Kauai, the wild ocean would sweep its penetrating arm into the bay and find itself impounded. Then it would leap like a caged animal high up the sides of the red cliff. Its topmost spray would poise there for a moment, then fall screaming down the sheer sides. To see such a storm at Hanakai was to see the ocean at its best. But to the north and east, from where the storms blew, there was a row of trees, not visible from the mansion, and it was upon these that the life of Hanakai depended, for they were the casuarina trees, and it was their needles that sifted out the salt and broke the back of the wild storm; they were the speechless, sighing workmen, and if the golden tree was the marvel of that part of Kauai, it existed solely because the casuarinas fought the storms on its behalf.

Within the protection of the casuarinas Wild Whip paused to review the beauty of his favorite spot in the islands. It had been given him by his doting grandfather, Captain Rafer Hoxworth, who had got it from the Alii Nui Noelani, and here Whip had brought his treasures from around the world. Hawaii's best mangoes grew at Hanakai, its most brilliant hibiscus and its best horses. As Whip now studied the red earth and heard the ocean growling at the cliffs he muttered, "Lucky Japanese who came here to work."

Kamejiro and his fellow laborers did not, of course, accompany Whip to the mansion. At the end of the lane Mr. Ishii, the interpreter, took them off in quite the opposite direction, toward the casuarina trees, and after half a mile he brought them to a long low wooden building consisting of a single room. It contained three doors, a few windows, half a dozen tables and some sagging wooden beds. Outside were two unspeakably foul toilets with a well between. There were no trees, no flowers, no amenities of any kind, but there was a copious amount of red mud, a thicket of wild plum from which firewood could be cut, and in all directions the green wilderness of growing sugar canes. This was the Ishii Camp, so known because of the interpreter who ran it.

In this particular camp, there were no women, no facilities for recreation, no doctor, and no church. There was lots of rice, for Wild Whip insisted that his men be fed well, and in each camp—for this was merely one of seven on Hanakai Plantation—one man was appointed fisherman, bringing to the table whatever he caught on the fruitful reefs of Kauai. It was Whip Hoxworth's full intention that any laborer whom he imported should work for him five or ten years, save his money, and return to Japan. There was thus no need for women or churches, and little need for doctors, since he hired only the ablest-bodied.

At Hanakai the Hoxworth laborers rose at four in the morning, ate a hot breakfast, hiked to the fields so as to be there at six and worked till six at night, hiking back to the Ishii Camp on their own time. For this they were paid sixty-seven cents a day, but they did get their food and a sagging bed. During harvest, of course, they worked nineteen hours a day for no extra money.

On the first workday Kamejiro Sakagawa marched home at dusk, feeling great strength in his bones, and looked about for some place in which to bathe, for like all Japanese he was fanatic in his attention to cleanliness, and he was dismayed to find that no provisions had been made. Water could be pumped from the well, but who could bathe properly in cold water? On this first night he had to make do, protestingly, and he listened to his mates growling as they recalled the sweet, hot baths of Hiroshima, and that night he went to see Ishii-san and said, "I think I will build a hot bath for the camp."

"There's no lumber," Ishii-san said. It was his job to protect the interests of Mr. Hoxworth and he did so.

"I saw some old boards at the edge of the sugar field," Kamejiro replied.

"You can have them, but there are no nails," Ishii-san warned.

"I saw some nails where the irrigation ditch was mended."

"Were they rusted?"

"Yes."

"You can have them."

On his second full day ashore in Hawaii, Kamejiro began building his hot bath. It was most tedious work, for he could not find lumber that fitted nor could he get hold of a piece of galvanized iron for the bottom, where the fire was to be built. At last he grabbed Ishii-san, who was skittish about the whole affair, and made the interpreter speak to Mr. Hoxworth—Hoxuwurtu, the Japanese men called him—and the tall boss growled, "What do you want galvanized iron for?"

"To take a bath," Kamejiro said.

"Use cold water. I do," Hoxworth snapped.

"I don't!" Kamejiro snapped back, and Hoxworth turned in his saddle to study the runty little man with the long arms that hung out from his body.

"Don't speak to me that way," Hoxworth said ominously, pointing his riding crop at him.

"We have to be clean," Kamejiro insisted, not drawing away from the crop.

"You have to work," Hoxworth said slowly.

"But after work we want to be clean," Kamejiro said forcefully.

"Are you looking for a fight?" Hoxworth cried, dropping from his horse and throwing his reins to an attendant. Ishii-san, the interpreter, began to sweat and mumbled his words, replying on behalf of Kamejiro, "Oh, no, sir! This man is fine workman!"

"Shut up!" Hoxworth snapped, pushing his little assistant aside. Striding up to Kamejiro he started to grab him by the shoulders, but as he did so he saw the enormous musculature of the stubborn workman, and he saw also that Kamejiro had no intention of allowing even the boss to touch him, and the two men stood in the cane field staring at each other. The other Japanese were terrified lest trouble start, but Kamejiro, to his surprise, was unconcerned, for he was studying the big American and thinking: "If he comes one step closer I will ram my head into his soft belly."

In mutual respect the tension dissolved, and Wild Whip asked Ishii-san, "What is it he wants?"

"He's building a bath for the camp," Ishii repeated.

"That's what I don't understand," Hoxworth replied.

"Japanese cannot live unless they have a bath each day," Kamejiro explained.

"Pump the water and take a bath," Whip said.

"A hot bath," Kamejiro replied.

For a long moment the two men stared at each other, after which Whip laughed easily and asked, "So you've got to have some corrugated iron?"

"Yes," Kamejiro said.

"You'll get it," Hoxworth replied. As if they were boys playing, Whip winked at Kamejiro, and chucked him under the chin with the whip. With one finger the Japanese laborer slowly moved the crop away, and the two men understood each other.

When the bath was built, a square tub four feet deep on stilts, Kamejiro rigged a triple length of bamboo which delivered water from the pump. Beneath the galvanized iron he built a fire with wild plum branches, and when the water was hot he clanged a piece of iron to summon the camp. Each man stripped, hung his clothes on a pole spiked with nails, and was allowed one panful of hot water with which to soap down outside the tub and rinse off. Then, mounting three wooden steps, he climbed into the steaming water and luxuriated for four minutes. While he was doing this, the next man was cleansing himself, and as the first crawled out reluctantly, the second climbed in eagerly. Kamejiro tended the fire and added new water as it was needed.

The first ten men to use the water paid a penny each, and cast lots to determine who had the right to climb in first. After the first ten, each man paid half a cent, and as many as wished used the water. Long after night had fallen, when the pennies were safely stowed away and the other men were eating their evening meal, Kamejiro himself would undress, place one more stick under the iron—for he liked his bath hotter than most—and after carefully soaping himself outside and washing off, he would climb into the remnants of the water. Its heat would encompass him and make him forget Hiroshima and the difficulties of the day. To the east the casuarina trees kept away the storm, and in the hot bath all was well.

When he returned to his bunk he invariably looked with deep respect at his only significant possession, the black-framed portrait of the Japanese emperor. Before this grim and bearded leader the little workman bowed; the one reality in his life was that the emperor personally knew of his daily behavior and was grieved when things went poorly. Each night before he went to sleep he weighed his day's actions and hoped that the emperor would approve.

In order to collect the firewood needed for the hot bath, Kamejiro rose at three-thirty each morning and worked while the others were eating. When the wood was safely stored, he grabbed two rice balls, a bit of pickle and part of a fish, munching them as he ran to the fields. At six, when the day's work ended, he dashed home ahead of the rest to get the fire started, and was not free to eat until the last bath had been taken. Then he accepted what was left and in this way he saved the money for the important step he was to take thirteen years later in 1915.

It was not easy to accumulate money, not even when one worked as hard as Kamejiro did. For example, in 1904 events transpired in Asia which were to eat up his savings, but no man worthy of the name would have done less than he did under the circumstances. For some months Japan had been having trouble with Russia, and the emperor's divine word to his people had reached even remote Kauai, where with trembling voice Ishii-san had read the rescript to all the assembled Japanese: "As it is Our heartfelt desire to maintain the peace of the East, We have caused Our government to negotiate with Russia, but We are now compelled to conclude that the Russian government has no sincere desire to maintain the peace of the East. We have therefore ordered Our government to break off negotiations with Russia and have decided to take free action for the maintenance of Our independence and self-protection."

"What does it mean?" Kamejiro asked.

"War," an older man explained.

Now Ishii-san's voice rose to an awed climax as he delivered the distant emperor's specific message to all loyal Japanese: "We rely upon your loyalty and valor to carry out Our object and thereby keep unsullied the honor of Our Empire."

"Banzai!" a former soldier shouted.

"Japan must win!" the workmen began to cry.

Ishii-san waited for the tumult to die down, then announced: "On Friday an officer of the emperor himself will come to Hanakai to collect money for the Imperial army. Let us show the world what loyal Japanese we are!" He hesitated a moment, then announced: "I will give eleven dollars."

A gasp went up from the crowd as men realized how much of his meager salary this represented, and another was inspired to cry, "I will give nineteen dollars." The crowd applauded, and as the ante rose, Kamejiro was swept up by the fervor of the moment. Japan was in danger. He could see his parents' fields overrun by Russian barbarians, and he thought how insignificant were his savings from the hot bath. In an ecstasy of emotion, seeing the grave, bearded emperor before him, he rose and cried in a roaring voice, "I will give all my bath money! Seventy-seven dollars."

A mighty cheer went up, and a Buddhist priest said, "Let us in our hearts resolve to protect the honor of Japan as Sakagawa Kamejiro has done this day." Men wept and songs were sung and Ishii-san shouted in his high, weak voice, "Let every man march by and swear allegiance to the emperor." Instinctively the workmen formed in orderly ranks and fell into martial rhythms as they marched past the place where the Buddhist priest stood. Pressing their hands rigidly to their knees, they bowed as if to the august presence itself and said, "Banzai! Banzai!"

When the excitement was over, and the emperor's emissary had left with the money, the camp settled down to the agony of waiting for war news. It was rumored that Russian troops had landed on the island of Kyushu, and Kamejiro whispered to Ishii-san at night, "Should we return to Honolulu and try to find a boat back to Japan?"

"No," Ishii said gravely. "After all, what we have heard is only a rumor."

"But Japan is in danger!" Kamejiro muttered.

"We must wait for more substantial news," Ishii-san insisted, and because he could read and write, people listened to him. And the year 1904 ended in apprehension.

But in January, 1905, his prudence was rewarded when word reached Kauai that the great Russian bastion at Port Arthur had surrendered to a Japanese siege. Kauai—that is, the Japanese living there—went wild with joy and a torchlight procession was held through the plantation town of Kapaa; and the celebrations had hardly ended when word came of an even more astonishing victory at Mukden, followed quickly by the climactic news from the Strait of Tsushima. A Russian fleet of thirty-eight major vessels had engaged the Japanese under Admiral Togo; nineteen were immediately sunk, five were captured, and of the remaining fourteen, only three got back to Russia. More than 10,000 of the enemy were drowned and 6,000 taken prisoner. For their part, the Japanese lost only three minor torpedo boats and less than 700 men. The Honolulu *Mail* called Tsushima "one of the most complete victories any nation has ever enjoyed at the expense of a major rival."

Kamejiro, listening to the stunning news, burst into tears and told his friend Ishii-san, "I feel as if my hot-bath money had personally sunk the Russian ships."

"It did," Ishii-san assured him. "Because it represented the undying spirit of the Japanese. Look at the poor Americans! Their president speaks to them, and nothing happens. No one pays attention. But when the emperor speaks to us, we hear even though we are lost at the end of the world."

Kamejiro contemplated this for a moment, then asked, "Ishii-san, do you feel proud today?"

"I feel as if my heart were a balloon carrying me above the trees," Ishii-san replied.

"I can feel guns going off in my chest every minute," Kamejiro confided. "They are the guns of Admiral Togo." Again tears came into his eyes and he asked, "Ishii-san, do you think it would be proper for us to say a prayer for that great admiral who saved Japan?"

"It would be better if the priest were here. That's his job."

"But wouldn't it be all right if we ourselves faced Japan and said a prayer?"

"I would like to do so," Ishii-san admitted, and the two laborers knelt in the red dust of Kauai and each thought of Hiroshima, and the rice fields, and the red torii looking out over the Japan Sea, and they prayed that their courageous country might always know victory.

By this time Kamejiro had saved, from his wages and the hot bath, an additional thirty-eight dollars, and the camp suspected this, so when word reached Kauai that a splendid victory celebration was to be held right in the heart of Honolulu, for all Hawaii to see, and that the island of Kauai was invited to send two men to march in Japanese uniforms and play the roles of immortal military leaders like Admiral Togo, everyone agreed that Kamejiro should be one of the men, because he could pay his own way, and a man named Hashimoto was the other, because he also had some savings, and in late May, 1905, the two stocky laborers set out on the inter-island boat *Kilauea* for Honolulu. There the committee provided them with handsome uniforms which local Japanese wives had copied from magazine pictures, and Kamejiro found himself a full colonel in memory of a leader who had personally thrown himself upon the Russian guns at the siege of Port Arthur. This Colonel Ito had been blown to pieces and into national immortality. It was with bursting pride that Colonel Sakagawa lined up on the afternoon of June 2, 1905, to march boldly through the streets of Honolulu and across the Nuuanu to Aala Park, where thousands of Japanese formed a procession that proceeded solemnly to the Japanese consulate, where a dignified man in frock coat and black tie nodded gravely. A workman from one of the Janders & Whipple plantations on Oahu was dressed in Admiral Togo's uniform, and from the steps of the consulate he led the Banzai and the formal marching broke up. Kamejiro and his fellow Kauai man, Hashimoto, walked back to Aala Park, where exhibitions of Japanese wrestling and fencing were offered to an appreciative crowd; but the victory celebration was to have overtones of another kind which Kamejiro would never forget, for at ten o'clock, when the crowd was greatest, a pathway was formed and eight professional geisha girls from one of the tea houses passed through the confusion to take their places on the dancing platform, and as they went one walked in her gently swaying manner quite close to Kamejiro and the powder in her hair brushed into his nostrils and he admitted, for the first time in three years, how desperately hungry he was for that girl Yoko back in Hiroshima.

A haze came over his eyes and he imagined that the mask was once more upon his face while he prepared to slip into her sleeping room. He could feel her arms about him and hear her voice in his ear. The crowd pressed in upon him but he was not part of it; he was in Hiroshima in the spring when the rice fields were a soft green, and a horrible thought took possession of him: "I shall never leave Kauai! I shall die here and never see Japan again! I shall live all my life without a woman!"

And he began, in his agony, to walk among the crowd and placed himself so that he might touch this Japanese wife or that. He did not grab at them or embarrass them; he wanted merely to see them and to feel their reality; and his glazed eyes stared at them. "I am so hungry," he muttered to himself as he moved so as to intercept a woman at least twenty years older than he. She shuffled along with her feet never leaving the ground, Japanese style, and the soft rustle of her passing seemed to him one of the sweetest sounds he had ever heard. Instinctively he reached out his hand and clutched at her arm, and the shuffling stopped. The housewife looked at him in amazement, pushed his hand down, and muttered, "You are a Japanese! Behave yourself! Especially when you wear such a uniform!"

Mortified, he fled the crowd and found Hashimoto, who said abruptly, "Those damned geisha girls are driving me loony. Let's find a good whorehouse."

The two Kauai laborers started probing the Aala region, but a stranger told them, "The houses you want are all in Iwilei," so they hurried to that quarter of the city, but the houses were filled with richer patrons and the two could gain no entrance.

"I'm going to grab any woman I see," Hashimoto said.

"No!" Kamejiro warned, remembering the admonition of the woman he had touched.

"To hell with you!" the other shouted. "Girl! Girls!" he shouted in Japanese. "Here I come to find you!" And he dashed down one of the Iwilei alleys. Kamejiro, now ashamed to be in such a place while dressed as Colonel Ito, who had sacrificed his life at Port Arthur, fled the area and returned to the park, where he sat for hours staring at the dancers. This time he kept away from women, and after a long time an old Japanese man came up to him with a bottle of sake and said, "Oh, Colonel! What a glorious war this was! And did you notice one thing tonight? Not one damned Chinese had the courage to appear on the streets while our army was marching! I tell you, Colonel! In 1895 we defeated the Chinese. And in 1905 we defeated the Russians. Two of the finest nations on earth. Who will we fight ten years from now? England? Germany?"

"All the world can be proud of Japan," Kamejiro agreed.

"What is more important, Colonel," the drunk continued, "is that here in Hawaii people have now got to respect us. The German lunas who beat us with whips. The Norwegian lunas who treat us with contempt. They have got to respect us Japanese! We are a great people! Therefore, Colonel, promise me one thing, and I will give you more sake. The next time a European luna dares to strike you in the cane fields, kill him! We Japanese will show the world."

It was a tremendous celebration, worthy of the impressive victory gained by the homeland, and even though it used up much of Kamejiro's savings and reminded him of how lonely he was, he felt it had been worthwhile; but it had one unfortunate repercussion which no one could have foreseen, and long after the celebration itself had faded into memory, this one dreadful result lived on in Kamejiro's mind.

It started in the whorehouses of Iwilei, after Kamejiro had abandoned his lusty friend Hashimoto to the alleys, for that young man had forced his way into one of the houses and had been soundly thrashed by half a dozen Germans who resented his intrusion. Thrown into one of the gutters, he had been found by a Hawaiian boy who did pimping for a group of girls, and this boy, in the custom of the islands, had lugged the bewildered Japanese home, where his sister had washed his bruises. They had been able to converse only in pidgin, but apparently enough had been said, for when Hashimoto returned to the Kauai ship, he had the sister in tow. She was a big, amiable, wide-eyed Hawaiian who carried with her only one bundle tied with string, but she seemed to like wiry, tough-minded Hashimoto and apparently intended to stay with him.

"I am going to marry her," Hashimoto stoutly informed Kamejiro, who still wore his colonel's uniform, and something about either the victory celebration or the uniform made Kamejiro especially patriotic that day, for as soon as his friend said the fatal words, "I am going to marry her," he sprang into action as if he were in charge of troops. Grabbing Hashimoto by the arm he warned,

"If you do such a thing, all Japan will be ashamed."

"I may not ever go back to Japan," Hashimoto said.

Impulsively, like a true colonel, Kamejiro struck Hashimoto across the face, shouting, "Don't ever speak like that! Japan is your home!"

Hashimoto was astonished at Colonel Sakagawa's unexpected behavior but he recognized that he deserved the rebuke, so he mumbled, "I'm tired of living without a woman."

This introduced a less military note into the discussion, and Kamejiro quit being an Imperial colonel and became once more a friend. "Hashimoto-san, it was bad enough to go to such a house, but to bring home one of the girls, and to marry her! You must put strength in your stomach and be a decent Japanese."

"She isn't from one of the houses," Hashimoto explained. "She's a good girl from a good hard-working family."

"But she's not Japanese!" Kamejiro argued.

He made no progress with Hashimoto, who was determined not to live alone any longer. Since there were no Japanese girls available on Kauai, he would live with his Hawaiian and marry her. But in his ardor for feminine companionship he had failed to consider the even greater ardor of the Japanese community, and when it was noised abroad what he had done, he experienced the full, terrible power of the sacred Japanese spirit.

"You have sullied the name of Japan," warned the older men, who had learned to live without women.

"You have disgraced the blood of Japan," others mourned.

"Have you no pride, no Yamato spirit?" younger men asked.

"Don't you realize that you bring disgrace upon us all?" his friends pleaded.

Hashimoto proved himself to be a man of fortitude. "I will not live alone any longer," he repeated stubbornly. "I am going to live with my wife, the way a man should."

"Then you will live forever apart from the Japanese community," a stern old man cried. He had been in Kauai for many years, also longing for a woman, but he had behaved himself as a decent Japanese should, and now on behalf of all the emperor's subjects he pronounced the ostracism: "Because you have been shameless, and because you have not protected the sacred blood of Japan, you must live apart. We don't want a man like you to work with us or to eat with us or to live with us. Get out."

Hashimoto began to feel the awful force of this sentence, and pleaded, "But a man needs a woman! What do you expect me to do?"

A fiery younger man replaced the one who had delivered the ostracism, and this one shouted belligerently, "We don't expect you to marry other women! You're no Chinese who is willing to marry anybody he can get his hands on. You're a Japanese!"

"What am I to do?" Hashimoto screamed. "Live alone all my life?"

"Use the prostitutes each month, like we do," the fiery young man cried, referring to the girls which the plantation bosses provided on paydays, moving them from camp to camp according to schedule.

"But the time comes when a man doesn't want prostitutes any longer," Hashimoto pleaded.

"Then live without them," an older man snapped. "Like Akagi-san. Eh, you Akagi-san? How many years you live without a woman?"

"Nineteen," a wiry veteran of the cane fields replied.

"And you, Yamasaki-san?"

"Seventeen," a sunburned Hiroshima man replied.

"They're decent, honest Japanese!" the younger man shouted. "They will wait here till they die, hoping for a Japanese wife, but if none arrives they would not think of marrying anyone else. In them the Japanese spirit is high. In you, Hashimoto, there is no honor. Now get out!"

So Hashimoto left Ishii Camp and lived with his Hawaiian wife in the town of Kapaa. He had to be fired by Hanakai Plantation, for other Japanese refused to work with an outcast who had sullied the blood of Japan. Sometimes when men from camp went into Kapaa to play a little pool or get drunk on okolehau, a potent illegal brew made from the root of the ti plant, they would meet their former friend Hashimoto, but they never spoke. He could not attend the Japanese church, nor any of the socials, nor play in Japanese games, nor listen to the heroic reciters who came from time to time from Tokyo, spending days among the camps, reciting the glories of Japanese history.

From all such normal intercourse Hashimoto was excluded, and although the dreadful example of his banishment was frequently recalled by other young men who may have wanted women and who were certainly tempted to marry Hawaiian or Chinese or drifting white girls, his proscribed name was never mentioned. Men hungry for girls did not warn each other: "Remember what happened to Hashimoto!" Instinctively they remembered, for of him it had once been said: "All Japan will be ashamed of what you have done." And the young men were convinced that throughout every village of Japan the evil word had been passed: "Hashimoto Sutekichi married a Hawaiian woman and all Japan is ashamed of him." What Honolulu thought of the marriage was unimportant, for Honolulu did not matter, but what Japan thought was of towering concern, for every man in Ishii Camp intended one day to return to Japan; and to take back with him any wife other than a decent Japanese was unthinkable.

THE YEARS FOLLOWING annexation had not been kind to Wild Whip Hoxworth. In business the more stodgy members of Hoxworth & Hale had kept him from assuming any position of leadership within the company, so that even though his sugar lands irrigated by artesian wells flourished and made him a millionaire several times over, he was denied for moral reasons the command of H & H to which his talents entitled him. So he had come to Kauai.

With driving energy he had imported hundreds of Japanese laborers and had built irrigation ditches, cleared land, and shown Kauai how to grow sugar by the most improved methods. He had erected his own mill and ground his own cane, filling the stubby cargo ships of the H & H line with his product.

With equal energy he had built the mansion at Hanakai, personally placing the croton bushes and the hibiscus. When the cut timbers arrived from China he supervised their erection, and it was he who added the idea of a broad area covered by flagstone through whose chinks grass grew, so that one walked both on the firmness of stone and the softness of grass. When he finished he had a magnificent house, perched on the edge of a precipice at whose feet the ocean thundered, but it was a house that knew no happiness, for shortly after Whip had moved in with his third wife, the Hawaiian-Chinese beauty Ching-ching, who was pregnant at the time, she had caught him fooling around with the brothel girls that flourished in the town of Kapaa. Without even a scene of recrimination, Ching-ching had simply ordered a carriage and driven back to the capital town of Lihue, where she boarded an H & H steamer for Honolulu. She divorced Whip but kept both his daughter Iliki and his yet-unborn son

John. Now there were two Mrs. Whipple Hoxworths in Honolulu and they caused some embarrassment to the more staid community. The two never met, but Hoxworth & Hale saw to it that each received a monthly allowance. The sums were generous, but not so much so as those sent periodically to Wild Whip's second wife, the fiery Spanish girl Aloma Duarte Hoxworth, whose name frequently appeared in New York and London newspapers.

During these early years of the twentieth century, Wild Whip lived alone at Hanakai, a driven, miserable man. Periodically he spent lost days in some back room of the Kapaa brothels, competing with his field hands for the favors of Oriental prostitutes. At other times he would pull himself together and organize the dreamlike sporting events that were a feature of Kauai. For example, he kept a large stable of quarter horses and a fine grassy oval on which to race them at meetings where Chinese and Hawaiian betters went wild and lost a year's wages on one race. Part of Whip's distrust of the Japanese stemmed from the fact that they did not bet madly on his horse races, for he said, "A man who can't get excited about a horse race is really no man at all, and you can have the little yellow bastards." But when it was pointed out that the Japanese enabled him to grow more cane than any other plantation in the islands, he always acknowledged that fact: "Work is their god and I respect them for it. But my love I reserve for men who like horses."

The highlight of any season came when Wild Whip organized one of his polo tournaments, for this was the conspicuous game of the islands, and he maintained a line of thirty-seven choice ponies. The games took place on a lovely grassy field edging the wild cliffs of Hanakai, but the high moment of any game occurred when a sudden shower would toss a rainbow above the players so that two riders fighting for the ball could pass mysteriously from shower into sunlight and back into the soft, misty rain. A polo game at Hanakai was one of the most beautiful sports a man could witness, and islanders often walked for miles to sit along the croton bushes.

Wild Whip played a fine game, and in order to maintain the quality of his team, always hired his lunas personally. Sitting carelessly in a deep chair, he watched the man approach down the long lanai and studied his gait. "Limber, supple, nice walk that one," he would muse. His first question was invariable: "Young man, have you a good seat?" If the man stuttered or failed to understand what a good seat implied, Whip courteously excused him from further consideration. But if the man said, "I've been riding since I was three," Whip proceeded with the interview. Traditionally, on Kauai, lunas were either German immigrants or Norwegians, and among themselves they circulated the warning: "Don't apply at Hanakai unless you're good at polo."

When he hired a man Whip laid down three requirements: "Polished boots that come to the knee, and I want them polished till they gleam. White riding breeches, and I want them white. And finally, lunas on Hanakai never strike the workmen."

Actually, few of the Germans and Norwegians were good at polo when they first started work, but Whip gave lessons every afternoon at four, and in time even the Japanese became proud when their boss and their lunas defended Hanakai's championship against all comers from Kauai.

But major excitement occurred periodically when a picked team from Honolulu, consisting mostly of Janderses and Whipples and Hewletts who had perfected their game at Yale—for many years in a row the stars of the Yale four came from Hawaii—chartered a boat to bring their ponies and their cheering section on an invasion of Kauai. Then haoles from all the local plantations moved out to Hanakai; enormous beds ten feet square were thrown along the lanai, with eight or ten haphazard people to the bed, and kitchens were set up behind the casuarina trees. In the evenings gala dances were held with men in formal dress and women brilliant in gowns from Paris and Canton. Frequently, tournaments were staged with four or five competing teams, and all lived at Hanakai for a week. Then life was glorious, with champagne and flirtations, and often Wild Whip succeeded in sequestering one of the visitors' wives in some darkened bedroom, so that over the polo games at Hanakai there hung always the ominous shadow of potential scandal.

There was another shadow, too, for if the polo field and the croton bushes were made possible only by the protecting rim of silent casuarina trees which kept away the storms and the killing salt, so the life of the haoles was protected by the rim of silent Japanese laborers who lived in the womanless huts and who kept away the sweat, the toil and the work of building the future.

It was curious that when the men of Hawaii returned to Yale for alumni celebrations, and when their former classmates who now lived in respectable centers like Boston and Philadelphia asked, "What holds a brilliant man like you in Hawaii?" the Janderses and the Hales and the Whipples usually replied longingly, "Have you ever seen a polo game at Hanakai? The ocean at your feet. The storms sweeping in with rainbows. When your pony slips, he leaves a bright red scar across the turf. You could live a hundred years in Philadelphia and never see anything like the polo season at Hanakai." The Yale men who had gone to live in Philadelphia never understood, but their former classmates who had played polo along the Hawaii circuit never forgot that Hawaii in those years provided one of the best societies on earth.

When the polo players had departed, when the field kitchens were taken down, and when the patient little Japanese gardeners were tending each cut in the polo turf as if it were a personal wound, Wild Whip would retire to his sprawling mansion overlooking the sea and get drunk. He was never offensive and never beat anyone while intoxicated. At such times he stayed away from the brothels in Kapaa and away from the broad lanai from which he could see the ocean. In a small, darkened room he drank, and as he did so he often recalled his grandfather's words: "Girls are like stars, and you could reach up and pinch each one on the points. And then in the east the moon rises, enormous and perfect. And that's something else, entirely different." It was now apparent to Whip, in his forty-fifth year, that for him the moon did not intend to rise. Somehow he had missed encountering the woman whom he could love as his grandfather had loved the Hawaiian princess Noelani. He had known hundreds of women, but he had found none that a man could permanently want or respect. Those who were desirable were mean in spirit and those who were loyal were sure to be tedious. It was probably best, he thought at such times, to do as he did: know a couple of the better girls at Kapaa, wait for some friend's wife who was bored with her husband, or trust that a casual trip through the more settled camps might turn up some workman's wife who wanted a little excitement. It wasn't a bad life and was certainly less expensive in the long run than trying to marry and divorce a succession of giddy women; but often when he had reached this conclusion, through the bamboo shades of the darkened room in which he huddled a light would penetrate, and it would be the great moon risen from the waters to the east and now passing majestically high above the Pacific. It was an all-seeing beacon, brilliant enough to make the grassy lawns of Hanakai a sheet of silver, probing enough to find any mansion tucked away beneath the casuarina trees. When this moon sought out Wild Whip he would first draw in his feet, trying like a child to evade it, but when it persisted he often rose, threw open the lanai screens, and went forth to meet it. He would stand in the shimmering brilliance for a long time, listening to the surf pound in below, and in its appointed course the moon would disappear behind the jagged hills to the west.

It was uncanny, at such moments, how the Hawaiian men who worked for Whip would sense his mood. In twos and threes, they would appear mysteriously with ukuleles, strumming them idly in subtle island harmonies, and Whip would hear them and cry, "Eh, you! Pupule, you come!" And the men would unostentatiously gather about him, and he would grab a ukulele and begin to chant some long-forgotten song his grandmother had taught him. He became a Hawaiian, moody, distant, hungry for the message of the night; and for hours he would sing with his men, one song after another. A field hand would grunt, "Eh, boss? You got some okolehau?" And Whip would open some whiskey, and the bottle would pass reflectively from mouth to mouth, and the old laments of Hawaii would continue. At dawn the men would inconspicuously shuffle away, one or two at a time, but the man whose ukulele Wild Whip had borrowed would linger on until at last he would have to say, "Mo bettah I go now, boss," and the long night would end.

After such interludes Wild Whip always turned to his pineapples. On a well-protected plateau about the size of two tennis courts, perched at the head of the Hanakai valley and about two hundred yards from the African tulip tree, he had constructed a special field and fertilized it for the propagation of pineapples, for it was Whip's belief that ultimately the growing of this fruit on high fields and sugar on low was the destiny of Hawaii. To anyone who would listen, he was eager to explain his theories.

"Look! The two things are natural partners. Sugar needs water, a ton of water for each pound of sugar. Pineapple doesn't. Sugar thrives on low fields, pineapples on high. At the very point on a hillside where it's no longer profitable to irrigate for sugar, that's where pineapple grows best. And if you have sugar growing down here and pineapple up there, when the fruit gets ripe you drench it in sugar, can it, and sell both at a huge profit.

"Why in hell do you suppose I came to Kauai? Because it offers an ideal combination of sugar lands and pineapple lands. Before I leave, I'll have the secret that'll make Hanakai the richest plantation in the world."

Whenever Whip looked at the land of Hawaii, with its fortunate combination of high dry fields and low wet ones, he became excited; but when he looked at his experimental pineapple beds, he became furious. For he had in his trial fields more than nineteen different kinds of pineapple, "and not one of them worth a goddamn." He showed his visitors all that he had found so far: "That one with the savage hooks along its leaves—they'd cut you into pieces trying to harvest in a field full of them—they're the Pernambuco and you can have every damned Pernambuco ever grown. The striped one is the Zebrina, looks good but the fruit's foul. That interesting one in three colors is the Bracteatus, and for a time I had hopes for it, but the fruit's too small. I have plants that look like rat tails, others that look like whips, some with teeth like sickles. The only two possibly worth bothering with are the Guatemala and the New Guinea, but they don't prosper here."

"That means you have nothing really worth working on?" agriculturists asked.

"Yep. Wouldn't try to grow any of 'em commercially."

"Then you conclude that pineapples aren't suited to Hawaii?"

"Well . . . I wouldn't admit that."

"You got something else in mind? Some new breed?"

"Maybe . . . maybe some day we'll find exactly the right fruit for these islands."

At such times Hoxworth became hard and secretive, for if he was no longer obsessed by any one woman, and if he had reached a reluctant truce with the standard patterns of love, he did entertain a positive lust for something he had once seen. In 1896 a Rio de Janeiro hotel had served him a Cayenne pineapple, and the instant he had seen that barrelshaped, sweet and heavy fruit he had known that this was the pineapple for Hawaii. He had expected that it would be simple to go to some agriculturist and say, "I'd like five thousand Cayenne plants," and he had tried to do so; but he quickly found that the French who controlled that part of the Guiana coast where this fortunate mutation of the pineapple family had developed were as excited about its prospects as he. No Cayenne plants were allowed outside the colony. At the seaport of Cayenne, outgoing luggage was minutely inspected, so that when Whipple Hoxworth and wife Ching-ching, from Rio, arrived in French Guiana, the government knew before they landed that he was the big planter from Hawaii and that he was going to try to steal some Cayenne plants. Consequently, with Gallic perfidy they served Whip an endless succession of perfect Cayenne pineapples, heavy, succulent and aromatic. But no Cayenne plant did he see. When he casually suggested a visit to one of the plantations, it rained. When he tried to bribe a scurrilous type to bring him some roots, the man was a government spy placed outside the hotel for that special purpose. And when in frustration he decided to go home empty-handed, the customs officials searched every cubic inch of his luggage with the smiling assurance that "we suspect attempts are being made to smuggle guns to the prisoners on Devil's Island." Whip smiled back and said, "I agree, you must be very careful." So he got no pineapple plants.

He bought substitutes and cared for them tenderly, for he realized that the Cayenne itself must have sprung from some chance cross-fertilization of two types which of themselves were nothing. Therefore, the meanest, rat-tailed, scrawny plant in Whip's experimental field received the same care as the best Guatemala; but the fruit that resulted fell so far short of a Cayenne that Whip became increasingly morbid on the subject. From Australia he imported plants that were supposed to be Cayennes, but they did not produce the smooth-skinned fruits he had known in South America. He could taste them now, and he imagined them being forced into cans cut to their size. He was haunted by this perfect pineapple, which he knew existed but which lay beyond his reach, and he became obsessed with the idea of acquiring a bundle of mother plants. For a time he considered a secret overland expedition from Paramaribo in Dutch Guiana, but discussions with geographers who knew the area convinced him that the intervening jungle was impenetrable. He tried suborning French colonial officials, but the government trusted its own subordinates no more than it trusted Whipple Hoxworth and checked them constantly, so that even though he poured some twenty thousand dollars' worth of bribes into Guiana, he got no pineapple plants in return.

And then one day a lanky Englishman named Schilling rode up to Hanakai on a wobbly horse, dismounted and asked for a whiskey soda. "I believe I am the man you are looking for," Schilling said in clipped accents.

"I don't need any more lunas," Whip replied, "and besides, you aren't husky enough."

"I have no intentions of working for a living," the lanky Englishman replied. "I have come to sell you something."

"I can think of nothing that I require," Whip snapped.

"I can think of something that you will want to pay a great deal of money for, Mr. Hoxworth."

"What?"

"Two thousand prime Cayenne crowns."

As if his hand had frozen, Whip stopped pouring the whiskey. He made no pretense of not being interested, and his Adam's apple moved up and down in his dry throat. He put the whiskey bottle down, turned, and looked steadily at his visitor. "Cayenne?" he asked.

"Prime crowns."

"How?"

"My father was a Dutchman before he became a British subject. He knows people in the Guianas."

"Are the crowns vital?"

"They're already growing in a hothouse in England."

Wildly Hoxworth grabbed the tall man's arm. "You're sure they're growing?"

"I've brought a photograph," Schilling replied, and he produced a snapshot of himself standing inside a greenhouse with pineapples growing about his feet, and from the hearts of several of the plants rose incontestably the distinctive Cayenne fruit.

"Mr. Schilling . . ." Whip began nervously.

"Dr. Schilling, botanist. I'll sell you the Cayennes, Mr. Hoxworth, but I want the job of raising them here in Hawaii."

"A deal!" Wild Whip agreed. "I'll send a special ship to pick them up. Can you keep them alive across the Atlantic and around the Horn?"

"I'm a botanist," Dr. Schilling replied.

While he waited for the Englishman's return, Wild Whip directed his feverish energy into laying out a special field to accommodate the two thousand crowns that Schilling had contracted to deliver, and as he worked he thought: "I'd like to find a man I could trust to care for these pineapples the way I'd do it." And he remembered the stocky Japanese field hand who had been willing to fight him over the matter of galvanized iron for the hot bath. "That's the kind of man I want," he mused. "Someone with guts."

He saddled his horse and rode out to the sugar fields until he spotted Kamejiro. "Eh, you one fella!" he shouted.

"You speak me?" the rugged little Japanese asked with a friendly grin.

"How you like work boss-man one field?" And the compact was sealed. Now Kamejiro ran each morning from the camp to till the pineapple field, pulverizing the earth with his hands. And each night he ran back to tend his hot bath. Wild Whip, seeing him always in a hurry, thought: "That one does the work of three men," and he raised his pay to seventy-five cents a day.

Under Whip's direction, Kamejiro plowed the land to a depth of two feet, and when its rich redness lay in the sunlight, Whip was pleased, for books had told him that above all else the pineapple required iron, and Kauai was practically solid iron. Every three months the field was turned again and special guano fertilizers were introduced to make it productive. Ditches were dug completely around the area to draw off unnecessary water, and a windbreak of wild plum and casuarina was planted to ward off any chance salt spray. Few brides have ever had homes arranged for them with the meticulous care that Wild Whip exercised in building this all-important seed bed. When it was done, he stood in the middle of its finely aerated soil and shouted to Kamejiro, "Bimeby all fields up there pineapple, eh?" And he pointed in all the upland directions as far as he could see, for he intended them all to be crowded with Cayenne plants, four thousand to the acre, and the money that he had so far made growing sugar would turn out to have been children's coins for playing store.

The first crop of Cayennes surpassed Whip's hopes. Dr. Schilling proved himself both a botanist and a dipsomaniac, and from the front room of the Hanakai mansion, which he obviously intended never to leave, the tall Englishman directed the successful propagation of the plants that were to revolutionize the Hawaiian economy. Of the first two thousand Cayennes which had been abducted from the fields of French Guiana, nearly nineteen hundred grew to luscious maturity, and these first pineapples were an astonishment to the citizens of Hawaii. Whip, as was his custom, gave the fruit away and told everyone, "Start tilling your upland fields now. Gold is about to drip out of them in a fragrant flow."

A pineapple plant produces slowly, only one fruit at the end of two years —technically it is a sorosis or bundle of fruits, each of the composite squares being the result of a separate flower—but when the fruit has matured, the plant offers four separate ways of propagating new plants: the crown of the pineapple fruit can be carefully torn off and planted; slips that have started growing from the base of the fruit can be lifted off and planted; suckers that have begun to spring out from the base of the plant can be used in the same way; or the stump itself can be cut up into chunks and planted like potatoes. From each surviving plant Dr. Schilling was thus able to recover one crown, three or four slips, two or three suckers, and two or three stump sections. By 1910 the pineapple industry was established in Hawaii.

But in 1911 it was overtaken by disaster, for the fields which Wild Whip had so carefully prepared stopped nourishing the plants, and they began to turn a sickly yellow. In panic Whip commanded Dr. Schilling to sober up and find out what was happening, but the drunken Englishman could not focus on the problem, so Whip stormed through the mansion which he now shared with Schilling and smashed all bottles containing alcohol. Then Dr. Schilling pulled himself together and spent some time in the fields. "I must make some experiments," he reported, and a corner of the mansion was given over to test tubes and beakers, but all Schilling was doing was using fresh pineapples for the distillation of a super-fine grade of alcohol which he liked better than whiskey, and he was soon incommunicado.

Wild Whip solved this impasse by beating the Englishman into insensibility, then throwing him into a cold bath. Apparently others had treated Schilling in this manner, for he took no great offense, shivering in the tub and whimpering like a child. "By God," Hoxworth shouted, "you brought these plants here and you'll find out what's wrong with them."

He dressed the gawky scientist, put his shoes on, and personally led the shaky man into the fields. "What's wrong with those plants?" he stormed.

"Look, Brother Hoxworth! You can't stand there and command me to find out what's happened. The human mind doesn't work that way."

"Yours will!" Hoxworth roared.

"Suppose I start to walk down the path and down that road and never look at these plants again. Then what?"

"Then by the time you get to the road, Dr. Schilling, you can't walk. Because both your legs are broken."

"I believe you would," the shaken Englishman said.

"You bet I would," Whip growled. "Now get to work." He stood back, stared in shock, and yelled, "Now what in hell are you doing?"

"I'm tasting the soil," Dr. Schilling replied.

"Oh, for Christ's sake," Whip snorted and left.

It took Dr. Schilling four weeks to make up his mind about the pineapple plants, and when he reported to his employer it was obvious that he himself scarcely believed his own conclusions. "This is extraordinary, Brother Hoxworth, and you won't believe it, but those plants are starved for iron."

"Ridiculous!" Hoxworth stormed. He was sick and tired of this infuriating Englishman and was at last ready to throw him off the plantation.

"No," Dr. Schilling replied soberly. "I'm convinced that they are about to die for lack of iron."

"That's preposterous!" Hoxworth stormed. "This goddamned island is practically solid iron. Look at the soil, man!"

"It's iron, that's true," Schilling agreed. "But I'm afraid it must be iron in some form that the plants cannot use."

"How can they stand in solid iron and not be able to use it?"

"That," Schilling said, "is why the universe will always be a mystery."

"Are you fooling with me?" Hoxworth asked ominously.

"Who would dare?" Schilling replied.

"What do you want us to do?" Hoxworth asked quietly.

"I want to sprinkle iron, in a different kind of solution, over these plants."

"No! It's totally preposterous. You get back out there and find out what's really wrong."

"It's iron," Schilling said stubbornly.

"How can you be sure?"

"I can taste it."

"Have you run any tests on it?"

"No. I don't have to."

"Well, run some tests. No! Don't! You'd just distill yourself some more alcohol. What kind of iron do you want?"

"Iron sulfate."

As a result of this decision, in late 1911 Kamejiro Sakagawa marched through the experimental fields of the Hanakai Pineapple Plantation lugging a bucket of spray, which he directed onto the yellow leaves of the perishing plants, and as he passed, the solution of sulfate of iron ran down the narrow leaves and penetrated to the red soil about the roots. As if by magic the sickly plants began to revive, and within four days the yellow leaves were returning to their natural color. The Cayennes were saved, and when it was proved, as Dr. Schilling suspected, that they had been standing in iron yet starving for iron, Wild Whip joyously gathered up an armful of ripe fruit and tossed it onto the mansion floor.

"Brew yourself some alcohol and stay drunk as long as you like," he commanded.

Sometimes Kamejiro, running to work and running back to tend his hot bath, would not see the tall Englishman for weeks at a time, and then as he cut the lawn he would find Schilling in a basket chair by the side of the cliff, staring down at the play of surf as it struck the opposite rocks.

Schilling was a surprising man, a drunken, besotted individual who could think. One day when he was driving into Kapaa with Whip in one of the first cars on Kauai, he spotted a junk yard and said, "You ought to buy that, Brother Hoxworth."

"That junk? Why?"

"You're paying a lot of money for iron sulfate, and that's what it is. Rusty junk to which sulphuric acid has been applied."

So Whip bought the junk yard and launched an iron sulfate factory, and in later years, when automobiles had become numerous, he bought all the old wrecks on Kauai for four dollars each, piled them up, drenched them with gasoline and burned away the rubber and the horse hair. When what was left had rusted he treated the junk with sulphuric acid and remarked, "Everyone who eats pineapple is eating the handiwork of Henry Ford, God bless him."

But in the growing of pineapple, which brought hundreds of millions of dollars into the territory, when one problem was licked, the next arose, for apparently the Cayenne did not enjoy growing in Hawaii and fell prey to one disaster after another. When the iron problem was solved, the mealy-bug arose, and once more the industry seemed doomed.

The ugly, louselike little bugs were moved from place to place by ants, who tended them like milch cows, living off their sweet, nutritious exudations. Particularly, the mealy-bugs loved pineapple, whose growth they destroyed, and it seemed an act of conscious malevolence when millions of ants hiked several miles to deposit their cows upon the precious pineapples. Dr. Schilling studied the problem for several months, while field after field of Wild Whip's choicest Cayennes wilted and died from the infestation. Then he hit upon a dual solution which halted the mealy-bugs: around each field he planted decoy rows of pineapple, and these intercepted the mealy-bugs and kept them from invading the productive areas; and around the entire field he laid long boards soaked repeatedly in creosote, and these fended off the ants and their ugly cows. After this victory over the little lice he subsided into a year-long lethargy of drunkenness, awaiting the next disaster.

It came when Whip's canning manager reported: "Because the Cayennes are so big we can't fit them into the cans, and waste forty per cent of the fruit trimming them down to can size."

"What in hell do you want me to do?" Whip snarled, wearied by the constant battle to keep his fields productive.

"What we've got to have is smaller Cayennes," the manager explained.

So Wild Whip stormed back to Hanakai, shook his English expert into reasonable sobriety, and said, "Dr. Schilling, you've got to make the pineapples smaller."

Through a golden haze that had been accumulating for thirteen months the scraggly Englishman said, "The mind of man can accomplish anything. Draw me the pineapple you want."

Whip went back to the canning manager, and together they drew on paper the specifications of the perfect pineapple. It had to be sufficiently barrel-shaped to leave a good rim of fruit when the core was cut out. It had to be juicy, acid, sweet, small, without barbs on the leaves, solid and golden in color. With a ruler and French curves the two men constructed the desired fruit, and when Whip thrust the paper at Schilling he said, "That's what we want."

Schilling, glad to have an alternative to drunkenness, replied, "That's what you'll get." He inspected every pineapple field on Kauai, comparing the available fruit against the ideal image, and whenever he found something close to the printed specifications, he marked that plant with a flag, and after four years of this infinitely patient work he announced, "We have built the perfect pineapple." When he delivered the first truckload to the cannery, the manager was ecstatic. "Our problems are over," he said.

"Until the next one," Schilling replied.

In 1911 a woman writer from New York, who had once stayed in Honolulu four weeks, wrote a rather scurrilous book about Hawaii in which she lamented three things: the influence of the missionaries who had maliciously killed off the Hawaiians by dressing them in Mother Hubbards; the criminality of companies like Janders & Whipple who had imported Orientals; and the avarice of missionary descendants like those in Hoxworth & Hale who had stolen the lush lands of Hawaii. After her book had created something of a sensation throughout America she returned to the islands and in triumph came to Kauai, where at a splendid polo tournament she was presented to Wild Whip Hoxworth. His team had just defeated Honolulu, and he was flushed with victory and should have been in a gracious mood, but as he was introduced to the lady author he thought he understood who she was and asked coldly, "Are you the good lady who wrote *Hawaii's Shame?*"

"Yes," she replied proudly. "I am," for she was accustomed to being fawned over. "What did you think of it?"

"Ma'am," Whip said, carefully placing his polo mallet on a rack lest he be tempted to use it in an unorthodox manner, "I thought your book was complete bullshit."

The polo players and their ladies recoiled from Whip's savage comment, and some began to offer the startled lady their apologies, but Whip interrupted. "No, there will be no apologies. Stand where you are, ma'am, and look in every direction. Whatever you see was brought into these islands by men like me. The sugar upon which our economy rests? My Grandfather Whipple, a missionary, brought that in. The pineapples? I'm the grandson of missionaries and I brought them in. The pine trees, the royal palms, the tulip trees, the avocados, the wild plum, the crotons, the house and the horses. We brought them all in. The Hoxworth mango, best fruit in the world, is named after me. And as for the Orientals. Heh, Kamejiro, you come, eh? This bandy-legged little man has done more work in Hawaii . . . he's built more and he will continue to build more than a dozen of the people you were wailing about. I brought him in here and I'm proud of it. I'm only sorry he doesn't intend to stay. Now, ma'am, if you have any more questions about Hawaii, I'd be glad to answer 'em. Because I hope you'll go home and write another book, and this time not be such a horse's ass."

He bowed and left her gagging. In Honolulu, of course, his polo-field speech, as it was termed, was a momentary sensation, since, as one of the Hale women explained, "If one were picking a man to defend the missionaries, he would hardly pick Wild Whip."

He and his drunken English friend lived on at Hanakai, with fairly frequent visits to the brothels at Kapaa. At the cliffside mansion he entertained a good deal, and in his leisurely talks over brandy he began to expound the first coherent theory of Hawaii: "What I visualize is an island community that treasures above all else its agricultural lands. On them it grows bulk crops of sugar and pineapple and ships them to the mainland in H & H ships. With the money we get we buy the manufactured goods our people need, things like iceboxes, automobiles, finished lumber, hardware and food. Thus the ships go one way loaded and come back loaded. That's the destiny of Hawaii, and anyone who disturbs that fine balance is an enemy of the islands.''

He was willing to identify the enemies of Hawaii: "Anyone who tampers with our shipping ought to be shot. Anyone who tries to talk radical ideas to our field hands ought to be run off the islands. Anyone who interferes with our assured supply of cheap labor from Asia strikes a blow at sugar and pineapple.''

Once he confided: "H & H have run the ships cheaply and faithfully. I see no reason why any radical changes are required. And I think you must admit that J & W have run the plantations well. Nobody can lodge a complaint against them. As long as these two firms continue to serve the islands justly, it seems to me the welfare of Hawaii is assured, and for outsiders like that goddamned woman author to go around raising a lot of questions is downright ingratitude.''

In 1912 the campaign for President on the mainland grew rather warm, and for the first time in some years Democrats felt that they had a good chance of sending their man, Woodrow Wilson, to the White House. Of course, citizens of Hawaii could not vote for the national offices, but in the island elections a few pathetic Democrats began to parrot the optimism existing on the mainland, and one misguided liberal even went so far as to appear before a mass meeting of six in the nearby town of Kapaa. Out of sheer curiosity over a human being who dared to be a Democrat in Hawaii, Wild Whip insinuated himself as the seventh listener and stood appalled as the man actually sought votes for his party: "There is a new spirit abroad in America, a clean, sharp wind from the prairies, an insistent voice from the great cities. Therefore I propose to do something that has never before been done in these islands. I, a Democrat and proud of the fact, am going to visit each of the sugar and pineapple plantations to explain in my words what the ideas of Woodrow Wilson and his adherents mean. Tell your friends that I'll be there.''

In some agitation Wild Whip rode home and carefully took down all the firearms he kept at Hanakai. Inspecting each, he summoned his lunas and said, "I just heard a Democrat say he was coming here to address our workmen. If he steps six inches onto Hanakai, shoot him.''

One of the lunas who had been through high school asked deferentially, "But doesn't he have the right to speak?''

"Right?" Whip thundered. "A Democrat have the right to step onto my plantation and spread his poison? My God! I say who shall come here and who shall not. This is my land and I'll have no alien ideas parading across it.''

Lunas in 1912 were not apt to be easily frightened, and this one stuck to his guns. "But if this man is a spokesman for one of the political parties . . .''

"Von Schlemm!" Whip roared in profound amazement. "I'm astonished at such talk from you. Can't you remember what that filthy Democrat, Grover Cleveland, did to Hawaii? Are you old enough to recall how those corrupted Democratic senators voted against us time and again? What surprises me is that somebody hasn't already shot this dirty little bastard. No Democrat has a place in Hawaii, and if one tries to walk onto my plantation he'll crawl home with broken legs.''

The aspiring politician did try to invade Hanakai, and Wild Whip, backed up by four heavily armed lunas, met him at the edge of the red-dust road. "You can't come in here, mister," Whip warned.

"I'm a citizen in pursuit of my political rights.''

"You're a Democrat, and there's no place for you in these islands.''

"Mr. Hoxworth, I'm coming to your plantation to speak to your men about the issues in the election.''

"My men don't want to hear the nonsense you talk.''

"Mr. Hoxworth, there's a new wind blowing across America. Woodrow Wilson is going to be elected President. And he promises a fair deal for all men. Even your workmen."

"I tell my workmen how to vote," Whip explained. "And they vote for the welfare of these islands. Now you go back to Honolulu and don't give me any more trouble." The four lunas moved in upon the visitor.

"How is it going to sound," the politician asked, "if I report to the press that I was forcibly thrown off Hanakai Plantation?"

Wild Whip, still lean and hard at fifty-five, reached forward, grabbed the offensive radical by the shoulders, and shook him as if he were a child. "No paper would publish such rubbish. Christ, if a rattlesnake tried to crawl onto my plantation and I shot it, I'd be a hero. I feel obligated to treat a Democrat the same way. Get out."

The visitor calmly smoothed his shirt, straightened his sleeves, and announced: "In pursuit of man's inalienable rights, I am going to come into your plantation."

"If you try it," Whip said, "you'll be thrown out on your inalienable ass."

The politician walked boldly onto the red soil of Hanakai and started for the lane of royal palms and Norfolk pines. He had gone only a few steps when the four lunas grabbed him, lifted him in the air, and threw him roughly back onto the road, where he fell heavily upon the inalienable portion of his anatomy, as Whip had predicted. While the surprised visitor sat in the red dust Whip advised him: "Go back to Honolulu. No Democrat will ever be allowed on this plantation."

But when the man had gone, Whip began to appreciate the real danger involved, so he summoned his lunas. "You are to tell every man on this plantation entitled to a vote that he is not to bother voting for this man or that. He's to vote the straight Republican ticket. One cross mark is all he needs."

"We can warn them," one luna pointed out, "but can we enforce it?"

"There's a way," Whip replied cryptically, and when the local elections came that year he stationed himself six feet from the Hanakai voting booth and as each of his qualified laborers approached he looked the man in the eye and said, "You know how to vote, don't you, Jackson?"

"Yes, sir, Mr. Hoxworth."

"See that you do it," Whip replied ominously, but he left nothing to chance. When Jackson was in the booth, with the protecting canvas about him so that no one could spy upon his ballot or the way he marked it, he reached for the voting pencil. It was tied to the end of a piece of string which led aloft, passing through an eyelet screwed into the ceiling of the booth, so that if he was about to mark his ballot Democratic, the string was ready to form a clear angle to the far right and thus betray his perfidy. But to make doubly sure, Whip had previously ordered that all pencils used for voting be of maximum hardness, and that the paper on the shelf in the voting booth be soft, so that when Jackson voted he was forced to punch his pencil strongly onto the ballot, leaving on the back side an easily read indication of how he had voted. Jackson folded his ballot and handed it to the Portuguese clerk, but that official paused before placing it in the box, and in that moment Wild Whip was free to inspect the back.

"All right, Jackson," Whip muttered as the man left.

As soon as the voting was over, Whip assembled his lunas and reported: "Jackson, Allingham and Cates voted Democratic. Get them out of here before midnight."

"What shall we tell them?"

"Nothing. They know the evil they've done."

And he stood in the shadows of the royal palms as the three traitors were thrown onto the public road, their bundles of goods under their arms.

It was as a result of this election, and the dangers represented by it—Wilson ruling in Washington, men like Jackson beginning to vote Democratic on Kauai—that Wild Whip made his decision. "I'm going back to Honolulu," he told Dr. Schilling. "You're welcome to live here and take care of the pineapples."

"What are you intending to do?" Schilling asked.

"There's a spirit of rebellion in the world. Crazy liberal thinking. Probably infected my own company. I'm going back to take over control of H & H."

"I thought they threw you out? Exiled you?"

"They did," Wild Whip confessed. "But in those days I didn't own the company."

"Do you now?"

"Yes, but the Yale men running it don't know it."

"You going to chop off a lot of heads?" Schilling asked with the fiendish joy of childhood.

"Not if they're good men," Whip replied, disappointing his permanent guest. And by Christmas Eve, 1912, he was in sole, dictatorial control of the great H & H empire, and although heads did not roll in the Schilling sense of the word, every man who was suspected of having voted Democratic was fired. "In Hawaii and in H & H," Whip explained without rancor, "there is simply no place for such men."

A NY GENERAL CONCLAVE of the great Kee hui was apt to be impressive. The older sons, like Asia, who ran the restaurant, retained their Chinese names—Kee Ah Chow—and wore pigtails and black sateen suits; but the younger sons cut their pigtails and wore contemporary American dress. They also preferred the English translations of their names, such as Australia Kee instead of Kee Oh Chow.

When the hui converged upon the ugly house up Nuuanu, they formed colorful processions. Some brought their wives and by 1908 were able to bring grown grandsons along with their pretty Chinese and Hawaiian wives. On festive occasions great-grandchildren appeared in number, tumbling about the grounds on which the family still grew taro and pineapples. The Kees, counting their wives and husbands, now numbered ninety-seven, but of course they were never able to convene at one time, because a dozen or so were apt to be at school on the mainland. Neither Yale nor Harvard had yet known a Kee, but Michigan, Chicago, Columbia and Pennsylvania did, and it was possible for a Chinese in Hawaii to be born, financed, protected at law, married, tended medically and buried—all at the hands of Kees. In addition, he could rent his land from them, and buy his vegetables, his meat and his clothes.

The most conspicuous member was still Nyuk Tsin. In 1908 she was sixty-one years old, and although she no longer lugged pineapples through the streets in her famous twin baskets, she still grew them and supervised others in the peddling. Year by year she grew shorter, thinner, balder, and although her face showed the wrinkling of age, her mind retained the resilience of youth. Her life consisted of purposeful ritual. Each year, with solemn dignity, she accompanied her brilliant son Africa to the tax office to pay her taxes. Twice a year she took eight or ten members of her family to the Punti store where they sent money to her husband's real wife in China. She had died in 1881, but the family in the Low Village continued to write letters of grateful acknowledgment on her behalf. Every two or three years Nyuk Tsin assembled as many of her family as possible for the trip to the leper colony at Kalawao, where they reported to their ancestor. And each fall, as if she were sending sacrifices to the gods, she took six or eight of her ablest grandsons down to the Hoxworth & Hale docks and bought them tickets for the mainland. The old woman conserved human resources just as carefully as she had the irrigated land of her first taro patch.

Therefore, it was she who now called the great hui into formal meeting, for two matters of prime importance, and far beyond the capacity of lawyer Africa to solve, had been brought to her attention; and while her great-grandchildren played in the dusty yard she talked to the thirty-odd elders who met with her.

The children of Africa Kee needed guidance, and Nyuk Tsin said, "Africa's oldest daughter, Sheong Mun, whom you prefer to call Ellen, is in deep perplexity, and I am not wise enough to counsel her."

"What has she done?" Asia's wife asked.

"She has fallen in love with a haole," Nyuk Tsin replied. A hush fell over the assembly, for although the Kees, under Nyuk Tsin's approval if not her outright urging, had always felt free to marry Hawaiians, none had yet made any signs of wanting to marry white Americans, and Ellen's bold proposal represented a jolt in family procedures. The clan turned to look at Africa's daughter, a bright-eyed, quick, handsome girl of twenty, and she looked back.

"Who is the white man?" Asia asked, exercising his prerogative as oldest son.

"Tell him, Sheong Mun," the old woman said.

In a soft voice taught her by the women teachers at the Episcopalian school, Ellen said, "He is a junior officer on one of the navy ships at Pearl Harbor."

A chorus of gasps came from the hui. A white man and a military man, too! This was indeed, as Wu Chow's Auntie had warned, a major problem, and Europe, who had married a Hawaiian girl, said, "It's bad enough to want to marry a white man, because they don't make good husbands and they take money out of the family. But to marry a military man is really indecent. No self-respecting girl . . ."

Australia interrupted: "We're not in China. I know some fine navy men."

Europe replied stiffly: "I don't."

Asia observed: "I had hoped never to see one of my family want to marry a soldier."

Australia snapped: "He's a sailor, and there's a big difference."

Europe said: "Military men are military men, and they make miserable husbands."

Australia cried: "Why don't you take those ideas back to China? That's where they came from."

At this, Nyuk Tsin intervened and said in her low, imperative voice, "It would be much better if Sheong Mun had fallen in love with a Chinese boy, or if she had come to me as a dutiful girl and said, 'Wu Chow's Auntie, find me a husband.' But she has done neither of these things."

"The worse for her," Asia said sadly. "In my restaurant I see many girls who stray from the old patterns, and they all suffer for it."

"Ridiculous!" Australia's wife snapped. "Asia! You know very well that when I was a girl I used to hide in your restaurant and kiss Australia behind the dried ducks. And nothing bad came of it except that I married your lazy brother."

"That was the beginning of what I'm talking about," Asia warned.

"Ridiculous!" Australia's wife, a high-spirited Ching beauty, laughed. "Because do you know who used to whistle at me to let me know your brother was waiting?" The Kees looked at the bright-eyed young wife, and with a dramatic gesture she pointed directly at Nyuk Tsin, sitting gray-haired and solemn at the head of the family. "That one did it! She's worse than any of us!"

The family roared at the old woman's embarrassment, and finally Nyuk Tsin wiped her blushing face and said softly, "I must admit I arranged it. But remember that Ching Siu Han was a Chinese girl. And a Hakka. And could be trusted. Today we are talking about something much different. A white man. And a soldier."

"Wu Chow's Auntie!" Ellen interrupted. "He's not a soldier. You must forget your old prejudices."

Asia asked, "Will he bring any land into our hui? Any money?"

"No," Ellen said resolutely. "In fact, he'll take money out. Because I have got to have two hundred dollars for clothes and more later for other things."

Together the Kees sucked in their breath and faced the day they had long feared. Sooner or later, some member of the family would want to marry a white man. Now it had come and those who dreaded the event suspected that Africa with the radical new ideas he had acquired at Michigan must somehow be at fault. Therefore, the older members of the family began staring at the lawyer, and he suffered from their harsh gaze. Finally Europe asked brusquely, "Tell us, Africa. What do you think of this?"

There was a long hush in the hot room, and voices of children could be heard. Finally Africa spoke. "I am humiliated," he said. "I am ashamed that it is my daughter who wants to marry outside our circle of acquaintance. I have given her a good education and her mother has tried to teach her to be a decent Hakka. I am humiliated and I do not know what to do." Suddenly the pressure upon him became great and he hid his face in his hands, sobbing quietly. The disgrace he had brought upon the family immobilized his speech, so his wife added, "He feels that he must accept the shame for what his daughter has done."

At this solemn moment Australia interjected a happier note. "Of course it's his responsibility. If a man goes to Michigan, he picks up foreign ways. I suppose that's why we sent him to Michigan. Remember, Asia, it was your sons who went to Pennsylvania. It was your sons who brought American friends into our homes, and it was one of those friends who met Sheong Mun. Bang! They're in love! Ellen, if your stingy father won't give you the two hundred dollars I will."

"It isn't the money that I want so much, Uncle Australia, as your blessing."

"You have mine!"

"And mine!" Australia's wife chimed.

"Have I yours, Wu Chow's Auntie?"

The family turned to look at Nyuk Tsin, sitting with her worn hands in her lap. "I am concerned with only one problem, Sheong Mun," the old woman said. "When your children are born they will be the children of a white man, and they will be lost to our family. Promise me that you will send me a letter each time you have a child, and I will go to the Punti scholar and find his true name, and we will write it in our book and send the name back to China, as we have always done."

"My sons will not want Chinese names," hard-headed Ellen countered.

"Later they will," the old woman said. "They will want to know who they are, and in the book the information will be waiting for them."

As the Kees dispersed over the face of the world, marrying with men who worked in strange lands, letters arrived constantly for Nyuk Tsin. Her sons would read them to her, and she would note the births of all children. For each son she got a proper name, and registered it in China, and as she predicted this day in 1908, the time did come when the boy so named would want to know what the Chinese half of his ancestry signified, and men would arrive in Honolulu whom you would not recognize as Chinese, and they would meet old Nyuk Tsin, and she would take down a book she could not read, and the interpreter would pick out the information and the Chinese-German-Irish-English boy would understand a little better who he was.

But on this particular day the old woman was concerned with Africa's children, and after it had been grudgingly agreed that the lawyer's daughter, Kee Sheong Mun, known locally as Ellen Kee, could marry her sailor, Nyuk Tsin coughed and said, "It is time we think again about getting Hong Kong into Punahou."

Asia groaned, America rose and left the room in disgust, and the rest of the family turned to stare at Africa's youngest son, a square-headed, wrinkle-eyed boy of fifteen. Among the family it was believed that young Koon Kong, who was known as Hong Kong, had inherited his father's intellectual brilliance. He was most able at figures, knew Punti, Hakka, English and Hawaiian well, and seemed unusually gifted at managing money, for he augmented whatever he got hold of by lending it out to his numerous cousins. His rate of interest was a standard, inflexible ten per cent a week which he enforced by meticulous collections on Friday after school. As his name Koon indicated, he was of the fourth generation—Koon Kong, Earth's Atmosphere—and he was of the earth. In his generation of Kees there were twenty-seven boys carrying the name Koon, one brother and twenty-six cousins, and he was the cleverest of them all. If any Kee was ever going to elbow his way into Punahou, Hong Kong was the one, and as the problem opened for discussion, the family grew tense.

"Will Hong Kong's mother tell us how her son is doing in school?" the matriarch began.

Mrs. Africa Kee, the older of the striking Ching girls, said, "His marks have been excellent. His behavior has been spirited but has brought no reprimand. I am proud of my son's accomplishment and feel that he merits the interest the family is taking in him."

"Does Hong Kong think he can do the work at Punahou . . . if he is accepted?" Nyuk Tsin asked.

The boy was embarrassed by the attention focused on him, but he yearned to get into Punahou, so he bore the indignity. Hunching up one shoulder he said, "If the Lum boy can do the work, I can do the work."

At the mention of the Lum boy, the Kees grew bitter. For a dozen years they had been trying to get one of their sons into Punahou, Hawaii's source of excellence, but for one reason or another they had never succeeded, even though they were a fairly wealthy family and could boast of Africa as a leading professional man. Yet the Lums, who really did not amount to much except that their father was a dentist and a man who loved to speak in public, had maneuvered one of their boys into the cherished haven.

Nyuk Tsin said, "I think that this time we really have a good chance. I have asked a dear old friend to counsel with us as to what we must do to get Hong

Kong accepted." She gave a signal and a grandson ran out to bring back a tall, bald Englishman with outrageous white mustaches and a flamboyant energy that projected him into the hot room, where he kissed Nyuk Tsin and cried in flowery Chinese: "Ah ha! We plot against the white people! Strike the tocsin! China shall rise!"

It was Uliassutia Karakoram Blake, the mad schoolteacher and the trusted friend of all Chinese. He was older and stouter but no more subdued, and now he locked his hands behind his neck, rocking to and fro as if he were going to fall over. "Beloved and prolific Kees," he said, "let us face the truth. There are good schools and there are great schools, and every family is entitled to send his ablest sons to the greatest. Iolani, where I slave for a pittance, is a good school. Punahou is a great school. It lends authority and glamour and caste. England is built on such foundations and so is Hawaii. Let a man use a wrong knife, and he is condemned to the Liberal Party for life."

"What's he talking about?" one of Australia's boys whispered.

"I'm talking about you!" Uliassutai Karakoram Blake shouted in English, flailing his arms out and thrusting his head a few inches from the face of the startled young Chinese. "Stand up!" Awkwardly the boy rose and Blake pointed at him as if he were an exhibit.

"Behold the scion of the Kee hui," he said in erudite Chinese. "He has done well at Iolani School, but he has not yet been accepted at Punahou. He is therefore limited to a perpetual secondary acceptance in Honolulu. He cannot associate with the men who rule the city. He cannot learn to speak with their inflections. He lacks their peculiar polish. And he must remain the rest of his life a Chinese peasant. Sit down!"

Blake turned his back on the boy and said to the elders, "The compassionate Buddha knows that at Iolani I have given you Chinese the salt of my blood and the convolutions of my brain, and I have raised you from ignorance into light, and the compassionate Buddha also knows that I wish I had done half as well with my light as you wonderful people have done with yours. If I had, I wouldn't now be toiling out the evening years of my life as an underpaid schoolmaster. Africa, how much did you earn last year?"

The Chinese loved this ridiculous man and his circumlocutions. With his British regard for proprieties and his Oriental love of bombast, he seemed Chinese, and now he got to the meat of his visit: "You might think that I, as an Iolani teacher who had brought Hong Kong to this point of his education, would object to the proposal that you now transfer him to Punahou. Not at all. A family like yours is entitled to have a son at the best school Hawaii can provide. There he will rub elbows with future lawyers, business giants, community leaders. If I were a Kee, I would suffer any humiliation to get my son into Punahou. Hong Kong, stand up. I tell you, Kees, there is as fine a boy as Hawaii has ever produced. He merits the best. Hong Kong, depart."

When the embarrassed boy had gone, Uliassutai Karakoram said, "Wu Chow's Auntie, it will be very difficult indeed for you to get that boy into Punahou. He's too intelligent, and your family is too able. The white people want to have one or two Chinese in their school, but not the best. They prefer slow, stolid boys of no great imagination. The Lum boy is ideal. Hong Kong is not, because even Buddha himself would refuse to prophesy what Hong Kong may one day accomplish. Africa, are you aware that you have sired a revolutionary genius?"

"Hong Kong has far more power than I ever had, Mr. Blake," Africa confessed to his old teacher.

"Wu Chow's Auntie!" Uliassutai Karakoram pleaded suddenly. "Would you not consider trying to get some other grandson into Punahou?"

"No," Nyuk Tsin replied evenly. "He is a brilliant boy. He deserves the best."

The big Englishman shrugged his shoulders and said, "If you're determined to go against my advice, let's see what evil tricks you ought to attempt this time. Who visited Punahou last time?"

Mrs. Africa Kee, a handsome, modern Chinese wife, raised her hand. "Stand up!" Blake snapped. He studied her carefully, dressed as she was in western style, and said, "Couldn't we send someone a little less . . . modern? White people feel safer when an Oriental looks more like a coolie."

There were some things the Kees would not tolerate, which was what made them a significant family, and now Africa said simply, "If my son applies to Punahou, his mother goes with him."

"May Buddha bless all stubborn people," Blake said magniloquently, "for without them this would be a most miserable world. But could not your wife dress a little more inconspicuously? She must look prosperous enough to pay the tuition, yet not so self-assured that she would ever say anything in a meeting of the children's parents. We want her to look unalterably Chinese, yet aspiring to become a decent American. We want her to look proud enough to clean her fingernails, yet humble enough to remain slightly stooped over as if she lugged baskets of pineapples about the town." He bowed grandly to Nyuk Tsin and said, "Do you think your son's wife can acquire the proper look of a Chinese appealing to white people for help?"

"No," Nyuk Tsin said coldly.

"I thought not," Blake said sadly. "Then you are prepared for Hong Kong to be rejected again?"

At this point America, whose two sons had tried in vain to enter Punahou, returned to the meeting and growled, "We are prepared to be rejected forever, Mr. Blake."

"I am sorry that you were not all born a little more stupid," the flamboyant Englishman said, "because then, with your money, you'd be accepted gracefully. But of course, if you had been more stupid . . . that one in particular," and he pointed at Nyuk Tsin, "why you wouldn't have the money you now have, and you would be kept out of Punahou on grounds of poverty."

"Do you think Hong Kong has a chance this time?" Nyuk Tsin pleaded.

"No," Blake said. "If I were a white man in Honolulu, I would never allow one of you damned Kees anywhere. You're smart. You work. You gang together. You're ambitious. First thing you know you'll be teaching your daughters to lure white men into marriage."

"Sheong Mun is going to marry a naval officer," Nyuk Tsin said softly.

In the hot room Uliassutai Karakoram Blake stopped ranting. He looked at the fresh, handsome child he had once taught. Little Ellen Kee, who could sing so charmingly. Gravely he went up to her, kissed her on the cheeks and said, quietly, "May the compassionate Buddha have mercy upon us all. The years of our lives are so short and the currents of the world are so strong. Good-bye, dear Kees. You will not get into Punahou . . . not this time."

When he was gone the elders of the family considered the many ideas he had proposed, and Nyuk Tsin said, "That strange man is right. Hong Kong's mother does look too modern, as if she were forcing her way upon the haoles. It will be too easy to reject her. This time we really must send someone else. How about Europe's wife? She's Hawaiian."

"No!" Africa cried. "He is my son, and he will report to Punahou with his own mother, and if they reject us again, let it be so."

"This time, then, I will go along," Nyuk Tsin announced. "I will be bare-footed and I will represent the old ways."

"No!" Africa protested again. "My wife, who will dress as she pleases, will take my son to Punahou and seek admission. I will tolerate no subterfuges."

"Africa," the old matriarch said softly, "the school has shown that it will accept one or two Chinese. Now it is terribly important that one of our boys be chosen. Please, this time allow me to arrange things."

"I have business on the Big Island," Africa said solemnly. "I shall go there and bear no part of this humiliation." He left the room and the clan breathed more easily, for he was a stubborn man.

"Now, when the Lums got their son into Punahou," Nyuk Tsin counseled, "the boy's mother wore a very plain dress, and her hair straight back, and she kept her eyes on the floor. I am therefore going to say flatly that Hong Kong's mother cannot go this time."

"I will go with my husband to the Big Island," Africa's wife announced, and she too left the plotters.

After much discussion, and after carefully studying the devices by which earlier Chinese families had managed to get sons into Punahou, the Kees hit upon an involved strategy. Barefoot Nyuk Tsin would go in smock and pants to give the proper coolie touch. Europe's wife would go as a pure-blooded Hawaiian to show that the Kees respected local traditions. And Australia's wife, the pretty Ching girl, would go in a very modest western-style dress to prove that the family knew how to eat with a knife and fork. The boy Hong Kong, who had an intellectual ability four levels higher than anyone then studying at Punahou, would tag along in a carefully selected suit that bespoke both the ability to pay tuition and a quiet gentility not common among newly rich Chinese families.

It was a hot day when the four Kees drove up to Punahou in a rented carriage, it having been decided that this was slightly more propitious than walking, and in the interview the three women played their roles to perfection, but Hong Kong squinted slightly and thought just a little too long before answering questions, brilliant though his replies were, and in due time the family got the news. "We regret that this year, due to overcrowded conditions, we can find no place for your son, whose marks and general deportment seemed other-wise acceptable."

The letter was delivered to Africa in his law offices, and he sat for a long time pondering it. At first he was consumed with rage at the humiliation his family had willingly undergone, and then he spent about an hour shoving the formal letter about his desk into this position and that. Finally he summoned his son and waited until the boy came in breathless from play along the river. In even, unimpassioned tones he said, "Hong Kong, you will not go back to school any more."

"I thought you said I was to go to Michigan."

"No. What you require to learn, son, you can learn right here. Tonight you will start reading this book on Hawaiian land systems. When you're through I'll give you your examination . . . sitting in that chair. Are those your school-books?"

"Yes."

"You'll never need them again." Slowly Africa Kee, who loved education, took the books and tore them apart. Throwing them into the wastebasket he said, "When you study your new book you are to memorize the end of every chapter. Hong Kong, you're going to get an education that no man in Hawaii has ever had before."

Ultimately, of course, the Kees did squeeze a boy into Punahou. It happened in a most peculiar way. In 1910 the Republican Party had difficulty finding the right man to run for the legislature from Chinatown and somebody made the radical proposal, "Why don't we run a Chinaman?"

"Oh, no!" one of the Hewlett boys protested. "I don't want that radical Africa Kee in government."

"I wasn't thinking of him. I was thinking of his brother Australia."

A hush fell over the caucus and smiles began to play upon the faces of the white men who ran the islands, for Australia was a man whom men could like. He wasn't too bright, played a good ukulele, was honest, didn't have too much education but did have a host of friends among both the Chinese and Hawaiians, with whom he had been reared. Furthermore, he had an appealing nickname, Kangaroo Kee, and without even taking a vote the caucus decided that he was their man.

Kangaroo Kee was elected by a huge majority and kept on getting elected, and in time he became the leading Chinese in the Republican Party, a man everyone loved and trusted. Fortunately, he had a son who like himself was gloriously average, and in 1912 Punahou felt that at last it had found a Kee who could be safely admitted to the school.

On the day this boy enrolled, Nyuk Tsin walked secretly to the entrance of the school and hid behind one of the palms to watch one of her grandsons at last enter the great school. As she saw the bright faces of the haole children gathering for the beginning of the new term, chatting of vacation experiences, she recognized here a Hale and there a Whipple, and thought: "The white people are crazy to allow Chinese in this school. This is the secret of how they rule the islands and they have a right to protect their interests."

Then, coming up the street, she saw her grandson walking with his father, the politician Kangaroo Kee, and she withdrew into the shadows, mumbling to herself, "This boy knows nothing. He is not worthy of this great school. But he is our beginning."

For THIRTEEN YEARS Kamejiro Sakagawa rose every morning at three-thirty to cut wild plum, storing it for his hot bath. He then ran to work, labored till sunset, ran home and lighted his fire. He now charged two cents for the first ten men to enjoy the clean hot water, a penny each for all who cared to follow. Over the course of a year he obviously earned quite a few dollars, and like all the Japanese laboring on Hanakai he watched with excitement as his hidden funds reached toward the mystic number: $400.

From the arrival of the first Japanese back in the 1880's, it had been agreed that a man who could return to Hiroshima with $400 in cash could thenceforth live like a samurai. "With four hundred dollars," the workmen assured one another, "a man could buy three good rice fields, build a large house, get all the kimonos you would ever need, and live in splendor." Every plantation laborer was determined that he would be the man to accumulate the $400, and almost none did.

It was appalling how the money slipped through the fingers of a well-intentioned man. In Kamejiro's case his weaknesses were neither gambling nor women nor alcohol; no, his were far more expensive—friendship and patriotism—and they kept depleting his funds. If a workman faced what appeared to be an insoluble crisis, he went at last to Kamejiro and said bluntly, "I have got to have eighty-one cents."

"Why don't you borrow from the Japanese money lender in Kapaa?" Kamejiro asked.

"In Kapaa if you borrow eighty-one cents, next payday you have to pay back the loan and eighty-one cents more," the workman explained, and he was correct. No white man in Hawaii ever abused Oriental labor as viciously as the Orientals themselves did. Men close to the Japanese consulate had organized a racket whereby incoming workmen were required to pay a deposit to safeguard their papers for eventual return to Japan, and the substantial sums of money were kept year after year with no interest, and when the time came to leave, the deposit often could not be found, and some Japanese became very rich. At every point, vicious practices gnawed away the financial security of the workmen, and interest rates of one hundred per cent a month were common. So usually, rugged little Kamejiro had to cough up the money for his friends.

Some of the Japanese men had begun to bring brides in from Japan, and this was always costly, throwing unusual burdens upon the whole community. There were photographs to be taken in Kapaa, fares to be paid, travel to Honolulu to complete the paper work, and store-bought black suits in which to be married. The amount of connubial bliss underwritten by stalwart Kamejiro was considerable; and this was a self-defeating game, because he found that as soon as a man and woman got together, there were apt to be babies which caused further financial crises. There was thus a constant drain upon his resources and at times it seemed as if he were paying for the family happiness of everyone but himself.

His biggest expenditures, however, arose from patriotism. If a priest came through Kauai telling of a new war memorial, Kamejiro was the man who contributed most heavily. When consular officials from Honolulu appeared to explain the great events transpiring in the homeland, Kamejiro paid their hotel bills. He contributed to the Japanese school, to the Japanese church, and above all to the Japanese reciters who passed through the islands periodically.

These men were the joy of Kamejiro's life, and whenever one was announced he worked with greater speed, impatient for the Sunday afternoon when the entire Japanese community would gather in some park of casuarina trees, sitting on beds of dried needles to wait for the appearance of the reciter. At one-thirty, after the Japanese had enjoyed their lunch of sushi and sashimi, a movable platform of boards, covered by a traditional cloth, was put into position, with a low lectern bearing a closed fan. A hush fell over the crowd, and the visitor from Japan, usually an elderly man with bald head and wide-shouldered starched uniform whose points swept out like butterfly wings, stepped onto the platform in white tabi, bowed many times, and sat on his haunches before the lectern. For some moments he seemed to pray that his voice would be strong, and then, as his audience waited breathless in the sunlight, he picked up the folded fan and began chanting.

"I . . . shall . . . speak . . . of . . . the . . . Battle . . . of . . . Ichi-no-tani," he cried in mournful voice, singing each pregnant word and holding onto it. In those first moments he seemed like an imprisoned volcano, about to burst into wild fury, and as the events of that battle, which had taken place more than seven hundred years before, began to unfold, the man's voice began to acquire new force. He projected himself into each of the characters in turn; he was the brave warrior Kumagai; he was the handsome youth Atsumori; he was the horse, the cliff, the flute; he was the brilliant hero Yoshitsune; and all the women. As his excitement grew, the veins of his head stood out as if they might burst and his neck muscles could be seen like pencils under the skin. At the various crises of the ancient battle, he roared and whispered, sobbed and screamed with joy; but when it came time for Atsumori to die—this bewitching young warrior playing a flute—the man reported grief as if it were a tangible thing, and the entire audience wept.

How terribly real was the heroism of Japan, there under the casuarina trees. How fair and loyal the women were, how brave the men. And as the battle drew to its tragic conclusion, with the plantation hands sobbing for the lost dead, the reciter added lines that were not originally part of the epic, but which he had been told were especially appropriate for distant colonies like this one on Kauai: "And . . . as . . . the . . . ghost . . . of . . . Atsumori . . . left . . . the . . . plain . . . of . . . Ichi-no-tani," the reciter cried mournfully, "he looked back upon the gallant warriors who had slain him and thought: 'These are the brave soldiers of Japan, and while they live there is no danger to the homeland. They can march for miles through hardship. They can live on nothing to support their emperor. They fear no enemy and withdraw from no storm. They are the bravest men on earth, fighting for just causes and the glory of Japan. How strong they are, how noble, how fine it is to see them on the battlefield. Oh, how I long to be with them again, the brave warriors of Japan.' "

A program consisted of four recitations, and since each lasted more than an hour, with famous ones like *Ichi-no-tani* requiring nearly two, the afternoon usually crept on toward darkness before the recital ended. How one man, taking so many varied parts and throwing his voice up and down the scale as if by magic, could last five hours was always a mystery, but in time a convention grew up at the Hanakai readings which made the last item on the program the best of all. It was initiated when a reciter announced: "Today I have a special reward! The story of Colonel Ito, who threw himself upon the Russian guns at Port Arthur." And someone remembered that their own Sakagawa Kamejiro had once played the role of Colonel Ito in the victory procession in Honolulu, and he was sent to fetch his uniform; so while the reciter told the impassioned story of Colonel Ito and the Russian guns, Kamejiro, five-feet-one-inch tall and with arms like hoops, stood rigidly at attention beside the platform, wearing the Imperial uniform which had been sewed up by the women of Honolulu. At such moments a strange thing occurred; he became Colonel Ito. He could see the Russian guns and smell their powder. When the emperor spoke as the troops were leaving Tokyo, Kamejiro could hear the august words, and when the colonel died, defending Japan against the barbarians, Kamejiro died, too, and entered the pantheon of heroes. Spiritually he was part of Japan, a warrior who had never yet borne arms, but who stood ready to die for his emperor. It was after such moments of exaltation that he contributed most heavily to war funds and military hospitals and all such good works.

The constant pull of Japan and its emotional history was so great that Kamejiro did not know one Japanese who intended remaining in Hawaii. All labored twelve hours a day for seventy-three cents, the pay having been raised, in hopes of returning to Hiroshima with $400 and a bright future, and although from the presence of an increasing number of white-haired men and women it was obvious that the majority never saved enough money to get home, not even the most despairing ever admitted that they had given up hope.

One night at the conclusion of a Japanese movie the Buddhist priest called for attention, and a spotlight was thrown upon him by the projectionist. "I want Sakagawa Kamejiro to step forth," the priest said, and the stocky little workman moved into the lights, blinking and keeping his left fist to his mouth. "His Imperial Majesty's consulate in Honolulu has directed me," the priest said, "to award this scroll to Sakagawa Kamejiro in recognition of his contributions on behalf of the brave sailors who lost their lives at the Fukushima catastrophe. All Japan is proud of this man."

To Kamejiro the last words were not an empty phrase. He believed that every village in Japan knew of his loyal behavior and he could visualize word of his deportment creeping to his parents' home, and he could see how happy they were that their son was a decent Japanese. All Japan was proud of him, and for Kamejiro that was sufficient.

For thirteen years he lived in this manner, excited by his recurring contacts with Japan and hopeful that one day soon he would accumulate the $400 plus the boat fare home; but one spring day in 1915, when the casuarina trees were throwing bright nodules at the tips of their needles, ready for the year's growth, and when blossoms were coming onto the pineapples nestling in the red earth, Kamejiro heard a bird cry. It was not a sea bird, for he knew their voices as they swept aloft on the spume thrown up by the cliffs. Perhaps it was from Tahiti, where it had been wintering; possibly it was merely crossing Kauai on its way to Alaska for the rich, insect-laden summer months; and Kamejiro never actually saw the bird, but he heard it winging past him and he stopped dead in the middle of the pineapple field and thought: "I am thirty-three years old and the years are flying past me."

He entered into a period of terrible depression, and a vision came to him which he could not expel: he saw Yoko waiting in Hiroshima, beside the rice fields, and birds were flying past her, too, and she held out her hands, and mists came from the Inland Sea and obliterated her pleading. For the first time he did not rise at three-thirty, and he failed to tend his hot baths, throwing the job onto a friend. He wandered about, gnawed at by an insatiable hunger, and he contemplated going to Kapaa and the brothels, but he rejected the idea, and at last he worked himself toward the decision that hundreds had made before him: "For a little while I shall forget about returning to Japan, but I will use my money to send for Yoko."

He was hoeing pineapple when he made this decision, and it was only two o'clock in the afternoon, but he dropped his hoe and walked in a kind of glorious daze out to the main highway and on into Kapaa, where the ostracized Hashimoto had a photograph shop and an agency for ships traveling to Japan. Smothering his pride and approaching the renegade, Kamejiro said, "I want to get my picture taken to send to Japan."

"Go home and shave," Hashimoto said bluntly. "And wear the dark suit."

"I have no suit."

"Ishii Camp has one. All the men use it."

"I don't want to wear a borrowed suit."

"What girl will want to marry you if you send a photograph without a dark suit?"

"Who said anything about girls?"

"Obviously, you want to get married. I'm glad for you and will take a fine picture. But shave first and wear the dark suit."

"How much will it all cost?" Kamejiro asked.

"Photograph three dollars. Boat fare for the girl seventy. Her train expenses and dresses and the feast back home, maybe seventy. Total one hundred forty-three dollars."

Such an amount would delay the accumulation of $400 by another three or four years at least, and Kamejiro hesitated. "I don't know about that," he said. "Please don't tell anybody."

"I take pictures. I talk to nobody."

"I may be back," Kamejiro said.

"You will be," Hashimoto predicted. Then, as he did with all the Japanese who had ostracized him, he added brutally, "You will marry the girl and you will never return to Japan. Make up your mind about that."

Kamejiro swallowed hard and avoided looking at the photographer. "I am going back to Japan," he said. "You have done me a favor, Hashimoto-san. For a moment I was hungry for a wife and thought: 'I will spend my money that way.' But you have shown me what that means. Good night. I won't be back."

But as he left the photographer's store, a brood of children, half-Japanese, half-Hawaiian, swept past him shouting in a language that no man living could understand—the wild, sweet pidgin of childhood, composed of all languages— and they bumped into him, and a little girl, her hair cut square in the Japanese fashion, cried, "Gomennasai!" and on the impulse of the moment Kamejiro stooped and caught the child, bringing her face to his, and for an instant she remained limp in his arms. Then she kicked free and cried in Hawaiian and Portuguese, "I must go with the others!" And from the doorway, Hashimoto, still hating the men who had driven him out, laughed and said, "It was my daughter you were holding. I have six children, four of them boys."

In great agitation Kamejiro walked home, and the smell of the little girl's hair burned his nostrils so that when he reached the camp and saw the long, bleak, womanless barracks in which he had been living for thirteen years, he rushed directly to Ishii-san and said, "You must write a letter home."

"Are you thinking of getting married?" the scribe asked, for he recognized the symptoms.

"Yes."

Unexpectedly, the thin little letter-writer grasped Kamejiro's hand and confided: "I have been thinking the same thing. What would it cost?"

"Not much!" Kamejiro cried excitedly. "Photograph three dollars. Fare seventy. Maybe a hundred and forty-three altogether."

"I am going to do it!" Ishii-san announced. "I've been thinking about it all this year."

"So have I," Kamejiro confessed, and he sat upon the floor as Ishii-san got out his brushes: "Dear Mother, I have decided to take a wife and later I will send you my photograph so that you can show it to Yoko-chan and she can see how I look now. When you tell me that she is willing to come to Hawaii, I will send the money. This does not mean that I am not going to come back home. It only means that I shall stay here a little longer. Your faithful son, Kamejiro."

It took nine weeks to receive an answer to this letter, and when it arrived Kamejiro was stunned by its contents, for his mother wrote: "You must be a stupid boy to think that Yoko-chan would still be waiting. She got married twelve years ago and already has five children, three of them sons. What made you suppose that a self-respecting girl would wait? But that is no loss, for as you can see I am sending you the photograph of a very fine young lady named Sumiko who has said that she would marry you. She is from this village and will make a lovely wife. Please send the money."

A photograph four inches by three fluttered to the bed, face down. For several moments Kamejiro allowed it to lie there, unable to comprehend that when he turned it over it would show not Yoko, whom he had kept enshrined in his memory, but some girl he had never known. Gingerly, and with two fingers, he lifted the edge of the picture and dropped his head sideways to peer at it. Suddenly he flipped it over and shouted, "Oh! Look at this beautiful girl! Look at her!"

A crowd gathered to study the photograph, and some protested: "That girl will never marry a clod like you, Kamejiro!"

"Tell them what the letter says!" Kamejiro instructed Ishii-san, and the scribe read aloud the facts of the case. The girl's name was Sumiko, and she was willing to marry Kamejiro.

"Is she a Hiroshima girl?" a suspicious man inquired.

"She's from Hiroshima-ken," Kamejiro replied proudly, and a sigh of contentment rose from the long bunkhouse.

On one person the photograph of Kamejiro's good luck had a depressing effect, for in an earlier mail Ishii-san had received a picture of the bride his parents had picked for him. She was a girl called Mori Yoriko, which was a pleasing name, but her photograph showed her to be one of those square-faced, stolid, pinch-eyed peasant girls that Japan seemed to produce in unlimited numbers. Ishii-san's mother assured him that Mori Yoriko could work better than a man and saved money, but the scribe felt that there was more to marriage than that, especially when, as in his case, the husband could read and write. He was patently disappointed and asked to see Kamejiro's picture again. Sumiko, as he studied her, appeared to have the classic type of beauty: gently slanted eyes, fine cheekbones, low forehead, pear-shaped face and delicate features. She looked like the girls whose pictures were painted on the sheets advertising Japanese historical movies, and Ishii-san said. "She's very pretty for a Hiroshima girl. Maybe she's from the city."

"No," Kamejiro assured him. "My mother would never send a city girl."

The next day the two would-be husbands borrowed Ishii Camp's publicly owned black suit, the tie that went with it, and the white shirt; they wrapped their treasure in a sheet, hired a taxi and drove into Kapaa, where Hashimoto the photographer told them, "Take turns with the suit, and be sure to comb your hair."

When Kamejiro climbed into the strange clothes, Hashimoto had to show him how to tie the tie, after which the stocky field hand plastered his hair down with a special grease Hashimoto provided for that purpose. Kamejiro then moved into range of the camera, posing rigidly and refusing to smile. The finished picture, even though it was properly styled and mounted, would have excited few prospective brides, and Hashimoto did not consider it one of his best. Nevertheless, Kamejiro mailed it with a fully paid ticket from Tokyo to Honolulu. Then he waited.

In late 1915 Ishii-san and Kamejiro received notice that their brides were arriving at Honolulu on the old Japanese freighter *Kyoto-maru*. The news did not occasion the joy that might have been expected, because it had been hoped at the camp that the two girls might arrive by separate ships, for then each husband, when he went to get his wife, could have worn the black suit, thus corresponding to the photographs sent to Japan. As things now stood, one man would wear the suit and not disappoint his bride, but the other would clearly have to wear his laboring clothes and stand before his bride as he really was. It was the character of Kamejiro to say quickly to his friend, "Since you can read and write, it is proper for you to wear the suit." And the camp agreed that this was the only logical solution.

The lovers, alternately ardent and afraid, left Lihue by the small ship *Kilauea* and went to Honolulu, where they took one room in a dingy Japanese inn on Hotel Street. Since they arrived on the evening before the *Kyoto-maru* was expected, they ate a meager supper of rice and fish, then hiked up Nuuanu and bowed low before the symbol of their emperor. As they were doing so an official in black cutaway hustled out on some important meeting and snapped: "Don't stand around here like peasants. Go about your work." Obediently the men left.

They were impressed by the big homes on Beretania Street but were shocked by the dirty alleys of Chinatown, where one miserable hovel leaned against the next. Ishii-san said, "They told me that fifteen years ago this whole neighborhood was burned down and the Chinese wanted to rebuild it like a proper city without alleys and mean houses, but the white people wanted it the way it was before, so it was built that way again." The two men, recalling the clean roads and immaculate homes of their childhood, shook their heads at the white man's ways.

Before they went to sleep that night Ishii-san spread before him the two photographs, and he spent a long time comparing them, and his disappointment at the tricks of fate became apparent in his features. "My mother didn't choose very well, I'm afraid," he said. "Isn't it strange, Kamejiro, to think that a great ship out there is bringing a woman with whom you will spend the rest of your life?"

"I'm nervous," Kamejiro confessed, but his nervousness that night was nothing to what he would experience during the next days; for when the *Kyoto-maru* docked, the seven Japanese men who had come to meet their picture brides were told, "We never let the women out of quarantine for three days."

"Can't we even see them?" Ishii-san implored.

"No contact of any kind," the immigration man warned.

Later, the ardent grooms found that if they bribed one of the attendants, they could press their faces against a hole the size of a half-dollar that had been bored into the door behind which the incoming brides were imprisoned, and the third man in line was Kamejiro. Squinting so as to make his eye smaller, he peered through the miserable peephole and saw seven women idly sitting and standing in groups. He looked from one to the other and was unable to detect which was Sumiko, and he looked back beseechingly at the guard who spoke no Japanese. Applying his eye once more to the circle, he looked avidly at the seven women, but again he could not isolate his intended wife, and in some confusion he turned the peephole over to his successor.

"Is she beautiful?" Ishii-san asked.

"Very," Kamejiro assured him.

"Did you see Yoriko?"

"I think so."

"Does she look pretty good?"

"She looks very healthy," Kamejiro said.

When Ishii-san left the peephole he was trembling. "She's a lot bigger than I am," he mumbled. "Damn my mother!"

"Oh, Ishii-san!" Kamejiro protested. "She's a Hiroshima girl. She's bound to make a good wife."

On the second and third days the men returned to spy upon their wives, and by a process of elimination Kamejiro discovered whom he was to marry. He had failed at first to find her because she was by all odds the loveliest of the girls and he had not been able to believe that she was intended for him. Commiserating with his friend Ishii-san's disappointment, he had the delicacy not to revel in the beauty of his own wife; but as the hours passed, leading up to the moment when the doors would be thrown open, he became frightfully nervous and excited.

"I am beginning to feel sick!" he told Ishii-san.

"I already am," the letter-writer confided.

"I think I may go away and come back later," Kamejiro whispered.

"Wait a minute!" one of the husbands snapped. "Look at the poor women!"

Kamejiro felt himself shoved to the peephole and for the last time he saw the seven brides. They knew that the hour of meeting was at hand, and the bravery that had marked their earlier behavior now fled. Without adequate water or combs, they made pathetic attempts to pretty themselves. They smoothed down one another's rumpled, sea-worn dresses, and tucked in ends of hair. One woman applied her fingertips to her forehead, as if she considered it ugly, and tried to spread its skin more smoothly over the heavy bones. In the corner one girl wept, and after a brief attempt at trying to console her, the others left her alone with her misery. But there was one thing that each girl in her final moments of panic did: she studied the photograph clutched in her hand and desperately tried to memorize the features of the man she was about to meet. She was determined that she would know him and that she would walk up to him unerringly and bow before him. But now all were weeping and the photographs were blurred.

A gong rang and Kamejiro jumped back from the door. Slowly the hinges swung open and the brides came forth. No tears were visible. The placid faces under the mounds of black hair looked steadily, inquiringly forward, and the first sound heard was a muffled gasp of pain. "Oh!" one of the brides sighed. "You are so much older than the picture."

"It was taken a long time ago," the man explained. "But I will be a good husband." He held out his hand, and the girl, controlling herself, bowed until her head almost touched his knees. They formed the first pair.

The next girl, the one who had been weeping alone in the corner, walked straight to her man, smiled and bowed low. "I am Fumiko," she said. "Your mother sends a thousand blessings." And she formed up the second pair.

The third girl was Mori Yoriko, Ishii-san's bride, and as he had feared, she was much more robust than he. She was a true Hiroshima country girl, red-cheeked, square-faced, squint-eyed. Knowing that she was less beautiful than any of the others, she made up for her deficiencies in stalwart courage and a burning desire to make herself into a good wife. She found Ishii-san and bowed low, her big hands held close to her knees. "Mr. Ishii," she whispered, "I bring you the love of your mother." Then, as if she knew reassurance was necessary, she quickly added in a halting whisper, "I will be a good wife."

The last girl to find her husband was Sumiko, the prettiest of the lot, and her recalcitrance sprang not from any lack of wit but from the shock she had received when she first saw Kamejiro. He did not wear the black suit in which he had been photographed, nor was his hair pasted down. His clothes were those of a mean peasant and his arms were brutally awkward. He was grim-faced, like an angry, stupid man, and he was twice as old as she had expected. Last in line, and with only one man unattached, Sumiko obviously knew who her husband was, but she refused to accept the fact.

"No!" she cried imperiously. "That one is not my man!"

"Oh!" Kamejiro gasped. "I am Sakagawa Kamejiro. I have your picture."

She slapped it from his hand and then threw hers upon it, stamping upon them. "I will not marry this man. I have been deceived."

At this outburst the first bride, who had also found a husband she did not want, shook Sumiko and cried in rapid Japanese, "Control yourself, you selfish little fool! In such an affair who expects to find a champion?"

"I will not marry this animal!" Sumiko wailed, whereupon the first bride, who had gracefully accepted her disappointment, delivered a solid slap across the girl's face.

"On the entire trip you were a mean, nasty child. You ought to be ashamed. Go to that good man and humble yourself before him." The first bride placed her hand in the middle of Sumiko's back and projected her across the hushed immigration room.

Sumiko would have stumbled except that from the astonished couples Ishii-san sprang forth to rescue her. He caught her by the waist and held her for a moment. Then, looking at Kamejiro and his own intended bride, he said with a frankness that startled even himself, "Kamejiro, you and Yoriko make a better pair. Give me Sumiko." And the beautiful girl, finding herself in the presence of a cultured man who wore a black suit, suddenly cried, "Yes, Kamejiro, you are too old for me. Please, please!"

In stolid bewilderment, Kamejiro looked down at the picture and recalled how deeply over the past months he had grown to love it. Then he looked up at square-faced, chapped-cheeked Mori Yoriko and thought: "She is not the girl in my picture. What are they doing to me?"

He hesitated, the room whirling about him, and then he felt on his arm the hand of the first bride, who had slapped Sumiko, and this quiet-voiced girl was saying, "I do not know your name, but I have lived with Yoriko for three weeks, and of all the brides here, I assure you that she will make the best wife. Take her."

The humiliated country girl, who had been so painfully rejected by her intended husband, found tears welling into her unpretty eyes, and she wanted to run to some corner, but she stood firm like the rock from which she had been hewn and bowed low before the stranger. "I will be a good wife," she mumbled, fighting to control her voice.

Kamejiro looked for the last time at the well-remembered picture on the floor, then picked it up and handed it to his friend Ishii-san. "It will be better this way," he said. Returning to the girl who still bowed, he said gently, "My name is Sakagawa Kamejiro. I am from Hiroshima-ken."

"My name is Mori Yoriko," the peasant girl answered. "I also am from Hiroshima."

"Then we will get married," he said, and the seven couples were completed.

D URING THE YEARS when Kamejiro Sakagawa and his bride Yoriko were discovering how lucky they were to have stumbled into their improvised marriage, the missionary families in Honolulu were experiencing a major shock, for one of their sons was proving to be a fiery radical, and reports of his behavior startled all Hawaii.

In these years Hawaii seemed filled with Hales and Whipples and Hewletts and Janderses and Hoxworths. In some classes at Punahou sixteen out of twenty-four students would bear these or related names. Only skilled genealogists tried to keep the blood lines straight, for Hales were Hoxworths and Hoxworths were Whipples, and fairly frequently a Hale would marry a Hale and thus intensify the complications, so that in time no child really understood who his various cousins were, and an island euphemism gained popularity: "He is my calabash cousin," which meant that if one went back far enough, some kind of blood relationship could be established.

Hawaii came to consider this Hale-Whipple-Hewlett-Janders-Hoxworth ménage simply as "the family" and to recognize its four salient characteristics: its children went to Punahou; its boys went to Yale; invariably it found some kind of good-paying job for every son and for the husband of every daughter; and members of the family tried to avoid scandal. Therefore, when one of the boys became a radical, the family was deeply jolted.

As long as he had stayed at Punahou, this renegade had done well, but this was not unusual, for the family expected its sons to prosper there. Take the case of Hoxworth Whipple, who gained international honors for his work on Polynesian history. He started his scholarly investigation while still at Punahou, although later he took his B.A. at Yale, his M.A. at Harvard, his Ph.D. from Oxford and his D.Litt. from the Sorbonne. He received honorary degrees from eleven major universities, but when he died in 1914 the Honolulu *Mail* announced simply: "The great scholar was educated at Punahou." None of the rest really mattered.

In the year that the great scholar died, crowded with honors, the young member of the family who was to become the radical was graduating from Punahou. He was Hoxworth Hale, in all outward respects a typical sixteen-year-old boy. He was neither tall nor short, fat nor thin. His hair was not black nor was it blond, and his eyes displayed no single prominent color. He was not at the top of his class nor yet at the bottom, and he was outstanding in no one scholastic accomplishment. He had played games moderately well but had never won fist fights against boys larger than himself.

Young Hoxworth Hale, named after the noted scholar, was most noted for the fact that he had uncommonly pretty sisters, Henrietta and Jerusha, and they lent him a spurious popularity which he would not otherwise have enjoyed. There was a good deal of chivvying to see which of his friends would win the favors of the charming sisters, and of course in later years his younger sister became engaged to one of her calabash cousins, a Whipple, whereupon Hoxworth's father told the family, "I think it's high time somebody married a stranger. Get some new blood into this tired old tree." His words were not taken in good grace, because he had married his cousin, a Hoxworth girl, and it was felt that he was casting aspersions upon her; nevertheless, when his oldest daughter began displaying outward tendencies and actually became engaged to a man named Gage from Philadelphia, he expressed his pleasure. But later Henrietta met a boy from New Hampshire named Bromley and the two discovered that way, way back her great-great-great-great-grandfather Charles Bromley and his great-great-great . . . well, anyway, she felt a lot more congenial with Bromley than she ever had with her fiancé Gage, so she married the former because, as she pointed out, "he seems more like one of the family."

When young Hoxworth Hale left Punahou it was understood that he would go on to Yale, and in New Haven this undistinguished youth was to explode into a prominence no one had anticipated. Not having wasted his limited intellectual reserves in preparatory school, he was ready to blossom in college and gradually became both a scholar and a polished gentleman. In his grades he did markedly better than boys who had surpassed him at Punahou, while in sports he captained the polo team and served as assistant manager of the basketball team. He acquired the lesser amenities and in politics ran successfully for president of his class.

It was this unlikely youth who became the radical. His commitment began one day in his junior year when a Professor Albers from Leipzig was ending a lecture on the theory of imperialism with this shrewd observation: "The Congregational-Church-cum-Boston-merchant invasion and capture of Hawaii is the exact counterpart of the Catholic-Church-cum-Paris-entrepreneur rape of Tahiti. The proof of this analogy lies, I think, in the demonstrated manner whereby the missionaries who went to Hawaii, though they did not call in the American gunboats as did their French cousins in Tahiti, nevertheless, by revolutionary means, stole the land from the Hawaiians and wound up possessors of the islands."

Professor Albers' class contained, in addition to young Hoxworth Hale, his calabash cousin Hewlett Janders, two Whipples and a Hewlett, but these other descendants of the missionaries were content to stare in embarrassment at their arm rests. Not so Hoxworth; he coughed once, coughed twice, then boldly interrupted: "Professor Albers, I'm sorry but I'm afraid you have your facts wrong."

"I beg your pardon," the German professor spluttered.

"I mean that whereas your facts on Tahiti may be correct, those on Hawaii are definitely in error."

"Don't you stand when you address remarks to your professor?" The Leipzig-trained scholar demanded, growing red. When Hoxworth got to his feet, Albers referred to his notes and began quoting an impressive list of sources: "The journals of Ellis, Jarves, Bird, the researches of Amsterfield, de Golier, Whipple. They all tell the same story."

"If they do," Hoxworth said, "they're all wrong."

Professor Albers flushed and asked, "What is your name, young man?"

"Hoxworth Hale, sir."

"Well!" Albers laughed. "Your testimony on this matter is hardly unimpeachable."

This contempt goaded Hale into making a reply that infuriated the professor: "You cited Jarves. Have you ever read Jarves?"

"I do not cite sources I have not read," Albers fumed.

"Jarves happened to be a friend of some of my ancestors, and they held him in keen regard because he was the first impartial observer to defend the missionaries, and I've read what he wrote, in the original papers in which he wrote it, and what he wrote, sir, simply doesn't support your thesis."

The class broke up in something of a scandal and for some weeks the word *missionary* had a curious force of its own at Yale. Professor Albers, goaded by his young tormentor, marshaled an impressive battery of anti-clerical critics whose gibes at all churches and their nefarious skill in capturing the land of backward countries pleased the young iconoclasts of that day, and for several biting weeks the professor carried the day, and the dormitories rang with the famous gibes against the Hawaiian missionaries: "They came to the island to do good, and they did right well." "No wonder the islands were lighter when they left; they stole everything in sight." "They taught the natives to wear dresses and sign leases." And most cutting of all: "Before the missionaries came to Hawaii, there were four hundred thousand happy, naked natives in the mountains killing each other, practicing incest, and eating well. After the missionaries had been there awhile, there were thirty thousand fully clothed, miserable natives, huddled along the shore, paying lip service to Christianity and owning nothing." In Professor Albers' classes such lines of reasoning became increasingly popular, and for the first time Yale, the source of missionaries, took a serious look at what they had really accomplished. In those exciting days it was downright unpleasant to be a Whipple or a Hewlett, for the fact was often cited that Dr. John Whipple had abandoned the church to become a millionaire, and that Hewlett had left to steal land from the defenseless natives.

In the fifth week of the intellectual investigation, Hoxworth Hale, then a junior, nineteen years old, asked for time to read to the class the results of some work he had been doing on his account, and in cold, dispassionate phrases he developed this thesis: "In the third decade of the last century a series of little ships brought missionaries to Hawaii. There were twelve ships in all, bearing a total of fifty-two ordained missionaries, brought to the islands at a cost of $1,220,000. At the end of nearly thirty years of religious and social service in the islands, the missionaries controlled practically no land, except in the case of one Abraham Hewlett who had married a Hawaiian lady and whose family lands have always been kept in her name for the welfare of her people. The Whipples owned no land whatever. Nor did the Hales except, in later days, a few building lots on which their homes have been built. In fact, in 1854 the Hawaiian government took cognizance of the unfortunate position of the mission families and passed a special law allowing those who had served the islands well to buy small parcels of land at favorable prices. And the government did this, Professor Albers, because they were afraid not that the missionaries would take over the islands, but that they would go back to America and take their children with them. The minutes of the government on this matter are explicit: 'June, 1851, the missionaries who have received and applied for lands have neither received nor applied for them without offering what they considered a fair compensation for them. So far as their applications have been granted, your Majesty's government have dealt with them precisely as they have dealt with other applications for land. It will not be contended that missionaries, because they are missionaries, have not the same right to buy land in the same quantities and at the same prices as those who are not missionaries. But, besides what is strictly due to them, in justice and in gratitude for large benefits conferred by them on your people, every consideration of sound policy, under the rapid decrease of the native population, is in favor of holding out inducements for them not to withdraw their children from these islands. We propose a formal resolution declaring the gratitude of this nation to the missionaries for the services they have performed, and making some provision to insure that their children remain in these islands.' "

At this point Hoxworth looked directly at his professor and continued: "Dr. Albers, the provisions of this resolution were carried out, and the investigating committee found that the missionaries who had worked so long in Hawaii had acquired so little that the community as a whole applauded when the government provided that any missionary who had served in the islands for eight years be allowed to buy 560 acres of government lands at a price of fifty cents an acre lower than what the average white newcomer would have to pay. Since the average price at that time was $1.45 an acre, this represents a reduction of exactly 34.5 per cent, or one per cent per year for arduous and faithful service. So far as I can find, the missionaries acquired land in absolutely no other way, and even so, most of them were then too poor to take advantage of the government's offer.

"Hawaii desperately wanted the mission families to stay in the islands, and it has been justly said that the most significant crop grown by the missionaries was not sugar, but their sons. Now, if you want to argue that the brilliant young mission sons who left Hawaii, studied here at Yale and then returned to the islands, usurped a disproportionate number of important jobs in medicine, law, government and management, you would be on good grounds, but if you do so argue, don't blame the missionaries. Blame Yale.

"I conclude that it is neither fair nor accurate to accuse these families of stealing land which they never came into possession of. It was the non-mission families, the New England sea rovers, who got the land. Then, the land having been obtained by these men, it is true that mission sons managed it, for a fee, but would you have had it lie fallow? The facts you cite apply to Tahiti. They simply do not apply to Hawaii."

He sat down, flushed with excitement, and expected the applause of his classmates for having dared argue with the arrogant professor, but what Hoxworth had said was not popular. It ran against the grain of the age and was not believed. Jokes about missionaries continued, and Hale saw that whereas he had gained nothing with his contemporaries he had placed himself at a serious disadvantage with the faculty. But what grieved him most was that his Punahou associates, Hewlett Janders and the others, felt rather ashamed that a subject which would have died with only momentary embarrassment had now been so thoroughly ventilated as to force all members of the class to be either anti-missionary or pro, and nearly everyone fell into the first category, and the Punahou men were infuriated that one of their own number had stirred up the mess.

So Hoxworth Hale's first venture into public argument backfired rather badly, but his studies had disclosed to him his ancestors, so that no matter how witty the gibes against missionaries became, he knew what the facts were, and this knowledge, in the subtle way that knowledge has, fortified him in many ways and made him a stronger man.

His preoccupation with researches into Hawaiian history developed an accidental concomitant which outraged all of Yale and led to his temporary withdrawal from the university. He was in the library one day, reading files of an early Honolulu newspaper, the *Polynesian,* for he wished to refresh his mind as to what that journal's excitable editor, James Jackson Jarves, had actually said about missionaries, and for a while he got bogged down in the story of how Jarves had protested when a French warship roared into Honolulu, insisting that French wines be imported in unlimited amounts, and of how the French authorities threatened to lash him through the streets with a cat-o'-nine-tails. Next he turned the yellowed pages to read of the time when the British consul actually did horsewhip poor Jarves for defending Hawaii against British intrusions into local affairs, and he began to laugh to himself: "Jarves must have been a wild-eyed young man . . . like me." And the conceit pleased him, and he felt sympathy for the strange, will-o'-the-wisp editor who had so befriended Hawaii and the missionaries, until he suddenly looked at the name again: James Jackson Jarves! Hadn't he heard that name in another context?

He hurried from the library and went to the exhibition hall where one of the glories of Yale University stood: the collection of early Italian masterpieces gathered together by a curious man named James Jackson Jarves, who had lived in Florence in the 1850's. Hoxworth hurried into the gallery and walked among the strange, faraway, gold and blue painting of an age he could not even begin to comprehend. He was unprepared to like the art he saw in the Jarves collection, and he did not try to do so, for it was in no way similar to the work of Raphael and Rembrandt, which he had been taught was true art; but as he gazed at the affectionate little paintings—more than a hundred of them—he sensed that they had been collected by someone who had loved them, and he asked an attendant, "Who was this man Jarves?" The man didn't know, so Hale sought out another, and finally the curator: "Who was Jarves?"

The curator had a brief memorandum on the forgotten donor and said, "An American writer on art who lived in Florence in the middle years of the last century. A close friend of Elizabeth and Robert Browning and John Ruskin. In his own way, an eminent man, and America's first writer on art."

"Did he ever live in Hawaii?"

"No. But late in life he did write the first book in English on Japanese art. He discovered prints as art forms, so he must have lived in the Orient, although I have no knowledge of the fact."

"Hawaii isn't in the Orient," Hale explained.

"Isn't it considered part of Asia?"

"No," Hale replied sharply and left. In those days he did not think much of faculty members.

He was puzzled. It seemed most unlikely that two men of such dissimilar natures as the rambunctious Hawaiian editor and the polished Italian art connoisseur could have been the same man, and yet there was the name: James Jackson Jarves; so he continued his researches and discovered at last that his Hawaiian Jarves had failed to make a living with his *Polynesian* and had fled in disgust to Florence, where he became the first great American collector of paintings, the first American art philosopher, and the first writer on Japanese aesthetics. He felt a proprietary interest in the strange man and thought: "That's not bad for a Hawaii boy!"

And then, as he looked into the peculiar circumstances whereby Yale acquired the Jarves paintings, he became appalled at the unsavory tricks the college had used to steal them, and he forgot all about missionaries and began digging into the events of 1871, when the former editor of the *Polynesian* was fifty-three years old and in sore need of money. Yale had loaned him $20,000 on his paintings, and he had been unable to repay the debt, so the college put the entire collection up for public auction, 119 masterpieces in all, worth $70,000 or $80,000 then . . . over a million dollars in 1917. But college authorities had quietly forewarned potential bidders that any buyer must take the entire collection in one lump, and the rumor had circulated that even if this were done, the college would not yield clear title to the pictures, so that any prospective buyer must beware of lawsuits; and on the day of the sale there were no bidders, and Yale acquired the collection for what Jarves owed the college.

"This is a scandal!" Hoxworth cried, and to his amazement he found himself deeply involved in art problems, and now when he passed through the Jarves collection, he thought: "These marvelous masterworks!" He wrote a long letter to the college paper, asking why a college with Yale's background should have conspired at such a nasty business, and hell broke loose.

Hoxworth was defamed on the Yale campus as a radical who had raped the reputation of his own college; but a Boston art critic wrote: "The general outline of the facts so patiently developed by young Mr. Hale have long been known in art circles but hitherto they have not been publicly aired, out of courtesy to a revered institution whose deportment otherwise has been above reproach." So once more one of the most essentially conservative young men Hawaii ever sent to Yale found himself the center of controversy, and this one far exceeded in general interest his spirited defense of the missionaries, for it involved the honor of the university itself.

At the height of the controversy the campus newspaper evolved a logical way for Hoxworth to apologize, but just as he had refused to accommodate himself to Professor Albers' erroneous data on Hawaii, so he now refused to condone what Yale had done to his favorite Hawaiian editor, James Jackson Jarves. Yale had stolen the pictures, and Hoxworth bluntly reiterated his charges. And then late one afternoon as he walked disconsolately through the collection a completely new thought came to him: "It really doesn't matter to Jarves now whether Yale stole the pictures or not, just as it doesn't matter whether the missionaries stole the land or not. What counts, and the only thing that counts is this: What good did the institution accomplish? If Yale had not picked up the pictures, forcibly perhaps, where would they be now? Could they possibly have served the wonderful purposes they serve here in New Haven? If the missionaries had stepped aside and allowed Hawaii to drift from one degeneracy to another, what good would have been accomplished? Yale is better by far for having had such a solid beginning for its art school, and Hawaii is better for having had the missionaries. The minor blemishes on the record are unimportant. It doesn't matter what an arrogant fool like Albers says. Janders and the rest were right to ignore him. The fact is that in Hawaii today there are sugar plantations, and pineapple, and deep reservoirs and a lot of different people living together reasonably well. If Yale stole the pictures, they're entitled to them because of the good use to which they put them. And I'm not going to argue with anyone any more about the missionaries stealing Hawaii. If they did, which I don't admit, they certainly put what they stole to good purposes." He saw then, that gloomy afternoon when he was being hammered by his friends, that there were many ways to judge the acts of an institution, and the pragmatic way was not the worst, by any means.

Thus he started his education, that marvelous, growing, aching process whereby a mind develops into a usable instrument with a collection of proved experience from which to function, and he was suddenly tired of Yale, and Punahou men, and professors trained at Leipzig, and problems relating to James Jackson Jarves. Consequently, he walked casually out of the gallery, nodded a grave farewell to the pictures he would never bother to see again, and reported to the New Haven post office where, on April 28, 1917, he enlisted in the army and went to France.

O N AUGUST 19, 1916, an event occurred which was to change the history of Hawaii, but as in the case of most such events, it was not so recognized at the time. It happened because one of the German lunas was both drunk and suffering from a toothache, the latter condition having occasioned the former.

Normally, the plantation lunas were a tough, cynical, reasonably well-behaved lot. Imported mostly from Germany and Norway—with one man sending for his brother and both calling upon a cousin, so that luna families were constantly being refreshed from the old country—they were employed by firms like Janders & Whipple to supervise field hands for two reasons. It was unthinkable that an Oriental could rise above minor roles, partly because few ever learned to speak English and partly because none intended to remain in Hawaii, but mostly because haoles could not visualize Chinese or Japanese in positions of authority. And from sad experience, the great plantation owners had discovered that the Americans they could get to serve as lunas were positively no good. Capable Americans expected office jobs and incapable ones were unable to control the Oriental field hands.

Therefore Hawaii was forced to import Europeans to run the plantations, and if the upper crust of Hawaiian society consisted of New England families like the Hales and the Whipples, the second and operating layer was built of Europeans who had once been lunas but who had now left the plantations for businesses of their own. Of the Europeans, the Germans were the greatest successes, both as lunas and as subsequent citizens, and it was ironic that the historical event of which I speak should have been precipitated by a German, but his toothache can probably be blamed.

He was on his way through Ishii Camp at six o'clock one morning, his boots polished and his white ducks freshly pressed. Of late he had been pestered by Japanese laborers in the long bunkhouses who had taken to guzzling large amounts of soy sauce in order to induce temporary fevers, which excused them from work that day; and he was determined to end this farce. If a man claimed a fever, he personally had to breathe in the face of the German luna, and God help him if he smelled of soy sauce.

In the nineteenth century, lunas had had a fairly free hand in abusing Oriental labor, and there were instances in which sadistic foremen lashed the pigtails of two Chinese together and tied the knot to a horse's tail, whipping the beast as he dragged the terrified Orientals through the red dust. Other lunas had formed a habit of beating either Chinese or Japanese as one would thrash a recalcitrant child, and by such methods the Europeans had maintained a ruthless dictatorship of the cane fields, but with the coming of pineapple, where an abused man seeking revenge could easily pass down a row of flowering plants and knock off hundreds of the tiny individual flowers, so that the resulting fruit would lack some of the small squares of which it should have been built, the lunas by and large surrendered their old prerogatives of lash and fist, and life in the plantations was not too bad.

But on August 19, 1916, this German luna found two of his Japanese suffering from "soy-sauce fever," and he cuffed them out to the fields, temperature or no. He then left the long barracks where bachelors stayed and entered the minute wooden house where Kamejiro Sakagawa and his wife Yoriko lived, and to his disgust he found the former in bed. The luna did not stop to recall that for fourteen years Kamejiro had never once requested a day off for illness, so that malingering was not likely. All the German saw was another Japanese in bed, claiming a fever.

"You breathe my face," he growled in thick pidgin.

Kamejiro, who did not even know of the soy-sauce trick, failed to grasp the instructions, which convinced the luna of his perfidy. Shaking the little laborer, he shouted again, "You breathe my face!" He leaned over the bed, and since the wife Yoriko had felt sorry for her stricken husband and had both bathed him and fed him some rice and soy sauce, the unmistakable odor of the strong black sauce struck the luna's nose, and something in what he interpreted as the mock-bewilderment of the little Japanese infuriated him, and with a judgment clouded by alcohol and his own substantial pain, he dragged the sick man from his bed and began thrashing him with the whip most lunas carried.

He had struck Kamejiro some dozen blows, none of them very effective because of the crowded nature of the cabin, when he realized from Mrs. Sakagawa's behavior and the flushed appearance of her husband that perhaps the man really was sick. But he had launched a specific course of action and found himself incapable of turning back. "Get dressed," he growled, and as bewildered Kamejiro, sick for the first time in Hawaii, climbed into his clothes, the luna stood over him, flexing the whip. He drove Kamejiro out of the cabin and into the pineapple fields, announcing to the others: "Soy-sauce pilikia pau! Plenty pau!"

Kamejiro, with a high fever, worked till noon and then staggered to one knee. "He's fainting!" the Japanese cried, and work stopped while they hauled him back to his cabin. The German luna, frightened by this twist of events, hurried for the plantation doctor and said, "You've got to say it was soy-sauce fever. We've got to stick together."

The doctor, an old hack who had proved himself unable to hold down any other job, understood, but he was nevertheless appalled at the high fever in the Japanese, and before he publicly announced that the man had been malingering, he dosed him well. Then he supported the luna and gave a stormy lecture in pidgin against the evils of drinking soy sauce. But when he rode back with the luna he warned: "The little bastard won't die this time, but sometimes they really are sick."

"How can you tell?" the German asked, and so far as he was concerned the incident was closed.

But not for Kamejiro Sakagawa. For fourteen years he had given his employer the kind of loyalty that all Japanese are expected to give their superiors. Every monologue delivered by the frenetic, bald-headed reciter dealt with the loyalty that an inferior owed his master. The suicides, the immolations and the feat of Colonel Ito at Port Arthur had all stemmed from this sense of obedience, and the reason that reciters came from Tokyo to such remote areas as Kauai was that the Imperial government wanted to remind all Japanese of their undying loyalty to superiors, in this case the emperor and his army. None had mastered the lesson more firmly than Kamejiro; to him loyalty and rectitude were inborn nature, and the high point of his life continued to be the moment when he dressed in Colonel Ito's uniform to stand at attention while the chanters screamed the story: "Colonel Ito and the Russian Guns at Port Arthur." In his dream life, Kamejiro was that colonel.

But what had happened to him now? When the fever abated he mumbled to his closest friends, "The worst part was not the whip, although it stung. But when I had fallen on the floor, he kicked me! With his shoe!"

If the German luna had been asked by a judge if this had truly happened, he would not have known, for to him the kick was of no significance. But to a Japanese it was an insult past enduring. It was no use to argue with Kamejiro that a kick was no worse than a thrashing from a whip. He knew that in Japanese recitations the most terrifying scene came when the villain, having knocked the hero down, takes off his zori and ceremoniously strikes the fallen hero, for then men like Kamejiro gasped, knowing that only death could avenge this ultimate insult.

"He kicked you?" one of the older men asked in a whisper.

"Yes."

"An ignorant, uneducated German kicked a Japanese?"

"Yes."

"All Japan will be ashamed of this day," the visitor mumbled and sharing this shame, departed.

When the Sakagawas were left alone, Kamejiro turned his face to the wall and began to sob. He could not understand what had happened, but he knew that revenge of some kind was imperative. As his visitor had clearly said, "All Japan will be ashamed."

His lumpy, square-faced wife understood the agony he felt and tried by various gentle means to placate him and poultice with kindness his festering sores, but she accomplished nothing, and at sunset her husband announced his plan: "I will borrow Ishii-san's sword, and after the darkness has fallen I will creep to the luna's house and on his front steps I will cut out my bowels. This will bring him great shame and the honor of Japan will be restored."

"No!" Yoriko pleaded. "This stupid German would not understand."

"When he stumbles upon my body in the morning, he will understand," Kamejiro replied.

"Oh, no!" Yoriko wept. She had not yet lived with her husband for a year, but she had found him to be one of the finest men she had ever known or heard of. He was kind and jovial. He saved his money and was generous with friends. He got drunk sometimes but fell into laughing fits when he did and had to lean on her to get home. And at all public gatherings of the Japanese, he represented the honor of the homeland. In his uniform of Colonel Ito he was as handsome a man as she had seen, and she did not want him, not even for the honor of his country, to commit hara-kiri before the house of a clod like the German luna.

"Kamejiro," she whispered. "Forget the sword. There is a better way. Wait till you are stronger. I will feed you rice and fish and you will become powerful as before. Then hide along the path, and when the luna comes along, leap at him and knock him down and then kick him with your zori."

"Germans are big men," Kamejiro reflected.

"Then get some of the others to help you," Yoriko plotted.

"I would not hide," Kamejiro replied. "That would offend the honor of Japan."

"Then walk up to him," Yoriko counseled, "and knock him down."

The German luna seemed rather bigger to Kamejiro than he did to Yoriko, so on his feverish bed the little laborer worked out an alternative plot that would both humiliate the luna and restore his own besmirched honor. He waited until his strength returned, bided his time while he spied on the luna, and then laid his trap. Planting himself along a road which the German had to traverse on his way to the overseers' quarters, he trembled with excitement as he saw the towering luna approach. When the German was almost abreast of him, he called sharply, "Mr. Von Schlemm!"

Startled, the luna stopped and drew his fists into a protective position. Then he saw that his accoster was the model workman Kamejiro, and he forgot that he had recently whipped the man. He dropped his guard slightly and asked, "What fo' you call?"

To his amazement, the little Japanese bent down, carefully took off his zori, stood erect like a major in a German play, and tapped the man facing him on the shoulder with the dusty Japanese shoe. At this moment Kamejiro expected to be knocked down by the luna, whereupon his friends hiding in the bushes were supposed to leap out and thrash the luna roundly.

But nothing happened. The big, bewildered German stared at his strange assailant, looked down at the one bare foot, and shrugged his shoulders. "You speak, Kamejiro?" he asked, unable to comprehend what was happening.

In disgust with a man so lacking in honor, Kamejiro turned his back and started hobbling with one shoe and one bare foot back to his quarters. The big luna, more perplexed than ever, watched him disappear, then shrugged his shoulders again and went along to his quarters, but as he walked he thought he heard in the sugar cane beside the road the muffled and derisive laughter of men, but when he turned suddenly to find them, he saw nothing but the waving cane.

That night Sakagawa Kamejiro was a hero among the Japanese of Ishii

Camp. "Tell us again how you humiliated the luna!" his admirers begged.

"I went up to him just as I told my wife I would and I called, 'Eh, you, Mr. Von Schlemm!' Then I took off my zori and struck him on the head with it."

"On the head?" asked the Japanese who had not been in the cane. "And he did nothing?"

One of the men who had been hiding in the cane explained: "He was astonished! He was afraid! I could see him tremble! What a sorry man he was that moment!"

"I think we had better celebrate with some sake," an older man suggested, proud of the manner in which Kamejiro had recovered the honor of Ishii Camp, but before the celebration could be properly launched, Ishii-san himself ran breathlessly in from Kapaa with shocking news. At first he could not speak, but then, with tears bursting from his bloodshot eyes, he blurted out: "My wife has run away!"

"Sumiko-san?" everyone cried.

"She has run away to Honolulu," the stricken man wailed. "She said she could not live in Kauai any longer."

"What was the matter?" one of the older men asked. "Weren't you able to pin her down in bed?"

"We had a good time in bed," Ishii-san explained, "but she laughed at me for having no suit. I pleaded with her . . . Maybe some of you heard the fights in our house."

He stood, a dejected man, ashamed of his fiasco and humiliated, and some of the men of Ishii Camp felt exceedingly sorry for him, for he could read and write and he had spent a good deal of money bringing a wife from Japan, and the one he finally got turned out to be the most beautiful Japanese girl in Hawaii, but he had not been able to hold her. There was a silence in the camp, and then Mrs. Sakagawa, the stocky, square-faced woman he had rejected, went up to him and said, "Forget this ill-mannered girl, Ishii-san. On the boat we grew to despise her and we knew she would never make a good wife. The blame is not yours. I announce to everyone here that the blame is not Ishii-san's."

The little scribe looked into the face of the rugged woman he had imported form Hiroshima, and in great dejection mumbled, "Then you forgive me, Yoriko-chan?"

"I forgave you long ago," the stocky peasant girl replied, "for you enabled me to find my true husband." She used the Japanese word Danna-san, Sir Master, and although she had never yet allowed Kamejiro to master her at anything, she sang the word in a lilting, wifelike manner and dropped her eyes, and all the men there thought: "How lucky Kamejiro was to make that swap."

In their own little house Kamejiro whispered to his wife, "Tonight I shivered to think that Sumiko might have been my wife."

"She would have run away from you, too."

"I was lucky! I was lucky!" Kamejiro chanted. "The four hundred thousand gods of Japan were looking out for me that day."

Yoriko looked down at her man and asked, "Did you truly strike Von Schlemm-san on the head with your zori?"

"I did."

"All Japan is proud of you, danna-san."

They fell together on the bed, and Kamejiro said, "It's very funny to me, but I knew little about girls and I thought that when a man and woman got married and slept together, babies always came along pretty quickly."

"Sometimes they do," Yoriko assured him.

"But not for us . . . it seems."

"We must work harder," Yoriko explained, and they blew out the oil lamp.

She also worked hard at other tasks. When the pineapples ripened, she helped harvest them at fifty-four cents a day. Later she would get a few days' employment stripping the crowns of unnecessary leaves so that when planted they would germinate faster. For this difficult and tedious work she got seventy-five cents a thousand crowns, and by applying a dogged concentration to the job, she learned to strip upwards of four thousand a day, so that she became the marvel of the plantation, and husbands in other camps asked their wives, "Why can't you strip crowns the way Kamejiro's wife does?" and the wives snapped, "Because we are human beings and not machines, that's why."

Yoriko also took over the cooking of meals for bachelors in the long house. They provided the food and she did the work. Now both she and her husband rose at three-thirty each day, he to gather wood both for his bath and for her stove, she to prepare the men's breakfasts, and together they earned substantial wages, but their goal of $400 clear in cash continued to slip away from them. There were military events in Japan to be underwritten, and various Imperial requests forwarded by the consulate in Honolulu. There were priests to support and schoolteachers who educated the young, for who would want to take children back to Hiroshima if they knew no Japanese? And although the Sakagawas had no children of their own, they helped those who did.

But most often the flight of dollars was accounted for by some personal tragedy within the camp community, as on the evening when Ishii-san burst into their home with a plea for thirty dollars. "I've got to go to Honolulu, right away," he mumbled, trying to keep back his tears.

"Sumiko?" Mrs. Sakagawa asked.

"Yes. Hashimoto-san, the photographer at Kapaa, was in Honolulu to buy another camera and he discovered that the man who took Sumiko away left her in the city and she . . ." He could not finish.

"And she's working in one of the brothels?" Yoriko asked coldly.

"Mmmmmmm," Ishii-san nodded, his face buried in his hands from humiliation.

"That is her destiny, Ishii-san," the Hiroshima woman assured him. "Leave her there. You can do nothing."

"Leave her there?" Ishii-san screamed. "She's my wife!"

"Believe me, Ishii-san," Mrs. Sakagawa asserted, "that one will be no wife, never."

"Then you won't let me have thirty dollars?" the little scribe pleaded.

"Of course we will," Kamejiro said, and although his wife protested at the waste, for she knew the trip to be useless, the passage money was delivered.

Five days later little Mr. Ishii, his eyes ashamed to meet those of his friends, returned alone to Kauai. For a long time no one questioned him about his wife and he went about his work with his head down, until finally at breakfast one morning in the long room Kamejiro banged the table and asked in a loud voice, "Ishii-san, is your wife still working in the brothel?"

"Yes," Ishii-san replied, happy that someone had openly asked the question.

"Then in due time you will divorce the no-good whore?"

"Yes," the scribe replied.

"You're better off that way," Kamejiro said, "but remember that you owe me thirty dollars." The men laughed and that was the last Ishii Camp heard of beautiful Sumiko, but sometimes at the dock Kamejiro, fascinated by the peril he had so narrowly escaped, inquired of sailors from Honolulu, "Whatever happened to that girl Sumiko?" and finally he learned, "She went back to Japan."

That night when he started to tell his wife Yoriko the news, he was interrupted by her own startling intelligence: "We are going to have a baby!"

Kamejiro dropped his hands and all thoughts of Sumiko vanished. "A baby!" he cried with explosive joy. "We'll name him Goro."

"Why Goro?" Yoriko asked in her practical way. "That's no name for a first son."

"I know," Kamejiro admitted. "But years ago I decided that my first son should be Goro. The name sounds good." And it was agreed.

I HAVE SAID that the heroic encounter between Kamejiro Sakagawa and the German luna Von Schlemm was one with historic consequences, and that is true, but they did not become apparent until forty years later. What followed immediately was that as soon as word of the affair reached Honolulu, Kamejiro's revenge was inflated into an incipient riot, and plantation managers whispered apprehensively about "that Japanese who kicked the bejeezus out of the German luna." Fortunately, Wild Whip was absent at the time, on vacation in Spain, but as soon as he climbed down off the H & H liner he was told about it.

His neck muscles tensed and blood rushed to the ugly scars across his cheek. "Who was the Jap?" he asked.

"Man named Kamejiro Sakagawa," an H & H official replied, and for several moments Wild Whip remained stationary on the dock, repeating the name "Kamejiro!" and looking off toward the Koolau Range. His tension increased, and on what seemed like an impulse he grabbed the reporting official by the collar.

"How soon can I get a boat to Kauai?" he rasped, and as the little interisland craft left for the Garden Island, the H & H official mumbled, "God help that poor Jap when Whip gets hold of him."

When the ferry reached Lihue, Wild Whip in great agitation leaped onto the dock, hired a taxi and went roaring out to Hanakai, where as soon as he reached his plantation he bellowed, "Bring me that goddamned Kamejiro who thinks he can kick my lunas around."

When Kamejiro approached, holding his cap in his hands, as was the custom when speaking to a white man, Whip rushed up to him and yelled, "I hear you smashed up my luna?"

Kamejiro did not understand what was happening, and thought: "I'm going to be fired. And with a baby girl to feed, what shall I do?"

"Well?" Whip growled. "Were you the one who did it?"

The little Japanese fumbled with his cap and said weakly, "I not hit the luna like you say . . . hontoni . . . Hoxuwortu. You b'lee me. I speak truth."

Suddenly Wild Whip grabbed Kamejiro by the shoulders and stuck his face close to his workman's. "Little man," he asked, "are you as tough as they say?"

"What is tough?" Kamejiro countered suspiciously.

"That day when we argued about the iron for your hot bath? Would you really have fought with me?"

Now Kamejiro understood, and since he was about to be fired anyway, he felt no caution. "Yes," he said, jabbing Whip in the stomach with his finger. "I going to smash you here . . . with my head."

"I figured that was your plan," Whip laughed evenly. "Do you know what my plan was? When you ducked your head, I was going to . . ." With a brutal uppercut of his right fist he swung at Kamejiro's head, stopping his knuckles an inch from the workman's nose. "I'd have killed you!"

Kamejiro glared back at his boss and replied, "Maybe I too quick for you. Maybe your fist never hit." He brought his own around with dreadful force, arresting it just short of Wild Whip's belly.

To his surprise, the boss exploded in gales of nervous laughter, embracing his gardener as if he had found a great treasure. "That settles it!" he shouted. "Kamejiro, you're a man I can respect." Jamming his strong hands under the little man's armpits, he danced the astonished Japanese up and down, crying, "Start to pack, you tough little bastard, because you and I have a date with a mountain."

Kamejiro broke free and studied Whip suspiciously. He had seen his boss before in these wild, fantastic moods and he assumed that Whip was either drunk or morbid over some pineapple problem. "Bimeby you be mo bettah," he assured him.

Whip laughed, grabbed his workman again, and dragged him onto the lawn, where he could point to the sweet, green mountains of Kauai. Gently he explained, "You and I are going over to Oahu, Kamejiro. And we're going to blast a puka right through the mountains. We'll get more water . . ."

"What you speak, Hoxuwortu?" the little Japanese asked.

"We're going to dynamite a tunnel right through the mountains, and you're going to do the dynamiting."

Kamejiro looked at his boss suspiciously. "Boom-boom?" he asked.

"Takusan boom-boom!" Whip replied.

"Sometime boom-boom kill," Sakagawa countered.

"That's why I wanted a man with guts," Whip shouted. "Good pay. One day one dollar."

"Mo bettah one dollar half," Kamejiro proposed.

Whip studied the tough little workman and laughed. "For you, Kamejiro, one dollar half."

He extended his hand to the stocky workman, but Kamejiro held back. "And one piece iron for hot bath?"

"All the iron you want. I hear you have a baby."

"One wahine," Kamejiro confessed with shame.

"Bring her along . . . and your wife," Whip cried, and the contract was confirmed.

The camp to which Kamejiro moved his family was high on the rainy side of the Koolau Range on Oahu, and to operate his hot bath for the Japanese workmen Kamejiro required a waterproof shed which he and Yoriko built at night. Yoriko also managed the commissary and by dint of literally endless work the two thrifty Japanese managed to acquire a considerable nest egg, but its size was due not primarily to their hard work but rather to the fact that in these inaccessible mountains the representatives of the consulate could not reach them, and so Kamejiro passed two full years without discovering how badly his homeland needed money.

He was occupied in the thrilling business of hauling great loads of dynamite deep into the tunnel, boring holes into which it was tamped, and then exploding it with dramatic effect. Technically, the job should have been simple and, if time-proved precautions were observed, free from real danger; but the Koolau Range presented perplexing features which made the job not only unpleasant but downright dangerous.

Millions of years before, the rocks of which the mountains were constructed had been laid down on a flat shoreline, with alternate layers of impermeable cap rock and easily permeable conglomerate. Later, a general uptilting had occurred, standing these alternate layers upright, with their ends exposed to the ceaseless rains. For millions of years torrential cascades had seeped down through the permeable layers and deep into the recesses of the island, thus feeding the underground reservoirs which Wild Whip and his driller, Mr. Overpeck, had tapped some thirty-five years before. Now, when inquisitive Kamejiro drove his drill into the impermeable cap rock all was well; but when he got to the permeable conglomerate it was as if he had pushed his drill into solid water, and often the drill would be washed from his hands as the impounded torrents gushed out. Eight million gallons of unexpected water a day flooded the tunnel, and Kamejiro, working in the middle of it, was constantly soaked; and since the water was a uniform sixty-six degrees, he was frequently threatened with pneumonia.

Wild Whip, watching him work, often thought: "He's the kind of man you could wish was an American."

Of course, the phrase was meaningless, for both the Americans and the Japanese clearly understood that none of the latter could become citizens. The law forbade it, and one of the reasons why the Japanese consulate kept such close check on its nationals was that America had said plainly: "They are your people, not ours." For example, when Japanese working on the tunnel found their food inedible they trudged in to their consulate, as was proper, and made their protest directly to the Japanese government. This accomplished nothing, for the consulate officials came from a class in Japan that exploited workers far worse than anyone in Hawaii would dare to; therefore the officials never presented protests to men like Wild Whip Hoxworth. Indeed, they marveled that he treated his Japanese as well as he did. When the tunnel workers had made their speeches, the consulate men replied abruptly: "Get back to work and don't cause trouble."

"But the food . . ."

"Back to work!" the Japanese officials roared, and the men went back. Of course, when in desperation they went to Wild Whip himself, he took one taste of the food and bellowed, "Who in hell calls this suitable for human beings?" And the diet was improved . . . just enough to forestall open rebellion.

But there was one aspect of dynamiting in the Koolau Range that involved real danger, and that was when an apparently normal charge hung fire. For some such failures there were detectable reasons: a fuse might be faulty; or the exploding charger had not delivered a proper spark; or a connection had torn loose. It might seem that these defects should have been easy to correct, but there was always an outside chance that a true hangfire existed: the fuse had been well lit and had started burning, but for some mysterious reason it had hesitated en route. At any moment it could resume its journey to the massive charge and any who happened to be investigating its momentary suspension would be killed.

Whenever a hang-fire occurred, anywhere in the tunnel, men shouted, "Eh, Kamejiro! What you think?" And he hurried up to take charge.

He had a feeling about dynamite. Men claimed he could think like a stick of TNT, and he seemed to know when to wait and when to go forward. So far he had seen four men killed as a result of ignoring his judgment, and in the later stages of drilling his word became final. If he said, "I'll look at the connection," men watched admiringly as he did so; but if he said, "Too much pilikia," everyone waited. Once he had held up operations for two hours, and in the end a thousand tons of basalt had suddenly been torn loose by a true hang-fire. Thanks to Kamejiro, no one was killed and that night one of the shaken workmen called from his hot bath: "Today, Mrs. Sakagawa, all Japan was proud of your husband!"

When the last remaining fragment of basalt was pierced, blown apart by Kamejiro's final concentration of dynamite, Hawaii began to appreciate what Wild Whip had accomplished. Twenty-seven million gallons of water a day poured down to join the artesian supplies developed earlier, and it became possible to bring into cultivation thousands of acres that had long lain arid and beyond hope. In the traditional pattern of Hawaii, the intelligence and dedication of one man had transformed a potential good into a realized one.

At the final celebration of the first great tunnel through the mountains, a speakers' platform was erected on which the governor sat, and three judges, and military leaders, and Wild Whip Hoxworth. Florid speeches were made congratulating the wise engineers who had laid out the plans, and the brave bankers who had financed it, and the sturdy lunas who had supervised the gangs; but there were no Japanese to be seen. It was as if, when the plans were formulated and the money provided, the puka had dug itself. But late that afternoon Wild Whip, who had a feeling for these things, sought out stocky little Kamejiro Sakagawa as he was tearing down the hot bath on the rainy side, and he said to the dynamiter, "Kamejiro, what you do now?"

"Maybe get one job dynamiter."

"They're hard to get." Whip kicked at the muddy earth and asked, "You like to work for me again, Hanakai?"

"Maybe stop Honolulu, maybe mo bettah."

"I think so, too," Whip agreed. "Tell you what, Kamejiro. I could never have built this tunnel without you. If I'd thought about it, I'd a had you on the platform today. But I didn't and that's that. Now I have a little plot of land in Honolulu, big enough for a garden. I'm going to give it to you."

"I don't want land," the little dynamiter said. "Pretty soon go back to Japan."

"Maybe that's best," Whip agreed. "I'll do this. Instead of the land, I'll give you two hundred dollars. And if you ever want to go back to Hanakai, let me know."

So Kamejiro turned down land, which if he had taken it, would one day have been worth $200,000. In its place he accepted $200, but this transaction was not so silly as it sounds, for this $200 plus what he and his wife had saved gave them at last the full funds they needed for a return to Japan.

They left the rainy hillside where they had worked so long and so miserably and turned joyously toward Honolulu and the offices of the *Kyoto-maru,* but when they got to the city they were immediately visited by officials from the consulate who were taking up a collection for the brave Imperial navy that had been fighting the Germans and a collection for the brave settlers who were going to the new colonies of Saipan and Yap. They were pounced on by Buddhist priests who were to build a fine temple up Nuuanu. And Mr. Ishii had come over from Kauai to try his luck in Honolulu and needed a hundred and fifty dollars.

"Kamejiro!" his wife pleaded. "Don't give that man any more money. He never pays it back."

"Whenever I look at poor Ishii-san, I am reminded that I stole his legitimate wife, and all my happiness is founded on his misfortune," Kamejiro said softly. "If he needs the money, he must have it."

So the return to Japan was momentarily delayed, and then Yoriko announced: "We are going to have another baby," and this time it was a boy, to be named Goro as planned. He was quickly followed by three brothers—Tadao in 1921, Minoru in 1922, and Shigeo in 1923—and the subtle bonds that tied the Sakagawas to Hawaii were more and more firmly tied, for the children, growing up in Hawaii, would speak English and laugh like Americans, and grow to prefer not rice but foods that came out of cans.

WHEN KAMEJIRO SAKAGAWA finished his work in the tunnel, and when the money he had saved dribbled through his hard hands in one way or another, he hoped, vainly as it proved, that he might find a similar job as dynamiter, but none developed. He therefore took his wife and two children to the artesian plantation west of Honolulu, the original Malama Sugar, and there he went to work, twelve hours a day for seventy-seven cents a day.

He was also given an old clapboard house twenty feet wide and fourteen feet deep, from which six square feet were cut for a porch. There was a sagging lean-to shed in which Yoriko did the cooking over an iron pan. The house stood on poles one foot high, providing an under space into which children could crawl on hot days. It was a dirty, cramped, unlovely living area, but fortunately it contained at the rear just enough space for Kamejiro to erect a hot bath, so that in spite of the meager income the family was somewhat better off than the neighbors, who had to pay to use the Sakagawa bath.

Furthermore, the family income was augmented by Mrs. Sakagawa, who worked in the sugar fields for sixty-one cents a day, leaving her children with neighbors. Each dusk there came a moment of pure joy when the family reconvened and the lively youngsters, their jet-black hair bobbed straight across their eyes, rushed out to meet their parents. But these moments of reunion were also apt to have overtones of confusion, for grudgingly the Sakagawas had to confess that they could not always understand what their children were saying. For example, one night when they asked in Japanese where a neighbor was, little Reiko-chan, a brilliant, limpid-eyed beauty, explained: "Him fadder pauhana konai," and her parents had to study the sentence, for *him fadder* was corrupted English, *pauhana* was Hawaiian for the end of work, and *konai* was good Japanese for has not come.

It therefore became apparent to Kamejiro that if he intended returning his daughter to Japan, and he did, he was going to have a hard time finding her a decent Japanese husband if she could not speak the language any better than that, so he enrolled her in the Japanese school, where a teacher from Tokyo kept strict order. Over his head loomed a great sign, with characters which Kamejiro could not read but which the teacher, a frail young man, explained: "Loyalty to the emperor." Added the instructor: "Here we teach as in Japan. If your child does not learn, she will suffer the consequences."

"You will teach her about the emperor and the greatness of Japan?" Kamejiro asked.

"As if she were back in Hiroshima-ken," the teacher promised, and from the manner in which he banged his knuckles against the heads of misbehaving boys, Kamejiro felt assured that he had put his child into good hands.

Actually, Reiko-chan required no discipline, for she learned both quickly and with joy. She was then the youngest child in school but also one of the ablest, and when she ran barefooted home at night, babbling in fine Japanese, Kamejiro felt proud, for she was learning to read and he could not.

There were other aspects of his life at Malama Sugar about which he was not happy, and these centered upon money. It was more expensive to live on Oahu than it had been on Kauai, yet his wages were lower. Rice, fish, seaweed and pickles had all gone up in price, yet there were now five children to feed, and the boys ate like pigs. Clothes too were more expensive, and although Yoriko was frugal, she did need a new visiting dress now and then. One morning, as the sun was beginning to rise, Kamejiro watched his hard-working wife setting out with her hoe and it occurred to him: "She's been wearing the same skirt, the same dotted blouse, the same white cloth about her face and the same straw hat for five years. And they're all in rags."

But when it came time for him to buy her a new outfit, he found that he did not have the money, and he realized that even with two adults working, the Sakagawa family was existing perilously close to the starvation level. He was therefore in a receptive frame of mind when an unusual visitor arrived at Malama Sugar. It was Mr. Ishii, who was now acting as traveling agent for the Japanese Federation of Labor, and his information was that after a series of talks with the big planters like Whipple Hoxworth, his organization was going to win decent wages for the Japanese.

"Listen to this!" he whispered to a group of workmen with whom he met secretly. "We are asking for one dollar and twenty-five cents a day for men, ninety-five cents for wahines. Can you imagine how that will improve your living? The workday will be cut back to eight hours, and there will be bonuses in December if the year has been a good one. If you have to work on Sundays, overtime. And for the wahines, they'll be allowed to quit work two weeks before the baby is born."

The men listened in awe as this vision of a new life dawned in the little hut, but before they had a chance to ascertain when all this was going to take place, a sentinel outside whistled, then ran up with frightening news: "Lunas! Lunas!"

Four big Germans burst into the meeting place, grabbed little Mr. Ishii before he could escape, and hauled him out into the dusty yard. They manhandled him no more than necessary, being content to give him a scare with three or four knocks, then kicked him onto the road leading back toward Honolulu. "Don't you come onto Malama Sugar with your radical ideas," they warned him. "Next time, plenty pilikia!"

While two of the lunas made sure that the little agitator left the plantation, the other two returned to the room where the clandestine meeting had been held. "Nishimura, Sakagawa, Ito, Sakai, Suzuki," one of the lunas recited while the other wrote. "A fine way to treat Mr. Janders and Mr. Whipple. Whose house is this? Yours, Inoguchi?" The biggest luna grabbed Inoguchi by the shirt and held him up. "I'll remember who the traitor was," the luna said, staring at the workmen. With a snort of disgust he threw the man back among his fellows, and the two Germans stamped out. But at the gate they stopped and said ominously, "You men go to your homes. No more meetings, understand?"

As Kamejiro left he whispered to Inoguchi, "Maybe a long time before we get what Ishi-san promised?"

"I think so, too," Inoguchi agreed.

From that night on, conditions at Malama Sugar grew increasingly tense. To everyone's surprise, little Mr. Ishii exhibited unforeseen reservoirs of heroism, for against really considerable odds, and in direct opposition to seven lunas, he managed time and again to slip back into the plantation to advise the men of how the negotiations were going. When he was caught, he was beat up, as he expected to be, and he lost one of his front teeth; but after twenty-two years of relative ineffectiveness in everything he attempted, he had at last stumbled upon an activity for which he was pre-eminently suited. He loved intrigue and rumor; he cherished the portrait of himself as a worker for the common good; so he came back again and again, until at last the lunas assembled all the field hands and said, "Anyone caught talking with the Bolshevik Ishii is going to be thrown out of his house and off the plantation. Is that clear?"

But the Japanese had caught a vision of what Mr. Ishii was trying to do, and at great danger to themselves they continued to meet with him, and one day in January he told them gravely, and with the sadness that comes from seeing fine plans destroyed, "The managers will not listen to our demands. We shall have to strike."

The next day Honolulu was marked by many pamphlets bearing the unmistakable touch of Mr. Ishii, his florid manner of expression and his hope: "Good men and ladies of Hawaii. We, the laborers who grow the sugar upon which you live, address you with humility and hope. Did you know, as you drive past our waving fields of cane, that the men who grow it receive only seventy-seven cents a day? On this money we raise our children and teach them good manners and teach them to be decent citizens. But on this money we also starve.

"We love Hawaii and consider it a great privilege and pride to live under the Stars and Stripes, which stands for freedom and justice. We are happy to be part of the great sugar industry and to keep the plantations running profitably.

"We love work. Thirty-five years ago when we first came to Hawaii the lands where we now work were covered with ohia and guava and wild grass. Day and night have we worked, cutting those parasites and burning the grass. Our work has made the plantations, but of course it is indisputable that we could not have succeeded were it not for the investments made by wealthy capitalists and the untiring efforts of the lunas and administrators. But Hawaii must not magnify the contributions of the capitalists and forget the equal contributions of the laborers who have served faithfully with sweat on their brows.

"Look at the silent tombstones in every locality. They are the last emblems of Hawaii's pioneers in labor. Why should they die in poverty while others get rich from their labors? Why should hard-working men continue to get seventy-seven cents a day? The other day a plantation manager said, 'I think of field hands as I do jute bags. Buy them, use them, buy others.' We think of ourselves as human beings and as members of the great human family. We want $1.25 a day for an eight-hour day. And in the interests of common humanity we deserve it."

THIS EXTRAORDINARY PREAMBLE to the workers' demands was received differently in four different quarters. When Kamejiro Sakagawa and his co-workers heard the flowery words read to them in Japanese, with lunas at hand to take down the names of everyone attending the meeting, Kamejiro listened with amazement that his friend Mr. Ishii should have caught so exactly the emotions that motivated the workers. With tears in his eyes he said, "Inoguchi-san? Have you ever heard a better piece of paper? He says that we are part of the great human family. Did you ever think of yourself that way before?"

"All I think," Inoguchi-san replied, "is that there's going to be trouble."

To his wife Yoriko, Kamejiro said, "When I heard Ishii-san's statement, I was glad for every dollar I ever loaned him. It looks as if we will get all we have asked for, because that is a very powerful bit of reasoning."

His stolid wife was more of Inoguchi's turn of mind. "We had better get ready to go hungry," she warned. And that day the strike began.

When the manifesto reached Wild Whip Hoxworth, the head of the planters' association gagged before he got to the end of it. "Mad Russian Bolshevism!" he bellowed. "Get the planters together!" When the leaders of the sugar industry were assembled, he went over the statement line by line. " 'We, the laborers,' " he read scornfully. "As if they had convened themselves into some kind of revolutionary tribunal. 'On this money we starve.' What a degrading, horrible play to the emotions. 'Good men and ladies of Hawaii!' As if by appealing to them they could by-pass those of us responsible for wages. By God, gentlemen, this document strikes at the very roots of society. It's rampant, red, pillaging Russianism, and if there is any man in this room who breaks ranks to give those little yellow bastards an inch, I'll personally knock him down and kick his weak-livered guts in. Is that understood?"

The other planters, who were perhaps more appalled by the Bolshevik-inspired manifesto than Wild Whip, for they had studied it in a calmer light and understood its implications better than he, showed no signs of disagreeing with their leader, and when he was satisfied on that point he passed to additional matters. "Now who in hell among you made that stupid statement about workmen and jute bags?" There was silence, and after a moment he slammed the paper on the table and growled, "It's true, and everyone here knows it's true. But don't say such things. Shut up. It's nobody's business what you and I do or think. Shut up. There's a dreadful spirit abroad in the world today, and I blame it all on Woodrow Wilson. Appealing to the people over the heads of their government. Just like this dirty sheet. From now on, I'll do the talking."

He summoned a secretary and dictated, while his astonished compatriots listened: "We have studied the statement of the Federation of Japanese Labor in Hawaii and are pleased to note its temperate tenor, its cautious manner of argument, and its refusal to stoop to violent or ill-founded reasoning. The men who wrote it are to be congratulated upon their restraint, which in previous similar disputes was not conspicuous.

"We regret, naturally, that a group of alien workmen, not citizens of this territory, should feel constrained to tell us how to manage the greatest industry in the islands, and it is our duty as loyal Americans to point out that in these years following a great war in which the principles of democracy were once more sustained against alien and unnatural enemies, the state of our economy, strained as it was by the war effort, simply cannot undertake any further aggravated expenses. A moment's analysis of what is requested in these demands will satisfy any impartial . . ."

He went on and on in a tone of sweet reasonableness, and when the secretary had left he said to the sugar men, "That's how we'll handle the little bastards. This is a strike of alien Japanese Bolsheviks against the bulwarks of American freedom, and by God don't let anybody forget . . . not for a minute. That's the ground we'll lick them on."

At the offices of the Honolulu *Mail* the workers' document had a staggering effect, for it was the first one in a long series of complaints to show any signs of mature composition. "Some fiendishly clever man wrote this!" the editor stormed. "Hell, if you didn't know what it was all about you might think Thomas Jefferson or Tom Paine had done it. In my opinion, this is the most dangerous document ever to have appeared in Hawaii, and it's got to be fought on that basis."

The entire staff was summoned to analyze the inflammatory document, after which the editor retired to his sanctum. Carefully, and with much polishing, he wrote: "This morning the citizens of Hawaii were at last able to comprehend what has been going on in the Japanese-language schools, in the Buddhist temples, and in the murky confines of the Imperial consulate. The manifesto of the Bolshevik Japanese labor union at last drew the gauze from before our eyes. Citizens of Hawaii, we are faced by no less than an organized attempt to make these islands a subsidiary part of the Japanese empire. Already the first loops of the tentacles have been swept about Kauai and Maui and Oahu. There is afoot an evil design to remove from positions of leadership those noble and hardworking sons of American pioneers who made these islands great and to supplant them with crafty Orientals whose sole purpose is not the betterment of their people but the aggrandizement of a distant and alien empire.

"The Japanese plotters appeal to the people of Hawaii to support their cause. This newspaper appeals to the people of Hawaii to consider what it will mean to each and every one of us if the present strike should be successful. In place of far-seeing men like the Whipples, the Janderses, the Hales and the Hoxworths who have built these islands to their present position of magnificence, we would have aliens attempting to run our industries. Sugar and pineapple would languish. No cargoes would move to the mainland. Our schools would wither and our churches would be closed.

"We must fight this strike to the end. Not a single concession must be granted. The entire citizenship of Hawaii must unite against this alien threat. For the issue at stake is brutally clear: Do we wish Hawaii to be part of America or part of Japan? There is no point in expressing the question in any other terms, and every American who has a streak of decency in him will know how to answer the terrible challenge that has been thrown down before him. This strike must fail! There must be no wavering, for any who do waver are traitors to their nation, their homes and their God.

"Lest there be any misunderstanding as to the position of this newspaper at this time of grave crisis we wish to say this: "If at any time in the process of this strike there is a choice between the total economic ruination of these islands and the turning of them over to the evil designs of the Japanese labor leaders, we unflinchingly declare that we will not only prefer but will encourage the former."

The fourth place in Honolulu where the manifesto occasioned an unexpectedly violent reaction was in the Japanese consulate, on Nuuanu. There the second secretary got a copy at about eight o'clock, read it, felt the blood leave his face, and rushed in to see his superior, who studied it with quivering hands. "Those fools! Those fools!" the consul cried. He had not yet seen the editorial in the Honolulu *Mail,* but he could visualize what was going to be said. Throwing the document down, he strode back and forth in his carpeted room, then shouted at his assistant, "Why don't those damned Japanese laborers learn to be content with what they have? The fools! Their wages here are twice what they'd be in Japan. And they get good treatment." He continued fuming, then assembled his entire staff.

"You have severe orders," he said coldly. "This consulate will do absolutely nothing to support the strikers. If a deputation marches on this consulate, as it has always done in the past, they are to be received with no warmth whatever. It is imperative that this strike be broken quickly."

"Suppose the strikers seek repatriation?" an underling asked.

"Their job is to stay here, work here, and send their money back home," the consul snapped.

"What shall we do if they appeal against police brutality?" the same underling pressed.

"Summon me. I'll make the usual formal protests, but we must avoid seeming to be on the side of the workmen. Remember, workmen do not govern Hawaii, and our responsibility is to people like Whipple Hoxworth who do."

"One more question, sir. Suppose the strikers ask for food?"

"Not to be granted. Gentlemen, this strike is a dangerous manifestation. If the phrases appearing in this document were to be used in Japan, those responsible would be jailed for life . . . or would be executed. I am appalled that decent Japanese field hands would dare to use such language. Our job is to force these men back to work. The strike must be broken, because if it isn't, the newspapers will begin to accuse the emperor of having fomented it."

THE STRIKE WAS broken, of course, but mainly by a series of adventitious developments, for on the day in February when the plantations evicted the Japanese laborers, telling them to live in the fields if necessary, by purest chance an influenza epidemic of the most virulent dimensions erupted, and in one crowded rural area where the strikers were living ten to a room or under trees, more than fifty of the workmen died. In all some five thousand strikers collapsed, many of them with no beds to sleep in and without hot food, and the subsequent death toll was interpreted by the superstitious as proof that the strike was against the will of God.

The Sakagawa family trudged twenty-six miles into Honolulu, hoping that Mr. Ishii could find them some place to stay, but he could not, and they at last took up residence with more than four hundred others in an abandoned sake brewery, where rats crawled over the children at night. There Reiko-chan caught the flu and it seemed that she was going to die. At first her mother was tempted to rail at Kamejiro for having supported the strike and having brought such misery upon his family, but when she saw with what passionate care he tended Reiko, even though she was a girl, the stolid woman forgave her husband and said, "Danna-san, we will win the strike this time, I am sure."

But next day the Board of Health met and listened to Wild Whip Hoxworth as he pointed out: "We're engaged in war, gentlemen, and in war you use every weapon you have. Every one. I passed by the old sake brewery last night, and it's a health menace. I want the people in there evicted, and I want it closed."

"Sir, there's a lot of children in there with the flu," a doctor protested.

"That's why it's got to be closed," Hoxworth replied.

"But these people will have no place to go," the doctor argued.

"I know. I want them to learn what it means to strike against the elements of law and order in a community."

"But, sir, we've got to think . . ."

"Close that goddamned brewery!" Hoxworth bellowed, and it was closed.

The temperature in Hawaii never indulges in extremes, except on the tops of the volcanic mountains, where snows persist through much of the year, but February nights can be miserably chilling, and for two influenza-ridden nights the Sakagawas slept on the ground near Iwilei. Kamejiro held the sick girl Reiko in his arms and his wife cradled Shigeo, the baby, and the nights were bad, but on the third day Mr. Ishii found them and said, "I have found a hut where an old woman died," and they wolfed down the food that she would have eaten had she lived.

For three weeks the epidemic raged and the deaths of exposed workmen reached toward the hundred mark. At the end of this time, Mr. Ishii, Kamejiro and Inoguchi-san organized a committee of sixteen who marched lawfully up Nuuanu to the Japanese consulate, seeking help in that quarter. They were met by an official in black-rimmed glasses, cutaway coat and nervous grin. Allowing Mr. Ishii to do their speaking, the men said, "We are being very poorly treated by the Americans, and we must come to the Imperial government for help."

"The Imperial government is protecting Japanese interests with studious care," the official assured the deputation. "Only yesterday His Excellency protested to the Chief of Police against keeping the Japanese from holding legal meetings."

"But they are throwing us out of our homes, and our men are dying in the fields," Mr. Ishii said quietly.

With equal calmness the spokesman explained, "His Excellency only last week looked into the law and found that the plantations have the right to expel you . . . if you strike."

"But there is a great sickness in these islands," Mr. Ishii protested.

"Then perhaps the strike ought to terminate," the spokesman suggested.

"But we can't live on seventy-seven cents a day."

"In Japan your brothers surely live on much less," the official assured the strikers, and the fruitless interview was concluded.

Another accident which worked against the strikers was the discovery, in early May, of a schoolbook used in the Japanese schools which had a long passage explaining what was meant by the phrase used by Japan's first emperor, "All the world under a roof of eight poles." Quite obviously, the book explained to the children of Japan—and it was never intended for use in Hawaii but had somehow got into the islands by mistake—it was the Emperor Jimmu Tenno's idea that all the world must some day be united into one great family paying homage to the sun goddess and obedience to the emperor, her lineal descendant. Cried the Honolulu *Mail:* "If anyone has wanted proof of the contentions of this newspaper that Japan intends one day to conquer the world, with Hawaii as the first step in the conquest, this evil little book proves the fact beyond contention. All the world under one roof! The local Japanese Bolsheviks have already taken the first step in that domination, and unless we remain steadfast and defeat their foul aspirations, we shall be the first foreign territory to be submerged beneath the Japanese roof." If sugar men were growing faint-hearted as the long strike headed for its sixth harrowing month, this timely discovery of what was being taught in Japan fortified them.

Finally, there was the disgraceful affair of dynamiting the home in which Inoguchi-san of Malama Sugar was living. No one was killed, fortunately, but when the Honolulu *Mail* disclosed that Inoguchi had been dynamited because he had been in secret negotiations with the sugar planters, telling them nightly what Mr. Ishii and the committee were planning next, the community had to acknowledge that the Japanese labor leaders really were a group of determined Bolsheviks. Swift police raids swept up nineteen of the leaders, including Mr. Ishii, and threw them into jail on charges of criminal conspiracy. Wild Whip Hoxworth visited the judges involved and pointed out that the charges might better be criminal syndicalism, and they thanked him for his interest in the case.

But now the question arose as to who had taught the committee how to handle dynamite, and a reporter remembered that Kamejiro Sakagawa, who had not yet been arrested, had learned the trade while working on the tunnel. He was known to be a friend of Mr. Ishii's, and so the police arrested him. He was thrown into jail, even though he had had nothing to do with the dynamiting, whereupon his wife Yoriko proved to the police that he had been at home caring for his sick children. The sugar committee, who were advising the district attorney as to how he should handle the case, refused to accept this alibi, pointing out: "A clever man like Sakagawa didn't have to be actually at the scene of the crime. He could well have prepared the sticks in advance and shown his fellow conspirators how to explode them. He is obviously guilty." And he was kept in jail.

Then the strike ended, with the workmen having gained little, and sugar was once more produced by some of the cheapest labor in America. H & H made millions carrying fresh cargoes to California, and J & W made more millions managing the plantations in the good old way. The conspirators were brought to trial and Mr. Ishii was sentenced to ten years in jail. He sagged when the words were thrown at him, falling backwards as if they had actually struck him, and from that day on he was never much of a man again. He grew to mumble and imagine things, and no one took much account of him.

Surprisingly, Kamejiro, the dynamiter by trade, was not convicted, for one day before the trial began he had a visitor in his cell. It was Wild Whip Hoxworth, lean and tall and handsome, flushed with victory. "Eh, you, Kamejiro. Boys say you plant dynamite. That true?"

"No, Mr. Hoxuwortu. No."

"Me, I think no too." And Wild Whip told the district attorney, "You better drop charges against Sakagawa. He wasn't involved."

"How do you know?" the young lawyer asked, nervous with excitement over the trial that was going to make his reputation.

"Because he told me so," Whip explained.

"And you're going to take his word?"

"He's the most honest man I know. Besides, his alibi is a good one."

"But I think we've got to convict the actual dynamiter, whether his alibi is good or not."

"Turn him loose!" Whip thundered. He was sixty-six years old and tired of arguing with fools.

So on the morning that the trial convened, Kamejiro was quietly set free. Of course, he was never again able to get a job at Malama Sugar, for the great plantations prudently maintained blacklists in order to keep out troublemakers, and he had now proved himself one who fought with lunas and supported Bolsheviks like Ishii. He found a small, rat-infested shack in the Kakaako area of Honolulu, from which he did odd jobs, principally the cleaning out of privies after midnight. Children whose fathers had better jobs called him "King of the Night Brigade," and indeed the name King was fitting, for whatever he was required to do, he did with the most earnest skill, so that in spite of the fact that he was surreptitiously known as Sakagawa the Dynamiter, the man who had tried to kill Inoguchi, people nevertheless continued to seek him out when their privies needed unloading, for he merited the title, "King of the Night Brigade."

IN 1926 THE disreputable old English botanist Dr. Schilling developed another striking idea about the growing of pineapple. Recovering from a four-month drunk, he turned fresh, if bloodshot, eyes upon the great fields of Kauai, and as he studied the swarms of Japanese women hoeing out the weeds from the red soil, he thought: "Why don't we spread paper over the whole damned field, punch holes in it where we plant the baby pineapple, and make it impossible for weeds to grow?"

He got some asphalt paper, rolled it across a trial field, and planted a crop of pineapple in the small holes he had punched in the black covering. To his surprise, the simple trick not only killed off all the weeds, saving hundreds of dollars in labor charges, but also provided two unforeseen advantages which proved to be more profitable than even the extermination of weeds: the paper trapped moisture and held it about the roots of the plants, and on sunny days it accumulated heat which was later dissipated exactly when the plants required it.

When Wild Whip saw the results of the experiment he gave an instant and dramatic order: "Hereafter all pineapple on our plantations will be grown under paper," and he worked diligently with Dr. Schilling and the California wood-pulp people in devising a special paper that resisted water for the first seven months of its life, then slowly disintegrated so that by the tenth month the field was clean. When the project was completed, Wild Whip reminded the pineapple men: "You can always find somebody from Yale who can accomplish anything you want. Treat them well, pay them a little, and call them Doctor. That's all they expect. But somebody with brains has got to set the problem for them."

And then, in 1927, this nonpareil of planters died at the brawling, bruising age of seventy. He died, as he had often predicted, of no ordinary disease but from an aggravated cancer of the prostate occasioned, the islands felt sure, by his numerous cases of gonorrhea and syphilis, plus cirrhosis of the liver brought on by endless overdoses of alcohol, all aggravated by the fact that the small airplane in which he was flying back from Hanakai Plantation to Honolulu flew into the mountain that he had pierced with his great tunnel. He had lain exposed in the cold rain for nearly twenty-four hours, but even under those conditions the vital old man fought a fairly even contest with death for a period of three weeks, during which he summoned to his hospital bed the leading members of H & H and J & W, including all who might logically aspire to his chairmanship.

Raising himself in pain to a sitting position, which appalled the nurses, he grunted, "We're entering a difficult period, and our job is to make half a dozen right decisions." He spoke as if he were to be with the managers for many years to come, and possibly forever. "I'm sure our present prosperity can't continue forever, and when there's a leveling off, sugar and pineapple will be hard hit. Thank God, it doesn't seem likely the Democrats will ever return to Washington, so we don't have to worry about radical communism. But we do have to worry about keeping our share of the market.

"We've got to have somebody heading up our enterprises who is clever enough to anticipate the future and bold enough to fight what's wrong. I've given a good deal of thought as to who that should be, and I've come up with only one solid conclusion. Don't ever, under any conceivable circumstances, allow either of my sons, Jesus Duarte or John, to meddle in this business. Pay them well, pay them regularly, and keep them to hell out of Hawaii. If my other son, Janders, had lived . . . well, that might have been a different story.

"Naturally I've thought a great deal about Mark Whipple. He has his father's brains and would have been my first choice, except that being a West Point man, he thinks he ought to stay with the army, and maybe he's right. But if he ever decides to resign his commission, get him back into the company quick.

"I've also given a good deal of consideration to Hewie Janders," and here the big, rugged, florid man who had starred as guard at Yale blushed, but Wild Whip continued, "and I fear that Hewie's attributes do not include intellectual force, which is what we need now.

"I've passed over as you can see, all the older fellows, because we need somebody who's going to give our firms a long, continued and strong leadership. So I've chosen as my executor, and the man to vote my shares as long as he remains intellectually and morally capable, this fellow." And he reached out and took the hand of Hoxworth Hale, then twenty-nine years old and aching for authority. The other directors could not protest the decision, nor had they any cause to do so, for Hale was obviously the man to take over at this juncture.

"Three rules, Hoxworth, and the rest of you listen. Don't ever sell sugar short. I went into pineapple, that's true, but only when I had a solid, secure base in sugar. You do the same. Protect sugar by research, protect your quotas by legislation, protect the plantations, protect your labor supply. Stay with sugar. It's better than money, more dependable than blood.

"Second, never allow labor to rear its head an inch. Study what's happened on the mainland. If a labor leader tries to get onto these islands, throw him back into the ocean and tell him to swim, but don't even show him which way California is. Be careful of the Japanese. They're making sounds like they wanted a union. Trust only the Filipinos, because nobody else can be trusted. But if the bolo-boys attempt any foolishness, bat them down.

"Third, you've got to keep mainland firms from forcing their way into our economy. Don't let the chain stores in. Don't let outfits like Gregory's and California Fruit onto these shores. We have a good system here, one that we've worked damned hard to perfect, and we don't want a lot of radical new ideas polluting it. If such gangsters try to invade, sell them no land, refuse to handle their shipping, tie them up on credit, strangle the bastards."

He had spoken rather forcefully and now fell back on his pillow, aching in the cancered prostrate, in his failing kidneys and in each of his four broken bones. The nurses dragooned a passing doctor, who cried, "Good God, gentlemen, you're most inconsiderate! Now you get out of here!"

Whip fell into a little sleep, and when in the later afternoon he woke, it was with considerable elation of spirit, for he was reviewing in imagination a series of pictures he had first invented with his wonderful old grandmother, Noelani, the Alii Nui from Lahaina. On her last trip to the Orient, Noelani had acquired a set of Japanese color prints showing what were called the eight loveliest scenes on earth. It contained a mountain in snow, boats returning to shore, wild geese descending, and sunset. "It is things like these," gracious old Noelani had told her grandchildren, "that are the real beauty of life." They had played a game: "Let's decide what the eight loveliest scenes of Hawaii are." And now Wild Whip, himself older than Noelani when she had umpired the contest, reviewed the permanent grandeurs of his islands.

For the mountain in the snow, they had chosen the great volcanoes of the big island, mysteriously clothed in white, yet standing within the tropics. Geologists considered them the highest single mountains in the world—19,000 feet below the ocean, almost 14,000 above. Nowhere in the world could boats returning to shore be lovelier than at Lahaina, where the roads were caught between islands. The wild geese descending were, of course, the single most glorious sight in Hawaii. "How beautiful they were," Whip thought. "How beautiful."

The evening glow, which the men who designated the eight supreme views liked especially, could be seen nowhere with finer effect than at the deep red canyon of Kauai, an incredible gash through fifty million years of scintillating rock; at dusk it seemed filled with demonic force. And as for night rain, much loved by the Japanese, where could it be seen to more poetic effect than on the gloomy lava beds of the big island, those confuted and tormented beds which had overrun the first settlers from Bora Bora?

The next two scenes were from Oahu, queen of the islands. Once Wild Whip had seen an autumn moon, gray and silver in radiance, shining on the plains that lay at the foot of the Pali, and he had been captivated by the subtle interplay of dark forms and moonlit shadows. The evening bell, which Chinese loved for its memories of home, Whip and his grandmother had assigned to Honolulu, for it was indeed memorable to sit on some broad lanai on a Honolulu hillside, listening to the evening bells of the churches and watching the lights of the city come on.

There was an eighth view, the sunset sky, the end of the day, the last glimpse of earth, and Whip could never recall where Noelani had placed this concluding view; but for himself, as he thought of his islands now, he could place it only at Hanakai. He saw the Norfolk pines and the royal palms, the trees and flowers he had brought in from all over the world. He saw the wild cliffs and the storms of winter leaping upon them, but most of all he saw beyond the grassy polo field the light green of sugar and higher up the dark blue-green of pineapple. How beautiful Hawaii was, how cherished by the ancient deities.

He died a Hawaiian, leaving his wild spirit to haunt the places he had loved. He was attended only by a pretty little Filipino girl he had picked up on Kauai. In his last minutes he tried to dictate a note to his seductive, brown-skinned playmate, but to his distress found she could not write, so he bellowed for a nurse, for he wanted to warn his successor: "Hoxworth, best way to keep labor controlled is to keep hand in legislature at all times." But when the nurse arrived to take this message, Wild Whip was dead, the builder of the islands who had been unable to build his own life, and the authorities spirited his little Filipino girl back to Kauai. The glowing sums of money old Whip had promised her she never got.

A T TWENTY-NINE HOXWORTH HALE assumed control of the vast holdings, and when he first took the chair that Wild Whip had occupied for fifteen years, he realized that he must seem like a boy presuming to do a man's work, but at least he was dressed correctly for his new role: a dark-blue four-button suit with tight vest, an Egyptian-cotton shirt with detachable stiff collar and a heavy blue and red tie. His cuff links were of gold and pearl, and his hair was parted severely on the right-hand side. He was clean-shaven and steady of mind, and he was determined to send forward the fortunes of the family.

He was not unaccustomed to command, for quick upon the heels of his impulsive enlistment in the American Expeditionary Force in 1917, he had become a sergeant, and in France had won a battlefield commission, demobilizing as a captain. His troops had great regard for him; he tried to be a brave, self-contained young leader, willing to assault any objective. His men also found him fun to be with, for he posed as having the insouciance that all young men in uniform like to think they have, and his company was one of the best.

After the war he completed his education at Yale, a quiet young man of twenty-two whose early radicalism had been abandoned somewhere in France, and he never once wandered back to see the notorious Jarves paintings. When he graduated he was already a conservative businessman, eager to make his contribution to Hoxworth & Hale, but in California on his way back to Hawaii he met a lovely girl whose father was a rancher with large land holdings. For a while it looked as if they were going to marry, but one night she spoke disparagingly of Honolulu and suggested that Hoxworth remain in California: "Hoxy! You could have your father assign you to the San Francisco office!"

His reply had been both cold and distant: "We send only nephews who aren't too bright to California." The courtship ended and after that no one ever called him Hoxy.

When he had been at work for some time in the head office in Honolulu he married his third cousin, Malama Janders, who was Hewie Janders' sister, and within a year he had a son Bromley, whom he prudently registered for both Punahou and Yale. It was true that whenever business took him to San Francisco, he experienced a sense of deep excitement when he first saw the California coastline, and he often wondered what had become of the pretty rancher's daughter; but that was about as errant a thought as he ever had.

Now, in 1927, Hoxworth Hale was these things, and in each he was an almost perfect exemplification of the archetype: he was a Hale, a Punahou graduate, a Yale man, the head of a great island firm, and a man married to his cousin. Therefore, when he spoke at his first meeting of the H & H board, his colleagues listened: "There is an unfortunate spirit of agitation in the world today, and I believe our first concern must be the protection of our position by exercising some kind of logical control over the legislature."

He outlined a sensible plan whereby his impressive cousin, big Hewie Janders, got himself elected president of the senate, while half a dozen assorted lawyers, treasurers and accountants who worked for the big firms ran for lesser seats. For speaker of the house Hoxworth shrewdly selected the jovial, relaxed Chinese politician Kangaroo Kee, to whom he offered several lucrative contracts; and so carefully did the new young leader plan that before long Hawaii passed into that secure and reasonable period when most of its legislation was decided upon first at quiet meetings held in the board room of H & H, whence it was sent to trusted representatives who could be depended upon to enact laws pretty much as proposed by Hoxworth Hale and his close associates.

The board room of H & H was on the second floor of a large, fortlike building that stood at the corner of Fort and Merchant, and from this combination of facts the powerful clique that ran Hawaii came to be known simply as The Fort. It included, of course, H & H and also J & W. The Hewletts were members, as were some of the lesser planters from the big island. Banks, railways, trust companies and large estate owners were represented, but exactly what The Fort consisted of no man could properly say; it was simply the group who by common consent were entitled to meet on the second floor of H & H, a close-knit, cohesive body of men who were determined to give Hawaii a responsible form of government.

The Fort rarely abused its power. If some crackpot legislator not subservient to it wanted to curry favor with his constituents by shouting, "I promised you I'd get a playground for Kakaako, and I'll get you a playground for Kakaako," they let him yell, and at one of their meetings Hoxworth Hale would ask, "Is there any reason why there shouldn't be a playground at Kakaako?" and if such a project did not imperil any fundamental interest of The Fort—and if its cost could be passed on to the general public without raising real estate taxes—the playground was allowed to go through. But if this same legislator subsequently shouted, "Last year plantation trains running without lights killed four people, so I insist upon lights where plantation trains cross public roads," then The Fort moved quietly but massively into action. "We've looked into costs of such lights," Hoxworth Hale would tell his directors, "and they would cut our sugar profits to the bone." Somehow such bills were ice-boxed in committee, and no amount of yelling by infuriated legislators could get them unfrozen.

Any major bill affecting either sugar, pineapple or land had to be actually drafted by The Fort itself; such bills were too important to be left to the whims of a legislature. But it was to Hoxworth Hale's credit that he did not allow grossly abusive bills to be proposed: "My interpretation of democracy is that business must never intrude into ordinary legislative processes, except where matters of vital importance are at stake and then never for selfish motives." At some sessions of the legislature forty-nine out of fifty bills were not interfered with in any way; but this was partly because the legislators had learned to ask, before proposing a bill, "Will The Fort go for this?" It was common prudence not to propose something that The Fort would automatically have to fight.

A fine example of Hoxworth Hale's statesmanship came one January when his wife, a Janders girl with a warm concern for human rights, said at breakfast, "Hoxworth, have you seen the casualty lists that resulted from the New Year's fireworks?"

"Were they bad, Malama?" he asked. One of the annual highlights in Hawaii was the Chinese New Year, when the Chinese practically blew the city apart with detonations of the most spectacular sort.

"This year one boy was killed and fourteen were seriously maimed," Malama reported. "Really, these fireworks must be outlawed."

Hoxworth, who agreed that the practice of blowing off arms and legs was ridiculous, told his wife, "If you can outlaw them by legal means, go ahead."

Consequently, Mrs. Hale enlisted a committee of fifty public-spirited ladies —all of them haole, unfortunately—who descended upon the legislature with a bill to halt the crippling of children. The first legislators approached thought: "Mrs. Hale! Probably got The Fort behind her. Better pass this bill." So the famous anti-fireworks bill was introduced.

And then all hell broke loose! By comparison, the New Year's pyrotechnic display was a subdued affair, for Chinese legislators shouted on the floor, "This is discrimination! We have always blown up fireworks on New Year's."

To everyone's surprise, the Chinese quickly gained support from the Hawaiians. "We love fireworks!" they protested.

A bombastic Portuguese legislator gave an impassioned plea for the right of little people to have their fun just one night a year, and a huge lobby of storekeepers, who made more than seventy per cent profit selling firecrackers, began to disrupt all customary legislative procedures.

At this point jovial Kangaroo Kee, speaker of the house and supposed to be a creature of The Fort, displayed leadership of an unexpected sort. Handing the gavel over to a friend, he descended to the floor of the house and delivered one of the most impassioned bits of oratory heard in Hawaii for many years. He shouted: "This evil bill is an attempt to deprive the Chinese of Hawaii of an inalienable right! It is religious persecution of the most abominable sort! Do the haole women who brought in this bill need fireworks for their religious ceremonies? No! But do Chinese need them for their ceremonies?"

He paused, and from the entire Chinese-Portuguese-Hawaiian contingent of the house went up a great throbbing cry in defense of religious freedom. So Kangaroo Kee continued: "I warn the people who have dared to bring this bill onto the floor of this house that if it is voted into law, I will instantly resign! I can stand political domination. I can stand economic retaliation. But I cannot stand religious persecution!" Men wept and the hall echoed with cheers.

That afternoon Hoxworth Hale summoned The Fort and asked glumly, "What in hell has happened around here? Why do we suddenly wind up as religious persecutors?"

"Your wife started it all by wanting to save children from fireworks," big

Hewie Janders reminded him. "And my wife, damn her bleeding heart, gave your wife support."

"All I know," Hoxworth growled, "is that the Chinese are threatening to start a new political party. The Hawaiians are charging religious persecution. The Portuguese have enlisted both of them behind that grade-crossing bill. And Kangaroo Kee submitted his resignation this morning. Says he'll suffer no more dictation from tyrants. Gentlemen, we better do something."

Hewie Janders suggested: "Could you make a formal statement? In defense of religious freedom and firecrackers?"

"Get a secretary," Hoxworth snapped, and when the young man arrived, the head of The Fort dictated his memorable announcement beginning: "The Islands of Hawaii have always known religious freedom, and among those who have defended this basic concern of all men none have excelled the Chinese. To think that unfeeling persons should have seen fit to trample upon one of the most cherished rituals of Chinese religion, namely, the explosion of fireworks at festive seasons, is repugnant."

At this point Hewie Janders pointed out: "But it was your wife and mine who did it, Hoxworth! If you release such a statement, they're going to boil."

To this Hale replied, "When the structure of society is endangered, I don't care whose feelings get hurt."

The upshot of his retreat was that Mrs. Hale and Mrs. Janders considered their husbands contemptible cowards, and said so; Kangaroo Kee, breaking down into a copious flow of tears, announced to the house that he had reconsidered his resignation because the leaders of Hawaii had magnanimously reaffirmed their belief in religious freedom; the dangerous Chinese-Hawaiian-Portuguese coalition was broken up; and merchants sold more fireworks than ever before. On the next Chinese New Year two children were blinded, a girl had three fingers blown off and there were sixteen cases of disfiguring burns; but the islands were happy. The Honolulu *Mail,* summarizing the wild night, called it a splendid manifestation of island charm. But Hoxworth Hale, whose wife pointed out that the blindings and maimings were exactly what her bill had been intended to prevent, remarked glumly to The Fort: "We must never again outrage the firecracker vote."

I T WAS UNDER Hale's direction that The Fort insinuated its men onto the public boards that controlled things like the university and the parks, and once when an outside writer took pains to cross-reference the 181 most influential board members in Hawaii, he found that only thirty-one men in all were involved, and that of them twenty-eight were Hales, Whipples, Hoxworths, Hewletts and Janderses . . . or their sons-in-law. "A very public-spirited group of people," the writer concluded, "but it is often difficult to tell one board from the other or any from the board of H & H."

The Honolulu *Mail* was owned by The Fort, but its function in the community was never blatantly abused. It was a good paper, Republican of course, and it frequently supported positions which The Fort could not have approved but which the general public did; but when an issue involved land, sugar or labor, the *Mail* wrote forceful editorials explaining how the public good was involved and how government ought to respond. Once when a *Mail* reporter was sent to fifteen different sugar-growing areas to write a series of articles proving how much better off the people of Hawaii were than laborers in Jamaica, Fiji and Queensland, his returning letters were first studied in The Fort, "to be sure he maintains the proper historical perspective." The *Mail* was scrupulously fair in reporting activities of the underground Democratic Party, but the articles were written as if a benevolent old man was chuckling over the actions of imbecile and delinquent children.

The endless chain of appointed office holders sent out from Washington— too often incompetent and gregarious politicians—was quickly absorbed into The Fort's genial social life: hunting trips to the big island, boating parties, picnics by the sea. Sometimes a newcomer could sit on the bench for six months without ever meeting a Chinese other than a defendant in a court case or a Japanese who was not dressed in white and serving sandwiches. Such officials could be forgiven if they came to think of Hawaii as The Fort and vice versa and to hand down their decisions accordingly.

But Hoxworth Hale's greatest contribution lay in a general principle which he propounded early in his regime, and it is to his credit that he perceived this problem long before any of his contemporaries, and his adroit handling of it earned *The Fort* millions upon millions of dollars. He announced his policy flatly: "No military man stationed in Hawaii above the rank of captain in the army or lieutenant in the navy is to leave these islands without having been entertained by at least three families in this room." Then he added, "And if you can include the lower ranks, so much the better!" As a result of this rule, the constant flow of military people who passed through Hawaii came to think of big Hewlett Janders and gracious Hoxworth Hale as the two commanders of the islands, men who could be trusted, men who were sound; and in the years that were about to explode, making Hawaii a bastion of the Pacific, it was very difficult for Washington to send any senior admiral or general to Honolulu who did not already know The Fort intimately. Therefore, when a contract was to be let, bids weren't really necessary: "Hewlett Janders, the fellow I went hunting with ten years ago, he can build it for us." More important, when the procurement and engineering offices in Washington began to assume major importance in America's rush program of military expansion, the rising young men who crowded those offices almost had to be the ones that Hoxworth Hale and Hewie Janders had entertained so lavishly in the previous decade.

Nothing Hoxworth accomplished was more important than this establishment of a personal pipeline direct to the sources of power in Washington. Again, he never abused his prerogatives. He never called generals on the phone, shouting, as did some, "Goddam it, Shelly, they're talking about eminent domain on three thousand acres of my choicest sugar fields." Usually this made Washington determined to go ahead with condemnation proceedings. Hoxworth Hale acted differently: "This you, Shelly? How's Bernice? We're fine out here. Say, Shelly, what I called about was the proposed air strip out Waipahu way. That's a good site, Shelly, but have your men studied what the landing pattern would be with those tall mountains at the end . . . Yes, Shelly, the ones we went hunting on that weekend . . . Yes, I just want to be sure your men have thought about that, because there's another strip of land a little farther makai . . . Yes, that means toward the sea in Hawaiian, and I was wondering . . . Yes, it's our land, too, so there's no advantage to me one way or the other . . . Be sure to give Bernice our best."

Hawaii in these years of benevolent domination by The Fort was one of the finest areas of the world. The sun shone, the trade winds blew, and when tourists arrived on the luxury H & H liners the police band played hulas and girls in grass skirts danced. Labor relations were reasonably good, and any luna who dared strike a worker would have been instantly whisked out of the islands. The legislature was honest, the judges sent out from the mainland handed down strict but impartial decisions, except in certain unimportant cases involving land, and the economy flourished. It is true that mainland firms like Gregory's and California Fruit protested: "My God, the place is a feudal barony! We tried to buy land for a store and they said, 'You can't buy any land in Hawaii. We don't want your kind of store in the islands.'"

It was also true that Chinese or Japanese who wanted to leave the islands to travel on the mainland had to get written permission to do so, and if The Fort felt that a given Oriental was not the kind of man who should represent the islands in America, because he tended toward communist ideas, speaking of labor unions and such, the authorities would not let him leave, and there was nothing he could do about it. Hewlett Janders in particular objected to the large number of young Chinese and Japanese who wanted to go to the mainland to become doctors and lawyers, and he personally saw to it that a good many of them did not get away, for, as he pointed out: "We've got fine doctors right here that we can trust, and if we keep on allowing Orientals to become lawyers, we merely create problems for ourselves. Educating such people above their station has got to stop."

Once in 1934, after Hoxworth and his team had performed miracles in protecting Hawaii from the fury of the depression—it fell less heavily on the islands than anywhere else on earth—he was embittered when a group of Japanese workers connived to have a labor man from Washington visit the islands, and Hale refused to see the visitor. "You'd think they'd have respect for what I've done keeping Hawaii safe from the depression. Every Japanese who got his regular pay check, got it thanks to me, and now they want me to talk with labor-union men!"

He refused three times to permit an interview, but one day the man from Washington caught him on the sidewalk and said hurriedly, "Mr. Hale, I respect your position, but I've got to tell you that under the new laws you are required to let labor-union organizers talk to your men on the plantations."

"What's that?" Hoxworth asked in astonishment. "Did you say . . ."

"I said," the visitor, an unpleasant foreign type, repeated slowly, "that under the law you are required to permit labor-union organizers access to your men on the plantations."

"I thought that's what you said," Hale replied. "Good heavens, man!" Then, taking refuge in a phrase he had often heard Wild Whip declaim, he said, "If I saw a rattlesnake crawling onto one of my plantations and I shot him, I'd be a hero. Yet you want me voluntarily to open my lands to labor organizers. Truly, you must be out of your mind." He turned abruptly and left.

"Mr. Hale!" the labor man called, catching up with him and grabbing his coat.

"Don't you ever touch me!" Hale stormed.

"I apologize," the man said contritely. "I just wanted to warn you that Hawaii's no different from the rest of America."

"Apparently you don't know Hawaii," Hale said, and left.

In his cold, efficient governance of The Fort he manifested only two peculiarities which could be construed as weaknesses. Whenever he had a major decision to make he spent some time alone in his office, pushing back and forth across his polished desk a reddish rock about the size of a large fist, and in the contemplation of its mysterious form he found intellectual reassurance. "The rock came from his great-great-grandmother on Maui," his secretary explained. "It's sort of a good-luck omen," she said, but what the good luck derived from she did not know and Hale never told her. Also, whenever The Fort started a new building Hale insisted that local kahunas be brought in to orient it. Once a mainland architect asked, "What's a man with a Yale degree doing with kahunas?" and Hale replied, "You'd be surprised. In our courts it's illegal to force a Hawaiian to testify if a known kahuna is watching in the courtroom." The architect asked, "You certainly don't believe such nonsense, do you?" and Hale replied evasively, "Well, if I were the judge, I would certainly insist that any known kahunas be barred from my courtroom. Their power is peculiar."

One unspoken rule regarding The Fort was observed by all: The Fort did not exist; it was a phrase never mentioned in public; Hale himself never spoke it; and it was banned from both newspaper and radio. The building in which the men met remained as it was during Wild Whip's tenancy: a rugged redstone commercial headquarters built like a fort and bearing a simple brass plate that read: Hoxworth & Hale, Shipmasters and Factors.

B ACK IN THE 1880's, when the Chinese vegetable peddler Nyuk Tsin decided to educate her five sons and to send one of them all the way to Michigan for a law degree, Honolulu had been amazed at her tenacity and instructed by the manner in which she forced four of her sons to support the fifth on the mainland. But what Hawaii was now about to witness in the case of Japanese families and their dedication to learning made anything that the Chinese had accomplished look both dilatory and lacking in conviction. Specifically, the penniless night-soil collector Kamejiro Sakagawa was determined that each of his five children must have nothing less than a full education: twelve years of public school, four years at the local university, followed by three at graduate school on the mainland. In any other nation in the world, such an ambition would have been insane; it was to the glory of America, and especially that part known as Hawaii, that such a dream on the part of a privy-cleaner was entirely practical, if only the family had the courage to pursue it.

From the Kakaako home each morning the five Sakagawa children set forth to school. They were clean. Their black hair was bobbed straight across their eyes and their teeth had no cavities. They walked with an eager bounce, their bright scrubbed faces shining in sunlight, for to them school was the world's great adventure. Their education did not come easily, for it was conducted in a foreign language: English. At home their mother spoke almost none and their father knew only pidgin.

But in spite of language difficulties, the five Sakagawas performed brilliantly and even teachers who might have begun with an animus against Japanese grew to love these particular children. Reiko-chan set the pattern for her brothers. In her first six grades she usually led her class, and when teachers had to leave the room to see the principal, they felt no compunction about turning their classes over to this adorable little girl with the delicately slanted eyes and the flawless skin. Reiko-chan was destined to be a teacher's pet, and early in life she decided that when she graduated from the university, she would be a teacher too.

The boys were a more rowdy lot, and no teacher in her right mind would have turned her class over to them. They specialized in the rougher games, for in accordance with the ancient rule that all who came to Hawaii were modified, the four Sakagawa boys were obviously going to be taller than their father, with better teeth, wider shoulders and straighter legs. It was noticeable that they threw like Americans and could knock bottles off fences with surprising accuracy, but their mastery of English fell markedly below their sister's, a fact of which they were proud, for in the Honolulu public schools anyone who spoke too well was censured and even tormented by his classmates. To be accepted, one had to speak pidgin like a moron, and above everything else, the Sakagawa boys wanted to be accepted.

The success of this family in the American school was the more noteworthy because when classes were over, and when haole children ran home to play, the five Sakagawas lined up and marched over to the Shinto temple, where the man who was a priest on Sundays appeared in a schoolteacher's black kimono to conduct a Japanese school. He was a severe man, much given to beating children, and since he was proud of the fact that he spoke no corrupting English and had only recently come from Tokyo, he tyrannized the children growing up in an alien land. "How can you ever become decent, self-respecting Japanese," he stormed, "If you do not learn to sit properly upon your ankles? Sakagawa Goro!" and the heavy rod fell harshly across the boy's back. "Do not fidget. Will you feel no shame when you return home and visit friends and fidget?" Bang, went the rod. Bang and bang again.

The priest was contemptuous of everything American and impressed upon his charges that they were in this alien land for only a few years until they took up their proper life, and when he described Japan, he eyes grew misty and a poetry came into his voice. "A land created by the immortal gods themselves!" he assured them. "In Japan there is no rowdyism like here. In Japan children are respectful to their parents. In Japan every man knows his place and all do reverence to the emperor. No man can predict what impossible things Japan will some day accomplish." He taught from the same books that were used in Tokyo, using the same inflections and the same stern discipline. For three hours each day, when other children were rollicking in the sun, the Sakagawas sat painfully on their ankles before the priest and received what he called their true education.

There was much agitation against the Japanese-language schools, as they were called, and there was no doubt that the priests taught an un-American, Shintoistic, nationalistic body of material, but in those years not a single child who attended the schools got into trouble with the police. Among the Japanese there was no delinquency. Parents were obeyed and teachers were respected. In the Japanese schools a severe rectitude was taught and enforced, and much of the civic responsibility that marked the adult Japanese community derived from these austere late-afternoon sessions; and it was a strange thing, but not a single child in later years ever remembered much of the jingoistic nonsense taught by the priests; few ever wanted to go back to Japan; but all learned respect for an established order of life. It was as if the great freedoms enjoyed in the American school in the first part of the day insulated the child against the nationalistic farrago of the afternoon, so that most Japanese children, like the Sakagawas, assimilated the best from both schools and were not marred by the worst of either.

Actually, their true education in these years took place at home. In their tiny Kakaako shack, which would have been cramped even for a family of three, their mother enforced the rigid rules of cleanliness that she had learned as a child. Nothing was left on the floor. No dish went unwashed. Chopsticks were handled so that no food dropped. Clothes were put away neatly, and the child who did not bathe completely at least once each day was a hopeless barbarian, no better than a Chinese. Their father's influence was more subtly felt. He saw the world as divided sharply into the good and the bad and he never hesitated long in defining where any given action fell. It was good to honor one's country, it was good to die heroically, it was good to attend to what one's superiors said, it was good to have education. He lived a life of the most fierce propriety in which stealing was bad, and gambling, and speaking back, and tearing one's clothes. He was a harsh disciplinarian, but he rarely struck his children, relying instead upon the force of his character. He loved his children as if they were mysterious angels that had been allowed to live with him for a little while, and if the mean little shack was sometimes barren of food, it was never lacking in love.

The children engaged in nonsensical jokes which their parents could not understand. Reiko-chan had a series of remarks which her brothers greeted with shouts no matter how often she recited them: "What did the hat say to the hatrack? You stay here and I'll go on a head." Six times a week the boys could scream with delight over that one. "What did the carpet say to the floor? Don't make a move, I got you covered!" And "What did the big toe say to the little toe? Don't look back, but we're being followed by a heel."

The boys had rougher games, including one in which Goro would grab a brother's ear and ask sweetly, "Do you want your ear any longer?" If the brother said no, Goro would pretend to twist it off. If the answer was yes, Goro would jerk vigorously on the ear and shout, "Then I'll make it longer!" This usually led to a fight, which was what Goro had intended.

But on two basic principles the Sakagawa children would permit no joking. No one was allowed to call them Japs. This was a word so offensive to the Japanese that it simply could not be tolerated, for throughout America it was being used in headlines and cartoons to depict sneaking, evil little men with buckteeth. No haole could appreciate the fervor with which Japanese combated the use of this word.

Nor were they to be called slant-eyes. They argued: "Our eyes are not slanted! It's only because we have no fold in our eyelids that they look slanted." But of course in this they were wrong. Reiko-chan's little eyes were delightfully slanted, low near the nose and tilting upward in saucy angles. It was she who came home with one of their best games. Putting her two fingers at the corners of her lovely eyes, she pulled them way up and chanted, "My mother's a Japanese." Then she pulled them far down and sang, "And my father's a Chinese." Then, moving her forefingers to the middle of her eyebrows and her thumbs below, she spread her eyes wide apart and shouted, "But I'm a hundred per cent American."

When Kamejiro first saw this trick, he rebuked his daughter and reminded her: "The proudest thing in your life is that you're a Japanese. Don't ever laugh about it." But at the same time he became vaguely aware that with the arrival of children his family had become entangled in values that were contradictory and mutually exclusive: he sent his offspring to American schools so that they would succeed in American life; but at the same time he kept them in Japanese school so that they would be prepared for their eventual return to Japan. The children felt this schizophrenia and one day at the close of the American school Goro went not to the Japanese teacher but directly home, where Kamejiro met him with the question, "Why are you home?"

"I'm not going to the Japanese school any longer."

Kamejiro held his temper and asked patiently, "Why not?"

"I don't want to be a Japanese. I want to be an American."

For several moments Kamejiro held his hands to his side, in self-discipline, but he could not do so for long. Suddenly he grabbed his oldest son, lifted him in the air, tucked him under one arm and ran with him furiously to the temple where after bowing ceremoniously to the priest, his son still under his arm, he threw the boy into the midst of the scholars. "He said he didn't want to be a Japanese!" he stammered in rage, then bowed and left.

Slowly the tall priest rose and reached for his rod. Moving silently in his bare feet to where Goro lay on the tatami, he began to flail the boy unmercifully. When he had finished he returned solemnly to his rostrum, sat meticulously upon the floor and cried in a quivering voice, "Sakagawa Goro, what are the first laws of life?"

"Love of country. Love of emperor. Respect for parents."

Even in their names, the Japanese children experienced this constant hauling in two directions. At the American school it was Goro Sakagawa; at the Japanese, Sakagawa Goro. And when the beating was over, Goro waited for an opportunity and whispered to his brother Tadao, "I will never go back to Japan."

"Who spoke?" the priest cried sharply.

"I did," Goro replied. For him to lie would have been unthinkable.

"What did you say?"

"I said that when I grow up I will never go back to Japan."

Ominously the priest reached for the rod once more, and this time the beating he delivered was both longer and more severe. At the end he asked, "Now will you go back to Japan?"

"No," Goro stubbornly replied.

That night the priest told Kamejiro, "We can have no boy like this in the Japanese school. He lacks the proper sincerity."

"He will be back on Monday," Kamejiro said dutifully, bowing before his intellectual superior. "Believe me, Sensei, he will be back."

That was Wednesday evening, and when bruised Goro started to go to bed his father caught his hand and said quietly, "Oh, no! You will not sleep tonight."

"But I must go to school tomorrow," Goro pleaded.

"No. For you there is no more school. Tonight you start to work with me." And Kamejiro made the boy dress in warm clothes and that night he took him on his rounds to clean out privies. Goro was appalled at the work his father did, at the humiliation of it, at the way late strolling drunks ridiculed him, at the stench. But bow-legged little Kamejiro said nothing. Hauling his son with him, he did his work, and at dawn the two night prowlers took their hot bath and breakfasted as the older children went to school.

On Thursday, Friday and Saturday nights young Goro continued to clean our privies, until he felt so sick that he was afraid even to walk beside his resolute father. At dawn on Sunday, as the brilliant tropical sun came over Diamond Head, Kamejiro said to his son, "This is the way men have to work when they do not have an education. Are you ready to apologize to the priest?"

"Yes."

"And you're ready to apply yourself . . . in both schools?"

"Yes."

On Monday afternoon Kamejiro took Goro back to the temple and stood in the doorway while his son announced to the entire class: "I apologize to all of Japan for what I said last Wednesday. I apologize to you, Sensei, for my evil behavior. I apologize to you, Father, for having been such an ungrateful son."

"Are you now willing to go back to Japan?" the priest asked.

"Yes, Sensei."

"Then sit down and we will resume our studies." After that experience, there were no more disturbances among the Sakagawa children.

THERE WAS ONE item of education which Kamejiro could delegate to no one. Whenever he took his family for a stroll through Kakaako he kept on the alert, and from time to time would grasp his left wrist with his right hand, and then his children knew. "Is that one?" the boys whispered.

"That's one," Kamejiro replied in hoarse, awe-struck tones, and in this way the Sakagawas learned to spot the Etas, those untouchables who had filtered into Hawaii. Mrs. Sakagawa lectured Reiko-chan concerning the worst fate that could befall any girl: "There was a girl in Kakaako named Itagaki, and without knowing it she married an Eta. Her family had to go to another island in disgrace."

There were ways a self-respecting family could protect itself from Etas, and Kamejiro often told his children, "When the time comes for you to marry, I'll go to the directive and he will tell me whether the other party is an Eta or an Okinawan." There were two such detectives in Hawaii, and since they kept dossiers on every Japanese family, few Etas or Okinawans were unknown to them. Their services were costly, but since they enabled prospective brides and grooms to avoid the shame of mismating, the general community was willing to pay their fee.

Then, as Reiko-chan approached the age when she must move on to a more advanced school, her father's attention was diverted from Etas and directed to a matter of more immediate importance. The haole citizens of Hawaii, properly disturbed by the abominable English spoken in the schools, united to demand at least one school on each island where all children would speak acceptable English, and out of this agitation the so-called English-standard school developed. To attain entrance a child had to undergo a verbal examination to prove that he was not corrupted by pidgin and would thus not contaminate his classmates, who were usually trying to gain entrance to some mainland college.

The basic concept of the English-standard school was meritorious, for in other schools there often appeared to be no standards at all and even teachers sometimes taught in pidgin; but the manner in which students were selected for these superior schools was one of the most shameful subterfuges ever permitted in the islands. Plantation managers soon let it be known that they would look with disfavor upon teachers who admitted to the preferred schools too many children of Oriental ancestry; so automatically the schools became costly private schools with superior facilities paid for out of general taxation but largely restricted to haole children. This discrimination was easy to enforce, for teachers who interviewed prospective enrollees were encouraged to disbar any child who evidenced even the slightest accent or the misuse of a single word; and a miserable mockery developed whereby teachers, who knew they were under the surveillance of plantation managers, conducted tests of Japanese and Filipino children, whose failures were ordained before they spoke a word. Of course, a few sons of Oriental doctors and lawyers were admitted, lest the abuse of tax dollars become too odious, but for the most part the English-standard school became another device to keep Orientals on the plantations, where they were supposed to belong. As Hoxworth Hale pointed out, when as a member of the Board of Education he encouraged the establishment of the schools: "We mustn't educate field hands beyond their capacity."

In Honolulu the English-standard school was Jefferson, a superb institution with superior playing fields, laboratories and teachers. With real anxiety Japanese fathers like Kamejiro Sakagawa watched the results of the first entrance tests at Jefferson. Almost no Japanese children gained admittance, and Kamejiro warned: "See! You lazy children who will not study. None of your friends got into the fine school! But you will get in, because from now on you will study twice as much as before." He launched an ingenious program whereby his five children attended two different Christian churches each Sunday, listening to the preacher use good English. At any free public lecture, there would be Kamejiro and his five children. He could not understand what was being said, but when he got the young students home he would seat them in a circle and make them repeat again and again what the speaker had said, and in the speaker's intonation. Before long, Reiko-chan and Goro were adept in English.

The Sakagawa children had now reached the apex of their educational schizophrenia. In their American school they learned that all people were created equal, but their father kept teaching them who the Etas were, and the Okinawans. In their Japanese school they learned formal Japanese and were beaten if they made mistakes, but at night they drilled one another in proper English. Their parents spoke little of the language, but they insisted that their children converse with each other in English. It was a crazy, conflicting world, but there was this refuge of assurance: when they were with other children like themselves they spoke only a wild, free pidgin whose syllables sang on the ear like the breaking of waves along the beach.

When Reiko-chan was a long-legged, flashing-eyed girl of twelve she was ready to take her all-important verbal examination for admission into the privileges of Jefferson. Her parents washed her with unusual care, dressed her in a white smock with ruffles, and polished her shoes. Kamejiro wanted to accompany her, but she begged him not to do so, only to find when she got to Jefferson that he was required to be with her. She ran back to get him, and when her mother saw how heated up she had become in doing so, she was given another bath, and with her father's apprehensive hand in hers she returned to Jefferson, where a teacher picked up the report from Reiko's elementary school and read silently: "Reiko Sakagawa. Grades A. Behavior A. Knowledge of American customs A. English A." The investigating teacher smiled and passed the report approvingly along to the other two members of the board, but one of these had at her elbow an additional report on the Sakagawa girl, and this said simply, "Father, privy cleaner."

"How do you spend your days this summer?" the first teacher asked.

In a sweet, clear voice Reiko-chan replied, with careful attention to each syllable, "I help my mother with the washing. And on Sundays I go to church. And when we have a picnic I help my brothers get dressed."

The three teachers were impressed with the precision of the little girl's speech. Obviously she was a girl who belonged in whatever excellent schools a community could provide, and the first teacher was about to mark the official ballot "Passed," when the third teacher whispered, "Did you see this? Her father?"

The damning paper was passed from hand to hand and the teachers nodded. "Failed," wrote the first. Then, smiling sweetly at Reiko-chan, she explained: "We are not going to accept you at Jefferson, my dear. We feel that you speak a little too deliberately . . . as if you had memorized."

There was no appeal. Kamejiro and his brilliant daughter were led away and in the summer sunlight the father asked in Japanese, "Did you get in?"

"No," she said, trying desperately not to cry.

"Why not?" her father asked in dumb pain.

"They said I spoke too slowly," she explained.

It was Kamejiro, and not Reiko-chan, who began to weep. He looked at the fine school, at the lovely grounds, and realized what a great boon his family had lost. "Why, why?" he pleaded. "At home you talk like a fire machine! Why do you talk slow today?"

"I wanted to be so careful," Reiko-chan explained.

Kamejiro felt that his daughter had failed the family through some conscious error, and his rage overcame him. Raising his arm he was about to punish her when he saw that tears were hanging in her eyes, so instead of thrashing her as he intended, he dropped on one knee and embraced her. "Don't worry," he said. "Goro will get in. Maybe it's even better that way, because he's a boy."

Then he grabbed his daughter lovingly by the hand and said, "We must hurry," and the event toward which he hurried proved how deeply confused he was, for after having tried with all his prayers to get Reiko-chan into Jefferson so that she could be even more American, he now rushed her back home and into a kimono so that she could join her brothers in demonstrating that she was perpetually a Japanese. For this was the emperor's birthday, and the community was assembling at the Japanese school. As each family entered, the parents bowed almost to the floor before the portrait of the august emperor, then led their children to an allotted place on the tatami, where they sat on their ankles. At eleven the teacher appeared, ashen-faced, so grave was his responsibility that day. A former army officer rose and explained, "In Japan today, if the teacher who reads the Imperial Rescript mispronounces even one word or stumbles once, he is required to commit hara-kiri. Let us pay attention as we hear the immortal words of the Emperor Meiji as to what makes a good Japanese."

Slowly, painfully, the teacher began reading. In Japanese life the Imperial Rescript was unlike anything that western nations knew. It had started out in 1890 as a simple announcement of what Japan's educational policy should be, but the nation had found its clear statement of citizenship so appealing that the Rescript had been made immortal. Children and soldiers had to memorize it and lead their lives according to its precepts. It taught love of country, complete subjugation to the divine will of the emperor, and obedience to all authority. In beautiful language it taught a staggering theory of life, and in humble attention to it, Japan had grown strong. When the teacher ended his reading of the terrifying words, huge drops of perspiration stood out on his forehead, and each member of his audience was freshly dedicated to Japan and willing to sacrifice his life at the command of the emperor.

The army officer rose and said, "Let us remember Japan!" And all bowed, thinking of that distant, sweet and lovely land.

The crowd now went outside, where an arena had been set up, and two enormous men visiting from Japan waited, stripped down to the merest loincloths, and after a priest had prayed over them, they went to their respective corners of the arena and grabbed handfuls of salt, which they scattered about the mat upon which they were to wrestle. Kamejiro whispered to his attentive boys, "Haoles who say Japanese are runty should see these men!" The preparations continued with painful deliberateness for forty minutes, then in a flash of speed, the two giants crashed into one another, groaned and hefted until one pushed the other across the boundary. The Japanese cheered, then burst into hilarious laughter as two of their own fatties, men from the plantations, appeared nearly naked to conduct their own wrestling match.

In the afternoon, officials from the consulate drove up in a black car and told the listeners, "Grave events are shaping up in Asia. The perpetual evil of China once more threatens us, and we cannot say what fearful measures our august emperor may be required to take. On this solemn day, may we rededicate our lives to the land we love." There was a great deal more about the ominous events that imperiled the homeland, but nobody was very clear as to what they were. However, a collection was taken to aid the emperor in this hour of need, and the Sakagawas contributed money that had been intended for a new dress for Reiko-chan. She was allowed to place the coins in the box, and she quivered with love of Japan as she did so.

Now the celebrants moved to the public square in Kakaako, where under a banyan tree they performed the ancient, ritualistic bon dances of Japan. The children were an important part of this dance, weaving in slow measures in and out, their colorful kimonos swaying in the soft night breezes, and one group of elderly ladies, who had learned their bon dances in villages thousands of miles from Hawaii, found tears in their eyes as they watched delicate Reiko-chan moving through the graceful figures. One old woman asked, "I wonder if she knows how beautiful she is? Such a flawless skin and her eyes so Japanese!"

Kamejiro, who overheard these words of praise, blushed and told the women, "We are training Reiko-chan so that when she returns to Japan she will be recognized as a fine Japanese."

"She is one now," the women said approvingly.

When the emperor's birthday celebration ended, the old confusions returned, and Kamejiro warned his sons, in one breath, "This sacred day should remind you of how important it is that we get our family back to Japan," and, "You boys saw that Reiko-chan missed getting into Jefferson. You are not to miss." So the tiny Sakagawa shack became a drill hall with all the children speaking English.

Even in its first year Jefferson demonstrated its success. With better teachers and better facilities it promised to turn out graduates who were proficient in English and who were sure to make good records at mainland colleges. Some of the plantation owners began to wonder if perhaps the English-standard schools weren't too good. Hoxworth Hale observed: "Why you get almost as fine an education at Jefferson as you do at Punahou. No tax-supported school has to be that good." But there were other protests of a more serious nature, for it had become apparent to laboring groups that their children were not going to be admitted to the superior schools, no matter how proficient their English, and some radical labor men began to argue: "We pay taxes to support these fine schools to educate those who don't need them. It is our own children who ought to be going to those schools, for then the differences between groups in the community would be diminished."

Sometimes at night, as Kamejiro listened to Reiko-chan drilling her brothers in English, he thought: "Everybody in Hawaii has it better than the Japanese. Look at those damned Kees! They have big stores and their sons go to Punahou. When the Chinese came to Hawaii, things were easy."

Now it was Goro's turn to try his luck at Jefferson, and like his sister he reported to the jury of three teachers. Like her he brought with him a rather striking report: "Grades A. Behavior B. Knowledge of American customs A. English A. This boy has unusual capacities in history." The test began, and he spoke with delightful fluency, explaining the Civil War to the teachers.

It looked as if they would have to accept him, when one teacher used a device that had been found effective in testing a child's real knowledge of

English. She slowly lifted a piece of paper and tore it in half.

"What did I do to the paper?" she asked.

"You broke it," Goro said promptly.

Again the teacher tore the paper and asked, "What did I do to it this time?"

"You broke it again," Goro said.

"We're sorry," the chairman announced. "She tore the paper. The word is tore." And Goro was rejected.

When his father heard the news he asked calmly, "What was the word again?"

Goro explained, "I said broke when I should have said tore."

"Broke!" Kamejiro cried in anguish. "Broke!" He did not know the word himself, but he was outraged that his son should have misused it. He began beating him about the shoulders, crying, "How many times have I told you not to say broke? You stupid, stupid boy!" And he continued hammering his son, not realizing that if it had not been the word *broke* it would have been some other, for the children of Japanese men who dug out privies were not intended to enter Jefferson.

I N 1936 KAMEJIRO Sakagawa faced a most difficult decision, for it became apparent that his grand design of educating five children from kindergarten through graduate school could not be attained. The hard-working family simply did not have the money to keep going. It was therefore necessary that some, at least, of the children quit school and go to work, and discussions as to the various courses open to the Sakagawas kept the family awake many nights.

The fault was not Kamejiro's. He would have been able to maintain the four boys in school and at the same time permit Reiko-chan to begin her university course except that news from China was increasingly bad. Time after time either the priest at the language school or the consular officials reported to the Japanese community that the emperor was facing the gravest crisis in Japanese history. "This sacred man," the priest intoned, "tries to sleep at night with the burden of all Japan on his shoulders. The very least you can do is to support our armies in their victorious march across China." The armies were always on the verge of victory, and certainly the Japanese newsreels showed the capture of one new province each week, but the Japanese forces never seemed to get anywhere, and in August of that year the consular official made a very blunt statement: "I want fifty thousand dollars sent from these islands to help save the Japanese army."

The Sakagawas contributed seventy of those dollars and that night assembled the family. "Reiko-chan cannot go to college," Kamejiro said bluntly. The brilliant little girl, president of the girls' club at McKinley and an honor student, sat primly with her hands in her lap. As a good Japanese daughter she said nothing, but Goro did. "She knows more than any of us. She's got to go to college. Then she can become a teacher and help pay our way."

"Girls get married," Kamejiro rationalized quietly. "Pretty girls get married right away, and the education and income are lost."

"She could promise not to get married," Goro suggested.

"It is boys who must be educated," Kamejiro pointed out, "though why both you and Tadao failed to get yourselves into Jefferson I cannot understand. Are you stupid? Why don't you learn to speak English right?" he fumed in Japanese.

"Please," the gentle girl begged, "you've seen that only the sons of people the plantation leaders like get into the good schools."

Kamejiro turned to look at his daughter. The idea she had suggested was startling to him and repugnant. "Is that right?" he asked.

"Of course it's right," Reiko-chan replied. "And Minoru and Shigeo won't get in, either."

"Nothing wrong with McKinley," Goro snapped, defending the wonderful rabbit-warren of a school where Orientals and Portuguese and indigent haloes went. It was a comfortable, congenial school, arrogant in its use of pidgin even in classrooms, and many of the islands' political leaders graduated from it, even if none of the business tycoons did. A boy could get his jaw broken at McKinley for speaking good English, but he could also get a good education, for the school always contained dedicated teachers who loved to see brilliant boys like Goro prosper.

"Forget McKinley," Kamejiro told his children. "What kind of job can Reiko-chan get that will bring in the most money?"

"Let her work for three years, then Tadao and I can get jobs," Goro suggested, "and she can go on to the university."

"No," Kamejiro corrected. "I have noticed that if boys stop, they never go back. Reiko-chan must work from now on."

It was at this point that the quiet girl almost sobbed, and her brothers saw the involuntary contraction of her shoulders. Goro, a big husky boy, larger than his father, went to his sister's chair and put his hand on her arm. "Pop's right," he said in English. "You'll get married. Pretty girl like you."

"We speak in Japanese!" Kamejiro rebuked. "Sit down. Now what kind of job?"

"I could be a typist," Reiko suggested.

"They pay nothing for Japanese typists," Kamejiro replied.

"Could she work for a doctor?" Tadao asked. He was a slim, wiry boy, taller than Goro but not nearly so rugged. "That's good pay."

"She's got to have training, and we have no money," Kamejiro replied. He waited for a moment, almost afraid to discuss openly what was in his mind. Then he swallowed and said, "I was talking with Ishii-san and he said . . ."

"Please, Father!" the boys interrupted. "Not Ishii-san! If you listen to what he says . . ."

"Ishii-san's a fool," Reiko laughed. "Everyone knows that."

"This family is indebted to Ishii-san," Kamejiro said forcefully. He often used this phrase, but he never explained to the children why they were indebted to the curious little man whose ideas got stranger each year. "And Ishii-san pointed out that the easiest way for a Japanese to make lots of money is . . ." He paused dramatically.

"Stealing!" Goro joked in English. His father knew something irreverent had been said, but not what, so he ignored his son.

"Ishii-san is going to lend me the money," Kamejiro explained with nervous excitement, "and I am going to open a small barbershop on Hotel Street where the sailors are. And all the chairs will have girl barbers."

Slowly, as if gripped by a nameless horror, the four boys turned to look at their pretty sister. She sat apart, watching her mother, who was washing rice, but in her silence the color left her cheeks, for she understood that her immediate destiny was not the university or nursing or stenography; she was going to be a lady barber. She knew that there was already one shop of lady barbers on Hotel Street, and men flocked in and whoever owned the shop was making a lot of money, and the girls were getting tips. "But who are the girls?" Reiko thought mutely. "They have hardly been through grammar school."

"So I have asked Sakai-san if he would allow his daughter Chizuko to work for me," Kamejiro reported, exuding hope, "and he said yes, if I watch her closely and prevent her from becoming familiar with strange men. And Rumiko Hasegawa will work with us too, so that with three chairs and with me to sweep up and shine shoes, we ought to do very well."

Unexpectedly, Goro threw his arms on the table and began to weep. When his father asked, "Now what's wrong?" the sixteen-year-old boy mumbled, "Reiko-chan is the best one of us all."

"Then she will be willing to help her brothers get their education," Kamejiro said quietly.

Now the mother, from her corner where she was preparing food, spoke, and she observed: "It is the duty of a Japanese girl to help her family. I helped mine when I was young, and it made me a better wife. If Reiko-chan works hard and earns her own money, she will appreciate it more when her husband gives her some to spend on her children. It is her duty."

"But a lady barber!" Goro cried through his sobs.

"As a barber she will earn more money," his mother replied.

Goro rushed to his sister and embraced her. "When I become a lawyer and make a million dollars," he said in rapid English, "it will all be yours." The tears coursed down his face. Then Tadao, who was doing exceptionally well in school, but not so well as his sister had done in the same classes, began to weep, and the two younger boys, who knew how their sister had dreamed of becoming a teacher, sobbed. This was too much for Kamejiro, whose cruel duty it had been to make this decision, and he began to find tears splashing down his cheeks.

Only Mrs. Sakagawa did not cry. "It is her duty," she assured her trembling menfolk, but then she saw the tears in her lovely daughter's eyes, and she could no longer hide the fact that duty is often too terrible to bear. Gathering her child to her bosom, she wept.

Kamejiro Sakagawa's barbershop was an immense success. It opened just as American military installations in Hawaii were beginning to boom, so that navy men from Pearl Harbor and army boys from Schofield Barracks crowded into Hotel Street to get tattooed by local artists and shaved by lady barbers. But the principal reason for Kamejiro's prosperity was the crystal-like beauty of the three Japanese girls who staffed his chairs. They were olive-skinned, dark-haired, soft-eyed young ladies who looked especially appealing in crisp white uniforms which they delighted in keeping clean. Men often dropped by just for an extra trim to watch the girls, for there was the double excitement of a lady barber who was also a Japanese. Before long, regular customers were begging the pretty girls for dates.

That was where Kamejiro came in. Early in the life of his barbershop he had taught his girls how to stab with their scissors fresh customers who were trying to feel their legs. He also showed them that one of the best ways to handle difficult suitors was to push a hot towel in the man's face just as he was making his proposal. He encouraged his girls to discourage persistent Lotharios by nicking them slightly with the razor, especially on the ear lobe where one bled freely, but this gambit sometimes had reverse results, for the girls usually felt repentance for this act and made over the wounded customer so prettily, daubing him with styptic and asking in a sweet voice, "Does it hurt?" that the men came back stronger than before.

At closing time each night there were loungers outside in Hotel Street waiting for the girls, but Kamejiro formed his barbers into a squad, marched them to the Sakai girl's home, and cried proudly, "Sakai-san! Here's your daughter safe and sound." He then marched to the Hasegawas' and cried, "Here's Rumiko, safe and sound." At the doorway to his own home he invariably informed his wife, "Here's our girl, safe at home." The Japanese community marveled at how well Kamejiro was doing, and all agreed that his Reiko-chan was a most excellent barber.

T HEN IN 1938, during Goro's last year at McKinley High, a real bombshell struck the Sakagawa family, an event so unanticipated that it left the household breathless. One afternoon in late July three men in blue suits came to the house in Kakaako and asked, "Mrs. Sakagawa, where's Tadao?"

Yoriko could speak little English, so she said, "Tadao, he not here."

"When he come home?" one of the men in a stiff white collar asked.

"Me not know."

"Tonight?"

"Hontoni, hontoni!" she nodded. "For sure."

"You tell him to wait here," the men said, and if they had smiled, as they should have done, they would have eased the apprehensions of the Sakagawa household enormously, but they did not, for Mrs. Sakagawa, hunched up from great work and somewhat wrinkled, scared them, and they stared at her as she stared at them.

When the family convened that night, Mrs. Sakagawa was the center of attraction. Four times she acted her role in the afternoon's ominous encounter, and everyone began pressing seventeen-year-old Tadao for the details of what offense he had committed, for the family assumed that the men were detectives. No other haoles in blue suits and white collars ever visited Japanese homes, and slowly the unincriminated members of the Sakagawa family began to coalesce against the first Sakagawa boy to have gotten into trouble. The awful, terrifying rectitude of the Japanese family asserted itself, and Reiko-chan cried, 'You, Tadao. What did you do? All day I work and see no-goods on Hotel Street. Is my brother to be one of these?'

"Tadao!" Kamejiro cried, banging the table. "What wrong thing have you done?"

The tall, quiet boy could not answer, so his stockier brother Goro shouted, "You and your damned foolishness! Suppose the police take you, no more teams at McKinley for you. And I'll be ashamed to go on the field. Tell us! What have you done?"

The guiltless and bewildered boy shivered before the anger of his family. So far as he knew he had done nothing, yet the men had been there. Kamejiro, who had worked desperately hard to keep his family decent Japanese of whom Hiroshima would be proud, saw that his efforts had come to naught, and began mumbling in his hands. "No man can bring children up right," he swore, his chin trembling with shame and sorrow.

There was a knock at the door, and the Sakagawas looked at each other with last-minute dismay. "You stand there!" Kamejiro whispered to his son, placing him where the men could reach him. There would be no running away in his family. Then, biting his lip to hide his disgrace, he opened the door.

"Mr. Sakagawa?" the leader asked. "I'm Hewlett Janders, and this is John Whipple Hoxworth, and this gentleman in back," and he laughed easily, "this is Hoxworth Hale. Good evening." The three business leaders of Hawaii entered the small room, stood awkwardly for a moment, then laughed when Reiko called in English, "Boys, get them some chairs!"

"We could use some," big Hewlett Janders laughed. "Mighty fine house you have here, Mr. Sakagawa. Rarely see such beautiful flowers any more. You must have a green thumb."

Goro translated rapidly and Kamejiro bowed. "Tell them I love flowers," he said. Goro translated this and apologized: "Father is ashamed of his English."

"You certainly handle the language well," Hewlett replied. "You're Goro, I take it?"

"Yes, sir."

The three men looked at him approvingly, and finally Hewlett said, jokingly, "You're the young fellow we hate."

Goro blushed, and Reiko-chan interrupted asking, "We thought it was Tadao you wanted to see. This is Tadao."

"We know, Miss Sakagawa. But this is the young rascal we worry about."

There was a moment's suspense. No one quite knew what was happening, nor what odd turn this strange meeting was going to take next. It was Hoxworth Hale, oldest and most prim of the visitors who spoke, and as always he tried to speak to the heart of the matter. "We are an informal alumni committee from Punahou School. We're sick and tired of seeing our team run over by first-class athletes like this Goro over here. Young man, you have a marvelous future. Basketball, baseball and most of all football. If you ever need any help, come see me."

"Then you didn't come to arrest one of us?" Reiko-chan asked.

"Good heavens no!" Hale replied. "Did we give that impression this afternoon?"

"My mother doesn't understand . . ." Reiko began, but the relief she felt was so great that she could not speak. She put her hand to her mouth to stop its quivering, then put her arm about Tadao.

"Good gracious no!" Hale continued. "Quite the contrary, Miss Sakagawa. In fact, we're so impressed by your family that we've come here tonight to offer your brother Tadao a full scholarship at Punahou, because we need a running halfback like him."

No one spoke. The older Sakagawas, not comprehending what was happening, looked at Goro for translation, but before he could begin, big Hewlett Janders clapped his arm about the boy's shoulder and said, "We wanted you, too, Goro, but we felt that since you're a senior, you probably ought to finish at McKinley. Besides, we have fairly good tackles at school. But you've got to promise one thing. In the Punahou game, don't tackle your brother."

"I'll tear him to shreds if he's Punahou," Goro laughed.

"You wrecked us for the past two years," Janders acknowledged, punching the boy in a friendly manner.

Now Tadao spoke. "How could I pay my way at Punahou?" he asked. "Besides the tuition, that is?"

"You'll be there two years," Hale explained. "No charges at all for tuition or books. You can have a job right now at H & H taking care of forms. And completely off the record, we would like to give you one hundred dollars, twenty now, the rest later, for some clothes and things like that."

John Whipple Hoxworth, a sharp-eyed, quick-minded man added, "Tell your father that we are doing this not only because you have great promise as a football player, but because we know you are a fine boy. If you were otherwise, we wouldn't want you at Punahou."

Hoxworth Hale said, "It won't be too easy for you, son. There aren't many Japanese at Punahou. You'll be alone and lonely."

Reiko-chan answered for her brother: "It's the best school in the islands. To go there would be worth anything."

"We think so," Hale replied. And the three men shook hands with Tadao, the new boy at Punahou.

When the men were gone, Kamejiro exploded. "What happened?" he shouted at Goro.

"Tadao has been accepted at Punahou," the interpreter replied.

"Punahou!" The name had rarely been mentioned in the Sakagawa household. It was a school that had no reality to the Japanese, a haole heaven, a forbidden land. A Japanese boy could logically aspire to Jefferson, and in recent years some were making it, but Punahou! Kamejiro sat down, bewildered. "Who applied to Punahou?" he mumbled.

"Nobody. The school came to him because he has good grades and can play football."

"How will he pay?"

"They have already paid him," Goro explained, pointing to Tadao's money.

It was at this point, as Kamejiro studied the twenty dollars, that the Sakagawa family as a whole acknowledged for the first time, openly and honestly, that the boys would probably not return to Japan; for they could see Tadao at Punahou, one of America's greatest schools, working with the finest people in the islands, and graduating and going on to college and university. He would become a doctor or a lawyer, and his life would be spent here in America; and the family looked at him in this moment of realization and they saw him as forever lost to Japan; for this was the power of education.

The three blue-suited alumni who visited that night had warned Tadao that life at Punahou would be difficult, but the source of the difficulty they failed to identify. It came not from Punahou, where Tadao's football prowess won respect, but from Kakaako, where the submerged people had long ago suspected Tadao because of his mastery of English. Now he was openly stigmatized as a haole-lover, and six times in September, Kakaako gangs waylaid him as he came home from football practice and beat him thoroughly. "We'll teach you to be better than we are!" they warned him. When he made three touchdowns against a team mainly of Japanese and other pidgin-speakers, they hammered him desperately, shouting, "You goddamned traitor! Who do you think you are, playing for Punahou?"

Tadao never tried to enlist Goro's aid. This punishment from Kakaako was something he had to absorb. He learned to keep his hands over his face so that his teeth would not be broken, and he quickly mastered the art of using his feet and knees as lethal weapons. By mid-October the assaults ended, especially since McKinley was having a good year with Goro as one of its brightest stars.

This football business in Honolulu was one of the strangest aberrations in the Pacific. Because Chinese, Japanese and Filipinos were mad about games, and because haoles like Janders, Hoxworth and Hale constantly recalled their days of glory at Punahou, the islands were sports-crazy and the easiest way to sell a newspaper was to work up a frenzy over football or basketball. Having no college league to focus on, the entire community bore down on the high schools. Radio commentators reported breathlessly that Akaiamu Kalania-naole had damaged a tendon in his right foot and would not be able to play Saturday for Hewlett Hall. Newspapers carried enormous photographs of fifteen-year-old boys, growling ferociously under captions like "Tiger Chung About to Tear into Punahou." Youths who should have been thinking of themselves as unshaven adolescents having trouble with the square roots of decimals, were forced to believe that they were minor Red Granges, and all the publicity that on the mainland was thrown at mature professional athletes, was in Hawaii directed at callow youths in high school. Consequently, from one year to the next, disgraceful scandals erupted in which adult gamblers bribed these boys to throw games. Then headlines moralized over the lack of character-training in the schools and occasionally some bewildered lad was actually thrown into jail for "corrupting the fabric of our sports world," while the adult gamblers who framed him went free.

At no time did this great Hawaiian nonsense flourish with more abandon than in the fall of 1938 when Goro Sakagawa was playing his last year at McKinley and his brother Tadao his first at Punahou. As the Thanksgiving Day classic between the two schools approached, all the local newspapers carried flamboyant stories about the two dramatic young men. The *Mail* got a fine shot of their father Kamejiro standing before his barbershop with a Punahou pennant in one hand, a McKinley banner in the other. "Impartial!" the caption read. It was one of the first pictures of a Japanese other than a criminal or an embassy official to appear outside the sports pages of a Honolulu newspaper.

On the day of the game there were two half-page spreads, one of Goro looking like an insane bullldog about to tear a squirrel apart and one of Tadao straight-arming an imaginary tackler. "Brother against Brother" read the headlines, two inches tall. It was a great game, and except for an extraordinary play by Goro in the last fifteen seconds, Tadao's three flaming touchdowns would have led Punahou to victory. That night, as he walked home through Kakaako, confused by the plaudits of the huge crowd who had eulogized him as the star of the Punahou team, he got his worst beating from the toughs. When they left him they warned: "Don't you never play like that against McKinley again!"

He stumbled home, his face bleeding from three different cuts, and Goro had had enough. "You know who did it?" he asked.

"Yes."

"Let's go!" They took sixteen-year-old Minoru and fifteen-year-old Shigeo along. Goro gave each a baseball bat or a railing from a picket fence, and they cruised Kakaako until they came upon seven members of the gang. "No mercy!" Goro whispered, and with deadly efficiency the four brothers moved in. Next morning the newspapers, writing of the game, called it, "Triumph of the Sakagawa Brothers," and when Goro saw the headline he told Tadao, "We didn't do so bad last night, either."

While the Sakagawa boys were thus clawing their way up the ladder of island life, boys of Hawaiian ancestry were enjoying quite a different experience. When old Abraham Hewlett on the island of Maui took as his second wife a handsome Hawaiian girl, he found that her family owned about half of what was to become the hotel area of Waikiki. Eventually the Hewlett lands were valued at over one million dollars an acre, and because of the far-sighted missionary generosity of old Abraham, the entire income was applied to Hewlett Hall, where boys and girls of Hawaiian blood were entitled to a free education. Under the guidance of a board usually composed exclusively of Hales, Hewletts and Whipples, the famous Hawaiian school developed into a marvelous institution. It had a sparkling band, one of the finest choruses in the islands, loving teachers and handsome dormitories. All was free, and an outsider looking casually at the school could have been forgiven if he had concluded: "Hewlett Hall has been the salvation of the Hawaiian race."

Actually, the facts were somewhat contrary. Physically, Hewlett Hall was about perfect, but intellectually it was limited by the vision of the great families who dominated its board. They sent their sons to Punahou and Yale. It never seriously occurred to them that Hawaiian boys had exactly the same capacities as haoles; consequently, they consciously forced Hewlett Hall into a trade-school mold; its directors, with the greatest love in the world, rationalized: "The Hawaiians are a delightful, relaxed race. They love to sing and play games. They make wonderful mechanics and chauffeurs. Their girls are excellent teachers. Let us encourage them to do these things even better." And the Hawaiians, by their own friends, were so encouraged.

Now in the old days when a brilliant Chinese boy had fallen under the wing of preposterous Uliassutai Karakoram Blake, he was told daily: "You are as great a human being as I have ever known. There is nothing of which you are not capable." And these boys grew into doctors, political leaders and bankers. When outstanding Japanese boys like Goro Sakagawa crammed themselves into McKinley High—called locally Mikado Prep—they invariably found some inspired woman teacher imported from Kansas or Minnesota who told them: "You have a mind that can accomplish anything. You could write great books or become a fine research doctor. You can do anything." So the Chinese boys and the Japanese battled their way to proficiency, but the Hawaiians were not so goaded. They were given everything free and were encouraged to become trustworthy mechanics, and no society has ever been ruled by trustworthy mechanics and loyal schoolteachers.

Back in 1907 when Dr. Hewlett Whipple was made a member of the board for Hewlett Hall, he had tried manfully to revitalize the curriculum and to find dynamic teachers like old Uliassutai Karakoram Blake, but the Hales and Hewletts stopped him: "We must not try to educate these fine Hawaiian children above their natural capacity." After three years of futile struggling, Dr. Whipple resigned, and on the night he quit he told his wife, "With love and money we have condemned these people to perpetual mediocrity. Hewlett Hall is the worst thing that has happened to the Hawaiians since the arrival of measles and the white man." So while the Chinese and Japanese learned to manipulate their society, the Hawaiians did not.

IN THE FALL of 1941 Honolulu was presented with evidence that Punahou, at least, was capable of producing young scholars who could turn out historical research of high literary merit. Proof appeared in the form of a mimeographed pamphlet late one Friday afternoon as school was dismissing, and by Friday night the entire haole community had heard of it, with widely varying reactions; even some of the Orientals, by habit indifferent to literary accomplishment, were chuckling.

No one reacted more violently than Hoxworth Hale, a sedate man, for by the time he had finished reading the fourth line of the manifesto he was apoplectic and felt, with reason, that a scandal had occurred which required action, a conclusion which the officials at Punahou had acted upon an hour earlier. Later, when he reviewed the matter, Hoxworth realized that he should have anticipated trouble, for he recalled that for some time his son Bromley had been behaving mysteriously.

With the aid of a professional carpenter, whom he paid out of his own funds, young Brom had erected a curious structure on the back lot, and when asked what it was, had repeatedly insisted: "A play pen for adults." It stood unrelated to anything else, a half-room, with no ceiling and only two wooden walls, into which were cut four small openings, in back of which were built little boxes. The ridiculous structure did have a wooden floor, five feet ten inches long by five feet one inch wide. Two-by-fours propped up the walls, and Hoxworth noted that several of his son's friends were working on the project. One day for example, crew-cut young Whipple Janders, with a new Leica picked up on his family's last trip to Germany, had called, "Hey, Mr. Hale. Would you help us a minute?"

"What can I do, Whip?"

"I want you to model this contraption."

"Only if you tell me what it is."

"Brom calls it a play pen for adults," Whipple had explained. "Some crazy idea of his."

"How do you want me to model it?" Hoxworth had asked.

"I want to see if a grown man could fit into one of our little boxes."

"You mean in there?"

"Yes. It's well braced."

"You want me to climb in?"

"Sure. Use the ladder."

Hoxworth was perpetually unprepared for the blasé manner in which modern children ordered their parents around, and with some misgivings he climbed into the bizarre box, stretched his legs out as far as they would reach, and laughed pleasantly at young Whipple Janders.

"I should have an Arrow collar on," he said.

"You're in sharp focus just as you are, sir," Whip replied, snapping several shots with his Leica. "Thank you very much, Mr. Hale."

Hoxworth, reading the inflammatory publication, thought back on those scenes and acknowledged that he had been tipped off. Whatever happened now was in part his fault. "But how can you anticipate children?" he groaned. The publication bore this title:

SEX ABOARD THE BRIGANTINE

or

They Couldn't Have Been Seasick All the Time

or

THERE WAS FRIGGIN' IN THE RIGGIN'

A speculative essay on missionaries by Bromley Whipple Hale

"It is acknowledged by my many and devoted friends at Punahou that I yield to no man in my respect for the missionary stock from which I, and many of my most intimate friends, derive. I count among my dearest possessions the time-worn memorials that have come down in my family, those treasured reminders of the hardships which my forebears suffered in Rounding the Horn in their thirst for salvation through good deeds. But more precious I count the blood of those stalwart souls as it courses through my veins and makes me the young man I am today. Therefore, when I speak of certain inquiries of a scientific nature which I have been conducting as an outgrowth of my studies in a revered school which itself has certain mission overtones, and where I have imbibed only the purest instruction, I speak as a Hale, a Whipple, a Bromley and a Hewlett. In fact, I may ask in all modesty, a trait for which I have been noted by my friends: Who of my generation, the sixth, could speak with greater propriety of mission matters? In equal modesty I would have to reply: No one.

"Bred as I was on missionary mythologies, I have always been profoundly impressed by several aspects of the long journey from Boston to Hawaii as undertaken by my ancestors. There was dreadful seasickness, from which almost all suffered constantly. There was binding biliousness which yellowed the eye and slowed the step, much as constipation does in our less euphemistic age. There were cramped quarters shared by eight where common decency required that there should have been only two. And there were the inconveniences of no fresh laundry, the same stinking clothes used week after week, and the uncontrollable boredom of life in unaccustomed quarters.

"No mission child has suffered more from a vicarious contemplation of these hardships than I. In fact, I have recently gone so far as to reconstruct the actual conditions under which my forebears struggled against the sea, and for several nights I have tried to live as they must have lived, endeavoring by these means to project myself into their reactions. In the first pictures that accompany this essay will be found my responses to the hardships borne by my ancestors."

Hoxworth Hale turned the page gingerly and found that Whipple Janders' Leica had been used to excellent effect. From the bunk leered Bromley Hale, his body contorted by the narrow quarters and . . .

"Good God!" Hoxworth gasped. "Isn't that Mandy Janders?" He studied the next photograph, which showed how husband and wife slept in the narrow bunks, and sure enough, there was his son Bromley Hale snoring while pretty, long-legged Amanda Janders, in a poke bonnet, lay beside him, staring in disgust. "Oh, my God! I'd better call Mandy's father right away," he said weakly, but the essay held him captive, just as it was imprisoning everyone in Honolulu lucky enough to possess one of the three hundred mimeographed copies accompanied by Whip Janders' glossy photos.

"As can be clearly seen," Bromley Hale's essay continued, "life aboard the brigantines must have been exactly as bad as our forebears have reported. But it has always seemed to me that our good ancestors were strangely silent on one important matter. Life on the brigantines was unadulterated hell, granted. But life went on. Oh, yes indeed, it went on. In fact, aided by the superb libraries resident in Honolulu, I have assembled certain statistics about just how fast life did go on. Take, for example, the brig *Thetis,* on which some of my ancestors, both on my father's side and on my mother's, reached these hospitable shores. The *Thetis* departed Boston on September 1, 1821 and reached Lahaina on March 26, 1822, after a passage of 207 storm-ridden days.

"Applying to these data certain facts which have been established beyond chance of successful contradiction in Botany 2, any child born to the eleven mission couples prior to May 27, 1822, must have been conceived—in holy wedlock to be sure—on land in New England, and any infant born after December 21, 1822 must by the same reasoning have been conceived on land in Hawaii. But surely, any child born to these particular mission families between May 27 and December 21, 1822, could have been conceived nowhere else but aboard the bouncing brig *Thetis.* Let us look at what happened to the occupants of one stateroom:

Parents	Offspring	Born
Abner and Jerusha Hale	son Micah	October 1, 1822
John and Amanda Whipple	son James	June 2, 1822

| Abraham and Urania Hewlett | son Abner | August 13, 1822 |
| Immanuel and Jeptha Quigley | daughter Lucy | July 9, 1822." |

Relying upon old records, Bromley Hale proved that of the eleven mission couples aboard the *Thetis,* nine had produced offspring within the critical period. In turn, he moved to each of the other revered missionary companies, establishing departure and arrival dates, against which he compared the birth records until at last he was able to present a fairly staggering array of statistical evidence. "Good God," Hoxworth groaned, "if a boy spent half as much ingenuity on something important . . ." But like the rest of Honolulu, he read eagerly on.

"Does not this amazing fecundity aboard the brigantines suggest rather directly that in the crowded staterooms there must have been one additional occupation whereby the idle time was whiled away, an occupation which our forefathers, through considerations of modesty, did not report to us? I think so.

"In what I am now about to discuss, I consider myself far from an expert, but from having hung around poolrooms and from arguments with my betters during football rallies, I think it fairly well established that for a human male to impregnate a human female—and God forbid that he try his tricks on any other—requires on the average not one act of intercourse but at least four. As I understand it, that is the normal experience of the human race, popular novels and sentimental movies that rely upon lucky coincidence notwithstanding. Therefore, it can be seen that for the nine pregnancies achieved aboard the *Thetis* . . ."

Hoxworth slumped in his chair. "This boy has a diseased mind," he groaned. "Now he's getting clinical!" Hoxworth was right: young Bromley had produced all sorts of hilarious statistical tables and at one point had fortified them with resounding rhetoric: "I think I may be allowed the privilege of at least taking into consideration the theories lately advanced by His Holiness in the Vatican, which theories establish beyond much doubt the fact that for the human female there is a period which the ecclesiastics designate as 'safe,' and although it is naturally repugnant for me, a Congregationalist, to rely upon the word of a Catholic dignitary in discussing the secret lives of a gang of Calvinists, and although the nicety of the situation is not lost upon me, nevertheless . . ."

The phone rang, the first of many calls that were to be made that night. It was Hewlett Janders and he was screaming, "Did you see that goddamned photograph that your goddamned son had of my daughter . . ."

"Don't roar, Hewlett! I just got the wretched thing."

"Have you finished it yet, Hoxworth?"

"No, I'm only on page five."

"Then you haven't got to the part yet where he says, and listen Hoxworth, I'm quoting your son. He adds up the total numbers of acts of sexual intercourse . . . Goddamn it, Hoxworth, what kind of monster have you reared?"

Later, after a dozen similar interruptions, Hoxworth reached his son's first conclusion: "So if we consider all these facts, which I hold to be statistically incontrovertible, we find that the brig *Thetis,* for sure, and all the other missionary ships probably, were not the angelic torture barges we have been taught, but —and I use the phrase literally—floating hells of concupiscence."

"No wonder they've been phoning," Hoxworth moaned. But his cup was far from running over, it had, in fact, reached not much over the sugar line in the bottom, for in succeeding pages Bromley discussed the heart of his investigations and shared his findings.

"What has always intrigued the scientific mind regarding the mission ships is the cramped nature of the staterooms. Again and again we have evidence that four men and four women, most of them married less than a week before entering the ship, and all of them total strangers, lived together in what could best be termed a rabbit warren. We know from incontrovertible testimony that months went by without either husband or wife ever removing his long red-flannel underwear, and we know that the heads of one couple had to be less than two feet from the heads of three other couples, with only a flimsy cloth barrier separating one family from another. Furthermore, as the following picture amply proves, an average-sized man could not stretch out full length . . ."

In anguish Hoxworth Hale turned to the picture, and his suspicion was correct. The average man whose knees were plainly doubled up was he, caught with a silly look on his face by young Whip Janders and his Leica.

Mercifully, the phone rang before he could digest the full ridiculousness of his situation. It was the headmaster at Punahou: "I suppose you've seen it, Hoxworth."

"How could such a thing have happened, Larry?" Hale groaned.

"We can never probe the minds of adolescents," the headmaster confessed.

"Does it seem as bad to you as it does to me?" Hoxworth asked.

"I haven't the time to judge degrees, Hoxworth. You realize, I'm sure, that this means . . ."

"He's got to go, Larry. I realize that."

"Thank you, Hoxworth. The important thing is, he's got to get into Yale. I've taken the liberty of dispatching a cable to my old friend Callinson at The Hill. There's a chance they'll take him. I've helped Callinson in the past."

"You think he can still make Yale?"

"We won't condemn the boy in our report, Hoxworth. Of that you can be sure."

"I appreciate this, Larry. But tell me, does this essay indicate a diseased mind?"

There was a pause, and the headmaster said reflectively, "I think we'd better leave it the way I said first. About adolescents, we can never know."

"Do you know where Bromley is?"

"No, Hoxworth, I don't."

The call ended and Hale sat in the lowering darkness. The phone immediately resumed jangling but Hoxworth let it ring. It would be some parent raising hell about what Bromley had said regarding their ancestors. "Damn them all!" Hoxworth cried in real confusion as he watched the lights of Honolulu come on, that nightly miracle that pleased him so much. His family had brought electricity to the city, just as they had brought so much more, but now that a Hale was in trouble, the vultures would want to rip him apart. Therefore, when the front doorbell rang insistently, Hoxworth was inclined to let it ring; he would not parade his hurt to the vultures. Let them pick the bones to their own ghoulish cackling.

The door opened and a cheery male voice cried, "Hey! Anybody in?" Hoxworth could hear footsteps crossing the first big room and he had a panicky thought: "It's some cheeky reporter!" And he started to run for it, when the voice called, "Hey, Mr. Hale. You're the one . . ."

"Who are you?" Hoxworth asked stiffly, turning unwillingly to see a brash-looking young man in flannel trousers and white linen coat. He carried three books under his arm, and looked disarmingly at ease.

"I'm Red Kenderdine. Brom's English teacher." He looked at a chair, and when Hale failed to respond, asked, "Mind if I sit down?"

"I don't want to talk about this thing, Mr. Kenderdine."

"Have you seen Brom yet?"

"No!" Hale snapped. "Where is he?"

"Good. I wanted very much to be the first to talk with you, Mr. Hale."

"Why?"

"I don't want you to make a serious mistake, Mr. Hale."

"What do you mean?"

"First, will you agree to honor what I'm about to say as coming from a personal friend . . . and not from a Punahou master?"

"I don't even know you," Hale replied stuffily. He had never liked educators. To him they were a mealy lot.

"But Bromley does."

Hale looked at the young man suspiciously. "Are you in any way involved . . ."

"Mr. Hale, I come here as a friend, not as a conspirator."

"Excuse me, Kenderdine. Bromley has spoken well of you."

"I'm glad," the young instructor said coldly. "I'm here to speak well of him."

"You're about the only one in Honolulu . . ."

"Exactly. Mr. Hale, have you read Brom's essay?"

"All I could stomach."

"Apart from the photograph of you, which is unforgivable, did you recognize your son's essay as a marvelous piece of irony."

"Irony! It was plain unadulterated filth. Sewer stuff."

"No, Mr. Hale, it was first rate compassionate irony. I wish I had the talent your son has."

"You wish . . ." Hoxworth sputtered and stared incredulously at his visitor. "You sound like one of the elements we're trying to control in this community."

Kenderdine blew air from his lower lip into his nose and took a patient respite before daring to answer. Then he handed Mr. Hale three books. "These are for you, sir."

"What do I want with them?" Hoxworth growled.

"They will help you understand the extraordinarily gifted young man who happens to be your son," Kenderdine explained.

"Never heard of them," Hale snorted, at which the young master lost his temper slightly and said something he immediately wished he could recall.

"I suppose you haven't sir. They happen to be three of the greatest novels of our time."

"Oh," Hale grunted, missing the sarcasm. "Well, I still never heard of them. What're they about?"

"Family histories, Mr. Hale. *A Lost Lady* is a great masterpiece. I wish everyone in Hawaii could read *The Grandmothers* by Glenway Wescott. It would explain so much about Honolulu and Punahou. And this last one should be read by everyone who comes from a large family with many mixed-up ramifications. Kate O'Brien's *Without My Cloak*. It's laid in Ireland, but it's about you and Bromley, Mr. Hale."

"You know, Kenderdine, I don't like you. I don't like your manner, and I think if the truth were known, Bromley probably got off on the wrong foot largely because of your bad influence. I don't know what Punahou's . . ."

"Mr. Hale, I don't like you either," the young instructor said evenly. "I don't like a man who can read one of the wittiest, most promising bits of writing I've ever known a schoolboy to write and not even recognize what his son has accomplished. Mr. Hale, do you know why Hawaii is so dreadfully dull, why it's such a wasteland of the human intellect? Because nobody speculates about these islands. Nobody ever writes about them. Aren't you ever perplexed over the fact Nebraskans write fine novels about Nebraska, and people in Mississippi write wonderful things about Mississippi? Why doesn't anybody ever write about Hawaii?"

"There was Stevenson," Hale protested, adding brightly, "and Jack London!"

"Complete junk," Kenderdine snapped disdainfully.

"Do you mean to sit there and tell me that you teach our children that Jack London . . ."

"What he wrote about Hawaii? Complete junk. What anybody else has written about Hawaii? Complete junk, Mr. Hale."

"Who are you to judge your betters?"

"I'm stating facts. And the biggest fact is that nobody writes about Hawaii because the great families, like yours, don't encourage their sons and daughters to think . . . to feel . . . and certainly not to report. You've got a good thing here, and you don't want any questions asked."

"Young man, I've heard enough from you," Hoxworth said stiffly. "I recognize you as a type too dangerous to work with young people. So, as a member of the board at Punahou . . ."

"You're going to fire me?"

"I would be derelict to my duty if I did otherwise, Mr. Kenderdine."

The young man relaxed insolently in the chair and stared at the lights of Pearl Harbor. "And I would be derelict to my duty as a human being who loves these islands, Mr. Hale, if I failed to tell you that I for one don't give a good goddamn what you do or when you do it. I've watched you try to hold education back. I've watched you try to hold labor back. I've watched you try to hold the legislature back. There was nothing I could do about those crimes against the larger community. But when you try to hold back a proven talent, your own son, who if he were encouraged could write the book that would illuminate these islands, then I object. I didn't know anything about your son's rare and wonderful essay until I saw it. I got my copy late, but I will always treasure it. When he becomes a great man, I'll treasure it doubly. I detect in it certain of my phrases, and I'm glad he learned at least something from me."

"You're through, Kenderdine! You're out!" Hale paced back and forth before the big windows, waiting for the insolent young man to leave, but the English teacher lit a cigarette, puffed twice, and slowly rose.

"I am through, Mr. Hale. But not because of your action. I was through when I came here. Because I won't tolerate your kind of crap a day longer. I've joined the navy."

"God help America if the navy takes men like you," Hale snorted.

"And when this war comes to Hawaii, Mr. Hale, as it inevitably must, not only will I be gone, but you will be, too. Everything you stand for. The labor you hate is going to organize. The Japanese you despise will begin to vote. And who knows, perhaps even your cozy little deal with the military, whereby you and they run the islands, will be blasted. I'm through for the time being, Mr. Hale. You're through forever."

He bowed gravely, jabbed his forefinger three times at the books and winked. But as he left the room he said gently, "I've allowed you to fire me, Mr. Hale. Now you do one thing for me. Read the essay again and discover the love your son holds for the missionaries. Only a mind steeped in true love can write irony. The others write satire." And he was gone.

Alone, Hoxworth decided to call the police to find where his son was, but he reconsidered. Then Hewlett Janders stormed over, big, robust, full of action and profanity. Hoxworth found the interview rather confusing because Hewlett on reconsideration didn't want to horsewhip Bromley at all. He thought the essay a damned good bit of skylarking and said it would probably do the mission families as much good as anything that had happened in years.

"Whole town's laughing their belly off," he roared. "I thought that picture of you in the bunk was downright killing, Hoxworth. And what about that paragraph where he sums up: 'So by projection we can assume . . .' Where's your copy, Hoxworth?" He glimpsed the mimeographed publication under a davenport pillow, picked it up and thumbed through it. "By God, Hoxworth, that picture of you in the bunk is worth ten thousand votes if you ever decide to run for office. Only thing you've ever done proves you're human. Here's the part I wanted. 'So by projection we can estimate that within an area less than six feet by five, during a voyage of 207 days, no less than 197 separate acts of sexual intercourse must have taken place under conditions which prevented any of the female participants from taking off their long flannel underwear or any of the men from stretching out full length in the bunks.' Now here's the part I like," Janders laughed robustly. " 'Against its will the mind is driven to haunting suspicions: What actually went on in those crowded staterooms? What orgies must have transpired? Out of delicate regard for the proprieties I shall not pursue the probabilities, for they are too harrowing to discuss in public, but I recommend that each reader develop this matter logically to its inevitable conclusions: What did go on?' " Big Hewlett Janders slammed the essay against his leg and shouted, "Y'know, Hoxworth, I often used to ask myself that very question. How the hell do you think the old folks did it?"

"How should I know?" Hoxworth pleaded.

"Damn it all, man, it was you they photographed hunched up in one of the bunks!" Janders roared.

"Does anyone know where Bromley is?" Hale asked stiffly.

"Sure," Janders laughed. "But don't change the subject. Don't you agree that the bit I just read is hilarious? By God, I can see prim Lucinda Whipple turning cartwheels when she reads that. One fellow at the club said your boy Brom must be a genius."

"Where is he?" Hale insisted.

"Whole gang of them are having chop suey at Asia Kee's. Every fifteen minutes somebody yells, 'Author! Author!' and Brom takes a bow. Then they all sing a dirge somebody made up, 'Farewell, Punahou!' I suppose you heard that my boy Whip also got expelled. For taking the pictures. Damned glad Mandy didn't, too. Posing like that with your boy." But his raucous laughter proved that he wasn't too concerned.

"Did you see them . . . at the chop suey place?" Hoxworth asked.

"Yeah, I stopped by . . . Well, hell, I figured, it's their big night, so I dropped off a couple bottles of Scotch."

"You gave these outrageous children . . ."

"What I stopped by to see you about, Hoxworth, is that I just called that

tutoring school near Lawrenceville, and they've agreed to take Whip and Brom
. . . if you want to send him . . . and guarantee to get them into Yale. That's the
only problem, really, Hoxworth. Get the boys into Yale."

"What school are you talking about?"

"What's the name? It's right near Lawrenceville. Mark Hewlett sent his boy
there when he got busted out of Punahou. They got him into Yale." Seeing the
three novels on the low table, Janders picked one up in the way men do who
never read books, and asked, "You drowning your sorrows in a good book?"

"Do you know an English master at Punahou named Kenderdine?"

"Yes. Crew-cut job."

"I had a fearful scene with him. He's at the root of this business, I'm
convinced."

"He's a troublemaker. Some jerkwater college like Wisconsin or Wesleyan.
I keep telling Larry, 'Get Yale men. They may not be so smart but in the long
run they give you less trouble.' But Larry always drags in some genius . . . Yes,
Kenderdine's Wisconsin."

"He's no longer Punahou."

"You fire him?"

"I certainly did. But you know, Hewlett, he said about the same thing you
did. Said Bromley's essay would do us all a lot of good. Get people laughing.
He said it was crystal-clear that Brom wrote the essay with love and affection
. . . that he wasn't lampooning the missionaries."

"That's what one of the judges at the club thought," Janders recalled. "But
I'll tell you what, Hoxworth. Seems it was my son who took the photo of you
in the bunk, proving that sex was impossible. Well, if you can handle him, you're
welcome to thrash hell out of him. I won't try because he can lick me."

The door banged and Hoxworth Hale was left alone in the big room
overlooking Honolulu. For a while he studied the never tedious pattern of
lights, as they came and went along the foreshores of the bay, and the bustling
activity at Pearl Harbor, and the starry sky to the south: his city, the city of his
people, the fruit of his family's energy. He leafed his son's startling essay and
saw again the provocative last sentence: "We can therefore conclude, I think,
that whereas our fathers often paced the deck of the *Thetis,* wrestling with their
consciences, they usually wound up by hustling below to the cramped bunks,
where they wrestled with their wives."

Idly he picked up the three books Kenderdine had left. Hefting the Irish
novel, he found it too heavy and put it aside. He looked at Willa Cather's slim
book, *A Lost Lady,* but its title seemed much too close to his own case, and he
did not want to read about lovely ladies who become lost, for it seemed to be
happening throughout his group. That left *The Grandmothers,* which was neither too heavy in bulk nor too close to home, although had he known when he
started reading, it was really the most dangerous of the three, for it was a barbed
shaft directed right at the heart of Honolulu and its wonderful matriarchies.

To his surprise, he was still reading the story of Wisconsin's rare old
women, when the lights of Honolulu sadly surrendered their battle against the
rising dawn. The door creaked open gingerly, and Bromley Whipple Hale,
flushed with pride of authorship and Uncle Hewlett's good whiskey, stumbled
into the room.

"Hi, Dad."

"Hello, Bromley."

The handsome young fellow, with indelible Whipple charm stamped on his bright features, slumped into a chair and groaned. "It's been quite a day, Dad."

Grudgingly, Hoxworth observed: "You seem to have cut quite a niche for yourself in the local mausoleum."

"Dad, I got thrown out of school."

"I know. Uncle Hewlett's already made plans for you and Whipple to get into one of the good cram schools. The one thing you have to safeguard is your Yale entrance."

"Dad, I was going to speak about this later, but I guess now's . . . I don't believe I want to go to Yale. Now wait a minute! I'd like to try either Alabama or Cornell."

"Alabama! Cornell!" Hoxworth exploded. "Those jerkwater . . . Good heavens, you might just as well go to the University of Hawaii."

"That's what I wanted to do . . . seeing as how I want to write about Hawaii. But Mr. Kenderdine says that Alabama and Cornell have fine classes in creative writing."

"Bromley, where did you ever get the idea that you want to be a writer? This isn't a job for a man. I've been relying on you to . . ."

"You'll have to rely upon somebody else, Dad. There's lots of good, bright young men from Harvard and Penn business schools who'd be glad . . ."

"What do you know about Harvard and Penn?"

"Mr. Kenderdine told us they were the best in the country . . . in business."

Hoxworth stiffened and growled, "I suppose your Mr. Kenderdine said that anyone who bothered to go into business . . ."

"Oh, no! He thinks business is the modern ocean for contemporary Francis Drakes and Jean Lafittes."

"Weren't they pirates?" Hoxworth asked suspiciously.

"They were adventurers. Mr. Kenderdine told Whip Janders he ought to try like the devil to get into Harvard Business School."

"But he didn't tell you that, did he?"

"No, Dad. He thinks I can write." There was a long pause in the big room as the pastel lights of morning spread across the city below, and one of those rare moments developed in which a son can talk to his father, and if Hoxworth Hale had growled in his customary manner, the moment would have passed, like the ghost of Pele ignoring one whom she considered not worth a warning, but Hoxworth's personal god sat heavily on his shoulder, and he said nothing so that his son continued: "You and your father and all your generations used to sit up here, Dad, and look down at Honolulu and dream of controlling it. Every streetcar that ran, every boat that came to port did so at your command. I appreciate that. It's a noble drive, a civilizing one. Sometimes I've caught a glimpse of such a life for myself. But it's always passed, Dad. I just don't have that vision, and you've got to find someone who has, or you and I will both go broke."

"Don't you have any vision at all?" Hoxworth asked quietly, back in the shadows.

"Oh, yes!" The handsome young fellow pointed to Honolulu, lying tribute beneath them, and confided for the first time to anyone: "I want to control this city too, Dad. But I want to bore into its heart to see what makes it run. Why the Chinese buy land and the Japanese don't. Why the old families like ours intermarry and intermarry until damned near half of them have somebody locked away in upstairs rooms. I want to know who really owns the waterfront, and what indignities a man must suffer before he can become an admiral at Pearl

Harbor. And when I know all these things, I'm going to write a book . . . maybe lots of them . . . and they won't be books like the ones you read. They'll be like *The Grandmothers* and *Without My Cloak,* books you never heard of. And when I know, and when I have written what I know, then I'll control Honolulu in a manner you never dreamed of. Because I'll control its imagination."

He was slightly drunk and fell back in his chair. His father watched him for some minutes, during which fragments of *The Grandmothers* repeated themselves in Hoxworth's agitated mind. Finally the father said, "I suppose you don't want to bundle off to the cram school?"

"No, Dad."

"What will you do?"

"There's no sweat getting into either Cornell or Alabama. I'll register Monday at McKinley High."

Hoxworth winced and asked, "Why McKinley?"

"The kids call it Manila Prep and I'd sort of like to know some Filipinos."

"You already know . . . Doesn't Consul Adujo's son go to Punahou?"

"I want to know real Filipinos, Dad."

Hoxworth Hale started to rear back, as if he were about to tell his son that he would tolerate no nonsense about McKinley High School, but as words began to formulate he saw his son etched against the pale morning light, and the silhouette was not of Bromley Hoxworth, the radical essayist who had outraged Hawaii, but of Hoxworth Hale, the radical art critic who had charged Yale University with thievery; and a bond of identity was established, and the father swallowed his words of reprimand.

"Tell me one thing, Bromley. This Mr. Kenderdine? Can his ideas be trusted?"

"The best, Dad. Unemotional, yet loaded with fire. You heard, I suppose, that we're losing him. Joining the navy. Says there's bound to be war."

There was a painful silence and the boy concluded: "Maybe that's why I want to go to McKinley now, Dad. There mayn't be too much time." He started to bed but realized that he owed his father some kind of apology, for the mimeographed essay had created a storm which he, the author, had not anticipated. "About that photograph of you, Dad . . . What I mean is, if I do become a writer, I'll be a good one." And he stumbled off to bed.

IN 1941 THE Thanksgiving Day football game was largely a replay of the 1938 classic, with Punahou pitted against McKinley, but this time two Sakagawa boys played for Punahou; for Hoxworth Hale and his committee of alumni had been so pleased with Tadao's performance that they had automatically extended scholarships to the younger boys, Minoru the tackle and Shigeo the halfback. Thus it was that the former privy cleaner Kamejiro sat in the stadium along with his wife and his two older boys—Goro was in army uniform—cheering for Punahou. A newspaperman remarked: "It's a revolution in Hawaii when Sakagawa the barber and Hoxworth Hale support the same team."

Throughout Hawaii these minor miracles of accommodation were taking place. When a child felt pain he said, "Itai, itai!" which was Japanese. When he finished work it was pauhana. He had aloha for his friends. He tried to avoid pilikia and when he flattered girls it was hoomalimali, all Hawaiian words. He rarely ate candy, but kept his pockets filled with seed, a delicious Chinese confection tasting like licorice, sugar and salt all at once and made of dried cherries or plums. After a dance he did not eat hot dogs; he ate a bowl of saimin,

Japanese noodles, with teriyaki barbecue. Or he had chop suey. For dessert he had a Portuguese malasada, a sweet, sticky fried doughnut, crackling with sugar. It was an island community and it had absorbed the best from many cultures. On this day, as Punahou battled McKinley in a game that was more thrilling to Honolulu than the Rose Bowl game was to California, Punahou, the haole heaven, fielded a team containing two Sakagawas, a Kee, two Kalanianaoles, a Rodriques and assorted Hales, Hewletts, Janderses and Hoxworths. That year Punahou won, 27-6, and Shigeo Sakagawa scored two of the touchdowns, so that as he went home through the streets of Kakaako the perpetual toughs taunted him contemptuously with being a haole-lover, but they no longer tried to assault the Sakagawa boys. They knew better.

Logically, the Sakagawas should have been able—what with the aid of scholarships for three of the boys—to retire Reiko-chan from the barbershop, allowing her to enroll in the university, but just as the family had enough money saved ahead for this, the consulate on Nuuanu Street convened the Japanese community and told them gravely, "The war in China grows more costly than ever. We have got to assist our homeland now. Please, please remember your vows to the emperor." And the fund had gone to help Japan resist the evil of China's aggression, though Goro asked his friends, "How can China be the aggressor when it's Japan that's done the invading?" He wanted to ask his father about this, but Kamejiro, in these trying days of late 1941, had pressing problems which he could not share with his children, nor with anyone else for that matter, except Mr. Ishii.

They began when Hawaii established a committee of American citizens whose job it was to visit all Japanese homes, beseeching the parents to write to Japan to have the names of their children removed from village registers, thus canceling their Japanese citizenship. Hoxworth Hale was the committee member who visited the Sakagawas, and with Reiko as interpreter he explained on the day after Thanksgiving: "Mr. Sakagawa, Japan is a nation that insists upon dual citizenship. But since your five fine children were born here, legally they're Americans. Emotionally they're Americans too. But because you registered their names in your Hiroshima village years ago they are also Japanese citizens. Suppose the war in Europe spreads. What if Japan and America get into it on opposite sides? Your sons might face serious difficulties if you allow them to retain two citizenships. To protect them, get it cleaned up."

The five children added their pleas. "Look, Pop," they argued. "We respect Japan, but we're going to be Americans." Their father agreed with them. He nodded. He told Mr. Hale that it ought to be done, but as always before, he refused to sign any papers. This the children could not understand and they sided with Mr. Hale when he said, "It really isn't right, Mr. Sakagawa, for you to penalize your sons, especially with three of them being Punahou boys."

But Sakagawa-san was adamant, and after Mr. Hale had left, and his family began hammering him with their arguments, he felt caged and finally kicked a chair and shouted, "I'm going away where a man can get some peace." He sought out Mr. Ishii and sat glumly with him.

"Our evil has caught up with us, old friend," he said.

"It was bound to, sooner or later," Mr. Ishii reflected sadly.

"The children are insisting that I write to Hiroshima and take their names off the village registry."

"You aren't going to do it, are you?" Mr. Ishii asked hopefully.

"How can I? And bring disgrace upon us all?"

The two men, now gray in their late fifties, sat moodily and thought of the shame in which they were involved. In their village Kamejiro had been legally married by proxy to the pretty girl Sumiko, by whom he had had five children, all duly reported; and Mr. Ishii had been legally married to Mori Yoriko, no children reported. Yet by convenient switching, Kamejiro had married Yoriko, American style, and she was the mother of the children; Mr. Ishii had likewise married Sumiko, and she had turned out to be a prostitute. How could they explain these things to the Japanese consulate on Nuuanu Street? How could they explain this accidental bigamy to the five children? Above all, how could they explain it to the village authorities in Hiroshima? "All Japan would be ashamed," Mr. Ishii said gloomily. "Kamejiro, we better leave things just as they are."

"But the children are fighting with me. Today even Mr. Hale came to the house. He had the papers in his hands."

"Of course he had the papers!" Mr. Ishii agreed. "But you watch his face when you try to explain who your wife is. Kamejiro, friend, let the matter drop."

But on Saturday, December 6, Mr. Hale returned to the shack and said, "You are the last holdout on my list, Mr. Sakagawa. Please end your sons' dual citizenship. With Goro here in the army, and Tadao and Minoru in the R.O.T.C., it's something you've got to do."

"I can't," Kamejiro said through his interpreter, Goro, who had a weekend pass from Schofield Barracks.

"I don't understand the old man," Goro said, smoothing out his army uniform, of which he was obviously proud. "He's loyal to Japan, but he's no great flag waver. I'll argue with him again when you're gone, Mr. Hale."

"His obstinacy looks very bad," Mr. Hale warned. "Especially with you in the army. I've got to report it, of course."

Goro shrugged his shoulders. "Have you ever tried to argue with a Japanese papa-san? My pop has some crazy fixed idea. But I'll see what I can do."

That Saturday night the entire Sakagawa family battled out this problem of dual citizenship, in Japanese. "I respect your country, Pop," Goro said. "I remember when I had the fight with the priest about going back to Japan. When I finally surrendered, I really intended to go. But you know what's happened, Pop. Football . . . now the army. Let's face it, Pop. I'm an American."

"Me too," Tadao agreed.

The sons hammered at him, and finally he said, "I want you to be Americans. When I put a newspaper picture like that over the sink, 'Four Sakagawa Stars,' don't you think I'm proud? Long ago I admitted you'd never again be Japanese."

"Then take our names off the citizenship registry in Japan."

"I can't," he repeated for the fiftieth time.

"Damn it, Pop, sometimes you make me mad!" Goro cried.

Kamejiro stood up. He stared at his sons and said, "There will be no shouting. Remember that you are decent Japanese sons." They came to attention, and he added sorrowfully, "There is a good reason why I cannot change the register."

"But why?" the boys insisted.

Through the long night the argument lasted, and stubborn Kamejiro was unable to explain why he was powerless to act; for even though his sons were American, he was forever Japanese, and he expected one day to return to Hiroshima; when he got there he could quietly tell his friends about the mix-up in Hawaii, but he could not do so by letter. He himself could not write, and he could not trust others to write for him. It was two o'clock in the morning when he went to bed, and as he pulled the covers up about his shoulders, on a group of aircraft carriers six hundred miles away, a task force of Japanese airmen, many of them from Hiroshima, prepared to bomb Pearl Harbor.

Shigeo, the youngest of the Sakagawas, rose early next morning and pedaled his bicycle down to Cable Wireless, where he worked on Sundays delivering cables that had accumulated during the night and those which would come in throughout the day. His first handful he got at seven-thirty and they were all addressed to people in the Diamond Head area like the Hales and the Whipples, who lived in big houses overlooking the city.

He had reached Waikiki when he heard from the vicinity of Pearl Harbor a series of dull explosions and he thought: "More fleet exercises. Wonder what it means?"

He turned his back on Pearl Harbor and pedaled up an impressive lane leading to the estate of Hoxworth Hale, and while waiting in the porte-cochere he looked back toward the naval base and saw columns of dense black smoke curling up into the morning sunlight. More explosions followed and he saw a series of planes darting and zigzagging through the bright blue overhead. "Pretty impressive," he thought.

He rang the Hale bell again, and in a moment Hoxworth Hale appeared in a dark business suit, wearing collar and tie, as if such a leader of the community were not allowed to relax. Shig noticed that the man's face was colorless and his hands trembling. The radio was making noises from a room Shig could not see, but what it was saying he could not determine. Gulping in a manner not common to the Hales, Hoxworth pushed open the screen door and said to the star of the Punahou eleven, "My God, Shig. Your country has declared war on mine."

For a moment Shig could not comprehend what had been said. Pointing back to Pearl Harbor he asked, "They having a make-believe invasion?"

"No," Hoxworth Hale replied in a hollow, terrified voice. "Japan is bombing Honolulu."

"Japan?" Shig looked up at the darting planes and saw that where they passed, explosions followed and that as the planes sped toward the mountains, puffs of gunfire traced them through the sky. "Oh, my God!" the boy gasped. "What's happened?"

Hoxworth held the door open, ignoring the cable, and indicated that Shig should come inside, and they went to the radio, whose announcer was repeating frantically, yet with a voice that tried to avoid the creation of panic: "I repeat. This is not a military exercise. Japanese planes are bombing Honolulu. I repeat. This is not a joke. This is war."

Hoxworth Hale covered his face with his hands and muttered, "How awful this is going to be." Looking at bright-eyed Shig, who was only a year older than his own son, he said, "You'll need all the courage you have, son."

Shig replied, "Outside you said, 'Your country has declared war on my country.' Yours and mine are both the same, Mr. Hale. I'm an American."

"I'm sorry, Shig. That's a mistake many of us will make in the next few days. God, look at that explosion!" The two watchers winced as an enormous thunder filled the air, accompanied by a slowly rising pillar of jet-black smoke that billowed and twisted upward from the ruins at Pearl Harbor. "Something terrible is taking place," Hale mumbled.

Then from a stairway behind him came a haunted voice, weak and piping like a child's, and he made as if to push Shigeo out the door, but before he could do so the person on the stairs had come down into the room and stood facing her husband and his visitor. It was Mrs. Hale, a frail and very beautiful woman of thirty-eight. She had light auburn hair and wide, level eyes that found difficulty in focusing. She wore a wispy dressing gown such as Shig had never seen before outside the movies, and she walked haltingly. "What is the great noise I hear, Hoxworth?" she asked.

"Malama, you shouldn't have come down here," her husband admonished.

"But I heard a shooting," she explained softly, "and I wondered if you were in trouble."

At this moment one of the bombing planes was driven off course by a burst of unexpected anti-aircraft fire, and it swerved from its planned escape route, winging swiftly over the Diamond Head area, and as it passed, Shig and Mr. Hale could see on its underbelly the red circle of Japan. "You'd better go now," Mr. Hale said.

"You haven't signed for the cable," Shig pointed out, and as Hoxworth took the cable and signed the receipt, his wife walked ghostlike to the door and looked toward Pearl Harbor, where the bombs were still exploding.

"Ahhhhhh!" she shrieked in a weird guttural cry. "It's war and my son will be killed." Throwing her filmy sleeves over her face, she ran to her husband, sobbing, "It's war, and Bromley will not come back alive."

Hale, holding his wife in his right arm, returned the receipt with his left hand and gripped Shigeo by the shoulder. "You must not speak of this," he said.

"I won't," Shigeo promised, not understanding exactly what it was that he was expected to keep secret.

Kamejiro had risen at six that morning and had gone down to the barbershop to sterilize everything again, for part of the success of his shop stemmed from his mania for cleanliness. Now he was back home waiting for his breakfast. His wife Yoriko, who never did her customers' laundry on Sunday, was leisurely preparing a meal, having already fed Shigeo. Goro, enjoying his pass, was sleeping late, but Tadao, who was in the R.O.T.C. at the university, had already risen. Reiko-chan was dressed and ready to go to an early service at the Community Church in Moiliili. Minoru, nineteen and already in training for basketball at Punahou, was also sleeping.

The first to comprehend what was happening was Goro, for when the bombs struck he thundered out of bed, ran in his shorts into the yard and shouted, "This is no game. Somebody's declared war!" He ran to the radio he had built for the family and heard official confirmation of his suspicions: "Enemy planes of unknown origin are bombing Pearl Harbor and Hickam Field." Turning to his family he announced in Japanese: "I think Japan has declared war against us."

The escape route used by those bombers who attacked the eastern segment of Pearl Harbor carried them across Kakaako, and now as they flashed by in triumph the Sakagawa family gathered on their minute lawn surrounded by flowers and watched the bright red rising sun of Japan dart by. As soon as the enemy was identified Goro shouted, "Tad! We better report right away!" Accordingly, he hurried into his army uniform and hitchhiked a ride out to Schofield Barracks, while Tadao and Minoru climbed into their R.O.T.C. uniforms, Tadao reporting to the university and Minoru to Punahou. But before the boys left, they bowed ceremoniously to their bewildered father.

The impact of these sudden happenings on Kamejiro staggered him. In an uncomprehending daze he sat down on the steps of his shack and stared at the sky, where puffs of ack-ack traced the departure of the Japanese planes. Three times he saw the red sun of his homeland flash past, and once he saw the evil snout of a low-flying Japanese fighter spewing machine-gun bullets ineffectively into the bay. He tried to focus his thoughts on what was happening and upon his sons' prompt departure for the American army; but the inchoate thoughts that were rising in his mind were not allowed to become words. Japan must have been in great trouble to have done such a thing. The boys must have been in great trouble if they left so promptly to defend America. That was as far as he could go.

At eleven o'clock that Sunday morning a group of four secret police, armed and with a black hearse waiting on Kakaako Street, rushed in the Sakagawa home and arrested Kamejiro. "Sakagawa," said one who spoke Japanese. "We've been watching you for a long time. You're a dynamiter, and you're to go into a concentration camp."

"Wait!" Reiko protested. "You know who the Sakagawa boys are. At Punahou. What's this about concentration camp?"

"He's a dynamiter, Miss Sakagawa. He gave money to Japan. And he refused to denationalize you. It's the pokey for him." The efficient team whisked bewildered Kamejiro into the hearse and it drove on, picking up other suspected seditionists.

At eleven-thirty Shigeo pedaled by on his Cable Wireless bicycle to share with the family the frightening things he had been seeing, but he said nothing of them, for Reiko's announcement that their father had been hauled away to concentration camp stunned him. This was really war, and he and all other Japanese were instantly involved. "Pop couldn't have been doing anything wrong, could he?"

The brother and sister looked at each other and it was Shigeo who formulated their doubt: "On the other hand, Pop used to prowl around every night."

"Shigeo!" Reiko-chan cried. "That's unworthy!"

"I'm only trying to think like the F.B.I.," Shig explained in justification.

They were further disturbed when Mr. Ishii, in a state of maximum excitement, ran up with this startling news: "The Japanese army is making a landing at the other end of the island. They've already captured Maui and Kauai."

"That's impossible!" Shigeo cried. "I've been all over Honolulu this morning, and I heard nothing like that."

"You'll see!" the quick little man assured them. "By tomorrow night Japan will be in complete control." To the amazement of the Sakagawa children, Mr. Ishii seemed positively exhilarated by the prospect, and Shigeo caught him by the arm.

"You be careful what you're saying, Mr. Ishii! The F.B.I. just arrested Pop."

"When the Japanese win he'll be a hero," the little man exulted. "Now everyone who laughs at Japanese will behave themselves. You watch what happens when the troops march into Honolulu." He waved a warning finger at them and dashed on down the street.

"I think he's out of his mind," Shigeo said sadly as he watched the community gossip disappear. As Mr. Ishii turned the corner, a patrol came through Kakaako, announcing with a loud-speaker: "All Japanese are under house arrest. Do not leave your homes. I repeat. Do not leave your homes."

Shigeo went up to them and said, "I'm the Sunday delivery boy for Cable Wireless."

There was a moment of hesitation, after which the patrol made the type of decision that was going to be made many times that day throughout Hawaii: the Japanese are all spies and they are all disloyal; they must be clamped into house arrest; but we know this particular Japanese and the work he is doing is essential, therefore he is excused. The patrol looked at Shig's bicycle with its clear marking, and one man asked, "Aren't you the kid who plays for Punahou?"

"Yes," Shig replied.

"You're all right. You go ahead."

"You got a pass I could use?" Shig asked. "I don't want to get shot at."

"Sure. Use this."

At two o'clock that afternoon, Shig reported to his main office for his fourth batch of telegrams and he was handed one addressed to General Lansing Hommer, but since Shig knew that the general lived at the extreme end of his route, he tucked that particular message into the bottom of his pile, and as he pedaled through the western part of Honolulu toward Pearl Harbor and saw the devastation he understood better than most what had happened and what was about to happen. From the porch of one house where he delivered a cable, he could see the anchorage at Pearl Harbor itself, and alongside the piers he saw the stricken ships, lying on their sides and belching flames.

The man to whom he had given the telegram said, "Well, the goddamned Japs hit everything they aimed at. Papers said Japs couldn't fly planes because they were cross-eyed. You ask me, we better get some cross-eyed pilots. And some gunners, too. I stood on this porch for three hours and I didn't see our men hit one goddamned Jap plane. What do you think of that?"

"You mean they all got away?"

"Every one of the bastards."

"Some monkey was telling me the Japanese have already landed," Shig said.

"They'll never make it," the man replied. "So far the Japs have hit only the navy, which is a bunch of do-nothings anyway. When they try to land they run up against the dogfaces. That'll be different. I got two sons in the infantry. Plenty tough. You got anyone in uniform?"

"Two brothers."

"Infantry, I hope?"

"Yep. They're plenty tough, too."

"I don't think the yellow bastards'll make it," the man said as he ripped open his telegram.

At four thirty-one that hot, terrifying afternoon Shigeo Sakagawa reached the end of his route, and he pedaled his Cable Wireless bicycle up on the long drive leading to the residence of General Hommer, where the ashen-faced military leader took the cable and scribbled his name in pencil across the receipt. His command had been virtually destroyed. The islands he was supposed to protect were at the mercy of the enemy. Even his own headquarters had been strafed with impunity. At the end of this debacle he was forced to receive cables from Washington, but this particular one was more than he could stomach. He read it, swore, crumpled it up, and threw it on the floor. As it slowly unfolded itself, Shig could read that it came from the War Department. It warned General Hommer that from secret sources Washington had concluded that Japan might attempt to attack Pearl Harbor. With all the instantaneous systems of communications available to the government, Washington could have rushed the message through in time to prevent the holocaust, but it had transmitted this most urgent of contemporary cables by ordinary commercial wireless. It arrived ten hours late, delivered on bicycle by a Japanese messenger boy.

The speed with which Goro and Tadao rushed to offer their services to America was not matched by America in accepting those services. The 298th Infantry Regiment, which Goro joined at Schofield Barracks, was composed mostly of Japanese enlisted men commanded by non-Japanese officers, and it was this unit which was dispatched to clean up the bomb damage at Hickam Field, where dozens of American aircraft had been destroyed by Japanese bombers. When the air corps men saw the truckload of local Japanese boys invading the wrecked air strip they yelled, "They're invading!" And some frightened guards started shooting.

"Knock it off!" the 298th shouted. "We're Americans!" and in the next three days of crisis the outfit put forth a remarkable effort, working eighteen and twenty hours a day to make the airfield operable. "Best crew on the island," one haole superior reported admiringly. "Not much question as to where their loyalty rests."

But on the night of December 10 somebody in Honolulu headquarters received a message from California pointing out how energetic California was in rounding up its criminal Japanese, and some senior officer pushed the panic button. So in the silent hours before dawn three companies of trustworthy haole soldiers were sent with an extra complement of machine guns to perform one of the war's most curious tasks, and when dawn broke, Goro Sakagawa was the first Japanese boy in the 198th to look out of his tent and cry, "Christ! We're surrounded!"

His mates tumbled out of their sacks and started to rush onto the parade ground when a stern voice, coming over an impersonal metallic loud-speaker, commanded: "You Japanese soldiers! Listen to me. Stay right where you are. Don't make one false move. You're surrounded by guns. Stay where you are!"

Then a different voice cried: "You Japanese soldiers. I want you to nominate one man from each ten to step outside. Quick!"

From his tent Goro stepped into the gathering light, wearing shorts and nothing more. Then the voice continued: "You Japanese soldiers inside the tents. Pass out your rifles, your revolvers, your grenades. Quick! You men outside, stack them."

When this was done the voice commanded: "If there are any non-Japanese soldiers in this encampment, they are to leave now. You have five minutes. Quick."

Friends, unable to look their Japanese partners in the eye, shuffled away, and when the five minutes were gone, only Japanese boys stood bewildered in the tents. "Does this mean prison camp?" one whispered.

"Who knows?" his mate shrugged.

What it meant the Japanese boys were now to discover. "Muster out here!" the tinny voice commanded. "As you are! As you are!" And when the bewildered troops were in line, the colonel who had spoken first advised them: "You have been disarmed as a precautionary measure. We cannot tell when your countrymen will try to attack us again and we cannot endanger our rear by having you carrying weapons among us. You will stay within this barbed-wire enclosure until you get further orders. My men have been given one simple command: If any Jap steps outside this compound, shoot!"

For three humiliating days, burdened with rumor and fear, the Japanese boys of the 198th looked out into machine-gun muzzles. Then their guard was relaxed and they were told, "You will be free to work on latrine duty, or paring potatoes, or picking up. But you'll never touch guns again. Now snap to." That took care of Goro, who went into permanent latrine duty.

When Tadao left home on December 7 he ran all the way to the university, where his unit of the R.O.T.C. had already formed up with men who lived in the dormitories, and he arrived breathless just in time to march with his outfit to repel a Japanese parachute landing that was reported to have taken place north of Diamond Head. Of course, no enemy had landed, but headquarters forgot to inform the R.O.T.C. of this, and the Japanese boys patrolled their areas for four days without relief. Japanese families in the area supplied them with rice balls into which salty pickled plums had been inserted, and the college boys kept to their lonely posts.

It was on this silent duty that Tadao Sakagawa thought out explicitly what he would do if Japanese Imperial soldiers came over the rise at him. "I'd shoot," he said simply. "They'd be the enemy and I'd shoot." At the water reservoir, Minoru Sakagawa, of the Punahou R.O.T.C., reached the same conclusion: "I'd shoot." Across Hawaii in those angry, aching days some fourteen thousand young Japanese Americans of military age fought out with themselves the same difficult question, and all came up with the same answer: "They're obviously the enemy, so obviously I'd shoot."

Then, after several weeks of distinguished duty, all Japanese boys in the R.O.T.C. were quietly told, "We no longer have any place for you in the outfit. Turn in your uniforms." They were given no reason, no alternative, so Tadao and Minoru turned in their hard-earned American uniforms and appeared next day in mufti. A haole soldier from Arkansas saw them walking along the street and jeered: "Why ain't you yellow-bellied bastards in uniform same as me? Why should I fight to protect you slant-eyes?"

Minoru, being a rather beefy tackle at Punahou, was always ready for a brawl, and he turned toward the Arkansas boy, but Tadao, a quieter type, caught his arm and dragged him along. "If you hit a soldier, they'd lynch you."

"I'll take so much," Minoru muttered, "and then somebody's going to get it."

But they were to find out that day just how much they would be required to take, for as they came down from the R.O.T.C. headquarters, where their pleas for reinstatement were rejected, they saw their mother in her customary black kimono and straw geta walking pin-toed along Kakaako, shuffling in her peasant style and bent forward from the hips. She looked, Minoru had to admit, extremely foreign, and he was not surprised therefore when a crowd gathered and began to shout at her, telling her in words which she couldn't understand that no slant-eyed Japanese were wanted in the streets of Honolulu with their filthy kimonos. And before the boys could get to their mother, rowdies were actually beginning to tear off her kimono.

"Why don't you wear shoes, like decent Americans?" the rowdies cried. They hectored her into a corner, without her understanding at all what was happening, and a big man kept kicking at the offensive zori. "Take 'em off, goddamn it. Take 'em off!"

Swiftly Minoru and Tadao leaped among the crowd to protect their mother, and some sports fan recognized them and shouted, "It's the Sakagawa boys." The incident ended without further embarrassment, but Tadao, who was a diplomat, whispered to his terrified mother, "Kick off your zori. That's what made them mad." Deftly she kicked away the Japanese shoes, and the crowd cheered. On the way home Tadao warned her, "You've got to stop coming out in public wearing your kimono."

"And buy some shoes!" Minoru snapped, for like all the boys of his age, he could not understand why his parents kept to their old ways.

In the following days Minoru and Tadao were to be repeatedly tested. Having been born in America, they were technically citizens and even eligible to become President; but they were also Japanese and were thus subjected to humiliations worse than those suffered by aliens. Several times they were threatened by drunken soldiers, and prudence told them to keep off the streets.

Nevertheless, animosity against all Japanese increased when Hawaii, staggered by the completeness with which Japan had defeated the local troops, understandably turned to any logical rationalization at hand. "You can't tell me the Japs could have bombed our ships unless the local slant-eyes were feeding them spy information," one man shouted in a bar.

"I know for a fact that plantation workers at Malama Sugar cut arrows across the cane fields, showing Nip fliers the way to Pearl Harbor," a luna reported.

"The F.B.I. has proved that almost every Jap maid working for the military was a paid agent of the Mikado," an official announced.

And the Secretary of the Navy himself, after inspecting the disaster, told the press frankly, "Hawaii was the victim of the most effective fifth-column work that has come out of this war, except in Norway."

It was therefore no wonder that many Japanese were arrested and thrown into hastily improvised jails, whereupon those not yet picked up were ready to believe the rumor that all Japanese in Hawaii were to be evacuated to tents on Molokai. But when the jails were jammed and ships actually appeared in the harbor to haul those already arrested to concentration camps in Nevada, an unusual thing happened, one which more than any other served to bind up the wounds caused by the attack on Pearl Harbor. Hoxworth Hale and Mrs. Hewlett Janders and Mrs. John Whipple Hoxworth and a maiden librarian named Lucinda Whipple went singly, and not as a result of concerted action, to the jails where the Japanese were being held. Being the leading citizens of the community, they were admitted, and as they walked through the corridors they said to the jailers, "I know that man well. He can't possibly be a spy. Let him go."

Mrs. Hewlett Janders even went so far as to bring her husband, big Hewie, to the jail in his naval uniform, and he identified half a dozen excellent citizens whom he had known for years. "It's ridiculous to keep those men in a concentration camp. They're as good Americans as I am."

"Will you vouch for them if we let them go?" the F.B.I. man asked.

"Me vouch for Ichiro Ogawa? I'd be proud to vouch for him. You come on out of there, Ichiro. Go back to work."

Some three hundred leading Japanese citizens were removed from jail by these voluntary efforts of the missionary descendants. It wasn't that they liked Japanese, or that they feared Imperial Japan less than their neighbors. It was just that as Christians they could not sit idly by and watch innocent people maltreated. In California, where the imaginary danger of trouble from potential fifth columnists was not a fraction of the real danger that could have existed in Hawaii, cruel and senseless measures were taken that would be forever an embarrassment to America: families of the greatest rectitude and patriotism were uprooted; their personal goods were stolen, their privacy was abused; and their pride as full-fledged American citizens outraged. Such things did not happen in Hawaii. Men like Hoxworth Hale and Hewlett Janders wouldn't allow them to happen; women like Miss Whipple and Mrs. Hoxworth personally went through the jails to protect the innocent.

But when Hoxworth Hale came to the cell in which Kamejiro Sakagawa sat, a more intricate moral problem presented itself, for at first Hale was not ready to swear to the F.B.I. men, "This fellow I know to be innocent." What Hale did know was this: Kamejiro was a known dynamiter who had been in trouble during the strike at Malama Sugar; he had obstinately refused to terminate the Japanese nationality of his children; he had been prowling about all of Honolulu at night some years before Pearl Harbor; and now he was running a barbershop with his own daughter as a lure to bring in sailors and soldiers. That was the debit side. But Hale also knew one other fact: of all the young Japanese boys in Honolulu, none were finer Americans than Kamejiro's sons. Therefore, instead of passing by the cell, Hale stopped and asked to be allowed to talk with this man Sakagawa. When the cell door was opened and he sat inside with Kamejiro he told the interpreter to ask: "Mr. Sakagawa, why did you refuse to allow me to end your sons' dual citizenship?"

The old stubborn light came into Kamejiro's eyes, but when he realized that if he did not speak the truth he might never again see his sons, he softened and said, "Will you promise never to tell my boys?"

"Yes," Hale said, for he had family problems of his own. He directed the interpreter to promise likewise.

"My wife and I are not married," Kamejiro began.

"But I saw the marriage certificate!" Hale interrupted.

"American yes, but it doesn't count," Kamejiro explained. "When I sent for a picture bride to Hiroshima-ken, a girl was picked out and she was married to me there, in proper Japanese style, and her name was put in the village book as my wife."

"Then what's the problem?" Hale asked.

Kamejiro blushed at his ancient indiscretion and explained, "So when she got here I didn't like her, and there was another man who didn't like his wife, either."

"So you swapped?" Hale asked. A smile came across his lips. It seemed rather simple.

"Yes. In each country I am married to a different woman."

"But of course this is your real country and this is what counts," Hale said.

"No," Kamejiro patiently corrected. "Japan is my real home, and I would be ashamed for my village to know the wrong thing I have done."

Hale was impressed by the man's forthright defense of Japan, even in such trying circumstances, and he said condescendingly, "I don't think it would really matter, at this distance of time."

"Ah, but it would!" Kamejiro warned. And what he said struck a vibrant chord in Hale's own memories. "Because the wife I got in the exchange turned out to be the best wife a man ever found. But the wife I gave my friend turned out to be a very bad woman indeed, and his life has been ruined and I have had to sit and watch it happen. My happiness came at his expense, and I will do nothing now to hurt him any further. At least in our village they think he is an honorable man, and I will leave it that way."

Hale clenched his hands and thought of his own reactions to just such problems and of his insistence, against the pressure of friends, that his wife Malama stay with him, even though her mind had wandered past the limits usually required for commitment to an asylum, and in that moment of loving a woman, and knowing apprehension about the fate of one's son in a time of war, Hale felt a close kinship to the little bow-legged Japanese sitting before him. To the F.B.I. man he said, "This one can surely go free." And Kamejiro returned to his family.

Of course, when the gardener Ichiro Ogawa, who had been saved from internment by Hewlett Janders, later insisted that he ought to get a raise from the $1.40 a day that Janders was paying him, big Hewie hit the roof and accused the little Japanese of being unpatriotic by demanding a raise at such a critical time in America's history. "I think of your welfare all the time, Ichiro," Hewie explained. "You must leave these things to me."

"But I can't live on $1.40 a day any more. War expense."

"Are you threatening me?" Janders boomed.

"I got to have more money," Ichiro insisted.

As soon as the Japanese had left, Janders called security at Pearl Harbor. "Lemuel," he spluttered, "I've got a workman out here whose loyalty I'm damned suspicious of. I think he ought to be carted off right now."

"What's his name?"

"Ichiro Ogawa, a real troublemaker."

And that night Ogawa was spirited away and committed to a concentration camp on the mainland, after which there was less agitation for increased wages.

NO ONE LIVING in Hawaii escaped the effect of Pearl Harbor, and on the morning of December 8 practically no one could have even dimly foreseen the changes he would undergo. For example, gruff Hewlett Janders became to his surprise a full captain in the navy with control over harbor facilities. He wore an expensive khaki, some of the finest braid in the Pacific and ultimately a presidential citation for having kept the port cleared for war material.

John Whipple Hewlett's wife was caught on the mainland and had to stay there for three years. Nineteen descendants of the old New Bedford sea captain, Rafer Hoxworth, saw service in uniform, including two girls who went into the WAVES. On the other hand, a total of nine female descendants of old Dr. John Whipple married military officers whom they happened to meet in Honolulu.

Of course, the most dramatic impact fell upon the Sakagawas, but I will save discussion of that till later, for it is important that everyone understand how this large family of Japanese aliens became, by virtue of the war, full-fledged Americans. It was ironic that years of pleading for citizenship had got the Japanese nowhere—good behavior availed them nothing—but as soon as the Japanese government destroyed Pearl Harbor and killed more than 4,000 men, everything the local Japanese had wanted was promptly given them; but as I said, I should like to postpone that ironic story for a while.

Apart from the Sakagawas, the impact of that dreadful day of bombing and defeat fell heaviest upon the sprawling Kee hui. Two days after the bombing had ended, Nyuk Tsin, then ninety-four, was taken on a tour of the city by her grandson, Hong Kong, and as she saw the confusion into which the white citizens of Honolulu had fallen, she perceived that the next half year was going to provide the Kee hui with a vital opportunity for material growth, and that if it failed this rare chance, the hui would have no further claim to consideration.

That night Nyuk Tsin summoned her sons and abler grandsons, and when her little house in Nuuanu was jammed, and the blackout curtains were in place, she said, "All over Honolulu the haoles are preparing to run away. Asia, do you think the Japanese are going to invade Hawaii?"

"No."

"They why are the haoles running away?"

"They may have better information than I do," careful Asia replied.

"Will the Japanese airplanes come back?" Nyuk Tsin pressed.

"I hear our airfields at Wheeler and Hickam were destroyed," Asia reported, "but a navy officer at the restaurant said that even so, next time we would drive the enemy planes away."

Nyuk Tsin thought about this for some time and pressed her wrinkled old hands against her sunken cheeks, then passed them back along her almost vanished hair. "Hong Kong, do you think the Japanese will be back?"

"They may try, but I don't think they'll succeed."

"Do you think Honolulu is a safe place for us to gamble in?" Nyuk Tsin asked. "I mean, will the Japanese be kept out?"

"Yes," Asia said.

"Does it matter?" Hong Kong asked. He was forty-eight, a hard, honest man who had been taught by his father, Africa Kee the lawyer, all the tricks of survival. Having been refused a standard education at Punahou, which would have softened his attitudes, he had acquired from his father a sure instinct for the jugular. As yet he was not well known in Hawaii, having been content to allow his popular uncles to stand before the community as ostensible leaders of the great Kee hui, but Nyuk Tsin, who ran the hui, knew that in Hong Kong she had a successor just as smart and diligent as herself. Therefore, when he asked, "Does it matter?" she listened.

"If Japan conquers Hawaii," Hong Kong pointed out, "we will all be executed as leading Chinese. So we don't have to worry about that. The F.B.I. won't allow us to escape to the mainland, so we don't have to worry about that, either. We've got to stay where we are, pray that the Japanese don't win, and work harder than ever before."

Nyuk Tsin listened, then dropped her thin hands into her lap. "Our adversity is our fortune," she whispered. "We can't run away, but the haoles can. Like frightened rabbits they will be leaving on every ship. And when they go, soldiers and sailors with lots of money will come in. When they arrive, we'll be here. This war will last a long time, and if we work hard, our hui can become stronger than ever before."

"What should we work at?" Asia asked.

"Land," Nyuk Tsin replied with the terrible tenacity of a Hakka peasant who had never known enough land. "As the frightened haoles run away, we must buy all the land they leave behind."

"We don't have enough money to do that," Hong Kong protested.

"I'm sorry," Nyuk Tsin apologized. "I didn't explain myself correctly. Of course we can't afford to buy. But we can put down small deposits and promise to pay later. Then we can work the land and earn the money to pay off the debts."

"But how can we get hold of enough money to start?" Hong Kong asked.

"We must spend every cent of cash we have," Nyuk Tsin replied. "Asia, you take charge of that. Turn everything into cash. Let us run the stores on Hotel Street, because that's where the soldiers will come. Put all our girls to work. Australia, could your granddaughters start a hot-dog stand in Waikiki?"

The hui laid plans to lure every stray nickel from passing military men, but the most important tactic was still to be discussed. "Tomorrow morning, every man who is able must report to Pearl Harbor," Nyuk Tsin directed. "If the shipyard was as badly damaged as they say, lots of men will be needed. They'll be afraid to employ Japanese, and our men will get good jobs. But every penny earned must be given to Asia."

The family agreed that this was the right procedure, so Nyuk Tsin turned next to Hong Kong: "Your job will be the most difficult. You are to take the money that Asia provides, and you are to buy land. That is, pay just enough to get control. And remember, when people are running away in fear, they'll accept almost any cash offer and trust in faith to get the balance."

Hong Kong listened, then asked, "Should I buy business land or private homes?"

There was some discussion of this, but Nyuk Tsin finally directed: "Later, when the war is over, the big money will be in industrial land. But right now, when the island fills with people, everybody'll want homes."

"So what should I do?" Hong Kong asked.

"Buy homes now, and as their rents come in, apply the money to business property," Nyuk Tsin advised. Then she looked at the senior members of the hui and said, "The next years will require courage. When the war ends, people will hurry back to Hawaii and say, 'Those damned Chinese stole our land from us.' They'll forget that they ran away in fear, and we didn't. But then what they say won't matter." She laughed tremulously and chided her men: "I've never seen grown men so afraid as you are tonight. If you could run away, too, you'd do so, everyone of you. But fortunately the F.B.I. won't let you. So we must all stay here and work."

From this night meeting behind bomb-proofed windows, three changes occurred in Honolulu. First, a good many of the small stores that catered to servicemen, selling them greasy food, soft drinks and candy bars, came to be operated by members of the Kee hui. Prices were kept reasonable, the stores were kept clean, and every establishment made money. Second, at Pearl Harbor, when the accelerated rebuilding of that damaged base began, a surprising number of the auditors, senior bookkeepers, expediters and managerial assistants were named Kee. Their wages were good, their work impeccable, and their behavior inconspicuous. When draft boards asked the navy, "Are you fellows out at Pearl hoarding manpower?" the navy apologetically released Mendoncas and Guerreros, but never a Kee, for the latter were essential to the war. Third, when the military began to fly in hundreds of civilian advisers, and in the case of senior officials, their families too, these men found that if they wanted to rent quarters they had to see Hong Kong Kee; even generals and admirals were told, "Better check with Hong Kong." As the war progressed and Hawaii became horribly overcrowded, with every house renting at triple premium and every store jammed with customers, only Nyuk Tsin and Hong Kong realized how inconspicuously the Kees were converting their rent money into commercial land sites.

THE MOST SUBTLE effect of the war fell upon Hoxworth Hale, who was only forty-three when it began. Of course he volunteered immediately, reminding the local generals of his World War I experience, but they replied that he was essential to H & H, many of whose activities tied in with military requirements. He was therefore not allowed to rejoin the army. Later, when he heard that a group of Yale men were organizing a submarine outfit, he fought to get into that, feeling that he was well fitted for submarine duty, but the navy rather stiffly pointed out that the Yale men involved were more nearly his son's age than his. He therefore had to stay in Honolulu, where he worked closely with Admiral

Nimitz and General Richardson, making a substantial contribution to the war effort. Along with his other duties he served as head of the draft board and chairman of the Office of Civilian Defense.

In the former capacity he was pleased at the forthright manner in which young Japanese in Hawaii volunteered for military duty, and thought that the Army's arbitrary rejection of the boys was unwarranted, and he wrote to President Roosevelt to tell him so: "I can speak of first-hand knowledge, sir, and these Japanese boys are among the most loyal citizens you will find in the nation. Why can't you order your people to form a combat team composed of Japanese intended for use in Europe only?"

On the other hand, he was distressed that so few Chinese stepped forward to bear arms in defense of America. "If they don't volunteer," he stormed one day, "I shall direct our draft boards to flush them out with cyanide of potassium. Where are they all?" When he had civil authorities look into the matter, he found that most of them were out at Pearl Harbor, and he asked Admiral Nimitz, "Do you mean to tell me that all those Chinese boys are essential to that war effort?" He was surprised when Nimitz looked into the matter and reported curtly: "Yes. We've got to have somebody out there who can use slide rules."

In early 1942 the air corps asked Hoxworth to join a group of senior officers who were flying to various South Pacific islands to study the possibilities for new airstrips, and he of course quickly consented, for with his wife in a depressed spell during which she could not converse intelligently, with his daughter in a mainland school, and his son in the air corps, he had no reason to stay at home, and the pleasure he got from climbing into uniform, with the simulated rank of colonel, was great.

His military contribution to the journey of inspection was not significant, but his sociological observations were of real import, and whenever the PBY started to descend at bases like Johnston Island, or Canton, or Nukufetau, and he saw from the cramped windows the crystal lagoons and the wide sweep of sand upon reef, he recalled all that one of his ancestors, Dr. John Whipple, had written about the tropics, and he was able to instruct the air corps men on many points. When he first stepped upon an atoll reef he had the peculiar sensation that he had come home, and although for years he had forgotten the fact that he was part-Polynesian, that ancient ancestry came flooding back upon him, and often while the officers were inspecting possible landing areas, he would remain upon the reef, looking out to sea, and long-submerged components of his blood came surging before his eyes, and he could see canoes and voyagers.

But these were not the subtle influences of which I spoke. They began when the PBY landed on Suva Bay, in the Fiji Islands. Hoxworth climbed into a small British boat and went ashore to meet the governor, a proper Englishman with an American wife, and the visit started out like any normal wartime trip to an island that might soon be invaded by the enemy; but as the group started looking into Fiji affairs, Hoxworth Hale began building up impressions that disturbed him deeply.

"Why are the Indians here kept apart?" he inquired.

"Oh, you can't do anything with an Indian!" the British secretary to the governor replied.

"Why not?" Hoxworth asked.

"Have you ever tried working with an Oriental?" the Englishman countered. Hale made no reply, but as he studied the sugar fields in Fiji, he found them exactly like the sugar fields in Hawaii, and he had certainly worked with Japanese in precisely such surroundings, and without too much trouble. He reflected: "Indians were imported into Fiji and Japanese were imported into Hawaii, for the same purposes at about the same time. But with what different results! In Hawaii the Japanese are reasonably good Americans. Here the Indians are totally undigested. What went wrong down here?"

"One good thing about it, though," the Englishman pointed out. "If you Johnnies want to pre-empt land for your airstrips, you don't have to worry about the bloody Indians. They're not allowed to own any."

"Why not?" Hoxworth asked.

"Orientals? Owning land?" the smart young man asked rhetorically, but to himself Hoxworth replied: "Bloody well why not? If I understand correctly, the Kees now own half the homes in Hawaii. Best thing ever happens to a Japanese is when he gets a little piece of land and starts to tidy it up. Makes him less radical and woos him away from labor unions."

"So the Indians own none of the land?" Hoxworth asked aloud.

"No, we restrict that very severely," the young man assured him. "Nor can they vote, so we won't have any trouble there, either."

"You mean, the ones born in India can't vote?" Hoxworth queried.

"Nor the ones born here," the aide explained, and Hoxworth thought: "How differently we've done things in Hawaii." And the more he saw of Fiji, the happier he was with the manner in which Hawaii's Orientals had been brought into full citizenship, with no real barriers hindering them. Did the Indians go to college? There were no colleges; but in Hawaii there were and God knows the Japanese went. Did the Indians own the land on which their crowded stores perched? No, but in Hawaii the Chinese and Japanese owned whatever they liked. Did the Indians participate in civil government? Heavens no, but in Hawaii their Oriental cousins were beginning to take over some branches. Did Indians serve as government clerks? No, but in Hawaii Chinese were sought after as government employees.

And so throughout his entire comparison of Fiji and Hawaii, Hoxworth Hale saw that what had been done to build the Orientals into Hawaiian life had been the right thing, and what the British in Fiji had done to keep the Indians a sullen, hateful half of the population was wrong; and it was from Fiji that Hale acquired his first insight into how fundamentally just the missionary descendants had been, for he concluded: "In Hawaii we have a sound base from which our islands can move into a constructive future: Japanese, Chinese, Filipinos, Caucasians and Hawaiians working together. But in Fiji, with the hatred I see between the races, I don't see how a logical solution will ever be worked out." Then he added grimly, but with humor, "By God, the next time I hear a Japanese sugar worker raising hell about a union, I'm going to say, 'Wantanabe-san, maybe you better go down to Fiji for a while and see how the Indians are doing.' He'd come back to Honolulu and cry at the wharf, 'Please, Mr. Hale, let me back on shore. I want to work in Hawaii, where things are good.'"

And then, when he was congratulating himself on the superior system evolved by his missionary ancestors, he attended a banquet given by Sir Ratu Salaka, a majestic black Fijian chief with degrees from Cambridge and Munich, and when this scion of a great Fijian family appeared dressed in a native lava-lava, with western shirt and jacket, enormous brown leather shoes, and medals of valor gained in World War I, Hale intuitively felt: "In Hawaii we have no natives like this man."

Sir Ratu Salaka was a powerfully oriented man. He spoke English faultlessly, knew of the progress of the war, and stood ready, although now well along in his fifties, to lead a Fijian expeditionary force against the Japanese.

"Remember, my good friends of the air corps," he said prophetically, "when you invade such islands as Guadalcanar and Bougainville, where I have been on ethnological expeditions, you will require as scouts men like myself. Our dark skins will be an asset in scouting, our knowledge of the jungle will enable us to go where you men could never penetrate, and our habit of secrecy in movement will allow us to creep up upon our opponents and kill them silently, while their companions sit ten yards away. When you need us, call, for we are ready."

"Will you have Indian troops with you?" Hale asked.

At this question the dark-skinned host exploded with laughter. "Indians?" he snorted contemptuously. "We put out a call for volunteers and out of our population of more than a hundred thousand Indians, do you know how many stepped forward? Two, and they did so with the firm stipulation that they never be required to leave Fiji. In fact, if I remember, they weren't even willing to go to the other islands of this group. No, Mr. Hale, we wouldn't use any Indians. They didn't volunteer, and we didn't expect them to."

Hale thought: "In Hawaii, from the same number of Japanese we could have got fifteen thousand volunteers . . . even to fight Japan. But here the Indians won't offer to fight an enemy with whom they have no ties of emotion whatever." And again he felt superior.

But when Sir Ratu Salaka finished his brandy, like the crusty English squire he was, he observed: "In Fiji, I assure you, we are not proud of the way in which we have failed to assimilate our Indian sugar workers. Some day we shall have to pay a terrible price for our neglect—civil disturbance, perhaps even blood-shed—and I as a Fijian leader am particularly aware of this tragedy. But when I visit Hawaii, and see how dismally the Polynesians have been treated there, how their lands have been stolen from them, how Japanese fill all the good governmental jobs, and how the total culture of a great people has been de-stroyed, I have got to say that even though our Indians are not so well situated as your Japanese, we Fijians are infinitely better off than your Hawaiians. We own our own land. I suppose that nine-tenths of the farm land you saw today belongs to Fijians. We also control the part of the government not held by Englishmen. Today our old patterns of life are stronger than they were fifty years ago. In all things we prosper, and I can think of no self-respecting Fijian who, aware of the paradise we enjoy here, would consent to trade places with a pitiful Hawaiian who had nothing left of his own. You Americans have treated the Hawaiians horribly."

A silence fell over the group, and finally Hoxworth said, "You may be surprised, Sir Ratu, and I suppose these officers will be too, but I am part-Hawaiian, and I do not feel as you suggest."

Sir Ratu was a tough old parliamentarian who rarely retreated, so he studied his guest carefully and said bluntly, "From appearances I should judge that the American half of you had prospered a good deal more than the Hawaiian half." Then he laughed gallantly and offered another round of brandy, saying to Hale, "We are talking of rather serious things, Mr. Hale, but I do think this question is sometimes worth considering: For whom do invaders hold an island in trust? Here the British have said, 'We hold these islands in trust for the Fijians,' and in doing so, they have done a great disservice, if not actual injustice, to the Indians whom they imported to work the sugar fields. But in Hawaii your missionaries apparently said, 'We hold these islands in trust for whomever we import to work our sugar fields,' and in saving them for the

Chinese, they did a grave injustice to all Hawaiians. I suppose if our ancestors had been all-wise, they would have devised a midway solution that would have pleased everybody. But you gentlemen are heading east to Tahiti. Study the problem there. You'll find the French did not do one damn bit better than the English here or the Americans in Hawaii."

To this Hale added, "At least, in Hawaii, we will never have civil war. We will never have bloodshed."

Sir Ratu, a giant of a man in all ways, could not let this pass, so he added, "And in a few years you'll have no bloody Hawaiians, either." And the party broke up.

It was with badly mixed emotions that Hoxworth Hale left Fiji, but when his PBY deposited the inspecting team in American Samoa he was propelled into an even more perplexing speculation. He arrived at Pago Pago the day before the islanders were scheduled to celebrate their annexation to America, which had occurred in 1900, and he was told that since a Japanese submarine had recently bombarded Samoa, the islanders this year wished to demonstrate in special ceremonies their loyalty to America. But when Hale rose next morning he saw that the forbidding peaks which surrounded Pago Pago had trapped a convoy of rain clouds, which were in the process of drenching the islands, and he assumed that the ceremonies would be cancelled.

But he did not know Samoans! At dawn the native marines stood in the rain and fired salutes. At eight the Fita Fita band, in splendid uniforms, marched to the "Stars and Stripes Forever," and by ten all citizens who could walk lined the soggy parade ground while Samoan troops executed festive maneuvers. Then a huge, golden-brown chief with a face like a rising sun and enough flesh for two men, moved to the foot of the flag pole and made an impassioned speech in Samoan, proclaiming his devotion to America. Others followed, and as they spoke, Hoxworth Hale began to catch words and finally whole phrases which he understood, and with these Polynesian tones reverberating in his memory he experienced a profound mental confusion, so that when the Fita Fita band played the "Star Spangled Banner" and the cannon roared, he did not hear the wild cheering of the crowd.

He was comparing what he had seen in Samoa with what he remembered of the way Hawaii celebrated its Annexation Day, and he was struck by the difference. In Samoa guns boomed; in Hawaii decent people maintained silence. In Samoa people cheered; in Hawaii many wept. In Samoa not even storms could daunt the islanders who wanted to watch once more their beloved new flag rising to the symbolic tip of the island; but in Hawaii the new flag was not even raised, for Hawaiians remembered that when their islands were joined to America, the act had been accomplished by trickery and injustice. In the inevitable triumph of progress, a people had been raped, a lesser society had been crushed into oblivion. It was understandable that in Samoa, Polynesians cheered Annexation Day, but in Hawaii they did not.

To Hoxworth Hale these reflections were particularly gloomy, for it had been his great-grandfather Micah who had engineered the annexation of Hawaii, and Hoxworth was always reminded by his family that the event had coincided with his own birth, so that friends said, "Hawaii is the same age as Hoxworth," thus making a family joke of what many considered a crime. But he could also remember his great-grandmother, the Hawaiian lady Malama, as she told him before she died: "My husband made me attend the ceremonies when the Hawaiian flag was torn down, and do you know what the haoles did with that flag, Hoxy? They cut it into little pieces and passed them around the crowd."

"What for?" he had asked.

"So they could remember the day," the old lady had replied. "But why they would want to remember it I never understood."

There were many Hawaiians, even in 1942, who preferred not to speak with a Hale and who refused to eat at the same table with one. But others remembered not stern Micah who had stolen their islands but his mother Jerusha who had loved the Hawaiians, and those who remembered her would eat with the Hales while the others would not. Now, in Samoa where the rains fell, Hoxworth Hale, the descendant of both Micah and Jerusha, felt their two natures warring in his sympathies, and he wished that something could be done to rectify the injustices of Hawaiian annexation so that his Polynesians would take as much pride in their new flag as the Samoans did in theirs; but he knew that this was not possible, and the old sorrow that had attacked him at Yale when he contemplated the stolen Jarves paintings returned and he thought: "Who can assess the results of an action?" And he found no joy in Samoa.

But when he reached Tahiti, that Mecca of the South Seas, and his seaplane landed in the small bay that lies off Papeete, between the island of Moorea and the Diademe of Tahiti, making it surely the loveliest seaplane base in the world, his spirits were again excited, for these were the islands from which his people had come. This was the storied capital of the seas, and it was more beautiful than he had imagined. He felt proud to be of a blood that had started from Tahiti.

He was disappointed in the legendary girls of the island, however, for few of them had teeth. Australian canned foods and a departure from the traditional fish diet had conspired to rob girls in their teens of their teeth, but, as one of the air corps majors said, "If a man goes for beautiful gums, he can have a hell of a time in Tahiti."

What interested Hoxworth most, however, was not the girls but the Chinese. The French governor pointed out that the Americans would find a secure base in Tahiti, because the Chinese were well in hand. They were allowed to own no land, were forbidden to enter many kinds of business, were severely spied on by currency control, and were in general so held down that the Americans could rest assured there would be no problems. Hoxworth started to say, "In Hawaii our island wealth is multiplied several times each year by the Chinese, who do own land and who do go into business. The only currency control we have is that all our banks would like to get hold of what the Chinese keep in their own banks." But as a visitor he kept his mouth shut and looked.

It seemed to him that Tahiti would be approximately ten times better off in all respects if the Chinese were not only allowed but encouraged to prosper. "You hear so much about Tahiti," he said in some disappointment to the general leading his party, "but compare their roads to Hawaii's."

"Shocking," the general agreed.

"Or their health services, or their stores, or their churches."

"Pretty grubby in comparison with what you fellows have done in Hawaii," the general agreed.

"Where are the Tahiti schools? Where is the university? Or the airport or the clean hospitals? You know, General, the more I see of the rest of Polynesia, the more impressed I am with Hawaii."

The general was concerned with other matters, and on the third day he

announced to his team: "It's incredible, but there simply isn't any place here in
Tahiti to put an airstrip. But there seems to be an island farther north where we
could probably flatten out one of the reefs and find ourselves with a pretty fine
landing strip."

"What island?" Hale asked.

"It's called Bora Bora," the general said, and early next morning he flew the
PBY up there, and Hoxworth Hale thus became the first part-Hawaiian ever to
see his ancestral island of Bora Bora from the air. He saw it on a bright sunny
day, when a running sea was breaking on the outer reef, while the lagoon was
a placid blue surrounding the dark island from which rose the tall mountains
and the solid, brutal block of basalt in the middle. He gasped at the sheer
physical delight of this fabled island, its deep-cut bays, its thundering surf, its
outrigger canoes converging near the landing area, and he thought: "No wonder
we still remember poems about this island," and he began to chant fragments
of a passage his great-great-grandfather Abner Hale had transcribed about Bora
Bora:

> "Under the bright red stars hides the land,
> Cut by the perfect bays, marked by the mountains,
> Rimmed by the reef of flying spume,
> Bora Bora of the muffled paddles!
> Bora Bora of the great navigators.

The other occupants of the PBY were equally impressed by the island, but
for other reasons. It possessed an enormous anchorage, and if necessary an
entire invasion fleet could find refuge within the lagoon; but more important, the
little islands along the outer reef were long, smooth and flat. "Throw a couple
of bulldozers there for three days, and a plane could land right now," an
engineer volunteered.

"We'll fly around once more," the general announced, "and see if we can
agree on which of the outer islands looks best." So while the military people
looked outward, to study the fringing reef, Hoxworth Hale looked inward, to
see the spires of rock and the scintillating bays that cut far inland, so that every
home on Bora Bora that he could spot lay near the sea. How marvelous that
island was, how like a sacred home in a turbulent sea.

Now the PBY leveled off and started descending toward the lagoon, and
Hoxworth thought how exciting it was to be within an airplane that had the
capacity to land on water, for this must have been the characteristic of the first
great beasts on earth who mastered flight. They must have risen from the sea
and landed on it, as the PBY now prepared to do. When it was near the water,
speeding along at more than a hundred miles an hour, Hoxworth realized for
the first time how swiftly this bird was flying, and as it reached down with its
underbelly step to find the waves, he caught himself straining with his buttocks,
adjusting them to insure level flight, and then seeking to let them down into the
waves, and he flew his bottom so well that soon the plane was rushing along the
tiptop particles of the sea, half bird, half fish, and then it lost its flight and
subsided into the primordial element, a plane that had conquered the Pacific and
come at last to rest upon it.

"Halloo, Joe!" a native cried at the door, and in a moment the plane was
surrounded by Bora Borans in their swift, small canoes.

Among the first to go ashore was Hale, because he knew a few words of
Polynesian and many of French, and as he sat precariously on the thwarts of one

of the canoes, and felt himself speeding across the limpid waters of the lagoon toward a sprawling, coconut-fringed village whose roofs were made of grass, he thought: "Hawaii has nothing to compare with this."

In a way he was right, for after the general and his staff had been fed with good sweet fish from the lagoon and red wine from Paris, the headman of the village approached with some embarrassment and said in French, which Hale had to interpret: "General, we people of Bora Bora know that you have come here to save us. God himself knows the French would do nothing to rescue us, because they hate Bora Borans, and do you know why? Because in all history we have never been conquered, not even by the French, and officially we are a voluntary part of their empire. They have never forgiven us for not surrendering peacefully like the others, but we say to hell with the French."

"Shut him up!" the general commanded. "The French have been damned good to us, Hale, and I want to hear no more of this sedition."

But the headman was already past his preamble and into more serious business. "So we Bora Borans want to help you in every way we can. You say you want to build an airstrip. Good! We'll help. You say you'll need water and food. Good! We'll help there too. But there is one matter you seem not to have thought about, and on this we will help too.

"While your flying boat sleeps in the lagoon, you will have to have some place to sleep on shore. We will put aside seven houses for you."

"Tell him we need only two," the general interrupted. "We don't want to disrupt native life."

The proud headman, dressed in a brown lava-lava and flowered wreath about his temples, did not allow the interruption to divert him: "The biggest house will be for the general, and the rest are about the same size. Now, because it is not comfortable for a man to sleep alone in such a house, we have asked seven of our young girls if they will take care of everything."

It was here that Hoxworth Hale, son of missionaries, began to blush, and when the maidens were brought forth, clean, shapely, dark-haired, barefoot girls in sarongs and flowers, he began to protest, but when the headman actually started apportioning the girls, the tallest and prettiest to the general, and a shy, slim creature of fifteen to him, Hale quite broke up and the translation stopped.

"What the hell is this?" the general asked, but then the tall, beautiful girl of seventeen who had been assigned to him, took him gently by the hand and started leading him toward his appointed house.

"My God!" the irreverent major cried. "In Bora Bora they got teeth!" And one of the girls must have known some English, for she laughed happily, and because these islanders were more primitive and ate more fish, their teeth were strong and white, and the major accepted his girl's hand and without even so much as looking at the general, disappeared.

"We can't allow this!" the general protested. "Tell them so."

But when Hale explained this decision the headman said, "We are not afraid of white babies. The island likes them." And after a while only Hoxworth Hale stood in the meeting shed, looking at his long-tressed, fifteen-year-old Polynesian guide. She was a year older than his own daughter, not quite so tall, but equally beautiful, and he was a totally confused man, and then she took his hand and said in French, "Monsieur le Colonel, your house is waiting. We had better go."

She led him along dark-graveled paths beneath breadfruit trees whose wide leaves hid the hot sun. They went along a row of coconut palms, bending toward the lagoon as they had done a thousand years before, and in time she came to a small house withdrawn from the others, and here she stopped at the trivial lintel that kept out the wandering pigs and chickens, and said, "This house is mine." She waited until he had entered, and then she joined him and untied a length of sennit that held up the woven door, and when it fell they were alone.

He stood rigid in acute embarrassment, holding onto a bundle of papers, as if he were a schoolboy, and these she took from him and then pushed him backwards slowly, until he sat on a bed with a wooden frame and a woven rope mattress, and he was as frightened as he had ever been in his life. But when she had thrown the papers into a corner she said, "My name is Tehani. And this is the house my father built me when I became fifteen. I plaited the roof of pandanus, but he built the rest."

Hoxworth Hale, then forty-four, was ashamed to be with a girl fifteen, but once when she passed where he was sitting on the bed, her long black hair moved past his face, and he smelled the fragrance of that sweetest of all flowers, the taire Tahiti, and he had never encountered that odor before, and automatically he reached up and caught at her hand, but she was moving rather swiftly, and he missed, but he did catch her right leg above the knee, and he felt her whole body stop at this command, and start to move willingly toward him. He kept hold of her leg and pulled her onto the bed, and she fell back happily and smiled up at him, with the taire flowers about her temples, and he took away the sarong and when she was naked she whispered, "I asked my father for you, for you were quieter than the others."

When the inspecting team convened late that afternoon around an improvised table under the breadfruit trees, by common but unspoken agreement, no one mentioned what had happened, and they proceeded to discuss where the airstrip should be, just as if nothing unusual had occurred, but as night fell and girls appeared with an evening meal, each officer instinctively brought his girl to the table beside him, and there was unprecedented tenderness in the way the older men saw to it that their young companions got a fair division of the food.

They had not finished eating when a group of young men, with long hair in their eyes and pareus about their hips, appeared with guitars and drums, and soon the Bora Bora night was filled with echoes. The audience waited until the general's tall, slim beauty leaped into the dancing ring and executed the wild, passionate dance of that island. This was a signal which permitted the other girls to do the same, and soon one had the cocky major in the ring with her, attempting a version of the dance, and he was followed by a colonel and then by the general himself. It became a wild, frenzied, delightful dance under the stars, and all the older people who were watching applauded.

Hoxworth Hale's girl, Tehani, did not ask him to dance, knowing from what had transpired in the grass house that he was a shy man, so finally an old woman with no teeth muscled her way through the crowd, stood before Hale and did a few lascivious steps. To the surprise of everyone, Hale leaped to his feet and swung into the Hawaiian hula, at which, like most of his Honolulu contemporaries, he was skilled. The audience stopped making noise and the military visitors sat down, tired as they were from their own exertions, while Hale and the old woman performed an admirable dance. Finally, when the astonishment was becoming vocal, the major shouted, "Hale for President!" and Hoxworth broke into a much swifter version while the old woman executed a downright lewd movement, to the howls of the crowd.

At this Tehani stepped forward, firmly pushed the old beldame away and took her place, and for a few minutes Hale and the delicately formed young girl, with streams of flowers in her hair, brought an ancient grace to the sands of

Bora Bora. He felt himself caught up in passions he had thought long dead, while the girl smiled softly to herself and, knowing that she was the envy of all the others for her man could dance, thought: "I got the best one of the group, and I was smart enough to ask for him."

The inspecting team lingered at Bora Bora for nine days, and every night during that time the entire community held an all-night celebration. From the nearby island of Raiatea, which in the old days had been known as Havaiki, the holy island of the Polynesians, a young French government official came over with a barrel of red wine which the general insisted on buying, although the gracious young man had intended it as a gift, and at dusk each day this barrel was cocked, and anyone who wished to drink could have one. The orchestra never stopped playing. In exhaustion men would drop their drums and others would pick them up. The seven girls who were tending the guests of honor rarely left them, so that in the end even at formal meetings of the inspection staff, the Polynesian girls would be there, not understanding a word that was being spoken, but each one proud whenever her man spoke forcefully on some point or other.

During the nine days no mention was made of sex, except once when the general remarked thoughtfully, "I am amazed at what a man of forty-nine can do." But he was taking a two-hour nap morning, afternoon, and evening.

Hoxworth preferred not even to think of Tehani as a real person. She was something that happened, a dream whose confines would never be appropriately known. Having experienced a normal Punahou and Yale education, he had been roughly aware of what sex was, but never accurately, and his marriage had been a family affair, which for a while had been formally proper, like going on an endless picnic with one's fully clothed sister, but soon even that had ended, and when at odd moments in the last few years he had thought about sex he had supposed that for him, at least, it had ended in his mid-thirties. Tehani Vahine, for that was her whole name, Miss Tehani of Bora Bora, had quite other intentions. She had been taught that men of Colonel Hale's age were those who enjoyed sex most, and who were often most proficient in it; and whereas she had been wrong in both guesses about Hale, for he was both afraid and unskilled, she had never known a man who could learn so fast.

They were days of listless, idle joy. He loved her best when she wore her sarong draped carelessly about her hips, her breasts bare and her long hair sparkling with flowers. He would lie endlessly upon the rope bed and watch her movements, as if he had never seen a girl before, and sometimes with a cry of joy he would leap up, catch her in his arms and carry her to the bed in a blizzard of kisses. Once he asked her, "Is it always like this in Bora Bora?" and she replied, "Usually we don't have so much good wine." And he thought: "In other parts of the world there is a war, and in Hawaii, nervous men are arguing with each other, and in New York girls are calculating, 'Should I let him tonight?' But in Bora Bora there's Tehani." Like the general, he was amazed at what a man of forty-four could do . . . if he had the right encouragement.

On the next-to-the-last day Tehani whispered, "Tell the others you won't be there tomorrow," and at dawn she sprinkled water on his face and cried, "You must get up and see the fish!"

She led him sleepily to a spot away from her house where she had a fresh tuna staked out and cleaned. "This is going to be the best dish you ever ate in your life," she assured him, "because it will be Bora Bora poisson cru. Watch me how I do it, so that when you are far away and want to remember me, you can make some and taste me in it."

She cut the fresh tuna into small fillets of about two inches in length and a quarter inch thick. These she placed in a large calabash, which she carried to the lagoon where no people came, and from the cold waters she dipped a few coconuts shells full of fresh salt water which she tossed on the fillets. Then she took a club and knocked down three limes, which she cut in half and squeezed into the calabash. Carefully seeking a place where the sun shone brightest, she put the fish there to steam through the long, hot morning, cooking itself in the lime juice and sea water.

"Now comes the part where you must help me!" she cried merrily as she pointed to a sloping palm that bent over the water, holding in its crest a bundle of ripe nuts. "I shall climb up there, but you must catch the nuts for me," and before he could stop her, she had tied her sarong about her hips, had caught hold of the tree with her hands and feet, and had bent-walked right up the tree to where the nuts clustered. Holding on with her left hand, she used her right to twist free a choice nut. Then, with a wide side-arm movement, she tossed it inland, where Hoxworth caught it. "Hooray!" she cried in glee and pitched another.

When she returned to earth she found a stout stick, jammed it in the earth, and showed her partner how to husk a coconut, and when he had done so, she knocked the two nuts together until they cracked open and their juices ran into a second calabash. Then she jammed into the ground a second stick, this time at an angle, and against its blunt edge she began scraping the coconut slowly and rhythmically, until white meat, dripping with nectar, began shredding down onto taro leaves placed on the ground. As her golden shoulders swayed back and forth in the sunlight, she sang:

> "Grating the coconut for my beloved,
> Shredding the sweet meat for him,
> Salting the fish,
> Under the swaying breadfruit tree,
> Under the rainless sky,
> I shred the sweet meat for my beloved."

When she finished grating she ignored Hoxworth, as if he were not there, and carefully gathered the shredded coconut, placing half in the calabash to join the captured coconut water, half in a tangle of brown fiber from the coconut husks, which she now caught in her slim hands and squeezed over a third calabash. As she twisted the coarse fibers, a fine rich liquor was forced out, and this was the sweet coconut milk that would complete the dish she was preparing.

Again and again Tehani squeezed the grated coconut, softly chanting her song, though now she spoke of twisting the meat for her beloved instead of grating it, and as the palms along the shore dipped toward the lagoon, Hoxworth Hale had a strikingly clear intuition: "From now on whenever I think of a woman, in the abstract . . . of womanliness, that is . . . I'll see this brown-skinned Bora Bora girl, her sarong loosely about her hips, working coconut and humming softly in the shadowy sunlight. Has she been here, under these bread-fruit trees, all these last empty years?" And he had a second intuition: that during the forthcoming even emptier years, she would still be there, a haunting vision of the other half of life, the womanliness, the caretaking symbol, the majestic, lovely, receptive other half.

Overcome by his vision of past and future, he desired to revel in the accidental now, and reached out from the shaded area where she had placed him, trying to catch her leg again, but she deftly evaded him and went to a pit where yams and taro had been baking, and she now proceeded to break the latter into small purplish pieces, rich in starch, while the yams she held in her hands for a moment, showing them to her lover. "These are what our sailors call the Little Eyes of Heaven," she laughed, pointing to the eyes of the yam, which clustered like the constellation whose rising in the east heralds the Polynesian New Year.

Finally, Tehani chopped the onions and then mixed all the vegetables in with the thick, rich coconut milk, and after she had washed her hands in the lagoon, she came back and sat cross-legged before Hale, her sarong pulled far up to expose soft brown thighs, and her breasts free in the sunlight. "It's a game we play," she explained, and with him in the shadows and she in the sunlight, she started slapping his shoulders, and as she hummed her coconut song, she indicated that he was to slap hers, and in this way she passed from his shoulders to his forearms, to his flanks, to his hips and finally to his thighs, and as the game grew more intense the slaps grew gentler and her song slower, until with a culminating gesture that started out to be a slap but which ended as an embrace, Hale caught her sarong and started pulling it away, but she cried softly in her own language, "Not in the sunlight, Hale-tane," and he understood, and swept her up in his arms and carried her into the grass house, where the game reached its intended conclusion.

Toward noon she asked him in French, "Do you like the way we make our poisson cru in Bora Bora?" And she brought in the fish, well saturated in sun and lime juice, and Hale saw that the tuna was no longer red but an inviting gray-white. Into it she mixed the prepared coconut milk with its burden of taro and onions and yams. Next she tossed in a few shellfish for flavor, and over the whole she sprinkled the freshly grated, juicy coconut. With her bare right hand she stirred the ingredients and finally offered her guest three fingers full of Bora Bora raw fish.

"This is how we feed our men on this island," she teased. "Can your girls do as well?" When Hale laughed, she pushed the dripping fish into his mouth and chuckled when the white milk ran down his chin and across his naked chest. "You are so sloppy!" she chided. "But you are such an adorable man, Hale-tane. You can laugh. You are tender. You dance like an angel. And you are strong in bed. You are a man any girl could love. Tell me," she begged, "do your girls at home love you?"

"Yes," he said truthfully, "they do."

"Do they sometimes play games like the slapping game with you, and then chase you around the house just for the fun of being with you?"

"No," he replied.

"I am sorry, Hale-tane," she said. "The years go by very fast and soon..." She pointed to an old woman searching for shellfish along the shore: "Then we play no more games." It was with the sadness of the world turning in space, or of the universe drifting madly through the darkness, that she said these words in island French: "Et bientôt c'est tout fini et nous ne jouons plus."

"Is that why your father builds you a house of your own when you're fifteen?" Hale asked. "So you can learn the proper games?"

"Yes," she explained. "No sensible man would want to marry me unless he knew that I understood how to make love properly. Men are happiest when a girl has proved she can have a baby, and do you know what I hope, Hale-tane? I hope that when you fly away tomorrow you leave in here a baby for me." She patted her flat brown stomach which looked as if it could never contain a child. "That is my wish."

And so they lazed the day away, and ate poisson cru, the best dish that any island ever invented, and played the silly games of love that Bora Borans had been teaching their daughters for nearly two thousand years, and in due time shadows crept across the lagoon, and night fell, and after the drums had been beating at the village dancing ground for some hours, Tehani wrapped herself in a sarong and said, "Come, Hale-tane, I should like the people of Bora Bora to see me dancing with you one more time. Then, if I do have your baby, they will remember that among all the Americans, you were the best dancer."

In the morning, as the inspection team piled into the PBY for takeoff and the return to Hawaii, no one spoke of the long-haired girls of Bora Bora, or of their flashing teeth, or of the games they knew how to play, for if anyone had spoken, all would have wanted to remain on the island for another day, another week; but when the plane had torn its bulk free from the waters of the lagoon and stood perched on what the aviators called "the step," the small after-portion on which the huge boat rode on the waves, until it finally soared into the air, Hale again felt the aesthetic moment, when men are half of the ocean and half of the air, and in this attitude the speeding PBY whipped across the lagoon until it finally soared aloft, and all were wholly of the sky.

It was then, as Bora Bora disappeared in the brilliance of morning sunlight, that the major observed bitterly, "To think! We're going to draft decent young American boys, tear them from their mother's arms, slam them into uniform and send them down to Bora Bora. God, it's inhuman." And for the rest of the war, and for many years thereafter, there would be a confraternity of men who met casually in bars, or at cocktail parties, or at business luncheons, and one would say, to the other, "They write mostly crap about the Pacific, but there's one island . . ."

"Are you speaking of Bora Bora?" the other would interrupt.

"Yes. Did you serve there?"

"Yep." Usually, nothing more was said, because if a man had served his hitch on Bora Bora nothing more was required to be said, but whenever Hoxworth Hale met such men he invariably went one step further: "Did you ever know a slim, long-haired girl of fifteen or sixteen? Lived by the mountain. Named Tehani."

Once he met a lieutenant-commander from a destroyer-escort who had known Tehani, and the destroyer man said, "Wonderful girl. Danced like an angel. She was the first one on the island to have an American baby."

"Was it a boy?" Hale asked.

"Yes, but she gave it to a family on Maupiti. Girls there had no chance to produce American babies, and the island wanted one."

And suddenly, in the smoke-filled bar, Hoxworth Hale saw a young girl dancing beside a lagoon, and he saw on the blue waters an ancient double-hulled canoe and he thought: "I am forever a part of Bora Bora, and my son lives on in the islands." Then the memory vanished and he heard a girl's voice lamenting: "The years go by very fast, and soon we play no more games."

In time, Hale's visit to the South Seas produced other fruit than his memory of Tehani Vahine, for in addition to her lilting song of the coconut-grater, he constantly recalled his conversation with Sir Ratu Salaka in Fiji, and he began to compare all aspects of Hawaii with similar conditions in Fiji and Tahiti, and he came to this unshakable conclusion: "In every respect but one we Americans have done a better job in Hawaii than the English have in Fiji or the French in Tahiti. Health, education, building and the creation of new wealth . . . we are really far ahead. And in the way we've integrated our Orientals into the very heart of our society, we're so far ahead that no comparisons are even permissible. But in the way we have allowed our Hawaiians to lose their land, their language, and their culture, we have been terribly remiss. We could have accomplished all our good and at the same time protected the Hawaiians." But whenever he reached this conclusion he would think of Joe Tom Char, who now presided as president of the senate, and he was half-Hawaiian, half-Chinese, or of the year's beauty queen, Helen Fukuda, half-Hawaiian, half-Japanese; or of the innumerable Kees who seemed to be running Pearl Harbor, many of whom were half-Hawaiian, half-Chinese. "Perhaps we're building something in Hawaii that will be infinitely better than anything Fiji or Tahiti ever produces." At any rate, Hale returned from his trip no longer apologetic for what the missionaries had accomplished.

WHEN IN THE early days of the war Japanese boys in Hawaii were removed from combat units and expelled from R.O.T.C., the islands supposed that this was the end of the matter. "No Jap can be trusted, so we kicked them all out," a general explained.

But to everyone's surprise, the Japanese boys stubbornly refused to accept this verdict. Humbly, quietly, but with an almost terrifying moral force, these boys began to press for their full rights as American citizens. "We demand the inalienable privilege of dying for the nation we love," they argued, and if anyone had asked the Sakagawa boys why they said this, they would have replied, "We were treated decently at McKinley and at Punahou. We were taught what democracy means, and we insist upon our right to defend it."

Committees of Japanese boys began hammering officials with petitions. One drawn up by Goro Sakagawa read: "We are loyal American citizens, and humbly request the right to serve our nation in its time of crisis. If you think you cannot trust us to fight against Japan, at least send us to Europe where this problem does not arise." The committees went to see generals and admirals, governors and judges: "We will do any national work you assign us. We will ask for no wages. We must be allowed to prove that we are Americans."

For eleven painful weeks the Japanese boys got nowhere, and then, because the three younger Sakagawas were Punahou boys, they were able to meet one of the most extraordinary men Hawaii was to produce in the twentieth century. His name was Mark Whipple, born in 1900, the son of the medical doctor who had ordered Chinatown burned, great-great-grandson of John Whipple who had helped Christianize Hawaii. This Mark Whipple was a West Point man and a colonel in the United States army. Most of his duty had been spent outside Hawaii, but recently he had been assigned to help the high command deal with the Japanese question; and in Washington it had been assumed that when he got to Hawaii he would quickly order the evacuation of all Japanese—none of whom could be trusted—to some concentration camp either in Nevada or on the island of Molokai: "This will include, of course, all the little yellow bastards who have infiltrated themselves into such units as the 298th Infantry and the local R.O.T.C. outfits."

Colonel Mark Whipple disappointed just about everybody, for when he reached Hawaii bearing very powerful directives specifically handed him by President Roosevelt, who knew his family, he gave no quick orders, paraded no insolence, but went swiftly to work. The first man he called in for a conference was the Honolulu head of the F.B.I., who reported, as Whipple had anticipated: "So far as we have presently ascertained, there was not a single case of espionage by any Japanese other than the registered and duly appointed agents of the Japanese consulate, all of whom were citizens of Japan."

"Then the Secretary of Navy's hasty report that Pearl Harbor was betrayed by local Japanese was all hogwash?" Whipple asked.

"Yes. But he can be forgiven. Excited admirals fed him the line. Now they know better."

"Any disloyalty now?" Whipple asked.

"Quite the contrary. The young Japanese seem to be burning to get into uniform. Had two of them in here the other day. Fine boys. Got kicked out of R.O.T.C. and now want us to use them as labor battalions, anything. They offer to serve with no pay."

"You got their names?"

"Right here."

Colonel Whipple hesitated before taking the paper. "I promise you that I will not write down what you reply to my next question. But I need guidance. Will you state categorically that the local Japanese have not engaged in sabotage of any kind?"

"I will state categorically that there has not been a single case of sabotage," the F.B.I. man said.

Whipple drummed his fingers. "I'd like to see those names. Can you get the boys in here?"

As a result of that meeting the Varsity Victory Volunteers were formed, with Tadao and Minoru Sakagawa as first members. The V.V.V. were all Japanese, all boys of the highest intelligence and patriotism. They foresaw that the entire future of their people in America depended upon what they did in this war against Japan, and they decided that if they were prevented by hysteria from bearing arms, they would bear shovels. They would dig out latrines, and pick up after white soldiers, and build bridges. There would be no work too menial for them, and they would do it all for $90 a month while their haole and Chinese schoolmates earned ten times that much working for the government in civilian jobs at Pearl Harbor. As Tadao told Colonel Whipple, "We will do anything to prove that we are Americans."

Colonel Whipple, when he recommended that the V.V.V. be established, drew a good deal of criticism from his fellow officers, but he pointed out that he carried a special command from Roosevelt to see exactly what could be done with the Japanese, and he was going to explore all possibilities; but when he next proposed that no Japanese be evacuated to prison camps, neither on Molokai nor anywhere else, the roof fell in.

"Do you mean to say . . ." a South Carolina admiral bellowed.

"I mean to say, sir, that these people are loyal Americans and no purpose would be served by placing them in prison camps."

"Why, goddamn it, California has shown us the way to handle these traitors."

"What California has done is its own affair. Here in Hawaii we won't do it that way."

"By God, Whipple! You're subversive!"

But Mark Whipple was not deviated one degree from the true course he had set himself. When a convocation of his own family warned him, "There's a good deal of apprehension about you, Mark. Military people say you're imperiling your whole career," he replied, "In this matter, I have a special burden to bear which only I can bear, and I would prefer to hear no more gossip of any kind. Because what I am about to propose next is going to tear this entire military community apart. Maybe you'd better fortify your tired nerves."

What he proposed was this: "I think we had better form, right now—this week—a special unit of the United States army composed solely of Japanese boys from Hawaii. Use them in Europe. Throw them against the Germans, and when they perform as I know they will, they'll not only re-establish their credentials here but in America. They will give all free men a propaganda victory over Naziism that will reverberate around the world. With their courage, they will prove Hitler wrong on every single count of his philosophy."

A gasp went up, which was duly reported by cable to Washington, where it was augmented: "Japanese troops in the American army? And a special unit at that? Ridiculous."

But one man did not think it ridiculous, the President of the United States, and when he had studied Colonel Whipple's report he issued a statement which read: "Patriotism is not a matter of the skin's color. It is a matter of the heart."

In Hawaii there was still vigorous opposition to the formation of such a unit, but when the President's order reached Honolulu in mid-May of 1942 grudging compliance was obligatory, and one gruff general asked, "Who'd want to march into battle with a regiment of Japs behind him?"

"I would," Colonel Whipple replied.

"You mean . . . you're volunteering for the job?"

"I am, sir."

"You've got it, and I hope you don't get shot in the back."

Colonel Whipple saluted and took prompt steps to assemble into one unit all the Japanese boys already in the army—men like Goro Sakagawa of the 298th Infantry—and to pave the way for later acceptance of others like those now in the V.V.V. or those like young Shigeo who were about ready for the draft. The Whipple family was distressed that their most brilliant son was imperiling his career by such imprudent action, but as he had told them earlier, in this matter he bore a special burden.

It arose from the fact that when he was a boy in Honolulu no Chinese would speak to him, for he was the son of the man who had burned Chinatown at the instigation of the haole merchants. He could never bring himself to believe that his gentle, courageous father, Dr. Whipple, had done such a thing, but the Chinese were certain that he had. To them the name of Whipple was ugly, and they were not reluctant to demonstrate this fact to young Mark. Finally, when his own haole playmates began to tease him, he accosted his father and had asked him point-blank: "Dad, did you burn Chinatown?"

"Well, in a manner of speaking, I did."

"In order to put the Chinese merchants out of business?"

His father had stopped and bowed his head. "So now you've heard that? What did they say?"

"They say there was a little sickness, and the haole storekeepers talked you into burning Chinatown and putting all the Chinese out of business."

"Now exactly who said this, son?"

"The haoles. The Chinese didn't say it because they won't even speak to me. But I know they think it."

Dr. Hewlett Whipple was then a man of forty, and about as successful a medical practitioner as one could hope to be in Honolulu, but the weight of his son's charge was very heavy indeed upon his soul. He led his twelve-year-old son to a grassy spot under a tree on the lawn of his Punchbowl home and said, "Now you ask me all the questions that worry you, Mark. And never forget what I reply."

"Did you burn Chinatown?"

"Yes."

"And did the Chinese lose all their stores?"

"Yes."

Mark had no further questions, so he shrugged his shoulders. His father laughed and said, "You aren't going to stop there, are you?"

"You've told me what I wanted to know," the boy replied.

"But aren't you concerned about the real truth? What really happened?"

"Well, like the boys said, you admitted burning the place."

"Mark, this is what truth is. Going behind what you hear first. Asking a hundred questions until you can make up your own mind on the basis of real evidence. Now let me ask the questions that you should have. All right?"

"Okay."

"*Dr. Whipple, why did you burn Chinatown?* Because a dreadful plague threatened the city.

"*Did burning Chinatown help save the city?* It saved ten thousand lives.

"*Did you intend to burn the Chinese stores?* No, the fire got out of hand. It ran away from us.

"*Did you do anything to help the Chinese?* I ran into the middle of the fire myself and helped them to safety.

"*Were you sorry that the fire got out of hand?* When I got home and looked back upon the destruction I sat down and wept.

"*Would you burn it again under the same circumstances?* I would."

A silence fell over the Whipples and they looked down at their city. Young Mark, in those moments, caught a glimmer of what truth was, but what his father said next exploded truth from a shimmering substance playing upon the edges of the mind into a radiant reality, for he said, "There are two other questions which have to be asked, and these require longer answers. Are you ready?"

"Yes."

"*Dr. Whipple, tell me honestly, were there not some haoles who were glad to see Chinatown burned?* Of course there were. And some Chinese, too. Any good action in the world will be used by some to their own economic advantage. Any misfortune will be used the same way. Therefore, you would expect some to profit from the burning and to be glad that it happened. When the fire was over, these same men rebuilt Chinatown exactly as it was before, so as to keep on making a little money from the hovels. So if your Chinese friends say there were some who were glad to see the Chinese stores destroyed, they are correct. But I was not one of them.

"*Dr. Whipple, can you not, even so, understand why the Chinese hate you?* Of course I understand. They believe falsehood, and it's always easier to accept a lie than to find out the truth. When I move through Honolulu, this is one of the burdens I am forced to bear. The Chinese hate me. But if they knew the truth, they would not."

As a colonel in the United States army, Mark Whipple often remembered that discussion with his father, and sometimes when he was required to make his men do brutal or unpleasant work, he knew that in ignorance they would hate him, whereas if they knew the truth they would not. So when he returned to Hawaii to deal with the Japanese problem, he was motivated by an acute desire that he, Mark Whipple, should, by dealing with the Japanese honestly, erase the stigma that his father Hewlett Whipple had suffered at the hands of the Chinese. In a sense, therefore, he did not volunteer to lead the Japanese troops; he was impelled by the entire history of his family to do so; for the Whipples of Hawaii were people who tried always to keep history straight.

His all-Japanese outfit, commanded by a cadre of haole officers, was known as the 222nd Combat Team, and it became a running joke in the unit for older men to ask newcomers, "What's your outfit, son?" And when the private replied, "The Two-Two-Two," the old-timers would shout, "Listen! He's playing train!" Later they would bellow, "What's your unit?" and when the private replied, "The Two-Two-Two," they would growl, "Speak up, son! Don't stutter."

The arm patch of the Two-Two-Two consisted of a blue sky against which rose a brown Diamond Head, at whose feet rested one palm tree and three white lines of rolling surf. Below in block letters stood the pidgin motto: "Mo Bettah." It was a handsome patch, and spoke of Hawaii, but the outfit did not appreciate how much Mo Bettah home was than some other places until they set up their basic training camp at Camp Bulwer in the boondocks of Mississippi.

On the first day in town Goro Sakagawa had to go to the toilet, and through ignorance stumbled into the "White" toilet. "Get out of here, you goddamned yellow-belly!" a native growled, and Goro backed out. Others had similar experiences, so that trouble threatened, but that night Colonel Mark Whipple showed the kind of man he was. Assembling the entire unit he shouted, "You men have only one job. Allow nothing whatever, neither death nor humiliation nor fear nor hunger, to deviate you from that job. You are here to prove to America that you are loyal citizens. You can do this only by becoming the finest soldiers in the American army and the most efficient fighters.

"If the people of Mississippi want to abuse you, they are free to do so. And you will keep your big mouths shut and take it. Because if any man in this outfit causes even one shred of trouble, I will personally ride him right to the gates of hell. Are there any questions?"

"Am I supposed to take it if some local yokel calls me a slant-eyed yellow-belly?"

"Yes!" Whipple stormed. "By God yes! Because if you're so sensitive that you are willing to imperil the future of all the Japanese in America for such a cause, then by God, Hashimoto, you are a slant-eyed yellow-belly. You're a creep. You're a damned Jap. You're what everybody accuses you of being, and in my eyes you're no man."

"Then we take it?" Goro asked in deep, stomach-churning fury. "Whatever they want to call us?"

"You take it," Whipple snarled. "Can't you add, you damned, stubborn buddha-heads?" As he said this he laughed, and the tension was broken. "For the insults that one accidental man throws at you, are you willing to put into jeopardy the future of three hundred thousand Japanese? Don't be idiots. For the love of Christ, don't be idiots."

From the rear ranks a sergeant grumbled, "I guess we can take it."

Then Colonel Whipple said, "Keep this vision in mind, men. As a unit you're going to strike the German army some day. And when you do, you're going to win. Of that there can be no doubt, for I have never led finer men. And when you win, you will triumph over bigotry at home, over Hitlerism abroad, over any insult you have ever borne. Your mothers and fathers and your children after you will lead better lives because of what you do. Aren't these stakes worth fighting for?"

Colonel Whipple laid down the most rigid rules and enforced them brutally: "Not a word of Japanese will be spoken in this outfit. You're Americans. Under no circumstances are you to ask a white girl for a date. It makes local people mad. You are absolutely forbidden to date a colored girl. That makes them even madder. And they have four long trains that haul beer into this state every week. You can't possibly drink it all."

Remorselessly Colonel Whipple drove his men according to West Point traditions of military behavior and his own family traditions of civil decency. In all America no unit in training suffered more disciplinary action than the Two-Two-Two, for their colonel held them responsible both on the post and off, and at the slightest infraction, he punished them. There was only one flare-up. After a great deal of heart-probing consultation the good people of Mississippi decided that so far as public toilets and buses were concerned, the Japanese soldiers were to be considered white men and were thus obligated to use white facilities; but where socializing with the community was concerned, it was better if they considered themselves halfway between the white and the Negro and off-limits to each.

This was too much, and Goro went to see Colonel Whipple. "I appreciate what you said, Colonel, and we've been abiding by your rules. But this directive on toilets is just too much. I can urinate like a white man but I've got to socialize like a Negro. The basic thing we're fighting for is human decency. Our men don't want the kind of concessions Mississippi is willing to make. We want to be treated like Negroes."

Colonel Whipple did not rant. He said quietly, "I agree with you, Sakagawa. Decency is one unbroken fabric without beginning or end. No man can logically fight for Japanese rights and at the same time ignore Negro rights. Logically he can't do it, but sometimes he's got to. And right now is one of those times."

"You mean we're to accept what Mississippi says, even though we know that given a chance they'd treat us worse than they do the Negroes?"

"That's the tactical situation you find yourself in."

"It's so illogical our men may not be able to take it."

Again Colonel Whipple failed to bellow. Instead he picked up an order and waved it at Goro, saying, "And the reason you'll take it is this paper. The army has agreed to accept all Japanese boys who want to volunteer. Your two brothers in the V.V.V. will be transferred to the outfit tonight. Now if trouble were to start in Mississippi, all that I've managed to acquire for you fellows would be lost. So, Goro, you urinate where the haoles tell you to."

In accordance with the new directive, the army announced that it would beef up the Two-Two-Two by adding 1,500 volunteers from Hawaii and 1,500 from the mainland, but the plan didn't work because in Honolulu 11,800 rushed forward to serve, stampeding the registration booths. Seven out of eight had to be turned down, including Shigeo Sakagawa, who wept. But on the mainland only 500 volunteered, leaving a thousand empty spaces. Quickly the army returned to Hawaii and filled the gaps left by the poor response of the mainland Japanese, and in this second draft, young Shig was accepted.

When President Roosevelt compared the contrasting reactions of the two groups, he ordered Colonel Whipple to submit an explanation of what had happened, and Whipple wrote: "Far from being a cause for concern, the differential should encourage us in our devotion to the perpetual effectiveness of democracy. If the result had been any different, I should have been worried. That the Hawaii Japanese behaved well and that the mainland boys did not is to me, and I think to America, reassuring.

"In Hawaii, Japanese were free to own land. In California they were not. In Hawaii they could become schoolteachers and government employees. In California they could not. In Hawaii they were accepted into our best schools, but not in California. In Hawaii they were built into our society and became a part of us, but in California they were rejected.

"More important, when war came the Japanese on the mainland were herded into concentration camps and their belongings were ruthlessly stripped from them at five cents on the dollar. In Hawaii there was some talk of this, but it was never permitted to go very far. Right after Pearl Harbor a good many Japanese in Hawaii were rounded up for concentration camps, but my aunt tells me that she personally, along with other Caucasian leaders of the community, went to the jail and effected the release of those she knew to be loyal. In short, the Japanese in Hawaii had every reason to fight for America; those on the mainland had none; and the basic difference lay not in the Japanese but in the way they were treated by their fellow citizens.

"So is it not logical that if you tell a group of Hawaiian Japanese who have not been thrown into camps or robbed of their belongings, 'You can volunteer to help us fight oppression,' that 11,800 should leap forward? And is it not logical that if you go through concentration camps and tell the brothers of these same men, 'We have abused you, imprisoned you, humiliated you, and stolen your belongings, but now we want you to volunteer to fight for us,' is it not logical that they should reply, 'Go to hell'? I am astonished that so many of the mainland Japanese volunteered. They must be very brave men, and I shall welcome them in my unit."

When President Roosevelt read the report he asked his aide, "Who is this Mark Whipple again?"

"You knew his father, Dr. Hewlett Whipple."

"The boy sounds intelligent. Is he the one who's leading the Japanese?"

"Yes. They're on their way to Italy now."

"We should expect some good news from that outfit," the President said.

One night in September, 1943, Nyuk Tsin asked her grandson Hong Kong, "Are we overextended?"

"Yes."

"If war ended tomorrow, would we be able to hold onto our properties?"

"No."

"What do you think we should do?" the old lady asked.

"I seem to have acquired your courage," Hong Kong replied. "I say. 'Hold onto our lands.' We'll pay off as much debt as we can, and when the war ends we'll tighten our belts and live on rice until the boom starts."

"How many bad years must we look forward to?" the old matriarch asked.

"Two very difficult years. Two reasonably dangerous. If we get through them, the hui will be prosperous."

"I'm worried," the old woman confessed, "but I agree with you that we must fight to a finish. However, I've been thinking that we might start to sell off a few of the houses, to relieve the pressure."

"The pressure is only on you and me," Hong Kong pointed out. "The others don't know about it. If you're not afraid, I'm not."

It was a curious thing for an old woman of ninety-six to be worrying about the future, but she was, and it was not her future that concerned her, but that of her great family, the on-going thing that she had started but which was now more powerful than she. Therefore she said, "It is not only our money we are gambling with, Hong Kong, but that of all the Kees, those who are working and the girls in the stores and the old people. Thinking of them, are you still willing to hold onto everything?"

"It is for them that I'm doing it," Hong Kong replied. "I know the delicate structure we've built. A house on top of a store on top of a job at Pearl Harbor on top of a little piece of land on top of an old man's savings. Maybe it's all going to crumble, but I'm willing to gamble that when it starts to totter, you and I will be smart enough to catch the falling pieces."

"I think it's beginning to totter now, Hong Kong," the old woman warned.

"I don't think it is," her grandson replied, and for once he ignored his grandmother's advice, and she said, "This is your decision, Hong Kong," and he replied, "We started our adventure when the haoles ran away from the war, and I'm not going to run away now," and she promised, "At least I won't tell the others of my fears."

He therefore held onto the fantastic, teetering structure—depending solely upon his own courage—and as Honolulu rents rose, and wages at Pearl Harbor, and profits from the stores, he applied the money Asia provided to further gambles, and the structure grew higher and more precarious, but he was never afraid of his perilous construction, and his old grandmother grew increasingly to realize that in Hong Kong she had developed a grandson she could truly admire. "In many ways," she reflected, thinking back to the High Village and the warm days of her youth, "he is like my father. He is bold, and willing to engage in great battles, and he will probably wind up with his head in a cage in the center of Honolulu." Then she thought of her father's grisly visage, staring, neckless, down upon the years, and she concluded: "Was it a bad way to die?" And the perilous gamble of the Kee hui continued.

WHILE THE FOUR Sakagawa boys were in uniform, fighting for an unqualified citizenship, their parents and their sister Reiko were experiencing grave contradictions and confusions. On the one hand, the older Sakagawas prayed for the safe return of their sons, and this implied an American victory, at least over the Germans, and accordingly they listened with gratification when Reiko-chan read them the local Japanese newspaper, the *Nippu Jiji,* which told of victory in Europe. But on the other hand, they continued to pray for Japanese victory in Asia, for their homeland was in trouble and they hoped that it would triumph, never admitting to themselves that American victory in Europe and Japanese victory in Asia were incompatible.

Then one day Mr. Ishii appeared furtively at the barbershop, whispering, "Tremendous news! I must stop by to see you tonight." And before Sakagawa-san could halt the little man, the latter had vanished into another Japanese store.

That evening, after Sakagawa had closed the barbershop and walked the girl barbers safely home, ignoring the whistles of American sailors who loafed on Hotel Street, Kamejiro said to Reiko, "You can be sure that Mr. Ishii has something very important for us," and the two hurried through the dark streets to the little cottage in Kakaako. There Mr. Ishii waited, and after the household was settled and the blinds drawn, he strode dramatically to the table where the day's issue of the *Nippu Jiji* lay and with fury tore it to bits, threw it on the floor, and spat on it.

"Thus I treat the enemies of Japan!" he cried.

"I haven't read it . . ." Reiko pleaded, trying to halt him.

"Never again will you read that filthy propaganda!" Mr. Ishii announced grandly. "I told you, didn't I, that it was all American lies? You laughed at me and said, 'What does Mr. Ishii know about war?' My friends, I will tell you what I know. I know what is really happening in the world. And in America all good Japanese know. It is only you fools who have to read the Hawaii newspapers who do not know."

Flamboyantly, he whipped out from his coat pocket a Japanese newspaper printed in Wyoming, the *Prairie Shinbun,* and there for Reiko to see were the exciting headlines: "Imperial Forces Defeat Americans in Bougainville." "Great Japanese Victory at Guadalcanal." "President Roosevelt Admits Japan Will Win the War." Most of the stories appearing on the front pages had been picked up from Japanese short-wave broadcasts emanating from military headquarters in Tokyo, and all purveyed the straight Japanese propaganda line. One story in particular infuriated the hushed group in the Sakagawa living room: "American Marines Confess Stabbing Helpless Japanese Soldiers with Bayonets." The story came from Tokyo and could not be doubted.

When the horror at American brutality subsided, Mr. Ishii proceeded with the important news, a story in which the Wyoming editors summarized, by means of Imperial releases, the progress of the war, and it was apparent to all in the little room that Japan was not only triumphing throughout the Pacific but that she must soon invade Hawaii. "And then, Sakagawa-san, what are you going to tell the emperor's general when he strides ashore at Honolulu and asks, 'Sakagawa, were you a good Japanese?' You, with four sons fighting against the emperor. And do you know what the general is going to say when he hears your reply? He's going to say, 'Sakagawa, bend down.' And when you have bent down, the general himself is going to unscabbard his sword and cut off your head."

None of the Sakagawas spoke. They looked at the newspaper dumbly, and Reiko picked out the headlines. It was a paper published openly in Wyoming, it had passed the United States censor, and what Mr. Ishii had read from it was true. Japan was winning the war and would soon invade Hawaii. In great pain of conscience Sakagawa-san looked at the paper which he could not read and asked Reiko-chan, "Is it true?" And his daughter said, "Yes."

It was one of the most exasperating anomalies of the war that whereas the F.B.I. and naval security kept very close watch on the Japanese newspapers in Hawaii, and saw that they printed only the strictest truth, with no stories at all datelined Tokyo, the Japanese-language newspapers in the states of Utah and Wyoming were free to print whatever they wished, it having been decided by the local military that the official Japanese communiqués were so ridiculous that they would in time defeat themselves, as indeed they did. So the mainland Japanese press, often edited by die-hard samurai types, kept pouring out an incredible mess of propaganda, rumor, anti-American sentiment and downright subversive lies, and when copies of the papers reached Hawaii, where rumors were apt to be virulent, their effect was shocking.

"I will tell the emperor's general," Sakagawa-san finally explained, "that my sons fought only in Europe. Never against Japan."

"It will do no good!" Mr. Ishii said sadly. "The emperor will never forgive you for what you have done."

Sakagawa-san felt weak. He had always had doubts about sending his sons to war, and now the Wyoming paper had fortified those doubts. Dumbly he looked at his old guide, and Mr. Ishii, after enjoying the moment of humiliation, finally said, "I will put in a good word for you with the general. I will tell him you have always been a good Japanese."

"Thank you, Mr. Ishii!" the dynamiter cried. "You are the only friend I can trust."

The Sakagawas went to bed that night in considerable torment, so the next day at her barber chair Reiko waited until an intelligent-looking young naval officer sat down, and when he had done so, she asked quietly, "Could you help me, please."

"Sure," the officer said. "Name's Jackson, from Seattle."

"A man told me last night that Japan might invade Hawaii at any moment. Is that true?"

The navy man's jaw dropped; he pulled the towel away from his neck and turned to look at Reiko, who was then twenty-six and at her prettiest. He smiled at her and asked, "Good God, woman! What have you been hearing?"

"I was told on good authority that Japanese ships might attack at any time."

"Look, lady!" the officer chided. "If you're a spy trying to get secrets . . ."

"Oh, no!" Reiko blushed. Then she saw her father approaching to enforce the rule against any conversation with customers. She retied the towel, jerking it back to muzzle the navy man, and started clipping. "We're not allowed to talk," she whispered.

"Where do you have lunch?" the officer asked.

"Senaga's," she whispered.

"I'll see you there, and tell you about the war."

"Oh, I couldn't!" Reiko blushed.

"Look, I'm from Seattle. I used to know lots of Japanese girls. Senaga's."

At the counter of the restaurant, run by the Okinawa pig-grower Senaga, Lieutenant Jackson surprised Reiko by ordering sushi and sashimi, which he attacked with chopsticks. "I served in Japan," he said. "If my skipper caught me eating with chopsticks I'd be courtmartialed. Unpatriotic."

"We all try to eat with forks," Reiko said.

"Now about this Jap invasion," Jackson said.

"Would you please not call us Japs?" Reiko asked.

"You're Japanese," Jackson laughed easily. "The enemy are Japs. What's your first name? Reiko, that's nice. Well, Reiko-chan . . ."

"Where did you learn Reiko-chan?"

"In Japan," he replied casually.

"Did you ever know a Reiko-chan?"

"I knew a Kioko-chan."

There was a long silence as they ate sushi, and Reiko wanted to ask many questions and Lieutenant Jackson wanted to make many comments, but neither spoke, until at the same moment Reiko pushed her fork toward the sashimi and the officer shoved his chopsticks at the raw fish. There was a clatter and laughter and Jackson said, "I was deeply in love with Kioko-chan, and she taught me some Japanese, and that's why I have my present job."

"What is it?" Reiko asked solemnly, her face flushed.

"Because I speak a little of your language . . . Well, you understand, I'm not really a navy officer. I'm a Seattle lawyer. I'm with the Adjutant General and my job is to visit Japanese families and tell them that their daughters should not marry American G.I.'s. I see about twenty families a week . . . You know how American men are, they see pretty girls and they want to marry 'em. My job is to see that they don't."

Suddenly he broke his chopsticks in half and his knuckles grew white with bitterness. "Each week, Reiko-chan, I see about twenty Japanese girls and argue with them, and every goddamned one of them reminds me of Kioko-chan, and pretty soon I'm going to go nuts."

He looked straight ahead, a man squeezed in a great vise, and he had no more appetite. Reiko, being a practical girl, finished the sashimi and said, "I must go back to work."

"Will you have lunch with me tomorrow?" the officer said.

"Yes," she said, but when he started to accompany her to the street, she gasped and said, "My father would die."

"Does he believe the Japanese fleet is coming soon?"

"Not he," she lied, "but his friend. What is the truth?"

"In one year or two we will destroy Japan."

That night Reiko-chan advised her father that there must be something wrong with the Wyoming newspaper, because Japan was not winning the war, but this infuriated Sakagawa-san, who had brought home a second copy of the *Prairie Shinbun,* more inflammatory than the first, and as Reiko patiently read it to him she herself began to wonder: "Who is telling the truth?"

Then proof came. President Roosevelt arrived in Honolulu aboard a naval ship, and the Sakagawas saw him with their own eyes and marked the way in which he rode through Honolulu, protected by dozens of secret-service men. To Sakagawa-san, this proved that America was strong, but he had not reckoned with Mr. Ishii's superior intellect, for scarcely had the long black automobiles sped by when the excited little man rushed into the barbershop with staggering news.

"Didn't I tell you?" he whispered. "Oh, tremendous! Come to Sakai's immediately."

Sakagawa turned the barbershop over to his daughter and slipped down a side street to Sakai's store, entering by a back door so as not to attract attention, for groups of Japanese were still prevented from assembling. In the back room Sakai, Mr. Ishii and several agitated older men stood discussing the exciting news. For a moment Sakagawa could not comprehend what it was all about, but soon Mr. Ishii explained everything.

"President Roosevelt has come to Hawaii on his way to Tokyo. He's going to surrender peacefully, be executed at the Yasukuni Shrine as a common war criminal, and the Japanese navy will be here in three days."

Mr. Ishii's stories always featured specific details and dates, and one would have thought that after a while his listeners would recall that for three years not one of his predictions had come to pass; but the hope of victory was so strong in the hearts of some of his audience that he was never called to task for his errors. "In three days!" he said. "Ships of the Imperial navy steaming into Pearl Harbor. But I will protect you, Sakagawa-san, and I will ask the emperor to forgive you for sending your sons to war."

When President Roosevelt left Honolulu for his execution in Tokyo, Mr. Ishii waited in a state of near-collapse for the battleships of his homeland to come steaming in from the west. For three nights he slept on his roof, waiting,

waiting, and in the little house in Kakaako, his friend Sakagawa also waited, in trepidation.

On the fourth day, when it was apparent that the Imperial navy was going to be temporarily delayed, Mr. Ishii dropped the whole subject and took up instead the rumor printed in the *Prairie Shinbun* that the Japanese had captured both Australia and New Zealand. He felt, he told the Sakagawas, that it might be a good idea to emigrate to Australia, for under Japanese control there would be good lands for all.

Reiko-chan discussed each of these rumors with Lieutenant Jackson, who listened patiently as the wide-eyed barber disclosed her apprehensions. Always he laughed, and once observed: "This Mr. Ishii must be quite a jerk," but Reiko apologized for the little man: "He came from Hiroshima long ago and has lived in darkness," whereupon the naval officer said, "He better watch out what he says. He could get into trouble." At this Reiko-chan laughed and said, "Nobody ever takes Mr. Ishii seriously. He's such a sweet, inoffensive little man."

It would be difficult to characterize as a love affair a series of meetings conducted in a barbershop under the hawklike eye of Kamejiro Sakagawa and in a crowded Okinawan restaurant run by the Senaga family, for between Reiko-chan and Lieutenant Jackson there were no crushing kisses or lingering farewells, but it was a love affair nevertheless, and on one bold Tuesday, Reiko extended her lunch hour till four in the afternoon, and that sunny day there were both kisses and enraptured embraces. One Wednesday night she slipped away from home and waited for Lieutenant Jackson's Chevrolet, and they drove out to Diamond Head and parked in a lovers' lane. Local people called this, "The midnight athletes watching the under-water submarine races under a full moon." But a shore patrol, inspecting the cars, called it country necking, and when they got to the Chevy they were astounded.

"What you doin' with a Jap, Lieutenant?"

"Talking."

"With a Jap?"

"Yes, with a Japanese."

"Let's see your papers."

"You didn't ask to see their papers."

"They're with white girls."

With a show of irritation Lieutenant Jackson produced his papers and the shore patrol shook their heads. "This beats anything," one of the sailors said. "She a local girl?"

"Of course."

"Can you speak English, lady?"

"Yes."

"Well, I guess it's all right, if a naval officer don't care whether he necks with a Jap or not."

"Look here, buddy . . ."

"You want to start something, sir?"

Lieutenant Jackson looked up at the two towering sailors and said, "No."

"We didn't think so. Good night, Jap-lover."

Lieutenant Jackson sat silent for some minutes, then said, "War is unbelievable. If those two boys live till we get to Tokyo, they'll probably fall in love with Japanese girls and marry them. With what confusion they will remember this night."

"Will our men get to Tokyo soon?" Reiko-chan asked.

The lieutenant was impressed by the manner in which she said "our men," and he asked, "Why did you say it that way?"

She replied, "I have four brothers fighting in Europe."

"You have . . ." he stopped, and on an uncontrollable impulse jumped out of the car and shouted, "Hey, shore patrol! Shore patrol!"

The two young policemen hurried back and asked, "What's the matter, Lieutenant? She turn out to be a spy?"

"Fellows, I want you to meet Miss Reiko Sakagawa. She has four brothers fighting in the American army in Italy. While you and I sit on our fat asses here in Hawaii. When you were here before, I didn't know."

"You got four men in the war?"

"Yes," she replied quietly.

"All army?"

"Yes. Japanese aren't allowed in the navy."

"Ma'am," one of the shore patrol said, a boy from Georgia, "I sure hope your brothers get home safe."

"Good night, miss," the other boy said.

"Night, fellows," Jackson muttered, and when the patrol wheeled down the road he stammered, "Reiko-chan, I think we ought to get married."

She sighed, clasped her hands very tightly, and said, "I thought your job was to keep men like you from marrying girls like me."

"It is, but have you ever noticed the way in which people in such jobs always fall prey to the very thing they are fighting against? It's uncanny. I've intervened in some three hundred cases like this, and almost every time the man has been from the Deep South."

"What has that to do with us?" Reiko-chan asked.

"You see, at home these Southern boys have been taught from birth that anyone with a different color is evil and to be despised. In their hearts they know this can't be true, so as soon as they get a fair chance to investigate a girl with a different color, they find her a human being and they suffer a compulsion to fall in love and marry her."

"Are you from the South, Lieutenant? Do you act from such a compulsion?"

"I'm from Seattle, but I have a compulsion greater than any of them. After Pearl Harbor my father, a pretty good man by and large, was the one who spearheaded the drive to throw all Japanese into concentration camps. He knew he was doing an evil thing. He knew he was giving false testimony and acting for his own economic advantage. But nevertheless, he went ahead. On the night he made his inflammatory speech over the radio I told him, 'Pop, you know what you said isn't true,' and he replied, 'This is war, son.' "

"So you want to marry me to get even with him?" Reiko asked. "I couldn't marry you on those terms."

"The compulsion is much deeper, Reiko-chan. Remember that I lived in Japan. No matter how old we both get, Reiko, never forget that at the height of the war I told you, 'When peace comes, Japan and America will be compatible friends.' I am positive of it. I am positive that my father, since he is essentially a good man, will welcome you graciously as his daughter. Because people have got to forget past errors. They have got to bind separated units together."

"You talk as if your father were the problem," Reiko said quietly.

"You mean yours is?"

"We will never get married," Reiko said sorrowfully. "My father would never permit it."

"Tell your father to go to hell. I told mine."

"But I am a Japanese," she said, kissing him on the lips.

* * *

Kamejiro Sakagawa first discovered his daughter's love affair with a haole when his good friend Sakai appeared at the barbershop one morning to say, "I am sorry, Kamejiro, but my daughter cannot work here any more."

Sakagawa gasped and asked, "Why not? I pay her well."

"Yes, and we need the money, but I can't risk having her work here another day. It might happen to her too. So many haoles coming in here."

"What might happen?" Sakagawa stammered.

"More better we go outside," Sakai said. There, along a gutter on Hotel Street, he said sorrowfully, "You have been a good friend, Kamejiro, and you have paid our girl well, but we cannot run the risk of her falling in love with a haole man, the way your Reiko has."

Little bulldog Kamejiro, his neck muscles standing out, grabbed his friend by the shoulders, rising on his toes to accomplish the feat. "What are you saying?" he roared.

"Kamejiro!" his friend protested, trying vainly to break loose from the frightening grip. "Ask anyone. Your daughter has lunch every day with the American . . . at Senaga's."

In a state of shock, little Kamejiro Sakagawa thrust his friend away and stared down Hotel Street at the Okinawa restaurant run by the pig-farmer, Senaga, and as he watched, that crafty Senaga entered the shop, taking with him a haole friend, and in this simple omen Sakagawa saw the truth of what his compatriot Sakai had charged. Reiko-chan, as good a daughter as a man ever had, strong and dutiful, had been visiting with a haole in an Okinawan restaurant. Shattered, the stocky little man, then sixty-one, leaned against a post, oblivious of the flow of sailors and soldiers about him.

It was ironic, he thought, that war should have catapulted two of the groups he hated most into such postures of success. The damned Chinese had all the good jobs at Pearl Harbor, and with the income they got, were buying up most of Honolulu. Their sons were not at war, and their arrogance was high. As allies, followers of the damnable Chiang Kai-shek, who had resisted decent Japanese overtures in China, they appeared in all the parades and made speeches over the radio. The Chinese, Sakagawa reflected that ugly morning, were doing very well.

But what was particularly galling was that the Okinawans were doing even better. Now, an Okinawan, Sakagawa mused in sullen anger as he studied Senaga's restaurant, is a very poor man to begin with, neither wholly Japanese nor wholly Chinese but making believe to be the former. An Okinawan cannot be trusted, must be watched every minute lest he set his daughters to trick a man's sons, and is a man who lacks the true Japanese spirit. There were few men in the world, Sakagawa felt, lower than an Okinawan, yet look at what had happened to them during the war!

Because in the years before 1941 they had not been accepted into Japanese society, they had banded together. Most of the garbage in Honolulu was collected by Okinawans. To get rid of the garbage they kept pigs, hundreds upon hundreds of pigs. So when the war came, and freighters were no longer available to carry fresh beef from California to Hawaii, where did everyone have to go for meat? To the Okinawans! Who opened up one restaurant after another, because they had the meat? The Okinawans! Who was going to come out of the war richer than even the white people? The Okinawans! It was a cruel jest, that an Okinawan should wind up rich and powerful and respected, just because he happened to own all the pigs.

It was with these thoughts that the little dynamiter, Kamejiro Sakagawa, hid among the crowd on Hotel Street and waited to spy upon his daughter Reiko, and as he waited he muttered to himself, "With a haole, in an Okinawan restaurant!" It was really more than he could comprehend.

At five minutes after twelve Lieutenant Jackson entered the restaurant and took a table which smiling Senaga-san had been reserving for him. The officer ordered a little plate of pickled radishes, which he ate deftly with chopsticks, and Sakagawa thought: "What's he doing eating tsukemono? With hashi?"

At ten minutes after twelve Reiko Sakagawa hurried into the restaurant, and even a blind man could have seen from the manner in which she smiled and the way in which her whole eager body bent forward that she was in love. She did not touch the naval officer, but her radiant face and glowing eyes came peacefully to rest a few inches from his. With a fork she began picking up a few pieces of radish, and her father, watching from the street, thought: "It's all very confusing. What is she doing with a fork?"

During the entire meal the little Japanese watched the miserable spectacle of his daughter having a date with a haole, and long before she was ready to leave, Kamejiro had hastened back down Hotel Street to his friend Sakai's store, asking, "Sakai, what shall I do?"

"Did you see for yourself?"

"Yes. What you said is true."

"Hasegawa is taking his daughter out of the barbershop, too."

"To hell with the barbershop! What shall I do about Reiko?"

"What you must do, Kamejiro, is find out who this haole is. Then go to the navy and ask that he be transferred."

"Would the navy listen to me?" Kamejiro pleaded.

"On such a matter, yes," Sakai said with finality. Then he added, "But your most important job, Kamejiro, is to find a husband for your daughter."

"For years I have been looking," the little dynamiter said.

"I will act as the go-between," Sakai promised. "But it will not be easy. Now that she has ruined herself with a haole."

"No! Don't say that. Reiko-chan is a good girl."

"But already everyone knows she has been going with a haole. What self-respecting Japanese family will accept her now, Kamejiro?"

"Will you work hard as the go-between, Sakai?"

"I will find a husband for your daughter. A decent Japanese man."

"You are my friend," Sakagawa said tearfully, but before he left he added prudently, "Sakai, could you please try to find a Hiroshima man? That would be better."

Mrs. Sakagawa had spent the morning at home making pickled cabbage and the afternoon at Mrs. Mark Whipple's rolling Red Cross bandages. The latter experience had been a trying one, for every woman in the room had at least one son in the Two-Two-Two except Mrs. Whipple, and her husband commanded it. Therefore, the conversation, which most of the Japanese women could not participate in, had to be about the war in Italy and the heavy casualties which the Japanese boys were suffering, but whenever grief began to stalk the room, Mrs. Whipple, one of the Hale girls, invariably brought up some new and cheering fact. Once she said, "President Roosevelt himself has announced that our boys are among the bravest that have fought under the Stars and Stripes." Later she said, *"Time* magazine this week reports that when our boys reached Salerno on leave, the other troops at the railway station cheered them as they disembarked." Mrs. Whipple always referred to the Japanese soldiers as "our boys," and other haoles in Hawaii were beginning to do the same.

So the afternoon had been an emotional one, regardless of whether the talk was of casualties or of triumphs, and Mrs. Sakagawa, whose feet were sore from the American shoes she felt obligated to wear, reached home eager for rest. Instead, she found her husband at home rather than in the barbershop, and she knew that something dire had happened. Before she could ask, Kamejiro shouted, "A fine daughter you raised! She's in love with a haole!"

The words were the harshest that Mrs. Sakagawa could have heard. There were some Japanese girls, she had to admit, who went openly with haoles, but they were not from self-respecting families, and there were a few who under the pressure of war had become prostitutes, but she suspected that these were really either Etas or Okinawans. It was unlikely that any Japanese girl, mindful of the proud blood that flowed in her veins . . .

"And Sakai took his daughter out of the barbershop lest she become contaminated too, and Hasegawa is removing his daughter tomorrow." He was about to cry, "We are ruined," but an even deeper concern overcame him, and he fell into a chair, sinking his head on his forearms and sobbing, "Our family has never known shame before."

Mrs. Sakagawa, who refused to believe that her daughter could have brought disgrace upon the family, kicked off her American shoes, wriggled her toes in comfort, and kneeled beside her distraught husband. "Kamejiro," she whispered, "we taught Reiko how to be a good Japanese. I am sure she will not disgrace us. Somebody has told you a great lie."

Violently the little dynamiter thrust his wife aside and strode across the room. "I saw them! She was almost kissing him in public. And I've been thinking. Where was she that afternoon she said she didn't feel well? Out with a haole. And where was she when she said she was going to a cinema? Riding in a dark car with a haole. I heard a car stop that night, but I was too stupid to put two and two together."

At this moment Reiko-chan, flushed with love and the brisk walk home, entered and saw immediately from her parents' faces that her secret had been discovered. Her father said simply, with a heartbreaking gasp, "My own daughter! With a haole!" Her mother was still ready to dismiss the whole scandal and asked, "It isn't true, is it?"

Reiko-chan, her dark eyes warm with the inner conviction that was to sustain her through the impending argument, replied, "I am in love, and I want to get married."

No one spoke. Kamejiro fell back into a chair and buried his face. Mrs. Sakagawa stared at her daughter in disbelief and then began to treat her with exaggerated solicitude, as if she were already illegally pregnant. Reiko smiled in quiet amusement, but then her stricken father gave an appalling gasp, and she knelt beside him, saying quickly, "Lieutenant Jackson is a wonderful man, Father. He's understanding, and he's lived in Japan. He has a good job in Seattle, but he thinks he may settle here after the war." She hesitated, for her words were not being heard, and then added, "Wherever he goes, I want to go with him."

Slowly her father pushed himself back from the table, withdrew from his daughter, and looked at her in shocked disbelief. "But you are a Japanese!" he cried in his misery.

"I am going to marry him, Father," his daughter repeated forcefully.

"But you're a Japanese," he reiterated. Taking her hand he said, "You have the blood of Japan, the strength of a great nation, everything . . ." He tried to explain how unthinkable her suggestion was, but could come back to only one paramount fact. "You're a Japanese!"

Reiko explained patiently, "Lieutenant Jackson is a respectable man. He has a much better job than any man here that I might possibly marry. He's a college graduate and has a good deal of money in the bank. His family is well known in Seattle. These things aren't of major importance, but I tell you so that you will realize what an unusual man he is."

Kamejiro listened in disgust at the rigmarole, and when it seemed likely that Reiko was going to add more, he slapped her sharply across the cheek. "It would be humiliating," he cried. "A permanent disgrace. Already even the rumor of your behavior has ruined the barbershop. The Sakai girl has quit. So has the Hasegawa. No self-respecting Japanese family will want to associate with us after what you have done."

Reiko pressed her hand to her burning cheek and said quietly, "Father, hundreds of decent Japanese girls have fallen in love with Americans."

"Whores, all of them!" Kamejiro stormed.

Ignoring him Reiko said, "I know, because that's Lieutenant Jackson's job. To talk with parents like you. And the girls are not . . ."

"Aha!" Kamejiro cried. "So that's what he does! Tomorrow I go see Admiral Nimitz."

"Father, I warn you that if you . . ."

"Admiral Nimitz will hear of this!"

The little dynamiter did not actually get to Nimitz. He was stopped first by an ensign, who was so enthralled by the stalwart, bow-armed Japanese that he passed him along to a full lieutenant who sent him on to a commodore who burst into the office of a rear admiral, with the cry: "Jesus, Jack! There's a little Japanese out here with the goddamnedest story you every heard. You gotta listen."

So a circle of captains, commodores and admirals interrupted their work to listen to Kamejiro's hilarious pidgin as he protested to the navy that one of their officers had wrecked his barbershop and had ruined his daughter.

"Is she pregnant?" one of the rear admirals asked.

"You watch out!" Kamejiro cried. "Mo bettah you know Reiko a good wahine!"

"I'm sorry, Mr. Sakagawa. In our language *ruined* means, well, *ruined.*"

When the officers heard who it was that ruined, or whatever, the girl Reiko, they almost exploded. "That goddamned Jackson!" one of them sputtered. "His job is to break up this sort of thing."

"I've told you a dozen times," another said. "Putting a civilian into uniform doesn't make him an officer."

"That's beside the point," the senior admiral said. "What I'd like to know, Mr. Sakagawa, is this. If the boy has a good reputation, a good job, a good income, and a good family back in Seattle . . . Well, what I'm driving at is this. Your daughter is a lady barber. It would seem to me that you would jump at the chance for such a marriage."

Little Kamejiro, who was shorter by nine inches than any man in the room, stared at them in amazement. "She's a Japanese!" he said to the interpreter. "It would be disgraceful if she married a haole."

"How's that?" the commodore asked.

"It would bring such shame on our family . . ."

"What the hell do you mean?" the commodore bellowed. "Since when is a Jap marrying a decent American a matter of shame . . . to the Jap?"

"Her brothers in Italy would be humiliated before all their companions," Kamejiro doggedly explained.

"What's that again?" the senior officer asked. "She got brothers in Italy?"

"My four boys are fighting in Italy," Kamejiro said humbly.

One of the rear admirals rose and came over to the little dynamiter. "You have four sons in the Two-Two-Two?"

"Yes."

"They all in Italy?"

"Yes."

There was a long silence, broken by the admiral, who said, "I got one son there. I worry about him all the time."

"I am worried about my daughter," the stubborn little man replied.

"And if she marries a white man, her four brothers won't be able to live down the disgrace?"

"Never."

"What do you want Admiral Nimitz to do?"

"Send Lieutenant Jackson away."

"He will go away this afternoon," the admiral said.

"May God bless Admiral Nimitz," Kamejiro said.

"That's an odd phrase," the admiral said. "You a Christian?"

"I'm Buddhist. But my children are all Christian."

When Kamejiro had been led outside, happy at the ease with which he had found a solution to his grave problem, the admiral shrugged his shoulders and said, "We'll beat the little bastards, but we'll never understand them."

Reiko-chan never saw Lieutenant Jackson again. In conformance with secret and high-priority orders he flew out of Hawaii that night, exiled to Bougainville, where, less than a week later, a body of Japanese infiltrators slipped through the jungle, attacked the headquarters in which he was serving, and lunged at him with bayonets. Knowing nothing of guns, the young lawyer tried to fight them off with a chair, but one Japanese soldier parried the chair, drove his bayonet through the lieutenant's chest, and left him strangling to death in the mud.

No one told Reiko that her lawyer was dead—there was no reason why anyone should—and she assumed that he had been fooling with her as men will, and that he had gone to other duties. When her father's barbershop had to close, because cautious Japanese families would not allow their daughters to work under a man who did not even protect his own daughter from disgrace of a haole love affair, Reiko went to work in another barbershop, and sometimes when a naval officer came in for a haircut, and she placed the towel about his neck and saw the railroad-track insignia on his shirt, she would for a moment feel dizzy. At other times, when brash enlisted men tried to feel her legs as she cut their hair, she would jab their hands with her scissors, as her father had taught her to do, but even as she did so, she felt confused by the great passion that can exist between men and women.

The forced closing of Kamejiro Sakagawa's barbershop was actually a considerable blessing to the family, although at the time it was not so recognized, for in the first weeks the stalwart little dynamiter could find no work other than caring for lawns, a job he did not like. Then the Okinawan restaurant keeper Senaga sent a messenger saying that he needed a busboy at a new restaurant he was opening in Waikiki, where a great many soldiers and sailors went, and he would like Sakagawa-san to take the job. Kamejiro's eyes blazed as he stared at the messenger. "If Senaga had been a friend, he would never have allowed a Japanese girl to talk with a haole in his restaurant. Tell him no." But to his wife, Kamejiro swore, "I would rather die of starvation than work for an Okinawan." Then, from a totally unexpected source, the Sakagawas received the financial aid which established them as one of the stronger and more prosperous Japanese families in Hawaii. It all happened because early in 1943 Hong Kong Kee had made a speech.

The inflamed oratory which provoked the loan took place before the Japanese boys of the Two-Two-Two had become the popular heroes they were later to be. When Hong Kong spoke, Japanese were still suspect, and a haole committee, seeking to whip up patriotism for war bonds, prevailed upon him to give a short speech explaining why the Chinese could be trusted and the Japanese could not. Since the committee of patriots contained many of the leaders of Honolulu, Hong Kong was naturally flattered by the invitation and spent some time in working out a rather fiery comparison of Chinese virtues as opposed to Japanese duplicity. Then, when he got on the speakers' platform, he became intoxicated by the crowd and deviated from his script, making his remarks rather more inclusive than he had planned. "The Japanese war lords have oppressed China for many years," he cried, "and it is with joy in our hearts that we watch the great American forces driving the evil Japanese from places where they have no right to be." He was astonished at the constant applause which the mass meeting threw back at him, and thus emboldened, he extended his remarks to include the Japanese in Hawaii. It was a very popular speech, sold a lot of war bonds, and got Hong Kong's picture in the papers under the caption "Patriotic Chinese Leader Flays Japs."

The affair was a big success except in one house. In her small, ugly clapboard shack up the Nuuanu, Hong Kong's grandmother, then ninety-six years old, listened appalled as one of her great-granddaughters read aloud the account of Hong Kong's oratory. "Bring him here at once!" she stormed, and when the powerful banker stood in her room she sent the others away, and when the door was closed she rose, stalked over to her grandson and slapped him four times in the face. "You fool!" she cried. "You fool! You damned, damned fool!"

Hong Kong fell back from the assault and covered his face to prevent further slappings. When he did this his fiery little grandmother began pushing him in the chest, calling him all the while "You fool!" until he stumbled backward against a chair and fell into it. Then she stopped, waited for him to drop his hands, and stared at him sorrowfully. "Hong Kong," she said, "Yesterday you were a great fool."

"Why?" he asked weakly.

She showed him the paper, with his picture grinning out from a semicircle of haole faces, and although she could not read, she could remember what her great-granddaughter had reported, and now she repeated the phrases with icy sarcasm: "We cannot trust the Japanese!" She spat onto her own floor. "They are deceitful and criminal men." Again she spat. Then she threw the paper onto the floor and kicked it, for her fury was great, and when this was done she shouted at her grandson, "What glory did you get from standing for a few minutes among the haoles?"

"I was asked to represent the Chinese community," Hong Kong fumbled.

"Who appointed you our representative, you stupid man?"

"I thought that since we are fighting Japan, somebody ought to . . ."

"You didn't think!" Nyuk Tsin stormed. "You have no brains to think. For a minute's glory, standing among the haoles, you have destroyed every good chance the Chinese have built up for themselves in Honolulu."

"Wait a minute, Auntie!" Hong Kong protested. "That's exactly what I was thinking about when I agreed to make the speech. It was a chance to make the Chinese look better among the haoles who run the islands."

Nyuk Tsin looked at her grandson in amazement. "Hong Kong?" she gasped. "Do you think that when the war is over, the haoles will continue to run Hawaii?"

"They have the banks, the newspapers . . ."

"Hong Kong! Who is doing the fighting? What men are in uniform? Who is going to come back to the islands ready to take over the political control? Tell me, Hong Kong."

"You mean the Japanese?" he asked weakly.

"Yes!" she shouted, her Hakka anger at its peak. "That's exactly who I mean. They are the ones who will win this war, and believe me, Hong Kong, when they take control they will remember the evil things you said yesterday, and every Kee in Honolulu will find life a little more difficult because of your stupidity."

"I didn't mean that . . ."

"Be still, you stupid man. After the war when Sam wants to build a store, who will sign the papers giving him the permit? Some Japanese. If Ruth's husband wants to run a bus line, who will give the permit? Some Japanese. And they will hate you for what you said yesterday. Already your words have been filled in their minds."

The shadow of a government building where all the permit signers were Japanese fell heavily upon Hong Kong, and he asked, "What ought we to do?" It was symptomatic of the Kees that when one of them took a bold step, he said of himself, "I did this," but when corrective measures had to be taken, he always consulted Wu Chow's Auntie and asked, "What must we do?"

The old woman said, "You must go through Honolulu and apologize to every Japanese you have ever known. Humble yourself, as you should. Then find at least twenty men who need money, and lend it to them. Help them start new businesses." She stopped, then added prudently, "It would be better if you lent the money to those who have a lot of sons in the war, for they will be the ones who are going to run Hawaii."

In the course of his apologies to the Japanese community, Hong Kong came in time to Sakai, the storekeeper, and Sakai said in English, "No, I don't need any money, but my good friend Sakagawa the dynamiter has lost his barber-shop, and he needs money to start a store of some kind."

"Where can I find him?" Hong Kong asked.

"He lives in Kakaako."

"By the way, any of his boys in the Two-Two-Two?"

"Four," Sakai replied.

"I will look him up," Hong Kong replied, and that afternoon he told Kamejiro, "I have come to apologize for what I said at the meeting."

"Mo bettah you be ashamed," Kamejiro said bluntly.

"Yes, with you having four sons in the battles."

"And all other Japanese, too."

"Kamejiro, I'm sorry."

"I sorry for you," the stocky little Japanese said, for he did not like Chinese.

"And I have come to lend you the money to start a store here in Kakaako."

Kamejiro drew back, for he had learned that anything either a Chinese or an Okinawan did was sure to be tricky. Surveying Hong Kong, he asked, "What for you lend me money?"

Humbly Hong Kong replied, "Because I've got to prove I am really sorry."

It was in this way that Kamejiro Sakagawa opened his grocery store, and because he was a frugal man and worked incredibly hard, and because his wife had a knack of waiting on Japanese customers and his barber daughter a skill in keeping accounts, the store flourished. Then, as if good fortune had piled up a warehouse full of beneficences, on New Year's Day, 1944, Sakai-san came running with breathless news.

"Pssst!" he called to Sakagawa as the latter sprayed his vegetables. "Come here."

"What?" the grocer shouted.

"Out here!"

Sakagawa left the store and allowed Sakai-san to lead him to an alley, where the latter said in awed tones, "I have found a husband for your daughter!"

"You have?" Sakagawa cried.

"Yes! A wonderful match!"

"A Japanese, of course?"

Sakai looked at his old friend with contempt. "What kind of baishakunin would I be if I even thought of proposing anyone but a Japanese?"

"Forgive me!" Sakagawa said. "You can understand, after the narrow escape we had."

"This man is perfect. A little house. More than a little money. Fine Japanese. And what else do you think!"

"Is he . . ." Sakagawa would not form the words, for this was too much to hope for.

"Yes! He's also a Hiroshima man!"

A thick blanket of positive euphoria settled over the two whispering men, for the go-between Sakai was just as pleased as Sakagawa that a fine Japanese girl had at last found a good husband, and a Hiroshima man at that. Finally Sakagawa got round to a question of lesser importance: "Who is he?"

"Mr. Ishii!" Sakai cried rapturously.

"Has he agreed to marry my daughter?" Kamejiro asked incredulously.

"Yes!" Sakai the baishakunin cried.

"Does he know about her . . . the haole?"

"Of course. I was honor-bound to tell him."

"And still he is willing to accept her?" Kamejiro asked in disbelief.

"Yes, he says it is his duty to save her."

"That good man," Sakagawa cried. He called his wife and told her, "Sakai has done it! He has found a husband for Reiko-chan."

"Who?" his practical-minded wife asked.

"Mr. Ishii!"

"A Hiroshima man!" And before Reiko-chan knew anything of her impending marriage, word that she had found a Hiroshima man flashed through the Japanese community and almost everybody was truly delighted with the girl's good fortune, especially since she had been mixed up with a haole man, but one girl, who had been through high school, reflected: "Mr. Ishii must be thirty-five years older than Reiko."

"What does it matter?" her mother snapped. "She's getting a Hiroshima man."

Reiko was in the barbershop on Hotel Street cutting the hair of a sailor when the news reached her. The girl at the next chair whispered in Japanese, "Congratulations, dear Reiko-chan."

"About what?" Reiko asked.

"Sakai-san has found you a husband."

The Japanese phrase fell strangely on Reiko's ears, for although she had long suspected that her parents had employed a baishakunin to find her a husband, she had never supposed that any solid arrangement would come to pass. Steadying herself against her chair, she asked casually, "Who did they say the man was?"

"Mr. Ishii! I think it's wonderful."

Reiko-chan kept mechanically moving her fingers, and the man in the chair warned: "Not too much off the sides, ma'am."

"I'm sorry," Reiko said. She wanted to run out of the barbershop, far from everyone, but she kept to her job. Patiently she trimmed the sailor's head just right, then lathered his neck and sideburns and asked, "You like them straight or on a little slant?"

"Any way looks best," the young man said. "You speak good English. Better'n me."

"I went to school," Reiko said quietly.

"Ma'am, do you feel well?" the sailor asked.

"Yes."

"You don't look so good. Look, ma'am . . ."

Reiko was about to faint, but with a tremendous effort she controlled herself and finished the lathering; but when she tried to grasp the razor she could not command it, and with great dismay she looked at the frightened sailor and asked softly, "Would you mind if I did not shave your neck this time? I feel dizzy."

"Ma'am, you ought to lie down," the sailor said, wiping the soap from his sideburns.

When he left, Reiko hung up her apron and announced, "I am going home," and on the long walk to Kakaako she tried not to compare Mr. Ishii with Lieutenant Jackson, but she could not keep her mind from doing so; then as she approached the family store she fortified herself with this consoling thought: "He's a crazy little man, and more like my father than a husband, but he is a proper Japanese and my father will be happy." Thinking no more of her absent Seattle lawyer, who had never even written to her, she went into the Sakagawa store, walked up to her father, and bowed. "I am grateful to you, Father."

"He is a Hiroshima man!" Sakagawa pointed out.

At the wedding, which was a highlight of the Japanese community in February of 1944, the baishakunin Sakai commanded everything. He told the family where to stand and the priest what to do and the groom how to behave. Mr. Ishii had spent the first part of the afternoon showing the assembly the latest copy of the *Prairie Shinbun,* which proved that valiant Imperial troops had finally driven all American marines off Guadalcanal and were about to launch a major invasion of Hawaii. One guest, who had two sons in Italy, whispered to his wife, "I think the old man's crazy!"

"Ssssh!" his wife said. "He's getting married."

When the crush was greatest, Reiko-chan, in old-style Japanese dress, happened to look at her bridegroom for the first time since her engagement had been announced, and she could not hide from herself the fact that he was a pathetic, cramped-up old man; and all her American education inspired her to flee from this insane ceremony, and great dizziness came upon her and she said to one of the girls near her, "This obi is too tight, I must get some air," and she was about to run away when the baishakunin Sakai cried, "We begin!" and the intricate, lovely Japanese wedding ceremony proceeded.

When it ended, women clustered about Reiko-chan and told her, "You were beautiful in your kimono. A true bride, with flushed cheeks and downcast eyes." Others said, "It's so wonderful to think that he is also a Hiroshima man." And the crush became so oppressive that she said, "This obi is really too tight. I must get some air," and she left the wedding feast and went alone to the porch, where she began to breathe deeply and where she arrived just in time to greet a messenger boy riding up on a bicycle.

At the next moment the guests inside heard a series of screams emanating from the porch, as if an animal had been mortally wounded, and they rushed out to find Reiko-chan screaming and screaming, and they could not stop her, for in her hand she held a message from the War Department advising the Sakagawa family of certain events that had recently transpired on a river bank in Italy.

O N SEPTEMBER 22, 1943, the Triple Two looked forward across the bow of their transport and saw rising in the misty dawn the hills of Italy, and Sergeant Goro Sakagawa thought: "I'll bet there's a German division hiding in there, waiting for us to step ashore."

He was right, and as the Japanese boys climbed down out of their transport to invade the beaches of Salerno, German planes and heavy artillery tried to harass them, but their aim was wild and all the units made it without casualty except one crop-headed private named Tashimoto, who sprained his ankle. The gang passed the word along with the acid comment, "Wouldn't you know it would be a guy from Molokai?"

Salerno lay southeast of Naples and had been chosen because it provided a logical stepping-off place for an encircling movement on Rome, some hundred and fifty miles distant, and on the day of landing, the Two-Two-Two started the long march north. The Germans, knowing both of their coming and of their composition, were determined to halt them. A specific order had been issued by Hitler: "To defeat the little yellow men who are traitors to our ally Japan and who are being cruelly used as propaganda by their Jewish masters in America, is obligatory. If these criminal little men should win a victory, it would be strongly used against us. They must be stopped and wiped out."

The Japanese boys from Hawaii did not know of this order, and after they had met one line of massive German resistance after another, they concluded: "These krauts must be the best fighters in the world. This is a lot tougher than they told us it was going to be." If the Two-Two-Two gained three miles, they did so against the most formidable German resistance: mines killed boys from Maui, tanks overran fighters from Molokai; gigantic shells exploded among troops from Kauai; and dogged, powerful ground forces contested every hill. Casualties were heavy, and the Honolulu *Mail* began carrying death lists with names like Kubokawa, Higa, and Moriguchi.

The furious efforts of the Germans to halt and humiliate the Japanese boys had an opposite effect to the one Hitler wanted; Allied war correspondents, both European and American, quickly discovered that whereas other fronts might not produce good stories, one could always get something exciting with the Two-Two-Two because they were the ones that were encountering the best the enemy could provide. Ernie Pyle, among others, marched for some days with the Hawaii troops, and wrote: "I have come to expect our American boys to continue fighting in the face of great odds, but these short, black-eyed little fighters are setting a new record. They continue slugging it out when even the bravest men would consolidate or withdraw. They form a terrific addition to our team, and dozens of boys from Texas and Massachusetts have told me, 'I'm glad they're on our side,' " So Hitler's determination to hit the Japanese so hard that they would be forced to collapse in shame, backfired because they fought on in glory.

Once Ernie Pyle asked Goro Sakagawa, "Sergeant, why did you push on against that cluster of houses? You knew it was crowded with Germans."

Goro replied in words that became famous both in Italy and American: "We had to. We fight double. Against the Germans and for every Japanese in America." Reported Pyle: "And they're winning both their wars."

September, October, November, December: the beautiful months, the months of poetry and rhythm, with nights growing colder and the soft mists of Italy turning to frost. How beautiful those months were when the boys from Hawaii first realized that they were as good fighting men as any in the world. "We fight double," they told themselves, and when they came to some Italian town, bathed in cloudless sunlight, standing forth against the hills like an etching, each tower clear in the bright glare, they attacked with fury and calculation, and bit by bit they drove the Germans back toward Rome. Colonel Whipple, delighted by the showing of his troops and pleased with the good reports they were getting in the American press, nevertheless warned his men: "It can't go on being as easy as this. Somewhere, the Germans are going to dig in real solid. Then we'll see if we're as good as they say."

In early December Hitler sent to the Italian front a fanatical Prussian colonel named Sep Seigl, unusual in that he combined a heritage of Prussian tradition and a loyalty to Naziism. Hitler told him simply, "Destroy the Japanese." And when he studied his maps he decided, "I shall do it at Monte Cassino." Colonel Seigl was a bullet-headed young man of thirty-seven whose promotion had been speeded because of his dedication to Hitler, and on three different battlefronts he had proved his capacities. At Monte Cassino he was determined to repeat his earlier performances. The Japanese would be humiliated.

So as December waned and as the Two-Two-Two slogged steadfastly up the leg of Italy toward Rome, they picked up many signs that their critical battle was going to be engaged somewhere near the old monastery of Monte Cassino, and belts tightened as they approached it. At the same time, from the north Colonel Sep Seigl was moving down to Cassino some of the ablest German units in Italy, but he did not intend to engage the Japanese on the slopes of the mountain. His troops were not permitted to construct their forward positions on that formidable pile of rock; they were kept down below along the banks of the Rapido River that here ran in a north-south direction, with the Japanese approaching from the east and the Germans dug in along the west. Surveying the German might he now had lined up along the Rapido, Colonel Seigl said, "We'll stop them at the river."

On January 22, 1944, Colonel Mark Whipple halted his Japanese troops along a line one mile east of the Rapido and told them, "Our orders are clear and simple. Cross the river . . . so that troops behind us can assault that pile of rocks up there. The Germans claim a rabbit can't get across the approaches without being shot at from six angles. But we're going across."

He dispatched a scouting party consisting of Sergeant Goro Sakagawa, his brother Tadao, who was good at sketching, and four riflemen, and at dusk on the twenty-second of January they crawled out of their hiding places and started on their bellies across the most difficult single battle terrain the Americans were to face in World War II. With meticulous care, Tadao Sakagawa drew maps of the route. Two hundred yards west of their present position the Two-Two-Two would come upon an irrigation ditch three feet wide and four feet deep. As they crawled out of it, they would be facing German machine guns and a marsh some thirty yards wide, beyond which lay another ditch. Thirty yards beyond hid a third ditch, twice as deep, twice as wide. As the men climbed out of this one, they would face a solid wall of machine-gun fire.

When they got this far in the darkness Goro Sakagawa licked his dry lips and asked his men, "What's that ahead?"

"Looks like a stone wall."

"Jesus," Goro whispered. "You can't expect our boys to negotiate those three ditches and then climb a wall. How high is it?"

"Looks about twelve feet high."

"This is impossible," Goro replied. "You fellows, split up. You go that way, we'll go this. Let's see if there's a break in the wall."

In the darkness they found none, only a stout, murderous stone wall, twelve feet high and with a jagged top. When they reassembled, Goro said in rasping whisper, "Christ, how can anybody get over that damned thing? With machine guns everywhere. Sssssh."

There was a sudden chatter of German guns, but the men firing them must have heard a sound in some other direction, for the firing did not come close to Goro and his men. "Well," he said when it ceased, "over we go."

Patiently and with skill, in the darkness of night, the six Japanese boys helped one another over the terrifying wall, and from it they dropped into the eastern half of the dry river bed of the Rapido. It was about seventy-five feet across, about fifteen feet deep, and every spot of its entire cross section was monitored by German machine guns. On their bellies, the six soldiers crept across the dry river and trusted that no searchlights would be turned on. In the cold night they were perspiring with fear.

But when they got to the other side of the Rapido they discovered what fear really was, for both machine guns and searchlights opened up, but the young Japanese managed to secrete themselves in crevices at the foot of the western bank; but what terrified them was not the imperative staccato of the guns or the probing fingers of light, but the monstrous nature of the river's west bank. It rose fairly straight up from the river bed, sixteen feet high, and was topped by a stout double fence of barbed wire which could be expected to contain mines at two-foot intervals.

"Are you getting this on paper?" Goro whispered to Tadao. "Cause when they see this, no general living would dare send men across this river." A passing light illuminated the wild and terrible tangles of barbed wire and then passed on. "You got it?" Goro asked. "Good. Hoist me up. I'm going through it."

Tadao grabbed his older brother's hand. "I have enough maps," he cautioned.

"Somebody's got to see what's over there."

His men hoisted him onto the top of the west bank of the river, where he spent fifteen perilous minutes picking his way inch by inch through the tangled barbed wire. He knew that at any moment he might explode a mine and not only kill himself but doom his five companions as well. He was no longer sweating.

He was no longer afraid. He had passed into some extraordinary state known only by soldiers at night or in the heat of unbearable battle. He was a crop-headed, tense-bellied Japanese boy from Kakaako in Honolulu, and the courage he was displaying in those fateful minutes no one in Hawaii would have believed.

He penetrated the wire, leaving on the barbs tiny shreds of cloth which would guide him safely back, and in the darkness he found himself on the eastern edge of a dusty road that led past the foot of Monte Cassino. Hiding himself in the ditch that ran alongside the road, he breathed deeply, trying to become a man again and not a nerveless automaton, and as he lay there, face up, a searchlight played across the countryside, hunting for him perhaps, and it passed on and suddenly illuminated the terrain that rose above him, and although he had seen it from a distance and knew its proportions, he now cried with pain: "Oh, Jesus Christ, no!"

For above him rose an unassailable rocky height, far, far into the sky, and at its crest clung an ancient monastery, and from where he lay Goro realized that he and his men were expected to cross all that he had seen tonight, and that when they got to this road in which he now huddled, other fellows from Hawaii were expected to forge ahead and climb those overpowering rocks that hung above him. In the lonely darkness he shivered with fright; then, as men do at such times, he effectively blocked out of his mind the realization of what Monte Cassino was like. It was not an unscalable height. It was not mined and inter-laced with machine guns. It was not protected by the Rapido River defenses, and a gang of Japanese boys was not required to assault it, with casualties that would have to mount toward the fifty-per-cent mark, or even the eighty. Goro Sakagawa, a tough-minded soldier, cleansed himself of this knowledge and crept back to his men, then back to his commanding officer.

"It'll be tough," he reported. "But it can be done."

As he spoke, Colonel Sep Seigl was reviewing the same terrain and he knew far more about it than Goro Sakagawa, for he had maps prepared by the famous Todt Labor Corps, which had built this ultimate defense of Rome. He could see that the first three ditches which the Japanese would have to cross were covered in every detail by mines and machinegun fire, and he told his men, "I suppose scouting parties are out there right now, but if they miss the mines, they'll be lucky." He saw the plans for defending the river itself, which presented one of the most formidable obstacles any army could encounter, and whereas Goro a few minutes before had been guessing as to where the mines and machine guns were, Seigl knew, and he knew that even his own soldiers, the finest in the world, could not penetrate that defense. And west of the river, of course, lay the exposed road which could be cut to shreds with mortar fire, and beyond that the cliffs of Monte Cassino up which no troops could move. At midnight Colonel Seigl concluded: "They'll try, but they'll never make it. Here is where we bloody the nose of the traitor Japanese. Tomorrow we'll watch them wilt under fire."

January 24, 1944, began with a cold, clear midnight and it was greeted with a thundering barrage of American gunfire which illuminated the bleak river but which did not dislodge the Germans. For forty minutes the barrage continued, and a beginner at warfare might have taken heart, thinking: "No man can live through that." But the dark-skinned men of the Two-Two-Two knew better;

they knew the Germans would be dug in and waiting.

At 0040 the barrage stopped and the whistles blew for advance. Goro clutched his brother by the arm and whispered, "This is the big one, kid. Take care of yourself." Progress to the first ditch was painful, for the Germans launched a counter-barrage and the first deaths at Monte Cassino occurred, but Goro and Tadao pushed stolidly ahead in the darkness, and when they had led their unit across the dangerous ditch and onto the edge of the marsh, they told their captain, "We'll take care of the mines," and they set out on their bellies, two brothers who could have been engaged in a tricky football play, and they crawled across the marsh, adroitly cutting the trip wires that would otherwise have detonated mines and killed their companions, and when they reached the second ditch Goro stood up in the night and yelled, "Mo bettah you come. All mines pau!" But as he sent the news his younger brother Tadao, one of the finest boys ever to graduate from Punahou, stepped upon a magnesium mine which exploded with a terrible light, blowing him into a thousand shreds of bone and flesh.

"Oh, Jesus!" Goro cried, burying his face in his hands. No action was required. None was possible. Tadao Sakagawa no longer existed in any conceivable form. Not even his shoes were recoverable, but where he had stood other Japanese boys swept over the marshy land and with battle cries leaped into the next ditch, and then into the next.

It took five hours of the most brutal fighting imaginable for the Japanese troops to reach the near bank of the Rapido and when dawn broke, Colonel Sep Seigl was slightly disturbed. "They should not have been able to cross those fields. They seem rather capable, but now the fight begins."

Against the troops for which he had a special hatred he threw a wall of bombardment that was almost unbelievable, and to his relief, the advance was halted. No human being could have penetrated that first awful curtain of shrapnel which greeted the Two-Two-Two at the Rapido itself. "Well," Colonel Seigl sighed, "at least they're human. They can be stopped. Now to keep them pinned down. The Japanese cannot absorb casualties. Kill half of them, and the other half will run."

But here Colonel Seigl was wrong. Half of Goro Sakagawa had already been killed; he had loved his clever brother Tadao as only boys who have lived in the close intimacy of poverty and community rejection can love, and now Tadao was dead. Therefore, when the German shelling was at its most intense, Goro said to his captain, "Let's move across that river. I know how."

"We'll dig in," the captain countermanded.

But when Colonel Whipple arrived to inspect the battered condition of his men, Goro insisted that the river could be crossed, and Whipple said, "Go ahead and try." At this point one of the lieutenants from Baker Company, Goro's commanding officer, and a fine young officer from Kansas, said, "If my men go, I go."

"All right, Lieutenant Shelly," Whipple said. "We've got to cross the river."

So Lieutenant Shelly led forty men, with Sergeant Sakagawa as guide, down into the bed of the Rapido, at nine o'clock on a crystal-clear morning, and they came within six yards of crossing the river, when a titanic German concentration of fire killed half the unit, including Lieutenant Shelly. The twenty who were left began to panic, but Goro commanded sternly, "Up onto that bank and through that barbed wire."

It was a completely insane thing to attempt. The Rapido River did not propose to allow any troops, led by Goro Sakagawa or otherwise, to violate it that day, and when his stubborn muddy fingers reached the barbed-wire embankment, such a furious load of fire bore down upon him that he had to drop back into the river. Three more times he endeavored vainly to penetrate the barbed wire, and each time Colonel Seigl screamed at his men, "Kill him! Kill him! Don't let them get started!" But although tons of ammunition were discharged in the general direction of Sakagawa and his determined men, somehow they were not killed. Huddling in the protection of the far bank of the river, the gallant twenty waited for their companions to catch up with them, when all together they might have a chance of crashing the barbed wire.

But the fire power of the Germans was so intense that the Japanese boys who were still on the eastern bank could not possibly advance. At times the wall of shrapnel seemed almost solid and it would have been complete suicide to move a man into it. "We've got to hold where we are," Colonel Whipple regretfully ordered.

"What about those twenty out there in the river?"

"Who's in charge? Lieutenant Shelly?"

"He was killed. Sergeant Sakagawa."

"Goro?"

"Yes, sir."

"He'll get his men out," Whipple said confidently, and at dusk, after a day of hell, Goro Sakagawa did just that. He brought all of his twenty men back across the river, up the dangerous eastern bank, back through the minefields and safely to headquarters.

"Colonel wants to see you," a major said.

"We couldn't make it," Goro reported grimly.

"No man ever tried harder, Lieutenant Sakagawa."

Goro showed no surprise at his battlefield commission. He was past fear, past sorrow, and certainly past jubilation. But when the bars were pinned to his tunic by the colonel himself, the rugged sergeant broke into tears, and they splashed out of his dark eyes onto his leathery yellow-brown skin. "Tomorrow we'll cross the river," he swore.

"We'll certainly try," Colonel Whipple said.

On January 26 the Japanese troops did try, but once more Colonel Sep Seigl's able gunners turned them back with dreadful casualties. On January 27 the Japanese tried for the third time, and although Lieutenant Goro Sakagawa got his men onto the road on the other side of the river, they were hit with such pulverizing fire that after forty-five minutes they had to withdraw. That night an Associated Press man wrote one of the great dispatches of the war: "If tears could be transmitted by cable, and printed by linotype, this story would be splashed with tears, for I have at last seen what they call courage beyond the call of duty. I saw a bunch of bandy-legged Japanese kids from Hawaii cross the Rapido River, and hold the opposite bank for more than forty minutes. Then they retreated in utter defeat, driven back by the full might of the German army. Never in victory have I seen any troops in the world achieve a greater glory, and if hereafter any American ever questions the loyalty of our Japanese, I am not going to argue with him. I am going to kick his teeth in."

On January 28, Lieutenant Sakagawa tried for the fourth time to cross the Rapido, and for the fourth time Colonel Sep Seigl's men mowed the Japanese down. Of the 1,300 troops with which Colonel Whipple had started four days earlier, 799 were now casualties. Dead Japanese bodies lined the fatal river, and men with arms and legs torn off were being moved to the rear. At last it became apparent that the Germans had effectively stopped the advance of the hated

Two-Two-Two. That night Colonel Seigl's intelligence reported: "Victory! The Japanese have been driven back. They're in retreat and seem to be leaving the line."

The report was partially correct. Lieutenant Goro Sakagawa's company, and the unit of which it was a part, was being withdrawn. The boys were willing to try again, but they no longer had enough men to maintain a cohesive company and they had to retreat to repair their wounds. As they passed back through a unit from Minnesota coming in to replace them, the Swedes, having heard of their tremendous effort, cheered them and saluted and one man from St. Paul yelled, "We hope we can do as good as you did."

"You will," a boy from Lahaina mumbled.

So the Germans stopped the Two-Two-Two . . . for a few hours, because in another part of the line other units from Hawaii were accumulating a mighty force, and on February 8 Colonel Sep Seigl's intelligence officer reported breathlessly, "The damned Japanese have crossed the river and are attacking the mountain itself!"

With a powerful surge the Japanese boys drove spearheads almost to the top of the mountain. They scaled heights that even their own officers believed impregnable, and they routed out more than two hundred separate machine-gun emplacements. Their heroism in this incredible drive was unsurpassed in World War II, and for a few breathless hours they caught a toehold on the summit of the mountain itself.

"Send us reinforcements!" they radioed frantically. "We've got them licked."

But reinforcements could not negotiate the cliffs, and one by one the Japanese victors were driven back from their dizzy pinnacles. As they stumbled down the steep flanks of Monte Cassino the Germans gunned them unmercifully, but at last the fragments of the force staggered back to camp and announced: "The Germans cannot be driven out." But one fact of triumph remained: the headquarters camp was now on the west bank of the Rapido. The river had been crossed. The way to Rome lay open.

It was in their bruising defeat at Monte Cassino that the Two-Two-Two became one of the most famous units of the war. "The Purple Heart Battalion" it was called, for it had suffered more casualties than any other similar-sized unit in the war. The Mo Bettahs won more honors, more decorations, more laudatory messages from the President and the generals than any other. But most of all they won throughout America a humble respect. Caucasians who fought alongside them reported back home: "They're better Americans than I am. I wouldn't have the guts to do what they do." And in Hawaii, those golden islands that the Japanese boys loved so deeply as they died in Italy, people no longer even discussed the tormenting old question: "Are the Japanese loyal?" Now men of other races wondered: "Would I be as brave?" So although the Prussian Nazi, Colonel Sep Seigl, did exactly what he had promised Hitler he would do—he crushed the Japanese at Monte Cassino—neither he nor Hitler accomplished what they had initially intended; for it was in defeat that the Japanese boys exhibited their greatest bravery and won the applause of the world.

Therefore it is strange to report that it was not at Monte Cassino that the Two-Two-Two won its greatest laurels. This happened by accident, in a remote corner of France.

After the Triple Two's had retired to a rear area in Italy, there to lick their considerable wounds and to re-form with fresh replacements from the States—

including First Lieutenant Goro Sakagawa's younger brothers Minoru and Shigeo—the Mo Bettah Battalion was shipped out of Italy and into Southern France, where it was allowed to march in a leisurely manner up the Rhone Valley. It met little German opposition, nor was it intended to, for the generals felt that after the heroic performance at Monte Cassino the Japanese boys merited something of a respite, and for once things went as planned. Then, accompanied by a Texas outfit that had also built a name for itself in aggressive fighting, the Two-Two-Two's swung away from the Rhone and entered upon routine mopping-up exercises in the Vosges Mountains, where the easternmost part of France touched the southernmost part of Germany.

The Triple Two's and the Texans moved forward with calculating efficiency until they had the Germans in what appeared to be a final rout. Lieutenant Sakagawa kept urging his men to rip the straggling German units with one effective spur: "Remember what they did to us at Cassino." Hundreds of bewildered Germans surrendered to him, asking pitifully, "Have the Japanese finally turned against us too? Like the Italians?" To such questions Goro replied without emotion: "We're Americans. Move through and back." But if he kept his hard face a mask of indifference, secretly he trembled with joy whenever he accepted the surrender of units from Hitler's master race.

It was understandable, therefore, that Goro Sakagawa, like his superiors, interpreted the Vosges campaign as the beginning of the end for Hitler. But this was a sad miscalculation, for if the young, untrained Nazi troops sometimes faltered, their clever Prussian generals did not. They were now charged with defending the German homeland, and from his epic success at Monte Cassino, Colonel Sep Seigl, now General Seigl, had arrived at the Vosges to organize resistance at that natural bastion. Therefore, if he allowed his rag-tag troops to surrender in panic to the Triple Two's, it was for a reason; and in late October of 1944 this reason became apparent, for on the twenty-fourth of that month General Seigl's troops appeared to collapse in a general rout, retreating helter-skelter through the difficult Vosges terrain; and in so doing they enticed the battle-hungry Texans to rush after them, moving far ahead of American tanks and into the neatest trap of the war.

General Seigl announced the springing of his trap with a gigantic barrage of fire that sealed the bewildered Texans into a pocket of mountains. "We will shoot them off one by one," Seigl ordered, moving his troops forward. "We'll show the Americans what it means to invade German soil." And he swung his prearranged guns into position and began pumping high explosives at the Texan camp. There without food or water or adequate ammunition, the gallant Texans dug in and watched the rim of fire creep constantly closer.

At this point an American journalist coined the phrase the "Lost Battalion," and in Texas radios were kept tuned around the clock. Whole villages listened to agonizing details as the sons of that proud state prepared to die as bravely as their circumstances would permit. A sob echoed across the prairies, and Texans began to shout, "Get our boys out of there! For Christssake, do something!"

Thus what had been intended as respite for the Triple Two suddenly became the dramatic high point of the war. A personal messenger from the Senate warned the Pentagon: "Get those Texans out of there or else." The Pentagon radioed SHAEF: "Effect rescue immediately. Top priority white." SHAEF advised headquarters in Paris, and they wirelessed General McLarney, at the edge of the Vosges. It was he who told Colonel Mark Whipple, "You will penetrate the German ring of firepower and rescue those men from Texas." Lest there be any misunderstanding, another general flew in from Paris, red-faced and bitter, and he said, "We're going to be crucified if we let those boys die. Get them, goddamn it, get them."

Colonel Whipple summoned Lieutenant Goro Sakagawa and said, "You've got to go up that ridge, Goro. You mustn't come back without them."

"We'll bring 'em out," Goro replied.

As he was about to depart, Mark Whipple took his hand and shook it with that quiet passion that soldiers know on the eve of battle. "This is the end of our road, Goro. The President himself has ordered this one. Win this time, and you win your war."

It was a murderous, hellish mission. A heavy fog enveloped the freezing Vosges Mountains, and no man could look ahead more than fifteen feet. As Baker Company filed into the predawn gloom, each Japanese had to hold onto the field pack of the boy in front, for only in this manner could the unit be kept together. From the big, moss-covered trees of the forest, German snipers cut down one Hawaiian boy after another, until occasionally some Japanese in despairing frustration would stand stubbornly with his feet apart, firing madly into the meaningless fog. At other times German machine guns stuttered murderously from a distance of twenty feet. But Goro became aware of one thing: firepower that an hour before had been pouring in upon the doomed Texans was now diverted.

To rescue the Lost Battalion, the Two-Two-Two had to march only one mile, but it was the worst mile in the world, and to negotiate it was going to require four brutal days without adequate water or food or support. The casualties suffered by the Japanese were staggering, and Goro sensed that if he brought his two younger brothers through this assault, it would be a miracle. He therefore cautioned them: "Kids, keep close to the trees. When we move from one to the other, run like hell across the open space. And when you hit your tree, whirl about instantly to shoot any Germans that might have infiltrated behind you."

At the end of the first day the Triple Twos had gained only nine hundred feet, and within the circle of steel wounded Texans were beginning to die from gangrene. Next morning the Japanese boys pushed on, a yard at a time, lost in cold fog, great mossy trees and pinnacles of rock. Almost every foot of the way provided General Seigl's riflemen with ideal cover, and they used it to advantage. With methodical care, they fired only when some Japanese ran directly into their guns, and they killed the Triple Two's with deadly accuracy. On that cold, rainy second day the Japanese troops gained six hundred feet, and nearly a hundred of the trapped Texans died from wounds and fresh barrages.

A curious factor of the battle was that all the world could watch. It was known that the Texans were trapped; it was known that the Two-Two-Two's were headed toward their rescue, and the deadly game fascinated the press. A Minnesota corporal who had fought with the Triple Two's in Italy told a newspaperman, "If anybody can get 'em, the slant-eyes will." In Honolulu newspapers that phrase was killed, but the entire community, sensing the awful odds against which their sons were fighting, prayed.

On the third day of this insane attempt to force the ring of fire, Baker Company was astonished to see trudging up the hill they had just traversed the familiar figure of Colonel Mark Whipple. The men well knew the basic rule of war: "Lieutenants lead platoons against the enemy. Captains stay back and encourage the entire company. Majors and light colonels move between headquarters and the companies. But chicken colonels stay put." Yet here was

Colonel Whipple, a West Point chicken colonel, breaking the rule and moving into the front lines. Instinctively the Japanese boys saluted as he passed. When he reached Goro he said simply, "We're going to march up that ridge and rescue the Texans today."

This was a suicidal approach and no one knew it better than Whipple, but it had been commanded by headquarters. "I can't order my boys into another Cassino," he had protested. "This is worse than Cassino," headquarters had admitted, "but it's got to be done." Whipple had saluted and said, "Then I must lead the boys myself." And there he was.

His inspiration gave the Japanese the final burst of courage they needed. With terrifying intensity of spirit the Two-Two-Two moved up the ridge. The fighting was murderous, with Germans firing pointblank at the rescuers. Barrages from hidden guns, planted weeks before at specific spots by General Seigl, cut down the Triple Two's with fearful effect, and at one faltering point Goro thought: "Why should we have to penetrate such firepower? We're losing more than we're trying to save."

As if he sensed that some such question might be tormenting his troops and halting their flow of courage, Colonel Whipple moved among them, calling, "Sometimes you do things for a gesture. This is the ultimate gesture. They're waiting for us, over that ridge." But the men of the Triple Two could not banish the ugly thought that haunted them: "Texans are important and have to be saved. Japanese are expendable." But no one spoke these words, for all knew that the Texas fighters didn't have to prove anything; the Japanese did.

When night fell on the twenty-ninth of October the Japanese troops were still four hundred yards short of their goal. They slept standing up, or leaning against frozen trees. There was no water, no food, no warmth. Outpost sentries, when relieved, muttered, "I might as well stay here with you." There was no bed. Men ached and those with minor wounds felt the blood throbbing in their veins. Hundreds were already dead.

At dawn a German sniper, hidden with Teutonic thoroughness, fired into the grim encampment and killed Private Minoru Sakagawa. For some minutes his brother Goro was not aware of what had happened, but then young Shigeo cried, "Jesus! They killed Minoru!"

Goro, hearing his brother's agonized cry, ran up and saw Minoru dead upon the frozen ground. This was too much to bear, and he began to lose his reason. "Achhhh!" he cried with a great rasping noise in his throat. Two of his brothers had now died while under his command, and the rest of his troops seemed doomed. His right hand began trembling while his voice continued to cry a meaningless "Achhhh."

Colonel Whipple, who knew what was happening, rushed up and clouted the young lieutenant brutally across the face. "Not now, Goro!" he commanded, using a strange phrase: *Not now,* as if later it would be permissible to go out of one's mind, as if at some later time all men might do so, including Whipple himself.

Goro fell back and his hand stopped trembling. Staring in dull panic at his colonel, he tried vainly to focus on the problems at hand, but failed. He could see only his brother, fallen on the pine needles of the Vosges. Then his cold reason returned, and he drew his revolver. Grabbing Shigeo by the shoulder he said, "You walk here." Then to his men he roared, in Japanese, "We won't stop!" And with appalling force he and his team marched in among the great trees.

It was a desperate, horrible hand-to-hand fight up the last thousand feet of the ridge. Shigeo, following the almost paralyzed fury of his brother, exhibited a courage he did not know he had. He moved directly onto German positions and grenaded them to shreds. He ducked behind trees like a veteran, and when the last roadblock stood ahead, ominous and spewing death, it was mild-mannered Shigeo, the quiet one of the Sakagawa boys—though there were now only two left—who with demonic craftiness went aginst it, drew its fire so that he could spot its composition, and then leaped inside with grenades and a Tommy gun. He killed eleven Germans, and when his companions moved past him to the ultimate rescue of the Texans he leaned out of the Nazi position and cheered like a schoolboy.

"You're a lieutenant!" Colonel Whipple snapped as he went forward to join the Texans, and a boy from Maui looked at Shig and said in pidgin, "Jeez, krauts all pau!"

In rough formation, with Lieutenant Goro Sakagawa at their head, the Japanese boys marched in to greet the Texans, and a tall Major Burns from Houston stumbled forward, his ankle in bad shape, and tried to salute, but the emotion of the moment was too great. He was famished and burning with thirst, and before he got to Goro he fell in the dust. Then he rose to his knees and said from that position, "Thank God. You fellows from the Jap outfit?"

"Japanese," Goro replied evenly. He stooped to help the Texan to his feet and saw that the man was at least a foot taller than he was. All the Texans, starving and parched though they were, were enormous men, and it seemed indecent that a bunch of runty little rice-eaters should have rescued them.

Against his will, for Major Burns was a very brave man and had kept his troops alive mainly through the force of his extraordinary character, the tall Texan began to weep. Then he was ashamed of himself, bit his lip till it nearly bled and asked, "Could my men have some water?" He turned to his troops and shouted, "Give these Japs a big welcome."

Goro grabbed the major as if they were two toughs back in Kakaako and said in sudden, surging anger, "Don't you call us Japs!"

"Goro!" Colonel Whipple shouted.

"What, sir?" He didn't remember what he had just said.

"All right," Whipple snapped. "Let's start down the hill."

The Japanese troops formed two lines at the entrance to the pocket in which the Texans had been trapped, and as the giant men passed to freedom between the pairs of stubby Triple Two's some of the Texans began to laugh, and soon the pocket was choked with merriment, in which big Texans began to embrace their rescuers and kiss them and jump them up into the air. "You little guys got guts," a huge fellow from Abilene shouted. "I thought we was done for."

Lieutenant Sakagawa did not join the celebration. He was watching his men, and estimated dully that of the original 1,200 Japanese boys that had set out to storm the ridge, fully two-thirds were now either dead or severely wounded. This terrible toll, including his brother Minoru, was almost more than he could tolerate, and he began mumbling, "Why did we have to lose so many little guys to save so few big ones?" It had cost 800 Japanese to rescue 341 Texans. Then his mind began to harden and to come back under control, and to discipline it he began checking off Baker Company, and he found that of the 183 men who had waded ashore with him at Salerno in September of 1943 only seven had managed to stick with the outfit through October of 1944. The rest —all 176 of them—were either dead or wounded.

Now Shigeo rushed up to advise his brother that Colonel Whipple had promoted him on the field of battle, a soldier's sweetest triumph, and the brilliant-eyed youth shouted, "Goro, I guess this time we really showed the world!" But Goro, counting the dead, wondered: "How much more do we have to prove?" And from the manner in which his mind jerked from one image to the next, he realized that he was close to mental collapse, but he was saved by a curious experience. From among the Texans a hysterical medic, his mind deranged by three shells that had exploded while he was trying to cut off a shattered leg, began moving from one Japanese to another, mumbling, "Greater love hath no man than this, that he lay down his life for his brother."

Major Burns heard the speech and yelled, "There goes that goddamned odd-ball again. Please, please, shut him up!"

But the medic had reached Goro, to whom he mumbled, "Lieutenant, indeed it is true. No man hath greater love than this, that he would march up such a fucking ridge to save a complete crock of shit like Major Burns." In his wildness the medic turned to face Burns, screaming hysterically, "I hate you! I hate you! You led us into this death trap, you crazy, crazy beast!"

Almost sadly, Major Burns, pivoting on his good leg, swung on the medic and knocked him out. "He was more trouble than the Germans," he apologized. "Somebody haul the poor bastard out."

Before any of the Texans could get to the capsized medic, Goro had compassionately pulled the unconscious fellow into his arms. A gigantic Texan came along to help, and the odd trio started down the bloody ridge, but when they had returned halfway to safety, General Seigl's last furious barrage enveloped them, and two shells bracketed Colonel Mark Whipple, killing him instantly. Goro, who witnessed the death, dropped his hold on the medic and started toward the man who had done so much for the Japanese, but at long last his nervous system gave way.

The awful "Achhhh" filled his throat, and his hands began trembling. His head jerked furiously as if he were an epileptic and his eyes went vacant like those of an imbecile. "Achhhh! Achhhh!" he began to shout hysterically, and he started falling to his right, but caught himself by clutching air. His voice cleared and he began screaming, "Don't you call me a Jap! Goddamn you big blond Texans, don't you call me a yellow-belly!"

In wild fury he began lashing out at his tormentors, stupidly, ineffectively. He kept shouting irrelevant threats at the Texans whom he had just saved, and was ready to fight even the biggest. One man from Dallas gently held him off as an adult would a child, and it was pathetic to see the stocky Japanese swinging wildly at the air, unable to reach his giant adversary. Finally he returned to the horrible achhhh sound, and at this point his brother Shigeo ran up to take command. He pinioned Goro's arms, and when the latter seemed about to break out once more, Shigeo smashed a hard right-cut to the jaw and slowed him down.

Now Goro began to whimper like a child, and two men from his outfit had the decency to cover him with a blanket, so that his disintegration would not be visible to his own troops, and in this condition they patiently led him, shivering and shuddering, out of the Vosges Mountains where the Texans had been trapped.

Toward the foothills they passed through a guard unit from their own battalion, and a young lieutenant from Able Company, a haole boy from Princeton asked, "Who you got under the blanket?" and Shigeo replied, "Lieutenant Sakagawa."

"Was he the one who got through to the Texans?"

"Who else?" Shig replied, and as the cortege of wounded and near-mad and starved and war-torn passed, the Princeton man looked at Goro Sakagawa's mechanically shuffling feet and muttered, "There goes an American."

VI

THE GOLDEN MEN

In 1946, when Nyuk Tsin was ninety-nine years old, a group of sociologists in Hawaii were perfecting a concept whose vague outlines had occupied them for some years, and quietly among themselves they suggested that in Hawaii a new type of man was being developed. He was a man influenced by both the west and the east, a man at home in either the business councils of New York or the philosophical retreats of Kyoto, a man wholly modern and American yet in tune with the ancient and the Oriental. The name they invented for him was the Golden Man.

At first I erroneously thought that both the concept and the name were derived from the fact that when races intermingled sexually, the result was apt to be a man neither all white nor all brown nor all yellow, but somewhere in between; and I thought that the Golden Man concept referred to the coloring of the new man—a blend of Chinese, Polynesian and Caucasian, for at this time Japanese rarely intermarried—and I went about the streets of Hawaii looking for the golden man of whom the sociologists spoke.

But in time I realized that this bright, hopeful man of the future, this unique contribution of Hawaii to the rest of the world, did not depend for his genesis upon racial intermarriage at all. He was a product of the mind. His was a way of thought, and not of birth, and one day I discovered, with some joy I may add, that for several years I had known the archetypes of the Golden Man, and if the reader has followed my story so far, he also knows three of them well and is about to meet the fourth, and it is interesting that none of these, in a direct sense, owed his golden quality to racial intermixtures. His awareness of the future and his rare ability to stand at the conflux of the world he owed to his understanding of the movements around him. I have known a good many golden men in the secondary, or unimportant, sense: fine Chinese-Hawaiians, excellent Portuguese-Chinese and able Caucasian-Hawaiians; but most of them had little concept of what was happening either in Hawaii or in the world. But the four men of whom I now wish to speak did know, and it is in reference to their knowledge that I wish to end my story of Hawaii, for they are indeed the Golden Men.

In 1946, when the war had ended and Hawaii was about to explode belatedly into the twentieth century, Hoxworth Hale was forty-eight years old; and one morning, when the trade winds had died away and the weather was unbearably sticky, he happened to look into his mirror while shaving, and the thought came to him: "This year I am as good a man as I shall ever be in this life. I have most of my teeth, a good deal of my hair, I'm not too much overweight, and my eyes are good enough to see distances without glasses, though close up I have a little trouble, and I suppose I'll have to see an oculist. I can still concentrate on a problem, and I derive pleasure from control of business. I like to go to work, even on mornings like this." He pummeled his midriff to start perspiration before entering the shower, and as the hot, muggy day closed in upon him he was forced to inspect the two areas in which he was no longer so good a man as he once had been.

First, there was the gnawing, never-ending pain that started when his son Bromley was shot down during the great fire of Tokyo in 1945, when the air corps practically destroyed the city. More than 70,000 Japanese had died in the great raids, and a city too, so that in one sense Bromley's death had contributed positive results, and after his raids victory for our side was assured. But Bromley Hale was a special young man. Everyone said so, and his departure left a gap both in the Hale family and in Hawaii that would never be filled, for in his last letters home, when capricious death had become so routine in his B-29 squadron as to depress all the fliers, he had spoken intimately of what he hoped to accomplish when the war ended, as soon it must.

He had written, from a hut on Iwo Jima: "We had to ditch our monstrous plane in the waters near here, and by the grace of God we were all saved, but in the going down, as I worked with the wheel I was not so much concerned about a perfect water landing as I was with my determination to do what years ago I had sworn to do while a senior at Punahou. I am determined to write a novel about—and this may stagger you, but bear with me—Aunt Lucinda Whipple. I shall have her sitting in the late afternoons in her house in Nuuanu Valley, and each day as the afternoon rains sweep down from the Pali and the white mildew grows on all things, she entertains the straggling members of our family. It has always seemed to me that Aunt Lucinda was everybody's aunt, and everybody comes to her and listens to her monotonous chatter about the old days, and nothing I write will make any sense at all— only an old woman's ceaseless vanity—until it begins to weave a spell, the kind of spell in which you and I have always lived. I shall show Aunt Lucinda exactly as she is, religious, family-proud, unseeing, unknowing, garrulous and unbelievably kind. She has become to me a web, a fatal emanation, an encroaching dream, and as our plane struck the water, I was listening not to my co-pilot, who was frantic as hell, but to dear old Aunt Lucinda. How she hated airplanes and fast automobiles and Japanese. As a matter of fact, if you took time to analyze it carefully, I guess she hated everybody but the Whipples, and the Janderses, and the Hales, and the Hewletts, and the Hoxworths. But even they gave her a lot of trouble, for she always took great pains to explain to visitors that she came from the branch of the Whipple family that had never had even a drop of Hawaiian blood, and she kept segregated in her mind those of her great family of whom this could not be said. She was suspicious of you and me because we were not pure English stock; and of course all the Hoxworths and half the Hewletts were contaminated, and often when I spoke with her she would hesitate, and I knew she was thinking: 'I'd better not tell him that, because after all, he is one of the contaminated.' "

"And from Aunt Lucinda's endless vagaries I want to construct an image of all Hawaii and the peoples who came to build it. I want to deal with the first volcano and the last sugar strike. You may not like my novel, but it will be accurate, and I think that counts for something. It is strange, I have been writing about Aunt Lucinda as if she were dead, but she is living and it may be I who shall be dead."

This dreadful hurt never left Hoxworth Hale's heart, and he started listening to Aunt Lucinda's meanderings, and he picked up the thoughts that his son had laid down: "We live in a web. Sugar cane, Hawaiian ghosts, pineapple, ships, streetcar lines, Japanese labor leaders, Aunt Lucinda's memories." The web became most tenuous, and at the same time most cruelly oppressive, when it involved the upstairs rooms where several of the great families kept the delicate women whose minds had begun to wander past even the accepted norm, and in one such room Hoxworth's own wife passed her days. In the 1920's, at Punahou, Malama Janders, as she was then, had been a laughing, poetic young lady, interested in music and boys, but as the years passed, and especially since the 1940's, her mind lost its focus and she preferred not to try understanding what had happened to her son Bromley or what her dashing daughter Noelani was doing. Her only joy came when someone drove her up Nuuanu Valley to Aunt Lucinda's, and there the two women would sit in the rainy afternoons talking of things that never quite got into sequence . . . and neither cared.

For generations the missionaries had railed against Hawaiians for having allowed brothers to marry sisters, and on no aspect of Hawaiian life was New England moral judgment sterner than on this. "It puts the Hawaiian outside the pale of civilized society," Lucinda Whipple's ancestors had stormed, particularly her great-grandfather Abner Hale, and yet the same curse had now overtaken her own great interlocking family. Whipples married Janderses, and Janderses married Hewletts, and if full brothers and sisters did not physically wed, intellectually and emotionally they did, so that a girl named Jerusha Hewlett Hoxworth was practically indistinguishable either in genes or ideas from a Malama Janders Hale, and each stayed mostly in an upstairs room.

In 1946, therefore, except for the death of his son, and the slow decline of his adored wife, Hoxworth Hale was truly as good a man as he would ever be, but those two bereavements oppressed him and prevented his enjoyment of the last powerful flowering of his talents. He therefore turned his whole attention to the government of the Hoxworth & Hale empire, and as the critical year started he relied more and more upon two stalwart resolves: "I will not give labor an inch, not another inch, especially when it's led by Japanese who don't really understand American ways. And we have got to keep Hawaii as it is. I will not have mainland firms like Gregory's elbowing their way in here and disrupting our Hawaiian economy." Behind him, to back up these two mighty resolves, he had the entire recourses of H & H, totaling some $260,000,000 and all the managerial strength of J & W, now worth more than $185,000,000. Lesser outfits like Hewlett and Son had to string along, for all saw in Hoxworth Hale the cool and able man, one above the passions of the moment, who could be depended upon to preserve their way of life.

Only in his understanding of what was happening should Hoxworth Hale be considered a Golden Man. Racially he was mostly haole. Emotionally he was all haole, and he thought of himself in that way. Actually, of course, he was one-sixteenth Hawaiian, inherited through the Alii Nui Noelani, who was his great-great-grandmother. He was also part-Arabian, for one of his European ancestors had married during the Crusades, part-African through an earlier Roman ancestor, part-Central Asian from an Austrian woman who had married a Hungarian in 1603, and part-American Indian through a cute trick that an early Hale's wife had pulled on him in remote Massachusetts. But he was known as pure haole, whatever that means.

In 1946 Hong Kong Kee was five years older than Hoxworth Hale, which made him exactly fifty-three, whereas his grandmother Nyuk Tsin was ninety-nine. This was not a particularly good year for Hong Kong, because in following his grandmother's urgent advice—"Buy every piece of land that frightened haoles want to sell"—he had somewhat over-extended himself and frankly did not know where he was going to find tax money to protect the large parcels of land on which he was sitting. Real estate had not been doing well; the anticipated boom in tourists had not yet materialized; and there was a prospect of long strikes in both sugar and pineapple. He had seven children in school, five in mainland colleges and two at Punahou, and for a while he considered abruptly cutting off their allowances and telling the boys to get to work and help pay taxes, but Nyuk Tsin would not hear of this. Her counsel was simple: "Every child must have the very best education possible. Every piece of land must be held as long as possible. If this means no automobiles and no expensive food, good! We won't ride and we won't eat!" The Kee hui was therefore on very short rations, and Hong Kong sent a form letter to all the Kees studying on the mainland—his own and others: "I will be able to pay only your tuition and books. If you are running an automobile, sell it and go to work. If you are faced by the prospect of spending two or even three more years in college under this plan, spend it, but for the time being there can be no more money from Hawaii!" The decision that hurt him most involved his youngest daughter, Judy. "You have to cut out private singing lessons," he told her, and it was sad to see her obey.

And then, when things were already difficult, Hong Kong surreptitiously heard that a well-known firm of mainland private detectives was investigating him. He picked up a rumor of this from one of the Ching clan who had been asked a good many questions about real-estate deals, and the interrogation had made no sense until a few days later when Lew Ching suddenly thought: "My God! Every one of those deals involved Hong Kong Kee!" And he felt obligated to lay this circumstantial evidence before his friend.

Hong Kong's first reaction was, "The income tax people are after me!" But reflection assured him that this was ridiculous, for certainly the government never used private detective agencies when they had such good ones of their own. This conclusion, however, left him more bewildered than ever, and gradually he came to suspect that The Fort had deduced that he might be overextended and was collecting evidence which would enable them to squeeze him out, once and for all. He judged that the mastermind was probably Hoxworth Hale.

His first substantial bit of evidence came, curiously, not from the Chinese, who were adroit in piecing together fragments of puzzles, but from his friend Kamejiro Sakagawa, whom he had helped establish in the supermarket business. Squat little Kamejiro bustled in one afternoon to announce bluntly: "Hong Kong, you bettah watch out, I t'ink you in big trouble. Dick from da mainland come to dis rock, ast me about you, how I git my land. Bimeby latah he go into da building H & H."

"This detective, he has no reason to bother you, Kamejiro," Hong Kong assured him. "Our deal is perfectly good."

"Whassamatta, dey ketch you from taxes?"

"Mine are okay. How about yours?"

"Mine okay too," Kamejiro assured him.

"Then don't you worry, Kamejiro. Let me worry. This has to do only with me."

"You in special trouble?" the Japanese asked.

"Everybody's always in trouble," Hong Kong assured him.

But what precise trouble he himself was in, Hong Kong could not discover. In succeeding days he caught various reports of the detectives and their work; all aspects of his varied business life were under surveillance. He never spotted any of the detectives himself, and then suddenly they vanished, and he heard no more about them. All he knew was: "Somebody knows almost as much about my business as I do. And they're reporting to Hoxworth Hale." He did not sleep easily.

In another sense, these were exciting times, for unless everything that Hong Kong and his grandmother had concluded from their studies was false, Hawaii had to be on the verge of startling expansion. Airplanes, no longer required for warfare, were going to ferry thousands of tourists to Hawaii, and many new hotels would be required. On the day that the boom started, the builders would have to come to Hong Kong, for he had the land, and he felt like a superb runner on the eve of an Olympics which would test him against athletes whom he had not previously encountered: he was a good runner, he was in tense condition, and he was willing to trust the morrow's luck. Even so, he took the precaution of discussing the detective mystery with his grandmother, and she pointed out to Hong Kong: "These are the years when we must sit tight. Wait, wait. That's always very difficult to do. Any fool can engage in action, but only the wise man can wait. It seems to me that if someone is spending so much money to investigate you, either he fears you very much, which is good, or he is weighing the prospects of joining you, which could be better. Therefore what you must do is wait, wait. Let him make the first move. If he is going to fight you, each day that passes makes you stronger. If he is going to join you, each day that you survive makes the cost to him a little greater. Wait."

So through most of 1946 Hong Kong waited, but without the confidence his grandmother commanded. Each day's mail tortured him, for he would sit staring at the long envelopes, wondering what bad news they brought; and he dreaded cables. But as he waited, he gathered strength, and as the year ended and his mind grew clearer and his financial position stronger, he began to resemble the Golden Man of whom the sociologists had spoken.

Hong Kong thought of himself as pure Chinese, for his branch of the family had married only Hakka girls, and whereas there were a good many Kees with Hawaiian and Portuguese and Filipino blood, he had none, a fact of which he was quietly proud. Of course, from past adventures of the Kee hui Hong Kong's ancestors had picked up a good deal of Mongolian blood, and Manchurian, and Tartar, plus a little Japanese during the wars of the early 1600's, plus some Korean via an ancestor who had traveled in that peninsula in 814, augmented by a good deal of nondescript inheritance from tribes who had wandered about southern China from the year 4000 B.C. on, but nevertheless he thought of himself as pure Chinese, whatever that means.

In 1946 young Shigeo Sakagawa was twenty-three years old, and now a full captain in the United States army. He was five feet six inches tall and weighed a lean 152 pounds. He did not wear glasses and was considerably better co-

ordinated than his stocky and somewhat awkward peasant father. He had a
handsome face with strong, clear complexion and very good teeth, but his most
conspicuous characteristic was a quick intellect which had marked him in whatever military duties he had been required to perform. The three citations that
accompanied his army medals spoke of courage beyond the call of duty, but
they were really awards for extraordinary ability to anticipate what was about
to happen.

In the memorable victory parade down Kapiolani Boulevard, Captain
Shigeo Sakagawa marched in the third file, behind the flag bearers and the
colonel. His feet, hardened from military life, strode over the asphalt briskly,
while his shoulders, accustomed to heavy burdens, were pulled back. This
brought his chin up, so that his slanted Japanese eyes were forced to look out
upon the community in which they had not previously been welcome. But when
he heard the thundering applause, and saw from the corner of his eye his bent
mother and his stocky, honest little father, accepted at last, he felt that the
struggle had been a good one. Tadao was dead in Italy, and Minoru the stalwart
tackle was buried in France. Goro was absent in Japan helping direct the
occupation, and the family would never be together again. The Sakagawas had
paid a terrible price to prove their loyalty, but it had been worth it. When the
marchers were well past the spot where the elder Sakagawas and other Japanese
were weeping with joy, the parade reached the old Iolani Palace, seat of Hawaii's government, and for the first time it looked to Shig Sakagawa like a
building which a Japanese might enter, just like anyone else. "This is my town,"
he thought as he marched.

But when he reached home after the parade and saw the photographs of
dead Tad and Minoru on the wall, he covered his face with his hands and
muttered, "If we Japanese are at last free, it was you fellows who did it. Jesus,
what a price!"

He was therefore embarrassed when his father, still fascinated by military
life, fingered his medals and said in English, "Like I tell b'fore, dey got no
soldiers mo bettah Japanese."

"I wasn't brave, Pop. I just happened to see what was going to happen."

"S'pose you saw, how come you not run away?" Kamejiro asked.

"I was Japanese, so I had to stay," Shig explained. "Too much at stake. I
swallowed my fear and for this they gave me medals."

"All Japan is proud of you," Kamejiro said in Japanese.

"I'm glad the emperor feels that way," Shig laughed, "because I'm on my
way to help him govern Japan."

Shigeo's mother screamed in Japanese, "You're not going away to war
again, are you? Goro's already in Japan, and I pray every night."

"There's no war!" her son explained warmly, clutching her affectionately by
the arm. "I'll be in no danger. Neither will Goro."

"No war?" Mrs. Sakagawa asked, startled. "Oh, Shigeo! Haven't you
heard? Mr. Ishii says . . ."

"Mother, don't bother me with what that crazy Mr. Ishii dreams up."

Nevertheless, Mrs. Sakagawa summoned her daughter and Mr. Ishii, and
after the wiry little labor leader had carefully inspected all the doors to be sure
no haoles were spying, he pulled down the shades and whispered in Japanese,
"What I told you last week is true, Kamejiro-san. Under no circumstances
should you allow a second son to go to Japan. He will be killed, just like Goro.
For everything we have heard is a lie. Japan is winning the war and may invade
Hawaii at any moment."

Shigeo thought his brain had become unhinged, and he caught Reiko's hand, asking, "Sister, do you believe your husband's nonsense?"

"Don't call it nonsense!" Mr. Ishii stormed in Japanese. "You have been fed a great collection of lies. Japan is winning the war and is accumulating strength."

"Reiko!" her brother insisted. "Do you believe this nonsense?"

"You'll have to forgive my husband," the dutiful wife explained. "He hears such strange reports at the meetings . . ."

"What meetings?" Shigeo demanded.

That night Mr. Ishii and his sister showed him. They took him to a small building west of Nuuanu where a meeting was in progress, attended by elderly Japanese. A fanatical religious leader, recently out of a concentration camp, was shouting in Japanese, "What they tell you about Hiroshima is all lies. The city was not touched. Tokyo was not burned. Our troops are in Singapore and Australia. Japan is more powerful than ever before!"

The audience listened intently, and Shigeo saw his brother-in-law, Mr. Ishii, nodding profoundly. At this moment Shigeo unfortunately tugged at his sister's sleeve, and the speaker saw him. "Ah!" he shouted. "I see we have a spy in our midst. A dirty dog of the enemy. You, Mrs. Ishii? Is he trying to tell you that Japan lost the war? Don't you believe him! He has been bought by the Americans! I tell you, he is a liar and a spy. Japan won the war!"

Against his own intelligence, Shigeo had to admit that many of the audience not only believed this crazy religious maniac, but they wanted to believe. When the meeting ended, many of the old people smiled sadly at Shigeo, who had criminally fought against Japan, and they hoped that when the emperor's troops landed they would deal kindly with him, for he had probably been seduced into his traitorous action. Many boys in Hawaii had been so tricked.

In a daze Shigeo started homeward. He wanted no more to do with Mr. Ishii and the pathetic old fools, but when he had walked some distance, he changed his mind and caught a bus that carried him down into the heart of Honolulu, and after some speculation as to what he should do he marched into the police station and asked to see one of the detectives. The haole knew him and congratulated him on his medals, but Shig laughed and said, "What I'm going to tell you, you may take them away."

"What's up?"

"You ever hear of the Katta Gumi Society? The Ever-Victorious Group?"

"You mean the Japan-Won screwballs? Yeah, we keep a fairly close watch on them."

"I just attended a meeting. Captain, I'm shook."

"The little hut back of the old mission school?"

"Yes."

"We check that regularly. Tony, did we have a man at the mission hut tonight?"

"We didn't bother tonight," the assistant replied.

"These people are out of their minds," Shig protested.

"It's pathetic," the detective agreed. "Poor old bastards, they were so sure Japan couldn't be licked that they believe whatever these agitators tell 'em. But they don't do any harm."

"Aren't you going to arrest them?" Shig asked.

"Hell no," the detective laughed. "We got six groups in Honolulu we check on regularly, and the Japan-Wons give us the least trouble. One group wants to murder Syngman Rhee. One wants to murder Chiang Kai-shek. One dupes old women out of all their money by predicting the end of the world on the first of each month. Last year we had one couple that prepared for the second coming of Christ on the first day of eleven succeeding months. They finally came to us and said that maybe something was wrong. So your crazy Japanese are only part of a pattern."

"But how can they believe . . . All the newspaper stories and newsreels? The men who were there?"

"Shig," the detective said, plopping his hands upright on the desk. "How can you believe for eleven successive months that Jesus Christ is coming down the Nuuanu Pali? You can be fooled once, I grant, but not eleven times."

When the time came for Shigeo to sail to his new job with General MacArthur in Japan, his mother wept and said, "If there is fighting when you get to Tokyo, don't get off the ship, Shigeo." Then, recalling more important matters, she told him, "Don't marry a northern girl, Shigeo. We don't want any zu-zu-ben in our family. And I'd be careful of Tokyo girls, too. They're expensive. Your father and I would be very unhappy if you married a Kyushu girl, because they don't fit in with Hiroshima people. And under no circumstances marry an Okinawan, or anyone who might be an Eta. What would be best would be for you to marry a Hiroshima girl. Such girls you can trust. But don't take one from Hiroshima City."

"I don't think Americans will be welcomed in Hiroshima," Shigeo said quietly.

"Why not?" his mother protested.

"After the bomb?" Shigeo asked.

"Shigeo!" his mother replied in amazement. "Nothing happened to Hiroshima! Mr. Ishii assured me . . ."

When Shig Sakagawa assembled with his Tokyo-bound outfit and marched through the streets of downtown Honolulu on his way to the transport that would take them to Yokohama, he was, without knowing it, a striking young man. He possessed a mind of steel, hardened in battle against both the Germans and the prejudices of his homeland. By personal will power he had triumphed against each adversary and had proved his courage as few men are required to do. No one recognized the fact that day, for then Shig was only twenty-three and had not yet acquired his lawyer's degree from Harvard, but he was the forward cutting edge of a revolution that was about to break over Hawaii. He was stern, incorruptible, physically hard and fearless. More important, so far as revolutions go, he was well organized and alert.

As he marched he passed, without either man's knowing it, Hoxworth Hale, who was walking up Bishop Street on his way to The Fort, and if in that moment Hale had had the foresight to stop the parade and to enlist Shig Sakagawa on his side, The Fort would surely have been able to preserve its prerogatives. Furthermore, if Hale, as an official of the Republican Party, had conscripted Shig and half a hundred other young Japanese like him, Republicanism in Hawaii would have been perpetually insured, for by their traditional and conservative nature the Japanese would have made ideal Republicans, and a combination of haole business acumen and Japanese industry would have constituted a strength that no adversary could have broken. But it was then totally impossible for Hoxworth Hale even to imagine such a union, and as he walked past the parade he had the ungracious thought: "If I hear any more about the brave Japanese boys who won the war for us, I'll vomit. Where's my son Bromley? Where's Harry Janders and Jimmy Whipple? They won the war, too, and they're dead." The crowd along Bishop Street cheered the Japanese boys, and the pregnant moment of history was lost. Hoxworth Hale went to The Fort and Shig Sakagawa went to Japan.

But if Hoxworth Hale failed to grasp the nettles of history, there was another who did, for as Hong Kong Kee walked down Bishop Street in the other direction he met Kamejiro Sakagawa proudly waving to his son, and Hong Kong asked, "Which one is your boy, Kamejiro?"

"Dat one ovah dere wid de medals," Kamejiro beamed.

Since most of the Japanese were wearing medals won in Europe, Hong Kong could not determine which one was Kamejiro's son. "Is he the one who has the red patch on his arm?" Hong Kong asked.

"Hai!" old Sakagawa agreed.

"I'd like to meet your boy," Hong Kong said, and when the troops broke ranks on the dock Kamejiro said to his son, "Dis Hong Kong Kee, berry good frien'. He give me da money fo' da stoah'."

With obvious gratitude, Captain Sakagawa thrust out his hand and said, "You had a lot of courage, Mr. Kee to gamble that way on my father. Especially during the war."

Hong Kong was tempted to bask in glory, but prudence had taught him always to anticipate trouble and to quash it in advance, so he said forthrightly, "Probably you didn't hear, but during the war I was stupid enough to make a very bad speech against the Japanese. Later, I was ashamed of myself and tried to make up."

"I know," Shig said. "My sister wrote me about your speech. But war's war."

"Things are much better now," Hong Kong said. "What I wanted to see you about, Shigeo. When you come home you ought to go to college. Maybe law school. You do well, maybe I'll have a job for you."

"You have a lot of sons of your own, Hong Kong."

"None of them is Japanese," Hong Kong laughed.

"You want a Japanese?" Shig asked, astounded.

"Of course," Hong Kong grunted. "You boys are going to run the islands."

Shig grew extraordinarily attentive. Standing directly in front of Hong Kong's metallic eyes, he studied the Chinese carefully and asked, "Do you really think there'll be changes?"

"Fantastic," Hong Kong replied. "I'd like to have a smart boy like you working for me."

"I may not work for anybody," Shig said slowly.

"That's good too," Hong Kong said evenly. "But everybody's got to have friends."

When Captain Sakagawa climbed aboard the transport he felt completely American. He had proved his courage, had been accepted by Honolulu, and now he was wanted by someone. In a sense, he was already a Golden Man, knowledgeable both in western and eastern values, for although he reveled in his newly won Americanism, he also took pride in being a pure-blooded Japanese. Of course this latter was ridiculous, for he contained inheritances from all those nameless predecessors who had once inhabited Japan: some of his genes came from the hairy Ainu to the north, from Siberian invaders, from the Chinese, from the Koreans amongst whom his ancestors had lived, and more particularly from that venturesome Indo-Malayan stock, half of whom had journeyed eastward to become Hawaiians while their brothers had moved northward along different islands to merge with the Japanese. Thus, of two ancient Malayan brothers starting from a point near Singapore, the northern traveler had become the ancestor of Shigeo Sakagawa, while the other had served as the progenitor of Kelly Kanakoa, the Hawaiian beachboy who now stood with a pretty girl watching the end of the parade.

Or, if one preferred looking north, of three ancient Siberian brothers, one bravely crossed the sea to Japan, where his genes found ultimate refuge in the body of Shigeo Sakagawa. Another crept along the Aleutian bridge toward Massachusetts, where his descendants wound up as Indian progenitors of Hoxworth Hale; while a third, less venturesome than his brothers, drifted southward along established land routes to central China, where he helped form the Hakka, thus serving as an ancestor to Hong Kong Kee. In truth, all men are brothers, but as generations pass, it is differences that matter and not similarities.

IN THE IRRELEVANT sense of the word, this Kelly Kanakoa of whom I just spoke was already a Golden Man, for at twenty-one he was slightly over six feet tall, weighed a trim 180, and had a powerful body whose muscles rippled in sunlight as if smeared with coconut oil. He was very straight and had unusually handsome features, marked by deep-set dark eyes, a gamin laugh, and a head of jet-black hair in which he liked to wear a flower. His manner was a mixture of relaxation and insolence, and although it was more than two years since he had knocked out two sailors on Hotel Street for calling him a nigger, he seemed always half ready for a brawl, but whenever one seemed about to explode, he tried to evade it: "Why you like beef wid me? I no want trobble. Let's shake and be blalahs again."

Now, as Kelly stood watching the departing parade, he held in his right hand the slim, well-manicured fingers of a Tulsa divorcee who had come to Honolulu from Reno, seeking emotional reorientation after her difficult divorce. At the ranch where she had stayed in Nevada a fellow divorcee had told her, "Rennie! If you go to Hawaii be sure to look up Kelly Kanakoa. He's adorable." So as soon as Rennie had disembarked from the H & H flagship, *Mauna Loa,* she had called the number her friend had given her, announcing: "Hello, Kelly? Maud Clemmens told me to look you up."

He had come sauntering around to the luxurious H & H hotel, the Lagoon, wearing very tight blue pants, a white busboy's jacket with only one button closed, sandals, a yachting cap, and a flower behind his ear. When she came down into the grandiose lobby, crisp and white in a new bathing suit edged in lace, he appraised her insolently and calculated: "This wahine's gonna screw the first night."

In his job as beachboy, which he had acquired by accident because he liked to surf and had a pleasant joking way with rich women customers, he had become expert in estimating how long it would take him to get into bed with any newcomer. Divorcees, he had found, were easiest because they had undergone great shock to their womanliness and were determined to prove that they, at least, had not been at fault in the breakup of their marriages. It rarely took Kelly more than two nights. Of course when they first met him they certainly had no intention of sleeping with him, but as he explained to the other fellows hanging around the beach, "S'pose da wahine not ride a surfboard yet, how she know what she really wanna do?" It was his job, and he got paid for it, to take divorcees and young widows on surfboards.

Ten minutes after Rennie met Kelly she was on her first surfing expedition, far out on the reef where the big waves were forming. She was excited by the exhilarating motion of the sea and felt that she would never be able to rise and stand on the board as it swept her toward shore, but when she felt Kelly's strong arms enveloping her from the rear she felt assured, and as the board gathered momentum she allowed herself to be pulled upright, always in Kelly's stout arms, until she stood daringly on the flying board. For a moment the spray blinded her, but she soon learned to tilt her chin high into the wind and break its force, so that soon she was roaring across the reef, with a thundering surf at her feet and the powerful shape of Diamond Head dominating the shore.

"How marvelous!" she cried as the comber maintained its rush toward the shore. Instinctively she drew Kelly's arm closer about her, pressed backward against him and reveled in his manliness. Then, when the crashing surf broke at last, she felt the board collapse into the dying waves, and she with it, until she was underwater with Kelly's arms still about her, and of her own accord she turned her face to his, and they kissed for a long time under the sea, then idly rose to the surface.

Now she climbed back upon the surfboard, and with Kelly instructing, started the long paddle out to catch the next wave, but when their board was well separated from the others, she relaxed backwards until she felt herself against the beachboy once more, and there she rested in his secure arms, paddling idly as his adept hands began their explorations beneath her new bathing suit. Sighing, she whispered, "Is this part of the standard instruction?"

"Not many wahine cute like you," Kelly replied gallantly, whereupon she shivered with joy and brought her body closer to his, where she could feel the muscles of his chest against her neck.

It was a long, exciting trip out to where the waves formed, and as they waited for the right one, Kelly asked, "You scared stand up dis time?"

"I'm game to try anything with you," Rennie said, and she showed remarkable aptitude on the long surge in, and when the surfboard finally subsided into the broken wave, and when they were underseas for a kiss, she found to her surprise that her hands were now inside his swimming suit, clutching passionately, hungrily. When they surfaced, his black hair in his eyes like a satyr's, he laughed and said approvingly, "Bimeby you numbah one surfer, get da trophy, Rennie."

"Do I do things right?" she asked modestly.

"You very right," he assured her.

"Shall we catch another wave?" she suggested.

"Why we not go on up your room?" he asked evenly, keeping his dark eyes directly on her.

"I think we'd better," she agreed, adding cautiously, "Are you allowed upstairs?"

"S'pose you forget your lauhala hat on de beach, somebody surely gotta bring it to you," he explained.

"Is that standard procedure?" Rennie asked coyly.

"Like mos' stuff," Kelly explained, "surfin's gotta have its own rules."

"We'll play by the rules," she agreed, squeezing his hand. And when he got to her room, holding the sun hat in his powerful hands, he found that she had already climbed into one of the skimpiest playsuits he had ever seen, and in his years on the beach he had seen quite a few.

"Hey, seestah! Wedder you wear muumuu or sundress or nuttin', you look beautiful," he said approvingly, and in her natural confusion over her divorce, this was exactly what she wanted to hear, and she dispensed with the customary formalities of such moments and held out her arms to the handsome beachboy.

"Normally I'd order a Scotch and soda, and we'd talk a while . . . Let's take up where we left off under water."

Kelly studied her for a long, delicious moment and suggested, "Alla time, dese badin' suit get wet too much." And he slipped his off, and when he stood before her in rugged, dark-skinned power she thought: "If I had married a man like this there'd have been no trouble."

Now, as the parade passed down Bishop Street, she was about to leave Hawaii, and she held his hand tightly in the last minutes before boarding the *Mauna Loa.* For nine days she had lived with Kelly passionately and in complete surrender to his amazing manliness. Once she told him, "Kelly, you should have seen the pathetic little jerk I was married to. God, what a waste of years." Now she whispered, in the bright sunlight, "If we hurried to the ship, would we have time for one more?"

"Whassamatta why not?" he asked, and they clambered aboard the big ship and sought out her stateroom, but her intended roommate was already unpacking, a tall, rather goodlooking girl in her late twenties. There were several embarrassed moments, after which Rennie whispered to Kelly, "What have I got to lose?"

She addressed the girl directly and said, "I'm sorry we haven't met, but would you think me an awful stinker if I borrowed the room for a little while?"

The tall girl slowly studied Rennie and then Kelly. They were an attractive couple, and she laughed, "A vacation's a vacation. How long you need?"

"About half an hour," Rennie replied. "They have a band upstairs."

"And a full orchestra right here," the girl laughed, and before she had climbed to the next deck, Rennie was undressed and in bed.

Later she confided, "For five days I've been imagining what it would be like to have you back in New York. How old are you, Kelly?"

"Twenty-one."

"Damn. I'm twenty-seven."

"You no seem twenty-seven yet, not in bed," the beachboy assured her.

"Am I good in bed?" she pleaded. "Really good."

"You numbah one wahine."

"Have you know many girls?"

"Surfin' is surfin'," he replied.

"For example, Maud Clemmens? Did you sleep with her?"

"How you like s'pose nex' week somebody ast me, 'How about Rennie? Dat wahine screw?' "

"Kelly! Such words!"

"Da whistle gonna blow, Rennie seestah," he warned her, climbing into his own clothes.

"I went down to the library, Kelly," she said softly. "And there it was, like you said. This big long book with the names written down by the missionary. It says that your family can be traced back for one hundred and thirty-four generations. It must make you feel proud."

"Don't make me feel notting," Kelly grunted.

"Why does a Hawaiian have the name Kelly?" she asked, slipping on her stockings.

"My kanaka name Kelolo, but nobody like say 'em."

"Kelly's a sweet name," she said approvingly. Then she kissed him and asked, "Why wouldn't you take me to your home?"

"It's nothing," he shrugged.

"You mean, your ancestors were kings and you have nothing for yourself?"

"I get guitar, I get surfboard, I get cute wahine like you."

"It's too damned bad," she said bitterly, kissing him again. "Kelly, you're the best thing in Hawaii." They went on deck and she made a quick sign to her roommate, thanking her. The tall girl laughed and winked. When the whistle blew for the last time, warning the various beachboys who had come down to see their haole wahines off, Rennie asked hesitantly, "If some of my friends decide to come to Hawaii . . . girl friends that is . . ." She paused.

"Sure, I look out for dem," Kelly agreed.

"You're a darling!" she laughed, kissing him ardently as he pulled away to run down the gangplank. In the departure shed the beachboy Florsheim—they called him that because sometimes he wore shoes—sidled up and asked, "Kelly blalah, da kine wahine da kine blonde, she good screwin'?"

"Da bes'," Kelly said firmly, and the two beachboys went amiably back to the Lagoon.

Once or twice as the year 1946 skipped away, Kelly had fleeting doubts which he shared with Florsheim: "Whassamatta me? Takin' care lotsa wahine, all mixed up. Where it gonna get me?" But such speculation was always stilled by the arrival of some new divorcee or widow, and the fun of working it around so that he got into bed with them, while they paid the hotel and restaurant bills, was so great that he invariably came around to Florsheim's philosophy: "Mo bettah we get fun now, while we young." So he maintained the routine: meet the ship, find the girl that someone had cabled about, take her surfing, live with her for eight days, kiss her good-bye on the *Moana Loa,* get some rest, and then meet the next ship. Sometimes he looked with admiration at Johnny Pupali, forty-nine years old and still giving the wahines what he called "Dr. Pupali's surfboard cure for misery."

One afternoon he asked Pupali about his surprising energy, and the dean of beachboys explained: "A man got energy for do four t'ings. Eat, work, surf, or make love. But at one time got stuff for only two. For me, surfin' and makin' love."

"You ever get tired?" Kelly asked.

"Surfin'? No. I gonna die on an incomin' wave. Wahines? Tell you da trufe, Kelly, sometime for about ten minutes after *Moana Loa* sail, I don' nevah wanna see da kine wahine no mo', but nex' day wen anudder ship blow anudder whistle, man, I'm strip for action."

In the lazy weeks between girls, Kelly found real joy in loafing on the beath with Florsheim, a big, sprawling man who wore his own kind of costume: enormous baggy shorts of silk and cotton that looked like underwear and fell two inches below his knees, a tentlike aloha shirt whose ends he tied about his middle, leaving a four-inch expanse of belly, Japanese slippers with a thong between his toes, and a coconut hat with a narrow brim and two long fibers reaching eight inches in the air and flopping over on one side. Florsheim always looked sloppy until he kicked off his clothes and stood forth in skin-tight bathing trunks, and then he looked like a pagan deity, huge, brown, long hair about his ears and a wreath of fragrant maile encircling his brow. Even the most fastidious mainland women reveled in this transformation and loved to lie on the sand beside him, tracing his rippling muscles with their red fingernails.

Kelly preferred Florsheim as a companion because the huge beachboy could sing the strange falsetto of the islands, and together they made a gifted pair, for Kelly had a fine baritone voice. He was also skilled at slack-key, a system of guitar playing peculiar to Hawaii, in which the strings were specially tuned to produce both plucked melody and strummed chords. Many people thought of Kelly's slack-key as the voice of the islands, for when he was in good form he gave his music an urgent sweetness that no other possessed. The melodies were swift and tremulous like an island bird, but the chords were slow and sure like the thundering of the surf. When the beachboys had nothing to do, they often called, "Kelly blalah. Play da kine sleck-key like dat." He was their troubadour, but he rarely played for visitors. "I doan' like waste time haole," he growled. "Dey doan' know sleck-key."

The other pastime that he and Florsheim loved was sakura, a crazy Japanese card game played with little black cards that came in a wooden box with a picture of cherry blossoms on the cover. Any beachboy was hailed as the day's hero who could scrape together enough money to buy a fresh box of sakura cards, and through the long hot days the gang would sit beneath coconut umbrellas, playing the silly game. No other was allowed, and if a man couldn't play sakura, he couldn't be a beachboy. Of course he must also speak degenerate pidgin, as on the afternoon when Kelly was protesting the price of cube steak at the corner drug store.

"Me t'ink high too much, da kine pipty cent," he mused.

"Kelly blalah, wha' da kine da kine you speak?" Florsheim asked idly.

"Whassamatta you, stoopid? You akamai good too much da kine da kine," Kelly growled, adding with a chopping motion of his right hand, "Da kine chop chop."

"Oh!" Florsheim sang in a high, descending wail of recognition. "You speak *da kine* da kine? Right, blalah, price too moch. Pipty cent too bloody takai." And they passed to other equally important topics.

As Kelly became better acquainted with American girls, he felt sorry for them. Invariably they confided how wretched their lives had been with their haole husbands, how the men were not interested in them and how unsatisfactory sex had been. This latter knowledge always astonished Kelly, for while the girls were with him they could think of little else, and if the world had women who were better at sex than the wahines who came over to Hawaii on the *Moana Loa,* he concluded they must be real tigers. One day he told Florsheim, "How some wahine gonna be any bettah than da kine wahine we get over heah? What you s'pose da mattah wid dese haole men?"

In 1947 he got a partial answer, because Florsheim married one of his young divorcees, a girl who had a lot of money and who gave him a Chevrolet convertible, and as long as they stayed in Hawaii things went rather well, but after three months in New York, they broke all to hell, and Florsheim came back alone to resume his job on the beach. On a day when there was little doing he explained to his companions, "Dese wahine da kine, seem like dey two people. Over here on a surfboard dey relax, dey screw like mad, dey don't gi'e a damn. Ova' heah I t'row my wahine in da jalopy and we go okolehau." He steered the imaginary car with his hands. "We have bes' time."

"Wha' hoppen?" Kelly asked.

"I tell you, Kelly blalah," Florsheim drawled. "She take me New York, she no like da way I dress. She no like da kine talk, and. She doan' like one goddamn t'ing, I t'ink. Allatime give me hell. No more time to go bed in de apternoon, when it's de bes'. So bimeby she tell me, 'Florsheim, you gotta go night school learn speak haole no kanaka,' and I tellem, 'Go to hell. I ketchem airplane Hawaii,' and she speak me, 'Wha' you gonna use money da kine?' and I tellem, 'Seven hunnerd dollars I scoop f'um you,' and she speak, 'You dirty boa', you filthy mountain pig!' and what I tellem den, I ain't gonna repeat."

"Da kine wahine turn out like dat?" Johnny Pupali mused. "Well, da's why I tell you boys, 'Screw 'em but doan' marry 'em.' "

Florsheim reflected: "Seem like dey good wahine ova' heah, but anudder kine back home."

"You gonna keep da kine Chevvy?" Kelly asked.

"Yeah," Florsheim said, adding, "I not halp so sorry for dem wahine like I was b'fore."

The sweet days rolled on and Kelly discovered what the older beachboys already knew: that the best wahines of all were those from the Deep South. They were gentler, kinder, and in memorable ways much more loving. They seemed fascinated by Kelly's dark-brown body, and on three different occasions Kelly stayed for days at a time in one suite or another with some adorable girl from the South, without ever leaving the room and often without dressing from one day to the next. At mealtime he would throw a small towel about his waist, tucking in the ends as if it were a sarong, and the wahine from Montgomery or Atlanta or Birmingham would admire him as he lolled about the davenport. Once such a girl said, "You're awfully close to a nigra, Kelly, and yet you aren't. It's fascinating."

"Hawaiians hate niggers," Kelly assured her, and she felt better.

"How do you make your living?" she asked softly, coming to lie beside him after the food had been pushed away.

"S'pose I learn you surfin', I get paid."

"You get paid for what you did on that surfboard?" she gasped.

"Whassamatta, you no look you bill? Clerk put 'im on dere."

"Do you get paid . . . for days like this?"

"Clerk put 'im on. Rules say I'm s'pose teachin' you somethin'."

"That you are," she said softly as they lapsed off into another nap.

In time the girls he slept with became fused in his memory, for one sent another who sent another, but they always seemed to be the same girl, someone he had first met during the war. But there were a few whom he remembered forever. Once a young widow from Baton Rouge flew into the islands, and when he met her he calculated: "Dis wahine t'ree nights da kine, maybe four." He had underestimated, for in her sorrow the young woman would accept no man, yet when they stood in her cabin aboard the departing *Moana Loa* she said in a soft southern drawl, "The world is such a goddamned lonely place, Kelly."

"S'pose you lose da kine man you love, I t'ink maybe so," he said.

"I never loved Charley," she confessed, blowing her nose. "But he was a decent man, a good human being, and the world is worse off now that he's gone."

"What you gonna do bimeby?" he asked her, lolling with one arm about the end of the bed.

"I don't know," she said. "How old are you, Kelly?"

"I twenty-two, las' week."

"You have your life ahead of you, Kelly. It should be so exciting. But never kid yourself, Kelly. The world is a very lonely place."

"People come, dey go," he said philosophically.

"But when a good one comes, hold onto the memory. It's almost time for the whistle, and I wonder if I might do one thing before you go?"

"Wha' dat?" Kelly asked suspiciously.

"Could I kiss you good-bye? You've been so kind and understanding." She started to say something more, but broke into tears and pressed her beautiful white face to his. "You are such a goddamned decent human being," she whispered. "More than anything in the world I needed to meet someone like you."

Biting her lip and sniffling away her tears, she pushed him back toward the door and said, "Kelly, do you understand even remotely how deeply a woman like me prays for the success of a strong young man like you? I wish the heavens could open and give you their glory. Kelly, make a good life for yourself. Don't be a bum. For you are one of the men whom Jesus loves." And she sent him away.

Often when the surf was breaking he contemplated her words and wondered how a man went about building a good life for himself. He suspected that it consisted neither in being an old stud horse like Johnny Pupali, fun though that was, nor in wasting one's energies on a Haole wife the way Florsheim had done. Yet all he knew how to do was lie in the sun, play slack-key and sakura, and teach wahines how to surf. So for the time being that had to be good enough.

In late 1947 however a night-club singer from New York arrived in the islands—a two-night wahine, she turned out to be—and she took such a boisterous joy in Kelly that one night she cried, "God, they ought to build a monument to you, Beachboy!"

She was outraged when she learned that the current popular song, "The Rolling Surf," was something Kelly had composed on the beach and had given away to whoever wanted it. A mainland musician had glommed onto it, added a few professional twists, and made a pile of money from it.

"You ought to sue the dirty bastard!" she yelled. Later she tested Kelly's voice and found it good. "Tomorrow night, Kelly Kanakoa, you're going to sing with me. In the dining room of the Lagoon."

"I no like singin'," Kelly protested, but she asked, "What's that lovely thing you and the falsetto boy were doing with your ukuleles?"

"You speak da kine 'Hawaiian Wedding Song'?" he asked.

"The one where you start low, and he comes in high?"

Casually, Kelly started singing "Ke Kali Ne Au," the greatest of all Hawaiian songs, a glorious, haunting evocation of the islands. At the moment he was wearing a Lagoon towel as a sarong, with a hibiscus flower in his hair, and as he sang, the night-club girl sensed his full power and cried, "Kelly, nothing can stop you."

After one day's rehearsal, for the girl was a real professional and learned quickly, Kelly Kanakoa, dressed in a red and white sarong, with one of his mother's whale-tooth hooks dangling from a silver chain about his neck, and with a flower in his hair, came onto the floor of the Lagoon and started singing with the voice that was to become famous throughout the islands. "The Wedding Song" was unusual in that it provided a powerful solo for a baritone voice and a high, soaring dreamlike melody for a soprano. It was a true art song, worthy of Schubert or Hugo Wolf, and although that night's audience had heard it often before, sung by blowzy baritones and worse sopranos, they had not really heard the full majesty of the lyric outcry. Kelly was a man in love, a muscular, bronzed god, and the slim blonde girl from New York was in all ways his counterfoil. It was a memorable evening, and as it ended, the singer called to Kelly while he washed down in her shower, "How'd you like to come to New York with me?"

"I doan' leave da rock," he called back.

"You don't have to marry me," she assured him, aware before he was of his apprehensions. "Just sing."

"Me 'n' da beach, we akamai," he said, and although she begged him several more times while they were in bed, he insisted that his place was in Hawaii. "See da kine wha' hoppen Florsheim!" he repeated.

"Well, anyway," she said as she dressed for the plane. "We taught one another a lot in a few days."

"You speak da trufe," Kelly agreed.

"You gonna keep on singing?" she asked.

"Skoshi singin', skoshi surfin'."

"Don't give up the surfing," she said sardonically. "You got a real good thing working for you there."

"Seestah, dis kanaka doan' aim to lose it," Kelly laughed.

"I'm sure you don't," she cracked. She was brassy, and her hair was dark at the roots, but she was a good clean companion, and Kelly appreciated her.

"I ain't able come out to da airport," he said apologetically.

"You took care of things here," she assured him, patting the bed, "and that's where it counts."

Then, in early 1948, when the tourist business was beginning to boom, he received a cable from some wahine in Boston named Rennie, but he couldn't remember who she was, but anyway she said, "MEET MOANA LOA MRS. DALE HENDERSON." And when the ship came in, Florsheim, barefooted and staring up at the railing, asked, "Which one you wahine, Kelly blalah?"

"Maybe da kine," he indicated with a shrug of his shoulder.

"You s'pose she gonna lay?" Florsheim asked, appraising the slim, handsomely groomed girl who appeared to be in her early thirties.

"She look maybe two nights, maybe four," Kelly calculated, for he had found that women who spent unusual care on their appearance were often more tardy in climbing into bed than their sisters who called to the world, "Here I am, windblown and happy!"

Kelly, who like the other beachboys was privileged to climb aboard the *Moana Loa* before disembarkation started, elbowed his way along the crowded deck and touched Mrs. Henderson on the arm. She turned and smiled at him, a clean, unconfused greeting. When he shook hands with her he asked, "You name Dale or somethin' else? Seem like nobody can't speak man's name, woman's name no more."

"My name is Mrs. Henderson. Elinor Henderson," she replied in the crisp and self-possessed voice of a New Englander. "I'm from Boston."

Kelly very much wanted to ask, "Who dis Rennie wahine cable me? I no remember nobody in Boston." But he didn't speak. One rule he had learned in his beachboy business: never mention one woman to another, so that even though most of the customers he met had been referred to him by others, often intimate friends, he never mentioned that fact. Culling his brain furiously, he still failed to recall who Rennie was and he did not refer to her cable. But Mrs. Henderson did.

"A college classmate of mine at Smith . . . ."

"Dat doan' sound like no wahine college, Smith."

"Rennie Blackwell, she told me to be sure to look you up."

Quickly Kelly composed his face as if he knew well who Rennie Blackwell was, and just as quickly Mrs. Henderson thought: "After all she told me, and he doesn't even remember her name." Wanting perversely to explore the situation further she added, "Rennie was the girl from Tulsa." Still Kelly could not place her among the nameless girls that populated his life, and now he was aware that Mrs. Henderson was playing a game with him, so he lapsed into his most barbarous pidgin and banged his head with his fist. "Sometime I no akamai da kine. Dis wahine Rennie I not collect."

Mrs. Henderson smiled and said, "She collects you, Kelly."

He was irritated with this secure woman and said, "S'pose one year pass, bimeby I say Florsheim, 'Cable here speak Elinor Henderson. Who dat one wahine?' Florsheim he doan' collect. I doan' collect."

"Who's Florsheim?" Elinor asked.

"Da kine beachboy yonder 'longside tall wahine," Kelly explained.

Mrs. Henderson laughed merrily and said, "Rennie told me you were the best beachboy in the business, but you must promise me one thing."

"Wha' dat?"

"You aren't required to talk pidgin to me any longer. I'll bet you graduated with honors from Hewlett Hall. You can probably speak English better than I can." She smiled warmly and asked, "Aren't you going to give me the lei?"

"I'm afraid to kiss you, Mrs. Henderson," he laughed, and handed her the flowers, but Florsheim saw this and rushed up, protesting, "Jeezus Criss! Kanaka handin' wahine flowers like New York?" He grabbed the lei, plopped it around Elinor's head and kissed her powerfully.

"Florsheim's been in New York," Kelly joked. "He knows how to act like a Hawaiian."

"Florsheim? In New York?" Mrs. Henderson reflected, studying the huge beachboy with the long hair and the wreath of maile leaves. "I'll bet the city'll never be the same."

"He married a society girl," Kelly explained. "Stayed with her three months and came back. He got a Chevvy convertible out of it. In fact, we're riding back to the hotel in it."

At this point Florsheim's girl from Kansas City hustled up, heavy with leis and mascara, and giggled: "My God! Aren't these men positively divine?" She grabbed Florsheim's dark-brown arm, felt the muscles admiringly and asked, "You ever hit a man with that fist, Florsheim?"

"Nevah," the beachboy replied. "Only wimmin."

His girl laughed outrageously, and when the various bits of luggage were piled into the Chevy, the two couples headed for the Lagoon, but when Florsheim drove up King Street and past the old mission houses, Elinor Henderson abruptly asked him to stop, and she studied the historic buildings carefully, explaining at last, "My great-great-grandmother was born in that house. Originally I was a Quigley."

"Never heard of them," Kelly said honestly.

"They didn't stay long. But I'm doing a biography of them . . . for my thesis. I teach at Smith, you know."

"You da kine wahine bimeby gonna write a book?" Florsheim asked as he resumed the trip.

"Tell him he doesn't have to talk pidgin," Elinor suggested.

"He can't talk anything else," Kelly laughed.

"I think pidgin's just adorable," the girl in front said, and Kelly thought: "Looks like I've got a four-nighter at best, and maybe not at all, but good old Florsheim better watch out or he's going to be layin' that babe in the lobby."

Kelly's suspicion about Elinor Henderson proved correct, for she was not a four-nighter or even a six. She loved surfing and felt secure in Kelly's arms, but that was all. Yet one night when Kelly borrowed Florsheim's convertible— for the Kansas City girl had said flatly, "Why go riding in a Chevvy when you can have so much fun in bed?"—he drove Elinor out to Koko Head, where they sat in darkness talking.

"In the islands we call this kind of date, 'Watching the midnight submarine races,' " he explained.

"Very witty," she laughed.

"How's the biography coming along?" he asked.

"I'm quite perplexed," she confessed.

"No good, eh?"

"I have been sorely tempted to put it aside, Kelly."

"Why?"

There was a long pause in the darkness as the late moon climbed out of the sea in the perpetual mystery of the tropics. Along the shore a coconut palm dipped out to meet it, and the night was heavy, bearing down on the world. Suddenly Elinor turned to Kelly and took his hands. "I have been driven mad by the desire to write about you, Kelly," she said.

The beachboy was astonished. "Me!" he cried. "What's there to write about me?"

She explained in clear, swift sentences, without allowing him to interrupt: "I have been haunted by Hawaii ever since I read my great-great-great-grandfather's secret journal. He stayed here only seven years. Couldn't take any more. And when he got back to Boston he wrote a completely frank account of his apprehensions. I can see his dear old handwriting still: 'I shall write as if God were looking over my shoulder, for since He ordained these things He must understand them.' "

"What did he write?" Kelly inquired.

"He said that we Christians had invaded the islands with the proper God but with an improper set of supporting values. It was his conviction that our God saved the islands, but our ideas killed them. Particularly the Hawaiians. And at one point, Kelly, he wrote a prophetic passage about the Hawaiian of the future. I copied it down, and last night I read it again, and he was describing you."

"Gloomy prophecy?" Kelly asked.

" 'The Hawaiian is destined to diminish year by year, dispossessed, distraught and confused.' That's what the old man wrote. He must have had you in mind, Kelly."

Kelly was twenty-three years old that night, and he realized that in Elinor Henderson he was mixed up with an entirely different kind of woman. She was thirty-one, he guessed, clean, honest and very appealing. Her hair was crisply drawn back, and her white chin was both determined and inviting. He put his left hand under it and slowly brought it up to his. There was enough moonlight for him to see the visitor's eyes, and he was captivated by their calm assurance, so that for some moments the missionaries' descendant and the dispossessed Hawaiian studied each other, and finally his hand relaxed and her chin was released, whereupon she took his powerful face in her soft white hands and brought it to hers, kissing him and confessing, "I have forgotten old missionaries, Kelly. When I start to write I see only you. Do you know what I wish to call my new biography? *The Dispossessed.*"

They talked for a long time, while other cars came to observe the midnight submarine races and depart. Elinor asked directly, "Do you call this a life, Kelly? Making love to one neurotic divorcee after another?"

"Who told you?"

"I can see Florsheim, can't I?"

"Florsheim's not me."

"That isn't what Rennie Blackwell told me."

"What did she tell you?" Kelly asked.

"She said it was the one good week of her life."

"Which one was she?" he asked directly.

"I knew you didn't remember. She was the one who told her roommate on the *Moana Loa . . ."*

"Of course! Look, I don't need to be ashamed of loving a girl like that," Kelly insisted.

"Do you suppose Florsheim's going to marry the Kansas City girl?" Elinor asked.

"She's doing her damnedest to make him," Kelly laughed. "He'll stay with her four or five months and come home with a Buick."

"Why haven't you ever tried it?" Elinor probed.

"I don't need the money. I sing a little, play a little slack-key, get a little money teaching girls like you. And if I need a convertible, somebody always has one."

"Is it a life?" Elinor asked.

Kelly thought a long time, then asked, "What makes you think you can write a book?"

"I can do anything I set my mind on," Elinor replied.

"How come you're divorced?"

"I'm not."

"Your husband dead?"

"One of the best, Kelly. One of the men God puts his special finger on."

"He die in the war?"

"Covered with medals. Jack would have liked you, Kelly. You'd have understood each other. He had a thing about happiness. God, if the world knew what that man knew about being happy."

They sat in silence for some time, and Kelly asked, "Why would you call your book *The Dispossessed?* I got everything I want."

"You don't have your islands. The Japanese have them. You don't have the money. The Chinese have that. You don't have the land. The Fort has that. And you don't have your gods. My ancestors took care of that. What do you have?"

Kelly laughed nervously and began to say something but fought back the impulse, for he knew it would lead to peril. Instead he wagged his finger in Elinor's face and said, "You'd be surprised at what we Hawaiians have. Truly, you'd be astounded."

"All right. Take the four pretty girls who do the hula at the Lagoon . . . in those fake cellophane skirts. What are their names? Tell me the truth."

"Well, the one with the beautiful legs is Gloria Ching."

"Chinese?"

"Plus maybe a little Hawaiian. The girl with the real big bosom, that's Rachel Fernandez. And the real beauty there . . . I sort of like her, except she's Japanese . . . that's Helen Fukuda, and the one on the end is Norma Swenson."

"Swedish?"

"Plus maybe a little Hawaiian."

"So what we call Hawaiian culture is really a girl from the Philippines, wearing a cellophane skirt from Tahiti, playing a ukulele from Portugal, backed up by a loud-speaker guitar from New York, singing a phony ballad from Hollywood."

"I'm not a phony Hawaiian," he said carefully. "In the library there's a book about me. More than a hundred generations, and when I sing a Hawaiian song it comes right up from my toes. There's lots you don't know, Elinor."

"Tell me," she persisted.

"No," he refused. Then abruptly he made the surrender which only a few minutes earlier he had recognized as perilous. "I'll do better . . . something I've never done before."

"What?" she asked.

"You'll see. Wear something cool and I'll pick you up about three tomorrow."

"Will it be exciting?"

"Something you'll never forget."

At three the next day he drove a borrowed car up to the Lagoon and waited idly in the driveway till she appeared. When she got into the Pontiac, crisp and cool in a white dress, he turned toward the mountains and drove inland from the reef until he came to a high board fence, behind which coconut palms rose in awkward majesty. He continued around the fence until he came to a battered gate which he opened by nosing the car against it. When he had entered the grounds, he adroitly backed the car into the gate and closed it. Then he raced the engine, spun the tires in the gravel, and brought the car up to a shadowy, palm-protected, weather-strained old wooden house built in three stories, with gables, wide verandas, fretwork and stained-glass windows.

"This is my home," he said simply. "No girl's ever been here before." He banged the horn, and at the rickety screen door appeared a marvelous woman, six feet two inches tall, almost as wide as the door itself, silver-haired and stately, with a great brown smile that filled her plastic face. "Is that you, Kelolo?" she asked in a perfectly modulated voice that contained a touch of New England accent.

"Hi, Mom. Prepare for a shock! I'm bringing' home a haole wahine." Lest his mother be aware of the changes he had undergone for this girl, Kelly lapsed into his worst pidgin.

His mother left the doorway, walked in stately fashion to the edge of the porch, and extended her hand: "We are truly delighted to welcome you to the Swamp."

"Muddah, dis wahine Elinor Henderson, Smith. Muddah's Vassar." The trim Bostonian and the huge Hawaiian shook hands, each respectful of the other, and the latter said in her soft voice, "I am Malama Kanakoa, and you are the first of Kelolo's haole friends he has ever brought here. You must be special."

"Eh, Muddah, watch out!" Kelly warned. "We not in love. Dis wahine mo eight years older dan me. She all fixed mo bettah in Boston."

"But she is special," Malama insisted.

"Special too much! She gotta brain da kine, akamai too good."

The trio laughed and each instinctively felt at ease with the other. Kelly helped by explaining, "Muddah, dis wahine she come from longtime mission pamily Quigley. I not speak dis pamily, but maybe you do."

"Immanuel Quigley!" Malama cried, taking her visitor's two hands. "He was the best of the missionaries. Only one who loved the Hawaiians. But he stayed only a short time."

"I think he transmuted all his love for Hawaii into his children, and I inherited it," Elinor said. She saw that she had entered a nineteenth-century drawing room, complete with chandelier, tiered crystal cases, an organ, a Steinway piano and a brown mezzotint of Raphael's "Ascent of the Virgin" in a massive carved frame. The ceiling was enormously high, which made the room unexpectedly cool, but Elinor was distracted from this fact by an object which hung inside an inverted glass bowl set in a mahogany base. "Whatever is it?" she cried.

"It's a whale's tooth," Malama explained. "Formed into a hook."

"But what's it hung on?" she asked.

"Human hair," Kelly assured her.

Malama interrupted, removing the glass cover and handing her visitor the precious relic. "My ancestor, the King of Kona, wore this when he fought as Kamehameha's general. Later he wore it when the first mission ship touched at Lahaina. I suppose that every hair in this enormous chain came from the head of someone my family cherished." She replaced the glass cover. Then she said, "Kelly, while you show Mrs. Henderson why we call this the Swamp, I'll be getting tea. Some of the ladies are coming in."

So Kelly took Elinor to the rear of the house, through a kitchen that had once prepared two hundred dinners for King Kalakaua, and soon they were in a fairyland of trees and flowers bordering a rush-lined swamp whose surface was covered with lilies. With some irony Kelly said, dropping his pidgin now that he was again alone with Elinor, "This was the only land the haoles didn't take. Now it's worth two million dollars. But of course Mom takes care of a hundred poor Hawaiians, and she's in hock up to her neck."

To Elinor, the scene of old decay was poignant, and as red-tufted birds darted through the swamp and perched on the tips of dancing reeds, she saw the complete motif for her biography. "You really are *The Dispossessed,*" she mused, fusing reality with her vision of it.

"No, I think you have it wrong," Kelly protested. "This is the walled-in garden that every Hawaiian knows, for he tends one in his own heart. Here no one intrudes."

"Then you're contemptuous of the haole girls you sleep with?" she asked.

"Oh, no! Sleeping is fun, Elinor. That's outside what we're talking about."

"You're right, and I apologize. What I meant was, insofar as they're haoles, you're contemptuous of them?"

Kelly thought about this for a long time, tossed a pebble at a swaying bird, and said, "I don't believe I would admit that. I'm not as tolerant as the missionaries were."

"Immanuel Quigley said almost the same thing."

"I think I would have liked old Quigley," Kelly admitted.

"He was young when he served here. He became old in Ohio. What a profound man he was."

"Mom's probably ready," Kelly suggested, and he led Elinor away from the swamp and back into the spacious drawing room, where four gigantic Hawaiian women, gray-haired and gracious, waited.

"This is Mrs. Leon Choy," Malama said softly. "And this is Mrs. Hideo Fukuda."

"Did I see your very pretty daughter dancing at the Lagoon?" Elinor inquired.

"Yes," the huge woman replied, bowing slightly and beaming with pleasure. "Helen loves to dance, as I did when I was younger."

"And this is Mrs. Liliha Mendonca," Malama continued. "Her husband owned the taxi company. And this poor little dwarf over here is Mrs. Jesus Rodriques," Malama laughed. Mrs. Rodriques was only five feet nine and weighed less than 190. "I've told the ladies that Mrs. Henderson is a descendant of dear old Immanuel Quigley. We hold him very warmly in our hearts, Elinor."

"I'm surprised you're not staying with the Hales or the Whipples," Mrs.

Mendonca said. "They came over on the same ship with your grandfather, or whatever he was."

"Our families were never close," Elinor explained. Each of the five Hawaiian women wanted desperately to explore this admission, but they were too well-bred to do so, and after a while Malama suggested, "I'm sure Mrs. Henderson would like to hear some of the old songs," and soon she had scraped together a couple of ukuleles and two guitars. The stately Hawaiian women preferred standing while they sang, and now along one edge of the room they formed a frieze of giants, and after a few preliminary plunks on their instruments, launched into a series of the most cherished Hawaiian melodies. They seemed like a professional chorus, so easily did their voices blend. Mrs. Choy, with marvelous darting eyes and gamin manner, sang the high parts, while Mrs. Rodriques and Mrs. Mendonca boomed massive chords that paved the musical structure. Each song contained dozens of verses, and as the last chords of one verse lingered in the air, Mrs. Fukuda in a sing-song falsetto enunciated the first words of the next. She owned a prodigious memory, and the other ladies did not enjoy singing unless she was along, for her monotonous setting of the next theme gave them much pleasure.

Dusk came over the Swamp and lamps were lit. The huge women, reminiscent of bygone splendors, stayed on, and Elinor listened enraptured to their soft conversation until Kelly interrupted brusquely and said, "I speak one kanaka play a little sleck-key tinnight. Da wahine 'n' me be goin'."

But when the women saw him about to leave, Mrs. Choy began casually humming the first bars of the "Hawaiian Wedding Song," so that Kelly stopped in the shadows by the door, and while light from the chandelier reflected upon him in variegated colors, he started softly into the great flowing passage of love. His voice was in excellent form, and he allowed it to expand to its fullest. When the time came for him to halt, Elinor wondered which of the five women would pick up the girl's part, and it was Malama. Standing vast like a monument with silvery hair, she soared into the sweeping lyric portion of the song, and after a while mother and son combined in the final haunting duet. It was an unusually fortunate rendition, and as the lingering chords died away, Mrs. Choy banged her ukulele several times and cried, "I could sing this way all night."

When Kelly and Elinor were back in the borrowed car he said, "They will, too."

Elinor asked, "When your mother came back from Vassar, what did she do?"

"In the hot afternoons she sang, and was good to the Hawaiians, and wasted her money. What else?"

Elinor began sniffling, and after a while said, "I'm bitterly tangled up, Kelly. I can't go back to the hotel."

"I have to sing," he said stubbornly.

"Do you get paid for it?" she asked between sniffles.

"Not tonight. For a friend."

"You lousy, defeated, wonderful people," she said. "Okay, take me back. For a friend you must do everything." She slumped against the door, then quickly jumped back beside Kelly. "Tell me, has this friend, as you call him, ever done anything for you?"

"Mmmmmm, well, no."

"So you sing your life away? For nothing?"

"Who's happier?" he countered. "Mom or the women you know back home?"

* * *

Early next morning Elinor Henderson reported at the library and asked Miss Lucinda Whipple for "that book which gives the genealogy of the Kanakoas." At this request Miss Whipple masked her contempt and studied Kelly's latest sleeping partner, for she had found that over the course of a year at least half a dozen awe-struck haole women, who by their ignorance of card catalogues proved they rarely saw a library, could be counted upon to ask for "that book about Kelly Kanakoa." Miss Whipple guessed that one girl probably told the next, for they appeared at regular intervals, and when they reverently returned the book, some gasped, "Gosh, his grandfather was a real king!" Miss Whipple never commented, but she did observe that with such women apparently the farthest back they could imagine was grandfather. Beyond that all was obscurity.

But this girl proved to be different. When she completed studying the long tables in the Missionary Museum publication, she asked Miss Whipple, "What authority substantiates this?"

Miss Whipple replied, "My great-grandfather, Abner Hale, transcribed this remarkable document from verbal traditions recited by a kahuna nui on Maui. A great deal of research has been done in both Tahiti and Hawaii, and the account seems to check out at most points."

"How many years do you accord each generation?" Mrs. Henderson asked.

"I suppose we ought to follow the dictionary and allot each one thirty years, but we feel that in a tropical climate, and judging from what we know to be true, twenty-two years is a safer estimate. Then, too, you will detect that what the genealogy calls two successive generations is often really one, for it was a case of brother succeeding brother rather than son succeeding father. By the way, you seem to have a substantial knowledge of Hawaii. May I ask what your interest is?"

"I am the great-great-great-granddaughter of Immanuel Quigley," Elinor explained.

"Oh, my goodness!" Miss Whipple said in a flurry. "We've never had a Quigley here before."

"No," Elinor said evenly. "As you know, my father had difficulties."

Recollection of old and bitter events did not diminish Lucinda Whipple's ardor, for her genealogical interests transcended unpleasantness, and she asked excitedly, "Shall you be in Honolulu on Saturday?"

"Yes," Elinor replied.

"Goodness, how wonderful!" Miss Whipple said. "It's the yearly anniversary of the missionaries' arrival, and I would be truly honored if you would accompany me. Imagine! A Quigley!" She went on to explain that each spring throughout her life she had attended the yearly meeting of the Mission Children's Society, and as the roll was called she had dutifully, and proudly, stood up for John Whipple, Abner Hale and Abraham Hewlett, each of whom had figured in her ancestry, as well as for the collateral line of Retire Janders, who, while not a missionary, had served with them.

"But we have never had anyone rise to honor the name of Quigley. Please, do come!"

So on a hot Saturday in April, Elinor Henderson sat among the mission offspring and sang the opening hymn, "From Greenland's icy mountains." When the exciting moment came to call the roll of those long-dead and honorable men and women who had served God in the islands, she felt a mounting excitement as the descendants of each couple rose. "Abner Hale and his wife Jerusha, brig *Thetis,* 1822," read the clerk, and there was a flurry of chairs pushing back, after which a varied crew of Hales stood at attention while the rest applauded.

"Dr. John Whipple and his wife Amanda, brig *Thetis,* 1822," the clerk intoned, and from the scraping, Elinor concluded that Dr. John must have been an unusually potent young medico, for many rose to honor him.

"Immanuel Quigley and his wife Jeptha, brig *Thetis,* 1822," called the clerk, and with a heart bursting with passion and history and the confused love of God, Elinor Henderson rose, the first Quigley ever to have done so in that society. Her rising must have inflamed bitter memories in the hearts of the Hales and the Hewletts and the Whipples, for although intractable Immanuel Quigley had suppressed his secret memoirs, which Elinor had found so damning, he had allowed enough of his ideas to escape so that his name was not a happy one among the mission families. Defiantly, his great-great-great-granddaughter stared ahead, and then she heard from the assembly a hammering of palms and wild applause. Continuing to stare ahead, for she was no more forgiving than her difficult ancestor had been, she resumed her seat as the clerk cried mournfully, "Abraham and Urania Hewlett, brig *Thetis,* 1822." Again there was a loud scraping of chairs, with many Hawaiians standing, for Abraham's offspring by Malia, his second wife, were numerous. Many of the missionary descendants considered it inappropriate for such people to rise as if they were the true descendants of blessed Urania Hewlett, but the Hawaiians got up anyway and nothing could be done about it.

That night Elinor Henderson told Kelly, "A visitor touches Hawaii at great risk. He never knows when the passions of the islands will engulf him."

"You think you know enough now to write the biography?" Kelly asked idly.

"Yes."

"You determined to call it *The Dispossessed?*"

"More than ever."

"Who do you think the dispossessed are?" Kelly taunted.

"You. Who else?"

"I thought maybe at the mission society you discovered that they were the real dispossessed," he argued.

"How do you mean?"

"They came here to bring Congregationalism, but we despised their brand of Christianity. Now most of us are Catholics or Mormons. Today we have nearly as many Buddhists in the islands as Congregationalists. Likewise, they came with a God they believed in. How many of them still have that God? And they had big ideas. Now all they have is money."

"You sound very bitter, Kelly. And in a way I'm glad."

"Do you know why the Mormons had so much success in these islands? They admit frankly. 'In heaven there are only white people.' I suppose you know that a nigger can't get a place to sleep in Salt Lake. So they tell us that if we are real good on earth and we love God, when we die God's going to make us white, and then we'll go to heaven and all will be hunky-dory."

"I don't believe Mormons think that, Kelly," she protested.

"It squares with the facts," he said carefully, but his anger was rising furiously and he was afraid of what he might say next. He tried to halt his words, but in spite of himself they rushed out: "Of course, the other Christians tell us that God loves all men, but we know that's bullshit!"

"Kelly!"

"We know it! We know it!" he stormed. "It's as clear as the mountains at dawn. God loves first white men, then Chinese, then Japanese, and after a long pause He accepts Hawaiians."

"Kelly, my darling boy, please!"

"But do you know the one consolation we got? Can you guess? We know for goddamn certain that He loves us better than He loves niggers. God, I'd hate to be a nigger."

Since Elinor Henderson had greater capacity for emotion than for logical control she was, of course, unable to write her book; in fact, she was prevented from even trying by one of those strange, wild occurrences that mark the tropics. At six-eighteen on the morning following her visit to the mission society she was still asleep, but in the deep waters of the Pacific, nearly three thousand miles to the north, an event of tremendous magnitude was taking place. The great shelf that lies off the Aleutian Chain was racked by a massive submarine earthquake, which in the space of a few minutes tumbled millions of tons of submerged ocean cliff down hidden mountainsides to a new resting place on the ocean floor. It was a titanic redisposal of the earth's crust, and the ocean in whose depths it occurred was shaken so violently that a mighty rhythmic wave was launched southward at an incomprehensible speed; but even though something like seven per cent of the entire ocean was affected, the resulting wave was physically inconspicuous, never more than four or five inches high.

Actually, one shipload of sailors passed right over it without knowing, for at seven-eighteen that morning a slight swell lifted a Japanese tanker some three inches higher than it had been a moment before, but no one noticed the event and it was not recorded in the log. But if the captain had been alert, and if he had known where the wave had originated only an hour before, he could have written: "Tsunami caused by an Alaskan submarine earthquake passed under our ship. Speed southward, 512 miles an hour." And if he had thought to flash a radio warning throughout the Pacific many lives would have been saved, but he neither saw nor thought, so the epic tsunami sped on unheralded at a speed approaching that of sound. If it encountered no stationary objects like islands, it would ultimately dissipate itself in the far Antarctic, but if it did come upon an island, its kinetic energy might pile waters more than seventy feet deep upon the land and then suck them back out to sea with demonic force. The coming in of the waters would destroy little, but their awful retreat would carry away all things.

While the tsunami was passing unnoticed under the Japanese tanker, Elinor Henderson was just rising to enjoy the last effects of dawn over the Pacific, and at nine she went down to the beach to watch the beachboys playing sakura. She was amused to hear them swearing in pidgin when the run of the black cards went against them, but this morning had a special attraction in that Florsheim appeared among the boys dressed in store clothes: polished tan shoes, a suit that was not quite big enough for his huge frame, a shirt that bound a little at the collar, a knitted tie that hung awry and a tropical straw hat. Beside him stood the rich girl from Kansas City, hardly able to keep her hands off him and crying to one group after another, "God, ain't he a hunk of man? We're gettin' married in St. Louis."

Florsheim grinned and handed his Chevvy keys to Elinor: "You, seestah, tell blalah Kelly take care of my jalopy." She said she would, and when she saw

Kelly she asked, "How long do you think Florsheim'll stay married this time?"

"Seem like blalah Florsheim gonna look funny Kansas City da kine. So bimeby dis wahine gonna find he doan' talk so good and she gonna gi'e him lotta wahine pilikia. So come late October you gonna see blalah Florsheim back on de beach wid a Buick convertible."

"This time it'll be a Cadillac! Want to bet?" She laughed and then an idea came to her: "Kelly! As long as we have the car, why don't we go on a picnic?" She insisted upon buying all the food, and at ten o'clock, when the tsunami was less than six hundred miles from Oahu, she pointed to a snug little valley on the north shore of the island and cried, "They saved this sandy beach for us!" And Kelly spread their blankets under a palm tree.

They went swimming, and when they were drying in the sun, Elinor said, "I'm going to leave Hawaii, Kelly. Don't speak. I'm falling in love with you, and I'm not the kind of woman who goes around robbing cradles."

"I'm old enough to teach you a lot," Kelly protested.

"I would never marry you, Kelly . . . eight years younger than I am. And I will not contribute to your delinquency."

"We could have a wonderful time," he insisted, pulling her toward him.

"I think it's immoral when a girl gets involved with a man she has no possibility of marrying. It's disgraceful, the way girls use you, Kelly."

He fell silent, then started pitching pebbles at a nearby rock. Finally he said, "If you ever go to another island, Mrs. Henderson, don't ask so many deep questions. Take it as it is."

"I'll stay away from islands," she promised. "I wanted to see why my ancestors couldn't stomach this one."

"Did you find out?" he asked.

"Yes, and I can't stand it either."

"Why not?" he asked drowsily.

"I always side with the dispossessed. You know, Immanuel Quigley got into great trouble in Ohio, aiding the Indians."

"I'm sorry I wrecked your book about Quigley. Will they be angry . . . at Smith?"

"The biography of one man is the biography of all men," she said. "In the passage of time, Kelly, we all become one person."

"Do you honestly think a kanaka like me is as good as a haole like you?" he asked.

"I was once taught that if a pebble falls in the Arabian desert, it affects me in Massachusetts. I believe that, Kelly. We are forever interlocked with the rest of the world."

She saw that he was sleepy, so she cradled his sun-browned shoulders in her lap, and he asked for his guitar so that he might play a little slack-key, and he picked out melodies that spoke of the sun-swept seashores that he loved. After a while the guitar fell from his hands, and he dozed.

Elinor, watching the panorama of sandy beach and palm trees, studied with interest what she thought was the changing of the tide, for the ocean waters seemed to be leaving the shore, until at last they stood far out to sea disclosing an emptier reef than any she had seen before, and she watched certain prominent puddles in which large fish, suddenly stranded, were whipping their tails in an attempt to escape. She began to laugh, and Kelly, forgetting where he was, asked drowsily, "Whassamatta you laff?" And she explained, "There's a fish trapped in a pool." And he asked, "How da heck he stuck in dis . . ."

In horror he leaped up, saw the barren reef and the withdrawn waters. "Oh,

Christ!" he cried in terror. "This is a big one!" He grabbed her in his strong arms and started dashing across the sand, past the useless Chevvy convertible and on toward higher land, but his effort was useless, for from the tormented sea the great tsunami that had sucked away the waters to feed its insatiable wave, now rushed forward at more than five hundred miles an hour.

It was not a towering wave but its oncoming force was incredible. It filled the reef. It kept coming relentlessly, across the sand, across the roads, across the fields. In low areas it submerged whole villages, but if it was not constricted and could spread out evenly, its destruction was moderate. However, when it was compressed into a narrowing wedge, as at the mouth of a valley, it roared in with accumulating fury until at last it stood more than seventy feet higher than along its accustomed shore.

In its first tremendous surge inward it trapped Kelly Kanakoa and Mrs. Henderson in their snug valley. It did not whip them about like an ordinary breaker, for it was not that kind of wave; it merely came on and on and on, bearing them swiftly inland until Kelly, who knew how awful the outgoing rush would be, shouted, "Elinor! Grab hold of something!"

Vainly she grabbed at bushes, at trees, at corners of houses, but the implacable wave swept her along, and she could hold nothing. "Grab something!" he pleaded. "When the wave sucks back out . . ."

He was struck in the neck by a piece of wood and started to sink, but she caught him and kept his head above the rushing waters. How terrifying they were, as they came on with endless force. She swept past the last house in the village and on up into the valley's tight confines, the most dangerous spot in the entire island from which to fight a retreating tsunami, for now the waters began to recede, slowly at first, then with speed and finally with uncontrollable fury.

She last saw Kelly almost unconscious, hanging instinctively to a kou tree upon whose branches she had placed his hands. She had tried to catch something for herself, too, but the waters were too powerful. At increasing speed she was sucked back over the route she had come, past the broken houses and the crushed Chevvy and the reef she had seen so strangely bare. As the last stones whipped past she thought: "This cursed island!" And she thought no more.

Now the drowsy life of the beachboy drifted from day to day, from week into week, and then into sleepy sun-swept months; the years of sand and sea crept on. In late November, when Florsheim drove his new Pontiac convertible off the *Moana Loa* and up to his old stand at the Lagoon, Kelly thought: "I wish I could tell Mrs. Henderson that it was neither a Buick nor a Cadillac," and the old hurt returned.

At the Swamp his mother Malama sang in the late afternoons with her Hawaiian friends: Mrs. Choy, Mrs. Fukuda, Mrs. Mendonca and Mrs. Rodriques, and they were never again bothered by Kelolo and his haole girls. For the most part he kept strictly to the Lagoon, where he sang a little, played some slack-key, and got a lot of cables. In time he found great consolation in Johnny Pupali's summary of sex: "It's the greatest thing in the world. You never get enough until you've just had some."

Once Florsheim remarked: "Kelly blalah, I t'ink dis one t'ing berry punny."

"Wha' dat?" Kelly asked.

"Allatime New York dey got pitchas wid' colors 'Come to Hawaii!' An' dey show dis rock wid wahines, grass skirts, flowahs in de hair, wigglin' de hips like to speak, 'You come to Hawaii, mister, we gonna screw till you dizzy.' "

"Ain' nuttin' wrong wid dat," Kelly reflected.

"But de punny t'ing, Kelly blalah, it ain' so easy to ketch a wahine on dis rock. It ain' dem mainland kanakas has de good time ovah heah, it's de wahines. You know what I t'ink, blalah?"

"You speak."

"I t'ink mo bettah dey get you 'n' me on de pitchas." And he fell into a exaggerated pose, his muscles flexed, his dark eyes staring out to sea past Diamond Head, and he made an ideal travel poster. Relaxing with laughter he yelled, "Kelly blalah, we de real attraction."

Later when Kelly was locked in a room with a red-hot divorcee from Los Angeles her father arrived unexpectedly and banged on the door, shouting, "Betty! I don't want you wrecking your life with any beachboy bum." But Kelly slipped out through a side hallway, so no real damage was done.

WHEN SHIG SAKAGAWA landed at Yokohama in early 1946, he studied his ancestral homeland with care, and when he saw the starving people, the bombed-out cities and the pathetic material base from which the Japanese had aspired to conquer the world, he thought: "Maybe Pop's right, and this is the greatest country on earth, but it sure don't look it." In his first letter home he tried to report faithfully what he was seeing, but when Kamejiro heard it read, he sent his son a stern reply which said: "Remember that you are a good Japanese, Shigeo, and do not say such things about your homeland." After that Shig wrote mostly generalities.

His first days in Japan were tremendously exciting, for the bustle of Tokyo was reviving, and hordes of little workmen, each of whom looked like his father, scrambled over the bombed ruins, cleaning up as they went. Shig had never before seen such national vitality, and in time he became impressed with Japan's unconquerable resilience. Along the streets he saw innumerable elderly women like his own mother, wearing baggy canvas pants, and they worked harder than the men, lugging away big baskets of rubble. Almost while he watched, Tokyo was cleaned up and prepared for a new cycle of life. "I have to admire such people," he wrote to his father, and old Kamejiro liked this letter better than the disloyal one that had reflected upon Japan's defeat.

Shig took great interest in his work as translator for the Harvard professor whom General MacArthur had brought over to advise the Occupation on land reform. Dr. Abernethy was a curious, lanky man of most acute insights, and although he had to depend upon Captain Sakagawa for actual translations of what the Japanese farmers told him, he relied ultimately upon his own perceptions, and for the first time in his life Shig was able to study at close hand a refined human mind at work. A rice farmer would tell Shig, "I have two hundred and forty tsubo for paddy," and Shig would translate this for Dr. Abernethy, but the latter seemed hardly to be listening, for he was surveying the land himself and judging its productive quotient; so that almost before either Shig or the farmer spoke, Dr. Abernethy knew what the land was worth, and if Shig's translated evidence contradicted his, Shig had to reconcile the facts, and usually Abernethy was right.

On long jeep trips through the countryside, while Shig drove, Abernethy expounded his theories of land reform. "What General MacArthur's up against here, Shig, is a classic medieval concept of land ownership. In each area half a dozen wealthy men control the land and parcel out portions of it according to their own economic interests. That's not a bad system, really.

Certainly it's a lot better than communism. But where the trouble comes is when personal economic interests, usually of an arbitrary nature, override national survival interest."

"Like what?" Shig asked, finding deep pleasure in Abernethy's willingness to talk to him on a mature, adult level. It was hell when well-meaning colonels insisted upon speaking pidgin.

"Well, like when a landowner in an area that needs more food holds back his land for other speculation, or doesn't use it at all."

"Does this happen?"

"Look around you! It's obvious that even during Japan's war for survival this landowner held his lands back. When such a thing occurs, to save your nation you ought to have a revolution. Throughout history that's been the inevitable concomitant of abusive land ownership. Fortunately, a land revolution can develop in either of two ways. In France the land was held so irrationally that the French Revolution was required before the whole rotten system could be swept away . . . with great loss of life. That's the poorest kind of revolution. In England, the same result was accomplished by taxation. In time the huge landholders simply couldn't hang onto their land any longer. Taxes were too high. So they were forced to sell, and so far as I know not a single human life was lost. That's the logical way to accomplish land reform."

"You think Japan faces the same problem as France and England?"

"All nations do," Abernethy said as they bounced along a rocky road in Shiba Prefecture. "The relationship of man to his land is simple and universal. Every nation began with land evenly distributed among producers. As a result of superior mentality or manipulative skill, able landlords begin to acquire large holdings, in which society confirms them. As long as there is no great pressure of population, these great holders are allowed to do pretty much as they wish. But when families multiply, their marriageable sons begin to look longingly at the expanse of idle land. For the moment all the conventions of society, religion, politics and custom support the large landholders, and in most nations those peasants who make the first protests are hanged. Here in Japan, when the first agitators asked for land, they were crucified, upside down. Later the pressures become greater, and you have a bloody revolution . . . unless you're smart, like the English, and then you accomplish the same end by adroitly applied taxes."

"And you think this cycle operates in all nations?" Shig pressed.

"I myself have witnessed five such revolutions at close hand. In Mexico the offenses against common sense were unbelievable, and so were the bloody reprisals. In England a smart bunch of legislators effected the change-over with marvelous simplicity. In Rumania the blood was ugly to see. Also Spain. In the western United States the cattlemen started to protect their immoral holdings with gunfire, but in time the common sense of the townspeople, applied through taxation, defeated them. No nation can avoid land reform. All it can do is determine the course it will take: blood revolution or taxation."

"It seems to me that here in Japan we have a third choice. Land reform by fiat."

"Of course," Abernethy quickly agreed. "What you and I finally decide to order done, General MacArthur will do, and it'll turn out to be his greatest accomplishment in Japan. For it will distribute land equitably and at the same time prevent a bloody revolution."

"Then there really is a third alternative?" Shig pressed.

"Yes," Abernethy replied, "but few nations are lucky enough to lose a war to the United States."

They drove in silence for more than two miles, looking for a country lane that led to the headquarters of one of the most illogical of the large land holdings that had imperiled Japan, and when they spotted the turning, Shig studied the relatively small area involved—small, that is, as compared with Hawaii—and he began to laugh. "What's the joke?" his lanky, dour companion asked.

"I was thinking how ironic it is!"

"What?" Abernethy asked, for he loved the ironies of history.

"Here we are, you and I, doing all this work in redistributing farm lands in defeated Japan, while, actually, the situation in my own home, Hawaii, is far worse."

Dr. Abernethy sat with his knees hunched up toward his chin and waited silently till Shig looked at him. Then he smiled slyly and asked, "What do you suppose I've been talking to you about?"

Shig was so startled that he slowed down the jeep, brought it to a complete halt, and turned formally to look at his commander. "You mean you've been talking to me about Hawaii?"

"Of course. I want you to appreciate what the alternatives are."

"How do you know anything about Hawaii?"

"Anyone interested in land reform knows Hawaii. Now that Hungary and Japan have faced their revolutions, Hawaii and China remain the most notorious remnants of medievalism in the world."

"Will both have to undergo revolutions?" Shig asked.

"Of course," Abernethy replied simply. "The hardest lesson in all history to learn is that no nation is exempt from history. China's revolution will probably end in bloody confiscation. Hawaii's will probably be accomplished by peaceful taxation." He paused and asked, "That is, if smart young fellows like you have any sense."

"I still think it's sardonic that I should be over here helping to save Japan," Shig reflected. "I should be doing the same job at home." He shifted gears and headed for the small house where the nervous Japanese landlords waited.

"As I said," Dr. Abernethy repeated dourly, "few nations are lucky enough to lose wars at the right time. Lucky Japan."

This fact was hammered home when Shig finally overtook his older brother Goro, who served as translator in General MacArthur's labor division. He had been in Nagoya when Shig landed, working on a long-range program for the unionization of Japanese industry, but instead of serving a quiet intellectual theorist like Dr. Abernethy of Harvard he was with a team of red-hot American labor organizers from the A.F. of L. "This job is driving me crazy!" stocky Goro cried, rubbing his crewcut stubble.

"Are the people you work for stupid?" Shig asked.

"Stupid! They're the smartest characters I ever met. What drives me nuts is that I work fifteen hours a day forcing Japanese into labor unions. I read them General MacArthur's statement that one of the strongest foundations of democracy is an organized laboring class, secure in its rights. And you know, I think MacArthur is right. It's the only way Japan will ever be able to combat the zaibatsu. Strong, determined unions. But by God it's maddening to be forcing onto the Japanese in Japan what the Japanese in Hawaii are forbidden to have."

"You mean unions?" Shig asked, as they drank Japanese beer in the Dai Ichi Hotel, where they were bunked.

"You're damned right I mean unions!" Goro fumed. "Let's be honest, Shig.

We practically fought a war to eliminate the zaibatsu in Japan. But you know the big firms here never controlled half as much as they do in Hawaii. You know, Shig, it's a crazy world when you fight a war to give the conquered what you refuse to give your own people back home."

Shig took refuge in a trick he often used when trying to think straight. He stopped talking and held his beer stein to his lips for a long time, but Goro used this interval to comment: "If unions are good in Japan, they're good in Hawaii. If the zaibatsu are bad in Japan, they're bad in Hawaii. Yet I'm forced to make the Japanese join unions here, and if I tried to do the identical thing in Hawaii I'd be arrested, beaten up, and thrown into jail. How bloody crazy can you get?"

"What you say is fascinating," Shig volunteered slowly. "The man I'm working for, this Dr. Abernethy, says exactly the same thing about the land problems. Only he always adds, 'A nation is lucky when it loses a war at the right time.' The more I look at what we're doing for Japan, the more I believe him."

Goro put down his beer and said solemnly, "When I get back to Honolulu, I'm going to introduce a new motto."

"What do you mean?"

" 'What's good enough for the vanquished, is good enough for the victor.' I'm going to see to it that a man in Hawaii has a right to join a union, too. Just like a man in Tokyo. And when I start, Hoxworth Hale better stand back. He won last time because labor was stupid. Next time I'll win because of what I'm learning in Japan."

"Don't commit yourself to trouble," Shig warned.

"If you don't do the same," Goro countered, "I'll be ashamed of you. You'll have wasted your war."

This was the first time Shig had heard the phrase that was to determine his behavior in the next few years. "Don't waste your war!" On this first enunciation of the basic law he said to his brother, "I've been wondering what I ought to do, Goro. Talking so much with Dr. Abernethy has convinced me of one thing. There isn't a single Japanese on Hawaii that's educated. Oh, there are smart men like Pop and medical doctors like Dr. Takanaga, but they don't really know anything."

"You're so right," Goro agreed sadly, slumping over his beer. "Have you ever talked to a real smart labor leader from New York?"

"So I thought maybe I'd go to Harvard Law School."

"What a marvelous idea!" Goro cried. "But look, kid, I don't want you to go there and just learn law."

"I have no intention of doing that," Shig replied carefully. "Dr. Abernethy suggested that maybe I'd like to live with him. His wife's a lawyer."

Goro became positively excited. "And you'd talk at night, and get a little polish and argue about world history. Shig! Take it. Look, I'd even help you with the money."

"Aren't you going on to graduate school?" Shig asked.

Goro blushed, toying with his beer, then looked at his watch. "I think I have other plans," he confessed. "I want you to meet her."

The Dai Ichi Hotel in Tokyo stood near the elevated loop that circled the city, and not far from the Shimbashi Station. In 1946 this area was filled each night with pathetic and undernourished Japanese girls, some of the most appealing prostitutes Asia had ever produced, and the tragedy of their near-starvation was that when they began to recover their health, and their cheeks filled out, they were so confirmed in streetwalking that they could not easily convert into any other occupation, and they continued at their old trade, mastering a few English words and sometimes moving into surreptitious army quarters with their G.I. lovers.

Now, as Shig and Goro walked through the bitter cold of a Tokyo January night, the horde of girls called to them in Japanese, "Nice Nisei G.I. Would you like to sleep with a real warm girl tonight?" Shig felt sick and tried not to look at the haunting, starved faces, but they pressed near him, begging, "Please, Nisei, I make you very happy for one night. I am a good girl."

They looked exactly like the prettier Japanese girls he had known in Hawaii, and as they tugged hungrily at his arms, he thought: "Maybe there's something about losing a war that Dr. Abernethy doesn't appreciate. Maybe it isn't so good."

In time the brothers broke away from the Shimbashi girls and turned left toward the Ginza, but they kept away from that broad street which M.P.'s patrolled and headed instead for the Nishi, or west, Ginza, where they entered into an exciting maze of alleys, one of which contained a very tiny bar, not much bigger than a bedroom, called Le Jazz Bleu. Ducking swiftly inside, they found the little room thick with smoke, bar fumes and the sound of an expensive gramophone playing Louis Armstrong. Three customers sat on minute bar-stools, while from the rear an extremely handsome girl in western clothes approached. She was no more than twenty, tall, thin from undereating, and with an unforgettably alert face. Extending a slim hand to Goro she cried in Japanese, "Welcome to our center of culture and sedition!" And with these words she introduced Shig into one of the most fascinating aspects of postwar Japan: the intellectual revolution.

With bad luck Akemi could have become, and she knew it, a Hershey-bar girl, cadging nylons and canned beef from G.I.'s at Shimbashi Station, but in the earliest days of the Occupation she had been lucky enough to meet Goro Sakagawa, and he was not a Hershey-bar boy. It is true that he gave her whatever food and money he could afford, but she gave him little in return except exciting talk, a knowledge of Japan and more spiritual love than he knew existed in the world. It took Shig about two minutes to see that this pair was going to get married.

"Why does she work in a bar?" he asked Goro when Akemi disappeared to serve some customers.

"She wants to work, and she likes the music," Goro explained.

"Is she an Edokko?" Shig inquired, referring to the old name for Tokyo.

"The purest modenne," Goro laughed. Postwar Japanese youth prided themselves on their use of French, and to be modenne—moderne—was their highest ambition. "This girl is a terrific brain," Goro confided.

"I'll bet she's not Hiroshima-ken?" Shig teased.

"Have you seen Hiroshima?" Goro asked. "Pppssskkk!" he went, leveling his hand over the floor. "I don't want anything to do with Hiroshima."

"Mom's going to be very unhappy," Shig warned. "You come all the way to Japan and don't have sense enough to get yourself a Hiroshima girl."

"This is the girl for me," Goro said as Akemi rejoined them, and when she came to a table, his or anyone's, she added a new dimension to it, for she contained within her slim body an electric vitality which marked many people in the new Japan.

At midnight she whispered, "Soon the customers will go, and then we have real fun." Patiently she waited for the wandering drinkers to empty their glasses, and to each straggler she said a warm good night, thus insuring their subsequent return, but when the last had gone and the proprietor was turning out the lights, she sighed and said, "I wish drinks cost less. Then men would guzzle them faster."

Opening the darkened door a crack she whispered, "No M.P.'s" and the trio ducked down a series of the smallest alleys in the world, barely wide enough for two to pass if one stood sideways, and finally they came to a darkened door which Akemi-san pushed slowly open, revealing a rather large room in which more than a dozen young men and women sat in the most rigid silence, for an imported gramophone was playing music that neither Shig nor Goro could recognize, but its name was obvious, for on a music stand, with a single shaft of light playing upon it, rested the album from which the records had been taken: Mahler's *Kindertotenlied* sung by a German group. Quietly the newcomers sank to the floor, and when the music ended and more lights were lit, they saw that they were among an intense Japanese group composed of handsome young men and pretty girls. When talk began, it was all about Paris and André Gide and Dostoevski. Much of it was in French, and since Shig had acquired a smattering of the language, he was well received.

Then talk returned to the new Japan: freedom for women, the breaking-up of large estates, the new role of labor, and both Shig and Goro were able to contribute much, but just as it seemed as if the old Japan were forever dead, Akemi appeared in a frail, tattered kimono which she kept by the gramophone, and the room grew deathly silent, with all assuming old, formal poses as Akemi began the tea ceremony, and as she moved through the curious and ancient ritual of making tea in a set way, and serving it just so, Shig sensed that these young Japanese were no different than he: they were caught in the changing of history, so that with part of their minds they embraced French words and everything modenne, while with the great anchors of the soul they held fast to the most inexplicable secrets of Japan. "Hawaii and Japan face the same problems," Shig mused, but when frail Akemi nodded that it was his turn, and another girl came creeping toward him on her knees, presenting him with the cup of bitter tea, he took it in both hands as he had been taught, turned the old cup until its most treasured edge was away from his unworthy lips, and drank.

When the ceremony ended, talk resumed and the girl who had brought him his bitter tea said, "American M.P.'s can destroy anything but the tea ceremony. No matter how hard you strike at our souls, you always seem to miss."

The statement irritated Shig and he said, "Not being an M.P., I wouldn't know. For myself, I bring freedom."

"What freedom?" the girl asked angrily.

"Land for the peasants," Shig said, and for a few minutes he was a hero, but then the lights lowered, the single shaft struck the music stand and Shig read: Bruckner, *The First Symphony*. This was a London recording, and he liked the music.

That night, as they made their way back through the remnant of Shimbashi girls that had caught no men for the evening, but who still hoped, not knowing what might turn up following a late brawl, Shig said, "I'd marry her, Goro. She's marvelous."

"I'm going to," his brother replied.

And in these strange ways the brothers Sakagawa discovered their ancestral homeland and saw how different it was from what their parents remembered, but they also discovered Hawaii, so that one night Goro slammed down his beer at the Dai Ichi Hotel and fumed: "It's insane that we should be here, Shig. We ought to be doing the same jobs at home." And as they worked in Japan, they thought of Hawaii.

IN 1947 THE great Kee hui faced memorable excitements, for Nyuk Tsin was one hundred years old and her family initiated a round of entertainments celebrating that fact, climaxed by a massive fourteen-course dinner at Asia's brassy restaurant. The little old matriarch, who now weighed ninety-one pounds, appeared at each celebration dressed in black, her sparse gray hair pulled severely back from her temples. She chatted with her huge family and felt proud of their accomplishments, being particularly pleased when Hong Kong's youngest daughter, Judy, brought a pianist from the university, where she was studying, to sing a series of songs in Chinese. Nyuk Tsin, watching Judy's animated face, thought: "She could be a girl from the High Village. I wonder what's happening there now?"

One hundred and forty-one great-great-grandchildren attended the festivities, and upon them Nyuk Tsin poured her special love. Whenever one was presented she would ask the child in Hakka, "And what is your name, my dear?" The child's mother would poke her offspring and say in English, "Tell Auntie your name." But if the child replied, "Harry Rodriques," Nyuk Tsin would correct him and insist upon his real name, and the child would reply, "Kee Doh Kong," and by decoding this according to the family poem, Nyuk Tsin understood who was standing before her.

With her own name she also had trouble, for now there was no one alive in the world who knew what it was. Even her remaining sons, now in their agile seventies and eighties, had never known her name, for she had submerged her own personality in this powerful hui of which she was now the head. She was content to rule as Wu Chow's Auntie, the concubine without a name, but when she thought of herself it was invariably as Char Nyuk Tsin, the daughter of a brave peasant who had risen to be a general. She was deeply moved, therefore, when the celebrations were ended and her sons Asia and Europe said to her, "Wu Chow's Auntie, I see no further reason why we should continue to send money to our mother in the Low Village. She must surely be dead by now, and her family has never done anything for us."

"On the other hand," Nyuk Tsin reasoned, "she may still be alive, just as I am, and if so she would need the money more than ever. After all, she is your mother and you owe her that respect."

Only one misfortune clouded her hundredth birthday: her principal grandson Hong Kong was obviously in trouble, for he was ill at ease, nervous and irritable. Nyuk Tsin guessed that he was having difficulty meeting payments on the various ventures into which she had goaded him, and she was sorry that it was he who had to bear the burden of these trying days and not she. Therefore, when the mammoth dinner at Asia's ended, the little old lady told the women about her that she wanted to talk with Hong Kong, and after she was taken home and had examined her body for leprosy, and had inspected her big graceful feet, she appeared in a black gown with buttons down the right side and asked in Hakka, "Hong Kong, are things so very bad?"

"Wu Chow's Auntie, the detectives are back again," he explained.

"But you don't know whether that means good or bad," she observed.

"Detectives are never good," he assured her.

"How do you know they're back?"

"Kamejiro Sakagawa said they were digging into his land deal again. They were also asking sly questions at Australia's."

"How are we fixed for taxes and mortgage payments?" she asked.

This was the one bright spot, and he said with some relief, "Not too bad. With the money we saved last year we're out of trouble."

"Then we'll be prudent and wait," she advised. "If someone wants to hurt you, Hong Kong, keep him off balance. Make him take the first step toward you, for then you can watch him coming and take precautions."

Four days later the first step came, in the person of a husky, quiet-spoken Irishman from Boston with huge, bushy-black eyebrows, who said that his name was McLafferty and who appeared in Hong Kong's office asking idle questions about real estate, and from the assured manner in which the visitor behaved, Hong Kong deduced: "This one has the detective reports in his pocket. He knows."

Not much happened that first day. Hong Kong probed: "You looking for a hotel site? You got something else in mind?"

"What hotel sites have you?" Mr. McLafferty parried, but it was obvious that he wasn't interested. "I'll be back," he said.

As soon as he was gone, Hong Kong started half a dozen Kees on his trail, but all they turned up was that he really was Mr. McLafferty and he was a lawyer from Boston, stopping at the Lagoon. Hong Kong took this information to his grandmother, and they carefully weighed the various possibilities that might bring a Boston lawyer to Hawaii, and Hong Kong was all for dispatching a cable to a Kee who was studying at Harvard asking for detailed information on McLafferty, but his grandmother told him to wait. "Don't get excited until he makes some specific move," she cautioned him.

Two days later Mr. McLafferty returned and said casually, "If my syndicate decided on one of the big hotel sites . . . at your price? Could you deliver title to the land?"

Hong Kong realized that considering the intricate Hawaiian system of land ownership, this apparently trivial question was a trap, so he answered slowly and cautiously, "Well, I'd better explain, Mr. McLafferty, that out here we don't sell land fee simple. What I'd be willing to do is guarantee you a fifty-year lease."

"You can't sell us any land outright?" McLafferty probed cautiously.

"My hui—are you familiar with the word hui?—well my hui has a little fee simple, but not choice hotel sites. What we do have is control of some of the best leases in Honolulu."

"Why don't you people sell fee simple?" McLafferty asked directly, but not bluntly. He was a careful operator.

Hong Kong decided not to waste time. "Mr. McLafferty, I don't think you're paying attention to land problems here. If you're far enough along to talk seriously about a hotel site you're bound to know that our estates never sell land. They lease it."

Mr. McLafferty liked this blunt answer, liked all he knew about Hong Kong, which was considerable, and felt that the propitious moment had come. "Could we send your secretary out? For maybe an hour?"

"Certainly," Hong Kong replied, his pulse hammering. He had learned that when this happened he must slow down . . . instantly. So he took some minutes giving his girl exaggerated instructions which Mr. McLafferty recognized as stalling. Then the wiry Chinese banker closed the door carefully, locked it, and returned to his desk, his pulse back to normal. In order to make his visitor think that he had been taken in by the hotel talk he said, "Now we have three wonderful hotel sites . . ."

"I'm not interested in hotels," the visitor said.

"What are you interested in?" Hong Kong asked evenly.

"I represent Gregory's."

The name literally exploded in the quiet office, ricocheted around Hong Kong's ears and left him stunned. Finally he asked, "You going to bull your way into the islands?"

"You have used exactly the right word," McLafferty said coldly. "Six months from now, Mr. Kee, we will have bulled our way into the biggest goddamned store right," and he whipped out a secret map of downtown Honolulu, "here." Forcefully he jabbed his finger at a prime intersection.

When Hong Kong saw the location he gasped. "The Fort will break you, Mr. McLafferty," he warned.

"Nope. We're too strong. We're ready to lose five million dollars the first three years. We have resources of nearly half a billion behind that. The Fort is not going to break us."

"But it won't let you buy that land, or lease it either. You simply aren't going to get in there."

"You're going to buy it for us, Mr. Kee."

"It's not for sale," Hong Kong protested.

"I mean, you're going to get the leases. You'll use an assumed name . . . a dozen assumed names. After today I won't see you again, but we'll arrange some system of keeping in contact. Gregory's is breaking into Honolulu, and don't you ever doubt it."

"If The Fort doesn't break you, it'll break whoever buys the land for you. It has great power to retaliate."

"We thought about that . . . a lot, Mr. Kee."

"Why don't you call me Hong Kong?"

"And we spent more than a year analyzing your position out here. If you keep in a solvent position, Hong Kong, nobody can hurt you. And if they try, we stand ready to spend a good deal of the five million we know we'll lose, shoring you up."

Hong Kong liked this daring, cold-blooded Boston Irishman, and after a moment's reflection asked, "You have to have that specific corner?"

"No other," the lawyer said.

"How long do I have?"

"Six months."

"You agree to pay fifty per cent above going rates?"

"We'll do better. You give us a strict accounting of actual costs, and we'll give you a hundred per cent commission."

"You know that if The Fort hears about this . . . ."

"We know. That's why we chose you to negotiate the leases."

Hong Kong leaned back. "You're certainly aware, Mr. McLafferty, that the profit to me is not very substantial. But nevertheless you're asking me to risk my business life in a head-on tangle with The Fort. How do you reason?"

"We say this. O. C. Clemmons wants to come into these islands, but The Fort won't let them. Won't sell them land. Won't provide shipping. Won't do anything. Same with Shea and Horner, same with California Fruit. The Fort has cold-bloodedly decided that no mainland firm will be allowed in Hawaii. They are determined to set their own prices, keep competition out, garner all profits to The Fort."

"I know all that," Hong Kong said evenly. "Maybe better than you. But why should I fight your battle?"

"For two simple reasons," the lawyer said. "You're right that we can't begin to pay you for the risks you'll be taking if The Fort decides to eliminate you, as they may. But remember this, Hong Kong. Here is the real estate you control." And on his map Mr. McLafferty pointed to almost every parcel Hong Kong then held. It was remarkable that the man knew so much. "Now if Gregory's comes in, and O. C. Clemmons, and Shea and Horner, the entire economic life of Hawaii gets a boost. Land is scarce. They have got to buy from you, and every inch you have will double and treble in value. Hong Kong, you've got to believe that an expanding economy is good for everyone, a stagnant economy is bad for us all. Your profits will come indirectly. And the irony of it is, if The Fort had let us in ten years ago when we first tried, for every dollar of profit we made, they would have made six, because we would have stirred up their whole economy for them."

"The Fort has no intention of allowing things to be stirred up," Hong Kong pointed out.

"And that's my second reason, Hong Kong. Anything that helps Gregory's or California Fruit helps you people, and by you people I mean the Japanese and the Chinese. Did your spies find out who my old man was? Look, I know you sent cables to Boston to check on me. Well, my old man was Black Jim McLafferty, a bull-necked Irishman from downtown Boston with ferocious eyebrows like mine, and every fight you Chinese have had in Hawaii, we Irishmen had twice as bad in Boston. But my old man . . . Hong Kong, he was a terror. Wound up governor till the local Fort put him in jail. Then he became mayor on a vindication ticket. I'm Black Jim's son, and I don't scare easy. Believe me when I tell you that you've got to do to The Fort what my old man did to the stiff-necked Protestants in Boston."

Hong Kong did not like the way the conversation was going, so he took it onto a higher level by observing, "Seems to me what you have to do sooner or later is get a bigger piece of land on the edge of the city where you can have lots of parking."

"We plan to, after we get our first operation working."

"What you ought to do, if you're smart, is buy the second piece of land right now before prices go up."

"Exactly what I wanted to discuss next. We've already settled on the location, and we expect you to buy it for us at the same time you get the downtown leases."

"Where?" Hong Kong asked.

"At the other end of town there's a fine piece of land inside a big fence. It's called the Swamp . . ."

"Oh, no!" Hong Kong laughed. "Can't be touched."

"We'd give two million for it."

"You'd give two million . . . I'd give two million . . . anybody would, but it can't be sold."

"It's owned by an elderly Hawaiian lady called . . ." He took out a piece of paper. "Malama Kanakoa, and she has one boy they call Kelly. He's a beachboy."

"Mr. McLafferty, you have remarkable judgment where land is concerned, but this parcel it tied up in a trust. To get it you've got to buck three trustees, appointed by the court. You know who they are in this case? First comes Hewlett Janders, from The Fort. Second, John Whipple Hoxworth, from The

Fort. And third, Harry Helmore, married to Abigail Hewlett, from The Fort. You think they're going to let you pick up that land?"

"We'll take it to court!" McLafferty stormed, and Hong Kong was pleased to see that the Irishman was in this fight to the finish.

"Good idea!" the Chinese agreed warmly. "And who do you suppose the judges will be who hear your appeal? Same ones who appointed the trustees. And what are the names of these judges? There's Judge Clements, married to a Whipple. There's Judge Harper, from Texas, came out a widower and married a Hoxworth. And there's Judge McClendin from Tennessee. He's not married to anybody, but his son is, to a Hale. How do you think they will hand down their decision in a case affecting The Fort?"

"Are they all crooks?" McLafferty asked bluntly.

"Not a one of them," Hong Kong replied. "In fifty years of pretty close watching The Fort I've never caught them in one crooked deal. They're very honest men, upright, trustworthy. They just happen to believe with all their hearts that only they know what is best for Hawaii. No judge ever hands down a dishonest decision. Never. They just study who's involved in the case, and if it's Hong Kong Kee versus Hoxworth Hale, why, on the face of it I've got to be wrong, because Hale is a man known to be honest, and whatever he wants to do is unquestionably for the welfare of Hawaii."

"They got it real sewed up, don't they?" McLafferty growled.

"But the best they've got is this trustee racket," Hong Kong continued. "You take this Malama Kanakoa. She has parcels of land worth ten million . . . at least. The judges say, 'Malama, you're a dear Hawaiian woman with no sense at all. We're going to put you on a spendthrift trust. Three fine haoles will look after your interests, protect you. All we're going to charge you for this service is fifty thousand dollars a year. You can have what's left.' And then the trustees, appointed by the courts, reason: 'Best way to keep a Hawaiian in line is keep 'em in debt.' So within a year poor Malama is so deep in debt to stores run by The Fort, and she owes the government so many back taxes she never can get her head above water. But year after year the trustees get their fees, before the stores, before the government, before Malama. They filter down a little money to her, and things go on and on."

"So by the trick of doing nothing and waiting, they steal the islands blind . . . but in an honest way."

Hong Kong studied this summary for some time, then cautiously observed: "I suppose so far The Fort has held us back two full generations. If we had paid labor a good wage twenty years ago, I suppose our gross island product would have increased maybe half a billion dollars each year."

"You don't call that stealing?" McLafferty asked.

"Technically you can't, if their intentions are honest. They may be dumb but they're not crooks."

"Then you'll get the land for us?" McLafferty asked.

"I have to consult my hui," Hong Kong countered, taking refuge in that word, for he knew that McLafferty would not understand if he said, "I must talk this over with my hundred-year-old grandmother."

"I needn't warn you," the Bostonian said, "that if any of your hui breathes a word of this . . ."

"My hui has been keeping secrets for almost a century," Hong Kong replied cryptically, and next day he reported: "My hui says that now's the time to strike. I have four Japanese, two Chinese and a Filipino starting to get your land. In six months you'll have it. How do I slip messages to you in Boston?"

McLafferty looked astonished. "Boston?" he repeated. "Didn't I tell you? I'm living here from now on. I'm part of the revolution that's about to hit these islands. Since I got my old man's eyebrows, I suppose that in the elections I'll be called Black Jim McLafferty. You see, I'm a working Democrat."

WHEN HOXWORTH HALE, back in 1946, succeeded in frustrating the attempt of California Fruit to open a string of supermarkets in Hawaii, he reported to the Fort: "Within the past year we have been faced by formidable challenges from the mainland. This was to have been expected after the dislocations of war, and for a while it looked as if the dangerous radical movements we have detected in the population might lead to California Fruit's success, for these outsiders came very close to snapping up several leases, and at one point I was afraid they might succeed in buying out Kamejiro Sakagawa, but we applied certain pressures on the little Japanese and forestalled that. So for the time being, at least, we have turned back a very dangerous enemy. But in a larger sense it seems to me that our real danger is going to come from Gregory's. They have tried twice now to penetrate our market, and only by the most resolute action have we forestalled them. We must remain extremely alert to keep them out of Hawaii, and I shall consider any member of our group derelict to his duty who does not keep us informed of Gregory's next move.

"As for O. C. Clemmons and Shea and Horner, I feel certain we have scared them off, so that unless something unforseen happens, we need expect no more challenges from them." Hoxworth looked steadily at his colleagues, as if to instill into each the courage to keep Hawaii free of alien influences, and the members left that meeting with added resolution, but in 1947 Hale had to summon his confreres again, and this time he reported: "Something is happening around here that I neither like nor understand. I was alerted some time ago by the clerk at the Lagoon to the fact that a Boston lawyer named James McLafferty was in our city and acting rather suspiciously. For example, he was caught talking a long time with the beachboy Kelly Kanakoa—that's Malama's rather worthless son. We put some people on Kelly and found out that this McLafferty had brought up the subject," and here Hoxworth paused for dramatic effect, "the subject of the Swamp."

A white-capped wave of excitement, marked by widely opened eyes, sped about the room, like a breaker heading for shore, and Hale continued: "So far as we can deduce from what Kelly was able to tell us, McLafferty had in mind the possibility of," again he dropped his voice to underline the enormity of what was going on, "a hotel." Once more the wave of opened eyes flashed about the room, for the owners of almost every important hotel sat that day in The Fort. "I've put tracers on this McLafferty and haven't come up with much. Hewlett, will you read us what we've found so far?"

Hewlett Janders coughed, picked up a sheet of paper, and read: "James McLafferty, B. A. Holy Cross 1921, Harvard Law School 1926. Practices law in Boston. Served as colonel in the Army Air Corps 1941–45 in charge of land procurement for airstrips in Africa, Italy and England. Author with Professor Harold Abernethy of Harvard *Land Procurement Policies of the U. S. Army Air Corps.* Son of the infamous Black Jim McLafferty, long-time Democratic politician who served a term in jail for malfeasance while governor. Roman Catholic and visited Rome twice while on duty overseas, which endeared him to his father's constituents. He himself has never run for office." Big Hewlett Janders stopped, then added, "No clue as to who is employing him for whatever he's doing in Hawaii." Hewlett threw the paper on the table as if to say, "If you think you can make anything out of this, you're welcome to try."

Hoxworth Hale said, "Well, what does it add up to? We find that a stranger who knows a lot about land procurement, who is obviously a radical of some sort from Harvard, is interested in the Swamp . . . for a hotel. It certainly looks to me as if he were the kind of man we've been trying to keep out of our city." The men about the table nodded, so Hale continued: "Do we have any of the Kanakoa Trust men among us?"

Hewlett Janders replied, "I'm on the board, so is John Whipple Hoxworth. The third member is Harry Helmore and he can certainly be trusted."

"Will you speak for Harry?" Hale asked.

"Well, he's married to my cousin Abigail," Hewlett pointed out. "I guess I can speak for him."

"It is agreed then that under no circumstances will Malama Kanakoa be allowed to sell the Swamp to McLafferty?"

"So far as I'm concerned," Hewlett replied. "How about you, John Hoxworth?"

"I would be criminal to admit a man like that into our city."

"Then it's agreed," Hoxworth announced, but his natural caution in these matters was not yet satisfied, so he asked, "Let's suppose for a minute that this talk about a hotel was a blind. Let's suppose that McLafferty was acting as front man for someone entirely different. Gentlemen, I think that's a fair supposition. Whom does this man really represent?"

The wily, practiced men of The Fort turned their whole attention to this problem. Slowly John Whipple Hoxworth, a thin, clever man with a typical Whipple intellect, reasoned: "The group that was most furious when we turned them back was California Fruit, but I think that out of natural vanity they would refuse to recruit an agent from Boston. It just wouldn't seem palatable to a Californian. I don't think O. C. Clemmons is going to fight again, and after two bad whippings I doubt that Gregory's will be back. Therefore I have to conclude that it's Shea and Horner. It's the kind of trick they'd pull, and after all, remember that Shea is a prominent Catholic."

"I wonder if it could be Gregory's after all?" Hoxworth mused. "Has anybody met this McLafferty yet?"

No one had, and the meeting ended with Hale's final warning: "I suppose you've all read that California Fruit has signed a contract with their labor unions? Gregory's entered into one three years ago, and you know the Shea and Horner stand. If you require any encouragement in this fight to keep men like McLafferty out of our city, keep the labor union angle in mind."

When the others had left The Fort, Hoxworth Hale sat brooding up the things they had been discussing, and he could not comprehend how any sensible man who loved Hawaii would even consider allowing an outfit like Gregory's entrance to the islands. "Why, damn it all!" he growled. "They're outsiders. They undercut established principles, and if they made a little money, what would they do with it? Siphon it off to New York. Does it ever do Hawaii any good? Not a penny of it." He looked out his window toward the Missionary Public Library, built with family funds, then toward the Missionary Art Museum, which his Grandfather Ezra had endowed with half a million dollars and a Rembrandt. In the distance lay the Missionary Natural History Museum, housing an unmatched collection of Hawaiian artifacts, and beyond it stood the rugged, magnificent memorial to old Abraham Hewlett's love of the Hawaiian people, Hewlett Hall, where Hawaiian boys and girls were given free a first-rate education. More important were the things that could not be seen: the family professorships at the university, the Missionary Foundation for Oceanic Research, the Missionary Fund for Retired Ministers. You could scarcely touch an aspect of Hawaii which had not been improved and nourished by some member of The Fort.

"Suppose we allowed Gregory's to come in and operate as they wished," Hoxworth mused. "Let's look at Honolulu fifty years from now. Is there going to be a Gregory's Museum, or a Gregory's School for Hawaiians? They will steal our money and give us nothing in return except lower prices for a little while. Will their executives raise large families here and put their children to work in the islands? They will not. We will have soulless absentee landlordism of the worse sort. If Gregory's ever do wedge their way into the islands . . . after my death I hope . . . they will bring us nothing . . . nothing."

He walked back and forth in real perplexity and came at last to the nexus of his thinking: "No, I'm wrong. They'll bring two things. They'll bring political unrest, because half of their people will be New Deal Democrats with radical ideas. And they'll bring labor unions." These two potentialities were so abhorrent that he paused to look out over the Honolulu he loved so well. "Why don't the people down there trust us to know what's best for these islands?" he asked in some bewilderment. "You'd think they'd bear in mind all we've done for Hawaii. Why, they ought to rise up as one man and kick outfits like Gregory's or California Fruit right into the ocean. But they never seem to appreciate what's best for them."

His secretary interrupted to say, "That young Japanese is trying to see you again," and Hale shook his head furiously.

"Not me! Negotiating with labor is Hewie's problem," and he ducked out a back door, calling for Hewlett Janders. When the big man appeared, Hale commissioned him: "See if you can handle this young troublemaker once and for all," and he felt some assurance as big Hewie hitched up his belt and went forth to battle.

When Janders entered the board room he found there a confident, crop-haired, smiling young man who extended his right hand across the table and said, "I'm Goro Sakagawa, sir. I remember how good you were to my brothers."

The gesture caught big Hewie Janders off guard, and for a fleeting instant he thought: "This is the brother we didn't take into Punahou. If we had, he'd never have grown up to be a labor leader." Then he dismissed the thought and said sternly, "What is it you wish to see me about, young man?" Pointedly, he did not ask Goro to sit down.

Displaying some of the polish he had acquired while serving General MacArthur in Japan, Goro ignored the fact that he had to remain standing and said, "They tell me your son Harry was killed on Bougainville."

"He was," Janders replied, and that made it necessary for him to ask, "Wasn't one of your brothers killed in Italy?"

"Two," Goro replied, and somehow each of the negotiators realized that Hewlett Janders of The Fort had been subtly brought down to Goro Sakagawa's level. They were equal, and Goro said, "You asked why I wanted to see you. I've been nominated by the men at Malama Sugar . . ."

"I won't discuss a labor union."

"I haven't said anything about a labor union," Goro pointed out, shifting from one foot to the other while Hewlett slumped back in his chair.

"What else would you want to talk about?" Janders snapped.

"All right, since you bring the matter up, Mr. Janders. Malama Sugar is going to organize . . ."

"Get out!" Janders said abruptly, his voice rising even though he remained seated.

Quietly Goro replied, "Malama Sugar is going to be organized, Mr. Janders. Under federal law we are entitled . . ."

"Out!" Janders shouted. Leaping to the door he called for his assistants, and when they had piled into the room he commanded: "Throw this communist out."

Goro, even stockier than he had been in high school, braced himself against the table and spoke quickly: "Mr. Janders, I'm not a communist and I'm not going to let your people throw me out, because if they did I'd have a court case against you. Then your position on the union would harden, and we'd have even more trouble discussing things intelligently. So call the dogs off."

"I will never accept a union," Janders cried. "And don't you ever come stomping back into this office."

"Mr. Janders, I promise you that the first plantation we organize will be Malama Sugar, and when we reach the final negotiations I will sit in this chair . . ." Goro reached for a chair, lifted it carefully and set it down in position. "This chair. Save it for me, Mr. Janders. The next time we meet here will be to sign papers. The name's Goro Sakagawa."

He left the room quietly and Janders dismissed his aides. Slumping into his chair he tried to understand what had happened: "A Japanese field hand stomped into my office and told me . . ." He collapsed in incredulity and called for Hoxworth Hale.

"How'd it go?" Hale asked.

"A Japanese field hand stomped into my office and told me . . ."

"Quit the dramatics, Hewie. What happened?"

"They're going to organize Malama Sugar."

"They'll never make it," Hale said firmly. He summoned The Fort and told his men, "Hewie's had a bad ten minutes. Young Sakagawa tipped his hand . . ."

"He stomped in here and tried to tell me . . ."

"Hewie!" Hale interrupted. "He didn't try to tell you. Damn it all, he told you."

"They're going to organize Malama Sugar," Janders repeated. "And if they succeed there . . . then they'll try the rest."

"This has come sooner than I expected," Hale observed. "When we beat back our Russian communists in the strikes of 1939 and 1946, I figured we had them licked. But apparently the dreadful Roosevelt virus has infected our entire society."

"But I never expected to see the day," Janders mumbled, "when a Japanese field hand could stomp into my office . . ."

Hard, competent Hoxworth Hale, who from behind the scenes had masterminded the two preceding fights against the union, now began marshaling his forces. Rapping on the table he said, "We shall present a unified force against them, and if anyone of you in this room wavers, we will show no mercy. On the one hand, the Japanese radicals will overwhelm you. And on the other, we'll ruin you. No credit. No common merchandising. No legal support. Gentlemen, you stick with us or you perish." He stopped, glared at the men, and asked, "Is that agreed?"

"Agreed," the plantation men muttered, and the strike was on.

When policies had been set and the meeting adjourned, the plantation owners stood nervously about the room, unwilling to leave, and Hale asked, "How did a decent young man like Goro Sakagawa, with three brothers in Punahou, become a communist?"

Janders replied, "I think he was assigned to the A.F. of L. in Japan."

A pall settled over The Fort. John Whipple Hoxworth mused: "To think that our government took a decent Japanese boy and instructed him in labor tactics!" Something of the world's maniacal contradiction seeped into the room and mocked the managers, and Hoxworth Hale asked sadly, "You mean that a boy who might have gone to Punahou was perverted by our own government?" On this gloomy note the first meeting of The Fort's strike committee ended.

Actually, when Hewlett Janders accused Goro Sakagawa of being a communist he was not far from the truth. When The Fort, in 1916, 1923, 1928, 1936, 1939 and 1946, refused point-blank even to discuss unionism and used every known device including force and subversion to block labor from attaining any of its legitimate ends, it made normal unionization of the islands impossible. The hard-hitting but completely American union organizers sent out from the mainland found that in Hawaii customary procedures got nowhere. Not even the vocabulary of unionism was understood, or acknowledged where it was understood, so that both The Fort and Honolulu *Mail* invariably referred to any union activity as communism; as a result, over the course of years Hawaii developed its own rather strange definition for terms which on the mainland were understood and accepted as logical parts of modern industrial life. In brief, unionism was subversion.

There were also physical difficulties. Oftentimes mainland men whom the course of history proved to have been rather moderate labor organizers were refused entrance to the islands. If they tried to talk to plantation hands they were bodily thrown off the premises. If they tried to hire a headquarters hall, none was allowed them. They were intimidated, vilified, abused and harassed by charges of communism.

In obedience to Gresham's Law of social change, when the moderates were driven out, the radicals moved in, and from 1944 on, a group of ultra-tough labor men quietly penetrated the islands and among them were many communists, for they had seen from afar that the situation in Hawaii made it a likely spot for the flowering of the communist creed. Among the leaders were a hefty, ugly Irish Catholic from New York named Rod Burke, who had joined the Party in 1927 and who had steadily risen in its ranks until he had reached a position of eminence from which he could be trusted to lead a serious attack upon Hawaii. His first step was to marry a Baltimore Nisei, and this Japanese girl, already a communist, was to prove of great assistance to him in his grand design for capturing the islands.

For example, when Rod Burke met Goro Sakagawa, returning to Hawaii after his instructive labor experiences in Japan, Burke instantly spotted the capable young army captain as the kind of person he required for the unionization and subsequently the communization of Hawaii. So Burke said to his Japanese wife, "Get young Sakagawa lined up," and the dedicated Nisei girl succeeded in enlisting Goro not as a communist but as a labor organizer, and through him Burke conscripted other Japanese and Filipinos without confiding to them his membership in the Communist Party. In this way a solid-core labor movement was founded which in 1947 stood ready to confront The Fort and fight to the rugged, island-breaking end.

In later years Goro Sakagawa often discussed these beginnings with his lawyer brother Shigeo, back from an honors degree at Harvard, and he allowed Shig to probe his motives and understandings as they existed in early 1947. "Did you know then that Rod Burke was a communist?" Shig asked.

"Well, I never knew for sure, but I guessed he was," Goro explained. "He never gave me any proof. But I recognized him as a tough-minded operator."

"If you had these suspicions, Goro, why were you willing to hook up with him?"

"I realized from experience that old-style methods would never break The Fort. We tried reasonable unionism and got nowhere. Burke knew how to apply power. That's the only thing The Fort understood."

"Did Burke ever try to sign you up in the Party?"

"No, he figured he could use me and then dump me in favor of the dumber Japanese and Filipinos he did sign up in the Party," Goro explained.

"How did he select his men?"

"Well, he picked them up where he could. Started enlisting Japanese who didn't know too much . . . Filipinos too. But they were just for support. The real guts of the Party was Rod Burke and his wife."

"Where did that leave you?" Shig explored.

"I figured just like Burke," Goro explained. "I figured I was smart enough to use him and then dump him."

"Must have been a very interesting period," Shig said wryly.

"There were no illusions on either side," Goro confessed. "Funny thing is that my wife, Akemi, figured the Burkes out the first time she saw them. She'd come up against a lot of communists in Japan, and she spotted Mrs. Burke instantly. And I think Mrs. Burke spotted her, so nobody was fooled," Goro assured his brother.

"Did Burke sign up any really good men?" Shig asked.

"Well, most of the Japanese were dopes, pure and simple, but Harry Akemi was as able a man as we ever produced in the islands."

"Looking back on it, Goro, do you think the alliance was necessary?"

Goro had often thought about this, especially since he had known so intimately the moderate A.F. of L. men on General MacArthur's team, and he concluded: "If you remember the position taken by The Fort . . . that even a discussion of labor was communism . . . Hell, Shig, I've told you about the time I went in to see Hewlett Janders. He made me stand like a peasant with my cap in my hands. Abused me, ridiculed me. Shig, there was no alternative."

"None?" his brother asked.

"None. Hawaii could never have moved into the twentieth century until the power of The Fort was broken. I alone couldn't have done it. The A.F. of L. men I knew in Japan couldn't have done it. Only a gutter fighter like Rod Burke could have accomplished it."

So when Hewlett Janders announced to the Honolulu *Mail* that mainland communists were endeavoring to capture the islands, he was right. And when he charged that Japanese had joined the Party under Rod Burke's leadership, he was also correct. But when he said that the leader of the plantation part of the strike, Goro Sakagawa, was also a communist, he was not right, but in those tense years the hatred of labor was so great that a relatively minor error like that didn't really matter.

* * *

The strike was a brutal, senseless, tearing affair, and it frightened Hawaii as nothing previous had ever done, not even the bombing of Pearl Harbor. Rod Burke moved swiftly to tie up the waterfront so that not a single H & H ship entered Hawaii for five and one half starving, agonizing months. The Fort retaliated by cutting credit, so that everyone in the islands felt the pinch.

Goro Sakagawa led his sugar-plantation workers out on strike. The Fort retaliated by suspending all sorts of benefits, so that soon it was not the workers who felt the cruelty of social warfare, but their families.

Rod Burke allowed no cargoes of either sugar or pineapple to leave the islands and no tourists to come in. The Fort retaliated by closing two of its hotels, and the maids and waiters thus thrown out of work were less able to weather the strike than were the hotel owners.

Goro Sakagawa got the pineapple workers to join the strike. The Fort coldly announced that its food-supply warehouses were nearly empty and it could no longer distribute to stores like Kamejiro Sakagawa's, so one shopkeeper after another faced bankruptcy.

No man can understand Hawaii who does not understand the great strike. It crippled the islands to the point of despair. Newsprint ran low and the existence of the papers was threatened. Food diminished to the one-week mark, and many families were hungry. Sugar plantations saw their crops rotting in the parching sunlight. Pineapple fields were untended, and millions upon millions of unrecoverable dollars were lost. Banks watched their normal flow of business halted. Big stores had neither new stocks nor old customers. Doctors went unpaid and dentists saw no patients. The major hotels could serve only inadequate foods, and the very life of the islands ground slowly to a halt.

For a strike in Hawaii was not like a strike in Florida. It was like nothing the mainland ever knew, for in Florida if the waterfront was tied up, food could be imported by train, and if the trains were closed down, men could use trucks, and if they were struck, hungry families could organize car caravans, and if they failed, a desperate man could walk. But in Hawaii when the docks were tied up, there were no alternatives, and the islands came close to prostration. Reasonable industrial relations having proved impractical, stupidity on the part of both capital and labor nearly destroyed the islands.

At the beginning of the sixth month Goro Sakagawa, attended by four assistants, marched into the board room of The Fort, waited for the directors of the great plantations to assemble, and then sat in precisely the chair he had promised Hewlett Janders he would one day occupy, and in that symbolic moment some of the intractable fight went out of him. It was curious that seating oneself in a chair that had been insolently forbidden should affect a man, as if there were hidden emotional channels that ran from his bottom to his brain, but that is what happened. Secure in his chair, Goro said in a conciliatory manner, "We think the strike has progressed long enough. We are sure you think the same. Is there not some way to end it?"

"I will not have a Japanese field hand stomp into my office . . ." Hewlett Janders began, but Hoxworth Hale looked at him in pity, as if the horrors of six months had been useless, in that Janders was using the same words he had used when the strike began.

Quietly Goro ignored him and addressed Hale, a tough negotiator: "Mr. Hale, my committee is not going to take cognizance of the fact that your negotiator, Mr. Hewlett Janders, has attacked us for being Japanese, because we know that your cousin, Colonel Mark Whipple, laid down his life that we might be free citizens. We're acting as free citizens, and I think you appreciate that fact."

The gracious tribute to Colonel Whipple softened the meeting, and all remembered what this same Goro Sakagawa, an army captain in those days, had said when it was proposed to bring Mark Whipple's body home from the Vosges Mountains: "Let them bring my brothers home, but Colonel Whipple should sleep in the heart-land of the world, where he died. No island is big enough to hold his spirit."

"What new terms have you in mind, Mr. Sakagawa?" Hale asked.

"We will never end the strike unless we get full union recognition," Goro replied, and Hewlett Janders slumped in his chair. He could see it coming: the others were willing to surrender. The communists were about to triumph. But before Hewie could speak, Goro quickly added, "Then, to match your concession, we'll accept ten cents an hour less."

"Gentlemen," Hoxworth Hale said with fresh hope, "I think Mr. Sakagawa's proposal gives us something to talk about." Subtly the spirit of Colonel Mark Whipple, who had died for these Japanese boys, invaded the room, and Hale asked quietly, "Goro, will you bring your men back in about three hours?"

"I will, Mr. Hale," the union leader assured him, but as the group started to leave, Hewie Janders asked sharply, "How do we know that communist Rod Burke'll allow us to open the piers?"

"That's what we've been negotiating about, Mr. Janders," Goro replied. "When I reach an agreement with you men, the piers are open. That's what negotiation means."

When the delegation left—three Japanese, a haole and two Filipinos—Hewlett Janders left his seat at the head of the table and said, "I cannot participate in what you men are about to do."

"I appreciate your position," Hale said coldly. "But will you bind yourself to accept what we decide?" At this question everyone turned to stare at Janders. If he refused to accept, in the same of J & W, the principal plantation operators, no one knew what the eventuality might be, and it was just possible that he might be big enough to resist both the unions and his own associates. Desperately he was tempted to fight this out to a Götterdämmerung conclusion, but he was prevented from doing so by cautious words from the man who twenty years before had taken the leadership of The Fort from him. Hoxworth Hale said slowly, "Hewie, your family and mine have always loved these islands. We cannot stand by and see them suffer any further."

The big man looked in dismay at his leader and was about to reject the proposals, but Hale reasoned: "If we must live with labor, and that seems to be the spirit of the times, let's do so with a certain grace. I'm going to call Sakagawa back and make the best . . ."

"I do not wish to be present," Janders said abruptly. He started to leave the room by the back door, but paused to warn his associates: "You're turning these islands over to the communists. I refuse to watch a Japanese field hand come stomping into my office and lay down . . ."

"But you will consider yourself bound by our decision?" Hale interrupted.

"Yes," Janders snapped grudgingly, and when Goro returned to ratify the mutual surrender, Hewlett Janders was not there.

When the great strike ended, three of Hale's plantation managers, men senior to himself, quit with these words: "We been doin' things our own way too long to be told by a bunch of slant-eyed Japs how to raise sugar." Younger men stepped forward to take their places—and it was a rueful moment when Hale discovered that he did not even know two of the replacements—and before the year ended, the new overseers were reporting: "We can work with the new system. Looks like we'll make more sugar than before." Hewie Janders snorted: "Something is eroding the character of America when young men are so eager to compromise with evil."

And then Hewie made his point. At a meeting of The Fort he rushed in with the news that one of the lesser communists had broken with Rod Burke and had signified his willingness to identify both Burke and his wife as card-carrying members of the Communist Party. This caused a flurry of excitement, which a series of substantiating phone calls raised to fever pitch. "I knew the whole lot of them were communists!" Hewie cried triumphantly. "To think that we allowed Goro Sakagawa to come stomping into this office . . ."

"I don't believe he's charged," Hale cautioned. "At least when I called Jasper he didn't . . ."

"They're all communists," Hewie warned. "I told you a year ago that Rod Burke was a red. And he was. I tell you now that Goro Sakagawa is a red. And he is."

John Whipple Hoxworth said icily, "Let's wait till they're indicted, then apply all our strength until they're convicted."

"Has anybody called the governor?" Janders asked.

"Not yet," John Whipple replied.

"I'd love to!" Janders gloated. "Last time I saw him about communism he said . . ."

"Nobody will call anybody," Hale interrupted. "A great thing has happened in our favor. Nobody must spoil it." And The Fort studied carefully how the new developments could be used to its advantage.

But the day's triumph was somewhat dampened by an assistant's report that while everyone's attention had been focused on the strike, something curious seemed to have been happening, something which he was unable to explain. Producing a map of downtown Honolulu, he pointed to certain areas hatched in red and explained: "This is the Rafer Hoxworth building, and the ground floor has been leased to a Japanese named Fujimoto. Nothing suspicious about that. He has the big dry-goods store in Kaimuki. Now this area is the restaurant whose building is owned by Ed Hewlett's widow. It's been leased to a Filipino who runs a restaurant in Wahiawa."

"What are you driving at, Charley?" Hoxworth asked impatiently.

"Look!" the assistant cried. "Within the past six months, every store in this block has been leased, except the big Joe Janders holding. Do you see what that means?"

Quiet descended over The Fort as the managers studied the map. Finally Hoxworth said, "If somebody has been leasing these sites under an assumed name . . ."

This ugly suspicion circulated, but it was soon stopped by robust Hewlett Janders, who said gruffly, "Hell, what are you worrying about? I've warned Cousin Joe a hundred times never to lease his building without clearing things with me. As long as he holds fast, there's not going to be any trouble. What could a person do, with just these little . . ."

"Call Joe," Hoxworth said imperatively.

An ominous silence surrounded bluff Hewlett as he cried warmly, "Hell-lo, Joe! This is Hewie. Joe, you haven't leased your big store site, have you?"

There was a ghastly silence, and Hewlett Janders, completely shaken, put down the phone. There was no cause to ask him what had happened; the news stood out from his sagging round face. "God damn!" Hoxworth Hale shouted, banging the table. "We've been outsmarted. Who did this?" he raged. "Hewlett, who leased that store?"

Big Hewlett Janders kept his head down, staring at the table. "I'm ashamed to say. Kamejiro Sakagawa."

"We'll break him!" Hoxworth stormed. "We'll not bring a single cargo of his into Honolulu. That man will starve on . . ."

Icy John Whipple Hoxworth was speaking: "The problem is two-fold. Who engineered this damnable thing? And for whom?"

There was a long discussion as to who could have accumulated enough capital and wisdom to have effected such a coup, and by a slow process of elimination all came to agree that only Hong Kong Kee could have swung it. "I'll challenge him right now," Hoxworth cried, and in a forthright manner he phoned Hong Kong and asked, "Did you buy up all the leases?" When the Chinese banker replied, Hoxworth nodded his head to his associates. "Whom were you representing, Hong Kong?" This time Hoxworth did not move his head, but listened in stunned silence. "Thank you, Hong Kong," he said, and put down the phone.

"California Fruit?" Janders asked.

"Gregory's," Hale replied.

There was an aching, dumb silence as an era came to an end. Finally one of the Hoxworths asked, "Can't we fight this in the courts?"

"I don't think so," Hale asked.

"Surely we could get Judge Harper to issue an injunction on one of these leases. He's married to my cousin and I could explain . . ."

"If Hong Kong Kee arranged those leases . . ." Hale could not go on. He dropped his head into his hands, thought for a long time and then asked his associates, "How could these people do this to us? Your family, Whipple, why they looked after the Kees. Damn it, the whole Kee hui got its start with that land Old Doc gave them. And those damned Sakagawas. Imagine Kamejiro showing such ingratitude! Buying leases behind our backs. How do you explain it? You'd think they'd feel some kind of loyalty to us. We brought them here, gave them land, looked after them when they were so damned poor they couldn't read or write. What's happening in the world when such people turn against you?"

"That's what McLafferty's been doing!" Janders shouted. "He threw us off the track, talking about that hotel."

Hale now had control of himself and said, "Gentlemen, this is the beginning of an endless fight. I personally am going to obstruct Gregory's and McLafferty at every turn. Not to keep them out of the islands, because if Hong Kong arranged these leases, they'll stand up in court . . ."

One of the Hoxworths interrupted: "You'd think that in view of all we've done for Judge Harper, we could at least rely on him to void one of the leases."

Hale ignored this stupid and unworthy observation, continuing: "We must fight for time. We'll establish branches of our own stores in Waikiki, in Waialae and across the Pali. Every one of you who controls a going concern, move a branch out into the suburbs. Multiply and tie everything up. By the time Gregory's gets here, we'll have our stores so prosperous they'll die on the vine."

So, in the curious way by which a deadly catfish, when thrown into a pool of trout, eats a few of the lazy fish but inspires the others to greater exertion, so that in the end there are more trout, and better, and all because of the evil catfish, the arrival of Gregory's into Hawaii, followed by California Fruit and Shea and Horner, drove the Hawaiian economy ahead by such spurts that soon The Fort was much better off than it had been before. In the same obtuse way, the increased wages that Goro Sakagawa's union had chiseled out of The Fort really made that establishment richer than ever, because much of the money filtered back into its enterprises, and the general prosperity of the islands multiplied.

Hale's determination to fight the mainland intruders with increased economic energy of his own had one unforeseen effect upon Hawaii, and in subsequent years this was often cited as the real revolution of that trying age: if The Fort was going to compete on an equal footing with outfits like Gregory's, it could no longer afford to promote into top positions inadequate nephews and cousins and gutless second sons. So under Hoxworth Hale's sharp eye, a good many Hales and Hoxworths and Janderses and Hewletts were weeded out. His policy was forthright: "Either give them minor jobs where they can't wreck the system, or give them substantial shares of stock on which they can live while real men run the companies." As a result, what crude Hewlett Janders called "the chinless wonders" found themselves with a lot of stock, a good yearly income and freedom to live either in France or Havana; while in their places appeared a flood of smart young graduates of the Wharton School, Stanford and Harvard Business. Some, out of sheer prudence, married Whipple girls or Hales or Hewletts, but most brought their own wives in from the mainland. And all Hawaii prospered.

But of the men who dominated The Fort, only shrewd, confused Hoxworth Hale, alternately fighting and surrendering, saw what the real menace of those days was. It was not the arrival of Gregory's, nauseating though that was, nor the triumph of the unions, seditious as that was: it lay in the fact that Black Jim McLafferty was a Democrat. His legal residence was now Hawaii. He no longer worked for Gregory's but had a small law practice of his own, which he combined with politicking, and whenever Hoxworth Hale passed McLafferty's office he studied the door with foreboding, for he knew that in the long run Democrats were worse than Gregory's or unions or communists.

He was therefore appalled one morning when he saw that McLafferty's door carried a new sign: McLafferty and Sakagawa, Shigeo was back from Harvard, an expert on land reform, a brilliant legalist, and thanks to Black Jim McLafferty's foresight, an official Democrat.

FOLLOWING THE STRIKE, two of the main protagonists were taken out of circulation by family problems, and for some time not much was heard of either Goro Sakagawa or Hoxworth Hale. At first it looked as if the former's troubles were the greater, for from that day in late 1945 when Goro had first met the slim and intense young Tokyo modenne, Akemi-san, their lives had been continuously complicated. First had come harassment by M.P.'s who had tried to enforce the no-fraternization edict of the Occupation, and it had been unpleasant to be dating a girl you loved when the M.P.'s had the right to intrude at any moment. Next had been the ridiculous difficulty faced by any American soldier who wanted to marry a Japanese girl, so that once Goro had remarked bitterly, "When good things are being passed out they never consider me an American, but when they're dishing out the misery I'm one of the finest Americans on record." The young lovers had evaded the anti-marriage edict by engineering a Shinto wedding at a shrine near the edge of Tokyo, and had later discovered that Goro couldn't bring a Shinto bride back to America, so there had been renewed humiliation at the consul's office, but in those trying periods Akemi-san had proved herself a stalwart girl with a saving sense of humor, and largely because she was so sweet to officialdom, her paper work was ultimately completed and by special connivance she found herself free to enter Hawaii.

In 1946, when the troop transport neared Honolulu, Akemi-san had been one of the most practical-minded brides aboard, suffering from few of the illusions whose shattering would mar the first days in America for many of the other girls. She had not been bedazzled by her young American, Goro Sakagawa. She had recognized that he was what modennes called a peasant type, stubborn, imperfectly educated and boorish; and even in the starving days when he had had access to the mammoth P.X.'s that blossomed across Japan, where his military pay had made him a millionaire compared to the Japanese, she had known that he was not a rich man. Furthermore, she had been specifically warned by friends who knew others who had lived in Hawaii that the islands were populated mostly by Hiroshima-ken people, who were clannish to a fault and not altogether contemporary. One lively Tokyo girl had whispered to her: "I've been to Hawaii. In the entire area, not one modenne." Akemi had no illusions about her new home, but even so she was not prepared for what faced her.

At the dock she was met by Mr. Sakagawa and his son-in-law Mr. Ishii, with their wives standing stolidly behind the stocky little men, and she thought: "This is the way families used to look in Japan thirty years ago." However, she took an instant liking to bulldog little Sakagawa-san, with his arms hanging out from knees, and thought, as she looked down at him: "He is like my father." But then she saw grim-faced Mrs. Sakagawa, iron-willed and conservative, and she shivered, thinking to herself: "She's the one to fear. She's the kind we had to fight against in Tokyo."

She was right. Mrs. Sakagawa never eased up. Gentle with her husband, she was a terror to her daughter-in-law. Long ago in Hiroshima, when a son brought home a wife to work the rice fields, it was his mother's responsibility to see that the girl was soon and ably whipped into the habits of a good farm wife, and Mrs. Sakagawa proposed to perform this task for Goro. In fact, as soon as she saw Akemi at the railing of the ship she realized that Goro had made a sad choice, for she whispered contemptuously to her daughter Reiko, "She looks like a city girl, and you know what expensive habits they have."

If Goro had had a well-paying job which permitted him to live away from home, things might have settled down to a mutual and smoldering disapproval in which the two women saw each other as little as possible and were then studiously polite for the sake of Goro, but this could not be, for Goro's salary at the union did not permit him to have his own home, so he stayed with his parents. Early in her battle to subdue Akemi, Mrs. Sakagawa established her theme: "When I came to Hawaii life was very difficult, and there is no reason why you should be pampered."

"Does she expect me to go out and chop a few fields of sugar each afternoon?" Akemi asked Goro one night, and in time he began to hate coming home, for each of his women would in turn try to grab him off to some corner to explain the faults of the other and the turmoil of that day.

What angered Akemi most was a little thing, yet so recurrent that it began eroding her happiness with Goro. The Sakagawas had not spoken the best Japanese even while growing up in Hiroshima, and their long imprisonment in Hawaii had positively corrupted their speech, so that they now used many Hawaiian, Chinese, haole and Filipino words, with a lilting melody to their speech borrowed from the Mexican. Much of their phraseology was incomprehensible to Akemi, but she said nothing and would have been polite enough never to have commented on this to the Sakagawas, for as she told another war bride whom she met at the store, "I find their horrible speech rather amusing," and the two girls had laughed pleasantly together.

The Sakagawas were not so considerate. They found Akemi's precise Japanese, with its careful inflection and pronunciations, infuriating. "She thinks she's better than we are," Mrs. Sakagawa stormed one night at Goro. "Always talking as if her mouth were full of beans which she didn't want to bite." Often when the family was gathered for evening meal, Akemi would make some casual observation and Mrs. Sakagawa would repeat one or two words, pronouncing them in the barbarous Hawaiian manner. Then everyone would laugh at Akemi, and she would blush.

She fell into the habit of waiting at the market till one or another of the war brides came in, and hungrily, like refugees in an alien land, they would talk with each other in fine Japanese without fear of being ridiculed. "It's like living in Japan a hundred years ago," Akemi said angrily one day. Then she broke into tears, and when the other girl handed her a mirror, so that she could make up her face and be presentable, she looked at herself a long time and said, "Fumiko, would you think that I had once been the leader of the modernes? I love Bruckner and Brahms. I was fighting to set the Japanese girl free. Now I'm in a worse prison than any of them, and do you know why it's worse? Because it's all so horribly ugly. Ugly houses, ugly speech, ugly thoughts. Fumiko, I haven't been to a concert or a play in over a year. Nobody I know, except you, has ever heard of André Gide. I think we've made a terrible mistake." Later, when alone at the Sakagawas, she thought: "I live for the few minutes I can talk with a sensible human being, but every time I do, I feel worse than before."

One night she said forcefully, "Goro, there's an orchestra concert tonight, and I think we should go." Awkwardly they went, but she did not enjoy it because Goro felt ill at ease, and the entire audience, except for a few students, were haoles. "Don't the Japanese ever go to plays or music?" she asked, but he interpreted this as the beginning edge of a complaint, so he mumbled, "We're busy working." "For what?" she snapped, and he said nothing.

When Akemi next met Fumiko at the market she asked, "What is it they're working for? In Japan, a man and woman will work like idiots to get tickets for the theater or to buy a beautiful ceramic. What do they work for here? I'll tell you what for. So that they can buy a big black automobile, and put the old mama-san in the back, and drive around Honolulu and say, 'Now I am as good as a haole.' I'm ashamed whenever I see Japanese doctors and lawyers in their big black automobiles."

"I am too," Fumiko confessed. "To think that they surrendered everything Japanese for such a set of values."

Things got a little better when Shigeo returned from Harvard with his honors degree in law for then Akemi had an intelligent person with whom she could talk and they had long discussions on politics and art. Akemi was astonished to find that Shig had been to visit the museums in Boston, but he explained: "I'd never have gone on my own account, but I was living with Dr. Abernethy and his wife, and they said that any Sunday on which you didn't do something to improve your mind was a Sunday wasted, and I had a great time with them."

"Tell me about the Boston Symphony," Akemi pleaded. "In Japan we think it's one of the best."

At this point shrewd Mrs. Sakagawa took Shigeo aside and said, "You must not talk any more with Akemi-san. She is your brother's wife, and not a good girl at all, and she will try to make you fall in love with her; and then we will have a tragedy in the family. I told both you and Goro that you ought to avoid city girls, but neither of you would listen, and now see what's happened."

"What has happened?" Shigeo asked.

"Goro has been trapped by a vain and silly girl," his mother explained. "Music, books, plays all day long. She wants to talk about politics. She is no good, that one."

The reasons his mother gave did not impress Shigeo, but the fact that Akemi was temptingly beautiful in her soft Japanese way did, and he stopped being alone with her, so that her life became even more desperate than before. It was rescued by the arrival one day of a young sociologist from the University of Hawaii, a Dr. Sumi Yamazaki, whose parents were also from Hiroshima. Dr. Yamazaki was a brilliant girl who was conducting three hundred interviews with Japanese girls married to G.I.'s, and she got to Akemi late in her study, when her findings had begun to crystallize.

Akemi, hoping that her intended visitor might be a woman of sophisticated intelligence, had first dressed in her most modenne Tokyo style, so that she looked almost as if she had come from Paris; but when she saw herself in the mirror she said, "Today I want to be very Japanese," and she had changed into a languorous pale blue and white shantung kimono with silver zori, and when she met Dr. Yamazaki, she found that it was the attractive young sociologist who was dressed like a real modenne, with bright eyes and quick intelligence to match. The two women liked each other immediately, and Dr. Yamazaki made a brief mental note that she would transcribe later: "Akemi Sakagawa appeared in formal kimono, therefore probably very homesick." And after two exploratory questions the sociologist was able to categorize her hostess with precision.

"Your kimono has told me all about you, Mrs. Sakagawa," she joked, in excellent Japanese.

"Call me Akemi, please."

"These are your complaints," the clever young sociologist said. "In Tokyo you were a modenne, fighting for women's rights. Here you find yourself in an ancient Japan that even your parents never knew. You find the local speech barbarous, the intellectual outlook bleak, and the aesthetic view of life nonexistent." Dr. Yamazaki hesitated, then added, "You feel that if this is America, you had better go back to something better."

Akemi-san gulped, for she had not yet formulated that bitter conclusion, though for some time she had suspected its inevitability. Now, through the soft speech of another, the frightening words had been spoken. "Do many feel as I do, Yamazaki-sensei?"

"Would it help you to know?" the young woman asked.

"Indeed it would!" Akemi cried eagerly.

"You understand that my figures are only tentative . . . ."

Akemi laughed nervously and said, "It's so good to hear a person use a word like *tentative.*"

"I'm afraid you're bitter," Dr. Yamazaki said reprovingly.

"Any more than the others?" Akemi asked.

"No."

"I think you reached me just at the right time," Akemi said eagerly.

"The general pattern is this," Dr. Yamazaki said, but before she could continue, Akemi interrupted and asked, "Would you think me a very silly girl, Yamazaki-sensei, if I said that I wanted to serve you tea? I am most terribly homesick."

The two women sat in silence as Akemi prepared tea in the ceremonial manner, and when the ritual was ended, Dr. Yamazaki continued: "Suppose that a hundred local soldiers married Japanese girls. Sixty of the husbands were Japanese. Thirty were Caucasians. Ten were Chinese."

"How have the marriages worked out?" Akemi-san asked.

"Well, if you take the thirty lucky girls who married Caucasians, about twenty-eight of them are quite happy. Some of the girls say they're deliriously happy. They say they wouldn't go back to Japan even if I gave them all of Hibiya Park."

"They wouldn't go back to Japan?" Akemi gasped. "Were they girls who were interested in books or plays or music?"

"Much like you. But you see, when a haole man marries a Japanese girl, his parents are so shocked that they make a true spiritual effort to like the girl. And when they meet someone like you, gentle, well-bred, sweet to their son, they overcompensate. They love her more than is required. They make her life a heaven on earth."

"Do such people listen to music?" Akemi asked.

"Usually a haole man hasn't the nerve to marry a Japanese girl unless he's rather sophisticated culturally. Such couples experience a very full spectrum."

Akemi looked glumly at the bleak walls of the Sakagawa home, with a four-tube radio invariably tuned to a station that alternated American Jazz with Japanese hillbilly songs. Whenever she and Goro went to a movie it was invariably a chanbara, a Japanese western in which the samurai hero fought sixty armed villains without suffering a wound.

"The Japanese girls who marry Chinese soldiers," Dr. Yamazaki continued, "face a different problem. The Chinese parents are totally disgusted and convinced that there is no possibility of their liking the unseen daughter-in-law, so they spend the time till she arrives hating her so much that when she finally gets here, they find she isn't anywhere near as bad as they had feared. When she demonstrates that she really loves their son, everyone reaches a plateau of mutual respect, and things go reasonably well."

"But the Japanese marriages?" Akemi asked. "You won't dare say they go well."

"Some do," Dr. Yamazaki assured her. "Where farm boys here have married farm girls from Hiroshima-ken, things work out rather well. But in a surprising number of cases, the Japanese-Japanese marriage does not do well. I think our figures are going to show that over fifty-five per cent of such marriages have run into trouble."

"Why?" Akemi pleaded.

"I was born in Hawaii myself," Dr. Yamazaki said. "From the very kind of family you married into. Stout Hiroshima peasants—and remember that even in modern Hiroshima our Hawaii people would seem very old fashioned. Anyhow, I'm partial to the local people. But the curious fact is this. The Caucasian mothers-in-law and the Chinese realize that they have to make a special effort to understand and love their strange new daughters. So they do so, and find happiness. The stolid Japanese mothers-in-law, and God help the Japanese girl who marries my brother and who has to put up with my mother . . . Well, it's obvious. They all think they're getting the kind of Japanese bride that used to flourish in southern Japan forty years ago. They make no effort to understand, so they haven't the slightest chance of finding happiness with their new daughters."

"Do you know what's killing my marriage?" Akemi asked bluntly. Dr. Yamazaki was not surprised at the forthrightness of the question, for she had watched the dissolution of several such marriages, but now Akemi paused, and it was apparent to Dr. Yamazaki that she was supposed to guess, so she volunteered: "In Japan young men are learning to accept new ways, but in Hawaii they have learned nothing."

"Yes," Akemi confessed. "Is that what the other girls say?"

"They all say the same thing," Dr. Yamazaki assured her. "But many of them outgrow their distaste, or somehow learn to modify their husbands."

"But do you know what will keep me from doing that?" Akemi asked. "What cuts me to the heart day after day?"

"What?" the sociologist asked professionally.

"The way they laugh at my correct speech. This I will not bear much longer."

Dr. Yamazaki thought of her own family and smiled bitterly. "I have the same problem," she laughed. "I have a Ph.D. degree." Then, imitating her mother, she asked, " 'Do you think you're better than we are, using such language?' So at home, in self-defense, I talk pidgin."

"I will not," Akemi said. "I am an educated Japanese who has fought a long time for certain things."

"If you love your husband," Dr. Yamazaki said, "you will learn to accommodate yourself."

"To certain things, never," Akemi said. Then she asked abruptly, "Have you ever been married, Yamazaki-sensei?"

"I'm engaged," the sociologist replied.

"To a local boy?"

"No, to a haole at the University of Chicago."

"I see. You wouldn't dare marry a local boy, would you?"

"No," Dr. Yamazaki replied carefully.

Akemi tapped the sociologist's notebook and laughed. "Now I'm embalmed in there."

"One of many," Dr. Yamazaki said.

"But can you guess where I'd like to be?"

"In a small coffee shop in the Nishi-Ginza, surrounded by exciting conversation on books and politics and music."

"How could you guess so accurately?" Akemi asked.

"Because I'd like to be there, too," Dr. Yamazaki confessed. "That's where I met my fiancé, so I know how lovely Japan can be. But I would say this, too. Hawaii can be just as exciting. To be a young Japanese here is possibly one of the most exhilarating experiences in the world."

"But you said you wouldn't marry one of them," Akemi-san reminded her.

"As a woman, seeking happiness in a relaxed home, I'll stick with my haole from Chicago. But as a pure intellect, if I were not involved as a woman, I would much prefer to remain in Hawaii."

"Tell me truthfully, Yamazaki-sensei, do you think that any society which has as its ideal a long, black automobile can ever be a good place to live?"

Dr. Yamazaki considered the question for some moments and replied: "You must understand that the visible symbols of success which our Japanese here in Hawaii are following are those laid down by the established haole society. A big home, a powerful car, a boy going to Yale whether he learns anything or not . . . these are the symbols people living in Hawaii must accept. You can't suddenly require the Japanese to prove themselves superior to the symbols upon which they've been raised."

"For three years I've hoped my husband would," Akemi said bitterly.

"Be patient," Dr. Yamazaki pleaded, "and you'll find Hawaii improving."

"I think not," Akemi said slowly. "It's a barren, stupid place and nothing will ever change it."

The two young women parted, and that night Dr. Yamazaki called Shig Sakagawa, whom she had known at Punahou and said, "Shig, it's none of my business, but your brother Goro is going to lose his wife."

"You think so?"

"I know so. She used every phrase the girls use before they catch the boat back to Japan. I've watched nineteen of them go back so far."

"What could he do?" Shig asked.

"Buy her three Beethoven symphonies," Dr. Yamazaki said, knowing that to blunt Goro such a step would be beyond the outer limits of imagination. Besides, Mrs. Sakagawa Senior would never allow such music in her house.

WHILE THE LABOR leader Goro Sakagawa faced these problems—or rather did not face them—Hoxworth Hale was concerned principally with the forthcoming marriage of his daughter Noelani to her cousin twice removed, Whipple Janders, the son of bold, straightforward Hewlett Janders, on whom Hoxworth had grown to depend so much in recent years. At one time, when Noelani was younger, Hoxworth had rather hoped that she might go outside The Fort and find herself a completely new kind of husband . . . somebody from Yale, of course, but perhaps an easterner who had never seen Hawaii. For a while when Noelani was a senior at Wellesley she dated an Amherst boy, which was almost as good as Yale, but nothing had come of it, and when young Whip Janders, who was belatedly completing his Yale education, asked her to a spring dance at New Haven, each of them instinctively knew that they ought to marry. After all, they had known each other at Punahou; they were from families who understood each other; and Whip had been the closest friend of Noelani's brother, who had been killed over Tokyo.

However, at one point in their engagement Noelani had experienced haunting doubts as to the propriety of their marriage, for Whipple had returned from the war somewhat changed. He was thinner, and his fashionable crew-cut did not entirely hide a tendency toward strongly individualistic behavior. Once at a Vassar dance he had appeared in formal dress but with a garish vest made of Hong Kong silk embroidered in purple dragons. He had been a sensation, but he had also been disturbing, for he had told one of the professors' wives, "Thorstein Veblen would have loved this vest," and she had stammered, "What?" and he had given his imitation of a dying tubercular patient, adding, "If you're going to have consumption, it ought to be conspicuous." It had been gruesomely funny, but unfortunately the professor's wife didn't catch on.

Now Whip and his crew-cut were back in Honolulu, dressed in Brooks Brothers' most austere fashion, and the wedding was about to take place. Shortly before the event, Noelani asked her father, for her mother was in one of her spells and could not comprehend questions, "Do you think it's proper for kids like us to go on intermarrying, Dad? I mean, frankly, what are the chances that our children will be more like Mother than like you?"

In considerable embarrassment, for this was the nagging fear that had made him hope that Noelani would marry some easterner, Hoxworth dodged the question and suggested: "Why don't we look into this with Aunt Lucinda. We always ask her about the family."

"Which family?" Noelani asked.

"The family . . . all of it," Hoxworth replied, and he drove his daughter up to see Aunt Lucinda in the mist-haunted house in Nuuanu Valley. When they arrived, they found that she was entertaining half a dozen ladies of nearly her own age, and most of them were drinking gin, so that the conversation wasn't exactly on focus, but there was a sweet, relaxed gentility about it.

"This is my great-niece, on my grandmother's side, Noelani Hale," Lucinda explained graciously, whisking her pale blue lace handkerchief toward the girl. "She's Malama Janders Hale's daughter, and on Saturday she's going to marry that fine young Whipple Janders, who is the great-grandson of Clement and Jerusha Hewlett."

At once, Noelani's place in the great succession was established, and the women smiled at her admiringly, one saying, "I knew your husband's great-grandmother Jerusha very well, Noelani. She was a marvelous woman and could play polo better than the men. If young Whipple has her blood, he'll be a stalwart man, I can assure you."

"What Noelani came to ask about," Aunt Lucinda explained, "is the extent to which she is related to Whip, and I would like to say right now that in my opinion it's a good deal safer to marry into a substantial island family, whose blood lines are known, than into some purely speculative mainland family whose backgrounds could have originated God knows where." The women all agreed to this, and a Japanese maid in crisp white took their cups for more tea or their glasses for more gin.

"The only possible question about the marriage of Noelani and Whip," Aunt Lucinda began, "is that each of them," and she lowered her voice, "does have a strain of Hawaiian blood. If you go back to her great-great-grandmother on her father's side, you find Malama Hoxworth, who was the daughter of Captain Rafer Hoxworth, who was not a missionary but who was a most marvelous and courtly gentleman of the finest character and breeding. Of course, he married Noelani Kanakoa, the last Alii Nui, but I think it safe to say that the Malama of whom we are speaking . . . the one that married the great Micah Hale, that is . . . well anyway . . ." and with an airy gesture she dismissed the whole matter. One of the most gratifying aspects of talking with Aunt Lucinda was that she threw out so many names that you didn't really have to listen, for when she found herself hopelessly involved in family lines she stopped and started over again. Now she switched abruptly and said, with no one able to guess how she arrived at the conclusion, "Anyway, no finer gentleman ever lived in Hawaii than Captain Rafer Hoxworth."

The Japanese maid brought back the drinks, and Aunt Lucinda asked, "Where was I? Oh, yes. So from that unfortunate marriage of Micah to the half-caste girl Malama . . . You know, I often wondered where Micah got the courage to appear in public so much when he was saddled with such a marriage. Well, anyway, our little Noelani here does have that strain of Hawaiian blood, but it's more than overcome, I should think by the Hale and Whipple strains, except that the Whipple girl her great-grandfather married was not from what I like to call the uncontaminated Whipples, to which I belong, but from the branch that married into the Hewletts, which as you know were also half-castes, except for the first boy who married Lucy Hale, from whom I am descended."

The mists from the Pali began to fill the valley, and a waterfall echoed mournfully as Aunt Lucinda continued her analysis of the family lines. Most of the meandering comments she made were meaningless to her listeners, but since all were descended from these early ancestors who had done so much to build Hawaii, each kept in the back of her mind some three or four specially prized progenitors to whom she attributed her character, and whenever Aunt Lucinda mentioned one of those names, that listener snapped to attention through the gin and nodded that three names in particular evoked veneration: it was best to be descended from Jerusha Bromley Hale, the great missionary mother; or from Rafer Hoxworth, the courtly and gracious sea captain; or from Dr. John Whipple, the patrician intellect. Aunt Lucinda, with modesty, could point out that she was descended from two of the three, and in a way she was happy that she was not related to Captain Hoxworth, for of course all his offspring were part Hawaiian.

"It's not that I'm against Hawaiians," she assured her visitors. "It's just that I get frightfully irritated at the hero-worship that goes on around here over the so-called Hawaiian royalty. I sit in the library and I can spot every malihini girl who is going to ask me, 'Do you have that book on Kelly Kanakoa?' I have to stop myself from warning them, 'You'll have to put your chewing gum away while you look at the pictures.' And when she hands the book back reverently she always says, 'Gee, his grandfather was a king!' As if that meant anything. I've always thought it was one of the most ridiculous aspects of Hawaiian life, the way they memorize these pathetic old lists of kings, as if a litany of imaginary names meant anything. You remember what Abner Hale, he was my great-grandfather, wrote about such ancestor worship: 'I think it impedes Hawaii as much as any other one thing, for the poor fools are so attentive to their past that they have no time to contemplate eternity.' And nothing makes me more irritated than the way a Hawaiian will point to some pathetic dregs of humanity and say accusingly, 'If the missionaries hadn't interfered, he would now be our king,' as if we had halted something fine and good. Do you know who the present king of Hawaii would be if the missionaries hadn't put a stop to such nonsense? The beachboy Kelly Kanakoa! Have you ever heard him speak? He insists on using a vocabulary of about ninety words, half of them *blalah*. Everybody Kelly likes is *blalah* except that he calls me his seestah."

Hoxworth coughed and his aunt collected her thoughts. "Oh yes, now about Whipple Janders. He went to Punahou and Yale, as you know, and had a very good record in the war. Handsome boy, but not so fleshy as his father, which is understandable, because Hewlett takes after the Hewlett side of the family, and they were always unprepossessing types, if you'll allow me to say so, Abigail, because as you know Abraham married a Hawaiian . . . well, he picked up a Hawaiian wahine after Urania died, but that's neither here nor there.

"I suppose what you're really interested in is how the intended bridegroom Whipple relates to the Hales. If you'll go back to Micah, who married the half-caste girl Malama Hoxworth, you'll remember that he had two children, Ezra and Mary, and Ezra of course was your great-grandfather, Noelani, and that takes care of that." The Japanese maid returned to pass coconut chips, toasted a delicious salty brown. "You may fill the glasses, too, Kimiko," Aunt Lucinda reminded her.

She never got back to Mary Hale, Micah's daughter, but the group understood that somehow Mary was related to Whipple Janders, but what Aunt Lucinda did say was perhaps of greater importance: "So you can see that Whipple comes from some of the finest stock in the islands. For three generations, Whipples have married Janderses, which accounts in part, I suppose, for the way in which their family fortunes have been conserved."

Turning directly to Noelani, the beautiful girl who was soon to be married, Lucinda said, "I can think of no one you could have chosen finer than Whipple Janders, and I am extremely happy for you, Noelani. When I look at your marvelous face I see your great-great-grandfather Micah Hale, the savior of these islands. You have his high forehead, his courage and his force of character. But your beauty comes from the Whipples. Isn't it strange," she asked the hushed group, "how the seed of one handsome man could have produced so much beauty in these islands? I know it's fashionable to laugh at old maids who haven't married, and I'm sure you'll think me vain if I claim that when I was young I too was a typical Whipple beauty. Kimiko, fetch me that portrait in the bedroom!" And the Japanese maid silently brought in one of the last great portraits completed by Sargent, and it showed a glowing young beauty in white, with lace and combs, and Lucinda said, "That's what I mean by the Whipple complexion. You have it, Noelani, and it's a great consolation to me to think that it will be reunited with the male side of the Whipple family. What handsome children you are bound to have!"

The maid stood awkwardly with the heavy picture, and Miss Lucinda said, "You may take it back, Kimiko." And when the maid was gone she confided: "Sargent did that of me when I was engaged to an Englishman, but Father felt that it would be better if I found a young man closer to home, and as you know I became engaged to my cousin Horace Whipple, but he . . ." She hesitated; then realizing that all of her listeners except perhaps Noelani knew the story anyway, she concluded: "Before the wedding Horace shot himself. At first it was suspected that he might have stolen money from J & W, but of course that was quickly disproved, for there has never been a case of theft in the family."

"Which family?" Noelani asked.

"The family. All of us," Aunt Lucinda replied, and when her nephew Hoxworth had departed with his attractive daughter, she summoned Kimiko to refill the glasses, remarking, "That Noelani is one of the loveliest these islands have ever produced. She did marvelously well at Wellesley, and I think we're lucky that she's come home to marry with her proper kind. After all, she comes from excellent stock."

It was a major characteristic of Hawaii that everyone claimed distinguished ancestors. In 1949 there were no Hawaiians who were not descended from kings. The Hales had constructed the myth that cantankerous old Abner from the miserable farm near Marlboro had been, were the truth known, of knightly ancestry dating far back in English history. The Kees never mentioned the fact that their progenitor was a shifty little gambler who had bought his concubine from a Macao whorehouse; he was, if you listened closely, something of a Confucian scholar. And even Mrs. Yoriko Sakagawa always loved to tell her children, "Remember that on your mother's side you come from samurai stock." Of all these gentle fables, only Mrs. Sakagawa's was true. In 1703 the great Lord of Hiroshima had had as one of his flunkies a stocky, stupid oaf whose principal job it was to stand with a feathered staff warning away chance intruders when his lord was going to the toilet. Technically, this male chambermaid was a samurai, but he had been too stupid even to hold the toilet signal well, and after a while had been discharged and sent back to his home village, where he married a local girl and became the ancestor of Yoriko Sakagawa; and if she, like the others in Hawaii, derived consolation from her supposed illustrious heritage, no harm was done.

The Hale-Janders wedding was a splendid affair, held in the flower-decked old missionary church, with Reverend Timothy Hewlett officiating; but as I said earlier, it only seemed that Goro Sakagawa was having more domestic trouble than his adversary, Hoxworth Hale, for Noelani and Whipple had been married only four months when Whipple suddenly announced, out of a clear blue sky if ever an announcement were so made: "I just don't love you, Noelani."

"What?" she asked in heartbroken astonishment.

"I'm going to live in San Francisco," he said simply.

"Is there some other girl?" Noelani pleaded, without shame.

"No. I guess I just don't like girls," he explained.

"Whip!"

"There's nothing wrong with you, Noe, but Eddie Shane and I are taking an apartment. He's the fellow I was with in the air corps."

"Oh, my God, Whip! Have you talked with anyone about this?"

"Look, Noe! Don't make a federal case of it, please. Marriage isn't for me, that's all."

"But you're willing to marry Eddie Shane, is that it?"

"If you want to put it that way, all right. I am."

He left Hawaii, and word filtered back that he and Eddie Shane had a large apartment in the North Beach area of San Francisco, where Eddie made ceramics which were featured in *Life* magazine, in color.

Aunt Lucinda loved to explain what had happened. She said, as Kimiko passed the gin, "Go back to Micah Hale's daughter, Mary. This girl was one-eighth Hawaiian, through her mother Malama Hoxworth, who was the daughter of Noelani Kanakoa, the last Alii Nui. Now that's bad enough, but as you know, Mary Hale married a Janders, and you'd expect that rugged stock to have counterbalanced the weak Hawaiian strain, but unfortunately she married into the Janders' line that had married one of the Hewlett girls, and as you know, they were Hawaiian. So poor Whipple Janders, when he ran off with the air corps man, was only doing what could be expected, because he had Hawaiian blood from both sides of his family."

But Hoxworth Hale, seeing the effect of this pathetic marriage on his high-strung daughter Noelani, thought: "Unless I can help her, there's going to be another woman sitting upstairs in the late afternoons." But what help he should offer, he did not know.

I N 1951 NYUK TSIN engineered her last big coup for the Kee hui, and in many ways it was her most typical accomplishment, for it derived from intelligence and was attained through courage. She was a hundred and four years old, sitting in her ugly house up Nuuanu listening to her grandson Harvey read the paper to her, when, in a shaky old voice, she interrupted: "What's that again?" Since Harvey was reading in English and speaking in Hakka, he could not be certain that he himself understood the confusing story, so phrase by phrase he repeated: "In American business today it is possible for a company which is losing money to be more valuable than it was a few years ago when it was making money."

Impetuously the old matriarch forced her grandson to read the strange concept three times, and when she had comprehended it she said in her piping voice, "That's exactly the kind of trick smart haoles think up for themselves and which we stupid Chinese never catch on to until it's too late." Accordingly, she summoned her great-grandson Eddie, Hong Kong's boy, whom she had sent to Harvard Law School, and told him: "I want a complete report on how this works."

At that time not much was known in Hawaii relating to this marriage of losing companies to those that were prosperous, but Eddie Kee applied himself to the task of assembling opinions from mainland tax courts, and within two months he was an expert in the field. Then with several tax reports airmailed in from New York he reported back to his great-grandmother in her little house, and when he came upon her she was picking lint from a shawl, and he thought: "How can she be so old and yet so interested?"

"Can you explain it now?" she asked in a high, cackling voice.

"Fundamentally," Eddie began in his best professional style, "it's an old law and a good one."

"I don't care whether it's good or bad," Nyuk Tsin interrupted, her voice suddenly lower. "What I want to know is how it works."

"Take the Janders Brewery. For years it's been losing money. Now suppose next year it makes money. It won't have to pay any taxes because recent years' losses can be used to offset next year's gains."

"Makes sense," Nyuk Tsin nodded.

"But look at what else we can do," Eddie lectured stolidly, as if addressing a class of legal students. "If the Kee hui buys the brewery, we can then add to its assets all of our old pineapple land. Then if the brewery sells the land, the profits will be offset by the past losses of the brewery. Do you see what that means, Wu Chow's Auntie?"

Little Nyuk Tsin did not reply. She sat in the late afternoon sun like a winsome old lady embroidered on a Chinese silk. She was smiling, and if an outsider had seen her beatific, wrinkled face he might have thought: "She's dreaming of an old love." But he would have been wrong. She was dreaming of the Janders Brewery, and she said, "How heavenly! We can use the Janders' losses to balance the Kee profits!"

"Wu Chow's Auntie!" Eddie cried. "You see exactly what I'm talking about."

"But I'm afraid you don't see what I've been talking about," Nyuk Tsin replied.

"What do you mean?" Eddie asked.

"Suppose that we do buy the Janders Brewery and do hide our pineapple lands inside it . . ." she began.

"That's what I've been explaining," Eddie said gently. It was the first sign that day that Wu Chow's Auntie was losing her acuity.

"But what I'm explaining," Nyuk Tsin said firmly, "is that after we have done this clever thing we will put some member of our family in charge of the brewery, and he will give it good management and he will turn what has been a loss into a profit."

Now the beatific smile passed over to Eddie's face and he said, "If you could arrange that, Wu Chow's Auntie, we'd make a fortune."

"That's what I had in mind," the old woman replied. "This law seems to have been expressly written for the Kee hui. It is our duty to use it sagaciously."

She summoned Hong Kong, and after discussing the theory of the law, told him abruptly, "Make us up a list of all the companies in Honolulu that are losing big money. Then write alongside each one the name of someone in our hui who could turn that loss into a profit."

"Where will we get the money to buy the sick companies?" Hong Kong parried.

"We don't have to buy them for cash," Nyuk Tsin replied, "but we'll need money for down payments. So we have to sell some of our holdings now and pay the taxes on our profits, but if the plan works we'll more than make up for those taxes in the end."

"Are you determined to go ahead on such a wild scheme?" Hong Kong asked. "Getting rid of profitable businesses in order to take a big gamble?"

Nyuk Tsin reflected a moment, then asked Eddie, "Does anyone else in Honolulu understand how this law works?"

"They must know," the Harvard man replied, "but they aren't doing anything about it."

Nyuk Tsin made up her mind. Clapping her hands sharply she said, "We'll go ahead. In six months everyone will know what we're doing, but by then there'll be nothing left to buy." And as Hong Kong and his son departed, old Nyuk Tsin looked at the back of the latter and thought: "I wonder what his education at Harvard cost us? It's been worth rubies and jade."

The next day Hong Kong returned to the weather-beaten old house up Nuuanu with his homework well done. Spreading papers which Nyuk Tsin could not read, he indicated all the businesses that had accumulated large losses: the brewery, a taxicab company, a chain of bakeries, some old office buildings, some stores. But now the perpetual drive of Nyuk Tsin manifested itself with unbroken force, and as each item was listed she asked simply, "How much fee-simple land does it have?" And if Hong Kong said that it owned no land of its own, she snorted: "Strike it off. Even better than accumulated back losses is land." So the final list that the Kees were going to buy contained only companies with big losses and bigger parcels of land.

But when Nyuk Tsin heard Hong Kong's second list—the Kee holdings that were to be liquidated to cover the new purchases—she perceived with displeasure that the biggest project of all was missing, and she wondered why. Beginning querulously and with a piping voice she said, "This is a good list, Hong Kong."

Hong Kong smiled and observed expansively: "Well, I thought we might as well get rid of the old projects."

"But if I heard your list correctly," Nyuk Tsin continued softly, "there was no suggestion that we sell the land upon which we are now sitting."

Hong Kong looked with some embarrassment at his son Eddie, but neither spoke, so Nyuk Tsin continued: "Surely, if we need money for new ventures, we ought to sell first of all this old taro patch. And everything on it. Didn't you think of that?"

In a burst of confidence Hong Kong said, "Of course we thought of it, Wu Chow's Auntie. But we considered this land too precious to you. We cannot sell it during your lifetime."

"Thank you, Hong Kong," the old woman replied, bowing her thin gray head. "But one of the reasons why this idea of selling old businesses to go into new is appealing to me is that we will not only make money but we will also be forced into many new operations. We will have to work and will not be allowed to grow lazy and fat." She folded her hands, smiled at her clever men and added, "have you noticed, Hong Kong, how every Chinese family that tries to hold on to old businesses loses everything in the end?"

"But you always preached to us, 'Hold on to the land!' " Hong Kong protested.

"Ah, yes!" Nyuk Tsin agreed. "But not always the same land." Then she added, "Old land and old ideas must be constantly surrendered."

A new concept had come into the room, a concept of change and going-forwardness, and for some moments Hong Kong and his son contemplated the old woman's vision of a great family always in flux and always working hard to profit from it. The silence was broken by Nyuk Tsin, who said, "So we must sell this precious old land, Hong Kong, and in our liquidation, let it be the first to go."

"The land we will sell," Hong Kong said quietly, "but we will keep the old house for a little while longer. I could not imagine you living anywhere else."

"Thank you, my dutiful grandson," Nyuk Tsin replied. Then, briskly, she added, "So we must start this day teaching Bill how to run a brewery. Sam must study how to make money from bakeries, and I want Tom to begin reading about new ideas in architecture for old buildings." She proposed ways by which every losing venture they were about to buy could be transformed into a money-maker, and she warned: 'Hong Kong, you must study carefully to see that we acquire only the best land. Eddie, organize everything in the best business procedure. I must depend upon you two to keep your eyes on everything."

As the meeting was about to break up, the old matriarch said, "It's very exciting to see a family launching out into bold new projects. You'll be proud of this day, but remember, Hong Kong, as you buy, be very secret, and do it all at once. And when you buy, always allow yourself to be forced into paying a little more than the seller has a right to hope for. When your plan is understood by all, nobody must feel he's been cheated." She paused, then added, "But don't pay too much more."

Three weeks later, at a meeting of The Fort, bluff Hewlett Janders laughed and said, "If we didn't follow the old missionary law about no alcohol here, I'd send out and buy drinks all around."

"Good news?" John Whipple Hoxworth asked.

"The best. Just managed to unload the brewery. What a millstone it's been. My sainted grandmother told me once, if she told me a hundred times, 'No good will come of a Hale going into the brewery business.' And she was so right."

"Get a good price for it?" Hoxworth Hale asked.

"I got thirty-five thousand more than I ever hoped to," Janders replied. "I've been wanting to stick Hong Kong Kee ever since he pulled that fast one in buying the Gregory leases."

"Did you say Hong Kong?" Hoxworth asked.

"Yes. He slipped this time. Nobody can make money from that brewery."

"That's odd," Hale said. "I just sold Hong Kong the old Bromley Block. It's been losing money for years."

At this point one of the Hewletts arrived with the good news that he had unloaded the taxicab company. "To Hong Kong Kee?" a chorus asked.

"Yes, and at a good price," young Hewlett replied.

A gray silence fell over the board room while Hale looked at Janders and Janders at Hewlett. "Have we been made fools of?" Hoxworth asked slowly.

Finally dour John Whipple Hoxworth said, glumly, "I guess it's my turn to confess. I just sold Hong Kong that chain of bakeries we started before the war. Big losers."

"What's he up to?" Hewlett Janders cried. "What's that tricky Chinaman up to?"

"It must be real estate. He's buying property just to get real estate."

"No," one of the young Hewletts interrupted. "Because he just sold the old Kee taro patch. For a million five."

"My God!" Janders choked. "He's selling, he's buying. What's that wily sonofabitch up to?" The men looked at one another in exasperation, not so much because they were angry at Hong Kong, as because they suspected that he had some clever deal cooking, one which they ought to have anticipated for themselves.

The deal was clever; in truth it was, but only the first half. Anyone, if he had had the advice of a hard-working lawyer like Eddie Kee, could have bought losing firms and sold prosperous ones, making a nice profit on the transaction. That was clever. But what really counted was the fact that Bill Kee, backstopped by his father Hong Kong and his smart brother Eddie, was learning how to brew fairly good beer.

It wasn't easy, and some of the first batches, introduced by a florid advertising hullabaloo featuring the slogan "Kee Beer, Your Key to Happiness," was dreadful stuff which the local population christened "Chinese arsenic." But soon, with the aid of a Swiss-German whom the hui flew in from St. Louis, the beer began to taste reasonably palatable, and since it sold for a nickel a can less than others, workingmen began acquiring a taste for it. So without even considering the $1,800,000 worth of real estate on which the old Janders Brewery had sat, the Kee hui made a very strong profit out of that particular tax purchase.

But the big money-maker, to everyone's surprise, turned out to be the bakeries. Each store brought with it enough real estate so that of itself the deal was favorable, but Sam Kee, at the age of sixty-four, discovered a real affinity for selling cakes, and he showed substantial profits on each unit in the chain.

Not all the projects turned out so well. For example, the taxicab company resisted every attempt to make it pay, and finally Hong Kong reported to his grandmother: "This one is no good."

"Give it away," Nyuk Tsin replied.

"I hate to surrender so easily," Hong Kong protested. "There ought to be some way to make money out of taxicabs."

"Somebody else probably can," Nyuk Tsin agreed. "But not the Kees. Anyway, I don't like taxis. They seem to aim at me whenever I go out. By the way, I saw what Tom is doing to the old Bromley Block, and he's making it into quite a handsome building. If we had traded even, giving away the taro patch for the Bromley Block, we'd still have been ahead. I like to see the family working," she said.

And as the year ended, her hundred and fourth, she sat in her little house at midnight, and with a flickering oil lamp she undressed, until she stood completely naked, a tremendously frail old woman made up mostly of bones, and with the lamp moving cautiously near her body she inspected herself for leprosy. There were no spots on her hands, none on her torso, none on her legs. Now she sat down and lifted in turn each of her ungainly big feet. There were no spots on the toes, none on the heel, none at the ankles. At peace for another night, she slipped into a flannel nightgown, blew out the lamp, and went to sleep.

The coup which Nyuk Tsin had engineered had one unexpected result. The Fort, after it had an opportunity to study exactly what Hong Kong Kee had accomplished by his revolutionary manipulations, concluded, in the words of Hoxworth Hale: "We could use a man like that on some of our boards," and everyone agreed that the man had a master intellect.

After one of the meetings of Whipple Oil Imports, Incorporated, Hoxworth asked his fellow board member, jokingly, "Hong Kong, now that the Gregory's deal is over and nobody got too badly hurt, are you happy that you sneaked the outfit into Hawaii?"

"What do you mean?" Hong Kong asked.

"Well," Hoxworth pointed out amiably, for he was growing to like the clever Chinese whose business judgments usually proved sound, "Gregory's has been here for nearly five years. They've taken enormous sums out of the Territory, but what have they done for Hawaii?"

"Like what?" Hong Kong asked.

"Like museums, schools, libraries, medical foundations."

Hong Kong thought a while and said in apparent seriousness, "Every year the manager of Gregory's has his picture in the paper handing the community drive a check for three hundred dollars." Hale looked at his new friend in astonishment, and saw that Hong Kong was laughing. "They don't do very much for Hawaii," the Chinese admitted.

"And as the years go by, Hong Kong, you'll see that they do even less. You have a lot of Kees in Hawaii, Hong Kong. How many?"

"We figure that the old grandmother has over two hundred great-great-grandchildren, but not all of them are in Hawaii."

"Have you ever thought that each one of them will be cheated just a little bit if there are no new museums or orchestras? Put it the other way, doesn't everyone of your family who grows up here go to college on the mainland a little bit stronger because of what the old families did for the islands?"

"You're right!" Hong Kong agreed hastily. "And nobody expects Gregory's to copy you. But it looks to me, Hoxworth, as if we're entering a new age. We don't have to have handouts from above any longer. We pay good wages. We tax. We get the economy moving real fast. Everybody is better off. Even you."

"Have you ever heard of an art museum financed by taxation? Do you think the smart young Japanese who are coming up so fast will put aside one penny for a good university or an orchestra? Will a dozen Gregory's ever make a decent society?"

"Hoxworth, you're going to be surprised," Hong Kong assured him. "When we get a functioning democracy here, our boys are going to vote for museums, universities, medical clinics. And they'll tax their own people like hell to pay for them. Hawaii will be the paradise people used to talk about."

"I can't believe it," Hoxworth argued. "The good society is always the reflection of a few men who had the courage to do the right thing. It is never voted into being. It is never accomplished if it's left to the Gregory's of the world." But when they parted he said something that would have been totally unthinkable two years earlier: "By the way, Hong Kong, if you spot any smart young Japanese who are as intelligent as you are, let me know."

"What do you have in mind?" Hong Kong asked.

"You're doing so well on our boards we thought it might be a good idea . . ."

"It would be," Hong Kong said quickly. "If you pick up young Shigeo Sakagawa, you'll be getting a winner."

"Isn't he running for senator . . . on the Democratic ticket?"

"Yes."

"How could I take such a man onto our boards?" Hoxworth asked.

"You won't find any good young Japanese running on the Republican ticket," Hong Kong said flatly.

"What are you, Hong Kong?" Hale asked.

"When I was poor, I was a Democrat. Now that I have responsibilities, I'm a Republican. But I make my campaign contributions only to smart young men like Shigeo . . . and they always seem to be Democrats."

"Let's talk about this again, after the election," Hoxworth said, and for the first time he started listening to Shigeo Sakagawa's campaign speeches. But as the campaign grew hotter, he heard Shig saying one night: "All over the world nations have had to fight for land reform. In England they accomplished it by the vote, and things went well. In France they had to have a bloody revolution, and all went badly. I have worked in Japan for General MacArthur, giving great landed estates to the peasants, and all the time I worked there I said to myself, 'I ought to be home in Hawaii, doing the same thing.' Because I knew what you know. Hawaii is generations behind the times. Our land is held by a few big families, and they lease it out to us in niggardly amounts as they see fit . . ."

"The young fool's a communist," Hale snorted as he turned off the radio, and there was no more talk about inviting Shigeo Sakagawa to join The Fort.

A FTER THE PRESIDENTIAL elections in 1952, Congressman Clyde V. Carter of the Thirty-ninth District in Texas appointed himself a committee of one to investigate—for the fourteenth time—Hawaii's fitness for statehood. He reached Honolulu in mid-December bearing with him only three minor prejudices: he hated to the point of nausea anyone who wasn't a white man; he knew from experience that rich men were the saviors of the republic; and he loathed Republicans. Thus he was not completely happy in Hawaii, where rich men were invariably Republicans, and where sixty per cent of the people he met were obviously not Caucasian. In the first five minutes he decided: "This place must never be a state."

He was therefore surprised when the welcoming committee, consisting of Hoxworth Hale, Whipple Janders and Black Jim McLafferty, head of the Democratic Party in the islands, gave florid but hard-hitting defenses of statehood. He was particularly impressed by what Hoxworth Hale cried over the loudspeaker: "We are an American community here, with American ideals, American standards of public behavior and a truly American system of education. Congressman Carter, we citizens of Hawaii want you to move among us as a brother. Stop anyone you see. Ask us any questions you please. We are here to be inspected. We have no secrets." The crowd applauded.

Black Jim McLafferty was also impressive. He said in a flowing brogue, "Today we citizens of God's fairest group of islands welcome a distinguished congressman from the great State of Texas. We know, Congressman Carter, that our terrain, magnificient though it is, would be lost in the confines of your vast kingdom of Texas. I am reminded, sir, of a story I heard while serving with the air corps in England, when a loyal son of Texas, somewhat under the influence of Scotch, that wonderful beverage, shouted in a local pub, 'Why, Texas is so big, you can get on a train at El Paso and travel all day and all night and all the next day and all the next night, and when you wake up the next morning, where are you? You're still in Texas!' And the Englishman replied, 'I know how it is, Jack. We got trains like that in England, too.' "

When the crowd chuckled, the congressman bowed graciously and raised his hand to Black Jim, whereupon the Democrat continued: "But what may surprise you about Hawaii, sir, is that although you have always heard that these islands are rock-ribbed Republican, which is probably why you voted against statehood at the last two sessions, I want to tell you here and now that the islands are going to be Democratic, and even though my good friend Hoxworth Hale is doing his very damnedest to keep them Republican, I'm doing just the opposite to make them Democratic, so that when you finally admit us to the Union, sir, you will be able to boast to your constituents, 'I'm responsible for bringin' Hawaii into the Union, yassuh. Best Democratic state in America, after Texas.' "

This prospect so intrigued the congressman that he asked if he could meet with McLafferty, so the Irishman, never one to miss the pregnant moment, volunteered: "Ride into town with me, and we can talk." To the dismay of the welcoming committee, who had planned things rather differently, big, comfortable Congressman Carter settled down beside Black Jim as the latter steered his 1949 Pontiac—"Never drive a better car than fifty per cent of the people who have to vote for you," his father had decided, and Black Jim had found it a good rule.

"Do the islands really want statehood?" Carter asked, glad to be in private with a practicing politician.

"Sir, you can believe this one fact. The islands want to be a state."

"Why?" Carter asked. "We treat them real well in Congress."

"I'm sure that's what George the Third said about the colonies. 'Parliament treats them decently. Why do they want self-government?' That's why we fought the Revolution."

This marvelous bit of sophistry was quite lost on Carter, for as a boy he had lived along the Mexican border and the word *revolution* had no appeal to him whatever; were he able to repeal American history he would have done so, and the Thirteen Colonies would have gained their independence by the efforts of gentlemen in powdered wigs who made polite speeches. "What would you have under statehood that you now don't have?" he asked coldly.

"People usually answer that with some statement about taxation without representation, or the fact that under statehood we'd elect our own governor. But I have only one explanation, sir. If we were a state, we'd either elect or appoint our own judges."

"Don't you do so now?" Carter asked, for like most visitors to the islands, he knew nothing about them.

"Indeed we don't," Black Jim said with feeling. "They're appointed from Washington, and even when we have Democratic presidents, they usually appoint worn-out mainland Republicans."

"How does that hurt you?" asked Carter, who had once been a judge himself.

"We're a feudal society here . . ." McLafferty began, but again he used the wrong word, for the South Texas which Carter represented was also feudal, and as he recalled his happy youth, he rather felt that this was one of the better patterns of life. As McLafferty droned on, the congressman reflected: "By God, under a benevolent feudalism you didn't have Mexicans trying to tell decent men . . ."

"So the one vital thing," McLafferty concluded, "is to have judges from the islands. Because in our peculiar society here in Hawaii, the judges decide all the things that really matter."

"What's so wrong about that?" Carter asked.

"Congressman!" Black Jim cried, as he dodged a truck. "Hey, you! Manuelo!" he shouted at the Filipino. "You look good next time, maybe, eh?" And the little brown man yelled something back, happily, for that evening he would be able to tell his friends at the sugar plantation: "This afternoon I had a talk with Black Jim McLafferty." All the plantation hands knew him.

"What I was saying," the Irishman continued, "was that as long as judges from the mainland control the great trusts and the land laws, it's easy for the rich local Republicans to control the judges. Well, not control them, because our judges have been reasonably honest men, legally speaking, but the rich Republicans get next to them, and court decisions usually follow their interests." The more Carter heard about Hawaii, the less need he saw for change. In Texas, too, society was subtly rigged so that rich Democrats stayed fairly close to judges and legislators and got things their way. "Frankly," Carter thought, "what's wrong with that?"

He was therefore not too pleased with McLafferty—had him tagged as one of those radical northerners who call themselves Democrats—when the biggest blow of the day came. Black Jim had his offices on the ground floor of a building on Hotel Street, at the grubby edge of Chinatown, where Japanese and Filipino workmen were not afraid to visit him, and as he brought his car to the curb, Carter gasped: "Why these people are all slant-eyes."

"Almost half of the people in the islands are," McLafferty said offhandedly. "Some of the best citizens you ever saw. Only trouble I find is that most of the damned Chinese are Republicans. But I'm trying to change that."

"Can they be trusted?" Carter asked in honest fear.

"Maybe you better meet one of them," McLafferty laughed. "And there's no better one to meet than my partner . . ."

But Carter did not hear the words, for he saw to his astonishment that McLafferty, the head of the Democratic Party in Hawaii, had as his partner a Japanese: McLafferty and Sakagawa. And when Black Jim kicked open the door, the congressman saw, from the big poster inside, that this Japanese was running for office: "Sakagawa for Senator." And finally, beneath the poster he saw the Japanese himself, a crisp, crew-cut young man with polished manners and quiet deportment. Shigeo Sakagawa stuck out his hand and said, with a slight Boston accent, "Congressman Carter, we are proud indeed to welcome you to Hawaii."

The next moment was an agonizing one, for Shig's hand stayed out; the congressman, who had never before seen a Japanese face-to-face, simply could not take it. His jaw dropped as if he had been hit over the head by a falling oil derrick, and he stared at the fearsome, curious man before him. The expression on Shig's handsome face did not change as he lowered his hand. Belatedly Carter started to accept the greeting, moving his right hand slightly, but by then he saw that Shig had dropped his. Black-browed McLafferty, whom nothing fazed, said brightly, "Young Shig's going to be our first Democratic senator. He's going to win the unexpired term in the Nineteenth District."

"Good luck," Carter said awkwardly. "We need Democrats." He backed out of the office into the street, where the passing Orientals frightened him as he had rarely been scared in his life. Then, with a sigh of profound relief, he saw the big black automobiles of Hoxworth Hale and Hewlett Janders swing into view on Hotel Street, and he ran up to the cars as if their occupants were his brothers.

"We'll go now," he gasped with relief. Quickly jumping in beside Hale, and feeling himself secure at last in the Cadillac, he waved professionally at McLafferty and called, "Best of luck in the campaign."

When the big black cars had moved away, Black Jim started laughing. Slapping his leg, he returned to his office and continued laughing. "Shig," he cried, "hold out your hand!" And as Shig did so, his partner gave a hilarious burlesque of an American congressman, the friend of the people, desperately afraid to touch one of the people. "Shig," he laughed, "there's one vote for statehood we better not count on. But don't you worry about it, son. Do you know why I hauled that fat-ass sonofabitch down here to our offices? Not to give him a pitch about statehood, because what he thinks concerns me not at all. Look at the crowds outside! They're impressed that a United States congressman came down to Hotel Street to see you. Now get out there and walk over to the mailbox, casually, and post something."

"What?" Shig asked.

"I don't give a damn what. Fold up a piece of paper and stick it in the mailbox, as if you had congressmen visiting you all the time. And speak pleasantly to everybody." So Shig walked out among his constituents and acquired great face.

In the meantime, one of the recurring miracles of Hawaii was taking place. In the Roosevelt-Truman years, from 1932 to 1952, thousands of important Democratic politicians and officials passed through the islands, but they rarely saw any Democrats. At the airport or the dock they were met by either Hoxworth Hale or Hewlett Janders or by trim little John Whipple Hoxworth, and they were whisked away to the big houses of The Fort. They were fed well, wined to perfection, and told what to believe. Sometimes when the Japanese maids, in crisp white uniforms, had withdrawn, a Roosevelt appointee would ask timorously, "These Japanese, can they be trusted?" And The Fort invariably replied, "We've had Sumiko for eighteen years, and we've never known a better or more loyal maid."

At such parties the Roosevelt appointees met military leaders and stout island judges and cool, sharp Hoxworth Hale. Together these people created the impression of a solid citizenry, one that avoided scandal, one that honestly intended doing well, and one that was certainly content with things as they were. At public meetings the two men who could always be counted upon to give rousing speeches on behalf of statehood for Hawaii were Hoxworth Hale and John Whipple Hoxworth, and visiting statesmen were impressed by the arguments marshaled by these advocates, but in the privacy of The Fort these very men, without saying anything, always managed to convey an impression exactly the opposite of their speeches.

Hale always found occasion to comment: "There is one thing about our islands that you must not overlook. We have the finest judges in America." He would pause and then add, "We would truly deplore the day when Oriental lawyers, untrained in American values, took over the judgeships. We fear that the American way of life would be terminated at that instant."

"Not that the Orientals aren't brilliant," John Whipple Hoxworth usually interposed. "Perhaps clever's the word I'm looking for. They're able men, clever, but they aren't schooled in American values."

For nine languorous, pleasant days Congressman Clyde V. Carter of Texas got the standard Fort treatment, not knowing that every incident in his entertainment was leading up to the two climactic experiences reserved for visiting dignitaries. On the morning of the last day Hoxworth Hale observed brightly: "Congressman, we've been monopolizing you for more than a week, and you haven't really seen the islands for yourself. So we've arranged to drop out of the picture today. We've got a tour car for you, and we want you to go exploring." A long black car was waiting in the driveway, and Hoxworth introduced the driver. "This is Tom Kahuikahela, and he knows more about Hawaii than anyone you've met so far. Tom, this is a very important visitor, Congressman Carter. Take mighty good care of him."

Later, as Carter climbed out of the car to enjoy the glorious Pali, he found

Tom Kahuikahela at his elbow, whispering, "It's to men like you, Congressman, that all of us look for the salvation of Hawaii."

"What do you mean?" Carter asked.

"Don't give us statehood, Congressman. Please," the robust Hawaiian begged.

"I thought everybody was for statehood," Carter gasped.

"Oh, no! The Hawaiians tremble for fear you'll give us statehood."

"Why?" Carter asked.

"The day we become a state, the Japanese will capture the islands."

For the rest of that day an appalled Congressman Carter listened as his driver told him the truth about Hawaii: how the local Japanese had plotted to destroy Pearl Harbor; how they were trying to marry all the Hawaiian girls so as to destroy the race; how they craftily bought all the land; how they controlled the stores and refused to extend credit to Hawaiians; how the young Japanese lawyers were planning to steal control of the islands; how truly desperate things were. "The only thing that saves us, sir, are the appointed governor and the judges."

Several times Carter interrupted. "I thought it was the Chinese who owned the land," he suggested.

"They buy it only for the sly Japanese," the driver assured him.

"It looked to me as if Black Jim McLafferty was the head of the Democratic Party here, but you say the Japanese . . ."

"They're using him for a front man . . . just for a while . . . then they take over."

"But why doesn't a man like Hoxworth Hale . . . Now surely, he must know everything you've told me. Why hasn't he told me these things?"

"He's scared to," the driver whispered ominously. "Everybody's scared of what's happening, and that's why we have to depend on good men like you to save us."

"Do all Hawaiians feel this way?" Carter asked.

"Every one," Tom Kahuikahela replied. "We dread statehood."

But Congressman Carter had not stayed on top of Texas politics for twenty-four years by being a fool, and he knew that you often found out what a man was really talking about only when he was done with his main pitch and had relaxed. Then you could sometimes slip in a fast question and dislodge the truth, so that it came tumbling out, and now Carter probed: "Just what kind of government would you like to see in the islands, Tom?"

"Well I'll tell you, sir!" the big man replied, adding a dimension beyond what his employers, Janders and Hale, had paid for. "What I'm working for is the return of the monarchy."

"What did you have in mind?" Carter asked in a confidential manner.

"Well, I'd like to see a king back on the throne, with a Hawaiian senate and the old nobles sort of running things. The big laws could be made in Washington, because we don't really need a legislature with a lot of lawyers arguing all the time. And the king would give big parties and the palace would be restored."

"Where would the United States come in?" Carter asked, and to his surprise Tom had a good answer.

"Well, like I said, we'd want you to pass the big laws, and coin our money for us, and you'd control all of our foreign policy. Our secretary of state would be appointed by your President, with approval of your Senate."

"You say my President. Isn't he yours, too?"

"To tell you the truth, sir, he isn't. My family boycotted the annexation. We keep a Hawaiian flag at home. We pray for the day when the alii come back."

"Were your family alii?" Carter asked.

"Yes, sir," Tom replied.

And Carter muttered, "I think I'm beginning to understand Hawaii."

The average people of the islands had a pretty shrewd idea of what occurred when congressmen were driven around Oahu, and they called this gambit "government by taxi driver," but they respected the device as the most effective lobby in Hawaii. But on this day a Democratic spy at a filling station phoned Black Jim McLafferty and reported: "They've got Congressman Carter going around the island today. Giving him the taxi-driver needle."

McLafferty slammed down the phone and stared at his partner. "Shig," he confided, "they're giving our boy the old 'government by taxi driver' routine. And that can hurt."

"What can we do?" Shig asked.

The two tacticians studied the problem for a long time, and finally the Irishman snapped: "Shig, one way or another I'm going to get hold of our congressman. I'm going to bring him down here, and you're going to take him home with you. Show him an average Japanese family. But, Shig, you run over there right now and see that your dad's service flag is hanging on the wall in the front room. The one with two gold stars. And you get your mother's box, the one with the glass cover and all the medals, and you see that every goddamned medal is polished, and lying flat so our boy can read them. Now get going, and be back here, waiting, in half an hour. Because I'm coming back with Congressman Carter, dead or alive."

It was in this way that Congressman Clyde V. Carter, of Texas, became one of the few Democrats ever to meet a Democratic family during a visit to Hawaii. Black Jim spotted the tour car returning to Honolulu along Nimitz Highway, and he elbowed it over to the shoulder, explaining, "Congressman, I've just got a damned interesting cable from Democratic Headquarters in Washington, I thought you ought to advise me as to how I should answer it." McLafferty had peeled off the date line, trusting that Carter would fail to notice this, and his luck held, so while Carter was reading the complex message, Black Jim politely eased him out of the taxi and into the old Pontiac. "We'd better answer it at the office," he said.

When Carter entered the door of McLafferty and Sakagawa, there stood Shigeo waiting, and the young man said bluntly, "While Mr. McLafferty's answering the cable, I thought you might like to see a Japanese home. Just an average place." And although this was the last wish in Carter's mind, he could find no graceful escape, and a few minutes later he was being hauled into the Sakagawa cottage. "This whole thing's a transparent trick," he decided.

At the front door he met old and bent Mrs. Sakagawa, who knew little English and who wore funny Japanese sandals with things between the toes. Shig did the interpreting and said, "Mom, this is a famous United States congressman." Mrs. Sakagawa sucked in her breath audibly, and bowed. "And this," Shig said proudly, "is my bow-legged, tough-minded little father, Kamejiro Sakagawa." The old man sucked in his breath and bowed.

"Is he an American citizen?" Carter asked.

"Not allowed become citizen," Kamejiro said belligerently.

"That's right," Shigeo explained. "I am, because I was born here. But people like my father and mother, they were born in Japan."

"And they can't become citizens?" Carter asked in surprise. "Mexicans can."

Little Kamejiro stuck out his jaw and wagged his finger at the congressman: "Mexicans okay. Colored people okay. Anybody okay but not Japanese. How do you like dat?"

Congressman Carter, looking away from the argumentative little man, saw the service flag, with two blue stars and two gold. As a professional politician he automatically grew reverent and asked quietly, "Were you in service Mr.—" He couldn't recall the name.

"I and my three brothers," Shig said.

"And two gave their lives for America?" Carter asked.

In Japanese Shigeo asked, "Mom, where's that picture of the four of us in football uniforms?" His mother, who prized this picture above all others, found it and jabbed it into Carter's hands.

"This one is Tadao," Shigeo said of the fleet young halfback. "He died in Italy. This one is Minoru," he added. "He died in France. This is my brother Goro, a labor-union man . . ." And the spell was broken. That was all Congressman Carter required to hear, and he drew away from the picture of four average American boys. He had voted against the Norris-La Guardia Act and all of its successors, and he felt that to be a labor-union man was worse, in many respects, than being a Russian communist, because the Russians, God forgive them, didn't know any better, whereas a decent, God fearing American who . . . The speech was running in his mind, and Shigeo knew it. The two men drew apart.

And then, by one of those lucky flukes that save some meetings and wreck others, Mrs. Sakagawa thrust into the congressman's hand her glass box of medals, and in Japanese said, "These are Minoru's. These are Tadao's. These are Goro's. And these five are Shigeo's," As she said the latter, she patted her son on his arm, and communion was reestablished.

Carter studied the medals and said, "Your family accomplished a great deal."

"Congressman," Shig began quietly, "each of us boys had to fight his way to get into uniform. We had to be better soldiers than anyone else in the world." He felt words coming into his mouth that he would be ashamed of later, but he could no longer hold them back. "We performed as perhaps no other family of boys did in the last war. We accumulated wounds and glory, and by God, sir, when you refused to shake my hand the other day I almost wept. Because whether you know it or not, Congressman, I'm one of your constituents, and by God I will never again accept such treatment from you."

"Constituent?" Carter gasped.

"Yes, sir. Congressman, have you heard of the Lost Battalion?"

Carter had not only heard of it, he had orated about it; and in relief the words came back to him: "It was one of the high water marks of Texas bravery, sir."

"How many of your men died there, Congressman?" Shigeo pressed.

"Too many," Carter replied sorrowfully. "The scars upon Texas are great."

"Do you know why any escaped?" There was a pause, and Shig asked harshly, "Well, do you?"

"I supposed that the gallant fighters of Texas . . ."

"Horse manure!" Shig snapped. "Your men of Texas live today, sir, because my dead brother Minoru, one of the finest men who ever touched earth, and Goro and I led a gang of Japanese boys to their rescue. We lost eight hundred men rescuing three hundred Texans!" He cried bitterly, "I want you to read this." And from his wallet he produced a treasured card, and Carter took it and read it, and he saw that it had been signed by a friend of his, a governor of Texas, and it stated that in gratitude for heroism beyond the call of duty, Shigeo Sakagawa was forever an honorary citizen of the State of Texas. Said the card: "On our day of desperate need, you succored us."

Gravely Carter handed back the card, but as he did so, he kept his hand extended, saying, "In all humility, Mr. Sakanawa, I should like to shake your hand."

"I should like to shake yours," Shig said, and the moment could have been extremely fruitful for Hawaii statehood, except that Mr. Ishii choose this instant to break into his father-in-law's house with momentous news.

The skinny little man with eyes like bowls of frightened tapioca saw the tall stranger, hesitated and started to back out, but his wife Reiko-chan blocked the doorway, and Carter, always careful to catch the eye of a pretty girl, bowed in a courtly manner and said, "Have you come with your father?"

"He is my husband," Reiko-chan said in perfect English.

"This is a congressman, from Texas!" Shig announced proudly, and at this news Reiko-chan, who knew what her husband was up to, tried to edge him out of the house, but he had heard the word *congressman,* and now asked with compassion, "You come to arrange the surrender?"

"What surrender?" Carter asked.

In desperate embarrassment, Reiko-chan tugged at Mr. Ishii's sleeve, but she could not silence him. "The surrender of Hawaii to Japan," Mr. Ishii explained.

"How's that?" Carter asked.

"See what the paper says!" Mr. Ishii cried joyously, flashing the Honolulu *Mail,* which headlined: "Japanese Fleet to Make Courtesy Visit to Islands." When the paper had passed from hand to hand the excited little man cackled, "Long time, sir, I tell them, 'Japan won the war.' But nobody listen, so I ask you. 'If Japan lose, how their fleet come to Hawaii?' "

"Is he saying what I think he's saying?" Carter asked.

"He is a poor old man," Reiko-chan said softly. "Don't listen to him, Congressman."

But now Mr. Ishii produced a worn photograph of the Japanese surrendering on board the *Missouri.* "You can see who won," he explained. "The Americans had to go to Tokyo. And see how all the American admirals are without neckties, while the Japanese have their swords. Of course Japan won."

"And what will happen when your fleet gets here?" Carter asked.

"Japanese very honorable men, sir. You see tonight when they come ashore. They behave good." He went to the door, threw it open and pointed down to the blue waters of the Pacific, where a squadron of five warships steamed under the bold red flag of the new Japan. Mr. Ishii's heart expanded, and he forgave his wife for her years of arguing against him. From his coat he whipped out a Japanese flag, long hidden, and waved encouragement to the conquerors as they came to take control of Pearl Harbor.

"I guess we'd better be going," Carter said. "I have to catch the plane." But he was not fooled by crazy old Mr. Ishii, he knew that in the Sakanawas, as he called them, he had seen a tremendous American family, and he was impressed, so that when he got McLafferty's message that the Hales would pick him up at the corner of Fort and Hotel on the way to the airport, he said, "I'd just like to stand outside and watch the people for a few minutes."

* * *

And as he stood there in the late afternoon, in the heart of Honolulu, watching the varied people of the island go past, he had a faint glimmer of the ultimate brotherhood in which the world must one day live: Koreans went by in amity with Japanese whom in their homeland they hated, while Japanese accepted Chinese, and Filipinos accepted both, a thing unheard of in the Philippines. A Negro passed by and many handsome Hawaiians whose blood was mixed with that of China or Portugal or Puerto Rico. It was a strange, new breed of men Congressman Carter saw, and grudgingly an idea came to him: "Maybe they've got something. Maybe I wasted my time here in Hawaii, living in the big houses of the white people. Maybe this is the pattern of the future. That Japanese boy today, he's as good . . . Look at that couple. I wonder who they are. I wonder if they would mind . . ." But before he could speak to them, a long black car driven not by a chauffeur but Hewlett Janders drove up, and Hoxworth Hale jumped out to whisk the congressman back into reality. Icy John Whipple Hoxworth shared the front seat, and as the car slowly crept away from the turmoil of Hotel Street, the three senior citizens of Hawaii provided their guests with the second climax of any official visit to the islands.

Coldly, and with no inflection in his voice, Hoxworth Hale laid it on the line. He spoke rapidly and looked the congressman right in the eye. "Carter, he said, "you've seen the islands, and you've heard each man in this car make public speeches in favor of statehood. Now we've got to get down to cases. If you're insane enough to give us statehood, you'll wreck Hawaii and do irreparable damage to the United States. Save us from ourselves, sir."

Carter gasped. "Is that your honest opinion, Hale?"

"It's the opinion of almost every person you met in Hawaii."

"But why don't you . . ."

"We're afraid to. Reprisals . . . I don't know."

"Give me the facts straight," Carter said. "What's wrong with statehood?"

"This is in confidence?" Hale asked.

"You understand," Janders threw back over his shoulder, "that if you were to betray us, we'd suffer."

"I understand," Carter said. "That's often the case in governing a democracy."

"Here are the facts," Hale said simply. "The white man in Hawaii is being submerged. He has some financial power left, a good idea, I suppose. He has the courts to defend him, and an appointed governor upon whom he can rely. Sir, if you change any one of those factors, Hawaii will become a toy in the hands of Japanese. They'll control the courts and start bringing in decisions against us. They'll upset our system of land holding. They'll elect their own governor and send Japanese to Congress. Do you want to serve with a Jap?"

There was a long silence in the car, and more in the way of eliciting further information than in disclosing his own conclusions Carter replied, "This afternoon I met a Japanese, a young man named Shig Sakanawa, and for a while I thought that maybe . . ."

Janders spoke. "Did he tell you that his brother, Goro, was the leading communist in Hawaii? A proved, card-carrying, subversive, filthy communist. That's the brother of the man who's running for senator from this district. That's a picture of Hawaii under Japanese rule."

"I must admit," Carter said, "that nobody told me about this brother."

"The leader of the communist movement in Hawaii," Janders reiterated.

Carter was somewhat shaken to think how nearly he had been taken in by the plausible young Japanese lawyer, so he decided to check additional items of information. "By the way," he asked casually, "what's the sentiment out here for a return of monarchy?"

Up front Hewie Janders and John Whipple Hoxworth stared at each other in amazement and muttered, "Monarchy?" while in the back Hoxworth Hale gasped. Then he said forcefully, "Congressman . . ." but Hewie was now recovered and blurted out, "Jesus Christ, nobody in his right mind pays any attention to those monarchy crackpots."

"What were you about to say, Hale?" Carter pressed.

"As you may know, I'm descended from the royal alii of Hawaii, and my great-great-great-grandmother was one of the noblest women I've ever heard of. Her daughter was quite a girl, too. Magnificent. But if one of those pathetic, incompetent alii ever tried to get back to the throne of Hawaii, I personally would take down my musket and shoot him through the head."

"I'd do it first," Hewie Janders interrupted. "You know, sir, that Hale's great-grandfather brought Hawaii into the Union?"

"He did?" Carter asked.

"Yes," Hale said simply. "Practically by force of his own character. But I'd like to add this, sir. I'm also descended from the missionaries. And if one of them tried to come back and govern in the harsh, bigoted old way, I'd shoot him through the head, too."

"Let me get it straight then, what is it you want?"

"We don't want royalty, we don't want missionaries, and we don't want Japanese," Hale summarized. "We want things to go along just as they are."

It was a very somber carload of men that finally pulled up at the airport, and Black Jim McLafferty, as he watched them disembark, thought: "I'll bet they've been pumping that one with a load of poison." He started to join the congressman, but when Carter saw him coming, he retreated to the safety of Hewlett Janders, for he did not want to be photographed with a man, even though he was leader of the Democratic Party, who had as his partner a Japanese whose brother headed the Communist Party in the islands. "In fact," he mused as he checked his tickets, "Hawaii's a lot like most parts of the north. You can travel from state to state and never find a Democrat you really like. They're all either tarred with labor or communism or atheism or Catholicism. I'll be glad to get back to Texas."

And as he climbed aboard the Stratoclipper and sank into his comfortable seat he thought: "Basically, it's the same everywhere. A handful of substantial, honest men govern and try to hold back the mobs. If you can get along with those men, you can usually find out what the facts of the case are." He stared out the window glumly as Japanese airport mechanics wheeled away the steps while other Japanese waved wands directing the big airplane on its way. He closed his eyes and thought, "Well, I found out what I wanted. These islands won't be ready for statehood in another hundred years." And that took care of Hawaii for the eighty-third session of Congress.

I N 1952, PASSAGE of the McCarran-Walter Immigration Act was greeted with joy in Hawaii, for the new law permitted persons born in the Orient to become American citizens. Schools were promptly opened in which elderly Chinese and Japanese were drilled in the facts of American government, and it was not uncommon in those days to see old men who had worked all their lives as field hands reciting stubbornly: "Legislative, executive, judicial."

By early 1953 hundreds of Orientals were applying for the citizenship that had so long been denied them, and as Black Jim McLafferty watched this impressive stream of potential Democratic voters entering political life he made a speech in which he cried: "They built the islands, but they were kept outside."

It is true that many of the applicants did not really appreciate what citizenship meant, but on the other hand it was impressive to see old, weather-stained faces light up when the solemn words were pronounced by the federal judge: "You are now a citizen of the United States of America." And it was not uncommon to see a sedate businessman suddenly grab his old Japanese mother and swing her into the air with a joyous cry of, "I knew you could make it, Mom!"

The real heroes of these exciting days were the old people who had refused to learn English, but who now had to learn or forgo American citizenship. Their children screamed at them: "Pop, I told you for twenty years, learn to speak English. But no, you were too smart! Now you can't become a citizen."

"But why should I become a citizen now?" these old people asked. "Only a few more years."

Often the children broke into tears and sniffled: "You must learn English, Pop, because I have always wanted you to be an American."

"For me it is nothing," the old people said, "but if it will make you happy."

"It will, Pop! It'll remove the last stigma. Please learn English."

With a fortitude that is difficult to believe, these stubborn old Orientals went to the language schools. All afternoon they practiced: "I see the man," and most of the night they recited: "Legislative, executive, judicial." That so many mastered the two difficult subjects was a credit to their persistence, and when they finally received certificates they understood their value. In succeeding years, at mainland elections only about sixty per cent of the eligible voters bothered to vote; in Hawaii more than ninety per cent voted. They knew what democracy was.

In two Honolulu families the McCarran-Walter Act struck with contrasting effect. When Goro and Shigeo Sakagawa proposed to their tough old father that he enroll in the English school and get a book which explained the legislative, executive and judicial functions he surprised them by saying in unusually formal Japanese, "I do not wish to become a citizen."

Goro protested: "It's the opportunity of a lifetime!"

Continuing with his precise Japanese, Kamejiro said, "They should have made this offer fifty years ago, when I arrived."

"Pop!" Shigeo reasoned. "It's a new world today. Don't hark back to fifty years ago."

"For fifty years we were told, 'You dirty Japs can never become Americans.' For fifty years we were told, 'Go back to Japan.' Now they come to me and say, 'You're a fine old man, Kamejiro, and at last we are willing to let you become an American.' Do you know what I say to them? 'You are fifty years too late.' "

His sons were astonished to discover the depth of their father's feeling, so they turned to their mother and endeavored to persuade her, but before she could react to their pressures, old Kamejiro said flatly, "Yoriko, you will not take the examination. All our lives we were good citizens and we don't need a piece of paper to prove it now."

Then Shigeo produced two reasons which threw quite a different light on the matter. First he said, "Pop, last time I almost lost the election because people brought up that nonsense about Mr. Ishii and his crazy Japanese flag when the fleet visited here. They pointed out that he was my brother-in-law and that I probably felt the same way too. Now if you turn down citizenship they're going to shout, 'That proves it! The whole damned family is pro-Japanese!' "

Old Kamejiro reflected on this, and Shig could see that his father was disturbed, for none of the old Japanese had been more delighted during the last election than Kamejiro. He had stood for hours in his store, staring at the big poster of his son. "There our boy was," he proudly told his wife, "asking people to vote for him." When Shig won, the old man had paraded up and down Kakaako announcing the fact to all Japanese families, assuring them that at last they had a personal protector in Iolani Palace.

While Kamejiro twisted this first bait about in his mouth, Shig dangled another, more tempting than the first: "Pop, if you and Mom become citizens, in 1954 you can march up to the election booth, say, 'Give us our ballots,' and march inside to give me two more votes." Now Shig could see his father imagining election day, with himself striding to the polls, his wife trailing four feet behind. The old man loved nothing more than the panoply and ritual of life, and Shig could remember from his earliest days the pride with which his father dressed in Colonel Ito's uniform to stand beside the reciter. This had been the highlight of Kamejiro's life, matched only by the days in World War II when he saw his four sons march off to their own war. Therefore Shig was not prepared for what happened next.

"I will not take citizenship," the old man said resolutely. "If this hurts you, Shigeo, I am sorry. If my vote and Mother's cause you to lose the election, I am sorry. But there is a right time to eat a pineapple, and if that time passes, the pineapple is bitter in the mouth. For fifty years I have been one of the best citizens in Hawaii. No boys in trouble. No back taxes. So for America to tell me now that I can have citizenship, at the end of my life, is insulting. America can go to hell."

He would not discuss the question again. Once Shig and Goro approached him with the news that Immigration had a new rule: "People who have lived in the islands for a long time don't have to take their examinations in English. What that means, Pop, is that you and Mom can now become citizens without bothering with the language school."

"It would be insulting," Kamejiro said, and the boys withdrew.

Shig talked the problem over with McLafferty, and his partner said, "Hell, your old man's right. It's as if they had told our people in Massachusetts, 'We kicked you Catholics around for two generations. Now you can all become Protestants and run for office.' Like he says, it would have been insulting."

"I don't think there's any analogy," Shig said coldly.

"Probably you're right," the Irishman agreed. "But it sounds good if the other guy doesn't listen too close."

"This may hurt me in the next election," Shig said carefully.

McLafferty boomed: "Shig, if your old man hadn't always been the way he is now, you wouldn't be the kind of guy you are. And if you weren't that kind of person, I wouldn't want you for a partner. What he's given you, nobody can take away."

"Yes, but he's become so provoked about this he says he's going back to Japan to live."

"He won't like it," McLafferty predicted.

"Wouldn't that hurt me in the election?" Shig pressed.

"My father found," McLafferty said, "that just a little scandal helped rather than hurt. It made the electorate feel that the candidate was human. That's why

I warned you about never disclosing in a lawsuit that a witness kept a mistress. For sure, somebody on the jury has either had a mistress—or if she's a woman, has been one—and your evidence is bound to backfire, because the juror says, 'Hell, I had a mistress, and I'm no scoundrel.' So if your old man acts up, Shig, it won't hurt you . . . not with the people whose votes we want . . . because their old folks act up too." And that was the end of Kamejiro Sakagawa's citizenship.

With Nyuk Tsin the case was quite different. From the day she had landed in Honolulu eighty-eight years before, she had forsworn forever the starving villages of China and had determined to become a permanent resident of Hawaii. When the United States annexed the islands, she desperately sought American citizenship, but to no avail. From her frail body had descended some seven hundred American citizens, and not one had so far been in jail. In a lockbox she still kept her tax receipts covering nearly a century, and when she heard that there was a chance that she might become an American citizen, truly and without limitation, she felt that she could know no greater joy.

She therefore had her Harvard-trained great-grandson, Eddie Kee, study the new law and heckle the Immigration authorities until she understood every nuance. When the first language class convened, she was present, and although she was well over a hundred years old at the time, she drove her eager brain to its extent, and in the evenings sat listening to the English-language radio. But she was so ingrained in Chinese thought that English escaped her, and one night she faced up to her failure. She told Hong Kong, "I can't learn the language now. Why didn't somebody force me to learn it years ago? Now I shall never become a citizen." And she looked disconsolately at her grandson.

But then Eddie arrived with the exciting news that certain elderly Orientals would be allowed to take the examinations in their own tongue, provided they were literate in it, and at this news Nyuk Tsin covered her old eyes for a moment, then looked up brightly and said, "I shall learn to write."

Hong Kong therefore hired a learned Chinese to teach the old woman what was undoubtedly the most difficult language in the world, but after a while it became apparent that she was simply too old to learn, so Eddie went to the Immigration authorities and said honestly, "My great-grandmother is a hundred and six, and she wants more than anything else in the world to become an American citizen. But she can't speak English . . ."

"No trouble!" the examiner explained. "Now she can be examined in Chinese."

"But she can't read and write Chinese," Eddie continued.

"Well!" The examiner studied this for a while, then went into the back office, and in a moment Mr. Brimstead, an official from Washington, appeared with one question: "You say this old woman is a hundred and six?"

"Yes, sir."

"She got a family?"

"Probably the biggest in Hawaii."

"Good! We've been looking for something dramatic. Pictures we could use for publicity in Asia. You get the family together. I'll give her the exam myself and we'll waive the literacy. But wait a minute. Is she able to answer questions. I mean, is she competent?"

"Wu Chow's Auntie is competent," her great-grandson assured him.

"Because on the questions I can't fudge. You know: legislative, executive, judicial."

"Can I accompany her, to give her moral support?"

"Sure, but our interpreters will report her answers, and they have to be right."

"She will be right," the young lawyer guaranteed.

He therefore entered upon a long series of cramming sessions with his great-grandmother, teaching her in the Hakka tongue the many intricacies of American government, and this time, with citizenship hanging like a silver lichee nut before her, she summoned her remarkable energies and memorized the entire booklet.

"The father of our country?" Eddie shouted at her.

"George Washington."

"Who freed the slaves?" Hong Kong drilled.

"Abraham Lincoln," the little old woman replied, and Eddie reflected: "It's difficult to believe, but she came to Hawaii in the year that Lincoln died."

On the day of her examination, the Immigration Department assembled several newsreel cameras, officials in white coats, and about two hundred members of the Kee hui, who were told to cheer when the old lady arrived in Hong Kong's Buick. When she stepped down, brushing aside Eddie's arm, she was very short, weighed less than ninety pounds, and was dressed in an old-style black Chinese dress above which her nearly bald head rose with its deep-set eyes, legendary wrinkles and anxious smile. She did not speak to her accumulated family, for she was repeating in her mind many litanies alien to ancient China: "The capital of Alabama is Montgomery; Arizona, Phoenix; Arkansas, Little Rock; California, Sacramento."

The cameras were moved into the examination room, and an announcer said in a hushed voice, "We are now going to listen in upon a scene that is taking place daily throughout the United States. A distinguished elderly Chinese woman, Mrs. Kee, after nearly ninety years of life in America, is going to try to pass her examination for citizenship. Mrs. Kee, good luck!"

"At the mention of her name, which in that form she did not recognize, Nyuk Tsin looked at the cameras, but her great-grandson said hurriedly, "Look over here. This is the examiner, Mr. Brimstead," and the announcer explained who the distinguished visitor from Washington was. The lights were adjusted; Nyuk Tsin began to sweat in nervous apprehension; and Mr. Brimstead, who was proving to be quite a ham on his first appearance before a camera, asked in a sweetly condescending voice, "Now tell us, Mrs. Kee, who was the father of our country?"

The official interpreter shot the question at the old lady in Hakka, and both Hong Kong and Eddie smiled superiorly, because they knew that Wu Chow's Auntie knew that one.

But there was silence. The cameras ground. Mr. Brimstead looked foolish and the Hakka interpreter shrugged his shoulders. "Wu Chow's Auntie!" Eddie whispered hoarsely. "You know. The father of our country!"

"Now, no coaching!" Mr. Brimstead rebuked. "This has got to be an honest examination."

"I wasn't coaching," Eddie pleaded.

"He didn't say nothing," the interpreter said in English.

"All right!" Mr. Brimstead snapped. "No coaching. Now, Mrs. Kee," and his voice was all honey again, "who was the father of our country?" Again the interpreter droned in Hakka and again there was silence. In agony Hong Kong stared at his grandmother and opened and shut his fingers by his mouth, signifying, "For God's sake, say something."

But the scene was too vital for old Nyuk Tsin to absorb. All her life she had wanted to belong: first to her brave and gallant father, whose head had perched in the village square; then to her Punti husband, who had scorned her big feet; then to her children, who were afraid of her possible leprosy; then to America, which had repulsed her as it did all Orientals. Now, when all that she hoped for was attainable, she fell mute. She heard no questions, saw no men, felt nothing. But she sensed inwardly that some golden moment, some crystal opportunity that would never come again was slipping by, and she looked up with mute anguish at the people about her.

She saw kindly Mr. Brimstead, almost wetting his pants in his eagerness for her to say something so that he could appear in the moving pictures. She saw bright young Eddie, who had coached her. She saw resolute Hong Kong, who must be praying for her to save the family reputation. And then over Hong Kong's shoulder she saw an official government etching of a long-dead hero with a determined chin and a three-cornered hat, and she heard as from a great distance the Hakka interpreter begging for the last time, "Mrs. Kee, tell the man, who was the founder of our country?" And with the floodgates of passion breaking over her, she rose, pointed at the etching of George Washington, and screamed, "That one!"

Then she started: "The capital of Alabama is Montgomery; Arizona, Phoenix; Arkansas, Little Rock; California, Sacramento . . ."

"Tell her that's enough!" Mr. Brimstead shouted. "I didn't ask that question yet."

"Keep those cameras grinding," the director shouted.

"You!" Hong Kong shouted at the interpreter. "Keep interpreting."

"The legislative passes the laws," Nyuk Tsin cried, "and the executive administers them and the judicial judges them against the Constitution."

"It's enough!" Mr. Brimstead shouted. "Tell her it's all right."

"And the Bill of Rights says that there shall be freedom of worship, and freedom of speech," Nyuk Tsin continued. "And no troops may search my house. And I may not be punished in cruel ways." She was determined to omit nothing that might swing the decision in her favor. "There are two houses in Congress," she insisted, "the Senate and the House . . ."

When she left the Immigration building, with her citizenship proved and in her hand, the Kees who had been waiting outside cheered, and she passed happily among them, speaking to each and asking, "What is your name?" and when they told her, she was able to place each one. And as she ticked off her great family she realized for the first time that they were neither Hakka nor Punti, for in Hawaii those old enmities had dissipated and all who had arrived in the *Carthaginian* had been transmuted into something new. In truth, the Kees were not even Chinese; they were Americans, and now Nyuk Tsin was an American too. Standing by Hong Kong's car she whispered, "When you are a citizen, the earth feels different."

But these fine words did not erase from Hong Kong's memory the anxiety he had suffered when in the examination room his auntie had sat in stolid silence like a Chinese peasant and now when he looked down at her citizenship paper, his former irritation returned and he protested with some petulance: "Oh, Wu Chow's Auntie! You didn't even pick up the right paper." He took the document from her and showed her where the strange name was written: Char Nyuk Tsin. But when he had read this name aloud to her, she said quietly and yet with great stubbornness, "I told the helpful man, 'Now that I am an American you must write on this paper my real name.' " And she climbed purposefully into the car, a small old woman who had made a great journey.

That night, terribly tired from the ordeal of citizenship, she lit her oil lamp, undressed, and inspected herself for leprosy. There were no lumps on her arms; her fingers were still good; her face was not deformed; and her legs were clean. Greatly relieved, she put the lamp on the floor so that she could examine her big feet, and in the morning Hong Kong found her there, a frail, naked, old dead body of bones, beside a sputtering lamp.

As thousands of once-proscribed Orientals gained citizenship and the vote, and as labor attained fresh power, haoles gloomily predicted that their day in Hawaii was ended, and no one felt this more strongly than Hoxworth Hale, for he was passing through a period of mist and fog, and his bearings were insecure: he was unable to understand his mercurial daughter or to communicate with his elfin-minded wife, who flitted from one inconsequential subject to the next. He tried diligently to maintain control of both H & H and of Hawaii, but he suspected that each was slipping away from him. Finally, the great pineapple crisis of 1953 struck and it looked as if Hawaii itself were crumbling.

The disaster first became known when a luna on Kauai inspected one of the far fields and discovered that all the plants which should have been a rich bluish green were now a sickly yellow. He immediately thought: "Some damn fool forgot to spray for nematodes." But when he consulted the records, he found that the field had been sprayed to control the tiny worms, so one of the pineapple botanists employed by The Fort flew over to inspect the dying plants and said, "This isn't nematodes. As a matter of fact, I don't know what it is."

In the second week of the blight, the once-sturdy plants fell over on their sides, as if some interior enemy had sapped their vitality, but there were no scars, no boring insects, nothing. The botanist became frightened and phoned Honolulu to discover that plants on scattered fields through the islands were beginning to show similar symptoms.

It would be an understatement to say that panic struck the pineapple industry. A raging fear swept the red fields and echoed in the Fort Street offices. Hoxworth Hale bore the brunt of the anxiety, because H & H had a good deal of its wealth in pineapples, while outfits like Hewlett's and J & W, who looked to him for leadership, were even more vulnerable. The loss in one year alone threatened to exceed $150,000,000, and still the botanists had no clue as to what was happening to their precious charges.

The famous Englishman, Schilling, who had licked mealybugs and nematodes, was now dead, but research scholars went through his papers to see if he had left any clues as to further apprehensions. But that was only a figure of speech, for the drunken expert had left no orderly papers and no suggestions. He had died one night in a fit of delirium tremens in a poverty ward on the island of Kauai, the nurses not recognizing who he was until after his death. Nevertheless, the botanists repeated all of Schilling's work on the pineapple and assured themselves that the fault lay not with iron, nor bugs, nor nematodes. They discovered nothing about the current disease except that hundreds of thousands of plants seemed determined to die.

In desperation, Hoxworth Hale suggested: "We know we're being attacked either by some invisible virus or by some chemical deficiency. It doesn't seem to be the former. Therefore, it's got to be the latter. I am willing to spray-feed every plant in the islands. But what with?"

A young chemist from Yale suggested: "We know the complete chemical component of the pineapple plant. Let's mix a spray which contains everything that might possibly be lacking. We'll shoot blind. At the same time, you fellows compare by analysis a hundred dead plants with a hundred unaffected ones. Maybe you can spot the deficiency."

The young man mixed a fantastic brew, a little of everything, and sprayed one of the dying fields. Almost as if by magic the hungry plants absorbed some tiny, unspecified element in the concoction, and within two days were both upright and back to proper color. It was one of the most dramatic recoveries in the history of pineapple culture, and that night for the first time in several months, Hoxworth Hale slept peacefully. In the morning his board asked him, "What was it that saved the crop?"

"Nobody knows. Now we're going to find out."

He encouraged the scientists, who withheld from the magic brew one component after another, but the fields responded dramatically no matter what was sprayed on them; and then one day zinc was omitted, and that day the plants continued to die.

"Zinc!" Hale shouted. "Who the hell ever heard of adding zinc to pineapple soils?"

Nobody had, but over the years the constant leaching of the soil and the introduction of chemical fertilizers had minutely depleted the zinc, whose presence to begin with no one was aware of, and when the critical moment was reached, the zinc-starved plants collapsed. "What other chemicals may be approaching the danger line?" Hale asked.

"We don't know," the scientists replied, but prudence warned him that if zinc had imperceptibly fled from the fields, other trace minerals must be doing so too, and he launched what became perhaps the most sophisticated development in the entire history of agriculture: "We are going to consider our famous red soil of Hawaii as a bank. From it we draw enormous supplies of things like calcium and nitrate and iron, and those are easy to replace. But we also seem to draw constant if minute supplies of things like zinc, and we haven't been putting them back. Starting today, I want the chemical components of every scrap of material harvested from our pineapple fields analyzed and their total weight calculated. If we take out a ton of nitrate, we'll put a ton back. And if we withdraw one-millionth of a gram of zinc, we're going to put the same amount back. This marvelous soil is our bank. Never again will we overdraw our account."

It was strange what depletions the scientists found: zinc, titanium, boron, cobalt, and many others. They were present in the soil only in traces, but if one vanished, the pineapple plants perished; and one night when balance had been restored to the vast plantations, and the economy of Hawaii saved, Hoxworth Hale, who had refused to surrender either to nematodes or to the depletion of trace minerals, suddenly had a vision of Hawaii as a great pineapple field: no man could say out of hand what contribution the Filipino or the Korean or the Norwegian had made, but if anyone stole from Hawaii those things which the tiniest component added to the society, perhaps the human pineapples would begin to perish, too. For a long time Hale stood at the edge of his fields, contemplating this new concept, and after that he viewed people like Filipinos and Portuguese in an entirely different light. "What vital thing do they add that keeps our society healthy?" he often wondered.

When Hong Kong Kee had served on various boards of The Fort for a testing period the unbelievable happened. He was summoned to the chambers of Judge Harper, who had married one of the Hoxworth girls, and was advised by that careful Texan: "Hong Kong, the judges have decided to appoint you one of the trustees of the Malama Kanakoa Estate."

Hong Kong stepped back as if the good judge had belted him across the face with a raw whip. "You mean that without applying, I've been appointed?"

"Yes. We felt that with Hawaii's commerce and politics falling more and more into the hands of our Oriental brothers, certain steps ought to be taken to recognize that fact."

In spite of his cynical knowledge of how The Fort and its ramifications operated, Hong Kong was visibly moved by the appointment, for he knew that when the evening papers revealed this story the extent of the Hawaii revolution could no longer be ignored. With bright young Japanese politicians taking over the legislature, the only remaining bulwark of the old order was the great trusteeships, and for The Fort voluntarily to relinquish one was an event of magnitude. Hong Kong was therefore inspired to complete frankness, for he wanted to be sure that Judge Harper knew what he was doing.

"I am deeply touched by this gesture, Judge Harper," he said with real humility. "I guess you know what it means to be the first Chinese on such a board. You judges are giving me an accolade I'll never forget. But do you know how I stand on land tenure? Leasehold? Breaking up the big estates that don't use their land creatively? You understand all those things, Judge?"

Big Judge Harper laughed and pointed to a paper on his desk. "Hong Kong, you apparently forget who your brother trustees will be. Hewlett Janders and John Whipple Hoxworth. You think they're going to let you run wild with any crazy idea?"

"But even with such men, Judge, ideas repeated often enough sometimes catch on . . . where you least expect them."

"We judges think you're the kind of man who will bring good new ideas, but we certainly aren't going to back you against your two fellow trustees."

"I'm not looking for a fight, Judge."

"We know. That's why we've appointed you. But before you take the job, Hong Kong—and I appreciate even better than you how signal an honor this is, because we have been petitioned for years to appoint some Oriental—I want you to understand with crystal clarity the nature of the task you're undertaking." The big man adjusted his considerable bulk in his judge's chair and told his secretary he didn't want to be interrupted.

"The very existence of Hawaii, Hong Kong, depends not upon what cynical outsiders like to term The Fort. The outsiders are wrong. It's not The Fort that controls Hawaii. It's the sanctity of the great trusts. They form the solid backbone of our society. The Fort is only the ribs and the people are our flesh. But the backbone has to be kept strong, and it is up to us judges to be its guardians.

"The trusts control the land and establish the systems of tenure. They control the sugar and the pineapple fields. They continue, where companies rise and fall. They remain productive while the families who profit from them subside into decay. Look at the one you're entering. It controls millions of dollars in the vital heart of Hawaii, for whom? For a dear old Hawaiian lady and her no-good beachboy son. We judges don't spend our time worrying about that trust because we're interested in those two poor Hawaiians. They aren't worth it. But the idea that Malama Kanakoa and her son Kelly are assured of a square deal from the courts is terribly important.

"What I have to say next, Hong Kong, I don't want to say sitting down." The big man rose, adjusted his dark brown suit, and pointed directly at his

Chinese visitor. "In the history of our great trusts, there has never been a scandal because some trustee stole money. There have been no defalcations, no illegal conversions, no overtrading for personal commissions, no theft. The trustees have often been accused of being too conservative, but in a trustee that's not a weakness. It's a virtue. Hong Kong, so long as we were satisfied to choose our trustees from the missionary families we enjoyed a spotlessly clean record. We're now branching out, and in a sense we're taking a risk. If you make one error, I personally will hound you out of the islands. The courts will never rest till you're behind bars. If you want to do one thing which will set the Orientals in Hawaii back three generations, abuse the Malama Kanakoa Trust." He sat down, smiled at Hong Kong, and added, "Of course, if you want to prove to our entire society that Orientals are as responsible as the missionaries ever were, you have that opportunity, too."

Hong Kong wished that his grandmother were alive to guide him at this moment, but he felt that she would have counseled courage, so he said bluntly, "What will you judges say when I recommend that Malama Kanakoa go mostly into some pretty radical investments?"

Judge Harper thought this one over a long time and finally said, "One of the reasons why we judges decided to appoint you to Malama's trust is that Hoxworth Hale told us about your investing ideas. He said they ought to be looked into, that maybe they were the answer to some of these trusts with vast back-tax structures."

"Then Hoxworth Hale got me this job?" Hong Kong asked.

"You misunderstand, Hong Kong. I appointed you."

The Chinese bowed slightly, but could not keep from smiling, and soon Judge Harper joined him. Rising from his desk and putting his arm about Hong Kong's shoulders, he said, "Let's put it this way. If you turn out badly, Hoxworth doesn't suffer the opprobrium. I do. Hong Kong, you are really going to be watched. By me."

"What do they call these Negroes who are the first to move into a white neighborhood?" Hong Kong laughed. "The blockbusters? Looks as if I'm the trustbuster."

"The word has an entirely different meaning," Judge Harper pointed out amiably, but when the able Chinese had gone he had a moment of nostalgic reflection, saying to himself, "He's probably right. Appointing him was probably the beginning of the end . . . at least of the safe, comfortable honest old system we knew."

Hong Kong drove immediately home and asked the cook, "Where is Judy?" and when he found that she was teaching at the conservatory, he drove there and went in to fetch her. Since the death of Nyuk Tsin, the oldest woman of his family, he had found himself drawing markedly closer to Judy, his youngest girl. He liked women's habits of thought, and he particularly appreciated Judy's cool, clean reasoning. After a few minutes she joined him, a sparkling, winsome Chinese girl of twenty-six, with two braids down her back, a starched pink dress and wide, clever eyes. She bounced into the Buick and asked, "What's up, Dad?"

"I want you to accompany me to a very important meeting. I've just been appointed a trustee for the Malama Kanakoa Trust."

"Are the judges out of their minds?" Judy chortled.

"The Fort has the ability to see the inevitable," her father said.

"Where are we going?" Judy asked.

"I want to see Malama. I'd like to find out what her ambitions are, her hopes for the land she owns, and at the same time doesn't own."

"Dad! You know Malama won't have any ideas."

"That's what everybody has said for years. But I suppose she's as bright as you and I, and I'd like to find out."

He drove toward Diamond Head until he crossed the Ala Wai canal, then turned into the gate at the board fence that surrounded the Swamp. When he drew up to the shingled house, with its spacious porch, Malama thrust open the screen door and appeared with a gigantic smile, her silver hair disheveled and her dress askew. "Hong Kong, the defender of my interests, come in! The judges told me last night!" With widespread arms she welcomed him, and Judy saw with some surprise that her father had had foresight enough to purchase a flower lei for his first visit. Graciously he bestowed it upon the woman who towered over him, then leaned up to give her two kisses while she beamed.

"Come in, my good friends!" she said expansively, adding, with the instinct that marked Hawaiians, "I never thought I should see the day when a distinguished Chinese banker was appointed one of my guardians. It is a happy day for me, Hong Kong. Your people and mine have blended well in the past, and I hope this is a good augury for the future."

"It's a new day in Hawaii, Malama," he replied.

"And is this your lovely daughter?" Malama asked, and when Hong Kong said that it was, she laughed and said, "In the old days I could never tell, when I saw a rich Chinese with a young girl, whether she was his daughter or his number four wife."

"I feel the same way when I go to a night club in New York," Hong Kong replied happily, "and see the haole bankers and their companions. We poor Chinese aren't allowed to get away with plural marriages any longer . . . only the haoles."

"I want you to meet my friends," Malama chuckled. "We gather now and then for some Hawaiian music. This is Mrs. Choy, Mrs. Fukuda, Mrs. Mendonca and Mrs. Rodriques."

Hong Kong bowed to each of the huge ladies and then returned to Mrs. Choy. "You the pretty girl named after the race horse?"

"Yes," Mrs. Choy laughed gaily. "My name is Carry-the-Mail. You see, Father won a lot of money on that horse."

"I know! My grandmother found out that my father had bet a lot of money on Carry-the-Mail, and she gave him hell, but the horse won. So my father and your father probably got drunk together, Mrs. Choy," Hong Kong said easily, and the women laughed.

"This is my daughter Judy, the musician. She has a job at the conservatory."

"How wonderful!" Malama cried, shoving a ukulele at the lovely Chinese girl, who slipped easily and without embarrassment into the great frieze of Hawaiian ladies who lined the wall of the chandeliered room. "You won't know the words, but you can hum." And the six women began an old Hawaiian song from the days when royalty lived at Lahaina, on Maui. It was true that Judy Kee knew none of the words, but she harmonized well, and once the others stopped singing while she vocalized a verse, and Mrs. Choy cried, "If we could do something about those slant-eyes, we could make her into a good Hawaiian."

The crowd laughed and Hong Kong asked easily, "What I'd like to find out, Malama, is what are the opinions of a Hawaiian who is placed on a spendthrift trust?" It was like asking the Pope his impressions of Martin Luther, but Hong Kong's blunt approach often proved best, and this was an occasion when it did, for all the Hawaiian ladies were interested in this question, which affected many of their friends.

"I'll tell you, Hong Kong," Malama confessed, as she asked Judy to help her serve tea. "I graduated from Vassar with very good grades, and I was shocked when the court said, 'You are not competent to handle your own affairs. We will pay three white men huge salaries to do it for you.' This was insulting, and I tried to fight back, but then I remembered what the sweet haole teachers had taught us at Hewlett Hall. I was Hawaiian. I was different. I was supposed to be incompetent, so I relaxed and found no shame in being judged a spendthrift. I love my friends, I love a guitar well played, I love the Swamp, so I have rather succumbed to the passing of the days. A little friendship, the birds in the Swamp . . . until I die. I am a spendthrift, so I suppose I deserve to be disciplined by a spendthrift trust."

Mrs. Fukuda said, "What always infuriates white men, and frugal Japanese like my husband, is the way a woman like Malama gives things to her friends. This they cannot understand. In their pinched and miserable hearts they can't understand it."

"What's money?" Malama asked.

"How much does the spendthrift trust allow you?" Hong Kong asked.

"I don't blame the trustees," Malama evaded. "When the courts stepped in I'd worked things around so that I owed the federal government $350,000 in back taxes. Somebody had to do something. So now all I get is $22,000 a year for myself."

"And all her friends," Mrs. Mendoca said. "After all, she is an alii nui and she does have some obligations."

"How do you like the system?" Hong Kong repeated.

"I neither understand it nor like it," Malama replied.

"Malama," Hong Kong said bluntly. "I'm going to make some radical investments for you. You'll have two very lean years, and you're going to make some kind of deal with the federal government, but if you behave, in three years you'll be off the spendthrift trust."

The faces of the five Hawaiian women bloomed like flowers after a providential rain, and Hong Kong could see them envisaging endless parties, good food, new automobiles and trips to Europe, like in the old days, but Hong Kong warned bleakly, "And when you're off the spendthrift trust, you'll be under my supervision, and you know a Chinese is ten times tougher than a haole judge."

The Hawaiians laughed, for this was the truth, and Malama cried, "I hope we can do it, Hong Kong." She kissed him on both cheeks as she placed over his head the lei he had previously given her. "I am not joking when I say that Hawaiians and Chinese have always been good for one another."

She was about to cite examples when she was interrupted by the screen door's banging open suddenly, then slamming shut as someone retreated down the porch. "Kelly!" Malama cried. "Come on in. It's only Hong Kong."

The tall beachboy shuffled into the room, barefoot, in his tight knee-length pants and waiter's jacket that failed to cover his rugged chest. He wore a yachting cap far back on his head, and his black hair was uncombed. "Apternoon, Hong Kong," he grunted.

"We've been talking about plans for the trust," Malama said graciously as she handed her son a cup of tea. He brushed it aside and plucked a few notes on his mother's ukulele.

"You da new trustee da kine?" Kelly said.

"Yes," Hong Kong said with obvious distaste for the pidgin.

"I speak true. You akamai dis trust, you fix heem up, you one damn good pella." He banged the ukulele and pointed at his mother, adding, "Because dis wahine spend, spend." He motioned with his uke to Mrs. Fukuda, who began strumming hers, and soon the women were singing, but as they entered into one of their most loved songs Kelly was aware of a Chinese voice, high and lyrical, and while he continued plunking his ukulele, he studied with approval the relaxed manner in which Hong Kong's daughter sang. Then he paid no more attention to her, but at the end of the song he grabbed a guitar and began a throbbing slack-key solo, to which the other instruments gradually joined in subdued harmonies. Finally, when the slack-key had ended, with its intricate fingerings echoing in the air, Kelly plucked the first few chords of the "Hawaiian Wedding Song," then threw the guitar to Mrs. Fukuda and rose to begin the majestic male solo. When it came time for the soprano to enter, he pushed his mother into the background, and with his right hand imperiously grabbed Judy and brought her to her feet. At the appropriate moment, he pointed at her, and for the first time in Hawaii an impressed audience heard the Chinese girl soar into the upper reaches of this passionate evocation of the islands. Her voice was like a clear bell in some inland church where a true wedding was being performed, and when it came time for Kelly to join her, he did not fool around with falsettos or effects; he projected his handsome baritone until it filled the old room and caused the chandelier to sway. In the final passages Malama and the four big Hawaiian women hummed softly, so that Hong Kong remained the only listener. Against his will, for he did not like his daughter singing Hawaiian songs, he had to applaud, and the four visiting women cheered and Kelly leaped into the other room and returned with a length of tapa, which he twisted about Judy's waist. He stuck three flowers into her braids and used his right forefinger as if it were a make-up pencil, dabbing it about her eyes.

"She gonna look more Hawaiian than I do," he cried. Then he pointed in turn at each of his mother's guests. "Choy!" he cried. "Fukuda, Mendonca, Rodriques, and you, Malama!" He stood back to survey them. "Tomorrow night. Your hair long. Old Muumuus. Flowers. Three ukuleles, two guitars. Da Lagoon gonna hear Hawaiian music like nevah bifore." He bowed to Judy and asked, "Seestah, you sing wit' me?"

"I will," she said simply.

Malama was an unusually outspoken woman, for a Hawaiian, and she asked, "Will it be taken with grace if a Chinese girl sings that particular song? It's so especially Hawaiian."

"Da kine people better get accustomed," Kelly snapped, "because dis wahine . . . a true meadowlark."

"What do you think, Hong Kong?" Malama asked.

It was apparent from his scowl that he was going to reserve his negative judgment until he got Judy alone, but his daughter said for him, "He'll be there, and so will I."

Back in the Buick, Hong Kong stormed: "I don't want my daughter singing in a night club!"

"But I want to sing," Judy said firmly.

"People will laugh, Judy. My daughter, singing in a club. You, a Chinese making believe you're Hawaiian."

"Dad, for a long time I've wanted to sing . . ."

"But Kelly Kanakoa! A no-good, broken-down Hawaiian!"

"What's wrong with a Hawaiian?" Judy snapped.

"I didn't raise a respectable Chinese girl to be messing around with a Hawaiian!"

"You're messing around, as you call it, with Malama."

"That's business, Judy. You're asking for trouble, girl."

"You be there tomorrow night, Dad. I want to see at least one friendly face."

The team of Kelly and Judy created a sensation in more ways than one. To the mainland tourists they were the first pair in the islands who showed any real sense of professional savoir-faire, and the five powerful gray-haired women who accompanied them on that first night were remarkable, for they set off the frail beauty of the girl and the lithe young masculinity of the baritone, so that if only the tourist had to be considered, the team was both an artistic and a financial success. But to the residents of Hawaii it was shocking on two counts. To the Chinese community it was inconceivable that on the very day that Hong Kong's appointment to the Malama Kanakoa Trust was announced, confirming as it were his respectability in the community, his well-trained daughter should appear in a public night club, her navel showing, singing and doing the hula with a man like Kelly Kanakora. At least four major Chinese families whose sons had been thinking of marrying the delectable music teacher said flatly, "We will never accept her as a daughter-in-law." But to the Hawaiian community it was an affront past understanding that an alii family like the Kanakoas would choose as Kelly's singing partner a pure Chinese girl, and for her to presume to dress like an honest Hawaiian and thus palm herself off to the public was morally outrageous.

So the Chinese boycotted Judy and the Hawaiians boycotted Kelly, but Manny Fineberg of Clarity Records heard them on the second night and signed them up to a profitable contract, but he did stipulate, "On the cover of the album, we got to have a pure Hawaiian girl. Judy can sing like an angel, but she can't get over them slant-eyes." As the young singers were driving home that night Judy said, "Kelly, I think that for our next album we ought to form our own company, right here in Hawaii." And that was the start of Island Records, which Judy Kee ran with an iron hand, seeking out fresh talent to sing famous old songs, so that before long, half the Hawaiian melodies played in America were produced by this clever Chinese girl.

She also devised the costume by which Kelly became famous in the island night clubs. She had a tailor make him skin-tight pants, one leg blue, the other red, with frayed ends reaching below the knee. For a top she found a subdued tapalike fabric from Java and had it made into a tight jacket with long ends that tied at the waist. His hat continued to be a yachting cap, worn on the back of his head, but his shoes were heavy leather sandals which she designed and which he could kick off when he wished to dance. "You must become a visual symbol," she insisted, and she did the same, with her exotic face framed in flowers and her two braids showing over an island sarong. But the thing that tourists remembered longest was the curious whale's tooth that Kelly wore on a silver chain about his neck. It became his trademark.

Judy made other changes in Kelly. When he spoke to her, he had to speak English, but when he was on stage she encouraged him to use a wild pidgin, as when in the middle of a performance he would suddenly halt Florsheim's guitar solo and cry, "Eh you, Florsheim blalah. Las' night I t'ink. More'n hunnerd years ago de missionary come dis rock and find my gradfadder you gradfadder wearin' nuttin', doin' nuttin', sleepin' under de palm tree, drinkin' okolehau, dey raise hell. Bimeby hunnerd years later you me kanaka we doin' all de work while de missionary kids sleepin' under de palm tree, drinkin' gin, wearin' almos' nuttin', and doin' nuttin'. Florsheim blalah, wha' in hell hoppen?"

It was Judy who insisted that Florsheim learn to play the steel guitar with an electronic booster, and she also encouraged the big slob to dress in disreputable costumes so as to set off Kelly's grandeur, but there were two problems concerning the huge Hawaiian that not even Judy could solve. If he was a member of a group, everyone unconsciously spoke pidgin, even Judy; and no one could keep the big man's girls straightened out. After a while Judy stopped trying, but one change she did make. She insisted that when Kelly got cables from divorcees on the mainland, he ignore them.

"You're an important artist, Kelly!" she hammered day after day. "You don't have to peddle yourself to every neurotic dame who sends you a distress signal."

"They're friends of my friends," he explained.

"Were they good for you, Kelly?" she asked bluntly.

"No," he said.

"Then cut it out," she said simply, and in time she even got Florsheim to stop running in breathlessly with the news: "Kelly blalah, I got dem two da kine wahine, one got convertible. Kelly blalah, you help me out, huh?"

There was one point on which Judy Kee never deceived herself. It was true that the financial success of her trio stemmed from her managerial ability, but its artistic reception derived solely from the infectious Polynesian charm of her two companions. When tourists saw handsome Kelly and ponderous Florsheim, they instinctively loved them, for the Hawaiians reminded them of an age when life was simpler, when laughter was easier, and when there was music in the air. No stranger to Hawaii ever loved the islands because Judy Kee and her astute father Hong Kong were making profound changes in the social structure; people loved Hawaii because of the Polynesians. All Judy did was make it possible for her two beachboys to live, for under her guidance they earned about $70,000 a year, with time off to go swimming almost every afternoon.

Two older people followed the regeneration of Kelly and Florsheim with interest. To Malama the arrival of the strongminded Chinese girl was a blessing from the old gods who had looked after Hawaiians. She told her tea-party friends, "I tried to make him grow up and failed. But this little Pake says jump, and he jumps. Always in the right direction."

"I hear she has the recording company in her name," Mrs. Rodriques probed.

"She does," Malama admitted. "But I suggested it. I didn't want Kelly free to shuffle out of his arrangements."

"Then if he wants to get his fair share of the company, he'll have to marry her, won't he?"

"Nothing could please me more," Malama said frankly. Then, looking sadly out over the swamp where the alii of a past age had boasted, she said softly, "By ourselves, we Hawaiians cannot maintain our position in the new world that surrounds us. I was staggering under frightful burdens till Hong Kong came along. He has such a peasant, earthy power that the boards of the porch seem a little firmer when he passes."

Mrs. Mendonca said, "I never thought to witness the day when you would approve the marriage of your son to a Chinese."

Malama continued looking out the window and said gravely, "You forget, Liliha, that she is not just a Chinese girl. She is the great-granddaughter of the Pake Kokua. When nobody else on this earth dared to help the Hawaiian lepers, that woman did. Any member of her family merits our special affection." Then she looked back into the room and asked, "Where would Kelly be today if it were not for the Pake girl? Do you think I was happy, the way he used to live? One divorced woman after another? I wish the world could somehow maintain just a little corner where Hawaiians could live as they liked and prosper, but since that is not the way of the world, the next best thing is to have a Chinese helping us. They can't hurt us any worse than the haoles did."

"Do you think they'll get married?" Mrs. Mendonca asked.

Malama evaded this question by volunteering a short speech: "I remember, Carry-the-Mail, when you married Leon Choy, and all the alii wept because a fine Hawaiian girl was marrying a Chinese, and I wept too, but as I recall, my father assured your father that it was all right, and that sometimes the Chinese were good people. How different things are now, because it is no longer a question of what we five elderly Hawaiian ladies think of such a marriage. The problem is: 'Will a leading Chinese family like Hong Kong Kee's allow their daughter to marry a Hawaiian?' We have fallen so swiftly on the slide of history." She strummed idly on her ukulele while her guests picked up an old song that had come down from better days.

The other older person who watched Kelly's new position with meticulous care was Hong Kong Kee, and one night he waited up till three in the morning to greet his beautiful, competent daughter. "Were you out there kissing him in the car?" he stormed.

"Yes."

"This is what the haoles call necking?"

"Yes."

"Well, don't let me catch you again."

"Then don't peek!" And she flounced up the stairs, but he trailed after her, protesting that the entire Chinese community was worried about her. Singing in a hotel was bad enough, but now it began to look as if . . .

"As if what?" she asked sternly, whirling about to face her anguished father.

"It begins to look as if you were thinking of marrying him," Hong Kong stammered.

"I am," Judy said.

"Oh, Judy!" her father gasped, and to her surprise the tough old warrior burst into tears. "You mustn't do this!" he pleaded. "You're a fine Chinese girl. You've got to think of your position in the community."

"Father!" Judy cried, pulling his hands down from his red eyes. "Kelly's a good boy. I love him and I think I'm going to marry him."

"Judy!" her father wept. "Don't do it." The noise awakened the rest of the family, and soon the hallway was filled with Kees, and when they heard Hong Kong's ominous warning that "Judy insists she's going to marry the Hawaiian," her brothers began to weep, too, and one said, "Judy, you can't bring this disgrace upon us."

For some time Judy had been aware of her family's apprehension about her growing friendship with Kelly, but she had considered it merely a normal expression of family concern. Now, as the weeping male members of her family stood about her, she realized that it was something much deeper. "You're a Chinese girl!" Brother Eddie stammered. "Don't you think that when I was at Harvard Law I met a lot of attractive haole girls? Even some I wanted to marry? But I didn't do it because I thought of the family here in Hawaii. And you can't do it, either."

"But Kelly's a settled-down citizen," Judy stubbornly repeated. "He makes more money than any of you, and if Dad can get the trust straightened out . . ."

"He's a Hawaiian," Mike said.

"You think I want my lovely daughter to marry a man with a vocabulary of seven hundred words, most of them *seestah* and *blalah?*" Hong Kong demanded.

"Kelly is an educated young man," Judy insisted.

"Very well," Hong Kong snapped. "If you marry him . . ."

"Don't say it, Father," Judy begged.

"If you insist upon bringing disgrace upon the whole Chinese community," Hong Kong said ominously, "we want nothing more to do with you. You're a lost girl."

The Kees went officially to bed, but through the night one after another crept to Judy's room to explain how deeply they opposed such a marriage. "It isn't that Kelly has a vocabulary of seven hundred words," one sister whispered. "It's that you're a fine Chinese girl, and he's a Hawaiian."

"Many Chinese married Hawaiians," Judy argued. "Look at Leon Choy."

"And whenever one did," the sister explained, "we all felt sorrowful. You're a Chinese, Judy. You can't do this."

"Would you feel the same way if Kelly were a haole?" Judy asked.

"Identically," the sister assured her. "You're a Chinese. Marry a Chinese."

But Judy Kee was a very tough-minded girl, and in spite of constantly renewed pressures from her entire family she came home one night at four and announced loudly: "Now hear this! Now hear this! Everybody wake up. The most precious flower of the Celestial Kingdom is going to marry Kelly Kanakoa. And what are you going to do about it?" She stomped off to bed and waited as one by one the family came to see if she were sober and in her right mind.

At first Hong Kong flatly refused to attend the wedding, as did many of the leading Chinese and some of the remaining Hawaiian alii, but Judy said bravely, "Tonight at the Lagoon, Kelly, we'll announce our engagement, and then we'll sing 'The Wedding Song' in our own honor." And they did, and among the tourists it was a very popular wedding, but among the affected citizens of Hawaii it was a catastrophe. At the last moment Hong Kong thought of his obligations to Malama Kanakoa, and out of respect for her, he attended the ceremony, but he would not walk down the aisle with his daughter.

But at The Fort, Hong Kong found that the disgrace he was suffering through his daughter's headstrong marriage brought him closer to his colleagues. Hewlett Janders, whose son Whip was still living with the air force man in San Francisco, said simply, "You can never tell about kids, Hong Kong." And Hoxworth Hale, whose daughter Noelani was still brooding about the house and trying to sneak in a divorce without publicity, clapped his Chinese friend on the shoulder and confided: "We all go through it, but by God I wish we didn't have to."

"You think I did right?" Hong Kong asked in a sudden longing to talk.

"I'd attend my daughter's wedding, no matter whom she married," Hoxworth said flatly.

"I'm glad I did," Hong Kong confessed. "But I can't bring myself to visit them."

"Wait till the first baby's born," Hoxworth wisely counseled. "It'll give you an excuse to retreat gracefully." And Hong Kong agreed, but he felt that he might not want to look at a grandchild that was only half Chinese.

To the Sakagawa family 1954 was a year that brought dislocation and frustration. It started in January when iron-willed Kamejiro, whose threats about leaving America no one had taken seriously, announced unexpectedly that he was sailing on Friday to spend the rest of his life in Hiroshima-ken. Consequently, on Friday he and his bent wife boarded a Japanese freighter and without even a round of farewell dinners departed for Japan. He told the boys, "The store will pay enough to feed me in Hiroshima. I worked hard in America, and Japan can be proud of the manner in which I conducted myself. I hope that when you're old you'll be able to say the same." Never a particularly sentimental man, he did not linger on deck gawking at the mountains he had pierced nor at the fields he had helped create. He led his wife below decks, where they had a sturdy meal of cold rice and fish, which they enjoyed.

It was usually overlooked in both Hawaii and the mainland that of the many Orientals brought to America, a substantial number preferred returning to their homelands, and in the years after World War II there was a heavy flow from America to Japan, of which the Sakagawas formed only an inconspicuous part. With their dollar savings such emigrants were able to buy, in the forgotten rural areas of Japan, fairly substantial positions in a poverty-stricken economy, and this Kamejiro intended doing. He would buy his Japanese relatives a little more land beside the Inland Sea and there it would wait, the family homestead in Hiroshima-ken, in case his boys Goro and Shigeo ever decided to return to their homeland.

The old folks' departure grieved Shigeo, because the more solidly American he became, with a seat in the senate and a canny man like Black Jim McLafferty as his partner, the more he appreciated the virtues old Kamejiro had inculcated in his sons; but Goro felt otherwise, for although he too treasured his father's moral teachings, he was glad to see his stern, unyielding mother go back to Japan, for he felt that this would give him a chance to keep his own wife, Akemi-san, in America. Accordingly, he and Shigeo gave Akemi a comfortable allowance, command of the Sakagawa house, and freedom from the old woman's tyranny. The brothers never laughed at Akemi's precise speech, and they showed her that they wanted her to stay.

But it was too late. One morning, as they were breakfasting, she said, "I am going back to Japan."

"Why?" Goro gasped.

"Where will you get the money?" Shigeo said.

"I've saved it. For a year I've bought nothing for myself and eaten mainly rice. I haven't cheated you," she insisted.

"No one's speaking of cheating, Akemi dear," Goro assured her. "But why are you leaving?"

"Because Hawaii is too dreadfully dull to live in," she replied.

"Akemi!" Goro pleaded.

She pushed back from the table and looked at the hardworking brothers. "In Hawaii I'm intellectually dead . . . decomposing."

"How can you say that?" Shig interrupted.

"Because it's true . . . and pitifully obvious to anyone from Japan."

"But don't you sense the excitement here?" Shig pleaded. "We Japanese are just breaking through to power."

"Do you know what real excitement is?" she asked sorrowfully. "The excitement of ideas? Quests? I'm afraid Hawaii will never begin to understand true intellectual excitement, and I refuse to waste my life here."

"But don't you find our arrival as a group of people exciting?" Shig pressed.

"Yes," she granted, "if you were going to arrive some place important it would be exciting. But do you know what your goal is? A big shiny black automobile. You'll never arrive at music or plays or reading books. You have a cheap scale of values, and I refuse to abide them any longer."

"Akemi!" Goro pleaded in real anguish. "Don't leave. Please."

"What will you do?" Shig asked.

"I'll get a job in a Nishi-Ginza bar where people talk about ideas," she said flatly, and that day she started to pack.

When it became obvious that she was determined to leave Hawaii, Goro disappeared from his labor office for several days, and Shigeo found him sitting dully at home, waiting for Akemi-san to return from the market, where she was informing her envious war-bride friends that she was sailing back to Japan. Goro's eyes were red, and his hands trembled. "Do you think that all we've been working at is useless, Shig?" he pleaded.

"Don't believe what this girl says," Shig replied, sitting with his brother.

"But I love her. I can't let her go!"

"Goro," Shigeo said quietly, "I love Akemi-san almost as much as you do, and if she walks out, I'm broken up, too. But I'm sure of one thing. You and I are working on something so big that she can't even dimly understand it. Give us another twenty years and we'll build here in Hawaii a wonderland."

Goro knew what his brother was speaking of, but he asked, "In the meantime, do you think we're as dull as she says?"

Shig thought several minutes, recalling Boston on a Friday night, and Harvard Law with its vital discussions, and Sundays at the great museums. "Hawaii's pretty bad," he confessed.

"Then you think Akemi-chan's justified?" Goro asked with a dull ache in his voice.

"She's not big enough to overlook the fact that we're essentially peasants," Shig replied.

"What do you mean?" Goro argued contentiously. "We got good educations."

"But fundamentally we're peasants," Shig reasoned. "Everybody who came to these islands came as illiterate peasants. The Chinese, the Portuguese, the Koreans, and now the Filipinos. We were all honest and hard-working, but, by God, we were a bunch of Hiroshima yokels."

Goro, lacerated by his wife's threatened desertion, would not accept this further castigation and cried, "Yokels or not, our people now get a decent wage in the sugar fields and our lawyers get elected to the legislature. I call that something."

"It's everything," Shig agreed, pressing his arm about his brother's shoulder. "The other things that Akemi-chan misses . . . they'll come later. It's our children who'll read books and listen to music. They won't be peasants."

Goro now changed from misery to belligerency and cried, "Hell, fifty years from now they'll put up statues to guys like you and me!" And he thought of many things he was going to tell his wife when she returned, but when he saw her come into the room, after carefully removing her geta at the door and walking pin-toed like a delicate Japanese gentlewoman, his courage collapsed and he pleaded, "Akemi-chan, please, please don't go."

She walked past him and into her room, where she completed her final packing and when she was ready to go to the boat she said softly, "I'm not running away from you, Goro-san. You were good to me and tender. But a girl has only one life and I will not spend mine in Hawaii."

"It'll grow better!" he assured her.

In precise Japanese the determined girl replied, "I would perish here." And that afternoon she sailed for Japan.

Mr. Ishii, of course, wrote a long letter in Japanese script to the Sakagawas in Hiroshima-ken, and when the local letter-reader had advised Mrs. Sakagawa of its contents, Goro began getting a series of delighted letters from his mother, which Ishii-san read to the boys, for although they could speak Japanese they could not read it: "I am so glad to hear that the superior-thinking young lady from Tokyo has gone back home. It's best for all concerned, Goro, and I have been asking through the village about suitable girls, and I have found several who would be willing to come to America, but you must send me a later picture of yourself, because the one I have makes you look too young, and the better girls are afraid that you are not well established in business. I am sending you in this letter pictures of three very fine girls. Fumiko-san is very strong and comes from a family I have known all my life. Chieko-san is from a very dependable family and when made-up looks rather sweet. Yuri-san is too short, but she has a heart which I know is considerate, for her mother, whom I knew as a girl, tells me that Yuri is the best girl in the village where taking care of a home is concerned. Also, since Shigeo now has a good job and ought to be looking for a wife, I am sending him two pictures of the schoolteacher in the village. She is well educated and would make a fine wife for a lawyer, because even though she went away to college, she is originally from this village. After the grave mistake Goro made with the girl from Tokyo, I am sure it would be better if you boys both found your wives at home."

The brothers spread the five photographs on the table and studied them gloomily. "It's too bad we're not raising sugar cane," Goro growled. "That quartet could hoe all the fields between here and Waipahu."

The next mail brought three more applicants, stalwart little girls with broad bottoms, gold teeth and backs of steel. Mr. Ishii, after reading the letters to the brothers, got great pleasure from studying the photographs and making therefrom his own recommendations. "Of all the things I have done in my life," he explained, "I am happiest that I married a Hiroshima girl. If you boys were wise, you would do the same thing."

Then came the letter that contained two better-than-average pictures, and as they fluttered out, Mr. Ishii studied the portraits with care and said, "I think these may be the ones," but his spirits were soon dampened by a passage from Mrs. Sakagawa which he could not find the courage to finish reading to the boys. It began, "Last week donna-san and I went to see Hiroshima City, a place we had not visited before, and I am ashamed to have to say that what the Americans reported is true. The city was bombed. It was mostly destroyed and you can still see the big black scars. Ishii-san, who will be reading this letter to you, ought to know that the damage was very bad and from looking at this city I don't see how anyone could believe any longer that Japan won the . . ."

Mr. Ishii's voice trailed off. For a long time he sat looking at the fatal pages.

Coming as they did, from his own mother-in-law, and a Hiroshima woman too, he could not doubt their veracity; but accepting her statement meant that all his visions for the past thirteen years since Pearl Harbor were fallacious, his life a mockery. The boys were considerate enough not to mention the facts which their mother had hammered home, and when the time came for them to go to work, they said good-bye to the little old man, their brother-in-law, and left him staring at the letter.

At about eleven that morning a Japanese man came running into the law offices of McLafferty and Sakagawa, shouting in English, "Jesus Christ! He did it on the steps of the Japanese Consulate."

Shig experienced a sinking feeling in his throat and mumbled, "Ishii-san?" and the informant yelled, "Yes. Cut his belly right open."

"I'll go with you," McLafferty called, and the two partners roared up Nuuanu to where, from the days of the first Japanese in Hawaii, the little bow-legged laborers had taken their troubles. At the consulate a group of police waited for an ambulance, which in due time screamed up, and Shig said, "I'm a relative. I'll go with him." But the little old labor leader was dead. He had felt that if his fatherland had indeed lost the war, the only honorable thing he could do was to inform the emperor of his grief, so he had gone to the emperor's building, and with the emperor's flag in his left hand, had behaved as his institutions directed. With his death, the Ever-Victorious Group died also, and the sadness of national defeat was at last brought home even to the farthest remnants of the Japanese community.

After the funeral Shigeo faced his first difficult decision of the year, for Goro hurried home late one afternoon with this dismaying news: "The communist trials begin next month, and Rod Burke wants you to defend him."

Shig dropped his head. "I knew it would come . . . sooner or later," he said. "But why does he have to ask me just as I'm getting ready to run for a full term as senator?"

Goro replied, "That's when the case was called. Will you take the job?"

Shig had anticipated that the communists would seek him as their counsel, and he had tried to formulate a satisfactory reply to the invitation; but whereas it is easy to prefabricate an answer to an expected question like "Shall we go to Lahaina next week?" it is not so easy to anticipate the moral and emotional entanglements involved in a more complex question like, "Am I, as a lawyer, obligated to provide legal aid to a communist?"

"I wish you hadn't asked me," Shig stalled.

"I wish Rod hadn't asked me," Goro countered.

"Are you determined to help him?" Shig asked.

"Yes, I'd have accomplished nothing without him."

"But you're sure he's guilty?"

"I suppose so," Goro granted. "But even a communist is entitled to a fair trial . . . and a defending lawyer."

"Why me?"

"Because you're my brother."

"I can't answer this one so fast, Goro."

"Neither could I at first," Goro said. "Take your time."

So Shigeo spent long hours walking the streets of Kakaako, wondering what he ought to do. He reasoned: "In Hawaii I have one overriding responsibility— the land laws. To do anything about these, I've got to keep getting re-elected. If I defend Rod Burke, I'll surely lose all the haole votes I apparently picked up last time, and that would mean I'd be licked in November. So from that point of view I ought to say no.

"But Rod Burke isn't the only defendant. There's his Japanese wife and two other Japanese. And if I go into court and give those people a stirring defense, I'll bind the Japanese vote to me forever, simply because I have dared to defend the underdog. So although I might lose this election, I'd probably be in stronger position next time, and the time after that.

"But are my personal interests the ones that ought to determine this decision? A man charged with a crime has a right to a lawyer, and when the community is most strongly against him, his right is morally greatest. Somebody has got to defend Rod Burke, and I suppose it ought to be me.

"But I am not just the average, non-attached lawyer of the case books. I'm the first Japanese to get into the senate from the Nineteenth. I'm the one who has a chance of getting in again. If my brother Goro has come to represent labor, then I represent a cross-section of all the Japanese. That's a major responsibility which I ought not destroy carelessly.

"But there are others in our family than Goro and me. There are Tadao and Minoru, and they gave their lives defending an ideal America. They never found it for themselves . . . certainly not here in Hawaii. But in Italy and France, fighting to defend America, they did find it. So did Goro and I. And what we found is definitely threatened by a communist conspiracy. How then can I go into court and defend identified communists?"

And then came the question of the age. It struck Shigeo as he was walking past a sashimi parlor on Kakaako Street, as it was striking hundreds of similar Americans in garages or at the movies or in church: "But if I turn my back on a supposed communist, how do I know that I am not turning my back on the very concept of liberty that I am seeking to protect? Honest men can always get someone to defend them. But what does justice mean if apparently dishonest men can find no one?"

So through this precise waltz the mind of Shigeo Sakagawa swayed, day after day. Finally he took his confusion to Black Jim McLafferty, asking, "How are you going to feel, Jim, first, as head of the Democratic Party, and second, as head of McLafferty and Sakagawa, if your partner defends the communists?"

Now it was Black Jim's turn to follow the devious paths of logic, emotion, politics, patriotism and self-interest. His two most interesting comments were stolen right from his father's Boston experiences: "It never hurts a Democratic lawyer to defend the underdog," and "As long as my half of our partnership is known to be Catholic, you're fairly free to defend whom you want to." Then, drawing from his Hawaiian experience, he added, "It would be a damned shame for the first Japanese elected from the Nineteenth to be thrown out of office on an irrelevancy." But prudently he refused to give a concrete recommendation.

With McLafferty's concepts adding to his confusion, Shigeo walked more miles, and the consideration which finally made up his mind for him was one that seemed at first wholly irrelevant. He recalled Akemi-san, his former sister-in-law, saying, on the day she left Hawaii, "In the entire Japanese community of Hawaii I have never encountered one idea." And Shig thought: "I have an idea. I have a concept that will move the entire community ahead," and he decided not to imperil his land-reform movement, so he refused his brother's request. "I won't defend the communists," he said, "and may God forgive me if it is cowardice."

"At least I do," Goro said.

This long travail explained why, when the electioneering season finally opened, Senator Shigeo Sakagawa spoke with unusual force and seriousness on the problem of land reform. He drew up charts showing how The Fort, and its members through their directorships on the great trusts, controlled the land of Hawaii. He pointed out how they released this land in niggardly amounts, not for social purposes, but to keep up values, "the way the diamond merchants of South Africa release an agreed-upon number of diamonds each year, to keep up prices. It's legitimate to do that with diamonds, which a man can buy or not, as he pleases, but is it right to do it with land, upon which we all exist or perish?"

His most damning chart was one which showed that certain families contrived to have their land, which they held back for speculation, assessed by a complaint government at two per cent of its real value, whereas three hundred typical shopkeepers with small holdings from which they lived had theirs assessed at fifty-one per cent of its real value. "You and I," Shig cried to his audience, "are subsidizing the big estates. We allow them to pay no taxes. We encourage them to hold their land off the market. We permit them a tax refuge under which they can speculate. I am not angry at these families. I wish I were as smart as they appear to be. Because you and I know that when they sold their last piece of land to Gregory's for the big new store, they sold it for $3,000,000. What value had they been paying taxes on? $71,000. Because you and I have been careless, we have allowed the Hewletts to keep valuable land off the market and pay taxes on it at one-fortieth of its real value."

In public parks, on the radio and on television Shigeo Sakagawa hammered home his dominant theme, and when citizens asked him if he was a radical, advocating the breaking up of landed estates the way they did in Russia, he kept his temper and replied, "No, I am a conservative English parliamentarian, trying to do in Hawaii what men like me accomplished in England one hundred years ago. Remember this. I am the conservative. It is the people who think that this problem can be endlessly postponed who are the radicals. Because their course leads to tragedy, mine to democracy."

But at every rally somebody sooner or later heckled: "Aren't you a communist, too, like your brother Goro?"

Shigeo had worked out a good answer to this question. He dropped his arms, looked off into space, and said quietly, "In any American election that's a fair question, and the voters have a right to an honest answer. I wonder in what form I can best give you my answer?" He seemed to be thinking, and after a moment, in a very relaxed voice he started speaking.

"Is the man who asked that question old enough to remember the McKinley-Punahou game of 1938? It was in the last fifteen seconds of the game, if you'll remember, and Punahou was trailing by four points, 18-14. Then, from a rather rough scrimmage, Punahou's star back broke loose, and I can see him now dashing down the sideline . . . ten yards, twenty, forty. He was going to score a magnificent touchdown and win the game, and I can remember even to this day how thrilled I was to see that run, because that runner was my brother Tadao Sakagawa, the first ordinary Japanese ever to get into Punahou and one of the greatest stars they ever had.

"But can you recall what happened next? From the McKinley players a tackle got up from one knee and started out like a fire engine after my brother, and although Tad could run fast, this McKinley man ran like the wind, and on the five-yard line, that close mind you, this McKinley man brought my brother down and saved the game. You all know who he was. He was my older brother, Goro, the one who had wanted to get into Jefferson and couldn't.

"Now the point of my story is this. Goro could have held back and let his brother Tad score the winning touchdown and be the biggest hero of the year, but he never wavered in his duty. He tackled his own brother on the five-yard line and saved the day. That's the way we Sakagawas were brought up by our parents. Duty, duty, duty.

"But the more important point of my story is this. Do you know where the great halfback Tadao Sakagawa is now? Buried beneath a military cross in the Punchbowl. He gave his life for America. And where is his brother, Minoru Sakagawa? Buried beneath a military cross in the Punchbowl. He also gave his life for his country. That is also the kind of boys we Sakagawas are. Tough, resolute, uncompromising fighters.

"I will tell you this. If my brother Goro Sakagawa was, as you charge, a communist, I would personally hound him out of the islands. I would never cease fighting him, I would tackle him down the way he tackled down Tadao, for I will make no compromise with communism."

Then his voice would take on a harder tone as he continued: "But Goro Sakagawa is not a communist. He is a very fine labor leader, and the good he has done for the working people of Hawaii is beyond calculation. I am for such labor leaders, and I want that fact to be widely known. Goro and I are two edges of the same sword, he in labor, I in politics. We are cutting away old and unfair practices. We are slashing at the relics of feudalism."

In conclusion his voice changed to one of exhortation: "And neither Goro nor I will stop, because we can remember the day our father took us to the old plantation camp on Kauai and showed us the barracks where the lunas used to tramp through with whips and lash the field hands, and we swore that that would stop. Now, sir, you who asked the question about communism, I want to ask you two questions in return: where were you when my brothers Minoru and Tadao were giving their lives for American democracy? What have you done comparable to what Goro and I have done to clean up the democracy they saved? Won't you please come up to see me after the rally, and if you have done half as much as we have done, I want to embrace you as a damned good American, because, brother, you are certainly not a communist, nor am I."

The audience always applauded madly at this point, and when Black Jim McLafferty first heard the reply he cried, "My God, we've got to plant somebody in the audience to ask that question every night. I never heard a better answer. Demagoguery at its best, and of course you know what they call demagoguery at its best? Oratory." But Shig refused to have anybody planted, because he was afraid that that might cut the edge of his conviction, because his answer had this merit: on more than half the occasions at which he used it, the questioner did come up afterwards to talk about old army days or the unhappy plantation experiences of his family, so that Shig's reply actually converted hecklers into supporters, which, as McLafferty pointed out, "is about the best you can expect of any answer."

But one thing that McLafferty said rankled in Shig's memory: the word *demagoguery*. "Am I guilty of that?" he asked himself, and as he analyzed each portion of his well-known reply, he could explain everything until he got to the part about the lunas, and then he always stumbled. "What actually happened?" he asked himself. "One day, one luna hit my father one time. The first time Pop told about it, he told the truth. 'Here is where the luna hit me that day.' Then our family constructed the legend: 'Here is where the lunas used to beat us.' And finally it comes out: 'Here is where the lunas used to beat all the Japanese.'" And he saw clearly that this conversion of the truth was indeed demagoguery of the worst sort, because it kept alive community hatreds, which, even if they had been legitimately founded were better dead in the graves of memory; but the speech did get votes, and one night after a particularly heated rally he put the problem frankly to Black Jim. "That part about the lunas beating the Japanese? Do you think I ought to keep saying that?"

Black Jim was tooling his old Pontiac down Kapiolani Boulevard and for some time said nothing. Then grudgingly he admitted, "It gets votes."

"What I asked was, 'What do you think of it?' " Shig pressed.

"Well, when I hear it coming, I usually go out in the alley," Black Jim confessed. "Just in case I have to vomit." So Shig dropped that part of his demagoguery, but he noticed that when Goro unveiled the murals at his labor headquarters, there was the plantation camp with lunas slashing their way through the laborers with bull whips, and Shigeo thought: "This is the greatest evil that grows out of a wrong act. Somebody always remembers it . . . in an evil way."

When the campaign reached its height, complicated by the trial of the communists, Shigeo received in his office a visitor he had never heard of and whose existence surprised him. It was a young haole woman, twenty-six years old and marked by a pallid beauty. She said nervously, "My name is Noelani Hale Janders. I'm divorced but I haven't taken back my maiden name. I like what you've been saying on the radio, and I wish to work in your campaign."

"What was the name again?" Shig asked.

"Noelani Hale is my real name," she explained.

"What Hale is that?" Shig asked.

"Hoxworth Hale is my father."

"Sit down," Shig said weakly. When he had caught control of himself he pointed out, "Are you sure you've heard what I've been saying, Mrs. Hale?"

"It's Mrs. Janders," Noelani said. "Didn't you read about my divorce? It was rather messy."

"I didn't," Shig apologized.

"I understand very well what you're saying, Senator Sakagawa, and your views coincide with my own."

"But have you heard what I said about land reform?" he pressed.

"That's what we're talking about," Noelani said in her precise Bostonian accent.

"You would hurt your father very much if you were active in my campaign," Shigeo warned. "As a matter of fact, you would probably hurt me, too."

"I studied politics at Wellesley," she replied firmly.

"Were you at Wellesley?" he asked.

"While you were at Harvard," she said. "Amy Fukugawa pointed you out one day, at the symphony."

"What's Amy doing?" he asked.

"She married a Chinese boy. Both their parents disowned them, so they're very happy in New York. He's a lawyer."

"Do you understand what I'm saying about land reform, Mrs. Janders? How what I say will affect your father, and his friends?"

"I want to know just one thing," Noelani said. "When you speak of breaking up the big estates . . ."

"I'm not sure I've ever used that phraseology," he corrected. "I say that the big estates must not be allowed to hold out of productive use the land they are not using for constructive agriculture."

Noelani sighed with relief and said, "But under your system would you permit lands that are being used legitimately for sugar and pineapple some kind of preferential treatment?"

"Look, Mrs. Janders," Shig cried. "Apparently I haven't made myself clear on this point."

"You haven't," she said, "and that's why I wanted to help, because I knew you were too smart not to have thought about the fundamental problem of land in Hawaii."

"What problem do you mean?" the expert asked.

She picked up two books and placed them on the desk. "Let's call this book Hawaii," she said, "and this one California. Now our problem is to get all the things we need, like food and building materials and luxuries, from California out here to Hawaii, and also to pay for them after we get them here. Let's call this inkwell our ship. We can fill it up in California every day of the year and haul to Hawaii the things we need. But how are we going to pay for them? And what is the ship going to carry back from Hawaii to California, so that it won't have to go back empty, which would double the freight costs on everything?"

She paused, and Shigeo plopped the inkwell down on the Hawaii book, saying, "I know very well that the ship has got to take back some bulk crop like sugar or pineapple. The sale of agricultural products provides the money on which we live. And the freight that sugar and pineapple pay going to the mainland helps pay the freight of food and lumber coming this way. I know that."

"You certainly haven't explained it to the people," Noelani said critically. "Because the important point is this. You fighting young Japanese have got to reassure Hawaii that legitimate farm lands will be protected for the welfare of everybody. As to the lands that have been hiding along the edges of the legitimate farms, held there for tax-free speculation, I think even my father knows they must be sold off to the people."

"You spoke of helping," Shig said. "What did you have in mind?"

"I'd like to help you put into words, for the radio and television, just what we've been talking about. It will insure your election."

"But why should Hoxworth Hale's daughter want to help a Japanese get elected?" Shig asked suspiciously.

"Because I love these islands, Senator. My people were here long before yours arrived, so I am naturally concerned about what happens to Hawaii."

"You ought to be a Republican," Shig said.

"For the time being, they're worn out," Noelani replied. "I've been living a long time with worn-out people, so I'm ready to accept new ideas."

Shig felt certain that when Hoxworth Hale saw his daughter's car with its bright-red bumper-banner, "Please Re-elect Senator Shigeo Sakagawa" the commander of The Fort would explode, but instead a most unexpected event transpired, for one afternoon Hong Kong Kee strolled into the McLafferty and Sakagawa offices and sat down with Shig. "I am in lots of trouble if my Republican friends see me down here," the Chinese said.

"What's up?" Shig inquired.

"I have a big surprise for you, Shigeo," Hong Kong confided.

"Trouble?" Shig asked, for in an election period every visitor brings anxiety.

"In a way," Hong Kong confessed. "Hoxworth Hale and his boys commissioned me to ask you how about coming on the board of Whipple Oil Imports, Incorporated. They figure a smart young Japanese on the board will help them sell more to Japanese customers."

Shig was quite unprepared for such a suggestion and studied Hong Kong carefully. He liked the shrewd Chinese, and appreciated what he had done for the Sakagawas, never mind the motives. But he was appalled that Hong Kong had consented to be used so crudely by The Fort in an attempt at political blackmail, and it was with difficulty that he restrained himself when he replied, coldly, "The Fort cannot buy me off on this land-reform business, and you can tell them so."

Hong Kong instantly realized the unfavorable position he appeared to be in, but instead of showing his embarrassment he said quietly, "Nobody at The Fort wants you, Shigeo, if your price is no higher than that. They know you're going to fight this land deal through to a conclusion. But what you don't know is, they're not too worried. They know it's inevitable."

"So they offer me a trivial directorship at such a time! It's contemptible."

"No, Shigeo, it's sensible. Two years ago they asked me to nominate some promising young Japanese. I said Shigeo. Last year they asked again. I said Shigeo. This is not a hasty idea. The Fort has had you in mind for a long time."

"I'd be false to my people if I joined up with their principal enemy," Shig said stubbornly.

"Maybe when you get elected one more time, Shigeo, you will stop talking about 'my people.' All the people in Hawaii are your people, and you better start thinking that way."

"If I took a job from The Fort, every Japanese in Hawaii would say I had turned traitor," Shig replied truthfully.

"I'll tell you this, Shigeo," the quick-minded Chinese corrected. "Until the time comes when you accept a job with The Fort, on your own terms, you are a traitor to your people. The whole purpose of you young Japanese getting elected to office, and you know how strong I work for you, is to bring you into the full society of Hawaii. You've got to get on the boards. You've got to get appointed trustees for the big estates."

"Trustees?" Shig laughed. "After what I've been shouting about the estates?"

"Exactly," Hong Kong replied. "Because if you show yourself interested, before the year ends you'll be suggested as a trustee."

"By whom?" the young senator asked contemptuously.

"By Hoxworth Hale and me," Hong Kong snapped. And as the young Japanese fell silent, the Chinese banker explained his view of Hawaii. He said: "The haoles are smarter than I used to think, Shigeo. First they worked the Hawaiians, and threw them out. Then they brought in my grandmother, and threw her out. Then they got your father, and dropped him when the Filipinos looked better. They always picked the winner, these haoles, and I respect them for it.

"So I work hard and show them I can run real estate better than they can, and they make me a partner. Other educated Chinese are breaking in, too. If you smart young Japanese don't pretty soon start joining up in the real running of Hawaii, it only means you aren't clever enough for anybody to want you. Getting elected is the easy part, Shigeo, because you can rely upon stupid people to do that for you, but getting onto the boards, and running the schools, and directing the trusts is the real test. Because there you have to be selected by the smartest people in Hawaii. Shigeo, I want you to join this board."

The young Japanese thought for a long time. If he were to join, he would be a spiritual traitor to his family and to his class. He could no longer say to his Japanese friends, "It was in the fields on Kauai that the lunas used to horsewhip our fathers. Well, those days are past." He would lose the sweet solidarity that he felt when he and Goro and the other young Japanese swore: "We are as good as the haoles." He would lose so much that had kept him fighting.

He temporized: "Hong Kong, you must know that no matter what The Fort offers me, I'm still going to fight for this land reform."

"Damn it!" Hong Kong cried. 'It's because you're going to fight for it that they want you. They know you're right, Shigeo."

"All right!" the young senator snapped. "Tell them that after the election I'll join."

"After the election it will have no moral force," Hong Kong pleaded.

"After the election," Shigeo repeated, and he applied himself with greater dedication to the campaign that was to alter life in Hawaii, for he and Black Jim McLafferty had whipped together a sterling slate of young Japanese veterans. All the boys were mainland-educated. Some appeared on the hustings lacking arms that had been lost in Italy or legs shot off in France, and if they had so desired, they could have appeared with their chests covered with medals. In contrast to former elections, the serious young men spoke on issues, and pressed home Senator Shigeo Sakagawa's figures on land reform. There was great excitement in the air, as if this October were an intellectual April with ideas germinating.

One night Noelani Janders said, as she drove Shigeo home from four outdoor rallies, "For a moment tonight, Shig, I had the fleeting sensation that we were going to win control of both the house and the senate. There's a real chance that a hell of a lot of you Japanese are going to be elected. It's terribly exciting."

Then the campaign, at least so far as Shigeo Sakagawa was concerned, fell completely apart, because one day without any previous announcement, old Kamejiro and his stooped wife climbed down off a Japanese freighter, took a bus out to Kakaako, and announced: "We have decided to live in America."

Goro and Shig embraced them as warmly as their stubborn, rocklike father would allow and tried to uncover the reasons for this sudden change of plans. All they could get from Kamejiro was this: "I'm too old to learn to use those goddamned Japanese toilets. I can't stay bent down that long." He would say no more.

Mrs. Sakagawa allowed several hints to fall. Once she observed: "The old man said he had grown so soft in America that he was no longer fit to be a real Japanese." At another time she said sorrowfully, "If you have been away from a farm for fifty-two years when you go back the fields look smaller." As for herself she said simply, "The Inland Sea is so terribly cold in winter."

Once, in late October when Shigeo was particularly nervous over the election, he snapped at his father: "I've seen a hundred of you people leave Hawaii, saying, 'I'm going back to the greatest land on earth!' But when you get there, you don't like it so much, do you?"

To his surprise old Kamejiro strode up to him, drew back and belted him severely across the face. "You're a Japanese!" he said fiercely. "Be proud of it!"

Mrs. Sakagawa had come home with several new photographs of Hiroshima-ken girls, and she arranged them on the kitchen table, admiringly, but when her boys showed no interest she sadly put them away. One night when she could not sleep she saw her youngest son come driving home with a haole girl, and it looked to her as if he had kissed the girl, and she called her husband and they confronted Shigeo, fearfully, and said, "Did you come home with a haole girl?"

"Yes," the young senator replied.

"Oh, no!" his mother groaned. "Kamejiro, speak to him."

The embittered session lasted for some hours, with old Kamejiro shouting, "If you get mixed up with a haole woman, all Japan will be ashamed!"

Mrs. Sakagawa held that it was the gods themselves who had inspired her return to America in time to save her son from such an irrevocable disgrace. She wept, "With all the fine girls I told you about from Hiroshima, why do you ride home with a haole?"

Strong threats were made, in the course of which Shigeo's mother cried, "It's almost as bad as if you married a Korean," at which Goro, who was now awake, pointed out, "Who said anything about getting married?" and Mrs. Sakagawa replied, "It's the same everywhere. Haole girls, Korean girls, Okinawa girls, Eta girls, all trying to trap decent Japanese boys."

This was too much for Goro, who suggested, "Mom, go to bed," but when she saw in Goro visible proof of the wreck her older son had made of his life she wept again and mourned, "You wouldn't listen to me. You went ahead and married a Tokyo girl, and see what happened. Let me warn you, Shigeo, haole girls are even worse than Tokyo girls. Much worse."

Goro pleaded ineffectively, "Shig, tell her that you're not marrying the girl."

"I saw him kissing her!" his mother cried.

"Mom," Goro cried. "I kissed a Filipino girl the other night. But I'm not marrying her."

Mrs. Sakagawa stopped her ranting. Dropping her arms she stared at her son and repeated dully, "A Filipino girl?" The idea was so completely repugnant that she could find no words with which to castigate it, so she turned abruptly on her heel and went to bed. Chinese girls, Okinawans, even Koreans you could fight. But a Filipino!

When the old people were gone, Goro asked quietly, "There's nothing between you and the haole, is there?"

"I don't think so," Shig replied.

"Look, blalah," Goro said, reverting to an old and dear phrase of their pidgin childhood, "she's a Hale, a Janders, a haole, a divorcee, all in one. Don't try it. You're strong, but you're not that strong."

Election Day, 1954, was one that will never be forgotten in Hawaii. Hula teams surrounded voting places. Candidates wearing mountainous flowered leis passed out sandwiches to haole voters and sushi to Japanese. Bands blared all day long, and trucks with long streamers ploughed through the streets. It was a noisy, gala, wonderful day, and that night when the votes were tallied, Hawaii realized with astonished pain that for the first time since the islands had joined America, Democrats were going to control both houses. The days were forever past when Republicans dominated by The Fort could rule the islands with impunity.

Then, toward midnight, when each specific contest approached final settlement, a second discovery was made, even more sobering than the first. Of the Democratic victors, the majority were going to be young Japanese. In the senate, out of fifteen seats, Japanese won seven. In the house, out of thirty seats, Japanese won fourteen. On the board that ran Honolulu, out of seven vacancies,

Japanese won four, and at midnight Hewie Janders, sitting glumly with John Whipple Hoxworth and the Hewlett boys, faced the unpalatable facts: "Gentlemen, we are now to be governed from Tokyo. And may God help us."

Black Jim McLafferty's team of brilliant young Japanese war veterans had swept into commanding power. Their average age was thirty-one. The average number of major wounds they had received in battle was two. Their average number of medals was four. They were honor graduates, of great mainland universities like Harvard, Columbia, Michigan and Stanford, and together they would compose the best-educated, most-decorated group of legislators elected that day in any of the forty-eight American states; there would be no finer legislature than that put together by the serious young Japanese lawyers of Hawaii.

Some pages back in this memoir I predicted that when, in 1916, the drunken luna Von Schlemm unfairly thrashed the sick Japanese field hand Kamejiro Sakagawa, the act was bound to have historic consequences which would not appear obvious for nearly forty years. Now, on Election Day of 1954, this old and almost forgotten event came home to roost. The Japanese, convinced that their laboring parents had been abused by the lunas, voted against the Republicans who had supervised that abuse. Von Schlemm's single blow had been transmuted by oratory into daily thrashings. In the early part of the campaign Senator Sakagawa, who should have known better, used this incident to lure the Japanese vote, but later he had the decency to drop such inflammatory rabble-rousing. In the labor troubles that haunted our islands, Goro Sakagawa originally used this same incident to inflame his workers, but later he also reconsidered and abandoned his irresponsible harangues. Nevertheless, for a few months in 1954 it looked as if a deep schism had been driven down the middle of our community, pitting Japanese against haole, but the Sakagawa boys had the courage to back away from that tempting, perilous course. They reconciled haole and Japanese, and it is to their credit that they did so. If there was one man in the history of Hawaii that I should have liked to strangle, it was that accidental, unthinking luna Von Schlemm. By the grace of God, our islands finally exorcised the evil that he so unwittingly initiated.

When the election returns were all in, toward two in the morning, and the Democratic victors were flushed with congratulations, Black Jim McLafferty leaned back in his chair at headquarters and warned Senator Sakagawa: "This victory is going to delay statehood. Last year our enemies rejected us on the grounds that Hawaii wasn't ready because the Japanese weren't Americanized. When they hear these returns, they'll reject us again because you Orientals are too damned well Americanized. But whether we ever become a state or not, we're going to build a great Hawaii."

His reflections were interrupted by the entrance into headquarters of a man whom no one expected to see there, for stern, black-coated Hoxworth Hale appeared bearing a maile lei whose fragrance was apparent even above the tobacco smoke and the shouting. The commander of The Fort looked gloomily about the unfamiliar terrain, then saw Shigeo Sakagawa among a group of cheering friends and noticed the bright-red lipstick on his yellow cheek, as if strangers had been kissing him. Moving toward the most important victor in the senatorial contests, Hoxworth extended his hand and said, "Congratulations." Then he placed the maile chain about the young Japanese boy's shoulders and said, "You'll forgive me if I don't kiss you."

"I'll do that for you, Dad," Noelani said, adding her lipstick to the collection.

Hoxworth studied the victorious senator for a moment and asked wryly, "How is it none of you smart young fellows are Republicans?"

"You never invited us," Shig replied with a nervous laugh.

In distinct tones that many could overhear, Hoxworth said, "Well, I want it on record this time, Senator Sakagawa. I'm inviting you to join the board of Whipple Oil. I would be proud to work with a man like you."

The crowd gasped, and Shigeo replied, "On the morning after I introduce my land-reform bill, I'll join you. That is, supposing you still want me."

"You'd be foolish to accept before," Hoxworth said, and with this the proud, lonely man, descendant of the missionaries and owner of the islands, excused himself from a celebration where he was not wholly at ease. When he was gone, Shig's friends cried, "My God! He asked a Japanese to join his board," but Noelani said, "That's not important. Look! He gave Shig a maile lei. Coming from my father that's better than a crown."

I can speak with a certain authority about these matters, because I participated in them. I knew these Golden Men: the lyric beachboy Kelly Kanakoa; the crafty Chinese banker Hong Kong Kee; and the dedicated Japanese politician Shigeo Sakagawa. I was there when they became vital parts of the new Hawaii.

It was I who engineered the coalition that defeated Senator Sakagawa's radical land reform. It was I who warned Noelani Janders against the needless folly of falling in love with a Japanese boy, and I told Shigeo Sakagawa frankly that he would damage his career if he allowed it; for in an age of Golden Men it is not required that their bloodstreams mingle, but only that their ideas clash on equal footing and remain free to cross-fertilize and bear new fruit.

So at the age of fifty-six I, Hoxworth Hale, have discovered that I, too, am one of those Golden Men who see both the West and the East, who cherish the glowing past and who apprehend the obscure future; and the things I have written of in this memoir are very close to my heart.

GENEALOGICAL CHARTS

Principal

(whose names appear in bold type on the following charts)

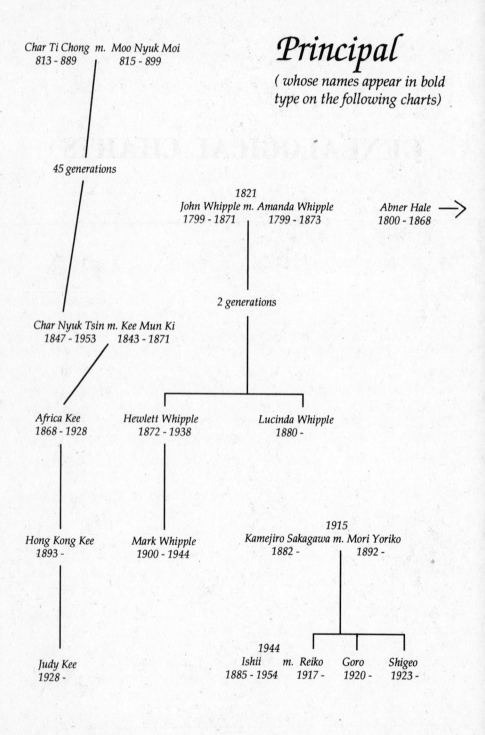

Char Ti Chong m. Moo Nyuk Moi
813 - 889   815 - 899

45 generations

1821
John Whipple m. Amanda Whipple
1799 - 1871   1799 - 1873

Abner Hale
1800 - 1868 →

2 generations

Char Nyuk Tsin m. Kee Mun Ki
1847 - 1953   1843 - 1871

Africa Kee
1868 - 1928

Hewlett Whipple
1872 - 1938

Lucinda Whipple
1880 -

Hong Kong Kee
1893 -

Mark Whipple
1900 - 1944

1915
Kamejiro Sakagawa m. Mori Yoriko
1882 -   1892 -

Judy Kee
1928 -

1944
Ishii   m. Reiko
1885 - 1954   1917 -

Goro
1920 -

Shigeo
1923 -

Characters

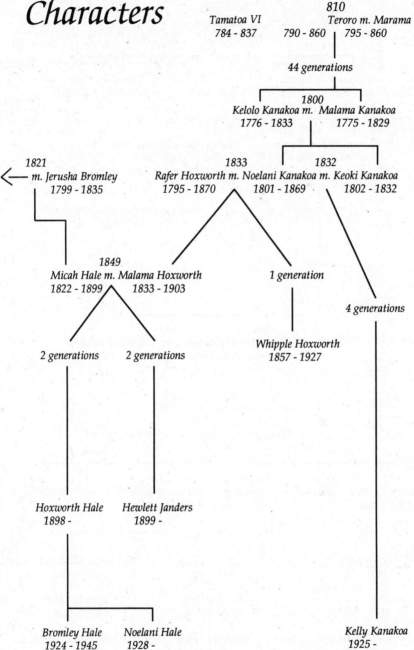

Tamatoa VI
784 - 837

810
Teroro m. Marama
790 - 860   795 - 860

44 generations

1800
Kelolo Kanakoa m. Malama Kanakoa
1776 - 1833   1775 - 1829

1821
← m. Jerusha Bromley
1799 - 1835

1833
Rafer Hoxworth m. Noelani Kanakoa m. Keoki Kanakoa
1795 - 1870   1801 - 1869   1802 - 1832

1832

1849
Micah Hale m. Malama Hoxworth
1822 - 1899   1833 - 1903

1 generation

4 generations

2 generations   2 generations

Whipple Hoxworth
1857 - 1927

Hoxworth Hale   Hewlett Janders
1898 -   1899 -

Bromley Hale   Noelani Hale
1924 - 1945   1928 -

Kelly Kanakoa
1925 -

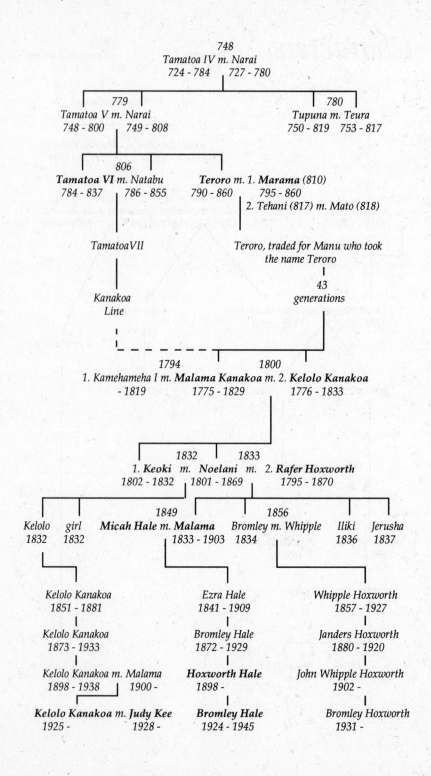

748
Tamatoa IV m. Narai
724 - 784   727 - 780

779
Tamatoa V m. Narai
748 - 800   749 - 808

780
Tupuna m. Teura
750 - 819   753 - 817

806
Tamatoa VI *m. Natabu*
784 - 837   786 - 855

Teroro *m.* 1. **Marama** *(810)*
790 - 860   795 - 860
2. *Tehani (817) m. Mato (818)*

TamatoaVII

Kanakoa
Line

Teroro, traded for Manu who took
the name Teroro

43
generations

1794   1800
1. *Kamehameha I m.* **Malama Kanakoa** *m.* 2. **Kelolo Kanakoa**
   - 1819   1775 - 1829   1776 - 1833

1832   1833
1. **Keoki** *m.* **Noelani** *m.* 2. **Rafer Hoxworth**
1802 - 1832   1801 - 1869   1795 - 1870

1849   1856
Kelolo *girl* **Micah Hale** *m.* **Malama** *Bromley m. Whipple* *Iliki* *Jerusha*
1832   1832   1833 - 1903   1834   1836   1837

Kelolo Kanakoa
1851 - 1881

Kelolo Kanakoa
1873 - 1933

Kelolo Kanakoa m. Malama
1898 - 1938   1900 -

Kelolo Kanakoa *m.* **Judy Kee**
1925 -   1928 -

Ezra Hale
1841 - 1909

Bromley Hale
1872 - 1929

Hoxworth Hale
1898 -

Bromley Hale
1924 - 1945

Whipple Hoxworth
1857 - 1927

Janders Hoxworth
1880 - 1920

John Whipple Hoxworth
1902 -

Bromley Hoxworth
1931 -

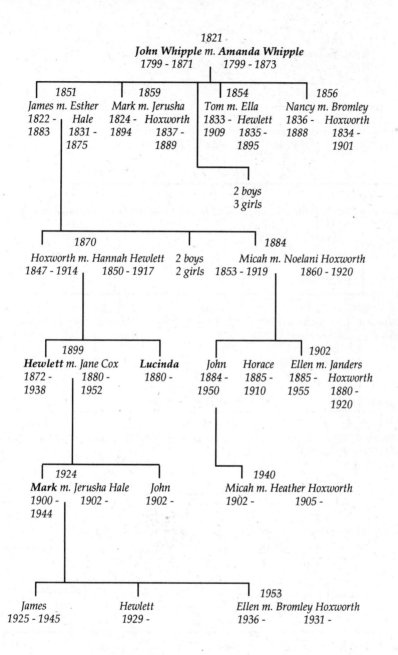

1821
John Whipple** m. **Amanda Whipple
1799 - 1871   1799 - 1873

1851
James m. Esther
1822 -   Hale
1883   1831 -
1875

1859
Mark m. Jerusha
1824 -   Hoxworth
1894   1837 -
1889

1854
Tom m. Ella
1833 - Hewlett
1909   1835 -
1895

1856
Nancy m. Bromley
1836 -   Hoxworth
1888   1834 -
1901

2 boys
3 girls

1870
Hoxworth m. Hannah Hewlett
1847 - 1914   1850 - 1917

2 boys
2 girls

1884
Micah m. Noelani Hoxworth
1853 - 1919   1860 - 1920

1899
***Hewlett** m. Jane Cox*
1872 -   1880 -
1938   1952

Lucinda
1880 -

John
1884 -
1950

Horace
1885 -
1910

1902
Ellen m. Janders
1885 -   Hoxworth
1955   1880 -
1920

1924
***Mark** m. Jerusha Hale*
1900 -   1902 -
1944

John
1902 -

1940
Micah m. Heather Hoxworth
1902 -   1905 -

James
1925 - 1945

Hewlett
1929 -

1953
Ellen m. Bromley Hoxworth
1936 -   1931 -

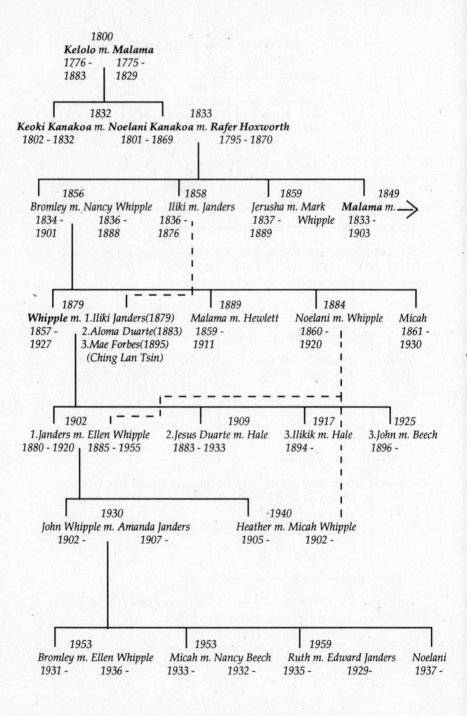

1800
Kelolo m. **Malama**
1776 -   1775 -
1883   1829

1832   1833
Keoki Kanakoa m. **Noelani Kanakoa** m. **Rafer Hoxworth**
1802 - 1832   1801 - 1869   1795 - 1870

1856   1858   1859   1849
Bromley m. Nancy Whipple   Iliki m. Janders   Jerusha m. Mark   **Malama** m. ⟶
1834 -   1836 -   1836 -   1837 -   Whipple   1833 -
1901   1888   1876   1889   1903

1879   1889   1884
Whipple m. 1.Iliki Janders(1879)   Malama m. Hewlett   Noelani m. Whipple   Micah
1857 -   2.Aloma Duarte(1883)   1859 -   1860 -   1861 -
1927   3.Mae Forbes(1895)   1911   1920   1930
    (Ching Lan Tsin)

1902   1909   1917   1925
1.Janders m. Ellen Whipple   2.Jesus Duarte m. Hale   3.Ilikik m. Hale   3.John m. Beech
1880 - 1920   1885 - 1955   1883 - 1933   1894 -   1896 -

1930   1940
John Whipple m. Amanda Janders   Heather m. Micah Whipple
1902 -   1907 -   1905 -   1902 -

1953   1953   1959
Bromley m. Ellen Whipple   Micah m. Nancy Beech   Ruth m. Edward Janders   Noelani
1931 -   1936 -   1933 -   1932 -   1935 -   1929-   1937 -

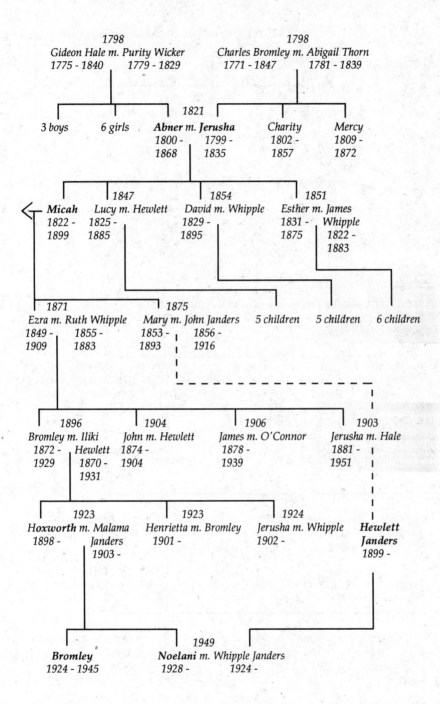

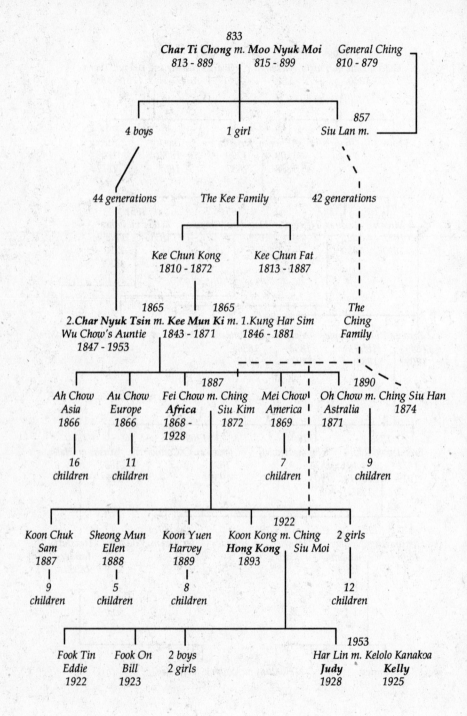

833
Char Ti Chong m. **Moo Nyuk Moi**   *General Ching*
813 - 889   *815 - 899*   *810 - 879*

4 boys   1 girl   857
                              Siu Lan m.

44 generations   *The Kee Family*   42 generations

Kee Chun Kong   *Kee Chun Fat*
1810 - 1872   *1813 - 1887*

1865   1865   *The*
2. Char Nyuk Tsin m. **Kee Mun Ki** m. 1. *Kung Har Sim*   *Ching*
Wu Chow's Auntie   *1843 - 1871*   *1846 - 1881*   *Family*
1847 - 1953

1887

Ah Chow   *Au Chow*   *Fei Chow* m. *Ching*   *Mei Chow*   *Oh Chow* m. *Ching Siu Han*
Asia   *Europe*   *Africa*   *Siu Kim*   *America*   *Astralia*   *1874*
1866   *1866*   *1868 -*   *1872*   *1869*   *1871*
                        1928   1890

16   11   7   9
children   children   children   children

1922

Koon Chuk   *Sheong Mun*   *Koon Yuen*   *Koon Kong* m. *Ching*   *2 girls*
Sam   *Ellen*   *Harvey*   *Hong Kong*   *Siu Moi*
1887   *1888*   *1889*   *1893*
                                                                    12
9   5   8   children
children   children   children

1953

Fook Tin   *Fook On*   *2 boys*   *Har Lin* m. *Kelolo Kanakoa*
Eddie   *Bill*   *2 girls*   **Judy**   **Kelly**
1922   *1923*   *1928*   *1925*

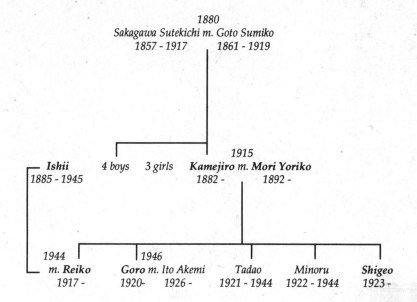

1880
Sakagawa Sutekichi *m.* Goto Sumiko
1857 - 1917   1861 - 1919

Ishii   4 boys   3 girls   **Kamejiro** *m.* **Mori Yoriko**
1885 - 1945   1882 -   1892 -

1944   1946
m. **Reiko**   **Goro** *m.* Ito Akemi   Tadao   Minoru   **Shigeo**
1917 -   1920-   1926 -   1921 - 1944   1922 - 1944   1923 -

ABOUT THE AUTHOR

Universally revered novelist JAMES A. MICHENER was forty before he decided on writing as a career. Prior to that, he had been an outstanding academic, an editor, and a U.S. Navy lieutenant commander in the Pacific Theater during World World II. His first book, *Tales of the South Pacific*, won a Pulitzer Prize and became the basis of the award-winning Rodgers and Hammerstein musical *South Pacific*. In the course of the next forty years Mr. Michener wrote such monumental bestsellers as *Sayonara*, *The Bridges at Toko-Ri*, *The Source*, *Iberia*, *Texas*, *Journey*, and *Caribbean*.

Decorated with America's highest civilian award, the Presidential Medal of Freedom, Mr. Michener has served on the Advisory Council to NASA, holds honorary doctorates in five fields from thirty leading universities, and has received an award from the President's Committee on the Arts and Humanities for his continuing commitment to art in America.